NON-CIRCULATING

USEFUL SUBJECT INDEX TERMS

Administration
- Agents
- Financial operations
    - Accounting
    - Funding
    - Payroll
    - Taxes
- Legal aspects
    - Censorship
    - Contracts
    - Copyright
    - Liabilities
    - Regulations
- Personnel
    - Labor relations
    - Unions
- Planning/operation
    - Producing
- Public relations
    - Advertising
    - Community relations
    - Marketing

Audience
- Audience composition
- Audience-performer relationship
- Audience reactions/comments

Basic theatrical documents
- Choreographies
- Film treatments
- Librettos
- Miscellaneous texts
- Playtexts
- Promptbooks
- Scores

Design/technology
- Costuming
- Equipment
- Lighting
- Make-up
- Masks
- Projections
- Properties
- Puppets
- Scenery
- Sound
- Special effects
- Technicians/crews
- Wigs

Institutions
- Institutions, associations
- Institutions, producing
- Institutions, research
- Institutions, service
- Institutions, social
- Institutions, special
- Institutions, training

Performance/production
- Acting
- Acrobatics
- Aerialists
- Aquatics
- Animal acts
- Choreography
- Clowning
- Dancing
- Directing
- Equestrian acts
- Equilibrists
- Instrumentalists
- Juggling
- Magic
- Martial arts
- Puppeteers

- Singing
- Staging

Performance spaces
- Amphitheatres/arenas
- Fairgrounds
- Found spaces
- Halls
- Religious structures
- Show boats
- Theatres
    - Auditorium
    - Foyer
    - Orchestra pit
    - Stage,
        - Adjustable
        - Apron
        - Arena
        - Proscenium
    - Support areas

Plays/librettos/scripts
- Adaptations
- Characters/roles
- Dramatic structure
- Editions
- Language
- Plot/subject/theme

Reference materials
- Bibliographies
- Catalogues
- Collected Materials
- Databanks
- Descriptions of resources
- Dictionaries
- Directories
- Discographies
- Encyclopedias
- Glossaries
- Guides
- Iconographies
- Indexes
- Lists
- Videographies
- Yearbooks

Relation to other fields
- Anthropology
- Economics
- Education
- Ethics
- Literature
- Figurative arts
- Philosophy
- Politics
- Psychology
- Religion
- Sociology

Research/historiography
- Methodology
- Research tools

Theory/criticism
- Aesthetics
- Deconstruction
- Dialectics
- Feminist criticism
- New historicism
- Phenomenology
- Reader response
- Reception
- Semiotics

Training
- Apprenticeship
- Teaching methods
    - Training aids

Other frequent subjects
- AIDS
- Alternative theatre
- Amateur theatre
- Archives/libraries
- Avant-garde theatre
- Awards
- Black theatre
- Broadway theatre
- Burlesque
- Casting
- Children's theatre
- Community theatre
- Computers
- Conferences
- Creative drama
- Educational theatre
- Elizabethan theatre
- Experimental theatre
- Farce
- Feminist theatre
- Festivals
- Folklore
- Fundraising
- Gay/Lesbian theatre
- Gender studies
- Health/safety
- Hispanic theatre
- Improvisation
- Indigenous theatre
- Jacobean theatre
- Jewish theatre
- Liturgical drama
- Management, stage
- Medieval theatre
- Metadrama
- Minstrelsy
- Monodrama
- Movement
- Multiculturalism
- Music hall
- Mystery plays
- Mythology
- Neoclassicism
- Off Broadway theatre
- Off-off Broadway theatre
- Open-air theatre
- Parody
- Passion plays
- Performance spaces
- Playhouses
- Playwriting
- Political theatre
- Popular entertainment
- Press
- Radio drama
- Regional theatre
- Religious theatre
- Renaissance theatre
- Restoration theatre
- Ritual-ceremony
- Satire
- Story-telling
- Street theatre
- Summer theatre
- Touring companies
- Transvestism
- Vaudeville
- Voice
- Women in theatre
- Workshops
- Yiddish theatre

INTERNATIONAL BIBLIOGRAPHY OF THEATRE: 1997

International Bibliography of Theatre: 1997

Published by the Theatre Research Data Center, Brooklyn College, City University of New York, NY 11210 USA.

© Theatre Research Data Center, 1999: ISBN 0-945419-08-2. All rights reserved.

This publication was made possible in part with in-kind support and services provided by Brooklyn College and the University Computing & Information Services of the City University of New York.

The paper used in this book complies with the Permanent Paper Standard issued by the National Information Standards Organization (Z39.48-1984).

THE THEATRE RESEARCH DATA CENTER

Rosabel Wang, Director

The Theatre Research Data Center at Brooklyn College houses, publishes and distributes the International Bibliography of Theatre. Inquiries about the bibliographies and the databank are welcome. Telephone (718) 951-5998; FAX (718) 951-4606; E-Mail RXWBC@CUNYVM.CUNY.EDU.

INTERNATIONAL BIBLIOGRAPHY OF THEATRE:1997

Benito Ortolani, Editor

Catherine Hilton, Executive Editor   Margaret Loftus Ranald, Associate Editor

Rosabel Wang, Systems Analyst

Rose Bonczek, Managing Editor   Helen Huff, Online Editor

Mickey Ryan, Research Editor

The International Bibliography of Theatre project is sponsored by:
The American Society for Theatre Research
The Theatre Library Association
The International Association of Libraries and Museums of the Performing Arts
in cooperation with
The International Federation for Theatre Research.

Theatre Research Data Center
New York 1999

QUICK ACCESS GUIDE

GENERAL

The Classed Entries are equivalent to library shelf arrangements.
The Indexes are equivalent to a library card catalogue.

SEARCH METHODS

By subject:

Look in the alphabetically arranged Subject Index for the relevant term(s), topic(s) or name(s): e.g., Feminist criticism; *Macbeth*; Shakespeare, William; Gay theatre; etc.
Check the number at the end of each relevant précis.
Using that number, search the Classed Entries section to find full information.

By country:

Look in the Geographical-Chronological Index for the country related to the *content* of interest.
    Note: Countries are arranged in alphabetical order and then subdivided chronologically.
Find the number at the end of each relevant précis.
Using that number, search the Classed Entries section to find full information.

By periods:

Determine the country of interest.
Look in the Geographical-Chronological Index, paying special attention to the chronological subdivisions.
Find the number at the end of each relevant précis.
Using that number, search the Classed Entries section to find full information.

By authors of listed books or articles:

Look in the alphabetically arranged Document Authors Index for the relevant names.
Using the number at the end of each Author Index entry, search the Classed Entries section to find full information.

SUGGESTIONS

Search a variety of possible subject headings.
Search the **most specific subject heading** first, e.g., if interested in acting in Ibsen plays, begin with Ibsen, Henrik, rather than the more generic Acting or Plays/librettos/scripts.
When dealing with large clusters of references under a single subject heading, note that items are listed in **alphabetical order of content geography** (Afghanistan to Zimbabwe). Under each country items are ordered alphabetically by author, following the same numerical sequence as that of the Classed Entries.

TABLE OF CONTENTS

ACKNOWLEDGMENTS

We are grateful to the many institutions and individuals who have helped us make this volume possible:

Brooklyn College: President Vernon Lattin, Professor Benito Ortolani, Professor Emeritus Irving M. Brown;

President Margaret Knapp, ASTR;

President Noëlle Guibert, SIBMAS;

President Josette Féral and the University Commission of FIRT;

Hedvig Belitska-Scholtz, National Széchényi Library, Budapest;

Magnus Blomkvist, Drottningholms Teatermuseum;

Ole Bøgh, University of Copenhagen, Denmark;

John Degen, Florida State University;

Elaine Fadden, Countway Library, Harvard University, Boston;

Temple Hauptfleisch, University of Stellenbosch;

Veronica Kelly, University of Queensland, Brisbane;

Danuta Kuźnicka, Polska Akademia Nauk, Warsaw;

Tamara Il. Lapteva, Russian State Library, Moscow;

Shimon Lev-Ari, Tel-Aviv University;

Anna McMullan, Trinity College, Dublin;

Lindsay Newman, University of Lancaster Library, and SIBMAS of Great Britain;

Louis Rachow, International Theatre Institute, New York;

Michael Ribaudo and Pat Reber, CUNY/Computing & Information Services, New York;

Willem Rodenhuis, Universiteit van Amsterdam;

Francka Slivnik, National Theatre and Film Museum, Ljubljana;

Jarmila Svobodová, Theatre Institute, Prague;

Alessandro Tinterri, Museo Biblioteca dell'Attore di Genova;

Sirkka Tukiainen, Central Library of Theatre and Dance, Helsinki;

And we thank our field bibliographers whose contributions have made this work a reality:

Jerry Bangham	Alcorn State Univ., Lorman, MS
Maria Olga Bieńka	Polska Akademia Nauk, Warsaw
Rose Bonczek	Brooklyn College, City Univ. of New York
Magdolna Both	National Széchényi Library, Budapest
Sarah Corner-Walker	University of Copenhagen, Denmark
Ekaterina Danilova	State Library of Russia, Moscow
Clifford O. Davidson	Western Michigan Univ., Kalamazoo, MI
Krystyna Duniec	Polska Akademia Nauk, Warsaw
Jayne Fenwick-White	Glyndebourne Festival Opera, Lewes
Ramona Floyd	Sandbox Theatre Productions, New York, NY
Steven H. Gale	Kentucky State University, Frankfort, KY
Carol Goodger-Hill	University of Guelph, ON
James Hatch	Hatch-Billops Collection, New York, NY
Catherine Hilton	University of Massachusetts, Amherst
Jane Hogan	TCI, Theatre Crafts International, New York, NY
Helen Huff	Graduate Center, City Univ. of New York
Valentina Jakushkina	State Library of Russia, Moscow
Gryegory Janikowski	Polska Akademia Nauk, Warsaw
Toni Johnson-Woods	University of Queensland, Brisbane
Marija Kaufman	National Theatre and Film Museum, Ljubljana
Aila Kettunen	Central Library of Theatre and Dance, Helsinki
Jarosław Komorowski	Polska Akademia Nauk, Warsaw
Joanna Krakowska-Narożniak	Polska Akademia Nauk, Warsaw
Clare MacDonald	University of Maryland, College Park
William L. Maiman	TCI, Theatre Crafts International, New York, NY
Margaret Majewska	Polish Centre of the International Theatre Institute, Warsaw;
Michaela Mertová	Theatre Institut, Prague
Alenka Mihalič-Klemenčič	University of Maribor Library, Slovenia
Clair Myers	Elon College, Elon, NC
Maria Napiontkowa	Polska Akademia Nauk, Warsaw
Danila Parodi	Museo Biblioteca dell'Attore di Genova
Michael Patterson	De Montfort University, UK
Miroslava Přikrylová	Theatre Institut, Prague
Margaret Loftus Ranald	Queens College, City Univ. of New York
Mickey Ryan	Synergy Ensemble Theatre Company, Islip, NY
James Shaw	Shakespeare Institute, University of Birmingham, UK
Heike Stange	Freie Universität Berlin
Juan Villegas	GESTOS Revista de Teoria y Practica del Teatro Hispanico, Univ. of Cal.-Irvine
David Whiteley	Université du Québec à Montréal
David Whitton	University of Lancaster, UK

A GUIDE FOR USERS

SCOPE OF THE BIBLIOGRAPHY

Materials Included

The *International Bibliography of Theatre: 1997* lists theatre books, book articles, dissertations, journal articles and miscellaneous other theatre documents published during 1997. It also includes items from prior years received too late for inclusion in earlier volumes. Published works (with the exceptions noted below) are included without restrictions on the internal organization, format, or purpose of those works. Materials selected for the Bibliography deal with any aspect of theatre significant to research, without historical, cultural or geographical limitations. Entries are drawn from theatre histories, essays, studies, surveys, conference papers and proceedings, catalogues of theatrical holdings of any type, portfolios, handbooks and guides, dictionaries, bibliographies, and other reference works, records and production documents.

Materials Excluded

Reprints of previously published works are usually excluded unless they are major documents which have been unavailable for some time. In general only references to newly published works are included, though significantly revised editions of previously published works are treated as new works. Purely literary scholarship is generally excluded, since it is already listed in established bibliographical instruments. An exception is made for material published in journals completely indexed by *IBT*. Studies in theatre literature, textual studies, and dissertations are represented only when they contain significant components that examine or have relevance to theatrical performance.

Playtexts are excluded unless they are published with extensive or especially noteworthy introductory material, or when the text is the first translation or adaptation of a classic from an especially rare language into a major language. Book reviews and reviews of performances are not included, except for those reviews of sufficient scope to constitute a review article, or clusters of reviews published under one title.

Language

There is no restriction on language in which theatre documents appear, but English is the primary vehicle for compiling and abstracting the materials. The Subject Index gives primary importance to titles in their original languages, transliterated into the Roman Alphabet where necessary. Original language titles also appear in Classed Entries that refer to plays in translation and in the précis of Subject Index items.

CLASSED ENTRIES

Content

The **Classed Entries** section contains one entry for each document analyzed and provides the user with complete information on all material indexed in this volume. It is the only place where publication citations may be found and where detailed abstracts are furnished. Users are advised to familiarize themselves with the elements and structure of the Taxonomy to simplify the process of locating items indexed in the **classed entries** section.

Organization

Entries follow the order provided in Columns I, II and III of the Taxonomy.

Column I classifies theatre into nine categories beginning with Theatre in General and thereafter listed alphabetically from "Dance" to "Puppetry." Column II divides most of the nine Column I categories into a number of subsidiary components. Column III headings relate any of the previously selected Column I and Column II categories to specific elements of the theatre. A list of Useful Subject Index Terms is also given (see frontpapers). These terms are also sub-components of the Column III headings.

Examples:

Items classified under "Theatre in General" appear in the Classed Entries before those classified under "Dance" in Column I, etc.

Items classified under the Column II heading of "Musical theatre" appear before those classified under the Column II heading of "Opera," etc.

Items further classified under the Column III heading of "Administration" appear before those classified under "Design/technology," etc.

Every group of entries under any of the divisions of the **Classed Entries** is printed in alphabetical order according to its content geography: e.g., a cluster of items concerned with plays related to Spain, classified under "Drama" (Column I) and "Plays/librettos/scripts" (Column III) would be printed together after items concerned with plays related to South Africa and before those related to Sweden. Within these country clusters, each group of entries is arranged alphabetically by author.

Relation to Subject Index

When in doubt concerning the appropriate Taxonomy category for a **Classed Entry** search, the user should refer to the **Subject Index** for direction. The **Subject Index** provides several points of access for each entry in the **Classed Entries** section. In most cases it is advisable to use the **Subject Index** as the first and main way to locate the information contained in the **Classed Entries**.

TAXONOMY TERMS

The following descriptions have been established to clarify the terminology used in classifying entries according to the Taxonomy. They are used for clarification only, as a searching tool for users of the Bibliography. In cases where clarification has been deemed unnecessary (as in the case of "Ballet", "Kabuki", "Film", etc.) no further description appears below. Throughout the Classed Entries, the term "General" distinguishes miscellaneous items that cannot be more specifically classified by the remaining terms in the Column II category. Sufficient subject headings enable users to locate items regardless of their taxonomical classification.

THEATRE IN GENERAL: Only for items which cannot be properly classified by categories "Dance" through "Puppetry," or for items related to more than one theatrical category.

DANCE: Only for items published in theatre journals that are indexed by *IBT*, or for dance items with relevance to theatre.

DANCE-DRAMA: Items related to dramatic genres where dance is the dominant artistic element. Used primarily for specific forms of non-Western theatre, e.g., *Kathakali, Nō.*

DRAMA: Items related to playtexts and performances where the spoken word is traditionally considered the dominant element. (i.e., all Western dramatic literature and all spoken drama everywhere). An article on acting as a discipline will also fall into this category, as well as books about directing, unless these endeavors are more closely related to musical theatre forms or other genres.

MEDIA: Only for media related-items published in theatre journals completely indexed by *IBT*, or for media items with relevance to theatre.

MIME: Items related to performances where mime is the dominant element. This category comprises all forms of mime from every epoch and/or country.

PANTOMIME: Both Roman Pantomime and the performance form epitomized in modern times by Étienne Decroux and Marcel Marceau. English pantomime is indexed under "Mixed Entertainment."

MIXED ENTERTAINMENT: Items related either 1) to performances consisting of a variety of performance elements among which none is considered dominant, or 2) to performances where the element of spectacle and the function of broad audience appeal are dominant. Because of the great variety of terminology in different circumstances, times, and countries for similar types of spectacle, such items as café-concert, quadrille réaliste, one-person shows, night club acts, pleasure gardens, tavern concerts, night cellars, saloons, Spezialitätentheater, storytelling, divertissement, rivistina, etc., are classified under "General", "Variety acts", or "Cabaret", etc. depending on time period, circumstances, and/or country.

Variety acts: Items related to variety entertainment of mostly unconnected "numbers", including some forms of vaudeville, revue, petite revue, intimate revue, burlesque, etc.

PUPPETRY: Items related to all kinds of puppets, marionettes and mechanically operated figures.

N.B.: Notice that entries related to individuals are classified according to the Column III category describing the individual's primary field of activity: e.g., a manager under "Administration," a set designer under "Design/technology," an actor under "Performance/production," a playwright under "Plays/librettos/scripts," a teacher under "Training," etc.

CITATION FORMS

Basic bibliographical information

Each citation includes the standard bibliographical information: author(s), title, publisher, pages, and notes, preface, appendices, etc., when present. Journal titles are usually given in the form of an acronym, whose corresponding title may be found in the **List of Periodicals**. Pertinent publication information is also provided in this list.

Translation of original language

When the play title is not in English, a translation in parentheses follows the original title. Established English translations of play titles or names of institutions are used when they exist. Names of institutions, companies, buildings, etc., unless an English version is in common use, are as a rule left untranslated. Geographical names are given in standard English form as defined by *Webster's Geographical Dictionary* (3rd ed. 1997).

Time and place

An indication of the time and place to which a document pertains is included wherever appropriate and possible. The geographical information refers usually to a country, sometimes to a larger region such as Europe or English-speaking countries. The geographical designation is relative to the time of the content: Russia is used before 1917, USSR to 1991; East and West Germany 1945-1990; Roman Empire until its official demise, Italy thereafter. When appropriate, precise dates related to the content of the item are given. Otherwise the decade or century is indicated.

Abstract

Unless the content of a document is made sufficiently clear by the title, the classed entry provides a brief abstract. Titles of plays not in English are given in English translation in the abstract, except for most operas and titles that are widely known in their original language. If the original title does not appear in the document title, it is provided in the abstract.

Spelling

English form is used for transliterated personal names. In the **Subject Index** each English spelling refers the users to the international or transliterated spelling under which all relevant entries are listed.

Varia

Affiliation with a movement and influence by or on individuals or groups is indicated only when the document itself suggests such information.

When a document belongs to more than one Column I category of the Taxonomy, the other applicable Column I categories are cross-referenced in the **Subject Index**.

Document treatment

"Document treatment" indicates the type of scholarly approach used in the writing of the document. The following terms are used in the present bibliography:

Bibliographical studies treat as their primary subject bibliographic material.

Biographical studies are articles on part of the subject's life.

Biographies are book-length treatments of entire lives.

Critical studies present an evaluation resulting from the application of criteria.

Empirical research identifies studies that incorporate as part of their design an experiment or series of experiments.

Historical studies designate accounts of individual events, groups, movements, institutions, etc., whose primary purpose is to provide a historical record or evaluation.

Histories-general cover the whole spectrum of theatre—or most of it—over a period of time and typically appear in one or several volumes.

Histories-specific cover a particular genre, field, or component of theatre over a period of time and usually are published as a book.

Histories-sources designate source materials that provide an internal evaluation or account of the treated subject: e.g. interviews with theatre professionals.

Histories-reconstruction attempt to reconstruct some aspect of the theatre.

Instructional materials include textbooks, manuals, guides or any other publication to be used in teaching.

Reviews of performances examine one or several performances in the format of review articles, or clusters of several reviews published under one title.

Technical studies examine theatre from the point of view of the applied sciences or discuss particular theatrical techniques.

Textual studies examine the texts themselves for origins, accuracy, and publication data.

Example with diagram

Here follows an example (in this case a book article) of a **Classed Entries** item with explanation of its elements:

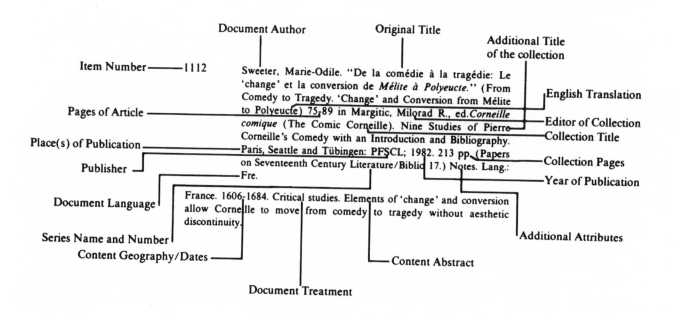

SUBJECT INDEX

Function

The Subject Index is a primary means of access to the major aspects of documents referenced by the **Classed Entries**.

Content

Each **Subject Index** item contains
- (a) subject headings, e.g., names of persons, names of institutions, forms and genres of theatre, elements of the theatre arts, titles of plays.
- (b) column III category indicating primary focus of the entry
- (c) short abstracts describing the items of the **Classed Entries** related to the subject heading
- (d) content country, city, time and language of document
- (e) the number of the **Classed Entry** from which each Subject Index item was generated.

Standards

Names of persons, including titles of address, are listed alphabetically by last names according to the standard established in *Anglo-American Cataloguing Rules* (Library of Congress, 2nd edition, 1978).

All names and terms originating in non-Roman alphabets, including Russian, Greek, Chinese and Japanese have been transliterated and are listed by the transliterated forms.

Geographical names are spelled according to *Webster's Geographical Dictionary* (3rd ed. 1997).

"SEE" references direct users from common English spellings or titles to names or terms indexed in a less familiar manner.

Example:

Chekhov, Anton
SEE
Čechov, Anton Pavlovič

Individuals are listed in the Subject Index when:

- (a) they are the primary or secondary focus of the document;
- (b) the document addresses aspects of their lives and/or work in a primary or supporting manner;
- (c) they are the author of the document, but only when their life and/or work is also the document's primary focus;
- (d) their lives have influenced, or have been influenced by, the primary subject of the document or the writing of it, as evidenced by explicit statement in the document.

This Subject Index is particularly useful when a listed individual is the subject of numerous citations. In such cases a search should not be limited only to the main subject heading (e.g., Shakespeare). A more relevant one (e.g., *Hamlet*) could bring more specific results.

"SEE" References

Institutions, groups, and social or theatrical movements appear as subject headings, following the above criteria. Names of theatre companies, theatre buildings, etc. are given in their original languages or transliterated. "See" references are provided for the generally used or literally translated English terms;

Example: "Moscow Art Theatre" directs users to the company's original title:

Moscow Art Theatre
SEE
Moskovskij Chudožestvennyj Akademičeskij Teat'r

No commonly used English term exists for "Comédie-Française," it therefore appears only under its title of origin. The same is true for *commedia dell'arte*, Burgtheater and other such terms.

Play titles appear in their original languages, with "SEE" references next to their English translations. Subject headings for plays in a third language may be provided if the translation in that language is of unusual importance.

Widely known opera titles are not translated.

Similar subject headings

Subject headings such as "Politics" and "Political theatre" are neither synonymous nor mutually exclusive. They aim to differentiate between a phenomenon and a theatrical genre. Likewise, such terms as "Feminism" refer to social and cultural movements and are not intended to be synonymous with "Women in theatre." The term "Ethnic theatre" is used to classify any type of theatrical literature or performance where the ethnicity of those concerned is of primary importance. Because of the number of items, and for reasons of accessibility, "African-American theatre," "Native American theatre" and the theatre of certain other ethnic groups are given separate subject headings.

Groups/movements, periods, etc.

Generic subject headings such as "Victorian theatre," "Expressionism," etc., are only complementary to other more specific groupings and do not list all items in the bibliography related to that period or generic subject: e.g., the subject heading "Elizabethan theatre" does not list a duplicate of all items related to Shakespeare, which are to be found under "Shakespeare," but lists materials explicitly related to the actual physical conditions or style of presentation typical of the Elizabethan theatre. For a complete search according to periods, use the **Geographical-Chronological Index**, searching by country and by the years related to the period.

Subdivision of Subject Headings

Each subject heading is subdivided into Column III categories that identify the primary focus of the cited entry. These subcategories are intended to facilitate the user when searching under such broad terms as "African-American theatre" or "*King Lear.*" The subcategory helps to identify the relevant cluster of entries. Thus, for instance, when the user is interested only in African-American theatre companies, the subheading "Institutions" groups all the relevant items together. Similarly, the subheading "Performance/production" groups together all the items dealing with production aspects of *King Lear*. It is, however, important to remember that these subheadings (i.e. Column III categories) are not subcategories of the subject heading itself, but of the main subject matter treated in the entry.

Printing order

Short abstracts under each subject heading are listed according to Column III categories. These categories are organized alphabetically. Short abstracts within each cluster, on the other hand, are arranged sequentially according to the item number they refer to in the Classed Entries. This enables the frequent user to recognize immediately the location and classification of the entry. If the user cannot find one specific subject heading, a related term may suffice, e.g., for Church dramas, see Religion. In some cases, a "SEE" reference is provided.

Example with diagram

Here follows an example of a **Subject Index** entry with explanation of its elements:

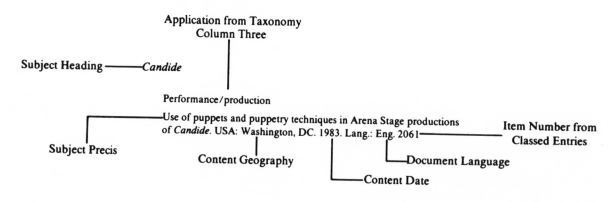

GEOGRAPHICAL-CHRONOLOGICAL INDEX

Organization

The **Geographical-Chronological Index** is arranged alphabetically by the country relevant to the subject or topic treated. The references under each country are then subdivided by date. References to articles with contents of the same date are then listed according to their category in the Taxonomy's Column III. The last item in each Geographical-Chronological Index listing is the number of the Classed Entry from which the listing was generated.

Example: For material on Drama in Italy between World Wars I and II, look under Italy, 1918-1939. In the example below, entries 2734, 2227 and 891 match this description.

Italy — cont'd

1907-1984.   **Theory/criticism.**
Cruelty and sacredness in contemporary theatre poetics.
Germany. France. Lang.: Ita.   2734

1914.   **Plays/librettos/scripts.**
Comparative study of *Francesca da Rimini* by Riccardo
Zandonai and *Tristan und Isolde* by Richard Wagner.
Lang.: Eng.   3441

1920-1936.   **Plays/librettos/scripts.**
Introductory analysis of twenty-one of Pirandello's plays
Lang.: Eng.   2227

1923-1936.   **Institutions.**
History of Teatro degli Indipendenti. Rome. Lang.; Ita.   891

1940-1984.   **Performance/production.**
Italian tenor Giuseppe Giacomini speaks of his career and
art. New York, NY. Lang.; Eng.   3324

Dates

Dates reflect the content period covered by the item, not the publication year. However, the publication year is used for theoretical writings and for assessments of old traditions, problems, etc. When precise dates cannot be established, the decade (e.g., 1970-1979) or the century (e.g., 1800-1899) is given.

Biographies and histories

In the case of biographies of people who are still alive, the year of birth of the subject and the year of publication of the biography are given. The same criterion is followed for histories of institutions such as theatres or companies which are still in existence. The founding date of such institutions and the date of publication of the entry are given—unless the entry explicitly covers only a specific period of the history of the institution.

Undatable content

No dates are given when the content is either theoretical or not meaningfully definable in time. Entries without date(s) print first.

DOCUMENT AUTHORS INDEX

The term "Document Author" means the author of the article or book cited in the **Classed Entries**. The author of the topic under discussion, e.g., Molière in an article about one of his plays, is *not* found in the **Document Authors Index**. (See Subject Index).

The **Document Authors Index** lists these authors alphabetically and in the Roman alphabet. The numbers given after each name direct the researcher to the full citations in the Classed Entries section.

N.B.: Users are urged to familiarize themselves with the Taxonomy and the indexes provided. The four-way access to research sources possible through consultation of the Classed Entries section, the Subject Index, the Geographical-Chronological Index and the Document Authors Index is intended to be sufficient to locate even the most highly specialized material.

CLASSED ENTRIES

THEATRE IN GENERAL

Administration

1   Fiscor, Mihály, Dr. "The Spring 1997 Horace S. Manges Lecture—Copyright for the Digital Era: The WIPO 'Internet' Treaties." *ColJL&A*. 1997 Spr/Sum; 21(3/4): 197-223. Notes. Lang.: Eng.

1997. Historical studies. ■Explains two treaties adopted by the World International Property Organization's diplomatic congress governing international copyright law with repect to current entertainment and information technologies.

2   Lucas, André. "Copyright Law and Technical Protection Devices." *ColJL&A*. 1997 Spr/Sum; 21(3/4): 225-238. Notes. Lang.: Eng.

1997. Critical studies. ■Artistic and literary property and the law governing the technical devices that protect from infringement.

3   Meyrick, Julian. "Accounting for the Arts in the Nineties: The Growth of Performing Arts Administration in Australia, 1975-1995." *JAML*. 1997 Win; 26(4): 285-307. Notes. Biblio. Tables. Lang.: Eng.

Australia. 1975-1995. Historical studies. ■The quest for accountability in arts, which led to increased administration, said to be a direct result of the failure of policy makers to define the performing arts. Maintains that the role of arts administration has increased and that of the artist has diminished.

4   Radbourne, Jennifer. "*Creative Nation*—A Policy for Leaders or Followers? An Evaluation of Australia's 1994 Cultural Policy Statement." *JAML*. 1997 Win; 26(4): 271-283. Notes. Lang.: Eng.

Australia. 1968-1997. Historical studies. ■Changes in arts and cultural industries reflected in government's cultural policy statement *Creative Nation*, which contained policy statements and objectives advocating renewed support for the arts and new financial allocations.

5   Jaumain, Michel. "Some Features of Cultural Policies Applied in Belgium, Particularly in the French-Speaking Community." *JAML*. 1997 Fall; 27(3): 205-225. Notes. Tables. Lang.: Eng.

Belgium. 1970-1997. Critical studies. ■Policy guidelines that perpetuate a common heritage in implementation of cultural policies, assessment of the means of implementation and the effects of cultural policies, and an overview of mechanisms for structural support for performing arts in the French-speaking community.

6   Bell, Karen. "It's All in the Marketing." *PAC*. 1997; 30(4): 6-7. Illus.: Photo. B&W. 2. Lang.: Eng.

Canada. 1992-1997. Historical studies. ■Profile of producers Jeffrey Follows and Lawrence Latimer, who specialize in mid-priced shows such as *Forever Plaid*. Their work in training producers and marketers.

7   Bell, Karen. "Corporate Sponsorship: A Suitable Match." *PAC*. 1997; 31(1): 9. Illus.: Photo. B&W. 1. Lang.: Eng.

Canada: Stratford, ON. 1953-1997. Critical studies. ■History of Bell Canada's financial support for the Stratford Festival since 1954. Present policies on investing in community and expectations of a 'payback'.

8   Fortier, Mark. "Ideals and Risks: An Interview with Steven Schipper." *CTR*. 1997 Win; 93: 10-15. Illus.: Photo. B&W. 2. Lang.: Eng.

Canada: Winnipeg, MB. 1996. Histories-sources. ■Schipper, artistic director of Manitoba Theatre Centre, describes factors in creating a regional theatre's season.

9   Gilbert, Leslie. "Refurbishing a Theatre and Revitalizing a Downtown Core." *PAC*. 1997; 31(2): 20-21. Illus.: Photo. B&W. 2. Lang.: Eng.

Canada: New Westminster, BC. 1927-1997. Historical studies. ■Fundraising efforts by the Raymond Burr Performing Arts Society to renovate the historic Columbia Theatre as a performing arts centre.

10   Vaïs, Michel. "Et M. pour le Message." (And M. For the Message.) *JCT*. 1997; 82: 152-155. Notes. Illus.: Dwg. Photo. B&W. 4. Lang.: Fre.

Canada: Montreal, PQ. 1962-1997. Historical studies. ■Suggests that Montreal theatre community is making International Day of Theatre increasingly nationalistic.

11   Vaïs, Michel. "Les Entrées libres de *Jeu*: Le théâtre privé sort de l'ombre." (*Jeu*'s Open Forums: Private Theatre Comes Out from the Shadows.) *JCT*. 1997; 83: 129-145. Notes. Illus.: Poster. Photo. B&W. 11. Lang.: Fre.

Canada: Montreal, PQ. 1997. Historical studies. ■Reports opinions expressed at a forum on unsubsidized theatre, held in Montreal on March 24, 1997.

12   Jindrová, Zuzana. "Z čeho žije české divadlo." (What Does Czech Theatre Live on.) *DiN*. 1997 June; 6 (13): 1, 4. Illus.: Photo. B&W. 1. Lang.: Cze.

Czech Republic. 1997. Critical studies. ■Model of financing for theatres in the Czech Republic.

13   Nielsen, Benedikte Hammershøy, comp.; Most, Henrik, comp. "Visioner for dansk teater." (Visions for Danish Theatre.) *TE*. 1997 Mar.; 83: 4-25. Illus.: Photo. B&W. 19. Lang.: Dan.

Denmark. 1997. Histories-sources. ■Short essays by theatre people speculating on the development of Danish theatre in the next century.

14   Olsen, Jakob Steen; Nielsen, Benedikte Hammershøy. "Stof til eftertanke og et spark i skridtet." (Something to Think About and a Kick Between the Legs.) *TE*. 1997 June; 84: 22-25. Illus.: Photo. B&W. 4. Lang.: Dan.

Denmark. 1992-1997. Historical studies. ■*Teater Et* awards Husets Teater in Copenhagen a prize for having an inventive and challenging repertoire. Presents the theatre's short history from it's founding in 1992.

15   Rottensten, Rikke. "Uden markedsføring ville teatret dø." (The Theatre Would Die without Marketing.) *TE*. 1997 Oct.; 85: 24-27. Illus.: Handbill. B&W. 4. Lang.: Dan.

Denmark. 1997. Histories-sources. ■Interviews with marketing consultants Christian Have and Jon Stephensen who work with the main the-

THEATRE IN GENERAL: —Administration

atres in Copenhagen. Includes examples of some of the posters created for Dr. Dante's Aveny and Gladsaxe Teater.

16   Bawcutt, N.W. "'Abstract of the Articles': an Early Restoration Theatre Agreement." *TN.* 1997; 51(2): 75-80. Notes. Lang.: Eng.

England: London. 1660-1663. Historical studies. ■Analyzes a legal agreement between Thomas Killigrew, William Davenant, and five actors of the Red Bull Company, as recorded by Joseph Haslewood in the early eighteenth century.

17   Ceresano, S.P. "Philip Henslowe, Simon Forman, and the Theatrical Community of the 1590s." *SQ.* 1993 Sum; 44(2): 145-158 . Notes. Illus.: Photo. B&W. 1. Lang.: Eng.

England: London. 1590-1600. Historical studies. ■Theatre manager Philip Henslowe's relationship with astrologer-conjurer Simon Forman and the theatrical community of London.

18   Corrigan, Brian Jay. "A Legal Dodge in the Business Practices of the Original Globe and Drury Lane Theatres." *TN.* 1997; 51(2): 72-74. Notes. Lang.: Eng.

England: London. 1599-1743. Historical studies. ■Demonstrates how the legal term 'use', which involves rights of ownership between two or more parties after the transfer of property, was employed by both theatres. Examines legal documents of 1599 and 1743.

19   Dutton, Richard. "Censorship." 287-304 in Cox, John D., ed.; Kastan, David Scott, ed. *A New History of Early English Drama.* New York, NY: Columbia UP; 1997. 565 pp. Index. Notes. Biblio. Lang.: Eng.

England. 1581. Critical studies. ■Argues that the contradictions found in censorship, specifically in the office of the Master of the Revels, served to stabilize as well as infringe upon a society.

20   Landro, Vincent. "Henslowe's Relocation to the North: Playhouse Management in Renaissance London." *ThS.* 1997 Nov.; 38 (2): 31-48. Tables. Lang.: Eng.

England: London. 1576-1616. Historical studies. ■Challenges traditional view of Henslowe's move from the Rose to the Fortune as motivated by Shakespeare's 'superior' company at the Globe and argues that the move was for more practical business purposes.

21   Powell, Rebekah Louise. *Culture, Capital and the State: Select Committee on Licensing and Regulating Theatres and Places of Public Entertainment.* Winnipeg, MB: The Univ. of Manitoba; 1997. 168 pp. [M.A. Thesis, Univ. Microfilms Order No. AAC MQ23462.] Lang.: Eng.

England: London. 1865-1867. Histories-specific. ■The rivalry between music halls and theatre as it unfolded before the Select Committee on Theatrical Licensing, in its cultural, social, and nationalistic context.

22   Burkhardt, Peter. "Neue Medien." (New Media.) *BtR.* 1997; 91(5): 26-27. Lang.: Ger.

Europe. 1997. Histories-sources. ■The coming information age and how theatre executives, administrative directors and technical leaders can prepare themselves. Includes discussion of new technology, email, worldwideweb, usenet, telebanking and videoconferencing that are already available.

23   Jentzen, Reinhold. "Kosten einer Theaterproduktion und welche Werte werden damit geschaffen." (Costs of a Theatre Production and Which Values Were Made With It.) *BtR.* 1997; 91(special issue): 8-14. Illus.: Photo. Graphs. Plan. B&W. Chart. 7. Lang.: Ger.

Europe. 1997. Critical studies. ■Reflections on the real costs of a theatre production including different working and repertory structures, space, personnel and contractual conditions at theatres not only in view of the pressure of present day economy but also regarding improved repertory planning and production preparation.

24   Roodhouse, Simon. "Interculturalism: The Relationship between Art and Industry." *JAML.* 1997 Fall; 27(3): 227-237. Notes. Biblio. Lang.: Eng.

Europe. 1992-1997. Historical studies. ■Relationship between artistic and industrial worlds in the last twenty years. Company sponsorship of art, results of surveys of artists and corporations discussing their perceptions of one another.

25   Kurki, Anneli. "Hello Hamlet, Lines Open to Collaboration." *FT.* 1997; 51: 2. Illus.: Photo. B&W. Lang.: Eng.

Finland. 1997. Historical studies. ■The campaign to create more theatrical performances for children, on the 125th anniversary of theatre in Finland.

26   Schlocker, Georges. "Kunst als Sozialfall." (Art as Hardship Case.) *DB.* 1997; 3: 30-32. Illus.: Photo. B&W. 2. Lang.: Ger.

France: Paris. 1997. Historical studies. ■Impressions from 110 venues in Paris and the working conditions of the artists there.

27   "Ist das Ensembletheater am Ende?" (Is Ensemble Performance at the End?) *THeute.* 1997; 10: 4-9. Illus.: Photo. B&W. 12. Lang.: Ger.

Germany. 1997. Histories-sources. ■Statements of theatre managers and dramatic advisers (Manfred Beilharz, Michael Wachsmann, Jürgen Flimm, Dieter Görne, Leander Haussmann, Ulrich Khuon, Günter Krämer, Thomas Langhoff, Dieter Sturm and Susanne Thelemann, Klaus Pierwoss, Michael Schindhelm and Friedrich Schirmer) about the meaning of ensembles.

28   Brandenburg, Detlef. "'Das Theater muss sich wichtig machen'." (Theatre Has to Be Self-Important.) *DB.* 1997; 10: 20-24. Illus.: Photo. B&W. 4. Lang.: Ger.

Germany: Bonn. 1997. Histories-sources. ■An interview with Generalintendant of opera and drama Manfred Beilharz about the future including reviews by Frieder Reininghaus of Richard Wagner's *Rheingold* directed by Siegfried Schoenbohm and by Birgit Eckes of *La Strada (The Street)* choreographed by Pavel Mikulastik.

29   Deuter, Ulrich. "Klinken putzen, Image polieren." (Going Door-to-Door to Promote One's Image.) *TZ.* 1997; 4: 50-52. Illus.: Photo. B&W. 1. Lang.: Ger.

Germany: Dusseldorf. 1997. Historical studies. ■A visit to Düsseldorfer Schauspielhaus, with emphasis on a meeting with Kurt Helbig, director of marketing.

30   Hoffmann, Hilmar. "Frankfurt ist überall." (Frankfurt Is Everywhere.) *DB.* 1997; 5: 22-25. Illus.: Photo. B&W. 3. Lang.: Ger.

Germany. 1997. Histories-sources. ■Former Kulturdezernent in Frankfurt on the problems of cultural policy relating to theatre. Includes a statement from his successor Linda Reisch.

31   Kahle, Ulrike. "Tod oder Theater, ist das hier die Frage?" (Death or Theatre, Is It the Question Here?) *THeute.* 1997; 12 : 32-38. Illus.: Photo. B&W. 5. Lang.: Ger.

Germany: Bremen. 1981-1997. Historical studies. ■A portrait of the theatre in Bremen, its history and development, about the current manager Klaus Pierwoss, its ensemble and concepts, and the threat of permanent closure.

32   Krug, Hartmut. "(K)ein Modell?" (A Model or None?) *DB.* 1997; 8: 21-23. Illus.: Photo. B&W. 4. Lang.: Ger.

Germany: Berlin. 1988-1997. Historical studies. ■A portrait of Hebbel-Theater and its program under the directorship of Nele Hertling since 1988, including a statement by Hertling about the relationship between Hebbel-Theater and free theatre scenes.

33   Lennartz, Knut. "Die Kunst, Feste zu feiern." (The Art to Celebrate.) *DB.* 1997; 9: 24-31. Illus.: Photo. B&W. 4. Lang.: Ger.

Germany: Bad Hersfeld, Weimar. 1997. Historical studies. ■Describes two theatre festivals: the traditional summer festival in Bad Hersfeld including an interview with its director Volker Lechtenbrink, and Kunstfest Weimar, including an interview with its director Bernd Kauffmann about traditions and spaces.

34   Lennartz, Knut. "Abschied von Illusionen." (Farewell to Illusions.) *DB.* 1997; 11: 10-15. Illus.: Photo. B&W. 4. Lang.: Ger.

Germany: Berlin. 1970-1997. Histories-sources. ■An interview with director Jürgen Schitthelm of Schaubühne about the present situation at his theatre on occasion of ensemble conflicts and participation in the beginning of the season.

35   Merck, Nikolaus. "Zwischenruf aus dem Parkett." (Interruption from the Stalls.) *TZ.* 1997; 2: 20-25. Illus.: Photo. B&W. 2. Lang.: Ger.

Germany. 1997. Critical studies. ■Describes the consequences of budget cuts and increasing closures of theatres on other theatres.

THEATRE IN GENERAL: —Administration

36 Merschmeier, Michael; Wille, Franz; Feuchtner, Bernd. "Landschaftsgärtner oder Totengräber?" (Landscape Gardener or Gravedigger?) *THeute.* 1997; 1: 30-34. Illus.: Photo. B&W. 4. Lang.: Ger.
Germany: Berlin. 1996-1997. Histories-sources. ■An interview with Peter Radunski, Senator for Science, Research and Culture in Berlin since spring 1996, about his own role, his support for a living culture in Berlin.

37 Kaán, Zsuzsa. "dr. Magyar Bálint művelődési és közoktatási miniszter: 'Csak úgy lehetnek klasszikus értékeink, ha újak is születnek!'." (Dr. Bálint Magyar, Minister of Culture and Education: 'Classical Values Will Be Fulfilled by Newly Emerging Values'.) *Tanc.* 1997; 28(4): 10-11. Illus.: Photo. B&W. 1. Lang.: Hun.
Hungary. 1994-1997. Histories-sources. ■The ministerial concept of direction, financial support, training and institutional background in the field of dance art from the aspect of top management.

38 Engert, Klaus. "Wo liegt Arkadien?" (Where Is Arcadia?) *DB.* 1997; 3: 24-27. Notes. Illus.: Photo. B&W. 2. Lang.: Ger.
Italy. 1867-1997. Historical studies. ■The structure of the present theatre situation in Italy with respect to the theatre crisis and the famous arenas in Verona and Taormina, stages in Venice and Milan.

39 Ginex, Giovanna, ed.; Lopez, Guido, ed.; Pallottino, Paola, ed. *Giorgio Tabet. Il fascino discreto dell'illustrazione.* (Giorgio Tabet: The Discreet Charm of Illustration.) Milan: Electa; 1997. 119 pp. Illus.: Photo. Dwg. Sketches. B&W. 184. Lang.: Ita.
Italy. 1904-1997. Histories-sources. ■Catalogue of an exhibition devoted to the work of illustrator Giorgio Tabet, including his playbills and cinema posters.

40 Trezzini, Lamberto. *Rapporto sull'economia dello spettacolo dal vivo in Italia (1980-1990).* (Report on the Economy of Live Performance in Italy, 1980-1990.) Rome: Bulzoni; 1997. 221 pp. Illus.: Graphs. Diagram. Lang.: Ita.
Italy. 1980-1990. Historical studies. ■The relationship between public funding and the theatres, opera companies, etc., that receive it.

41 Ruf, Wolfgang. "... Europe ist das Vorbild." (Europe Is the Idol.) *DB.* 1997; 4: 39-43. Illus.: Photo. B&W. 7. Lang.: Ger.
Mexico. 1996-1997. Historical studies. ■Reviews the contemporary situation of theatre in Mexico, with attention to cultural politics, dwindling finances, and audience and performances from the traditional to the pseudo-avantgarde. Also considers the relationship between Germany and Mexico.

42 Maanen, Hans van. *Het Nederlandse Toneelbestel van 1945 tot 1995.* (Dutch Theatre Policy, 1945-1995.) Amsterdam: Amsterdam UP; 1997. 422 pp. Pref. Notes. Biblio. Gloss. Index. Tables. Illus.: Diagram. Graphs. Lang.: Dut.
Netherlands. 1945-1995. Histories-specific. ■Fifty years of Dutch cultural policy as it relates to theatre: funding and criteria, evaluation of the structure.

43 Rueschemeyer, Marilyn Shattner. "Art, Artists' Associations, and the State in Norway." *JAML.* 1997 Fall; 27(3): 187-204. Notes. Tables. Lang.: Eng.
Norway. 1960-1997. Critical studies. ■Public support for the arts in Norway, with special focus on painting and sculpture. Historical development of cultural policy, role of artists' associations, recent development in relationships between artists' associations and government.

44 Ciesileska, Magdalena. "Artists Talk about Themselves." *TP.* 1997; 39(1): 29-38. Illus.: Photo. Poster. Color. B&W. 13. Lang.: Eng, Fre.
Poland. 1931-1997. Histories-sources. ■Interviews with theatrical poster artists Waldemar Świerzy, Franciszek Starowieyski, Andrzej Pągowski, Wiesław Wałkuski on their techniques, influences, symbolism.

45 Drewniak, Bogusław. "Organizacja niemieckiego życia teatralnego na obszarach okupowanej Polski w latach II-ej wojny światowej." (The Organization of German Theatre in Occupied Poland During World War II.) *PaT.* 1997; 46(1-4): 460-503. Notes. Illus.: Poster. B&W. 5. Lang.: Pol.
Poland. 1939-1944. Historical studies. ■Includes discussion on the repertory of German theatre groups, directors and actors, audience reactions, excerpts from reviews.

46 Got, Jerzy. "Pięć teatrów Stanisława Skarbka." (Five Theatres of Stanisław Skarbek.) 26-33 in Kuchtówna, Lidia, ed. *Teatr polski we Lwowie.* Studia i materiały do dziejów teatru polskiego. t. XXV (37). Warsaw: Instytut Sztuki Polskiej Akademii Nauk; 1997. 293 pp. Lang.: Pol.
Poland: Lvov. 1818-1842. Historical studies. ■Stanisław Skarbek's efforts to obtain Austrian authorities' permission to build theatres in Lvov.

47 Jarecka, Dorota. "Symbol vs. Description." *TP.* 1997; 39(1): 16-18. Illus.: Photo. Poster. B&W. 10. Lang.: Eng, Fre.
Poland. 1949-1997. Historical studies. ■Polish theatre poster art after 1945. Styles, artistic schools, focus on the poster art of Henryk Tomaszewski.

48 Kłossowicz, Jan. "Showcasing the Theatre." *TP.* 1997; 39(1): 41-43. Illus.: Poster. B&W. 2. Lang.: Eng, Fre.
Poland. 1960-1997. Histories-sources. ■Author's personal experience in attempting to present the theatre in exhibitions. Visual attractiveness, documentary values, use of photographs, video and film.

49 Michalik, Jan. *Dzieje teatru w Krakowie w latach 1865-1893. Przedsiębiorstwa teatralne.* (History of Theatre in Cracow, 1865-1893: Theatre Enterprises.) Cracow: Wydawnictwo Literackie; 1996. 490 pp. Pref. Index. Illus.: Design. Photo. Poster. B&W. 32. Lang.: Pol.
Poland: Cracow. 1865-1893. Histories-specific. ■Activity of theatre enterpreneurs in the late nineteenth century, with attention to legal aspects and principles of organization of theatres, subsidization, and working conditions. Reference to work of Adam Skorupka, Stanisław Koźmian, Józef Rychter, and Jakub Glikson.

50 Martinsson, Maria. "Kulturraseriet kämpar för barnkulturen." (The Culture Rage Fights For Children's Culture.) *Tningen.* 1997; 21(5): 39-40. Illus.: Photo. B&W. Lang.: Swe.
Sweden: Gothenburg. 1997. Historical studies. ■Protests by Teater Uno and Backa Teatern against funding cuts for theatre performances for schoolchildren. Includes interviews with Kerste Broberg and Lena Fridell.

51 Müller, Peter. "Die grosse Wut der Direktorin." (The Director's Great Rage.) *TZ.* 1997; 6: 4-6. Illus.: Photo. B&W. 1. Lang.: Ger.
Switzerland. 1917-1997. Historical studies. ■A historical review of the relationship between money and theatre in Switzerland.

52 Benecke, Patricia. "Survival of the Fittest." *THeute.* 1997; 4: 28-31. Illus.: Photo. B&W. 7. Lang.: Ger.
UK-England: London. 1948-1997. Critical studies. ■Reviews the development of 'fringe' theatre, the current situation of these sixty-one houses that get no financial support and their influences on mainstream theatre.

53 Forbes, Derek. "Colour and Decoration on Nineteenth-Century Playbills." *TN.* 1997; 51(1): 26-41. Notes. Illus.: Handbill. Poster. B&W. 9. Lang.: Eng.
UK-England. 1804-1850. Historical studies. ■Explores the design of playbills and how they functioned as both poster and program. Topics discussed include colored inks, expanded text, colored paper, emblems, dingbats, and framing.

54 Moore, Dick. "Equity, British AEA, Producers Discuss Exchange Program at London Meetings." *EN.* 1997 Oct.; 82(8): 1. Lang.: Eng.
UK-England: London. USA. 1997. Historical studies. ■Leaders of British and American Equity and producers from both countries discuss the actor exchange program, in effect since 1981.

55 Auslander, Philip. "Legally Live: Performance in/of the Law." *TDR.* 1997 Sum; 41(2): 9-29. Notes. Biblio. Lang.: Eng.
USA. 1975-1997. Historical studies. ■Performance in relation to American law with focus on copyright and what the rules of evidence reveal about legal proceedings as performance.

THEATRE IN GENERAL: —Administration

56   Baird, John A., Jr. "The Three R's of Fund Raising." *FundM*. 1997 Mar.; 28(1): 14-17. Lang.: Eng.
USA. 1997. Critical studies. ■The importance of research, reach, and reward in meeting fundraising goals.

57   Bogan, Neill. "Vetoed School Play Won't Disappear." *AmTh*. 1997 Oct.; 14(8): 78-79. Illus.: Photo. B&W. 1. Lang.: Eng.
USA: Ridgewood, NJ. 1997. Historical studies. ■School officials' censorship of *Labor Play*, developed by fourth graders and their teacher Maria Sweeney, and its eventual production on Broadway directed by Scott Ellis. Play focuses on child labor in third world countries, and exploitation of child labor by American companies such as Nike.

58   Cargo, Russell A. "Changing Fiduciary Responsibilities for Nonprofit Boards." *JAML*. 1997 Sum; 27(2): 123-138. Notes. Lang.: Eng.
USA. 1997. Historical studies. ■How corporation law limits fiduciary responsibility for members of nonprofit boards of directors and creates dilemmas within the nonprofit sector.

59   Chach, Maryann; Magliozzi, Ron; McNamara, Brooks, ed.; Swartz, Mark, ed. "An Industry Unto Himself: An Interview with George Fenmore, Part II." *PasShow*. 1997 Spr/Sum; 20(1): 2-18. Lang.: Eng.
USA: New York, NY. 1961-1997. Histories-sources. ■Interview with long-time Broadway product-placement maven George Fenmore that covers his career from the early sixties to the present.

60   Chach, Maryann; Fletcher, Reagan; Kueppers, Brigitte; McNamara, Brooks; Schoenfeld, Gerald; Swartz, Mark. "Editor's Note." *PasShow*. 1997 Fall/Win, 1998 Spr/Sum; 20/21(1/2): 2-12. Lang.: Eng.
USA: New York, NY. 1977-1997. Histories-sources. ■Personal reminiscences of individuals instrumental to the Shubert Archive's formation and success on the occasion of the Archive's and *The Passing Show*'s twentieth anniversary. Goals for the Archive, location of space, obtaining archival material, organization and planning.

61   Dattuso, Greg. "Investing for the Small Non-Profit." *FundM*. 1997 Feb.; 27(12): 30-31. Illus.: Photo. B&W. 1. Lang.: Eng.
USA. 1997. Critical studies. ■Investment advice for the small non-profit organization on how to optimize its capital for future use.

62   De Shields, André. "Equity Celebrates African American Heritage Month 1997." *EN*. 1997 May; 82(4): 4-5, 8. Illus.: Photo. 31. Lang.: Eng.
USA. 1997. Historical studies. ■Historical look at Black entertainers and contributions to American entertainment.

63   Dowell, Teresa Annette. *The African American Theatre Producer as the African American 'Griot'*. Long Beach, CA: California State Univ; 1997. 87 pp. Notes. Biblio. [M.F.A. Dissertation, Univ. Microfilms Order No. AAC 1387676.] Lang.: Eng.
USA. 1996. Histories-sources. ■Account of an African-American producer's presentation of Dowell's *Paper or Plastic: A Homeless Round Up*, performed by Prymari Colors Theatre Company and presented at the California Repertory Theatre at California State University.

64   Gaupp, Andrew Christopher. "Founder's Syndrome: The New Theatre's Dilemma." *TD&T*. 1997 Spr; 33(2): 48-55. Notes. Lang.: Eng.
USA. 1997. Critical studies. ■A discussion of the pitfalls facing the founders of new theatres once success has been achieved: common problems and strategies to avoid the obstacles to furthering a founder's vision for a company.

65   Goodale, Toni K. "Changes In Giving and Volunteering." *FundM*. 1997 Feb.; 27(12): 28-29. Lang.: Eng.
USA. 1990-1997. Historical studies. ■Monitors both the good and bad changes that have taken place in the fundraising field during the nineties.

66   Graham, Paul Stuart. *Finding the Big Gift—Now! A Case Study of an Advisory Board's Fundraising Campaign to Name a New Theatre Building: The Allan Tebbetts Theatre*. Long Beach, CA: California State Univ; 1997. 53 pp. Notes. Biblio. [M.A. Thesis, Univ. Microfilms Order No. AAC 1385567.] Lang.: Eng.

USA: Long Beach, CA. 1996-1997. Historical studies. ■California Repertory Theatre's advisory board's search for a major donor after whom the building was to be named.

67   Greengrass, Andrew. "Take My Joke ... Please! *Foxworthy v. Custom Tees* and the Prospects for Ownership of Comedy." *ColJL&A*. 1997 Spr/Sum; 21(3/4): 273-288. Notes. Lang.: Eng.
USA. 1995. Critical studies. ■Protection of comedic intellectual property in the US, focusing on *Foxworthy v. Custom Tees, Inc*, a case involving comedian Jeff Foxworthy.

68   Hulbert, Dan. "Lisa Mount." *AmTh*. 1997 Feb.; 14(2): 44-45. Illus.: Photo. B&W. 1. Lang.: Eng.
USA: Atlanta, GA. 1989-1997. Biographical studies. ■Managing director of 7 Stages theatre and her fundraising efforts that revitalized the company.

69   Jensen, Sharon. "Non-Traditional Casting Project Continues to Seek Solutions to Problems of Exclusion in the Entertainment Industry." *EN*. 1997 Mar.; 82(2): 2. Lang.: Eng.
USA. 1997. Historical studies. ■Report on latest activities of Equity's Non-Traditional Casting Project, identifying the problem, outlining possible solutions, current work, and future possibilities.

70   Karas, Sandra. "1996 Tax Law Changes May Affect You." *EN*. 1997 Jan/Feb.; 82(1): 1-2. Lang.: Eng.
USA. 1997. Historical studies. ■New tax rules for 1997 and how they will affect actors and others in the entertainment industry.

71   Karas, Sandra. "A Performer's Tax Program." *EN*. 1997 Mar.; 82(2): 1. Lang.: Eng.
USA. 1997. Historical studies. ■On putting together an appropriate tax program for theatre personnel.

72   Karas, Sandra. "So, You're Audited ... What's the Dif?" *EN*. 1997 Apr.; 82(3): 1. Lang.: Eng.
USA. 1997. Historical studies. ■How to deal with audits and the IRS: a guide for actors.

73   Kelly, Colleen. "John Corker: Balancing Art and Business in *Rent*." *SoTh*. 1997 Sum; 38(3): 18-19. Illus.: Photo. B&W. 1. Lang.: Eng.
USA: New York, NY. 1997. Historical studies. ■Career of John Corker, a Broadway general manager (currently of *Rent*): his career advancement, the duties of a general manager, and his views on the significance of *Rent*.

74   Kimbis, Thomas Peter. "Surviving the Storm: How the National Endowment for the Arts Restructured Itself to Serve a New Constituency." *JAML*. 1997 Sum; 27(2): 139-158. Notes. Tables. Lang.: Eng.
USA: Washington, DC. 1996-1997. Historical studies. ■Restructuring of the NEA shows how a federal agency can shift constituencies to compensate for a shortage in financial and political support.

75   La Varco, Valerie. "'The Show Must Go On' Psychosis or Things You Should Know About Workers' Compensation and Salary Continuance." *EN*. 1997 Nov.; 82(9): 1. Lang.: Eng.
USA. 1997. Instructional materials. ■Equity representative in charge of Workers' Compensation outlines the application process.

76   Lazio, Rick. "The Power of Consensus." *AmTh*. 1997 Apr.; 14(4): 15. Illus.: Photo. B&W. 1. Lang.: Eng.
USA: Washington, DC. 1996. Histories-sources. ■Letter by Congressional Representative, co-signed by other Republican house members, to House Speaker Newt Gingrich asking for continued support for the National Endowment for the Arts.

77   Leichtman, David. "Unemployment Insurance for Artists: Prats, Pitfalls and Solutions for Artists and Arts Organizations." *ColJL&A*. 1997 Win; 21(2): 129-141. Notes. Lang.: Eng.
USA. 1997. Critical studies. ■Examines the availability of unemployment insurance for artists, an area of law in which arts organizations, particularly non-profits, also have a stake.

78   Lewis, Herschell Gordon. "Direct Mail Fund Raising Techniques." *FundM*. 1997 July; 28(5): 17-19. Lang.: Eng.

THEATRE IN GENERAL: —Administration

USA. 1997. Critical studies. ▪Pros and cons of direct-mail fundraising and the most effective techniques.

79 McCord, Keryl E. "The Challenge of Change." *AfAmR.* 1997 Win; 31(4): 601-609. Biblio. Lang.: Eng.

USA. 1997. Critical studies. ▪Response to playwright August Wilson and critic/director Robert Brustein's debate on the state of Black theatre in the US, with an emphasis on innovative Black approaches to setting up theatre companies and discarding outmoded white models.

80 Miller, Barbara. "Creative Brainstorming with Your Board." *FundM.* 1997 Jan.; 27(11): 18-20. Lang.: Eng.

USA. 1997. Critical studies. ▪Importance of brainstorming sessions to the motivational vitality and fundraising creativity of non-profit boards of directors.

81 Moore, Dick. "New Three-Year TYA Contract Improves Salaries, Working Conditions." *EN.* 1997 Jan/Feb.; 82(1): 1. Lang.: Eng.

USA. 1997. Historical studies. ▪Equity negotiates for a new Theatre for Young Audiences (TYA) contract.

82 Moore, Dick. "1998 National Council Election Gets Underway: 16 Seats Are Open." *EN.* 1997 Dec.; 82(10): 1-2. Lang.: Eng.

USA. 1997. Historical studies. ▪Information on Equity national and regional elections.

83 Moore, Dick. "Organizing the Non-Union Tours: Arguments for and Against." *EN.* 1997 Dec.; 82(10): 1-2. Lang.: Eng.

USA. 1997. Historical studies. ▪Debate on Equity's involvement with non-union touring companies.

84 Moore, Dick. "Optical Plan Added to Health Benefits." *EN.* 1997 Oct.; 82(8): 1. Lang.: Eng.

USA. 1997. Historical studies. ▪Comprehensive vision care benefits become available to Equity members covered by the health plan.

85 Moore, Dick. *Nothing Like a Dame II* Coming to NY February 24, 1997 at the Marquis Theatre." *EN.* 1997 Jan/Feb.; 82(1) : 1. Lang.: Eng.

USA: New York, NY. 1997. Historical studies. ▪Preview of benefit in support of the Equity-sponsored Phyllis Newman Women's Health Initiative, which is committed to the good health of women in the entertainment industry, to be held at the Marquis Theatre.

86 Moore, Dick. "Equity's Bonding Policy and How It Works." *EN.* 1997 Jan/Feb.; 82(1): 2. Lang.: Eng.

USA. 1997. Historical studies. ▪Explanation of changes in Equity's bonding policy.

87 Moore, Dick. "A Walk Down 42nd Street Shows Activity and Change." *EN.* 1997 Jan/Feb.; 82(1): 3. Illus.: Maps. 1. Lang.: Eng.

USA: New York, NY. 1997. Historical studies. ▪Overview and progress report on changes in the theatre district made by the 42nd Street Development Land Use Improvement Project, the largest development project ever undertaken by the City and State of New York.

88 Moore, Dick. "Tenth Annual BC/EFA Holiday Appeal Raises $1,488,000." *EN.* 1997 Jan/Feb.; 82(1): 4-5. Illus.: Photo. 8. Lang.: Eng.

USA. 1996. Historical studies. ▪Tenth annual benefit fundraiser for Broadway Cares/Equity Fights AIDS. Events held simultaneously all over the country.

89 Moore, Dick. "John Holly Appointed Western Regional Director." *EN.* 1997 Mar.; 82(2): 1. Illus.: Photo. 1. Lang.: Eng.

USA: Los Angeles, CA. 1997. Historical studies. ▪On the appointment of John Holly as Equity's Western Regional Director.

90 Moore, Dick. "Guest Artist Agreement Adds Tiers to Become More User-Friendly." *EN.* 1997 May; 82(4): 2. Lang.: Eng.

USA. 1997. Historical studies. ▪Equity's creation of a tiered structure in its new guest artist contract.

91 Moore, Dick. "New Study Confirms that Unemployment Continues to Plague the Arts." *EN.* 1997 Mar.; 82(2): 1. Lang.: Eng.

USA. 1997. Historical studies. ▪On the recent study *Employment and Earnings of Performing Artists, 1970-1990*, prepared for the National Endowment for the Arts. Study shows that unemployment for theatre artists is still far higher than the national average.

92 Moore, Dick. "Equity, Livent Reach Agreement." *EN.* 1997 Apr.; 82(3): 1-2. Lang.: Eng.

USA. 1997. Historical studies. ▪Final contract negotiation approved between Actors' Equity and Live Entertainment (Livent), Broadway producer. Benefits to actors.

93 Moore, Dick. "Membership Meetings in All Regions Kick Off New Season." *EN.* 1997 Sep.; 82(7): 1. Lang.: Eng.

USA. 1997. Historical studies. ▪Announcements for regional meetings of Actors' Equity Association: Eastern, Central and Western.

94 Moore, Dick. "Labor Board to Rule on Proposed Changes in Equity's Audition System." *EN.* 1997 Apr.; 82(3): 1. Lang.: Eng.

USA. 1997. Historical studies. ▪The National Labor Relations Board's proposal to modify settlement agreements covering the audition provisions of Equity's collective bargaining agreements.

95 Moore, Dick. "Actors' Work Program Joins the Actors' Fund." *EN.* 1997 Apr.; 82(3): 2. Lang.: Eng.

USA. 1997. Historical studies. ▪The Actors' Work Program, the non-profit career counseling and job training center for entertainment industry professionals, unites with the Actors' Fund.

96 Moore, Dick. "1997 Candidates Submit Statements." *EN.* 1997 Apr.; 82(3): 3-7. Lang.: Eng.

USA. 1997. Historical studies. ▪Candidates for local and national Equity elections submit their statements for consideration by members.

97 Moore, Dick. "NY State Senate Takes Aim at NYC's Cultural Community and Economy." *EN.* 1997 May; 82(4): 1. Lang.: Eng.

USA. 1997. Historical studies. ▪On the 1997 rent negotiations in New York City. Author examines the huge impact of housing changes on actors and other theatre personnel.

98 Moore, Dick. "Open Letter to Equity Members from NYC Council Member Tom Duane." *EN.* 1997 May; 82(4): 1. Lang.: Eng.

USA. 1997. Historical studies. ▪Transcript of a letter from City Councilman Tom Duane to members of the theatrical community on his support for affordable housing initiatives in New York City.

99 Moore, Dick. "Boys Choir of Harlem and Its Founder Receive Annual Rosetta LeNoire Award." *EN.* 1997 May; 82(4): 2. Illus.: Photo. 1. Lang.: Eng.

USA. 1997. Historical studies. ▪Dr. Walter J. Turnbull and the Boys Choir of Harlem receive Equity's 1997 Rosetta LeNoire Award honoring outstanding achievements in non-traditional or affirmative casting.

100 Moore, Dick. "New Category Created in CORST Agreement." *EN.* 1997 May; 82(4): 2. Lang.: Eng.

USA. 1997. Historical studies. ▪Equity creates a new company category in the recently negotiated Council of Resident Stock Theatres agreement to give special consideration to theatres with a potential gross below $35,000.

101 Moore, Dick. "Labor Board Approves Equity-Only Auditions." *EN.* 1997 June; 82(5): 1, 7. Lang.: Eng.

USA. 1997. Historical studies. ▪The National Labor Relations Board approves Equity-only auditions in a landmark decision.

102 Moore, Dick. "Salaries, Safety, Stage Managers Addressed in New Outdoor Drama Pact." *EN.* 1997 May; 82(4): 6. Lang.: Eng.

USA. 1997. Historical studies. ▪On Equity's negotiations with Outdoor Drama producers resulting in a new three-year agreement featuring improvements in many areas.

103 Moore, Dick. "Council Holds First Plenary." *EN.* 1997 June; 82(5): 1. Illus.: Photo. 1. Lang.: Eng.

USA. 1997. Historical studies. ▪Account of the first Council Plenary held by Actors' Equity, attended by over one hundred councillors, officers, and regional staff members.

104 Moore, Dick. "House Votes to Kill NEA Funding." *EN.* 1997 July/Aug.; 82(6): 1. Lang.: Eng.

THEATRE IN GENERAL: —Administration

USA. 1997. Historical studies. ■Account of the US House of Representatives's vote to kill funding for the National Endowment for the Arts. Equity had campaigned hard for funding to be restored.

105 Moore, Dick. "Actors' Fund Breaks Ground on Low Cost Housing for Persons with HIV/AIDS in West Hollywood." *EN.* 1997 July/Aug.; 82(6): 8. Lang.: Eng.

USA: Hollywood, CA. 1997. Historical studies. ■The Actors' Fund of America, the West Hollywood Community Housing Corporation, and Housing for Entertainment Professionals, break ground on a low-cost housing facility to be built entirely for persons with HIV/AIDS.

106 Moore, Dick. "Showdown Near on Arts Foundation." *EN.* 1997 Sep.; 82(7): 1. Lang.: Eng.

USA. 1997. Historical studies. ■New developments in Equity's fight to restore and maintain the National Endowment for the Arts.

107 Moore, Dick. "Los Angeles Office Moving to Museum Square." *EN.* 1997 Sep.; 82(7): 1. Lang.: Eng.

USA: Los Angeles, CA. 1997. Historical studies. ■New California location for Actors' Equity.

108 Moore, Dick. "AFTRA Convention Okays Referendum on Merger with SAG." *EN.* 1997 Sep.; 82(7): 1. Lang.: Eng.

USA. 1997. Historical studies. ■Delegates to the Convention of the American Federation of Television and Radio Artists endorse the plan for merger with the Screen Actors Guild. Only remaining obstacles are pension fund administration and funding.

109 Moore, Dick. "Non-Traditional Casting Project Fields Growing Number of Requests for Assistance, Artist Files." *EN.* 1997 Oct.; 82(8): 3. Lang.: Eng.

USA. 1997. Historical studies. ■Increased requests for the Artist Files of Equity's Non-Traditional Casting Project.

110 Moore, Dick. "Broadway Flea Market, Grand Auction Bring In More than $425,000 for BC/EFA." *EN.* 1997 Oct.; 82(8): 7. Illus.: Photo. 2. Lang.: Eng.

USA: New York, NY. 1997. Historical studies. ■The 11th Annual Broadway Flea Market raises over $425,000 from over sixty Broadway and Off Broadway shows, theatrical guilds and unions, as well as more than seventy of the theatre and daytime television's biggest stars. Money raised is given to Broadway Cares/Equity Fights AIDS.

111 Moore, Dick. "NYC Tax Abatement Helps Theatre." *EN.* 1997 Nov.; 82(9): 1. Illus.: Photo. 1. Lang.: Eng.

USA: New York, NY. 1997. Historical studies. ■A new New York State law exempting commercial theatrical productions from paying New York City's 4.2 percent share of sales tax on the construction and upkeep of sets and costumes.

112 Moore, Dick. "President Silver Renews Request to Include AEA in Merger Talks." *EN.* 1997 Nov.; 82(9): 1. Illus.: Photo. 1. Lang.: Eng.

USA. 1997. Historical studies. ■Equity President Ron Silver calls for Equity to be included in talks between AFTRA and SAG on merger.

113 Moore, Dick. "Broadway Initiatives Working Group Adopts By-Laws, Establishes New Labor/Management Organization." *EN.* 1997 July/Aug.; 82(6): 3. Lang.: Eng.

USA. 1997. Historical studies. ■The Broadway Initiatives Working Group agrees to establish a new not-for-profit public benefit corporation for the betterment of New York theatre.

114 Nunns, Stephen. "NEA Grants, Round One." *AmTh.* 1997 Feb.; 14(2): 52. Illus.: Sketches. B&W. 1. Lang.: Eng.

USA: Washington, DC. 1997. Historical studies. ■Announcement of first round of grants by the National Endowment for the Arts after enduring a forty percent budget cut by Congress. List of award winners and amounts.

115 Nunns, Stephen. "The Force Is With Her." *AmTh.* 1997 Apr.; 14(4): 20-23, 52-53. Illus.: Photo. B&W. 1. Lang.: Eng.

USA: Washington, DC. 1989-1996. Historical studies. ■Profile of arts advocate Lee Kessler, executive director of the American Arts Alliance, and her efforts to gain support for the National Endowment for the Arts in Congress. History of controversy between Congress and the NEA.

116 Nunns, Stephen. "The News Vs. the Muse." *AmTh.* 1997 Dec.; 14(10): 24-25. Illus.: Sketches. B&W. 1. Lang.: Eng.

USA: Washington, DC. 1997. Historical studies. ■Media representation of the National Endowment for the Arts' paper 'American Canvas', written by Gary O. Larson, which reported on the agency's wealth and future.

117 Pace, Guy. "1996-97 Banner Year Sets All-Time Employment Record." *EN.* 1997 Dec.; 82(10): 3-8. Illus.: Graphs. CH. Diagram. 6. Lang.: Eng.

USA. 1997. Historical studies. ■Actors' Equity's 1997 Annual Report on employment in the entertainment industry.

118 Reis, George R. "The 1998 Non-Profit Software Directory." *FundM.* 1997 Oct.; 28(8): 6-16. Lang.: Eng.

USA. 1997. ■Directory of available software for non-profit organizations.

119 Reiss, Alvin H. "Smaller Arts Groups Remain Committed Despite Growing Economic Difficulties." *FundM.* 1997 Feb.; 27(12): 34-35. Illus.: Photo. B&W. 1. Lang.: Eng.

USA. 1997. Critical studies. ■Successful fundraising strategies of small theatre groups and arts alliances in an era of decreased government funding and private patronage.

120 Reiss, Alvin H. "Are You Having Any Funds?" *FundM.* 1997 Apr.; 28(2): 31. Lang.: Eng.

USA: New York, NY. 1997. Critical studies. ■Humorous excerpts from Reiss's otherwise sober treatise *Cash In! Funding and Promoting the Arts!*.

121 Reiss, Alvin H. "Technical Aid Helps Smaller Arts Groups Develop Funding and Marketing Skills." *FundM.* 1997 Dec.; 28 (10): 34-36. Lang.: Eng.

USA. 1997. Critical studies. ■The use of volunteers to help small organizations develop funding and marketing strategies.

122 Reiss, Alvin H. "Arts Need National Marketing Plan to Engender Interest and Support." *FundM.* 1997 Aug.; 28(6): 32. Lang.: Eng.

USA. 1997. Critical studies. ■Stresses the need for a cohesive marketing plan by arts organizations on a national scale, in order to generate interest from government and personal sources of funding for their needs.

123 Samuels, Steven. "Courage & Conviction." *AmTh.* 1997 Apr.; 14(4): 16-19. Illus.: Photo. B&W. 1. Lang.: Eng.

USA. 1965-1996. Historical studies. ■History of not-for-profit theatre and government subsidy in the US. Founding of the National Endowment for the Arts, how regional theatres benefited and the need for the NEA today.

124 Shank, Theodore. "Scott Kellman." *MimeJ.* 1991/92; 15: 74-92. Illus.: Photo. B&W. 9. Lang.: Eng.

USA: Los Angeles, CA. 1982-1991. Histories-sources. ■Interview with producer/performer Kellman regarding his influences and willingness to take chances as a producer.

125 Swarbrick, Carol. "How an Equity Regional Director Is Selected." *EN.* 1997 July/Aug.; 82(6): 4. Lang.: Eng.

USA. 1997. Historical studies. ■An Equity regional Vice President describes the process of selection for regional officers.

126 Thompson, Joe Bill. *A Marketing Model for the Texas Tech University Department of Theatre and Dance Graduate Program: A Professional Problem.* Lubbock, TX: Texas Tech Univ; 1997. 182 pp. [Ph.D. Dissertation, Univ. Microfilms Order No. AAC 9718500.] Lang.: Eng.

USA: Lubbock, TX. 1994-1996. Empirical research. ■Argues that a marketing methodology can assist performing arts programs in analyzing and evaluating their student recruitment program and can identify the performing arts program's market position, potential target market, competition, students' wants and needs, and graduate students' perceptions of the program.

127 Vimuktamon, Atisaya. "Non-Profits and the Internet." *FundM.* 1997 Oct.; 28(8): 25-28. Illus.: Photo. Dwg. Color. B&W. 3. Lang.: Eng.

USA. 1997. Critical studies. ■The crucial importance of the internet for not-for-profit organizations.

128 Viola, Tom. "Easter Bonnet Competition Raises $1,474, 272." *EN.* 1997 May; 82(4): 3. Illus.: Photo. 6. Lang.: Eng.

THEATRE IN GENERAL: —Administration

USA. 1997. Historical studies. ■The 11th Annual Easter Bonnet Competition, the two-day Broadway spectacular featuring singing, dancing and hats, raised $1,474,272 and involved fifty-three participating Broadway, Off Broadway and national touring companies. Money is given to Broadway Cares/Equity Fights AIDS.

129 White, George C.; Duncan, Louise L. "The Art for Art's Sake." *JAML.* 1997 Sum; 27(2): 119-122. Lang.: Eng.
USA. 1978-1997. Historical studies. ■Changes in copyright laws that protected the rights of authors and their heirs after 1978, and differences in how the rules apply to corporate owners.

130 Winick, Raphael. "Intellectual Property, Defamation and the Digital Alteration of Visual Images." *ColJL&A.* 1997 Win; 21 (2): 143-196. Notes. Lang.: Eng.
USA. 1997. Critical studies. ■Examines whether current state of the law sufficiently protects persons depicted in altered images, and whether the law must develop new doctrines to ensure that the public receives accurate information from the media.

131 Witham, Barry B. "Censorship in the Federal Theatre." *THSt.* 1997; 17: 3-14. Illus.: Photo. 1. Lang.: Eng.
USA. 1935-1936. Historical studies. ■The operation of censorship in the Federal Theatre Project. Author focuses on two specific areas of conflict—the administrative structure of the arts projects and the attempted influence of the Legion of Decency, a watchdog arm of the Catholic Church.

Audience

132 Hadamczik, Dieter. "Das Musical boomt, die Klassik bleibt." (The Musical Booms, the Classic Flops.) *DB.* 1997; 4: 35-38. Illus.: Photo. Graphs. B&W. 10. Lang.: Ger.
Austria. Germany. Switzerland. 1995-1996. Empirical research. ■Analyzes statistical trends of the German speaking theatre based on the publication of 'Werkstatistik' (statistics of performances) 1995/96 by Deutscher Bühnenverein. Discusses the difference between offered plays and genres and the preferences of the audience.

133 Cook, Ann Jennalie. "Audiences: Investigation, Interpretation, Invention." 305-320 in Cox, John D., ed.; Kastan, David Scott, ed. *A New History of Early English Drama.* New York, NY: Columbia UP; 1997. 565 pp. Index. Notes. Biblio. Lang.: Eng.
England. 1500-1642. Historical studies. ■Examines the audiences of early English theatre. Argues for an infinite variety of audience configurations.

134 Fouquet, Ludovic. "Lettre de France de Ludovic Fouquet." (Letter from France from Ludovic Fouquet.) *JCT.* 1997; 85: 141-145. Illus.: Photo. B&W. 2. Lang.: Fre.
France: Paris. 1997. Historical studies. ■Spectator's impressions of productions of various disciplines at Festival d'Automne.

135 Giacché, Piergiorgio. "Consumare teatro." (Consuming Theatre.) *TeatroS.* 1997; 12(19): 349-369. Notes. Lang.: Ita.
Italy. 1997. Critical studies. ■Shifts and uncertainties in the role of spectator/consumer in contemporary theatre.

136 Axer, Erwin. "Theatre and Its Audience." *TP.* 1997; 39(2): 12-13. Illus.: Photo. B&W. 1. Lang.: Eng, Fre.
Poland. 1949-1989. Historical studies. ■Audience development for the theatre in Poland before and after World War II.

137 Pelias, Ronald J. "A Theatre Week in New York City." *JDTC.* 1997 Spr; 11(2): 141-146. Lang.: Eng.
USA: New York, NY. 1995-1996. Critical studies. ■Author recounts a week spent in New York City viewing theatre. Using a theoretical framework, he analyzes audience reception of the events he attended.

Design/technology

138 Pannell, Sylvia J. Hillyard. "The Vision of Design and Technology in the Next Century." *TD&T.* 1997 Sum; 33(3): 17-20. Biblio. Illus.: Photo. B&W. 5. Lang.: Eng.
1997. Historical studies. ■Addresses given by set designer Michael Levine, set/light designer Claude-André Roy, lighting designer Jennifer Tipton, film and theatre director Laurie-Shawn Borzovoy and actor/director Robert Lepage on theatre's role after the millennium during the opening of the OISTAT tenth World Congress.

139 Brophy, Charles P. "Light, Sound, Computers." *LDim.* 1997 Jan/Feb.; 21(1): 68-72. Illus.: Photo. Color. 3. Lang.: Eng.
Australia. 1997. Technical studies. ■LSC Electronics and their development of lighting desks, dimmers and DMX distribution equipment. History of company, facilities.

140 Brophy, Charles P. "Jands' Grand Tour." *LDim.* 1997 Apr.; 21(3): 90-93. Illus.: Photo. Color. 2. Lang.: Eng.
Australia. 1973-1997. Technical studies. ■History, current projects and products of Jands Electronics lighting company.

141 Kull, Gustaf. "OISTAT's utbildningsmöte i Varna." (The Conference of Training of OISTAT at Varna.) *ProScen.* 1997; 21(3): 64-65. Illus.: Photo. B&W. Lang.: Swe.
Bulgaria: Varna. 1997. Historical studies. ■A report from the meeting with reference to the theatre festival of Varna and the plans for the future.

142 Binnie, Eric. "Theatrical Design." 366-392 in Plant, Richard, ed.; Saddlemyer, Ann, ed. *Later Stages: Essays in Ontario Theatre from the First World War to the 1970s.* Toronto, ON: Univ of Toronto P; 1997. 496 pp. (The Ontario Historical Studies Series.) Index. Notes. Biblio. Illus.: Photo. 16. Lang.: Eng.
Canada. 1914-1979. Historical studies. ■On the evolution and development of theatre design (sets, costumes, lighting) in Ontario theatre.

143 Chesney, William. "Design By Example: Teaching Design and Production As Part Of A Liberal Arts Education." *CTR.* 1997 Sum; 91: 9-12. Illus.: Photo. B&W. 2. Lang.: Eng.
Canada: Waterloo, ON. 1997. Histories-sources. ■The author's approach to teaching in an institution with limited course offerings.

144 Clunes, Amaya; Fournier, Alain; Guzman, Patricio, photo.; Guzman, Rosaura, photo.; Whiteley, David, transl. "Spaces of Scenography." *CTR.* 1997 Sum; 91: 25-31. Illus.: Photo. B&W. 10. Lang.: Eng.
Canada: Montreal, PQ. 1997. Histories-sources. ■Photo essay representing exposition of scenography at Salle Beverly Webster Rolph, Musée d'art contemporain de Montréal, January 23 to March 2, 1997, curator: Mario Bouchard.

145 Eagan, Michael. "Defining a National Scenographic Style at the National Theatre School of Canada." *CTR.* 1997 Sum; 91: 22-24. Illus.: Photo. B&W. 1. Lang.: Eng.
Canada: Montreal, PQ. 1997. Histories-sources. ■Head of Scenography Program at National Theatre School of Canada reflects on stylistic impact of bicultural nature of his program.

146 Fedoruk, Ronald. "The Cosmopolitan Classroom." *CTR.* 1997 Sum; 91: 5-8. Notes. Illus.: Photo. B&W. 3. Lang.: Eng.
Canada: Vancouver, BC. 1997. Critical studies. ■The effects of cross-cultural influences on classroom teaching of design at University of British Columbia, Vancouver.

147 Gardiner, Robert. "Design Training at UBC: Snapshots and Notes." *CTR.* 1997 Sum; 91: 41-46. Illus.: Photo. B&W. 8. Lang.: Eng.
Canada: Vancouver, BC. 1986-1997. Historical studies. ■Looks at the past ten years of University of British Columbia's MFA Design program, and speculates about the future.

148 Hume, Charles. "The Apprenticeship Program of Associated Designers of Canada: Charles Hume in Conversation with Bill Corcoran, Laura Lisowsky and Arun Srinivasan." *CTR.* 1997 Sum; 91: 37-40. Lang.: Eng.
Canada. 1997. Histories-sources. ■Three young designers describe their apprenticeship experience with Associated Designers of Canada.

149 Lesage, Marie-Christine. "L'art du déséquilibre: David Gaucher, scénographe." (The Art of Imbalance: David Gaucher, Scenographer.) *JCT.* 1997; 85: 124-133. Notes. Illus.: Sketches. Photo. B&W. 10. Lang.: Fre.
Canada: Montreal, PQ. 1992-1997. Biographical studies. ■Distortion of reality and imbalance in set designs of David Gaucher, and their impact on spectators and actors.

150 McCullough, Douglas T. "The Curricular Catherine Wheel." *CTR.* 1997 Sum; 91: 32-36. Illus.: Dwg. Photo. B&W. 4. Lang.: Eng.

THEATRE IN GENERAL: —Design/technology

Canada. 1997. Critical studies. ■Proposes an unorthodox curriculum to prepare young designers for training in technique.

151 Noiseaux-Gurik, Renée. "French Language Studies in Scenography and Stagecrafts in Quebec." *CTR.* 1997 Sum; 91: 1995. Tables. Notes. [First published in special issue of *Actualité de la scénographie* on 'La scénographie au Québec', 1995.] Lang.: Eng.

Canada. 1997. Historical studies. ■Outlines and compares current scenographic training in Quebec.

152 Watts, Allan. "Design, Computers, and Teaching." *CTR.* 1997 Sum; 91: 18-21. Biblio. Lang.: Eng.

Canada. USA. 1997. Critical studies. ■Reviews emerging technologies in the field of design/scenography and offers concerned observations about its teaching.

153 Salzer, Beeb. "Friends." *TD&T.* 1997 Spr; 33(2): 24-27. Illus.: Photo. Color. 5. Lang.: Eng.

Chile. USA. 1955-1997. Biographical studies. ■A friend and classmate's obituary for Chilean lighting/set designer Bernardo Trumper.

154 Svoboda, Joseph; De Angeli, Elena, ed. *I segreti dello spazio teatrale.* (The Secrets of Theatrical Space.) Milan: Ubulibri; 1997. 219 pp. Lang.: Ita.

Czechoslovakia. 1920-1997. Histories-sources. ■Italian translation of the autobiography of the scenographer Josef Svoboda (*Tajemství divadelního prostoru*, 1992).

155 Bergeron, David M. "Inigo Jones, Renaissance Visual Culture, and English Outer Darkness." *RORD.* 1997; 36: 97-104. Lang.: Eng.

England. 1605-1995. Critical studies. ■Critical review of John Peacock's *The Stage Designs of Inigo Jones: The European Context* (Cambridge UP, 1995). Examines approach to and power of the masque, questions Peacock's assumptions about the genre and its audiences.

156 Egan, Gabriel. "Ariel's Costume in the Original Staging of *The Tempest*." *TN.* 1997; 51(2): 62-72. Notes. Lang.: Eng.

England: London. 1570-1612. Historical studies. ■Discusses costuming possibilities with reference to the First Folio staging directions, a contemporary pamphlet by Anthony Munday, and recent criticism on the subject.

157 Epp, Garrett P.J.; MacIntyre, Jean. "'Cloathes worth all the rest': Costumes and Properties." 269-286 in Cox, John D., ed.; Kastan, David Scott, ed. *A New History of Early English Drama.* New York, NY: Columbia UP; 1997. 565 pp. Index. Notes. Biblio. Lang.: Eng.

England. 1100-1500. Critical studies. ■The uses, significance, and importance of stage costumes in English Renaissance theatre.

158 Jackson, Allan S. "*Pizarro*, Bridges, and the Gothic Scene." *TN.* 1997; 51(2): 81-91. Notes. Illus.: Photo. Pntg. Lang.: Eng.

England: London. 1750-1899. Historical studies. ■The theatrical vogue for, and lasting influence of, atmospheric and picturesque set design. Discussion of John Philip Kemble's *Pizarro*, with designs by Loutherbourg (1804).

159 Grund, Uta. "Edward Gordon Craigs 'Scene'. Zur Wechselbeziehung der Künste um 1900." (Edward Gordon Craig's 'Scene': Towards the Correlation of Arts Around 1900.) 11-61 in Fiebach, Joachim, ed.; Mühl-Benninghaus, Wolfgang, ed.; Humboldt-Universität zu Berlin, Institut für Theaterwissenschaft/Kulturelle Kommunikation. *Theater und Medien an der Jahrhundertwende.* Berlin: Vistas Verlag; 1997. 214 pp. (Berliner Theaterwissenschaft 3.) Notes. Illus.: Design. Dwg. Photo. B&W. 14. Lang.: Ger.

Europe. 1872-1966. Historical studies. ■Discusses Craig's theory of 'scene' from an art historian's point of view. Her analyses are based on Craig's theoretical essays, unpublished notebooks, set designs, and on influences by other artists (Beggarstaff, Isadora Duncan).

160 Schierenberg, Olaf. "Abwärmenutzung bei Bühnenscheinwerfern." (Use of Spotlights' Waste Heat.) *BtR.* 1997; 91(5): 34-36. Illus.: Plan. Detail. Schematic. 5. Lang.: Ger.

Europe. 1997. Technical studies. ■Investigates whether more careful handling of energy resources in the lighting field will be possible and how this could be technically realized.

161 Tarrant, Naomi. *The Development of Costume.* New York, NY: Routledge; 1996. 176 pp. Notes. Index. Biblio. Illus.: Photo. 72. Lang.: Eng.

Europe. 250 B.C.-1995 A.D. Histories-specific. ■Examination of the structure of western European dress, focusing on the actual shape and fabrication of clothing and how raw materials, human ingenuity, and the need for self-expression all play vital roles in the development of costume.

162 Takala, Kimmo. "Tila, jonka aika lävistää." (A Space Pierced by Time.) *Teat.* 1997; 52(8): 8-10. Illus.: Photo. B&W. 2. Lang.: Fin.

Finland: Tampere. 1997. Histories-sources. ■Interview with stage designer Kimmo Viskari.

163 Goeres-Petry, Jürgen. "Theater als Ausbildungsstätte." (Theatre as a Training Site.) *BtR.* 1997; 91(5): 40-47. Lang.: Ger.

Germany: Berlin. 1997. Histories-sources. ■Discusses a new dual profession: Medium Designer for Image and Sound, a work with a creative and a technical side, with participating specialists (Mathias Nitsche, Mathias Laermanns, Karl-Heinz Weber, Florian von Hofen) during a platform discussion at ShowTech on June 4, 1997. Continued in *BtR* 91:6 (1997), 43-45.

164 Holmén, Helga. "Helga först i Dresden." (Helga the First at Dresden.) *ProScen.* 1997; 21(3): 54-55. Illus.: Photo. Color. Lang.: Swe.

Germany: Dresden. 1996. Histories-sources. ■Personal impressions of the first term as student of theatrical painting at Hochschule für Bildende Kunst.

165 Nobling, Torsten. "ShowTech Internationale Fachmesse für Veranstaltungstechnik." (ShowTech International Fair of Performance Technology.) *ProScen.* 1997; 21(3): 42-47. Illus.: Photo. B&W. Lang.: Swe.

Germany: Berlin. 1997. Technical studies. ■A report from this year's exhibition of scene technologies at Berlin.

166 Pfüller, Volker. "Text und Bild auf der Bühne—verlorene Liebesmüh." (Text and Image on Stage—that Is Futile.) *SJW.* 1997; 133: 98-108. Lang.: Ger.

Germany. 1990-1997. Histories-sources. ■Problems of set design in relationship to new media by a set designer and professor of set design.

167 Poppenhäger, Annette. "Theater goes online." *DB.* 1997; 4: 44-47. Illus.: Diagram. Photo. B&W. 3. Lang.: Ger.

Germany. 1997. Historical studies. ■Reviews the contemporary use of virtual reality, cyberspace and internet in the context of theatre, including homepages of theatres, set designs that are simulated by computers, training by computers and reference books.

168 Tretow, Christine. "Caspar Neher–'Graue Eminenz hinter der Brecht-Gardine. Zum 100. Geburtstag eines bekannten Unbekannten." (Caspar Neher—the 'Eminence Grise' behind Brecht's Curtain: Towards the 100th Birthday of a Well-Known Stranger.) *FMT.* 1997; 12(2): 175-194. Notes. Lang.: Ger.

Germany. 1897-1962. Biographical studies. ■Caspar Neher's formative influence on Brecht's characteristic theatre form which he developed in association with Brecht.

169 Winkelsesser, Karin. "Theater per Mausklick." (Theatre by Mouseclick.) *BtR.* 1997; 91(5): 14-21. Illus.: Photo. Color. 8. Lang.: Ger.

Germany: Berlin. 1997. Historical studies. ■Discusses ShowTech '97, Europe's most extensive congress in the field of performance technology, its conception, the boom of the event technology and new demands on work such as flexibility and minimalism. Describes a tour of the fair where different fields of work are represented including supporting acts, management workshops, the technology, training and further education.

170 Bőgel, József. "Antinekrológ. Fehér Miklós: Álomvárás." (Anti-Necrology: Miklós Fehér: Waiting for Dreams.) *Sz.* 1997; 30(12): 46-47. Illus.: Photo. B&W. 1. Lang.: Hun.

THEATRE IN GENERAL: —Design/technology

Hungary. 1929-1994. Biographical studies. ■Commemoration of a major stage designer of the post-war Hungarian theatre with the help of a recently published volume of his collected writings.

171 Bőgel, József. "Thália, Melpomené, Terpszikhoré 1996 nyarán." (Thalia, Melpomene, Terpsichore in Summer of 1996.) *SFo.* 1996/1997; 23/24(3/4-1/2): 41-46. Illus.: Photo. B&W. 2. Lang.: Hun.

Hungary. 1996. Critical studies. ■Open-air productions of summer 1996.

172 Bőgel, József. "Az élet illusztrátora. Vogel Eric (1907-1996)." (The Illustrator of Life: Eric Vogel, 1907-1996.) *Sz.* 1997; 30(2): 44-45. Illus.: Photo. B&W. 2. Lang.: Hun.

Hungary. 1907-1996. Biographical studies. ■Career of Vogel, a theatrical artist, graphic designer, and painter, who died while working on the sets of a new operetta production in Szolnok.

173 Róna, Katalin. "A színpad építésze: Csikós Attila." (The Architect of the Stage: Attila Csikós.) *ZZT.* 1997; 4(3): 11-12. Lang.: Hun.

Hungary. 1960-1997. Histories-sources. ■Summing up a successful career with architect, stage and costume designer Attila Csikós, chief designer of the Budapest Opera House.

174 Bignami, Paola, ed.; Azzaroni, Giovanni, ed. *Gli oggetti nello spazio del teatro. Atti dei Convegni: 'Spazi del teatro, idee e luoghi di spettacolo' e 'Il teatro degli oggetti, gli oggetti di teatro'.* (Objects in Theatrical Space: Proceedings of the Meetings on 'Spaces of Theatre, Ideas and Places of Entertainment' and 'Theatre of Objects, Objects of Theatre'.) Rome: Bulzoni; 1997. 242 pp. (Biblioteca Teatrale 96.) Illus.: Photo. B&W. Lang.: Ita.

Italy. 1994. Critical studies. ■Proceedings of two meetings on scenery and the use of objects in the theatre.

175 Clark, Mike. "Avant-Garde Artistry." *LDim.* 1997 Apr.; 21(3): 68-75. Illus.: Photo. Color. 6. Lang.: Eng.

Italy. 1982-1997. Biographical studies. ■Training and career of lighting designer Fabrizio Crisafulli and his work in experimental theatre and dance.

176 Clark, Mike. "Artistic Attaché." *LDim.* 1997 Sep.; 21(8): 70-73. Illus.: Photo. Color. 5. Lang.: Eng.

Italy. 1960-1997. Historical studies. ■Lighting designer Pepi Morgia's work in the concert and theatrical fields, and cinematic overtones of his designs.

177 Iwai, Tatsuya. "Street Culture." *LD&A.* 1996 Jan.; 26(1): 32-35. Illus.: Diagram. Photo. Color. B&W. 5. Lang.: Eng.

Japan: Hachioji City. 1996. Technical studies. ■Urban themed interior lighting design for the Hachioji City Art and Cultural Hall.

178 Boepple, Leanne. "Theory of Evolution." *TCI.* 1997 Jan.; 31(1): 18-21. Illus.: Photo. Sketches. 7. Lang.: Eng.

North America. Europe. 1996-1997. Historical studies. ■Lighting designer/set consultant Michael Ledesma's work on the most recent world tour of pop star Gloria Estefan.

179 Berezkin, V. "Scenografija-97: na vystavke i na scene." (Scenography '97: On Display and on Stage.) *TeatZ.* 1997; 8: 26-33. Lang.: Rus.

Russia: Moscow. 1996-1997. Historical studies. ■Scenography of the 1996-97 Moscow theatre season, and the critics' rating.

180 Brandesky, Joe. "Boris Anisfeld and the Theatre." *TD&T.* 1997 Win; 34(1): 46-54. Illus.: Design. Photo. Dwg. Color. B&W. 17. Lang.: Eng.

Russia: St. Petersburg. USA. 1994-1997. Historical studies. ■Exhibit of the sketches, renderings, and costumes of designer Boris I. Anisfeld, presently seen in St. Petersburg, and soon to tour in the US.

181 Bul', Ž. *Epós 'Džangar' i kalmyckij sceničeskij kostjum.* (The Džanger Epic and Kalmuck Theatrical Costume.) Elista: Kalmickoe izdatel'stvo; 1997. 80 pp. Lang.: Rus.

Russia. 1990-1997. Historical studies. ■Theatrical costumes of Kalmykija.

182 Glinskij, N. "Moja žizn'–ves' XX vek: vospominanija teatral'nogo chudoznika." (My Life–The Whole Twentieth Century: Recollections of a Theatre Artist.) *Volga.* 1997; 5-6: 152-176. Lang.: Rus.

Russia. 1900-1997. Histories-sources. ■Memoirs of scenographer N. Glinskij.

183 Kirsanova, R.M. *Sceničeskij kostjum i teatral'naja publika.* (Stage Costume and the Theatrical Audience.) Moscow: Artist. Režisser. Teat'r; 1997. 384 pp. Lang.: Rus.

Russia. 1700-1950. Histories-specific. ■The actor, the costume, and the audience.

184 Zolotnickaja, T. "Žitie chudožnika Igorja Ivanova, ili Put' k sebje." (The Artistic Life of Igor Ivanov, or the Path to the Self.) *PTZ.* 1997; 14: 15-21. Lang.: Rus.

Russia: St. Petersburg. 1990-1997. Historical studies. ■The work of scenographer Igor Ivanov.

185 Guillemaut, Alf. "Tarzan–en teaterarbetare med rätt att fixa." (Tarzan–a Theatre-Worker With License To Fix.) *ProScen.* 1997; 21(2): 9-11. Illus.: Photo. B&W. Lang.: Swe.

Sweden. Cuba. South Africa, Republic of. 1976. Biographical studies. ■A presentation of the technician and factotum Gert-Ove Vågstam, with references to his background and career at the alternative theatre groups, AVAB lighting equipment company, and abroad.

186 Nygård, Berit. "Jättebilder från datorn–komplement i scenografin." (Big Images From Computers–a Complement To Scenography.) *ProScen.* 1997; 21(3): 35-37. Illus.: Photo. Color. Lang.: Swe.

Sweden: Täby. 1987. Technical studies. ■A presentation of Big Image Systems and its director Werner Schäfer, with reference to all its cooperation with theatres and scenographers.

187 Söderberg, Olle. "Festspel i Ramsberg." (Festival At Ramsberg.) *ProScen.* 1997; 21(3): 10-11. Illus.: Photo. Color. Lang.: Swe.

Sweden: Ramsberg. 1997. Historical studies. ■A report from the community play about Ramsberg's history from 1589 until today, with reference to the technical design.

188 Söderberg, Olle. "Besök hos Woodlite i Karlstad." (A Visit To Woodlite at Karlstad.) *ProScen.* 1997; 21(3): 24. Illus.: Photo. B&W. Lang.: Swe.

Sweden: Karlstad. 1997. Technical studies. ■A presentation of the lighting company Woodlite and one of the partners Magnus Jansson.

189 Söderberg, Olle. "Nytt styrsystem på Malmö Stadsteater." (A New Control System At Malmö Stadsteater.) *ProScen.* 1997; 21(3): 31. Illus.: Photo. Color. Lang.: Swe.

Sweden: Malmö. 1997. Technical studies. ■A report of how the old revolving stage at Malmö Stadsteater was put in order by Stage Technology.

190 Westerlund, Erik. "En ledstjärna för alla–maskindirektivet för tillverkarna." (A Guiding Star For All–A Directive For the Manufacture of Machines.) *ProScen.* 1997; 21(1): 22-23. Illus.: Photo. B&W. Lang.: Swe.

Sweden. 1995. Historical studies. ■A presentation of the directive *Maskiner och vissa andra tekniska anordningar (Machines and Some Other Technical Devices)* from the Swedish Board for Occupational Safety and Health.

191 Maurer, Silvia. "Jetzt sind die Theater gefordert." (Now Theatres Are Called Upon.) *BtR.* 1997; 91(special issue): 27-29 . Illus.: Photo. Color. 10. Lang.: Ger.

Switzerland: Zurich. 1989-1997. Historical studies. ■History of the Swiss Technical College for Women that has trained women tailors and dressers for theatre since 1989. The training has been restructured to include a professional component that takes orders from theatres.

192 Johnson, David. "Simon Corder." *TCI.* 1997 Aug/Sep.; 31(7): 74-77. Illus.: Photo. 12. Lang.: Eng.

UK-England: London. 1997. Historical studies. ■On the work of English lighting designer Simon Corder. Discusses his work in the US and in London, where he designed the lighting for Sir Peter Hall's production of Tennessee Williams' *A Streetcar Named Desire* at the Theatre Royal, Haymarket.

193 Lampert-Gréaux, Ellen. "Anthony J. Douglas-Beveridge." *LDim.* 1997 Mar.; 21(2): 20. Illus.: Photo. B&W. 1. Lang.: Eng.

THEATRE IN GENERAL: —Design/technology

UK-England. 1997. Biographical studies. ■Profile and career of the Standards Officer of PLASA, the UK-based Professional Lighting and Sound Association.

194   Moles, Steve. "Reforming the Brits." *LDim*. 1997 May; 21(4): 70-71, 86. Illus.: Photo. Color. 3. Lang.: Eng.
UK-England. 1980-1997. Historical studies. ■Professional design created for the Brit Awards for music. Equipment used by lighting designer Mike Sutcliffe, challenges of lighting the stage presentation that is then telecast.

195   Moles, Steve. "Blazing Saddles." *LDim*. 1997 Sep.; 21(8): 68-69, 115. Illus.: Photo. Color. 4. Lang.: Eng.
UK-England. 1997. Historical studies. ■Simon Sidi's theatrical lighting design for the camp pop group Erasure's tour. Special effects, scenic elements, equipment.

196   Moles, Steve. "The Colour and the Sound." *TCI*. 1997 Aug/Sep.; 31(7): 78-79. Illus.: Photo. 3. Lang.: Eng.
UK-England. 1997. Historical studies. ■Two engineers for the rock music band, Foo Fighters—Craig Overbay and Ian Beveridge—on their work as the band prepares for a US tour.

197   "1994 IESNA Survey of Illuminance and Luminance Meters." *LD&A*. 1994 June; 24(6): 31-42. Tables. Lang.: Eng.
USA. 1994. Technical studies. ■Rates meters for gauging illuminance and luminance: contains performance table and list of participating manufacturers.

198   "1994 IESNA Software Survey." *LD&A*. 1994 July; 24(7): 24-32. Tables. Lang.: Eng.
USA. 1994. Technical studies. ■Performance and value rating of available lighting design software with list of participating manufacturers.

199   "1994 Lighting Equipment & Accessories Directory." *LD&A*. 1994 Feb.; 24(2): 24-118. Lang.: Eng.
USA. 1994. Technical studies. ■Source directory for lighting equipment. Manufacturers are listed alphabetically, geographically, and by equipment type.

200   "1995 Lighting Equipment & Accessories Directory." *LD&A*. 1995 Feb.; 25(2): 17-106. Lang.: Eng.
USA. 1995. Technical studies. ■Source directory for lighting equipment. Manufacturers are listed alphabetically, geographically, and by equipment type.

201   IESNA Progress Committee. "Progress Report." *LD&A*. 1995 Nov.; 25(11): 32-52. Illus.: Photo. Color. 128. Lang.: Eng.
USA. 1995. Technical studies. ■Report on the state of the lighting industry regarding new developments and innovations in application, technology and equipment.

202   "1996 Lighting Equipment & Accessories Directory." *LD&A*. 1996 Mar.; 26(3): 27-138. Lang.: Eng.
USA. 1996. Technical studies. ■Source directory for lighting equipment. Manufacturers are listed alphabetically, geographically, and by equipment type.

203   "1996 IESNA Software Survey." *LD&A*. 1996 Sep.; 26(9): 39-47. Tables. Lang.: Eng.
USA. 1996. Technical studies. ■Performance and value rating of available lighting design software with list of participating manufacturers.

204   IESNA Progress Committee. "1996 Progress Report." *LD&A*. 1996 Nov.; 26(11): 32-61. Illus.: Photo. Color. B&W. 122. Lang.: Eng.
USA. 1996. Technical studies. ■Report on the state of the lighting industry regarding new developments and innovations in application, technology, and equipment.

205   "Queen of the Mississippi." *LD&A*. 1997 Mar.; 27(3): 38-41. Illus.: Photo. Color. 7. Lang.: Eng.
USA. 1997. Technical studies. ■Designers Katherine Abernathy, Randall Burkett, Ronald Kurtz's lighting for the steamboat *American Queen*, a floating hotel for retirees. Includes the Grand Saloon theatre.

206   "1997 Iesna Software Survey." *LD&A*. 1997 July; 27(7): 41-50. Tables. Lang.: Eng.
USA. 1997. Technical studies. ■Survey of best available computer software for lighting design application.

207   "IESNA: 1997-98 Society Committees." *LD&A*. 1997 Oct.; 27(10): 1-14. Lang.: Eng.
USA: New York, NY. 1997. Technical studies. ■Committee and membership directory for the Illuminating Engineering Society of North America. Includes membership application.

208   IESNA Progress Committee. "Progress Report." *LD&A*. 1997 Nov.; 27(11): 31-48. Illus.: Photo. Color. B&W. 86. Lang.: Eng.
USA. 1997. Technical studies. ■Survey of the latest in lighting technology and equipment, and also on the newest developments in the design field as compiled by the Illuminating Engineering Society of North America's Progress Committee.

209   "Industry Resources." *LDim*. 1997 Dec.; 21(11): 31-272. Lang.: Eng.
USA. 1997. ■Comprehensive listing of companies, products, contact information for the lighting industry.

210   "Industry Resources Websites Directory." *LDim*. 1997 Dec.; 21(11): 27-30. Lang.: Eng.
USA. 1997. ■List of websites for lighting resources.

211   "Orlando Magic." *LDim*. 1997 Jan/Feb.; 21(1): 48-51, 82-118. Illus.: Photo. Color. 9. Lang.: Eng.
USA: Orlando, FL. 1997. Technical studies. ■Lighting Dimensions International 96: companies represented, products and equipment featured, awards. Includes comprehensive list of all exhibitors and description of their product.

212   "Special Report: 30 Years of TCI." *TCI*. 1997 Aug/Sep.; 31(7): 62-69. Illus.: Photo. 16. Lang.: Eng.
USA. 1967-1997. Historical studies. ■Focus on TCI's expanded coverage from theatre alone to the design and technology of theatre, film, architecture, concerts, theme parks, television, opera, and more.

213   "Industry Resources 1997-1998." *TCI*. 1997 Dec.; 31(10): 1-218. Lang.: Eng.
USA. 1997. ■Guide to resources for design industry for media, theatre, and film.

214   "Industry Resources, 1997-1998." *TCI*. 1997 June/July; 31(6): 1-204. Lang.: Eng.
USA. 1997. ■Guide to resources in the design industry for media, film, and theatre.

215   USITT Engineering Commission. "USITT S3-1997: Standard for Stage Pin Connectors." *TD&T*. 1997 Fall; 33(5): 49-61. Append. Illus.: Diagram. 9. Lang.: Eng.
USA. 1997. Technical studies. ■Guidelines for dimensional and other requirements for stage pin connectors as set forth by USITT's Engineering Commission.

216   "Professional Development Workshops: Long Beach '98." *TD&T*. 1997 Fall; 33(5): 9-11. Illus.: Photo. Sketches. Color. 5. Lang.: Eng.
USA: Long Beach, CA. 1997. Technical studies. ■Preview of the workshops at the 1998 Professional Development Workshop to be held at the 1998 USITT conference.

217   "Lighting Equipment and Accessories Directory." *LD&A*. 1997 Mar.; 27(3): 42-132. Lang.: Eng.
USA. 1997. ■Directory listing manufacturers of lighting equipment and related products.

218   "1995 IESNA Software Survey." *LD&A*. 1995 July; 25(7): 22-30. Tables. Lang.: Eng.
USA. 1995. Technical studies. ■Performance and value rating of available lighting design software with a list of participating manufacturers.

219   "Education." *TCI*. 1997 Oct.; 31(8): 44-47, 52-59. Illus.: Photo. 17. Lang.: Eng.
USA. 1997. Historical studies. ■Report on education and training programs available for design throughout the US. Also, how design teachers balance a design career in addition to their teaching.

220   IESNA Progress Committee. "Progress Report '94." *LD&A*. 1994 Nov.; 24(11): 22-40. Illus.: Photo. Color. 103. Lang.: Eng.
USA. 1994. Technical studies. ■Report on the state of the lighting industry regarding new developments and innovations in equipment, technology and application.

THEATRE IN GENERAL: —Design/technology

221 Albertová, Helena; Bonds, Alexandra; Brookfield, Kathie; Brown, Pat; Gallagher, Martin John; Garl, Mike; Keyser, Dan; Raphael, Nanalee; Ruskai, Martha. "The Sessions." *TD&T*. 1997 Sum; 33(3): 25-37. Illus.: Photo. Graphs. Diagram. B&W. 22. Lang.: Eng.

USA: Pittsburgh, PA. 1997. Technical studies. ▪Thumbnail sketches of what was available at the USITT Conferences and Stage Expo: classes on wigmaking and theatrical miking, demonstrations of truss systems, and a retrospective on the work of designer Josef Svoboda.

222 Arnold, Richard; Bellman, Willard; Blausen, Whitney; Brockman, Bruce; Byrnes, William, Jr.; Funicello, Ralph; Hale, David; Hill, Larry; Hite, Maribeth; Jones, Ellen E.; Phillips, Van; Rodger, David; Schmidt, Jack; Will, David. "The People." *TD&T*. 1997 Sum; 33(3): 38-48. Illus.: Photo. B&W. 8. Lang.: Eng.

USA: Pittsburgh, PA. 1997. Historical studies. ▪Awards recipients and description of their accomplishments at the USITT Conference and Stage Expo.

223 Barbour, David. "The Master Dealer." *LDim*. 1997 Oct.; 21(9): 82-89. Illus.: Photo. B&W. 1. Lang.: Eng.

USA: North Creek, NY. 1970-1997. Technical studies. ▪History of Creative Stage Lighting company and their focus on mail order and distribution.

224 Barbour, David. "Jeff Nellis." *LDim*. 1997 July; 21(6): 12. Illus.: Photo. B&W. 1. Lang.: Eng.

USA: New York, NY. 1997. Biographical studies. ▪Career of lighting designer Nellis, and most recent work on two one-man shows, *My Italy Story* by Joseph Gallo and *Men on the Verge of a His-Panic Breakdown* by Guillermo Reyes, both presented at Off Broadway's 47th Street Playhouse.

225 Barbour, David. "Showstoppers." *LDim*. 1997 Oct.; 21(9): 94-95, 173. Illus.: Photo. B&W. 2. Lang.: Eng.

USA: New York, NY. 1977-1997. Historical studies. ▪Author looks back on first issue of *Lighting Dimensions* (June 1977), and quotes from an interview with lighting designer Tharon Musser to use as a gauge for the changes in theatrical lighting design over the last twenty years.

226 Baymiller, Joanna; Block, Dick; Boone, Steve; Davis, Robert; Dorn, Dennis; Hoffer, Heidi; Kelly, Timothy; Morsette, Zoe; Mundell, Anna; Saternow, Tim; Weaver, Arden. "The Events." *TD&T*. 1997 Sum; 33(3): 50-65. Illus.: Photo. B&W. 35. Lang.: Eng.

USA: Pittsburgh, PA. 1997. Historical studies. ▪Survey and review of events, lectures, and exhibits at the USITT conference.

227 Blomquist, Kurt. "Framtidens teater och teaterteknik." (The Theatre and the Theatre Technology of the Future.) *ProScen*. 1997; 21(2): 24-27. Illus.: Photo. B&W. Lang.: Swe.

USA: Pittsburgh. 1997. Historical studies. ▪A report from the OISTAT's Tenth Conference with the theme The Vision of the Future, Design and Technology in the Next Century, with reference to the light-designer Jennifer Tipton, the director Robert Lepage, the scenographer Michael Levine and the multi-media designer Laurie-Shawn Borzovoy.

228 Boone, Mary Callahan. "Jean Rosenthal's Light: Making Visible the Magician." *TTop*. 1997 Mar.; 7(1): 77-92. Illus.: Photo. 2. Lang.: Eng.

USA: New York, NY. 1932-1969. Historical studies. ▪Lighting designer Jean Rosenthal, one of the early pioneers in lighting design for the Broadway theatre. Argues that Rosenthal's aesthetic goals for the theatrical use of light were limited and shaped by cultural expectations of her gender.

229 Brauner, Leon I. "Making the Conference." *TD&T*. 1997 Sum; 33(3): 10-13. Illus.: Photo. B&W. 9. Lang.: Eng.

USA. 1997. Critical studies. ▪Vice president of Conferences for USITT describes what is behind the project of putting together its yearly conference, site location, theme, product expositions, etc.

230 Brockman, Bruce. "Revisiting the Twin City Scenic Collection." *TD&T*. 1997 Win; 34(1): 18-32. Biblio. Illus.: Photo. Color. B&W. 37. Lang.: Eng.

USA: Minneapolis, MN. 1896-1997. Technical studies. ▪A visit to the collection of the Twin City Scenic Company, housed at the University of Minnesota, with a look at its work from the formation of the company to its demise in 1980.

231 Cashill, Robert. "Turned On." *LDim*. 1997 Mar.; 21(2): 47-49, 88-95. Illus.: Photo. Color. 7. Lang.: Eng.

USA: Houston, TX. 1997. Technical studies. ▪Theatrical lighting designs for nightclub settings created by Tim Hannum, project designer of On Design Group. Lists lighting and video equipment used, budgets.

232 Cashill, Robert, ed. "*Lighting Dimensions* Buyers Guide." *LDim*. 1997 Aug.; 21(7): 10-270. Illus.: Photo. Color. B&W. 250. Lang.: Eng.

USA: New York, NY. 1997. Technical studies. ▪Annual guide to lighting products. Includes manufacturers list, descriptions and photos of products, classified and ad index.

233 Cleveland, Elbin. "Karl Eigsti Shares Insight on Scene Design." *SoTh*. 1997 Sum; 38(3): 27, 29, 32. Illus.: Photo. B&W. 1. Lang.: Eng.

USA. 1962-1997. Histories-sources. ▪Interview with scene designer Karl Eigsti, discussing his response to some contemporary designs, his use of 'white models' and his transition to teaching.

234 de Jongh, James. "Bernard Johnson." *BlackM*. 1997 Feb/Mar.; 12(3): 15. Lang.: Eng.

USA: New York, NY. 1997. Biographical studies. ▪Obituary for costumer/director/choreographer and teacher Bernard Johnson.

235 Dorn, Dennis. "Tech Expo '97." *TD&T*. 1997 Fall; 33(5): 27-39. Tables. Illus.: Photo. Plan. Plan. 13. Lang.: Eng.

USA: Pittsburgh, PA. 1997. Technical studies. ▪The Tech Expo '97 award-winning exhibits, including ones for projection, fly system, costuming, turntable, trapdoor.

236 Durst, Richard. "The OISTAT World Congress." *TD&T*. 1997 Sum; 33(3): 14-15. Illus.: Photo. B&W. 4. Lang.: Eng.

USA: Pittsburgh, PA. 1997. Historical studies. ▪Survey of the tenth OISTAT World Congress.

237 Durst, Richard. "A World Theatre Conference: Pittsburgh '97." *TD&T*. 1997 Win; 34(1): 10-13. Illus.: Photo. B&W. 5. Lang.: Eng.

USA: Pittsburgh, PA. 1997. Historical studies. ▪Preview of the upcoming USITT Annual Conference and Stage Expo and the tenth OISTAT World Congress, both to be hosted in Pittsburgh, PA.

238 Erhardt, Louis. "Views on the Visual Environment." *LD&A*. 1994 Jan.; 24(1): 6-7. Lang.: Eng.

USA. 1994. Technical studies. ▪Effects of recreating natural light in interior venues. Its implication on visual communication.

239 Gold, Richard. "Quiet, Heavy-Duty Traveler Track." *TechB*. 1997 Jan.: 1-3. Illus.: Plan. B&W. 4. [TB 1293.] Lang.: Eng.

USA. 1997. Technical studies. ▪Traveler track system used for moving scenic elements too heavy for traditional systems.

240 Green, Richard; Schwendinger, Leni; Dupuy, Robert; Noell, Eunice. "Lightfair International Seminar Preview." *LD&A*. 1997 Apr.; 27(4): 65-81. Illus.: Photo. Color. 17. Lang.: Eng.

USA: New York, NY. 1997. Technical studies. ▪Preview of the Lightfair International Seminar: a look at events and products to be offered.

241 Hall, Delbert L. "Internet: Latest Technology Provides Fast, Economical Way for Theatre Design Staffs to Communicate." *SoTh*. 1997 Fall; 38(4): 10-11. Illus.: Photo. B&W. 1. Lang.: Eng.

USA. 1997. Technical studies. ▪Freelance consultant Hall discusses communication among production staff members in diverse locations through such internet technologies as email, File Transfer protocol, AutoCAD transfers and conferencing software.

242 Harrison, William C., Jr. "Inexpensive MR16 Lamp Holders." *TechB*. 1997 Apr.: 1-2. Illus.: Plan. B&W. 1. [TB 1295.] Lang.: Eng.

USA. 1997. Technical studies. ▪Construction, mounting, wiring of and safety precautions for a small lamp holder.

243 Hartung, Tim. "USITT Architecture Awards Program." *TD&T*. 1997 Spr; 33(2): 9-14. Illus.: Photo. Color. 8. Lang.: Eng.

THEATRE IN GENERAL: —Design/technology

USA. 1997. Historical studies. ■The winners of the 1997 USITT Awards for outstanding architectural design: lists the eight winners and names all forty-one nominees.

244 Hendrickson, Alan. "A Hand-Driven Endless-Loop Turntable Drive." *TechB*. 1997 Apr.: 1-3. Illus.: Plan. B&W. 3. [TB 1297.] Lang.: Eng.

USA. 1997. Technical studies. ■Manual device to rotate lightly loaded turntables onstage. Includes information for determining drive sheave diameter.

245 Hendrickson, Alan. "Roller Chain Turntable Drives." *TechB*. 1997 Jan.: 1-3. Illus.: Plan. B&W. 3. [TB 1292.] Lang.: Eng.

USA. 1997. Technical studies. ■Construction, advantages and disadvantages of a roller chain device used for driving a turntable on stage.

246 Heslin, Kevin. "A Toon With a View." *LD&A*. 1994 Jan.; 24(1): 15-18. Illus.: Photo. Color. 5. Lang.: Eng.

USA: Anaheim, CA. 1994. Technical studies. ■Lighting design for the newest addition to Disneyland, 'Mickey's Toontown'.

247 Hill, Philip. "Doug Berky: The Mime and His Masks." *SoTh*. 1997 Spr; 38(2): 20-25. Illus.: Photo. B&W. 8. Lang.: Eng.

USA. 1996. Technical studies. ■Berky's use and designing of masks, including basic design considerations and building techniques.

248 Hogan, Jane. "The Process of *Evolution*." *LDim*. 1997 Mar.; 21(2): 21. Illus.: Photo. Color. 1. Lang.: Eng.

USA: New York, NY. 1997. Historical studies. ■R.J. Tolan's lighting design and direction for Shadow Productions' *Evolution*, a touring performance-rock piece presented at Tribeca Arts Center.

249 Hopper, Elizabeth W. "Freddy Wittop: Artist, Costume Designer, Dancer." *SoTh*. 1997 Sum; 38(3): 26, 28. Illus.: Photo. B&W. 1. Lang.: Eng.

USA. 1911-1997. Biographical studies. ■Career of costume designer Freddy Wittop, who discusses his favorite designs.

250 Johnson, David. "From Bullrings to Boardrooms." *LDim*. 1997 Jan/Feb.; 21(1): 34-41. Illus.: Photo. B&W. Color. 7. Lang.: Eng.

USA: Dallas, TX. 1997. Technical studies. ■History of Vari-Lite Inc. and future plans for development of lighting equipment. Designs for rock concerts, instruments, patents, personnel.

251 Johnson, David. "Life's Work." *LDim*. 1997 Mar.; 21(2): 53-55, 114. Illus.: Photo. Color. LP. 3. Lang.: Eng.

USA: New York, NY. 1997. Historical studies. ■Michael Fink of Magical Designs and Ted Doumazios of State of the Art Lighting and their architectural and entertainment lighting for the former Village Gate, renamed Life, a multi-use performance space.

252 Johnson, David. "Golden Years." *LDim*. 1997 June; 21(5): 42-49. Illus.: Photo. Color. B&W. 4. Lang.: Eng.

USA: New York, NY. 1997. Technical studies. ■History and future plans of Barbizon Electric. Equipment, personnel, work for film and television.

253 Johnson, David. "Found in Yonkers." *LDim*. 1997 Sep.; 21(8): 38-41. Illus.: Photo. Color. 4. Lang.: Eng.

USA: Yonkers, NY. 1997. Historical studies. ■History and current projects of Altman Stage Lighting company. Technology and equipment developed and marketed, expansion from theatrical to television and film lighting.

254 Jowitt, Deborah. "Beverly Emmons." *AmTh*. 1997 July/Aug.; 14(6): 44-45. Illus.: Photo. B&W. 1. Lang.: Eng.

USA: New York, NY. 1960-1997. Biographical studies. ■Career of lighting designer Emmons: her current work on the musical *Jekyll & Hyde*, differences between lighting for theatre and other media.

255 King, Dave. "A Sure-Shot Fireball Launcher." *TechB*. 1997 Jan.: 1-3. Illus.: Photo. Plan. B&W. 5. [TB 1291.] Lang.: Eng.

USA. 1997. Technical studies. ■Design and construction of an inexpensive, safe, actor-controlled pyrotechnic device to simulate a flash and fireball.

256 Klein, Stephen Lars. "Scene Shop Tuffets." *TechB*. 1997 Oct.: 1. Illus.: Plan. B&W. 1. [TB 1301.] Lang.: Eng.

USA. 1997. Technical studies. ■Style of tuffet used for low floor work which facilitates movement of the stage technician.

257 Klein, Stephen Lars. "Handrail Armatures for a Grand Staircase." *TechB*. 1997 Apr.: 1-3. Illus.: Photo. Plan. B&W. 5. [TB 1298.] Lang.: Eng.

USA. 1997. Technical studies. ■Design and installation of curved handrails for large staircases.

258 Lampert-Gréaux, Ellen. "Winner Take All." *LDim*. 1997 Sep.; 21(8): 82-83. Lang.: Eng.

USA: Las Vegas, NV. 1997. Technical studies. ■Preview of Lighting Dimensions International entertainment and design trade show and conference. Workshop sessions, presentations.

259 Lampert-Gréaux, Ellen. "Backstage LDI." *LDim*. 1997 Oct.; 21(9): 100-101, 175-177. Illus.: Photo. B&W. Color. 11. Lang.: Eng.

USA. 1987-1997. Historical studies. ■Retrospective of the history of LDI's past trade shows on the occasion of its tenth anniversary.

260 Lampert-Gréaux, Ellen. "Rhythm of the Night." *LDim*. 1997 Oct.; 21(9): 126-127, 147. Illus.: Photo. Color. 3. Lang.: Eng.

USA: Anaheim, CA. 1997. Technical studies. ■Technology, design, special effects and equipment used by lighting designer Brian Gale for Disneyland's theme entertainment show *Light Magic*.

261 Levy, Adriane M. "A Motorized, Mirrored Rain Effect." *TechB*. 1997 Oct.: 1-3. Illus.: Plan. B&W. 3. [TB 1300.] Lang.: Eng.

USA. 1997. Technical studies. ■Creation of a stylized lighting effect to simulate a downpour of rain.

262 Liao, Pater. "A Durable, Rough Texture Coating for Scenery and Props." *TechB*. 1997 Jan.: 1-2. Illus.: Photo. B&W. 2. [TB 1294.] Lang.: Eng.

USA. 1997. Technical studies. ■Formula and application of a texture coating that can easily be built up into rich relief and has greater durability than other mixtures.

263 Mackay, Pat. "Richard Durst Elected New President of OISTAT." *TD&T*. 1997 Sum; 33(3): 16. Illus.: Photo. B&W. 2. Lang.: Eng.

USA. 1997. Historical studies. ■OISTAT presidential candidate Maija Pekkanen's defeat by Richard Durst for the post.

264 Maiman, William L. "Small Wonders." *LDim*. 1997 Jan/Feb.; 21(1): 74-75. Illus.: Photo. Color. 1. Lang.: Eng.

USA. 1997. Technical studies. ■Product review of two fully-featured, easy-to-program lighting consoles produced by Leprecon.

265 Maiman, William L. "Fusion's Bright Idea." *LDim*. 1997 May; 21(4): 28-29. Illus.: Photo. Color. 1. Lang.: Eng.

USA. 1997. Technical studies. ■Development of Fusion Lighting Solar 1000, an electrodeless lamp which can produce brilliant light without consuming great wattage.

266 Maiman, William L. "Vegas Engagements." *LDim*. 1997 Oct.; 21(9): 128-133. Illus.: Photo. B&W. Color. 4. Lang.: Eng.

USA: Las Vegas, NV. 1997. Technical studies. ■New equipment featured by manufacturers at LDI97 lighting conference. Includes companies, location at conference, description of instruments.

267 Maiman, William L. "Higher Learning." *LDim*. 1997 May; 21(4): 42-47. Illus.: Photo. Color. 2. Lang.: Eng.

USA: Troy, NY. 1988-1997. Historical studies. ■Profile of Lighting Research Center, a non-profit research and education center, which provides information and support regarding new product developments and health, energy, environmental and regulatory issues.

268 McHugh, Catherine. "Rock and Roll—and Beyond." *LDim*. 1997 Apr.; 21(3): 42-45, 97-101. Illus.: Photo. Color. 8. Lang.: Eng.

USA. 1975-1997. Technical studies. ■History of the company Light and Sound Design (LSD), which specializes in lighting rock concerts, including the use of Icon automated luminaire and control system.

269 McHugh, Catherine. "Age of Destruction." *LDim*. 1997 Apr.; 21(3): 54-59, 109-111. Illus.: Photo. Color. 10. Lang.: Eng.

USA. 1988-1997. Historical studies. ■John Broderick's intricate lighting design for the rock band Metallica's *Load* world tour. Instruments used,

THEATRE IN GENERAL: —Design/technology

pyrotechnic effects, spotlights, audience lights, past shows and band's involvement in design process.

270 McHugh, Catherine. "Kenny G and Toni B." *LDim.* 1997 May; 21(4): 74-84. Illus.: Photo. Color. LP. 6. Lang.: Eng.
USA. 1997. Historical studies. ■Valerie Groth and Justin Collie's lighting design for concert tour of musicians Kenny G and Toni Braxton. Equipment and systems used.

271 McHugh, Catherine. "Rock and Roll Circus." *LDim.* 1997 Sep.; 21(8): 42-49. Illus.: Photo. Color. LP. 5. Lang.: Eng.
USA. 1997. Historical studies. ■Butch Allen's innovative lighting design for rock musician Ozzy Osbourne's touring show. Equipment, special effects, video support.

272 McHugh, Catherine. "Rush Service Normal." *LDim.* 1997 Oct.; 21(9): 64-74. Illus.: Photo. Color. B&W. 6. Lang.: Eng.
USA. 1970-1997. Technical studies. ■History and work of TMB Associates, providing lighting equipment and services to professionals worldwide including touring musicians, film companies and theatrical ventures.

273 McHugh, Catherine. "Minimalism to Margaritaville." *LDim.* 1997 Nov.; 21(10): 80-83, 122-126. Illus.: Photo. Color. B&W. LP. 7. Lang.: Eng.
USA. 1974-1997. Technical studies. ■Training and career of lighting designer Sid Strong, his use of lighting design for singer Jimmy Buffett's tour which made use of theatrical sets.

274 McHugh, Catherine. "Wild Majesty." *LDim.* 1997 Nov.; 21(10): 52-57. Illus.: Photo. Color. B&W. LP. 5. Lang.: Eng.
USA: New York, NY. 1997. Technical studies. ■Alexandre Parra's dramatic lighting design for the musical group Gipsy Kings at Radio City Music Hall. Brief overview of Parra's training and career in lighting for theatre and dance.

275 Millhone, John P. "Partners for Change." *LD&A.* 1994 May; 24(5): 52-61. Tables. Lang.: Eng.
USA. 1994. Critical studies. ■The relationship between federal and local governments and the lighting industry regulations concerning equipment, safety and research.

276 Moles, Steve. "Beyond Rock and Roll." *LDim.* 1997 Oct.; 21(9): 76-80. Illus.: Photo. Color. B&W. 4. Lang.: Eng.
USA. 1993-1997. Technical studies. ■Lighting designer Patrick Woodroffe's work in dance, rock music, theatre and banquets.

277 Moles, Steve. "Four for Tina: The Queen of Rock's Wildest Dreams Tour." *TCI.* 1997 Mar.; 31(3): 44-49. Illus.: Photo. Lighting. 10. Lang.: Eng.
USA. 1996. Historical studies. ■Collaboration on pop singer Tina Turner's latest tour: production designer Mark Fisher, lighting designer LeRoy Bennett, sound engineer Dave Natale, and video director Christine Strand.

278 Nobling, Torsten. "USITT's seminarier och utställningen i Pittsburgh." (USITT's Seminars and the Exhibition at Pittsburgh.) *ProScen.* 1997; 21(3): 39-41. Illus.: Photo. B&W. Color. Lang.: Swe.
USA: Pittsburgh, PA. 1997. Historical studies. ■A report from USITT's conference and exhibtion.

279 Patterson, Michael. "Self-Trimming Flown Units." *TechB.* 1997 Apr.: 1-3. Illus.: Plan. B&W. 3. [TB 1296.] Lang.: Eng.
USA. 1997. Technical studies. ■Construction of a self-masking and trim-correcting flat and foot design for smooth operation of scenery that must be flown in onstage.

280 Payne, Darwin Reid. "Design Conferences in Cyberspace." *TD&T.* 1997 Win; 34(1): 41-44. Illus.: Photo. Color. B&W. 9. Lang.: Eng.
USA. 1997. Technical studies. ■The use of computers to communicate design concepts quickly and cheaply: what's presently feasible, and what may be available in the future.

281 Rodger, David, ed. "1997-1998 USITT Membership Directory." *TD&T.* 1997/98; 33(4): 1-172. Lang.: Eng.
USA. 1997-1998. ■Membership directory for the United States Institute for Theatre Technology (USITT).

282 Rosen, Steven. "Jurassic PARs." *LDim.* 1997 Nov.; 21(10): 66-69, 120. Illus.: Photo. Color. B&W. LP. 4. Lang.: Eng.

USA: New York, NY. 1997. Technical studies. ■Author's use of theatrical lighting rig for traveling museum exhibit *The Lost World: The Life and Death of Dinosaurs.* Special effects, equipment, rigging.

283 Royan, Kevin; Serame, Arnold, contrib. "The Mighty MAC 600." *LDim.* 1997 Nov.; 21(10): 90-92. Illus.: Photo. Color. 1. Lang.: Eng.
USA: New York, NY. 1997. Technical studies. ■Review of the MAC 600 fresnel lighting instrument, manufactured by Martin Professional and the author's experiences using it during a tour.

284 Rubin, Joel E., Dr.; Grosser, Helmut. "The OISTAT Gold Pin." *TD&T.* 1997 Sum; 33(3): 21-23. Illus.: Photo. B&W. 2. Lang.: Eng.
USA: Pittsburgh, PA. 1997. Historical studies. ■Former presidents of OISTAT Rubin and Grosser receive OISTAT's Gold Pin for activism and honor one another in their essays.

285 Ruling, Karl G. "Does Pouncing a Gel Make Any Difference?" *TD&T.* 1997 Spr; 33(2): 28-31. Illus.: Photo. Graphs. Color. B&W. 4. Lang.: Eng.
USA. 1997. Empirical research. ■Results of an experiment to determine whether 'pouncing' gels, the practice of poking holes in them, makes a gel last longer than one that is not treated in this manner.

286 Ruzika, Donna. "Long Beach." *TD&T.* 1997 Sum; 33(3): 66-67. Illus.: Photo. B&W. Color. 4. Lang.: Eng.
USA: Long Beach, CA. 1997. Historical studies. ■Critique of Long Beach, CA, chosen host of the 1998 USITT conference and Stage Expo.

287 Sammler, Ben, ed.; Harvey, Don, ed. "Index." *TechB.* 1997 Apr.: 1-5. [TB 1227-1298.] Lang.: Eng.
USA. 1997. Technical studies. ■Index for *TechB* volumes 11-16 categorized by subject: costumes, lighting, lighting effects, painting, props, rigging, safety, scenery, sound.

288 Schreiber, Loren. "A Self-Paging Cable Tray." *TechB.* 1997 Oct.: 1-2. Illus.: Plan. B&W. 2. [TB 1299.] Lang.: Eng.
USA: San Diego, CA. 1997. Technical studies. ■Inexpensive solution for distributing power to a wagon or slip-stage.

289 Schwartzman, Eric. "UV: New and Groovy." *LD&A.* 1995 June; 25(6): 23-27. Illus.: Photo. Color. 5. Lang.: Eng.
USA. 1995. Technical studies. ■Application of ultraviolet backlight in all spheres of entertainment and art.

290 Terry, Steve. "Where Is 'Common Ethernet'?" *LDim.* 1997 Mar.; 21(2): 74-78. Lang.: Eng.
USA. 1997. Technical studies. ■Need for an advanced common-protocol, high-speed network for the lighting industry. Equipment, manufacturers.

291 Terry, Steve. "Power Play." *LDim.* 1997 Sep.; 21(8): 84-93. Tables. Lang.: Eng.
USA. 1990-1997. Technical studies. ■Considerations for feeding permanent dimmer-per-circuit systems in theatres and similar locations. Discusses past and current changes in the National Electrical Code.

292 Thompson, Richard D. "Is It Listed?" *TD&T.* 1997 Win; 34(1): 14-17. Lang.: Eng.
USA. 1997. Critical studies. ■Urges the entertainment industry to involve itself in the drafting of safety standards for its electrical equipment before others with little experience relating to the field overreact when a mishap occurs.

293 van der Heide, Rogier. "All the World's a Stage." *LD&A.* 1995 July; 25(7): 38-41. Illus.: Photo. Color. 6. Lang.: Eng.
USA. 1995. Technical studies. ■Application of theatrical lighting techniques in non-theatrical venues such as restaurants, museums, retail stores, etc.

294 Walton, Tony. "Mesmerised by Mielziner: A Designer's Thank-You." *AmTh.* 1997 Apr.; 14(4): 39-40. Illus.: Sketches. B&W. 2. Lang.: Eng.
USA. 1936-1960. Historical studies. ■Career of scenic designer Jo Mielziner and his influence on the author.

295 Wengrow, Arnold. "Tony Walton, Protean of American Design." *TD&T.* 1997 Spr; 33(2): 32-46. Illus.: Photo. Sketches. Color. B&W. 25. Lang.: Eng.

THEATRE IN GENERAL: —Design/technology

USA. UK-England. 1934-1997. Biographical studies. ■The life and career of Broadway scene designer Tony Walton, including a brief portfolio of some of his designs with the designer's own reflections on them.

296 Wieder, Don. "Wiliam H. Grant III: Lighting the Stages of the World." *BlackM.* 1997 June/July; 12(4): 5-6, 15. Illus.: Photo. B&W. 1. Lang.: Eng.

USA. 1950-1997. Biographical studies. ■Influences on the professional career of the lighting designer.

Institutions

297 Kékesi Kun, Árpád. "Az érzékelés ünnepe. Bécsi ünnepi Hetek." (The Festival of Sensation: The Wiener Festwochen.) *Sz.* 1997; 30(11): 7-13. Illus.: Photo. B&W. 5. Lang.: Hun.

Austria: Vienna. 1997. Reviews of performances. ■Survey of several Swiss, German and Italian perfomances, directed by Luc Bondy, Peter Zadek, Romeo Castellucci and Heiner Goebbels as the outstanding productions of this year's festival.

298 Koltai, Tamás. "A rendező az úr. Salzburgi ünnepi Játékok." (The Director Is the Master: The Salzburger Festspiele.) *Sz.* 1997; 30(11): 2-7. Illus.: Photo. B&W. 5. Lang.: Hun.

Austria: Salzburg. 1997. Reviews of performances. ■Having been present at the festival the critic Tamás Koltai reviews some drama and opera performances, directed by Sam Mendes, François Abu Salem, Peter Stein and Peter Sellars.

299 Heliodora, Barbara. "Grupo Galpão: A Brazilian Street Theatre." *TheatreF.* 1997 Win/Spr; 10: 4-10. Illus.: Photo. 9. Lang.: Eng.

Brazil: Belo Horizonte. 1982-1997. Historical studies. ■How the Grupo Galpão street theatre group create and perform their work, both with improvisation and scripted works. Focuses on their recent work *Romeo & Juliet.*

300 Bell, Karen. "Not the Only Game in Town Anymore." *PAC.* 1997; 30(4): 4-5. Illus.: Photo. B&W. 2. Lang.: Eng.

Canada: Toronto, ON. 1997. Historical studies. ■Profile of the O'Keefe Centre for the performing arts, which has brought world famous artists including singers, comedians and large scale musicals to Toronto.

301 Colbert, François. "Changes in Marketing Environment and Their Impact on Cultural Policy." *JAML.* 1997 Fall; 27(3): 177-186. Notes. Biblio. Lang.: Eng.

Canada. 1957-1997. Critical studies. ■How the creation of the Canada Council for the Arts affected government involvement in high and popular art, including film, radio and television, and how this resulted in an increased demand for the performing arts.

302 Defraeye, Piet. "Theatre (in) New Brunswick." *CTR.* 1997 Win; 93: 27-31. Notes. Biblio. Illus.: Photo. B&W. 1. Lang.: Eng.

Canada: Fredericton, NB. 1996. Historical studies. ■State of theatre companies in New Brunswick, with particular attention to Theatre New Brunswick.

303 Paventi, Eza. "L'improvisation, à la manière de Robert Gravel." (Improvisation, Robert Gravel-Style.) *JCT.* 1997; 82: 94-97. Illus.: Photo. B&W. 6. Lang.: Fre.

Canada: Montreal, PQ. 1977-1997. Historical studies. ■Institutionalization of Robert Gravel's improv games, through Ligue National d'Improvisation and other Montreal improv leagues.

304 Telenko, Sherri. "Why Is Sharon Pollock so Dissatisfied with the State of Canadian Theatre?" *PAC.* 1997; 30(4): 14-15. Illus.: Photo. B&W. 1. Lang.: Eng.

Canada: Calgary, AB. 1981-1997. Historical studies. ■Director and playwright Pollock and her efforts to create a community theatre that reflects diversity in poor neighborhoods in Calgary.

305 Burian, Jarka M. "Laterna Magika as a Synthesis of Theatre and Film: Its Evolution and Problematics." *THSt.* 1997; 17: 33-62. Illus.: Photo. 16. Lang.: Eng.

Czechoslovakia: Prague. 1959-1997. Historical studies. ■Aesthetic and practical evolution of Laterna Magika. Focuses on its principles of mixed live and filmed action, short revue format, and its emphasis on spectacle rather than text.

306 Turner, Jane. "Prospero's Floating Island: ISTA 1995." *ATJ.* 1997 Spr; 14(1): 120-125. Biblio. Lang.: Eng.

Denmark: Holstebro. 1995. Historical studies. ■Report on 1995 session at Eugenio Barba's International School of Theatre Anthropology. Barba's theatre, rehearsals of his work *Theatrum Mundi.*

307 Lowerre, Kathryn J. *Music in the Productions at London's Lincoln's Inn Fields Theater, 1695-1705.* Durham, NC: Duke Univ; 1997. 888 pp. [Ph.D. Dissertation, Univ. Microfilms Order No. AAC 9727379.] Lang.: Eng.

England. 1695-1705. Historical studies. ■Covers music from brief songs in stock comedies to extensive and elaborate fully-musical productions such as dramatic operas and masques. Analyzes numerous composers including John Eccles, Gottfried Finger, John Lenton and William Corbett and singers such as Richard Elford.

308 Söderberg, Olle. "Ett fönster mot framtiden." (A Window Towards the Future.) *ProScen.* 1997; 21(3): 68-69. Lang.: Swe.

Finland: Tampere. 1987. Historical studies. ■Profile of Teatterikorkeakoulu's department of lighting and sound design, located in Tampere, and the Center for Development of Theatre Technology.

309 Söderberg, Olle. "Teaterfestival i Tammerfors." (Theatre Festival at Tampere.) *ProScen.* 1997; 21(3): 50. Illus.: Photo. B&W. Lang.: Swe.

Finland: Tampere. 1997. Historical studies. ■A report from the festival with references to Teatr Biuro Podróży's *Carmen Funèbre* and Teater Galeasen's production of Steven Berkoff's *Kvetch* directed by Linus Tunström.

310 Campanelli, Claudia. "Strategie di sopravvivenza di un teatro di Boulevard tra Impero e Restaurazione: la scene di Porte Saint-Martin, una vicenda emblematica." (Strategies for Survival of a Boulevard Theatre Between the Empire and the Restoration: The Theatre of Porte Saint-Martin, an Emblematic History.) *IlCast.* 1997; 10(30): 97-113. Notes. Lang.: Ita.

France: Paris. 1802-1830. Historical studies. ■History of the Théâtre de Porte Saint-Martin through a study of unpublished documents, said to be an example of the relationship between a boulevard theatre and the French state.

311 Decock, Jean. "Avignon: The Russians Are Coming." *WES.* 1997 Fall; 9(3): 5-14. Illus.: Photo. 5. Lang.: Eng.

France: Avignon. 1997. Historical studies. ■Review of the 1997 Avignon Festival: productions, financial operations, and especially the prominence of Russian theatre companies represented.

312 Féral, Josette. "Le droit et la reconnaissance: Congrès mondial de l'UNESCO sur le statut de l'artiste." (Rights and Recognition: UNESCO World Congress on the Status of the Artist.) *JCT.* 1997; 83: 150-152. Lang.: Fre.

France: Paris. 1997. Historical studies. ■Reports main themes of UNESCO's World Congress on the Status of the Artist, Paris 1996.

313 Hammerstein, Dorothee. "Götter, Helden und Geschmähte." (Gods, Heroes and Abused Ones.) *THeute.* 1997; 9: 4-9. Illus.: Photo. B&W. 5. Lang.: Ger.

France: Avignon. 1997. Historical studies. ■Impressions from the Festival d'Avignon. Describes *Nathan* by Gotthold Ephraim Lessing directed by Denis Marleau, *Le Visage d'Orphée (The Face of Orpheus)* written and directed by Olivier Py, *Contention* by Didier-Georges Gabily directed by Stanislas Nordey, *Pereira Prétend (Pereira Claims)* after Antonio Tabucchi directed by Didier Bezace.

314 Ley, Graham. "French Theatre Schools & Performances." *STP.* 1997 Dec.; 16: 141-146. Lang.: Eng.

France: Paris. 1997. Histories-sources. ■The author describes the results of a fact-finding visit to Paris to gather information on French theatre schools and related performances.

315 Margolies, Eleanor. "The Present of Memory: Théâtre Demodesastr in Performance." *PerfR.* 1997 Spr; 2(1): 2-10. Notes. Biblio. Illus.: Photo. Dwg. B&W. 4. Lang.: Eng.

France. 1995. Critical studies. ■Analysis of the site-specific performance *La Porte*, by Théâtre Demodesastr in relation to the theatre practice and concepts of Kantor and Brecht.

THEATRE IN GENERAL: —Institutions

316   Nelson, Robert. *"Le Théâtre du Peuple*—International Events in a French Popular Theatre." *STP.* 1997 Dec.; 16: 26-34. Notes. Biblio. Illus.: Photo. B&W. 2. Lang.: Eng.
France: Bussang. 1895-1997. Historical studies. ■The work of Le Théâtre du Peuple, founded by Maurice Pottecher in an attempt to promote reconciliation and a humanitarian vision in a troubled region. Describes the coming together of theatre students in *Les Réalisations de Jeunes 1997*, documenting three different approaches to the staging of the ending of Sophocles' *Electra* by groups from Greece, England and Portugal.

317   Schlocker, Georges. "Saturnalien in Avignon." (Saturnalia in Avignon.) *DB.* 1997; 9: 36-38. Illus.: Photo. B&W. 1. Lang.: Ger.
France: Avignon. 1997. Historical studies. ■Impressions from the theatre festival in Avignon. Describes a city in theatre fascination, but also the difficulties of the festival, the lower local subsidy in spite of profits from tourism.

318   Bender, Ruth. "Hamburgs rebellischer Ort." (Hamburg's Rebellious Place.) *DB.* 1997; 8: 28-30. Illus.: Photo. B&W. 2. Lang.: Ger.
Germany: Hamburg. 1997. Historical studies. ■Describes Kampnagel-Fabrik, a central performance space of Hamburg's free theatre scene. There meet productions made in Hamburg and international theatre avant-garde.

319   Heine, Beate. "Die Nomaden werden sesshaft." (The Nomads Settle Down.) *DB.* 1997; 8: 16-20. Illus.: Photo. B&W. 3. Lang.: Ger.
Germany: Berlin. 1997. Critical studies. ■Reviews the free theatre scene in Berlin and its changes, the necessity of continuous theatre work within a certain budget and firm organizational rules.

320   Krusche, Friedemann. "Revolution? Keine Sache für Sachsen!" (Revolution? No Matter for Saxony!) *THeute.* 1997; 5: 4-6 . Illus.: Photo. B&W. 5. Lang.: Ger.
Germany: Dresden. 1949-1997. Historical studies. ■Describes the current significance of Dresdner Staatsschauspiel, its former important role in GDR history, the audience and the relationship to politics and politicians.

321   Merschmeier, Michael; Wille, Franz. "Vor der Zerreissprobe." (Before the Ordeal.) *THeute.* 1997; 6: 22-24. Illus.: Photo. B&W. 1. Lang.: Ger.
Germany: Freiburg. 1997. Histories-sources. ■An interview with Gerhard Jörder, the chief editor of the feature section of the newspaper *Badische Zeitung* about coverage of the arts and especially regional alternative theatre.

322   Merschmeier, Michael; Wille, Franz. "Lustvolle Aufklärung." (Enlightenment With Pleasure.) *THeute.* 1997; 8: 30-31. Illus.: Photo. B&W. 1. Lang.: Ger.
Germany: Hamburg. 1997. Histories-sources. ■Interview with Thomas Schmid, assistant editor of *Hamburger Morgenpost*, about the responsibility of a newspaper to provide not only an arts calendar but information and coverage of cultural issues.

323   Peter, Wolf-Dieter. "Neue Ansichten, neue Aussichten." (New Opinions, New Views.) *DB.* 1997; 12: 18-21. Illus.: Photo. B&W. 6. Lang.: Ger.
Germany: Munich. 1997. Historical studies. ■A portrait of Nationaltheater under the directorship of Peter Jonas for five years. Describes the program of first performances and contemporary directing concepts, modernism in marketing and management.

324   Quilitzsch, Frank; Jung, Matthias, photo. "Die Rolle im hohen Alter." (The Role in One's Old Age.) *TZ.* 1997; 2: 38-43. Illus.: Photo. B&W. 7. Lang.: Ger.
Germany: Weimar. 1893-1997. Historical studies. ■A portrait of Marie-Seebach-Stift, the only retirement home especially for actors in Germany, and of its founder.

325   Radunski, Peter; Schitthelm, Jürgen; Siebenhaar, Klaus. "Berlin: Die Krisenhauptstadt." (Berlin: The Capital of Crisis.) *DB.* 1997; 5: 28-34. Illus.: Photo. B&W. 8. Lang.: Ger.
Germany: Berlin. 1997. Histories-sources. ■Statements about the difficult theatre situation in the capital from different points of view by Kultursenator (Minister of the arts) Peter Radunski, director Jürgen

Schitthelm at Schaubühne and the public relations director Klaus Siebenhaar at Deutsches Theater.

326   Stammen, Silvia. "Verblasste Mythen." (Paled Myths.) *DB.* 1997; 8: 24-27. Illus.: Photo. B&W. 3. Lang.: Ger.
Germany: Munich. 1997. Historical studies. ■Reviews the situation of free theatre groups under financial pressure in Munich.

327   Stumpfe, Mario. "Standortbestimmung." (Definition of a Position.) *TZ.* 1997; 1: 47-51. Illus.: Photo. B&W. 4. Lang.: Ger.
Germany: Berlin. 1997. Histories-sources. ■A meeting of independent theatres (Nov. 22, 1996), including a public discussion of the aesthetics of the free theatre scene.

328   Bőhm, Judit; Gárdos, Katalin; Jakobi, Nóra; Svéd, Tamás; Kádár, Kata, photo. "Hogyan hat? Kolibri-előadások vizsgálata." (What Kind of Reception? Analysis of the Productions by the Kolibri Theatre.) *Sz.* 1997 ; 30(9): 29-32. Illus.: Photo. B&W. 4. Lang.: Hun.
Hungary: Budapest. 1997. Critical studies. ■A team of four analyzes, on the basis of interviews and questionnaires, the impression made by several productions of the Colibri Theatre on their young public.

329   Csáki, Judit; Izsák, Éva, photo.; Kaczur, György, photo. "A csúf jövő. Országos Gyerekszínházi Találkozó." (Unpromising Future: The Festival of Hungarian Children's Theatre.) *Sz.* 1997; 30(9): 26-28. Illus.: Photo. B&W. 2. Lang.: Hun.
Hungary: Budapest. 1997. Critical studies. ■Summary of the experiences of the author, a critic, at the children's theatre festival.

330   Enyedi, Sándor. "Erdélyi színiiskolák." (Theatre Education in Transylvania.) *Sz.* 1997; 30(9): 44. Illus.: Dwg. B&W. 1. Lang.: Hun.
Hungary. Romania. 1792-1997. Historical studies. ■Account of the history of theatre education in Transylvania, once a part of Hungary and now belonging to Romania.

331   Enyedi, Sándor. "Szabadtéri előadások Erdélyben." (Open-Air Performances in Transylvania.) *Sz.* 1997 ; 30(12): 43-44. Illus.: Photo. B&W. 1. Lang.: Hun.
Hungary. Romania. 1800-1940. Historical studies. ■The chronicle of Hungarian open-air performances in Transylvania from the beginnings, at the end of eighteenth century, up to the 1940s.

332   Forgách, András. "A 'Mészáros'—Egy műfaj határán." (The 'Mészáros'—On the Dividing Line of a Genre.) *Sz.* 1997; 30(11): 31-32. Illus.: Photo. B&W. 1. Lang.: Hun.
Hungary: Budapest. 1982-1996. Critical studies. ■Some remarks on critic Tamás Mészáros' *A Katona: Egy korszak határán* (Budapest: Pesti Szalon, 1977), a collection of interviews and reviews concerned with the history and perspectives of Budapest's famous Katona József Theatre.

333   Kelemen, István; Fábián, Imre, ed.; Szabó, József, epilogue. *Várad színészete.* (The Theatre of Nagyvárad.) Oradea: Literator-Charta; 1997. 256 pp. Index. Notes. Illus.: Photo. B&W. 15. Lang.: Hun.
Hungary: Nagyvárad. Romania: Oradea. 1798-1975. Histories-specific. ■Kelemen's 1975 monograph published on the 200th anniversary of Hungarian professional theatre in Nagyvárad/Oradea (a part of Romania since 1918).

334   Koltai, Tamás. "Ceterum censeo." *Sz.* 1997; 30(4): 1. Lang.: Hun.
Hungary. 1989-1997. Critical studies. ■Changes in values and quality in Hungarian theatre since the historic turning-point of 1989 summarized by the editor-in-chief of the *Színház*. Contesting the view of certain critics who reject entirely this new stage, he attributes the changes partly to the new social and economic conditions but also to the appearance of a new generation of artists who adopt new and different attitudes about the function of theatre.

335   Mátai, Györgyi; Kanyó, Béla, photo. "'Miért ne nyáriasíthatnánk az Operaházat? Az ötletgazda: Bán Teodóra és Kevehézi Gábor." ('Why Could We Not Have the Opera Open in Summer?' Originators: Teodóra Bán and Gábor Kevehézi.) *Tanc.* 1997; 28(3): 12-13. Illus.: Photo. B&W. 1. Lang.: Hun.

THEATRE IN GENERAL: —Institutions

Hungary: Budapest. 1991-1997. Histories-sources. ■A talk with the ballet dancer couple on their theatrical venture, 'Budafest', which is an annual Summer Opera and Ballet Festival.

336 Nánay, István; Gombos, Gabriella, photo. "Tíz év után. Beszélgetés Huszti Péterrel." (After Ten Years: An Interview with Péter Huszti.) *Sz.* 1997; 30(9): 2-5. Illus.: Photo. B&W. 2. Lang.: Hun.
Hungary: Budapest. 1987-1997. Histories-sources. ■A conversation of actor-director Péter Huszti, rector of Budapest's High School of Theatre Arts, focusing on the problems of theatre high school education.

337 Nánay, István; Simara, László, photo. "Állapotrajz." (The State of Affairs.) *Sz.* 1997; 30(9): 21-26. Illus.: Photo. B&W. 4. Lang.: Hun.
Hungary: Budapest. 1997. Historical studies. ■Survey of the recent festival of children's and youth theatre organized by the Hungarian Centre of ASSITEJ (10-15 April, 1997).

338 Nánay, István. "Dwa bratanki." *Sz.* 1997; 30(1): 1. Lang.: Hun.
Hungary. Poland. 1989-1996. Critical studies. ■Report on a round-table conference organized at the Polish Centre in Budapest with the participation of theatre managers and critics of both countries focusing on similar issues and problems in this period of radical changes and uncertainty.

339 Rajnai, Edit. "Színházfoglaló, 1945. Egy vállalkozás végjátéka." (Dispossession, 1945: The Endgame of a Theatrical Venture.) *Sz.* 1997; 30(10): 20-28. Notes. Illus.: Photo. B&W. 6. Lang.: Hun.
Hungary: Budapest. 1911-1949. Historical studies. ■The dispossession of private theatre owner Elemér Wertheimer after the Communist takeover in Hungary in the middle of the forties. Includes relevant documents.

340 Róna, Katalin; Koncz, Zsuzsa, photo. "Hármas szerepben. Beszélgetés Balikó Tamással." (In Threefold Quality: An Interview with Tamás Balikó.) *Sz.* 1997; 30(4): 30-32. Illus.: Photo. B&W. 3. Lang.: Hun.
Hungary. 1980-1996. Histories-sources. ■A talk with actor, director and manager of the Pécs National Theatre summing up his activity as a manysided theatre man.

341 Upor, László. "Felszállt a léghajó." (The Airship Has Flown Up.) *Sz.* 1997; 30(8): 1. Notes. Lang.: Hun.
Hungary: Szeged. 1997. Critical studies. ■An account of the annual National Theatre Meeting held at Szeged in June, 1997.

342 Black, Annette. "The Children's Ark." *IW.* 1997 Nov/Dec.; 46(6): 36-40. Illus.: Photo. Sketches. B&W. Color. 19. Lang.: Eng.
Ireland: Dublin. 1982-1997. Historical studies. ■History and development of children's cultural centre, The Ark. Director Martin Drury, former director of the Druid Theatre, discusses children's programs in music, drama, poetry and crafts, and adult artists who work with the children.

343 Becchi, Lorenza, ed.; Campogalliani, Francesco, ed.; Signoretti, Aldo, ed. *Accademia Teatrale Francesco Campogalliani della città di Mantova. 1946-1997 ... il catalogo è questo.* (The Francesco Campogalliani Theatrical Academy of Mantua, 1946-1997: The Catalogue.) Mantua: Casa del Mantegna; 1997. 237 pp. Illus.: Photo. Sketches. B&W. Color. Lang.: Ita.
Italy: Mantua. 1946-1997. Histories-sources. ■The repertory of the amateur company Accademia Teatrale Francesco Campogalliani on its fiftieth anniversary.

344 Guarino, Raimondo, ed. "Nuovi teatri, nuova eloquenza (con una note di Raimondo Guarino)." (New Theatres, New Eloquence—with a Note from Raimondo Guarino.) *TeatroS.* 1997; 12(19): 371-381. Notes. Lang.: Ita.
Italy. 1997. Histories-sources. ■Collection of writings of emerging Italian theatre groups, focusing on self-definition and sense of history.

345 Liszka, Tamás; Ilovszky, Béla, photo. "A semmi birodalmában. MittelFest—Cividale del Friuli." (In the Empire of Nothing: MittelFest—Cividale del Friuli.) *Sz.* 1997; 30(11): 20-22. Illus.: Photo. B&W. 3. Lang.: Hun.
Italy: Cividale del Friuli. 1997. Critical studies. ■Overview of the recent productions at the Italian festival which became the meeting place for Central European countries in the past seven years.

346 Nerbano, Mara. "Cultura materiale nel teatro delle confraternite umbre." (Material Culture and the Theatre of Umbrian Confraternities.) *TeatroS.* 1997; 12(19): 293-346. Notes. Lang.: Ita.
Italy. 1300-1578. Historical studies. ■Analysis of unpublished documents of confraternities in an effort to determine the theatrical qualities of the performance of dramatic lauds.

347 Scano, Gaetana, ed. *Periodici italiani e stranieri nella biblioteca della Fondazione Marco Besso.* (Italian and Foreign Periodicals in the Library of the Marco Besso Foundation.) Rome: Fondazione Marco Besso; 1997. 217 pp. Pref. Index. Tables. Illus.: Photo. B&W. Color. Lang.: Ita.
Italy: Rome. 1830-1997. Histories-sources. ■Catalogue of periodicals available in the foundation library, including theatre-related publications.

348 Dmitrievskaja, Ekaterina. "'Sata-97' v Nerjungri." (Sata-97 in Nerjungri.) *TeatZ.* 1997; 5-6: 23-25. Lang.: Rus.
Jakutija. 1996. Historical studies. ■Third theatre festival in the Republic of Sacha.

349 Sonnen, Arthur; Herwijnen, Karin van. *Van Schommelzang tot Licht: Tien Jaar Theaterfestival 1987-1996.* (From Rocking Chair Song to Light: Ten Years of Theaterfestival.) Amsterdam: Express-20; 1997. 252 pp. Pref. Biblio. Index. Illus.: Photo. B&W. Color. 178. Lang.: Dut.
Netherlands: Amsterdam. 1987-1996. Histories-specific. ■History of the annual Theaterfestival, with an overview of the next season's productions.

350 Voeten, Jessica. *Een Nederlands Wonder. Vijftig jaar Holland Festival.* (A Dutch Miracle: Fifty Years of the Holland Festival.) Amsterdam: Stichting Holland Festival; 1997. 239 pp. Pref. Biblio. Gloss. Index. Illus.: Graphs. Poster. Photo. B&W. Color. 208. Lang.: Dut.
Netherlands. 1947-1997. Histories-specific. ■Jubilee volume for the Holland Festival, with coverage of programming, international productions in theatre, dance, and opera.

351 Fryz-Więcek, Agnieska. "Around the Press." *TP.* 1997; 39(2): 40-42. Illus.: Photo. B&W. 1. Lang.: Eng, Fre.
Poland: Cracow. 1996. Historical studies. ■Overview of productions at the Fifth Festival of the Union of Theatres of Europe, critical responses.

352 Gruszczyński, Piotr. "The 25th Warsaw Theatre Meetings." *TP.* 1997; 39(2): 17-19. Illus.: Photo. B&W. 1. Lang.: Eng, Fre.
Poland: Warsaw. 1997. Historical studies. ■Overview of the best Polish theatre performances (distinguished with awards) from other festivals and presented to the Warsaw public. Trends in material presented, productions and companies represented.

353 Koltai, Tamás. "A színház mint metafora. Unió-fesztivál Krakkóban." (The Theatre as Metaphor: The UNIO Festival in Cracow.) *Sz.* 1997; 30(1): 44-48. Illus.: Photo. B&W. 5. Lang.: Hun.
Poland: Cracow. 1996. Critical studies. ■Account of the latest Festival of the European Theatre Union held in Cracow.

354 Lajos, Sándor. "Visztula-parti esték. Kontakt'97 Toruńban." (Theatre Evenings on the Banks of the Vistula: Kontakt '97 in Toruń.) *Sz.* 1997; 30(11): 17-20. Illus.: Photo. B&W. 4. Lang.: Hun.
Poland: Toruń. 1997. Reviews of performances. ■Notes on the interesting contribution of the Baltic theatres to the festival and analysis of a performance of T. S. Eliot's *Murder in the Cathedral* produced by the Hungarian National Theatre from Ukraine.

355 Meils, Cathy. "Seven Years After the Revolutions." *AmTh.* 1997 Oct.; 14(8): 90-92. Illus.: Photo. B&W. 2. Lang.: Eng.
Poland: Toruń. 1990-1997. Historical studies. ■Kontakt international theatre festival: impact of political and social upheaval on development of theatre culture, representation of Lithuania at the festival.

356 Nánay, István. "Színházi gyors. Lengyel vendégjátékok." ('Polonia Express': Polish Guest Performances.) *Sz.* 1997; 30(5): 26-28. Illus.: Photo. B&W. 2. Lang.: Hun.

THEATRE IN GENERAL: —Institutions

Poland. Hungary: Budapest. 1996. Historical studies. ■Summary of a festival of modern Polish art, entitled 'Polonia Express', organized by the Institute for Polish Culture in Budapest.

357 Spiegel, Krystyna. "The Poster Museum in Wilanów." *TP*. 1997; 39(1): 45-46. Illus.: Poster. B&W. 1. Lang.: Eng, Fre.
Poland: Wilanów. 1966-1997. Critical studies. ■World's first poster museum: archives, conservation studios, permanent displays, historical presentations.

358 Taranienko, Zbigniew; Urbański, Leon, designer. *Gardzienice. Praktyki teatralne Włodzimierza Staniewskogo.* (Gardzienice: Włodzimierz Staniewski's Theatrical Practices.) Lublin: Wydawnictwo Test; 1997. 132 pp. Pref. Index. Tables. Append. Illus.: Photo. Maps. B&W. Color. Architec. Detail. Grd.Plan. R.Elev. Fr.Elev. Schematic. 133. Lang.: Pol.
Poland: Gardzienice. 1976-1996. Histories-specific. ■Twenty years of the activities of Staniewski's experimental theatre group Ośrodek Praktyk Teatralnych, located in the village of Gardzienice in the Lublin region: performances, gatherings, anthropological research, training, acting method, and the search for 'a new ecology of theatre'.

359 Tyszka, Juliusz; Cynkutis, Jolanta, transl.; Randolph, Tom, transl. "The School of Being Together: Festivals as National Therapy during the Polish 'Period of Transition'." *NTQ*. 1997; 13(50): 171-182. Notes. Illus.: Photo. B&W. 11. Lang.: Eng.
Poland. 1989-1995. Historical studies. ■Surveys the numerous theatre festivals that, despite economic stringency, have sprung up or renewed themselves since the end of the Cold War and sees their success as a form of national celebration.

360 Vaïs, Michel. "Séoul, où S? C'est où l'horizon critique s'élargit?" (Seoul, Where iS it? It's Where the Critical Horizon Is Expanded.) *JCT*. 1997; 85: 149-157. Notes. Illus.: Poster. Photo. B&W. 6. Lang.: Fre.
Poland. Uruguay. Finland. South Korea. 1992-1997. Historical studies. ■Developments at meetings of the International Association of Theatre Critics in Warsaw '92, Montevideo '94, Helsinki '96 and Seoul '97.

361 Visky, András; Koncz, Zsuzsa, photo. "Hermészi szerepben. A dramaturg és a szöveg." (In the Role of Hermes: The Dramaturg and the Playtext.) *Sz*. 1997; 30(7): 30-33. Illus.: Photo. B&W. 3. Lang.: Hun.
Romania: Bucharest. Hungary. 1997. Critical studies. ■Edited version of the Hungarian lecture at the Bucharest conference of AICT, the international federation of theatre critics. Visky, literary manager of the Hungarian State Theatre of Kolozsvár/Cluj-Napoca, Romania, expounded his views on the present functions of a literary manager or dramaturg.

362 Berezkin, V. "Plastičeskij teat'r: avangardnaja eres' ili drugoe iskusstvo?" (Plastic Theatre: Avant-Garde Nonsense or a Different Art?)*TeatZ*. 1997; 1: 35-39. Lang.: Rus.
Russia. 1996. Historical studies. ■Thoughts on the plastic art of contemporary theatre, with respect to the festival Konfrontacja-96.

363 Bespal'ceva, G. "Ot 'Kon'ka-Gorbunka' do 'Lolity'." (From Kon'ka-Gorbunka to Lolity.) *Otčij kraj*. 1997; 2: 138-143. Lang.: Rus.
Russia: Volgograd. 1997. Historical studies. ■Profile of Volgogradskij Teat'r Junogo Zritelja (Volgograd Youth Theatre).

364 Dubnova, E. "Leonid Andrejév, novaja žizn'." (Leonid Andrejév: A New Life.) *SovD*. 1997; 2: 183-192. Lang.: Rus.
Russia: Orel. 1996. Historical studies. ■Report on the festival of Russian theatres, dedicated to the 125th anniversary of the birth of writer Leonid Andrejév.

365 Gauss, Rebecca Banker. *Studios of the Moscow Art Theatre from 1905-1927.* Boulder, CO: Univ. of Colorado; 1997. 260 pp. Notes. Biblio. [Ph.D. Dissertation, Univ. Microfilms Order No. AAC 9725731.] Lang.: Eng.
Russia. 1905-1927. Critical studies. ■Argues that the studios offered new approaches to staging, explored new dramatic literature, and provided a fertile ground for the 'new' acting theories of Stanislavskij.

366 Gvozdeva, A. "Bol'šoj teat'r malenkogo goroda." (Big Theatre in a Small City.) *NasSovr*. 1997; 248(10): 253. Lang.: Rus.
Russia. 1997. Historical studies. ■First all-Russian festival of theatres from small Russian cities, held in Vušnij Voloček in the Tversky district.

367 Kirillova, Natalija. "Teatral'nyj bum konca XX veka." (Theatrical High Point at the Sunrise of the Twentieth Century.) *TeatZ*. 1997; 11-12: 19-20. Lang.: Rus.
Russia: Moscow. 1996-1997. Histories-sources. ■Interview with Anatolij Smeljanski regarding the work of theatre artists who have won the Zolotoj maski (Golden Mask) and the festival dedicated to their work.

368 Novikova, Lidija. "Dom, gde sogrevajutsja serdca." (The House that Warms the Heart.) *TeatZ*. 1997; 9-10: 40-42. Lang.: Rus.
Russia: Moscow. 1990-1997. Historical studies. ■Profile of the Dom Aktera (Actors' House), directed by Margarita Eskina.

369 Soldatina, Ja. "Pomoč' i zaščitit'." (To Help and Protect.) *TeatZ*. 1997; 9-10: 54-55. Lang.: Rus.
Russia: Moscow. 1990-1997. Histories-sources. ■Interview with A. Majakovskij, director of the Russian Theatre Union (Sojuz Teatral'nych Dejatelej), about current economic conditions.

370 *The European Cultural Month Ljubljana 1997.* Ljubljana: Municipality of Ljubljana; 1997. 199 pp. Illus.: Photo. B&W. Color. Lang.: Eng.
Slovenia: Ljubljana. 1997. Histories-sources. ■Program for the European Cultural Month held in Ljubljana May 15 to July 5, 1997.

371 Kač, Tatjana. "Igralo se je, pelo in plesalo—skratka zabavalo." (There Was Singing and Dancing, In Short, Much Merriment.) *CZN*. 1997; 30: 45-70. Lang.: Slo.
Slovenia: Celje. 1896-1914. Historical studies. ■The role of Celje's National Cultural Center in Slovene life and resistance to Germanization, with emphasis on the beginnings of amateur theatre before the establishment of professional companies.

372 Potočnik, Dragan. "Ljubiteljski odri v Mariboru v obdobju od 1918 do 1941." (Amateur Stages in Maribor, 1918-1941.) *CZN*. 1997; 68(1): 79-91. Lang.: Slo.
Slovenia: Maribor. 1918-1941. Historical studies. ■History of the amateur theatre groups that existed alongside the National Theatre in Maribor.

373 Šuligoj, Ljubica. "Ptujska čitalnica in njen Narodni dom." (The Ptuj Reading Society and its National Cultural Center.) *CZN*. 1997; 30: 115-134. Lang.: Slo.
Slovenia: Ptuj. 1864-1942. Historical studies. ■Theatrical activities in Ptuj within the context of the Reading Society, an important prewar Slovene institution that was instrumental in the struggle to preserve ethnic identity and a national consciousness.

374 Van Daele, Koen, ed. *Mesto žensk.* (City of Women.) Ljubljana: Open Society Fund; 1997. 33 pp. Illus.: Photo. B&W. Lang.: Slo.
Slovenia: Ljubljana. 1997. Histories-sources. ■Program for the International Festival of Contemporary Arts City of Women.

375 Varga, Sándor. *A szlovéniai magyarok műkedvelő tevékenysége 1920-1970.* (The Hungarian Amateur Theatre in Slovenia (Yugoslavia) 1920-1970.) Lendva-Győr: Magyar Nemzetiségi Művelődési Intézet-Hazánk; 1997. 135 pp. Illus.: Photo. B&W. 111. Lang.: Hun.
Slovenia. 1920-1970. Histories-specific. ■A history of the Hungarian-language amateur acting in Slovenia.

376 Bain, Keith. "Berkoff, Boerwors and Box-Office Betrayal: Standard Bank National Arts Festival." *SATJ*. 1997 May/Sep.; 11 (1/2): 238-258. Biblio. Illus.: Photo. B&W. 2. Lang.: Eng.
South Africa, Republic of: Grahamstown. 1997. Historical studies. ■Report on the 1997 Standard Bank National Arts Festival.

377 Blumer, Arnold. "The Future of the Performing Arts Councils in a New South Africa." 260-271 in Davis, Geoffrey V., ed.; Fuchs, Anne, ed. *Theatre and Change in South Africa.* Amsterdam: Harwood Academic Publishing; 1996. (Contemporary Theatre Studies 12.) Notes. Index. Append. Lang.: Eng.
South Africa, Republic of. 1963-1995. Critical studies. ■On the future political and social changes in South African Performing Arts Councils.

THEATRE IN GENERAL: —Institutions

378 Davis, Geoffrey V.; Fuchs, Anne. "'It's Time to Have a South African Culture': An Interview with Ramolao Makhene." 272-297 in Davis, Geoffrey V., ed.; Fuchs, Anne, ed. *Theatre and Change in South Africa.* Amsterdam: Harwood Academic Publishing; 1996. (Contemporary Theatre Studies 12.) Notes. Index. Append. Lang.: Eng.
South Africa, Republic of. 1976-1996. Histories-sources. ■Interview with Ramolao Makhene, a founder of Performing Arts Workers Equity (PAWE) and his work with creating arts agencies.

379 Steinberg, Carol. "PACT: Can the Leopard Change Its Spots?" 246-259 in Davis, Geoffrey V., ed.; Fuchs, Anne, ed. *Theatre and Change in South Africa.* Amsterdam: Harwood Academic Publishing; 1996. (Contemporary Theatre Studies 12.) Notes. Index. Append. Biblio. Lang.: Eng.
South Africa, Republic of. 1963-1995. Critical studies. ■Explores the origins and current strategies of the Performing Arts Council of the Transvaal (PACT), a government-funded agency for the arts. Calls for radical restructuring to decolonize the performing arts in South Africa.

380 van Zyl, Johan. "Afrikaners en Andere: Die Klein Karoo Nasionale Kunstefees." (Afrikaaners and Others: The Little Karoo National Arts Festival.) *SATJ.* 1997 May/Sep.; 11(1/2): 216-225. Biblio. Illus.: Photo. B&W. 2. Lang.: Afr.
South Africa, Republic of: Oudtshoorn. 1997. Historical studies. ■Survey of the 1997 Little Karoo National Arts Festival.

381 Carlsson, Hasse. "Från Kapten Zoom till Ulf Kjell Gür." (From Captain Zoom To Ulf Kjell Gür.) *Tningen.* 1997 ; 21(5): 36-38. Illus.: Photo. B&W. Lang.: Swe.
Sweden. 1977-1997. Historical studies. ■A survey of the twenty years of the publication *Nya Teatertidningen.*

382 Fransson, Emma. "Vem försvarar teater?" (Who Defends the Theatre?) *Tningen.* 1997; 21(5): 10-11. Illus.: Dwg. B&W. Lang.: Swe.
Sweden. 1997. Histories-sources. ■An interview with two theatre researchers, Jenny Fogelquist and Magnus Kirchhoff, about the situation of the Swedish theatres today and the estrangement between the active theatre and the establishment.

383 Hallin, Ulrika. "Ryms världskulturen på Södra Teatern?" (Will There Be Room For the Cultures of the World In the Södra Teatern?) *Tningen.* 1997; 21(5): 45-47. Illus.: Photo. Color. Lang.: Swe.
Sweden: Stockholm. 1997. Historical studies. ■A presentation of the transforming of Södra Teatern into a forum for the cultures of the world, with reference to the report by Lars Enqvist and the newly appointed director, Ozan Sunar.

384 D'Anna-Huber, Christine. "Jenseits des 'Röstigraben'." (Beyond the 'Röstigraben'.) *TZ.* 1997; 6: 14-17. Illus.: Photo. B&W. 3. Lang.: Ger.
Switzerland. 1989-1997. Historical studies. ■Portraits of the theatres Comédie (Genf) and Théâtre Vidy (Lausanne).

385 Engelhardt, Barbara. "Zugluft in der Zentralschweiz." (Draught in Central Switzerland.) *TZ.* 1997; 6: 7-12. Illus.: Photo. B&W. 9. Lang.: Ger.
Switzerland: Zurich. 1997. Historical studies. ■Impressions from a week in Zurich. Describes the Zürcher Schauspielhaus, Theater Neumarkt and Theater in der Gessnerallee.

386 Brock, Susan. "International Shakespeare Association Approaches Silver Anniversary." *ShN.* 1997 Win; 47(4): 65, 76. Notes. [Number 235.] Lang.: Eng.
UK-England: Stratford. 1997. Historical studies. ■Overview of history of ISA, their activities, goals, contact information.

387 Davidson, Geoff. "Marie Tempest: The End of Her Story." *TN.* 1997; 51(1): 23-25. Lang.: Eng.
UK-England: London. 1935-1937. Historical studies. ■Campaign for a hospital ward devoted to the care of actors, for which Tempest raised funds until her death in 1937. Ward opened in 1935 and survived in her name until 1980 when the hospital was relocated.

388 Nobling, Torsten. "London bjöd på intressanta möten." (London Offered Interesting Encounters.) *ProScen.* 1997; 21(1): 12-15. Illus.: Photo. B&W. Lang.: Swe.
UK-England: London. 1996. Historical studies. ■A report from OISTAT's meeting of the commission of architects, where they discussed the Prague Quadrennial and were shown the new Glyndebourne Opera House.

389 Nobling, Torsten. "Rapport från Arkitekturkommisionens möte i London." (A Report From the Meeting of the Commission of Architects at London.) *ProScen.* 1997; 21(2): 13-15. Illus.: Dwg. Photo. B&W. Lang.: Swe.
UK-England: London. 1996. Historical studies. ■A continuation of the report from OISTAT's meeting with reference to the New Globe Theatre and what was dealt with in the five different sessions.

390 "Scottish and Brave." *Econ.* 1997 Aug 30-Sep 5; 344(8032): 65-66. Illus.: Photo. B&W. 1. Lang.: Eng.
UK-Scotland: Edinburgh. 1947-1997. Critical studies. ■Success of Edinburgh festival on occasion of its fiftieth anniversary. Brief mention of productions and revivals featured.

391 Benecke, Patricia. "Perfekte Momente, lustvolles Chaos." (Perfect Moments, Chaos With Pleasure.) *THeute.* 1997; 10: 29-33. Illus.: Photo. B&W. 4. Lang.: Ger.
UK-Scotland: Edinburgh. 1997. Critical studies. ■Impressions from the Edinburgh Festival including *Timeless* by David Greig directed by Graham Eatough and played by the company Suspect Culture, *East Palace, West Palace* written and directed by Zhang Yuan, *Cegada de Amor (Blinded by Love)* directed by Jordi Milan and played by company La Cubana and *Blue Heart* by Caryl Churchill directed by Max Stafford-Clark at Traverse.

392 Fisher, Mark. "Scottish Theatres Run by Women." *TheatreF.* 1997 Sum/Fall; 11: 49-54. Illus.: Photo. 5. Lang.: Eng.
UK-Scotland. 1996. Historical studies. ■Profiles Irina Brown at Tron Theatre in Glasgow, Cathie Boyd at Theatre Cryptic, Nicola McCartney at LookOut, Gerda Stevenson at Stellar Quines, Mariela Stevenson at fActional Theatre, Muireann Kelly at Theatre Galore.

393 Loney, Glenn. "Festival and Fringe in Edinburgh." *WES.* 1997 Fall; 9(3): 27-36. Illus.: Photo. 5. Lang.: Eng.
UK-Scotland: Edinburgh. 1997. Historical studies. ■Report on the final three weeks of the Edinburgh Festival, including the Fringe Festival.

394 "1997-98 Season Schedules." *AmTh.* 1997 Oct.; 14(8): 27-55. Illus.: Photo. B&W. 9. Lang.: Eng.
USA. 1997-1998. Historical studies. ■Comprehensive listing of productions, dates and directors at Theatre Communications Group constituent theatres nationwide.

395 "'97 Summer Festivals." *AmTh.* 1997 May/June; 14(5): 19-29. Illus.: Photo. B&W. 11. Lang.: Eng.
USA. Europe. Asia. 1997. Histories-sources. ■Comprehensive list of national and international summer festivals: dates, productions, directors, contact information. Includes separate list of Shakespeare festivals.

396 Berson, Misha. "The Other Side of the Rainbow." *AmTh.* 1997 Oct.; 14(8): 18-23, 94-95. Illus.: Photo. B&W. 14. Lang.: Eng.
USA: Seattle, WA. 1980-1997. Historical studies. ■Theatrical renaissance in Seattle beginning around 1980. Artistic directors Sharon Ott (Seattle Repertory), Gordon Edelstein (Contemporary Theatre), Warner Shook (Intiman Theatre) and Eddie Levi Lee (Empty Space) discuss audience development, productions, challenges in producing, theatrical missions. Sidebar articles describe the current state of theatre in Los Angeles, CA, Austin, TX, Atlanta, GA and Providence, RI.

397 Brown, Abena Joan. "Developing Black Performing Arts Institutions." *AfAmR.* 1997 Win; 31(4): 611-615. Lang.: Eng.
USA: Chicago, IL. 1996. Histories-sources. ■ETA Creative Arts Foundation's president's views on developing institutions for the Black performing arts, culled from a 1996 video interview.

398 Coen, Stephanie. "Paradise North." *AmTh.* 1997 Jan.; 14(1): 60-63. Illus.: Photo. B&W. 3. Lang.: Eng.
USA: Poughkeepsie, NY. 1930-1997. Historical studies. ■New York Stage and Film theatre company in residence at Vassar College. Founders and producing directors Max Mayer, Leslie Urdang and Mark Linn-Baker discuss goals of company, past and current productions.

THEATRE IN GENERAL: —Institutions

399   Crestani, Eliana. *Traveling Actress and Manager in the Nineteenth Century: The Western Career of Nellie Boyd, 1879-1888.* Tucson, AZ: Univ. of Arizona; 1997. 152 pp. [M.A. Thesis, Univ. Microfilms Order No. AAC 1384552.] Lang.: Eng.
USA. 1879-1888. Historical studies. ■The activity of the Nellie Boyd Dramatic Company, which performed exclusively in the western U.S., pioneering several southwestern territories. Analyzes the company's impact on the life of particular western towns, the organization of the company, its repertoire and the possible significance of Boyd's choice of roles, and critical reception.

400   Gold, Sylvaine. "The Disney Difference." *AmTh.* 1997 Dec.; 14(10): 14-18, 50-53. Illus.: Photo. Sketches. B&W. 12. Lang.: Eng.
USA: New York, NY. 1990-1997. Historical studies. ■Disney Corporation's investment in theatres and real estate on Broadway and its impact on community and Broadway theatre. Success of their productions of *Beauty and the Beast* and *The Lion King*, reactions from other Broadway and Off Broadway theatre companies.

401   Kimbis, Thomas Peter. "Planning to Survive: How the National Endowment for the Arts Restructured Itself to Serve a New Constituency." *ColJL&A.* 1997 Spr/Sum; 21(3/4): 239-272. Notes. Lang.: Eng.
USA: Washington, DC. 1979-1997. Historical studies. ■Comprehensive picture of the NEA during its restructuring process, illustrating its priorities and its mechanisms for determining those priorities.

402   Lennartz, Knut. "Im Schatten von Hollywood." (In Hollywood's Shadow.) *DB.* 1997; 2: 36-38. Illus.: Photo. B&W. 5. Lang.: Ger.
USA: Los Angeles, CA. 1996-1997. Historical studies. ■A portrait of the Colony Theatre in Los Angeles, one of 200 not-for-profit theatre groups in the USA who joined together in the Theatre Communication Group, and the working conditions.

403   McDonald, Arthur. "Spoleto: Theatre Takes Many Forms at U.S. Festival." *SoTh.* 1997 Win; 38(1): 4-11. Illus.: Photo. B&W. 4. Lang.: Eng.
USA: Charleston, SC. 1976-1996. Historical studies. ■Overview of the attractions presented at the 1996 Spoleto Festival in Charleston, SC, with sidebars on 'Piccolo Spoleto: The 'Fringe' of Spoleto' and a brief history of the Festival.

404   Moore, Dick. "Candlelight Goes Out in Chicago." *EN.* 1997 July/Aug.; 82(6): 2. Lang.: Eng.
USA: Chicago, IL. 1997. Historical studies. ■The Candlelight Dinner Theatre, the nation's oldest dinner theatre, closes its doors due to financial difficulties.

405   Moore, Maureen. "There Is a Doctor in the House: An Interview with Dr. Barry Kohn." *EN.* 1997 Oct.; 82(8): 3. Illus.: Photo. 2. Lang.: Eng.
USA: New York, NY. 1997. Histories-sources. ■Interview with Dr. Barry Kohn, founder of Physician Volunteers for the Arts, a non-profit corporation that provides free medical and allergy care for the performing community in New York City and Los Angeles.

406   Nunns, Stephen. "NEA Wins Vote, Loses Alexander." *AmTh.* 1997 Nov.; 14(9): 70-71. Illus.: Photo. B&W. 1. Lang.: Eng.
USA: Washington, DC. 1997. Historical studies. ■Preservation of the National Endowment for the Arts by the House and Senate, resignation of NEA's chairman Jane Alexander. Includes sidebar article on public funding disputes over controversial plays in Charlotte, NC.

407   Palmer, Caroline. "A Bridled Anarchy." *AmTh.* 1997 Sep.; 14(7): 50-53. Illus.: Photo. B&W. 6. Lang.: Eng.
USA. 1984-1997. Historical studies. ■Origins, work and funding of National Performance Network which provides partnership opportunities to artists and organizations whose work lies outside the mainstream, and links up primary sponsors and performing artists from around the country. Includes sidebar article on companies which have benefitted from NPN's efforts.

408   Reiss, Alvin H. "Arts Presenters Confronting a Constantly Changing Scene." *FundM.* 1997 Mar.; 28(1): 38-39. Illus.: Photo. B&W. 1. Lang.: Eng.
USA: New York, NY. 1997. Historical studies. ■Overview of the forty-ninth annual conference of International Society for the Performing Arts and the fortieth annual conference of Association of Performing Arts Presenters, held in New York City.

409   Reiss, Alvin H. "For Long Term NEA Survival, Arts Must Reach Unreached Constituencies." *FundM.* 1997 June; 28(4): 36-37. Illus.: Photo. B&W. 1. Lang.: Eng.
USA: Washington, DC. 1997. Critical studies. ■Differences between advocates of government funding of the arts through the NEA and their opponents in Congress.

410   Reiss, Alvin H. "Partnership Boosts Local Cultural Activities to Woo Theme Park Tourists and Conventioneers." *FundM.* 1997 Sep.; 28(7): 20-21. Illus.: Photo. B&W. 1. Lang.: Eng.
USA: Orlando, FL. 1997. Critical studies. ■Strategies employed by the Orlando/Peabody Alliance for the Arts and Culture to draw an audience from among the tourists and conventioneers.

411   Samuels, Steven; Dineen, Jennifer; Valade, David S. "Theatre Facts 1996." *AmTh.* 1997 Dec.; 14(10): 26-30. Tables. Lang.: Eng.
USA. 1996. Historical studies. ■Results of Theatre Communications Group annual fiscal survey of regional theatres. How changes in National Endowment for the Arts and the Financial Accounting Standards Board policies are affecting theatres, attendance figures, income.

412   Tsuruta, Dorothy Randall. "The African-American Drama Company: Twenty Years of Cultural Work." *BlackM.* 1997 Feb/Mar.; 12(3): 7-8. Illus.: Photo. B&W. 2. Lang.: Eng.
USA: Santa Clara, CA. 1977-1997. Historical studies. ■The AADC's twenty years of bringing lives and cultures of African Americans to theatres and campuses across the nation.

413   Walker, Victor Leo, II. "The National Black Theatre Summit 'On Golden Pond'—March 2-7, 1998." *AfAmR.* 1997 Win; 31(4): 621-627. Biblio. Notes. Lang.: Eng.
USA. 1997. Historical studies. ■The upcoming National Black Theatre Summit being held at Dartmouth College to discuss specific strategies for maintaining, building and funding Black theatre companies and institutions nationwide.

Performance spaces

414   Jordan, Robert. "The Georgian Theatre in Sydney: Some Facts and Problems." *TN.* 1997; 51(3): 128-146. Notes. Illus.: Maps. Dwg. B&W. Lang.: Eng.
Australia: Sydney. 1796-1820. Historical studies. ■Study of the Sydney Theatre built by convicts from Britain. Drawing on the limited primary resources available the author focuses on the site, duration and financiers of the theatre.

415   "Curtain Up! Light the Lights!" *LD&A.* 1997 Mar.; 27(3): 58-63. Illus.: Photo. Color. 7. Lang.: Eng.
Canada: Vancouver, BC. 1997. Technical studies. ■The lighting in Suzanne Powadiuk's overall design for the Ford Centre for the Performing Arts.

416   Brickenden, Jack. "The Long-Awaited Guelph Civic Centre Is Now a Reality." *PAC.* 1997; 30(4): 34-35. Illus.: Photo. B&W. 2. Lang.: Eng.
Canada: Guelph, ON. 1997. Historical studies. ■The new Guelph Civic Centre which has been in planning stages for many years and its facilities for over fifty organizations.

417   Eley, Wallace G.; Waite, Duane R. "Command Performance." *LD&A.* 1995 Feb.; 25(2): 107-109. Illus.: Photo. Color. 4. Lang.: Eng.
Canada: Toronto, ON. 1994. Technical studies. ■House lighting design for the newly built Princess of Wales Theatre.

418   Vigeant, Louise. "La nouvelle Maison Théâtre." (The New Maison Théâtre.) *JCT.* 1997; 85: 134-136. Illus.: Photo. B&W. 3. Lang.: Fre.
Canada: Montreal, PQ. 1997. Historical studies. ■Architectural changes to Maison Théâtre, performance space for Montreal children's theatre companies.

419   Maxa, Miloslav. "Das Prager Theater Spirála." (Prague's 'Spirala' Theatre.) *BtR.* 1997; 91(2): 18-21. Illus.: Photo. Plan. Color. Schematic. 11. Lang.: Ger.

THEATRE IN GENERAL: —Performance spaces

Czech Republic: Prague. 1991-1997. Historical studies. ■Description of the cylindrical theatre in which there are three levels for performance and several levels for spectators. Includes description of lighting and projection system.

420 Bawcutt, N.W. "Documents of The Salisbury Court Theatre in the British Library." *MRDE.* 1997; 9(1): 179-193. Notes. Lang.: Eng.
England: London. 1629-1639. Historical studies. ■Overview of documents relating to the Salisbury Court Theatre, the last theatre to be built in London before the outbreak of civil war.

421 Berry, Herbert. "The First Public Playhouses, Especially the Red Lion." *SQ.* 1989 Sum; 40(2): 133-148. Notes. Append. Illus.: Dwg. B&W. 1. Lang.: Eng.
England: London. 1567-1576. Historical studies. ■Discusses history of the first public theatres in London, specifically the Red Lion.

422 Elliott, John R., Jr.; Nelson, Alan H. "The Universities: Early Staging in Cambridge and Oxford." 59-76 in Cox, John D., ed.; Kastan, David Scott, ed. *A New History of Early English Drama.* New York, NY: Columbia UP; 1997. 565 pp. Notes. Biblio. Index. Grd.Plan. 3. Lang.: Eng.
England: Oxford, Cambridge. 1540-1620. Historical studies. ■Analysis of English Renaissance academic theatres as playing spaces. Examines the spaces themselves and also plays for staging directions.

423 Garlick, A.G.G. *Neo-Classicism and English Theatre Architecture, 1775-1843.* Unpublished Ph.D. thesis, Univ. of Exeter: 1996. Notes. Biblio. Illus.: Dwg. B&W. [Abstract in *Index to Theses,* 46-9203.] Lang.: Eng.
England. 1775-1843. Histories-specific. ■Based on a visual analysis of contemporary English and continental theatre drawings and engravings, together with a detailed study of contemporary architectural treatises and descriptive accounts, this thesis attempts to assess the extent to which English theatres reflected neo-classical practices in Europe.

424 Orrell, John. "The Theaters." 93-112 in Cox, John D., ed.; Kastan, David Scott, ed. *A New History of Early English Drama.* New York, NY: Columbia UP; 1997. 565 pp. Notes. Biblio. Index. Illus.: GP. 2. Lang.: Eng.
England. 1600-1650. Historical studies. ■Analysis of theatrical spaces in early modern England, with focus on three areas: the court theatre, the private theatres such as Blackfriars, the early public playhouses such as the Rose and the two great public playhouses, the Globe and the Fortune.

425 Stern, Tiffany. "Was *Totus Mundus Agit Histrionem* Ever the Motto of the Globe Theatre?" *TN.* 1997; 51(3): 122-127. Notes. Lang.: Eng.
England: London. 1599-1720. Historical studies. ■Factual evidence suggests that *Totus...* was used as a motto by Drury Lane Theatre until the early eighteenth century. All attempts to link the phrase with the Globe, first forwarded by Edmund Malone, are based on conjecture and stem largely from associations with the 'All the World's a Stage' speech in *As You Like It* (II, vii).

426 Wasson, John M. "The English Church as Theatrical Space." 25-38 in Cox, John D., ed.; Kastan, David Scott, ed. *A New History of Early English Drama.* New York, NY: Columbia UP; 1997. 565 pp. Notes. Biblio. Index. Lang.: Eng.
England. 1100-1300. Critical studies. ■Using historical archival records, examines the different stages throughout England and theorizes possible staging practices from the records and from stage directions in several of the plays such as the anonymous *Adam* and *The Play of the Sacrament.*

427 Westfall, Suzanne. "'A Commonty a Christmas gambold or a tumbling trick': Household Theater." 39-58 in Cox, John D., ed.; Kastan, David Scott, ed. *A New History of Early English Drama.* New York, NY: Columbia UP; 1997. 565 pp. Notes. Biblio. Lang.: Eng.
England. 1400-1550. Historical studies. ■Analysis of early English household theatre, including revels and entertainments, considering the household as 'stage,' resident household personnel as performers, the aristocratic producer, the audiences, and the performers themselves.

428 Longman, Stanley V. "The Idea of the Playhouse." 9-14 in Castagno, Paul C., ed. *Theatrical Spaces and Dramatic Places: The Reemergence of the Theatre Building in the Renaissance.* Tuscaloosa, AL: Univ of Alabama P; 1996. 151 pp. (Southeastern Theatre Conference Theatre Symposium 4.) Biblio. Lang.: Eng.
Europe. 1995. Historical studies. ■Introductory essay of symposium on Renaissance stages.

429 Mohler, Frank. "A Brief Shining Moment: An Effect That Disappeared from the Illusionistic Stage." 83-90 in Castagno, Paul C., ed. *Theatrical Spaces and Dramatic Places: The Reemergence of the Theatre Building in the Renaissance.* Tuscaloosa, AL: Univ of Alabama P; 1996. 151 pp. (Southeastern Theatre Conference Theatre Symposium 4.) Biblio. Illus.: Photo. Dwg. 5. Lang.: Eng.
Europe. 1600-1700. Historical studies. ■On the spectacular celestial effects of the seventeenth-century European stage. Examines the decline of a specific machine that enabled a device to travel through the sky from upstage to downstage, then expand to fill the stage.

430 Staub, August W.; Justice-Malloy, Rhona. "Gothic and Post-Gothic Theatre: Cities, Paradise, *Corrales,* Globes, and Olimpico." 132-139 in Castagno, Paul C. *Theatrical Spaces and Dramatic Places: The Reemergence of the Theatre Building in the Renaissance.* Tuscaloosa, AL: Univ of Alabama P; 1996. 151 pp. (Southeastern Theatre Conference Theatre Symposium 4.) Biblio. Lang.: Eng.
Europe. 1300-1650. Historical studies. ■Reassessing the impact of the roofed theatre. Argues that this form was part of a long evolution from the theatre space of the Middle Ages and that earlier theatres could have been roofed, but theatre builders and practitioners chose not to do so.

431 Scott, Virginia. "'My Lord, the Parterre': Space, Society, and Symbol in the Seventeenth-Century French Theatre." 62-75 in Castagno, Paul C., ed. *Theatrical Spaces and Dramatic Places: The Reemergence of the Theatre Building in the Renaissance.* Tuscaloosa, AL: Univ of Alabama P; 1996. 151 pp. (Southeastern Theatre Conference Theatre Symposium 4.) Biblio. Lang.: Eng.
France. 1600-1700. Historical studies. ■Traces the history of the parterre, both the physical space within the theatre and the audience members that peopled it. Author traces its evolution and its effect on French theatre.

432 Daberto, Reinhold. "Kurhaustheater Göggingen." *BtR.* 1997; 91(special issue): 30-39. Append. Illus.: Dwg. Photo. Plan. B&W. Color. Explod.Sect. Fr.Elev. Grd.Plan. 16. Lang.: Ger.
Germany: Göggingen. 1885-1997. Historical studies. ■Describes the Kurhaustheater (Health Resort Theatre) which was built in 1885 with a modern architectural language, functionality, spatial effects and technical standards, the design in advance of its time. Concerns itself with construction history, with the past and present architectural and restoration solutions.

433 Ehrlich, Willi. "Das Goethe-Theater in Bad Lauchstädt." (The Goethe Theatre in Bad Lauchstädt.) *BtR.* 1997; 91 (2): 12-18. Illus.: Photo. Dwg. Plan. B&W. Color. Detail. Explod. Sect. Grd.Plan. Schematic. 23. Lang.: Ger.
Germany: Bad Lauchstädt. 1768-1997. Historical studies. ■Reports on the history of this house, which represents an architectural and technical monument in the tradition of Goethe.

434 Gerling, Kurt. "Prinzregententheater München." (Prinzregententheater in Munich.) *BtR.* 1997; 91(3): 8-14. Illus.: Dwg. Photo. Plan. B&W. Color. Explod.Sect. Detail. Grd. Plan. 16. Lang.: Ger.
Germany: Munich. 1901-1997. Historical studies. ■The history and reconstruction of the technology as well as the new installations of the Prinzregententheater, built in 1901 by Max Littman.

435 Grundmann, Ute. "Wo der Wellbaum ächzt..." (Where the Tree Creaks...)*DB.* 1997; 9: 32-35. Illus.: Photo. B&W. 4. Lang.: Ger.
Germany: Bad Lauchstädt, Gotha. 1681-1997. Historical studies. ■Profile of the Goethe-Theater of Bad Lauchstädt and the Ekhof-

THEATRE IN GENERAL: —Performance spaces

Theater of Gotha: the architecture, equipment, and audience appeal of these traditional theatres.

436 Mercouris, Spyros. *Mia Skene Gia Ton Dionyso. Theatrikós Chóros & Archaío Dráma.* (A Stage for Dionysos: Theatrical Space & Ancient Drama.) Thessaloniki: Kapon; 1997. 215 pp. Pref. Index. Biblio. Tables. Illus.: Design. Pntg. Diagram. Photo. Plan. Dwg. Maps. B&W. Color. 160. Lang.: Eng, Gre. Greece. 1997. Histories-specific. ■An exhibition on Greek and Roman amphitheatres and their reconstruction, on the occasion of Thessaloniki's being declared a Cultural Capital for 1997.

437 Wiles, David. *Tragedy in Athens: Performance Space and Theatrical Meaning.* Cambridge: Cambridge UP; 1997. 230 pp. Index. Notes. Biblio. Illus.: Photo. 13. Lang.: Eng. Greece. 500-100 B.C. Historical studies. ■Examines the theatrical performance space in Greek theatre: the center point, the chorus and its use of space, and the iconography of sacred space.

438 Vargha, Mihály, ed.; Nádai, Ferenc, designer. *Nemzeti Színház tervpályázat.* (National Theatre Architectural Competition.) Budapest: Gyorsjelentés; 1997. 126 pp. (Magyar építészet könyvek.) Append. Biblio. Illus.: Photo. B&W. Color. Architec. Detail. Grd.Plan. Explod.Sect. R.Elev. Fr. Elev. Schematic. 362. Lang.: Hun. Hungary: Budapest. 1996-1997. Technical studies. ■Introducing the competition with detailed presentation of the seventy-three projects (competition entries). The richly illustrated book was published on the 160th anniversary of the opening of Hungarian National Theatre's first building.

439 *Roma splendidissima e magnifica. Luoghi di spettacolo a Roma dall'umanesimo ad oggi.* (Splendid and Magnificent Rome: Performance Spaces in Rome from the Humanist Period to the Present.) Milan: Electa; 1997. 232 pp. Biblio. Illus.: Pntg. Plan. Dwg. Photo. B&W. Color. Lang.: Ita. Italy: Rome. 1350-1997. Historical studies. ■Catalogue of an exhibition devoted to Roman performance spaces.

440 *Il Teatro Sociale di Alba. Modernità e tradizione.* (Alba's Teatro Sociale: Modernity and Tradition.) Turin: Celid; 1997. 131 pp. Illus.: Photo. Plan. B&W. Color. Lang.: Ita. Italy: Alba. 1932-1997. Historical studies. ■The reconstruction of the Teatro Sociale, which was condemned in 1932 and reopened in 1997.

441 Allegri, Luigi; Longman, Stanley V., transl. "On the Rebirth of the Theatre, or of the *Idea* of Theatre, in Humanistic Italy." 51-61 in Castagno, Paul C., ed. *Theatrical Spaces and Dramatic Places: The Reemergence of the Theatre Building in the Renaissance.* Tuscaloosa, AL: Univ of Alabama P; 1996. 151 pp. (Southeastern Theatre Conference Theatre Symposium 4.) Biblio. Lang.: Eng. Italy. 1550-1650. Historical studies. ■The development of theatrical stage space in Renaissance Italy and its eventual dissemination throughout Europe.

442 Baffi, Giulio. *Teatri di Napoli. Origini, vicende, personaggi e curiosità dei teatri di prosa.* (Neapolitan Theatres: Origins, Vicissitudes, Characters, and Curiosities of the Playhouses.) Rome: Newton & Compton; 1997. 63 pp. (Tascabili Economici Newton: Napoli Tascabili 63.) Biblio. Illus.: Dwg. Lang.: Ita. Italy: Naples. 1850-1997. Histories-specific. ■A brief history of the theatres of Naples.

443 Devoti, Luigi. *Teatri e anfiteatri di Roma antica.* (Theatres and Amphitheatres of Ancient Rome.) Rome: Newton & Compton; 1997. 61 pp. (Tascabili Economici Newton: Roma Tascabili 74.) Illus.: Plan. Dwg. Lang.: Ita. Italy: Rome. 179 B.C.-476 A.D. Histories-specific. ■History of performance spaces used by acting companies and for gladiatorial combat.

444 Giacomelli, Milva. "La casa d'arte Bragaglia di Virgilio Marchi." (The Bragaglia Casa d'Arte of Virgilio Marchi.) *Quasar.* 1997; 17: 73-84. Illus.: Photo. B&W. 17. Lang.: Ita. Italy: Rome. 1921-1923. Historical studies. ■The work of architect and scenographer Virgilio Marchi in the Futurist-inspired restoration of the Casa d'Arte Bragaglia.

445 Pallen, Thomas A. "Decking the Hall: Italian Renaissance Extension of Performance Motifs into Audience Space." 91-100 in Castagno, Paul C., ed. *Theatrical Spaces and Dramatic Places: The Reemergence of the Theatre Building in the Renaissance.* Tuscaloosa, AL: Univ of Alabama P; 1996. 151 pp. (Southeastern Theatre Conference Theatre Symposium 4.) Biblio. Illus.: Photo. 2. Lang.: Eng. Italy. 1500-1700. Historical studies. ■On the unified nature of the Renaissance Italian stage and auditorium (hall). Examines how the decorated auditorium contributed to this unified vision.

446 Staccioli, Paola. *I teatri di Roma dal Rinascimento ai giorni nostri.* (Roman Theatres from the Renaissance to the Present.) Rome: Newton & Compton; 1997. 64 pp. (Tascabili Economici Newton: Roma Tascabili 82.) Lang.: Ita. Italy: Rome. 1500-1997. Historical studies. ■Short history of Rome's theatres and theatrical life.

447 Król-Kaczorowska, Barbara. "O budynku teatru skarbkowskiego." (On the Building of Skarbek's Theatre.) 16-26 in Kuchtówna, Lidia, ed. *Teatr polski we Lwowie. Studia i materiały do dziejów teatru polskiego. t. XXV (37).* Warsaw: Instytut Sztuki Polskiej Akademii Nauk; 1997. 293 pp. Lang.: Pol. Poland: Lvov. 1842-1902. Historical studies. ■The building of Teatr im. Fr. Skarbka, offered as a gift to the city of Lvov by Stanisław Skarbek.

448 Maxa, Miloslav. "Rekonstruktion des Theaters 'Horácké divadlo' in Jihlava." (Reconstruction of the Horácké divadlo Theatre Building in Jihlava.) *BtR.* 1997; 91(1): 14-18. Illus.: Photo. Plan. Color. Explod.Sect. Grd.Plan. 11. Lang.: Ger. Slovakia: Jihlava. 1995. Histories-specific. ■Describes the reconstruction of 'Horácké divadlo' in 1995, the situation, the scope of work, the equipment and the architectural conception. Erected 1630, the building was used as a monastery, a church and a warehouse until it was rebuilt as a theatre in 1850.

449 Allen, John J. "The Reemergence of the Playhouse in the Renaissance: Spain, 1550-1750." 27-38 in Castagno, Paul C., ed. *Theatrical Spaces and Dramatic Places: The Reemergence of the Theatre Building in the Renaissance.* Tuscaloosa, AL: Univ of Alabama P; 1996. 151 pp. (Southeastern Theatre Conference Theatre Symposium 4.) Biblio. Illus.: Photo. 6. Lang.: Eng. Spain. 1550-1750. Historical studies. ■The evolution of staging areas in Renaissance Spain from pageant wagons and city squares to outdoor platform stages, innyards, and hospital patios.

450 Dowling, John. "The Spanish Buen Retiro Theatre, 1638-circa 1812." 124-131 in Castagno, Paul C. *Theatrical Spaces and Dramatic Places: The Reemergence of the Theatre Building in the Renaissance.* Tuscaloosa, AL: Univ of Alabama P; 1996. 151 pp. (Southeastern Theatre Conference Theatre Symposium 4.) Biblio. Illus.: Photo. 1. Lang.: Eng. Spain: Madrid. 1638-1812. Historical studies. ■Historical examination of the Buen Retiro theatrical space and its evolution.

451 Söderberg, Olle. "Skall Riksteatern ha Ensamrätt till Spelplatsregistret?" (Should Riksteatern Have Sole Right To the Directory of Performance Spaces?) *ProScen.* 1997; 21(3): 22. Lang.: Swe. Sweden. 1990. Historical studies. ■A presentation of the Swedish Directory of Performance Spaces, which is kept and owned by Riksteatern.

452 Waites, Aline. "Focus On Fringe." *PlPl.* 1997 Aug/Sep.; 515: 19. Lang.: Eng. UK-England: London. 1993-1997. Historical studies. ■Renovating Rosemary Branch pub into a fringe theatre venue and launching a first season of performances.

453 "Symposium Discussion." 76-82 in Castagno, Paul C., ed. *Theatrical Spaces and Dramatic Places: The Reemergence of the Theatre Building in the Renaissance.* Tuscaloosa, AL: Univ of Alabama P; 1996. 151 pp. (Southeastern Theatre Conference Theatre Symposium 4.) Biblio. Lang.: Eng. USA. 1995. Histories-sources. ■Comments of panelists from the Theatre Symposium on Theatrical Spaces and Dramatic Places.

THEATRE IN GENERAL: —Performance spaces

454 "The new New Amsterdam." *Econ.* 1997 June 7-13; 343(8020): 87-88. Lang.: Eng.
USA: New York, NY. 1920-1997. Historical studies. ■The effect of the Times Square Redevelopment project on Broadway theatres, renovation of the New Amsterdam theatre by the Disney Corporation.

455 Burgess, Randy. "California Dreaming." *LD&A.* 1997 May; 27(5): 32-35. Illus.: Photo. Color. 8. Lang.: Eng.
USA: Escondido, CA. 1997. Technical studies. ■Lighting design of the California Center for the Arts. Designers were the firm of Moore, Ruble Yudell.

456 Davis, Lee. "The Magnificent Dramatic Temple." *ShowM.* 1997 Sum; 13(2): 31-34, 61-62. Illus.: Photo. B&W. 9. Lang.: Eng.
USA: New York, NY. 1903-1997. Historical studies. ■Broadway's New Amsterdam Theatre, its opening, its attractions, its decline, and its reconstruction.

457 Fliotsos, Anne. "From Vaudeville to Talkies: A Case Study in Our Nation's Capital, Earle Theatre, 1924-1928." *TheatreS.* 1997; 42: 21-32. Notes. Biblio. Illus.: Photo. Poster. B&W. 5. Lang.: Eng.
USA: Washington, DC. 1924-1992. Historical studies. ■Examination of the weekly performance roster from the *Washington Post* and using the Earle Theatre (renamed the Warner Theatre in 1947) to illuminate performances of the vaudeville era. Architecture, productions and performers, impact of popularity of film on theatres, and its renovation and restoration in 1992.

458 Haddah, Sonya. "The New Amsterdam: A Theater Is Reborn." *OpN.* 1997 Aug.; 62(2): 30-31. Illus.: Photo. Color. 6. Lang.: Eng.
USA: New York, NY. 1903-1997. Historical studies. ■The history and restoration of the New Amsterdam Theatre, West 42nd Street, New York by Hugh Hardy and Hardy Holzman Peiffer Associates. Original designs were by Henry Herts and Hugh Tallant.

459 Pollock, Steve. "Jesse Jones Redux." *TD&T.* 1997 Spr; 33(2): 15-23. Illus.: Diagram. Photo. Color. 6. Lang.: Eng.
USA: Houston, TX. 1966-1997. Historical studies. ■The renovation of the Jesse H. Jones Hall for the Performing Arts, a multi-use performing arts center designed by George Izenour.

460 Smith, Patrick J. "Viewpoint: Building for the Arts." *OpN.* 1997 Jan 25; 61(9): 4. Lang.: Eng.
USA: College Park, MD. 1997. Histories-sources. ■Brief note on the Maryland Performing Arts Center, under construction at the University of Maryland, College Park, Maryland. Comments on its training mission and the diminution of public funds for the arts.

Performance/production

461 Blumberg, Marcia. "Staging AIDS: Activating Theatres." *SATJ.* 1997 May/Sep.; 11(1/2): 155-181. Notes. Biblio. Lang.: Eng.
1980-1997. Critical studies. ■Representations of AIDS in various staging venues: educational, quiltings, dance and drama.

462 Drain, Richard, ed. *Twentieth-Century Theatre: A Sourcebook.* London/New York, NY: Routledge; 1995. 387 pp. Pref. Index. Biblio. Lang.: Eng.
1890-1994. Critical studies. ■Collection of original writings on theatre theory and practice by directors, playwrights, performers, and designers, covering the entire twentieth century.

463 Finter, Helga. "Antonin Artaud and the Impossible Theatre: The Legacy of the Theatre of Cruelty." *TDR.* 1997 Win; 41(4): 15-40. Notes. Biblio. Illus.: Photo. B&W. 7. Lang.: Eng.
1920-1997. Historical studies. ■Compares contemporary experimental theatre to Artaud's late theatre of cruelty to explore relationship between symbolic and imaginary, relationship of voice to text, and to question relevance of Artaud's theories and the function of the manifest presence of the Real.

464 Girard, Dale Anthony. *Actors on Guard: A Practical Guide for the Use of the Rapier and Dagger for Stage and Screen.* New York, NY/London: Routledge; 1997. 511 pp. Biblio. Pref. Append. Gloss. Illus.: Dwg. Sketches. 314. Lang.: Eng.

1996. Instructional materials. ■Guide to practical training techniques for stage combat with sword, rapier, and dagger routines for the stage, the illusions needed for stagework and actual rehearsing notes. Appendices include suppliers, stage combat associations, maintenance information and a glossary of terms.

465 Rozik, Eli. "Mask and Disguise in Ritual, Carnival and Theatre." *SATJ.* 1997 May/Sep.; 11(1/2): 183-198. Notes. Biblio. Lang.: Eng.
1997. Critical studies. ■Masks as used in ritual, carnival and theatre. Suggests a set of definitions to establish what the different functions of the mask are in these divergent domains.

466 Diakhaté, Ousmane; Eyoh, Hansel Ndumbe. "Of Inner Roots and External Adjuncts." 17-29 in Rubin, Don, ed.; Diakhaté, Ousmane, ed.; Eyoh, Hansel Ndumbe, ed. *The World Encyclopedia of Contemporary Theatre: Africa.* Vol. 3. London/New York, NY: Routledge; 1997. 426 pp. Biblio. Index. Lang.: Eng.
Africa. 1800-1996. Historical studies. ■On the tradition of African theatre: rooted in traditional forms, yet assimilating European and American theatre traditions. Examines religion, ritual, music, and dance in African theatrical forms, including Francophone and Anglophone Africa.

467 Mensah, Atta Annan. "The Great Ode of History: Music and Dance in Africa." 30-37 in Rubin, Don, ed.; Diakhaté, Ousmane, ed.; Eyoh, Hansel Ndumbe, ed. *The World Encyclopedia of Contemporary Theatre: Africa.* Vol. 3. London/New York, NY: Routledge; 1997. 426 pp. Biblio. Index. Lang.: Eng.
Africa. 1800-1996. Historical studies. ■The role of music and dance in forming Africa's initial performative history and its presence as other theatrical forms are integrated into African theatre.

468 Quayson, Ato. "African Theatre and the Question of History." 41-44 in Rubin, Don, ed.; Diakhaté, Ousmane, ed.; Eyoh, Hansel Ndumbe, ed. *The World Encyclopedia of Contemporary Theatre: Africa.* Vol. 3. London/New York, NY: Routledge; 1997. 426 pp. Biblio. Index. Lang.: Eng.
Africa. 1800-1996. Historical studies. ■Examines the indigenous roots and resources of African theatre and situates them within a historical context.

469 Rubin, Don. "African Theatre in a Global Context." 14-16 in Rubin, Don, ed.; Diakhaté, Ousmane, ed.; Eyoh, Hansel Ndumbe, ed. *The World Encyclopedia of Contemporary Theatre: Africa.* Vol. 3. London/New York, NY: Routledge; 1997. 426 pp. Biblio. Lang.: Eng.
Africa. 1800-1996. Critical studies. ■African theatre and paratheatrical forms compared to theatre as interpreted in the rest of the world.

470 Riccio, Thomas. "N!ngongaio: People Come Out of Here: Making a New Story with the !Xuu and Khwe Bushmen." *TheatreF.* 1997 Win/Spr; 10: 45-59. Illus.: Photo. 9. Lang.: Eng.
Angola. South Africa, Republic of. 1993-1996. Histories-sources. ■Account of the author's participation in the creation of a tourist show with the arts workshop of the !Xuu and Khwe Cultural Project, with ethnographic analysis of the workshop.

471 Tanitch, Robert. "Theatre Down Under." *PlPl.* 1997 June/July; 514: 48-49. Illus.: Photo. Color. 2. Lang.: Eng.
Australia: Sydney. 1997. Historical studies. ■Theatre and dance seen at various venues in Sydney and Australia's Northern Territory.

472 Hrvatin, Emil; Hoffman, Irene, transl. "The Scream." *PerfR.* 1997 Spr; 2(1): 82-91. Notes. Biblio. Lang.: Eng.
Belgium. 1985-1996. Critical studies. ■Focuses on metaphors of voice and voicelessness in theatre work of Jan Fabre, with related discussion of a variety of contemporary film and theatre.

473 Rosa, M.A.C. *The Nature Roots and Relevance of the Folk Theatre of the North-East of Brazil.* Unpublished Ph.D. thesis, Univ. of Warwick; 1995. Notes. Biblio. [Abstract in *Index to Theses*, 46-3157.] Lang.: Eng.
Brazil. 1500-1995. Histories-specific. ■Examines the origins, relevant characteristics, and contemporary meaning of four folk theatre forms which are still performed in Brazil: the *Bumbo-meu-Boi*, the *Cheganca*,

THEATRE IN GENERAL: —Performance/production

the *Pastoril* and the *Mamulengo*, stressing the aspects which they share with other folk theatre forms worldwide.

474 Loney, Glenn. "Varna: Festival on the Black Sea." *SEEP*. 1997 Fall; 17(3): 54-63. Illus.: Photo. 4. Lang.: Eng.
Bulgaria: Varna. 1992-1997. Histories-sources. ■Account of the 5th Annual Varna Summer Theatre Festival.

475 Lavoie, Pierre. "'Une certaine connivence'." ('A Certain Connivance'.) *JCT*. 1997; 82: 83-86. Notes. Illus.: Dwg. Photo. B&W. 5. Lang.: Fre.
Canada: Montreal, PQ. 1977-1996. Biographical studies. ■Iconoclastic projects in theatre and improvisation of actor/writer Robert Gravel.

476 Lévesque, Solange. "Il n'y a pas de mystère, il y a du travail: Entretien avec Monique Miller." (There Is No Mystery, There Is Work: Interview with Monique Miller.) *JCT*. 1997; 84: 86-102. Illus.: Photo. B&W. 19. Lang.: Fre.
Canada: Montreal, PQ. 1940-1997. Histories-sources. ■Actress Monique Miller's career in radio, television and theatre.

477 MacDougall, Jill. *Performing Identities on the Stages of Quebec.* New York, NY: Peter Lang; 1997. 231 pp. (Francophone Cultures and Literature 15.) Pref. Notes. Index. Biblio. Illus.: Photo. 22. Lang.: Eng.
Canada. 1901-1995. Historical studies. ■Examines performance and identity politics on the stages of Quebec—national, local, and global—as identity rituals.

478 Mann, Martha. "Amateur Theatre." 260-304 in Plant, Richard, ed.; Saddlemyer, Ann, ed. *Later Stages: Essays in Ontario Theatre from the First World War to the 1970s.* Toronto, ON: Univ of Toronto P; 1997. 496 pp. (The Ontario Historical Studies Series.) Index. Notes. Biblio. Illus.: Photo. 18. Lang.: Eng.
Canada. 1914-1979. Historical studies. ■Amateur and community theatre in Ontario, including religious and church theatre.

479 Nunns, Stephen. "You Can't Go Home Again." *AmTh.* 1997 Sep.; 14(7): 59-61. Illus.: Photo. B&W. 2. Lang.: Eng.
Canada: Montreal, PQ. 1997. Histories-sources. ■The author's personal experiences attending the Festival de Théâtres des Amériques on the eve of Canadian federal elections. Discusses his perspective on political and cultural change as a native Montrealer.

480 Pedneault, Hélène. "Robert Gravel: Esquisse d'un homme de théâtre baveux." (Robert Gravel: Sketch of a Crass Man of the Theatre.) *JCT*. 1997; 82: 66-82. Illus.: Dwg. Photo. B&W. 20. Lang.: Fre.
Canada: Montreal, PQ. 1976-1996. Biographical studies. ■Actor/playwright Robert Gravel's career in improvisation and experimental theatre.

481 Plante, Raymond. "Le cheval indompté." (The Untamed Horse.) *JCT*. 1997; 82: 87-90. Illus.: Photo. B&W. 5. Lang.: Fre.
Canada: Montreal, PQ. 1973-1996. Biographical studies. ■Importance of play in career and private life of actor Robert Gravel.

482 Popovic, Pierre. "La maldonne des gravelures." (Misunderstood Obscenities.) *JCT*. 1997; 82: 91-93. Illus.: Photo. B&W. 3. Lang.: Fre.
Canada. Belgium. 1973-1996. Critical studies. ■Argues that material judged obscene in improvisations and writings of actor/playwright Robert Gravel actually served as social criticism.

483 Scott, Robert B. "Professional Performers and Companies." 13-120 in Plant, Richard, ed.; Saddlemyer, Ann, ed. *Later Stages: Essays in Ontario Theatre from the First World War to the 1970s.* Toronto, ON: Univ of Toronto P; 1997. 496 pp. (The Ontario Historical Studies Series.) Index. Notes. Biblio. Illus.: Photo. Dwg. 21. Lang.: Eng.
Canada. 1914-1979. Historical studies. ■Professional performers and companies in Ontario from 1914 to 1979.

484 Stuart, Ann; Stuart, Ross. "University Theatre." 305-332 in Plant, Richard, ed.; Saddlemyer, Ann, ed. *Later Stages: Essays in Ontario Theatre from the First World War to the 1970s.* Toronto, ON: Univ of Toronto P; 1997. 496 pp. (The Ontario Historical Studies Series.) Index. Notes. Biblio. Illus.: Photo. 11. Lang.: Eng.

Canada. 1914-1979. Historical studies. ■University theatre as a training ground for Canadian theatre.

485 Stuart, Ross. "Summer Festivals and Theatres." 224-259 in Plant, Richard, ed.; Saddlemyer, Ann, ed. *Later Stages: Essays in Ontario Theatre from the First World War to the 1970s.* Toronto, ON: Univ of Toronto P; 1997. 496 pp. (The Ontario Historical Studies Series.) Index. Notes. Biblio. Illus.: Photo. Dwg. 13. Lang.: Eng.
Canada. 1914-1979. Historical studies. ■On the evolution of summer theatre and festivals in Ontario. Includes the history of the Stratford Festival.

486 Wickham, Philip. "Le personnage, miroir des multiples faces de la nature humaine." (The Character, Mirror of the Multiple Faces of Human Nature.) *JCT*. 1997; 83: 93-101. Notes. Illus.: Pntg. Photo. B&W. 6. Lang.: Fre.
Canada: Montreal, PQ. 1997. Histories-sources. ■Recounts explanations given by Montreal actors on interpreting dramatic characters.

487 Rodden, John. "'I am inventing myself all the time': Isabel Allende and the Literary Interview as Public Performance." *TextPQ.* 1997 Jan.; 17(1): 1-24. Notes. Biblio. Lang.: Eng.
Chile. 1972-1995. Critical studies. ■How celebrities occasionally use the role of interviewee for autobiographical purposes, treating the interview as an opportunity to perform and shape a personal narrative. Uses novelist Allende's interview history as a case history.

488 Budde, Antje. "Zentrales Experimentiertheater." (Central Experimental Theatre.) *TZ.* 1997; 1: 14-19. Illus.: Dwg. Photo. B&W. 14. Lang.: Ger.
China: Beijing. 1900-1997. Historical studies. ■Reviews the 40-year-old history of the 'Experimental Theatre', the historical context of its founding, its development and program.

489 Hui-ling, Chou. "Striking Their Own Poses: The History of Cross-Dressing on the Chinese Stage." *TDR.* 1997 Sum; 41(2): 130-152. Notes. Biblio. Illus.: Photo. B&W. 10. Lang.: Eng.
China. 1200-1997. Historical studies. ■Examines practice of cross-dressing onstage and in life, tracing the history of the performance of gender in Chinese society before the May Fourth Movement. Maps out women's changing place in theatre in relation to ancient practice of cross-dressing before the first Chinese cultural revolution. Society's ideas of gender performance, theatre reform movement of the twentieth century.

490 Bai, Di. *A Feminist Brave New World: The Cultural Revolution Model Theater Revisited.* Columbus, OH: Ohio State Univ; 1997. 205 pp. [Ph.D. Dissertation, Univ. Microfilms Order No. AAC 9813214.] Lang.: Eng.
China, People's Republic of. 1965-1976. Historical studies. ■Argues that the 'model theatre' of Cultural Revolution was significant in subverting hegemonic Communist Party ideology because of its feminist literary production model, heroic women's images, and appropriation of class and political identities to escape subordinate gender identities.

491 Riley, Jo. *Chinese Theatre and the Actor in Performance.* Cambridge: Cambridge UP; 1997. 348 pp. (Cambridge Studies in Modern Theatre.) Gloss. Index. Notes. Biblio. Illus.: Photo. Diagram. 120. Lang.: Eng.
China, People's Republic of. 1980-1996. Historical studies. ■Creating presence on the Chinese stage: *jingju*, puppet theatre, and iconography of performance. Focuses on one of the best known *jingju* performers, Mei Lanfang.

492 Tansi, Sony Labou. "Theatre in Africa: The Art and Heart of Living." 45-46 in Rubin, Don, ed.; Diakhaté, Ousmane, ed.; Eyoh, Hansel Ndumbe, ed. *The World Encyclopedia of Contemporary Theatre: Africa.* Volume 3. London/New York, NY: Routledge; 1997. 426 pp. Biblio. Index. Lang.: Eng.
Congo. 1995. Historical studies. ■Congolese playwright Sony Labou Tansi's historical overview of theatre in the Congo, both traditional and modern, including his work with the Rocado Zulu Theatre in Brazzaville.

493 Graubard, Allan; McGee, Caroline. "Theatre in Croatia: The 1997 Summer Festivals in Dubrovnik and Split." *SEEP.* 1997 Fall; 17(3): 48-53. Illus.: Photo. 2. Lang.: Eng.

THEATRE IN GENERAL: —Performance/production

Croatia: Dubrovnik, Split. 1950-1997. Histories-sources. ■Theatrical and operatic offerings of the 47th Annual Dubrovnik Summer Festival and the Split Summer Festival.

494 Nikčević, Sanja. "Historical Plays in Search of National Identity in Croatian Theatre Today." *SEEP.* 1997 Sum; 17(2): 21-26. Illus.: Photo. 1. Lang.: Eng.
Croatia. 1900-1996. Historical studies. ■The pressures of politics vs. mythic consciousness in the historical plays of Croatian theatre. Author examines this genre throughout the twentieth century, highlighting major plays.

495 Senker, Boris. "Changes in the Croatian Theatre After 1990." *SEEP.* 1997 Sum; 17(2): 32-40. Illus.: Photo. 2. Lang.: Eng.
Croatia. 1990-1996. Historical studies. ■The practical effects of war on Croatian theatre: themes of plays, damage to theatres, the siege mentality, and the differing responses of theatre artists. Changes in the economy, funding for the theatre, and training and education of theatre professionals are also examined.

496 Vrgoč, Dubravka. "The Return of Melodrama in Recent Croatian Theatre." *SEEP.* 1997 Sum; 17(2): 41-46. Illus.: Photo. 2. Lang.: Eng.
Croatia. 1995-1996. Historical studies. ■The reemergence of melodrama and its sentimental conclusions on the Croatian stage in the aftermath of war. Author examines *Medea 1995* by Josip Vela, performed by the Zagrebačko Kazalište Mladih (Zagreb Youth Theatre), directed by Leo Katunarić.

497 Barba, Eugenio. "An Amulet Made of Memory: The Significance of Exercises in the Actor's Dramaturgy." *TDR.* 1997 Win; 41 (4): 127-132. Notes. Illus.: Photo. B&W. 4. Lang.: Eng.
Denmark: Holstebro. 1950-1997. Critical studies. ■Founder/director of the International School of Theatre Anthropology discusses physical work, subtext, and use of exercises for the actor and in actor training.

498 Beck-Nielsen, Claus. "Brat beretning fra ingenmandsland." (A Short Report from No-Man's-Land.) *TE.* 1997 Oct.; 85: 4-7. Illus.: Photo. B&W. 2. Lang.: Dan.
Denmark. 1997. Biographical studies. ■Claus Beck-Nielsen reflects on his two different professions, acting and reviewing. He believes that it is possible to combine the two different jobs.

499 Rottensten, Rikke. "En verden i sig selv." (A World of Its Own.) *TE.* 1997 June; 84: 16-18. Illus.: Photo. B&W. 3. Lang.: Dan.
Denmark. 1985-1997. Biographical studies. ■A short biography of Bo Hr. Hansen, a Danish writer of poetry, screenplays and drama.

500 Astington, John H. "Rereading Illustrations of the English Stage." *ShS.* 1997; 50(1): 151-170. Notes. Illus.: Handbill. Sketches. Poster. 12. Lang.: Eng.
England. 1580-1642. Historical studies. ■Examines illustrations of the English stage for authenticity in relation to their subject: do they really represent the stage or are they unrelated.

501 Bristol, Michael D. "Theater and Popular Culture." 231-250 in Cox, John D., ed.; Kastan, David Scott, ed. *A New History of Early English Drama.* New York, NY: Columbia UP; 1997. 565 pp. Notes. Biblio. Index. Lang.: Eng.
England. 1590-1610. Historical studies. ■The social constructs reflected in English Renaissance theatre. Uses Bakhtinian analysis to examine how popular culture expressed a resistance to social control and rigid hierarchies, and how this resistance operated in the theatre.

502 Burling, William J. "New London Cast Listings, 1696-1737, with Other Additions and Corrections to *The London Stage.*" *TN.* 1997; 51(1): 42-54. Notes. Lang.: Eng.
England: London. 1696-1737. Histories-sources. ■Contains updates and additions to *The London Stage, 1660-1800,* including partial cast variants, new cast listings, and information on dates and locations.

503 Greenfield, Peter H. "Touring." 251-268 in Cox, John D., ed.; Kastan, David Scott, ed. *A New History of Early English Drama.* New York, NY: Columbia UP; 1997. 565 pp. Notes. Biblio. Index. Lang.: Eng.
England. 1590-1642. Historical studies. ■Positive aspects of early English touring companies: argues that the companies actually benefited from touring in profits, reputation, and patronage.

504 Knutson, Roslyn L. "The Repertory." 461-480 in Cox, John D., ed.; Kastan, David Scott, ed. *A New History of Early English Drama.* New York, NY: Columbia UP; 1997. 565 pp. Index. Notes. Biblio. Lang.: Eng.
England. 1595-1603. Critical studies. ■On the importance of a company repertory in early English theatre. Argues that a study of repertory reveals new perspectives on the economics of playing, prevailing cultural attitudes, and commercial relations in the theatrical industry.

505 McGee, C.E.; Meagher, John C. "Preliminary Checklist of Tudor and Stuart Entertainments: 1625-1634." *RORD.* 1997; 36: 23-95. Lang.: Eng.
England. 1625-1634. Historical studies. ■List of Stuart and Tudor masques, pastorals, pageants, and entertainments that includes description of event, participants, and archival source for the material.

506 McLuskie, Kathleen E. "Patronage and the Economics of Theater." 423-440 in Cox, John D., ed.; Kastan, David Scott, ed. *A New History of Early English Drama.* New York, NY: Columbia UP; 1997. 565 pp. Index. Notes. Biblio. Lang.: Eng.
England. 1580-1610. Critical studies. ■On the social relations of patronage and the economic relations of a commercial theatre. Argues that patronage was slowly replaced by a system of regular fees and ticket prices.

507 Milhous, Judith; Hume, Robert D. "Thomas Doggett at Cambridge in 1701." *TN.* 1997; 51(3): 147-165. Notes. Lang.: Eng.
England: Cambridge. 1690-1701. Historical studies. ■The suppression of Doggett's troupe of strolling players by the Cambridge University, with new evidence supplied from two equity lawsuits discovered in the Public Record Office.

508 Osborne, Laurie E. "The Rhetoric of Evidence: The Narration and Display of Viola and Olivia in the Nineteenth-Century." 124-143 in Pechter, Edward, ed. *Textual and Theatrical Shakespeare: Questions of Evidence.* Iowa City, IA: Univ of Iowa P; 1997. 267 pp. (Studies in Theatre History and Culture.) Notes. Illus.: Photo. 2. Lang.: Eng.
England. 1808-1850. Critical studies. ■Examines two different nineteenth-century 'performances' of Shakespeare's *Twelfth Night* to argue that the performances are not transparent windows through which to study the text, but objects of study in themselves, reflecting cultural conditions. The two performances are singer Maria Tree's singing as Viola in Henry Bishop's opera of the same name, and magazine illustrations of Olivia's first-act unveiling.

509 Pascoe, Judith. *Romantic Theatricality: Gender, Poetry, and Spectatorship.* Ithaca, NY/London: Cornell UP; 1997. 251 pp. Index. Notes. Illus.: Dwg. Photo. 23. Lang.: Eng.
England. 1790-1850. Historical studies. ■Performative aspects of early Romantic literary culture as reflected in the theatrical representations of female poets. Examines Sarah Siddons and the performative female in society, women and the 'courtroom theatre' of the 1794 treason trials, Marie Antoinette as a 'theatricalized female subject,' and the poet Letitia Landon and her representations of dying women.

510 Pilkinton, Mark C., ed. *Records of Early English Drama: Bristol.* Toronto, ON: Univ of Toronto P; 1997. xxxii, 382 pp. Notes. Index. Biblio. Append. Gloss. Illus.: Maps. Sketches. 4. Lang.: Eng.
England: Bristol. 1255-1642. Histories-sources. ■Compilation of records taken from civic, guild, church, and legal sources. Includes political and economic historical background material, local drama and public entertainments, school drama, touring entertainments, performance spaces, and minstrels.

511 Rasmussen, Eric. "The Revision of Scripts." 441-460 in Cox, John D., ed.; Kastan, David Scott, ed. *A New History of Early English Drama.* New York, NY: Columbia UP; 1997. 565 pp. Index. Notes. Biblio. Lang.: Eng.
England. 1590-1615. Critical studies. ■How revision and textual versions were conceived and carried out in early English theatre performance.

THEATRE IN GENERAL: —Performance/production

Argues that versions and revisions reflected theatrical performance cutting and additions. Examines Shakespeare's *Midsummer Night's Dream* and *Troilus and Cressida*.

512 Streitberger, W.R. "Personnel and Professionalization." 337-356 in Cox, John D., ed.; Kastan, David Scott, ed. *A New History of Early English Drama*. New York, NY: Columbia UP; 1997. 565 pp. Index. Notes. Biblio. Lang.: Eng.
England. 1550-1620. Historical studies. ■Development of the professional theatre company in early English theatre. Author examines the growth of these companies, the importance of patronage in the system, financial backing, and shifts in personnel matters.

513 Thomson, Peter. "Rogues and Rhetoricians: Acting Styles in Early English Drama." 321-336 in Cox, John D., ed.; Kastan, David Scott, ed. *A New History of Early English Drama*. New York, NY: Columbia UP; 1997. 565 pp. Index. Notes. Biblio. Lang.: Eng.
England. 1595-1615. Critical studies. ■Examines the role of character in early English acting.

514 Rähesoo, Jaak. "An Unknown Revolution: The Estonian Theatre of the 1960s and 1970s." *SEEP*. 1997 Sum; 17(2): 47-62. Illus.: Photo. 6. Lang.: Eng.
Estonia. 1960-1979. Historical studies. ■Examines the nationalistic fervor in Estonian theatre: history, influences, theory, and dramatic structure as well as historical reconstructions of performance.

515 Counsell, Colin. *Signs of Performance: An Introduction to Twentieth-Century Theatre*. London/New York, NY: Routledge; 1996. 242 pp. Index. Biblio. Lang.: Eng.
Europe. North America. 1900-1995. Critical studies. ■Theatre as a signifying practice. Considers the work of Stanislavskij, Strasberg, Brecht, Beckett, Peter Brook, and Robert Wilson, as well as postmodernism and performance art.

516 Dean, Roger T.; Smith, Hazel. *Improvisation, Hypermedia and the Arts Since 1945*. Amsterdam: Harwood Academic Publishing; 1997. 334 pp. (Performing Arts Series 4.) Index. Biblio. Append. Illus.: Graphs. Diagram. Dwg. Sketches. 18. Lang.: Eng.
Europe. North America. 1945-1996. Historical studies. ■Examines developments in improvisation in the arts since 1945, with emphasis on process and technique. Attempts to expand on the nature of improvisation in figurative arts such as architecture's use of public space.

517 Féral, Josette. "Performance and Theatricality: The Subject Demystified." 289-300 in Murray, Timothy, ed. *Mimesis, Masochism, and Mime: The Politics of Theatricality in Contemporary French Thought*. Ann Arbor, MI: Univ. of Michigan P; 1997. 328 pp. (Theater: Theory/Text/Performance.) Notes. [1982.] Lang.: Eng.
Europe. USA. 1960-1979. Critical studies. ■Feminist interpretation of performance in the 1960s and 70s in the US and Europe. Focuses on gendered representations and spatial representations.

518 Greenfield, Peter. "Census of Medieval Drama Productions." *RORD*. 1997; 36: 179-205. Lang.: Eng.
Europe. North America. 1996-1997. Historical studies. ■List of productions of medieval theatre including title, author, venue, director, designers, dates, brief description of productions.

519 Kłossowicz, Jan. "Pokazywanie teatru." (Demonstrations of Theatre.) *DialogW*. 1997; 4: 105-122. Lang.: Pol.
Europe. Asia. 1959-1997. Histories-sources. ■Describes the author's work in organizing photographic, film, and multi-media exhibitions in Europe and Asia relating to Polish theatre.

520 Lehmann, Hans-Thies. "From Logos to Landscape: Text in Contemporary Dramaturgy." *PerfR*. 1997 Spr; 2(1): 55-60. Notes. Biblio. Illus.: Diagram. 1. Lang.: Eng.
Europe. 1970-1996. Critical studies. ■Analysis of contemporary theatre with reference to the Aristotelian concepts of 'logos' and 'opsis', describing a movement away from 'logos' and toward 'opsis'.

521 Wesemann, Arnd. "Jan Fabre: Belgian Theatre Magician." *TDR*. 1997 Win; 41(4): 41-62. Notes. Biblio. Illus.: Photo. B&W. 15. Lang.: Eng.
Europe. 1958-1997. Biographical studies. ■Career and productions of director Fabre: his radical approach to creating theatre, use of physical

expression vs. text, his work at Teatro Carlo Goldoni and Theater am Turm, and his direction of operas.

522 Aaltojärvi, Pia. "Tradition alustalla post-kehässä, näkökulmia teatterin tutkimiseen." (In a Post-Circle based on Tradition: Thoughts about Theatrical Research.) *TeatterT*. 1997; 1: 44-51. Illus.: Photo. B&W. 3. Lang.: Fin.
Finland. 1997. Histories-sources. ■Thoughts on the actors' identity and the research on artists' work.

523 Auslander, Philip. "The Second *Helsinki Act*, May 1997." *WES*. 1997 Fall; 9(3): 79-82. Illus.: Photo. 2. Lang.: Eng.
Finland: Helsinki. 1997. Historical studies. ■Covers the 'Helsinki Act', a bi-annual event organized by the Continuing Education Centre of the Theatre Academy, Finland's national professional training school, combining a performance festival with symposia and workshops.

524 Groth, Anna. "Matkalla täydelliseen läsnäoloon." (On the Way to the Complete Presence.) *Teat*. 1997; 52(4): 13-14. Illus.: Photo. B&W. 1. Lang.: Fin.
Finland. 1997. Histories-sources. ■Interview with actor Marcus Groth on the work of a director and use of gestalt psychology.

525 Helavuori, Hanna. "Vallan uusijako, laumassa herkkyys tiivistyy." (New Division of Power, Sensitivity Gets Condensed in the Crowd.) *Teat*. 1997; 52(6): 4-7. Illus.: Photo. B&W. 5. Lang.: Fin.
Finland. 1997. Histories-sources. ■Experiences from the theatre laboratory project 'Mans and Orlovski' and new levels of communication between actor and director.

526 Hotinen, Juha-Pekka. "Työnäytös, iloa tarkoituksettomuudesta." (Demonstration: Joy from Uselessness.) *Teat*. 1997; 52(1): 12-16. Illus.: Photo. B&W. 4. Lang.: Fin.
Finland: Helsinki. 1997. Histories-sources. ■Excerpts from the diary of theatre researcher and teacher Juha-Pekka Hotinen: her work at The Theatre Academy (Teatterikokeakoulu) and her plans for an experimental theatrical performance called *Demonstration*.

527 Jänicke, Tuija. "Monologiteatteri on itsetuntolaji." (Monologue Requires Self-Confidence.) *Teat*. 1997; 52(6): 11-13. Illus.: Photo. B&W. 4. Lang.: Fin.
Finland. 1997. Historical studies. ■The philosophy and requirements of doing one-person shows.

528 Martikainen, Anita. "Granada, lihaan sidotujen saaga." (Granada—Tied in the Flesh.) *Teat*. 1997; 52(1): 17-19. Illus.: Photo. B&W. 1. Lang.: Fin.
Finland: Tampere. 1997. Histories-sources. ■Cross-cultural actors' training project at University of Tampere titled *Granada*.

529 Niemi, Irmeli. "Esko Salminen, Every Inch an Actor." *FT*. 1997; 51: 5-6. Illus.: Photo. B&W. 4. Lang.: Eng.
Finland: Helsinki. 1971-1996. Historical studies. ■Profile and career of Finnish actor Salminen.

530 Vähäpassi, Sara. "Mahtuuko tanssi teatteriin." (Is There Room for Dance in the Future.) *Teat*. 1997; 52(8): 4-6. Illus.: Photo. B&W. 4. Lang.: Fin.
Finland. 1997. Historical studies. ■Integrating physical expression dance, dancers and choreography to the established Finnish theatre.

531 Decroux, Etienne. "Decroux on Artaud." *MimeJ*. 1997; 19: 108-110. Lang.: Eng.
France: Paris. 1920-1945. Histories-sources. ■Decroux discusses his relationship with Antonin Artaud, excerpted from a 1980 lecture.

532 Kuharski, Allen J. "Jerzy Grotowski's First Lecture at the Collège de France." *SEEP*. 1997 Sum; 17(2): 16-20. Illus.: Photo. 2. Lang.: Eng.
France: Paris. 1997. Historical studies. ■The first theatrical director/theorist to be named to the Collège, Grotowski departed from tradition and held his lecture in Peter Brook's Théâtre aux Bouffes du Nord. The lecture provided a critical overview of his theoretical and practical work with actors.

533 Osiński, Zbigniew. "Grotowski at the Collège de France: Lesson One." *TP*. 1997; 39(3): 17-19. Lang.: Eng, Fre.
France: Paris. 1997. Historical studies. ■Report on lecture given by director/teacher Jerzy Grotowski at Théâtre aux Bouffes du Nord in which he discussed the organic process and artificiality in theatre art.

THEATRE IN GENERAL: —Performance/production

534 Schoemaker, George Henry. *Contemporary Shadow Theater in France: Performance and the Politics of Culture.* Bloomington, IN: Indiana Univ; 1997. 314 pp. [Ph.D. Dissertation, Univ. Microfilms Order No. AAC 9805398.] Lang.: Eng.
France. 1750-1995. Historical studies. ■History of *théâtre d'ombres* or shadow play, formerly a court entertainment. Traces the decline of the genre following the advent of cinema and the recent resurgence of interest, with attention to political processes that have contributed to the construction of French shadow theatre.

535 Tanitch, Robert. "Spring In Paris." *PlPl.* 1997 May; 513: 42. Illus.: Photo. B&W. 1. Lang.: Eng.
France: Paris. 1997. Historical studies. ■English perspective on Parisian performances and performance spaces seen in spring 1997.

536 Balme, Christopher. "Persephone at the Olympics: Robert Wilson in Munich." *WES.* 1997 Fall; 9(3): 47-50. Illus.: Photo. 2. Lang.: Eng.
Germany: Munich. 1997. Historical studies. ■Critical review of Robert Wilson's new performance piece, *Persephone*, produced on Munich's Olympic Lake in an amphitheatre.

537 Brandt, Ellen. "Der Kampf um die Zuschauer." (The Struggle for Audience.) *DB.* 1997; 1: 28-30. Illus.: Photo. B&W. 5. Lang.: Ger.
Germany. 1997. Histories-sources. ■Discussion of public relations and the dramaturg at the annual conference of Dramaturgische Gesellschaft, the dramaturgs' professional organization.

538 Dermutz, Klaus. "Die Tour der Leiden und der Freuden." (The Tour of Joys and Sorrows.) *THeute.* 1997; 11: 22-27. Illus.: Photo. B&W. 2. Lang.: Ger.
Germany. Austria. 1970-1997. Historical studies. ■Reports of a journey through Germany and Austria. Describes the free theatre scene including a reflection on its history and the changes of themes.

539 Kuhns, David F. *German Expressionist Theatre: The Actor and the Stage.* Cambridge: Cambridge UP; 1997. 311 pp. Index. Notes. Biblio. Lang.: Eng.
Germany. 1916-1921. Histories-specific. ■Examines the stylized and anti-realistic qualities of symbolic acting on the German Expressionist stage. Relates the development of the style to specific cultural crises that enveloped Germany at the time, and examines and analyzes the acting itself.

540 Manthei, Fred. "'Die Ganze Welt ist eine Bühne'. Ein Portrait der Bremer Shakespeare Company." ('All the World's a Stage'. A Portrait of the Bremer Shakespeare Company.) *SJW.* 1997; 133: 166-177. Append. Lang.: Ger.
Germany: Bremen. 1983-1997. Histories-sources. ■An interview with Norbert Kentrup who is organizer, actor and director/producer since the beginning of the Bremer Shakespeare Company about the company's history and future, concepts and acting.

541 Merschmeier, Michael; Wille, Franz. "Richard langweilt sich nicht." (Richard Is Not Boring.) *THeute.* 1997; 12: 4-9. Illus.: Photo. B&W. 6. Lang.: Ger.
Germany: Munich. 1961-1997. Histories-sources. ■An interview with the actor Thomas Holtzmann about his main roles, the competition between theatre and film, about classical and modern plays, the conflict between directing and acting theatre.

542 Peiseler, Christian; Rischbieter, Henning. "Aufbrechen—nicht, um anzukommen." (To Start Out—Not to Arrive.) *THeute.* 1997; 2: 34-37. Illus.: Photo. B&W. 4. Lang.: Ger.
Germany: Mülheim, Bremen. 1996. Historical studies. ■Discusses impressions of 'Impulse 1996', a festival of free theatre at Mülheim including a report of the 3rd Bremen festival 'Politik im Freien Theater' (Politics in Free Theatre).

543 Price, Henry Paschal, III. *From the Life of a Wandering Actor: A Translation of the Memoirs of Jakob Neukaufler.* Claremont, CA: Claremont Graduate Univ; 1997. 49 pp. Biblio. Notes. [D.M.A. Thesis, Univ. Microfilms Order No. AAC 9814021.] Lang.: Eng.
Germany. 1774-1825. Histories-sources. ■Neukaufler's early training, his work with the troupe of Emanuel Schikaneder, life as a traveling actor, and politics of his time.

544 Rouse, John. "The 33rd Berlin *Theatertreffen*, May 1996." *WES.* 1997 Spr; 9(2): 5-12. Illus.: Photo. 7. Lang.: Eng.
Germany: Berlin. 1996. Historical studies. ■Coverage of the 1996 Berlin Theatre Festival, under the auspices of the Berliner Festspiele. Reviews of productions, account of the financial difficulties in this year's festival, and themes of the festival are included.

545 Schlueter, June. "Who Was John Wobster? New Evidence Concerning the Playwright/Minstrel in Germany." *MRDE.* 1996; 8(1): 165-175. Notes. Illus.: Photo. B&W. 2. Lang.: Eng.
Germany: Kassel. 1596. Historical studies. ■Attempts to identify the individual referred to as John Wobster, who may have been playwright John Webster or minstrel/actor George Webster who accompanied Robert Browne (of eponymous acting troupe) to Germany in August of 1596.

546 Schwind, Klaus. "'No Laughing!' Autonomous Art and the Body of the Actor in Goethe's Weimar." *ThS.* 1997 Nov.; 38(2): 89-108. Lang.: Eng.
Germany: Weimar. 1793-1808. Historical studies. ■Using Foucault's theoretical framework, author examines Goethe's abusive treatment of actors at Weimar. He argues that the idealistic aestheticism celebrated by theatre historians came at a high cost.

547 Shafer, Yvonne. "Opera and Theatre in Berlin." *WES.* 1997 Fall; 9(3): 59-64. Illus.: Photo. 5. Lang.: Eng.
Germany: Berlin. 1997. Historical studies. ■On the current state of opera and theatre in Berlin including *Ithaka* by Botho Strauss, directed by Thomas Langhoff at the Deutsches Theater.

548 Stephan, Erika. "Sozialarbeiter oder Supervisor." (Social Worker or Supervisor.) *DB.* 1997; 1: 24-27. Illus.: Photo. B&W. 4. Lang.: Ger.
Germany. 1997. Histories-sources. ■Report on the annual conference of the dramaturgs' association, Dramaturgische Gesellschaft, covering discussion of the dramaturgs' role and training.

549 Calame, Claude; Collins, Derek, transl.; Orion, Jane, transl. *Choruses of Young Women in Ancient Greece: Their Morphology, Religious Role, and Social Functions.* Lanham, MD: Rowman and Littlefield; 1997. 282 pp. (Greek Studies: Interdisciplinary Approaches 15.) Biblio. Notes. Index. Lang.: Eng.
Greece. 500-100 B.C. Critical studies. ■Examination of choral odes written specifically for female choruses in ancient Greek theatre, with consideration of the makeup of the lyric chorus and the role and importance of ritual.

550 Holmstrand, Kjell. "Europas kulturhuvudstad 1997." (The Capital of Culture of Europe 1997.) *Tningen.* 1997; 21(2): 45-46 . Illus.: Photo. Color. Lang.: Swe.
Greece: Thessaloniki. 1997. Historical studies. ■A survey of the events of Thessaloniki's year as cultural capital.

551 Fazekas, Valéria. *Egy asszony meg a fia (Beszélgetések Varga Magdával és Cserhalmi Györggyel).* (A Woman and Her Son: A Conversation with Magda Varga and György Cserhalmi.) Debrecen: Fazekas Valéria; 1997. 90 pp. Illus.: Photo. B&W. 35. Lang.: Hun.
Hungary. 1922-1996. Histories-sources. ■Series of interviews with opera singer Magda Varga and her son, actor György Cserhalmi.

552 Koltai, Tamás. *Mab királyné (Álomszínház).* (Queen Mab: Dream Theatre.) Budapest: Osiris; 1997. 327 pp. Lang.: Hun.
Hungary. 1986-1996. Reviews of performances. ■A collection of writings on the theatre by a renowned critic in the series of 'dreams' (on Shakespeare, the past, the century, the Hungarian drama, the National Theatre etc.).

553 Nánay, István. "Nyár, piac, művészet." (Summer, Market, Art.) *Sz.* 1997; 30(11): 1. Lang.: Hun.
Hungary. 1997. Critical studies. ■Summary of Hungarian summer theatre offerings, suggesting that under the new conditions the character and audience of summer productions remain yet to be discovered.

554 Püspöki, Péter; Strassburger, Alexandra, photo.; Koncz, Zsuzsa, photo. "Egy évad a motelban. Kísérleti előadás-sorozat Miskolcon." (A Season at the Motel: Series

THEATRE IN GENERAL: —Performance/production

of Experimental Performances at Miskolc.) *Sz.* 1997; 30(8): 9-14. Illus.: Photo. B&W. 4. Lang.: Hun.

Hungary: Miskolc. 1996-1997. Historical studies. ■An interesting and much discussed experimental season under the direction of Zoltán Kamondi at a new Miskolc venue, Csarnok Kultusz Motel.

555 Woods, Leigh; Gunnarsdóttir, Ágústa. *Public Selves, Political Stages: Interviews with Icelandic Women in Government and Theatre.* Amsterdam: Harwood Academic Publishers; 1997. 285 pp. (Contemporary Theatre Studies 18.) Biblio. Index. Illus.: Photo. 21. Lang.: Eng.

Iceland. 1980-1996. Histories-sources. ■Interviews with women of the Icelandic theatre—actors, directors—who also function as government officials, including the current President of Iceland, former theatre director Vigdís Finnbogadóttir. Includes a critical historical overview of Icelandic theatre and women in Iceland.

556 Emigh, John. *Masked Performance: The Play of Self and Other in Ritual and Theatre.* Philadelphia, PA: Univ. of Pennsylvania P; 1997. 359 pp. Notes. Index. Biblio. Lang.: Eng.

India. Papua New Guinea. Indonesia. 1800-1995. Histories-specific. ■Examines details of non-Western ritual performance. Author argues that the use of the mask and subsequent 'trance' states reveal character in these societies, as opposed to the West, where the mask conceals.

557 Richmond, Farley. *Kutiyattam: Sanskrit Theater of India.* Ann Arbor, MI: Univ. of Michigan P; 1997. Biblio. [CD-ROM format.] Lang.: Eng.

India. 1000-1997. Critical studies. ■Interactive, multimedia visual presentation of the Indian performance style *kutiyattam.* CD features text and graphics on the acting, costume, makeup, music, and architecture of the form, audio and video clips of actual performances and training, and an extensive scholarly bibliography.

558 Bodden, Michael H. "Teater Koma's *Suksesi* and Indonesia's New Order." *ATJ.* 1997 Fall; 14(2): 259-280. Notes. Biblio. Illus.: Photo. Color. B&W. 4. Lang.: Eng.

Indonesia: Jakarta. 1977-1993. Critical studies. ■Political and social events surrounding Teater Koma's (headed by N. and Ratna Riantiarno) production of *Suksesi* by poet/playwright Rendra, and the resultant conflict between artists and government regarding censorship issues.

559 Barth, Diana. "Visit to Galway." *WES.* 1997 Fall; 9(3): 83-86. Illus.: Photo. 1. Lang.: Eng.

Ireland: Galway. 1997. Historical studies. ■Report on the Fourth International Women Playwrights Conference, held in Galway. Includes discussion of a coproduction of Martin McDonagh's *The Beauty Queen of Leenane* by Druid Theatre of Galway and the Royal Court Theatre of London.

560 Quick, Andrew. "Performing Displacement: desperate optimists and the Arts of Impropriety." *PerfR.* 1997 Fall; 2(3): 25-29. Notes. Biblio. Illus.: Photo. B&W. 2. Lang.: Eng.

Ireland: Dublin. 1993-1997. Critical studies. ■Theatre and the politics of place in the work of the group desperate optimists and their focus on themes of oppression, nationhood, security, and sanctuary.

561 Bentoglio, Alberto. *Giuseppe Patroni Griffi e il suo teatro.* (Giuseppe Patroni Griffi and His Theatre.) Rome: Bulzoni; 1997. 519 pp. (Quaderni di Gargnano: I protagonisti del teatro contemporaneo 7.) Pref. Index. Lang.: Ita.

Italy. 1948-1997. Critical studies. ■Collection of essays on Patroni Griffi's stagings for theatre, television, and radio. Includes a list of his plays.

562 Cambiaghi, Mariagabriella, ed. *Mario Missiroli e il suo teatro.* (Mario Missiroli and His Theatre.) Rome: Bulzoni; 1997. 310 pp. (Quaderni di Gargnano: I protagonisti del teatro contemporaneo 5.) Pref. Index. Biblio. Lang.: Ita.

Italy. 1956-1995. Critical studies. ■Collection of essays on Mario Missiroli's stagings for theatre, television, and opera.

563 Deriu, Fabrizio. *Gian Maria Volonté: il lavoro d'attore.* (Gian Maria Volonté: The Actor's Work.) Rome: Bulzoni; 1997. 454 pp. (Biblioteca teatrale 91.) Pref. Index. Append. Lang.: Ita.

Italy. 1933-1994. Critical studies. ■Analysis of Volonté's interpretations for theatre, television, and film. Includes a chronology of his roles and productions.

564 Günsberg, Maggie. *Gender and the Italian Stage: From the Renaissance to the Present Day.* Cambridge: Cambridge UP; 1997. 275 pp. Pref. Notes. Index. Biblio. Illus.: Photo. Dwg. 6. Lang.: Eng.

Italy. 1526-1995. Histories-specific. ■Feminist analysis of the representation of gender on the Italian stage from the patriarchal comedies of the Renaissance to the one-woman satires of Franca Rame. Considers social categories of class, age, and family to produce a feminist reading.

565 Pretini, Giancarlo. *Spettacolo leggero: dal music hall al varietà alla rivista al musical.* (Entertainment: From Music Hall to Variety to Revue to Musical.) Udine: Trapezio; 1997. 436 pp. Biblio. Gloss. Index. Illus.: Photo. Dwg. Poster. B&W. Color. Lang.: Ita.

Italy. 1850-1996. Histories-specific. ■Italian light entertainment, including music, dance, comedy, and the production of American and English musicals.

566 Schachenmayr, Volker. "Emma Lyon, the Attitude, and Goethean Performance Theory." *NTQ.* 1997; 13(49): 3-17. Notes. Biblio. Illus.: Pntg. Dwg. B&W. 4. Lang.: Eng.

Italy: Naples. Germany. 1786-1791. Critical studies. ■Re-evaluates the *tableau vivant,* investigating how far or in what ways a static pose, or attitude, can be a theatrical performance. Uses as example Emma Lyon and analyzes Goethe's critical response to her work, which he saw as an exciting experiment fusing stage performance and visual art.

567 Coaldrake, A. Kimi. *Women's Gidayu and the Japanese Theatre Tradition.* New York, NY/London: Routledge P; 1997. (Routledge Japanese Studies 5.) [CD-ROM format.] Lang.: Eng.

Japan. 1888-1997. Critical studies. ■CD-ROM devoted to the women's performance genre *gidayu.* Introduces performers, their musical narratives and the politics of their survival within Japanese performing culture, in light of Japanese notions of gender, culture, and society.

568 Koike, Misako. "Breaking the Mold: Women in Japanese Theatre." *AmTh.* 1997 Apr.; 14(4): 42-45. Illus.: Photo. B&W. 2. Lang.: Eng.

Japan: Tokyo. 1970-1996. Critical studies. ■Kaitaisha theatre company's production of *Tokyo Ghetto December 1996* and its depiction of women in Japanese society. Women's roles in Japanese theatre history, mention of the few representative female voices in contemporary Japanese theatre.

569 Leiter, Samuel L., ed. *Japanese Theater in the World.* New York, NY: The Japan Society; 1997. 196 pp. Index. Biblio. Illus.: Photo. Pntg. Sketches. Poster. B&W. Color. 538. Lang.: Eng.

Japan. 1997. Historical studies. ■Exhibition catalogue of Japanese theatre, with essays on the influence and place of Japanese theatre in the world.

570 Zeltiņa, Guna. "Latvian Theatre in the 90s: Trends, Repertoire, Personalities." *SEEP.* 1997 Spr; 17(1): 37-48. Illus.: Photo. 5. Lang.: Eng.

Latvia. 1990-1995. Critical studies. ■Struggle, disillusion, and changes in recent theatre in Latvia since its independence from Russia.

571 Konijn, Elly; Westerbeek, Astrid. *Acteren en Emoties: Vorm Geven aan Emoties op het Toneel.* (Acting and Emotions: Giving Shape to Emotions on Stage.) Amsterdam: Boom; 1997. 253 pp. Pref. Biblio. Index. Tables. Lang.: Dut.

Netherlands. USA. 1997. Empirical research. ■Psychological study of the influence of role playing on actors' private lives, with respect to personal and social relationships.

572 Afzal-Khan, Fawzia. "Street Theatre in Pakistani Punjab: The Case of Ajoka, Lok Rehas, and the Woman Question." *TDR.* 1997 Fall; 41(3): 39-62. Notes. Biblio. Illus.: Photo. B&W. 9. Lang.: Eng.

Pakistan. 1979-1996. Critical studies. ■The Parallel Theatre Movement and its representation of the citizen-state and male-female relations. Focuses on plays about abuses of women's rights, written by Shahid Naheem and produced by Ajoka.

573 Abramow-Newerly, Jarosław. "Janusz Warmiński: The Power of Taste." *TP.* 1997; 39(1): 10-11. Illus.: Photo. B&W. 1. Lang.: Eng, Fre.

THEATRE IN GENERAL: —Performance/production

Poland. 1944-1997. Biographical studies. ■Reflection on the career of theatre director Warmiński upon his recent death. Productions, artistic direction of Teatr Ateneum.

574 Burzyński, Tadeusz. "Grotowski's Come-back." *TP.* 1997; 39(3): 6-8. Illus.: Photo. B&W. 1. Lang.: Eng, Fre.
Poland: Wrocław. 1982-1997. Historical studies. ■Theatre director and teacher Jerzy Grotowski's return to Wrocław to present his piece *Action (Akcja)* at the Library of Zakład Narodowy im. Ossolińskich. Argues whether *Action* can be seen as a true play, techniques and approaches of Grotowski.

575 Chojka, Joanna. "Ten Years of Theatre of Expression." *TP.* 1997; 39(3): 24-27. Illus.: Photo. B&W. Color. 3. Lang.: Eng, Fre.
Poland: Sopot. 1987-1997. Critical studies. ■Wojciech Misiuro's founding of Teatr Ekspresji, which combines techniques of dance, movement and acting as a formula of creation. Past productions *Passion (Pasja)*, *The Dead Can Dance (Umarli potrafią tańczyć)* and their themes.

576 Chojnacka, Anna. "Kronika teatru lwowskiego." (Chronicle of Theatre in Lvov.) 238-271 in Kuchtówna, Lidia, ed. *Teatr polski we Lwowie. Studia i materiały do dziejów teatru polskiego. t. XXV (37).* Lang.: Pol.
Poland: Lvov. 1583-1945. Historical studies. ■Chronicle of major theatre events in Lvov, including premieres and guest performances, and discussion of important directors and legal aspects of theatre in Lvov.

577 Dziewulska, Małgorzata. "'Cult' or How To Become More Real." *TP.* 1997; 39(2): 7-9. Illus.: Photo. B&W. 1. Lang.: Eng, Fre.
Poland. 1920-1997. Historical studies. ■Followers of the work of Antonin Artaud, Joseph Chaikin, Krystian Lupa: communal living, political beliefs, beliefs of theatre as community.

578 Dziewulska, Małgorzata. "Wrocław Revisited." *TP.* 1997; 39(3): 12-13. Lang.: Eng, Fre.
Poland: Wrocław. 1975-1997. Historical studies. ■Brief history of the development and work of Jerzy Grotowski's Theatre Laboratory. His current presentation of *Action (Akcja)*.

579 Hernik Spalińska, Jagoda. "Życie teatralne Wilna podczas II wojny światowej." (Theatre Life in Vilna During the Second World War.) *PaT.* 1997; 46(1-4): 585-684. Notes. Append. Illus.: Handbill. Photo. B&W. 8. Lang.: Pol.
Poland: Vilna. 1939-1945. Historical studies. ■Wartime theatre activity under the successive occupations of the Soviet Army, the Lithuanians, and the Nazis.

580 Horbatowski, Piotr. "Życie teatralne we Lwowie w latach 1939-1946." (Theatrical Life in Lvov, 1939-1946.) *PaT.* 1997 ; 46(1-4): 685-734. Notes. Append. Illus.: Handbill. Photo. B&W. 6. Lang.: Pol.
Poland: Lvov. 1939-1946. Historical studies. ■Wartime theatre activities in the city, which was occupied in turn by Soviets, Nazis, and Soviets again.

581 Konabrodzki, Mateusz. *Dziecięcy język teatru.* (The Childish Language of Theatre.) Lodz: ŁDK-TKT; 1997. 60 pp. Notes. Append. Lang.: Pol.
Poland. 1964-1992. Critical studies. ■Analysis of Jerzy Grotowski's *Apocalypsis cum figuris* with respect to modern psychology, anthropology, and the work of other directors, including Kantor, Jarocki, and Swinarski.

582 Kuharski, Allen J. "The Third International Gombrowicz Festival." *SEEP.* 1997 Fall; 17(3): 37-47. Illus.: Photo. 6. Lang.: Eng.
Poland: Radom. 1997. Critical studies. ■Critical review of the International Gombrowicz Festival. The festival covers productions of Gombrowicz's plays from Poland and abroad, as well as art exhibits, film screenings, and international symposia.

583 Maresz, Barbara. *Występy gościnne w teatrze polskim. Z dziejów życia teatralnego Krakowa, Lwowa i Warszawy.* (Guest Performances in Polish Theatre: On the History of Theatre in Cracow, Lvov, and Warsaw.) Cracow: Universitas; 1997. 346 pp. Pref. Biblio. Index. Illus.: Photo. Poster. 8. Lang.: Pol.

Poland: Cracow, Lvov, Warsaw. 1810-1915. Histories-specific. ■Influence of guest performances on the main theatre centers of Poland and the different acting styles. Reference to Adelaide Ristori, Sarah Bernhardt, Helena Modjeska, Wincenty Rapacki, Bolesław Ładnowski, Helena Marcello, Józef Kotarbiński, Maria Wisnowska, Kazimierz Kamiński, and Mieczysław Frenkiel.

584 Pleśniarowicz, Krzysztof; Adamus, Grzegorz, designer. *Kantor. Artysta końca wieku.* (Kantor: The Artist of the End of the Century.) Wrocław: Wydawnictwo Dolnośląskie; 1997. 349 pp. (A to Polska właśnie.) Biblio. Index. Tables. Filmography. Illus.: Design. Graphs. Pntg. Dwg. Poster. Photo. Sketches. B&W. Color. 456. Lang.: Pol.
Poland. 1915-1992. Critical studies. ■Tadeusz Kantor's idea of theatre and art, with analysis of performances, exhibitions, and Happenings, the history of Cricot 2 and Kantor's life. Includes texts of Kantor's artistic manifestos.

585 Porębski, Mieczysław. *T. Kantor. Świadectwa. Rozmowy. Komentarze.* (Tadeusz Kantor: Records, Conversations, Commentary.) Warsaw: Muzeum Sztuki w Łodzi/Murator Wydawnictwo; 1997. 229 pp. Pref. Index. Illus.: Pntg. Dwg. Photo. B&W. Color. 81. Lang.: Pol.
Poland: Cracow. 1943-1997. Histories-sources. ■Archival material concerning relations of the author, an art historian and critic, with director and theatre artist Tadeusz Kantor: letters, records of their conversations, photos of Kantor's paintings and drawings, and Porębski's comments on their exchange of ideas.

586 Somerville, Paul. *The Monumental Theatre of Leon Schiller.* New York, NY: City Univ. of New York; 1997. 270 pp. Notes. Biblio. [Ph.D. Dissertation, Univ. Microfilms Order No. AAC 9720144.] Lang.: Eng.
Poland. 1907-1954. Critical studies. ■Director Leon Schiller's concept of 'monumental theatre' in the style of Appia and Craig, and his stagings of the plays of Adam Mickiewicz, Juliusz Słowacki, Zygmunt Krasiński.

587 Styk, Maria Barbara. *Teatr amatorski w Lublinie i na Lubelszczyźnie w latach 1866-1918.* (Amateur Theatre in the District of Lublin, 1866-1918.) Lublin: Redakcja Wydawnictw Katolickiego Uniwersytetu Lubelskiego; 1997. 257 pp. Pref. Biblio. Index. Illus.: Dwg. Photo. Maps. B&W. 56. Lang.: Pol.
Poland: Lublin. 1866-1918. Histories-specific. ■The importance of amateur theatre productions in the Lublin district for Polish cultural identity during the partitions. Considers performers, repertory, stage design, music, critical and audience reception.

588 Woźniakowski, Krzysztof. "Jawne polskie życie teatralne w okupowanym Krakowie 1939-1945." (Official Polish Theatre Life in Occupied Cracow, 1939-1945.) *PaT.* 1997; 46(1-4): 410-459. Notes. Illus.: Photo. B&W. 1. Lang.: Pol.
Poland: Cracow. 1939-1945. Historical studies. ■The repertory of the official (not underground) Polish theatres during World War II. Includes analysis of various forms of variety and popular theatre, opera, and guest performances of Warsaw troupes, and reviews in underground newspapers.

589 Bespal'ceva, G. "S ljubov'ju pro ljubov': Tjuzovskie portrety." (With Love for Love: Portraits of Youth Theatre.) *Otčij kraj.* 1997; 5: 142-152. Lang.: Rus.
Russia: Volgograd. 1990-1997. Historical studies. ■Portraits of three actors in children's theatre: V. Bondarenko, V. Kameneckij, and E. Jefimovskaja.

590 Cirpons, I., comp. *Aktery, roli, zriteli.* (Actors, Roles, Spectators.) Pskov: Izdatel'skij dom 'Sterch'; 1997. 132 pp. Lang.: Rus.
Russia: Pskov. 1800-1900. Histories-specific. ■From the history of theatrical life of Pskov.

591 Gerould, Daniel. "Pages from the Past: Jasieński, Lunacharsky, Moor, and *The Mannequin's Ball.*" *SEEP.* 1997 Spr; 17(1): 54-71. Illus.: Dwg. Photo. 8. Lang.: Eng.
Russia. 1931. Historical studies. ■Using the drawings of the playwright, author examines a theatrical event from the past, poet Bruno Jasieński's play *Bal Manekinov (The Mannequin's Ball,* with an introduction by Anatolij Lunačarskij, and illustrations by Moor (Dmitri Stakciévič

THEATRE IN GENERAL: —Performance/production

Orlov). This political satire was soon attacked by the Communist Party and Jasieński and Lunačarskij were persecuted.

592 Gerould, Daniel. "Chronology of the Life and Work of Bruno Jasieński." *SEEP.* 1997 Spr; 17(1): 72-75. Lang.: Eng.
Russia. 1901-1977. Biographical studies. ■The career of poet Bruno Jasieński, author of *Bal Manekinov (The Mannequin's Ball)*.

593 Golub, Spencer. "Moscow Is Watching." *SEEP.* 1997 Spr; 17(1): 28-36. Lang.: Eng.
Russia: Moscow. 1995. Critical studies. ■Author's recent experiences of attending theatre in Moscow.

594 Gromov, Ju.I. *Tanec i ego rol' v vospitanii plastičeskoj kul'tury aktera.* (Dance and its Role in the Development of the Actor's Physical Culture.) St. Petersburg: Gumanitarny Universitet Profsoyuzov; 1997. 256 pp. Lang.: Rus.
Russia. 1997. Historical studies. ■The role of dance in the actor's development.

595 Hančin, V. *Nosil on sovest' blizko k serdcu: Vysockij v Kujbyševe 1967 g.* (Close to the Heart: Vysockij in Kujbyshev, 1967.) Samara: Parus; 1997. 144 pp. Lang.: Rus.
Russia: Kujbyshev. 1967. Historical studies. ■The actor Vladimir Vysockij's work in Kujbyshev.

596 Krylov, A.E.; Žukov, B.B., ed. *Mir Vysockogo. Issledovanija i materialy. Al'manach. Vyp. I.* (Vysockij's World: Findings and Materials, Almanac, Volume 1.) Moscow: Gosudarstvénnyj kul'turnij cent'r/Muzej V.S. Vysockogo; 1997. 536 pp. Lang.: Rus.
Russia. 1938-1980. Histories-sources. ■Collection of materials related to actor and singer Vladimir Vysockij.

597 Lunacharsky, Anatolii; Gerould, Daniel, transl. "Anatolii Lunacharsky's Introduction to the 1931 Moscow Edition of *The Mannequin's Ball*." *SEEP.* 1997 Spr; 17(1): 76-77. Lang.: Eng.
Russia. 1931. Historical studies. ■English translation of Lunačarskij's essay on *Bal Manekinov (The Mannequin's Ball)*.

598 Maksimov, V. "S večnostju naedine." (Alone with Eternity.) *TeatZ.* 1997; 9-10: 19-22. Lang.: Rus.
Russia: Moscow. 1950-1997. Historical studies. ■Profile of actor and national artist of the USSR Michajl Ul'janov on the occasion of his seventieth birthday.

599 Šach-Azizova, T. "Sezon, ili dialektika na teatre." (The Season, or A Dialectic on the Theatre.) *TeatZ.* 1997; 8: 2-8. Lang.: Rus.
Russia: Moscow. 1996-1997. Reviews of performances. ■Review of the Moscow theatre season.

600 Savčenko, B. *Moskovskaja estrada v licach.* (Moscow Theatre in Personalities.) Moscow: MKO Estrada; 1997. 432 pp. Lang.: Rus.
Russia. Historical studies. ■Artists of the Moscow stage.

601 Stanislavskij, Konstantin S.; Guerrieri, Gerardo, ed. *Il lavoro dell'attore su se stesso.* (The Actor's Work on Himself.) Rome/Bari: Laterza; 1997. li, 600 pp. (Biblioteca Universale Laterza 45.) Pref. Notes. Append. Illus.: Photo. B&W. Lang.: Ita.
Russia. 1863-1938. Instructional materials. ■Italian translation of Stanislavskij's acting text.

602 Starosel'skaja, Natalija. "Marafon dlinoju v četyre goda." (A Four-Year Marathon.) *TeatZ.* 1997; 11-12: 32-39. Lang.: Rus.
Russia. 1993-1997. Historical studies. ■From the history of the professional theatre award Zolotoj maski (The Golden Mask).

603 Berger, Aleš. *Novi ogledi in pogledi.* (New Views and Reviews.) Ljubljana: Slovenian Literary Society; 1997. 261 pp. Lang.: Slo.
Slovenia. 1984-1996. Reviews of performances. ■Collection of previously published newspaper reviews of plays produced in Slovenian theatres.

604 Marin, Marko; Matić, Dragan; Slivnik, Francka; Pušić, Barbara; Lukan, Blaž. *O nevzvišenem v gledališču.* (On the Non-

Sublime in Theatre.) Ljubljana: KUD France Prešeren/AGRFT; 1997. 131 pp. (Vesela znanost.) Illus.: Photo. B&W. Lang.: Slo.
Slovenia. 1765-1914. Historical studies. ■Five articles on practical problems of theatre, including founding a theatre, building a theatre, costuming, and acting.

605 Esterhuizen, Johan. "Cinderella Goes Shopping: A Response to the Standard Bank International Conference on the Economic Benefits of Arts and Culture: Grahamstown, South Africa 11-13 June 1997." *SATJ.* 1997 May/Sep.; 11(1/2): 232-237. Lang.: Afr.
South Africa, Republic of: Grahamstown. 1996. Historical studies. ■Report on the Standard Bank International Conference held in Grahamstown.

606 Horn, Peter. "What Is a Tribal Dress? The 'Imbongi' (Praise-Singer) and the 'People's Poet.' Reactivation of a Tradition in the Liberation Struggle." 115-131 in Davis, Geoffrey V., ed.; Fuchs, Anne, ed. *Theatre and Change in South Africa.* Amsterdam: Harwood Academic Publishing; 1996. 324 pp. (Contemporary Theatre Studies 12.) Index. Notes. Append. Lang.: Eng.
South Africa, Republic of. 1980-1989. Critical studies. ■Poetry in South African popular culture, both indigenous and postcolonial, focusing on the *imbongi*, or oral poet.

607 "Selected Theatre Listings in Madrid and Barcelona, 1996-97." *WES.* 1997 Win; 9(1): 21-22. Lang.: Eng.
Spain: Barcelona, Madrid. 1996-1997. Histories-sources. ■Listing of theatrical activity in Madrid and Barcelona for 1996 and 1997, listing production, theatre venue, and director.

608 Feldman, Sharon G. "Theatrical Politics and Political Theatrics in Barcelona." *WES.* 1997 Win; 9(1): 17-20. Lang.: Eng.
Spain: Barcelona. 1996. Historical studies. ■Current theatre in Barcelona, emphasizing the political content of its theatrical practice, including Els Joglars *Ubú President*, directed by Albert Boadella, at the Teatro Lliure.

609 Leonard, Candyce. "Andalusian Theatre." *WES.* 1997 Fall; 9(3): 69-72. Illus.: Photo. 1. Lang.: Eng.
Spain: Seville. 1997. Historical studies. ■Current state of theatrical activities in the Spanish region of Andalusia, concentrating on the Centro Andaluz de Teatro, a centralized theatre, archive and research facility.

610 Lera, Fernández. "The Night and the Dreams: a Conversation with Esteve Graset." *PerfR.* 1997 Spr; 2(1): 106-113. Notes. Biblio. Illus.: Photo. B&W. 3. Lang.: Eng.
Spain. 1978-1996. Biographical studies. ■An interview with Graset just before his death in 1996. Includes an introduction summarizing his contribution to Spanish and European art and theatre. Focuses on the relationship between installation and scenography and the audience's experience in relation to the process of composition.

611 Villegas, Juan. "XI Festival Iberoamericano de Teatro de Cádiz." (Eleventh Spanish-American Theatre Festival in Cádiz.) *Gestos.* 1997 Apr.; 12(23): 169-176. Lang.: Spa.
Spain: Cádiz. 1996. Historical studies. ■Report on the eleventh Spanish-American Theatre Festival in Cádiz.

612 Zatlin, Phyllis. "Women Directors: An Important Force Throughout Spain's Theatre World." *WES.* 1997 Win; 9(1): 37-42. Illus.: Photo. 4. Lang.: Eng.
Spain. 1990-1996. Historical studies. ■The presence of women in Spanish theatre, from professional directors to heads of theatre schools. Includes directors such as Zulema Katz, Patsy Fuller, Sara Molina, Elena Cánovas, Ana Diosdado, among others.

613 Hallin, Ulrika. "Var är alla gästpel?" (Where Are All the Guest Performances?)*Tningen.* 1997; 21(3): 11-14. Illus.: Photo. B&W. Lang.: Swe.
Sweden. 1980. Critical studies. ■A survey of the shrinking interest in Sweden for international guests, with interviews with Chris Torch from Intercult, Björn Westeson from Swedish Institute and Ann Mari Engel from Svenska Teaterförbundet.

614 Romanus, Linda. "Robert Wilson, närmast okänd världskändis på besök." (Robert Wilson, a Visit of an

THEATRE IN GENERAL: —Performance/production

Almost an Unknown World Famous Person.) *Entré*. 1997; 24(2): 39-40. Illus.: Photo. B&W. Lang.: Swe.
Sweden: Stockholm. USA. 1976. Biographical studies. ■A presentation of Robert Wilson and his forthcoming guest production at Stockholms Stadsteater.

615 DiGaetani, John Louis. "Report from London: Winter 1997." *WES*. 1997 Spr; 9(2): 23-28. Illus.: Photo. 3. Lang.: Eng.
UK-England: London. 1997. Historical studies. ■Report on current theatre, opera, and ballet in London: performances, actors, venues, and financial information.

616 Goodall, Jane. "Transferred Agencies: Performance and the Fear of Automatism." *TJ*. 1997 Dec.; 49(4): 441-454. Notes. Lang.: Eng.
UK-England. 1870-1954. Historical studies. ■Argues that the display of women's bodies in popular performance mediates a cultural anxiety in response to newly developing industrial technologies. Examines performances of the Tiller Girls, a dance troupe in England in the late nineteenth century.

617 Müller, Péter, P. "Megtörtént esetek." (True Stories.) *Sz*. 1997; 30(4): 44-48. Illus.: Photo. B&W. 2. Lang.: Hun.
UK-England: Cambridge, Stratford-on-Avon. 1996. Historical studies. ■A report on interesting novelties at the Cambridge Grass Roots 2 Festival and at Stratford-on-Avon's two experimental theatres, the Swan and The Other Place.

618 Newey, Katherine. "Melodrama and Metatheatre: Theatricality in the Nineteenth Century Theatre." *JDTC*. 1997 Spr; 11(2): 85-100. Lang.: Eng.
UK-England. 1840-1900. Critical studies. ■Metatheatricality in nineteenth-century melodrama as the result of the extremes of expression in character and structure inherent in the genre. Two plays are used as examples: *True Love, or, The Interlude Interrupted* by Edward Geoghegan, and Charles Selby's *Behind the Scenes, or, Actors by Lamplight*.

619 Read, Alan. "No Hiding Place." *PerfR*. 1997 Fall; 2(3): 65-74. Notes. Biblio. Illus.: Photo. B&W. 5. Lang.: Eng.
UK-England. 1960-1997. Critical studies. ■Space as a dynamic element of social relations and as gendered territory in site-specific performance. Considers Christopher Heighes and Ewan Forster's *Preliminary Hearing*, Platform's *Homeland*, Neil Bartlett's *The Seven Sacraments of Nicolas Poussin*, the writings of Iain Sinclair, such as *Downriver* and *Lights Out for the Territory*, and the films of Patrick Keiller, *London* and *Robinson in Space*.

620 Roberts, Philip. "George Devine's Visit to Edward Gordon Craig." *TN*. 1997; 51(1): 14-23. Notes. Lang.: Eng.
UK-England. 1951-1956. Historical studies. ■Includes extracts from Devine's private memorandum recording Craig's observations on various aspects of theatre following their meeting in 1951. Includes discussion on Henry Irving and Isadora Duncan.

621 Sokalski, Joseph. "From Screen to Stage: A Case Study of the Paper Print Collection." *NCT*. 1997 Win; 25(2): 115-138. Illus.: Photo. B&W. 3. Lang.: Eng.
UK-England. France. USA. 1863-1903. Historical studies. ■The documentation of the relationship between nineteenth-century theatre and film in the Paper Print Collection of the Library of Congress, Washington, DC. Includes a CD-ROM with seventeen illustrations for this essay.

622 Toek, Barry. "Kids Stuff." *PIPl*. 1997 Dec.; 514: 8-9. Illus.: Photo. B&W. 1. Lang.: Eng.
UK-England. 1938-1997. Historical studies. ■Anecdotes regarding child actors in England.

623 Trowsdale, Jo. "'Identity—Even if it is a Fantasy': The Work of Carran Waterfield." *NTQ*. 1997; 13(51): 231-247. Biblio. Illus.: Photo. B&W. 5. Lang.: Eng.
UK-England: Coventry. 1978-1997. Historical studies. ■Describes growth of Carran Waterfield's multi-disciplinary, mostly solo performance pieces, which bear an organic relationship to her own life and that of her community.

624 Zareckaja, Z. "Muzyka prežde vsego... (Muzykal'nyje postanovki v tvorčestve Edvarda Gordona Kreg." (Music Before All: Musical Play in the Work of Edward Gordon Craig.) *Skripičnyj ključ*. 1997; 1: 56-62. Lang.: Rus.

UK-England. 1872-1966. Critical studies. ■Musical aspects of Craig's work as a director.

625 "Non-Traditional Casting Project: Putting Artists On-Line." *BlackM*. 1997 June/July; 12(4): 14. Illus.: Photo. B&W. 1. Lang.: Eng.
USA. 1997. Critical studies. ■Introduces the Non-Traditional Casting Project Artists Files On-Line as a way for actors to obtain auditions.

626 Ábrahám, Eszter; Regős, János, photo. "Bábel után. Beszélgetés Peter Schumann-nal." (After Babel: A Conversation with Peter Schumann.) *Sz*. 1997; 30(10): 45. Illus.: Photo. B&W. 1. Lang.: Hun.
USA. 1997. Histories-sources. ■Interview with Peter Schumann of Bread and Puppet Theatre on the creation of a street performance based on the Biblical story of the Tower of Babel.

627 Auslander, Philip. *From Acting to Performance: Essays on Modernism and Postmodernism*. New York, NY/London: Routledge P; 1997. 184 pp. Biblio. Notes. Index. Lang.: Eng.
USA. 1960-1990. Critical studies. ■Examines the changes in acting and performance during the transition from the theatre of the Vietnam era to the postmodern era of the 1980s. Author argues that traditional theatre and contemporary performance studies are united by shared concerns and critical approaches.

628 Bérczes, László. "A Broadway felé. Egy hónap New Yorkban." (Towards Broadway: A Month in New York.) *Sz*. 1997; 30(9): 37-43. Illus.: Photo. B&W. 5. Lang.: Hun.
USA: New York, NY. 1997. Critical studies. ■A critic's impressions of the New York stage as sampled during a stay of some weeks in this city.

629 Bérczes, László. "Üres tér, középen." (In the Middle of Empty Spaces.) *Sz*. 1997; 30(5): 1. Lang.: Hun.
USA: New York, NY. 1996. Reviews of performances. ■Report on a recent trip to the US by drawing some general conclusions from the seventeen theatre productions seen.

630 Bianchi, Ruggero; De Martini, Roberta, ed. "Tecnologia, visione olistica del mondo, differenza et identità etnica al servizio di un teatro totale." (Technology, a Holistic Vision of the World, Difference, and Ethnic Identity in the Service of a Total Theatre.) *IlCast*. 1997; 10(29): 33-60. Notes. Illus.: Photo. B&W. Lang.: Ita.
USA. 1985. Histories-sources. ■Interview with theatre artist Ping Chong about the artistic language he has developed on the basis of his cultural (Asian) background.

631 Bianchi, Ruggero; Caglianone, Maria, ed. "Ricevere, trasformare, trasmettere: il teatro come 'spazio radio'." (Receiving, Transforming, Transmitting: Theatre as 'Radio Space'.) *IlCast*. 1997; 10(29): 61-82. Notes. Illus.: Photo. B&W. Lang.: Ita.
USA. 1985. Histories-sources. ■Interview with Christopher Hardman about his theatrical experiments with Snake Theatre and the Antenna Group. Discussion of technology as a means of reinventing theatre with social and psychological implications.

632 Bowman, Ruth Laurion. "'Joking' with the Classics: Using Boal's Joker System in the Performance Classroom." *TTop*. 1997 Sep.; 7(2): 139-151. Lang.: Eng.
USA. 1995-1996. Histories-sources. ■The author's experience using the 'joker' system of Augusto Boal's Theatre of the Oppressed in directing students in a university production of Euripides' *Bákchai (The Bacchae)*. Focus is on the pedagogical value of such an approach.

633 Brooks, Daphne Ann. *The Show Must Go On: Race, Gender and Nation in Nineteenth Century Trans-Atlantic Performance Culture*. Los Angeles, CA: Univ. of California; 1997. 367 pp. Notes. Biblio. [Ph.D. Dissertation, Univ. Microfilms Order No. AAC 9803519.] Lang.: Eng.
USA. Europe. 1855-1902. Historical studies. ■Examines African-American theatre and political activism, and constructions of race, gender, and the body in performance. Considers popular works including Dion Boucicault's *The Octoroon*, American stage adaptations of *Dr. Jekyll and Mr. Hyde*, the 'racially-ambiguous' actress Adah Isaacs Menken, the Bert Williams and George Walker production of *In Dahomey*, and actress/dancer Aida Overton Walker.

THEATRE IN GENERAL: —Performance/production

634 Bryan, Vernanne. *Laura Keene: A British Actress on the American Stage, 1826-1873.* Jefferson, NC/London: McFarland; 1997. 222 pp. Notes. Biblio. Index. Illus.: Photo. 27. Lang.: Eng.
USA. UK. 1826-1873. Biographical studies. ■Biography of actress/manager Laura Keene.

635 Cheng, Meiling. "Sacred Naked Nature Girls." *TheatreF.* 1997 Sum/Fall; 11: 5-13. Illus.: Photo. 11. Lang.: Eng.
USA. 1996. Historical studies. ■On *Home: The Last Place I Ran to Just About Killed Me* by the Sacred Naked Nature Girls, presented by Highways Performance Space. Focuses on their collaboration and improvisational style.

636 Cosson, Steven. "*Tailings*: A Collaboration Between Erik Ehn and Smart Mouth Theatre." *TheatreF.* 1997 Sum/Fall; 11: 86-93. Illus.: Photo. 7. Lang.: Eng.
USA: San Francisco, CA. 1995-1997. Histories-sources. ■The artistic director of Smart Mouth Theatre describes the group's collaboration with Erik Ehn in the production of *Tailings*, presented at Intersection for the Arts. Author publishes his journal focusing on collaboration, rehearsal and performance.

637 Eileraas, Karina. "Witches, Bitches & Fluids: Girl Bands Performing Ugliness as Resistance." *TDR.* 1997 Fall; 41(3): 122-139. Notes. Biblio. Illus.: Photo. B&W. 8. Lang.: Eng.
USA. 1970-1996. Critical studies. ■Use of symbolism in female rock bands: representations of rebelliousness, appropriation and use of negative female iconography for self-empowerment, voice and vocal techniques for cathartic expression.

638 Freeberg, Debra L. "Wandering Thespians: Performance Across the Liberal Arts Curriculum." *TTop.* 1997 Sep.; 7(2): 93-102 . Lang.: Eng.
USA: Pittsburgh, PA. 1995-1996. Historical studies. ■On the work of the Wandering Thespians, a group of college theatre students who perform in classrooms across the Calvin College campus. This innovative solution to several practical problems fulfills theatre department needs for performance experience for their students as well as serving larger needs of the college.

639 Frick, John W. "Anti-Intellectualism and Representations of 'Commonness' in the Nineteenth-Century American Theatre." *JADT.* 1997 Spr; 9(2): 2-22. Notes. Lang.: Eng.
USA. 1920-1940. Critical studies. ■The persistent and recurring pattern of anti-intellectualism in American popular culture as reflected on the nineteenth-century stage in melodramas, minstrel shows and drawing room comedies.

640 Fricker, Karen. "Adam & Anthony Rapp." *AmTh.* 1997 Jan.; 14(1): 50-51. Illus.: Photo. B&W. 1. Lang.: Eng.
USA. 1997. Biographical studies. ■Actor Anthony Rapp and his brother playwright/novelist Adam Rapp: personal relationship, careers, Anthony's success in the musical *Rent* by Jonathan Larson.

641 Gottschild, Brenda Dixon. *Digging the Africanist Presence in American Performance: Dance and Other Contexts.* Westport, CT/London: Greenwood; 1996. 189 pp. (Contributions in Afro-American and African Studies 179.) Index. Biblio. Illus.: Photo. 18. Lang.: Eng.
USA. 1840-1995. Histories-specific. ■Examines the Africanist influences on and components of American theatre, from minstrelsy to hip-hop and performance studies.

642 Hamilton, Marybeth. *When I'm Bad, I'm Better: Mae West, Sex, and American Entertainment.* New York, NY: Harper Collins; 1995. 307 pp. Biblio. Notes. Index. Lang.: Eng.
USA. 1913-1943. Critical studies. ■Traces history of performer Mae West's public persona, the process of theatrical experimentation by which she constructed and promoted herself through vaudeville, Broadway, and in film. Argues the social history of sex as a commodity.

643 Harrison, Paul Carter. "The Crisis of Black Theatre Identity." *AfAmR.* 1997 Win; 31(4): 567-578. Biblio. Lang.: Eng.
USA. 1997. Critical studies. ■A call to Black theatre artists to ressuscitate Black theatre from its current state.

644 Hartnett, John Thomas. *Cultural Pluralism in Drama Curriculum Development in the American Repertory Theater: Oneself as Another.* San Francisco, CA: Univ. of San Francisco;

1997. 209 pp. [Ph.D. Dissertation, Univ. Microfilms Order No. AAC 9735452.] Lang.: Eng.
USA. 1994-1996. Historical studies. ■Examination of traditional vs. non-traditional theatre casting and the implications of new thinking on repertory theatre. Calls for a new 'morality' of casting across racial and cultural barriers in order to resolve conflicts within local communities.

645 Heaton, Daniel Weaver. *Postmodern Messiah: A Critical Ethnography of Elvis Presley as a Site of Performance.* Baton Rouge, LA: Louisiana State Univ. and Agricultural and Mechanical College; 1997. 279 pp. [Ph.D. Dissertation, Univ. Microfilms Order No. AAC 9808746.] Lang.: Eng.
USA. 1997. Critical studies. ■Argues that cultural identity, authority, and representation are contextualized within the cultural practices of Elvis fans and others who use Elvis as the basis for their cultural performances.

646 Highland, Nathalie M. *Performing the Single Voice: The One-Woman Show in America.* Bowling Green, OH: Bowling Green State Univ; 1997. 237 pp. [Ph.D. Dissertation, Univ. Microfilms Order No. AAC 9820904.] Lang.: Eng.
USA. 1890-1995. Historical studies. ■A materialist feminist analysis of female solo performers, including platform readers Anna Cora Mowatt, Fanny Kemble, and Charlotte Cushman, monologists Ruth Draper, Cornelia Otis Skinner, Dorothy Sands, and Cissie Loftus, the poem-dramas of Black playwrights Beah Richards and Sonia Sanchez, and the contemporary performances of Anna Deavere Smith, Whoopi Goldberg, and Lily Tomlin.

647 Jackson, Shannon. "White Privilege and Pedagogy: Nadine Gordimer in Performance." *TTop.* 1997 Sep.; 7(2): 117-138. Lang.: Eng.
USA. 1995-1996. Histories-sources. ■The author's experience directing an adaptation of Nadine Gordimer's short story *The Smell of Death and Flowers* into a play for students at Northwestern University. Uses Gordimer's text and the adaptation process as a basis for theorizing relationships amongst postcolonial theory, critical pedagogy, and performance and theatre studies.

648 Kaufman, Will. *The Comedian as Confidence Man: Studies in Irony Fatigue.* Detroit, MI: Wayne State UP; 1997. 270 pp. (Humor in Life and Letters.) Pref. Biblio. Lang.: Eng.
USA. 1960-1967. Critical studies. ■The comedian as critic—the use of humor and irony to create cultural criticism in the works of Lenny Bruce and others.

649 Kaye, Nick. *Art Into Theatre: Performance Interviews and Documents.* Amsterdam: Harwood; 1996. 281 pp. (Contemporary Theatre Studies 16.) Illus.: Photo. Graphs. Sketches. Diagram. Plan. Dwg. 69. Lang.: Eng.
USA. 1952-1994. Histories-sources. ■Concepts of performance and performance practices which delineate a wide range of interdisciplinary exchanges in art and theatre, for example 'non-theatrical' practices such as painting, sculpture, music, and site-related art, video, and film. Artists include John Cage, Carolee Schneemann, Dennis Oppenheim, Joan Jonas, Richard Foreman, Michael Kirby and his Structuralist Workshop, Ping Chong, Richard Schechner, and Elizabeth LeCompte and the Wooster Group.

650 Kendig, Daun. "Transforming Gender Scripts: Life After *You Just Don't Understand.*" *TextPQ.* 1997 Apr.; 17(2): 197-210. Biblio. Lang.: Eng.
USA. 1997. Critical studies. ■Examines how working collaboratively through improvisational performance offers a way to explore the dominant culture's gender scripts and transform them. Uses examples from Deborah Tannen's self-help book *You Just Don't Understand*, and suggests that Augusto Boal's forum theatre provides a framework for disrupting dominant scripts and generating alternatives.

651 Krämer, Peter. "A Slapstick Comedian at the Crossroads: Buster Keaton, the Theater, and the Movies in 1916/17." *THSt.* 1997; 17: 133-146. Lang.: Eng.
USA. 1916-1917. Historical studies. ■Explores the early stage career of Buster Keaton, arguing that this has been neglected and that it contains vital clues to understanding Keaton's later career in film, and understanding the larger issue of the relationship between stage and screen at particular historical moments.

THEATRE IN GENERAL: —Performance/production

652 Krasner, David. *Resistance, Parody, and Double Consciousness in African-American Theatre, 1895-1910.* New York, NY: St. Martin's P; 1997. 218 pp. Index. Biblio. Notes. Lang.: Eng.
USA. 1895-1910. Critical studies. ■Explores African-American theatre with an emphasis on its resistance to racism, the emergence of parody and the use of a double consciousness to offer resistance. Specifically examines the work of Aida Overton Walker and 'cakewalking' and Bert Williams's and George Walker's *Abyssinia.*

653 Kuftinec, Sonja. "*Odakle Ste?* (Where Are You From?): Active Learning and Community-Based Theatre in Former Yugoslavia and the US." *TTop.* 1997 Sep.; 7(2): 171-186. Illus.: Photo. 2. Lang.: Eng.
USA. Croatia. Serbia. 1995-1996. Historical studies. ■How the community-based performance process lends itself to active learning techniques, through the performance of theatre pieces situated in the context of a war focused on identity. Includes a brief description of how these techniques have been usefully adapted to teaching in the United States.

654 Lavin, Suzanne. *Women and Comedy in Solo Performance: Phyllis Diller, Lily Tomlin, and Roseanne.* Boulder, CO: Univ. of Colorado; 1997. 170 pp. Notes. Biblio. [Ph.D. Dissertation, Univ. Microfilms Order No. AAC 9725756.] Lang.: Eng.
USA. 1950-1995. Critical studies. ■Changes in American women's comedy performance, focusing on the traditional vaudevillian standup style of Phyllis Diller, the satiric comedy of Roseanne, and the character comedy of Lily Tomlin.

655 Lee, Joann F. J. *Changing Shades of the 'Yellow Peril': Asian American Actors in the 1990's: An Ethnographic Case Study.* New York, NY: New York Univ; 1997. 285 pp. [Ph.D. Dissertation, Univ. Microfilms Order No. AAC 9737468.] Lang.: Eng.
USA. 1990-1997. Historical studies. ■Narratives from veteran and aspiring Asian American actors provide insights into how the group is coping with shifts in opportunities, attitudes, and constraints in film, television, and theatre.

656 Mackay, Carol Hanbery. "'Both Sides of the Curtain': Elizabeth Robins, Synaesthesia, and the Subjective Correlative." *TextPQ.* 1997 Oct.; 17(4): 299-316. Notes. Biblio. Lang.: Eng.
USA. 1862-1952. Critical studies. ■Actress/playwright/novelist Robins' creation of a new form of performance from autobiography, enabling reader/viewer to experience creation of a new 'multiple self'. Her performances of Ibsen's 'new women' characters, involvement in the women's movement.

657 Mamet, David. "Business is Business." *AmTh.* 1997 Nov.; 14(9): 16-17. Illus.: Sketches. B&W. 1. Lang.: Eng.
USA. 1997. Critical studies. ■Reprinted from Mamet's book *True and False: Heresy and Common Sense for the Actor,* the playwright suggests specific approaches to creation of a character, and to succeeding in the business of acting.

658 McKinley, Jesse. "Steve Park: Actor and Advocate." *AmTh.* 1997 Sep.; 14(7): 46-47. Illus.: Photo. B&W. 1. Lang.: Eng.
USA. 1997. Biographical studies. ■Career and political activism of actor Park. His work on behalf of Asian actors, and account of his published statement in the *Los Angeles Times* regarding alleged racism in the Hollywood community.

659 Moore, Dick. "Lansbury, Robards Receive National Arts Medals." *EN.* 1997 Nov.; 82(9): 2. Illus.: Photo. 1. Lang.: Eng.
USA. 1997. Historical studies. ■Actors Angela Lansbury and Jason Robards are presented the National Medal of Arts.

660 Moore, Dick. "Equity Foundation Presents Three Awards." *EN.* 1997 Jan/Feb.; 82(1): 2. Illus.: Photo. 1. Lang.: Eng.
USA: New York, NY. 1997. Historical studies. ■Equity presents the Shakespeare Award to actor Nicholas Kepros, and two Callaway Awards to actors Kathleen Chalfant and Frank Langella.

661 Moore, Dick. "Never Give Up, Never Give In: Frank Langella Tells Performers' Seminar." *EN.* 1997 Apr.; 82(3): 8, 11. Lang.: Eng.

USA. 1997. Histories-sources. ■Transcript of seminar by Frank Langella, in which the actor speaks of the hardship of an actor's life, his recent role in Strindberg's *The Father (Fadren)* at the Roundabout Theatre, and influences on his career.

662 Mukhi, Sunita Sunder. *Performing Indianness in New York City.* New York, NY: New York Univ; 1997. 466 pp. Notes. Biblio. [Ph.D. Dissertation, Univ. Microfilms Order No. AAC 9731422.] Lang.: Eng.
USA: New York, NY. 1994-1996. Historical studies. ■Examination of the Indian Independence Day Parade and Cultural Program, the Deepavali Festival at the South Street Seaport, the Sindhi Hindu Divali celebrations, and the productions of New York University based South Asian Organization, Shruti. All are staged performances of stories about how Asian Indians residing in the United States perform their Indianness, as well as assimilate into American life.

663 Nunns, Stephen. "Karen Kandel." *AmTh.* 1997 Feb.; 14(2): 42-43. Illus.: Photo. B&W. 2. Lang.: Eng.
USA: New York, NY. 1977-1997. Biographical studies. ■Career of performer Kandel. Her work with Mabou Mines including *Lear* and their current production *Peter and Wendy,* an adaptation of J.M. Barrie's story featuring puppets and music, directed by Lee Breuer.

664 Olf, Julian M. "Reading the Dramatic Text for Production." *TTop.* 1997 Sep.; 7(2): 153-169. Lang.: Eng.
USA. 1995-1996. Histories-sources. ■The author's approach to integrating intellectual discourse and emotional connection to texts in university teaching, with emphasis on an entry-level graduate course.

665 Pelias, Ronald J. "Confessions of Apprehensive Performer." *TextPQ.* 1997 Jan.; 17(1): 25-32. Lang.: Eng.
USA. 1988. Histories-sources. ■Personal narrative on stage fright.

666 Pollock, Della. "Origins in Absence: Performing Birth Stories." *TDR.* 1997 Spr; 41(1): 11-42. Notes. Biblio. Lang.: Eng.
USA. 1997. Critical studies. ■Stories of childbirth that challenge the comic-heroic norm of birth story-telling. Argues that these tales slip categories of death, difference and normality into a performative framework within which death may be relived. Includes excerpts from transcripts of women telling the stories.

667 Poole, Richard L. "Tent Rep vs. the Movies: The Dirty Business of Show Business." *THSt.* 1997; 17: 121-131. Illus.: Photo. 2. Lang.: Eng.
USA. 1920-1929. Historical studies. ■Competition between tent repertory theatre and movie houses for audiences in its historical context.

668 Rodden, John. "Giving Voice to Vision: An Interview with Marge Piercy." *TextPQ.* 1997 Oct.; 17(4): 366-381. Lang.: Eng.
USA. 1973-1997. Histories-sources. ■Interview with poet Piercy discussing her views about poetry readings and their performances. Reviews her past works and collections of her poetry.

669 Rose, Heidi M. "Julianna Fjeld's *The Journey:* Identity, Production in an ASL Performance." *TextPQ.* 1997 Oct.; 17(4): 331-342. Notes. Biblio. Lang.: Eng.
USA. 1997. Critical studies. ■The enactment of subjectivity in Fjeld's autobiographical work performed in American Sign Language.

670 Rosenberg, Scott. "A Byte of Blake." *AmTh.* 1997 Apr.; 14(4): 36-37. Illus.: Photo. B&W. 2. Lang.: Eng.
USA: Berkeley, CA. 1997. Critical studies. ■Director George Coates's use of three-dimensional slides and video projections to create a multimedia theatre design for his production of *20/20 Blake,* with music composed by Adlai Alexander.

671 Russell, Martin Richard. *Tom O'Horgan, Staging the Outrageous: A Chronological Study of His Theatre.* New York, NY: City Univ. of New York; 1997. 325 pp. Notes. Biblio. [Ph.D. Dissertation, Univ. Microfilms Order No. AAC 9807994.] Lang.: Eng.
USA. 1950-1996. Historical studies. ■Examines the career of the American experimental director Tom O'Horgan, especially the avant-garde theatre scene of the 1960s.

672 Sell, Michael Thomas. *Performing Crisis: Countercultural Theater and the 60s.* Ann Arbor, MI: Univ. of Michigan;

THEATRE IN GENERAL: —Performance/production

1997. 263 pp. [Ph.D. Dissertation, Univ. Microfilms Order No. AAC 9722087.] Lang.: Eng.
USA. 1960-1970. Historical studies. ■Analysis of the Living Theatre, the 'Happening,' Black theatre artists such as Adrienne Kennedy, Larry Neal, and Ed Bullins, and the Otrabanda Company and suggests a paradigm of cultural and literary studies that explains previously unexplored textual, critical, and performance traditions.

673   Shank, Theodore. "TForum: Michael Kirby Remembered." *TheatreF.* 1997 Sum/Fall; 11: 99-103. Lang.: Eng.
USA. 1935-1996. Historical studies. ■Eulogy for theatre artist/critic Michael Kirby.

674   Shank, Theodore. "Reza Abdoh." *MimeJ.* 1991/1992; 15: 10-27. Illus.: Photo. B&W. 11. Lang.: Eng.
USA: Los Angeles, CA. 1980-1992. Histories-sources. ■Director Reza Abdoh discusses influences on his approach to the theatre, including working and performing in Los Angeles.

675   Shaw, Catherine M. "Edwin Booth's *Richard II* and the Divided Nation." 144-163 in Pechter, Edward, ed. *Textual and Theatrical Shakespeare: Questions of Evidence.* Iowa City, IA: Univ of Iowa P; 1997. 267 pp. (Studies in Theatre History and Culture.) Notes. Lang.: Eng.
USA. 1865-1875. Critical studies. ■Booth's post-Civil War production of Shakespeare's *Richard II* and its different reception in northern and southern cities, as reflected in rhetorical and anecdotal accounts of the production.

676   Sheingorn, Pamela. "Reception and the Fleury Mary Magdalene at the Cloisters." *EDAM.* 1997 Fall; 20(1): 45-47. Lang.: Eng.
USA: New York, NY. 1997. Historical studies. ■Analysis of the Ensemble for Early Music's production of the Fleury Mary Magdalene play at The Cloisters, with attention to the influence of a different time, place, and audience on the play's presentation and, possibly, genre.

677   Silver, Andrew Brian. *Minstrel Shows and Whiteface Conventions: The Politics of Popular Discourse and the Transformation of Southern Humor, 1835-1939.* Atlanta, GA: Emory Univ; 1997. 229 pp. [Ph.D. Dissertation, Univ. Microfilms Order No. AAC 9725079.] Lang.: Eng.
USA. 1835-1939. Histories-specific. ■Argues that Southern humor represents an effort to negotiate middle-class identity through the stylized language and gestures of lower-class whites and African-Americans, incorporating aspects of popular theatre, journalism, religion, and political narratives. Examines texts of Erskine Caldwell, Mark Twain, and blackface minstrelsy.

678   Smith, Iris L. "The 'Intercultural' Work of Lee Breuer." *TTop.* 1997 Mar.; 7(1): 37-58. Illus.: Photo. 2. Lang.: Eng.
USA: New York, NY. 1980-1995. Histories-sources. ■Discourses of interculturalism in the work of Lee Breuer. Argues that Breuer's work, particularly with Mabou Mines, stages genealogies of cultural stereotypes, especially gender stereotypes.

679   Sörenson, Margareta. "Meditativa levande bilder." (Meditative Living Images.) *Danst.* 1997; 7(1): 3-5, 16-17. Illus.: Photo. B&W. Color. Lang.: Swe.
USA. Europe. 1960-1996. Biographical studies. ■A short presentation of the writer and director Robert Wilson, in connection with his receiving the Premio Europa per il teatro 1996.

680   Stovall, Count. "Cynthia Belgrave-Farris." *BlackM.* 1997 Feb/Mar.; 12(3): 15. Lang.: Eng.
USA: New York, NY. 1997. Biographical studies. ■Obituary for director/actress/producer Cynthia Belgrave-Farris.

681   Taylor, Don. *Directing Plays.* New York, NY/London: Routledge; 1997. 200 pp. Biblio. Lang.: Eng.
USA. 1997. Instructional materials. ■Explores both the theory and practice of directing plays, with emphasis on textual interpretation.

682   Viola, Tom. "Remembering Colleen Dewhurst." *EN.* 1997 Nov.; 82(9): 3, 8. Illus.: Photo. 3. Lang.: Eng.
USA. 1997. Biographical studies. ■Historical remembrances of the late actress Colleen Dewhurst recounting her life and career.

683   Wainscott, Ronald H. *The Emergence of the Modern American Theatre, 1914-1929.* New Haven, CT: Yale UP; 1997.

288 pp. Index. Notes. Biblio. Pref. Illus.: Photo. 18. Lang.: Eng.
USA. 1914-1929. Critical studies. ■Examines the conflicting artistic tastes and cultural, economic, and political events of the modern American theatre from World War I to the stock market crash. Some specific topics include the theatre tax rebellion of 1919, the role of women in popular sex farces, censorship battles, the drama's treatment of commercialism, and theatrical responses to the Russian Revolution.

684   Weiner, Wendy. "John Collins: Accidents Will Happen." *AmTh.* 1997 Sep.; 14(7): 48-49. Illus.: Photo. B&W. 1. Lang.: Eng.
USA: New York, NY. 1991-1997. Biographical studies. ■Profile of artistic and technical director of theatre company Elevator Repair Service. His training, work as a sound designer, and original plays developed through his own company.

685   Welker, Linda S.; Goodall, H.L., Jr. "Representation, Interpretation, and Performance. Opening the Text of *Casing a Promised Land.*" *TextPQ.* 1997 Jan.; 17(1): 109-122. Notes. Biblio. Lang.: Eng.
USA. 1997. Histories-sources. ■The development of the production *Casing a Promised Land: The Autobiography of an Organizational Detective as Cultural Ethnographer*, directed by Welker and based on texts by Goodall (*Casing a Promised Land* and *Living in the Rock n Roll Mystery*), in which he presents his ethnographic research in story form. The production took place at Southern Illinois University.

686   Yalowitz, William Cantor. *Community Performance, Historical Fictions and Intercultural Transactions:* Joshua's Wall *in Mount Airy, Philadelphia.* Philadelphia, PA: Temple Univ; 1997. 355 pp. [Ph.D. Dissertation, Univ. Microfilms Order No. AAC 9724302.] Lang.: Eng.
USA: Philadelphia, PA. 1994-1995. Historical studies. ■Description of a two-phase community movement-theatre performance cycle, *Joshua's Wall*, created by a combination of artists and community performers. Analyzes the role of intercultural dynamics such as race, class, religion, ethnicity, age, and gender.

687   Zarrilli, Phillip B. "Acting 'at the nerve ends': Beckett, Blau, and the Necessary." *TTop.* 1997 Sep.; 7(2): 103-116. Illus.: Photo. 3. Lang.: Eng.
USA. 1995-1996. Histories-sources. ■Author's experiences using psychophysiological training for actors in the university environment, specifically in a production of Beckett's *Act Without Words I*.

688   Kosiński, Dariusz. "Polskie życie teatralne w obozach, więzieniach i miejscach zsyłek na terenie ZSRR i Litwy 1939-1947." (Polish Theatrical Life in Camps, Prisons, and in Exile in the Territories of the USSR and Lithuania, 1939-1947.) *PaT.* 1997; 46(1-4): 735-756. Notes. Illus.: Handbill. Photo. B&W. 4. Lang.: Pol.
USSR. Lithuania. Poland. 1939-1947. Historical studies. ■Polish theatrical activities in Soviet camps and prisons.

689   Diamond, Catherine. "The Pandora's Box of 'Doi Moi': the Open-Door Policy and Contemporary Theatre in Vietnam." *NTQ.* 1997; 13(52): 372-385. Notes. Biblio. Illus.: Photo. B&W. 10. Lang.: Eng.
Vietnam. 1986-1997. Historical studies. ■While the popularity of traditional theatre forms has been reduced in urban areas by foreign videos, television, and films, those that address contemporary issues play to large audiences in Saigon and Hanoi. Many dramatists have broken away from the socialist realist ideal and are looking towards the West and China for new artistic developments.

Plays/librettos/scripts

690   Del Colle, Tonino. "I personaggi delle storie e gli archetipi junghiani." (Literary Characters and Jungian Archetypes.) *BiT.* 1997; 44: 157-177. Notes. Lang.: Ita.
Critical studies. ■Jungian archetypes are compared with Propp functions and with characters from literature, theatre, and film, demonstrating the analogy between the Jungian approach and the basic rules of writing fiction or drama.

691   Soyinka, Wole. "African Theatre: From *Ali Baba* to *Woza Albert!*." 11-13 in Rubin, Don, ed.; Diakhaté, Ousmane, ed.; Eyoh, Hansel Ndumbe, ed. *The World Encyclopedia of Con-*

THEATRE IN GENERAL: —Plays/librettos/scripts

temporary Theatre: Africa. Vol. 3. London/New York, NY: Routledge; 1997. 426 pp. Biblio. Index. Lang.: Eng.
Africa. 1800-1996. Historical studies. ■Nigerian playwright Wole Soyinka gives an historical overview of African theatre.

692 Soledad, Lagos de Kassai/M. "Zur Poetik des Marginalen im chilenischen Theater der neunziger Jahre am Beispiel des Teatro La Memoria." (Toward a Poetics of Marginalization in Chilean Theatre in the 1990s from Teatro La Memoria.) *FMT.* 1997; 12(2): 195-208. Notes. Lang.: Ger.
Chile. 1986-1997. Historical studies. ■The *Trilogía Testimonial* of Alfredo Castro, director of Teatro La Memoria—performances based on statements and narratives of marginalized people.

693 Mayer, David. "Parlour and Platform Melodrama." 211-234 in Hays, Michael, ed.; Nikolopoulou, Anastasia, ed. *Melodrama: The Cultural Emergence of a Genre.* New York, NY: St. Martin's P; 1996. 288 pp. Notes. Illus.: Photo. 1. Lang.: Eng.
England. 1840-1900. Historical studies. ■On the private performance nature of the parlour melodrama of the late nineteenth century.

694 Łabędzka, Izabella. "Artaud, Yeats, Brecht, i teatry wschodu." (Artaud, Yeats, Brecht, and Oriental Theatres.) *DialogW.* 1997; 5: 142-149. Lang.: Pol.
Europe. Asia. 1915-1997. Critical studies. ■The influence of Asian theatre on European theatre artists, with consideration of the intercultural aspect of modern theatre.

695 Burckhardt, Barbara. "'Nur Dummköpfe beschäftigen sich mit Politik'." ('Only Fools Deal with Politics.') *THeute.* 1997; 7: 31-32. Pref. Illus.: Photo. B&W. 1. Lang.: Ger.
Hungary. 1964-1997. Histories-sources. ■An interview with playwright Ákos Németh about politics and everyday life in Hungary.

696 Campbell, Charles Lewis. *Investigations of Representational Practices in Mid-Twentieth Century 'Avant-Garde' Works.* Minneapolis, MN: Univ. of Minnesota; 1997. 183 pp. [Ph.D. Dissertation, Univ. Microfilms Order No. AAC 9811257.] Lang.: Eng.
North America. Europe. 1950-1990. Critical studies. ■Analysis of the diverse modes of representation seen in modern avant-garde works, from Samuel Beckett's *Waiting for Godot* and *Endgame*, to the theatre of Tadeusz Kantor and Allan Kaprow.

697 Ratajczakowa, Dobrochna. "Lwów w dramacie polskim XVIII, XIX i XX wieku." (Lvov in the Polish Drama of the Eighteenth, Nineteenth, and Twentieth Centuries.) 104-121 in Kuchtówna, Lidia, ed. *Teatr polski we Lwowie.* Studia i materiały do dziejów teatru polskiego. t. XXV (37). Warsaw: Instytut Sztuki Polskiej Akademii Nauk; 1997. 293 pp. Lang.: Pol.
Poland. 1700-1939. Critical studies. ■Images of Lvov in Polish drama, including the idyllic images in comedy, vaudeville, and music drama of German origin after the first partition of Poland in 1771 and the myth of the city as an invincible fortress after the war between Poland and the Soviet Union in 1920. Considers plays of Fredro and productions by Bogusławski and Kamiński.

698 Allsopp, Ric. "Writing-Text-Performance." *PerfR.* 1997 Spr; 2(1): 45-52. Notes. Biblio. Illus.: Photo. Design. B&W. 5. [Transcript of a keynote address to the seminar Words: Theatre, Dialogue, Copenhagen, November, 1996.] Lang.: Eng.
UK-England. USA. 1980-1996. Critical studies. ■The relation between performance and enduring textual evidence, changes in the relationship among writing, text and performance in the last decade, and current writing practice which extends the possibilities of performance into video, installation and other forms of time-based art. Considers work of Forced Entertainment, Richard Kostelanetz, Gary Hill, Caroline Bergvall, Marina Abramović, and Robert Wilson.

699 Saakana, A.S. *Sites of Conflict Identity, Sexuality, Reproduction: European Mythological Imaging of the African on the London Stage, 1908-1939.* Unpublished Ph.D. thesis, Univ. of London: Goldsmith's College; 1996. Notes. Biblio. [Abstract in *Index to Theses,* 46-3159.] Lang.: Eng.

UK-England: London. Africa. 1908-1939. Histories-specific. ■Examines selected plays in which Africans were portrayed by actors of European descent and shows that all conformed to stereotypes.

700 Tanitch, Robert. "Wilde About Oscar." *PlPl.* 1997 Dec.; 514: 28-29. Illus.: Photo. B&W. 1. Lang.: Eng.
UK-England. 1997. Historical studies. ■Observes recent interest in life and trials of Oscar Wilde, and describes various works about Wilde, including Brian Gilbert's film *Wilde* and Moisés Kaufman's play *Gross Indecency.*

701 Bank, Rosemarie K. *Theatre Culture in America, 1825-1860.* Cambridge: Cambridge UP; 1997. 292 pp. (Cambridge Studies in American Theatre and Drama 7.) Index. Notes. Biblio. Illus.: Dwg. Sketches. Maps. Photo. 27. Lang.: Eng.
USA. 1825-1860. Histories-specific. ■The staging of American culture before the Civil War. Explores issues of race, class, and gender and advances the idea that cultures are performances that take place inside and outside of playhouses.

702 Barnwell, Michael. "A Novel Approach." *AmTh.* 1997 Oct.; 14(8): 72-76. Illus.: Photo. B&W. 4. Lang.: Eng.
USA. 1997. Critical studies. ■Adaptations of novels to the stage: *The Cider House Rules* by John Irving, adapted by Peter Parnell, *The Joy Luck Club* by Amy Tan, adapted by Susan Kim, *Ragtime* by E.L. Doctorow, adapted by Terrence McNally, Stephen Flaherty composer, Lynn Ahrens lyricist, and *Jane Eyre* by Charlotte Brontë, adapted by composer Paul Gordon and director John Caird.

703 Ellwell, Jeffrey Scott. "The Electronic Hustle: Using the Internet to Market Your Plays." *DGQ.* 1997 Spr; 34(1): 26-29. Lang.: Eng.
USA. 1997. Instructional materials. ■Examines the effectiveness of the internet as a tool for playwrights to market their work.

704 O'Quinn, Jim. "The Subject that Won't Go Away." *AmTh.* 1997 Apr.; 14(4): 38. Illus.: Photo. B&W. 1. Lang.: Eng.
USA: Key West, FL. 1984-1997. Historical studies. ■Key West Literary Seminar focusing on writing about the AIDS epidemic. Key speakers included playwrights Larry Kramer and Tony Kushner.

705 Singer, Dana. *Stage Writers Handbook: A Complete Business Guide for Playwrights, Composers, Lyricists and Librettists.* New York, NY: Theatre Communications Group; 1997. 302 pp. Index. Lang.: Eng.
USA. 1997. Instructional materials. ■Business guide for stagewriters includes information on copyright, collaboration, underlying rights, marketing and self-promotion, production contracts, representation (agents and lawyers), publishers, and developing areas for business.

706 Strauss, Alix. "Schmoozing Without Losing: The Art of Networking." *DGQ.* 1997 Spr; 34(1): 10-14. Lang.: Eng.
USA. 1997. Instructional materials. ■Strategies for the hopeful playwright in the art of networking and making contacts, a necessary facet of furthering one's writing career.

707 Weyhrauch, Peter William. *Guiding Interactive Drama.* Pittsburgh, PA: Carnegie-Mellon Univ; 1997. 183 pp. [Ph.D. Dissertation, Univ. Microfilms Order No. AAC 9802566.] Lang.: Eng.
USA. 1996. Technical studies. ■Examination of computer-based interactive drama, which allows a user to interact with simulated worlds inhabited by complex autonomous characters and shaped by a flexible story. Describes a computer architecture designed to provide dramatic guidance.

Reference materials

708 Pavice, Patrice; Lampret, Igor, transl. *Gledališki slovar.* (Theatre Dictionary.) Ljubljana: Ljubljana City Theatre; 1997. 879 pp. (Ljubljana City Theatre Library 124.) Pref. Biblio. Index. Lang.: Slo.
■Slovene translation of Pavis' *Dictionnaire du théâtre.*

709 Rubin, Don. "An Introduction: Of Nations and Their Theatres." 3-10 in Rubin, Don, ed.; Diakhaté, Ousmane, ed.; Eyoh, Hansel Ndumbe, ed. *The World Encyclopedia of Contemporary Theatre: Africa.* Vol. 3. London/New York, NY: Routledge; 1997. 426 pp. Biblio. Index. Lang.: Eng.

THEATRE IN GENERAL: —Reference materials

Africa. 1790-1996. Histories-specific. ■Introductory article to *Volume 3: Africa* of the *World Encyclopedia of Contemporary Theatre*.

710 Rubin, Don, ed.; Diakhaté, Ousmane, ed.; Eyoh, Hansel Ndumbe, ed. *The World Encyclopedia of Contemporary Theatre: Africa.* London/New York, NY: Routledge; 1997. 426 pp. Biblio. Index. Illus.: Photo. 235. [Vol. 3.] Lang.: Eng.
Africa. 1700-1996. ■Encyclopedia of contemporary theatre in Africa. Includes geographical regions, bibliography, further reading on each country.

711 McCallum, Heather. "Resources for Theatre History." 424-435 in Plant, Richard, ed.; Saddlemyer, Ann, ed. *Later Stages: Essays in Ontario Theatre from the First World War to the 1970s.* Toronto, ON: Univ of Toronto P; 1997. 496 pp. (The Ontario Historical Studies Series.) Lang.: Eng.
Canada. 1914-1979. Historical studies. ■Archives and resource libraries for theatre history in Ontario.

712 Hageman, Elizabeth H. "Recent Studies in the English Renaissance." *ELR.* 1997 Spr; 27(2): 281-326. Notes. Biblio. Illus.: Dwg. B&W. 1. Lang.: Eng.
Europe. North America. 1945-1996. Bibliographical studies. ■Bibliographic survey of the material features of manuscripts including topics related to codicology and paleography and the part played by manuscripts in the transmission of texts.

713 Müller, Wiebke, ed. *Performing Arts Yearbook for Europe 1998.* London: Arts Publishing International; 1997. x, 716 pp. Pref. Index. Notes. Illus.: Photo. Color. B&W. 150. [9th edition revised.] Lang.: Eng.
Europe. 1997. Histories-sources. ■Focuses on major and medium-sized companies, with selected notable small subsidized and young people's or children's theatre companies. Adds national and support organizations, festivals, venues, promoters, agents, media, competitions, publications, training, and services.

714 Antonucci, Giovanni. *Storia del teatro antico: Grecia e Roma.* (History of Ancient Theatre: Greece and Rome.) Rome: Newton & Compton; 1997. 96 pp. (Tascabili Economici Newton: Il sapere 140.) Notes. Biblio. Lang.: Ita.
Greece. Rome. 500 B.C.-476 A.D. Histories-specific. ■Brief history of ancient Greek and Roman theatre, including dramaturgy, staging, scenography, and criticism.

715 *Il Patalogo venti. Annuario 1997 dello spettacolo. Teatro.* (The Patalogo 20: 1997 Entertainment Yearbook—Theatre.) Milan: Ubulibri; 1997. 285 pp. Illus.: Photo. B&W. Lang.: Ita.
Italy. 1997. ■Yearbook of Italian theatre, festivals, and seasons with brief critical notations.

716 Vergani, Orio. *Birignao: piccolo lessico del palcoscenico.* (A Brief Lexicon of the Stage.) Udine: Casamassima; 1997. 68 pp. Illus.: Dwg. Photo. B&W. Lang.: Ita.
Italy. 1923-1960. ■Brief dictionary of traditional Italian theatrical terms.

717 Engelander, Ruud; Gaal, Rob van. *Nederlands Theaterjaarboek 1996-1997.* (Netherlands Theatre Year Book, 1996-97.) Amsterdam: Theater Instituut Nederland; 1997. 463 pp. Pref. Biblio. Gloss. Index. Illus.: Design. Graphs. Pntg. Diagram. Dwg. Photo. Photo. CP. 154. Lang.: Dut.
Netherlands. 1996-1997. ■Covers all professional productions in the performing arts.

718 Vevar, Štefan; Kocijančič, Katarina; Petek, Danica. *Slovenski gledališki letopis: 1995/1996.* (Slovene Theatre Annual, 1995-96.) Ljubljana: SGFM; 1997. 223 pp. (9th expanded edition of the Repertoire of Slovene Theatres 1867/1967.) Pref. Index. Lang.: Slo.
Slovenia. 1995-1996. ■List of productions of drama, opera, ballet, and puppet theatre in Slovenia, including all professional and some amateur theatres. Includes a bibliography of press reviews.

719 Barbour, Sheena, ed. *British Performing Arts Yearbook 1998/99.* London: Rhinegold; 1997. x, 594 pp. Pref. Index. Notes. [11th ed.] Lang.: Eng.
UK-England. 1996-1997. Histories-sources. ■Concentrates on venues, with a large section for companies and solo performers (dance, drama, community, puppets, mixed entertainment, opera and music). Other sec-

tions cover official and support organizations, suppliers, arts festivals, and education.

720 "A Look Back at *The Passing Show:* An Index to Volumes I-XX." *PasShow.* 1997 Fall/Win, 1998 Spr/Sum; 20/21(1/2): 13-39. Lang.: Eng.
USA: New York, NY. 1977-1997. Histories-sources. ■Complete index with introduction describing origins of the newsletter.

721 Peterson, Bernard L., Jr., ed. *The African-American Theatre Directory, 1816-1960: A Comprehensive Guide to Early Black Theatre Organizations, Theatres, and Performing Groups.* Westport, CT/London: Greenwood; 1997. 301 pp. Index. Pref. Append. Lang.: Eng.
USA. 1824-1960. ■African-American theatre groups and companies prior to 1960.

Relation to other fields

722 Armstrong, Gordon. "Theatre as a Complex Adaptive System." *NTQ.* 1997; 13(51): 277-288. Notes. Biblio. Lang.: Eng.
Historical studies. ■Argues that the functioning of human consciousness in interpreting and staging a theatrical performance is a highly selective and adaptive operation.

723 Okagbue, Osita. "When the Dead Return: Play and Seriousness in African Masked Performances." *SATJ.* 1997 May/Sep.; 11 (1/2): 89-107. Biblio. Lang.: Eng.
Africa. 1997. Critical studies. ■Attempts to divine the philosophy behind traditional African masked performances specifically the rich and diverse masks of the Igbo people.

724 Fanon, Frantz. "Algeria Unveiled." 259-274 in Murray, Timothy, ed. *Mimesis, Masochism, and Mime: The Politics of Theatricality in Contemporary French Thought.* Ann Arbor, MI: Univ. of Michigan P; 1997. 328 pp. (Theater: Theory/Text/Performance.) Notes. Lang.: Eng.
Algeria. 1967. Critical studies. ■Women and the veil in colonial Algeria.

725 Taylor, Diana. *Disappearing Acts: Spectacles of Gender and Nationalism in Argentina's 'Dirty War'.* Durham, NC/London: Duke UP; 1997. 309 pp. Index. Biblio. Notes. Pref. Lang.: Eng.
Argentina. 1976-1983. Critical studies. ■The performance of gender, nationality, and motherhood. Includes discussion of Griselda Gambaro's *Antígona* and Teatro Alberto, a series of one-act plays devoted to resistance, written by Osvaldo Dragún, Ricardo Monti, Diana Raznovich, and others.

726 Munk, Erika. "Notes from a Trip to Sarajevo." *ThM.* 1993; 24(3): 14-30. Illus.: Photo. B&W. 10. Lang.: Eng.
Bosnia: Sarajevo. 1993. Histories-sources. ■The effect of war on the culture and art, specifically theatre, in Sarajevo.

727 Kerr, David. "Drama as a Forum of Action Research: The Experience of UBR423 at the University of Botswana." *SATJ.* 1997 May/Sep.; 11(1/2): 133-154. Biblio. Illus.: Photo. B&W. 3. Lang.: Eng.
Botswana: Serowe. 1997. Histories-sources. ■Analysis of a drama course, taught by the author at the University of Botswana, to show how performing arts can help provide links between two incompatible methods of investigation: the ratiocinative and the existential.

728 Breon, Robin. "Noises Off-Right: Theatre in the Toronto Region." *CTR.* 1997 Win; 93: 16-22. Notes. Biblio. Illus.: Photo. B&W. 4. Lang.: Eng.
Canada: Toronto, ON. 1980-1997. Historical studies. ■The weave of cultural contexts that contribute to theatre within the greater Toronto region.

729 Cloutier, Joseph Leonard. *Popular Theatre, Education, and Inner City Youth.* Edmonton, AB: Univ. of Alberta; 1997. 239 pp. [Ph.D. Dissertation, Univ. Microfilms Order No. AAC NQ21558.] Lang.: Eng.
Canada: Edmonton, AB. 1994-1996. Empirical research. ■Explores the pedagogy of popular theatre in a long-term participatory action research project with a small group of former street youth. Argues that theatre gives young people the means to understand and empower themselves.

THEATRE IN GENERAL: —Relation to other fields

730 Barroll, Leeds. "Defining 'Dramatic Documents'." *MRDE.* 1997; 9(1): 112-126. Notes. Lang.: Eng.
England. 1605. Historical studies. ■The complex intersection of politics, precedence and governance that defined theatrical commerce in Stuart England, with emphasis on the relationship between James I and the operation of the early modern companies and players.

731 Burling, William J. "An Unknown Backstage Painting: Nixon's 'A Peep Behind the Scenes, Covent Garden Theatre'." *TN.* 1997; 51(3): 166-169. Notes. Illus.: Pntg. B&W. Lang.: Eng.
England: London. 1750-1802. Historical studies. ■Examines John Nixon's painting of backstage during a performance of Colman's *The Poor Gentleman*, including named actors. No record of such a performance exists.

732 Burwick, Frederick. "'Shakespeare Gallery' and the Stage." Append. Notes. Illus.: Dwg. 17. Lang.: Eng.
England. 1757-1772. Historical studies. ■Comparing the artwork of John Boydell's 'Shakespeare Gallery' with stage settings, costuming and acting, especially gesture and expression, of the contemporary theatre to show that they were not influenced only by reading Shakespeare.

733 Cerasano, S.P. "The Telling of Rumor: John Chamberlain's Theatrical Reports." *MRDE.* 1997; 9(1): 19-33. Notes. Lang.: Eng.
England: London. 1597-1626. Historical studies. ■Analysis of letters from London written by John Chamberlain, an ironmonger's son, that refer to theatre among other things.

734 Duncan-Jones, Katherine. "What Are Shakespeare's Sonnets Called?" *ECrit.* 1997 Jan.; 47(1): 1-12. Notes. Lang.: Eng.
England. 1595-1609. Critical studies. ■Examines the question of the title of Shakespeare's sonnets.

735 MacLean, Sally-Beth. "Festive Liturgy and the Dramatic Connection: A Study of Thames Valley Parishes." *MRDE.* 1996; 8(1) : 49-62. Notes. Illus.: Maps. B&W. 2. Lang.: Eng.
England. 1450-1560. Historical studies. ■Explores late medieval change and variation in Christian drama and custom using church records of Thames Valley parishes.

736 Reynolds, Bryan. "The Devil's House, 'or worse': Transversal Power and Antitheatrical Discourse in Early Modern England." *TJ.* 1997 May; 49(2): 142-167. Notes. Illus.: Dwg. 2. Lang.: Eng.
England. 1583-1615. Historical studies. ■Argues for the disruptive potential of theatre by examining the anti-theatrical discourses of the period, with particular focus on the debate on female-to-male transvestism.

737 Plastow, Jane. "Theatre of Conflict in the Eritrean Independence Struggle." *NTQ.* 1997; 13(50): 144-154. Notes. Illus.: Photo. B&W. 5. Lang.: Eng.
Eritrea. 1940-1991. Historical studies. ■Considers the history of Eritrean theatre in relation to colonial cultural and political constraints. Against that background explores the role of text-based drama in the emerging country's fight for independence and the attempts to mold this alien genre into a public voice. Continued in *NTQ* 1997. 13 (51): 221-230.

738 Plastow, Jane. "The Eritrea Community-Based Theatre Project." *NTQ.* 1997; 13(52): 386-395. Illus.: Photo. B&W. 3. Lang.: Eng.
Eritrea. 1992-1996. Histories-sources. ■Describes three-month project with a wide variety of trainees which was intended to encourage a syncretised theatre, using both indigenous and foreign concepts of performance to make issue-based theatre within a distinctively Eritrean aesthetic.

739 Warwick, Paul. "Theatre and the Eritrean Struggle for Freedom: the Cultural Troupes of the People's Liberation Front." *NTQ.* 1997; 13(51): 221-230. Notes. Illus.: Photo. B&W. 3. Lang.: Eng.
Eritrea. 1972-1995. Historical studies. ■Documents the theatrical activities of the People's Liberation Front, which served as both propaganda and education for rural communities.

740 Kershaw, Baz. "Fighting in the Streets: Dramaturgies of Popular Protest, 1968-1989." *NTQ.* 1997; 13(51): 255-276. Notes. Biblio. Illus.: Photo. B&W. 10. Lang.: Eng.
Europe. USA. China, People's Republic of. 1968-1989. Historical studies. ■Considers protest as an action which has become increasingly theatricalized, partly through its own tactics, and partly through the ways in which media coverage creates its own version of politics as performance.

741 Oldoni, Massimo. "L'artificio meraviglioso. Dedali e labirinti di un teatro medievale." (The Marvelous Artifice: Mazes and Labyrinths of a Medieval Theatre.) *Ariel.* 1997; 12(2): 79-89. Notes. Lang.: Ita.
Europe. 850-1552. Critical studies. ■Labyrinths in medieval theatre and travel literature as a metaphor of the extension of human knowledge and relationship with nature and God.

742 Selbach, Peter. "Theater im Freien." (Theatre in the Open Air.) *S&B.* 1997; 2: 4-7. Illus.: Photo. B&W. 7. Lang.: Ger.
Europe. 1750-1997. Histories-general. ■An historical review of the development of open-air theatre since 1750 based on Rousseau's words 'back to nature'.

743 Häkkänen, Juha. "Teatteri ja alue." (Theatre and the Region.) *Teat.* 1997; 52(2): 10-13. Illus.: Photo. B&W. 4. Lang.: Fin.
Finland. 1990-1997. Histories-sources. ■Thoughts on the regional theatre policy by an actor working in northern Finland.

744 Kirkkopelto, Esa. "Teatteri ja hulluus." (Theater and Madness.) *Teat.* 1997; 52(7): 35-37. Lang.: Fin.
Finland. 1997. Histories-sources. ■Speech given at the one hundredth anniversary of the Finnish Mental Health Association regarding the helpful role of theatre in the treatment of mental illness.

745 Mikkola, Kaisu. "Theatre Is Part of Even Small Town Finnish Life/Le théâtre est inhérent á la vie d'une petite ville." *NFT.* 1997; 51: 11-13. Illus.: Photo. B&W. 4. Lang.: Eng, Fre.
Finland. 1997. Critical studies. ■It is not uncommon for small Finnish communities to have their own professional companies.

746 Hansen, Joel. "Seeing Without Subject: Reading *III Seen III Said*." *JBeckS.* 1997; 6(2): 63-84. Notes. Lang.: Eng.
France. 1997. Critical studies. ■The autonomy of the word in Beckett's *III Seen III Said*.

747 Obregón, Osvaldo. "III Coloquio internacional de Perpignan: teatro, público y sociedad." (3rd Perpignan International Conference: Theatre, the Public and Society.) *Gestos.* 1997 Apr.; 12(23): 166-168. Lang.: Spa.
France: Perpignan. 1996. Historical studies. ■Report on the conference regarding the relationship of theatre to an audience and its ramifications in society at large.

748 Badstübner-Gröger, Sibylle. "Sie hat sich die Berliner Theaterlandschaft mit der Zeichenfeder erobert." (She Took the Berlin Theatre Scene With a Drawing Pen.) *KSGT.* 1997; 39: 73-77. Illus.: Dwg. 6. [Ingeborg Voss und Paul Gehring.] Lang.: Ger.
Germany: Berlin. 1970-1997. Biographical studies. ■The work of theatre draughtsman Ingeborg Voss and the effect of the reunification of Germany on her work.

749 Hahn, Ines. "Es kommt halt nichts ohne weiteres auf einen zu—Paul Gehring 1917-1992." (Nothing Comes Directly: Paul Gehring 1917-1992.) *KSGT.* 1997; 39: 28-36. Notes. Illus.: Dwg. 19. [Ingeborg Voss und Paul Gehring.] Lang.: Ger.
Germany: Berlin. 1917-1992. Biographical studies. ■Profile of theatre draughtsman Paul Gehring.

750 Hahn, Ines; Schirmer, Lothar. "Er liebte das Theater, und er liebte die Schauspieler, und es machte ihm Spass." (He Loved Theatre, and He Loved the Actors, and It Amused Him.) *KSGT.* 1997; 39: 37-41. Append. Notes. Illus.: Dwg. 6. [Ingeborg Voss und Paul Gehring.] Lang.: Ger.
Germany: Berlin. 1946-1981. Histories-sources. ■An interview with critic Heinz Ritter about theatre draughtsman Paul Gehring.

751 Hahn, Ines. "35 Jahre Theaterzeichnungen für den 'Abend'." (35 Years of Theatre Drawings for *Abend*.)

THEATRE IN GENERAL: —Relation to other fields

KSGT. 1997; 39: 42-57. Notes. Illus.: Dwg. 30. [Ingeborg Voss and Paul Gehring.] Lang.: Ger.

Germany: Berlin. 1946-1981. Biographical studies. ■Berlin Stadtmuseum's collection of 1300 theatre drawings by Paul Gehring for the newspaper *Abend.*

752 Hahn, Ines; Louis, Petra; Reissmann, Bärbel. "Ich liebe das Theater leidenschaftlich. Ein Gespräch mit Ingeborg Voss." (I Love Theatre Passionately: An Interview with Ingeborg Voss.) *KSGT.* 1997; 39: 60-68. Append. Illus.: Dwg. 10. [Ingeborg Voss und Paul Gehring.] Lang.: Ger.

Germany. 1922-1997. Histories-sources. ■An interview with theatre draughtsman Ingeborg Voss about her life, training, working method, the work at Deutsches Kammerspiele (Berlin) and for the press.

753 Hesse, Ulrich. "Schritte in vermintes Terrain." (Steps into Mined Terrain.) *SuT.* 1997; 159: 27-29. Illus.: Photo. B&W. 1. Lang.: Ger.

Germany. 1935-1940. Historical studies. ■Educational and political aspects of the amateur play movement and its representatives at the end of the 1920s.

754 Kuhla, Holger. "Theater und Krieg. Betrachtungen zu einem Verhältnis. 1914-1918." (Theatre and War: Reflections on this Relationship, 1914-1918.) 63-115 in Fiebach, Joachim, ed.; Mühl-Benninghaus, Wolfgang, ed.; Humboldt-Universität zu Berlin, Institut für Theaterwissenschaft/ Kulturelle Kommunikation. *Theater und Medien an der Jahrhundertwende.* Berlin: Vistas Verlag; 1997. 214 pp. (Berliner Theaterwissenschaft 3.) Notes. Lang.: Ger.

Germany. 1914-1918. Historical studies. ■Discusses intention, function and meaning of theatre in the First World War: correlation between war and theatre from writers' engagement in war, laws and practice of censorship during the war, repertory of Deutsches Theater, and discussions about the future theatre by press.

755 Rabanus, Winfried E. "Licht und Szene." (Light and Scene.) *DB.* 1997; 12: 31-33. Illus.: Photo. B&W. 4. Lang.: Ger.

Germany: Munich. 1950-1997. Histories-sources. ■The Munich theatre photographer describes the problems of the profession from his point of view and his experiences.

756 Reissmann, Bärbel. "Zeichnungen von ungemein sympathischer Ausstrahlung." (Drawings of Immense Sympathic Magnetism.) *KSGT.* 1997; 39: 69-72. Append. Illus.: Dwg. 5. [Ingeborg Voss und Paul Gehring.] Lang.: Ger.

Germany: Berlin. 1960-1990. Histories-sources. ■An interview with critic Rolf-Dieter Eichler about the theatre draughtsman Ingeborg Voss.

757 Reissmann, Bärbel. "Vier Jahrzehnte gezeichnete Theatergeschichte." (Four Decades Drawing Theatre History.) *KSGT.* 1997; 39: 78-98. Notes. Illus.: Dwg. Photo. 36. [Ingeborg Voss and Paul Gehring.] Lang.: Ger.

Germany: Berlin. 1962-1996. Biographical studies. ■Berlin Stadtmuseum's collection of 4,000 theatre drawings by Ingeborg Voss.

758 Roth, Wilhelm. "Theater und Fotografie." (Theatre and Photography.) *DB.* 1997; 10: 14-17. Illus.: Photo. B&W. 7. Lang.: Ger.

Germany. 1938-1997. Historical studies. ■Describes theatre photography that contains documentation, art and public relations. Portraits of four photographers: Mara Eggert, Stefan Odry, Friedemann Simon and Matthias Horn.

759 Rühle, Günther. "Scharfzüngiger Kritiker und lebensverliebter Flaneur." (A Critic With a Sharp Tongue and a Flaneur Who Loves Life.) *THeute.* 1997; 9: 34-40. Illus.: Photo. B&W. 7. Lang.: Ger.

Germany. 1890-1919. Biographical studies. ■An essay about the young critic Alfred Kerr, his 'Berliner Briefe' (Berlin letters) on turn-of-the-century society.

760 Schelling, Franke. "Vom Jugendspiel zum Fronttheater, Teil 2." (From Youth Play to Vanguard Theatre, Part 2.) *SuT.* 1997 ; 159: 27-29. Illus.: Photo. B&W. 1. Lang.: Ger.

Germany. 1935-1940. Historical studies. ■Notes on the development of the amateur play movement during the National Socialist period.

761 Schirmer, Lothar. "Theater—Gezeichnet 1843-1993." (Theatre—Drawn 1843-1993.) *KSGT.* 1997; 39: 4-25. Notes.

Illus.: Dwg. 31. [Ingeborg Voss and Paul Gehring.] Lang.: Ger.

Germany: Berlin. 1843-1993. Historical studies. ■The professional draughtsmen who specialized in theatrical productions and actors in Berlin: their work and working conditions with the press.

762 Schneider, Hansjörg. "Enttäuschte Hoffnung. Erich Ponto als Generalintendant im Nachkriegs-Dresden." (Disappointed Hope: Erich Ponto as Theatre Director in Postwar Dresden.) *MuK.* 1997; 39(1): 61-102. Notes. Illus.: Photo. B&W. 7. Lang.: Ger.

Germany: Dresden. 1945-1947. Historical studies. ■Ponto's tenure as director of theatre, opposition both from the press and the municipal government, and his letter of resignation (December 31, 1946).

763 Sheppard, Richard W. "'Der Schauspieler greift in die Politik'. Five Actors and the German Revolution 1917-1922." ('The Actor Reaches into Politics': Five Actors and the German Revolution.) *MuK.* 1997; 39(1): 23-60. Notes. Lang.: Eng.

Germany. 1917-1922. Historical studies. ■Political activities of actors Alexander Moissi, Max Weber, Ernst Hoferichter, Albert Florath, and Ernst Friedrich.

764 Vince, Ronald W. "The Ritual and Performative Basis of Greek Combat Sport and Hoplite Warfare." *TA.* 1997; 50: 72-82. Notes. Lang.: Eng.

Greece. Historical studies. ■Sublimation of the warrior impulse through combat style athletics and dance in ancient Greece.

765 Vrečko, Janez. "Aristotel, mimesis in estetski doživljaj." (Aristotle, Mimesis, and the Aesthetic Experience.) *Slavr.* 1997; 45(1/2): 225-238. Lang.: Slo.

Greece. 500-400 B.C. Critical studies. ■Argues that the conflict between poetry and philosophy posited by Plato is fictitious.

766 Jenkins, Ron; Nyoman Catra, I. "Taming the Tourists: Balinese Temple Clowns Preserve Their Village Traditions." *PerfR.* 1997 Sum; 2(2): 22-26. Illus.: Photo. B&W. 1. Lang.: Eng.

Indonesia-Bali: Singapadu. 1996. Critical studies. ■How Balinese village people extend the meanings of traditional performances to include tourists and so minimize the negative effects of tourism on village culture, a sign of Balinese village culture's vitality and resistance to threat.

767 Schechner, Richard. "Believed-In Theatre." *PerfR.* 1997 Sum; 2(2): 76-91. Notes. Illus.: Photo. B&W. 5. Lang.: Eng.

Israel: Akko. USA. 1994-1997. Critical studies. ■The role of theatre in enabling the celebration and problematizing of history, with emphasis on the Akko Theatre Center's exploration of the Holocaust and American community-based theatre groups such as Swamp Gravy. Argues that the boundaries between viewing and doing theatre have changed and that theatre is moving away from entertainment and towards efficacy in the contemporary world.

768 Crispolti, Enrico, ed.; Sborgi, Franco, ed. *Futurismo: i grandi temi 1909-1944.* (Futurism: The Major Themes, 1909-1944.) Milan: Mazzotta; 1997. 336 pp. Index. Illus.: Pntg. Dwg. Lang.: Ita.

Italy. 1909-1944. Histories-sources. ■Catalogue of an exhibition held in Genoa at the Palazzo Ducale, 1997-1998.

769 Gurgul, Monika. *Teatr Daria Fo w latach 1959-1975.* (The Theatre of Dario Fo, 1959-1975.) Cracow: TAIWPN Universitas; 1997. 209 pp. Pref. Notes. Biblio. Tables. Append. Lang.: Pol.

Italy. 1959-1975. Historical studies. ■Fo's life and theatrical activities, with emphasis on the social and political context of his work in the period covered.

770 Ragazzi, Franco, ed. *Liguria futurista.* (Liguria and Futurism.) Milan: Mazzotta; 1997. 150 pp. Pref. Biblio. Illus.: Pntg. Dwg. Poster. Photo. B&W. Lang.: Ita.

Italy: Genoa. 1920-1942. Histories-sources. ■Catalogue of an exhibition held at the Palazzo Ducale in Genoa beginning in 1997 regarding the Futurist movement in Liguria.

771 Ngugi, Wa Thiongo. "Enactments of Power: The Politics of Performance Space." *TDR.* 1997 Fall; 41(3): 11-30. Biblio. Lang.: Eng.

THEATRE IN GENERAL: —Relation to other fields

Kenya: Nairobi. 1938-1997. Critical studies. ∎Examines conflicts between the power of performance in the arts and the performance of power by the state, and defines the primary area of struggle as the definition, delimitation and regulation of the actual performance space. Censorship, special focus on state intervention in production of the play *The Trial of Dedan Kmathi* by the author and Mcere Mūgo.

772 Pesek, Michael. "Geschichte und Performance in Lamu, Kenia (1800-1925)." (History and Performance in Lamu, Kenya, 1800-1925.) 117-167 in Fiebach, Joachim, ed.; Mühl-Benninghaus, Wolfgang, ed.; Humboldt-Universität zu Berlin, Institut für Theaterwissenschaft/Kulturelle Kommunikation. *Theater und Medien an der Jahrhundertwende.* Berlin: Vistas Verlag; 1997. 214 pp. (Berliner Theaterwissenschaft 3.) Notes. Lang.: Ger.
Kenya: Lamu. 1800-1925. Historical studies. ∎Reviews the history and the regional culture in Lamu, and its relationship to colonialism.

773 Westermann, Martine Henriette. *The Amusements of Jan Steen: Comic Painting in the Seventeenth Century.* New York, NY: New York Univ; 1997. 654 pp. [Ph.D. Dissertation, Univ. Microfilms Order No. AAC 9717808.] Lang.: Eng.
Netherlands. 1640-1690. Historical studies. ∎The influence of theatre on the comic paintings of Dutch painter Jan Steen.

774 Hera, Janina. "Losy aktorów w Generalnym Gubernatorstwie (wrzesień 1939-1 sierpnia 1944)." (Vicissitudes of Actors in German-Occupied Poland, September 1939 to August 1, 1944).) *PaT.* 1997; 46(1-4): 315-398. Notes. Illus.: Handbill. Photo. B&W. 17. Lang.: Pol.
Poland. 1939-1944. Historical studies. ∎The first comprehensive and documented representation of the effect of war on Polish actors and their attitudes under German occupation.

775 Koecher-Hensel, Agnieszka. "Władysław Daszewski— prowokator czy ofiara sowieckiej prowokacji?" (Władysław Daszewski: Agent Provocateur or Victim of Soviet Provocation?) *PaT.* 1997; 46(1-4): 225-278. Notes. Illus.: Photo. B&W. 2. Lang.: Pol.
Poland: Lvov. 1940. Historical studies. ∎The Soviet action targeted at Polish writers in occupied Lvov, with emphasis on the role of stage designer Władysław Daszewski.

776 Krasiński, Edward. "Działalność Komisji Weryfikacyjnych ZASP 1945-1949." (The Activity of the Verification Boards of the Polish Theatre Association, 1945-1949.) *PaT.* 1997; 46(1-4): 36-112. Notes. Append. Illus.: Photo. B&W. 10. Lang.: Pol.
Poland. 1940-1950. Historical studies. ∎Attitudes of Polish actors toward working in official theatres during the occupation and on Soviet territory, and description of the Verification Boards of the theatre association after the war.

777 Kruger, Loren. "'An die Nachgeborenen'." (To Future Generations.) *TZ.* Yb: 25-27. Lang.: Ger.
South Africa, Republic of. 1930-1997. Historical studies. ∎The influence of Brecht's theatre on political theatre in South Africa since 1963, and the earlier influences of European and American workers' theatres, unions and communist parties, and South African traditions.

778 Naidoo, Muthal. "The Search for a Cultural Identity: A Personal View of South African 'Indian' Theatre." *TJ.* 1997 Mar.; 49(1): 29-40. Notes. Lang.: Eng.
South Africa, Republic of. 1950-1995. Historical studies. ∎Historical account of the South African Indian community's negotiation of competing claims on its members' cultural affiliation, including classical Indian performance, Western literary drama, and the protest theme of anti-apartheid theatre.

779 García Martinez, Manuel. "Theatre in Galicia." *WES.* 1997 Win; 9(1): 51-52. Illus.: Photo. 1. Lang.: Eng.
Spain. 1996. Historical studies. ∎Current theatre in the Galician region of Spain, focusing on social and political issues particular to the region.

780 Torkelson, Eva. *Expert- Och Deltagarperspektiv pa stress hos schenartister.* (Expert and Participatory Perspectives on Stress in Stage Artists.) Lund, Sweden: Lunds Universitet; 1997. 206 pp. [FILDR Dissertation available from Department of Psychology, Lunds University, S-223 50 Lund, Sweden. hh.] Lang.: Swe.
Sweden. 1997. Empirical research. ∎Examines how to control work environments and provide social support systems to combat stress in stage artists.

781 Theissen, Hermann. "Auf des Messers Schneide." (On the Razor's Edge.) *THeute.* 1997; 9: 26-33. Illus.: Photo. B&W. 8. Lang.: Ger.
Turkey: Istanbul. 1997. Historical studies. ∎Impressions from theatre in Turkey, about fundamentalism, politics and concepts of theatre. Reports of the 9th International Theatre Festival in Istanbul.

782 Barker, Howard; Olsen, Jakob Steen, transl. "Infektionens hus." (The House of Infection.) *TE.* 1997 Mar.; 83: 30-33. Illus.: Photo. B&W. 2. Lang.: Dan.
UK-England. Germany. 1996. Histories-sources. ∎Danish translation of Howard Barker's speech at the Technical University in Dresden, October 1996: contrasts the contemporary wish to understand and illuminate everything with the darkness of the tragic theatre.

783 Barstow, Susan Torrey. "Ellen Terry and the Revolt of the Daughters." *NCT.* 1997 Sum; 25(1): 5-32. Notes. Illus.: Photo. B&W. 3. Lang.: Eng.
UK-England: London. 1880-1909. Biographical studies. ∎The import of actress Terry on late Victorian women in their search for an alternative to the prevailing ideals of marriage and motherhood.

784 Garfinkel, Sharon. "Drama in the House: Edwina Currie MP talks to Sharon Garfinkel." *PlPl.* 1997 Feb.; 511: 8. Illus.: Photo. Color. 1. Lang.: Eng.
UK-England: London. 1997. Histories-sources. ∎British Member of Parliament Edwina Currie likens politicians to actors.

785 Hodgdon, Barbara. "'Here Apparent': Photography, History, and the Theatrical Unconscious." 181-209 in Pechter, Edward, ed. *Textual and Theatrical Shakespeare: Questions of Evidence.* Iowa City, IA: Univ of Iowa P; 1997. 267 pp. (Studies in Theatre History and Culture.) Notes. Illus.: Photo. 11. Lang.: Eng.
UK-England. 1951-1991. Critical studies. ∎Examines photos of stars and pictures of actors in rehearsal and performance, and argues to challenge photography's privileged position as epistemological evidence. Argues that photographic evidence is 'contaminated' by the presence of the photographer.

786 O'Sullivan, Maurice J. "Shakespeare's Other Lives." *SQ.* 1987 Sum; 38(2): 133-153. Notes. Biblio. Lang.: Eng.
UK-England. 1987. Critical studies. ∎Survey of fictional and dramatic treatments of Shakespeare as a character and comparison with biographical treatments.

787 Read, Alan. "A-Z: (R-T): A Conversation with Iain Sinclair." *PerfR.* 1997 Fall; 2(3): 85-90. Lang.: Eng.
UK-England. 1997. Histories-sources. ∎Interview with poet Iain Sinclair about the influence of geography and topography on various art forms, including theatre.

788 Seymour, A. *The Communal Experience of Theatre.* Unpublished Ph.D. thesis, Univ. of Manchester: 1996. Notes. Biblio. [Abstract in *Index to Theses,* 46-3160.] Lang.: Eng.
UK-England. 1960-1995. Histories-specific. ∎Contends that all theatre, whether at an intellectual, emotional or experiential level, is a communal experience. Addresses theoretical perspectives of Marxism and postmodernism, but is primarily concerned with current theatrical phenomena, which are assessed in the light of 'communal' processes.

789 "Beyond Black & White. 'On Cultural Power': 13 Commentaries." *AmTh.* 1997 May/June; 14(5): 14-17, 59-62. Illus.: Photo. B&W. 13. Lang.: Eng.
USA. 1997. Histories-sources. ∎Response of thirteen theatre artists to the recent public debate between playwright August Wilson and critic and director Robert Brustein, moderated by Anna Deavere Smith, on multiculturalism, Black theatre in America and color blind casting: dramaturg James Leverett, critics and authors Michele Wallace and Gordon Rogoff, playwright Eduardo Machado, performance artist Robbie McCauley, teachers Gitta Honegger and Una Chaudhuri, directors Kenny Leon, Dudley Cocke, Carole Rothman, Zelda Fichandler, Ricardo Khan, Woodie King, Jr.

THEATRE IN GENERAL: —Relation to other fields

790 "Beyond the Wilson-Brustein Debate." *TheaterM*. 1997; 27(2/3): 9-13. Lang.: Eng.
USA: New York, NY. 1997. Historical studies. ■Introduction by editors to series of articles focusing on the Robert Brustein-August Wilson public debate on issues of multiculturalism, African-American theatre and non-traditional casting. Gives history of the conflict between the artists and events leading up to the public debate sponsored by Theatre Communications Group and moderated by actress Anna Deavere Smith.

791 "War of the Words: An Interview with Margo Jefferson." *TheaterM*. 1997; 27(2/3): 13-20. Lang.: Eng.
USA: New York, NY. 1960-1997. Historical studies. ■Interview with Jefferson, a theorist, critic, and teacher of theatre, focusing on her reaction to the Robert Brustein-August Wilson debate on Black culture, African-American theatre, multiculturalism and nontraditional casting. Discusses Wilson's call for separate Black theatres, racial divisions.

792 "Ibsen and Art: A Visual Essay." *INC*. 1997; 17(1): 27. Lang.: Eng.
USA: New York, NY. 1996. Historical studies. ■Account of a meeting of the Ibsen Society of America relating to the writer's affinity for the visual arts.

793 Ambush, Benny Sato. "Culture Wars." *AfAmR*. 1997 Win; 31(4): 579-586. Biblio. Lang.: Eng.
USA: New York, NY. 1996-1997. Historical studies. ■Debate on the condition and future of professional Black theatre in the US between playwright August Wilson and critic/director Robert Brustein, beginning with Wilson's keynote address at the Eleventh Biennial National Theatre Conference in 1996 through a public debate at Town Hall moderated by actress/playwright Anna Deavere Smith.

794 Aronson, Arnold. "Theatre Technology and the Shifting Aesthetic." *NETJ*. 1997; 8: 1-10. Biblio. Lang.: Eng.
USA. 1997. Critical studies. ■Gauging a society's shifting tastes from the technology present in its art forms, with a specific look at how theatre reflects this idea.

795 Bellamy, Lou. "The Colonization of Black Theatre." *AfAmR*. 1997 Win; 31(4): 587-590. Lang.: Eng.
USA: St. Paul, MN, Princeton, NJ. 1996-1997. Critical studies. ■Support of playwright August Wilson's views on the future of Black theatre in the US as expressed in his keynote address at the National Theatre Conference. Author is artistic director of the Penumbra Theatre Company.

796 Bello, Richard. "The Contemporary Rise of Louisiana Voices and Other Neo-Chautauquas: A Return to Oral Performance." *TextPQ*. 1997 Apr.; 17(2): 182-196. Notes. Biblio. Lang.: Eng.
USA. 1874-1996. Historical studies. ■Describes and analyzes ongoing rise of neo-Chautauquas, with special focus on Louisiana Voices. Compares and contrasts traditional Chautauqua with newer forms, argues that neo-Chautauqua phenomenon can be explained by society's shift to condition of secondary orality characterized by saturation of mass media and computer technologies.

797 Bergeron, David M. "Teaching Practices." *SQ*. 1997 Win; 48(4): 458-461. Lang.: Eng.
USA. 1612-1997. Historical studies. ■Examines Thomas Heywood's *An Apology for Actors* and theorist Leslie Heywood's *Dedication to Hunger: The Anorexic Aesthetic in Modern Culture* to illustrate conflicts in teaching literary criticism and theory.

798 Berkeley, Anne. "Changing Theories of Collegiate Curricula, 1900-1945." *JAE*. 1997 Fall; 31(3): 77-90. Notes. Lang.: Eng.
USA. 1900-1945. Historical studies. ■Innovations in collegiate theatrical instuction in the United States, and its effect on the legitimization of theatre as an academic field of study.

799 Bianchi, Ruggero. "Verso un nuovo nuovo?" (Toward a New Kind of New?)*IlCast*. 1997; 10(29): 5-11. Notes. Lang.: Ita.
USA. 1995-1996. Critical studies. ■Argues that the 'new theatre' compares itself not with other theatrical genres but with other arts and media.

800 Bousquet, Marc. *The Practice of Association*. New York, NY: City Univ. of New York; 1997. 355 pp. [Ph.D. Dissertation, Univ. Microfilms Order No. AAC 9807908.] Lang.: Eng.

USA. 1800-1900. Historical studies. ■The theatricality of everyday life in nineteenth-century America, with discussion of Masonic temples, barrooms, workplaces, streets, churches, schools and homes and events such as voluntary performances to raise money and amateur lodge productions.

801 Broda-Bahm, Christine. "Resisting Museums as Cultural Authority: Theatricality and the Windy City Art Blues." *TA*. 1997; 50: 83-101. Notes. Illus.: Photo. B&W. 3. Lang.: Eng.
USA: Chicago, IL. 1988-1997. Critical studies. ■The theatrical nature of protests regarding exhibitions at the Art Institute of Chicago.

802 Brown, Cynthia Lynn. *Longevity and the Secondary Theatre Arts Teacher: A Case Study*. Tucson, AZ: Arizona State Univ; 1997. 107 pp. [Ph.D. Dissertation, Univ. Microfilms Order No. AAC 9812456.] Lang.: Eng.
USA. 1994-1996. Empirical research. ■Study of the personal characteristics and external support systems which may lead to longevity in the careers of theatre arts teachers. Interviews with teachers, students and colleagues. Classroom and rehearsal observations were conducted to obtain results and analyze strategies to assist teachers of drama.

803 Clark, Nancy G. *An Assessment of Secondary Theatre Teachers in Mississippi*. University, MS: The Univ. of Mississippi; 1997. 112 pp. [Ph.D. Dissertation, Univ. Microfilms Order No. AAC 9816959.] Lang.: Eng.
USA. 1996-1997. Empirical research. ■Study of secondary-school theatre instructors and their instructional techniques. Explores ways to make arts programs stronger by improving administrative and financial support, classroom space and maintenance, and additional training courses and workshops for retraining.

804 Cohen, David S. "736 New Grants Complete NEA Cycle." *AmTh*. 1997 May/June; 14(5): 48-49. Lang.: Eng.
USA: Washington, DC. 1997. Historical studies. ■Comprehensive list of National Endowment for the Arts grant recipients for the 1997 funding cycle.

805 Colaresi, Judith McColl. *A Case Study of a High School Theatre Teacher: Planning, Teaching, and Reflecting*. College Park, MD: Univ. of Maryland; 1997. 270 pp. [Ph.D. Dissertation, Univ. Microfilms Order No. AAC 9736541.] Lang.: Eng.
USA. 1995. Empirical research. ■Focuses on the teacher's knowledge of content and pedagogy when he plans, teaches, and reflects on an introductory acting class.

806 Colter-Antczak, Leslie. *Existential Drama Therapy: Journey Through Darkness*. San Francisco, CA: California Institute of Integral Studies; 1997. 57 pp. [M.A. Thesis, Univ. Microfilms Order No. AAC 1385157.] Lang.: Eng.
USA. 1997. Critical studies. ■The application of existentialist philosophy and existential/phenomenological psychology to the field of drama therapy.

807 Crouch, Stanley. "Who's Zooming Who?" *TheaterM*. 1997; 27(2/3): 20-23. Lang.: Eng.
USA: New York, NY. 1997. Historical studies. ■Analysis of playwright August Wilson's speech 'The Ground on Which I Stand' given at the Theatre Communications Group annual conference in which he called for a separate Black theatre in America. Argues that speech contained weaknesses and cliches not found in Wilson's dramas.

808 Davis, Clinton Turner. "Non-Traditional Casting (an open letter)." *AfAmR*. 1997 Win; 31(4): 591-594. Lang.: Eng.
USA. 1997. Critical studies. ■Letter to white theatre artists asking them to examine racist policies and to work with Black artists to achieve greater equality in hiring practices.

809 DeCosta, Louise. *Paradox and the Psychological World of the Performing Artist*. Cincinnati, OH: Union Institute; 1997. 120 pp. [Ph.D. Dissertation, Univ. Microfilms Order No. AAC 9804163.] Lang.: Eng.
USA. 1994-1996. Critical studies. ■Psychological study of the world of the performing artist examines how individuals develop the capacity to bridge multiplicity and integrate paradoxical dissonance during psychotherapy treatment.

THEATRE IN GENERAL: —Relation to other fields

810   Dolan, Jill. "Advocacy and Activism: Identity, Curriculum and Theatre Studies in the Twenty-First Century." *TTop.* 1997 Mar.; 7(1): 1-10. Lang.: Eng.
USA. 1996. Histories-sources. ■The author's year of working on the Advocacy Committee of the Association for Theatre in Higher Education. The association's relationship to arts advocacy and educational advocacy, and the ways in which theatre studies straddle the arts and education.

811   Doyle, Daniel F. *Freedom and Responsibility: The Interface of Drama Therapy and Existentialism.* San Francisco, CA: California Institute of Integral Studies; 1997. 76 pp. [M.A. Thesis, Univ. Microfilms Order No. AAC 1387982.] Lang.: Eng.
USA. 1997. Critical studies. ■Existentialism's concepts of freedom and responsibility and their relevance for drama therapy.

812   Fleche, Anne. "Echoing Autism: Performance, Performativity, and the Writing of Donna Williams." *TDR.* 1997 Fall; 41(3): 107-121. Notes. Biblio. Lang.: Eng.
USA. 1964-1996. Critical studies. ■Examines *Nobody Nowhere: The Extraordinary Autobiography of an Autistic* and *Somebody Somewhere: Breaking Free of Autism* by Donna Williams to show contradictory ways in which it is possible to embody a self by performing autism, by vocalizing the need to embody a self, and showing the link between performance and performativity.

813   Fuchs, Elinor. "Theater as Shopping." *ThM.* 1993; 23(1): 19-30. Illus.: Photo. B&W. 2. Lang.: Eng.
USA. 1987. Critical studies. ■Effects of the shopping culture on theatre, with respect to the marketing techniques of *Tamara: The Living Movie* an interactive show by John Krizanc, dir. by Richard Rose and presented at the 66th Street Armory.

814   Fuoss, Kirk W. *Striking Performances/Performing Strikes.* Jackson, MI: UP of Mississippi; 1997. 203 pp. (Performance Studies: Expressive Behavior in Culture.) Index. Biblio. Notes. Lang.: Eng.
USA: Flint, MI, Elizabeth, NJ. 1936-1937. Critical studies. ■Cultural performance, contestation, and community in the seizure of the New Jersey State Assembly by members of the Worker's Alliance of America and in the United Auto Workers' sit-down strike.

815   Gainer, Brenda. "Marketing Arts Education: Parental Attitudes toward Arts Education for Children." *JAML.* 1997 Win; 26 (4): 253-268. Biblio. Tables. Lang.: Eng.
USA. 1980-1997. Empirical research. ■Study of parental concerns about arts and arts education to assist in the strategy and content of social marketing campaigns directed at attitude change.

816   Hay, Samuel A. "Escaping the Tar-and-Feather Future of African American Theatre." *AfAmR.* 1997 Win; 31(4): 617-620. Lang.: Eng.
USA. 1997. Critical studies. ■Focus on how Black artists can best free themselves from the cultural ropes that bind them, and allow for a more vibrant African American theatre.

817   Hill, Randall T.G. "Performance and the 'Political Anatomy' of Pioneer Colorado." *TextPQ.* 1997 July; 17(3): 236-255. Notes. Biblio. Lang.: Eng.
USA: Sand Creek, CO. 1860-1997. Critical studies. ■Examines how pioneer inhabitants of the Colorado Territory used performance as a means of initiating, celebrating, and ultimately defending the Sand Creek Massacre of Native Americans.

818   Houle, Ann. *Rehearsing Courage: The Use of Drama Therapy in Teaching Self-Defense for Women.* San Francisco, CA: California Institute of Integral Studies; 1997. 110 pp. [M.A. Thesis, Univ. Microfilms Order No. AAC 1383629.] Lang.: Eng.
USA. 1997. Critical studies. ■Examines the structure of the Bay Area Model Mugging (BAMM) course for women from the perspectives of self-defense, theatre, and the metaphor of the hero's journey to illuminate the processes that provide the students an experience of courage in facing the threat of assault.

819   Jones, Joni L. "sista docta: Performance as Critique of the Academy." *TDR.* 1997 Sum; 41(2): 51-67. Notes. Biblio. Illus.: Photo. B&W. 6. Lang.: Eng.

USA. 1994-1997. Histories-sources. ■Explores ways that performance in general, and the author's performance piece *sista docta* specifically, challenges the academy's philosophy of inclusion and the academy's predilection for print scholarship. Autobiographical performance, African American women in academia, author's performance of the piece at the Second Annual Performance Studies Conference.

820   Joseph, May. "Alliances Across the Margins." *AfAmR.* 1997 Win; 31(4): 595-599. Biblio. Lang.: Eng.
USA. 1997. Critical studies. ■Playwright August Wilson and critic/ director Robert Brustein's debate on the present state of Black theatre in the US and its future.

821   King, W.D. "'Shadow of a Mesmeriser': The Female Body on the 'Dark' Stage." *TJ.* 1997 May; 49(2): 189-206. Notes. Illus.: Photo. 3. Lang.: Eng.
USA. 1840-1901. Historical studies. ■Argues that late-nineteenth spiritualism and mesmerism were played out on the stage through gender construction, or literal performance through the female body.

822   Krane-Calvert, Judith A. "A Twentieth-Century Analogue of *The Play of the Sacrament.*" *EDAM.* 1997 Fall; 20(1): 24-27. Lang.: Eng.
USA. England. 1400-1997. Historical studies. ■Account of a tale analogous to the fifteenth-century *Play of the Sacrament* told by Gary, Indiana, schoolchildren after World War II and traced to nuns from Poland.

823   Kumar, Shefali. *Shedding Skin, Shedding Light: Drama Therapy as a Means of Reaching the Empowered Self.* San Francisco, CA: California Institute of Integral Studies; 1997. 82 pp. [M.A. Thesis, Univ. Microfilms Order No. AAC 1384140.] Lang.: Eng.
USA. 1997. Critical studies. ■Feminist psychological literature and 'Goddess' archetypal psychology are examined and related to the field of drama therapy, particularly to the concepts of role embodiment, aesthetic distance and creative enactment. An original self-revelatory performance piece created by the author is included.

824   MacNeil, Robert. "Who Needs Artists?" *AmTh.* 1997 Apr.; 14(4): 10-14. Illus.: Sketches. Photo. B&W. 3. Lang.: Eng.
USA. 1996. Historical studies. ■Media commentator discusses role of art and artists in America, current political hostility towards art. Includes excerpt from a speech given by author Victor Hugo to the French Assembly, 1848.

825   Munk, Erika. "Up Front." *TheaterM.* 1997; 27(2/3): 5-8. Lang.: Eng.
USA. 1997. Historical studies. ■Report on Town Hall debate between playwright August Wilson and critic/director Robert Brustein on issues of multiculturalism, non-traditional casting and African-American theatre.

826   Mutima, Niamani. "Face to Face: The Wilson/Brustein Discussion." *BlackM.* 1997 Feb/Mar.; 12(3): 9, 15. Illus.: Photo. B&W. 5. Lang.: Eng.
USA. 1995-1997. Critical studies. ■Essay on the debate between August Wilson and Robert Brustein on the African-American presence in American theatre: continued in *BlackM* 12:4 (1997 June/July), p 9.

827   Navvab, Mojtaba. "Never Mind the Bollards ... Here's the Rock and Roll Hall of Fame." *LD&A.* 1996 Feb.; 26(2): 24-28. Illus.: Diagram. Photo. Color. B&W. 15. Lang.: Eng.
USA: Cleveland, OH. 1996. Technical studies. ■Discusses flaws and strengths of I.M. Pei's overall design for the Rock and Roll Hall of Fame.

828   Nesmith, Eugene. "Present, Past, Future." *TheaterM.* 1997; 27(2/3): 23-30. Lang.: Eng.
USA. 1926-1997. Historical studies. ■Analysis of debate between playwright August Wilson and critic Robert Brustein regarding condition and future of Black theatre and culture in America. Briefly examines history of Black theatre in America and W.E.B. Dubois's definition of Negro theatre.

829   Nicholson, James. "Cissy Lacks." *AmTh.* 1997 Mar.; 14(3): 34-35. Illus.: Photo. B&W. 1. Lang.: Eng.
USA: St. Louis, MO. 1994-1997. Historical studies. ■Controversy and legal battle surrounding teacher Cissy Lacks' work with inner city students after she videotaped their creative works on gang violence, drugs and other teen issues. Tapes were confiscated and debate ensued over First Amendment rights vs. exploitation of the young students.

THEATRE IN GENERAL: —Relation to other fields

830   Nunns, Stephen. "Wilson, Brustein & the Press." *AmTh.*
       1997 Mar.; 14(3): 17-19. Illus.: Photo. B&W. 3. Lang.: Eng.
USA: New York, NY. 1997. Historical studies. ■Public debate between
director Robert Brustein and playwright August Wilson (moderated by
actress/playwright Anna Deavere Smith) on issues of multiculturalism,
the nature of art and social consciousness. Includes excerpts from the
national press critiquing the event.

831   Nunns, Stephen. "Stormy Season Ahead." *AmTh.* 1997 Jan.;
       14(1): 66. Lang.: Eng.
USA: Washington, DC. 1997. Historical studies. ■Projected impact of
recent national elections on the arts and not-for-profit organizations.

832   Nunns, Stephen. "The Reverend and the Representative."
       AmTh. 1997 May/June; 14(5): 44-45. Illus.: Photo. B&W. 1.
       Lang.: Eng.
USA: Washington, DC. 1997. Historical studies. ■Influence of religious
extremists on politicians and their support for the National Endowment
for the Arts. Controversy on NEA's support for gay and lesbian arts with
focus on filmmaker Cheryl Dunye's *The Watermelon Woman*.

833   Nunns, Stephen. "Storming the Hill." *AmTh.* 1997 May/
       June; 14(5): 46-45. Illus.: Photo. B&W. 1. Lang.: Eng.
USA: Washington, DC. 1997. Historical studies. ■Political and entertainment celebrity supporters of the National Endowment for the Arts
on Arts Advocacy Day. Reauthorization process.

834   Nunns, Stephen. "A Sunburst of Art on the Capitol Lawn."
       AmTh. 1997 July/Aug.; 14(6): 56-57. Illus.: Photo. B&W. 1.
       Lang.: Eng.
USA: Washington, DC. 1997. Historical studies. ■ARTNOW's national
demonstration and celebration of art in support of arts funding in Washington.

835   O'Sullivan, John; Pollitt, Katha; Hart, Jeffrey; Navasky, Vic-
       tor. "The Nation vs. National Review." *AmTh.* 1997 Sep.;
       14 (7): 18-21, 62-65. Illus.: Photo. B&W. 5. Lang.: Eng.
USA. 1981-1997. Histories-sources. ■Writers for the journal *The Nation*
and for *National Review* debate virtues and drawbacks of public art support. Article is transcript of participants' positions in the order they were
delivered in the public forum held at Berkshire Theatre Festival.

836   Reiss, Alvin H. "State Assemblies Growing Arts Presence."
       FundM. 1997 May; 28(3): 36-37. Illus.: Photo. B&W. 4.
       Lang.: Eng.
USA. 1997. Historical studies. ■Arts funding in the states of Texas, New
York, and Kansas.

837   Reiss, Alvin H. "Texas Panhandle Pride Boosts Cultural
       Support." *FundM.* 1997 Nov.; 28(9): 32-34. Illus.: Photo.
       B&W. 4. Lang.: Eng.
USA: Amarillo, TX. 1966-1997. Critical studies. ■Cultural pride as
prime motivator of funding and support from the community for the
Panhandle-Plains Museum, which has produced in Palo Duro Canyon
Park for thirty-two years the drama, *Texas*, by Paul Green.

838   Romero, Emily L. *Artists-in-Residence: A Qualitative Study
       of a Rural Arts Program.* Denver, CO: Univ. of Denver;
       1997. 426 pp. [Ph.D. Dissertation, Univ. Microfilms Order
       No. AAC 9804077.] Lang.: Eng.
USA. 1997. Empirical research. ■Analysis of the Young Audiences and
the Artist-in-Residence program, bringing theatre, dance, and music to
rurual school districts. Argues for national standards for arts education
as a way of keeping arts programs funded.

839   Rowlands, Judith Gail. *A Modified Delphi Study: Survey of
       the Fine and Performing Arts Programs at the New Jersey
       Community Colleges.* Chester, PA: Widener Univ; 1997. 309
       pp. [Ph.D. Dissertation, Univ. Microfilms Order No. AAC
       9819486.] Lang.: Eng.
USA. 1994-1996. Empirical research. ■Investigates to what extent and
in what ways New Jersey community colleges have addressed specific
recommendations put forth by the State of New Jersey Board of Higher
Education to examine the status and role of educational fine and performing arts programs. Based on interviews and surveys of teachers and
coordinators.

840   Schonmann, Shifra. "How to Recognize Dramatic Talent
       When You See It: And Then What?" *JAE.* 1997 Win; 31(4):
       7-21. Notes. Lang.: Eng.

USA. 1997. Critical studies. ■Explores, in the context of aesthetic education, the notion of recognizing children with dramatic talent and ways
for the teacher to assign meaning to it.

841   Sorgenfrei, Carol Fisher. "Desperately Seeking Asia: A Sur-
       vey of Theatre History Textbooks." *ATJ.* 1997 Fall; 14(2):
       223-258. Notes. Lang.: Eng.
USA. 1720-1994. Critical studies. ■Evaluates Asian sections of major
theatre history texts and concludes that Eurocentric bias continues to
thrive in much of American academia.

842   Trevens, Francine L. "Playwrights Who Teach: Challenges
       and Rewards of Leading a Double Life." *DGQ.* 1997 Win;
       34(4): 40-45. Lang.: Eng.
USA. 1997. Critical studies. ■Reviews the advantages teaching affords
the playwright, both artistically and spiritually.

843   Turner, Beth. "Erotica and the Black Image." *BlackM.* 1997
       June/July; 12(4): 4. Illus.: Photo. B&W. 1. Lang.: Eng.
USA. 1997. Critical studies. ■Black sexuality as an area of exploration
for the Black artist.

844   Vierk, Janice Marie. *The Use of Pedagogy and Theatre of the
       Oppressed and Interactive Theatre Exercises in the Commu-
       nity College Composition Classroom.* Lincoln, NB: Univ. of
       Nebraska; 1997. 176 pp. [Ph.D. Dissertation, Univ. Micro-
       films Order No. AAC 9812363.] Lang.: Eng.
USA. 1994-1996. Empirical research. ■Examines a teacher research
project determining the effectiveness of using pedagogy and Boal's Theatre of the Oppressed teaching methods along with interactive theatre
exercises in community colleges.

845   Voorberg, Petronella F. *Black Velvet: Uncovering True Self
       Through the Use of a Transitional Object.* San Francisco, CA:
       California Institute of Integral Studies; 1997. 62 pp. [M.S.
       Thesis, Univ. Microfilms Order No. AAC 1385156.] Lang.:
       Eng.
USA. 1997. Critical studies. ■The use of theatre props to access hidden
aspects of the self in the process of creating and performing a self-
revelatory theatre piece during drama therapy.

846   Waggoner, Catherine Egley. "The Emancipatory Potential
       of Feminine Masquerade in Mary Kay Cosmetics." *TextPQ.*
       1997 July ; 17(3): 256-272. Notes. Biblio. Lang.: Eng.
USA. 1993-1997. Critical studies. ■The role of feminine masquerade for
members of the Mary Kay cosmetics company and the way in which the
company formalized representations of itself as a culture.

847   Weigel, Julie K. *Drama Therapy Is Spiritual Healing.* San
       Francisco, CA: California Institute of Integral Studies; 1997.
       150 pp. [M.A. Thesis, Univ. Microfilms Order No. AAC
       1387721.] Lang.: Eng.
USA. 1997. Critical studies. ■The belief structure of spiritual healing, the
principles of drama therapy, and their intersection in practice.

848   Weinstock, Jeffrey A. "Virus Culture." *SPC.* 1997 Oct.;
       20(1): 83-97. Biblio. Lang.: Eng.
USA. 1997. Critical studies. ■Fear of infection (i.e. AIDS, computer
viruses) and its influence upon popular art and culture in the US.

849   Zimmerman, Mark. "Nan Goldin and Lyle Ashton Harris."
       PerAJ. 1997 Jan.; 19(1): 38-45. Illus.: Photo. B&W. 5. [Num-
       ber 55.] Lang.: Eng.
USA: New York, NY. 1996-1997. Critical studies. ■Performative cri-
tique of separate photographic exhibits of Nan Goldin and Lyle Ashton
Harris delving into the narrative inconsistencies in their work.

Research/historiography

850   Brannen, Anne. "Creating a Dramatic Record: Reflections
       on Some Drunken Ghosts." *EDAM.* 1997 Fall; 20(1): 16-24.
       Lang.: Eng.
Critical studies. ■The problem of distinguishing dramatic and other
forms of activity when collecting dramatic records, with reference to a
sixteenth-century incident in which a group of men impersonated a ghost.

851   Geldner, Georg. *Der Milde Knabe, oder Die Natur eines
       Berufenen: Ein Wissenschaftlicher Ausblick, Oskar Pausch
       zum Eintritt in den Ruhestand Gewidmet.* (The Gentleman,
       or the Nature of a Vocation: A Scientific Perspective, Dedi-
       cated to Oskar Pausch on the Occasion of His Retirement.)

THEATRE IN GENERAL: —Research/historiography

Vienna: Böhlau; 1997. 333 pp. Pref. Notes. Illus.: Design. Pntg. Plan. Dwg. Poster. Photo. Maps. 160. Lang.: Ger, Fre, Eng.
1997. Critical studies. ■A *liber amicorum* for Pausch, the former president of SIBMAS and managing director of the Österreichisches Theatermuseum, containing articles on museology, research on collections, computer applications and technology in the field of the performings arts archives, libraries and museums.

852 Meyer, Moe; Bede-Fagbamila, Baba Ogunda; Drewal, Margaret Thompson, intro. "Ifa and Me: A Divination of Ethnography." *TextPQ*. 1997 Jan.; 17(1): 33-57. Notes. Biblio. Illus.: Photo. B&W. 6. Lang.: Eng.
Africa. 1997. Histories-sources. ■Proposes an experimental solution to problems of conventional ethnography (the nature of textualization, ethnographic authority, and power relations between ethnographer and informant) that allows the subject to determine the form and content of the ethnography. Explores practice of ritual Ifa divination and sacrifices.

853 Kobialka, Michal. "Medieval Representations: An Introduction." *ThS*. 1997 May; 38(1): 1-8. Lang.: Eng.
Europe. 1208-1400. Historical studies. ■Introductory essay to special volume on medieval historiography. Emphasis is on new strategies and current concerns in the field.

854 Gajdó, Tamás. *A színháztörténet-írás módszerei.* (A Methodology Theatre Historiography.) Veszprém: Veszprémi Egyetemi Kiadó; 1997. 217 pp. Append. Illus.: Photo. B&W. 29. Lang.: Hun.
Hungary. 1960-1990. Critical studies. ■A comprehensive survey of works by theatre historians and presentation of a scientific approach to theatre historiography organized with respect to special collections and museums of performing arts.

855 McConachie, Brian. "Cultural Systems and the Nation State: Paradigms for Writing National Theatre History." *NETJ*. 1997; 8: 29-44. Biblio. Lang.: Eng.
USA. 1997. Critical studies. ■Attempts to establish a narrative paradigm for the theatre historian eager to incorporate a multicultural perspective in writing a national theatre history.

856 Ryder, Andrew David. *Between Relativism and Realism: Postpositivist Theatre History Writing in the United States Since 1974.* Bowling Green, OH: Bowling Green State Univ; 1997. 232 pp. [Ph.D. Dissertation, Univ. Microfilms Order No. AAC 9820920.] Lang.: Eng.
USA. 1974-1997. Historical studies. ■Similarities and differences between the positivist and postpositivist approaches to the writing of history, particularly theatre history, with emphasis on the postpositivist theatre historiography of Tracy C. Davis, Bruce A. McConachie, and Joseph R. Roach.

Theory/criticism

857 Johansson, Ola. "Gårsdagens kritik om dagens teater." (The Critique of Yesterday on the Theatre of Today.) *TE*. 1997 Oct.; 85: 36-39. Illus.: Photo. B&W. 2. Lang.: Dan.
500 B.C.-1997 A.D. Histories-specific. ■A short history of criticism with examples from the history of theatre from ancient Greece to modern American performances.

858 Marin, Louis. "The Utopic Stage." 115-135 in Murray, Timothy, ed. *Mimesis, Masochism, and Mime: The Politics of Theatricality in Contemporary French Thought.* Ann Arbor, MI: Univ. of Michigan P; 1997. 328 pp. (Theater: Theory/ Text/Performance.) Notes. Lang.: Eng.
1984. Critical studies. ■Myth as ritual, theatre as the scene of representation, and utopia in tragedy.

859 Watson, Ian. "Naming the Frame: the Role of the Pre-Interpretive in Theatrical Reception." *NTQ*. 1997; 13(50): 161-170. Notes. Biblio. Lang.: Eng.
1977-1993. Critical studies. ■Uses *La Muerte y la doncella (Death and the Maiden)* by Ariel Dorfman, *Circe and Bravo* by Harold Pinter, and the Invisible Theatre of Augusto Boal to investigate the first, pre-interpretive part of the two-part process of reception.

860 Mauldin, Michael. "The Uncertain Path to Discovery: An Examination of Averroes' Concept of Uncertainty as a Cata-

lyst for Effective Audience Engagement." *TheatreS*. 1997; 42: 45-55. Notes. Biblio. Lang.: Eng.
Arabia. 1126-1997. Critical studies. ■Analysis of Averroës' commentary on Aristotle's *Poetics*.

861 Beckey, Christopher. "Hom(m)oerotics? Or to Queer the Male Body on Stage." *ADS*. 1997 Oct.; 31: 33-47. Notes. Illus.: Photo. B&W. 1. Lang.: Eng.
Australia. 1997. Critical studies. ■Representation of the male body onstage and the effect of a queer point of view on ideas of sexuality.

862 Bollen, Jonathan. "'What a queen's gotta do' and the Rhetorics of Performance." *ADS*. 1997 Oct.; 31: 106-123. Notes. Lang.: Eng.
Australia. 1997. Critical studies. ■Uses of the terms 'performance' and 'performativity' and investigates some of the problems tied up with the notion of queer performativity and its relation to performance, queer or otherwise.

863 Tait, Peta. "Interpreting Bodily Functions in Queer Performance." *ADS*. 1997 Oct.; 31: 48-56. Notes. Lang.: Eng.
Australia. 1997. Critical studies. ■A queer theorist's view of the stage function of bodily functions in gay performance.

864 Brask, Per. "Towards an Ontological-Democratic Theatre: A Manifesto." *CTR*. 1997 Win; 93: 68-69. Notes. Lang.: Eng.
Canada. 1997. Histories-sources. ■Playwright/director/critic sets forth principles of 'ontological-democratic' theatre, an 'interpretive stance' devoted to authenticity and ethics of interdependence.

865 Stephenson, Anthony. "Theatre Criticism." 393-423 in Plant, Richard, ed.; Saddlemyer, Ann, ed. *Later Stages: Essays in Ontario Theatre from the First World War to the 1970s.* Toronto, ON: Univ of Toronto P; 1997. 496 pp. (The Ontario Historical Studies Series.) Index. Notes. Biblio. Lang.: Eng.
Canada. 1914-1979. Historical studies. ■On the evolution and development of theatre criticism in Ontario.

866 Vaïs, Michel. "Les Entrées libres de *Jeu*: Théâtre et médias." (*Jeu*'s Free Admission Series: Theatre and the Media.) *JCT*. 1997; 84: 34-48. Notes. Illus.: Photo. B&W. 7. Lang.: Fre.
Canada: Montreal, PQ. 1997. Historical studies. ■Report on round-table discussion on level and nature of representation of Montreal theatre in the media.

867 Chen, Jingsong. "To Make People Happy, Drama Imitates Joy: The Chinese Theatrical Concept of *Mo*." *ATJ*. 1997 Spr; 14 (1): 38-55. Notes. Biblio. Lang.: Eng.
China. 1918-1982. Critical studies. ■Significance of *mo* in traditional Chinese theatre, its emphasis on theatricality. Examines the history of the word's usage and defines its place in Chinese drama in terms of its similarities and differences from Western realism.

868 Osolsobě, Ivo; Procházka, Miroslav. "Zichovo pozapomenuté paralipomenon (Několik poznámek o pořádku, Otakaru Zichovi, jeho PTD i EDU)." (Zich's Almost Forgotten Paralipomenon: Some Notes on the Zich Study.) *DivR*. 1997; 8(1): 3-11. Illus.: Dwg. B&W. 1. Lang.: Cze.
Czechoslovakia. 1922. Critical studies. ■Introduction to Otakar's Zich's study of dramaturgy, written in 1922 and printed here for the first time.

869 Zich, Otakar. "Principy teoretické dramaturgie." (Principles of Theoretical Dramaturgy.) *DivR*. 1997; 8(1): 12-24. Lang.: Cze.
Czechoslovakia. 1922. Critical studies. ■Zich's dramaturgical study from 1922, printed here for the first time.

870 Brask, Per. "Niels Bohr's Pre-Ramble to a Dramaturgical Theory: A Monologue Intended Only for Reading." *CTR*. 1997 Fall; 92: 82-86. Notes. Biblio. Illus.: Photo. B&W. 2. Lang.: Eng.
Denmark. 1997. Critical studies. ■Argues need for coherent communication in theatre, using principles from the work of Niels Bohr and Peter Zinkernagel.

871 Christensen, Anne Flindt. "Får teaterkritikken overhovedet lov til at mene noget?" (Are the Critics Allowed an Opinion?) *TE*. 1997 Oct.; 85: 12-15. Lang.: Dan.

THEATRE IN GENERAL: —Theory/criticism

Denmark. 1997. Critical studies. ■An essay by a theatre/dance critic on the current situation in Danish critique. Argues for a more daring critique with the courage to have strong opinions.

872 Garsdal, Lise. "Kritikkens problem—det er kritikkens eget." (The Problem of Criticism Is Its Own.) *TE.* 1997 Oct.; 85: 8-11. Illus.: Photo. B&W. 2. Lang.: Dan.

Denmark. 1997. Histories-sources. ■The critic Lise Garsdal interviews playwright Peter Asmussen on the subject of crticism. Asmussen is not interested in a dialogue between the critics and the artists and argues that reviews of performances are written solely for the readers, not for the theatres or the artists.

873 Davidson, Clifford. "Carnival, Lent, and Early English Drama." *RORD.* 1997; 36: 123-142. Notes. [Medieval Supplement.] Lang.: Eng.

England. 1513-1556. Historical studies. ■Argues that applying idea of Carnival as a device to interpret late medieval religious plays may do them a disservice.

874 Diller, Hans-Jürgen. "Code-Switching in Medieval English Drama." *CompD.* 1997 Win; 31(4): 506-537. Notes. Tables. Lang.: Eng.

England. 1300-1600. Critical studies. ■Attempts to apply sociolinguistic concept of code-switching to the analysis of medieval English drama.

875 Evrard, Yves. "Democratizing Culture or Cultural Democracy." *JAML.* 1997 Fall; 27(3): 167-175. Notes. Biblio. Lang.: Eng.

Europe. 1970-1997. Critical studies. ■Presentation of two paradigms said to be at the heart of all cultural debate: the democratization of culture and cultural democracy. How this conflict may be viewed in light of the transition from modernity to postmodernity.

876 Kattenbelt, Chiel. "Theater als Artefakt, ästhetisches Objekt und szenische Kunst." (Theatre as Artifact, Aesthetic Object and Scenic Art.) *FMT.* 1997; 12(2): 132-159. Notes. Lang.: Ger.

Europe. 1800-1997. Critical studies. ■Theatre from point of view of communications theory, with reference to work of Habermas and Seel.

877 Lehmann, Hans-Thies. "Theater und Gedächtnis." (Theatre And Memory.) *TZ.* 1997; 5: VI-XI. Illus.: Photo. B&W. 14. Lang.: Ger.

Europe. 1997. Critical studies. ■A lecture about the relationship between theatre and memory given February 22nd, 1997.

878 Phelan, Peggy. *Mourning Sex: Performing Public Memories.* London/New York, NY: Routledge; 1997. 187 pp. Index. Notes. Biblio. Illus.: Dwg. Photo. Maps. Sketches. 9. Lang.: Eng.

Europe. North America. 1993-1995. Critical studies. ■Injured or traumatized bodies and their critical analysis. Includes the archaeological excavation of the Rose Theatre as an example of an 'unearthed body' and its impact on architecture, theatre, the representation of the body, and Renaissance theatre architecture.

879 Walter, Klaus. "Reimen & Stehlen." (Rhyming & Stealing.) *TZ.* 1997; Yb: 97-101. Illus.: Photo. B&W. 3. Lang.: Ger.

Europe. 1993-1997. Critical studies. ■Compares Brecht's theory and methods with the practice of Hip-Hop, pointing to similarities in the notion of realism, their self-referential and demonstrative nature, use of found language material, orientation toward intertextuality and multimediality, and the processual character of the production.

880 Hotinen, Juha-Pekka. "Tekstuaalista häirintää—seksi/porno." (Textual Harassment—Sex/Porn.) *TeatterT.* 1997; 1: 52-55. Lang.: Fin.

Finland. 1997. Histories-sources. ■Theatrical performance and its relation to sex and pornography.

881 Kirkkopelto, Esa. "Teatteri yhteisönä—ei kenelle tahansa." (Theatre as Community—Not for Anyone.) *Teat.* 1997; 52(3): 6-8. Illus.: Photo. B&W. 2. Lang.: Fin.

Finland. 1997. Histories-sources. ■Director Esa Kirkkopelto's views on the impact of a theatrical performance.

882 Derrida, Jacques. "The Theater of Cruelty and the Closure of Representation." 40-62 in Murray, Timothy, ed. *Mimesis, Masochism, and Mime: The Politics of Theatricality in Contemporary French Thought.* Ann Arbor, MI: Univ. of Michi-

gan P; 1997. 328 pp. (Theater: Theory/Text/Performance.) Notes. [1978.] Lang.: Eng.

France. 1935-1949. Critical studies. ■Theoretical musings on Antonin Artaud's theatre of cruelty and its representation of closure.

883 Durand, Régis. "The Disposition of the Voice." 301-310 in Murray, Timothy, ed. *Mimesis, Masochism, and Mime: The Politics of Theatricality in Contemporary French Thought.* Ann Arbor, MI: Univ. of Michigan P; 1997. 328 pp. (Theater: Theory/Text/Performance.) Notes. Lang.: Eng.

France. 1977. Critical studies. ■The voice in theatrical representation.

884 Foucault, Michel. "Theatrum Philosophicum." 216-238 in Murray, Timothy, ed. *Mimesis, Masochism, and Mime: The Politics of Theatricality in Contemporary French Thought.* Ann Arbor, MI: Univ. of Michigan P; 1997. 328 pp. (Theater: Theory/Text/Performance.) Notes. Lang.: Eng.

France. 1977. Critical studies. ■On the nature of illusion—from Plato to Deleuze.

885 Green, André. "The Psycho-analytic Reading of Tragedy." 136-162 in Murray, Timothy, ed. *Mimesis, Masochism, and Mime: The Politics of Theatricality in Contemporary French Thought.* Ann Arbor, MI: Univ. of Michigan P; 1997. 328 pp. (Theater: Theory/Text/Performance.) Notes. Lang.: Eng.

France. 1979. Critical studies. ■Argues that it is the unconscious doubleness in the theatre that attracted Freud to its study and examines doubleness in tragedy.

886 Irigaray, Luce. "The Stage Setup." 63-86 in Murray, Timothy, ed. *Mimesis, Masochism, and Mime: The Politics of Theatricality in Contemporary French Thought.* Ann Arbor, MI: Univ. of Michigan P; 1997. 328 pp. (Theater: Theory/Text/Performance.) Notes. Lang.: Eng.

France. 1985. Critical studies. ■French feminist thought on mimesis and the lack of femaleness in Plato's thoughts on mimesis.

887 Kristeva, Julia. "Modern Theater Does Not Take (a) Place." 277-281 in Murray, Timothy, ed. *Mimesis, Masochism, and Mime: The Politics of Theatricality in Contemporary French Thought.* Ann Arbor, MI: Univ. of Michigan P; 1997. 328 pp. (Theater: Theory/Text/Performance.) Notes. Lang.: Eng.

France. 1977. Critical studies. ■The impact of language and semiotics on theatrical representation.

888 Lacoue-Labarthe, Philippe. "Theatrum Analyticum." 175-196 in Murray, Timothy, ed. *Mimesis, Masochism, and Mime: The Politics of Theatricality in Contemporary French Thought.* Ann Arbor, MI: Univ. of Michigan P; 1997. 328 pp. (Theater: Theory/Text/Performance.) Notes. Lang.: Eng.

France. 1942-1977. Critical studies. ■Analysis of a text by Freud, 'Psychopathic Characters on the Stage,' originally published in 1942. Focuses on the relation of psychoanalysis to theatricality, or, more generally, to representation.

889 Lyotard, Jean-François. "The Unconscious as *Mise-en-Scène.*" 163-174 in Murray, Timothy, ed. *Mimesis, Masochism, and Mime: The Politics of Theatricality in Contemporary French Thought.* Ann Arbor, MI: Univ. of Michigan P; 1997. 328 pp. (Theater: Theory/Text/Performance.) Notes. Lang.: Eng.

France. 1977. Critical studies. ■Staging, the unconscious, and the Freudian interpretation of dreams.

890 Lyotard, Jean-François. "The Tooth, the Palm." 282-288 in Murray, Timothy, ed. *Mimesis, Masochism, and Mime: The Politics of Theatricality in Contemporary French Thought.* Ann Arbor, MI: Univ. of Michigan P; 1997. 328 pp. (Theater: Theory/Text/Performance.) Notes. Lang.: Eng.

France. 1977. Critical studies. ■On the theory of semiotics as reflected in theatrical representation. Uses the theories of Zeami, Brecht, Artaud, Freud, and Marx to examine signs in theatricality.

891 Murray, Timothy. "Introduction: The *Mise-en-Scène* of the Cultural." 1-26 in Murray, Timothy, ed. *Mimesis, Masochism, and Mime: The Politics of Theatricality in Contemporary French Thought.* Ann Arbor, MI: Univ. of Michigan P; 1997. 328 pp. (Theater: Theory/Text/Performance.) Notes. Lang.: Eng.

THEATRE IN GENERAL: —Theory/criticism

France. 1967-1997. Critical studies. ■Introduction to a volume of essays by French poststructuralists, mostly written in the 1970s, regarding theatricality and critical thought.

892 Pavis, Patrice; Szántó, Judit, transl.; Fodor, Géza, intro. "A ritmus szerepe a rendezésben." (The Role of Rhythm in the Direction of Plays.) *Sz.* 1997; 30(5): 44-48. Biblio. Lang.: Hun.

France. 1985. Critical studies. ■Translation of Pavis' essay, previously published in his collection *Voix et images de la scène* (Lille, 1985), with an introductory essay by Fodor.

893 Varisco, Robert A. "Anarchy and Resistance in Tristan Tzara's *The Gas Heart*." *MD.* 1997 Spr; 15(1): 139-148. Notes. Lang.: Eng.

France. 1916. Critical studies. ■Influence of Dadaism on absurdist theatre and on Tzara's *Le Coeur à Gaz* and its anarchic elements.

894 Fiebach, Joachim. "Vordenker der Moderne." (Mentor of Modern Age.) *DB.* 1997; 1: 19-21. Notes. Illus.: Photo. B&W. 3. Lang.: Ger.

Germany. 1924-1930. Historical studies. ■Fifty years after his death, describes László Moholy-Nagy's theories and works for modern theatre that changed the use of light, sound, film and video in the 1920s.

895 Flemming, Willi; Szántó, Judit, transl.; Fodor, Géza, intro. "Színház, dráma, szövegkönyv." (Theatre, Drama, Playtext.) *Sz.* 1997; 30(3): 33-36. Lang.: Hun.

Germany. 1960. Critical studies. ■Translation of Flemming's article on aspects of drama, with an introduction by theatre researcher Géza Fodor.

896 Jhering, Herbert; Szántó, Judit, transl.; Fodor, Géza, intro. "Der Kampf ums Theater und andere Streitschriften." (Fight Around the Theatre and Other Polemic Essays.) *Sz.* 1997; 30(10): 29-39. Illus.: Photo. Dwg. B&W. 8. Lang.: Hun.

Germany. 1918-1933. Critical studies. ■Translation of three essays on theatre criticism and directing, introduced by theatre researcher Géza Fodor.

897 Kahane, Arthur; Szántó, Judit, transl.; Fodor, Géza, intro. "A színésznő." (The Actress.) *Sz.* 1997; 30(7): 36-41. Illus.: Photo. B&W. 5. Lang.: Hun.

Germany. 1872-1932. Critical studies. ■Publication of two essays by Arthur Kahane, literary manager of Max Reinhardt, on the nature and specific features of actresses and actors introduced by theatre researcher Géza Fodor.

898 Kerr, Alfred; Szántó, Judit, transl.; Fodor, Géza, intro. "Die Welt im Drama." (The World as Reflected in Dramas.) *Sz.* 1997; 30(8): 38-45. Notes. Lang.: Hun.

Germany. 1904-1917. Critical studies. ■Hungarian translation of two essays by a prominent early twentieth-century critic. Includes a lengthy preface by researcher Géza Fodor.

899 Netenjakob, Egon. "Henningway." *THeute.* 1997; 3: 34-37. Illus.: Photo. B&W. 5. Lang.: Ger.

Germany. 1927-1997. Biographical studies. ■A portrait of the theatre critic, author and founder of *Theater Heute* Henning Rischbieter on occasion of his 70th birthday.

900 Tian, Min. "'Alienation-Effect' for Whom? Brecht's (Mis) interpretation of the Classical Chinese Theatre." *ATJ.* 1997 Fall; 14(2): 200-222. Notes. Biblio. Gloss. Lang.: Eng.

Germany. 1925-1959. Critical studies. ■Brecht's understanding of Mei Lanfang's acting as a foundation for his theory of the 'alienation effect'. Author's examination of Brecht's interpretation of Chinese theatre and argument that his perceptions were incorrect.

901 Ferenc, Kerényi. "Mikszáth Kálmán és korának színházi élete. 150 éve született Mikszáth Kálmán." (Kálmán Mikszáth and the Theatrical Life of His Age: Kálmán Mikszáth Was Born 150 Years Ago.) *SzSz.* 1997(32): 143-156. Append. Notes. Lang.: Hun.

Hungary. 1847-1907. Historical studies. ■The writer's work as a theatre critic and his relationship with theatre.

902 Kékesi Kun, Árpád. "A theoretikusnak állapotja." (The Position of a Theoretician.) *Sz.* 1997; 30(12): 1. Lang.: Hun.

Hungary. 1997. Critical studies. ■Continuation of a discussion begun in *Színház* 30:7 (1997), pp. 22-29, and 30:9 (1997), p. 1, on the role of theory in the analysis of directorial work.

903 Koltai, Tamás. "Az új teatralitás és a kritika." (The New Theatricality and Criticism.) *Sz.* 1997; 30(9) : 1. Lang.: Hun.

Hungary. 1990. Critical studies. ■Critique of Árpád Kékesi Kun's article in *Színház* 30:7 (1997), pp 22-29, on the work of young Hungarian directors. Argues that Kékesi Kun's approach is excessively theoretical.

904 Bharucha, Rustom. "Negotiating the 'River': Intercultural Interaction and Interventions." *TDR.* 1997 Fall; 41(3): 31-38. Notes. Biblio. [Originally keynote address at the IDEA '95 congress in Brisbane.] Lang.: Eng.

India. 1938-1997. Critical studies. ■The river as a metaphor of cultural exchange in the larger context of intracultural interactions and interventions in theatre.

905 Cohen, Marilyn. "Beyond Boundaries: Towards an Interdisciplinary Irish Studies." *Eire.* 1996 Spr/Sum; 31(1&2): 137-162. Notes. Lang.: Eng.

Ireland. 1991-1997. Critical studies. ■Reflects upon the possible research agendas for the integration of Irish experience and neglected categories of Irish people into comparative theoretical debates. Argues for the need for interdisciplinary scholarship.

906 Fasoli, Doriano. *La stanza delle passioni. Dialoghi sulla letteratura francese e italiana.* (The Room of Passions: Dialogues on French and Italian Literature.) Venice: Marsilio; 1997. 111 pp. (Gli specchi della memoria.) Lang.: Ita.

Italy. France. 1997. Histories-sources. ■Interview with literary critic Giovanni Macchia on literature, theatre, and cinema.

907 Maggi, Armando. "Performing/Annihilating the Word: Body as Erasure in the Visions of a Florentine Mystic." *TDR.* 1997 Win; 41(4): 110-126. Notes. Biblio. Illus.: Pntg. B&W. 1. Lang.: Eng.

Italy: Florence. 1584-1585. Critical studies. ■Argues that *I colloqui (The Dialogues)*, mystical monologues of Saint Maria Maddalena de' Pazzi, question the meaning of text and genre, the word's intrinsic performativity, relationship between authorship and readership/audience, and the connection between gendered/sexual presence and discourse.

908 Scappaticci, Tommaso. "Matilde Serao e il teatro." (Matilde Serao and the Theatre.) *Ariel.* 1997; 12(2): 91-112. Notes. Lang.: Ita.

Italy. 1899-1912. Biographical studies. ■Analysis of journalist and writer Matilde Serao's newspaper reviews and theatrical themes in her novels.

909 Jones, Joni L. "Performing Osun without Bodies." *TextPQ.* 1997 Jan.; 17(1): 69-93. Notes. Biblio. Illus.: Photo. Sketches. Dwg. 18. Lang.: Eng.

Nigeria. 1993-1996. Critical studies. ■An experiment in translating performance events into ethnographic scholarship drawing on both verbal and visual means of communication. Attempts to create an interaction between text about the Yoruba goddess Osun and reader, and to give them the experience of the Osun festival.

910 Norén, Kjerstin. "Teaterns motiv." (The Motive of the Theatre.) *Tningen.* 1997; 21(3): 30-34. Illus.: Photo. B&W. Lang.: Swe.

Sweden. Denmark. France. 1992. Critical studies. ■Essay on the possibility of real, lived theatre today, with references to Grotowski and Institutet för Scenkonst.

911 Balme, Christopher. "Beyond Style: Typologies of Performance Analysis." *ThR.* 1997; 22(1): 24-30. Notes. Lang.: Eng.

UK-England. USA. 1963-1997. Critical studies. ■Uses the film version of Peter Brook's *Marat/Sade* and Karen Finley's *The Constant State of Desire* to demonstrate the unacknowledged historicity of performance typologies of Patrice Pavis and Hans-Thies Lehmann.

912 Billington, Michael; Olsen, Jakob Steen, transl. "Kritik der draeber." (Criticism that Kills.) *TE.* 1997 Oct.; 85: 32-35 . Illus.: Photo. B&W. 2. Lang.: Dan.

UK-England. 1877-1994. Historical studies. ■Argument for a more sober dialogue between critics and artists, based on the case of artist R.B. Kitaj, who claims that bad reviews of his Tate Gallery show in 1994 caused his wife's death.

THEATRE IN GENERAL: —Theory/criticism

913 Roberts, David. "Towards a Study of Theatre Journalism." *STP*. 1997 Dec.; 16: 129-138. Biblio. Lang.: Eng.
UK-England. 1992-1997. Critical studies. ■Considers the limitations of newspaper reviews of theatrical productions, with Irving Wardle's 1992 *Theatre Criticism*, and urges further academic study of theatre journalism.

914 Austin, Gayle; Klein, Jeanne; Zeder, Suzan. "A Feminist Dialogue on Theatre for Young Audiences Through Suzan Zeder's Plays." *JDTC*. 1997 Spr; 11(2): 115-139. Lang.: Eng.
USA. 1995-1996. Critical studies. ■The presence and impact of feminism on children's theatre, examined through the work of playwright Suzan Zeder. Plays discussed are *Step on a Crack*, *Mother Hicks*, and *Do Not Go Gentle*.

915 Corey, Frederick C.; Nakayama, Thomas K. "Sextext." *TextPQ*. 1997 Jan.; 17(1): 58-68. Biblio. Lang.: Eng.
USA. 1997. Critical studies. ■A fictional account of text and body as fields of pleasure. Textualizes ephemeral nature of desire in the context of gay-male pornography using theories of Roland Barthes.

916 Erickson, Peter. "Rewriting the Renaissance, Rewriting Ourselves." *SQ*. 1987 Fall; 38(3): 327-337. Notes. Lang.: Eng.
USA. UK-England. 1987. Critical studies. ■Assesses, from a feminist standpoint, the relations between new historicism and feminist criticism, and the prospects for future interactions between these disciplines to further the understanding of male/female roles in Renaissance literature.

917 Fischlin, Daniel. "Theatre, Theory and the Shaping Fantasies of Early Modern Criticism: A Review Essay." *ET*. 1997; 15 (2): 239-246. Notes. Biblio. Lang.: Eng.
USA. UK-England. 1988-1995. Critical studies. ■The purpose and place of theatrical representation in early modern England. Comparison of two recent books on the subject: *The Place of the Stage: License, Play, and Power in Renaissance England* by Steven Mullaney (Chicago: Univ of Chicago P, 1988, reprinted Univ of Michigan P, 1995) and *The Purpose of Playing Shakespeare and Cultural Politics in the Elizabethan Theatre* by Louis Montrose (Chicago: Univ of Chicago P, 1996).

918 Hollander, Judd. "Tribute to Theaterweek 1987-1997." *PlPl*. 1997 Feb.; 511: 25. Lang.: Eng.
USA: New York, NY. 1987-1997. Historical studies. ■Recalls *Theaterweek*'s contribution to New York theatre culture and mourns its ceasing of publication, January 1997.

919 Ishida, Yuichi. "'Force' und 'Rolle': Über die 'Kraft' der Sprache und das Theater in der Neuzeit." ('Force' and 'Role': Towards the 'Illocutionary' of Language and Theatre in Modern Times.) *FMT*. 1997; 12(1): 3-18. Notes. Lang.: Ger.
USA. 1955-1997. Critical studies. ■Connections between the history of philosophy of language and theatre based on John L. Austin's lectures 'How to Do Things with Words' delivered at Harvard University in 1955. Discusses the important term 'performance' in the second half of the twentieth century which ignores the dividing line between everyday life and theatre.

920 Kempinski, Tom. "John Keats V Bob Dylan: The Judge's Verdict." *PlPl*. 1997 Feb.; 511: 20-21. Lang.: Eng.
USA. UK-England. 1997. Critical studies. ■Argues superiority of 'high art' over 'popular art' using reflection of society as objective measure of artistic value.

921 Lancaster, Kurt. "When Spectators Become Performers: Contemporary Performance-Entertainments Meet the Needs of an 'Unsettled' Audience." *JPC*. 1997 Spr; 30(4): 75-88. Notes. Lang.: Eng.
USA. 1997. Critical studies. ■Importance of audience need to participate in entertainments. Cites the communal and cathartic nature of theatre of the ancients, said to have been repressed in the modern era.

922 Latham, Angela J. "Performance, Ethnography, and History: An Analysis of Displays by Female Bathers in the 1920s." *TextPQ*. 1997 Apr.; 17(2): 170-181. Notes. Biblio. Lang.: Eng.
USA. 1997. Critical studies. ■Proposes historical performance ethnography to study cultures whose remoteness is a matter of time rather than place, with emphasis on transgressive displays by women in the sport-leisure ritual of public bathing to illustrate the ways in which cultural values are exhibited, endorsed, defied, mediated and transformed in the female body.

923 McGrath, John Edward. "Intimate Screaming: The Sound of Surveillance." *WPerf*. 1997; 9(2): 81-93. Notes. Biblio. [Number 18.] Lang.: Eng.
USA. 1997. Critical studies. ■The performativity of language and sound, with respect to surveillance tapes and videos and their appearance in the courtroom.

924 Peterson, Eric E.; Langellier, Kristin M. "The Politics of Personal Narrative Methodology." *TextPQ*. 1997 Apr.; 17(2): 135-152. Notes. Biblio. Lang.: Eng.
USA. 1997. Critical studies. ■Uses an excerpt from an interview with a breast cancer survivor to examine the methodological implications of the assumption that personal narrative is not a performance but a text that can be fully transcribed and analyzed.

925 Pittenger, Elizabeth. "The Practice of Theory." *SQ*. 1997 Win; 48(4): 461-464. Lang.: Eng.
USA. 1997. Historical studies. ■Uses Pierre Bourdieu's *Outline of a Theory of Practice* to examine questions of theory and practice.

926 Rice, Joseph Charles. *The Development of Performance Studies: The Impact of Interdisciplinarity and Interculturalism*. Austin, TX: Univ. of Texas; 1997. 263 pp. [Ph.D. Dissertation, Univ. Microfilms Order No. AAC 9803005.] Lang.: Eng.
USA. 1890-1996. Historical studies. ■The impact of interdisciplinarity and interculturalism on the development of American Performance Studies. Focus on nineteenth-century professional schools of training and early academic theatre departments as well as late twentieth-century interdisciplinary approaches to performance studies.

927 Richardson, Brian. "Beyond Poststructuralism: Theory of Character, the Personae of Modern Drama, and the Antinomies of Critical Theory." *MD*. 1997 Spr; 15(1): 86-99. Notes. Lang.: Eng.
USA. 1997. Critical studies. ■Argues for more comprehensive form of literary theory as well as a more capacious approach to the concept of character. Brief survey of critical theories without implying progess or regress in history of recent critical theory.

928 Smith, Edward Barton. *The Low and Open World: Mimesis and the Staging of Reality in Contemporary Performance*. Austin, TX: Univ. of Texas; 1997. 317 pp. [Ph.D. Dissertation, Univ. Microfilms Order No. AAC 9803029.] Lang.: Eng.
USA. 1990-1997. Critical studies. ■The role of ideas about mimesis in critical response to performance practices that stage the 'real'. Works examined include those of Anna Deavere Smith and Spalding Gray and television shows *Cops* and *America's Most Wanted*.

Training

929 De Marinis, Marco. "Rifare il corpo. Lavoro su se stessi e ricerca sulle azioni fisiche dentro e fuori del teatro nel Novecento." (Rebuilding the Body: Work on the Self and Research on Physical Action Within and Outside Twentieth-Century Theatre.) *TeatroS*. 1997; 12(19): 161-182. Lang.: Ita.
Europe. 1900-1997. Historical studies. ■Introduction to the theatrical context of work on the physical body, with emphasis on Mejerchol'd, Decroux, Gurdjieff, and Steiner.

930 Hotinen, Juha-Pekka. "Tekstuaalista häirintää—opettaminen." (Textual Harassment—Teaching.) *TeatterT*. 1997; 2: 42-29. Lang.: Fin.
Finland: Helsinki. 1997. Histories-sources. ■Polemical views and visions on teaching theatre at the Theatre Academy.

931 Petrini, Armando. "'Artifex versus pontifex'. Ovvero: dell'autenticità e della sincerità, appunti su di un seminario di Jerzy Grotowski." ('Artifex vs. Pontifex' or On Authenticity and Sincerity: Notes on a Seminar by Jerzy Grotowski.) *LadB*. 1997; 1(1): 35-57. Notes. Lang.: Ita.
Poland. Italy. 1959-1991. Historical studies. ■The themes of Grotowski's 1991 seminar at the University of Turin and a survey of his career.

THEATRE IN GENERAL: —Training

932 Sidorow, Sonja. "Att stärka den sceniska närvaron." (To Strengthen the Scenic Presence.) *Danst.* 1997; 7(2): 6-9 . Illus.: Photo. B&W. Lang.: Swe.
Russia. Sweden. 1920-1996. Historical studies. ■A report from Gennadij Bogdanov's workshop on bio-mechanics at Sotenäs Teateratelje, with reference to V.E. Mejerchol'd.

933 Boston, Jane. "Voice: The Practitioners, their Practices, and their Critics." *NTQ.* 1997; 13(51): 248-254. Notes. Biblio. Lang.: Eng.
UK-England. USA. 1973-1994. Histories-sources. ■Joins the debate in previous issues of *NTQ* and argues that the apparently opposed viewpoints of scholars and working practitioners derive partly from semantic misunderstanding.

934 Gilbey, Liz. "So You Want to Act?" *PI.* 1997 Nov.; 13(3): 14-15. Illus.: Photo. B&W. 2. Lang.: Eng.
UK-England. 1997. Instructional materials. ■Overview of possibilities for training in acting as well as other aspects of theatre, information on choosing a drama school.

935 Eek, Dr. Nathaniel S. "The History Doctor: A Tribute to Dr. John McDowell." *TheatreS.* 1997; 42: 57-58. Illus.: Photo. B&W. 1. Lang.: Eng.
USA. 1997. Biographical studies. ■Profile of theatre history teacher McDowell on occasion of his death. Teaching methods, his approach to classical material.

936 Himes, Franklin John. *The Janus Paradigm: An Historical and Critical Study Toward Administrative and Curricular Reform in College and University Theatre Pedagogy and Practice.* Bowling Green, OH: Bowling Green State Univ; 1997. 237 pp. [Ph.D. Dissertation, Univ. Microfilms Order No. AAC 9820905.] Lang.: Eng.
USA. 1997. Historical studies. ■Addresses the legitimation crisis in American academic theatre and supports a cooperative system of interdisciplinary theory and coordinated practice.

937 Margolin, Deb. "A Perfect Theatre for One: Teaching 'Performance Composition'." *TDR.* 1997 Sum; 41(2): 68-81. Lang.: Eng.
USA: New York, NY. 1997. Critical studies. ■An educator's approach to teaching performance composition at New York University: definition of performance, techniques in working with students and their original creations, description of exercises used and excerpts of the students' writing.

938 McCaw, Dick. "Breathing Creatively." *DTJ.* 1997; 13(3): 32-33. Illus.: Photo. B&W. 1. Lang.: Eng.
USA. UK-England. 1968-1997. Histories-sources. ■Acting, dance and martial arts teacher Henry Smith relates his experiences with the Open Theatre, choreographer Anna Sokolow, and as artistic director of the Solaris Lakota Dance Theatre Company.

939 Nunns, Stephen. "Student Survey: A View from the Trenches of Training." *AmTh.* 1997 Jan.; 14(1): 38-44, 94. Illus.: Photo. Sketches. B&W. 6. Lang.: Eng.
USA. 1997. Critical studies. ■Students in theatre training programs nationwide respond to *American Theatre* survey asking why they have undertaken training for the theatre at a time when work in other entertainment media seems more profitable.

DANCE

General

Design/technology

940 Shank, Theodore. "Design and Collaboration: An Interview with Peter Pabst." *TheatreF.* 1997 Win/Spr; 10: 79-83. Illus.: Photo. 4. Lang.: Eng.
Germany: Wuppertal. 1996. Histories-sources. ■Interview with designer Peter Pabst on his stage design for Tanztheater Wuppertal's latest work *Nur Du (Only You)*.

941 Róna, Katalin. "Gombár, Judit a színházi ember." (Judit Gombár, the Theatre Artist.) *ZZT.* 1997; 4(2) : 27-29. Illus.: Design. B&W. 2. Lang.: Hun.

Hungary. 1955-1996. Histories-sources. ■A conversation with costume designer, pedagogue, and manysided artist of Hungarian theatre on her career working with choreographers home and abroad.

942 Lampert-Gréaux, Ellen. "Healing Light." *LDim.* 1997 Sep.; 21(8): 11. Illus.: Photo. Color. 2. Lang.: Eng.
USA: New York, NY. 1997. Historical studies. ■Thomas Hase's lighting design for Ping Chong's impressionistic dance performance piece *After Sorrow (Viet Nam)* at La MaMa, with projections by Chong and Jan Hartley.

Institutions

943 Grundmann, Ute. "Tanz-Träume." (Dance Dreams.) *DB.* 1997; 2: 23-25. Illus.: Photo. B&W. 3. Lang.: Ger.
Germany: Leipzig. 1990-1997. Historical studies. ■A portrait of choreographer Irina Pauls who established a dance company at Schauspielhaus (Leipzig) seven years ago, about her successes and the danger of the company's dissolving because of budget cuts.

944 Poppenhäger, Annette. "Was vom Tanze übrigblieb." (The Remains of the Dance.) *DB.* 1997; 10: 48-50. Illus.: Photo. B&W. 3. Lang.: Ger.
Germany: Cologne. 1997. Historical studies. ■Describes the Deutsches Tanzarchiv Köln that shows shoes, photographs, paintings, drawings, engravings and properties in an exhibition. It also presents its collected materials in archives and library.

945 Scheier, Helmut. "'Im Wind der Zeit'." ('In the Wind of Time'.) *Tanzd.* 1997; 36(1): 23-24. Illus.: Photo. B&W. 1. Lang.: Ger.
Germany: Cologne. 1992-1997. Critical studies. ■Reviews the dance exhibitions shown by Deutsches Tanzarchiv Köln for the last five years. Its photograph collection contains 80,000 positives and 50,000 original negatives.

946 Servos, Norbert. "Berlin tanzt ins Ungewisse." (Berlin Dances Into the Unknown.) *DB.* 1997; 7: 34-37. Illus.: Photo. B&W. 3. Lang.: Ger.
Germany: Berlin. 1997. Critical studies. ■Impressions from the current dance theatre in Berlin, about the competition among the dance companies of the three opera houses, the indifferent productions of the free scene, and the absence of political decision.

947 Fritzsche, Dietmar. "Zwischen Idealismus und Ideologie." (Between Idealism and Ideology.) *Tanzd.* 1997; 36(1): 25-26. Illus.: Photo. B&W. 1. Lang.: Ger.
Germany, East. 1949-1956. Historical studies. ■Report on an exhibition by Tanzarchiv Leipzig in cooperation with students of theatre studies. It deals with dance in East Germany from 1949 until 1956.

948 Körtvélyes, Géza. "Külföldi együttesek vendégjátéka, 1970-1977." (Guest Performances of Foreign Companies in Hungary Between 1970 and 1977.) *ZZT.* 1997; 4(5): 25-28. Illus.: Photo. B&W. 1. Lang.: Hun.
Hungary: Budapest. 1969-1978. Historical studies. ■Summary of the guest performances of world's leading ballet and dance companies in Budapest in the 1970s and adaptation of foreign choreographies in the program of the Hungarian ballet ensemble.

949 Szabó Durucz, Zsuzsa. "Bemutatjuk a Táncművészeti Főiskolát." (Introducing the Hungarian Dance Academy.) *ZZT.* 1997; 4(3): 7-10. Illus.: Photo. B&W. 5. Lang.: Hun.
Hungary: Budapest. 1950-1997. Historical studies. ■A brief history of the training school for dancers, Magyar Táncművészeti Főiskola.

950 Hongell, Johanna. "Dansfestival i Chennai." (A Dance Festival At Chennai.) *Danst.* 1997; 7(3): 18. Illus.: Photo. B&W. Lang.: Swe.
India: Chennai. 1996. Historical studies. ■A report from the sixteenth Natya Kala Conference, with references to Chitra Wisweswaran, Anita Ratna and Ramli Ibrahim.

951 Kaán, Zsuzsa; Leslie-Spinks, Lesley, photo.; Skoog, Martin, photo. "A holland csoda ...—Gyorsfénykép az 50. Holland Fesztiválról - 1. rész." (The Dutch Miracle—A Snapshot of the 50th Holland Festival—Part I.) *Tanc.* 1997; 28 (4): 30-31. Illus.: Photo. B&W. 2. Lang.: Hun.
Netherlands. 1947-1997. Critical studies. ■A brief historical survey of the festival focusing on this year's program.

DANCE: General—Institutions

952   Satin, Leslie. *Legacies of the Judson Dance Theater: Gender and Performing Autobiography.* New York, NY: New York Univ; 1997. 350 pp. [Ph.D. Dissertation, Univ. Microfilms Order No. AAC 9808335.] Lang.: Eng.

USA. 1960-1965. Historical studies. ■The early history of Judson Dance Theatre and its primary form, dancing autobiography. Traces the integration of dancing autobiography and gender and the influence of the form on Yvonne Rainer, Carolee Schneemann, Deborah Hay, Sally Gross, and Meredith Monk.

Performance/production

953   Vasiljeva, T.K., comp. *Sekret tanca.* (The Secret of Dance.) St. Petersburg: Djamaket/Zolotoj Vek; 1997. 480 pp. Lang.: Rus.

Instructional materials. ■Dance history textbook covering ballet, modern and folk dance, as well as the dance of south and southeast Asia.

954   Baim, Jo. *The Tango: Icon of Culture, Music, and Dance in Argentina, Europe, and the United States from 1875 to 1925.* Cincinnati, OH: Univ. of Cincinnati; 1997. 245 pp. Notes. Biblio. [Ph.D. Dissertation, Univ. Microfilms Order No. AC 9818591.] Lang.: Eng.

Argentina. USA. 1875-1925. Historical studies. ■The tango's early history, with reference to Argentinian cultural history, society's reaction to the new ballroom dances, tango as a form of dance and music and as source material for composers of art music.

955   Laermans, Rudi. "Cultural Unconsciousness in Meg Stuart's Allegorical Performances." *PerfR.* 1997 Fall; 2(3): 97-102. Biblio. Illus.: Photo. B&W. 1. Lang.: Eng.

Belgium. 1991-1997. Critical studies. ■The work of American-born choreographer Meg Stuart.

956   Sponsler, Claire. "Writing the Unwritten: Morris Dance and the Study of Medieval Theatre." *ThS.* 1997 May; 38(1): 73-95. Lang.: Eng.

England. 1570-1590. Historical studies. ■Morris dance as a cultural performance in medieval England. Author explores the patterns of appropriation, recuperation, and revival that construct the relationship between past performance and its subsequent historiographic reproductions.

957   Bryson, Norman. "Cultural Studies and Dance History." 55-80 in Desmond, Jane C., ed. *Meaning in Motion: New Cultural Studies of Dance.* Durham, NC/London: Duke UP; 1997. 398 pp. (Post-Contemporary Interventions.) Index. Notes. Illus.: Photo. 5. Lang.: Eng.

Europe. 1675-1900. Historical studies. ■Calls for an interdisciplinary approach to dance history. Focusing on the court of Louis XIV and European modernism, gives examples of how an informed use of cultural studies can enlarge the field of dance research. Uses art history, film, and comparative literature.

958   Kirchmann, Kay. "'Welcher Körper singt nun das Lied?'." ('Which Body Sings the Song Now?'.) *Tanzd.* 1997; 39(4): 12-17. Append. Lang.: Ger.

Europe. USA. 1980-1995. Critical studies. ■Analysis of the working methods of choreographers Merce Cunningham and Pina Bausch with respect to myth, undersood as a principle of order beyond abstract thought.

959   Macaulay, Alistair. "Further Notes on Dance Classicism." *DTJ.* 1997; 13(3): 24-30. Notes. Illus.: Photo. B&W. 4. Lang.: Eng.

Europe. 1997. Critical studies. ■Argues for the importance of dance classicism as a key component to the beauty of the form. Searches for examples in modern dance and ballet.

960   Stöckemann, Patricia. "Den menschlichen Körper vergessen machen." (To Make Us Forget the Human Body.) *Tanzd.* 1997; 37(2): 12-15. Illus.: Photo. B&W. 6. Lang.: Ger.

Europe. South America. 1927-1997. Biographical studies. ■A portrait of the dancer, choreographer and teacher Jean Cébron and his working methods basically influenced by the Jooss-Leeder method.

961   Ojala, Raija. "Dance Comes In from the Cold/La danse émerge de sa marginalisation." *NFT.* 1997; 51: 17-18. Illus.: Photo. B&W. 5. Lang.: Eng, Fre.

Finland. 1980-1997. Critical studies. ■Diversification of dance disciplines in Finland since 1980, including more varied training for the performer as opposed to strict balletic techniques.

962   Rouhiainen, Leena. "Matka Tanssinmerkityksiin ja niiden tutkimiseen." (A Trip to the Meanings of Dance and Their Research.) *TeatterT.* 1997; 2: 36-41. Illus.: Photo. B&W. 4. Lang.: Fin.

Finland. 1997. Histories-sources. ■Report and experiences from the 'Researching of Dance' seminar, focusing especially on the teaching of Karen Bond and Sue Stinson.

963   Hill, Constance Valis. "Jazz Modernism." 227-244 in Morris, Gay, ed. *Moving Words: Re-writing Dance.* London/New York, NY: Routledge; 1996. 343 pp. Index. Notes. Biblio. Illus.: Photo. 1. Lang.: Eng.

France. 1920-1930. Critical studies. ■Jazz music and dance and their influence on French culture.

964   Bausch, Pina; Farabough, Laura, intro. "Casebook: Pina Bausch: *Nur Du (Only You)*, A Piece by Pina Bausch." *TheatreF.* 1997 Win/Spr(10): 60-62. Illus.: Photo. 1. Lang.: Eng.

Germany: Wuppertal. 1996. Histories-sources. ■On the creation of Bausch's *Nur Du (Only You)*, presented in Wuppertal and in the US.

965   Draeger, Volkmar. "'Sinnliche Subversion'." ('Sensuous Subversion'.) *TZ.* 1997; 1: 10-13. Pref. Illus.: Photo. B&W. 5. Lang.: Ger.

Germany. 1967-1997. Histories-sources. ■An interview with director and producer Thomas Guggi who was choreographer of the first free dance company in East Germany.

966   Farabough, Laura. "A Conversation with Matthias Schmiegelt." *TheatreF.* 1997 Win/Spr; 10: 63-66. Illus.: Photo. 4. Lang.: Eng.

Germany: Wuppertal. 1996. Histories-sources. ■Interview with company manager Matthias Schmiegelt of Tanztheater Wuppertal on Pina Bausch's new piece *Nur Du (Only You)*.

967   Luzina, Sandra; McClung, Michael, transl. "Sasha Waltz and Guests: *Travelogue*." *TheatreF.* 1997 Win/Spr; 10: 38-43. Illus.: Photo. 6. Lang.: Eng.

Germany. 1993-1996. Historical studies. ■Examines the work of dance theatre artist Sasha Waltz focusing on *Twenty to Eight* and *Travelogue*.

968   Ochaim, Brygida. "Die Barfusstänzerin Olga Desmond." (The Barefoot Dancer Olga Desmond.) *Tanzd.* 1997; 39(4): 18-21. Append. Notes. Illus.: Photo. B&W. 3. Lang.: Ger.

Germany: Berlin. 1891-1964. Biographical studies. ■A portrait of the barefoot dancer Olga Desmond and her work.

969   Orr, Shelley. "The American West Inspires Tanztheater Wuppertal." *TheatreF.* 1997 Win/Spr; 10: 67-73. Illus.: Photo. 5. Lang.: Eng.

Germany: Wuppertal. 1996. Historical studies. ■Account of the creation of Pina Bausch's new piece *Nur Du*, from a dramaturgical standpoint.

970   Servos, Norbert. "Der Tod tanzt um sein Leben." (Death Dances for its Life.) *THeute.* 1997; 4: 4-10. Illus.: Photo. B&W. 6. Lang.: Ger.

Germany. 1980-1997. Historical studies. ■Reports of the German dance theatre mainly influenced by choreographers such as Pina Bausch and Johann Kresnik for the last twenty-five years. Describes how these important choreographers react to social changes and transform them into a contemporary dance theatre.

971   Sieben, Irene. "*Angst & Geometrie* — 3D Gerhard Bohner." *Tanzd.* 1997; 39(4): 7-11. Illus.: Photo. B&W. 3. Lang.: Ger.

Germany. 1936-1997. Historical studies. ■Analyzing the important meaning of Bohner's choreographies and their influences on dancers today from the performance of Bohner's *Fear and Geometry* at Komische Oper (Berlin).

972   Stöckemann, Patricia; Witzeling, Klaus. "'Tanz ist eine Bewusstseinsfrage'." ('Dance Is a Question of Consciousness'.) *Tanzd.* 1997; 37(2): 4-7. Pref. Illus.: Photo. B&W. 3. Lang.: Ger.

Germany: Dresden. 1989-1997. Histories-sources. ■An interview with choreographer Stephan Thoss about his studies, his working methods,

DANCE: General—Performance/production

influences by the Jooss-Leeder method and the possibilities of working like this in theatre.

973 Thorausch, Thomas. "Emmy Sauerbeck." *Tanzd.* 1997; 39(4): 22-23. Notes. Pref. Illus.: Photo. B&W. 4. Lang.: Ger.
Germany. 1894-1974. Biographical studies. ■A portrait of the dancer, choreographer and dance teacher Emmy Sauerbeck by her successor at Deutsches Tanzarchiv in Cologne.

974 Williams, Faynia. "Working with Pina Bausch: A Conversation with Tanztheater Wuppertal." *TheatreF.* 1997 Win/Spr; 10: 74-78. Illus.: Photo. 4. Lang.: Eng.
Germany: Wuppertal. 1996. Histories-sources. ■Interviews with Tanztheater Wuppertal personnel on the creation of *Nur Du (Only You)*: Pina Bausch, Dominique Mercy, Julie Shanahan, Peter Pabst, Matthias Schmiegelt, and Jann Perry.

975 Breuer, Péter. "Magyar táncos a Batsheva élén." (A Hungarian Dancer Heading the Batsheva in Israel.) *Tanc.* 1997; 28(1/2): 48-49. Lang.: Hun.
Hungary. Israel: Tel Aviv. 1994-1996. Histories-sources. ■An interview with the new star of the Batsheva Dance Group, István Juhos, who has been a member of the company since August 1996.

976 Königer, Miklós. "Táncoló színészcsodák—1. rész." (Dancing Actor-Wonders, Part I.) *Tanc.* 1997; 28(4): 35-36. Illus.: Photo. B&W. 7. Lang.: Hun.
Hungary. 1929-1945. Historical studies. ■Hungarian dancers' film careers in Europe and the U.S. Continued in *Tanc* 28:5/6, p. 52.

977 Körtvélyes, Géza. "Tendenciák a magyar táncművészetben 1964-1970." (Tendencies in Hungarian Dance Art Between 1964 and 1970.) *ZZT.* 1997; 4(1): 14-16. Illus.: Photo. B&W. 2. Lang.: Hun.
Hungary. 1964-1970. Historical studies. ■Introducing a period of innovation in Hungarian dance art concept, institutional basis, traditions, program policy, training and important productions of the seasons in the late sixties.

978 Arnadóttir, Gudbjörg. "Dansen på Island." (The Dance In Iceland.) *Danst.* 1997; 7(2): 20-21. Illus.: Photo. Color. Lang.: Swe.
Iceland: Reykjavik. 1952. Historical studies. ■A survey of the position of dance in Iceland, with reference to Íslenski Dansflokkurinn.

979 Hongell, Johanna. "Att koreografera Bharata Natyam." (To Put Choreography to Bharata Natyam.) *Danst.* 1997; 7(5): 14-15. Illus.: Photo. B&W. Lang.: Swe.
India. 1997. Biographical studies. ■The dancer Johanna Hongell speaks about how you can create new dances in the *Bharata Natyam* form, with reference to her teacher Savrithri Jagannatha Rao and Kalanidhi Narayanan.

980 Gelencsér, Ágnes. "A Batsheva-táncegyüttes vendégjátéka 1989-ben." (The Guest Performance of Batsheva Dance Company in 1989.) *ZZT.* 1997; 4(4): 33. Lang.: Hun.
Israel: Tel Aviv. Hungary: Budapest. 1963-1989. Reviews of performances. ■Notes on the guest performance of the Israeli dance company.

981 Pontremoli, Alessandro, ed. *Drammaturgia della danza. Percorsi coreografici del secondo Novecento.* (Dramaturgy of Dance: A Choreographic Journey through the Late Twentieth Century.) Milan: Euresis Edizioni; 1997. 166 pp. Index. Illus.: Photo. Sketches. B&W. Lang.: Ita.
Italy. USA. 1950-1997. Historical studies. ■The work of Alwin Nikolais, Enzo Cosimi, Fabrizio Monteverde, Lucia Latour, and Virgilio Sieni.

982 Sinisi, Silvana. "La nuova coreografia italiana: percorsi tra la danza, l'arte, la scena." (The New Italian Choreography: Travels Between Dance, Art, and Stage.) *Ariel.* 1997; 12(1): 43-49. Illus.: Photo. B&W. 1. Lang.: Ita.
Italy. 1970-1997. Critical studies. ■Brief survey of recent Italian choreographers and the close relationship among dance, the visual arts, and experimental theatre.

983 Hentschel, Beate. "Jeder Moment besitzt seine eigene Zeit." (Every Moment Has Its Own Time.) *Tanzd.* 1997; 39(4): 4-6. Illus.: Photo. B&W. 2. Lang.: Ger.

Japan. Europe. 1992-1997. Histories-sources. ■An interview with dancer and choreographer Saburo Teshigawara about his performances and thoughts of quality in dance and movement.

984 Guimaraes, Daniel Tercio Ramos. *The History of Dance in Portugal. From the Patio Comedies to the Founding of the S. Carlos Theatre.* Lisbon: Universidade Tecnica de Lisboa; 1997. 666 pp. Lang.: Por.
Portugal. 1660-1793. Historical studies. ■History of dance in Portugal, focusing on change in the court, elite society, and the wider society. Interprets the spaces for the practice and representation of dance, and areas of ideological confrontation.

985 Laakkonen, Johanna. "Mitä tanssija voi tehdä aktiiviuran jälkeen." (The Possibilities for the Dancer after the Active Career.) *Tanssi.* 1997; 18(1): 18-19. Lang.: Fin.
Scandinavia. 1997. Historical studies. ■Support services for older and/or retiring dancers in Nordic countries with special focus on career and personal counseling.

986 Azta. "Träningskläder—slitna och svettiga älskningar." (Practice Wear—Shabby and Sweaty Darlings.) *Danst.* 1997; 7(6): 10-11. Illus.: Photo. B&W. Lang.: Swe.
Sweden: Stockholm. 1997. Historical studies. ■A short survey of the clothing habits of the dancer's workday.

987 Harryson, Lotta. "Jazzen steppar upp igen." (Jazz Steps Up Again.) *Danst.* 1997; 7(1): 14-15. Illus.: Photo. B&W. Lang.: Swe.
Sweden. 1900. Critical studies. ■A survey of the jazz dance in Sweden, with reference to the new Modern Jazzdans Ensemble.

988 Olsson, Irène. "Den mångsidige Håkan Mayer." (The Versatile Håkan Mayer.) *Danst.* 1997; 7(3): 22-23. Illus.: Photo. B&W. Lang.: Swe.
Sweden. 1970. Histories-sources. ■An interview with Håkan Mayer about his career, from a classical dancer to a free lance as modern dancer and choreographer for operas.

989 Sörenson, Margareta. "Dans för barn och frågan om ett pedagogiskt alibi." (Dance For Children and the Question of a Pedagogical Alibi.) *Danst.* 1997; 7(3): 10-11. Illus.: Photo. B&W. Lang.: Swe.
Sweden. 1990. Critical studies. ■A survey of the poor repertory of modern dance performances for children in Sweden.

990 Wrange, Ann-Marie. "En dansare tar ton." (A Dancer Takes to Music.) *Danst.* 1997; 7(6): 13-15. Illus.: Photo. B&W. Color. Lang.: Swe.
Sweden: Stockholm. 1981. Histories-sources. ■An interview with the dancer Rennie Mirro about his background and the years as ballet dancer at Kungliga Operan, and now as singing and dancing actor in musicals.

991 Nenander, Fay. "Hur ser framtiden ut för den klassiska dansen?" (What Is the Future of Classical Dance?) *Danst.* 1997; 7(4): 24-26. Lang.: Swe.
Switzerland: Lausanne. 1997. Historical studies. ■A report from a conference held in Lausanne, 29-31 January where the want of new creativity among the classical dance companies was discussed.

992 Dodds, Sherril. "'Televisualised': Bodies and Changing Perspectives." *DTJ.* 1997; 13(4): 44-47. Notes. Illus.: Photo. B&W. 4. Lang.: Eng.
UK-England. 1997. Critical studies. ■Examines the relationship of video dance and criticism. Suggests that criteria for stage choreography are inappropriate when appraising dance created for video.

993 Flood, Philip. "In the Silence and Stillness." *DTJ.* 1997; 13(4): 36-39. Notes. Illus.: Sketches. B&W. 8. Lang.: Eng.
UK-England. 1997. Histories-sources. ■Composer Flood discusses the difficulties and rewards of collaborating with a choreographer.

994 Koritz, Amy. "Dancing the Orient for England: Maud Allan's *The Vision of Salome*." 133-152 in Desmond, Jane C., ed. *Meaning in Motion: New Cultural Studies of Dance.* Durham, NC/London: Duke UP; 1997. 398 pp. (Post-Contemporary Interventions.) Index. Notes. Illus.: Photo. 1. Lang.: Eng.
UK-England: London. USA. 1908. Critical studies. ■The relationship of gender to the production of English nationalism as seen in American

DANCE: General—Performance/production

dancer Maud Allan's notorious depiction of *The Vision of Salome* in England at the Palace Theatre. Uses the analytical model of cultural critic Edward Said to frame analysis of dominant discourses, reception, and shaping of the performance event.

995 McPherson, Katrina. "A Passion for Screen Dance." *DTJ.* 1997; 13(4): 48-50. Notes. Illus.: Photo. B&W. 2. Lang.: Eng.
UK-England. 1997. Biographical studies. ■Tribute to late video choreographer Michele Fox.

996 Albright, Ann Cooper. *Choreographing Difference: The Body and Identity in Contemporary Dance.* Hanover, NH: UP of New England; 1997. 244 pp. Biblio. Index. Illus.: Photo. 26. Lang.: Eng.
USA. 1985-1995. Critical studies. ■Choreographing bodies as a source of cultural identity, with attention to the work of Bill T. Jones, Cleveland Ballet Dancing Wheels, Zab Maboungou, David Dorfman, Marie Chouinard, Jawole Willa Jo Zollar, and others.

997 Banes, Sally. *Dancing Women: Female Bodies on Stage.* New York, NY/London: Routledge; 1997. 208 pp. Notes. Biblio. Index. Illus.: Photo. 25. Lang.: Eng.
USA. Europe. 1801-1997. Critical studies. ■Feminist analysis of dance performance in specific socio-political and cultural contexts. Demonstrates that choreographers have created representations of women that are shaped by, and in turn shape, society's continuing debates on sexuality and female identity.

998 Bull, Cynthia Jean Cohen. "Sense, Meaning, and Perception in Three Dance Cultures." 269-288 in Desmond, Jane C., ed. *Meaning in Motion: New Cultural Studies of Dance.* Durham, NC/London: Duke UP; 1997. 398 pp. (Post-Contemporary Interventions.) Index. Notes. Illus.: Photo. 3. Lang.: Eng.
USA. Ghana. 1995-1997. Critical studies. ■Examination of dance practices to reveal cultural constructions, beliefs and concepts. Examines dance training, performance, and audience perception in three different contemporary settings: ballet and contact improvisation in North America, and West African Ghanaian dance.

999 Caglianone, Maria. "I percorsi spazio/temporali di Meredith Monk." (Meredith Monk's Time/Space Journeys.) *IlCast.* 1997; 10(29): 13-32. Notes. Illus.: Photo. B&W. 3. Lang.: Ita.
USA. 1970-1988. Historical studies. ■The evolution of Meredith Monk's choreography, in which each performance is described as a journey through time and space with the aim of revealing the circularity of existence.

1000 Climenhaga, Royd. "Performance in Review: Pina Bausch, Tanztheater Wuppertal in a Newly Commissioned Piece: *Nur Du (Only You).*" *TextPQ.* 1997 July; 17(3): 288-298. Notes. Biblio. Lang.: Eng.
USA. 1960-1991. Critical studies. ■Dancer/choreographer Bausch and her dance/theatre company's recent presentation of new piece on a rare U.S. tour, and the opportunity it presented to audiences and artists to view her work first hand. Bausch's training and background, her combination of dance and theatre techniques.

1001 Daniels, Don. "Urban Renewal." *BR.* 1997 Spr; 25(1): 60-64. Illus.: Photo. B&W. 2. Lang.: Eng.
USA: New York, NY. 1997. Critical studies. ■Survey of recent dance performances: Doug Elkins' *Cross My Heart* for Dance Theater Workshop, Mark Dendy's *Afternoon of the Fawns* at the club Mother, and Aleksand'r Blok's *Balagančik (The Puppet Show)* staged at La MaMa by Roger Babb and Rocky Bornstein.

1002 Erdman, Joan L. "Dance Discourses: Rethinking the History of the 'Oriental Dance'." 288-305 in Morris, Gay, ed. *Moving Words: Re-writing Dance.* London/New York, NY: Routledge; 1996. 343 pp. Index. Notes. Biblio. Lang.: Eng.
USA. 1920-1990. Critical studies. ■Examines the interweavings of Indian and Western 'oriental' dance in the twentieth century.

1003 Fischer, Dagmar. "Wie die Arbeit eines Detektivs." (Like a Detective's Work.) *Tanzd.* 1997; 38(3): 4-7. Pref. Illus.: Photo. B&W. 2. Lang.: Ger.
USA. 1929-1997. Histories-sources. ■An interview with Ernestine Stodelle, a former student of Doris Humphrey, about her reconstructions of Humphrey's dances and the teaching methods she uses in workshops.

1004 Goldberg, Marianne. "Homogenized Ballerinas." 305-320 in Desmond, Jane C., ed. *Meaning in Motion: New Cultural Studies of Dance.* Durham, NC/London: Duke UP; 1997. 398 pp. (Post-Contemporary Interventions.) Index. Notes. Illus.: Photo. 10. Lang.: Eng.
USA. 1987-1997. Critical studies. ■A 'performance lecture,' in which author combines words, visuals, and choreography on the page and presents it in a two-dimensional format. Examines questions of dance, history, representation, spectatorship, and gender.

1005 Lobenthal, Joel. "New York." *BR.* 1997 Sum; 25(2): 9-13. Illus.: Photo. B&W. 1. Lang.: Eng.
USA: New York, NY. 1981-1997. Biographical studies. ■Mikhail Baryshnikov's tenure as artistic director of American Ballet Theatre and his present work with his modern dance troupe White Oak Dance Project.

1006 Marion, Sheila. *Notation Systems and Dance Style: Three Systems Recording and Reflecting One Hundred Years of Western Theatrical Dance.* New York, NY: New York Univ; 1997. 308 pp. [Ph.D. Dissertation, Univ. Microfilms Order No. AAC 9717774.] Lang.: Eng.
USA. 1700-1995. Historical studies. ■Comparison of the dance notation systems devised by Benesh, Laban, and Stepanov, with emphasis on the ways in which their structures and vocabularies reflect movement concepts and dance style.

1007 Mason, Francis. "Forewords and Afterwords." *BR.* 1997 Spr; 25(1): 4-13. Illus.: Photo. B&W. 4. Lang.: Eng.
USA: New York, NY. 1996-1997. Historical studies. ■Account of events, classes, books and television programs that enriched dance in the greater New York area from August 1996 to February 1997.

1008 McRobbie, Angela. "Dance Narratives and Fantasies of Achievement." 207-234 in Desmond, Jane C., ed. *Meaning in Motion: New Cultural Studies of Dance.* Durham, NC/London: Duke UP; 1997. 398 pp. (Post-Contemporary Interventions.) Index. Notes. Lang.: Eng.
USA. 1980-1990. Critical studies. ■The representation of social dancing in contemporary mass media. Uses urban dance halls, the television series *Fame* and the movie *Flashdance*, directed by Adrian Lyne, to argue that class, race, and gender social contexts are all present in social dance.

1009 Nielsen, Eric Brandt. "Dance: SETC Auditions Provide Rare Opportunity for Performers to Show Skills, Find Work." *SoTh.* 1997 Fall; 38(4): 4-8. Illus.: Photo. B&W. 4. Lang.: Eng.
USA. 1997. Instructional materials. ■Audition choreographer for the Southeast Theatre Conference describes the evaluation process in dance auditions, tells potential auditioners what to expect, and advises non-dancers and dancers alike what to do in the audition process.

1010 Ochaim, Brygida. "Vom Verschwinden des Körpers." (Toward the Disappearance of the Body.) *Tanzd.* 1997; 37(2): 16-21. Notes. Pref. Illus.: Photo. B&W. 7. Lang.: Ger.
USA. Europe. 1892-1996. Critical studies. ■Dancer/choreographers Loie Fuller and Oskar Schlemmer and the influence on their work of film and its techniques such as cut, flashback, repetition, editing, slow-motion.

1011 Sannuto, John. *On Contemporary Musical Dance Theatre: The Creation and Production of an Original Work.* New York, NY: New York Univ; 1997. 346 pp. [Ph.D. Dissertation, Univ. Microfilms Order No. AAC 9810497.] Lang.: Eng.
USA. 1995. Historical studies. ■Examines the creative process for a contemporary musical dance theatre event, *Cry of the Earth*, performed at New York University, which blends contemporary modern dance, music, and theatre and borrows elements from the realms of performance art and musical theatre.

1012 Schneider, Katja. "Die eigene Stimme finden." (To Find Your Own Voice.) *Tanzd.* 1997; 37(2): 8-11. Append. Illus.: Photo. B&W. 2. Lang.: Ger.
USA. 1972-1995. Biographical studies. ■A portrait of the American dancer, choreographer and pedagogue Karen Bamonte on occasion of her workshop at 'Hasting Studio für Tanz und Bewegung' ('Hasting Studio for Dance and Movement') in Munich in August 1997.

DANCE: General—Performance/production

1013 Scott, Anna Beatrice. "Spectacle and Dancing Bodies That Matter: Or, If It Don't Fit, Don't Force It." 259-268 in Desmond, Jane C., ed. *Meaning in Motion: New Cultural Studies of Dance.* Durham, NC/London: Duke UP; 1997. 398 pp. (Post-Contemporary Interventions.) Index. Notes. Illus.: Photo. 1. Lang.: Eng.
USA: San Francisco, CA. 1996. Critical studies. ■Examination of a 'bloco afro' rehearsal by dancers of different racial, ethnic, and national backgrounds. Uses this rehearsal to examine issues of race, gender, and class in dance.

Plays/librettos/scripts

1014 Richard, Christine. "Wieviel Leere braucht der Wahnsinn..." (How Much Emptiness Does Madness Need...) *Thsch.* 1997; 11: 142-149. Illus.: Photo. B&W. 1. Lang.: Ger, Fre, Dut, Eng.
Switzerland: Basel. 1990-1997. Histories-sources. ■An interview with choreographer Joachim Schlömer about his dance adaptations.

Relation to other fields

1015 Sinibaldi, Clara. "Il corpo spirituale. Sulle tracce della danza sacra contemporanea." (The Spiritual Body: On the Trail of Contemporary Sacred Dance.) *TeatroS.* 1997; 12(19): 131-159. Notes. Lang.: Ita.
Europe. 1970-1997. Critical studies. ■Analysis of the Catholic Church's recent interest in the involvement of the body in prayer, from liturgical gestures to sacred dance.

1016 Brandt-Knack, Olga. "Zu Aufgaben und Zielen des Tanzes im Nachkriegsdeutschland." (Towards Tasks and Purposes of Dance in Postwar Germany.) *Tanzd.* 1997; 36(1): 19-22. Append. Pref. Illus.: Photo. B&W. 5. Lang.: Ger.
Germany. 1951. Histories-sources. ■Text of an address on the necessity of political engagement for dance and its value in society with respect to unionization, given during a congress of dancers in Recklinghausen on July 12th, 1951.

1017 Lipp, Nele. "Befreiung von Farbe und Form." (Emancipation from Color and Form.) *Tanzd.* 1997; 36(1): 27-28. Illus.: Photo. B&W. 2. Lang.: Ger.
Germany: Bremen. 1900-1925. Critical studies. ■Reviews exhibitions of Kunsthalle Bremen dealing with dance and describes especially the last exhibition 'Tanz in der Moderne. Von Schlemmer bis Matisse' ('Dance in the Modern Age. From Schlemmer to Matisse').

1018 Johnson, Eyvind. "Dansen är som fåglarnas sång och fåglarnas flykt: den äro." (The Dance Is Like the Song of the Birds and the Flight of the Birds: It Just Is.) *Danst.* 1997; 7(4): 7-10. Illus.: Dwg. B&W. Lang.: Swe.
Sweden: Stockholm. 1940-1941. Histories-sources. ■Excerpt from Eyvind Johnson's novel *Grupp Krilon (The Group Krilon)* that deals with dance and has a character who is a ballerina.

1019 Vasarhelyi, Lilian Karina; Sundberg, Sonja. "Att lära av danshistorien." (To Learn of the History of Dance.) *Danst.* 1997; 7(2): 22-23. Lang.: Swe.
Sweden. Germany. 1911-1945. Historical studies. ■A discussion about the situation of the dancers during Nazism in Germany and in Sweden during the war, with reference to the book *Tanz unterm Hakenkreuz.*

1020 Gibson, Gwen Askin. *Producing a High School Dance Concert as a Means to Improve Students' Performance Ability and Creative Confidence.* Long Beach, CA: California State Univ; 1997. 30 pp. [M.A. Thesis, Univ. Microfilms Order No. AAC 1385561.] Lang.: Eng.
USA: Long Beach, CA. 1996. Empirical research. ■Study of the production of a successful high school dance concert, based on how well the dancers performed during the concert and how much they progressed technically, creatively, and as a cohesive group. Choreography by author.

1021 Smith, Colleen Altaffer. *Collaboration: A Dancer's Phenomenological Study of the Combined Vision in Art-Making.* Denton, TX: Texas Woman's Univ; 1997. 179 pp. [Ph.D. Dissertation, Univ. Microfilms Order No. AAC 9733477.] Lang.: Eng.
USA. 1996. Critical studies. ■Examines decisions, patterns, and integration of elements in dance collaboration and uses philosophy as a way to investigate the collaborative process in creative and performing arts. Based on interviews with dancers.

1022 Taylor, Marsha Natalie. *'Shoutin': The Dance of the Black Church.* Cleveland, OH: Case Western Reserve Univ; 1997. 128 pp. [Ph.D. Dissertation, Univ. Microfilms Order No. AAC 9818209.] Lang.: Eng.
USA. 1700-1995. Histories-specific. ■Describes the 'ring shout' dance practiced by African-Americans in worship rituals as sacred dance, with roots going back to ancient Greek theatre and worship.

Research/historiography

1023 Desmond, Jane C. "Embodying Difference: Issues in Dance and Cultural Studies." 29-54 in Desmond, Jane C., ed. *Meaning in Motion: New Cultural Studies of Dance.* Durham, NC/London: Duke UP; 1997. 398 pp. (Post-Contemporary Interventions.) Index. Notes. Lang.: Eng.
USA. 1990-1997. Historical studies. ■Calls for a new engagement between cultural studies and dance scholarship. Dance historian author examines social and theatrical dance styles from ballet to hip hop and tango to analyze new forms of representation transcending race, class, and national boundaries.

1024 Veroli, Patrizia. "Die Tanzgeschichtsforschung als ständige Herausforderung." (Dance Research as Permanent Challenge.) *Tanzd.* 1997; 39(4): 35-37. Lang.: Ger.
USA. 1977-1997. Histories-sources. ■An interview with Lynn Garafola about the current dance research at universities in USA and its development during the last twenty years.

Theory/criticism

1025 Jooss, Kurt. "Gedanken über Stilfragen." (Thoughts about Questions of Style.) *Tanzd.* 1997; 38(3): 26-29. Pref. Illus.: Photo. B&W. 2. Lang.: Ger.
Europe. 1600-1957. Histories-sources. ■A lecture on dance history and various styles to his students at Folkwangschule on September 23rd, 1957.

1026 Ness, Sally Ann. "Observing the Evidence Fail: Difference Arising from Objectification in Cross-Cultural Studies of Dance." 245-269 in Morris, Gay, ed. *Moving Words: Re-writing Dance.* London/New York, NY: Routledge; 1996. 343 pp. Index. Notes. Biblio. Illus.: Maps. 1. Lang.: Eng.
Europe. North America. 1995. Critical studies. ■Examines anthropological models to identify different ways of categorizing dance.

1027 Wolff, Janet. "Reinstating Corporeality: Feminism and Body Politics." 81-100 in Desmond, Jane C., ed. *Meaning in Motion: New Cultural Studies of Dance.* Durham, NC/London: Duke UP; 1997. 398 pp. (Post-Contemporary Interventions.) Index. Notes. Lang.: Eng.
Europe. 1980-1995. Critical studies. ■Feminist study of postmodern dance. Uses feminist theories of Julia Kristeva, Luce Irigaray, Hélène Cixous and others.

1028 Tawast, Minna. "Vartioinko minä täällä, tanssikriitikot kirjoittavat työstään." (Am I Standing Guard Here?) *Tanssi.* 1997; 18(5): 18-21. Lang.: Fin.
Finland. 1997. Critical studies. ■Dance critics write about their profession.

1029 Kozel, Susan. "'The Story Is Told as a History of the Body': Strategies of Mimesis in the Work of Irigaray and Bausch." 101-109 in Desmond, Jane C., ed. *Meaning in Motion: New Cultural Studies of Dance.* Durham, NC/London: Duke UP; 1997. 398 pp. (Post-Contemporary Interventions.) Index. Illus.: Photo. 2. Lang.: Eng.
Germany: Wuppertal. 1978-1991. Critical studies. ■New visions for feminist dance theory. Author examines work of Pina Bausch and theories of feminist theorist Luce Irigaray to demonstrate how one mimetically informs the other. Works of Wuppertal Dance Theater include *Kontakthof* and *Tanzabund II.*

1030 Nagura, Miwa. "Cross-Cultural Differences in the Interpretation of Merce Cunningham's Choreography." 270-287 in Morris, Gay, ed. *Moving Words: Re-writing Dance.* London/New York, NY: Routledge; 1996. 343 pp. Index. Notes. Biblio. Illus.: Photo. 1. Lang.: Eng.

DANCE: General—Theory/criticism

Japan. USA. 1970-1979. Critical studies. ■Analysis of Japanese studies of choreography by Merce Cunningham, demonstrating an Asian view of Western culture.

1031 Harryson, Lotta. "Kropp, kön och teori." (Body, Sex and Theory.) *Danst.* 1997; 7(6): 8. Illus.: Photo. B&W. Lang.: Swe.

Sweden: Stockholm. 1997. Historical studies. ■A report from the seminar *Body and Sex* (Kropp och kön), arranged by Dramatiska Institutet, where practice had confronted theory.

1032 Olsson, Irène. "Dans med röst och teater med dans." (Dance With the Voice and Theatre With the Dance.) *Danst.* 1997; 7(6): 24-25. Illus.: Photo. B&W. Lang.: Swe.

Sweden: Stockholm. 1997. Historical studies. ■A report from the seminar 'Exit text?' about the relationship between the dancing and the text, and between dance and theatre.

1033 Nugent, Ann. "Choreography, Criticism and Community." *DTJ.* 1997; 13(4): 26-30. Notes. Illus.: Photo. B&W. 1. Lang.: Eng.

UK-England. 1997. Critical studies. ■Examines the relationship between choreography and criticism, described as divergent diciplines with the common aim of communication.

1034 Burch, Steven Dedalus. "Imitation of Life: A Meditation on 'Victim Art'." *JDTC.* 1997 Fall; 12(1): 121-131. Lang.: Eng.

USA. 1997. Critical studies. ■A critical response to the controversy in the dance world over 'victim art,' initially set off by an article by dance critic Arlene Croce in the December 1994 *New Yorker*.

1035 Gottschild, Brenda Dixon. "Some Thoughts on Choreographing History." 167-178 in Desmond, Jane C., ed. *Meaning in Motion: New Cultural Studies of Dance*. Durham, NC/London: Duke UP; 1997. 398 pp. (Post-Contemporary Interventions.) Index. Notes. Lang.: Eng.

USA. 1990-1996. Critical studies. ■How the cultural and social values of critics and scholars bear on topics and methodologies. Calls for intertextual studies that recognize dominant aesthetic hierarchies and make room for 'content-specific' intertextual studies.

1036 Jordan, Stephanie. "Musical/Choreographic Discourse: Method, Music Theory, and Meaning." 15-28 in Morris, Gay, ed. *Moving Words: Re-writing Dance*. London/New York, NY: Routledge; 1996. 343 pp. Biblio. Notes. Index. Lang.: Eng.

USA. 1995. Critical studies. ■Outlines an analytical method for examining the relationships between music and dance.

1037 Martin, Carol. "High Critics/Low Arts." 320-333 in Morris, Gay, ed. *Moving Words: Re-writing Dance*. London/New York, NY: Routledge; 1996. 343 pp. Index. Notes. Biblio. Illus.: Photo. 1. Lang.: Eng.

USA. 1995-1996. Critical studies. ■Examines problems that arise when differing notions of what constitutes dance are not acknowledged. Examines Arlene Croce's critique of Bill T. Jones's *Still/Here*, a work that focuses on people with life-threatening illnesses.

1038 Martin, Randy. "Dance Ethnography and the Limits of Representation." 321-344 in Desmond, Jane C., ed. *Meaning in Motion: New Cultural Studies of Dance*. Durham, NC/London: Duke UP; 1997. 398 pp. (Post-Contemporary Interventions.) Index. Notes. Lang.: Eng.

USA. 1997. Critical studies. ■On the relationship of theory and practice. Argues that performance should come first to reveal methodological insights into cultural contexts and the performative nature of history.

Training

1039 Artus, Hans-Gerd. "Zur Selbsterfahrung in der Tanzpädagogik." (On Self-awareness in Dance Education.) *Tanzd.* 1997; 38(3): 16-19. Notes. Lang.: Ger.

Europe. 1997. Histories-general. ■Discusses aspects of self-awareness and its possible use in dance teaching from general psychological and educational points of view.

1040 Brotherus, Hanna. "Keski-ikäisen naistanssijan tie on auki." (An Open Road for the Middle-Aged Female Dancer.) *Tanssi.* 1997; 18(4): 19-21. Illus.: Photo. B&W. 2. Lang.: Fin.

Finland. 1997. Historical studies. ■The long-time collaboration of choreographers and dancers Soile Lahdenperä and Ervi Siren on teaching and choreography.

1041 Melis, Veronica. "François Delsarte: frammenti da un insegnamento." (François Delsarte: Fragments of a Master Class.) *TeatroS.* 1997; 12(19): 37-65. Notes. Lang.: Ita.

France. 1846-1871. Historical studies. ■Delsarte's artistic personality and teaching methods.

1042 Franco, Susanne. "Ginnastica e corpo espressivo. Il metodo Bode." (Gymnastics and the Expressive Body: the Bode Method.) *TeatroS.* 1997; 12(19): 67-96. Notes. Lang.: Ita.

Germany. 1881-1971. Historical studies. ■The 'expressive gymnastics' of Rudolf Bode, a pupil of Dalcroze, which attracted the attention of Eisenstein and Tretjakov.

1043 Witzeling, Klaus; Stöckemann, Patricia. "Nicht Schritte vermitteln, sondern Bewegungsbewusstsein." (Not Teaching Steps but Awareness of Movement.) *Tanzd.* 1997; 38(3): 20-25. Pref. Illus.: Photo. B&W. 3. Lang.: Ger.

Germany: Essen. 1927-1997. Histories-sources. ■An interview with Lutz Förster, director of the dance department at Folkwang-Hochschule, about historical and contemporary aspects of dance training at Folkwang-Hochschule.

1044 Johansson, Kerstin. "Ett träningssystem för sig." (A System of Training By Itself.) *Danst.* 1997; 7(3): 6-9. Illus.: Photo. B&W. Lang.: Swe.

Sweden: Stockholm. USA: New York, NY. 1992. Histories-sources. ■An interview with the dancer and pedagogue Karin Jameson about the Kleintechnique, the special training method by Susan Klein, and her future plans in Sweden.

1045 Hobson, William. "Releasing Sensibilities." *DTJ.* 1997; 13(3): 34-37. Illus.: Photo. B&W. 2. Lang.: Eng.

UK-England: London. 1996. Histories-sources. ■Conversation between Joan Skinner and teacher/choreographer Gaby Agis regarding Skinner's 'releasing technique', which integrates the mind/body complex in the act of dancing.

1046 Foster, Susan Leigh. "Dancing Bodies." 235-258 in Desmond, Jane C., ed. *Meaning in Motion: New Cultural Studies of Dance*. Durham, NC/London: Duke Univ P; 1997. 398 pp. (Post-Contemporary Interventions.) Index. Notes. Illus.: Photo. 6. Lang.: Eng.

USA. 1990-1996. Critical studies. ■New approaches in dance training. Calls for more analysis of other practices that 'cultivate the body,' sports, etiquette, and acting techniques. Examines several dance training methods in detail.

Ballet

Administration

1047 Snow, Leida. "Miami." *BR.* 1997 Spr; 25(1): 13-15. Lang.: Eng.

USA. 1997. Critical studies. ■Discusses the ever-weakening funding support for classical forms of art, specifically ballet. Edward Villella of the Miami City Ballet also expresses his concern regarding the 'anti-intellectual' mood of the country.

Design/technology

1048 "Designing Diaghilev." *BR.* 1997 Sum; 25(2): 59-60. Illus.: Design. Photo. B&W. 13. Lang.: Eng.

Russia. France. 1909-1929. Histories-specific. ■Costume and set designs for Serge Diaghilev's Ballets Russes productions on view at Wadsworth Atheneum in Hartford, CT.

1049 Slingerland, Amy L. "Dance Macabre: Houston Ballet Presents the Voluptuous Horror of Dracula." *TCI.* 1997 Apr.; 31(4): 28-31. Illus.: Photo. Sketches. 10. Lang.: Eng.

USA: Houston, TX. 1897-1997. Historical studies. ■The centennial of the publication of Bram Stoker's *Dracula* is celebrated by the Houston Ballet (choreographer/director Ben Stevenson) in a coproduction with Pittsburgh Ballet Theatre. Examines ballet's costumes by Judanna Lynn, sets by Thomas Boyd, and lighting by Timothy Hunter.

DANCE: Ballet

Institutions

1050 Suhonen, Tiina. "The Finnish National Ballet is Celebrating its 75th Anniversary." *Tanssi*. 1997; 18(3): 16-18. Illus.: Photo. B&W. 3. Lang.: Eng.
Finland: Helsinki. 1923-1997. Historical studies. ■History of the Finnish National Ballet, Suomen Kansallisbaletti, and its current works and programs.

1051 Gelencsér, Ágnes; Kanyó, Béla, photo. "Balettvizsga'97—A Magyar Táncművészeti Főiskola végzőseinek koncertje az Operaházban." (Graduation Concert '97—The Concert of the Graduating Class of Hungarian Dance Academy at the Opera.) *Tanc*. 1997; 28(4): 16-17. Illus.: Photo. B&W. 4. Lang.: Hun.
Hungary: Budapest. 1997. Historical studies. ■Account of the graduation performance of the young ballet dancers.

1052 Jálics, Kinga; Schuch, József, photo. "'Tényleg boldogok lehetünk'—Afonyi éva és Kiss János." ('We Can Really Be Happy'—Éva Afonyi and János Kiss.) *Tanc*. 1997; 28(1/2): 14-15. Illus.: Photo. B&W. 3. Lang.: Hun.
Hungary: Győr. 1970-1997. Histories-sources. ■Meeting János Kiss, the artistic director of Győr Ballet and Éva Afonyi, his wife, who is a soloist of the ensemble.

1053 Kaán, Zsuzsa; Waldman, Max, photo.; Péres, Louis, photo. "'európaS'-díjas: 'Egészséges néha, ha van vetélytársunk!'." ('europaS' Award-Winning Artist Iván Nagy: 'Having Rivals Is Healthy!'.) *Tanc*. 1997; 28(1/2): 10-11. Illus.: Photo. B&W. 2. Lang.: Hun.
Hungary. Chile: Santiago. 1970-1996. Histories-sources. ■Interview with dancer, pedagogue and manager Iván Nagy, director of the Ballet de Santiago, who has already had a five-year directorship with this company between 1981 and 1985. (In the meantime he was the director of the English National Ballet).

1054 Körtvélyes, Géza. "Korszerű tendenciák a magyar táncművészetben, 1964-1970." (Modern Tendencies in Hungarian Dance Art Between 1964-1970.) *ZZT*. 1997; 4(2): 23-25. Illus.: Photo. B&W. 2. Lang.: Hun.
Hungary: Pécs, Szeged. 1964-1970. Historical studies. ■Survey of Hungarian ballet ensemble's of the sixties through their productions, with emphasis on the Pécsi Balett and the Szegedi Kortárs Balett.

1055 Körtvélyes, Géza. "Az operaházi balett, 1970-1977." (The Ballet Ensemble of the Budapest Opera House, 1970-1977.) *ZZT*. 1997; 4(4): 30-33. Illus.: Photo. B&W. 1. Lang.: Hun.
Hungary: Budapest. 1969-1978. Historical studies. ■The development of the ballet ensemble of Budapest Opera House in the 1970s: program policy, choreography, music, genre and style .

1056 Szász, Anna; Kaán, Zsuzsa, photo. "'Ma már tudom, hogy öt perccel előbb hagytam abba!'—Beszélgetés Nagy Ivánnal, a chilei Santiago de Ballet igazgatójával." ('Today I Already Know That I Finished It Five Minutes Too Early'—Interview with Iván Nagy, the Director of the Ballet de Santiago in Chile.) *Tanc*. 1997; 28 (5/6): 12-13. Illus.: Photo. B&W. 5. Lang.: Hun.
Hungary. Chile: Santiago. 1943-1997. Histories-sources. ■A conversation with the globe-trotting Hungarian dancer, choreographer, director Iván Nagy on his international career.

1057 Alovert, N. *Balet Mariinskogo teatra: včera, segodnja, XXI vek...: Al'bom*. (Ballet of the Mariinskij Theatre: Yesterday, Today, and in the Twentieth Century.) St. Petersburg: 1997. 40 pp. Illus.: Photo. Lang.: Rus.
Russia: St. Petersburg. 1800-1997. Histories-specific. ■Illustrated portrait of the Mariinskij Ballet, formerly known as the Kirov.

1058 Häger, Bengt. "Kirov i London." (Kirov In London.) *Danst*. 1997; 7(5): 16-18. Illus.: Photo. Color. Lang.: Swe.
Russia: St. Petersburg. UK-England: London. 1995. Historical studies. ■A report from the ballet company's guest performances in London and their future policy with reference to their new director Machar Vaziev.

1059 Jacobson, Daniel. "Royal Gypsies." *BR*. 1997 Fall; 25(3): 34-46. Illus.: Photo. B&W. 6. Lang.: Eng.
UK-England: London. 1997. Critical studies. ■The touring repertoire of the Royal Ballet, while the Royal Opera House undergoes renovations.

1060 Kaán, Zsuzsa. "Szakmai kapcsolatok Budapest és Elmhurst között." (Professional Links Between Elmhurst and Budapest.) *Tanc*. 1997; 28(5/6): 50-51. Lang.: Hun.
UK-England. Hungary. 1996-1997. Histories-sources. ■Connections between the English Elmhurst Ballet School and the Hungarian Dance Academy in Budapest, beginning autumn 1996 with scholarships and visits from both sides.

1061 Parish, Paul. "San Francisco." *BR*. 1997 Sum; 25(2): 15-18. Lang.: Eng.
USA: San Francisco, CA. 1997. Critical studies. ■Critical assessment of some of the leading dancers and the dances offered by the San Francisco Ballet.

1062 Tallchief, Maria. "The Beginning of the New York City Ballet." *BR*. 1997 Spr; 25(1): 45-59. Lang.: Eng.
USA: New York, NY. 1946. Histories-sources. ■Excerpt from Maria Tallchief's autobiography *Maria Tallchief: America's Prima Ballerina* on the origins of the New York City Ballet with a George Ballanchine/Igor Stravinskij collaboration on the ballet *Orpheus*.

Performance/production

1063 Simonsen, Majbrit. "Mere hael end tå." (More Heel than Toe.) *TE*. 1997 Mar.; 83: 26-29. Illus.: Photo. B&W. 3. Lang.: Dan.
Denmark. 1994-1996. Critical studies. ■Critique of Royal Danish Ballet's performances during Copenhagen's year as Cultural City (1996), when Peter Schaufuss was director.

1064 Arkin, Lisa C.; Smith, Marian. "National Dance in the Romantic Ballet." 11-68 in Garafola, Lynn, ed. *Rethinking the Sylph: New Perspectives on the Romantic Ballet*. Hanover, NH/London: UP of New England/Wesleyan UP; 1997. 287 pp. Index. Notes. Biblio. Illus.: Photo. Dwg. 20. Lang.: Eng.
Europe. 1830-1850. Historical studies. ■The influence of folk-derived forms on the stage and dance floor.

1065 Ojala, Raija. "A Long Dance on the Thin Line between the Body and the Mind." *Tanssi*. 1997; 18(3): 24-26. Illus.: Photo. B&W. 4. Lang.: Eng.
Finland: Helsinki. 1980-1997. Historical studies. ■History of the dance group Zodiak Presents.

1066 Räsänen, Auli. "Haavoittuvuus, mystisyys, eroottisuus, linnun hahmoa tulkitaan modernin androgyynisyyden kautta." (Vulnerability, Mysticism, Eroticism. The Bird Interpreted through Modern Androgyny.) *Tanssi*. 1997; 18(2): 14-17. Illus.: Photo. B&W. 6. Lang.: Fin.
Finland: Helsinki. 1997. Historical studies. ■Various possibilities for stage interpretations of the ballet *Lebedinoje osero (Swan Lake)* by Čajkovskij.

1067 Alderson, Evan. "Ballet as Ideology: *Giselle*, Act 2." 121-132 in Desmond, Jane C., ed. *Meaning in Motion: New Cultural Studies of Dance*. Durham, NC/London: Duke UP; 1997. 398 pp. (Post-Contemporary Interventions.) Index. Notes. Lang.: Eng.
France. 1800-1900. Critical studies. ■Gender construction and the aesthetic gaze of desire in classical ballet, especially the Romantic period. Focuses on *Giselle* and its reception and history to analyze dominant notions of what is 'beautiful'.

1068 Banes, Sally; Carroll, Noël. "Marriage and the Inhuman: *La Sylphide*'s Narratives of Domesticity and Community." 91-106 in Garafola, Lynn, ed. *Rethinking the Sylph: New Perspectives on the Romantic Ballet*. Hanover, NH/London: UP of New England/Wesleyan UP; 1997. 287 pp. Index. Notes. Biblio. Illus.: Sketches. Dwg. 11. Lang.: Eng.
France. 1830-1835. Critical studies. ■Cultural examination of the cult of domesticity, women's place in the community, and the role of marriage in society as reflected in Filippo Taglioni's *La Sylphide* (music by Jean-Madeleine Schneitzhoeffer, libretto by Adolphe Nourrit).

1069 Batson, Charles Richard. *Words Into Flesh: Parisian Dance Theater, 1911-1924*. Urbana-Champaign, IL: Univ. of Illinois; 1997. 256 pp. Notes. Biblio. [Ph.D. Dissertation, Univ. Microfilms Order No. AAC 9812527.] Lang.: Eng.

DANCE: Ballet—Performance/production

France. 1911-1924. Historical studies. ▪Artistic collaboration in Paris, focusing on the role of the body and gender in performance and the work of writers, painters, choreographers, and musicians, including Serge de Diaghilev's Ballets Russes, Ida Rubinstein, Jean Cocteau, Blaise Cendrars, Vaclav Nižinskij and Jean Borlin, and the Ballets Suédois.

1070 Bruner, Jody. "Redeeming *Giselle*: Making a Case for the Ballet We Love to Hate." 107-120 in Garafola, Lynn, ed. *Rethinking the Sylph: New Perspectives on the Romantic Ballet*. Hanover, NH/London: UP of New England/Wesleyan UP; 1997. 287 pp. Index. Notes. Biblio. Illus.: Photo. 7. Lang.: Eng.

France. 1830-1835. Critical studies. ▪The victimization of women in the ballet *Giselle* (ballet conceived by Théophile Gautier, choreography by Jean Coralli and Jules Perrot, music by Adolphe Charles Adam). Uses the theoretical work of Julia Kristeva to make sense of the work in light of its modern contradictions and conflicts for audiences.

1071 Chazin-Bennahum, Judith. "Women of Faint Heart and Steel Toes." 121-130 in Garafola, Lynn, ed. *Rethinking the Sylph: New Perspectives on the Romantic Ballet*. Hanover, NH/London: UP of New England/Wesleyan UP; 1997. 287 pp. Index. Notes. Biblio. Illus.: Photo. Sketches. Dwg. 19. Lang.: Eng.

France. 1830-1850. Historical studies. ▪The effect of changes in costume and clothing on ballet technique. Charts the fashion changes for both men and women and links these changes to the ballet through visual documentation. Also examines how the visual image affected ballet, as seen in the increased manufacture of lithographs.

1072 Hézső, István. "Balettestek Párizsban." (Ballet Evenings in Paris.) *Tanc*. 1997; 28(1/2): 46-47. Illus.: Photo. B&W. 1. Lang.: Hun.

France: Paris. 1996. Reviews of performances. ▪Notes on two performances of the ballet company of the Opéra de Paris: a Balanchine-Stravinskij evening and Čajkovskij's *The Nutcracker* produced in December, 1996.

1073 Hézső, István; Moatti, Jacques, photo. "John Neumeier *Sylviá*-ja a Garnier Palotában." (John Neumeier's *Sylvia* at the Palais Garnier.) *Tanc*. 1997; 28(4): 32-33. Illus.: Photo. B&W. 2. Lang.: Hun.

France: Paris. 1997. Critical studies. ▪A critical analysis of Neumeier's choreography to music of Delibes with a short account of significant productions by noted choreographers from the première of the classic ballet in 1876 at the Garnier Opera.

1074 Kaplan, Larry. "Les Étoiles." *BR*. 1997 Win; 25(4): 12-19. Illus.: Photo. B&W. 6. Lang.: Eng.

France: Paris. 1983-1997. Critical studies. ▪Principal dancers and soloists of the Paris Opera Ballet, some of whom came of age under the tutelage of former artistic director Rudolf Nureyev: Elisabeth Platel, Isabelle Guerin, Laurent Hilaire, Manuel Legris, Stéphane Phavorin, and Marie-Agnès Gillot.

1075 Kútszegi, Csaba; Slobodian, Michael, photo. "Kicsoda ön Myriam Naisy?" (Who Are You, Myriam Naisy?) *Tanc*. 1997; 28(1/2): 28. Illus.: Photo. B&W. 1. Lang.: Hun.

France. 1997. Histories-sources. ▪A conversation with the French choreographer on the occasion of a training course and her guest performance as a choreographer in Budapest.

1076 Meglin, Joellen A. "Feminism or Fetishism: *La Révolte des femmes* and Women's Liberation in France in the 1830s." 69-90 in Garafola, Lynn, ed. *Rethinking the Sylph: New Perspectives on the Romantic Ballet*. Hanover, NH/London: UP of New England/Wesleyan UP; 1997. 287 pp. Index. Notes. Biblio. Illus.: Sketches. Dwg. 4. Lang.: Eng.

France. 1830-1840. Critical studies. ▪Feminist elements in the Romantic ballet *La Révolte des femmes (The Revolt of the Women)*, choreographed by Filippo Taglioni for his daughter, Marie. Analysis of critiques of the ballet with respect to the situation of women in France of the period.

1077 Gilpin, Heidi. "Shaping Critical Spaces: Issues in the Dramaturgy of Movement Performance." 83-87 in Jonas, Susan, ed.; Proehl, Geoffrey S., ed. *Dramaturgy in American Theatre: A Sourcebook*. New York, NY: Harcourt Brace College Pub; 1997. 590 pp. Pref. Notes. Biblio. Index. Lang.: Eng.

Germany: Frankfurt. 1993-1997. Histories-sources. ▪Author's dramaturgical work with Frankfurt Ballet and the sensibility she perceives as common to all her work.

1078 Árva, Eszter; Papp, Dezső, photo. "Imre Zoltán (1943-1997)." (Zoltán Imre 1943-1997.) *Tanc*. 1997; 28(4) : 12. Illus.: Photo. B&W. 1. Lang.: Hun.

Hungary. 1943-1997. Biographical studies. ▪A portrait-sketch of the dancer-choreographer, deceased recently, who had gained success all over the world as member of famous ballet companies from 1969. After returning home in 1986 he worked with the reorganized Szeged Ballet as a choreographer and between 1990 and 1993 as a director.

1079 Gelencsér, Ágnes. "Dokumentumok, emlékek a '*Giselle*' 1996. évi felújításához." (Documents and Memories of the Revival of Adolphe Adam's *Giselle* in 1996.) 8-13 in Kővágó, Zsuzsa, ed. *Tánctudományi Tanulmányok 1996/1997*. Budapest: Magyar Tánctudományi Társaság; 1997. 173 pp. Lang.: Hun.

Hungary: Budapest. 1841-1996. Historical studies. ▪A brief survey of the career of Adam's classic ballet on the Hungarian stage, including two documents related to the 150th anniversary of *Giselle* in Hungary.

1080 Gelencsér, Ágnes. "A Pécsi Balett a Tavaszi Fesztiválon." (The Pécs Ballet at the Spring festival.) *ZZT*. 1997; 4(4): 26-27. Lang.: Hun.

Hungary: Pécs. 1997. Reviews of performances. ▪Analysis of Béla Bartók's *Blubeard's Castle (A kékszakállú herceg vára)* adapted for the ballet stage and his dance drama, *The Miraculous Mandarin (A csodálatos mandarin)* performed by the Pécs Ballet at Budapest's Spring Festival (Choreogapher: István Herczog).

1081 Gelencsér, Ágnes; Körtvélyes, Géza; Kanyó, Béla, photo. "'Táncot kívánnék látni...'—Balettest Pongor Ildikó tiszteletére az Erkel Színházban." ('It Is Dance I Would Like to See'—A Ballet Evening in Ildikó Pongor's Honor at the Erkel Theatre.) *Tanc*. 1997; 28(3): 18-19. Illus.: Photo. B&W. 2. Lang.: Hun.

Hungary. 1997. Critical studies. ▪Notes on a dance performance of leading foreign choreographers' works at a jubilee concert for the 25th anniversary of Ildikó Pongor's dance career with Budapest Opera House.

1082 Gelencsér, Ágnes; Papp, Dezső, photo. "Pongor Ildikó jutalomjátéka. Pártay-Csajkovszkij: *Anna Karenina*." (Ildikó Pongor's Testimonial Performance. Lilla Pártay-Čajkovskij: *Anna Karenina*.) *Tanc*. 1997; 28(3): 28-29. Illus.: Photo. B&W. 2. Lang.: Hun.

Hungary: Budapest. 1997. Critical studies. ▪Tolstoj's novel adapted for the ballet stage by choreographer Lilla Pártay with Čajkovskij's music and performed by Ildikó Pongor with the Hungarian Opera House's ballet ensemble.

1083 Gelencsér, Ágnes; Kanyó, Béla, photo. "Don Quijote—magyar változatban." (*Don Quijote* by Petipa-Minkus—Hungarian Version.) *Tanc*. 1997; 28(5/6): 16-18. Illus.: Photo. B&W. 6. Lang.: Hun.

Hungary: Budapest. 1997. Historical studies. ▪Analysis of the first night of the classic ballet at Budapest Opera House.

1084 Gelencsér, Ágnes; Kanyó, Béla, photo.; Papp, Dezső, photo. "Balanchine-est az Operaházban." (Balanchine-Première at the Opera.) *Tanc*. 1997; 28(5/6): 19-21. Illus.: Photo. B&W. 6. Lang.: Hun.

Hungary: Budapest. 1997. Critical studies. ▪An essay on the ballet evening of the famous choreographer George Balanchine's work performed by the Hungarian National Ballet.

1085 Kaán, Zsuzsa; Kanyó, Béla, photo. "Fülöp Viktor (1929-1997)." (Viktor Fülöp, 1929-1997.) *Tanc*. 1997; 28(4): 13. Illus.: Photo. B&W. 1. Lang.: Hun.

Hungary. 1929-1997. Biographical studies. ▪Commemoration of the late soloist of the Hungarian State Opera's ballet company.

1086 Kaán, Zsuzsa. "Az ifjúság édes madarai—A Magyar Fesztivál Balett második bemutatója." (The Sweet Birds of Youth—A New Programme by the Hungarian Festival Ballet.) *Tanc*. 1997; 28(3): 16-17. Illus.: Photo. B&W. 2. Lang.: Hun.

DANCE: Ballet—Performance/production

Hungary: Budapest. 1997. Historical studies. ■Production of Magyar Fesztivál Balett of Iván Markó's *A Magányos zongoro (The Solitary Piano)* and *A Dzsungel (The Jungle)*.

1087 Körtvélyes, Géza. "A Pécsi Balett 1970-1977." (The Pécs Ballet, 1970-1977.) *ZZT.* 1997; 4(6): 34-38. Lang.: Hun.
Hungary: Pécs. 1977-1978. Historical studies. ■Choreographer Imre Eck's adaptations of works by Hungarian composers for the ballet stage. The guest choreographers of the period are also mentioned in the article.

1088 Körtvélyes, Géza; Kanyó, Béla, photo. "A Pécsi Balett Bartók-estje." (A Bartók Evening with the Pécs Ballet.) *Tanc.* 1997; 28(1/2): 34-35. Illus.: Photo. B&W. 3. Lang.: Hun.
Hungary: Pécs. 1992-1997. Reviews of performances. ■A production of Béla Bartók's stage works, *A kékszakállú herceg vára (Bluebeard's Castle)* and *A csodálatos mandarin (The Miraculous Mandarin)*, adapted for ballet from works of Béla Bartók, presented by Pécs Ballet with choreography by István Herczog.

1089 Kővágó, Zsuzsa. "Milloss Aurél szólóestjei és a *Magyar Csupajáték*." (Aurél Milloss' Solo Nights and the *Hungarian All-Play*.) 55-62 in Kővágó, Zsuzsa, ed. *Tánctudományi Tanulmányok 1996/1997.* Budapest: Magyar Tánctudományi Társaság; 1997. 173 pp. Append. Notes. Lang.: Hun.
Hungary. 1906-1942. Critical studies. ■Less known activities of Aurél Milloss as a teacher, choreographer and performer, with emphasis on the transition between Milloss' early artistic activities and his creations staged in the 'Roman period'.

1090 Kővágó, Zsuzsa. "Fülöp Viktor emlékére (1929-1997)." (In Memoriam Viktor Fülöp, 1929-1997.) *ZZT.* 1997; 4(6): 5. Illus.: Photo. B&W. 1. Lang.: Hun.
Hungary. 1929-1997. Biographical studies. ■Commemorating the great dancer of the ballet ensemble of Budapest Opera House, recently deceased.

1091 Kútszegi, Csaba. "Mendelssohn-Seregi: *Szentivánéji álom* (Egy balettpremier Kelet-Európa történelmi pillanatában)." (F.B. Mendelssohn-László Seregi: *A Midsummer Night's Dream*—A Ballet Premiere in a Historic Moment of East Europe.) 29-38 in Kővágó, Zsuzsa, ed. *Tánctudományi Tanulmányok 1996/1997.* Budapest: Magyar Tánctudományi Társaság; 1997. 173 pp. Notes. Lang.: Hun.
Hungary: Budapest. 1864-1989. Critical studies. ■Historical background and reception of Seregi's choreography for Mendelssohn's music.

1092 Mátai, Györgyi; Mezey, Béla, photo.; Kanyó, Béla, photo. "'Művészi alázat nélkül a lélek nem mozdul meg a színpadon'—Beszélgetés Erényi Bélával." ('Without Artistic Humility the Soul Does Not Move on the Stage'—An Interview with Béla Erényi.) *Tanc.* 1997; 28(1/2): 12-13. Illus.: Photo. B&W. 6. Lang.: Hun.
Hungary: Budapest. 1974-1997. Histories-sources. ■Interview with dancer Béla Erényi summarizing his career.

1093 Mátai, Györgyi; Kanyó, Béla, photo. "Két világ—A Győri Balett vendégjátéka." (Two Worlds—The Guest Performance of Győr Ballet.) *Tanc.* 1997; 28(1/2): 36-37. Illus.: Photo. B&W. 6. Lang.: Hun.
Hungary. 1997. Critical studies. ■Notes on the guest performance of the Győri Balett at the Hungarian Dance Panorama '97.

1094 Pór, Anna; Kanyó, Béla, photo. "Újító szellemmel vissza a forráshoz. Robert North *Carmen*-je Győrött." (Back to the Origins in the Spirit of Reformation—*Carmen* by Robert North in Győr.) *Tanc.* 1997; 28(5/6): 24-25. Illus.: Photo. B&W. 5. Lang.: Hun.
Hungary: Győr. 1997. Reviews of performances. ■Győr Ballet's performance of Robert North's choreography, set to music of Christopher Benstead and based on the original story of *Carmen* by Prosper Mérimée.

1095 Cavalletti, Lavinia. "Salvatore Taglioni, King of Naples." 181-196 in Garafola, Lynn, ed. *Rethinking the Sylph: New Perspectives on the Romantic Ballet.* Hanover, NH/London: UP of New England/Wesleyan UP; 1997. 287 pp. Index. Notes. Biblio. Illus.: Dwg. 2. Lang.: Eng.

Italy: Naples. 1830-1860. Historical studies. ■The work of Salvatore Taglioni, dancer, choreographer, and composer for the ballet: his involvement with the Teatro San Carlo, the many works he produced, and the non-Romantic elements in his ballets.

1096 Celi, Claudia. "The Arrival of the Great Wonder of Ballet, or Ballet in Rome from 1845 to 1855." 165-180 in Garafola, Lynn, ed. *Rethinking the Sylph: New Perspectives on the Romantic Ballet.* Hanover, NH/London: UP of New England/Wesleyan UP; 1997. 287 pp. Index. Notes. Biblio. Illus.: Sketches. Dwg. 8. Lang.: Eng.
Italy: Rome. 1845-1855. Historical studies. ■The effect of foreign dancers on Italian dancers and Italian ballet.

1097 Poesio, Giannandrea. "Blasis, the Italian *Ballo*, and the Male Sylph." 131-142 in Garafola, Lynn, ed. *Rethinking the Sylph: New Perspectives on the Romantic Ballet.* Hanover, NH/London: UP of New England/Wesleyan UP; 1997. 287 pp. Index. Notes. Biblio. Illus.: Photo. Dwg. 4. Lang.: Eng.
Italy. 1830-1850. Historical studies. ■Stylistic canons of nineteenth-century Italian ballet, the tradition of male dancers and the most important figure of dance in Italy at the time, Carlo Blasis, who codified dance vocabulary.

1098 Pudelek, Janina. "Ballet Dancers at Warsaw's Wielki Theater." 143-164 in Garafola, Lynn, ed. *Rethinking the Sylph: New Perspectives on the Romantic Ballet.* Hanover, NH/London: UP of New England/Wesleyan UP; 1997. 287 pp. Index. Notes. Biblio. Illus.: Sketches. Dwg. 6. Lang.: Eng.
Poland: Warsaw. 1830-1850. Historical studies. ■The Wielki (Grand) Theatre's ballet school. Examines the dancers that came from the school and their influence on Polish ballet.

1099 Calobanova, V. "Baletnaja imperija Borisa Ejfmana." (The Ballet Empire of Boris Ejfman.) *TeatZ.* 1997; 5-6: 63-65. Lang.: Rus.
Russia: St. Petersburg. 1997. Historical studies. ■Ejfman's ballet *Krasnaja Žizel' (Red Giselle)*, about the tragic fate of ballerina O. Spesivceva.

1100 Daniels, Don. "V-Day." *BR.* 1997 Win; 25(4): 42-48. Illus.: Photo. B&W. 6. Lang.: Eng.
Russia: Moscow. 1997. Biographical studies. ■Profile of Kirov Ballet dancer Diana Višnjeva.

1101 Gershenzon, Pavel; Scholl, Tim, transl. "Gabriela Komleva: *Symphony in C* in Leningrad." *BR.* 1997 Fall; 25(3): 18-21. Illus.: Photo. B&W. 1. Lang.: Eng.
Russia: St. Petersburg. 1997. Histories-sources. ■Interview with ballerina and choreographer Komleva regarding Bizet's ballet *Symphony in C* using Balanchine's choreography. Originally appeared in *Marinskij teatr.*

1102 Gershenzon, Pavel; Scholl, Tim, transl. "Sergei Vikharev: Rehearsing *Symphony in C*." *BR.* 1997 Fall; 25(3): 22-27. Illus.: Photo. B&W. 4. Lang.: Eng.
Russia: St. Petersburg. 1997. Histories-sources. ■Interview with dancer Sergej Vicharév regarding George Balanchine's choreography for Bizet's *Symphony in C* for the Maryinsky Ballet. Originally appeared in *Marinskij teatr.*

1103 Gershenzon, Pavel; Scholl, Tim, transl.; Klyagin, Irina, transl. "*Symphony in C*: An Obscure Object of Desire." *BR.* 1997 Fall; 25(3): 28-33. Lang.: Eng.
Russia. 1997. Critical studies. ■The cult status of George Balanchine's staging of Bizet's *Symphony in C* among Russia's ballet aficionados.

1104 Gladkova, O. "'Vo vsech teatrach, krome Marijinskogo, pora zapretit' Petipa'." (In All Theatres but the Mariinskij, It Is Time to Prohibit Petipa.) *Skripičnyj ključ.* 1997; 1: 13. Lang.: Rus.
Russia. 1990-1997. Histories-sources. ■Interview with N. Zozulina about the current status of choreography in Russian state theatres.

1105 Gladkova, O. "'Protivno rabotat' dlja sytych i ravnodušnych'." (It's Unpleasant to Work for the Well Fed and People Who Just Don't Care.) *Skripičnyj ključ.* 1997; 1: 15-16. Lang.: Rus.
Russia: St. Petersburg. 1990-1997. Histories-sources. ■Interview with N. Bojarčikov, chief ballet instructor of the Mussorgskij Theatre, about the

DANCE: Ballet—Performance/production

situation of his dancers, his work outside Russia, and contemporary ballet culture.

1106 Karp, P. *Mladšaja muza.* (The Youngest Muse.) Moscow: Sovremennik; 1997. 236 pp. Lang.: Rus.
Russia. ■The art of the ballet.

1107 Kolesova, Natasja; Sidorow, Sonja, transl. "En helt egen Svansjö." (A Quite Odd Swan Lake.) *Danst.* 1997; 7(1): 18-19. Illus.: Photo. B&W. Lang.: Swe.
Russia: Moscow. 1996. Critical studies. ■Vladimir Vasiljėv's new version of *Lebedinoje osero (Swan Lake)* at the Bolšoj Teat'r.

1108 Neubauer, Henrik. *Razvoj baletne umetnosti v Sloveniji. I.* (The Development of the Art of Ballet in Slovenia, I.) Ljubljana: Forma 7; 1997. 292 pp. Pref. Biblio. Index. Illus.: Photo. B&W. Lang.: Slo.
Slovenia. 1635-1944. Histories-specific. ■The history of ballet in Slovenia, which was almost entirely performed by traveling German and Italian troupes. Reference to the ballet *Možiček (Jumping Jack)* by Josip Ipavec (1912).

1109 Ångström, Anna. "Han vågar vidga rummet." (He Dares To Enlarge the Room.) *Danst.* 1997; 7(5): 3-5. Illus.: Photo. B&W. Lang.: Swe.
Sweden: Stockholm. 1978. Biographical studies. ■The dancer Anders Nordström speaks about his career and his attitude towards dance—rather be creative than just best.

1110 Hellström Sveningson, Lis. "Michiyo Hayashi—poetisk månren." (Michiyo Hayashi—a Poetic Moondeer.) *Danst.* 1997; 7(2): 12-13. Illus.: Photo. Color. Lang.: Swe.
Sweden: Gothenburg. 1997. Histories-sources. ■An interview with the dancer Michiyo Hayashi about her Japanese background and her career at GöteborgsOperan, with reference to *Månrenen* by Birgit Cullberg.

1111 Olsson, Irène. "Levande dans från alla tider." (Living Dance From All Times.) *Danst.* 1997; 7(4): 22-23. Illus.: Photo. B&W. Lang.: Swe.
Sweden: Stockholm. 1950. Histories-sources. ■An interview with the former dancer and now rehearser Gunilla Roempke, about her stagings of ballets by Birgit Cullberg.

1112 Rosen, Astrid von. "Elsa Marianne von Rosen—ett barnbarnsbarn till Bournonville." (Elsa Marianne von Rosen—A Great-Grandchild of Bournonville.) *Danst.* 1997; 7(6): 6-7. Illus.: Photo. B&W. Lang.: Swe.
Sweden. Denmark. 1936. Biographical studies. ■A presentation of Elsa Marianne von Rosen, her career as dancer and choreographer, with reference to her stagings of the ballets by August Bournonville.

1113 Sörensen, Margareta. "Carina Ari." *Danst.* 1997; 7(5): 6-9. Illus.: Photo. B&W. Lang.: Swe.
Sweden. France. 1918-1970. Histories-sources. ■An interview with Bengt Häger about the career of Carina Ari, both as dancer and choreographer.

1114 Sörenson, Margareta. "En man med karaktärsdans." (A Man With Character Dance.) *Danst.* 1997; 7(3): 3-5. Illus.: Photo. Color. Lang.: Swe.
Sweden: Stockholm. 1940. Histories-sources. ■An interview with the teacher of character dance at Svenska Balettskolan i Stockholm (The Swedish Ballet School at Stockholm), Pierre de Olivo, about his early career as an artist and the importance of training in real character dance.

1115 Ståhle, Anna-Greta. "Lulli Svedins många år inom dansen." (Lulli Svedin's Many Years Of Dance.) *Danst.* 1997 ; 7(2): 15. Illus.: Photo. B&W. Lang.: Swe.
Sweden: Stockholm. 1920. Biographical studies. ■A survey of the career of Lulli Svedin as a modern dancer and teacher of ballet for the last forty years.

1116 Christiansen, Rupert. "Kenneth MacMillan and the Roughing-up of Ballet." *DTJ.* 1997; 13(3): 10-13. Illus.: Photo. B&W. 1. Lang.: Eng.
UK-England: London. 1955-1992. Biographical studies. ■Reassessment of the work of the late choreographer during his tenure at the Royal Ballet.

1117 Croce, Arlene. "The Loves of His Life." *NewY.* 1997 19 May: 78-87. Illus.: Photo. B&W. 2. Lang.: Eng.

UK-England. 1904-1988. Biographical studies. ■Profile of choreographer Frederick Ashton and his career with the Royal Ballet.

1118 Pjaseckaja, A. "Kogda vstrečajutsja zvezdy." (When the Stars Meet.) *EchoP.* 1997; 50: 29-30. Lang.: Rus.
UK-England. 1962-1997. Biographical studies. ■The life and artistic partnership of Rudolf Nureyev and Margot Fonteyn at the Royal Ballet.

1119 Wolf, Matt. "Matthew Bourne." *AmTh.* 1997 May/June; 14(5): 33-34. Illus.: Photo. B&W. 2. Lang.: Eng.
UK-England: London. 1997. Biographical studies. ■Profile of choreographer Bourne and his production of *Swan Lake (Lebedinoje osero)* at Sadlers Wells Theatre and in London's West End which included an all-male corps de ballet and has a gay perspective.

1120 "Ashton's Legacy." *BR.* 1997 Sum; 25(2): 20-31. Illus.: Photo. B&W. 1. Lang.: Eng.
USA: New York, NY. 1992. Histories-sources. ■Interview with choreographer Michael Somes regarding his staging of Frederick Ashton's *Symphonic Variations* for ABT. Interjections by his assistants Wendy Ellis and Judy Thomas during the interview are included.

1121 Bird, Dorothy; Greenberg, Joyce, ed. "Bird's Eye View—2." *BR.* 1997 Sum; 25(2): 71-86. Lang.: Eng.
USA: New York, NY. 1930-1937. Critical studies. ■Excerpt from the author's *Bird's Eye View* in which the dancer recounts her relationship and break with Martha Graham.

1122 Csillag, Pál. "A zene és a tánc kapcsolatának vizsgálata Franz Schubert-Robert North: *A Halál és a Leányka* c. táncművében." (Links Between Music and Choreography in Robert North's *Death and the Maiden.*) 14-28 in Kővágó, Zsuzsa, ed. *Tánctudományi Tanulmányok 1996/1997.* Budapest: Magyar Tánctudományi Társaság; 1997. 173 pp. Append. Biblio. Lang.: Hun.
USA. 1945-1992. Critical studies. ■Analysis of North's choreography for Schubert's *Death and the Maiden.*

1123 Daniels, Don. "Stiefel at ABT." *BR.* 1997 Sum; 25(2): 67-70. Illus.: Photo. B&W. 3. Lang.: Eng.
USA: New York, NY. 1997. Critical studies. ■Assesses the initial performances of new American Ballet Theatre dancer Ethan Stiefel.

1124 Fay, Anthony. "Leon Danielian (1920-1997)." *BR.* 1997 Fall; 25(3): 79-83. Illus.: Photo. B&W. 5. Lang.: Eng.
USA. 1920-1997. Biographical studies. ■Obituary for classical ballet dancer Danielian.

1125 Goldschmidt, Hubert. "Patricia Ruanne on Nureyev." *BR.* 1997 Sum; 25(2): 87-95. Lang.: Eng.
USA. 1997. Histories-sources. ■Interview with dancer Ruanne concerning her experiences working with Rudolf Nureyev.

1126 Gorman, Paul. "*Agon* and Its Music." *BR.* 1997 Fall; 25(3): 47-51. Lang.: Eng.
USA. 1959. Critical studies. ■Examines the rhythms and melodies of Stravinskij's ballet *Agon.*

1127 Kaán, Zsuzsa. "Nicolas Petrov-'Viletta Verdy önként jött a társulathoz'." (Nicolas Petrov-'Violetta Verdi Joined My Company Voluntarily!'.) *Tanc.* 1997; 28(1/2): 49-52. Illus.: Photo. B&W. 12. Lang.: Hun.
USA. 1996. Histories-sources. ■A portrait of the dancer, choreographer, director and pedagogue Nicolas Petrov.

1128 Kokich, Kim Alexandra. "A Conversation with Maria Tallchief." *BR.* 1997 Spr; 25(1): 22-44. Illus.: Photo. B&W. 21. Lang.: Eng.
USA: Washington, DC. 1997. Histories-sources. ■Interview with ballerina Tallchief regarding her life and work in ballet. Included is a gallery of photographs at various stages of her career.

1129 Tchernichova, Elena; Lobenthal, Joel. "*Giselle.*" *BR.* 1997 Win; 25(4): 23-34. Illus.: Photo. B&W. 5. Lang.: Eng.
USA. 1950-1997. Histories-sources. ■Choreographer Tchernichova reminisces about various productions of the ballet *Giselle* by Adolphe Adam with which she has been involved.

1130 Witchel, Leigh. "Four Decades of *Agon.*" *BR.* 1997 Fall; 25(3): 52-78. Illus.: Photo. B&W. 20. Lang.: Eng.

DANCE: Ballet—Performance/production

USA. 1959-1997. Historical studies. ■A look at the performance history of Balanchine's and Stravinskij's ballet *Agon*, including stage and film treatments.

Relation to other fields

1131 Servos, Norbert. "Die Faszination der Ballets Russes." (The Fascination of the Ballets Russes.) *Tanzd.* 1997; 37(2): 24-25. Illus.: Photo. B&W. 1. Lang.: Ger.
Europe. 1909-1929. Historical studies. ■Discusses the exhibition and catalog 'Die Ballets Russes und die Künste' ('The Ballets Russes and the Arts') shown and published in Berlin in 1997.

Theory/criticism

1132 Daly, Ann. "Classical Ballet: A Discourse of Difference." 111-120 in Desmond, Jane C., ed. *Meaning in Motion: New Cultural Studies of Dance.* Durham, NC/London: Duke UP; 1997. 398 pp. (Post-Contemporary Interventions.) Index. Notes. Illus. 1. Lang.: Eng.
Europe. 1700-1990. Critical studies. ■Gender difference as an aesthetic virtue in classical ballet history. Examines how this bipolarity has produced the pleasure found in ballet.

1133 Schneider, Katja. "Schlank, biegsam, grazil..." (Slim, Flexible, Willowy...) *Tanzd.* 1997; 36(1): 10-18. Notes. Illus.: Photo. B&W. 3. Lang.: Ger.
Europe. 1909-1997. Historical studies. ■The development of the body image in classical dance, with reference to the Ballets Russes, Georges Balanchine, Maurice Béjart, Hans van Manen and William Forsythe.

1134 Bergner, Gwen; Plett, Nicole. "Uncanny Women and Anxious Masters: Reading *Coppélia* Against Freud." 159-182 in Morris, Gay, ed. *Moving Words: Re-writing Dance.* London/New York, NY: Routledge; 1996. 343 pp. Index. Notes. Biblio. Illus.: Photo. 1. Lang.: Eng.
France. 1870. Critical studies. ■Feminist analysis of *Coppélia*, choreography by Arthur Saint-Léon, scenario by Charles Nuitter and Saint-Léon, score by Léo Delibes.

1135 Chapman, John V. "Jules Janin: Romantic Critic." 197-241 in Garafola, Lynn, ed. *Rethinking the Sylph: New Perspectives on the Romantic Ballet.* Hanover, NH/London: UP of New England/Wesleyan UP; 1997. 287 pp. Index. Notes. Biblio. Illus.: Dwg. Sketches. 13. Lang.: Eng.
France. 1832-1850. Historical studies. ■Analysis of a collection of essays by dance critic Jules Janin, which is included.

Training

1136 Kovács, Judit; Kaán, Zsuzsa, photo. "'Pedagógiát nem lehet tanulni, arra születni kell!' Portré Nagyné Sárközy Viola balettmesterről." ('You Cannot Learn to Become a Pedagogue—You Must Be Born for it'—Portrait of Viola Sárközy, Mrs. Nagy, Ballet Mistress.') *Tanc.* 1997; 28(5/6): 10-11. Illus.: Photo. B&W. 5. Lang.: Hun.
Hungary: Debrecen. 1914-1997. Histories-sources. ■Interview with Viola Nagy-Sárközy, a dance teacher and the mother of dancer and director Iván Nagy.

1137 Szabó Durucz, Zsuzsa. "A főiskolai tanár: Kékesi Mária." (The Academy Teacher: Mária Kékesi.) *ZZT.* 1997; 4(3): 30-31. Illus.: Photo. B&W. 1. Lang.: Hun.
Hungary. 1950-1997. Histories-sources. ■Portrait of the ballet mistress of the Hungarian Dance Academy, a one-time soloist of the ballet ensemble of Hungarian State Opera House.

1138 Szabó Durucz, Zsuzsa. "Forgách József, a Táncművészeti Főiskola balettmestere." (József Forgách, Ballet-Master of the Hungarian Dance Academy.) *ZZT.* 1997; 4(4): 13-14. Illus.: Photo. B&W. 1. Lang.: Hun.
Hungary. 1941-1970. Histories-sources. ■Life and career of the former soloist of the ballet ensemble of Budapest Opera House who made his début recently as a choreographer.

1139 Boal, Peter. "Richard Rapp." *BR.* 1997 Win; 25(4): 49-51. Lang.: Eng.
USA: New York, NY. 1997. Biographical studies. ■Salute to recently retired classical ballet teacher Richard Rapp, who taught at the School of American Ballet.

1140 Wilkins, Darrell A. "Stanley Williams." *BR.* 1997 Fall; 25(3): 4-7. Illus.: Photo. B&W. 1. Lang.: Eng.
USA: New York, NY. 1997. Biographical studies. ■Obituary for one of the most influential teachers of classical ballet, the School of American Ballet's Stanley Williams.

Ethnic dance

Design/technology

1141 Moles, Steve. "Flamenco with Flair." *LDim.* 1997 June; 21(5): 18-19. Illus.: Photo. Color. 1. Lang.: Eng.
Spain: Madrid. 1995-1997. Historical studies. ■Patrick Woodroffe and VariLite programmer Belloqui's lighting design for flamenco dancer Joaquim Cortes and his troupe's *Gypsy Passion (Pasión Gitana)*.

Institutions

1142 Timár, Sándor. "A magyar tánc ünnepe Sao-Paulóban." (The Festival of Hungarian Dance in Sao Paulo.) *Tanc.* 1997; 28(5/6): 50. Lang.: Hun.
Brazil: São Paulo. 1997. Historical studies. ■The 6th Hungarian Folk Dance Festival in South America including training courses and workshops.

1143 Körtvélyes, Géza. "Néptáncművészet és mozgalom." (Folk Dance Art and Movement.) *ZZT.* 1997; 4(3): 22-26. Illus.: Photo. B&W. 3. Lang.: Hun.
Hungary. 1964-1970. Historical studies. ■An essay on the Hungarian folk dance ensembles of the sixties in the series of 'Modern tendencies in Hungarian dance art, 1964-1970'.

Performance/production

1144 Kevin, Jonna. "Resa med lätt bagage." (Travel Light.) *Danst.* 1997; 7(2): 3-5, 16-17. Illus.: Photo. B&W. Color. Lang.: Swe.
Cuba: Havana. 1700. Critical studies. ■A short survey of the Afro-Caribbean religious dances for the gods of Los Orishai.

1145 Sandberg, Helen. "En afrikansk panter." (An African Panther.) *Danst.* 1997; 7(3): 12-15. Illus.: Photo. Color. Lang.: Swe.
Guinea. 1957-1997. Histories-sources. ■Interview with choreographer Secouba Camara about his career and work with the traditional dances of Guinea.

1146 Ramsey, Kate. "Vodou, Nationalism, and Performance: The Staging of Folklore in Mid-Twentieth-Century Haiti." 345-378 in Desmond, Jane C., ed. *Meaning in Motion: New Cultural Studies of Dance.* Durham, NC/London: Duke UP; 1997. 398 pp. (Post-Contemporary Interventions.) Index. Notes. Illus. 3. Lang.: Eng.
Haiti. 1940-1960. Critical studies. ■How nations generate history through performance. Uses Haitian folklore performance and its formulations influenced by such political conditions as U.S. intervention, tourism, and the search for a local Haitian national representation in service of self- government. The romanticization of the staging of folklore offers a critical focus for scholarly research.

1147 Allen, Matthew Harp. "Rewriting the Script for South Indian Dance." *TDR.* 1997 Fall; 41(3): 63-100. Notes. Biblio. Illus.: Dwg. B&W. 2. Lang.: Eng.
India. 1904-1996. Historical studies. ■Investigation of Pan-Asian patterns of revival in dance and intellectual influences from outside South Asia. Focus on dancer Rukmini Devi (founder of preeminent dance training institution in the region) and her role in revival, her influence on others, and symbol of god Nataraja and its representation of the dance and nationalist movement.

1148 Zalán, Magda. "Riverdance—Poszt-népi és neo-etnikus táncegyüttesek Washingtonban—1. rész." (Riverdance—Post-Folkloric and Neo-Ethnic Folkdance in Washington—Part 1.) *Tanc.* 1997; 28(5/6): 48-49. Illus.: Photo. B&W. 1. Lang.: Hun.
Ireland. USA: Washington, DC. 1997. Reviews of performances. ■Michael Flatley's *Riverdance* at Wolf Trap.

DANCE: Ethnic dance—Performance/production

1149 Berggren, Klara. "Bröllopsfest i Bamako." (A Wedding Party At Bamako.) *Danst.* 1997; 7(6): 16-17. Illus.: Photo. Color. Lang.: Swe.
Mali: Bamako. 1997. Historical studies. ■A description of a typical wedding and its dances in a city of Mali.

1150 Kudaev, M.Č. *Drevnije tancy balkarcev i karacaevcev.* (Ancient Dances of the Balkarcevs and Karacaevcevs.) Nalchik: El'brys; 1997. 144 pp. Lang.: Rus.
Russia. Histories-specific. ■The national dance tradition of the Balkarcevs and Karacaevcevs.

1151 Malefyt, Timothy Dwight Dewaal. *Gendered Authenticity: The Invention of Flamenco Tradition In Seville, Spain.* Providence, RI: Brown Univ; 1997. 289 pp. Notes. Biblio. [Ph.D. Dissertation, Univ. Microfilms Order No. AAC 9738592.] Lang.: Eng.
Spain: Seville. 1975-1995. Historical studies. ■Analysis of flamenco performance with respect to cultural construction of Andalusian identity, the invention of tradition, gender, and the resistance to cultural commodification.

1152 Leask, Josephine. "Ecstatic Rituals." *DTJ.* 1997; 13(3). Notes. 38-39. Lang.: Eng.
Syria: Damascus. 1996. Critical studies. ■Profile of the Whirling Dervishes of Damascus. Relates what is necessary to achieve the ecstasy such dancing can bring.

1153 Desmond, Jane C. "Invoking 'The Native': Body Politics in Contemporary Hawaiian Tourist Shows." *TDR.* 1997 Win; 41(4): 83-109. Notes. Biblio. Illus.: Photo. B&W. 9. Lang.: Eng.
USA. 1950-1997. Critical studies. ■Examines the 'hula' dance as an embodied social practice to reveal complex relationships among bodies, social identity, and performative practice, and that these relationships have important implications for theorizations of social categorization. Looks at the performance of hula within and outside of the tourist arena.

1154 Harris, Max. "The Return of Moctezuma: Oaxaca's *Danza de la Pluma* and New Mexico's *Danza de los Matachines.*" *TDR.* 1997 Spr; 41(1): 106-134. Notes. Biblio. Illus.: Photo. B&W. 15. Lang.: Eng.
USA. Mexico: Oaxaca. 1550-1997. Historical studies. ■Illustrates the interplay of public and hidden transcripts by way of study of two traditional dances, the public transcripts generally featuring defeat of Moctezuma and his people, the hidden transcripts reversing that outcome. Folk performances, Native American traditions, ritual representations.

Relation to other fields

1155 Brennan, Mary. "Knowing the Elephant." *DTJ.* 1997; 13(4): 14-17. Illus.: Photo. B&W. 3. Lang.: Eng.
Africa. 1997. Critical studies. ■Discusses the development of dance in Africa, and its relevance in the current surge in popularity of ethnic dance.

1156 Dox, Donnalee. "Thinking Through Veils: Questions of Culture, Criticism and the Body." *ThR.* 1997; 22(2): 150-161. Notes. Illus.: Photo. B&W. 8. Lang.: Eng.
USA. 1851-1993. Historical studies. ■Cultural borrowing in relation to history of belly dancing in USA. Includes analysis of Middle Eastern dance at a Turkish-American wedding in Wisconsin.

1157 Vail, June Adler. "Balkan Tradition, American Alternative: Dance, Community, and the People of the Pines." 306-319 in Morris, Gay, ed. *Moving Words: Re-writing Dance.* London/New York, NY: Routledge; 1996. 343 pp. Index. Notes. Biblio. Illus.: Photo. 1. Lang.: Eng.
USA. 1980-1996. Critical studies. ■Examines how dance created culture for a group of Americans who formed a Balkan dance troupe, Borovčani, in Maine in the 1970s.

Modern dance

Design/technology

1158 Ervasti, Tarja. "Dance with Northern Lights." *Tanssi.* 1997; 18(3): 28-30. Illus.: Photo. B&W. 3. Lang.: Eng.
Finland. 1997. Historical studies. ■The collaboration between modern Finnish choreographers and lighting designers.

1159 Slingerland, Amy L. "Blind Faith." *LDim.* 1997 Mar.; 21(2): 32-39. Illus.: Photo. Color. LP. 8. Lang.: Eng.
USA: New York, NY. 1997. Historical studies. ■Improvisational lighting design concept for dance piece *Spectral Hoedown* at St. Mark's Church Danspace created by David Fritz, Roma Flowers, Carol Mullins, and Philip Sandström. Discusses challenges of dancers following lighting instead of vice versa.

Institutions

1160 "Zodiak, Centre for Contemporary Dance." *FinnishT.* 1997; 51: 19. Illus.: Photo. B&W. Lang.: Eng.
Finland: Helsinki. 1986-1996. Historical studies. ■Profile of Zodiak Presents, which has developed into Zodiak Center for Contemporary Dance.

1161 Bóta, Gábor; Papp, Dezső, photo. "'Nem próbálunk hasonlítani senkihez'—Riportalany a Sámán Táncszínház: Magyar éva és Horváth Csaba." ('We Do Not Try to Resemble Anyone'— Report on the Shaman Theatre: Éva Magyar and Csaba Horváth.) *Tanc.* 1997; 28(3): 14-15. Illus.: Photo. B&W. 2. Lang.: Hun.
Hungary. 1993-1997. Histories-sources. ■Profile of Sámán Színház, the dance group of Éva Magyar and Csaba Horváth, which has recently won awards at dance festivals.

1162 Felletár, Béla. "A Szegedi Kortárs Balett házatájáról." (The Szeged Contemporary Ballet.) *ZZT.* 1997; 4(4): 27-28. Illus.: Photo. B&W. 1. Lang.: Hun.
Hungary: Szeged. 1987-1997. Historical studies. ■A brief history of the ensemble, reorganized by choreographer Zoltán Imre after his return from England in 1987. In 1993 Tamás Juronics became the artistic director of the company.

1163 Kaán, Zsuzsa; Papp, Dezső, photo. "A Tisza, a Themze vagy a Hudson folyó partjáról? Tízéves a Szegedi (Kortárs) Ballet." (From the Bank of River Tisza, Thames or Hudson? The Szeged (Contemporary) Ballet Is 10 Years Old.) *Tanc.* 1997; 28(3): 30-31. Illus.: Photo. B&W. 2. Lang.: Hun.
Hungary: Szeged. 1987-1997. Historical studies. ■The chronicle of the reorganized ballet company of Szeged National Theatre, Szegedi Kortárs Balett, led by choreographer Imre Zoltán until 1993 and Tamás Juronics since 1994.

1164 Gelencsér, Ágnes. "A holland 'modernek'." (The Dutch Centers of Modern Dance.) *ZZT.* 1997; 4(3): 27-28. Lang.: Hun.
Netherlands: Amsterdam, The Hague. 1959-1989. Historical studies. ■Profile of Nederlands Dans Theater, Sonja Gaskell, artistic director, and Het National Ballet, directed by Jiri Kylián.

1165 Kunst, Bojana, ed. *En-knap Dance Company.* Ljubljana: En-knap; 1997. 24 pp. Illus.: Photo. Color. Lang.: Eng.
Slovenia: Ljubljana. 1993-1997. Histories-sources. ■Pictorial history of the Slovene modern dance group.

1166 Johnson, Robert. "New York." *BR.* 1997 Fall; 25(3): 12-17. Lang.: Eng.
USA: New York, NY. 1997. Reviews of performances. ■Critique of Tharp!, Twyla Tharp's new dance group debuting at City Center.

1167 Kaán, Zsuzsa; Schartz, Howard, photo. "Mitől friss a gomba? A 25 éves Pilobulus Együttes újabb művei a New York-i Joyce Theatre-ben—2. rész." (What Makes a Mushroom Fresh? New Pieces by the 25-Year-Old Pilobolus Ensemble at the Joyce Theatre—Part 2.) *Tanc.* 1997; 28(1/2): 43-45. Illus.: Photo. B&W. Color. 4. Lang.: Hun.
USA: New York, NY. 1971-1996. Critical studies. ■Profile of Pilobulus Dance Theatre.

1168 Reiss, Alvin H. "Foundation Support, Board Upgrading Help Top Dance Troupe Achieve Stability." *FundM.* 1997 Jan.; 27(11) : 34-35. Illus.: Photo. B&W. 1. Lang.: Eng.
USA: New York, NY. 1989-1997. Historical studies. ■Fundraising strategies and board of directors changes that enabled the Alvin Ailey American Dance Theatre to find economic and artistic stability after the death of its founder Alvin Ailey.

1169 Sheare, Sybil. "Chicago." *BR.* 1997 Spr; 25(1): 15-17. Lang.: Eng.

CLASSED ENTRIES

DANCE: Modern dance—Institutions

USA: Chicago, IL. 1997. Historical studies. ■Survey of the Fall Festival of Dance in Chicago, focusing on the work of Stephen Petronio as a harbinger of the future of modern dance.

1170 Skånberg, Ami. "Den moderna dansens Mecka." (The Mecca of the Modern Dance.) *Danst.* 1997; 7(5): 22-23. Illus.: Photo. B&W. Lang.: Swe.

USA: Durham, NC. 1997. Historical studies. ■A report from American Dance Festival at Duke University, with reference to Ann Halprin.

1171 Zalán, Magda; Mitchel, Jack, photo.; Greenfield, Lois, photo. "Az életre kelt szójáték—A Paul Taylor Dance Company Washingtonban." (Play on Words Come Alive—The Paul Taylor Dance Company in Washington.) *Tanc.* 1997; 28(3): 34-35. Illus.: Photo. B&W. 2. Lang.: Hun.

USA: New York, NY. 1950-1997. Historical studies. ■Portrait of the American choreographer and his company on the occasion of its guest performance in Washington, April 1997.

1172 Zalán, Magda. "Fekete America titkos kincse—Találkozás Garth Fagan táncaival." (The Secret Treasure of Black America—Meeting Garth Fagan's Dances.) *Tanc.* 1997; 28(4): 28-29. Illus.: Photo. B&W. 3. Lang.: Hun.

USA: Washington, DC. 1997. Historical studies. ■A production by Garth Fagan Dance at the Kennedy Center's 'African Odyssey' series.

Performance/production

1173 Brennan, Mary. "Eurocrash—the Bane of Physical Theatre." *DTJ.* 1997; 13(3): 4-5. Illus.: Photo. B&W. 1. Lang.: Eng.

Belgium. 1989-1997. Historical studies. ■Influence of Belgian choreographer Wim Vandekeybus on the young dancemakers of the Eurocrash movement.

1174 Meisner, Nadine. "Circular Moves." *DTJ.* 1997; 13(4): 10-13. Notes. Illus.: Photo. B&W. 2. Lang.: Eng.

Belgium: Brussels. 1980-1997. Biographical studies. ■Profile of Flemish choreographer Anne Teresa De Keersmaeker.

1175 Massoutre, Guylaine. "La clé des apparences: L'automne 1996 en danse." (The Key to Appearances: Autumn 1996 in Dance.) *JCT.* 1997; 82: 118-129. Notes. Illus.: Photo. B&W. 12. Lang.: Fre.

Canada: Montreal, PQ. 1996. Historical studies. ■Trends in local and touring dance productions seen in Montreal, fall 1996.

1176 Massoutre, Guylaine. "Villes et voyages: L'hiver 1997 en danse." (Cities and Travels: Winter 1997 in Dance.) *JCT.* 1997; 84: 151-160. Notes. Illus.: Photo. B&W. 10. Lang.: Fre.

Canada: Montreal, PQ. 1997. Historical studies. ■Diversity of dance shows presented around Montreal, in the winter of 1997.

1177 Simonsen, Majbrit. "Veteran med pubertetsenergien i behold." (A Veteran with His Youthful Energy Still Intact.) *TE.* 1997 June; 84: 26-29. Illus.: Photo. B&W. 5. Lang.: Dan.

Denmark. 1964-1997. Historical studies. ■*Teater Et* awards choreographer Eske Holm a prize for his many performances. He had his debut in 1964 with *Tropismer*, a dance performance inspired by twelve-tone music.

1178 Daly, Ann. "Isadora Duncan e la 'distinzione' della danza." (Isadora Duncan and the 'Distinction' of Dance.) *TeatroS.* 1997; 12(19): 11-36. Notes. Lang.: Ita.

Europe. 1899-1927. Critical studies. ■Duncan's strategies of distinction by which she intended to raise the level of dance from a simple entertainment to an art.

1179 Manning, Susan. "The Female Dancer and the Male Gaze: Feminist Critiques of Early Modern Dance." 153-166 in Desmond, Jane C., ed. *Meaning in Motion: New Cultural Studies of Dance.* Durham, NC/London: Duke UP; 1997. 398 pp. (Post-Contemporary Interventions.) Index. Notes. Illus.: Photo. 2. Lang.: Eng.

Europe. USA. 1906-1930. Critical studies. ■Analyzes work of Isadora Duncan, Maud Allan, and Ruth St. Denis and argues a new theoretical and representational point of view, a historically-based kinesthetic experience for dance reception.

1180 Tawast, Minna. "From Urban Rage to Abstract Movement—or ... ?" *Tanssi.* 1997; 18(3): 12-13. Illus.: Photo. B&W. 2. Lang.: Eng.

Finland: Helsinki. 1997. Historical studies. ■Career and works of choreographer Kenneth Kvarnström.

1181 Sándor, L. István; Dusa, Gábor, photo. "Nagy József: *Habakuk-kommentárok.*" (Josef Nadj: *The Habakuk Variations.*) *Sz.* 1997; 30(12): 24-27. Illus.: Photo. B&W. 4. Lang.: Hun.

France. Hungary: Budapest. 1997. Historical studies. ■Hungarian-born József Nagy, having become as Josef Nadj a leading personality in modern French dance theatre, gave a guest perfomance of his company in Budapest.

1182 Schaik, Eva van. *Hans van Manen. Leven & Werk.* (Hans van Manen: Life and Work.) Amsterdam: Arena; 1997. 615 pp. Pref. Biblio. Gloss. Index. Append. Illus.: Photo. B&W. 35. Lang.: Dut.

Netherlands. 1932-1997. Biographies. ■The life of choreographer Hans van Manen.

1183 Sörenson, Margareta. "En Ek som växer ut i världen." (An Oak That Is Growing All Over the World.) *Danst.* 1997; 7(4): 3-5. Illus.: Photo. Color. Lang.: Swe.

Netherlands: The Hague. 1997. Historical studies. ■A report from the first performance of Mats Ek's *A Sort of* danced by the Netherlands Dance Theatre.

1184 Andersson, Gerd; Jonsson, Per; Engdahl, Horace; Roos, Cecilia; Sörenson, Margareta; Wrange, Ann-Marie. "Dansens korta minne." (The Short Memory of the Dance.) *Danst.* 1997; 7(1): 6-10. Illus.: Photo. B&W. Lang.: Swe.

Sweden. 1950. Critical studies. ■A discussion about the poor conditions for the creation of new dance works and the impossibility of preserving them for a wider audience.

1185 Harryson, Lotta. "Att ge sig hän åt en obeskrivlig längtan." (To Give Oneself Up To an Indescribable Longing.) *Danst.* 1997; 7(4): 14-17. Illus.: Photo. B&W. Lang.: Swe.

Sweden: Örebro, Stockholm. 1997. Critical studies. ■A presentation of the choreographer Lena Josefsson and her ways of creating dances, with reference to her *Om smekningar (About Caresses)* where dance and texts are combined.

1186 Höglund, Christina. "Ung koreografi i Norden." (Young Choreography of the Nordic Countries.) *Danst.* 1997; 7(4): 12-13. Illus.: Photo. B&W. Color. Lang.: Swe.

Sweden. 1997. ■A report from performances on TV by Jo Strömgren, Jens Österberg with his *Obsessions of a Puzzled Breed*, and Juho Saarinen in his *Dansaren och tystnaden på 100 decibel (The Dancer and the Silence of 100 Decibles).*

1187 Sörensen, Margareta. "Dans med blicken på orden." (Dance With a Look at the Words.) *Danst.* 1997; 7(5): 24-26. Illus.: Photo. B&W. Lang.: Swe.

Sweden: Gothenburg. 1970. Histories-sources. ■An interview with the dancer and choreographer Gunilla Witt about her joint works with dance and words, with reference to her solo *Perforera honom (Perforate Him).*

1188 Sörenson, Margareta. "Anne Külper—koreografi i ett givet sceneri." (Anne Külper—Choreography In a Given Scenery.) *Danst.* 1997; 7(6): 3, 5. Illus.: Photo. B&W. Lang.: Swe.

Sweden: Stockholm. 1968-1997. Histories-sources. ■An interview with Anne Külper about her background and current work with the dance group Tiger, as a chief choreographer.

1189 Bakht, Natasha. "Shobana Jeyasingh and Cultural Issues, Part II: Rewriting the Culture." *DTJ.* 1997; 13(4): 8-9. Notes. Illus.: Photo. B&W. 1. Lang.: Eng.

UK-England. 1997. Histories-sources. ■Bakht, a dancer with Jeyasingh, reveals the company's difficulties in overcoming stereotypes.

1190 Dodds, Sherril. "The Momentum Continues." *DTJ.* 1997; 13(3): 6-9. Illus.: Photo. B&W. 2. Lang.: Eng.

UK-England. 1976-1997. Biographical studies. ■Career of choreographer Rosemary Butcher.

1191 Dodds, Sherril; Adshead-Lansdale, Janet. "Gesture, Pop Culture, and Intertextuality in the Work of Lea Anderson." *NTQ.* 1997; 13(50): 155-160. Notes. Biblio. Illus.: Photo. B&W. 1. Lang.: Eng.

DANCE: Modern dance—Performance/production

UK-England. 1984-1994. Historical studies. ■Lea Anderson co-founded the all-female group The Cholmondeleys and its all-male counterpart The Featherstonehaughs. Article explores the intertextual elements in her work, which make it accessible, distinctive, and postmodern.

1192 Horta, Rui. "The Critical Distance." *DTJ.* 1997; 13(3): 14-15. Notes. Lang.: Eng.

UK-England. 1997. Histories-sources. ■Choreographer expresses her uneasiness about working in an overly technological world. Questions the place of dance and representation of the body in such a world.

1193 Kay, Graeme. "Lost for Words." *DTJ.* 1997; 13(4): 24-25. Notes. Illus.: Photo. B&W. 1. Lang.: Eng.

UK-England: London. 1997. Critical studies. ■Audience reception of the Mark Morris Dance Group's *L'Allegro, il Penseroso ed il Moderato* at the Coliseum.

1194 Nugent, Ann. "Two Tall Women." *DTJ.* 1997; 13(3): 22-23. Illus.: Photo. B&W. 1. Lang.: Eng.

UK-England. USA. 1997. Critical studies. ■Comparison of the choreographic styles of Twyla Tharp and Rosemary Butcher.

1195 Roy, Sanjoy. "Shobana Jeyasingh and Cultural Issues, Part I: Multiple Choices." *DTJ.* 1997; 13(4): 4-7. Notes. Illus.: Photo. B&W. 3. Lang.: Eng.

UK-England. 1988-1997. Biographical studies. ■Profile of choreographer Shobana Jeyasingh: the influences of Indian dance styles, her own modernism. Includes a list of her choreographies.

1196 Russ, Claire. "Delivering Dance." *DTJ.* 1997; 13(3): 16-17. Illus.: Photo. B&W. 1. Lang.: Eng.

UK-England. 1997. Histories-sources. ■Choreographer Russ discusses her influences and artistic goals.

1197 Albright, Ann Cooper. "Auto-Body Stories: Blondell Cummings and Autobiography in Dance." 179-206 in Desmond, Jane C., ed. *Meaning in Motion: New Cultural Studies of Dance.* Durham, NC/London: Duke UP; 1997. 398 pp. (Post-Contemporary Interventions.) Index. Notes. Illus.: Photo. 1. Lang.: Eng.

USA. Europe. 1910-1990. Critical studies. ■The solo performances and audience reception of choreographers Isadora Duncan and Blondell Cummings. Examines the categories of race and gender as they are read off the body.

1198 Calamita, Claudia. "Il 'dancedrama' di Martha Graham: figure femminili del ciclo greco." (Martha Graham's Dancedrama: Female Figures of the Greek Cycle.) *BiT.* 1997; 44: 117-155. Notes. Lang.: Ita.

USA. 1926-1991. Critical studies. ■Analysis of *Clytemnestra, Dark Meadows,* and *Cave of the Heart.* Compares Graham's performances to ancient ritual, which uses the trained body to convey the struggles of the inner self.

1199 Copeland, Roger. "Mark Morris, Postmodernism, and History Recycled." *DTJ.* 1997; 13(4): 18-23. Notes. Illus.: Photo. B&W. 2. Lang.: Eng.

USA. 1997. Critical studies. ■Discusses how history influences the work of choreographer Mark Morris.

1200 Daly, Ann. "Finding the Logic of Difference." *DTJ.* 1997; 13(3): 18-21. Illus.: Photo. B&W. 3. Lang.: Eng.

USA: New York, NY. 1997. Historical studies. ■Assesses the 1997 Altogether Different dance series at the Joyce Theatre. Criticizes New York City dance fare in general.

1201 DeFrantz, Thomas. "Simmering Passivity: The Black Male Body in Concert Dance." 107-120 in Morris, Gay, ed. *Moving Words: Re-writing Dance.* London/New York, NY: Routledge; 1996. 343 pp. Index. Notes. Biblio. Illus.: Photo. 1. Lang.: Eng.

USA. 1980-1995. Historical studies. ■Examines ways in which African American men have depicted themselves on the concert stage. Looks at Alvin Ailey and his company, among others.

1202 Dunn, Robert Ellis; Chin, Daryl, ed. "Robert Ellis Dunn: In Memoriam." *PerAJ.* 1997 Sep.; 19(3): 11-20. Illus.: Photo. B&W. 1. [Number 57.] Lang.: Eng.

USA: Milwaukee, WI. 1945-1997. Histories-sources. ■Two brief statements on dance made at conferences, a draft of an essay 'Evaluating

Choreography', and text of an untitled video-dance installation in collaboration with Matthew Chernov, by the recently deceased choreographer Robert Ellis Dunn.

1203 Franko, Mark. "Some Notes on Yvonne Rainer, Modernism, Politics, Emotion, Performance, and the Aftermath." 289-304 in Desmond, Jane C., ed. *Meaning in Motion: New Cultural Studies of Dance.* Durham, NC/London: Duke UP; 1997. 398 pp. (Post-Contemporary Interventions.) Index. Notes. Lang.: Eng.

USA. 1968. Critical studies. ■Analyzes Yvonne Rainer's performance dance piece *Trio A* from a performance theory viewpoint.

1204 Franko, Mark. "Nation, Class, and Ethnicities in Modern Dance of the 1930s." *TJ.* 1997 Dec.; 49(4): 475-492. Notes. Illus.: Photo. 4. Lang.: Eng.

USA. 1930-1940. Historical studies. ■The formation of female beauty as constructed by female dancers, with emphasis on the work of Martha Graham, Jane Dudley, and Asadata Dafora.

1205 Manning, Susan. "Cultural Theft—or Love?" *DTJ.* 1997; 13(4): 32-35. Notes. Illus.: Photo. B&W. 1. Lang.: Eng.

USA. 1997. Critical studies. ■Explores connections between Black dance, white dance, and the work of Twyla Tharp.

1206 Morris, Gay. "'Styles of the Flesh': Gender in the Dances of Mark Morris." 141-158 in Morris, Gay, ed. *Moving Words: Re-writing Dance.* London/New York, NY: Routledge; 1996. 343 pp. Index. Notes. Biblio. Illus.: Photo. 1. Lang.: Eng.

USA. 1980-1995. Critical studies. ■Analysis of gender in Mark Morris's *Dido and Aeneas* and *The Hard Nut.*

1207 Prevots, Naima. "Benjamin Zemach (1902-1997)." *BR.* 1997 Win; 25(4): 56-59. Lang.: Eng.

USA. 1902-1997. Biographical studies. ■Obituary for dancer/actor/choreographer Zemach.

1208 Satin, Leslie. "Being Danced Again: Meredith Monk, Reclaiming the Girlchild." 121-140 in Morris, Gay, ed. *Moving Words: Re-writing Dance.* London/New York, NY: Routledge; 1996. 343 pp. Index. Notes. Biblio. Illus.: Photo. 1. Lang.: Eng.

USA. 1980-1995. Critical studies. ■Feminist theory and autobiography in Meredith Monk's *Education of the Girlchild.*

1209 Whitaker, Rick; Daniels, Don. "A Conversation with Neil Greenberg." *BR.* 1997 Spr; 25(1): 67-89. Illus.: Photo. B&W. 7. Lang.: Eng.

USA: New York, NY. 1997. Histories-sources. ■Interview with choreographer Neil Greenberg concerning his work with Merce Cunningham and his career in choreography.

Relation to other fields

1210 Burns, Judy. "The Culture of Nobility/The Nobility of Self-Cultivation." 203-226 in Morris, Gay, ed. *Moving Words: Re-writing Dance.* London/New York, NY: Routledge; 1996. 343 pp. Index. Notes. Biblio. Illus.: Photo. 1. Lang.: Eng.

USA. 1910-1920. Historical studies. ■Examines women's adoption of Delsarte principles and practice to reinforce status and gain freedom in dance and in society.

1211 Forman, Catlyn. *Introducing Dance to Academic Curriculum Through Production.* Long Beach, CA: California State Univ; 1997. 42 pp. [M.A. Thesis, Univ. Microfilms Order No. AAC 1388698.] Lang.: Eng.

USA: Long Beach, CA. 1997. Histories-sources. ■Account of the creation of a dance project, *Building Shared Vision: A Dance Concert,* performed at the Martha B. Knoebel Dance Theatre at California State University, Long Beach, on February 7, 1997, choreographed by the author, Laura Gordon Sammons, and Marjeritta Phillips.

1212 Phillips, Marjeritta. *Dancing in the Spirit: A Choreographic Project for the Students From Compton Community College and the Kollege for Kids Outreach Dance Program.* Long Beach, CA: California State Univ; 1997. 53 pp. [M.A. Thesis, Univ. Microfilms Order No. AAC 1387767.] Lang.: Eng.

DANCE: Modern dance—Relation to other fields

USA: Long Beach, CA. 1997. Histories-sources. ■Account of the creation of a dance project, *Building Shared Vision: A Dance Concert*, performed at the Martha B. Knoebel Dance Theatre at California State University, Long Beach, on February 7, 1997, choreographed by the author, Catlyn Forman, and Laura Gordon Sammons.

1213   Sammons, Laura Gordon. *Building Shared Vision: Lifelong Learning in Dance Education*. Long Beach, CA: California State Univ; 1997. 36 pp. [M.A. Thesis, Univ. Microfilms Order No. AAC 1388726.] Lang.: Eng.

USA: Long Beach, CA. 1997. Histories-sources. ■Account of the creation of a dance project, *Building Shared Vision: A Dance Concert*, performed at the Martha B. Knoebel Dance Theatre at California State University, Long Beach, on February 7, 1997, choreographed by author, Catlyn Forman, and Marjeritta Phillips.

Theory/criticism

1214   Caprioli, Christina; Redbark-Wallander, Ingrid. "Talking Talking Dancing." *Danst.* 1997; 7(6): 18-19, 21. Illus.: Photo. B&W. Lang.: Swe.

Sweden: Stockholm. USA. 1997. Historical studies. ■A discussion about the postmodern dance of America, the problems of reconstruction and performing the dances from the 1970s, with reference to Yvonne Rainer and the seminar *Talking Dancing* at Dansens Hus.

1215   Franko, Mark. "Five Theses On *Laughter After All*." 43-62 in Morris, Gay, ed. *Moving Words: Re-writing Dance*. London/New York, NY: Routledge; 1996. 343 pp. Biblio. Notes. Index. Illus.: Photo. 8. Lang.: Eng.

USA. 1995. Critical studies. ■Examines theory and interpretation in Paul Sanasardo and Donya Feuer's 1960 dance *Laughter After All*.

1216   Koritz, Amy. "Re/Moving Boundaries: From Dance History to Cultural Studies." 88-106 in Morris, Gay, ed. *Moving Words: Re-writing Dance*. London/New York, NY: Routledge; 1996. 343 pp. Biblio. Notes. Index. Lang.: Eng.

USA. 1913-1933. Critical studies. ■Dance history within the context of cultural studies, exemplified by analysis of race, nation, self, and performance in plays of Eugene O'Neill and choreographies of Martha Graham.

1217   Manning, Susan. "*American Document* and American Minstrelsy." 183-202 in Morris, Gay, ed. *Moving Words: Re-writing Dance*. London/New York, NY: Routledge; 1996. 343 pp. Index. Notes. Biblio. Illus.: Photo. 1. Lang.: Eng.

USA. 1938. Critical studies. ■Race and gender in Martha Graham's *American Document*.

1218   Siegel, Marcia B. "Visible Secrets: Style Analysis and Dance Literacy." 29-42 in Morris, Gay, ed. *Moving Words: Re-writing Dance*. London/New York, NY: Routledge; 1996. 343 pp. Biblio. Notes. Index. Illus.: Photo. 1. Lang.: Eng.

USA. 1995. Critical studies. ■Examines the use of movement analysis to critique Western modern dance. Looks at Paul Taylor's *Speaking in Tongues*: structure and individual dances.

1219   Thomas, Helen. "Do You Want to Join the Dance? Postmodernism/Poststructuralism, the Body, and Dance." 63-87 in Morris, Gay, ed. *Moving Words: Re-writing Dance*. London/New York, NY: Routledge; 1996. 343 pp. Biblio. Notes. Index. Lang.: Eng.

USA. 1995. Critical studies. ■Critique of feminist theory as applied to dance.

Training

1220   Kästner, Irmela. "'Ist das Tanz?'." ('Is This Dance?'.) *Tanzd.* 1997; 38(3): 12-15. Notes. Lang.: Ger.

Germany: Hamburg. 1992-1993. Histories-sources. ■Describes the research project 'Schule in Bewegung' (School in Movement) which was carried out by the author who also teaches modern dance in Hamburg.

1221   Devecseri, Veronika. "Berczik Sára egyetemes táncművész." (Sára Berczik—A Universal Dancer.) 39-54 in Kővágó, Zsuzsa, ed. *Tánctudományi Tanulmányok 1996/1997*. Budapest: Magyar Tánctudományi Társaság; 1997. 173 pp. Append. Lang.: Hun.

Hungary. 1906-1996. Biographical studies. ■The author, second-generation pupil of dancer and pedagogue Sára Berczik, describes her

method in terms of recent research. Includes biographical data on Berczik and information on dance and movement of the 1930s.

1222   Postuwka, Gabriele. "Aufbruch in die Moderne." (Emergence into the Modern Age.) *Tanzd.* 1997; 38(3): 8-11. Notes. Illus.: Photo. B&W. 3. Lang.: Ger.

USA. Europe. 1920-1929. Critical studies. ■Reviews concepts of dance education and dance training in Europe and USA which were developed and accepted in correlation with modern dance.

DANCE-DRAMA

General

Performance/production

1223   Varley, Julia. "Sanjukta danza per gli dei." (Sanjukta Dances for the Gods.) *TeatroS.* 1997; 12(19): 97-130. Notes. Lang.: Ita.

India. 1952-1996. Histories-sources. ■A collection of autobiographical material from the Indian dancer Sanjukta Panigrahi and the comments of the author, a member of Odin Teatret.

1224   Ortolani, Benito. "From Shamanism to *Buto*: Continuity and Innovation in Japanese Theater History." 15-24 in Leiter, Samuel L., ed. *Japanese Theater in the World*. New York, NY: The Japan Society; 1997. 196 pp. Notes. Illus.: Photo. B&W. Color. 6. Lang.: Eng.

Japan. 500-1997. Historical studies. ■Factors that shaped the birth and influenced the development and aesthetic continuity of Japanese theatrical genres over fifteen centuries.

1225   Erkvist, Ingela Britt. *The Performance of Tradition: An Ethnography of Hira Gasy Popular Theatre in Madagascar*. Uppsala: Uppsala Universitet; 1997. 200 pp. [ISBN: 91-554-4070-3. Available from Department of Cultural Anthropology and Ethnology, Tradgardsgatau 18, S-753 09 Uppsala, Sweden.] Lang.: Swe.

Madagascar. 1800-1995. Historical studies. ■Ethnographic study of the performance, actors, and audiences of the popular theatre form *Hira Gasy*, developed from a court to a rural performance during the last two centuries, and influenced by the British and French presence in the country. Argues that Hira Gasy performances provide a forum in which the problems of identification and belonging are discussed.

Plays/librettos/scripts

1226   Burgoyne, Lynda. "L'utopie mène le théâtre et mène le monde: Entretien avec Lük Fleury." (Utopia Leads the Theatre and Leads the World: Interview with Lük Fleury.) *JCT.* 1997; 83: 8-17. Illus.: Dwg. Photo. B&W. 6. Lang.: Fre.

Canada: Montreal, PQ. 1993-1997. Histories-sources. ■Content of Lük Fleury's *Choeur des silences (Chorus of Silence)* and his experience creating the text with Théâtre Kafala.

1227   Compton, June. *The Kyogen Women: A Comparative Analysis and Classification of the Female Characters in Japan's Classical Comedies*. Boulder, CO: Univ. of Colorado; 1997. 764 pp. Notes. Biblio. [Ph.D. Dissertation, Univ. Microfilms Order No. AAC 9725717.] Lang.: Eng.

Japan. Critical studies. ■Identifies elements of characterization that distinguish and individualize various female roles, defines motivations of characters, and explores relationships between character types and social positions.

Relation to other fields

1228   Bharucha, Rustom. "When 'Eternal India' Meets the YPO." *PerfR.* 1997 Sum; 2(2): 34-40. Illus.: Photo. B&W. 1. [Transcript of a talk given at the Performance, Tourism and Identity Conference, Wales, September 1996.] Lang.: Eng.

India: Mumbai. 1996. Critical studies. ■Analysis of a performance sponsored by the humanitarian organization Sarthi for members of the Young Presidents Organisation. Explores the inherent contradictions involved in creating such a spectacle for this audience.

DANCE-DRAMA: *Kabuki*

Kabuki

Design/technology

1229 Leiter, Samuel L. "'What Really Happens Backstage': A Nineteenth-Century *Kabuki* Document." *ThS.* 1997 Nov.; 38(2): 109-128. Illus.: Dwg. 12. Lang.: Eng.

Japan. 1858-1859. Historical studies. ▪Recently discovered text of a two-volume work on stage effects in the *kabuki* theatre. Text includes drawings of the stagecraft with brief explanations of their purposes.

Performance spaces

1230 Leiter, Samuel L. "The Kanamaru-za: Japan's Oldest *Kabuki* Theatre." *ATJ.* 1997 Spr; 14(1): 56-92. Notes. Biblio. Illus.: Photo. Sketches. B&W. Color. 50. Lang.: Eng.

Japan: Kotohira. 1830-1995. Historical studies. ▪Historical introduction to the playhouse, home of an annual *kabuki* festival, built in the 1830s and recently restored. Provides guided tour of space with groundplans and numerous detail photographs. Originally presented in shorter form in August 1996 at conference of the Association for Theatre in Higher Education in New York.

Nō

Performance/production

1231 Kaán, Zsuzsa. "A No-színház korszerűsége–Gyorsfénykép az 50. Holland Fesztiválról–2. rész." (The Up-to-Date Feature of the *Nō* Theatre–A Snapshot of the 50th Holland Festival–Part 2.) *Tanc.* 1997; 28(5/6): 45. Illus.: Photo. B&W. 14. Lang.: Hun.

Japan. Netherlands. 1997. Critical studies. ▪Analysis of the special interpretation of traditional *nō* theatre in the context of today's theatre at the festival.

Plays/librettos/scripts

1232 Lim, Beng Choo. *Kanze Kojiro Nobumitsu and Furyu Noh: A Study of the Late Muromachi Noh Theater.* Ithaca, NY: Cornell Univ; 1997. 298 pp. [Ph.D. Dissertation, Univ. Microfilms Order No. AAC 9731995.] Lang.: Eng.

Japan. 1500-1600. Critical studies. ▪Examines the life and works of Kanze Kojiro Nobumitsu and his importance in the *Furyu Nō* theatre style. Argues for the unconventionality of Nobumitsu's works.

DRAMA

Administration

1233 Vigeant, Louise. "Théâtre et collégialité: deux passions, un itinéraire: Entretien avec Pierre MacDuff." (Theatre and Collegial Structure: Two Passions, One Path: Interview with Pierre MacDuff.) *JCT.* 1997; 82: 22-32. Notes. Illus.: Photo. B&W. 8. Lang.: Fre.

Canada: Montreal, PQ, Quebec, PQ. 1960-1997. Histories-sources. ▪Retraces Pierre MacDuff's work promoting and producing québécois theatre, most recently as general manager of Deux Mondes.

1234 Olsen, Jakob Steen. "Et teater ligger hvor det ligger–interview med Klaus Hoffmeyer." (An Interview with Klaus Hoffmeyer.) *TE.* 1997 Oct.; 85: 16-20. Illus.: Photo. B&W. 3. Lang.: Dan.

Denmark. 1997. Histories-sources. ▪An interview with Klaus Hoffmeyer, head of the dramatic arts department at The Royal Theatre of Copenhagen, on the surprising repertoire planned for the 1997-98 season, which includes seven new Danish plays.

1235 Gurr, Andrew. "Three Reluctant Patrons and Early Shakespeare." *SQ.* 1993 Sum; 44(2): 159-174. Notes. Lang.: Eng.

England: London. 1592-1594. Historical studies. ▪Effect of policies of three different Lords Chamberlain upon the early development of Shakespeare.

1236 MacLean, Sally-Beth. "The Politics of Patronage: Dramatic Records in Robert Dudley's Household Books." *SQ.* 1993 Sum; 44 (2): 175-182. Notes. Lang.: Eng.

England. 1584-1586. Historical studies. ▪Examines household account book of Robert Dudley, Earl of Leicester, patron of Leicester's Men acting company, for clues to the extent of his involvement with the troupe.

1237 Runnalls, Graham A. "Sponsorship and Control in Medieval French Religious Drama: 1402-1548." *FS.* 1997 July; 51(3): 257-266. Notes. Lang.: Eng.

France: Paris. 1402-1548. Historical studies. ▪Analysis of two decrees that gave the Paris Confrérie de la Passion the right to perform religious plays and then revoked that right.

1238 Deuter, Ulrich. "Reise ins Schaffeland." (Journey to the Working Land.) *TZ.* 1997; 1: 20-26. Illus.: Photo. B&W. 5. Lang.: Ger.

Germany: Stuttgart. 1993-1997. Historical studies. ▪The current situation at Württembergische Staatstheater under the directorship of Friedrich Schirmer.

1239 Koch, Stefan. "Joint Venture für die Kunst." (Joint Venture for Fine Art.) *DB.* 1997; 6: 33-35. Illus.: Photo. B&W. 3. Lang.: Ger.

Germany: Mannheim. 1996-1997. Biographical studies. ▪A portrait of Ulrich Schwab, director of Mannheimer Nationaltheater, and his concepts of marketing to improve the relationship between great theatre tradition and faithful audience.

1240 Quilitzsch, Frank. "Förderschwerpunkte statt Fusion für Erfurt und Weimar." (Main Supports Instead of Amalgamation of Erfurt And Weimar.) *TZ.* 1997; 4: 8-10. Illus.: Photo. B&W. 3. Lang.: Ger.

Germany: Erfurt, Weimar. 1997. Histories-sources. ▪Describes the current situation of theatres in Erfurt and Weimar including an interview with Günther Beelitz, director (*Generalintendant*) of Deutsches Nationaltheater.

1241 Kristoffersson, Birgitta; Grönstedt, Olle. "Rivstart på teatern?" (A Flying Start at the Theatre?) *Dramat.* 1997; 5(1): 12-16. Illus.: Photo. Color. Lang.: Swe.

Sweden: Gothenburg, Stockholm. 1997. Histories-sources. ▪Interviews with the new managers of Göteborgs Stadsteater and Kungliga Dramatiska Teatern, Ronny Danielsson and Ingrid Dahlberg, about the severe financial situations for institutional theatres.

1242 Billington, Michael; Cramer, Franz, transl. "Wir sind am Scheideweg." (We Are at the Crossroads.) *THeute.* 1997; 1: 37-40. Illus.: Photo. B&W. 4. Lang.: Ger.

UK-England. 1995-1997. Historical studies. ▪Report on the current situation of the English theatre scene, with a focus on small budgets and young playwrights.

1243 Hunter, Robin. "Like Father—Like Son." *PlPl.* 1997 June/ July; 514: 27. Lang.: Eng.

UK-England: London. 1940-1954. Biographical studies. ▪Details of personal life of theatre manager Anthony Hawtrey.

Audience

1244 Belzil, Patricia. "Odeur de cinoche: *Un air de famille* aux Variétés." (Smells Like the Movies: *Un air de famille* at the Variétés.) *JCT.* 1997; 82: 175-177. Notes. Illus.: Photo. B&W. 2. Lang.: Fre.

Canada: Montreal, PQ. 1997. Historical studies. ▪Mixed audience of theatregoers, filmgoers and variety show fans create unusual atmosphere for Agnès Jaoui and Jean-Pierre Bacri's production of *Un air de famille (A Family Resemblance)* at Théâtre des Variétés, directed by Daniel Roussel, produced by Sortie 22 in 1997.

1245 Camerlain, Lorraine. "Ouvertures." (Overtures.) *JCT.* 1997; 82: 156-159. Illus.: Photo. B&W. 3. Lang.: Fre.

Canada: Quebec, PQ. 1996. Critical studies. ▪Open letter explaining author's enjoyment of live theatre to a book-reader, with reference to Serge Denoncourt's staging of Michel Tremblay's *Messe solennelle pour une pleine lune d'été (Solemn Mass for a Full Moon in Summer)* at Théâtre du Trident, 1996.

1246 Lieblein, Leanore. "Theatre Archives at the Intersection of Production and Reception: The Example of Québécois

DRAMA: —Audience

Shakespeare.'' 164-180 in Pechter, Edward, ed. *Textual and Theatrical Shakespeare: Questions of Evidence.* Iowa City, IA: Univ of Iowa P; 1997. 267 pp. (Studies in Theatre History and Culture.) Notes. Lang.: Eng.

Canada. 1978-1993. Critical studies. ■Examines the unique audience reception during fifteen years of Shakespeare production in Quebec.

1247 Levin, Richard. "Women in the Renaissance Theatre Audience." *SQ.* 1989 Sum; 40(2): 165-174. Notes. Lang.: Eng.

England. 1567-1642. Historical studies. ■Discusses high proportion of women attending plays during the English Renaissance.

1248 Lindroth, Mary Claire. *The Mixed Audiences and Comic Practices of Early Modern English Drama.* Iowa City, IA: Univ. of Iowa; 1997. 256 pp. [Ph.D. Dissertation, Univ. Microfilms Order No. AAC 9731832.] Lang.: Eng.

England. 1590-1615. Critical studies. ■The presence of both upper and lower classes in Elizabethan England's public and private theatres. Uses the comedies of Shakespeare, Peele, Beaumont and Jonson to analyze cultural constructs of playgoing.

1249 Thoret, Yves. "Lettre de France d'Yves Thoret." (Letter from France from Yves Thoret.) *JCT.* 1997; 85: 146-147. Illus.: Photo. B&W. 146-147. Lang.: Fre.

France: Paris. 1997. Historical studies. ■Spectator's impression of Robert Wilson's staging of Marguerite Duras' *La Maladie de la Mort (The Sickness of Death)* and a debate featuring actors from that production, at Festival d'Automne, Paris 1997.

1250 Torres-Reyes, Maria Luisa. "Theatre as an Encounter of Cultures." *ThR.* 1997; 22(1 Supplement): 61-68. Notes. Lang.: Eng.

Philippines. 1905-1993. Historical studies. ■Historical and contemporary cultural role of theatre in Philippines. Includes discussion of productions of *Pilipinas: Circa 1907* and Rody Vera's *Ang Paglakbay ni Radya Mangandiri (The Journey of Radya Mangandiri).*

1251 Franzon, Johan. "Publiken spelar roll." (The Audience Plays a Part.) *Entré.* 1997; 24(8): 12-19. Illus.: Photo. B&W. Lang.: Swe.

Sweden. USSR. 1900. Critical studies. ■A survey of the tradition in which the audience is involved in the performance, with references to experiments in the Soviet Union, theatre in education and Teater Uno.

1252 Holdsworth, Nadine. "Good Nights Out: Activating the Audience with 7:84 (England)." *NTQ.* 1997; 13(49): 29-40. Notes. Biblio. Illus.: Photo. B&W. 3. Lang.: Eng.

UK-England. 1971-1985. Historical studies. ■Considers the importance of the audience for this touring, popular theatre company and identifies some of the strategies used to attract and retain radical working-class spectators.

1253 Jackson, Anthony. "Positioning the Audience: Inter-Active Strategies and the Aesthetic in Educational Theatre." *ThR.* 1997; 22(1 Supplement): 48-60. Notes. Lang.: Eng.

UK-England. 1960-1994. Critical studies. ■Proposes a theory of aesthetic distance for examining the relationship between reality and fictionality in Theatre in Education.

Basic theatrical documents

1254 Klinkenberg, Rob; Oberman, Hanna. *Nu Benik Alleen. 101 Monologen Uit de Toneelliteratuur.* (Now I Am Alone: 101 Theatrical Soliloquies.) Amsterdam: International Theatre & Film Books; Pref. Index. Biblio. Lang.: Dut.

■Excerpts of monologues and soliloquies.

1255 Benzie, Tim. "*Personal Fictions.*" *ADS.* 1997 Oct.; 31: 129-174. Lang.: Eng.

Australia. 1994. ■Complete text of Benzie's play.

1256 Gerdes, Brigitte Simone. *Johann Nestroy's Der Talisman: An English Performance Translation.* Edmonton, AL: Univ. of Alberta; 1997. 202 pp. [M.A. Thesis, Univ. Microfilms Order No. AAC MQ21131.] Lang.: Eng.

Austria. 1833-1849. ■Performance translation of Johann Nestroy's *Der Talisman oder die Schicksalsperucken (The Talisman or the Wigs of Fate)*. Includes discussion of the numerous influences on the translation: critical works, audio and video recordings, drawings and paintings, the-

atrical tradition, the play's original source, and the effects of Nestroy's acting ensemble on the play.

1257 de Vries, Marion. "*big face.*" *CTR.* 1997 Fall; 92: 68-81. Illus.: Photo. B&W. 2. Lang.: Eng.

Canada. 1995. ■Complete playtext with notes. One-woman show.

1258 Gardner, Mary Lu Anne. *Margaret Durham, with Afterword.* Guelph, ON: Univ. of Guelph; 1997. 112 pp. [M.A. Thesis, Univ. Microfilms Order No. AAC MM16658.] Lang.: Eng.

Canada. 1996. ■Text of the play with an afterword that explores aspects of working with dramatic voice and dramatic structure.

1259 Garnhum, Ken. "*One Word.*" *CTR.* 1997 Sum; 91: 47-60. Illus.: Dwg. Photo. B&W. 4. Lang.: Eng.

Canada. 1997. ■Complete playtext with prop drawings and photos from production at Tarragon Theatre, Extra Space.

1260 Garnhum, Ken. "*New Art Book*: A Picture Monologue by Ken Garnhum." *CTR.* 1997 Sum; 91: 61-62. Lang.: Eng.

Canada. 1997. ■Monologue, no production notes.

1261 Sherman, Jason. "None is Too Many." *CTR.* 1997 Win; 93: 42-67. Illus.: Photo. B&W. 2. Lang.: Eng.

Canada. 1997. ■Complete playtext with notes. Based on book by Irving Abella and Harold Troper.

1262 Taylor, Drew Hayden. "*Girl Who Loved Her Horses*: A One-Act Play for Young Audiences." *TDR.* 1997 Fall; 41(3): 153-181. Illus.: Photo. Poster. B&W. 6. Lang.: Eng.

Canada. 1990-1997. ■Complete playscript with introduction describing author's influences and early production of play.

1263 Díaz, Jorge. "*El memoricido.*" (The Memory-Killer.) *Gestos.* 1997 Apr.; 12(23): 131-148. Illus.: Handbill. Photo. B&W. 5. Lang.: Spa.

Chile. 1994. ■Text of Díaz' play.

1264 Chen, Fan Pen, intro., transl. "*Reunion with Son and Daughter in Kingfisher Red County.* A Yuan Drama." *ATJ.* 1997 Fall ; 14(2): 157-199. Notes. Biblio. Gloss. Lang.: Eng.

China. 1280-1994. ■English translation, with an introduction including description of genre, historical and theatrical context of play, contemporary interest in play.

1265 Johnson, Charles. "*Love in a Forest.*" 81-132 in Tomarken, Edward, ed. *As You Like It from 1600 to the Present.* New York, NY: Garland; 1997. 672 pp. (Shakespeare Criticism 17.) Lang.: Eng.

England. 1723. ■Text of *Love in a Forest*, Johnson's adaptation of Shakespeare's *As You Like It*. Includes analysis.

1266 Lehtola, Juha. "*Mind Speak.*" *FT.* 1997; 51: 22-30. Illus.: Photo. B&W. 3. Lang.: Eng.

Finland. 1997. ■English translation of *Mielen Kieli*, including notes on the playwright and production.

1267 Aubert, Gérald. "*Le Voyage.*" (The Journey.) *AST.* 1996 15 June; 992: 2-38. Illus.: Photo. B&W. 12. Lang.: Fre.

France. 1996. ■Text of Aubert's play as produced by La Compagnie des Champs-Elysées directed by Michel Fagadou. Includes profiles of the author, director, and actors, an essay on Aubert's work, and excerpts from press reviews.

1268 Bauer, Jean-Louis. "*Page 27.*" *AST.* 1996 15 July; 994: 2-57. Illus.: Photo. B&W. 28. Lang.: Fre.

France. 1996. ■Text of Bauer's play as directed by Pierre Santini, who also starred, at Théâtre Tristan Bernard. Includes profiles of the author, Santini and other members of the cast, and the theatre, as well as an interview with Bauer. The text of Bauer's libretto for *Gédéon*, a brief musical play by Polish composer Piotr Moss, is also included.

1269 Doutreligne, Louise. "*L'Esclave du démon.*" (Slave of the Devil.) *AST.* 1996 1 Nov.; 997: 3-50. Illus.: Photo. B&W. 19. Lang.: Fre.

France. Spain. 1612-1996. ■Text of Doutreligne's play, which is based on (and includes a French verse translation of) a seventeenth-century text of Antonio Mira de Amescua. The play, originally produced in an earlier version as *Un Faust espagnol*, was directed by Jean-Luc Paliès at Théâtre de l'Épée de Bois-Cartoucherie. Includes profiles of the authors, the venue, and the Compagnie Influence Fievet-Paliès, as well as an essay by the director and excerpts from press reviews.

DRAMA: —Basic theatrical documents

1270 Fenwick, Jean-Noël. *"Potins d'enfer."* (Hellish Gossip.) *AST.* 1996 15 Feb.; 984: 2-42. Illus.: Photo. B&W. 20. Lang.: Fre.

France: Paris. 1996. ■Text of Fenwick's play, which reexamines the basic premise of Sartre's *Huis Clos (No Exit)*, as produced by Théâtre Rive Gauche, directed by Fenwick. Includes an interview with Fenwick, profiles of the actors, photos of other productions, and a note on Alain Maillet, director of Théâtre Rive Gauche.

1271 Feydeau, Georges. *"La Puce à l'Oreille."* (A Flea in Her Ear.) *AST.* 1996 15 Oct.; 996: 2-84. Illus.: Photo. B&W. 18. Lang.: Fre.

France. 1902-1996. ■Text of Feydeau's farce as directed by Bernard Murat at Théâtre des Variétés. Includes profiles of the author and personnel of the production and a history of previous productions, with photographs.

1272 Gallaire, Fatima. *"Les Richesses de l'hiver."* (The Riches of Winter.) *AST.* 1996 1 June; 991: 2-42. Illus.: Photo. B&W. 11. Lang.: Fre.

France: Ajaccio. 1996. ■Text of Gallaire's play as presented by Théâtre Point of Corsica, directed by Francis Aïqui. Includes profiles of the author, actors, the company, and the Parisian venue (Théâtre de Proposition), an interview with the director, and excerpts from press reviews.

1273 Gleizes, Gilles, adapt. *"Le Secret de l'Aiguille creuse—Une aventure d'Arsène Lupin."* (The Secret of the Hollow Needle, An Arsène Lupin Adventure.) *AST.* 1996 15 Nov.; 998: 2-41. Illus.: Photo. B&W. 17. Lang.: Fre.

France. 1996. ■Text of Gleizes' play, which he also directed for the Théâtre des Jeune Spectateurs of the Centre Dramatique National of Montreuil, based on a novel by Maurice Leblanc. Includes profiles of Gleize, other personnel of the production, and the children's theatre company of the Centre Dramatique National, essays on the play and Leblanc's Arsène Lupin mystery novels with bibliography.

1274 Métayer, Alex. *"Aimez-moi les uns les autres."* (Love Me One and All.) *AST.* 1996 15 May; 990: 2-44. Illus.: Photo. B&W. 15. Lang.: Fre.

France. 1996. ■Text of Métayer's comedy as directed by Gil Galliot. Includes profiles of author and actors, an essay on Métayer's comedies, and excerpts from press reviews.

1275 Poudérou, Robert. *"Les Oiseaux d'Avant."* (The Birds from Before.) *AST.* 1996 1 Feb.; 983: 2-39. Illus.: Photo. B&W. 18. Lang.: Fre.

France. 1996. ■Text of Poudérou's play, set in the year 2000, as presented by Théâtre de la fenêtre ouverte, directed by Jacques Clancy. Includes profiles of the author, director, actors, company, and theatre, as well as an essay on Poudérou's work, photographs of other plays by him, and notes from the director.

1276 Simon, Yoland. *"Couleur de cerne et de lilas."* (The Color of Bruises and Lilac.) *AST.* 1996 1 Mar.; 985: 2-40. Illus.: Photo. B&W. 23. Lang.: Fre.

France. 1996. ■Text of Simon's play, the third part of the trilogy *Chroniques villageoises (Village Chronicles)* which also includes *Je l'avais de si près tenu (So Closely Held)* and *Imprécations*, as produced by La Compagnie Derniers Détails directed by Didier Perrier. Includes profiles of author, director, actors, and the theatre building.

1277 Vinaver, Michel; de Haan, Christopher, transl.; Schoëvaërt, Marion, transl.; Berg, Andrew, transl. *"The Interview."* *ThM.* 1997; 28(1): 79-116. Illus.: Photo. B&W. 5. Lang.: Eng.

France. 1994. ■English translation of *La Demande d'emploi.*

1278 Büchner, Georg; Hartman, Bruno, transl.; Kranjc, Mojca, transl.; Udovič, Jože, transl. *Drame in proza.* (Plays and Prose.) Ljubljana: Mladinska knjiga; 1997. 279 pp. (Knjižnica Kondor 281.) Notes. Lang.: Slo.

Germany. 1835-1837. ■Includes Slovene translations of *Dantons Tod (Danton's Death), Lenz, Leonce und Lena (Leonce and Lena),* and *Woyzeck.*

1279 Büchner, Georg; Regnault, François, transl.; Demarcy-Mota, Emmanuel, transl. *"Léonce et Léna."* (Leonce and Lena.) *AST.* 1996 1 July; 993: 2-40. Illus.: Photo. B&W. 20. Lang.: Fre.

Germany. France. Belgium. 1838-1996. ■French translation of *Leonce und Lena* as coproduced by the companies of Théâtre des Millefontaines, Théâtre de la Commune Pandora, and Théâtre d'Esch-sur-Alzette, directed by Emmanuel Demarcy-Mota. Includes profiles of the author, companies, translators, and director, an essay by the director on comic aspects of the play, and some songs of Musset, one of which was included in the production.

1280 Fassbinder, Rainer Werner; Calandra, Denis, transl.; Calandra, Brendan, transl. *"Just a Slice of Bread."* *PerAJ.* 1997 May; 19(2): 100-114. [Number 56.] Lang.: Eng.

Germany. 1971. ■English translation of *Nur eine Scheibe Brot*, a recently discovered early play.

1281 Handke, Peter; Honegger, Gitta, transl. *"The Hour We Knew Nothing of Each Other."* *ThM.* 1993; 23(1): 93-105. Illus.: Photo. B&W. 4. Lang.: Eng.

Germany. 1992. ■English translation of *Die Stunde da wir nichts voneinander wussten.*

1282 Lange-Müller, Katja. *"Schneewittchen im Eisblock. Ein Spiegelbild."* (Snow White in the Block of Ice: A Reflection.) *TZ.* 1997; 1: 78-80. Biblio. Illus.: Photo. B&W. 1. Lang.: Ger.

Germany. 1997. ■A playtext including the playwright's biography and bibliography.

1283 Schleef, Einar. *"Totentrompeten II."* (Dead Trumpets II.) *TZ.* 1997; 2: 75-103. Pref. Illus.: Photo. B&W. 1. Lang.: Ger.

Germany. 1997. ■A playtext including the playwright's biography and bibliography.

1284 Schürer, Ernst, ed. *German Expressionist Plays.* New York, NY: Continuum; 1997. 322 pp. Biblio. Lang.: Eng.

Germany. 1900-1920. ■Translations of German expressionist plays: Oskar Kokoschka's *Mörder, Hoffnung der Frauen (Murderer, The Women's Hope)*, 1907, August Stramm's *Sancta Susanna (St. Susannah)*, 1914, Gottfried Benn's *Ithaka (Ithaca)*, 1914, Carl Sternheim's *Die Hose (The Bloomers)*, 1911, Walter Hasenclever's *Der Sohn (The Son)*, 1915, Georg Kaiser's *Von Morgens bis Mitternachts (From Morning to Midnight)*, 1916, Ernst Toller's *Masse Mensch (Masses and Man)*, 1919, and Georg Kaiser's *Gas I* and *Gas II*, 1918 and 1920. Volume includes a critical introduction to the plays and the historical period.

1285 McGuinness, Frank; Long, Joseph, transl.; Poulain, Alexandra, transl. *"Regarde les fils de l'Ulster marchant vers la Somme."* (Observe the Sons of Ulster Marching Towards the Somme.) *AST.* 1996 1 May; 989: 2-68. Illus.: Photo. Maps. B&W. 33. Lang.: Fre.

Ireland. France. 1985-1996. ■French translation of McGuinness' play, which was presented at the Théâtre de l'Odéon by Abbey Theatre, directed by Patrick Mason. Includes profiles of the author, translators and Abbey Theatre, songs with music, as well as materials created by Abbey Theatre, including essays on the playwright, Ulster, Irish history and World War I, and the renewal of Irish theatre.

1286 Molloy, Christine; Lawlor, Joe. *"Photogrammetry."* *PerfR.* 1997 Fall; 2(3): 17-24. Illus.: Design. Photo. B&W. 21. Lang.: Eng.

Ireland: Dublin. 1997. ■Scenario for a performance by the group desperate optimists.

1287 Lunari, Luigi; Snelling, Clive, transl. *"An Uncomfortably Close Encounter."* *PI.* 1997 Mar.; 12(8): 34-46. Lang.: Eng.

Italy. 1995. ■English translation of *Incontro Ravvicinato di Tipo Estremo.*

1288 Pulci, Antonia; Cook, James Wyatt, transl. *Florentine Drama for Convent and Festival: Seven Sacred Plays.* Chicago, IL/London: Univ of Chicago P; 1996. 281 pp. (The Other Voice in Early Modern Europe.) Notes. Biblio. Index. Lang.: Eng.

Italy. 1452-1501. ■English translations of *The Play of Saint Francis, The Play of Saint Domitilla, The Play of Saint Guglielma, The Play of the Prodigal Son, The Play of Saint Anthony the Abbot, The Play of Saint Theodora,* and *The Play and Festival of Rosana.* Includes critical analysis of each play's themes, and a biography of the author.

1289 Tordi, Anne Wilson, ed., transl. *La festa et storia di Sancta Caterina: A Medieval Italian Religious Drama.* New York, NY: Peter Lang; 1997. 300 pp. (Studies in the Humanities:

DRAMA: —Basic theatrical documents

Literature—Politics—Society 25.) Notes. Biblio. Append. Illus.: Photo. 2. Lang.: Eng.

Italy. 1380-1400. ■English translation of Medieval Italian religious play *La festa et storia di Sancta Caterina sopra l'altre divota et bella (The Feast and History of Saint Catherine, Beautiful and Devout above All Others)*, with critical introduction giving history of the legend, the genre, and notes on previous editions of the work.

1290 Betsuyaku, Minoru; Yuasa, Masako, intro., transl. *"A Corpse with Feet."* *ATJ.* 1997 Spr; 14(1): 1-37. Notes. Biblio. Illus.: Photo. B&W. Grd.Plan. 12. Lang.: Eng.

Japan. 1937-1995. ■English translation of *Ashi no aru shitai.* Introduction focuses on playwright's work with Katatsumuri no Kai (Snail Theatre Company), including complete production list from 1978-1995, and his long-term collaboration with director Murai Shimako and his wife, actress Kusunoki Yūko.

1291 Salas, Teresa Cajiao, ed.; Vargas, Margarita, ed. *Women Writing Women: An Anthology of Spanish American Theater of the 1980s.* Albany, NY: State Univ of New York P; 1997. 468 pp. (SUNY Series in Latin American and Iberian Thought and Culture.) Pref. Index. Biblio. Lang.: Eng.

Latin America. 1981-1989. ■English translations of plays by Latin American Spanish-speaking women: *Altarpiece of Yumbel (Retablo de Yumbel)* by Isidora Aguirre, *Yankee (Yanqui)* by Sabina Berman, *The Great USkrainian Circus (El gran circo Eukraniano)* by Myrna Casas, *Evening Walk (Paseo al atardecer)* by Teresa Marichal, *Dial-a-Mom (Casa matriz)* by Diana Raznovich, *Waiting for the Italian (Esperando al italiano)* by Mariela Romero, *7 Times Eva (7 veces Eve)* by Teresa Cajiao Salas and Margarita Vargas and *A Woman, Two Men, and a Gunshot (Una mujer, dos hombres y un balazo)* by Maruxa Vilalta.

1292 Al-Shaykh, Hannan; Cobham, Catherine, transl. *"Paper Husband."* *PI.* 1997 May; 12(10): 38-45. Lang.: Eng.

Middle East. 1997. ■English translation of an Arabic original. Continued in *PI* 12:11 (1997 June), 38-46.

1293 Warmerdam, Alex van. *Alex van Warmerdam: Verzameld Theaterwerk. 1982-1996.* (Collected Plays, 1982-96.) Amsterdam: Thomas Rap; 1997. 423 pp. Illus.: Dwg. Photo. B&W. 53. Lang.: Dut.

Netherlands. 1982-1996. ■Includes seven plays with brief accounts of performances and playbills.

1294 Ibsen, Henrik; Moder, Janko, transl. *Brand.* Maribor: Obzorja; 1997. 248 pp. Notes. Lang.: Slo.

Norway. 1865. ■Slovene translation of Ibsen's *Brand.*

1295 Filatov, Leonid. *Ljubov' k trem apel'sinam: Skazki, povesti, parodii. Kinoscenarii.* (The Love for Three Oranges: Fairy Tales, Novels, Parodies—Scenario.) Moscow: Truen; 1997. 416 pp. Lang.: Rus.

Russia. 1960-1997. ■Writings by a renowned stage and film actor.

1296 Gluvić, Goran. *Šest iger.* (Six Plays.) Grosuplje: Mondena; 1997. 173 pp. (Zbirka Ésprit slovène 2.) Lang.: Slo.

Slovenia. 1980-1997. ■Includes *Borutovo poletje (Borut's Summer), Video klub (Video Club), Stanovanje (The Flat), Carlos, Jam session,* and *Norma.*

1297 Jančar, Drago. *Halštat.* (Halstatt.) Ljubljana: Nova revija; 1996. 90 pp. (Samorog.) Lang.: Slo.

Slovenia. 1994. ■Text of Jančar's Grum award-winning play about an archaeological excavation.

1298 Jesih, Milan. *Štiri igre za otroke.* (Four Plays for Children.) Ljubljana: Mladinska knjiga; 1997. 140 pp. (Zbirka Mladi oder.) Lang.: Slo.

Slovenia. 1997. ■Complete texts of four children's theatre plays.

1299 Jovanović, Dušan. *Balkanska trilogija.* (The Balkan Trilogy.) Ljubljana: Cankarjeva založba; 1997. 151 pp. Pref. Lang.: Slo.

Slovenia. 1997. ■Texts of Jovanović's last three plays: *Antigona (Antigone), Uganka korajže (The Enigma of Courage),* and *Kdo to poje Sizifa (Who's Singing Sisyphus?),* all of which confront the Balkan and European worlds.

1300 Partljič, Tone. *Komedije.* (Comedies.) Ljubljana: Pisanica; 1997. 161 pp. Pref. Illus.: Photo. B&W. Lang.: Slo.

Slovenia. 1997. ■Three comedies concerning the current political and social conditions in Slovenia.

1301 Predan, Alja, ed. *Contemporary Slovenian Drama.* Ljubljana: Slovene Writers' Association; 1997. 432 pp. (Le livre slovène XXXV, 90.) Illus.: Photo. B&W. Lang.: Eng.

Slovenia. 1980-1997. ■Translations of plays by Evald Flisar, Drago Jančar, Dušan Jovanović, Ivo Svetina, Rudi Šeligo, and Dane Zajc.

1302 Svetina, Ivo. *Tako je umrl Zaratuštra.* (Thus Died Zarathustra.) Ljubljana: Slovene National Theatre; 1997. 76 pp. Illus.: Photo. B&W. Lang.: Slo.

Slovenia. 1995. ■Text of Svetina's Grum award-winning play, a demystification of Nietzschean nihilism.

1303 Svetina, Ivo; Hribar, Darja, transl.; Križman, Mirko, transl. *Babylon.* Maribor: Plays of the Slovene National Theatre; 1996. 43 pp. Illus.: Photo. B&W. Lang.: Eng, Ger.

Slovenia. 1997. ■English and German translations of Svetina's verse drama evoking the world of the hanging gardens of Babylon.

1304 Zupančič, Matjaž. *"Vladimir."* *Sodob.* 1997; 45(8/9): 669-707. Lang.: Slo.

Slovenia. 1997. ■Text of Grum award-winning play about violence among young people.

1305 Zupančič, Mirko. *Tri drame.* (Three Plays.) Novo mesto: Novo mesto/Dolenjska; 1997. 140 pp. Lang.: Slo.

Slovenia. 1997. ■Texts of Zupančič's *Elektrino maščevanje (Electra's Revenge), Čarobnice (The Enchantresses),* and *Potovalci (The Travelers).*

1306 Uys, Pieter-Dirk. *"No Space on Long Street."* *SATJ.* 1997 May/Sep.; 11(1/2): 325-362. Illus.: Photo. B&W. 2. Lang.: Eng.

South Africa, Republic of. 1997. ■Text of Uys' one-man play.

1307 Escudero Baztan, Juan Manual. *El Alcalde de Zalamea, Versiones de Lope de Vega (Atribuida) y Calderón de la Barca: Edición Crítica, Estudio y Notas.* (The Mayor of Zalamea, Versions of Lope de Vega (Attributed) and Calderón de la Barca: Critical Editions, Analysis, and Notes.) Navarra: Universidad de Navarra; 1997. 896 pp. Notes. Biblio. Index. [D.R. Dissertation available from Faculty of Arts, Universidad de Navarra, E-31080 Pamplona, Spain.] Lang.: Spa.

Spain. 1642. ■A critical edition of two versions of the play. Includes an introductory study covering authorship, date of composition, sources, characters, plots, structures and performances of both plays.

1308 Salom, Jaime; Zatlin, Phyllis, transl. *Una Hoguera en al amanecer.* (Bonfire at Dawn.) University Park, PA: Estreno; 1992. 59 pp. (Contemporary Spanish Plays I.) Lang.: Eng.

Spain. 1986-1992. ■First English translation of Salom's play.

1309 Strindberg, August; Balzamo, Elena, transl. *"Mademoiselle Julie/ La Plus Forte."* (Miss Julie/The Stronger.) *AST.* 1996 15 Mar.; 986: 3-34. Illus.: Photo. B&W. 31. Lang.: Fre.

Sweden. France. 1888-1996. ■French translations of *Fröken Julie* and *Den Starkare* as presented by Théâtre de Chartres, directed by Jacques Kraemer. Includes the director's pre-rehearsal notes, profiles of the director, actors, Théâtre de Chartres, and other productions.

1310 Ayckbourn, Alan; Blanc, Michel, transl., adapt. *"Temps variable en soirée."* (Communicating Doors.) *AST.* 1996 1 Oct.; 995: 2-68. Illus.: Photo. B&W. 22. Lang.: Fre.

UK-England. France. 1995. ■French translation of Ayckbourn's *Communicating Doors* as directed by Stephan Meldegg at Théâtre de la Renaissance. Includes profiles of personnel.

1311 Brown, Ben. *"All Things Considered."* *PI.* 1997 Sep.; 13(1): 36-45. Illus.: Photo. B&W. 1. Lang.: Eng.

UK-England. 1996. ■Continued in *Plays International* 13:2 (1997), 36-46.

1312 Furse, Anna. *Augustine (Big Hysteria).* Amsterdam: Harwood Academic Publishers; 1997. 49 pp. (Contemporary Theatre Studies 20.) Illus.: Photo. 4. Lang.: Eng.

UK-England. 1991. ■Text of Furse's *Augustine (Big Hysteria).* Includes a critical introduction and notes on the original staging (at the Plymouth Theatre Royal by Drum Theatre, directed by author).

1313 Goulding, Philip. *"Went Down to the Crossroads."* *PI.* 1997 Apr.; 12(9): 34-45. Lang.: Eng.

DRAMA: —Basic theatrical documents

UK-England. 1997. ■Complete playtext.

1314 Ney, Diane. "*Fastia.*" *PI.* 1997 Nov.; 13(3): 36-45. Lang.: Eng.
UK-England. 1997. ■Play continued in *Plays International* 13:4 (1997), 40-46.

1315 Penhall, Joe. "*Love and Understanding.*" *PI.* 1997 July; 12(12): 38-51. Lang.: Eng.
UK-England. 1997. ■Text of Penhall's play.

1316 Pinter, Harold. "Early Typed Draft, *The Homecoming.*" *PintR.* 1997: 16-27. Lang.: Eng.
UK-England. 1965. ■Early pages from typed draft of *The Homecoming* with corrections and notes.

1317 Pinter, Harold. "Early Draft, *The Homecoming*: Amended Version." *PintR.* 1997: 200-207. Lang.: Eng.
UK-England. 1964. ■Section of an early holograph version of Harold Pinter's play *The Homecoming.*

1318 Saunders, James; Guedj, Attica, transl.; Meldegg, Stephan, transl. "*Le Refuge.*" (Retreat.) *AST.* 1996 15 Jan.; 982: 3-40. Illus.: Photo. B&W. 25. Lang.: Fre.
UK-England. France: Paris. 1995. ■French translation of *Retreat* as produced by Théâtre La Bruyère directed by Stephan Meldegg. Includes profile of the author and actors.

1319 von Henning, Marc; Mount, Kevin, illus. "*After the Hunt*: After Ovid." *PerfR.* 1997 Fall; 2(3): 39-44. Illus.: Photo. B&W. 5. Lang.: Eng.
UK-England. 1997. ■Text of von Henning's verse piece about the death of Actaeon.

1320 Wilde, Oscar; Déprats, Jean-Michel, transl. "*L'Importance d'être constant.*" (The Importance of Being Earnest.) *AST.* 1996 1 Jan.; 981: 3-62. Illus.: Photo. Sketches. B&W. 19. Lang.: Fre.
UK-England. France: Paris. 1895-1996. ■French translation of Wilde's comedy as performed by Théâtre National de Chaillot directed by Jérôme Savary. Includes profile of the author, translator, and actors, an essay on the play, and the reactions of French contemporaries to Oscar Wilde.

1321 Clark, Phil, ed. *Act One Wales: Thirteen One-Act Plays.* Bridgend: Seren P; 1997. 271 pp. (Seren Drama.) Pref. Lang.: Eng.
UK-Wales. 1952-1996. ■Collection of thirteen one-act plays by Welsh playwrights: *Return Journey* by Dylan Thomas (1952), *The Sound of Stillness* by Trevor C. Thomas (1959), *Gazooka* by Gwyn Thomas (1960), *The Eccentric* by Dannie Abse (1959), *Sailing to America* by Duncan Bush (1989), *Redemption Song* by Alan Osborne (1980), *The Drag Factor* by Frank Vickery (1994), *Looking Out to See* by Charles Way (1996), *Hiraeth* by Edward Thomas (1994), *The Old Petrol Station* by Tim Rhys (1994), *The Ark* by Helen Griffin (1994), *A Night Under Canvas* by Lisa Hunt (1990), and *The Ogpu Men* by Ian Rowlands (1992).

1322 Algarín, Miguel, ed.; Griffith, Lois, ed. *Action: The Nuyorican Poets Cafe Theatre Festival.* New York, NY: Touchstone; 1997. 551 pp. Lang.: Eng.
USA: New York, NY. 1973-1990. ■Collection of plays performed at the Nuyorican Poets Cafe. Includes short historical introduction. Works include Wesley Brown's *Life During Wartime*, Ishmael Reed's *Hubba City*, Peter Spiro's *Howya Doin' Franky Banana*, Amiri Baraka's *The Election Machine Warehouse*, Miguel Piñero's *Playland Blues*, Dennis Moritz's *Just the Boys*, Gloria Feliciano's *Between Blessings*, Lois Elaine Griffith's *White Sirens*, and *The Goong Hay Kid* by Alvin Eng.

1323 Davis, David. "*Five Exits.*" *SoTh.* 1997 Fall; 38(4): 12-26. Illus.: Photo. B&W. 1. Lang.: Eng.
USA. 1995. ■Complete playtexts by Davis, preceded by an interview with the playwright by Jeffrey Scott Elwell, in which Davis discusses his career and his views on playwriting.

1324 Diamond, Betty. "*Thanksgiving.*" *DGQ.* 1997 Fall; 34(3): 46-47. Lang.: Eng.
USA. 1997. ■Text of Betty Diamond's one-minute play *Thanksgiving.*

1325 Elovich, Richard. "*Someone Else from Queens Is Queer.*" *ThM.* 1993; 24(2): 53-66. Illus.: Photo. B&W. 4. Lang.: Eng.

USA. 1992. ■Complete text of Elovich's one-man play.

1326 Foreman, Richard. "*Pearls for Pigs.*" *ThM.* 1997; 28(1): 35-57. Lang.: Eng.
USA. 1995. ■Complete text of Foreman's play.

1327 Foreman, Richard. "Script: *The Universe.*" *TheatreF.* 1997 Win/Spr; 10: 24-37. Illus.: Photo. 7. Lang.: Eng.
USA. 1996. ■Text of *The Universe* presented in performance at St. Mark's Church by the Ontological-Hysteric Theatre.

1328 Fusco, Coco; Bustamante, Nao. "*Stuff.*" *TDR.* 1997 Win; 41(4): 63-82. Lang.: Eng.
USA. 1997. ■Complete playtext with introduction decsribing origins of script and premiere production.

1329 Gingrich-Philbrook, Craig. "Autobiographical Performance Scripts: *Refreshment.*" *TextPQ.* 1997 Oct.; 17(4): 352-360. Notes. Biblio. Lang.: Eng.
USA. 1997. ■Complete text and specific stage directions of this autobiographical performance text, *Refreshment.*

1330 Jenkin, Len. "Script: *Like I Say.*" *TheatreF.* 1997 Sum/Fall; 11: 57-84. Illus.: Photo. 11. Lang.: Eng.
USA. 1997. ■Text of *Like I Say* by Len Jenkin.

1331 Kaufman, Moisés. "*Gross Indecency: The Three Trials of Oscar Wilde.*" *AmTh.* 1997 Nov.; 14(9): 23-45. Illus.: Photo. B&W. 4. Lang.: Eng.
USA: New York, NY. 1997. ■Complete playtext accompanied by brief interview with playwright by Jesse McKinley.

1332 Kornblatt, Marc. "*Eulogies.*" *DGQ.* 1997 Fall; 34(3): 45. Lang.: Eng.
USA. 1997. ■Text of Marc Kornblatt's one-minute play.

1333 Kushner, Tony; Wajcman, Gérard, transl.; Lichtenstein, Jacqueline, transl. "*Angels in America: Fantaisie gay sur des thèmes nationaux. Deuxième partie: Perestroïka.*" (Angels in America, A Gay Fantasy on National Themes, Part II: Perestroika.) *AST.* 1996 1-15 Apr.; 987-988: 2-108. Illus.: Photo. B&W. 33. Lang.: Fre.
USA. France: Paris. 1996. ■French translation of Kushner's play as produced by Théâtre de la Commune Pandora and Comédie de Genève, directed by Brigitte Jacques. Includes profiles of the author, director, translators, and actors, the author's notes and acknowledgements, notes on characters, an essay on the play's historical context, and a glossary of American terms.

1334 Lounsbury, Richard C., ed. *Louisa S. McCord: Selected Writings.* Charlottesville, VA/London: UP of Virginia; 1997. 306 pp. (The Publications of the Southern Texts Society.) Illus.: Pntg. Photo. Dwg. 12. Lang.: Eng.
USA. 1810-1879. ■Writings of Louisa McCord, including her only play *Caius Gracchus.*

1335 McNally, Terrence. "*A Perfect Ganesh.*" *PI.* 1997 Jan.; 12(6): 32-45. Lang.: Eng.
USA. 1993. ■Text of play, continued in *PI* 12:7 (1997 Feb), 34-45.

1336 Moore, Kym. "*The Date.*" *AfAmR.* 1997 Win; 31(4): 639-646. Lang.: Eng.
USA. 1997. ■Text of Kym Moore's play with an introduction.

1337 Parks, Suzan-Lori. "*Imperceptible Mutabilities in the Third Kingdom.*" *ThM.* 1993; 24(3): 88-115. Illus.: Photo. B&W. 5. Lang.: Eng.
USA. 1989. ■Complete text of Parks' play.

1338 Perkins, Kathy A., ed.; Uno, Roberta, ed. *Contemporary Plays by Women of Color.* London: Routledge; 1996. 323 pp. Index. Illus.: Photo. 12. Lang.: Eng.
USA. 1992-1996. ■Anthology of plays by contemporary women writers including Anna Deavere Smith's *Twilight: Los Angeles, 1992*, Marga Gomez's *Memory Tricks*, Glenda Dickerson and Breena Clark's *Re(m)embering) Aunt Jemima: A Menstrual Show*, Diana Son's *R.A.W. ('Cause I'm a Woman)*, Brenda Wong Aoki's *The Queen's Garden*, Migdalia Cruz's *The Have-Little*, and Cherríe Moraga's *Heroes and Saints.*

1339 Peters, Emma Gene. *Southern Bells: Voices of Working Women. A Telling in Three Parts.* Cincinnati, OH: Union Institute; 1997. 114 pp. [Ph.D. Dissertation, Univ. Microfilms Order No. AAC 9812108.] Lang.: Eng.

DRAMA: —Basic theatrical documents

USA. 1997. ■Playtext in the form of a 'storytelling performance piece', including *Anthelia's Letters, The Labor Organizer,* and *Miracle on Coon Creek* by Emma Gene Peters.

1340 Rabe, David. *"A Question of Mercy."* AmTh. 1997 July/ Aug.; 14(6): 21-43. Illus.: Photo. B&W. 5. Lang.: Eng.
USA: New York, NY. 1997. ■Complete text of play adapted from the essay by Richard Selzer. Includes brief interview with Rabe by Stephanie Coen.

1341 Sakamoto, Edward. *Hawaii No Ka Oi—The Kamiya Family Trilogy.* Honolulu, HI: Univ of Hawaii P; 1995. 142 pp. Notes. Gloss. Lang.: Eng.
USA. 1993-1994. ■Collection of three plays by Hawaiian-American playwright Edward Sakamoto: *The Taste of Kona Coffee, Mānoa Valley* and *The Life of the Land.* Includes a short critical introduction to the plays and the history of Japanese-Americans in Hawaii.

1342 Silverman, Jeffry Lloyd. *What Comes From Hitting Sticks and Other Plays.* Anchorage, AK: University of Alaska; 1997. 126 pp. [M.A. Thesis, Univ. Microfilms Order No. AAC 1386996.] Lang.: Eng.
USA. 1994-1996. ■Text of Silverman's original play.

1343 Spry, Tami. *"Skins:* A Daughter's (Re)Construction of Cancer. A Performative Autobiography." TextPQ. 1997 Oct.; 17(4): 361-365. Lang.: Eng.
USA. 1993. ■Complete text with introduction by author describing subject material and development of piece.

1344 Stephens, Thomas W. *"Miserere, Passing Through."* SoTh. 1997 Win; 38(1): 12-26. Illus.: Photo. B&W. 1. Lang.: Eng.
USA. 1994-1996. ■Complete text of Thomas W. Stephens' play, preceded by an interview with the playwright by Jeffery Scott Elwell in which he discusses the evolution of the play.

1345 Vogel, Paula. *"The Mineola Twins."* AmTh. 1997 Feb.; 14(2): 23-41. Illus.: Photo. B&W. 5. Lang.: Eng.
USA. 1995-1997. ■Complete text of play. Includes brief interview with playwright by Kathy Sova.

1346 Wasserstein, Wendy. *"An American Daughter."* AmTh. 1997 Sep.; 14(7): 23-43. Illus.: Photo. B&W. 4. Lang.: Eng.
USA. 1997. ■Complete playtext including interview with playwright by Stephanie Coen.

1347 Wellman, Mac. *"Cat's-Paw."* ThM. 1997; 27(2/3): 96-135. Illus.: Photo. B&W. 4. Lang.: Eng.
USA. 1997. ■Complete text of play which is a 'meditation on the Don Juan theme'.

1348 Wellman, Mac. *"The Difficulty of Crossing a Field."* ThM. 1997; 27(2/3): 64-86. Illus.: Photo. B&W. 2. Lang.: Eng.
USA. 1997. ■Complete playtext with music by David Laing.

1349 Wellman, Mac. *"The Land of Fog and Whistles."* ThM. 1993; 23(1): 43-51. Lang.: Eng.
USA. 1992. ■Text of Wellman's play.

1350 West, Mae; Schlissel, Lillian, ed. *Three Plays by Mae West.* New York, NY/London: Routledge; 1997. 256 pp. Notes. Illus.: Photo. 8. Lang.: Eng.
USA. 1926-1928. ■Texts of *Sex, The Drag,* and *Pleasure Man.* Includes an introduction on the life and career of the actress and playwright.

1351 Wilder, Thornton; O'Neil, F.J., ed. *"The Rivers Under the Earth."* AmTh. 1997 Mar.; 14(3): 25-30. Illus.: Photo. B&W. 3. Lang.: Eng.
USA. 1897-1997. ■Complete playtext. Includes interview with play's editor F.J. O'Neil conducted by Stephen Nunns.

1352 Wilson, Erin Cressida. *"Script: Hurricane."* TheatreF. 1997 Sum/Fall; 11: 20-37. Illus.: Photo. 10. Lang.: Eng.
USA. 1996. ■Text of Wilson's performance piece.

1353 Yankowitz, Susan, ed. *"1969 Terminal 1996: An Ensemble Work."* PerAJ. 1997 Sep.; 19(3): 80-106. Illus.: Photo. B&W. 2. [Number 57.] Lang.: Eng.
USA: New York, NY. 1969-1996. ■Updated text of the play originally conceived by the Open Theatre with an introduction and notes on the approach a director and performers should take when presenting it.

Design/technology

1354 Garnhum, Ken. *"A Setting for Frida K."* CTR. 1997 Sum; 91: 62. Lang.: Eng.
Canada: Toronto, ON. 1997. Histories-sources. ■Poem written by Garnhum as inspiration for his scene design for *Frida K.* by Gloria Montero, directed by Peter Hinton at Tarragon Theatre's Extra Space.

1355 Howard, Ruth. *"Holding On and Letting Go."* CTR. 1997 Spr; 90: 15-19. Illus.: Dwg. Photo. B&W. 13. Lang.: Eng.
Canada. 1990-1997. Histories-sources. ■Designer Ruth Howard describes her efforts to create effective design teams for community theatre productions.

1356 Lampert-Gréaux, Ellen. *"François Melin."* LDim. 1997 Jan/ Feb.; 21(1): 22. Illus.: Photo. B&W. 1. Lang.: Eng.
France: Paris. 1997. Biographical studies. ■Profile and career of chief electrician for Comédie-Française.

1357 Dózsa, Katalin, F. *"A kulisszáktól a stilizált színpadig. Mégegyszer a Tragédia 1883-1915 közötti díszletterveiről."* (From Behind Scenes to the Stylized Stage: The Stage Designs of Imre Madách's *Tragedy* Between 1883 and 1915.) SzSz. 1997(32): 33-48. Illus.: Photo. B&W. 5. Lang.: Hun.
Hungary: Budapest. 1883-1915. Historical studies. ■A survey of the stage designs for Imre Madách's *Az ember tragédija (The Tragedy of Man)* by renowned designers of the period.

1358 Heinrich, Manfred. *"Bühnenbild ohne Umbau."* (A Set Without Scene Changes.) BtR. 1997; 91(2): 33-37. Illus.: Design. Photo. Plan. Color. Grd.Plan. 11. Lang.: Ger.
Sweden: Stockholm. 1800-1997. Histories-sources. ■Historical account of projections and contemporary techniques, equipment, control systems from Tony Kushner's *Angels in America* directed by Peter Lundquist at Stockholms Stadsteater.

1359 Söderberg, Olle. *"Patronerna på Ahlquittern."* (The Squires at Ahlquittern.) ProScen. 1997; 21(3): 14. Illus.: Photo. B&W. Lang.: Swe.
Sweden: Bjurtjärn. 1997. Historical studies. ■A report from Bjurtjärns teaterförening's production of *Patronerna på Ahlquittern (The Squires at Ahlquittern)* with references to the technical solutions for an out door show.

1360 Lampert-Gréaux, Ellen. *"National Treasure."* LDim. 1997 Apr.; 21(3): 32-35. Illus.: Photo. Color. 7. Lang.: Eng.
UK-England: London. 1997. Biographical studies. ■Career of lighting designer Mark Jonathan, head of the lighting department at the Royal National Theatre.

1361 Lampert-Gréaux, Ellen. *"Joanna Town."* LDim. 1997 Sep.; 21(8): 20. Illus.: Photo. B&W. 1. Lang.: Eng.
UK-England: London. 1986-1997. Biographical studies. ■Profile of Joanna Town, head lighting designer of the Royal Court Theatre. Career, current work on *The Steward of Christendom* by Sebastian Barry directed by Max Stafford-Clark.

1362 Aronson, Arnold. *"Richard Foreman as Scenographer."* TheatreF. 1997 Win/Spr; 10: 17-23. Illus.: Photo. 5. Lang.: Eng.
USA. 1990-1996. Historical studies. ■Director Richard Foreman's sets and scenography and their importance to his vision as playwright and director. Examines *Eddie Goes to Poetry City, I've Got the Shakes, Major Problems, My Head Was a Sledgehammer,* and *Permanent Brain Damage (Risk It! Risk It!).*

1363 Aronson, Arnold. *"Design for Angels in America:* Envisioning the Millennium." 213-226 in Geis, Deborah R., ed.; Kruger, Steven F., ed. *Approaching the Millennium: Essays on Angels in America.* Ann Arbor, MI: Univ. of Michigan P; 1997. 352 pp. Notes. Illus.: Photo. 2. Lang.: Eng.
USA: New York, NY, Los Angeles, CA. UK-England: London. 1992-1994. Critical studies. ■Staging and scenery to present the 'idea of America' in three productions of Tony Kushner's play: The London production, designed by Nick Ormerod, directed by Declan Donnellan for the Royal National Theatre at the Cottesloe. The New York production designed by Robin Wagner, directed by George C. Wolfe on Broadway. The Los Angeles production, designed by John Conklin, directed by Oskar Eustis at the Mark Taper Forum.

DRAMA: —Design/technology

1364   Barbour, David. "Night and Day." *LDim.* 1997 Jan/Feb.; 21(1): 13. Illus.: Photo. Color. 2. Lang.: Eng.
USA: New York, NY. 1997. Historical studies. ■Lighting designer Kenneth Posner's work for Michael Cristofer's *The Blues Are Running* and Leslie Ayvazian's *Nine Armenians*, both at Manhattan Theatre Club.

1365   Barbour, David. "Derek McLane." *TCI.* 1997 Feb.; 31(2): 36-39. Illus.: Photo. Sketches. 15. Lang.: Eng.
USA: New York, NY. 1996-1997. Historical studies. ■Set designer Derek McLane's latest work on Broadway, Noël Coward's *Present Laughter*, directed by Scott Elliott, starring Frank Langella at the Walter Kerr Theatre.

1366   Barbour, David. "The Light of History." *LDim.* 1997 Jan/Feb.; 21(1): 17. Illus.: Photo. Color. 1. Lang.: Eng.
USA: New York, NY. 1997. Historical studies. ■Howell Binkley's lighting design for Ronald Harwood's *Taking Sides* which ran on Broadway at the Brooks Atkinson theatre.

1367   Barbour, David. "The War Between Men and Women." *LDim.* 1997 May; 21(4): 15. Illus.: Photo. Color. 2. Lang.: Eng.
USA: New York, NY. 1997. Historical studies. ■Peter Mumford's lighting design for Broadway productions of Pam Gems' *Stanley* at Circle in the Square Theatre and Ibsen's *A Doll's House (Et Dukkehjem)*, adapted by Frank McGuinness. Both productions originated on London's West End.

1368   Barbour, David. "The Dying of the Light." *LDim.* 1997 June; 21(5): 15. Illus.: Photo. Color. 1. Lang.: Eng.
USA: New York, NY. 1978-1997. Historical studies. ■Kirk Bookman's lighting design for the revival of D.L. Coburn's *The Gin Game* on Broadway, directed by Charles Nelson Reilly.

1369   Barbour, David. "Illuminating the Universe." *LDim.* 1997 June; 21(5): 22. Illus.: Photo. Color. 1. Lang.: Eng.
USA: New York, NY. 1997. Historical studies. ■Dennis Parichy's lighting design for Lanford Wilson's *Sympathetic Magic* at Second Stage Theatre, directed by Marshall Mason. Parichy's past collaborations with Wilson and Mason.

1370   Barbour, David. "Lighting Up Louisville." *LDim.* 1997 July; 21(6): 26-33. Illus.: Photo. Color. 2. Lang.: Eng.
USA: Louisville, KY. 1997. Historical studies. ■Ed McCarthy and Greg Sullivan's lighting designs for the 1997 Humana Festival of New American Plays for Actors' Theatre of Louisville. Productions included Benjie Aerenson's *Lighting Up the Two-Year-Old*, Steven Dietz's *Private Eyes*, Richard Dresser's *Gunshy* and Naomi Iizuka's *Polaroid Stories*.

1371   Barbour, David. "Beat the Clock." *LDim.* 1997 Dec.; 21(11): 20-21. Illus.: Photo. Color. 1. Lang.: Eng.
USA: New York, NY. 1997. Technical studies. ■Jeffrey S. Koger's lighting design for Signature Theatre Company's revival of Arthur Miller's *The American Clock*, directed by James Houghton. Challenges faced by renovation of space.

1372   Barbour, David. "Robert Brill." *TCI.* 1997 May; 31(5): 46-49. Illus.: Photo. 14. Lang.: Eng.
USA: New York, NY. 1997. Historical studies. ■On the work of set designer Robert Brill in Craig Lucas' new play *God's Heart* at the Mitzi Newhouse Theatre at Lincoln Center.

1373   Barbour, David. "Neil Patel." *TCI.* 1997 Jan.; 31(1): 26-29. Illus.: Photo. 13. Lang.: Eng.
USA. 1996. Historical studies. ■Patel's designs for three off-Broadway productions: *The Model Apartment* by Donald Margulies, directed by Lisa Peterson at Primary Stages, *The Grey Zone* by Tim Blake Nelson, directed by Doug Hughes at Manhattan Class Company, and Doug Wright's *Quills* directed by Howard Shalwitz at New York Theatre Workshop.

1374   Cochran, Kathleen Claire. *Costume Design for Shirley Gee's 'Warrior'.* Long Beach, CA: California State Univ; 1997. 59 pp. Notes. Biblio. [M.F.A. Thesis, Univ. Microfilms Order No. AAC 1385526.] Lang.: Eng.
USA: Long Beach, CA. 1997. Historical studies. ■On designing costumes for a production of Shirley Gee's *Warrior* at California Repertory Company, California State University.

1375   Everding, Robert G. "William Saroyan and the Growth of Impressionist Stage Setting." *TA.* 1997; 50: 102-108. Notes. Lang.: Eng.
USA. 1939-1943. Historical studies. ■Saroyan's insistence on realistic stage sets for his plays as a means of expressing his vision. Focus on *The Time of Your Life* and *My Heart's in the Highlands*.

1376   Hogan, Jane. "Dreamweaver." *LDim.* 1997 July; 21(6): 13. Illus.: Photo. Color. 1. Lang.: Eng.
USA: New York, NY. 1997. Historical studies. ■Charlie Spickler's lighting design for *An Obituary—Heiner Müller: A Man Without a Behind* at the Castillo Theatre.

1377   Hogan, Jane. "Running Wilde." *LDim.* 1997 May; 21(4): 30. Illus.: Photo. Color. 1. Lang.: Eng.
USA: New York, NY. 1997. Historical studies. ■Betsy Adams' lighting design for Tectonic Theater Project, Inc.'s production of *Gross Indecency: The Three Trials of Oscar Wilde*, written and directed by Moisés Kaufman.

1378   Istel, John. "Paul Owen." *AmTh.* 1997 Apr.; 14(4): 29-31. Illus.: Photo. B&W. 2. Lang.: Eng.
USA: Louisville, KY. 1997. Biographical studies. ■Career of set designer Owen, collaboration with director Jon Jory, and his current work for the Humana Festival of New American Plays produced at Actors' Theatre of Louisville.

1379   Lampert-Gréaux, Ellen. "*Silents* and Sound." *LDim.* 1997 July; 21(6): 11. Illus.: Photo. Color. 1. Lang.: Eng.
USA: New York, NY. 1997. Historical studies. ■Mimi Jordan Sherin's use of old instruments for the lighting design of *American Silents* presented at The Raw Space and *The Medium*, presented at Miller Theatre of Columbia University, both directed by Anne Bogart.

1380   Walton, Tony. "Light Up the Sky." *AmTh.* 1997 July/Aug.; 14(6): 18-20. Illus.: Photo. B&W. 3. Lang.: Eng.
USA: New York, NY. 1956-1997. Critical studies. ■Designer Walton pays tribute to his mentor, lighting designer Abe Feder who died in 1997. Feder's work in opera and theatre, personal relationship.

Institutions

1381   Kaye, Nick, ed. "Jan Lauwers/Needcompany: Snakesong/Le Désir." *PerfR.* 1997 Spr; 2(1): 23-30. Index. Illus.: Photo. B&W. 6. Lang.: Eng.
Belgium: Antwerp. 1996. Histories-sources. ■Composite text of interviews with Needcompany members and texts from *Snakesong Trilogy*.

1382   Laermans, Rudi. "The Essential Theatre of Needcompany." *PerfR.* 1997 Spr; 2(1): 14-22. Illus.: Photo. B&W. 4. Lang.: Eng.
Belgium: Antwerp. 1996. Critical studies. ■Analysis of the work of director Jan Lauwers and his group Needcompany in relation to voyeurism and exhibitionism, the ethics of communication and politics of language. Focuses on the company's *Snakesong Trilogy*.

1383   Bell, Karen. "Centaur New Leader Gordon McCall." *PAC.* 1997; 31(1): 5-6. Illus.: Photo. B&W. 2. Lang.: Eng.
Canada: Montreal, PQ. 1997. Biographical studies. ■McCall's background in Canadian theatre and how it prepared him to assume the directorship of Montreal's Centaur Theatre.

1384   Belzil, Patricia. "Quelques crocs-en-jambe au réel." (Pulling Some Fast Ones on Reality.) *JCT.* 1997; 84: 116-124. Notes. Illus.: Photo. B&W. 7. Lang.: Fre.
Canada: Montreal, PQ. 1997. Historical studies. ■Young theatre artists questioning the world observed in a cross-section of plays at Festival de Théâtre des Amériques, 1997 edition.

1385   Burgoyne, Lynda. "Préparer le public de demain: La Compagnie de Théâtre Longue Vue." (Preparing the Public of Tomorrow: The Compagnie de Théâtre Longue Vue.) *JCT.* 1997; 83: 32-35. Notes. Illus.: Photo. B&W. 3. Lang.: Fre.
Canada: Montreal, PQ. 1995-1997. Historical studies. ■Montreal-based Compagnie de Théâtre Longue Vue seeks to attract a new audience to theatre through populist treatment of classics and workshops for students.

1386   Falkenstein, Len. "Edmonton's Citadel Theatre: A Changing of the Guards or Just Soldiering On?" *CTR.* 1997 Win; 93: 5-9. Biblio. Notes. Illus.: Photo. B&W. 1. Lang.: Eng.

DRAMA: —Institutions

Canada: Edmonton, AB. 1965-1997. Historical studies. ■Attempts to redefine the role of Citadel Theatre as regional theatre.

1387 Fouquet, Ludovic. "Lettre de France." (Letter from France.) *JCT.* 1997; 84: 145-149. Notes. Illus.: Photo. B&W. 3. Lang.: Fre.

Canada: Montreal, PQ. 1997. Historical studies. ■Lessons for a Frenchman attending Festival de Théâtre des Amériques, 1997 edition.

1388 Godin, Jean-Cléo. "La 'dramaturgie nationale' au Théâtre du Nouveau Monde." (The 'National Play Repertoire' at the Théâtre du Nouveau Monde.) *AnT.* 1997 Spr; 22: 43-56. Biblio. Notes. Lang.: Fre.

Canada: Montreal, PQ. 1949-1997. Historical studies. ■Place of plays by québécois playwrights and premiere productions of québécois plays in Théâtre du Nouveau Monde programming from its foundation to present day.

1389 Graham, Catherine. "Speaking as Part of Canada: An Interview with Gordon McCall about Centaur Theatre." *CTR.* 1997 Win; 93: 23-26. Lang.: Eng.

Canada: Montreal, PQ. 1997. Histories-sources. ■Artistic director Gordon McCall on running Centaur Theatre as English-language theatre in Quebec.

1390 Jones, Heather. "Rising Tide Theatre and/in the Newfoundland Cultural Scene." *CTR.* 1997 Win; 93: 38-41. Biblio. Illus.: Photo. B&W. 1. Lang.: Eng.

Canada: Trinity, NF. 1973-1997. Historical studies. ■History of Rising Tide Theatre in context of Newfoundland cultural policy.

1391 Lafon, Dominique. "Molière au Théâtre du Nouveau Monde: du bon usage des classiques." (Molière at the Théâtre du Nouveau Monde: Good Use of the Classics.) *AnT.* 1997 Spr; 22: 23-42. Notes. Tables. Lang.: Fre.

Canada: Montreal, PQ. 1951-1997. Historical studies. ■Place of Molière's plays in Théâtre du Nouveau Monde's programming from its foundation to present day.

1392 Lesage, Marie-Christine. "Monologues." *JCT.* 1997; 84: 130-135. Illus.: Photo. B&W. 4. Lang.: Fre.

Canada: Montreal, PQ. 1997. Historical studies. ■Solo performances at the Festival de Théâtre des Amériques by William Yang (*The North*), Pol Pelletier (*Or*), Urbi et Orbi (*Dits et Inédits*), the Ronnie Burkett Theatre of Marionettes (*Tinka's New Dress*), and Robert Marinier of Théâtre de la Vieille 17 (*L'insomnie*).

1393 Marsolais, Gilles. "Dis-moi où tu loges.: Témoignage." (Tell Me Where You Are Staying.: Witness.) *AnT.* 1997 Spr ; 22: 13-22. Notes. Biblio. Lang.: Fre.

Canada: Montreal, PQ. 1951-1997. Historical studies. ■History of Théâtre du Nouveau Monde told through studies of the four theatre spaces it has occupied: Gésù, Orpheum, Port-Royal and Comédie Canadienne.

1394 Partington, Richard. "The Juniper Theatre's Canadian Content and the Critics." *JCT.* 1997 Spr; 18(1): 59-88. Notes. Biblio. Lang.: Eng.

Canada: Toronto, ON. 1951-1954. Historical studies. ■Measures Juniper Theatre's contribution to Canadian theatre through studies of Canadian-written plays it produced and critical reception they received. Appendices list Juniper productions and casts of their Canadian plays.

1395 Shantz, Valerie. "Products of the Canadian Imagination: An Interview with Joey Tremblay and Jonathan Christenson of Catalyst Theatre." *CTR.* 1997 Spr; 90: 78-82. Notes. Illus.: Photo. B&W. 3. Lang.: Eng.

Canada: Edmonton, AB. 1995-1996. Histories-sources. ■Structural and artistic changes to Catalyst Theatre under co-artistic directors Joey Tremblay and Jonathan Christenson.

1396 Stapleton, David. "Theatre Cambrian." *PAC.* 1997; 31(1): 32-33. Illus.: Photo. B&W. 3. Lang.: Eng.

Canada: Sudbury, ON. 1985-1997. Historical studies. ■Theatre Cambrian involves a cross section of the community and has invigorated Sudbury theatre.

1397 Wickham, Philip; Legault, Yannick. "L'éternité entre l'heure zéro et la fin du millénaire." (The Eternity Between Zero Hour and the End of the Millennium.) *JCT.* 1997; 84: 136-144. Notes. Illus.: Photo. B&W. 6. Lang.: Fre.

Canada: Montreal, PQ. 1997. Historical studies. ■Mixing genres and forms in experimental and theatre productions of Festival de Théâtre des Amériques, 1997 edition.

1398 Wickham, Philip. "Pouvoir lire le théâtre: Dramaturges Éditeurs." (The Ability to Read Theatre: Dramaturges Éditeurs.) *JCT.* 1997; 84: 171-176. Illus.: Photo. B&W. 4. Lang.: Fre.

Canada. 1996-1997. Historical studies. ■Dramaturges Éditeurs, publishing house launched by Claude Champagne and Yvan Bienvenue, fills gap in québécois play publishing.

1399 Winston, Iris. "The Centaur Theatre." *PAC.* 1997; 31(1): 4. Illus.: Photo. B&W. 1. Lang.: Eng.

Canada: Montreal, PQ. 1969-1997. Historical studies. ■The Centaur Theatre, Montreal's oldest English-language theatre, its importance as one of Canada's most prominent theatres, and its management by artistic director Maurice Podbrey for twenty-eight years.

1400 Heje, Alice Bryrup; Lewin, Jan, transl. "Är elefanten räddningen?" (Is the Elephant the Solution?)*Entré.* 1997; 24(5): 44-45. Illus.: Photo. B&W. Lang.: Swe.

Denmark: Copenhagen. 1997. Historical studies. ■A report from the theatres of Copenhagen and the problem with too many unions, with reference to Annisette and Thomas Koppel's *Bella Vita* at Gladsaxe Teater, produced by three succesive directors: Kristiana Korf, Tommy Karter and Thomas Koppel.

1401 Dmitrevskaja, Marina; Witt, Susanne, transl. "Huset som Sonnenschein byggde." (The House That Sonnenschein Built.) *Tningen.* 1997; 21(3): 16-19. Illus.: Photo. B&W. Lang.: Swe.

Estonia: Tallinn. 1967. Historical studies. ■A presentation of the Tallinna Linnateater and its artistic director Elmo Nüganen.

1402 Kennedy, Dennis. "The Language of the Spectator." *ShS.* 1997; 50(1): 29-40. Notes. Lang.: Eng.

Europe. USA. Canada. 1946-1997. Historical studies. ■Post-War rise of Shakespeare festivals as one means of international recovery, and audience reception of Shakespeare's language through the last half-century.

1403 Didong, Paola. "Pojkarna i Avignon." (The Boys At Avignon.) *Entré.* 1997; 24(5): 40-42. Illus.: Photo. B&W. Lang.: Swe.

France: Avignon. 1997. Historical studies. ■A report from this year's festival at Avignon, with references to the directors Stanislas Nordey, Laurent Pelly and Olivier Py, and his production *Le Visage d'Orphée.*

1404 Engelhardt, Barbara. "Grenzverkehr." (Border Traffic.) *TZ.* 1997; 5: 12-17. Illus.: Photo. B&W. 5. Lang.: Ger.

France: Strasbourg. 1900-1997. Histories-general. ■A portrait and the history of Théâtre National de Strasbourg.

1405 Holm, Brent. "Picture and Counter-Picture: An Attempt to Involve Context in the Interpretation of Théâtre Italien Iconography." *ThR.* 1997; 22(3): 219-233. Notes. Illus.: Dwg. B&W. 12. Lang.: Eng.

France: Paris. 1653-1697. Historical studies. ■Analysis of iconography of Théâtre Italien in seventeenth-century Paris, revealing presence of official (royalist) and unofficial (obscene) imagery.

1406 Spindler, Fredrika. "Äntligen nyskapande förmågor." (At Last Innovative Talents.) *Dramat.* 1997; 5(3): 25. Illus.: Photo. B&W. Lang.: Swe.

France: Avignon. 1997. Historical studies. ■A report from the Avignon Festival, with reference to Olivier Py's production of *Le Visage d'Orphée (The Face of Orpheus).*

1407 Williams, David. ""A Grain of Sand in the Works': Continuity and Change at the Théâtre du Soleil." *PerfR.* 1997 Sum; 2(2): 102-107. Notes. Biblio. Lang.: Eng.

France: Paris. 1970-1997. Critical studies. ■The development of the Théâtre du Soleil and the way in which it has tried to contest the ways in which we are invited to live under capitalism. Focuses on the open letter that the company sent to their hosts on being invited to perform in Jeruslaem in 1988 as an example of the company's political and artistic strategy.

DRAMA: —Institutions

1408 Brandenburg, Detlef. "Von der grossen Verdumpfung." (About the Great Dullness.) *DB*. 1997; 7: 19-23. Illus.: Photo. B&W. 2. Lang.: Ger.
Germany: Berlin. 1997. Histories-sources. ■An interview with Michael Merschmeier, speaker of the jury of Berliner Theatertreffen, about the present situation of stages and the objections to this year's selection.

1409 Burckhardt, Barbara. "Treue und Neugier." (Faith and Curiosity.) *THeute*. 1997; 5: 19-20. Illus.: Photo. B&W. 2. Lang.: Ger.
Germany: Stuttgart. 1993-1997. Histories-sources. ■An interview with Friedrich Schirmer who is manager at Schauspiel Stuttgart about his directorship since 1993 and plans for the future.

1410 Burckhardt, Barbara. "Vier Wände und ein Dach." (Four Walls And a Roof.) *THeute*. 1997; Yb: 48-59. Illus.: Photo. B&W. 6. Lang.: Ger.
Germany: Hamburg. Switzerland: Zurich. 1997. Historical studies. ■Portraits of Deutsches Schauspielhaus and Theater Neumarkt, chosen as theatres of the year by critics of *Theater Heute*, with description of the management of each theatre.

1411 Burckhardt, Barbara; Wille, Franz. "Demokratie als Liebe des Despoten." (Democracy as the Despot's Love.) *THeute*. 1997; 10: 10-15. Illus.: Photo. B&W. 6. Lang.: Ger.
Germany: Berlin. 1979-1997. Histories-sources. ■Interview with actor Peter Simonischek about his work at Schaubühne, his collaboration with Peter Stein and other directors, and the functioning of an ensemble.

1412 Franke, Eckhard. "All They Need Is Love." *THeute*. 1997; 1: 34-36. Illus.: Photo. B&W. 2. Lang.: Ger.
Germany: Darmstadt. 1996-1997. Historical studies. ■The season at Staatstheater Darmstadt under the new directorship of Gerd-Theo Umberg. Includes discussion on *Familie Schroffenstein (The Feud of the Schroffensteins)* by Heinrich von Kleist directed by Thomas Krupa, *Die Unvernünftigen sterben aus (The Reckless Are Dying Out)* by Peter Handke directed by Thomas Janssen and *Liliom* by Ferenc Molnár directed by Michael Gruner.

1413 Grund, Stefan. "'Mehr Funken schlagen'." (To Raise More Sparks.) *TZ*. 1997; 5: 8-11. Illus.: Photo. B&W. 2. Lang.: Ger.
Germany: Bremen. 1997. Histories-sources. ■An interview with Klaus Pierwoss, manager at Bremer Schauspielhaus, including a statement about efficient structures by dramaturg Ulrich Fuchs.

1414 Hass, Ulrike. "Die Kunst, in der Fremde zu bleiben." (The Skill of Staying in Foreign Parts.) *TZ*. 1997; 4: 11-15. Illus.: Photo. B&W. 4. Lang.: Ger.
Germany: Jena. 1986-1997. Historical studies. ■Describes the concepts and aesthetics of Theaterhaus and the actors who left Berlin to go to Jena.

1415 Höbel, Wolfgang. "Das Normale ist doch schon unangenehm genug." (The Normal Is Just Unpleasant Enough.) *THeute*. 1997; 8: 33-36. Pref. Illus.: Photo. B&W. 3. Lang.: Ger.
Germany: Hannover. 1997. Histories-sources. ■A published speech in which he reflects the way he chose new plays to perform on occasion of the IIIrd 'Autorentage' (Hannover).

1416 Klaić, Dragan. "Reconnecting in the Ruhr." *ThM*. 1993; 24(2): 112-115. Illus.: Photo. B&W. 1. Lang.: Eng.
Germany: Mülheim. 1992. Critical studies. ■Profile of Roberto Ciulli and his company Theater an der Ruhr.

1417 Kohse, Petra. "Staat im Staatstheater." (A State Within the State Theatre.) *TZ*. 1997; 6: 22-25. Illus.: Photo. B&W. 5. Lang.: Ger.
Germany: Berlin. 1997. Historical studies. ■A portrait of Baracke, a venue of Deutsches Theater (Berlin), under the management of director Thomas Ostermeier and dramaturg Jens Hillje.

1418 Lennartz, Knut. "Düsseldorf bleibt Düsseldorf." (Dusseldorf Remains Dusseldorf.) *DB*. 1997; 6: 26-29. Illus.: Photo. B&W. 5. Lang.: Ger.
Germany: Dusseldorf. 1996-1997. Histories-sources. ■An interview with Anna Badora, the first female director of Düsseldorfer Schauspielhaus for the last season, about her start and program.

1419 Lysell, Roland. "Tysk teater vågar—men inte kritiken." (The German Theatre Dares—But Criticism Doesn't.) *Entré*. 1997; 24(4): 41-42. Illus.: Photo. B&W. Lang.: Swe.
Germany: Berlin. 1997. Historical studies. ■A report from Theatertreffen in Berlin, with reference to Elfriede Jelinek's *Stecken, Stab und Stangl (Stick, Rod, and Pole)* directed by Thirza Bruncken.

1420 Merck, Nikolaus. "'Theater ist wunderbar und unentbehrlich'." ('Theatre Is Wonderful And Indispensable'.) *TZ*. 1997; 5: 4-7. Illus.: Photo. B&W. 2. Lang.: Ger.
Germany: Dresden. 1997. Histories-sources. ■An interview with Dieter Görne, manager of Staatsschauspiel Dresden, about the task and function of theatre in society.

1421 Mufson, Daniel. "Performing Space and History: Theater der Welt '96." *ThM*. 1997; 27(2/3): 147-154. Illus.: Photo. B&W. 5. Lang.: Eng.
Germany: Dresden. 1996. Historical studies. ■Analysis of Theater der Welt's 1996 season.

1422 Pietzsch, Ingeborg. "Theater im Feuerwehrturm." (Theatre in the Fire Tower.) *TZ*. 1997; 43: 58-61. Illus.: Photo. B&W. 5. Lang.: Ger.
Germany: Mannheim. 1996. Historical studies. ■A portrait of Schnawwl, a children's theatre, under the new directorship of Brigitte Dethier since 1996.

1423 Quasthoff, Michael. "Pfadfinder im Weltgetriebe." (Scouts in the World System.) *TZ*. 1997; 4: 4-5. Illus.: Photo. B&W. 1. Lang.: Ger.
Germany: Hannover. 1997. Histories-sources. ■An interview with Ulrich Khuon, manager of Staatsschauspiel Hannover, about ideas and successes.

1424 Raddatz, Franz. "Die Ebene des Dritten geht verloren." (The Level of the Third Gets Lost.) *TZ*. 1997; 2: 4-8. Illus.: Photo. B&W. 1. Lang.: Ger.
Germany: Berlin. 1989-1997. Histories-sources. ■An interview with actor and manager Martin Wuttke at Berliner Ensemble about Heiner Müller, politics and culture.

1425 Rischbieter, Henning. "Die Wonnen der Gewöhnlichkeit." (The Delights of Commonness.) *THeute*. 1997; 8: 24-29. Illus.: Photo. B&W. 6. Lang.: Ger.
Germany: Cologne. 1985-1997. Historical studies. ■Kölner Schauspiel under the directorship by Günter Krämer. Describes Krämer's directions of *Faust I* by Johann Wolfgang von Goethe, *Mephisto* by Ariane Mnouchkine, *Zur schönen Aussicht (Belle Vue)* by Ödön von Horváth.

1426 Rischbieter, Henning. "Die Abseitsfalle." (The Offside Trap.) *THeute*. 1997; 3: 23-29. Illus.: Photo. B&W. 7. Lang.: Ger.
Germany: Berlin. 1996-1997. Historical studies. ■A current portrait of Schaubühne, the last big theatre in West Berlin. Reports of *Der Hausbesuch (The Visit)* by Rudolf Borchardt directed by Edith Clever, *Madame de Sade (Sado koshaku fujin)* by Yukio Mishima directed by Yoshi Oida and *The Birds (Ornithes)* by Aristophanes directed by Andrea Breth.

1427 Roth, Wilhelm. "Netzwerk der Avantgarde." (Network of the Avant-garde.) *DB*. 1997; 8: 31-33. Illus.: Photo. B&W. 3. Lang.: Ger.
Germany: Frankfurt/Main. 1997. Historical studies. ■A portrait of Theater am Turm, which works and produces together with the few comparable institutions in European avantgarde-theatre.

1428 Schmitz-Burckhardt, Barbara. "Menschen, an sich selbst gefesselt." (Men Tied to Themselves.) *THeute*. 1997; 1: 22-29. Append. Illus.: Photo. B&W. 9. Lang.: Ger.
Germany: Berlin. 1996-1997. Historical studies. ■Deutsches Theater under the directorship of Thomas Langhoff in the winter season 1996/97 including a statement by Michael Eberth, former dramaturg.

1429 Selling, Jan. "Berliner Ensemble i permanent kris." (The Berliner Ensemble In a Permanent Crisis.) *Tningen*. 1997; 21(2): 11-15. Illus.: Photo. B&W. Lang.: Swe.
Germany: Berlin. 1989. Historical studies. ■A survey of financial and ideological troubles at Berliner Ensemble, with an interview with the just retired actor and director Martin Wuttke.

DRAMA: —Institutions

1430 Selling, Jan. "Hovnarren Frank Castorf." (The Court-jester Frank Castorf.) *Tningen.* 1997; 21(4): 41-46. Illus.: Photo. Color. Lang.: Swe.
Germany: Berlin. 1990. Histories-sources. ■An interview with the artistic director of Volksbühne, Frank Castorf, about the German theatre today and the policy of Volksbühne.

1431 Stoll, Dieter. "Triumph im Mittelmass." (Triumph of Mediocrity.) *THeute.* 1997; 3: 32-33. Illus.: Photo. B&W. 1. Lang.: Ger.
Germany: Nuremberg. 1997. Historical studies. ■Describes the management of the Schauspiel Nürnberg and analyzes two of its productions: *Death of a Salesman* by Arthur Miller and *Macbeth* by William Shakespeare, directed by Holger Berg.

1432 Stumm, Reinhardt. "Wieso Zypern?" (Why Cyprus?)*TZ.* 1997; 3: 8-13. Illus.: Photo. B&W. 9. Lang.: Ger.
Germany: Konstanz. 1609-1997. Historical studies. ■A portrait of Stadttheater Konstanz, from its beginning in 1609 until the directorship of Rainer Mennicken since 1993/1994.

1433 Stumpfe, Mario. "Sturm im Wasserglas?" (A Tempest in a Teapot?)*TZ.* 1997; 2: 48-50. Illus.: Photo. B&W. 1. Lang.: Ger.
Germany: Berlin. 1997. Historical studies. ■Reports of a discussion at Theater Hallesches Ufer. The free theatre scene thinks and talks about new promotion models.

1434 Theissen, Hermann. "Depression im Nachkrieg." (Depression in Postwar.) *THeute.* 1997; 12: 26. Illus.: Photo. B&W. 1. Lang.: Ger.
Germany: Mülheim. 1997. Historical studies. ■Theater an der Ruhr's festival of theatre from the former Yugoslavia.

1435 Wille, Franz. "Ihr müsst wissen, was ihr tut." (You Must Know What You Are Doing.) *THeute.* 1997; 10: 1-2. Illus.: Photo. B&W. 2. Lang.: Ger.
Germany: Hamburg. 1997. Histories-sources. ■An interview with Frank Baumbauer, manager of Deutsches Schauspielhaus, about ensembles, stars and contracts.

1436 Zimmermann, Marie. "Nachrichten aus der Beziehungsfalle." (News from the Trap of a Relationship.) *THeute.* 1997; Yb: 118-121. Illus.: Photo. B&W. 1. Lang.: Ger.
Germany. 1980-1997. Historical studies. ■The difficult relationship between theatres and newspapers, with reference to the Jörder case, in which a popular theatre reviewer was fired and later rehired by *Badische Zeitung.*

1437 Burckhardt, Barbara. "Sprachspiele im Komödienstadl." (Language Games in the 'Komödienstadl'.) *THeute.* 1997; 7: 23-27. Illus.: Photo. B&W. 6. Lang.: Ger.
Hungary. 1997. Critical studies. ■Impressions from a congress on current Hungarian drama. Describes *Búcsúszimfónia (Farewell Symphony)* by Peter Esterházy directed by Sándor Zsóter during the festival.

1438 Gajdó, Tamás. "Színháztörténeti képeskönyv. Százéves a kecskeméti színház." (A Pictorial Book of Theatre History: The Hundred-Year-Old Theatre of Kecskemét.) *Sz.* 1997; 30(12): 45-46. Illus.: Photo. B&W. 2. Lang.: Hun.
Hungary: Kecskemét. 1896-1996. Historical studies. ■Comments on the jubilee album published by Kecskemét's Katona József Theatre on the occasion of its centenary.

1439 Mészáros, Tamás. *'A Katona' (Egy korszak határán).* ('The Katona': On the Dividing Line of an Era.) Budapest: Pesti Szalon; 1997. 251 pp. Lang.: Hun.
Hungary: Budapest. 1982-1996. Critical studies. ■Introducing the Katona József Theatre through a series of interviews and reviews by the author.

1440 Scarlat, Ana; Schulz, Wilfried; Golinska, Justyna; Dobák, Lívia; Upor, László. "Találkozások." (Meetings.) *Sz.* 1997; 30(7): 15-17. Illus.: Photo. B&W. 3. Lang.: Hun.
Hungary. 1997. Critical studies. ■Recently Budapest played host to a festival of contemporary Hungarian playwriting. Some opinions of visiting Polish, German and Romanian theatre experts.

1441 Veres, Dóra, ed.; Simon, Attila, ed.; Haiman, Ágnes, designer. *R.S.9. 1990-1997.* Budapest: Dezső Dobay, Astoria

Színházi Egyesület; 1997. 47 pp. Illus.: Photo. B&W. Color. 103. Lang.: Hun.
Hungary: Budapest. 1990-1997. Historical studies. ■A pictorial history of alternative theatre company R.S.9. Introduces the repertory by seasons with reviews and summary of the productions in English as well.

1442 Veress, Anna, ed.; Guelmino, Sándor, comp.; Sediánszky, Nóra, comp. *Katona József Színház 1982-97—Kamra 1991-97.* (Katona József Theatre 1982-97—The Chamber 1991-97.) Budapest: Katona József Színház Alapítvány; 1997. 112 pp. Append. Illus.: Photo. B&W. 152. Lang.: Hun.
Hungary: Budapest. 1982-1997. Historical studies. ■A pictorial history of one of the most significant theatre companies of Budapest of the eighties and nineties: a chronicle of fifteen seasons and a collection of data on the programs of its two performance spaces.

1443 Toibín, Colm. "Extraordinary Playful Druids." *IW.* 1996 May/June; 45(3): 36-40. Illus.: Photo. B&W. Color. 11. Lang.: Eng.
Ireland: Galway. 1982-1997. Historical studies. ■History of the Druid Theatre Company: past productions, promotion of new plays and playwrights, touring productions, influence on the growth of the arts in Galway, artistic direction of Garry Hynes.

1444 Lagerström, Cecilia. "Om dynamikens dramaturgi." (About the Dramaturgy of Dynamics.) *Tningen.* 1997; 21(1): 13-16. Illus.: Photo. B&W. Lang.: Swe.
Italy: Pontremoli. 1971. Historical studies. ■A presentation of Institutet för Scenkonst, about its method and training of actors in a more free dramaturgy and performance.

1445 Quazzolo, Paolo. *Vent'anni di Contrada.* (Twenty Years of Contrada.) Trieste: Lint; 1997. 371 pp. Illus.: Photo. B&W. Lang.: Ita.
Italy: Trieste. 1976-1996. Historical studies. ■The activities of the company La Contrada at the Teatro Cristallo.

1446 Romeo, Ignazio. *La scuola di Michele Perriera: diario di un laboratorio teatrale.* (The School of Michele Perriera: Diary of a Theatre Workshop.) Palermo: Edizioni della Battaglia; 1997. 124 pp. (Insula sic(!) 9.) Pref. Lang.: Ita.
Italy: Palermo. 1995-1996. Histories-sources. ■The author's diary of a year spent studying with playwright and director Michele Perriera.

1447 Persson, Inger. "Att se sitt liv gestaltat." (To See One's Own Life Performed.) *Dramat.* 1997; 5(4): 38-40. Illus.: Photo. B&W. Lang.: Swe.
Mozambique: Maputo. 1987-1997. Historical studies. ■A presentation of the theatre group Mutembela Gogo, its background and policy, with reference to director Henning Mankell.

1448 Luwes, Nico. "International Theatreschool Festival: Amsterdam 21-30 June 1996." *SATJ.* 1997 May/Sep.; 11(1/2): 226-231. Lang.: Afr.
Netherlands: Amsterdam. 1996. Historical studies. ■Survey of the 1996 International Theatreschool Festival held in Amsterdam.

1449 Thielemans, Johan. "De Vriendelijke Dwang van Guy Cassiers. Het RO-Theater Heeft een Nieuwe Artistiek Leider." (The Friendly Compulsion of Guy Cassiers, New Artistic Director of RO-Theater.) *Theatermaker.* 1997; 1(5/6): 48-52. Illus.: Photo. B&W. 4. Lang.: Dut.
Netherlands: Rotterdam. 1997. Historical studies. ■Profile of RO-Theater's new artistic director Guy Cassiers.

1450 Czuj, Łukasz; Pászt, Patrícia, transl. "Intézményes segítség." (State Support.) *Sz.* 1997; 30 (11): 29-30. Illus.: Photo. B&W. 2. Lang.: Hun.
Poland: Cracow. 1995-1997. Historical studies. ■Introducing Cracow's Centre for Polish Drama, an institution concerned with providing information, publishing services and occasions for discussion and workshop activities to Polish playwrights.

1451 Kruk, Stefan. *Teatr Miejski w Lublinie 1918-1939.* (The Miejski Theatre, Lublin, 1918-1939.) Lublin: Wydawnictwo Uniwersytetu Marii Curie-Skłodowskiej; 1997. 256 pp. Pref. Notes. Index. Illus.: Poster. Photo. B&W. 37. Lang.: Pol.
Poland: Lublin. 1918-1939. Histories-specific. ■Teatr Miejski as an institution during the interwar period: its management, repertory, and audience, with discussion of selected productions.

DRAMA: —Institutions

1452 Pályi, András; Koncz, Zsuzsa, photo. "Az eltűnt Gombrowicz. Nemzetközi találkozó Radomban." (The Disappeared Gombrowicz: International Meeting at Radom.) *Sz.* 1997; 30(11): 13-17. Illus.: Photo. B&W. 4. Lang.: Hun.
Poland: Radom. 1997. Critical studies. ■Analysis of productions of the third Gombrowicz Festival. Argues that the staging of adaptations of Gombrowicz's nondramatic works dilutes or deforms the essence of the writer's personality.

1453 Pawlowski, Roman. "Teatr Biuro Podrozy from Poland: Mystery Plays for the 21st Century." *TheatreF.* 1997 Win/Spr; 10 : 84-89. Illus.: Photo. 6. Lang.: Eng.
Poland: Poznań. 1988-1996. Historical studies. ■On the theatre company Teatr Biuro Podrózy, and its founder Pawel Szkotak. Work examined includes *Einmal ist Keinmal (One Time Is Nothing)*, *Lagodny koniec smierci (The Gentle End of Death)*, *Giordano*, and *Carmen Funèbre*.

1454 "In a Spin." *Econ.* 1997 July 5-11; 344(8024): 81. Illus.: Photo. B&W. 1. Lang.: Eng.
Russia: St. Petersburg. 1997. Historical studies. ■Departure of Bolšoj Theatre's artistic director Jurij Grigorovič after a tenure of thirty years. Impact on Bolšoj reputation, recent productions.

1455 Chejfec, Leonid. "Prekrasnje i jarostnje ljudi." (Wonderful and Violent People.) *TeatZ.* 1997; 7: 10-12. Lang.: Rus.
Russia: Moscow. 1990-1997. Histories-sources. ■A director's view of director training at Rossiskaja Akademija Teatral'nogo Iskusstva (formerly known as the Lunačarskij Institute or GITIS).

1456 Gončarov, Andrej. "Živaja škola ličnogo opyta." (A Living School of Personal Experiences.) *TeatZ.* 1997; 7: 7-8. Lang.: Rus.
Russia: Moscow. 1997. Histories-sources. ■Gončarov, the artistic director of the Majakovskij Theatre, on director training at Rossiskaja Akademija Teatral'nogo Iskusstva (formerly known as the Lunačarskij Institute or GITIS).

1457 Gudkova, A. "'Fomjata'." *TeatZ.* 1997; 7: 27-28. Lang.: Rus.
Russia: Moscow. 1990-1997. Historical studies. ■The students of Pětr Fomenko at Rossiskaja Akademija Teatral'nogo Iskusstva.

1458 Ignatjuk, O. "O 'molodych teatrach' Moskvy." (On Moscow's 'Young Theatres'.) *Mosk.* 1997; 12: 154-154. Lang.: Rus.
Russia: Moscow. 1990-1997. Historical studies. ■Profiles of two newly established theatres, Teat'r na Pokrovke and Masterskaja Petra Fomenko.

1459 Jakubova, N. "A ešče..." (And...) *TeatZ.* 1997; 1: 18-23. Lang.: Rus.
Russia: Moscow. 1986-1996. Historical studies. ■The actors of Pětr Fomenko's theatre, Masterskaja Petra Fomenko.

1460 Kirillova, Natalija. "Moe sčactje i moe opravdanie." (My Happiness and My Excuses.) *TeatZ.* 1997; 3: 27-28. Lang.: Rus.
Russia: Moscow. 1977-1997. Histories-sources. ■Interview with Valerij Beljakovič, director of Teat'r na Jugo-Zapade, on the occasion of the theatre's twentieth anniversary.

1461 Krečetova, R. "Teat'r dlja ljudej." (A Theatre for People.) *TeatZ.* 1997; 5-6: 12-14. Lang.: Rus.
Russia: Moscow. 1990-1997. Histories-sources. ■Interview with Sergej Ženovač, executive director of Teat'r na Maloj Bronnoj.

1462 Kuchta, E. "'Ljudi, l'vy, orly i kuropatki...'." (People, Lions, Eagles, and Partridges.) *TeatZ.* 1997; 2: 6-9. Lang.: Rus.
Russia. 1996. Historical studies. ■Account of international theatre festival featuring productions of Čechov's *Čajka (The Seagull)* by several different companies.

1463 Lebedina, L. "Strannye pticy s černoj otmetinoj." (Strange Birds with Black Marks.) *TeatZ.* 1997; 5-6: 16-17. Lang.: Rus.
Russia: Moscow. 1996. Historical studies. ■Account of the youth play *Groza (The Storm)*, based on work of Ostrovskij, directed by Genrietta Janovskaja at Teat'r Junogo Zritelja.

1464 Nikitin, A. "Prazdnik na budščee." (Holiday for the Future.) *TeatZ.* 1997; 8: 34-36. Lang.: Rus.
Russia: Perm. 1927-1997. Historical studies. ■Profile of Permskij Teat'r Dramy on its seventieth anniversary.

1465 Shevtsova, Maria. "Resistance and Resilience: an Overview of the Maly Theatre of St. Petersburg." *NTQ.* 1997; 13(52): 299-317. Illus.: Photo. B&W. 7. Lang.: Eng.
Russia: St. Petersburg. 1983-1996. Historical studies. ■Surveys the development of the Maly Dramatic Theatre (founded 1944) under its current artistic director Lev Dodin, whose productions have toured the UK on six occasions since 1988. Those singled out for analysis here include the epic *Brothers and Sisters (Bratja i sestry)*, *The Devils (Besy)*, *The Cherry Orchard (Višněvyj sad)*, and *Stars in the Morning Sky (Zvezdy na rassvete, zvezdy v utrennom nebe)*.

1466 Smeljanskij, A.M.; Solovjeva, I.N. "'Sjuzet' Chudožestvennogo teatra." (Subject: Art Theatre.) 209-217 in *Vestnik Rossiskogo gumanitarnogo chaučnogo fonda.* Moscow: Vestnik Rossiskogo gumanitarnogo chaučnogo fonda; 1997. Lang.: Rus.
Russia: Moscow. 1897-1997. Historical studies. ■Dictionary of the Moscow Art Theatre created by the theatre's research division.

1467 Starosel'skaja, Natalija. "Anšlag." (Sold Out.) *TeatZ.* 1997; 3: 1-3. Lang.: Rus.
Russia: Moscow. 1980-1997. Historical studies. ■Profile of Valerij Beljakovič's Teat'r na Jugo-Zapade.

1468 Starosel'skaja, Natalija. "Imja goedinjajuščee." (The Name that Makes the Connection.) *TeatZ.* 1997; 9-10: 30-32 . Lang.: Rus.
Russia: Irkutsk. 1996. Historical studies. ■Account of the festival dedicated to the work of dramatist Aleksand'r Vampilov, on the occasion of his sixtieth birthday.

1469 *32. Borštnikovo srečanje. Program BS 97.* (The 32nd Borštnik's Meeting, 1997: Program.) Maribor: Borštnikovo srečanje; 1997. 45 pp. Illus.: Photo. B&W. Lang.: Slo.
Slovenia. 1997. Histories-sources. ■Program of the competition of Slovene theatres, Borštnikovo srečanje.

1470 Hartman, Bruno. "Delež slovenske dramatike v repertoarju Narodnega gledališča v Mariboru med vojnama." (The Role of Slovene Drama in the Repertoire of the National Theatre, Maribor, between the Two World Wars.) 197-206 in Pogačnik, Jože, ed. *Zbornik ob sedemdesetletnici Franceta Bernika.* Ljubljana: Znanstvenoraziskovalni center SAZU; 1997. 584 pp. Lang.: Slo.
Slovenia: Maribor. 1919-1941. Historical studies. ■The professional and nationalistic development of the National Theatre in Maribor, with emphasis on the large number of Slovene plays presented.

1471 Purkey, Malcolm. "Productive Misreadings." *TZ.* 1997; Yb: 13-18. Append. Illus.: Photo. B&W. 3. Lang.: Eng.
South Africa, Republic of: Johannesburg. 1976-1997. Histories-sources. ■The founder and director of Junction Avenue Theatre Company describes how the company created a political and popular theatre, using Brecht's 'Aesthetics and Politics'.

1472 Wallström, Catharina. "Det är på tiden att våra liv blir synliggjorda." (It's Time That Our Lives Are Visualized.) *Entré.* 1997; 24(6): 39-43. Illus.: Photo. B&W. Lang.: Swe.
South Africa, Republic of: Johannesburg. 1975. Histories-sources. ■An interview with the director and actor Pule Hlatshwayo about the Market Theatre, its history and ideology, with reference to their performance of *Gomorrah!*.

1473 Björkstén, Ingmar. "Telia hjälper dramaten—och tvärtom." (Telia Helps Dramaten—And Vice Versa.) *Dramat.* 1997; 5(1): 26-27. Illus.: Photo. Color. Lang.: Swe.
Sweden: Stockholm. 1997. Histories-sources. ■An interview with Peter Mossberg, representing Telia telecommunications and Ingrid Dahlberg, the manager of Kungliga Dramatiska Teatern company, about the sponsoring of cultural institutions, with reference to Kungliga Dramatiska Teatern.

1474 Buck, Yvonne. "Riddarhyttans industriteater." *Tningen.* 1997; 21(2): 37-40. Illus.: Photo. B&W. Lang.: Swe.
Sweden: Riddarhyttan. 1985. Historical studies. ■A survey of Riddarhyttans industriteater from the small Rödgruveensemblen to the activities of today, with an interview with the artistic director Anders Olsson.

DRAMA: —Institutions

1475 Englund, Claes. "Projektcirkusen slår sönder teatern." (The Circus of Projects Destroys the Regional Theatre.) *Entré.* 1997; 24(2): 2-3. Illus.: Photo. B&W. Lang.: Swe.
Sweden: Kalmar. 1975-1997. Critical studies. ■The manager of Byteatern, Bertil Hertzberg, speaks about the changing condition of funding that in the long run will destroy all the regional theatres and the culture for everyone.

1476 Guillemaut, Alf; Lengstrand, Björn; Olsson, Jimmy. "Vad pågår egentligen i Göteborg?" (What's On in Gothenburg?) *ProScen.* 1997; 21(3): 7-9. Illus.: Photo. B&W. Lang.: Swe.
Sweden: Gothenburg. 1997. Technical studies. ■Four different views from technicians on the threatened shutdown of Göteborgs Stadsteater.

1477 Haglund, Birgitta. "Tribunalen." (Tribunal.) *Tningen.* 1997; 21(3): 43-45. Illus.: Photo. Color. Lang.: Swe.
Sweden: Stockholm. 1995. Histories-sources. ■An interview with the director Richard Turpin and the actor Henrik Dahl, both founders of Teater Tribunal, about their ambition to be a true political theatre.

1478 Hoogland, Rikard. "Först kommer moralen." (The Moral Comes First.) *Tningen.* 1997; 21(2): 41-44. Illus.: Photo. B&W. Color. Lang.: Swe.
Sweden: Luleå. 1997. Historical studies. ■A report from the Third Theatre Biennale, with references to the author Bengt Pohjanen and seminars on the future of the theatre.

1479 Hoogland, Rikard. "Göteborgs Stadsteater, dinosauris eller dynamo?" (Göteborgs Stadsteater, a Dinosaur Or a Dynamo?) *Tningen.* 1997; 21(4): 12. Lang.: Swe.
Sweden: Gothenburg. 1997. Critical studies. ■A report from the one-man investigation into the financial crisis of Göteborgs Stadsteater, with a lot of critical commentary.

1480 Hoogland, Rikard. "Det är en stor sorg." (It Is a Great Grief.) *Tningen.* 1997; 21(5): 12-15. Lang.: Swe.
Sweden: Gothenburg. 1996. Historical studies. ■A short survey of vicissitudes of Göteborgs Stadsteater, and an interview with the director Ronny Danielsson about the closing of the theatre.

1481 Kristoffersson, Birgitta. "I Skövde gillar man teater." (They Like Theatre in Skövde.) *Dramat.* 1997; 5(1): 36-37. Illus.: Photo. Color. Lang.: Swe.
Sweden: Skövde. 1964. Histories-sources. ■A presentation of Länsteatern i Skövde, its repertory, with interview with the artistic manager Hans Berndtsson.

1482 Kristoffersson, Birgitta; Hjulström, Lennart; Holm, Staffan Valdemar; Josephson, Erland; Kalmér, Åsa. "Teaterns hot och möjligheter." (The Threat and Possibilities of the Theatre.) *Dramat.* 1997; 5(3): 18-19. Illus.: Photo. B&W. Lang.: Swe.
Sweden: Gothenburg. 1997. Critical studies. ■Different points of view regarding the threat to close down Göteborgs Stadsteater.

1483 Lagercrantz, Ylva. "Teater utan bidrag, en svår konst." (Theatre Without Funding, a Difficult Task.) *Dramat.* 1997; 5(3): 42-44. Illus.: Photo. Color. Lang.: Swe.
Sweden: Stockholm. 1989-1997. Historical studies. ■A presentation of the independent theatre group Teater Satori, with reference to the funding of Statens Kulturråd (The Swedish National Council for Cultural Affairs).

1484 Långbacka, Ralf. "Går ensembleteatern mot sin undergång?" (Is the Ensemble Theatre Heading For Ruin?) *Entré.* 1997; 24(7): 14-17. Illus.: Photo. B&W. Lang.: Swe.
Sweden: Gothenburg. Germany. 1900. Historical studies. ■Some reflections about the ensemble and its ruin with reference to Schaubühne and Göteborgs Stadsteater.

1485 Lewin, Jan. "Skapande utifrån grannskapets villkor." (Creativity On the Terms of the Neighborhood.) *Entré.* 1997 ; 24(3): 32-36. Illus.: Photo. B&W. Lang.: Swe.
Sweden: Gothenburg. 1980. Historical studies. ■A presentation of Angered Nya Teater and its young director Niklas Hjulström, with reference to their ambition to be a theatre for and of the habitants of the suburb Angered.

1486 Lewin, Jan. "Osthyveln fungerar inte längre." (The Salami Tactics Don't Work Any More.) *Entré.* 1997; 24(3): 1-5 . Illus.: Photo. B&W. Lang.: Swe.
Sweden: Gothenburg. 1997. Histories-sources. ■An interview with Ronny Danielsson, the new manager of Göteborgs Stadsteater, about the financial problems and the possible solutions.

1487 Lewin, Jan. "Malmö AmatörteaterForum." *Entré.* 1997; 24(2): 16-19. Illus.: Photo. B&W. Lang.: Swe.
Sweden: Malmö. 1995. Historical studies. ■A presentation of the new amateur theatre organization Malmö AmatörteaterForum, which open a way to professional life for the unemployed youths, with an interview with Calle Lindbom Kolstad.

1488 Lewin, Jan. "Drama i fem akter (i väntan på den femte)." (A Drama In Five Acts: Waiting For the Fifth.) *Entré.* 1997; 24(6): 1-7. Illus.: Photo. B&W. Lang.: Swe.
Sweden: Gothenburg. 1995. Historical studies. ■The impending closing of Göteborgs Stadsteater, with reference to artistic director Ronny Danielsson and consultant Stefan Pettersson.

1489 Lewin, Jan. "Fjärde teaterhögskolan på plats i femte hamnmagasinet." (The Fourth College of Theatre In Place In the Fifth Port Warehouse.) *Entré.* 1997; 24(4): 2-5. Illus.: Photo. B&W. Lang.: Swe.
Sweden: Luleå. 1995. Historical studies. ■A presentation of the youngest and smallest college for actors, Luleå's Teaterhögskolan.

1490 Lewin, Jan. "På spaning efter den rätta modellen." (Be On the Look-out For the Correct Model.) *Entré.* 1997; 24(8): 2-11. Illus.: Photo. B&W. Lang.: Swe.
Sweden. 1990. Histories-sources. ■Interviews with Jarl Lindahl, artistic director of Borås Stadsteater, and Hans Sjöberg of Dalateatern about coping with financial difficulties. Continued in *Entre* 24:8 (1997), 2-11, with interviews with Peter Wahlqvist, artistic director of Stockholms Stadsteater, and Peter Oskarson of Folkteatern i Gävleborg.

1491 Löfgren, Lars. "Den enda lojaliteten ska vara mot teatern." (The Only Loyalty Should Be to the Theatre.) *Dramat.* 1997; 5(3): 28-29. Illus.: Photo. Color. Lang.: Swe.
Sweden: Stockholm. 1986-1997. Histories-sources. ■Lars Löfgren looks back on his eleven years as manager of Kungliga Dramatiska Teatern.

1492 Mörtberg, Johanna. "Teatern som redskap i tillvaron." (The Theatre As a Tool of Existence.) *Entré.* 1997; 24 (2): 12-16. Illus.: Photo. B&W. Lang.: Swe.
Sweden: Luleå. 1979. Historical studies. ■A presentation of Rosteriet, an institute for healing youths with problems through creative drama, including interviews with the founder Christer Engberg and some of the students, and references to the School of Arts in Liverpool and the new Teater Vildängeln, an offspring of Rosteriet.

1493 Ruthström, Maria. "Teatern lever trots allt." (The Theatre Is Living After All.) *Tningen.* 1997; 21(3): 38-40. Illus.: Photo. B&W. Lang.: Swe.
Sweden: Stockholm. 1997. Historical studies. ■A report from the 'Teaterdagar i Hallunda (Theatredays at Hallunda)' with the title *Spela för framtiden (Play for the Future)*, organized by Riksteatern, where the young generation of Scandinavian playwrights was discussed, with reference to the Danish playwright Line Knutzon.

1494 Szalczer, Eszter. "The 1996 Strindberg Festival in Stockholm." *WES.* 1997 Spr; 9(2): 43-46. Illus.: Photo. 3. Lang.: Eng.
Sweden: Stockholm. 1996. Historical studies. ■Coverage of the 1996 Strindberg Festival. Includes descriptions of performances, both staged and on film, seminars and public debates on several aspects of his work including acting and the future of Swedish theatre, exhibits, concerts, and staged walks through the city.

1495 Ehrnrooth, Albert. "Första säsongen för Shakespeares nya Globe." (The First Season of Shakespeare's New Globe.) *Tningen.* 1997; 21(2): 34-35. Illus.: Photo. B&W. Lang.: Swe.
UK-England: London. 1996. Historical studies. ■A survey of the first season of the Globe Theatre, with an interview with the director Richard Olivier.

1496 Ley, Graham. "Theatre of Migration and the Search for a Multicultural Aesthetic: Twenty Years of Tara Arts." *NTQ.*

DRAMA: —Institutions

1997; 13(52): 349-371. Biblio. Illus.: Photo. B&W. 6. Lang.: Eng.

UK-England. 1977-1997. Histories-sources. ■Interview with director Jatinder Verma about the British-Asian company Tara Arts from its origins in outrage at a racist murder, through changing perceptions of how multicultural identity can best find its dramatic expression, to Verma's own recent work for Contact Theatre and the National Theatre.

1497 McGill, Stewart. "Old Vic—Good News." *PlPl*. 1997 Feb.; 511: 14. Lang.: Eng.

UK-England: London. 1997. Histories-sources. ■Artistic director Peter Hall discusses the Old Vic's 1997 season of classic and new drama.

1498 Raab, Michael. "Avantgarde an der Basis." (Avant-garde at the Foundation.) *DB*. 1997; 10: 44-47. Illus.: Photo. B&W. 4. Lang.: Ger.

UK-England: London. 1953-1997. Historical studies. ■Portrait and history of Theatre Royal, Stratford East under the directorship of its founder Joan Littlewood and since 1979 Philip Hedley.

1499 Shenton, Mark. "The Olivier Goes Round." *PI*. 1997 May; 12(10): 8-9, 46. Illus.: Photo. B&W. 2. Lang.: Eng.

UK-England: London. 1997. Historical studies. ■Richard Eyre's project for a National Theatre Company season of theatre in the round at the Olivier. Simon McBurney will direct Brecht's *Kaukasische Kreidekreis (The Caucasian Chalk Circle)* and Jeremy Sams will direct *Marat/Sade*.

1500 Zettner, Maria. "Richard Eyre's 'Golden Age' at the National Theatre: A Look Back." *FMT*. 1997; 12(2): 209-217. Notes. Lang.: Eng.

UK-England: London. 1960-1997. Biographical studies. ■Eyre's career, his directorship of the Royal National Theatre, its repertory, his cooperation with the press, his successes.

1501 Bernstein, Charles; Danto, Arthur; Foreman, Richard; Lotringer, Sylvère; Michelson, Annette. "Beyond Sense and Nonsense: Perspectives on the Ontological at 30." *ThM*. 1997; 28(1): 22-34. Lang.: Eng.

USA: New York, NY. 1997. Histories-sources. ■Transcript of a panel discussion regarding Richard Foreman's Ontological-Hysteric Theatre and its resonance within other artistic disciplines.

1502 Black, Cheryl. "Pioneering Theatre Managers: Edna Kenton and Eleanor Fitzgerald of the Provincetown Players." *JADT*. 1997 Fall; 9(3): 40-58. Notes. Illus.: Photo. 2. Lang.: Eng.

USA: New York, NY. 1916-1924. Historical studies. ■Examines the careers of two women theatre managers of the Provincetown Players, Edna Kenton and Eleanor Fitzgerald.

1503 Connelly, Stacey. "Playing for Time: Nelson Jewell and the HIV Ensemble." *TTop*. 1997 Mar.; 7(1): 59-76. Illus.: Photo. 1. Lang.: Eng.

USA: New York, NY. 1993-1996. Historical studies. ■The mission and performance aesthetic of the HIV Ensemble, founded by Nelson Jewel, which seeks to entertain, but also to educate and inform audiences on the AIDS epidemic. Includes reconstruction of the Ensemble's first production *Working Out with Leona*.

1504 Kenton, Edna. "The Provincetown Players and the Playwright's Theatre 1915-1922." *EOR*. 1997 Spr/Fall; 21(1&2): 1-160. Pref. Illus.: Photo. B&W. 1. Lang.: Eng.

USA: Provincetown, MA, New York, NY. 1915-1922. Histories-sources. ■History of the Provincetown Players from previously unpublished manuscript by one of the company's managers, Edna Kenton.

1505 Mooney, Theresa R. "Southern Repertory Theatre Strives to Capture the 'Legend of Southern Life'." *SoTh*. 1997 Fall; 38 (4): 28-32. Illus.: Photo. B&W. 4. Lang.: Eng.

USA: New Orleans, LA. 1986-1997. Historical studies. ■Profile of Southern Repertory Theatre in New Orleans including history, policies, seasons and facilities.

1506 Morales, Donald M. "Do Black Theatre Institutions Translate into Great Drama?" *AfAmR*. 1997 Win; 31(4): 633-637. Biblio. Notes. Lang.: Eng.

USA: New York, NY. 1997. Critical studies. ■Critique of Black institutions' ability to produce great drama because of lack of funding, audience or support to nurture work. Focus on the Negro Ensemble Company.

1507 Palmer, Caroline. "Carlos Questa: A New Head for the Playwright's Center." *DGQ*. 1997 Win; 34(4): 14-17. Illus.: Photo. B&W. 1. Lang.: Eng.

USA: Minneapolis, MN. 1997. Critical studies. ■A look at the new head of the Playwright's Center, his background and plans for the institution.

1508 Pendleton, Thomas A. "The Shakespeare Society: New Association Founded in New York City." *ShN*. 1997 Win; 47(4): 75. [Number 235.] Lang.: Eng.

USA: New York, NY. 1997. Historical studies. ■Establishment of The Shakespeare Society, Inc., an organization dedicated to encouraging the growth of Shakespeare studies and performance. Contact information, founders, goals.

1509 Pettengill, Richard. "Educational and Community Programs at the Goodman Theatre, 1996." 205-208 in Jonas, Susan, ed.; Proehl, Geoffrey S., ed. *Dramaturgy in American Theatre: A Sourcebook*. New York, NY: Harcourt Brace College Pub; 1997. 590 pp. Pref. Notes. Biblio. Index. Lang.: Eng.

USA: Chicago, IL. 1996-1997. Historical studies. ■Educational initiatives offered by the Goodman Theatre, collaborations between dramaturgs and professional communities.

1510 Rosales, Gerardo Piña. "Entrevista a José Cheo Oliveras y La Compañía Teatro Círculo de Nueva York." (Interview with José Cheo Oliveras and the Compañía Teatro Círculo of New York.) *Gestos*. 1997 Apr.; 12(23): 149-156. Illus.: Handbill. Photo. B&W. 1. Lang.: Spa.

USA: New York, NY. 1996. Histories-sources. ■Interview with the artistic director of the Teatro Círculo regarding the group's artistic aims and their on the work of Cervantes.

1511 Ryen, Dag. "Humana: Role of Director Takes Center Stage at 21st Annual Festival." *SoTh*. 1997 Sum; 38(3): 6-8. Illus.: Photo. B&W. 2. Lang.: Eng.

USA: Louisville, KY. 1997. Critical studies. ■Critical summary of the offerings at the 1997 Humana Festival of New American Plays at the Actors' Theatre of Louisville, considering as well the role of the directors in the success or failure of the plays.

1512 Schloff, Aaron Mack. "Sundance Puts a New Foot Forward." *AmTh*. 1997 Nov.; 14(9): 56-62. Illus.: Photo. B&W. 5. Lang.: Eng.

USA: Salt Lake City, UT. 1997. Historical studies. ■Artistic mission of Sundance Institute Playwright's Lab to develop new works. Current projects include Sybille Pearson's *True Stories*, directed by Michael Mayer, Jessica Hagedorn's *Dogeaters* directed by Loretta Greco, and Martha Clarke's *Martha Clarke's Narrative Project*.

1513 Simons, Tad. "Joe Dowling: Oh, Lucky Man." *AmTh*. 1997 Oct.; 14(8): 68-70. Illus.: Photo. B&W. 1. Lang.: Eng.

USA: Minneapolis, MN. Ireland: Dublin. 1963-1997. Biographical studies. ■Guthrie Theatre's new artistic director, Irish director Joe Dowling: artistic policies, productions, community outreach, increase in financial stability under his stewardship, comparison to previous artistic administrations.

1514 Smith, Jill Niemczyk. "Minutes of the Columbia University Seminar on Shakespeare." *ShN*. 1997 Win; 47(4): 81-82. [Number 235.] Lang.: Eng.

USA: New York, NY. England. 1997. Histories-sources. ■Record of events at meetings dedicated to Shakespearean studies: 'Sound Reason for Enjoying Shakespeare: The Acoustic Design of Plays for the Globe and Blackfriars', and 'Shakespeare 1916: *Caliban by the Yellow Sands* and the New Dramas of Democracy'.

1515 Smith, Jill Niemczyk. "Minutes of the Columbia University Seminar on Shakespeare." *ShN*. 1997 Sum/Fall; 47(2/3): 54-56. Notes. [Number 233/234.] Lang.: Eng.

USA: New York, NY. 1997. Histories-sources. ■Record of events of four meetings of Shakespearean scholars at Columbia in which the topics were the text and editorial tradition of *Romeo and Juliet*, 'Shakespeare and Hollywood: Kenneth Branagh's *Much Ado About Nothing*', 'Shifting Blame: Perspectives of the Rape of Lucrece in St. Augustine and Shakespeare,' and 'Interrogating Triplicity: the *Henry VI* Plays'.

1516 Sundgaard, Arnold. "Susan Glaspell and The Federal Theatre Revisited." *JADT*. 1997 Win; 9(1): 1-10. Lang.: Eng.

DRAMA: —Institutions

USA: Chicago, IL. 1936-1938. Historical studies. ■Historical account of the Midwest Play Bureau of the Federal Theatre project and its first director, Susan Glaspell.

1517 Thompson, Garland Lee. "Hal DeWindt." *BlackM.* 1997 Aug/Sep.; 12(5): 9. Lang.: Eng.

USA. 1934-1997. Biographical studies. ■Obituary for the founder of the American Theatre of Harlem.

Performance spaces

1518 Brandesky, Joe. "South Bohemian Jewels: Two Faces of Theatre in Český Krumlov." *SEEP.* 1997 Spr; 17(1): 19-27. Illus.: Photo. 2. Lang.: Eng.

Czech Republic: Český Krumlov. 1995. Critical studies. ■The production, during the Prague Quadrennial, of František Hrubín's *Kráska a Zvíře (Beauty and the Beast)*, designed by Jaroslav Malina and directed by Miroslav Krobot, in the revolving auditorium theatre Měsíčník Ceských Divadel.

1519 Unruh, Delbert; Christilles, Dennis. "The Revolving Auditorium Theatre of Český Krumlov." *TD&T.* 1997 Win; 34(1) : 33-39. Illus.: Photo. B&W. 13. Lang.: Eng.

Czech Republic: Český Krumlov. 1947-1996. Historical studies. ■The use of the revolving auditorium theatre Měsíčník Ceských Divadel and its use in a production of *Kráska a Zvíře (Beauty and the Beast)* by František Hrubín, designed by Jaroslav Malina and directed by Miroslav Krobot.

1520 Foakes, R.A. "Shakespeare's Elizabethan Stages." 10-22 in Bate, Jonathan, ed.; Jackson, Russell, ed. *Shakespeare: An Illustrated Stage History.* Oxford: Oxford UP; 1996. 253 pp. Index. Notes. Biblio. Illus.: Maps. Sketches. Dwg. 5. Lang.: Eng.

England. 1590-1615. Historical studies. ■The life of Shakespeare's plays on Elizabethan stages. Takes fragments of historical documents such as contracts, letters, pamphlets, comments in diaries, etc. to examine the theatrical world of the Rose Theatre, the Swan Theatre, actors Edward Alleyn and Richard Burbage, the companies of the time, the economics, and how the plays may have been staged.

1521 Gurr, Andrew. "The Social Evolution of Shakespeare's Globe." 15-27 in Castagno, Paul C., ed. *Theatrical Spaces and Dramatic Places: The Reemergence of the Theatre Building in the Renaissance.* Tuscaloosa, AL: Univ of Alabama P; 1996. 151 pp. (Southeastern Theatre Conference Theatre Symposium 4.) Biblio. Notes. Lang.: Eng.

England. 1599-1613. Historical studies. ■Structural antecedents to the Globe Theatre and their culmination in Shakespeare's theatre.

1522 Gurr, Andrew. "Shakespeare's Globe: A History of Reconstructions and Some Reasons for Trying." 27-47 in Mulryne, J.R., ed.; Shewring, Margaret, ed. *Shakespeare's Globe Rebuilt.* Cambridge: Cambridge UP; 1997. 189 pp. Index. Notes. Biblio. Illus.: Sketches. Photo. Dwg. 13. Lang.: Eng.

England: London. 1599-1995. Historical studies. ■Attempts to reconstruct the Globe Theatre from Edmond Malone's attempt in 1790, to Karl Theodore Gaedertz, a Berlin librarian, to George Bernard Shaw, and finally to Sam Wanamaker's long but successful twentieth-century attempt using archaeological findings.

1523 Hildy, Franklin J. "Oppositional Staging in Shakespeare's Theatre." 101-108 in Castagno, Paul C., ed. *Theatrical Spaces and Dramatic Places: The Reemergence of the Theatre Building in the Renaissance.* Tuscaloosa, AL: Univ of Alabama P; 1996. 151 pp. (Southeastern Theatre Conference Theatre Symposium 4.) Biblio. Lang.: Eng.

England. 1590-1613. Historical studies. ■On the size of Elizabethan stages. Argues that a particular size influenced the staging of Shakespeare's plays, specifically oppositional staging (sword fights, etc.).

1524 Lusardi, James P. "The Pictured Playhouse: Reading the Utrecht Engraving of Shakespeare's London." *SQ.* 1993 Sum; 44(2): 202-227. Notes. Append. Illus.: Dwg. Sketches. B&W. 12. Lang.: Eng.

England: London. 1597. Historical studies. ■Examines an engraved panorama of London (c.1597) for clues as to modes of representation of theatres in sixteenth and seventeenth century drawn views.

1525 Nelsen, Paul. "Posting Pillars at the Globe." *SQ.* 1997 Fall; 48(3): 324-335. Illus.: Photo. B&W. 1. Lang.: Eng.

England: London. 1599-1995. Historical studies. ■Controversy over stage design and pillars at rebuilt Shakespeare's Globe Theatre. Debates between theatre historians and theatre practitioners on construction, architecture, and placement. Reviews original Philip Henslowe plans for Fortune Playhouse and the Hope.

1526 Orrell, John. "Building the Fortune." *SQ.* 1993 Sum; 44(2): 127-144. Notes. Lang.: Eng.

England: London. 1600. Historical studies. ■Chronicles the building of the Fortune Theatre.

1527 Vince, Ronald. "Historicizing the Sixteenth-Century Playhouse." 39-50 in Castagno, Paul C., ed. *Theatrical Spaces and Dramatic Places: The Reemergence of the Theatre Building in the Renaissance.* Tuscaloosa, AL: Univ of Alabama P; 1996. 151 pp. (Southeastern Theatre Conference Theatre Symposium 4.) Biblio. Lang.: Eng.

Europe. 1500-1600. Historical studies. ■Historical methods in studying sixteenth-century European playhouses, especially the Globe Theatre and Teatro Olimpico.

1528 Connolly, Thomas F. "Academic Theatricality and the Transmission of Form in the Italian Renaissance." 140-148 in Castagno, Paul C. *Theatrical Spaces and Dramatic Places: The Reemergence of the Theatre Building in the Renaissance.* Tuscaloosa, AL: Univ of Alabama P; 1996. 151 pp. (Southeastern Theatre Conference Theatre Symposium 4.) Biblio. Lang.: Eng.

Italy. 1500-1700. Historical studies. ■Examines the *commedia erudita*, or learned comedy, of the Italian Renaissance. Examines the impact of this form on theatrical design and stage use.

1529 Söderberg, Olle. "Slut på sjunkande förscen." (Stop For a Sinking Fore-Stage.) *ProScen.* 1997; 21(3): 34. Illus.: Photo. Color. Lang.: Swe.

Sweden: Stockholm. 1997. Technical studies. ■A report on repairs to the control system of the elevating stages of Kungliga Dramatiska Teatern.

1530 Söderberg, Olle. "Elverket—en ny spännande scen i Stockholm." (The Power Station—a New Exciting Stage at Stockholm.) *ProScen.* 1997; 21(3): 32-33. Illus.: Photo. Color. Lang.: Swe.

Sweden: Stockholm. 1997. Technical studies. ■A presentation of the stage of Kungliga Dramatiska Teatern at Elverket.

1531 "Intimate Magnificence." *Econ.* 1997 Sep 20-26; 344(8035): 97-98. Illus.: Photo. B&W. 1. Lang.: Eng.

UK-England: London. 1997. Historical studies. ■How the stage and structural design of Shakespeare's rebuilt Globe Theatre enhances actor/audience relationship.

1532 Blatherwick, Simon. "The Archaeological Evaluation of the Globe Playhouse." 67-80 in Mulryne, J.R., ed.; Shewring, Margaret, ed. *Shakespeare's Globe Rebuilt.* Cambridge: Cambridge UP; 1997. 189 pp. Index. Notes. Biblio. Illus.: Maps. 6. Lang.: Eng.

UK-England: London. 1989. Historical studies. ■A record of the excavation of the original Globe Theatre. Problems and revelations.

1533 Brooks, David; Tonks, Matthew; Godden, Jerry. "Savoy Rises from the Ashes." *LD&A.* 1994 Jan.; 24(1): 20-25. Illus.: Photo. Color. 10. Lang.: Eng.

UK-England: London. 1990-1994. Technical studies. ■Report on the reconstruction of the Savoy Theatre which was destroyed by fire, with emphasis on the new lighting system.

1534 Gauntlet, Mark. "The Interests of the Theatre: Stephen Greenblatt on Shakespeare's Stage." *ET.* 1997; 16(1): 53-66. Notes. Biblio. Lang.: Eng.

UK-England. 1590-1610. Historical studies. ■Discussion of Greenblatt's research on Elizabethan culture and theatre, with reference to the concept of power.

1535 Greenfield, Jon. "Design as Reconstruction: Reconstruction as Design." 81-96 in Mulryne, J.R., ed.; Shewring, Margaret, ed. *Shakespeare's Globe Rebuilt.* Cambridge: Cambridge UP; 1997. 189 pp. Index. Notes. Biblio. Illus.: Design. Photo. 18. Lang.: Eng.

DRAMA: —Performance spaces

UK-England: London. 1980-1995. Historical studies. ■The design process for the rebuilding of the Globe Theatre: from its earliest planning stages of the frame, walls, and thatch to actual designs and renderings.

1536 Greenfield, Jon. "Timber Framing, the Two Bays and After." 97-117 in Mulryne, J.R., ed.; Shewring, Margaret, ed. *Shakespeare's Globe Rebuilt.* Cambridge: Cambridge UP; 1997. 189 pp. Index. Notes. Biblio. Illus.: Design. Photo. Sketches. 13. Lang.: Eng.

UK-England: London. 1992-1996. Historical studies. ■The timber roof, the frame of the galleries, and jointing details of the rebuilt Globe Theatre from beginnings to finishing details.

1537 Gurr, Andrew. "Staging at the Globe." 159-168 in Mulryne, J.R., ed.; Shewring, Margaret, ed. *Shakespeare's Globe Rebuilt.* Cambridge: Cambridge UP; 1997. 189 pp. Index. Notes. Biblio. Illus.: Photo. 4. Lang.: Eng.

UK-England: London. 1995-1996. Historical studies. ■Musings on possible future stagings at the rebuilt Globe. While keeping history in mind, actors and directors will experiment with various staging techniques. Examines uses of central opening, entrances, and exits, the use of *frons* and balcony, descents, stage hangings, stage posts, the use of cross-dressing, and the challenges of staging the plays.

1538 Keenan, Siobhan; Davidson, Peter. "The Iconography of the Globe." 147-156 in Mulryne, J.R., ed.; Shewring, Margaret, ed. *Shakespeare's Globe Rebuilt.* Cambridge: Cambridge UP; 1997. 189 pp. Index. Notes. Biblio. Illus.: Photo. 2. Lang.: Eng.

UK-England: London. 1992-1996. Historical studies. ■Iconography in the Globe reconstruction: research and implementation on the Heavens, the scene fronts, painted cloths and hangings, and the Lords' Rooms.

1539 Mahon, John W. "New Globe Opens with *Henry V, The Winter's Tale*, and Two More Plays." *ShN.* 1997 Sum/Fall; 47(2/3): 25, 41. [Number 233/234.] Lang.: Eng.

UK-England: London. 1997. Historical studies. ■Inaugural season of the rebuilt Shakespeare's Globe Theatre. Features of the performance space, audience response.

1540 Milhous, Judith. "A Dissenter's View of the New Globe." *WES.* 1997 Fall; 9(3): 65-68. Illus.: Photo. 2. Lang.: Eng.

UK-England: London. 1997. Critical studies. ■Author gives her opinion on Shakespeare's Globe Theatre criticizing the theatre's architecture.

1541 Mörtberg, Johanna. "Nya The Globe." (The New Globe.) *Entré.* 1997; 24(5): 29-39. Illus.: Photo. B&W. Color. Lang.: Swe.

UK-England: London. 1970. Historical studies. ■A presentation of Sam Wanamaker's project come true: Shakespeare's Globe Theatre, the theatre building, with references to the musical director Claire van Kampen and *The Winter's Tale* in David Freeman's production, and Richard Olivier's *The Life of Henry the Fifth.*

1542 Orrell, John. "Designing the Globe: Reading the Documents." 51-65 in Mulryne, J.R., ed.; Shewring, Margaret, ed. *Shakespeare's Globe Rebuilt.* Cambridge: Cambridge UP; 1997. 189 pp. Index. Notes. Biblio. Illus.: Photo. Dwg. 5. Lang.: Eng.

UK-England: London. 1979. Histories-sources. ■Author's experience as historical adviser to American actor/director Sam Wanamaker's rebuilding project. His consultation of the historical documents and the archaeological digs of the Rose and the Globe informed how designers and architects went about rebuilding the theatre.

1543 Ronayne, John. "Totus Mundus Agit Histrionem (The Whole World Moves the Actor): The Interior Decorative Scheme of the Bankside Globe." 121-146 in Mulryne, J.R., ed.; Shewring, Margaret, ed. *Shakespeare's Globe Rebuilt.* Cambridge: Cambridge UP; 1997. 189 pp. Index. Notes. Biblio. Append. Illus.: Dwg. Photo. 22. Lang.: Eng.

UK-England: London. 1992-1996. Historical studies. ■Chronicle of researching, designing, and implementing interiors for new Globe Theatre: decoration, facades, carving, illusionist painting, the actual stage and its levels, and materials used. Painting techniques are included in appendix.

1544 Rylance, Mark. "Playing the Globe: Artistic Policy and Practice." 169-178 in Mulryne, J.R., ed.; Shewring, Margaret, ed.

Shakespeare's Globe Rebuilt. Cambridge: Cambridge UP; 1997. 189 pp. Index. Notes. Biblio. Illus.: Photo. 5. Lang.: Eng.

UK-England: London. 1996. Histories-sources. ■Globe artistic director on the artistic policy and practice at the rebuilt theatre. Addresses the challenges of live theatre in an old space, acting, costuming, the presence of the pit, etc.

1545 Schra, Emile. "The Wooden O: Een Ring van Energie." (The Wooden O: An Energy Ring.) *Theatermaker.* 1997; 1(3): 20-27. Illus.: Photo. Dwg. B&W. 5. Lang.: Dut.

UK-England: London. 1985-1997. Historical studies. ■Overview of the reconstruction of the Globe Theatre in London.

1546 Stasio, Marilyn. "Wanamaker's Wild Idea Takes Wing." *AmTh.* 1997 Sep.; 14(7): 54-55. Illus.: Photo. B&W. 2. Lang.: Eng.

UK-England: London. 1997. Historical studies. ■Actor, director, producer Wanamaker's efforts to resurrect and rebuild Shakespeare's Globe Theatre. Fundraising, political opposition and eventual success of the project is recalled by his daughter, actress Zoë Wanamaker.

1547 Vigeant, Louise. "Visite au Globe, tel qu'en Shakespeare." (A Visit to the Globe, As In Shakespeare.) *JCT.* 1997; 85: 162-166. Illus.: Dwg. Photo. B&W. 4. Lang.: Fre.

UK-England: London. 1997. Historical studies. ■History of the original Globe Theatre and the reconstruction inaugurated in April, 1997.

Performance/production

1548 Moten, Fred. "The Dark Lady and the Sexual Cut: Sonnet Record/Frame/Shakespeare Jones Eisenstein." *WPerf.* 1997; 9(2): 143-161. Notes. Biblio. [Number 18.] Lang.: Eng.

1997. Critical studies. ■Concepts of framing, montage and race in works of Shakespeare, LeRoi Jones (Amiri Baraka) and filmmaker Sergej Eisenstein.

1549 Scanlan, Robert. "The Proper Handling of Beckett's Plays." 160-163 in Oppenheim, Lois, ed.; Buning, Marius, ed. *Beckett On and On....* Madison, NJ: Fairleigh Dickinson UP; 1996. 289 pp. Notes. Lang.: Eng.

1996. Histories-sources. ■The 'purist' position on allowable latitude in the performance of plays by Samuel Beckett. Explains the author's own methods of determining what does and does not, in his view, respect Beckett's intentions.

1550 Senelick, Laurence. *The Chekhov Theatre: A Century of the Plays in Performance.* Cambridge: Cambridge UP; 1997. 441 pp. Index. Notes. Illus.: Photo. 46. Lang.: Eng.

1880-1995. Histories-specific. ■Cross-cultural study of Cechov plays in production, from initial performance in Russia to most recent postmodern deconstructions, and analyzes how the reception of the plays reflect social, political, and aesthetic attitudes in specific countries. Also focuses on Cechov's influence on major twentieth-century directors.

1551 Solomon, Alisa. *Re-dressing the Canon: Essays on Theatre and Gender.* New York, NY/London: Routledge; 1997. 192 pp. Notes. Biblio. Index. Lang.: Eng.

250 B.C.-1995 A.D. Critical studies. ■Essays on the relationship between gender and performance in texts from Aristophanes' *Lysistrata* to contemporary performances such as Split Britches' *Belle Reprieve.* Author uses current debates in feminism and queer theory to formulate a new reading of these texts.

1552 Williams, Gary Jay. *Our Moonlight Revels: A Midsummer Night's Dream* in the Theatre. Iowa City, IA: Univ of Iowa P; 1997. 344 pp. (Studies in Theatre History and Culture.) Index. Append. Notes. Illus.: Photo. Pntg. Sketches. Dwg. 74. Lang.: Eng.

1594-1995. Histories-specific. ■Production history of Shakespeare's *A Midsummer Night's Dream*, with historical overview of the myth of Theseus, the ritual of marriage, the nature of empire, the play's Italian heritage, and the fairy world of Shakespeare. Recounts production throughout history of play, from eighteenth-century opera to modern stagings.

1553 Worthen, W.B. *Shakespeare and the Authority of Performance.* Cambridge: Cambridge UP; 1997. 255 pp. Index. Notes. Biblio. Lang.: Eng.

DRAMA: —Performance/production

1590-1997. Histories-specific. ■Examines how both Shakespeare's text and performances of Shakespearean plays are construed as vessels of authority, with attention to three areas of negotiation between dramatic texts and stage performances: directing, acting, and scholarship.

1554 Kennedy, Dennis. "Shakespeare Without His Language." 133-148 in Bulman, James C., ed. *Shakespeare, Theory, and Performance.* London/New York, NY: Routledge; 1996. 218 pp. Notes. Biblio. Index. Lang.: Eng.
Asia. Africa. Europe. 1975-1995. Critical studies. ■Explores translations and non-English-language productions, including film versions of Shakespeare over the last twenty years. Argues that translation liberates the performance from its reliance on language and frees up directors to focus on visual elements of performance.

1555 Salter, Denis. "Acting Shakespeare in Postcolonial Space." 113-132 in Bulman, James C., ed. *Shakespeare, Theory, and Performance.* London/New York, NY: Routledge; 1996. 218 pp. Notes. Biblio. Index. Lang.: Eng.
Asia. Africa. 1975-1995. Critical studies. ■The interpretation of Shakespeare's texts in postcolonial societies. Suggests that Shakespeare's texts articulate imperialistic values.

1556 Babcock, Keiryn. "'Pleasure, danger and genderfucking': An Interview with Moira Finucane." *ADS.* 1997 Oct.; 31: 22-32. Illus.: Photo. B&W. 2. Lang.: Eng.
Australia: Melbourne. 1997. Histories-sources. ■Interview with the genderbending actress regarding her approach to character and her collaboration with director Jackie Smith, with a chronology of her performance history.

1557 Bilton-Smith, Philip. "'Because they're my people': An Interview with Alex Harding and Barry Lowe." *ADS.* 1997 Oct.; 31: 57-70. Notes. Lang.: Eng.
Australia: Sydney. 1997. Histories-sources. ■Tandem interview with playwright Barry Lowe and actor/composer/writer Alex Harding regarding their work and the state of gay theatre in Australia, with a chronology of their work.

1558 Devlin-Glass, Frances. "An Interview with John Bell." *ADS.* 1997 Apr.; 30: 27-42. Notes. Lang.: Eng.
Australia: Melbourne. 1995. Histories-sources. ■Interview with the director regarding his philosophies toward Shakespearean staging and performing.

1559 Rogers, Meredith. "Pathology & Pedagogy: Directing Student Actors in John Ford's *The Broken Heart*." *STP.* 1997 Dec.; 16: 64-75. Biblio. Lang.: Eng.
Australia: La Trobe. 1997. Histories-sources. ■Author describes his own production of *The Broken Heart* with drama students at La Trobe University, emphasizing the value of student productions and relating the process to general psychological processes, as described in the work of D.W. Winnicott.

1560 Rowlands, Shane. "Textualities and Sexualities of Bodies in Motion: An Interview with Gail Kelly." *ADS.* 1997 Oct.; 31: 92-105. Lang.: Eng.
Australia: Sydney. 1997. Histories-sources. ■Interview with director and co-founder of The Party Line regarding her career.

1561 Fritsch, Sibylle. "Gegen den Strom." (Against the Current.) *DB.* 1997; 2: 10-14. Illus.: Photo. B&W. 3. Lang.: Ger.
Austria: Vienna. 1975-1997. Histories-sources. ■An interview with the actor Gert Voss about acting, theatre and its possibilities on the occasion of the first performance of Peter Handke's *Zurüstungen für die Unsterblichkeit (Preparations for Immortality)* directed by Claus Peymann at Burgtheater.

1562 Fritsch, Sibylle. "'It's not my cup of tea'." *DB.* 1997; 9: 10-12. Illus.: Photo. B&W. 1. Lang.: Ger.
Austria: Vienna. 1997. Histories-sources. ■An interview with director George Tabori about directing Elfriede Jelinek's *Stecken, Stab und Stangl (Stick, Rod, and Pole)* and his work on his autobiography.

1563 Grund, Stefan. "Theaterhauptstadt Wien." (Theatre Capital Vienna.) *TZ.* 1997; 4: 28-31. Illus.: Photo. B&W. 3. Lang.: Ger.
Austria: Vienna. 1997. Historical studies. ■Important performances of the season, including Bertolt Brecht's *Die heilige Johanna der Schlachthöfe (Saint Joan of the Stockyards)* directed by Frank-Patrick

Steckel at Akademietheater, Horváth's *Kasimir und Karoline (Kasimir and Karoline)* directed by Matthias Hartmann at Burgtheater, and *Endlich Schluss (At Last the End)* by Peter Turrini and directed by Claus Peymann.

1564 Honegger, Gitta. "Trying to Like Salzburg, the Festival." *ThM.* 1993; 24(3): 80-85. Illus.: Photo. B&W. 2. Lang.: Eng.
Austria: Salzburg. 1993. Historical studies. ■Survey of the 1993 Salzburg Festival.

1565 Leyko, Małgorzata. "'Jedermann' Hugo von Hofmannsthala w reżyserii Maxa Reinhardta." (Hugo von Hofmannsthal's *Everyman* Directed by Max Reinhardt.) 11-34 in Pleśniarowicz, Krzysztof, ed.; Sugiera, Małgorzata, ed. *Arcydzieła inscenizacji od Reinhardta do Wilsona.* Cracow: Księgarnia Akademicka; 1997. 139 pp. (Wielkie dzieła teatralne.) Pref. Notes. Index. Lang.: Pol.
Austria: Salzburg. Germany: Berlin. 1911-1920. Historical studies. ■Reconstruction of Reinhardt's 1920 staging in Salzburg, analysis of Hofmannsthal's text, and comparison with Reinhardt's earlier production in Berlin (1911).

1566 Löffler, Sigrid. "Wachgeküsst und unterworfen." (Awakened With a Kiss and Conquered.) *THeute.* 1997; 9: 10-13. Illus.: Photo. B&W. 3. Lang.: Ger.
Austria: Salzburg. 1997. Historical studies. ■Analysis of *Libussa* by Franz Grillparzer directed by Peter Stein, his last performance during his artistic management of Salzburger Festspiele.

1567 Wille, Franz. "Handke! Krausser! Enzensberger!" *THeute.* 1997; 3: 6-12. Illus.: Photo. B&W. 5. Lang.: Ger.
Austria. Germany. 1996-1997. Reviews of performances. ■Describes premieres of *Zurüstungen für die Unsterblichkeit (Preparations for Immortality)* by Peter Handke directed by Claus Peymann at Burgtheater, *Spät Weit Weg (Late Far Away)* by Helmut Krausser directed by Thomas Krupa at Darmstadt and *Voltaires Neffe (Voltaire's Nephew)* by Hans Magnus Enzensberger directed by Piet Drescher at Renaissance-Theater.

1568 Burgoyne, Suzanne; McDaniel, Carol. "Making the Invisible Visible: Julien Roy on Staging Maeterlinck." *WES.* 1997 Fall; 9(3): 99-106. Illus.: Photo. 1. Lang.: Eng.
Belgium: Brussels. 1997. Histories-sources. ■Interview with Julien Roy on his experiences in directing Maeterlinck's *Pelléas et Mélisande* at the Paris-Bruxelles Exhibition.

1569 Hugo, Daniel. "Die man wat vlug vir die Nobel Prys: Gedagtes rondom Hugo Claus en sy besoek aan Suid-Afrika." (The Man Who Flees the Nobel Prize: Thoughts around Hugo Claus and His Visit to South Africa.) *SATJ.* 1997 May/Sep.; 11(1/2): 286-288. Lang.: Afr.
Belgium. 1997. Biographical studies. ■Salute to Flemish playwright/dramaturg director Hugo Claus.

1570 Muinzer, Louis. "Maeterlinck and Ibsen in Brussels." *WES.* 1997 Fall; 9(3): 93-98. Illus.: Photo. 5. Lang.: Eng.
Belgium: Brussels. 1997. Historical studies. ■Two productions at the Paris-Bruxelles Exhibition: Ibsen's *An Enemy of the People (En Folkefiende)*, directed by Lorent Wanson, and Maeterlinck's *Pelléas et Mélisande*, directed by Julien Roy, both staged at Théâtre National.

1571 Lagercrantz, Ylva. "Livsviktig teater." (A Vital Theatre.) *Dramat.* 1997; 5(2): 41-42. Illus.: Photo. B&W. Lang.: Swe.
Bosnia: Sarajevo. 1992-1997. Histories-sources. ■Some interviews with Bosnian actors Narda Niksé and Jasna Diklié about their views as actors during the war.

1572 Munk, Erika. "Reports from the 21st Century: A Sarajevo Interview." *ThM.* 1993; 24(3): 9-13. Lang.: Eng.
Bosnia: Sarajevo. 1993. Histories-sources. ■Interview with members of the Sarajevo Youth Theater performing in *Alcestis* and *Waiting for Godot.*

1573 Munk, Erika. "Only the Possible: Interview with Susan Sontag." *ThM.* 1993; 24(3): 31-36. Lang.: Eng.
Bosnia: Sarajevo. 1993. Histories-sources. ■Interview with Susan Sontag regarding her Sarajevan production of *Waiting for Godot.*

DRAMA: —Performance/production

1574 de Sousa, Geraldo U. "*The Merchant of Venice*: Brazil and Cultural Icons." *SQ*. 1994 Win; 45(4): 469-474. Notes. Illus.: Photo. B&W. 1. Lang.: Eng.

Brazil: Brasília. 1993. Historical studies. ■Review of the 151 Theatre Group's production of *The Merchant of Venice* directed by Cláudio Torres Gonzaga at Teatro Dulcina. Notes the increasing popularity of Shakespeare in Brazil.

1575 Reidler, Carl-Eric. "Ingen teater utan stjärnor från TV." (No Theatre Without Stars From TV.) *Entré*. 1997; 24(8): 42-44. Illus.: Photo. B&W. Lang.: Swe.

Brazil. 1967. Histories-sources. ■An interview with the actress and producer Regina Braga about her career and the situation of a free lance in Brazil.

1576 Bell, Karen. "Al Waxman on Stage." *PAC*. 1997; 31(1): 7. Illus.: Photo. B&W. 1. Lang.: Eng.

Canada: Stratford, ON. 1967-1997. Biographical studies. ■Actor Waxman and his return to the stage in the lead role of Arthur Miller's *Death of a Salesman*. His previous work performing roles on television.

1577 Brask, Per. "Kierkegaard and the Art in Ross McMillan's *Fever*." *CTR*. 1997 Fall; 92: 23-26. Notes. Biblio. Illus.: Photo. B&W. 2. Lang.: Eng.

Canada: Winnipeg, MB. 1997. Historical studies. ■Interiority and authenticity in Ross McMillan's performance of Wallace Shawn's monodrama *The Fever*.

1578 Brooks, Daniel. "Some Thoughts about Directing *Here Lies Henry*." *CTR*. 1997 Fall; 92: 42-45. Illus.: Photo. B&W. 4. Lang.: Eng.

Canada: Toronto, ON. 1994-1995. Histories-sources. ■Daniel Brooks on co-creating and directing one-man show *Here Lies Henry* with Daniel MacIvor.

1579 Burgoyne, Lynda. "France Dansereau, pompière passionnée de la petite enfance." (France Dansereau, Firefighter Impassioned of Little Children.) *JCT*. 1997; 82: 170-173. Notes. Illus.: Photo. B&W. 4. Lang.: Fre.

Canada: Montreal, PQ. 1974-1997. Biographical studies. ■France Dansereau's career as an actor in children's theatre.

1580 Burgoyne, Lynda. "Le théâtre pour dire les vraies choses: Entretien avec Louisette Dussault." (Theatre for Saying Real Things: Interview with Louisette Dussault.) *JCT*. 1997; 84: 50-57. Notes. Illus.: Photo. B&W. 11. Lang.: Fre.

Canada: Montreal, PQ. 1979-1997. Histories-sources. ■Actress Louisette Dussault on her career and especially on performing her one-woman show *Moman (Mommy)*.

1581 Burgoyne, Lynda. "Une minute silvouplè une dernière pour le manke damour." (Jus' a sec please one las' one for the lack of luv.) *JCT*. 1997; 85: 83-87. Notes. Illus.: Photo. B&W. 4. Lang.: Fre.

Canada: Montreal, PQ. 1997. Critical studies. ■Divorcing theatre from realism in order to go beyond the banal in Anita Picchiarini's staging of Jean-François Caron's *Aux hommes de bonne volonté (To Men of Good Will)* (Théâtre Sirocco production at Théâtre de Quat'Sous, 1997).

1582 Elson, Brigid. "The State of the Monarchy." *PAC*. 1997; 31(2): 10-11. Illus.: Photo. B&W. 3. Lang.: Eng.

Canada: Niagara-on-the-Lake, ON. 1997. Critical studies. ■Contemporary interpretation of Shaw's comedy *In Good King Charles's Golden Days* in the Court House Theatre at the Shaw Festival, directed by Allen MacInnis, designed by Charlotte Dean, and featuring Andrew Gillies.

1583 Godin, Diane. "La parole du corps." (The Body's Speech.) *JCT*. 1997; 84: 125-129. Notes. Illus.: Photo. B&W. 4. Lang.: Fre.

Canada: Montreal, PQ. 1997. Critical studies. ■The text through the body in productions of the Festival de Théâtre des Amériques: *Les Trois derniers jours de Fernando Pessoa (The Three Last Days of Fernando Pessoa)* directed by Denis Marleau for Théâtre UBU, Cechov's *Three Sisters (Tri sestry)* directed by Eimuntas Nekrošius, *Orestea (Una commedia organica?) (Oresteia, An Organic Comedy?)* by Societas Raffaello Sanzio directed by Romeo Castellucci, and *Matines: Sade au petit déjeuner (Matins: Sade at Breakfast)*, an early morning production at Espace Libre by Nouveau Théâtre Expérimental.

1584 Knowles, Richard Paul. "Focus, Faithfulness, Shakespeare, and the Shrew: Directing as Translation as Resistance." *ET*. 1997; 16(1): 33-52. Notes. Biblio. Lang.: Eng.

Canada: Montreal, PQ. 1995-1997. Critical studies. ■Argues that the negative critical reception of Marco Micone's *La Mégère de Padova (The Shrew of Padua)*, an adaptation of Shakespeare's *The Taming of the Shrew* produced at Théâtre du Nouveau Monde, may have been rooted in Quebec politics.

1585 Lavoie, Pierre. "Cultiver l'instant présent: Entretien avec Sylvie Drapeau." (Cultivating the Present Moment: Interview with Sylvie Drapeau.) *JCT*. 1997; 84: 58-71. Notes. Illus.: Photo. B&W. 14. Lang.: Fre.

Canada: Montreal, PQ. 1967-1997. Histories-sources. ■Sylvie Drapeau on her experiences becoming an actress and working with established Montreal directors.

1586 Lévesque, Solange. "Gaston Talbot et Jean-Louis Millette: contrepoint onirique." (Gaston Talbot and Jean-Louis Millette: Dreamlike Counterpoint.) *JCT*. 1997; 83: 66-69. Illus.: Photo. B&W. 3. Lang.: Fre.

Canada: Montreal, PQ. 1996. Histories-sources. ■Jean-Louis Millette's comments from an interview on performing Larry Tremblay's one-man show *The Dragonfly of Chicoutimi* juxtaposed with quotations from the playtext.

1587 Lévesque, Solange. "La méthode, c'est le chemin parcouru: Entretien avec Gilles Pelletier." (The Method is the Path Taken: Interview with Gilles Pelletier.) *JCT*. 1997; 83: 109-127. Illus.: Photo. B&W. 21. Lang.: Fre.

Canada: Montreal, PQ. 1950-1997. Histories-sources. ■Actor Gilles Pelletier reviews his career and gives opinions on acting.

1588 Lynde, Denyse. "Wanaba. A Native Word Meaning 'Place of First Light'." *CTR*. 1997 Win; 93: 32-37. Biblio. Illus.: Photo. B&W. 5. Lang.: Eng.

Canada: Bell Island, NF. 1996. Historical studies. ■Describes production of collective creation *Place of First Light* (First Light Productions, 1996), a theatrical tour relating history of Bell Island to tourists.

1589 Mendel, Tessa. "Home at Last: Nova Scotia, 1996: A Journal of a Community Theatre Experience." *CTR*. 1997 Spr; 90: 32-35. Illus.: Photo. B&W. 2. Lang.: Eng.

Canada: Halifax, NS. 1996. Histories-sources. ■Selections from director Tessa Mendel's personal journal regarding her production of Christopher Heide's *Home at Last* with the Women's Theatre and Creativity Centre.

1590 Metcalfe, Robin. "*The Company Store*." *ArtsAtl*. 1997; 15(1): 53. Illus.: Photo. B&W. 1. Lang.: Eng.

Canada: Halifax, NS. 1996-1997. Critical studies. ■Production of Sheldon Currie's *The Company Store*, considered part of a genre called Maritime Gothic, at Malgrave Road Theatre directed by Cliff LeJeune.

1591 Oram, Jon. "The Art of the Community Play." *CTR*. 1997 Spr; 90: 5-9. Biblio. Illus.: Photo. B&W. 2. Lang.: Eng.

Canada: UK-England. 1997. Histories-sources. ■Oram, artistic director of the Colway Theatre Trust, explains his philosophy and methodology of creating art through directing community theatre.

1592 Page, Malcolm. "*Betrayal* in Vancouver." *PintR*. 1997: 189-191. Lang.: Eng.

Canada: Vancouver, BC. 1996. Historical studies. ■Production of Pinter's *Betrayal* at The Playhouse, directed by Susan Cox.

1593 Paventi, Eza. "Albertine en cinq voix." (Albertine in Five Voices.) *JCT*. 1997; 83: 70-74. Illus.: Photo. B&W. 4. Lang.: Fre.

Canada: Montreal, PQ. 1995. Historical studies. ■Staging the tragic element of a character interpreted by five actors in Michel Tremblay's *Albertine en cinq temps (Albertine in Five Times)*, directed by Martine Beaulne at Espace GO.

1594 Pochhammer, Sabine. "Shakespeare's Technical Genius." *Thsch*. 1997; 11: 72-79. Illus.: Photo. B&W. 2. Lang.: Ger, Fre, Dut, Eng.

Canada. 1992-1997. Histories-sources. ■An interview with director Robert Lepage about his adaptations of Shakespeare's plays.

DRAMA: —Performance/production

1595 Salter, Denis. "Between Wor(l)ds: Lepage's *Shakespeare Cycle*." *ThM*. 1993; 24(3): 61-70. Illus.: Photo. B&W. 3. Lang.: Eng.
Canada: Quebec, PQ. 1993. Critical studies. ■Robert Lepage's approach to Shakespeare in his productions of *Macbeth*, *The Tempest* and *Coriolanus*.

1596 Salter, Denis. "Borderlines: An Interview with Robert Lepage and Le Théâtre Repère." *ThM*. 1993; 24(3): 71-79. Illus.: Photo. B&W. 5. Lang.: Eng.
Canada: Quebec, PQ. 1993. Histories-sources. ■Interview with director Robert Lepage, actresses Anne-Marie Cadieux and Marie Brassard, composer Guy Laramée and musical arranger Louise Simard, members of Théâtre Repère, regarding the group's productions of *Macbeth*, *Coriolanus*, and *The Tempest*.

1597 Taylor, Drew Hayden. "Native Theatre: The Growth of Native Theatre in Canada." *TDR*. 1997 Fall; 41(3): 140-152. Illus.: Photo. Poster. B&W. 10. Lang.: Eng.
Canada. 1979-1997. Historical studies. ■The success of Native Canadian playwrights. Work of the De-Ba-Jeh-Mu-Jig Theatre Group, playwright Tomson Highway and his plays *The Rez Sisters* and *Dry Lips Oughta Move to Kapuskasing*, and author's own work *Someday*.

1598 Vaïs, Michel. "Janine Sutto-Deyglun: Entretien." (Janine Sutto-Deyglun: Interview.) *JCT*. 1997; 84: 72-85. Illus.: Photo. B&W. 15. Lang.: Fre.
Canada: Montreal, PQ. 1921-1997. Histories-sources. ■Actress Janine Sutto-Deyglun on her life, her career in the theatre and her method of acting.

1599 Vaïs, Michel. "Un gouffre au bord du pays: Entretien avec Martin Faucher." (A Chasm at the Edge of the Country: Interview with Martin Faucher.) *JCT*. 1997; 85: 105-116. Illus.: Photo. B&W. 7. Lang.: Fre.
Canada: Montreal, PQ. 1996-1997. Histories-sources. ■Director Martin Faucher describes process of creating French version of Edward Thomas' *House of America*, presented as *La Maison Amérique* by Théâtre de la Manufacture, 1997.

1600 Vaïs, Michel. "Les Entrées libres de *Jeu* Questions sur le réalisme." (*Jeu*'s Free Admission Series: Questions About Realism.) *JCT*. 1997; 85: 42-52. Notes. Illus.: Photo. B&W. 8. Lang.: Fre.
Canada: Montreal, PQ. 1997. Historical studies. ■Account of roundtable on realism, from the point of view of actors and of spectators. Discussion held October 6, 1997 in Montreal.

1601 Vigent, Louise. "De Tartuffe en Tartuffe." (From Tartuffe to Tartuffe.) *JCT*. 1997; 83: 58-65. Notes. Illus.: Dwg. Photo. B&W. 7. Lang.: Fre.
Canada: Montreal, PQ, Quebec, PQ. 1996-1997. Critical studies. ■Ideological consequences of interpretation of characters in Benno Besson's *Tartuffe* at the Carrefour international de théâtre de Québec, 1996 and Lorraine Pintal's *Tartuffe* at Théâtre du Nouveau Monde, 1997.

1602 Wagner, Vit. "*One Word*." *ArtsAtl*. 1997; 15(1): 46. Illus.: Photo. B&W. 1. Lang.: Eng.
Canada. 1994-1997. Critical studies. ■Ken Garnhum's *One Word*, a sequel to his work *Pants on Fire*, directed by Andy McKim at the Tarragon Theatre.

1603 Wagner, Vit. "*The Soldier Dreams*." *ArtsAtl*. 1997; 15(1): 46-47. Illus.: Photo. B&W. 1. Lang.: Eng.
Canada: Toronto, ON. 1997. Critical studies. ■Production of Daniel MacIvor's play *The Soldier Dreams* at Canadian Stage Company directed by Daniel Brooks.

1604 Wehle, Philippa. "Christoph Marthaler's *Stunde Null oder Die Kunst des Servierens*." *WES*. 1997 Fall; 9(3): 53-54. Illus.: Photo. 1. Lang.: Eng.
Canada: Montreal, PQ. Germany: Berlin. 1997. Historical studies. ■Account of Christoph Marthaler's *Stunde Null oder Die Kunst des Servierens* (Zero Hour or the Art of Public Service) presented by the Deutsches Schauspielhaus Hamburg at the Festival de Théâtre des Amériques.

1605 Whiteley, David. "Of Mothers and Dragonflies: Two Montreal Solo Performances." *CTR*. 1997 Fall; 92: 34-38. Biblio. Illus.: Photo. B&W. 4. Lang.: Eng.
Canada: Montreal, PQ. 1997. Historical studies. ■Primacy of the actor in Quebec monodramas, exemplified by Louisette Dussault's *Moman (Mommy)* at Nouvelle Compagnie Théâtrale, directed by Pierre Rousseau, and Larry Tremblay's *The Dragonfly of Chicoutimi*, performed by Jean-Louis Millette at Théâtre d'Aujourd'hui and directed by the author.

1606 Winston, Iris. "*The Piano Man's Daughter*." *PAC*. 1997; 31(1): 36. Illus.: Photo. B&W. 2. Lang.: Eng.
Canada: Ottawa, ON. 1995-1997. Critical studies. ■Account of a production of *The Piano Man's Daughter*, based on the novel by Timothy Findley. The production was directed by Paul Thompson and featured Victoria Tennant.

1607 Stillmark, Alexander. "Erinnern in Chile." (Remember in Chile.) *DB*. 1997; 3: 33-35. Illus.: Photo. B&W. 2. Lang.: Ger.
Chile: Santiago. 1996-1997. Histories-sources. ■The German director describes his impressions from working in Chile and the political context of directing Heiner Müller's *Der Auftrag (The Mission)* with the group La Memoria. Includes a review of the guest performance at Berliner Ensemble by Ellen Brandt.

1608 Booker, Margaret. "Building 'Fences' in Beijing." *AmTh*. 1997 May/June; 14(5): 50-52. Illus.: Photo. B&W. 2. Lang.: Eng.
China, People's Republic of: Beijing. 1983-1997. Histories-sources. ■Director's personal account of her experience directing August Wilson's *Fences* at the National Theatre of China. Rehearsal process, cultural and societal differences.

1609 Císař, Jan. "Setkání dvou věků." (The Meeting of Two Ages.) *Svet*. 1997; 8(2): 84-91. Illus.: Photo. B&W. 2. Lang.: Cze.
Czech Republic. 1997. Historical studies. ■Stage interpretations of three Czech classics: *Její pastorkyňa (Jenůfa)* by Gabriela Preissová, staged by J.A. Pitinský at the Municipal Theatre Zlín (Městské divadlo) and by V. Morávek at Hradec Králové in Klipcera, *Naši furianti (Our Swaggerers)* by L. Stroupežnický, staged by P. Lébl at Divadlo na Zábradlí, *Maryša* by A.V. Mrštíkovi, staged by V. Morávek at Divadlo Husa na Provázku and at Divadlo na Zábradlí.

1610 Day, Barbara; Slavíková, Jitka, transl. "Případ Abrahámův: otázka víry." (The Abraham Affair: a Question of Faith.) *DivR*. 1997; 8(2): 36-43. Lang.: Cze.
Czech Republic. 1968-1997. Critical studies. ■The current status of Czech theatre, said to have been 'normalized' after the suppression of reforms in 1968.

1611 Kerbr, Jan. "Jaurés, Frézy, Lucerna, jak se to rýmuje ... Poznámky k inscenacím českých textů v České republice." (Jaurés, Cutting Machine, The Lantern ...)*Svet*. 1997; 8(6): 92-101. Illus.: Photo. B&W. 6. Lang.: Cze.
Czech Republic. 1990-1997. Critical studies. ■The staging of older Czech dramatic texts on Czech stages in recent years.

1612 Kohout, Pavel. "Marťan s lidskou tváří. Dvanáct zastavení v čase." (Martian with a Human Face: Twelve Stoppages in Time.) *DiN*. 1997 Apr.; 6(7): 1, 7. Illus.: Photo. B&W. 3. Lang.: Cze.
Czech Republic. 1924-1997. Biographical studies. ■Remembrance of stage director Luboš Pistorius on the occasion of his death.

1613 Merritt, Susan Hollis. "*Moonlight* and *The Homecoming* in Prague." *PintR*. 1997: 171-179. Notes. Biblio. Lang.: Eng.
Czech Republic: Prague. 1994-1996. Historical studies. ■Production of Pinter's *The Homecoming* directed by Ivo Krobot at Divadlo pod Palmovkou, and *Moonlight* directed by Karel Lňz at PenKlub.

1614 Patočková, Jana. "O časových posunech, míjení a setkávání (Strehler a české divadlo)." (On the Shifting of Time, Missings and Meetings: Strehler and the Czech Theatre.) *DivR*. 1997; 8(3): 18-24. Lang.: Cze.
Czech Republic. 1958. Historical studies. ■The significance of a single guest performance of Giorgio Strehler's Piccolo Teatro.

1615 Roubal, Jan. "Dvě alternativní tendence Nedivadla Ivana Vyskočila." (Two Alternative Features of Ivan Vyskočil's Nontheatre.) *DivR*. 1997; 8(4): 30-46. Lang.: Cze.

DRAMA: —Performance / production

Czech Republic: Prague. 1963-1990. Historical studies. ■Actor, psychologist and teacher Vyskočil's Nedivadlo (Nontheatre) examined in its context.

1616 Žantovská, Kristina. "Český mýtus věčného Žida." (The Czech Myth of the Eternal Jew.) *Svet.* 1997; 8(5): 138-144. Illus.: Photo. B&W. 2. Lang.: Cze.
Czech Republic. 1997. Critical studies. ■Jewish themes on Czech stages in recent years.

1617 Dahl, Kirsten. "Lad os kalde det fantastisk realisme." (Let us Call it Fantastic Realism.) *TE.* 1997 June; 84: 12-15. Illus.: Photo. B&W. 3. Lang.: Dan.
Denmark. 1997. Histories-sources. ■A discussion with writer and director Hans Rønne on his play *Napoleonskrigen (The Napoleonic War)*, and a general discussion on style in modern Danish theatre.

1618 Rottensten, Rikke. "Teater tiltiden—om tiden." (Theatre on Time—about Time.) *TE.* 1997 June; 84: 8-11. Illus.: Photo. B&W. 2. Lang.: Dan.
Denmark: Copenhagen. 1997. Histories-sources. ■An interview with theatre manager at Dr.Dante's Aveny, Nikolaj Cederholm, about his play *Paradis (Paradise)*.

1619 Crane, Mary Thomas. "Linguistic Change, Theatrical Practice, and the Ideologies of Status in *As You Like It.*" *ELR.* 1997 Fall; 27(3): 361-392. Notes. Illus.: Dwg. B&W. 1. Lang.: Eng.
England: London. 1594-1612. Historical studies. ■The move of the Chamberlain's Men to the Globe Theatre in 1599, and their production of *As You Like It*, possibly the first play produced there. Issues of social status, the suppression of 'jigs' at the end of the play, and the replacement of clown actor Will Kempe by the more 'refined' Robert Armin.

1620 Dawson, Anthony B. "Performance and Participation: Desdemona, Foucault, and the Actor's Body." 29-45 in Bulman, James C., ed. *Shakespeare, Theory, and Performance.* London/New York, NY: Routledge; 1996. 218 pp. Notes. Biblio. Index. Lang.: Eng.
England. 1589-1613. Critical studies. ■Argues that the affective power of the body on stage, its capacity to arouse an audience's passions, resists cultural inscription.

1621 Dessen, Alan C. "Conceptual Casting in the Age of Shakespeare: Evidence from *Mucedorus.*" *SQ.* 1992 Spr; 43(1): 67-70. Notes. Lang.: Eng.
England. 1598-1610. Historical studies. ■Considers the doubling and tripling of casting on the early modern stage, including Shakespeare, based on an examination of the 1598 and 1610 quartos of the anonymous *Mucedorus*, which contain breakdowns for actors.

1622 Dessen, Alan C. "Recovering Elizabethan Staging: A Reconsideration of the Evidence." 44-65 in Pechter, Edward, ed. *Textual and Theatrical Shakespeare: Questions of Evidence.* Iowa City, IA: Univ of Iowa P; 1997. 267 pp. (Studies in Theatre History and Culture.) Notes. Lang.: Eng.
England. 1628-1633. Critical studies. ■Using a recently discovered, unexamined Jacobean printed quarto containing John Fletcher's *Love's Cure*, Philip Massinger's *Believe As You List* (1631), and Fletcher and Massinger's *Sir John Van Olden* (1628), with playhouse annotations, examines what original playgoers may have actually seen while they watched given scenes and articulates possible problems with this approach.

1623 Dobson, Michael. "Improving on the Original: Actresses and Adaptations." 45-68 in Bate, Jonathan, ed.; Jackson, Russell, ed. *Shakespeare: An Illustrated Stage History.* Oxford: Oxford UP; 1996. 253 pp. Index. Notes. Biblio. Illus.: Photo. Maps. Sketches. Dwg. 14. Lang.: Eng.
England: London. 1660-1740. Historical studies. ■The transformation of Shakespeare's plays by the advent on the Renaissance stage of actresses such as Hannah Pritchard, and the age of the great adaptations of Garrick, Betterton, Kemble, and changes in theatre space.

1624 Friedman, Michael D. "'O, let him marry her!': Matrimony and Recompense in *Measure for Measure.*" *SQ.* 1995 Win; 46(4): 454-464. Notes. Lang.: Eng.

England. 1604. Critical studies. ■Discusses possible stagings of the Duke's proposal of marriage to Isabella at the end of *Measure for Measure.*

1625 Gurr, Andrew. "Intertextuality at Windsor." *SQ.* 1987 Sum; 38(2): 189-200. Notes. Lang.: Eng.
England: London. 1594-1600. Historical studies. ■Influence of competition, rivalry, and imitation between acting companies on dramatic texts. Focuses on the Chamberlain's Men and the Admiral's Company.

1626 Gurr, Andrew. "*Measure for Measure*'s Hoods and Masks: the Duke, Isabella, and Liberty." *ELR.* 1997 Win; 27(1): 89-105. Notes. Illus.: Dwg. B&W. 1. Lang.: Eng.
England: London. 1555-1604. Historical studies. ■Roles of hoods and masks in the original staging of Shakespeare's play. Speculates on Shakespeare's original intentions for costuming and particular use of the friar's hood, historical details of nunneries and possible influences of local orders on the play.

1627 Holland, Peter. "The Age of Garrick." 69-91 in Bate, Jonathan, ed.; Jackson, Russell, ed. *Shakespeare: An Illustrated Stage History.* Oxford: Oxford UP; 1996. 253 pp. Index. Notes. Biblio. Illus.: Photo. Sketches. 10. Lang.: Eng.
England. 1747-1776. Historical studies. ■Changes in Shakespeare production under David Garrick, especially *A Midsummer Night's Dream*, *King Lear*, and *Macbeth*. Also examines the crucial role of the actresses who performed with Garrick: Hannah Pritchard (Lady Macbeth) and Susannah Cibber (Cordelia).

1628 Lynch, Kathleen. "The Dramatic Festivity of *Bartholomew Fair.*" *MRDE.* 1996; 8(1): 128-145. Notes. Lang.: Eng.
England. 1600-1608. Historical studies. ■Places Jonson's *Bartholomew Fair* in its original festive context examining several dramatic conditions of the initial performances of the play.

1629 Mulryne, Ronnie; Shewring, Margaret. "The Once and Future Globe." 15-26 in Mulryne, J.R., ed.; Shewring, Margaret, ed. *Shakespeare's Globe Rebuilt.* Cambridge: Cambridge UP; 1997. 189 pp. Pref. Notes. Illus.: Sketches. Maps. Dwg. 3. Lang.: Eng.
England: London. 1599-1613. Historical studies. ■The Globe Theatre and the plays performed there. Examines what the space was like, inside and out, the city of London, other playhouses and theatrical spaces in London, staging in the Globe, and the challenge to rebuild it in the 1990s.

1630 Osborne, Laurie E. "Antonio's Pardon." *SQ.* 1994 Spr; 45(1): 108-114. Notes. Lang.: Eng.
England. 1600-1601. Critical studies. ■Discusses various ways to stage the final scene of *Twelfth Night* in regards to the fate of Antonio.

1631 Pascoe, David. "Marston's Childishness." *MRDE.* 1997; 9(1): 92-111. Notes. Lang.: Eng.
England. 1598-1634. Biographical studies. ■Playwright John Marston's involvement with children's theatres such as the Children of St. Paul and the Blackfriars boys for whom he wrote *The Malcontent.*

1632 Peck, James. "Anne Oldfield's Lady Townly: Consumption, Credit, and the Whig Hegemony of the 1720s." *TJ.* 1997 Dec.; 49 (4): 397-416. Notes. Illus.: Dwg. 1. Lang.: Eng.
England. 1720-1730. Historical studies. ■The body of the actress in the performance of character, with emphasis on Anne Oldfield's characterization of Lady Townly in Colley Cibber's *The Provoked Husband.* Argues that the actress participated in articulating a version of the aristocratic female at a moment of crisis for Whig political economy.

1633 Price, Diane. "SHAXICON and Shakespeare's Acting Career: A Reply to Donald Foster." *ShN.* 1997 Spr; 47(1): 11, 14. Notes. [Number 232.] Lang.: Eng.
England. 1996. Critical studies. ■Continuation of an exchange with Foster (*ShN* Fall 1996) regarding lexical patterns said to reveal that Shakespeare remembered roles better than others. Examines evidence in First Folio and other archival evidence.

1634 Ripley, John. "*Coriolanus*'s Stage Imagery on Stage, 1754-1901." *SQ.* 1987 Fall; 38(3): 338-350. Notes. Lang.: Eng.
England. 1754-1901. Historical studies. ■Stage imagery in productions of Shakespeare's *Coriolanus*, based on notes from productions by Thomas Sheridan, William Charles Macready, John Philip Kemble, Samuel Phelps, Edwin Forrest, and Henry Irving.

DRAMA: —Performance/production

1635 Scullion, Adrienne. "'Forget Scotland': Plays by Scots on the London Stage, 1667-1715." *CompD.* 1997 Spr; 31(1): 105-128 . Notes. Lang.: Eng.
England: London. Scotland. 1667-1715. Historical studies. ■Discusses Thomas St. Serfe's *Tarugo Wiles*, David Crawford's *Courtship à-la-mode* and *Love at First Sight*, Newburgh Hamilton's *The Petticoat Plotter* and *The Doating Lover*, and Catharine Trotter's version of *Agnes de Castro*.

1636 Sedinger, Tracey. "'If sight and shape be true': The Epistemology of Crossdressing on the London Stage." *SQ.* 1997 Spr; 48(1): 63-79. Notes. Lang.: Eng.
England. 1599. Historical studies. ■Based on Shakespeare's *As You Like It*, analyzes stage transvestism as the failure of the dominant epistemology that subtended the politics of sex and gender in the early modern period.

1637 Wiggins, Martin. "The King's Men and After." 23-44 in Bate, Jonathan, ed.; Jackson, Russell, ed. *Shakespeare: An Illustrated Stage History.* Oxford: Oxford UP; 1996. 253 pp. Index. Notes. Biblio. Illus.: Maps. Sketches. Dwg. 3. Lang.: Eng.
England. 1605-1640. Historical studies. ■The stage history of Shakespeare's plays during the Jacobean and Carolinian periods. Examines the King's Men company, the role of King and Parliament in the culture, and private theatres such as Blackfriars.

1638 Womack, Mark. *Shakespearean Delights: A Poetics of Pleasure.* Austin, TX: Univ. of Texas; 1997. 171 pp. [Ph.D. Dissertation, Univ. Microfilms Order No. AAC 9803069.] Lang.: Eng.
England. 1590-1613. Critical studies. ■Examines how Shakespeare's dramas provide pleasure for audiences. Analyzes poetic rhythm, audience engagement, patterned repetitions, and moments of contradiction.

1639 Ashagrie, Aboneh. "Popular Theatre in Ethiopia." *Ufa.* 1997 Spr/Fall; 24(2/3): 32-41. Notes. Lang.: Eng.
Ethiopia: Addis Ababa. 1996. Critical studies. ■How community-based, development-oriented plays could best aid the furtherance of Ethiopian society, using examples of plays developed by peasants, workers and students.

1640 Bots, Pieter. "Med Urbs Vie. A Cultural Exchange Programme Between Rotterdam, Lille, Cairo, Casablanca and Istanbul/Project d'Échange Culturel entre Rotterdam, Lille, le Caire, Casablanca et Istanbul." *Carnet.* 1997 Mar.; 13: 20-24. Illus.: Photo. B&W. 2. Lang.: Eng, Fre.
Europe. North Africa. 1996-1997. Historical studies. ■Survey of a project, financed by Rotterdam, of a cultural exchange project involving cities that are major seaports and/or have a significant Turkish, Moroccan, or Egyptian population.

1641 Davidson, Clifford. "Sacred Blood and the Medieval Stage." *CompD.* 1997 Fall; 31(3): 436-458. Notes. Lang.: Eng.
Europe. 1400-1550. Historical studies. ■The depiction of religious scenes in the Passion on the later Medieval stage, also discusses the Wycliffite *Tretise of Miraclis Pleyinge*.

1642 Ferrone, Siro; Mamone, Sara. "Il Teatro." (The Theatre.) 377-397 in Cavallo, Guglielmo, ed. *Lo spazio letterario del Medioevo. vol. 4 L'attualizzazione del testo.* Rome: Salerno Editore; 1997. Lang.: Ita.
Europe. 1900-1997. Critical studies. ■The reconstruction of medieval plays and productions in the twentieth century.

1643 Finter, Helga; Griffin, Matthew, transl. "The Body and its Doubles: on the (De-)Construction of Femininity on Stage." *WPerf.* 1997; 9(2): 119-141. Notes. Biblio. Illus.: Photo. B&W. 2. [Number 18.] Lang.: Eng.
Europe. 1923-1997. Critical studies. ■Analysis of Jutta Lampe and Isabelle Huppert's performances in Robert Wilson's German and French productions of Virginia Woolf's *Orlando* to demonstrate ways in which performance deconstructs femininity in a multiple subject, and how performance generates a manifold potential body from the visible body of the performer.

1644 Gámez, Luis. "Introduction." *CompD.* 1997 Spr; 31(1): 1-6. Notes. Lang.: Eng.
Europe. 1640-1800. Historical studies. ■Introduction to issue devoted to drama and opera of the Enlightenment.

1645 Kagel, Martin; Merck, Nikolaus. "Brecht Files." *TZ.* 1997; Yb: 70-75. Illus.: Photo. B&W. 4. Lang.: Eng.
Europe. North America. 1947-1997. Histories-sources. ■Interview with director George Tabori about his relationship with Bertolt Brecht, both personal and artistic. Covers Tabori's translations of Brecht's plays, his direction of the plays in Europe and the U.S., and includes a 1962 letter to Helene Weigel.

1646 Klaić, Dragan. "Out of Friedrichswald." *ThM.* 1993; 23(1): 106-110. Illus.: Photo. B&W. 2. Lang.: Eng.
Europe. 1992. Critical studies. ■Discusses the state of the theatre and its future in Western Europe.

1647 Kotzamani, Marina Anastasia. *'Lysistrata', Playgirl of the Western World: Aristophanes on the Early Modern Stage.* New York, NY: City Univ. of New York; 1997. 437 pp. Notes. Biblio. [Ph.D. Dissertation, Univ. Microfilms Order No. AAC 9807953.] Lang.: Eng.
Europe. USA. 1892-1930. Historical studies. ■Early modern theatrical interpretations of Aristophanes' *Lysistrata*: Maurice Donnay's *Lysistrata*, a boulevard spectacle featuring Gabrielle Rejane in the lead role, Max Reinhardt's interpretation in Berlin, Nemirovič-Dančenko's politicized version for the Moscow Art Theater's Musical Studio, and Norman Bel Geddes Broadway version.

1648 Larsson, Stellan. "Ärlighet, tillit och disciplin." (Honesty, Confidence and Discipline.) *Tningen.* 1997; 21(1): 10-11. Illus.: Photo. B&W. Lang.: Swe.
Europe. Guatemala. 1967. Histories-sources. ■An interview with the actor, director and teacher Mario Gonzales about his career, his work with Théâtre du Soleil and at Conservatoire National Supérieur d'Art Dramatique, with reference to Project Commedia in Malmö.

1649 Merschmeier, Michael. "Kindertheater der Grausamkeit." (Children's Theatre of Cruelty.) *THeute.* 1997; 7: 9-13. Illus.: Photo. B&W. 6. Lang.: Ger.
Europe. 1997. Historical studies. ■Current performances of Elizabethan theatre: Shakespeare's *Richard III* directed by Peter Zadek and produced by Wiener Kammerspiele and Wiener Festwochen, Branagh's film adaptation of *Hamlet*, and *The Revenger's Tragedy* by Cyril Tourneur directed by Stefan Bachmann at Münchner Schauspielhaus.

1650 Rothwell, Kenneth S. "In Search of Nothing: Mapping *King Lear*." 135-147 in Boose, Lynda E., ed.; Burt, Richard, ed. *Shakespeare, the Movie: Popularizing the Plays on Film, TV, and Video.* London/New York, NY: Routledge; 1997. 277 pp. Index. Notes. Biblio. Lang.: Eng.
Europe. USA. 1909-1994. Historical studies. ■The use of the map in England in the first scene of several productions of Shakespeare's *King Lear*. Discusses staged productions by Adrian Noble (1982, 1994) and Nicholas Hytner (1990) for RSC, film versions by William V. Ranous (1909), Gerolamo Lo Savio (*Re Lear*, 1910), Grigorij Kozincev (1970), Peter Brook (1971), and Jean-Luc Godard (1987), and television adaptations by Peter Brook and Orson Welles (1953), Jonathan Miller (BBC, 1982), and Michael Elliott (Grenada, 1983).

1651 Thomson, Peter. *Brecht: Mother Courage and Her Children.* Cambridge: Cambridge UP; 1997. 206 pp. (Plays in Production 5.) Index. Notes. Biblio. Pref. Illus.: Design. Photo. 10. Lang.: Eng.
Europe. USA. Africa. 1949-1995. Histories-specific. ■Analysis of *Mutter Courage und ihre Kinder*: sources, the first production by Brecht at Berliner Ensemble, and the transmission of the play to the English-speaking world. Includes historical accounts of several productions throughout the world of the play and its continued importance in light of the war in the former Yugoslavia.

1652 Worthen, W.B. "Invisible Bullets, Violet Beards: Reading Actors Reading." 210-230 in Pechter, Edward, ed. *Textual and Theatrical Shakespeare: Questions of Evidence.* Iowa City, IA: Univ of Iowa P; 1997. 267 pp. (Studies in Theatre History and Culture.) Notes. Lang.: Eng.
Europe. North America. 1985-1996. Critical studies. ■The relationship between Shakespearean actors and academic critics as a place where

DRAMA: —Performance/production

negotiations between theatrically and non-theatrically based commentaries can be made.

1653 "To Finland for its Festivals/Découvrez les festivals Finlandais." *NFT*. 1997; 51: 31-32. Illus.: Photo. B&W. 3. Lang.: Eng, Fre.
Finland. 1997. Historical studies. ■Survey of the various performing arts festivals offered throughout Finland.

1654 Harju, Hannu. "Lengthy Productions from the Dustbin of History/Longues pièces recueillies de la poubelle de l'histoire." *NFT*. 1997; 51: 6-10. Illus.: Photo. B&W. 8. Lang.: Eng, Fre.
Finland: Helsinki, Tampere. 1997. Critical studies. ■Report on Finnish stage productions: Ibsen's *Brand* directed by Kristian Smeds at Teatteri Takomo, Esa Kirkkopelto's *Kostumassinfonia (Kostumas Symphony)* for Helsinki Youth Theatre, and Tampere Theatre's production of *Isänmaan miehet (Men of the Fatherland)* by Yrjö Isohella and Heikki Vihinen, directed by Vihinen.

1655 Knight, Alan E. "Faded Pageant: The End of Mystery Plays in Lille." *JMMLA*. 1996 Spr; 29(1): 3-14. Notes. Biblio. Lang.: Eng.
Flanders: Lille. 1480-1690. Historical studies. ■Examines the gradual extinction of mystery play performances in Lille.

1656 Althusser, Louis. "The 'Piccolo Teatro': Bertolazzi and Brecht—Notes on a Materialist Theater." 199-215 in Murray, Timothy, ed. *Mimesis, Masochism, and Mime: The Politics of Theatricality in Contemporary French Thought*. Ann Arbor, MI: Univ. of Michigan P; 1997. 328 pp. (Theater: Theory/Text/Performance.) Notes. Lang.: Eng.
France: Paris. Italy: Milan. 1977. Critical studies. ■Theoretical criticism of Bertolazzi's *El Nost Milan*, presented at the Théâtre des Nations by Piccolo Teatro. Further relates the materialist aspect of the production to the plays of Brecht.

1657 Brown, Gregory Stephen. *A Field of Honor: The Cultural Politics of Playwriting in Eighteenth Century France*. New York, NY: Columbia Univ; 1997. 651 pp. Notes. Biblio. [Ph.D. Dissertation, Univ. Microfilms Order No. AAC 9728158.] Lang.: Eng.
France. 1700-1800. Historical studies. ■Examines the encounter between the royal court and an emerging commercial public in eighteenth-century France, through the experience of playwrights for the Comédie-Française.

1658 Burgoyne, Suzanne. "Claude Régy Directs Maeterlinck's *La Mort de Tintagiles*: The Actor as Shadow Puppet." *WES*. 1997 Fall; 9(3): 89-92. Lang.: Eng.
France. Belgium: Ghent. 1997. Historical studies. ■Critical review of a production that is part of the Paris-Bruxelles Exhibition, which is devoted to artistic and literary exchanges between France and Belgium. Focuses on Claude Régy's production of Maeterlinck's *La Mort de Tintagiles* presented at the Théâtre Gérard-Philippe.

1659 Carlson, Marvin. "Two *Peer Gynts* in Paris." *WES*. 1997 Spr; 9(2): 35-38. Illus.: Photo. 2. Lang.: Eng.
France: Paris. 1996. Historical studies. ■Report on two Paris productions of Ibsen's *Peer Gynt* produced during the Autumn Festival. The foreign production, from Italy's Teatro Centrale, was directed by Luca Ronconi. The native production was directed by Stéphane Braunschweig from the Théâtre de Gennevilliers.

1660 Carney, Benjamin. "Didier Bezace and *Pereira Prétend*." *WES*. 1997 Fall; 9(3): 21-26. Lang.: Eng.
France. 1997. Historical studies. ■Didier Bezace and the Théâtre de l'Aquarium's production of *Pereira Prétend (Pereira Claims)*, adapted from the novel by Antonio Tabucchi, presented at the Avignon Festival.

1661 Dasgupta, Gautam. "Remembering Artaud." *PerAJ*. 1997 May; 19(2): 1-5. [Number 56.] Lang.: Eng.
France. 1897-1997. Historical studies. ■Paean to Antonin Artaud on the one-hundreth anniversary of his birth: his still resonant influence on modern drama.

1662 Di Lella, Livia. "Drammaturgia e spazio scenico nei Karamazov di Jacques Copeau." (Dramaturgy and Scenic Space in Copeau's *Brothers Karamazov*.) *TeatroS*. 1997; 12(19): 201-228. Notes. Lang.: Ita.

France. 1908-1911. Critical studies. ■Analysis of Copeau's adaptation of Dostojévskij's novel *Bratja Karamazov* for clues to staging and spatial structure.

1663 Didong, Paola. "Grandios och rörande tilltro till teatern." (A Grandiose and Touching Confidence in the Theatre.) *Tningen*. 1997; 21(1): 17-21. Illus.: Photo. B&W. Lang.: Swe.
France: Paris. 1997. Historical studies. ■A presentation of Olivier Py's twenty-four-hour performance of *La Servante*, with an interview with one of the actors: Jean-Damien Barbin.

1664 Didong, Paola. "Maeterlinck åter på scen." (Maeterlinck On the Stage Again.) *Entré*. 1997; 24(3): 50-52. Illus.: Photo. B&W. Lang.: Swe.
France: Paris. 1997. Critical studies. ■A short presentation of Maurice Maeterlinck and his plays with reference to Claude Régy's production of *La Mort de Tintagiles (The Death of Tintagiles)* at Théâtre Gérard-Philippe, Olivier Werner's *Pelléas et Mélisande* at Théâtre de l'Athénée, and Robert Wilson's production of Claude Debussy's *Pelléas et Mélisande* at l'Opéra de Paris.

1665 Féral, Josette. "*Nathan the Wise*: A Tranquil Force: Denis Marleau in Avignon." *WES*. 1997 Fall; 9(3): 15-20. Illus.: Photo. 1. Lang.: Eng.
France: Avignon. 1997. Historical studies. ■Analytical review of Denis Marleau's production of Lessing's *Nathan der Weise* at the Avignon Festival.

1666 Fortin, Christine Annie. *Théâtre Forain, Culture Française*. College Park, MD: Univ. of Maryland; 1997. 458 pp. Biblio. Notes. [Ph.D. Dissertation, Univ. Microfilms Order No. AAC 9816460.] Lang.: Fre.
France. 1700-1730. Historical studies. ■Examines 'théâtre de la foire,' or fair theatre, a popular theatre form: detailed analysis of several plays, as well as archival sources, tracing the sometimes difficult social, legal and commercial contexts in which the fair theatre developed.

1667 George, B. *The Work of André Benedetto at the Théâtre des Carmes, Avignon, 1961-1991*. Unpublished Ph.D. thesis, Univ. of Wales: Swansea; 1995. Notes. Biblio. [Abstract in *Index to Theses*, 46-198.] Lang.: Eng.
France: Avignon. 1961-1991. Histories-specific. ■Critical assessment of the techniques and achievements of Benedetto as both dramatist and director. A chronological survey of his career reveals him as a left-wing playwright who moved from a conventional framework to street and community theatre, as well as festivals.

1668 Hammerstein, Dorothea. "Marx—neu herausgebracht? Nora—endlich begraben?" (Marx—re-Performed? Nora—Finally Buried?) *THeute*. 1997; 6: 10-15. Illus.: Photo. B&W. 5. Lang.: Ger.
France: Paris. 1996-1997. Historical studies. ■The theatre season in Paris: *Le Radeau de la Méduse (The Raft of the Medusa)* written and directed by Roger Planchon at Théâtre National de la Colline, *Zakat (Sunset)* by Isaak Babel directed by Bernard Sobel, *Karl Marx* compiled and directed by Jean-Pierre Vincent at Théâtre des Amandiers, *Nora (Et Dukkehjem)* by Henrik Ibsen directed by Deborah Warner at Théâtre de L'Europe and *Tartuffe* by Molière at Comédie Française.

1669 Hammerstein, Dorothee. "Die Wiederkehr der Geister." (The Return of the Ghosts.) *THeute*. 1997; 12: 10-15. Illus.: Photo. B&W. 4. Lang.: Ger.
France: Paris. 1997. Historical studies. ■History and politics on the Paris stage: *Nathan* by Gotthold Ephraim Lessing directed by Alexander Lang at Comédie-Française, *Histoire de France (History of France)* written and directed by Michel Deutsch and Georges Lavaudant at Odéon de Gaulle, *L'héritage (Inheritance)* by Bernard-Marie Koltès directed by Catherine Marnas at Théâtre de la Ville.

1670 Ho, Christopher. "Antonin Artaud: From Center to Periphery, Periphery to Center." *PerAJ*. 1997 May; 19(2): 6-22. Notes. Illus.: Photo. B&W. 7. [Number 56.] Lang.: Eng.
France. 1897-1997. Biographical studies. ■Life, career, and influences of Antonin Artaud.

1671 McCarthy, Gerry. "Rehearsals for the End of Time: Indeterminacy and Performance in Beckett." 148-159 in Oppenheim, Lois, ed.; Buning, Marius, ed. *Beckett On and On....*

DRAMA: —Performance/production

Madison, NJ: Fairleigh Dickinson UP; 1996. 289 pp. Notes. Lang.: Eng.
France. Ireland. 1960-1973. Critical studies. ■Open-endedness in interpretation, the rehearsal process, and the role of the director in Beckett's *Not I* and *Krapp's Last Tape*. Argues for more latitude and openness in the staging of Beckett's plays.

1672 Melrose, Susan. "Rehearsing Reconciliations: Mnouchkine's Molière." *PerfR*. 1997 Sum; 2(2): 108-111. Notes. Lang.: Eng.
France: Paris. 1996. Critical studies. ■The treatment of French colonialism in Théâtre du Soleil's production of Molière's *Tartuffe*. Raises questions about who is the audience for the production.

1673 Pfaff, Walter. "The Ant and the Stone: Learning Kutiyattam." *TDR*. 1997 Win; 41(4): 133-162. Notes. Biblio. Illus.: Photo. B&W. 15. Lang.: Eng.
France. India. 1989-1997. Histories-sources. ■Statement by the founder of Parate Labor, a French group dedicated to the study and performance of the traditional Sanskrit temple theatre form *kutiyattam*.

1674 Proust, Sophie. "Interview with Stéphane Braunschweig." *WES*. 1997 Spr; 9(2): 39-42. Lang.: Eng.
France: Paris. 1996. Histories-sources. ■Interview with director Stéphane Braunschweig, during which he discusses his current production of Ibsen's *Peer Gynt* at the Autumn Festival.

1675 Rysiak-Vallet, Anna. "Klasyk poprzez Brechta odczytany: 'Grzegorz Dyndała' Rogera Planchona." (A Brecht-Inspired Reading of a Classic: Roger Planchon's *Georges Dandin*.) 70-86 in Pleśniarowicz, Krzysztof, ed.; Sugiera, Małgorzata, ed. *Arcydzieła inscenizacji od Reinhardta do Wilsona*. Cracow: Księgarnia Akademicka; 1997. 139 pp. (Wielkie dzieła teatralne.) Pref. Notes. Index. Lang.: Pol.
France: Villeurbanne. 1958. Historical studies. ■Reconstruction of Planchon's staging of Molière's play. Considers the influence of a 1951 production of Brecht's *Mother Courage* directed by Jean Vilar and a guest performance of the Berliner Ensemble at the Théâtre des Nations.

1676 Salter, Denis. "Hand Eye Mind Soul: Théâtre du Soleil's *Les Atrides*." *ThM*. 1993; 23(1): 59-65. Illus.: Photo. B&W. 2. Lang.: Eng.
France: Paris. 1992. Critical studies. ■Analysis of Théâtre du Soleil's *Les Atrides*, directed by Ariane Mnouchkine, which combines the work of Euripides and Aeschylus.

1677 Salter, Denis. "Théâtre du Soleil: *Les Atrides*." *ThM*. 1993; 23(1): 66-74. Illus.: Photo. B&W. 3. Lang.: Eng.
France: Paris. 1992. Histories-sources. ■Group interview with some of the performers in the Théâtre du Soleil production *Les Atrides*, directed by Ariane Mnouchkine: Simon Abkarian, Nirupama Nityanandan, Juliana Carneiro da Cunha, Brontis Jodorowsky, and Catherine Schaub.

1678 Shevtsova, Maria. "Sociocultural Analysis: National and Cross-Cultural Performance." *ThR*. 1997; 22(1): 4-18. Notes. Illus.: Photo. B&W. 5. Lang.: Eng.
France. 1993-1994. Critical studies. ■Outlines a sociocultural approach to performance analysis, illustrated by analyses of mono- and cross-cultural chronotopes in Jacques Lassalle's productions of Molière's *Dom Juan*, Jean-Luc Paliès's production of Doutreligne's *Don Juan d'origine* and Nika Kossenkova and Pascal Larue's production of Čechov's *Three Sisters (Tri sestry)*.

1679 Singleton, Brian. "Receiving *Les Atrides* Productively: Mnouchkine's Intercultural Signs as Intertexts." *ThR*. 1997; 22 (1): 19-23. Notes. Lang.: Eng.
France: Paris. 1990-1997. Critical studies. ■Analysis of intercultural signs in Ariane Mnouchkine's production of *Les Atrides* illustrating the application of a theory of productive reception.

1680 Spindler, Fredrika. "Knivskarpa tolkningar." (Knifesharp Renderings.) *Dramat*. 1997; 5(2): 40. Illus.: Photo. B&W. Lang.: Swe.
France: Paris. 1997. Historical studies. ■A report from the performances in Paris, with special reference to Dominique Blanc's staging of Ibsen's *Et Dukkehjem (A Doll's House)* at Théâtre de l'Odéon.

1681 Spindler, Fredrika. "Det andliga sökandets flyende." (The Fugitive of the Spiritual Searching.) *Dramat*. 1997; 5(4): 44-46. Illus.: Photo. B&W. Lang.: Swe.

France. 1995-1997. Histories-sources. ■An interview with the French director Olivier Py, with reference to his own ideas about essential theatre and its situation in France.

1682 Fjellner Patlakh, Irina. "Georgiens teater ytterst vital också efter kriget." (The Theatre of Georgia Is Quite Vital Even After the War.) *Entré*. 1997; 24(2): 41-44. Illus.: Photo. B&W. Lang.: Swe.
Georgia: Tbilisi. 1993. Historical studies. ■Reports that theatrical activity is intense, but that the domestic play is lacking. With reference to the directors Robert Sturua and David Doishvili.

1683 Balme, Christopher B. "Interpreting the Pictorial Record: Theatre Iconography and the Referential Dilemma." *ThR*. 1997; 22(3): 190-201. Notes. Illus.: Dwg. Photo. B&W. 4. Lang.: Eng.
Germany. UK-England. 1608-1918. Critical studies. ■Iconographic analysis of three visual records of actors (the play *Niemandt und Jemandt*, David Garrick and Frank Wedekind) as examples of multiple levels of aesthetic and social representation.

1684 Banu, Georges; Müry, Andres, transl. "Das Knarren des Bühnenbodens in Musik verwandeln." (Changing the Creaking of the Stage Floor Into Music.) *THeute*. 1997; 3: 30-31. Illus.: Photo. B&W. 2. Lang.: Ger.
Germany. France. 1948-1997. Histories-sources. ■An interview with Luc Bondy, theatre and film director in Paris and director at Schaubühne, in which he reflects his current dream of theatre.

1685 Buck, Elmar. "Die Neuberin—ein Theatermythos." (Neuberin—a Theatre Myth.) *DB*. 1997; 4: 24-27. Illus.: Dwg. 4. Lang.: Ger.
Germany. 1697-1760. Biographical studies. ■The life of actress Caroline Neuber, owner and founder of the Leipziger Schule, an early representative of female emancipation and a theatre director with a dream of a theatre of her own, on the occasion of the 300th anniversary of her birth. Includes a description of the Neuberin Museum in Reichenbach.

1686 Buhre, Traugott. "'Ich bin ein Dinosaurier'." ('I Am a Dinosaur'.) *THeute*. 1997; 4: 32-37. Illus.: Photo. B&W. 4. Lang.: Ger.
Germany. 1949-1997. Biographical studies. ■A portrait of the actor Traugott Buhre, his training and his important roles at German and Austrian theatres.

1687 Burckhardt, Barbara. "Lauter Königsspieler." (Nothing But King Actors.) *THeute*. 1997; 5: 16-18. Illus.: Photo. B&W. 2. Lang.: Ger.
Germany: Stuttgart. 1997. Critical studies. ■Important performances of Schauspiel Stuttgart: *Oidípous Týrannos (Oedipus the King)* by Sophocles directed by Martin Kusej and *Einfach kompliziert (Simply Complicated)* by Thomas Bernhard directed by Elmar Goerden with respect to the role of the kings.

1688 Burckhardt, Barbara. "Augen auf und durch!" (Open Your Eyes And Through!) *THeute*. 1997; 10: 20-25. Illus.: Photo. B&W. 3. Lang.: Ger.
Germany: Hamburg. 1997. Reviews of performances. ■Describes the start of the season at Deutsches Schauspielhaus: from *Peer Gynt* by Henrik Ibsen directed by Matthias Hartmann, *American Psycho*, adapted from the novel by Brett Easton Ellis directed by Thirza Bruncken and Stefanie Carp and *Indien (India)* by Josef Hader directed by Lars-Ole Walburg.

1689 Buselmeier, Michael. "Der Chef kocht gerne selbst." (The Chef Himself Likes to Cook.) *THeute*. 1997; 6: 25-28. Illus.: Photo. B&W. 4. Lang.: Ger.
Germany: Mannheim. 1996-1997. Historical studies. ■Describes productions of Bruno Klimek who is also the manager of the drama at Mannheimer Nationaltheater: *Die Jungfrau von Orleans (The Maid of Orleans)* by Schiller and *Višněvyj sad (The Cherry Orchard)* by Čechov.

1690 Carlson, Marvin. "Report from Berlin." *WES*. 1997 Spr; 9(2): 13-18. Illus.: Photo. 6. Lang.: Eng.
Germany: Berlin. 1996. Historical studies. ■In-depth account of the 1996 Berlin Theatre Festival. Focuses on Carl Zuckmayer's *Des Teufels General (The Devil's General)*, from the Volksbühne Theatre, directed by Frank Castorf, and other contemporary German plays.

DRAMA: —Performance/production

1691 Carp, Stefanie. "Vom produktiven Leerlauf..." (Towards Productive Idleness...)*THeute.* 1997; Yb: 30-36. Illus.: Photo. B&W. 3. Lang.: Ger.
Germany. 1985-1997. Histories-sources. ■An interview with actor Josef Bierbichler, about his work with director Christoph Marthaler.

1692 Carp, Stefanie. "Langsames Leben ist lang." (Slow Life Is Long.) *Thsch.* 1997; 12: 65-77. Illus.: Photo. B&W. 4. Lang.: Ger, Fre, Dut, Eng.
Germany. 1980-1997. Histories-sources. ■The theatre of Christoph Marthaler as giving a voice to the powerless, with attention to his productions of *Murx den Europäer! Murx ihn! Murx ihn! Murx ihn ab! (Kill the European! Kill Him! Kill Him! Kill Him Off!)* at Volksbühne, and *Kasimir und Karoline (Kasimir and Karoline)* by Ödön von Horváth at Deutsches Schauspielhaus.

1693 Dermutz, Klaus. "Glauben an den Lebensatem." (Believing in the Breath of Life.) *THeute.* 1997; 9: 14-19. Illus.: Photo. B&W. 5. Lang.: Ger.
Germany. 1960-1997. Biographical studies. ■A portrait of the actress Andrea Clausen, her work with director Andrea Breth, and important roles.

1694 Deuter, Ulrich. "Ich würde mich mit Brechts Erben wunderbar verstehen." (I Understand Brecht's Heirs All Too Well.) *TZ.* 1997; Yb: 8-11. Append. Illus.: Photo. B&W. 2. Lang.: Ger.
Germany: Bochum. 1997. Histories-sources. ■An interview with actor and director Leander Haussmann, since 1995 director at Schauspielhaus, about Brecht's influences on theatre.

1695 Erenstein, Robert L.; Ogden, Dunbar H. "*At Hathui's Tomb* and *The Lions' Den*: Resurrection Dramas in the Medieval Church." *JDTC.* 1997 Fall; 12(1): 161-174. Illus.: Photo. Dwg. 5. Lang.: Eng.
Germany: Gernrode. Netherlands: Maastricht. 1500-1996. Critical studies. ■Comparative study of two stagings in medieval churches, parallel in their death-and-resurrection stories, in their use of ecclesiastical architecture, and in their messages to their audiences. The first, *At Hathui's Tomb* (from *Visitatio sepulchri*), was performed in a German convent in 1500, the other, *The Lions' Den* (from the medieval *Visitatio Mariae Magdalenae*), in Maastricht in 1996.

1696 Fiebach, Joachim. "Bilder der grossen Kapitulation." (Images of the Grand Capitulation.) *TZ.* 1997; Yb: 170-172. Append. Illus.: Photo. B&W. 2. Lang.: Ger.
Germany: Berlin. 1949. Critical studies. ■Discusses Brechts's deconstructive potential based on the fourth scene of *Mutter Courage und ihre Kinder (Mother Courage and Her Children)* directed by Brecht himself and Erich Engel at Deutsches Theater.

1697 Franke, Eckhard. "Hoffnungsträger Zwiebelmesser." (Onion Knife as a Subject of Hope.) *THeute.* 1997; 11: 30-31. Illus.: Photo. B&W. 2. Lang.: Ger.
Germany: Mannheim. 1997. Historical studies. ■Describes premieres of *Klistier (Enema)* by Kerstin Hensel directed by Corinna Bethge and *Geheimnis des Lebens (Secret of Life)* by Barbara Frey directed by Bettina Meyer at Nationaltheater.

1698 Funke, Christoph. "Krieg mit Krähe und Uhu." (War with Owl and Crow.) *THeute.* 1997; 6: 32-33. Illus.: Photo. B&W. 2. Lang.: Ger.
Germany: Berlin. Israel. 1997. Historical studies. ■Israeli guest performances during the 4th 'Deutsches Kinder- und Jugendtheatertreffen'.

1699 Garforth, Julian A. "'Unsere wichtigste Entdeckung für die deutsche Bühne?': Critical Reaction to the German Premieres of Samuel Beckett's Stage Plays." *FMT.* 1997; 12(1): 75-90. Append. Notes. Lang.: Eng.
Germany. 1953-1976. Historical studies. ■The relationship among the German press, society and Beckett, who became an accepted figure mainly based on his directions of plays in postwar Germany.

1700 Hansell, Sven. "Jag vill irretera, men om möjligt för utsälda huso." (I Want To Irritate, But With Full Houses If Possible.) *Entré.* 1997; 24(5): 8-17. Illus.: Photo. B&W. Lang.: Swe.
Germany: Berlin. Sweden: Stockholm. 1976. Critical studies. ■A presentation of the director Frank Castorf about his background and career, with references to Ibsen's *Fruen fra havet (The Lady From the Sea)* and Zuckmayer's *Des Teufels General (The Devil's General)* both at Volksbühne, and Strindberg's *Svarta fanor (Black Banners)* at Stockholms Stadsteater.

1701 Heeg, Günther. "Herr und Knecht, Furcht und Arbeit, Mann und Frau." (Master and Servant, Fear and Labor, Man and Woman.) *TZ.* 1997; Yb: 147-152. Append. Illus.: Photo. B&W. 3. Lang.: Ger.
Germany: Berlin. 1996. Critical studies. ■Einar Schleef's archaeological approach to the dialectic of master and servant in his production of Brecht's *Herr Puntila und sein Knecht Matti (Mr. Puntila and His Man Matti)* at Berliner Ensemble.

1702 Heine, Beate. "Sternschnuppe oder Fixstern?" (Shooting Star or Fixed Star?)*DB.* 1997; 11: 33-35. Illus.: Photo. B&W. 1. Lang.: Ger.
Germany. 1967-1997. Biographical studies. ■A portrait of playwright and director Daniel Call born in 1967.

1703 Höfele, Andreas. "A Theatre of Exhaustion? 'Posthistoire' in Recent German Shakespearean Production." *SQ.* 1992 Spr; 43(1): 80-86. Notes. Lang.: Eng.
Germany. 1989-1992. Historical studies. ■German approach to productions of Shakespeare post-Berlin Wall.

1704 Hortmann, Wilhelm. "Berlin–Zürich–Düsseldorf: Aspects of German Theatre During the Nazi Period and After." *STP.* 1997 Dec.; 16: 5-25. Notes. Biblio. Lang.: Eng.
Germany: Berlin, Dusseldorf. Switzerland: Zurich. 1933-1952. Historical studies. ■The development of German-language theatre from Hitler's take-over to the immediate post-war years. Discusses opposition to the regime in work of Gründgens and Hilpert, the role of the Schauspielhaus in Zurich as a home for exiles, return of exiles like Kortner, the spiritual humanism of post-war German theatre.

1705 Huber, Alfred. "Die Glücksucherin." (She Is Looking for Luck.) *DB.* 1997; 11: 40-41. Illus.: Photo. B&W. 2. Lang.: Ger.
Germany. 1961-1997. Biographical studies. ■A portrait of the playwright Kerstin Hensel.

1706 Jörder, Gerhard. "Verpanzert in Lebenstrauer." (Armored in Sorrow of Life.) *THeute.* 1997; 2: 11-13. Illus.: Photo. B&W. 2. Lang.: Ger.
Germany: Dusseldorf, Stuttgart. 1996-1997. Historical studies. ■Describes two performances of Čechov's *Ivanov* directed by Anna Badora at Düsseldorfer Schauspielhaus and by Elmar Goerden at Schauspiel Stuttgart.

1707 Kahle, Ulrike. "Die Rolle als einzige Haut." (The Role as the Only Skin.) *THeute.* 1997; Yb: 27-28. Illus.: Photo. B&W. 1. Lang.: Ger.
Germany: Hamburg. 1997. Biographical studies. ■A portrait of Josef Bierbichler, the actor of the year, chosen by *Theater Heute* for his role as Kasimir in *Kasimir und Karoline (Kasimir and Karoline)* by Ödön von Horváth directed by Christoph Marthaler.

1708 Koerbl, Jörg-Michael. "Theater–das grösste Geheimnis." (Theatre–the Biggest Secret.) *TZ.* 1997; 1: 4-5. Illus.: Photo. B&W. 3. Lang.: Ger.
Germany: Berlin. 1997. Histories-sources. ■An interview with Dagmar Manzel, actress at Deutsches Theater, about art as resistance.

1709 Krumbholz, Martin. "Sein & Schein im Ernst und weiter!" (Reality and Appearance: In Earnest And So On!)*THeute.* 1997; 12: 22-24. Illus.: Photo. B&W. 1. Lang.: Ger.
Germany: Wiesbaden. 1997. Historical studies. ■Describes the beginning of the season under the new directorship of Daniel Karasek at Staatstheater Wiesbaden. Reports of *Questa sera si recita a soggetto (Tonight We Improvise)* by Luigi Pirandello directed by Daniel Karasek and *Woyzeck* by Georg Büchner directed by Elke Lang.

1710 Krusche, Friedemann. "Woyzeck aus Ungarn meets Lenin in Zürich an der Elbe." (Woyzeck from Hungary Meets Lenin in Zurich-on-Elbe.) *THeute.* 1997; 7: 28-30. Illus.: Photo. B&W. 3. Lang.: Ger.
Germany: Magdeburg. 1989. Critical studies. ■Describes plays from Russia, Hungary and Bulgaria performed at Kammerspiele: *Die grünen Wangen des April (The Green Cheeks of April)* by Michajl Ugarov

DRAMA: —Performance/production

directed by Axel Richter, *Júlia és a hadnagy avagy holtomiglan-holtodiglan (Julia and Her Lieutenant, or Till Death Do Us Part)* by Ákos Németh directed by Hermann Schein and *Persifedron* by Konstantin Pavlov directed by Wolf Bunge.

1711 Krusche, Friedemann. "Das Theater der Grausamkeit." (Theatre of Cruelty.) *THeute.* 1997; 2: 26-28. Append. Illus.: Photo. B&W. 2. Lang.: Ger.

Germany: Rostock. 1994-1997. Historical studies. ■Describes *Macbeth* directed by Christina Emig-Könning at Schauspielhaus Rostock. Also discusses the directorship of Manfred Straube, cultural politics, and budget cuts.

1712 Krusche, Friedemann. "Im fallenden Herzen die kalte Glut." (The Cold Fire in the Falling Heart.) *THeute.* 1997; 4: 22-25 . Illus.: Photo. B&W. 2. Lang.: Ger.

Germany: Leipzig. 1996-1997. Reviews of performances. ■Modern version of the classics: Goethe's *Clavigo* directed by Wolfgang Engel and Friedrich Schiller's *Kabale und Liebe (Intrigue and Love)* directed by Konstanze Lauterbach at Schauspiel Leipzig.

1713 Krusche, Friedemann. "Aus deutschen Hinterwald." (From the German Backwoods.) *THeute.* 1997; 12: 27-28. Illus.: Photo. B&W. 1. Lang.: Ger.

Germany: Leipzig. 1997. Historical studies. ■Describes the performances of *Fidibus* by Frank Sporkmann directed by Armin Petras and *Richard's Cork Leg* by Brendan Behan directed by Konstanze Lauterbach at Schauspiel Leipzig.

1714 Kümmel, Peter. "Bis die Endorphine strömen." (Until the Endorphine Is Streaming.) *THeute.* 1997; 8: 20-23. Illus.: Photo. B&W. 3. Lang.: Ger.

Germany: Stuttgart. 1967-1997. Biographical studies. ■A portrait of the actor Samuel Weiss and his acting at Stuttgart Schauspiel.

1715 Kümmel, Peter. "'Das hat eing'schlagen da drunten!'." ('This Has Stroken Down There!) *THeute.* 1997; 12: 20-22. Illus.: Photo. B&W. 1. Lang.: Ger.

Germany: Stuttgart. 1997. Critical studies. ■Performances of *Der Gehülfe (The Assistant)* by Robert Walser directed by Marcus Mislin and Deborah Epstein and *Geier-Wally (Vulture-Wally)* by Wilhelmine von Hillern directed by Martin Kusej at Schauspiel Stuttgart at the beginning of the season.

1716 Lennartz, Knut. "Kinder der Unschuld." (Children of Innocence.) *DB.* 1997; 4: 10-14. Illus.: Photo. B&W. 5. Lang.: Ger.

Germany. 1996-1997. Critical studies. ■Productions of plays by Schiller, the most frequently performed classic playwright of the season: *Don Carlos* directed by Karl-Dirk Schmidt at Maxim Gorki Theater and Barbara Bilabel at Bremer Theater, *Die Jungfrau von Orleans (The Maid of Orleans)* directed by Katja Paryla at Deutsches Nationaltheater and by Beverly Blankenship at Saarländisches Staatstheater.

1717 Lennartz, Knut. "In Bewegung bleiben." (To Keep Moving.) *DB.* 1997; 6: 10-14. Illus.: Photo. B&W. 6. Lang.: Ger.

Germany. 1985-1997. Biographical studies. ■Director Andreas Kriegenburg, whose Bayerisches Staatsschauspiel production of Borchert's *Draussen vor der Tür (The Man Outside)* has been selected for presentation at Theatertreffen.

1718 Lennartz, Knut. "Von Stücken und Tücken." (On Plays and Difficulties.) *DB.* 1997; 7: 28-31. Illus.: Photo. B&W. 4. Lang.: Ger.

Germany: Mülheim. 1997. Reviews of performances. ■Discusses the German speaking contemporary drama on occasion of Mülheimer Theatertage. Reviews of *Stecken, Stab und Stangl (Stick, Rod, and Pole)* by Elfriede Jelinek directed by Thirza Bruncken, Deutsches Schauspielhaus, and *Top Dogs* by Urs Widmer directed by Ulrich Hesse, Theater Neumarkt.

1719 Lord, Mark. "The Dramaturgy Reader." 88-101 in Jonas, Susan, ed.; Proehl, Geoffrey S., ed. *Dramaturgy in American Theatre: A Sourcebook.* New York, NY: Harcourt Brace College Pub; 1997. 590 pp. Pref. Notes. Biblio. Index. Lang.: Eng.

Germany: Frankfurt. 1997. Histories-sources. ■Essay/poem challenging assumptions about production dramaturgy.

1720 Lysell, Roland. "Den skapande restaurationen." (The Creative Restoration.) *Tningen.* 1997; 21(2): 7-10. Illus.: Photo. B&W. Color. Lang.: Swe.

Germany: Munich. 1996. Historical studies. ■A presentation of Botho Strauss' *Ithaka* in the production of Dieter Dorn at Münchner Kammerspiele.

1721 Merschmeier, Michael. "Dandies, Diven, Menschenfresser." (Dandies, Divas, Cannibals.) *THeute.* 1997; 3: 12-17. Illus.: Photo. B&W. 7. Lang.: Ger.

Germany. 1996-1997. Reviews of performances. ■German performances of plays by Terrence McNally and Nicky Silver: McNally's *Love! Valour! Compassion!* directed by Gustav Peter Wöhler at Deutsches Schauspielhaus and *Master Class* directed by Niels Peter Rudolph at Thalia Theater, by Gerd Heinz at Cuvilliès Theater, and by John Dew at Theater Dortmund, Silver's *Raised in Captivity* directed by Harald Demmer at Theater Dortmund, *The Food Chain* directed by Christiane Buhre at Hannover and *Fat Men in Skirts* directed by Thomas Ostermeier at Deutsches Theater/Baracke.

1722 Merschmeier, Michael. "Die Stunden der Wahrheit." (The Hours of Truth.) *THeute.* 1997; 2: 4-10. Illus.: Photo. B&W. 7. Lang.: Ger.

Germany. Austria. 1996-1997. Critical studies. ■Recent productions of Ödön von Horváth's plays. Compares *Kasimir und Karoline (Kasimir and Karoline)* directed by Christoph Marthaler at Deutsches Schauspielhaus and by Matthias Hartmann at Burgtheater, and *Geschichten aus dem Wiener Wald (Tales from the Vienna Woods)* directed by Hans Neuenfels at Residenztheater.

1723 Merschmeier, Michael; Wille, Franz; Feuchtner, Bernd. "Die Gesprächsprobe." (Trial of Talk.) *THeute.* 1997; Yb: 6-24 . Illus.: Photo. B&W. 10. Lang.: Ger.

Germany. Switzerland. 1980-1997. Histories-sources. ■An interview with Christoph Marthaler and Anna Viebrock, who were chosen by critics of *Theater Heute* as director and set and costume designer of the year for their work on *Kasimir und Karoline (Kasimir and Karoline)* by Ödön von Horváth about the 'Marthaler method' including statements of Frank Baumbauer, manager at Hamburger Schauspielhaus, and of actor André Jung.

1724 Mihan, Jörg. "'Ich bin kein Mensch der Keule'." ('I Am Not a Clubman'.) *TZ.* 1997; 5: 18-22. Illus.: Photo. B&W. 5. Lang.: Ger.

Germany. 1996-1997. Biographical studies. ■A portrait of the actor and director Matthias Brenner and his working methods.

1725 Müller, Christoph. "Einladung zum Salat." (Invitation for Salad.) *THeute.* 1997; Yb: 112. Illus.: Photo. B&W. 1. Lang.: Ger.

Germany. 1988-1997. Historical studies. ■A portrait of Claudia Jahn, young actress of the year chosen by critics of *Theater Heute*.

1726 Müller, Christoph. "Deutschland, deine gaffgierigen Schwaben." (Germany, Your Swabians With Greedy Eyes.) *THeute.* 1997; 9: 20-25. Illus.: Photo. B&W. 6. Lang.: Ger.

Germany: Stuttgart. 1997. Historical studies. ■The most successful performances of the season in Swabia: *Der Totmacher (The Killer)* by Romuald Karmakar directed by Christian Pade, *Medea* by Euripides directed by Hans-Ulrich Becker, *Stella* by Goethe directed by Marcel Keller at Stuttgart and *Feurio* by Bernhard Blume, and directed by Heike Beutel played by Melchinger Lindenhof.

1727 Neubert-Herwig, Christa. "Einengung ist selten produktiv." (Constriction Is Seldom Productive.) *TZ.* 1997; 6: 18-20. Illus.: Photo. B&W. 4. Lang.: Ger.

Germany. Switzerland. 1949-1997. Histories-sources. ■An interview with director Benno Besson about staging and working with actors including statements of the actors Elsa Grube-Deister, Fred Düren und Käthe Reichel about Besson's working methods.

1728 Nordmann, Alfred; Wickert, Hartmut. "The Impossible Representation of Wonder: Space Summons Memory." *ThR.* 1997; 22(1): 38-48. Notes. Illus.: Photo. B&W. 5. Lang.: Eng.

Germany: Hannover. 1993. Critical studies. ■Analysis of Hartmut Wickert's production of *Die Stunde da wir nichts voneinander wussten (The*

DRAMA: —Performance/production

Hour We Knew Nothing of Each Other) by Peter Handke, at Schauspiel Hannover, 1993.

1729 Pietzsch, Ingeborg. "Wir suchen, was uns eint." (We Look for Common Interests.) *TZ.* 1997; 3: 36-37. Illus.: Photo. B&W. 2. Lang.: Ger.
Germany. 1970-1997. Biographical studies. ■Portraits of the directors Tom Kühnel and Robert Schuster, common interests and concepts, and their training.

1730 Preusser, Gerhard. "Vatermord, Ehekrieg, Mordsfrau." (Patricide, Marriage War and Mortal Woman.) *THeute.* 1997; 5: 22-24 . Illus.: Photo. B&W. 2. Lang.: Ger.
Germany: Bochum. 1997. Reviews of performances. ■Reviews Niklas Frank and Yehoshua Sobol's adaptation of Strindberg's *Fadren (The Father)*, directed by Uwe Dag Berlin, *Kamraterna (Comrades)* by August Strindberg directed by film director Detlef Buck and *Macbeth* by William Shakespeare directed by Jürgen Kruse at Bochumer Schauspielhaus. Analyzes how the tragedies were transformed into comedies.

1731 Preusser, Gerhard. "Wohin geht die Fahrt?" (Where Is the Trip Going?)*THeute.* 1997; 11: 13-14. Illus.: Photo. B&W. 2. Lang.: Ger.
Germany: Dusseldorf. 1997. Historical studies. ■Describes the start of the season at Düsseldorfer Schauspielhaus: *The Tempest* by William Shakespeare directed by Anna Badora and *Top Dogs* by Urs Widmer directed by Peter Hailer.

1732 Rischbieter, Henning. "Fanpost aus der Mördergrube." (Fan Mail from the Den of Cutthroats.) *THeute.* 1997; 2: 29-33. Illus.: Photo. B&W. 2. Lang.: Ger.
Germany: Bochum. 1995-1997. Historical studies. ■Discusses performances at the Bochumer Schauspielhaus from the aspect of developing a style to the house. Analyzes *Marquis de Sade* by Charles Méré directed by Frank Castorf, *The Taming of the Shrew* by William Shakespeare directed by Leander Haussmann, *Zimmerschlacht (Home Front)* by Martin Walser directed by Dimiter Gotscheff, *A Midsummer Night's Dream* by William Shakespeare directed by Peter Fitz and *Knife* by John Cassavetes directed by Jürgen Kruse.

1733 Schwind, Klaus. "Dramatisch-Theatralisches. Prolegomena zu einem theatralen Begriff der Intonation." (Dramatic-Theatricality: Prolegomena to the Theatrical Term Intonation.) *FMT.* 1997; 12(1): 19-28. Notes. Lang.: Ger.
Germany. 1806-1991. Critical studies. ■Discusses different aspects of the term 'intonation' from Heinrich von Kleist's *Amphitryon* directed by Klaus Michael Grüber at Schaubühne (Berlin) in 1991. Describes 'intonation' also as exercise and theatrical communication structures.

1734 Shafer, Yvonne. "Interview with Frank Castorf." *WES.* 1997 Fall; 9(3): 55-58. Illus.: Photo. 1. Lang.: Eng.
Germany: Berlin. 1997. Histories-sources. ■Interview with Volksbühne director Frank Castorf.

1735 Skasa, Michael. "Der Löwe schläft nicht, wenn der Dschungel ruft." (The Lion Will Not Sleep If the Jungle Calls.) *THeute.* 1997; Yb: 37-44. Illus.: Photo. B&W. 6. Lang.: Ger.
Germany. 1989-1997. Biographical studies. ■A portrait of Corinna Harfouch, actress of the year chosen by critics of *Theater Heute*.

1736 Stephan, Erika. "Mordspiele." (Killing Games.) *THeute.* 1997; 4: 25-27. Illus.: Photo. B&W. 2. Lang.: Ger.
Germany: Leipzig. 1996-1997. Critical studies. ■Discusses contemporary plays performed at Schauspiel Leipzig *Stecken, Stab und Stangl (Stick, Rod, and Pole)* by Elfriede Jelinek directed by Kazuko Watanabe and *Life According to Agfa* after the film by Assi Dayan directed by Wolfgang Engel.

1737 Stoll, Dieter. "Classic light." *THeute.* 1997; 12: 30-31. Illus.: Photo. B&W. 1. Lang.: Ger.
Germany. 1997. Critical studies. ■Describes the performances of classical plays in Franconia like William Shakespeare's *Twelfth Night* directed by Andreas Hänsel at Markgrafentheater (Erlangen) and *As You Like It* directed by Oliver Karbus at Landestheater (Coburg), and Friedrich Schiller's *Don Carlos* directed by Holger Berg at Schauspiel Nürnberg.

1738 Stryk, Lydia. "Marthaler Meets Chekhov: *Three Sisters*, Volksbühne Premiere." *WES.* 1997 Fall; 9(3): 51-52. Lang.: Eng.

Germany: Berlin. 1997. Historical studies. ■Critical review of Christoph Marthaler's latest production, Čechov's *Tri sestry* at the Volksbühne am Rosa-Luxemburg-Platz.

1739 Stumpfe, Mario. "Jo Fabian." *TZ.* 1997; 3: 40-43. Illus.: Photo. B&W. 4. Lang.: Ger.
Germany: Berlin. 1987-1997. Critical studies. ■Analysis of Fabian's directorial style through a study of twenty-six productions. Describes Fabian's aesthetics as between avant-garde and mannerism.

1740 Sugiera, Małgorzata. "Teatr epicki, realizm i modele: 'Matka Courage i jej dzieci' Bertolda Brechta." (Epic Theatre, Realism, and Models: Brecht's *Mother Courage and Her Children*.) 53-69 in Pleśniarowicz, Krzysztof, ed.; Sugiera, Małgorzata, ed. *Arcydzieła inscenizacji od Reinhardta do Wilsona*. Cracow: Księgarnia Akademicka; 1997. 139 pp. (Wielkie dzieła teatralne.) Pref. Notes. Index. Lang.: Pol.
Germany: Berlin. 1949. Historical studies. ■Reconstruction of the Berlin production, with analysis of Brecht's models and his relations with Stanislavskij.

1741 Theissen, Hermann. "Warten auf den nächsten Bus Stop." (Waiting for the Next Bus Stop.) *THeute.* 1997; 8: 5-10. Illus.: Photo. B&W. 6. Lang.: Ger.
Germany. Austria. 1969-1997. Biographical studies. ■A portrait of the actress Traute Hoess from her beginning at Falkenbergschule until today, about her work within Theaterkollektiv 'Rote Rübe' and cooperation with directors Rainer Werner Fassbinder, Günter Krämer, Werner Schroeter.

1742 Tóth, Tas. "McNally mesterkurzusa Münchenben." (Terrence McNally's *Master Class* in Munich.) *ZZT.* 1997; 4(4): 34. Illus.: Photo. B&W. 1. Lang.: Hun.
Germany: Munich. 1997. Reviews of performances. ■Elisabeth Rath's performance as Maria Callas in Terrence McNally's *Master Class* at Cuvilliés Theater.

1743 Vogler, Werner Simon. "Aufbruch am Ende der Hoffnung." (Start at the End of Hope.) *THeute.* 1997; 12: 28-30. Illus.: Photo. B&W. 1. Lang.: Ger.
Germany: Mainz. 1997. Critical studies. ■Describes the concepts from the opening of a new venue of Stadttheater Mainz. Reports of *Na dně (The Lower Depths)* by Maksim Gorkij directed by Michael Helle and *Johann Gabriel Borkman* by Henrik Ibsen directed by Thomas Bischoff.

1744 Weber, Manfred. "Die Zeit ist nicht die Uhr." (Time Is Not an Hour of Day.) *Thsch.* 1997; 12: 124-141. Illus.: Photo. B&W. 2. Lang.: Ger, Fre, Dut, Eng.
Germany: Berlin. 1989-1997. Histories-sources. ■An interview with director Jo Fabian about history, repetitions and perceptions.

1745 Wille, Franz. "Richard For President?" *THeute.* 1997; 1: 16-21. Illus.: Photo. B&W. 5. Lang.: Ger.
Germany. Switzerland. 1996. Critical studies. ■Compares the performances of *Richard III* by William Shakespeare directed by Peter Löscher at Basler Theater, by Wolfgang Engel at Leipzig Schauspiel, and by Martin Kusej at Volksbühne. Describes the acting of Jürgen Maurer, Ulrich Wildgruber and Bruno Cathomas as Richard III.

1746 Wille, Franz. "Gnade des Vergessens." (Mercy of Oblivion.) *THeute.* 1997; 5: 34-37. Illus.: Photo. B&W. 3. Lang.: Ger.
Germany: Berlin, Frankfurt. 1996-1997. Historical studies. ■Reports of the most discussed plays that were performed again this season. Describes *Ithaka* by Botho Strauss directed by Thomas Langhoff at Deutsches Theater and *Zurüstungen für die Unsterblichkeit (Preparations for Immortality)* by Peter Handke directed by Hans Hollmann at Frankfurter Schauspiel.

1747 Wille, Franz. "Der Preis der Revolution ist der Bürger." (The Revolution's Price Is the Citizen.) *THeute.* 1997; 11: 6-9. Illus.: Photo. B&W. 3. Lang.: Ger.
Germany: Bochum. 1997. Historical studies. ■Reports of the start of the season at Bochumer Schauspielhaus with *Dantons Tod (Danton's Death)* by Georg Büchner directed by Leander Haussmann and *Maria Magdalena* by Friedrich Hebbel directed Jürgen Kruse.

1748 Wille, Franz. "Harry Heines Nachfahren." (Harry Heine's Issue.) *THeute.* 1997; 12: 39-42. Illus.: Photo. B&W. 3. Lang.: Ger.

DRAMA: —Performance/production

Germany. 1968-1997. Historical studies. ■Describes the play *Harrys Kopf (Harry's Head)* by Tankred Dorst and Ursula Ehler, and its first performances directed by Wilfried Minks at Düsseldorfer Schauspielhaus and directed by Jürgen Flimm at Thalia Theater.

1749 Di Benedetto, Vincenzo; Medda, Enrico. *La tragedia greca sulla scena. La tragedia greca in quanto spettacolo teatrale.* (Greek Tragedy on Stage: Greek Tragedy as Theatrical Performance.) Turin: Einaudi; 1997. xv, 422 pp. (Piccola Biblioteca Einaudi 639.) Notes. Index. Lang.: Ita.
Greece: Athens. 500 B.C. Critical studies. ■Analysis of the visual component of ancient Greek theatre, with consideration of the scenic space of the tragedies, the theatre of Dionysos in Athens, as well as the scenery, acting, and disposition of the chorus and actors.

1750 Rutter, Carol Chillington. "Harrison, Herakles, and Wailing Women: *Labourers* at Delphi." *NTQ.* 1997; 13(50): 133-143. Notes. Biblio. Illus.: Photo. B&W. 2. [Report from the eighth International Meeting on Ancient Greek Drama at the European Cultural Centre, Delphi.] Lang.: Eng.
Greece: Delphi. 1995. Reviews of performances. ■*The Labourers of Herakles* is a new play by Tony Harrison, with a female chorus of cement mixers and set on a building site, which uses textual fragments from the past to pose a question about the future.

1751 Wilson, Peter. "Leading the Tragic *Khoros*: Tragic Prestige in the Democratic City." 81-108 in Pelling, Christopher, ed. *Greek Tragedy and the Historian.* Oxford: Clarendon; 1997. 268 pp. Notes. Biblio. Index. Lang.: Eng.
Greece. 500-400 B.C. Historical studies. ■The significance of the role of the *khoregos*, or choral leader, a position awarded to a patron or prestigious member of the community.

1752 Bérczes, László; Koncz, Zsuzsa, photo. "Így lett. Beszélgetés Végvári Tamással." (Things Happened Like This: A Conversation with Tamás Végvári.) *Sz.* 1997; 30(8): 30-34. Illus.: Photo. B&W. 5. Lang.: Hun.
Hungary. 1958-1997. Historical studies. ■Tamás Végvári's appearance at the club of the publishing house Osiris, which hosts monthly meetings with outstanding theatre personalities.

1753 Bérczes, László; Benda, Iván, photo.; Koncz, Zsuzsa, photo. "A szerző szándéka, a szöveg szándéka. Beszélgetés Kiss Csabával és Parti Nagy Lajossal." (The Intention of the Playwright and the Interpretation of the Text: A Conversation with director Csaba Kiss and playwright Lajos Parti Nagy.) *Sz.* 1997; 30(1): 28-32. Illus.: Photo. B&W. 4. Lang.: Hun.
Hungary. 1980-1996. Historical studies. ■The appearance of author Lajos Parti Nagy and director Csaba Kiss, recipients of a 1997 critics' award, at the club of the publishing house Osiris, which hosts monthly meetings with outstanding theatre personalities. They discussed Kiss's production of *Macbeth* and the production of Parti Nagy's *Mauzóleum (Mausoleum)* by Gábor Máté.

1754 Bérczes, László; Koncz, Zsuzsa, photo. "Létra, fal, mese. Beszélgetés Gothár Péterrel." (Ladder, Wall, Tale: An Interview with Péter Gothár.) *Sz.* 1997; 30(2): 36-39. Illus.: Photo. B&W. 3. Lang.: Hun.
Hungary. 1947-1997. Histories-sources. ■A conversation with film and theatre director Péter Gothár on his career and future plans in both fields of his activity.

1755 Bérczes, László; Koncz, Zsuzsa, photo. "Tegnap és ma. Színház-est Ács Jánossal." (Past and Present: A Theatre Evening with János Ács.) *Sz.* 1997; 30(3): 37-45. Illus.: Photo. B&W. 5. Lang.: Hun.
Hungary. 1960-1997. Histories-sources. ■A conversation with one of the significant Hungarian directors of the eighties with focus on his views on present-day Hungarian theatre.

1756 Bérczes, László; Koncz, Zsuzsa, photo. "Bő esztendők. Beszélgetés Valló Péterrel." (Substantial Years: A Conversation with Péter Valló.) *Sz.* 1997; 30(4): 25-30. Illus.: Photo. B&W. 4. Lang.: Hun.
Hungary. 1970-1997. Histories-sources. ■Career of the director with a summary of his important productions in the eighties and nineties.

1757 Bérczes, László; Koncz, Zsuzsa, photo. "Édes fájás. Beszélgetés Csákányi Eszterrel." (Sweet Pain: An Interview with Eszter Csákányi.) *Sz.* 1997; 30(7): 18-21. Illus.: Photo. B&W. 5. Lang.: Hun.
Hungary. 1990-1997. Histories-sources. ■The actress speaks about her recent roles and a guest performance in Vienna.

1758 Bérczes, László; Koncz, Zsuzsa, photo. "Valami történik. Beszélgetés Szász Jánossal." (Something Happens: A Conversation with János Szász.) *Sz.* 1997; 30(12): 28-31. Illus.: Photo. B&W. 4. Lang.: Hun.
Hungary. 1980-1997. Histories-sources. ■Interviewing the successful young theatre and film director on his life and career.

1759 Bódis, Mária. "Mimikai tanulmányok. Rakodczay Pál (1856-1921)." (Mimic Studies: Pál Rakodczay (1856-1921).) *Sz.* 1997; 30(2): 41-43. Illus.: Photo. B&W. 9. Lang.: Hun.
Hungary. 1856-1921. Historical studies. ■Evoking the pathetic figure of Pál Rakodczay, an actor-manager of the late nineteenth century.

1760 Bódis, Mária. "Apraxin Júlia (1830-1917)." (Júlia Apraxin, 1830-1917.) *Sz.* 1997; 30(12): 41-43. Illus.: Photo. B&W. 6. Lang.: Hun.
Hungary. 1830-1917. Historical studies. ■Profile and photographs of Hungarian actress Júlia Apraxin.

1761 Dömötör, Adrienne; Koncz, Zsuzsa, photo. "Egy civil színész. Beszélgetés László Zsolttal." (A Civil Actor: An Interview with Zsolt László.) *Sz.* 1997; 30(3): 45-48. Illus.: Photo. B&W. 2. Lang.: Hun.
Hungary. 1990-1997. Histories-sources. ■Meeting a young leading actor of Budapest New Theatre (Új Színház).

1762 Enyedi, Sándor. "*Az ember tragédiája*-jának vidéki előadásai, 1884-1918." (The Provincial Performances of Imre Madách's *The Tragedy of Man*, 1884-1918.) *SzSz.* 1997(32): 132-140. Lang.: Hun.
Hungary. 1884-1918. Historical studies. ■The stage career of Madách's play in the provinces with a collection of data on productions.

1763 Fábri, Magda, B., ed.; Avar, István, contrib.; Cseke, Csilla, photo. *A tanár úr—Vámos László emlékkönyv.* (The Teacher—In Honor of László Vámos.) Budapest: Gemini; 1997. 202 pp. Append. Illus.: Photo. B&W. 171. Lang.: Hun.
Hungary. 1928-1996. Biographical studies. ■Memory of a significant personality of the post-war Hungarian theatre introduced by recollections of his colleagues. László Vámos was a director, pedagogue at the Budapest Academy of Drama and Film, and the secretary general of the Hungarian Theatre Association (1981-1990). His proficiency was highly esteemed home and abroad by various awards and guest performances.

1764 Gábor, Miklós. *Sánta szabadság.* (Awkward Freedom.) Budapest: Magvető; 1997. 579 pp. Lang.: Hun.
Hungary. 1955-1957. Histories-sources. ■Continuation of the actor's diary during the age of restricted freedom.

1765 Gerold, László. "A *Tragédia* színházi és irodalmi utóélete a Vajdaságban." (The Presence of Imre Madách's *Tragedy* in Literature and in the Theatre in Voivodship.) *SzSz.* 1997(32): 101-110. Notes. Lang.: Hun.
Hungary. Yugoslavia. 1884-1965. Historical studies. ■Stage career of Imre Madách's *Az ember tragédiája (The Tragedy of Man)* in Voivodship, which became part of Yugoslavia in 1918.

1766 Gervai, András. "Természetes volt, hogy maradok. Beszélgetés Lohinszky Lóránddal." (It Was Obvious to Stay: A Talk with Lóránd Lohinszky.) *Sz.* 1997; 30(12): 32-35. Illus.: Photo. B&W. 5. Lang.: Hun.
Hungary. Romania: Târgu-Mureş. 1946-1997. Histories-sources. ■Interview with a leading actor of the Hungarian ethnic minority theatre in Transylvania, celebrating the 50th anniversary of his career, about his motivations for having remained in Romania.

1767 Janovics, Jenő; Enyedi, Sándor, ed., intro. "Janovics Jenő és a *Tragédia*." (Jenő Janovics and Imre Madách's *Tragédia*.) *SzSz.* 1997(32): 111-131. Lang.: Hun.
Hungary: Kolozsvár. Romania: Cluj. 1894-1945. Historical studies. ■Transylvanian productions of *Az ember tragédiája (The Tragedy of Man)* staged by Janovics (actor, director, manager and publicist).

DRAMA: —Performance / production

Includes excerpts from the Janovics' writings on the drama and its productions.

1768 Kaizinger, Rita. "Erkel Gyula kísérőzenéje a *Tragédia* ősbemutatójára." (Gyula Erkel's Music for the Première of Imre Madách's *Tragedy*.) *SzSz*. 1997(32): 49-52. Notes. Lang.: Hun.
Hungary: Budapest. 1883. Critical studies. ■The importance of music in the premiere of Madách's *Az ember tragédiája (The Tragedy of Man)* directed by Ede Paulay at the National Theatre. Based on the director's copy and original scores by Erkel preserved at the Theatre History and Music Collection of the National Széchényi Library.

1769 Kékesi Kun, Árpád; Koncz, Zsuzsa, photo.; Strassburger, Alexandra, photo.; Benda, Iván, photo. "A reprezentáció játékai. A kilencvenes évek magyar rendezői színháza." (The Plays of Representation: The Director's Theatre in Hungary in the 90s.) *Sz*. 1997; 30(7): 22-29. Notes. Illus.: Photo. B&W. 6. Lang.: Hun.
Hungary. 1990-1997. Critical studies. ■Survey of trends among young Hungarian directors in the nineties.

1770 Koltai, Gábor; Ikládi, László, photo.; Fábián, József, photo. "Elromlott románc. *Troilus és Cressida*-olvasat." (Spoilt Romance: The Interpretation of Shakespeare's *Troilus and Cressida*.) *Sz*. 1997; 30(11): 33-40. Illus.: Photo. B&W. 7. Lang.: Hun.
Hungary. 1970-1980. Critical studies. ■Analyzing the unique mixture of tragedy and bitter farce in Shakespeare's play through various productions.

1771 Kovács, Dezső; Ilovszky, Béla, photo. "Kocsis Etelka: Fullajtár Andrea—Csalog Zsolt: *Csendet akarok*." (Etelka Kocsis: Andrea Fullajtár in Zsolt Csalog's *I Want Silence*.) *Sz*. 1997; 30(5): 25. Illus.: Photo. B&W. 1. Lang.: Hun.
Hungary: Budapest. 1996. Critical studies. ■Analysis of the interpretation given by Academy student Andrea Fullajtár in Zsolt Csalog's one-woman show dealing with a homeless person. (Katona József Theatre, Chamber—directed by Gábor Zsámbéki).

1772 Lévai, Balázs; Koncz, Zsuzsa, photo. "Csodák, kis hibával." (Miracles with Small Mistake.) *Sz*. 1996; 30 (3): 25-27. Illus.: Photo. B&W. 2. Lang.: Hun.
Hungary: Budapest. 1996. Reviews of performances. ■Ferenc Molnár's *The Good Fairy (A jó tündér)* at the Radnóti Theatre directed by István Verebes.

1773 Mácsai, Pál, intro.; Sas, György, intro. *Tábori Nóra.* (Nóra Tábori.) Budapest: Pallas Stúdió; 1997. 48 pp. (Örökös tagság.) Append. Filmography. Illus.: Photo. B&W. 50. Lang.: Hun.
Hungary. 1928-1996. Histories-sources. ■An album of the Hungarian actress including a conversation with her on the occasion of receiving the 'life membership' award.

1774 Márton, Gábor. *Rózsahegyi Kálmán.* (Kálmán Rózsahegyi.) Budapest: Xénia; 1997. 175 pp. (Nagy magyar színészek.) Illus.: Photo. B&W. 20. Lang.: Hun.
Hungary. 1873-1961. Biographies. ■Life and career of the famous actor and pedagogue of the Hungarian theatre.

1775 Róna, Katalin; Koncz, Zsuzsa, photo. "Gödrök közt ugrálva. Beszélgetés Garas Dezsővel." (Jumping Across Pits: Interview with Dezső Garas.) *Sz*. 1997; 30(8): 34-37. Illus.: Photo. B&W. 3. Lang.: Hun.
Hungary. 1960-1997. Histories-sources. ■Interview with a prominent actor of Hungarian theatre: his career and views on acting and directing.

1776 Róna, Katalin; Koncz, Zsuzsa, photo. "Csak az alkotás jelent örömet. Beszélgetés Jordán Tamással." (Only Creation Can Bring Joy: A Conversation with Tamás Jordán.) *Sz*. 1997; 30(2): 33-36. Illus.: Photo. B&W. 4. Lang.: Hun.
Hungary. 1960-1997. Histories-sources. ■A talk with actor-manager Tamás Jordán, founder of Budapest's Merlin Theatre (1991-), about his life, his ambitions and plans, and his ideas on acting.

1777 Róna, Katalin; Koncz, Zsuzsa, photo. "Kelepce-interjú. Beszélgetés Mácsai Pállal." (A 'Trap-Interview' with Pál Mácsai.) *Sz*. 1997; 30(5): 42-43. Illus.: Photo. B&W. 1. Lang.: Hun.

Hungary. 1980-1997. Histories-sources. ■A brief survey of a career with actor-director Pál Mácsai.

1778 Róna, Katalin; Koncz, Zsuzsa, photo. "Erős érzelmek kellenek. Beszélgetés Sinkó Lászlóval." (Strong Emotions Are Needed: A Talk with László Sinkó.) *Sz*. 1997; 30(10): 16-19. Illus.: Photo. B&W. 4. Lang.: Hun.
Hungary. 1960-1997. Histories-sources. ■The leading actor of Budapest's New Theatre (Új Színház) speaks about the nature of his profession sharing his views on acting.

1779 Székely, György. "A Tragédia ősbemutatójának problémái." (Problems of the First Night of Imre Madách's *The Tragedy of Man*.) *SzSz*. 1997(32): 6-22. Notes. Illus.: Photo. B&W. 6. Lang.: Hun.
Hungary: Budapest. 1883. Critical studies. ■Dramaturgical analysis of the first performance of the drama (National Theatre, September 21, 1883) under Ede Paulay's direction based on director's copy, archival material, photo, score, etc.

1780 Kapadia, Parmita. *Bastardizing the Bard: Appropriations of Shakespeare's Plays in Postcolonial India.* Amherst, MA: Univ. of Massachusetts; 1997. 198 pp. [Ph.D. Dissertation, Univ. Microfilm Order No. AAC 9737547.] Lang.: Eng.
India. 1880-1995. Histories-specific. ■Examines how Indian directors and scholars have appropriated and adapted the Shakespeare canon to suit their individual needs, argues that these contemporary interpretations allow a simultaneous assertion and disruption of colonial authority and postcolonial influence.

1781 Mee, Erin B. "Contemporary Indian Theatre: Three Different Views." *PerAJ*. 1997 Jan.; 19(1): 1-26. Notes. Illus.: Photo. B&W. 4. [Number 55.] Lang.: Eng.
India. 1997. Histories-sources. ■Interviews with three Indian playwright/directors, Kavalam Narayana Pannikkar, Tripurari Sharma, and Mahesh Dattani, on the state of theatre in their country.

1782 O'Yeah, Zac. "Mot kastväsendet, med teatern som vapen." (Against the Caste System With the Theatre As Weapon.) *Entré*. 1997; 24(1): 30-48. Illus.: Photo. B&W. Lang.: Swe.
India: New Delhi, Heggodu. 1970. Historical studies. ■A presentation of the director Prasanna, leader of Kavi-Kavya at Heggodu, a combination of theatre, cutural center and a textile factory, and the theatre school Ninasam, with references to his work at National School of Drama at New Delhi and the staging of *Agni aur Barkha (The Fire and the Rain)* by Girish Karnad.

1783 Seizer, Susan. *Dramatic License: Negotiating Stigma On and Off the Tamil Popular Stage.* Chicago, IL: Univ. of Chicago; 1997. 489 pp. Notes. Biblio. [Ph.D. Dissertation, Univ. Microfilms Order No. AAC 9800637.] Lang.: Eng.
India. 1950-1995. Historical studies. ■Ethnographic study of the lives of artists in Southern India who perform 'Special Drama', a genre of modern popular theatre that has a low reputation among Tamil performing arts for reasons pertaining to nature of the art and to the way of life of its practitioners. Focus on comic aspect of 'Special Drama'.

1784 Singleton, Brian. "K. N. Pannikkar's *Teyyateyyam*: Resisting Interculturalism Through Ritual Practice." *ThR*. 1997; 22 (2): 162-169. Notes. Illus.: Photo. B&W. 6. Lang.: Eng.
India: Trivandrum. 1993. Historical studies. ■Performance analysis of *Teyyateyyam* by K. N. Pannikkar, a writer and director from the Sopanam Institute of Performing Arts.

1785 Beresford-Plummer, Michael. "The Self as an I/Eye: Rehearsal Reflections on the Playing of Samuel Beckett." *JBeckS*. 1997; 6(1): 71-79. Biblio. Lang.: Eng.
Ireland. France. USA. 1978-1997. Critical studies. ■Explores the concept that the perception of the actor and audience become informed by their own interior 'eye/I' when approaching such later Beckett plays such as *Footfalls* and *Rockaby*.

1786 Bernstein, George. "Two Plays in Dublin, Summer 1997." *WES*. 1997 Fall; 9(3): 87-88. Lang.: Eng.
Ireland: Dublin. 1997. Historical studies. ■Two recent productions of Peacock Theatre: Connall Morrison's adaptation of Patrick Kavanaugh's novel *Tarry Flynn*, directed by Morrison, and Jimmy Murphy's *A Piece of Paradise*, directed by David Byrne.

DRAMA: —Performance/production

1787 Cullingford, Elizabeth Butler. "National Identities in Performance: The Stage Englishman of Boucicault's Irish Drama." *TJ*. 1997 Oct.; 49(3): 287-300. Notes. Lang.: Eng.
Ireland. 1850-1890. Historical studies. ■Irish nationalism and postcolonialism reflected in the English characters created by playwright Dion Boucicault. Argues that these characters negotiated and mediated social and political conflict of the period for audiences.

1788 Johansson, Ola. "Irland—regn, nationalism och teater." (Ireland—Rain, Nationalism and Theatre.) *Entré*. 1997; 24(6): 44-46. Illus.: Photo. B&W. Lang.: Swe.
Ireland: Sligo, Dublin. 1997. Historical studies. ■A report from Irish theatres, with references to Yeats's *The Dreaming of the Bones* and *The Words Upon the Window-Pane*, O'Casey's *Juno and the Paycock*, and Tom Gallacher's *Mr. Joyce Is Leaving Paris*.

1789 O'Hara, J.D. "Savagely Damned to Fame." *JBeckS*. 1997; 6(1): 137-143. Biblio. Lang.: Eng.
Ireland. France. 1550-1997. Biographical studies. ■Traces Beckett's quote that he was 'damned to fame' to the English writer Richard Savage.

1790 O'Toole, Fintan. "Recent Theatre." *IW*. 1996 Nov/Dec.; 45(5): 20-23. Illus.: Photo. B&W. Color. 4. Lang.: Eng.
Ireland: Dublin. 1990-1996. Critical studies. ■The present state of Irish theatre, with consideration of its focus on the audience in Ireland rather than abroad, the commitment of its artists to remain in Ireland, the increase in the number of theatre companies, and new voices in playwriting.

1791 Blum, Bilha. "Interaction of Style and Meaning in Drama and Performance." *ThR*. 1997; 22(1): 63-69. Notes. Illus.: Photo. B&W. 3. Lang.: Eng.
Israel: Tel Aviv. 1990. Critical studies. ■Analysis of Hanan Snir's HaBimah production of García Lorca's *Blood Wedding (Bodas de sangre)* focusing on its relation to Israeli context and highlighting stylistic divergences of performance and text.

1792 Kaynar, Gad. "The Actor as Performer of the Implied Spectator's Role." *ThR*. 1997; 22(1): 49-62. Notes. Illus.: Photo. B&W. 12. Lang.: Eng.
Israel: Tel Aviv. 1993. Critical studies. ■Analysis of Omri Nitzan's production of *The Servant of Two Masters (Il Servitore di due padroni)* for HaBimah and Hillel Mittelpunkt's production of his own *Gorodish—The Seventh Day*, Kameri Theatre.

1793 Alemanno, Roberto, ed.; Lombardi, Angelo, ed. *...Un pò per non morire. Ettore Petrolini a sessant'anni dalla scomparsa.* (Ettore Petrolini Sixty Years After His Death.) Rome: Bulzoni; 1997. 104 pp. Illus.: Photo. B&W. Lang.: Ita.
Italy. 1886-1936. Critical studies. ■Essays on the work of comic actor Ettore Petrolini.

1794 Ault, Thomas. "Classical Humanist Drama in Transition: The First Phase of Renaissance Theatre in Ferrara." *TA*. 1997; 50 : 17-39. Notes. Lang.: Eng.
Italy: Ferrara. 1486-1502. Historical studies. ■Using two epistolary sources and an anonymous diarist, attempts to relate the atmosphere surrounding classical theatrical performances in early Renaissance Ferrara.

1795 Barbieri, Claudia. "'They live from the heat': gli italiani nell'immaginario di Tennessee Williams." (Tennessee Williams' Images of Italians.) *BiT*. 1997; 42: 141-151. Notes. Lang.: Ita.
Italy. 1996. Critical studies. ■The first Italian production of *The Rose Tattoo* at the Bevenuto festival, directed by Gabriele Vacis and starring Valeria Moriconi in the role of Serafina. Includes consideration of Williams's view of Italians.

1796 Bellavia, Sonia. "Un insuccesso emblematico: il Lear del 1908 allo Stabile di Roma." (An Emblematic Failure: The 1908 *King Lear* at Teatro Stabile in Rome.) *Ariel*. 1997; 12(2): 39-51. Notes. Lang.: Ita.
Italy: Rome. 1908. Critical studies. ■Analysis of the production of Shakespeare's *King Lear* by Teatro Stabile di Roma under the direction of actor Mario Fumagalli who also played the title role.

1797 Bentoglio, Alberto. "Interpretazioni registiche della *Figlia di Iorio* sulle scene italiane del Novecento." (Directorial Interpretations of *Iorio's Daughter* on the Twentieth-Century Italian Stage.) *Ariel*. 1997; 12(1): 51-57. Notes. Lang.: Ita.
Italy. 1904-1983. Critical studies. ■The staging of D'Annunzio's play, with reference to productions by Guido Salvini (Teatro Lirico, Milan, 1936), Corrado Pavolini (Pescara, 1949, designed by Virgilio Marchi), Luigi Squarzina (1957), and Roberto De Simone (1982).

1798 De Monticelli, Roberto. *Le mille notti del critico. Trentacinque anni di teatro vissuti e raccontati da uno spettatore di professione.* (The Critic's Thousand Nights: Thirty-Five Years of Theatre Lived and Reported by a Professional Spectator.) Rome: Bulzoni; 1997. (Biblioteca teatrale 93.) Index. [Vol. 2.] Lang.: Ita.
Italy. 1964-1973. Critical studies. ■Collection of reviews for *Il Giorno* and *Epoca*.

1799 Di Nocera, Antonella. "Leo De Berardinis Directs *King Lear*." *WES*. 1997 Spr; 9(2): 19-22. Illus.: Photo. 2. Lang.: Eng.
Italy: Naples. 1996. Historical studies. ■Critical reception of Shakespeare's *King Lear* at the Teatro Mercadante, directed by Leo De Berardinis.

1800 Gazzara, Giovanni. *Anna Maria Guarnieri. Ritratto d'attrice del teatro in Italia della seconda metà del Novecento.* (Anna Maria Guarnieri: Portrait of a Late Nineteenth-Century Italian Theatre Actress.) Rome: Black Hole; 1997. 127 pp. Illus.: Photo. B&W. Lang.: Ita.
Italy. 1954-1996. Biographies. ■Brief biography of actress Anna Maria Guarnieri with a chronology of her interpretations and awards.

1801 Giacché, Piergiorgio. *Carmelo Bene. Antropologia di una 'macchina attoriale'.* (Carmelo Bene: Anthropology of an Acting Machine.) Milan: Bompiani; 1997. xxiii, 185 pp. (Studi Bompiani.) Pref. Notes. Biblio. Index. Lang.: Ita.
Italy. 1937-1997. Biographical studies. ■The art and craft of Carmelo Bene, actor, playwright, and director.

1802 Grande, Maurizio. "La follia teatrale." (Theatrical Madness.) *IlCast*. 1997; 10(28): 125-127. Lang.: Ita.
Italy: Rome. 1995. Critical studies. ■Analysis of Luca Ronconi's production of Shakespeare's *King Lear* (Teatro Argentina), in which madness is extended to all the characters, who become caricatures of themselves.

1803 Guardenti, Renzo. "Fra Stanislavskij e Shakespeare: Giulio Cesare o la crudeltà della retorica." (Between Stanislavskij and Shakespeare: Julius Caesar or the Cruelty of Rhetoric.) *BiT*. 1997; 42: 53-66. Notes. Lang.: Ita.
Italy: Prato. 1997. Critical studies. ■Analysis of the staging at Teatro Fabbricone of Shakespeare's *Julius Caesar* by Societas Raffaello Sanzio, directed by Romeo Castellucci as a tragedy of rhetoric and with allusions to Stanislavskij's early twentieth-century production.

1804 Iannuzzi, Maria. "In principio era Brecht." (In the Beginning Was Brecht.) *Ariel*. 1997; 12(2): 53-58. Illus.: Photo. B&W. 2. Lang.: Ita.
Italy: Messina. 1995. Critical studies. ■Review of Brecht's *Im Dickicht der Städte (In the Jungle of Cities)* performed by I Magazzini company of Teatro Vittorio Emanuele under the direction of Federico Tiezzi.

1805 Klett, Renate. "Exerzitien und Exzesse." (Exercises And Excesses.) *THeute*. 1997; 10: 34-37. Illus.: Photo. B&W. 4. Lang.: Ger.
Italy: Volterra, Pontedera. 1986-1997. Historical studies. ■Impressions from a visit to Pontedera where Jerzy Grotowski works with the director Thomas Richards and six actors. Describes the Festival at Volterra with Compagnia della Fortezza who played *The Brig (Le Bagne)* and *The Blacks (Les Nègres)* by Jean Genet, both directed by Armando Punoz.

1806 Lapini, Lia. "*La ragione degli altri* di Massimo Castri." (Massimo Castri's *The Reason of the Others*.) *IlCast*. 1997; 10(30): 117-122. Notes. Illus.: Photo. B&W. 2. Lang.: Ita.
Italy: Messina. 1996-1997. Critical studies. ■Castri's staging of Pirandello's play at the Teatro Stabile dell'Umbria.

1807 Lapini, Lia. "Il ritorno di Brecht, o un nuovo Brecht?" (The Return of Brecht, or a New Brecht?) *BiT*. 1997; 42: 91-100. Notes. Lang.: Ita.

DRAMA: —Performance/production

Italy: Messina. 1995. Critical studies. ■Federico Tiezzi's production at Teatro Vittorio Emanuele of *Im Dickicht der Städte (In the Jungle of Cities)* by Bertolt Brecht.

1808 Mango, Lorenzo. "Amleto tra grottesco e sublime." (Hamlet between the Grotesque and the Sublime.) *IlCast.* 1997; 10(28): 113-124. Lang.: Ita.
Italy. 1995. Critical studies. ■Comparison of Robert Wilson's *Hamlet: A Monologue* as staged at the 1995 Biennale di Venezia, and Benno Besson's production of *Hamlet* as staged at the Teatro Argentina in Rome. Argues that both directors propose an essential dramaturgical rewriting of Shakespeare's text without compromising its identity.

1809 Mazzocchi, Federico, ed.; Bertoglio, Alberto, ed. *Giorgio Strehler e il suo teatro.* (Giorgio Strehler and His Theatre.) Rome: Bulzoni; 1997. 403 pp. (Quaderni di Gargnano: I protagonisti del teatro contemporaneo 6.) Index. Lang.: Ita.
Italy: Milan. 1943-1995. Critical studies. ■Collection of essays on the work of director Giorgio Strehler and his Piccolo Teatro.

1810 Molinari, Cesare. "Il male oscuro: *L'Oreste* di Massimo Castri." (The Obscure Illness: Massimo Castri's *Orestes.*) *BiT.* 1997; 42: 11-34. Lang.: Ita.
Italy: Prato. 1995. Critical studies. ■Massimo Castri's staging of Euripides' *Orestes* at Teatro Fabbricone.

1811 Mori, Lucia. "Gli ultimi Giganti di Strehler." (Strehler's Last Giants.) *BiT.* 1997; 42: 101-139. Notes. Lang.: Ita.
Italy: Milan. 1966-1994. Critical studies. ■Giorgio Strehler's last staging of Pirandello's *I Giganti della montagna (The Mountain Giants)* at Piccolo Teatro.

1812 Perrelli, Franco. "Paolo Sperati: un musicista piemontese per Ibsen." (Paolo Sperati, Ibsen's Piedmontese Musician.) *IlCast.* 1997; 10(28): 75-87. Notes. Lang.: Ita.
Italy. Norway. 1856. Biographical studies. ■Portrait of Sperati, who worked as a musician in the theatres of Christiania and composed the music for Ibsen's *Gildet på Solhoug (The Feast at Solhoug).* The music, previously unpublished, is reproduced here.

1813 Pietrini, Sandra. "Iago o dell'invidia della creazione. L'*Otello* di Gabriele Lavia." (Iago or the Envy of Creation: Gabriele Lavia's *Othello.*) *BiT.* 1997; 42: 67-90. Notes. Lang.: Ita.
Italy: Novara. 1995. Critical studies. ■Lavia's production of Shakespeare's *Othello* at Teatro Coccia in a modern military environment with Iago as the hero. A coproduction of Teatro degli Incamminati and Teatro Eliseo.

1814 Price, Amanda; Meredith, Peter. "*Mankind* in Camerino (continued): Dramatising the Word. Playing the Very Devil and Other Matters." *STP.* 1997 Dec.; 16: 76-92. Biblio. Illus.: Sketches. 2. Lang.: Eng.
Italy: Camerino. 1996. Histories-sources. ■Director outlines how performers in this 1996 production of *Mankind* created their roles through understanding and embodying the language. The actor who played the devil-figure Titivillus describes his entrance via an exploding pulpit and reflects on the difficulties of creating a figure that is at once trivial and dangerous.

1815 Rose, Margaret. "Notes on a Lecture-Workshop on Pinter's *Monologue.*" *PintR.* 1997: 85-89. Notes. Lang.: Eng.
Italy: Bologna. 1973-1994. Critical studies. ■Discussion of a staging of Pinter's play *Monologue,* British Council of Teachers' Conference in Bologna.

1816 Sgroi, Alfredo. "Del teatro non teatrale: due lettere inedite di Bragaglia a Savarese." (On Non-Theatrical Theatre: Two Unpublished Letters from Bragaglia to Savarese.) *Ariel.* 1997; 12(2): 177-182. Notes. Lang.: Ita.
Italy. 1926. Histories-sources. ■Two letters from director Anton Giulio Bragaglia to playwright Nino Savarese after Bragaglia's production of *Il principe pauroso (The Timid Prince)* by Savarese.

1817 Sinisi, Silvana. "La scena della fiaba: Hansel e Gretel della Raffaello Sanzio." (The Scene of the Fairy Tale: Raffaello Sanzio's *Hansel and Gretel.*) *Ariel.* 1997; 12(3): 35-37. Lang.: Ita.

Italy: Cesena. 1997. Critical studies. ■Brief analysis of the staging for children of Grimm's fairy tale *Hansel and Gretel* by Societas Raffaello Sanzio.

1818 Sinisi, Silvana. "Un omaggio al Dadaismo: *Eternity Lasts Longer* della compagnia norvegese Passage Nord Theatre." (Homage to Dadaism: *Eternity Lasts Longer* by the Norwegian Company Passage Nord.) *Ariel.* 1997; 12(3): 37-39. Lang.: Ita.
Italy: Rome. 1997. Critical studies. ■Review of a production by Passage Nord, inspired by the work of avant-garde writer Kurt Schwitters and directed by Kjetil Skoien at Teatro Vascello.

1819 Tamiozzo Goldmann, Silvana. *Giuliano Scabia: ascolto e racconto, con antologia di testi inediti e rari.* (Giuliano Scabia: Listening and Telling, with an Anthology of Rare Unpublished Texts.) Rome: Bulzoni; 1997. 127 pp. (Biblioteca di cultura 536.) Notes. Biblio. Index. Lang.: Ita.
Italy. 1935-1997. Critical studies. ■The work of Scabia, a writer and director of the Italian avant-garde theatre of the 1960s.

1820 Valentini, Valentina; Rankin, Tom, transl. "The *Oresteia* of the Societas Raffaello Sanzio." *PerfR.* 1997 Fall; 2(3) : 58-64. Biblio. Illus.: Photo. B&W. 4. Lang.: Eng.
Italy: Cesena. 1981-1997. Critical studies. ■Societas Raffaello Sanzio's use of language to recreate the world through the power of the voice. Focus on their production of Aechylus' *Oresteia.*

1821 Valentini, Valentina. "*L'Orestea* della Societas Raffaello Sanzio." (Societas Raffaello Sanzio's *Oresteia.*) *BiT.* 1997; 42: 35-46. Notes. Lang.: Ita.
Italy: Cesena. 1995. Critical studies. ■The staging of Euripides' *Oresteia* by Societas Raffaello Sanzio, directed by Romeo Castellucci.

1822 Mori, Mitsuya. "Noh, Kabuki and Western Theatre: An Attempt of Schematizing Acting Styles." *ThR.* 1997; 22(1 Supplement) : 14-21. Notes. Illus.: Diagram. B&W. 15. Lang.: Eng.
Japan. Europe. 1150-1997. Critical studies. ■Difference and similarities between Western and Eastern acting styles, with attention to the relationship of actor, character, and spectator as practiced in *nō* and *kabuki* and as defined by Artaud and Brecht.

1823 Tanaka, Mariko Hori. "Special Features of Beckett's Performances in Japan." 226-239 in Oppenheim, Lois, ed.; Buning, Marius, ed. *Beckett On and On....* Madison, NJ: Fairleigh Dickinson UP; 1996. 289 pp. Notes. Lang.: Eng.
Japan. 1960-1994. Historical studies. ■The performance of Samuel Beckett's plays in Japan, with emphasis on culturally-based adaptations of the texts and staging. Includes a list of major productions.

1824 Binnerts, Paul. "Jan Joris Lamers—A True 'Homo Universalis' of the Theatre/Un véritable 'Homo universalis' du théâtre." *Carnet.* 1997 Mar.; 13: 2-11. Illus.: Photo. B&W. 4. Lang.: Eng, Fre.
Netherlands. 1968-1997. Biographical studies. ■Career of the director and influence on contemporary theatre style.

1825 Callens, Johan. "Epistemologies of Loss: *Buried Child, The American Dream,* and *A Lie of the Mind* in Flanders." *WES.* 1997 Spr; 9(2): 61-66. Illus.: Photo. 4. Lang.: Eng.
Netherlands: Ghent. 1996. Historical studies. ■Critical reception of three plays produced at the Nederlands Toneel Gent, all directed by Guy Cassiers: Shepard's *A Lie of the Mind* and *Buried Child* and Albee's *The American Dream.*

1826 Drukman, Steven. "Tomatoes and Their Consequences." *AmTh.* 1997 Nov.; 14(9): 64-68. Illus.: Photo. B&W. 3. Lang.: Eng.
Netherlands: Amsterdam. 1969-1997. Critical studies. ■New artistic director of the Holland Festival, Ivo van Hove, the Belgian artistic director of Het Zuidelij Toneel, his adaptation of John Cassavetes' film *Faces* (*Koppen*) for the festival, and his version of O'Neill's *More Stately Mansions* which was brought to New York Theatre Workshop.

1827 Hummelen, W. M. H. "Doubtful Images." *ThR.* 1997; 22(3): 202-218. Notes. Illus.: Dwg. B&W. 15. Lang.: Eng.
Netherlands. 1555-1637. Historical studies. ■Census of extant visual records of early Dutch outdoor theatre performances. Argues that depictions are influenced by visual arts and contain misleading elements.

DRAMA: —Performance/production

1828 Hummelen, Willem M.H. "Performers and Performance in the Earliest Secular Plays in the Netherlands." *CompD.* 1992 Spr; 26(1): 19-23. Notes. Lang.: Eng.
Netherlands. 1405-1410. Historical studies. ■Examines the Hulthem manuscript, a collection of ten vernacular plays from the fifteenth century, for clues about how they were performed. Argues that they were done by masked professional actors on a stage with a tiring house with two entrances.

1829 Kock, Petra de. "Total Theatre on an Eggshell. Firm Reiks Swarte/Théâtre total dans une coquille. Le Firme Rieks Swarte." *Carnet.* 1997 Mar.; 13: 30-36. Illus.: Photo. B&W. 3. Lang.: Eng, Fre.
Netherlands. 1989-1997. Critical studies. ■The image-directed work of director Rieks Swarte, who manipulates props and actors.

1830 Ibsen, Henrik. *A Doll's House.* New York, NY/London: Routledge; 1997. [CD-ROM format.] Lang.: Eng.
Norway. USA. 1879-1997. Critical studies. ■Videodisc of Ibsen's *Et Dukkehjem* combining performance and commentary. Topics covered include body language and camera angles, rehearsal compared to performance, set design, costume and makeup, and the historical context of the play.

1831 Muinzer, Louis. "1996 Ibsen Stage Festival." *INC.* 1997; 17(1): 10-12. Lang.: Eng.
Norway: Oslo. 1996. Historical studies. ■Survey of the 1996 Ibsen Stage Festival.

1832 Templeton, Joan. "The 1996 Ibsen Stage Festival in Oslo." *WES.* 1997 Spr; 9(2): 53-56. Illus.: Photo. 3. Lang.: Eng.
Norway: Oslo. 1996. Historical studies. ■Coverage of the 1996 Ibsen Stage Festival, focusing on the National Theatre's production of Ibsen's *The Pretenders (Kongsemnerne),* directed by Terry Hands.

1833 "Shakespeare on Polish Stages 1993-1997." *TP.* 1997; 39(4): 41-45. Illus.: Photo. B&W. Color. 5. Lang.: Eng, Fre.
Poland. 1993-1997. Historical studies. ■Comprehensive list of Shakespearean productions in Poland: includes directors, translators, designers, theatres.

1834 Baniewicz, Elżbieta. "Shakespeare's Difficult Comedies." *TP.* 1997; 39(4): 21-25. Illus.: Photo. B&W. 3. Lang.: Eng, Fre.
Poland. 1997. Critical studies. ■Analysis of recent productions of *The Tempest* at Stary Teatr, directed by Rudolf Zioło, *As You Like It* at Teatr Dramatyczny directed by Piotr Cieślak and *The Merchant of Venice* at Teatr Ateneum directed by Waldemar Śmigasiewicz.

1835 Baniewicz, Elżbieta. *Ona to ja.* (She Is Me.) Warsaw: Twój Styl; 1997. 160 pp. Append. Illus.: Photo. B&W. Color. 100. Lang.: Pol.
Poland: Cracow. 1950-1997. Biographies. ■Anna Dymna, a leading actress of the Stary Teatr: her most important roles, work with directors Konrad Swinarski, Andrzej Wajda, and Jerzy Jarocki, analysis of her acting style, and a listing of her roles on stage as well as in film and television.

1836 Chojka, Joanna. "W poszukiwaniu zagubionego pisma." (Searching for Lost Writing.) *DialogW.* 1997; 10: 144-156. Lang.: Pol.
Poland. 1983-1995. Critical studies. ■Tadeusz Bradecki's activity as an actor, director, and playwright, including analysis of his Stary Teatr productions and his work as artistic director of that theatre.

1837 Chojnacka, Anna. "Leon Schiller. Losy wojenne i powojenne okarżenia." (Leon Schiller: War Vicissitudes and Postwar Accusations.) *PaT.* 1997; 46(1-4): 127-184. Notes. Append. Illus.: Photo. Plan. Sketches. B&W. 9. Lang.: Pol.
Poland. 1939-1950. Biographical studies. ■The theatrical projects, literary works, and political activities during World War II of director Leon Schiller, who was later accused of collaboration with the Nazis.

1838 Duda, Artur. "Struś, herbata i piła tarczowa nad Elsynorem." (Ostrich, Tea, and Circular over Elsinore.) *DialogW.* 1997; 8: 134-142. Lang.: Pol.
Poland. Lithuania. 1997. Historical studies. ■Ghosts in three productions: *Hamlet* directed by Eimuntas Nekrošius, *I Love You* at Teatr Porywaczy Ciał, Anskij's *Dibuk (The Dybbuk)* at Towarzystwo Wierszalin Teatr.

1839 Górska-Damięcka, Irena. *Wygrałam życie. Pamiętnik aktorki.* (I Won the Life: The Diary of an Actress.) Warsaw: Prószyński i S-ka; 1997. 411 pp. Index. Append. Illus.: Photo. B&W. 75. Lang.: Pol.
Poland. 1910-1996. Histories-sources. ■Actress's autobiography, including her forty-six years on stage, with lists of her roles and plays she directed.

1840 Gruszczyński, Piotr. "People and Artists." *TP.* 1997; 39(3): 30-33. Illus.: Photo. B&W. Color. 5. Lang.: Eng, Fre.
Poland: Warsaw. 1997. Critical studies. ■Production of Peter Handke's *The Hour We Knew Nothing of Each Other (Die Stunde da wir nichts voneinander wussten)* directed by Zbigniew Brzoza at Teatr Studio. Brzoza's direction of the piece, stage design.

1841 Gruszczyński, Piotr. "In Search of an Original Idiom." *TP.* 1997; 39(4): 33-36. Illus.: Photo. B&W. Color. 3. Lang.: Eng, Fre.
Poland: Poznań. 1997. Critical studies. ■Production of *The Winter's Tale* by Shakespeare, directed by Krysztof Warlikowski at Teatr Nowy. Staging, directorial interpretation, set design by Małgorzata Szczęśniak .

1842 Guczalska, Beata. "Ślub czyli teatr Jerzego Jarockiego." (*The Wedding* or the Theatre of Jerzy Jarocki.) *DialogW.* 1997; 10: 131-143. Lang.: Pol.
Poland. 1960-1991. Critical studies. ■Analysis of Jarocki's six productions of Gombrowicz's play, representing his essential characteristics as a director.

1843 Howard, Tony. "Behind the Arras, Through the Wall: Wajda's *Hamlet* in Krakow, 1989." *NTQ.* 1997; 13(49): 53-68. Notes. Illus.: Photo. B&W. 6. Lang.: Eng.
Poland: Cracow. 1989. Historical studies. ■Celebrated production at the Stary Theatre in which Hamlet is played by actress Teresa Budzisz-Krzyzanowska, discussed in the context of its socio-political cultural background and that of its director Andrzej Wajda.

1844 Kosiński, Dariusz. *Sztuka aktorska Wandy Siemaszkowej.* (Wanda Siemaszkowa's Art of Acting.) Cracow: Universitas; 1997. 200 pp. Pref. Biblio. Append. Lang.: Pol.
Poland: Cracow, Lvov, Warsaw. 1887-1946. Biographical studies. ■The development of the actress's craft during the 'Young Poland' period, with an attempt to reconstruct her best roles.

1845 Kubikowski, Tomasz. "Floating Island." *TP.* 1997; 39(2): 23-25. Illus.: Photo. B&W. 2. Lang.: Eng, Fre.
Poland: Wrocław. 1997. Critical studies. ■Analysis of text and staging of *Immanuel Kant* by Thomas Bernhard, adapted and directed by Krystian Lupa, music by Jacek Ostaszewski at Teatr Polski.

1846 Kulczyński, Jan. *Rozbieranie Hamleta.* (Stripping Hamlet.) Warsaw: Akademia Teatralna im. A. Zelwerowicza/Krąg; 1997. 338 pp. Pref. Lang.: Pol.
Poland: Warsaw. 1997. Histories-sources. ■The author's work with his directing students at the Theatre Academy in Warsaw, describing how they analyze the text and search for directing clues.

1847 Norén, Kjerstin. "Skådespelaren Ryszard Cieslak, 1937-1990." (The Actor Ryszard Cieslak, 1937-1990.) *Tningen.* 1997; 21(3): 35-37. Illus.: Photo. B&W. Lang.: Swe.
Poland. 1937-1990. Biographical studies. ■A portrait of the actor Ryszard Cieslak.

1848 Osterloff, Barbara. "Ksiądz Robak. Wojenne lata Aleksandra Zelwerowicza." (Priest Robak: Aleksander Zelwerowicz in Wartime.) *PaT.* 1997; 46(1-4): 185-224. Notes. Illus.: Photo. B&W. 9. Lang.: Pol.
Poland. 1925-1979. Biographical studies. ■Focuses on the wartime and postwar activities of the Polish actor and director, including underground theatre and assistance to Jews.

1849 Taborski, Roland. "Die Rezeption Max Reinhardts im polnischen Theaterleben bis zum Ersten Weltkrieg." (Max Reinhardt's Reception in Polish Theatre Life until the First World War.) *MuK.* 1997; 39(1): 7-22. Notes. Lang.: Ger.
Poland. 1903-1914. Historical studies. ■The influences and effects of Reinhardt's style of directing on theatre people such as Arnold Szyfman and Ryszard Ordyński.

DRAMA: —Performance/production

1850 Walaszek, Joanna. "Jan Nowicki w Starym Teatrze." (Jan Nowicki at Stary Teatr.) *DialogW.* 1997; 1: 152-161. Lang.: Pol.

Poland: Cracow. 1939-1997. Biographical studies. ■The work of actor Jan Nowicki at Stary Teatr with such directors as Andrzej Wajda and Jerzy Jarocki.

1851 Węgrzyniak, Rafal. "Sprawa Michala Weicherta." (The Case of Michal Weichert.) *PaT.* 1997; 46(1-4): 279-314. Notes. Illus.: Photo. B&W. 6. Lang.: Pol.

Poland. 1939-1958. Biographical studies. ■The life of the eminent director of Jewish theatre during and after World War II, who was indicted for collaboration with the Nazis in connection with his charitable activities.

1852 Zawistowski, Wladyslaw. "Between Politics and the Disco." *TP.* 1997; 39(4): 37-39. Illus.: Photo. B&W. 3. Lang.: Eng, Fre.

Poland. 1610-1997. Critical studies. ■Impact of new translations by Stanislaw Barańczak on Shakespearean productions in recent Polish theatre. Audience response to productions of *Macbeth*, *Antony and Cleopatra* and *Hamlet*. Brief overview of history of staging Shakespeare in Poland.

1853 Zielińska, Maryla. "The Tropics." *TP.* 1997; 39(3): 37-39. Illus.: Photo. B&W. 2. Lang.: Eng, Fre.

Poland: Warsaw. 1997. Critical studies. ■Productions of *Tropical Madness (Bzik Tropikalny)* based on *Mister Price or Tropical Madness (Mister Price, czyli Bzik tropikalny)* and *The New Deliverance (Nowe Wyzwolenie)* by Stanisław Ignacy Witkiewicz, adapted and directed by Grzegorz Horst d'Albertis at Teatr Rozmaitości. Staging, interpretation.

1854 Zielińska, Maryla. "Opus Minorum." *TP.* 1997; 39(2): 33-36. Illus.: Photo. Color. B&W. 4. Lang.: Eng, Fre.

Poland: Wroclaw. 1993-1997. Critical studies. ■Comparison of two productions of *Platonov—akt pominięty (Platonov—The Omitted Act)* by Anton Čechov, both adapted and directed by Jerzy Jarocki at Teatr Polski. Jarocki describes his appoach to the play, stage design.

1855 Bérczes, László; Járó, S. Tibor, photo. "A folyó neve. Beszélgetés Maia Morgensternnel." (The Name of the River: An Interview with Maia Morgenstern.) *Sz.* 1997; 30(10): 46-48. Illus.: Photo. B&W. 4. Lang.: Hun.

Romania: Bucharest. Hungary: Győr. 1997. Histories-sources. ■Maia Morgenstern, famous Romanian actress, member of Bucharest's Jewish Theatre, who recently gave a guest performance in Győr.

1856 "Director, Spare That Play." *Econ.* 1997 Nov 1; 345(8041): 89-90. Illus.: Photo. B&W. 1. Lang.: Eng.

Russia: Moscow. 1940-1997. Critical studies. ■Current revivals of Čechov's plays focusing on Oleg Jéfremov's *Tri sestry (Three Sisters)* at the Moscow Art Theatre and Galina Volček's *Višnëvyj sad (The Cherry Orchard)* at Sovremennik. Contemporary influences, comedy and class conflict.

1857 Annenkov, Nikolaj. "'Ja sčastliv, čto javl'jajus' naslednikom Sčepkina'." (I Am Glad to Be an Heir of Sčepkin.) *TeatZ.* 1997; 9-10: 12-14. Lang.: Rus.

Russia: Moscow. 1990-1997. Histories-sources. ■National artist of the USSR Annenkov's reflections on himself, his acting career, his teachers, and his students.

1858 Antarova, K. *Na odnoj tvorčeskoj trope: Besedy K.S. Stanislavskogo.* (On the Same Creative Path: Discussions of K.S. Stanislavskij.) Moscow: Garmonya; 1997. 352 pp. Lang.: Rus.

Russia. 1863-1938. Histories-sources. ■Memories of Stanislavskij and his method of working with actors.

1859 Borisov, Oleg. "Bez znakov prepinanija." (Without Punctuation Marks.) *PTZ.* 1997; 13: 10-16. Lang.: Rus.

Russia: St. Petersburg. 1970-1989. Histories-sources. ■Excerpts from the diary of actor Oleg Borisov covering five different periods of his life.

1860 Cekinovskij, B. "Puškin v rossijskoj glubinke." (Puškin in a Russian Village.) *TeatZ.* 1997; 8: 24-26. Lang.: Rus.

Russia: Skopina. 1990-1997. Historical studies. ■Account of an amateur theatre production, directed by V. Del, of *Mocart i Saljeri (Mozart and Salieri)* on the 200th anniversary of Puškin's birth.

1861 Dmitrevskaja, M. "Vtoraja real'nost'." (Another Reality.) *PTZ.* 1997; 13: 4-9. Lang.: Rus.

Russia: Moscow. Estonia: Tallinn. 1996-1997. Historical studies. ■Two Moscow Art Theatre productions: Ingmar Bergman's *Efter repetitionen (After the Rehearsal)* directed by Vjačeslav Dolgačev and designed by Marija Demjanova, and *Odna-edinstvennaja žizn' (One and Only One Life)*, performed by Tallinn Municipal Theatre, written and directed by Janus Rochumaa and designed by Aimé Unt.

1862 Dmitrevskaja, M. "'Mu vse smertel'no raneny'." (We Are All Being Injured.) *PTZ.* 1997; 12: 74-76. Lang.: Rus.

Russia: St. Petersburg. 1996. Historical studies. ■Production of Jean Anouilh's *Antigone*, directed by Temur Čcheidze, with scene design by V. Kuvarin at the G.A. Tovstonogov Bolšoj Drama Theatre.

1863 Dmitrevskaja, M. "Ta-ta-ta-tam!" *PTZ.* 1997; 12: 60-67. Lang.: Rus.

Russia: St. Petersburg, Moscow. 1997. Historical studies. ■Two productions of *Tanja-Tanja* by Ol'ga Muchina: one directed by Pëtr Fomenko at Masterskaja Petra Fomenko, and one by V. Tumanov by Teat'r Satiry of St. Petersburg.

1864 Evans, Charles. "Pinter in Russia." *PintR.* 1997: 41-53. Lang.: Eng.

Russia: Moscow. 1996. Historical studies. ■Russian productions of the plays of Harold Pinter, including *The Dumb Waiter* directed by Michajl Makejëv (1989), *Betrayal* directed by Andrei Rossinskij (1992), and *The Caretaker* directed by Grigorij Zalkin (1994).

1865 Frolova, L.A. *Stichotvornoe slovo v tvorčestve režissera i ispolnitelja.* (The Poetic Word in the Artistic Work of the Director and Performer.) Moscow: Moskovskij gosudarstvénnyj universitet kul'turi; 1997. 76 pp. Lang.: Rus.

Russia. 1997. Historical studies. ■Speech training as part of the training of directors.

1866 Gafarova, E. "Pjat' večerov v teatre Farida Bikčantajeva." (Five Evenings in the Theatre of Farid Bikčantejév.) *PTZ.* 1997; 13: 64-67. Lang.: Rus.

Russia: Kazan. 1997. Historical studies. ■The work of director Farid Bikčantajёv of Tatarskij Teat'r im. Kamala.

1867 Gaft, Valentin. *'... Ja postepenno poznaju'.* (I Am Slowly Getting to Know.) Nizhni Novgorod: Dekom; 1997. 288 pp. Lang.: Rus.

Russia. 1960-1997. Histories-sources. ■Book of verse, epigrams, and prose by an actor of stage and screen.

1868 Ganelin, Jévgenij; Bogdanov, Vladimir. *Dela akterskije.* (The Actor's Business.) St. Petersburg: Izdatel'stvo Sankt-Peterburgskij gosudarstvennyj techničeskij universitet; 1997. 55 pp. Lang.: Rus.

Russia: St. Petersburg. 1960-1997. Histories-sources. ■Notes and comments made over many years in connection with the author's master class for actors.

1869 Gilman, Richard. "Following Chekhov." *ThM.* 1993; 23(1): 75-81. Lang.: Eng.

Russia: Moscow. 1989. Critical studies. ■A description of Čechov's home-turned-museum and ruminations on his place among the literary lions.

1870 Glučarjov, Jevgenij. "Frihetens olidliga lätthet." (The Unbearable Lightness Of Freedom.) *Dramat.* 1997; 5(2): 38-39. Illus.: Photo. B&W. Lang.: Swe.

Russia: Moscow. 1997. Critical studies. ■A report from the situation of the theatre in Moscow today, with references to the many Swedish plays that are now running.

1871 Gončarov, A.A. *Moj teatral'nje pristrastija.* (My Theatrical Bias.) Moscow: Iskusstvo; 1997. 334 pp., 205 pp. [2 vols.] Lang.: Rus.

Russia: Moscow. 1970-1997. Histories-sources. ■Director Andrej Gončarov of the Majakovskij Academic Theatre on his career.

1872 Gvozdickij, V. "Ešče mgnovenje—i isčeznet." (A Second Longer, and It Will Disappear.) *PTZ.* 1997; 13: 25-29. Lang.: Rus.

Russia: St. Petersburg. 1990-1997. Biographical studies. ■Artistic portrait of actress E.A. Uvarova of the Comedy Theatre.

CLASSED ENTRIES

DRAMA: —Performance/production

1873 Jakubova, N. "'Mesjac v derevne' ili 'Dvadcat' let pod krovat u'." (*A Month in the Country* or *Twenty Years Under the Bed.*) *TeatZ*. 1997; 1: 16-17. Lang.: Rus.
Russia: Moscow. 1996. Historical studies. ■Sergej Ženovač's production of *Mesjac v derevne (A Month in the Country)* by Turgenjév at Masterskaja Petra Fomenko.

1874 Jéfremov, Oleg N.; Smeljanskij, A.A. *O teatre i o sebe.* (About the Theatre—and Himself.) Moscow: Izdatel'stvo: Moskovskij Chudožestvénnyj Akademičéskij Teat'r; 1997. 246 pp. Lang.: Rus.
Russia. 1960-1997. Histories-sources. ■Moscow Art Theatre director on his work, his actors, and his productions.

1875 Kaminskaja, N. "Chrjukin živ!" (Chrjukin Lives.) *TeatZ*. 1997; 5-6: 60-61. Lang.: Rus.
Russia: Moscow. 1996. Historical studies. ■Sovremennik's production of *Anomalja (Anomaly)*, written and directed by Aleksand'r Galin.

1876 Kaz'mina, N. "Slučaj, skazka, anekdot." (Episode, Fairy Tale, Anecdote.) *TeatZ*. 1997; 1: 14-16. Lang.: Rus.
Russia: Moscow. 1996. Historical studies. ■Pétr Fomenko's production of *Pikovaja Dama (Queen of Spades)* by Puškin at the Vachtangov Theatre.

1877 Kazinirovskaja, Natalia. "Trots allt är jag nöjd med mitt liv." (I'm Content With My Life In Spite Of All.) *Dramat*. 1997; 5(4): 30-32. Illus.: Photo. B&W. Lang.: Swe.
Russia. Sweden. 1957-1997. Histories-sources. ■An interview with the actor Sergej Jurskij about his experiences of theatrical life in Russia and his impressions of Kungliga Dramatiska Teatern.

1878 Kazmina, Natalija. "Djavoljada." *TeatZ*. 1997; 3: 7-9. Lang.: Rus.
Russia: Moscow. 1996. Historical studies. ■Account of a production by Teat'r na Jugo-Zapade, directed by Valerij Beljakovič, based on plays of Bulgakov, including *Mol'jer (Molière)* and *Master i Margarita (The Master and Margarita)*.

1879 Kazmina, Natalija. "Sonečka, Levitin i Kazanova." (Sonečka, Levitin, and Casanova.) *TeatZ*. 1997; 5-6: 9-11. Lang.: Rus.
Russia: Moscow. 1996. Historical studies. ■Teat'r Ermitaž's production of *Sonečka i Kazanova (Sonečka and Casanova)* by Marina Cvetajeva, directed by Michajl Levitin.

1880 Kuržnov, Jurij. "Ja vstretil Vas... Zametki ob artiste P.P. Pankove." (I Met You: Notes on the Artist P.P. Pankov.) *PTZ*. 1997; 13: 17-24. Lang.: Rus.
Russia: St. Petersburg. 1970-1997. Biographical studies. ■Artistic portrait of Bolšoj Drama Theatre actor P.P. Pankov.

1881 Kuznecov, E. "Vladimir Anšon i ego 'Pianola'." (Vladimir Anšon and his 'Pianola'.) *PTZ*. 1997; 14: 30-38. Lang.: Rus.
Russia: St. Petersburg. 1995. Historical studies. ■Anšon's direction of Čechov's *Pianola* for Tallinn Municipal Theatre.

1882 Lific, E. "'A v Vologde—Granatov'." (Oh, in Vologda, Granatov.) *PTZ*. 1997; 13: 61-63. Lang.: Rus.
Russia: St. Petersburg. 1980-1997. Historical studies. ■Profile of Boris Granatov, a director with Vologodskij Youth Theatre.

1883 Matonina, E. "Vspominaja Smoktunovskogo." (Remembering Smoktunovskij.) *Smena*. 1997; 11: 14-31. Lang.: Rus.
Russia. 1925-1994. Biographical studies. ■Life of the stage and screen actor Innokentij Smoktunovskij.

1884 Mirkes, A. "Dochodnoje mesto bluždajuščich zvezd." (The Profitable Place of the Wandering Stars.) *PTZ*. 1997 ; 12: 70-72. Lang.: Rus.
Russia: Novosibirsk. 1997. Historical studies. ■A production of Ostrovskij's *Žadov i drugie (Žadov and Others)* at the Globus, directed by Venjamin Fil'štinskij.

1885 Orechanova, G. "Razve v nas serdca okameneli?" (Have Our Hearts Been Turned to Stone?)*NasSovr*. 1997; 195(9): 198. Lang.: Rus.
Russia: Moscow. 1997. Historical studies. ■Performance of Ostrovskij's *Kozma Zacharič Minin, Suchoruk (Kozma Zacharič Minin)* by Moscow Art Theatre, directed by V. Beljakovič.

1886 Pavlova, I. "Teatral'nyj roman." (Theatre Novel.) *TeatZ*. 1997; 5-6: 41-45. Lang.: Rus.
Russia: St. Petersburg. 1990-1997. Historical studies. ■Work of director Vladislav Pazi.

1887 Pesočinskij, N. "Režissura kak technika i filosofija." (Directing as Technique and Philosophy.) *PTZ*. 1997; 13: 48-52. Lang.: Rus.
Russia: St. Petersburg. 1980-1997. Historical studies. ■Plays directed by Aleksand'r Galibin, a student of Vasiljév, in various St. Petersburg theatres.

1888 Rajkina, E., comp. *Arkadij Rajkin v vospominanijach sovremennikov.* (Arkadij Rajkin in the Memories of His Contemporaries.) Moscow: ACT-LTD; 1997. 400 pp. Lang.: Rus.
Russia. 1911-1987. Histories-sources. ■Collection of materials about the actor by his daughter, who is an actress herself.

1889 Rudnev, Pavel. "Sposobnost' zit' s udovol'stviem." (The Ability to Live with Joy.) *TeatZ*. 1997; 8: 44-45. Lang.: Rus.
Russia: Moscow. 1990-1997. Histories-sources. ■Interview with actor A. Mežulis of the Mossovét Theatre.

1890 Ruseva, L. "Jarkaja kometa." (The Bright Comet.) *Smena*. 1997; 11: 176-186. Lang.: Rus.
Russia: Moscow. 1849-1934. Biographical studies. ■The life and career of actress Anna Brenko of the Maljy Theatre.

1891 Šarko, Zinajda. "Moe sčastje." (My Luck.) *PTZ*. 1997; 12: 5-15. Lang.: Rus.
Russia: St. Petersburg. 1960-1989. Histories-sources. ■Bolšoj Drama Theatre actress on the work of the theatre's artistic director Georgij Tovstonogov.

1892 Schechter, Joel. "The Post-Soviet Politician as Clown: Notes on Joseph Brodsky's *Democracy*." *SEEP*. 1997 Spr; 17(1): 49-53. Lang.: Eng.
Russia. 1988-1995. Critical studies. ■Notes on the author's experiences viewing European and American performances of Joseph Brodsky's *Demokracija*.

1893 Schuler, Catherine. *Women in Russian Theatre: The Actress in the Silver Age.* New York, NY/London: Routledge; 1997. 272 pp. (Gender in Performance 6.) Biblio. Index. Notes. Illus.: Photo. 10. Lang.: Eng.
Russia. 1845-1916. Critical studies. ■Feminist analysis argues that the Russian actress had a previously unexplored impact on the development of modernist theatre.

1894 Senelick, Laurence. "Recovering the Theatre's Memory." *SEEP*. 1997 Spr; 17(1): 17-18. Lang.: Eng.
Russia. 1996. Critical studies. ■On the recent publication of the first volume of neglected materials on Russian performance and theatre, *Mnemozina. Dokumenty i fakty iz istorii russkogo teatra XX veka (Mnemosyne. Documents and Data from the History of Twentieth-Century Russian Theatre)*, under the auspices of the Russian Academy of Sciences, the Ministry of Culture, and GITIS. Volume contains fragments of plays, manifestos, and excerpts from production notebooks.

1895 Sorokina, N. "On smotrit na čelovečeskie istorii, budto dostig vozrasta mudrosti." (He Looks at People's Stories as if He Had Reached the Age of Wisdom.) *TeatZ*. 1997; 7: 29. Lang.: Rus.
Russia: Moscow. 1996. Historical studies. ■A production by Pétr Fomenko's students at Rossiskaja Akademija Teatral'nogo Iskusstva of *Garpagonida*, based on work of Varinov.

1896 Svobodin, A. *Teat'r v licach.* (Theatre in the Personalities of the Actors.) Moscow: Znanie; 1997. 192 pp. Lang.: Rus.
Russia. 1960-1997. Biographical studies. ■Essays and portraits of film and stage actors including Jévgenij Jévstignejév, Michajl Ul'janov, and Jévgenij Leonov.

1897 Taršis, N. "'Antigona'-96, BDT." (*Antigone* 1996 at the Bolšoj.) *PTZ*. 1997; 12: 73-76. Lang.: Rus.
Russia: St. Petersburg. 1996. Historical studies. ■Production of Anouilh's *Antigone* directed by Temur Čcheidze and designed by V. Kuvarin at the Bolšoj Drama Theatre.

DRAMA: —Performance/production

1898 van de Water, Manon. "Mister Twister or Goodbye America!: The Interdependence of Meanings and Material Conditions." *ET.* 1997; 16(1): 85-93. Notes. Biblio. Lang.: Eng.
Russia. 1933-1996. Critical studies. ■Pre- and post-perestrojka productions of *Gudbai Amerika (Goodbye America)*, a satirical adaptation by A. Nedzvetskij of the anti-American children's poem 'Mister Tvister' by Samuil Maršak, with reference to Moscow Youth Theatre.

1899 Vovsi-Michoéls, N. *Moj otec Solomon Michoéls: Vospominanije o žizni i gibeli.* (My Father, Solomon Michoéls: Memories of His Life and Death.) Moscow: Vozvrašenie; 1997. 238 pp. Lang.: Rus.
Russia: Moscow. 1890-1948. Histories-sources. ■The well-known director and actor Solomon Michoéls as remembered by his son.

1900 Žitinkin, Andrej. "Don Žuan režissera." (Don Juan the Director.) *Smena.* 1997; 12: 110-117. Lang.: Rus.
Russia: Moscow. 1990-1997. Histories-sources. ■The director of Mossovét Theatre on his life and work.

1901 Zverev, Aleksej. "'Tragedija smechotvorna?'." (Tragedy Is Funny?)*TeatZ.* 1997; 3: 3-5. Lang.: Rus.
Russia: Moscow. 1996. Historical studies. ■Teat'r na Jugo-Zapade's production of *Rhinocéros* by Eugène Ionesco, directed by Valerij Beljakovič.

1902 Luterkort, Ingrid. "En drömd framtid." (A Dreamed Future.) *Tningen.* 1997; 21(1): 44-46. Illus.: Photo. Color. Lang.: Swe.
Serbia: Belgrade. 1996. Historical studies. ■A report from BITEF (Belgrade International Theatre Festival).

1903 Jakopec, Miloš. *Matičkovi odmevi leta 1848 v Novem mestu.* (Echoes of Matiček in Novo Mesto in 1848.) Novo mesto: Municipality; 1997. 8 pp. Lang.: Slo.
Slovenia: Novo mesto. 1848. Historical studies. ■The performance in Novo mesto of the comedy *Ta veseli dan ali Matiček se ženi (This Merry Day, or Matiček Gets Married)*, (1790) by Anton Tomaž Linhart, the first Slovene playwright.

1904 Korun, Mile. *Režiser in Cankar.* (The Director and Cankar.) Ljubljana: Ljubljana City Theatre; 1997. 375 pp. Illus.: Photo. B&W. Lang.: Slo.
Slovenia. 1965-1995. Histories-sources. ■Excerpts from the diary of a theatre director regarding his productions of plays by Ivan Cankar over a period of thirty years.

1905 Kralj, Lado. "Teatrski škandal zaradi 'Veselega vinograda'." (The Theatrical Scandal of *The Happy Vineyard.*) 150-158 in Vodopivec, Peter, ed; Mahnič, Joža, ed. *Slovenska trideseta leta.* Ljubljana: Slovenian Literary Society; 1997. 252 pp. Lang.: Slo.
Slovenia: Ljubljana. 1932. Historical studies. ■Account of an incident in which young, mainly Catholic intellectuals interrupted a performance of Zuckmayer's *Der fröhliche Weinberg* and demanded that it be removed from the repertoire.

1906 Pandur, Livia, ed.; Božac, Angelo, photo. *Pandur's Theatre of Dreams.* Maribor: Seventheaven; 1997. 334 pp. Pref. Biblio. Illus.: Photo. B&W. Color. Lang.: Eng, Ger.
Slovenia. 1989-1996. Histories-sources. ■Pictorial history of director Tomaž Pandur's productions at the Mladinsko in Ljubljana and the National Theatre in Maribor.

1907 Vevar, Štefan. *Sem, torej igram. Prispevki za psihosociološki portret slovenskega igralstva.* (I Exist, Therefore I Perform: A Contribution to the Psychosociological Portrait of Slovene Acting.) Ljubljana: SGFM; 1997. 148 pp. (Documents SGFM 32, 66-67.) Pref. Index. Illus.: Photo. B&W. Lang.: Slo.
Slovenia. 1880-1970. Historical studies. ■Portrayal of Slovene acting based on manuscripts in the Slovene Theatre and Film Museum, consisting mainly of correspondence.

1908 Barnes, Hazel. "Theatre for Reconciliation: *Desire* and South African Students." *TJ.* 1997 Mar.; 49(1): 41-52. Notes. Illus.: Photo. 2. Lang.: Eng.
South Africa, Republic of: Pietermaritzburg. 1993-1995. Historical studies. ■Examines the fusion of theatrical practice and the public ritual of confession and reconciliation through a performance of David Lan's *Desire* by drama students at the University of Natal, directed by the author.

1909 Fleishman, Mark. "Physical Images in South African Theatre." *SATJ.* 1997 May/Sep.; 11(1/2): 199-214. Notes. Biblio. Lang.: Eng.
South Africa, Republic of. 1997. Critical studies. ■Importance of movement in South African theatre, and the place of the physical image.

1910 Fleishman, Mark. "Physical Images in the South African Theatre." 173-182 in Davis, Geoffrey V., ed.; Fuchs, Anne, ed. *Theatre and Change in South Africa.* Amsterdam: Harwood Academic Publishing; 1996. (Contemporary Theatre Studies 12.) Notes. Index. Append. Illus.: Photo. 1. Lang.: Eng.
South Africa, Republic of. 1996. Critical studies. ■Examines the use of 'physical images' in South African theatre—the physical body as a site of transformation and metaphor.

1911 Krouse, Matthew. "My Life in the Theatre of War: The Development of an Alternative Consciousness." 101-114 in Davis, Geoffrey V., ed.; Fuchs, Anne, ed. *Theatre and Change in South Africa.* Amsterdam: Harwood Academic Publishing; 1996. 324 pp. (Contemporary Theatre Studies 12.) Index. Notes. Append. Illus.: Photo. 1. Lang.: Eng.
South Africa, Republic of. 1982. Critical studies. ■Author's experience as an actor in the entertainment corps of the South African Defence Force and its influence upon his later acting career. Comments on censorship in South Africa under apartheid.

1912 Orkin, Martin. "Whose Popular Theatre and Performance?" 49-64 in Davis, Geoffrey V., ed.; Fuchs, Anne, ed. *Theatre and Change in South Africa.* Amsterdam: Harwood Academic Publishing; 1996. 324 pp. (Contemporary Theatre Studies 12.) Index. Notes. Append. Lang.: Eng.
South Africa, Republic of. 1976-1994. Critical studies. ■Attempts to construct and nurture a 'popular' theatre in South Africa.

1913 Purkey, Malcolm. "*Tooth and Nail*: Rethinking Form for the South African Theatre." 155-172 in Davis, Geoffrey V., ed.; Fuchs, Anne, ed. *Theatre and Change in South Africa.* Amsterdam: Harwood Academic Publishing; 1996. (Contemporary Theatre Studies 12.) Notes. Index. Append. Illus.: Photo. 4. Lang.: Eng.
South Africa, Republic of: Johannesburg. 1988-1989. Histories-sources. ■Founder of Junction Avenue Theatre Company describes its earlier *Tooth and Nail*, and compares it to *Sophiatown* arguing that this comparison sheds light on the ongoing evolution of South Africa.

1914 Gabriele, John. "Interview with Alberto Miralles." *WES.* 1997 Win; 9(1): 27-32. Illus.: Photo. 2. Lang.: Eng.
Spain: Barcelona, Madrid. 1950-1996. Histories-sources. ■Interview with Alberto Miralles, playwright, director and founder of Cátaro Theatre Group. Currently living in Madrid, he continues to write and direct plays.

1915 Holt, Marion P. "Angel García Moreno: Director-Impresario of the Teatro Fígaro." *WES.* 1997 Win; 9(1): 23-26. Illus.: Photo. 2. Lang.: Eng.
Spain: Madrid. 1996. Historical studies. ■The life and career of Angel García Moreno, currently artistic director of Teatro Fígaro.

1916 Lamartina-Lens, Iride. "Paloma Pedrero: A Profile." *WES.* 1997 Win; 9(1): 53-54. Illus.: Photo. 1. Lang.: Eng.
Spain. 1957-1996. Historical studies. ■On the work of director Paloma Pedrero: influences on her career, recent work.

1917 Leonard, Candyce. "Diversity in Contemporary Spanish Theatre: Three Directors." *WES.* 1997 Win; 9(1): 33-36. Illus.: Photo. 2. Lang.: Eng.
Spain. 1975-1996. Historical studies. ■Changes in Spanish theatre since the death of Franco as seen in the work of three directors, José Luis Gómez, José Sanchis Sinisterra, and Etelvino Vázquez.

1918 Leonard, Candyce. "Interview with Playwright Fermín Cabal." *WES.* 1997 Win; 9(1): 47-50. Illus.: Photo. 3. Lang.: Eng.
Spain. 1948-1996. Histories-sources. ■Interview with playwright Fermín Cabal on his life and career.

DRAMA: —Performance/production

1919   Zatlin, Phyllis. "The Catalans Invade the Madrid Stage."
WES. 1997 Win; 9(1): 5-8. Illus.: Photo. 3. Lang.: Eng.
Spain: Madrid. 1996. Historical studies. ■Discussion of *¡Hombres!*
(Men!), a collection of skits by assorted authors, directed by Sergi Belbel
at Teatro Marquina, Els Joglars's *Ubú President*, written and directed by
Albert Boadella at the Teatro Nuevo Apolo, and others.

1920   Zatlin, Phyllis. "...And the Madrilenians Fight Back." *WES*.
1997 Win; 9(1): 9-12. Illus.: Photo. 3. Lang.: Eng.
Spain: Madrid. 1996. Historical studies. ■Spanish theatre on the stages
of Madrid, with emphasis on Jorge Márquez's *La tuerta suerte de Perico
Galápago (The One-Eyed Luck of Perico Galápago)* at the Teatro Olimpia, directed by Juan Margallo.

1921   Gunawardana, A. J. "Is It the End of History for Asia's Modern Theatres?" *ThR*. 1997; 22(1 Supplement): 73-80. Notes.
Lang.: Eng.
Sri Lanka. 1956-1997. Historical studies. ■Overview of tendencies in
contemporary Asian theatre, with focus on modernization, relationship
to pre-modern theatre and cultural globalization.

1922   Amble, Lolo. "När generationerna befruktar varandra."
(When the Generations Fertilize Each Other.) *Dramat*.
1997; 5 (4): 26-29. Illus.: Photo. Color. Lang.: Swe.
Sweden: Stockholm. 1934-1997. Histories-sources. ■An interview with
the actors Sif Ruud and Thorsten Flinck about the different attitudes
toward rhetoric and audibility among actors.

1923   Bromee, Anna. "Johan Ulveson och hans många komiska
karaktärer." (Johan Ulveson and His Many Comical Characters.) *Dramat*. 1997; 5(3): 6. Illus.: Photo. Color. Lang.:
Swe.
Sweden: Stockholm. 1997. Historical studies. ■A presentation of the
actor Johan Ulveson's many different parts during this year.

1924   Bromee, Anna. "Vad händer efter succén?" (What Happens
After the Success?)*Dramat*. 1997; 5(4): 42-43. Illus.: Photo.
Color. Lang.: Swe.
Sweden: Stockholm. 1997. Histories-sources. ■An interview with actors
Jan Myrbrand and My Holmsten about the current situation of the free
lance actor, and the difference between an institution like Kungliga Dra-
matiska Teatern and an independent group.

1925   Case, Sue-Ellen. "Sex and Gender in Stockholm." *WES*.
1997 Spr; 9(2): 47-52. Illus.: Photo. 5. Lang.: Eng.
Sweden: Stockholm. 1996. Historical studies. ■Sex and gender in Dra-
maten production of Euripides's *Bákchai (The Bacchae)* directed by Ing-
mar Bergman, and Stockholms Stadsteater production of Tony
Kushner's *Angels in America, Part II: Perestroika*, and Unga Klara's
Syrener (Lilacs) by Eva Ström and *Irina's Nya Liv (Irina's Book)* by
Irina von Martens, both directed by Suzanne Osten.

1926   Fant, Kenne. "Jalle, Kenne och när allt började." (Jalle,
Kenne And When Everything Started.) *Dramat*. 1997; 5 (4):
36-37. Illus.: Photo. B&W. Lang.: Swe.
Sweden: Stockholm. 1945. Histories-sources. ■Excerpts from the book
Nära bilder (Close Images) by Kenne Fant, about the admission examination to Dramatens Elevskola, with reference to Jarl Kulle as an
apprentice.

1927   Franzon, Johan. "Flyktingsöde som teater." (The Fates of
Refugees As Theatre.) *Tningen*. 1997; 21(3): 7-10. Illus.:
Photo. Color. Lang.: Swe.
Sweden: Gothenburg. 1997. Historical studies. ■A presentation of three
plays based on authentic material of refugees, Cecillia Parkert's *Vittne
(Witness)* staged by Jasenko Selimovic, *Lava* staged by Gunilla Eriksson
with fifteen unemployed youths and *Transit* staged by Niklas Hjulström,
with interviews with the directors.

1928   Gislén, Ylva. "Staffan Valdemar Holm." *Entré*. 1997;
24(1): 2-18. Illus.: Photo. B&W. Lang.: Swe.
Sweden: Malmö. Denmark: Copenhagen. 1984-1997. Histories-sources.
■An interview with the artistic director of Malmö Dramatiska Ensemble,
Staffan Valdemar Holm, about his education at Statens Teaterskole in
Copenhagen, his career in Denmark and since 1992 in Sweden, with ref-
erences to his productions of German plays at Malmö and his *Carmen*
at Folkoperan.

1929   Hägglund, Kent. "Johan Ulveson." *Entré*. 1997; 24(3):
22-38. Illus.: Photo. B&W. Lang.: Swe.

Sweden: Stockholm. 1977. Histories-sources. ■An interview with the
actor Johan Ulveson, about his background and career, and the differences between playing comic parts and dramatic characters.

1930   Haglund, Birgitta. "Svensk teater har något ängsligt över
sig." (The Swedish Theatre Has Some Anxiety About Itself.)
Tningen. 1997; 21(1): 4-6. Illus.: Photo. Color. Lang.: Swe.
Sweden: Stockholm. 1993. Histories-sources. ■An interview with the
actor Dan Johansson about his career and the ensemble at Fria Teatern.

1931   Hoogland, Rikard. "Skilda världar." (Separate Worlds.)
Tningen. 1997; 21(5): 8-9. Illus.: Photo. B&W. Lang.: Swe.
Sweden. 1990-1997. Histories-sources. ■An interview with the actor
Tommy Andersson about the work with independent theatre groups and
his reevaluation of the institutions.

1932   Huss, Pia. "Lena Fridell—en teaterföreställning är en stor
händelse." (Lena Fridell—A Theatrical Performance Is a
Great Occasion.) *Entré*. 1997; 24(6): 26-38. Illus.: Photo.
B&W. Lang.: Swe.
Sweden: Gothenburg. 1985-1997. Histories-sources. ■Interview with
dramaturg Lena Fridell about children's theatre, Kultur i Förskolan (a
preschool program), and the theatres En Trappa Ner and Backa Teater.

1933   Huss, Pia. "Staffan Valdemar Holm låter kvinnan besegra
Strindberg." (Staffan Valdemar Holm Lets the Woman
Defeat Strindberg.) *Dramat*. 1997; 5(2): 18-21. Illus.: Photo.
B&W. Color. Lang.: Swe.
Sweden: Stockholm. 1997. Histories-sources. ■An interview with the
director Staffan Valdemar Holm about his new production of August
Strindberg's *Fadren (The Father)* at Kungliga Dramatiska Teatern.

1934   Kjoller, Merete. *Bergman e Shakespeare*. (Bergman and
Shakespeare.) Rome: Bulzoni; 1997. 122 pp. (Piccola Biblioteca Shakespeariana 14.) Pref. Notes. Lang.: Ita.
Sweden. Germany. 1944-1994. Critical studies. ■Analysis of Ingmar Bergman's direction of works by Shakespeare, including *Macbeth* (1944,
1948), *Twelfth Night* (1975, 1979), *Hamlet* (1986), and *The Winter's
Tale* (1994).

1935   Kristoffersson, Birgitta. "Allan Edwall." *Dramat*. 1997;
5(1): 22-23. Illus.: Photo. B&W. Lang.: Swe.
Sweden: Stockholm. 1949-1997. Biographical studies. ■An homage to
the actor Allan Edwall, with reference to Kungliga Dramatiska Teatern,
and his own theatre Brunnsgatan Fyra.

1936   Kristoffersson, Birgitta. "I motsatta roller." (In Opposing
Parts.) *Dramat*. 1997; 5(3): 34-35. Illus.: Photo. B&W.
Lang.: Swe.
Sweden: Stockholm. 1970-1997. Biographical studies. ■A presentation
of the actor Björn Granath, with references to his career and cooperation
with Ingmar Bergman, Thorsten Flinck and his views on acting.

1937   Kristoffersson, Birgitta. "Jarl Kulle och hans reskamrater."
(Jarl Kulle and His Travel Companions.) *Dramat*. 1997;
5(4) : 35. Illus.: Photo. Color. Lang.: Swe.
Sweden. 1997. Historical studies. ■A presentation of the actor Jarl
Kulle's last one-man-show *Reskamraten (The Traveling Companion)*.

1938   Lagercrantz, Ylva. "Rock'n'roll-regissören och stillheten i
Körsbärsträdgården." (The Director of Rock'n'Roll and the
Stillness of The Cherry Orchard.) *Dramat*. 1997; 5(2): 44-47.
Illus.: Photo. Color. Lang.: Swe.
Sweden: Stockholm. 1997. Histories-sources. ■An interview with the
Danish director Peter Langdal about his staging of Čechov's *Višněvyj sad
(The Cherry Orchard)* at Kungliga Dramatiska Teatern.

1939   Lahger, Håkan. "En repetition kring ett minne." (A
Rehearsal about a Memory.) *Dramat*. 1997; 5(1): 20-21.
Illus.: Photo. Color. Lang.: Swe.
Sweden: Stockholm. 1974-1997. Historical studies. ■A presentation of
the actor and director Peter Luckhaus and his career, with reference to
his production of Brian Friel's *Molly Sweeney* at Kungliga Dramatiska
Teatern.

1940   Lahger, Håkan. "En dag växer man upp och tar av sig cow-
boystövlarna." (One Day You Grow Up and Take Off Your
Cowboy Boots.) *Dramat*. 1997; 5(1): 42-44. Illus.: Photo.
Color. Lang.: Swe.

DRAMA: —Performance/production

Sweden: Stockholm. 1965. Histories-sources. ■An interview with the actor Per Mattsson about his career, with references to his parts in the productions of Ingmar Bergman and his parts in plays by Sam Shepard.

1941 Lahger, Håkan. "Mycket av allting." (Plenty of Everything.) *Dramat.* 1997; 5(3): 20-23. Illus.: Photo. Color. Lang.: Swe.
Sweden: Stockholm. 1970-1997. Histories-sources. ■An interview with director Peter Dalle about his background, his opinions about cultural policy, his cooperation with Thorsten Flinck, and his staging of Martin McDonagh's *The Cripple of Inishmaan* at Kungliga Dramatiska Teatern.

1942 Lahger, Håkan. "Samtal med Lars Norén." (A Conversation With Lars Norén.) *Dramat.* 1997; 5(4): 14-18. Illus.: Photo. B&W. Lang.: Swe.
Sweden: Stockholm. 1980-1997. Histories-sources. ■An interview with the author and director Lars Norén about his views on the play versus the novel, his *Personkrets 3:1 (Personal Circle 3:1)* and his political views.

1943 Lewin, Jan. "Från konstnärligt ankare till ängslig hantverkareo." (From An Artistic Anchor To An Anxious Artisan.) *Entré.* 1997; 24(5): 2-7. Illus.: Photo. B&W. Lang.: Swe.
Sweden: Stockholm, Gothenburg. 1990. Histories-sources. ■An interview with the director Ragnar Lyth about the turbulent situation of the Swedish theatre institutions and specially the position of the directors, with references to Teaterförbundet.

1944 Magnusson, Anna. "Stor nu!" (Big Now!)*Dramat.* 1997; 5(4): 10-13. Illus.: Photo. B&W. Color. Lang.: Swe.
Sweden: Stockholm. 1985. Histories-sources. ■An interview with the actress Melinda Kinnaman about her background and career, with references to the author Lars Norén and his staging of his plays *En Sorts Hades (A Kind of Hades)* and *Personkrets 3:1 (Personal Circle 3:1)*, and the director Bo Widerberg and Kungliga Dramatiska Teatern.

1945 Olzon, Janna. "Teatern håller på att K-märkas." (The Theatre Is Becoming an Historic Monument.) *Tningen.* 1997; 21(5): 4-5. Illus.: Photo. Color. Lang.: Swe.
Sweden: Malmö. 1997. Histories-sources. ■An interview with the young acting student Rasmus Lindgren about the joy of acting and the importance of a present theatre.

1946 Olzon, Janna. "Nu vill jag välja sammanhang." (Now I Like To Choose the Circumstances.) *Tningen.* 1997; 21(5): 6-7. Illus.: Photo. Color. Lang.: Swe.
Sweden: Stockholm. 1981. Histories-sources. ■An interview with the actress Lina Pleijel about her career, experiences in soap operas, and the urge to be involved in real theatre.

1947 Rokem, Freddie. "The Production of *Hamlet* at the Västanå Theatre in Sweden." *WES.* 1997 Spr; 9(2): 57-60. Illus.: Photo. 2. Lang.: Eng.
Sweden: Värmland. 1996. Historical studies. ■Critical reception of Shakespeare's *Hamlet*, directed by Leif Stinnerbom at the Västanå Theatre.

1948 Romanus, Lina. "Tom Fjordefalk." *Entré.* 1997; 24(4): 29-39. Illus.: Photo. B&W. Lang.: Swe.
Sweden: Stockholm. 1972-1997. Histories-sources. ■An interview with Tom Fjordefalk about his background and training at Institutet för Scenkonst, and in *kathakali* in India, as well as the career as an actor at Odin Teatret, Teater Schahrazad and now director of Tyst Teater, a company for deaf actors.

1949 Romanus, Linda. "Man ska inte vika sig för ungdomen." (You Shouldn't Give In To Youth.) *Entré.* 1997; 24(2): 4-11. Illus.: Photo. B&W. Lang.: Swe.
Sweden: Stockholm, Uppsala. 1995-1997. Histories-sources. ■Interviews with set designer Karin Lind, playwright Sofia Fredén and actress Alexandra Mörner about how they like to vitalize the theatre and involve the youth audiences.

1950 Ruthström, Maria. "Skådespelaren, en sanningssägare." (The Actor, a Teller of Truths.) *Tningen.* 1997; 21(2) : 4-6. Illus.: Photo. Color. Lang.: Swe.
Sweden: Stockholm. 1985-1997. Histories-sources. ■An interview with the actor Olle Jansson about his career and his ideas about acting.

1951 Ruthström, Maria. "Försök att fånga nuet." (Try To Catch The Now.) *Tningen.* 1997; 21(3): 4-6. Illus.: Photo. Color. Lang.: Swe.
Sweden: Stockholm. 1986-1997. Histories-sources. ■An interview with the director Kajsa Isakson about her plays and stagings, with reference to her own *Rundgång (Vicious Circle)* at Teater Salieri.

1952 Söderberg, Olle. "3 små gummor i Mora." (Three Little Old Ladies at Mora.) *ProScen.* 1997; 21(3): 18-19. Illus.: Photo. Color. Lang.: Swe.
Sweden: Mora. 1997. Historical studies. ■A presentation of the semi-professional, semi-community production of Maria Lang's crime play *3 små gummor (Three Little Old Ladies)*, shown in a tent, directed by Peter Krantz.

1953 Sörenson, Elisabeth. "Jarl Kulle och en bunt bilder." (Jarl Kulle And A Bunch of Pictures.) *Dramat.* 1997; 5(1): 28-33. Illus.: Photo. B&W. Lang.: Swe.
Sweden: Stockholm. 1950-1995. Histories-sources. ■An interview with the actor Jarl Kulle about his many parts, with reference to photos of the parts.

1954 Sörenson, Elisabeth. "En halv sekund av tvekan." (Half a Second of Doubt.) *Dramat.* 1997; 5(2): 36-37. Illus.: Photo. Color. Lang.: Swe.
Sweden: Stockholm. 1980-1997. Histories-sources. ■An interview with the actor Sven Lindberg about his recent acting experiences.

1955 Sörenson, Elisabeth. "Bilder av Jarl Kulle." (Pictures of Jarl Kulle.) *Dramat.* 1997; 5(4): 33-34. Lang.: Swe.
Sweden: Malmö, Stockholm. 1972. Historical studies. ■Some memories of the actor Jarl Kulle, with reference to his version on Strindberg's *Carl XII*, directed by Gösta Folke at Malmö Stadsteater.

1956 Sunding, Monika. "Med Frida i Glasriket." (With Frida at Glasriket.) *Entré.* 1997; 24(3): 46-49. Illus.: Photo. B&W. Lang.: Swe.
Sweden: Småland. 1997. Histories-sources. ■An inside view of a tour in the southern highlands of Sweden with Friteatern.

1957 Szalczer, Eszter. "Spring Stages in Stockholm: Two Strindberg Productions." *WES.* 1997 Fall; 9(3): 43-46. Illus.: Photo. 3. Lang.: Eng.
Sweden: Stockholm. 1997. Historical studies. ■Analysis of two productions of the annual Strindberg festival at Stockholms Stadsteater. Strindberg's novel *Svarta fanor (Black Banners)* staged by individuals from Berliner Volksbühne: Thomas Martin, adapter, Hartmut Meyer, scene and costume designer, and Frank Castorf, director. *Pelikanen (The Pelican)* staged by the 'Backstage' ensemble of Stadsteater: Anders Paulin, adaptor and director, and Karin Lind, designer.

1958 Vogel, Viveka. "Marie Göranzon, klok syster ur vår egen tid." (Marie Göranzon, A Wise Sister of Our Own Time.) *Dramat.* 1997; 5(3): 30-32. Illus.: Photo. Color. Lang.: Swe.
Sweden: Stockholm. 1964-1997. Histories-sources. ■An interview with the actress Marie Göranzon about her career and many collaborations with her husband, the actor Jan Malmsjö, with reference to her return to Kungliga Dramatiska Teatern.

1959 Wallström, Catharina. "Det handlar om kärlek och lust." (It's About Love and Joy.) *Entré.* 1997; 24(8): 35-41. Illus.: Photo. B&W. Lang.: Swe.
Sweden. Mozambique. 1997. Histories-sources. ■An interview with the director Eva Bergman, the author Henning Mankell and the actress Lucrécia Paco about their joint production *Berättelse på tidens strand (A Tale on the Shore of Time)*, with references to the contacts between Backa Teater and Teatro Avenida.

1960 Westman, Nancy. "Före och efter Solveig." (Before and After Solveig.) *Danst.* 1997; 7(1): 11-13. Illus.: Photo. B&W. Color. Lang.: Swe.
Sweden: Gothenburg. 1996. Biographical studies. ■A presentation of Birgitta Egerbladh, about her shifting activities as choreographer, composer and director, with reference to her *Varför kysser alla Solveig? (Why Does Everyone Kiss Solveig)* at Göteborgs Stadsteatern.

1961 Wigardt, Gaby. "Solveig & Börje." *Dramat.* 1997; 5(2): 8-11. Illus.: Photo. Color. Lang.: Swe.

DRAMA: —Performance/production

Sweden: Stockholm. 1967. Historical studies. ■A presentation of the actors Solveig Tärnström's and Börje Ahlstedt's parts together, with reference to *Änkeman Jarl* and *Marknadsafton* by Vihelm Moberg.

1962   Karsai, György. "Látványköltészet. Robert Wilson Duras-rendezése." (The Poetry of Vision: Marguerite Duras' *La Maladie de la mort* Directed by Robert Wilson.) *Sz.* 1997; 30(7): 33-35. Illus.: Photo. B&W. 1. Lang.: Hun.

Switzerland: Lausanne. 1970-1997. Critical studies. ■Essay on the latest production by Robert Wilson performed by the Théâtre Vidy-Lausanne at various international festivals.

1963   Richard, Christine. "Im Reich des Abstrusen." (In the World of Abstruseness.) *THeute.* 1997; 3: 18-20. Illus.: Photo. B&W. 2. Lang.: Ger.

Switzerland: Zurich, Basel. 1995-1997. Critical studies. ■Describes and compares the performances *Swiss Christmas* by Katharina Thanner directed by Maya Fanke at Theater in der Gessnerallee and *Mütternacht (Mothers' Night)* by Lisa Engel directed by Barbara Neureiter at Basler Theater.

1964   Richard, Christine. "Faust light und Hamlet heavy." *THeute.* 1997; 5: 14-15. Illus.: Photo. B&W. 1. Lang.: Ger.

Switzerland: Zurich. 1997. Critical studies. ■Compares performances of *Faust II* by Johann Wolfgang von Goethe directed by Stephan Müller at Theater Neumarkt and *Hamlet* by William Shakespeare directed by Uwe Eric Laufenberg at Zürcher Schauspielhaus.

1965   Simon, John. "A Woman Scorned: Friedrich Dürrenmatt's *The Visit*, the Source for Gottfried von Einem's Opera, Is a Masterful Study in Vengeance and Greed." *OpN.* 1997 Apr 5; 61(14): 24-26, 28. Illus.: Photo. B&W. Color. 5. Lang.: Eng.

Switzerland. 1921-1990. Critical studies. ■Argues that Maurice Valency's American adaptation of *Der Besuch der alten Dame (The Visit)* by Friedrich Dürrenmatt omitted the element of expressionism in the play. Discussion of various stage and film productions as well as other plays by Dürrenmatt.

1966   Fuchs, Elinor. "Istanbul Looking West: Art or Politics?" *AmTh.* 1997 Dec.; 14(10): 40-47. Illus.: Photo. B&W. 4. Lang.: Eng.

Turkey: Istanbul. 1980-1997. Historical studies. ■Productions at the International Istanbul Theatre Festival and how they mirror the nation's cultural crisis. Productions include the Royal National Theatre's *King Lear* directed by Richard Eyre, Heiner Müller's Berliner Ensemble staging of Brecht's *The Resistible Rise of Arturo Ui (Der aufhaltsame Aufstieg des Arturo Ui)*, and Piccolo Teatro's *The Island of Slaves (L'île des esclaves)* by Marivaux.

1967   "Reviews of Productions." *TR.* 1997; 17(6): 331-338. Lang.: Eng.

UK-England: London. 1997. ■*Hurlyburly* by David Rabe, dir by Wilson Milam at the Old Vic: rev by Bassett, Billington, Butler, Cavendish, Coveney, de Jongh, Gross, Morley, Nathan, Nightingale, Peter, Smith, Taylor, Usher. *Exposition* by Tom Minter, dir by Areta Breeze at the Arts: rev by Christopher, Curtis, Marlowe, Marmion, Taylor. *St. Joan* by Julia Pascal, dir by Pascal at the New End: rev by Cavendish, Christopher, Hewison, Nathan.

1968   "The Inaccessible Bard." *Econ.* 1997 Feb 15; 342(8004): 81-82. Illus.: Photo. B&W. 2. Lang.: Eng.

UK-England: London. 1997. Critical studies. ■Explores accessibility of Shakespeare's plays to contemporary audiences: modern film adaptations of Shakespeare's plays including those of Kenneth Branagh. Also looks at the RSC's current production of *Troilus and Cressida*.

1969   "Reviews of Productions." *TR.* 1997; 17(13): 804-805. Lang.: Eng.

UK-England: London. 1997. ■*Daddy Come Home* by Noli, dir by Noli at BAC Main: rev by Christopher, Curtis, Marlowe, Turpin, Tushingham. *Philoctetes* by Sophocles, transl by Eleanor Brown, dir by Georgina Van Welie at the Cockpit: rev by Cavendish. *On the Couch with Chrissie* by Vanessa Brooks, dir by Brooks at the Orange Tree: rev by McPherson, Stratton.

1970   "Reviews of Productions." *TR.* 1997; 17(7): 402-408. Lang.: Eng.

UK-England: London. 1997. ■*Popcorn* by Ben Elton, dir by Laurence Boswell at the Apollo: rev by Bassett, Benedict, Butler, Christopher, Coveney, Curtis, Edwardes, Gardener, Gross, Hagerty, Morley, Nathan, Nightingale, Peter, Smith, Taylor, Wareham, Wilson. *The Censor* by Anthony Neilson, dir by Neilson at the Finborough: rev by Gardner, Stratton. *Surfing* by Robert Young, by Lisa Goldman at the Finborough: rev by McPherson, Stratton, Taylor, Woddis.

1971   "Reviews of Productions." *TR.* 1997; 17(1/2): 7-11. Lang.: Eng.

UK-England: London. 1997. ■*Beef, No Chicken* by Derek Walcott, dir by Yvonne Brewster at the Tricycle: rev by Bassett, Billington, Butler, Curtis, Gross, Hemming, Nathan, Peter, Sierz, Stratton, Usher, Williams. *A Quick Eternity* by Robert Hamilton, dir by Pet Darling at the Etcetera: rev by Williams. *Saltimbanco* performed and created by Cirque du Soleil, dir by Franco Dragone at the Royal Albert Hall: rev by Gore-Langton, Hassell, Sacks, Spencer.

1972   "Reviews of Productions." *TR.* 1997; 17(1/2): 11-16. Lang.: Eng.

UK-England: London. 1997. ■*Sex for the Masses*, book, music and lyrics by Henry Lewis, dir by Simon Bell at the Etcetera: rev by Foss, Stratton. *Elsinore (Elsineur)* by Robert Lepage with Pierre Bernier, adapted from *Hamlet* by William Shakespeare, dir by Lepage at the Lyttelton: rev by Brown, Curtis, Edwardes, Macauley, Nathan, Nightingale, Smith. *I'll Be Your Dog* by Robbie McCallum, dir by Andrea Brooks at the Old Red Lion: rev by Gardner, Stevens.

1973   "Reviews of Productions." *TR.* 1997; 17(1/2): 17-28. Lang.: Eng.

UK-England: London. 1997. ■*The Cripple of Inishmaan* by Martin McDonagh, dir by Nicholas Hytner at the Cottesloe: rev by Billington, Brown, Butler, Coveney, de Jongh, Gore-Langton, Gross, Hagerty, Macauley, Nathan, Nightingale, Peter, Smith, Spencer, Stratton, Taylor. *Lord of the Dance* by Michael Flatley, dir by Flatley at the Wembley Arena: rev by Gibbons, Sacks. *The White Devil* by John Webster, dir by Gale Edwards for the RSC at the Pit: rev by Bassett, Brown, Curtis, Gardner, Kingston, Logan, Shuttleworth, Smith.

1974   "Reviews of Productions." *TR.* 1997; 17(1/2): 28-32. Lang.: Eng.

UK-England: London. 1997. ■*Absolution* by Robert William Sherwood, dir by Brennan Street at the White Bear: rev by Godfrey-Faussett, Ives, Reade. *The Fever* by Wallace Shawn, dir by Clare Coulter at the Royal Court Upstairs Circle: rev by Butler, Cavendish, Coveney, de Jongh, Gross, Hagerty, Macauley, Nathan, Nightingale, Peter, Smith, Spencer, Taylor, Usher. *Sketches by Boz* by Charles Dickens, adapted and dir by Robert Butler at Wimbledon Studio: rev by McPherson, Tushingham.

1975   "Reviews of Productions." *TR.* 1997; 17(18): 1109-1113. Lang.: Eng.

UK-England: London. 1997. ■*The Comedy of Errors* by Shakespeare, dir by Tim Supple for the RSC at the Young Vic: rev by Billington, de Jongh, Edwardes, Macauley, Milne, Nathan, Nightingale, Peter, Rosenthal, Smith, Spencer, Usher, Woddis. *Timon of Athens* by Shakespeare, dir by Andrew Jarvis at the Brixton Shaw Theatre: rev by Marlowe, Marmion. *A Tainted Dawn* by Sudha Buchar and Kristine Landon-Smith, dir by Landon-Smith at the Tricycle: rev by Edwardes, Gross, Woddis.

1976   "Reviews of Productions." *TR.* 1997; 17(18): 1114-1122. Lang.: Eng.

UK-England: London. 1997. ■*Heartbreak House* by G.B. Shaw, dir by David Hare at the Almeida: rev by Billington, Brown, Clapp, de Jongh, Edwardes, Gore-Langton, Hagerty, Macauley, Milne, Morley, Nathan, Nightingale, Peter, Rosenthal, Sierz, Smith, Spencer, Taylor, Usher, Woddis. *Canterbury Tales* by Richard Hope, from Chaucer, dir by John Cotgrave at the New End: rev by Kingston, Logan. *Wound to the Face* by Howard Barker, dir by Stephen Wrentmore at Riverside 3: rev by Cooper, Fisher, Logan, Peter, Shuttleworth, Turpin.

1977   "Reviews of Productions." *TR.* 1997; 17(18): 1122-1131. Lang.: Eng.

UK-England: London. 1997. ■*Glub! Glub!* devised by clown troupe Yllana, dir by David Ottone at the Hackney Empire: rev by Brennan, Edwardes, Hutera, Logan. *Chips with Everything* by Arnold Wesker, dir by Howard Davies for the Royal National at the Lyttelton: rev by Billington, Brown, Clapp, de Jongh, Foss, Grant, Hagerty, Macauley,

DRAMA: —Performance/production

Milne, Morley, Nathan, Nightingale, Peter, Rosenthal, Sierz, Spencer, Taylor, Usher, Woddis. *Disco Pigs* by Enda Walsh, dir by Pat Kiernan at the Bush: rev by Butler, de Jongh, Edwardes, Fisher, Gross, Hagerty, Hemming, Higgins, Kingston, Peter, Rubnikowicz, Williams.

1978   "Reviews of Productions." *TR.* 1997; 17(18): 1131-1134. Lang.: Eng.

UK-England: London. 1997. ■*Which Way the Cat Jumps* by Robert Hamilton, dir by Robert McIntosh at the Grace: rev by Godfrey-Faussett, McPherson. *The Censor* by Anthony Neilson, dir by Neilson at the Royal Court Upstairs: rev by Benedict, Billington, Butler, Morley, Nathan, Nightingale, Peter, Spencer, Taylor. *Candides* from Voltaire by Cirque Baroque, dir by Mauricio Celedon at Three Mills Island: rev by Brennan, Cavendish, Noth, Rubnikowicz.

1979   "Reviews of Productions." *TR.* 1997; 17(18): 1135-1138. Lang.: Eng.

UK-England: London. 1997. ■*Do You Come Here Often?* by Sean Foley, Hamish McColl and Josef Houben, dir by Houben at the Lyric Studio: rev by Benedict, Cooper, Coveney, Edwardes, Games, R.L. Parry, Rubnikowicz. *The Hanging Tree* by Nicola McCartney, dir by McCartney at BAC 2: rev by Cavendish, Logan, Shuttleworth, Stevens. *One Night* by Prabjot Dolly Dhingra, dir by Keith Khan at Theatre Royal, Stratford East: rev by Bassett, Billington, Curtis, Foss, Stratton.

1980   "Reviews of Productions." *TR.* 1997; 17(1/2): 33-37. Lang.: Eng.

UK-England: London. 1997. ■*Blood and Ice* by Liz Lochhead, dir by John Link at the New End: rev by Christopher, Clanchy, Kingston, Marmion, Turpin, Williams. *Ladies in Retirement* by Edward Percy and Reginald Denham, dir by Jamila Awar at the Riverside: rev by McPherson. *Showstopper* by Dan Rebellato, dir by Sarah Frankcom at the Arts: rev by Butler, Christopher, Curtis, Darvell, Gore-Langton, Gross, Hagerty, Nathan, Shuttleworth, Taylor.

1981   "Reviews of Productions." *TR.* 1997; 17(1/2): 37-40. Lang.: Eng.

UK-England: London. 1997. ■*Entertaining Angels* by Nicola McCartney and Lucy McLellan, dir by McCartney at BAC: rev by Curtis, Stevens. *Snowshow* by Slava Polunin, dir by Victor Kramer at the Peacock: rev by Brennan, Brown, Christopher, Hagerty, Lockerbie, Nathan, Parry, Peter, Reade, Sacks, Spencer. *The Sash (My Father Wore)* by Hector MacMillan, dir by Dawn Lintern at the Finborough: rev by Logan, Stevens.

1982   "Reviews of Productions." *TR.* 1997; 17(1/2): 41-49. Lang.: Eng.

UK-England: London. 1997. ■*The Storm (Oväder)* by August Strindberg, dir by Wils Wilson, *After the Fire (Brända tomten)* by Strindberg, dir by Loveday Ingram, and *The Ghost Sonata (Spöksonaten)* by Strindberg, dir by Georgina Van Welie at the Gate: rev by Billington, Coveney, Curtis, Gross, Macauley, McPherson, Nightingale, Peter, Spencer, Taylor, Tushingham. *The Snail Inside* by Gerard Foster, dir by Robin Dashwood at Hen & Chickens: rev by Edwardes, Parry. *All of You Mine* by Richard Cameron, dir by Simon Usher at the Bush: rev by Benedict, Billington, Brown, Butler, Cavendish, Coveney, de Jongh, Gore-Langton, Gross, Hagerty, Marlowe, Nathan, Nightingale, Peter, Shuttleworth, Sierz, Spencer, Usher.

1983   "Reviews of Productions." *TR.* 1997; 17(1/2): 49-54. Lang.: Eng.

UK-England: London. 1997. ■*Wuthering Heights* adapt by Mandy Adams from the novel by Emily Brontë, dir by Mark Civil at the Riverside: rev by Williams. *Light Shining in Buckinghamshire* by Caryl Churchill, dir by Mark Wing-Davey at the Cottesloe: rev by Bassett, Brown, Butler, Coveney, Curtis, Gross, Hanks, Kingston, Logan, Macauley, Marlowe, Morley, Nightingale, Peter, Sierz, Usher. *New Territories* by David K.S. Tse, dir by Tse at the Oval House: rev by Abdulla, Dowden, Gardner, Kingston.

1984   "Reviews of Productions." *TR.* 1997; 17(1/2): 55-59. Lang.: Eng.

UK-England: London. 1997. ■*Black Bread and Cucumber* by Caroline Blakiston, dir by Blakiston at the Jermyn Street: rev by Abdulla, Bassett, Benedict, Nightingale, Shuttleworth, Smith. *Between the Lines* by Alan Ayckbourn and Paul Todd, dir by Todd at the Wimbledon Studio: rev by McPherson. *The Shift* by Clare Bayley, dir by Andy Lavender at the

Young Vic: rev by Billington, Butler, Curtis, Marlowe, Marmion, Nathan, Nightingale, Spencer, Turpin.

1985   "Reviews of Productions." *TR.* 1997; 17(1/2): 59-62. Lang.: Eng.

UK-England: London. 1997. ■*Dracula* by Bram Stoker, adapt by Jonathan Rigby, dir by Harry Meacher at Pentameters: rev by Foss, Godfrey-Faussett. *One Last Surviving* by Alex Mermekides, dir by Annie Siddons at the Lyric Studio: rev by Cavendish, Curtis, McPherson, Nightingale. *Flesh* by Spencer Hazel, dir by Frantic Assembly at BAC 1: rev by Curtis, Hemming, Nightingale, Stevens.

1986   "Reviews of Productions." *TR.* 1997; 17(1/2): 62-73. Lang.: Eng.

UK-England: London. 1997. ■*The Magic Door* by Alison Davis, at the Grace: rev by Cavendish, McPherson, Nightingale. *It, Wit, Don't Give a Shit Girls* by Fascinating Aida (Dillie Keane, Adele Anderson, Issy van Randwyck), dir by Nica Burns at the Vaudeville: rev by Darvell, Edwardes, Games, Hagerty, Hemming, Kingston, Morley, Nathan, Rampton, Spencer, Usher. *The Homecoming* by Harold Pinter, dir by Roger Michell at the Lyttelton: rev by Brown, Butler, Christopher, Coveney, de Jongh, Gardner, Gore-Langton, Grant, Gross, Hagerty, Hassell, Macauley, Morley, Nathan, Peter, Sierz, Spencer, Taylor, Usher.

1987   "Reviews of Productions." *TR.* 1997; 17(1/2): 73-81. Lang.: Eng.

UK-England: London. 1997. ■*Paper Husband* by Hannan Al-Shaykh, dir by Gemma Bodinetz at the Hampstead: rev by Billington, Butler, Coveney, de Jongh, Foss, Gross, Morley, Nathan, Nightingale, Peter, Reade, Spencer, Stratton, Taylor. *Three Hours After Marriage* by John Gay, Alexander Pope and John Arbuthnot, dir by Richard Cottrell for the RSC at the Barbican: rev by Curtis, Foss, Gardner, Hagerty, Logan, Macauley, Nightingale. *A Midsummer Night's Dream* by William Shakespeare, dir by Jatinder Verma at the Lyric Hammersmith: rev by Billington, Butler, Coveney, Davé, de Jongh, Gross, Hemming, Kingston, Peter, Spender, Stratton, Taylor.

1988   "Reviews of Productions." *TR.* 1997; 17(1/2): 82-89. Lang.: Eng.

UK-England: London. 1997. ■*One Word Improv* by Eddie Izzard, Neil Mullarkey, Stephen Frost and Suki Webster at the Albery: rev by Billington, David, Dessau, Games, Hagerty, Nathan, Rampton, Shuttleworth, Spender, Taylor. London International Mime Festival 1997: *The Last Hallucination of Lucas Cranach the Elder* by Compagnie Mossoux-Bonté, dir by Nicole Mossoux and Patrick Bonté at the Purcell Room: rev by Christopher, Gilbert, Peter, Stratton. *The Seed Carriers* by Stephen Mottram's Animata, dir by Mottram at ICA: rev by Gilbert, Kingston. *70 Hill Lane* by Phelim McDermott, Guy Dartnell and Steve Tiplady, dir by Lee Simpson and Julian Crouch and *Animo* by McDermott, Simpson and Crouch, dir by Simpson and Crouch at BAC: rev by Bassett, Constanti, Kingston, Marmion, Turpin.

1989   "Reviews of Productions." *TR.* 1997; 17(1/2): 115-119. Lang.: Eng.

UK-England: London. 1997. ■*Beatrix* adapt by Patrick Garland and Judy Taylor, from the writings of Beatrix Potter, dir by Garland at the Greenwich: rev by Bayley, Hemming, Hewison, Marlowe, Marmion, Spencer, Usher. *The Seal Wife* by Sue Glover, dir by Jenny Lee at the Warehouse, Croydon: rev by McPherson, Stratton, Turpin, Woddis. *The Tempest* by William Shakespeare, dir by Nancy Meckler at the Richmond: rev by Gardner, Kingston, Nathan, Peter, Taylor.

1990   "Reviews of Productions." *TR.* 1997; 17(1/2): 119-121. Lang.: Eng.

UK-England: London. 1997. ■*I Am (The Space)* from Gaston Bachelard's *Poetics of Space*, devised by Reflective Theatre, dir by Gari Jones at White Bear: rev by Cavendish, McPherson. *What Do I Get?* by Alan Pollock, dir by Jake Lushington at the Old Red Lion: rev by Christopher, Coveney, Curtis, Gilbey, Parry, Reade. *Untitled... Naturally* devised and performed by the Divine David at the Albany: rev by Marmion.

1991   "Reviews of Productions." *TR.* 1997; 17(1/2): 122-130. Lang.: Eng.

UK-England: London. 1997. ■*Henry IV, Part 1* and *Henry IV, Part 2* by William Shakespeare, dir by Stephen Unwin at the Old Vic: rev by Bassett, Brown, Butler, de Jongh, Edwardes, Gross, Hagerty, Kingston, Morley, Murray, Nathan, Smith, Usher. *Everybody Knows All Birds Have*

DRAMA: —Performance/production

Wings by Randhi McWilliams, dir by McWilliams, at the Pleasance: rev by Christopher, Gardner, Godfrey-Faussett, Gore-Langton, Loup-Nolan, Peter, Taylor. *Airswimming* by Charlotte Jones, dir by Anna Mackmin at BAC 2: rev by Abdulla, Gardner, Kingston, Marlowe, Peter, Turpin.

1992 "Reviews of Productions." *TR.* 1997; 17(4): 201-204. Lang.: Eng.

UK-England: London. 1997. ■*Hard Times* by Charles Dickens, adapted by Dennis Saunders, dir by Sue Pomeroy at the Richmond: rev by Christopher. *American Buffalo* by David Mamet, dir by Lindsay Posner at the Young Vic: rev by Benedict, Billington, de Jongh, Hagerty, Hewison, Macauley, Morley, Nathan, Nightingale, Spencer, Stratton, Woddis. *Fishtank* by Clive Saunders, dir by Saunders at the Finborough: rev by Cavendish.

1993 "Reviews of Productions." *TR.* 1997; 17(1/2): 131-135. Lang.: Eng.

UK-England: London. 1997. ■*East Is East* by Ayub Khan-Din, dir by Kristine Landon-Smith at Theatre Royal, Stratford East: rev by Coveney, Darvell, Gross, Hanks, Kingston. *Backpay* by Tamantha Hammerschlag, dir by Mary Peate, and *Cockroach Who?* by Jess Walters, dir by Caroline Hall at the Royal Court Upstairs: rev by Billington, Coveney, Curtis, Foss, Hanks, Hemming, Hewison, Nightingale, Spencer, Stratton, Taylor, Usher. *Spinning* by Tenebris Light, dir by Struan Leslie at the Oval House: rev by Abdulla.

1994 "Reviews of Productions." *TR.* 1997; 17(1/2): 136-141. Lang.: Eng.

UK-England: London. 1997. ■*Kitchensink* by Paul Mercier, dir by Mercier at the Tricycle: rev by Billington, Coveney, Curtis, Edwardes, Foss, Gross, Hanks, Hemming, Kingston, Nathan, Peter, Spencer, Turpin, Usher. *David Strassman*, solo ventriloquist show at the Apollo: rev by Billington, Games, Gross, Hagerty, Nightingale, Rampton, Spencer, Stevens, Wareham. *The Newly Weds (De Nygifte)* by Björn Björnson, dir by T.J. Gilbreath at the Rosemary Branch: rev by Allan, Marmion.

1995 "Reviews of Productions." *TR.* 1997; 17(1/2): 142-147. Lang.: Eng.

UK-England: London. 1997. ■*When God Wanted a Son* by Arnold Wesker, dir by Spencer Butler at the New End: rev by Bassett, Benedict, Billington, Brown, Coveney, Darvell, de Jongh, Edwardes, Gross, Nathan, Nightingale, Peter, Usher. *Danny and Me* solo show by Ted Rogers, with material by Eric Davidson, dir by Joe McGrath at the Arts: rev by Foss, Hagerty, Nathan. *Babycakes* by Armistead Maupin, adapt for the stage by John Binnie, dir by Ian Brown at the Drill Hall: rev by Brennan, Cooper, de Jongh, Donald, Gardner, Hewison, Stratton, Woddis.

1996 "Reviews of Productions." *TR.* 1997; 17(3): 148-150. Lang.: Eng.

UK-England: London. 1997. ■*The Jewess of Toledo (La Judía de Toledo)* by Lope de Vega, transl by Michael Jacobs, dir by Colin Ellwood at the Bridewell: rev by Billington, Christopher, Curtis, McPherson, Nathan, Reade, Turpin. *The World's Not Over Until the Fat Man Dances* by Gerry Marsh, at the Bird's Nest: rev by Tushingham. *Shakuntala* by Kalidasa, tranl by Peter Oswald, dir by Indhu Rubasingham at the Gate: rev by Curtis, Kingston, Loup-Nolan, Marmion.

1997 "Reviews of Productions." *TR.* 1997; 17(4): 199-201. Lang.: Eng.

UK-England: London. 1997. ■*Euphoria* devised by Theatre Pur, dir by Lisa Baraitser and Simon Bayly at the Young Vic Studio: rev by Tushingham, Woddis. *The Seal Wife* by Sue Glover, dir by Jenny Lee at the Wimbledon Studio: rev by Kingston. *Luv* by Murray Schisgal, dir by Neil Marcus at the Jermyn Street: rev by Abdulla, Coveney, Hagerty, Hassell, Kingston, Nathan, Reade, Usher.

1998 "Reviews of Productions." *TR.* 1997; 17(3): 151-155. Lang.: Eng.

UK-England: London. 1997. ■*The School for Wives (L'École des femmes)* by Molière, transl by Ranjit Bolt, dir by Peter Hall at the Piccadilly: rev by Billington, Brown, Christopher, Coveney, Dowden, Edwardes, Gore-Langton, Gross, Hagerty, Hanks, Hewison, Morley, Murray, Nathan, Nightingale, Spencer, Taylor, Usher. *Hunger* devised by Primitive Science from the stories of Franz Kafka, dir by Marc von Henning at the Purcell Room: rev by Tushingham. *The Rivals* by Richard Brinsley

Sheridan, dir by Mark Clements at the Derby Playhouse: rev by Coveney, Gardner, Gore-Langton, Peter.

1999 "Reviews of Productions." *TR.* 1997; 17(4): 177-186. Lang.: Eng.

UK-England: London. 1997. ■*Cardiff East* by Peter Gill, dir by Gill at the Cottesloe: rev by Billington, Brown, Clanchy, Coveney, de Jongh, Edwardes, Gore-Langton, Gross, Hagerty, Hanks, Hewison, Marlowe, Morley, Murray, Nathan, Nightingale, Spencer, Taylor, Usher. *Seventy Scenes of Halloween* by Jeffrey M. Jones, dir by John Guerrasio at Pentameters: rev by Cavendish, Stevens, Stratton. *Heathcliff*, book by Cliff Richard and Frank Dunlop, lyrics by Tim Rice, music by John Farrar, dir by Dunlop at Labatt's Apollo: rev by Hagerty, Logan, Morley, Nightingale, Shuttleworth, Smith.

2000 "Reviews of Productions." *TR.* 1997; 17(4): 205-208. Lang.: Eng.

UK-England: London. 1997. ■*The General from America* by Richard Nelson, dir for the RSC by Howard Davies at The Pit: rev by Curtis, Edwardes, Foss, Hemming, Kingston, Morley, Usher. *Swaggers* by Mick Mahoney, dir by Mahoney at BAC 1: rev by Curtis, Gardner, Hanks, Hemming, Hewison, Kingston, Marlowe. *Natural World* by Joyoti Grech, dir by Anne Edyvean at the Oval House: rev by Godfrey-Faussett.

2001 "Reviews of Productions." *TR.* 1997; 17(4): 186-198. Lang.: Eng.

UK-England: London. 1997. ■*When Five Years Pass (Así que Pasen Cinco Años)* by Federico García Lorca, transl by Pilar Orti, dir by Phillip Hoffman at Chelsea Centre: rev by Godfrey-Faussett. *The Shallow End* by Doug Lucie, dir by Robin Lefevre at the Royal Court Downstairs: rev by Billington, Brown, Butler, Coveney, de Jongh, Edwardes, Gore-Langton, Gross, Hagerty, Hewison, Macaulay, Morley, Nathan, Nightingale, Sierz, Smith, Spencer, Taylor, Usher. *Ivanov* by Anton Cechov, transl by David Hare, dir by Jonathan Kent at the Almeida: rev by Billington, Brown, Butler, Coveney, de Jongh, Edwardes, Gore-Langton, Gross, Hagerty, Hewison, Macaulay, Morley, Nathan, Nightingale, Smith, Spencer, Taylor, Usher.

2002 "Reviews of Productions." *TR.* 1997; 17(4): 209-215. Lang.: Eng.

UK-England: London. 1997. ■*The Slow Drag* by Carson Kreitzer, dir by Lisa Forrell at the Freedom: rev by Abdulla, Andersen, Butler, de Jongh, Foss, Gross, Hagerty, Kingston, Morley, O'Farrell, Spencer, Taylor, Usher. *Under Glass* devised by Bouge-de-là and Andrew Dawson, dir by Dawson at BAC 2: rev by Cavendish, McPherson, Turpin. *St. Nicholas* by Conor McPherson, dir by McPherson at the Bush: rev by Billington, Butler, Coveney, Curtis, Gore-Langton, Gross, Hassell, Macaulay, Marmion, Morley, Nathan, Nightingale, Peter, Spencer, Taylor, Usher.

2003 "Reviews of Productions." *TR.* 1997; 17(4): 215-218. Lang.: Eng.

UK-England: London. 1997. ■*Ivan* by Fouad Zloof and Eva Lynn, dir by Hugh Beardesmore-Billings at the Riverside: rev by Bayley, Reade. *Inheritors* by Susan Glaspell, dir by Sam Walters at the Orange Tree: rev by Benedict, Billington, Curtis, Hewison, Kingston, McPherson, Stratton. *Get Out of Here* devised by Commotion, dir by Rick Zoltowski at BAC Main: rev by Cavendish, Gardner, Logan, Williams.

2004 "Reviews of Productions." *TR.* 1997; 17(4): 219-220. Lang.: Eng.

UK-England: London. 1997. ■*La Tulipe Noire* by Edward Kemp, from the novel by Alexandre Dumas, dir by Simon Bolton at the Turtle Key: rev by Marlowe, Stratton. *Sea of Faces* by Daniel Jamieson, dir by Nikki Sved at the Warehouse, Croydon: rev by Cavendish, Saddler. *Falstaff* by David Buck, from the novel by Robert Nye, dir by David Delve at the Grace: rev by Logan, Turpin.

2005 "Reviews of Productions." *TR.* 1997; 17(5): 235-242. Lang.: Eng.

UK-England: London. 1997. ■*Faust*, text by Mark Ravenhill from the work by Goethe, dir by Nick Philippou at the Lyric Studio: rev by Bassett, Coveney, de Jongh, Foss, Hanks, Hemming, Kingston, Peter, Stratton, Usher. *It Took More Than One Man* by Ivan Cartwright, dir by Brendan Murray at the Albany: rev by Cavendish, Tushingham. *Women on the Verge of HRT* by Marie Jones, dir by Pam Brighton at the Vaude-

DRAMA: —Performance/production

ville: rev by Billington, Brown, Butler, Cooke, Coveney, de Jongh, Foss, Gore-Langton, Gross, Hagerty, Macaulay, Nathan, Nightingale, Peter, Spencer, Stratton, Taylor, Treadwell, Usher.

2006 "Reviews of Productions." *TR*. 1997; 17(5): 243-247. Lang.: Eng.

UK-England: London. 1997. ▪*Golden Own Goal* by Paul Pavitt, dir by Ken McClymont at the Old Red Lion: rev by Christopher, Foss, Godfrey-Faussett: *The Message* by Nigel Charnock from texts by Tony Harrison, Fergal Keane, Primo Levi, H.H. Munro, Charles Resnikoff and William Shakespeare, dir by Charnock at the Lyric Hammersmith: rev by Cavendish, *Guardian* (unattributed), Kingston, McPherson, J. Parry, Shuttleworth, Stratton. *The Troubled Man* by Dazz Dean, dir by Colin Sinclair at the Etcetera: rev by Abdulla.

2007 "Reviews of Productions." *TR*. 1997; 17(9): 536-540. Lang.: Eng.

UK-England: London. 1997. ▪*The Mai* by Marina Carr, dir by Nicolas Kent at the Tricycle: rev by Billington, Coveney, de Jongh, Edwardes, Foss, Hanks, Hemming, Nathan, Nightingale, Peter, Spencer, Taylor, Woddis. *Easy* by Nicola McCartney, dir by McCartney at BAC 2: rev by McPherson, Turpin, Tushingham. *Absent Friends* by Alan Ayckbourn, dir by Michael Simkins at the Greenwich: rev by Curtis, Foss, Kingston, Logan, Shuttleworth.

2008 "Reviews of Productions." *TR*. 1997; 17(5): 248-254. Lang.: Eng.

UK-England: London. 1997. ▪*The Positive Hour* by April De Angelis, dir by Max Stafford-Clark at the Hampstead: rev by Bassett, Billington, Butler, Coveney, Curtis, Edwardes, Gross, Hassell, *Independent* (unattrib), Kingston, Nathan, Peter, Shuttleworth. *Autumn and Winter (Höst och vinter)* by Lars Norén, transl by Gunilla Anderman, dir by Ramin Gray at the Man in the Moon: rev by Cavendish, Logan. *The Little Comedy* and *Summer Share*, two one-act musicals, book and lyrics by Barry Harman, music by Keith Herrmann, dir by Steven Dexter at the Gielgud: rev by Abdulla, Benedict, Darvell, Gore-Langton, Gross, Hagerty, Nightingale, Spencer, Treadwell, Usher.

2009 "Reviews of Productions." *TR*. 1997; 17(5): 254-258. Lang.: Eng.

UK-England: London. 1997. ▪*Card Tricks and Close-Up Magic* devised by Jerry Sadowitz at the Etcetera: rev by Dessau, Games. *Birdy* by Naomi Wallace from the novel by William Wharton, dir by Kevin Knight at the Comedy: rev by Brown, Butler, Coveney, de Jongh, Gore-Langton, Gross, Hagerty, Hemming, Hewison, Logan, Nathan, Nightingale, Smith, Spencer, Usher. *The Mysteries* by Richard Williams, dir by Williams at the Arts: rev by Hassell, Hayden, Taylor.

2010 "Reviews of Productions." *TR*. 1997; 17(5): 259-262. Lang.: Eng.

UK-England: London. 1997. ▪*Viper's Opium* and *Road Movie* by Godfrey Hamilton, dir by Lorenzo Mele at the Drill Hall: rev by Abdulla, Cavendish, Kingston, Marlowe, Shuttleworth. *Being There with Peter Sellars* by Richard Braine, dir by David Grindley at the Pleasance: rev by Abdulla, Cavendish, Foss. *The Wolves* by Michael Punter, dir by Simon Usher at Bridewell: rev by Benedict, Cavendish, Gardner, McPherson, Taylor.

2011 "Reviews of Productions." *TR*. 1997; 17(5): 262-268. Lang.: Eng.

UK-England: London. 1997. ▪*Rabenthal* by Jorg Graser, transl by David McClintock, dir by Caroline Smith at Theatro Technis: rev by Godfrey-Faussett. In Extremis, Moments of Survival, short plays: *Bella's Tale, Janek's Tale*, and *Susan's Tale* compiled by Leona Heimfeld, *Eisgeist* by Peter Wolf, *You* by Bonnie Greer from *The Hassidic Tales of the Holocaust* by Yaffa Eliach, *Miracle in a Potato Field* compiled by Heimfeld from Maggie O'Kane's *Guardian* dispatches, *Green Rabbi* by Bernard Kops, dir by Heimfeld at the Young Vic Studio: rev by Cavendish, Gardner, Ives, Nathan, Tushingham. *Live and Kidding* by Maureen Lipman, dir by Alan Strachan at the Duchess: rev by Bassett, Benedict, Brown, Coveney, Dessau, Gross, Hagerty, Kingston, Logan, Macaulay, Nathan, Peter, Smith, Usher.

2012 "Reviews of Productions." *TR*. 1997; 17(5): 268-277. Lang.: Eng.

UK-England: London. 1997. ▪*'I Doubt It', Says Pauline* by D'Unbelievables (Jon Kenny and Pat Shortt), dir by Kenny and Shortt

at the Tricycle: rev by Christopher, Marlowe, Marmion. *Waking* by Lin Coghlan, dir by Abigail Morris at 21 Dean Street: rev by Billington, Curtis, Hassell, Hemming, Nathan, Nightingale, Spencer, Stratton, Taylor. *Lady in the Dark* by Moss Hart, lyrics by Ira Gershwin, music by Kurt Weill, dir by Francesca Zambello at the Lyttelton: rev by Billington, Butler, Coveney, de Jongh, Edwardes, Gore-Langton, Gross, Hagerty, Macaulay, Nathan, Nightingale, Peter, Smith, Spencer, Taylor, Usher.

2013 "Reviews of Productions." *TR*. 1997; 17(5): 277-282. Lang.: Eng.

UK-England: London. 1997. ▪*Tenerife* by Richard Hayton, dir by Alistair Barrie at the Duke of Cambridge: rev by Tushingham: *So Saddle Like a Horse Why Don't You?* by Will Harrison, dir by Paul Farrar at the White Bear: rev by Godfrey-Faussett. *Cymbeline* by William Shakespeare, dir by Adrian Noble for the RSC at the Royal Shakespeare, Stratford: rev by Billington, Brown, Butler, Coveney, de Jongh, Edwardes, Gore-Langton, Gross, Hagerty, Macaulay, Nathan, Nightingale, Peter, Spencer, Taylor, Woddis.

2014 "Reviews of Productions." *TR*. 1997; 17(5): 283-292. Lang.: Eng.

UK-England. 1997. ▪*Camino Real* by Tennessee Williams, dir by Steven Pimlott for the RSC at the Swan: rev by Billington, Butler, Coveney, de Jongh, Gore-Langton, Gross, Hagerty, Logan, Nathan, Nightingale, Peter, Spencer, Taylor, Usher, Woddis. *The Mysteries: Part One: The Creation, Part Two: The Passion* by Edward Kemp with Katie Mitchell, dir by Mitchell for the RSC at The Other Place, Stratford: rev by Billington, Butler, Coveney, Curtis, Edwardes, Gore-Langton, Macaulay, Nightingale, Peter, Spencer, Taylor.

2015 "Reviews of Productions." *TR*. 1997; 17(6): 338-340. Lang.: Eng.

UK-England: London. 1997. ▪*Raw Women and Cooked Men* based on 'A Lover's Discourse' by Roland Barthes, dir by Firenza Guidi at the Warehouse, Croydon: rev by Bayley, Marmion, McPherson. *The Fall of the House of Usherettes* by the Brittonioni Brothers (Chris and Tim Britton, and Ed Jobling) at the Lyric Studio: rev by Curtis, Kingston, Shuttleworth, Stevens. *The Boys Next Door* by Tom Griffin, dir by Sarah Esdaile at the Grace: rev by Cavendish.

2016 "Reviews of Productions." *TR*. 1997; 17(6): 311-316. Lang.: Eng.

UK-England: London. 1997. ▪*Attempts on Her Life* by Martin Crimp, dir by Tim Albery at the Royal Court Downstairs: rev by Billington, Butler, Coveney, de Jongh, Edwardes, Foss, Gross, Macaulay, Nightingale, Peter, Taylor, Usher. *Badfinger* by Simon Harris, dir by Michael Sheen at Donmar Warehouse: rev by Bassett, Coveney, Curtis, Foss, Gardner, Hemming, Kingston, Peter, Taylor, Treadwell, Tushingham. *Street Cries* by Mitch Binns with music by Moveable Feast, dir by Lynne Kendrick at the Camden People's: rev by Williams.

2017 "Reviews of Productions." *TR*. 1997; 17(6): 319-330. Lang.: Eng.

UK-England: London. 1997. ▪*In the Solitude of the Cotton Fields (Dans la solitude des champs de coton)* by Bernard-Marie Koltès, transl by Kimon Koufogiannis, dir by Koufogiannis at the Gate: rev by Bruce, Cavendish, Logan, Kingston, Murphy. *Waste* by Harley Granville-Barker, dir by Peter Hall at the Old Vic: rev by Billington, Brown, Butler, Coveney, de Jongh, Edwardes, Gross, Hagerty, Macaulay, Nathan, Nightingale, Peter, Sierz, Smith, Spencer, Taylor, Treadwell, Usher. *Cloud Nine* by Caryl Churchill, dir by Tom Cairns at the Old Vic: rev by Billington, Brown, Butler, Coveney, Darvell, de Jongh, Gore-Langton, Gross, Hagerty, Logan, Macaulay, Nathan, Nightingale, Peter, Spencer, Taylor, Treadwell, Usher.

2018 "Reviews of Productions." *TR*. 1997; 17(6): 341-346. Lang.: Eng.

UK-England: London. 1997. ▪*The Importance of Being Oscar* by Michael MacLiammoir, dir by Patrick Garland at the Savoy: rev by Billington, Butler, Coveney, de Jongh, Edwardes, Foss, Gross, Hagerty, Macaulay, Morley, Nathan, Nightingale, Peter, Spencer, Taylor, Usher. *The Fundraisers* by Tony Marchant, dir by Phil Willmott at the Finborough: rev by Marmion, Stevens, Turpin. *Tickets and Ties: The African Tale* by Sesan Ogunledun and Femi Elufowoju, Jr., dir by Elufowoju at Theatre Royal, Stratford East: rev by Abdulla, R.L. Parry.

DRAMA: —Performance/production

2019 "Reviews of Productions." *TR.* 1997; 17(6): 346-347. Lang.: Eng.

UK-England: London. 1997. ■*Rosmersholm* by Henrik Ibsen, transl by David Rudkin, dir by Jenny Lee at Wimbledon Studio: rev by McPherson. *Lickers and Kickers* by Emil Braginsky, transl by Julia Munrow, dir by Munrow at Etcetera: rev by Godfrey-Faussett, Turpin. *The Impressionist* devised by Mari Natsuki, dir by Natsuki at ICA: rev by Smith, Turpin.

2020 "Reviews of Productions." *TR.* 1997; 17(6): 348-351. Lang.: Eng.

UK-England: London. 1997. ■*Mourning Song* by Denise Wong and The Black Mime Theatre, dir by Wong at the Cochrane: rev by Gardner, Kingston, Stratton, Turpin, Williams. *The Comic Mysteries (Mistero Buffo)* by Dario Fo, transl by Ed Emery, dir by John Retallack at the Greenwich: rev by Bassett, Coveney, Curtis, Gardner, Hagerty, Hanks, Hemming, Nightingale, R.L. Parry, Reade. *The Outside* by Susan Glaspell, dir by Martin Wylde at the Orange Tree Room: rev by Kingston, McPherson.

2021 "Reviews of Productions." *TR.* 1997; 17(7): 409-417. Lang.: Eng.

UK-England: London. 1997. ■*Cigarettes and Chocolate* by Anthony Minghella, dir by Christopher G. Sandford at the Man in the Moon: rev by Bassett, Edwardes, Gardner, Gore-Langton, Kingston, Peter, Turpin, Williams. *Language Roulette* by Daragh Carville, dir by Tim Loane at the Bush: rev by Bassett, Butler, Coveney, Curtis, Gardner, Gross, Marlowe, Nightingale, Peter, Reade, Taylor. *Noise* by Alex Jones, dir by Mark Brickman at 21 Dean Street: rev by Curtis, Foss, Gardner, Hemming, Logan, Peter, Spencer, Taylor.

2022 "Reviews of Productions." *TR.* 1997; 17(6): 352-355. Lang.: Eng.

UK-England: London. 1997. ■*Honestly* by Hoipolloi Theatre with Mick Barnfather and Marine Benech, dir by Barnfather and Benech at the Young Vic Studio: rev by Godfrey-Faussett, Lavender, McPherson, Shuttleworth, Turpin, Usher. *Skank* by Steve Livermore, dir by Livermore at the Old Red Lion: rev by Christopher. *Much Revue About Nothing!* by Rexton Bunnett and Michael Lavine, dir by Philip George at King's Head: rev by Butler, Foss, Gross, Hagerty, Marmion, Nathan, Nightingale, Reade, Spencer. *Don't Ask for the Moon* by Martyn Edward Hesford, with additional material by Earl Grey, dir by Hesford at the Albany: rev by Cavendish.

2023 "Reviews of Productions." *TR.* 1997; 17(7): 379-388. Lang.: Eng.

UK-England: London. 1997. ■*Summer Begins* by David Eldridge, dir by Jonathan Lloyd at the Donmar Warehouse: rev by Bassett, Benedict, Butler, Coveney, Curtis, Foss, Gardner, Hagerty, Logan, Nightingale, Peter. *East Is East* by Ayub Khan-Din, dir by Kristine Landon-Smith at the Royal Court Downstairs: rev by Smith. *King Lear* by William Shakespeare, dir for the Royal National by Richard Eyre at the Cottesloe: rev by Bassett, Billington, Butler, Carlowe, Coveney, de Jongh, Gross, Hagerty, Hassell, Macaulay, Morley, Nightingale, Peter, Stratton, Taylor, Usher.

2024 "Reviews of Productions." *TR.* 1997; 17(7): 418-423. Lang.: Eng.

UK-England: London. 1997. ■*Oblomov* by Stephen Sharkey, dir by Erica Whyman at the Pleasance: rev by Cavendish, Godfrey-Faussett, R.L. Parry, Woddis. *Marlene* by Pam Gems, dir by Sean Mathias at the Lyric: rev by Brown, Burston, Butler, Coveney, Darvell, Gross, Hagerty, Morley, Murray, Nathan, Nightingale, Peter, Usher.

2025 "Reviews of Productions." *TR.* 1997; 17(7): 388-394. Lang.: Eng.

UK-England: London. 1997. ■*Ungrateful Dead* by Parv Bancil, dir by Harmage Singh Kalirai at the Watermans: rev by Marmion. *Rhinoceros* by Eugène Ionesco, transl by Derek Prouse, dir by Andrea Brooks at Riverside 3: rev by Abdulla. *Then Again.* a revue dir by Neil Bartlett at the Lyric Hammersmith: rev by Bassett, Benedict, Billington, Butler, Carlowe, Coveney, Foss, Games, Gross, Hagerty, Kingston, Marmion, Peter, Taylor, Usher. *The Art of Seduction* by Ranjit Bolt from *La Double Inconstance* by Marivaux, dir by David Hankinson at the Duke of Cambridge: rev by Cavendish, Tushingham.

2026 "Reviews of Productions." *TR.* 1997; 17(7): 395-401. Lang.: Eng.

UK-England: London. 1997. ■*Kings* adapt by Christopher Logue from Homer's *Iliad*, dir by Liane Aukin at the Tricycle: rev by Cavendish, Curtis, Gardner, Gore-Langton, Gross, Hanks, Hassell, Hemming, Kingston, Usher. *Gloomy Sunday: Rudi Seress's Farewell Performance*, a musical by Peter Mueller, dir by Caroline Smith at Theatro Technis: rev by Carlowe, Tushingham. *Lady Windermere's Fan* by Oscar Wilde, dir by Braham Murray at Theatre Royal, Haymarket: rev by Bassett, Benedict, Brown, Butler, Christopher, Coveney, Darvell, de Jongh, Gardner, Gross, Hagerty, Hemming, Logan, Morley, Nihgtingale, Taylor.

2027 "Reviews of Productions." *TR.* 1997; 17(8): 437-442. Lang.: Eng.

UK-England: London. 1997. ■*Halloween Night* by Declan Hughes, dir by Lynne Parker at Donmar Warehouse: rev by Butler, Clancy, Coveney, Curtis, Edwardes, Foss, Gardner, Gross, Macauley, Moroney, Spencer. *The Miser (L'Avare)* by Molière, transl by Alan Drury, dir by Robert Thorogood at the Etcetera: rev by Marmion. *Princess Sharon* by Andrzej Sadowski, adapt from Witold Gombrowicz' *Princess Yvonne (Iwona, Księżniczka Burgundia)* dir by Katarzyna Deszcz at the Purcell Room: rev by Cavendish, Gardner, Godfrey-Faussett, Lavender, Peter.

2028 "Reviews of Productions." *TR.* 1997; 17(8): 443-447. Lang.: Eng.

UK-England: London. 1997. ■*Antony and Cleopatra* by Shakespeare, dir by Carol Metcalfe at the Bridewell: rev by Albasini, Bayley, Cavendish, Taylor, Williams. *Captain of the Birds* by Edward Carey, dir by Louise Stafford Charles at the Young Vic Studio: rev by Stratton, Turpin. *The Power of Darkness (Vlast Tmy)* by Leo Tolstoj, transl by Anthony Clark, dir by Sean Holmes at the Orange Tree: rev by Bayley, Butler, Cavendish, Curtis, Hemming, McPherson, Spencer, Taylor.

2029 "Reviews of Productions." *TR.* 1997; 17(8): 458-464. Lang.: Eng.

UK-England: London. 1997. ■*The Tempest* by Shakespeare, dir by Richard Hurst at the Grace: rev by McPherson, Turpin. *Animal Farm* by George Orwell, adapt by Ian Woolridge, dir by Alan Lyddiard at the Young Vic: rev by Bassett, Benedict, Curtis, Godfrey-Faussett, Hemming, Kingston, McPherson. *Cracked* by Daniel Hill, dir by Terry Johnson at the Hampstead: rev by Billington, Booth, Butler, Coveney, de Jongh, Edwardes, Gross, Hagerty, Morley, Nathan, Nightingale, Peter, Shuttleworth, Spencer, Taylor, Usher.

2030 "Reviews of Productions." *TR.* 1997; 17(8): 447-457. Lang.: Eng.

UK-England: London. 1997. ■*Super-Beasts* by Emlyn Williams from the stories of Saki (H.H. Munro), dir by Dee Hart at the Jermyn Street: rev by Curtis, Foss, Kingston. *Tom and Clem* by Stephen Churchett, dir by Richard Wilson at the Aldwych: rev by Billington, Brown, Butler, Coveney, Deedes, de Jongh, Gore-Langton, Grant, Gross, Hagerty, Hassell, Morley, Nathan, Nightingale, Peter, Shuttleworth, Spencer, Taylor, Usher. *Stones of Kolin* by Judy Herman, dir by Jacqui Somerville at the New End: rev by Darvell, Nathan, Tushingham.

2031 "Reviews of Productions." *TR.* 1997; 17(8): 464-467. Lang.: Eng.

UK-England: London. 1997. ■*Oh Sweet Sita* by Ravi Kapoor, dir by Kapoor at the Oval House: rev by Gardner. *The Herbal Bed* by Peter Whelan, dir by Michael Attenborough, for the RSC at the Duchess: rev by Coveney, Davé, de Jongh, Hagerty, Morley, Murray, Nightingale, Peter, Stratton, Usher. *Find Me* by Olwen Wymark, dir by Clive Perrott at Pentameters: rev by Abdulla, Christopher.

2032 "Reviews of Productions." *TR.* 1997; 17(8): 468-474. Lang.: Eng.

UK-England: London. 1997. ■*The Goodbye Girl* by Neil Simon, music by Marvin Hamlisch, lyrics by Don Black, dir by Rob Bettinson at the Albery: rev by Brown, Butler, Coveney, de Jongh, Edwardes, Gardner, Gross, Hagerty, Macauley, Morley, Nathan, Nightingale, Peter, Smith, Spencer, Taylor, Usher. *70 Hill Lane* by Phelim McDermott, dir by McDermott at the Lyric Studio: rev by Marlowe. *King Ubu (Ubu Roi)* by Alfred Jarry, transl by Kenneth McLeish, dir by John Wright at the Gate: rev by Billington, Hemming, Kingston, Marmion, Smith.

DRAMA: —Performance/production

2033 "Reviews of Productions." *TR.* 1997; 17(8): 485-487. Lang.: Eng.

UK-England. 1997. ▪*The Admirable Crichton* by J.M. Barrie, dir by Michael Rudman at the Chichester Festival: rev by Curtis, Gore-Langton, Hagerty, Kingston, Peter, Shuttleworth, Spencer, Taylor. *The Amen Corner* by James Baldwin, dir by Paulette Randall at Theatre Royal, Bristol: rev by Martin, Morse.

2034 "Reviews of Productions." *TR.* 1997; 17(8): 474-482. Lang.: Eng.

UK-England: London. 1997. ▪*What's To Be Done with Algernon?* by Michael Allen, dir by David Lavender at the Warehouse, Croydon: rev by Foss, Logan. *The Caucasian Chalk Circle (Der Kaukasische Kreidekreis)* by Bertolt Brecht, transl by Frank McGuinness, dir by Frank McBurney for the Royal National at the Olivier: rev by Billington, Brown, Butler, Coveney, de Jongh, Gore-Langton, Macauley, Nightingale, Peter, Smith, Spencer, Stratton, Taylor, Wardle. *Under Milkwood* by Dylan Thomas and *Animal Farm* by George Orwell, adapt by Guy Masterson, both dir by Tony Boncza at the Arts: rev by Curtis, Godfrey-Faussett, Rampton.

2035 "Reviews of Productions." *TR.* 1997; 17(8): 483-484. Lang.: Eng.

UK-England: London. 1997. ▪*Waiting to Inhale* by Geoff Schumann, with additional material by Andrew Murrell, dir by Angie Le Mar at Theatre Royal, Stratford: rev by Christopher, Foss, Rampton. *The Man of Destiny* and *Annajanska, The Bolshevik Empress* by G.B. Shaw, dir by Massimiliano Farau at the Wimbledon Studio: rev by McPherson. *Heinrich Heine vs. Nikolai Gogol* by Tom Kempinski, dir by Kempinski at the New End: rev by Nathan.

2036 "Reviews of Productions." *TR.* 1997; 17(8): 492-505. Lang.: Eng.

UK-England: London. 1997. ▪*The Stronger (Den Starkare)* by August Strindberg, transl by Michael Meyer and *The Lover* by Harold Pinter, dir by Michael Billington at BAC Main: rev by Billington, Daldry, Marlowe, Morley, Noble, Ravenhill. *Traveller Without Luggage (Le Voyageur sans bagage)* by Jean Anouilh, transl by John Whiting, dir by Nicholas de Jongh at BAC Main: rev by Daldry, de Jongh, Edwardes, Herring, Kelly, Marlowe, Morley. *Albertine in Five Times (Albertine en cinq temps)* by Michel Tremblay, dir by Jeremy Kingston at BAC 1: rev by Burns, Doughty, Hall, Horne, Kingston, Marlowe, Stratton. *The Shoe Shop of Desire* by Robert Young, dir by James Christopher at BAC 2: rev by Christopher, Croft, de Jongh, Dromgoole, Marlowe, Nightingale, Posner, Stafford-Clark.

2037 "Reviews of Productions." *TR.* 1997; 17(9): 523-532. Lang.: Eng.

UK-England: London. 1997. ▪*Bailegangaire* by Tom Murphy, dir by James Macdonald at the Royal Court Upstairs: rev by Butler, Coveney, de Jongh, Edwardes, Gardner, Hemming, Nightingale, Peter, Spencer, Taylor, Wardle, Woddis. *Mad for Love (La Dama boba)* by Lope de Vega, transl John Farndon, dir by Farndon at the Riverside 3: rev by Christopher, McPherson, Turpin. *Out Cry* by Tennessee Williams, dir by Timothy Walker at the Lyric Hammersmith: rev by Billington, Brown, Butler, Coveney, Curtis, Hagerty, Hassell, Kingston, Macauley, Morley, Peter, Spencer, Stratton, Taylor, Wardle.

2038 "Reviews of Productions." *TR.* 1997; 17(9): 532-535. Lang.: Eng.

UK-England: London. 1997. ▪*Goldmines* by Lavinia Murray, dir by Nadia Molinari at the Etcetera: rev by Abdulla, Loup-Nolan. *Frankly Scarlett* by Peter Morris and Philip George, dir by George at the King's Head: rev by Coveney, Foss, Gross, Hagerty, Logan, Morley, Nightingale, Peter, Turpin, Usher. *Last Bus from Bradford* by Tim Fountain, dir by Fountain at Chelsea Centre: rev by Cavendish, Turpin, Williams.

2039 "Reviews of Productions." *TR.* 1997; 17(9): 541-546. Lang.: Eng.

UK-England. 1997. ▪*Tucson* by Lisa Perotti, dir by Janet Gordon at the Finborough: rev by Marmion, McPherson. *Doña Rosita the Spinster (Doña Rosita la Soltera)* by Federico García Lorca, transl by Peter Oswald, dir by Phyllida Lloyd at the Almeida: rev by Bassett, Billington, Coveney, Davé, de Jongh, Edwardes, Gore-Langton, Gross, Hagerty, Hanks, Hewison, Macauley, Morley, Nathan, Nightingale, Taylor, Usher. *Hungry for It* by Hi Ching, dir by Ching at the Albany, Deptford: rev by Tushingham.

2040 "Reviews of Productions." *TR.* 1997; 17(9): 547-550. Lang.: Eng.

UK-England: London. 1997. ▪*Children in Uniform* by Barbara Burnham, adapt from *Mädchen in Uniform* by Christa Winsloe, dir by Sean O'Connor at BAC 1: rev by Abdulla, Nathan, Turpin, Usher, Williams. *Mad Dog Killer Leper Fiend* by Tim Plester, dir by Robert Pepper at the Man in the Moon: rev by Marmion, Stevens, Turpin. *Love and Understanding* by Joe Penhall, dir by Mike Bradwell at the Bush: rev by Billen, Billington, Christopher, de Jongh, Hanks, Logan, Nathan, Peter, Taylor, Woddis.

2041 "Reviews of Productions." *TR.* 1997; 17(10): 583-586. Lang.: Eng.

UK-England: London. 1997. ▪*Fat Janet Is Dead* by Simon Smith, dir by Jessica Dromgoole at the Warehouse, Croydon: rev by Christopher, Foss, Marmion, Turpin. *The People Downstairs* by Deirdre Strath, dir by Rufus Norris at the Young Vic Studio: rev by Foss, Stratton, Turpin. *The Cracked Comic* by Stewart Permutt, dir by Sonia Fraser at the New End: rev by Abdulla, Carlowe, Curtis, Foss, Turpin.

2042 "Reviews of Productions." *TR.* 1997; 17(9): 551-559. Lang.: Eng.

UK-England: London. 1997. ▪*Spring Awakening (Frühlings Erwachen)* by Frank Wedekind, dir by Margarete Forsyth at BAC: rev by Curtis, R.L. Parry, Stratton, Turpin. *Gabriel* by Moira Buffini, dir by Fiona Buffini at 21 Dean Street: rev by Benedict, Butler, Christopher, Curtis, Smith, Tushingham. *Master Class* by Terrence McNally, dir by Leonard Foglia at the Queens: rev by Billen, Billington, Brown, Butler, de Jongh, Gore-Langton, Gross, Hagerty, Hassell, Lister, Logan, Macauley, Nightingale, Peter, Spencer, Taylor, Usher.

2043 "Reviews of Productions." *TR.* 1997; 17(9): 559, 569-570. Lang.: Eng.

UK-England. 1997. ▪*Whale Riding Weather* by Bryden MacDonald, dir by Graham Callan at the Drill Hall: rev by Benedict, Godfrey-Faussett, Marlowe. *Lady Windermere's Fan* by Oscar Wilde, dir by Richard Cottrell at the Chichester Festival: rev by Christopher, Curtis, Hewison, Shuttleworth.

2044 "Reviews of Productions." *TR.* 1997; 17(10): 586-593. Lang.: Eng.

UK-England: London. 1997. ▪*The Duel* by Tim Marchant, based on Čechov's short story as transl by Roger Ringrose, dir by Marchant at the Lyric Studio: rev by Christopher, Stratton, Williams. *The Seagull (Čajka)* by Čechov, version Tom Stoppard from a literal transl by Joanna Wright, dir by Peter Hall at the Old Vic: rev by Billington, Brown, Butler, Coveney, Davé, de Jongh, Gross, Hagerty, Kellaway, Morley, Murray, Nathan, Nightingale, Peter, Reade, Spencer, Taylor. *Restless Heart (La Sauvage)* by Jean Anouilh, transl by Lucienne Hill, dir by Amy Kassai at Riverside 3: rev by Tushingham.

2045 "Reviews of Productions." *TR.* 1997; 17(10): 594-601. Lang.: Eng.

UK-England: London. 1997. ▪*An Evening with Jack Dee* by Dee at the Gielgud: rev by Christopher, Davis, Dessau, Games, Hagerty, Rampton, Thompson, Wareham. *Life Is a Dream (La Vida es sueño)* by Calderón, transl by Edward Fitzgerald, dir by Kenneth McClellan and Trevor Rawlins at the Grace: rev by Godfrey-Faussett, McPherson. *The Fix* book and lyrics by John Dempsey, music by Dana P. Rowe, dir by Sam Mendes, at the Donmar Warehouse: rev by Billington, Brown, Coveney, de Jongh, Edwardes, Gore-Langton, Hagerty, Kellaway, Macauley, Morley, Nathan, Nightingale, Peter, Smith, Spencer, Taylor. *Marcel Marceau* at the Royal Festival Hall: rev by Lavender.

2046 "Reviews of Productions." *TR.* 1997; 17(10): 602-610. Lang.: Eng.

UK-England: London. 1997. ▪*My Mother Said I Never Should* by Charlotte Keatley, dir by Dominic Cooke at the Young Vic: rev by Abdulla, Christopher, Curtis, C. Donald, M. Donald, Marlowe, Murray, Sierz, Turpin. *A Glass of Water* by Ljudmila Petruševskaja, transl by Stephen Mulrine, dir by Phil Tinline at the Orange Tree Room: rev by McPherson. *Beauty and the Beast* book by Linda Woolverton, music by Alan Menken, lyrics by Tim Rice and Howard Ashman, dir by Robert Jess Roth at the Dominion: rev by Billington, Brown, Coveney, de Jongh, Gross, Hagerty, Kellaway, Logan, Macauley, Morley, Nathan, Nightingale, Peter, Smith, Spencer, Taylor.

DRAMA: —Performance/production

2047   "Reviews of Productions." *TR*. 1997; 17(10): 610-612. Lang.: Eng.

UK-England: London. 1997. ■*Three Sisters (Tri sestry)* by Čechov, transl by Michael Frayn, dir by Lucy Pittman-Wallace at Southwark Playhouse: rev by Curtis, Edwardes. *A Little Satire on the 1997 General Election* by Gregory Motton, dir by Motton and David Farr at the Gate: rev by Christopher, Curtis, McPherson, Stratton. *Black Dove* by Robin Keys, dir by Ken McClymont at the Old Red Lion: rev by Christopher, Foss, Godfrey-Faussett.

2048   "Reviews of Productions." *TR*. 1997; 17(10): 613-623. Lang.: Eng.

UK-England: London. 1997. ■*Marat/Sade* by Peter Weiss, transl by Geoffrey Skelton, verse adaptation by Adrian Mitchell, dir by Jeremy Sams for the Royal National at the Olivier: rev by Billington, Brown, Butler, Coveney, de Jongh, Edwardes, Gore-Langton, Gross, Hagerty, Kellaway, Macauley, Marlowe, Nathan, Nightingale, Peter, Spencer, Taylor. *Steaming* by Nell Dunn, dir by Ian Brown at the Piccadilly: rev by Benedict, Brown, Butler, Coveney, de Jongh, Foss, Gardner, Gore-Langton, Gross, Hagerty, Hemming, Kellaway, Logan, Morley, Nathan, Nightingale, Peter, Spencer. *The Yeats Season* 5 Plays by W.B. Yeats: *The Words Upon the Window-Pane* and *Purgatory* dir by Diana Maxwell, *On Baile's Strand, The Dreaming of the Bones* and *The Cat and the Moon* dir by Seamus Newham at the Pentameters: rev by Godfrey-Faussett, Marmion, R.L. Parry, Taylor.

2049   "Reviews of Productions." *TR*. 1997; 17(10): 623-630. Lang.: Eng.

UK-England: London. 1997. ■*Da* by Hugh Leonard, dir by Denis Quilligan at the White Bear: rev by Cavendish, Godfrey-Faussett. *Prayers of Sherkin* by Sebastian Barry, dir by John Dove at the Old Vic: rev by Bassett, Billington, Butler, Christopher, Coveney, Curtis, Edwardes, Gore-Langton, Gross, Hassell, Kingston, Macauley, Nathan, Peter, Taylor. *Titus Andronicus* by Shakespeare, performed by the National Theatre of Craiova in Romanian, dir by Silviu Purcarete at the Lyric Hammersmith: rev by Billington, Butler, Christopher, Curtis, Gore-Langton, Kingston, Macauley, Peter, Taylor.

2050   "Reviews of Productions." *TR*. 1997; 17(11): 683, 686-688. Lang.: Eng.

UK-England. 1997. ■*The Crime* by Doug Rollins and *Now There's Just the Three of Us* by Michael Weller, dir by Rollins at the Man in the Moon: rev by Marlowe. *The Cherry Orchard (Višněvyj sad)* by Čechov, a new version by Janet Suzman from the South African adapt by Roger Martin, dir by Suzman at the Birmingham Rep: rev by Benedict, A. Billen, Butler, Christopher, Coveney, Peter, Shuttleworth, Spencer.

2051   "Reviews of Productions." *TR*. 1997; 17(10): 631-640. Lang.: Eng.

UK-England. 1997. ■*The Spanish Tragedy* by Thomas Kyd, dir by Michael Boyd for the RSC at the Swan: rev by Billington, Curtis, Grant, Hagerty, Macauley, Nightingale, Peter, Taylor. *Hamlet* by Shakespeare, dir by Matthew Warchus for the RSC at Theatre Royal, Stratford: rev by Billen, Billington, Brown, Butler, de Jongh, Gore-Langton, Grant, Gross, Hagerty, Macauley, Nathan, Nightingale, Peter, Spencer, Taylor, Treadwell.

2052   "Reviews of Productions." *TR*. 1997; 17(11): 663-666. Lang.: Eng.

UK-England: London. 1997. ■*A Midsummer Night's Dream* by Shakespeare, dir by Niall Henry at Riverside 2: rev by Cavendish, Clancy, Curtis. *Throwaway* by Danny Miller, dir by Kate Williams at the Theatre Royal, Stratford East: rev by Bassett, Marmion, Nathan. *Beach Blanket Babylon* by Steve Silver, dir by Kenny Mazlowe at the Arts: rev by Benedict, Christopher, Edwardes, Foss, Thorncroft.

2053   "Reviews of Productions." *TR*. 1997; 17(11): 666-670. Lang.: Eng.

UK-England: London. 1997. ■*The Last Threads* by Ann Kerr, dir by David Peacock at the Machine Room: rev by Godfrey-Faussett. *People on the River* by Judy Upton, dir by Lisa Goldman at the Finborough: rev by Gardner, McPherson, Turpin, Tushingham. *A Midsummer Night's Dream* by Shakespeare, dir by Rachel Kavanaugh at the Open Air, Regent's Park: rev by Abdulla, Bassett, Billen, Brown, Butler, Cavendish, Coveney, Gross, Hassell, Kingston, Nathan, Peter.

2054   "Reviews of Productions." *TR*. 1997; 17(11): 671-673. Lang.: Eng.

UK-England: London. 1997. ■*Albert Camus, What's the Score?* by Nick Whitfield and Wes Williams, dir by Williams at the Lyric Studio: rev by Curtis, Marmion, McPherson, Turpin. *The Birds (Ornithes)* by Aristophanes, adapt by Stephen Greenhorn from transl by Michael Brunstrom, dir by Gaynor Macfarlane at the Gate: rev by Christopher, Curtis, Edwardes, Gardner, Hewison, Marlowe. *The Woman Who Thought She Was a Dog* by Nick Joseph, dir by Brennan Street at BAC 2: rev by Abdulla, Davé.

2055   "Reviews of Productions." *TR*. 1997; 17(11): 674-681. Lang.: Eng.

UK-England: London. 1997. ■*Closer* by Patrick Marber, dir by Marber for the Royal National at the Cottesloe: rev by Benedict, A. Billen, N. Billen, Billington, Brown, Butler, Coveney, Curtis, Edwardes, Gross, Hagerty, Kingston, Macauley, Nathan, Peter, Smith, Spencer. *Skeleton* by Tanika Gupta, dir by Jonathan Lloyd at 21 Dean Street: rev by Billington, Butler, Curtis, Kingston, R.L. Parry, Spencer, Taylor, Tushingham. *Not Just an Asian Babe* by Parminder Sekhon and Shakila Maan, dir by James Neale-Kennerly at the Etcetera: rev by Godfrey-Faussett.

2056   "Reviews of Productions." *TR*. 1997; 17(11): 682-683. Lang.: Eng.

UK-England: London. 1997. ■*Amphitryon* by Molière, adapt by David Cottis, dir by Cottis at the Etcetera: rev by Godfrey-Faussett. *Coffee* by Edward Bond at Royal Court Upstairs: rev by Turpin. *Someone Whistled* by Benjamin Till, dir by Till at the Pleasance: rev by Cavendish.

2057   "Reviews of Productions." *TR*. 1997; 17(12): 707-714. Lang.: Eng.

UK-England: London. 1997. ■*Damn Yankees* by George Abbott and Douglass Wallop, lyrics and music by Richard Adler and Jerry Ross, dir by Jack O'Brien at the Adelphi: rev by Benedict, Billington, Brown, Butler, Christopher, Coveney, Curtis, Foss, Grant, Gross, Hagerty, Morley, Nathan, Nightingale, Peter, Spencer, Taylor. *A Passionate Englishman* by Kate Glover, dir by Amanda Hill at the Hen & Chickens: rev by Tushingham. *The Censor* by Anthony Neilson, dir by Neilson at the Royal Court Downstairs: rev by Christopher, Coveney, *Daily Telegraph* (unattrib), Gross, Kingston, Macauley, Marmion, Peter, Smith.

2058   "Reviews of Productions." *TR*. 1997; 17(12): 760-765. Lang.: Eng.

UK-England. 1997. ■*Nocturne for Lovers* by Bruno Villien, transl by Gavin Lambert, dir by Kado Kostzer at the Chichester Minerva: rev by Bassett, Gardner, Kingston, Marmion, Morley, Peter, Shuttleworth. *Blithe Spirit* by Noël Coward, dir by Tim Luscombe at the Chichester Festival: rev by Butler, Coveney, de Jongh, Gardner, Gore-Langton, Gross, Hagerty, Nathan, Nightingale, Shuttleworth, Spencer, Taylor.

2059   "Reviews of Productions." *TR*. 1997; 17(12): 714-721. Lang.: Eng.

UK-England: London. 1997. ■*Dearly Beloved* book and lyrics by Robert Styles, music by Timothy Higgs, dir by Styles, *The Great Big Radio Show* a musical by Philip Glassborow, dir by Angela Hardcastle, and *Hogarth*, music and lyrics by David Malin and Nick Hogarth, book by Mark Eden, dir by Clive Paget at the Bridewell: rev by Foss. *Somewhere* by the Pet Shop Boys (Neil Tennant and Chris Lowe), dir by Sam Taylor-Wood at the Savoy: rev by Barber, Cheal, Clark, Dalton, Flett, Miller, O'Sullivan, Thorncroft. *Voices from Theresienstadt* by Ellen Foyn Bruun and Bente Kahan, transl by Dahlia Pfeffer and David Keir Wright, dir by Foyn Bruun at the New End: rev by Abdulla, Broughton, Nathan, Stevens.

2060   "Reviews of Productions." *TR*. 1997; 17(12): 721-730. Lang.: Eng.

UK-England: London. 1997. ■*Life's a Dream (La Vida es sueño)* by Calderón, transl by Adrian Mitchell and John Barton, dir by Ruth Levin at the Old Red Lion: rev by Godfrey-Faussett. *The Winter's Tale* by Shakespeare, dir by David Freeman at Shakespeare's Globe: rev by Billington, Butler, Curtis, Edwardes, Gross, Hassell, Macauley, Nightingale, Spencer. *Henry V* by Shakespeare, dir by Richard Olivier at Shakespeare's Globe: rev by Billington, Brown, Butler, Clapp, Coveney, Gross, Hagerty, Macauley, Marmion, Morley, Nathan, Nightingale, Peter, Sierz, Smith, Spencer, Taylor.

DRAMA: —Performance/production

2061 "Reviews of Productions." *TR.* 1997; 17(12): 731-733. Lang.: Eng.

UK-England: London. 1997. ■*What the Butler Saw* by Joe Orton, dir by Ewan Marshall at the Oval House: rev by Logan. *Flyin' West* by Pearl Cleage, dir by Yvonne Brewster at the Drill Hall: rev by Cavendish, Christopher, McPherson, Woddis. *Love Me Slender* by Vanessa Brooks, dir by Auriol Smith at the Orange Tree: rev by Abdulla, Billington, Christopher, McPherson.

2062 "Reviews of Productions." *TR.* 1997; 17(12): 734-744. Lang.: Eng.

UK-England: London. 1997. ■*All Things Considered* by Ben Brown, dir by Alan Strachan at the Hampstead: rev by Benedict, Billington, Butler, Coveney, Curtis, Edwardes, Gross, Hagerty, Morley, Nathan, Nightingale, Peter, Smith, Spencer, Taylor. *Always*, musical by William May and Jason Sprague, add'l book by Frank Hauser, dir by Hauser and Thommie Walsh at the Victoria Palace: rev by Brown, Butler, Clapp, Coveney, Curtis, Darvell, Edwardes, Gardner, Gore-Langton, Gross, Hagerty, Hewison, Macauley, Morley, Nathan, Nightingale, Spencer, Taylor. *After October* by Rodney Ackland, dir by Keith Baxter at the Greenwich: rev by Billington, Butler, Clapp, Foss, Logan.

2063 "Reviews of Productions." *TR.* 1997; 17(12): 745-749. Lang.: Eng.

UK-England: London. 1997. ■*Live from Boerassic Park* by Pieter-Dirk Uys, dir by Uys at the Tricycle: rev by Cowan, Dessau, Edwardes, Hewison, Nightingale, Rampton, Stevens, S. Taylor. *All's Well That Ends Well* by Shakespeare, dir by Helena Kaut-Howson at the Open Air, Regent's Park: rev by Brown, Coveney, Curtis, Davé, Edwardes, Gore-Langton, Hagerty, Hanks, Nightingale, Spencer. *An Error in Judgement* by the Strathcona Theatre Company, dir by Ann Cleary and Ian McCurrach at the Young Vic Studio: rev by Stratton.

2064 "Reviews of Productions." *TR.* 1997; 17(12): 750-756. Lang.: Eng.

UK-England: London. 1997. ■*The Winter's Tale* by William Shakespeare, dir by Mike Alfreds at the Lyric Hammersmith: rev by Bassett, Benedict, Gardner, Kingston, Marlowe, Peter, Stratton, Turpin. *Ghosts (Gengangere)* by Ibsen, dir by Mike Alfreds at the Lyric Hammersmith: rev by Bassett, Benedict, Hassell, Kingston, Marmion, Peter, Stratton, Turpin. *Wishbones* by Lucinda Coxon, dir by Simon Usher at the Bush: rev by Butler, de Jongh, Gardner, Gross, Logan, Nathan, Nightingale, Peter, Shuttleworth, Spencer, Williams.

2065 "Reviews of Productions." *TR.* 1997; 17(12): 759. Lang.: Eng.

UK-England: London. 1997. ■*In the Jungle of Cities (Im Dickicht der Städe)* by Brecht, transl by Gerhard Nelhaus, dir by Mehmet Ergen at Southwark Playhouse: rev by Logan. *The Silent Time* by Rhiannon Tyse, dir by Timothy Hughes at the Brockley Jack: rev by Godfrey-Faussett, Woddis. *Me and My Friend* by Gillian Plowman, dir by Dawn Lintern at the White Bear: rev by Abdulla.

2066 "Reviews of Productions." *TR.* 1997; 17(12): 779-785. Lang.: Eng.

UK-England: London. 1997. ■*The Wood Demon (Lešji)* by Čechov, transl by Nicholas Saunders and Frank Dwyer, dir by Anthony Clark at the Playhouse: rev by Billington, Butler, Clapp, Coveney, de Jongh, Edwardes, Foss, Gore-Langton, Gross, Hagerty, Murray, Nathan, Nightingale, Peter, Spencer, Taylor. *The Twilight of the Golds* by Jonathan Tolins, dir by Polly James at the Arts: rev by Bassett, de Jongh, Foss, Hagerty, Hewison, Kingston, Morley, Nathan, Shuttleworth, Stratton, Taylor. *As You Like It* by Shakespeare, dir by Robert Shaw at the Prince: rev by R.L. Parry.

2067 "Reviews of Productions." *TR.* 1997; 17(13): 786-797. Lang.: Eng.

UK-England: London. 1997. ■*Amy's View* by David Hare, dir by Richard Eyre at the Lyttelton: rev by Billington, Brown, Butler, Clapp, Coveney, Edwardes, Gore-Langton, Gross, Hagerty, Macauley, Morley, Nathan, Nightingale, Peter, Sierz, Smith, Spencer, Taylor, Woddis. *The Blue Garden* by Peter Moffat, dir by Ted Craig at the Warehouse, Croydon: rev by Basset, Billington, Christopher, Foss, Godfrey-Faussett, Turpin. *Bread and Water* by Chris Ballance, *Baked Alaska* by Michael Bourdages, *Love Bites* by Dominic Leggett, *Hello Pizza* by Anthony Teague, *False Feeding* by Mark O'Thomas and *Fishy Fingers* by Alison

Watt, dir by Mark Brickman for Soho Theatre Co. at the Soho: rev by Cavendish, Christopher, Foss, Taylor.

2068 "Reviews of Productions." *TR.* 1997; 17(13): 798-803. Lang.: Eng.

UK-England: London. 1997. ■*Elvis—The Musical* by Jack Good and Ray Cooney, dir by Keith Strachan and Carole Todd at the Piccadilly: rev by Gore-Langton, Hassell, Stratton. *The Maids (Les Bonnes)* by Jean Genet, transl by David Rudkin, dir by John Crowley at Donmar Warehouse: rev by Bassett, Benedict, Butler, Clapp, Coveney, de Jongh, Gore-Langton, Gross, Hagerty, Hemming, Hewison, Logan, Morley, Nathan, Nightingale, Stratton, Woddis. *Inherit the Wind* by Jerome Lawrence and Robert E. Lee, dir by Phil Willmott at BAC Courtyard: rev by Logan, McPherson, Turpin.

2069 "Reviews of Productions." *TR.* 1997; 17(13): 806-814. Lang.: Eng.

UK-England: London. 1997. ■*Shopping and Fucking* by Mark Ravenhill, dir by Max Stafford-Clark at the Gielgud: rev by Billington, Butler, Clapp, Coveney, Curtis, Davé, Grant, Gross, Macauley, Nathan, Nightingale, Sierz, Spencer. *Waiting for Godot (En attendant Godot)* by Samuel Beckett, dir by Peter Hall at the Old Vic: rev by Billington, Brown, Butler, Clapp, Coveney, de Jongh, Edwardes, Gore-Langton, Gross, Hassell, Hewison, Macauley, Morley, Nathan, Nightingale, Spencer, Taylor. *Teenage Vitriol* by Justin Chubb, dir by Paul Jepson at the Finborough: rev by Marmion, McPherson.

2070 "Reviews of Productions." *TR.* 1997; 17(13): 815-820. Lang.: Eng.

UK-England: London. 1997. ■*Skylight* by David Hare, dir by Richard Eyre at the Vaudeville: rev by Benedict, Brown, Coveney, Curtis, Edwardes, Gore-Langton, Gross, Hassell, Hewison, Morley, Nathan, Nightingale, Spencer. *Monsters* by Martin Green, dir by Green at the Grace: rev by Abdulla: *The Seven Sacraments of Nicolas Poussin* by Neil Bartlett, dir by Bartlett at the Royal London Hospital: rev by Billington, Curtis, Feaver, Hewison, Kingston, O'Farrell, Shuttleworth, Spencer, Woddis.

2071 "Reviews of Productions." *TR.* 1997; 17(13/Suppl): 2-6. Lang.: Eng.

UK-England: London. 1997. ■London International Festival of Theatre: *Oraculos* by Enrique Vargas, dir by Vargas at The Former Coach Station: rev by Albasini, Coveney, Curtis, Gardner, Spencer, Stratton. *Journey to the East* by Zuni Icosahedron (Hong Kong) at ICA: rev by Nightingale, Spencer, Taylor, Woddis. *K'Far* by Joshua Sobol, dir by Yevgeny Arye for the Gesher Theatre at the Lyric, Hammersmith: rev by Bassett, Kingston, Lavender, Macauley, Nathan, Peter, Turpin.

2072 "Reviews of Productions." *TR.* 1997; 17(13): 821-822, 831-835. Lang.: Eng.

UK-England. 1997. ■*Permanent Brain Damage* by Richard Foreman, dir by Foreman at the Royal Festival Hall: rev by Cavendish, Curtis. *It's a Slippery Slope* by Spalding Gray at Royal Festival Hall: rev by Davis. *Ivor Cutler* at Queen Elizabeth Hall: rev by Games. *What Ever* by Heather Woodbury, dir by Woodbury at the Purcell Room: rev by Hanks. *Tallulah* by Sandra Ryan Heyward, dir by Michael Rudman, at the Chichester Minerva: rev by Butler, Clapp, Coveney, de Jongh, Gore-Langton, Gross, Hagerty, Morley, Nathan, Nightingale, Smith, Spencer, Taylor, Thorncroft, Wark.

2073 "Reviews of Productions." *TR.* 1997; 17(13/Suppl): 7-9. Lang.: Eng.

UK-England: London. 1997. ■London International Festival of Theatre: *The Geography of Haunted Places* by Josephine Wilson, dir by Erin Hefferon at the Royal Court Upstairs: rev by Bassett, Gardner, Turpin, Woddis. *The 7 Stages of Grieving* by Wesley Enoch and Deborah Mailman, dir by Enoch at BAC: rev by Stratton, Woddis. *A Little More Light (Un Peu Plus de Lumière)* by Eric Noel, pyrotechnical theatre show dir by Christophe Bertonneau at Battersea Park: rev by Gardner, Woddis. *Khol Do* by Maya Krishna Rao, dir by Rao at BAC: rev by Shuttleworth. *The Feast of the Five Senses (La Feria de los cinco sentidos)* by Alicia Rios, dir by Rios at BAC: rev by Gardner, Shuttleworth.

2074 "Reviews of Productions." *TR.* 1997; 17(13/Suppl): 9-13. Lang.: Eng.

UK-England: London. 1997. ■London International Festival of Theatre: *Zero Hour (Stunde Null)* by Christoph Marthaler, dir by Marthaler

DRAMA: —Performance/production

at Queen Elizabeth Hall: rev by Billington, Kingston, Taylor, Woddis. *Things Fall Apart* by Biyi Bandele from the novel by Chinua Achebe, dir by Chuck Mike at the Royal Court Upstairs: rev by Cavendish, Coveney, Stevens. *Cirque Ici* dir and perf by Johann Le Guillerm at Clapham Common: rev by Clapp, Smith, Tushingham, Woddis.

2075   "Reviews of Productions." *TR.* 1997; 17(14): 845-849. Lang.: Eng.

UK-England: London. 1997. ■*King Lear* by Shakespeare, dir by Helena Kaut-Howson at the Young Vic: rev by de Jongh, Foss, Hemming, Kingston, Sierz, Stratton, Woddis. *Candide* by Murray Gold, adapt from Voltaire, dir by David Farr at the Gate: rev by Albasini, Curtis, Edwardes, Gross, Hewison, Nightingale, Sierz, Taylor, Williams. *Drinking in Circles* by Robert William Sherwood, dir by Michael Kingsbury at the White Bear: rev by Cavendish, Shuttleworth.

2076   "Reviews of Productions." *TR.* 1997; 17(13/Suppl): 13-18. Lang.: Eng.

UK-England: London. 1997. ■London International Festival of Theatre: *Periodo Villa Villa* realised by Fabio D'Aquila, perf by De La Guarda at Three Mills Island: rev by Bassett, Conrad, Gardner, Hemming, Renton, Stratton, Viddi, Williams. *I Was Real—Documents* by Saburo Teshigawara, dir by Teshigawara at Queen Elizabeth Hall: rev by I. Brown, Mackrell, Percival. *Ramzy Abdul Majd* adapt by George Ibrahim from *Sizwe Bansi Is Dead* by Athol Fugard, dir by Mohammad Bakri at Royal Court Upstairs: rev by Curtis, Nightingale.

2077   "Reviews of Productions." *TR.* 1997; 17(13/Suppl): 19. Lang.: Eng.

UK-England: London. 1997. ■London International Festival of Theatre: *This Is a Chair*, scenes by Caryl Churchill, dir by Stephen Daldry at the Royal Court Downstairs: rev by Billington, Kingston, Spencer, *Time Out* (unattrib). *Tides of Night* by Ghasir El-Leil, dir by Hassan El-Geretly at the Royal Court Upstairs: rev by Woddis.

2078   "Reviews of Productions." *TR.* 1997; 17(14): 850-861. Lang.: Eng.

UK-England: London. 1997. ■*The Provok'd Wife* by Sir John Vanbrugh, dir by Lindsay Posner at the Old Vic: rev by Billington, Brown, Butler, Clapp, Coveney, de Jongh, Foss, Gore-Langton, Gross, Hagerty, Hewison, Logan, Morley, Nathan, Nightingale, Shuttleworth, Spencer, Taylor. *Israel* by Michael J. Austin, dir by Peter Moreton at the Man in the Moon: rev by Carlowe, Marmion. *Grace Note* by Samuel Adamson, dir by Dominic Dromgoole at the Old Vic: rev by Benedict, Billington, Butler, Clapp, Coveney, de Jongh, Gore-Langton, Gross, Hagerty, Hemming, Hewison, Morley, Nathan, Nightingale, Smith, Spencer, Stratton.

2079   "Reviews of Productions." *TR.* 1997; 17(14): 869-870. Lang.: Eng.

UK-England: London. 1997. ■*Ready or Not* by Robert McKewley and Adeshegun Ikoli, dir by Jo Martin at Theatre Royal, Stratford East: rev by Foss, Kingston, Marmion, Tushingham. *She Knows, You Know!* by Jean Fergusson, dir by Christopher Wren at the Bridewell: rev by Darvell, Marmion. *Soldiers Dancing* by Trevor Walker, dir by Walker at the Onion Shed, SW9: rev by Logan.

2080   "Reviews of Productions." *TR.* 1997; 17(14): 861-868. Lang.: Eng.

UK-England: London. 1997. ■*1000 Fine Lines* by Emilia di Girolamo, dir by Charlotte Conquest at the Machine Room: rev by Stratton. *Summer Holiday* by Michael Gyngell and Mark Haddigan, songs by Peter Myers, Ronnie Cass et al, dir by Ultz at Labatt's Apollo: rev by Baum, Benedict, Butler, Coveney, Foss, Gore-Langton, Gross, Hagerty, Hattenstone, Hewison, Logan, Marmion, Morley, Nightingale, Shuttleworth, Spencer, Wareham. *Headstate* devised by Boilerhouse and Irvine Welsh, dir by Paul Pinson at the Trinity Buoy Wharf: rev by Gardner, Marmion, Nightingale, Smith, Spencer.

2081   "Reviews of Productions." *TR.* 1997; 17(14): 871-878. Lang.: Eng.

UK-England: London. 1997. ■*The Weir* by Conor McPherson, dir by Ian Rickson at the Royal Court Upstairs: rev by Billington, Butler, Clapp, Coveney, Edwardes, Gore-Langton, Gross, Hewison, Macauley, Marlowe, Nathan, Nightingale, Sierz, Spencer, Turpin. *Fairy Tales* by Eric Lane Barnes, dir by Ken Caswell at the Drill Hall: rev by Kingston, Logan, Marmion. *Assassins*, musical by Stephen Sondheim, book by John Weidman, dir by Sam Buntrock at the New End: rev by Abdulla,

Benedict, Christopher, Coveney, Hagerty, Hewison, Morley, Nathan, Shuttleworth, Smith.

2082   "Reviews of Productions." *TR.* 1997; 17(14): 878-883, 885-889. Lang.: Eng.

UK-England. 1997. ■*Mum's the Word* by Emma Kilbey, Posy Miller, and Symantha Simcox, dir by Kilbey at the Old Red Lion: rev by Abdulla. *The Cenci* by Giorgio Battistelli after Antonin Artaud, with text by Battistelli and Nick Ward from English version by David Parry, dir by Ward at the Almeida: rev by Christiansen, Clements, Driver, Hanks, Maddocks, Milnes, Murray, Rosenthal. *Divorce Me, Darling!*, musical by Sandy Wilson, dir by Paul Kerryson at the Chichester Festival: rev by Billington, Benedict, Coveney, de Jongh, Gross, Hagerty, Morley, Nathan, Nightingale, Rosenthal, Shuttleworth, Spencer.

2083   "Reviews of Productions." *TR.* 1997; 17(15): 899-907. Lang.: Eng.

UK-England: London. 1997. ■*Chimps* by Simon Block, dir by Gemma Bodinetz at the Hampstead: rev by Benedict, Billington, Clapp, Coveney, de Jongh, Gross, Hagerty, Hemming, Hewison, Morley, Nathan, Nightingale, Rosenthal, Sierz, Spencer, Stratton, Woddis. *Molly and the Captain* by Paul Thomas, dir by David Stuttard at the Turtle Key: rev by Abdulla. *The Prince* adapt by Simon Blake from Machiavelli, dir by Blake at the Young Vic Studio: rev by Albasini, Curtis, Foss, Hewison, Nightingale, Rosenthal, Tushingham.

2084   "Reviews of Productions." *TR.* 1997; 17(16): 968-977. Lang.: Eng.

UK-England: London. 1997. ■*The Greenhouse Effect* by Paul Prescott, dir by Chris Barnfield at Riverside 3: rev by Abdulla, Marmion, McPherson. *Life Support* by Simon Gray, dir by Harold Pinter at the Aldwych: rev by Billington, Brown, Butler, Clapp, Coveney, de Jongh, Edwardes, Gross, Hagerty, Hassell, Macauley, Morley, Nathan, Nightingale, Peter, Spencer, Taylor. *An Ideal Husband* by Oscar Wilde, dir by Peter Hall at Theatre Royal, Haymarket: rev by Coveney, de Jongh, Foss, Godfrey-Faussett, Holland, Kingston, Macauley.

2085   "Reviews of Productions." *TR.* 1997; 17(15): 908-911. Lang.: Eng.

UK-England: London. 1997. ■*Her Sister's Tongue* by Janet Goddard, dir by Jacquetta May at the Lyric Studio: rev by Benedict, Cavendish, Gardner, Hewison, Kingston, Marmion, Williams. *Goodnight Desdemona (Good Morning Juliet)* by Ann-Marie MacDonald, dir by Michael Cowie at the Grace: rev by Christopher, Logan, McPherson, Rampton. *Once Upon a Time Very Far From England* by Farhana Sheikh from 'Plain Tales from the Hills' by Rudyard Kipling, dir by Adrian Jackson for London Bubble in the open air at Greenwich Park: rev by Butler, Haydon, Tushingham.

2086   "Reviews of Productions." *TR.* 1997; 17(15): 912-920. Lang.: Eng.

UK-England: London. 1997. ■*Kiss Me, Kate*, musical by Cole Porter, book by Bella and Samuel Spewack, dir by Ian Talbot at Regent's Park, Open Air: rev by Bassett, Billington, Brown, Butler, Clapp, Coveney, Curtis, Gore-Langton, Gross, Hagerty, Hewison, Marmion, Morley, Nightingale, Taylor, Thorncroft. *Lovers* by Brian Friel, dir by Yvonne A.K. Johnson at Riverside 3: rev by Albasini, Christopher, Hewison, Stratton. *Goliath* by Bryony Lavery, based on Beatrix Campbell's synonomous book, dir by Annie Castledine at the Bush: rev by Christopher, Curtis, Foss, Gardner, Gross, Hagerty, Hemming, Hewison, Kingston, Marmion, Morley, Nathan, Taylor.

2087   "Reviews of Productions." *TR.* 1997; 17(15): 920-929. Lang.: Eng.

UK-England: London. 1997. ■*The Light House* devised by Bateau Ivre from Cechov's *The Three Sisters*, dir by Antona Mirto at Wimbledon Studio: rev by Godfrey-Faussett, McPherson. *The Leenane Trilogy: The Beauty Queen of Leenane, A Skull in Connemara* and *The Lonesome West* all by Martin McDonagh, dir by Garry Hynes for the Druid Theatre at the Royal Court, Downstairs: rev by Billington, Brown, Butler, Clancy, Clapp, Coveney, de Jongh, Gore-Langton, Gross, Macauley, Moroney, Nightingale, Peter, Sierz, Smith, Spencer, Stratton, Taylor, Woddis. *Palestinian Nights* and *Left Breastless* by Gideon Dodi, dir by Rachel Board and Dodi at the Etcetera: rev by Abdulla.

2088   "Reviews of Productions." *TR.* 1997; 17(15): 930-939. Lang.: Eng.

DRAMA: —Performance/production

UK-England: London. 1997. ■*Pygmalion* by Shaw, dir by Ray Cooney at the Albery: rev by Bassett, Butler, Christopher, Coveney, Darvell, de Jongh, Gardner, Gross, Hagerty, McCauley, Marmion, Morley, Nathan, Nightingale, Peter, Taylor. *Side By Side By Sondheim* by Stephen Sondheim, book by Ned Sherrin, additional music by Leonard Bernstein, Mary Rodgers, Richard Rodgers, and Jule Styne, dir by Matthew Francis at the Greenwich: rev by Bassett, Benedict, Brown, Christopher, Coveney, Curtis, Darvell, Gore-Langton, Hagerty, Kingston, Logan, McKie, Nathan, Peter, Shuttleworth. *Dreams of Anne Frank* by Bernard Kops, dir by Rachel Lasserson at Stables Antique Market: rev by Godfrey-Faussett, Jacobus, Kingston, Taylor, Williams.

2089 "Reviews of Productions." *TR.* 1997; 17(16): 940-945, 948-952. Lang.: Eng.

UK-England: London. 1997. ■1997 Channel 4 Sitcom Festival: *Always On My Mind* by Hugh Costello, dir by Jonathan Lloyd, *Fort Beaver* by Ray Brennan, dir by Richard Georgeson, *No Place Like Home* by Owen O'Neill, dir by Audrey Cooke, *Thicker Than Water* by Greg Keen, dir by Lloyd, *Family Values* by Chris Neil, dir by Cooke, *Eat This!* by Dan Gaster and Paul Powell, dir by Paulette Randall, *The Adventures of Mummy's Boy* by Iain Heggie, dir by Georgeson, *Cock and Bull* by Gordon Steel, dir by Steel and William Burdett-Coutts, and *School Daze* by Susan Nickson, dir by Randall at Riverside Studios: rev by Games, Gardner, S. Taylor. *'Art'* by Yasmina Reza, dir by Matthew Warchus at Wyndham's: rev by Butler, Foss, Gross, Macauley, Morley, Nightingale, Stratton. *Suzanna Adler* by Marguerite Duras, dir by Lindy Davies at the Minerva Chichester: rev by Bassett, Benedict, Billington, Butler, Clapp, de Jongh, Gore-Langton, Gross, Hagerty, Hewison, Nightingale, Taylor.

2090 "Reviews of Productions." *TR.* 1997; 17(16): 961-967. Lang.: Eng.

UK-England: London. 1997. ■*Last Letters from Stalingrad* by Matthew Mills, dir by Chattie Salaman at the Bridewell: rev by Cavendish, Marlowe, Nathan, Nightingale, Shuttleworth. *Approaching Zanzibar* by Tina Howe, dir by Brennan Street at Southwark Playhouse: rev by Stratton, Taylor. *Umabatha: The Zulu Macbeth* by Welcome Msomi, dir by Msomi at Shakespeare's Globe: rev by Butler, Curtis, Gardner, Hanks, Nightingale. *Romeo and Juliet* by Shakespeare, dir by Dan Crawford at King's Head: rev by Christopher, Foss, Godfrey-Faussett.

2091 "Reviews of Productions." *TR.* 1997; 17(16): 977-981. Lang.: Eng.

UK-England: London. 1997. ■*Grave Plots* by David Kane, dir by Ken McClymont at the Old Red Lion: rev by Christopher, Edwardes, Williams. *A Lot of Living!: The Songs of Charles Strouse* conceived by Barbara Simon, dir by Simon at the Jermyn Street: rev by Abdulla, Christopher, Clapp, Coveney, Darvell, Gross, Hagerty, Morley. *Carnaby Street*, musical by James Hall, dir by Terry John Bate at the Arts: rev by Barker, Cavendish, Hagerty, Marlowe, Nightingale, Sullivan.

2092 "Reviews of Productions." *TR.* 1997; 17(16): 986-990. Lang.: Eng.

UK-England. 1997. ■*Talk Radio* by Eric Bogosian at Man in the Moon: rev by Cavendish. *New Anatomies* by Timberlake Wertenbaker, dir by Diane Maguire at the Hen & Chickens: rev by Stratton. *Our Betters* by W. Somerset Maugham, dir by Michael Rudman at the Chichester Festival: rev by Curtis, Kingston, Nathan, O'Connor, Woddis.

2093 "Reviews of Productions." *TR.* 1997; 17(16): 981-985. Lang.: Eng.

UK-England: London. 1997. ■*Brace's Benefit* and *Ooh ... War!* by Alexander Kirk and Simon Messingham, at the Etcetera: Godfrey-Faussett. *The Mysterious Mr. Love* by Karoline Leach, dir by Bob Tomson at the Comedy: rev by N. Billen, Butler, Coveney, Curtis, Gross, Hagerty, Marmion, Morley, Nathan, Nightingale, R.L. Parry, Spencer, Taylor, Thorncroft. *Much Ado About Nothing* and *Measure for Measure* by Shakespeare, dir by George Thompson at Lincoln's Inn: rev by Godfrey-Faussett, Stratton.

2094 "Reviews of Productions." *TR.* 1997; 17(17): 1005-1010. Lang.: Eng.

UK-England: London. 1997. ■*The Bible: The Complete Word of God (Abridged)* by the Reduced Shakespeare Company with additional material by Matthew Croke, dir by Reed Martin, Adam Long and Austin Tichenor at the Gielgud: rev by Cavendish, Foss, Gross, Hagerty, Kingston, Morley, Nathan, Thorncroft. *The Seagull (Čajka)* by Čechov, transl by Stephen Mulrine, dir by Stephen Unwin at the Donmar Warehouse: rev

by Butler, Clapp, de Jongh, Gardner, Hanks, Kingston, Macauley, Marlowe, Marmion, Nathan, Peter, Spencer. *The Sound of Silence (Le Bel indifférent)* by Jean Cocteau, dir by Judd Bachelor at the Man in the Moon: rev by McPherson.

2095 "Reviews of Productions." *TR.* 1997; 17(17): 1011-1012. Lang.: Eng.

UK-England: London. 1997. ■*Anton Chekov* by Michael Pennington, dir by Peter Hall at the Old Vic: rev by Kellaway, Kingston, Marmion, Smith. *My Native Land* by Rodney Clark, dir by Ezra Hjalmarsson at the Lyric Studio: rev by Booth, Godfrey-Faussett, Kingston.

2096 "Reviews of Productions." *TR.* 1997; 17(17): 1077-1080. Lang.: Eng.

UK-England: London. 1997. ■*Family Circles* by Alan Ayckbourn, dir by Sam Walters at the Orange Tree: rev by Abdulla, McPherson, Nightingale. *Macbeth—Stage of Blood*, Manipuri version by Somerendra Arambam, dir by Lokendra Arambam at the Watermans: rev by Cartwright, Kingston. *Eve of Retirement (Vor dem Ruhestand)* by Thomas Bernhard, transl by Gitta Honegger, dir by David Fielding at the Gate: rev by Billington, Edwardes, Nathan, Nightingale, Stevens, Taylor.

2097 "Reviews of Productions." *TR.* 1997; 17(18): 1099-1104. Lang.: Eng.

UK-England: London. 1997. ■*Hurlyburly* by David Rabe, dir by Wilson Milam at the Queen's: rev by de Jongh, Edwardes, Foss, Gore-Langton, Gross, Hagerty, Hanks, Morley, Murray, Nathan, Nightingale, Peter, Sierz, Spencer, Usher. *Sleeping Nightie* by Victoria Hardie, dir by Robert Wolstenholme at the White Bear: rev by Abdulla. *Lucky Stiff* book and lyrics by Lynn Ahrens, music by Stephen Flaherty, dir by Steven Dexter at the Bridewell: rev by Christopher, Gardner, Gross, Hagerty, Logan, McPherson, Morley, Nathan, Usher.

2098 "Reviews of Productions." *TR.* 1997; 17(17): 1080-1090. Lang.: Eng.

UK-England. 1997. ■*Bury the Duck* by Michael Chapman, dir by Harry Pearce at the Etcetera: rev by Abdulla. *The Maid's Tragedy* by Francis Beaumont and John Fletcher, dir by Lucy Bailey at Shakespeare's Globe: rev by Curtis, Edwardes, Gardner, Gross, Hagerty, Nathan, Nightingale, Smith, Usher, Woddis. *A Chaste Maid in Cheapside* by Thomas Middleton, dir by Malcolm McKay at Shakespeare's Globe: rev by Benedict, Curtis, Gardner, Gore-Langton, Grant, Gross, Hagerty, Kellaway, Macauley, Nathan, Nightingale, Spencer, Usher, Wark, Woddis. *Misalliance* by Shaw, dir by Frank Hauser at Minerva Studio, Chichester: rev by Hagerty, Hewison, Macauley, Nathan, Nightingale.

2099 "Reviews of Productions." *TR.* 1997; 17(18): 1104-1108. Lang.: Eng.

UK-England: London. 1997. ■*Terry Titter's Full Length* by Terry Kilkelly, dir by Kilkelly at the New End: rev by Abdulla. *The Odd Couple* by Neil Simon, dir by Andrew O'Connor and *Biloxi Blues* by Simon dir by Edward Wilson for the National Youth Theatre at the Arts: rev by Cowan, Curtis, Logan, Woddis. *Romeo and Juliet* by Shakespeare, dir by Gwenda Hughes for the National Youth Theatre at the Bloomsbury: rev by Abdulla. *The Beggar's Opera* by John Gay, dir by Jeremy James Taylor and Frank Whatley for the National Youth Music Theatre at the Lyric Hammersmith: rev by Kimberly.

2100 "Reviews of Productions." *TR.* 1997; 17(18): 1138-1144. Lang.: Eng.

UK-England: London. 1997. ■*Double* by Julia Rayner, dir by Rayner, *One* by Emi Slater and *Two* by Jim Cartwright, dir by Slater at the Finborough: rev by Godfrey-Faussett, McPherson. *The Prince of West End Avenue* by Kerry Shale from the novel by Alan Isler, dir by Sonia Fraser at the Hampstead: rev by Cavendish, Clapp, Coveney, Gardner, Gross, Hagerty, Kingston, Levitt, Lockerbie, Macauley, Morley, Murray, Smith. *Flowers of the Dead Red Sea* by Edward Thomas, dir by Patrick Wilde at the Canal Cafe: rev by Marmion, Stevens. *The False Hairpiece* by John Constable, dir by Chris Baldwin at Southwark Playhouse: rev by Dowden, Godfrey-Faussett.

2101 "Reviews of Productions." *TR.* 1997; 17(19): 1159-1169. Lang.: Eng.

UK-England: London. 1997. ■*The Farmer's Bride* by Ged McKenna, dir by Polly Irvin at BAC: rev by Clapp, Hemming, Logan, Marlowe. *An Enchanted Land* by Dale Wasserman, dir by Joseph Blatchley at the Riverside: rev by Booth, Marmion, Peter. *Playhouse Creatures* by April De

DRAMA: —Performance/production

Angelis, dir by Lynne Parker at the Old Vic: rev by Billington, Butler, Clapp, de Jongh, Gross, Hagerty, Kingston, Logan, Morley, Nathan, Peter, Shuttleworth, Sierz, Smith, Spencer, Taylor.

2102 "Reviews of Productions." *TR.* 1997; 17(19): 1169-1170. Lang.: Eng.

UK-England: London. 1997. ∎*The Promise (Moj bednyj Marat)* by Aleksei Arbuzov, transl by Ariadne Nicolaeff, dir by Dalia Ibelhauptaite at the Old Red Lion: rev by Stratton. *Stories from the Bleedhinder* by Mason Ball, dir by Ball at the Machine Room: rev by Godfrey-Faussett. *Fool House* by Joff Chafer and Toby Wilsher, dir by Chafer and Wilsher at the Purcell Room: rev by Brennan, Butler, Gardner, Hanks.

2103 "Reviews of Productions." *TR.* 1997; 17(19): 1171-1180. Lang.: Eng.

UK-England: London. 1997. ∎*Othello* by Shakespeare, dir by Sam Mendes for the Royal National at the Olivier: rev by Billington, Brown, Butler, Clapp, Edwardes, Gross, Hagerty, Kingston, Morley, Nathan, Nightingale, Peter, Smith, Spencer, Taylor. *Enter the Guardsman* music by Craig Bohmler, lyrics by Marion Adler, book by Scott Wentworth based on the play by Ferenc Molnár, dir by Jeremy Sams at the Donmar Warehouse: rev by Billington, Butler, Clapp, de Jongh, Edwardes, Foss, Gross, Hagerty, Macauley, Nathan, Nightingale, Spencer, Taylor. *Caliban* by Marcos Azevedo, adapt from Shakespeare by Azevedo and Eduardo Bonito, text transl by Bonito, Fabiana Guglielmetti and Susan Betts, dir by Betts at the Riverside: rev by Farrell, Kingston.

2104 "Reviews of Productions." *TR.* 1997; 17(19): 1181-1189. Lang.: Eng.

UK-England: London. 1997. ∎*The Wasp Factory* by Malcolm Sutherland from the novel by Iain Banks, dir by Sutherland at the Lyric, Hammersmith: rev by Cavendish, Christopher, Curtis, Hemming, Marlowe, Peter. *Love Song of the Apocalypse* by Dave Weiner, dir by Andrew Grosso at the Etcetera: rev by Godfrey-Faussett. *An Enemy of the People (En Folkefiende)* by Ibsen, transl by Christopher Hampton, dir by Trevor Nunn for the Royal National at the Olivier: rev by Billington, Brown, Butler, Clapp, Coveney, de Jongh, Edwardes, Gore-Langton, Gross, Hagerty, Macauley, Morley, Nathan, Nightingale, Peter, Smith, Spencer, Taylor.

2105 "Reviews of Productions." *TR.* 1997; 17(19): 1189-1196. Lang.: Eng.

UK-England: London. 1997. ∎*The Boys in the Band* by Mart Crowley, dir by Kenneth Elliott at the King's Head: rev by Cavendish, de Jongh, Foss, Nathan, Nightingale. *Blue Heart: Heart's Desire/Blue Kettle*, two plays by Caryl Churchill, dir by Max Stafford-Clark at the Royal Court Downstairs: rev by Billington, Brown, Butler, Clapp, Cooper, Coveney, Curtis, Gross, Hagerty, Hemming, Marlowe, Morley, Nathan, Nightingale, Peter, Shuttleworth, Spencer, Stratton, Taylor. *To Blusher with Love* by Judy Upton, dir by Philip Dart at the Man in the Moon: rev by Godfrey-Faussett, McPherson.

2106 "Reviews of Productions." *TR.* 1997; 17(25/26): 1608-1610. Lang.: Eng.

UK-England: London. 1997. ∎*Think No Evil of Us: My Life with Kenneth Williams* by David Benson, at the Lyric Studio: rev by Benedict, Billington, Christopher. *Snowshow* a clown show by Slava Polunin at the Old Vic: rev by Davé, Dessau, Hemming, Hewison, Kingston, Marmion. *Eleemosynary* by Lee Blessing, dir by Victoria Moss at the Etcetera: rev by North.

2107 "Reviews of Productions." *TR.* 1997; 17(19): 1196-1197. Lang.: Eng.

UK-England: London. 1997. ∎*Andy and Edie* by Anton Binder, dir by Polly Wiseman at the Man in the Moon: rev by Logan. *Squirrels* by David Mamet, dir by Ali Robertson at the Canal Cafe: rev by McPherson, Stratton. *The Hairy Ape* by O'Neill, dir by Rhys Thomas at the Brockley Jack: rev by *Time Out* (unattrib). *She'll Be Wearing Silk Pyjamas* by Kate O'Riordan, dir by Phil Tinline at the Orange Tree Room: rev by McPherson.

2108 "Reviews of Productions." *TR.* 1997; 17(20): 1262-1264. Lang.: Eng.

UK-England: London. 1997. ∎*Salvador* by Mark O'Thomas, dir by John Burton at the Man in the Moon: rev by Godfrey-Faussett, Marlowe. *Jump to Cow Heaven* by Gill Adams, dir by William Kerley at the River-

side: rev by Booth, Coveney, Godfrey-Faussett, Kingston, Spencer. *Shelf Life* musical by David Haines, additional script by Tom Payne, dir by David Evans Rees at Southwark Playhouse: rev by Marmion, McPherson.

2109 "Reviews of Productions." *TR.* 1997; 17(19): 1198-1210. Lang.: Eng.

UK-England. 1997. ∎*Cyrano de Bergerac* by Edmond Rostand, dir by Gregory Doran for the RSC at the Swan, Stratford: rev by Billington, Brown, Clapp, Coveney, de Jongh, Edwardes, Gore-Langton, Gross, Hagerty, Nathan, Nightingale, Peter, Spencer, Taylor, Treadwell, Woddis. *Henry V* by Shakespeare, dir by Ron Daniels for the RSC at the Royal Shakespeare, Stratford: rev by Billington, Brown, Butler, Clapp, Coveney, de Jongh, Edwardes, Gore-Langton, Macauley, Peter, Spencer, Taylor, Treadwell. *Electra* by Sophocles, transl by Frank McGuinness, dir by David Leveaux at the Minerva, Chichester: rev by Albasini, Billington, Clapp, Coveney, Curtis, Hagerty, Nathan, Nightingale, Peter, Spencer, Taylor.

2110 "Reviews of Productions." *TR.* 1997; 17(20): 1231-1240. Lang.: Eng.

UK-England: London. 1997. ∎*King Lear* by Shakespeare, dir by Peter Hall at the Old Vic: rev by Billington, Brown, Clapp, Coveney, Gore-Langton, Gross, Hassell, Logan, Morley, Murray, Nathan, Nightingale, Peter, Spencer, Taylor. *Swan Song* by Jonathan Harvey, dir by Richard Osborne at the Hampstead: rev by Clapp, Fisher, Foss, Gardner, Gore-Langton, Gross, Nightingale, Peter, Rubnikowicz, L. Spencer, Stratton, Walsh. *Danton's Death (Dantons Tod)* by Georg Büchner, transl by David Farr, dir by Farr at the Gate: rev by Billington, Christopher, Curtis, Davé, Edwardes, Murray, Peter, Taylor, Woddis.

2111 "Reviews of Productions." *TR.* 1997; 17(21): 1325-1327. Lang.: Eng.

UK-England: London. 1997. ∎*Jane Eyre* by Polly Teale from Charlotte Brontë, dir by Teale at the Young Vic: rev by Christopher, Edwardes, Gardner, Hewison, Kellaway, Marmion, Sierz, Smith, Spencer. *Moon* by Jacqueline Hale, dir by Christopher Hynes at Southwark Playhouse: rev by Logan. *Noël and Gertie* by Sheridan Morley, dir by Morley at the Jermyn Street: rev by Darvell.

2112 "Reviews of Productions." *TR.* 1997; 17(20): 1240-1249. Lang.: Eng.

UK-England: London. 1997. ∎*As You Like It* by Shakespeare, dir by David Terence at the Bridewell: rev by Driver, Godfrey-Faussett. *Dorian* by David Reeves, dir by Mehmet Ergen at the Arts: rev by Christopher, Curtis, Darvell, Hagerty, Hemming, Stratton, Turpin. *Maddie* music by Stephen Keeling, lyrics by Shaun McKenna, book by McKenna and Steven Dexter, based on the novel by Jack Finney, dir by Martin Connor at the Lyric: rev by Bassett, Billington, Brown, Butler, Coveney, de Jongh, Edwardes, Gore-Langton, Hagerty, Macauley, McPherson, Morley, Nathan, Nightingale, Peter, Taylor, Wardle.

2113 "Reviews of Productions." *TR.* 1997; 17(20): 1249-1253. Lang.: Eng.

UK-England: London. 1997. ∎*Scapin's Tricks (Les Fourberies de Scapin)* by Molière, transl by Kenneth McClellan, dir by Melissa Holston at Wimbledon Studio: rev by McPherson. *Les fausses confidences (The False Confessions)* by Marivaux, dir by Jean-Pierre Miquel for Comédie-Française at the Lyttelton: rev by Billington, Butler, Clapp, Coveney, de Jongh, Edwardes, Gore-Langton, Macauley, Nightingale, Spencer, Taylor, Wardle. *Surfing* and *Obsession* by Robert Young, dir by Lisa Goldman at BAC 1: rev by Christopher, Curtis, Marlowe, McPherson.

2114 "Reviews of Productions." *TR.* 1997; 17(20): 1254-1262. Lang.: Eng.

UK-England: London. 1997. ∎*The Invention of Love* by Tom Stoppard, dir by Richard Eyre for the Royal National at the Cottesloe: rev by Billington, Brown, Butler, Clapp, Coveney, de Jongh, Edwardes, Gore-Langton, Hagerty, Hassell, Lister, Macauley, Morley, Nathan, Nightingale, Peter, Spencer, Taylor, Wardle. *Frost Flower (Isblomst)* by Terje Nordby, transl by Kim Dambaek, dir by Peter Craze, and *Unleashed in the USSR (Mugg)* by Marit Tusik, transl by Julian Garner, dir by Kate Hall at the White Bear: rev by Abdulla. *The Murder of Edgar Allan Poe* by Sophia Kingshill, dir by Joe Cushley at the Finborough: rev by Logan, Marlowe.

DRAMA: —Performance/production

2115 "Reviews of Productions." *TR.* 1997; 17(20): 1265-1270. Lang.: Eng.

UK-England: London. 1997. ■*Kat and the Kings* by David Kramer and Taliep Petersen, dir by Kramer at the Tricycle: rev by Bassett, Clapp, Curtis, Davé, Gardner, Hemming, Hewison. *Independent* (unattrib), rev by Kingston, Marmion, Morley, Woddis. *Mackerel Sky* by Hilary Fanning, dir by Mike Bradwell at the Bush: rev by Billington, Butler, Clapp, Coveney, Godfrey-Faussett, Gore-Langton, Gross, Macauley, Marlowe, Nightingale, Peter, Spencer, Taylor. *If Mr. Frollo Finds Out* by Middleton Mann, dir by Mann at the Old Red Lion: rev by Logan.

2116 "Reviews of Productions." *TR.* 1997; 17(20): 1280-1281. Lang.: Eng.

UK-England: London. 1997. ■*Richard II* by Shakespeare, dir by Phillip Joseph at the Pleasance: rev by Albasini, Edwardes. *Queen Christina* by Pam Gems, dir by Andrew Pratt at BAC 1: rev by Marlowe. *Ripley Bogle* by Richard Hurst from Robert McLiam Wilson's novel, dir by Hurst at the Grace: rev by Logan, McPherson.

2117 "Reviews of Productions." *TR.* 1997; 17(20): 1271-1280. Lang.: Eng.

UK-England: London. 1997. ■*Overboard (Par-dessus bord)* by Michel Vinaver, transl by Gideon Lester, dir by Sam Walters at the Orange Tree: rev by Billington, Butler, Curtis, Edwardes, Kingston, McPherson, Peter, Spencer, Taylor, Woddis. *Warrior* by Shirley Gee, dir by Giles Burton at the Tabard: rev by Marmion. *Cinderella* ballet by Matthew Bourne, music by Prokofieff, dir by Bourne at the Piccadilly: rev by I. Brown, Christiansen, Coveney, Craine, Crisp, Darvell, Dougill, Dromgoole, Gilbert, Hagerty, Kyle, Levine, Mackrell, J. Parry, Poesio, Sacks.

2118 "Reviews of Productions." *TR.* 1997; 17(21): 1307-1316. Lang.: Eng.

UK-England: London. 1997. ■*HRH* by Snoo Wilson, dir by Simon Callow at the Playhouse: rev by Billington, Brown, Butler, Clapp, Coveney, *Evening Standard* (unattrib), Foss, Gore-Langton, Grant, Gross, Hagerty, Morley, Nathan, Nightingale, Peter, Shuttleworth, Sierz, Taylor, Woddis. *Elsa Edgar* by Bob Kingdom with Neil Bartlett, dir by Robert Gillespie at the Lyric Studio: rev by Nightingale, North, R.L. Parry. *Bernadetje* by Alain Platel and Arne Sierens, transl by Rebecca Prichard, dir by Sierens at the Round House: rev by Clapp, Gore-Langton, Kingston, Taylor.

2119 "Reviews of Productions." *TR.* 1997; 17(21): 1316-1320. Lang.: Eng.

UK-England: London. 1997. ■*Jocasta* by Josephine Corcoran, dir by Corcoran at Chelsea Centre: rev by Godfrey-Faussett. *150 Cigarettes* by Michael Bourdages, dir by Tamsin Hoare at the Machine Room: ref by Abdulla. *My Boy Jack* by David Haig, dir by John Dove at the Hampstead: rev by Butler, Clapp, Curtis, Edwardes, Gardner, Gross, Hanks, Hassell, Hemming, Hewison, Kingston, Morley, Nathan, Sierz.

2120 "Reviews of Productions." *TR.* 1997; 17(21): 1320-1324. Lang.: Eng.

UK-England: London. 1997. ■*Othello* by Shakespeare, dir by Yvonne Brewster at the Drill Hall: rev by Cavendish, Marlowe. *Snake in the Grass* by Roy MacGregor, dir by Dominic Dromgoole at the Old Vic: rev by Bassett, Billington, Butler, Coveney, de Jongh, Gross, Hagerty, Kellaway, Morley, Nightingale, Peter, Smith, Stratton. *Coming Up* by James Martin Charlton, dir by Ted Craig at the Warehouse, Croydon: rev by Foss, Kingston, Marmion.

2121 "Reviews of Productions." *TR.* 1997; 17(20): 1282, 1290-1293. Lang.: Eng.

UK-England: London. 1997. ■*The Seagull (Čajka)* by Čechov, transl by Harry Meacher, dir by Meacher at Pentameters: rev by Abdulla, Driver. *Off the Wall* by David Glass, dir by Glass at the Polka: rev by Gardner. *The Magistrate* by Arthur Wing Pinero, dir by Nicholas Broadhurst at the Chichester Festival: rev by Brown, Butler, Coveney, Curtis, Gore-Langton, Gross, Hagerty, Macauley, Nathan, Nightingale, Peter, Spencer, Taylor.

2122 "Reviews of Productions." *TR.* 1997; 17(21): 1338-1336. Lang.: Eng.

UK-England: London. 1997. ■*Faith* by Meredith Oakes, dir by John Burgess at the Royal Court Upstairs: rev by Billington, Butler, de Jongh, Hemming, Nightingale, R.L. Parry, Peter, Taylor. *A Letter of Resignation* by Hugh Whitemore, dir by Christopher Morahan at the Comedy:

rev by Brown, Butler, Clapp, de Jongh, Gardner, Gore-Langton, Grant, Gross, Hagerty, Hassell, Jacobus, Morley, Nightingale, Peter, Shuttleworth, Sierz, Spencer, Taylor. *Theatre Stories* by Ken Campbell, dir by Colin Watkeys at the Cottesloe: rev by Foss, Gore-Langton, Kingston, Logan, Marmion, Shuttleworth, Taylor.

2123 "Reviews of Productions." *TR.* 1997; 17(23): 1454-1456. Lang.: Eng.

UK-England: London. 1997. ■*Unlucky for Some* by Paul Tucker, dir by Timothy Hughes at the Southwark Playhouse: rev by Benedict, Stratton. *Dear Brutus* by J.M. Barrie, dir by Stephanie Sinclair Crawford at the King's Head: rev by Gross, Hassell, Kingston, Morley, Stratton. *An Evening with Kate's Gang* by Clare Summerskill, dir by Kate Crutchley at the Oval House: rev by Miller.

2124 "Reviews of Productions." *TR.* 1997; 17(21): 1337-1349. Lang.: Eng.

UK-England: London. 1997. ■*Glorious* by Eddie Izzard, dir by Izzard at Labatt's Apollo: rev by Barber, Bassett, Brown, Games, Hagerty, Hawkins, Hay, Smith, S. Taylor. *She Knows, You Know!* by Jean Fergusson, dir by Christopher Wren at the Vaudeville: rev by Coveney, Foss, Gore-Langton, Gross, Hagerty, Hewison, Marmion, Nightingale, Shuttleworth, Spencer, Taylor. *A Delicate Balance* by Edward Albee, dir by Anthony Page at the Theatre Royal, Haymarket: rev by Billington, Brown, Butler, Coveney, de Jongh, Donald, Edwardes, Fisher, Gore-Langton, Gross, Hagerty, Hassell, Hewison, Kellaway, Morley, Murray, Nathan, Nightingale, Spencer, Taylor.

2125 "Reviews of Productions." *TR.* 1997; 17(21): 1349-1353, 1358-1360. Lang.: Eng.

UK-England. 1997. ■*You Are My Mother (U Bent Mijn Moeder)* by Joop Admiraal, transl by Catherine Holland-Cunningham, dir by Dorothea Alexander at the Etcetera: rev by Abdulla, Affleck. *Macbeth* by Shakespeare, dir by George Costigan at the Theatre Royal, Bristol: rev by Albasini, Bassett, Brown, Christopher, Clapp, Coveney, Logan, Morse, Peter. *Shintoku-Maru* by Shuji Terayama, adapt by Rio Kishida for performance in Japanese by the Ninagawa Company, dir by Yukio Ninagawa at the Barbican: rev by Billington, Butler, Clapp, Coveney, de Jongh, Nightingale, Shuttleworth, Spencer, Taylor.

2126 "Reviews of Productions." *TR.* 1997; 17(22): 1371-1376. Lang.: Eng.

UK-England: London. 1997. ■*Scissor Happy* adapt by Neil Mullarkey, Lee Simpson and Jim Sweeney from *Sheer Madness*, dir by Mullarkey at the Duchess: rev by Billington, de Jongh, Foss, Hagerty, Kellaway, Kingston, Logan, Nathan, Shuttleworth, Spencer, Taylor. *A View from the Bridge* by Arthur Miller, dir by Rachel Kavanaugh at the Greenwich: rev by Christopher, Gardner, Godfrey-Faussett, Gore-Langton, Hanks, Marlowe, Marmion, Sierz. *The Reckless Are Dying Out (Die Unvernünftigen sterben aus)* by Peter Handke, transl by Penny Black, dir by Gordon Anderson at the Lyric Studio: rev by Abdulla, Booth.

2127 "Reviews of Productions." *TR.* 1997; 17(22): 1377-1380. Lang.: Eng.

UK-England: London. 1997. ■*Electra* by Sophocles, transl by Frank McGuinness, dir by David Leveaux at Donmar Warehouse: rev by Brown, Butler, Cavendish, Gross, Stothard. *Vortigern* by William Henry Ireland, dir by Joe Harmston at the Bridewell: rev by Gardner, Hanks, Kingston, Logan. *Redemption* by Michael Skelly, dir by Ken McClymont at the Old Red Lion: rev by Foss, Godfrey-Faussett. *Centralia*, music by Clement Ishmael, book and lyrics by Sam Snape, dir by Snape and Charles Augins at the Brixton Shaw Theatre: rev by Edwardes.

2128 "Reviews of Productions." *TR.* 1997; 17(24): 1542-1546. Lang.: Eng.

UK-England: London. 1997. ■*Heritage* by Stephen Churchett, dir by Mark Rayment at the Hampstead: rev by Billington, Clapp, Coveney, de Jongh, Edwardes, Gore-Langton, Gross, Hagerty, Hanks, Macauley, Morley, Nathan, Nightingale, Peter, Spencer, Taylor, Woddis. *The Suitcase Kid* by Sam Snape, from the novel by Jacqueline Wilson, dir by Snape at the Brix: rev by Butler. *27* by John Keates, dir by Keates at the Oval House: rev by Abdulla.

2129 "Reviews of Productions." *TR.* 1997; 17(22): 1383-1386. Lang.: Eng.

UK-England: London. 1997. ■*Tales My Lover Told Me* book and lyrics by Chris Burgess, music by Sarah Travis, dir by Burgess at the King's

DRAMA: —Performance/production

Head: rev by Christopher, Foss, Godfrey-Faussett, Marmion, Nathan. *Absolution* by Robert Sherwood, dir by Brennan Street at BAC 1: rev by Christopher, Gardner. *Woyzeck* by Georg Büchner, transl by William Fiennes, dir by Sarah Kane at the Gate: rev by Bassett, Cavendish, Clapp, Edwardes, Hewison, Kingston, Marlowe, Marmion, Woddis.

2130 "Reviews of Productions." *TR.* 1997; 17(22): 1407-1409. Lang.: Eng.

UK-England: London. 1997. ∎*Sunstroke* by Lesley Coburn, dir by Coburn at the Grace: rev by McPherson. *Crazyhorse* by Parv Bancil, dir by Vicky Featherstone at BAC 2: rev by Christopher, Morse, Stratton, Williams. *The Goodwoman of Sharkville* by Gcina Mhlophe and Janet Suzman, adapt from Brecht's *The Good Person of Setzuan (Der Gute Mensch von Sezuan)*, dir by Suzman at the Hackney empire: rev by Curtis.

2131 "Reviews of Productions." *TR.* 1997; 17(22): 1387-1393. Lang.: Eng.

UK-England: London. 1997. ∎*The Milk Train Doesn't Stop Here Anymore* by Tennesee Williams, dir by Philip Prowse at the Lyric Hammersmith: rev by Billington, Brown, Butler, Clapp, de Jongh, Edwardes, Gross, Hagerty, Holland, Kingston, Morley, Murray, Nathan, Peter, Sierz, Spencer, Taylor, Usher, Woddis. *Marking Time* by Mike Snelgrove, dir by Snelgrove at the Man in the Moon: rev by Godfrey-Faussett. *The Optimist's Daughter* by Chris Lee, dir by Mervyn Millar and *Double Effect* by Simon Warne, dir by Tristan Brolly at the Finborough: rev by Marlowe, North.

2132 "Reviews of Productions." *TR.* 1997; 17(22): 1394-1400. Lang.: Eng.

UK-England: London. 1997. ∎*Stepping Out* book by Richard Harris, music by Denis King, lyrics by Mary Stewart-David, dir by Julia McKenzie at the Albery: rev by Abdulla, Benedict, N. Billen, Brown, Butler, Curtis, Gardner, Gross, Hagerty, Hewison, Kingston, McPherson, Morley, Nathan, Spencer, Usher. *Reach* by Sharon Swyer, Scott Baker, and Patrick Davey, dir by Davey at Pentameters: rev by Miller. *The Boys in the Band* by Mart Crowley, dir by Kenneth Elliott at the Aldwych: rev Benedict, Edwardes, Gardner, Gross, Hewison, Murray, R.L. Parry, Spencer.

2133 "Reviews of Productions." *TR.* 1997; 17(22): 1401-1407. Lang.: Eng.

UK-England: London. 1997. ∎*The Dispute (La Dispute)* by Marivaux, *Contention* by Didier-Georges Gabily, *The Consequences of the Very Real Nature of Dying (Conséquences de la réalité des morts)* by Vincent Ravalec and *The Fable of the Sheath and the Knife* by Diderot, dir by Stanislas Nordey at the Peacock: rev by Benedict, Christopher, Johnson. *Dirty Tricks* book and lyrics by Stephen Chance, music by Paul Barker, dir by Christopher Newell at the Spitalfields Opera: rev by Allison. *Tongue of a Bird* by Ellen McLaughlin, dir by Peter Gill at the Almeida: rev by Benedict, Billington, Butler, Clapp, Coveney, de Jongh, Macauley, Marlowe, Morley, Nathan, Nightingale, Peter, Spencer, Stratton.

2134 "Reviews of Productions." *TR.* 1997; 17(22): 1410-1414, 1425-1430. Lang.: Eng.

UK-England: London. 1997. ∎*Beckett Shorts: Footfalls, Rockaby, Not I, Embers, A Piece of Monologue, That Time* by Beckett, dir by Katie Mitchell for the RSC at The Other Place, Stratford: rev by Billington, Butler, Clapp, Curtis, Holland, Kingston, Morley, Peter, Spencer, Stratton, Taylor, Treadwell, Woddis. *BAC Festival of Visual Theatre*: critical overview of the event by Bassett, Cavendish, Christopher, Clapp, Edwardes, Johnson, Kingston, McPherson, Palmer, Smith.

2135 "Reviews of Productions." *TR.* 1997; 17(23): 1448-1454. Lang.: Eng.

UK-England: London. 1997. ∎*Hello and Goodbye* by Athol Fugard, dir by Ilse van Hemert at BAC Main: rev by Costa, Marlowe. *The Slow Drag* by Carson Kreitzer, dir by Lisa Forrell at the Whitehall: rev by Benedict, Christopher, Coveney, de Jongh, Driver, Gore-Langton, Gross, Hemming, Marmion, Nathan. *The Sickness of Death (La Maladie de la Mort)* by Marguerite Duras, dir by Robert Wilson at the Peacock: rev by Billington, Butler, Clapp, Johnson, Kingston, Spencer.

2136 "Reviews of Productions." *TR.* 1997; 17(23): 1439-1448. Lang.: Eng.

UK-England: London. 1997. ∎*The Neighbours (Les Voisins)* by Michel Vinaver, transl by Paul Antal, dir by Geoffrey Beevers and *Dissident,*

Goes Without Saying (Dissident, Va Sans Dire) by Vinaver, transl by Peter Meyer, dir by Auriol Smith at the Orange Tree: rev by Kingston, Logan, McPherson. *Romeo and Juliet* by Shakespeare, dir by Michael Attenborough for the RSC at The Pit: rev by Benedict, Billington, Brown, Butler, Clapp, Coveney, Curtis, Edwardes, Gore-Langton, Hagerty, Macauley, Nathan, Nightingale, Peter, Smith, Spencer. *Henry V* by Shakespeare, dir by Ron Daniels for the RSC at the Barbican: rev by de Jongh, Foss, Gross, Hagerty, Morley, Nathan, Nightingale.

2137 "Reviews of Productions." *TR.* 1997; 17(23): 1457-1462. Lang.: Eng.

UK-England: London. 1997. ∎*Shining Souls* by Chris Hannan, dir by Hannan at the Old Vic: rev by Bassett, Benedict, Billington, Butler, Coveney, Curtis, Edwardes, Foss, Gross, Hagerty, Macauley, Nathan, Nightingale, Peter, Sierz. *The Opium Eaters* devised by Brouhaha, dir by Paul Hunter at the Young Vic Studio: rev by Logan, Stevens. *Fame* by David de Silva, music by Steven Margoshes, lyrics by Jacques Levy, dir by de Silva at Victoria Palace: rev by Williams.

2138 "Reviews of Productions." *TR.* 1997; 17(23): 1462-1466. Lang.: Eng.

UK-England: London. 1997. ∎*Riverdance* dance spectacular w/ music by Bill Whelan at Labatt's Apollo: rev by Smith. *The Popular Mechanicals* by Keith Robinson, Shakespeare, and Tony Taylor (sic), dir by Geoffrey Rush at the Arts: rev by Bassett, Cavendish, Curtis, Hemming, Marlowe, Nightingale, Peter. *Angels and Demons* story tellers Simon Thorp and Emma Cater, dir by Rebecca Wolman at the Tricycle: rev by Christopher, Curtis, Edwardes, Gardner, Marlowe, Nathan, Woddis.

2139 "Reviews of Productions." *TR.* 1997; 17(23): 1466-1469. Lang.: Eng.

UK-England: London. 1997. ∎*The Birth of Pleasure* by Jehane Markham, dir by Penny Cherns at the Rosemary Branch: rev by Gardner. *Caravan* by Helen Blakeman, dir by Gemma Bodinetz at the Bush: rev by Benedict, Billington, Butler, Curtis, Davé, Hagerty, Kingston, Morley, Nathan, Peter, Stratton, Woddis. *School for Buffoons (L'École des Bouffons)* by Michel de Ghelderode, dir by Victor Sobchak at the Bird's Nest: rev by Godfrey-Faussett.

2140 "Reviews of Productions." *TR.* 1997; 17(23): 1470-1477. Lang.: Eng.

UK-England: London. 1997. ∎*Chicago* music by John Kander, lyrics by Fred Ebb, book by Ebb and Bob Fosse, dir by Walter Bobbie at the Adelphi: rev by Billington, Brown, Butler, Clapp, Coveney, de Jongh, Edwardes, Gross, Hagerty, Lister, Macauley, Morley, Nathan, Nightingale, Peter, Smith, Spencer, Taylor. *Top Girls* by Caryl Churchill, dir by Peter Craze at the Chelsea Centre: rev by Cavendish. *Three Viewings* by Jeffrey Hatcher, dir by Mark Clements at the New End: rev by Cavendish, Kingston.

2141 "Reviews of Productions." *TR.* 1997; 17(23): 1478-1479. Lang.: Eng.

UK-England: London. 1997. ∎*Srebrenica* by Nicholas Kent, dir by Kent at the Olivier: rev by Billington, Butler, Macauley. *Hope Deferred* by Chris Ballance, dir by Tom Downes at the Machine Room: rev by Edwardes, Logan. *Saucy Jack and the Space Vixens*, book by Charlotte Mann, music by Robin Forrest and Jonathan Croese, additional lyrics by Michael Fidler, additional music by Adam Megiddo, dir by Keith Strachan at the Hackney Empire: rev by Judah.

2142 "Reviews of Productions." *TR.* 1997; 17(23): 1479, 1481-1485. Lang.: Eng.

UK-England. 1997. ∎*The Middle-Class Tendency* by David Simons, dir by Simons at the Etcetera: rev by Costa. *Big Girls* by Colin Davids and Christopher Lillicrap, dir by Lillicrap at Wimbledon Studio: rev by McPherson. *Sive* by John B. Keane, dir by Ben Barnes at the Palace, Watford: rev by Billington, Butler, Clapp, Curtis, Gore-Langton, Kingston, Pearse.

2143 "Reviews of Productions." *TR.* 1997; 17(24): 1499-1508. Lang.: Eng.

UK-England: London. 1997. ∎*The End of the Affair* by Rupert Goold and Caroline Butler, from the novel by Graham Greene, dir by Goold at the Bridewell: rev by Godfrey-Faussett, Logan, Shuttleworth, Williams. *Madame de Sade (Sado Koshaku fujin)* by Yukio Mishima, transl by Brian Powell from orig English transl by Donald Keen, dir by William Glynne at Riverside 3: rev by Bayley, Booth, Logan. *One More Wasted*

DRAMA: —Performance/production

Year by Christophe Pellet, transl by Martin Crimp, *Bazaar (Bazar)* by David Planell, transl by John Clifford and *Stranger's House (Fremdes Haus)* by Dea Loher, transl by David Tushingham, dir by Mary Peate and Roxanna Silbert at Royal Court Upstairs: rev by Billington, Cavendish, Christopher, Clapp, Curtis, Edwardes, Foss, Godfrey-Faussett, Hemming, Macauley, Peter, Taylor, Woddis.

2144 "Reviews of Productions." *TR.* 1997; 17(24): 1509-1516. Lang.: Eng.
UK-England: London. 1997. ■*Orpheus* by Kenneth McLeish, dir by Nick Philippou at the Lyric Studio: rev by Christopher, Curtis, McPherson, Stratton, Taylor. *The Castle Spectre* by M.G. 'Monk' Lewis, dir by Melissa Holston at the Grace: rev by Logan, McPherson. *Mutabilitie* by Frank McGuinness, dir by Trevor Nunn, for the Royal National at the Cottesloe: rev by Billington, Brown, Butler, Clapp, Coveney, de Jongh, Foss, Gore-Langton, Gross, Hagerty, Macauley, Morley, Nathan, Nightingale, Peter, Spencer, Stratton, Taylor, Woddis.

2145 "Reviews of Productions." *TR.* 1997; 17(24): 1533-1538. Lang.: Eng.
UK-England: London. 1997. ■*Lone Star* by James McLure, dir by Russell Boulter at the Old Red Lion: rev by Christopher, Foss, Stratton. *Oh Les Beaux Jours (Happy Days)* by Beckett, French text, dir by Peter Brook at the Riverside: rev by Billington, Clapp, Coveney, Edwardes, Gross, Hanks, Lockerbie, Macauley, Marlowe, Nightingale, Peter, Spencer. *All in the Wrong* by Arthur Murphy, dir by Sam Walters at the Orange Tree: rev by Curtis, Kingston, Marmion, McPherson.

2146 "Reviews of Productions." *TR.* 1997; 17(24): 1516-1519. Lang.: Eng.
UK-England: London. 1997. ■*Beyond the Blue Horizon* by David Horne, dir by Toby Wilsher at Queen Elizabeth Hall: rev by Butler. *Bugsy Malone* by Paul Williams and Alan Parker, dir by Russel Labey and Jeremy James Taylor for the National Youth Music Theatre at the Queen's: rev by Butler, Cavendish, de Jongh, Gore-Langton, Gross, Hagerty, Hewison, Morley, Nathan, Nightingale, Robinson, Spencer. *New World (El nuevo mundo)* by Carlos Somigliana, *Third Person Included* by Eduardo Pavlovsky, *Cumbia Morena Cumbia* by Mauricio Kartun, and *Grey Song of Absence (Gris de ausencia)* by Roberto Cossa, all four transl by Michael Jacobs, dir by Colin Ellwood at the Finborough: rev by Logan, Sierz, Williams.

2147 "Reviews of Productions." *TR.* 1997; 17(24): 1520-1526. Lang.: Eng.
UK-England: London. 1997. ■*Autumn Music* by Bernardo Stella, dir by Nicky Flack at Pentameters: rev by Costa, Marlowe. *A Little Fight Music* by Philip Pellew, music by Anthony Ingle, dir by Pellew at The Canal Cafe: rev by Godfrey-Faussett, R.L. Parry. *The Chairs (Les Chaises)* by Ionesco, transl by Martin Crimp, dir by Simon McBurney at Royal Court Downstairs: rev by Billington, Brown, Clapp, Coveney, de Jongh, Gore-Langton, Gross, Hagerty, Hanks, Macauley, Morley, Nathan, Nightingale, Peter, Sierz, Smith, Spencer, Stratton, Taylor.

2148 "Reviews of Productions." *TR.* 1997; 17(24): 1539-1541. Lang.: Eng.
UK-England: London. 1997. ■*Leonce and Lena* by Georg Büchner, transl by Lee Hall, dir by Ace McCarron at the Gate: rev by Billington, Cavendish, Davé, de Jongh, Edwardes, Gross, Hanks, Nightingale, Peter. *Measure for Measure* by Shakespeare, dir by Gregory Thompson at BAC: rev by Marlowe. *The Empire Writes Back* by Dominic Flynn and Joshua Morris, dir by Morris at the Man in the Moon: rev by McPherson.

2149 "Reviews of Productions." *TR.* 1997; 17(24): 1527-1532. Lang.: Eng.
UK-England: London. 1997. ■*A Grand Night Out: Wallace & Gromit Alive on Stage* by Andrew Dawson and Bob Baker, inspired by animated films created by Nick Park, dir by Martin Lloyd-Evans at the Peacock: rev by Barker, Christopher, Curtis, Fisher, Gardner, Gilbert, Gore-Langton, Hagerty, Hassell, Nathan, Shuttleworth, Wilson. *The Birds (Ornithes)* by Aristophanes, transl by Peter Meineck, dir by Robert Richmond at the Pleasance: rev by Godfrey-Faussett, R.L. Parry. *Cyrano de Bergerac* by Edmond Rostand, transl by Anthony Burgess, dir by Gregory Doran for the RSC at the Lyric: rev by Christopher, Curtis, Logan, Morley, Murray, Smith.

2150 "Reviews of Productions." *TR.* 1997; 17(24): 1547-1557. Lang.: Eng.
UK-England. 1997. ■*Twelfth Night* by Shakespeare, dir by Adrian Noble for the RSC at the Royal Shakespeare, Stratford: rev by Billington, Brown, Clapp, Coveney, de Jongh, Edwardes, Gore-Langton, Gross, Hagerty, Hanks, Macauley, Nathan, Nightingale, Peter, Spencer, Taylor, Treadwell, Woddis. *Roberto Zucco* by Bernard-Marie Koltès, transl by Martin Crimp, dir by James Macdonald for the RSC at the Other Place, Stratford: rev by Clapp, Coveney, de Jongh, Edwardes, Gross, Hanks, Macauley, Nightingale, Peter, Spencer, Taylor, Treadwell.

2151 "Reviews of Productions." *TR.* 1997; 17(25/26): 1575-1582. Lang.: Eng.
UK-England: London. 1997. ■*The Spanish Tragedy* by Thomas Kyd, dir by Michael Boyd for the RSC at the Pit: rev by de Jongh, Hanks, Hemming, Kingston, Marlowe, Nathan, Stratton. *Hamlet* by Shakespeare, dir by Matthew Warchus at the Barbican: rev by Billington, Bassett, Coveney, de Jongh, Edwardes, Hassell, Kingston, Macauley, Morley, Nightingale, Sierz. *Sive* by John B. Keane, dir by Ben Barnes at the Tricycle: rev by Benedict, Cavendish, Coveney, Hanks, Nathan, Peter, Spencer.

2152 "Reviews of Productions." *TR.* 1997; 17(25/26): 1582-1586. Lang.: Eng.
UK-England: London. 1997. ■*Ready or Not* by Jim O'Hanlon, dir by O'Hanlon at the Man in the Moon: rev by Cavendish. *Chicks with Flicks* by Jackie Clune, dir by Clune at the King's Head: rev by Clapp, Games, Hagerty, North, R.L. Parry. *The Sound of Music* by Rodgers and Hammerstein, book by Lindsay and Crouse, dir by Phil Willmott at BAC Main: rev by Albasini, Benedict, Christopher, Curtis, Gardner, Logan, McPherson.

2153 "Reviews of Productions." *TR.* 1997; 17(25/26): 1586-1588. Lang.: Eng.
UK-England: London. 1997. ■*A Bill of Divorcement* by Clemence Dane, dir by Kate Bannister at the Prince: rev by Abdulla. *The Castle Spectre* by M.G. 'Monk' Lewis, dir by Ted Craig at the Warehouse, Croydon: rev by Cavendish, Costa, Curtis, Foss, Kingston. *Hysteric Studs* by Charlotte Mann, dir by Mann at BAC 1: rev by Godfrey-Faussett, R.L. Parry.

2154 "Reviews of Productions." *TR.* 1997; 17(25/26): 1589-1597. Lang.: Eng.
UK-England: London. 1997. ■*Cinderella* by Cheryl Moch, from original idea by Moch and Holly Gewandter, dir by Nona Shepphard at the Drill Hall: rev by Albasini, Curtis, Foss, Hewison, Kingston, Marmion. *The House of Desires* by Sor Juana Inés de la Cruz, transl by Peter Oswald, dir by Gaynor Macfarlane at BAC 2: rev by Marlowe, Stratton. *More Grimm Tales* by the Brothers Grimm, adapt by Carol Ann Duffy, dir by Tim Supple at the Young Vic: rev by Brown, Clapp, Coveney, Curtis, Gardner, Gore-Langton, Gross, Hagerty, Hanks, Hewison, Logan, Macauley, Nathan, Nightingale, O'Reilly, Smith, Spencer, Taylor.

2155 "Reviews of Productions." *TR.* 1997; 17(25/26): 1597-1601. Lang.: Eng.
UK-England: London. 1997. ■*Change of Heart* adapt from Hans Christian Andersen's 'The Snow Queen' by Strathcona Theatre Company, dir by Ann Cleary and Ian McCurrach at the Young Vic Studio: rev by Christopher, Costa. *David Copperfield* adapt by Matthew Francis from Dickens, dir by Francis at the Greenwich: rev by Billington, Coveney, de Jongh, Dowden, Gross, Hagerty, Haydon, Hemming, Kingston, Marmion, Nathan, Spencer, Woddis. *The Magistrate* by Arthur Wing Pinero, dir by Nicholas Broadhurst at the Savoy: rev by Kingston, Smith, Stratton.

2156 "Reviews of Productions." *TR.* 1997; 17(25/26): 1602-1607. Lang.: Eng.
UK-England: London. 1997. ■*Treasure Island* adapt by Neil Bartlett from Robert Louis Stevenson, dir by Bartlett at the Lyric, Hammersmith: rev by Benedict, Brown, Gardner, Godfrey-Faussett, Gore-Langton, Gross, Hagerty, Hanks, Hewison, Marlowe, Nathan. *Dearest Daddy ... Darling Daughter* by Peter Whittle, dir by Gari Jones at the Young Vic Studio: rev by Christopher. *What's On* (unattrib). *Julian Clary—Special Delivery* by Julian Clary, at the Vaudeville: rev by Barber, Bassett, Dessau, Games, Gross, Hagerty, Marlowe, Nightingale, Peter, Rampton, Shuttleworth, Turpin.

DRAMA: —Performance/production

2157 "Reviews of Productions." *TR.* 1997; 17(25/26): 1611-1621. Lang.: Eng.

UK-England: London. 1997. ∎*The Waste Land* T.S. Eliot's poem performed by Fiona Shaw, dir by Deborah Warner at the Wilton's: rev by Cavendish, Clapp, Coveney, Gardner, Gore-Langton, Gross, Macauley, Nathan, Nightingale, Peter, Spencer, Taylor, Woddis. *The Wizard of Oz* by L. Frank Baum, adapt by Louise Gilbert, dir by Anat Raphael and Titania Krimpas at the New End: rev by Abdulla, R.L. Parry. *The Front Page* by Ben Hecht and Charles MacArthur, dir by Sam Mendes at the Donmar Warehouse: rev by Benedict, Billington, Brown, Butler, Clapp, Coveney, de Jongh, Dowden, Edwardes, Gore-Langton, Gross, Hagerty, Macauley, Nathan, Nightingale, Peter, Sierz, Spencer.

2158 "Reviews of Productions." *TR.* 1997; 17(25/26): 1622-1636. Lang.: Eng.

UK-England: London. 1997. ∎*Little Eyolf (Lille Eyolf)* by Ibsen, transl by Michael Meyer, dir by Adrian Noble for the RSC at The Pit: rev by Bassett, Curtis, Kingston, Nathan, Smith, Stratton. *Peter Pan* by J.M. Barrie in a new version by John Caird and Trevor Nunn, dir by Caird and Fiona Caird at the Olivier: rev by Billington, Brown, Butler, Clapp, Coveney, de Jongh, Edwardes, Gore-Langton, Gross, Hagerty, Hassell, Hewison, Macauley, Morley, Nathan, Nightingale, O'Reilly, Spencer, Taylor. *The Government Inspector (Revizor)* by Nikolai Gogol, transl by John Byrne from a literal transl by Alex Wilbraham, dir by Jonathan Kent at the Almeida: rev by Billington, Butler, Clapp, Coveney, de Jongh, Edwardes, Gore-Langton, Gross, Hagerty, Macauley, Nathan, Nightingale, Peter, Smith, Spencer, Taylor, Woddis.

2159 "Reviews of Productions." *TR.* 1997; 17(25/26): 1636-1642. Lang.: Eng.

UK-England: London. 1997. ∎*William Tell* by John Abulafia from an original scenario by Ralph Oswick and Brian Popay, dir by Abulafia at the Purcell Room: rev by Nightingale. *The Merry Wives of Windsor* by Shakespeare, dir by Ian Judge for the RSC at the Barbican: rev by Bassett, Cavendish, Christopher, Curtis, Gross, Marlowe. *Saturday Night* musical by Stephen Sondheim, book by Julius and Philip Epstein, dir by Carol Metcalfe and Clive Paget at the Bridewell: rev by Bassett, Benedict, Billington, Clapp, Curtis, Darvell, Godfrey-Faussett, Gross, Hagerty, Kingston, Nathan, Peter, Taylor, White.

2160 "Reviews of Productions." *TR.* 1997; 17(25/26): 1642-1646. Lang.: Eng.

UK-England: London. 1997. ∎*Ali Baba and the Forty Thieves* pantomime by Jonathan Petherbridge, dir by Petherbridge at the Albany: rev by Haydon. *Aladdin*, pantomime by John David, dir by David at the Hackney Empire: rev by Butler, Foss, Gore-Langton, Nightingale, Rampton. *Macbeth and the Beanstalk* by David Mitchell and Robert Webb, music by Mark Etherington, lyrics by Jonathan Dryden Taylor, dir by Taylor at the Pleasance: rev by Davé, Games, Kingston, North, Thorncroft.

2161 "Reviews of Productions." *TR.* 1997; 17(25/26): 1647-1649. Lang.: Eng.

UK-England: London. 1997. ∎*Babes in the Wood* adapt and dir by Maurice Browning and Geoffrey Brown from original pantomime by H.J. Byron at the Players: rev by Curtis, Darvell, Kingston, Williams. *Giselle* book and lyrics by Steven Hirst, music by Hirst and Robert Sterne, dir by Hirst and *A Grand Night For Singing* conceived by Walter Bobbie, the songs of Rodgers and Hammerstein, musical arrangements by Fred Wells. dir by Timothy Sheader at the Grace: rev by Marmion, McPherson. *Puss in Boots* by Philip Pullman, dir by Vicky Ireland at the Polka: rev by Haydon, Hewison, Nightingale, H. Taylor.

2162 "Reviews of Productions." *TR.* 1997; 17(25/26): 1650-1655. Lang.: Eng.

UK-England: London. 1997. ∎*Hansel and Gretel* by Patrick Prior, dir by Karen Rabinowitz at Theatre Royal, Stratford East: rev by Darvell, Hagerty, Holland, Kingston, Marmion, Stout. *Cinderella*, Stuart Paterson's pantomime, dir by Tony Graham at the Unicorn (Arts): rev by Haydon, Hewison, Sebag-Montefiore, Spencer. Overall pantomime Round-up by Coveney, Farrell, Gore-Langton, Kingston, Lockerbie, Shuttleworth, Spencer, Watkins.

2163 "Reviews of Productions." *TR.* 1997; 17(25/26): 1659-1670. Lang.: Eng.

UK-England. 1997. ∎*Bartholomew Fair* by Ben Jonson, dir by Laurence Boswell for the RSC at the Swan, Stratford: rev by Billington, Clapp,

Gore-Langton, Hanks, Marmion, Nathan, Nightingale, Peter, Spencer, Taylor. *The Merchant of Venice* by Shakespeare, dir by Gregory Doran for the RSC at the Royal Shakespeare, Stratford: rev by Billington, Brown, Clapp, Coveney, de Jongh, Edwardes, Gore-Langton, Gross, Hagerty, Hanks, Macauley, Nathan, Nightingale, Peter, Spencer, Taylor, Treadwell. *Goodnight Children Everywhere* by Richard Nelson, dir by Ian Brown for the RSC at The Other Place, Stratford: rev by Brown, Clapp, Coveney, de Jongh, Edwardes, Gross, Macauley, Peter, Spencer, Taylor, Woddis.

2164 Baluch, Wojciech. "'Mahabharata' Brooka: Teatr jako opowiadanie historii." (Brook's *Mahabharata*: Theatre as Story-Telling.) 103-119 in Pleśniarowicz, Krzysztof, ed.; Sugiera, Małgorzata, ed. *Arcydzieła inscenizacji od Reinhardta do Wilsona.* Cracow: Księgarnia Akademicka; 1997. 139 pp. (Wielkie dzieła teatralne.) Pref. Notes. Index. Lang.: Pol.

UK-England. France. 1985. Historical studies. ∎Reconstruction of Peter Brook's staging of *The Mahabharata*, which premiered at the Avignon Festival, and consideration of the place of that play in Brook's work.

2165 Banfield, Chris. "Memory Play: Role-Play or Leucotome? The Case of Rose Williams and *Suddenly Last Summer.*" *STP.* 1997 Dec.; 16: 47-63. Notes. Biblio. Illus.: Photo. B&W. 3. Lang.: Eng.

UK-England: Birmingham. 1996. Histories-sources. ∎Author's interpretation of *Suddenly Last Summer* in a production with drama students at Birmingham University. He related the characters of the play to Tennessee Williams's own family and argues that the play shows how the reliving of events in drama could provide more effective therapy than neurosurgery.

2166 Bate, Jonathan. "The Romantic Stage." 92-111 in Bate, Jonathan, ed.; Jackson, Russell, ed. *Shakespeare: An Illustrated Stage History.* Oxford: Oxford UP; 1996. 253 pp. Index. Notes. Biblio. Illus.: Sketches. Dwg. 10. Lang.: Eng.

UK-England. 1800-1840. Historical studies. ∎Changes in Shakespeare production during the Romantic age: Sarah Siddons and Eliza O'Neill, Edmund Kean, John Philip Kemble until the advent of Macready.

2167 Benecke, Patricia. "Shakespeare Is a Universe." *Thsch.* 1997; 11: 131-141. Illus.: Photo. B&W. 2. Lang.: Ger, Fre, Dut, Eng.

UK-England: London. 1990-1997. Histories-sources. ∎Interview with director Deborah Warner regarding her adaptations of Shakespeare's plays and her emphasis on actors and acting.

2168 Borreca, Art. "'Dramaturging' the Dialectic: Brecht, Benjamin, and Declan Donnellan's Production of *Angels in America.*" 245-260 in Geis, Deborah R., ed.; Kruger, Steven F., ed. *Approaching the Millennium: Essays on Angels in America.* Ann Arbor, MI: Univ. of Michigan P; 1997. 352 pp. Notes. Lang.: Eng.

UK-England: London. 1992. Critical studies. ∎Examines the play's complex social and theatrical dialectics through both Brechtian epic theatre and Benjamin-influenced anti-Brechtian spectacle. Uses Declan Donnellan's National Theatre production to examine the elements of epic theatre and develop a dramaturg's protocol for a staging of the play.

2169 Buonanno, G. *A Stage Under Petticoat Government: Italian International Actresses in the Age of Queen Victoria.* Unpublished Ph.D. thesis, Univ. of Warwick: 1995. Notes. Biblio. [Abstract in *Index to Theses*, 46-6268.] Lang.: Eng.

UK-England. 1850-1900. Histories-specific. ∎Documents the English careers of Adelaide Ristori and Eleonora Duse, within the context of the debate on their roles and natures, as well as the reception of foreign stars on the English stage.

2170 Canaris, Volker. "'All the Text's a Stage'." *SJW.* 1997; 133: 11-28. Lang.: Ger.

UK-England. Germany. 1958-1995. Critical studies. ∎Non-literary realism in Shakespeare productions: *As You Like It* directed by Karl Heinz Stroux at Düsseldorfer Schauspielhaus, *Romeo and Juliet* directed by Franco Zeffirelli at Old Vic, *King Lear* directed by Peter Brook at Royal Shakespeare Company, *Othello* and *Richard III* directed by Fritz Kortner at Münchner Kammerspiele, *The Moor of Venice, King Lear, Othello, Hamlet* directed by Peter Zadek in Bochum and Hamburg, *Romeo and*

DRAMA: —Performance/production

Juliet, The Moor of Venice, A Midsummer Night's Dream by Karin Beier at Düsseldorfer Schauspielhaus.

2171 Canaris, Volker. "Von Adam und Eva zu Jedermann." (From Adam and Eve to Everyman.) *THeute.* 1997; 6: 16-21. Illus.: Photo. B&W. 3. Lang.: Ger.
UK-England: Stratford. 1996-1997. Critical studies. ■Analysis of two Royal Shakespeare Company productions based on medieval texts: Katie Mitchell's adaptation of Kemp's *The Mysteries: Part One: The Creation, Part Two: The Passion* and the anonymous *Everyman*, directed by Kathryn Hunter and Marcello Magni.

2172 Caretti, Laura. "Rosencrantz e Guildenstern in primo piano." (Rosencrantz and Guildenstern in the Foreground.) *BiT.* 1997; 42: 153-174. Notes. Lang.: Ita.
UK-England: London. Italy: Forlì. 1966-1996. Critical studies. ■Comparison of two productions of Tom Stoppard's *Rosencrantz and Guildenstern Are Dead*: the Royal National Theatre production in 1966 and the recent Teatro dell'Arca production, directed by Letizia Quintavalla and Bruno Stori, in which actors interact with images from Stoppard's film version.

2173 Courtney, Richard. "Beerbohm Tree and G. Wilson Knight." *NTQ.* 1997; 13(50): 183-185. Lang.: Eng.
UK-England. 1904-1952. Histories-sources. ■Author was a pupil of scholar-actor Knight and recalls the latter's performances in Shakespeare's plays. He demonstrates the influence on him of the actor-manager Herbert Beerbohm Tree.

2174 Cummings, Derek. "'Enter a Throng of Citizens': Extras at the Royal Shakespeare Theatre." *TN.* 1997; 51(1): 8-13. Notes. Lang.: Eng.
UK-England: Stratford. 1879-1995. Historical studies. ■Charts the practice of using amateur actors in the first 65 years of the theatre. Records tell us the number of actors, dates, and payments, but little is known of the theatrical effect. Author documents the critical reaction when the practice was revived in the 1994 and 1995 seasons.

2175 Davies, Anthony. "From the Old Vic to Gielgud and Olivier." 139-159 in Bate, Jonathan, ed.; Jackson, Russell, ed. *Shakespeare: An Illustrated Stage History.* Oxford: Oxford UP; 1996. 253 pp. Index. Notes. Biblio. Illus.: Photo. 12. Lang.: Eng.
UK-England. 1914-1959. Historical studies. ■Shakespeare's plays as treated by companies established in the early half of the twentieth century, before the age of national subsidy: The Old Vic, managed by Lilian Baylis, and Birmingham Repertory, managed by Barry Jackson. Also examines the most important actors to come out of these theatres: John Gielgud, Laurence Olivier, and Donald Wolfit, and director Tyrone Guthrie, as well as the establishment of the Shakespeare Memorial Theatre in 1930 and the beginning of the National Theatre.

2176 de Jongh, Nicholas. "Representing Sex on the British Stage: The Importance of *Angels in America*." 261-270 in Geis, Deborah R., ed.; Kruger, Steven F., ed. *Approaching the Millennium: Essays on Angels in America.* Ann Arbor, MI: Univ. of Michigan P; 1997. 352 pp. Notes. Lang.: Eng.
UK-England: London. 1992. Critical studies. ■The significance of Declan Donnellan's production of Tony Kushner's *Angels in America* for the National Theatre Company with respect to the British aversion to representing sex on stage.

2177 Dench, Judi. "A Career in Shakespeare." 197-210 in Bate, Jonathan, ed.; Jackson, Russell, ed. *Shakespeare: An Illustrated Stage History.* Oxford: Oxford UP; 1996. 253 pp. Index. Notes. Biblio. Illus.: Photo. 9. Lang.: Eng.
UK-England: London. 1957-1995. Historical studies. ■Actor/director Judi Dench describes her thirty-five year career performing and directing Shakespeare, from her debut in 1957 in *Hamlet* to her 1988 direction of *Much Ado About Nothing* at the Renaissance Theatre Company and her performance as Cleopatra in *Antony and Cleopatra*, directed by Peter Hall at the National.

2178 Dusinberre, Juliet. "Squeaking Cleopatras: Gender and Performance in *Antony and Cleopatra*." 46-67 in Bulman, James C., ed. *Shakespeare, Theory, and Performance.* London/New York, NY: Routledge; 1996. 218 pp. Notes. Biblio. Index. Lang.: Eng.
UK-England. North America. 1827-1987. Critical studies. ■Reviewers' reactions to modern productions of Shakespeare's *Antony and Cleopatra*, with emphasis on discomfort with Cleopatra's sensuality. Considers reactions to productions by Peter Hall and Michael Langham and performances by Judi Dench, Barbara Jefford, Janet Suzman, Peggy Ashcroft, and Vivian Leigh.

2179 Eccles, Christine. "What's Post Feminism?" *PI.* 1997 Apr.; 12(9): 6-7. Illus.: Photo. B&W. 1. Lang.: Eng.
UK-England: London. 1997. Historical studies. ■Profile of Vicky Featherstone, the new artistic director of Paines Plough.

2180 Ewbank, Inga-Stina. "European Cross-Currents: Ibsen and Brecht." 128-138 in Bate, Jonathan, ed.; Jackson, Russell, ed. *Shakespeare: An Illustrated Stage History.* Oxford: Oxford UP; 1996. 253 pp. Index. Notes. Biblio. Illus.: Photo. Dwg. 5. Lang.: Eng.
UK-England. 1900-1960. Historical studies. ■Brechtian and Ibsenian influences on the staging of Shakespeare's plays.

2181 Fisher, James. "The First Woman Stage Manager: Edy Craig and the Pioneer Players." *NETJ.* 1997; 8: 73-94. Notes. Biblio. Append. Illus.: Photo. B&W. 3. Lang.: Eng.
UK-England: London. 1907-1947. Biographical studies. ■Craig, first woman director on record, her influence on the British theatre, and her involvement with the Pioneer Players.

2182 Gilbey, Liz. "A Stratford Debut." *PI.* 1997 Feb.; 12(7): 13. Lang.: Eng.
UK-England: Stratford. 1997. Historical studies. ■Film actor Leslie Phillips' debut, at the age of 72, with the Royal Shakespeare Company, playing in *The Merry Wives of Windsor* and *Camino Real*.

2183 Gilbey, Liz. "A Colossus of a Play." *PI.* 1997 May; 12(10): 12-13. Illus.: Photo. B&W. 2. Lang.: Eng.
UK-England: Stratford. 1997. Historical studies. ■Michael Boyd's production of Kyd's *Spanish Tragedy* for the RSC at the Swan.

2184 Gilbey, Liz. "An Irish Ophelia." *PI.* 1997 June; 12(11): 14-15. Illus.: Photo. B&W. 2. Lang.: Eng.
UK-England: Stratford. 1997. Historical studies. ■Irish actress Derbhle Crotty, playing Ophelia in Matthew Warchus' production of *Hamlet* for the RSC at the Stratford.

2185 Gilbey, Liz. "Believe It or Forget It." *PI.* 1997 Christmas; 13(4): 12-13. Illus.: Photo. B&W. 2. Lang.: Eng.
UK-England: London. 1997. Biographical studies. ■Profile of Black actor Ray Fearon, playing Romeo in Michael Attenborough's production of *Romeo and Juliet*, Royal Shakespeare Company.

2186 Goldman, Jill. "Accentuate The Positive: Des Barrit talks to Jill Goldman." *PlPl.* 1997 June/July; 514: 33. Illus.: Photo. B&W. 1. Lang.: Eng.
UK-England: London. 1977-1997. Histories-sources. ■Actor Desmond Barrit reviews his career and describes working on the revue *Then Again.*, directed by Neil Bartlett at London's Lyric Theatre.

2187 Gurr, Andrew. "The First Plays at the New Globe." *TN.* 1997; 51(1): 4-7. Lang.: Eng.
UK-England: London. 1996. Critical studies. ■Argues that the prologue season at Shakespeare's Globe Theatre, which included *The Two Gentlemen of Verona*, shed no light on the staging methods of the original Globe Theatre, and that the commercial success of the season was due to the theatre itself rather than the performances. The only exception was *A Midsummer Night's Dream* by the touring company, Northern Broadsides.

2188 Hankey, Julie. "Victorian Portias: Shakespeare's Borderline Heroine." *SQ.* 1994 Win; 45(4): 426-448. Notes. Lang.: Eng.
UK-England. 1832-1903. Historical studies. ■Victorian notions of womanhood as conveyed through the portrayal of Portia in *The Merchant of Venice*.

2189 Hodgdon, Barbara. "Looking for Mr. Shakespeare After 'The Revolution': Robert Lepage's Intercultural *Dream Machine*." 68-91 in Bulman, James C., ed. *Shakespeare, Theory, and Performance.* London/New York, NY: Routledge; 1996. 218 pp. Notes. Biblio. Index. Lang.: Eng.
UK-England: London. 1992-1993. Critical studies. ■Explores the problem of reception posed by an intercultural and culturally confrontational

DRAMA: —Performance / production

production of *A Midsummer Night's Dream* at the National Theatre, directed by Robert Lepage.

2190 Holland, Peter. *English Shakespeares: Shakespeare on the English Stage in the 1990s.* Cambridge: Cambridge UP; 1997. 295 pp. Index. Pref. Notes. Illus.: Photo. 29. Lang.: Eng.

UK-England. 1989-1997. Histories-specific. ■Historical account of contemporary performances of Shakespeare in England. Focuses on the Royal Shakespeare Company, the National, the populist work of the Swan Theatre, and also explores productions of Shakespeare by non-British companies from other countries.

2191 Hunter, Robin. "Ralph Lynn—A Farcical Genius." *PlPl.* 1997 May; 513: 19. Illus.: Diagram. Photo. B&W. 2. Lang.: Eng.

UK-England: London. 1953. Histories-sources. ■Recalls comedian Ralph Lynn's antics working on Ben Travers' farce *Wild Horses*, Aldwych Theatre, 1953.

2192 Hunter, Robin. "Exploding Boots." *PlPl.* 1997 Aug/Sep.; 515: 7. Illus.: Photo. B&W. 1. Lang.: Eng.

UK-England. 1970-1997. Biographical studies. ■Memories of moments in personal life of actor Don Henderson.

2193 Jackson, Russell. "Actor-Managers and the Spectacular." 112-127 in Bate, Jonathan, ed.; Jackson, Russell, ed. *Shakespeare: An Illustrated Stage History.* Oxford: Oxford UP; 1996. 253 pp. Index. Notes. Biblio. Illus.: Photo. Dwg. 12. Lang.: Eng.

UK-England. 1840-1914. Historical studies. ■Shakespeare in the age of actor-managers such as Charles Kean, the Bancrofts, William Macready, Beerbohm Tree, Henry Irving and Ellen Terry, William Poel, and Harley Granville-Barker.

2194 Jackson, Russell. "Shakespeare in Opposition: From the 1950s to the 1990s." 211-230 in Bate, Jonathan, ed.; Jackson, Russell, ed. *Shakespeare: An Illustrated Stage History.* Oxford: Oxford UP; 1996. 253 pp. Index. Notes. Biblio. Illus.: Photo. 10. Lang.: Eng.

UK-England. 1950-1995. Historical studies. ■Modern changes in Shakespeare performance: modern redressings, new ways of speaking the text, and new social issues.

2195 Jays, David. "Hurrah for Repertoire." *PI.* 1997 July; 12(12): 12-13. Illus.: Photo. B&W. 2. Lang.: Eng.

UK-England: London. 1997. Historical studies. ■Actor Dominic West and his role in *The Seagull (Čajka)*, directed by Peter Hall at the Old Vic.

2196 Jays, David. "Studies in Misogyny." *PI.* 1997 Oct.; 13(2): 10-11. Illus.: Photo. B&W. 3. Lang.: Eng.

UK-England: London. 1997. Biographical studies. ■Recent roles of Michael Pennington at the Old Vic under the direction of Peter Hall in *The Provok'd Wife* by Vanbrugh, *The Seagull (Čajka)* by Čechov, and *Waste* by Granville-Barker, as well as his own one-man Čechov evening, *Anton Chekov*.

2197 Jays, David. "Wearing Two Hats." *PI.* 1997 Mar.; 12(8): 10-11. Illus.: Photo. B&W. 1. Lang.: Eng.

UK-England: London. 1997. Historical studies. ■Profile of Mark Rylance, artistic director and lead actor at Shakespeare's Globe in its first full season.

2198 Jays, David. "A Passion for New Writing." *PI.* 1997 May; 12(10): 10-11. Illus.: Photo. B&W. 2. Lang.: Eng.

UK-England: London. 1997. Historical studies. ■Michael Attenborough's production of *The Herbal Bed* by Peter Whelan for the RSC.

2199 Kalmér, Åsa. "Unga regissörer söker nya vägar." (Young Directors On the Look-Out For New Paths.) *Dramat.* 1997; 5(3): 24. Illus.: Photo. Color. Lang.: Swe.

UK-England: Stratford. 1997. Historical studies. ■A report from a meeting of young directors from Europe at Royal Shakespeare Company, with reference to the director Katie Mitchell.

2200 Kempinski, Tom. "Ignorance is Bliss (as long as you avoid the furniture)." *PlPl.* 1997 May; 513: 37. Lang.: Eng.

UK-England. 1997. Critical studies. ■Argues that ignorance of psychology among English actors and directors leads to shallow interpretations.

2201 Knowles, Richard Paul. "Shakespeare, Voice, and Ideology: Interrogating the Natural Voice." 92-112 in Bulman, James C., ed. *Shakespeare, Theory, and Performance.* London/New York, NY: Routledge; 1996. 218 pp. Notes. Biblio. Index. Lang.: Eng.

UK-England. North America. 1975-1995. Critical studies. ■Critique of vocal training as practiced by Cicely Berry, Kristin Linklater, and Patsy Rodenburg and analysis of voice training as an ideologically coded theatrical practice in contemporary Shakespearean production.

2202 Mariani, Laura. "Chi è Miriam Rooth? La Musa Tragica di Henry James." (Who Is Miriam Rooth? Henry James's Tragic Muse.) *TeatroS.* 1997; 12(19): 245-254. Notes. Lang.: Ita.

UK-England. 1890. Historical studies. ■Hypotheses about the model for the protagonist of James's novel *The Tragic Muse*, who may have been Sarah Siddons, Julia Bartet, Sarah Bernhardt, or Rachel.

2203 Mazer, Cary M. "Historicizing Alan Dessen: Scholarship, Stagecraft, and the 'Shakespeare Revolution'." 149-167 in Bulman, James C., ed. *Shakespeare, Theory, and Performance.* London/New York, NY: Routledge; 1996. 218 pp. Notes. Biblio. Index. Lang.: Eng.

UK-England. 1905-1979. Critical studies. ■Twentieth-century English theatre's use of Elizabethan stage semiotics, emphasizing Poel's supposedly historically accurate productions of Shakespeare early in the century, Peter Brook's 'Elizabethan' staging of *A Midsummer Night's Dream* in 1967, and Richard Barton's RSC production of *Richard II* in 1973.

2204 Meech, Tony; Upton, Carole-Anne. "Botho Strauss on the British Stage." *STP.* 1997 Dec.; 16: 35-46. Lang.: Eng.

UK-England. 1996. Histories-sources. ■Description of the authors' production of *Time and the Room (Die Zeit und das Zimmer)* with drama students at Hull University, in which the playfulness of Strauss's text challenged the performers to abandon preconceptions of character and motivation and 'to experiment with what may be the nearest the stage can aspire to abstraction, to pure form'.

2205 Merrit, Susan Hollis. "Pinter Playing Pinter: *The Hothouse*." *PintR.* 1997: 73-84. Notes. Lang.: Eng.

UK-England: Chichester. 1996. Critical studies. ■Harold Pinter's performance in his own play *The Hothouse* at the Minerva Studio Theatre.

2206 Oliva, Judy Lee. "Directing David Hare's *The Secret Rapture*: Issues Toward a New Aesthetic Praxis." *JDTC.* 1997 Spr; 11(2): 101-114. Illus.: Diagram. 2. Lang.: Eng.

UK-England. 1988-1995. Histories-sources. ■The author's experience in directing Hare's *The Secret Rapture*, in light of what it reveals about stage practice and the development of aesthetics. She examines how this kind of dramaturgy is realized on stage, what specifically informs a director's decisions, and what changes might be warranted in the development of the directing experience.

2207 Owen, Robert. "She Knows Hylda You Know." *PI.* 1997 Oct.; 13(2): 14-15. Illus.: Photo. B&W. 1. Lang.: Eng.

UK-England. 1996-1997. Historical studies. ■Jean Fergusson's one-woman show *She Knows, You Know!*, about music-hall star Hylda Baker.

2208 Patterson, Michael. "Fighting Woman's Revenge." *STP.* 1997 Dec.; 16: 140. Lang.: Eng.

UK-England. 1593-1750. Histories-sources. ■The author speculates, in the light of a personal experience, whether the pre-nineteenth century practice of distributing roles individually to actors, without accompanying stage-directions, may have led to violent misunderstandings.

2209 Schafer, Elizabeth. "Census of Renaissance Drama Productions." *RORD.* 1997; 36: 105-119. Lang.: Eng.

UK-England. 1996-1997. Historical studies. ■List of recent productions of Renaissance authors: includes play, author, venue, director, dramaturg, dates.

2210 Shaughnessy, Robert. "'Ragging the Bard': Terence Gray, Shakespeare, and *Henry VIII*." *TN.* 1997; 51(2): 92-111. Notes. Illus.: Photo. B&W. 1. Lang.: Eng.

UK-England: Cambridge. 1925-1940. Historical studies. ■Artistic principles behind controversial director Terence Gray's work and his subsequent critical reputation. Includes an extended account of *Henry VIII*, presented at the Cambridge Festival Theatre in 1931.

DRAMA: —Performance / production

2211 Shenton, Mark. "Returning to One's Roots." *PI.* 1997 Oct.; 13(2): 12-13. Illus.: Photo. B&W. 1. Lang.: Eng.
UK-England: London. 1997. Biographical studies. ■Director Anthony Page's current project: Albee's *A Delicate Balance* at the Theatre Royal, Haymarket.

2212 Shenton, Mark. "Like Father Like Son?" *PI.* 1997 Jan.; 12(6): 8-9. Illus.: Photo. B&W. 1. Lang.: Eng.
UK-England: London. 1997. Historical studies. ■Profile of actors Timothy and Sam West, father and son, who are playing Falstaff and Hal, respectively, in Shakespeare's *Henry IV* parts 1 and 2, directed by Stephen Unwin for the English Touring Theatre.

2213 Shenton, Mark. "Grown Up Talents." *PI.* 1997 Feb.; 12(7): 10-12. Illus.: Photo. B&W. 1. Lang.: Eng.
UK-England: London. 1997. Historical studies. ■Profile of Dominic Dromgoole, former artistic director of the Bush Theatre, now programming the season of new plays for Peter Hall at the Old Vic.

2214 Shenton, Mark. "Popcorn's Progress." *PI.* 1997 Apr.; 12(9): 10-11. Illus.: Photo. B&W. 1. Lang.: Eng.
UK-England: London. 1997. Historical studies. ■Profile of Laurence Boswell, director of *Popcorn* by Ben Elton at the Apollo.

2215 Shenton, Mark. "Crossing the Thames." *PI.* 1997 Christmas; 13(4): 10-11, 39. Illus.: Photo. B&W. 1. Lang.: Eng.
UK-England: London. 1997. Historical studies. ■John Caird's adaptation of *Peter Pan* with Ian McKellen and its move from RSC to the National at Olivier Theatre.

2216 Shrubsall, Anthony; Pitches, Jonathan. "Two Perspectives on the Phenomenon of Biomechanics in Contemporary Performance: an Account of Gogol's *The Government Inspector* in Production." *STP.* 1997 Dec.; 16: 93-128. Notes. Biblio. Illus.: Diagram. Photo. B&W. Grd.Plan. 6. Lang.: Eng.
UK-England: Northampton. 1997. Histories-sources. ■Director and the actor of the title-role describe work on their production of *The Government Inspector (Revizor)* at Nene College, Northampton, employing Mejerchol'd's techniques. Preparation included workshops using 'stick work' to develop balance, spatial awareness and instantaneous reaction, which resulted in strongly physical performances at several removes from Stanislavskij's psychological realism.

2217 Smallwood, Robert. "Directors' Shakespeare." 176-196 in Bate, Jonathan, ed.; Jackson, Russell, ed. *Shakespeare: An Illustrated Stage History*. Oxford: Oxford UP; 1996. 253 pp. Index. Notes. Biblio. Illus.: Photo. 7. Lang.: Eng.
UK-England. 1964-1993. Historical studies. ■The effect of the director on Shakespeare's plays and the effect of Shakespeare on the 'century of the director.' Examination ranges from open vs. interpretive direction to experiments and epics.

2218 Teschke, Holger. "Waiting for the End of the Copyright Laws." *TZ.* 1997; Yb: 30-32. Illus.: Photo. B&W. 2. Lang.: Eng.
UK-England: London. 1983-1997. Histories-sources. ■An interview with actor and director Simon McBurney, director of Théâtre de Complicité, about ensemble acting and his production of *Der Kaukasische Kreidekreis (The Caucasian Chalk Circle)* in 1997.

2219 Thomas, Sue. "Sexual Matter and *Votes for Women*." *PLL.* 1997 Win; 33(1): 47-70. Notes. Biblio. Lang.: Eng.
UK-England: London. 1907. Historical studies. ■Significance of Elizabeth Robins' play *Votes for Women! A Dramatic Tract* to the suffragette movement, with analysis of its performance and reception at the Court Theatre.

2220 Thomson, Peter. "Shakespeare and the Public Purse." 160-175 in Bate, Jonathan, ed.; Jackson, Russell, ed. *Shakespeare: An Illustrated Stage History*. Oxford: Oxford UP; 1996. 253 pp. Index. Notes. Biblio. Illus.: Photo. 7. Lang.: Eng.
UK-England. 1960-1988. Historical studies. ■The effect of nationalization, the Arts Council and subsidy on Shakespeare's plays and their reception. Follows versions of *The Taming of the Shrew*, *Hamlet*, and *A Midsummer Night's Dream* through the National and Royal Shakespeare Company's first three decades to chart the effect.

2221 Tulloch, John; Burvill, Tom; Hood, Andrew. "Reinhabiting *The Cherry Orchard*: Class and History in Performing Chekhov." *NTQ.* 1997; 13(52): 318-328. Notes. Lang.: Eng.
UK-England. 1977-1995. Critical studies. ■Compares two productions of *The Cherry Orchard (Višněvyj sad)*: Richard Eyre and Trevor Griffiths (1977) and Adrian Noble (1995), suggesting that whereas the latter referenced class in his rehearsal style and staging, the former embodied the intra-class mobility of the Thatcher era.

2222 van Werson, Gerard. "Getting Paid for Your Hobby." *PI.* 1997 Feb.; 12(7): 14-15. Illus.: Photo. B&W. 1. Lang.: Eng.
UK-England: London. 1997. Historical studies. ■Profile of actor David Bradley, appearing in *The Homecoming* at the National.

2223 van Werson, Gerard. "Playing the Baddie." *PI.* 1997 Mar.; 12(8): 14-15. Illus.: Photo. B&W. 1. Lang.: Eng.
UK-England: London. 1997. Historical studies. ■Actor James Laurenson's return to his role as Benedict Arnold in Richard Nelson's *The General from America*, Royal Shakespeare Company.

2224 Waites, Aline. "Stewart Permutt in Conversation: with Aline Waites." *PlPl.* 1997 June/July; 514: 40-41. Illus.: Photo. B&W. 1. Lang.: Eng.
UK-England: London. 1950-1997. Histories-sources. ■Actor-playwright Stewart Permutt reviews his career and discusses his latest play, *The Cracked Comic*.

2225 Wells, Stanley; Szántó, Judit, transl.; Csutkai, Csaba, photo.; Simara, László, photo. "Az erőszak szervessége. A *Titus Andronicus* rehabilitálása." (The Nature of Violence: The Rehabilitation of Shakespeare's *Titus Andronicus*.) *Sz.* 1997; 30(11): 40-47. Illus.: Photo. B&W. 6. Lang.: Hun.
UK-England. USA. 1955-1995. Critical studies. ■Analysis of productions directed by Robert Atkins, Peter Brook, Gerald Freedman, Deborah Warner, Jonathan Miller, and Jane Howell, as well as productions of the Oregon and New Jersey Shakespeare festivals.

2226 Wille, Franz. "Das Theater und seine Doubles." (Theatre and its Doubles.) *THeute.* 1997; 7: 14-18. Illus.: Photo. B&W. 4. Lang.: Ger.
UK-England: London. 1997. Historical studies. ■Discusses Brecht's old-fashioned alienation and a modern version of his *Der Kaukasische Kreidekreis (The Caucasian Chalk Circle)* directed by Simon McBurney and played by Théâtre de Complicité.

2227 Young, Stuart. "Sleeping with the Mainstream: Gay Drama and Theatre in Britain Moves in from the Margins." *ADS.* 1997 Oct.; 31: 71-91. Notes. Illus.: Photo. B&W. 1. Lang.: Eng.
UK-England. 1986-1997. Critical studies. ■Examines the growing acceptance of gay drama in Britain's mainstream theatre.

2228 Ziółkowski, Grzegorz. "Teatr moralnego niepokoju: 'Król Lear' w reżyserii Petera Brooka." (The Theatre of Moral Deliberation: Peter Brook's *King Lear*.) 87-102 in Pleśniarowicz, Krzysztof, ed.; Sugiera, Małgorzata, ed. *Arcydzieła inscenizacji od Reinhardta do Wilsona*. Cracow: Księgarnia Akademicka; 1997. 139 pp. (Wielkie dzieła teatralne.) Lang.: Pol.
UK-England: Stratford, London. 1970. Historical studies. ■Reconstruction of the RSC production with Paul Scofield.

2229 Ziter, Edward. *The Invention of the Middle East in British Scene Painting and Mise en Scène: 1798-1853*. Santa Barbara, CA: Univ. of California; 1997. 385 pp. Notes. Biblio. [Ph.D. Dissertation, Univ. Microfilms Order No. AAC 9804296.] Lang.: Eng.
UK-England. 1798-1853. Critical studies. ■Characterizes British stage practice as a 'colonial geography in the making'. Examines a range of stage productions, optical shows, and exhibitions from the first half of the century that center on depictions of the Middle East.

2230 "Reviews of Productions." *TR.* 1997; 17(17): 1016-1026. Lang.: Eng.
UK-Scotland: Edinburgh. 1997. ■*Measure for Measure* by Shakespeare, dir by Stéphane Braunschweig at the Royal Lyceum: rev by Billington, Butler, Clapp, Coveney, de Jongh, Donald, Fisher, Gore-Langton, Gross, Macauley, Nightingale, Peter, Smith, Spencer, Taylor. *Blinded by Love (Cegada de Amor)* by Jordi Milan w/Joaquim Oristell, José Cor-

DRAMA: —Performance/production

bacho and Fernando Colomo, dir by Milan for La Cubana at the Edinburgh International Conference Centre: rev by Billington, Butler, Clapp, Coveney, de Jongh, Donald, Gore-Langton, Gross, Nightingale, Peter, Shuttleworth, Smith, Spencer, Taylor, Wareham. *A Tainted Dawn* by Sudha Buchar and Kristine Landon-Smith, dir by Landon-Smith at the Gateway: rev by Clapp, Coveney, de Jongh, Nightingale, Peter, Shuttleworth, Taylor, Wilson.

2231 "Reviews of Productions." *TR.* 1997; 17(17): 1026-1036. Lang.: Eng.

UK-Scotland: Edinburgh. 1997. ■*Le Bourgeois Gentilhomme* by Molière, transl by Jeremy Sams, and *Ariadne auf Naxos* by Richard Strauss, libretto by Hugo von Hofmannsthal, dir by Martin Duncan at the Festival: rev by Ashley, Canning, Christiansen, Coveney, Donal, Fisher, Kennedy, Miller, Milnes, Monelle, Murray, Tumelty. *East Palace, West Palace* by Zhang Yuan, dir by Zhang at the Gateway: rev by Cooper, Donald, Fisher, Peter, Shuttleworth, Spencer. *The Cocktail Party* by T.S. Eliot, dir by Philip Franks at the King's: rev by Bassett, Clapp, Donald, Fisher, Nightingale, Peter, Shuttleworth, Turpin.

2232 "Reviews of Productions." *TR.* 1997; 17(17): 1037-1044, 1050-1052. Lang.: Eng.

UK-Scotland: Edinburgh. 1997. ■*Timeless* by David Grieg, music by Nick Powell, dir by Graham Eatough at the Gateway: rev by Bassett, Billington, Clapp, Donald, Fisher, Kingston, Peter, Shuttleworth, Taylor. *The Cherry Orchard (Višněvyj sad)* by Čechov, dir in German by Peter Stein (Salzburg Festival production): rev by Billington, Clapp, de Jongh, Donald, Kingston, Macauley, Spencer, Taylor. *Anna Weiss* by Mike Cullen, dir by Vicky Featherstone at the Traverse: rev by Butler, Clapp, Coveney, de Jongh, Edwardes, Gore-Langton, Gross, Macauley, Nightingale, Peter, Spencer, Turpin. *Massage* by Steven Berkoff, dir by Berkoff at the Assembly Rooms: rev by Cooper, Coveney, Curtis, Donald, Peter, Shuttleworth.

2233 Malague, Rose. "Two Festivals, Three Plays: Caryl Churchill in London and Edinburgh." *WES.* 1997 Fall; 9(3): 37-42. Illus.: Photo. 2. Lang.: Eng.

UK-Scotland: Edinburgh. UK-England: London. 1997. Historical studies. ■Critical review of Caryl Churchill's *This Is a Chair* directed by Stephen Daldry at the Royal Court Theatre, and *Heart's Desire* and *Blue Kettle*, also by Churchill, presented at the Edinburgh Fringe Festival, directed by Max Stafford-Clark at the Traverse.

2234 Selavie, Sasha. "Puttin' On The Glitz: Sian Phillips talks to Sasha Selavie." *PlPl.* 1997 June/July; 514: 8-9. Illus.: Photo. Color. 1. Lang.: Eng.

UK-Wales. UK-England: London. 1930-1997. Histories-sources. ■Actor Sian Phillips' life and career, from performing Bible stories in Wales to portraying Marlene Dietrich in Pam Gems' *Marlene* in London's West End.

2235 "How to Talk to a Playwright: Panel Discussion with Steve Carter, Constance Congdon, John Glore, Philip Kan Gotanda, Eric Overmyer, and Sandy Shiner." 180-189 in Jonas, Susan, ed.; Proehl, Geoffrey S., ed. *Dramaturgy in American Theatre: A Sourcebook.* New York, NY: Harcourt Brace College Pub; 1997. 590 pp. Pref. Notes. Biblio. Index. Lang.: Eng.

USA. 1990. Histories-sources. ■Partial proceedings of a Literary Managers and Dramaturgs of America (LMDA) conference. Dramaturgs and playwrights explore ways in which culture, gender, and terminology affect their collaboration.

2236 "A Conversation with Mame Hunt, Dramaturg-Artistic Director, and Susan Mason, Dramaturg-Academic, 19 August 1994, Oakland." 421-430 in Jonas, Susan, ed.; Proehl, Geoffrey S., ed. *Dramaturgy in American Theatre: A Sourcebook.* New York, NY: Harcourt Brace College Pub; 1997. 590 pp. Pref. Notes. Biblio. Index. Lang.: Eng.

USA. 1994. Histories-sources. ■Interview with Hunt of Magic Theatre and Mason of California State University, exploring the role of literary managers, dramaturgs, and artistic directors in working with new plays and shaping the aesthetic/ideological function of a specific theatre.

2237 Albright, William. "Annalee Jefferies." *AmTh.* 1997 Mar.; 14(3): 32-33. Illus.: Photo. B&W. 4. Lang.: Eng.

USA: Houston, TX. 1986-1997. Biographical studies. ■Career and training of actress Jefferies including past productions and her work with the Alley Theatre company.

2238 Arata, Luis O. "Performing the Maya Vision from the *Popol Vuh.*" *Gestos.* 1997 Apr.; 12(23): 115-129. Notes. Biblio. Lang.: Eng.

USA: New York, NY. 1995. Critical studies. ■Analysis of Ralph Lee's production of Cherríe Moraga's *Heart of the Earth, A Popol Vuh Story*, derived from the Mayan book of creation, and presented at INTAR.

2239 Aronson, Arnold. "Like First-Class Advertising." *TZ.* 1997; Yb: 88-92. Append. Illus.: Photo. B&W. 2. Lang.: Eng.

USA. 1950-1997. Histories-sources. ■An interview with director, playwright, designer and producer Richard Foreman regarding the influence of Brecht on his early development.

2240 Ballet, Arthur. "Why in the Hell Are We So Serious?" 78-82 in Jonas, Susan, ed.; Proehl, Geoffrey S., ed. *Dramaturgy in American Theatre: A Sourcebook.* New York, NY: Harcourt Brace College Pub; 1997. 590 pp. Pref. Notes. Biblio. Index. Lang.: Eng.

USA. 1965-1997. Histories-sources. ■Author recounts his personal experience as a dramaturg.

2241 Bly, Mark. "Bristling with Multiple Possibilities." 48-55 in Jonas, Susan, ed.; Proehl, Geoffrey S., ed. *Dramaturgy in American Theatre: A Sourcebook.* New York, NY: Harcourt Brace College Pub; 1997. 590 pp. Pref. Notes. Biblio. Index. Lang.: Eng.

USA. 1997. Historical studies. ■On maintaining the questioning nature of dramaturgy.

2242 Borreca, Art. "Dramaturging New Play Dramaturgy: The Yale and Iowa Ideals." 56-69 in Jonas, Susan, ed.; Proehl, Geoffrey S., ed. *Dramaturgy in American Theatre: A Sourcebook.* New York, NY: Harcourt Brace College Pub; 1997. 590 pp. Pref. Notes. Biblio. Index. Lang.: Eng.

USA. 1997. Historical studies. ■Compares/contrasts two influential centers of dramaturgical activity and training, Yale University and University of Iowa.

2243 Boyd, Deanna Patrice. *Breaking the Roles of Gender and Class: An Acting Analysis of Fran in 'An O. Henry Christmas'.* Long Beach, CA: California State Univ; 1997. 88 pp. Notes. Biblio. [M.F.A. Thesis, Univ. Microfilms Order No. AAC 1387563.] Lang.: Eng.

USA: Long Beach, CA. 1994-1996. Histories-sources. ■On the author's creation and performance of the character Fran in Howard Burman's adaptation of *An O. Henry Christmas*, produced by the California Repertory Company and performed at California State University, Long Beach.

2244 Boyd, J. Caleb; Gagnon, Pauline. "Olympics: Theatre Series Showcases Atlanta Theatre, But Fails to Win Gold Medal." *SoTh.* 1997 Win; 38(1): 28-31. Illus.: Photo. B&W. 3. Lang.: Eng.

USA: Atlanta, GA. 1996. Critical studies. ■The plays produced at the Theatre Series of the 1996 Olympic Arts Festival in Atlanta, with an assessment of how well they fulfilled the goals of the organizing committee.

2245 Bredbeck, Gregory W. "'Freeing the Erotic Angels': Performing Liberation in the 1970s and 1990s." 271-290 in Geis, Deborah R., ed.; Kruger, Steven F., ed. *Approaching the Millennium: Essays on Angels in America.* Ann Arbor, MI: Univ. of Michigan P; 1997. 352 pp. Notes. Lang.: Eng.

USA. 1992-1994. Critical studies. ■Tony Kushner's *Angels in America* in the context of queer performance history, with emphasis on Charles Ludlam's production of *Bluebeard* with the Ridiculous Theatrical Company.

2246 Brockett, Oscar G. "Dramaturgy in Education: Introduction." 42-47 in Jonas, Susan, ed.; Proehl, Geoffrey S., ed. *Dramaturgy in American Theatre: A Sourcebook.* New York, NY: Harcourt Brace College Pub; 1997. 590 pp. Pref. Notes. Biblio. Index. Lang.: Eng.

DRAMA: —Performance/production

USA. 1997. Historical studies. ■On the role of dramaturgy in the university, emphasizing its relationship to the role of the director in American theatre.

2247 Brustein, Robert. "From 'The Future of an Un-American Activity'." 33-36 in Jonas, Susan, ed.; Proehl, Geoffrey S., ed. *Dramaturgy in American Theatre: A Sourcebook.* New York, NY: Harcourt Brace College Pub; 1997. 590 pp. Pref. Notes. Biblio. Index. Lang.: Eng.

USA. 1997. Historical studies. ■The transformation of dramatic criticism at Yale University from an adversarial position outside the rehearsal process to a collaborative role within it.

2248 Cattaneo, Anne. "Dramaturgy: An Overview." 3-15 in Jonas, Susan, ed.; Proehl, Geoffrey S., ed. *Dramaturgy in American Theatre: A Sourcebook.* New York, NY: Harcourt Brace College Pub; 1997. 590 pp. Pref. Biblio. Notes. Index. Lang.: Eng.

USA. 1997. Historical studies. ■Brief history of performance dramaturgy, including European and American precursors, detailed description of role of the dramaturg in American theatre.

2249 Chetta, Peter N. "The Shakespeare Marathon: A Personal Perspective." *ShN.* 1997 Sum/Fall; 47(2/3): 25, 32, 38, 42. [Number 233/234.] Lang.: Eng.

USA: New York, NY. 1997. Historical studies. ■Overview of the New York Shakespeare Festival's production of the Shakespeare canon initiated by producer Joseph Papp (beginning in 1987) upon the recent completion of the project. Year by year analysis of productions presented, actors, directors, audience response.

2250 Clark, Susan F. "Solo Black Performance before the Civil War: Mrs. Stowe, Mrs. Webb and *The Christian Slave.*" *NTQ.* 1997; 13(52): 339-348. Notes. Illus.: Handbill. Dwg. B&W. 2. Lang.: Eng.

USA. 1853-1857. Historical studies. ■The role of melodramatic stage adaptations of *Uncle Tom's Cabin* in creating a stereotype Negro slave. Emphasis on Harriet Beecher Stowe's own dramatization of her novel, which was to be performed solely by Mrs. Mary E. Webb, a mulatto dramatic reader.

2251 Coen, Stephanie. "The Fascination of What's Difficult." *AmTh.* 1997 Mar.; 14(3): 12-16. Illus.: Photo. B&W. 6. Lang.: Eng.

USA. UK-England. 1980-1997. Histories-sources. ■Interview with actress Fiona Shaw and director Deborah Warner: their collaboration on adapting T.S. Eliot's *The Waste Land* and their experience performing it in New York at the Liberty Theatre, produced by Jedediah Wheeler and site-specific En Garde Arts. Includes sidebar article 'A Clearing of the Boards' on Fiona Shaw's residency at University of Missouri-Kansas City and her work with acting students.

2252 Coen, Stephanie. "Peter Schickele." *AmTh.* 1997 Apr.; 14(4): 31. Illus.: Photo. B&W. 1. Lang.: Eng.

USA: New York, NY. 1965-1997. Histories-sources. ■Brief interview with composer/musician Schickele (also known as P.D.Q. Bach) about his score for Elizabeth Huddle's production of Richard Brinsley Sheridan's *The Rivals.*

2253 Connelly, Stacey. "Brecht's Out-of-Town Tryout: The World Premiere of *The Caucasian Chalk Circle.*" *THSt.* 1997; 17: 93-119. Illus.: Photo. 5. Lang.: Eng.

USA: Northfield, MN. 1948. Historical studies. ■The world premiere performance of Brecht's *Der Kaukasische Kreidekreis* directed by Henry Goodman at Carleton College. Author examines the extraordinary historical aspects of this production as well as partially reconstructing the performance itself.

2254 Coppenger, Royston; Preston, Travis. "The Way We Work." 165-175 in Jonas, Susan, ed.; Proehl, Geoffrey S., ed. *Dramaturgy in American Theatre: A Sourcebook.* New York, NY: Harcourt Brace College Pub; 1997. 590 pp. Pref. Biblio. Index. Lang.: Eng.

USA. 1983-1997. Histories-sources. ■Director Travis Preston and dramaturg Royston Coppenger reflect on their work together, especially the rehearsal process.

2255 Crum, Jane Ann. "Toward a Dramaturgical Sensibility." 70-77 in Jonas, Susan, ed.; Proehl, Geoffrey S., ed. *Drama-*

turgy in American Theatre: A Sourcebook. New York, NY: Harcourt Brace College Pub; 1997. 590 pp. Pref. Notes. Biblio. Index. Lang.: Eng.

USA. 1997. Instructional materials. ■Pedagogical applications of dramaturgy: author gives methods and exercises for training dramaturgs, as well as suggestions on a 'dialogue' between dramaturgs and directors.

2256 Devin, Lee. "Conceiving the Forms: Play Analysis for Production Dramaturgs." 209-219 in Jonas, Susan, ed.; Proehl, Geoffrey S., ed. *Dramaturgy in American Theatre: A Sourcebook.* New York, NY: Harcourt Brace College Pub; 1997. 590 pp. Pref. Notes. Biblio. Index. Lang.: Eng.

USA. 1997. Critical studies. ■Examines a shared vocabulary between directors and dramaturgs. Argues that collaboration requires a language that will describe their undertakings and allow them to communicate more effectively.

2257 Dixon, Michael Bigelow. "The Dramaturgical Dialogue: New Play Dramaturgy at Actors' Theatre of Louisville." 412-420 in Jonas, Susan, ed.; Proehl, Geoffrey S., ed. *Dramaturgy in American Theatre: A Sourcebook.* New York, NY: Harcourt Brace College Pub; 1997. 590 pp. Pref. Notes. Biblio. Index. Lang.: Eng.

USA: Louisville, KY. 1972-1995. Historical studies. ■Examines the work of Actors' Theatre of Louisville, one of the leaders in producing new plays for American theatre.

2258 Driscoll, F. Paul. "Going to the Opera ... with Zoe Caldwell and Robert Whitehead." *OpN.* 1997 Sep.; 62(3): 28-31. Illus.: Photo. B&W. 3. Lang.: Eng.

USA: New York, NY. 1996. Histories-sources. ■Actor Zoe Caldwell and her husband, producer Robert Whitehead, discuss *Master Class* by Terrence McNally, based on the 1971 master classes offered by Maria Callas at the Juilliard School of Music.

2259 Eccles, Christine. "Having a Voice." *PI.* 1997 July; 12(12): 14-15. Illus.: Photo. B&W. 1. Lang.: Eng.

USA. 1997. Historical studies. ■Profile of Patsy Rodenburg, voice coach for the National Theatre.

2260 Elam, Harry J., Jr. *Taking It to the Streets: The Social Protest Theater of Luis Valdez and Amiri Baraka.* Ann Arbor, MI: Univ. of Michigan P; 1997. 192 pp. Notes. Biblio. Index. Illus.: Photo. 10. Lang.: Eng.

USA. 1965-1975. Critical studies. ■Comparison of the performance methodologies, theories, and practices of Luis Valdez's Teatro Campesino, and Amiri Baraka's Black Revolutionary Theatre, two social protest theatre groups. Author argues that the performances of these groups linked the political, the cultural, and the spiritual with community, while agitating against the dominant power structure.

2261 Erdman, Harley. *Staging the Jew: The Performance of an American Ethnicity, 1860-1920.* New Brunswick, NJ/ London: Rutgers UP; 1997. 224 pp. Notes. Index. Biblio. Lang.: Eng.

USA. 1860-1920. Critical studies. ■Exploration of the performance of Jewish characters by both Jews and Gentiles on the American stage. Uses ethnicity and gender as analytical tools to analyze the construction of discourse and its relation to power.

2262 Esslin, Martin. "Towards an American Drama: Adapting the Function of Dramaturgy to U.S. Conditions." 25-30 in Jonas, Susan, ed.; Proehl, Geoffrey S., ed. *Dramaturgy in American Theatre: A Sourcebook.* New York, NY: Harcourt Brace College Pub; 1997. 590 pp. Pref. Biblio. Notes. Index. Lang.: Eng.

USA. 1997. Historical studies. ■Comparison of the function of the dramaturg in contemporary Europe with its American counterpart.

2263 Falls, Robert; Pettengill, Richard; Bilderback, Walter. "Production Dramaturgy of a Classic: Molière's *The Misanthrope* at La Jolla Playhouse and the Goodman Theatre." 308-316 in Jonas, Susan, ed.; Proehl, Geoffrey S., ed. *Dramaturgy in American Theatre: A Sourcebook.* New York, NY: Harcourt Brace College Pub; 1997. 590 pp. Pref. Notes. Biblio. Index. Lang.: Eng.

USA: La Jolla, CA, Chicago, IL. 1989-1990. Histories-sources. ■Director Robert Falls and dramaturgs Richard Pettengill and Walter Bilderback

DRAMA: —Performance/production

examine their work on Molière's *The Misanthrope* at La Jolla Playhouse and the Goodman Theatre. Focuses on the process of translation and adaptation.

2264 Fearnow, Mark. *The American Stage and the Great Depression: A Cultural History of the Grotesque.* Cambridge: Cambridge UP; 1997. 212 pp. (Cambridge Studies in American Theatre and Drama, 6.) Notes. Index. Biblio. Illus.: Photo. 9. Lang.: Eng.
USA. 1929-1940. Histories-specific. ■Argues that a surge in the grotesque during the Depression represents the cultural contradictions of the time. Plays examined include Robert Sherwood's *Idiot's Delight* and *Reunion in Vienna*, Clare Boothe Luce's *Kiss the Boys Goodbye* and Joseph Kesselring's *Arsenic and Old Lace*.

2265 Finque, Susan. "Making Theater from a Queer Aesthetic." 461-471 in Jonas, Susan, ed.; Proehl, Geoffrey S., ed. *Dramaturgy in American Theatre: A Sourcebook.* New York, NY: Harcourt Brace College Pub; 1997. 590 pp. Pref. Notes. Biblio. Index. Lang.: Eng.
USA. 1997. Histories-sources. ■Argues for a reconsideration of supposed gender and sexual roles by dramaturgs.

2266 Fjelde, Rolf. "An Evening with Austin Pendleton." *INC.* 1997; 17(1): 1-4. Lang.: Eng.
USA. 1980-1995. Histories-sources. ■Interview with actor/director Pendleton regarding his 1980 production of Ibsen's *Johan Gabriel Borkman*, with E.G. Marshall and Irene Worth: what was lacking and what was successful about the production.

2267 Frieze, James. "Channelling Rubble: *Seven Streams of the River Ota* and *After Sorrow.*" *JDTC.* 1997 Fall; 12(1): 133-142. Lang.: Eng.
USA: New York, NY. 1996-1997. Critical studies. ■Death in two contemporary productions: Ex Machina's *Les Sept branches de la Rivière Ota (The Seven Streams of the River Ota)* by Robert Lepage, performed at Brooklyn's Academy of Music, and Ping Chong's *After Sorrow (Viet Nam)*, performed at La MaMa.

2268 Galloway, Terry. "Taken: The Philosophically Sexy Transformations Engendered in a Woman by Playing Male Roles in Shakespeare." *TextPQ.* 1997 Jan.; 17(1): 94-100. Notes. Lang.: Eng.
USA. 1971-1997. Histories-sources. ■The author's experience playing male roles in *Henry IV, Part I* and *A Midsummer Night's Dream*.

2269 Garner, Shirley Nelson. "Shakespeare in My Time and Place." 287-306 in Garner, Shirley Nelson, ed.; Sprengnether, Madelon, ed. *Shakespearean Tragedy and Gender.* Bloomington, IN: Indiana UP; 1996. 326 pp. Index. Notes. Biblio. Lang.: Eng.
USA. 1996. Histories-sources. ■Author's personal experiences of Shakespeare's tragedies in her work teaching and directing. She concludes that the works need to be located firmly within Shakespeare's time and place while simultaneously recognizing the claims of her own.

2270 Garrett, Shawn-Marie. "Dummied Down: *Pearls for Pigs* at the Hartford Stage." *ThM.* 1997; 28(1): 15-21. Lang.: Eng.
USA: Hartford, CT. 1995. Critical studies. ■Analysis of the Ontological-Hysteric Theatre's Hartford Stage production of Richard Foreman's play.

2271 Garrett, Shawn-Marie. "Heavenly Creatures." *AmTh.* 1997 Feb.; 14(2): 4. Illus.: Photo. B&W. 1. Lang.: Eng.
USA. China. 1997. Critical studies. ■Mary Zimmerman's adaptation of the sixteenth-century Chinese epic *Journey to the West* for the American stage. Origins of original fable, other adaptations, characters, audience response.

2272 Gates, Henry Louis, Jr. "The Chitlin Circuit." *NewY.* 1997 3 Feb.: 44-55. Illus.: Photo. B&W. 2. Lang.: Eng.
USA. 1997. Critical studies. ■With reference to playwright August Wilson's call for a separate African-American theatre, Gates briefly discusses the work of such groups as Crossroads Theatre and the Negro Ensemble Company, then describes a performance by a touring company presenting melodramatic productions with gospel music to all-Black audiences.

2273 Gillen, Francis. "*Moonlight* in New York." *PintR.* 1997: 180-183. Lang.: Eng.
USA: New York, NY. 1994-1996. Critical studies. ■Production of Pinter's play *Moonlight* at the Roundabout Theatre, directed by Karel Reisz.

2274 Grant, Nathan L. "Extending the Ladder: A Remembrance of Owen Dodson." *Callaloo.* 1997 Sum; 20(3): 640-645. Lang.: Eng.
USA. 1914-1983. Biographical studies. ■A look back at the life and work of the poet/playwright/director with particular attention to his poetry.

2275 Gunter, Gregory. "Exploration through Imagery: Gregory Gunter Talks About Working with Anne Bogart." 176-179 in Jonas, Susan, ed.; Proehl, Geoffrey S., ed. *Dramaturgy in American Theatre: A Sourcebook.* New York, NY: Harcourt Brace College Pub; 1997. 590 pp. Pref. Notes. Biblio. Index. Lang.: Eng.
USA. 1995-1997. Histories-sources. ■Interview with dramaturg author on his collaboration with director Anne Bogart working with images, pictures, colors, and shapes instead of words.

2276 Haring-Smith, Tori. "The Dramaturg as Androgyne: Thoughts on the Nature of Dramaturgical Collaboration." 137-143 in Jonas, Susan, ed.; Proehl, Geoffrey S., ed. *Dramaturgy in American Theatre: A Sourcebook.* New York, NY: Harcourt Brace College Pub; 1997. 590 pp. Pref. Notes. Biblio. Index. Lang.: Eng.
USA. 1997. Historical studies. ■Examines the roles of dramaturg and director in light of production models absorbed from the culture around us.

2277 Harrington, John P. *The Irish Play on the New York Stage, 1874-1966.* Lexington, KY: UP of Kentucky; 1997. 192 pp. Index. Notes. Illus.: Photo. 19. Lang.: Eng.
USA: New York, NY. Ireland. 1874-1966. Critical studies. ■The Irish play and Irish characters on the American stage. Examines playwrights such as Dion Boucicault, George Bernard Shaw, John Millington Synge, James Joyce, Sean O'Casey, Samuel Beckett, and Brian Friel.

2278 Harrison, Paul Carter. "*The Black Star Line*: The De-Mystification of Marcus Garvey." *AfAmR.* 1997 Win; 31(4): 713-716. Lang.: Eng.
USA: Chicago, IL. 1997. Critical studies. ■The Goodman Theatre's production of Charles Smith's *The Black Star Line*.

2279 Hayes, Steve. "Lisa Peterson." *AmTh.* 1997 Apr.; 14(4): 28-29. Illus.: Photo. B&W. 1. Lang.: Eng.
USA: Los Angeles, CA. 1997. Biographical studies. ■Director Peterson and her work on *Ikebana* by Alice Tuan, presented at East West Players and *Collected Stories* by Donald Margulies at South Coast Rep.

2280 Hayford, Justin. "Babette on the Barricades." *AmTh.* 1997 Mar.; 14(3): 6. Illus.: Photo. B&W. 1. Lang.: Eng.
USA: Chicago, IL. 1950-1997. Critical studies. ■Theater Oobleck's *Babette's Feast*, an adaptation of Isak Dinesen's short story. Brief history of the company and their political activism.

2281 Hyman, Colette A. *Staging Strikes: Workers' Theatre and the American Labor Movement.* Philadelphia, PA: Temple UP; 1997. 210 pp. (Critical Perspectives on the Past.) Notes. Index. Biblio. Illus.: Photo. 5. Lang.: Eng.
USA. 1929-1940. Histories-specific. ■The effect of working-class theatre on national and local labor movements. Argues that audiences saw performances as visions of social justice which gave them a sense of empowerment. The impact of race and gender on workers' theatre are examined through the work of the Federal Theatre project.

2282 Jones, Chris. "Iphigenia Illuminated." *AmTh.* 1997 Dec.; 14(10): 32-34. Illus.: Photo. B&W. 1. Lang.: Eng.
USA: Chicago, IL. 1990-1997. Critical studies. ■JoAnne Akalaitis's Court Theatre production of *The Iphigenia Cycle* by Euripides. The director's modernized interpretation, design concepts.

2283 Jones, Chris. "Bogart Pins Strindberg to the Mat." *AmTh.* 1997 Apr.; 14(4): 34-35. Illus.: Photo. B&W. 1. Lang.: Eng.
USA: Louisville, KY. 1888-1997. Critical studies. ■Anne Bogart's direction of Strindberg's *Miss Julie (Fröken Julie)* for Actors' Theatre of Louisville.

2284 Kalb, Jonathan. "Notes for a Definition." 37 in Jonas, Susan, ed.; Proehl, Geoffrey S., ed. *Dramaturgy in American Theatre: A Sourcebook.* New York, NY: Harcourt Brace Col-

DRAMA: —Performance/production

lege Pub; 1997. 590 pp. Pref. Notes. Biblio. Index. Lang.: Eng.

USA. 1997. Historical studies. ■Short note on the role of dramaturgy and its integration with current cultural affairs.

2285   Kaplan, Deborah. "Learning 'to Speak the English Language': *The Way of the World* on the Twentieth-Century American Stage." *TJ.* 1997 Oct.; 49(3): 301-322. Notes. Lang.: Eng.

USA. 1924-1991. Historical studies. ■Twentieth-century performances of William Congreve's *The Way of the World* reveal moments of transition and transformation in theatrical representations of national and gender identity.

2286   Kashi, Charles; Turner, Beth. "Billy Graham." *BlackM.* 1997 Aug/Sep.; 12(5): 15. Lang.: Eng.

USA. 1997. Biographical studies. ■Obituary for the actor, playwright, director, producer, comedian, who was also the first Black comic book artist hired by Marvel Comics.

2287   Katz, Leon. "The Compleat Dramaturg." 115-120 in Jonas, Susan, ed.; Proehl, Geoffrey S., ed. *Dramaturgy in American Theatre: A Sourcebook.* New York, NY: Harcourt Brace College Pub; 1997. 590 pp. Pref. Notes. Biblio. Index. Lang.: Eng.

USA. 1997. Historical studies. ■Overview of characteristics that best describe the ideal dramaturg.

2288   Kennedy, Allen. "Professional Theatre and Education: Contexts for Dramaturgy." 190-204 in Jonas, Susan, ed.; Proehl, Geoffrey S., ed. *Dramaturgy in American Theatre: A Sourcebook.* New York, NY: Harcourt Brace College Pub; 1997. 590 pp. Pref. Notes. Biblio. Index. Lang.: Eng.

USA. 1990-1996. Historical studies. ■Educational initiatives involving play production and dramaturgs at theatres such as the Guthrie, the Huntington, and People's Light and Theatre Company.

2289   Kocher, Eric. "The Early Tennessee: A 'Memory Piece'." *DGQ.* 1997 Sum; 34(2): 34-41. Lang.: Eng.

USA. 1941-1942. Histories-sources. ■Playwright Eric Kocher relates his early experiences with colleague Tennessee Williams in various social situations.

2290   Koszyn, Jayme. "The Dramaturg and the Irrational." 276-282 in Jonas, Susan, ed.; Proehl, Geoffrey S., ed. *Dramaturgy in American Theatre: A Sourcebook.* New York, NY: Harcourt Brace College Pub; 1997. 590 pp. Pref. Notes. Biblio. Index. Lang.: Eng.

USA: Boston, MA, Philadelphia, PA. 1992-1995. Histories-sources. ■Examines a new approach for finding new contexts and making new performances out of old plays. Author's work with Euripidean drama at Huntington Theatre and with director Harriet Power and her production of Caryl Churchill's *Mad Forest* at Venture Theatre are used as examples.

2291   Kuharski, Allen. "Joseph Chaikin and the Presence of the Dramaturg." 144-158 in Jonas, Susan, ed.; Proehl, Geoffrey S., ed. *Dramaturgy in American Theatre: A Sourcebook.* New York, NY: Harcourt Brace College Pub; 1997. 590 pp. Pref. Notes. Biblio. Index. Lang.: Eng.

USA: New York, NY. 1963-1990. Histories-sources. ■Examines author's role as dramaturg working with director Joseph Chaikin. Explores the emergence of production dramaturgy in Chaikin's Open Theatre and winter program.

2292   London, Todd. "Open Call: A Year in the Lives of 15 Actors Starting Out in New York." *AmTh.* 1997 Jan.; 14(1): 32-36, 76-94. Illus.: Photo. Sketches. B&W. 18. Lang.: Eng.

USA: New York, NY. 1994-1997. Biographical studies. ■A year in the lives of American Repertory Theatre's graduating class of 1995, their move from training programs to professional careers. Continued in *AmTh* 14:2 (1997 Feb), 16-20, 58-81, and 14:3 (1997 Mar), 20-24, 50-55.

2293   Luczak, Raymond. "Hands Onstage: Notes of a Deaf Playwright." *DGQ.* 1997 Sum; 34(2): 14-17. Lang.: Eng.

USA. 1997. Histories-sources. ■Deaf playwright Luczak's views on the future of Deaf theatre and Deaf playwrights in the United States.

2294   Lupu, Michael. "There Is Clamor in the Air." 109-114 in Jonas, Susan, ed.; Proehl, Geoffrey S., ed. *Dramaturgy in*

American Theatre: A Sourcebook. New York, NY: Harcourt Brace College Pub; 1997. 590 pp. Pref. Notes. Biblio. Index. Lang.: Eng.

USA. 1997. Histories-sources. ■Author recounts his aesthetic for dramaturgy as a fundamental part of theatremaking.

2295   Lutterbie, John H. "Theory and the Practice of Dramaturgy." 220-243 in Jonas, Susan, ed.; Proehl, Geoffrey S., ed. *Dramaturgy in American Theatre: A Sourcebook.* New York, NY: Harcourt Brace College Pub; 1997. 590 pp. Pref. Notes. Biblio. Index. Lang.: Eng.

USA. 1997. Historical studies. ■Examines the tension between theory and practice in American theatre. Argues that dramaturgs can relieve this tension.

2296   MacAdams, Susannah. *Reflections of the Heart: The Duenna in Edmond Rostand's 'Cyrano de Bergerac'.* Long Beach, CA: California State Univ; 1997. 52 pp. Notes. Biblio. [M.F.A. Thesis, Univ. Microfilms Order No. AAC 1385616.] Lang.: Eng.

USA. 1995. Histories-sources. ■The author's creation and performance of the character of the duenna in Edmond Rostand's *Cyrano de Bergerac.* The play was produced by the California Repertory Theatre at California State University.

2297   Macdonald, Robert. "All 36: A Marathon Journal." *ShN.* 1997 Sum/Fall; 47(2/3): 33-36. [Number 233/234.] Lang.: Eng.

USA: New York, NY. 1987-1997. Histories-sources. ■Author's journal excerpts recounting personal memories of attending the New York Shakespeare Festival's presentation of Shakespeare's canon beginning in 1987, first begun by producer Joseph Papp. Productions, actors, personal anecdotes.

2298   Mahon, John W. "A Derek Jacobi Fest." *ShN.* 1997 Spr; 47(1): 1, 6, 8, 12. [Number 232.] Lang.: Eng.

USA: Washington, DC. 1997. Historical studies. ■Actor Sir Derek Jacobi's reception of the Sir John Gielgud Award for Excellence in the Dramatic Arts. Festivities sponsored by the Shakespeare Guild and the Folger Library. Jacobi discussed acting, his career, *Hamlet* and his collaboration with actor Kenneth Branagh.

2299   Mahon, John W. "NYSF's Classic Colloquium." *ShN.* 1997 Sum/Fall; 47(2/3): 43. [Number 233/234.] Lang.: Eng.

USA: New York, NY. 1997. Historical studies. ■New York Shakespeare Festival/Joseph Papp Public Theatre's presentation of 'Speak the Speech: the Language of Shakespeare in Contemporary America', a colloquium of theatre artists and critics discussing language, contemporary productions of Shakespeare and their interpretations.

2300   Margolis, Ellen Marie. *Recoveries: A History of Laurette Taylor.* Santa Barbara, CA: Univ. of California; 1997. 297 pp. Notes. Biblio. [Ph.D. Dissertation, Univ. Microfilms Order No. AAC 9819578.] Lang.: Eng.

USA. 1884-1946. Biographies. ■Actress Laurette Taylor, the creation of the mythology around her career, especially her most famous role, Amanda, in Tennessee Williams's *The Glass Menagerie.* Focuses on issues of celebrity, gender, and identity.

2301   Marks, Jonathan. "On Robert Brustein and Dramaturgy." 31-32 in Jonas, Susan, ed.; Proehl, Geoffrey S., ed. *Dramaturgy in American Theatre: A Sourcebook.* New York, NY: Harcourt Brace College Pub; 1997. 590 pp. Pref. Biblio. Notes. Index. Lang.: Eng.

USA. 1997. Historical studies. ■On Robert Brustein and his leadership in the field of production dramaturgy.

2302   Marowitz, Charles. "Shakespeare Recycled." *SQ.* 1987 Win; 38(4): 467-478. Lang.: Eng.

USA. 1987. Histories-sources. ■Director Charles Marowitz on his approach to directing Shakespeare. Originally presented as an adress to the Deutsche Shakespeare-Gesellschaft-West.

2303   Mazer, Cary M. "Rebottling: Dramaturgs, Scholars, Old Plays, and Modern Directors." 292-307 in Jonas, Susan, ed.; Proehl, Geoffrey S., ed. *Dramaturgy in American Theatre: A Sourcebook.* New York, NY: Harcourt Brace College Pub; 1997. 590 pp. Pref. Notes. Biblio. Index. Lang.: Eng.

DRAMA: —Performance/production

USA. 1995-1997. Histories-sources. ■Examines the importance of new theoretical insights in rehearsal and production. Author uses his own work on Webster's *The Duchess of Malfi* at the University of Pennsylvania as an example of how directors and dramaturgs can approach old works.

2304 McCauley, Robbie; Munk, Erika. "Mississippi Freedom: South and North." *ThM.* 1993; 24(2): 88-98. Illus.: Photo. B&W. 5. Lang.: Eng.
USA. 1990-1992. Histories-sources. ■McCauley's diary outlining the development of her play *Mississippi Freedom* and its reception in the north and south of the US ending in an interview with playwright regarding her goals as a dramatist.

2305 Mehta, Xerxes. "Ghosts." *ThM.* 1993; 24(3): 37-48. Illus.: Photo. B&W. Lang.: Eng.
USA. 1993. Histories-sources. ■Mehta's approach to directing Beckett, particularly later plays such as *Not I, Ohio Impromptu, Play, Rockaby,* and *Footfalls.*

2306 Mishler, William; Nadon, Daniel R.; Sheffield, Clarence Burton, Jr.; Templeton, Joan. "Ibsen on Stage." *INC.* 1997; 17 (1): 4-9. Lang.: Eng.
USA. France. UK-England. 1996-1997. Critical studies. ■Critical examination of various Ibsen plays as presented in North America and Europe, including *A Doll's House (Et Dukkehjem), When We Dead Awaken (Når vi døde vågner), Johan Gabriel Borkman, Peer Gynt* and *The Lady from the Sea (Fruen fra havet).*

2307 Moore, Dick. "A Wilder Year: L.A.'s Colony Studio Theatre Participates in Thornton Wilder Centenary." *EN.* 1997 Oct.; 82 (8): 2. Lang.: Eng.
USA. Los Angeles, CA. 1997. Historical studies. ■The Colony Theatre joins in the celebration of playwright Thornton Wilder's 100th birthday. The theatre produces Wilder's *The Matchmaker*, directed by Barbara Beckley.

2308 Morrison, Michael A. "The Voice Teacher as Shakespearean Collaborator: Margaret Carrington and John Barrymore." *ThS.* 1997 Nov.; 38(2): 129-158 ia. Illus.: Photo. 4. Lang.: Eng.
USA. 1919-1923. Historical studies. ■Examines the contribution to actor John Barrymore's career of his vocal coach, Margaret Carrington, whose work on coaching Barrymore for his famous productions of *Richard III* and *Hamlet* has been ignored by scholars. Traditional scholarly work has focused on the actor and his director, Arthur Hopkins.

2309 Murray, Timothy. *Drama Trauma: Specters of Race and Sexuality in Performance, Video and Art.* New York, NY/London: Routledge; 1997. 272 pp. Notes. Biblio. Index. Lang.: Eng.
USA. Europe. 1590-1995. Critical studies. ■Examines the artistic struggle over the subjects of race, gender, sexuality, and power. Author covers a wide range of interdisciplinary subjects and periods, from Shakespeare to recent political projects in performance and video by women and minorities.

2310 Niesen, Jim. "Textual Collidings: Group Dramaturgy and the Irondale Ensemble Project." 283-291 in Jonas, Susan, ed.; Proehl, Geoffrey S., ed. *Dramaturgy in American Theatre: A Sourcebook.* New York, NY: Harcourt Brace College Pub; 1997. 590 pp. Pref. Notes. Biblio. Index. Lang.: Eng.
USA: New York, NY. 1986-1989. Histories-sources. ■Author recounts his experience as dramaturg at Irondale Ensemble and explores the company's reworking of Shakespeare's *As You Like It.* Focuses on Irondale's unique approach to production dramaturgy, requiring all members to serve as dramaturgs.

2311 Nunns, Stephen. "Bunny Love." *AmTh.* 1997 Jan.; 14(1): 22. Illus.: Photo. B&W. 1. Lang.: Eng.
USA: Seattle, WA. 1979-1996. Critical studies. ■Seattle Children Theatre's production of James and Deborah Howe's book *Bunnicula*, adapted by playwright Jon Klein, music composed by Chris Jeffries, directed by Rita Giomi.

2312 Nunns, Stephen. "Regarding 'Henry': Two Directors Talk Shop." *AmTh.* 1997 Mar.; 14(3): 44-47. Illus.: Photo. B&W. 4. Lang.: Eng.

USA: New York, NY, Washington, DC. 1950-1996. Histories-sources. ■Directors Michael Kahn and Karin Coonrod discuss their approaches to staging and interpretation of characters in Shakespeare's *Henry VI* at the Shakespeare Theatre and New York's Public Theatre, respectively.

2313 Nunns, Stephen. "Rock & Roll Richelieu." *AmTh.* 1997 Nov.; 14(9): 20-21. Illus.: Photo. B&W. 1. Lang.: Eng.
USA: New York, NY. 1990-1997. Critical studies. ■Robert Myers's one-person play *Lee Atwater: Fixin' to Die* starring Bruce McIntosh, directed by George Furth, performing Off Broadway after a national tour. McIntosh's portrayal of the controversial former chairman of the Republican National Committee, audience response.

2314 O'Connor, Jacqueline. "*The Strangest Kind of Romance*: Tennessee Williams and His Broadway Critics." 255-264 in Roudané, Matthew C., ed. *The Cambridge Companion to Tennessee Williams.* Cambridge: Cambridge UP; 1997. 277 pp. (Cambridge Companions to Literature.) Index. Notes. Biblio. Lang.: Eng.
USA: New York, NY. 1944-1982. Historical studies. ■Critical reception of Williams' plays on Broadway.

2315 Orr, Shelley. "Len Jenkin: A Landscape of Language." *TheatreF.* 1997 Sum/Fall; 11: 55-56. Illus.: Photo. 1. Lang.: Eng.
USA: San Diego, CA. 1997. Historical studies. ■On Len Jenkin's new play *Like I Say* produced at the University of California, San Diego, directed by Robert Egan.

2316 Palmer, Caroline. "Mutiny with a Mission." *AmTh.* 1997 Jan.; 14(1): 20-21. Illus.: Photo. B&W. 2. Lang.: Eng.
USA: Milwaukee, WI. 1996. Historical studies. ■Milwaukee Repertory Theatre's adaptation of *Benito Cereno* (novel by Herman Melville, play adaptation by Robert Lowell) by director Edward Morgan in collaboration with Ferne Caulker, founder and artistic director of Ko-Thi Dance Company. Incorporation of modern viewpoint, African and Haitian elements, dance and drumming.

2317 Paran, Janice. "Heiress Apparent." *AmTh.* 1997 May/June; 14(5): 10-13. Illus.: Photo. B&W. 5. Lang.: Eng.
USA: Washington, DC. 1992-1996. Biographical studies. ■Personal life, training and career of actress Cherry Jones. Past work on *The Heiress* on Broadway, and current work on Tina Howe's *Pride's Crossing* at the Old Globe Theatre, directed by Jack O'Brien.

2318 Pettengill, Richard. "Dramaturging Education." 102-108 in Jonas, Susan, ed.; Proehl, Geoffrey S., ed. *Dramaturgy in American Theatre: A Sourcebook.* New York, NY: Harcourt Brace College Pub; 1997. 590 pp. Pref. Notes. Biblio. Index. Lang.: Eng.
USA: Chicago, IL. 1990-1997. Histories-sources. ■Author's career as a dramaturg from graduate school to position at the Goodman Theatre. Gives insights into the daily workings of a dramaturg at a major regional theatre.

2319 Power, Harriet. "Re-imagining the Other: A Multiracial Production of *Mad Forest*." 355-372 in Jonas, Susan, ed.; Proehl, Geoffrey S., ed. *Dramaturgy in American Theatre: A Sourcebook.* New York, NY: Harcourt Brace College Pub; 1997. 590 pp. Pref. Notes. Biblio. Index. Lang.: Eng.
USA: Philadelphia, PA. 1992. Historical studies. ■Author recounts her experience as dramaturg and director on Caryl Churchill's *Mad Forest* at Venture Theatre.

2320 Proehl, Geoffrey S. "The Images Before Us: Metaphors for the Role of the Dramaturg in American Theatre." 124-136 in Jonas, Susan, ed.; Proehl, Geoffrey S., ed. *Dramaturgy in American Theatre: A Sourcebook.* New York, NY: Harcourt Brace College Pub; 1997. 590 pp. Pref. Notes. Biblio. Index. Lang.: Eng.
USA. 1967-1997. Historical studies. ■Examines ways in which dramaturgs have written about their place in the process over the past thirty years.

2321 Rafalowicz, Mira. "Dramaturgy in Collaboration with Joseph Chaikin." 159-164 in Jonas, Susan, ed.; Proehl, Geoffrey S., ed. *Dramaturgy in American Theatre: A Sourcebook.* New York, NY: Harcourt Brace College Pub; 1997. 590 pp. Pref. Notes. Biblio. Index. Lang.: Eng.

DRAMA: —Performance/production

USA: New York, NY. 1963-1973. Histories-sources. ■On collaborating in the director/dramaturg dynamic as illustrated in Joseph Chaikin's Open Theatre.

2322 Ramírez, Elizabeth C. "Multicultural Approaches in Dramaturgy: A Case Study." 331-341 in Jonas, Susan, ed.; Proehl, Geoffrey S., ed. *Dramaturgy in American Theatre: A Sourcebook.* New York, NY: Harcourt Brace College Pub; 1997. 590 pp. Pref. Notes. Biblio. Index. Lang.: Eng.

USA: Tucson, AZ. 1992. Histories-sources. ■Author's experience as dramaturg for a multicultural adaptation of Beaumarchais' *Le Mariage de Figaro (The Marriage of Figaro)* as *One Crazy Day*, translated by Roger Downey and directed by David Ira Goldstein for Arizona Theatre Company. The production was set in nineteenth-century Mexico, now Arizona.

2323 Rehlin, Gunnar. "Dustin Hoffman återvänder alltid till teatern." (Dustin Hoffman Always Returns To the Theatre.) *Dramat.* 1997; 5(3): 17. Illus.: Photo. Color. Lang.: Swe.

USA. UK-England. 1997. Biographical studies. ■Dustin Hoffman's views on theatre versus film.

2324 Reinelt, Janelle. "Notes on *Angels in America* as American Epic Theater." 234-244 in Geis, Deborah R., ed.; Kruger, Steven F., ed. *Approaching the Millennium: Essays on Angels in America.* Ann Arbor, MI: Univ. of Michigan P; 1997. 352 pp. Notes. Illus.: Photo. 2. Lang.: Eng.

USA. 1992-1995. Critical studies. ■Examines Tony Kushner's *Angels in America* in light of Brechtian epic theatre. Focus on the 1994 production by American Conservatory Theatre, directed by Mark Wing-Davey and designed by Kate Edmunds, with brief comments on George C. Wolfe's 1993 New York production.

2325 Richardson, Brian. "*Old Times* in Washington." *PintR.* 1997: 184-185. Lang.: Eng.

USA: Washington, DC. 1994. Critical studies. ■Production of Pinter's play *Old Times* at the Washington Stage Guild theatre, directed by John MacDonald.

2326 Rogoff, Gordon. "Angels in America, Devils in the Wings." *ThM.* 1993; 24(2): 21-29. Illus.: Photo. B&W. 6. Lang.: Eng.

USA: New York, NY. UK-England. 1992-1993. Critical studies. ■Analysis of Tony Kushner's *Angels in America, Part I: Millennium Approaches* with a comparison of the London production directed by Declan Donnellan and George C. Wolfe's New York production.

2327 Román, David. "November 1, 1992: AIDS/*Angels in America.*" 40-55 in Geis, Deborah R., ed.; Kruger, Steven F., ed. *Approaching the Millennium: Essays on Angels in America.* Ann Arbor, MI: Univ. of Michigan P; 1997. 352 pp. Notes. Illus.: Photo. 1. Lang.: Eng.

USA: Los Angeles, CA. 1992. Critical studies. ■The delayed opening in Los Angeles of Tony Kushner's *Angels in America*'s because of the Presidential election.

2328 Rowell, Charles H. "An Interview with Owen Dodson." *Callaloo.* 1997 Sum; 20(3): 627-639. Lang.: Eng.

USA. 1975. Histories-sources. ■Previously unpublished 1975 interview with playwright/director Owen Dodson regarding his life and philosophy.

2329 Ryan, Kate Moira. "Hearing the Laughter: How Moss Hart Can Light Up the Stage in the '90's." *DGQ.* 1997 Sum; 34(2): 18-22. Illus.: Photo. B&W. 1. Lang.: Eng.

USA: Chicago, IL. 1997. Histories-sources. ■Interview with director David Petrarca regarding his upcoming revival of Moss Hart's *Light Up the Sky* at the Goodman Theatre.

2330 Rybkowski, Radosław. "Broadwayowski teatr reżysera: 'Tramwaj zwany pożądaniem' w inscenizacji Ellii Kazana." (Director's Theatre on Broadway: Elia Kazan's Staging of *A Streetcar Named Desire*.) 35-52 in Pleśniarowicz, Krzysztof, ed.; Sugiera, Małgorzata, ed. *Arcydzieła inscenizacji od Reinhardta do Wilsona.* Cracow: Księgarnia Akademicka; 1997. 139 pp. (Wielkie dzieła teatralne.) Pref. Notes. Index. Lang.: Pol.

USA: New York, NY. 1947. Historical studies. ■Reconstruction of Kazan's production of the play by Tennessee Williams, with analysis of the relationship between the written text and the staging.

2331 Saivetz, Deborah. "Releasing the 'Profound Physicality of Performance'." *NTQ.* 1997; 13(52): 329-338. Notes. Illus.: Photo. B&W. 3. Lang.: Eng.

USA. 1970-1996. Histories-sources. ■Interview with director JoAnne Akalaitis about her artistic encounters with Beckett, Brecht, and Genet, her thoughts on the relationship between art and politics, and her belief in the connection between the physical and the emotional in performance.

2332 Salaam, Kalamu ya. "Black Theatre—The Way It Is: An Interview with Woodie King, Jr." *AfAmR.* 1997 Win; 31(4): 647-658. Lang.: Eng.

USA: Detroit, MI, New York, NY. 1937-1997. Histories-sources. ■Interview with actor/director Woodie King, touching on his life, career and the state of Black theatre.

2333 Sanford, Tim. "The Dramaturgy of Reading: Literary Management Theory." 431-440 in Jonas, Susan, ed.; Proehl, Geoffrey S., ed. *Dramaturgy in American Theatre: A Sourcebook.* New York, NY: Harcourt Brace College Pub; 1997. 590 pp. Pref. Notes. Biblio. Index. Lang.: Eng.

USA. 1984-1996. Histories-sources. ■Artistic director/literary manager Tim Sanford describes his work at Playwrights Horizons and argues for the importance of theoretical foundations in the job.

2334 Schechter, Joel. "In the Beginning There Was Lessing ... Then Brecht, Müller, and Other Dramaturgs." 16-24 in Jonas, Susan, ed.; Proehl, Geoffrey S., ed. *Dramaturgy in American Theatre: A Sourcebook.* New York, NY: Harcourt Brace College Pub; 1997. 590 pp. Pref. Biblio. Notes. Index. Lang.: Eng.

USA. 1997. Historical studies. ■Detailed history of production dramaturgy from Lessing to Brecht and Müller. Author sees the dramaturg as a person actively involved in cultural and political affairs of the day.

2335 Schecter, Joel. "Zapatistas Take the Stage." *AmTh.* 1997 Mar.; 14(3): 4-5. Illus.: Photo. B&W. 1. Lang.: Eng.

USA: San Francisco, CA. 1997. Critical studies. ■Creation of *13 Días/13 Days*, an exploration of Mexico's rebel Zapatistas by San Francisco Mime Troupe members Joan Holden, Paula Loera, Daniel Nugent and Eva Tessler. Bilingual production featured songs by Bruce Barthol and Eduardo Lopez Martinez, was directed by Dan Chumley and toured nationally.

2336 Scheie, Timothy. "'Questionable terms': Shylock, Céline's *L'Eglise*, and the Performative." *TextPQ.* 1997 Apr.; 17 (2): 153-169. Notes. Biblio. Lang.: Eng.

USA: Santa Cruz, CA. France: Paris. 1992-1997. Critical studies. ■Performative theory and potentially offensive characterizations, with emphasis on Shakespeare's *The Merchant of Venice* performed by Shakespeare Santa Cruz, directed by Danny Scheie, and Jean-Louis Martinelli's direction of Céline's *L'Église (The Church)* at the Théâtre des Amandiers. Audience response, censorship, controversy.

2337 Schloff, Aaron Mack. "Dear Adolf." *AmTh.* 1997 Jan.; 14(1): 24. Illus.: Photo. B&W. 1. Lang.: Eng.

USA: New York, NY. 1938-1996. Critical studies. ■Director Tuvia Tenenbom on his staging of *Love Letters to Adolf Hitler*, taken from actual letters written by German women, for the Jewish Theatre of New York. Audience response, challenges in theatricalizing the controversial material.

2338 Selig, Paul. "Morgan Jenness Tells the Truth to Paul Selig: An Interview." 401-411 in Jonas, Susan, ed.; Proehl, Geoffrey S., ed. *Dramaturgy in American Theatre: A Sourcebook.* New York, NY: Harcourt Brace College Pub; 1997. 590 pp. Pref. Notes. Biblio. Index. Lang.: Eng.

USA. 1979-1996. Histories-sources. ■Interview with Morgan Jenness, dramaturg for new play development at the New York Shakespeare Festival/Public Theatre.

2339 Sentilles, Renee Marie. *Performing Menken: Adah Isaacs Menken's American Odyssey.* Williamsburg, VA: The College of William and Mary; 1997. 341 pp. [Ph.D. Dissertation, Univ. Microfilms Order No. AAC 9805158.] Lang.: Eng.

USA. 1835-1868. Biographies. ■Examines the life and writings of actress Adah Isaacs Menken.

DRAMA: —Performance/production

2340   Shafer, Yvonne. "Marsden Revisited." *EOR*. 1997 Spr/Fall; 21(1&2): 163-171. Lang.: Eng.

USA. 1998. Histories-sources. ■Chat with actor Edward Petherbridge regarding his experience playing Charles Marsden in *Strange Interlude*.

2341   Shank, Theodore. "Jude Narita." *MimeJ*. 1991/92; 15: 160-175. Illus.: Photo. B&W. 8. Lang.: Eng.

USA: Los Angeles, CA. 1987-1989. Histories-sources. ■Interview with Narita regarding her one-woman show *Coming Into Passion/Song for a Sansei* relating the experiences of five different Asian women.

2342   Sheehy, Catherine. "Silents Are Golden." *AmTh*. 1997 Oct.; 14(8): 65-66. Illus.: Photo. B&W. 1. Lang.: Eng.

USA: New York, NY. 1997. Historical studies. ■Comparison of *American Silents*, conceived and directed by Anne Bogart, presented at Raw Space, and *The First Picture Show*, written and directed by Ain and David Gordon, presented at Playhouse at St. Clement's. Use of silent movies as subject material, characters and themes.

2343   Sheehy, Helen. "Making a Difference: Eva Le Gallienne: Actor, Director, Translator, Theatre Pioneer." *EN*. 1997 June; 82 (5): 3. Illus.: Photo. 1. Lang.: Eng.

USA. 1997. Biographical studies. ■Historical account of actress, director Eva Le Gallienne.

2344   Sheehy, Helen. "Missing Le Gallienne." *AmTh*. 1997 Jan.; 14(1): 30-31. Illus.: Photo. B&W. 1. Lang.: Eng.

USA. 1920-1996. Histories-sources. ■Author of biography *Eva Le Gallienne* discusses process of working on the book, personal experiences with Le Gallienne, and love of her subject.

2345   Shepard, John. *An Analysis of Saint-Claude as Dürrenmatt's Mouthpiece*. Long Beach, CA: California State Univ; 1997. 57 pp. Notes. Biblio. [M.F.A. Thesis, Univ. Microfilms Order No. AAC 1385683.] Lang.: Eng.

USA: Long Beach, CA. 1996. Histories-sources. ■The author's creation of the characters of Frederic Rene Saint-Claude in Friedrich Dürrenmatt's *The Marriage of Mr. Mississippi* for California Repertory Company.

2346   Shewey, Don. "Sam Shepard's Identity Dance." *AmTh*. 1997 July/Aug.; 14(6): 12-17, 61. Illus.: Photo. B&W. 7. Lang.: Eng.

USA: New York, NY. 1976-1997. Critical studies. ■Signature Theatre Company's (artistic director James Houghton) decision to devote its season to the works of playwright Sam Shepard. Choices of plays, critical response to productions of *Curse of the Starving Class*, his one-acts *Chicago*, *The Sad Lament of Pecos Bill on the Eve of Killing His Wife*, *Killer's Head*, and the revised version of *The Tooth of Crime* subtitled 'Second Dance'.

2347   Solomon, Alisa. "A New York (Theater) Diary, 1992." *ThM*. 1993; 23(1): 7-18. Illus.: Photo. B&W. 11. Lang.: Eng.

USA: New York, NY. 1991-1992. Reviews of performances. ■Jeff Weiss's serial drama *Hot Keys* and Robbie McCauley's *Sally's Rape* at the Kitchen.

2348   Stoudt, Charlotte. "Ollie's Follies." *AmTh*. 1997 Feb.; 14(2): 5-6. Illus.: Photo. B&W. 1. Lang.: Eng.

USA: Arlington, VA. 1986-1997. Critical studies. ■John Strand's *Three Nights in Tehran*, a political comedy premiering at Signature Theatre, directed by Kyle Donnelly. Use of contemporary American politics for subject material, audience response.

2349   Sullivan, Esther Beth. "The Dimensions of Pearl Cleage's *Flyin' West*." *TTop*. 1997 Mar.; 7(1): 11-22. Illus.: Photo. 2. Lang.: Eng.

USA. 1994-1995. Histories-sources. ■The development of community-based dramaturgy, or 'staging community' in contemporary theatre productions, with emphasis on an early production of Pearl Cleage's *Flyin' West* at the Intiman Theatre in Seattle. Discussion includes not only the community represented in the play, but the audience reception of the Intiman's production.

2350   Taylor, Zanthe. "Singing for Their Supper: The Negro Units of the Federal Theatre Project and Their Plays." *ThM*. 1997; 27(2/3): 42-59. Biblio. Illus.: Photo. Poster. 4. Lang.: Eng.

USA: Washington, DC, New York, NY. 1935. Historical studies. ■Political and social effects of the Federal Theatre Project on Black actors and writers. Includes discussion of Orson Welles' all-Black 'voodoo' *Macbeth* and Theodore Ward's *Big White Fog*.

2351   Uldall-Jessen, Gritt. "Det indrammede teater." (The Framed Theatre.) *TE*. 1997 Mar.; 83: 37-39. Illus.: Photo. B&W. 2. Lang.: Dan.

USA. 1968-1997. Histories-sources. ■Richard Foreman's directing methods. Some history on his Ontological-Hysterical Theatre founded in 1968 and situated in New York. The author has been assistant director on Richard Foreman's latest performance titled *Permanent Brain Damage*.

2352   Vilga, Edward. *Acting Now: Conversations on Craft and Career*. New Brunswick, NJ/London: Rutgers UP; 1997. 215 pp. Index. Pref. Notes. Illus.: Photo. 15. Lang.: Eng.

USA. 1997. Histories-sources. ■Interviews with leading actors, teachers, and directors on contemporary acting, especially on the practical difficulties of the career and the harsh realities of the modern entertainment industry. Includes Stella Adler, Tanya Berezin, André Bishop, Robert Falls, Ellen Burstyn, Spalding Gray, and Austin Pendleton.

2353   Weber, Carl. "Foreign Drama in Translation: Some Reflections on Otherness, Xenophobia, the Translator's Task, and the Problems They Present." 266-275 in Jonas, Susan, ed.; Proehl, Geoffrey S., ed. *Dramaturgy in American Theatre: A Sourcebook*. New York, NY: Harcourt Brace College Pub; 1997. 590 pp. Pref. Notes. Biblio. Index. Lang.: Eng.

USA. 1997. Historical studies. ■Examines the state of translation in American theatre.

2354   Weiner, Wendy. "Eve Ensler." *AmTh*. 1997 May/June; 14(5): 31-33. Illus.: Photo. B&W. 1. Lang.: Eng.

USA: New York, NY. 1980-1997. Biographical studies. ■Career and activism of playwright/performer Ensler, with special focus on her solo work *The Vagina Monologues*.

2355   Werner, Derek Whitney. *Toward a Model of Performance-Based Critical Reading: A Study of Ensemble Rehearsal and Performance in a Production of William Gibson's 'Neuromancer'*. Evanston, IL: Northwestern Univ; 1997. 483 pp. [Ph.D. Dissertation, Univ. Microfilms Order No. AAC 9814337.] Lang.: Eng.

USA: Santa Fe, NM. 1996. Historical studies. ■The adaptation and performance of Gibson's novel under the auspices of Red Shoes Variety Productions.

2356   Williams, John. "Nilo Cruz: A Bright New Bi-Cultural Voice." *BlackM*. 1997 Aug/Sep.; 12(5): 7-8, 15. Illus.: Photo. B&W. 2. Lang.: Eng.

USA: San Francisco, CA. 1995-1997. Histories-sources. ■Interview with Afro-Cuban playwright Nilo Cruz about his influences and work.

2357   Wilson, Erin Cressida. "*Hurricane*: A Journal in Three Short Chapters." *TheatreF*. 1997 Sum/Fall(11): 14-19. Illus.: Photo. 3. Lang.: Eng.

USA. 1996. Histories-sources. ■On the creation of author's performance piece *Hurricane*, produced at Campo Santo Theatre directed by Delia MacDougall.

2358   Wilson, Mary Louise. "Where Are the Witty Bitches?" *AmTh*. 1997 Oct.; 14(8): 24-25. Illus.: Photo. B&W. 1. Lang.: Eng.

USA: New York, NY. 1997. Histories-sources. ■Actress describes challenges of finding good roles as an actress ages, and personal inspiration for creating her one-woman show *Full Gallop*.

2359   Winston, Hattie. "Frances Foster." *BlackM*. 1997 Aug/Sep.; 12(5): 9. Illus.: Photo. B&W. 1. Lang.: Eng.

USA. 1924-1997. Biographical studies. ■Obituary for the veteran stage, film and television actress.

2360   Worthen, W.B. "Staging América: The Subject of History in Chicano/a Theatre." *TJ*. 1997 May; 49(2): 101-120. Notes. Lang.: Eng.

USA. 1964-1995. Historical studies. ■History in recent Chicano/a theatre, with respect to the historical construction of identity categories and the specific history of the US-Mexico border. Plays examined include Carlos Morton's *Los Dorados* and *Rancho Hollywood*, Luis Valdez's *The Shrunken Head of Pancho Villa* and *Bandido!*, and Cherríe Moraga's *Heroes and Saints*.

DRAMA: —Performance/production

2361 Zeder, Suzan L. "The Once and Future Audience: Dramaturgy and Children's Theatre." 447-460 in Jonas, Susan, ed.; Proehl, Geoffrey S., ed. *Dramaturgy in American Theatre: A Sourcebook.* New York, NY: Harcourt Brace College Pub; 1997. 590 pp. Pref. Notes. Biblio. Index. Lang.: Eng.
USA. 1997. Histories-sources. ■Explores emerging models for developing plays for young audiences and the role production dramaturgy in these programs.

2362 Zimmerman, Scott Alan. *Representative Stages: American Theatre and National Identity.* Minneapolis, MN: Univ. of Minnesota; 1997. 264 pp. Notes. Biblio. [Ph.D. Dissertation, Univ. Microfilms Order No. AAC 9817675.] Lang.: Eng.
USA. 1910-1940. Historical studies. ■The development of modern American theatre, focusing on commercial centralization, academic experimentation, and financial endowment processes that reveal ongoing tensions over America's national identity. Examines the Theatre Guild, the Civic Repertory Theatre, the Provincetown Players, the Group Theatre, and the WPA's Federal Theatre Project, to reveal several different strands of development strategies.

2363 Kazimirovskaja, Natalia. "Kvinnan med det ljusa leendet." (The Woman With the Bright Smile.) *Tningen.* 1997; 21(5): 32-34. Illus.: Photo. B&W. Lang.: Swe.
USSR. 1950-1997. Histories-sources. ■An interview with the former concentration camp actress Tamara Petkevich about her experiences, with reference to the director Aleksander Gavronski.

Plays/librettos/scripts

2364 Burnett, Linda. "Margaret Clarke's Gertrude & Ophelia: Writing Revisionist Culture, Writing a Feminist 'New Poetics'." *ET.* 1997; 16(1): 15-32. Notes. Biblio. Lang.: Eng.
1993-1997. Critical studies. ■*Gertrude and Ophelia*, Clarke's revision of *Hamlet*, by concentrating on the women in the play, changes our perception of the original. It also draws attention to existing paternal structures and reviews the changing attitudes of critics towards women.

2365 Charnes, Linda. "Shakespeare, Paranoia, and the Logic of Mass Culture." *SQ.* 1997 Spr; 48(1): 1-16. Notes. Lang.: Eng.
1600-1996. Critical studies. ■Analysis of Shakespeare's *Hamlet* as a revenge tragedy and as an antecedent of classic and *noir* detective fiction. Discusses Zeffirelli's 1990 film version and Steve Martin's film *L.A. Story* regarding their *noir* elements and postmodern sensibilities.

2366 Chedgzoy, Kate. *Shakespeare's Queer Children: Sexual Politics and Contemporary Culture.* Manchester/New York, NY: Manchester UP; 1995. 229 pp. Index. Notes. Illus.: Photo. 2. Lang.: Eng.
1590-1995. Critical studies. ■The appropriation of Shakespearean texts by the dispossessed and marginalized. Emphasis on gay themes in performances by Gay Sweatshop and film adaptations by Derek Jarman (*The Tempest*, Marlowe's *Edward II*) as well as readings by Edward Bond, Oscar Wilde, and several twentieth-century female novelists.

2367 Poniž, Denis. *Na poti h komediji.* (On the Way to Comedy.) Ljubljana: The 2000 Society; 1997. 56 pp. Lang.: Slo.
Histories-specific. ■Essay on the characteristics of comedy, its components, characters, periods, and language.

2368 Sörenson, Elisabeth. "Shakespeare—samtida efter 400 år." (Shakespeare—A Contemporary After 400 Years.) *Dramat.* 1997; 5(1): 8-10. Illus.: Photo. Color. Lang.: Swe.
1564-1997. Histories-sources. ■An interview with the dramaturg Magnus Florin about the popularity of Shakespeare through the ages, with reference to *The Taming of the Shrew.*

2369 Vigouroux-Frey, Nicole. "Greeks in Drama: Four Contemporary Issues." 3-14 in Boireau, Nicole, ed. *Drama on Drama: Dimensions of Theatricality on the Contemporary British Stage.* New York, NY: St. Martin's; 1997. 256 pp. Pref. Notes. Index. Biblio. Lang.: Eng.
1970-1990. Critical studies. ■The classical Greek world of great myths as reflected in four major contemporary plays: Wole Soyinka's *The Bacchae of Euripides* (1973), Edward Bond's *The Woman* (1978), Steven Berkoff's *Greek* (1980), and Seamus Heaney's *The Cure at Troy* (1990).

2370 Weeks, Stephen. "How to Do It: A Brief History of Professional Advice." 385-397 in Jonas, Susan, ed.; Proehl, Geoffrey S., ed. *Dramaturgy in American Theatre: A Sourcebook.* New York, NY: Harcourt Brace College Pub; 1997. 590 pp. Pref. Notes. Biblio. Index. Lang.: Eng.
350 B.C.-1997 A.D. Historical studies. ■The history of works devoted to teaching the craft of playwriting, and their failure to adapt to modernism.

2371 Okagbue, Osita. "The Strange and the Familiar: Intercultural Exchange Between African and Caribbean Theatre." *ThR.* 1997 ; 22(2): 120-129. Notes. Lang.: Eng.
Africa. Caribbean. 1970-1997. Critical studies. ■Structural types and modes of representation and story-telling as reflections of cultural interchange between African and Caribbean theatre.

2372 Benér, Theresa. "Teater är tyvärr olyckans konstart." (The Theatre Is Unfortunately the Art of Unhappiness.) *Tningen.* 1997; 21(4): 7-11. Illus.: Photo. B&W. Color. Lang.: Swe.
Algeria. 1990. Histories-sources. ■An interview with the Algerian playwright Slimane Benaissas, now in exile in France, about his plays and the severe situation of the theatre in Algeria.

2373 Parker, Robert. "Gods Cruel and Kind: Tragic and Civic Theology." 143-160 in Pelling, Christopher, ed. *Greek Tragedy and the Historian.* Oxford: Clarendon; 1997. 268 pp. Notes. Biblio. Index. Lang.: Eng.
Ancient Greece. 500-250 B.C. Historical studies. ■Argues that the active benevolence as well as cruelty of the gods in Greek tragedy reflects religious ambivalence and offers another interpretation of the works.

2374 Camara, Elena. *Del realismo exasperante de Eduardo Pavlovsky.* (On the Exasperating Realism of Eduardo Pavlovsky.) Chapel Hill, NC: Univ. of North Carolina; 1997. 262 pp. [Ph.D. Dissertation, Univ. Microfilms Order No. AAC 9730498.] Lang.: Spa.
Argentina. 1962-1993. Critical studies. ■Analysis of the writing style of political playwright Eduardo Pavlovsky in *La mueca (The Grimace), El señor Galindez, Telarañas (Spiderwebs), Camara lenta, Potestad (Power), Paso de dos (Pas de deux), Pablo* and *Rojos globos rojos (Red Globes Red).*

2375 Bemrose, Anna. "E.W. O'Sullivan's *Coo-ee, or, Wild Days in the Bush*: People's Theatre or Political Circus?" *ADS.* 1997 Apr.; 30: 87-103. Notes. Illus.: Dwg. Poster. B&W. 2. Lang.: Eng.
Australia: Sydney. 1906. Critical studies. ■Analysis of politician and journalist Edward William O'Sullivan's melodrama, focusing on its conformity to the genre of 'bush melodrama' and its use as an electoral instrument to project the author's nationalistic views.

2376 Carroll, Dennis. "Some Defining Characteristics of Australian Aboriginal Drama." *MD.* 1997 Spr; 15(1): 100-110. Notes. Lang.: Eng.
Australia. 1967-1997. Historical studies. ■Development and characteristics of Aboriginal drama from *The Cherry Pickers* by Kevin Gilbert, which marked beginning of Aboriginal drama. Focus on *Kullark (Home)* by Jack Davis, and his trilogy *The First Born* which includes *No Sugar, The Dreamers,* and *Barungin (Smell the Wind).*

2377 Davis, Jim. "The Empire Right or Wrong: Boer War Melodrama on the Australian Stage, 1899-1901." 21-38 in Hays, Michael, ed.; Nikolopoulou, Anastasia, ed. *Melodrama: The Cultural Emergence of a Genre.* New York, NY: St. Martin's P; 1996. 288 pp. Notes. Illus.: Photo. 2. Lang.: Eng.
Australia. 1899-1901. Historical studies. ■Argues that melodrama was the site of Australia's break with its colonial legacy and search for a separate cultural identity.

2378 Kiernander, Adrian. "Making Things Up As We Go Along: An Introduction to Tim Benzie's *Personal Fictions*." *ADS.* 1997 Oct.; 31: 124-128. Lang.: Eng.
Australia. 1997. Critical studies. ■Introduction to Tim Benzie's play *Personal Fictions.*

2379 Romeril, John. "Ringing Heaven: the Second Rex Cramphorn Memorial Lecture." *ADS.* 1997 Apr.; 30: 17-26. Lang.: Eng.

DRAMA: —Plays/librettos/scripts

Australia: Melbourne. 1996. Histories-sources. ▪Text of playwright Romeril's speech on the state of Australian theatre and culture given at the Merlyn Playhouse, Melbourne, on November 1, 1996.

2380 Tompkins, Joanne. "Breaching the Body's Boundaries: Abjected Subject Positions in Postcolonial Drama." *MD.* 1997 Win; 40 (4): 502-513. Notes. Lang.: Eng.

Australia. Ireland. Samoa. 1997. Critical studies. ▪Identity in colonial subjects through the staging of several actors playing the same character or aspects of that character, with emphasis on Louis Nowra's *Summer of the Aliens*, Brian Friel's *Dancing at Lughnasa* and John Kneubuhl's *Think of a Garden*.

2381 Honegger, Gitta. "Fools on the Hill: Thomas Bernhard's Mise-en-Scène." *PerAJ.* 1997 Sep.; 19(3): 34-48. Notes. [Number 57.] Lang.: Eng.

Austria. 1931-1989. Biographical studies. ▪The influence of opera and Austria on the novelist and playwright Thomas Bernhard.

2382 Jelinek, Elfriede. "Sinn egal. Körper zwecklos." (Meaning Immaterial. Body Useless.) *Thsch.* 1997; 11: 22-33. Lang.: Ger, Fre, Dut, Eng.

Austria. 1750-1997. Histories-sources. ▪Playwright Elfriede Jelinek describes her method of using citations from philosophers in foreign or contrasting contexts in her plays.

2383 Yates, W.E. "Sex in the Suburbs: Nestroy's Comedy of Forbidden Fruit." *MLR.* 1997 Apr.; 92(2): 379-391. Notes. Lang.: Eng.

Austria: Vienna. 1841-1995. Critical studies. ▪Argues that *Das Mädl aus der Vorstadt (The Girl from the Suburbs)* within the constraints imposed both by the convention of commercial theatre and by censorship laws, presents a satire of double standards of morality. Original audience response, career overview of Nestroy.

2384 Carlotti, Edoardo Giovanni. "Foreste di simboli e serre d'allegorie. Vista e visione in *Les Aveugles* di Maeterlinck." (Forests of Symbols and Hothouses of Allegory: Sight and Vision in Maeterlinck's *The Blind*.) *IlCast.* 1997; 10(30): 43-55. Notes. Lang.: Ita.

Belgium. 1890. Critical studies. ▪Analysis of *Les Aveugles (The Blind)* by Maurice Maeterlinck.

2385 Friche, Michèle. "La Balade du Grand Macabre de Michel de Ghelderode." (Michel de Ghelderode's *The Grand Macabre's Stroll*.) *ASO.* 1997 Nov/Dec.; 180: 90-93. Illus.: Dwg. B&W. 3. Lang.: Fre.

Belgium. 1934. Critical studies. ▪Analysis of Ghelderode's farce as background to Ligeti's opera *Le Grand Macabre*. Includes a sidebar on the process of creating a score.

2386 Vigeant, Louise. "Amélie Nothomb, Antigone ou Cassandre?" (Amélie Nothomb, Antigone or Cassandra?) *JCT.* 1997; 83 : 162-165. Notes. Illus.: Photo. B&W. 3. Lang.: Fre.

Belgium. 1994. Critical studies. ▪Themes of literature and violence in Amélie Nothomb's *Les Combustibles (The Combustibles)*. Brief biography of playwright.

2387 Damasceno, Leslie H. *Cultural Space and Theatrical Conventions in the Works of Oduvaldo Vianna Filho.* Detroit, MI: Wayne State UP; 1996. 290 pp. (Latin American Literature and Culture Series.) Index. Notes. Biblio. Illus.: Photo. 20. Lang.: Eng.

Brazil. 1934-1974. Histories-specific. ▪English translation of *Espaço cultural e conveções teatrais na obra de Oduvaldo Vianna Filho* (UNICAMP, 1994). Analysis of Vianna Filho's work with Teatro de Arena and his engagement with contemporary culture and politics. Only plays that were produced shortly after their writing are discussed, with emphasis on *Rasga coração (Rend Your Heart)*.

2388 Tancheva, Kornelia. "Melodramatic Contingencies: Tendencies in the Bulgarian Drama and Theatre of the Late Nineteenth Century." 61-82 in Hays, Michael, ed.; Nikolopoulou, Anastasia, ed. *Melodrama: The Cultural Emergence of a Genre.* New York, NY: St. Martin's P; 1996. 288 pp. Notes. Lang.: Eng.

Bulgaria. 1880-1910. Historical studies. ▪The reflection of Bulgarian revolution and independence in melodrama. Argues that melodrama also reveals national class structure and difference.

2389 Archambault, François. "Le jeu de la vérité." (The Truth Game.) *JCT.* 1997; 85: 73-75. Illus.: Photo. B&W. 1. Lang.: Fre.

Canada: Montreal, PQ. 1997. Histories-sources. ▪Playwright François Archambault discusses realism, in general and in his play *15 Secondes (15 Seconds)*.

2390 Bell, Karen. "Beth French." *PAC.* 1997; 30(4): 19. Illus.: Photo. B&W. 1. Lang.: Eng.

Canada: Toronto, ON. 1989-1997. Biographical studies. ▪French's new play *Life Sentences*, written in a monologue style with no stage directions, and its production at the Factory Theatre.

2391 Bell, Lindsay Dale-Ann. *Priest, from Screen to Stage: A Dramaturgical Transposition of Jimmy McGovern's Screenplay.* Edmonton, AB: Univ. of Alberta; 1997. 111 pp. [M.A. Thesis, Univ. Microfilms Order No. AAC MQ21125.] Lang.: Eng.

Canada. 1996. Histories-sources. ▪Chronicle of project in which Jimmy McGovern's screenplay *Priest* was adapted, workshopped and produced for the 'New Play' production requirement of the MFA Directing program at the University of Alberta. Documents the dramaturgical decisions and challenges of adapting this work from screen to stage.

2392 Bondar, Alanna F. "'Life Doesn't Seem Natural:' Ecofeminism and the Reclaiming of the Feminine Spirit in Cindy Cowan's *A Woman from the Sea*." *JCT.* 1997 Spr; 18(1): 18-26. Biblio. Lang.: Eng.

Canada. 1986. Critical studies. ▪Argues that Cindy Cowan's play *A Woman from the Sea* outlines liberating potential of ecofeminism and female spirituality.

2393 Brunner, Astrid. "*Whylah Falls*." *ArtsAtl.* 1997; 15(1): 55. Illus.: Photo. B&W. 1. Lang.: Eng.

Canada. 1997. Critical studies. ▪Analysis of George Elliott Clarke's *Whylah Falls*: its theme of racism, author's previous work as a poet.

2394 Camerlain, Lorraine. "Julie Fiction." *JCT.* 1997; 83: 153-156. Illus.: Photo. B&W. 1. Lang.: Fre.

Canada: Montreal, PQ. 1997. Critical studies. ▪Fiction and reality in Yvan Bienvenue's *Dits et Inédits (Tales and Unpublished Stories)*.

2395 Caton, Jacolyn. "Mansel Robinson." *PAC.* 1997; 31(1): 31. Illus.: Photo. B&W. 1. Lang.: Eng.

Canada. 1993-1997. Critical studies. ▪Political themes in plays of Robinson, their productions and his receipt of several playwriting awards.

2396 Classen, Sigrid Ulrike. *The Black Madonna Figure as a Source of Female Empowerment in the Works of Four Italian-Canadian Authors.* Sherbrooke, PQ: Université de Sherbrooke; 1997. 130 pp. [M.A. Thesis, Univ. Microfilms Order No. AAC MQ21732.] Lang.: Eng.

Canada. 1950-1990. Critical studies. ▪The presence of a pre-Christian female deity in Vittorio Rossi's play *The Last Adam* and Marco Micone's play *Addolorata* as well as novels by Nina Ricci and Frank Paci.

2397 David, Gilbert. "Dispositifs (post)modernes." ((Post) Modern Forms.) *AnT.* 1997 Spr; 21: 144-157. Notes. Biblio. Lang.: Fre.

Canada. 1981-1988. Critical studies. ▪Autoreflexivity as element of modernism and postmodernism of québécois plays of 1980s. Examples drawn from Normand Chaurette's *Provincetown Playhouse, juillet 1919, j'avais 19 ans (Provincetown Playhouse, July 1919, I Was 19 Years Old)*, Claude Poissant's *Passer la nuit (Spending the Night)* and Normand Canac-Marquis's *Le syndrome de Cézanne (The Cézanne Syndrome)*.

2398 de Guevara, Lina. "Sisters/Strangers: A Community Play about Immigrant Women." *CTR.* 1997 Spr; 90: 28-31. Lang.: Eng.

Canada: Victoria, BC. 1994. Histories-sources. ▪Lina de Guevara describes writing and producing her *Sisters/Strangers*, a play reflecting experiences of immigrant women in British Columbia.

2399 Dolbec, Nathalie. "Une Stratégie descriptive dans *La Sagouine* d'Antonine Maillet: l'énumération." (A Descriptive Strategy in Antonine Maillet's *The Slattern*: Enumeration.) *JCT.* 1997 Spr; 18(1): 27-41. Notes. Biblio. Lang.: Fre.

Canada. 1971. Critical studies. ▪Examines and explains significance of enumerative descriptions in Antonine Maillet's one-woman show *La Sagouine (The Slattern)*.

DRAMA: —Plays/librettos/scripts

2400 Downton, Dawn Rae. "*Here Lies Henry.*" *ArtsAtl.* 1997; 15(1): 53-54. Lang.: Eng.
Canada: Halifax, NS. 1990-1997. Critical studies. ■Profile of playwright Daniel MacIvor: his receipt of the Chalmers award, international response to his work, and his one-person play *Here Lies Henry.*

2401 Falck, Joanna Grace. *Graceful Penetration: Judith Thompson and Her Audience.* Edmonton, AL: Univ. of Alberta; 1997. 79 pp. [M.A. Thesis, Univ. Microfilms Order No. AAC MQ21130.] Lang.: Eng.
Canada. 1984-1991. Critical studies. ■The 'penetrative effect' on the audience of *White Biting Dog*, *I Am Yours*, and *Lion in the Streets* by Judith Thompson.

2402 Forsyth, Louise H. "A Clash of Symbols: When I Put on What I Want to Put on." *CTR.* 1997 Fall; 92: 27-33. Notes. Biblio. Illus.: Photo. B&W. 7. Lang.: Eng.
Canada: Montreal, PQ. 1970-1993. Historical studies. ■Surveys feminist solo performance in Quebec, along with its reception and reputation.

2403 Forsyth, Louise H. "Relire le théâtre-femmes. *Encore cinq minutes* de Françoise Loranger." (Rereading Women's Theatre. *Five More Minutes* by Françoise Loranger.) *AnT.* 1997 Spr; 21: 43. Notes. Biblio. Lang.: Fre.
Canada. 1967. Critical studies. ■Elements of early feminism in Françoise Loranger's play *Encore cinq minutes (Five More Minutes).*

2404 Fralic, Michael Lloyd. *Marginalization and the Active Margins in the Plays of Ray Guy.* St. John's, NF: Memorial Univ. of Newfoundland; 1997. 160 pp. [M.A. Thesis, Univ. Microfilms Order No. AAC MQ23136.] Lang.: Eng.
Canada. 1948-1951. Historical studies. ■Political, economic, and cultural marginalization of human populations in the plays of Ray Guy, including *Young Triffie's Been Made Away With*, *Frog Pond*, and *The Swinton Massacre.*

2405 Gilbert, Reid. "'You'll Become Part of Me': Solo Performance." *CTR.* 1997 Fall; 92: 5-9. Notes. Biblio. Illus.: Photo. B&W. 3. Lang.: Eng.
Canada: Vancouver, BC, Victoria, BC. 1997. Critical studies. ■Speculates on varieties of solo performance and maps their manifestations in Vancouver and Victoria, BC.

2406 Godin, Diane. "*38: Shakespeare Graffiti.*" *JCT.* 1997; 82: 165-169. Notes. Illus.: Dwg. Photo. B&W. 5. Lang.: Fre.
Canada: Montreal, PQ. 1996. Critical studies. ■Searching for traces of Shakespeare in *38*, co-production of Théâtre d'Aujourd'hui and Théâtre Urbi et Orbi presenting thirty-eight texts inspired by Shakespeare, September 1996.

2407 Gross, Robert F. "Offstage Sounds: The Permeable Playhouse of Charles Charles." *TRC.* 1997 Spr; 18(1): 3-17. Notes. Biblio. Lang.: Eng.
Canada. 1982. Critical studies. ■Thematic interplay of sameness and difference in Normand Chaurette's *Provincetown Playhouse, juillet 1919, j'avais 19 ans (Provincetown Playhouse, July 1919, I Was 19 Years Old)* as means of critiquing homophobia and masculinist ideology.

2408 Hadfield, Dorothy. "The Role Power Plays in George F. Walker's Detective Trilogy." *ET.* 1997; 16(1): 67-83. Notes. Biblio. Lang.: Eng.
Canada. 1980-1997. Critical studies. ■Analysis of *The Power Plays* by George F. Walker.

2409 Harvie, Jennifer. "The Nth Degree: An Interview with Guillermo Verdecchia." *CTR.* 1997 Fall; 92: 46-49. Illus.: Photo. B&W. 3. Lang.: Eng.
Canada. 1993-1997. Histories-sources. ■Writer/actor Guillermo Verdecchia discusses playwriting, solo performance and cultural dialogue.

2410 Hulslander, Kenneth. "L'espace comme signe identitaire dans *El Clavadista* de Colleen Curran." (Space as Sign of Identity in *El Clavadista* by Colleen Curran.) *AnT.* 1997 Spr; 21: 132-143. Notes. Biblio. Lang.: Fre.
Canada. 1990. Critical studies. ■Interprets use of space in Colleen Curran's *El Clavadista (The Cliffdiver)* as means of expressing problematic of Anglo-Quebec identity.

2411 Kaplan, Jon. "The Royal Family." *AmTh.* 1997 Mar.; 14(3): 9. Illus.: Photo. B&W. 1. Lang.: Eng.

Canada: Toronto, ON. 1980-1997. Histories-sources. ■Writer/performer Linda Griffiths and director Paul Thompson's revival of their play *Maggie & Pierre* at Passe Muraille.

2412 Knowles, Richard Paul; Lane, Harry. "Solo Performance." *CTR.* 1997 Fall; 92: 3-4. Lang.: Eng.
Canada. 1980-1997. Historical studies. ■Observes the increase in solo performance texts in Canada since 1980 and notes important features.

2413 Laliberté, Hélène. "Espaces et territoires dans *Being at home with Claude* de René-Daniel Dubois." (Spaces and Territories in *Being at Home With Claude* by René-Daniel Dubois.) *AnT.* 1997 Spr; 21: 119-131. Notes. Biblio. Lang.: Fre.
Canada. 1986. Critical studies. ■References to space, both literal and figurative, in René-Daniel Dubois' *Being at Home with Claude.*

2414 Leggatt, Alexander. "Plays and Playwrights." 333-365 in Plant, Richard, ed.; Saddlemyer, Ann, ed. *Later Stages: Essays in Ontario Theatre from the First World War to the 1970s.* Toronto, ON: Univ of Toronto P; 1997. 496 pp. (The Ontario Historical Studies Series.) Index. Notes. Biblio. Illus.: Photo. 2. Lang.: Eng.
Canada. 1914-1979. Historical studies. ■Evolution and development of playwriting in Ontario.

2415 Levasseur, Jean. "Histoire et historicité, intertextualité et réception dans *Louis Mailloux* (1975) de Calixte Duguay et Jules Boudreau." (History and Historicity, Intertextuality and Reception in *Louis Mailloux* (1975) by Calixte Duguay and Jules Boudreau.) *JCT.* 1997 Spr; 18(1): 89-106. Notes. Biblio. Lang.: Fre.
Canada. 1975. Critical studies. ■Intertextual study of Calixte Duguay and Jules Boudreau's *Louis Mailloux* with historical source documents. Concludes that authors avoided concept of national hero in favor of collective hero.

2416 Lévesque, Solange. "Penser le monde: Entretien avec Marie-Line Laplante." (Imagining the World: Interview with Marie-Line Laplante.) *JCT.* 1997; 82: 34-41. Illus.: Photo. B&W. 4. Lang.: Fre.
Canada: Montreal, PQ. 1991-1997. Histories-sources. ■Sources of inspiration for playwright Marie-Line Laplante.

2417 Lévesque, Solange. "Éclaircie dans l'été des théâtres." (Brighter Skies for Summer Theatres.) *JCT.* 1997; 85: 167-170. Illus.: Poster. 2. Lang.: Fre.
Canada. 1997. Critical studies. ■Argues that summer theatres in francophone Quebec are improving by staging plays with richer, more three-dimensional characters, such as those in Carole Tremblay's *Jeune femme cherche homme, désespérément (Young Woman Desperately Seeking Man)* and Michel Marc Bouchard's *Pierre et Marie. et le démon (Pierre and Marie. And the Demon).*

2418 Little, Edward. "Aesthetic Morality in the Blyth and District Community Play: A Festival Hosts a Celebration." *CTR.* 1997 Spr; 90: 20-27. Biblio. Illus.: Photo. B&W. 2. Lang.: Eng.
Canada: Blyth, ON. 1993. Historical studies. ■Ideology and the absence of contentious issues in collaborative community plays such as *Many Hands* at Blyth Festival, 1993.

2419 Loffree, Carrie. "La nouvelle dramaturgie et l'informatique. Stratégies de réception communes." (The New Playwriting and Computing: Common Reception Strategies.) *AnT.* 1997 Spr; 21: 102-118. Notes. Biblio. Lang.: Fre.
Canada. 1997. Historical studies. ■Approaches to reading playtexts and performance texts inspired by non-linearity of computer age information systems.

2420 Massoutre, Guylaine. "Des tortionnaires à foison." (Torturers Galore.) *JCT.* 1997; 83: 26-28. Illus.: Photo. B&W. 2. Lang.: Fre.
Canada: Montreal, PQ. 1996-1997. Historical studies. ■Differing treatments of theme of overcoming childhood fears in Emmanuel Bilodeau's *Simone avait des ailes (Simone Had Wings)* and Réjane Charpentier's *Coeur à coeur (Heart-to-Heart).*

2421 Melançon, Benoît. "Moderniser les Lumières." (Modernizing the Enlightenment.) *JCT.* 1997; 83: 44-50. Illus.: Photo. B&W. 4. Lang.: Fre.

DRAMA: —Plays/librettos/scripts

Canada: Montreal, PQ. France. 1997. Critical studies. ▪Different approaches to adapting classics for contemporary audiences with Lorraine Côté's version of Voltaire's *Candide* (Théâtre du Sous-Marin Jaune, directed by Antoine Laprise, 1997) and Alice Ronfard's staging of Marivaux's *La Seconde Surprise de l'amour (The Second Surprise of Love)* (Espace GO, 1997).

2422 Mercier, Martin. "La rhétorique du mensonge." (The Rhetoric of the Lie.) *JCT*. 1997; 83: 29-31. Illus.: Photo. B&W. 1. Lang.: Fre.
Canada: Quebec, PQ. 1997. Historical studies. ▪Michel Nadeau's play *Terrains vagues (Wastelands)* adapts Akira Kurosawa's film *Rashomon* for Quebec theatres and contemporary québécois society.

2423 Moss, Jane. "Larry Tremblay et la dramaturgie de la parole." (Larry Tremblay and the Dramaturgy of Language.) *AnT*. 1997 Spr; 21: 62-83. Notes. Biblio. [Originally published in English in *The American Review of Canadian Studies* vol 25, no 2-3, p 251-267.] Lang.: Fre.
Canada. 1989-1995. Critical studies. ▪Language use as dominant feature of monodramas by Larry Tremblay: *Le déclic du destin (The Click of Destiny)*, *Leçon d'anatomie (Anatomy Lesson)* and *The Dragonfly of Chicoutimi*.

2424 Perkins, Don. "Shifting Loyalties: The Indigenous and Indigenisation in Canadian Historical Drama of Cultural Contacts." *ET*. 1997; 16(2): 151-162. Notes. Biblio. Lang.: Eng.
Canada. 1886-1997. Critical studies. ▪The role of indigenous peoples in Canadian history plays of the 1970s as compared to similar plays of the late nineteenth century: *Daulac* by Wilfred Campbell, *De Roberval* by John Hunter-Duvar, *Tecumseh* by Charles Mair, *Sainte-Marie Among the Hurons* by James Nichol, *The Great Wave of Civilization* by Herschel Hardin, and *On the Rim of the Curve* by Michael Cook.

2425 Perkins, Don. "Recreating/Re-enacting a Dream: Rhonda Trodd, Frank Moher, and *Supreme Dream*." *CTR*. 1997 Fall; 92: 19-22. Illus.: Photo. B&W. 2. Lang.: Eng.
Canada: Toronto, ON. 1997. Histories-sources. ▪Playwright Frank Moher and actress Rhonda Trodd describe the process of writing *Supreme Dream*, based on Trodd's experience with The Supremes.

2426 Quevillon, Michel. "La figure de Stavroguine: la voie entre le roman et la scène." (The Face of Stavrogin: The Route from Novel to Stage.) *JCT*. 1997; 83: 102-107. Notes. Illus.: Photo. B&W. 4. Lang.: Fre.
Canada: Montreal, PQ. 1997. Critical studies. ▪Director Téo Spychalski's version of Dostoévskij's *The Demons* (Groupe la Veillée, 1997) adapts novel for stage by centering action on character of the Prince.

2427 Riendeau, Pascal. "Sense et science à la dérive dans *Fragments d'une lettre d'adieu lus par des géologues*." (Meaning and Science Adrift in *Fragments of a Farewell Letter Read by Geologists*.) *AnT*. 1997 Spr; 21: 84-101. Notes. Biblio. Lang.: Fre.
Canada. 1986. Critical studies. ▪Literary, scientific and otherwise non-theatrical discourse in Normand Chaurette's *Fragments d'une lettre d'adieu lus par des géologues (Fragments of a Farewell Letter Read by Geologists)*.

2428 Robert, Lucie. "(D)écrire le corps." (Describing/Writing the Body.) *AnT*. 1997 Spr; 21: 28-42. Notes. Biblio. Lang.: Fre.
Canada. 1986-1992. Critical studies. ▪Changes in power relations of author, director and actors in 'authority' of playwrights over staging of their plays. Discusses Robert Claing's *La femme d'intérieur (The Woman Inside)*, Marie Laberge's *L'homme gris (The Tipsy Man)* and Larry Tremblay's *Leçon d'anatomie (Anatomy Lesson)*.

2429 Salverson, Julie. "The Art of Witness in Popular Theatre." *CTR*. 1997 Spr; 90: 36-39. Biblio. Notes. Lang.: Eng.
Canada: Toronto, ON. 1997. Critical studies. ▪Explores potential of popular theatre to be an 'art of witness' and a tool for describing and healing trauma.

2430 Stowe, Lisa Roxanne. *Thompson's Family Values: Judith Thompson's Rupturing of the Traditional Family Unit.* St. John's, NF: Memorial Univ. of Newfoundland; 1997. 116 pp. [M.A. Thesis, Univ. Microfilms Order No. AAC MQ23175.] Lang.: Eng.
Canada. 1980-1997. Critical studies. ▪The theme of family in plays Judith Thompson: plays covered are *The Crackwalker*, *White Biting Dog*, and *I Am Yours*.

2431 Turp, Gilbert. "Écrire pour le corps." (Writing for the Body.) *AnT*. 1997 Spr; 21: 161-172. Notes. Biblio. Lang.: Fre.
Canada: Montreal, PQ. 1992-1996. Histories-sources. ▪Extract of round-table discussion featuring Quebec playwrights Larry Tremblay, Serge Boucher, Carole Fréchette, Wajdi Mouawad, Élizabeth Bouget discussing theme of body in their plays.

2432 Vaillancourt, Lise. "Où il est question de machine, de pantoufle et de gouffre." (It's a Matter of Machines, Slippers, Abysses.) *JCT*. 1997; 83: 84-87. Illus.: Dwg. 1. Lang.: Fre.
Canada. 1997. Histories-sources. ▪Playwright Lise Vaillancourt on the process of creating characters.

2433 Vaïs, Michel. "La voie politique." (The Political Lane.) *JCT*. 1997; 85: 8-10. Notes. Illus.: Poster. Photo. B&W. 3. Lang.: Fre.
Canada: Montreal, PQ. 1997. Historical studies. ▪Michel Monty's *Lettre de Cantos (Letter from Cantos)* as a rare example of political theatre in Quebec.

2434 Van Fossen, Rachael. "Writing for the Community Play Forum." *CTR*. 1997 Spr; 90: 10-14. Illus.: Photo. B&W. 3. Lang.: Eng.
Canada: Fort Qu'Appelle, SK, Regina, SK. 1990-1997. Histories-sources. ▪Playwright Rachael Van Fossen dispels myths surrounding writing community-theatre scripts and explains her own process writing *The Gathering* and *A North Side Story (or two)*.

2435 Vigeant, Louise. "Regard de l'autre ou regard sur soi." (The View of the Other or the View of Oneself.) *JCT*. 1997; 85: 26-29. Notes. Illus.: Photo. B&W. 2. Lang.: Fre.
Canada: Montreal, PQ. 1997. Critical studies. ▪Difference in metaphoric content between personal reading of Franz Kafka's *Der Prozess* and interpretation implied by Elizabeth Albahaca's adaptation, *Le Procès (The Trial)* produced by Groupe de la Veillée, 1997.

2436 Wickham, Philip. "Des personnages étrangement familiers." (Strangely Familiar Characters.) *JCT*. 1997; 85: 117-122. Illus.: Photo. B&W. 5. Lang.: Fre.
Canada. UK-Wales. 1997. Historical studies. ▪Study of the characters in Edward Thomas' *House of America* in French translation by René-Daniel Dubois (*La Maison Amérique*).

2437 Wilson, Ann. "Lying and Dying: Theatricality in *Here Lies Henry*." *CTR*. 1997 Fall; 92: 39-41. Biblio. Illus.: Photo. B&W. 2. Lang.: Eng.
Canada. 1994-1996. Critical studies. ▪Relates themes of lying and fear of death in *Here Lies Henry*, monodrama by Daniel MacIvor and Daniel Brooks.

2438 Wylie, Herb. "'Painting the Background': Metadrama and the Fabric of History in Sharon Pollock's *Blood Relations*." *ET*. 1997; 15(2): 191-205. Notes. Biblio. Lang.: Eng.
Canada. 1892-1997. Historical studies. ▪Pollock's treatment of the Lizzie Borden theme in *Blood Relations* compared to contemporary media accounts and other historical accounts.

2439 Diago, Nel. "Elogio de la traición: *Malinche* de Inés M. Stanger y *Opus primum, un conte de guerra* de Hadi Kurich." (Eulogy for Treason: *Malinche* by Inés M. Stanger and *Opus primum, A Story of War* by Hadi Kurich.) *Gestos*. 1997 Apr.; 12(23): 157-162. Lang.: Spa.
Chile. Spain. 1993. Critical studies. ▪Thematic comparison between the play *Malinche* by Chilean playwright Stanger and Bosnian playwright Kurich's *Opus primum*, which he wrote in the language of his adopted country, Spain.

2440 Luonan, Ding. "At the Intersection of Eastern and Western Theatre: Forms and Concepts of Chinese Theatre in the 1980s." *ThR*. 1997; 22(1 Supplement): 69-72. Notes. Lang.: Eng.
China, People's Republic of. 1980-1989. Historical studies. ▪Summary of modernization and nationalization of Chinese spoken theatre resulting from intercultural exchange between East and West in 1980s.

DRAMA: —Plays/librettos/scripts

2441 Garavito, C. Lucía. "Dramaturgia e ideologia en *Siete lunas y un espejo* de Albalucía Angel." (Dramaturgy and Ideology in *Seven Moons and a Looking Glass* by Albalucía Angel.) *Gestos.* 1997 Apr.; 12(23): 85-96. Notes. Biblio. Lang.: Spa.
Colombia. 1991. Critical studies. ■Feminist analysis of the play by the controversial playwright and novelist.

2442 Schille, Candy B.K. "Rereading 'The Maid's Soliloquy'." *ELN.* 1997 June; 34(4): 22-29. Notes. Lang.: Eng.
Colonial America. England. 1713-1753. Critical studies. ■Popularity of Addison's play *Cato* in the North American colonies, one of Cato's speeches being the source of a popular anonymous poem 'The Maid's Soliloquy'.

2443 Lukić, Darko. "Contemporary Croatian War Plays." *SEEP.* 1997 Sum; 17(2): 27-31. Illus.: Photo. 1. Lang.: Eng.
Croatia. 1990-1996. Historical studies. ■The reflection of war in current Croatian theatre. Author divides approximately thirty plays into groups of five that examine specific war-oriented themes.

2444 Linares-Ocanto, Luis. *La doble magía: Teatro y religión en Cuba en el siglo XX.* (Double Magic: Theatre and Religion in Twentieth-Century Cuba.) Iowa City, IA: Univ. of Iowa; 1997. 185 pp. [Ph.D. Dissertation, Univ. Microfilms Order No. AAC 9731831.] Lang.: Spa.
Cuba. 1925-1990. Critical studies. ■The 'Black Madonna' and cultural and religious manifestations associated with this figure through the representation of Afro-Cuban religious ceremonies in twentieth-century Cuban theatre. Analysis of *Juana Revolico* by Flora Diaz Parrado, *El peine y el espeio (The Comb and the Mirror)* by Abelardo Estorino, *Requiem por Yarini* by Carlos Felipe, *Santa Camila de la Habana vieja* by José Brene, *Mamico Omi Omo* by José Milian, *Maria Antonia* by Eugenio Hernandez Espinoza.

2445 Meche, Jude R. "Female Victims and the Male Protagonist in Václav Havel's Drama." *MD.* 1997 Win; 40(4): 468-476. Notes. Lang.: Eng.
Czech Republic. 1963-1997. Critical studies. ■Havel's presentation and use of secretaries and victimized female characters as foils for male protagonists in his plays *Pokoušení (Temptation)*, *Zahradní slavnost (The Garden Party)* and *Ztížená možnost soustředění (The Increased Difficulty of Concentration)*.

2446 Erben, Joan Marie. *The Spirit from Below: A Critical Approach to Václav Havel's Temptation.* Boise, ID: Idaho State Univ; 1997. 35 pp. Notes. Biblio. [D.A. Dissertation, Univ. Microfilms Order No. AAC 9735249.] Lang.: Eng.
Czechoslovakia. 1985. Critical studies. ■The treatment of the Faust themes in Havel's *Pokoušení (Temptation)* as well as temes of government harassment, personal self-reflection and philosophical contemplation.

2447 Langkilde, Nicole Maria. "Taenkende teater og alfonsvirksomhed." (Meaningful Theatre and Pimping.) *TE.* 1997 June; 84: 4-7. Illus.: Photo. B&W. 3. Lang.: Dan.
Denmark. 1997. Histories-sources. ■An interview with director Katrine Wiedemann about her realization of Jokum Rohde's play *Fantomsmerter—Det virkelige liv 2 (Phantom Pains—Real Life 2)*.

2448 "The Crisis of Counsel in Early Jacobean Political Tragedy." *RenD.* 1993; 24: 57-81. Notes. Biblio. Lang.: Eng.
England: London. 1603-1610. Critical studies. ■The reflection of King James' domination at the hands of his counsellors in Samuel Daniel's *The Tragedy of Philotas*, Ben Jonson's *The Tragedy of Sejanus*, and Fulke Greville's *Mustapha*.

2449 Adelman, Janet. "'Born of Woman': Fantasies of Maternal Power in *Macbeth*." 105-134 in Garner, Shirley Nelson, ed.; Sprengnether, Madelon, ed. *Shakespearean Tragedy and Gender.* Bloomington, IN: Indiana UP; 1996. 326 pp. Index. Notes. Biblio. Lang.: Eng.
England. 1606. Critical studies. ■The co-existence of an absolute, destructive female power and the simultaneous escape from it in Shakespeare's play. Order is restored at the end, but at the expense of the women in the play, all of whom are killed.

2450 Adelman, Janet. "Iago's Alter Ego: Race as Projection in *Othello*." *SQ.* 1997 Sum; 48(2): 125-144. Notes. Lang.: Eng.

England. 1604. Critical studies. ■Play's representation of Othello's experience of race as it comes to dominate his sense of self, and function of Othello's race for Iago. Attempts to test applicability of psychoanalytic theory to problems of race.

2451 Agan, Cami D. *Frances Sheridan and Mid-Eighteenth Century Drama Reconsidered and Recontextualized.* Pittsburgh, PA: Duquesne Univ; 1997. 334 pp. [Ph.D. Dissertation, Univ. Microfilms Order No. AAC 9725218.] Lang.: Eng.
England. 1740-1780. Critical studies. ■Critical analysis of six newly-staged comedies—Arthur Murphy's *The Way to Keep Him* and *All in the Wrong*, George Colman's *The Jealous Wife*, William Whitehead's *The School For Lovers* and George Colman and David Garrick's *The Clandestine Marriage*, with focused attention on Frances Sheridan's *The Discovery*, in order to reevaluate its importance in the larger scheme of eighteenth-century theatre.

2452 Alfar, Cristina Leon. *'Evil' Women: Patrilineal Fantasies in Early Modern Tragedy.* Seattle, WA: Univ. of Washington; 1997. 323 pp. [Ph.D. Dissertation, Univ. Microfilms Order No. AAC 9736234.] Lang.: Eng.
England. 1590-1613. Critical studies. ■The portrayal of 'evil' women in Shakespeare's *Romeo and Juliet*, *King Lear*, *Macbeth*, and *The Winter's Tale*, Beaumont and Fletcher's *The Maid's Tragedy*, and Webster's *The White Devil*.

2453 Amis, Margaret. *Three Couples Talking: Doing It with Words in Restoration Comedy.* Santa Cruz, CA: Univ. of California; 1997. 203 pp. [Ph.D. Dissertation, Univ. Microfilms Order No. AAC 9823025.] Lang.: Eng.
England. 1660-1700. Critical studies. ■Applies language game theory to conversations of the 'Wit' couples in George Etherege's *The Man of Mode*, John Dryden's *Marriage à la Mode*, and William Congreve's *The Way of the World*.

2454 Anderson, Kathleen Kay. *'Talk Not of Paradise or Creation, But Mark the Show': Christopher Marlowe's Plays in Performance.* Athens, GA: Univ. of Georgia; 1997. 174 pp. [Ph.D. Dissertation, Univ. Microfilms Order No. AAC 9817782.] Lang.: Eng.
England. 1585-1593. Critical studies. ■Examines Marlowe's plays—*Doctor Faustus*, *Tamburlaine the Great*, *The Jew of Malta*, and *Edward II*—to differentiate his dramaturgy from that of Shakespeare.

2455 Andrew, Martin. "'Cut So Like Her Character': Preconstructing Celia in *Volpone*." *MRDE.* 1996; 8(1): 94-118. Notes. Lang.: Eng.
England. 1607. Critical studies. ■Attempts to defend the character of Celia in Jonson's *Volpone* from historical and contemporary critical misconceptions.

2456 Anzi, Anna. *Storia del teatro inglese dalle origini al 1660.* (History of English Theatre from the Origins to 1660.) Turin: Einaudi; 1997. xii, 362 pp. (Piccola Biblioteca Einaudi 641.) Biblio. Index. Append. Illus.: Dwg. 19. Lang.: Ita.
England. 965-1660. Histories-specific. ■Covers liturgical theatre of the Middle Ages, the Elizabethan period, the closing of the theatres, and the Restoration.

2457 Appelbaum, Robert. "'Standing to the wall:' The Pressures of Masculinity in *Romeo and Juliet*." *SQ.* 1997 Fall; 48(3): 251-272. Notes. Lang.: Eng.
England. 1595. Critical studies. ■Argues that in the world of Shakespeare's play the regime of masculinity is constituted as a system from which there is no escape, but in which there is also no experience of masculine satisfaction.

2458 Archer, John Michael. "Antiquity and Degeneration in *Antony and Cleopatra*." 145-164 in MacDonald, Joyce Green, ed. *Race, Ethnicity, and Power in the Renaissance.* Madison, NJ: Fairleigh Dickinson UP; 1997. 187 pp. Notes. Index. Lang.: Eng.
England. 1607-1707. Critical studies. ■Issues of race and gender in Shakespeare's *Antony and Cleopatra* and critical discourses written about the text during the one hundred years after its publication.

2459 Ashizu, Kaori. "'Pardon Me?' Judging Barnardine's Judge." *EnSt.* 1997 Sep.; 78(5): 417-429. Notes. Lang.: Eng.

DRAMA: —Plays/librettos/scripts

England. 1604. Critical studies. ■The dramatic function of the prisoner Barnardine in Shakespeare's *Measure for Measure* and how his plight reflects upon the behavior of Duke Vincentio.

2460   Ayers, P.K. "Reading, Writing, and *Hamlet*." *SQ.* 1993 Win; 44(4): 423-439. Notes. Lang.: Eng.

England. 1600-1601. Critical studies. ■Focuses on the literal and metaphorical texts involved in *Hamlet* and the various reading practices they generate.

2461   Badir, Patricia. "Representations of the Resurrection at Beverley Minster circa 1208: Chronicle, Play, Miracle." *ThS.* 1997 May; 38(1): 9-41. Lang.: Eng.

England. 1208. Historical studies. ■Explores an account of a play of the Resurrection of Christ appended to a twelfth-century *vita* of St. John of Beverley. Argues that the body of Christ was a site where community and constituency negotiated and regulated social terms.

2462   Baker, Anthony Douglas. *Truth, Moralization, and Narrativity in Tudor Murder Plays.* Louisville, KY: Univ. of Louisville; 1997. 97 pp. [M.A. Thesis, Univ. Microfilms Order No. AAC 1387068.] Lang.: Eng.

England. 1591-1599. Critical studies. ■Spousal homicide in the anonymous *Arden of Faversham* and *A Warning for Fair Women*. Argues that while the dramas are grounded in historical fact, they also function as morality plays.

2463   Baker, Susan. "Personating Persons: Rethinking Shakespearean Disguises." *SQ.* 1992 Fall; 43(3): 303-316. Notes. Lang.: Eng.

England. 1590-1613. Critical studies. ■Function of disguise in Shakespeare's plays.

2464   Baldwin, T.W. "Brave New World." 101-124 in Miola, Robert S., ed. *The Comedy of Errors: Critical Essays.* New York, NY: Garland; 1997. 592 pp. (Shakespeare Criticism 18.) Lang.: Eng.

England. 1594. Critical studies. ■Analysis of Shakespeare's *The Comedy of Errors* (1965).

2465   Banerjee, Rita. *The Ideology of John Fletcher's Tragicomedies.* DeKalb, IL: Northern Illinois Univ; 1997. 255 pp. [Ph.D. Dissertation, Univ. Microfilms Order No. AAC 9818105.] Lang.: Eng.

England. 1579-1625. Critical studies. ■Study of the neglected plays of John Fletcher, both solo plays and those written in collaboration with Philip Massinger.

2466   Barker, Roberta Ellen. *Knaves and Shape-Shifters: Webster's Malcontents, Class and Theatricality in Early Modern England.* Halifax, NS: Dalhousie Univ; 1997. 156 pp. [M.A. Thesis, Univ. Microfilms Order No. AAC MQ24797.] Lang.: Eng.

England. 1600-1634. Critical studies. ■Early modern responses to the social power of theatricality and John Webster's characterization of malcontents in *The Malcontent* (written with John Marston), *The White Devil* and *The Duchess of Malfi.*

2467   Bennett, Alexandra Gay. *Invisible Acts: Female Dramatists and the Writing of Women's Agency in England, 1590-1660.* Waltham, MA: Brandeis Univ; 1997. 249 pp. [Ph.D. Dissertation, Univ. Microfilms Order No. AAC 9729349.] Lang.: Eng.

England. 1590-1660. Critical studies. ■Plays written by women before the reopening of London's public theatre and subsequent rise of professional female dramatists. Explores this neglected 'closet drama' in the works of Joanna Baillie and others.

2468   Berger, Harry, Jr.; Erickson, Peter, ed. *Making Trifles of Terrors: Redistributing Complicities in Shakespeare.* Stanford, CA: Stanford UP; 1997. 487 pp. Notes. Index. Lang.: Eng.

England. 1588-1616. Critical studies. ■Collection of essays, 1960-1992, by Harry Berger. All major plays are covered.

2469   Bergeron, David M. "Fletcher's *The Woman's Prize*, Transgression, and 'Querelle des Femmes'." *MRDE.* 1996; 8(1): 146-164. Notes. Lang.: Eng.

England. 1633. Critical studies. ■Examines John Fletcher's *The Woman's Prize* for its possible subversion of male expectation of a woman's role in society.

2470   Bernstein, Seymour. "Hamlet's Horatio: The Devil's Advocate Convinced." *ShN.* 1997 Spr; 47(1): 15-16, 18. [Number 232.] Lang.: Eng.

England. 1604. Critical studies. ■Examines character Horatio from *Hamlet* and his motivations for accompanying Marcellus and Bernardo to watch for the ghost.

2471   Berry, Herbert. "Shylock, Robert Miles, and Events at the Theatre." *SQ.* 1993 Sum; 44(2): 183-201. Notes. Append. Lang.: Eng.

England: London. 1588-1596. Historical studies. ■History of litigation between James Burbage and Robert Miles. Conjectures that Shakespeare used Miles as a model for Shylock in *The Merchant of Venice.*

2472   Berry, Philippa. "Hamlet's Ear." *ShS.* 1997; 50(1): 57-64. Notes. Lang.: Eng.

England. 1600-1601. Critical studies. ■Hamlet's wordplay and ironic use of iteration as an effective means of fomenting disorder in Shakespeare's play.

2473   Bertinetti, Paolo. *Storia del teatro inglese dalla Restaurazione all'Ottocento 1660-1895.* (History of English Theatre from the Restoration to the Nineteenth Century, 1660-1895.) Turin: Einaudi; 1997. 303 pp. (Piccola Biblioteca Einaudi 642.) Notes. Biblio. IZ. Illus.: Plan. 1. Lang.: Ita.

England. 1668-1895. Histories-specific. ■History of English dramatic literature.

2474   Bevington, David. "*The Comedy of Errors* in Dramatic Context." 313-337 in Miola, Robert S., ed. *The Comedy of Errors: Critical Essays.* New York, NY: Garland; 1997. 592 pp. (Shakespeare Criticism 18.) Notes. Illus.: Photo. 2. Lang.: Eng.

England. 1594. Critical studies. ■Theatrical antecedents in Shakespeare's *The Comedy of Errors.*

2475   Birkenstock, Susan-Marie. *Gesturing Toward the Renaissance Woman.* Gainesville, FL: Univ. of Florida; 1997. 241 pp. [Ph.D. Dissertation, Univ. Microfilms Order No. AAC 9824026.] Lang.: Eng.

England. 1450-1600. Critical studies. ■Dramatic representations of early modern women in Renaissance England by boy actors. Examines the semiotics of language, gesture, and culture.

2476   Blayney, Peter W.M. "The Publication of Playbooks." 383-422 in Cox, John D., ed.; Kastan, David Scott, ed. *A New History of Early English Drama.* New York, NY: Columbia UP; 1997. 565 pp. Index. Notes. Biblio. Lang.: Eng.

England. 1583-1642. Historical studies. ■Relationship between early English theatre and the book trade: how plays were published and sold.

2477   Booth, Stephen. "Shakespeare's Language and the Language of Shakespeare's Time." *ShS.* 1997; 50(1): 1-17. Notes. Lang.: Eng.

England. 1589-1612. Critical studies. ■Shakespeare's strategic use of uncommon language.

2478   Brandes, Georg. "William Shakespeare: A Critical Study." 411-422 in Tomarken, Edward, ed. *As You Like It from 1600 to the Present.* New York, NY: Garland; 1997. 672 pp. (Shakespeare Criticism 17.) Lang.: Eng.

England. 1598. Critical studies. ■Possible sources of Shakespeare's *As You Like It*, theme of rural festivity (1898).

2479   Breitenberg, Mark. "The Anatomy of Masculine Desire in *Love's Labor's Lost*." *SQ.* 1992 Win; 43(4): 430-449. Notes. Lang.: Eng.

England. 1593. Critical studies. ■Heterosexual male desire in Shakespeare's comedies examined from the point of view of Montaigne's essay on Virgil.

2480   Brooks, Harold F. "Themes and Structure in *The Comedy of Errors*." 94-99 in Miola, Robert S., ed. *The Comedy of Errors: Critical Essays.* New York, NY: Garland; 1997. 592 pp. (Shakespeare Criticism 18.) Lang.: Eng.

England. 1594. Critical studies. ■Criticism of Shakespeare's *The Comedy of Errors* (1961).

DRAMA: —Plays/librettos/scripts

2481 Brown, John Russell. "Representing Sexuality in Shakespeare's Plays." *NTQ.* 1997; 13(51): 205-213. Notes. Lang.: Eng.

England. 1594-1608. Critical studies. ■Explores Shakespeare's arts of sexual obliquity, whether in silence, prevarication, or kindled imagination and their relationship with more direct forms of allusion and with an audience's response.

2482 Bruster, Douglas. "Female-Female Eroticism and the Early Modern Stage." *RenD.* 1993; 24: 1-32. Notes. Biblio. Lang.: Eng.

England. 1594-1632. Critical studies. ■Female homoeroticism in the plays of Shakespeare, Jonson, Lyly, Middleton and Brome.

2483 Bruster, Douglas. "The Jailer's Daughter and the Politics of Madwomen's Language." *SQ.* 1995 Fall; 46(3): 277-300. Notes. Lang.: Eng.

England. 1612-1613. Critical studies. ■Analysis of Shakespeare and Fletcher's *The Two Noble Kinsmen* with attention to the speeches of the Jailer's Daughter and what they reveal about power in the play, social relations in the playhouse, and transformation in Jacobean society.

2484 Burbery, Timothy John. *Milton as a Dramatist.* Stony Brook, NY: State Univ. of New York; 1997. 201 pp. [Ph.D. Dissertation, Univ. Microfilms Order No. AAC 9807378.] Lang.: Eng.

England. 1630-1660. Critical studies. ■Examines poet John Milton's dramatic works *Arcades, A Masque at Ludlow Castle,* and *Samson Agonistes.*

2485 Burnett, Mark Thornton. "'Strange and Woonderfull Syghts': *The Tempest* and the Discourses of Monstrosity." *ShS.* 1997; 50(1): 187-199. Notes. Illus.: Handbill. Sketches. Poster. B&W. 7. Lang.: Eng.

England. 1611. Critical studies. ■Questions of monstrosity and portentous occurence in *The Tempest.*

2486 Burroughs, Catherine B. *Closet Stages: Joanna Baillie and the Theater Theory of British Romantic Women Writers.* Philadelphia, PA: Univ. of Pennsylvania P; 1997. 264 pp. Notes. Index. Biblio. Lang.: Eng.

England. 1790-1820. Histories-specific. ■Drawing on journals, letters, diaries as well as celebrity memoirs and autiobiographies, author examines 'closet drama' as an alternative theatrical site for women such as Joanna Baillie, Hannah More, Mary Berry, Sarah Siddons, and Elizabeth Craven. Feminist, queer, and performance theories are used to analyze this social and performative space.

2487 Cain, James. "Putting on the Girls: Cross-Dressing as a Performative Strategy in the Twelfth-Century Latin Comedy *Alda.*" *ThS.* 1997 May; 38(1): 43-71. Lang.: Eng.

England. 1159. Critical studies. ■Critical issues in the overlooked medieval comedy *Alda* by William of Blois revealing political concerns about gender and social mobility during the period.

2488 Calder, Alison. "'I am unacquainted with that language, Roman': Male and Female Experiences of War in Fletcher's *Bonduca.*" *MRDE.* 1997; 8(1): 211-226. Notes. Lang.: Eng.

England. 1613. Critical studies. ■Masculine martial symbolism and the marginalization of the feminine in Fletcher's play.

2489 Calderwood, James L. "Speech and Self in *Othello.*" *SQ.* 1987 Fall; 38(3): 293-303. Notes. Lang.: Eng.

England. 1604. Critical studies. ■Othello's use of verse and prose in Shakespeare's play as indications of his character.

2490 Callens, Johan. *From Middleton and Rowley's* Changeling *to Sam Shepard's* Bodyguard: *A Contemporary Appropriation of a Renaissance Drama.* Lewiston, NY: Edwin Mellen P; 1997. 177 pp. (Studies in Comparative Literature 7.) Index. Biblio. Notes. Lang.: Eng.

England. USA. 1622-1971. Critical studies. ■Analysis of Shepard's early adaptation of the play into a never produced filmscript, *The Bodyguard.* Discusses the adaptation process and the interculturalism aspect of adapting a seventeenth-century Jacobean tragedy into the twentieth-century world.

2491 Candido, Joseph. "Dining Out in Ephesus: Food in *The Comedy of Errors.*" 224-248 in Miola, Robert S., ed. *The*

Comedy of Errors: Critical Essays. New York, NY: Garland; 1997. 592 pp. (Shakespeare Criticism 18.) Lang.: Eng.

England. 1594. Critical studies. ■On the significance of food in Shakespeare's *The Comedy of Errors.*

2492 Canfield, J. Douglas. *Tricksters and Estates: On the Ideology of Restoration Comedy.* Lexington, KY: UP of Kentucky; 1997. 315 pp. Pref. Notes. Index. Biblio. Lang.: Eng.

England. 1660-1710. Critical studies. ■Cultural ideas, values, and power relations of English Restoration comedy, both upholding the status quo and opposing it. Works studied include Aphra Behn's *The False Count,* Nahum Tate's *A Duke and No Duke,* William Wycherley's *The Plain Dealer,* and many others.

2493 Capell, Edward. "Notes to *As You Like It.*" 235-250 in Tomarken, Edward, ed. *As You Like It from 1600 to the Present.* New York, NY: Garland; 1997. 672 pp. (Shakespeare Criticism 17.) Lang.: Eng.

England. 1598. Critical studies. ■Criticism of Shakespeare's *As You Like It* (1779).

2494 Carroll, William C. "'The Base Shall Top Th' Legitimate': The Bedlam Beggar and the Role of Edgar in *King Lear.*" *SQ.* 1987 Win; 38(4): 426-441. Notes. Lang.: Eng.

England. 1605-1606. Critical studies. ■The development of Edgar's character and its significance to Shakespeare's play.

2495 Charles, Casey. "Gender Trouble in *Twelfth Night.*" *TJ.* 1997 May; 49(2): 121-141. Notes. Lang.: Eng.

England. 1600. Historical studies. ■Examination of gender categories in Shakespeare's *Twelfth Night,* particularly seen in its elements of cross-dressing and gender ambiguity.

2496 Charnes, Linda. "What's Love Got to Do with It? Reading the Liberal Humanist Romance in *Antony and Cleopatra.*" 268-286 in Garner, Shirley Nelson, ed.; Sprengnether, Madelon, ed. *Shakespearean Tragedy and Gender.* Bloomington, IN: Indiana UP; 1996. 326 pp. Index. Notes. Biblio. Lang.: Eng.

England. 1607. Critical studies. ■Argues that a reading of Shakespeare's *Antony and Cleopatra* reveals the sociopolitical meanings obscured in the play, freeing it from its traditional gender role interpretation.

2497 Charney, Maurice. "The Voice of Marlowe's Tamburlaine in Early Shakespeare." *CompD.* 1997 Sum; 31(2): 213-223. Notes. Lang.: Eng.

England. 1587-1616. Critical studies. ■Marlowe's *Tamburlaine the Great* and its resonance in Shakespeare's plays.

2498 Churchward, Dale. "Hamlet's Editors and Gertrude's Closet: Putting Polonius in His Place." *ET.* 1997; 15(2): 221-238. Notes. Biblio. Lang.: Eng.

England. 1603-1997. Textual studies. ■Analysis of editions of Shakespeare's *Hamlet,* including early printed texts, to reveal ambiguity about the slaying of Polonius.

2499 Cirrone, Steven F. *Shakespeare's Magic: Gender-based Occult Value in Midsummer Night's Dream, I Henry VI and Macbeth.* Claremont, CA: Claremont Graduate Univ; 1997. 230 pp. [Ph.D. Dissertation, Univ. Microfilms Order No. AAC 9730908.] Lang.: Eng.

England. 1590-1613. Critical studies. ■Gender ideology and the occult in Shakespeare's plays.

2500 Clark, Cumberland. "Shakespeare and Psychology." 467-468 in Tomarken, Edward, ed. *As You Like It from 1600 to the Present: Critical Essays.* New York, NY: Garland; 1997. 672 pp. (Shakespeare Criticism 17.) Notes. Lang.: Eng.

England. 1598. Critical studies. ■On the presence of psychological theory in Shakespeare's *As You Like It* (1936).

2501 Clark, Ira. "The Marital Double Standard in Tudor and Stuart Lives and Writing: Some Problems." *MRDE.* 1997; 9(1): 34-55 . Lang.: Eng.

England. 1598-1650. Critical studies. ■Complexity of the sexual double standard in Tudor and Stuart England and its reflection in such plays as Brome's *A Mad Couple Well Match'd* and the anonymous *Looke About You.*

2502 Clark, Marlene. *Aging Queens in/and Shakespeare's Drama.* New York, NY: City Univ. of New York; 1997. 221 pp.

DRAMA: —Plays/librettos/scripts

[Ph.D. Dissertation, Univ. Microfilms Order No. AAC 9807917.] Lang.: Eng.

England. 1590-1613. Critical studies. ■The cultural place and power of Shakespeare's older women characters and their potential for subverting patriarchy. Some characters examined are Gertrude in *Hamlet*, Hermione in *The Winter's Tale*, and Cleopatra in *Antony and Cleopatra*. Argues that adult males may have played these roles in Shakespeare's theatre.

2503   Clegg, Cyndia Susan. "'By the choise and inuitation of al the realme': *Richard II* and Elizabethan Press Censorship." *SQ*. 1997 Win; 48(4): 432-448. Notes. Lang.: Eng.

England. 1595. Historical studies. ■Suggests that the paradigm for investigating *Richard II*'s potential censorship during the reign of Elizabeth I be relocated in the local history of texts certainly censored and the practices that suppressed them rather than in the prevailing narratives of political hegemony of authority and subversion.

2504   Clubb, Louise George. "Commedia Grave and *The Comedy of Errors*." 200-222 in Miola, Robert S., ed. *The Comedy of Errors: Critical Essays*. New York, NY: Garland; 1997. 592 pp. (Shakespeare Criticism 18.) Lang.: Eng.

England. 1594. Critical studies. ■On the role of *commedia* in Shakespeare's *The Comedy of Errors*.

2505   Coleridge, Samuel Taylor. "A Poetical Farce." 70-76 in Miola, Robert S., ed. *The Comedy of Errors: Critical Essays*. New York, NY: Garland; 1997. 592 pp. (Shakespeare Criticism 18.) Lang.: Eng.

England. 1594. Critical studies. ■Early criticism of Shakespeare's *The Comedy of Errors* (1836).

2506   Collier, J. Payne. "The Works of William Shakespeare." 283-286 in Tomarken, Edward, ed. *As You Like It from 1600 to the Present*. New York, NY: Garland; 1997. 672 pp. (Shakespeare Criticism 17.) Lang.: Eng.

England. 1598. Critical studies. ■Textual history of Shakespeare's *As You Like It* and discussion of a source, Thomas Lodge's 1590 novel, *Rosalynde*.

2507   Colombo, Claire Miller. *'You All May Boast the Censor's Art': Censorship and Authority in Romantic Drama*. Austin, TX: Univ. of Texas; 1997. 282 pp. [Order No: AAC 9822573 ProQuest—Dissertation Abstracts.] Lang.: Eng.

England. 1790-1820. Critical studies. ■Dramatists' use of prefaces to printed versions of their plays to speak about censorship and self-authorization. Considers prefaces to Hannah More's *The Fatal Falsehood*, Joanna Baillie's *DeMonfort*, and Samuel Taylor Coleridge's *Remorse*.

2508   Comensoli, Viviana. *'Household Business': Domestic Plays of Early Modern England*. Toronto, ON: Univ of Toronto P; 1996. 238 pp. (The Mental and Cultural World of Tudor and Stuart England.) Index. Biblio. Notes. Lang.: Eng.

England. 1590-1633. Critical studies. ■Domestic conflict in the plays of Thomas Heywood, Thomas Dekker, and the early prototypes in the cycle play. How these plays reveal cultural constructs of marriage, gender, and other sociopolitical life.

2509   Cook, Albert. "The Transmutation of Heroic Complexity: Plutarch and Shakespeare." *CML*. 1996 Fall; 17(1): 31-43. Notes. Lang.: Eng.

England. 1599-1608. Historical studies. ■The influence of Plutarch's *Lives* as source material for Shakespeare's Roman plays *Julius Caesar*, *Antony and Cleopatra* and *Coriolanus*.

2510   Cook, Carol. "The Fatal Cleopatra." 241-267 in Garner, Shirley Nelson, ed.; Sprengnether, Madelon, ed. *Shakespearean Tragedy and Gender*. Bloomington, IN: Indiana UP; 1996. 326 pp. Index. Biblio. Lang.: Eng.

England. 1607. Critical studies. ■Analysis of punning language in Shakespeare's *Antony and Cleopatra*, said to call into question the gender and power politics of the play.

2511   Cooperman, Robert. "Expanding Upon Nothing: *A Slight Ache* and *King Lear*." *PintR*. 1997: 143-151. Biblio. Notes. Lang.: Eng.

England. 1623-1961. Critical studies. ■A comparison between 'fool' characters in Shakespeare's *King Lear* and Pinter's play *A Slight Ache*.

2512   Cotton, Nancy. "Castrating (W)itches: Impotence and Magic in *The Merry Wives of Windsor*." *SQ*. 1987 Fall; 38(3): 320-326. Notes. Lang.: Eng.

England. 1597. Critical studies. ■Female power, witchcraft, and male disempowerment in Shakespeare's play.

2513   Cox, John D.; Kastan, David Scott. "Introduction: Demanding History." 1-6 in Cox, John D., ed.; Kastan, David Scott, ed. *A New History of Early English Drama*. New York, NY: Columbia UP; 1997. 565 pp. Notes. Biblio. Index. Lang.: Eng.

England. 1100-1500. Critical studies. ■Introduces the volume's critical and theoretical methodology and describes the works as contested sites of meaning with a plurality of meanings inherent in the texts.

2514   Craig, Martha J. *Feminine Virtue in Shakespeare's England: The Power of Submission in Spenser, Sidney, Shakespeare, and Leigh*. West Lafayette, IN: Purdue Univ; 1997. 244 pp. [Ph.D. Dissertation, Univ. Microfilms Order No. AAC 9818935.] Lang.: Eng.

England. 1580-1615. Critical studies. ■The representation of female virtue in early modern England.

2515   Cunningham, Karen. "Female Fidelities on Trial: Proof in the Howard Attainder and *Cymbeline*." *RenD*. 1994; 25: 1-31. Notes. Biblio. Lang.: Eng.

England. 1542-1610. Historical studies. ■Comparison of Katherine Howard's attainder for treason in 1542 with Imogen's metaphorical trial for promiscuity in Shakespeare's *Cymbeline*.

2516   Curran, John E., Jr. "Royalty Unlearned, Honor Untaught: British Savages and Historiographical Change in *Cymbeline*." *CompD*. 1997 Sum; 31(2): 277-303. Notes. Lang.: Eng.

England: London. 1608. Critical studies. ■Attempts to reconcile two traditional camps' views on Shakespeare's *Cymbeline*, one viewing it as pure romance, while the other approaches it looking for its allegorical or topical significance.

2517   Daalder, Joost. "Perspectives of Madness in *Twelfth Night*." *EnSt*. 1997 Mar.; 78(2): 105-110. Notes. Lang.: Eng.

England. 1600-1601. Critical studies. ■Discusses Shakespeare's perspective on madness through a reading of *Twelfth Night*.

2518   Darby, Barbara. "Feminism, Tragedy, and Frances Burney's *Edwy and Elgiva*." *JDTC*. 1997 Spr; 11(2): 3-24. Lang.: Eng.

England. 1752-1840. Critical studies. ■Argues that the play should be examined in light of new feminist criticism and considered as both a text and a script for performance.

2519   Dash, Irene G. *Women's Worlds in Shakespeare's Plays*. Newark, DE/London: Univ of Delaware P/Assoc Univ Presses; 1997. 304 pp. Index. Notes. Biblio. Illus.: Dwg. Photo. 22. Lang.: Eng.

England. 1590-1613. Histories-specific. ■Feminist analysis of the place of women in *All's Well That Ends Well*, *A Midsummer Night's Dream*, *Hamlet*, *Macbeth*, and *Twelfth Night*. Argues that the plays accurately reflect women's place in Elizabethan culture, politics, and economics.

2520   de Grazia, Margareta; Stallybrass, Peter. "The Materiality of the Shakespearean Text." *SQ*. 1993 Fall; 44(3): 255-283. Notes. Lang.: Eng.

England. 1623-1993. Textual studies. ■Using the quarto and folio versions of *King Lear*, attempts to distinguish between Shakespeare's text and editorial mangling.

2521   de Grazia, Margreta. "World Pictures, Modern Periods, and the Early Stage." 7-24 in Cox, John D., ed.; Kastan, David Scott, ed. *A New History of Early English Drama*. New York, NY: Columbia UP; 1997. 565 pp. Notes. Biblio. Index. Lang.: Eng.

England. 1100-1500. Critical studies. ■New historical/ideological perspectives on early English drama. Establishes an 'epochal' framework of chronology and then situates the theatre within a time/space binary, applying a philosophical analysis of the drama.

2522   Deats, Sara Munson. *Sex, Gender, and Desire in the Plays of Christopher Marlowe*. Newark, DE/London: Univ of Delaware P/Associated Univ Presses; 1997. 297 pp. Index. Biblio. Notes. Lang.: Eng.

DRAMA: —Plays/librettos/scripts

England. 1587-1593. Critical studies. ▪Examines sex/gender discourses in the plays of Christopher Marlowe. Uses feminist theoretical methods to examine *Dido, Queen of Carthage, Tamburlaine, Parts I and II, Edward II,* and *Doctor Faustus.*

2523 DeRitter, Jones. "'Wonder not, princely Gloster, at the notice this paper brings you': Women, Writing, and Politics in *Jane Shore.*" *CompD.* 1997 Spr; 31(1): 86-104. Notes. Lang.: Eng.

England. 1714. Critical studies. ▪Nicholas Rowe's *Tragedy of Jane Shore* as a conservative valediction on the end of the reign of Queen Anne, an era when gender stereotypes and political realities were in open conflict.

2524 Desper, Richard. "An Alternative Solution to the Funeral Elegy." *ERev.* 1997 Fall; 5(2): 79-92. Notes. Biblio. Lang.: Eng.

England. 1612. Historical studies. ▪Examines new evidence bearing on Shakespeare authorship in the form of a poem 'A Funeral Elegy for Master William Peter'.

2525 Dessen, Alan C. "Massed Entries and Theatrical Options in *The Winter's Tale.*" *MRDE.* 1996; 8(1): 119-127. Notes. Lang.: Eng.

England. 1602. Critical studies. ▪Exploration of several key scenes for theatrical options that have been screened out by assumptions of massed entries.

2526 Detmer, Emily. *The Politics of Telling: Women's Consent and Accusations of Rape in English Renaissance Drama.* Oxford, OH: Miami Univ; 1997. 266 pp. [Ph.D. Dissertation, Univ. Microfilms Order No. AAC 9813089.] Lang.: Eng.

England. 1550-1630. Critical studies. ▪Argues that representations of women's increased authority to claim rape also reflect cultural anxieties produced by women's gaining such power. Examines Shakespeare's *Titus Andronicus, All's Well That Ends Well,* and *Measure for Measure,* Heywood's *The Rape of Lucrece,* Middleton's *Women Beware Women* and *The Spanish Gypsie,* and Fletcher's *The Queen of Corinth.*

2527 Detmer, Emily. "'Civilizing Subordination': Domestic Violence and *The Taming of the Shrew.*" *SQ.* 1997 Fall; 48(3): 275-294. Notes. Lang.: Eng.

England. 1551-1594. Critical studies. ▪Argues that the play signals a shift toward a 'modern' way of managing the subordination of wives by legitimizing domination as long as it is not physical. England's attempts to make wife-beating reforms, and Kate and Petruchio's relationship as a reflection of the new ideologies.

2528 Diehl, Huston. *Staging Reform, Reforming the Stage: Protestantism and Popular Theatre in Early Modern England.* Ithaca, NY/London: Cornell UP; 1997. 238 pp. Biblio. Index. Notes. Illus. Photo. 16. Lang.: Eng.

England. 1559-1612. Histories-specific. ▪The presence of Protestantism in early English drama, said to have staged and reflected the religious crisis. Plays and genres examined include the revenge tragedies of Kyd, Shakespeare and Middleton, *Othello,* Stuart love tragedies, and Webster's *The Duchess of Malfi.*

2529 Dillon, Janette. "Is There a Performance in This Text?" *SQ.* 1994 Spr; 45(1): 74-86. Notes. Lang.: Eng.

England. 1603. Textual studies. ▪Analysis of the first quarto of *Hamlet* to determine its performability as a means to ascertain whether it is 'the' authoritative text.

2530 Dolan, Frances E. "The Subordinate('s) Plot: Petty Treason and the Forms of Domestic Rebellion." *SQ.* 1992 Fall; 43(3): 317-340. Notes. Lang.: Eng.

England. 1605. Historical studies. ▪Rebellious wives' and servants' treatment in Shakespeare's *The Tempest* and the anonymous *Arden of Faversham.* Also discusses transcript of trial of the Earl of Castlehaven to illuminate the difference when the transgressor is master/husband.

2531 Dox, Donnalee. "Medieval Drama as Documentation: 'Real Presence' in the Croxton *Conversion of Ser Jonathas the Jewe by the Myracle of the Blissed Sacrament.*" *ThS.* 1997 May; 38(1): 97-115. Lang.: Eng.

England. 1400-1500. Historical studies. ▪The image of five Jews who desecrate the host in the play and medieval European stereotypes about Jews.

2532 Eaton, Sara. "A Woman of Letters: Lavinia in *Titus Andronicus.*" 54-74 in Garner, Shirley Nelson, ed.; Sprengnether, Madelon, ed. *Shakespearean Tragedy and Gender.* Bloomington, IN: Indiana UP; 1996. 326 pp. Index. Notes. Biblio. Lang.: Eng.

England. 1593-1594. Critical studies. ▪Argues that Shakespeare's character Lavinia is expressive of the anxieties she generates as an educated, and hence potentially unruly, woman and that her rape and mutilation make evident the nature of her social function as an object of exchange among men.

2533 Eggleston, Robert. "A Sentimental Appeal to Reason: The Fun Never Stops: Young Tom Fashion's Role in Sir John Vanbrugh's *The Relapse.*" *Restor.* 1997 Win; 12(2): 1-14. Notes. Lang.: Eng.

England. 1677-1696. Critical studies. ▪Analysis of a neglected secondary character as a reflection of the the the 'Lord of Misrule'.

2534 Elam, Keir. "'I'll Plague Thee for That Word': Language, Performance and Communicable Diseases." *ShS.* 1997; 50(1): 19-27. Notes. Lang.: Eng.

England. 1603-1607. Critical studies. ▪Language, performance, and bubonic plague epidemic in Shakespeare's early Jacobean drama, particularly *Timon of Athens.*

2535 Elliott, G.R. "Weirdness in *The Comedy of Errors.*" 78-92 in Miola, Robert S., ed. *The Comedy of Errors: Critical Essays.* New York, NY: Garland; 1997. 592 pp. (Shakespeare Criticism 18.) Lang.: Eng.

England. 1594. Critical studies. ▪Analysis of Shakespeare's *The Comedy of Errors.*

2536 Enders, Jody. "Emotion Memory and the Medieval Performance of Violence." *ThS.* 1997 May; 38(1): 139-160. Lang.: Eng.

England. 1400-1600. Historical studies. ▪Violence and spectacularity in the language of medieval law, politics, and theology. Late medieval works such as the *Mystère de Saint Christofle* and other mystery plays are examined.

2537 Enterline, Lynn. "'You speak a language that I understand not': The Rhetoric of Animation in *The Winter's Tale.*" *SQ.* 1997 Spr; 48(1): 17-44. Notes. Lang.: Eng.

England. 1610-1611. Critical studies. ▪Analysis of the 'female voice' in Shakespeare's *The Winter's Tale.* Considers relationship between the trope of the female voice in the Ovidian-Petrarchan tradition and the rhetorical concerns through which the play reads that tradition, turning it into theatrical metacommentary.

2538 Evans, Robert C. "Contemporary Contexts of Jonson's *The Devil Is an Ass.*" *CompD.* 1992 Sum; 26(2): 140-176. Notes. Lang.: Eng.

England. 1616. Critical studies. ▪Examines Jonson's play in its context, with particular attention to the status of his career and the fluid politics of the Jacobean court.

2539 Faucit, Helena. "Some of Shakespeare's Female Characters." 343-394 in Tomarken, Edward, ed. *As You Like It from 1600 to the Present.* New York, NY: Garland; 1997. 672 pp. (Shakespeare Criticism 17.) Lang.: Eng.

England. 1598-1893. Critical studies. ▪Actress author discusses playing Rosalind in Shakespeare's *As You Like It* and other female characters.

2540 Finin-Farber, Kathryn R. *Justice, Language, and the Female Body in Early Modern English Drama.* Binghamton, NY: State Univ. of New York; 1997. 177 pp. [Ph.D. Dissertation, Univ. Microfilms Order No. AAC 9724868.] Lang.: Eng.

England. 1590-1640. Critical studies. ▪Gendered power relations in representations of law and revenge in Shakespeare's *Titus Andronicus* and *The Merchant of Venice,* Middleton's *The Revenger's Tragedy,* and Webster's *The White Devil.*

2541 Finin-Farber, Kathryn R. "Framing (the) Woman: *The White Devil* and the Deployment of Law." *RenD.* 1994; 25: 219-245. Notes. Biblio. Lang.: Eng.

England. 1609-1612. Critical studies. ▪How the character Vittoria calls into question the predetermined frames of reference which determine the outcome of legal proceedings in Webster's play.

DRAMA: —Plays/librettos/scripts

2542 Fischer, Sandra K. "'He means to pay': Value and Metaphor in the Lancastrian Tetralogy." *SQ.* 1989 Sum; 40(2): 149-164. Notes. Lang.: Eng.
England. 1595-1599. Critical studies. ■Analyzes characters' use of economic metaphor in *Richard II*, *Henry IV* and *Henry V*.

2543 Fitzhenry, William John. *Vernacularity and Theater: Gender and Religious Identity in East Anglian Drama.* Durham, NC: Duke Univ; 1997. 260 pp. [Ph.D. Dissertation, Univ. Microfilms Order No. AAC 9727359.] Lang.: Eng.
England. 1400-1500. Critical studies. ■Representations of community and religious identity in the *N-Town Plays*, the Digby *Mary Magdalene*, Arundel's *Constitutions*, and Nicholas Love's *Mirror of the Blessed Life of Jesus Christ.* Traces the relations between vernacular drama and the political uses of the English language.

2544 Flanigan, Tom. "Everyman or Saint? Doubting Joseph in the Corpus Christi Cycle." *MRDE.* 1996; 8(1): 19-48. Notes. Lang.: Eng.
England. 1440-1550. Historical studies. ■Uses the character of Joseph to explore the range of popular conceptions about the saint, the variety and vitality of medieval cycle drama, and the differences within various English cycle dramas.

2545 Franceschina, John. *Homosexualities in the English Theatre: From Lyly to Wilde.* Westport, CT/London: Greenwood; 1997. 340 pp. (Contributions in Drama and Theatre Studies 79.) Index. Biblio. Notes. Pref. Lang.: Eng.
England. 1680-1900. Critical studies. ■The reflection of homosexual behavior or attraction in English theatre through various historical periods.

2546 Freeburg, Victor O. "Disguise Plots in Elizabethan Drama." 435-436 in Tomarken, Edward, ed. *As You Like It from 1600 to the Present.* New York, NY: Garland; 1997. 672 pp. (Shakespeare Criticism 17.) Lang.: Eng.
England. 1598. Critical studies. ■On Shakespeare's *As You Like It* as a disguise play. Author investigates the theatricality of disguise situations (1915).

2547 Freedman, Barbara. "Shakespearean Chronology, Ideological Complicity, and Floating Texts: Something is Rotten in Windsor." *SQ.* 1994 Sum; 45(2): 190-210. Notes. Lang.: Eng.
England. 1597-1602. Textual studies. ■Debate over the date of authorship for Shakespeare's *The Merry Wives of Windsor.*

2548 Freedman, Barbara. "Reading Errantly: Misrecognition and the Uncanny in *The Comedy of Errors.*" 264-289 in Miola, Robert S., ed. *The Comedy of Errors: Critical Essays.* New York, NY: Garland; 1997. 592 pp. (Shakespeare Criticism 18.) Notes. Biblio. Lang.: Eng.
England. 1594. Critical studies. ■Feminist criticism of Shakespeare's *The Comedy of Errors.*

2549 Gallardo, Ximena. *Representing Shakespeare's 'Brave New World': Latin American Appropriations of The Tempest.* Shreveport, LA: Louisiana State Univ. and Agricultural and Mechanical College; 1997. 354 pp. [Ph.D. Dissertation, Univ. Microfilms Order No. AAC 9808741.] Lang.: Eng.
England. Latin America. Caribbean. 1612-1994. Critical studies. ■Latin American and Caribbean reworkings and appropriations of Shakespeare's *The Tempest*, including those of José Enrique Rodo, Roberto Fernandez Retamar, Edward Kamau Brathwaite, Aimé Césaire and George Lamming. Also examines productions of Shakespeare's play by El Conventillo (Chile, 1989), La Bordada (Chile, 1994), Grupo Rajatabla (Caracas, 1991), and Por Amor Al Arte (Mexico, 1992) and analyzes the connection between the appropriations and the culture and literature of Latin America.

2550 Gamer, Michael. "National Supernaturalism: Joanna Baillie, Germany, and the Gothic Drama." *ThS.* 1997 Nov.; 38(2): 49-88 . Lang.: Eng.
England. 1789-1825. Historical studies. ■How playwright Joanna Baillie negotiated the boundaries between melodrama and high romantic drama, between British and German national drama, and between closet drama and theatre.

2551 Gentleman, Francis. "The Dramatic Censor, or, Critical Companion." 225-234 in Tomarken, Edward, ed. *As You Like It from 1600 to the Present.* New York, NY: Garland; 1997. 672 pp. (Shakespeare Criticism 17.) Lang.: Eng.
England. 1598. Critical studies. ■Criticism of Shakespeare's *As You Like It* (1770).

2552 Gibbons, Brian. "Erring and Straying Like Lost Sheep: *The Winter's Tale* and *The Comedy of Errors.*" *ShS.* 1997; 50(1) : 111-123. Notes. Lang.: Eng.
England. 1591-1611. Critical studies. ■Comparison of *The Winter's Tale* and *The Comedy of Errors*: focus on some unexpected similarities.

2553 Gildon, Charles. "Remarks on the Plays of Shakespeare." 79-80 in Tomarken, Edward, ed. *As You Like It from 1600 to the Present.* New York, NY: Garland; 1997. 672 pp. (Shakespeare Criticism 17.) Lang.: Eng.
England. 1598. Critical studies. ■Early criticism of Shakespeare's *As You Like It* (1710).

2554 Goetz, Lisa M. *The Influence on Audience Members of Late Medieval and Early Tudor Drama.* Pittsburgh, PA: Duquesne Univ; 1997. 362 pp. [Ph.D. Dissertation, Univ. Microfilms Order No. AAC 9809034.] Lang.: Eng.
England. 1400-1550. Critical studies. ■Argues that the plays are rhetorically structured to implicate audience members in transgression, allow them moral awareness and the ability to reason. In this way, medieval playwrights could elicit support for political agendas of prevailing authority, ensuring and reinforcing cultural hegemony.

2555 Gordon, George. "Shakespearian Comedy and Other Studies." 469-474 in Tomarken, Edward, ed. *As You Like It from 1600 to the Present: Critical Essays.* New York, NY: Garland; 1997. 672 pp. (Shakespeare Criticism 17.) Notes. Lang.: Eng.
England. 1598. Critical studies. ■On the characters in Shakespeare's *As You Like It* (1944).

2556 Green, Douglas E. "Interpreting 'her martyr'd signs': Gender and Tragedy in *Titus Andronicus.*" *SQ.* 1989 Fall; 40(3): 317-326. Notes. Lang.: Eng.
England. 1590-1594. Critical studies. ■Focuses on Tamora and Lavinia in *Titus Andronicus* to illustrate how gender both marks and is marked by this revenge tragedy. Argues it is largely through and on the female characters that the character Titus is constructed and his tragedy inscribed.

2557 Grindon, Rosa E. "Shakespeare and His Plays from a Woman's Point of View." 455-462 in Tomarken, Edward, ed. *As You Like It from 1600 to the Present.* New York, NY: Garland; 1997. 672 pp. (Shakespeare Criticism 17.) Lang.: Eng.
England. 1598. Critical studies. ■A female critic's view of Shakespeare's *As You Like It* (1930).

2558 Grosman, Meta; Rot, Veronika. *Šolska ura s Hamletom.* (An Hour with *Hamlet*.) Ljubljana: Zavod Republike Slovenije za šolstvo; 1997. 47 pp. Biblio. Lang.: Slo.
England. 1600. Instructional materials. ■Analysis of Shakespeare's *Hamlet.*

2559 Haar, Eric Imler. *An Examination of Social Status in Dramas by Medwall, Sheridan, and Tyler.* Warrensburg, MO: Central Missouri State Univ; 1997. 33 pp. [M.A. Thesis, Univ. Microfilms Order No. AAC 1387352.] Lang.: Eng.
England. Colonial America. 1500-1700. Critical studies. ■Analyzes Henry Medwall's *Fulgens and Lucres*, Richard Brinsley Sheridan's *The School for Scandal*, and Royall Tyler's *The Contrast.*

2560 Hackel, Heidi Brayman. "'Rowme' of Its Own: Printed Drama in Early Libraries." 113-132 in Cox, John D., ed.; Kastan, David Scott, ed. *A New History of Early English Drama.* New York, NY: Columbia UP; 1997. 565 pp. Notes. Biblio. Index. Lang.: Eng.
England. 1600-1650. Historical studies. ■The lack of native drama in early English library collections. Examines the reasons for its exclusion and its relegation to home collections. Also analyzes early reading spaces and how drama was treated in these early library prototypes.

DRAMA: —Plays/librettos/scripts

2561 Hamlin, William M. "Skepticism and Solipsism in *Doctor Faustus.*" *RORD.* 1997; 36: 1-22. Notes. Lang.: Eng.
England. 1551-1616. Critical studies. ∎Analysis of doubt and solipsism in Marlowe's play.

2562 Harrawood, Michael Steven. *Figures of Icarian Flight and Fall in Shakespeare's* Henry VI *Plays: A Study in Power, Persona and Social Performance.* Berkeley, CA: Univ. of California; 1997. 252 pp. [Ph.D. Dissertation, Univ. Microfilms Order No. AAC 9828716.] Lang.: Eng.
England. 1589-1595. Critical studies. ∎Shakespeare's use of the Icarus metaphor in his *Henry* plays to examine the individual and failure, society and culture.

2563 Harris, Diane. "'Downy Lawns of Fruitful Bliss': Marriage in Colley Cibber's Original Comedies." *Restor.* 1997 Sum; 12 (1): 40-57. Notes. Lang.: Eng.
England. 1696-1730. Critical studies. ∎Cibber's portrayal of marriage as a source of emotional and sensual satisfaction and of the model wife as a woman who transgressed traditional boundaries of female behavior. Focus on his early plays *Love's Last Shift, The Lady's Last Stake* and *The Careless Husband.*

2564 Harris, Jonathan Gil. "'Narcissus in thy face': Roman Desire and the Difference it Fakes in *Antony and Cleopatra.*" *SQ.* 1994 Win; 45(4): 408-425. Notes. Lang.: Eng.
England. 1607. Critical studies. ∎Examines the relation between Elizabethan versions of Ovid's Narcissus myth and Shakespeare's *Antony and Cleopatra.*

2565 Hatcher, Judy L. *Gender and Patriarchy in Shakespeare's* Othello *and* The Winter's Tale*: A Feminist Perspective.* Clear Lake, TX: Univ. of Houston; 1997. 78 pp. [M.A. Thesis, Univ. Microfilms Order No. AAC 1387991.] Lang.: Eng.
England. 1604-1613. Critical studies. ∎Argues that Shakespeare dramatizes harmful effects of gender bias not only on female characters, but on the male characters as well.

2566 Hatlen, Burton. "The 'Noble Thing' and the 'Boy of Tears': *Coriolanus* and the Embarrassments of Identity." *ELR.* 1997 Fall; 27(3): 393-420. Notes. Lang.: Eng.
England. 1608. Critical studies. ∎Identity and shame in Shakespeare's *Coriolanus.* Argues that the play demonstrates that identity is impossible because any form of selfhood is already implicated in otherness, socially, linguistically and psychologically.

2567 Hayne, Victoria. *Performing Social Practice: Theatrical Representation of Social Convention and Conflict in Tudor-Stuart Drama.* Los Angeles, CA: Univ. of California; 1997. 433 pp. [Ph.D. Dissertation, Univ. Microfilms Order No. AAC 9807632.] Lang.: Eng.
England. 1571-1670. Critical studies. ∎Aspects of social practice, convention, and conflict, with emphasis on practices of marriage formation and sexual regulation in Shakespeare's *Measure for Measure,* moneylending in Shakespeare's *The Merchant of Venice* and other plays, and political and religious conflict in Nathaniel Lee's *Lucius Junius Brutus.*

2568 Hayne, Victoria. "Performing Social Practice: The Example of *Measure for Measure.*" *SQ.* 1993 Spr; 44(1): 1-29. Notes. Lang.: Eng.
England. 1604. Critical studies. ∎The representational exchanges by which Shakespeare transformed social practices of his time into elements of theatrical meaning in *Measure for Measure.*

2569 Healy, Robert Michael. *Homoerotic Desire and Narrative Dilation in Elizabethan England.* Coral Gables, FL: Univ. of Miami; 1997. 219 pp. [Ph.D. Dissertation, Univ. Microfilms Order No. AAC 9805963.] Lang.: Eng.
England. 1580-1620. Critical studies. ∎Representations of unorthodox sexuality in Elizabethan drama with emphasis on Shakespeare's *Richard II* and *The Merry Wives of Windsor,* and other texts.

2570 Heller, Herbert Jack. *Penitent Brothellers: Grace, Sexuality, and Genre in Thomas Middleton's City Comedies.* Shreveport, LA: Louisiana State Univ. and Agricultural and Mechanical College; 1997. 316 pp. [Ph.D. Dissertation, Univ. Microfilms Order No. AAC 9808749.] Lang.: Eng.
England. 1604-1611. Critical studies. ∎Middleton's Calvinism and the theme of repentance and conversion in his city comedies *A Mad World,*

My Masters, The Widow, A Chaste Maid in Cheapside, A Trick to Catch the Old One, and *Michaelmas Term,* as well as *The Roaring Girl* (written in collaboration with Thomas Dekker).

2571 Henderson, Diana E. "The Theater and Domestic Culture." 173-194 in Cox, John D., ed.; Kastan, David Scott, ed. *A New History of Early English Drama.* New York, NY: Columbia UP; 1997. 565 pp. Notes. Biblio. Index. Lang.: Eng.
England. 1592-1621. Historical studies. ∎The reflection of domestic culture as a site of social struggle in Elizabethan theatre. Uses contemporary feminist theory to explore social and cultural constructs reflected in plays such as *Arden of Faversham,* Heywood's *A Woman Killed with Kindness,* and Middleton's *A Chaste Maid in Cheapside.*

2572 Hendricks, Margo. "'The Moor of Venice,' or the Italian on the Renaissance English Stage." 193-209 in Garner, Shirley Nelson, ed.; Sprengnether, Madelon, ed. *Shakespearean Tragedy and Gender.* Bloomington, IN: Indiana UP; 1996. 326 pp. Index. Notes. Biblio. Lang.: Eng.
England. 1605. Critical studies. ∎Gender and racial politics in Shakespeare's *Othello.* Argues that the play is a complex study of radically unstable divisions within the Venice of the time (an ideal image of the well-governed state vs. a site of political and sexual corruption), which are embodied in Othello and Desdemona.

2573 Henke, Robert. *Pastoral Transformations: Italian Tragicomedy and Shakespeare's Late Plays.* London: Associated Univ Presses; 1997. 239 pp. Index. Biblio. Notes. Illus.: Dwg. 1. Lang.: Eng.
England. 1609-1613. Critical studies. ∎The pastoral element in Shakespeare's late plays, *Cymbeline, The Winter's Tale,* and *The Tempest.*

2574 Henley, W.E. "'The Graphic' Gallery of Shakespeare's Heroines." 341-342 in Tomarken, Edward, ed. *As You Like It from 1600 to the Present.* New York, NY: Garland; 1997. 672 pp. (Shakespeare Criticism 17.) Lang.: Eng.
England. 1598. Critical studies. ∎Criticism of Shakespeare's *As You Like It* and its heroines, Rosalind and Celia (1888).

2575 Herford, C. "The Culminating Comedies." 425-426 in Tomarken, Edward, ed. *As You Like It from 1600 to the Present.* New York, NY: Garland; 1997. 672 pp. (Shakespeare Criticism 17.) Lang.: Eng.
England. 1598. Critical studies. ∎The wit of the female characters in Shakespeare's *As You Like It* and the contrast of court and country (1912).

2576 Hill Vasquez, Heather Lee. *The Possibilities of Performance: Mediatory Styles in Middle English Religious Drama.* Seattle, WA: Univ. of Washington; 1997. 294 pp. [Ph.D. Dissertation, Univ. Microfilms Order No. AAC 9736395.] Lang.: Eng.
England. 1400-1550. Critical studies. ∎Audience participation in Middle English religious drama. Focuses on figures who acknowledge an audience's role in performance in works such as the Chester cycle, the Digby plays, Lewis Wager's *The Life and Repentaunce of Marie Magdalene,* the Croxton *Play of the Sacrament,* the Brome and Northampton versions of *Abraham and Isaac,* and the York cycle.

2577 Hillman, David. "The Gastric Epic: *Troilus and Cressida.*" *SQ.* 1997 Fall; 48(3): 295-313. Notes. Lang.: Eng.
England. 1601-1602. Critical studies. ∎Argues that Shakespeare's *Troilus and Cressida* enacts a restoration of words, and of the ideals created out of them, to their sources inside the body, both in the play and in Shakespeare's cultural milieu.

2578 Hillman, Richard. "Antony, Hercules, and Cleopatra: 'the bidding of the gods' and 'the subtlest maze of all'." *SQ.* 1987 Win; 38(4): 442-451. Notes. Lang.: Eng.
England. 1607. Critical studies. ∎Analysis of Shakespeare's *Antony and Cleopatra* as a romance rather than a tragedy.

2579 Hillman, Richard. *Self-Speaking in Medieval and Early Modern English Drama: Subjectivity, Discourse, and the Stage.* New York, NY: St. Martin's; 1997. 309 pp. Index. Notes. Biblio. Lang.: Eng.
England. 1250-1642. Critical studies. ∎Examines theatrical techniques such as soliloquies, monologues, asides, and silences to analyze a fictional interiority in a sociohistorical context. Author examines *The Span-*

DRAMA: —Plays/librettos/scripts

ish Tragedy, Richard II, Doctor Faustus and The Second Shepherd's Play.

2580 Holahan, Michael. "'Look, her lips': Softness of Voice, Construction of Character in *King Lear*." *SQ*. 1997 Win; 48(4): 406-431. Notes. Lang.: Eng.
England. 1605. Critical studies. ■Speech and characterization in Shakespeare's play.

2581 Holmer, Joan Ozark. "'Draw, if you be men': Saviolo's Significance for *Romeo and Juliet*." *SQ*. 1994 Sum; 45(2): 163-189. Notes. Illus.: Dwg. Sketches. B&W. 5. Lang.: Eng.
England. 1595-1596. Textual studies. ■Asserts the year 1595 as the year of *Romeo and Juliet*'s writing, citing Vincentio Saviolo's fencing manual as the source for both the comic and tragic elements in Shakespeare's use of fencing in the play.

2582 Hopkins, Lisa. "Spartan Boys: John Ford and Philip Sydney." *CML*. 1997 Spr; 17(3): 217-229. Notes. Lang.: Eng.
England. 1629. Critical studies. ■Focuses on the use of common motifs in pointedly different ways in the work of John Ford and Philip Sidney. Key comparison between Ford's *The Broken Heart* and Sidney's prose work *The Countess of Pembroke's Arcadia (The Old Arcadia).*

2583 Hopkins, Lisa. "Beguiling the Master of the Mystery: Form and Power in *The Changeling*." *MRDE*. 1997; 9(1): 149-161. Notes. Lang.: Eng.
England. 1622. Critical studies. ■Male and female power strategies and their tragic results in Middleton and Rowley's *The Changeling*.

2584 Hopkins, Lisa. "Household Words: *Macbeth* and the Failure of Spectacle." *ShS*. 1997; 50(1): 101-110. Notes. Lang.: Eng.
England. 1606. Critical studies. ■Argues that the contrast between the mundanity of the language and the theatricality within *Macbeth* leads to its ultimate failure as a 'spectacle of banality'.

2585 Howard, Skiles. "Hands, Feet, and Bottoms: Decentering the Cosmic Dance in *A Midsummer Night's Dream*." *SQ*. 1993 Fall; 44(3): 325-342. Notes. Lang.: Eng.
England. 1594-1595. Critical studies. ■Examines the multifarious nature of Shakespeare's use of dance in his plays focusing on *A Midsummer Night's Dream*.

2586 Hughes, Derek. "Who Counts in Farquhar." *CompD*. 1997 Spr; 31(1): 7-27. Notes. Lang.: Eng.
England. 1677-1707. Critical studies. ■Significance of numbers and counting, in relation to certain characters' use of them in the plays of George Farquhar.

2587 Hughes, Derek. "Body and Ritual in Farquhar." *CompD*. 1997 Fall; 31(3): 414-435. Notes. Lang.: Eng.
England. 1660-1700. Critical studies. ■George Farquhar's use of the individual body as a symbol of numerical significance, a unit of material exchange, in such plays as *The Twin Rivals*, *The Recruiting Officer*, and *Love and a Bottle*.

2588 Hunt, Maurice. "Shakespeare's *King Richard III* and the Problematics of Tudor Bastardy." *PLL*. 1997 Spr; 33(2): 115-141 . Notes. Biblio. Lang.: Eng.
England. 1593. Historical studies. ■Shakespeare's handling of legitimacy and illegitimacy in *Richard III*.

2589 Hunt, Maurice. "Slavery, English Servitude, and *The Comedy of Errors*." *ELR*. 1997 Win; 27(1): 31-56. Notes. Illus.: Dwg. B&W. 1. Lang.: Eng.
England. 1590. Critical studies. ■The ambiguous servant/slave status and rough treatment of the Dromios in Shakespeare's play, the focus on the institution of marriage and the individual's ordering of his/her inner faculties. Questions whether the reunions and festive releases at the play's end includes a remedy for slavery.

2590 Hynes, Peter. "Against Theory? Knowledge and Action in Wycherley's Plays." *MP*. 1996 Nov.; 94(2): 163-189. Notes. Lang.: Eng.
England. 1671-1676. Critical studies. ■The relationship between action and theoretical knowledge in *The Way of the World, Love in a Wood, The Country Wife*, and *The Plain Dealer*.

2591 Ilsemann, Hartmut. "Radicalism in the Melodrama of the Early Nineteenth Century." 191-210 in Hays, Michael, ed.;

Nikolopoulou, Anastasia, ed. *Melodrama: The Cultural Emergence of a Genre.* New York, NY: St. Martin's P; 1996. 288 pp. Notes. Lang.: Eng.
England. 1820-1832. Historical studies. ■Examines the impact of domestic concerns on the political and economic conflict in John Walker's melodrama *The Factory Lad.*

2592 Jackson, Justin Andrew. *Transcending Ben Jonson's Reputation and Discovering His Work.* Fresno, CA: California State Univ; 1997. 133 pp. [M.A. Thesis, Univ. Microfilms Order No. AAC 1386283.] Lang.: Eng.
England. 1598-1637. Critical studies. ■Rhetorical and stylish devices in Ben Jonson's *Every Man in His Humour*, *The Alchemist*, and *Epicoene, or, The Silent Woman.*

2593 Jankowski, Theodora A. "'The scorne of Savage people': Virginity as 'Forbidden Sexuality' in John Lyly's *Love's Metamorphosis*." *RenD*. 1993; 24: 123-153. Notes. Biblio. Lang.: Eng.
England. 1599. Critical studies. ■The transitory power and autonomy of the virgin characters in Lyly's play.

2594 Jardine, Lisa. "Cultural Confusion and Shakespeare's Learned Heroines: 'These are old paradoxes'." *SQ*. 1987 Spr; 38(1): 1-18. Notes. Lang.: Eng.
England. 1596-1603. Critical studies. ■Examines the ambivalence toward educated women in early modern society through Shakespeare's *The Merchant of Venice* and *All's Well That Ends Well.*

2595 Jenkins, Harold. "Much adoe about Nothing." *ShN*. 1997; Extra Issue: 5-7, 16. Notes. Illus.: Dwg. B&W. 2. [Previously unpublished lecture delivered at the University of Newcastle-upon-Tyne, May 1982.] Lang.: Eng.
England. 1598. Critical studies. ■Critical analysis of the plot and characters of Shakespeare's *Much Ado About Nothing*: double plot of the two couples, the reunion motif of this and other plays of Shakespeare, importance of minor characters to the story.

2596 Jenkins, Harold. "As you Like it." *ShN*. 1997; Extra Issue: 9-11, 19-20. Notes. Illus.: Dwg. B&W. 2. [Lecture to the Shakespeare Conference at Stratford-upon-Avon, August 1953.] Lang.: Eng.
England. 1599. Critical studies. ■Argues that *As You Like It* exhibits most clearly of all the comedies Shakespeare's characteristic excellence in this genre. Suggests that Shakespeare took this comedy as far as he could, and that it represents his readiness to change his course as an author.

2597 Jenkins, Harold. "Twelfe Night, Or what you will." *ShN*. 1997; Extra Issue: 13-15, 17-18. Notes. Illus.: Dwg. B&W. 2. [Lecture at the Rice Institute, Houston, TX, March 1958.] Lang.: Eng.
England. 1594-1602. Critical studies. ■Examines features of Shakespeare's comic art through his play *Twelfth Night*, and comparison to his earlier play *The Two Gentlemen of Verona.*

2598 Johnson, Gerald D. "*The Merry Wives of Windsor*, Q1: Provincial Touring and Adapted Texts." *SQ*. 1987 Sum; 38(2): 154-165. Notes. Tables. Lang.: Eng.
England. 1597-1619. Textual studies. ■Possible explanations for the 'bad quartos' of *The Merry Wives of Windsor*: the result of the transcriber's faulty memory or abridged texts for touring in the provinces.

2599 Johnson, Samuel. "The Plays of William Shakespeare." 133-224 in Tomarken, Edward, ed. *As You Like It from 1600 to the Present.* New York, NY: Garland; 1997. 672 pp. (Shakespeare Criticism 17.) Notes. Lang.: Eng.
England. 1598. Critical studies. ■Noted critic's thoughts on Shakespeare's *As You Like It* and his printing of the play (1765).

2600 Jordan, Constance. "Contract and Conscience in *Cymbeline*." *RenD*. 1994; 25: 33-58. Notes. Biblio. Lang.: Eng.
England. 1608-1610. Critical studies. ■Meanings generated by the terms of verbal contracts and their engagement with conscience in Shakespeare's *Cymbeline.*

2601 Kachur, B.A. "Etherege's *She Would If She Could*: Rereading the Libertines." *Restor*. 1997 Win; 12(2): 40-60. Notes. Biblio. Lang.: Eng.

DRAMA: —Plays/librettos/scripts

England. 1670. Critical studies. ■The inception of the comedy of manners in the young lover characters of Etherege's play.

2602 Kahan, Jeffrey. "A Further Gloss on *The Alchemist.*" *ELN.* 1997 Mar.; 34(3): 21-23. Notes. Lang.: Eng.
England. 1593-1632. Critical studies. ■Analysis of the reference to a 'madam with a dildo' in Jonson's play.

2603 Kahn, Coppélia. "'Magic of Bounty': *Timon of Athens,* Jacobean Patronage, and Maternal Power." 135-167 in Garner, Shirley Nelson, ed.; Sprengnether, Madelon, ed. *Shakespearean Tragedy and Gender.* Bloomington, IN: Indiana UP; 1996. 326 pp. Index. Notes. Biblio. Lang.: Eng.
England. 1607-1608. Critical studies. ■Explores the way in which the fantasy of an all-bountiful yet ultimately rejecting mother underlies the system of male patronage in Shakespeare's *Timon of Athens.* Originally appeared in *SQ* 38:1 (1987 Spr), 34-57.

2604 Kaplan, M. Lindsay; Eggert, Katherine. "'Good queen, my lord, good queen': Sexual Slander and the Trials of Female Authority in *The Winter's Tale.*" *RenD.* 1994; 25: 89-118. Notes. Biblio. Lang.: Eng.
England. 1536-1610. Historical studies. ■A gendered legal history of early modern England with respect to the slander of women as represented in Shakespeare's *The Winter's Tale.*

2605 Kastan, David Scott. "Is There a Class in This (Shakespearean) Text." *RenD.* 1993; 24: 101-121. Notes. Biblio. Lang.: Eng.
England. 1592-1616. Critical studies. ■Representations of class and sex in the language of Shakespeare's plays.

2606 Kates, Ronald E. *'Invent the Means': Re-presenting* The Shoemaker's Holiday *Through Rowland Lacy's Manipulations.* Atlanta, GA: Georgia State Univ; 1997. 183 pp. [Ph.D. Dissertation, Univ. Microfilms Order No. AAC 9821969.] Lang.: Eng.
England. 1599. Critical studies. ■Argues that character of Rowland Lacy in Thomas Dekker's *The Shoemaker's Holiday,* by dominating the play, provides the play with a narrative that heightens all levels.

2607 Kathman, David. "Why I'm Not an Oxfordian." *ERev.* 1997 Spr; 5(1): 32-48. Notes. Biblio. Lang.: Eng.
England. 1590-1616. Historical studies. ■Challenges the theory that Edward de Vere, Seventeenth Earl of Oxford, was the true author of the plays of Shakespeare.

2608 Kehler, Dorothea. "The First Quarto of *Hamlet*: Reforming Widow Gertred." *SQ.* 1995 Win; 46(4): 398-413. Notes. Lang.: Eng.
England. 1600-1604. Textual studies. ■Compares the more sympathetic Gertred of the First Quarto with the incarnations of the character in Second Quarto and First Folio.

2609 Keller, Michelle Margo. *A Study of Pathological Narcissism in Renaissance English Tragic Drama.* Tucson, AZ: Univ. of Arizona; 1997. 350 pp. [Ph.D. Dissertation, Univ. Microfilms Order No. AAC 9729505.] Lang.: Eng.
England. 1450-1580. Critical studies. ■Focuses on William Shakespeare's *Coriolanus,* Cyril Tourneur's *The Revenger's Tragedy,* Christopher Marlowe's *Edward II,* and Thomas Heywood's *A Woman Killed with Kindness.*

2610 Kendall, Gillian Murray. "Overkill in Shakespeare." *SQ.* 1992 Spr; 43(1): 33-50. Notes. Lang.: Eng.
England. 1604-1611. Critical studies. ■Excessive violence as metaphor of the limits of political power in *Measure for Measure, Macbeth,* and *The Winter's Tale.*

2611 Kendall, Gillian Murray. "'Lend me thy hand': Metaphor and Mayhem in *Titus Andronicus.*" *SQ.* 1989 Fall; 40(3): 299-316 . Notes. Lang.: Eng.
England. 1590-1594. Critical studies. ■The disjunction between metaphor and reality in Shakespeare's play.

2612 Kermode, Lloyd Edward. "Destination Doomsday: Desires for Change and Changeable Desires in *The Roaring Girl.*" *ELR.* 1997 Fall; 27(3): 421-442. Notes. Lang.: Eng.
England. 1610. Critical studies. ■Analysis of Middleton and Dekker's *The Roaring Girl* that takes into account the viewpoints of other charac-

ters. Attempts to show that Moll exists as both a representative of a type of Londoner in her public social quest, and as a unique individual.

2613 Kerrigan, John. "Secrecy and Gossip in *Twelfth Night.*" *ShS.* 1997; 50(1): 65-80. Notes. Lang.: Eng.
England. 1602. Critical studies. ■Rennaissance England's ideas of privacy and gossip as reflected in the language of the play.

2614 Kezar, Dennis Dean, Jr. *Renaissance Killing Poems: The Subject of Death and Its Literary Executions in Early Modern England.* Charlottesville, VA: Univ. of Virginia; 1997. 283 pp. [Ph.D. Dissertation, Univ. Microfilms Order No. AAC 9738812.] Lang.: Eng.
England. 1590-1610. Critical studies. ■The representation of violence in selected Renaissance texts, including John Skelton's *Phyllyp Sparowe,* Edmund Spenser's *The Faerie Queene,* William Shakespeare's *Julius Caesar,* John Donne's *Anniversaries,* and John Milton's *Samson Agonistes.*

2615 Kim, Kang. *Shakespeare's Roman Trilogy: Contemporary Readings of History and Politics.* Buffalo, NY: State Univ. of New York; 1997. 216 pp. [Ph.D. Dissertation, Univ. Microfilms Order No. AAC 9801312.] Lang.: Eng.
England. 1599-1608. Critical studies. ■Examines Shakespeare's Roman history plays—*Julius Caesar, Antony and Cleopatra, Coriolanus*—in the historical context of Eliabethan and Jacobean England.

2616 Kinney, Arthur F. "Shakespeare's *The Comedy of Errors* and the Nature of Kinds." 174-197 in Miola, Robert S., ed. *The Comedy of Errors: Critical Essays.* New York, NY: Garland; 1997. 592 pp. (Shakespeare Criticism 18.) Lang.: Eng.
England. 1594. Critical studies. ■The nature of doubles in Shakespeare's *The Comedy of Errors.*

2617 Kinservik, Matthew Jon. *Disciplining Satire: The Plays of Fielding, Foote, and Macklin.* University Park, PA: Pennsylvania State Univ; 1997. 353 pp. [Ph.D. Dissertation, Univ. Microfilms Order No. AAC 9732304.] Lang.: Eng.
England. 1710-1789. Critical studies. ■The effects of the State Licensing Act of 1737 on satiric drama, with emphasis on the work of three controversial and heavily-censored satiric dramatists: Henry Fielding, Samuel Foote, and Charles Macklin.

2618 Kline, Daniel T. "Structure, Characterization, and the New Community in Four Plays of Jesus and the Doctors." *CompD.* 1992/93 Win; 26(4): 394-357. Notes. Lang.: Eng.
England: York, Towneley, Coventry. 1420-1500. Critical studies. ■Examines the structure and placement of the Jesus and the Doctors plays within the Chester, York, Coventry, and Towneley cycles.

2619 Knowles, Richard. "Revision Awry in Folio *Lear* 3.1." *SQ.* 1995 Spr; 46(1): 32-46. Notes. Lang.: Eng.
England. 1605-1623. Textual studies. ■Considers the special importance of the textual variants between the quarto and folio versions of *King Lear* III.i.

2620 Knowles, Richard. "Cum Notis Variorum: Sex in the Variorums." *ShN.* 1997 Spr; 47(1): 3-4, 18, 20. Notes. [Number 232.] Lang.: Eng.
England. 1598-1997. Historical studies. ■Examines the censorship and editing of sexual language and bawdy terms in early variorum editions of Shakespeare's plays. Aesthetic versus moral reasons for edits.

2621 Knutson, Roslyn. "Falconer to the Little Eyases: A New Date and Commercial Agenda for the 'Little Eyases' Passage in *Hamlet.*" *SQ.* 1995 Spr; 46(1): 1-31. Notes. Tables. Lang.: Eng.
England. 1601-1709. Textual studies. ■Argues for a later date than generally accepted for the addition of the 'little eyases' passage to the text of *Hamlet.* Uses example from quarto and first folio versions.

2622 Ko, Yu Jin. "The Comic Close of *Twelfth Night* and Viola's *Noli me tangere.*" *SQ.* 1997 Win; 48(4): 391-405. Notes. Lang.: Eng.
England. 1601-1602. Critical studies. ■Examines Viola's command to Sebastian 'do not embrace me' by looking at Shakespeare's allusion to, and manipulation of, its antecedents in dramatic and literary tradition.

2623 Kolbe, Frederick C. "Shakespeare's Way." 463-466 in Tomarken, Edward, ed. *As You Like It from 1600 to the*

DRAMA: —Plays/librettos/scripts

Present: Critical Essays. New York, NY: Garland; 1997. 672 pp. (Shakespeare Criticism 17.) Notes. Lang.: Eng.
England. 1590-1593. Critical studies. ■1930 essay comparing Shakespeare's *As You Like It* with Thomas Lodge's 1590 novel *Rosalynde.*

2624 Kurland, Stuart M. "'A beggar's book/Outworth's a noble's blood': The Politics of Faction in *Henry VIII.*" *CompD.* 1992 Fall; 26(3): 237-253. Notes. Lang.: Eng.
England. 1612-1613. Critical studies. ■Analysis of Shakespeare's play with respect to the debasement of honorable titles through James I's wholesale distribution of knighthoods.

2625 Lahiri, Jhumpa. *Accursed Palace: The Italian Palazzo on the Jacobean Stage (1603-1625).* Boston, MA: Boston Univ; 1997. 319 pp. [Ph.D. Dissertation, Univ. Microfilms Order No. AAC 9809110.] Lang.: Eng.
England. 1603-1625. Histories-specific. ■Examines John Marston's *The Malcontent,* Cyril Tourneur's *The Revenger's Tragedy* and *Women Beware Women,* and John Webster's *The Duchess of Malfi.*

2626 Lander, Jesse M. "'Faith in Me unto this Commonwealth': *Edward IV* and the Civic Nation." *RenD.* 1996; 27: 47-78. Notes. Biblio. Lang.: Eng.
England: London. 1599-1600. Critical studies. ■Civic pride in the anonymous *Edward IV 1 and 2.*

2627 Lanier, Douglas. "'Stigmatical in Making': The Material Character of *The Comedy of Errors.*" 291-311 in Miola, Robert S., ed. *The Comedy of Errors: Critical Essays.* New York, NY: Garland; 1997. 592 pp. (Shakespeare Criticism 18.) Notes. Lang.: Eng.
England. 1594. Critical studies. ■Feminist criticism of Shakespeare's *The Comedy of Errors.*

2628 Latham, Grace. "Miss Grace Latham on Rosalind, Celia, and Helen." 323-340 in Tomarken, Edward, ed. *As You Like It from 1600 to the Present.* New York, NY: Garland; 1997. 672 pp. (Shakespeare Criticism 17.) Lang.: Eng.
England. 1598. Critical studies. ■1892 essay analyzing the characters Rosablind, Celia, and Helen in Shakespeare's *As You Like It.*

2629 Lee, Brian S. "'Well done of rash Virginius': Renaissance Transformations of Livy's Account of the Fall of the Decemvirs." *ELR.* 1997 Fall; 27(3): 331-360. Notes. Illus.: Dwg. B&W. 1. Lang.: Eng.
England. 1569-1624. Historical studies. ■Renaissance authors' handling of Livy's story of Appius and Virginia: its influence on Shakespeare's *Titus Andronicus,* George Peele's melodrama *Alphonsus Emperor of Germany* and Thomas Heywood's *Gynaikeion, or The History of Women.*

2630 Leggatt, Alexander. "Shakespeare's Comedy of Love: *The Comedy of Errors.*" 144-172 in Miola, Robert S., ed. *The Comedy of Errors: Critical Essays.* New York, NY: Garland; 1997. 592 pp. (Shakespeare Criticism 18.) Lang.: Eng.
England. 1594. Critical studies. ■Criticism of Shakespeare's *The Comedy of Errors* (1891).

2631 Leinwand, Theodore B. "Shakespeare and the Middling Sort." *SQ.* 1993 Fall; 44(3): 284-303. Notes. Lang.: Eng.
England: London. 1590-1613. Critical studies. ■Representation of class, specifically 'the commons', in the work of Shakespeare.

2632 Leventhal, Melvyn R. "Cressida at the Tailhook Convention: 'A woeful Cressid 'mongst the merry Greeks!'." *ShN.* 1997 Spr ; 47(1): 5, 20. Notes. [Number 232.] Lang.: Eng.
England. 1600. Critical studies. ■Analysis of Shakespeare's *Troilus and Cressida* in the light of recent cases of sexual assault. Examines various versions of the text to argue that Cressida is not promiscuous but a victim of sexual assault.

2633 Levin, Harry. "Two Comedies of Error." 126-142 in Miola, Robert S., ed. *The Comedy of Errors: Critical Essays.* New York, NY: Garland; 1997. 592 pp. (Shakespeare Criticism 18.) Lang.: Eng.
England. 1594. Critical studies. ■The double plot structure of Shakespeare's *The Comedy of Errors* (1966).

2634 Levin, Richard A. "That I Might Hear Thee Call Great Caesar 'Ass Unpolicied'." *PLL.* 1997 Sum; 33(3): 244-264. Notes. Biblio. Lang.: Eng.

England. 1607. Critical studies. ■The death of Cleopatra in Shakespeare's *Antony and Cleopatra* with emphasis on her adversarial relationship with Octavius Caesar.

2635 Levine, Nina. "Lawful Symmetry: The Politics of Treason in *2 Henry VI.*" *RenD.* 1994; 25: 197-218. Notes. Biblio. Lang.: Eng.
England. 1585-1592. Historical studies. ■The relationship between theatre and treason trials, with consideration of Shakespeare's *Henry VI, part 2.*

2636 Liebler, Naomi Conn. "Getting It All Right: *Titus Andronicus* and Roman History." *SQ.* 1994 Fall; 45(3): 263-278. Notes. Lang.: Eng.
England. 1550-1594. Textual studies. ■Argues that Herodian's history *De imperatorum Romanorum praeclara gesta* is the most likely source for Shakespeare's play.

2637 Lief, Madelon; Radel, Nicholas F. "Linguistic Subversion and the Artifice of Rhetoric in *The Two Noble Kinsmen.*" *SQ.* 1987 Win; 38(4): 405-425. Notes. Lang.: Eng.
England. 1612-1613. Critical studies. ■Argues that Fletcher and Shakespeare deliberately undercut the play's rhetoric, reflecting the increasingly cynical worldview of the times.

2638 Lister, Rebecca Crow. *Wild Thro' the Woods I'le Fly: Female Mad Songs in Seventeenth-Century English Drama.* Tallahassee, FL: Florida State Univ; 1997. 190 pp. [D.M. Dissertation, Univ. Microfilms Order No. AAC 9725009.] Lang.: Eng.
England. 1685-1700. Critical studies. ■The gendered use of 'mad' songs and their cultural and dramatic contexts. Examines songs by John Eccles from Thomas D'Urfey's *The Comical History of Don Quixote, Part Two* and John Banks's *Cyrus the Great,* and by Henry Purcell from *The Comical History of Don Quixote, Part Three,* and Nathaniel Lee's *Sophonisba.*

2639 Little, Arthur L., Jr. "'An essence that's not seen': The primal Scene of Racism in *Othello.*" *SQ.* 1993 Fall; 44(3): 304-324. Notes. Lang.: Eng.
England. 1604. Critical studies. ■Psychoanalysis of racism in *Othello.*

2640 Loughlin, Marie H. *Hymeneutics: Interpreting Virginity on the Early Modern Stage.* London: Associated Univ Presses; 1997. 226 pp. Index. Biblio. Pref. Notes. Lang.: Eng.
England. 1490-1650. Critical studies. ■Representations of virginity in works ranging from Shakespeare's *Cymbeline,* Fletcher's *The Faithful Shepherdess* and *Philaster,* and Beaumont and Fletcher's *The Queen of Corinth, Valentinian,* and *The Loyal Subject.*

2641 Lucking, David. "'And All Things Change Them to the Contrary': *Romeo and Juliet* and the Metaphysics of Language." *EnSt.* 1997 Jan.; 78(1): 8-18. Notes. Lang.: Eng.
England. 1595-1596. Critical studies. ■Discusses the possible reasons for Shakespeare's frequent use of the oxymoron in *Romeo and Juliet.*

2642 Luckyj, Christina. "'A Moving Rhetoricke': Women's Silences and Renaissance Texts." *RenD.* 1993; 24: 33-56. Notes. Biblio. Lang.: Eng.
England. 1601-1613. Critical studies. ■Argues that feminine silence in Shakespeare's *King Lear, Troilus and Cressida,* and Webster's *The Duchess of Malfi* represents misogyny and the perception of danger rather than an ideal of womanly decorum. Cites John Barton's three Royal Shakespeare Company productions of *Troilus and Cressida* of the 1960s and 1970s that reflect this interpretation.

2643 Mack, Robert L. "'Stand, Sir, and Deliver Up Your Muse': Some Observations on John Dryden's *Albumazar* Prologue and the Decorum of Poetic Appropriation in the 'Early Augustan Battleground'." *Restor.* 1997 Win; 12(2): 61-67. Notes. Lang.: Eng.
England. 1612-1668. Critical studies. ■Analysis of John Dryden's prologue for a revival of Thomas Tomkis's university comedy *Albumazar.* Dryden mistakenly thought this play to have been the source for Ben Jonson's *The Alchemist* and drew on elaborate contrasts between the plays.

2644 Magnusson, A. Lynne. "The Rhetoric of Politeness and *Henry VIII.*" *SQ.* 1992 Win; 43(4): 391-409. Notes. Lang.: Eng.

DRAMA: —Plays/librettos/scripts

England. 1612-1613. Critical studies. ■Function of politeness, the social strategy of maintenance and repair, in *Henry VIII*.

2645 Magnusson, Lynn. "'Voice Potential': Language and Symbolic Capital in *Othello*." *ShS*. 1997; 50(1): 91-99. Notes. Lang.: Eng.

England. 1604. Critical studies. ■Language as a symbol of power in *Othello*.

2646 Maguire, Laurie. "The Girls from Ephesus." 339-352 in Miola, Robert S., ed. *The Comedy of Errors: Critical Essays*. New York, NY: Garland; 1997. 592 pp. (Shakespeare Criticism 18.) Notes. Biblio. Lang.: Eng.

England. 1594. Critical studies. ■Feminist critique of Shakespeare's *The Comedy of Errors*.

2647 Marshall, Cynthia. "Man of Steel Done Got the Blues: Melancholic Subversion of Presence in *Antony and Cleopatra*." *SQ*. 1993 Win; 44(4): 385-408. Notes. Lang.: Eng.

England. 1607. Critical studies. ■Determines that what the melancholy Antony feels is actually 'the blues' which express the loss of control with which love threatens masculine identity.

2648 Masefield, John. "William Shakespeare." 423-424 in Tomarken, Edward, ed. *As You Like It from 1600 to the Present*. New York, NY: Garland; 1997. 672 pp. (Shakespeare Criticism 17.) Lang.: Eng.

England. 1598. Critical studies. ■Poet's 1911 essay on Shakespeare's *As You Like It*, with emphasis on Jacques' wisdom.

2649 Masten, Jeffrey. *Textual Intercourse: Collaboration, Authorship, and Sexualities in Renaissance Drama*. Cambridge: Cambridge UP; 1997. 223 pp. (Cambridge Studies in Renaissance Literature and Culture 14.) Index. Biblio. Notes. Illus.: Photo. Dwg. 14. Lang.: Eng.

England. 1550-1620. Critical studies. ■Argues that writing for the theatre in Renaissance England shifted from a model of homoerotic collaboration toward singular authorship on a 'patriarchal-absurdist' model. Examines the work of Shakespeare, Fletcher, Beaumont, Margaret Cavendish, and others.

2650 Masten, Jeffrey. "Playwriting: Authorship and Collaboration." 357-382 in Cox, John D., ed.; Kastan, David Scott, ed. *A New History of Early English Drama*. New York, NY: Columbia UP; 1997. 565 pp. Index. Notes. Biblio. Lang.: Eng.

England. 1580-1610. Critical studies. ■Argues that the collective form of playwriting—collaboration—was the standard mode of operation in the early English theatre, and single-authored plays were the exception.

2651 Matheson, Mark. "*Hamlet* and 'A Matter Tender and Dangerous'." *SQ*. 1995 Win; 46(4): 383-397. Notes. Lang.: Eng.

England. 1601. Critical studies. ■Analysis of the religious content in *Hamlet*.

2652 Matthews, Brander. "Shakespeare as a Playwright." 427-434 in Tomarken, Edward, ed. *As You Like It from 1600 to the Present*. New York, NY: Garland; 1997. 672 pp. (Shakespeare Criticism 17.) Lang.: Eng.

England. 1598. Critical studies. ■1913 essay on the structure of Shakespeare's *As You Like It*.

2653 Maurer, Kathleen M. *The Clothes That Make the Man: The Assumption of Male Disguise in Three 17th-Century Dramas*. Milwaukee, WI: Marquette Univ; 1997. 325 pp. [Ph.D. Dissertation, Univ. Microfilms Order No. AAC 9823985.] Lang.: Eng.

England. 1602-1674. Critical studies. ■Women disguised as men in Shakespeare's *Twelfth Night*, Middleton and Dekker's *The Roaring Girl*, and Wycherley's *The Plain Dealer*.

2654 Maurer, Margaret. "Facing the Music in Arden: 'Twas I, But 'Tis Not I'." 475-509 in Tomarken, Edward, ed. *As You Like It from 1600 to the Present: Critical Essays*. New York, NY: Garland; 1997. 672 pp. (Shakespeare Criticism 17.) Notes. Lang.: Eng.

England. 1598-1723. Critical studies. ■Comparison of Shakespeare's *As You Like It* and Charles Johnson's adaptation *Love in a Forest*.

2655 McCandless, David. "Helena's Bed-trick: Gender and Performance in *All's Well That Ends Well*." *SQ*. 1994 Win; 45(4): 449-468. Notes. Lang.: Eng.

England. 1602-1603. Critical studies. ■Representations of female sexual desire and male sexual dread in Shakespeare's comedy.

2656 McEachern, Claire. "*Henry V* and the Paradox of the Body Politic." *SQ*. 1994 Spr; 45(1): 33-56. Notes. Lang.: Eng.

England. 1599. Historical studies. ■The idea of nationhood in Shakespeare's *Henry V*, including the association of Henry with the Elizabethan personification of the crown.

2657 McLuskie, Kathleen E. "The Shopping Complex: Materiality and the Renaissance Theatre." 86-101 in Pechter, Edward, ed. *Textual and Theatrical Shakespeare: Questions of Evidence*. Iowa City, IA: Univ of Iowa P; 1997. 267 pp. (Studies in Theatre History and Culture.) Notes. Lang.: Eng.

England. 1580-1620. Critical studies. ■Relations between early and modern economic markets and their influence on the Renaissance theatre. Examines the marketplace as reflected in the theatre and the larger marketplace for theatrical products.

2658 Meagher, John C. *Shakespeare's Shakespeare: How the Plays Were Made*. New York, NY: Continuum; 1997. 240 pp. Pref. Notes. Lang.: Eng.

England. 1590-1613. Critical studies. ■Principles of Shakespearean dramaturgy, with reference to *A Midsummer Night's Dream*, *As You Like It*, *Richard II*, *Henry IV, Part 1*, *Romeo and Juliet*, *Hamlet*, and *King Lear*.

2659 Meyer, Constance J. Luby. *Business in The Merchant of Venice*. Arlington, TX: Univ. of Texas; 1997. 154 pp. [Ph.D. Dissertation, Univ. Microfilms Order No. AAC 9825560.] Lang.: Eng.

England. 1596. Critical studies. ■Arranged marriage, usury, law, and the new commerce in Shakespeare's *The Merchant of Venice*.

2660 Micheli, Linda McJ. "'Sit By Us': Visual Imagery and the Two Queens in *Henry VIII*." *SQ*. 1987 Win; 38(4): 452-466. Notes. Lang.: Eng.

England. 1612-1613. Critical studies. ■Visual and nonverbal elements associated with the two queens, Anne and Katherine, in Shakespeare's *Henry VIII*.

2661 Mikalachki, Jodi. "Gender, Cant, and Cross-talking in *The Roaring Girl*." *RenD*. 1994; 25: 119-143. Notes. Biblio. Lang.: Eng.

England. 1608-1611. Historical studies. ■The relationship between Moll Frith's languge in Dekker and Middleton's play and the policing of disorderly and criminal behavior among the vagrant population.

2662 Mikalachki, Jodi. "The Masculine Romance of Roman Britain: *Cymbeline* and Early Modern English Nationalism." *SQ*. 1995 Fall; 46(3): 301-322. Notes. Lang.: Eng.

England. 1609-1610. Critical studies. ■Analysis of Shakespeare's play in terms of the issues of gender and sexuality, taking both as constitutive of the nationalism the play articulates.

2663 Miles, Gary B. "How Roman are Shakespeare's Romans?" *SQ*. 1989 Fall; 40(3): 257-283. Notes. Illus.: Photo. B&W. 11. Lang.: Eng.

England. 1599-1608. Critical studies. ■The depiction of Roman characters and their accuracy in Shakespeare's *Julius Caesar*, *Antony and Cleopatra*, and *Coriolanus*.

2664 Miller, Jo E. "'And All This Passion for a Boy?': Cross-Dressing and the Sexual Economy of Beaumont and Fletcher's *Philaster*." *ELR*. 1997 Win; 27(1): 129-150. Notes. Lang.: Eng.

England. 1609. Critical studies. ■Analysis of the character Bellario, a woman disguised as a man, and her activity outside the love story.

2665 Miola, Robert. "The Play and the Critics: Works Consulted." 3-68 in Miola, Robert S., ed. *The Comedy of Errors: Critical Essays*. New York, NY: Garland; 1997. 592 pp. (Shakespeare Criticism 18.) Biblio. Lang.: Eng.

England. 1594. Critical studies. ■Introductory essay to a collection of criticism of Shakespeare's *The Comedy of Errors*.

DRAMA: —Plays/librettos/scripts

2666   Morel, Michel. "*Women Beware Women* by Howard Barker (with Thomas Middleton): The 'Terrible Consistency'." 59-71 in Boireau, Nicole, ed. *Drama on Drama: Dimensions of Theatricality on the Contemporary British Stage*. New York, NY: St. Martin's; 1997. 256 pp. Pref. Notes. Index. Biblio. Lang.: Eng.
England. 1621-1986. Critical studies. ■Semiotic analysis and comparison of Thomas Middleton's *Women Beware Women* and Howard Barker's version with the same title. Examines the nature of collaboration at such an historical distancing.

2667   Morelli, Annamaria. *La scena della visione. L'eccesso barocco e la teatralità shakespeariana.* (The Scene of Vision: Baroque Excess and Shakespearean Theatricality.) Rome: Bulzoni; 1997. 177 pp. (Università degli Studi di Roma 'La Sapienza': Studi e ricerche 53.) Notes. Biblio. Lang.: Ita.
England. 1600-1606. Critical studies. ■The poetics of vision in Shakespeare's *Hamlet, Othello*, and *King Lear*.

2668   Morey, James H. "The Death of King John in Shakespeare and Bale." *SQ.* 1994 Fall; 45(3): 327-331. Notes. Illus.: Dwg. B&W. 6. Lang.: Eng.
England. 1539-1596. Textual studies. ■Compares depictions of the death of King John from Shakespeare's eponymous play and John Bale's *King Johan* for their similarities.

2669   Mossman, Judith. "*Henry V* and Plutarch's *Alexander*." *SQ.* 1994 Spr; 45(1): 57-73. Notes. Lang.: Eng.
England. 1599. Historical studies. ■Compares the flawed characters of Henry V and Alexander the Great from Shakespeare's play and *Plutarch's Lives*, respectively.

2670   Mowat, Barbara A. "The Theater and Literary Culture." 213-230 in Cox, John D., ed.; Kastan, David Scott, ed. *A New History of Early English Drama*. New York, NY: Columbia UP; 1997. 565 pp. Notes. Biblio. Index. Lang.: Eng.
England. 1595-1620. Historical studies. ■How printed plays were received in the literary world, who read them, and who 'performed' them, ultimately arguing that print precedes performance.

2671   Muir, Kenneth. "Shakespeare and the Metamorphosis of the Pentameter." *ShS.* 1997; 50(1): 147-150. Notes. Lang.: Eng.
England. 1598-1997. Critical studies. ■Development of iambic pentameter and the actor's approach to its delivery in the works of Shakespeare and other Elizabethan dramatists.

2672   Mullaney, Steven. "Mourning and Misogyny: *Hamlet, The Revenger's Tragedy*, and the Final Progress of Elizabeth I, 1600-1607." *SQ.* 1994 Sum; 45(2): 139-162. Notes. Lang.: Eng.
England. 1600-1607. Historical studies. ■Using the last days of the reign of Elizabeth to reflect the ambivalent attitude of realm toward a female sovereign. Cites examples in *Hamlet* and Middleton's *Revenger's Tragedy*.

2673   Müller, Klaus Peter. "Cultural Transformations of Subversive Jacobean Drama: Contemporary Sub-Versions of Tragedy, Comedy, and Tragicomedy." 30-58 in Boireau, Nicole, ed. *Drama on Drama: Dimensions of Theatricality on the Contemporary British Stage*. New York, NY: St. Martin's; 1997. 256 pp. Pref. Notes. Index. Biblio. Lang.: Eng.
England. 1604-1986. Critical studies. ■Revisions or adaptations of plays as cultural transformations of specific forms of meaning. Examines three representative Jacobean plays and their contemporary revisions: Thomas Middleton's *Women Beware Women* (1621) and Howard Barker's 1986 version, Middleton's *A Mad World, My Masters* (1605-1607) and Barrie Keeffe's 1977 version, and Shakespeare's *Measure for Measure* (1604) and Howard Brenton's 1972 version.

2674   Murray, Catherine Teresa. *Grassi, Historicity, and Rhetorical Presence in John Ford's Perkin Warbeck*. Denton, TX: Texas Woman's Univ; 1997. 117 pp. [Ph.D. Dissertation, Univ. Microfilms Order No. AAC 9733475.] Lang.: Eng.
England. 1634. Critical studies. ■Examines rhetorical presences (playwright, audience, director, actors) in John Ford's *Perkin Warbeck* and analyzes historical data about Warbeck and compares it to Ford's version.

2675   Muth, Benita Huffman. *Examining Authority: Forced Marriage Plots in Early Modern Drama*. Chapel Hill: Univ. of North Carolina; 1997. 231 pp. [Ph.D. Dissertation, Univ. Microfilms Order No. AAC 9730571.] Lang.: Eng.
England. 1584-1642. Critical studies. ■Argues that the forced marriage plot in plays by Shakespeare, Lyly, Dekker, Beaumont, Fletcher, Middleton, Shirley, and Ford sheds light on political and domestic authority in Elizabethan England.

2676   Myhill, Nova. *'Judging Spectators': Dramatic Representations of Spectatorship in Early Modern London, 1580-1642.* Los Angeles, CA: Univ. of California; 1997. 277 pp. [Ph.D. Dissertation, Univ. Microfilms Order No. AAC 9807676.] Lang.: Eng.
England: London. 1580-1642. Critical studies. ■Examines the relationship between theatre audiences and plays through dramatic representations of spectatorship. Considers Thomas Kyd's *The Spanish Tragedy* and Shakespeare's *Measure for Measure*.

2677   Neely, Carol Thomas. "'Documents in Madness': Reading Madness and Gender in Shakespeare's Tragedies and Early Modern Culture." 75-104 in Garner, Shirley Nelson, ed.; Sprengnether, Madelon, ed. *Shakespearean Tragedy and Gender*. Bloomington, IN: Indiana UP; 1996. 326 pp. Index. Notes. Biblio. Lang.: Eng.
England. 1589-1613. Critical studies. ■Shakespeare's contribution to the process by which madness came to be secularized, medicalized, and psychologized as well as gendered, with reference to *Hamlet, Macbeth*, and *King Lear*. Focuses on the contrast between the way in which male and female characters behave in states of psychic extremity.

2678   Neill, Michael. "Broken English and Broken Irish: Nation, Language and the Optic of Power in Shakespeare's Histories." *SQ.* 1994 Spr; 45(1): 1-32. Notes. Illus.: Photo. B&W. 2. Lang.: Eng.
England. 1590-1599. Historical studies. ■English view of the Irish during the Elizabethan and Jacobean eras, and the surfacing of these feelings in Shakespeare's history plays.

2679   Neill, Michael. "Unproper Beds: Race, Adultery and the Hideous in *Othello*." *SQ.* 1989 Win; 40(4): 383-412. Notes. Illus.: Pntg. Dwg. B&W. 6. Lang.: Eng.
England. 1604. Critical studies. ■Analysis of the racial and sexual overtones of *Othello*, and the shocking nature of the final scene.

2680   Newman, Karen. "Portia's Ring: Unruly Women and Structures of Exchange in *The Merchant of Venice*." *SQ.* 1987 Spr; 38 (1): 19-33. Lang.: Eng.
England. 1596. Critical studies. ■Women as a commodity to be traded to enhance the bonding between men in Shakespeare's *The Merchant of Venice*.

2681   Nikolopoulou, Anastasia. "Historical Disruptions: The Walter Scott Melodrama." 121-146 in Hays, Michael, ed.; Nikolopoulou, Anastasia, ed. *Melodrama: The Cultural Emergence of a Genre*. New York, NY: St. Martin's P; 1996. 288 pp. Notes. Lang.: Eng.
England. 1810-1830. Historical studies. ■Comparison between the novels of Walter Scott and stage adaptations such as *Guy Mannering*, adapted by Daniel Terry, and *The Bride of Lammermoor*, adapted by John William Calcraft. Argues that the stage versions highlighted social issues while the novels suppressed them.

2682   Nilsen, Don L.F. *Humor in British Literature, From the Middle Ages to the Restoration: A Reference Guide*. Westport, CT/London: Greenwood; 1997. 226 pp. Pref. Index. Lang.: Eng.
England. 1300-1700. Bibliographical studies. ■Humor and wit in English literature and theatre, with sections on significant dramatists of the period.

2683   Noble, Richmond. "Shakespeare's Use of Song." 437-442 in Tomarken, Edward, ed. *As You Like It from 1600 to the Present*. New York, NY: Garland; 1997. 672 pp. (Shakespeare Criticism 17.) Lang.: Eng.
England. 1598. Critical studies. ■1923 essay on the use of music and song in Shakespeare's *As You Like It*.

DRAMA: —Plays/librettos/scripts

2684　Norland, Howard B. "'Lamentable tragedy mixed ful of pleasant mirth': The Enigma of *Cambises.*" *CompD.* 1992/93 Win; 26 (4): 330-343. Notes. Lang.: Eng.
England. 1564-1569. Critical studies. ■Analysis of Thomas Preston's *Cambyses,* considered the Elizabethan paragon of bad taste and dramatic ineptitude.

2685　O'Donnell, Brennan. "The Errors of the Verse: Metrical Reading and Performance of *The Comedy of Errors.*" 353-371 in Miola, Robert S., ed. *The Comedy of Errors: Critical Essays.* New York, NY: Garland; 1997. 592 pp. (Shakespeare Criticism 18.) Notes. Lang.: Eng.
England. 1594. Critical studies. ■The use of poetry and meter in Shakespeare's *The Comedy of Errors.*

2686　O'Rourke, James. "'Rule in Unity' and Otherwise: Love and Sex in *Troilus and Cressida.*" *SQ.* 1992 Sum; 43(2): 139-158. Notes. Lang.: Eng.
England. 1601-1602. Critical studies. ■Corruption of sexuality within a patriarchal social order in Shakespeare's play.

2687　Orlin, Lena Cowen. "Desdemona's Disposition." 171-192 in Garner, Shirley Nelson, ed.; Sprengnether, Madelon, ed. *Shakespearean Tragedy and Gender.* Bloomington, IN: Indiana UP; 1996. 326 pp. Index. Notes. Biblio. Lang.: Eng.
England. 1605. Critical studies. ■The reflection of early modern discourses of marriage and race in Shakespeare's *Othello.* Examines the moral import of physical behavior in early texts dealing with wifely conduct and argues that Desdemona embodies this construct of female behavior and feminine response, which exposes the patriarchal assumptions underlying the action.

2688　Osborne, Laurie E. *The Trick of Singularity:* Twelfth Night *and the Performance Editions.* Iowa City, IA: Univ of Iowa P; 1996. 206 pp. (Studies in Theatre History and Culture.) Notes. Biblio. Index. Lang.: Eng.
England. 1774-1992. Critical studies. ■Examines promptbooks of Shakespeare's *Twelfth Night* as performance editions and traces their history from the late 1700s to recent video editions. Includes bibliography of all editions.

2689　Osborne, Laurie E. "Rethinking the Performance Editions: Theatrical and Textual Productions of Shakespeare." 168-186 in Bulman, James C., ed. *Shakespeare, Theory, and Performance.* London/New York, NY: Routledge; 1996. 218 pp. Notes. Biblio. Index. Lang.: Eng.
England. 1589-1613. Critical studies. ■The significance of early performance editions of Shakespeare's plays as a 'set of possibilities' for material realization.

2690　Owens, Margaret E. "Desperate Juggling Knacks: The Rehearsal of the Grotesque in *Doctor Faustus.*" *MRDE.* 1996; 8(1): 63-93. Notes. Lang.: Eng.
England. 1604. Critical studies. ■Ritual sacrifice, dismemberment and juggling in Marlowe's *Doctor Faustus,* and the decline of morality drama and the rise of tragedy.

2691　Pace, Thomas Bruton. *Passionate Development: The Embodiment of the Lyric Voice in Shakespearean Narrative.* Louisville, KY: Univ. of Louisville; 1997. 65 pp. [M.A. Thesis, Univ. Microfilms Order No. AAC 1387094.] Lang.: Eng.
England. 1590-1613. Critical studies. ■Elizabethan dramatic narrative and the use of love lyrics by female characters in several of Shakespeare's comic plays including *As You Like It, Twelfth Night,* and *The Merchant of Venice.*

2692　Palmer, Daryl W. "Jacobean Muscovites: Winter, Tyranny, and Knowledge in *The Winter's Tale.*" *SQ.* 1995 Fall; 46(3): 323-339. Notes. Lang.: Eng.
England. Russia. 1610-1611. Critical studies. ■References in Shakespeare's *The Winter's Tale* to Russia, which had only recently come into regular contact with England.

2693　Palmer, Daryl W. "Merchants and Miscegenation: *The Three Ladies of London, The Jew of Malta,* and *The Merchant of Venice.*" 36-66 in MacDonald, Joyce Green, ed. *Race, Ethnicity, and Power in the Renaissance.* Madison, NJ: Fairleigh Dickinson UP; 1997. 187 pp. Notes. Index. Lang.: Eng.
England. 1590-1650. Critical studies. ■Analysis of Renaissance plays to examine the phenomenon of 'selling' racial and national meanings.

2694　Parker, Barbara L. "'A Thing Unfirm': Plato's *Republic* and Shakespeare's *Julius Caesar.*" *SQ.* 1993 Spr; 44(1): 29-43 . Notes. Lang.: Eng.
England. 1599. Critical studies. ■Influence of Plato's *Republic* upon Shakespeare's play.

2695　Parker, Patricia. "Preposterous Events." *SQ.* 1992 Sum; 43(2): 186-213. Notes. Lang.: Eng.
England. 1593. Critical studies. ■The idea of what should follow what in Shakespeare's *Love's Labour's Lost.*

2696　Paster, Gail Kern. "'In the spirit of men there is no blood': Blood as Trope of Gender in *Julius Caesar.*" *SQ.* 1989 Fall; 40(3): 284-298. Notes. Lang.: Eng.
England. 1599. Critical studies. ■Shakespeare's use of the bodily signs of blood and bleeding in *Julius Caesar* in order to both decipher the complex annotation of gender difference in unambiguously gendered characters and write the body into cultural history.

2697　Patterson, Steven J. *Pleasure's Likeness: The Politics of Homosexual Friendship in Early Modern England.* Philadelphia, PA: Temple Univ; 1997. 284 pp. [Ph.D. Dissertation, Univ. Microfilms Order No. AAC 9724266.] Lang.: Eng.
England. 1595-1613. Critical studies. ■Argues that male friendship is represented as an ethical form of erotic bonding in Shakespeare's *The Merchant of Venice* and *The Winter's Tale,* Marlowe's *Edward II,* Shakespeare and Fletcher's *The Two Noble Kinsmen.*

2698　Pearlman, E. "The Invention of Richard of Gloucester." *SQ.* 1992 Win; 43(4): 410-429. Notes. Lang.: Eng.
England. 1590-1593. Textual studies. ■Shakespeare's characterization of Richard of Gloucester in *Richard III* and *Henry VI.*

2699　Peterson, Whitney Anne. *A Critical Edition of Thomas Heywood's The First and Second Partes of King Edward the Fourth.* Lincoln, NB: Univ. of Nebraska; 1997. 264 pp. [Ph.D. Dissertation, Univ. Microfilms Order No. AAC 9815904.] Lang.: Eng.
England. 1600-1626. Critical studies. ■Comparative study of several quarto editions of Thomas Heywood's *King Edward the Fourth.* Includes a critical introduction, notes on content and context, a table of substantive variants, an historical timeline, and a selected bibliography.

2700　Phelan, William Jeffrey. *The Vale of Years: Early Modern Aging, Gender, and Shakespearean Tragedy.* Los Angeles, CA: Univ. of California; 1997. 431 pp. [Ph.D. Dissertation, Univ. Microfilms Order No. AAC 9811490.] Lang.: Eng.
England. 1590-1613. Critical studies. ■Examines aging and its use in Shakespeare's plays, from the 'seven ages of man' speech in *As You Like It,* to a specific focus on age as an overt theme in *King Lear, Othello,* and *Antony and Cleopatra.*

2701　Poole, Kristen. "Saints Alive! Falstaff, Martin Marprelate, and the Staging of Puritanism." *SQ.* 1995 Spr; 46(1): 47-75. Notes. Illus.: Photo. B&W. Lang.: Eng.
England. 1596-1599. Textual studies. ■Argues that Shakespeare's grotesque characterization of Falstaff in the Henriad was intended as a satire on Puritanism.

2702　Priestley, J.B. "The English Comic Characters." 443-454 in Tomarken, Edward, ed. *As You Like It from 1600 to the Present: Critical Essays.* New York, NY: Garland; 1997. 672 pp. (Shakespeare Criticism 17.) Notes. Lang.: Eng.
England. 1598. Critical studies. ■1925 essay on the comic character of Touchstone in Shakespeare's *As You Like It.*

2703　Prior, Roger. "'Runnawayes Eyes': A Genuine Crux." *SQ.* 1989 Sum; 40(2): 191-195. Notes. Lang.: Eng.
England. 1595-1596. Textual studies. ■Offers opinion as to the correct reading of the 'runnawayes eyes' in line 6 of Juliet's soliloquy in III.ii of *Romeo and Juliet.*

2704　Rackin, Phyllis. "History into Tragedy: The Case of *Richard III.*" 31-53 in Garner, Shirley Nelson, ed.; Sprengnether, Madelon, ed. *Shakespearean Tragedy and Gender.* Bloomington, IN: Indiana UP; 1996. 326 pp. Index. Notes. Biblio. Lang.: Eng.

DRAMA: —Plays/librettos/scripts

England. 1589-1613. Critical studies. ■Argues that Shakespeare's shift from the loose chronicle form of his early history plays to the tightly focused structure of tragedy restricted the range of possible roles for women.

2705 Raley, Marjorie. "Claribel's Husband." 95-119 in MacDonald, Joyce Green, ed. *Race, Ethnicity, and Power in the Renaissance.* Madison, NJ: Fairleigh Dickinson UP; 1997. 187 pp. Notes. Index. Lang.: Eng.

England. 1611. Critical studies. ■Argues that through the dynastic marriage event that sets *The Tempest* in action, Shakespeare explores race, gender, and sexuality.

2706 Ransom, Nona Ann. *Supreme Gifts, Valuable Commodities: A Study of the Interaction of Two Competing Discourses in Shakespearean Drama.* Washington, DC: George Washington Univ; 1997. 245 pp. [Ph.D. Dissertation, Univ. Microfilms Order No. AAC 9726670.] Lang.: Eng.

England. 1590-1613. Critical studies. ■Study of the gift and money economies in Shakespearean drama, with particular attention to how they pertain to marriage. Examines *The Merchant of Venice, The Taming of the Shrew, As You Like It,* and *The Winter's Tale.*

2707 Rasmussen, Eric. "Shakespeare's Hand in *The Second Maiden's Tragedy.*" *SQ.* 1989 Spr; 40(1): 1-26. Notes. Illus.: Photo. B&W. 2. Lang.: Eng.

England. 1611-1991. Textual studies. ■Debates the issue of Shakespearean authorship of revisions made in Thomas Middleton's *The Second Maiden's Tragedy.*

2708 Read, David. "Losing the Map: Topographical Understanding in the *Henriad.*" *MP.* 1997 May; 94(4): 475-495. Notes. Lang.: Eng.

England. 1596-1599. Critical studies. ■Argues that notions of physical orientation in the world are crucial to Shakespeare's presentation of the main characters in the second tetralogy and especially to their presentation as historical actors.

2709 Relihan, Constance C. "Erasing the East from *Twelfth Night.*" 80-94 in MacDonald, Joyce Green, ed. *Race, Ethnicity, and Power in the Renaissance.* Madison, NJ: Fairleigh Dickinson UP; 1997. 187 pp. Notes. Index. Lang.: Eng.

England. 1600-1601. Critical studies. ■Examines the representations of nonwhite characters in Shakespeare's *Twelfth Night,* with emphasis on the idea of the 'east' through which nationality and sexuality are seen.

2710 Rhu, Lawrence. "Agons of Interpretation: Ariostan Source and Elizabethan Meaning in Spenser, Harington, and Shakespeare." *RenD.* 1993; 24: 171-188. Notes. Biblio. Lang.: Eng.

England. 1591. Critical studies. ■John Harington's English translation of Ariosto's *Orlando Furioso* as a source for Edmund Spenser's *Faerie Queen* and Shakespeare's *Much Ado About Nothing.*

2711 Riddell, James A. "Jonson and Stansby and the Revisions of *Every Man in His Humour.*" *MRDE.* 1997; 9(1): 81-91. Notes. Lang.: Eng.

England: London. 1601-1616. Historical studies. ■History of the printings of Jonson's *Every Man in His Humour.*

2712 Ripley, John. "*Coriolanus* as Tory Propaganda." 102-123 in Pechter, Edward, ed. *Textual and Theatrical Shakespeare: Questions of Evidence.* Iowa City, IA: Univ of Iowa P; 1997. 267 pp. (Studies in Theatre History and Culture.) Notes. Lang.: Eng.

England. 1682. Critical studies. ■Examines the adaptation of Shakespeare's *Coriolanus* by Nahum Tate as *The Ingratitude of a Commonwealth,* as an example of how adaptations reflect different cultural contexts.

2713 Rogerson, Margaret. "The Coventry Corpus Christi Play: A 'Lost' Middle English Creed Play?" *RORD.* 1997; 36: 143-177. Notes. Lang.: Eng.

England. 1535-1568. Historical studies. ■Search for a Middle English Creed Play in Coventry: examines documentary information, text remnants, performance records, and suggests that Coventry *Corpus Christi* play was a dramatic expression of the Apostles' Creed.

2714 Rollins, John Bowrell. *Dramatic Satire of the Exclusion Crisis: 1680-1683.* Houston, TX: Univ. of Houston; 1997. 94 pp.

[M.A. Thesis, Univ. Microfilms Order No. AAC 1384085.] Lang.: Eng.

England. 1680-1683. Critical studies. ■Theatre's participation in cultural debate over the exclusion crisis and the deep political involvement of playwrights. Works examined include Elkanah Settle's *The Female Prelate,* Thomas Shadwell's *The Lancashire Witches,* John Dryden's *The Spanish Fryar,* Thomas D'Urfey's *Sir Barnaby Whigg,* Aphra Behn's *The Roundheads* and *The City Heiress,* Thomas Otway's *Venice Preserv'd,* Dryden and Lee's *The Duke of Guise,* and John Crowne's *The City Politiques.*

2715 Rose, Mary Beth. "The Heroics of Marriage in *Othello* and *The Duchess of Malfi.*" 210-238 in Garner, Shirley Nelson, ed.; Sprengnether, Madelon, ed. *Shakespearean Tragedy and Gender.* Bloomington, IN: Indiana UP; 1996. 326 pp. Index. Notes. Biblio. Lang.: Eng.

England. 1605-1613. Critical studies. ■Compares the treatment of women in Webster's *The Duchess of Malfi* and Shakespeare's *Othello.* Author argues that both plays locate their female characters in the field of Protestant discourse concerning marriage, that of women being spiritually and socially equal to their husbands yet expected to be subordinate.

2716 Rosen, Alan. "The Rhetoric of Exclusion: Jew, Moor, and the Boundaries of Discourse in *The Merchant of Venice.*" 67-79 in MacDonald, Joyce Green, ed. *Race, Ethnicity, and Power in the Renaissance.* Madison, NJ: Fairleigh Dickinson UP; 1997. 187 pp. Notes. Index. Lang.: Eng.

England. 1596. Critical studies. ■Argues that the racial constructs of colonialism are reflected in the language of the nonwhite characters in Shakespeare's play.

2717 Rosenfield, Kirstie Gulick. *Theatricks, Theatrix, Theatrics: Witchcraft, Female Sexuality, and Antitheatricality in Shakespeare's Plays.* Stanford, CA: Stanford Univ; 1997. 252 pp. [Ph.D. Dissertation, Univ. Microfilms Order No. AAC 9802109.] Lang.: Eng.

England. 1590-1613. Critical studies. ■Relationships between the history of witchcraft and early modern constructions of gender, sexuality, and power as represented in Shakespeare's *Henry VI, Part 2, The Winter's Tale, Othello, A Midsummer Night's Dream, Henry V,* and *Pericles.*

2718 Ross, Charles Stanley. "Shakespeare's *Merry Wives* and the Law of Fraudulent Conveyance." *RenD.* 1994; 25: 145-169. Notes. Biblio. Lang.: Eng.

England. 1596-1603. Historical studies. ■The law of fraudulent conveyance and its representation in Shakespeare's *The Merry Wives of Windsor.*

2719 Ross, Lawrence J. *On* Measure for Measure*: An Essay in Criticism of Shakespeare's Drama.* Newark, DE/London: Univ of Delaware P/Associated Univ Presses; 1997. 182 pp. Index. Biblio. Notes. Pref. Illus.: Pntg. 1. Lang.: Eng.

England. 1604. Critical studies. ■Critical essay on Shakespeare's *Measure for Measure.* Argues for a produceable interpretation—that is, one based on performance, not text.

2720 Rowe, Katherine A. "Dismembering and Forgetting: *Titus Andronicus.*" *SQ.* 1994 Fall; 45(3): 279-303. Notes. Illus.: Dwg. Sketches. 7. Lang.: Eng.

England. 1590-1594. Critical studies. ■Discusses the meanings of dismemberment, particularly of the hands, in Shakespeare's violent play.

2721 Rubinstein, Frankie. "They Were Not Such Good Years." *SQ.* 1989 Spr; 40(1): 70-74. Notes. Lang.: Eng.

England. 1590-1616. Textual studies. ■Argues that Shakespeare's use of the word 'goodyear' refers to diseases of lechery.

2722 Saenger, Michael. "A Reference to Ovid in *Coriolanus.*" *ELN.* 1997 Mar; 34(3): 18-20. Notes. Lang.: Eng.

England. 1607. Critical studies. ■Compares Coriolanus' reversal outside the walls of Rome in Shakespeare's play to Mars's transformation in Ovid's *Metamorphoses.*

2723 Sanders, Julie. "The Collective Contract Is a Fragile Structure: Local Government and Personal Rule in Jonson's *A Tale of a Tub.*" *ELR.* 1997 Fall; 27(3): 443-467. Notes. Illus.: Dwg. B&W. 1. Lang.: Eng.

DRAMA: —Plays/librettos/scripts

England. 1633. Critical studies. ■Explores potential for reading Jonson's play as a critique or subversion of Carolinian personal rule. Explores ramifications and hierarchies of local government, and the implicit questioning of absolutism in the play.

2724 Sanderson, Richard K. "Suicide as Message and Metadrama in English Renaissance Tragedy." *CompD.* 1992 Fall; 26(3): 199-217. Notes. Lang.: Eng.
England. 1590-1625. Critical studies. ■The communicative, self-dramatizing, and self-fashioning dimension of suicide in Shakespeare's *Hamlet,* Heywood's *The Rape of Lucrece,* Fletcher's *Valentinian,* and Tourneur's *The Revenger's Tragedy.*

2725 Schalkwyk, David. "'She never told her love': Embodiment, Textuality, and Silence in Shakespeare's Sonnets and Plays." *SQ.* 1994 Win; 45(4): 381-407. Notes. Lang.: Eng.
England. 1591-1616. Critical studies. ■Reading Shakespeare's plays and sonnets for what they may reveal about the author, and in the case of the sonnets for what they may reveal about their subject.

2726 Scherb, Victor I. "Frame Structure in *The Conversion of St. Paul.*" *CompD.* 1992 Sum; 26(2): 124-139. Notes. Lang.: Eng.
England. 1500. Critical studies. ■Argues that the dramatic power of *The Conversion of St. Paul* can be apprehended only when the play is viewed from a medieval perspective, that is, in the context of medieval staging.

2727 Seligmann, Raphael. *The Functions of Song in the Plays of Thomas Middleton.* Waltham, MA: Brandeis Univ; 1997. 378 pp. [Ph.D. Dissertation, Univ. Microfilms Order No. AAC 9729356.] Lang.: Eng.
England. 1580-1627. Critical studies. ■Middleton's use of music to clarify ideological tensions in his plays. Uses semiotic theory to analyze how meaning is generated.

2728 Selleck, Nancy Gail. *Coining the Self: Language, Gender, and Exchange in Early Modern English Literature.* Princeton, NJ: Princeton Univ; 1997. 254 pp. [Ph.D. Dissertation, Univ. Microfilms Order No. AAC 9809180.] Lang.: Eng.
England. 1580-1620. Critical studies. ■The idea of selfhood in the English Renaissance with emphasis on the works of Spenser, Shakespeare, Jonson, and Donne.

2729 Shand, G.B. "Lear's Coronet: Playing the Moment." *SQ.* 1987 Spr; 38(1): 78-82. Notes. Lang.: Eng.
England. 1605-1606. Critical studies. ■Analysis of the line 'This coronet part between you' (*King Lear* I.i.) with reference to misconceptions in recent productions.

2730 Sharon, Louise. *'When Wit's More Ripe': A Defense of Shakespeare's Pericles.* Milwaukee, WI: Marquette Univ; 1997. 149 pp. [Ph.D. Dissertation, Univ. Microfilms Order No. AAC 9811399.] Lang.: Eng.
England. 1607-1609. Critical studies. ■Argues that *Pericles* is an important transition play to the later romantic tragedies that follow it.

2731 Shattuck, Sim Bryam. *The Cross-Dressed Heroine and Female Mobility in The Faerie Queene and The Merchant of Venice.* Hattiesburg, MS: Univ. of Southern Mississippi; 1997. 233 pp. [Ph.D. Dissertation, Univ. Microfilms Order No. AAC 9809160.] Lang.: Eng.
England. 1590-1596. Critical studies. ■Argues that the presence of cross-dressed female characters in Spenser's *The Faerie Queene* and Shakespeare's *The Merchant of Venice* not only reflects Renaissance cultural humanism but also, perhaps unwittingly, undermined patriarchal control.

2732 Simmons, J. L. "Masculine Negotiations in Shakespeare's History Plays: Hal, Hotspur, and 'the foolish Mortimer'." *SQ.* 1993 Win; 44(4): 440-463. Notes. Tables. Lang.: Eng.
England. 1590-1599. Critical studies. ■Masculinity and feminine disruption in *Henry IV, Henry V, Henry VI, Richard II, Richard III.*

2733 Simonds, Peggy Muñoz. "'My charms crack not': The Alchemical Structure of *The Tempest.*" *CompD.* 1997 Win; 31(4): 538-570. Notes. Illus.: Dwg. B&W. 7. Lang.: Eng.
England: London. 1600-1610. Critical studies. ■Examines *The Tempest* as a response to Ben Jonson's satirical *The Alchemist.*

2734 Sinfield, Alan. "*Poetaster,* the Author, and the Perils of Cultural Production." *RenD.* 1996; 27: 3-18. Notes. Biblio. Lang.: Eng.
England. 1601. Critical studies. ■Ben Jonson's view of himself as an artist reflected in the character Horace in his play *The Poetaster.*

2735 Skura, Meredith. "Marlowe's *Edward II*: Penetrating Language in Shakespeare's *Richard II.*" *ShS.* 1997; 50(1): 41-55. Notes. Lang.: Eng.
England. 1592-1597. Critical studies. ■Sexual, political and linguistic comparison of Marlowe's *Edward II* and Shakespeare's *Richard II.*

2736 Slights, Camille Wells. "Slaves and Subjects in *Othello.*" *SQ.* 1997 Win; 48(4): 377-390. Notes. Lang.: Eng.
England. 1604. Historical studies. ■Emerging ideas of selfhood and slavery as reflected in Shakespeare's *Othello.*

2737 Snider, Denton J. "System of Shakespeare's Dramas." 315-322 in Tomarken, Edward, ed. *As You Like It from 1600 to the Present.* New York, NY: Garland; 1997. 672 pp. (Shakespeare Criticism 17.) Lang.: Eng.
England. 1598. Critical studies. ■1877 essay on the contrast between the actual and idyllic worlds in Shakespeare's *As You Like It.*

2738 Snyder, Susan. "'The King's not here': Displacement and Deferral in *All's Well That Ends Well.*" *SQ.* 1992 Spr; 43(1): 20-32. Notes. Lang.: Eng.
England. 1599-1600. Critical studies. ■Function of substitution and delay in Shakespeare's play.

2739 Snyder, Susan. "Naming Names in *All's Well That Ends Well.*" *SQ.* 1992 Fall; 43(3): 265-279. Notes. Lang.: Eng.
England. 1602-1603. Critical studies. ■Importance and unimportance of character names, particularly the Lords, Steward, and Clown in *All's Well That Ends Well.*

2740 Sofer, Andrew. "Felt Absences: The Stage Properties of *Othello*'s Handkerchief." *CompD.* 1997 Fall; 31(3): 367-393. Notes. Lang.: Eng.
England. 1605. Critical studies. ■The liminal status of Desdemona's handkerchief in *Othello,* both as itself and other than itself: an object as well as a symbol.

2741 Spear, Gary. "Shakespeare's 'Manly' Parts: Masculinity and Effeminacy in *Troilus and Cressida.*" *SQ.* 1993 Win; 44(4): 409-422. Notes. Lang.: Eng.
England. 1601-1602. Critical studies. ■Early modern view of masculine and feminine men in Shakespeare's play.

2742 Spiró, György. *Shakespeare szerepösszevonásai.* (The Doubling of Parts in Shakespeare's Plays.) Budapest: Európa; 1997. 277 pp. (Mérleg.) Notes. Lang.: Hun.
England. 1588-1613. Critical studies. ■The concept and practice of double casting in the plays of Shakespeare.

2743 Sprengnether, Madelon. "The Gendered Subject of Shakespearean Tragedy." 1-30 in Garner, Shirley Nelson, ed.; Sprengnether, Madelon, ed. *Shakespearean Tragedy and Gender.* Bloomington, IN: Indiana UP; 1996. 326 pp. Index. Notes. Biblio. Lang.: Eng.
England. 1589-1613. Critical studies. ■Introductory essay to text on feminist analyses of the female subject in Shakespeare's tragedies.

2744 Stewart, Ann Marie. "Rape, Patriarchy, and the Libertine Ethos: The Function of Sexual Violence in Aphra Behn's 'The Golden Age' and *The Rover, Part I.*" *Restor.* 1997 Win; 12(2): 26-39. Notes. Lang.: Eng.
England. 1660. Critical studies. ■Argues that in *The Rover* men attempt to rape women in order to curb their potential for power and freedom, and that it does not represent violation of a female body but signifies the capacity for women to usurp male authority.

2745 Sticpewich, Margaret M. *Sexual Discourse in the Jacobean Theater of Social Mobility.* Houston, TX: Rice Univ.; 1997. 205 pp. [Ph.D. Dissertation, Univ. Microfilms Order No. AAC 9727614.] Lang.: Eng.
England. 1618-1640. Critical studies. ■Social mobility and its effects on the gentry in Shakespeare's *All's Well That Ends Well,* Massinger's *The Maid of Honour* and *The Bondman,* and Middleton's *The Changeling.*

DRAMA: —Plays/librettos/scripts

2746 Stierstorfer, Klaus. "A Sentimental Appeal to Reason: *The London Merchant.*" *Restor.* 1997 Sum; 12(1): 1-17. Notes. Lang.: Eng.

England: London. 1731. Critical studies. ■Biblical and literary influences on Lillo's *The London Merchant*: how they help highlight Lillo's focus and establish a wider context to our understanding of the play.

2747 Stroffolino, Louis Christopher, Jr. *Complications of Closure in Shakespeare's Middle Comedies.* Albany, NY: State Univ. of New York; 1997. 364 pp. [Ph.D. Dissertation, Univ. Microfilms Order No. AAC 9809294.] Lang.: Eng.

England. 1595-1605. Critical studies. ■Literary 'closure' in Shakespeare's *A Midsummer Night's Dream, The Merchant of Venice, Much Ado About Nothing,* and *As You Like It.*

2748 Sullivan, Garrett A., Jr. "'All Things Come into Commerce': Women, Household Labor, and the Spaces of Marston's *The Dutch Courtesan.*" *RenD.* 1996; 27: 19-46. Notes. Biblio. Lang.: Eng.

England. 1604. Critical studies. ■Commodification of sex and its relation to the household labor of women in Marston's play.

2749 Tanner, Virginia Elizabeth Dally. *Comitatus: Shakespeare's Joust with Convention in Love's Labor's Lost.* Kingsville, TX: Texas A&M Univ; 1997. 84 pp. [M.S. Thesis, Univ. Microfilms Order No. AAC 1385453.] Lang.: Eng.

England. 1593. Critical studies. ■Argues that Shakespeare was the first English Renaissance writer to create, in *Love's Labour's Lost,* an original male-female relationship that resisted gender inequality, thus going against traditional literary relationships of comitatus and courtly love.

2750 Tassi, Marguerite. "Shakespeare and Beckett Revisited: A Phenomenology of Theatre." *CompD.* 1997 Sum; 31(2): 248-276. Notes. Lang.: Eng.

England. Ireland. France. 1606-1958. Critical studies. ■*King Lear* as a possible inspiration for *Fin de partie (Endgame).*

2751 Taylor, A.B. "Shakespeare Rewriting Ovid: Olivia's Interview with Viola and the Narcissus Myth." *ShS.* 1997; 50(1): 81-89. Notes. Lang.: Eng.

England. 1602. Critical studies. ■Viola's interview with Olivia in *Twelfth Night* as an example of Shakespeare's language of imitation, whereby he closely follows the model of a section of Ovid's *Metamorphoses.*

2752 Thatcher, David. "Reading Timon's Epitaphs." *ShN.* 1997 Sum/Fall; 47(2/3): 31. Notes. [Number 233/234.] Lang.: Eng.

England. 1607. Critical studies. ■How lack of punctuation in Shakespeare's *Timon of Athens* affects character interpretation and performance of the ending.

2753 Thompson, Peggy. "'Strange Animation and Vigour': Self-Representation in Frances Burney's *The Witlings.*" *Restor.* 1997 Win; 12(2): 15-25. Notes. Lang.: Eng.

England. 1778. Historical studies. ■Argues that the play predicts and explains its own suppression, examines the role of women and the representation of the author in the play.

2754 Thomson, Leslie. "A Quarto 'Marked for Performance': Evidence of What?" *MRDE.* 1996; 8(1): 176-210. Notes. Append. Illus.: Photo. B&W. 8. Lang.: Eng.

England. 1620. Textual studies. ■The annotations of two bookkeepers on a quarto of *The Two Merry Milkmaids* by J.C., and what light they shed on the staging practices of the era.

2755 Tiffany, Grace. "Falstaff's False Staff: 'Jonsonian' Asexuality in *The Merry Wives of Windsor.*" *CompD.* 1992 Fall; 26(3): 254-270. Notes. Lang.: Eng.

England. 1597. Critical studies. ■Based on the asexual nature of the character Falstaff, argues that Shakespeare's play is an early attempt at comedy of humors.

2756 Time, Victoria Mesode. *The Fictional Criminal: An Analysis of Selected Shakespearean Plays.* Indiana, PA: Indiana Univ. of Pennsylvania; 1997. 223 pp. [Ph.D. Dissertation, Univ. Microfilms Order No. AAC 9721017.] Lang.: Eng.

England. 1590-1613. Critical studies. ■The themes of law and justice in Shakespeare's plays and their relevance to historical as well as contemporary criminological thinking. Plays examined include *Measure for*

Measure and *The Merchant of Venice, Othello* and *Macbeth, Richard III* and *Henry IV, Part One.*

2757 Turner, Dorothy. "Restoration Drama in the Public Sphere: Propaganda, The Playhouse, and Published Drama." *Restor.* 1997 Sum; 12(1): 18-39. Notes. Lang.: Eng.

England. 1678-1683. Critical studies. ■Relationship between printed propaganda and published plays during the Restoration with particular reference to the tragedies published during the Popish Plot. Claims that drama formed a part of the published debates and helped shape the early public sphere.

2758 Ulrici, Hermann P. "Shakespeare's Dramatic Art." 305-314 in Tomarken, Edward, ed. *As You Like It from 1600 to the Present.* New York, NY: Garland; 1997. 672 pp. (Shakespeare Criticism 17.) Lang.: Eng.

England. 1598. Critical studies. ■1876 essay on the nature of the fanciful in the plot and characters of Shakespeare's *As You Like It.*

2759 Upham, Cathy G. *The Role of Rhetorical Inquiry in Shakespeare's Troilus and Cressida.* Carbondale, IL: Southern Illinois Univ; 1997. 186 pp. [Ph.D. Dissertation, Univ. Microfilms Order No. AAC 9738091.] Lang.: Eng.

England. 1601-1602. Critical studies. ■The role of rhetoric in the characterization and structure of Shakespeare's *Troilus and Cressida.*

2760 Vaughan, Virginia Mason. "The Construction of Barbarism in *Titus Andronicus.*" 165-180 in MacDonald, Joyce Green, ed. *Race, Ethnicity, and Power in the Renaissance.* Madison, NJ: Fairleigh Dickinson UP; 1997. 187 pp. Notes. Index. Lang.: Eng.

England. 1590-1594. Critical studies. ■Racial aspects of colonialism in Shakespeare's *Titus Andronicus.* Argues that the play reveals European tensions and ambivalence about contact with other peoples.

2761 Vaughn, Jennifer Renee. *To 'Be' a Woman: Elizabeth Cary and the Tragedy of Mariam: The Fair Queen of Jewry.* Fresno, CA: California State Univ; 1997. 46 pp. [M.A. Thesis, Univ. Microfilms Order No. AAC 1388803.] Lang.: Eng.

England. 1695. Critical studies. ■Gender ideology in Elizabeth Cary's *The Tragedy of Mariam: The Fair Queen of Jewry.*

2762 Velz, John W. "'Some shall be pardon'd, and some punished': Medieval Dramatic Eschatology in Shakespeare." *CompD.* 1992/93 Win; 26(4): 312-329. Notes. Lang.: Eng.

England. 1590-1616. Critical studies. ■Themes of death, immortality and punishment in the plays of Shakespeare.

2763 Waith, Eugene M. "Concern for Villains." *RenD.* 1993; 24: 155-170. Notes. Biblio. Lang.: Eng.

England. 1594-1621. Critical studies. ■Discusses the complexity of sympathetic villains on the early modern stage. *Richard III, Titus Andronicus, King Lear, The White Devil* are cited as examples.

2764 Walker, Jarret. "Voiceless Bodies and Bodiless Voices: The Drama of Human Perception in *Coriolanus.*" *SQ.* 1992 Sum; 43 (2): 170-185. Notes. Lang.: Eng.

England. 1608. Critical studies. ■Examines the conflict between body and speech in *Coriolanus.*

2765 Wall, Wendy. "Forgetting and Keeping: Jane Shore and the English Domestication of History." *RenD.* 1996; 27: 123-156. Notes. Biblio. Lang.: Eng.

England. 1599-1600. Critical studies. ■Memory and remembrance in the anonymous *The First and Second Parts of Edward IV,* attributed by this writer to Thomas Heywood.

2766 Walworth, Alan Marshall. *Displacing Desires in Early Modern Drama.* Urbana-Champaign, IL: Univ. of Illinois; 1997. 263 pp. [Ph.D. Dissertation, Univ. Microfilms Order No. AAC 9812800.] Lang.: Eng.

England. 1590-1619. Critical studies. ■Transvestism, desire, and psychosexual displacement in early modern theatre, with emphasis on Shakespeare and Fletcher's *The Two Noble Kinsmen,* and Dekker and Middleton's *The Roaring Girl.*

2767 Ward, David. "The King and *Hamlet.*" *SQ.* 1992 Fall; 43(3): 280-302. Notes. Lang.: Eng.

England. 1600-1623. Textual studies. ■Historical reasons for the differences between versions of Shakespeare's *Hamlet* in the First and Second

DRAMA: —Plays/librettos/scripts

Quartos and First Folio, especially the Second Quarto version, published during the reign of James I (1604).

2768 Weimann, Robert. "Performance-Game and Representation in *Richard III.*" 66-87 in Pechter, Edward, ed. *Textual and Theatrical Shakespeare: Questions of Evidence.* Iowa City, IA: Univ of Iowa P; 1997. 267 pp. (Studies in Theatre History and Culture.) Notes. Lang.: Eng.

England. 1592-1593. Critical studies. ■The concepts of *locus*, the place of representation of history, and *platea*, the place of theatrical performance, and their interaction in Shakespeare's *Richard III.*

2769 White, Paul Whitfield. "Theater and Religious Culture." 133-152 in Cox, John D., ed.; Kastan, David Scott, ed. *A New History of Early English Drama.* New York, NY: Columbia UP; 1997. 565 pp. Notes. Biblio. Index. Lang.: Eng.

England. 1620-1642. Historical studies. ■The representation of religion on Renaissance English stages. Representations of religion in theatre and how these representations reflected tensions between religion and society.

2770 Whiter, Walter. "A Specimen of a Commentary on Shakespeare." 251-282 in Tomarken, Edward, ed. *As You Like It from 1600 to the Present.* New York, NY: Garland; 1997. 672 pp. (Shakespeare Criticism 17.) Lang.: Eng.

England. 1598. Critical studies. ■1794 essay on Shakespeare's *As You Like It.*

2771 Whittier, Gayle. "The Sonnet's Body and the Body Sonnetized in *Romeo and Juliet.*" *SQ.* 1989 Spr; 40(1): 27-41. Notes. Lang.: Eng.

England. 1595-1596. Critical studies. ■Relationship of poetry and physical action in Shakespeare's play.

2772 Whitworth, Charles. "Rectifying Shakespeare's *Errors*: Romance and Farce in Bardeditry." 250-262 in Miola, Robert S., ed. *The Comedy of Errors: Critical Essays.* New York, NY: Garland; 1997. 592 pp. (Shakespeare Criticism 18.) Notes. Illus.: Photo. 2. Lang.: Eng.

England. 1594. Critical studies. ■Shakespeare's use of farce in *The Comedy of Errors.*

2773 Wikander, Mathew H. "The Protean Prince Hal." *CompD.* 1992/93 Win; 26(4): 295-311. Notes. Lang.: Eng.

England. 1596-1597. Critical studies. ■Analysis of Prince Hal's transformation and political agenda in both parts of *Henry IV.*

2774 Williams, Carolyn. "'This Effeminate Brat': Tamburlaine's Unmanly Son." *MRDE.* 1997; 9(1): 56-80. Notes. Lang.: Eng.

England. 1587. Critical studies. ■Elizabethan ideas of masculinity as seen through Tamburlaine's killing of his son Calyphas for cowardice in Marlowe's *Tamburlaine, Part II.*

2775 Williams, George Walton. "Continuing the Story—From *Part Two* to *Henry V.*" *ShN.* 1997 Win; 47(4): 67-68, 82. Tables. [Number 235.] Lang.: Eng.

England. 1596-1599. Historical studies. ■Argues that the popularity of the character Falstaff in *Henry IV, Part One* led to the creation of a sequel, and that an original version, which did not set up characters for the sequel, may exist. Considers *Henry IV* parts one and two, *Henry V.*

2776 Wilson, Luke. "Promissory Performances." *RenD.* 1994; 25: 59-87. Notes. Biblio. Lang.: Eng.

England. 1592-1616. Critical studies. ■The evolution of the word 'performance' and 'perform' in the plays of Shakespeare, from a legal or quasi-legal term to one with a theatrical connotation.

2777 Wilson, Richard. "'Like the old Robin Hood': *As You Like It* and the Enclosure Riots." *SQ.* 1992 Spr; 43(1): 1-19. Notes. Lang.: Eng.

England. 1598-1600. Historical studies. ■Famine, enclosure, and social resistance in Shakespeare's play.

2778 Wingate, Charles. "Shakespeare's Heroines." 395-410 in Tomarken, Edward, ed. *As You Like It from 1600 to the Present.* New York, NY: Garland; 1997. 672 pp. (Shakespeare Criticism 17.) Lang.: Eng.

England. 1598-1895. Critical studies. ■On actresses who have played Rosalind in Shakespeare's *As You Like It.*

2779 Wright, George T. "An Almost Oral Art: Shakespeare's Language on Stage and Page." *SQ.* 1992 Sum; 43(2): 159-169. Notes. Lang.: Eng.

England. 1590-1613. Critical studies. ■Debates the differences between reading Shakespeare and hearing Shakeapeare.

2780 Yachnin, Paul. "The Politics of Theatrical Mirth: *A Midsummer Night's Dream, A Mad World, My Masters* and *Measure for Measure.*" *SQ.* 1992 Spr; 43(1): 51-66. Notes. Lang.: Eng.

England. 1594-1605. Critical studies. ■Social and political implications of mirth-making in Shakespeare's and Middleton's plays.

2781 Zunder, William. "Shakespeare and the End of Feudalism: *King Lear* as Fin-de-Siècle Text." *EnSt.* 1997 Nov.; 78(6): 513-521. Notes. Lang.: Eng.

England. 1605. Critical studies. ■Argues that Shakespeare wrote *King Lear* as a commentary on the death of Elizabeth I and the accession of the Stuarts.

2782 Barker, Francis. "Nationalism, Nomadism and Belonging in Europe: *Coriolanus.*" 233-265 in Joughin, John J., ed. *Shakespeare and National Culture.* Manchester: Manchester UP; 1997. 343 pp. Notes. Index. Lang.: Eng.

Europe. 1990-1994. Critical studies. ■The cultural ideal of nationalism in current European politics and its reflection in Shakespeare's *Coriolanus.*

2783 Bauer, Agnes Sophie. *Play-within-a-Play and Audience-Response Theory: A Comparative Analysis of Contagious Dramas by Gatti, Stoppard, and Weiss.* West Lafayette, IN: Purdue Univ; 1997. 277 pp. [Ph.D. Dissertation, Univ. Microfilms Order No. AAC 9818915.] Lang.: Eng.

Europe. 1964-1982. Critical studies. ■Examines the concept of theatrical 'contagion' and metatheatrical technique in Peter Weiss' *Marat/Sade*, Armand Gatti's *Chant public devant deux chaises électriques*, and *The Real Thing* by Tom Stoppard.

2784 Bertini, Ferruccio. *Plauto e dintorni.* (Around Plautus.) Rome/Bari: Laterza; 1997. 232 pp. (Quadrante 88.) Biblio. Lang.: Ita.

Europe. 259 B.C.-1997 A.D. Critical studies. ■The influence of Plautus and his comic themes, with attention to Renaissance theatre. Includes a bibliographical essay for Italy, 1950-1970.

2785 Campbell, Julie Delynn. *Renaissance Women Writers: The Beloved Speaks Her Part.* Kingsville, TX: Texas A&M Univ; 1997. 284 pp. [Ph.D. Dissertation, Univ. Microfilms Order No. AAC 9729168.] Lang.: Eng.

Europe. 1400-1590. Histories-specific. ■The works of Italian, French, and English male and female Renaissance writers, and the theatricality of salon etiquette. Considers works by Isabella Andreini, Ludovico Ariosto, Louise Labé, Pierre de Ronsard, Etienne Jodelle, Edmund Spenser, Philip Sidney, William Shakespeare, and Ben Jonson.

2786 Canfield, J. Douglas. "The Classical Treatment of Don Juan in Tirso, Molière, and Mozart: What Cultural Work Does It Perform." *CompD.* 1997 Spr; 31(1): 42-64. Notes. Lang.: Eng.

Europe. 1612-1787. Critical studies. ■The character of Don Juan as an affirmation of a system of shared power between men at the expense of women and oppressed classes in *Don Giovanni*, Molière's *Don Juan* and Tirso's *Burlador de Sevilla.*

2787 Carandini, Silvia, ed. *Chiarezza e verosimiglianza. La fine del dramma barocco.* (Evidence and Verisimilitude: The End of Baroque Drama.) Rome: Bulzoni; 1997. 222 pp. (I libri dell'Associazione Sigismondo Malatesta.) Pref. Notes. Biblio. Lang.: Ita.

Europe. 1600-1699. Critical studies. ■Collection of essays on the drama of the late Baroque period.

2788 Healy, Thomas. "Past and Present Shakespeares: Shakespearian Appropriations in Europe." 206-232 in Joughin, John J., ed. *Shakespeare and National Culture.* Manchester: Manchester UP; 1997. 343 pp. Notes. Index. Lang.: Eng.

Europe. 1870-1994. Critical studies. ■Cultural reception and traditions of Shakespeare in Europe.

DRAMA: —Plays/librettos/scripts

2789 Isser, Edward R. *Stages of Annihilation: Theatrical Representations of the Holocaust.* Madison, NJ: Fairleigh Dickinson UP; 1997. 260 pp. Index. Notes. Biblio. Lang.: Eng.
Europe. North America. 1950-1996. Histories-specific. ■History and critical analysis of worldwide drama featuring representations of the Holocaust, divided into sections on Britain, America, Germany, and France, with special sections on feminist American drama, the work of George Bernard Shaw and Arthur Miller, and current work combining the Holocaust with gay themes and the AIDS crisis.

2790 Kowalczykowa, Alina. *Dramat i teatr romantyczny.* (Romantic Drama and Theatre.) Warsaw: Instytut Badań Literackich; 1997. 268 pp. Lang.: Pol.
Europe. 1800-1851. Historical studies. ■The relation between the written text and performance in the Romantic period. Considers works of Schlegel, Goethe, Mickiewicz, Słowacki, Krasiński, Norwid, Hugo, Dumas, and Shakespeare.

2791 Lehmann, Hans Thies. "Zeitstrukturen/Zeitskulpturen: zu einigen Theaterformen am Ende des 20. Jahrhunderts." (Time Structures/Time Sculptures: On Some Theatrical Forms at the End of the Twentieth Century.) *Thsch.* 1997; 12: 28-47. Illus.: Photo. B&W. 3. Lang.: Ger, Fre, Dut, Eng.
Europe. 1990-1997. Critical studies. ■Theoretical discussion of temporality as both theme and mode of presentation of recent theatrical productions, including Einar Schleef's production of Oscar Wilde's *Salomé* at Düsseldorfer Schauspielhaus. Includes brief mentions of productions by Christoph Marthaler, Robert Wilson, Tadeusz Kantor, Jan Lauwers, and Heiner Müller.

2792 Londré, Felicia Hardison. *Love's Labour's Lost: Critical Essays.* London/New York, NY: Garland; 1997. 476 pp. (Shakespeare Criticism 13.) Notes. Biblio. Illus.: Photo. 9. Lang.: Eng.
Europe. North America. 1598-1994. Critical studies. ■Collection of over fifty previously published essays, reviews, notes, remarks, and miscellaneous writings on Shakespeare's *Love's Labour's Lost.*

2793 Meldolesi, Claudio. "Dal nō Taniko a Il Consenziente e Il Dissenziente. Chiarimenti della drammaturgia d'autore, anche sui confini dell'*Opera da tre soldi* e di *Godot.*" (From the Nō Play *Taniko* to *He Who Says Yes* and *He Who Says No*: The Dramaturgy of the Author and the Frontiers of *The Three Penny Opera* and *Waiting for Godot.*) *TeatroS.* 1997; 12 (19): 185-200. Notes. Lang.: Ita.
Europe. 1900-1993. Critical studies. ■The dramaturgical reelaboration of texts of the past in the work of contemporary authors, including Bertolt Brecht and Samuel Beckett.

2794 Neely, Kent. "Death: (Re)Presenting Mortality and Moribundity. PRAXIS: An Editorial Statement." *JDTC.* 1997 Fall; 12(1): 97-101. Lang.: Eng.
Europe. 1997. Critical studies. ■The uniqueness of theatre in depicting representations of death and dying.

2795 Pearce, Howard. *Human Shadows Bright as Glass: Drama as Speculation and Transformation.* London: Associated Univ Presses; 1997. 271 pp. Index. Biblio. Notes. Lang.: Eng.
Europe. North America. 1590-1920. Critical studies. ■On the nature of drama. Examines six facets of the dramatic event: spectacle, mimesis, audience and author, the outer world, the play itself, and the imagination.

2796 Pochhammer, Sabine. "'Fair is foul, and foul is fair' Shakespeare Is a Paradox." *Thsch.* 1997; 11: 80-111. Illus.: Photo. B&W. 7. Lang.: Ger, Fre, Dut, Eng.
Europe. 1985-1997. Histories-sources. ■An interview with author, director and designer Jan Lauwers and literature professor and German Shakespeare translator Klaus Reichert about Shakespeare's actuality within the immediate context of Lauwer's production of *Macbeth*, performed by Needcompany.

2797 Rokem, Freddie. "From One-Point Perspective to Circular Vision: Some Spatial Themes and Structures in the Modern Theatre." *FMT.* 1997; 12(1): 29-36. Notes. Lang.: Eng.
Europe. 1900-1956. Critical studies. ■Changes in the dialectical interactions between the objective and the subjective modes of visual perception from Ibsen to Strindberg to Brecht.

2798 Sugiera, Małgorzata. *Wariacje szekspirowskie w powojennym dramacie europejskim.* (Shakespearean Variations in Postwar European Drama.) Cracow: TAIWPN Universitas; 1997. 209 pp. Pref. Notes. Index. Lang.: Pol.
Europe. 1965-1995. Critical studies. ■Variations on Shakespearean themes in plays by Stoppard, Brešan, Żurek, Głowacki, Césaire, Bond, Ionesco, Müller, Groński, Dürrenmatt, and Schwab and productions by Kresnik and Beier.

2799 Trubey, Todd Roger. *Classical Romans, Renaissance Italians, and Shakespeare: An Intertextual Study of the Relationship Between Individuals and Social Systems in Literary Texts.* Evanston, IL: Northwestern Univ.yr 1997; 438 pp. [Ph.D. Dissertation, Univ. Microfilms Order No. AAC 9814329.] Lang.: Eng.
Europe. 200 B.C.-1610 A.D. Critical studies. ■Analysis of classical Roman, Renaissance Italian, and Shakespearean versions of three story lines—twins dramas, variations on Lucretia's rape, and bed-trick narratives—that revolve around replacement or substitution of characters. Examines Plautus's *Menaechmi*, Livy and Ovid's Lucretia narratives, Machiavelli's *Mandragola* and *Clizia*, Bibbiena's *La Calandria*, and Shakespeare's *The Comedy of Errors, Twelfth Night,* and *Cymbeline* to distinguish different ideals of social interaction proposed by the authors.

2800 Jääskinen, Hanna. "Writer, Director Juha Lehtola: 'Looking for the Moment of Realization'/Juha Lehtola, écrivain, metteur en scène: 'Je cherche le moment de la révélation'." *NFT.* 1997; 51: 20-21. Illus.: Photo. B&W. 1. Lang.: Eng, Fre.
Finland. 1997. Histories-sources. ■The playwright and director discusses his influences and artistic goals.

2801 Shepherd-Barr, Kirsten. *Ibsen and Early Modernist Theatre, 1890-1900.* Westport, CT/London: Greenwood; 1997. 200 pp. (Contributions in Drama and Theatre Studies 78.) Index. Notes. Pref. Biblio. Lang.: Eng.
Finland. 1885-1905. Histories-specific. ■Henrik Ibsen's reception in England and France as a cross-cultural phenomenon which encouraged early modernist ideas about art, literature and language. Uses semiotics to critique theatrical production and audience reception. Plays studied are *Et Dukkehjem (A Doll's House), Rosmersholm, Hedda Gabler* and *Bygmester Solness (The Master Builder).*

2802 Templeton, Joan. *Ibsen's Women.* Cambridge: Cambridge UP; 1997. 386 pp. Index. Notes. Pref. Biblio. Illus.: Dwg. Photo. 22. Lang.: Eng.
Finland. 1855-1905. Histories-specific. ■Feminist study traces patterns of gender throughout Ibsen's plays and examines how the women in Ibsen's life influenced the women in his plays.

2803 "Molière and Authority: From *Querelle de l'École des Femmes* to the *Affaire Tartuffe.*" *RQ.* 1997 Spr; 44(2): 80-92. Notes. Lang.: Eng.
France. 1660-1666. Critical studies. ■Authenticity and Molière's *Tartuffe* and *L'Ecole des femmes.*

2804 Armani, Ada Speranza. *Intorno all'amour tyrannique. Drammaturgia e retorica nella Francia del Seicento.* (On 'Amour Tyrannique': Dramaturgy and Rhetoric in Seventeenth-Century France.) Rome: Bulzoni; 1997. 152 pp. (Biblioteca di cultura 526.) Notes. Index. Lang.: Ita.
France. 1600-1699. Critical studies. ■The theme of love in theatre and other literary genres compared with the themes of honor and the dynamics of power.

2805 Bishop, Tom. *From the Left Bank: Reflections on the Modern French Theatre and Novel.* New York, NY/London: New York UP; 1997. 298 pp. Index. Notes. Pref. Illus.: Photo. 9. Lang.: Eng.
France. 1937-1989. Critical studies. ■Collection of essays, articles, and interviews dealing with French culture, especially French theatre and fiction. Focuses on avant-garde French theatre, including Jean Giraudoux, Jean Cocteau, Jean Anouilh, Jean-Louis Barrault, Eugène Ionesco, François Tilly, Jean-Paul Sartre, and Samuel Beckett.

2806 Bradby, David. "Bernard-Marie Koltès: Chronology, Contexts, Connections." *NTQ.* 1997; 13(49): 69-90. Biblio. Illus.: Photo. B&W. 4. Lang.: Eng.

DRAMA: —Plays/librettos/scripts

France. 1948-1989. Historical studies. ∎Outlines the life and work of Koltès and includes an interview with Patrice Chéreau, who produced all his major plays.

2807 Brand, Genevieve. *Jean Cocteau and Federico García Lorca: The Search for Identity.* Boca Raton, FL: Florida Atlantic Univ; 1997. 67 pg. [M.A. Thesis, Univ. Microfilms Order No. AAC 1387287.] Lang.: Eng.

France. Spain. 1930-1937. Critical studies. ∎Gendered identity as performance in *Les Chevaliers de la Table Ronde (Knights of the Round Table)* by Jean Cocteau and *El público (The Public)* by Federico García Lorca.

2808 Campbell, John. "Tragedy and Time in Racine's *Mithridate.*" *MLR.* 1997 July; 92(3): 590-598. Notes. Biblio. Lang.: Eng.

France. 1673. Critical studies. ∎Defense of Racine's *Mithridate* against charges that its dramatic structure is flawed. Considers the unity of tragic time and the play's divergences from the classical model of tragedy.

2809 Cixous, Hélène. "Mimesis Imposed: Machineries of Representation." 29-39 in Murray, Timothy, ed. *Mimesis, Masochism, and Mime: The Politics of Theatricality in Contemporary French Thought.* Ann Arbor, MI: Univ. of Michigan P; 1997. 328 pp. (Theater: Theory/Text/Performance.) Notes. Lang.: Eng.

France. 1991. Histories-sources. ∎Interview with Hélène Cixous conducted by the journal *Hors Cadre* about how she approaches writing and her reaction to media and culture.

2810 Cooper, Barbara T. "The Return of Martin Guerre in an Early Nineteenth-Century French Melodrama." 103-120 in Hays, Michael, ed.; Nikolopoulou, Anastasia, ed. *Melodrama: The Cultural Emergence of a Genre.* New York, NY: St. Martin's P; 1996. 288 pp. Notes. Lang.: Eng.

France. 1800-1850. Historical studies. ∎The adaptation of the story of the French peasant Martin Guerre into melodrama in nineteenth-century France. Argues that the story illustrates melodrama's ability to enfold complex ideological and social issues.

2811 Cujec, Carol A. "Modernizing Antiquity: Jean Cocteau's Early Greek Adaptations." *CML.* 1996 Fall; 17(1): 45-56. Notes. Lang.: Eng.

France. 1922-1937. Historical studies. ∎Examination of Cocteau's adaptations of Sophocles' *Antigone* and *Oidípous Týrannos (Oedipus the King).* He also collaborated on an operatic version of *Oedipus the King* with Igor Stravinskij.

2812 D'Angeli, Concetta. "La fondazione del potere in *Le Balcon* di Jean Genet." (The Foundation of Power in Genet's *Le Balcon.*) *TeatroS.* 1997; 12(19): 229-244. Notes. Lang.: Ita.

France. 1956. Critical studies. ∎Images of power and the role of the public as an actor in *Le Balcon (The Balcony)* by Jean Genet.

2813 Davis, Peter. "Rewriting Seneca: Garnier's *Hippolyte.*" *CML.* 1997 Sum; 17(4): 293-318. Notes. Lang.: Eng.

France. 1635. Critical studies. ∎Contrasts Seneca's *Phaedra* with Robert Garnier's *Hippolyte.*

2814 Deprats, Jean-Michel. "The 'Shakespearian Gap' French." *ShS.* 1997; 50(1): 125-133. Notes. Lang.: Eng.

France. UK-England. 1997. Critical studies. ∎Strategic approaches and suggestions to French translators of Shakespeare.

2815 Hawcroft, Michael. "French Classical Drama and the Tension of Utterance: Racine, Molière, and Madame de Saint-Balmon." *FS.* 1997 Oct.; 51(4): 395-411. Notes. Lang.: Eng.

France. 1601-1700. Critical studies. ∎The function of language to set emotional tone and propel characterization in the plays of Racine, Molière and Madame de Saint-Balmon.

2816 Isley, Edwin Lewis. *Noël Le Breton de Hauteroche: Seventeenth-Century Comic Playwright and Actor.* Columbus, OH: Ohio State Univ; 1997. 459 pp. Notes. Biblio. [Ph.D. Dissertation, Univ. Microfilms Order No. AAC 9813280.] Lang.: Eng.

France. 1620-1680. Historical studies. ∎The works and career of Noël Le Breton, known as Hauteroche, actor, theatre manager, and playwright. Focuses on his work at the Hôtel de Bourgogne and his importance as an innovator of the one-act form in France.

2817 Jones, Richard. "Audience and Otherness in *La Dame aux Camélias.*" *NETJ.* 1997; 8: 111-126. Notes. Biblio. Lang.: Eng.

France. 1848. Critical studies. ∎Marguerite Gautier, the protagonist of Dumas *fils'* play, as the representative of a sexualized, commodified femininity that was a threat to the nineteenth-century bourgeois audience.

2818 Klaver, Elizabeth. "Entering Beckett's Postmodern Space." 111-126 in Oppenheim, Lois, ed.; Buning, Marius, ed. *Beckett On and On....* Madison, NJ: Fairleigh Dickinson UP; 1996. 289 pp. Notes. Biblio. Lang.: Eng.

France. Ireland. USA. 1942-1982. Critical studies. ∎Considers whether Samuel Beckett's plays may be considered 'postmodern'.

2819 Lester, Gideon. "Industrial Art: The Theatre of Michel Vinaver." *ThM.* 1997; 28(1): 69-73. Notes. Biblio. Illus.: Photo. B&W. 1. Lang.: Eng.

France. 1997. Critical studies. ∎Introduction of the French playwright to an American audience.

2820 Maskell, David. "Corneille's *Examens* Examined: The Case of *Horace.*" *FS.* 1997 July; 51(3): 267-280. Notes. Lang.: Eng.

France. 1660. Critical studies. ∎Corneille's own critique of his work, particularly in the individual introductions to his plays, with emphasis on *Horace.*

2821 Maskell, David. "The Aesthetics of Farce: *La Jalousie du Barbouillé.*" *MLR.* 1997 July; 92(3): 581-589. Notes. Biblio. Lang.: Eng.

France. 1450-1820. Critical studies. ∎An attempt to prove Molière's authorship of *The Jealousy of Barbouillé* through exploration of the aesthetics of farce in three interconnected readings—generic, carnival, and theatrical.

2822 Mazet, Veronique. *Love as Theater: A Study of Pierre Corneille's Early Comedies, 1628-1638.* Notes. Biblio. [Ph.D. Dissertation, Univ. Microfilms Order No. AAC 9802953.]

France. 1628-1638. Critical studies. ∎Argues that Corneille's early comic plays were a new style of comedy in French theatre.

2823 Mazzaro, Jerome. "The *Mystère d'Adam* and Christian Memory." *CompD.* 1997 Fall; 31(3): 481-505. Notes. Lang.: Eng.

France. 1146-1175. Historical studies. ∎The mnemonic and devotional thrust of the passion *Mystère d'Adam* and its wider focus beyond the events of the life of Christ.

2824 Mehta, Binita. *India as Spectacle: The Representation of India in French Theater.* New York, NY: City Univ.of New York; 1997. 362 pp. [Ph.D. Dissertation, Univ. Microfilms Order No. AAC 9720115.] Lang.: Eng.

France. India. 1700-1995. Critical studies. ∎Examines how India was used by French dramatists, both to express their misgivings toward their own society as well as to establish India's aesthetic relationship to their own work.

2825 Metayer, Léon. "What the Heroine Taught, 1830-1870." 235-244 in Hays, Michael, ed.; Nikolopoulou, Anastasia, ed. *Melodrama: The Cultural Emergence of a Genre.* New York, NY: St. Martin's P; 1996. 288 pp. Notes. Lang.: Eng.

France. 1830-1870. Historical studies. ∎Examines representations of women in the melodrama theatres of Paris—the Ambigu, Gaîté, and Porte Saint-Martin.

2826 Miranda, Giovanna. "Alle origini della Lulù di Frank Wedekind: la 'clownesse danseuse' di Félicien Champsaur." (At the Origin of Wedekind's *Lulu*: Félicien Champsaur's 'clownesse danseuse'.) *BiT.* 1997; 44: 79-115. Notes. Lang.: Ita.

France. Germany. 1888-1904. Critical studies. ∎Comparison of Wedekind's heroine Lulu and the character of the same name in pantomimes and a novel by Félicien Champsaur. Argues that the character Lulu represents a desire to bring *commedia dell'arte* to life.

2827 Moore, Nancy Gaye. *Valentine de St.-Point: 'La femme intégrale' and Her Quest for a Modern Tragic Theatre in L'Agonie de Messaline (1907) and La Métachorie (1913).* Evanston, IL: Northwestern Univ; 1997. 257 pp. [Ph.D. Dis-

DRAMA: —Plays/librettos/scripts

sertation, Univ. Microfilms Order No. AAC 9814273.] Lang.: Eng.

France. 1875-1953. Critical studies. ■The life and works of Futurist playwright Valentine de St.-Point. Focus on her tragic drama *L'Âme Imperiale ou L'Agonie de Messaline* and her 'geometric dance' *La Métachorie*.

2828 Newman, Karen. "Corneille's City Comedy: Courtship and Consumption in Early Modern Paris." *RenD*. 1996; 27: 105-122. Notes. Biblio. Illus.: Dwg. B&W. 2. Lang.: Eng.

France: Paris. 1631-1640. Critical studies. ■The comedies of Pierre Corneille, with emphasis on *La galerie du palais (The Palace Gallery)*.

2829 Posner, David M. "Le dernier des Justes: Suréna and the End of Nobility." *RenD*. 1993; 24: 83-99. Notes. Biblio. Lang.: Eng.

France. 1674. Critical studies. ■The conflict between the heroic and the political in Corneille's *Suréna, général des Parthes*.

2830 Pucci, Suzanne R. "The Nature of Domestic Intimacy and Sibling Incest in Diderot's *Fils Naturel*." *ECS*. 1997 Spr; 30 (3): 271-287. Notes. Lang.: Eng.

France. 1757. Critical studies. ■Explores elements of incest and familial taboos in Diderot's play.

2831 Ryngaert, Jean-Pierre. "Pour un 'scénario d'action'." (Towards a 'Scenario of Actions'.) *AnT*. 1997 Spr; 21: 17-27. Notes. Biblio. Lang.: Fre.

France. 1997. Critical studies. ■Proposes creation of lists of actions of dramatic characters as method of scene analysis for critics and playwrights.

2832 Shevtsova, Maria. "Interculturalism, Aestheticism, Orientalism: Starting from Peter Brook's *Mahabharata*." *ThR*. 1997; 22(2): 98-104. Notes. Lang.: Eng.

France: Paris. 1988-1992. Critical studies. ■Argues for cultural specificity of all theatre, and discusses its implications for analysis of interculturalism in productions by Mnouchkine and Brook.

2833 Spreen, Constance Susan. *The Politics of Escapism: Theatrical Reform and Fascism in France*. Chicago, IL: Univ. of Chicago; 1997. 245 pp. [Ph.D. Dissertation, Univ. Microfilms Order No. AAC 9729887.] Lang.: Eng.

France. 1930-1945. Critical studies. ■Examination of the writings of avant-garde theatre reformers Antonin Artaud, Jacques Copeau, and Gaston Baty in their historical and ideological context to demonstrate the convergence of avantgardism and fascism in escapist aesthetics.

2834 Toma, Oana G. *Producing and Performing Identities: Theoretical, Cultural, and Practical Articulations of Jean Genet's Concept of Self*. Edmonton, AL: Univ. of Alberta; 1997. 116 pp. [M.A. Thesis, Univ. Microfilms Order No. AAC MQ22558.] Lang.: Eng.

France. 1950-1975. Critical studies. ■Analysis of *Les Nègres (The Blacks)* and *Les Paravents (The Screens)* by Jean Genet with attention to the playwright's concept of self as a dynamic process of becoming, constitutive and performative in nature.

2835 Vinaver, Michel; de Haan, Christopher, transl. "A Reflection of My Works." *ThM*. 1997; 28(1): 74-78. Illus.: Photo. B&W. 2. Lang.: Eng.

France. 1996. Histories-sources. ■Playwright Michel Vinaver on the themes of his work.

2836 Bowyer, T.H. "Warren Hastings in the Drama of Lion Feuchtwanger and Bertolt Brecht: Contexts and Connections." *CompD*. 1997 Fall; 31(3): 394-413. Notes. Lang.: Eng.

Germany. 1916-1927. Critical studies. ■The portrayal of Hastings in *Warren Hastings, Gouverneur von Indien (Warren Hastings, Governor of India)* by Lion Feuchtwanger and in *Kalkutta, 4. Mai. (Calcutta, May 4)* by Feuchtwanger and Bertolt Brecht.

2837 Buselmeier, Michael. "Aussenseiter der Vergangenheit." (Outsider of the Past.) *THeute*. 1997; 7: 35-37. Illus.: Photo. B&W. 3. Lang.: Ger.

Germany. 1997. Critical studies. ■New German plays with historical themes: *Maienschlager (A May Pop-Song)* by Katharina Gericke directed by Janek Starczewskiat at Stückemarkt and *Zwischen zwei Feuern (Between Two Fires)* by Albert Ostermaier directed by Christoph Biermeier at Mannheimer Nationaltheater.

2838 Case, Sue-Ellen. "'Wer raucht, sieht kaltblütig aus'." (Who Smokes Looks Cold-Blooded.) *TZ*. 1997; Yb: 163-169. Append. Illus.: Photo. B&W. 4. Lang.: Eng.

Germany: Berlin. 1923-1996. Critical studies. ■The different images of Bertolt Brecht and Heiner Müller, who often appeared with a cigar in mouth or hand, making it a signature symbol of the radical German playwright.

2839 Davies, Cecil. *The Plays of Ernst Toller: A Revaluation*. Amsterdam: Harwood Academic Publishers; 1996. 685 pp. (Contemporary Theatre Studies 10.) Biblio. Index. Notes. Append. Illus.: Photo. 5. Lang.: Eng.

Germany. 1893-1939. Critical studies. ■Critical overview of the plays of Ernst Toller. Includes a bibliography of audio tapes and archives, and related materials.

2840 Devlin, Eugene J. "The *Regnum Humanitatis* Trilogy: A Humanist Manifesto." *CompD*. 1992 Spr; 26(1): 58-72. Notes. Lang.: Eng.

Germany. 1585-1600. Critical studies. ■Renaissance humanism and religious sensitivity in *Regnum Humanitatis (The Reign of Humanity)* by Jesuit playwright Jacob Grester.

2841 Ercolani, Daniela. "Giuditta, donna demoniaca e santa. La vicenda biblica e le tragedie di Frierich Hebbel e Jean Giraudoux." (Judith, Demonic and Saintly Woman: Biblical Vicissitude and the Tragedies of Friedrich Hebbel and Jean Giraudoux.) *BiT*. 1997; 44: 39-78. Notes. Lang.: Ita.

Germany. France. 1841-1931. Critical studies. ■The treatment of the Biblical character Judith in plays by Hebbel and Giraudoux, both titled *Judith*.

2842 Garforth, Julian A. "Translating Beckett's Translations." *JBeckS*. 1997; 6(1): 49-70. Notes. Lang.: Eng.

Germany. 1967-1978. Critical studies. ■Examines the German translations of *Endgame, Krapp's Last Tape, Happy Days, Waiting for Godot, Footfalls, Play*, and *That Time*.

2843 Grazioli, Cristina. "Una declinazione della marionetta grottesca: maschera e automa in *Matusalemme o l'eterno borghese* di Iwan Goll." (A Variation on Puppet Grotesque: Mask and Automaton in Iwan Goll's *Methuselah or the Eternal Bourgeois*.) *IlCast*. 1997; 10(30): 57-93. Notes. Lang.: Ita.

Germany. 1918-1927. Critical studies. ■Analysis of Goll's satiric drama *Methusalem oder der ewige Bürger*, in which Biblical references and grotesque elements are intertwined.

2844 Honegger, Gitta. "Seeing Through the Eyes of the Word." *ThM*. 1993; 23(1): 87-92. Illus.: Photo. B&W. 2. Lang.: Eng.

Germany. 1992. Critical studies. ■Analysis of Peter Handke's play without words *Die Stunde da wir nichts voneinander wussten (The Hour We Knew Nothing of Each Other)*.

2845 Jahnke, Manfred. "Sehnsucht nach starken Geschichten." (Desire for Strong Stories.) *DB*. 1997; 6: 48-49. Illus.: Photo. B&W. 2. Lang.: Ger.

Germany: Berlin. 1997. Reviews of performances. ■Impressions from the 4th Deutsche Kinder- und Jugendtheatertreffen. Reviews of Wolf Erlbruch's *Die fürchterlichen Fünf (The Terrible Five)* by Landestheater Tübingen, Ignace Cornelissen's *Heinrich V. (Henry V.)*, adapted from William Shakespeare, performed by Theater Triebwerk, and Christian Tschirner's *Der Baron auf den Bäumen (The Baron in the Trees)* directed by Roland Bertschi at Hans Otto Theater.

2846 Jörder, Gerhard. "Die Globalisierung frisst ihre Kinder." (Globalization Eats its Children.) *THeute*. 1997; Yb: 113-116. Illus.: Photo. B&W. 3. Lang.: Ger.

Germany: Berlin. 1997. Histories-sources. ■Text of Jörder's speech on the occasion of the award received by Widmer's *Top Dogs* directed by Volker Hesse at Theater Neumarkt at Berliner Theatertreffen 1997.

2847 Kaiser, Anne. "Der nicht-alltägliche Alltag: Zur intendierten Wirkung des dramatischen Werkes von Georg Seidel." (The Not-Daily Everyday Life: Towards Intended Effects of Georg Seidel's Dramatic Work.) *FMT*. 1997; 12(1): 54-74. Notes. Illus.: Graphs. 3. Lang.: Ger.

Germany. 1980-1990. Critical studies. ■Discusses Seidel's plays *Kondensmilchpanorama, Carmen Kittel* and *Villa Jugend* in correlation to the

DRAMA: —Plays/librettos/scripts

East German society and culture. Defines Seidel's dramatic style and his situation in the socialist tradition.

2848 Kümmel, Peter. "Ein Roman in Stimmen." (A Novel in Voices.) *THeute.* 1997; 3: 21-22. Illus.: Photo. B&W. 1. Lang.: Ger.
Germany. 1933-1997. Biographical studies. ■English author B.S. Johnson and the performance of Jonson's life in *Lebensabend (Life's Evening)* directed by Hans-Ulrich Becker at Stuttgarter Staatstheater.

2849 Leskinen, Mika. "Nykydramatiikan sunnuntailapset." (Sunday Children of Modern Drama.) *Teat.* 1997; 52(3): 14-15. Illus.: Photo. B&W. 3. Lang.: Fin.
Germany. 1997. Histories-sources. ■Playwrights Tankred Dorst and Ursula Ehler interviewed by theatre director Mika Leskinen.

2850 Niccolini, Elisabetta. "Darstellung einer 'Landschaft jenseits des Todes': *Bildbeschreibung* von Heiner Müller oder der entfremdete Blick auf die fremdgewordene Natur." (Description of a 'Landscape Beyond Death': Heiner Müller's *Bildbeschreibung* or the Alienated Look at Estranged Nature.) *FMT.* 1997; 12(2): 160-174. Notes. Lang.: Ger.
Germany. 1985. Critical studies. ■Analysis of nature, history and language in Heiner Müller's *Bildbeschreibung (Description of a Picture).*

2851 Pietzsch, Ingeborg. "'Mein Schreiben ist gerichtet auf ein Du'." ('My Writing Is Directed Towards a 'Du'.) *TZ.* 1997; 1: 42-46. Illus.: Photo. B&W. 4. Lang.: Ger.
Germany. 1947-1997. Histories-sources. ■An interview with Rudolf Herfurthner on occasion of the award 'Deutscher Kindertheaterpreis 1996' for his play *Waldkinder (Children of the Wood).*

2852 Schachenmayr, Volker. "Edited to the Point of Performativity: Strategies for Engaging the *Woyzeck Faksimileausgabe.*" *JDTC.* 1997 Fall; 12(1): 57-76. Append. Lang.: Eng.
Germany. 1875-1981. Critical studies. ■Survey of the many manuscript, published, and performed versions of Büchner's *Woyzeck*, with particular attention to a facsimile edition by Gerhard Schmid.

2853 Stammen, Sylvia. "Schreiben zwischen Macht und Ohnmacht." (Writing between Power and Faint.) *DB.* 1997; 10: 38-41. Illus.: Photo. B&W. 2. Lang.: Ger.
Germany. 1967-1997. Biographical studies. ■A portrait of the playwright Albert Ostermaier on occasion of his successes at Berliner Stückemarkt, Autorentage and the performance of his new play *Zuckersüss und Leichenbitter (Sugar-Sweet and Mournful)* directed by Udo Samel at Marstall Theater.

2854 Sugiera, Małgorzata. "Elfriede Jelinek—demontaż powszednich mitów." (Elfriede Jelinek: Destruction of Everyday Myths.) *DialogW.* 1997; 3: 176-189. Lang.: Pol.
Germany. Austria. 1989-1997. Critical studies. ■Feminist aspects of Jelinek's plays, with consideration of language, psychology, and philosophy.

2855 Wailes, Stephen L. *The Rich Man and Lazarus on the Reformation Stage: A Contribution to the Social History of German Drama.* London: Associated Univ Presses; 1997. 359 pp. Index. Biblio. Notes. Lang.: Eng.
Germany. 1529-1600. Critical studies. ■The social turmoil and theological struggles of the Reformation as reflected in ten dramatic treatments of the biblical story of Lazarus and the rich man.

2856 Walther, Lutz. "Apel, Kind, Wilson: Aspekte des Freischützstoffes." (Apel, Kind, Wilson: Aspects of the 'Freischütz' Theme.) *FMT.* 1997; 12(1): 91-99. Notes. Lang.: Ger.
Germany. 1811-1990. Critical studies. ■The relationship between the character Max and nature in Johann August Apel's *Der Freischütz. Eine Volkssage*, Friedrich Kind's libretto to Carl Maria von Weber's *Der Freischütz* and Robert Wilson, Tom Waits and William Burroughs' *The Black Rider.*

2857 Weimann, Robert. "A Divided Heritage: Conflicting Appropriations of Shakespeare in (East) Germany." 173-205 in Joughin, John J., ed. *Shakespeare and National Culture.* Manchester: Manchester UP; 1997. 343 pp. Notes. Index. Lang.: Eng.

Germany. 1960-1996. Critical studies. ■On the shifting adaptation and appropriation of Shakespeare in Germany, contradictions in cultural practice.

2858 Whitinger, Raleigh. *Johannes Schlaf and German Naturalist Drama.* Columbia, SC: Camden House; 1997. 193 pp. Index. Biblio. Lang.: Eng.
Germany. 1888-1892. Critical studies. ■Playwright Johannes Schlaf (1862-1941) and his contributions to German naturalism. Focuses on his collaboration with fellow playwright Arno Holz (1861-1929) and their works *Die Familie Selicke (The Selicke Family)* and *Papa Hamlet*, and Schlaf's solo work *Meister Oelze (Master Oelze).*

2859 Wille, Franz. "Die Könige der Sandburgen." (The Kings of Sand Castles.) *THeute.* 1997; Yb: 62-75. Illus.: Photo. B&W. 8. Lang.: Ger.
Germany. Austria. Switzerland. 1997. Critical studies. ■Discusses trends in plays of Peter Handke, Botho Strauss, Einar Schleef, Urs Widmer, Thomas Hürlimann, Elfriede Jelinek, Elfriede Müller, the playwrights of the year chosen by critics of *Theater Heute.*

2860 Wille, Franz. "Tatzenhiebe in die Zeitgeschichte." (Blows With a Paw into Contemporary History.) *THeute.* 1997; 4: 11-15 . Illus.: Photo. B&W. 3. Lang.: Ger.
Germany. 1945-1997. Reviews of performances. ■Postwar German portrayals of customs in West and East Germany in *St. Pauli Saga* by Dagobert Lindlau directed by Wilfried Minks at Deutsches Schauspielhaus and *Drei Alte tanzen Tango (Three Old People Do the Tango)* by Einar Schleef directed by Ernst Binder at Staatstheater Schwerin.

2861 Wille, Franz. "'Ich bin wie ich bin'." ('I Am What I Am'.) *THeute.* 1997; 8: 38-39. Illus.: Photo. B&W. 1. Lang.: Ger.
Germany. 1997. Histories-sources. ■An interview with Albert Ostermaier, a young playwright, about writing and his play *Tatar Titus.*

2862 Wille, Franz. "Schöne neue Fernsehwelt." (Beautiful New World of Television.) *THeute.* 1997; 9: 41-44. Illus.: Photo. B&W. 5. Lang.: Ger.
Germany. 1967-1997. Biographical studies. ■A portrait of the young playwright Daniel Call and his plays *Der Teufel kommt aus Düsseldorf (The Devil Comes from Dusseldorf)*, *Gärten des Grauens (Garden of Horror)* and *Wetterleuchten (Sheet Lightning)*. Discusses whether these plays are organized according to aesthetic of TV.

2863 Wille, Franz. "Reden Sie mal mit einem Penner." (Just Speak to a Tramp.) *THeute.* 1997; 10: 38. Pref. Illus.: Photo. B&W. 1. Lang.: Ger.
Germany. 1997. Histories-sources. ■An interview with playwright Oliver Bukowski about work and his latest play *Nichts Schöneres (Nothing Nicer).*

2864 Wille, Franz. "'Pseudonym?—Da hätte ich Thea Wacker genommen'." ('Pseudonym?—Then I Would Have Chosen Thea Wacker'.) *THeute.* 1997; 11: 35-37. Illus.: Photo. B&W. 4. Lang.: Ger.
Germany. 1990-1997. Biographical studies. ■A portrait of the young playwright Theresia Walser. Describes the first performances of *Kleine Zweifel (Little Doubts)* directed by Dieter Dorn at Münchner Kammerspiele and *Restpaar (Pair of Remains)* at Theater die Rampe (Stuttgart).

2865 Zähringer, Norbert. "Auf Autoren zugehen..." (To Approach Authors...) *TZ.* 1997; 2: 26-29. Illus.: Photo. B&W. 1. Lang.: Ger.
Germany. 1997. Histories-sources. ■An interview with Uwe B. Carstensen, manager of the theatre and media department of the publishing house S. Fischer Verlag, about contemporary drama, its promotion and aesthetic.

2866 Barber, Karin; Collins, John; Ricard, Alain. *West African Popular Theatre.* Bloomington/Indianapolis, IN: Indiana UP; 1997. 285 pp. Notes. Index. Illus.: Photo. 5. Lang.: Eng.
Ghana. Togo. Nigeria. 1995-1997. Histories-specific. ■Analysis of popular theatre in West Africa featuring three popular plays: *Orphan Do Not Glance* by Jaguar Jokers of Ghana, *The African Girl* by Happy Star of Togo, and *The Secret Is Out* by Eda Theatre, a popular Nigerian Yoruba theatre. Texts of these plays are included, preceded by a critical introduction. Includes a chapter analyzing the social and cultural background.

2867 Albini, Umberto. *Riso alla greca. Aristofane o la fabbrica del comico.* (Laughter Greek Style: Aristophanes or the Comedy

DRAMA: —Plays/librettos/scripts

Factory.) Milan: Garzanti; 1997. 141 pp. (Saggi blu.) Lang.: Ita.

Greece. 445-399 B.C. Critical studies. ■The language and scenic structures used by Aristophanes to entertain his audience, described as varied and hard to please.

2868 Bauers, Shelley Ann. *Aeschylus'* Oresteia*: A Vehicle for Questioning the Status of Women.* Fresno, CA: California State Univ; 1997. 43 pp. [M.A. Thesis, Univ. Microfilms Order No. AAC 1386264.] Lang.: Eng.

Greece. 500 B.C. Critical studies. ■The position of women in Aeschylus' *Oresteia.* Argues that Aeschylus' portrayal of strong women in the plays contradicts the traditional view of women in Greek society as weak and powerless.

2869 Bers, Victor. *Speech in Speech: Studies in Incorporated* Oratio Recta *in Attic Drama and Oratory.* Lanham, MD: Rowman and Littlefield; 1997. 249 pp. (Greek Studies: Interdisciplinary Approaches 12.) Index. Biblio. Notes. Pref. Illus.: Graphs. 12. Lang.: Eng.

Greece. 400 B.C.-100 A.D. Critical studies. ■Representing another's speech (quoting a speaker) in Greek Attic drama. Examines the work of Aeschylus, Sophocles, Euripides, and Aristophanes.

2870 Bowie, A.M. "Tragic Filters for History: Euripides' *Supplices* and Sophocles' *Philoctetes.*" 39-62 in Pelling, Christopher, ed. *Greek Tragedy and the Historian.* Oxford: Clarendon; 1997. 268 pp. Notes. Biblio. Index. Lang.: Eng.

Greece. 400-200 B.C. Historical studies. ■The construction of history in Euripides' *Hikétides (The Suppliant Women)* and Sophocles' *Philoctetes.* Argues that Greek history is filtered through religious and literary models which make possible a complex series of audience reactions.

2871 Clausen, Bruce. *Euripidean Rhetoric: A Formal and Literary Study.* Vancouver, BC, Canada: Univ. of British Columbia; 1997. 314 pp. [Ph.D. Dissertation, Univ. Microfilms Order No. AAC NN19566.] Lang.: Eng.

Greece. 500-300 B.C. Critical studies. ■Explores elements of persuasive speech in Euripidean drama, and ways in which the balanced arguments and abstract speculations of Euripidean characters contribute to the construction of plots, themes and characters. Plays are *Phaedra, Hikétides (The Suppliant Women)*, and *Iphigéneia he en Aulíde (Iphigeneia in Aulis).*

2872 Compton-Engle, Gwendolyn Leigh. *Sudden Glory:* Acharnians *and the First Comic Hero.* Ithaca, NY: Cornell Univ; 1997. 130 pp. [Ph.D. Dissertation, Univ. Microfilms Order No. AAC 9738190.] Lang.: Eng.

Greece. 425 B.C. Critical studies. ■Study of Aristophanes' *Acharnês (The Acharnians)*, focusing on its protagonist, Dicaeopolis.

2873 Connolly, Joy. *Vile Eloquence: Performance and Identity in Greco-Roman Rhetoric.* Philadelphia, PA: Univ. of Pennsylvania; 1997. 221 pp. [Ph.D. Dissertation, Univ. Microfilms Order No. AAC 9800854.] Lang.: Eng.

Greece. Roman Empire. 450-350 B.C. Critical studies. ■Explores the multiple identity of rhetoric, said to be an essential element of ancient political activity and a suspect discourse with intrinsically feminine aspects, in the Greek world. Author explores the work of Euripides, Aristophanes and Plato to critique rhetoric as a practice with the power to destabilize natural categories of gender.

2874 Easterling, P.E. "Constructing the Heroic." 21-37 in Pelling, Christopher, ed. *Greek Tragedy and the Historian.* Oxford: Clarendon; 1997. 268 pp. Notes. Biblio. Index. Lang.: Eng.

Greece. 500-400 B.C. Historical studies. ■Argues that the cultural construction of the hero in Greek tragedy reveals how the Greeks felt about their world. Contemporary audiences must learn to read these specific signs.

2875 Erp Taalman Kip, Maria van. *Bokkenzang. Over Griekse Tragedies.* (Goat Song: On Greek Tragedy.) Amsterdam: Athenaeum—Polak & Van Genner; 1997. 156 pp. Pref. Biblio. Index. Illus.: Graphs. Dwg. 3. Lang.: Dut.

Greece. 500-400 B.C. Critical studies. ■The objectives of Greek tragedy, with a close analysis of *Oidípous Týrannos (Oedipus the King)* by Sophocles.

2876 Girard, René. "From Mimetic Desire to the Monstrous Double." 87-111 in Murray, Timothy, ed. *Mimesis, Masochism, and Mime: The Politics of Theatricality in Contemporary French Thought.* Ann Arbor, MI: Univ. of Michigan P; 1997. 328 pp. (Theater: Theory/Text/Performance.) Notes. [1977.] Lang.: Eng.

Greece. 500-400 B.C. Critical studies. ■Greek drama and its focus on violence, ritual, and masks and their place in the interpretation of mimesis.

2877 Halliwell, Stephen. "Between Public and Private: Tragedy and Athenian Experience of Rhetoric." 121-141 in Pelling, Christopher, ed. *Greek Tragedy and the Historian.* Oxford: Clarendon; 1997. 268 pp. Notes. Biblio. Index. Lang.: Eng.

Greece. 500-250 B.C. Historical studies. ■Greek ambivalence about rhetoric as reflected in *Hepta epì Thebas (Seven Against Thebes)* by Aeschylus and *Oidípous Týrannos (Oedipus the King)* by Sophocles.

2878 Ippaso, Katia. "Elettra e Oreste: elaborazioni drammaturgiche e letterarie del tema della sorellanza." (Electra and Orestes: Literary and Dramatic Elaborations of the Theme of Sisterhood.) *BiT.* 1997; 44: 7-38. Notes. Lang.: Ita.

Greece. 458 B.C. Critical studies. ■Aeschylus' characters Electra and Orestes considered as archetypes which are still used by twentieth-century writers and playwrights.

2879 McClure, Laura. "Clytemnestra's Binding Spell (A.G. 958-974)." *ClassJ.* 1997 Dec/Jan.; 92(2): 123-140. Notes. Lang.: Eng.

Greece. 458 B.C. Critical studies. ■Magic and the dangers of unregulated feminine utterances as a fundamental concern in Aeschylus' *Agamemnon.*

2880 Morrell, Kenneth Scott. "The Fabric of Persuasion: Clytaemnestra, Agamemnon, and the Sea of Garments." *ClassJ.* 1997 Dec/Jan.; 92(2): 141-165. Notes. Biblio. Lang.: Eng.

Greece. 458 B.C. Critical studies. ■References to garments in the confrontation between Clytemnestra and Agamemnon in the third episode of Aeschylus' *Agamemnon.*

2881 Nardo, Don, ed. *Readings on Sophocles.* San Diego, CA: Greenhaven; 1997. 176 pp. (The Greenhaven Press Literary Companion to World Authors.) Biblio. Index. Append. Lang.: Eng.

Greece. 496-406 B.C. Histories-specific. ■Previously published essays on Sophocles divided into three sections: Sophocles the dramatist, his play *Oidípous Týrannos (Oedipus the King)*, and production of his plays.

2882 Parker, Janet Elaine. *Approaching Homer and Greek Tragedy Through Translation: Key Words, Elusive Utterance.* London: Open Univ; 1997. [Ph.D. Dissertation, No order number available.] Lang.: Eng.

Greece. 458-400 B.C. Critical studies. ■Pedagogical implications of the use of classical Greek and Homeric translations in which key words are transliterated, leading to more active reading and a greater awareness of cultural difference. Focuses on Homer, Aeschylus' *Oresteia,* Sophocles' *Antigone, Oedipus Rex,* and *Philoctetes,* Euripides' *Medea, Hippolytos,* and the *Bákchai (The Bacchae).*

2883 Pelling, Christopher. "Aeschylus' *Persae* and History." 1-20 in Pelling, Christopher, ed. *Greek Tragedy and the Historian.* Oxford: Clarendon; 1997. 268 pp. Notes. Biblio. Index. Lang.: Eng.

Greece. 500-450 B.C. Historical studies. ■Aeschylus' version of the historical battle of Salamis as reflected in his *Persai (The Persians).* Argues that history is fashioned and elaborated in the tragedy to meet Greek stylistic conventions and audience expectation.

2884 Petruskevich, Joni. *Silence, Suicide, and Sacrifice: Women in Classical Drama.* Edmonton, AB: Univ. of Alberta; 1997. 93 pp. [M.A. Thesis, Univ. Microfilms Order No. AAC MQ22550.] Lang.: Eng.

Greece. 500-200 B.C. Critical studies. ■Feminist study of the depiction of female characters in Greek classical drama and its implications for Aristotelian theory.

2885 Rocco, Christopher. *Tragedy and Enlightenment: Athenian Political Thought and the Dilemmas of Modernity.* Berkeley,

DRAMA: —Plays/librettos/scripts

CA: Univ of California P; 1997. 228 pp. (Classics and Contemporary Thought 4.) Notes. Index. Biblio. Lang.: Eng.
Greece. 500-100 B.C. Critical studies. ■Argues that the plays of Sophocles and Aeschylus reveal the formation of political theory and inform the tradition of Western political thought.

2886 Scafuro, Adele C. *The Forensic Stage: Settling Disputes in Graeco-Roman New Comedy.* Cambridge: Cambridge UP; 1997. 512 pp. Index. Biblio. Notes. Pref. Append. Lang.: Eng.
Greece. Rome. 500 B.C.-200 A.D. Critical studies. ■How legal disputes are settled out of court in Athens, both on and off the comic stage. Examines these issues in the works of Menander, Plautus, and Terence.

2887 Sommerstein, Alan H. "The Theatre Audience, the *Demos*, and the *Suppliants* of Aeschylus." 63-79 in Pelling, Christopher, ed. *Greek Tragedy and the Historian.* Oxford: Clarendon; 1997. 268 pp. Notes. Biblio. Index. Lang.: Eng.
Greece. 500-400 B.C. Historical studies. ■Problems of historical interpretation in Greek tragedy and comedy. Argues that the Greek audience, or *demos*, is the most crucial element in understanding the history, especially in Aeschylus' *Hikétides*.

2888 Sourvinou-Inwood, Christiane. "Tragedy and Religion: Constructs and Readings." 161-186 in Pelling, Christopher, ed. *Greek Tragedy and the Historian.* Oxford: Clarendon; 1997. 268 pp. Notes. Biblio. Index. Lang.: Eng.
Greece. 500-250 B.C. Historical studies. ■Warns contemporary scholars against creating meanings different from those constructed by Greek tragedians and shared by their contemporaries. Argues that understanding the religious assumptions of ancient Greece will lead to new strategies for reading the plays.

2889 Venturi, Ippolita. *Dionisio e la democrazia ateniese.* (Dionysus and Athenian Democracy.) Rome: Bulzoni; 1997. 294 pp. (Chi siamo 24.) Notes. Biblio. Index. Lang.: Ita.
Greece. 600-400 B.C. Critical studies. ■The myth of Dionysus in Greek literature and theatre, with attention to Euripides' *Bákchai (The Bacchae).*

2890 Vidal-Naquet, Pierre. "The Place and Status of Foreigners in Athenian Tragedy." 109-119 in Pelling, Christopher, ed. *Greek Tragedy and the Historian.* Oxford: Clarendon; 1997. 268 pp. Notes. Biblio. Index. Lang.: Eng.
Greece. 400-250 B.C. Historical studies. ■Examines the status of foreigners in the Greek world as reflected in Greek tragedy.

2891 Vrečko, Janez. "Klitajmestra kot subjekt." (Clytemnestra as Subject.) 547-563 in Pogačnik, Jože, ed. *Zbornik ob sedemdesetletnici Franceta Bernika.* Ljubljana: Znanstvenoraziskovalni center SAZU; 1997. 584 pp. Lang.: Slo.
Greece. 525-456 B.C. Critical studies. ■Analysis of Aeschylus' *Oresteia* with attention to the role of Clytemnestra.

2892 Vrečko, Janez. *Atiška tragedija.* (Attic Tragedy.) Maribor: Obzorja; 1997. 386 pp. Pref. Biblio. Lang.: Slo.
Greece. 600-300 B.C. Critical studies. ■A comparative anthropological approach to the study of tragedies by Sophocles, Euripides, and Aeschylus.

2893 White, Richard Lloyd. *Nomos and Physis: Callicles and Euripides' Cyclops.* Halifax, NS: Dalhousie Univ; 1997. 65 pp. [M.A. Thesis, Univ. Microfilms Order No. AAC MQ24943.] Lang.: Eng.
Greece. 450-425 B.C. Critical studies. ■The dialectic of laws and customs (*nomoi*) vs laws of nature (*physis*) in Euripides' *Cyclops* and other Greek writings.

2894 Bíró, Béla; Ikládi, László, photo.; Németh, Juli, photo. "A tragikum tragédiája." (The Tragedy of Tragicality.) *Sz.* 1997; 30(7): 42-48. Illus.: Photo. B&W. 6. Lang.: Hun.
Hungary. Romania. 1960-1970. Critical studies. ■Analysis of the typical features of Hungarian drama in Romania during the seventies.

2895 Csáki, Judit; Koncz, Zsuzsa, photo. "Beszélgetés Spiró Györggyel." (An Interview with György Spiró.) *Sz.* 1997; 30(5): 37-41. Illus.: Photo. B&W. 4. Lang.: Hun.
Hungary. 1980-1997. Histories-sources. ■A conversation with playwright, author, translator, manager, critic György Spiró on his many-sided activity in the field of literature as well as in theatrical life.

2896 Király, Gyula. "Utópia és tragikum. Kísérlet Dosztojevszkij és Madách poétikájának összehasonlítására." (Utopia and the Tragic: An Attempt at the Comparative Analysis of Poetics in Dostoévskij and Madách's Works.) *SzSz.* 1997(32): 75-88. Lang.: Hun.
Hungary. 1860-1900. Critical studies. ■Compares structure, character motivation, and theme of ideas impossible to realize in the novels of Dostojévskij and Imre Madách's play *Az ember tragédiája (The Tragedy of Man).*

2897 Nánay, István. "Magyar dráma exportra." (Hungarian Drama Abroad.) *Sz.* 1997; 30(7): 1. Lang.: Hun.
Hungary. 1990-1997. Critical studies. ■Possibilities for arousing interest abroad for new Hungarian plays, with respect to the Festival of Contemporary Hungarian Drama organized in April 1997 in Budapest.

2898 Striker, Sándor. "Stílus és gondolat." (Style and Thought.) *SzSz.* 1997(32): 67-74. Lang.: Hun.
Hungary. 1842-1862. Critical studies. ■Poet János Arany's revisions to Imre Madách's text of *Az ember tragédiája (The Tragedy of Man).*

2899 Tóth, Éva. "Éva és Ádám." (Eve and Adam.) *SzSz.* 1997(32): 53-58. Lang.: Hun.
Hungary. 1824. Critical studies. ■Analysis of the female character of Imre Madách's *Az ember tragédiája (The Tragedy of Man).*

2900 Varga, Pál, S. *Két világ közt választani. Világkép és többszólamúság Az ember tragédiá-jában.* (Between Two Worlds: World Concept and Polyphony in *The Tragedy of Man* by Imre Madách.) Budapest: Argumentum; 1997. 171 pp. (Irodalomtörténeti füzetek 141.) Notes. Lang.: Hun.
Hungary. 1850-1860. Histories-specific. ■A history of reception and structural analysis of Imre Madách's drama.

2901 Visky, András; Fábián, József, photo.; Máthé, András, photo. "Mítosz vagy zsáner? Tamási Áron és a magyar színházi tradíció." (Myth or a Special Character? Aron Tamási and the Tradition of Hungarian Theatre.) *Sz.* 1997; 30(9): 45-48. Notes. Illus.: Photo. B&W. 2. Lang.: Hun.
Hungary. Romania: Sfintu-Gheorghe. 1897-1997. Critical studies. ■The relation of Áron Tamási, a Hungarian playwright of Transylvanian origin, to the Hungarian drama on the occasion of the coming centennial celebration of his birth at the Tamási Áron Theatre (Sepsiszentgyörgy/Sfintu-Gheorghe).

2902 Loomba, Ania. "Shakespearian Transformations." 109-141 in Joughin, John J., ed. *Shakespeare and National Culture.* Manchester: Manchester UP; 1997. 343 pp. Notes. Index. Illus.: Photo. 11. Lang.: Eng.
India. 1850-1980. Critical studies. ■The interpretation of identity in Shakespeare as seen in the cross-cultural adaptations on the Parsi stages of Bombay. Author argues for the complexity of these cultural exchanges and resists reducing them to a colonialist/anti-colonialist view.

2903 Acheson, James. *Samuel Beckett's Artistic Theory and Practice: Criticism, Drama, and Early Fiction.* London/New York, NY: Macmillan/St. Martin's P; 1997. 254 pp. Pref. Index. Notes. Biblio. Lang.: Eng. ■The theoretical development of playwright Samuel Beckett. Evaluates Beckett's early critical and theoretical essays and argues that these early themes help define his later work, both plays and fiction.
Ireland. France. 1929-1989. Critical studies.

2904 Adams, Ann Marie. "The Sense of an Ending: The Representation of Homosexuality in Brendan Behan's *The Hostage.*" *MD.* 1997 Fall; 40(3): 414-421. Notes. Lang.: Eng.
Ireland. 1958. Critical studies. ■Negative stereotyping of the homosexual characters Rio Rita and Grace in Behan's play, and its association with 'closet drama'.

2905 Becker, Joachim. "Boogie-Woogie der Existenz: Zu Samuel Becketts *Eleutheria.*" (Boogie-Woogie of Existence: On Samuel Beckett's *Eleutheria.*) *FMT.* 1997; 12(1): 37-41. Notes. Lang.: Ger.
Ireland. France. 1947-1986. Critical studies. ■The theme of failure and its cathartic effect in Beckett's first play *Eleutheria* (first published in 1995), and its connection to later plays.

2906 Bjørnerud, Andreas. "Beckett's Model of Masculinity: Male Hysteria in *Not I.*" 27-35 in Oppenheim, Lois, ed.; Buning,

DRAMA: —Plays/librettos/scripts

Marius, ed. *Beckett On and On....* Madison, NJ: Fairleigh Dickinson UP; 1996. 289 pp. Biblio. Lang.: Eng.
Ireland. USA. 1973. Critical studies. ■Investigates femininity in Samuel Beckett's *Not I* and its relation to Beckett's figuring of masculinity.

2907 Bradby, David. "'Note and/or query'." *STP.* 1997 Dec.; 16: 139. Lang.: Eng.
Ireland. France. 1953-1995. Critical studies. ■A parallel is drawn between the concern of Estragon about his boots in *Waiting for Godot* and the opening narration of James Kelman's novel *How Late It Was, How Late.*

2908 Bryden, Mary. "Gender in Beckett's Music Machine." 36-43 in Oppenheim, Lois, ed.; Buning, Marius, ed. *Beckett On and On....* Madison, NJ: Fairleigh Dickinson UP; 1996. 289 pp. Notes. Lang.: Eng.
Ireland. France. USA. 1955-1989. Critical studies. ■The metaphorical function of music and the evolution of gender inscription as binaries in the plays of Samuel Beckett.

2909 Carter, Steven. "Estragon's Ancient Wound: A Note on *Waiting for Godot*." *JBeckS.* 1997; 6(1): 125-133. Notes. Biblio. Lang.: Eng.
Ireland. France. 1953. Critical studies. ■Estragon's leg and foot wounds in *En attendant Godot (Waiting for Godot)*, in the context of Western literary tradition.

2910 Castle, Gregory. "Staging Ethnography: John M. Synge's *Playboy of the Western World* and the Problem of Cultural Translation." *TJ.* 1997 Oct.; 49(3): 265-286. Notes. Lang.: Eng.
Ireland. 1898-1918. Historical studies. ■Argues that the Anglo-Irish Revival's fascination with the 'primitive' culture of the Gaelic west was reflected in Synge's play, and that the title character is both the successor and destroyer of the stereotyped stage Irishman.

2911 Cohn, Ruby. "Now Converging, Now Diverging: Beckett's Metatheatre." 91-107 in Boireau, Nicole, ed. *Drama on Drama: Dimensions of Theatricality on the Contemporary British Stage.* New York, NY: St. Martin's; 1997. 256 pp. Pref. Notes. Index. Biblio. Lang.: Eng.
Ireland. France. 1947-1989. Critical studies. ■Argues that metatheatre as a theatre experience in a continuous present tense gives Beckett an overarching 'performativity of experience'.

2912 Colomba, Sergio, ed. *Le ceneri della commedia. Il teatro di Samuel Beckett.* (The Ashes of Comedy: The Theatre of Samuel Beckett.) Rome: Bulzoni; 1997. 479 pp. (La Fenice dei Teatri 5.) Notes. Biblio. Lang.: Ita.
Ireland. France. 1906-1996. Critical studies. ■Collection of essays on Beckett's plays and productions, including a contribution by Beckett himself.

2913 Falkenstein, Leonard Robert. *Renovating the Kitchen: Irishness, Nationalism, and Form in the Theatre of John B. Keane, Tom Murphy, Hugh Leonard, Brian Friel, and Thomas Kilroy.* Edmonton, AB: Univ. of Alberta; 1997. 162 pp. [Ph.D. Dissertation, Univ. Microfilms Order No. AAC NQ21567.] Lang.: Eng.
Ireland. 1959-1993. Histories-specific. ■Irish drama as a reflection of radical transformations in Irish culture and society. Considers works of John B. Keane, Tom Murphy, Hugh Leonard, Brian Friel, and Thomas Kilroy.

2914 Gleitman, Claire. "'Like Father, Like Son': *Someone Who'll Watch Over Me* and the Geopolitical Family Drama." *Eire.* 1996 Spr; 31(1/2): 78-88. Biblio. Lang.: Eng.
Ireland. 1992. Critical studies. ■Analysis of the three characters in Frank McGuinness' play in terms of Ireland's political situation. Includes a brief comparison with Beckett's *En attendant Godot (Waiting for Godot)*.

2915 Gordon, David J. "Au Contraire: The Question of Beckett's Bilingual Text." 164-177 in Oppenheim, Lois, ed.; Buning, Marius, ed. *Beckett On and On....* Madison, NJ: Fairleigh Dickinson UP; 1996. 289 pp. Notes. Biblio. Lang.: Eng.
Ireland. France. USA. 1958-1989. Critical studies. ■Beckett and the use of two languages, with discussion of his self-translations, variations, and authoritative translations of his works.

2916 Hill, Leslie. "'Fuck Life': *Rockaby*, Sex, and the Body." 19-26 in Oppenheim, Lois, ed.; Buning, Marius, ed. *Beckett On and On....* Madison, NJ: Fairleigh Dickinson UP; 1996. 289 pp. Notes. Lang.: Eng.
Ireland. USA. 1981. Critical studies. ■Gender in Samuel Beckett's *Rockaby* and the play's pairing of unstable binaries.

2917 Knowlson, James. *Damned to Fame: The Life of Samuel Beckett.* London: Bloomsbury; 1996. 872 pp. Biblio. Index. Pref. Notes. Illus.: Photo. Dwg. 61. Lang.: Eng.
Ireland. France. 1906-1989. Biographies. ■Life and work of playwright Samuel Beckett. Focuses on early influences and great epochs of his plays.

2918 Kumar, K. Jeevan. "The Chess Metaphor in Samuel Beckett's *Endgame*." *MD.* 1997 Win; 40(4): 540-552. Notes. Lang.: Eng.
Ireland. France. 1957. Critical studies. ■The chess metaphor in *Fin de partie* as a unifying element, linking the other symbols and integrating movements and decor in the play and, in the process, presenting the existential angst of man through the uncertainty of the last phase of a game of chess.

2919 Kundert-Gibbs, John L. "What Is a Birth Astride a Grave?: *Ohio Impromptu* as Zen Koan." *MD.* 1997 Spr; 15(1): 38-56. Notes. Illus.: Dwg. 1. Lang.: Eng.
Ireland. USA. 1997. Critical studies. ■A Zen interpretation of the structure and text of Beckett's *Ohio Impromptu*.

2920 Lawley, Paul. "Samuel Beckett's Relations." *JBeckS.* 1997; 6(2): 1-61. Notes. Lang.: Eng.
Ireland. France. 1935-1984. Critical studies. ■Examines the relationship of the the narrative act with the figures of father and mother in the work of Samuel Beckett.

2921 Levy, Shimon. "Does Beckett 'Admit the Chaos'?" *JBeckS.* 1997; 6(1): 81-95. Notes. Biblio. Lang.: Eng.
Ireland. France. 1997. Critical studies. ■Elements of religion and chaos throughout Beckett's theatrical canon.

2922 Locatelli, Carla. "'My Life Natural Order More or Less in the Present More or Less': Textual Immanence as the Textual Impossible in Beckett's Works." 127-147 in Oppenheim, Lois, ed.; Buning, Marius, ed. *Beckett On and On....* Madison, NJ: Fairleigh Dickinson UP; 1996. 289 pp. Notes. Biblio. Lang.: Eng.
Ireland. France. USA. 1950-1989. Critical studies. ■Open-endedness in the texts of Beckett. Argues for new habits of reading and strategies for understanding Beckett.

2923 Lydon, Mary. "Stretching the Imagination: Samuel Beckett and the Frontier of Writing." *JMMLA.* 1996 Spr; 30(1/2): 1-15. Notes. Illus.: Photo. B&W. 2. Lang.: Eng.
Ireland. France. 1941-1953. Critical studies. ■Possible explanations for Beckett's creative surge between 1941 and 1953.

2924 Malkin, Jeanette R. "Matters of Memory in *Krapp's Last Tape* and *Not I*." *JDTC.* 1997 Spr; 11(2): 25-39. Lang.: Eng.
Ireland. France. 1958-1972. Critical studies. ■Memory and self in two plays by Beckett.

2925 Martin, Matthew John. *Drama North and South: The Irish Plays of Brian Friel and Tom Murphy.* Ann Arbor, MI: Univ. of Michigan; 1997. 253 pp. [Ph.D. Dissertation, Univ. Microfilms Order No. AAC 9722037.] Lang.: Eng.
Ireland. UK-Ireland. 1961-1995. Critical studies. ■Argues that the plays of Friel and Murphy reflect their cultural backgrounds in different parts of Ireland.

2926 Mehta, Xerxes. "Shapes of Suffering: Image/Narrative/Impromptu in Beckett's *Ohio Impromptu*." *JBeckS.* 1997; 6(1): 97-118. Notes. Lang.: Eng.
Ireland. France. USA. 1984. Critical studies. ■Paralleling a writer's fears with those of his audience in Samuel Beckett's *Ohio Impromptu*.

2927 Merriman, Vic. "Centering the Wanderer: Europe as Active Imaginary in Contemporary Irish Theatre." *IUR.* 1997 Spr/Sum; 27(1): 55-68. Lang.: Eng.
Ireland. 1984-1989. Critical studies. ■Examines the figure of the returning migrant/exile in Dermot Bolger's *The Lament for Arthur Cleary*, and

DRAMA: —Plays/librettos/scripts

argues that the perspective of the Irish-European migrant reveals issues of marginalization and exclusion in Irish society.

2928 Moorjani, Angela. "Mourning, Schopenhauer, and Beckett's Art of Shadows." 83-101 in Oppenheim, Lois, ed.; Buning, Marius, ed. *Beckett On and On....* Madison, NJ: Fairleigh Dickinson UP; 1996. 289 pp. Notes. Biblio. Lang.: Eng.

Ireland. France. USA. 1976-1981. Critical studies. ■Philosophical and psychoanalytic analysis of *Ohio Impromptu, Footfalls,* and *Rockaby* by Samuel Beckett.

2929 Ostmeier, Dorothee. "Dramatizing Silence: Beckett's Shorter Plays." 187-198 in Oppenheim, Lois, ed.; Buning, Marius, ed. *Beckett On and On....* Madison, NJ: Fairleigh Dickinson UP; 1996. 289 pp. Notes. Lang.: Eng.

Ireland. France. USA. 1960-1981. Critical studies. ■Tension between language and silence in the shorter plays of Samuel Beckett such as *Play, Krapp's Last Tape,* and *Rockaby.*

2930 Sandblad, Fia Adler. "Nyskriven dramatik som ställer det vanliga sättet att se och tänka på huvudet." (Newly Written Plays That turn the Ordinary Way of Seeing And Thinking Upside Down.) *Tningen.* 1997; 21(4): 37-39. Illus.: Photo. B&W. Lang.: Swe.

Ireland: Galway. 1997. Historical studies. ■A report from the International Women Playwrights Conference, with references to the playwrights Laura Ruohonen, Ratna Sarumpaet and Alison Lyssas.

2931 Schmitt, Natalie Crohn. "The Landscape Play: W.B. Yeats's *Purgatory.*" *IUR.* 1997 Aut/Win; 27(2): 262-275. Lang.: Eng.

Ireland. 1938. Critical studies. ■Argues that Yeats's *Purgatory* was inspired by specific big houses, in particular the ruined Foxborough House, ancestral home of Lady Gregory. Underlines the importance of landscape infused with the supernatural in Yeats's drama.

2932 Schmitt, Natalie Crohn. "'Haunted by Places': Landscape in Three Plays by W.B. Yeats." *CompD.* 1997 Fall; 31(3): 337-366 . Notes. Illus.: Photo. B&W. 14. Lang.: Eng.

Ireland. 1916-1919. Critical studies. ■The influence of landscape and mystical places in Yeats's *At the Hawk's Well, The Cat and the Moon,* and *The Dreaming of the Bones.*

2933 Schrank, Bernice, ed.; Demastes, William W., ed. *Irish Playwrights, 1880-1995: A Research and Production Sourcebook.* Westport, CT/London: Greenwood; 1997. 454 pp. Index. Pref. Biblio. Lang.: Eng.

Ireland. 1880-1995. Bibliographical studies. ■Performance history of Irish dramatists. Includes biographical overview, major plays, lesser plays, assessment of playwright's career, archival sources and bibliographies for each playwright.

2934 Thompson, Kirill O. "Beckett's Dramatic Vision and Classical Taoism." 212-225 in Oppenheim, Lois, ed.; Buning, Marius, ed. *Beckett On and On....* Madison, NJ: Fairleigh Dickinson UP; 1996. 289 pp. Notes. Lang.: Eng.

Ireland. France. 1953. Critical studies. ■Parallels between Beckett's dramatic vision and classical Taoism as reflected in *En attendant Godot (Waiting for Godot).*

2935 Upton, Carole-Anne. "Visions of the Sightless in Friel's *Molly Sweeney* and Synge's *The Well of the Saints.*" *MD.* 1997 Fall; 40(3): 347-358. Notes. Lang.: Eng.

Ireland. UK-Ireland. 1997. Critical studies. ■Comparison of Friel and Synge's plays: similarities in plot, geography, themes of blindness and vision.

2936 van Slooten, Johanneke. "Beckett's Irish Rhythm Embodied in His Polyphony." 44-60 in Oppenheim, Lois, ed.; Buning, Marius, ed. *Beckett On and On....* Madison, NJ: Fairleigh Dickinson UP; 1996. 289 pp. Lang.: Eng.

Ireland. France. 1955-1989. Critical studies. ■The multiplicity of voices and the presence of Irish rhythms in the plays of Samuel Beckett.

2937 Watt, Stephen; Williams, Julia. "Representing a 'Great Distress': Melodrama, Gender, and the Irish Famine." 245-266 in Hays, Michael, ed.; Nikolopoulou, Anastasia, ed. *Melodrama: The Cultural Emergence of a Genre.* New York, NY: St. Martin's P; 1996. 288 pp. Notes. Illus.: Dwg. 2. Lang.: Eng.

Ireland. 1879-1886. Historical studies. ■Examines three melodramas based on the Irish famine: Hubert O'Grady's *The Eviction, Emigration,* and *The Famine,* and the melodramatic heroine that drives the plots of all three.

2938 Yi, Hyangsoon. *The Traveler in Modern Irish Drama.* University Park, PA: Pennsylvania State Univ; 1997. 374 pp. [Ph.D. Dissertation, Univ. Microfilms Order No. AAC 9732406.] Lang.: Eng.

Ireland. 1910-1930. Critical studies. ■The character of the traveler, drawn from folk culture and history, in the works of Irish Renaissance playwrights P.T. McGinley, Douglas Hyde, Lady Gregory, John Millington Synge, Seamus O'Kelly, and William Butler Yeats.

2939 Zeifman, Hersh. "The Syntax of Closure: Beckett's Late Drama." 240-254 in Oppenheim, Lois, ed.; Buning, Marius, ed. *Beckett On and On....* Madison, NJ: Fairleigh Dickinson UP; 1996. 289 pp. Notes. Lang.: Eng.

Ireland. USA. 1980-1990. Critical studies. ■The development of closure in Samuel Beckett's plays of his final decade compared with the denial of closure in his earlier work.

2940 *Angelo Beolco detto Ruzante.* (Angelo Beolco, Known as Ruzante.) Padua: Pepergraf; 1997. 348 pp. Lang.: Ita.

Italy. 1500-1542. Critical studies. ■Proceedings of a conference on playwright Angelo Beolco.

2941 Alonge, Roberto. "La cifra ambigua (e l'ambiguità delle cifre) del *Sogno d'un tramonto d'autunno.*" (The Ambiguous Cipher, and the Ambiguity of Ciphers, in *Dream of an Autumn Sunset.*) *IlCast.* 1997; 10(28): 55-71. Notes. Lang.: Ita.

Italy. 1898. Critical studies. ■Analysis of *Sogno di un tramonto d'autunno (Dream of an Autumn Sunset)* by Gabriele D'Annunzio, with emphasis on the female characters, described as the articulations of a female ego struggling to find itself.

2942 Artioli, Umberto. "Il primo *Sogno* dannunziano, o della circolarità impossibile." (D'Annunzio's First *Dream,* or the Impossible Circle.) *IlCast.* 1997; 10(28): 15-27. Lang.: Ita.

Italy. 1895-1900. Critical studies. ■Analysis of *Sogno d'un mattino di primavera (A Spring Morning's Dream)* by Gabriele D'Annunzio.

2943 Barbina, Alfredo. "Le 'incompiute' di Pirandello." (Pirandello's Unfinished.) *Ariel.* 1997; 12(1): 101-112. Notes. Lang.: Ita.

Italy. 1886-1895. Bibliographical studies. ■Unfinished plays, rough copies, ideas, titles, and plans for plays of Luigi Pirandello. Continued in *Ariel* 12:2 (1997), 165-175 and 12:3 (1997), 83-89.

2944 Bartolazzi, Marita. "Pirandello e la caricatura." (Pirandello and Caricature.) *Ariel.* 1997; 12(1): 113-121. Notes. Lang.: Ita.

Italy. 1910-1936. Histories-sources. ■A selection of caricatures of Luigi Pirandello originally published in *Almanacco letterario* and *Il becco giallo.*

2945 Bassi, Adriano. *Caro maestro.* (Dear Maestro.) Genoa: De Ferrari; 1997. 205 pp. Biblio. Lang.: Ita.

Italy. 1904-1939. Histories-sources. ■Collection of letters from playwright Gabriele D'Annunzio to the famous musicians of his time.

2946 Beniscelli, Alberto, ed. *Naturale e artificiale in scena nel secondo Settecento.* (The Natural and the Artificial on the Late Eighteenth-Century Stage.) Rome: Bulzoni; 1997. 287 pp. (La Fenice dei Teatri 6.) Lang.: Ita.

Italy. 1750-1800. Critical studies. ■Proceedings of a meeting held in Venice, 1996, dealing with the complex relationship between nature and artifice in Italian plays of the second half of the eighteenth century.

2947 Castellucci, Romeo. "The *Oresteia* through the Looking-Glass." *Thsch.* 1997; 11: 191-199. Illus.: Photo. B&W. 2. Lang.: Ger, Fre, Dut, Eng.

Italy: Cesena. 1995. Histories-sources. ■Director explains his radical interpretation of the *Oresteia* of Aeschylus for Societas Raffaello Sanzio.

2948 Cesarotti, Melchiorre; Ranzini, Paola, ed. *Drammaturgia universale antica e moderna.* (Universal Dramaturgy, Ancient and Modern.) Rome: Bulzoni; 1997. 305 pp. (Le

CLASSED ENTRIES

DRAMA: —Plays/librettos/scripts

fonti dello spettacolo teatrale 3.) Pref. Notes. Biblio. Index. Lang.: Ita.

Italy. 1795-1800. Bibliographical studies. ■Previously unpublished list of titles compiled by Cesarotti in the late eighteenth century.

2949 Cotticelli, Francesco. "Raffaele Viviani: suggestioni e proposte di lettura." (Raffaele Viviani: Suggestions and Proposed Readings.) *Ariel.* 1997; 12(2): 113-128. Notes. Lang.: Ita.

Italy: Naples. 1888-1950. Critical studies. ■Analysis of dramatic works of Neapolitan actor-playwright Raffaele Viviani.

2950 De Matteis, Tiberia. "*Quaderno proibito* di Alba De Céspedes: un diario in scena." (*Forbidden Notebook* by Alba De Céspedes: A Diary on Stage.) *Ariel.* 1997; 12(1): 93-100. Notes. Lang.: Ita.

Italy. 1952. Critical studies. ■Analysis of De Céspedes' stage adaptation of her own novel.

2951 De Matteis, Tiberia. "Eduardo e il sogno del lotto in *Non ti pago.*" (Eduardo and the Dream of the Lottery in *I Don't Pay You.*) *Ariel.* 1997; 12(3): 63-71. Notes. Lang.: Ita.

Italy. 1940-1997. Critical studies. ■Analysis of *Non ti pago (I Don't Pay You)* by Eduardo De Filippo.

2952 De Troja, Elisabetta. *Goldoni, la scrittura, le forme.* (Goldoni, Writing, and Form.) Rome: Bulzoni; 1997. 175 pp. (Biblioteca di cultura 525.) Pref. Notes. Index. Lang.: Ita.

Italy: France. 1761-1793. Critical studies. ■The influence of French culture on the plays of Carlo Goldoni.

2953 Defendi, Adrienne Stefania. *Spectacles of Medusa: Exploring a Medusean Poetics in the Works of D'Annunzio, Graf, and Marinetti.* New Haven, CT: Yale Univ; 1997. 211 pp. Biblio. Notes. [Ph.D. Dissertation, Univ. Microfilms Order No. AAC 9732501.] Lang.: Ita.

Italy. 1909-1935. Critical studies. ■Analyzes the Medusa myth and its concurrent theme of 'fragmentation' in d'Annunzio's *La Gioconda, La città morta,* and *La Gloria* and in his poetry, in the work of the leading Futurist, Filippo Tommaso Marinetti, and in poet Arturo Graf's *Medusa.*

2954 Doni, Carla. *Il mito greco nelle tragedie di Ugo Foscolo: Tieste e Aiace.* (Greek Mythology in the Tragedies of Ugo Foscolo: Thyestes and Ajax.) Rome: Bulzoni; 1997. 119 pp. (Biblioteca di cultura 531.) Notes. Index. Lang.: Ita.

Italy. 1795-1811. Critical studies. ■Analysis of the poet Foscolo's two tragedies, *Tieste* and *Aiace.*

2955 Fratta, Arturo. *Salvatore Di Giacomo. La vita, la poesia, le canzoni, la prosa.* (Salvatore Di Giacomo: His Life, Poetry, Songs, Prose.) Rome: Newton & Compton; 1997. 60 pp. (Tascabili Economici Newton: Napoli Tascabile 62.) Biblio. Illus.: Dwg. Lang.: Ita.

Italy: Naples. 1860-1934. Biographies. ■Brief biography of poet, writer, and playwright Salvatore Di Giacomo.

2956 Gallucci, Mary Margaret. *The Erotics of Witchcraft and the Politics of Desire in Renaissance Florence.* Storrs, CT: Univ. of Connecticut; 1997. 271 pp. Notes. Biblio. [Ph.D. Dissertation, Univ. Microfilms Order No. AAC 9810509.] Lang.: Eng.

Italy: Florence. 1500-1600. Historical studies. ■The complex intersections of sexuality and power in sixteenth- century Florence as represented in the comic characters of witches in *La Spiritata* and *La Strega,* both by Antonfrancesco Grazzini. Also explores materials of a non-literary nature: handbooks, trial transcripts, medical treatises, legal codes, and marriage manuals.

2957 Giordano Gramegna, Anna. "La leggenda di Didone: amore e tragedia." (The Legend of Dido: Love and Tragedy.) *Ariel.* 1997 ; 12(1): 63-77. Notes. Lang.: Ita.

Italy. Spain. 1542-1616. Critical studies. ■The figure of Dido in works of the Italian Renaissance and Spanish Golden Age, including *Didone* by Giovanni Battista Giraldi Cinthio (1542), *Didone* by Ludovico Dolce (1547), *Elisa Dido* by Cristóbal de Virués (1581) and *Dido y Eneas* by Guillén de Castro.

2958 Iermano, Toni. "Il poeta e il pittore: lettere di Salvatore Di Giacomo a Luca Postiglione." (The Poet and the Painter: Letters from Salvatore Di Giacomo to Luca Postiglione.) *Ariel.* 1997; 12(3): 91-140. Illus.: Photo. Dwg. B&W. 18. Lang.: Ita.

Italy. 1908-1927. Histories-sources. ■Collection of thirty-five letters from Di Giacomo, a poet and playwright, to the painter Postiglione, who created stage designs for Di Giacomo's works.

2959 Lopez, Guido. "Federico De Roberto e Sabatino Lopez cent'anni fa." (Federico De Roberto and Sabatino Lopez One Hundred Years Ago.) *Belfagor.* 1997; 111(309): 322-340. Lang.: Ita.

Italy: Catania. 1896-1897. Biographical studies. ■The friendship between playwright Sabatino Lopez and writer Federico De Roberto.

2960 Marko, Susanne. "Med en gycklare skämtar man inte ostraffat." (You Don't Make Fun of a Jester With Impunity.) *Entré.* 1997; 24(7): 2-13. Illus.: Photo. B&W. Lang.: Swe.

Italy. 1952-1972. Biographical studies. ■A presentation of Dario Fo's background and earlier career.

2961 Martinuzzi, Paola. *Le Martyre de Saint Sebastien* fra mito e archetipo (Per superare una nozione acquisita di ambiguità del teatro di D'Annunzio rituale)." (*The Martyrdom of Saint Sebastian* from Myth to Archetype: Overcoming the Received Notion of the Ambiguity of D'Annunzio's Ritual Theatre.) *Ariel.* 1997; 12(1): 79-91. Notes. Lang.: Ita.

Italy. 1911. Critical studies. ■Analysis of *Le Martyre de Saint Sébastien (The Martyrdom of Saint Sebastian)* by Gabriele D'Annunzio.

2962 Mazzaro, Jerome. "Memory and Madness in Pirandello's *Enrico IV.*" CompD. 1992 Spr; 26(1): 34-57. Notes. Lang.: Eng.

Italy. 1922. Critical studies. ■Function of amnesia and schizophrenia in Pirandello's play.

2963 Nesi, Lorenzo. "Den italienska teatern går mot sin död." (The Italian Theatre Is Heading For Death.) *Tningen.* 1997; 21(1): 7-9. Illus.: Photo. B&W. Lang.: Swe.

Italy. 1990. Histories-sources. ■An interview with the playwright Luigi Lunari, with reference to his comedy *Tre sull'altalena (Three on the Swing).*

2964 Parussa, Sergio. *L'Eros Onnipotente: Omoerotismo, Letteratura e Impegno nell'Opera di Pier Paolo Pasolini e Jean Genet.* (Eros Omnipotent: Homoeroticism, Literature, and Commitment in the Works of Pier Paolo Pasolini and Jean Genet.) Providence, RI: Brown Univ; 1997. 201 pp. [Ph.D. Dissertation, Univ. Microfilms Order No. AAC 9738608.] Lang.: Ita.

Italy. 1942-1950. Critical studies. ■The work of writer and filmmaker Pier Paolo Pasolini and playwright Jean Genet , both of whom are said to have challenged the boundaries of bourgeois society.

2965 Pirandello, Luigi; Tozzi, Silvia, ed. "'Ho qui nello studio il ritratto di lui, che mi guarda...'." (I Have Here in My Study His Portrait, Looking at Me.) *Ariel.* 1997; 12(2): 155-175. Tables. Lang.: Ita.

Italy. 1917-1920. Histories-sources. ■A letter from Pirandello to the widow of writer Federigo Tozzi.

2966 Pirandello, Luigi; Andreoli, Annamaria, ed. *Taccuino segreto.* (The Secret Notebook.) Milan: Mondadori; 1997. 215 pp. Lang.: Ita.

Italy. 1867-1936. Histories-sources. ■First publication of a notebook of Luigi Pirandello.

2967 Santoli, Carlo. *Gabriele D'Annunzio. La musica i musicisti.* (Gabriele D'Annunzio: Music and Musicians.) Rome: Bulzoni; 1997. 645 pp. (Biblioteca di cultura 527.) Pref. Biblio. Index. Tables. Illus.: Photo. B&W. 126. Lang.: Ita.

Italy. 1874-1938. Critical studies. ■Comprehensive study of the relationship between playwright Gabriele D'Annunzio, his work, and music and musicians.

2968 Sinisi, Silvana. "I colori del sogno." (The Colors of the Dream.) *IlCast.* 1997; 10(28): 43-53. Notes. Lang.: Ita.

Italy. 1898. Critical studies. ■Analysis of *Sogno di un tramonto d'autunno (Dream of an Autumn Sunset)* by Gabriele D'Annunzio, with emphasis on the two female characters Pantheà and Gradeniga as complementary aspects of an eternal feminine archetype.

DRAMA: —Plays/librettos/scripts

2969 Tacchini, Cristina. "Francesco Saverio Salfi, un teorico 'd'avanguardia' nel panorama teatrale italiano sette-ottocentesco." (Francesco Saverio Salfi, an 'Avant-Garde' Theoretician in the Panorama of Eighteenth and Nineteenth-Century Italian Theatre.) *Ariel.* 1997; 12(3): 41-61. Notes. Lang.: Ita.
Italy. 1759-1832. Critical studies. ■Essay on Salfi, a playwright, theoretician, and leading Italian exponent of Jacobin theatre, committed to the ideals of the French Revolution.

2970 Taffon, Giorgio. *Lo scrivano, gli scarrozzanti, i templi. Giovanni Testori e il teatro.* (The Copyist, the Carriage Rides, the Temples: Giovanni Testori and the Theatre.) Rome: Bulzoni; 1997. 233 pp. (Biblioteca di cultura 547.) Index. Lang.: Ita.
Italy. 1923-1993. Critical studies. ■The works of playwright Giovanni Testori and his relationship with the theatre and the stage.

2971 Trebbi, Fernando. "Mascheramenti e giochi metamorfici sulla scena del Sogno di un mattino di primavera." (Masking and Metamorphic Games on the Stage of *A Spring Morning's Dream.*) *IlCast.* 1997; 10(28): 29-41. Lang.: Ita.
Italy. 1898. Critical studies. ■Vision, transparency, and representation in *Sogno d'un mattino di primavera (A Spring Morning's Dream)* by Gabriele D'Annunzio.

2972 Venturini, Valentina. "Schegge di Davila." (Splinters of Davila.) *Ariel.* 1997; 12(2): 59-72. Notes. Lang.: Ita.
Italy. 1997. Critical studies. ■Analysis of *Davila Roa* by Alessandro Baricco, commissioned by Luca Ronconi, who subsequently directed it.

2973 Bixler, Jacqueline E. *Convention and Transgression: The Theatre of Emilio Carballido.* London: Associated Univ Presses; 1997. 256 pp. Index. Biblio. Notes. Pref. Gloss. Lang.: Eng.
Mexico. 1925-1996. Critical studies. ■Critical evaluation of the artistic career of Mexican playwright Emilio Carballido, according to stylistic patterns of his work and forms.

2974 Abrahamse, Wouter. *Het Toneel van Theodore Rodenburgh.* (The Theatre of Theodore Rodenburgh.) Amsterdam: AD&L; 1997. 218 pp. Pref. Notes. Biblio. Index. Illus.: Graphs. Diagram. Dwg. 15. Lang.: Dut.
Netherlands. 1574-1644. Biographies. ■Doctoral thesis on the life and work of diplomat and playwright Theodore Rodenburgh.

2975 Engen, Max van. "Hollandse Nieuwe, of Hoe de Multiculturele Praktijk de Beleidsmakers Achter zich Laat." (Dutch Fresh, or How Multicultural Practice Leaves Policymakers Behind.) *Theatermaker.* 1997; 1(9/10): 25-29. Illus.: Photo. B&W. 11. Lang.: Dut.
Netherlands. 1990-1997. Critical studies. ■Reaction to the recent publication of works by immigrant playwrights: argues that there is a gap between practice and official governmental policy toward immigrants.

2976 Gompes, Loes. "Alex van Warmerdam: Wat Heb ik aan een Gelukkig Gezin?" (Alex van Warmerdam: Who Cares about a Happy Family?) *Theatermaker.* 1997; 1(5/6): 62-66. Illus.: Photo. B&W. 3. Lang.: Dut.
Netherlands. 1980-1997. Critical studies. ■Survey of the work of playwright Alex van Warmerdam.

2977 Otten, Willem-Jan. "De Droom van Echt. Aantekeningen in Afwachting van een Première." (The Dream of Reality: Notes in Anticipation of a Premiere.) *Theatermaker.* 1997; 1(1): 42-47. Illus.: Photo. B&W. 6. Lang.: Dut.
Netherlands. 1996-1997. Histories-sources. ■Playwright describes his attitude toward the theatre on the occasion of the rehearsal of his play *Een Sneeuw (Snow).*

2978 Ozick, Cynthia. "Who Owns Anne Frank?" *NewY.* 1997 6 Oct.: 76-87. Illus.: Photo. B&W. 3. Lang.: Eng.
Netherlands. USA. 1945-1997. Historical studies. ■The history of adaptations of the diary of Anne Frank, beginning with the expurgated edition published by her father, with attention to the stage version by Frances Goodrich and Albert Hackett and a production directed by Garson Kanin (1955) and allusions to an upcoming revival.

2979 Stachurski, Christina. "Scenes of the Crime: Returning to the Past." *MD.* 1997 Spr; 15(1): 111-122. Notes. Illus.: Photo. B&W. 1. Lang.: Eng.
New Zealand. 1954-1996. Historical studies. ■Artistic works inspired by true-life murder committed by two teenage girls, with special focus on play *Daughters of Heaven* by Michelanne Forster. Premiere production at Court Theatre, interpretation of relationships, gender roles.

2980 Byam, Dale. "Art, Exile and Resistance." *AmTh.* 1997 Jan.; 14(1): 26-29. Illus.: Photo. B&W. 5. Lang.: Eng.
Nigeria. 1986-1996. Histories-sources. ■Interview with playwright and activist Wole Soyinka on his process, political views, Yoruba culture, his current state of exile, and his plays *The Beatification of Area Boy* and *Open Sore of a Continent.*

2981 Ojewuyi, Olesegun; Garrett, Shawn-Marie. "A World of Amusement and Pity." *ThM.* 1997; 28(1): 61-68. Illus.: Photo. B&W. 1. Lang.: Eng.
Nigeria. 1997. Histories-sources. ■Interview with the playwright Wole Soyinka regarding his world view and his body of work.

2982 Ojewuyi, Olesegun. "Wole Soyinka: The Hunter, The Hunt." *ThM.* 1997; 28(1): 58-60. Illus.: Photo. B&W. 1. Lang.: Eng.
Nigeria. 1997. Critical studies. ■Introduction to interview with the Nigerian playwright.

2983 Lingard, Lorelei. "The Daughter's Double Bind: The Single-Parent Family as Cultural Analogue in Two Turn-of-the-Century Dramas." *MD.* 1997 Spr; 15(1): 123-138. Notes. Lang.: Eng.
Norway. Sweden. 1888-1890. Critical studies. ■Compares diverse social commentaries enacted through a dramatic focus on a type of single-parent family in Ibsen's *Hedda Gabler* and Strindberg's *Fröken Julie (Miss Julie).* Absence of mother, role of father, fate of daughters.

2984 Godin, Diane. "Witold Gombrowicz: grand artificier du monde." (Witold Gombrowicz: Great Pyrotechnist of the World.) *JCT.* 1997; 85: 158-161. Notes. Illus.: Photo. B&W. 2. Lang.: Fre.
Poland. 1935-1969. Biographical studies. ■Introduces Polish playwright Witold Gombrowicz through extracts of his plays and personal journal.

2985 Majcherek, Janusz; Weksler, Jacek; Semil, Małgorzata; Pászt, Patrícia, transl. "Párbeszéd a lengyel színházzal." (A Dialog with the Polish Theatre.) *Sz.* 1997; 30(11): 25-26. Illus.: Photo. B&W. 4. Lang.: Hun.
Poland. Hungary. 1990-1997. Critical studies. ■Budapest Institute for Polish Culture's series of events related to contemporary Polish playwriting. Critic Janusz Majcherek, theatre manager Jacek Weksler and literary manager Małgorzata Semil introduce the recent developments in Polish drama.

2986 Pászt, Patrícia. "A gyermekarcú halál. Grzegorz Nawrocki bulvárdrámái." (*Death with a Young Face*: Grzegorz Nawrocki's Plays.) *Sz.* 1997; 30(11): 27-29. Illus.: Photo. B&W. 2. Lang.: Hun.
Poland. 1996-1997. Critical studies. ■Analysis of a performance by Teatr Współczesny of Nawrocki's three one-act plays concerned with youth criminality.

2987 Zwolińska, Emilia. *Molier po polsku. Casus Tartuffe'a.* (Molière in Polish: The Case of Tartuffe.) Poznan: Abedik; 1997. 228 pp. Pref. Notes. Biblio. Lang.: Pol.
Poland. 1664-1973. Critical studies. ■Analysis of Polish translations of plays by Molière.

2988 Damon, Cynthia. *The Mask of the Parasite: A Pathology of Roman Patronage.* Ann Arbor, MI: Univ. of Michigan P; 1997. 270 pp. Notes. Index. Biblio. Illus.: Photo. 3. Lang.: Eng.
Roman Empire. 200-500. Critical studies. ■Examines the Greco-Roman parasite character in comedy and in culture. Examines extant plays of the late Greek and Roman periods, as well as the use of the parasite in other literary works and in cultural relationships.

2989 Chan, May. *The Political Phases of Literary Amicitia in Rome from the Third Century BC to the Second Century AD.* Kingston, ON: Queen's Univ; 1997. 160 pp. [M.A. Thesis, Univ. Microfilms Order No. AAC MQ22281.] Lang.: Eng.

CLASSED ENTRIES

DRAMA: —Plays/librettos/scripts

Rome. 400 B.C.-200 A.D. Critical studies. ■Early origins of literary patronage, and the role of drama in the development of Latin literature.

2990   Bloom, Harold. "'Simpler, More Truthful, More Himself'." *ThM*. 1993; 23(1): 82-86. Lang.: Eng.
Russia. 1993. Critical studies. ■Attempts to discern elements of Čechov's personality from his plays, including *Diadia Vania (Uncle Vanya)*, *Višnĕvyj sad (The Cherry Orchard)*, *Čajka (The Seagull)* and *Tri sestry (Three Sisters)*.

2991   Bulgakov, Michajl A.; Losev, V., ed. *Dnevnik. Pis'ma 1914-1940.* (Diary: Letters 1914-1940.) Moscow: Sovremennik pisatel'; 1997. 640 pp. Lang.: Rus.
Russia. 1914-1940. Histories-sources. ■Journals and letters of the playwright.

2992   Cousin, Geraldine. "Revisiting the Prozorovs." *MD*. 1997 Fall; 40(3): 325-336. Notes. Lang.: Eng.
Russia. UK-England. 1901-1997. Critical studies. ■Influence of Čechov's *Tri sestry (Three Sisters)* on Andrzej Sadowski's *The Sisters* produced at Scarlet Theatre, directed by Katarzyna Deszcz, and Timberlake Wertenbaker's *The Break of Day* produced by Out of Joint in tandem with *Three Sisters*, both directed by Max Stafford-Clark. Comparison of characters and themes.

2993   Fjellner Patlakh, Irina. "Finns det några levande dramatiker?" (Are There Any Living Playwrights?)*Tningen*. 1997; 21 (1): 24-32. Illus.: Photo. B&W. Lang.: Swe.
Russia: Moscow. 1960-1997. Historical studies. ■A survey of the new young playwrights of Russia, who are opposing both Chekhovian realism and the new wave of the 1980s, with reference to Michajl Ugarov, Xenia Dragunskaja, Marija Arbarovas, Ivan Saveljév, Olga Michajlova and Oleg Bogaev.

2994   Gel'man, Aleksand'r. "Desjat' let—sčast'ja njet." (Ten Years Pass—No Happiness.) *TeatZ*. 1997; 8: 9-11. Lang.: Rus.
Russia. 1996. Histories-sources. ■A playwright's account of the meeting of dramatists in Šelkogo Kostromskoj, the birthplace of Ostrovskij.

2995   Gul'čenko, V. "'Treplev bolit'." (Treplev Hurts.) *TeatZ*. 1997; 2: 13-17. Lang.: Rus.
Russia. 1896. Critical studies. ■Reflections on the character of Treplev in *Čajka (The Seagull)* by Anton Čechov.

2996   Lejderman, N.L. *Dramaturgija Nikolaja Koljady: kritičeskij očerk.* (The Dramaturgy of Nikolaj Koljada: Critical Essay.) Kamensk-Uralskij: Kalan; 1997. 160 pp. Lang.: Rus.
Russia. 1980-1997. Critical studies. ■Analysis of plays by Nikolaj Koljada.

2997   Nemčenko, Larisa. "'Nado vse eto prozit'—inace ničego ne polučitsja'." (We Have to Live Through Everything, Otherwise Nothing Will Happen.) *PTZ*. 1997; 13: 36-41. Lang.: Rus.
Russia: St. Petersburg. 1990-1997. Histories-sources. ■Interview with playwright Nikolaj Koljada.

2998   O'Malley, Lurana Donnels. "Masks of the Empress: Polyphony of Personae in Catherine the Great's *Oh, These Times!*." *CompD*. 1997 Spr; 31(1): 65-85. Notes. Lang.: Eng.
Russia: St. Petersburg. 1772. Critical studies. ■How the characters in Catherine the Great's first play *O vremja! (Oh, These Times!)* were disguises for her personal views and ideas, much in keeping with eighteenth-century playwriting conceits.

2999   Peterdi Nagy, László. "Mikor született a *Sirály*? Levél Moszkvából." (On the Genesis of Čechov's *The Seagull*: A Letter from Moscow.) *Sz*. 1997; 30(1): 11-16. Illus.: Photo. B&W. 4. Lang.: Hun.
Russia. 1892-1996. Critical studies. ■The genesis and stage career of Čichov's *Čajka*.

3000   Šach-Azizova, T. "Večnoe dvizenie." (Constant Movement.) *TeatZ*. 1997; 3: 2-5. Lang.: Rus.
Russia. 1896-1997. Historical studies. ■Reflections of a theatre critic on the fate of Čechov's *Čajka (The Seagull)*.

3001   Sokolov, B. *Tri žizni Michajla Bulgakova.* (The Three Lives of Michajl Bulgakov.) Moscow: Ellis; 1997. 432 pp. Lang.: Rus.

Russia. 1891-1940. Biographies. ■The life and work of dramatist Michajl Bulgakov.

3002   Spiró, György; Keleti, Éva, photo. "Csehov szerepei." (The Characters of Čechov's Plays.) *Sz*. 1997; 30 (1): 16-17. Illus.: Photo. B&W. 1. Lang.: Hun.
Russia. 1880-1900. Critical studies. ■Essay on some specific features of the Čechovian figures by playwright György Spiró.

3003   Stinchcomb, Janice Marion. *Aleksandr Ostrovskij: Domestic Drama and National Identity.* Austin, TX: Univ.of Texas; 1997. 257 pp. [Ph.D. Dissertation, Univ. Microfilms Order No. AAC 9803036.] Lang.: Eng.
Russia. 1823-1886. Historical studies. ■Playwright Aleksand'r Ostrovskij's efforts to build a national theatre. Uses social and cultural history and theories of gender and culture to argue for Ostrovskij's contribution to modern Russian theatre.

3004   Zorin, Leonid. *Avanscena: Memuarnyj roman.* (Proscenium: A Memoir in Novel Form.) Moscow: Slovo; 1997. 526 pp. Lang.: Rus.
Russia. 1934-1994. Histories-sources. ■Dramatist's memoirs recalling his meetings with people in the arts and culture.

3005   Ambrož, Darinka; Poznanović, Mojca. *Antigona in Hamlet za maturante.* (Antigone and Hamlet for the Matura Exam.) Ljubljana: Rokus; 1997. 145 pp. Pref. Illus.: Photo. B&W. Lang.: Slo.
Slovenia. 500 B.C.-1960 A.D. Instructional materials. ■Analysis of Sophocles *Antigone*, Dominik Smole's *Antigona*, and Shakespeare's *Hamlet*.

3006   Faganel, Jože. "Verzni prestop v drami Voranc Daneta Zajca." (Verse Enjambment in Dane Zajc's *Voranc*.) 97-106 in Pogačnik, Jože, ed. *Zbornik ob sedemdesetletnici Franceta Bernika.* Ljubljana: Znanstvenoraziskovalni center SAZU; 1997. 584 pp. Lang.: Slo.
Slovenia. 1960. Critical studies. ■Analysis of enjambment in Zajc's verse play *Voranc*.

3007   Javoršek, Jan Jona. "Elementi Maeterlinckove dramske tehnike v Cankarjevi dramatiki." (Elements of Maeterlink's Dramatic Techniques in the Plays of Cankar.) *Primk*. 1997; 1: 63-84. Lang.: Slo.
Slovenia. Critical studies. ■Analysis of Ivan Cankar's *Jakob Ruda* and *Lepa Vida* to determine the nature and extent of Maeterlinck's influence.

3008   Kermauner, Taras. *Blodnja. Knj. 1.* (The Maze: Book 1.) Ljubljana: SGFM; 1997. 282 pp. Lang.: Slo.
Slovenia. 1900-1996. Critical studies. ■Analysis of *Gabrijel in Mihael (Gabriel and Michael)* by Jože Snoj and *Tako je umrl Zaratuštra (Thus Died Zarathustra)* by Ivo Svetina.

3009   Kermauner, Taras. *Dramatika slovenske politične emigracije. 1: Sveta vojna.* (The Drama of Slovene Political Emigration, 1: The Holy War.) Ljubljana: SGFM; 1997. 280 pp. Lang.: Slo.
Slovenia. Argentina. 1945-1996. Critical studies. ■Analysis of the works of Slovene-Argentine playwrights about military events and the consequences of World War II.

3010   Kermauner, Taras; Kavčič, Vladimir. *Trije despotje. 1: Diktator Aleksander Veliki.* (Three Despots, 1: Dictator Alexander the Great.) Ljubljana: SGFM; 1997. 256 pp. Lang.: Slo.
Slovenia. 1900-1996. Critical studies. ■Analysis of *Aleksander pranih rok (Alexander Empty-Hands)* by Vitomil Zupan and *Aleksander Veliki (Alexader the Great)* by Vladimir Kavčič.

3011   Kermauner, Taras. *Blodnja. Knj. 2: Človek in nič.* (The Maze, Book 2: Man and Nothing.) Ljubljana: SGFM; 1997. 281 pp. Lang.: Slo.
Slovenia. 1900-1996. Critical studies. ■Analysis of *Potohodec (The Roadwalker)* by Dane Zajc, arguing that it is Zajc's best work after 1945.

3012   Kermauner, Taras. *Slovenski plemenski junaki. Del 3: Tugomer.* (Slovene Tribal Heroes, Part 3: Tugomer.) Ljubljana: SGFM; 1997. 271 pp. Lang.: Slo.
Slovenia. 1875-1996. Critical studies. ■Analysis of plays about the Slovene tragic hero Tugomer by Fran Levstik and by Josip Jurčič.

CLASSED ENTRIES

DRAMA: —Plays/librettos/scripts

3013 Kermauner, Taras. *Blato v izviru in izteku. 1: Premagovanje blata.* (Mud in Spring and in Flux, 1: The Vanquishing of the Mud.) Ljubljana: SGFM; 1997. 259 pp. Lang.: Slo.
Slovenia. 1884-1996. Critical studies. ■Social morality in the works of Catholic playwrights Janez Evangelist Krek and Fran Saleški Finžgar. Argues that only Christianity can save the nation from chaos and fratricide.

3014 Kermauner, Taras; Kavčič, Vladimir. *Trije despotje. 2: Grof Tahi, škof Hren.* (Three Despots, 2: Count Tahi, Bishop Hren.) Ljubljana: SGFM; 1997. 270 pp. Lang.: Slo.
Slovenia. 1976-1996. Critical studies. ■Morality in feudal times as represented in *Spolno življenje grofa Franja Tahija (The Sexual Life of Count Franjo Tahi)*, *Škof Tomaž Hren (Bishop Tomaž Hren)*, and *Štiftarji (The Štiftarji)* by Denis Poniž.

3015 Kermauner, Taras. *Slovenski plemenski junaki. 1: Črtomir.* (Slovene Tribal Heroes, 1: Črtomir.) Ljubljana: SGFM; 1997. 265 pp. Lang.: Slo.
Slovenia. 1836-1996. Critical studies. ■Analysis of *Karantanska tragedija (Carinthian Tragedy)* by Radivoj Rehar, compared to the Romantic poem 'Krst pri Savici (Baptism by the Savica)' by France Prešeren to argue for the necessity of religion in the prevention of war.

3016 Kermauner, Taras. "Projekt etičnega kapitalizma." (The Project of Ethical Capitalism.) 271-288 in Pogačnik, Jože, ed. *Zbornik ob sedemdesetletnici Franceta Bernika.* Ljubljana: Znanstvenoraziskovalni center SAZU; 1997. 584 pp. Lang.: Slo.
Slovenia. 1920. Critical studies. ■Analysis of Anton Funtek's *Kristalni grad (The Crystal Castle)* and comparison with plays of Ivan Cankar in which capitalism was rejected on grounds of inhumanity.

3017 Koruza, Jože. *Slovenska dramatika od začetkov do sodobnosti.* (Slovenian Drama from its Origins to the Present.) Ljubljana: Mihelač; 1997. 231 pp. Pref. Lang.: Slo.
Slovenia. 1789-1975. Histories-specific. ■Essays on Slovenian drama.

3018 Kosi, Tina, ed.; Poniž, Denis, ed.; Zavrl, Mateja, ed. *Postmoderna in sodobna slovenska drama. Zbornik dramaturških razprav.* (Postmodernism and Contemporary Slovene Drama: A Collection of Dramaturgical Papers.) Ljubljana: AGRFT, Drama Dept.; 1997. 204 pp. Lang.: Slo.
Slovenia. 1972-1996. Critical studies. ■Collection of essays resulting from a group project of drama students determining the nature and extent of postmodern elements in the work of contemporary Slovene playwrights.

3019 Medved-Udovič, Vida; Glušič, Helga. *Šolska ura z Jančarjevim Velikim briljantnim valčkom.* (An Hour with Jančar's *Grande Polonaise Brillante.*) Ljubljana: Zavod Republike Slovenije za šolstvo; 1997. 44 pp. Pref. Biblio. Lang.: Slo.
Slovenia. 1985. Instructional materials. ■Analysis of Drago Jančar's *Veliki briljantni valček (Grande Polonaise Brillante).*

3020 Pacheiner-Klander, Vlasta. "Verzna podoba Kalidasovih dram v Glaserjevih prevodih." (Kalidasa's Verse Dramas in Glaser's Translations.) 405-435 in Pogačnik, Jože, ed. *Zbornik ob sedemdesetletnici Franceta Bernika.* Ljubljana: Znanstvenoraziskovalni center SAZU; 1997. 584 pp. Lang.: Slo.
Slovenia. 1885-1908. Critical studies. ■Analysis of various European translations of the Indian verse dramas of Kalidasa, with emphasis on the work of Slovene Indologist Karl Glaser and the treatment of the versification.

3021 Schmidt, Goran. "Evropski literarni in filozofski vplivi ter kritična distanca do domače tradicije v dramskem prvencu Stanka Majcna." (European Literary and Philosophical Influences and a Critical Distance from Slovene Tradition in Stanko Majcen's First Play.) 463-480 in Pogačnik, Jože, ed. *Zbornik ob sedemdesetletnici Franceta Bernika.* Ljubljana: Znanstvenoraziskovalni center SAZU; 1997. 584 pp. Lang.: Slo.
Slovenia. 1912. Critical studies. ■Analysis of *Alenčica, kraljica Ogrska (Alenčica, Queen of Hungary)*, in which Majcen is said to have challenged national views on literature, philosophy, and religion.

3022 Akerman, Anthony. "Theatre in Exile." 89-100 in Davis, Geoffrey V., ed.; Fuchs, Anne, ed. *Theatre and Change in South Africa.* Amsterdam: Harwood Academic Publishing; 1996. 324 pp. (Contemporary Theatre Studies 12.) Index. Notes. Append. Illus.: Photo. 1. Lang.: Eng.
South Africa, Republic of. UK-England. 1973. Histories-sources. ■Expatriate South African author/playwright describes his experience, and that of other artists, as well as his return to South Africa in 1990.

3023 Blumberg, Marcia. "Two Continents, No Refuge: Engendering the Problematics of Home." *PerfR.* 1997 Fall; 2(3): 30-38. Notes. Biblio. Lang.: Eng.
South Africa, Republic of. 1990. Critical studies. ■Analysis of Reza De Wet's epistolary play *Worm in the Bud*, set in the South Africa of the early 1900s. Explores the gender and racial tensions of the period in which the play is set.

3024 Crow, Brian. "'A Truly Living Moment': Acting and the Statements Plays." 13-24 in Davis, Geoffrey V., ed.; Fuchs, Anne, ed. *Theatre and Change in South Africa.* Amsterdam: Harwood Academic Publishing; 1996. 324 pp. (Contemporary Theatre Studies 12.) Index. Notes. Append. Lang.: Eng.
South Africa, Republic of. 1960-1974. Critical studies. ■The acting of everyday life in three 'statement' plays of South African playwright Athol Fugard: *Sizwe Bansi Is Dead*, *The Island*, and *Statements After an Arrest Under the Immorality Act.*

3025 David, Geoffrey V.; Fuchs, Anne. "'An Interest in the Making of Things': An Interview with William Kentridge." 140-154 in Davis, Geoffrey V., ed.; Fuchs, Anne, ed. *Theatre and Change in South Africa.* Amsterdam: Harwood Academic Publishing; 1996. 324 pp. (Contemporary Theatre Studies 12.) Index. Notes. Append. Lang.: Eng.
South Africa, Republic of. 1986-1994. Critical studies. ■Interview with South African playwright/filmmaker William Kentridge: career, training, workshop theatre, apartheid, puppets and audiences.

3026 Davis, Geoffrey V.; Fuchs, Anne. "'I Will Remain an African': An Interview with Maishe Maponya." 183-192 in Davis, Geoffrey V., ed.; Fuchs, Anne, ed. *Theatre and Change in South Africa.* Amsterdam: Harwood Academic Publishing; 1996. (Contemporary Theatre Studies 12.) Notes. Index. Append. Illus.: Photo. 1. Lang.: Eng.
South Africa, Republic of. 1996. Histories-sources. ■Playwright Maishe Maponya discusses his commitment to teaching a 'new' South African theatre at the university level.

3027 Davis, Geoffrey V.; Fuchs, Anne. "'This Compost Heap of a Country': An Interview with Barney Simon." 225-241 in Davis, Geoffrey V., ed.; Fuchs, Anne, ed. *Theatre and Change in South Africa.* Amsterdam: Harwood Academic Publishing; 1996. (Contemporary Theatre Studies 12.) Notes. Index. Append. Lang.: Eng.
South Africa, Republic of. 1976-1992. Histories-sources. ■Interview with playwright/actor Barney Simon on his history in South African theatre.

3028 Dike, Fatima. "*So What's New?* The Story Behind the Play." 242-245 in Davis, Geoffrey V., ed.; Fuchs, Anne, ed. *Theatre and Change in South Africa.* Amsterdam: Harwood Academic Publishing; 1996. (Contemporary Theatre Studies 12.) Notes. Index. Append. Lang.: Eng.
South Africa, Republic of. 1990. Histories-sources. ■Playwright Fatima Dike recounts the origins of her play *So What's New?*.

3029 Duggan, Carolyn Richards. "Gabbling Like a Thing Most Brutish: The Postcolonial Writer and Language, with Reference to the Early Plays of Zakes Mda." *SATJ.* 1997 May/Sep.; 11(1/2): 109-132. Notes. Biblio. Lang.: Eng.
South Africa, Republic of. 1979-1996. Critical studies. ■Focuses on *Dark Voices Ring*, *Dead End*, *The Hill* and *We Shall Sing for the Fatherland.*

3030 McLaren, Robert. "'The Many Individual Wills': From *Crossroads* to *Survival*. The Work of Experimental Theatre Workshop '71." 25-48 in Davis, Geoffrey V., ed.; Fuchs, Anne, ed. *Theatre and Change in South Africa.* Amsterdam: Harwood Academic Publishing; 1996. 324 pp. (Contemporary Theatre Studies 12.) Index. Notes. Append. Lang.: Eng.

DRAMA: —Plays/librettos/scripts

South Africa, Republic of: Johannesburg. 1972-1976. Histories-sources. ■Author recounts his experiences with the Experimental Theatre Workshop '71 and two works it created, *Crossroads* and *Survival*.

3031 Mda, Zakes. "Politics and the Theatre: Current Trends in South Africa." 193-218 in Davis, Geoffrey V., ed.; Fuchs, Anne, ed. *Theatre and Change in South Africa*. Amsterdam: Harwood Academic Publishing; 1996. (Contemporary Theatre Studies 12.) Notes. Index. Append. Illus.: Photo. 1. Lang.: Eng.

South Africa, Republic of. 1990-1996. Critical studies. ■Theatre practitioner Zakes Mda writes on current developments in South African theatre.

3032 Orkin, Martin. "Whose Things of Darkness? Reading/Representing *The Tempest* in South Africa After April 1994." 142-169 in Joughin, John J., ed. *Shakespeare and National Culture*. Manchester: Manchester UP; 1997. 343 pp. Notes. Index. Lang.: Eng.

South Africa, Republic of. 1994. Critical studies. ■Language and the implementation of political order as seen in the study and reception of Shakespeare's *The Tempest*.

3033 Sitas, Ari. "The Workers' Theatre in Natal." 132-139 in Davis, Geoffrey V., ed.; Fuchs, Anne, ed. *Theatre and Change in South Africa*. Amsterdam: Harwood Academic Publishing; 1996. 324 pp. (Contemporary Theatre Studies 12.) Index. Notes. Append. Lang.: Eng.

South Africa, Republic of. 1986-1994. Critical studies. ■Critical treatise on workers' theatre in Natal province.

3034 Rynarzewska, Ewa. "Przesiąknięci samotnością i strachem." (Permeated by Loneliness and Fear.) *DialogW*. 1997; 1: 107-115. Lang.: Pol.

South Korea. 1961-1997. Critical studies. ■Analysis of plays by Lee Kang-Baek, including *Al (Egg)*, *Chokpo (Origins)*, and *Pomnal (Spring Day)*: their relation to Korean and European traditions, and the influence of contemporary politics.

3035 Dlugos, Joan Johnson. *The Theater of Violence in Post-Civil War Spain*. Storrs, CT: Univ. of Connecticut; 1997. 232 pp. Notes. Biblio. [Ph.D. Dissertation, Univ. Microfilms Order No. AAC 9821901.] Lang.: Eng.

Spain. 1939-1975. Historical studies. ■Violence in post-Civil War Spanish drama by Antonio Buero Vallejo, Alfonso Sastre, José Martín Recuerda, and Fernando Arrabal.

3036 Erdocia, Carolina. *Hacia una poética de la representación sacramental del siglo de oro Español: Las loas sacramentales de Calderón de la Barca y la celebración del Corpus Christi.* (Toward a Poetics of Sacramental Representation in the Spanish Golden Age: Calderón's *loas sacramentales* and the Celebration of *Corpus Christi*.) Princeton, NJ: Princeton Univ; 1997. 411 pp. Notes. Biblio. [Ph.D. Dissertation, Univ. Microfilms Order No. AAC 9734240.] Lang.: Spa.

Spain. 1630-1681. Critical studies. ■Argues that an analysis of the *loas*, or dramatic prologues to the *autos sacramentales* celebrating *Corpus Christi* reveals Calderón's poetics of representation in regard to the *Corpus Christi* performances in particular and to drama in general.

3037 Gabriele, John. "A Conversation with Rodrigo García." *WES*. 1997 Win; 9(1): 55-60. Illus.: Photo. 3. Lang.: Eng.

Spain. 1964-1996. Histories-sources. ■Interview with playwright Rodrigo García.

3038 Gomez, Roberto Agustin. *El Pensamiento de Fray Benito Jerónimo Feijoo.* (The Thought of Brother Benito Jerónimo Feijoo.) Albany, NY: State Univ. of New York; 1997. 191 pp. Notes. Biblio. [Ph.D. Dissertation, Univ. Microfilms Order No. AAC 9724439.] Lang.: Spa.

Spain. 1950-1990. Critical studies. ■Examines the body of work of theatre critic and writer Fray Benito Jerónimo Feijoo. Author specifically focuses on Feijoo's theme of humanism.

3039 Graf, Eric Clifford. *Urgent Fury. Exemplary Dissent in Cervantes's* La Numancia: *Towards an Ideological Etiology of Quixotic Desire*. Charlottesville, VA: Univ. of Virginia; 1997. 235 pp. Biblio. Notes. [Ph.D. Dissertation, Univ. Microfilms Order No. AAC 9724694.] Lang.: Eng.

Spain. 1580-1598. Critical studies. ■The themes of religion and politics in *El Cerco de Numancia (The Siege of Numancia)* and the sonnet *Al túmulo del rey Felipe II en Sevilla* by Cervantes.

3040 Hitchcock, Albert David. *Versions of the Self: The Search for Identity in the Drama of Francisco Nieva*. Ithaca, NY: Cornell Univ; 1997. 246 pp. Notes. Biblio. [Ph.D. Dissertation, Univ. Microfilms Order No. AAC 9738176.] Lang.: Eng.

Spain. 1947-1990. Critical studies. ■The concept of selfhood in the plays of Francisco Nieva.

3041 Holt, Marion. "A Homage to Buero-Vallejo at 80." *WES*. 1997 Win; 9(1): 13-14. Illus.: Photo. 2. Lang.: Eng.

Spain: Madrid. 1916-1996. Biographical studies. ■The life and career of playwright Antonio Buero Vallejo.

3042 Holt, Marion. "José López Rubio, 1903-1996." *WES*. 1997 Win; 9(1): 15-16. Illus.: Photo. 1. Lang.: Eng.

Spain. 1903-1996. Biographical studies. ■The life and career of playwright José López Rubio.

3043 Levin, Leslie A. *Signs of the Times: Metaphors of Conversion in Selected Dramas of Tirso de Molina and Calderón de la Barca*. Providence, RI: Brown Univ; 1997. 308 pp. [Ph.D. Dissertation, Univ. Microfilms Order No. AAC 9738587.] Lang.: Eng.

Spain. 1600-1681. Critical studies. ■The representation of the conversion experience in Spanish Golden Age drama through the use of figurative language. Analyzes *Los lagos de San Vicente* and *El condenado por desconfiado* by Tirso de Molina, and *El purgatorio de San Patricio* and *El mágico prodigioso* by Calderón de la Barca.

3044 London, John. *Reception and Renewal in Modern Spanish Theatre: 1939-1963*. London: W.S. Maney & Son; 1997. 273 pp. (Modern Humanities Research Associates: Texts and Dissertations 45.) Index. Notes. Biblio. Illus.: Dwg. Photo. 14. Lang.: Eng.

Spain. UK-England. USA. 1939-1963. Histories-specific. ■Argues that the 'cross-fertilization' of 'foreign' theatre, primarily English and American, in pre-Civil War Spain influenced audience reception and contributed to the worldview of later Spanish dramatists Antonio Buero Vallejo and Fernando Arrabal.

3045 Martínez Thomas, Monique. "El *didascalos* escenógrafo: *El tragaluz* de Antonio Buero Vallejo." (Scenographic 'Stage Direction': *The Skylight* by Antonio Buero Vallejo.) *Gestos*. 1997 Apr.; 12(23): 67-84. Notes. Lang.: Spa.

Spain. 1967. Critical studies. ■Analysis of the spatial relationships in Buero Vallejo's play.

3046 Ostlund, DeLys. *The Re-creation of History in the Fernando and Isabel Plays of Lope de Vega*. New York, NY: Peter Lang; 1997. 129 pp. (Ibérica 18.) Notes. Index. Biblio. Lang.: Eng.

Spain. 1579-1626. Historical studies. ■Examines plays of Lope de Vega that deal with Spain's age of empire, the reign of Fernando and Isabel. Analyzes the role and place of history in the plays and how they use the characters of the monarchs in *El mejor mozo de España (The Best Youth in Spain)*, *Fuente ovejuna*, *El cerco de Santa Fé (The Siege of Santa Fe)*, *El nuevo mundo descubierto por Cristóbal Colón (The New World Discovered by Christopher Columbus)*, and *Las cuentas del Gran Capitán (The Accounts of the Grand Captain)*.

3047 Pirraglia, Elvira I. *Parodia y discurso subversivo en las obras de Valle-Inclán.* (Parody and Subversive Discourse in the Works of Valle-Inclán.) New York, NY: City of New York; 1997. 519 pp. Biblio. Notes. [Ph.D. Dissertation, Univ. Microfilms Order No. AAC 9732961.] Lang.: Spa.

Spain. 1899-1936. Critical studies. ■Narrative and theatrical voice as a strategy of parody in plays by Ramón del Valle-Inclán.

3048 Podol, Peter. "Interview with Fernando Arrabal." *WES*. 1997 Win; 9(1): 61-66. Illus.: Photo. 2. Lang.: Eng.

Spain. 1932-1996. Histories-sources. ■Interview with playwright and director Fernando Arrabal on his life and career.

3049 Ríos-Font, Wadda C. *Rewriting Melodrama: The Hidden Paradigm in Modern Spanish Theater*. London: Associated Univ Presses; 1997. 233 pp. Index. Biblio. Notes. Lang.: Eng.

DRAMA: —Plays/librettos/scripts

Spain. 1870-1900. Critical studies. ■Argues that the melodrama genre in Spanish theatre, as seen in the work of José Echegaray, led to twentieth-century Spanish drama.

3050 Sanchez Basterra, Gabriela. *The Choreography of Fate: García Lorca's Reconfigurations of the Tragic.* Cambridge, MA: Harvard Univ; 1997. 272 pp. Notes. Biblio. [Ph.D. Dissertation, Univ. Microfilms Order No. AAC 9733397.] Lang.: Eng.

Spain. 1920-1936. Critical studies. ■The reconfiguration of narrative in García Lorca's *Bodas de sangre (Blood Wedding)* and *Yerma*.

3051 Simerka, Barbara. "Early Modern Skepticism and Unbelief and the Demystification of Providential Ideology in *El burlador de Sevilla*." *Gestos.* 1997 Apr.; 12(23): 39-66. Notes. Biblio. Lang.: Eng.

Spain. 1622. Critical studies. ■Connection between ideology and aesthetics in Tirso de Molina's play, and what it relates about its society at the time it was written.

3052 Harris, Max. "A Catalan Corpus Christi Play: *The Martyrdom of St. Sebastian with the Hobby Horses and the Turks*." *CompD.* 1997 Sum; 31(2): 224-247. Notes. Illus.: Photo. Sketches. B&W. 6. Lang.: Eng.

Spain-Catalonia. 1437-1997. Historical studies. ■Traces the history of *Martiri de S. Sebastiá ab los caballs cotoners é ab los turchs*, still performed in various parts of Catalonia.

3053 Carlson, Harry G. *Out of Inferno: Strindberg's Reawakening as an Artist.* Seattle, WA: Univ. of Washington P; 1996. 390 pp. Index. Biblio. Illus.: Photo. 16. Lang.: Eng.

Sweden. 1889-1897. Historical studies. ■Argues that August Strindberg's return to his painting during the period known as the Inferno Crisis provided him with a framework to develop a new view of the role of the visual imagination in the arts. This new view is reflected in his post-Inferno plays.

3054 Davy, Daniel. "Strindberg's Unknown Comedy." *MD.* 1997 Fall; 40(3): 305-324. Notes. Lang.: Eng.

Sweden. 1888. Critical studies. ■Analysis of and influences on Strindberg's *Brott och brott (Crimes and Crimes)*. Negative public response, review of contemporary critical analysis of play.

3055 Fransson, Emma. "Schizofreni som hobby." (Schizophrenia As a Hobby.) *Tningen.* 1997; 21(4): 4-6. Illus.: Photo. Color. Lang.: Swe.

Sweden: Stockholm. 1994-1997. Histories-sources. ■An interview with Erik Uddenberg about his first year as playwright, with reference to his play *Husmonstret (The Monster of the House)*.

3056 Gislén, Ylva. "Lära genom att skriva under stor press." (To Learn By Writing Under Great Stress.) *Entré.* 1997; 24(4): 6-9. Illus.: Photo. B&W. Lang.: Swe.

Sweden: Malmö. 1995-1997. Histories-sources. ■An interview with the two playwrights Lars Arrhed and Klas Abrahamsson about their plays for Ensembleteatern, with references to *Anklagad (Accused)*, *Martin Keller* and *Skådespelarnas klassiker (Actors' Classics)*.

3057 Olzon, Janna. "Teater måste angå, annars är den inte viktig!" (The Theatre Must Be Relevant, Otherwise It Isn't Important!) *Tningen.* 1997; 21(3): 46-47. Illus.: Photo. Color. Lang.: Swe.

Sweden: Stockholm. 1992-1997. Histories-sources. ■An interview with the playwright Camilla Wittmos, about her career and her views on theatre.

3058 Sörenson, Elisabeth. "Det ska fan vara dramatiker." (I'm a Playwright, Damn It!) *Dramat.* 1997; 5(2): 13-15. Illus.: Photo. B&W. Lang.: Swe.

Sweden: Stockholm. 1931-1942. Historical studies. ■An essay about the correspondence between the author Vilhelm Moberg and the manager Pauline Brunius at Kungliga Dramatiska Teatern.

3059 Sörenson, Elisabeth; Florin, Magnus; Josephson, Erland; Kleberg, Lars; Hedlund, Magnus. "Att göra det omöjliga." (To Do the Impossible.) *Dramat.* 1997; 5(3): 36-41. Illus.: Photo. B&W. Color. Lang.: Swe.

Sweden. 1847-1997. Critical studies. ■A discussion about the problems and possibilities of translating drama, with reference to Carl August Hagberg's translation of Shakespeare.

3060 Sörenson, Margareta. "En sträng estet fyller 90." (A Severe Aesthete Turns 90.) *Dramat.* 1997; 5(4): 20-23. Illus.: Dwg. Photo. Color. Lang.: Swe.

Sweden. 1944-1997. Histories-sources. ■A presentation of the author Astrid Lindgren, including interviews with the literary researcher Vivi Ekström and the author Kristina Lugn, about Astrid Lindgren's fairy tales, with reference to Hans Klinga's new staging of *Mio, min Mio (Mio, My Mio)* at Kungliga Dramatiska Teatern.

3061 Stockenström, Göran. "August Strindberg: A Modernist in Spite of Himself." *CompD.* 1992 Sum; 26(2): 95-123. Notes. Lang.: Eng.

Sweden. 1894-1907. Critical studies. ■The paradox of Strindberg's traditionalist theatrical precepts with the modernism of his later plays, including *Till Damaskus (To Damascus)*, *Svarta fanor (Black Banners)*, *Ett Drömspel (A Dream Play)* and *Spöksonaten (The Ghost Sonata)*.

3062 Szalczer, Eszter. *Strindberg's Cosmic Theatre: Theosophical Impact and the Theatrical Metaphor.* New York, NY: City Univ. of New York; 1997. 272 pp. Notes. Biblio. [Ph.D. Dissertation, Univ. Microfilms Order No. AAC 9808011.] Lang.: Eng.

Sweden. 1880-1912. Critical studies. ■Explores connections between the theosophical interests and the dramatic-theatrical innovations of Swedish playwright August Strindberg.

3063 Vogel, Viveka. "Jösses flickor, vilken tjej!" (Bless Me, What a Girl!) *Dramat.* 1997; 5(2): 28-30. Illus.: Photo. B&W. Color. Lang.: Swe.

Sweden: Stockholm. 1960-1997. Histories-sources. ■An interview with Margareta Garpe about her background and career as author and director, with references to feminist theatre and Henrik Ibsen.

3064 Löb, Ladislaus. "'Insanity in the Darkness': Anti-Semitic Stereotypes and Jewish Identity in Max Frisch's *Andorra* and Arthur Miller's *Focus*." *MLR.* 1997 July; 92(3): 545-558. Notes. Biblio. Lang.: Eng.

Switzerland. 1961. Critical studies. ■Jewish persecution and identity in Frisch's play and the possible influence of Arthur Miller's 1945 novel.

3065 Widmer, Urs. "Königs Ende." (King's End.) *THeute.* 1997; Yb: 4-5. Pref. Illus.: Photo. B&W. 1. Lang.: Ger.

Switzerland. 1997. Histories-sources. ■A statement by Urs Widmer, who was chosen by critics of *Theater Heute* as playwright of the year, about Shakespeare's *Richard III*.

3066 Wille, Franz. "Vom Saft der autonomen Zitrone." (On Juice of the Autonomous Lemon.) *THeute.* 1997; 2: 38-41. Append. Illus.: Photo. B&W. 38-41. Lang.: Ger.

Switzerland: Zurich. 1996. Historical studies. ■Describes the background of Urs Widmer's play *Top Dogs*. Describes his anthropological studies in behavior of managers who became unemployed, the cooperation with director Volker Hesse and the actors at Theater Neumarkt. Includes a statement by Urs Widmer.

3067 Angel-Perez, Elisabeth. "The Revival of Medieval Forms in Recent Political Drama." 15-29 in Boireau, Nicole, ed. *Drama on Drama: Dimensions of Theatricality on the Contemporary British Stage.* New York, NY: St. Martin's; 1997. 256 pp. Pref. Notes. Index. Biblio. Lang.: Eng.

UK-England. 1970-1990. Critical studies. ■Themes and practices of medieval theatre in British drama of the 1970s and 80s, with emphasis on non-illusion. Plays examined include: David Edgar's *O Fair Jerusalem*, Peter Barnes's *Red Noses* and *Sunset and Glories*, and Howard Barker's *The Castle* and *The Last Supper*.

3068 Aragay, Mireia. "Writing, Politics, and *Ashes to Ashes*: An Interview with Harold Pinter." *PintR.* 1997: 4-15. Lang.: Eng.

UK-England. 1996. Histories-sources. ■Interview with playwright Pinter: his plays presented at a festival in Barcelona, especially *Ashes to Ashes*. Politics, audience response, literary history considered.

3069 Arndt, Susanne. "'We're all free to do as we're told': Gender and Ideology in Tom Stoppard's *The Real Thing*." *MD.* 1997 Win; 40(4): 489-501. Notes. Lang.: Eng.

UK-England. 1983. Critical studies. ■Proposes an interpretation of Stoppard's play that unsettles underlying assumptions privileging the concept of a male subject as a universal, transcendent self, and simultaneously

DRAMA: —Plays/librettos/scripts

rendering woman as a subordinate being. Also examines other critical analyses of the play.

3070 Boireau, Nicole. "Tom Stoppard's Metadrama: The Haunting Repetition." 136-151 in Boireau, Nicole, ed. *Drama on Drama: Dimensions of Theatricality on the Contemporary British Stage.* New York, NY: St. Martin's; 1997. 256 pp. Pref. Notes. Index. Biblio. Lang.: Eng.

UK-England. 1967-1995. Critical studies. ■Postmodernism and metatheatricality in the plays of Tom Stoppard.

3071 Booth, Michael. "Soldiers of the Queen: Drury Lane Imperialism." 3-20 in Hays, Michael, ed.; Nikolopoulou, Anastasia, ed. *Melodrama: The Cultural Emergence of a Genre.* New York, NY: St. Martin's P; 1996. 288 pp. Notes. Illus.: Photo. 1. Lang.: Eng.

UK-England. 1850-1900. Historical studies. ■Melodrama as a staging of cultural tensions in the age of British imperialism. Argues that audiences identified with the state through melodrama's show of patriotic sentiment and heroic characters.

3072 Carlson, Marvin. "He Never Should Bow Down to a Domineering Frown: Class Tensions and Nautical Melodrama." 147-166 in Hays, Michael, ed.; Nikolopoulou, Anastasia, ed. *Melodrama: The Cultural Emergence of a Genre.* New York, NY: St. Martin's P; 1996. 288 pp. Notes. Lang.: Eng.

UK-England. 1804-1850. Historical studies. ■On the necessity of submitting to traditional authority structures, as seen in nautical melodramas such as Jerrold's *Mutiny at the Nore.*

3073 Castle, Terry. *Noël Coward and Radclyffe Hall: Kindred Spirits.* New York, NY: Columbia UP; 1996. 150 pp. (Between Men—Between Women: Lesbian and Gay Studies.) Notes. Index. Biblio. Illus.: Photo. Dwg. 56. Lang.: Eng.

UK-England. 1880-1940. Historical studies. ■Playwright Noël Coward's life as a gay man, marked by social danger and secrecy, compared with the life of lesbian novelist Radclyffe Hall.

3074 Clausius, C. "Specialized Time in Harold Pinter's *Silence.*" *PintR.* 1997: 28-40. Biblio. Lang.: Eng.

UK-England. 1971-1993. Critical studies. ■How silence affects meaning in Pinter's plays, with emphsis on the play *Silence.*

3075 Clum, John M. "'Myself of Course': J.R. Ackerly and Self-Dramatization." *ThM.* 1993; 24(2): 76-87. Biblio. Lang.: Eng.

UK-England. 1925. Critical studies. ■Analysis of J.R. Ackerly's gay drama *The Prisoners of War.*

3076 Coppa, Francesca. "Coming Out in the Room: Joe Orton's Epigrammatic Re/Vision of Harold Pinter's Menace." *MD.* 1997 Spr; 15(1): 11-22. Notes. Lang.: Eng.

UK-England. 1998. Critical studies. ■Textual analysis of Orton's *The Ruffian on the Stair*: themes of homosexuality, incest, and application of journalistic conventions on text, influence of Pinter's work on Orton.

3077 Cousin, Geraldine. *Women in Dramatic Place and Time: Contemporary Female Characters on Stage.* London/New York, NY: Routledge; 1996. 211 pp. Index. Biblio. Lang.: Eng.

UK-England. 1980-1995. Critical studies. ■Detailed analyses of plays by British women including Pam Gems's *Queen Christina,* Charlotte Keatley's *My Mother Said I Never Should,* Louise Page's *Real Estate,* Timberlake Wertenbaker's *The Grace of Mary Traverse,* Winsome Pinnock's *Leave Taking,* Caryl Churchill's *The Skriker,* and Anne Devlin's *After Easter.*

3078 Cox, Jeffrey N. "The Ideological Tack of Nautical Melodrama." 167-190 in Hays, Michael, ed.; Nikolopoulou, Anastasia, ed. *Melodrama: The Cultural Emergence of a Genre.* New York, NY: St. Martin's P; 1996. 288 pp. Notes. Lang.: Eng.

UK-England. 1794-1830. Historical studies. ■Examines social and political issues and the function of ideological discourse in nautical melodramas.

3079 Dymkowski, Christine. "'The Play's the Thing': The Metatheatre of Timberlake Wertenbaker." 121-135 in Boireau, Nicole, ed. *Drama on Drama: Dimensions of Theatricality*

on the Contemporary British Stage. New York, NY: St. Martin's; 1997. 256 pp. Pref. Notes. Index. Biblio. Lang.: Eng.

UK-England. 1988-1995. Critical studies. ■Studies metatheatricality in two plays of Timberlake Wertenbaker, *Our Country's Good* and *The Love of the Nightingale.*

3080 Egan, Gabriel. "Myths and Enabling Fictions of 'Origin' in the Editing of Shakespeare." *NTQ.* 1997; 13(49): 41-47. Notes. Lang.: Eng.

UK-England. 1592-1996. Textual studies. ■Continues the debate on editorial practice and responds in detail to Andrew Spong's defense of the 'Shakespeare Originals' project (*NTQ* 1996: 12 (45): 65-70), arguing that explained editorial interference is essential.

3081 Ehrnrooth, Albert. "Våldsam och livaktig." (Violent and Vigorous.) *Tningen.* 1997; 21(2): 17-23. Illus.: Photo. B&W. Lang.: Swe.

UK-England. 1990. Critical studies. ■A presentation of the plays by the young playwrights of Britain, with references to Nick Grosso, Judy Upton, David Eldridge, Jez Butterworth, Martin McDonagh and Joe Penhall.

3082 Fietz, Lothar. "On the Origins of the English Melodrama in the Tradition of Bourgeois Tragedy and Sentimental Drama: Lillo, Schröder, Kotzebue, Sheridan, Thompson, Jerrold." 83-102 in Hays, Michael, ed.; Nikolopoulou, Anastasia, ed. *Melodrama: The Cultural Emergence of a Genre.* New York, NY: St. Martin's P; 1996. 288 pp. Notes. Lang.: Eng.

UK-England. 1800-1880. Historical studies. ■Argues that sentimentalism in English melodrama illuminates politics, economy and larger social issues of value and behavior.

3083 Fuchs, Anne. "Devising Drama on Drama: The Community and Theatre Traditions." 184-195 in Boireau, Nicole, ed. *Drama on Drama: Dimensions of Theatricality on the Contemporary British Stage.* New York, NY: St. Martin's; 1997. 256 pp. Pref. Notes. Index. Biblio. Lang.: Eng.

UK-England. 1989. Critical studies. ■Analysis of 'devised' theatre—theatre that creates a work based on the experiences of a community of more than one person. Uses *Heartlanders* by Stephen Bill, Anne Devlin, and David Edgar, and Caryl Churchill's *Fen,* written with Joint Stock Theatre Group, as examples to explore the relationship between the work and the originators.

3084 Gallant, Desmond. "Brechtian Sexual Politics in the Plays of Howard Barker." *MD.* 1997 Fall; 40(3): 403-413. Notes. Lang.: Eng.

UK-England. 1987-1997. Critical studies. ■Influence of Brecht on the treatment of human sexuality in the plays of Barker: poetic use of sexuality, complexity of human desire. Focus on Barker's *The Castle* and Brecht's *Mutter Courage (Mother Courage)* and *Die Gute Mensch von Sezuan (Good Person of Szechwan).*

3085 Gardner, Julia D. *Sensational Technologies: Victorian Stagings of Gender and Sexuality.* Riverside, CA: Univ. of California; 1997. 204 pp. [Ph.D. Dissertation, Univ. Microfilms Order No. AAC 9804261.] Lang.: Eng.

UK-England. 1830-1900. Critical studies. ■Issues of gender and sexuality in Victorian melodrama represented by fallen women, ghostly apparitions, and the racial other. Examines stage adaptations of Mary Braddon's novel *Lady Audley's Secret* and C.H. Hazelwood's play version of *Aurora Floyd,* among others.

3086 Garner, Stanton B. "Rewriting Europe: Pentecost and the Crossroads of Migration." *ET.* 1997; 16(1): 3-14. Notes. Biblio. Lang.: Eng.

UK-England: Stratford. 1994-1997. Critical studies. ■Analysis of David Edgar's *Pentecost,* described as a comment on the politics and culture of post-Cold-War Europe.

3087 Ghilardi-Santacatterina, Maria; Sierz, Aleks. "Pinter and the Pinteresque: An Author Trapped by His Own Image?" 108-120 in Boireau, Nicole, ed. *Drama on Drama: Dimensions of Theatricality on the Contemporary British Stage.* New York, NY: St. Martin's; 1997. 256 pp. Pref. Notes. Index. Biblio. Lang.: Eng.

DRAMA: —Plays/librettos/scripts

UK-England. 1980-1993. Critical studies. ■Intertextuality as a complex cultural experience in the plays of Harold Pinter. Examines this idea in the plays as they developed chronologically.

3088 Gillen, Francis; Gale, Steven H. "Introduction." *PintR*. 1997: xiii-xv. Lang.: Eng.

UK-England. USA. 1993-1996. Critical studies. ■Introduction to contents of *The Pinter Review: 1995 and 1996*.

3089 Glaap, Albert-Reiner. "Translating, Adapting, Rewriting: Three Facets of Christopher Hampton's Work as a Playwright." 215-230 in Boireau, Nicole, ed. *Drama on Drama: Dimensions of Theatricality on the Contemporary British Stage*. New York, NY: St. Martin's; 1997. 256 pp. Pref. Notes. Index. Biblio. Lang.: Eng.

UK-England. 1967-1994. Critical studies. ■Analysis of Hampton's work.

3090 Goodman, Lizbeth. "Representing Gender/Representing Self: A Reflection on Role Playing in Performance Theory and Practice." 196-214 in Boireau, Nicole, ed. *Drama on Drama: Dimensions of Theatricality on the Contemporary British Stage*. New York, NY: St. Martin's; 1997. 256 pp. Pref. Notes. Index. Biblio. Lang.: Eng.

UK-England. 1982-1995. Critical studies. ■Role playing in relation to feminist theatre work which examines its own 'role' in culture. Caryl Churchill's *Top Girls*, Sarah Daniels' *Blow Your House Down*, and Joan Lipkin's *Small Domestic Acts*.

3091 Granger, Judith. *The Widening Scope of the Shavian Heroine*. New York, NY: City Univ. of New York; 1997. 149 pp. [Ph.D. Dissertation, Univ. Microfilms Order No. AAC 9807937.] Lang.: Eng.

UK-England. 1893-1923. Critical studies. ■Woman's historical experience and expanding role in society at the turn of the twentieth century, as reflected in Shaw's major plays including *Candida, Man and Superman, Mrs. Warren's Profession, Pygmalion, Major Barbara*, and *Saint Joan*.

3092 Herold, Christopher Terrence. *'What's Going On Here': The Actor and the Phenomenon of Mystery in the Plays of Harold Pinter*. Berkeley, CA: Univ. of California, Berkeley; 1997. 209 pp. Notes. Biblio. [Ph.D. Dissertation, Univ. Microfilms Order No. AAC 9828728.] Lang.: Eng.

UK-England. 1965-1995. Critical studies. ■Mystery in the plays of Harold Pinter from the perspective of the actor. Works examined include *The Dumb Waiter, The Birthday Party*, and *Old Times*.

3093 Jensen, Phebe. "The Textual Politics of *Troilus and Cressida*." *SQ*. 1995 Win; 46(4): 414-423. Notes. Lang.: Eng.

UK-England. 1995. Textual studies. ■Enters debate whether the Quarto or Folio is the more authoritative version of the play.

3094 Köppen, Ulrich. "Modern and Postmodern Theatres." *NTQ*. 1997; 13(50): 99-105. Notes. Lang.: Eng.

UK-England. 1966-1996. Histories-sources. ■Interview with playwright Edward Bond about his concept of Theatre Events, which he believes have replaced the Brechtian alienation effect in his work. Discusses his published aesthetic theory as well as his plays.

3095 Kramer, Jeffrey; Kramer, Prapassaree. "Stoppard's *Arcadia*: Research, Time, Loss." *MD*. 1997 Spr; 15(1): 1-10. Notes. Lang.: Eng.

UK-England. 1988-1998. Critical studies. ■Realism, surrealism, uses of scientific theories (particularly chaos theory) in concepts of time and reality in Stoppard's play *Arcadia*. Influence on characters and themes.

3096 Lamb, Charles. *Howard Barker's Theatre of Seduction*. Amsterdam: Harwood Academic Publishers; 1997. 153 pp. (Contemporary Theatre Studies 19.) Index. Biblio. Notes. Pref. Lang.: Eng.

UK-England. 1975-1994. Critical studies. ■Analysis of Barker's *Judith* and *The Castle* with respect to irrational love in the form of seduction.

3097 Langford, Larry L. "The Unsocial Socialism of John Osborne." *EnSt*. 1997 May; 78(3): 237-257. Notes. Lang.: Eng.

UK-England. 1950-1997. Biographical studies. ■Political background and life of John Osborne.

3098 MacMurraugh, Kavanagh. "Culture, Chameleons ... and Critics." *PI*. 1997 Christmas; 13(4): 14-15, 23. Illus.: Photo. B&W. 1. Lang.: Eng.

UK-England. 1996. Histories-sources. ■Interview with playwright Peter Shaffer. Continued in *Plays International* 13:5 (1998), 12-14: 'Myth-Making and Breaking'.

3099 Mann, Susan Gail. *Salieri and Mozart: Historical Accuracy in 'Amadeus'*. Long Beach, CA: California State Univ; 1997. 113 pp. Notes. Biblio. [M.A. Thesis, Univ. Microfilms Order No. AAC 1385623.] Lang.: Eng.

UK-England. 1979. Critical studies. ■Analysis of the characters Mozart and Salieri in Peter Shaffer's *Amadeus*.

3100 Montañes Brunet, Elvira Maria. *La literatura como lengua: hacia un análisis lingüístico integrador del discurso dramático*. (Literature as Language: Towards an Integrative Linguistic Analysis of Dramatic Discourse.) Valencia: Universitat de Valencia; 1997. 422 pp. [Ph.D. Dissertation available from Servicio de Publicaciones, Universitat de Valencia, C. de la Nave, 2, E-46003 Valencia, Spain.] Lang.: Spa.

UK-England. 1956-1984. Critical studies. ■Analysis of Shelagh Delaney's *A Taste of Honey*, Harold Pinter's *The Birthday Party*, Joe Orton's *Entertaining Mr. Sloane*, and Pam Gems's *Loving Women* with emphasis on the analysis, description, and interpretation of dicourse.

3101 Moore, Peter R. "The Abysm of Time: The Chronology of Shakespeare's Plays." *ERev*. 1997 Fall; 5(2): 24-60. Notes. Lang.: Eng.

UK-England. 1911-1930. Historical studies. ■Analysis of Sir Edmund Chambers' published chronology of the Shakespearean canon.

3102 Peacock, D. Keith. *Harold Pinter and the New British Theatre*. Westport, CT/London: Greenwood P; 1997. 227 pp. (Contributions in Drama and Theatre Studies, Lives of the Theatre 77.) Index. Biblio. Append. Pref. Illus.: Photo. 12. Lang.: Eng.

UK-England. 1957-1996. Critical studies. ■Pinter's career as one of the 'new' twentieth-century British playwrights. Examines Pinter's work and his politics.

3103 Peters, Sally. *Bernard Shaw: The Ascent of the Superman*. New Haven, CT: Yale UP; 1996. 328 pp. Notes. Pref. Index. Biblio. Illus.: Photo. 26. Lang.: Eng.

UK-England. 1890-1950. Biographies. ■Critical biography of playwright George Bernard Shaw from his beginnings in Ireland to his playwriting career in London. Concentrates on his construction of the Superman and Don Juan character in his own life and career.

3104 Pinter, Harold. "Harold Pinter: *A Speech of Thanks*." *PintR*. 1997: 1-3. Lang.: Eng.

UK-England. 1995. Histories-sources. ■Pinter's speech of thanks on receiving the David Cohen British Literature prize of 1995, recalling his literary background.

3105 Prunet, Monique. "Japanese Theatrical Forms in Edward Bond's *The Bundle* and *Jackets*." 72-88 in Boireau, Nicole, ed. *Drama on Drama: Dimensions of Theatricality on the Contemporary British Stage*. New York, NY: St. Martin's; 1997. 256 pp. Pref. Notes. Index. Biblio. Lang.: Eng.

UK-England. 1980-1990. Critical studies. ■Examines Japanese theatrical and stylistic elements—primarily *nō* and *kabuki*—in Bond's plays.

3106 Redondo, M. Susana. "Realism and the Female Subject in Jacqueline Rudet's *Basin*." *MD*. 1997 Win; 40(4): 477-488. Notes. Lang.: Eng.

UK-England. 1985-1997. Critical studies. ■The effect of the play's realistic features on the determination of positions for women, through the characters and the narrative movement.

3107 Saltz, David Z. "Radical Mimesis: The 'Pinter Problem' Revisited." *CompD*. 1992 Fall; 26(3): 218-236. Notes. Lang.: Eng.

UK-England. 1960-1997. Critical studies. ■The problem of finding descriptive terms for the use of language in plays by Harold Pinter.

3108 Sierz, Aleks. "'About Now' in Birmingham." *NTQ*. 1997; 13(51): 289-290. [*NTQ* Reports and Announcements.] Lang.: Eng.

DRAMA: —Plays/librettos/scripts

UK-England. 1990-1996. Historical studies. ■Reports on the Eighth Birmingham Theatre Conference, hosted by David Edgar, who argued that masculinity was a dominant theme of the new playwriting and that young authors owed a great deal to sympathetic artistic directors as well as to regional self-help groups.

3109 Silverstein, Marc. "'My skin used to wrap me up': Staging the Body in A Mouthful of Birds." *ET.* 1997; 16(2): 177-190. Notes. Biblio. Lang.: Eng.

UK-England. 1986-1997. Critical studies. ■Analysis of *A Mouthful of Birds* by Caryl Churchill, with attention to hermaphroditic imagery and gender theory.

3110 Simard, Jean-Pierre. "*Watching for Dolphins* by John McGrath: The Single Voicing of a Multiple Voice Performance." 171-183 in Boireau, Nicole, ed. *Drama on Drama: Dimensions of Theatricality on the Contemporary British Stage.* New York, NY: St. Martin's; 1997. 256 pp. Pref. Notes. Index. Biblio. Lang.: Eng.

UK-England. 1991. Critical studies. ■Argues that McGrath's single-character play contains many voices as a result of fragmentation.

3111 Stirling, Grant. "Ortonesque/Carnivalesque: The Grotesque Realism of Joe Orton." *JDTC.* 1997 Spr; 11(2): 41-63. Lang.: Eng.

UK-England. 1964-1967. Critical studies. ■The application of Bakhtinian concepts of the carnivalesque and grotesque realism to the dramaturgy of playwright Joe Orton.

3112 Stuart, Ian, ed. *Edward Bond: Letters, III.* Amsterdam: Harwood; 1996. 211 pp. (Contemporary Theatre Studies 14.) Index. Notes. Pref. Lang.: Eng.

UK-England. 1984-1994. Histories-sources. ■Third volume of letters of playwright Edward Bond. Divides book into seven sections: writing, translation, general correspondence, revivals, new plays, and television plays. Letters cover only part of his career.

3113 Su, John J. "Nostalgic Rapture: Interpreting Moral Commitments in David Hare's Drama." *MD.* 1997 Spr; 15(1): 23-37. Notes. Lang.: Eng.

UK-England: London. 1947-1997. Critical studies. ■English postwar nostalgia and moral response of characters to political problems in plays of Hare: *Plenty, The Secret Rapture, Racing Demon, The Absence of War* and *Murmuring Judges.*

3114 Tyler, Lisa. "Charting Pinter's Itinerary: Literary Allusions in *A Kind of Alaska.*" *PintR.* 1997: 90-100. Biblio. Notes. Lang.: Eng.

UK-England. 1994. Critical studies. ■Literary allusions in Pinter's one-act play *A Kind of Alaska,* based on a true psychological case study in Oliver Sacks' book *Awakenings.*

3115 Upor, László; Koncz, Zsuzsa, photo. "Wesker ölte meg Mostelt. Beszélgetés az angol drámaíróval." (Wesker Killed Mostel: Interview with the English Playwright Arnold Wesker.) *Sz.* 1997; 30(9): 33-36. Notes. Illus.: Photo. B&W. 4. Lang.: Hun.

UK-England. 1958-1997. Histories-sources. ■A talk with playwright Arnold Wesker during his recent visit to Budapest.

3116 Walshe, Eibhear. "'Angels of Death': Wilde's Salomé and Shaw's *Saint Joan.*" *IUR.* 1997 Spr/Sum; 27(1): 24-32. Lang.: Eng.

UK-England. Ireland. 1891-1923. Critical studies. ■Argues that the female protagonists of Wilde's *Salomé* and Shaw's *Saint Joan* usurp male privileges and are punished by the patriarchal order.

3117 Wardle, Irving. "Thieves and Parasites: on Forty Years of Reviewing in England." *NTQ.* 1997; 13(50): 119-132. [Originally presented as a talk at the Banff Centre for the Arts.] Lang.: Eng.

UK-England. 1959-1995. Historical studies. ■Retired drama critic of *The Times* and the *Independent on Sunday,* Wardle surveys successive decades of new English playwriting, when actors were dethroned by writers and directors, and evaluates the response of drama reviewers to these changes.

3118 Werstine, Paul. "Plays in Manuscript." 481-498 in Cox, John D., ed.; Kastan, David Scott, ed. *A New History of Early English Drama.* New York, NY: Columbia UP; 1997. 565 pp. Index. Notes. Biblio. Lang.: Eng.

UK-England. 1906-1996. Critical studies. ■Examines twentieth-century attempts to classify, edit, and disseminate early English play manuscripts.

3119 Wilson, Ann. "Hauntings: Ghosts and the Limits of Realism in *Cloud Nine* and *Fen* by Caryl Churchill." 152-167 in Boireau, Nicole, ed. *Drama on Drama: Dimensions of Theatricality on the Contemporary British Stage.* New York, NY: St. Martin's; 1997. 256 pp. Pref. Notes. Index. Biblio. Lang.: Eng.

UK-England. 1980-1990. Critical studies. ■Feminist analysis of the use of ghosts in Churchill's plays as a way of making audiences reconsider theatrical realism with particular attention to the implications of its ideological investment in patriarchy.

3120 Yacowar, Maurice. "Shakespeare's 'Appearance' in *The Herbal Bed.*" *ShN.* 1997 Sum/Fall; 47(2/3): 37, 48. [Number 233/234.] Lang.: Eng.

UK-England. 1997. Critical studies. ■Shakespeare's multiple meanings in Peter Whelan's play *The Herbal Bed,* in which the central figure is Shakespeare's daughter Susanna.

3121 Krause, David. "The Failed Words of Brian Friel." *MD.* 1997 Fall; 40(3): 359-373. Notes. Lang.: Eng.

UK-Ireland. 1994-1997. Critical studies. ■Examination of *Molly Sweeney, Dancing at Lughnasa* and *Wonderful Tennessee* to reveal a pattern of recurring problems with the language of the plays. Discusses staging of the plays as well as text.

3122 Richards, Shawn. "Placed Identities for Placeless Times: Brian Friel and Post-Colonial Criticism." *IUR.* 1997 Spr/Sum; 27(1): 55-68. Lang.: Eng.

UK-Ireland. 1980-1994. Critical studies. ■Situates Brian Friel's dramas, particularly *Dancing at Lughnasa, Wonderful Tennessee* and *Molly Sweeney* in relation to post-modern and post-colonial concepts of identity, and argues that Friel's search for placed identities challenges post-modern depthlessness and placelessness.

3123 Lazaridès, Alexandre. "Edward Thomas, dramaturge de l'absence." (Edward Thomas, Playwright of Absence.) *JCT.* 1997; 85: 89-97. Notes. Illus.: Photo. B&W. 4. Lang.: Fre.

UK-Wales. 1988-1992. Critical studies. ■Aesthetics of unity and arbitrariness in Edward Thomas' Welsh trilogy *House of America, Flowers of the Dead Red Sea* and *East from the Gantry.*

3124 Abbotson, Susan Claire Whitfield. *Towards a Humanistic Democracy: The Balancing Acts of Arthur Miller and August Wilson.* Storrs, CT: Univ. of Connecticut; 1997. 388 pp. [Ph.D. Dissertation, Univ. Microfilms Order No. AAC 9821891.] Lang.: Eng.

USA. 1980-1996. Critical studies. ■Argues that both playwrights explore moral responsibility toward the self and others, balancing the needs of the individual with the needs of the group.

3125 Adler, Thomas P. "Before the Fall—and After: *Summer and Smoke* and *The Night of the Iguana.*" 114-127 in Roudané, Matthew C., ed. *The Cambridge Companion to Tennessee Williams.* Cambridge: Cambridge UP; 1997. 277 pp. (Cambridge Companions to Literature.) Notes. Biblio. Index. Illus.: Photo. 1. Lang.: Eng.

USA. 1948-1961. Critical studies. ■The intertextuality of Tennessee Williams's *Summer and Smoke* and *The Night of the Iguana.*

3126 Adler, Thomas P. "Conscience and Community in *An Enemy of the People* and *The Crucible.*" 86-100 in Bigsby, Christopher, ed. *The Cambridge Companion to Arthur Miller.* Cambridge: Cambridge UP; 1997. 277 pp. (Cambridge Companions to Literature.) Index. Notes. Illus.: Photo. 1. Lang.: Eng.

USA. 1950-1984. Historical studies. ■Compares ideas of community and conscience in Ibsen's *An Enemy of the People (En Folkefiende),* which playwright Arthur Miller adapted for television, and his own *The Crucible.* Also covers Miller's legal conflict with the Wooster Group over the deconstructive use of *The Crucible.*

DRAMA: —Plays/librettos/scripts

3127 Almeida, Diane. "Four Saints in Our Town: A Comparative Analysis of Works by Gertrude Stein and Thornton Wilder." *JADT.* 1997 Fall; 9(3): 1-23. Notes. Lang.: Eng.

USA. 1934-1938. Historical studies. ■Historical account of the friendship between Gertrude Stein and Thornton Wilder, reflected in the writings of each. Specifically focuses on Stein's *Four Saints in Three Acts*, score by Virgil Thomson, and Wilder's *Our Town.*

3128 Bak, John S. "From '10' to 'Quarter Past Eight Foot': Tennessee Williams and William Inge, 1957." *AmerD.* 1997 Fall; 7 (1): 18-29. Notes. Biblio. Lang.: Eng.

USA. 1943-1957. Historical studies. ■Personal and professional relationship of Inge and Williams. The strains in the friendship, influence on one another's writing, comparison of Williams' *Orpheus Descending* and Inge's *The Dark at the Top of the Stairs.*

3129 Balakian, Jan. "*Camino Real*: Williams's Allegory About the 1950s." 67-94 in Roudané, Matthew C., ed. *The Cambridge Companion to Tennessee Williams.* Cambridge: Cambridge UP; 1997. 277 pp. (Cambridge Companions to Literature.) Notes. Biblio. Index. Illus.: Photo. 1. Lang.: Eng.

USA. 1953-1990. Critical studies. ■Analyzes elements of Tennessee Williams's *Camino Real*, including the play's surrealism both in its original production and key landmark productions over the years.

3130 Balakian, Jan. "Two Interviews with Wendy Wasserstein." *JADT.* 1997 Spr; 9(2): 58-84. Lang.: Eng.

USA. 1995-1996. Histories-sources. ■Two interviews with playwright Wendy Wasserstein. Discussion ranges from her adaptations of other writers' work to her emphasis on women in her plays.

3131 Balakian, Janet N. "The Holocaust, the Depression, and McCarthyism: Miller in the Sixties." 115-138 in Bigsby, Christopher, ed. *The Cambridge Companion to Arthur Miller.* Cambridge: Cambridge UP; 1997. 277 pp. (Cambridge Companions to Literature.) Index. Notes. Illus.: Photo. 3. Lang.: Eng.

USA. 1960-1969. Historical studies. ■Social issues of the 1960s in the plays of Arthur Miller, including *After the Fall*, *Incident at Vichy* and *The Price* and his film *The Misfits.* Focuses on denial as a social issue in race relations and the Vietnam War.

3132 Banks, Michael Lawrence. *George S. Kaufman: American Social Critic on Stage.* St. Louis, MO: St. Louis Univ; 1997. 289 pp. Notes. Biblio. [Ph.D. Dissertation, Univ. Microfilms Order No. AAC 9803746.] Lang.: Eng.

USA. 1889-1961. Historical studies. ■Plays of George S. Kaufman in their historical, cultural, and ideological contexts. Focuses on how Kaufman's plays reflect and comment on the values of American family life, business, and politics. Plays considered are *Beggar On Horseback* (1924), *The Royal Family* (1927), *You Can't Take It With You* (1936), *The Man Who Came To Dinner* (1939), *The Late George Apley* (1944) and *The Solid Gold Cadillac* (1953).

3133 Barbera, Jack. "The Emotion of Multitude and David Rabe's *Streamers.*" *AmerD.* 1997 Fall; 7(1): 50-66. Notes. Biblio. Lang.: Eng.

USA. 1976. Critical studies. ■Argues that play evokes the emotion by its characters, language, themes of difficulty of communication and through overriding images of exposure and enclosure.

3134 Barnes-McLain, Noreen. "Death and Desire: The Evolution of the AIDS Play." *JDTC.* 1997 Fall; 12(1): 113-120. Illus.: Photo. 1. Lang.: Eng.

USA. 1997. Critical studies. ■The issue of death and dying in AIDS plays. Focuses on Larry Kramer's *The Normal Heart*, Tony Kushner's *Angels in America* and others.

3135 Barnett, Claudia. "A Prison of Object Relations: Adrienne Kennedy's *Funnyhouse of a Negro.*" *MD.* 1997 Fall; 40(3): 374-384. Notes. Lang.: Eng.

USA. 1964. Critical studies. ■Examines how characters of Kennedy's play attempt to order their anxieties by splitting and projecting them onto persecutory and ideal objects. Focus on character of Sarah and her 'selves'.

3136 Becker, Becky K. "Women Who Choose: The Theme of Mothering in Selected Dramas." *AmerD.* 1997 Spr; 6(2): 43-57. Biblio. Lang.: Eng.

USA. 1996. Critical studies. ■Focuses on *The Abdication* by Ruth Wolff, *Machinal* by Sophie Treadwell and *The Heidi Chronicles* by Wendy Wasserstein.

3137 Bennett, Elizabeth; Frisch, Norman; Weems, Marianne. "Dramaturgy on the Road to Immortality: Inside the Wooster Group." 483-494 in Jonas, Susan, ed.; Proehl, Geoffrey S., ed. *Dramaturgy in American Theatre: A Sourcebook.* New York, NY: Harcourt Brace College Pub; 1997. 590 pp. Pref. Notes. Biblio. Index. Lang.: Eng.

USA: New York, NY. 1982-1988. Histories-sources. ■Authors recount their work as dramaturgs with the Wooster Group, delineating the role of the dramaturg in experimental theatre.

3138 Bernard, Louise. "The Musicality of Language: Redefining 'History' in Suzan-Lori Parks's *The Death of the Last Black Man in the Whole Entire World.*" *AfAmR.* 1997 Win; 31(4): 687-698. Notes. Biblio. Lang.: Eng.

USA. 1995. Critical studies. ■Examines Parks's play as an intricate blues riff on the 'complexities of identity and subjectivity' within the cultural realm of African Americans.

3139 Bernstein, Melissa Salz. "Emily Mann: Having Her Say." *AmerD.* 1997 Spr; 6(2): 81-99. Biblio. Lang.: Eng.

USA: Princeton, NJ. 1981-1996. Histories-sources. ■Interview with author/director Emily Mann on her latest projects, documentary theatre and American politics. Introduction by author discusses emergence of documentary theatre and Mann's work in that genre through her plays *Still Life, Execution of Justice, Greensboro: A Requiem* and *Having Our Say.*

3140 Bethune, Brian D. *Remaindered Subjects: A Lacanian Reading of Selected Plays by Lee Blessing.* Bowling Green, OH: Bowling Green State Univ; 1997. 241 pp. [Ph.D. Dissertation, Univ. Microfilms Order No. AAC 9820892.] Lang.: Eng.

USA. 1989-1991. Critical studies. ■The protagonist as a remaindered subject seeking recognition, meaning or affirmation in *Two Rooms, Down the Road*, and *Fortinbras.*

3141 Bianchi, Ruggero; Gobbato, Cristiana, ed. "Il futuro del teatro americano è l'onestà intellettuale." (Intellectual Integrity Is the Future of American Theatre.) *IlCast.* 1997; 10(29): 103-125. Notes. Illus.: Photo. B&W. Lang.: Ita.

USA. 1985. Histories-sources. ■Interview with playwright Gina Wendkos about American theatre of the 1980s and the importance in gaining distance from European models and focusing on the American experience, which includes television.

3142 Bianchi, Ruggero; Gobbato, Cristiana, ed. "*Location* and *Performer*: la loro memoria diventa memorabile." (*Location* and *Performer*: Their Memory Becomes Memorable.) *IlCast.* 1997; 10(29): 83-102. Illus.: Photo. B&W. Lang.: Ita.

USA. 1985. Histories-sources. ■Interview with playwright Laura Farabough about her work, with special attention to site-specific theatre and her use of video and film technology.

3143 Bigsby, C.W.E. "Entering *The Glass Menagerie.*" 29-44 in Roudané, Matthew C., ed. *The Cambridge Companion to Tennessee Williams.* Cambridge: Cambridge UP; 1997. 277 pp. (Cambridge Companions to Literature.) Notes. Biblio. Index. Illus.: Photo. 1. Lang.: Eng.

USA. 1934-1944. Critical studies. ■The reflection of Tennessee Williams's 'apprenticeship' years in *The Glass Menagerie.*

3144 Bigsby, Christopher. "The Early Plays." 21-47 in Bigsby, Christopher, ed. *The Cambridge Companion to Arthur Miller.* Cambridge: Cambridge UP; 1997. 277 pp. (Cambridge Companions to Literature.) Index. Notes. Lang.: Eng.

USA. 1940-1950. Historical studies. ■Early efforts of playwright Arthur Miller and their evolution into later plays and themes.

3145 Bigsby, Christopher. "Miller in the Nineties." 168-183 in Bigsby, Christopher, ed. *The Cambridge Companion to Arthur Miller.* Cambridge: Cambridge UP; 1997. 277 pp. (Cambridge Companions to Literature.) Index. Notes. Illus.: Photo. 3. Lang.: Eng.

USA. 1990-1997. Historical studies. ■Examines a prolific period in playwright Arthur Miller's career, as he kept current with political and social

DRAMA: —Plays/librettos/scripts

developments reflected in his plays *The Ride Down Mount Morgan, The Last Yankee,* and *Broken Glass.*

3146 Bliss, Matt. "'So happy for a time:' A Cultural Poetics of Eugene O'Neill's *Long Day's Journey Into Night.*" *AmerD.* 1997 Fall; 7(1): 1-17. Biblio. Lang.: Eng.
USA. 1939-1941. Critical studies. ■Comparison of the Irish immigrant experience in the US to characters in O'Neill's play. Uses approach of New historicism to interpret play as dramatic literature rather than autobiography.

3147 Bottoms, Stephen J. "'Language is the Motor': Maria Irene Fornes's *Promenade* as Text and Performance." *NETJ.* 1997; 8: 45-71. Notes. Biblio. Illus.: Photo. B&W. 2. Lang.: Eng.
USA. 1969-1994. Critical studies. ■Analysis of Fornes' play, and the evolution of the play through performance.

3148 Bradbury, Malcolm. "Arthur Miller's Fiction." 211-229 in Bigsby, Christopher, ed. *The Cambridge Companion to Arthur Miller.* Cambridge: Cambridge UP; 1997. 277 pp. (Cambridge Companions to Literature.) Index. Notes. Lang.: Eng.
USA. 1940-1995. Historical studies. ■Examines the fiction of playwright Arthur Miller and compares style and theme to his plays.

3149 Branyon, Alexandra. "William Luce: Putting Biography Onstage." *DGQ.* 1997 Sum; 34(2): 23-33. Lang.: Eng.
USA. 1997. Histories-sources. ■Interview with playwright William Luce discussing his fascination with literary and dramatic figures in his biographical plays *Barrymore, The Belle of Amherst* and *Lillian.*

3150 Burchard, Rachael C. "What's an 'Apostroplay'?" *DGQ.* 1997 Fall; 34(3): 35-38. Lang.: Eng.
USA. 1997. Critical studies. ■Proposes to call the one-person short play 'apostroplay', to distinguish it from the broader term 'monologue'.

3151 Burke, Sally. *American Feminist Playwrights: A Critical History.* New York, NY: Twayne; 1997. 270 pp. (Twayne's Critical History of American Drama 5.) Notes. Biblio. Index. Illus.: Photo. 8. Lang.: Eng.
USA. 1772-1995. Critical studies. ■Critical essays on American feminist playwrights including Mercy Otis Warren, Susanna Rowson, Anna Cora Mowatt, Rachel Crothers, Susan Glaspell, Marsha Norman, Wendy Wasserstein, and Maria Irene Fornes.

3152 Burkman, Katherine H. "The Myth of Narcissus: Shepard's *True West* and Mamet's *Speed-the-Plow.*" *JADT.* 1997 Spr; 9(2) : 23-32. Notes. Lang.: Eng.
USA. 1980-1988. Critical studies. ■Examines the myth of the Hollywood cinema in two contemporary American plays, David Mamet's *Speed-the-Plow* and Sam Shepard's *True West.* Compares this American mythology to the myth of Narcissus.

3153 Burton, Jennifer Susan. *Creative Expections: Hope as a Literary and Political Tool in American Prose and Performance from World War I Until the Crash (1914-1929).* Cambridge, MA: Harvard Univ; 1997. 190 pp. [Ph.D. Dissertation, Univ. Microfilms Order No. AAC 9733251.] Lang.: Eng.
USA. 1914-1929. Critical studies. ■Study of the theme of hope in personal and social change. Examines the Harlem Renaissance, suffragist political theatre, the modern clown, and the street as the symbolic setting for struggles regarding social mobility and exchange. Plays analyzed in detail include Angelina Weld Grimké's *Rachel,* Marita Bonner's *The Purple Flower,* Eugene O'Neill's one-act *Abortion,* Mary P. Burrill's *They That Sit in Darkness,* Charlotte Perkins Gilman's *Something to Vote For,* Zona Gale's *Miss Lulu Bett,* and Elmer Rice's *Street Scene.* Also considers Sherwood Anderson's *Winesburg, Ohio,* the films of Chaplin and Keaton, and novels by F. Scott Fitzgerald and Ernest Hemingway.

3154 Cadden, Michael. "Strange Angel: The Pinklisting of Roy Cohn." 78-89 in Geis, Deborah R., ed.; Kruger, Steven F., ed. *Approaching the Millennium: Essays on Angels in America.* Ann Arbor, MI: Univ. of Michigan P; 1997. 352 pp. Notes. Lang.: Eng.
USA. 1992-1994. Critical studies. ■Considers treatment of character Roy Cohn in Tony Kushner's *Angels in America.* Argues that this 'outing' of a complex historical figure can aid in moving toward a new community based on solidarity between old and new lines of group identification.

3155 Callens, Johan. "'We Trespass, We Plagiarize, We Steal'." *Thsch.* 1997; 11: 173-188. Illus.: Photo. B&W. 2. Lang.: Ger, Fre, Dut, Eng.
USA: New York, NY. 1975-1997. Critical studies. ■Analysis of the specific reworkings of the classics by the Wooster Group.

3156 Carr, C. "No Trace of the Bland: Interview with Playwright Holly Hughes." *ThM.* 1993; 24(2): 67-75. Illus.: Photo. B&W. 3. Lang.: Eng.
USA. 1990-1993. Histories-sources. ■Interview with lesbian playwright Holly Hughes about her plays *No Trace of the Blonde, World Without End* and her views on sexuality.

3157 Castagno, Paul C. "New Play Development and the 'New' Dramaturg: The Dramaturg's Approach to the First Draft." 441-446 in Jonas, Susan, ed.; Proehl, Geoffrey S., ed. *Dramaturgy in American Theatre: A Sourcebook.* New York, NY: Harcourt Brace College Pub; 1997. 590 pp. Pref. Notes. Biblio. Index. Lang.: Eng.
USA. 1996-1997. Histories-sources. ■Training new dramaturgs by working with new playwrights: collaboration and challenge.

3158 Centola, Steven R. "*All My Sons.*" 48-59 in Bigsby, Christopher, ed. *The Cambridge Companion to Arthur Miller.* Cambridge: Cambridge UP; 1997. 277 pp. (Cambridge Companions to Literature.) Index. Notes. Lang.: Eng.
USA. 1947. Historical studies. ■Examines playwright Arthur Miller's first major theatrical success, *All My Sons*: history, structure, etc.

3159 Chambers, Jonathan. "How Hollywood Led John Howard Lawson to Embrace Communism and How He Turned Hollywood Red." *THSt.* 1997; 17: 15-32. Lang.: Eng.
USA. 1933-1947. Historical studies. ■The development of political consciousness in playwright John Howard Lawson's work for both stage and screen. Focuses on his work with the Screen Writers Guild and his participation in the Communist Party.

3160 Classon, H. Lin. "Re-Evaluating *Color Struck*: Zora Neale Hurston and the Issue of Colorism." *TheatreS.* 1997; 42: 4-18 . Notes. Illus.: Photo. B&W. 12. Lang.: Eng.
USA. 1891-1995. Critical studies. ■Content and structure of Hurston's prize-winning play *Color Struck,* techniques employed, and the social and cultural significance of the play. Hurston's choice of topic, colorism, and author's argument for Hurston's place as a pioneer in African American drama of social commentary.

3161 Clum, John M. "The Sacrificial Stud and the Fugitive Female in *Suddenly Last Summer, Orpheus Descending,* and *Sweet Bird of Youth.*" 128-146 in Roudané, Matthew C., ed. *The Cambridge Companion to Tennessee Williams.* Cambridge: Cambridge UP; 1997. 277 pp. (Cambridge Companions to Literature.) Notes. Biblio. Index. Illus.: Photo. 1. Lang.: Eng.
USA. 1956-1959. Critical studies. ■The erotic in three plays by Tennessee Williams: *Suddenly Last Summer, Orpheus Descending,* and *Sweet Bird of Youth.* Argues that Williams presented a new sex/gender system that revolutionized theatre.

3162 Coen, Stephanie. "Kia Corthron: Taking Sides." *DGQ.* 1997 Spr; 34(1): 22-25. Illus.: Photo. B&W. 1. Lang.: Eng.
USA. 1997. Histories-sources. ■Interview with playwright Corthron regarding her newest play *Seeking the Genesis.*

3163 Coen, Stephanie. "Writers and Their Work: Constance Congdon." *DGQ.* 1997 Win; 34(4): 25-36. Lang.: Eng.
USA. 1997. Histories-sources. ■Interview with the playwright touching on her plays *Tales of the Lost Formicans, Casanova, No Mercy,* and *Dog Opera,* and the direction she perceives theatre is going.

3164 Cohen, Sarah Blacher, ed. *Making a Scene: The Contemporary Drama of Jewish-American Women.* Syracuse, NY: Syracuse UP; 1997. 370 pp. Biblio. Illus.: Photo. 7. Lang.: Eng.
USA. 1985-1995. ■Includes Wendy Wasserstein's *Isn't It Romantic,* Barbara Lebow's *A Shayna Maidel,* Sarah Blacher Cohen's *The Ladies Locker Room,* Lois Roisman's *Nobody's Gilgul,* Barbara Kahn's *Whither Thou Goest,* Hindi Brooks' *The Night the War Came Home,* and Merle Feld's *Across the Jordan.*

3165 Cohn, Ruby. "Tennessee Williams: The Last Two Decades." 232-243 in Roudané, Matthew C., ed. *The Cambridge Com-*

panion to Tennessee Williams. Cambridge: Cambridge UP; 1997. 277 pp. (Cambridge Companions to Literature.) Index. Notes. Biblio. Lang.: Eng.
USA. 1966-1983. Historical studies. ■Examines the merits of Tennessee Williams's less-known works later works such as *The Chalky White Substance, Small Craft Warnings, Vieux Carré, A House Not Meant to Stand,* and *Something Cloudy, Something Clear.*

3166 Congdon, Constance. "The Science Was Beautiful." *AmTh.* 1997 Mar.; 14(3): 8. Illus.: Photo. B&W. 1. Lang.: Eng.
USA: Evanston, IL. 1984-1997. Histories-sources. ■Interview with playwright/director Russell Vandenbroucke on his new play *Atomic Bombers* and its focus on physicist Richard Feynmann.

3167 Crandell, George W. *The Critical Response to Tennessee Williams.* Westport, CT/London: Greenwood; 1996. 307 pp. (Critical Responses in Arts and Letters.) Index. Notes. Lang.: Eng.
USA. 1940-1982. Historical studies. ■Collection of critical reviews and essays covering playwright Tennessee Williams' career from his earliest play *Battle of Angels* to *A House Not Meant to Stand.*

3168 Crandell, George W. "Misrepresentation and Miscegenation: Reading the Racialized Discourse of Tennessee Williams's *A Streetcar Named Desire.*" *MD.* 1997 Fall; 40(3): 337-346. Notes. Lang.: Eng.
USA. 1911-1983. Critical studies. ■Absence or underrepresentation of African-American characters in the plays of Williams, and theory that Stanley in *Streetcar* is ascribed the features of a racial 'Other'.

3169 Cummings, Scott T. "Garden or Ghetto? The Paradoxy of New Play Development." 376-384 in Jonas, Susan, ed.; Proehl, Geoffrey S., ed. *Dramaturgy in American Theatre: A Sourcebook.* New York, NY: Harcourt Brace College Pub; 1997. 590 pp. Pref. Notes. Biblio. Index. Lang.: Eng.
USA. 1960-1996. Historical studies. ■The history and problems of new play development in the United States.

3170 Debusscher, Gilbert. "Creative Rewriting: European and American Influences on the Dramas of Tennessee Williams." 167-188 in Roudané, Matthew C., ed. *The Cambridge Companion to Tennessee Williams.* Cambridge: Cambridge UP; 1997. 277 pp. (Cambridge Companions to Literature.) Index. Notes. Biblio. Lang.: Eng.
USA. 1944-1980. Historical studies. ■European and American influences on playwright Tennessee Williams. Explores primary figures such as Oscar Wilde, Hart Crane, Bertolt Brecht, Federico García Lorca, and Jean Cocteau, but insists on the originality of Williams.

3171 Dee, Edward Martin. *The Travel to the Past in Twentieth-Century Anglo-American Drama.* New York, NY: City Univ. of New York; 1997. 295 pp. Notes. Biblio. [Ph.D. Dissertation, Univ. Microfilms Order No. AAC 9732910.] Lang.: Eng.
USA. Canada. UK-England. 1908-1993. Critical studies. ■Travel to the past in the work of J.M. Barrie (*The Admirable Crichton, Peter Pan, Dear Brutus,* and *Mary Rose*), John L. Balderston's *Berkeley Square,* Maxwell Anderson's *The Star Wagon,* Thornton Wilder's *Our Town,* Ann-Marie MacDonald's *Goodnight Desdemona (Good Morning Juliet),* and Marsha Norman's *Daniel Boone* among others.

3172 Dellamora, Richard. "Tony Kushner and the 'Not Yet' of Gay Existence." *JADT.* 1997 Fall; 9(3): 73-101. Notes. Lang.: Eng.
USA. 1988-1996. Historical studies. ■The reflection of current cultural debates in Tony Kushner's *Angels in America.* Focuses specifically on the debate of social decadence and conservatives' fear of contagion in the AIDS epidemic.

3173 Demastes, William W. "Miller's 1970s 'Power' Plays." 139-151 in Bigsby, Christopher, ed. *The Cambridge Companion to Arthur Miller.* Cambridge: Cambridge UP; 1997. 277 pp. (Cambridge Companions to Literature.) Index. Notes. Lang.: Eng.
USA. 1970-1979. Historical studies. ■Social issues of the 1970s in the works of playwright Arthur Miller including *A Memory of Two Mondays, Fame, The Reason Why, The Creation of the World and Other Business,*

The Archbishop's Ceiling and the musical *Up from Paradise* (musical version of *The Creation of the World and Other Business*).

3174 Devlin, Albert J. "Writing in 'A Place of Stone': *Cat on a Hot Tin Roof.*" 95-113 in Roudané, Matthew C., ed. *The Cambridge Companion to Tennessee Williams.* Cambridge: Cambridge UP; 1997. 277 pp. (Cambridge Companions to Literature.) Notes. Biblio. Index. Illus.: Photo. 1. Lang.: Eng.
USA. 1955. Critical studies. ■Proposes a new reading of plot, character and theme of Tennesse Williams' play and gives background information on the original composition of the play, different versions of the third act, and why revisions were made.

3175 Diamond, Betty. "The One-Minute Play: Gimmick or Theatrical Haiku?" *DGQ.* 1997 Fall; 34(3): 39-44. Lang.: Eng.
USA. 1997. Critical studies. ■Argues in favor of the legitimacy of the one-minute play form.

3176 Diamond, Elin. *Unmaking Mimesis: Essays on Feminism and Theater.* New York, NY/London: Routledge; 1997. 224 pp. Notes. Biblio. Index. Lang.: Eng.
USA. 1997. Critical studies. ■Analysis of the concept of mimesis in relation to feminism, theatre, and performance. Author combines psychoanalytic, semiotic, and materialist strategies with readings of plays such as Ibsen's *A Doll's House (Et Dukkehjem),* Brecht's *Good Woman of Szechuan (Der Gute Mensch von Sezuan),* Aphra Behn's *The Rover,* Caryl Churchill's *The Skriker,* and the work of Peggy Shaw of Split Britches.

3177 Diamond, Liz. "Perceptible Mutability in the Word Kingdom." *ThM.* 1993; 24(3): 86-87. Lang.: Eng.
USA. 1993. Critical studies. ■Introduction to the text of Suzan-Lori Parks' play *Imperceptible Mutabilities in the Third Kingdom.*

3178 Dickey, Jerry. *Sophie Treadwell: A Research and Production Sourcebook.* Westport, CT: Greenwood; 1997. 288 pp. Notes. Index. Biblio. Lang.: Eng.
USA. 1885-1970. Histories-specific. ■Assessment of works by, and scholarship about, playwright Sophie Treadwell. Includes plot summaries of all of Treadwell's plays.

3179 Downing, Michael John. *Restoring the Myths: Converting Stereotype to Archetype in Five Plays of August Wilson.* Indiana, PA: Indiana Univ. of Pennsylvania; 1997. 202 pp. [Ph.D. Dissertation, Univ. Microfilms Order No. AAC 9731976.] Lang.: Eng.
USA. 1982-1995. Critical studies. ■Explores Wilson's role in constructing a cultural mythology for African Americans. Plays examined are *Ma Rainey's Black Bottom, Fences, Joe Turner's Come and Gone, The Piano Lesson,* and *Two Trains Running.*

3180 Drukman, Steven. "Julie Jensen." *AmTh.* 1997 Jan.; 14(1): 52-53. Illus.: Photo. B&W. 2. Lang.: Eng.
USA: Las Vegas, NV. 1970-1997. Biographical studies. ■Profile and career of playwright Jensen. Influence of living in Las Vegas on her writing, her plays *Stray Dogs* and *The Lost Vegas Series.*

3181 Drukman, Steven. "Writers and Their Work: Paula Vogel." *DGQ.* 1997 Sum; 34(2): 4-13. Illus.: Photo. B&W. 2. Lang.: Eng.
USA: New York, NY. 1997. Histories-sources. ■Interview with playwright Paula Vogel, centering on the future of women writers in the theatre and her plays *The Mineola Twins, How I Learned to Drive* and *And Baby Makes Seven.*

3182 Durang, Christopher. "Day by Day with Christopher Durang." *DGQ.* 1997 Spr; 34(1): 34-44. Illus.: Photo. B&W. 1. Lang.: Eng.
USA: New York, NY. 1997. Histories-sources. ■A five-day diary composed by Durang during the closing of his play *Sex and Longing.* Originally commissioned for *Slate,* an on-line magazine.

3183 Engle, Sherry D. "Desperately Seeking a Poe: Sophie Treadwell's *Plumes in the Dust.*" *AmerD.* 1997 Spr; 6(2): 25-42. Notes. Biblio. Lang.: Eng.
USA. 1917-1936. Historical studies. ■Examination of Treadwell's process as playwright from conception to production using *Poe* as a case study. Her legal action against actor John Barrymore for piracy of the play, the change of its name to *Plumes in the Dust,* its eventual production with actor Henry Hull, directed by Arthur Hopkins for Broadway.

DRAMA: —Plays/librettos/scripts

3184 Evell, Kim. "Signifyin(g) Ritual: Subverting Stereotypes, Salvaging Icons." *AfAmR*. 1997 Win; 31(4): 667-675. Biblio. Lang.: Eng.
USA. 1986-1997. Critical studies. ■Beginning with George C. Wolfe's *The Colored Museum*, explores contemporary Black playwrights' continuing exorcism of entrenched stereotypes through subversive approaches to character, exemplified by *I Ain't Yo Uncle* by Robert Alexander, *King of Coons* by Michael Henry Brown and *Porch Monkey* by Kim Dunbar.

3185 Farfan, Penny. "Feminism, Metatheatricality, and *Mise-en-scène* in Maria Irene Fornes's *Fefu and Her Friends*." *MD*. 1997 Win; 40(4): 442-453. Notes. Lang.: Eng.
USA: New York, NY. 1977-1997. Critical studies. ■Argues that in reconfiguring the conventional performer-spectator relationship, the play realizes in theatrical terms an alternative model for interaction with the universe external to the self such as that proposed by one of the characters. Play posits postmodern feminist theatre practice as a constructive response to the psychic dilemmas of the characters.

3186 Fleche, Anne. *Mimetic Disillusion: Eugene O'Neill, Tennessee Williams, and U.S. Dramatic Realism*. Tuscaloosa, AL: Univ of Alabama P; 1997. 134 pp. Index. Notes. Biblio. Lang.: Eng.
USA. 1913-1980. Critical studies. ■The limitations of classical mimesis in *The Iceman Cometh* and *Long Day's Journey Into Night* by Eugene O'Neill and *The Glass Menagerie* and *A Streetcar Named Desire* by Tennessee Williams.

3187 Foerster, Marjorie Lonora. *Freedom's Inauguration: The Evolution of Patriotism in Early American Drama*. San Jose, CA: San Jose State Univ; 1997. 120 pp. [M.A. Thesis, Univ. Microfilms Order No. AAC 1388192.] Lang.: Eng.
USA. 1775-1817. Critical studies. ■The developing definition of patriotism as seen in Mercy Otis Warren's *The Group*, Hugh Henry Brackenridge's *The Battle of Bunker's-Hill*, Royall Tyler's *The Contrast*, and William Dunlap's *Andre* and *The Glory of Columbia: Her Yeomanry!*.

3188 Franklin, Nancy. "The Time of Her Life." *NewY*. 1997 14 Apr.: 62-71. Illus.: Photo. B&W. 1. Lang.: Eng.
USA: New York, NY. 1997. Historical studies. ■Profile of Playwright Wendy Wasserstein at the start of rehearsals for her *An American Daughter*.

3189 Frantzen, Allen J. "Prior to the Normans: The Anglo-Saxons in *Angels in America*." 134-150 in Geis, Deborah R., ed.; Kruger, Steven F., ed. *Approaching the Millennium: Essays on Angels in America*. Ann Arbor, MI: Univ. of Michigan P; 1997. 352 pp. Notes. Lang.: Eng.
USA. 1992-1994. Critical studies. ■Focuses on ethnicity in Tony Kushner's *Angels in America*, specifically, the character of Prior Walter and his identity as a white, Anglo-Saxon Protestant.

3190 Frederic, Cheryl. "George S. Kaufman and Moss Hart's *Merrily We Roll Along*: The Cuckoo in the Nest?" *THSt*. 1997; 17: 63-77. Illus.: Photo. 2. Lang.: Eng.
USA. 1934. Historical studies. ■Historical reasons for Kaufman and Hart's uncharacteristically pessimistic serious play *Merrily We Roll Along*. Author examines the early writing collaboration of Kaufman and Hart for clues to later stylistic change as well as contemporary social and cultural events.

3191 Freeman, Roger. "Narrative and Anti-Narrative: Televisual Representation and Non-Causal Linearity in Contemporary Drama." *JDTC*. 1997 Fall; 12(1): 39-55. Lang.: Eng.
USA. 1990-1997. Critical studies. ■Examines the partial rejection of causal narrative and the use of a televisual dramaturgy in several works by contemporary playwrights, such as Eric Overmyer's *In Perpetuity Throughout the Universe*, Craig Lucas's *Reckless*, and Len Jenkin's *Gogol, A Mystery Play*.

3192 Gargano, Cara. "The Starfish and the Strange Attractor: Myth, Science, and Theatre as Laboratory in Maria Irene Fornes' *Mud*." *NTQ*. 1997; 13(51): 214-220. Notes. Biblio. Lang.: Eng.
USA. 1983-1995. Critical studies. ■Compares divergent critical interpretations of *Mud* and suggests that Fornes uses the theatrical space as her laboratory—a place to explore the interface between society's construction of the world and our evolving scientific vision.

3193 Garner, Stanton B., Jr. "*Angels in America*: the Millennium and Postmodern Memory." 173-184 in Geis, Deborah R., ed.; Kruger, Steven F., ed. *Approaching the Millennium: Essays on Angels in America*. Ann Arbor, MI: Univ. of Michigan P; 1997. 352 pp. Notes. Lang.: Eng.
USA. 1992-1994. Critical studies. ■Places Tony Kushner's *Angels in America* in the context of postmodern rhetoric and the preoccupations with 'millenarianism'.

3194 Geis, Deborah R. "Werewolves, Fractals and Forbidden Knowledge." *ThM*. 1997; 27(2/3): 87-95. Illus.: Design. Photo. B&W. 4. Lang.: Eng.
USA. 1997. Histories-sources. ■Interview with playwrigth Mac Wellman regarding his work and career.

3195 Geis, Deborah R. "'The Delicate Ecology of Your Illusions': Insanity, Theatricality, and the Thresholds of Revelation in Kushner's *Angels in America*." 199-212 in Geis, Deborah R., ed.; Kruger, Steven F., ed. *Approaching the Millennium: Essays on Angels in America*. Ann Arbor, MI: Univ. of Michigan P; 1997. 352 pp. Notes. Lang.: Eng.
USA. 1992-1994. Critical studies. ■Insanity and prophecy in Tony Kushner's *Angels in America*. Focuses on Harper and Prior, the two characters in the play most consistently associated with revelation.

3196 Gener, Randy. "Minutes from the Donaghy Route." *DGQ*. 1997 Win; 34(4): 8-13. Illus.: Photo. B&W. 1. Lang.: Eng.
USA. 1997. Histories-sources. ■Interview with playwright Tom Donaghy regarding his new work *Minutes from the Blue Route*.

3197 Giles, Freda Scott. "The Motion of Herstory: Three Plays by Pearl Cleage." *AfAmR*. 1997 Win; 31(4): 709-712. Notes. Biblio. Lang.: Eng.
USA: Atlanta, GA. 1992-1997. Critical studies. ■View of Black female cultural history in three plays by Cleage: *Flyin' West*, *Blues for an Alabama Sky*, and *Bourbon at the Border*.

3198 Gluck, David. "Leslie Ayvazian." *AmTh*. 1997 Dec.; 14(10): 37-39. Illus.: Photo. B&W. 2. Lang.: Eng.
USA: New York, NY. 1995-1997. Biographical studies. ■Ayvazian's move from a career in acting to playwriting. Her play *Nine Armenians*, training in acting and writing, and most recent work *Singer's Boy*.

3199 Godin, Diane. "Deux fois le monde." (Two Times the World.) *JCT*. 1997; 83: 18-24. Notes. Illus.: Photo. B&W. 5. Lang.: Fre.
USA. Romania. 1997. Critical studies. ■Theme of mystification and the individual's place in society in Eric Bogosian's *Sex, Drugs, Rock & Roll* and Matéi Visniec's *Théâtre décomposé ou l'Homme-poubelle (Decomposed Theatre or the Human Garbage Can)*.

3200 Goggans, Thomas H. "Laying Blame: Gender and Subtext in David Mamet's *Oleanna*." *MD*. 1997 Win; 40(4): 433-441. Notes. Lang.: Eng.
USA. 1992-1997. Critical studies. ■Suggests a new interpretation of the actions of the character of Carol in Mamet's play about sexual harassment to dispel criticisms that she is 'one-sided'. Argues that the character undergoes a true dramatic progression.

3201 Gross, Robert F. "O'Neill's Queer Interlude: Epicene Excess and Camp Pleasures." *JDTC*. 1997 Fall; 12(1): 3-22. Lang.: Eng.
USA. 1926-1927. Critical studies. ■The public success of O'Neill's *Strange Interlude* contrasted with the scorn it received from critics. Both are said to result from the play's transgression of cultural modes of masculinity.

3202 Gross, Robert F. "The Pleasures of Brick: Eros and the Gay Spectator in *Cat on a Hot Tin Roof*." *JADT*. 1997 Win; 9(1): 11-25. Notes. Lang.: Eng.
USA. 1955. Critical studies. ■Gay erotics in Tennessee Williams's *Cat on a Hot Tin Roof*.

3203 Haedicke, Susan. "Arthur Miller: A Bibliographic Essay." 245-266 in Bigsby, Christopher, ed. *The Cambridge Companion to Arthur Miller*. Cambridge: Cambridge UP; 1997. 277 pp. (Cambridge Companions to Literature.) Index. Notes. Lang.: Eng.
USA. 1940-1997. Bibliographical studies. ■Includes bibliographies, critical studies and interdisciplinary approaches, fiction and screenplays.

DRAMA: —Plays/librettos/scripts

3204 Hale, Allean. "Early Williams: The Making of a Playwright." 11-28 in Roudané, Matthew C., ed. *The Cambridge Companion to Tennessee Williams*. Cambridge: Cambridge UP; 1997. 277 pp. (Cambridge Companions to Literature.) Notes. Biblio. Index. Illus.: Photo. 1. Lang.: Eng.

USA. 1911-1944. Biographical studies. ■Tennessee Williams's life and career before *The Glass Menagerie*, including home life, early influences, and more than forty-five short stories, essays, and plays.

3205 Hanes, Mary. "Spinning a Crimson Thread." *DGQ.* 1997 Win; 34(4): 4-7. Lang.: Eng.

USA. 1997. Histories-sources. ■Playwright Mary Hanes relates her inspiration for her play *The Crimson Thread*.

3206 Harries, Martin. "Flying the Angel of History." 185-198 in Geis, Deborah R., ed.; Kruger, Steven F., ed. *Approaching the Millennium: Essays on Angels in America*. Ann Arbor, MI: Univ. of Michigan P; 1997. 352 pp. Notes. Lang.: Eng.

USA. 1992-1994. Critical studies. ■Theoretical analysis of the supernatural aspects of Tony Kushner's *Angels in America*.

3207 Hilton, Melissa. *The Political Ideologies of Roy Cohn and Prior Walter: Tony Kushner's Political Vision in Angels in America: A Gay Fantasia on National Themes*. San Angelo, TX: Angelo State Univ; 1997. 88 pp. [M.A. Thesis, Univ. Microfilms Order No. AAC 1386100.] Lang.: Eng.

USA. 1994-1996. Critical studies. ■Examines the AIDS crisis and characters in Tony Kushner's *Angels in America: A Gay Fantasia on National Themes*.

3208 Hsiu-chen, Lin. "Staging Orientalia: Dangerous 'Authenticity' in David Henry Hwang's *M. Butterfly*." *JADT.* 1997 Win; 9 (1): 26-35. Notes. Lang.: Eng.

USA. 1988. Critical studies. ■The success of David Henry Hwang's *M. Butterfly* as a historical and critical phenomenon. Warns of the potential stereotyping of 'authenticity' in the reception of the play.

3209 Jackson, Pamela Faith. "Ed Bullins: From Minister of Culture to Living Legend." *BlackM.* 1997 Aug/Sep.; 12(5): 5-6. Illus.: Photo. B&W. 2. Lang.: Eng.

USA. 1968-1997. Biographical studies. ■Politics and professional career of the playwright.

3210 Jonas, Susan. "Aiming the Canon at Now: Strategies for Adaptation." 244-265 in Jonas, Susan, ed.; Proehl, Geoffrey S., ed. *Dramaturgy in American Theatre: A Sourcebook*. New York, NY: Harcourt Brace College Pub; 1997. 590 pp. Pref. Notes. Biblio. Index. Lang.: Eng.

USA. 1997. Historical studies. ■Examines specific strategies for a radical re-contextualization of canonical texts for contemporary production.

3211 Jonas, Susan. "Tony Kushner's Angels: An Interview with Tony Kushner Conducted by Susan Jonas." 472-482 in Jonas, Susan, ed.; Proehl, Geoffrey S., ed. *Dramaturgy in American Theatre: A Sourcebook*. New York, NY: Harcourt Brace College Pub; 1997. 590 pp. Pref. Notes. Biblio. Index. Lang.: Eng.

USA. 1989-1995. Histories-sources. ■Interview with playwright Tony Kushner regarding his history of collaboration with dramaturgs. Argues for a strong ideological and political foundation.

3212 Jones, Chris. "Blues Elixir." *AmTh.* 1997 Jan.; 14(1): 12-14. Illus.: Photo. B&W. 2. Lang.: Eng.

USA. 1995-1996. Critical studies. ■Keith Glover's play *Thunder Knocking on the Door*: influence of blues music on its structure, current productions. Brief overview of Glover's previous works.

3213 Katz, Leon. "Mea Culpa, Nostra Culpa." 398-400 in Jonas, Susan, ed.; Proehl, Geoffrey S., ed. *Dramaturgy in American Theatre: A Sourcebook*. New York, NY: Harcourt Brace College Pub; 1997. 590 pp. Pref. Notes. Biblio. Index. Lang.: Eng.

USA. 1960-1997. Critical studies. ■Critique of the process of play development in the United States.

3214 Kearns, Michael. "Getting Your Solo Act Together: The Genres." *DGQ.* 1997 Fall; 34(3): 29-34. Illus.: Photo. B&W. 1. Lang.: Eng.

USA. 1997. Instructional materials. ■Excerpt from actor/playwright Kearns' book *Getting Your Solo Act Together*, discussing subject matter and approach for young solo artists.

3215 King, W.D. *Writing Wrongs: The Work of Wallace Shawn*. Philadelphia, PA: Temple UP; 1997. 242 pp. (American Subjects.) Append. Biblio. Index. Notes. Illus.: Photo. 4. Lang.: Eng.

USA. 1970-1996. Critical studies. ■Critical examination of plays by Wallace Shawn, including *Marie and Bruce, The Music Teacher, My Dinner with André, Aunt Dan and Lemon, The Fever, Vanya on 42nd Street*, and *The Designated Mourner*. Includes an interview with the playwright.

3216 Klaver, Elizabeth. "Ronald Ribman's *Buck*, Unsolved Mysteries, and the Television Simulators." *AmerD.* 1997 Fall; 7(1): 82-98. Biblio. Lang.: Eng.

USA. 1983. Critical studies. ■Comparison of the play *Buck* which examines the complexity of television simulations, and the crime reenactment television show *Unsolved Mysteries*. Epistemological questions that are raised with the literary and cultural movement of postmodernism.

3217 Kolin, Philip C. "'It's only a paper moon': The Paper Ontologies in Tennessee Williams's *A Streetcar Named Desire*." *MD.* 1997 Win; 40(4): 454-467. Notes. Lang.: Eng.

USA. 1940-1996. Critical studies. ■Cultural and sexual significance of paper in Williams's play: its symbolism, and how a character's power or instability is tracked through the medium of paper.

3218 Kondo, Dorinne. *About Face: Performing 'Race' in Fashion and Theater*. New York, NY/London: Routledge; 1997. 288 pp. Notes. Biblio. Index. Illus.: Photo. 12. Lang.: Eng.

USA. 1990-1997. Critical studies. ■Representations of Asia, especially in the theatre. Author analyzes the politics of pleasure, the performance of racial identities, and the possibility of intervention in political and economic systems through works such as David Henry Hwang's *M. Butterfly*.

3219 Konkle, Lincoln. "American Jeremiah: Edward Albee as Judgement Day Prophet in *The Lady From Dubuque*." *AmerD.* 1997 Fall; 7(1): 30-49. Notes. Biblio. Lang.: Eng.

USA. 1980. Critical studies. ■Argues that Albee uses the Puritan concept of Judgement Day and filters it through a postmodern sensibility in *The Lady from Dubuque* and other plays.

3220 Kritzer, Amelia Howe. "Mary Carr Clarke's Dramas of Working Women, 1815-1833." *JADT.* 1997 Fall; 9(3): 24-39. Notes. Lang.: Eng.

USA. 1815-1833. Historical studies. ■Examines the three extant plays of Mary Carr Clarke, *The Fair Americans, The Benevolent Lawyers*, and *Sarah Maria Cornell, or, The Fall River Murder*.

3221 Kruger, Steven F. "Identity and Conversion in *Angels in America*." 151-172 in Geis, Deborah R., ed.; Kruger, Steven F., ed. *Approaching the Millennium: Essays on Angels in America*. Ann Arbor, MI: Univ. of Michigan P; 1997. 352 pp. Notes. Lang.: Eng.

USA. 1992-1994. Critical studies. ■Explores how identities can change in Kushner's *Angels in America* and the larger meanings of cultural transformation.

3222 Lahr, John. "Fortress Mamet." *NewY.* 1997 17 Nov.: 70-82. Illus.: Photo. B&W. 2. Lang.: Eng.

USA. 1947-1997. Biographical studies. ■Profile of playwright David Mamet.

3223 Lampe, Eelka. "Disruptions in Representation: Anne Bogart's Creative Encounter with East Asian Performance Traditions." *ThR.* 1997; 22(2): 105-110. Notes. Illus.: Photo. B&W. 3. Lang.: Eng.

USA. 1984-1994. Critical studies. ■Discusses influence of East Asian aesthetics and philosophy on Anne Bogart's writing and directing.

3224 Langkilde, Nicole Maria. "Nicky Silvers univers." (Nicky Silver's Universe.) *TE.* 1997 June; 84: 34-35. Illus.: Photo. B&W. 3. Lang.: Dan.

USA. Denmark. 1994-1997. Critical studies. ■The American dramatist Nicky Silver has been succesful in Denmark since 1994 when Teater Får302 Copenhagen staged his play *Fat Men in Skirts*.

DRAMA: —Plays/librettos/scripts

3225 Lee, Josephine. *Performing Asian America: Race and Ethnicity on the Contemporary Stage.* Philadelphia, PA: Temple UP; 1997. 241 pp. Notes. Index. Biblio. Illus.: Photo. 21. Lang.: Eng.
USA. 1970-1997. Critical studies. ■Analysis of Asian-American drama including Frank Chin's *The Year of the Dragon*, David Henry Hwang's *Family Devotions*, R.A. Shiomi's *Yellow Fever*, Philip Kan Gotanda's *Yankee Dawg You Die*, and Darrell Lum's *Oranges Are Lucky*, among others.

3226 Lerner, Gail. "For Playwrights Only." *AmTh.* 1997 Mar.; 14(3): 37-38. Illus.: Photo. B&W. 1. Lang.: Eng.
USA. 1930-1996. Critical studies. ■Playwrights' alliances created by Robert Menna in Seattle, John Sherman and Douglas Post in Chicago, and Kate Robin, Colette Burson and Jennifer Farber in New York.

3227 Londré, Felicia Hardison. "A Streetcar Running Fifty Years." 45-66 in Roudané, Matthew C., ed. *The Cambridge Companion to Tennessee Williams.* Cambridge: Cambridge UP; 1997. 277 pp. (Cambridge Companions to Literature.) Notes. Biblio. Index. Illus.: Photo. 1. Lang.: Eng.
USA. 1947. Critical studies. ■Analysis of Tennessee Williams's *A Streetcar Named Desire*, in its historical context. Examines its theatrical and cultural impact and gives a new reading of the play by analyzing all eleven scenes.

3228 Lopez, Tiffany Ana. *Bodily Inscriptions: Representations of the Female Body as Cultural Critique in United States Latina Drama.* Santa Barbara, CA: Univ. of California; 1997. 207 pp. [Ph.D. Dissertation, Univ. Microfilms Order No. AAC 9800471.] Lang.: Eng.
USA. 1980-1991. Critical studies. ■Study of the work of three Latina-American playwrights, Maria Irene Fornes, Cherríe Moraga, and Migdalia Cruz, working at the Hispanic Playwright's Lab at INTAR in New York City. Focuses on Latina/o issues, sexual violence, and the role of the body in explorations of women's history and memory. Plays examined are Fornes's *The Conduct of Life*, Moraga's *Giving Up the Ghost*, and Cruz's *Miriam's Flowers*.

3229 Lutterbie, John H. *Hearing Voices: Modern Drama and the Problem of Subjectivity.* Ann Arbor, MI: Univ. of Michigan P; 1997. 192 pp. Notes. Index. Biblio. Lang.: Eng.
USA. Europe. 1940-1990. Critical studies. ■Subjectivity, ethics, and the body in plays of Heiner Müller, Eric Bogosian, Jean Genet, Sam Shepard, and Samuel Beckett.

3230 Magruder, James. "Love Has Entered My Vocabulary: A Cautionary Tale." 317-330 in Jonas, Susan, ed.; Proehl, Geoffrey S., ed. *Dramaturgy in American Theatre: A Sourcebook.* New York, NY: Harcourt Brace College Pub; 1997. 590 pp. Pref. Notes. Biblio. Index. Lang.: Eng.
USA: Baltimore, MD. 1986-1995. Histories-sources. ■Author recounts his work as translator of Marivaux's *Le Triomphe de l'amour (The Triumph of Love)* from his first draft as a student at Yale to its premiere at Baltimore's Center Stage.

3231 Marino, Stephen A. *Arthur Miller's Language: The Poetic in the Colloquial.* New York, NY: Fordham Univ; 1997. 249 pp. [Ph.D. Dissertation, Univ. Microfilms Order No. AAC 9730101.] Lang.: Eng.
USA. 1940-1995. Critical studies. ■Argues that Miller uses the figurative devices of metaphor, symbol, and imagery to give poetic significance to the common man's dialect.

3232 McDonough, Carla J. *Staging Masculinity: Male Identity in Contemporary American Drama.* Jefferson, NC/London: McFarland; 1997. 186 pp. Index. Notes. Biblio. Lang.: Eng.
USA. 1915-1995. Histories-specific. ■Masculinity in the works of Sam Shepard, David Mamet, David Rabe, and August Wilson. Includes brief historical overview of O'Neill, Williams, Miller, and Baraka.

3233 McDonough, Carla J. "God and the Owls: The Sacred and the Profane in Adrienne Kennedy's *The Owl Answers*." *MD.* 1997 Fall; 40(3): 385-402. Lang.: Eng.
USA. 1965-1997. Critical studies. ■Symbolism, identity, social and racial ideologies, characters and themes in Kennedy's play. Tendency to overlook this play in favor of her earlier work *Funnyhouse of a Negro*.

3234 Melnick, Ralph. *The Stolen Legacy of Anne Frank: Meyer Levin, Lillian Hellman, and the Staging of the Diary.* New Haven, CT: Yale UP; 1997. 304 pp. Biblio. Index. Illus.: Photo. 13. Lang.: Eng.
USA. 1947-1950. Critical studies. ■Meyer Levin's stage adaptation of the diary of Anne Frank and the influence of Lillian Hellman and Otto Frank, Anne's father, on a drastically revised version by Francis Goodrich and Albert Hackett, said to have reduced the overtly Jewish content in favor of a more universal appeal.

3235 Miller, James. "Heavenquake: Queer Anagogies in Kushner's America." 56-77 in Geis, Deborah R., ed.; Kruger, Steven F., ed. *Approaching the Millennium: Essays on Angels in America.* Ann Arbor, MI: Univ. of Michigan P; 1997. 352 pp. Notes. Illus.: Photo. 1. Lang.: Eng.
USA. 1992-1994. Historical studies. ■Situates Tony Kushner's *Angels in America* in relation to the history of the AIDS crisis.

3236 Minwalla, Framji. "When Girls Collide: Considering Race in *Angels in America*." 103-117 in Geis, Deborah R., ed.; Kruger, Steven F., ed. *Approaching the Millennium: Essays on Angels in America.* Ann Arbor, MI: Univ. of Michigan P; 1997. 352 pp. Notes. Lang.: Eng.
USA. 1992-1994. Critical studies. ■Representations of race and gender in Tony Kushner's *Angels in America*.

3237 Mitra, Mita. *The Role of Silence in Edward Albee's Plays.* New York, NY: City Univ. of New York; 1997. 145 pp. [Ph.D. Dissertation, Univ. Microfilms Order No. AAC 9720119.] Lang.: Eng.
USA. 1928-1996. Critical studies. ■Examines specific 'linguistic silences' as well as the actor's use of tone and gesture to make these silences 'heard' to explore Albee's themes of communication breakdown and problems in family relationships.

3238 Mufson, Daniel. "Sexual Perversity in Viragos." *ThM.* 1993; 23(1): 111-113. Lang.: Eng.
USA. 1992. Critical studies. ■Critical response to the misogynistic point of view in David Mamet's *Oleanna*.

3239 Mufson, Daniel. "Quipping Boy." *ThM.* 1993; 24(2): 116-119. Lang.: Eng.
USA. 1992. Critical studies. ■Analysis of Paul Rudnick's play *Jeffrey*.

3240 Murphy, Brenda. "The Tradition of Social Drama: Miller and His Forebears." 10-20 in Bigsby, Christopher, ed. *The Cambridge Companion to Arthur Miller.* Cambridge: Cambridge UP; 1997. 277 pp. (Cambridge Companions to Literature.) Index. Notes. Lang.: Eng.
USA. 1915-1996. Historical studies. ■The influence of Greek drama on playwright Arthur Miller, focusing on *A View from the Bridge* as the best example of classical Greek structure in his plays. Also examines Ibsen's influence on Miller's *The Man Who Had All the Luck*, *All My Sons*, and his television adaptation of Ibsen's *An Enemy of the People (En Folkefiende)*.

3241 Murphy, Brenda. "Seeking Direction." 189-203 in Roudané, Matthew C., ed. *The Cambridge Companion to Tennessee Williams.* Cambridge: Cambridge UP; 1997. 277 pp. (Cambridge Companions to Literature.) Index. Notes. Biblio. Lang.: Eng.
USA. 1944-1980. Historical studies. ■The relationship between playwright Tennessee Williams and directors, including Elia Kazan, Eddie Dowling, Margo Jones, and José Quintero. Explores elements such as artistic integrity, authorial control, and commercial viability, as well as Williams's own ambivalent relationship with his directors.

3242 O'Connor, Jacqueline. "Words on Williams: A Bibliographic Essay." 244-254 in Roudané, Matthew C., ed. *The Cambridge Companion to Tennessee Williams.* Cambridge: Cambridge UP; 1997. 277 pp. (Cambridge Companions to Literature.) Index. Notes. Biblio. Lang.: Eng.
USA. 1963-1995. Bibliographical studies. ■Survey of major critical statements on playwright Tennessee Williams from biographical studies, past and current bibliographies, and collections of critical essays.

3243 Oha, Obododimma. "Her Dissonant Selves: The Semiotics of Plurality and Bisexuality in Adrienne Kennedy's *Funny-*

DRAMA: —Plays/librettos/scripts

house of a Negro.'' *AmerD.* 1997 Spr; 6(2): 67-80. Notes. Biblio. Lang.: Eng.
USA. 1964. Critical studies. ■Analyzes Kennedy's pluralization of the African-American character Sarah and signification of bisexual polyphony in *Funnyhouse.*

3244 Owen/Penomee, Dr. Kari Ann. "Stages: A DisAbled Playwright Speaks.'' *DGQ.* 1997 Spr; 34(1): 19-21. Lang.: Eng.
USA. 1997. Histories-sources. ■The author's play *Terms of Surrender,* about a gay priest with AIDS, and its relationship to her own disabilities.

3245 Palmer, R. Barton. "Hollywood in Crisis: Tennessee Williams and the Evolution of the Adult Film.'' 204-231 in Roudané, Matthew C., ed. *The Cambridge Companion to Tennessee Williams.* Cambridge: Cambridge UP; 1997. 277 pp. (Cambridge Companions to Literature.) Index. Notes. Biblio. Lang.: Eng.
USA. 1950-1969. Historical studies. ■Examines playwright Tennessee Williams's major contributions to Hollywood film. Examines *Cat on a Hot Tin Roof, A Streetcar Named Desire, The Rose Tattoo, Sweet Bird of Youth, Suddenly Last Summer* and *Baby Doll.*

3246 Parker, Brian. "A Provisional Stemma for Drafts, Alternatives, and Revisions of Tennessee Williams's *The Rose Tattoo* (1951).'' *MD.* 1997 Sum; 40(2): 279-294. Notes. Lang.: Eng.
USA. 1937-1997. Critical studies. ■Drawing from archival materials from private collections and the Billy Rose Collection at Lincoln Center Library for the Performing Arts, author creates a chronological, detailed listing of source materials and script changes for the text and its drafts.

3247 Paulin, Diana. "Representing Forbidden Desire: Interracial Unions, Surrogacy, and Performance.'' *TJ.* 1997 Dec.; 49(4): 417-440. Notes. Lang.: Eng.
USA. 1882-1893. Historical studies. ■Analysis of Black and white characters in Bartley Campbell's play *The White Slave* and William Dean Howells's novel *An Imperative Duty.* Author argues that these transracial stereotypes reveal norms of contemporary society.

3248 Pawley, Thomas D. "Eugene O'Neill and American Race Relations.'' *JADT.* 1997 Win; 9(1): 66-88. Notes. Lang.: Eng.
USA. 1920-1940. Critical studies. ■Examines the role of Black characters in three plays of Eugene O'Neill: *The Dreamy Kid,* a one-act, *All God's Chillun Got Wings,* and *The Iceman Cometh.*

3249 Pearce, Michael. "Yeats and the Women Who Loved Him.'' *AmTh.* 1997 Feb.; 14(2): 7. Illus.: Sketches. B&W. 1. Lang.: Eng.
USA: Atlanta, GA. 1997. Critical studies. ■Sandra Deer's historical play *Sailing to Byzantium* premiering at Actor's Express, directed by Chris Coleman, focusing on lovers of William Butler Yeats.

3250 Perloff, Carey. "Seven Avenues Towards the Heart of a Mystery.'' *ThM.* 1997; 27(2/3): 60-63. Lang.: Eng.
USA. 1997. Critical studies. ■Introduction to Mac Wellman's play *The Difficulty of Crossing a Field.*

3251 Phelan, Peggy. "Tim Miller's *My Queer Body:* An Anatomy in Six Sections.'' *ThM.* 1993; 24(2): 30-34. Notes. Lang.: Eng.
USA: New York, NY. 1993. Critical studies. ■Analysis of Miller's play for its ideas about politics, sexuality, and the need for community.

3252 Piggford, George. "Looking into Black Skulls: Amiri Baraka's *Dutchman* and the Psychology of Race.'' *MD.* 1997 Spr; 15 (1): 74-85. Notes. Lang.: Eng.
USA. 1964-1997. Critical studies. ■Illuminating race relations in the US through psychological case study of Baraka's play *The Dutchman.* Baraka's focus on white dominance and revolution.

3253 Postlewait, Thomas. "From Melodrama to Realism: The Suspect History of American Drama.'' 39-60 in Hays, Michael, ed.; Nikolopoulou, Anastasia, ed. *Melodrama: The Cultural Emergence of a Genre.* New York, NY: St. Martin's P; 1996. 288 pp. Notes. Lang.: Eng.
USA. 1880-1915. Historical studies. ■Ideological criticism of melodrama and its impact on the developing form of realism in the United States.

3254 Proehl, Geoffrey S. *Coming Home Again: American Family Drama and the Figure of the Prodigal Son.* London: Associated Univ Presses; 1997. 221 pp. Pref. Notes. Biblio. Index. Append. Lang.: Eng.
USA. 1946-1962. Critical studies. ■The figure of the prodigal son in *Long Day's Journey Into Night* by Eugene O'Neill, *Death of a Salesman* and *All My Sons* by Arthur Miller, *A Streetcar Named Desire* by Tennessee Williams, *A Raisin in the Sun* by Lorraine Hansberry, and *Who's Afraid of Virginia Woolf?* by Edward Albee.

3255 Rabillard, Sheila. "Crossing Cultures and Kinds: Maria Irene Fornes and the Performance of a Post-Modern Sublime.'' *JADT.* 1997 Spr; 9(2): 33-43. Notes. Lang.: Eng.
USA. 1990-1993. Critical studies. ■Postmodern dramaturgical techniques in Maria Irene Fornes' latest play *Enter the Night.*

3256 Radavich, David. "The Incredible Shrinking Theatre.'' *DGQ.* 1997 Win; 34(4): 37-39. Lang.: Eng.
USA. 1997. Critical studies. ■Criticism of one-minute and ten-minute play contests, said to be indicative of the present theatre culture.

3257 Ràfols, Wilfredo de. "Nonworded Words and Unmentionable *Pharmaka* in O'Neill and Valle-Inclán.'' *CompD.* 1997 Sum; 31(2): 193-212. Notes. Lang.: Eng.
USA. Spain. 1926-1959. Critical studies. ■The art of word avoidance and eventual disclosure of a word in O'Neill's *Long Day's Journey Into Night* and Rámon del Valle-Inclán's *Esperpento de las galas del difunto (The Dead Man's Duds).*

3258 Raymond, Gerard. "Peter Hedges: Production and Reproduction.'' *DGQ.* 1997 Spr; 34(1): 15-18. Lang.: Eng.
USA. 1997. Histories-sources. ■Interview with playwright/novelist Peter Hedges focusing on his two new plays *Baby Anger* and *Good as New.*

3259 Raymond, Gerard. "Charles Busch: Dramatist and Diva.'' *DGQ.* 1997 Fall; 34(3): 18-24. Illus.: Photo. B&W. 2. Lang.: Eng.
USA. 1997. Histories-sources. ■Interview with drag actor/playwright Charles Busch about his new play *Queen Amarantha:* his evolution as a playwright, his ideas on advancing the art of performing in drag.

3260 Raynor, Deirdre Joyce. *Concurrent Dialogue in Novels and Plays by African-American Women from the Harlem Renaissance to the Present.* Seattle, WA: Univ. of Washington; 1997. NA. [Ph.D. Dissertation, no DAI number available.] Lang.: Eng.
USA. 1900-1993. Critical studies. ■Intersections of race, class, gender, and sexuality as seen through simultaneous discourse in works by Georgia Douglas Johnson, Mary P. Burrill, May Miller, Eulalie Spence, and Zora Neale Hurston, as well as contemporary novelists Toni Morrison, Alice Walker, and Gloria Naylor.

3261 Richardson, Kym Blaise. "Margaret Wilkerson's Journey.'' *BlackM.* 1997 Feb/Mar.; 12(3): 5-6. Illus.: Photo. B&W. 1. Lang.: Eng.
USA. 1982-1997. Biographical studies. ■Account of the fifteen-year writing of the biography of playwright Lorraine Hansberry by Wilkerson, who was also chairing Berkeley's African-American studies program and department of dramatic arts.

3262 Robinson, Marc. "Richard Foreman Loses His Head.'' *ThM.* 1997; 28(1): 5-14. Illus.: Photo. B&W. 2. Lang.: Eng.
USA. 1995. Critical studies. ■Analysis of Foreman's play *Pearls for Pigs.*

3263 Robinson, Marc. "Four Writers.'' *ThM.* 1993; 23(1): 31-42. Lang.: Eng.
USA. 1993. Critical studies. ■Analysis of plays by Wallace Shawn, Suzan-Lori Parks, David Greenspan, and Mac Wellman, and how they follow the playwriting principles of Gertrude Stein.

3264 Rosenberg, Rachel A. *Dramas of Collaboration in Twentieth-Century Women's Theatre and Fiction.* Evanston, IL: Northwestern Univ; 1997. 490 pp. [Ph.D. Dissertation, Univ. Microfilms Order No. AAC 9814300.] Lang.: Eng.
USA. UK-England. 1930-1990. Historical studies. ■The collaborations of women in theatre including Zora Neale Hurston (with Langston Hughes on *Mule Bone* and Dorothy Waring on *Polk County*), Michelene Wandor (with theatre collectives Gay Sweatshop on *Care* and Monstrous Regiment on *Floorshow,* and with Sara Maitland on *Arky Types*), and

CLASSED ENTRIES

DRAMA: —Plays/librettos/scripts

Caryl Churchill's collaboration with Joint Stock Theatre Company to produce *Cloud Nine.*

3265 Roudané, Matthew C. "*Death of a Salesman* and the Poetics of Arthur Miller." 60-87 in Bigsby, Christopher, ed. *The Cambridge Companion to Arthur Miller.* Cambridge: Cambridge UP; 1997. 277 pp. (Cambridge Companions to Literature.) Index. Notes. Illus.: Photo. 1. Lang.: Eng.
USA. 1949. Historical studies. ■Examines Miller's masterpiece *Death of a Salesman* and seeks to establish a historical and cultural framework for the play that marks it as distinctly American.

3266 Roudané, Matthew C. "Introduction." 1-10 in Roudané, Matthew C., ed. *The Cambridge Companion to Tennessee Williams.* Cambridge: Cambridge UP; 1997. 277 pp. (Cambridge Companions to Literature.) Notes. Biblio. Index. Lang.: Eng.
USA. 1911-1988. Historical studies. ■Introductory essay to collection of book articles on the work of American playwright Tennessee Williams.

3267 Roudané, Matthew C. *American Drama Since 1960: A Critical History.* New York, NY: Twayne; 1997. 298 pp. (Twayne's Critical History of American Drama 4.) Notes. Biblio. Index. Illus.: Photo. 12. Lang.: Eng.
USA. 1960-1997. Critical studies. ■Critical essays on the work of twenty-four American dramatists including Alice Childress, Edward Albee, Lorraine Hansberry, Megan Terry, Maria Irene Fornes, Marsha Norman, Beth Henley, Wendy Wasserstein, Arthur Kopit, Lanford Wilson, David Rabe, David Mamet, Sam Shepard, and Arthur Miller.

3268 Samuels, Steve. "Finding the Future in Dayton." *AmTh.* 1997 Oct.; 14(8): 86-88. Lang.: Eng.
USA: Dayton, OH. 1997. Histories-sources. ■Author's personal experience as an adjudicator for community theatre Dayton Playhouse's FutureFest new plays competition. Casting from the community, selection process, commitment of audiences.

3269 Sander, Lucia Vieira. *Double Exposure: Gender, Genre, and the Plays of Susan Glaspell.* Stony Brook, NY: State Univ. of New York; 1997. 303 pp. [Ph.D. Dissertation, Univ. Microfilms Order No. AAC 9809046.] Lang.: Eng.
USA. 1876-1948. Critical studies. ■Gender analysis of the neglected plays of Susan Glaspell including *Trifles, The Outside,* and *The Verge.* Specifically explores gender implications of generic conventions.

3270 Savran, David. "Ambivalence, Utopia, and a Queer Sort of Materialism: How *Angels in America* Reconstructs the Nation." 13-39 in Geis, Deborah R., ed.; Kruger, Steven F., ed. *Approaching the Millennium: Essays on Angels in America.* Ann Arbor, MI: Univ. of Michigan P; 1997. 352 pp. Notes. Lang.: Eng.
USA. 1992-1994. Critical studies. ■The popularity and critical reception of Tony Kushner's *Angels in America,* the influence of Walter Benjamin and Mormonism, and the play's construction of American history.

3271 Scapp, Ron. "The Vehicle of Democracy: Fantasies toward a (Queer) Nation." 90-102 in Geis, Deborah R., ed.; Kruger, Steven F., ed. *Approaching the Millennium: Essays on Angels in America.* Ann Arbor, MI: Univ. of Michigan P; 1997. 352 pp. Notes. Lang.: Eng.
USA. 1992-1994. Critical studies. ■Analysis of the last scene in Tony Kushner's *Angels in America, Part II: Perestroika.* Argues that it is an allegory for American fantasies of democracy, self-determination, and progress.

3272 Schlueter, June. "Miller in the Eighties." 152-167 in Bigsby, Christopher, ed. *The Cambridge Companion to Arthur Miller.* Cambridge: Cambridge UP; 1997. 277 pp. (Cambridge Companions to Literature.) Index. Notes. Lang.: Eng.
USA. 1980-1989. Historical studies. ■Playwright Arthur Miller's collaboration with his wife Inge Morath on *The American Clock, Some Kind of Love Story, Elegy for a Lady, Playing for Time* and *Danger: Memory!* (consisting of *I Can't Remember Anything* and *Clara*), as well as regional theatre productions of his classics.

3273 Schmidt, Paul. "Translating Chekhov All Over Again." *DGQ.* 1997 Win; 34(4): 18-23. Lang.: Eng.

USA. 1994-1997. Histories-sources. ■Playwright Schmidt discusses the advantages and disadvantages of translating Čechov while neglecting his own work.

3274 Selmon, Michael. "'Like ... so many small theatres': The Panoptic and the Theatric in *Long Day's Journey into Night.*" *MD.* 1997 Win; 40(4): 526-539. Notes. Lang.: Eng.
USA. 1939-1941. Critical studies. ■The interaction of gazes in the play and the tension generated when the domestic surveillance in the play becomes an object of audience scrutiny. Particular focus on Mary's loneliness under the onstage gaze and how it replicates isolation felt offstage as well.

3275 Seymour, James C. *The Theatre of Romulus Linney, 1967-1995: Holy Ghosts and Hidden Histories.* New York, NY: City Univ. of New York; 1997. 257 pp. Notes. Biblio. [Ph.D. Dissertation, Univ. Microfilms Order No. AAC 9732971.] Lang.: Eng.
USA. 1967-1995. Critical studies. ■Linney's connection to the American regional theatre movement and his debt to European and American roots. Plays examined include *The Sorrows of Frederick, Democracy, The Death of King Philip, Childe Byron, Three Poets, Oscar Over Here, Holy Ghosts, Heathen Valley,* and various one-act plays.

3276 Shafer, Yvonne. "August Wilson and the Contemporary Theatre." *JDTC.* 1997 Fall; 12(1): 23-38. Illus.: Photo. 3. Lang.: Eng.
USA. 1985-1997. Histories-sources. ■Interview with playwright August Wilson. Focuses on his plays, especially his latest *Jitney,* and on his controversial debate with critic and director Robert Brustein on multiculturalism.

3277 Shannon, Sandra G. "A Transplant That Did Not Take: August Wilson's Views on the Great Migration." *AfAmR.* 1997 Win; 31 (4): 659-666. Biblio. Lang.: Eng.
USA. 1997. Critical studies. ■August Wilson's opinion that Blacks would have been a culturally stronger people if they had remained in the south, as reflected in his plays *Jitney, Joe Turner's Come and Gone, Ma Rainey's Black Bottom, The Piano Lesson, Fences, Two Trains Running* and *Seven Guitars.*

3278 Shewey, Don. "Ballyhoo and Daisy, Too." *AmTh.* 1997 Apr.; 14(4): 24-27, 54-55. Illus.: Photo. B&W. 3. Lang.: Eng.
USA. 1987-1996. Histories-sources. ■Career of playwright Alfred Uhry and his collaborative relationship with actress Dana Ivey. Includes interview with Ivey and Uhry in which they discuss their work on *Driving Miss Daisy* and Uhry's current play on Broadway *The Last Night of Ballyhoo.*

3279 Smith, Susan Harris. *American Drama: The Bastard Art.* Cambridge, UK: Cambridge UP; 1997. 248 pp. (Cambridge Studies in American Theatre and Drama 14.) Index. Biblio. Illus.: Maps. Lang.: Eng.
USA. 1710-1995. Critical studies. ■Examines the state of American drama as it is currently configured in higher education. Author argues that it is marginalized in favor of European models and is often neglected in productions.

3280 Solomon, Alisa. "Wrestling with *Angels*: A Jewish Fantasia." 118-133 in Geis, Deborah R., ed.; Kruger, Steven F., ed. *Approaching the Millennium: Essays on Angels in America.* Ann Arbor, MI: Univ. of Michigan P; 1997. 352 pp. Notes. Lang.: Eng.
USA. 1992-1994. Critical studies. ■Exploration of Jewish identity in Tony Kushner's *Angels in America*—going beyond stereotypes.

3281 Splawn, P. Jane. "Re-Imaging the Black Woman's Body in Alexis De Veaux's *The Tapestry.*" *MD.* 1997 Win; 40(4): 514-525. Notes. Lang.: Eng.
USA. 1976-1997. Critical studies. ■The visual representation of the body of the Black woman as a signifier of strength and survival in De Veaux's play.

3282 Stacy, James R. "Making the Grave Less Deep: A Descriptive Assessment of Sam Shepard's Revisions to *Buried Child.*" *JADT.* 1997 Fall; 9(3): 59-72. Notes. Lang.: Eng.
USA. 1975-1996. Critical studies. ■Analysis of the effectiveness of the revisions in plot, character, language, and imagery between the original

DRAMA: —Plays/librettos/scripts

1975 version of playwright Sam Shepard's *Buried Child* and his revised version staged on Broadway in 1996.

3283 Staub, August W. "Public and Private Thought: The Enthymeme of Death in Albee's *Three Tall Women*." *JDTC*. 1997 Fall; 12(1): 149-158. Lang.: Eng.

USA. 1993-1994. Critical studies. ■Analysis of a contemporary portrait of death and dying, Edward Albee's *Three Tall Women*.

3284 Stephens, Judith L. "Lynching, American Theatre, and the Preservation of a Tradition." *JADT*. 1997 Win; 9(1): 54-65. Notes. Illus.: Photo. 1. Lang.: Eng.

USA. 1858-1994. Critical studies. ■Examines the social conditions surrounding the creation and preservation of 'lynching drama' and calls for further investigation into this unexamined tradition in American theatre. Plays examined include Langston Hughes's *Mulatto*.

3285 Stephens, Thomas W. "Christopher Durang 'Explains It All' in Miami." *SoTh*. 1997 Sum; 38(3): 20-24. Illus.: Photo. B&W. 1. Lang.: Eng.

USA. 1971-1997. Histories-sources. ■Account of playwright Durang's presentation at the 1997 SETC convention, with an excerpt from his address and highlights from the subsequent question and answer session. Discusses the negative critical response to his play *Sex and Longing*, his reactions to the conservative assault on the National Endowment for the Arts, the inspiration behind several of his plays, and the motivation and influences that led him to become a playwright.

3286 Striff, Erin. "Lady Killers: Feminism and Murder in Sharon Pollock's *Blood Relations* and Wendy Kesselman's *My Sister in This House*." *NETJ*. 1997; 8: 95-109. Notes. Biblio. Lang.: Eng.

USA. Canada. 1982-1984. Critical studies. ■The oppression of women and the murderous impulse as reflected in plays of Kesselman and Pollock.

3287 Svich, Caridad. "A Prayer for Abundance." *DGQ*. 1997 Fall; 34(3): 25-28. Lang.: Eng.

USA. 1997. Critical studies. ■Argues that women playwrights should have a broader palate of subjects.

3288 Taav, Michael. *A Body Across the Map: The Father-Son Plays of Sam Shepard*. New York, NY: City Univ. of New York; 1997. 208 pp. Notes. Biblio. [Ph.D. Dissertation, Univ. Microfilms Order No. AAC 9720145.] Lang.: Eng.

USA. 1965-1993. Critical studies. ■The father-son conflict as central to all of Shepard's plays.

3289 Tavel, Ronald. "Disputing the Canon of American Dramatic 'Literature'." *NTQ*. 1997; 13(49): 18-28. Notes. Biblio. Lang.: Eng.

USA. 1938-1996. Critical studies. ■Argues that the commercial American theatre, endorsed by the educational system and theatrical establishment, never visualized the scripted play as art, nor, consequently, produced a single example of it.

3290 Tedford, Harold. "Playwriting: Romulus Linney on 'Sublime Gossip'." *SoTh*. 1997 Spr; 38(2): 26-30, 32. Illus.: Photo. B&W. 1. Lang.: Eng.

USA. 1948-1996. Histories-sources. ■Interview with playwright Linney, discussing his career, his body of work, his affinity for the South, and his advice to young playwrights, with a biographical sidebar on Linney by Harold Tedford.

3291 Tischler, Nancy M. "Romantic Textures in Tennessee Williams's Plays and Short Stories." 147-166 in Roudané, Matthew C., ed. *The Cambridge Companion to Tennessee Williams*. Cambridge: Cambridge UP; 1997. 277 pp. (Cambridge Companions to Literature.) Notes. Biblio. Index. Illus.: Photo. 1. Lang.: Eng.

USA. 1944-1983. Historical studies. ■Romantic elements in the plays and short stories of Tennessee Williams. Includes biographical details, his own presence in the works, and his view of the human condition.

3292 Tomc, Sandra. "David Mamet's Oleanna and the Way of the Flesh." *ET*. 1997; 16(2): 163-175. Notes. Biblio. Lang.: Eng.

USA. 1993. Critical studies. ■Examines sexual harassment in modern society and the role of controversy in counterculture theatre in relation to Mamet's play *Oleanna*.

3293 Vacca, V. John. "Telling Women's Lives: African-American One-Person Plays." *AmerD*. 1997 Spr; 6(2): 58-66. Biblio. Lang.: Eng.

USA. 1972-1996. Critical studies. ■Using one-person shows *A Black Woman Speaks* and *Chain* by Beah Richards, *Sister Son/ji* by Sonia Sanchez and *Pretty Fire* by Charlayne Woodard, examines how form which originally depended on devices of traditional poetry has evolved to incorporate elements of traditional theatre and performance art.

3294 Vorlicky, Robert, ed. *Tony Kushner in Conversation*. Ann Arbor, MI: Univ. of Michigan P; 1997. 280 pp. Index. Illus.: Photo. 7. Lang.: Eng.

USA. 1989-1997. Histories-sources. ■Compilation of playwright Tony Kushner's interviews, tracing his career from its early years to his maturing artistic and political visions.

3295 Wade, Leslie A. *Sam Shepard and the American Theatre*. Westport, CT/London: Greenwood; 1997. 188 pp. (Contributions in Drama and Theatre Studies 76: Lives of the Theatre 5.) Index. Notes. Biblio. Lang.: Eng.

USA. 1943-1996. Biographies. ■Primary focus is on Shepard's position as an uniquely American playwright. Situates his work in postwar United States and its shifting conditions of production, and its tensions between anxiety and ambition.

3296 Walker, Craig Stewart. "Three Tutorial Plays: *The Lesson, The Prince of Naples* and *Oleanna*." *MD*. 1997 Spr; 15(1): 149-162. Notes. Lang.: Eng.

USA. Canada. France. 1951-1997. Critical studies. ■The dramatization of cultural tension in plays about teachers and students: focus on George F. Walker's *The Prince of Naples*, Eugène Ionesco's *The Lesson (La Leçon)* and David Mamet's *Oleanna*.

3297 Walker, Victor Leo, II. "*The Old Settler* is Far from Settled." *AfAmR*. 1997 Win; 31(4): 717-721. Lang.: Eng.

USA. 1997. Critical studies. ■Looks at the potential of John Henry Redwood's play *The Old Settler* which was presented as part of the Silver Anniversary for the Intiman Theatre.

3298 Warshauer, Susan Claire. *The Rhetoric of Victimization in Tennessee Williams'* The Glass Menagerie*: The Development, Performance and Reception of Laura Wingfield's Characterization*. Austin, TX: Univ. of Texas; 1997. 231 pp. [Ph.D. Dissertation, Univ. Microfilms Order No. AAC 9803059.] Lang.: Eng.

USA. 1945-1994. Critical studies. ■The construction of the character Laura by playwright, performers, and audience in productions of *The Glass Menagerie* for both stage and screen.

3299 Watson, Charles S. *The History of Southern Drama*. Lexington, KY: UP of Kentucky; 1997. 259 pp. Index. Notes. Biblio. Pref. Illus.: Photo. Dwg. 12. Lang.: Eng.

USA. 1681-1997. Histories-specific. ■Comprehensive history of drama written in the South and about the South. Focuses on historical significance rather than on literary analysis.

3300 Weber, Carl M.; Scheidler, Antje, transl. "Ich werde immer wieder zu Brecht zurückfinden." (I Always Come Back to Brecht.) *TZ*. 1997; 6: 42-46. Illus.: Photo. B&W. 1. Lang.: Ger.

USA. 1997. Histories-sources. ■An interview with Tony Kushner and the influences of Bertolt Brecht on his theatre works.

3301 Wertheim, Albert. "*A View from the Bridge*." 101-114 in Bigsby, Christopher, ed. *The Cambridge Companion to Arthur Miller*. Cambridge: Cambridge UP; 1997. 277 pp. (Cambridge Companions to Literature.) Index. Notes. Lang.: Eng.

USA. 1955-1956. Historical studies. ■Examines possible sources and influences on playwright Arthur Miller's *A View from the Bridge*.

3302 Wertheim, Albert. "Hollywood's Moral Landscape: Clifford Odets' *The Big Knife*." *AmerD*. 1997 Fall; 7(1): 67-81. Notes. Biblio. Lang.: Eng.

USA. 1930-1949. Biographical studies. ■Analysis of *The Big Knife*, which Odets considered a morality play, with respect to the effect of the move from New York to Hollywood on Odets' work and personal life.

CLASSED ENTRIES

DRAMA: —Plays/librettos/scripts

3303 Wetzsteon, Ross. "Wallace Shawn, Subversive Moralist." *AmTh.* 1997 Sep.; 14(7): 12-17. Illus.: Photo. B&W. 6. Lang.: Eng.
USA. 1981-1997. Critical studies. ■Career of playwright/actor Shawn with focus on his plays *The Designated Mourner, Marie and Bruce, Aunt Dan and Lemon*, and *The Fever*. Shawn's approach to writing, political and philosophical viewpoints. Includes partial transcript of interview between Shawn and author.

3304 Wilkins, John Robinson. *The Problem of the American Playwright: The Successes and Failures of e. e. cummings, Arthur Miller and Sam Shepard.* Berkeley, CA: University of California, Berkeley; 1997. 342 pp. Notes. Biblio. [Ph.D. Dissertation, Univ. Microfilms Order No. AAC 9827153.] Lang.: Eng.
USA. 1940-1995. Critical studies. ■Examines the attempts of three extremely different playwrights—e.e. cummings, Arthur Miller, and Sam Shepard—to create an authentic American theatrical aesthetic.

3305 Williams, Megan. "Nowhere Man and the Twentieth-Century Cowboy: Images of Identity and American History in Sam Shepard's *True West*." *MD.* 1997 Spr; 15(1): 57-73. Notes. Lang.: Eng.
USA. 1997. Critical studies. ■Argues that Shepard's work as a whole engages and illustrates theories of the postmodern, while the character of Lee in *True West* challenges the postmodern assumption that contemporary man's loss of subjectivity and history must be a negative experience.

3306 Wolf, Sara. "Luis Alfaro." *AmTh.* 1997 Nov.; 14(9): 52-54. Illus.: Photo. B&W. 1. Lang.: Eng.
USA: Los Angeles, CA. 1991-1997. Biographical studies. ■Alfaro's plays and community activism, current work *Straight as a Line*, and his response to being a recent recipient of a MacArthur 'genius award'.

3307 Wood, Gerald C. "Horton Foote's Politics of Intimacy." *JADT.* 1997 Spr; 9(2): 44-57. Notes. Lang.: Eng.
USA. 1943. Critical studies. ■Examines the 'hidden' social and political agenda in playwright Horton Foote's dramaturgy as reflected in his single Broadway play *Only the Heart*.

3308 Woodard, Charlayne. "Show & Tell." *DGQ.* 1997 Spr; 34(1): 31-33. Illus.: Photo. B&W. 1. Lang.: Eng.
USA: New York, NY. 1997. Histories-sources. ■Author's account of how she wrote her solo shows *Pretty Fire* and *Neat*.

3309 Young-Minor, Ethel A. *To Redeem Her Body: Performing Womanist Liberation.* Bowling Green, OH: Bowling Green State Univ; 1997. 159 pp. [Ph.D. Dissertation, Univ. Microfilms Order No. AAC 9820930.] Lang.: Eng.
USA. 1840-1994. Historical studies. ■Explores works by African-American women from the nineteenth century, including the anonymous *A Colored Minister of the Gospel* and Harriet Powers' *Bible Quilt*, including Zora Neale Hurston's *Color Struck*, May Miller's *Harriet Tubman*, Ntozake Shange's *for colored girls who have considered suicide/when the rainbow is enuf*, and Anna Deavere Smith's *Twilight: Los Angeles, 1992*.

3310 Young, Jean. "The Re-Objectification and Re-Commodification of Saartjie Baartman in Suzan-Lori Parks's *Venus*." *AfAmR.* 1997 Win; 31(4): 699-708. Notes. Biblio. Lang.: Eng.
USA. 1996. Critical studies. ■Analysis of the central character in the play with respect to the historical accuracy of her portrayal and her complicity in her own exploitation.

Reference materials

3311 *500 dramskih zgodb.* (500 Theatre Stories.) Ljubljana: Mladinska knjiga; 1997. 573 pp. (Cicero Collection.) Pref. Index. Lang.: Slo.
500 B.C.-1997 A.D. ■Encyclopedia of dramatic plots from ancient Greek theatre to the present.

3312 Harner, James L., ed. "World Shakespeare Bibliography 1992." *SQ.* 1993 Win; 44(5): 520-930. Index. Lang.: Eng.
1992. ■1992 bibliography of materials pertaining to the study of Shakespeare.

3313 Harner, James L., ed. "World Shakespeare Bibliography 1994." *SQ.* 1995 Win; 46(4): 506-877. Notes. Lang.: Eng.

3314 Harner, James L., ed. "World Shakespeare Bibliography, 1993." *SQ.* 1994 Win; 45(5): 506-912. Index. Lang.: Eng.
1993. ■1993 Bibliography of materials pertaining to the study of Shakespeare.

3315 Merritt, Susan Hollis. "Harold Pinter Bibliography, 1993-1994." *PintR.* 1997: 208-228. Lang.: Eng.
1993-1994. Bibliographical studies. ■Annual bibliography of works by and about Harold Pinter, including all aspects of his writing (plays, films, television, poetry, prose) and performances, as well as his acting and directing.

3316 Meserole, Harrison T., ed.; Harner, James L., ed. "Shakespeare: Annotated World Bibliography for 1991." *SQ.* 1992 Win; 43(5): 516-885. Index. Lang.: Eng.
1991. ■1991 bibliography of materials pertaining to the study of Shakespeare.

3317 Meserole, Harrison T., ed. "Shakespeare: Annotated World Bibliography for 1986." *SQ.* 1987; 38(5): 550-915. Index. Lang.: Eng.
1986. ■Annotated bibliography of material related to the study of Shakespeare and his works.

3318 Pottie, Lisa M.. "Modern Drama Studies: An Annual Bibliography." *MD.* 1997 Sum; 40(2): 183-278. Lang.: Eng.
North America. 1899-1997. Bibliographical studies. ■Record of current scholarship, criticism and commentary focusing on dramatic literature and theatre history. Includes all playwrights who lived past 1899 and influential theatre figures other than performers.

3319 Knowles, Ronald. "From London: Harold Pinter 1994-95 and 1995-96." *PintR.* 1997: 152-167. Lang.: Eng.
UK-England. 1994-1996. Historical studies. ■Review of events and performances related to playwright Harold Pinter which took place in the United Kingdom 1994 through 1996.

3320 Bennett, Suzanne; Peterson, Jane T. *Women Playwrights of Diversity: A Bio-Bibliographical Sourcebook.* Westport, CT/London: Greenwood P; 1997. 399 pp. Index. Biblio. Append. Pref. Lang.: Eng.
USA. 1970-1996. ■Sourcebook on female African American, Asian American, Latina, and lesbian playwrights. Includes short introductory passages to each section of playwrights. Each playwright receives a short biography, play descriptions, production history, play availability, awards, and critical essays.

3321 Hischak, Thomas S. *The Theatregoer's Almanac: A Collection of Lists, People, History, and Commentary on the American Theatre.* Westport, CT/London: Greenwood; 1997. 345 pp. Index. Biblio. Pref. Lang.: Eng.
USA. 1870-1995. Histories-specific. ■A compendium of various historical and anecdotal facts about American theatre. Organizes book by: Broadway, plays, players, playwrights, musicals, awards, and 'odds and ends'.

3322 Vanden Heuvel, Michael. *Elmer Rice: A Research and Production Sourcebook.* Westport, CT/London: Greenwood; 1996. 242 pp. (Modern Dramatists Research and Production Sourcebooks 9.) Pref. Index. Biblio. Illus.: Photo. 1. Lang.: Eng.
USA. 1892-1967. ■Sourcebook on playwright Elmer Rice, including chronology of plays, plot synopses and critical reviews, cast lists, bibliography of reviews and archival sources, and short biography.

Relation to other fields

3323 Colbert, François; Valée, Luc; Beauregard, Caroline. "Aller au théâtre, c'est trop cher?" (Is Going to the Theatre Too Expensive?)*JCT.* 1997; 82: 134-138. Biblio. Notes. Illus.: Dwg. 2. Lang.: Fre.
Canada: Montreal, PQ. 1995. Empirical research. ■Summary of poll recording demographics and attitudes of Montreal theatregoers.

3324 Wickham, Philip. "Observations sur le théâtre amateur." (Observations on Amateur Theatre.) *JCT.* 1997; 83: 169-173. Illus.: Photo. B&W. 4. Lang.: Fre.

DRAMA: —Relation to other fields

Canada: Montreal, PQ. 1997. Historical studies. ∎Role of amateur theatre in contemporary Quebec theatrical production.

3325 Astington, John H. "The 'Unrecorded Portrait' of Edward Alleyn." *SQ.* 1993 Spr; 44(1): 73-86. Notes. Illus.: Sketches. Dwg. B&W. 10. Lang.: Eng.
England. 1603. Historical studies. ∎Discusses engraving of actor Edward Alleyn in his Tamburlaine costume that is contained in Richard Knolles' *The General Historie of the Turkes*.

3326 Belsey, Catherine. "Love as Trompe-l'oeil: Taxonomies of Desire in *Venus and Adonis*." *SQ.* 1995 Fall; 46(3): 257-276. Notes. Lang.: Eng.
England. 1593. Critical studies. ∎Lust and degrees of desire in Shakespeare's poem.

3327 Bevis, Richard. "Canon, Pedagogy, Prospectus: Redesigning 'Restoration and Eighteenth-Century English Drama'." *CompD.* 1997 Spr; 31(1): 178-191. Notes. Lang.: Eng.
England. 1701-1800. Critical studies. ∎Argues for a new, more comprehensive, anthology of eighteenth-century English drama, to be applied to undergraduate studies of this subject.

3328 Brownlow, F.W. "John Shakespeare's Recusancy: New Light on an Old Document." *SQ.* 1989 Sum; 40(2): 187-191. Notes. Lang.: Eng.
England: Stratford, Warwickshire. 1592. Historical studies. ∎Examines the 'Recusancy of Warwickshire' of 1592 in which Shakespeare's father John is listed as a non-attendee at church, and what light this sheds on John's life.

3329 Chandler, David. "'New Significance': Owen's 'Strange Meeting' and *Richard III*." *ELN.* 1997 June; 34(4): 48-52. Notes. Lang.: Eng.
England. 1593-1919. Critical studies. ∎Wilfred Owen's poem 'Strange Meeting' and the debt it owes to Shakespeare's play.

3330 Coleridge, Samuel Taylor. "Shakespeare's *Venus and Adonis*." 69-72 in Kolin, Philip C., ed. *Venus and Adonis: Critical Essays*. New York, NY: Garland; 1997. 448 pp. (Shakespeare Criticism 16.) Lang.: Eng.
England. 1593. Critical studies. ∎Early criticism (1817) on Shakespeare's 'Venus and Adonis'.

3331 Dillon, Janette. "'Is Not All the World Mile End, Mother?': The Blackfriars Theatre, the City of London, and *The Knight of the Burning Pestle*." *MRDE.* 1997; 9(1): 127-148. Notes. Lang.: Eng.
England: London. 1607. Historical studies. ∎The staging of *The Knight of the Burning Pestle* by the Blackfriars Theatre and its contentious reception by London's city fathers.

3332 Foster, Donald W. "'Shall I Die' Post Mortem: Defining *Shakespeare*." *SQ.* 1987 Spr; 38(1): 58-77. Notes. Illus.: Dwg. B&W. 1. Lang.: Eng.
England. 1604-1637. Critical studies. ∎Disputes recent attribution of the lyric poem 'Shall I Die' to Shakespeare.

3333 Gervinus, G.G. "*Venus and Adonis*." 75-76 in Kolin, Philip C., ed. *Venus and Adonis: Critical Essays*. New York, NY: Garland Pub; 1997. 448 pp. (Shakespeare Criticism 16.) Lang.: Eng.
England. 1593. Critical studies. ∎1849 essay on Shakespeare's 'Venus and Adonis'.

3334 Gordon, Christine Mack. *Dreaming in Shakespeare: Pedagogy, Performance, Dramaturgy, Fiction*. Minneapolis, MN: Univ. of Minnesota; 1997. 213 pp. [Ph.D. Dissertation, Univ. Microfilms Order No. AAC 9728949.] Lang.: Eng.
England. 1997. Empirical research. ∎Collection of essays and exercises that explore ways in which the work of Shakespeare can be vividly brought to life within the context of the college classroom. Examines various pedagogical methods.

3335 J., Y. "Shakespeare's Poems." 73-74 in Kolin, Philip C., ed. *Venus and Adonis: Critical Essays*. New York, NY: Garland; 1997. 448 pp. (Shakespeare Criticism 16.) Lang.: Eng.
England. 1593. Critical studies. ∎Analysis of Shakespeare's 'Venus and Adonis'.

3336 Kaufman, Robert. "The Sublime as Super-Genre of the Modern, or *Hamlet* in Revolution: Caleb Williams and His Problems." *SiR.* 1997 Win; 36(4): 541-574. Notes. Lang.: Eng.
England. 1600-1794. Critical studies. ∎Argues that William Godwin's novel *Caleb Williams* is informed by *Hamlet* and presents itself as product and harbinger of the inexpressibly new, or 'modern'.

3337 Kolin, Philip C. "Venus and/or Adonis Among the Critics." 3-65 in Kolin, Philip C., ed. *Venus and Adonis: Critical Essays*. New York, NY: Garland; 1997. 448 pp. (Shakespeare Criticism 16.) Biblio. Lang.: Eng.
England. 1593. Critical studies. ∎Introduction to collection of essays on Shakespeare's 'Venus and Adonis' outlining the methodology of the book.

3338 Levin, Richard. "What's Wrong with His Feet and Tail and Her Face and Back?" *ShN.* 1997 Sum/Fall; 47(2/3): 29. Notes. Illus.: Dwg. B&W. 1. [Number 233/234.] Lang.: Eng.
England. 1588-1677. Historical studies. ∎The connection between physical and moral deformity in several of Shakespeare's plays and the distinction between natural and supernatural deformity in woodcut images and text from *The Life and Death of Mother Shipton* by Richard Head.

3339 Martin, Christopher. "Retrieving Jonson's Petrarch." *SQ.* 1994 Spr; 45(1): 89-92. Notes. Illus.: Dwg. B&W. 1. Lang.: Eng.
England. 1581-1994. Historical studies. ∎Report on the recovery of an item thought lost from Ben Jonson's personal library, Petrarch's *Opera omnia*.

3340 McCune, Pat. "Order and Justice in Early Tudor Drama." *RenD.* 1994; 25: 171-196. Notes. Biblio. Lang.: Eng.
England. 1490-1550. Historical studies. ∎Transformation of English drama from religious pieces dealing with the struggle of vices and virtues to a form with a distinct secular ideology of justice which valued retribution over reconciliation.

3341 McGuire, Philip C. "Shakespeare's Non-Shakespearean Sonnets." *SQ.* 1987 Fall; 38(3): 304-319. Notes. Lang.: Eng.
England. 1599-1616. Critical studies. ∎Attempts to ascertain Shakespearean authorship of the sonnets by breaking down the rhyme scheme.

3342 Newman, Jane O. "'And Let Mild Women to Him Lose Their Mildness': Philomela, Female Violence, and Shakespeare's *Rape of Lucrece*." *SQ.* 1994 Fall; 45(3): 304-326. Notes. Lang.: Eng.
England. 1592-1595. Critical studies. ∎Shakespeare's poem and the uneasiness over violent women in patriarchal society.

3343 Pressly, William L. "The Ashbourne Portrait of Shakespeare: Through the Looking-Glass." *SQ.* 1993 Spr; 44(1): 54-72. Notes. Illus.: Photo. Pntg. Sketches. B&W. 9. Lang.: Eng.
England. 1611-1979. Historical studies. ∎History of the Ashbourne portrait whose subject was once considered to be William Shakespeare but proven to be another while undergoing restoration in 1979.

3344 Radel, Nicholas F. "Homoeroticisim, Discursive Change, and Politics: Reading 'Revolution' in Seventeenth-Century English Tragicomedy." *MRDE.* 1997; 9(1): 162-178. Notes. Lang.: Eng.
England. 1601-1700. Critical studies. ∎Tragicomedy and its relationship to social and historical change: how dramatic works can effect social change through alteration of strategic discursive positions in an ongoing social struggle.

3345 Rollett, John M. "The Dedication to Shakespeare's Sonnets." *ERev.* 1997 Fall; 5(2): 93-122. Notes. Biblio. Lang.: Eng.
England. 1609. Historical studies. ∎Attempts to determine the identity of 'Mr. W.H.' by examining the dedication on the second leaf of the 1609 quarto containing Shakespeare's sonnets.

3346 Skura, Meredith. "Elizabeth Cary and Edward II: What Do Women Want to Write?" *RenD.* 1996; 27: 79-104. Notes. Biblio. Lang.: Eng.
England. 1627. Historical studies. ∎Debate over the authorship of the prose historical account of the life of Edward II published in 1627 by

DRAMA: —Relation to other fields

'E.F.': was it Henry Cary, first Viscount Falkland, or his wife, playwright Elizabeth Cary?.

3347 Somerset, Alan. "Damnable Deconstructions: Vice Language in the Interlude." *CompD.* 1997 Win; 31(4): 571-588. Notes. Lang.: Eng.

England. 1561-1580. Critical studies. ■Reasons for the rise in anti-theatrical polemics in the mid-sixteenth century, and how some clergymen like William Wager became playwrights to extend their anti-drama ideas to the stage.

3348 Trousdale, Marion. "Reading the Early Modern Text." *ShS.* 1997; 50(1): 135-145. Notes. Lang.: Eng.

England. 1595-1750. Critical studies. ■Close relationship of language and social formation reflected in the work of Shakespeare.

3349 Vitkus, Daniel J. "Turning Turk in *Othello*: The Conversion and Damnation of the Moor." *SQ.* 1997 Sum; 48(2): 145-176. Notes. Illus.: Dwg. B&W. 2. Lang.: Eng.

England. 1453-1604. Historical studies. ■How the creation and perception of characters such as Shakespeare's Othello was influenced by English fears of colonization resulting from the expansion of the Islamic and Ottoman Empires and their perceived threat to Christendom.

3350 Klaić, Dragan. "Letter from Europe: A Week in the Memory." *ThM.* 1997; 27(2/3): 136-146. Illus.: Photo. B&W. 2. Lang.: Eng.

Europe. 1997. Histories-sources. ■Author's observations while traveling through Europe to take part in symposia and conferences, confronting Europe's diversity as the continent shifts towards integration.

3351 Erpenbeck, John. "Widersacher." (Adversaries.) *TZ.* 1997; Yb: 123-127. Append. Illus.: Photo. B&W. 3. Lang.: Ger.

Germany: Berlin. 1920-1956. Histories-sources. ■The son of actor Fritz Erpenbeck and playwright Hedda Zinner describes their relationship with Bertolt Brecht. As communists they thought of him as a worldly but politically irresponsible writer.

3352 Hein, Christoph; Teschke, Holger. "'Wir haben es schwerer, wir sind Dialektiker'." (We Have a Harder Time, We're Dialectical Thinkers.) *TZ.* 1997; Yb: 128-131. Append. Illus.: Photo. B&W. 5. Lang.: Ger.

Germany: Berlin. 1943-1956. Histories-sources. ■An interview with Hans Mayer, emeritus professor of German literature, about Bertolt Brecht and his existential disgust with bureaucratic and politico-cultural quarrels.

3353 Hörnigk, Therese; Hörnigk, Frank. "Begegnungen mit Brecht." (Encounters with Brecht.) *TZ.* 1997; Yb: 104-108. Append. Illus.: Photo. B&W. 4. Lang.: Ger.

Germany: Berlin. 1953-1997. Histories-sources. ■An interview with the novelist Günter Grass about Brecht, expressing his disappointment with Brecht's relationship to the events of June 17, 1953, and to Stalinism.

3354 Müller-Schöll, Nikolaus. "Der Eingriff ins Politische." (Intervention Into Politics.) *TZ.* 1997; Yb: 113-117. Illus.: Photo. B&W. 4. Lang.: Ger.

Germany. 1920-1940. Critical studies. ■Discusses numerous traces of Carlo Schmitt's writings in Brecht's work mainly in *Die Geschäfte des Julius Caesar (The Transactions of Julius Caesar)* and his *Lehrstücke* in which he transformed Schmitt's theory of dictatorial resolution into 'dictatorship on stage'.

3355 Stephan, Alexander. "'Der Pass ist der edelste Teil von einem Menschen'." (A Passport Is the Most Noble Part of a Human Being.) *TZ.* 1997; Yb: 132-136. Append. Illus.: Photo. B&W. 4. Lang.: Ger.

Germany. USA. 1933-1947. Biographical studies. ■Discusses Brecht's expatriation upon the denial of his German citizenship in 1935 and the renewal of his passport in New York in spite of FBI surveillance since Brecht's contacts with the Soviet Union in 1936.

3356 Schleef, Einar. "Staat und Sprache." (State and Speech.) *THeute.* 1997; 5: 30-32. Illus.: Photo. B&W. 2. Lang.: Ger.

Germany, East. 1964-1997. Histories-sources. ■Director describes his life in East Germany and the consequences of the East German system and its language for intellectuals and dissidents.

3357 Osborne, Robin. "The Ecstasy and the Tragedy: Varieties of Religious Experience in Art, Drama, and Society." 187-211

in Pelling, Christopher, ed. *Greek Tragedy and the Historian.* Oxford: Clarendon; 1997. 268 pp. Notes. Biblio. Index. Illus.: Photo. 16. Lang.: Eng.

Greece. 500-250 B.C. Historical studies. ■Representations of tragedy, not just in dramatic form but also in representations of classical scenes displayed on Athenian pots of the period. Considers whether these visual representations relate to representations in drama, and whether scholars might be able to use these representations to write a history of religious experience in ancient Greece.

3358 Vicentini de Azevedo, Ana. *The Names of the Name: The Paternal Metaphor in Psychoanalysis and Literature.* New York, NY: City Univ. of New York; 1997. 280 pp. [Ph.D. Dissertation, Univ. Microfilms Order No. AAC 9720147.] Lang.: Eng.

Greece. 458 B.C. Critical studies. ■Comparison of psychoanalytic and literary discourse with respect to the general principle that presides over cultural, linguistic, and psychic structures, as applied to Aeschylus's *Oresteia.*

3359 Ackerley, Chris. "'Do Not Despair': Samuel Beckett and Robert Greene." *JBeckS.* 1997; 6(1): 119-124. Notes. Lang.: Eng.

Ireland. France. 1938. Critical studies. ■Identifies Elizabethan poet Robert Greene's pastoral *Menaphon* as the source of a particular allusion in Beckett's novel *Murphy.*

3360 Balzano, Wanda. "Re-mythologizing Beckett: the Metaphors of Metafiction in *How It Is.*" 102-110 in Oppenheim, Lois, ed.; Buning, Marius, ed. *Beckett On and On....* Madison, NJ: Fairleigh Dickinson UP; 1996. 289 pp. Notes. Biblio. Lang.: Eng.

Ireland. France. 1961. Critical studies. ■Examines Beckett's novel *Comment c'est (How It Is)* and its transgressive notion of genre.

3361 Caselli, Daniela. "Looking It Up in My Big Dante: A Note on 'Sedendo et Quiesc(i)endo'." *JBeckS.* 1997; 6(2): 85-93. Notes. Lang.: Eng.

Ireland. France. 1932. Textual studies. ■Traces the source of the phrase 'sedendo et quiesciendo' which appears in Beckett's *Dream of Fair to Middling Women.* Points out that it is an old, persistent misprint of 'sedendo et quiscendo' from Dante's *Divine Comedy.*

3362 Caselli, Daniela. "Beckett's Intertextual Modalities of Appropriation: The Case of Leopardi." *JBeckS.* 1997; 6(1): 1-24. Notes. Lang.: Eng.

Ireland. France. 1929-1985. Critical studies. ■Influence of the poetry of Giacomo Leopardi on Beckett's work.

3363 Clissold, Bradley D. "Fingerpondering Shakespeare, Swinburne, and the Concentration Camps." *ShN.* 1997 Sum/Fall; 47(2/3) : 47-48. Notes. [Number 233/234.] Lang.: Eng.

Ireland. 1920. Historical studies. ■James Joyce's references to Swinburne and *Hamlet* in his novel *Ulysses* in relation to the politics of British colonialism in South Africa and Ireland.

3364 Duffy, Brian. "*Malone meurt*: The Comfort of Narrative." *JBeckS.* 1997; 6(1): 25-47. Notes. Lang.: Eng.

Ireland. France. 1951. Critical studies. ■The precise and calculated use of narrative in Beckett's novel *Malone meurt (Malone Dies),* and its context within his trilogy, which includes *Molloy* and *L'Innommable (The Unnameable).*

3365 Goldstein, Gary. "Who Was Joyce's Shakespeare?" *ERev.* 1997 Spr; 5(1): 26-31. Notes. Lang.: Eng.

Ireland. 1900-1939. Critical studies. ■James Joyce's theories about the true authorship of Shakespeare's plays as evidenced in Joyce's work.

3366 Kiely, Declan D. "'The termination of this solitaire': A Textual Error in *Murphy.*" *JBeckS.* 1997; 6(1): 135-136. Notes. Lang.: Eng.

Ireland. France. 1938. Textual studies. ■Points to an inconsistency that can only be found in the English language editions of Beckett's novel *Murphy,* an illegal chess move.

3367 Mahon, Derek. "Euphorion in Ely Place." *IW.* 1997 May/June; 46(3): 30-35. Illus.: Photo. Pntg. Maps. B&W. Color. 10. Lang.: Eng.

Ireland: Dublin. UK-England: London. 1852-1933. Biographical studies. ■Personal life and career of English novelist/playwright George

DRAMA: —Relation to other fields

Moore, his commitment to the Irish language, collaboration with Yeats on the play *Diarmuid and Grania*, and his trilogy *Hail and Farewell* which chronicled his years in Dublin and satirized his colleagues Yeats, George Russell and Edward Martyn.

3368 Matton, Frank. "Beckett's Trilogy and the Limits of Autobiography." 69-82 in Oppenheim, Lois, ed.; Buning, Marius, ed. *Beckett On and On....* Madison, NJ: Fairleigh Dickinson UP; 1996. 289 pp. Notes. Lang.: Eng.
Ireland. France. 1947-1979. Critical studies. ■Autobiographical elements in Samuel Beckett's trilogy of novels: *L'innomable (The Unnameable)*, *Molloy*, and *Malone meurt (Malone Dies)*.

3369 Pilling, John. "A Short Statement with Long Shadows: *Watt*'s Arsene and His Kind(s)." 61-68 in Oppenheim, Lois, ed.; Buning, Marius, ed. *Beckett On and On....* Madison, NJ: Fairleigh Dickinson UP; 1996. 289 pp. Notes. Lang.: Eng.
Ireland. France. 1942-1963. Critical studies. ■Examines the structure of Beckett's novel *Watt*.

3370 Tseng, Li-Ling. "Undoing and Doing: Allegories of Writing in the *Trilogy*." 199-211 in Oppenheim, Lois, ed.; Buning, Marius, ed. *Beckett On and On....* Madison, NJ: Fairleigh Dickinson UP; 1996. 289 pp. Notes. Lang.: Eng.
Ireland. France. 1960-1965. Critical studies. ■Textuality, theatricality, and the Western intellectual tradition in the fiction trilogy of Samuel Beckett: *L'innommable (The Unnameable)*, *Molloy*, and *Malone meurt (Malone Dies)*.

3371 Vandervlist, Harry. "'A Voice from Elsewhere': Impossible Survivals and the Annihilating Power of Language in Beckett's Fiction." 178-186 in Oppenheim, Lois, ed.; Buning, Marius, ed. *Beckett On and On....* Madison, NJ: Fairleigh Dickinson UP; 1996. 289 pp. Notes. Biblio. Lang.: Eng.
Ireland. France. 1930-1985. Critical studies. ■Examines the relation of the speaker to speech, or the authenticity of expression versus the impossibility of the author's task in the fiction of playwright Samuel Beckett.

3372 Scolnicov, Hanna. "An Intertextual Approach to Teaching Shakespeare." *SQ.* 1995 Sum; 46(2): 210-219. Notes. Illus.: Photo. B&W. 1. Lang.: Eng.
Israel: Tel Aviv. 1993-1995. Histories-sources. ■Author shares her experiences and her approaches to teaching Shakespeare while working with graduate students at the University of Tel Aviv.

3373 Yogev, Michael. "'How shall we find the concord of this discord?': Teaching Shakespeare in Israel, 1994." *SQ.* 1995 Sum; 46(2): 157-164. Notes. Lang.: Eng.
Israel: Haifa. 1994. Histories-sources. ■Primary account of a teacher's experience teaching Shakespeare at the University of Haifa during a time of great political disturbance.

3374 Bartoli, Francesco. "Figure della melanconia e dell'ardore: il Botticelli di D'Annunzio." (Images of Melancholy and Passion: D'Annunzio's Conception of Botticelli.) *IlCast.* 1997; 10(28): 5-13. Notes. Lang.: Ita.
Italy. 1895-1897. Critical studies. ■Comparison of Gabriele D'Annunzio's *Sogno d'un mattino di primavera (A Spring Morning's Dream)* with Botticelli's painting *Primavera*, demonstrating that the theatrical text is inspired by some neoplatonic figures of the painting.

3375 Levy, Jonathan. "Theatre and Moral Education." *JAE.* 1997 Fall; 31(3): 65-75. Notes. Lang.: Eng.
Italy. England. 1551-1997. Historical studies. ■Theatre as a central part of European education for over four hundred years with attention to Latin Jesuit school plays in Messina, and the use of plays as a teaching tool in sixteenth-century English schools.

3376 Kermauner, Taras. *Blagor blata. Knj. 3: Bratovski, objem blata.* (The Welfare of Mud, Book 3: Mud's Brotherly Embrace.) Ljubljana: SGFM; 1997. 283 pp. Lang.: Slo.
Slovenia. 1900-1996. Critical studies. ■Based on an analysis of contemporary Slovene drama, argues that all sociopolitical models other than Christianity lead inevitably to fratricide or holy war on the one hand, or to narcissism and delusion on the other.

3377 Mazibuko, Doreen. "Theatre: The Political Weapon in South Africa." 219-224 in Davis, Geoffrey V., ed.; Fuchs, Anne, ed. *Theatre and Change in South Africa.* Amsterdam:

Harwood Academic Publishing; 1996. (Contemporary Theatre Studies 12.) Notes. Index. Append. Lang.: Eng.
South Africa, Republic of. 1910-1992. Historical studies. ■The political history of theatre in South Africa from the Afrikaners and English to changes in the 1990s.

3378 Brovik, Ingela. "Ventilsystem i segregationen." (A Pressure Valve for Segregation.) *Entré.* 1997; 24(3): 39-45. Illus.: Photo. B&W. Lang.: Swe.
Sweden: Malmö. 1996. Historical studies. ■Account of a competition for the best new play, scenography and music, involving immigrants, as a means to address the social problems of the immigrant-dominated suburbs, with reference to the promoter Elizabeta Zemljic.

3379 Licht, Fred, ed. *Füssli pittore di Shakespeare. Pittura e teatro 1775-1825.* (Füssli as Painter of Shakespeare: Painting and Theatre, 1775-1825.) Milan: Electa; 1997. 237 pp. Biblio. Illus.: Dwg. Pntg. Lang.: Ita.
Switzerland. 1775-1825. Histories-sources. ■Catalogue of an exhibition held at the Fondazione Magnani Rocca, Parma, 1997, on paintings and drawings of Shakespearean subjects by Johann Heinrich Füssli.

3380 Fiebach, Joachim. "Ebrahim Hussein's Dramaturgy: A Swahili Multiculturalist's Journey in Drama and Theatre." *RAL.* 1997 Win; 28(4): 19-37. Notes. Biblio. Lang.: Eng.
Tanzania. 1966-1997. Critical studies. ■African attitudes toward multiculturalism as reflected in the work of playwright Ebrahim Hussein.

3381 Barker, Simon. "Re-loading the Canon: Shakespeare and the Study Guides." 42-57 in Joughin, John J., ed. *Shakespeare and National Culture.* Manchester: Manchester UP; 1997. 343 pp. Notes. Index. Lang.: Eng.
UK-England. 1990-1996. Critical studies. ■The alleged failure of study guides to impart critical theory to students of Shakespeare.

3382 Domenichelli, Mario. "'L'anima dell'uomo sotto il socialismo'. La filosofia politica di Oscar Wilde." (*The Soul of Man Under Socialism*: Oscar Wilde's Political Philosophy.) *LadB.* 1997; 1(1): 11-33. Notes. Lang.: Ita.
UK-England. 1890. Historical studies. ■Analysis of *The Soul of Man Under Socialism* by Oscar Wilde.

3383 Holderness, Graham; Murphy, Andrew. "Shakespeare's England: Britain's Shakespeare." 19-41 in Joughin, John J., ed. *Shakespeare and National Culture.* Manchester: Manchester UP; 1997. 343 pp. Notes. Index. Lang.: Eng.
UK-England. 1990. Historical studies. ■The 1990 attempt to establish a core curriculum in England including compulsory exams on Shakespeare. Examines the significance of this ideological contestation with Shakespeare at its center and analyzes why and if Shakespeare represents 'Englishness'.

3384 Maley, Willy. "'This sceptred isle': Shakespeare and the British Problem." 83-108 in Joughin, John J., ed. *Shakespeare and National Culture.* Manchester: Manchester UP; 1997. 343 pp. Notes. Index. Lang.: Eng.
UK-England. 1990-1996. Critical studies. ■Questions of British national identity, both current and past. Focuses on the 'Englishness' of Shakespeare as constructed within a British context and against other national identities.

3385 Sawyer, Robert Eugene. *Mid-Victorian Appropriations of Shakespeare: George Eliot, A.C. Swinburne, and Robert Browning.* Athens, GA: Univ. of Georgia; 1997. 256 pp. [Ph.D. Dissertation, Univ. Microfilms Order No. AAC 9817832.] Lang.: Eng.
UK-England. 1840-1870. Critical studies. ■The influence of Shakespeare's works on nineteenth-century authors Charles Lamb, George Eliot, A.C. Swinburne, and Robert Browning.

3386 Wilson, Richard. "NATO's Pharmacy: Shakespeare by Prescription." 58-80 in Joughin, John J., ed. *Shakespeare and National Culture.* Manchester: Manchester UP; 1997. 343 pp. Notes. Index. Lang.: Eng.
UK-England. 1990-1996. Critical studies. ■Political analysis of the current place of the Royal Shakespeare Company in British culture and how Shakespeare has been reconstructed as a panacea for national ills and to serve a political ideology.

DRAMA: —Relation to other fields

3387 Ackerman, Alan Louis, Jr. *Displaced Theatre and American Literature*. Cambridge, MA: Harvard Univ; 1997. 281 pp. [Ph.D. Dissertation, Univ. Microfilms Order No. AAC 9733220.] Lang.: Eng.
USA. 1850-1910. Historical studies. ■Investigates the relationship between theatre and the literary imagination in Walt Whitman, Herman Melville, William Dean Howells, Louisa May Alcott, and Henry James, who are said to have thought deeply about the theatre and represented it in literature, both in the prolific and innovative use of theatrical metaphors and in aspects of literary form which represent dramaturgical assumptions of the melodramatic and, later, the realist stage.

3388 Andreas, James R. "Writing Down, Speaking Up, Acting Out, and Clowning Around in the Shakespeare Classroom." 25-34 in Salomone, Ronald E., ed.; Davis, James E., ed. *Teaching Shakespeare Into the Twenty-First Century*. Athens, OH: Ohio UP; 1997. 290 pp. Pref. Biblio. Lang.: Eng.
USA. 1997. Instructional materials. ■Examines wordplay and vulgarity in Shakespeare focusing on the character of Dogberry in *Much Ado About Nothing*. Argues that examination of the clowns in Shakespeare engages students' interest and leads them to a discussion of philosophic purpose and thematic structure.

3389 Baker, Susan. "Shakespearean Authority in the Classic Detective Story." *SQ*. 1995 Win; 46(4): 424-448. Notes. Append. Lang.: Eng.
USA. UK-England. 1995. Critical studies. ■The influence of Shakespeare on classic detective fiction, and the genre's approach to the subject of Shakespearean authority.

3390 Beehler, Sharon A. "Making Media Matter in the Shakespeare Classroom." 247-254 in Salomone, Ronald E., ed.; Davis, James E., ed. *Teaching Shakespeare Into the Twenty-First Century*. Athens, OH: Ohio UP; 1997. 290 pp. Pref. Biblio. Lang.: Eng.
USA. 1997. Instructional materials. ■The nature and uses of media for future classrooms, including the strengths and weaknesses of some common audio-visual materials, elements of film criticism, the availability and use of CD-ROMs and laserdiscs, and sets of questions and exercises.

3391 Brent, Harry. "Different Daggers: Versions of *Macbeth*." 215-221 in Salomone, Ronald E., ed.; Davis, James E., ed. *Teaching Shakespeare Into the Twenty-First Century*. Athens, OH: Ohio UP; 1997. 290 pp. Pref. Biblio. Lang.: Eng.
USA. 1997. Instructional materials. ■Using a series of writing assignments to teach Shakespeare's *Macbeth*. Author delineates the assignments, which require students to compare different video versions of the play.

3392 Buhler, Stephen M. "Text, Eyes, and Videotape: Screening Shakespeare Scripts." *SQ*. 1995 Sum; 46(2): 236-244. Notes. Lang.: Eng.
USA. 1995. Critical studies. ■Debates the pros and cons of using film and videotape when teaching Shakespeare.

3393 Christel, Mary T.; Heckel-Oliver, Christine. "Role-Playing: *Julius Caesar*." 18-24 in Salomone, Ronald E., ed.; Davis, James E., ed. *Teaching Shakespeare Into the Twenty-First Century*. Athens, OH: Ohio UP; 1997. 290 pp. Pref. Biblio. Lang.: Eng.
USA. 1997. Instructional materials. ■The importance of role-playing and journal writing in teaching Shakespeare's *Julius Caesar* and other works.

3394 Christenbury, Leila. "Problems with *Othello* in the High School Classroom." 182-192 in Salomone, Ronald E., ed.; Davis, James E., ed. *Teaching Shakespeare Into the Twenty-First Century*. Athens, OH: Ohio UP; 1997. 290 pp. Pref. Biblio. Lang.: Eng.
USA. 1997. Instructional materials. ■The difficult issue of race in teaching Shakespeare's *Othello*. Suggests techniques to aid instructors and students.

3395 Collins, Michael J. "Teaching *King Lear*." 166-171 in Salomone, Ronald E., ed.; Davis, James E., ed. *Teaching Shakespeare Into the Twenty-First Century*. Athens, OH: Ohio UP; 1997. 290 pp. Pref. Biblio. Lang.: Eng.
USA. 1997. Instructional materials. ■Examines the myriad and often contradictory meanings in Shakespeare's *King Lear*. Encourages instruc-

tors to help students recognize that there is no one 'right reading' for the text.

3396 Collins, Michael J. "Using Films to Teach Shakespeare." *SQ*. 1995 Sum; 46(2): 228-235. Notes. Append. Lang.: Eng.
USA. 1995. Critical studies. ■Recommends the use of film as a way of enhancing student understanding of Shakespeare.

3397 Coursen, H.R. *Teaching Shakespeare with Film and Television: A Guide*. Westport, CT/London: Greenwood; 1997. 193 pp. Pref. Notes. Biblio. Index. Lang.: Eng.
USA. 1985-1996. Instructional materials. ■Ways of using media to teach Shakespeare. Book is in two sections: theory, techniques, and resources, and applications, both using examples from contemporary films.

3398 Coursen, H.R. "Uses of Media in Teaching Shakespeare." 193-200 in Salomone, Ronald E., ed.; Davis, James E., ed. *Teaching Shakespeare Into the Twenty-First Century*. Athens, OH: Ohio UP; 1997. 290 pp. Pref. Biblio. Lang.: Eng.
USA. 1997. Instructional materials. ■The use of media in teaching Shakespeare. Suggests using different video and film versions of a play to examine issues and conflicts. Focuses on Othello's murder of Desdemona and suggests videotaping students' performances for further discussion and analysis.

3399 Crowl, Samuel. "'Our Lofty Scene': Teaching Modern Film Versions of *Julius Caesar*." 222-231 in Salomone, Ronald E., ed.; Davis, James E., ed. *Teaching Shakespeare Into the Twenty-First Century*. Athens, OH: Ohio UP; 1997. 290 pp. Pref. Biblio. Lang.: Eng.
USA. 1997. Instructional materials. ■The use of video in teaching Shakespeare's *Julius Caesar*. Author delineates his experience using two different versions to facilitate small-group classroom discussion.

3400 de Grazia, Margreta. "The Question of the One and the Many: The Globe Shakespeare, The *Complete King Lear*, and the New Folger Library Shakespeare." *SQ*. 1995 Sum; 46(2): 245-251. Notes. Lang.: Eng.
USA. 1995. Critical studies. ■Review of the efficacy for classroom use of three texts: *The Globe Shakespeare*, *The New Folger Shakespeare*, and the *Complete King Lear 1608-1623* compiled by Michael Warren, which has four different versions of the play.

3401 Elliott, Ward E.Y.; Valenza, Robert J. "Glass Slippers and Seven-League Boots: C-Prompted Doubts About Ascribing *A Funeral Elegy* and *A Lover's Complaint* to Shakespeare." *SQ*. 1997 Sum; 48(2): 177-207. Notes. Tables. Lang.: Eng.
USA: Claremont, CA. 1997. Textual studies. ■Computer-aided exclusion and inclusion tests developed or adapted by Claremont Shakespeare Clinic examine whether 'A Lover's Complaint' or 'A Funeral Elegy' can be ascribed to Shakespeare. Methods of testing, results, test criteria.

3402 Figgins, Margo A. "Mirrors, Sculptures, Machines, and Masks: Theater Improvisation Games." 65-80 in Salomone, Robert E., ed.; Davis, James E., ed. *Teaching Shakespeare Into the Twenty-First Century*. Athens, OH: Ohio UP; 1997. 290 pp. Pref. Biblio. Lang.: Eng.
USA. 1997. Instructional materials. ■The value and use of improvisational theatre games to teach Shakespeare. Uses *Much Ado About Nothing* to illustrate technique.

3403 Flachmann, Michael. "Professional Theater People and English Teachers: Working Together to Teach Shakespeare." 57-64 in Salomone, Robert E., ed.; Davis, James E., ed. *Teaching Shakespeare Into the Twenty-First Century*. Athens, OH: Ohio UP; 1997. 290 pp. Pref. Biblio. Lang.: Eng.
USA. 1997. Histories-sources. ■Author's experience as company dramaturg for the Utah Shakespearean Festival, with reflections on how theatre professionals and teachers of English literature can work together.

3404 Flannagan, Roy. "Beyond the Gee Whiz Stage: Computer Technology, the World Wide Web, and Shakespeare." 262-270 in Salomone, Ronald E., ed.; Davis, James E., ed. *Teaching Shakespeare Into the Twenty-First Century*. Athens, OH: Ohio UP; 1997. 290 pp. Pref. Biblio. Lang.: Eng.
USA. 1997. Instructional materials. ■The use of the World Wide Web in teaching Shakespeare. Provides information on constructing home pages, searching databases, and also what is on the Web.

DRAMA: —Relation to other fields

3405 Frey, Charles H. "Making Sense of Shakespeare: A Reader-Based Response." 96-103 in Salomone, Robert E., ed.; Davis, James E., ed. *Teaching Shakespeare Into the Twenty-First Century.* Athens, OH: Ohio UP; 1997. 290 pp. Pref. Biblio. Lang.: Eng.

USA. 1997. Instructional materials. ■Examines the use of reader-response methodology in teaching Shakespeare. Explores the idea that words can engage emotions through analysis of *Romeo and Juliet* and *Macbeth.*

3406 Fritsch, Sibylle. "Die rote Spur." (The Red Trace.) *DB.* 1997; 8: 43-45. Illus.: Photo. B&W. 2. Lang.: Ger.

USA. 1991-1997. Historical studies. ■Describes and analyzes the influences of AIDS on new plays, including Tony Kushner's *Angels in America* and Nicky Silver's *Pterodactyls.*

3407 Gathergood, William J. "Computers in the Secondary Classroom." 255-261 in Salomone, Ronald E., ed.; Davis, James E., ed. *Teaching Shakespeare Into the Twenty-First Century.* Athens, OH: Ohio UP; 1997. 290 pp. Pref. Biblio. Lang.: Eng.

USA. 1997. Instructional materials. ■The uses of the computer in teaching Shakespeare, such as the Internet and email. Uses *Hamlet* as an example and describes activities and exercises he has used.

3408 Giese, Loreen L. "Images of *Hamlet* in the Undergraduate Classroom." 172-176 in Salomone, Ronald E., ed.; Davis, James E., ed. *Teaching Shakespeare Into the Twenty-First Century.* Athens, OH: Ohio UP; 1997. 290 pp. Pref. Biblio. Lang.: Eng.

USA. 1997. Instructional materials. ■Feminist and performance techniques for teaching Shakespeare's *Hamlet.* Argues that a discussion of gender roles in the play, different video versions of a specific scene, and small classroom performances can aid students in understanding and being interested in Shakespeare.

3409 Griffin, C.W. "Textual Studies and Teaching Shakespeare." 104-111 in Salomone, Robert E., ed.; Davis, James E., ed. *Teaching Shakespeare Into the Twenty-First Century.* Athens, OH: Ohio UP; 1997. 290 pp. Pref. Biblio. Lang.: Eng.

USA. 1997. Instructional materials. ■Identifies ways that modern Shakespearean texts are 'cleaned up' for the reader and why teachers of Shakespeare should encourage students to explore how the texts were first produced, marketed, and received.

3410 Hallett, Charles A. "Scene versus Sequence: Distinguishing Action from Narrative in Shakespeare's Multipartite Scenes." *SQ.* 1995 Sum; 46(2): 183-195. Notes. Lang.: Eng.

USA. 1995. Instructional materials. ■Outlines strategy of analyzing the action in Shakespeare as a way of significantly enhancing the student's ability to perceive and enjoy the dramatic substructure of his plays.

3411 Helphinstine, Frances L. "Using Playgrounding to Teach *Hamlet.*" 50-56 in Salomone, Robert E., ed.; Davis, James E., ed. *Teaching Shakespeare Into the Twenty-First Century.* Athens, OH: Ohio UP; 1997. 290 pp. Pref. Biblio. Lang.: Eng.

USA. 1997. Instructional materials. ■The use of playgrounding, a theatrical sports analogy, in the classroom, said to give students a fresh awareness of all facets of theatrical experience and production. Focuses on *Hamlet* to illustrate techniques.

3412 Herold, Niels. "Pedagogy, *Hamlet,* and the Manufacture of Wonder." *SQ.* 1995 Sum; 46(2): 125-134. Notes. Lang.: Eng.

USA. UK-England. 1995. Critical studies. ■Instilling a sense of wonder in students reading Shakespeare's *Hamlet.*

3413 Howlett, Kathy M. "Team-Teaching Shakespeare in an Interdisciplinary Context." 112-119 in Salomone, Robert E., ed.; Davis, James E., ed. *Teaching Shakespeare Into the Twenty-First Century.* Athens, OH: Ohio UP; 1997. 290 pp. Pref. Biblio. Lang.: Eng.

USA. 1997. Instructional materials. ■The author's experience teaching Shakespeare's *Henry V* in a team-taught, interdisciplinary environment.

3414 Johannessen, Larry R. "Enhancing Response to *Romeo and Juliet.*" 154-165 in Salomone, Ronald E., ed.; Davis, James E., ed. *Teaching Shakespeare Into the Twenty-First Century.* Athens, OH: Ohio UP; 1997. 290 pp. Pref. Biblio. Lang.: Eng.

USA. 1997. Instructional materials. ■Non-traditional approaches to teaching Shakespeare's *Romeo and Juliet.* Gives specific examples, such as activities and writing assignments.

3415 Johnson, Robert Carl. "What Happens in the Mousetrap: Versions of *Hamlet.*" 177-181 in Salomone, Ronald E., ed.; Davis, James E., ed. *Teaching Shakespeare Into the Twenty-First Century.* Athens, OH: Ohio UP; 1997. 290 pp. Pref. Biblio. Lang.: Eng.

USA. 1997. Instructional materials. ■A pedagogical approach to teaching Shakespeare's *Hamlet* via the mousetrap scene. Advocates an approach using four different productions shown on video giving four different interpretations of the particular scene. Encourages students to develop individual interpretations.

3416 Kahn, Coppélia. "Shakespeare: Reading/Text/Theory." *SQ.* 1997 Win; 48(4): 455-458. Lang.: Eng.

USA. 1997. Historical studies. ■Methods of teaching close reading through theoretical concepts and vice versa. Argues that Shakespeare is still extremely popular as subject matter for students.

3417 Kissler, Linda. "Teaching Shakespeare through Film." 201-208 in Salomone, Ronald E., ed.; Davis, James E., ed. *Teaching Shakespeare Into the Twenty-First Century.* Athens, OH: Ohio UP; 1997. 290 pp. Pref. Biblio. Lang.: Eng.

USA. 1997. Instructional materials. ■The use of videotapes in teaching Shakespeare's *Henry V.* Gives specific video clips she uses, homework assignments, mock interviews of character and other activities.

3418 Lennartz, Knut. "Fluchtpunkt L.A." (Vanishing Point L.A.) *DB.* 1997; 1: 14-18. Illus.: Photo. Handbill. B&W. 9. Lang.: Ger.

USA: Los Angeles, CA. Germany: Berlin. 1921-1997. Biographical studies. ■A portrait of the actor, director and theatre director Walter Wicclair who emigrated from Kreuzburg to Los Angeles in 1933, the founding there of a German stage called Freie Bühne, and his failed attempts to reestablish himself as a director in postwar Germany.

3419 Liston, William T. "Paraphrasing Shakespeare." 11-17 in Salomone, Ronald E., ed.; Davis, James E., ed. *Teaching Shakespeare Into the Twenty-First Century.* Athens, OH: Ohio UP; 1997. 290 pp. Pref. Biblio. Lang.: Eng.

USA. 1997. Instructional materials. ■On the benefits of practicing daily paraphrasing of Shakespeare with students.

3420 Maher, Mary Z. "Shakespeare in Production." 35-42 in Salomone, Ronald E., ed.; Davis, James E., ed. *Teaching Shakespeare Into the Twenty-First Century.* Athens, OH: Ohio UP; 1997. 290 pp. Pref. Biblio. Lang.: Eng.

USA. 1997. Instructional materials. ■Examines the possibilities and limitations of performance as applied in the college classroom. Analyzes the use of film and video as ways to explore performance further.

3421 McDonald, Russ. "Shakespeare Goes to High School: Some Current Practices in the American Classroom." *SQ.* 1995 Sum; 46 (2): 145-156. Lang.: Eng.

USA. 1995. Histories-sources. ■Unscientific survey conducted in questionnaire form of several high school teachers on what approaches they use when teaching Shakespeare.

3422 McManus, Eva B. "Shakespeare Festivals: Materials for the Classroom." 232-246 in Salomone, Ronald E., ed.; Davis, James E., ed. *Teaching Shakespeare Into the Twenty-First Century.* Athens, OH: Ohio UP; 1997. 290 pp. Pref. Biblio. Lang.: Eng.

USA. 1997. Instructional materials. ■Based on the author's own two-year study, examines the use of educational programs at festivals and theatres to teach Shakespeare. Offers suggestions to teachers about accessibility and resources.

3423 Moore, Dick. "Robeson Award Goes to Athol Fugard." *EN.* 1997 Nov.; 82(9): 1. Illus.: Photo. 1. Lang.: Eng.

USA: New York, NY. 1997. Historical studies. ■The 1997 Paul Robeson Award honoring those who struggle for justice and equality is awarded to South African playwright Athol Fugard.

3424 O'Brien, Peggy. "'And Gladly Teach': Books, Articles, and a Bibliography on the Teaching of Shakespeare." *SQ.* 1995 Sum; 46(2): 165-172. Notes. Biblio. Lang.: Eng.

DRAMA: —Relation to other fields

USA. 1995. Critical studies. ■Review of literature specific to the teaching of Shakespeare: includes a bibliography of material recommended.

3425 Pierce, Robert B. "Teaching the Sonnets with Performance Techniques." 43-49 in Salomone, Robert E., ed.; Davis, James E., ed. *Teaching Shakespeare Into the Twenty-First Century.* Athens, OH: Ohio UP; 1997. 290 pp. Pref. Biblio. Lang.: Eng.
USA. 1997. Instructional materials. ■The use of performance techniques to teach Shakespeare's sonnets, said to encourage students to pay attention to sounds and to connect rhythm, meaning, and interpretation.

3426 Plasse, Marie A. "An Inquiry-Based Approach." 120-126 in Salomone, Robert E., ed.; Davis, James E., ed. *Teaching Shakespeare Into the Twenty-First Century.* Athens, OH: Ohio UP; 1997. 290 pp. Pref. Biblio. Lang.: Eng.
USA. 1997. Instructional materials. ■Author's approach to teaching students how to develop their own inquiries into Shakespeare's plays, rather than forcing her own agenda.

3427 Radavich, David. "Western Drama and the New Frontier." *AmerD.* 1997 Fall; 7(1): 99-120. Notes. Biblio. Lang.: Eng.
USA. 1939-1997. Critical studies. ■Examines sociological, political, regional and environmental reasons for marginalization of drama on the literature and life of the American West with special focus on the frontier myth, narrative of the west and melodrama.

3428 Riggio, Milal C. "The Universal is Specific: Deviance and Cultural Identity in the Shakespeare Classroom." *SQ.* 1995 Sum ; 46(2): 196-209. Notes. Lang.: Eng.
USA. 1995. Critical studies. ■How the multicultural makeup of a classroom leads to the need to redesign approaches to the in-class performance of Shakespeare.

3429 Rocklin, Edward L. "Shakespeare's Script as a Cue for Pedagogic Invention." *SQ.* 1995 Sum; 46(2): 135-144. Notes. Lang.: Eng.
USA. 1995. Critical studies. ■Argues that teachers should approach teaching Shakespeare in a dramatic fashion to enhance appreciation of the subject.

3430 Rozett, Martha Tuck. "Creating a Context for Shakespeare with Historical Fiction." *SQ.* 1995 Sum; 46(2): 220-227. Notes. Lang.: Eng.
USA. 1985. Instructional materials. ■Giving students a context for Elizabethan and Jacobean times by assigning historical fiction. Approach enhances students' appreciation of Shakespeare's work.

3431 Saeger, James P. "The High-Tech Classroom: Shakespeare in the Age of Multimedia, Computer Networks, and Virtual Space." 271-283 in Salomone, Ronald E., ed.; Davis, James E., ed. *Teaching Shakespeare Into the Twenty-First Century.* Athens, OH: Ohio UP; 1997. 290 pp. Pref. Biblio. Lang.: Eng.
USA. 1997. Instructional materials. ■Survey of some future technological innovations and resources available. Focuses on three methods for teaching Shakespeare: the World Wide Web, computerized video presentations, and text-based virtual classrooms.

3432 Sauer, David Kennedy. "'Speak the Speech, I pray you', Or Suiting the Method to the Moment: A Theory of Classroom Performance of Shakespeare." *SQ.* 1995 Sum; 46(2): 173-182. Notes. Biblio. Lang.: Eng.
USA. 1995. Critical studies. ■Discusses the benefits of performing Shakespeare in the classroom.

3433 Schevera, Nicholas. *Theatricality in the Fiction of Henry James.* New York, NY: New York Univ; 1997. 509 pp. [Ph.D. Dissertation, Univ. Microfilms Order No. AAC 9717795.] Lang.: Eng.
USA. 1870-1910. Critical studies. ■James's early involvement in theatre and the ways in which the characters in his fiction manipulate and control one another through the deliberate creation or termination of 'scenes'.

3434 Shurgot, Michael W. "'So Quick Bright Things Come to Confusion': Shakespeare in the Heterogeneous Classroom." 139-146 in Salomone, Robert E., ed.; Davis, James E., ed. *Teaching Shakespeare Into the Twenty-First Century.* Athens, OH: Ohio UP; 1997. 290 pp. Pref. Biblio. Lang.: Eng.

USA. 1997. Instructional materials. ■Encourages teachers to be open to the possibility of multiple interpretations of Shakespearean texts, with particular references to *A Midsummer Night's Dream* and *Othello.*

3435 Skrebels, Paul. "Transhistoricizing *Much Ado About Nothing:* Finding a Place for Shakespeare's Work in the Postmodern World." 81-95 in Salomone, Robert E., ed.; Davis, James E., ed. *Teaching Shakespeare Into the Twenty-First Century.* Athens, OH: Ohio UP; 1997. 290 pp. Pref. Biblio. Lang.: Eng.
USA. 1997. Instructional materials. ■Examines the use of transhistoricism, a critical approach comparing one historical epoch with a contemporary one, in the teaching of Shakespeare. Demonstrates the approach with *Much Ado About Nothing.*

3436 Smith, Bruce R. "Teaching the Resonances." *SQ.* 1997 Win; 48(4): 451-455. Lang.: Eng.
USA: Washington, DC. 1997. Historical studies. ■Controversy surrounding Georgetown University's decision to drop Shakespeare from its curriculum. The author, a professor at the University, argues for a dialectic between past and present and to teach the work of new historicists as well as that of Shakespeare.

3437 Styan, J.L. "The Writing Assigment: The Basic Question." 3-10 in Salomone, Ronald E., ed.; Davis, James E., ed. *Teaching Shakespeare Into the Twenty-First Century.* Athens, OH: Ohio UP; 1997. 290 pp. Pref. Biblio. Lang.: Eng.
USA. 1997. Instructional materials. ■On the difficulty of generating effective writing assignments in teaching Shakespeare. Suggests a simple assignment that promotes close reading, encourages visualization of performance activities, and calls for critical judgements by students.

3438 Swope, John Wilson. "A Whole-Language Approach to *A Midsummer Night's Dream.*" 127-138 in Salomone, Robert E., ed.; Davis, James E., ed. *Teaching Shakespeare Into the Twenty-First Century.* Athens, OH: Ohio UP; 1997. 290 pp. Pref. Biblio. Lang.: Eng.
USA. 1997. Instructional materials. ■Calls for more concentration on Shakespeare's comedies in the high school classroom. Author delineates his experiences teaching *A Midsummer Night's Dream* and suggests a whole-language approach to facilitate better reading skills in students.

3439 Warner, Christine D. "Building Shakespearean Worlds in the Everyday Classroom." 147-153 in Salomone, Ronald E., ed.; Davis, James E., ed. *Teaching Shakespeare Into the Twenty-First Century.* Athens, OH: Ohio UP; 1997. 290 pp. Pref. Biblio. Lang.: Eng.
USA. 1997. Instructional materials. ■The instructor as facilitator in teaching Shakespeare. Recommends group improvisation strategies called process drama, activities that explore an improvised dramatic world.

3440 Wilson, August. "National Black Theatre Festival, 1997." *Callaloo.* 1997 Sum; 20(3): 483-492. Lang.: Eng.
USA: Winston-Salem, NC. 1997. Histories-sources. ■Speech delivered by August Wilson on the state of Black theatre at the National Black Theatre Festival.

3441 Wilson, August. "The Ground on Which I Stand." *Callaloo.* 1997 Sum; 20(3): 493-503. Lang.: Eng.
USA. 1996. Histories-sources. ■Reprint of Wilson's controversial address to the TCG national conference regarding the role of the Black artist in American theatre.

3442 Young, Debra Bailey. *'A Woman's Pen Presents You with a Play': The Influence of Drama and the Theater on the Life and Writings of Louisa May Alcott.* Indiana, PA: Indiana Univ. of Pennsylvania; 1997. 244 pp. [Ph.D. Dissertation, Univ. Microfilms Order No. AAC 9816760.] Lang.: Eng.
USA. 1832-1888. Critical studies. ■The fiction and dramatic adaptations of Louisa May Alcott and the influence of the theatre and acting on her work. Argues that the influence of theatre and drama, which Alcott used to characterize her work, has been underestimated by critics.

3443 Koljazin, Wladimir; Berger, Johannes, transl. "Bertolt Brecht im Visier der Stalinschen Geheimpolizei." (Bertolt Brecht Under Surveillance by Stalin's Secret Police.) *TZ.* 1997; Yb: 118-122. Illus.: Photo. B&W. 4. Lang.: Ger.
USSR. 1932-1954. Biographical studies. ■Describes the police surveillance of Brecht by the Ljubjanka and NKVD, and his apparent indiffer-

DRAMA: —Relation to other fields

ence to the terror under Stalin and the arrest and conviction of close friends like Tretyakov, Neher, and Lacis.

3444 Lunga, Violet Bridget. *An Examination of an African Post-colonial Experience of Language, Culture, and Identity: Amakhosi Theatre, Ako Bulawayo, Zimbabwe.* Burnaby, BC: Simon Fraser Univ; 1997. 272 pp. [Ph.D. Dissertation, Univ. Microfilms Order No. AAC NQ24330.] Lang.: Eng.
Zimbabwe. 1960-1997. Empirical research. ■A cultural and ethnographic study of the Amakhosi theatre tradition of Zimbabwe. Author explores postcolonial identity as found in intersections of colonial (English) language and indigenous (Ndebele) language and analyzes the plays of the Amakhosi theatre to reveal the contradictions of postcolonial identity and culture.

Research/historiography

3445 Aliverti, Maria Ines. "Major Portraits and Minor Series in Eighteenth-Century Theatrical Portraiture." *ThR.* 1997; 22(3) : 234-254. Notes. Illus.: Dwg. B&W. 12. Lang.: Eng.
England. France. 1700-1800. Historical studies. ■Account of main series of eighteenth-century actors' portraits, with comparative analysis of patterns of representation in England and France. Reference to Michel Baron, Adrienne Lecouvreur, Mlle du Clos, and David Garrick.

3446 Clare, Janet. "Historicism and the Question of Censorship in the Renaissance." *ELR.* 1997 Spr; 27(2): 155-176. Notes. Illus.: Dwg. B&W. 1. Lang.: Eng.
England: London. 1588-1980. Critical studies. ■Location of censorship in Renaissance drama and limitations of current historical method. Suggests a more inclusive historicist approach to the literary Renaissance. Focus on *Henry IV* and *Richard II*.

3447 Erenstein, Robert L. "Theatre Iconography: An Introduction." *ThR.* 1997; 22(3): 185-189. Notes. Lang.: Eng.
Europe. 1600-1995. Critical studies. ■Overview of research in theatre iconography. Summarizes selection of papers given at Wassenaar symposium in 1995.

3448 Pelling, Christopher. "Conclusion: Tragedy as Evidence." 213-235 in Pelling, Christopher, ed. *Greek Tragedy and the Historian.* Oxford: Clarendon; 1997. 268 pp. Notes. Biblio. Index. Lang.: Eng.
Greece. 500-250 B.C. Historical studies. ■The use of Greek tragedy as historical evidence, with emphasis on the reconstruction of civic ideology.

3449 Vince, Ronald. "The Aristotelian Theatrical Paradigm as Cultural-Historic Construct." *ThR.* 1997; 22(1 Supplement): 38-47. Notes. Lang.: Eng.
Greece: Athens. 600-300 B.C. Historical studies. ■Discusses historiographical processes in relation to performative aspects of Athenian culture in fourth century B.C. and proposes a performative reading of Aristotle's *Poetics.*

3450 Pilkington, Lionel. "'Every Crossing Sweeper Thinks Himself a Moralist': The Critical Role of Audiences in Irish Theatre History." *IUR.* 1997 Spr/Sum; 27(1): 152-165. Lang.: Eng.
Ireland: Dublin. 1897-1907. Critical studies. ■Investigates tendency of Irish theatre criticism to focus on textual analysis of drama, rather than on the specific and historical occasion of theatrical peformance. Discusses the significance of the 1902 production of Yeats and Lady Gregory's *Cathleen ni Houlihan.*

3451 Senelick, Laurence. "Early Photographic Attempts to Record Performance Sequence." *ThR.* 1997; 22(3): 255-264. Notes. Illus.: Photo. B&W. 14. Lang.: Eng.
Russia. USA. 1865-1900. Historical studies. ■Describes nineteenth-century attempts to record performance sequence photographically, with illustrations of Adah Menken in *Child of the Sun* by John Brougham, and actor Viktor Andrejév-Burlak in Gogol's *Diary of a Madman.*

3452 Dawson, Giles E. "A Seventh Signature for Shakespeare." *SQ.* 1992 Spr; 43(1): 72-79. Notes. Illus.: Photo. B&W. 11. Lang.: Eng.
USA: Washington, DC. 1938-1992. Historical studies. ■The debate over whether a signature on a document in the possession of the Folger Library is in fact that of William Shakespeare.

Theory/criticism

3453 Bretzius, Stephen. *Shakespeare in Theory: The Postmodern Academy and the Early Modern Theater.* Ann Arbor, MI: Univ. of Michigan P; 1997. 160 pp. Notes. Index. Biblio. Illus.: Photo. 4. Lang.: Eng.
1997. Critical studies. ■Survey of postmodern Shakespearean criticism.

3454 Bristol, Michael D. "How Good Does Evidence Have to Be?" 22-43 in Pechter, Edward, ed. *Textual and Theatrical Shakespeare: Questions of Evidence.* Iowa City, IA: Univ of Iowa P; 1997. 267 pp. (Studies in Theatre History and Culture.) Pref. Notes. Index. Lang.: Eng.
1997. Critical studies. ■The different ways evidence functions to structure critical inquiry and justify its claims in Shakespeare's plays.

3455 Bulman, James C. "Introduction: Shakespeare and Performance Theory." 1-11 in Bulman, James C., ed. *Shakespeare, Theory, and Performance.* London/New York, NY: Routledge; 1996. 218 pp. Notes. Biblio. Index. Lang.: Eng.
1996. Critical studies. ■Introduction to a collection of essays regarding contemporary critical perspectives regarding practical questions of performing Shakespeare.

3456 de Marinis, Marco; Chiampi, James T., transl. "From Script to Hypertext: *Mise en Scène* and the Notation of Theatrical Production in the Twentieth Century." *Gestos.* 1997 Apr.; 12(23): 9-37. Notes. Biblio. Lang.: Eng.
1901-1997. Historical studies. ■Discusses methods of notation used in the twentieth century for recording the staging of theatrical productions.

3457 De Sousa, Geraldo U. "'Paradigm Lost'? The Fate of Literature in the Age of Theory." *SQ.* 1997 Win; 48(4): 449-451. Lang.: Eng.
1997. Historical studies. ■Introduction to series of papers from the special plenary session 'Paradigm Lost?' at the annual meeting of the Shakespeare Association of America. Session considered the impact of theory on the teaching of Shakespeare and the extent to which the collective theoretical debates are redefining the role and responsibilities of educators.

3458 Fuchs, Barbara. "'Conquering Islands': Contextualizing *The Tempest.*" *SQ.* 1997 Spr; 48(1): 45-62. Notes. Illus.: Dwg. B&W. 1. Lang.: Eng.
1997. Critical studies. ■Argues that the context of colonialist ideology in the sixteenth and seventeenth centuries can and should be revealed by a multiple historical interpretation of Shakespeare's play. Discusses American criticism and the role of England in Ireland.

3459 Kos, Janko. "K vprašanju o bistvu komedije." (On the Problem of the Essence of Comedy.) *Slavr.* 1997; 45(1/2): 292-305. Lang.: Slo.
1997. Critical studies. ■Explores the possibilities for a contemporary definition of comedy, with consideration of the theories of Aristotle and Hegel, as well as works of Aristophanes, Plautus, Gogol, Cankar, and Ionesco.

3460 Pechter, Edward. "Textual and Theatrical Shakespeare: Questions of Evidence." 1-21 in Pechter, Edward, ed. *Textual and Theatrical Shakespeare: Questions of Evidence.* Iowa City, IA: Univ of Iowa P; 1997. 267 pp. (Studies in Theatre History and Culture.) Pref. Notes. Index. Lang.: Eng.
1997. Critical studies. ■Introductory essay on gaps in contemporary scholarship between the theatrical performance of Shakespeare's plays and the literary and cultural analysis of Shakespeare's texts.

3461 Skura, Meredith Anne. "Discourse and the Individual: The Case of Colonialism in *The Tempest.*" *SQ.* 1989 Spr; 40(1): 42-69. Notes. Lang.: Eng.
1985-1989. Historical studies. ■Scrutinizes the recent new historicist criticism regarding *The Tempest.*

3462 Vigeant, Louise. "Visages du réalisme à travers l'histoire du théâtre." (Faces of Realism Through the History of Theatre.) *JCT.* 1997; 85: 56-64. Notes. Illus.: Photo. B&W. 8. Lang.: Fre.
Historical studies. ■Role of reality and realism in theatre from the Greeks through to contemporary Quebec drama.

3463 Worthen, W.B. "Staging 'Shakespeare': Acting, Authority, and the Rhetoric of Performance." 12-28 in Bulman, James

DRAMA: —Theory/criticism

C., ed. *Shakespeare, Theory, and Performance*. London/New York, NY: Routledge; 1996. 218 pp. Notes. Biblio. Index. Lang.: Eng.
1977-1996. Critical studies. ■Challenges the notion that contemporary performance practices reflect an 'authentic Shakespearean' theatre experience.

3464 Godin, Jean Cléo. "Les avatars du réalisme québécois." (The Avatars of Quebec Realism.) *JCT*. 1997; 85: 65-72. Notes. Illus.: Poster. Photo. B&W. 11. Lang.: Fre.
Canada. 1904-1997. Historical studies. ■Realism in Quebec drama from the turn of the century to the present.

3465 Knowles, Richard Paul. "Shakespeare, 1993, and the Discourses of the Stratford Festival, Ontario." *SQ*. 1994 Sum; 45(2): 211-225. Lang.: Eng.
Canada: Stratford, ON. 1993. Critical studies. ■Critic discusses his review approach to the season at the Stratford Festival, an approach informed by the precepts of critics Stark Young and Eric Bentley.

3466 Laprise, Michel. "L'inconnu/le quotidien." (The Unknown/The Everyday.) *JCT*. 1997; 85: 76-82. Illus.: Photo. B&W. 3. Lang.: Fre.
Canada: Montreal, PQ. 1997. Histories-sources. ■Playwright/director Michel Laprise on realism, reality and truthfulness in theatre.

3467 Lévesque, Solange. "La grande illusion ou Les pépins de la réalité." (The Great Illusion or The Seeds of Reality.) *JCT*. 1997; 85: 53-55. Illus.: Photo. B&W. 3. Lang.: Fre.
Canada. 1997. Critical studies. ■Limits of reality in realism and difficulties of theorizing on realism.

3468 Vaïs, Michel. "Les Entrées libres de *Jeu*: Théâtre et société: quels rapports." (*Jeu*'s Open Forums: Theatre and Society: What Connections?)*JCT*. 1997; 82: 8-21. Notes. Illus.: Photo. B&W. 14. Lang.: Fre.
Canada. France. Belgium. 1974-1996. Historical studies. ■Social discourse in francophone theatre, from 1970s Brechtianism to contemporary theatre of images. Account of public forum held in Montreal, December 8th 1996.

3469 Cannan, Paul Dietrich. *The Generation of a Critic: The Emergence of Dramatic Criticism in England, 1660-1715*. University Park, PA: Pennsylvania State Univ; 1997. 301 pp. [Ph.D. Dissertation, Univ. Microfilms Order No. 9817444.] Lang.: Eng.
England. 1660-1715. Historical studies. ■Methods and aims of four different types of critics: authors (e.g,, John Dryden), 'professional' critics (Thomas Rymer, John Dennis, and Charles Gildon), moralistic critics (Jeremy Collier), and journalistic critics (Joseph Addison and Richard Steele).

3470 Cummings, Brian. "Swearing in Public: More and Shakespeare." *ELR*. 1997 Spr; 27(2): 197-232. Notes. Illus.: Dwg. B&W. 1. Lang.: Eng.
England: London. 1215-1622. Historical studies. ■Based on Sir Thomas More's investigation into statements made by a condemned man at his execution, and censorship of Shakespeare's *Othello*, ostensibly because of profanity, examines interpretation of swearing in public, problems relating the public to private thoughts and whether a public utterance can convey to its listeners a private meaning.

3471 Forster, Antonia. "Eighteenth-Century Shakespeare: Samuel Badcock, A Would-Be Editor." *SQ*. 1993 Spr; 44(1): 44-53. Notes. Lang.: Eng.
England. 1779-1789. Biographical studies. ■Career of literary critic and reviewer of volumes of Shakespeare's plays for periodicals, Samuel Badcock.

3472 Holbrook, Peter. "Nietzsche's *Hamlet*." *ShS*. 1997; 50(1): 171-186. Notes. Lang.: Eng.
England. Germany. 1601-1997. Critical studies. ■Nietzsche's interpretation of *Hamlet*: the play's resonance within his own life, and its influence on twentieth-century criticism.

3473 Orkin, Martin. "Othello and the 'plain face' of Racism." *SQ*. 1987 Sum; 38(2): 166-188. Notes. Lang.: Eng.
England. South Africa, Republic of. 1604-1987. Critical studies. ■Attitudes toward race in Shakespeare's England and *Othello*, with emphasis on how the silence about racism in South African *Othello* criticism supports racist doctrine and practice.

3474 Sherbo, Arthur. "Notes: John Kynaston (1728-83), A Neglected Shakespearean." *SQ*. 1997 Spr; 48(1): 80-90. Lang.: Eng.
England. 1728-1783. Biographical studies. ■Profile of literary critic for *Gentlemen's Magazine* with focus on his extensive Shakespearean criticism.

3475 Shershow, Scott Cutler. "Windings and Turnings: The Metaphoric Labyrinth of Restoration Dramatic Theory." *CompD*. 1992 Spr; 26(1): 1-18. Notes. Lang.: Eng.
England. 1650-1700. Historical studies. ■Development of dramatic theory in Restoration England.

3476 Buse, Peter. "Stage Remains: Theatre Criticism and the Photographic Archive." *JDTC*. 1997 Fall; 12(1): 77-96. Illus.: Photo. 3. Lang.: Eng.
Europe. 1890-1970. Critical studies. ■The role of photographs in theatre criticism. Argues that they are valuable not only to theatre but as artifacts of cultural history.

3477 Dox, Donnalee. "And All Was Cold As Any Stone: Death and the Critique of Representation." *JDTC*. 1997 Fall; 12(1): 103-111. Lang.: Eng.
Europe. 1997. Critical studies. ■Theatrical representations of death in current theoretical contexts. Author concentrates on a materialist reading of Shakespeare's *Hamlet*.

3478 Groenveld, Leanne Michelle. *The Medieval Theatre of Cruelty: Antonin Artaud and Corpus Christi Drama*. Edmonton, AB: Univ. of Alberta; 1997. 398 pp. [Ph.D. Dissertation, Univ. Microfilms Order No. AAC NQ22988.] Lang.: Eng.
Europe. 1400-1950. Critical studies. ■Theorist/playwright Antonin Artaud's views on medieval theatre, his theory of cruelty and Passion plays as represented through bodies subject to disease, death, and decay.

3479 Joughin, John J. "Shakespeare, National Culture and the Lure of Transnationalism." 269-294 in Joughin, John J., ed. *Shakespeare and National Culture*. Manchester: Manchester UP; 1997. 343 pp. Notes. Index. Lang.: Eng.
Europe. 1990-1994. Critical studies. ■The influence of the new media and the current debate on the nature and course of nationalism and transnationalism in Shakespeare criticism. Warns that institutional conformity must be resisted.

3480 Malekin, Peter; Yarrow, Ralph. *Consciousness, Literature and Theatre*. London/New York, NY: Macmillan/St. Martin's P; 1997. 197 pp. Pref. Index. Biblio. Append. Lang.: Eng.
Europe. North America. 1900-1996. Critical studies. ■Spirituality and the working consciousness in literature and dramatic texts. William Shakespeare, Eugène Ionesco, Augusto Boal and his 'theatre of liberation,' and other theatre practitioners are examined.

3481 Pavis, Patrice; Engelhardt, Barbara, transl. "Der Gestus bei Brecht." (Brecht's Gestus.) *TZ*. 1997; Yb: 42-45. Append. Illus.: Photo. B&W. 2. Lang.: Ger.
Europe. 1934-1997. Critical studies. ■Discusses Brecht's concept of 'Gestus', which cannot be reduced to a single definition and also relativizes the social function of a particular presentation. In relationship to concepts like 'body techniques' (Marcel Mauss), 'habitus' (Pierre Bourdieu) and the 'gendered body' (Elin Diamond), the concept is said to offer possibilities for an ongoing discussion.

3482 Pokling, James Nathan. *Casting Spells from the Stage: Magic and Ideology in the Modern Theatre*. Atlanta, GA: Emory Univ; 1997. 182 pp. [Ph.D. Dissertation, Univ. Microfilms Order No. AAC 9725073.] Lang.: Eng.
Europe. 1910-1950. Critical studies. ■Magic as a defining trope of modern drama in the theatrical theories of Stanislavskij, Yeats, Artaud, and Brecht.

3483 Sauter, Wilmar. "Approaching the Theatrical Event: The Influence of Semiotics and Hermeneutics on European Theatre Studies." *ThR*. 1997; 22(1 Supplement): 4-13. Notes. Lang.: Eng.
Europe. 1900-1997. Critical studies. ■Positions contemporary reception theory in relation to main trends in theatre research, and distinguishes

three levels of audience reception: the sensory, the artistic and the fictional.

3484 Lévesque, Solange. "Trois questions pour la critique: Congrès de l'Association internationale des critiques de théâtre à Helsinki." (Three Questions for Criticism: Congress of the International Association of Theatre Critics at Helsinki.) *JCT.* 1997; 83: 146-149. Notes. Illus.: Poster. Photo. B&W. 6. Lang.: Fre.
Finland: Helsinki. 1996. Historical studies. ■1996 Helsinki congress of International Association of Theatre Critics posed three theme-questions: Strategies for survival? New forms, old language? and Precariousness or permanence?.

3485 "Per Bernard Dort." (For Bernard Dort.) *BiT.* 1997; 43: 11-23. Notes. Lang.: Ita.
France. 1929-1994. Biographical studies. ■Issue devoted to the late theatre critic and essayist Bernard Dort.

3486 Banu, Georges. "L'écrit et l'oral ou l'entre-deux du théâtre." (Theatre: Written and Oral or Between the Two.) *JCT.* 1997; 82: 139-151. Notes. Illus.: Dwg. Photo. B&W. 7. Lang.: Fre.
France. 1997. Critical studies. ■Transitions from speech to writing in theatre rehearsal, in books on theatre and in theatre criticism.

3487 Berry, R.M. "Beckett in Theory." *JBeckS.* 1997; 6(2): 97-110. Notes. Lang.: Eng.
France. 1997. Critical studies. ■Value of post-postmodernist criticism when evaluating the work of Samuel Beckett.

3488 Deleuze, Gilles. "One Less Manifesto." 239-258 in Murray, Timothy, ed. *Mimesis, Masochism, and Mime: The Politics of Theatricality in Contemporary French Thought.* Ann Arbor, MI: Univ. of Michigan P; 1997. 328 pp. (Theater: Theory/Text/Performance.) Notes. Lang.: Eng.
France. 1997. Critical studies. ■The relationship between theatre and its critique, or original plays and their derivatives. Uses Carmelo Bene's adaptation of *Romeo and Juliet* as a prototype.

3489 Ufer, Marianne. "Frank Wedekind e la modernità. Recenti contributi critici all'opera dell'autore." (Frank Wedekind and Modernity: Recent Critical Contributions on the Author's Work.) *TeatroS.* 1997; 12(19): 255-267. Lang.: Ita.
Germany. 1891-1994. Critical studies. ■Summary of essays on Wedekind's plays presented at a conference in Dresden, October, 1994.

3490 Perrelli, Franco. "La prima fortuna di Strindberg sulle scene italiane." (Strindberg's Early Reception on the Italian Stage.) *IlCast.* 1997; 10(30): 5-42. Notes. Lang.: Ita.
Italy. 1885-1964. Historical studies. ■Analysis of unpublished documents and press reviews regarding the production of Strindberg's plays. Emphasis on the virtuosity of actors including Achille Vitti and Ermete Zacconi.

3491 Rossiskij institut istorii iskusstv. *Mejerchol'd v russkoj teatral'noj kritike. 1892-1918.* (Mejerchol'd in Russian Theatre Criticism, 1892-1918.) Moscow: Artist. Režisser. Teat'r; 1997. 527 pp. Lang.: Rus.
Russia. 1892-1918. Histories-sources. ■Theatre criticism of V.E. Mejerchol'd's productions, with comments by the editors.

3492 Sherbo, Arthur. "Lord Hailes, Shakespeare Critic." *SQ.* 1989 Sum; 40(2): 175-185. Notes. Lang.: Eng.
Scotland: Edinburgh. 1778-1791. Historical studies. ■Contributions made to Shakespeare criticism by Lord Hailes (Sir David Dalrymple) who wrote under the pseudonym Lucius. Contains entire text of 'Critical Remarks' that was published in *Edinburgh Magazine* in November 1786.

3493 Kos, Janko. "Vprašanje o dramatiki." (The Drama Question.) 289-305 in Pogačnik, Jože, ed. *Zbornik ob sedemdesetletnici Franceta Bernika.* Ljubljana: Znanst, venoraziskovalni center SAZU; 1997. 584 pp. Lang.: Slo.
Slovenia. 1996. Critical studies. ■The essential nature of drama as compared to lyric and epic.

3494 Banning, Yvonne. "(Re)viewing *Medea*: Cultural Perceptions and Gendered Consciousness in Reviewers' Responses to New South African Theatre." *SATJ.* 1997 May/Sep.; 11(1/2): 54-87. Notes. Biblio. Illus.: Photo. B&W. 3. Lang.: Eng.
South Africa, Republic of. 1994-1996. Critical studies. ■Analyzes the reviews in daily and weekly newspapers of Mark Fleishman and Jenny Reznek's production of Euripides' *Medea* at Nico Arena Theatre, Market Theatre, and the National Festival of Art in Grahamstown. Examines the complex mediations that occur in reception of 'new' or innovative theatrical ideas and prevailing popular perceptions.

3495 Sörenson, Margareta. "Teaterkritiken." (Theatre Criticism.) *Dramat.* 1997; 5(1): 38-41. Illus.: Photo. Color. Lang.: Swe.
Sweden. 1950-1997. Critical studies. ■Eight points of view of the reviewer and his reviews.

3496 Challinor, A.M. "Controversy Among Gentlemen." *ERev.* 1997 Fall; 5(2): 61-78. Notes. Biblio. Lang.: Eng.
UK-England. 1908-1930. Historical studies. ■Looks at the differing opinions of two early twentieth-century literary critics, George Greenwood and J.M. Robertson, regarding Shakespearean authorship.

3497 Davis, Lloyd. "Queer Criticism of Shakespeare." *ADS.* 1997 Oct.; 31: 5-21. Notes. Lang.: Eng.
UK-England. 1997. Critical studies. ■Cites gay, lesbian and queer criticism as having expanded the cultural and critical significance of Shakespearean sexuality.

3498 Barker, Stephen. "Critic, Criticism, Critics." 230-244 in Bigsby, Christopher, ed. *The Cambridge Companion to Arthur Miller.* Cambridge: Cambridge UP; 1997. 277 pp. (Cambridge Companions to Literature.) Index. Notes. Lang.: Eng.
USA. 1940-1995. Historical studies. ■Critical history of playwright Arthur Miller: his role as critic, other critics' views of his work, and the types of criticism over the years concerning his work.

3499 Fortier, Mark. *Theory/Theatre: An Introduction.* New York, NY/London: Routledge; 1997. 208 pp. Notes. Biblio. Index. Lang.: Eng.
USA. Europe. 1997. Instructional materials. ■Introductory text that examines the relationship between the application and relation of literary theory to theatre. Author uses nine categories of theory: semiotics, phenomenology, deconstruction, psychoanalysis, feminism and gender theory, reader-response, materialism, postmodernism, and post-colonialism.

3500 Greene, Gayle. "Leaving Shakespeare." 307-316 in Garner, Shirley Nelson, ed.; Sprengnether, Madelon, ed. *Shakespearean Tragedy and Gender.* Bloomington, IN: Indiana UP; 1996. 326 pp. Index. Notes. Biblio. Lang.: Eng.
USA. 1950-1956. Histories-sources. ■Feminist critic recounts her early love of and later disenchantment with Shakespeare and her growing sense of identity with female playwrights.

3501 Haverkamp, Anselm. "Perpetuum Mobile: Shakespeares fotwährende Renaissance." (Perpetuum Mobile: Shakespeare's Continual Renaissance.) *Thsch.* 1997; 11: 34-49. Notes. Lang.: Ger, Fre, Dut, Eng.
USA. 1800-1997. Critical studies. ■The reception of Shakespeare from the Romantic period to the present. Shakespeare's theatre described as haunted and driven by the spirit of history in which not only his characters but the audience too find ourselves situated.

3502 McNulty, Charles. "The Queer as Drama Critic." *ThM.* 1993; 24(2): 12-20. Biblio. Lang.: Eng.
USA. 1993. Critical studies. ■Ramifications of queer theory for theatre critics.

3503 Mufson, Daniel. "Interpret *This*." *ThM.* 1993; 24(3): 116-119. Lang.: Eng.
USA. 1993. Critical studies. ■The diminishing role of the drama critic and the expanding place of the dramaturg in today's theatrical world.

3504 Nester, Nancy L. "The Agoraphobic Imagination: The Protagonist Who Murders and the Critics Who Praise Her." *AmerD.* 1997 Spr; 6(2): 1-24. Notes. Biblio. Lang.: Eng.
USA. 1922-1997. Critical studies. ■Critics' perceptions of violent female protagonists in *My Sister in This House* by Wendy Kesselman, Susan Glaspell's *The Verge* and Sophie Treadwell's *Machinal.*

3505 Solomon, Alissa. "Not Just a Passing Fancy: Notes on Butch." *ThM.* 1993; 24(2): 35-46. Biblio. Illus.: Photo. B&W. 5. Lang.: Eng.

DRAMA: —Theory/criticism

USA. 1993. Critical studies. ■The theatricality of 'butchness' and what it reveals about the performativity of gender. Considers what kind of theatre metaphor works best for describing butchness and of gender presentation in general.

3506 Walker, Craig Stewart. "Reckoning with States on the Phenomenology of Theatre." *JDTC.* 1997 Spr; 11(2): 65-83. Lang.: Eng.

USA. 1964-1967. Critical studies. ■An examination of phenomenology, semiotics, and the work of theorists Michael Kirby and Bert States.

3507 Wellman, Mac. "A Chrestomathy of 22 Answers to 22 Wholly Unaskable and Unrelated Questions Concerning Political and Poetic Theater." *ThM.* 1993; 23(1): 43-51. Lang.: Eng.

USA. 1993. Critical studies. ■Playwright's views on the place of political and poetic theatre.

Training

3508 Berry, Cicely; Rodenburg, Patsy; Linklater, Kristin. "Shakespeare, Feminism, and Voice: Responses to Sarah Werner." *NTQ.* 1997; 13(49): 48-52. Lang.: Eng.

UK-England. USA. 1973-1994. Histories-sources. ■Three leading Anglo-American voice teachers respond with passion to the article by Sarah Werner (*NTQ* 1996: 12 (47): 249-258), arguing that it was not founded on the reality of practical voice work but exemplifies the split between academics and professional theatre.

3509 Werner, Sarah. "Voice Training, Shakespeare, and Feminism." *NTQ.* 1997; 13(50): 183. Lang.: Eng.

UK-England. USA. 1973-1994. Histories-sources. ■Brief reply to article by voice teachers Cicely Berry, Patsy Rodenburg, and Kristin Linklater in *NTQ* 1997: 13 (49): 48-52 to the effect that academics and theatre practitioners should each use their own tools to help each other.

MEDIA

General

Performance/production

3510 Lanier, Douglas. "Drowning the Book: *Prospero's Books* and the Textual Shakespeare." 187-209 in Bulman, James C., ed. *Shakespeare, Theory, and Performance.* London/New York, NY: Routledge; 1996. 218 pp. Notes. Biblio. Index. Lang.: Eng.

UK-England. 1979-1991. Critical studies. ■The possibility of video and film performances to solidify new performance texts as stable artifacts instead of ephemeral experiences. Uses the films *Prospero's Books* (1991) by Peter Greenaway and *The Tempest* (1979), by Derek Jarman (both adaptations of Shakespeare's *The Tempest*).

Plays/librettos/scripts

3511 Hollinger, Karen. "'Respeaking' Sisterhood." *SPC.* 1997 Oct.; 20(1): 53-64. Biblio. Lang.: Eng.

USA. 1986-1996. Critical studies. ■Sisterhood and female bonding in Bruce Beresford's film of Beth Henley's play *Crimes of the Heart* and the television show *Sisters*.

Relation to other fields

3512 Sun, William H. "TDR Comment: Performative Politics and International Media." *TDR.* 1997 Win; 41(4): 5-10. Notes. Biblio. Lang.: Eng.

China, People's Republic of. 1989-1997. Historical studies. ■International, particularly Western, media coverage of political change and protest in China. Impact of the coverage in China, author's belief that media plays into hands of politicians.

Theory/criticism

3513 Meyer, Petra Maria. "Theaterwissenschaft als Medienwissenschaft." (Theatre Studies as Media Studies.) *FMT.* 1997; 12(2): 115-131. Notes. Lang.: Ger.

Europe. 1600-1997. Critical studies. ■Analysis of Erika Fischer-Lichte's theory of theatre semiotics and suggests a theory of media transforma-

tion which uses the latest research in theatre studies, philosophy and memory theory.

Audio forms

Basic theatrical documents

3514 Verdecchia, Guillermo. "*The Terrible But Incomplete Journals of John D.*" *CTR.* 1997 Fall; 92: 50-67. Illus.: Photo. B&W. 1. Lang.: Eng.

Canada: Vancouver, BC. 1996. ■Complete text of radioplay for actor, cello and soundscape.

Institutions

3515 Danielsen, Allan. "Der er noget i luften!" (There is Something in the Air!)*TE.* 1997 June; 84: 36-39. Illus.: Photo. B&W. 1. Lang.: Dan.

Denmark: Copenhagen. 1928-1997. Historical studies. ■History of Radioteatret, with emphasis on the most recent season of radio drama.

Performance/production

3516 Bénard, Johanne. "Écouter le théâtre." (Listening to Theatre.) *JCT.* 1997; 84: 24-28. Notes. Illus.: Photo. B&W. 2. Lang.: Fre.

Canada. 1995-1997. Critical studies. ■Semiotic analysis of audio recordings of Michel Marc Bouchard's *Les Muses orphelines (The Orphan Muses)* and Michel Tremblay's *Albertine en cinq temps (Albertine in Five Times)* (Société Radio-Canada series 'Coups de théâtre', produced by Line Meloche).

3517 Gammon, John Raymond. *Creating for the Audience of One: An Ethnography of a Radio Drama.* Montreal, PQ: Concordia Univ; 1997. 112 pp. Notes. Biblio. [MA Thesis, Univ. Microfilms Order No. AAC MQ25975.] Lang.: Eng.

Canada. 1920-1995. Historical studies. ■On the production of Canadian radio drama, within the historical context of governmental regulation of broadcasting and promotion of a unified national identity. Focuses on the drama production team, the Canadian Broadcasting Corporation, the broadcast radio drama, and the audience.

3518 Bryden, Mary. "*The Proust Screenplay* on BBC Radio." *PintR.* 1997: 186-188. Notes. Lang.: Eng.

UK-England: London. 1995-1996. Historical studies. ■Performance of Pinter's *The Proust Screenplay*, adapted by Michael Bakewell and directed by Ned Chaillet on BBC Radio.

Plays/librettos/scripts

3519 Hillel, John. "Screenplays for Radio: The Radio Drama of Louis Nowra." *ADS.* 1997 Apr.; 30: 68-86. Notes. Lang.: Eng.

Australia: Sydney. 1975-1993. Critical studies. ■The radio plays of playwright Louis Nowra and their part in changing the face of drama on the air in a post-television media landscape.

3520 Gontarski, S.E. "Unediting Beckett, or Restoring 'The ... Ruins'." *JBeckS.* 1997; 6(2): 95-96. Lang.: Eng.

France: St. Lô. Ireland: Dublin. 1946-1997. Historical studies. ■The 'mystery, confusion and error' surrounding *The Capital of the Ruins*, a report about the Irish hospital at St. Lô that Beckett prepared for broadcast on Irish radio in 1946, ever since the piece was discovered in 1983.

3521 Hill, Mary Louise. "Women's Time/Radio Time: Time, Translation and Transgression." *WPerf.* 1997; 9(2): 25-51. Notes. Biblio. [Number 18.] Lang.: Eng.

USA. 1967-1997. Critical studies. ■Examines Ilse Aichinger's radio play *The Sisters Jouet*: how it provides a practical-theoretical text which exemplifies how the *mise en jeu* of radio may aid in the development of women's language and consciousness, and how it embodies the time-nexus of radio.

Film

Administration

3522 Cassidy, John. "Chaos in Hollywood." *NewY.* 1997 31 Mar.: 36-44. Illus.: Dwg. Color. 1. Lang.: Eng.

USA. 1997. Historical studies. ■Account of research using chaos theory to try to explain why certain films are hits.

MEDIA: Film—Administration

3523 Regester, Charlene. "Oscar Micheaux the Entrepreneur: Financing *The House Behind the Cedars.*" *JFV.* 1997 Spr/Sum; 49 (1/2): 17-27. Illus.: Photo. B&W. 2. Lang.: Eng.

USA. 1920-1922. Historical studies. ■How Micheaux, an African-American filmmaker, was able to arrange financing for his work, focusing on his adaptation of a novel by Charles W. Chesnutt (1900).

Basic theatrical documents

3524 Barrett, Shirley. "*Love Serenade.*" *Scenario.* 1997; 3(2): 110-148. Illus.: Pntg. Color. 4. Lang.: Eng.

Australia. 1997. ■Text of Barrett's screenplay, which she also directed.

3525 Egoyan, Atom. "*The Sweet Hereafter.*" *Scenario.* 1997; 3(4): 6-37. Illus.: Pntg. Color. 5. Lang.: Eng.

Canada. 1997. ■Screenplay for Egoyan's film, which he also directed.

3526 Hoolboom, Mike; Baughman, Cynthia, intro. "Three Scripts." *JFV.* 1997 Fall; 49(3): 38-47. Illus.: Photo. B&W. 3. Lang.: Eng.

Canada. 1984-1994. ■Brief scripts for Hoolboom's experimental films, including one without visual images.

3527 Denis, Claire; Fargeau, Jean-Pôl. "*I Can't Sleep.*" *Scenario.* 1997; 3(2): 52-83. Illus.: Pntg. Color. 4. Lang.: Eng.

France. 1994. ■English translation of the filmscript *J'ai pas sommeil.*

3528 Amini, Hossein. "*The Wings of the Dove.*" *Scenario.* 1997; 3(2): 6-48. Illus.: Pntg. Color. 4. Lang.: Eng.

UK-England. 1995-1997. ■Text of Amini's film script, an adaptation of the novel by Henry James.

3529 Attanasio, Paul. "*Donnie Brasco.*" *Scenario.* 1997; 3(2): 4-46. Illus.: Pntg. Color. 4. Lang.: Eng.

USA. 1997. ■Text of Attanasio's screenplay.

3530 Eszterhas, Joe. "*Telling Lies in America.*" *Scenario.* 1997; 3(4): 105-150. Illus.: Pntg. Sketches. B&W. Color. 6. Lang.: Eng.

USA. 1997. ■Text of Eszterhas' screenplay.

3531 Goldsmith, Martin. "*Detour.*" *Scenario.* 1997; 3(2): 132-178. Illus.: Photo. Color. 4. Lang.: Eng.

USA. 1945. ■Text of Goldsmith's screenplay.

3532 Gordon, Robert. "*Addicted to Love.*" *Scenario.* 1997; 3(2): 88-127. Illus.: Pntg. Color. 5. Lang.: Eng.

USA. 1997. ■Text of Gordon's screenplay.

3533 Greiff, Jason. "*One Crash, Three Accidents.*" *Scenario.* 1997; 3(4): 158-192. Illus.: Pntg. Color. 4. Lang.: Eng.

USA. 1996. ■The winning script of the student screenplay competition.

3534 Isherwood, Christopher; Bachardy, Don. "*The Beautiful and Damned.*" *Scenario.* 1997; 3(2): 154-191. Illus.: Pntg. Color. 4. Lang.: Eng.

USA. 1975. ■Text of Isherwood and Bachardy's filmscript.

3535 Lehman, Ernest. "*North by Northwest.*" *Scenario.* 1997; 3(1): 146-207. Illus.: Pntg. Color. 4. Lang.: Eng.

USA. 1959. ■Lehman's script for the film that was directed by Alfred Hitchcock.

3536 Mankiewicz, Joseph L. "*All About Eve.*" *Scenario.* 1997; 3(2): 54-103. Illus.: Pntg. Color. 4. Lang.: Eng.

USA. 1950. ■Script of Mankiewicz filmscript.

3537 Poirier, Gregory. "*Rosewood.*" *Scenario.* 1997; 3(1): 6-50. Illus.: Pntg. Color. 5. Lang.: Eng.

USA. 1997. ■Text of Poirier's filmscript.

3538 Rainer, Yvonne. "*Murder and murder.*" *PerAJ.* 1997 Jan.; 19(1): 76-117. [Number 55.] Lang.: Eng.

USA. 1996. ■Text of Rainer's screenplay.

3539 Salt, Waldo. "*Midnight Cowboy.*" *Scenario.* 1997; 3(4): 46-87. Illus.: Photo. B&W. 6. Lang.: Eng.

USA. 1969. ■Screenplay for the film, which was directed by John Schlesinger.

3540 Tesich, Steve. "*Breaking Away.*" *Scenario.* 1997; 3(1): 56-94. Illus.: Pntg. Color. 5. Lang.: Eng.

USA. 1979. ■Text of Tesich's screenplay.

3541 Williamson, Kevin. "*Scream.*" *Scenario.* 1997; 3(1): 100-139. Illus.: Pntg. Color. 4. Lang.: Eng.

USA. 1996. ■Text of Williamson's film script.

Design/technology

3542 Calhoun, John. "Emotional Landscapes." *LDim.* 1997 Oct.; 21(9): 112-115, 165-171. Illus.: Photo. Color. B&W. 11. Lang.: Eng.

Canada. 1997. Technical studies. ■Cinematographer Paul Sarossy's lighting design for the film *The Sweet Hereafter* directed by Atom Egoyan.

3543 Calhoun, John. "Disaster, Italian Style." *TCI.* 1997 Feb.; 31(2): 40-43. Illus.: Photo. 9. Lang.: Eng.

Italy: Rome. 1996. Historical studies. ■Production designer Benjamin Fernandez's recent work on the film *Daylight*, directed by Rob Cohen, starring Sylvester Stallone, produced by Universal Pictures. The movie was filmed on a studio lot in Rome.

3544 Sheehan, Thomas W. "The Production of a Woman in Andrei Tarkovsky's *The Sacrifice.*" *WPerf.* 1997; 9:2(18): 199-210. Biblio. Lang.: Eng.

Russia. 1932-1986. Critical studies. ■Use of sound and soundtrack in Tarkovsky's *Offret (The Sacrifice)*: audio and visual representation of woman, and impact of actress Susan Fleetwood's performance on the director's vision.

3545 Calhoun, John. "Night Moves." *LDim.* 1997 Mar.; 21(2): 58-61, 100-104. Illus.: Photo. Color. 7. Lang.: Eng.

USA. 1997. Historical studies. ■Lighting design and special lighting needs for director Richard Linklater's film adaptation of Eric Bogosian's play *subUrbia.*

3546 Calhoun, John. "Madonna with Cinematographer." *LDim.* 1997 Jan/Feb.; 21(1): 56-61, 78. Illus.: Photo. Color. 13. Lang.: Eng.

USA. 1997. Biographical studies. ■Cinematographer Darius Khondji and his work on the film adaptation of the musical *Evita.* Technical choices, past work on other films.

3547 Calhoun, John; Johnson, David; Cashill, Robert. "Lights, Camera, Color." *LDim.* 1997 June; 21(5): 51-67, 93. Illus.: Photo. Color. B&W. 33. Lang.: Eng.

USA. 1997. Historical studies. ■Series of articles which focus on lighting and cinematography of upcoming summer films: *Batman and Robin*, *Men in Black, Face/Off, The Pillow Book* and *When the Cat's Away.* Special effects lighting, equipment.

3548 Calhoun, John. "Myers' Way." *TCI.* 1997 Oct.; 31(8): 32-35. Illus.: Photo. 12. Lang.: Eng.

USA. 1997. Historical studies. ■Costume designer Ruth Myers and her recent work in film on *LA Confidential*, directed by Curtis Hanson and starring Kim Basinger and Kevin Spacey, and *A Thousand Acres*, directed by Jocelyn Moorhouse and starring Jessica Lange and Michelle Pfeiffer.

3549 Calhoun, John. "The Crucible." *TCI.* 1997 Jan.; 31(1): 22-25. Illus.: Photo. 8. Lang.: Eng.

USA. 1995-1996. Historical studies. ■Production designer Lilly Kilvert and costume designer Bob Crowley recreate Puritan New England for the first English-language film version of Arthur Miller's play *The Crucible* directed by Nicholas Hytner.

3550 Calhoun, John. "Raising Rosewood." *TCI.* 1997 Mar.; 31(3): 40-43. Illus.: Photo. 7. Lang.: Eng.

USA. 1996. Historical studies. ■Production designer Paul Sylbert's experiences recreating an entire vanished town in the film *Rosewood*, directed by John Singleton, produced by Warner Brothers, starring Ving Rhames and Jon Voight.

3551 Cashill, Robert. "Collision Course." *LDim.* 1997 May; 21(4): 72-73, 106-109. Illus.: Photo. Color. 3. Lang.: Eng.

USA. 1997. Historical studies. ■Technical challenges faced by Peter Suschitzky in shooting the film *Crash* directed by David Cronenberg. Negative public response to the film adapted from a novel by J.G. Ballard.

3552 Cole, Holly. "Costuming for Film." *TD&T.* 1997 Fall; 33(5): 41-48. Tables. Illus.: Photo. B&W. 3. Lang.: Eng.

USA. 1997. Instructional materials. ■Instructions and advice for the novice costume designer when trying to break into film or television.

MEDIA: Film—Design/technology

3553 Levin, Steve. "Give Me That Old Time Projection." *MarqJTHS*. 1997 1st Qtr; 29(1): 26-27. Illus.: Photo. B&W. 2. Lang.: Eng.
USA: San Francisco, CA. 1937-1989. Historical studies. ■A discussion of traditional projection practices prior to the introduction of the automated projection booth.

Performance spaces

3554 Burgess, Randy; Levinson, Roslyn G. "Arthouse Revival." *LD&A*. 1997 Feb.; 27(2): 36-41. Illus.: Photo. Color. 11. Lang.: Eng.
USA: Louisville, KY. 1996-1997. Technical studies. ■The refurbishing of the Palace Theatre, a Louisville movie house, focusing on the delicate antique fixtures and the strategies applied in handling them during renovation.

3555 DuciBella, Joseph R. "Vertical Signs 1997." *MarqJTHS*. 1997 1st Qtr; 29(1): 24-25. Illus.: Photo. Sketches. B&W. 12. Lang.: Eng.
USA: Chicago, IL. 1925-1997. Historical studies. ■The Uptown Theatre's simple vertical sign and designs submitted for a more elaborate sign.

3556 Gallegos, Patrick. "Broadway Goes Hollywood." *LD&A*. 1995 June; 25(6): 37-41. Illus.: Photo. Color. 7. Lang.: Eng.
USA: New York, NY. 1995. Technical studies. ■Theatrical nature of the house lighting design in the Sony Theatres at Lincoln Square movie complex.

3557 Klugh, Terra; Boucher, Jack, photo. "Birmingham's Magic Star." *MarqJTHS*. 1997 4th Qtr; 29(4): 1, 4-9, 32. Illus.: Photo. B&W. Color. 15. Lang.: Eng.
USA: Birmingham, AL. 1927-1997. Historical studies. ■History of the Alabama Theatre, originally a cinema, now called the Alabama Theatre for the Performing Arts.

3558 Levin, Steve. "Keith-Albee Palace Rochester New York." *MarqJTHS*. 1997 4th Qtr; 29(4): 14-17. Illus.: Photo. Handbill. B&W. 11. [Photo Feature.] Lang.: Eng.
USA: Rochester, NY. 1928-1965. Historical studies. ■History of the theatre, which was demolished in 1965.

3559 Levin, Steve. "Conclave Preview Utah, Idaho & Montana." *MarqJTHS*. 1997 1st Qtr; 29(1): 1, 4-17, 29, 32. Illus.: Photo. B&W. 44. Lang.: Eng.
USA. 1905-1997. Historical studies. ■Guide to theatres to be visited on the Theatrical Historical Society's 1997 tour of Utah, Idaho and Montana.

3560 Levin, Steve. "Gone but not Forgotten." *MarqJTHS*. 1997 1st Qtr; 29(1): 18-23. Illus.: Photo. Dwg. B&W. 15. Lang.: Eng.
USA: Salt Lake City, UT, Ogden UT. 1890-1989. Historical studies. ■Brief histories, with photos, of eight Utah theatres that will not be visited during the Theatre Historical Society's 1997 Conclave because they been demolished or altered from their original design.

3561 Levin, Steve. "Peery's Egyptian Theatre David Eccles Conference Center Ogden, Utah." *MarqJTHS*. 1997 3rd Qtr; 29(3): 6-9, 32. Illus.: Photo. Handbill. B&W. Color. Grd. Plan. 10. Lang.: Eng.
USA: Ogden, UT. 1924-1997. Historical studies. ■History of Peery's Egyptian Theatre, built as a movie palace in 1924 and reopened as the David Eccles Conference Center in 1997.

3562 Levin, Steve. "Grauman's Egyptian Theatre 75th Anniversary 1922-1997." *MarqJTHS*. 1997 3rd Qtr; 29(3): 3,10-19. Illus.: Photo. Plan. Handbill. B&W. 19. Lang.: Eng.
USA: Los Angeles, CA. 1922-1997. Historical studies. ■A collection of photographs of Grauman's Egyptian Theatre. There are also a cross-section and plan of the building and a copy of the program of the dual premieres of the films *Sparrows* and *The Black Pirate*.

3563 Levin, Steve. "Tennessee Theatre Knoxville Tennessee." *MarqJTHS*. 1997 4th Qtr; 29(4): 10-13. Illus.: Photo. B&W. 8. [Photo Feature.] Lang.: Eng.
USA: Knoxville, TN. 1929-1997. Historical studies. ■History of the Tennessee Theatre, which is still in use.

3564 Levin, Steve, ed. "Balaban & Katz Oriental Theatre Chicago Illinois C. W. & George L. Rapp Architects." *MarqJTHS*. 1997 Annual; A24: 1-36. Tables. Illus.: Handbill. Photo. B&W. 65. [Theatre Historical Society of America Annual No. 14-1997.] Lang.: Eng.
USA: Chicago, IL. 1926-1997. Historical studies. ■History of the Oriental Theatre which closed in 1982 but was renovated with reopening scheduled for 1998.

3565 Olson, Bryan. "Radio City-Minnesota Theatre." *MarqJTHS*. 1997 4th Qtr; 29(4): 18-27. Illus.: Photo. Handbill. B&W. Grd.Plan. 11. [Second Place, 1995 Jeffery Weiss Literary Prize Competition.] Lang.: Eng.
USA: Minneapolis, MN. 1928-1997. Historical studies. ■History of the Minneapolis Theatre, renamed Radio City Theatre in 1944 and mostly destroyed in 1959.

3566 Swett, Naomi. "Egyptian Theatre, Portland Oregon, Built in 90 Days." *MarqJTHS*. 1997 3rd Qtr; 29(3): 20-24. Illus.: Photo. B&W. Grd.Plan. 10. [From *American Builder*, March 1925.] Lang.: Eng.
USA: Portland, OR. 1924. Historical studies. ■Reprint of 1925 article describing the construction of Graeper's Egyptian Theatre, now used as a warehouse.

Performance/production

3567 Jays, David. "Why Film the Bard?" *PI*. 1997 June; 12(11): 12-13. Illus.: Photo. B&W. 2. Lang.: Eng.
1990-1997. Critical studies. ■Brief survey of recent Shakespearean films.

3568 Harris, Kristine Marie. *Silent Speech: Envisioning the Nation in Early Shanghai Cinema*. New York, NY: Columbia Univ; 1997. 395 pp. [Ph.D. Dissertation, Univ. Microfilms Order No. AAC 9809723.] Lang.: Eng.
China, People's Republic of: Shanghai. 1896-1937. Histories-specific. ■Development of cinema in China, with special attention to the active role of Shanghai filmmakers in constructing a discourse of the modern nation. Examines political, economic, artistic, and social concerns, including classical dramatic forms, evolving technology, censorship, and representation of women.

3569 Thompson, Ann. "Asta Nielsen and the Mystery of *Hamlet*." 215-224 in Boose, Lynda E., ed.; Burt, Richard, ed. *Shakespeare, the Movie: Popularizing the Plays on Film, TV, and Video*. London/New York, NY: Routledge; 1997. 277 pp. Index. Notes. Biblio. Illus.: Photo. 1. Lang.: Eng.
Denmark. 1920. Historical studies. ■Analyzes the performance of Danish silent film star Asta Nielsen, who played Hamlet as a woman disguised as a man in the film directed by Svend Gade and Heinz Schall.

3570 Boose, Lynda E.; Burt, Richard. "Introduction: Shakespeare, the Movie." 1-7 in Boose, Lynda E., ed.; Burt, Richard, ed. *Shakespeare, the Movie: Popularizing the Plays on Film, TV, and Video*. London/New York, NY: Routledge; 1997. 277 pp. Index. Notes. Biblio. Lang.: Eng.
Europe. USA. 1922-1995. Critical studies. ■Introductory essay to volume on film adaptations of Shakespeare plays in the twentieth century from *Richard III* to *King Lear*.

3571 Salter, James. "Passionate Falsehoods." *NewY*. 1997 4 Aug.: 56-63. Illus.: Photo. B&W. 5. Lang.: Eng.
Europe. 1954-1968. Histories-sources. ■The author, a novelist, screenwriter, and director, on the European film scene.

3572 Bíró, Yvette. "Caryatids of Time: Temporality in the Cinema of Agnès Varda." *PerAJ*. 1997 Sep.; 19(3): 1-10. Illus.: Photo. B&W. 2. [Number 57.] Lang.: Eng.
France. 1997. Critical studies. ■Varda's use of time as a character, particularly in her *Cléo de 5 à 7 (Cleo from 5 to 7)*.

3573 Chin, Daryl. "The Antonin Artaud Film Project." *PerAJ*. 1997 May; 19(2): 23-28. [Number 56.] Lang.: Eng.
France. 1993. Critical studies. ■Analysis of films by Gérard Mordillat and Jérôme Prieur on the subject of Artaud, including a lengthy documentary, a narrative film, and a brief videotape.

3574 Calhoon, Kenneth S. "Emil Jannings, Falstaff, and the Spectacular of the Body Natural." *MLQ*. 1997 Mar.; 58(1): 83-109. Notes. Biblio. Illus.: Photo. B&W. 3. Lang.: Eng.

MEDIA: Film—Performance/production

Germany. 1929-1945. Historical studies. ■Roles of film actor Jannings including *Der alte und der junge König (The Old and the Young King), Der blaue Engel (The Blue Angel)* and *Henry IV.* His imposing physical size used to examine place of the body as symbolism in the history of modern domination, particular focus on the Third Reich.

3575   Elsaesser, Thomas. *Fassbinder's Germany: History Identity Subject.* Amsterdam: Amsterdam UP; 1997. 400 pp. Biblio. Index. Illus.: Photo. 3. Lang.: Eng.

Germany. 1945-1989. Critical studies. ■A reading of Rainer Werner Fassbinder's films as a single oeuvre in the context of Germany and its recent history.

3576   Merschmeier, Michael. "Abschied von Gestern." (Farewell From Yesterday.) *THeute.* 1997; Yb: 77-91. Illus.: Photo. B&W. 12. Lang.: Ger.

Germany. 1941-1997. Histories-sources. ■Discusses possibilities and difficulties of actors and actresses with working for stage, film and television. A conversation with Hannelore Elsner, Stefan Kurt, Ulrich Matthes, Otto Sander and Rosel Zech who have played in various media forms including a short biography of each person.

3577   Wayne, Valerie. "*Shakespeare Wallah* and Colonial Specularity." 95-102 in Boose, Lynda E., ed.; Burt, Richard, ed. *Shakespeare, the Movie: Popularizing the Plays on Film, TV, and Video.* London/New York, NY: Routledge; 1997. 277 pp. Index. Notes. Biblio. Lang.: Eng.

India. UK-England. 1965. Critical studies. ■Analysis of the early Merchant Ivory film *Shakespeare Wallah*, about the reception of Shakespeare's plays, presented by a British acting troupe, in India.

3578   Mac Reamoinn, Laoise. "Ireland on Screen." *IW.* 1996 Nov/Dec.; 45(6): 20-25. Illus.: Photo. B&W. Color. 25. Lang.: Eng.

Ireland: Dublin. 1896-1996. Historical studies. ■History of filmmaking in Ireland on the occasion of cinema's centenary in Dublin. Increased funding from the Irish Film Board, award-winning work of directors Jim Sheridan and Neil Jordan, international productions.

3579   Hapgood, Robert. "Popularizing Shakespeare: The Artistry of Franco Zeffirelli." 80-94 in Boose, Lynda E., ed.; Burt, Richard, ed. *Shakespeare, the Movie: Popularizing the Plays on Film, TV, and Video.* London/New York, NY: Routledge; 1997. 277 pp. Index. Notes. Biblio. Lang.: Eng.

Italy. 1966-1990. Historical studies. ■The international reception of director Franco Zeffirelli's Shakespeare films *The Taming of the Shrew, Romeo and Juliet,* and *Hamlet.*

3580   Mastroianni, Marcello; Tatò, Francesco, ed. *Mi ricordo, si, io mi ricordo.* (I Remember, Yes, I Do Remember.) Milan: Baldini & Castoldi; 1997. 185 pp. (I Saggi 93.) Illus.: Photo. B&W. Lang.: Ita.

Italy. 1924-1996. Histories-sources. ■The transcribed oral recollections of actor Marcello Mastroianni.

3581   Okome, Onookome. "The Context of Film Production in Nigeria: The Colonial Heritage." *Ufa.* 1997 Spr/Fall; 24(2/3): 42-62 . Notes. Lang.: Eng.

Nigeria. 1997. Critical studies. ■Problems inherent in making a film in Nigeria, and the enduring colonial legacy.

3582   Liebman, Stuart. "'I Was Always in the Epicenter of Whatever Was Going On...': An Interview with Wanda Jakubowska." *SEEP.* 1997 Fall; 17(3): 16-30. Illus.: Photo. 2. Lang.: Eng.

Poland. 1948-1997. Histories-sources. ■Interview with Polish filmmaker Wanda Jakubowska, focusing on her most famous work *Ostatni Etap (The Last Stop)*, a film about the Holocaust and her experiences in the Auschwitz concentration camp.

3583   Stachówna, Grażyna. "Bogusław Linda—nasz współdzesny." (Bogusław Linda Our Contemporary.) *DialogW.* 1997; 2: 116-123. Lang.: Pol.

Poland. 1952-1997. Biographical studies. ■The popular actor who began his work in theatre before changing to film, where he became a leading man.

3584   Frolov, I. *Orlova v grime i bez grima.* (Orlova With and Without Make-Up.) Moscow: Panorama; 1997. 272 pp. Lang.: Rus.

Russia. 1902-1975. Biographies. ■The life and work of Mossovét Theatre actress Ljubov' Orlova.

3585   Hillman, Roger. "Tarkovsky's Odes to ... Joy?" *SEEP.* 1997 Fall; 17(3): 31-36. Lang.: Eng.

Russia. 1979-1983. Histories-sources. ■The use of music by Wagner, Bach, and Beethoven in the films *Nostalghia* and *Stalker* by Andrej Tarkovskij.

3586   Rjazanov, El'dar A. *Nepodvedennye itogi.* (Incomplete Results.) Moscow: Vagrius; 1997. 576 pp. Lang.: Rus.

Russia: Moscow. 1950-1997. Histories-sources. ■Well-known film director on his work in film with stage actors.

3587   Botha, Martin. "My Involvement in the Process Which Led to the White Paper on South African Cinema." *SATJ.* 1997 May/Sep.; 11(1/2): 269-285. Notes. Lang.: Eng.

South Africa, Republic of. 1996-1997. Histories-sources. ■Background to the ongoing debate on the restructuring of South African cinema and an indirect response to an article in *SATJ* 10:2 (1996) by Keyan Tomaselli and Arnold Shepperson critical of a document of proposals on said restructuring of the RSA film industry.

3588   Ngakane, Lionel. "Thoughts On My Life in Film." *SATJ.* 1997 May/Sep.; 11(1/2): 261-268. Lang.: Eng.

South Africa, Republic of. 1997. Histories-sources. ■Text of speech given by Ngakane reflecting on his life in film, and the future of the South African film industry.

3589   "From Script to Film: *The Wings of the Dove.* A Talk with Director Iain Softley." *Scenario.* 1997; 3(2): 53, 201-202. Lang.: Eng.

UK-England. 1995-1997. Histories-sources. ■Interview with the director of *The Wings of the Dove*, based on the novel by Henry James.

3590   Crowl, Samuel. "Changing Colors Like the Chameleon: Ian McKellen's *Richard III* from Stage to Screen." *PS.* 1997 Fall; 17(1): 53-63. Notes. Biblio. Illus.: Photo. B&W. 4. Lang.: Eng.

UK-England. 1995-1996. Historical studies. ■Differences between the cinematic and staged version of Shakespeare's *Richard III* by Ian Mckellen and Richard Loncraine.

3591   Donaldson, Peter S. "Shakespeare in the Age of Post-Mechanical Reproduction: Sexual and Electronic Magic in *Prospero's Books.*" 169-185 in Boose, Lynda E., ed.; Burt, Richard, ed. *Shakespeare, the Movie: Popularizing the Plays on Film, TV, and Video.* London/New York, NY: Routledge; 1997. 277 pp. Index. Notes. Biblio. Lang.: Eng.

UK-England. 1991. Critical studies. ■Gender in *Prospero's Books*, Peter Greenaway's film version of Shakespeare's *The Tempest*, starring John Gielgud. Argues that the new media of digital image technology links the work to the Renaissance.

3592   Fry, Stephen. "Playing Oscar." *NewY.* 1997 16 June: 82-88. Lang.: Eng.

UK-England. 1997. Histories-sources. ■The author's experience playing Oscar Wilde in the film *Wilde* directed by Brian Gilbert.

3593   Hedrick, Donald K. "War Is Mud: Branagh's Dirty Harry V and the Types of Political Ambiguity." 45-66 in Boose, Lynda E., ed.; Burt, Richard, ed. *Shakespeare, the Movie: Popularizing the Plays on Film, TV, and Video.* London/New York, NY: Routledge; 1997. 277 pp. Index. Notes. Biblio. Lang.: Eng.

UK-England. USA. 1989. Critical studies. ■The theatricalization of war in Kenneth Branagh's *Henry V.* Also explores the transnational nature of directing Shakespeare films.

3594   Henderson, Diana E. "A Shrew for the Times." 148-168 in Boose, Lynda E., ed.; Burt, Richard, ed. *Shakespeare, the Movie: Popularizing the Plays on Film, TV, and Video.* London/New York, NY: Routledge; 1997. 277 pp. Index. Notes. Biblio. Lang.: Eng.

UK-England. USA. 1908-1966. Historical studies. ■Analysis of several film and television adaptations of Shakespeare's *The Taming of the Shrew*, with a focus on gender issues.

3595   Lehmann, Courtney. "Kenneth Branagh at the Quilting Point: Shakespearean Adaptation, Postmodern Auteurism,

MEDIA: Film—Performance/production

and the (Schizophrenic) Fabric of 'Everyday Life'." *PS.* 1997 Fall; 17(1): 6-27. Biblio. Illus.: Photo. B&W. 4. Lang.: Eng.

UK-England. 1989. Critical studies. ■Argues that Branagh's film adaptation of Shakespeare's *Henry V* evokes the postmodern schizophrenic experience of society and questions how the contemporary artist can confront aesthetic chaos.

3596 Loehlin, James N. "'Top of the World, Ma': *Richard III* and Cinematic Convention." 67-79 in Boose, Lynda E., ed.; Burt, Richard, ed. *Shakespeare, the Movie: Popularizing the Plays on Film, TV, and Video.* London/New York, NY: Routledge; 1997. 277 pp. Index. Notes. Biblio. Illus.: Photo. B&W. 3. Lang.: Eng.

UK-England. USA. 1993-1996. Critical studies. ■Analysis of the film adaptation of Shakespeare's *Richard III* by Richard Loncraine and Ian McKellen.

3597 Meier, Paul. "Kenneth Branagh: With Utter Clarity." *TDR.* 1997 Sum; 41(2): 82-89. Illus.: Photo. B&W. 5. Lang.: Eng.

UK-England: London. 1989-1997. Histories-sources. ■Interview with director/actor Branagh on his current film adaptation of Shakespeare's *Hamlet*: focus on his use of language, comparison between British and American acting approaches, his work on his film *Henry V*, shifts in acting styles.

3598 Royal, Derek. "Shakespeare's Kingly Mirror: Figuring the Chorus in Olivier's and Branagh's *Henry V*." *LFQ.* 1997; 25(2) : 104-110. Notes. Biblio. Illus.: Photo. B&W. 1. Lang.: Eng.

UK-England. 1944-1989. Critical studies. ■Compares the depiction of the chorus in Laurence Olivier's and Kenneth Branagh's film versions of *Henry V.*

3599 "Directing *Scream*: A Talk with Wes Craven." *Scenario.* 1997; 3(1): 143-144. Lang.: Eng.

USA. 1996. Histories-sources. ■Interview with film director about his work on *Scream*, written by Kevin Williamson.

3600 "Directing *Breaking Away*: A Talk with Peter Yates." *Scenario.* 1997; 3(1): 97-99. Lang.: Eng.

USA. 1929-1997. Histories-sources. ■Interview with the film director, primarily about his work on the 1979 film written by Steve Tesich.

3601 "Directing *Midnight Cowboy*: A Talk with John Schlesinger." *Scenario.* 1997; 3(4): 98-101, 206. Illus.: Sketches. B&W. Color. 3. Lang.: Eng.

USA. 1969. Histories-sources. ■Interview with the director.

3602 "Producing *Midnight Cowboy*: A Talk with Jerome Hellman." *Scenario.* 1997; 3(4): 93-97, 205-206. Illus.: Sketches. B&W. Color. 5. Lang.: Eng.

USA. 1969. Histories-sources. ■Interview with the producer of the film, written by Waldo Salt and directed by John Schlesinger.

3603 "On Filming *Angels*: An Interview." 227-233 in Geis, Deborah R., ed.; Kruger, Steven F., ed. *Approaching the Millennium: Essays on Angels in America.* Ann Arbor, MI: Univ. of Michigan P; 1997. 352 pp. Notes. Lang.: Eng.

USA. 1995. Histories-sources. ■Interview with film director Robert Altman on his plans for a movie version of Tony Kushner's *Angels in America.*

3604 Abramson, Leslie H. *In the Eye of the Director: Self-Reflexivity in the Films of Alfred Hitchcock.* Chicago, IL: Univ. of Chicago; 1997. 322 pp. [Ph.D. Dissertation, Univ. Microfilms Order No. AAC 9811833.] Lang.: Eng.

USA. 1936-1980. Critical studies. ■Analyzes Hitchcock's work in the broader context of cultural studies.

3605 Anderson, Lisa M. *Mammies No More: The Changing Image of Black Women on Stage and Screen.* Lanham, MD: Rowman and Littlefield; 1997. 147 pp. Index. Biblio. Illus.: Photo. 11. Lang.: Eng.

USA. 1939-1995. Critical studies. ■Examines cultural representations of Black women on stage and screen. Focuses on the iconic 'Black mammy' character, the 'tragic' mulatta, and the myth of the 'jezebel' whore.

3606 Bartels, Emily C. "Shakespeare to the People." *PerAJ.* 1997 Jan.; 19(1): 58-60. Illus.: Photo. B&W. 1. [Number 55.] Lang.: Eng.

USA. 1996. Critical studies. ■Analysis of actor/director Al Pacino's approach to *Richard III* in his film *Looking for Richard.*

3607 Burt, Richard. "The Love That Dare Not Speak Shakespeare's Name: New Shakesqueer Cinema." 240-268 in Boose, Lynda E., ed.; Burt, Richard, ed. *Shakespeare, the Movie: Popularizing the Plays on Film, TV, and Video.* London/New York, NY: Routledge; 1997. 277 pp. Illus.: Photo. 8. Lang.: Eng.

USA. UK-England. 1977-1991. Historical studies. ■Representations of queerness in Shakespearean films and films in which Shakespeare is discussed, played, or adapted. Covers a wide range of films.

3608 Chin, Daryl. "Festivals, Markets, Critics: Notes on the State of the Art Film." *PerAJ.* 1997 Jan.; 19(1): 58-60. [Number 55.] Lang.: Eng.

USA. 1996-1997. Critical studies. ■Appraisal of the current trends in independent 'art' cinema and festivals.

3609 Cohen, Allen; Lawton, Harry. *John Huston: A Guide to References and Resources.* New York, NY: G.K. Hall; 1997. 827 pp. (A Reference Publication in Film.) Pref. Index. Filmography. Lang.: Eng.

USA. 1906-1987. Bibliographical studies. ■Guide to references and bibliographies for film actor/director John Huston. Includes critical overview of career, film chronology, filmography, annotated bibliography, reviews, interviews, awards, collections, archives, theatrical activity, discography, and media sources (CDs, Internet, etc.).

3610 Croce, Arlene. "Golden Girl." *NewY.* 1997 22 Sep.: 130-138. Illus.: Dwg. B&W. 1. Lang.: Eng.

USA. 1893-1979. Critical studies. ■The life of actress Mary Pickford, with reference to a biography by Eileen Whitfield.

3611 Donaldson, Peter. "Liz White's *Othello*." *SQ.* 1987; 38(4): 482-495. Notes. Illus.: Photo. B&W. 19. Lang.: Eng.

USA. 1980. Critical studies. ■Analysis of Liz White's screen version of Shakespeare's *Othello.*

3612 Durang, Christopher. "'We Talked in Sentences Then!'." *Scenario.* 1997; 3(2): 4-5, 207-208. Lang.: Eng.

USA. 1950. Critical studies. ■Playwright's thoughts on dialogue in films of the 1940s and 1950s, with emphasis on Joseph Mankiewicz's *All About Eve.*

3613 Eggert, Katherine. "Age Cannot Wither Him: Warren Beatty's Bugsy as Hollywood Cleopatra." 198-214 in Boose, Lynda E., ed.; Burt, Richard, ed. *Shakespeare, the Movie: Popularizing the Plays on Film, TV, and Video.* London/New York, NY: Routledge; 1997. 277 pp. Index. Notes. Biblio. Lang.: Eng.

USA. 1991. Historical studies. ■The reproduction of characters and plots of Shakespeare's *Antony and Cleopatra* in Warren Beatty's film *Bugsy* (directed by Barry Levinson). Argues that Beatty's presence represents Cleopatra as femme fatale and sexual object.

3614 Fuller, Karla Rae. *Hollywood Goes Oriental: Caucasian Performance in American Cinema.* Evanston, IL: Northwestern Univ; 1997. 358 pp. [Ph.D. Dissertation, Univ. Microfilms Order No. AAC 9731258.] Lang.: Eng.

USA. 1930-1969. Histories-specific. ■Analyzes cartoon images, B films, and blockbusters to argue that the physical embodiment of Asian characters by the non-Asian actors displays patently artificial and theatrical features, but nevertheless offers a site for the projection of displaced desires and fears of the West.

3615 Gardner, Colin Raymond. *Time Without Pity: Immanence and Contradiction in the Films of Joseph Losey.* Los Angeles, CA: Univ. of California; 1997. 1305 pp. [Ph.D. Dissertation, Univ. Microfilms Order No. AAC 9737352.] Lang.: Eng.

USA. 1909-1984. Critical studies. ■Theoretical exploration of the work of American film director Joseph Losey.

3616 Gopnik, Adam. "The Contrarian Comic." *NewY.* 1997 8 Sep.: 80-84. Illus.: Dwg. B&W. 1. Lang.: Eng.

USA. 1880-1946. Critical studies. ■Review of a biography of actor W.C. Fields by Simon Louvish.

MEDIA: Film—Performance/production

3617 Heffernan, Kevin Joseph S. *The Horror Genre and the American Film Industry, 1953-1968.* Madison, WI: Univ. of Wisconsin; 1997. 617 pp. [Ph.D. Dissertation, Univ. Microfilms Order No. AAC 9727996.] Lang.: Eng.
USA. 1953-1968. Histories-specific. ▪Examines the economic, aesthetic, technological, and cultural forces responsible for the success of horror films in the American motion picture market. Films include William Castle's *The Tingler* and George Romero's *The Night of the Living Dead.*

3618 Hertzberg, Hendrik. "Theatre of War." *NewY.* 1997 27 July: 30-33. Illus.: Dwg. 1. Lang.: Eng.
USA. 1997. Historical studies. ▪Analysis of Steven Spielberg's film *Saving Private Ryan.*

3619 Lane, Jim. "The Career and Influence of Ed Pincus: Shifts in Documentary Epistemology." *JFV.* 1997 Win; 49(4): 3-17. Illus.: Photo. B&W. 3. Lang.: Eng.
USA. 1967-1981. Biographical studies. ▪The work of documentary filmmaker Pincus, with emphasis on his autobiographical film *Diaries.*

3620 Lobenthal, Joel. "Marilyn Miller at the Elm Tree Inn." *BR.* 1997 Spr; 25(1): 65-66. Illus.: Photo. B&W. 1. Lang.: Eng.
USA. 1929. Historical studies. ▪Broadway musical comedy/dance star Marilyn Miller with emphasis on her appearance in the musical film *Sally.*

3621 Miller, Lynn C. "A *TPQ* Interview: (Un)documenting History: An Interview with Filmmaker Jill Godmilow." *TextPQ.* 1997 July; 17(3): 273-287. Notes. Lang.: Eng.
USA. 1967-1997. Histories-sources. ▪Writer/producer/director Godmilow discusses film, theatre, performance, and strategies she employed in the film *Roy Cohn/Jack Smith* performed by Ron Vawter and written by Vawter and Gary Indiana based on speeches by Cohn, and *Waiting for the Moon,* a fictional portrayal of the lives of Gertrude Stein and Alice B. Toklas.

3622 Seabrook, John. "Why Is the Force Still With Us?" *NewY.* 1997 6 Jan.: 40-53. Illus.: Dwg. Photo. B&W. Color. 9. Lang.: Eng.
USA. 1997. Historical studies. ▪Filmmaker and producer George Lucas and his work at Skywalker Ranch, with emphasis on the continuing popularity of the film *Star Wars* and its spinoffs to other media.

3623 Singer, Mark. "Sal Stabile, For Real." *NewY.* 1997 11 Aug.: 42-49. Illus.: Pntg. Color. 1. Lang.: Eng.
USA. 1974-1997. Historical studies. ▪Profile of young independent filmmaker Sal Stabile.

3624 Sragow, Michael. "Godfatherhood." *NewY.* 1997 24 Mar.: 44-52. Illus.: Photo. B&W. 1. Lang.: Eng.
USA. 1972-1997. Historical studies. ▪Director Francis Ford Coppola, his thoughts on making *The Godfather,* and its effect on later Hollywood films.

3625 Starks, Lisa S. "An Interview with Michael Maloney." *PS.* 1997 Fall; 17(1): 79-87. Notes. Illus.: Photo. B&W. 1. Lang.: Eng.
USA. 1995. Histories-sources. ▪Interview with the actor regarding his experiences playing in filmed adaptations of Shakespeare such as *Hamlet, Othello,* and *Henry V.*

3626 Weales, Gerald. "What Sartre Saw in Salem." *AmTh.* 1997 Apr.; 14(4): 51. Illus.: Photo. B&W. 1. Lang.: Eng.
USA. 1957-1996. Critical studies. ▪Film adaptations of Arthur Miller's play *The Crucible.* French director Raymound Rouleau's *Les Sorcières de Salem* with a screenplay adapted by Jean-Paul Sartre, and brief mention of Nicholas Hytner's current film adaptation.

3627 Welsh, Jim. "Postmodern Shakespeare: Strictly *Romeo.*" *LFQ.* 1997; 25(2): 152-153. Illus.: Photo. B&W. 1. Lang.: Eng.
USA. 1997. Reviews of performances. ▪Review of Baz Luhrmann's gender-confused, ethnically mixed film version of Shakespeare's *Romeo and Juliet.*

3628 Wilinsky, Barbara Jean. *Selling Exclusivity: The Emergence of Art Film Theatres in Post World War II United States Culture.* Evanston, IL: Northwestern Univ; 1997. 256 pg. [Ph.D. Dissertation, Univ. Microfilms Order No. AAC 9731364.] Lang.: Eng.
USA. 1946-1970. Histories-specific. ▪The socioeconomic and industrial context of the post-war art film house movement and the role of art cinema as an alternative to Hollywood cinema.

3629 Wiseman, Susan. "The Family Tree Motel: Subliming Shakespeare in *My Own Private Idaho.*" 225-239 in Boose, Lynda E., ed.; Burt, Richard, ed. *Shakespeare, the Movie: Popularizing the Plays on Film, TV, and Video.* London/New York, NY: Routledge; 1997. 277 pp. Index. Notes. Biblio. Lang.: Eng.
USA. 1993. Historical studies. ▪Analyzes elements of Shakespeare's *Henry IV* and *Henry V* in Gus Van Sant's film *My Own Private Idaho.*

3630 Livio, Gigi. "Ejzenstein-Stanislavskij, Majakovskij-Lunacarskij, e Zdanov." *LadB.* 1997; 1(1): 59-83. Notes. Lang.: Ita.
USSR. 1917-1958. Critical studies. ▪The actor in Russian film as compared to the stage actor. The importance of the director in Russian cinema.

Plays/librettos/scripts

3631 Strain, Ellen. "Snapshots of Greece: *Never on Sunday* and the East/West Politics of the 'Vacation Film'." *JFV.* 1997 Spr/Sum; 19(1/2): 80-93. Illus.: Photo. B&W. 3. Lang.: Eng.
1962-1991. Critical studies. ▪The creation of a mythic Greece through exoticism and eroticism in film, including *Never on Sunday, Zorba the Greek,* and *Summer Lovers* and the political ramifications of this myth.

3632 "Writing and Directing *Love Serenade*: A Talk with Shirley Barrett." *Scenario.* 1997; 3(2): 149-153, 205-207. Illus.: Sketches. B&W. 1. Lang.: Eng.
Australia. 1997. Histories-sources. ▪Interview with Barrett about *Love Serenade.*

3633 "Writing and Directing *The Sweet Hereafter*: A Talk with Atom Egoyan." *Scenario.* 1997; 3(4): 38-43, 197-202. Lang.: Eng.
Canada. 1997. Histories-sources. ▪Interview with the screenwriter and director.

3634 Banks, Russell. "A Wonderful Reversal." *Scenario.* 1997; 3(4): 44-45, 203-204. Lang.: Eng.
Canada. 1997. Histories-sources. ▪Interview: comments on Atom Egoyan's film *The Sweet Hereafter* by the author of the novel on which the film was based.

3635 Belzil, Patricia. "*Lilies* ou la répétition d'un nouveau drame romantique." (*Lilies* or the Rehearsal of a New Romantic Drama.) *JCT.* 1997; 83: 174-178. Notes. Illus.: Photo. B&W. 2. Lang.: Fre.
Canada. 1996. Historical studies. ▪Changes in style and substance in adapting Michel Marc Bouchard's *Les Feluettes (Lilies)* to film version *Lilies,* directed by John Greyson.

3636 Kane, Jill. "From the Baroque to *Wabi*: Translating Animal Imagery from Shakespeare's *King Lear* to Kurosawa's *Ran.*" *LFQ.* 1997; 25(2): 146-151. Biblio. Lang.: Eng.
England. Japan. 1605-1984. Critical studies. ▪Significance of animal imagery in *King Lear* and Akira Kurosawa's film adaptation *Ran.*

3637 Breight, Curtis. "Elizabethan World Pictures." 295-325 in Joughin, John J., ed. *Shakespeare and National Culture.* Manchester: Manchester UP; 1997. 343 pp. Notes. Index. Lang.: Eng.
Europe. 1990-1994. Critical studies. ▪The connection between globalism and cultural imperialism as seen in the proliferation of multi-national film adaptations of Shakespeare.

3638 Giammarco, Maurizio Mercedes. *Angle of Vision: Reaccentuating the Literary Past Through Adaptation.* Philadelphia, PA: Temple Univ; 1997. 187 pp. [Ph.D. Dissertation, Univ. Microfilms Order No. AAC 9737946.] Lang.: Eng.
Europe. USA. 1915-1995. Critical studies. ▪The nature of film adaptation: how filmmakers engage narrational, thematic, and ideological features inscribed in classic literature so that their adaptations resonate for contemporary audiences.

MEDIA: Film—Plays/librettos/scripts

3639 Pochhamer, Sabine; Runde, Andreas. "Towards a Post-James Joycean Filmmaking." *Thsch*. 1997; 11: 50-71. Illus.: Photo. B&W. 4. Lang.: Ger, Fre, Dut, Eng.
Europe. 1995. Histories-sources. ■An interview with Peter Greenaway about his film *Prospero's Books* and his text adaptation.

3640 "Writing and Directing *I Can't Sleep*: A Talk with Claire Denis." *Scenario*. 1997; 3(2): 84-87, 185-187. Illus.: Sketches. B&W. 1. Lang.: Eng.
France. 1994. Histories-sources. ■Interview with the writer (with Jean-Pôl Fargeau) of the film *J'ai pas sommeil*.

3641 Buzzard, Sharon. "Scripting for a Viewer Response: Woolrich, Truffaut, and *The Bride Wore Black*." *JFV*. 1997 Fall; 49 (3): 15-27. Illus.: Photo. B&W. 2. Lang.: Eng.
France. 1967. Historical studies. ■François Truffaut's adaptation of the novel by Cornell Woolrich (William Irish), with attention to audience reception, suspense, the effect of feminism, and the failure of contemporary critics to understand the film.

3642 Yarza, Alejandro. "En el nombre del padre: la reescritura de la narrativa edípica en ¿Qué he hecho yo para merecer esto?." (In the Name of the Father: The Restructuring of the Oedipal Narrative in *What Have I Done to Deserve This?*.) *Gestos*. 1997 Apr.; 12(23): 97-113. Notes. Biblio. Lang.: Spa.
Spain. 1984. Critical studies. ■Patriarchy and social politics in Pedro Almodóvar's screenplay.

3643 "Adapting *The Wings of the Dove*: A Talk with Hossein Amini." *Scenario*. 1997; 3(2): 49-52, 199-201. Illus.: Sketches. B&W. 1. Lang.: Eng.
UK-England. 1995-1997. Histories-sources. ■Interview with the writer of the film adaptation of Henry James' novel.

3644 Buhler, Stephen M. "Double Takes: Branagh Gets to *Hamlet*." *PS*. 1997 Fall; 17(1): 43-52. Biblio. Illus.: Photo. B&W. 2. Lang.: Eng.
UK-England. 1995-1996. Critical studies. ■Branagh's two cinematic views of *Hamlet*: *A Midwinter's Tale* about an ad hoc theatre troupe's attempt to put on the play, and the play itself.

3645 Burnett, Mark Thornton. "The 'Very Cunning of the Scene': Kenneth Branagh's *Hamlet*." *LFQ*. 1997; 25(2): 78-82. Notes. Biblio. Illus.: Photo. B&W. 1. Lang.: Eng.
UK-England. 1996. Critical studies. ■Analysis of Branagh's film adaptation of Shakespeare's *Hamlet*.

3646 Cavecchi, Mariacristina. "Peter Greenaway's *Prospero's Books*: A Tempest Between Word and Image." *LFQ*. 1997; 25(2): 83-89. Notes. Biblio. Illus.: Photo. B&W. 1. Lang.: Eng.
UK-England. 1991. Critical studies. ■How Greenaway's reorganizations of events in his film version of Shakespeare's *The Tempest* elicits imaginative responses into the viewers.

3647 Gale, Steven H.; Hudgins, Christopher C. "The Harold Pinter Archives II: a Description of the Filmscript Material in the Archive in the British Library." *PintR*. 1997: 101-142. Biblio. Notes. Lang.: Eng.
UK-England. 1963-1994. Historical studies. ■Description of Pinter's filmscript material held in the British Library.

3648 Griffin, C.W. "Henry V's Decision: Interrogative Texts." *LFQ*. 1997; 25(2): 99-103. Biblio. Illus.: Photo. B&W. 1. Lang.: Eng.
UK-England. 1989. Critical studies. ■Analyzes the contradiction inherent in *Henry V*'s eponymous hero, focusing on Branagh's film adaptation because of its emphasis on the play's ambiguities.

3649 Harris, Diana; Jackson, MacDonald. "Stormy Weather: Derek Jarman's *The Tempest*." *LFQ*. 1997; 25(2): 90-98. Notes. Biblio. Illus.: Photo. B&W. 1. Lang.: Eng.
UK-England. 1979. Critical studies. ■Re-evaluation of Jarman's screen version of Shakespeare's *The Tempest*.

3650 Hudgins, Christopher C. "Harold Pinter's *The Comfort of Strangers*: Fathers and Sons and Other Victims." *PintR*. 1997: 54-72. Notes. Lang.: Eng.
UK-England. 1990. Critical studies. ■Analysis of Pinter's film script *The Comfort of Strangers*.

3651 Mitchell, Deborah. "*Richard III*: Tonypandy in the Twentieth Century." *LFQ*. 1997; 25(2): 133-145. Notes. Biblio. Illus.: Photo. B&W. 1. Lang.: Eng.
UK-England. 1995. Critical studies. ■Historical accuracy and Richard Loncraine and Ian McKellen's depiction of Shakespeare's *Richard III* in their film adaptation of their stage production.

3652 "Writing *Rosewood*: A Talk with Gregory Poirier." *Scenario*. 1997; 3(1): 51-55, 213-216. Illus.: Sketches. B&W. 1. Lang.: Eng.
USA. 1997. Histories-sources. ■Interview with the screenwriter and author of *Rosewood*.

3653 "Steve Tesich (1942-1996)." *Scenario*. 1997; 3(1): 95-96. Illus.: Sketches. B&W. 1. Lang.: Eng.
USA. 1942-1996. Biographical studies. ■Brief biography of the screenwriter, playwright, and novelist, excerpted from a 1982 article in the *New York Times Magazine*.

3654 "Writing *Scream*: A Talk with Kevin Williamson." *Scenario*. 1997; 3(1): 140-142, 145, 216-220. Lang.: Eng.
USA. 1996. Histories-sources. ■Interview with the screenwriter.

3655 "Writing *Donnie Brasco*: A Talk with Paul Attanasio." *Scenario*. 1997; 3(2): 47-51, 182-185. Illus.: Sketches. B&W. 1. Lang.: Eng.
USA. 1997. Histories-sources. ■Interview with the screenwriter.

3656 "Martin Goldsmith (1913-1994)." *Scenario*. 1997; 3(2): 179. Lang.: Eng.
USA. 1913-1994. Biographical studies. ■Profile of the writer who left television and film to pursue a career as a stage playwright and novelist.

3657 "Writing *Addicted to Love*: A Talk with Robert Gordon." *Scenario*. 1997; 3(2): 128-131, 188-192. Illus.: Sketches. B&W. 1. Lang.: Eng.
USA. 1997. Histories-sources. ■Interview with the screenwriter.

3658 "Auteur Detour." *Scenario*. 1997; 3(2): 180-181. Lang.: Eng.
USA. 1945. Historical studies. ■Argues that while credit for the style of the film *Detour* usually goes to director Edgar G. Ulmer, it is screenwriter Martin Goldsmith who should be credited. Includes an excerpt from Goldsmith's unpublished memoirs.

3659 "Joseph L. Mankiewicz (1909-1993)." *Scenario*. 1997; 3(2): 104-109, 202-205. Illus.: Sketches. B&W. 1. Lang.: Eng.
USA. 1909-1993. Biographical studies. ■Profile of director and screenwriter Mankiewicz, with excerpt from a 1972 interview with him, as well as interviews with his son Tom Mankiewicz, also a screenwriter, and actress Celeste Holm who appeared in *All About Eve*.

3660 "Adapting *The Beautiful and Damned*: A Talk with Don Bachardy." *Scenario*. 1997; 3(2): 192-198. Illus.: Sketches. B&W. 3. Lang.: Eng.
USA. 1975. Histories-sources. ■Interview with Bachardy, adapter of Christopher Isherwood's play for film.

3661 "Waldo Salt (1914-1987)." *Scenario*. 1997; 3(4): 88-93. Illus.: Sketches. B&W. Color. 6. Lang.: Eng.
USA. 1914-1987. Biographical studies. ■Profile of the blacklisted screenwriter.

3662 "My Father, Waldo Salt: A Talk with Jennifer Salt." *Scenario*. 1997; 3(4): 102-105. Illus.: Sketches. B&W. Color. 3. Lang.: Eng.
USA. 1969. Histories-sources. ■The daughter of the writer of *Midnight Cowboy* describes her father's work on the film, in which she also had a role.

3663 "Writing *Telling Lies in America*: A Talk with Joe Eszterhas." *Scenario*. 1997; 3(4): 151-157, 206-208. Illus.: Sketches. B&W. 2. Lang.: Eng.
USA. 1997. Histories-sources. ■Interview with the screenwriter.

3664 "Writing *One Crash, Three Accidents*: A Talk with Jason Greiff." *Scenario*. 1997; 3(4): 193-195. Lang.: Eng.
USA. 1996. Histories-sources. ■Interview with the winner of the student screenplay competition.

3665 Alvarado, Sonya Yvette. *Dark Visions of America: David Mamet's Adaptation of Novels and Plays for the Screen*. Lubbock, TX: Texas Tech Univ; 1997. 176 pp. [Ph.D. Disserta-

MEDIA: Film—Plays/librettos/scripts

tion, Univ. Microfilms Order No. AAC 9725925.] Lang.: Eng.
USA. 1981-1996. Historical studies. ■Focuses on four screenplays adapted by Mamet—*The Postman Always Rings Twice*, *The Verdict*, *Glengarry Glen Ross* and *American Buffalo*—that best represent how he remains true to the theme of the original literary text while at the same time adding his strong materialist critique of the world.

3666   Baitz, John Robin. "A Wedding of Worlds." *AmTh*. 1997 Mar.; 14(3): 48-49. Illus.: Photo. B&W. 1. Lang.: Eng.
USA. 1989-1996. Histories-sources. ■Playwright Baitz discusses challenges and process for adapting his play *The Substance of Fire* for film.

3667   Braverman, Douglas. "*The Last of Sheila*: Sondheim as Master Game-Player." 85-92 in Gordon, Joanne, ed. *Stephen Sondheim: A Casebook*. New York, NY/London: Garland; 1997. 259 pp. (Casebooks on Modern Dramatists.) Notes. Biblio. Index. Lang.: Eng.
USA. 1973. Critical studies. ■Stephen Sondheim's love of games and puzzles as reflected in his filmscript *The Last of Sheila*, co-authored with Anthony Perkins.

3668   Christensen, Ann C. "Petruchio's House in Postwar Suburbia: Reinventing the Domestic Woman Again." *PS*. 1997 Fall; 17(1) : 28-42. Biblio. Illus.: Photo. B&W. 3. Lang.: Eng.
USA. 1929-1966. Critical studies. ■Representation of Petruchio's house and Katherine's housewifery in three versions of *The Taming of the Shrew*: the musical *Kiss Me, Kate*, Zeffirelli's 1966 adaptation, and an uncredited, silent version from 1929.

3669   Debona, Guerric. "The Canon and Cultural Studies: Culture and Anarchy in Gotham City." *JFV*. 1997 Spr/Sum; 49(1/2): 52-65. Illus.: Photo. B&W. 2. Lang.: Eng.
USA. 1989. Critical studies. ■High and low culture and political allegory in the recent film *Batman*.

3670   Engel, Joel. "Writing *North by Northwest*: A Talk with Ernest Lehman." *Scenario*. 1997; 3(1): 208-212. Illus.: Sketches. B&W. 1. Lang.: Eng.
USA. 1995. Histories-sources. ■Interview with the screenwriter about his work with director Alfred Hitchcock. Excerpt from Engel's *Screenwriters on Screenwriting* (Hyperion, 1995).

3671   Gehring, Wes D. *American Dark Comedy: Beyond Satire*. Westport, CT: Greenwood P; 1997. 194 pp. (Contributions to the Study of Popular Culture 55.) Index. Biblio. Illus.: Photo. 24. Lang.: Eng.
USA. 1850-1996. Historical studies. ■Traces the development of satire and 'dark comedy' in America from its roots in mid-nineteenth century literature such as Melville's short novel *The Confidence Man* to films of the twentieth century ranging from Chaplin's early silents to Robert Altman's Hollywood satire, *The Player*.

3672   Haspel, Jane Seay. *Dirty Jokes and Fairy Tales: David Mamet and the Narrative Capability of Film*. Denton, TX: Univ. of North Texas; 1997. 239 pp. [Ph.D. Dissertation, Univ. Microfilms Order No. AAC 9727782.] Lang.: Eng.
USA. 1975-1995. Historical studies. ■Playwright David Mamet as screenwriter and director. Analyzes *House of Games*, *Things Change*, *Homicide*, and *Oleanna* as reflections of Mamet's ideas on the best ways of conveying a story on film.

3673   Kunz, Don. "Oliver Stone's *Talk Radio*." *LFQ*. 1997; 25(1): 62-67. Notes. Illus.: Photo. B&W. 1. Lang.: Eng.
USA: Hollywood, CA. 1988. Critical studies. ■Film adaptation by Oliver Stone and Eric Bogosian of Bogosian's play *Talk Radio*.

3674   Li Lan, Yong. "'The Very Painting of Your Fear'." *SJW*. 1997; 133: 109-117. Notes. Lang.: Eng.
USA. 1971. Critical studies. ■The cinematic adaptation of Shakespeare's *Macbeth* by Roman Polanski, with discussion of the cultural re-possesion of high-brow English art by the film itself and the thriller genre.

3675   McCombe, John P. "Toward an Objective Correlative: The Problem of Desire in Franco Zeffirelli's *Hamlet*." *LFQ*. 1997; 25(2): 125-131. Biblio. Lang.: Eng.
USA. 1990. Critical studies. ■Argues that Zeffirelli oversimplifies political ambiguity in his film adaptation of Shakespeare's play, thus reducing it to a dysfunctional family melodrama.

3676   Mortimer, Barbara. "Portraits of the Postmodern Person in *Taxi Driver*, *Raging Bull*, and *The King of Comedy*." *JFV*. 1997 Spr/Sum; 49(1/2): 28-38. Illus.: Photo. B&W. 2. Lang.: Eng.
USA. 1976-1982. Critical studies. ■Analysis of films by Martin Scorsese and starring Robert De Niro, with attention to questions of identity. Argues that postmodernism is undercut by a male/female dialectic in which women are perceived as a threat to men.

3677   Palmer, R. Barton. "Arthur Miller and the Cinema." 184-210 in Bigsby, Christopher, ed. *The Cambridge Companion to Arthur Miller*. Cambridge: Cambridge UP; 1997. 277 pp. (Cambridge Companions to Literature.) Index. Notes. Lang.: Eng.
USA. 1960-1997. Historical studies. ■Examines cinematic versions of Arthur Miller's plays including both theatrical films and televised versions. Author examines his career from the 1960s to his latest screenplay in 1995 for *The Crucible*.

3678   Rosenthal, Alan. "The Politics of Passion: An Interview with Anthony Thomas." *JFV*. 1997 Spr/Sum; 49(1/2): 94-102. Lang.: Eng.
USA. 1980-1997. Histories-sources. ■Interview with the creator of docudramas, whose credits include *Death of a Princess* (1980).

3679   Russ, Jeff; Baughman, Cynthia. "Language as Narrative Voice: The Poetics of the Highly Inflected Screenplay." *JFV*. 1997 Fall; 49(3): 28-37. Illus.: Photo. B&W. Lang.: Eng.
USA. 1998. Critical studies. ■Analysis of the dramatic and narrative voices in screenplay, as distinguished from shooting script. Brief references to several films.

3680   Simmons, James R., Jr. "'In the Rank Sweat of an Enseamed Bed': Sexual Aberration and the Paradigmatic Screen *Hamlet*s." *LFQ*. 1997; 25(2): 111-118. Notes. Biblio. Illus.: Photo. B&W. 1. Lang.: Eng.
USA. UK-England. 1920-1996. Critical studies. ■Treatment of issues of sexual aberrance in numerous film adaptations of Shakespeare's *Hamlet*.

3681   Stachówna, Grażyna. "Dzieje zadłuzenia." (The History of Indebtedness.) *DialogW*. 1997; 12: 133-147. Lang.: Pol.
USA. 1951-1972. Critical studies. ■Film's debt to live theatre: analysis of films based on *A Streetcar Named Desire* by Tennessee Williams directed by Elia Kazan, *Who's Afraid of Virginia Woolf?* by Edward Albee directed by Mike Nichols, and *Play It Again, Sam* by Woody Allen directed by Herb Ross.

3682   Starks, Lisa S. "Educating Eliza: Fashioning the Model Woman in the 'Pygmalion Film'." *PS*. 1997 Win/Spr; 16(2): 44-55. Notes. Biblio. Illus.: Photo. B&W. 6. Lang.: Eng.
USA. 1938. Critical studies. ■The perfect woman and cinematic treatment of the Pygmalion myth in such films as *My Fair Lady*, *Pygmalion*, *Pretty Woman*, and *Sabrina*.

3683   Starks, Lisa S. "The Veiled (Hot) Bed of Race and Desire: Parker's *Othello* and the Stereotype as Screen Fetish." *PS*. 1997 Fall; 17(1): 64-78. Notes. Biblio. Illus.: Photo. B&W. 11. Lang.: Eng.
USA. 1995. Critical studies. ■Examines Oliver Parker's eroticized filming of *Othello* for its play on the audience's expectations.

3684   Starks, Lisa S. "Introduction." *PS*. 1997 Fall; 17(1): 3-5. Notes. Biblio. Lang.: Eng.
USA. 1997. Critical studies. ■Introduction to issue devoted to Shakespeare and film adaptations.

3685   Varnell, Margaret A. "A Note on *Richard III* (1912)." *PS*. 1997 Fall; 17(1): 88-90. Biblio. Filmography. Illus.: Photo. B&W. 4. Lang.: Eng.
USA. 1912. Historical studies. ■Examines the oldest surviving complete film in America: M.B. Dudley's silent *Richard III*.

3686   Veitch, Jonathan. "The Politics and Paradoxes of Censorship: *Miss Lonelyhearts* in Hollywood." *JFV*. 1997 Fall; 49(3): 6-14. Lang.: Eng.
USA. 1933. Historical studies. ■Leonard Praskins' adaptation of Nathanael West's novel.

MEDIA: Film—Plays/librettos/scripts

3687 Wellec, Philip. "Freud's Footprints in Films of *Hamlet*." *LFQ*. 1997; 25(2): 119-125. Notes. Biblio. Illus.: Photo. B&W. 1. Lang.: Eng.
USA. UK-England. 1910-1996. Critical studies. ■Presence of Freudian psychology in film adaptations of Shakespeares's *Hamlet*.

3688 Welsch, Tricia. "At Work in the Genre Laboratory: Brian De Palma's *Scarface*." *JFV*. 1997 Spr/Sum; 49(1/2): 39-51. Illus.: Photo. B&W. 2. Lang.: Eng.
USA. 1932-1983. Critical studies. ■The use of generic hybridization with other forms—horror, comedy, musical, *film noir*—in recent gangster films to contain the threat of cultural difference.

Reference materials

3689 Díaz-Fernández, José Ramón. "Shakespeare on Film: A Bibliography of Critical Studies." *PS*. 1997 Fall; 17 (1): 91-104. Lang.: Eng.
USA. 1997. ■Bibliography of criticism of Shakespearean film and adaptation broken into three headings.

3690 Keller, Gary D., comp. *A Biographical Handbook of Hispanics and United States Film*. Tempe, AZ: Bilingual; 1997. 322 pp. Biblio. Index. Illus.: Photo. 125. Lang.: Eng.
USA. 1911-1995. ■A biographical directory of Hispanic presence in American film.

3691 Klotman, Phyllis R., comp.; Gibson, Gloria J., comp. *Frame by Frame II: A Filmography of the African American Image, 1978-1994*. Bloomington, IN: Indiana UP; 1997. 771 pp. Index. Biblio. Lang.: Eng.
USA. 1978-1994. ■African-American presence in American films.

Relation to other fields

3692 Tomaselli, Keyan G.; Shepperson, Arnold. "Course File for 'Documentary Film, Visual Anthropology, and Visual Sociology'." *JFV*. 1997 Win; 49(4): 44-57. Lang.: Eng.
South Africa, Republic of. 1997. Histories-sources. ■Detailed course description including readings, screenings, and assignments.

3693 Boose, Lynda E.; Burt, Richard. "Totally Clueless? Shakespeare Goes Hollywood in the 1990s." 8-22 in Boose, Lynda E., ed.; Burt, Richard, ed. *Shakespeare, the Movie: Popularizing the Plays on Film, TV, and Video*. London/New York, NY: Routledge; 1997. 277 pp. Index. Notes. Biblio. Lang.: Eng.
USA. 1990-1997. Critical studies. ■American cultural ambivalence about Shakespeare, seen in acknowledged and unacknowledged Shakespearean presence in recent commercial films.

3694 Clark, Ginger. "Cinema of Compromise: *Pinky* and the Politics of Post War Film Production." *WJBS*. 1997 Fall; 21(3): 180-189. Notes. Biblio. Lang.: Eng.
USA. 1948. Historical studies. ■The influence of Hollywood's political and social atmosphere on the making of Elia Kazan's 'problem' film *Pinky* whoch focused on a young girl dealing with life in the racist south.

3695 Rush, Jeff. "Course File for 'Narrative Film: Theory and Practice'." *JFV*. 1997 Fall; 49(3): 48-67. Lang.: Eng.
USA. 1997. Histories-sources. ■Detailed description of graduate seminar, including topics, exercises, screenings, readings, and assignments.

3696 Sklar, Zachary. "Child of the Blacklist." *Scenario*. 1997; 3(4): 4-5, 195-197. Lang.: Eng.
USA. 1947-1987. Histories-sources. ■The author, a screenwriter and the son of a blacklisted screenwriter, assesses the impact of the House Unamerican Activities Committee on the film industry and discusses the recent restoration of credit to blacklisted writers.

Theory/criticism

3697 Kalisch, Eleonore. "Vom Schneeball-Effekt zur thrill-comedie." (From Snowball-Effect to Thrill-Comedy.) 191-212 in Fiebach, Joachim, ed.; Mühl-Benninghaus, Wolfgang, ed.; Humboldt-Universität zu Berlin, Institut für Theaterwissenschaft/Kulturelle Kommunikation. *Theater und Medien an der Jahrhundertwende*. Berlin: Vistas Verlag; 1997. 214 pp. (Berliner Theaterwissenschaft 3.) Notes. Lang.: Ger.

Europe. 1928-1983. Critical studies. ■Concepts of gestures and comedy from Bergson's philosophy of decentered image-understanding and its interpretation by Gilles Deleuze.

3698 Mühl-Benninghaus, Wolfgang. "Frühes Kino und Theater. Versuch einer Annäherung." (Early Cinema and Theatre: An Attempt at Approximation.) 169-190 in Fiebach, Joachim, ed.; Mühl-Benninghaus, Wolfgang, ed.; Humboldt-Universität zu Berlin, Institut für Theaterwissenschaft/Kulturelle Kommunikation. *Theater und Medien an der Jahrhundertwende*. Berlin: Vistas Verlag; 1997. 214 pp. (Berliner Theaterwissenschaft 3.) Notes. Lang.: Ger.
Germany: Berlin. 1900-1913. Historical studies. ■Similarities and differences of theatre and film in the early 20th century with respect to theoretical discussions, censorship, acting arts and commercial development.

3699 Mayer, David. "Learning to See in the Dark." *NCT*. 1997 Win; 25(2): 92-114. Lang.: Eng.
UK-England. France. USA. 1895-1910. Historical studies. ■An attack on the prevailing theory of the relationship between theatre and film in the late Victorian and Edwardian periods with particular attention to Nicholas Vardac and his study, *From Stage to Screen*. Includes a CD-ROM with illustrations for this essay.

3700 Meyer, Moe. "Rethinking *Paris Is Burning*: Performing Social Geography in Harlem Drag Balls." *TA*. 1997; 50: 40-71. Notes. Lang.: Eng.
USA. 1991. Critical studies. ■Analysis of the written critiques of Jennie Livingston's documentary on drag balls in Harlem.

3701 Rothman, William; Keane, Marian. "Toward a Reading of *The World Viewed*." *JFV*. 1997 Spr/Sum; 49(1/2): 5-16. Illus.: Photo. B&W. 2. Lang.: Eng.
USA. 1968-1997. Historical studies. ■Theories of film study, with emphasis on *The World Viewed* by Stanley Cavell (1971).

Mixed media

Design/technology

3702 Saltz, David Z. "Beckett's Cyborgs: Technology and the Beckettian Text." *TheatreF*. 1997 Sum/Fall; 11: 38-48. Illus.: Photo. 21. Lang.: Eng.
USA. 1996. Histories-sources. ■On a technologically-mediated performance installation, *Beckett Space: A Modernist Carnival*, based on several short Beckett plays, directed by author and presented at SUNY-Stony Brook. Piece consisted of live actors, computers, video projectors, video cameras, and motion tracking devices. Author focuses on new technologies and how they affect traditional works and the interaction between technology and performance.

3703 White, Benjamin. "Flight." *LD&A*. 1996 Jan.; 26(1): 28-31. Illus.: Photo. Color. 10. Lang.: Eng.
USA: Chicago, IL. 1996. Technical studies. ■The author's design for the Chicago Museum of Science & Industry's 'flight simulator' exhibit. Discusses how use of theatrical projectors to achieve artificial takeoff.

3704 Wodiczko, Krzysztof. "Open Transmission." *PerfR*. 1997 Fall; 2(3): 1-8. Illus.: Photo. B&W. 8. [Edited transcript of a talk given at the Institute for Contemporary Arts, London, as part of the series 'Spaced Out 3—Smart Practices in a Complex World', March, 1997.] Lang.: Eng.
USA. Europe. 1997. Histories-sources. ■The development of a performance art and technology project in which the author created a prosthetic device called the Alien Staff based on a traditional walking stick with a video addition, to be used by immigrants and strangers to a city to tell stories and raise issues about identity, communication and the sharing of space by many peoples.

Plays/librettos/scripts

3705 Garrand, Timothy. "Scripting Narrative for Interactive Multimedia." *JFV*. 1997 Spr/Sum; 49(1/2): 66-79. Illus.: Photo. Chart. 6. Lang.: Eng.
USA. 1997. Instructional materials. ■Guidelines for the creation of classical linear narrative plots for interactive multimedia.

MEDIA: Mixed media

Relation to other fields

3706 Auslander, Philip. "Against Ontology: Making Distinctions between the Live and the Mediatized." *PerfR.* 1997 Fall; 2(3): 50-55. Notes. Biblio. Lang.: Eng.
Canada. USA. 1977-1997. Critical studies. ■Theatre and media as rivals in the era of the televisual. Reviews theories of performance in relation to production, and challenges the accepted theoretical opposition between the live and the mediatized in a world where there is a continuing incursion of media into the live event. Discusses the work of several artists, including Anna Deveare Smith (*Twilight: Los Angeles, 1992*) and Christine Kozlov (*Information: No Theory*).

3707 Ho, Christopher. "The Illusion of Illumination." *PerAJ.* 1997 Jan.; 19(1): 28-37. Notes. Illus.: Photo. B&W. 4. [Number 55.] Lang.: Eng.
USA: New York, NY. 1996. Critical studies. ■Shift of museums from didactic presenters of cultural norms into a forum for comparative textualization, using the Guggenheim Museum Soho's *Mediascape* exhibition of video art as an example of this process.

Video forms

Administration

3708 Murray, Matthew John. *Broadcast Content Regulation and Cultural Limits, 1920-1962.* Madison, WI: Univ. of Wisconsin; 1997. 332 pp. Notes. Biblio. [Ph.D. Dissertation, Univ. Microfilms Order No. AAC 9737016.] Lang.: Eng.
USA. 1920-1965. Historical studies. ■Developments in radio and television censorship, focusing on the processes of self-regulation employed by the broadcast networks.

3709 Speiss, Thomas J., III. "'Heigh Ho, Heigh Ho': A Sychronization License Granted to Use Musical Compositions on Film and on Television Does Not Include Videocassettes." *JAML.* 1997 Sum; 27(2): 101-117. Notes. Lang.: Eng.
USA. 1997. Historical studies. ■Examining recent court case involving the Disney Corporation, discusses copyright assignments of ownership, copyright licenses, and the roles of attorneys and arts managers.

3710 Weinberg, Jonathan. "Cable TV, Indecency and the Court." *ColJL&A.* 1997 Win; 21(2): 95-128. Notes. Lang.: Eng.
USA. 1995. Historical studies. ■The First Amendment impact of the Supreme Court decision in the *Denver Area Educational Tele-Communications Consortium v. FCC* case.

Design/technology

3711 Calhoun, John. "Filming in Vancouver." *TCI.* 1997 Apr.; 31(4): 36-41. Illus.: Photo. 14. Lang.: Eng.
Canada: Vancouver, BC. 1996. Historical studies. ■Filming of television production, *Millennium* (creator/producer Chris Carter, production designer Mark Freeborn), in Vancouver. A diverse geography, solid infrastructure, and favorable exchange rate make the area a popular one for television and film production.

3712 Boepple, Leanne. "Lifetime Commitment." *LDim.* 1997 Sep.; 21(8): 74-77. Illus.: Photo. Color. 4. Lang.: Eng.
USA: New York, NY. 1997. Technical studies. ■Use of motorized DeSisti lighting system and grid in television studios for fast and convenient changes. Technology, equipment, use by Lifetime Studios in New York.

3713 Calhoun, John. "Lighting to Deadline." *LDim.* 1997 Apr.; 21(3): 60-63, 107-108. Illus.: Photo. Color. 4. Lang.: Eng.
USA: New York, NY. 1997. Technical studies. ■Special lighting needs designed by New York City Lites for television news program that is located in studio with exterior windows allowing in natural light.

3714 McHugh, Catherine. "Comic Relief." *LDim.* 1997 June; 21(5): 32-41. Illus.: Photo. Color. 5. Lang.: Eng.
USA: Aspen, CO. 1997. Historical studies. ■Allen Branton's lighting design for HBO cable television's third annual US Comedy Festival, which featured sixty performers in over seventy different shows in nine different venues.

Institutions

3715 Reis, George R. "Reel Concern: American Movie Classics' Fifth Annual Film Preservation Festival." *FundM.* 1997 Aug.; 28 (6): 24-27. Illus.: Photo. Color. B&W. 5. Lang.: Eng.
USA. 1997. Critical studies. ■American Movie Classic's fifth annual televised fund-raising campaign directed at raising money for the restoration of films.

Performance/production

3716 Moran, Albert. "Try and Try Again: *The Restless Years* and Nationalising Television Drama." *ADS.* 1997 Apr.; 30: 57-67. Notes. Lang.: Eng.
Australia. Germany. 1977-1993. Critical studies. ■Analysis of the television serial *The Restless Years* for its Australian cultural significance and its adaptation to another country's *zeitgeist*: that of Germany.

3717 Chaîné, Francine. "Collage, assemblage, bricolage ou la mise en scène dans l'installation-vidéo." (Collage, Assemblage, Tinkering or Staging Techniques in Video Installations.) *JCT.* 1997 Spr; 18(1): 42-58. Notes. Biblio. Illus.: Photo. B&W. 6. Lang.: Fre.
Canada. 1978-1997. Historical studies. ■Techniques used in creating a video installation, and similarities with theatre staging techniques.

3718 Lavoie, Pierre. "Chapeau!" (Hats Off!) *JCT.* 1997; 82: 160-164. Illus.: Photo. B&W. 8. Lang.: Fre.
Canada. 1997. Historical studies. ■Québécois actor Olivier Guimond is remembered in four-part televised series *Cher Olivier (Dear Olivier)*, directed by André Melançon, produced by Productions Avanti Ciné Vidéo.

3719 Lévesque, Solange. "Un autre regard sur le théâtre: Entretien avec Jean Faucher." (Another Perspective on the Theatre: Interview with Jean Faucher.) *JCT.* 1997; 82: 100-116. Notes. Illus.: Photo. B&W. 17. Lang.: Fre.
Canada. 1952-1997. Histories-sources. ■Quebec television director Jean Faucher retraces his career and explains his directing methods.

3720 Krakowska-Narożniak, Joanna. "Teatr w krzywym zwierciadle dokumentacji filmowej." (Theatre in the Distorting Mirror of Film.) *DialogW.* 1997; 4: 123-132. Lang.: Pol.
Europe. 1912-1997. Historical studies. ■The difficulties of recording and preserving live theatrical performance on video from both theoretical and practical standpoints.

3721 Rozett, Martha Tuck. "When Images Replace Words: Shakespeare, Russian Animation, and the Culture of Television." 208-214 in Salomone, Ronald E., ed.; Davis, James E., ed. *Teaching Shakespeare Into the Twenty-First Century.* Athens, OH: Ohio UP; 1997. 290 pp. Pref. Biblio. Lang.: Eng.
Russia. 1997. Critical studies. ■*Shakespeare: The Animated Tales*, adaptations of Shakespearean plays, directed by Leon Farfield. Focus on the ability of images to communicate the plays.

3722 Opperud, Inger Marie. "När teater blir TV." (When Theatre Turns To TV.) *Dramat.* 1997; 5(2): 22-26. Illus.: Photo. Color. Lang.: Swe.
Sweden: Stockholm. 1996. Critical studies. ■A discussion about transferring a stage production to TV, and pro and con of adaptation and broadcasting, with references to Björn Melander's staging of Albee's *Three Tall Women* and interview with the actress Lill Terselius.

3723 Osborne, Laurie E. "Poetry in Motion: Animating Shakespeare." 103-120 in Boose, Lynda E., ed.; Burt, Richard, ed. *Shakespeare, the Movie: Popularizing the Plays on Film, TV, and Video.* London/New York, NY: Routledge; 1997. 277 pp. Index. Notes. Biblio. Lang.: Eng.
UK. Russia. 1992. Critical studies. ■Analysis of British/Russian series on Shakespeare for children, *Shakespeare: The Animated Tales.*

3724 "Ronnie Fraser 1930-1997." *PlPl.* 1997 May; 513: 29. Illus.: Photo. B&W. 1. Lang.: Eng.
UK-England. 1930-1997. Biographical studies. ■Life and career of television actor Ronnie Fraser.

3725 Boose, Lynda E. "Grossly Gaping Viewers and Jonathan Miller's *Othello*." 186-197 in Boose, Lynda E., ed.; Burt, Richard, ed. *Shakespeare, the Movie: Popularizing the Plays*

MEDIA: Video forms—Performance/production

on Film, TV, and Video. London/New York, NY: Routledge; 1997. 277 pp. Index. Notes. Biblio. Lang.: Eng.
UK-England. 1981. Historical studies. ■Gender in Jonathan Miller's BBC version of Othello. Author focuses on voyeuristic position of audience.

3726   Hodgdon, Barbara. "Race-ing Othello, Re-Engendering White-Out." 23-44 in Boose, Lynda E., ed.; Burt, Richard, ed. Shakespeare, the Movie: Popularizing the Plays on Film, TV, and Video. London/New York, NY: Routledge; 1997. 277 pp. Index. Notes. Biblio. Lang.: Eng.
UK-England. 1987-1996. Critical studies. ■Analysis of two television versions of Othello, directed by Janet Suzman/1987 and Trevor Nunn/1989, with reference to the O.J. Simpson murder trial, often compared to the plot of Shakespeare's play.

3727   Lord, Angela. "Life After Soap: Sarah Lancaster talks to Angela Lord." PlPl. 1997 May; 513: 6-7. Illus.: Photo. B&W. Color. 3. Lang.: Eng.
UK-England. 1997. Histories-sources. ■Actor Sarah Lancaster discusses leaving Coronation Street to work on drama series Where the Heart Is.

3728   Lord, Angela. "Happy To Be Single: Stephen Billington talks to Angela Lord." PlPl. 1997 June/July; 514: 36. Illus.: Photo. Color. 1. Lang.: Eng.
UK-England. 1997. Historical studies. ■Actor Stephen Billington on his career and on playing Lysander in television adaptation of Jilly Cooper's novel The Man Who Made Husbands Jealous.

3729   Mullin, Michael. "Stage and Screen: The Trevor Nunn Macbeth." SQ. 1987 Fall; 38(3): 350-359. Notes. Illus.: Photo. B&W. 3. Lang.: Eng.
UK-England. 1976-1978. Critical studies. ■Analysis of Trevor Nunn's production for television of Shakespeare's Macbeth, which is a record of his stage version.

3730   Howard, Tony. "When Peter Met Orson: The 1953 CBS King Lear." 121-134 in Boose, Lynda E., ed.; Burt, Richard, ed. Shakespeare, the Movie: Popularizing the Plays on Film, TV, and Video. London/New York, NY: Routledge; 1997. 277 pp. Index. Notes. Biblio. Lang.: Eng.
USA. 1953. Historical studies. ■The television adaptation of King Lear by Peter Brook and Orson Welles: critical and audience reaction, the attempt to adapt the play to a new medium.

3731   Keyes, Daniel Joseph. The Performance of Testimonial Television on Daytime Talk Shows. Toronto, ON: York Univ; 1997. 535 pp. Notes. Biblio. [Ph.D. Dissertation, Univ. Microfilms Order No. AAC NQ22913.] Lang.: Eng.
USA. 1985-1996. Critical studies. ■The cultural significance and political implications of testimonial performance in television talk shows.

3732   McHugh, Catherine. "Attention Shoppers." TCI. 1997 Nov.; 31(9): 42-47. Illus.: Photo. 24. Lang.: Eng.
USA. 1997. Historical studies. ■The use of video screen and interactive technology in rock group U2's latest tour POPMART.

3733   Montgomery, Elizabeth Joann. Talkshow Performance Practices and the Display of Identity. Evanston, IL: Northwestern Univ; 1997. 249 pp. Notes. Biblio. [Ph.D. Dissertation, Univ. Microfilms Order No. AAC 9814271.] Lang.: Eng.
USA. 1985-1996. Critical studies. ■Performance as a theatrical event and as constitutive of identity in television talk shows.

Plays/librettos/scripts

3734   Lavoie, Pierre. "Un miroir sur la scène ou 'Une chanson d'amour endormie dans une taverne'." (A Mirror on the Stage or 'A Love Song Asleep in a Tavern'.) JCT. 1997; 83: 157-161. Notes. Illus.: Photo. B&W. 4. Lang.: Fre.
Canada. 1997. Historical studies. ■Documentary video Un miroir sur la scène (A Mirror on the Stage), directed by Jean-Claude Coulbois, recounts history of Quebec theatre.

3735   Drewniak, Łukasz. "Wstręt spod lądy." (Disgust from under the Counter.) DialogW. 1997; 10: 102-116. Lang.: Pol.
Poland. 1929-1997. Critical studies. ■Portrayals of Polish reality in Polish television plays: commercialism in Ketchup Schroedera (Schroeder's Ketchup) by Roman Nowakowski, directed by Filip Zylber, and every-

day poverty in Der Aufhaltsame Aufstieg des Arturo Ui (The Resistible Rise of Arturo Ui) by Bertolt Brecht, directed by Piotr Szulkin.

Reference materials

3736   Baxter, Joan. Television Musicals: Plots, Critiques, Casts, and Credits for 222 Shows Written for and Presented on TV, 1944-1996. Jefferson, NC/London: McFarland; 1997. 204 pp. Index. Pref. Biblio. Illus.: Photo. 26. Lang.: Eng.
USA. 1944-1996. ■Directory of original musicals written for and presented on television.

Relation to other fields

3737   Burch, Elizabeth. "Getting Closer to Folk TV Production: Nontraditional Uses of Video in the U.S. and Other Cultures." JFV. 1997 Win; 49(4): 18-29. Lang.: Eng.
1990-1997. Historical studies. ■The use of video among native or marginalized groups around the world, activist video, the growth of 'real-life programming' on commercial television, and the stylistic influence of home video on conventional programming and advertising.

3738   Martin-Smith, Alistair; Zatzman, Belarie Hyman. "Crossing Boundaries: Drama in the Electric Age." NETJ. 1997; 8: 11-25. Notes. Biblio. Lang.: Eng.
Canada. UK-England. 1997. Critical studies. ■Examines Electric Bedroom, a video conference held between England and Canada, in which teenagers crossed cultural boundaries to focus on role playing and framing. Points to this mediation between drama and technology as a tool to explore constructing and sharing identities.

3739   Bourden, Pierre; Serra, Alessandro, transl. Sulla televisione. (On Television.) Milan: Feltrinelli; 1997. 122 pp. (Elementi/Feltrinelli.) Notes. Append. Lang.: Ita.
Europe. 1997. Critical studies. ■Italian translation of Sur la télévision. The relation between television journalism and politics.

3740   Jenkins, Ron. "Stand Back, Johannesburg." AmTh. 1997 Nov.; 14(9): 18-19, 71-72. Illus.: Photo. B&W. 9. Lang.: Eng.
South Africa, Republic of: Johannesburg. 1981-1997. Historical studies. ■Satirist Pieter-Dirk Uys's drag performances in theatre and on television as the character Evita Bezuidenhout. Political content of his material, influence of Uys on political figures.

3741   Boltz, Ingeborg. "Shakespeare. 'The Animated Tales'. Vom Trickfilmstudio in die Schule." (Shakespeare, 'The Animated Tales': From the Trick Film Studio to School.) SJW. 1997; 133: 118-133. Append. Illus.: Dwg. 6. Lang.: Ger.
UK. Russia. 1991-1997. Critical studies. ■Introduces twelve of Shakespeare: The Animated Tales which were adapted from Shakespeare to videos. Describes genesis and educational aims, length and use of Shakespeare's original language for the script by Leon Garfield and suggests the video's use for teaching and course-work.

MIME

General

Institutions

3742   Reidinger, Jiří. "O tom, jak se stan proměnil ve fotoparát. Divadlo Mimů Alfred ve dvoře začíná." (How the Tent Changed into a Camera. The Early Mime Theatre 'Alfred ve dvoře'.) DiN. 1997 May; 6(10): 3. Illus.: Photo. B&W. 2. Lang.: Cze.
Czech Republic: Prague. 1961-1996. Historical studies. ■History of and current trends in the Czech pantomime theatre 'Alfred ve dvoře'.

3743   Rea, Kenneth. "The Cutting Edge." PlPl. 1997 May; 513: 29. Lang.: Eng.
UK-England: London. 1997. Historical studies. ■Performances at the 1997 London International Mime Festival.

Performance/production

3744   Panovová, Olga. "Ctibor Turba na Slovensku (1975-1982) (Transformácia cirkusovej klauniády vo filme a na javisku)." (Ctibor Turba in Slovakia (1975-1982): The Transformation of Circus Buffoonery in the Film and Theatre.) *DivR*. 1997; 8(4): 47-61. Illus.: Photo. B&W. 12. Lang.: Cze.

Czechoslovakia. 1975-1982. Historical studies. ■Creative activity of the Czech mime artist, director and educator Turba in Slovakia.

3745 de Marinis, Marco. "Copeau, Decroux and the Birth of Corporeal Mime." *MimeJ*. 1997; 19: 24-43. Notes. Biblio. Lang.: Eng.

France: Paris. 1920-1992. Historical studies. ■The differences and similarities between work of mime Jacques Copeau and Etienne Decroux, pointing to Decroux as the real father of 'corporeal', or modern, mime.

3746 Leabhart, Thomas. "An Interview with Maximilien Decroux." *MimeJ*. 1997; 19: 44-57. Illus.: Photo. B&W. 2. Lang.: Eng.

France: Paris. 1945-1987. Histories-sources. ■Interview with Etienne Decroux's son Maximilien about his father's influence on his life and career.

Theory/criticism

3747 Barba, Eugenio. "The Hidden Master." *MimeJ*. 1997; 19: 6-13. Lang.: Eng.

France. Denmark. 1966-1997. Histories-sources. ■The influence of the late mime teacher and theorist Etienne Decroux on Barba's theories and approaches to theatre.

3748 Decroux, Etienne. "Decroux on Dance, the Personality, and Categories of Corporeal Mime." *MimeJ*. 1997; 19: 111-114. Illus.: Photo. B&W. 1. Lang.: Eng.

France. 1975. Critical studies. ■Decroux discusses his theories relating to a spectrum of performance disciplines, excerpted from a 1975 lecture.

3749 Sklar, Deidre. "Passing Through the Oblique: The Embodied Thinking of Etienne Decroux." *MimeJ*. 1997; 19: 58-77. Biblio. Notes. Illus.: Photo. B&W. 1. Lang.: Eng.

France. 1997. Critical studies. ■Argues that movement is a conceptual as well as a kinesthetic process, and points to Decroux's idea of the physical expression of thought, that the body be the 'vanguard' of thoughts in motion.

Training

3750 Leabhart, Thomas. "The Man Who Preferred to Stand—Megalomaniac or Genius?" *MimeJ*. 1997; 19: 3-5. Biblio. Lang.: Eng.

France. 1945-1992. Historical studies. ■Introduction to the focus of this volume, mime teacher and theorist Etienne Decroux, and his place in twentieth-century theatre.

3751 Leabhart, Thomas. "Friday Night Pearls of Wisdom." *MimeJ*. 1997; 19: 98-107. Notes. Illus.: Photo. B&W. 1. Lang.: Eng.

France: Paris. 1968-1972. Histories-sources. ■The author's experiences at Etienne Decroux's mime academy L'École du Vieux-Colombier.

3752 Soum, Corinne. "Decroux the Ungraspable: or Different Categories of Acting—Man of Sport, Man of the Drawing Room, Mobile Statuary, Man of Reverie." *MimeJ*. 1997; 19: 14-23. Notes. Illus.: Photo. B&W. 1. Lang.: Eng.

France. UK-England. 1997. Histories-sources. ■Former student of Decroux and co-founder of Théâtre de l'Ange Fou celebrates the vagueness of Decroux's methods, and the inability of academics to codify him.

3753 Wylie, Kathyrn. "The Body Politic of Corporeal Mime: A Modern Redesign of 'Le Corps Civilisé' from Below." *MimeJ*. 1997; 19: 78-97. Biblio. Notes. Illus.: Photo. B&W. 1. Lang.: Eng.

France. 1945-1992. Critical studies. ■Etienne Decroux's desire to train a generation of 'super' mimes in order to retheatricalize a lethargic, and almost dormant, theatre clinging to outmoded forms.

English pantomime

Plays/librettos/scripts

3754 Holland, Peter. "The Play of Eros: Paradoxes of Gender in English Pantomime." *NTQ*. 1997; 13(51): 195-204. Notes. Biblio. Illus.: Photo. B&W. 3. [Revised version of a paper read at the conference on *Eros e commedia sulla scene inglese*, Terza Università, Rome, 1995.] Lang.: Eng.

UK-England. 1870-1995. Historical studies. ■Distinctive typology of crossed-dressed characters, with a Principal Boy, who is a girl, and a Dame, who is a male, is discussed in the light of recent developments in sexual politics and critical approaches to gender.

MIXED ENTERTAINMENT

General

Administration

3755 Crowhurst, Andrew. "Big Men and Big Business: The Transition from 'Caterers' to 'Magnates' in British Music-Hall Entrepreneurship, 1850-1914." *NCT*. 1997 Sum; 25(1): 33-59. Notes. Lang.: Eng.

UK-England: London. 1850-1914. Historical studies. ■Analysis of the shift from the publican-entrepreneur to the professional magnate in the British music hall with comparisons to the fundamental economic changes in the society at large.

Audience

3756 Lancaster, Kurt. "When Spectators Become Performers: Contemporary Performance-Entertainments Meet the Needs of an 'Unsettled' Audience." *JPC*. 1997 Spr; 30(4): 75-88. Notes. Biblio. Lang.: Eng.

USA. 1988-1997. Critical studies. ■Participatory communal relationship between spectator and performer in historical and contemporary theatre: catharsis, community bonding, transformation of spectator to performer examined through movie theme parks, karaoke, and participatory theatre.

Design/technology

3757 "Beautiful Noise." *LD&A*. 1997 Feb.; 27(2): 28-31. Illus.: Photo. Color. 8. Lang.: Eng.

USA. 1996-1997. Technical studies. ■Marilynn Lowey's lighting design for singer Neil Diamond's Tennessee Moon concert tour.

3758 Peck, Marty. "Burning Down the Block." *LD&A*. 1994 Oct.; 24(10): 32-35. Illus.: Photo. Color. B&W. 3. Lang.: Eng.

USA: Milwaukee, WI. 1994. Technical studies. ■Report on the lighting used in recreating the 'Great Milwaukee Fire' of 1892 to celebrate its one-hundredth anniversary.

Institutions

3759 Heijden, Laurens van der. *Dogtroep. Photographs 1991-1996*. Amsterdam: Dogtroep/ITFB; 1997. 45 pp. Illus.: Photo. B&W. Color. 50. Lang.: Dut, Eng.

Netherlands: Amsterdam. 1991-1996. Historical studies. ■Pictorial overview of the street theatre group's work, inspired by the plastic arts.

3760 Coleman, Bud. "The Jewel Box Revue: America's Longest-Running, Touring Drag Show." *THSt*. 1997; 17: 79-92. Illus.: Photo. 4. Lang.: Eng.

USA: Miami, FL. 1939-1975. Historical studies. ■History of the Jewel Box Revue, a theatre devoted to gender impersonation. Based in Miami, the Revue began touring early in its history and toured successively for over thirty years.

3761 Plimpton, George. "I Played the Apollo." *NewY*. 1997 20 Jan.: 55-59. Illus.: Photo. B&W. 1. Lang.: Eng.

USA: New York, NY. 1966-1997. Histories-sources. ■Profile of the Apollo Theatre's amateur nights, including the author's recollection of his own performance there in the 1960s.

Performance spaces

3762 Siemens, Elena. "Theatre Square." *PerfR*. 1997 Sum; 2(2): 92-101. Notes. Illus.: Photo. B&W. 10. Lang.: Eng.

Russia: Moscow. 1996. Histories-sources. ■The author's performance as a walker in her home town of Moscow.

3763 Biley, Scott. "The Tacoma Theatre." *MarqJTHS*. 1997 2nd Qtr; 29(2): 4-17, 30. Notes. Illus.: Photo. Handbill. B&W. Architec. 16. [First Place, 1995, Jeffery Weiss Literary Prize Contest.] Lang.: Eng.

MIXED ENTERTAINMENT: General—Performance spaces

USA: Tacoma, WA. 1888-1963. Historical studies. ■History of the Tacoma Theatre (1890), renamed the Fox Broadway in 1927 and the Music Box in 1930, destroyed by fire in 1963.

3764   del Valle, Cezar. "Grand Prospect Hall." *MarqJTHS*. 1997 2nd Qtr; 29(2): 18-22. Notes. Illus.: Photo. Handbill. B&W. 6. Lang.: Eng.

USA: Brooklyn, NY. 1892-1997. Historical studies. ■History of Prospect Hall.

3765   King, Donald C. "The Boston Bijou, 1836-1943." *MarqJTHS*. 1997 2nd Qtr; 29(2): 1, 23-27. Illus.: Photo. Plan. B&W. 6. Lang.: Eng.

USA: Boston, MA. 1836-1943. Historical studies. ■History of the theatre, named at various times the Lion, the Mechanics Institute, the Melodeon, the Gaiety, the Bijou, the Bijou Opera House, and the Bijou Dream.

3766   Stockinger, Herb. "Prologue: Egyptian Theatres in the United States." *MarqJTHS*. 1997 3rd Qtr; 29(3): 1, 4-5, 24-26. Tables. Illus.: Photo. B&W. 9. Lang.: Eng.

USA. 1899-1988. Historical studies. ■A general introduction to a special issue dealing with Egyptian-style theatres. There is a table listing forty-five Egyptian-style theatres built in the United States.

Performance/production

3767   Granasztói, Péter. "Tömegszórakozás a Városligetben—A Vurstli." (Popular Entertainment in the City Park—The Fun-Fair.) *BudN*. 1997; 6(2/3): 163-190. Notes. Illus.: Photo. B&W. 15. Lang.: Hun.

Hungary: Budapest. 1860-1938. Historical studies. ■A historical survey of various types of spectacles and shows at the fun-fair of Budapest's City Park.

3768   Fagiolo Dell'Arco, Maurizio. *La festa barocca.* (The Baroque Feast.) Rome: De Luca; 1997. 607 pp. (Corpus delle Feste a Roma 1.) Biblio. Pref. Index. Illus.: Dwg. Sketches. Lang.: Ita.

Italy: Rome. 1585-1700. Histories-sources. ■Analysis of 300 feasts, each listed with descriptions, illustrations, and information dating from the period.

3769   Fagiolo, Marcello, ed. *Il Settecento e l'Ottocento.* (The Eighteenth and Nineteenth Centuries.) Rome: De Luca; 1997. 478 pp. (Corpus delle Feste a Roma 2.) Biblio. Illus.: Dwg. Sketches. Lang.: Ita.

Italy: Rome. 1700-1870. Histories-sources. ■Catalogue of an exhibition on the most significant Roman feasts.

3770   Rislund, Staffan. "Teater utan publik." (Theatre Without Any Audience.) *Tningen*. 1997; 21(1): 36-43. Illus.: Photo. Color. Lang.: Swe.

Sweden. 1990. Historical studies. ■Presentation of an interactive, role-playing theatre form in which a group performs a story in reconstructed historical surroundings without an audience. Reference to the medieval theme of *Trenne byar (Three Villages)*.

3771   Davis, Brook. "Let the Children Speak: *The Pageant of Sunshine and Shadow*, A Child Labor Pageant by Constance D'Arcy Mackay." *TheatreS*. 1997; 42: 33-44. Notes. Biblio. Illus.: Sketches. B&W. 2. Lang.: Eng.

USA. 1900-1918. Historical studies. ■Examination of *The Pageant of Sunshine and Shadow* (later titled *The Child Labor Pageant*) to illustrate Mackay's transformation of a pageant from a children's play to anti-child labor propaganda. Choice to use children in the pageant, American pageantry movement, child labor laws and violations, social changes.

3772   Dennett, Andrea Stulman. *Weird and Wonderful: The Dime Museum in America.* New York, NY/London: New York UP; 1997. 200 pp. Pref. Notes. Index. Biblio. Append. Illus.: Photo. Dwg. 26. Lang.: Eng.

USA. 1841-1868. Histories-specific. ■History of the dime museum as it developed from a cabinet of curiosities to an integrated 'entertainment palace' that included theatrical performances, including Barnum's American Museum and Wood's Museum in New York, and the Boston Museum.

3773   Gilbert, Joanne R. "Performing Marginality: Comedy, Identity, and Cultural Critique." *TextPQ*. 1997 Oct.; 17(4): 317-330 . Notes. Biblio. Lang.: Eng.

USA. 1985-1997. Critical studies. ■The potentially subversive use of self-deprecating humor by comedians Phyllis Diller and Roseanne Barr, the construction of themselves and others as the butt of jokes, and aspects of autobiographical performance.

Plays/librettos/scripts

3774   Bach, Rebecca Ann. "Bearbaiting, Dominion, and Colonialism." 19-35 in MacDonald, Joyce Green, ed. *Race, Ethnicity, and Power in the Renaissance.* Madison, NJ: Fairleigh Dickinson UP; 1997. 187 pp. Notes. Index. Lang.: Eng.

England. 1450-1600. Critical studies. ■Examines the links between the popular English sport of bearbaiting and English colonialism.

3775   Hall, Kim F. "'Troubling Doubles': Apes, Africans, and Blackface in *Mr. Moore's Revels*." 120-144 in MacDonald, Joyce Green, ed. *Race, Ethnicity, and Power in the Renaissance.* Madison, NJ: Fairleigh Dickinson UP; 1997. 187 pp. Notes. Index. Illus.: Photo. 2. Lang.: Eng.

England. 1636. Critical studies. ■Examines race and gender in *Mr. Moore's Revels*, an 'entertainment' that marks a transition from anti-masque to the masque.

Relation to other fields

3776   "Architecture: Sports Venues—Introduction." *TCI*. 1997 May; 31(5): 31-32. Illus.: Photo. 1. Lang.: Eng.

USA. 1996-1997. Historical studies. ■Introductory essay on the annual architecture issue. Theme of this year's issue is sports architecture.

3777   Miller, Michele Lynne. *The Charms of Exposed Flesh: Reginald Marsh and the Burlesque Theater.* Philadelphia, PA: Univ. of Pennsylvania; 1997. 264 pp. [Ph.D. Dissertation, Univ. Microfilms Order No. AAC 9818060.] Lang.: Eng.

USA. 1920-1950. Historical studies. ■Examination and interpretation of paintings and prints of the burlesque theatre produced by Reginald Marsh (1898-1954) during the 1920s, 1930s, and early 1940s. Argues that these paintings not only reveal the history of burlesque but serve as cultural artifacts, revealing social attitudes towards gender, sexuality, and class.

Cabaret

Institutions

3778   Ščul'c, S.S. *'Brodjacaja sobaka'.* (Street Dog.) St. Petersburg: OO Almaz; 1997. 190 pp. Lang.: Rus.

Russia: St. Petersburg. 1912-1915. Histories-specific. ■Profile of Brodjacaja sobaka, a literary-artistic cabaret founded by V.K. Pronyn and frequented by Mejerchol'd, among others.

Performance/production

3779   Eriksson, Torbjörn. "Ute Lemper." *MuD*. 1997; 19(2): 8-9. Illus.: Photo. B&W. Lang.: Swe.

Germany. 1986. Biographical studies. ■A presentation of Ute Lemper during a recording session, and her views on the German cabarets of the twenties and thirties.

3780   Buckley, Michael. "Put Down the Knitting..." *ShowM*. 1997/98 Win; 13(4): 39-42, 69. Illus.: Photo. Dwg. B&W. 11. Lang.: Eng.

USA. 1975-1997. Historical studies. ■The careers of successful cabaret performers Steve Ross, Marcia Lewis, Cameron Silver, Tom Andersen, Charles Cermele, Lee Lessack, Marilyn Volpe, and Amanda McBroom. Focus on how to put together a cabaret act, the choice of material, and the various venues.

Carnival

Basic theatrical documents

3781   Jenkin, Len; Arnone, John. "*Doctor Divine Presents: Baby Zoe Midway Spectacular and Cabinet of Curiosities*." *ThM*. 1993; 24(3): 49-60. Illus.: Dwg. B&W. 10. Lang.: Eng.

USA. 1993. ■Scenario developed by Jenkin and Arnone for an interactive traveling carnival for people of all ages.

MIXED ENTERTAINMENT: Carnival

Performance/production

3782 Castelli, Franco, ed.; Grimaldi, Piercarlo, ed. *Maschere e corpi. Tempi e luoghi del Carnevale.* (Masks and Bodies: Time and Place in Carnival.) Rome: Metelmi; 1997. 213 pp. (Gli Argonauti 30.) Notes. Lang.: Ita.

Europe. Critical studies. ■Collection of essays on carnival-related forms and performances.

3783 *Il Carnevale napoletano. Storia, maschere e rituali dal XVI al XIC secolo.* (Neapolitan Carnival: History, Masks, and Rituals from the Sixteenth to the Nineteenth Centuries.) Rome: Newton & Compton; 1997. 62 pp. (Tascabili Economici Newton: Napoli Tascabile 53.) Lang.: Ita.

Italy: Naples. 1500-1800. Histories-specific. ■History of Neapolitan carnival, including the balls and feasts of the aristocracy, the guild parades, and the popular celebrations of the common people.

Circus

Institutions

3784 *Sankt-Peterburgskij gosudarstvĕnnyj cirk. 120 let: 1877-1997 g. Prospekt.* (The St. Petersburg Circus: One Hundred Twenty Years, 1877-1997: Prospect.) St. Petersburg: 1997. 34 pp. Lang.: Rus.

Russia: St. Petersburg. 1877-1997. Histories-specific. ■History of the circus, Sankt-Peterburgskij gosudarstvĕnnyj cirk.

3785 Lindström, Dick. "Barnen i centrum på Norsholms Ungdomscirkus." (Children Are Central at Norsholm Youth Circus.) *ProScen.* 1997; 21(3): 16-17. Illus.: Photo. B&W. Lang.: Swe.

Sweden: Norsholm. 1979. Technical studies. ■A presentation of the Norsholms Ungdomscirkus, with references to the technology of a touring circus and their plans for the future.

Reference materials

3786 Kartaškin, A.S. *Fokusy. Zanimatel'naja enciklopedija.* (Tricks: Amusing Encyclopedia.) Moscow: Izdatel'skij dom 'Iskatel'; 1997. 544 pp. Lang.: Rus.

Russia. 1997. ■Encyclopedia of original circus genres.

Theory/criticism

3787 Fensham, Rachel. "'Making-real' the Body: A Subordinate Reading of the Female Performer in Nineteenth-Century Australian Circus." *ADS.* 1997 Apr.; 30: 3-16. Notes. Illus.: Photo. B&W. 1. Lang.: Eng.

Australia. 1801-1900. Historical studies. ■Analyzes the corporeal struggles of the female body with the Australian circus as another mode of constructing a performance history. Reclaiming the subordinate position to tell a new and gendered account of the nineteenth-century circus performer.

Commedia dell'arte

Audience

3788 Henke, Robert. "Toward Reconstructing the Audiences of the *Commedia dell'Arte*." *ET.* 1997; 15(2): 207-220. Notes. Biblio. Illus.: Dwg. B&W. 1. Lang.: Eng.

Italy. 1565-1620. Historical studies. ■Profile of *commedia* audiences, divided into 'apologists' and 'antitheatricalists'.

Basic theatrical documents

3789 Gambelli, Delia. *Arlecchino a Parigi. Lo scenario di Domenico Biancolelli.* (Arlequin in Paris: The Scenario of Domenico Biancolelli.) Rome: Bulzoni; 1997. 874 pp. Pref. Biblio. Index. Illus.: Dwg. [2 vol.] Lang.: Ita.

France: Paris. 1662-1668. ■First publication of the scenarios by Biancolelli, the Arlequin of the Comédiens du Roi de la troupe Italienne. The original Italian manuscript was lost: this reconstruction is based on a contemporary French translation.

Performance spaces

3790 Castagno, Paul C. "The Mannerist Space in Early *Commedia dell'Arte* Iconography." 109-123 in Castagno, Paul C. *Theat-*

rical Spaces and Dramatic Places: The Reemergence of the Theatre Building in the Renaissance. Tuscaloosa, AL: Univ of Alabama P; 1996. 151 pp. (Southeastern Theatre Conference Theatre Symposium 4.) Biblio. Illus.: Photo. 6. Lang.: Eng.

Italy. 1520-1620. Historical studies. ■Definition of the mannerist style of theatrical performance space in early *commedia* and its distinction from other Renaissance iconographic styles.

Performance/production

3791 Berthold, Margot. "Hefe im Sauerteig des Theaters." (The Yeast in the Sourdough of Theatre.) *S&B.* 1997; 1: 4-11. Illus.: Dwg. Photo. B&W. 9. Lang.: Ger.

Italy. 1520-1997. Histories-general. ■Describes the history and development of *commedia dell'arte* and the family of harlequins that give new impulses and ideas to amateur theatre.

3792 Henke, Robert. "The Italian Mountebank and the *Commedia dell'Arte*." *ThS.* 1997 Nov.; 38(2): 1-30. Append. Illus.: Photo. 1. Lang.: Eng.

Italy. 1550-1620. Historical studies. ■Uses civic documents to articulate performance practices of the mountebank in Italian society and their relations to *commedia*.

3793 Tylus, Jane. "Women at the Windows: *Commedia dell'Arte* and Theatrical Practice in Early Modern Italy." *TJ.* 1997 Oct.; 49(3): 323-342. Notes. Lang.: Eng.

Italy. 1545-1650. Historical studies. ■The impact of the theatrical emergence, through *commedia*, of women in early modern Italy. Argues that this privileged and relatively secure site allowed women to exert authority over social as well as theatrical space, and thus earn the right to participate in social drama.

3794 Bowles, Norma. "From Gags to Riches: The Uses and Abuses of Commedia." *WES.* 1997 Win; 9(1): 43-46. Illus.: Photo. 2. Lang.: Eng.

Spain: Barcelona. 1996. Historical studies. ■On the *commedia* tradition in contemporary Spain. Author examines the recent work of four companies: Vol Ras, Tricicle, Melody Sisters, and Narren Treppe, all touring companies.

Court entertainment

Performance/production

3795 Parry, Graham. "Entertainments at Court." 195-212 in Cox, John D., ed.; Kastan, David Scott, ed. *A New History of Early English Drama.* New York, NY: Columbia UP; 1997. 565 pp. Notes. Biblio. Index. Lang.: Eng.

England. 1490-1660. Historical studies. ■Argues that court entertainments of early Renaissance England, from the reign of Elizabeth I to the early Restoration, changed in form to reflect the political interests of the current ruler.

3796 Piazza, Gary L. *A Conductor's Performance Guide to the Stuart Masque.* Tallahassee, FL: Florida State Univ; 1997. 350 pp. [Ph.D. Dissertation, Univ. Microfilms Order No. AAC 9812340.] Lang.: Eng.

England. 1500-1640. Instructional materials. ■Guide includes a historical perspective of the masque form, the role of dance in the masque, stage and costuming for the masque, instrumental accompaniment, and vocal considerations.

3797 Felibien, André; Ausoni, Alberto, ed. *Le feste di Versailles.* (The Feasts of Versailles.) Rome: Salerno; 1997. 115 pp. Pref. Notes. Gloss. Index. Illus.: Pntg. 11. Lang.: Ita.

France: Versailles. 1668. Historical studies. ■Chronicle of a 'great royal entertainment' at Versailles, including descriptions of a comedy, a ball, and fireworks.

3798 Ortolani, Benito. "To Court and Shrine from the World: *Gigaku* and *Bugaku*." 38-42 in Leiter, Samuel L., ed. *Japanese Theater in the World.* New York, NY: The Japan Society; 1997. 196 pp. Pref. Notes. Illus.: Photo. B&W. Color. 4. Lang.: Eng.

Japan. 646-1997. Historical studies. ■Examination of two Japanese ceremonial theatrical forms developed for performance in the imperial court and within shrines: *gigaku* which disappeared after the fourteenth century, and *bugaku* which is still performed today.

Pageants/parades

Performance/production

3799 Higgins, Anne. "Streets and Markets." 77-92 in Cox, John D., ed.; Kastan, David Scott, ed. *A New History of Early English Drama.* New York, NY: Columbia UP; 1997. 565 pp. Notes. Biblio. Index. Illus.: Maps. 1. Lang.: Eng.
England: York. 1456-1501. Critical studies. ■Analysis of processional theatre on the street and in the markets of York. Author examines how power was negotiated between civic and ecclesiastical groups for dominance in the town.

3800 Kipling, Gordon. "Wonderfull Spectacles: Theater and Civic Culture." 153-172 in Cox, John D., ed.; Kastan, David Scott, ed. *A New History of Early English Drama.* New York, NY: Columbia UP; 1997. 565 pp. Notes. Biblio. Index. Lang.: Eng.
England. 1392-1599. Historical studies. ■Civic pageants and processionals and their development in England, with attention to ritual function, liturgical imagery, symbolism, and dramatic form.

3801 Weissengruber, Erik Paul. "The Corpus Christi Procession in Medieval York: A Symbolic Struggle in Public Space." *ThS.* 1997 May; 38(1): 117-138. Lang.: Eng.
England. 1419-1490. Historical studies. ■Explores a neglected aspect of the *Corpus Christi* celebrations, a procession of torches honoring the sacrament of the Eucharist as a representation of social hierarchy.

3802 Staccioli, Paola. *Feste romane. Quattro secoli di festeggiamenti religiosi e civili dal Rinascimento all'Italia unita.* (Roman Feasts: Four Centuries of Religious and Civic Festivities from the Renaissance to the Unification of Italy.) Rome: Newton & Compton; 1997. 63 pp. (Tascabili Economici Newton: Roma Tascabile 80.) Lang.: Ita.
Italy: Rome. 1500-1860. Histories-specific. ■Includes discussion of Roman Carnival, Holy Week rituals, Roman May, and the night of San Giovanni, among others.

3803 Webster, Susan Verdi. "The Descent from the Cross in Sixteenth-Century New Spain." *EDAM.* 1997 Spr; 19(2): 69-85. Illus.: Photo. B&W. 4. Lang.: Eng.
Mexico. 1600-1997. Historical studies. ■Public enactments of the Descent from the Cross in Mexico date from the sixteenth century. The presentations are in pantomime, but with full costumes and gestures. Evidence is derived from documentary sources and works of art in Mexican churches.

3804 Maingard, Jacqueline. "Imag(in)ing the South African Nation: Representations of Identity in the Rugby World Cup 1995." *TJ.* 1997 Mar.; 49(1): 15-28. Notes. Illus.: Photo. 3. Lang.: Eng.
South Africa, Republic of. 1910-1995. Historical studies. ■Critical analysis of the opening and closing ceremonies of the 1995 Rugby World Cup, hosted by South Africa. Author argues that this performative event shows the continuity of motifs and format between a 'postapartheid' celebration of the 'rainbow nation' and the pageants celebrating Union (1910).

3805 Merrington, Peter. "Masques, Monuments, and Masons: The 1910 Pageant of the Union of South Africa." *TJ.* 1997 Mar.; 49 (1): 1-14. Notes. Illus.: Photo. 1. Lang.: Eng.
South Africa, Republic of. 1910. Historical studies. ■Theoretical analysis of the South African Pageant of Union in 1910, and the local drama of conflict and reconciliation of the 'white races,' Boer and Briton. Author sets this event against the backdrop of Masonic ritual and worldwide British imperial iconography.

3806 McNamara, Brooks. *Day of Jubilee: The Great Age of Public Celebrations in New York, 1788-1909.* New Brunswick, NJ/London: Rutgers UP; 1997. 209 pp. Notes. Index. Biblio. Illus.: Photo. 88. Lang.: Eng.
USA: New York, NY. 1788-1909. Critical studies. ■Analysis of parades, banquets, balls, and workers' marches.

3807 Roarty, Robert C. "Fun To Be Free: Intervention Takes the Stage." *JADT.* 1997 Win; 9(1): 36-53. Notes. Lang.: Eng.
USA: New York, NY. 1941. Historical studies. ■The historical/political war pageant 'Fun To Be Free,' staged in Madison Square Garden. Author delineates how typical theatrical constructions operated within the context of political rallies, and how the propagandistic nature of the rally reveals differences between theatrical representation and political reality. The core of the pageant was scripted by Ben Hecht and Charles MacArthur.

3808 Sponsler, Claire. "Brooklyn's Giglio and the Negotiation of Ethnicity." *ET.* 1997; 16(2): 137-150. Notes. Biblio. Illus.: Photo. B&W. 2. Lang.: Eng.
USA: Brooklyn, NY. 1880-1997. Historical studies. ■The history and social aspects of the Giglio, an annual ethnic religious street celebration.

3809 Wade, Leslie A. "New Orleans' Theatre of the Dead." *JDTC.* 1997 Fall; 12(1): 175-183. Lang.: Eng.
USA: New Orleans, LA. 1867-1996. Critical studies. ■A site-specific reading of a New Orleans Day of the Dead ritual (the celebration of All Saints' Day at St. Roch's Cemetery) and its motifs of memory, lineage, and intercession.

Relation to other fields

3810 Noyes, Dorothy. "Reciprocal Tourism and the Fear of the Floating Local: Networkers and Integristes in a Catalan Provincial Town." *PerfR.* 1997 Sum; 2(2): 54-63. Notes. Illus.: Photo. B&W. 3. Lang.: Eng.
Spain-Catalonia. 1950-1997. Critical studies. ■The negotiation of identity and cultural exchange in collective performances at Catalan festivals, particularly the Patum of Berga, and the participants' performative strategies for dealing with tourists. Examines the development of reciprocal tourism between Spain and other nations, fostered through workers' and political networks.

3811 Kirshenblatt-Gimblett, Barbara; Lemley, Mary, photo. "Afterlives." *PerfR.* 1997 Spr; 2(1): 1-9. Notes. Illus.: Photo. B&W. 27. [A reworked transcript of the keynote address given at the Performance, Tourism and Identity Conference, Wales, September 1996.] Lang.: Eng.
UK-Wales. 1994-1996. Critical studies. ■The performance of heritage tourism in Wales today in the light of theories of space, place and identity. Concludes that heritage tourism is implicated in the construction of that which it seeks to represent.

Research/historiography

3812 Guarino, Raimondo. "Storiografia umanistica e spettacolo del Rinascimento." (Humanist Historiography and Renaissance Theatre.) *TeatroS.* 1997; 12(19): 271-291. Notes. Lang.: Ita.
Italy. 1400-1499. Historical studies. ■Focuses on contemporary descriptions of pageants in fifteenth-century Naples, Reggio Emilia, and Venice to argue that humanist historiography was an agent for change in the perception of public life and spectacle in the Italian Renaissance.

Performance art

Basic theatrical documents

3813 Callaghan, Stacey. "*still raw.*" *ADS.* 1997 Oct.; 31: 176-199. Notes. Lang.: Eng.
Australia. 1994. ■Text of the performance piece with an introduction by the author.

3814 Dempsey, Shawna; Millan, Lorri. "*Object/Subject of Desire.*" *CTR.* 1997 Fall; 92: 17-18. Illus.: Photo. B&W. 2. Lang.: Eng.
Canada. 1987. ■Text of monologue, with introduction describing performance history.

Performance/production

3815 Hamilton, Margaret. "Open City: A Field of Linguistic Possibilities." *ADS.* 1997 Apr.; 30: 43-56. Notes. Illus.: Photo. B&W. 1. Lang.: Eng.
Australia: Sydney. 1987-1997. Historical studies. ■Language and the performance pieces of Open City. Examines founder Keith Gallasch and

CLASSED ENTRIES

MIXED ENTERTAINMENT: Performance art—Performance/production

Virginia Baxter's collaborations on *Photoplay, Tokyo Two, Sense* and *Sum of the Sudden.*

3816 Hall, Lynda. "Bodies in Sight: Shawna Demsey (Re) Configures Desire." *CTR.* 1997 Fall; 92: 10-16. Notes. Biblio. Illus.: Photo. B&W. 7. Lang.: Eng.
Canada. 1992-1997. Critical studies. ■Desire treated as spectacle and subject of social critique in Shawna Dempsey's solo performances.

3817 Erkkilä, Helena. "Taide, teatterillisuus ja performanssi." (Art, Theatricality, and Performance.) *Teat.* 1997; 52(7) : 41-43. Illus.: Photo. B&W. 1. Lang.: Fin.
Finland. 1997. Historical studies. ■Discusses present state of performance art and compares it to the relationship between theatre and performance art in the 1980s.

3818 Dreyblatt, Arnold. "The Memory Work." *PerfR.* 1997 Fall; 2(3): 91-96. Biblio. Illus.: Photo. B&W. 3. Lang.: Eng.
Germany. 1997. Histories-sources. ■American expatriate performance and video installation artist on the influence of memory on his art and that of others.

3819 Mesch, Ulrike Claudia. *Problems of Remembrance in Post-War German Performance Art.* Chicago, IL: Univ. of Chicago; 1997. 392 pp. [Ph.D. Dissertation, Univ. Microfilms Order No. AAC 9800624.] Lang.: Eng.
Germany. 1960-1987. Historical studies. ■Examination of the work of performance artists Wolf Vostell and Joseph Beuys with attention to the ways in which each artist deployed performance art to explore the dynamics of individual and collective memory.

3820 Winderlich, Kirsten; Brandes, Kerstin, transl.; Amendinger, Jürgen, transl. "Who is Lili Fischer?" *PerfR.* 1997 Fall ; 2(3): 45-49. Notes. Biblio. Illus.: Photo. B&W. 3. Lang.: Eng.
Germany. 1989-1997. Critical studies. ■The methodologies of performance artist Lili Fischer: her presentation of the self in performance and her transformation of the meanings of ordinary acts and objects in her performance work, which focuses on utilitarian actions such as cleaning and scrubbing.

3821 Gómez-Peña, Guillermo. "From Chiapas to Wales." *PerfR.* 1997 Sum; 2(2): 64-75. Notes. Illus.: Photo. B&W. 4. Lang.: Eng.
Mexico. UK-Wales. 1996. Histories-sources. ■Excerpt from the forthcoming *Two Chicanos on the Road* in which Gómez-Peña describes his travels with performance artist Roberto Sifuentes in Chiapas and in Wales for the conference on performance, tourism, and identity.

3822 Gómez-Peña, Guillermo. "Mexican Beasts and Living Santos." *TDR.* 1997 Spr; 41(1): 135-146. Notes. Biblio. Illus.: Photo. B&W. 9. Lang.: Eng.
Mexico. 1994-1997. Histories-sources. ■Selection of 'confessions' obtained during the performance/installation piece *The Temple of Confessions*, both written and recorded. Piece combined format of pseudo-ethnographic diorama with that of religious dioramas. Created by Roberto Sifuentes and author.

3823 Phillips, Andrea. "'A Path is Always Between Two Points'." *PerfR.* 1997 Fall; 2(3): 9-16. Notes. Biblio. Illus.: Photo. B&W. 4. Lang.: Eng.
UK-England: London. Germany: Kassel. 1997. Critical studies. ■Space, place, and travel in performance art and installations by Francis Alÿs, Gordana Stanisic, Danielle Vallet Kleiner and Penny Yassour, who use walking and traveling both metaphorically and actually to communicate progress.

3824 Kirshenblatt-Gimblett, Barbara. "Alicia Rios: Tailor of the Body's Interior." *TDR.* 1997 Sum; 41(2): 90-110. Notes. Illus.: Photo. B&W. Detail. Grd.Plan. 14. Lang.: Eng.
UK-Wales. 1994-1997. Histories-sources. ■Interview with performance artist Rios: her use of food in performance, history as a restaurateur, her production of *A Temperate Meal* during conference titled 'Points of Contact: Performance, Food, and Cookery'. Introduction describes performance in detail, architectural plans for performance space.

3825 "The Real Charles Atlas: An Interview." *PerAJ.* 1997 Sep.; 19(3): 21-33. Illus.: Photo. B&W. 5. [Number 57.] Lang.: Eng.
USA: New York, NY. 1990-1997. Histories-sources. ■Interview with video and performance artist Charles Atlas regarding his work.

3826 Bergengren, Charles. "Febrile Fiber Phantoms: Ken Jacobs at the C.I.A." *TDR.* 1997 Spr; 41(1): 72-85. Notes. Biblio. Illus.: Photo. B&W. 7. Lang.: Eng.
USA: Cleveland, OH. 1945-1995. Histories-sources. ■Description of author's viewing of Ken and Flo Jacobs' performance piece *Febrile Fiber Phantoms*. Visual images, technical effects, music, three-dimensional shadow techniques which artist refers to as 'Apparitions Theatre'.

3827 Fischer-Lichte, Erika. "Performance Art and Performative Culture: Theatre as Cultural Model." *ThR.* 1997; 22(1 Supplement): 22-37. Notes. Lang.: Eng.
USA. Austria. 1952-1975. Critical studies. ■Theatre, art and performative culture, with analysis of performance art events: Cage's 1952 'untitled event', Nitsch's *Orgy Mystery Theatre*, Beuys's *Coyote: I Like America and America Likes Me* and Abramović's *Lips of Thomas*.

3828 Gómez-Peña, Guillermo. "Guillermo Gómez-Peña." *MimeJ.* 1991/92; 15: 42-73. Illus.: Photo. B&W. 11. Lang.: Eng.
USA: Los Angeles, CA. 1979-1989. Histories-sources. ■Excerpts from Gómez-Peña's performance diary chronicling his growth as an artist.

3829 Graver, David. "The Actor's Bodies." *TextPQ.* 1997 July; 17(3): 221-235. Notes. Biblio. Lang.: Eng.
USA. 1997. Critical studies. ■Argues that the actor on stage establishes seven ontologically distinct bodies. Uses Ron Vawter's *Roy Cohn/Jack Smith*, Robbie McCauley's *Sally's Rape*, Holly Hughes's *World Without End* as examples.

3830 Johansson, Ola. "Brother Theodore—off off Broadways okända legend." (Brother Theodore—the Unknown Legend of Off-Off Broadway.) *Entré.* 1997; 24(4): 43-44. Illus.: Photo. B&W. Lang.: Swe.
USA: New York, NY. 1980-1997. Historical studies. ■A report about an avant-garde performance by Brother Theodore.

3831 Kaprow, Allan. "Just Doing." *TDR.* 1997 Fall; 41(3): 101-106. Notes. Illus.: Dwg. B&W. 4. Lang.: Eng.
USA. 1980-1996. Histories-sources. ■Keynote address for 'Performance, Art, Culture, and Pedagogy' held at Pennsylvania State University. Author's experiences in creating Happenings, and perceptions on experimental art. Includes quotes from author's past writings.

3832 MacCannell, Dean. "Virtual Reality's Place." *PerfR.* 1997 Sum; 2(2): 10-21. Notes. Illus.: Photo. B&W. 1. Lang.: Eng.
USA. 1993-1996. Critical studies. ■The development of virtual travel, in which participants explore film-world locations, and instances of performance art and installation that seek to raise the viewer's critical awareness of Virtual Reality, conluding that Virtual Reality is the death of entertainment.

3833 McKenzie, Jon. "Laurie Anderson for Dummies." *TDR.* 1997 Sum; 41(2): 30-50. Notes. Biblio. Illus.: Photo. B&W. 7. Lang.: Eng.
USA. 1960-1997. Historical studies. ■Guide to performance artist Anderson's current work. Focusing on links between various work, article is designed as a 'hyperguide', may be used while navigating Anderson's performance, listening to her CD's, reading her books, playing her CD-ROM or visiting her homepage.

3834 Minwalla, Framji. "Performing Richard Elovich." *ThM.* 1993; 24(2): 47-52. Illus.: Photo. B&W. 2. Lang.: Eng.
USA. 1993. Histories-sources. ■Profile of solo artist Richard Elovich: his work, his politics, his influences.

3835 O'Dell, Kathy. "Fluxux Feminus." *TDR.* 1997 Spr; 41(1): 43-60. Notes. Biblio. Illus.: Photo. B&W. 14. Lang.: Eng.
USA. 1960-1996. Critical studies. ■Influences on women artists whose activities came to be known as 'Fluxus'. Describes work and artists featured at Fluxus retrospective, focus on exclusionary practices of Fluxus artists, and the relationship in the work between body and text.

3836 Ryan, Katy. "A Body's Mind Experience in Tim Miller's Workshop." *TTop.* 1997 Sep.; 7(2): 205-207. Lang.: Eng.
USA. 1995-1996. Histories-sources. ■Author's experience in performance artist Tim Miller's workshop at the Performance Art, Culture and Pedagogy Symposium at Pennsylvania State University.

MIXED ENTERTAINMENT: Performance art—Performance/production

3837 Schneider, Rebecca. *The Explicit Body in Performance.* New York, NY/London: Routledge; 1997. 256 pp. Index. Biblio. Notes. Illus.: Photo. 10. Lang.: Eng.

USA. Europe. 1960-1995. Critical studies. ■Controversy surrounding the use of the female body in performance art. Examines the work of Karen Finley, Spiderwoman Theater, Carolee Schneemann, and Annie Sprinkle.

3838 Shank, Theodore. "Tim Miller." *MimeJ.* 1991/92; 15: 122-142. Illus.: Photo. B&W. 10. Lang.: Eng.

USA: Los Angeles, CA. 1991. Histories-sources. ■Interview with solo artist Miller concerning his work and career.

3839 Shank, Theodore. "John Fleck." *MimeJ.* 1991/1992; 15: 28-41. Illus.: Photo. B&W. 7. Lang.: Eng.

USA: Los Angeles, CA. 1991. Histories-sources. ■Solo artist Fleck discusses his work, his fears and what keeps him in Los Angeles.

3840 Shank, Theodore. "John Malpede." *MimeJ.* 1991/92; 15: 94-120. Illus.: Photo. B&W. 15. Lang.: Eng.

USA: Los Angeles, CA, New York, NY. 1972-1991. Histories-sources. ■Interview with John Malpede regarding his career working in New York and Los Angeles. Discusses his group the Los Angeles Poverty Department, the nation's first group of homeless performers.

3841 Shank, Theodore. "Jan Munroe." *MimeJ.* 1991/92; 15: 144-158. Illus.: Photo. B&W. 9. Lang.: Eng.

USA: Los Angeles, CA. 1991. Histories-sources. ■Interview with movement and performance artist Munroe regarding his life and career.

3842 Shank, Theodore. "Rachel Rosenthal." *MimeJ.* 1991/92; 15: 176-200. Illus.: Photo. B&W. 1. Lang.: Eng.

USA: Los Angeles, CA. 1926-1991. Histories-sources. ■Interview with Rosenthal, a teacher of dance and acting, about her work as a performance artist.

3843 Shank, Theodore. "Kedric Wolfe." *MimeJ.* 1991/92; 15: 202-229. Illus.: Photo. B&W. 16. Lang.: Eng.

USA: Los Angeles, CA. 1983-1991. Histories-sources. ■Interview with writer/actor Wolfe regarding his career as a performance artist.

3844 Takemoto, Tina. "Performativity and Difference: The Politics of Illness and Collaboration." *JAML.* 1997 Spr; 27(1): 7-22 . Notes. Illus.: Photo. B&W. 8. Lang.: Eng.

USA. 1991-1997. Critical studies. ■Collaboration between the author and performer Angela Ellsworth on *Her/She Senses Imag(in)ed Malady* as a response to Ellsworth's illness and its impact on their lives. History of their collaborative relationship, past productions.

3845 Wheeler, Britta B. "The Performance of Distance and the Art of Catharsis: Performance Art, Artists, and Audience Response." *JAML.* 1997 Spr; 27(1): 37-49. Notes. Biblio. Lang.: Eng.

USA. 1977-1997. Critical studies. ■The expression of emotion by performance artists and its reception by audiences.

3846 Wilcox, Dean. "Karen Finley's *Hymen*." *ThR.* 1997; 22(1): 31-37. Notes. Lang.: Eng.

USA. 1988-1990. Critical studies. ■Performance analysis of excerpt from Finley's *The Constant State of Desire* contained in the film *Mondo New York.*

3847 Wilcox, Dean. "A Complex Tapestry of Text and Imagery: Karen Finley, *The American Chestnut*, Cornell University, May 10, 1996." *JDTC.* 1997 Fall; 12(1): 143-148. Illus.: Photo. 1. Lang.: Eng.

USA. 1997. Critical studies. ■Critical performance review of Karen Finley's newest work *The American Chestnut*, in an early performance at Cornell University.

3848 Wolford, Lisa. "Oppositional Performance/Critical Pedagogy: A Report from the Penn State Symposium." *TTop.* 1997 Sep.; 7 (2): 187-203. Illus.: Photo. 1. Lang.: Eng.

USA. 1995-1996. Historical studies. ■Report on the Performance Art, Culture and Pedagogy Symposium held at Pennsylvania State University in 1996. The Symposium gave opportunities for students and participants to engage with featured artists in various forms of practical work.

Plays/librettos/scripts

3849 Gómez-Peña, Guillermo. *The New World Border: Prophecies, Poems and Loqueras for the End of the Century.* San Francisco, CA: City Lights; 1996. 258 pp. Lang.: Eng.

USA. 1985-1995. Critical studies. ■Collection of writings of performance artist Guillermo Gómez-Peña on the nature of intercultural collaboration.

Relation to other fields

3850 MacDonald, Claire. "Stepping into the Light." *PerfR.* 1997 Fall; 2(3): 75-84. Notes. Biblio. Illus.: Photo. B&W. 2. Lang.: Eng.

UK-England. 1980-1997. Critical studies. ■The relationship of space to feminist performance art and politics. Discusses political protests, including recent road protests and the feminist protest at the Greenham Common missile base, as performance, and relates political space to the ways space is used within the work of artists, focusing on the work of Rose Garrard which is collected in her publication *Archiving My Own History.*

Research/historiography

3851 Pearson, Mike; Shanks, Michael. "Performing a Visit: Archaeologies of the Contemporary Past." *PerfR.* 1997 Sum; 2(2): 41-53. Notes. Illus.: Photo. B&W. 15. Lang.: Eng.

UK-Wales. 1997. Critical studies. ■Proposes an integration of approaches to place which combines archaeology and performance, expanding conventions of travel writing with performance analysis.

Theory/criticism

3852 Cronn-Mills, Kristin Jean. *Performance and Problematization in Rhetorical Culture: The Example of Laurie Anderson.* Ames, IA: Iowa State Univ; 1997. 222 pp. [Ph.D. Dissertation, Univ. Microfilms Order No. AAC 9814634.] Lang.: Eng.

USA. 1990-1995. Critical studies. ■Articulates a theory of performance incorporating performance studies, rhetoric, narrative, and visual theory into the language theories of Foucault and applies it to performance artist Laurie Anderson's film piece *Home of the Brave.*

3853 O'Dell, Kathy. "Displacing the Haptic: Performance Art, the Photographic Document, and the 1970s." *PerfR.* 1997 Spr; 2 (1): 73-81. Notes. Biblio. Illus.: Photo. B&W. 4. Lang.: Eng.

USA. Europe. 1970-1979. Historical studies. ■Traces the history and definition of the term Performance art to the early 1970s and the practices to which it refers in earlier 20th century art, as well as the role of photographic documentation. Details the work of two artists, Vito Acconci and Gina Pane, drawing on psychoanalytic theory.

Variety acts

Design/technology

3854 Moen, Debi. "Phantom of the Mega-Musical." *LD&A.* 1996 June; 26(6): 36-39. Illus.: Photo. Color. 7. Lang.: Eng.

USA: Las Vegas, NV. 1996. Technical studies. ■Technical elements of the production *EFX!* at the MGM Grand Hotel. Lighting and effects designed by Natasha Katz and the director is Scott Faris.

Performance/production

3855 Gardner, David. "Variety." 121-223 in Plant, Richard, ed.; Saddlemyer, Ann, ed. *Later Stages: Essays in Ontario Theatre from the First World War to the 1970s.* Toronto, ON: Univ of Toronto P; 1997. 496 pp. (The Ontario Historical Studies Series.) Index. Notes. Biblio. Illus.: Photo. 20. Lang.: Eng.

Canada. 1914-1979. Historical studies. ■Theatrical offerings in Ontario: circus, medicine shows, minstrel shows, vaudeville, burlesque, cabaret, musical comedy, and revues.

3856 Ruf, Elizabeth. "¡Qué linda es Cuba!: Issues of Gender, Color, and Nationalism in Cuba's Tropicana Nightclub Performance." *TDR.* 1997 Spr; 41(1): 86-105. Notes. Biblio. Illus.: Photo. B&W. 7. Lang.: Eng.

Cuba: Havana. 1959-1997. Critical studies. ■History of the Tropicana Nightclub, the fascination with the *mulata* in Cuban culture, racial and gender stereotypes in performance spectacles that highlight *mulata*

MIXED ENTERTAINMENT: Variety acts—Performance/production

showgirls, and their role in the country's tourism, origins of musical revue in Cuba.

3857 Holloway, Myles. "Music Hall in Johannesburg: 1886-1896." *SATJ.* 1997 May/Sep.; 11(1/2): 15-53. Notes. Biblio. Lang.: Eng.

South Africa, Republic of: Johannesburg. 1886-1896. Historical studies. ■Evolution of music hall in Johannesburg and its significance as a social institution in the wider spheres of government and society.

3858 Lieberfeld, Daniel. "Pieter-Dirk Uys: Crossing Apartheid Lines." *TDR.* 1997 Spr; 41(1): 61-71. Notes. Illus.: Photo. B&W. 7. Lang.: Eng.

South Africa, Republic of. 1945-1994. Histories-sources. ■Interview with political satirist Uys: his use of cross-dressing to create satirical characters for television, skits and revues, his approach to political theatre and his true life associations with political figures and their response to his work.

3859 Söderberg, Olle. "Skrattrevyn i Brevens Bruk." (The Revue of Laughter at Brevens Bruk.) *ProScen.* 1997; 21(3): 15. Illus.: Photo. B&W. Lang.: Swe.

Sweden: Brevens Bruk. 1993. Historical studies. ■A presentation of how *Skrattrevyn i Brevens Bruk (The Brevens Bruk Revue)* was produced at Folkets Hus with Lon Satton from London as star, with reference to the simple but effective technology.

3860 Tanitch, Robert. "David Strassman." *PlPl.* 1997 May; 513: 26. Lang.: Eng.

UK-England: London. 1997. Historical studies. ■Description of David Strassman's ventriloquism act at the Apollo Theatre.

3861 Tyndall, C. Patrick. "Blacks in Minstrelsy: The Grand Paradox." *BlackM.* 1997 June/July; 12(4): 7-8, 15. Illus.: Photo. B&W. 1. Lang.: Eng.

USA. 1821-1915. Historical studies. ■The paradoxical entry of African-American performers into the genre of blackface minstrelsy, an extremely popular form of entertainment.

Relation to other fields

3862 Kandyba, V.M. *Estradnyj gipnoz: Čudesa na scene. Učebnik.* (Stage Hypnosis: Magic on Stage—Textbook.) St. Petersburg: Lan'; 1997. 640 pp. Lang.: Rus.

Russia. 1997. Critical studies. ■On the role of hypnosis onstage: its effects on artists and subjects.

MUSIC-DRAMA

General

Institutions

3863 Salzman, Eric. "*La Prière du Loup* at the Scène Nationale de Quimper." *TheatreF.* 1997 Sum/Fall; 11: 94-98. Illus.: Photo. 5. Lang.: Eng.

France: Quimper. 1995-1996. Historical studies. ■On the creation of a musical-theatre piece *La Prière du Loup (The Prayer of the Wolf)* by Eric Salzman and the Scène Nationale de Quimper, artistic director Michel Rostain. Focuses on using local community and history to create the piece.

Performance/production

3864 Jakubcová, Alena. "'... a melodramy zaplavily svět.' (K předpokladům vzniku melodramu Circe Václava Praupnera, 1789)." ('... and melodramas flooded the world.' Assumptions for the Creation of the Melodrama *Circe* by Václav Praupner, 1789.) *DivR.* 1997; 8(1): 39-54. Notes. Append. Lang.: Cze.

Austro-Hungarian Empire: Prague, Bohemia. 1700-1799. Historical studies. ■Melodramas of Prague composer Václav Praupner, including *Circe*.

3865 Starr, Floyd Favel. "The Artificial Tree: Native Performance Culture Research 1991-1996." *CTR.* 1997 Spr; 90: 83-85. Lang.: Eng.

Canada. 1991-1996. Histories-sources. ■Author's efforts, as artistic director of Takwakin Theatre, to develop a methodology of theatrical creation based on native performance culture.

3866 Linders, Jan. "Time Has No Concept." *Thsch.* 1997; 12: 79-95. Illus.: Dwg. Photo. B&W. 8. Lang.: Ger, Fre, Dut, Eng.

Europe. 1969-1997. Histories-sources. ■An interview with Robert Wilson about his stage productions and constructions in time and space.

3867 Paris, Heidi; Gente, Peter. "Klänge in der Zeit." (The Sounds of Time.) *Thsch.* 1997; 12: 107-123. Illus.: Photo. B&W. 3. Lang.: Ger, Fre, Dut, Eng.

Europe. 1978-1997. Histories-sources. ■An interview with composer Hans Peter Kuhn who has collaborated with Robert Wilson for years about the relationship between time and music.

3868 Kuusisaari, Harri. "Teatterimusiikissakin se on huomattu." (Even in Stage Music, the Best Source of the Voice Is Human.) *Teat.* 1997; 52(7): 10-12. Illus.: Photo. B&W. 4. Lang.: Fin.

Finland. 1997. Histories-sources. ■Finnish stage composers on audience reaction to music that is live rather than taped or recorded.

3869 "Salut, Broadway." *Econ.* 1997 Nov 15; 345(8043): 92-94. Lang.: Eng.

France. 1855-1997. Critical studies. ■Brief history of reception of operas and musicals in France, current season of musical productions.

3870 Iversen, Gunilla. "*O Virginitas, in regali thalamo stas*: New Light on the *Ordo Virtutum*: Hildegard, Richardis, and the Order of the Virtues." *EDAM.* 1997 Fall; 20(1): 1-16. Lang.: Eng.

Germany. 1100-1200. Historical studies. ■Suggests that the motivation for Hildegard's writing of the *Ordo Virtutum* may have been the departure of the nun Richardis to become abbess at another convent.

3871 Puthussery, Joly. "Chavittunatakam: A Music-Drama of Kerala Christians." *EDAM.* 1997 Spr; 19(2): 93-104. Illus.: Photo. B&W. 6. Lang.: Eng.

India: Kerala. 1500-1997. Historical studies. ■*Chavittunátakam* is a form of music drama brought to Kerala by Portuguese missionaries in the sixteenth century and thereafter adapted to the forms of Indian music and dance. The plays center on topics similar to European liturgical drama with the addition of plays on the Charlemagne story. Continued in *EDAM* 20:1 (Fall 1997), 27-33.

3872 Boer, Nienke de. "*Ludus Danielis* in Maastricht." *EDAM.* 1997 Spr; 19(2): 121-123. Lang.: Eng.

Netherlands: Maastricht. 1996. Reviews of performances. ■A performance, in Maastricht's Church of Our Lady, of the twelfth-century Beauvais *Ludus Danielis (The Play of Daniel)* by Nova Schola Cantorum of Amsterdam, musical direction by Marcel Zijlstra, dramatic direction by Dunbar H. Ogden. The performance was a historical reconstruction that used the entire interior space of the church.

3873 Erenstein, Robert L. "*Ludus Danielis* in Maastricht." *WES.* 1997 Spr; 9(2): 67-70. Illus.: Photo. 2. Lang.: Eng.

Netherlands: Maastricht. 1996. Critical studies. ■Critical reception of a performance at the Music Sacra Festival in Maastricht: a collaborative reconstruction of the twelfth-century Beauvais *Ludus Danielis (The Play of Daniel)* by Nova Schola Cantorum (Marcel Zijlstra, music director) and the drama department of the University of California at Berkeley (Dunbar H. Ogden, dramatic director). The performance was staged in the local cathedral.

3874 Kolsteeg, Johan. "'Where Do We Go From Here? Towards Theatre' Music Theatre in the Netherlands/Le Théâtre lyrique aux Pays-Bas." *Carnet.* 1997 Mar.; 13: 10-16. Illus.: Photo. B&W. 5. Lang.: Eng, Fre.

Netherlands. 1990-1997. Historical studies. ■Overview of recent developments in opera and musical theatre in the Netherlands.

3875 Bardijewska, Liliana. "Life after Life." *TP.* 1997; 39(2): 28-29. Illus.: Photo. B&W. 2. Lang.: Eng, Fre.

Poland: Zusno. 1997. Critical studies. ■Analysis of production of *Gaja (Gaia)*, written and directed by Krysztof Rau, music by Robert Łuczak, choreography by Tadeusz Wiśniewski at Teatr 3/4. Use of puppets and actors.

MUSIC-DRAMA: General—Performance/production

3876 Beljakov, A. *Alla, Allочka, Alla Borisovna: Roman-biografija.* (Alla, Allochka, Alla Borisovna: Novel-Biography.) Moscow: Zacharov-Vagrius; 1997. 352 pp. Lang.: Rus.
Russia. 1970-1997. Biographies. ■The artistic life of singer Alla Pugačeva.

3877 Pojurovskij, B.M., ed. *Alla Pugačeva glazami druzej i nedrugov. V 2-ch knigach.* (Alla Pugačeva as Seen by Her Friends and Enemies.) Moscow: Centrpoligraf; 1997. 424 pp., 377 pp. [2 vols.] Lang.: Rus.
Russia. 1970-1997. Histories-sources. ■Collection of materials relating to singer Alla Pugačeva.

3878 Dowling, John. "Fortunes and Misfortunes of the Spanish Lyric Theatre in the Eighteenth Century." *CompD.* 1997 Spr; 31 (1): 129-157. Notes. Lang.: Eng.
Spain. 1701-1800. Historical studies. ■Various changes in form and popularity of the Spanish lyric theatre during the eighteenth century.

3879 Traubner, Richard. "¿Qué Pasa? ¿Zarzuela?" *OpN.* 1997 July; 62(1): 20-22, 24-27. Illus.: Photo. B&W. Color. 14. Lang.: Eng.
Spain. Latin America. 1600-1997. Historical studies. ■The history and development of *zarzuela*, with emphasis on shifts of style.

3880 Blier, Steven. "Seduced by Zarzuela." *OpN.* 1997 July; 62(1): 10. Illus.: Photo. B&W. 1. Lang.: Eng.
USA: New York, NY. 1997. Histories-sources. ■Accompanist Steven Blier discusses the inclusion of *zarzuela* in the annual Festival of Song recital series he runs with Michael Barrett at the 92nd Street Y.

3881 Cockrell, Dale. *Demons of Disorder: Early Blackface Minstrels and Their World.* Cambridge: Cambridge UP; 1997. 236 pp. (Cambridge Studies in American Theatre and Drama 11.) Pref. Notes. Biblio. Index. Illus.: Photo. Diagram. 14. Lang.: Eng.
USA. 1800-1875. Histories-specific. ■Examination of the blackface minstrelsy form, focusing on issues of race and class. Investigates the roots of songs such as 'Zip Coon,' 'Jim Crow,' 'Dan Tucker,' and Black minstrelsy performer George Washington Tucker.

3882 Koger, Alicia Kae. "Dramaturgical Criticism: A Case Study of *The Gospel at Colonus.*" *TTop.* 1997 Mar.; 7(1): 23-35. Illus.: Photo. 1. Lang.: Eng.
USA. 1983-1990. Histories-sources. ■Analysis of *The Gospel at Colonus* by Lee Breuer, music by Bob Telson, as performed in New York, Chicago, and Philadelphia productions, with attention to the balance of the play's cultural and dramaturgical aesthetic.

3883 Quadri, Franco; Bertoni, Franco; Stearns, Robert. *Robert Wilson.* Florence: Contini; 1997. 240 pp. Illus.: Dwg. Photo. Sketches. B&W. Color. Lang.: Ita.
USA. Europe. 1964-1996. Biographical studies. ■Illustrated volume devoted to the theatrical productions of Robert Wilson. Includes a chronology.

3884 Vought, Joy Michelle. *Nancy Van de Vate: Her Theatrical Vocal Music.* Cincinnati, OH: Univ. of Cincinnati; 1997. 120 pp. Notes. Biblio. [D.M.A. Dissertation, Univ. Microfilms Order No. AAC 9734941.] Lang.: Eng.
USA. 1945-1995. Critical studies. ■Includes a brief biographical sketch, analysis of Van de Vate's style, and analysis of her work including *A Night in the Royal Ontario Museum, Cocaine Lil, In the Shadow of the Glen,* and *Nemo: Jenseits von Vulkania.*

3885 Zinger, Pablo. "The Spanish Songbook." *OpN.* 1997 July; 62(1): 12-14,18-19. Illus.: Poster. Photo. B&W. Color. 3. Lang.: Eng.
USA. 1980-1997. Histories-sources. ■The present state of the *zarzuela* music theatre genre in the United States, with brief discussions of individual works and notes on recent and upcoming performances.

Plays/librettos/scripts

3886 Waterman, Ellen Frances. *R. Murray Schafer's Environmental Music Theatre: A Documentation and Analysis of Patria, the Epilogue and And Wolf Shall Inherit the Moon.* San Diego, CA: Univ. of California; 1997. 512 pp. Notes. Biblio.

[Ph.D. Dissertation, Univ. Microfilms Order No. AAC 9732703.] Lang.: Eng.
Canada. 1966-1996. Critical studies. ■Analysis of Schafer's plays and his concept of Theatre of Confluence.

3887 Powers, David M. "Perceptions of Non-Europeans in Early French Musical Dramas: Parisian Society and the African *Other.*" *OJ.* 1997 Mar.; 30(1): 2-13. Notes. Tables. Lang.: Eng.
France. Africa. 1600. Historical studies. ■Ways in which France contributed to the concept of the Other in Africa through its musical dramas and other performance media. Influences on characterizations of African personages, study includes verbal ballets and operas.

Relation to other fields

3888 Newark, Cormac; Wassenaar, Ingrid. "Proust and Music: The Anxiety of Competence." *COJ.* 1997; 9(2): 163-183. Notes. Lang.: Eng.
France: Paris. 1897-1927. Textual studies. ■Literary manifestations of music in Marcel Proust's *A la recherche du temps perdu.* Discusses the difficulty of reconstructing music in literature and uses two examples: a 'petite phrase' based on Saint-Saëns and Wagner's *Tristan und Isolde,* to illustrate Proust's differing approaches to making musicality within textuality meaningful.

3889 Tambling, Jeremy. "Towards a Psychopathology of Opera." *COJ.* 1997; 9(3): 263-279. Notes. Lang.: Eng.
USA. Europe. 1884-1985. Critical studies. ■Applies psychoanalytic theories, particularly Freudian, to musical theatre and opera. Considers whether musical such as *Show Boat* attempt to establish an American ego-psychology and whether the same could be applied to Western opera. Distinctions between sound and meaning, and the notion of sound as a representation of ego are considered, with particular reference to the female voice in opera.

Chinese opera

Design/technology

3890 Bonds, Alexandra. "Beijing Opera Costumes." *TD&T.* 1997 Fall; 33(5): 13-26. Notes. Tables. Biblio. Illus.: Photo. Dwg. Color. 22. Lang.: Eng.
China, People's Republic of: Beijing. 1996. Technical studies. ■Costume as a visual code, as important as language, in Beijing opera.

Performance/production

3891 Sussman, Sally; Day, Tony. "*Orientalia,* Orientalism, and the Peking Opera Artists as 'Subject' in Contemporary Australian Performance." *ThR.* 1997; 22(2): 130-149. Notes. Illus.: Photo. B&W. 8. Lang.: Eng.
Australia. 1988-1996. Histories-sources. ■Sussman's work learning, teaching, and adapting traditional Chinese *xiqu* to Australian performance.

3892 Chang, Huei-Yuan Belinda. "A Theatre of Taiwaneseness: Politics, Ideologies, and Gezaixi." *TDR.* 1997 Sum; 41(2): 111-129. Notes. Biblio. Illus.: Photo. B&W. 9. Lang.: Eng.
China: Taiwan. 1895-1997. Historical studies. ■*Gezaixi,* Taiwanese opera, as culturally representative of the people, compared to Beijing opera, or *jingju.* Culture and history that gave rise to both forms, focus on language it is performed in, criticisms of the form, government censorship, increased popularity of the form and its embodiment of Taiwanese history and tradition.

3893 Luo, Qin. *Kunju, Chinese Classical Theater and Its Revival in Social, Political, Economic, and Cultural Contexts.* Kent, OH: Kent State Univ; 1997. 279 pp. [Ph.D. Dissertation, Univ. Microfilms Order No. AAC 9816205.] Lang.: Eng.
China, People's Republic of. 1950-1960. Historical studies. ■A history and analysis of *kunju* musical and cultural foundations, and a case study of a *kunju* actor Zhou Chuanying, the Zhejiang Kunju Troupe, and the politics of the *kunju* revival.

MUSIC-DRAMA

Musical theatre

Administration

3894 Lahr, John. "The High Roller." *NewY.* 1997 2 June: 70-77. Illus.: Sketches. Color. 1. Lang.: Eng.
Canada. 1997. Historical studies. ■Profile of producer Garth Drabinsky.

3895 Cummings, Scott T. "Larson's Intent Key in *Rent* Case." *AmTh.* 1997 Oct.; 14(8): 80-81. Illus.: Photo. B&W. 1. Lang.: Eng.
USA: New York, NY. 1991-1997. Historical studies. ■Court ruling that dramaturg Lynn Thomson was not a co-author of Jonathan Larson's *Rent* and dismissal of her complaint that she had made copyrightable contributions to the script and was due royalties. Includes sidebar article on alleged theft of Joe Mantello's original direction of McNally's *Love! Valour! Compassion!* by Michael Hall of Caldwell Theatre Company.

3896 Grode, Eric. "Trading Faces: Broadway's Constant Gamble." *ShowM.* 1997 Fall; 13(3): 17-22, 72. Illus.: Photo. B&W. 22. Lang.: Eng.
USA: New York, NY. 1952-1977. Historical studies. ■Consideration of the problems inherent in recasting star roles when the stars leave and need to be replaced, with a historical survey of replacements for stars in Broadway musicals. Sidebar article on the work of Betsy D. Bernstein, the director of casting for the 1990s Broadway revival of *Grease* which rotated minor 'stars' in half a dozen roles.

3897 Grode, Eric. "Rights & Reason: Licensing Agents Must Redefine Themselves as They Market Both New Shows and Classics." *ShowM.* 1997/98 Win; 13(4): 25-26, 66-67. Illus.: Dwg. B&W. 1. Lang.: Eng.
USA. 1997. Critical studies. ■Representatives of major licensing agencies (Rodgers and Hammerstein Library, Tams-Witmark, Music Theatre International, and Samuel French) discuss trends, policies, and the impact of Broadway revivals on amateur rights.

3898 Moore, Dick. "Equity Continues Protests of Non-Union Shows in Philadelphia." *EN.* 1997 Jan/Feb.; 82(1): 1. Lang.: Eng.
USA: Philadelphia, PA. 1997. Historical studies. ■Equity leads a protest against a non-union production of the musical *Grease* being presented at the Merriam Theatre.

3899 Moore, Dick. "Equity Protests Non-Union *State Fair*." *EN.* 1997 June; 82(5): 1. Lang.: Eng.
USA. 1997. Historical studies. ■Contract talks break off between Actors' Equity and Kenneth Gentry, producer of the upcoming tour of *State Fair*.

3900 Moore, Dick. "*State Fair* Goes Equity." *EN.* 1997 July/Aug.; 82(6): 1. Lang.: Eng.
USA. 1997. Historical studies. ■After intense negotiations, Equity and the producers of *State Fair*, including Kenneth Gentry, reach an agreement allowing the tour to proceed under an Equity contract.

3901 Stasio, Marilyn. "The Selling of Ragtime." *AmTh.* 1997 Dec.; 14(10): 20-23, 54-55. Illus.: Photo. Poster. B&W. 6. Lang.: Eng.
USA: New York, NY. Canada: Toronto, ON. 1997. Historical studies. ■Producer Garth Drabinsky's advertising and marketing campaigns for the Broadway production of *Ragtime*. Includes sidebar article on Drabinsky and his personal approach to his work.

3902 Swarbrick, Carol. "The *State Fair* Contract: A Bold Step." *EN.* 1997 Oct.; 82(8): 2. Lang.: Eng.
USA. 1997. Historical studies. ■Regional Vice President examines the recently negotiated contract for *State Fair*.

Basic theatrical documents

3903 Van Fossen, Rachael; Morton, Billy; Wildcat, Darrel; Herrell, Heather. "*Ka'ma'mo'pi cik/The Gathering*." *CTR.* 1997 Spr ; 90: 40-77. Illus.: Photo. B&W. 1. Lang.: Eng.
Canada: Fort Qu'Appelle, SK. 1997. ■Complete playtext with lyrics (music by Billy Morton not included).

3904 Riis, Thomas L. *The Music and Scripts of In Dahomey*. Madison, WI: A-R Editions; 1996. 245 pp. (Recent Researches in American Music 25: Music of the United States of America 5.) Append. Discography. Illus.: Photo. 3. Lang.: Eng.
USA. 1903. Histories-sources. ■Music and libretto for *In Dahomey*, composed by Will Marion Cook and Alex Rogers, book by Jesse Shipp. Includes history of production and historical context.

Design/technology

3905 Barbour, David. "Syncopated Illumination." *LDim.* 1997 Apr.; 21(3): 64-67, 102-106. Illus.: Photo. Color. 7. Lang.: Eng.
Canada: Toronto, ON. 1975-1997. Historical studies. ■Lighting designers Jules Fisher and Peggy Eisenhauer's work for the musical *Ragtime* (book by Terrence McNally, music and lyrics by Stephen Flaherty and Lynn Ahrens) based on E.L. Doctorow's novel, directed by Frank Galati at the Ford Centre for the Performing Arts.

3906 Garnhum, Ken. "A Setting for *The House of Martin Guerre*." *CTR.* 1997 Sum; 91: 62. Lang.: Eng.
Canada. 1997. Histories-sources. ■Poem by Garnhum, composed as inspiration for creating his scenography.

3907 Schob, Ivo. "Szenische Maschinensteuerung für Musical-, Theater- und andere Produktionen." (Scenic Machine Control System for Musical, Theatre and Other Productions.) *BtR.* 1997; 91(3): 16-19. Illus.: Photo. Graphs. Color. 6. Lang.: Ger.
Germany: Essen. 1997. Historical studies. ■The technical production director of the Colosseum discusses his experiences in the field of machine control systems and the permanent changes in electronic branches using the examples of *Miss Saigon* and *Les Misérables* by Claude-Michel Schönberg, and *Joseph and the Amazing Technicolor Dreamcoat* by Andrew Lloyd Webber.

3908 Lampert-Gréaux, Ellen. "Lady Luck." *LDim.* 1997 June; 21(5): 14. Illus.: Photo. Color. 3. Lang.: Eng.
UK-England: London. 1941-1997. Historical studies. ■Rick Fisher's lighting design for a revival of the Moss Hart/Ira Gershwin/Kurt Weill musical *Lady in the Dark*, directed by Francesca Zambello at the Lyttelton Theatre.

3909 Moles, Steve. "Resurrecting *Jesus Christ Superstar*." *LDim.* 1997 Apr.; 21(3): 17. Illus.: Photo. Color. 1. Lang.: Eng.
UK-England: London. 1997. Historical studies. ■David Hersey's lighting design for revival of Andrew Lloyd Webber and Tim Rice's musical at the Lyceum Theatre.

3910 Shenton, Mark. "Breaking Out." *PI.* 1997 July; 12(12): 10-11. Illus.: Photo. B&W. 1. Lang.: Eng.
UK-England: London. 1997. Historical studies. ■Designer Hildegard Bechter, best known for her collaborations with director Deborah Warner, and her first design for a musical, *Always* written by William May and Jason Sprague, at Victoria Palace.

3911 Barbour, David. "Billington Strikes Again." *LDim.* 1997 July; 21(6): 44-47, 89-94. Illus.: Photo. Color. 6. Lang.: Eng.
USA: New York, NY. 1997. Biographical studies. ■Award winning lighting designer Ken Billington's recent Broadway productions including *Candide* by Leonard Bernstein, *Annie* and *Dream*. Scheduling challenges, previous experience with the shows, equipment.

3912 Barbour, David. "John Lasiter." *LDim.* 1997 May; 21(4): 22. Illus.: Photo. B&W. 1. Lang.: Eng.
USA: New York, NY. 1991-1997. Biographical studies. ■Profile, training and career of theatrical lighting designer Lasiter with focus on his design for the Off Broadway musical *Dreamstuff*.

3913 Barbour, David. "Independence Day." *LDim.* 1997 Oct.; 21(9): 14. Illus.: Photo. Color. 1. Lang.: Eng.
USA: New York, NY. 1969-1997. Technical studies. ■Brian Nason's lighting design for Roundabout Theatre's revival of the musical *1776* on Broadway.

3914 Barbour, David. "Godspeed, Titanic." *TCI.* 1997 Aug/Sep.; 31(7): 70-73. Illus.: Photo. 15. Lang.: Eng.
USA: New York, NY. 1997. Historical studies. ■The set and costume designs of Stewart Laing seen on Broadway in *Titanic*, by Peter Stone (book) and Maury Yeston (music and lyrics), directed by Richard Jones at the Lunt-Fontanne Theatre.

3915 Barbour, David. "A Hell of a Town." *TCI.* 1997 Nov.; 31(9): 48-51. Illus.: Photo. Sketches. 10. Lang.: Eng.

MUSIC-DRAMA: Musical theatre—Design/technology

USA: New York, NY. 1997. Historical studies. ■Design elements in *On the Town* (book and lyrics by Betty Comden and Adolph Green, music by Leonard Bernstein) at the Delacorte Theatre, directed by George C. Wolfe as part of the summer season of the New York Shakespeare Festival. Focuses on work of set designer Adrianne Lobel and costume designer Paul Tazewell.

3916 Halliday, Robert. "Revisiting *Les Misérables.*" *LDim.* 1997 Oct.; 21(9): 54-62. Illus.: Photo. Color. 6. Lang.: Eng.
USA: New York, NY. 1987-1997. Technical studies. ■Refurbishment of lighting design by David Hersey for the musical *Les Misérables* on the occasion of its tenth anniversary on Broadway. Equipment, special effects.

3917 Hogan, Jane. "Raising *Titanic.*" *LDim.* 1997 Nov.; 21(10): 86-89. Illus.: Photo. Color. B&W. LP. 11. Lang.: Eng.
USA: New York, NY. 1992-1997. Technical studies. ■Paul Gallo, David Weiner and Vivien Leone's lighting design for the Broadway musical *Titanic.* Challenges in lighting the moving set, equipment used.

3918 Lampert-Gréaux, Ellen. "City Lights." *LDim.* 1997 July; 21(6): 48-51, 76-78. Illus.: Photo. Color. LP. 9. Lang.: Eng.
USA: New York, NY. 1997. Historical studies. ■Richard Pilbrow's lighting design of the Cy Coleman-Ira Gasman musical *The Life* on Broadway. Challenges, equipment used.

3919 Newman, Mark A. "Lollapalooza of Broadway." *LD&A.* 1997 Feb.; 27(2): 22-26. Illus.: Photo. Color. 7. Lang.: Eng.
USA: New York, NY. 1996-1997. Technical studies. ■Blake Burba's lighting design for *Rent* at the Nederlander theatre, directed by Michael Greif.

3920 Newman, Mark A. "Whistling Dixie." *LD&A.* 1997 July; 27(7): 34-37. Illus.: Photo. Color. 4. Lang.: Eng.
USA: Washington, DC. 1997. Technical studies. ■Howell Binkley's atmospheric lighting design for Andrew Lloyd Webber's *Whistle Down the Wind*, lyrics by Jim Steinman, text by Patricia Knopf and directed by Hal Prince at the National Theatre.

3921 Phillips, Michael. "Harlem Nights." *LDim.* 1997 Apr.; 21(3): 10. Illus.: Photo. Color. 1. Lang.: Eng.
USA: San Diego, CA. 1997. Historical studies. ■Technical designs for new musical *Play On!*, an adaptation of Shakespeare's *Twelfth Night* by Cheryl L. West, directed by Sheldon Epps.

3922 Pilbrow, Richard. "He Just Keeps Rolling." *LD&A.* 1995 June; 25(6): 19-21. Illus.: Photo. Color. 9. Lang.: Eng.
USA: New York, NY. 1994. Histories-sources. ■The author's lighting design for Harold Prince's revival of *Show Boat* at the Gershwin Theatre.

3923 Ramage, Fred. "A Plausible, Practical Raft." *TechB.* 1997 Oct.: 1-3. Illus.: Photo. Plan. B&W. 3. [TB 1302.] Lang.: Eng.
USA. 1997. Technical studies. ■Creating an effective raft with locking system for a production of the musical *Big River.*

3924 Sandla, Robert. "Transformations." *LDim.* 1997 Sep.; 21(8): 60-61, 112-113. Illus.: Photo. Color. 3. Lang.: Eng.
USA: New York, NY. 1886-1997. Historical studies. ■Beverly Emmons' lighting design for the Broadway musical *Jekyll & Hyde: The Musical*, book and lyrics by Leslie Bricusse and score by Frank Wildhorn, directed by Robin Phillips, adapted from *The Strange Case of Dr. Jekyll and Mr. Hyde* by Robert Louis Stevenson.

3925 Scher, Herb. "Sound Concerns—A Critical Report on Sound in Today's Musical Theatre." *ShowM.* 1997 Spr; 13(1): 41-44. Illus.: Photo. B&W. 6. Lang.: Eng.
USA. 1961-1997. Historical studies. ■A critical consideration of the history, use and techniques of amplified sound in the Broadway musical theatre, including comments from critics, directors, and sound designers Abe Jacob and Tony Meola.

Institutions

3926 Winston, Iris. "Orpheus: 90 and Still Going Strong." *PAC.* 1997; 31(2): 36-37. Illus.: Photo. B&W. 2. Lang.: Eng.
Canada: Ottawa, ON. 1917-1997. Historical studies. ■Profile of the Orpheus Musical Theatre Society, the oldest musical theatre group in North America: how it has developed through the years and its current presentation of Broadway-style musicals.

3927 Injachin, A. "Muzyka duši moej." (The Music of My Soul.) *TeatZ.* 1997; 7: 20-23. Lang.: Rus.

Russia: Moscow. 1996. Historical studies. ■Plays of the musical comedy program of the Rossiskaja Akademija Teatral'nogo Iskusstva.

3928 Reiss, Alvin H. "Will Success Spoil the Theatre that Produced Rent?" *FundM.* 1997 Oct.; 28(8): 40-41. Illus.: Photo. B&W. 1. Lang.: Eng.
USA: New York, NY. 1996-1997. Critical studies. ■Examines problems faced by the New York Theatre Workshop after the success of Jonathan Larson's *Rent* in which the theatre was actually a minor producer.

Performance spaces

3929 Hansen, Walter. "Musical *Space Dream* in Berlin." *BtR.* 1997; 91(4): 10-14. Illus.: Photo. Plan. Color. Explod.Sect. GR. 10. Lang.: Ger.
Germany: Berlin. 1997. Historical studies. ■Discusses the performance place, a hangar of Berlin's Tempelhof Airport, and the completely new spatial and technical dimensions of the performance of *Space Dream* by Harry Schürer, directed by Burkhard Jahn.

3930 Sonntag-Kunst, Helga. "Das Colosseum in Essen—Industriehalle wird zum Theater." (The Coliseum in Essen—An Industrial Hall Becomes a Theatre.) *BtR.* 1997; 91(2): 22-30. Illus.: Photo. Plan. B&W. Color. Explod.Sect. 17. Lang.: Ger.
Germany: Essen. 1900-1997. Technical studies. ■The history of the Colosseum, its new interior design, and the technical and artistic details for Andrew Lloyd Webber's musical *Joseph and the Amazing Technicolor Dreamcoat*, directed by Steven Pimlott und Nicola Treherne.

3931 Weathersby, William, Jr. "Resurrection: London's Long-Dormant Lyceum Theatre Is Renovated as a Home for *Jesus Christ Superstar.*" *TCI.* 1997 Apr.; 31(4): 32-35. Illus.: Photo. 7. Lang.: Eng.
UK-England: London. 1904-1997. Historical studies. ■Account of the renovation of the 1904 Lyceum Theatre last used as a theatre in 1939, in time for a production of Tim Rice and Andrew Lloyd Webber's *Jesus Christ Superstar.* The $25 million renovation restored the theatre to its turn-of-the-century opulence, with enhanced staging capabilities and remapped support and hospitality spaces.

Performance/production

3932 Douglas, James B. "Eyre In Ragtime." *PlPl.* 1997 May; 513: 41. Illus.: Photo. B&W. 2. Lang.: Eng.
Canada: Toronto, ON. 1997. Historical studies. ■Comparison of two musical productions: *Ragtime*, produced by Garth Drabinsky at the Ford Centre for the Performing Arts (Toronto), directed by Frank Galati, book by Terrence McNally, music by Stephen Flaherty, lyrics by Lynn Ahrens. *Jane Eyre*, produced by David Mirvish, music by Paul Gordon, book and direction by John Caird.

3933 Gruber, HK. "Simplicity Is the Richness: HK Gruber Talks about Performing Kurt Weill." *KWN.* 1997 Spr; 15(1): 10-12. Illus.: Photo. B&W. 1. Lang.: Eng.
Germany. 1997. Histories-sources. ■Interview with the German composer, conductor and chansonnier in which he discusses his experiences performing Kurt Weill's music and his own theory of singing.

3934 Lenya, Lotte; Davis, George. "Weill and His Collaborators." *KWN.* 1997 Spr; 15(1): 4-9. Illus.: Photo. B&W. 13. Lang.: Eng.
Germany: Berlin. USA: New York, NY. 1927-1945. Biographical studies. ■Excerpt from a biography in progress of Kurt Weill, detailing his methods of collaboration with playwrights Bertolt Brecht and Maxwell Anderson, among others.

3935 Fábri, Péter; Halasi, Imre; Horváth, Péter; Kerényi, Miklós Gábor; Maklári, László; Szolnoki, Tibor; Váradi, Katalin; Vas, Zoltán Iván; Iklády, László, photo.; Keleti, Éva, photo. "Nyolcak a zenés színházról." (Eight Views on the Musical Theatre.) *Sz.* 1997; 30(3): 10-14. Illus.: Photo. B&W. 4. Lang.: Hun.
Hungary. 1900-1990. Histories-sources. ■Introducing eight projects by the competitors for the vacant managerial post of the Budapest Operetta Theatre: author-directors Péter Fábri and Péter Horváth, directors Imre Halasi (final winner of the competition), Miklós Gábor Kerényi and Zoltán Iván Vas, actor Tibor Szolnoki and conductors László Maklári and Katalin Váradi.

MUSIC-DRAMA: Musical theatre—Performance/production

3936 Lajos, Sándor; Koncz, Zsuzsa, photo.; Máthé, András, photo.; Szoboszlai, Gábor, photo. "Maugli-hullám. Dés-Geszti-Békés: A dzsungel könyve." (Mowgli-Wave: László Dés-Péter Geszti-Pál Békés: *The Jungle Book.*) *Sz.* 1997; 30(8): 25-29. Illus.: Photo. B&W. 4. Lang.: Hun.
Hungary. 1996-1997. Critical studies. ■A comparative analysis of four productions of the highly successful youth musical *A Dzsungel könyve*, based on Rudyard Kipling's *The Jungle Book* (music by László Dés, songs by Péter Geszti, playtext by Pál Békés). Directors: Géza Hegedűs D. at Budapest, István Pinczés at Debrecen, József Bal at Kecskemét, Zsuzsa Dávid at Eger.

3937 Macher, Szilárd; Kanyó, Béla, photo. "Árnyak és fények. A Fővárosi Operettszínház tánckara és a Madách Táncműhely közös estje." (Shades and Lights: A Joint Musical Evening by the Dance Company of Budapest Operetta Theatre and the Madách Dance Workshop.) *Tanc.* 1997; 28(1/2): 18-19. Illus.: Photo. B&W. Color. 5. Lang.: Hun.
Hungary: Budapest. 1996-1997. Historical studies. ■A successful joint production of two theatrical dance workshops in the field of musical productions.

3938 Kantor, G.M. *Muzykal'nyj teat'r v Kazani XIX-nacala XX v.: Issledovanie.* (Musical Theatre in Kazan in the Nineteenth and Early Twentieth Centures: An Exploration.) Kazan: Karpol; 1997. 186 pp. Lang.: Rus.
Russia. 1800-1997. Histories-specific. ■Musical theatre in Tatarstan.

3939 Parin, A. "V ožidanii bol'ščich peremen." (Waiting for Big Changes.) *TeatZ.* 1997; 11-12: 21-25. Lang.: Rus.
Russia. 1990-1997. Critical studies. ■Survey of Russian musical theatre, its development and conditions.

3940 Petrov, V. "Vertinskij v Šanchae." (Vertinskij in Shanghai.) *Smena.* 1997; 12: 190-195. Lang.: Rus.
Russia. 1889-1957. Biographical studies. ■On the well-known Russian singer Aleksand'r Vertinskij.

3941 Balme, Christopher. "The Performance Aesthetics of Township Theatre: Frames and Codes." 65-84 in Davis, Geoffrey V., ed.; Fuchs, Anne, ed. *Theatre and Change in South Africa.* Amsterdam: Harwood Academic Publishing; 1996. 324 pp. (Contemporary Theatre Studies 12.) Index. Notes. Append. Illus.: Photo. 4. Lang.: Eng.
South Africa, Republic of. 1976-1994. Critical studies. ■Examines the genre of the Black musical theatre form from South African townships. Author examines three works: *Woza Albert!* by Percy Mtwa, Mbongeni Ngema, and Barney Simon, *Asinamali!* by Mbongeni Ngema, and *Bopha!* by Percy Mtwa.

3942 Mofokeng, Jerry. "Theatre for Export: The Commercialization of the Black People's Struggle in South African Export Musicals." 85-88 in Davis, Geoffrey V., ed.; Fuchs, Anne, ed. *Theatre and Change in South Africa.* Amsterdam: Harwood Academic Publishing; 1996. 324 pp. (Contemporary Theatre Studies 12.) Index. Notes. Append. Lang.: Eng.
South Africa, Republic of. 1996. Critical studies. ■The question of authenticity with respect to the use of musical theatre as a cultural export in South Africa.

3943 Lahger, Håkan. "Black rider." *Dramat.* 1997; 5(3): 10-15. Illus.: Photo. Color. Lang.: Swe.
Sweden: Stockholm. 1990-1997. Critical studies. ■Director Rickard Günther and his staging at Dramaten of *The Black Rider* by Robert Wilson, William S. Burroughs, and Tom Waits.

3944 Ford, Piers. "Atlantic Overtures—'Lost Musicals' Resurfaces at London's Barbican." *ShowM.* 1997 Spr; 13(1): 25-28. Illus.: Photo. B&W. 5. Lang.: Eng.
UK-England: London. 1990-1997. Historical studies. ■The 'Discover the Lost Musicals' series, founded and produced by Ian Marshall Fisher, of concert versions of neglected American musicals.

3945 Ford, Piers. "Making Up Her Mind." *ShowM.* 1997 Fall; 13(3): 37-40. Illus.: Photo. B&W. 6. Lang.: Eng.
UK-England: London. 1983-1997. Biographical studies. ■Profile of the musical theatre career of English actress/singer Maria Friedman, currently starring in *Lady in the Dark* in London, with her thoughts on Stephen Sondheim, in whose *Sunday in the Park with George* and *Passion* she appeared in London.

3946 Shenton, Mark. "How Beauty Was Born." *PI.* 1997 June; 12(11): 10-11, 46. Illus.: Photo. B&W. 1. Lang.: Eng.
UK-England: London. 1997. Historical studies. ■Profile of Robert Jess Roth, the director of *Beauty and the Beast* in New York and now in London.

3947 Shenton, Mark. "Multi-Cultured Lady." *PI.* 1997 Mar.; 12(8): 12-13. Illus.: Photo. B&W. 1. Lang.: Eng.
UK-England: London. 1997. Historical studies. ■Francesca Zambello's directorial debut at the National with the London premiere of *Lady in the Dark* (1941) by Weill, Gershwin, and Hart.

3948 Shenton, Mark. "Making It With Maddie?" *PI.* 1997 Sep.; 13(1): 10-11, 46. Illus.: Photo. B&W. 1. Lang.: Eng.
UK-England. 1997. Historical studies. ■Account of *Maddie*, a new musical by Stephen Keeling, Shaun McKenna, and Steven Dexter, directed in its West End premiere by Martin Connor. The play is based on Jack Finney's novel *Marion's Well*.

3949 Angelo, Gregory. "Lillias White: This Is Your Life." *ShowM.* 1997 Fall; 13(3): 23-25, 69. Illus.: Photo. B&W. 5. Lang.: Eng.
USA: New York, NY. 1981-1997. Biographical studies. ■Career of actress/singer Lillias White, on the occasion of her critically acclaimed performance in the 1997 Broadway musical *The Life*, with music by Cy Coleman.

3950 Brown, Stuart. "The 1990s Radio Hour." *ShowM.* 1997 Sum; 13(2): 27-30. Illus.: Photo. Dwg. B&W. 5. Lang.: Eng.
USA. 1997. Critical studies. ■Survey of radio programs on stations devoted to playing recordings of stage musicals.

3951 Craig, David. "On Performing Sondheim: *A Little Night Music* Revisited." 93-106 in Gordon, Joanne, ed. *Stephen Sondheim: A Casebook.* New York, NY/London: Garland; 1997. 259 pp. (Casebooks on Modern Dramatists.) Notes. Biblio. Index. Lang.: Eng.
USA. 1973. Histories-sources. ■Author recounts his experiences re-staging the score of Stephen Sondheim's *A Little Night Music*.

3952 Davis, Lee. "From Ragtime to Riches." *ShowM.* 1997/98 Win; 13(4): 18-24, 64-65. Illus.: Photo. Dwg. B&W. 12. Lang.: Eng.
USA. 1970-1997. Biographical studies. ■Careers of composer Stephen Flaherty and lyricist Lynn Ahrens and the Broadway production of their latest musical, *Ragtime*.

3953 Flahaven, Sean Patrick. "The Bard Meets the Duke." *ShowM.* 1997 Sum; 13(2): 45-46, 63. Illus.: Photo. B&W. 4. Lang.: Eng.
USA: New York, NY. 1997. Historical studies. ■The development of the 1997 Broadway musical *Play On!*, a musical adaptation by Cheryl L. West of Shakespeare's *Twelfth Night*, reset in 1940s Harlem, using the music of Duke Ellington, with extensive commentary of director/conceiver Sheldon Epps, brief discussions of Ellington's theatre music and other musical versions of Shakespeare's plays.

3954 Flinn, Denny Martin. *Musical! A Grand Tour.* New York, NY: Schirmer; 1997. 556 pp. Notes. Biblio. Index. Append. Filmography. Illus.: Photo. 144. Lang.: Eng.
USA. UK-England. 1912-1995. Historical studies. ■The great age of the American musical and its antecedents. Includes sections on the English musical, the rock musical, and landmark musical theatre productions such as *Oklahoma!* and *A Chorus Line.*

3955 Gitkin, Matthew Todd. *In Preparation for* Jacques Brel Is Alive and Well and Living in Paris*: An Application of David Craig's Technique.* Long Beach, CA: California State Univ; 1997. 62 pp. Notes. Biblio. [M.F.A. Thesis, Univ. Microfilms Order No. AAC 1385563.] Lang.: Eng.
USA: Long Beach, CA. 1996. Historical studies. ■On the creation and performance of Eric Blau's and Mort Shuman's *Jacques Brel Is Alive and Well and Living in Paris*, produced by the California Repertory Theatre at California State University.

MUSIC-DRAMA: Musical theatre—Performance/production

3956 Grode, Eric. "Susan Stroman: Woman of Steel." *ShowM.* 1997 Spr; 13(1): 37-39, 55-59. Illus.: Photo. B&W. 8. Lang.: Eng.
USA: New York, NY. 1975-1997. Historical studies. ■Choreographer Susan Stroman, and her latest project, John Kander, Fred Ebb, and David Thompson's *Steel Pier.*

3957 Grode, Eric. "Songs of Bernadette." *ShowM.* 1997 Sum; 13(2): 21-26, 67. Illus.: Photo. B&W. Color. 14. Lang.: Eng.
USA. 1961-1997. Historical studies. ■A survey of the stage and film career of actress/singer Bernadette Peters, with extensive commentary by Ms. Peters.

3958 Howard, Jessica Harrison. *America's Hometown: Performance and Entertainment in Branson, Missouri.* New York, NY: New York Univ; 1997. 327 pp. Notes. Biblio. [Ph.D. Dissertation, Univ. Microfilms Order No. AAC 9731404.] Lang.: Eng.
USA: Branson, MO. 1906-1996. Historical studies. ■Focuses on the tourist phenomenon of Branson, a small town in southwest Missouri that is known for its music shows and for its location in the scenic Ozark hills. Analyzes history of area and examines the 'production' of culture, tourism, and entertainment.

3959 Hulbert, Dan. "Outlaw *Oklahoma!* Has to Toe the Mark." *AmTh.* 1997 May/June; 14(5): 40-41. Illus.: Photo. B&W. 1. Lang.: Eng.
USA: Atlanta, GA. 1997. Historical studies. ■Unauthorized version of the Rodgers and Hammerstein musical *Oklahoma!* directed by Chris Coleman for Actor's Express. Questions of artistic license and legal aspects.

3960 Kellow, Brian. "Sound Bites: David Sabella." *OpN.* 1997 Feb 8; 61(10): 10-11. Illus.: Photo. Color. 1. Lang.: Eng.
USA: New York, NY. 1996. Biographical studies. ■Brief profile of Handelian countertenor David Sabella, currently playing 'Mary Sunshine' on Broadway in the musical *Chicago* by John Kander and Fred Ebb.

3961 Latham, Angela J. "The Right to Bare: Containing and Encoding American Women in Popular Entertainments of the 1920s." *TJ.* 1997 Dec.; 49(4): 455-474. Notes. Illus.: Photo. 2. Lang.: Eng.
USA. 1920-1930. Historical studies. ■Representations of female bodies in the construction of female beauty in the Ziegfeld Follies and other forms of popular entertainment. Focuses on the interaction between economic and ideological systems.

3962 Lynch, Richard C. "For the Record: Anthony Newley (Part 1)." *ShowM.* 1997/98 Win; 13(4): 43-46, 68. Illus.: Photo. Dwg. B&W. 7. Lang.: Eng.
USA: New York, NY. 1945-1967. Biographical studies. ■First half of a profile of career of actor, singer, composer and lyricist Anthony Newley, with a discography of his recordings.

3963 Lynch, Richard C. "For the Record: Liliane Montevecchi." *ShowM.* 1997 Sum; 13(2): 47-48, 65. Illus.: Photo. Dwg. B&W. 5. Lang.: Eng.
USA. France. UK-England. 1933-1996. Biographical studies. ■Brief profile of the career of singer/actress Liliane Montevecchi, with a discography of her recordings.

3964 Lynch, Richard C. "For the Record: Ron Husmann." *ShowM.* 1997 Fall; 13(3): 47-49. Illus.: Photo. Dwg. B&W. 6. Lang.: Eng.
USA: New York, NY. 1956-1997. Biographical studies. ■Profile of singer/actor Ron Husmann, with a discography of his recordings.

3965 Maslon, Laurence. "With a Song In My Art: Dramaturgy and the American Musical Theater." 342-354 in Jonas, Susan, ed.; Proehl, Geoffrey S., ed. *Dramaturgy in American Theatre: A Sourcebook.* New York, NY: Harcourt Brace College Pub; 1997. 590 pp. Pref. Notes. Biblio. Index. Lang.: Eng.
USA. 1992-1993. Critical studies. ■Explores issues of community and the re-staging of the musical theatre canon. Argues that musical theatre requires the same dramaturgical care given to new plays and standard plays.

3966 McNicholl, BT. "Al Hirschfeld: Between the Lines." *ShowM.* 1997 Sum; 13(2): 39-44, 60. Illus.: Dwg. Photo. B&W. 26. Lang.: Eng.
USA: New York, NY. 1903-1997. Histories-sources. ■Examples of .u Hirschfeld's caricature illustrations of historic musicals over his seventy-year career.

3967 Nesmith, N. Graham. "Luoyong Wang." *AmTh.* 1997 Jan.; 14(1): 54. Illus.: Photo. B&W. 1. Lang.: Eng.
USA: New York, NY. 1984-1997. Biographical studies. ■Training and career of first Asian actor to portray the Eurasian engineer in *Miss Saigon* on Broadway.

3968 Scheper, Jeanne. "'Take Black or White': Libby Holman's Sound." *WPerf.* 1997; 9(2): 94-118. Notes. Biblio. Illus.: Photo. B&W. 3. [Number 18.] Lang.: Eng.
USA: New York, NY. 1920-1995. Biographical studies. ■Career and recordings of music hall and musical theatre singer Holman: racial and sexual context of her sound, personal history, performances playing mixed race characters. Includes chronological list of her performances.

3969 Shank, Theodore. "*Rent*: Uptown and Downtown: An Interview with Director Michael Greif." *TheatreF.* 1997 Win/Spr; 10: 11-16. Illus.: Photo. 4. Lang.: Eng.
USA. 1996-1997. Histories-sources. ■Interview with Michael Greif, director of musical *Rent.* Focuses on early creation of the work.

3970 Sheehan, John D. "Lost Boys." *OpN.* 1997 May; 61(16): 56-57. Illus.: Photo. B&W. 1. Lang.: Eng.
USA: New York, NY. 1938-1997. Histories-sources. ■The difficulty experienced by Larry Moore in reconstituting the Hans Spialeck orchestration for the revival of *The Boys from Syracuse,* by Richard Rodgers and Moss Hart, with vocal arrangements by Hugh Martin, for performance by Encores! at the New York City Center.

3971 Shenton, Mark. "Actor into Director." *PI.* 1997 Nov.; 13(3): 10-11. Illus.: Photo. B&W. 1. Lang.: Eng.
USA. UK-England. 1971-1997. Biographical studies. ■Profile of Walter Bobbie, directing *Chicago* in London.

3972 Sherman, Howard. "From Melonville to Broadway: The Riotous Rise of Andrea Martin." *ShowM.* 1997 Spr; 13(1): 29-32. Illus.: Photo. Dwg. B&W. 7. Lang.: Eng.
USA: New York, NY. 1947-1997. Biographical studies. ■The career of actress/singer Andrea Martin, both in television and in musicals, and her upcoming appearance in Harold Prince's 1997 Broadway revival of *Candide.*

3973 Stasio, Marilyn. "Luther Henderson." *AmTh.* 1997 May/June; 14(5): 30. Illus.: Photo. B&W. 1. Lang.: Eng.
USA: New York, NY. 1997. Biographical studies. ■Profile of Broadway orchestrator Henderson: past productions, influence of blues and jazz on his work.

3974 Viagas, Robert. "Always a Different Tune." *ShowM.* 1997/98 Win; 13(4): 27-30, 67. Illus.: Photo. Dwg. B&W. 3. Lang.: Eng.
USA. 1995-1997. Histories-sources. ■Interview with director/choreographer/performer Tommy Tune, discussing his injury which forced the closing of *Busker Alley,* the writing of his memoirs *Footnotes,* his recent touring and recording, and his plans for the upcoming *Easter Parade.*

3975 Vitaris, Paula. "The Unsinkable Maury Yeston." *ShowM.* 1997 Spr; 13(1): 17-23. Illus.: Photo. B&W. Color. 9. Lang.: Eng.
USA: New York, NY. 1945-1997. Historical studies. ■A survey of the career of composer/lyricist Maury Yeston, providing biographical background and a discussion of his musicals from *Nine* through *Titanic.*

3976 Vitaris, Paula. "More Than a Beauty." *ShowM.* 1997/98 Win; 13(4): 35-38. Illus.: Photo. B&W. 6. Lang.: Eng.
USA: New York, NY. 1991-1997. Historical studies. ■Career of singer/actress Susan Egan, tracing her early touring, her work for Disney (notably as the first Belle in the stage version of *Beauty and the Beast*) and the development of her latest show *Triumph of Love* by James Magruder, Jeffrey Stock, and Susan Birkenhead.

3977 Wilkinson, Alec. "The Flame." *NewY.* 1997 8 Dec.: 96-99. Illus.: Photo. B&W. 1. Lang.: Eng.

MUSIC-DRAMA: Musical theatre—Performance/production

USA. 1968-1997. Biographical studies. ■Profile of salsa singer Marc Anthony with emphasis on his leading role in Paul Simon's musical *The Capeman.*

3978 Wolf, Stacy. "'Never Gonna Be a Man/Catch Me If You Can/I Won't Grow Up': A Lesbian Account of Mary Martin as Peter Pan." *TJ.* 1997 Dec.; 49(4): 493-510. Notes. Illus.: Photo. 2. Lang.: Eng.

USA. 1950-1959. Critical studies. ■The body of performer Mary Martin in her signature musical theatre performance in *Peter Pan* (original story by J.M. Barrie, book by Carolyn Leigh, music by Mark Charlap, directed by Vincent Donehue, choreographed by Jerome Robbins, additional lyrics by Betty Comden and Adolph Green, additional music by Jule Styne). Argues that her subjective spectatorship makes visible a politics of the subject which allows for seeing non-normative representations through the dominant system of representation.

3979 Wolf, Stacy. "Desire in Evidence." *TextPQ.* 1997 Oct.; 17(4): 343-351. Notes. Biblio. Lang.: Eng.

USA. 1913-1997. Critical studies. ■Raises questions about gay and lesbian historiography, the status of evidence, and the possible lesbianism of musical theatre actress Mary Martin.

3980 Zinger, Pablo. "Son of Zarzuela." *OpN.* 1997 July; 62(1): 16. Illus.: Photo. B&W. Color. 3. Lang.: Eng.

USA. 1941-1997. Histories-sources. ■Interview with Plácido Domingo on his plans to develop interest in *zarzuela* and continue the work of his parents.

Plays/librettos/scripts

3981 "Writers and Their Work: Peter Stone." *DGQ.* 1997 Fall; 34(3): 4-17. Illus.: Photo. B&W. 3. Lang.: Eng.

USA: New York, NY. 1997. Histories-sources. ■Interview with playwright Peter Stone, current president of the Dramatists Guild about the 1997 theatre season, during which *1776*, for which he wrote the book, was revived and he won the Tony Award for the book of *Titanic.*

3982 Bonahue, Edward T., Jr. "Portraits of the Artist: *Sunday in the Park with George* as 'Postmodern' Drama." 171-186 in Gordon, Joanne, ed. *Stephen Sondheim: A Casebook.* New York, NY/London: Garland; 1997. 259 pp. (Casebooks on Modern Dramatists.) Notes. Biblio. Index. Lang.: Eng.

USA. 1984. Critical studies. ■The post-modern themes and structure of Stephen Sondheim's *Sunday in the Park with George.*

3983 Clarke, Kevin. "'But the Poet of Them All, Who Will Start 'em Simply Ravin', Is the Poet People Call the Bard of Stratford-on-Avon': Shakespeare als Musical." *SJW.* 1997; 133: 134-149. Notes. Lang.: Ger.

USA. 1938-1997. Historical studies. ■Describes how the three 'classic' musicals *The Boys from Syracuse* by Richard Rodgers and Lorenz Hart, *Kiss Me, Kate* by Cole Porter and *West Side Story* by Leonard Bernstein transform the original Shakespearean text into musicals and their specific and artistic possibilities for years.

3984 Cronin, Mari. "Sondheim: The Idealist." 143-152 in Gordon, Joanne, ed. *Stephen Sondheim: A Casebook.* New York, NY/London: Garland; 1997. 259 pp. (Casebooks on Modern Dramatists.) Notes. Biblio. Index. Lang.: Eng.

USA. 1956-1996. Critical studies. ■How the theme of idealism drives the work of Stephen Sondheim.

3985 Deutsch, Didier C. "John Kander, Fred Ebb, Maury Yeston: Broadway's Tony Trio." *BMI.* 1997 Fall; 3: 24-29. Illus.: Photo. Color. 7. Lang.: Eng.

USA: New York, NY. 1997. Histories-sources. ■Interviews with *Chicago*'s authors Kander and Ebb and *Titanic*'s author Maury Yeston, regarding their Tony-winning shows.

3986 Elsom, John. "Les Enfants de Parodie: The Enlightened Incest of Anglo-American Musicals." 231-245 in Boireau, Nicole, ed. *Drama on Drama: Dimensions of Theatricality on the Contemporary British Stage.* New York, NY: St. Martin's; 1997. 256 pp. Pref. Notes. Index. Biblio. Lang.: Eng.

USA. UK-England. 1727-1990. Critical studies. ■Argues that parody and satire of the 'art forms of Old Europe' are inherent in the musical-theatre genre. Includes discussion of *The Beggar's Opera* by John Gay and *City of Angels* by Gelbart, Coleman, and Zippel.

3987 Fink, Bert. "All Singing! All Dancing! All Shakespeare!: Musicalizing the Bard On and Off-Broadway." *DGQ.* 1997 Spr; 34 (1): 3-9. Illus.: Photo. B&W. 2. Lang.: Eng.

USA: New York, NY. 1938-1997. Historical studies. ■Skims the Broadway and Off Broadway history of musical adaptations of Shakespeare from *The Boys from Syracuse* to *Play On!*, an adaptation of *Twelfth Night*, conceived by Sheldon Epps, book by Cheryl L. West with the score a compilation of Duke Ellington songs.

3988 Fisher, James. "Nixon's America and *Follies*: Reappraising a Musical Theater Classic." 69-84 in Gordon, Joanne, ed. *Stephen Sondheim: A Casebook.* New York, NY/London: Garland; 1997. 259 pp. (Casebooks on Modern Dramatists.) Notes. Biblio. Index. Lang.: Eng.

USA. 1971. Critical studies. ■Socio-political themes in Stephen Sondheim's *Follies.* Explores parallels between then-President Richard M. Nixon and his career and the characters of the musical, reflecting the disillusionment of the era.

3989 Flahaven, Sean Patrick. "Three's a Crowd." *ShowM.* 1997 Fall; 13(3): 27-30, 70-71. Illus.: Photo. B&W. 7. Lang.: Eng.

USA: New York, NY. 1964-1997. Historical studies. ■Survey of one- or two-character stage musicals which played on or Off-Broadway, from Harvey Schmidt and Tom Jones' *I Do, I Do* to Andrew Lippa and Tom Greenwald's *John & Jen* (1995), including Skip Kennon and Ellen Fitzhugh's *Herringbone* (1982), Polly Pen and Peggy Harmon's *Goblin Market* (1985), and Andrew Lloyd Webber and Don Black's *Sing and Dance* as adapted by director Richard Maltby, Jr. (1985).

3990 Fleischer, Leonard. "'More Beautiful Than True' or 'Never Mind a Small Disaster': The Illusion in *Pacific Overtures.*" 107-124 in Gordon, Joanne, ed. *Stephen Sondheim: A Casebook.* New York, NY/London: Garland; 1997. 259 pp. (Casebooks on Modern Dramatists.) Notes. Biblio. Index. Lang.: Eng.

USA. 1976. Critical studies. ■Analysis of Stephen Sondheim's *Pacific Overtures.*

3991 Fraser, Barbara Means. "Revisiting Greece: The Sondheim Chorus." 223-250 in Gordon, Joanne, ed. *Stephen Sondheim: A Casebook.* New York, NY/London: Garland; 1997. 259 pp. (Casebooks on Modern Dramatists.) Notes. Biblio. Index. Lang.: Eng.

USA. 1962-1996. Critical studies. ■The nature of the Chorus in musicals by Stephen Sondheim compared to its use in classical Greek drama.

3992 Hanson, Laura. "Broadway Babies: Images of Women in the Musicals of Stephen Sondheim." 13-34 in Gordon, Joanne, ed. *Stephen Sondheim: A Casebook.* New York, NY/London: Garland; 1997. 259 pp. (Casebooks on Modern Dramatists.) Notes. Biblio. Index. Lang.: Eng.

USA. 1956-1996. Critical studies. ■Argues that these increasingly complex women in Sondheim's musicals explore the tensions and anxieties of ambiguous relationships in the modern world.

3993 Kivesto, Lois. "Comedy Tonight! *A Funny Thing Happened on the Way to the Forum.*" 35-46 in Gordon, Joanne, ed. *Stephen Sondheim: A Casebook.* New York, NY/London: Garland; 1997. 259 pp. (Casebooks on Modern Dramatists.) Notes. Biblio. Index. Lang.: Eng.

USA. 1962. Critical studies. ■Reconstruction of creation of composer/lyricist Stephen Sondheim's first solo success, *A Funny Thing Happened on the Way to the Forum.* Focuses on the role of classical Roman comedy in the musical.

3994 Konas, Gary. "*Passion*: Not Just Another Simple Love Story." 205-222 in Gordon, Joanne, ed. *Stephen Sondheim: A Casebook.* New York, NY/London: Garland; 1997. 259 pp. (Casebooks on Modern Dramatists.) Notes. Biblio. Index. Lang.: Eng.

USA. 1994. Critical studies. ■The theme of love, internal structure, musical line, and psychological spirit of Stephen Sondheim's musical *Passion.*

3995 Miller, Scott. "*Assassins* and the Concept Musical." 187-204 in Gordon, Joanne, ed. *Stephen Sondheim: A Casebook.* New York, NY/London: Garland; 1997. 259 pp. (Casebooks on Modern Dramatists.) Notes. Biblio. Index. Lang.: Eng.

MUSIC-DRAMA: Musical theatre—Plays/librettos/scripts

USA. 1970-1991. Critical studies. ∎Stephen Sondheim's two 'concept musicals' *Company* and *Assassins*.

3996 Milner, Andrew. "'Let the Pupil Show the Master': Stephen Sondheim and Oscar Hammerstein II." 153-170 in Gordon, Joanne, ed. *Stephen Sondheim: A Casebook.* New York, NY/London: Garland; 1997. 259 pp. (Casebooks on Modern Dramatists.) Notes. Biblio. Index. Lang.: Eng.

USA. 1945-1968. Critical studies. ∎On the relationship between composer/lyricist Stephen Sondheim and his early mentor Oscar Hammerstein II.

3997 Olson, John. "*Company*—25 Years Later." 47-68 in Gordon, Joanne, ed. *Stephen Sondheim: A Casebook.* New York, NY/London: Garland; 1997. 259 pp. (Casebooks on Modern Dramatists.) Notes. Biblio. Index. Lang.: Eng.

USA. 1970. Critical studies. ∎Why Stephen Sondheim's *Company*, with its specific appeal to its 1970 audience, is seldom revived. Discusses theme, action and situations, period references, production design, and changes in audience perspective.

3998 Pickle, Deborah Laureen. *Crossing Bridges: The Roles in the Works of Stephen Sondheim for Classically Trained Soprano.* Tempe, AZ: Arizona State Univ; 1997. 181 pp. Notes. Biblio. [D.M.A. Thesis, Univ. Microfilms Order No. AAC 9725327.] Lang.: Eng.

USA. 1959-1996. Critical studies. ∎Roles are examined for their tessitura, range, use of legitimate technique, and difficulty both musically and vocally, as well as the character's function within the plot, participation in ensembles, and analysis of her solo songs. A brief plot synopsis of each show is provided, as well as significant historical information about performances.

3999 Schlesinger, Judith. "Psychology, Evil, and *Sweeney Todd* or, 'Don't I Know You, Mister'." 125-142 in Gordon, Joanne, ed. *Stephen Sondheim: A Casebook.* New York, NY/London: Garland; 1997. 259 pp. (Casebooks on Modern Dramatists.) Notes. Biblio. Index. Lang.: Eng.

USA. 1976. Critical studies. ∎The effect on audiences of psychological themes in Stephen Sondheim's *Sweeney Todd.*

4000 Sherman, Harold. "Broadway's Forbidden History." *ShowM.* 1997 Fall; 13(3): 41-46. Illus.: Photo. B&W. 8. Lang.: Eng.

USA: New York, NY. 1981-1997. Historical studies. ∎Parodist Gerard Alessandrini, who wrote and produced nine editions of *Forbidden Broadway* between 1981 and 1997. Includes lyrics from nine songs from the shows with Alessandrini's comments on them.

4001 Stasio, Marilyn. "The Difference between Kander and Ebb." *AmTh.* 1997 Feb.; 14(2): 10-14. Illus.: Photo. B&W. 5. Lang.: Eng.

USA: New York, NY. 1927-1997. Biographical studies. ∎Career and collaborative partnership of lyricist Fred Ebb and composer John Kander. Focus on current revival of their musical *Chicago* and upcoming Broadway opening of *Steel Pier* directed by Scott Ellis. Includes complete list of their theatre, film and television credits.

4002 Terry-Morgan, Elmo. "*Noise/Funk*: Fo' Real Black Theatre on 'Da Great White Way." *AfAmR.* 1997 Win; 31(4): 677-686. Lang.: Eng.

USA: New York, NY. 1996-1997. Critical studies. ∎Hails *Bring in 'Da Noise, Bring in 'Da Funk*, created by Savion Glover and George C. Wolfe, book by Reg E. Gaines, music by Ann Duquesnay, Zane Mark and Daryl Waters, as a play that captures most fully the Black experience, populated with Black characters that Black audiences know in an historical context.

Opera

Administration

4003 Pfalzer, Janina. "Det kollektiva mordet på en konstart." (The Collective Murder Of an Artform.) *MuD.* 1997; 19(4): 8-9. Illus.: Photo. B&W. Lang.: Swe.

Europe. USA. 1960. Critical studies. ∎A discussion about the increasing fees for jet-set singers at the expense of the more ordinary singer, with reference to Norman Lebrecht's book *When the Music Stops.*

4004 Diquinzio, Mary Elizabeth. *Opera in the Duchy of Lucca, 1817-1847.* Washington, DC: Catholic Univ. of America; 1997. 210 pp. Biblio. Notes. [Ph.D. Dissertation, Univ. Microfilms Order No. AAC 9726486.] Lang.: Eng.

Italy: Lucca. 1817-1847. Historical studies. ∎State patronage and control of opera, with emphasis on the high level of subsidization and the social, political and economic rationale for state support. Also reconstructs the activities of impresario Alessandro Lanari, whose career was launched in Lucca and who maintained close ties with the Duchy for decades.

4005 Reiss, Alvin H. "Opera Woos Audience and Donors with Innovative Marketing Approaches." *FundM.* 1997 July; 28(5): 40-41. Illus.: Photo. B&W. 2. Lang.: Eng.

USA. 1997. Historical studies. ∎Marketing techniques of opera companies including Houston Grand Opera's brochure designed by Maurice Sendak and Opera Pacific's use of Warner Brothers cartoon characters.

4006 Vilmányi, Zita. "Látogatóban az Opera News-nál." (A Visit to *Opera News.*) *OperaL.* 1997; 6(1): 28-29. Illus.: Photo. B&W. 1. Lang.: Hun.

USA: New York, NY. 1933-1997. Histories-sources. ∎A historical survey of the popular opera-related magazine introduced by the editor-in-chief Patrick J. Smith.

Audience

4007 Orbaum, Jack; Roberts, Don; Heintzman, Joseph R.; Walsh, Philip; Yates, Joyce. "*Opera Canada*'s Readers Go to the Opera." *OC.* 1997 Sum; 38(2): 18-21. Illus.: Photo. B&W. 4. Lang.: Eng.

Canada. USA. 1997. Histories-sources. ∎Publication of winning entries in a contest in which readers relate their most memorable moments attending opera.

Basic theatrical documents

4008 Ligeti, György; Meschke, Michael; Michel, Pierre, ed.; Vittoz, Michel, transl.; Skelton, Geoffrey, transl. "Le Grand Macabre." *ASO.* 1997 Nov/Dec.; 180: 3-85. Notes. Illus.: Photo. B&W. Lang.: Fre, Eng.

Europe. 1978-1997. ∎Ligeti and Meschke's libretto, in English and French translations from the original Swedish version, for Ligeti's opera *Le Grand Macabre*, which is based on *La Balade du Grand Macabre (The Grand Macabre's Stroll)* by Michel de Ghelderode and influenced by playwright Alfred Jarry. Includes plot and musical analysis, commentary, numerous photos.

4009 Boieldieu, François Adrien; Scribe, Eugène; Colas, Damien, ed. "La Dame Blanche." (The Lady in White.) *ASO.* 1997 Mar/Apr.; 176: 3-87. Notes. Illus.: Photo. Dwg. B&W. Lang.: Fre.

France. 1825. ∎Text of Scribe's libretto for Boieldieu's opera, with extensive analysis, commentary, and illustration.

4010 Donizetti, Gaetano; Bayard, Jean-François; Vernoy de Saint-Georges, J.H.; Campos, Rémy, ed. "La Fille du régiment." (The Daughter of the Regiment.) *ASO.* 1997 Sep/Oct.; 179: 3-67. Illus.: Dwg. Photo. B&W. Lang.: Fre.

France. 1840. ∎The libretto by Bayard and Vernoy de Saint-Georges for Donizetti's opera. Includes plot and musical analysis, commentary, illustration.

4011 Brasch, Thomas. "*Der Sprung.*" (The Jump.) *TZ.* 1997; 5: 82-85. Illus.: Photo. B&W. 6. Lang.: Ger.

Germany. 1997. Histories-sources. ∎A libretto including the playwright's biography and bibliography.

4012 Bellini, Vincenzo; Romani, Felice; Mancini, Claudio, transl.; Boukobza, Jean-François, ed. "La Somnambule." (The Sleep Walker.) *ASO.* 1997 July/Aug.; 178: 3-54. Illus.: Photo. Dwg. B&W. Lang.: Fre, Ita.

Italy. 1831. ∎Romani's libretto for Bellini's opera *La sonnambula.* Includes notes, commentary, detailed plot and musical analysis, and numerous illustrations.

4013 Cimarosa, Domenico; Bertati, Giovanni; Mancini, Claudio, transl.; Campos, Rémy, ed. "Le Mariage secret." (The Secret Marriage.) *ASO.* 1997 Jan/Feb.; 175: 3-84. Notes. Tables. Illus.: Photo. B&W. Lang.: Fre, Ita.

MUSIC-DRAMA: Opera—Basic theatrical documents

Italy. 1792. ■Text of Bertati's libretto for Cimarosa's opera *Il matrimonio segreto* in Italian with French translation. Includes analysis of music and plot, numerous illustrations.

4014 Falla, Manuel de; Fernández Shaw, Carlos; Boukobza, Jean-François, ed.; Milliet, Paul, transl. "La vie brève." (Life Is Short.) *ASO.* 1997 May/June; 177: 12-42. Notes. Illus.: Photo. B&W. Lang.: Fre, Spa.
Spain. 1913-1914. ■Fernández Shaw's libretto, with translation into French, for Falla's opera *La vida breve*. Includes introduction, plot and musical analysis, extensive illustration.

4015 Falla, Manuel de; Martínez Sierra, Gregorio; Boukobza, Jean-François, ed.; Hoffelé, Jean-Charles, intro. "L'amour sorcier." (Love, the Magician.) *ASO.* 1997 May/June; 177: 52-78. Notes. Illus.: Photo. B&W. Lang.: Fre, Spa.
Spain. 1915-1916. ■Falla and Martínez Sierra's libretto to Falla's opera *El amor brujo*, with French translation, musical and plot analysis, abundant illustration and commentary. Includes accounts of the 1916 ballet version.

4016 Falla, Manuel de; Hoffelé, Jean-Charles, ed.; Ramirez, B.&C., transl.; Jean-Aubry, G., transl. "Les Tréteaux de Maître Pierre." (The Play of Master Pedro.) *ASO.* 1997 May/June; 177: 88-111. Illus.: Photo. B&W. Lang.: Fre, Spa.
Spain. 1923. ■Text of Falla's libretto, based on Cervantes' *Don Quixote*, for his opera *El retablo de Maese Pedro*.

4017 Fornes, Maria Irene. "*Terra Incognita*." *ThM.* 1993; 24(2): 99-111. Illus.: Photo. B&W. 6. Lang.: Eng.
USA. 1992. ■Text of Fornes' libretto for Roberto Sierra's opera.

Design/technology

4018 Radon, Florian. "*Maschinist Hopkins*." *BtR.* 1997; 91(special issue): 20-22. Tables. Illus.: Photo. Color. 5. Lang.: Ger.
Austria: Vienna. 1997. Historical studies. ■Describes the stage sets and their technical realization as well as spatial-acoustical problems of Max Brand's *Maschinist Hopkins*, directed by Peter Pawlik, the history and its performance by Neue Oper Wien at Wiener Messepalast including a short biography of the composer.

4019 Lasker, David. "Reality by Design." *OC.* 1997 Sum; 38(2): 10-13. Illus.: Photo. B&W. 4. Lang.: Eng.
Canada: Toronto, ON. USA: New York, NY. 1975-1997. Critical studies. ■Critique of the minimalist design movement in opera, including the Met's 1975 production of *Eugene Onegin* designed by Michael Levine and directed by Robert Carsen and John Conklin's design for the Canadian Opera Company's *Il Re Pastore*.

4020 *Sogno e deliria. Scenografie d'opera della Bibliothèque National de France—Bibliothèque Musée de l'Opéra de Paris.* (Dream and Frenzy: Opera Stage Designs from the Bibliothèque National's Library and Museum of the Paris Opera.) Milan: Electa; 1997. 93 pp. Illus.: Dwg. Sketches. Lang.: Ita.
France: Paris. 1850-1997. Histories-sources. ■Catalogue of an exhibition, held at the French Academy in Rome in 1997, of sketches and watercolors belonging to the Paris Opera Museum and Library.

4021 Butzmann, Volker. "Märchenhafte Objektwelt in der Semperoper." (Magical World of Objects at the Semper Opera.) *BtR.* 1997; 91(6): 10-16. Illus.: Photo. Plan. B&W. Color. Explod.Sect. Grd.Plan. 21. Lang.: Ger.
Germany: Dresden. 1997. Histories-sources. ■The technical director describes from an exclusively technical viewpoint the set and costume designs created by Rosalie for Richard Strauss' *Die Frau ohne Schatten*, directed by Hans Hollmann at Semperoper (Dresden).

4022 Heckelmann, Susanne. "Schlachthof V–Die Simultanbühne im neuen Gewand." (*Slaughterhouse 5*–The Simultaneous Stage in New Appearance.) *BtR.* 1997; 91(1): 8-12. Illus.: Photo. Color. 8. Lang.: Ger.
Germany: Munich. 1997. Historical studies. ■Reports on the first performance of the opera *Schlachthof 5* by Hans Jürgen Bose and directed by Eike Gramss at Bayerische Staatsoper. The dramaturgical conception uses a simultaneous stage with light-pads by designer Gottfried Pilz.

4023 Meilhaus, Andrea. "Idomeneo." *BtR.* 1997; 91(special issue): 40-44. Illus.: Photo. Plan. Sketches. B&W. Color. Detail. Grd.Plan. 22. Lang.: Ger.

Germany: Munich. 1996. Histories-sources. ■A scenic assistant describes the development and final course of Mozart's *Idomeneo* directed by Andreas Homoki at Bayerische Staatsoper. It concerns a unit, enclosed space, fixed at the proscenium area but able to open to all sides.

4024 Csák, P. Judit. "Díszlettervező: Kádár János Miklós." (Stage-Designer: János Miklós Kádár.) *OperaL.* 1997; 6(3): 27-28. Lang.: Hun.
Hungary. 1954-1997. Histories-sources. ■A conversation with the stage-designer of Mozart's *Don Giovanni*, presented by the Debrecen Csokonai Theatre under György Lengyel's direction in April, 1997.

4025 Bucci, Moreno, ed.; Bartoletti, Chiara, ed. *Felice Casorati per il teatro.* (Felice Casorati and His Theatre.) Florence: Ente Autonomo Teatro Comunale Firenze; 1997. 221 pp. Biblio. Illus.: Photo. Sketches. B&W. Lang.: Ita.
Italy. 1933-1954. Histories-sources. ■Catalogue of an exhibition devoted to the work of painter and scenographer Felice Casorati.

4026 Topor, Roland. "Un frisson de vraie trouille." (A Shiver of True Terror.) *ASO.* 1997 Nov/Dec.; 180: 108. Illus.: Dwg. B&W. 6. Lang.: Fre.
Italy: Bologna. 1979. Histories-sources. ■Costume designer of Giorgio Pressburger's production of *Le Grand Macabre* by Ligeti describes his work.

4027 Blomqvist, Kurt. "Höga krav på dekorhantering." (High Demands For Handling the Decor.) *ProScen.* 1997; 21(1): 20-21. Illus.: Photo. Color. Lang.: Swe.
Sweden: Stockholm. 1995. Technical studies. ■A short presentation of the new transport system for sets between the opera house Kungliga Operan and the workshops just outside Stockholm.

4028 Forssén, Michael. "Det slitstarka marmorgolvet." (The Durable Marble Floor.) *ProScen.* 1997; 21(2): 17. Illus.: Photo. Color. Lang.: Swe.
Sweden: Gothenburg. 1996. Technical studies. ■Report on the construction of a faux-marble floor made of painted PVC-plates at GöteborgsOperan.

4029 Nilsson, Göran. "Helgonet på Bleecker Street på YstadsOperan." (*The Saint of Bleecker Street* at YstadsOperan.) *ProScen.* 1997; 21(3): 13. Illus.: Photo. B&W. Lang.: Swe.
Sweden: Ystad. 1997. Historical studies. ■Report on the technical aspects of Richard Bark's summer production of Menotti's opera.

4030 Ståhle, Anna-Greta. "Operans gömda skatter." (The Hidden Treasures of the Royal Opera.) *Danst.* 1997; 7(3): 20-21. Illus.: Photo. Color. Lang.: Swe.
Sweden: Stockholm. 1954-1997. Historical studies. ■A presentation of the former wardrobe manager of the Royal Swedish Opera, Börje Edh, and his investigations of the rich collections of costumes from the eighteenth century onwards.

4031 Svensson, Niklas; Efraimsson, Lars-Magnus. "Ett lättare liv med sandwichkonstruktioner." (An Easier Life With Sandwich Constructions.) *ProScen.* 1997; 21(3): 28-29. Illus.: Diagram. Photo. B&W. Lang.: Swe.
Sweden: Gothenburg. 1996. Technical studies. ■A presentation of a sandwich technology using Divinycell as core for construction of a grand stairway, with reference to Staffan Aspegren's staging of Puccini's *Tosca* at GöteborgsOperan, with scenography by Lars Östbergh.

4032 Barbour, David. "Nights at the Opera." *LDim.* 1997 Mar.; 21(2): 13. Illus.: Photo. Color. 2. Lang.: Eng.
UK-England. 1997. Historical studies. ■Giuseppe Di Iorio's lighting design for two operas produced by the English Touring Opera company: *Les Pêcheurs de perles* by Bizet and *Rigoletto* by Verdi.

4033 Lampert-Gréaux, Ellen. "Russian Roulette." *LDim.* 1997 May; 21(4): 18-19. Illus.: Photo. Color. 2. Lang.: Eng.
USA: New York, NY. 1997. Historical studies. ■Jean Kalman's lighting design for production of Čajkovskij's *Eugene Onegin* at the Metropolitan Opera, directed by Robert Carsen.

4034 Lampert-Gréaux, Ellen. "Revolutionary Lighting." *LDim.* 1997 Nov.; 21(10): 15. Illus.: Photo. Color. 2. Lang.: Eng.
USA: New York, NY, Cooperstown, NY. 1997. Technical studies. ■Robert Wierzel's lighting design for Verdi's *Macbeth* at New York City Opera, directed by Leon Major, and Mark McCullough's lighting design

MUSIC-DRAMA: Opera—Design/technology

for Rossini's *L'Italiana in Algeri* at Glimmerglass Opera, directed by
Christopher Alden.

4035   Lampert-Gréaux, Ellen. "Martin Pakledinaz." *TCI.* 1997
Nov.; 31(9): 38-41. Illus.: Photo. 18. Lang.: Eng.
USA: Santa Fe, NM, New York, NY. 1997. Historical studies. ■Costume
designer Martin Pakledinaz uses 15th to 19th-century Indian silhouettes
to clothe characters in *Ashoka's Dream* at the Santa Fe Opera (directed
by Stephen Wadsworth, music by Peter Lieberson, libretto by Douglas
Penick), and at the New York City Opera in Handel's *Xerxes*, also
directed by Wadsworth.

4036   Winn, Steven. "Lotfi Ambitions." *TCI.* 1997 Feb.; 31(2):
32-35. Illus.: Photo. 9. Lang.: Eng.
USA: San Francisco, CA. 1996. Historical studies. ■Sound designer
Roger Gans' collaboration with San Francisco Opera general director
Lotfi Mansouri, and conductor and music director Donald C. Runnicles.
The Opera is temporarily housed at the Bill Graham Civic Auditorium
while the War Memorial Opera House is under repair for earthquake
damage. Addresses sound problems at this temporary housing.

Institutions

4037   Csernay, László. "A bécsi Staatsoper krónikája." (The
Chronicle of the Viennese State Opera House.) *OperaL.*
1997; 6(2): 29-30. Lang.: Hun.
Austria: Vienna. Hungary. 1945-1995. Critical studies. ■Review of
Hevard Hoyer's *Chronic der Wiener Staatsoper* published in 1995, with
emphasis on the book's listing of seventy five Hungarian and Hungarian-
born artists among the renowned personalities.

4038   Citron, Paula. "A Delicate Balance." *OC.* 1997 Fall; 38(3):
20-23. Illus.: Photo. B&W. 3. Lang.: Eng.
Canada. 1997. Histories-sources. ■Interviews with the general directors
of the Canadian Opera Company, Vancouver Opera, L'Opéra de Montréal, Calgary Opera and Ottawa Lyra Opera, regarding the planning of
an opera season.

4039   Lazaridès, Alexandre. "Une saison à l'opéra (1996-1997)."
(A Season at the Opera, 1996-1997.) *JCT.* 1997; 84 : 161-
167. Notes. Illus.: Photo. B&W. 3. Lang.: Fre.
Canada: Montreal, PQ. 1996-1997. Historical studies. ■Reviews 96-97
season offered by Opéra de Montréal.

4040   McLean, Sandy. "Un-Sung Heroes." *OC.* 1997 Fall; 38(3):
10-15. Illus.: Photo. B&W. 9. Lang.: Eng.
Canada. 1997. Critical studies. ■Directory of small Canadian opera companies nationwide, with descriptions of mission and product.

4041   Scott, Iain. "Why *Opera Canada* Matters: Celebrating 150
Issues of Service to Opera in Canada." *OC.* 1997 Spr; 38(1):
10-13. Illus.: Photo. B&W. 24. Lang.: Eng.
Canada: Toronto, ON. 1960-1997. Historical studies. ■Honoring the
publication's thirty-eight years of covering opera in Canada.

4042   Huang, Chun-Zen. *Traveling Opera Troupes in Shanghai,
1842-1949.* Washington, DC: Catholic Univ. of America;
1997. 272 pp. Notes. Biblio. [Ph.D. Dissertation, Univ.
Microfilms Order No. AAC 9728641.] Lang.: Eng.
China: Shanghai. 1842-1949. Historical studies. ■Traveling Western
opera troupes in Shanghai and their eventual impact on Chinese culture.
Details the touring companies, their repertoire, impresarios, singers, the
theatres where they performed and, where possible, the quality of their
performance.

4043   Sørensen, Lilo. "Mod alle odds—pris til Holland House."
(Against All Odds—Prize to Holland House.) *TE.* 1997 June;
84: 30-33. Illus.: Photo. B&W. 7. Lang.: Dan.
Denmark. 1988-1997. Historical studies. ■*Teater Et* awards the music
theatre Holland House and director Jacob F. Schokking for its excellent
opera productions.

4044   Tranberg, Sören. "Att våga vara genial—inom givna ramar."
(To Dare To Be Brilliant—Within Given Frames.) *MuD.*
1997; 19(2): 16-17. Illus.: Photo. B&W. 4. Lang.: Swe.
Denmark: Copenhagen. 1980. Histories-sources. ■An interview with the
opera manager at Det Kongelige Teater: Elaine Padmore, about her policy of repertory and casting.

4045   Raiskinen, Juhani. "The Rise of Opera." *FT.* 1997; 51:
14-16. Illus.: Photo. B&W. 4. Lang.: Eng.

Finland: Helsinki. 1990-1996. Historical studies. ■Development of Finnish National Opera, Suomen Kansallisoopera, throughout the 1990s.

4046   Brandenburg, Detlef. "Wie sieht das Opernhaus der Zukunft
aus?" (How Does the Opera of the Future Look?) *DB.* 1997;
12: 12-17. Illus.: Photo. B&W. 5. Lang.: Ger.
Germany: Hamburg. 1997. Histories-sources. ■An interview with Albin
Hänseroth, director of Staatsoper about programs and concepts.

4047   Brandenburg, Detlef. "Im Opernhaus zum Goldnen Hirsch-
en." (In the Opera Toward the Golden Stag.) *DB.* 1997; 5:
10-15. Illus.: Photo. B&W. 5. Lang.: Ger.
Germany: Hannover. 1996-1997. Biographical studies. ■A portrait of
Andreas Delfs, General Music Director at Niedersächsische Staatsoper
since 1996 and his success conducting *König Hirsch* by Hans Werner
Henze directed by Hans-Peter Lehmann.

4048   Kranz, Dieter. "Millionen und Donnerkeile." (Millions and
Flintstones.) *DB.* 1997; 12: 22-26. Illus.: Photo. B&W. 5.
Lang.: Ger.
Germany: Berlin. 1997. Historical studies. ■Describes the current situa-
tion of the three opera houses (Deutsche Oper, Deutsche Staatsoper and
Komische Oper) in Berlin in view of increasing budget cuts.

4049   Dalos, László. "Volt egyszer egy Vígopera." (Once Upon a
Time There Was the Comic Opera.) *OperaL.* 1997; 6(3) :
29-31. Lang.: Hun.
Hungary: Budapest. 1946-1948. Historical studies. ■Profile of Vígopera,
which produced mainly comic chamber opera unfamiliar to the Hungarian audience of the time, using young singers (most later engaged by the
Hungarian State Opera House) under the direction of composer-
conductor Béla Endre.

4050   Mátyus, Zsuzsa, comp., ed.; Mezey, Béla, photo. *Magyar
Állami Operaház és Erkel Színház, 112. évad, 1995-1996.*
(The Hungarian State Opera House and Erkel Theatre,
112th Season, 1995/96.) Budapest: Magyar Állami
Operaház; 1996. 146 pp. Illus.: Photo. B&W. Color. 126.
Lang.: Hun.
Hungary: Budapest. 1995-1996. Histories-sources. ■Annual of the activ-
ity of Budapest's Opera House summing up the premieres, revivals, guest
performances, competitions and other events with collection of data on
the company.

4051   Mátyus, Zsuzsa, comp., ed.; Mezey, Béla, photo. *Magyar
Állami Operaház és Erkel Színház, 113. évad, 1996-1997.*
(The Hungarian State Opera House and Erkel Theatre,
113th Season, 1996/1997.) Budapest: Magyar Állami
Operaház; 1997. 148 pp. Illus.: Photo. B&W. Color. 135.
Lang.: Hun.
Hungary: Budapest. 1996-1997. Histories-sources. ■Annual of the activ-
ity of Budapest's Opera House (and its other performance space, the
Erkel Theatre) summing up the premières, revivals, guest performances,
competititons, gala concerts and other events with a collection of data on
the company.

4052   Suèr, Henk; Meurs, Josine. *Geheel in de Geest van Wagner.
De Wagner-vereeniging in Nederland 1883-1959.* (Totally
Devoted to Wagner: The Wagner Society in the Nether-
lands, 1883-1959.) Amsterdam: Theater Instituut Neder-
land; 1997. 302 pp. Pref. Notes. Biblio. Index. Append. Illus.:
Photo. Dwg. B&W. Color. 120. Lang.: Dut.
Netherlands. 1883-1959. Histories-sources. ■Archival materials of the
Wagner-vereeniging, which was vital to the development of opera pro-
duction in the Netherlands in the early twentieth century.

4053   Djakova, L. *Teatral'naja sjuita: Permskij akademičeskij
teat'r opery i baleta—v licach, vstrečach i razmyšlenijach.*
(Theatrical Suite: Perm's Academic Opera and Ballet Theatre, in Faces, Meetings, and Discussions.) Perm: Puška;
1997. 120 pp. Lang.: Rus.
Russia: Perm. 1945-1997. Historical studies. ■Portrait of the theatre.

4054   "Noises Off." *Econ.* 1997 Nov 22; 345(8044): 101. Illus.:
Photo. B&W. 1. Lang.: Eng.
Spain: Madrid. 1997. Historical studies. ■Managerial conflicts at the
newly refurbished Teatro Real Opera House. Budgetary problems, architecture of the new building, acoustics.

MUSIC-DRAMA: Opera—Institutions

4055 Bergfors, P-G. "Milleniumskifte med mjukvaror." (A Turn Of the Millenium With Software.) *MuD*. 1997; 19(2): 18. Illus.: Photo. B&W. Lang.: Swe.
Sweden: Gothenburg. 1997. Historical studies. ■A presentation of the plans of GöteborgsOperan for the coming three seasons.

4056 Pfalzer, Janina. "Björling bor i Borlänge." (Björling Lives In Borlänge.) *MuD*. 1997; 19(3): 43. Illus.: Photo. B&W. Lang.: Swe.
Sweden: Borlänge. 1994. Historical studies. ■A presentation of the new Jussi Björling Museum, constructed by Harald Henrysson.

4057 Pfalzer, Janina. "Satsa eller ta konsekvenserna!" (Invest Or Take the Consequences!)*MuD*. 1997; 19(4): 10. Illus.: Photo. B&W. Lang.: Swe.
Sweden: Gothenburg, Stockholm. 1994. Critical studies. ■A comparison of the funding of Kungliga Operan, GöteborgsOperan and Folkoperan.

4058 Crawford, Bruce. "Toward the 21st Century." *OpN*. 1997 Dec 6; 62(6): 44-45. Illus.: Photo. Color. 1. Lang.: Eng.
USA: New York, NY. 1997. Histories-sources. ■Interview with Metropolitan Opera President, Bruce Crawford, about challenges for the arts in the new millennium.

4059 Driscoll, F. Paul. "Let's Get Small." *OpN*. 1997 Aug.; 62(2): 24-29. Illus.: Photo. B&W. Color. 5. Lang.: Eng.
USA. 1997. Histories-sources. ■Comments on downsizing by directors of regional operas, summer festivals, and musical institutions on their operatic aims and production policies. Interviewees are: Charles Mackay, Opera Theatre of St. Louis. Peter Russell, Wolf Trap Opera Company. Mark Tiarks, Chicago Opera Theater. Gordon Ostrowski, Manhattan School of Music. Susan MacLennan, Tri-Cities Opera. Paul Kellogg, Glimmerglass Opera. New York City Opera. Kevin MacDowell, Academy of Vocal Arts. Joseph LoSchiavo, The Vineyard Theatre. Richard Marshall, Center for Contemporary Opera. Elaine Bookwalter, Indiana Opera Theater.

4060 Marsh, Robert C. "The Ravinia Opera, 1912-1931." *OQ*. 1997 Spr; 13(3): 97-116. Notes. [Reprinted from the Chicago Opera Project of the Newberry Library, 1995.] Lang.: Eng.
USA: Chicago, IL. 1904-1931. Historical studies. ■History of the Ravinia Opera: construction of theatre and pavilion, audience response, its evolution from a concert series to an opera festival, productions, artists, conductors.

4061 Nix, John. "Coach's Notebook: An Interview with Robert Spillman." *OJ*. 1997 Dec.; 30(4): 31-41. Lang.: Eng.
USA: Boulder, CO. 1940-1997. Histories-sources. ■Interview with music director of Lyric Theatre program and chair of piano at University of Colorado: his teaching methods with singers, early piano training, discussion of relationship between singers and accompanists, career development options for singers and pianists.

4062 Pearlman, Richard. "Close Encounters." *OpN*. 1997 Aug.; 62(2): 18-23. Illus.: Photo. B&W. Color. 6. Lang.: Eng.
USA. 1997. Histories-sources. ■Pearlman, director of the Lyric Opera of Chicago's Lyric Opera Center for American Artists, recounts his experience with chamber opera in the United States.

4063 Rosenfeld, Lorraine, comp. "Summer Magic: a Guide to Festival Opera in the U.S." *OpN*. 1997 June; 61(17): 36-44. Illus.: Photo. Color. B&W. 10. Lang.: Eng.
USA. Canada. 1997. Histories-sources. ■List of summer 1997 opera festivals in the United States and Canada.

4064 Sevilla-Gonzaga, Marylis. "Pearls of the Golden West." *OpN*. 1997 Nov.; 62(5): 32-34. Illus.: Photo. B&W. Color. 5. Lang.: Eng.
USA: Santa Barbara, CA. 1946-1997. Historical studies. ■Development of the summer school voice program of the Music Academy of the West. Notes the influence of Lotte Lehmann, Martial Singher, and Marilyn Horne, the current director. Emphasizes the 1997 performance of *Il Viaggio a Reims* by Rossini, Christopher Mattaliano, director.

Performance spaces

4065 Aronson, Arnold; Karin Winkelser, transl. "Avantgarde-Oper und szenischer Raum." (Avant-garde Opera and Scenic Space.) *BtR*. 1997; 91(4): 35-38. Lang.: Ger.
Europe. 1900-1997. Critical studies. ■Argues that proscenium architecture is a 'gigantic chasm', which has assimilated its audience over 400 years of theatre tradition and has devoured all attempts at renewal.

4066 Schmitz-Gielsdorf. "Der venezianische Phönix." (The Venetian Phoenix.) *DB*. 1997; 3: 19-23. Illus.: Photo. B&W. 4. Lang.: Ger.
Italy: Venice. 1792-1997. Historical studies. ■Describes the historical and future meaning of Teatro La Fenice and its burning in 1996.

4067 Blomquist, Kurt. "Stockholmsoperan har fått nya repetitionslokaler." (The Stockholm Opera Has Got New Rehearsal Premises.) *ProScen*. 1997; 21(2): 20-21. Illus.: Photo. Color. Lang.: Swe.
Sweden: Stockholm. 1996. Technical studies. ■How the opera's new rehearsal space was planned along with the performance space.

4068 Söderberg, Olle. "Från väveri till moderna lokaler." (From Weaving Mill To Modern Localities.) *ProScen*. 1997; 21(1): 8-10. Illus.: Photo. B&W. Lang.: Swe.
Sweden: Karlstad. 1996. Historical studies. ■A presentation of Musikteater i Värmland's new workshop and spaces for rehearsals in an old weaving mill.

4069 Söderberg, Olle. "Vacker pärla vid Klarälvens strand." (A Beautiful Pearl on the Beach at Klarälven.) *ProScen*. 1997; 21(1): 17-19. Illus.: Photo. B&W. Color. Lang.: Swe.
Sweden: Karlstad. 1876. Historical studies. ■A presentation of the newly restored Karlstad Teater.

4070 Hagman, Bertil. "Covent Garden—en ansiktslyftning." (Covent Garden—a Face Lift.) *MuD*. 1997; 19(1): 24-25. Illus.: Dwg. B&W. Lang.: Swe.
UK-England: London. 1997. Technical studies. ■A short presentation of the plans to rebuild the Royal Opera House, Covent Garden.

4071 Crickhowell, Nicholas. *Opera House Lottery: Zaha Hadid and the Cardiff Bay Project*. Cardiff: Univ of Wales P; 1997. 175 pp. Index. Illus.: Design. 7. Lang.: Eng.
UK-Wales: Cardiff. 1986-1995. Historical studies. ■Examines conflicts in the construction and management of a new performing arts complex, the Cardiff Bay Opera House, home of the Welsh National Opera. Examines its ten-year history, government funding background, the politics involved, both local and regional, and town planning and urban renewal agendas.

Performance/production

4072 "Les différentes versions de 'L'Amour sorcier'." (The Different Versions of *El amor brujo*.) *ASO*. 1997 May/June; 177: 86. Lang.: Fre.
1915-1924. Historical studies. ■Traces the various versions of Falla's opera for ballet, orchestral suites, etc.

4073 Bannon, David. "Point and Click Opera! Top Web Sites for the Opera Fan." *OpN*. 1997 Nov.; 62(5): 48-49. Illus.: Photo. Color. Lang.: Eng.
1997. Histories-sources. ■An evaluative weblist guide for opera lovers.

4074 Bégaud, Josée. "L'oeuvre à l'affiche." (The Work on Stage.) *ASO*. 1997 Mar/Apr.; 176: 94-96. Illus.: Photo. Dwg. B&W. 7. Lang.: Fre.
1825-1997. Historical studies. ■Productions of Boieldieu's *La Dame Blanche*.

4075 Bégaud, Josée. "L'oeuvre à l'affiche." (The Work on Stage.) *ASO*. 1997 Jan/Feb.; 175: 108-115. Illus.: Photo. B&W. 15. Lang.: Fre.
1792-1996. Historical studies. ■List of worldwide productions of Cimarosa's opera *Il matrimonio segreto*.

4076 Bégaud, Josée. "L'oeuvre à l'affiche." (The Work on Stage.) *ASO*. 1997 May/June; 177: 48-51. Illus.: Photo. Dwg. B&W. 9. Lang.: Fre.
1913-1995. Historical studies. ■Listing and brief description of productions worldwide of Manuel de Falla's opera *La vida breve*.

4077 Bégaud, Josée. "L'oeuvre à l'affiche." (The Work on Stage.) *ASO*. 1997 May/June; 177: 116-117. Illus.: Dwg. Photo. B&W. 5. Lang.: Fre.
1923-1993. Historical studies. ■Listing and evaluation of productions of Manuel de Falla's opera *El retablo de Maese Pedro*.

MUSIC-DRAMA: Opera—Performance/production

4078   Bégaud, Josée. "L'oeuvre à l'affiche." (The Work on Stage.) *ASO*. 1997 July/Aug.; 178: 78-85. Illus.: Photo. Dwg. B&W. 13. Lang.: Fre.
1831-1994. Historical studies. ■Productions world wide of Bellini's opera *La sonnambula*.

4079   Bégaud, Josée; Soldini, Elisabetta. "L'oeuvre à l'affiche." (The Work on Stage.) *ASO*. 1997 Sep/Oct.; 179: 88-95. Illus.: Dwg. Photo. B&W. 18. Lang.: Fre.
1840-1996. Historical studies. ■Worldwide productions of Donizetti's *La Fille du régiment* since its premiere.

4080   Bégaud, Josée. "L'oeuvre à l'affiche." (The Work on Stage.) *ASO*. 1997 Nov/Dec.; 180: 112-115. Illus.: Photo. B&W. 3. Lang.: Fre.
1978-1998. Historical studies. ■Productions world wide of Ligeti's opera *Le Grand Macabre*.

4081   Blier, Steven. "Waiting for Gaetano." *OpN*. 1997 Nov.; 62(5): 36-37, 40-43. Illus.: Photo. B&W. Color. 7. Lang.: Eng.
1997. Historical studies. ■Questions why so few of Donizetti's thirty operas are performed today, two hundred years after his birth, with reference to the planned revival of some little-known works.

4082   Cabourg, Jean. "Profil des voix." (Profile of Voices.) *ASO*. 1997 July/Aug.; 178: 66-71. Illus.: Photo. Dwg. B&W. 7. Lang.: Fre.
1831-1984. Historical studies. ■Outstanding singers who have performed in Bellini's opera *La sonnambula*, with emphasis on Giuditta Pasta and Maria Callas in the role of Amina. Briefer comments on male roles, sidebar articles on performances by Callas.

4083   Cabourg, Jean. "Discographie." (Discography.) *ASO*. 1997 July/Aug.; 178: 72-77. Illus.: Dwg. B&W. 1. Lang.: Fre.
1899-1996. Historical studies. ■Bellini's opera *La sonnambula*, both complete recordings and individual arias.

4084   Cometta, Sandro; Soldini, Elisabetta. "Discographie." (Discography.) *ASO*. 1997 Jan/Feb.; 175: 104-107. Lang.: Fre.
1949-1992. Historical studies. ■Listing and evaluation of complete recordings of Cimarosa's opera *Il matrimonio segreto*.

4085   Cometta, Sandro; Soldini, Elisabetta. "Discographie." (Discography.) *ASO*. 1997 Sep/Oct.; 179: 78-84. Illus.: Photo. B&W. 5. Lang.: Fre.
1940-1989. Historical studies. ■Listing and evaluation of complete recordings of *La Fille du régiment* by Donizetti, both the original French version and the later Italian translation.

4086   Flinois, Pierre. "Vidéographie." (Videography.) *ASO*. 1997 Sep/Oct.; 179: 85. Illus.: Photo. B&W. 1. Lang.: Fre.
1965-1986. Historical studies. ■Brief commentary on several available performances of Donizetti's *La Fille du régiment* on video.

4087   Flinois, Pierre. "Discographie." (Discography.) *ASO*. 1997 Nov/Dec.; 180: 110-111. Illus.: Photo. B&W. 1. Lang.: Fre.
1979-1998. Historical studies. ■Listing and evaluation of complete and partial recordings of Ligeti's opera *Le Grand Macabre*.

4088   Hoffelé, Jean-Charles. "Discographie." (Discography.) *ASO*. 1997 May/June; 177: 112-115. Lang.: Fre.
1953-1975. Historical studies. ■Complete recordings of Manuel de Falla's opera *El retablo de Maese Pedro*.

4089   Merlin, Christian. "Discographie." (Discography.) *ASO*. 1997 May/June; 177: 80-85. Lang.: Fre.
1945-1995. Historical studies. ■Recordings of Falla's *El amor brujo*, including the 1915 and 1916 versions, as well as the orchestral suites.

4090   Rosenfeld, Lorraine. "Opera News International Opera Forecast, 1997-1998." *OpN*. 1997 Sep.; 62(3): 33-59. Lang.: Eng.
1996-1997. Histories-sources. ■List of 1997-1998 worldwide scheduled opera performances.

4091   van Moere, Didier. "Discographie." (Discography.) *ASO*. 1997 Mar/Apr.; 176: 92-93. Lang.: Fre.
1961-1996. Historical studies. ■Listing and evaluation of complete recordings of Boieldieu's *La Dame Blanche*.

4092   van Moere, Didier. "Discographie." (Discography.) *ASO*. 1997 May/June; 177: 44-46. Illus.: Photo. B&W. 1. Lang.: Fre.
1913-1995. Historical studies. ■Listing and evaluation of complete recordings of Falla's opera *La vida breve*.

4093   Varnay, Astrid; Arthur, Donald. "Valhalla on the Hudson: an Excerpt from the New Memoir *55 Years in 5 Acts*." *OpN*. 1997 June; 61(17): 18-20, 22, 24, 26-27. Illus.: Photo. B&W. 9. Lang.: Eng.
1918-1997. Histories-sources. ■Excerpt from the memoir of soprano Astrid Varnay with comments on the many roles she sang, singers and conductors with whom she performed.

4094   "Thoroughly Modern Salzburg." *Econ*. 1997 Aug 30-Sep 5; 344(8032): 63-64. Illus.: Photo. B&W. 1. Lang.: Eng.
Austria: Salzburg. 1997. Historical studies. ■Contemporary influences on the Salzburg festival under the artistic directorship of Gérard Mortier. Audience response and success of producing twentieth century operas.

4095   Barry, Barbara R. "Inversional Symmetry in *The Magic Flute*." *OJ*. 1997 Mar.; 30(1): 14-27. Notes. Tables. Lang.: Eng.
Austria. 1791. Critical studies. ■Structural symmetry and inversional redefinition of character in Mozart's *Die Zauberflöte* with focus on the Queen, Sarastro and Tamino.

4096   Brandenburg, Detlef. "Salzburg edel, Salzburg light." (Salzburg Noble, Salzburg Light.) *DB*. 1997; 9: 14-19. Illus.: Photo. B&W. 5. Lang.: Ger.
Austria: Salzburg. 1997. Histories-sources. ■Impressions from the Salzburger Festspiele under the directorship of Gérard Mortier. Describes György Ligeti's *Le Grand Macabre* directed by Peter Sellars and Mozart's *Die Zauberflöte (The Magic Flute)* directed by Achim Freyer.

4097   Brandenburg, Detlef. "Gefässe für den Geist der Musik." (Vessels for the Spirit of Music.) *DB*. 1997; 9: 20-22. Illus.: Photo. B&W. 1. Lang.: Ger.
Austria: Salzburg. 1997. Histories-sources. ■An interview with director and set designer Achim Freyer on occasion of his direction of Mozart's *Die Zauberflöte*.

4098   Loney, Glenn. "*Porgy and Bess* on Lake Constance." *WES*. 1997 Fall; 9(3): 73-78. Illus.: Photo. 2. Lang.: Eng.
Austria: Bregenz. 1997. Historical studies. ■Gershwin's *Porgy and Bess* presented in the huge open-air amphitheatre on Lake Constance, performed in English, directed by Götz Friedrich.

4099   Perroux, Alain. "Les nouvelles aventures du Grand Macabre." (The Further Adventures of the Grand Macabre.) *ASO*. 1997 Nov/Dec.; 180: 100-106. Illus.: Photo. B&W. 7. Lang.: Fre.
Austria: Salzburg. 1997. Historical studies. ■Peter Sellars' production of Ligeti's opera *Le Grand Macabre* at the 1997 Salzburg Festival. Includes excerpts from press reviews.

4100   Pines, Roger; Höslinger, Clemens, intro. "*Wiener Staatsoper Live*: A Survey of the Historic Koch Schwann Series." *OQ*. 1997 Fall; 14(1): 45-66. Notes. Illus.: Photo. B&W. 4. Lang.: Eng.
Austria: Vienna. 1928-1943. Critical studies. ■Detailed review of the forty-eight disk set in Schwann's *Wiener Staatsoper*: best of the live performances, conductors, productions, singers. Special focus on works by Wagner and Strauss.

4101   Swain, Joseph P. "Musical Disguises in Mozart's Late Comedies." *OQ*. 1997 Sum; 13(4): 47-58. Notes. Lang.: Eng.
Austria. 1786-1790. Historical studies. ■In depth study of musical passages from *Le Nozze di Figaro*, *Don Giovanni* and *Così fan tutte* that focus on character's deceptions and inherent problems encountered in those passages.

4102   Smith, Patrick J. "Worth the Wait?" *OpN*. 1997 Feb 8; 61(10): 16-17. Illus.: Dwg. 1. Lang.: Eng.
Austro-Hungarian Empire: Vienna. 1786-1997. Critical studies. ■The operatic and structural logic of the 'procession of arias' in the final act of Mozart's *Le Nozze di Figaro*.

4103   Baker, Paul G. "Quilico on Quilico." *OC*. 1997 Spr; 38(1): 14-17. Illus.: Photo. B&W. 3. Lang.: Eng.

MUSIC-DRAMA: Opera—Performance/production

Canada. 1970-1997. Biographical studies. ∎Baritone Gino Quilico's nineteen years on the international operatic stage.

4104 Charles, John. "Frances Ginzer: The Calgary Born Soprano Makes the Leap from Coloratura to Wagner." *OC.* 1997 Spr; 38(1) : 9. Illus.: Photo. B&W. 1. Lang.: Eng.
Canada. 1995-1997. Biographical studies. ∎Profile of the soprano Frances Ginzer.

4105 Crory, Neil. "Irene Jessner 1901-1994: Great Canadian Musical Figures." *OC.* 1997 Spr; 38(1): 8. Illus.: Photo. B&W. 1. Lang.: Eng.
Canada. 1901-1994. Biographical studies. ∎Profile of late soprano and voice teacher Jessner.

4106 deVrij, Robert. "James Milligan 1928-1961: Great Canadian Musical Figures." *OC.* 1997 Fall; 38(3): 8. Illus.: Photo. B&W. 1. Lang.: Eng.
Canada. 1928-1961. Biographical studies. ∎Profile of the charismatic Canadian baritone, James Milligan.

4107 Eatock, Colin. "Béatrice La Palme: Great Canadian Musical Figures." *OC.* 1997 Win; 38(4): 8. Illus.: Photo. B&W. 1. Lang.: Eng.
Canada. 1898-1919. Biographical studies. ∎Short professional career of opera singer who gave up singing at the pinnacle of her artistry.

4108 Fraser, Hugh. "Debut: Daniel Taylor: A Countertenor Wins High Marks on the International Scene." *OC.* 1997 Fall; 38(3): 9. Illus.: Photo. B&W. 1. Lang.: Eng.
Canada. 1997. Biographical studies. ∎Profile of the countertenor as he takes to the international concert and oratorio circuit.

4109 Gooding, Wayne. "World Class." *OC.* 1997 Win; 38(4): 10-13. Illus.: Photo. B&W. 5. Lang.: Eng.
Canada. 1977-1997. Biographical studies. ∎Career of Canadian lyric tenor Michael Schade.

4110 Krsek, Barbora. "Festivals and Summer Stock." *OC.* 1997 Spr; 38(1): 18-21. Lang.: Eng.
Canada. USA. Europe. 1997. Historical studies. ∎*Opera Canada's* annual listing of summer opera festivals in the US, Canada and Europe.

4111 Levin, David J. "Operatic School for Scandal." *PerAJ.* 1997 Jan.; 19(1): 52-57. Illus.: Photo. B&W. 1. [Number 55.] Lang.: Eng.
Canada: Toronto, ON. 1996. Critical studies. ∎Analysis of filmmaker Atom Egoyan's staging of *Salome* for the Canadian Opera Company.

4112 Lindgren, Allana Christine. *Opera Atelier's Dido and Aeneas*: Baroque Performance Conventions Meet Contemporary Innovations. North York, ON: York Univ; 1997. 143 pp. [M.A. Thesis, Univ. Microfilms Order No. AAC MM20401.] Lang.: Eng.
Canada: Toronto, ON. 1994-1995. Historical studies. ∎Analysis of the way in which Opera Atelier, founded by Marshall Pynkoski and Jeannette Zingg, combined Baroque and contemporary performance conventions in its interpretation of Henry Purcell and Nahum Tate's opera, *Dido and Aeneas*, the company's most widely acclaimed production.

4113 Midgette, Anne. "Bare Essence: Canadian Director Robert Carsen Specializes in Paring Operas Down to the Core." *OpN.* 1997 Dec 6; 62(6): 54-57. Illus.: Photo. Color. 2. Lang.: Eng.
Canada. Europe. 1995-1997. Biographical studies. ∎Profile of Canadian director Robert Carsen, said to offer a minimalist distillation of the essence of opera. Discussion of his work in Canada and Europe.

4114 So, Joseph. "Manon Feubel: The Quebec Soprano Makes a Brilliant Entrance." *OC.* 1997 Sum; 38(2): 9. Illus.: Photo. B&W. 1. Lang.: Eng.
Canada. 1996. Biographical studies. ∎Ontario debut of Quebec-born soprano Manon Feubel, at a performance of Verdi's *Requiem* with the Kitchener-Waterloo Symphony.

4115 So, Joseph. "Soprano Isabel Bayrakdarian Brings a Scientist's Sensibility to Her Burgeoning Art." *OC.* 1997 Win; 38(4): 9. Illus.: Photo. B&W. 1. Lang.: Eng.
Canada. 1997. Biographical studies. ∎Profile of the first Canadian soprano since Teresa Stratas to win the Metropolitan Opera auditions.

4116 Thompson, Brian. "Calixa Levallée: 1842-1891: Great Canadian Musical Figures of the Past." *OC.* 1997 Sum; 38(2): 8. Illus.: Photo. B&W. 1. Lang.: Eng.
Canada. 1842-1891. Biographical studies. ∎Profile of the influential musician and band leader who composed the anthem *O Canada*.

4117 Dibbern, Mary. "Coach's Notebook: *Carmen* in Shanghai." *OJ.* 1997 Sep.; 30(3): 13-23. Illus.: Photo. B&W. 3. Lang.: Eng.
China, People's Republic of: Beijing. 1982-1997. Histories-sources. ∎Vocal coach for a Beijing production of Bizet's *Carmen* at Shanghai Opera House, conduted by Yu Long, describes experience of teaching Asian singers to perform in French using International Phonetic Alphabet. Rehearsals, approach to character.

4118 Havlíková, Helena. "Janáček? Janáček?? Janáček??? 1. čast: Dramaturgické jistoty, hubední hledání." (Janáček? Janáček?? Janáček??? Part 1: Dramaturgical Confidences, Musical Searching.) *Svet.* 1997; 8(4): 92-99. Illus.: Photo. B&W. 10. Lang.: Cze.
Czech Republic. 1854-1928. Historical studies. ∎The problems encountered with the staging of Janáček's works in Czech opera companies. Continued in *Svet* 8:5, 28-40. Part 2: Directorial Grouping.

4119 Hrdinová, Radmila. "Luděk Vele: 'Chtěl bych, aby o mně lidi neříkali, že jsem byl špatnej chlap'." (Luděk Vele: 'I wish people wouldn't say that I was a bad chap'.) *DiN.* 1997 May; 6(11): 3. Illus.: Photo. B&W. 1. Lang.: Cze.
Czech Republic. 1951-1997. Biographical studies. ∎Life and career of opera singer Luděk Vele.

4120 Phillips, Harvey E. "Running Wild." *OpN.* 1997 Nov.; 62(5): 44-47. Illus.: Photo. Color. 2. Lang.: Eng.
Denmark: Copenhagen. 1997. Biographical studies. ∎Soprano Constance Hausman's performance in Berg's *Lulu*, performed at the Royal Riding School of the Christianborg Palace, with reference to her acting style.

4121 Sevilla-Gonzaga, Marylis. "Cophenhagen Sings." *OpN.* 1997 May; 61(16): 14-16, 17. Illus.: Photo. Color. 6. Lang.: Eng.
Denmark: Copenhagen. 1997. Historical studies. ∎Opera and culture in Copenhagen and surrounding area. Profiles the Royal Danish Opera, artistic director Elaine Padmore, formerly of the Wexford National Opera, Den Andern Oper, headed by Jesper Lützøft, the Musikteatret Albertslund, managing director Torben Holm Larsen, and the Arken museum of art and architecture at Ishøj, among others.

4122 Kaufman, Tom. "The Grisi-Viardot Controversy: 1848-1852." *OQ.* 1997/98 Win; 14(2): 7-22. Notes. Lang.: Eng.
England: London. 1848-1852. Historical studies. ∎Investigates charges that soprano Giulia Grisi attempted to sabotage soprano Pauline Viardot's career: the damage to both their reputations, alleged jealousies. Author examines charges from both sides of the conflict, and proposes that accusations were an attempt by Viardot to gain coveted roles.

4123 McKee, David. "Navy Blues: Why Are the Officers in *Billy Budd* So Terrified of Mutiny?" *OpN.* 1997 Mar 8; 61(12): 22-25 . Illus.: Photo. Color. B&W. 4. Lang.: Eng.
England. 1797. Histories-sources. ∎Background study of living and disciplinary conditions in the Royal Navy of King George III of England in the year of mutinies, 1797, with respect to the opera *Billy Budd* by Benjamin Britten, based on the novella by Herman Melville, and its account of the navy of Rear Admiral Horatio Nelson.

4124 "Entretien avec Marc Minkowski." (Interview with Marc Minkowski.) *ASO.* 1997 Mar/Apr.; 176: 90-91. Illus.: Photo. B&W. 1. Lang.: Fre.
Europe. 1997. Histories-sources. ∎Interview with Minkowski, who is conducting a new integral recording of Boieldieu's opera *La Dame Blanche*.

4125 Baxter, Robert. "*Hochdramatische Zwillingsschwestern*: Astrid Varnay and Birgit Nilsson." *OQ.* 1997 Fall; 14(1): 7-24. Notes. Illus.: Photo. B&W. 3. Lang.: Eng.
Europe. 1918-1973. Historical studies. ∎Comparison of the careers and singing talents of sopranos Nilsson and Varnay: their dominance as Wagnerian sopranos, personal background, productions, roles, training.

MUSIC-DRAMA: Opera—Performance/production

4126 Bergström, Gunnel. "Prima primadonnor." (First-Class Prima Donnas.) *MuD.* 1997; 19(2): 20-22. Illus.: Photo. B&W. Lang.: Swe.
Europe. 1597-1997. Critical studies. ■An essay about the opera singer's dilemma between the demands of the music and the stage director, with reference to the inadequate training of the singers today.

4127 Bruder, Harold. "Manuel García the Elder: His School and His Legacy." *OQ.* 1997 Sum; 13(4): 19-46. Notes. Discography. Illus.: Photo. Dwg. Pntg. 5. Lang.: Eng.
Europe. 1817-1943. Biographical studies. ■Career and roles of tenor Manuel García drawing on memoirs of Rev. John Edmund Cox who wrote extensively about the singer's performances. García's musical training, his influence on his son Manuel García the younger, and the younger's career as a teacher of opera singers. Includes discography of artists who studied with him.

4128 Crutchfield, Will. "The Bel Canto Connection." *OpN.* 1997 July; 62(1): 30-35, 51. Illus.: Photo. B&W. Color. 7. Lang.: Eng.
Europe. 1705-1997. Historical studies. ■Compares the Baroque style of Handel's operas to the Romantic operas of Rossini, Bellini, and Donizetti, and argues that the stylistic similarities outweigh the differences. Considers cadenzas, coloratura, ornamentation, portamento, legato, etc.

4129 Hamilton, David. "Pitching on the High C's: ... the Thorny Question of Transposition." *OpN.* 1997 Feb 8; 61(10): 18-21, 51. Illus.: Photo. B&W. 7. Lang.: Eng.
Europe. 1900-1997. Historical studies. ■Is transposition of pitch a form of cheating, or is it permissible to 'tweak'? A non-judgmental treatment. Lists such practitioners as Enrico Caruso, Marcella Sembrich, Rosa Ponselle, Lotte Lehmann, Zinka Milanov, Helen Traubel, Lily Pons, Richard Tucker, Mario del Monaco, Jussi Bjoerling. Examines Mapleson cylinders, recorded and broadcast versions.

4130 Hermansson, Jan. "En hymn till galenskapen." (An Anthem For Madness.) *MuD.* 1997; 19(1): 12-19. Discography. Illus.: Photo. B&W. Lang.: Swe.
Europe. 1937-1995. Critical studies. ■A discussion around the characters Elektra, Chrysostemis and Klytämnestra in Richard Strauss' opera *Elektra*, with references to all records now avaible.

4131 McKee, David. "Cut-and-Paste: The Checkered History of *Don Carlo* at the Met." *OpN.* 1997 Dec 20; 62(7): 12-14, 50. Illus.: Photo. B&W. Color. 7. Lang.: Eng.
Europe. USA. 1867-1997. Historical studies. ■The international production history of the frequently-revised opera *Don Carlo* by Giuseppe Verdi. Emphasizes its career at the Metropolitan Opera 1920-1997, including a list of conductors, singers, and producers.

4132 Michel, Pierre. "Mon opéra est une sort de farce noire." (My Opera Is a Sort of Black Farce.) *ASO.* 1997 Nov/Dec.; 180: 96-99. Illus.: Photo. Dwg. B&W. 2. Lang.: Fre.
Europe. 1997. Histories-sources. ■Interview with György Ligeti, composer and librettist (with Michael Meschke) of *Le Grand Macabre*.

4133 Samuel, Claude. "Ligeti, le clin d'oeil au happening." (Ligeti: Winking at the Happening.) *ASO.* 1997 Nov/Dec.; 180: 94-95. Lang.: Fre.
Europe. 1923-1997. Biographical studies. ■Profile of composer György Ligeti, with emphasis on his opera *Le Grand Macabre*.

4134 Sevilla-Gonzaga, Marylis, comp. "Voices of Summer: *Opera News* Spotlights the Top European Festivals Abroad." *OpN.* 1997 May; 61(16): 40-51. Illus.: Photo. Color. 9. Lang.: Eng.
Europe. Asia. 1997. Histories-sources. ■List of summer 1997 opera festivals in Europe, Scandinavia, Russia, Turkey.

4135 Freeman, John W. "Finland's Turn." *OpN.* 1997 May; 61(16): 22-25. Illus.: Photo. B&W. Color. 6. Lang.: Eng.
Finland. 1997. Historical studies. ■Over fifty performing arts festivals in Finland. Emphasis on opera festivals and Savonlinna.

4136 "New from Old." *Econ.* 1997 Nov 15; 345(8043): 94. Illus.: Photo. B&W. 1. Lang.: Eng.
France. 1717-1997. Historical studies. ■Brief history of opera-ballet as a genre, past production and audience response, recent experiments in restaging them for contemporary audiences.

4137 Blier, Steven. "Reverse Angle." *OpN.* 1997 Jan 25; 61(9): 10-14. Illus.: Photo. B&W. Color. 6. Lang.: Eng.
France: Paris. 1835. Historical studies. ■Recreates the historical atmosphere in Paris, January 1835, when Rossini's *I Puritani* received its premiere at the Théâtre Italien. Its stars were Giulia Grisi, Antonio Tamburini, and Luigi Lablache. Lists other operas and their stars in performance at that time. Argues that opera at that time was superior to the musical theatre of today and has more to offer the audience.

4138 Choukroun, Patrick; Dibbern, Mary, transl. "Jacques Leguerney (1906-1997): The Celebration of French Song." *OJ.* 1997 Dec.; 30(4): 42-46. Lang.: Eng.
France. 1906-1997. Biographical studies. ■Personal background and career of composer Leguerney recalled upon his death. Training, compositions, influences on his work.

4139 Conlon, James. "The Carmen Myth." *OpN.* 1997 Mar 22; 61(13): 8-9. Illus.: Photo. B&W. 6. Lang.: Eng.
France: Paris. USA: New York, NY. 1875-1997. Critical studies. ■Essay on the character of Bizet's heroine Carmen. Includes photographs of Emma Calvé, Geraldine Farrar (with Pedro de Cordoba), Jean Madeira, Risë Stevens, Grace Bumbry, Régine Crespin, and Marilyn Horne.

4140 Crichton, Ronald. "Old Sweet Song." *OpN.* 1997 Apr 5; 61(14): 16-18. Illus.: Photo. B&W. Color. 5. Lang.: Eng.
France: Paris. 1818-1893. Biographical studies. ■The background, career, and reputation of French opera composer Charles Gounod, particularly *Faust*, *Roméo et Juliette*, *La Nonne Sanglante*, *Sapho*, and *Mireille*.

4141 García Martínez, Manuel. "Jacques Nichet Directs Cocteau." *WES.* 1997 Spr; 9(2): 29-34. Illus.: Photo. 1. Lang.: Eng.
France: Paris. 1996. Historical studies. ■Account of the staging by Jacques Nichet of the opera based on Cocteau's *L'épouse injustement soupçonnée*, music by Valérie Stephan, at the Théâtre de la Ville in Paris.

4142 Loomis, George. "À L'Italienne." *OpN.* 1997 Jan 25; 61(9): 23-25. Illus.: Photo. B&W. Color. 8. Lang.: Eng.
France: Paris. 1801-1878. Historical studies. ■History of the Théâtre Italien begun by the impresario Marguerite Brunet, also known as La Montansier. Discusses the overall repertoire and relationship to politics, the most important operas and artists.

4143 Suschitzky, Anya. "*Ariane et Barbe-Bleue*: Dukas, the Light and the Well." *COJ.* 1997; 9(2): 133-161. Notes. Illus.: Pntg. Dwg. 5. Lang.: Eng.
France. 1885-1936. Historical studies. ■Examination of Paul Dukas' opera *Ariane et Barbe-Bleue* showing the influences of Maeterlinck and Perrault on the text, Debussy and d'Indy on the music, and events such as the Dreyfus Affair and contemporary notions of truth on the theme. The opera is described as an embodiment of a post-Wagnerian aesthetic.

4144 Turnbull, Michael T.R.B. "Mary Garden, Debuts and Debussy: 1900-1903." *OQ.* 1997 Sum; 13(4): 5-18. Notes. [Third chapter of the author's recent biography *Mary Garden*. Reprinted from Amadeus Press.] Lang.: Eng.
France: Paris. 1875-1957. Biographical studies. ■Career, role and training of singer Garden: special focus on her performance in Charpentier's *Louise* at the Opéra-Comique, *La Marseillaise* directed by Albert Carré, Debussy's *Pelléas et Mélisande*, and her work with composer/conductor André Messager.

4145 Baker, David J. "*Wozzeck*'s Greatest Hits." *OpN.* 1997 Feb 22; 61(11): 24-27, 53. Illus.: Photo. B&W. 6. Lang.: Eng.
Germany. USA. 1923-1996. Historical studies. ■Musical evaluation of *Wozzeck* by Alban Berg, emphasizing the role of Marie and some of its famous interpreters. Discusses the use of *Sprechstimme*. Includes excerpts from the score.

4146 Brandenburg, Detlef. "Lebenspartien." (Parts of Life.) *DB.* 1997; 1: 10-13. Illus.: Photo. B&W. 5. Lang.: Ger.
Germany: Berlin. 1997. Histories-sources. ■An interview with opera singer Noemi Nadelmann about singing, roles and her famous title part in *Lucia di Lammermoor*, directed by Harry Kupfer at Komische Oper.

4147 Brandenburg, Detlef. "Gesucht: Die Opernkrise." (Wanted: The Crisis of Opera.) *DB.* 1997; 5: 43-45. Illus.: Photo. B&W. 2. Lang.: Ger.

MUSIC-DRAMA: Opera—Performance/production

Germany. 1997. Reviews of performances. ■Impressions from a journey through German cities looking for the crisis of opera. Describes a lively scene from Massenet's *Manon* directed by Christof Loy at Deutsche Oper am Rhein, *Tosca* directed by Christine Mielitz at Theater Essen, Wagner's *Parsifal* directed by Günter Krämer at Oper Bonn, Wagner's *Der Fliegende Holländer* directed by Götz Friedrich at Deutsche Oper, Alban Berg's *Wozzeck* directed by Peter Stein at Festspielhaus Salzburg.

4148 Brandenburg, Detlef. "Aus alten Märchen winkt es..." (It Waves From Old Fairytales.) *DB.* 1997; 6: 15-19. Illus.: Photo. B&W. 4. Lang.: Ger.
Germany: Munich. 1997. Reviews of performances. ■Impressions from the performances at the Munich Biennale at the end of the directorship of its founder Hans Werner Henze. Reviews of *Helle Nächte (Bright Nights)* by Moritz Eggert directed by Tilman Knabe, *The Juniper Tree* by Roderick Watkins directed by David McVicar (a co-production with Almeida Opera) and Gerd Baumann's *Merge opera* directed by Ian MacNaughton.

4149 Breiholz, Jochen. "All in the Music." *OpN.* 1997 Feb 22; 61(11): 16-18. Illus.: Photo. B&W. Color. 3. Lang.: Eng.
Germany. 1997. Histories-sources. ■Interview with baritone Falk Struckman on the role of Wozzeck.

4150 Cerf, Steven R.; Folkman, Benjamin. "*Rheingold*'s Curse." *OpN.* 1997 Mar 22; 61(13): 20-23, 27. Illus.: Photo. B&W. 6. Lang.: Eng.
Germany: Munich, Bayreuth. 1869-1876. Historical studies. ■The production problems attendant on *Der Ring des Nibelungen* were many, but the 1869 premiere of *Das Rheingold*, caused scandal, as well.

4151 Downer, Gregory. "'cause I'm a Wanderer: Postcard from Bayreuth." *OpN.* 1997 Dec 6; 62(6): 62-63. Illus.: Photo. B&W. 2. Lang.: Eng.
Germany: Bayreuth. 1997. Historical studies. ■Comments on the conducting by James Levine of Wagner's *Der Ring des Nibelungen* at the Bayreuther Festspiele. Also comments on individual singers and the designer Erich Wonder.

4152 Eckert, Nora. "Das schöne Tier—ein Theaterleben." (The Beautiful Animal—a Theatre Life.) *TZ.* 1997; 5: 46-49. Illus.: Photo. B&W. 1. Lang.: Ger.
Germany. 1997. Critical studies. ■Current interpretations of the character Lulu in various performances of Alban Berg's opera directed by Annegret Ritzel at Städtische Bühnen, Margarethe von Trotta at Staatstheater Stuttgart and Peter Mussbach at Staatsoper Berlin.

4153 Gurewitsch, Matthew. "Explorer." *OpN.* 1997 Mar 22; 61(13): 10-12, 62. Illus.: Photo. B&W. Color. 5. Lang.: Eng.
Germany. 1957-1997. Biographical studies. ■Profile of German soprano Waltraud Meier, emphasizing her interpretation of Carmen.

4154 Heed, Sven-Åke. "Passionen—den förbrännande Kupfers Lucia di Lammermoor." (Passion: Kupfer's Scorching *Lucia de Lammermoor*.) *MuD.* 1997; 19(2): 14-15. Illus.: Photo. B&W. Lang.: Swe.
Germany: Berlin. 1997. ■A presentation of Harry Kupfer's staging of Donizetti's *Lucia di Lammermoor* at Komische Oper.

4155 Hoelen, H. *Symboliek en Werkelijkheid in de Werken van Richard Wagner.* (Symbolism and Reality in the Works of Richard Wagner.) Assen: Van Gorcum; 1997. 268 pp. Pref. Biblio. Illus.: Photo. B&W. 1. Lang.: Dut.
Germany. 1813-1883. Critical studies. ■The motives and inspirations of Wagner's operas.

4156 Löhlein, Heinz-Harald. "Zeitgenössischen Konstellationen." (Contemporary Constellations.) *DB.* 1997; 2: 15-19. Biblio. Illus.: Photo. B&W. 4. Lang.: Ger.
Germany: Hamburg. 1921-1997. Historical studies. ■Reviews the history of Hans Werner Henze's modern music theatre on occasion of the first performance of *Das Mädchen mit den Schwefelhölzern (The Little Match Girl)* directed by Achim Freyer at Staatsoper, including a statement by Detlef Brandenburg about the first performance of *Venus and Adonis* directed by Pierre Audi at Bayerische Staatsoper.

4157 Márton, Dávid. "Interjú Korondi Annával." (An Interview with Anna Korondi.) *OperaL.* 1997; 6(2): 22-26. Illus.: Photo. B&W. 4. Lang.: Hun.

Germany: Berlin. 1990-1997. Histories-sources. ■Interview with the Hungarian soprano, who has been offered a permanent engagement with the Komische Oper after her début there in Mozart's *Don Giovanni*.

4158 Marx, Robert. "A Soldier's Tale." *OpN.* 1997 Feb 22; 61(11): 20-23, 51. Illus.: Photo. B&W. Color. 8. Lang.: Eng.
Germany: Berlin. 1914-1997. Historical studies. ■Historical, dramatic and musical introduction to *Wozzeck* by Alban Berg, with reference to its source in the play *Woyzeck*, by Georg Büchner, emphasizing its revolutionary sociopolitical aspects. Includes production history of the opera.

4159 Meyer, Stephen. "*Das wilde Herz*: Interpreting Wilhelmine Schröder-Devrient." *OQ.* 1997/98 Win; 14(2): 23-40. Notes. Lang.: Eng.
Germany. 1804-1863. Biographical studies. ■Study of the mythology surrounding the life of singer Schröder-Devrient and its political, social and aesthetic meanings during the nineteenth century.

4160 Paris, Barry. "The Force." *OpN.* 1997 Apr 5; 61(14): 8-10, 12, 14. Illus.: Photo. Color. 6. Lang.: Eng.
Germany. 1997. Histories-sources. ■Profile, interview with German Wagnerian soprano Hildegard Behrens who deserted law for opera.

4161 Petty, Jonathan Christian. "Sieglinde's 'Long Day's Journey Into Night'." *OJ.* 1997 June; 30(2): 11-35. Biblio. Notes. Append. Lang.: Eng.
Germany. 1853-1874. Critical studies. ■Linear harmonal analysis of musical structure, and tonal language of the character Sieglinde from Wagner's *Ring* and impact on the narrative of the story.

4162 Smith, Patrick J. "Musical Legend." *OpN.* 1997 June; 61(17): 12, 14, 16. Illus.: Photo. B&W. Color. 6. Lang.: Eng.
Germany. 1917-1997. Historical studies. ■History of and critical introduction to the opera *Palestrina* by Hans Pfitzner, first performed in 1917. The Royal Opera House (Covent Garden) performed it at the Metropolitan Opera, July 1997.

4163 Steinberg, Michael. "Berg and Büchner." *OpN.* 1997 Feb 11; 61(11): 8-18, 12-15. Illus.: Photo. B&W. 5. Lang.: Eng.
Germany. Austria: Vienna. 1925. Historical studies. ■The historical background of Alban Berg's *Wozzeck* and its source, *Woyzeck* by Georg Büchner.

4164 Balogh, Gyula. "Fiatalok: Pánti Anna." (Young Singers: Anna Pánti.) *OperaL.* 1997; 6(3): 25-26. Illus.: Photo. B&W. 1. Lang.: Hun.
Hungary. 1980-1997. Histories-sources. ■A conversation with the young coloratura soprano on her eight seasons at the Budapest Opera House.

4165 Boros, Attila. "Száz éve született Németh Mária." (Mária Németh Was Born 100 Years Ago.) *OperaL.* 1997; 6(2): 8-9. Illus.: Photo. B&W. 2. Lang.: Hun.
Hungary. 1897-1967. Biographical studies. ■Life and career of the dramatic soprano.

4166 Boros, Attila; Szkárossy, Zsuzsanna, photo. "Portré: Csavlek Etelka." (A Portrait of Etelka Csavlek.) *OperaL.* 1997; 6(3): 8-14. Illus.: Photo. B&W. Color. 5. Lang.: Hun.
Hungary. 1980-1997. Histories-sources. ■The career of the ceramist who went on the operatic stage at the age of thirty-five.

4167 Boros, Attila. "Az Operaház örökös tagjai: Szőnyi Olga." (Life Members of the Opera House: Olga Szőnyi.) *OperaL.* 1997; 6(5): 12-16. Illus.: Photo. B&W. 6. Lang.: Hun.
Hungary. 1933-1997. Histories-sources. ■A conversation with a prominent mezzo-soprano of post-war opera life in Budapest regarding her early success and international career.

4168 Csák, P. Judit. "*A csengőtől a Figaró házasságáig.* Beszélgetés Galgóczy Judittal." (From Donizetti's *Il Campanello* to Mozart's *Le Nozze di Figaro*—An Interview with Judit Galgóczy.) *OperaL.* 1997; 6(5): 29-31. Lang.: Hun.
Hungary. 1987-1997. Histories-sources. ■Survey of a ten-year career with stage-director Judit Galgóczy from her first staging, Donizetti's opera at the Budapest Opera House to her present production, Mozart's Figaro at the Erkel Theatre.

4169 Dalos, László. "Egy operaénekes házaspár: Mátray Ferenc–Vámos Ágnes." (An Opera Singer Couple: Ferenc Mátray and Ágnes Vámos.) *OperaL.* 1997; 6(1): 13-17. Illus.: Photo. B&W. 5. Lang.: Hun.

MUSIC-DRAMA: Opera—Performance/production

Hungary. 1943-1990. Biographical studies. ■Portrait of the retired tenor-soprano couple and their successful career.

4170   Dalos, László; Kotnyek, Antal, photo. "Isten veled, Bánk!" (Farewell Bánk!)*OperaL.* 1997; 6(2): 2-3. Illus.: Photo. Color. 1. Lang.: Hun.
Hungary. 1917-1997. Biographical studies. ■Commemoration of the tenor József Simándy, best known for his interpretation of the title role of Ferenc Erkel's *Bánk bán* which he performed 147 times.

4171   Dalos, László. "Tinóditól Turandotig. Pályaképféle Szabó Miklósról, a magyar tenoristák korelnökéről." (From Tinódi to Turandot: Miklós Szabó, Senior of Hungarian Tenors.) *OperaL.* 1997; 6(4): 25-28. Lang.: Hun.
Hungary. 1930-1989. Histories-sources. ■The 87-year-old artist recalls his 60-year stage career, and his translation of numerous opera librettos into Hungarian.

4172   Hollósi, Zsolt; Veréb, Simon, photo; Hernádi, Oszkár, photo. "Portrévázlat Gyimesi Kálmánról." (A Portrait Sketch of Kálmán Gyimesi.) *OperaL.* 1997; 6(4): 17-20 ia. Illus.: Photo. B&W. 4. Lang.: Hun.
Hungary. 1945-1997. Histories-sources. ■The 70-year-old life member of the Szeged National Theatre speaks about present-day Szeged opera performances and future plans including teaching.

4173   Huszár, Klára. "Márkus László emlékezete." (The Heritage of László Márkus.) *OperaL.* 1997; 6(1): 18-20. Illus.: Photo. B&W. 1. Lang.: Hun.
Hungary: Budapest. 1923-1944. Biographical studies. ■The wide-ranging theatrical career of Márkus, a director, theatrical designer, dramaturg and musician who worked at several repertory theatres in Budapest. In 1923 he became the chief stage-director and from 1935 the general director of the Royal Hungarian Opera House up to 1944.

4174   Kertész, Iván. "Az Operaház örökös tagjai: Kálmán Oszkár." (Life-Members of the Opera House: Oszkár Kálmán.) *OperaL.* 1997; 6(3): 18-20. Illus.: Photo. B&W. 3. Lang.: Hun.
Hungary: Budapest. 1887-1971. Biographical studies. ■The forty-one-year career of bass Oszkár Kálmán in Hungary and abroad.

4175   Kertész, Iván. "Halmos János emlékezete." (Commemorating János Halmos.) *OperaL.* 1997; 6(4): 21-22. Lang.: Hun.
Hungary. 1887-1954. Biographical studies. ■The unusual career of Halmos, the leading tenor of the Budapest Opera 1928-1954, who as a young singer and actor appeared in operas, popular folk-operettas and spoken drama.

4176   Mátai, Györgyi; Szántó, György, photo. "Egy operaénekes nem élhet szertelenül. Pályakép Berczelly Istvánról." (An Opera Singer Must Not Live Immoderately: A Portrait of István Berczelly.) *OperaL.* 1997; 6(1): 21-23. Illus.: Photo. B&W. 4. Lang.: Hun.
Hungary. 1960-1996. Histories-sources. ■An interview with the leading baritone of the Hungarian State Opera, presently in the revival of the *Ring* cycle as Wotan.

4177   Mátai, Györgyi. "Születésnapi interjú Ilosvay Róberttel." (Róbert Ilosvay: A Birthday Interview.) *OperaL.* 1997; 6(4): 4-8. Illus.: Photo. B&W. 7. Lang.: Hun.
Hungary. 1946-1997. Histories-sources. ■The famous tenor celebrating his 70th birthday has been member of the Budapest Opera since 1954 and he gained success as permanent guest performer of the Cologne Opera for twenty-two years as well.

4178   Mátai, Györgyi. "Bemutatjuk Gémes Katalint." (Introducing Katalin Gémes.) *OperaL.* 1997; 6(5): 26-28. Lang.: Hun.
Hungary. 1988-1997. Histories-sources. ■Career of the young mezzo-coloratura of the Budapest Opera.

4179   Meixner, Mihály. "Anthes György emlékezete." (Commemorating György Anthes.) *OperaL.* 1997; 6(5): 17-19. Illus.: Photo. B&W. 6. Lang.: Hun.
Hungary. 1863-1922. Biographical studies. ■Profile of Anthes, a major opera personality at the turn of the century, and the heroic tenor of former Royal Hungarian Opera House. Following his retirement he became the leading stage-director of the Opera House.

4180   Szomory, György. "Bemutatjuk Kertesi Ingridet." (Introducing Ingrid Kertesi.) *OperaL.* 1997; 6(4): 12-16. Illus.: Photo. B&W. Color. 4. Lang.: Hun.
Hungary. 1970-1997. Biographical studies. ■Profile of the young coloratura soprano, recently awarded the Liszt Prize, who performs with the Budapest Opera and the Dusseldorf Opera.

4181   Szomory, György. "Vendégünk volt: Laki Krisztina." (Krisztina Laki Was Our Guest.) *OperaL.* 1997; 6(1): 2-7. Illus.: Photo. B&W. Color. 9. Lang.: Hun.
Hungary. 1970-1996. Biographical studies. ■The career of the soprano in German-speaking Switzerland, Germany and Austria. Her repertoire consists of a nucleus of Mozart's and Strauss' works.

4182   Szomory, György; Földi, Imre, photo. "A Budapesti Opera-barátok Egyesületének díszelőadása a millecentenárium évében." (The Millecentennial Gala of the Association of the Budapest Opera-Friends.) *OperaL.* 1997; 6(1): 8-11. Illus.: Photo. Color. 13. Lang.: Hun.
Hungary: Budapest. 1996. Historical studies. ■The gala was part of Hungary's millecentennial celebration with Hungarian artists living inside and outside the borders of Hungary, including singers unknown to Hungarian audiences.

4183   Szomory, György. "Ismét itthon Carelli Gábor." (Meeting Gábor Carelli in Budapest.) *OperaL.* 1997; 6(2): 15-18. Lang.: Hun.
Hungary. USA: New York, NY. 1916-1997. Histories-sources. ■Conversation with Gábor Carelli, New York-based Hungarian singer and pedagogue who sang with the Metropolitan Opera from 1950 to 1975.

4184   Szomory, György. "Mozgásba oltott zene—Beszélgetés Kerényi Miklós Gáborral *A bolygó hollandi* ról—és más egyébről." (Music Blended with Movement—An Interview with the Stage-Director of Wagner's *The Flying Dutchman*.) *OperaL.* 1997; 6(3): 2-6. Illus.: Photo. B&W. 1. Lang.: Hun.
Hungary: Budapest. 1997. Histories-sources. ■The revival of Richard Wagner's *Der Fliegende Holländer* at the Budapest Opera House under the direction of Miklós Gábor Kerényi, stage design by Péter Makai.

4185   Szomory, György. "Beszélgetés a *Turandot* rendezőjével." (An Interview with the Stage-Director of Puccini's *Turandot*.) *OperaL.* 1997; 6(5): 4-7. Illus.: Photo. B&W. 2. Lang.: Hun.
Hungary: Budapest. 1995-1997. Histories-sources. ■A new production of Puccini's opera at Budapest Erkel Theatre directed by the young Balázs Kovalik compared to his former staging of the opera at Szeged Theatre in 1995. (He graduated from the Munich College of Musical Arts in 1996).

4186   Baker, David J. "Desperate Measure: The Trouble with 'Sempre Libera'." *OpN.* 1997 Jan 11; 61(8): 14-17, 53. Illus.: Photo. B&W. 4. Lang.: Eng.
Italy. USA: New York, NY. 1886-1996. Critical studies. ■Jean de Reszke, Julian Budden, Will Crutchfield, Frank Corsaro, George Martin, Charles Osborne, and sopranos Anna Moffo, Beverly Sills, Ashley Putnam, Joan Sutherland, Renata Scotto, discuss the difficulty of the cabaletta 'Sempre Libera' from *La Traviata* by Giuseppe Verdi. Includes comments on performances by Rosa Ponselle and Patricia Brooks, and the English National Opera translation.

4187   Casali, Patrick Vincent. "The Pronunciation of Turandot: Puccini's Last Enigma." *OQ.* 1997 Sum; 13(4): 77-91. Notes. Append. Illus.: Photo. B&W. 1. Lang.: Eng.
Italy. 1867-1957. Critical studies. ■Speculation on the correct pronunciation of Turandot's name, what Puccini might have done with the unfinished portions of the opera had he lived to complete the writing, and composer Franco Alfano's music written to fill in incomplete sections of the opera. Past performances and recordings consulted for the pronunciations.

4188   Csák, P. Judit. "Fél évszázad után újra Budapesten—Fedora Barbieri." (Fedora Barbieri Again In Budapest After Half a Century.) *OperaL.* 1997; 6(3): 15-17. Illus.: Photo. B&W. 1. Lang.: Hun.

MUSIC-DRAMA: Opera—Performance/production

Italy. Hungary. 1940-1997. Biographical studies. ■The opera singer's return, as a member of the jury of the international singing competition, to Budapest, where she made her operatic debut in 1942.

4189 Duncan, Scott. "Buon Marcello: Rebirth of a Tenor." *OpN.* 1997 Jan 11; 61(8): 24-25. Illus.: Photo. Color. 1. Lang.: Eng.
Italy. 1965-1997. Histories-sources. ■Tenor Marcello Giordano appears to have overcome his vocal problems.

4190 Handt, Herbert. "Bohemian Quartet: How *La Bohème* Reflects Puccini's Early Days in Milan." *OpN.* 1997 Jan 11; 61(8) : 10-12, 53. Illus.: Dwg. Photo. B&W. Color. 7. Lang.: Eng.
Italy: Milan. 1894-1898. Biographical studies. ■Influence of Pietro Mascagni, Ruggero Leoncavallo, Alberto Franchetti, on the opera *La Bohème*, by Giacomo Puccini.

4191 Innaurato, Albert. "The Last Prima Donna." *OpN.* 1997 Apr 19; 61(15): 8-10, 12-15. Illus.: Photo. Color. B&W. 8. Lang.: Eng.
Italy. 1935-1997. Biographical studies. ■Playwright Albert Innaurato reports on his interviews with soprano Mirella Freni and other singers concerning her long career as a diva.

4192 Innaurato, Albert. "Coda: Baritone Gems." *OpN.* 1997 Feb 8; 61(10): 54. Illus.: Photo. B&W. 2. Lang.: Eng.
Italy. 1996. Critical studies. ■Playwright Albert Innaurato analyzes and criticizes a new CD entitled 'Famous Italian Baritones'.

4193 Kaufman, Tom. "Mercadante and Verdi." *OQ.* 1997 Spr; 13(3): 41-56. Notes. Tables. [Revised and expanded version of a paper read at the 'Conferenza su tematiche Mercadantiane December 1995.] Lang.: Eng.
Italy. 1852-1995. Biographical studies. ■Attributes the neglect of composer Saverio Mercadante to reviews written by Verdi scholars. Includes comparison of compositions by Verdi and Mercadante.

4194 Petty, Jonathan Christian. "The Ravished Flower: A Major Poetics in *Madama Butterfly*." *OJ.* 1997 Dec.; 30(4): 2-20. Lang.: Eng.
Italy. 1836. Critical studies. ■Analysis of Puccini's A major music in *Madama Butterfly* and its poetic coherence elsewhere in Puccini and in opera generally. Explores which textual elements are 'associative' with respect to keys chosen to present them.

4195 Phillips-Matz, Mary Jane. "Royal Portrait." *OpN.* 1997 Dec 20; 62(7): 16-21. Illus.: Photo. B&W. Color. 7. Lang.: Eng.
Italy. 1813-1901. Historical studies. ■Verdi's revision and interpretation of Spanish history. Emphasizes *Don Carlo* but also discusses influences on *Il Trovatore, Ernani, La Forza del Destino, I deliri di Saul, Giovanna d'Arco, I Masnadieri* and *Luisa Miller*.

4196 Piemonti, Anita. "Zwei Operninszenierungen von Erwin Piscator." (Two Opera Productions by Erwin Piscator.) *MuK.* 1997; 39(1): 103-121. Notes. Illus.: Photo. B&W. 6. Lang.: Ger.
Italy: Florence. 1963-1964. Historical studies. ■Characteristics of Piscator's late theatre work and his permanent style, based on performances of *I Masnadieri* by Giuseppe Verdi and *Salome* by Richard Strauss.

4197 Rosen, David. "First Edition." *OpN.* 1997 Feb 8; 61(10): 12-14. Illus.: Photo. Dwg. B&W. Color. 4. Lang.: Eng.
Italy: Milan. 1856-1888. Textual studies. ■Examination of the original production book of *Un Ballo in Maschera* published by Casa Ricordi, Milan. Compares the treatment of librettist Antonio Somma with *Gustave III* by Eugène Scribe.

4198 Scherer, Barrymore Laurence. "Passion Flower." *OpN.* 1997 Apr 19; 61(15): 16-19. Illus.: Photo. B&W. 6. Lang.: Eng.
Italy. 1898-1997. Historical studies. ■The checkered reputation of *Fedora* by *verismo* composer Umberto Giordano, based on a melodrama by Victorien Sardou.

4199 Tommasini, Anthony. "The Last of the Prima Donnas? Mirella Freni and the Italian Tradition." *New York Times.* 1997 May 1, 1997: C13-14. Illus.: Photo. B&W. 4. Lang.: Eng.
Italy. 1935-1997. Biographical studies. ■Profile, evaluation of the flowering of Mirella Freni into a great Italian prima donna. Discusses the recorded legacy of Freni and numerous prima donnas, including Maria Callas.

4200 Bruls, Willem. "De vernietigende Hamer van Richard Wagner. De Ring van Pierre Audi." (The Destroying Hammer of Richard Wagner: Pierre Audi's *Ring*.) *Theatermaker.* 1997; 1(5/6): 26-30. Illus.: Photo. B&W. 2. Lang.: Dut.
Netherlands: Amsterdam. 1997. Critical studies. ■Nederlandse Opera's production of *Der Ring des Nibelungen*, with attention to the artistic principles of its director Pierre Audi.

4201 Tranberg, Sören. "Oddbjørn Tennfjord Vandraren." (Oddbjørn Tennfjord The Wanderer.) *MuD.* 1997; 19(1): 20-22 . Illus.: Photo. B&W. Color. Lang.: Swe.
Norway: Oslo. 1970. Histories-sources. ■An interview with the bass singer Oddbjørn Tennfjord about his career and the operatic life in Norway.

4202 Scherer, Barrymore Laurence. "Alto Rhapsody." *OpN.* 1997 June; 61(17): 30-31, 45. Illus.: Photo. B&W. Color. 2. Lang.: Eng.
Poland. 1997. Histories-sources. ■Profile, interview with Polish contralto Ewa Podleś.

4203 Allison, John. "Angela's Way." *OpN.* 1997 Mar 22; 61(13): 24-26. Illus.: Photo. Color. 4. Lang.: Eng.
Romania. 1997. Biographical studies. ■Profile of Romanian soprano, Angela Gheorghiu, wife of French tenor Roberto Alagna.

4204 Dyer, Richard. "Arkhipova at Last." *OpN.* 1997 Apr 19; 61(15): 34-35. Illus.: Photo. B&W. Color. 5. Lang.: Eng.
Russia: Moscow. 1925-1997. Biographical studies. ■The long career of Russian mezzo soprano Irina Archipova.

4205 Pokrovskij, Boris A. *Puteštvie v stranu 'opera'.* (The Voyage to the Country 'Opera'.) Moscow: Sovremennik; 1997. 238 pp. Lang.: Rus.
Russia. 1980-1997. Histories-sources. ■Opera director on his work.

4206 Robinson, Harlow. "Into the West." *OpN.* 1997 Apr 19; 61(15): 25-27. Illus.: Photo. Color. 3. Lang.: Eng.
Russia: St. Petersburg. 1962-1997. Biographical studies. ■Profile, interview and analysis of the burgeoning career of Russian soprano Galina Gorčakova.

4207 Šaljapin, Fëdor. *Maska i duša.* (Mask and Soul.) Moscow: Vagrius; 1997. 320 pp. Lang.: Rus.
Russia. France. 1873-1938. Histories-sources. ■Memoirs of the Russian opera star Fëdor Šaljapin.

4208 Stenning Edgecomb, Rodney. "Wagnerian Elements in Tchaikovsky's *Mazeppa*." *OJ.* 1997 Dec.; 30(4): 21-30. Lang.: Eng.
Russia. 1877-1884. Critical studies. ■Influence of Wagner on Čajkovskij's compositions: compares Wagnerian operas to *Orleanskaja Deva (The Maid of Orleans)* and *Burja (The Tempest)*, critical reception of these works and further influences of French and Austrian opera.

4209 Teachout, Terry. "A Quiet Place." *OpN.* 1997 Apr 19; 61(15): 20-23. Illus.: Photo. Color. B&W. 6. Lang.: Eng.
Russia. 1879-1997. Historical studies. ■An analysis of the opera *Eugene Onegin* by Pëtr Iljič Čajkovskij, based on the novel by Aleksand'r Sergejëvič Puškin. It is more popular in Russia than elsewhere.

4210 Breiholz, Jochen. "Botha's Bow." *OpN.* 1997 Jan 25; 61(9): 26-27. Illus.: Photo. Color. 2. Lang.: Eng.
South Africa, Republic of. 1996. Histories-sources. ■Interview with South African tenor Johan Botha.

4211 Hoffelé, Jean-Charles. "Don Manuel et l'opéra." (Don Manuel and the Opera.) *ASO.* 1997 May/June; 177: 4-7. Illus.: Photo. B&W. 5. Lang.: Fre.
Spain. 1876-1946. Biographical studies. ■Life of composer Manuel de Falla.

4212 Nectoux, Jean-Michel. "Manuel de Falla: Un itinéraire spirituel." (Manuel de Falla: A Spiritual Itinerary.) *ASO.* 1997 May/June; 177: 5-11. Notes. Lang.: Fre.
Spain. 1876-1926. Critical studies. ■The development of Falla's music.

4213 Sevilla-Gonzaga, Marylis; Heliotis, Harry. "Sound Bites: Aïnhoa Artetoa." *OpN.* 1997 Jan 25; 61(9): 8-9. Illus.: Photo. Color. 1. Lang.: Eng.

MUSIC-DRAMA: Opera—Performance/production

Spain. 1997. Histories-sources. ■Introduces the new Spanish soprano Aïnhoa Artetoa, who sang in *La Traviata* and *Fedora* this season at the Metropolitan Opera.

4214 Sevilla-Gonzaga, Marylis. "The Master Touch." *OpN.* 1997 July; 62(1): 28-29. Illus.: Photo. B&W. Color. 4. Lang.: Eng.
Spain. 1990-1997. Histories-sources. ■The Alfredo Kraus International Competition 1990-1997. Photographs of winners and comments on Kraus's interest in *zarzuela*.

4215 Kellow, Brian. "Fire and Ice: The Art of Anne Sofie von Otter." *OpN.* 1997 May; 61(16): 8-12. Illus.: Photo. B&W. Color. 4. Lang.: Eng.
Sweden: Stockholm. 1997. Histories-sources. ■Profile, interview, and assessment of the work of Swedish mezzo-soprano Anne Sofie von Otter.

4216 Kellow, Brian. "Songs on a Summer's Night." *OpN.* 1997 May; 61(16): 30-32, 34, 57. Illus.: Photo. B&W. Color. 9. Lang.: Eng.
Sweden. 1997. Histories-sources. ■Summer opera and musical entertainments available in Sweden, particularly at the Kungliga Operan, Drottningholmsteatern, the Vadstena Summer Opera Festival, and Dalhalla.

4217 Nilsson, Gunnar. "Med otryggheten som drivkraft." (With Risk as a Driving Force.) *MuD.* 1997; 19(4): 12-14. Illus.: Photo. B&W. Color. Lang.: Swe.
Sweden: Stockholm. 1980. Histories-sources. ■An interview with the tenor Lars Cleveman about his background as a member of a rock group and career as an opera singer.

4218 Pfalzer, Janina. "Sångare—ett riskyrke." (The Singers—a Profession of Risks.) *MuD.* 1997; 19(1): 36-37. Illus.: Photo. B&W. Lang.: Swe.
Sweden. 1995. Critical studies. ■A presentation of a dissertation about the problems and fears of an opera singer of today by Maria Sandgren.

4219 Smith, Patrick J. "Tenor for the Ages." *OpN.* 1997 May; 61(16): 35. Illus.: Photo. B&W. Color. Lang.: Eng.
Sweden. 1926-1997. Histories-sources. ■Profile of Swedish-Russian tenor Nicolai Gedda.

4220 Stensson, Ola. "Realismen på Operan." (Realism at the Opera.) *MuD.* 1997; 19(1): 40-41. Illus.: Photo. B&W. Lang.: Swe.
Sweden: Stockholm. 1862-1997. Critical studies. ■A presentation of Göran Gademan'a dissertation *Realismen på Operan (Realism at the Opera)* about the new realistic stagings at Kungliga Operan.

4221 Tranberg, Sören. "'Satsa på sången, flicka lilla!o'." ('Go In For the Singing, My Girl!o'.) *MuD.* 1997; 19 (3): 8-11. Illus.: Photo. B&W. Lang.: Swe.
Sweden. Europe. 1979. Histories-sources. ■An interview with the singer Hillevi Martinpelto about her background and career.

4222 McKee, David. "Belated Visit." *OpN.* 1997 Apr 5; 61(14): 20-23. Illus.: Photo. B&W. 5. Lang.: Eng.
Switzerland. 1918-1996. Biographical studies. ■Analysis and performance history of *Der Besuch der alten Dame* by Gottfried von Einem, based on the play by Friedrich Dürrenmatt, to be presented this year by the New York City Opera.

4223 "From Oberto to Falstaff." *Econ.* 1997 Aug 2-8; 344(8028): 69. Illus.: Photo. B&W. 1. Lang.: Eng.
UK-England: London. 1997. Critical studies. ■Goals of the Royal Opera House's Verdi festival led by associate musical director Sir Edward Downes: productions, challenges, audience response.

4224 "The Best Has Yet to Sing." *Econ.* 1997 Jan 25; 342(8001): 75-76. Illus.: Photo. B&W. 1. Lang.: Eng.
UK-England. USA. 1997. Historical studies. ■Examines lack of big, dramatic voices in current generation of singers and young artists programs at American opera houses, compares training of singers in America and the UK.

4225 Driscoll, F. Paul; Barda, Clive. "Full Sail." *OpN.* 1997 Mar 8; 61(12): 26-31. Illus.: Photo. Color. 5. Lang.: Eng.
UK-England: London. 1997. Biographical studies. ■Career of lyric tenor Philip Langridge who combines singing and acting skills in interpreting roles in operas by Benjamin Britten, including Captain Vere in *Billy Budd*, and Aschenbach in *Death in Venice*.

4226 Kellow, Brian. "Sound Bites: Susannah Waters." *OpN.* 1997 Nov.; 62(5): 50-51. Illus.: Photo. Color. 2. Lang.: Eng.
UK-England. 1997. Biographical studies. ■Profile and discussion of the performance of soprano Susannah Waters in such roles as Romilda in *Xerxes* by Handel. Her brother is Mark Rylance, the Shakespearean actor.

4227 Sutcliffe, Tom. "British Journal." *OpN.* 1997 Dec 6; 62(6): 64-65. Lang.: Eng.
UK-England: London. UK-Wales: Cardiff. 1996-1997. Histories-sources. ■Accounts of performances and turmoil at the Royal Opera House, Covent Garden, the English National Opera, the Welsh National Opera, and Glyndebourne.

4228 Teachout, Terry. "Coda: Do the Wrong Thing." *OpN.* 1997 Mar 8; 61(12): 54. Lang.: Eng.
UK-England. Austro-Hungarian Empire. 1790-1951. Critical studies. ■Moral conflicts in *Così fan tutte* by Mozart and *Billy Budd* by Benjamin Britten.

4229 Eriksson, Torbjörn. "Efter Pavarotti—här kommer Tafferotti!" (After Pavarotti—Here Comes Tafferotti!)*MuD.* 1997; 19(3): 13-15. Illus.: Photo. B&W. Color. Lang.: Swe.
UK-Wales. 1989. Histories-sources. ■An interview with Bryn Terfel about his background and career.

4230 New York City Opera. "Telecast Performance." *OpN.* 1997; 61. Illus.: Diagram. Dwg. Photo. Color. B&W. [*La Bohème* (Mar 22): 60.] Lang.: Eng.
USA: New York, NY. 1997. Histories-sources. ■Photograph, list of principals, conductor, production staff, telecast performance.

4231 Lyric Opera of Chicago. "Lyric Opera of Chicago: Radio Broadcast Performances." *OpN.* 1997; 61. Discography. Illus.: Design. Diagram. Dwg. Photo. Color. B&W. [*Il Trittico, Il Tabarro, Suor Angelica, Gianni Schicchi*, (May): 53, *The Consul, Don Carlo* (May): 54, *Un Re in Ascolto, Die Zauberflöte* (May): 55, *Norma* (June): 53, *Salome* (June): 50, *Turandot* (June): 50.] Lang.: Eng.
USA: Chicago, IL. 1997. Histories-sources. ■Photographs, lists of principals, conductors, production staff, Lyric Opera of Chicago radio broadcast performances.

4232 Juilliard Opera. "Telecast Performance." *OpN.* 1997; 62. Illus.: Diagram. Dwg. Photo. Color. B&W. [*Hänsel und Gretel* (Dec 6): 80.] Lang.: Eng.
USA: New York, NY. 1997. Histories-sources. ■Photograph, list of principals, conductor, production staff, telecast performance.

4233 Metropolitan Opera. "Telecast Performance." *OpN.* 1997; 62. Illus.: Diagram. Dwg. Photo. Color. B&W. [*Fedora* (Oct): 66, *Carmen* (Dec. 20): 51.] Lang.: Eng.
USA: New York, NY. 1997. Histories-sources. ■Photograph, list of principals, conductor, production staff, Metropolitan Opera telecast performance.

4234 Metropolitan Opera. "Telecast Performance." *OpN.* 1997; 62. Illus.: Design. Diagram. Dwg. Photo. Color. B&W. [*Fedora* (October 29, 1997): 66.] Lang.: Eng.
USA: New York, NY. 1997. Histories-sources. ■Photograph, list of principals, conductor, production staff, telecast performance.

4235 Allison, John. "The Accidental Conductor." *OpN.* 1997 Dec 20; 62(7): 8-11, 52. Illus.: Photo. Color. Lang.: Eng.
USA: New York, NY. 1953-1997. Histories-sources. ■Profile, interview with Korean-born international opera conductor, Myung-Whun Chung.

4236 Baldridge, Charlene. "American Inquisition." *OpN.* 1997 Feb 22; 61(11): 28-30. Illus.: Photo. B&W. 3. Lang.: Eng.
USA: San Diego, CA. 1997. Historical studies. ■The background of *The Conquistador*, Myron Fink, composer, libretto by Donald Moreland, to be presented by the San Diego Opera in March 1997. Based on *The Martyr: The Story of a Secret Jew and the Mexican Inquisition*, by Martin A. Cohen (1973), it centers on Luis de Carvajal, a sixteenth-century conquistador of Jewish ancestry. The role of Carvajal will be played by Jerry Hadley.

4237 Bergman, Beth; Davidson, Erika; Elbers, Johan; Schiller, Beatriz; Klotz, Winnie. "Radio Broadcast Performances." *OpN.* 1997; 62. Discography. Illus.: Diagram. Dwg. Photo.

Color. B&W. [*La Clemenza di Tito* (Dec 6): 30-32, 34, *Turandot* (Dec 6): 36-38, 40, *Il Barbiere di Siviglia* (Dec 10): 26-29, *Don Carlo* (Dec 20): 30-33.] Lang.: Eng.
USA: New York, NY. 1997-1997. Histories-sources. ■Photographs, lists of principals, conductors, production staff, biographies, synopses, discographies.

4238 Bergman, Beth; Davidson, Erika; Elbers, Johan; Schiller, Beatriz; Klotz, Winnie. "Radio Broadcast Performances." *OpN.* 1997; 61. Discography. Illus.: Design. Diagram. Dwg. Photo. Color. B&W. [*La Bohème* (Jan 11): 30-33, *La Traviata* (Jan 11): 34-37, *Cavalleria Rusticana* and *Pagliacci* (Jan 25): 34-37, *I Puritani* (Jan 25): 38-41, *Le Nozze di Figaro* (Feb 8): 32-35, *Un Ballo in Maschera* (Feb 8): 36-39, *Wozzeck* (Feb 22): 32-35, *Aida* (Feb 22): 36-39, *Billy Budd* (Mar 8): 32-35, *Così fan tutte* (Mar 8): 36-39, *Carmen* (March 22): 40-43, *Das Rheingold* (March 22): 44-47, *Faust* (Apr 5): 32-35, *Die Walküre* (Apr 5): 34-39, *Eugene Onegin* (Apr 19): 36-39, *Fedora* (Apr 19): 40-43.] Lang.: Eng.
USA: New York, NY. 1997. Histories-sources. ■Photographs, lists of principals, conductors, production staff, biographies, synopses, discographies, radio broadcast performances.

4239 Buchau, Stephanie von. "Home Again." *OpN.* 1997 Sep.; 62(3): 24-26. Illus.: Photo. Color. 5. Lang.: Eng.
USA: San Francisco, CA. 1996. Historical studies. ■The San Francisco Opera celebrates its seventy-fifth Season Gala Concert in the repaired and refurbished War Memorial Opera House, damaged by earthquake and fire 1995-1996.

4240 Crutchfield, Will; Kapuszta, Janusz, illus. "The Well-Tempered Cut." *OpN.* 1997 Dec 6; 62(6): 23-24, 26-27, 84. Illus.: Dwg. 1. Lang.: Eng.
USA. 1997. Critical studies. ■Examines and evaluates the reasons for abridging a composer's score for performance. Examples are drawn from the works of Wolfgang Amadeus Mozart, Giuseppe Verdi, Richard Wagner, George Frideric Handel, Ludwig van Beethoven, Gaetano Donizetti, Fromental Halévy.

4241 Davidson, Justin. "*Ashoka*'s Dreamer." *OpN.* 1997 June; 61(17): 28-29. Illus.: Dwg. Photo. B&W. 3. Lang.: Eng.
USA: New York, NY. 1947-1997. Biographical studies. ■Brief biography of American composer Peter Lieberson on the occasion of the premiere of his opera *Ashoka's Dream*, libretto by Douglas Penick, at the Santa Fe Opera.

4242 Davidson, Justin. "Slave Ship." *OpN.* 1997 Oct.; 62(4): 38. Illus.: Photo. Color. 1. Lang.: Eng.
USA: Chicago, IL. 1997. Histories-sources. ■Anthony Davis' opera *Amistad*, libretto by Thulani Davis, and its Lyric Opera of Chicago premiere.

4243 Davis, Peter G. "Call of Fire." *OpN.* 1997 Mar 22; 61(13): 14-19, 27. Illus.: Photo. B&W. 5. Lang.: Eng.
USA. 1851-1929. Biographical studies. ■The major international opera career of Minnie Hauk (born Amalia Mignon Hauck) in a variety of soprano roles.

4244 Di Stefano Miller, Marie; Thorendahl, Erik; Bellardo, Samuel J. "The 40th Anniversary of a Star: Antonietta Stella." *OJ.* 1997 Mar.; 30(1): 29-38. Illus.: Photo. B&W. 2. Lang.: Eng.
USA: New York, NY. 1954-1997. Biographical studies. ■Personal life and career of soprano Stella: her debut at the Metropolitan Opera, her signature role in Verdi's *Aida*, critical response to her performances, early training, later work as a singing teacher.

4245 Drake, James A. "A Perfect Voice: Ponselle in *Norma*." *OQ.* 1997 Fall; 14(1): 67-77. Notes. [Excerpt from *Rosa Ponselle: A Centenary Biography* (Amadeus Press, 1997).] Lang.: Eng.
USA: New York, NY. 1920-1927. Biographical studies. ■Impact of the demands of the lead roles in *La vestale* by Spontini and *Norma* on personal life and career of Rosa Ponselle. Critical response, popularity of *Norma* by Bellini.

4246 Driscoll, F. Paul. "Going to the Opera: with Liza Moran Maloy." *OpN.* 1997 Jan 11; 61(8): 8, 53. Illus.: Photo. Color. 1. Lang.: Eng.
USA: New York, NY. 1988-1997. Critical studies. ■The Metropolitan Opera, New York, NY through the eyes and ears of eight-year-old Liza Moran Maloy on her first visit to the opera to hear *La Bohème* by Giacomo Puccini.

4247 Driscoll, F. Paul. "Trial by Fire." *OpN.* 1997 Feb 8; 61(10): 22, 53. Illus.: Photo. B&W. 1. Lang.: Eng.
USA: New York, NY. 1979. Histories-sources. ■Tenor Jerry Hadley recalls his disaster-ridden New York City Opera debut September 14, 1979, as Arturo in *Lucia di Lammermoor* after less than a week's notice and no stage rehearsal.

4248 Driscoll, F. Paul. "Going to the Opera: ... with André Bishop." *OpN.* 1997 Apr 5; 61(14): 40-41, 51. Illus.: Photo. B&W. 2. Lang.: Eng.
USA: New York, NY. 1997. Critical studies. ■André Bishop, artistic director of Lincoln Center Theatre since 1992, offers his personal reactions to opera.

4249 Driscoll, F. Paul. "Going to the Opera ... with Susan Orlean: *Così fan tutte*." *OpN.* 1997 June; 61(17): 32-33, 61. Illus.: Photo. B&W. 1. Lang.: Eng.
USA: New York, NY. 1997. Critical studies. ■The reaction of *New Yorker* writer Susan Orlean to a Metropolitan Opera performance of *Così fan tutte* by Mozart, particularly the aria 'Per pietà' as sung by American soprano Renée Fleming.

4250 Driscoll, F. Paul. "Going to the Opera ... with Ira Levin." *OpN.* 1997 Oct.; 62(4): 36-37, 64. Illus.: Photo. B&W. Color. 2. Lang.: Eng.
USA: New York, NY. 1997. Critical studies. ■The reaction of Ira Levin, author of thrillers and plots for musicals, to a production of Gounod's *Faust* at the Metropolitan Opera.

4251 Driscoll, F. Paul. "Going to the Opera ... with Sam Waterston. *Eugene Onegin*." *OpN.* 1997 Dec 6; 62(6): 16-18. Illus.: Photo. B&W. Color. 2. Lang.: Eng.
USA: New York, NY. 1996-1997. Critical studies. ■The reaction of actor Sam Waterston to the performance of *Eugene Onegin* by Pětr Iljič Čajkovski.

4252 Gooding, Wayne. "The Angel and the Dog." *OC.* 1997 Fall; 38(3): 16-19. Illus.: Photo. B&W. 2. Lang.: Eng.
USA. UK-England. 1897-1997. Historical studies. ■Salute to a century of recordings of great opera singers on the RCA Victor and EMI labels.

4253 Gurewitsch, Matthew. "Wide Horizons." *OpN.* 1997 Apr 19; 61(15): 28-32. Illus.: Photo. B&W. 4. Lang.: Eng.
USA. 1960-1997. Biographical studies. ■The career of American-born opera conductor Antonio Pappano, from his beginnings at the New York City Opera to international demand.

4254 Haddad, Sonya. "Lili in Bloom." *OpN.* 1997 Mar 22; 61(13): 48-51, 62. Illus.: Photo. Color. B&W. 7. Lang.: Eng.
USA: Chicago, IL. 1921-1997. Biographical studies. ■Profile, biography of contralto Lili Chookasian.

4255 Haddad, Sonya. "Remembering 'The Last Great Impresario'." *OpN.* 1997 Nov.; 62(5): 10-12, 14. Illus.: Photo. B&W. 7. Lang.: Eng.
USA: New York, NY. 1950-1972. Histories-sources. ■Selected comments by singers and management staff of the Metropolitan Opera on the tenure of Rudolf Bing as General Manager.

4256 Hamilton, David. "*The Ring* on ROM." *OpN.* 1997 Oct.; 62(4): 10-22, 27. Illus.: Photo. 2. Lang.: Eng.
USA. 1996. Critical studies. ■Evaluative analysis of the digital CD-ROM set of *Der Ring des Nibelungen*, noting its characteristics and the absence of cast lists.

4257 Hamilton, David; Kapuszta, Janusz, illus. "Choices: ... Criteria for Picking What to Read and Hear." *OpN.* 1997 Dec 6; 62(6): 28. Illus.: Dwg. B&W. Lang.: Eng.
USA: New York, NY. 1997. Critical studies. ■Criteria for recommending printed and audio aids to the understanding of opera.

MUSIC-DRAMA: Opera—Performance/production

4258 Honig, Joel. "Is It Curtains for American Chamber Opera?" *OpN*. 1997 Aug.; 62(2): 10-12, 14, 16-17. Illus.: Dwg. Photo. B&W. Color. 5. Lang.: Eng.

USA. 1868-1997. Historical studies. ■A brief history of chamber opera, with emphasis on American performance and compositions. Considers Stephen Glover's *Beauty and the Beast* (1868, with W.F. Vandervell), *The Medium, The Old Maid and the Thief* by Gian Carlo Menotti, and *The Tender Land* by Aaron Copland as well as Jack Beeson's *Lizzie Borden, Hello Out There, Sorry, Wrong Number, My Heart's in the Highlands*. The importance of the Columbia Opera Workshop.

4259 Jay, Cynthia Lee. *A Production of Gian Carlo Menotti's Opera* The Medium*: A Performance Project Directed and Produced by Cynthia L. Jay.* College Park, MD: Univ. of Maryland; 1997. 339 pp. [D.M.A. Dissertation, Univ. Microfilms Order No. AAC 9808688.] Lang.: Eng.

USA. 1996. Histories-sources. ■Production guide for *The Medium* including casting decisions, rehearsal process, and design decisions for the production presented in this dissertation performance project. Includes biographical sketch of the composer and an analysis of the female roles.

4260 Jennings, Harlan. "Grand Opera Comes to Denver: 1864-1881." *OQ*. 1997 Spr; 13(3): 57-84. Notes. Lang.: Eng.

USA: Denver, CO. 1864-1881. Historical studies. ■Early artists and opera companies that performed in Denver: geographical isolation, development of audience interest, critical response, Horace Tabor's construction of a permanent opera house and his selection of prima donna Emma Abbott and her Grand English Opera Company to open the inaugural season.

4261 Keller, James M. "American Classic." *OpN*. 1997 Oct.; 62(4): 10-12, 14, 64. Illus.: Photo. Color. 5. Lang.: Eng.

USA. 1959-1997. Biographical studies. ■Profile, analysis, interview, with soprano Renée Fleming.

4262 Kellow, Brian. "Coda: The High Road." *OpN*. 1997 Jan 11; 61(8): 54. Illus.: Photo. B&W. 1. Lang.: Eng.

USA. 1904-1996. Biographical studies. ■The work of opera critic, novelist and biographer Marcia Davenport, author of the first American biography of Mozart, and the daughter of soprano Alma Gluck.

4263 Kellow, Brian. "Making Her Point." *OpN*. 1997 Sep.; 62(3): 14-16, 18, 20, 22. Illus.: Photo. Color. 6. Lang.: Eng.

USA. 1958-1997. Biographical studies. ■Profile, interview with soprano Lauren Flanigan.

4264 Kellow, Brian; Prall, Sarah, photo. "Bus and Truck Bohème: On the Road with New York City Opera's National Company." *OpN*. 1997 Nov.; 62(5): 16-18, 20, 22, 24-26, 28, 30-31. Illus.: Photo. Color. 17. Lang.: Eng.

USA. 1994. Histories-sources. ■New York City Opera's seventy-city tour of *La Bohème*.

4265 Kerner, Leighton. "Schubert's Last Stand: The 92nd Street Y's Ten-Year Schubertiade Reaches Its Conclusion." *OpN*. 1997 Mar 8; 61(12): 18-21. Illus.: Dwg. Photo. Color. 4. Lang.: Eng.

USA: New York, NY. 1988-1998. Historical studies. ■An account of the ten-year Schubertiade, originally planned to offer lectures on, and performance of, the entire canon of the music of Franz Schubert. The dream of baritone Hermann Prey, it was begun by Omus Hirshbein, Director of the 92nd Street Y, but met with considerable difficulty and subsequent reorganization.

4266 Kravitz, Herman. "Titan: The Bing Years at the Met." *OpN*. 1997 Nov.; 62(5): 6. Illus.: Photo. B&W. Lang.: Eng.

USA: New York, NY. 1950-1972. Historical studies. ■Short evaluation of the tenure of Rudolf Bing as General Manager of the Metropolitan Opera.

4267 Marsh, Robert C. "The Annals of the Ravinia Opera." *OQ*. 1997 Spr; 13(3): 107-116. Notes. [Reprinted from the Chicago Opera Project of the Newberry Library, 1995.] Lang.: Eng.

USA: Chicago, IL. 1912-1926. Histories-sources. ■Listing of productions, singers, conductors, dates, directors represented at Ravinia Opera from 1912-1916. Continued in *OQ* 13:4 (1997), 123-139 (1917-1921), 14:1 (1997), 80-101 (1922-1926), and 14:2 (1997), 57-82 (1927-1931).

4268 Marshbrook, William. "Nelson Eddy's Career in Opera." *OQ*. 1997 Spr; 13(3): 7-18. Notes. Illus.: Photo. B&W. 3. Lang.: Eng.

USA. 1901-1967. Biographical studies. ■Movie actor Eddy's career as an opera singer: training, roles and productions, opera companies he was employed by, critical response, concert tours.

4269 McKee, David. "You've Come a Long Way, Baby Doe." *OpN*. 1997 Jan 11; 61(8): 26-27, 43, 51. Illus.: Photo. B&W. Color. 6. Lang.: Eng.

USA. 1957-1997. Historical studies. ■After forty years, *The Ballad of Baby Doe* by Douglas Moore may well be the quintessential American opera with its rags-to-riches theme.

4270 Miller, Sarah Bryan. "Zen Master." *OpN*. 1997 Jan 25; 61(9): 32-33. Illus.: Photo. Color. 3. Lang.: Eng.

USA: Houston, TX. 1997. Biographical studies. ■The career of opera conductor Christoph Eschenbach and the unusual qualities he brings to his work.

4271 Pearson, Edward Hagelin. "Victor Herbert's *Madeleine*." *OQ*. 1997 Sum; 13(4): 59-75. Notes. Illus.: Photo. Poster. B&W. 7. Lang.: Eng.

USA: New York, NY. 1907-1995. Historical studies. ■Casting, rehearsal and premiere at the Metropolitan Opera House of Herbert's one-act opera *Madeleine*, directed by Jules Speck. Audience and critical response, later studies of the opera and significant revivals.

4272 Peters, Alton E. "Metropolitan Opera Guild Annual Report." *OpN*. 1997 Oct.; 62(4): 46, 67. Illus.: Photo. B&W. 1. Lang.: Eng.

USA: New York, NY. 1996-1997. Histories-sources. ■President of the Metropolitan Opera Guild, reports on guild activities for the year 1996-97.

4273 Phillips-Matz, Mary Jane. "Sister Act: The Vaudeville Roots of Carmela and Rosa Ponselle." *OpN*. 1997 Jan 11; 61(8): 18-23. Illus.: Photo. B&W. 7. Lang.: Eng.

USA: New York, NY. 1889-1981. Biographical studies. ■The vaudeville career of Carmela Ponselle (original name Ponzillo) and her more famous sister, Rosa Ponselle, who starred at the Metropolitan Opera.

4274 Plotkin, Fred. "Coda: Marie's First Child." *OpN*. 1997 Feb 22; 61(11): 54. Illus.: Photo. B&W. 1. Lang.: Eng.

USA: New York, NY. 1959. Histories-sources. ■Reminiscences of the New York premiere of Berg's *Wozzeck* at the Metropolitan Opera, where the role of Marie was played by Eleanor Steber and the child by Alice Plotnick (sister of the author), later a Broadway star named Alice Playten.

4275 Smith, Patrick J. "Viewpoint: Nixon Revisited." *OpN*. 1997 Mar 22; 61(13): 4. Lang.: Eng.

USA: New York, NY. 1987-1997. Critical studies. ■The concert performance, January 22, 1997, by the Eos Ensemble of *Nixon in China* (Act III), by John Adams.

4276 Smith, Patrick J.; Heliotis, Harry; Umans, Mary. "Under New Management: Paul Kellogg Kicks off the Next Era at New York City Opera." *OpN*. 1997 Mar 8; 61(12): 10-12, 14, 16. Illus.: Photo. B&W. Color. 5. Lang.: Eng.

USA: New York, NY. 1996. Histories-sources. ■Interview with Paul Kellogg, former director of the Glimmerglass Opera, and now manager of the New York City Opera: his career to date, future scheduling at the New York City Opera, and his continuing connection with Glimmerglass and Santa Fe Opera.

4277 Smith, Patrick J. "This Side of Heaven." *OpN*. 1997 Sep.; 62(3): 8-10, 12. Illus.: Photo. Color. 6. Lang.: Eng.

USA: New York, NY. 1950-1997. Historical studies. ■The development of the Metropolitan Opera Orchestra from the 1950s emphasizing the work of conductor James Levine.

4278 Stearns, David Patrick. "The Right Box." *OpN*. 1997 Oct.; 62(4): 16-18. Illus.: Photo. Color. 2. Lang.: Eng.

USA. 1996. Historical studies. ■History of advances in luxury record packaging, notably the 1996 CD-ROM collection of Leontyne Price recordings.

MUSIC-DRAMA: Opera—Performance/production

4279 Zeger, Brian; Heliotis, Harry. "Helping Hands: The Life of a Rehearsal Pianist." *OpN.* 1997 Jan 25; 61(9): 28, 30, 52. Illus.: Photo. B&W. 2. Lang.: Eng.
USA: New York, NY. 1996. Biographical studies. ■The duties and difficulties of a rehearsal pianist in the opera house, discussed by a member of the Metropolitan Opera staff.

Plays/librettos/scripts

4280 Brown, Kristi Ann. *A Critical Study of the Female Characters in Mozart's Don Giovanni and Die Zauberflöte.* Berkeley, CA: Univ. of California; 1997. 262 pp. Notes. Biblio. [Ph.D. Dissertation, Univ. Microfilms Order No. AAC 9803138.] Lang.: Eng.
Austria. 1756-1791. Critical studies. ■Draws from historical sources, traditions of critical reception, feminist theory, and reader-response theory to understand the character 'type' and to evaluate the relationship between these representations of women and present-day ethical concerns and cultural attitudes about femininity, sexuality, and power.

4281 Russell, Charles C. "Confusion in the Act I Finale of Mozart and Da Ponte's *Don Giovanni*." *OQ.* 1997 Fall; 14(1): 25-44. Notes. Append. Lang.: Eng.
Austria. 1787. Textual studies. ■Lack of clarity in stage directions at the end of Act I in *Don Giovanni*, usually resulting in their being modified or ignored. Lists stage directions with floor plan, and includes the section being examined in four separate published libretto texts including all original errors. Also examines whether story and its protagonist were considered comic or heroic.

4282 Baker, David J. "The Reluctant Ruler: Does Tito's Persistent Clemency Make Mozart's Final Opera Seria Less than Convincing?" *OpN.* 1997 Dec 6; 62(6): 12-15, 80-81. Illus.: Photo. B&W. Color. 6. Lang.: Eng.
Austro-Hungarian Empire. 1791-1997. Historical studies. ■Analysis of Mozart's final opera *La Clemenza di Tito* with respect to his choice of libretto (a shortened version by Mazzolà rather than the original 1734 text by Metastasio), the historical context of the opera's composition, and the current perception of the genre as dated.

4283 Beaton, Virginia. "Inside *Ashoka's Dream*." *OC.* 1997 Sum; 38(2): 14-17. Illus.: Photo. B&W. 3. Lang.: Eng.
Canada. 1997. Critical studies. ■Peter Lieberson's upcoming opera *Ashoka's Dream*, the second of a proposed four-opera cycle. The first was *King Gesar*. His librettist is Douglas Penick.

4284 Scott, Iain. "The Perfect 10." *OC.* 1997 Win; 38(4): 18-23. Illus.: Photo. B&W. 7. Lang.: Eng.
Canada. 1997. Histories-sources. ■The author's approach to the task of naming the ten greatest operas yet written, including mailing out questionnaires and assigning the question in class.

4285 Balázs, István. "La fin du monde vue d'en-bas." (The End of the World as Seen from Below.) *ASO.* 1997 Nov/Dec.; 180: 86-87. Lang.: Fre.
Europe. 1978-1990. Critical studies. ■Translation of an excerpt from a 1990 article by Balázs, included as supplementary commentary on *Le Grand Macabre* by György Ligeti, the topic of this issue of *ASO*.

4286 Enckell, Pierre. "Petite promenade somnambulique." (A Little Sleep Walk.) *ASO.* 1997 July/Aug.; 178: 62-65. Lang.: Fre.
Europe. 1831. Historical studies. ■Background information on Bellini's opera *La Sonnambula* regarding somnambulism, nightmares, and other sleep disorders, and a brief description of the source play by Scribe.

4287 Grim, William E. "The Male Heroine in Opera." *OJ.* 1997 Sep.; 30(3): 2-12. Notes. Lang.: Eng.
Europe. 1607-1997. Critical studies. ■Argues that opera, because it challenges the modes of expression of spoken drama, does not reinforce gender stereotypes. Uses Monteverdi's *L'Orfeo*, Mozart's *Don Giovanni* and Wagner's *Die Götterdämmerung* as examples.

4288 Liszt, Franz. "La Dame Blanche de Boieldieu." (Boieldieu's Lady in White.) *ASO.* 1997 Mar/Apr.; 176: 88-89. Illus.: Dwg. B&W. 2. Lang.: Fre.
Europe. 1825-1854. Historical studies. ■Liszt's reaction to Boieldieu's opera *La Dame Blanche*, in which he wonders whether it will still be popular one hundred years after its composition.

4289 Singler-Wilson, Juliette Clare. *Prima le Parole: A Look at the Methodologies Involved in Creating Effective Opera Libretti.* Claremont, CA: Claremont Graduate Univ; 1997. 48 pp. [D. M.A. Dissertation, Univ. Microfilms Order No. AAC 9730920.] Lang.: Eng.
Europe. 1770-1915. Critical studies. ■Analysis of Arrigo Boito's libretto for Verdi's *Otello*, adapted from Shakespeare's *Othello*, Da Ponte's libretto for Mozart's *Le Nozze di Figaro*, based on *Le Mariage de Figaro (The Marriage of Figaro)* by Beaumarchais, and Gertrude Stein's original libretto for Virgil Thomson's *Four Saints in Three Acts*.

4290 Dietrich, Charles. "Les Opéras Parfumés: Aspects of Orientalism in Nineteenth-Century French Opera." *ThR.* 1997; 22(2): 111-120. Notes. Lang.: Eng.
France. 1863-1894. Critical studies. ■The representation of the Orient in Bizet's *Les pêcheurs de perles*, Berlioz's *Les Troyens*, Massenet's *Esclarmonde* and *Thaïs*, Saint-Saëns' *Samson et Dalila*, Meyerbeer's *L'Africaine*, and Delibes' *Lakmé*.

4291 Thomas, Downing A. "Opera, Dispossession, and the Sublime: The Case of *Armide*." *TJ.* 1997 May; 49(2): 168-188. Notes. Illus.: Dwg. 2. Lang.: Eng.
France. 1686. Historical studies. ■The effectiveness of Lully and Quinault's *tragédie en musique* in defending the contemporary discourse on gender in which desire and loss are left 'to the woman as her lot'.

4292 Yon, Jean-Claude. "La Fille du régiment, opéra français et patriotique." (The Daughter of the Regiment: A Patriotic French Opera.) *ASO.* 1997 Sep/Oct.; 179: 68-73. Notes. Illus.: Dwg. B&W. 4. Lang.: Fre.
France. 1840. Critical studies. ■The extreme 'Frenchness' and patriotism of the opera despite its having been written by the Italian composer Gaetano Donizetti. Analysis of the opera as a reflection of its time and place, discussion of politics and stereotypes.

4293 Brandenburg, Detlef. "Schönheit, um zu überleben." (Beauty for Survival.) *DB.* 1997; 4: 20-23. Illus.: Photo. B&W. 5. Lang.: Ger.
Germany: Munich. 1997. Histories-sources. ■An interview with composer Moritz Eggert on occasion of the first performance of *Helle Nächte (Bright Nights)* directed by Tilman Knabe at the Munich Biennale.

4294 Brandenburg, Detlef. "'Ein grosser Schatz...'." (A Great Treasure...) *DB.* 1997; 4: 15-19. Illus.: Photo. B&W. 6. Lang.: Ger.
Germany: Munich. 1996. Histories-sources. ■An interview with composer Michael Obst on occasion of the first performance of *Solaris* directed by Anja Sündermann at the Munich Biennale.

4295 Bromander, Lennart. "Wagners säck i Hitlers påse." (The Sack of Wagner In Hitler's Bag.) *MuD.* 1997; 19(3): 16-19. Illus.: Photo. B&W. Lang.: Swe.
Germany: Bayreuth. 1849. Critical studies. ■An essay about Hitler's obsession with Wagner's ideas and music.

4296 Eckert, Nora. "Happy new ears oder Das Ende der Oper." (Happy New Ears, Or, The End of the Opera.) *TZ.* 1997; 1: 36-40. Illus.: Photo. B&W. 2. Lang.: Ger.
Germany. 1970-1997. Historical studies. ■The development of non-literary operas and new plays of sight and sound, with reference to Mauricio Kagel's *Staatstheater (State Theatre)* (1971) and Heiner Goebbels' *Die Wiederholung (The Repetition)* (1995).

4297 Hart, Beth. "Hugo von Hofmannsthal's Ideal Woman: A Psychoanalytic Perspective." *OQ.* 1997 Sum; 13(4): 93-121. Notes. Illus.: Photo. B&W. 12. Lang.: Eng.
Germany. 1860-1965. Critical studies. ■Psychoanalytic analysis of primary female characters and themes in Hofmannsthal and Strauss's *Arabella*. Political climate and its influences on the writing, popular misconceptions regarding the opera, relationship between Hofmannsthal and Strauss.

4298 Petty, Jonathan Christian. "Sieglinde and the Moon." *OQ.* 1997/98 Win; 14(2): 41-56. Notes. Illus.: Dwg. B&W. 8. Lang.: Eng.
Germany. 1853-1874. Critical studies. ■Symbolism and mythology in the characters and actions in Wagner's *Ring*, particularly *Die Walküre*. The symbolism of Wagner's choices of musical keys for each character.

MUSIC-DRAMA: Opera—Plays/librettos/scripts

4299 Richards, Walter William. *Nature as a Symbolic Element in Richard Wagner's Treatment of Myth*. Tallahassee, FL: Florida State Univ; 1997. 210 pp. [Ph.D. Dissertation, Univ. Microfilms Order No. AAC 9817319.] Lang.: Eng.
Germany. 1832-1883. Critical studies. ■Argues that Wagner's use of myth and nature was inspired by ancient Greek drama and integrated myth in such a way as to allow the viewer/listener to participate in myth at both an intellectual and intuitive level simultaneously.

4300 Spångberg, Mårten. "Heiner Maskin—Hamlet Müller." (Heiner Machine—Hamlet Müller.) *MuD.* 1997; 19(2): 24-25. Illus.: Photo. B&W. Lang.: Swe.
Germany. 1978. Historical studies. ■A presentation of Wolfgang Rihm's opera version of Heiner Müller's *Die Hamletmaschine*.

4301 Barber, Patrick. "Le Mariage secret ou l'autre 'folle journée'." (The Secret Marriage or Another 'Crazy Day'.) *ASO.* 1997 Jan/Feb.; 175: 86-91. Illus.: Dwg. B&W. 4. Lang.: Fre.
Italy. 1792. Critical studies. ■The conventions and character types of the Neapolitan comic genre as used in operas by Cimarosa, Paisiello, Rossini, and Donizetti.

4302 Cabourg, Jean. "Entre buffo et serio." (Between 'buffo' and 'serio'.) *ASO.* 1997 Jan/Feb.; 175: 102-103. Illus.: Dwg. B&W. 1. Lang.: Fre.
Italy. 1792. Critical studies. ■Argues that the classification of Cimarosa's opera *Il matrimonio segreto* as *opera buffa* does not do it justice.

4303 Deldonna, Anthony Robert. *The Operas of Pietro Alessandro Guglielmi (1728-1804): The Relationship of His Dialect Operas to His Opere Serie*. Washington, DC: Catholic Univ. of America; 1997. 338 pp. Notes. Biblio. [Ph.D. Dissertation, Univ. Microfilms Order No. AAC 9828863.] Lang.: Eng.
Italy. 1750-1804. Critical studies. ■Examines representative surviving musical manuscripts, libretti, and contemporary accounts of this work that demonstrate this cross-fertilization of genres.

4304 Di Profio, Alessandro. "Un sujet à la mode. *Il matrimonio segreto* et ses emprunts." (A Fashionable Subject: *Il matrimonio segreto* and Its Borrowings.) *ASO.* 1997 Jan/Feb.; 175: 92-101. Notes. Illus.: Dwg. B&W. 7. Lang.: Fre.
Italy. 1766-1792. Critical studies. ■Sources for the libretto by Giovanni Bertati for Cimarosa's opera *Il matrimonio segreto*, including *The Clandestine Marriage* by George Colman and David Garrick (itself based on Hogarth's 'Marriage à la mode' series) and several French translations and adaptations. Analysis of late eighteenth-century treatments of the secret marriage theme.

4305 Koran, Thomas Noel. *A Performance Translation of* La Cecchina, ossia la buona figliuola *by Niccolò Piccinni Based on the English Translation by Edward G. Toms (1766) with an Historical Introduction*. Austin, TX: Univ. of Texas; 1997. 169 pp. [D.M.A. Dissertation, Univ. Microfilms Order No. AAC 9803087.] Lang.: Eng.
Italy. USA. 1766-1996. Histories-sources. ■Introduction examines the historical significance of Piccinni's opera, libretto by Carlo Goldoni, said to be an important bridge between early Italian comic opera and the mature comic works of Mozart and his librettist, Lorenzo Da Ponte. In addition, author includes his own adaptation of *The Accomplish'd Maid*, an eighteenth-century English translation of the opera by Edward G. Toms, written for a production at London's Covent Garden Theatre.

4306 McClymonds, Maria Petzoldt. "*Bianca de'Rossi* as Play, Ballet, Opera: Contours of 'Modern' Historical Tragedy in the 1790s." *CompD.* 1997 Spr; 31(1): 158-177. Notes. Lang.: Eng.
Italy. 1790-1799. Historical studies. ■Sources of Vittorio Trento's popular opera *Bianca de'Rossi*, including a play by Pierantonio Meneghelli and a ballet by Giuseppe Trafieri.

4307 Yon, Jean-Claude. "L'arrivée d'un nouveau seigneur, ou *La Somnambule* avant Bellini." (The Arrival of a New Lord, or *La Sonnambula* before Bellini.) *ASO.* 1997 July/Aug.; 178: 56-61 aa no. Illus.: Dwg. B&W. 6. Lang.: Fre.
Italy. France. 1831. Historical studies. ■Thematic antecedents in theatre and ballet, borrowings, and unacknowledged translations of a play by

Scribe were the sources of Bellini's opera *La Sonnambula* and its libretto by Felice Romani.

4308 Zweifel, P.F. "The Three Faces of 'Eve': A Second-Person Analysis of Italian Opera." *OQ.* 1997 Spr; 13(3): 85-95. Notes. Lang.: Eng.
Italy. 1864-1881. Textual studies. ■Subtleties in interpersonal relationships revealed through analysis of different forms of address in the second person in Mozart's *Don Giovanni* and Verdi's *La Bohème*.

4309 Morrison, Simon Alexander. *Russian Opera and Symbolist Poetics*. Princeton, NJ: Princeton Univ; 1997. 277 pp. [Ph.D. Dissertation, Univ. Microfilms Order No. AAC 9801198.] Lang.: Eng.
Russia. 1890-1930. Historical studies. ■The influence of Russian Symbolist poetics on operatic composition. Focuses on four important trends in Symbolist aesthetics as evidenced in Čajkovskij's *Pique Dame (The Queen of Spades)*, Rimskij-Korsakov's *Skazanie o nevidimom grade Kiteže (Legend of the Invisible City of Kitezh and the Maiden Fevroniya)*, Aleksand'r Skriabin's incomplete *Mysterium (and Preparatory Act)*, and Sergei Prokofiev's *Ognennyi angel (The Fiery Angel)*.

4310 Bergström, Gunnel. "'Jag skulle gråta om en text jag skrivit gick förlorad som Kerstins." ('I Would Cry If a Text Of My Own Was Lost Like the One by Kerstin.) *MuD.* 1997; 19(2): 47. Lang.: Swe.
Sweden: Malmö. 1997. Critical studies. ■A report from a conference about musical dramaturgy, with reference to Hans Gefors' opera *Vargen kommer (The Wolf Arrives)* with libretto by Kerstin Klein-Perski.

4311 Gademan, Göran. "Sveriges meste operalibrettist?" (The Most Active Librettist in Sweden?)*MuD.* 1997; 19(4): 16-18. Illus.: Dwg. Photo. B&W. Lang.: Swe.
Sweden: Stockholm. 1828-1908. Biographical studies. ■A presentation of the Swedish author, director, playwright and manager Frans Hedberg.

4312 Ligeti, György. "À propos de la genèse de mon opéra." (On the Genesis of My Opera.) *ASO.* 1997 Nov/Dec.; 180: 88-89. Lang.: Fre.
Sweden. 1978. Histories-sources. ■The composer and librettist's account of how *Le Grand Macabre* came to be written, with reference to the process of 'Jarrycizing' the libretto, based on Ghelderode's *La Balade du Grand Macabre (The Grand Macabre's Stroll)*, and the influence of Breughel.

4313 Peterson, Hans-Gunnar. "Alltid på upptäcksfärd." (Always On Expeditions.) *MuD.* 1997; 19(1): 10-11. Illus.: Photo. B&W. Lang.: Swe.
Sweden. 1985-1997. Historical studies. ■A presentation of Thomas Jennefelt's new opera *Farkosten*.

4314 "New Mozarts Wanted: Mortals Should also Apply." *Econ.* 1997 Nov 15; 345(8043): 91-92. Illus.: Photo. B&W. 2. Lang.: Eng.
UK-England: London. 1960-1997. Historical studies. ■Examines where material for new operas can be found. Brief discussion of contemporary opera *Jackie O* by Michael Daugherty.

4315 Chen, Shu-Ling. *Music and Language in Two Twentieth-Century American Operas: Virgil Thomson/Gertrude Stein's 'The Epilogue,' from* The Mother of Us All, *and Robert Ashley's 'The Park,' Episode One from* Perfect Lives, *an Opera for Television*. College Park, MD: Univ. of Maryland; 1997. 321 pp. [Ph.D. Dissertation, Univ. Microfilms Order No. AAC 9808588.] Lang.: Eng.
USA. 1925-1980. Critical studies. ■Analyzes both the text and music of the two operas and applies the linguistic theories of Stein to one scene from each opera.

4316 Herold, Christian. "The Other Side of Echo: The Adventures of a Dyke-Mestiza-Chicana-Marimacha Ranchera Singer in (Robert) Ashleyland." *WPerf.* 1997; 9(2): 162-197. Notes. Biblio. Illus.: Photo. B&W. 2. [Number 18.] Lang.: Eng.
USA. 1961-1994. Critical studies. ■Argues that main character in Robert Ashley's avant-garde opera *Now Eleanor's Idea* projects a world with little real interaction between people and cultures.

4317 Sala, Emilio. "On the Track of *La pie voleuse*." *OQ.* 1997 Spr; 13(3): 20-40. Notes. Illus.: Sketches. B&W. 1. Lang.: Eng.

MUSIC-DRAMA: Opera—Plays/librettos/scripts

USA. 1815. Historical studies. ■Reconstruction of the features of the famous *mélodrame historique* that is the source of the libretto for Rossini's *La gazza ladra*: a play titled *La pie voleuse, ou La servante de Palaiseau (The Thieving Magpie or the Maid of Palaiseau)* by Caigniez and d'Aubigny. Discovery of music by Alexandre Piccini that accompanied the play according to the traditions of the popular *mélodrame*.

4318 Santore, Jonathan C. "Attitudes Toward Sexuality and the Tonal Structure of Hindemith's *Sancta Susanna*." *OJ*. 1997 June; 30(2): 2-10. Notes. Biblio. Lang.: Eng.
USA. 1922-1997. Critical studies. ■Interpretation of poet August Stramm's libretto for Paul Hindemith's one-act opera.

Reference materials

4319 Boukobza, Jean-François; Hoffelé, Jean-Charles. "Glossaire de termes musicaux espagnols." (Glossary of Spanish Musical Terms.) *ASO*. 1997 May/June; 177: 118-119. Lang.: Fre.
Spain. 1923. ■Explanation of Spanish musical terms, with reference to short operas by Manuel de Falla.

4320 Milnes, Rodney, ed. *Opera Index 1997*. London: Opera; 1997. 98 pp. Lang.: Eng.
UK-England. Europe. 1997. Histories-sources. ■General subject index to volume 48 of *Opera*, with additional separate indexes to operas, artists, and contributors.

Relation to other fields

4321 Aspden, Suzanne. "'An Infinity of Factions': Opera in Eighteenth-Century Britain and the Undoing of Society." *COJ*. 1997 ; 9(1): 1-19. Notes. Illus.: Sketches. B&W. 2. Lang.: Eng.
England: London. 1698-1737. Historical studies. ■Considers ways in which opera represented and encouraged declining social tastes and morality in a manner that undermined systems of government. Emphasis on Samuel Johnson's opera *Hurlothrumbo* and the use of *castrati*.

4322 Noble, Yvonne. "Castrati, Balzac, and Barthe*S/Z*." *CompD*. 1997 Spr; 31(1): 28-41. Notes. Lang.: Eng.
France. 1830-1970. Critical studies. ■Critical perception of *castrato* singers and their representation in Balzac's short story *Sarrasine*.

4323 Ahlquist, Karen. *Democracy at the Opera: Music, Theater, and Culture in New York City, 1815-1860*. Urbana/Chicago: Univ of Illinois P; 1997. 248 pp. (Music in American Life.) Index. Biblio. Pref. Notes. Lang.: Eng.
USA: New York, NY. 1815-1860. Histories-specific. ■Examines the cultural and specific historical circumstances behind the development of opera in New York. Delineates development from early days of English opera, through theatrical reform and the emergence of the new Italian opera, to the split between high and low culture as the 'new' opera became associated with society's elite.

4324 Finger, Anke Karen. *The Poetics of Cultural Unity: Gesamtkunstwerk and the Discourse on National Arts in German and American Culture*. Waltham, MA: Brandeis Univ; 1997. 223 pp. [Ph.D. Dissertation, Univ. Microfilms Order No. AAC 9729368.] Lang.: Eng.
USA. Germany. 1875-1920. Histories-specific. ■Focuses on Richard Wagner's influence on cultural and political changes and argues that unity in the arts is closely aligned with cultural politics and nationality.

Research/historiography

4325 Winn, James A. "Heroic Song: A Proposal for a Revised History of English Theater and Opera, 1656-1711." *ECS*. 1996/97 Win; 30(2): 113-137. Notes. Lang.: Eng.
England. 1639-1711. Historical studies. ■Proposes a more unified account of the variety of dramatic forms in this period stressing *The Siege of Rhodes*, written by Sir William Davenant, and produced by him as a fully sung opera and regarded by Dryden as the original model for the rhymed heroic play. Examines musical scenes that occur in many heroic plays.

Theory/criticism

4326 Kareda, Urjo. "A Moving Target." *OC*. 1997 Win; 38(4): 14-17. Illus.: Photo. B&W. 5. Lang.: Eng.

Canada. 1997. Critical studies. ■Discusses the opera maven's need to keep opera separate from other forms of musical theatre such as operetta, comic opera, zarzuela, and singspiel.

4327 Berio, Luciano; Osmond-Smith, David, transl. "Of Sounds and Images." *COJ*. 1997; 9(3): 295-299. [Text of a lecture delivered in November 1995 at the University of Siena.] Lang.: Eng.
Europe. 1880-1995. Critical studies. ■Text of a speech by Berio on the relationship between operatic music and its dramatic realization, with particular reference to Wagner.

4328 Condé, Gérard. "Un modèle pour l'opérette française? À propos de la réaction de Berlioz." (A Model for French Operetta? The Reaction of Berlioz.) *ASO*. 1997 Sep/Oct.; 179: 74-77. Illus.: Dwg. Photo. B&W. 3. Lang.: Fre.
France. 1840. Critical studies. ■Analysis of the apparently nationalistic grounds for the negative response of composer and critic Hector Berlioz to Donizetti's opera *La Fille du régiment*. Argues for the work's compositional superiority to the work of French composers of the period.

4329 Henson, Karen. "In the House of Disillusion: Augusta Holmès and *La Montagne noire*." *COJ*. 1997; 9(3): 233-262. Notes. Illus.: Photo. B&W. 1. Lang.: Eng.
France: Paris. 1881-1901. Critical studies. ■How contemporary perceptions of Holmès intertwine her personality with her work. Analyzes her opera *La Montagne noire* in detail with particular comment about the nationalism evident in the piece.

4330 Bergström, Gunnel. "Opera efter Auschwitz." (Opera Post Auschwitz.) *MuD*. 1997; 19(1): 6-8. Illus.: Photo. B&W. Lang.: Swe.
Germany. 1955. Critical studies. ■A presentation of the ideas of Theodor W. Adorno about the opera, based on his lecture at Darmstadt 1955.

4331 Lazaridès, Alexandre. "De l'oeuvre d'art totale aux spectacles multimédias." (From Total Art Work to Multimedia Spectacles.) *JCT*. 1997; 84: 169-174. Illus.: Photo. B&W. 4. Lang.: Fre.
Germany: Bayreuth. 1850-1997. Historical studies. ■Draws line from Wagnerian *Gesamtkunstwerk* to contemporary multimedia shows, as suggested by Denis Bablet's essay collection *L'Oeuvre d'art totale (The Total Art Work)*.

4332 Levin, David J. "Reading a Staging/Staging a Reading." *COJ*. 1997; 9(1): 47-71. Notes. Illus.: Design. Photo. 7. Lang.: Eng.
Germany. USA. 1885-1989. Critical studies. ■Compares conservative, literalist readings of Wagner's *Meistersinger* to radical critical readings. Both styles can be interpreted as adhering to Wagner's original intentions and yet have produced two diametrically opposed camps of Wagner production.

4333 Teachout, Terry. "Coda: I Don't Do Wagner." *OpN*. 1997 Apr 5; 61(14): 54. Illus.: Photo. B&W. 1. Lang.: Eng.
Germany. 1997. Histories-sources. ■Reviewer explains his reservations about the operas of Richard Wagner.

4334 Bergström, Gunnel. "Dramma per musica—renässansen upptäcker passionen." (Dramma per musica—the Renaissance Discovers Passion.) *MuD*. 1997; 19(4): 19-21. Illus.: Photo. B&W. Lang.: Swe.
Italy: Florence. 1598-1610. Critical studies. ■A presentation of the birth of the opera, the Camerata Fiorentina and the members of the camerata.

4335 Abel, Sam. *Opera in the Flesh: Sexuality in Operatic Performance*. Boulder, CO: Westview; 1996. 235 pp. Index. Biblio. Pref. Notes. Illus.: Dwg. Sketches. 5. Lang.: Eng.
USA. Europe. 1996. Critical studies. ■The erotics of and in opera. Examines the embodiment of opera, the desire of the public for opera, the homoerotic appeal of opera, and how sexual desire and power operate in opera. Also examines issues of sexual transgression and gender constructs in opera history such as the *castrati* and cross-dressed characters.

Operetta

Institutions

4336 Gajdó, Tamás. "Meg nem írt színházi regény. Bános Tibor: *A Csárdáskirálynő vendégei*." (An Unwritten Theatrical

MUSIC-DRAMA: Operetta—Institutions

Novel: Tibor Bános: *The Guests of the Czardas Queen*.) *Sz.* 1997; 30(3): 31-32. Illus.: Photo. B&W. 1. Lang.: Hun.
Hungary. 1945-1960. Critical studies. ▪Analysis of Bános' study of the effect of the Communist regime on Hungarian theater (Budapest: Cserépfalvi, 1996).

4337 Ward, Robert. "A Light Touch: Ohio Light Opera Keeps the Spirit of Operetta Alive." *OpN.* 1997 June; 61(17): 47. Illus.: Photo. B&W. Color. Lang.: Eng.
USA: Wooster, OH. 1968-1997. Historical studies. ▪The work of James Stuart in the founding and nurturing of the Ohio Light Opera Company from 1968, now holding summer seasons at the Freedlander Theatre at the College of Wooster.

Performance/production

4338 Molnár Gál, Péter. *Honthy Hanna és kora.* (Hanna Honthy and Her Age.) Budapest: Magvető; 1997. 225 pp. Illus.: Photo. B&W. 10. Lang.: Hun.
Hungary. 1893-1950. Critical studies. ▪Essays on operetta, cabaret and related entertainments, focusing on the life and career of performer Hanna Honthy.

Plays/librettos/scripts

4339 Hanák, Péter. "A bécsi és a budapesti operett kultúrtörténeti helye." (The Operetta in Vienna and Budapest in the Development of Cultural History.) *BudN.* 1997; 5(2/3): 9-30. Notes. Illus.: Photo. B&W. 10. Lang.: Hun.
Austro-Hungarian Empire: Vienna, Budapest. 1850-1930. Historical studies. ▪The development of the genre.

4340 Koltai, Tamás. "Több szólamban." (Polyphony.) *Sz.* 1997; 30(3): 8-9. Illus.: Photo. B&W. 2. Lang.: Hun.
Hungary. 1900-1990. Critical studies. ▪Some pertinent ideas on the special features and characters of the operetta in theatre history exposed by composer Emil Petrovics, director Tamás Ascher and critic Péter Molnár Gál in a TV interview.

Theory/criticism

4341 Fritsch, Sibylle. "Wo das Förstermädel mit dem Kaiser tanzt." (Where the Ranger Girl Dances with the Kaiser.) *DB.* 1997; 5: 49-51. Illus.: Photo. B&W. 3. Lang.: Ger.
Austria: Vienna. 1997. Historical studies. ▪Discusses the meaning of the genre operetta and its revival, including an interview with Klaus Bachler, director of the Volksoper, about the Viennese operetta and artists.

PUPPETRY

General

Design/technology

4342 Götz, Eva Maria. "Von Menschen und Puppen." (Of Men and Puppets.) *DB.* 1997; 8: 40-42. Illus.: Photo. B&W. 4. Lang.: Ger.
Germany: Berlin. 1997. Historical studies. ▪A portrait of Suse Wächter, puppeteer and puppet designer.

4343 Varl, Breda. *Maske.* (Masks.) Šentilj: Aristej; 1997. 36 pp. (Moje lutke 6.) Illus.: Photo. Dwg. B&W. Color. Lang.: Slo.
Slovenia. 1996. Instructional materials. ▪Basic handbook for amateur puppeteers and teachers on the construction of masks for the faces, heads, and whole bodies of puppets.

4344 Varl, Breda. *Ročne lutke.* (Hand Puppets.) Šentilj: Aristej; 1997. 36 pp. (Moje lutke 3.) Illus.: Dwg. Photo. B&W. Color. Lang.: Slo.
Slovenia. 1997. Instructional materials. ▪Basic handbook for the construction of hand puppets, intended for amateur puppeteers and teachers.

4345 Varl, Breda. *Ploske lutke.* (Flat Puppets.) Šentilj: Aristej; 1997. 36 pp. (Moje lutke 4.) Illus.: Photo. Dwg. B&W. Color. Lang.: Slo.
Slovenia. 1997. Instructional materials. ▪Basic handbook for amateur puppeteers and teachers on the construction of flat puppets.

4346 Christopher, Dan. "Everything You Wanted to Know About PA Systems ... But Didn't Know Who To Ask!" *PuJ.* 1997 Sum; 48(4) : 23-24. Illus.: Photo. B&W. 1. Lang.: Eng.
USA. 1997. Instructional materials. ▪A professional's advice to the amateur puppeteer regarding working with public address systems.

Institutions

4347 Exnarová, Alena. "The Puppet Museum/Musée de la marionnette." *CT/TC.* 1997; 13: 72-80. Illus.: Photo. B&W. 12. Lang.: Eng, Fre.
Czech Republic: Chrudim. 1972-1997. Historical studies. ▪History of the Museum of Puppeteer Cultures, Muzeum loutkářských kultur.

4348 Brendenal, Silvia. "Anderes Theater." (An Other Theatre.) *TZ.* 1997; 4: 53-57. Illus.: Photo. B&W. 6. Lang.: Ger.
Germany. 1997. Historical studies. ▪Reports of the 10th 'Internationales Figurentheaterfestival' in Erlangen, Nuremberg Fürth and Schwabach in 1997.

4349 Konnerth, Karen. "III Bienal Internacional de Titeres de Puerto Rico (October 11 to 26, 1996): A Rich Experience in Community and Communication." *PuJ.* 1997 Spr; 48(3): 13-15. Illus.: Photo. B&W. 2. Lang.: Eng.
Puerto Rico: Caguas. 1996. Historical studies. ▪Survey of the third biennial puppetry festival from an Anglo perspective.

4350 *Poletni lutkovni pristan.* (Puppets' Summer Home.) Maribor: Puppet Theatre; 1997. 38 pp. Illus.: Photo. B&W. Lang.: Slo.
Slovenia: Maribor. 1997. Histories-sources. ▪Program of eighth international puppetry festival in Maribor.

4351 *Lutke '97.* (Puppets '97.) Ljubljana: Puppet Theatre; 1997. 79 pp. Illus.: Photo. B&W. Lang.: Slo.
Slovenia: Ljubljana. 1997. Histories-sources. ▪Program of the international puppet festival in Ljubljana, introducing the groups participating.

4352 Mlakar-Adamič, Jana. *Lutke in lutkarji. Amatersko lutkovno gledališče iz Hrastnika.* (Puppets and Puppeteers: The Amateur Puppet Theatre of Hrastnik.) Hrastnik: District Museum; 1997. 36 pp. Biblio. Illus.: Photo. B&W. Color. Lang.: Slo.
Slovenia: Hrastnik. 1947-1997. Historical studies. ▪The thirty-year history of the now-defunct amateur puppet theatre Amatersko lutkovno gledališče. The puppets are on exhibit in the Hrastnik District Museum.

4353 Sörenson, Margareta. "Dockteater Tittut 20 år." (Peek-a-Boo Puppet Theatre Turns Twenty.) *Tningen.* 1997; 21(5): 41-44. Illus.: Photo. Color. Lang.: Swe.
Sweden: Stockholm. 1977. Historical studies. ▪A presentation of Dockteater Tittut, the only exclusive children's puppet theatre of Sweden, with reference to Ing-Mari Tirén, Eva Grytt and Michael Meschke.

4354 Berty, Chuck; Berty, Joyce. "P of A National Festival '97— 'Kaleidoscope of Puppetry'." *PuJ.* 1997 Sum; 48(4): 2-3. Illus.: Photo. B&W. 4. Lang.: Eng.
USA: Toledo, OH. 1997. Historical studies. ▪Survey of the 1997 Puppeteers of America National Festival.

4355 Levin, Jordan. "The Resurrection Circus and Me." *AmTh.* 1997 Oct.; 14(8): 62-64. Illus.: Photo. B&W. 2. Lang.: Eng.
USA: Plainfield, VT. 1972-1997. Histories-sources. ▪Author's personal experiences participating in performances and workshops hosted by Bread and Puppet Theatre, artistic directors and founders Peter and Elka Schumann, with focus on annual circus weekend and the volunteers from local community who participate.

4356 Manning, Bill. "She's New, She's Young, and She's Serious." *PuJ.* 1997 Sum; 48(4): 5-6. Illus.: Photo. B&W. 1. Lang.: Eng.
USA: Boston, MA. 1997. Historical studies. ▪A look at the new executive director of the Puppet Showplace Theatre, Kristen McLean, who succeeds founder Mary Churchill, and the changes she may implement.

4357 Solomons, Gus, Jr. "New York." *BR.* 1997 Spr; 25(1): 17-18. Lang.: Eng.
USA: New York, NY. 1997. Historical studies. ▪Survey of the International Festival of Puppet Theatre.

4358 Thompson, Barney. "Clowns, Nerds, Snakes, and Foodi-Bob-in-a-Box." *PuJ.* 1997 Spr; 48(3): 18-19. Illus.: Photo. B&W. 3. Lang.: Eng.

PUPPETRY: General—Institutions

USA: Ft. Wayne, IN. 1997. Histories-sources. ■Founder describes the work of Bob-in-a-Box Puppet Theatre, in which he, his wife, and their children perform.

Performance/production

4359 Jurkowski, Henryk. "African Puppets and Masks: Links in a Historical Chain." 38-40 in Rubin, Don, ed.; Diakhaté, Ousmane, ed.; Eyoh, Hansel Ndumbe, ed. *The World Encyclopedia of Contemporary Theatre: Africa*. Vol. 3. London/New York, NY: Routledge; 1997. 426 pp. Biblio. Index. Lang.: Eng.
Africa. 1800-1996. Historical studies. ■African puppetry and its ritualistic use of statuettes, dolls, and masks. Compares it to European and Asian forms.

4360 Makonj, Karel. "Theatre of Josef Skupa/Le théatre de Josef Skupa." *CT/TC*. 1997; 13: 49-55. Illus.: Photo. Dwg. B&W. 7. Lang.: Eng, Fre.
Bohemia. 1892-1957. Biographical studies. ■Profile and career of Josef Skupa, puppeteer, scenic designer, director and author of puppet plays.

4361 Coad, Luman. "Ronnie Burkett's *Tinka's New Dress*." *PuJ*. 1997 Sum; 48(4): 4-5. Lang.: Eng.
Canada: Winnipeg, MB. 1997. Reviews of performances. ■Review of Ronnie Burkett's play *Tinka's New Dress* which weaves a story of two puppeteers and the puppets they create in relation to their oppressive surroundings. It has played in many venues across Canada.

4362 Bílková, Marie. "The Puppet through the Eyes of Visual artist/La Marionnette vue par les artistes." *CT/TC*. 1997; 13: 2-20. Illus.: Photo. Graphs. Dwg. Color. B&W. 21. Lang.: Eng, Fre.
Czech Republic. 1912-1997. Histories-specific. ■History of Czech puppet theatre from 1912 to the present.

4363 Král, Karel. "Jací jsme? Část 1: Národ sám o sobě." (Who Are We? Part I: A Nation Talks About Itself.) *Svet*. 1997; 8(3): 18-25. Illus.: Photo. B&W. 12. Lang.: Cze.
Czech Republic. 1997. Critical studies. ■Essay about the Czech character as reflected in contemporary puppet plays. Continued in *Svet* 8:4, 10-21: Part 2: The Dovelike Character and Heroes.

4364 Novotný, J.A. "Puppetmaker (Reflections on Discussion with Jiří Trnka)/Marionnettiste (Reminiscences d'entretiens avec Jiří Trnka)." *CT/TC*. 1997; 13: 56-67. Illus.: Photo. Dwg. Color. 20. Lang.: Eng, Fre.
Czech Republic. 1912-1969. Biographical studies. ■Life and career of Jiří Trnka, a puppeteer, film director and illustrator.

4365 Mészáros, Emőke. "*Az ember tragédiája* bábszínpadon." (*The Tragedy of Man* on the Puppet Stage.) *SzSz*. 1997(32): 59-66. Notes. Lang.: Hun.
Hungary. 1918-1954. Historical studies. ■A study in the adaptation of Imre Madách's classic play by painter and puppet artist Géza Blattner, who had a great success with the French-language production of the puppet-play at the Paris World Exhibition awarded the Grand Prix in 1937.

4366 Law, Jane Marie. *Puppets of Nostalgia: The Life, Death, and Rebirth of the Japanese Awaji ningyō Tradition*. Princeton, NJ: Princeton UP; 1997. 322 pp. Index. Biblio. Notes. Illus.: Photo. Dwg. 37. Lang.: Eng.
Japan: Awaji. 1600-1995. Histories-specific. ■The history of the *Awaji ningyō* puppet tradition, from its earliest forms to its near extinction in World War II to its postwar preservation. Examines cultural issues in the form's creation using rituals and effigies, the puppet forms of the genre, and the current revival.

4367 Bespal'ceva, G. "Magija kukol." (Puppet Magic.) *Otčij kraj*. 1997; 4: 202-206. Lang.: Rus.
Russia: Volgograd. 1960-1997. Historical studies. ■Puppet theatre in Volgograd.

4368 Ivanova, A. "Kukol'nik." (Puppeteer.) *PTZ*. 1997; 14: 49-51. Lang.: Rus.
Russia: St. Petersburg. 1990-1997. Historical studies. ■Master puppeteer Viktor Antonov.

4369 Resetnikova, N. "Andrej Jefimov. Kukol'nik." (Andrej Jefimov, Puppeteer.) *PTZ*. 1997; 14: 40-44. Lang.: Rus.

Russia: Ekaterinburg. 1990-1997. Historical studies. ■Profile of Jefimov, director with the Ekaterinburg Puppet Theatre.

4370 Hume, Alice. "The Best of British: A Visit with John & Barbara Styles." *PuJ*. 1997 Spr; 48(3): 10-13. Illus.: Photo. B&W. 6. Lang.: Eng.
UK-England: Sidcup. 1995-1996. Histories-sources. ■Magician/puppeteer John Styles and his wife Barbara: their collection of Punch puppets from several eras.

4371 "Gordon Murdock." *PuJ*. 1997 Sum; 48(4): 24-25. Lang.: Eng.
USA. 1996. Biographical studies. ■Obituary for the puppeteer, who was co-creator of the 'The Standwells' hand puppets.

4372 Bell, John. "Landscape and TEETH Masks: Understanding Bread and Puppet Pageants." *TA*. 1997; 50: 1-16. Notes. Illus.: Photo. B&W. 4. Lang.: Eng.
USA: Plainfield, VT. 1970-1997. Historical studies. ■Meaning of Bread and Puppet Theater's annual *Our Domestic Resurrection Circus* pageant.

4373 Bell, John. "Puppets and Performing Objects in the Twentieth Century." *PerAJ*. 1997 May; 19(2): 29-46. Illus.: Photo. B&W. 12. [Number 56.] Lang.: Eng.
USA: New York, NY. 1996. Historical studies. ■Survey of the 1996 International Festival of Puppet Theatre.

4374 Blumenthal, Eileen. "The Life and Death of Puppets." *AmTh*. 1997 Jan.; 14(1): 16-19. Illus.: Photo. B&W. 2. Lang.: Eng.
USA. 1996. Historical studies. ■Comparison of live actors and created figures in puppet theatre. Increase in popularity of puppetry in contemporary theatre, audience responses, upcoming International Festival of Puppet Theatre.

4375 Gussow, Mel. "Morey Bunin." *PuJ*. 1997 Sum; 48(4): 25. Lang.: Eng.
USA. 1997. Biographical studies. ■Obituary for early television pioneer who created the puppets for *The Adventures of Lucky Pup* show.

4376 Hughes, Raylynn. "Interview With a Monster." *PuJ*. 1997 Spr; 48(3): 2-6. Illus.: Photo. B&W. 5. Lang.: Eng.
USA: Atlanta, GA. 1996. Histories-sources. ■Interview with puppeteer John Ludwig on his adaptation of *Frankenstein* which he wrote and directed at the Center for Puppetry Arts in Atlanta, GA.

4377 Ritchard, Dan. "'Puppetry or Puppetry, Which is Better for Me?'." *PuJ*. 1997 Sum; 48(4): 17-18. Lang.: Eng.
USA. 1997. Critical studies. ■Essay discussing ventriloquism's place in the multi-disciplinary field of puppetry.

4378 Schandelmeier, Cathleen. "Puppets for the Medicis (Although This is a True Story, Names May Have Been Changed)." *PuJ*. 1997 Sum; 48(4): 7-8. Illus.: Photo. B&W. 1. Lang.: Eng.
USA: Melrose Park, CA. 1997. Histories-sources. ■Author's experience compromising her art to create a puppet play for a wealthy child's party.

4379 Stockman, Todd. "In Memoriam: Dick Weston." *PuJ*. 1997 Spr; 48(3): 32-33. Illus.: Photo. B&W. 1. Lang.: Eng.
USA. 1997. Biographical studies. ■Obituary for veteran night club performer whose trademark was to have two of his 'dummies' sing harmony.

4380 Skipitares, Theodora. "Vietnam Journal." *PerAJ*. 1997 May; 19(2): 64-80. Illus.: Photo. Dwg. B&W. 8. [Number 56.] Lang.: Eng.
Vietnam: Hanoi. 1996-1997. Histories-sources. ■Journal account of Skipitares' trip, accompanied by Ellen Stewart of La Mama E.T.C., to Vietnam to collaborate with the Vietnamese National Puppetry Theatre and the National Theatre of Vietnam.

Plays/librettos/scripts

4381 Kovyčeva, E.I. "Nekotorye razmyšlenija o proischozdenii Petruški." (Some Thoughts on the Origins of Petruška.) 19-40 in *Vestnik Udmurskogo Universiteta*. Ižensk: Izdatel'stvo Udmurskogo Universiteta; 1996. Lang.: Rus.
Russia. Historical studies. ■The origin of the Russian puppet character Petruška.

Reference materials

4382   Vranc, Danilo. *Repertoarni kažipot za lutkarje, lutkovne sku-pine ali lutkovna gledališča. Seznam lutkovne literature.* (Repertoire Directory for Puppeteers, Puppetry Groups, and Puppet Theatres: A List of Puppetry Literature.) Maribor: Society of Cultural Organizations; 1997. 34 pp. Lang.: Slo.
Slovenia. 1942-1997. ■Bibliography of scripts for puppet plays in Slovene.

Relation to other fields

4383   Stuber, Petra. "Zinnober. Die erste freie Theatergruppe der DDR." (Zinnober. The First Free Theatre Company in the GDR.) *FMT.* 1997; 12(1): 42-53. Notes. Lang.: Ger.
Germany: Berlin. 1980-1997. Historical studies. ■Describes the history of Zinnober, founded by a group of puppeteers and drop-outs. Analyzes the reactions of the political system to Zinnober's refusal to separate theatre and life.

4384   Listorti, John. "'What is an Otto Clave?'." *PuJ.* 1997 Spr; 48(3): 23. Lang.: Eng.
USA. 1997. Histories-sources. ■Discusses the author's use of a puppet character for getting the attention of his high school science class.

Research/historiography

4385   Kurten, Allelu. "Stan Stack." *PuJ.* 1997 Spr; 48(3): 33-34. Lang.: Eng.
USA. 1997. Biographical studies. ■Obituary of puppetry historian Stan Stack.

Training

4386   Regős, János. "Kenyér és báb. Peter Schumann Kec-skeméten." (Bread and Puppet: Peter Schumann at Kec-skemét.) *Sz.* 1997; 30(10): 40-44. Illus.: Photo. B&W. 5. Lang.: Hun.
USA: Plainfield, VT. Hungary: Kecskemét. 1963-1997. Critical studies. ■Report on a workshop for young Hungarian theatre people at Kec-skemét directed by Peter Schumann, founder and director of Bread and Puppet Theatre, illustrated by the author's photos.

Marionettes

Basic theatrical documents

4387   Geiser, Jamie. "*Evidence of Floods.*" *PerAJ.* 1997 May; 19(2): 47-63. Illus.: Photo. Dwg. B&W. 12. [Number 56.] Lang.: Eng.
USA. 1994. ■Complete scenario in storyboard form of Geiser's play for marionettes, *Evidence of Floods.*

Performance/production

4388   Plowright, Poh Sim. "The Birdwoman and the Puppet King: a Study of Inversion in Chinese Theatre." *NTQ.* 1997; 13(50): 106-118. Notes. Biblio. Illus.: Photo. B&W. 5. Lang.: Eng.
China: Quanzhou, Fujian. 714-1994. Historical studies. ■Contemporary theatre in this region of South China, whose origins can be traced to the eighth century Pear Garden Theatre, is rooted in the practice of ancestor worship through which most performances become sacrificial offerings.

4389   "In Memoriam: Rev. Grant Melville Selch." *PuJ.* 1997 Spr; 48(3): 33-34. Lang.: Eng.
USA. 1997. Biographical studies. ■Obituary for 'The Puppeteering Parson', a founding member of the Puppeteers of America in 1937.

4390   "Nellie Braithwaite." *PuJ.* 1997 Sum; 48(4): 25. Lang.: Eng.
USA: Cleveland, OH. 1997. Biographical studies. ■Obituary for the co-creator of the Mayfair Marionettes.

4391   Coad, Luman. "Biography: Meredith Bixby." *PuJ.* 1997 Spr; 48(3): 8-10, 6-7. Illus.: Photo. B&W. 3. Lang.: Eng.
USA: Detroit, MI, New York, NY. 1930-1997. Biographical studies. ■Overview of longtime marionettist Meredith Bixby's life and work including his entrance into the craft of puppet-making and performing.

4392   Herzog, David. "'That's Christmas'." *PuJ.* 1997 Spr; 48(3): 16-17. Illus.: Photo. Dwg. B&W. 3. Lang.: Eng.

USA: Chicago, IL. 1996. Reviews of performances. ■Review of the puppetry elements of Chicago's holiday extravaganza *That's Christmas.* Focus on Phillip Huber and his Huber Marionettes.

4393   Michaelson, Vera; Harms, Carl. "The Sicilian Marionettes at the Kaye Playhouse." *PuJ.* 1997 Sum; 48(4): 11-12. Lang.: Eng.
USA: New York, NY. 1997. Critical studies. ■Examination of Coopera-tivo Teatroarte Cuticchio's performance at the Kaye Playhouse.

Plays/librettos/scripts

4394   Lévesque, Solange. "Bon voyage, Candide et Loup Bleu!" *JCT.* 1997; 83: 166-168. Notes. Illus.: Photo. B&W. 2. Lang.: Fre.
Canada: Montreal, PQ. 1997. Critical studies. ■Lorraine Côté's adaptation of Voltaire's *Candide* for Sous-Marin Jaune puppet theatre fulfils mandate to produce iconoclastic mini-theatre.

Relation to other fields

4395   Louis, Alan. "Marionettes: A New Medium for Character Education." *PuJ.* 1997 Sum; 48(4): 9-10. Illus.: Photo. B&W. 5. Lang.: Eng.
USA: Atlanta, GA. 1996. Historical studies. ■Alan Louis' experience with students at the Mary Lin Elementary School helping them create marionettes based on historical characters.

Muppets

Design/technology

4396   Varl, Breda. *Mimične lutke.* (Muppets.) Šentilj: Aristej; 1997. 35 pp. (Moje lutke 5.) Illus.: Photo. Dwg. B&W. Color. Lang.: Slo.
Slovenia. 1997. Instructional materials. ■Basic handbook for amateur puppeteers and teachers on the construction of muppets.

Performance/production

4397   "*The Wubbulous World of Dr. Seuss.*" *PuJ.* 1997 Spr; 48(3): 6-7. Illus.: Photo. B&W. 1. Lang.: Eng.
USA: New York, NY. 1997. Critical studies. ■Profile of *The Wubbulous World of Dr. Seuss,* a television series of Nickelodeon and Jim Henson Productions, using puppets working against computer generated backgrounds to bring Dr. Seuss's characters to life.

4398   Henson, Cheryl; Geiss, Tony; Oz, Frank; Robinson, Martin. "Jon Stone." *PuJ.* 1997 Sum; 48(4): 25-26. Illus.: Photo. B&W. 1. Lang.: Eng.
USA: New York, NY. 1997. Biographical studies. ■Obituary for writer, director, producer of *Sesame Street,* a position he held for twenty-five years.

Rod puppets

Performance/production

4399   Weintraub, Andrew Noah. *Constructing the Popular: Super-stars, Performance, and Cultural Authority in Sundanese Wayang Golek Purwa of West Java, Indonesia.* Berkeley, CA: Univ. of California; 1997. 277 pp. Notes. Biblio. [Ph.D. Dissertation, Univ. Microfilms Order No. AAC 9827148.] Lang.: Eng.
Indonesia. 1994-1995. Historical studies. ■Focuses on the relationship between performers, performance, and the commercial, cultural, and official apparatuses that promote and regulate the production and reception of *wayang golek purwa.* Studies individual star puppeteers, professional troupes, and the increasing influence of the mass media in modern Indonesia.

Shadow puppets

Performance/production

4400   Blackburn, Stuart. *Inside the Drama-House: Rama Stories and Shadow Puppets in South India.* Berkeley, CA: Univ. of California P; 1997. 304 pp. Notes. Index. Biblio. Illus.: Photo. 7. Lang.: Eng.

PUPPETRY: Shadow puppets—Performance/production

India. 1500-1995. Histories-specific. ■The *tol pava kuttu* form of Indian shadow puppetry, which is performed without an audience, said to turn the focus of the performers inward and to enrich the relationships among characters, texts, and performers.

4401   Cohen, Matthew Isaac. *An Inheritance from the Friends of God: The Southern Shadow Puppet Theater of West Java, Indonesia.* New Haven, CT: Yale Univ; 1997. 433 pp. [Ph.D. Dissertation, Univ. Microfilms Order No. AAC 9731005.] Lang.: Eng.

Indonesia. 1900-1995. Historical studies. ■Examination of *wayang kulit* (shadow puppet theater), specifically the Kidulan or 'Southern' shadow puppet theater which developed in the first decades of the twentieth century as a popular form shunned by the elite. Examines this form's history as a protest against the dominant group's religious and cultural oppression, and as a medium for the exploration of Islamic Javanese identity.

4402   Terrence, John Thomas. *The Psychocultural Significance of the Balinese Shadow Theater from the Perspective of Its Master Practitioners.* Los Angeles, CA: Univ. of California; 1997. 234 pp. Notes. Biblio. [Ph.D. Dissertation, Univ. Microfilms Order No. AAC 9725999.] Lang.: Eng.

Indonesia. 1300-1995. Critical studies. ■Changes in the centuries-old tradition of *wayang kulit* shadow puppet theatre. Argues that the form formerly served as a didactic tool for civic regulation, a moral guide for society, and a religious ritual.

4403   Sitar, Jelena; Cvetko, Igor, illus. *Primeri detektiva Karla Loota. Skrivnost v galeriji ali Zgodba o senčnih lutkah.* (Detective Carl Loot's Cases: Mysteries of the Gallery or The Shadow Puppets' Story.) Ljubljana: DZS; 1997. 64 pp. (Umetnost igre 2.) Illus.: Pntg. Dwg. Photo. B&W. Color. Lang.: Slo.

Slovenia. 1997. Instructional materials. ■An illustrated detective story that introduces shadow puppet theatre.

SUBJECT INDEX

Acting: Part 1 — cont'd

Stage imagery in productions of Shakespeare's *Coriolanus*. England. 1754-1901. Lang.: Eng. 1634

Interview with actor, director, and teacher Mario Gonzales. Europe. Guatemala. 1967. Lang.: Swe. 1648

Interviews with the cast of Théâtre du Soleil's *Les Atrides*. France: Paris. 1992. Lang.: Eng. 1677

Actress, theatre director, and teacher Caroline Neuber. Germany. 1697-1760. Lang.: Ger. 1685

Actor Traugott Buhre. Germany. 1949-1997. Lang.: Ger. 1686

Productions of Schauspiel Stuttgart. Germany: Stuttgart. 1997. Lang.: Ger. 1687

Interview with actor Josef Bierbichler. Germany. 1985-1997. Lang.: Ger. 1691

Actress Andrea Clausen. Germany. 1960-1997. Lang.: Ger. 1693

Actor Josef Bierbichler. Germany: Hamburg. 1997. Lang.: Ger. 1707

Interview with actress Dagmar Manzel. Germany: Berlin. 1997. Lang.: Ger. 1708

Portrait of actor Samuel Weiss. Germany: Stuttgart. 1967-1997. Lang.: Ger. 1714

Actor and director Matthias Brenner. Germany. 1996-1997. Lang.: Ger. 1724

Profile of actress Claudia Jahn. Germany. 1988-1997. Lang.: Ger. 1725

Profile of actress Corinna Harfouch. Germany. 1989-1997. Lang.: Ger. 1735

Profile of actress Traute Hoess. Germany. Austria. 1969-1997. Lang.: Ger. 1741

Elisabeth Rath's performance in Terrence McNally's *Master Class*. Germany: Munich. 1997. Lang.: Hun. 1742

Comparison of productions of Shakespeare's *Richard III*. Germany. Switzerland. 1996. Lang.: Ger. 1745

Visual performance aspects of Greek tragedy. Greece: Athens. 500 B.C. Lang.: Ita. 1749

Excerpts from the diary of actor Miklós Gábor. Hungary. 1955-1957. Lang.: Hun. 1764

Biography of actor Kálmán Rózsahegyi. Hungary. 1873-1961. Lang.: Hun. 1774

Comic actor Ettore Petrolini. Italy. 1886-1936. Lang.: Ita. 1793

Actress Anna Maria Guarnieri. Italy. 1954-1996. Lang.: Ita. 1800

Actor, director, and playwright Carmelo Bene. Italy. 1937-1997. Lang.: Ita. 1801

Visit to Grotowski and Compagnia della Fortezza. Italy: Volterra, Pontedera. 1986-1997. Lang.: Ger. 1805

Analysis of manuscript containing ten vernacular plays. Netherlands. 1405-1410. Lang.: Eng. 1828

Biography of actress Anna Dymna. Poland: Cracow. 1950-1997. Lang.: Pol. 1835

Tadeusz Bradecki's activity as an actor, director, and playwright. Poland. 1983-1995. Lang.: Pol. 1836

Autobiography of actress Irena Górska-Damięcka. Poland. 1910-1996. Lang.: Pol. 1839

Actress Wanda Siemaszkowa. Poland: Cracow, Lvov, Warsaw. 1887-1946. Lang.: Pol. 1844

Profile of actor Ryszard Cieslak. Poland. 1937-1990. Lang.: Swe. 1847

Wartime and postwar activities of actor and director Aleksander Zelwerowicz. Poland. 1925-1979. Lang.: Pol. 1848

Actor Jan Nowicki. Poland: Cracow. 1939-1997. Lang.: Pol. 1850

Actor Nikolaj Annenkov. Russia: Moscow. 1990-1997. Lang.: Rus. 1857

Recollections of director K.S. Stanislavskij. Russia. 1863-1938. Lang.: Rus. 1858

Excerpts from the diary of actor Oleg Borisov. Russia: St. Petersburg. 1970-1989. Lang.: Rus. 1859

Writings of actor Valentin Gaft. Russia. 1960-1997. Lang.: Rus. 1867

Notes from the actors' master class of Jévgenij Ganelin and Vladimir Bogdanov. Russia: St. Petersburg. 1960-1997. Lang.: Rus. 1868

Actress E.A. Uvarova of Teat'r Komedii. Russia: St. Petersburg. 1990-1997. Lang.: Rus. 1872

Interview with Sergej Jurskij. Russia. Sweden. 1957-1997. Lang.: Swe. 1877

Actor P.P. Pankov of the Bolšoj Drama Theatre. Russia: St. Petersburg. 1970-1997. Lang.: Rus. 1880

Actor Innokentij Smoktunovskij. Russia. 1925-1994. Lang.: Rus. 1883

Recollections of actor Arkadij Rajkin. Russia. 1911-1987. Lang.: Rus. 1888

Interview with actor A. Mežulis. Russia: Moscow. 1990-1997. Lang.: Rus. 1889

Actress Anna Brenko of Malyj Teat'r. Russia: Moscow. 1849-1934. Lang.: Rus. 1890

Actress Zinajda Šarko on the work of director G.A. Tovstonogov. Russia: St. Petersburg. 1960-1989. Lang.: Rus. 1891

Portraits of stage and film actors. Russia. 1960-1997. Lang.: Rus. 1896

Actor and director Solomon Michoéls remembered by his son. Russia: Moscow. 1890-1948. Lang.: Rus. 1899

The psychology and sociology of Slovene acting. Slovenia. 1880-1970. Lang.: Slo. 1907

Matthew Krouse, formerly an actor in the entertainment corps of the South African Defence Force. South Africa, Republic of. 1982.Lang.: Eng. 1911

Interview with actors Sif Ruud and Thorsten Flinck. Sweden: Stockholm. 1934-1997. Lang.: Swe. 1922

Comic actor Johan Ulveson. Sweden: Stockholm. 1997. Lang.: Swe. 1923

Interview with actors Jan Mybrand and My Holmstein about free-lance acting. Sweden: Stockholm. 1997. Lang.: Swe. 1924

Actor Jarl Kulle as a student at Dramatens Elevskola. Sweden: Stockholm. 1945. Lang.: Swe. 1926

Interview with actor Johan Ulveson. Sweden: Stockholm. 1977. Lang.: Swe. 1929

Interview with actor Dan Johansson of Fria Teatern. Sweden: Stockholm. 1993. Lang.: Swe. 1930

Interview with actor Tommy Andersson. Sweden. 1990-1997. Lang.: Swe. 1931

Actor Allan Edwall and his theatre Brunnsgatan Fyra. Sweden: Stockholm. 1949-1997. Lang.: Swe. 1935

Actor Björn Granath. Sweden: Stockholm. 1970-1997. Lang.: Swe. 1936

Jarl Kulle's one-man show *Reskamraten (The Traveling Companion)*. Sweden. 1997. Lang.: Swe. 1937

Interview with actor Per Mattsson. Sweden: Stockholm. 1965. Lang.: Swe. 1940

Interview with actress Melinda Kinnaman. Sweden: Stockholm. 1985. Lang.: Swe. 1944

Interview with acting student Rasmus Lindgren. Sweden: Malmö. 1997. Lang.: Swe. 1945

Interview with actress Lina Pleijel. Sweden: Stockholm. 1981. Lang.: Swe. 1946

Interview with actor and director Tom Fjordefalk. Sweden. 1972-1997. Lang.: Swe. 1948

Involving youth audiences in theatre. Sweden: Stockholm, Uppsala. 1995-1997. Lang.: Swe. 1949

Interview with actor Olle Jansson. Sweden: Stockholm. 1985-1997. Lang.: Swe. 1950

Interview with actor Jarl Kulle. Sweden: Stockholm. 1950-1995. Lang.: Swe. 1953

Interview with actor Sven Lindberg. Sweden: Stockholm. 1980-1997. Lang.: Swe. 1954

Memories of actor Jarl Kulle. Sweden: Malmö, Stockholm. 1972. Lang.: Swe. 1955

Interview with actress Marie Göranzon. Sweden: Stockholm. 1964-1997. Lang.: Swe. 1958

The work together of actors Solveig Tännström and Börje Ahlstedt. Sweden: Stockholm. 1967. Lang.: Swe. 1961

Productions of plays by Shakespeare and Goethe at Zürcher Schauspielhaus and Theater Neumarkt. Switzerland: Zurich. 1997. Lang.: Ger. 1964

Staging Shakespeare in the Romantic period. UK-England. 1800-1840. Lang.: Eng. 2166

Interview with director Deborah Warner. UK-England: London. 1990-1997. Lang.: Ger, Fre, Dut, Eng. 2167

The Shakespearean acting and directing career of Judi Dench. UK-England: London. 1957-1995. Lang.: Eng. 2177

Reactions to modern performances of *Antony and Cleopatra*. UK-England. North America. 1827-1987. Lang.: Eng. 2178

Acting: Part 1 — cont'd

Polish actors and their work during the occupation of Poland and on Soviet territory. Poland. 1940-1950. Lang.: Pol. 776

Actress Ellen Terry's effect on women's roles. UK-England: London. 1880-1909. Lang.: Eng. 783

Case study of a high school theatre teacher. USA. 1995. Lang.: Eng. 805

The psychology of the performing artist. USA. 1994-1996. Lang.: Eng. 809

Training

Work on the body in its theatrical context. Europe. 1900-1997. Lang.: Ita. 929

The career of Jerzy Grotowski and notes on one of his seminars. Poland. Italy. 1959-1991. Lang.: Ita. 931

Gennadij Bogdanov's workshop on biomechanics, Sotenäs Teateratelje. Russia. Sweden. 1920-1996. Lang.: Swe. 932

Information on theatre training. UK-England. 1997. Lang.: Eng. 934

Acting: Part 2

Administration

Analysis of a legal agreement involving the Red Bull Company. England: London. 1660-1663. Lang.: Eng. 16

The British-U.S. Actors' Equity actors' exchange. UK-England: London. USA. 1997. Lang.: Eng. 54

Report on unemployment among theatre artists. USA. 1997. Lang.: Eng. 91

Institutions

Account of a visit to French theatre schools. France: Paris. 1997. Lang.: Eng. 314

Interview with Tamás Balikó, actor, director, and manager of Pécs National Theatre. Hungary. 1980-1996. Lang.: Hun. 340

Actress Marie Tempest's campaign for a hospital ward for actors. UK-England: London. 1935-1937. Lang.: Eng. 387

Profile of the National Performance Network. USA. 1984-1997. Lang.: Eng. 407

Report on Strindberg festival. Sweden: Stockholm. 1996. Lang.: Eng. 1494

Performance/production

Interview with actress Monique Miller. Canada: Montreal, PQ. 1940-1997. Lang.: Fre. 476

Work of Robert Gravel in improvisation and experimental theatre. Canada: Montreal, PQ. 1976-1996. Lang.: Fre. 480

Actor Robert Gravel. Canada: Montreal, PQ. 1973-1996. Lang.: Fre. 481

Obscenity as social criticism in work of Robert Gravel. Canada. Belgium. 1973-1996. Lang.: Fre. 482

Actors on the interpretation of character. Canada: Montreal, PQ. 1997. Lang.: Fre. 486

Cross-dressing in Chinese theatre and society. China. 1200-1997. Lang.: Eng. 489

Physical work in actor training. Denmark: Holstebro. 1950-1997. Lang.: Eng. 497

The suppression of Thomas Doggett's troupe of strolling players. England: Cambridge. 1690-1701. Lang.: Eng. 507

The development of the professional theatre company. England. 1550-1620. Lang.: Eng. 512

Acting styles in early English drama. England. 1595-1615. Lang.: Eng. 513

Analysis of Jerzy Grotowski's Collège de France lecture at Théâtre aux Bouffes du Nord. France: Paris. 1997. Lang.: Eng. 532

Goethe's aestheticism and his abuse of actors. Germany: Weimar. 1793-1808. Lang.: Eng. 546

CD-ROM presentation of all aspects of *kutiyattam*. India. 1000-1997. Lang.: Eng. 557

Community movement in theatre. Poland. 1920-1997. Lang.: Eng, Fre. 577

Anecdotes about child actors. UK-England. 1938-1997. Lang.: Eng. 622

Modernism and postmodernism in American theatre. USA. 1960-1990. Lang.: Eng. 627

The brothers Rapp: actor Anthony and playwright Adam. USA. 1997. Lang.: Eng. 640

The early stage career of actor Buster Keaton. USA. 1916-1917. Lang.: Eng. 651

Autobiographical performances of Elizabeth Robins. USA. 1862-1952. Lang.: Eng. 656

Excerpt from *True and False: Heresy and Common Sense for the Actor* by David Mamet. USA. 1997. Lang.: Eng. 657

Political activism of actor Steve Park. USA. 1997. Lang.: Eng. 658

Transcript of seminar by actor Frank Langella. USA. 1997. Lang.: Eng. 661

Career of performer Karen Kandel. USA: New York, NY. 1977-1997. Lang.: Eng. 663

The phenomenon of stage fright. USA. 1988. Lang.: Eng. 665

Life and career of actress Colleen Dewhurst. USA. 1997. Lang.: Eng. 682

Psychophysiological training of actors in a production of Beckett's *Act Without Words I*. USA. 1995-1996. Lang.: Eng. 687

Student production of John Ford's *The Broken Heart*. Australia: La Trobe. 1997. Lang.: Eng. 1559

Actor Al Waxman. Canada: Stratford, ON. 1967-1997. Lang.: Eng. 1576

Ross McMillan's performance of *The Fever* by Wallace Shawn. Canada: Winnipeg, MB. 1997. Lang.: Eng. 1577

Children's theatre actress France Dansereau. Canada: Montreal, PQ. 1974-1997. Lang.: Fre. 1579

Interview with actress and solo performer Louisette Dussault. Canada: Montreal, PQ. 1979-1997. Lang.: Fre. 1580

The body and the text in productions of the Festival de Théâtre des Amériques. Canada: Montreal, PQ. 1997. Lang.: Fre. 1583

Interview with actress Sylvie Drapeau. Canada: Montreal, PQ. 1967-1997. Lang.: Fre. 1585

Jean-Louis Millette's performance in Larry Tremblay's one-man show *The Dragonfly of Chicoutimi*. Canada: Montreal, PQ. 1996. Lang.: Fre. 1586

Interview with actor Gilles Pelletier. Canada: Montreal, PQ. 1950-1997. Lang.: Fre. 1587

Interview with actress Janine Sutto-Deyglun. Canada: Montreal, PQ. 1921-1997. Lang.: Fre. 1598

Realism from the viewpoints of actors and audience. Canada: Montreal, PQ. 1997. Lang.: Fre. 1600

As You Like It and the Chamberlain's Men's move to the Globe. England: London. 1594-1612. Lang.: Eng. 1619

Anne Oldfield's performance as Lady Townly in *The Provoked Husband* by Colley Cibber. England. 1720-1730. Lang.: Eng. 1632

As You Like It, transvestism, and early modern sexual politics. England. 1599. Lang.: Eng. 1636

The deconstruction of femininity in Jutta Lampe and Isabelle Huppert's performances of *Orlando*. Europe. 1923-1997. Lang.: Eng. 1643

Shakespearean commentary and the relationship between actors and academics. Europe. North America. 1985-1996. Lang.: Eng. 1652

Life, career, and influences of Antonin Artaud. France. 1897-1997. Lang.: Eng. 1670

Iconographic analysis of visual records of actors. Germany. UK-England. 1608-1918. Lang.: Eng. 1683

Conversation with actor Tamás Végvári. Hungary. 1958-1997. Lang.: Hun. 1752

Interview with actress Eszter Csákányi. Hungary. 1990-1997. Lang.: Hun. 1757

Actor-manager Pál Rakodczay. Hungary. 1856-1921. Lang.: Hun. 1759

Photographs of actress Júlia Apraxin. Hungary. 1830-1917. Lang.: Hun. 1760

Interview with actor Zsolt László of Új Színház. Hungary. 1990-1997. Lang.: Hun. 1761

Interview with actor Lóránd Lohinszky. Hungary. Romania: Târgu-Mureş. 1946-1997. Lang.: Hun. 1766

Andrea Fullajtár's performance in *Csendet akarok (I Want Silence)* by Zsolt Csalog. Hungary: Budapest. 1996. Lang.: Hun. 1771

Album devoted to actress Nóra Tábori. Hungary. 1928-1996. Lang.: Hun. 1773

Interview with actor Dezső Garas. Hungary. 1960-1997. Lang.: Hun. 1775

Interview with actor Tamás Jordán, founder of Merlin Színház. Hungary. 1960-1997. Lang.: Hun. 1776

Interview with actor-director Pál Mácsai. Hungary. 1980-1997. Lang.: Hun. 1777

Interview with actor László Sinkó of Új Színház. Hungary. 1960-1997. Lang.: Hun. 1778

Acting: Part 2 — cont'd

The interior I/eye in later plays of Samuel Beckett. Ireland. France. USA. 1978-1997. Lang.: Eng. 1785

The role of the implied spectator in productions of Omri Nitzan and Hillel Mittelpunkt. Israel: Tel Aviv. 1993. Lang.: Eng. 1792

Creating roles in medieval theatre in the absence of psychological motivation. Italy: Camerino. 1996. Lang.: Eng. 1814

Contrast and comparison of Eastern and Western acting styles. Japan. Europe. 1150-1997. Lang.: Eng. 1822

Visual records of early outdoor performances. Netherlands. 1555-1637. Lang.: Eng. 1827

Analysis of Andrzej Wajda's Stary Theatre production of *Hamlet*. Poland: Cracow. 1989. Lang.: Eng. 1843

Interview with actress Maia Morgenstern. Romania: Bucharest. Hungary: Győr. 1997. Lang.: Hun. 1855

The actress in Russian theatre. Russia. 1845-1916. Lang.: Eng. 1893

English acting careers of Eleonora Duse and Adelaide Ristori. UK-England. 1850-1900. Lang.: Eng. 2169

The influence of Herbert Beerbohm Tree on G. Wilson Knight. UK-England. 1904-1952. Lang.: Eng. 2173

The use of amateurs as extras at the Royal Shakespeare Theatre. UK-England: Stratford. 1879-1995. Lang.: Eng. 2174

Interview with actor Desmond Barrit. UK-England: London. 1977-1997. Lang.: Eng. 2186

Comedian Ralph Lynn's work on *Wild Horses* by Ben Travers. UK-England: London. 1953. Lang.: Eng. 2191

Actor Don Henderson. UK-England. 1970-1997. Lang.: Eng. 2192

Ignorance of psychology among English actors and directors. UK-England. 1997. Lang.: Eng. 2200

A student production of *Time and the Room (Die Zeit und das Zimmer)* by Botho Strauss. UK-England. 1996. Lang.: Eng. 2204

Possible misunderstandings arising from role distribution practices. UK-England. 1593-1750. Lang.: Eng. 2208

Use of Mejerchol'd's techniques in a production of Gogol's *The Government Inspector (Revizor)*. UK-England: Northampton. 1997. Lang.: Eng. 2216

Actor/playwright Stewart Permutt. UK-England: London. 1950-1997. Lang.: Eng. 2224

Interview with actress Sian Phillips. UK-Wales. UK-England: London. 1930-1997. Lang.: Eng. 2234

Actress Annalee Jefferies. USA: Houston, TX. 1986-1997. Lang.: Eng. 2237

Deborah Warner and Fiona Shaw on their adaptation of *The Waste Land* by T.S. Eliot. USA. UK-England. 1980-1997. Lang.: Eng. 2251

Zoe Caldwell and Robert Whitehead on Terrence McNally's *Master Class*. USA: New York, NY. 1996. Lang.: Eng. 2258

Interview with actor/director Austin Pendleton. USA. 1980-1995. Lang.: Eng. 2266

The experience of cross-gender role-playing. USA. 1971-1997. Lang.: Eng. 2268

A year in the lives of fifteen actors recently graduated from American Repertory Theatre's training program. USA: New York, NY. 1994-1997. Lang.: Eng. 2292

Derek Jacobi's reception of the Gielgud Award. USA: Washington, DC. 1997. Lang.: Eng. 2298

Colony Theatre production of *The Matchmaker* by Thornton Wilder. USA: Los Angeles, CA. 1997. Lang.: Eng. 2307

John Barrymore's vocal coach Margaret Carrington. USA. 1919-1923. Lang.: Eng. 2308

Interview with director JoAnne Akalaitis. USA. 1970-1996. Lang.: Eng. 2331

Interview with actor/director Woodie King, Jr. USA: Detroit, MI, New York, NY. 1937-1997. Lang.: Eng. 2332

Actress and director Eva Le Gallienne. USA. 1997. Lang.: Eng. 2343

Eva Le Gallienne's biographer on her work. USA. 1920-1996. Lang.: Eng. 2344

Film actor Emil Jannings. Germany. 1929-1945. Lang.: Eng. 3574

Interview with actor/director Kenneth Branagh. UK-England: London. 1989-1997. Lang.: Eng. 3597

The TV series *Cher Olivier (Dear Olivier)* on actor Olivier Guimond. Canada. 1997. Lang.: Fre. 3718

Life and career of television actor Ronnie Fraser. UK-England. 1930-1997. Lang.: Eng. 3724

Interview with television actress Sarah Lancaster. UK-England. 1997. Lang.: Eng. 3727

Interview with actor Stephen Billington. UK-England. 1997. Lang.: Eng. 3728

Subversive potential in comedy of Phyllis Diller and Roseanne Barr. USA. 1985-1997. Lang.: Eng. 3773

Interview with performance artist Alicia Rios. UK-Wales. 1994-1997. Lang.: Eng. 3824

Performance art, theatre, and performative culture. USA. Austria. 1952-1975. Lang.: Eng. 3827

The body of the actor on stage. USA. 1997. Lang.: Eng. 3829

Current work of performance artist Laurie Anderson. USA. 1960-1997. Lang.: Eng. 3833

Angela Ellsworth and Tina Takemoto's *Her/She Senses Imag(in)ed Malady*. USA. 1991-1997. Lang.: Eng. 3844

Performance analysis of *The Constant State of Desire* by Karen Finley. USA. 1988-1990. Lang.: Eng. 3846

Sally Sussman's adaptation of *xiqu* to Australian performance. Australia. 1988-1996. Lang.: Eng. 3891

Profile of actor Luoyong Wang. USA: New York, NY. 1984-1997. Lang.: Eng. 3967

Actress Mary Martin and gay/lesbian historiography. USA. 1913-1997. Lang.: Eng. 3979

Plays/librettos/scripts
Interview with writer/actor Guillermo Verdecchia. Canada. 1993-1997. Lang.: Eng. 2409

Actress Helena Faucit on playing Rosalind in Shakespeare's *As You Like It*. England. 1598-1893. Lang.: Eng. 2539

On actresses who have played Rosalind in Shakespeare's *As You Like It*. England. 1598-1895. Lang.: Eng. 2778

Playwright Leslie Ayvazian. USA: New York, NY. 1995-1997. Lang.: Eng. 3198

Interview with drag actor and playwright Charles Busch. USA. 1997. Lang.: Eng. 3259

Playwright and actor Wallace Shawn. USA. 1981-1997. Lang.: Eng. 3303

Relation to other fields
English Member of Parliament on similarities between acting and politics. UK-England: London. 1997. Lang.: Eng. 784

Joni L. Jones's performance piece *sista docta*. USA. 1994-1997. Lang.: Eng. 819

Controversy over the videotaping of creative works by students. USA: St. Louis, MO. 1994-1997. Lang.: Eng. 829

Political satire of Pieter-Dirk Uys. South Africa, Republic of: Johannesburg. 1981-1997. Lang.: Eng. 3740

Research/historiography
Eighteenth-century theatrical portraits. England. France. 1700-1800. Lang.: Eng. 3445

Early attempts to record performance photographically. Russia. USA. 1865-1900. Lang.: Eng. 3451

Theory/criticism
Hungarian translation of essays on acting by Max Reinhardt's literary manager Arthur Kahane. Germany. 1872-1932. Lang.: Hun. 897

Brecht's misunderstanding of Chinese theatre as interpreted by Mei Lanfang. Germany. 1925-1959. Lang.: Eng. 900

Training
Vocal training and the split between academics and practitioners. UK-England. USA. 1973-1994. Lang.: Eng. 933

The teaching of performance composition. USA: New York, NY. 1997. Lang.: Eng. 937

Voice teachers defend their work. UK-England. USA. 1973-1994. Lang.: Eng. 3508

Voice training, Shakespeare, and feminism. UK-England. USA. 1973-1994. Lang.: Eng. 3509

Actor-managers
Performance/production
Actor-manager Pál Rakodczay. Hungary. 1856-1921. Lang.: Hun. 1759

Shakespearean production in the age of actor-managers. UK-England. 1840-1914. Lang.: Eng. 2193

Actor's Express (Atlanta, GA)
Performance/production
Actor's Expression production of an unauthorized version of the musical *Oklahoma!*. USA: Atlanta, GA. 1997. Lang.: Eng. 3959

Adaptations — cont'd

Basic theatrical documents

Text of *None Is Too Many* by Jason Sherman. Canada. 1997. Lang.: Eng. 1261

Text of *Le Secret de l'Aiguille creuse (The Secret of the Hollow Needle)*, Gilles Gleizes' adaptation of an Arsène Lupin mystery novel. France. 1996. Lang.: Fre. 1273

Text of *A Question of Mercy* by David Rabe. USA: New York, NY. 1997. Lang.: Eng. 1340

Text of Hossein Amini's film adaptation of *The Wings of the Dove* by Henry James. UK-England. 1995-1997. Lang.: Eng. 3528

Design/technology

Work of cinematographer Darius Khondji on film adaptation of musical *Evita*. USA. 1997. Lang.: Eng. 3546

Institutions

Criticism of productions of Gombrowicz festival. Poland: Radom. 1997. Lang.: Hun. 1452

Performance/production

Performances of Shakespeare's *Twelfth Night* as objects of study. England. 1808-1850. Lang.: Eng. 508

Race, gender, and nation in nineteenth-century performance. USA. Europe. 1855-1902. Lang.: Eng. 633

Directing a stage adaptation of *The Smell of Death and Flowers* by Nadine Gordimer. USA. 1995-1996. Lang.: Eng. 647

Ildikó Pongor's performance in the ballet *Anna Karenina*. Hungary: Budapest. 1997. Lang.: Hun. 1082

Budapest production of the ballet *Don Quijote* by Marius Petipa and Leon Minkus. Hungary: Budapest. 1997. Lang.: Hun. 1083

Imre Eck's ballets for works by Hungarian composers. Hungary: Pécs. 1977-1978. Lang.: Hun. 1087

Negative reception of Marco Micone's adaptation of Shakespeare, *La Mégère de Padova (The Shrew of Padua)*. Canada: Montreal, PQ. 1995-1997. Lang.: Eng. 1584

Interview with director and adaptor Robert Lepage. Canada. 1992-1997. Lang.: Ger, Fre, Dut, Eng. 1594

Actresses and the adaptation of Shakespeare. England. 1660-1740. Lang.: Eng. 1623

Théâtre de l'Aquarium's production of *Pereira Prétend (Pereira Claims)* directed by Didier Bezace. France. 1997. Lang.: Eng. 1660

Jacques Copeau's stage adaptation of *The Brothers Karamazov*. France. 1908-1911. Lang.: Ita. 1662

Appropriations of Shakespeare's plays in postcolonial India. India. 1880-1995. Lang.: Eng. 1780

Report on recent Dublin productions. Ireland: Dublin. 1997. Lang.: Eng. 1786

Japanese productions of plays by Samuel Beckett. Japan. 1960-1994. Lang.: Eng. 1823

Čechov's *Platonov* adapted by Jerzy Jarocki, Teatr Polski. Poland: Wrocław. 1993-1997. Lang.: Eng, Fre. 1854

The accessibility of Shakespeare's plays to today's audiences. UK-England: London. 1997. Lang.: Eng. 1968

Interview with director Deborah Warner. UK-England: London. 1990-1997. Lang.: Ger, Fre, Dut, Eng. 2167

John Caird's adaptation of *Peter Pan*. UK-England: London. 1997. Lang.: Eng. 2215

Stage adaptations of *Uncle Tom's Cabin*. USA. 1853-1857. Lang.: Eng. 2250

Deborah Warner and Fiona Shaw on their adaptation of *The Waste Land* by T.S. Eliot. USA. UK-England. 1980-1997. Lang.: Eng. 2251

Director and dramaturgs on translating, adapting and producing Molière's *Misanthrope*. USA: La Jolla, CA, Chicago, IL. 1989-1990. Lang.: Eng. 2263

Mary Zimmerman's adaptation of the Chinese epic *Journey to the West*. USA. China. 1997. Lang.: Eng. 2271

Theater Oobleck's collective production of *Babette's Feast*. USA: Chicago, IL. 1950-1997. Lang.: Eng. 2280

Roles of director and dramaturg in updating plays for contemporary performance. USA. 1995-1997. Lang.: Eng. 2303

Seattle Children's Theatre's production of *Bunnicula*. USA: Seattle, WA. 1979-1996. Lang.: Eng. 2311

Milwaukee Repertory Theatre and Ko-Thi Dance Company's adaptation of *Benito Cereno*. USA: Milwaukee, WI. 1996. Lang.: Eng. 2316

The dramaturg and *One Crazy Day*, an adaptation of Beaumarchais' *The Marriage of Figaro*. USA: Tucson, AZ. 1992. Lang.: Eng. 2322

Rehearsal and performance of a stage adaptation of *Neuromancer* by William Gibson. USA: Santa Fe, NM. 1996. Lang.: Eng. 2355

Film adaptations of Shakespearean plays. Europe. USA. 1922-1995. Lang.: Eng. 3570

Franco Zeffirelli's film adaptations of Shakespearean plays. Italy. 1966-1990. Lang.: Eng. 3579

Interview with director Iain Softley. UK-England. 1995-1997. Lang.: Eng. 3589

Loncraine and McKellen's *Richard III* from stage to screen. UK-England. 1995-1996. Lang.: Eng. 3590

The theatricalization of war in Kenneth Branagh's film version of Shakespeare's *Henry V*. UK-England. USA. 1989. Lang.: Eng. 3593

Screen adaptations of Shakespeare's *The Taming of the Shrew*. UK-England. USA. 1908-1966. Lang.: Eng. 3594

Analysis of Kenneth Branagh's film adaptation of Shakespeare's *Henry V*. UK-England. 1989. Lang.: Eng. 3595

Analysis of *Richard III*, film version by Loncraine and McKellen. UK-England. 1993-1996. Lang.: Eng. 3596

The film *Bugsy* as an adaptation of Shakespeare's *Antony and Cleopatra*. USA. 1991. Lang.: Eng. 3613

Film adaptations of *The Crucible* by Arthur Miller. USA. 1957-1996. Lang.: Eng. 3626

The power of images to communicate the plays in *Shakespeare: The Animated Tales*. Russia. 1997. Lang.: Eng. 3721

Transferring a stage production to television. Sweden: Stockholm. 1996. Lang.: Swe. 3722

Analysis of cartoon adaptation for children: *Shakespeare: The Animated Tales*. UK. Russia. 1992. Lang.: Eng. 3723

Voyeurism in Jonathan Miller's TV version of Shakespeare's *Othello*. UK-England. 1981. Lang.: Eng. 3725

Television versions of Shakespeare's *Othello*. UK-England. 1987-1996. Lang.: Eng. 3726

The television adaptation of Shakespeare's *King Lear* by Peter Brook and Orson Welles. USA. 1953. Lang.: Eng. 3730

The development of *Play On!*, a musical adaptation of Shakespeare's *Twelfth Night*. USA: New York, NY. 1997. Lang.: Eng. 3953

Géza Blattner's puppet adaptation of *Az ember tragédiája (The Tragedy of Man)* by Madách. Hungary. 1918-1954. Lang.: Hun. 4365

Interview with puppeteer John Ludwig. USA: Atlanta, GA. 1996. Lang.: Eng. 4376

Plays/librettos/scripts

Stage adaptations of novels. USA. 1997. Lang.: Eng. 702

Dance adaptations of Joachim Schlömer. Switzerland: Basel. 1990-1997. Lang.: Ger, Fre, Dut, Eng. 1014

Hamlet, revenge tragedy, and *film noir*. 1600-1996. Lang.: Eng. 2365

La Balade du Grand Macabre by Ghelderode and its operatic adaptation by György Ligeti. Belgium. 1934. Lang.: Fre. 2385

Account of stage adaptation of Jimmy McGovern's screenplay *Priest*. Canada. 1996. Lang.: Eng. 2391

Adaptations of French classics for contemporary audiences. Canada: Montreal, PQ. France. 1997. Lang.: Fre. 2421

Terrains Vagues (Wastelands), Michel Nadeau's stage adaptation of *Rashomon*. Canada: Quebec, PQ. 1997. Lang.: Fre. 2422

Téo Spychalski's production of *Les Démons (The Demons)*. Canada: Montreal, PQ. 1997. Lang.: Fre. 2426

Elizabeth Albahaca's *Le Procès (The Trial)* an adaptation of Kafka's *Der Prozess*. Canada: Montreal, PQ. 1997. Lang.: Fre. 2435

Sam Shepard's unproduced film adaptation of *The Changeling* by Middleton and Rowley. England. USA. 1622-1971. Lang.: Eng. 2490

Shakespearean text and editorial mangling in versions of *King Lear*. England. 1623-1993. Lang.: Eng. 2520

New world adaptations of Shakespeare's *The Tempest*. England. Latin America. Caribbean. 1612-1994. Lang.: Eng. 2549

The 'bad quartos' of *The Merry Wives of Windsor* as abridged touring editions. England. 1597-1619. Lang.: Eng. 2598

Shakespeare's *As You Like It* and Thomas Lodge's novel *Rosalynde*. England. 1590-1593. Lang.: Eng. 2623

Comparison of Shakespeare's *As You Like It* and Charles Johnson's adaptation *Love in a Forest*. England. 1598-1723. Lang.: Eng. 2654

Analysis of Middleton's *Women Beware Women* and its adaptation by Howard Barker. England. 1621-1986. Lang.: Eng. 2666

Adaptations — cont'd

Twentieth-century adaptations of Jacobean plays. England. 1604-1986. Lang.: Eng. 2673

Analysis of melodramas based on novels of Walter Scott. England. 1810-1830. Lang.: Eng. 2681

Possible revisions by Shakespeare to *The Second Maiden's Tragedy* by Thomas Middleton. England. 1611-1991. Lang.: Eng. 2707

Analysis of Nahum Tate's adaptation of Shakespeare's *Coriolanus*. England. 1682. Lang.: Eng. 2712

Contemporary playwrights and the adaptation process. Europe. 1900-1993. Lang.: Ita. 2793

Director and translator on the actuality of Shakespeare. Europe. 1985-1997. Lang.: Ger, Fre, Dut, Eng. 2796

Shakespearean themes in contemporary plays and productions. Europe. 1965-1995. Lang.: Pol. 2798

Jean Cocteau's adaptations of works of Sophocles. France. 1922-1937. Lang.: Eng. 2811

Garnier's *Hippolyte* and its source, Seneca's *Phaedra*. France. 1635. Lang.: Eng. 2813

Brook, Mnouchkine and intercultural theatre. France: Paris. 1988-1992. Lang.: Eng. 2832

Analysis of German translations of plays by Samuel Beckett. Germany. 1967-1978. Lang.: Eng. 2842

Nature in Apel's *Der Freischütz* and its operatic adaptations. Germany. 1811-1990. Lang.: Ger. 2856

German adaptations and appropriations of Shakespeare. Germany. 1960-1996. Lang.: Eng. 2857

Cross-cultural adaptations of Shakespeare on the Parsi stage. India. 1850-1980. Lang.: Eng. 2902

Romeo Castellucci's adaptation of the *Oresteia*. Italy: Cesena. 1995. Lang.: Ger, Fre, Dut, Eng. 2947

Analysis of Alba De Céspedes' stage adaptation of her novel *Quaderno proibido (Forbidden Notebook)*. Italy. 1952. Lang.: Ita. 2950

Adaptations of the diary of Anne Frank. Netherlands. USA. 1945-1997. Lang.: Eng. 2978

Author Astrid Lindgren. Sweden. 1944-1997. Lang.: Swe. 3060

Gender and sexuality on the Victorian stage. UK-England. 1830-1900. Lang.: Eng. 3085

Christopher Hampton—playwright, translator, and adaptor. UK-England. 1967-1994. Lang.: Eng. 3089

Comparison of Arthur Miller's *The Crucible* and his adaptation of Ibsen's *An Enemy of the People*. USA. 1950-1984. Lang.: Eng. 3126

The Wooster Group's adaptations of classic plays. USA: New York, NY. 1975-1997. Lang.: Ger, Fre, Dut, Eng. 3155

Strategies for recontextualizing classic theatrical texts. USA. 1997. Lang.: Eng. 3210

The influence of Ibsen and Greek tragedy on the plays of Arthur Miller. USA. 1915-1996. Lang.: Eng. 3240

Paul Schmidt on translating and adapting plays of Čechov. USA. 1994-1997. Lang.: Eng. 3273

Sisterhood and female bonding in *Crimes of the Heart* and *Sisters*. USA. 1986-1996. Lang.: Eng. 3511

Reactions to *The Sweet Hereafter* by the author of the novel on which the film was based. Canada. 1997. Lang.: Eng. 3634

John Greyson's film adaptation of *Les Feluettes (Lilies)* by Michel Marc Bouchard. Canada. 1996. Lang.: Fre. 3635

Animal imagery in *King Lear* and Akira Kurosawa's film adaptation *Ran*. England. Japan. 1605-1984. Lang.: Eng. 3636

Film adaptations of Shakespeare and cultural imperialism. Europe. 1990-1994. Lang.: Eng. 3637

The nature of film adaptation. Europe. USA. 1915-1995. Lang.: Eng. 3638

Interview with director Peter Greenaway. Europe. 1995. Lang.: Ger, Fre, Dut, Eng. 3639

Interview with Hossein Amini, author of the filmscript *The Wings of the Dove*. UK-England. 1995-1997. Lang.: Eng. 3643

Analysis of Kenneth Branagh's films *A Midwinter's Tale* and *Hamlet*. UK-England. 1995-1996. Lang.: Eng. 3644

Analysis of Kenneth Branagh's film adaptation of *Hamlet*. UK-England. 1996. Lang.: Eng. 3645

Analysis of Peter Greenaway's film adaptation of *The Tempest*, *Prospero's Books*. UK-England. 1991. Lang.: Eng. 3646

The ambiguity of Shakespeare's *Henry V* in Kenneth Branagh's film adaptation. UK-England. 1989. Lang.: Eng. 3648

Re-evaluation of Jarman's screen version of *The Tempest*. UK-England. 1979. Lang.: Eng. 3649

Richard Loncraine and Ian McKellen's film adaptation of *Richard III*. UK-England. 1995. Lang.: Eng. 3651

David Mamet's film adaptations of plays and novels. USA. 1981-1996. Lang.: Eng. 3665

Jon Robin Baitz on the film adaptation of his play *The Substance of Fire*. USA. 1989-1996. Lang.: Eng. 3666

Film adaptations of Shakespeare's *The Taming of the Shrew*. USA. 1929-1966. Lang.: Eng. 3668

Film adaptation of Eric Bogosian's *Talk Radio*. USA: Hollywood, CA. 1988. Lang.: Eng. 3673

Polanski's *Macbeth* and the reclamation of high art by the thriller genre. USA. 1971. Lang.: Eng. 3674

Critique of Franco Zeffirelli's film adaptation of *Hamlet*. USA. 1990. Lang.: Eng. 3675

Film adaptations of plays by Arthur Miller. USA. 1960-1997. Lang.: Eng. 3677

Sexual aberration in film adaptations of *Hamlet*. USA. UK-England. 1920-1996. Lang.: Eng. 3680

Cinematic versions of the Pygmalion myth. USA. 1938. Lang.: Eng. 3682

Analysis of Oliver Parker's screen adaptation of *Othello*. USA. 1995. Lang.: Eng. 3683

Introduction to issue on Shakespeare and film adaptation. USA. 1997. Lang.: Eng. 3684

M.B. Dudley's film adaptation of Shakespeare's *Richard III*. USA. 1912. Lang.: Eng. 3685

The film adaptation of Nathanael West's *Miss Lonelyhearts*. USA. 1933. Lang.: Eng. 3686

Freudian psychology in film adaptations of *Hamlet*. USA. UK-England. 1910-1996. Lang.: Eng. 3687

Analysis of musical adaptations of Shakespearean plays. USA. 1938-1997. Lang.: Ger. 3983

Survey of musical adaptations of Shakespeare. USA: New York, NY. 1938-1997. Lang.: Eng. 3987

Analysis of opera librettos by Boito, Da Ponte, and Gertrude Stein. Europe. 1770-1915. Lang.: Eng. 4289

Wolfgang Rihm's operatic adaptation of *Die Hamletmaschine (Hamletmachine)* by Heiner Müller. Germany. 1978. Lang.: Swe. 4300

Piccinni's *La Cecchina*: English translations and analysis. Italy. USA. 1766-1996. Lang.: Eng. 4305

Lorraine Côté's adaptation of Voltaire's *Candide* for Sous-Marin Jaune puppet theatre. Canada: Montreal, PQ. 1997. Lang.: Fre. 4394

Reference materials
Bibliography of Shakespearean film. USA. 1997. Lang.: Eng. 3689

Relation to other fields
The influence of theatre on novelist and adapter Louisa May Alcott. USA. 1832-1888. Lang.: Eng. 3442

Shakespeare, Hollywood, and American cultural ambivalence. USA. 1990-1997. Lang.: Eng. 3693

Addicted to Love
Basic theatrical documents
Script of *Addicted to Love* by Robert Gordon. USA. 1997. Lang.: Eng. 3532

Plays/librettos/scripts
Interview with screenwriter Robert Gordon. USA. 1997. Lang.: Eng. 3657

Addison, Joseph
Plays/librettos/scripts
Addison's *Cato* as the source of the poem *The Maid's Soliloquy*. Colonial America. England. 1713-1753. Lang.: Eng. 2442

Addolorata
Plays/librettos/scripts
The 'Black Madonna' in works of Italian-Canadian authors. Canada. 1950-1990. Lang.: Eng. 2396

Adelphi Theatre (London)
Performance/production
Collection of newspaper reviews by London theatre critics. UK-England: London. 1997. Lang.: Eng. 2057

Collection of newspaper reviews by London theatre critics. UK-England: London. 1997. Lang.: Eng. 2140

Aesthetics — cont'd

Afonyi, Éva

Institutions

Africaine, L'

Plays/librettos/scripts

African Girl, The

Plays/librettos/scripts

African-American Drama Company (Santa Clara, CA)

Institutions

African-American theatre

SEE ALSO

Black theatre.

Administration

Basic theatrical documents

Design/technology

Institutions

Performance/production

Plays/librettos/scripts

African-American theatre — cont'd

Playwright August Wilson's views on the northward migration of Blacks. USA. 1997. Lang.: Eng. 3277

The Black woman's body in *The Tapestry* by Alexis De Veaux. USA. 1976-1997. Lang.: Eng. 3281

The evolution of solo performance in African-American one-person plays. USA. 1972-1996. Lang.: Eng. 3293

Analysis of *The Old Settler* by John Henry Redwood. USA. 1997. Lang.: Eng. 3297

The voices of African-American women. USA. 1840-1994. Lang.: Eng. 3309

Analysis of *Venus* by Suzan-Lori Parks. USA. 1996. Lang.: Eng. 3310

Bring in 'Da Noise, Bring in 'Da Funk and the Black audience. USA: New York, NY. 1996-1997. Lang.: Eng. 4002

Reference materials
Directory of African-American theatre. USA. 1824-1960. Lang.: Eng. 721

Sourcebook on women playwrights of diversity. USA. 1970-1996. Lang.: Eng. 3320

Filmography of African-Americans. USA. 1978-1994. Lang.: Eng. 3691

Relation to other fields
Theatre artists' responses to the debate on multiculturalism of August Wilson and Robert Brustein. USA. 1997. Lang.: Eng. 789

Introduction to articles on the Wilson-Brustein debate. USA: New York, NY. 1997. Lang.: Eng. 790

Theatre critic and theorist Margo Jefferson on the Robert Brustein/August Wilson debate. USA: New York, NY. 1960-1997. Lang.: Eng. 791

Commentary on the Wilson-Brustein debate. USA: New York, NY. 1996-1997. Lang.: Eng. 793

Support for August Wilson's views on Black American theatre. USA: St. Paul, MN, Princeton, NJ. 1996-1997. Lang.: Eng. 795

Critique of August Wilson's call for a separate Black American theatre. USA: New York, NY. 1997. Lang.: Eng. 807

Call for white directors to examine their casting policies. USA. 1997. Lang.: Eng. 808

The future of African-American theatre. USA. 1997. Lang.: Eng. 816

Joni L. Jones's performance piece *sista docta*. USA. 1994-1997. Lang.: Eng. 819

Analysis of the Wilson-Brustein debate. USA. 1997. Lang.: Eng. 820

The debate on multiculturalism of August Wilson and Robert Brustein. USA. 1997. Lang.: Eng. 825

The Wilson/Brustein debate on African-Americans and theatre. USA. 1995-1997. Lang.: Eng. 826

August Wilson and the history of African-American theatre. USA. 1926-1997. Lang.: Eng. 828

Robert Brustein and August Wilson debate multiculturalism. USA: New York, NY. 1997. Lang.: Eng. 830

Sexuality and the Black artist. USA. 1997. Lang.: Eng. 843

The 'ring shout' dance of African-American churches and its roots. USA. 1700-1995. Lang.: Eng. 1022

August Wilson's address to the National Black Theatre Festival. USA: Winston-Salem, NC. 1997. Lang.: Eng. 3440

August Wilson's TCG speech on the Black artist in American theatre. USA. 1996. Lang.: Eng. 3441

After Easter
Plays/librettos/scripts
Female characters in plays of contemporary British women. UK-England. 1980-1995. Lang.: Eng. 3077

After October
Performance/production
Collection of newspaper reviews by London theatre critics. UK-England: London. 1997. Lang.: Eng. 2062

After Sorrow (Viet Nam)
Design/technology
Thomas Hase's lighting design for *After Sorrow (Viet Nam)* by Ping Chong and Company. USA: New York, NY. 1997. Lang.: Eng. 942

Performance/production
Death in productions by Robert Lepage and Ping Chong. USA: New York, NY. 1996-1997. Lang.: Eng. 2267

After the Fall
Plays/librettos/scripts
Social issues of the sixties in plays and films of Arthur Miller. USA. 1960-1969. Lang.: Eng. 3131

After the Hunt
Basic theatrical documents
Text of *After the Hunt* by Marc von Henning. UK-England. 1997. Lang.: Eng. 1319

Agamemnon
Performance/production
Théâtre du Soleil's *Les Atrides*. France: Paris. 1992. Lang.: Eng. 1676

Interviews with the cast of Théâtre du Soleil's *Les Atrides*. France: Paris. 1992. Lang.: Eng. 1677

Intercultural signs in Mnouchkine's *Les Atrides (The Atridae)*, Théâtre du Soleil. France: Paris. 1990-1997. Lang.: Eng. 1679

Plays/librettos/scripts
Clytemnestra's binding spell in Aeschylus' *Agamemnon*. Greece. 458 B.C. Lang.: Eng. 2879

References to clothing in Aeschylus' *Agamemnon*. Greece. 458 B.C. Lang.: Eng. 2880

Agents
Plays/librettos/scripts
Business guide to writing for the stage. USA. 1997. Lang.: Eng. 705

Networking for playwrights. USA. 1997. Lang.: Eng. 706

Agis, Gaby
Training
Conversation between teacher Joan Skinner and choreographer Gaby Agis. UK-England: London. 1996. Lang.: Eng. 1045

Agitprop theatre
Performance/production
Constance D'Arcy Mackay's *The Pageant of Sunshine and Shadow*. USA. 1900-1918. Lang.: Eng. 3771

Plays/librettos/scripts
Analysis of *The Big Knife* by Clifford Odets. USA. 1930-1949. Lang.: Eng. 3302

Agnes de Castro
Performance/production
Scottish plays on the London stage. England: London. Scotland. 1667-1715. Lang.: Eng. 1635

Agni aur Barkha (Fire and the Rain, The)
Performance/production
Profile of Prasanna, director and teacher. India: New Delhi, Heggodu. 1970. Lang.: Swe. 1782

Agon
Performance/production
Musicological analysis of Stravinskij's ballet *Agon*. USA. 1959. Lang.: Eng. 1126

Performance history of the ballet *Agon* by Stravinskij and Balanchine. USA. 1959-1997. Lang.: Eng. 1130

Aguirre, Isidora
Basic theatrical documents
Anthology of Latin American women's plays. Latin America. 1981-1989. Lang.: Eng. 1291

Ahlstedt, Börje
Performance/production
The work together of actors Solveig Tännström and Börje Ahlstedt. Sweden: Stockholm. 1967. Lang.: Swe. 1961

Ahrens, Lynn
Design/technology
Lighting design for *Ragtime* at the Ford Centre for the Performing Arts. Canada: Toronto, ON. 1975-1997. Lang.: Eng. 3905

Performance/production
Collection of newspaper reviews by London theatre critics. UK-England: London. 1997. Lang.: Eng. 2097

Comparison of productions of *Ragtime* and *Jane Eyre*. Canada: Toronto, ON. 1997. Lang.: Eng. 3932

Stephen Flaherty and Lynn Ahrens, composer and lyricist of *Ragtime*. USA. 1970-1997. Lang.: Eng. 3952

Plays/librettos/scripts
Stage adaptations of novels. USA. 1997. Lang.: Eng. 702

Aiace (Ajax)
Plays/librettos/scripts
Greek mythology in tragedies of Ugo Foscolo. Italy. 1795-1811. Lang.: Ita. 2954

Aichinger, Ilse
Plays/librettos/scripts
Ilse Aichinger's radio play *The Sisters Jouet*. USA. 1967-1997. Lang.: Eng. 3521

Aida
Performance/production
Background material on Metropolitan Opera radio broadcast performances. USA: New York, NY. 1997. Lang.: Eng. 4238

Aida — cont'd

Soprano Antonietta Stella. USA: New York, NY. 1954-1997. Lang.: Eng. 4244

AIDS
Administration
Tenth annual benefit fundraiser for Broadway Cares/Equity Fights AIDS. USA. 1996. Lang.: Eng. 88

Actors' Fund support of low-cost housing for people with HIV/AIDS. USA: Hollywood, CA. 1997. Lang.: Eng. 105

The Broadway Flea Market fundraiser for Broadway Cares/Equity Fights AIDS. USA: New York, NY. 1997. Lang.: Eng. 110

The Easter Bonnet competition, a fundraiser for Broadway Cares/Equity Fights AIDS. USA. 1997. Lang.: Eng. 128

Institutions
Profile of the educational theatre group HIV Ensemble. USA: New York, NY. 1993-1996. Lang.: Eng. 1503

Performance/production
Staged representations of AIDS. 1980-1997. Lang.: Eng. 461

Plays/librettos/scripts
Account of seminar on writing about AIDS. USA: Key West, FL. 1984-1997. Lang.: Eng. 704

Theatrical representations of the Holocaust. Europe. North America. 1950-1996. Lang.: Eng. 2789

Death and dying in plays about AIDS. USA. 1997. Lang.: Eng. 3134

Social debate reflected in Tony Kushner's *Angels in America*. USA. 1988-1996. Lang.: Eng. 3172

Analysis of *Angels in America* by Tony Kushner. USA. 1994-1996. Lang.: Eng. 3207

Tony Kushner's *Angels in America* and the AIDS crisis. USA. 1992-1994. Lang.: Eng. 3235

Kari Ann Owen/Penomee on her play *Terms of Surrender*. USA. 1997. Lang.: Eng. 3244

Relation to other fields
The fear of infection in American popular art and culture. USA. 1997. Lang.: Eng. 848

The effect of AIDS on contemporary drama. USA. 1991-1997. Lang.: Ger. 3406

Ailey, Alvin
Institutions
Alvin Ailey American Dance Theatre: how it achieved stability after Ailey's death. USA: New York, NY. 1989-1997. Lang.: Eng. 1168

Performance/production
The Black male body in concert dance. USA. 1980-1995. Lang.: Eng. 1201

Aimez-moi les uns les autres (Love Me One and All)
Basic theatrical documents
Text of *Aimez-moi les uns les autres (Love Me One and All)* by Alex Métayer. France. 1996. Lang.: Fre. 1274

Aïqui, Francis
Basic theatrical documents
Text of *Les Richesses de l'hiver (The Riches of Winter)* by Fatima Gallaire. France: Ajaccio. 1996. Lang.: Fre. 1272

Air de famille, Un (Family Resemblance, A)
Audience
The audience for Sortie 22's *Un air de famille (A Family Resemblance)*. Canada: Montreal, PQ. 1997. Lang.: Fre. 1244

Airswimming
Performance/production
Collection of newspaper reviews by London theatre critics. UK-England: London. 1997. Lang.: Eng. 1991

Ajoka (Punjab)
Performance/production
Street theatre in Punjab province. Pakistan. 1979-1996. Lang.: Eng. 572

Akademičeskij Teat'r Opery i Baleta im. S.M. Kirova (St. Petersburg)
Institutions
Illustrated portrait of the Mariinskij, or Kirov, Ballet Theatre. Russia: St. Petersburg. 1800-1997. Lang.: Rus. 1057

The Kirov Ballet's guest performances in London. Russia: St. Petersburg. UK-England: London. 1995. Lang.: Swe. 1058

Performance/production
Diana Višnjeva of the Kirov Ballet. Russia: Moscow. 1997. Lang.: Eng. 1100

Interview with ballerina Gabriela Komleva. Russia: St. Petersburg. 1997. Lang.: Eng. 1101

Interview with dancer Sergej Vicharév. Russia: St. Petersburg. 1997. Lang.: Eng. 1102

Soprano Galina Gorčakova. Russia: St. Petersburg. 1962-1997. Lang.: Eng. 4206

Akademietheater (Vienna)
Performance/production
Major productions of the Vienna theatre season. Austria: Vienna. 1997. Lang.: Ger. 1563

Akalaitis, JoAnne
Performance/production
Court Theatre's production of *The Iphigenia Cycle*, based on Euripides. USA: Chicago, IL. 1990-1997. Lang.: Eng. 2282

Interview with director JoAnne Akalaitis. USA. 1970-1996. Lang.: Eng. 2331

Akcja (Action)
Performance/production
Jerzy Grotowski's *Akcja (Action)*. Poland: Wrocław. 1982-1997. Lang.: Eng, Fre. 574

History of Grotowski's Teatr Laboratorium. Poland: Wrocław. 1975-1997. Lang.: Eng, Fre. 578

Akerman, Anthony
Plays/librettos/scripts
Expatriate South African playwright Anthony Akerman. South Africa, Republic of. UK-England. 1973. Lang.: Eng. 3022

Akko Theatre Center (Acre)
Relation to other fields
The movement of theatre from entertainment to 'efficacy'. Israel: Akko. USA. 1994-1997. Lang.: Eng. 767

Al-Shaykh, Hannan
Basic theatrical documents
English translation of *Paper Husband* by Hannan Al-Shaykh. Middle East. 1997. Lang.: Eng. 1292

Performance/production
Collection of newspaper reviews by London theatre critics. UK-England: London. 1997. Lang.: Eng. 1987

Alabama Theatre (Birmingham, AL)
Performance spaces
History of the Alabama Theatre. USA: Birmingham, AL. 1927-1997. Lang.: Eng. 3557

Aladdin
Performance/production
Collection of newspaper reviews by London theatre critics. UK-England: London. 1997. Lang.: Eng. 2160

Alagna, Roberto
Performance/production
Soprano Angela Gheorghiu. Romania. 1997. Lang.: Eng. 4203

Albahaca, Elizabeth
Plays/librettos/scripts
Elizabeth Albahaca's *Le Procès (The Trial)* an adaptation of Kafka's *Der Prozess*. Canada: Montreal, PQ. 1997. Lang.: Fre. 2435

Albany Theatre (Deptford)
Performance/production
Collection of newspaper reviews by London theatre critics. UK-England. 1997. Lang.: Eng. 2039

Albany Theatre (London)
Performance/production
Collection of newspaper reviews by London theatre critics. UK-England: London. 1997. Lang.: Eng. 1990

Collection of newspaper reviews by London theatre critics. UK-England: London. 1997. Lang.: Eng. 2005

Collection of newspaper reviews by London theatre critics. UK-England: London. 1997. Lang.: Eng. 2022

Collection of newspaper reviews by London theatre critics. UK-England: London. 1997. Lang.: Eng. 2160

Albee, Edward
Performance/production
Plays by Shepard and Albee at Nederlands Toneel Gent. Netherlands: Ghent. 1996. Lang.: Eng. 1825

Collection of newspaper reviews by London theatre critics. UK-England: London. 1997. Lang.: Eng. 2124

Anthony Page's production of *A Delicate Balance* by Edward Albee. UK-England: London. 1997. Lang.: Eng. 2211

Transferring a stage production to television. Sweden: Stockholm. 1996. Lang.: Swe. 3722

Plays/librettos/scripts
Postmodern view of Judgement Day in Albee's *The Lady from Dubuque*. USA. 1980. Lang.: Eng. 3219

Silence in the plays of Edward Albee. USA. 1928-1996. Lang.: Eng. 3237

Amor brujo, El
Basic theatrical documents
Libretto for Falla's opera *El amor brujo*. Spain. 1915-1916. Lang.: Fre, Spa.   4015

Performance/production
Versions of Falla's *El amor brujo*. 1915-1924. Lang.: Fre.   4072

Recordings of Falla's *El amor brujo*. 1945-1995. Lang.: Fre.   4089

Amphitheatres/arenas
Performance spaces
Greek and Roman amphitheatres and their reconstruction: exhibition catalogue. Greece. 1997. Lang.: Eng, Gre.   436

Theatres and amphitheatres of ancient Rome. Italy: Rome. 179 B.C.-476 A.D. Lang.: Ita.   443

Performance/production
Visual performance aspects of Greek tragedy. Greece: Athens. 500 B.C. Lang.: Ita.   1749

Amphitryon
Performance/production
The term 'intonation' in German theatrical theory and practice. Germany. 1806-1991. Lang.: Ger.   1733

Collection of newspaper reviews by London theatre critics. UK-England: London. 1997. Lang.: Eng.   2056

Amusement parks
Design/technology
Lighting design for 'Mickey's Toontown' at Disneyland. USA: Anaheim, CA. 1994. Lang.: Eng.   246

Amy's View
Performance/production
Collection of newspaper reviews by London theatre critics. UK-England: London. 1997. Lang.: Eng.   2067

Ancient Greek theatre
SEE ALSO
Geographical-Chronological Index under Greece 600 BC-100 AD.

Performance spaces
The meaning of performance space in ancient Greek theatre. Greece. 500-100 B.C. Lang.: Eng.   437

Performance/production
Odes for female choruses in Greek theatre. Greece. 500-100 B.C. Lang.: Eng.   549

Visual performance aspects of Greek tragedy. Greece: Athens. 500 B.C. Lang.: Ita.   1749

The honorary position of *khoregos* or choral leader in Greek tragedy. Greece. 500-400 B.C. Lang.: Eng.   1751

Plays/librettos/scripts
Religious ambivalence in Greek tragedy. Ancient Greece. 500-250 B.C. Lang.: Eng.   2373

Comic techniques of the playwright Aristophanes. Greece. 445-399 B.C. Lang.: Ita.   2867

Strong women in the *Oresteia* of Aeschylus. Greece. 500 B.C. Lang.: Eng.   2868

Speech within speech in Attic drama. Greece. 400 B.C.-100 A.D. Lang.: Eng.   2869

Greek history as interpreted in plays of Sophocles and Euripides. Greece. 400-200 B.C. Lang.: Eng.   2870

Rhetoric in Euripidean drama. Greece. 500-300 B.C. Lang.: Eng.   2871

Analysis of Aristophanes' *Acharnēs (The Acharnians)*. Greece. 425 B.C. Lang.: Eng.   2872

Attitudes about rhetoric in Greek and Roman drama. Greece. Roman Empire. 450-350 B.C. Lang.: Eng.   2873

The cultural construction of the hero in Greek tragedy. Greece. 500-400 B.C. Lang.: Eng.   2874

Greek drama and mimesis. Greece. 500-400 B.C. Lang.: Eng.   2876

Ambivalence about rhetoric in Greek tragedy. Greece. 500-250 B.C. Lang.: Eng.   2877

Clytemnestra's binding spell in Aeschylus' *Agamemnon*. Greece. 458 B.C. Lang.: Eng.   2879

Collection of essays on Sophocles as a dramatist. Greece. 496-406 B.C. Lang.: Eng.   2881

Translation and the study of Greek tragedy. Greece. 458-400 B.C. Lang.: Eng.   2882

History and Aeschylus' *Persai (The Persians)*. Greece. 500-450 B.C. Lang.: Eng.   2883

The depiction of women in ancient Greek theatre. Greece. 500-200 B.C. Lang.: Eng.   2884

Problems of historical interpretation in Greek tragedy and comedy. Greece. 500-400 B.C. Lang.: Eng.   2887

Ancient Greek tragedy and religion. Greece. 500-250 B.C. Lang.: Eng.   2888

Foreigners in Athenian tragedy. Greece. 400-250 B.C. Lang.: Eng.   2890

Comparative anthropological approach to Greek tragedy. Greece. 600-300 B.C. Lang.: Slo.   2892

Analysis of Euripides' *Cyclops*. Greece. 450-425 B.C. Lang.: Eng.   2893

The Greco-Roman parasite character. Roman Empire. 200-500. Lang.: Eng.   2988

The influence of Ibsen and Greek tragedy on the plays of Arthur Miller. USA. 1915-1996. Lang.: Eng.   3240

Myth and nature in Wagnerian opera. Germany. 1832-1883. Lang.: Eng.   4299

Reference materials
History of ancient Greek and Roman theatre. Greece. Rome. 500 B.C.-476 A.D. Lang.: Ita.   714

Relation to other fields
The 'ring shout' dance of African-American churches and its roots. USA. 1700-1995. Lang.: Eng.   1022

Visual representations of Greek drama. Greece. 500-250 B.C. Lang.: Eng.   3357

Psychoanalysis and Aeschylus' *Oresteia*. Greece. 458 B.C. Lang.: Eng.   3358

Research/historiography
Using Greek tragedy as a historical source. Greece. 500-250 B.C. Lang.: Eng.   3448

Ancient Roman theatre
Plays/librettos/scripts
The Greco-Roman parasite character. Roman Empire. 200-500. Lang.: Eng.   2988

Latin literature, drama, and patronage. Rome. 400 B.C.-200 A.D. Lang.: Eng.   2989

Reference materials
History of ancient Greek and Roman theatre. Greece. Rome. 500 B.C.-476 A.D. Lang.: Ita.   714

And Baby Makes Seven
Plays/librettos/scripts
Interview with playwright Paula Vogel. USA: New York, NY. 1997. Lang.: Eng.   3181

And Wolf Shall Inherit the Moon
Plays/librettos/scripts
The environmental music theatre of R. Murray Schafer. Canada. 1966-1996. Lang.: Eng.   3886

Andern Oper, Den (Copenhagen)
Performance/production
Opera and culture in Copenhagen area. Denmark: Copenhagen. 1997. Lang.: Eng.   4121

Andersen, Tom
Performance/production
Successful cabaret performers and their techniques. USA. 1975-1997. Lang.: Eng.   3780

Anderson, Adele
Performance/production
Collection of newspaper reviews by London theatre critics. UK-England: London. 1997. Lang.: Eng.   1986

Anderson, Gordon
Performance/production
Collection of newspaper reviews by London theatre critics. UK-England: London. 1997. Lang.: Eng.   2126

Anderson, Laurie
Performance/production
Current work of performance artist Laurie Anderson. USA. 1960-1997. Lang.: Eng.   3833

Theory/criticism
Performance theory applied to Laurie Anderson's *Home of the Brave*. USA. 1990-1995. Lang.: Eng.   3852

Anderson, Lea
Performance/production
Lea Anderson, founder of The Cholmondeleys and The Featherstonehaughs. UK-England. 1984-1994. Lang.: Eng.   1191

Anderson, Maxwell
Performance/production
Kurt Weill's collaborations with playwrights. Germany: Berlin. USA: New York, NY. 1927-1945. Lang.: Eng.   3934

Plays/librettos/scripts
Time travel in English-language drama. USA. Canada. UK-England. 1908-1993. Lang.: Eng.   3171

Andersson, Tommy
Performance/production
Interview with actor Tommy Andersson. Sweden. 1990-1997. Lang.:
Swe. 1931
Andorra
Plays/librettos/scripts
Jewish persecution and identity in works of Max Frisch and Arthur
Miller. Switzerland. 1961. Lang.: Eng. 3064
Andre
Plays/librettos/scripts
Patriotism in early American drama. USA. 1775-1817. Lang.: Eng. 3187
Andreini, Isabella
Plays/librettos/scripts
Male and female Renaissance writers. Europe. 1400-1590. Lang.: Eng.
2785
Andrejév-Burlak, Viktor Nikolaj
Research/historiography
Early attempts to record performance photographically. Russia. USA.
1865-1900. Lang.: Eng. 3451
Andrejév, Leonid Nikolajévič
Institutions
Festival of Russian theatres dedicated to the work of Leonid Andrejév.
Russia: Orel. 1996. Lang.: Rus. 364
Andy and Edie
Performance/production
Collection of newspaper reviews by London theatre critics. UK-England:
London. 1997. Lang.: Eng. 2107
Ang Paglakbay ni Radya Mangandiri (Journey of Radya Mangandiri, The)
Audience
The role of theatre in Philippine culture. Philippines. 1905-1993. Lang.:
Eng. 1250
Angel, Albalucía
Plays/librettos/scripts
Analysis of *Siete lunas y un espejo (Seven Moons and a Looking Glass)*
by Albalucía Angel. Colombia. 1991. Lang.: Spa. 2441
Angels and Demons
Performance/production
Collection of newspaper reviews by London theatre critics. UK-England:
London. 1997. Lang.: Eng. 2138
Angels in America
Design/technology
Projection techniques for *Angels in America* at Stockholms Stadsteater.
Sweden: Stockholm. 1800-1997. Lang.: Ger. 1358
Design for three productions of Tony Kushner's *Angels in America*.
USA: New York, NY, Los Angeles, CA. UK-England: London. 1992-
1994. Lang.: Eng. 1363
Performance/production
Analysis of Declan Donnellan's production of *Angels in America* by
Tony Kushner. UK-England: London. 1992. Lang.: Eng. 2168
Sexuality on stage in the National Theatre production of Tony
Kushner's *Angels in America*. UK-England: London. 1992. Lang.: Eng.
2176
Tony Kushner's *Angels in America* in the context of queer performance.
USA. 1992-1994. Lang.: Eng. 2245
Tony Kushner's *Angels in America* as epic theatre. USA. 1992-1995.
Lang.: Eng. 2324
The presidential election and the Los Angeles premiere of *Angels in
America*. USA: Los Angeles, CA. 1992. Lang.: Eng. 2327
Interview with director Robert Altman on filming *Angels in America*.
USA. 1995. Lang.: Eng. 3603
Plays/librettos/scripts
Death and dying in plays about AIDS. USA. 1997. Lang.: Eng. 3134
The character Roy Cohn in Tony Kushner's *Angels in America*. USA.
1992-1994. Lang.: Eng. 3154
Social debate reflected in Tony Kushner's *Angels in America*. USA.
1988-1996. Lang.: Eng. 3172
Ethnicity in Tony Kushner's *Angels in America*. USA. 1992-1994. Lang.:
Eng. 3189
Tony Kushner's *Angels in America*, postmodernism, and millenarianism.
USA. 1992-1994. Lang.: Eng. 3193
Insanity and prophecy in Tony Kushner's *Angels in America*. USA.
1992-1994. Lang.: Eng. 3195
The supernatural in Tony Kushner's *Angels in America*. USA. 1992-
1994. Lang.: Eng. 3206
Analysis of *Angels in America* by Tony Kushner. USA. 1994-1996.
Lang.: Eng. 3207

Identity, cultural transformation, and Tony Kushner's *Angels in
America*. USA. 1992-1994. Lang.: Eng. 3221
Tony Kushner's *Angels in America* and the AIDS crisis. USA. 1992-
1994. Lang.: Eng. 3235
Representations of race and gender in Tony Kushner's *Angels in
America*. USA. 1992-1994. Lang.: Eng. 3236
Tony Kushner's *Angels in America* and U.S. history. USA. 1992-1994.
Lang.: Eng. 3270
Jewish identity in *Angels in America* by Tony Kushner. USA. 1992-
1994. Lang.: Eng. 3280
Relation to other fields
The effect of AIDS on contemporary drama. USA. 1991-1997. Lang.:
Ger. 3406
Angels in America, Part I: Millennium Approaches
Performance/production
Comparison of productions of Tony Kushner's *Angels in America, Part
I: Millennium Approaches*. USA: New York, NY. UK-England. 1992-
1993. Lang.: Eng. 2326
Angels in America, Part II: Perestroika
Basic theatrical documents
French translation of Tony Kushner's *Angels in America, Part II:
Perestroika*. USA. France: Paris. 1996. Lang.: Fre. 1333
Performance/production
Sex and gender in recent Stockholm productions. Sweden: Stockholm.
1996. Lang.: Eng. 1925
Plays/librettos/scripts
Analysis of the final scene of *Angels in America, Part II: Perestroika* by
Tony Kushner. USA. 1992-1994. Lang.: Eng. 3271
Angered Nya Teater (Gothenburg)
Institutions
Profile of Angered Nya Teater, Niklas Hjulström, director. Sweden:
Gothenburg. 1980. Lang.: Swe. 1485
Angst & Geometrie (Fear and Geometry)
Performance/production
Gerhard Bohner's choreography *Angst & Geometrie (Fear and Geometry)*.
Germany. 1936-1997. Lang.: Ger. 971
Anholt, Christien
Performance/production
Harold Pinter's performance in his own play *The Hothouse*. UK-
England: Chichester. 1996. Lang.: Eng. 2205
Animal Farm
Performance/production
Collection of newspaper reviews by London theatre critics. UK-England:
London. 1997. Lang.: Eng. 2029
Collection of newspaper reviews by London theatre critics. UK-England:
London. 1997. Lang.: Eng. 2034
Animata (London)
Performance/production
Collection of newspaper reviews by London theatre critics. UK-England:
London. 1997. Lang.: Eng. 1988
Animation
Performance/production
The power of images to communicate the plays in *Shakespeare: The
Animated Tales*. Russia. 1997. Lang.: Eng. 3721
Profile of television series *The Wubbulous World of Dr. Seuss*. USA:
New York, NY. 1997. Lang.: Eng. 4397
Relation to other fields
Shakespeare: The Animated Tales: educational videos, based on
Shakespeare's plays. UK. Russia. 1991-1997. Lang.: Ger. 3741
Animo
Performance/production
Collection of newspaper reviews by London theatre critics. UK-England:
London. 1997. Lang.: Eng. 1988
Anisfeld, Boris I.
Design/technology
Costume designs of Boris I. Anisfeld, soon to be exhibited. Russia: St.
Petersburg. USA. 1994-1997. Lang.: Eng. 180
Änkeman Jarl (Widower Jarl, The)
Performance/production
The work together of actors Solveig Tännström and Börje Ahlstedt.
Sweden: Stockholm. 1967. Lang.: Swe. 1961
Anklagad (Accused)
Plays/librettos/scripts
Interview with playwrights Lars Arrhed and Kjell Abrahamsson.
Sweden: Malmö. 1995-1997. Lang.: Swe. 3056
Anna Karenina
Performance/production
Ildikó Pongor's performance in the ballet *Anna Karenina*. Hungary:
Budapest. 1997. Lang.: Hun. 1082

Anna Weiss
Performance/production
Collection of newspaper reviews by London theatre critics. UK-Scotland: Edinburgh. 1997. Lang.: Eng. 2232

Annajanska, The Bolshevik Empress
Performance/production
Collection of newspaper reviews by London theatre critics. UK-England: London. 1997. Lang.: Eng. 2035

Anne Frank: The Diary of a Young Girl
Plays/librettos/scripts
Adaptations of the diary of Anne Frank. Netherlands. USA. 1945-1997. Lang.: Eng. 2978

Annenkov, Nikolaj Aleksandrovič
Performance/production
Actor Nikolaj Annenkov. Russia: Moscow. 1990-1997. Lang.: Rus. 1857

Annie
Design/technology
Lighting designer Ken Billington. USA: New York, NY. 1997. Lang.: Eng. 3911

Anomalja (Anomaly)
Performance/production
Galin's *Anomalja (Anomaly)* at Sovremennik. Russia: Moscow. 1996. Lang.: Rus. 1875

Anouilh, Jean
Performance/production
Bolšoj Drama Theatre production of Anouilh's *Antigone*. Russia: St. Petersburg. 1996. Lang.: Rus. 1862
Anouilh's *Antigone* at the Bolšoj Drama Theatre. Russia: St. Petersburg. 1996. Lang.: Rus. 1897
Collection of newspaper reviews by London theatre critics. UK-England: London. 1997. Lang.: Eng. 2036
Collection of newspaper reviews by London theatre critics. UK-England: London. 1997. Lang.: Eng. 2044
Plays/librettos/scripts
Collection of articles on French avant-garde culture, including theatre. France. 1937-1989. Lang.: Eng. 2805

Anskij, Solomon
Performance/production
Ghosts in theatrical productions. Poland. Lithuania. 1997. Lang.: Pol. 1838

Anšon, Vladimir
Performance/production
Vladimir Anšon's production of Čechov's *Pianola*. Russia: St. Petersburg. 1995. Lang.: Rus. 1881

ANTA
SEE
American National Theatre and Academy.

Antenna Theatre (San Francisco, CA)
Performance/production
Interview with experimental theatre artist Christopher Hardman. USA. 1985. Lang.: Ita. 631

Anthelia's Letters
Basic theatrical documents
Text of *Southern Bells: Voices of Working Women* by Emma Gene Peters. USA. 1997. Lang.: Eng. 1339

Anthes, György
Performance/production
Profile of tenor and opera stage director György Anthes. Hungary. 1863-1922. Lang.: Hun. 4179

Anthony, Marc
Performance/production
Marc Anthony's role in *The Capeman*. USA. 1968-1997. Lang.: Eng. 3977

Anthropology
Institutions
Włodzimierz Staniewski's experimental theatre group Ośrodek Praktyk Teatralnych. Poland: Gardzienice. 1976-1996. Lang.: Pol. 358
Performance/production
Ethnographic analysis of the creation of a tourist show. Angola. South Africa, Republic of. 1993-1996. Lang.: Eng. 470
Analysis of Jerzy Grotowski's *Apocalypsis cum figuris*. Poland. 1964-1992. Lang.: Pol. 581
The popular theatre genre of *Hira Gasy*. Madagascar. 1800-1995. Lang.: Swe. 1225
Renaissance theatre performances in Ferrara. Italy: Ferrara. 1486-1502. Lang.: Eng. 1794
Analysis of television serial *The Restless Years*. Australia. Germany. 1977-1993. Lang.: Eng. 3716

Performance, mass media, and the regulation of *wayang golek purwa*. Indonesia. 1994-1995. Lang.: Eng. 4399
The southern form of *wayang kulit* shadow puppet theatre. Indonesia. 1900-1995. Lang.: Eng. 4401
Plays/librettos/scripts
Brook, Mnouchkine and intercultural theatre. France: Paris. 1988-1992. Lang.: Eng. 2832
Comparative anthropological approach to Greek tragedy. Greece. 600-300 B.C. Lang.: Slo. 2892
Relation to other fields
Small-town Finnish theatre. Finland. 1997. Lang.: Eng, Fre. 745
Ritual and performance in ancient Greek sport and warfare. Greece. Lang.: Eng. 764
The development of dance in Africa and the popularity of ethnic dance. Africa. 1997. Lang.: Eng. 1155
The culture and ethnography of the Amakhosi theatre tradition. Zimbabwe. 1960-1997. Lang.: Eng. 3444
Description of course on film and visual anthropology and sociology. South Africa, Republic of. 1997. Lang.: Eng. 3692
Identity, cultural exchange, and tourism. Spain-Catalonia. 1950-1997. Lang.: Eng. 3810
Anthropological analysis of stage hypnosis. Russia. 1997. Lang.: Rus. 3862
Theory/criticism
Audience participation and the catharsis of theatre. USA. 1997. Lang.: Eng. 921
Anthropological models for ways to categorize dance. Europe. North America. 1995. Lang.: Eng. 1026

Antígona
Relation to other fields
Performance of gender, nationality, and motherhood in various Argentine plays. Argentina. 1976-1983. Lang.: Eng. 725

Antigona
Basic theatrical documents
Text of Dušan Jovanović's Balkan trilogy. Slovenia. 1997. Lang.: Slo. 1299
Plays/librettos/scripts
Analysis of Sophocles' and Smole's treatments of Antigone and Shakespeare's *Hamlet*. Slovenia. 500 B.C.-1960 A.D. Lang.: Slo. 3005

Antigone
Performance/production
Bolšoj Drama Theatre production of Anouilh's *Antigone*. Russia: St. Petersburg. 1996. Lang.: Rus. 1862
Anouilh's *Antigone* at the Bolšoj Drama Theatre. Russia: St. Petersburg. 1996. Lang.: Rus. 1897
Plays/librettos/scripts
Jean Cocteau's adaptations of works of Sophocles. France. 1922-1937. Lang.: Eng. 2811
Translation and the study of Greek tragedy. Greece. 458-400 B.C. Lang.: Eng. 2882
Analysis of Sophocles' and Smole's treatments of Antigone and Shakespeare's *Hamlet*. Slovenia. 500 B.C.-1960 A.D. Lang.: Slo. 3005

Anton Chekov
Performance/production
Collection of newspaper reviews by London theatre critics. UK-England: London. 1997. Lang.: Eng. 2095

Antonov, Viktor
Performance/production
Master puppeteer Viktor Antonov. Russia: St. Petersburg. 1990-1997. Lang.: Rus. 4368

Antony and Cleopatra
Performance/production
Collection of newspaper reviews by London theatre critics. UK-England: London. 1997. Lang.: Eng. 2028
The Shakespearean acting and directing career of Judi Dench. UK-England: London. 1957-1995. Lang.: Eng. 2177
Reactions to modern performances of *Antony and Cleopatra*. UK-England. North America. 1827-1987. Lang.: Eng. 2178
The film *Bugsy* as an adaptation of Shakespeare's *Antony and Cleopatra*. USA. 1991. Lang.: Eng. 3613
Plays/librettos/scripts
Race and gender in Shakespeare's *Antony and Cleopatra*. England. 1607-1707. Lang.: Eng. 2458
Shakespeare's *Antony and Cleopatra* as a romance. England. 1607. Lang.: Eng. 2496

Arsenic and Old Lace
Performance/production
The grotesque on the American stage during the Depression. USA.
1929-1940. Lang.: Eng. 2264

'Art'
Performance/production
Collection of newspaper reviews by London theatre critics. UK-England:
London. 1997. Lang.: Eng. 2089

Art of Seduction, The
Performance/production
Collection of newspaper reviews by London theatre critics. UK-England:
London. 1997. Lang.: Eng. 2025

Artaud, Antonin
Performance/production
Contemporary experimental theatre and Artaud's theatre of cruelty.
1920-1997. Lang.: Eng. 463

The relationship of Antonin Artaud and Etienne Decroux. France: Paris.
1920-1945. Lang.: Eng. 531

Community movement in theatre. Poland. 1920-1997. Lang.: Eng, Fre.
577

Antonin Artaud's continuing influence on modern drama. France. 1897-
1997. Lang.: Eng. 1661

Life, career, and influences of Antonin Artaud. France. 1897-1997.
Lang.: Eng. 1670

Contrast and comparison of Eastern and Western acting styles. Japan.
Europe. 1150-1997. Lang.: Eng. 1822

Collection of newspaper reviews by London theatre critics. UK-England.
1997. Lang.: Eng. 2082

Films about Antonin Artaud by Gérard Mordillat and Jérome Prieur.
France. 1993. Lang.: Eng. 3573

Plays/librettos/scripts
Asian influence on European theatre. Europe. Asia. 1915-1997. Lang.:
Pol. 694

The convergence of fascism and avant-garde theatre aesthetics. France.
1930-1945. Lang.: Eng. 2833

Theory/criticism
Derrida's analysis of the theatre of cruelty. France. 1935-1949. Lang.:
Eng. 882

Signs in theatrical representation. France. 1977. Lang.: Eng. 890

Artaud's theatre of cruelty and the passion play. Europe. 1400-1950.
Lang.: Eng. 3478

Magic as defining trope of modern drama. Europe. 1910-1950. Lang.:
Eng. 3482

Artetoa, Aïnhoa
Performance/production
Soprano Aïnhoa Artetoa. Spain. 1997. Lang.: Eng. 4213

Arts Council of Canada (Canada)
SEE
Canada Council.

Arts in education
Institutions
Profile of children's cultural center The Ark. Ireland: Dublin. 1982-
1997. Lang.: Eng. 342

Relation to other fields
Parental attitudes toward arts education for children. USA. 1980-1997.
Lang.: Eng. 815

Arts Theatre (London)
Performance/production
Collection of newspaper reviews by London theatre critics. UK-England:
London. 1997. Lang.: Eng. 1967

Collection of newspaper reviews by London theatre critics. UK-England:
London. 1997. Lang.: Eng. 1980

Collection of newspaper reviews by London theatre critics. UK-England:
London. 1997. Lang.: Eng. 1995

Collection of newspaper reviews by London theatre critics. UK-England:
London. 1997. Lang.: Eng. 2009

Collection of newspaper reviews by London theatre critics. UK-England:
London. 1997. Lang.: Eng. 2034

Collection of newspaper reviews by London theatre critics. UK-England:
London. 1997. Lang.: Eng. 2052

Collection of newspaper reviews by London theatre critics. UK-England:
London. 1997. Lang.: Eng. 2066

Collection of newspaper reviews by London theatre critics. UK-England:
London. 1997. Lang.: Eng. 2091

Collection of newspaper reviews by London theatre critics. UK-England:
London. 1997. Lang.: Eng. 2099

Collection of newspaper reviews by London theatre critics. UK-England:
London. 1997. Lang.: Eng. 2112

Collection of newspaper reviews by London theatre critics. UK-England:
London. 1997. Lang.: Eng. 2138

Collection of newspaper reviews by London theatre critics. UK-England:
London. 1997. Lang.: Eng. 2162

Arye, Yevgeny
Performance/production
Collection of newspaper reviews by London theatre critics. UK-England:
London. 1997. Lang.: Eng. 2071

As You Like It
Basic theatrical documents
Text of *Love in a Forest*, an adaptation of *As You Like It* by Charles
Johnson. England. 1723. Lang.: Eng. 1265

Performance/production
As You Like It and the Chamberlain's Men's move to the Globe.
England: London. 1594-1612. Lang.: Eng. 1619

As You Like It, transvestism, and early modern sexual politics. England.
1599. Lang.: Eng. 1636

Performances of the classics in Franconia. Germany. 1997. Lang.: Ger.
1737

Recent productions of plays by Shakespeare. Poland. 1997. Lang.: Eng,
Fre. 1834

Collection of newspaper reviews by London theatre critics. UK-England:
London. 1997. Lang.: Eng. 2066

Collection of newspaper reviews by London theatre critics. UK-England:
London. 1997. Lang.: Eng. 2112

Non-literary realism in Shakespeare productions. UK-England.
Germany. 1958-1995. Lang.: Ger. 2170

The dramaturg and Irondale Ensemble Project's *As You Like It*. USA:
New York, NY. 1986-1989. Lang.: Eng. 2310

Plays/librettos/scripts
Analysis of Shakespeare's *As You Like It*. England. 1598. Lang.: Eng.
2478

Notes on Shakespeare's *As You Like It* by an eighteenth-century critic.
England. 1598. Lang.: Eng. 2493

Psychological theory in Shakespeare's *As You Like It*. England. 1598.
Lang.: Eng. 2500

Shakespeare's *As You Like it* and its source. England. 1598. Lang.: Eng.
2506

Actress Helena Faucit on playing Rosalind in Shakespeare's *As You
Like It*. England. 1598-1893. Lang.: Eng. 2539

Shakespeare's *As You Like It* as a disguise play. England. 1598. Lang.:
Eng. 2546

Eighteenth-century criticism of Shakespeare's *As You Like It*. England.
1598. Lang.: Eng. 2551

Eighteenth-century criticism of Shakespeare's *As You Like It*. England.
1598. Lang.: Eng. 2553

The characters of Shakespeare's *As You Like It*. England. 1598. Lang.:
Eng. 2555

A female critic's view of Shakespeare's *As You Like It*. England. 1598.
Lang.: Eng. 2557

The heroines of Shakespeare's *As You Like It*. England. 1598. Lang.:
Eng. 2574

Court and country in Shakespeare's *As You Like It*. England. 1598.
Lang.: Eng. 2575

Analysis of Shakespeare's *As You Like It*. England. 1599. Lang.: Eng.
2596

Samuel Johnson on Shakespeare's *As You Like It*. England. 1598.
Lang.: Eng. 2599

Shakespeare's *As You Like It* and Thomas Lodge's novel *Rosalynde*.
England. 1590-1593. Lang.: Eng. 2623

Female characters in Shakespeare's *As You Like It*. England. 1598.
Lang.: Eng. 2628

Poet John Masefield's analysis of Shakespeare's *As You Like It*.
England. 1598. Lang.: Eng. 2648

The structure of Shakespeare's *As You Like It*. England. 1598. Lang.:
Eng. 2652

Comparison of Shakespeare's *As You Like It* and Charles Johnson's
adaptation *Love in a Forest*. England. 1598-1723. Lang.: Eng. 2654

Principles of Shakespearean dramaturgy. England. 1590-1613. Lang.:
Eng. 2658

Audience reactions/comments — cont'd

Community-based dramaturgy and Pearl Cleage's *Flyin' West* at Intiman Theatre. USA. 1994-1995. Lang.: Eng. 2349

The production of Canadian radio drama. Canada. 1920-1995. Lang.: Eng. 3517

Voyeurism in Jonathan Miller's TV version of Shakespeare's *Othello*. UK-England. 1981. Lang.: Eng. 3725

Performance art and catharsis. USA. 1977-1997. Lang.: Eng. 3845

The audience and live music on stage. Finland. 1997. Lang.: Fin. 3868

Plays/librettos/scripts
Religious ambivalence in Greek tragedy. Ancient Greece. 500-250 B.C. Lang.: Eng. 2373

The plays of Judith Thompson and their effect on audiences. Canada. 1984-1991. Lang.: Eng. 2401

The use of dramatic structures to reinforce political and cultural hierarchies. England. 1400-1550. Lang.: Eng. 2554

Ibsen and early modernist theatre. Finland. 1885-1905. Lang.: Eng. 2801

Greek history as interpreted in plays of Sophocles and Euripides. Greece. 400-200 B.C. Lang.: Eng. 2870

The cultural construction of the hero in Greek tragedy. Greece. 500-400 B.C. Lang.: Eng. 2874

Ambivalence about rhetoric in Greek tragedy. Greece. 500-250 B.C. Lang.: Eng. 2877

History and Aeschylus' *Persai (The Persians)*. Greece. 500-450 B.C. Lang.: Eng. 2883

Problems of historical interpretation in Greek tragedy and comedy. Greece. 500-400 B.C. Lang.: Eng. 2887

Ancient Greek tragedy and religion. Greece. 500-250 B.C. Lang.: Eng. 2888

The role of 'foreign' theatre on the Spanish stage. Spain. UK-England. USA. 1939-1963. Lang.: Eng. 3044

O'Neill's *Strange Interlude* and its critical and popular reception. USA. 1926-1927. Lang.: Eng. 3201

Authenticity and stereotype in David Henry Hwang's *M. Butterfly*. USA. 1988. Lang.: Eng. 3208

The rhetoric of victimization in *The Glass Menagerie* by Tennessee Williams. USA. 1945-1994. Lang.: Eng. 3298

Viewer response and François Truffaut's *The Bride Wore Black*. France. 1967. Lang.: Eng. 3641

Psychological themes in Stephen Sondheim's *Sweeney Todd* and their effect on audiences. USA. 1976. Lang.: Eng. 3999

Relation to other fields
Visual representations of Greek drama. Greece. 500-250 B.C. Lang.: Eng. 3357

Theory/criticism
Speech and writing in various aspects of theatre. France. 1997. Lang.: Fre. 3486

Reflections on theatre reviews. Sweden. 1950-1997. Lang.: Swe. 3495

Audience-performer relationship
Audience
The role of the spectator/consumer in contemporary theatre. Italy. 1997. Lang.: Ita. 135

The audience for Sortie 22's *Un air de famille (A Family Resemblance)*. Canada: Montreal, PQ. 1997. Lang.: Fre. 1244

The role of theatre in Philippine culture. Philippines. 1905-1993. Lang.: Eng. 1250

The involvement of the audience in performance. Sweden. USSR. 1900. Lang.: Swe. 1251

Reality and fictionality in theatre in education. UK-England. 1960-1994. Lang.: Eng. 1253

The participatory communal relationship between spectator and performer. USA. 1988-1997. Lang.: Eng. 3756

Anecdotes by opera audience members. Canada. USA. 1997. Lang.: Eng. 4007

Performance spaces
The structural design of Shakespeare's Globe. UK-England: London. 1997. Lang.: Eng. 1531

Performance/production
Interview with installation artist Esteve Graset. Spain. 1978-1996. Lang.: Eng. 610

Problems of creating and preserving new dance works. Sweden. 1950. Lang.: Swe. 1184

The honorary position of *khoregos* or choral leader in Greek tragedy. Greece. 500-400 B.C. Lang.: Eng. 1751

The role of the implied spectator in productions of Omri Nitzan and Hillel Mittelpunkt. Israel: Tel Aviv. 1993. Lang.: Eng. 1792

Space, place, and travel in performance art and installations. UK-England: London. Germany: Kassel. 1997. Lang.: Eng. 3823

Plays/librettos/scripts
Changing relationships of writing, text and performance. UK-England. USA. 1980-1996. Lang.: Eng. 698

Relation to other fields
Performance of gender, nationality, and motherhood in various Argentine plays. Argentina. 1976-1983. Lang.: Eng. 725

The inclusion of tourism in Balinese village traditional performance. Indonesia-Bali: Singapadu. 1996. Lang.: Eng. 766

The movement of theatre from entertainment to 'efficacy'. Israel: Akko. USA. 1994-1997. Lang.: Eng. 767

Analysis of a performance for the Young Presidents Organization. India: Mumbai. 1996. Lang.: Eng. 1228

The distinction between the live and the mediatized. Canada. USA. 1977-1997. Lang.: Eng. 3706

Identity, cultural exchange, and tourism. Spain-Catalonia. 1950-1997. Lang.: Eng. 3810

Space in feminist performance art and political protest. UK-England. 1980-1997. Lang.: Eng. 3850

Research/historiography
Archaeology and performance in site-specific productions. UK-Wales. 1997. Lang.: Eng. 3851

Theory/criticism
Audience participation and the catharsis of theatre. USA. 1997. Lang.: Eng. 921

Audio forms
SEE ALSO
Classed Entries under MEDIA—Audio forms.
Administration
Censorship and self-censorship on American television. USA. 1920-1965. Lang.: Eng. 3708

Design/technology
Work of engineers for rock band Foo Fighters. UK-England. 1997. Lang.: Eng. 196

Performance/production
Rock group U2's use of video and interactive technology. USA. 1997. Lang.: Eng. 3732

Review of live performance recordings from Staatsoper. Austria: Vienna. 1928-1943. Lang.: Eng. 4100

Review of a new CD entitled 'Famous Italian Baritones'. Italy. 1996. Lang.: Eng. 4192

Analysis of a digital CD-ROM of Wagner's *Ring*. USA. 1996. Lang.: Eng. 4256

Opera and luxury record packaging. USA. 1996. Lang.: Eng. 4278

Plays/librettos/scripts
Critical survey of works by playwright Ernst Toller. Germany. 1893-1939. Lang.: Eng. 2839

Auditions
Administration
The National Labor Relations Board's approval of Equity-only auditions. USA. 1997. Lang.: Eng. 101

Performance/production
The dance audition—the evaluation process and advice for auditioners. USA. 1997. Lang.: Eng. 1009

Auditorium
Performance spaces
History of the parterre and the audience that occupied it. France. 1600-1700. Lang.: Eng. 431

The unity of decor in the Renaissance Italian stage and hall. Italy. 1500-1700. Lang.: Eng. 445

Theatre structures used at Prague Quadrennial. Czech Republic: Český Krumlov. 1995. Lang.: Eng. 1518

Profile of Měsíčník Ceských Divadel, a revolving auditorium theatre. Czech Republic: Český Krumlov. 1947-1996. Lang.: Eng. 1519

The history of the Colosseum and its new interior design. Germany: Essen. 1900-1997. Lang.: Ger. 3930

Aufhaltsame Aufstieg des Arturo Ui, Der (Resistible Rise of Arturo Ui, The)
Performance/production
Productions of the International Istanbul Theatre Festival. Turkey: Istanbul. 1980-1997. Lang.: Eng. 1966

Ballets Russes (Paris) — cont'd

Performance/production
The body and gender in Parisian dance performance. France. 1911-1924. Lang.: Eng.   1069

Relation to other fields
The Ballets Russes and the arts. Europe. 1909-1929. Lang.: Ger.   1131

Ballets Suédois (Paris)

Performance/production
The body and gender in Parisian dance performance. France. 1911-1924. Lang.: Eng.   1069

Ballo in Maschera, Un

Performance/production
Analysis of the original production book of *Un Ballo in Maschera*. Italy: Milan. 1856-1888. Lang.: Eng.   4197

Background material on Metropolitan Opera radio broadcast performances. USA: New York, NY. 1997. Lang.: Eng.   4238

Balzac, Honoré de

Relation to other fields
Representation and reception of the *castrato*. France. 1830-1970. Lang.: Eng.   4322

BAM

SEE
Brooklyn Academy of Music.

Bamonte, Karen

Performance/production
Profile of dancer and choreographer Karen Bamonte. USA. 1972-1995. Lang.: Ger.   1012

Bán, Teodóra

Institutions
Interview with Teodóra Bán and Gábor Keveházi about summer opera festival. Hungary: Budapest. 1991-1997. Lang.: Hun.   335

Bancil, Parv

Performance/production
Collection of newspaper reviews by London theatre critics. UK-England: London. 1997. Lang.: Eng.   2025

Collection of newspaper reviews by London theatre critics. UK-England: London. 1997. Lang.: Eng.   2130

Bancroft, Marie

Performance/production
Shakespearean production in the age of actor-managers. UK-England. 1840-1914. Lang.: Eng.   2193

Bancroft, Squire

Performance/production
Shakespearean production in the age of actor-managers. UK-England. 1840-1914. Lang.: Eng.   2193

Bandele, Biyi

Performance/production
Collection of newspaper reviews by London theatre critics. UK-England: London. 1997. Lang.: Eng.   2074

Bandido!

Performance/production
History in recent Chicano/a theatre. USA. 1964-1995. Lang.: Eng.   2360

Bánk bán

Performance/production
Tenor József Simándy. Hungary. 1917-1997. Lang.: Hun.   4170

Banks, Iain

Performance/production
Collection of newspaper reviews by London theatre critics. UK-England: London. 1997. Lang.: Eng.   2104

Banks, John

Plays/librettos/scripts
Female 'mad' songs in seventeenth-century English drama. England. 1685-1700. Lang.: Eng.   2638

Bannister, Kate

Performance/production
Collection of newspaper reviews by London theatre critics. UK-England: London. 1997. Lang.: Eng.   2153

Baraitser, Lisa

Performance/production
Collection of newspaper reviews by London theatre critics. UK-England: London. 1997. Lang.: Eng.   1997

Baraka, Imamu Amiri (Jones, LeRoi)

Basic theatrical documents
Text of plays performed at the Nuyorican Poets Cafe. USA: New York, NY. 1973-1990. Lang.: Eng.   1322

Performance/production
Framing, montage, and race in works of Shakespeare, Baraka, and Eisenstein. 1997. Lang.: Eng.   1548

The social protest theatre of Luis Valdez and Amiri Baraka. USA. 1965-1975. Lang.: Eng.   2260

Plays/librettos/scripts
Male identity in contemporary American drama. USA. 1915-1995. Lang.: Eng.   3232

Baraka's *The Dutchman* and American race relations. USA. 1964-1997. Lang.: Eng.   3252

Barańczak, Stanisław

Performance/production
Effect of new translations of Shakespeare on Polish theatre. Poland. 1610-1997. Lang.: Eng, Fre.   1852

Barba, Eugenio

Institutions
Report on the 1995 season of ISTA. Denmark: Holstebro. 1995. Lang.: Eng.   306

Performance/production
Physical work in actor training. Denmark: Holstebro. 1950-1997. Lang.: Eng.   497

Theory/criticism
The influence of Etienne Decroux on Eugenio Barba. France. Denmark. 1966-1997. Lang.: Eng.   3747

Barber of Seville, The (opera)

SEE
Barbiere di Siviglia, Il.

Barbican Theatre (London)

SEE ALSO
Royal Shakespeare Company.

Performance/production
Collection of newspaper reviews by London theatre critics. UK-England: London. 1997. Lang.: Eng.   1987

Collection of newspaper reviews by London theatre critics. UK-England. 1997. Lang.: Eng.   2125

Collection of newspaper reviews by London theatre critics. UK-England: London. 1997. Lang.: Eng.   2136

Collection of newspaper reviews by London theatre critics. UK-England: London. 1997. Lang.: Eng.   2151

Collection of newspaper reviews by London theatre critics. UK-England: London. 1997. Lang.: Eng.   2159

Barbiere di Siviglia, Il

Performance/production
Background material on Metropolitan Opera radio broadcast performances. USA: New York, NY. 1997-1997. Lang.: Eng.   4237

Barbieri, Fedora

Performance/production
Opera singer Fedora Barbieri. Italy. Hungary. 1940-1997. Lang.: Hun.   4188

Barbin, Jean-Damien

Performance/production
Jean-Damien Barbin in Olivier Py's *La Servante (The Servant)*, a twenty-four-hour performance. France: Paris. 1997. Lang.: Swe.   1663

Baricco, Alessandro

Plays/librettos/scripts
Analysis of *Davila Roa* by Alessandro Baricco. Italy. 1997. Lang.: Ita.   2972

Bark, Richard

Design/technology
Technical aspects of YstadsOperan's production of *The Saint of Bleecker Street*. Sweden: Ystad. 1997. Lang.: Swe.   4029

Barker, Howard

Performance/production
Collection of newspaper reviews by London theatre critics. UK-England: London. 1997. Lang.: Eng.   1976

Plays/librettos/scripts
Analysis of Middleton's *Women Beware Women* and its adaptation by Howard Barker. England. 1621-1986. Lang.: Eng.   2666

Twentieth-century adaptations of Jacobean plays. England. 1604-1986. Lang.: Eng.   2673

Medieval theatre as reflected in contemporary drama. UK-England. 1970-1990. Lang.: Eng.   3067

Brecht's influence on the plays of Howard Barker. UK-England. 1987-1997. Lang.: Eng.   3084

Analysis of *Judith* and *The Castle* by Howard Barker. UK-England. 1975-1994. Lang.: Eng.   3096

Relation to other fields
Howard Barker on illumination and tragedy. UK-England. Germany. 1996. Lang.: Dan.   782

Barker, Paul

Performance/production
Collection of newspaper reviews by London theatre critics. UK-England: London. 1997. Lang.: Eng.   2133

Barnes, Ben
Performance/production
Collection of newspaper reviews by London theatre critics. UK-England.
1997. Lang.: Eng.   2142

Collection of newspaper reviews by London theatre critics. UK-England:
London. 1997. Lang.: Eng.   2151

Barnes, Eric Lane
Performance/production
Collection of newspaper reviews by London theatre critics. UK-England:
London. 1997. Lang.: Eng.   2081

Barnes, Hazel
Performance/production
Confession, reconciliation, and David Lan's *Desire*. South Africa,
Republic of: Pietermaritzburg. 1993-1995. Lang.: Eng.   1908

Barnes, Peter
Plays/librettos/scripts
Medieval theatre as reflected in contemporary drama. UK-England.
1970-1990. Lang.: Eng.   3067

Barnfather, Mick
Performance/production
Collection of newspaper reviews by London theatre critics. UK-England:
London. 1997. Lang.: Eng.   2022

Barnfield, Chris
Performance/production
Collection of newspaper reviews by London theatre critics. UK-England:
London. 1997. Lang.: Eng.   2084

Baron auf den Bäumen, Der (Baron in the Trees, The)
Plays/librettos/scripts
Children's theatre festival productions. Germany: Berlin. 1997. Lang.:
Ger.   2845

Baron, Michel
Research/historiography
Eighteenth-century theatrical portraits. England. France. 1700-1800.
Lang.: Eng.   3445

Baroque opera
Performance/production
Opera Atelier's production of Purcell's *Dido and Aeneas*. Canada:
Toronto, ON. 1994-1995. Lang.: Eng.   4112

Stylistic similarities in Baroque and nineteenth-century opera. Europe.
1705-1997. Lang.: Eng.   4128

Baroque theatre
SEE ALSO
Geographical-Chronological Index under Europe, and other European
countries, 1594-1702.
Plays/librettos/scripts
Essays on late Baroque drama. Europe. 1600-1699. Lang.: Ita.   2787

Barr, Roseanne
Performance/production
Subversive potential in comedy of Phyllis Diller and Roseanne Barr.
USA. 1985-1997. Lang.: Eng.   3773

Barrault, Jean-Louis
Plays/librettos/scripts
Collection of articles on French avant-garde culture, including theatre.
France. 1937-1989. Lang.: Eng.   2805

Barrett, Shirley
Basic theatrical documents
Script of *Love Serenade* by Shirley Barrett. Australia. 1997. Lang.: Eng.
                                                                     3524
Plays/librettos/scripts
Interview with screenwriter and director Shirley Barrett. Australia. 1997.
Lang.: Eng.   3632

Barrie, Alistair
Performance/production
Collection of newspaper reviews by London theatre critics. UK-England:
London. 1997. Lang.: Eng.   2013

Barrie, James M.
Performance/production
Collection of newspaper reviews by London theatre critics. UK-England.
1997. Lang.: Eng.   2033

Collection of newspaper reviews by London theatre critics. UK-England:
London. 1997. Lang.: Eng.   2123

Collection of newspaper reviews by London theatre critics. UK-England:
London. 1997. Lang.: Eng.   2158

A lesbian reading of Mary Martin's performance as Peter Pan. USA.
1950-1959. Lang.: Eng.   3978
Plays/librettos/scripts
Time travel in English-language drama. USA. Canada. UK-England.
1908-1993. Lang.: Eng.   3171

Barrit, Desmond
Performance/production
Interview with actor Desmond Barrit. UK-England: London. 1977-1997.
Lang.: Eng.   2186

Barry, Sebastian
Design/technology
Joanna Town, head lighting designer of the Royal Court Theatre. UK-
England: London. 1986-1997. Lang.: Eng.   1361
Performance/production
Collection of newspaper reviews by London theatre critics. UK-England:
London. 1997. Lang.: Eng.   2049

Barrymore
Plays/librettos/scripts
Interview with playwright William Luce. USA. 1997. Lang.: Eng.   3149

Barrymore, John
Performance/production
John Barrymore's vocal coach Margaret Carrington. USA. 1919-1923.
Lang.: Eng.   2308
Plays/librettos/scripts
Sophie Treadwell and her play *Plumes in the Dust*. USA. 1917-1936.
Lang.: Eng.   3183

Bársony, Rózsi
Performance/production
Film careers of Hungarian dancers. Hungary. 1929-1945. Lang.: Hun.
                                                                      976

Bartered Bride, The
SEE
Prodana Nevĕsta.

Bartet, Julia
Performance/production
Actresses who may have been the model for Henry James's character
Miriam Rooth. UK-England. 1890. Lang.: Ita.   2202

Barthes, Roland
Performance/production
Collection of newspaper reviews by London theatre critics. UK-England:
London. 1997. Lang.: Eng.   2015

Barthol, Bruce
Performance/production
San Francisco Mime Troupe's *13 Días/13 Days*. USA: San Francisco,
CA. 1997. Lang.: Eng.   2335

Bartholomew Fair
Performance/production
The festive context of Jonson's *Bartholomew Fair*. England. 1600-1608.
Lang.: Eng.   1628

Collection of newspaper reviews by London theatre critics. UK-England.
1997. Lang.: Eng.   2163

Bartlett, Neil
Performance/production
Space in site-specific performance. UK-England. 1960-1997. Lang.: Eng.
                                                                      619

Collection of newspaper reviews by London theatre critics. UK-England:
London. 1997. Lang.: Eng.   2025

Collection of newspaper reviews by London theatre critics. UK-England:
London. 1997. Lang.: Eng.   2070

Collection of newspaper reviews by London theatre critics. UK-England:
London. 1997. Lang.: Eng.   2118

Collection of newspaper reviews by London theatre critics. UK-England:
London. 1997. Lang.: Eng.   2156

Interview with actor Desmond Barrit. UK-England: London. 1977-1997.
Lang.: Eng.   2186

Bartók, Béla
Performance/production
Pécsi Balett's performance of choreographies by István Herczog to music
of Bartók. Hungary: Pécs. 1997. Lang.: Hun.   1080

Bartók's stage works presented by Pécsi Balett. Hungary: Pécs. 1992-
1997. Lang.: Hun.   1088

Barton, John
Plays/librettos/scripts
Women's silence in Renaissance drama. England. 1601-1613. Lang.:
Eng.   2642

Barton, Richard
Performance/production
Elizabethan stage semiotics in twentieth-century Shakespearean
productions. UK-England. 1905-1979. Lang.: Eng.   2203

Barungin (Smell the Wind)
Plays/librettos/scripts
Analysis of Aboriginal drama. Australia. 1967-1997. Lang.: Eng.   2376

Baryshnikov, Mikhail
Performance/production
The career of dancer and choreographer Mikhail Baryshnikov. USA: New York, NY. 1981-1997. Lang.: Eng. 1005

Basement, The
Plays/librettos/scripts
British Library holdings of filmscript material of Harold Pinter. UK-England. 1963-1994. Lang.: Eng. 3647

Basin
Plays/librettos/scripts
Analysis of *Basin* by Jacqueline Rudet. UK-England. 1985-1997. Lang.: Eng. 3106

Basler Theater (Basel)
Performance/production
Comparison of productions of Shakespeare's *Richard III*. Germany. Switzerland. 1996. Lang.: Ger. 1745

Productions of plays by Katharina Thanner and Lisa Engel. Switzerland: Zurich, Basel. 1995-1997. Lang.: Ger. 1963

Bate, Terry John
Performance/production
Collection of newspaper reviews by London theatre critics. UK-England: London. 1997. Lang.: Eng. 2091

Bateau Ivre Theatre Company (London)
Performance/production
Collection of newspaper reviews by London theatre critics. UK-England: London. 1997. Lang.: Eng. 2087

Batman
Plays/librettos/scripts
Political allegory in the film *Batman*. USA. 1989. Lang.: Eng. 3669

Batsheva Dance Group (Tel Aviv)
Performance/production
Interview with István Juhos of the Batsheva Dance Group. Hungary. Israel: Tel Aviv. 1994-1996. Lang.: Hun. 975

Budapest guest performance of the Batsheva Dance Group. Israel: Tel Aviv. Hungary: Budapest. 1963-1989. Lang.: Hun. 980

Battersea Arts Centre (London)
Performance/production
Collection of newspaper reviews by London theatre critics. UK-England: London. 1997. Lang.: Eng. 1969

Collection of newspaper reviews by London theatre critics. UK-England: London. 1997. Lang.: Eng. 1979

Collection of newspaper reviews by London theatre critics. UK-England: London. 1997. Lang.: Eng. 1981

Collection of newspaper reviews by London theatre critics. UK-England: London. 1997. Lang.: Eng. 1985

Collection of newspaper reviews by London theatre critics. UK-England: London. 1997. Lang.: Eng. 1988

Collection of newspaper reviews by London theatre critics. UK-England: London. 1997. Lang.: Eng. 1991

Collection of newspaper reviews by London theatre critics. UK-England: London. 1997. Lang.: Eng. 2000

Collection of newspaper reviews by London theatre critics. UK-England: London. 1997. Lang.: Eng. 2002

Collection of newspaper reviews by London theatre critics. UK-England: London. 1997. Lang.: Eng. 2003

Collection of newspaper reviews by London theatre critics. UK-England: London. 1997. Lang.: Eng. 2007

Collection of newspaper reviews by London theatre critics. UK-England: London. 1997. Lang.: Eng. 2036

Collection of newspaper reviews by London theatre critics. UK-England: London. 1997. Lang.: Eng. 2040

Collection of newspaper reviews by London theatre critics. UK-England: London. 1997. Lang.: Eng. 2042

Collection of newspaper reviews by London theatre critics. UK-England: London. 1997. Lang.: Eng. 2054

Collection of newspaper reviews by London theatre critics. UK-England: London. 1997. Lang.: Eng. 2068

Collection of newspaper reviews by London theatre critics. UK-England: London. 1997. Lang.: Eng. 2073

Collection of newspaper reviews by London theatre critics. UK-England: London. 1997. Lang.: Eng. 2101

Collection of newspaper reviews by London theatre critics. UK-England: London. 1997. Lang.: Eng. 2113

Collection of newspaper reviews by London theatre critics. UK-England: London. 1997. Lang.: Eng. 2116

Collection of newspaper reviews by London theatre critics. UK-England: London. 1997. Lang.: Eng. 2129

Collection of newspaper reviews by London theatre critics. UK-England: London. 1997. Lang.: Eng. 2130

Collection of newspaper reviews by London theatre critics. UK-England: London. 1997. Lang.: Eng. 2134

Collection of newspaper reviews by London theatre critics. UK-England: London. 1997. Lang.: Eng. 2135

Collection of newspaper reviews by London theatre critics. UK-England: London. 1997. Lang.: Eng. 2148

Collection of newspaper reviews by London theatre critics. UK-England: London. 1997. Lang.: Eng. 2152

Collection of newspaper reviews by London theatre critics. UK-England: London. 1997. Lang.: Eng. 2153

Collection of newspaper reviews by London theatre critics. UK-England: London. 1997. Lang.: Eng. 2154

Battersea Latchmere Theatre (London)
SEE
Latchmere Theatre (London).

Battistelli, Giorgio
Performance/production
Collection of newspaper reviews by London theatre critics. UK-England. 1997. Lang.: Eng. 2082

Battle of Bunker's-Hill, The
Plays/librettos/scripts
Patriotism in early American drama. USA. 1775-1817. Lang.: Eng. 3187

Baty, Gaston
Plays/librettos/scripts
The convergence of fascism and avant-garde theatre aesthetics. France. 1930-1945. Lang.: Eng. 2833

Bauer, Jean-Louis
Basic theatrical documents
Text of *Page 27* by Jean-Louis Bauer. France. 1996. Lang.: Fre. 1268

Baum, L. Frank
Performance/production
Collection of newspaper reviews by London theatre critics. UK-England: London. 1997. Lang.: Eng. 2157

Baumann, Gerd
Performance/production
Productions at the Munich Biennale. Germany: Munich. 1997. Lang.: Ger. 4148

Baumbauer, Frank
Performance/production
Interview with director Christoph Marthaler and set designer Anna Viebrock. Germany. Switzerland. 1980-1997. Lang.: Ger. 1723

Bausch, Pina
Design/technology
Peter Pabst's stage design for Tanztheater Wuppertal's *Nur Du (Only You)*. Germany: Wuppertal. 1996. Lang.: Eng. 940
Performance/production
The choreography of Merce Cunningham and Pina Bausch. Europe. USA. 1980-1995. Lang.: Ger. 958

Analysis of Pina Bausch's *Nur Du (Only You)*. Germany: Wuppertal. 1996. Lang.: Eng. 964

Interview with Matthias Schmiegelt, company manager of Tanztheater Wuppertal. Germany: Wuppertal. 1996. Lang.: Eng. 966

The creation of Pina Bausch's *Nur Du (Only You)*. Germany: Wuppertal. 1996. Lang.: Eng. 969

The influence of Pina Bausch and Johann Kresnik on German choreography. Germany. 1980-1997. Lang.: Ger. 970

Interviews with members of Tanztheater Wuppertal. Germany: Wuppertal. 1996. Lang.: Eng. 974

Review of U.S. tour of Pina Bausch's *Nur Du (Only You)*. USA. 1960-1991. Lang.: Eng. 1000
Theory/criticism
Feminist theory and choreographer Pina Bausch. Germany: Wuppertal. 1978-1991. Lang.: Eng. 1029

Bavarian State Opera
SEE
Bayerische Staatsoper im Nationaltheater.

Baxter, Keith
Performance/production
Collection of newspaper reviews by London theatre critics. UK-England: London. 1997. Lang.: Eng. 2062

Baxter, Virgina
Performance/production
Performance pieces of Open City. Australia: Sydney. 1987-1997. Lang.: Eng. 3815

Berlin, Uwe Dag
Performance/production
Reviews of Bochumer Schauspielhaus productions. Germany: Bochum.
1997. Lang.: Ger. 1730
Berliner Ensemble (Berlin)
Institutions
Interview with Martin Wuttke of Berliner Ensemble. Germany: Berlin.
1989-1997. Lang.: Ger. 1424

Problems at Berliner Ensemble. Germany: Berlin. 1989. Lang.: Swe.
1429
Performance/production
Alexander Stillmark on directing Müller's *Der Auftrag (The Mission)*.
Chile: Santiago. 1996-1997. Lang.: Ger. 1607

The history of *Mutter Courage und ihre Kinder (Mother Courage and
Her Children)* by Bertolt Brecht. Europe. USA. Africa. 1949-1995. Lang.:
Eng. 1651

Roger Planchon's production of *Georges Dandin* by Molière. France:
Villeurbanne. 1958. Lang.: Pol. 1675

Einar Schleef's Berliner Ensemble production of Brecht's *Herr Puntila*.
Germany: Berlin. 1996. Lang.: Ger. 1701

Brecht's production of *Mother Courage*. Germany: Berlin. 1949. Lang.:
Pol. 1740

Productions of the International Istanbul Theatre Festival. Turkey:
Istanbul. 1980-1997. Lang.: Eng. 1966
Berliner Stückemarkt, Autorentage (Hannover)
Institutions
Statement of one of the jurors for the Autorentage theatre festival.
Germany: Hannover. 1997. Lang.: Ger. 1415
Plays/librettos/scripts
Playwright Albert Ostermaier. Germany. 1967-1997. Lang.: Ger. 2853
Berlioz, Hector
Plays/librettos/scripts
Representations of the Orient in nineteenth-century French opera.
France. 1863-1894. Lang.: Eng. 4290
Theory/criticism
The reaction of Hector Berlioz to Donizetti's *La Fille du régiment*.
France. 1840. Lang.: Fre. 4328
Berman, Sabina
Basic theatrical documents
Anthology of Latin American women's plays. Latin America. 1981-1989.
Lang.: Eng. 1291
Bernadetje
Performance/production
Collection of newspaper reviews by London theatre critics. UK-England:
London. 1997. Lang.: Eng. 2118
Berndtsson, Hans
Institutions
Profile of Länsteatern i Skövde. Sweden: Skövde. 1964. Lang.: Swe.
1481
Bernhard, Thomas
Performance/production
Productions of Schauspiel Stuttgart. Germany: Stuttgart. 1997. Lang.:
Ger. 1687

Krystian Lupa's production of *Immanuel Kant* by Thomas Bernhard.
Poland: Wrocław. 1997. Lang.: Eng, Fre. 1845

Collection of newspaper reviews by London theatre critics. UK-England:
London. 1997. Lang.: Eng. 2096
Plays/librettos/scripts
Operatic and Austrian influences on the work of Thomas Bernhard.
Austria. 1931-1989. Lang.: Eng. 2381
Bernhardt, Sarah
Performance/production
Guest performances in Polish cities. Poland: Cracow, Lvov, Warsaw.
1810-1915. Lang.: Pol. 583

Actresses who may have been the model for Henry James's character
Miriam Rooth. UK-England. 1890. Lang.: Ita. 2202
Bernier, Pierre
Performance/production
Collection of newspaper reviews by London theatre critics. UK-England:
London. 1997. Lang.: Eng. 1972
Bernstein, Betsy D.
Administration
Recasting star roles in Broadway musicals. USA: New York, NY. 1952-
1977. Lang.: Eng. 3896
Bernstein, Leonard
Performance/production
Collection of newspaper reviews by London theatre critics. UK-England:
London. 1997. Lang.: Eng. 2088

Plays/librettos/scripts
Analysis of musical adaptations of Shakespearean plays. USA. 1938-
1997. Lang.: Ger. 3983
Berry, Cicely
Performance/production
Critique of voice training in contemporary Shakespearean production.
UK-England. North America. 1975-1995. Lang.: Eng. 2201
Training
Vocal training and the split between academics and practitioners. UK-
England. USA. 1973-1994. Lang.: Eng. 933

Voice teachers defend their work. UK-England. USA. 1973-1994. Lang.:
Eng. 3508
Berry, Mary
Plays/librettos/scripts
Women's Romantic 'closet' drama as an alternative theatrical space.
England. 1790-1820. Lang.: Eng. 2486
Bertati, Giovanni
Basic theatrical documents
Text of the libretto to *Il matrimonio segreto* by Domenico Cimarosa.
Italy. 1792. Lang.: Fre, Ita. 4013
Plays/librettos/scripts
Analysis of Cimarosa's opera *Il matrimonio segreto*. Italy. 1792. Lang.:
Fre. 4302

Cimarosa's *Il matrimonio segreto* and the clandestine marriage on the
eighteenth-century stage. Italy. 1766-1792. Lang.: Fre. 4304
Bertolazzi, Carlo
Performance/production
Materialism in Brecht's plays and a Piccolo Teatro performance. France:
Paris. Italy: Milan. 1977. Lang.: Eng. 1656
Bertonneau, Christophe
Performance/production
Collection of newspaper reviews by London theatre critics. UK-England:
London. 1997. Lang.: Eng. 2073
Bertschi, Roland
Plays/librettos/scripts
Children's theatre festival productions. Germany: Berlin. 1997. Lang.:
Ger. 2845
Besson, Benno
Performance/production
Productions of Molière's *Tartuffe* by Benno Besson and Lorraine Pintal.
Canada: Montreal, PQ, Quebec, PQ. 1996-1997. Lang.: Fre. 1601

Interview with director Benno Besson. Germany. Switzerland. 1949-
1997. Lang.: Ger. 1727

Treatments of Shakespeare's *Hamlet* by Robert Wilson and Benno
Besson. Italy. 1995. Lang.: Ita. 1808
Besuch der alten Dame, Der
Performance/production
Gottfried von Einem's opera *Der Besuch der alten Dame*. Switzerland.
1918-1996. Lang.: Eng. 4222
Besuch der alten Dame, Der (Visit, The)
Performance/production
Dürrenmatt's *Der Besuch der alten Dame (The Visit)* and its American
adaptation. Switzerland. 1921-1990. Lang.: Eng. 1965
Besy (Devils, The)
Institutions
Malyj Dramatic Theatre under Lev Dodin. Russia: St. Petersburg. 1983-
1996. Lang.: Eng. 1465
Bethge, Corinna
Performance/production
World premieres at Mannheimer Nationaltheater. Germany: Mannheim.
1997. Lang.: Ger. 1697
Betrayal
Performance/production
Susan Cox's production of Pinter's *Betrayal* at The Playhouse. Canada:
Vancouver, BC. 1996. Lang.: Eng. 1592

Russian productions of plays by Harold Pinter. Russia: Moscow. 1996.
Lang.: Eng. 1864
Plays/librettos/scripts
British Library holdings of filmscript material of Harold Pinter. UK-
England. 1963-1994. Lang.: Eng. 3647
Betsuyaku, Minoru
Basic theatrical documents
English translation of *Ashi no Aru Shitai (A Corpse with Feet)* by
Minoru Betsuyaku. Japan. 1937-1995. Lang.: Eng. 1290
Betterton, Thomas
Performance/production
Actresses and the adaptation of Shakespeare. England. 1660-1740.
Lang.: Eng. 1623

Bettinson, Rob
  Performance/production
    Collection of newspaper reviews by London theatre critics. UK-England:
    London. 1997. Lang.: Eng.   2032
Betts, Susan
  Performance/production
    Collection of newspaper reviews by London theatre critics. UK-England:
    London. 1997. Lang.: Eng.   2103
Between Blessings
  Basic theatrical documents
    Text of plays performed at the Nuyorican Poets Cafe. USA: New York,
    NY. 1973-1990. Lang.: Eng.   1322
Between Life and Death
  Performance/production
    Sally Sussman's adaptation of *xiqu* to Australian performance. Australia.
    1988-1996. Lang.: Eng.   3891
Between the Lines
  Performance/production
    Collection of newspaper reviews by London theatre critics. UK-England:
    London. 1997. Lang.: Eng.   1984
Between Two Women
  SEE
    Fausse suivante, La.
Beutel, Heike
  Performance/production
    Significant productions in Swabia. Germany: Stuttgart. 1997. Lang.: Ger.
                                                                 1726
Beuys, Joseph
  Performance/production
    The performance art of Wolf Vostell and Joseph Beuys. Germany. 1960-
    1987. Lang.: Eng.   3819
    Performance art, theatre, and performative culture. USA. Austria. 1952-
    1975. Lang.: Eng.   3827
Beveridge, Ian
  Design/technology
    Work of engineers for rock band Foo Fighters. UK-England. 1997.
    Lang.: Eng.   196
Beyond the Blue Horizon
  Performance/production
    Collection of newspaper reviews by London theatre critics. UK-England:
    London. 1997. Lang.: Eng.   2146
Bezace, Didier
  Institutions
    Impressions of the Festival d'Avignon. France: Avignon. 1997. Lang.:
    Ger.   313
  Performance/production
    Théâtre de l'Aquarium's production of *Pereira Prétend (Pereira Claims)*
    directed by Didier Bezace. France. 1997. Lang.: Eng.   1660
Bharata Natyam
  Performance/production
    Choreography and *Bharata Natyam*. India. 1997. Lang.: Swe. 979
Bianca de'Rossi
  Plays/librettos/scripts
    Trento's opera *Bianca de'Rossi* and its sources. Italy. 1790-1799. Lang.:
    Eng.   4306
Biancolelli, Domenico
  Basic theatrical documents
    The *commedia* scenarios of Domenico Biancolelli. France: Paris. 1662-
    1668. Lang.: Ita.   3789
Bibbiena, Bernardo Davizi da
  Plays/librettos/scripts
    Comparison of classical Roman, Renaissance Italian, and Shakespearean
    treatments of similar stories. Europe. 200 B.C.-1610 A.D. Lang.: Eng.
                                                                 2799
Bible Quilt
  Plays/librettos/scripts
    The voices of African-American women. USA. 1840-1994. Lang.: Eng.
                                                                 3309
Bible: The Complete Word of God (Abridged), The
  Performance/production
    Collection of newspaper reviews by London theatre critics. UK-England:
    London. 1997. Lang.: Eng.   2094
Bibliographies
  Performance/production
    Guide to references and bibliographies on the acting and directing
    career of John Huston. USA. 1906-1987. Lang.: Eng.   3609
  Plays/librettos/scripts
    Critical survey of works by playwright Ernst Toller. Germany. 1893-
    1939. Lang.: Eng.   2839

    Sourcebook of Irish playwrights. Ireland. 1880-1995. Lang.: Eng. 2933
    Pirandello's unfinished plays. Italy. 1886-1895. Lang.: Ita.   2943
    Repertory of titles of plays compiled in the eighteenth century. Italy.
    1795-1800. Lang.: Ita.   2948
    Arthur Miller bibliography. USA. 1940-1997. Lang.: Eng.   3203
    Bibliography of Tennessee Williams criticism. USA. 1963-1995. Lang.:
    Eng.   3242
  Reference materials
    Bibliography of recent Renaissance drama studies. Europe. North
    America. 1945-1996. Lang.: Eng.   712
    1992 Shakespeare bibliography. 1992. Lang.: Eng.   3312
    1994 Shakespeare bibliography. 1994. Lang.: Eng.   3313
    1993 Shakespeare bibliography. 1993. Lang.: Eng.   3314
    Annual bibliography of works by and about Harold Pinter. 1993-1994.
    Lang.: Eng.   3315
    1991 Shakespeare bibliography. 1991. Lang.: Eng.   3316
    1986 annual Shakespeare bibliography. 1986. Lang.: Eng.   3317
    Annual bibliography of modern drama studies. North America. 1899-
    1997. Lang.: Eng.   3318
    Sourcebook on women playwrights of diversity. USA. 1970-1996. Lang.:
    Eng.   3320
    Bibliography of Shakespearean film. USA. 1997. Lang.: Eng.   3689
    Bibliography of scripts for puppet plays in Slovene. Slovenia. 1942-1997.
    Lang.: Slo.   4382
Bienvenue, Yvan
  Institutions
    Profile of Quebec play publishing house Dramaturges Éditeurs. Canada.
    1996-1997. Lang.: Fre.   1398
  Plays/librettos/scripts
    Analysis of *Dits et Inédits (Tales and Unpublished Stories)* by Yvan
    Bienvenue. Canada: Montreal, PQ. 1997. Lang.: Fre.   2394
Bierbichler, Josef
  Performance/production
    Interview with actor Josef Bierbichler. Germany. 1985-1997. Lang.: Ger.
                                                                 1691
    Actor Josef Bierbichler. Germany: Hamburg. 1997. Lang.: Ger. 1707
Biermeier, Christoph
  Plays/librettos/scripts
    Account of new German plays with historical themes. Germany. 1997.
    Lang.: Ger.   2837
big face
  Basic theatrical documents
    Text of *big face* by Marion de Vries. Canada. 1995. Lang.: Eng. 1257
Big Girls
  Performance/production
    Collection of newspaper reviews by London theatre critics. UK-England.
    1997. Lang.: Eng.   2142
Big Knife, The
  Plays/librettos/scripts
    Analysis of *The Big Knife* by Clifford Odets. USA. 1930-1949. Lang.:
    Eng.   3302
Big River
  Design/technology
    A raft for use in a production of the musical *Big River*. USA. 1997.
    Lang.: Eng.   3923
Big White Fog
  Performance/production
    Black actors and writers and the Negro Units of the Federal Theatre
    Project. USA: Washington, DC, New York, NY. 1935. Lang.: Eng. 2350
Bijou Theatre (Boston, MA)
  Performance spaces
    History of the oft-renamed Bijou Theatre. USA: Boston, MA. 1836-
    1943. Lang.: Eng.   3765
Bikčantajév, Farid
  Performance/production
    Director Farid Bikčantajév of Teat'r im. Kamala. Russia: Kazan. 1997.
    Lang.: Rus.   1866
Bilabel, Barbara
  Performance/production
    Recent productions of plays by Schiller. Germany. 1996-1997. Lang.:
    Ger.   1716
Bildbeschreibung (Description of a Picture)
  Plays/librettos/scripts
    Analysis of Heiner Müller's *Bildbeschreibung (Description of a Picture)*.
    Germany. 1985. Lang.: Ger.   2850

Bilderback, Walter
Performance/production
Director and dramaturgs on translating, adapting and producing Molière's *Misanthrope*. USA: La Jolla, CA, Chicago, IL. 1989-1990. Lang.: Eng.						2263
Bílková, Marie
Performance/production
History of Czech puppet theatre. Czech Republic. 1912-1997. Lang.: Eng, Fre.						4362
Bill Graham Civic Auditorium (San Francisco, CA)
Design/technology
Sound design problems of San Francisco Opera's temporary home. USA: San Francisco, CA. 1996. Lang.: Eng.						4036
Bill of Divorcement, A
Performance/production
Collection of newspaper reviews by London theatre critics. UK-England: London. 1997. Lang.: Eng.						2153
Bill, Stephen
Plays/librettos/scripts
The relationship of creators and their work in devised theatre. UK-England. 1989. Lang.: Eng.						3083
Billington, Ken
Design/technology
Lighting designer Ken Billington. USA: New York, NY. 1997. Lang.: Eng.						3911
Billington, Michael
Performance/production
Collection of newspaper reviews by London theatre critics. UK-England: London. 1997. Lang.: Eng.						2036
Billington, Stephen
Performance/production
Interview with actor Stephen Billington. UK-England. 1997. Lang.: Eng.						3728
Billy Bishop Goes to War
Plays/librettos/scripts
Survey of one- or two-character musicals. USA: New York, NY. 1964-1997. Lang.: Eng.						3989
Billy Budd
Performance/production
Background on Britten's opera *Billy Budd*. England. 1797. Lang.: Eng.						4123
Lyric tenor Philip Langridge. UK-England: London. 1997. Lang.: Eng.						4225
Moral conflicts in Mozart's *Così fan tutte* and Britten's *Billy Budd*. UK-England. Austro-Hungarian Empire. 1790-1951. Lang.: Eng.						4228
Background material on Metropolitan Opera radio broadcast performances. USA: New York, NY. 1997. Lang.: Eng.						4238
Bilodeau, Emmanuel
Plays/librettos/scripts
Childhood fears in children's plays of Emmanuel Bilodeau and Réjane Charpentier. Canada: Montreal, PQ. 1996-1997. Lang.: Fre.						2420
Biloxi Blues
Performance/production
Collection of newspaper reviews by London theatre critics. UK-England: London. 1997. Lang.: Eng.						2099
Binder, Anton
Performance/production
Collection of newspaper reviews by London theatre critics. UK-England: London. 1997. Lang.: Eng.						2107
Binder, Ernst
Plays/librettos/scripts
Postwar German portrayals of customs in East and West Germany. Germany. 1945-1997. Lang.: Ger.						2860
Bing, Rudolf
Performance/production
Colleagues recall Metropolitan Opera general manager Rudolf Bing. USA: New York, NY. 1950-1972. Lang.: Eng.						4255
Rudolf Bing's tenure as general manager of the Metropolitan Opera. USA: New York, NY. 1950-1972. Lang.: Eng.						4266
Binkley, Howell
Design/technology
Howell Binkley's lighting design for *Taking Sides* by Ronald Harwood. USA: New York, NY. 1997. Lang.: Eng.						1366
Howell Binkley's lighting design for *Whistle Down the Wind* at the National Theatre. USA: Washington, DC. 1997. Lang.: Eng.						3920
Binnie, John
Performance/production
Collection of newspaper reviews by London theatre critics. UK-England: London. 1997. Lang.: Eng.						1995

Binns, Mitch
Performance/production
Collection of newspaper reviews by London theatre critics. UK-England: London. 1997. Lang.: Eng.						2016
Bird, Dorothy
Performance/production
Dancer Dorothy Bird and her work with Martha Graham. USA: New York, NY. 1930-1937. Lang.: Eng.						1121
Bird's Nest Theatre (London)
Performance/production
Collection of newspaper reviews by London theatre critics. UK-England: London. 1997. Lang.: Eng.						1996
Collection of newspaper reviews by London theatre critics. UK-England: London. 1997. Lang.: Eng.						2139
Birdy
Performance/production
Collection of newspaper reviews by London theatre critics. UK-England: London. 1997. Lang.: Eng.						2009
Birkenhead, Susan
Performance/production
Singer/actress Susan Egan. USA: New York, NY. 1991-1997. Lang.: Eng.						3976
Birmingham Repertory Theatre
Performance/production
Collection of newspaper reviews by London theatre critics. UK-England. 1997. Lang.: Eng.						2050
Shakespearean production before national subsidy. UK-England. 1914-1959. Lang.: Eng.						2175
Birth of Pleasure, The
Performance/production
Collection of newspaper reviews by London theatre critics. UK-England: London. 1997. Lang.: Eng.						2139
Birthday Party, The
Plays/librettos/scripts
Mystery in the plays of Harold Pinter. UK-England. 1965-1995. Lang.: Eng.						3092
Linguistic analysis of plays by Delaney, Pinter, Orton, and Gems. UK-England. 1956-1984. Lang.: Spa.						3100
Bischoff, Thomas
Performance/production
Performances at Staattheater Mainz's new venue. Germany: Mainz. 1997. Lang.: Ger.						1743
Bishop, André
Performance/production
Interviews on acting with actors, teachers, and directors. USA. 1997. Lang.: Eng.						2352
André Bishop, artistic director of Lincoln Center Theatre, and his personal reactions to opera. USA: New York, NY. 1997. Lang.: Eng.						4248
Bishop, Henry
Performance/production
Performances of Shakespeare's *Twelfth Night* as objects of study. England. 1808-1850. Lang.: Eng.						508
BITEF (Belgrade)
Performance/production
Report from Belgrade International Theatre Festival. Serbia: Belgrade. 1996. Lang.: Swe.						1902
Bixby, Meredith
Performance/production
Marionette artist Meredith Bixby. USA: Detroit, MI, New York, NY. 1930-1997. Lang.: Eng.						4391
Bizet, Georges
Design/technology
Giuseppe Di Iorio's lighting designs for the English Touring Opera. UK-England. 1997. Lang.: Eng.						4032
Performance/production
Interview with ballerina Gabriela Komleva. Russia: St. Petersburg. 1997. Lang.: Eng.						1101
Interview with dancer Sergej Vicharév. Russia: St. Petersburg. 1997. Lang.: Eng.						1102
The popularity of Balanchine's choreography to Bizet's *Symphony in C*. Russia. 1997. Lang.: Eng.						1103
Beijing production of Carmen's *Bizet*. China, People's Republic of: Beijing. 1982-1997. Lang.: Eng.						4117
Interpreters of Bizet's heroine Carmen. France: Paris. USA: New York, NY. 1875-1997. Lang.: Eng.						4139
Soprano Waltraud Meier. Germany. 1957-1997. Lang.: Eng.						4153

Bizet, Georges — cont'd

Background material on Metropolitan Opera telecast performance. USA: New York, NY. 1997. Lang.: Eng.   4233

Background material on Metropolitan Opera radio broadcast performances. USA: New York, NY. 1997. Lang.: Eng.   4238

Plays/librettos/scripts

Representations of the Orient in nineteenth-century French opera. France. 1863-1894. Lang.: Eng.   4290

Björling, Jussi
Institutions

Profile of the Jussi Björling Museum. Sweden: Borlänge. 1994. Lang.: Swe.   4056

Björnson, Björn
Performance/production

Collection of newspaper reviews by London theatre critics. UK-England: London. 1997. Lang.: Eng.   1994

Black Bread and Cucumber
Performance/production

Collection of newspaper reviews by London theatre critics. UK-England: London. 1997. Lang.: Eng.   1984

Black Dove
Performance/production

Collection of newspaper reviews by London theatre critics. UK-England: London. 1997. Lang.: Eng.   2047

Black Mime Theatre (London)
Performance/production

Collection of newspaper reviews by London theatre critics. UK-England: London. 1997. Lang.: Eng.   2020

Black Revolutionary Theatre (New York, NY)
Performance/production

The social protest theatre of Luis Valdez and Amiri Baraka. USA. 1965-1975. Lang.: Eng.   2260

Black Rider, The
Performance/production

Interview with director Richard Günther. Sweden: Stockholm. 1990-1997. Lang.: Swe.   3943

Plays/librettos/scripts

Nature in Apel's *Der Freischütz* and its operatic adaptations. Germany. 1811-1990. Lang.: Ger.   2856

Black Star Line, The
Performance/production

The Goodman Theatre production of *The Black Star Line* by Charles Goodman. USA: Chicago, IL. 1997. Lang.: Eng.   2278

Black theatre
SEE ALSO

African-American theatre.

Performance/production

Race, gender, and nation in nineteenth-century performance. USA. Europe. 1855-1902. Lang.: Eng.   633

Jazz music and dance in Paris. France. 1920-1930. Lang.: Eng.   963

Profile of actor Ray Fearon. UK-England: London. 1997. Lang.: Eng.   2185

Township musical, the Black musical theatre genre. South Africa, Republic of. 1976-1994. Lang.: Eng.   3941

Plays/librettos/scripts

Interview with playwright Wole Soyinka. Nigeria. 1986-1996. Lang.: Eng.   2980

Black Woman Speaks, A
Plays/librettos/scripts

The evolution of solo performance in African-American one-person plays. USA. 1972-1996. Lang.: Eng.   3293

Black, Don
Performance/production

Collection of newspaper reviews by London theatre critics. UK-England: London. 1997. Lang.: Eng.   2032

Blackfriars Theatre (London)
Institutions

Record of Shakespearean studies seminar. USA: New York, NY. England. 1997. Lang.: Eng.   1514

Performance spaces

Early modern performance spaces. England. 1600-1650. Lang.: Eng.   424

Performance/production

John Marston and children's theatres. England. 1598-1634. Lang.: Eng.   1631

Shakespeare on the Jacobean and Caroline stage. England. 1605-1640. Lang.: Eng.   1637

Relation to other fields

The staging and reception of *The Knight of the Burning Pestle*. England: London. 1607. Lang.: Eng.   3331

Blake, Simon
Performance/production

Collection of newspaper reviews by London theatre critics. UK-England: London. 1997. Lang.: Eng.   2083

Blakeman, Helen
Performance/production

Collection of newspaper reviews by London theatre critics. UK-England: London. 1997. Lang.: Eng.   2139

Blakiston, Caroline
Performance/production

Collection of newspaper reviews by London theatre critics. UK-England: London. 1997. Lang.: Eng.   1984

Blanc, Dominique
Performance/production

Report on the Paris theatre scene. France: Paris. 1997. Lang.: Swe.   1680

Blankenship, Beverly
Performance/production

Recent productions of plays by Schiller. Germany. 1996-1997. Lang.: Ger.   1716

Blasis, Carlo
Performance/production

Carlo Blasis and the male dancer in Italian ballet. Italy. 1830-1850. Lang.: Eng.   1097

Blatchley, Joseph
Performance/production

Collection of newspaper reviews by London theatre critics. UK-England: London. 1997. Lang.: Eng.   2101

Blattner, Géza
Performance/production

Géza Blattner's puppet adaptation of *Az ember tragédiája (The Tragedy of Man)* by Madách. Hungary. 1918-1954. Lang.: Hun.   4365

Blau, Eric
Performance/production

Production of *Jacques Brel Is Alive and Well...*, California State University. USA: Long Beach, CA. 1996. Lang.: Eng.   3955

Blaue Engel, Der (Blue Angel, The)
Performance/production

Film actor Emil Jannings. Germany. 1929-1945. Lang.: Eng.   3574

Blessing, Lee
Performance/production

Collection of newspaper reviews by London theatre critics. UK-England: London. 1997. Lang.: Eng.   2106

Plays/librettos/scripts

Lacanian reading of plays by Lee Blessing. USA. 1989-1991. Lang.: Eng.   3140

Blithe Spirit
Performance/production

Collection of newspaper reviews by London theatre critics. UK-England. 1997. Lang.: Eng.   2058

Block, Simon
Performance/production

Collection of newspaper reviews by London theatre critics. UK-England: London. 1997. Lang.: Eng.   2083

Blok, Aleksand'r Aleksandrovič
Performance/production

Survey of recent dance performances. USA: New York, NY. 1997. Lang.: Eng.   1001

Blood and Ice
Performance/production

Collection of newspaper reviews by London theatre critics. UK-England: London. 1997. Lang.: Eng.   1980

Blood Relations
Plays/librettos/scripts

Historical background of *Blood Relations* by Sharon Pollock. Canada. 1892-1997. Lang.: Eng.   2438

Feminism and murder in plays of Wendy Kesselman and Sharon Pollock. USA. Canada. 1982-1984. Lang.: Eng.   3286

Bloomsbury Theatre (London)
Performance/production

Collection of newspaper reviews by London theatre critics. UK-England: London. 1997. Lang.: Eng.   2099

Blow Your House Down
Plays/librettos/scripts

Role playing in feminist theatre. UK-England. 1982-1995. Lang.: Eng.   3090

Blue Garden, The
Performance/production

Collection of newspaper reviews by London theatre critics. UK-England: London. 1997. Lang.: Eng.   2067

Blue Heart
Institutions
Impressions of the Edinburgh Festival. UK-Scotland: Edinburgh. 1997.
Lang.: Ger. 391

Blue Kettle
Performance/production
Collection of newspaper reviews by London theatre critics. UK-England:
London. 1997. Lang.: Eng. 2105

Productions of plays by Caryl Churchill. UK-Scotland: Edinburgh. UK-
England: London. 1997. Lang.: Eng. 2233

Bluebeard
Performance/production
Tony Kushner's *Angels in America* in the context of queer performance.
USA. 1992-1994. Lang.: Eng. 2245

Bluebeard's Castle
SEE
Kékszakállú herceg vára, A.

Blues Are Running, The
Design/technology
Work of lighting designer Kenneth Posner. USA: New York, NY. 1997.
Lang.: Eng. 1364

Blues for an Alabama Sky
Plays/librettos/scripts
Black female culture in plays of Pearl Cleage. USA: Atlanta, GA. 1992-
1997. Lang.: Eng. 3197

Blume, Bernhard
Performance/production
Significant productions in Swabia. Germany: Stuttgart. 1997. Lang.: Ger.
1726

Boadella, Albert
Performance/production
Politics in Barcelona theatre. Spain: Barcelona. 1996. Lang.: Eng. 608

Catalan drama on the Madrid stage. Spain: Madrid. 1996. Lang.: Eng.
1919

Boal, Augusto
Performance/production
Use of Boal's 'joker' system in a production of Euripides' *Bákchai (The
Bacchae)*. USA. 1995-1996. Lang.: Eng. 632

Augusto Boal's forum theatre and the transformation of gender scripts.
USA. 1997. Lang.: Eng. 650
Relation to other fields
Theatre of the Oppressed in the classroom. USA. 1994-1996. Lang.:
Eng. 844
Theory/criticism
The role of the pre-interpretive in theatrical reception. 1977-1993.
Lang.: Eng. 859

Spirituality and consciousness in Western theatre. Europe. North
America. 1900-1996. Lang.: Eng. 3480

Board, Rachel
Performance/production
Collection of newspaper reviews by London theatre critics. UK-England:
London. 1997. Lang.: Eng. 2087

Boards of directors
Administration
The fiduciary responsibilities of nonprofit boards. USA. 1997. Lang.:
Eng. 58

Brainstorming techniques for boards of directors. USA. 1997. Lang.:
Eng. 80
Institutions
Alvin Ailey American Dance Theatre: how it achieved stability after
Ailey's death. USA: New York, NY. 1989-1997. Lang.: Eng. 1168

Bob-in-a-Box Puppet Theatre (Ft. Wayne, IN)
Institutions
Profile of Bob-in-a-Box Puppet Theatre. USA: Ft. Wayne, IN. 1997.
Lang.: Eng. 4358

Bobbie, Walter
Performance/production
Collection of newspaper reviews by London theatre critics. UK-England:
London. 1997. Lang.: Eng. 2140

Collection of newspaper reviews by London theatre critics. UK-England:
London. 1997. Lang.: Eng. 2161

Profile of director Walter Bobbie. USA. UK-England. 1971-1997. Lang.:
Eng. 3971

Bochumer Schauspielhaus (Bochum)
Performance/production
Interview with actor/director Leander Haussmann on Brecht's influence.
Germany: Bochum. 1997. Lang.: Ger. 1694

Reviews of Bochumer Schauspielhaus productions. Germany: Bochum.
1997. Lang.: Ger. 1730

The style of productions at Bochumer Schauspielhaus. Germany:
Bochum. 1995-1997. Lang.: Ger. 1732

The new season at Bochumer Schauspielhaus. Germany: Bochum. 1997.
Lang.: Ger. 1747

Non-literary realism in Shakespeare productions. UK-England.
Germany. 1958-1995. Lang.: Ger. 2170

Bodas de sangre (Blood Wedding)
Performance/production
Hanan Snir's productions of Lorca's *Blood Wedding (Bodas de sangre)*.
Israel: Tel Aviv. 1990. Lang.: Eng. 1791
Plays/librettos/scripts
Analysis of *Bodas de sangre (Blood Wedding)* and *Yerma* by Federico
García Lorca. Spain. 1920-1936. Lang.: Eng. 3050

Bode, Rudolf
Training
The gymnastic training methods of Rudolf Bode. Germany. 1881-1971.
Lang.: Ita. 1042

Bodinetz, Gemma
Performance/production
Collection of newspaper reviews by London theatre critics. UK-England:
London. 1997. Lang.: Eng. 1987

Collection of newspaper reviews by London theatre critics. UK-England:
London. 1997. Lang.: Eng. 2083

Collection of newspaper reviews by London theatre critics. UK-England:
London. 1997. Lang.: Eng. 2139

Bodyguard, The
Plays/librettos/scripts
Sam Shepard's unproduced film adaptation of *The Changeling* by
Middleton and Rowley. England. USA. 1622-1971. Lang.: Eng. 2490

Bogaev, Oleg
Plays/librettos/scripts
Profile of young Russian playwrights. Russia: Moscow. 1960-1997.
Lang.: Swe. 2993

Bogart, Anne
Design/technology
Mimi Jordan Sherin's lighting design and use of old instruments for
American Silents and *The Medium*. USA: New York, NY. 1997. Lang.:
Eng. 1379
Performance/production
Interview with dramaturg Gregory Gunter on his collaboration with
Anne Bogart. USA. 1995-1997. Lang.: Eng. 2275

Anne Bogart's production of Strindberg's *Miss Julie* at Actors' Theatre.
USA: Louisville, KY. 1888-1997. Lang.: Eng. 2283

The use of silent films in theatrical productions. USA: New York, NY.
1997. Lang.: Eng. 2342
Plays/librettos/scripts
East Asian influences on writing and directing of Anne Bogart. USA.
1984-1994. Lang.: Eng. 3223

Bogdanov, Gennadij
Training
Gennadij Bogdanov's workshop on biomechanics, Sotenäs Teateratelje.
Russia. Sweden. 1920-1996. Lang.: Swe. 932

Bogdanov, Vladimir
Performance/production
Notes from the actors' master class of Jévgenij Ganelin and Vladimir
Bogdanov. Russia: St. Petersburg. 1960-1997. Lang.: Rus. 1868

Bogosian, Eric
Design/technology
Lighting design for film adaptation of Eric Bogosian's *subUrbia*. USA.
1997. Lang.: Eng. 3545
Performance/production
Collection of newspaper reviews by London theatre critics. UK-England.
1997. Lang.: Eng. 2092
Plays/librettos/scripts
Analysis of plays by Eric Bogosian and Matéi Visniec. USA. Romania.
1997. Lang.: Fre. 3199

Subjectivity, ethics, and the body in contemporary drama. USA. Europe.
1940-1990. Lang.: Eng. 3229

Film adaptation of Eric Bogosian's *Talk Radio*. USA: Hollywood, CA.
1988. Lang.: Eng. 3673

Boguslawski, Wojciech
Plays/librettos/scripts
The image of Lvov in Polish drama. Poland. 1700-1939. Lang.: Pol. 697

Bohème, La
Performance/production
The influence of Mascagni, Leoncavallo, and Franchetti on Puccini's *La
Bohème*. Italy: Milan. 1894-1898. Lang.: Eng. 4190

Bohème, La — cont'd

Background material on New York City Opera telecast performance of *La Bohème*. USA: New York, NY. 1997. Lang.: Eng. 4230

Background material on Metropolitan Opera radio broadcast performances. USA: New York, NY. 1997. Lang.: Eng. 4238

A child's first visit to the Metropolitan Opera. USA: New York, NY. 1988-1997. Lang.: Eng. 4246

New York City Opera's seventy-city tour of *La Bohème*. USA. 1994. Lang.: Eng. 4264

Plays/librettos/scripts
Direct address in *Don Giovanni* and *La Bohème*. Italy. 1864-1881. Lang.: Eng. 4308

Bohmler, Craig
Performance/production
Collection of newspaper reviews by London theatre critics. UK-England: London. 1997. Lang.: Eng. 2103

Bohner, Gerhard
Performance/production
Gerhard Bohner's choreography *Angst & Geometrie (Fear and Geomety)*. Germany. 1936-1997. Lang.: Ger. 971

Boieldieu, François Adrien
Basic theatrical documents
Scribe's libretto for Boieldieu's opera *La Dame Blanche*. France. 1825. Lang.: Fre. 4009
Performance/production
Productions of Boieldieu's *La Dame Blanche*. 1825-1997. Lang.: Fre. 4074

Listing and evaluation of complete recordings of Boieldieu's *La Dame Blanche*. 1961-1996. Lang.: Fre. 4091

Interview with conductor Marc Minkowski. Europe. 1997. Lang.: Fre. 4124
Plays/librettos/scripts
Franz Liszt's comments on *La Dame Blanche* by Boieldieu. Europe. 1825-1854. Lang.: Fre. 4288

Boilerhouse Theatre (London)
Performance/production
Collection of newspaper reviews by London theatre critics. UK-England: London. 1997. Lang.: Eng. 2080

Boito, Arrigo
Plays/librettos/scripts
Analysis of opera librettos by Boito, Da Ponte, and Gertrude Stein. Europe. 1770-1915. Lang.: Eng. 4289

Bojarčikov, N.
Performance/production
Interview with N. Bojarčikov, chief ballet instructor of the Mussorgskij Theatre. Russia: St. Petersburg. 1990-1997. Lang.: Rus. 1105

Bolger, Dermot
Plays/librettos/scripts
Analysis of *The Lament for Arthur Cleary* by Dermot Bolger. Ireland. 1984-1989. Lang.: Eng. 2927

Bolshoi Theatre (Leningrad/St. Petersburg)
SEE
Bolšoj Dramatičéskij Teat'r.

Bolshoi Theatre (Moscow)
SEE
Gosudarstvénnyj Akademičéskij Bolšoj Teat'r.

Bolšoj Dramatičéskij Teat'r im. G.A. Tovstonogova (St. Petersburg)
Performance/production
Bolšoj Drama Theatre production of Anouilh's *Antigone*. Russia: St. Petersburg. 1996. Lang.: Rus. 1862

Actor P.P. Pankov of the Bolšoj Drama Theatre. Russia: St. Petersburg. 1970-1997. Lang.: Rus. 1880

Actress Zinajda Šarko on the work of director G.A. Tovstonogov. Russia: St. Petersburg. 1960-1989. Lang.: Rus. 1891

Anouilh's *Antigone* at the Bolšoj Drama Theatre. Russia: St. Petersburg. 1996. Lang.: Rus. 1897

Bolšoj Dramatičéskij Teat'r im. M. Gorkogo (BDT, St. Petersburg)
Institutions
Departure of Bolšoj Theatre's artistic director Jurij Grigorovič. Russia: St. Petersburg. 1997. Lang.: Eng. 1454

Bolt, Ranjit
Performance/production
Collection of newspaper reviews by London theatre critics. UK-England: London. 1997. Lang.: Eng. 2025

Bolton, Simon
Performance/production
Collection of newspaper reviews by London theatre critics. UK-England: London. 1997. Lang.: Eng. 2004

Boncza, Tony
Performance/production
Collection of newspaper reviews by London theatre critics. UK-England: London. 1997. Lang.: Eng. 2034

Bond, Edward
Performance/production
Collection of newspaper reviews by London theatre critics. UK-England: London. 1997. Lang.: Eng. 2056
Plays/librettos/scripts
Greek myth in contemporary drama. 1970-1990. Lang.: Eng. 2369

Shakespearean themes in contemporary plays and productions. Europe. 1965-1995. Lang.: Pol. 2798

Interview with playwright Edward Bond. UK-England. 1966-1996. Lang.: Eng. 3094

Nō and *kabuki* elements in plays of Edward Bond. UK-England. 1980-1990. Lang.: Eng. 3105

Letters of playwright Edward Bond. UK-England. 1984-1994. Lang.: Eng. 3112

Bond, Karen
Performance/production
Report on dance research seminar. Finland. 1997. Lang.: Fin. 962

Bondarenko, V.
Performance/production
Portraits of actors in children's theatre. Russia: Volgograd. 1990-1997. Lang.: Rus. 589

Bondman, The
Plays/librettos/scripts
Social mobility in Jacobean drama. England. 1618-1640. Lang.: Eng. 2745

Bonduca
Plays/librettos/scripts
Masculine and feminine in *Bonduca* by John Fletcher. England. 1613. Lang.: Eng. 2488

Bondy, Luc
Performance/production
Interview with director Luc Bondy. Germany. France. 1948-1997. Lang.: Ger. 1684

Bonito, Eduardo
Performance/production
Collection of newspaper reviews by London theatre critics. UK-England: London. 1997. Lang.: Eng. 2103

Bonner, Marita
Plays/librettos/scripts
The theme of hope in postwar American theatre and writing. USA. 1914-1929. Lang.: Eng. 3153

Bonnes, Les (Maids, The)
Performance/production
Collection of newspaper reviews by London theatre critics. UK-England: London. 1997. Lang.: Eng. 2068

Bonté, Patrick
Performance/production
Collection of newspaper reviews by London theatre critics. UK-England: London. 1997. Lang.: Eng. 1988

Booker, Margaret
Performance/production
Margaret Booker on directing August Wilson's *Fences* in Beijing. China, People's Republic of: Beijing. 1983-1997. Lang.: Eng. 1608

Bookman, Kirk
Design/technology
Kirk Bookman's lighting design for *The Gin Game* directed by Charles Nelson Reilly. USA: New York, NY. 1978-1997. Lang.: Eng. 1368

Booth, Edwin
Performance/production
Northern and southern reactions to Edwin Booth's production of Shakespeare's *Richard II*. USA. 1865-1875. Lang.: Eng. 675

Boothe, Clare
SEE
Luce, Clare Boothe.

Bopha!
Performance/production
Township musical, the Black musical theatre genre. South Africa, Republic of. 1976-1994. Lang.: Eng. 3941

Borchardt, Rudolf
Institutions
Recent productions of Schaubühne. Germany: Berlin. 1996-1997. Lang.: Ger. 1426

Borchert, Wolfgang
Performance/production
Director Andreas Kriegenburg. Germany. 1985-1997. Lang.: Ger. 1717

Brecht, Bertolt — cont'd

Performance/production

Twentieth-century theatre as a signifying practice. Europe. North America. 1900-1995. Lang.: Eng.   515

Major productions of the Vienna theatre season. Austria: Vienna. 1997. Lang.: Ger.   1563

Interview with director George Tabori about Bertolt Brecht. Europe. North America. 1947-1997. Lang.: Eng.   1645

The history of *Mutter Courage und ihre Kinder (Mother Courage and Her Children)* by Bertolt Brecht. Europe. USA. Africa. 1949-1995. Lang.: Eng.   1651

Materialism in Brecht's plays and a Piccolo Teatro performance. France: Paris. Italy: Milan. 1977. Lang.: Eng.   1656

Roger Planchon's production of *Georges Dandin* by Molière. France: Villeurbanne. 1958. Lang.: Pol.   1675

Interview with actor/director Leander Haussmann on Brecht's influence. Germany: Bochum. 1997. Lang.: Ger.   1694

The 'deconstructive potential' of Brecht's own production of *Mother Courage*. Germany: Berlin. 1949. Lang.: Ger.   1696

Einar Schleef's Berliner Ensemble production of Brecht's *Herr Puntila*. Germany: Berlin. 1996. Lang.: Ger.   1701

Brecht's production of *Mother Courage*. Germany: Berlin. 1949. Lang.: Pol.   1740

I Magazzini's production of Brecht's *Im Dickicht der Städte (In the Jungle of Cities)*. Italy: Messina. 1995. Lang.: Ita.   1804

Federico Tiezzi's production of Brecht's *Im Dickicht der Städte (In the Jungle of Cities)*. Italy: Messina. 1995. Lang.: Ita.   1807

Contrast and comparison of Eastern and Western acting styles. Japan. Europe. 1150-1997. Lang.: Eng.   1822

Productions of the International Istanbul Theatre Festival. Turkey: Istanbul. 1980-1997. Lang.: Eng.   1966

Collection of newspaper reviews by London theatre critics. UK-England: London. 1997. Lang.: Eng.   2034

Collection of newspaper reviews by London theatre critics. UK-England: London. 1997. Lang.: Eng.   2065

Collection of newspaper reviews by London theatre critics. UK-England: London. 1997. Lang.: Eng.   2130

The influence of Ibsen and Brecht on Shakespearean staging. UK-England. 1900-1960. Lang.: Eng.   2180

Simon McBurney on his production of *The Caucasian Chalk Circle*, Théâtre de Complicité. UK-England: London. 1983-1997. Lang.: Eng.   2218

Bertolt Brecht's influence on Richard Foreman. USA. 1950-1997. Lang.: Eng.   2239

The world premiere of Brecht's *The Caucasian Chalk Circle*. USA: Northfield, MN. 1948. Lang.: Eng.   2253

Interview with director JoAnne Akalaitis. USA. 1970-1996. Lang.: Eng.   2331

The dramaturg and cultural and political affairs. USA. 1997. Lang.: Eng.   2334

HK Gruber on songs of Kurt Weill. Germany. 1997. Lang.: Eng.   3933

Kurt Weill's collaborations with playwrights. Germany: Berlin. USA: New York, NY. 1927-1945. Lang.: Eng.   3934

Plays/librettos/scripts

Asian influence on European theatre. Europe. Asia. 1915-1997. Lang.: Pol.   694

Contemporary playwrights and the adaptation process. Europe. 1900-1993. Lang.: Ita.   2793

Dialectical interaction and visual perception in Ibsen, Strindberg, and Brecht. Europe. 1900-1956. Lang.: Eng.   2797

Portrayals of colonial governor Warren Hastings in plays of Feuchtwanger and Brecht. Germany. 1916-1927. Lang.: Eng.   2836

Brecht, Müller, and the cigar. Germany: Berlin. 1923-1996. Lang.: Eng.   2838

Brecht's influence on the plays of Howard Barker. UK-England. 1987-1997. Lang.: Eng.   3084

Interview with playwright Edward Bond. UK-England. 1966-1996. Lang.: Eng.   3094

Mimesis, feminism, theatre, and performance. USA. 1997. Lang.: Eng.   3176

Interview with playwright Tony Kushner on the influence of Brecht. USA. 1997. Lang.: Ger.   3300

Analysis of plays shown on Polish television. Poland. 1929-1997. Lang.: Pol.   3735

Relation to other fields

Bertolt Brecht and South African political theatre. South Africa, Republic of. 1930-1997. Lang.: Ger.   777

The Communist view of Brecht. Germany: Berlin. 1920-1956. Lang.: Ger.   3351

Brecht's disgust with bureaucracy and political quarrels. Germany: Berlin. 1943-1956. Lang.: Ger.   3352

Interview with novelist Günter Grass about Bertolt Brecht. Germany: Berlin. 1953-1997. Lang.: Ger.   3353

The influence of Carlo Schmitt on the plays of Bertolt Brecht. Germany. 1920-1940. Lang.: Ger.   3354

Brecht as an expatriate. Germany. USA. 1933-1947. Lang.: Ger.   3355

Brecht and Stalin. USSR. 1932-1954. Lang.: Ger.   3443

Theory/criticism

Brecht and Hip-Hop. Europe. 1993-1997. Lang.: Ger.   879

Signs in theatrical representation. France. 1977. Lang.: Eng.   890

Brecht's misunderstanding of Chinese theatre as interpreted by Mei Lanfang. Germany. 1925-1959. Lang.: Eng.   900

Brecht's concept of 'Gestus'. Europe. 1934-1997. Lang.: Ger.   3481

Magic as defining trope of modern drama. Europe. 1910-1950. Lang.: Eng.   3482

Breeze, Areta

Performance/production

Collection of newspaper reviews by London theatre critics. UK-England: London. 1997. Lang.: Eng.   1967

Bregenzer Festspiele (Bregenz)

Performance/production

Götz Friedrich's production of Gershwin's *Porgy and Bess*. Austria: Bregenz. 1997. Lang.: Eng.   4098

Bregvadze, Boris

Performance/production

Budapest production of the ballet *Don Quijote* by Marius Petipa and Leon Minkus. Hungary: Budapest. 1997. Lang.: Hun.   1083

Bremer Schauspielhaus (Bremen)

Institutions

Interview with Klaus Pierwoss of Bremer Schauspielhaus. Germany: Bremen. 1997. Lang.: Ger.   1413

Bremer Shakespeare Company (Bremen)

Performance/production

Interview with Norbert Kentrup of Bremer Shakespeare Company. Germany: Bremen. 1983-1997. Lang.: Ger.   540

Bremer Theater (Bremen)

Administration

Profile of Bremer Theater. Germany: Bremen. 1981-1997. Lang.: Ger.   31

Performance/production

Recent productions of plays by Schiller. Germany. 1996-1997. Lang.: Ger.   1716

Brene, José

Plays/librettos/scripts

The 'Black Madonna' in Cuban theatre. Cuba. 1925-1990. Lang.: Spa.   2444

Brenko, Anna

Performance/production

Actress Anna Brenko of Malyj Teat'r. Russia: Moscow. 1849-1934. Lang.: Rus.   1890

Brennan, Ray

Performance/production

Collection of newspaper reviews by London theatre critics. UK-England: London. 1997. Lang.: Eng.   2089

Brenner, Matthias

Performance/production

Actor and director Matthias Brenner. Germany. 1996-1997. Lang.: Ger.   1724

Brenton, Howard

Plays/librettos/scripts

Twentieth-century adaptations of Jacobean plays. England. 1604-1986. Lang.: Eng.   2673

Brešan, Ivo

Plays/librettos/scripts

Shakespearean themes in contemporary plays and productions. Europe. 1965-1995. Lang.: Pol.   2798

Breth, Andrea

Institutions

Recent productions of Schaubühne. Germany: Berlin. 1996-1997. Lang.: Ger.   1426

Broadway theatre — cont'd

Lighting design for *Show Boat*, Gershwin Theatre. USA: New York, NY. 1994. Lang.: Eng.   3922

Beverly Emmons' lighting design for the Broadway musical *Jekyll & Hyde*. USA: New York, NY. 1886-1997. Lang.: Eng.   3924

Amplified sound and the Broadway musical. USA. 1961-1997. Lang.: Eng.   3925

Institutions
The impact of the Disney Corporation on Broadway. USA: New York, NY. 1990-1997. Lang.: Eng.   400

Performance spaces
The New Amsterdam Theatre and the redevelopment of Times Square. USA: New York, NY. 1920-1997. Lang.: Eng.   454

Profile of Broadway's New Amsterdam Theatre. USA: New York, NY. 1903-1997. Lang.: Eng.   456

Performance/production
The public persona of actress Mae West. USA. 1913-1943. Lang.: Eng.   642

Transcript of seminar by actor Frank Langella. USA. 1997. Lang.: Eng.   661

Early modern interpretations of Aristophanes' *Lysistrata*. Europe. USA. 1892-1930. Lang.: Eng.   1647

Tennessee Williams on Broadway—critical response. USA: New York, NY. 1944-1982. Lang.: Eng.   2314

Reconstruction of Elia Kazan's production of *A Streetcar Named Desire* by Tennessee Williams. USA: New York, NY. 1947. Lang.: Pol.   2330

Broadway and musical film dancer Marilyn Miller. USA. 1929. Lang.: Eng.   3620

The development of *Play On!*, a musical adaptation of Shakespeare's *Twelfth Night*. USA: New York, NY. 1997. Lang.: Eng.   3953

Profile of actor Luoyong Wang. USA: New York, NY. 1984-1997. Lang.: Eng.   3967

Broadway orchestrator Luther Henderson. USA: New York, NY. 1997. Lang.: Eng.   3973

Marc Anthony's role in *The Capeman*. USA. 1968-1997. Lang.: Eng.   3977

Plays/librettos/scripts
Playwright Alfred Uhry. USA. 1987-1996. Lang.: Eng.   3278

Analysis of Sam Shepard's revisions to *Buried Child*. USA. 1975-1996. Lang.: Eng.   3282

Analysis of *Only the Heart* by Horton Foote. USA. 1943. Lang.: Eng.   3307

Interviews with authors of Tony Award-winning shows. USA: New York, NY. 1997. Lang.: Eng.   3985

Parody and satire in musical theatre. USA. UK-England. 1727-1990. Lang.: Eng.   3986

Survey of musical adaptations of Shakespeare. USA: New York, NY. 1938-1997. Lang.: Eng.   3987

Survey of one- or two-character musicals. USA: New York, NY. 1964-1997. Lang.: Eng.   3989

Bring in 'Da Noise, Bring in 'Da Funk and the Black audience. USA: New York, NY. 1996-1997. Lang.: Eng.   4002

Reference materials
Almanac of American theatre. USA. 1870-1995. Lang.: Eng.   3321

Broberg, Kerste

Administration
Protests against budget cuts affecting children's theatre. Sweden: Gothenburg. 1997. Lang.: Swe.   50

Brockley Jack Theatre (London)

Performance/production
Collection of newspaper reviews by London theatre critics. UK-England: London. 1997. Lang.: Eng.   2065

Collection of newspaper reviews by London theatre critics. UK-England: London. 1997. Lang.: Eng.   2107

Broderick, John

Design/technology
John Broderick's lighting design for the rock band Metallica. USA. 1988-1997. Lang.: Eng.   269

Brodjacaja sobaka (St. Petersburg)

Institutions
Profile of the literary-artistic cabaret Brodjacaja sobaka. Russia: St. Petersburg. 1912-1915. Lang.: Rus.   3778

Brodsky, Joseph

Performance/production
Productions of *Demokracija (Democracy)* by Joseph Brodsky. Russia. 1988-1995. Lang.: Eng.   1892

Broken Glass

Plays/librettos/scripts
Recent work of playwright Arthur Miller. USA. 1990-1997. Lang.: Eng.   3145

Broken Heart, The

Performance/production
Student production of John Ford's *The Broken Heart*. Australia: La Trobe. 1997. Lang.: Eng.   1559

Plays/librettos/scripts
John Ford's *The Broken Heart* and the prose of Sir Philip Sidney. England. 1629. Lang.: Eng.   2582

Brolly, Tristan

Performance/production
Collection of newspaper reviews by London theatre critics. UK-England: London. 1997. Lang.: Eng.   2131

Brome, Richard

Plays/librettos/scripts
Female homoeroticism on the early English stage. England. 1594-1632. Lang.: Eng.   2482

Theatrical reflections of the marital double standard. England. 1598-1650. Lang.: Eng.   2501

Brontë, Charlotte

Performance/production
Collection of newspaper reviews by London theatre critics. UK-England: London. 1997. Lang.: Eng.   2111

Brontë, Emily

Performance/production
Collection of newspaper reviews by London theatre critics. UK-England: London. 1997. Lang.: Eng.   1983

Brook, Peter

Performance/production
Twentieth-century theatre as a signifying practice. Europe. North America. 1900-1995. Lang.: Eng.   515

Analysis of Jerzy Grotowski's Collège de France lecture at Théâtre aux Bouffes du Nord. France: Paris. 1997. Lang.: Eng.   532

The map of England in productions of Shakespeare's *King Lear*. Europe. USA. 1909-1994. Lang.: Eng.   1650

Collection of newspaper reviews by London theatre critics. UK-England: London. 1997. Lang.: Eng.   2145

Peter Brook's production *The Mahabharata*. UK-England. France. 1985. Lang.: Pol.   2164

Non-literary realism in Shakespeare productions. UK-England. Germany. 1958-1995. Lang.: Ger.   2170

Elizabethan stage semiotics in twentieth-century Shakespearean productions. UK-England. 1905-1979. Lang.: Eng.   2203

Productions of Shakespeare's *Titus Andronicus*. UK-England. USA. 1955-1995. Lang.: Hun.   2225

Peter Brook's RSC production of Shakespeare's *King Lear*. UK-England: Stratford, London. 1970. Lang.: Pol.   2228

The television adaptation of Shakespeare's *King Lear* by Peter Brook and Orson Welles. USA. 1953. Lang.: Eng.   3730

Plays/librettos/scripts
Brook, Mnouchkine and intercultural theatre. France: Paris. 1988-1992. Lang.: Eng.   2832

Theory/criticism
Typologies of performance analysis. UK-England. USA. 1963-1997. Lang.: Eng.   911

Brooklyn Academy of Music (BAM, New York, NY)

Performance/production
Death in productions by Robert Lepage and Ping Chong. USA: New York, NY. 1996-1997. Lang.: Eng.   2267

Brooks, Andrea

Performance/production
Collection of newspaper reviews by London theatre critics. UK-England: London. 1997. Lang.: Eng.   1972

Collection of newspaper reviews by London theatre critics. UK-England: London. 1997. Lang.: Eng.   2025

Brooks, Daniel

Performance/production
Daniel Brooks on his collaboration with Daniel MacIvor on *Here Lies Henry*. Canada: Toronto, ON. 1994-1995. Lang.: Eng.   1578

Daniel Brooks' production of *The Soldier Dreams* by Daniel MacIvor. Canada: Toronto, ON. 1997. Lang.: Eng.   1603

Plays/librettos/scripts
Analysis of *Here Lies Henry* by Daniel MacIvor and Daniel Brooks. Canada. 1994-1996. Lang.: Eng.   2437

Büchner, Georg — cont'd

Collection of newspaper reviews by London theatre critics. UK-England: London. 1997. Lang.: Eng. 2110

Collection of newspaper reviews by London theatre critics. UK-England: London. 1997. Lang.: Eng. 2129

Collection of newspaper reviews by London theatre critics. UK-England: London. 1997. Lang.: Eng. 2148

Introduction to *Wozzeck* by Alban Berg. Germany: Berlin. 1914-1997. Lang.: Eng. 4158

Background of the opera *Wozzeck* by Alban Berg. Germany. Austria: Vienna. 1925. Lang.: Eng. 4163

Plays/librettos/scripts

The numerous versions of Büchner's *Woyzeck*. Germany. 1875-1981. Lang.: Eng. 2852

Buck

Plays/librettos/scripts

Television simulation and Ronald Ribman's *Buck*. USA. 1983. Lang.: Eng. 3216

Buck, David

Performance/production

Collection of newspaper reviews by London theatre critics. UK-England: London. 1997. Lang.: Eng. 2004

Buck, Detlef

Performance/production

Reviews of Bochumer Schauspielhaus productions. Germany: Bochum. 1997. Lang.: Ger. 1730

Búcsúszimfónia (Farewell Symphony)

Institutions

A congress on current Hungarian drama. Hungary. 1997. Lang.: Ger. 1437

Budapest Opera

SEE

Magyar Állami Operaház.

Budden, Julian

Performance/production

The difficulty of performing 'Sempre Libera' in Verdi's *La Traviata*. Italy. USA: New York, NY. 1886-1996. Lang.: Eng. 4186

Budzisz-Krzyzanowska, Teresa

Performance/production

Analysis of Andrzej Wajda's Stary Theatre production of *Hamlet*. Poland: Cracow. 1989. Lang.: Eng. 1843

Buen Retiro (Madrid)

Performance spaces

The theatrical space of the Buen Retiro. Spain: Madrid. 1638-1812. Lang.: Eng. 450

Buero Vallejo, Antonio

Plays/librettos/scripts

Violence in Spanish drama after the Civil War. Spain. 1939-1975. Lang.: Eng. 3035

The life and career of playwright Antonio Buero Vallejo. Spain: Madrid. 1916-1996. Lang.: Eng. 3041

The role of 'foreign' theatre on the Spanish stage. Spain. UK-England. USA. 1939-1963. Lang.: Eng. 3044

Analysis of *El Tragaluz (The Skylight)* by Antonio Buero Vallejo. Spain. 1967. Lang.: Spa. 3045

Buffini, Fiona

Performance/production

Collection of newspaper reviews by London theatre critics. UK-England: London. 1997. Lang.: Eng. 2042

Buffini, Moira

Performance/production

Collection of newspaper reviews by London theatre critics. UK-England: London. 1997. Lang.: Eng. 2042

Bugaku

Performance/production

The development of Japanese theatrical genres. Japan. 500-1997. Lang.: Eng. 1224

Ceremonial theatrical forms *gigaku* and *bugaku*. Japan. 646-1997. Lang.: Eng. 3798

Bugsy

Performance/production

The film *Bugsy* as an adaptation of Shakespeare's *Antony and Cleopatra*. USA. 1991. Lang.: Eng. 3613

Bugsy Malone

Performance/production

Collection of newspaper reviews by London theatre critics. UK-England: London. 1997. Lang.: Eng. 2146

Buhre, Christiane

Performance/production

German productions of plays by Terrence McNally and Nicky Silver. Germany. 1996-1997. Lang.: Ger. 1721

Buhre, Traugott

Performance/production

Actor Traugott Buhre. Germany. 1949-1997. Lang.: Ger. 1686

Bukowski, Oliver

Plays/librettos/scripts

Interview with playwright Oliver Bukowski. Germany. 1997. Lang.: Ger. 2863

Bulgakov, Michajl Afanasjévič

Performance/production

Teat'r na Jugo-Zapade's production of work based on plays of Bulgakov. Russia: Moscow. 1996. Lang.: Rus. 1878

Plays/librettos/scripts

Journals and letter of Michajl Bulgakov. Russia. 1914-1940. Lang.: Rus. 2991

The life and work of dramatist Michajl Bulgakov. Russia. 1891-1940. Lang.: Rus. 3001

Bullins, Ed

Performance/production

Analysis of countercultural theatre. USA. 1960-1970. Lang.: Eng. 672

Plays/librettos/scripts

Politics and playwright Ed Bullins. USA. 1968-1997. Lang.: Eng. 3209

Bumbry, Grace

Performance/production

Interpreters of Bizet's heroine Carmen. France: Paris. USA: New York, NY. 1875-1997. Lang.: Eng. 4139

Bundle, The

Plays/librettos/scripts

Nō and *kabuki* elements in plays of Edward Bond. UK-England. 1980-1990. Lang.: Eng. 3105

Bunge, Wolf

Performance/production

Russian, Hungarian and Bulgarian plays at Kammerspiele. Germany: Magdeburg. 1989. Lang.: Ger. 1710

Bunin, Morey

Performance/production

Obituary for television puppeteer Morey Bunin. USA. 1997. Lang.: Eng. 4375

Bunnett, Rexton

Performance/production

Collection of newspaper reviews by London theatre critics. UK-England: London. 1997. Lang.: Eng. 2022

Buntrock, Sam

Performance/production

Collection of newspaper reviews by London theatre critics. UK-England: London. 1997. Lang.: Eng. 2081

Burba, Blake

Design/technology

Blake Burba's lighting design for *Rent*. USA: New York, NY. 1996-1997. Lang.: Eng. 3919

Burbage, James

Performance spaces

London's first public theatres. England: London. 1567-1576. Lang.: Eng. 421

Burbage, Richard

Performance spaces

Shakespeare's plays on the Elizabethan stage. England. 1590-1615. Lang.: Eng. 1520

Performance/production

Rivalry between acting companies and its influence on plays. England: London. 1594-1600. Lang.: Eng. 1625

Burdett-Coutts, William

Performance/production

Collection of newspaper reviews by London theatre critics. UK-England: London. 1997. Lang.: Eng. 2089

Burgess, Chris

Performance/production

Collection of newspaper reviews by London theatre critics. UK-England: London. 1997. Lang.: Eng. 2129

Burgess, John

Performance/production

Collection of newspaper reviews by London theatre critics. UK-England: London. 1997. Lang.: Eng. 2122

Burgtheater (Vienna)

Performance/production

Interview with actor Gert Voss. Austria: Vienna. 1975-1997. Lang.: Ger. 1561

Major productions of the Vienna theatre season. Austria: Vienna. 1997. Lang.: Ger. 1563

Cartwright, Ivan
Performance/production
Collection of newspaper reviews by London theatre critics. UK-England: London. 1997. Lang.: Eng. 2005
Cartwright, Jim
Performance/production
Collection of newspaper reviews by London theatre critics. UK-England: London. 1997. Lang.: Eng. 2100
Carville, Daragh
Performance/production
Collection of newspaper reviews by London theatre critics. UK-England: London. 1997. Lang.: Eng. 2021
Cary, Elizabeth
Plays/librettos/scripts
Analysis of *The Tragedy of Mariam* by Elizabeth Cary. England. 1695. Lang.: Eng. 2761
Relation to other fields
Playwright Elizabeth Cary and the historical account of King Edward II. England. 1627. Lang.: Eng. 3346
Casa d'Arte Bragaglia (Rome)
Performance spaces
The work of Virgilio Marchi in the restoration of the Casa d'Arte Bragaglia. Italy: Rome. 1921-1923. Lang.: Ita. 444
Casa matriz (Dial-a-Mom)
Basic theatrical documents
Anthology of Latin American women's plays. Latin America. 1981-1989. Lang.: Eng. 1291
Casanova
Plays/librettos/scripts
Interview with playwright Constance Congdon. USA. 1997. Lang.: Eng. 3163
Casas, Myrna
Basic theatrical documents
Anthology of Latin American women's plays. Latin America. 1981-1989. Lang.: Eng. 1291
Casing a Promised Land: The Autobiography of an Organizational Detective as Cultural Ethnographer
Performance/production
The development of the production *Casing a Promised Land* by Linda Welker and H.L. Goodall. USA. 1997. Lang.: Eng. 685
Casorati, Felice
Design/technology
Opera scenography of Felice Casorati. Italy. 1933-1954. Lang.: Ita. 4025
Cass, Ronnie
Performance/production
Collection of newspaper reviews by London theatre critics. UK-England: London. 1997. Lang.: Eng. 2080
Cassavetes, John
Performance/production
The style of productions at Bochumer Schauspielhaus. Germany: Bochum. 1995-1997. Lang.: Ger. 1732
Cassiers, Guy
Institutions
Profile of RO-Theater's new artistic director Guy Cassiers. Netherlands: Rotterdam. 1997. Lang.: Dut. 1449
Performance/production
Plays by Shepard and Albee at Nederlands Toneel Gent. Netherlands: Ghent. 1996. Lang.: Eng. 1825
Castellucci, Claudia
Performance/production
The *Oresteia* of Aeschylus as performed by Societas Raffaello Sanzio. Italy: Cesena. 1981-1997. Lang.: Eng. 1820
Castellucci, Romeo
Performance/production
The body and the text in productions of the Festival de Théâtre des Amériques. Canada: Montreal, PQ. 1997. Lang.: Fre. 1583
Societas Raffaello Sanzio's production of Shakespeare's *Julius Caesar*. Italy: Prato. 1997. Lang.: Ita. 1803
The *Oresteia* of Aeschylus as performed by Societas Raffaello Sanzio. Italy: Cesena. 1981-1997. Lang.: Eng. 1820
Societas Raffaello Sanzio's production of the *Oresteia* of Euripides. Italy: Cesena. 1995. Lang.: Ita. 1821
Plays/librettos/scripts
Romeo Castellucci's adaptation of the *Oresteia*. Italy: Cesena. 1995. Lang.: Ger, Fre, Dut, Eng. 2947
Casting
Administration
Recent activities of the Non-Traditional Casting Project. USA. 1997. Lang.: Eng. 69

Increased requests for the Artist Files of Equity's Non-Traditional Casting Project. USA. 1997. Lang.: Eng. 109
Recasting star roles in Broadway musicals. USA: New York, NY. 1952-1977. Lang.: Eng. 3896
Institutions
Interview with Elaine Padmore, opera manager of Det Kongelige Teater. Denmark: Copenhagen. 1980. Lang.: Swe. 4044
Performance/production
Updates and additions to *The London Stage, 1660-1800*. England: London. 1696-1737. Lang.: Eng. 502
The Non-Traditional Casting Project's on-line artist files. USA. 1997. Lang.: Eng. 625
Nontraditional casting and the resolution of conflict in communities. USA. 1994-1996. Lang.: Eng. 644
Constraints and opportunities for Asian-American actors. USA. 1990-1997. Lang.: Eng. 655
Political activism of actor Steve Park. USA. 1997. Lang.: Eng. 658
The doubling and tripling of casting on the early modern stage. England. 1598-1610. Lang.: Eng. 1621
Possible misunderstandings arising from role distribution practices. UK-England. 1593-1750. Lang.: Eng. 2208
Production guide for a performance of *The Medium* by Gian Carlo Menotti. USA. 1996. Lang.: Eng. 4259
Relation to other fields
Commentary on the Wilson-Brustein debate. USA: New York, NY. 1996-1997. Lang.: Eng. 793
Support for August Wilson's views on Black American theatre. USA: St. Paul, MN, Princeton, NJ. 1996-1997. Lang.: Eng. 795
Call for white directors to examine their casting policies. USA. 1997. Lang.: Eng. 808
The Wilson/Brustein debate on African-Americans and theatre. USA. 1995-1997. Lang.: Eng. 826
August Wilson's address to the National Black Theatre Festival. USA: Winston-Salem, NC. 1997. Lang.: Eng. 3440
August Wilson's TCG speech on the Black artist in American theatre. USA. 1996. Lang.: Eng. 3441
Castle Spectre, The
Performance/production
Collection of newspaper reviews by London theatre critics. UK-England: London. 1997. Lang.: Eng. 2144
Collection of newspaper reviews by London theatre critics. UK-England: London. 1997. Lang.: Eng. 2153
Castle Theatre (Budapest)
SEE
Várszinház.
Castle Theatre (Gyula)
SEE
Gyulai Várszinház.
Castle Theatre (Kisvárda)
SEE
Kisvárdai Várszinház.
Castle Theatre (Kőszeg)
SEE
Kőszegi Várszinház.
Castle, The
Plays/librettos/scripts
Medieval theatre as reflected in contemporary drama. UK-England. 1970-1990. Lang.: Eng. 3067
Brecht's influence on the plays of Howard Barker. UK-England. 1987-1997. Lang.: Eng. 3084
Analysis of *Judith* and *The Castle* by Howard Barker. UK-England. 1975-1994. Lang.: Eng. 3096
Castle, William
Performance/production
The horror genre and the American film industry. USA. 1953-1968. Lang.: Eng. 3617
Castledine, Annie
Performance/production
Collection of newspaper reviews by London theatre critics. UK-England: London. 1997. Lang.: Eng. 2086
Castorf, Frank
Institutions
Interview with Frank Castorf, artistic director of Volksbühne. Germany: Berlin. 1990. Lang.: Swe. 1430
Performance/production
Castorf's production of *Des Teufels General (The Devil's General)* at Theatertreffen festival. Germany: Berlin. 1996. Lang.: Eng. 1690

Castorf, Frank — cont'd

Director Frank Castorf. Germany: Berlin. Sweden: Stockholm. 1976.
Lang.: Swe. 1700

The style of productions at Bochumer Schauspielhaus. Germany:
Bochum. 1995-1997. Lang.: Ger. 1732

Interview with director Frank Castorf. Germany: Berlin. 1997. Lang.:
Eng. 1734

Two productions of the annual Strindberg festival at Stockholms
Stadsteater. Sweden: Stockholm. 1997. Lang.: Eng. 1957

Castrati
Relation to other fields
Opera and social decline. England: London. 1698-1737. Lang.: Eng.
4321

Representation and reception of the *castrato*. France. 1830-1970. Lang.:
Eng. 4322
Theory/criticism
Opera and eroticism. USA. Europe. 1996. Lang.: Eng. 4335

Castri, Massimo
Performance/production
Massimo Castri's production of *La Ragione degli altri (The Reason of
the Others)* by Pirandello. Italy: Messina. 1996-1997. Lang.: Ita. 1806

Massimo Castri's staging of Euripides' *Orestes* at Teatro Fabbricone.
Italy: Prato. 1995. Lang.: Ita. 1810

Castro, Alfredo
Plays/librettos/scripts
The *Trilogía Testimonial (Trilogy of Witness)* of Alfredo Castro, Teatro
La Memoria. Chile. 1986-1997. Lang.: Ger. 692

Castro, Guillén de
Plays/librettos/scripts
The figure of Dido in works of the Italian Renaissance and Spanish
Golden Age. Italy. Spain. 1542-1616. Lang.: Ita. 2957

Caswell, Ken
Performance/production
Collection of newspaper reviews by London theatre critics. UK-England:
London. 1997. Lang.: Eng. 2081

Cat and the Moon, The
Performance/production
Collection of newspaper reviews by London theatre critics. UK-England:
London. 1997. Lang.: Eng. 2048
Plays/librettos/scripts
Landscape in plays of W.B. Yeats. Ireland. 1916-1919. Lang.: Eng. 2932

Cat on a Hot Tin Roof
Plays/librettos/scripts
Analysis of *Cat on a Hot Tin Roof* by Tennessee Williams. USA. 1955.
Lang.: Eng. 3174

Gay eroticism in Tennessee Williams' *Cat on a Hot Tin Roof.* USA.
1955. Lang.: Eng. 3202

Tennessee Williams' plays on film. USA. 1950-1969. Lang.: Eng. 3245

Cat's-Paw
Basic theatrical documents
Text of *Cat's-Paw* by Mac Wellman. USA. 1997. Lang.: Eng. 1347

Català, Víctor
SEE
Albert, Caterina.

Catalogues
Performance/production
Exhibition catalogue and essays on the influence of Japanese theatre.
Japan. 1997. Lang.: Eng. 569

Catalyst Theatre (Edmonton, AB)
Institutions
Interview with Joey Tremblay and Jonathan Christenson. Canada:
Edmonton, AB. 1995-1996. Lang.: Eng. 1395

Cátaro (Barcelona)
Performance/production
Interview with Alberto Miralles of the theatre group Cátaro. Spain:
Barcelona, Madrid. 1950-1996. Lang.: Eng. 1914

Cater, Emma
Performance/production
Collection of newspaper reviews by London theatre critics. UK-England:
London. 1997. Lang.: Eng. 2138

Catherine the Great, Empress of Russia
Plays/librettos/scripts
Analysis of *O vremja! (Oh, These Times!)* by Catherine the Great.
Russia: St. Petersburg. 1772. Lang.: Eng. 2998

Cathleen ni Houlihan
Research/historiography
Irish theatre critics' focus on text rather than performance. Ireland:
Dublin. 1897-1907. Lang.: Eng. 3450

Cathomas, Bruno
Performance/production
Comparison of productions of Shakespeare's *Richard III.* Germany.
Switzerland. 1996. Lang.: Ger. 1745

Cato
Plays/librettos/scripts
Addison's *Cato* as the source of the poem *The Maid's Soliloquy.*
Colonial America. England. 1713-1753. Lang.: Eng. 2442

Caucasian Chalk Circle, The
SEE
Kaukasische Kreidekreis, Der.

Caulker, Ferne
Performance/production
Milwaukee Repertory Theatre and Ko-Thi Dance Company's
adaptation of *Benito Cereno.* USA: Milwaukee, WI. 1996. Lang.: Eng.
2316

Cavalleria Rusticana
Performance/production
Background material on Metropolitan Opera radio broadcast
performances. USA: New York, NY. 1997. Lang.: Eng. 4238

Cave of the Heart
Performance/production
Analysis of Martha Graham's Greek cycle of dance dramas. USA. 1926-
1991. Lang.: Ita. 1198

Cavendish, Margaret
Plays/librettos/scripts
Collaboration and authorship of Renaissance drama. England. 1550-
1620. Lang.: Eng. 2649

Čcheidze, Temur
Performance/production
Bolšoj Drama Theatre production of Anouilh's *Antigone.* Russia: St.
Petersburg. 1996. Lang.: Rus. 1862

Anouilh's *Antigone* at the Bolšoj Drama Theatre. Russia: St. Petersburg.
1996. Lang.: Rus. 1897

Cébron, Jean
Performance/production
Profile of dancer and choreographer Jean Cébron. Europe. South
America. 1927-1997. Lang.: Ger. 960

Cecchina, ossia la buona figliuola, La
Plays/librettos/scripts
Piccinni's *La Cecchina*: English translations and analysis. Italy. USA.
1766-1996. Lang.: Eng. 4305

Čechov, Anton Pavlovič
Institutions
Theatre festival devoted to productions of *Čajka (The Seagull)* by
Anton Čechov. Russia. 1996. Lang.: Rus. 1462

Malyj Dramatic Theatre under Lev Dodin. Russia: St. Petersburg. 1983-
1996. Lang.: Eng. 1465
Performance/production
History of Čechov's plays in production world-wide. 1880-1995. Lang.:
Eng. 1550

The body and the text in productions of the Festival de Théâtre des
Amériques. Canada: Montreal, PQ. 1997. Lang.: Fre. 1583

Sociocultural analysis of recent French productions. France. 1993-1994.
Lang.: Eng. 1678

Productions of Bruno Klimek at Mannheimer Nationaltheater.
Germany: Mannheim. 1996-1997. Lang.: Ger. 1689

Recent productions of Čechov's *Ivanov.* Germany: Dusseldorf, Stuttgart.
1996-1997. Lang.: Ger. 1706

Christoph Marthaler's production of Čechov's *Tri sestry (Three Sisters).*
Germany: Berlin. 1997. Lang.: Ger. 1738

Čechov's *Platonov* adapted by Jerzy Jarocki, Teatr Polski. Poland:
Wrocław. 1993-1997. Lang.: Eng, Fre. 1854

Current productions of plays by Čechov. Russia: Moscow. 1940-1997.
Lang.: Eng. 1856

Anton Čechov and his museum. Russia: Moscow. 1989. Lang.: Eng.
1869

Vladimir Anšon's production of Čechov's *Pianola.* Russia: St.
Petersburg. 1995. Lang.: Rus. 1881

Peter Langdahl's production of *The Cherry Orchard* at Dramaten.
Sweden: Stockholm. 1997. Lang.: Swe. 1938

Collection of newspaper reviews by London theatre critics. UK-England:
London. 1997. Lang.: Eng. 2001

Collection of newspaper reviews by London theatre critics. UK-England:
London. 1997. Lang.: Eng. 2044

Čechov, Anton Pavlovič — cont'd

Collection of newspaper reviews by London theatre critics. UK-England: London. 1997. Lang.: Eng. 2047

Collection of newspaper reviews by London theatre critics. UK-England. 1997. Lang.: Eng. 2050

Collection of newspaper reviews by London theatre critics. UK-England: London. 1997. Lang.: Eng. 2066

Collection of newspaper reviews by London theatre critics. UK-England: London. 1997. Lang.: Eng. 2087

Collection of newspaper reviews by London theatre critics. UK-England: London. 1997. Lang.: Eng. 2094

Collection of newspaper reviews by London theatre critics. UK-England. 1997. Lang.: Eng. 2121

Actor Dominic West. UK-England: London. 1997. Lang.: Eng. 2195

Recent roles of actor Michael Pennington. UK-England: London. 1997. Lang.: Eng. 2196

Social class in English productions of Čechov's *Višněvyj sad (The Cherry Orchard)*. UK-England. 1977-1995. Lang.: Eng. 2221

Collection of newspaper reviews by London theatre critics. UK-Scotland: Edinburgh. 1997. Lang.: Eng. 2232

Plays/librettos/scripts
Čechov's personality as discerned through his plays. Russia. 1993. Lang.: Eng. 2990

The influence of Čechov's *Tri sestry (Three Sisters)* on plays of Sadowski and Wertenbaker. Russia. UK-England. 1901-1997. Lang.: Eng. 2992

The character Treplev in Čechov's *Čajka (The Seagull)*. Russia. 1896. Lang.: Rus. 2995

The genesis and stage history of Čechov's *Čajka (The Seagull)*. Russia. 1892-1996. Lang.: Hun. 2999

The fate of Čechov's *Čajka (The Seagull)*. Russia. 1896-1997. Lang.: Rus. 3000

The characters of Čechov's plays. Russia. 1880-1900. Lang.: Hun. 3002

Paul Schmidt on translating and adapting plays of Čechov. USA. 1994-1997. Lang.: Eng. 3273

Cederholm, Nikolaj
Performance/production
Interview with Nikolaj Cederholm of Dr. Dante's Aveny. Denmark: Copenhagen. 1997. Lang.: Dan. 1618

Cegada de Amor (Blinded by Love)
Institutions
Impressions of the Edinburgh Festival. UK-Scotland: Edinburgh. 1997. Lang.: Ger. 391

Performance/production
Collection of newspaper reviews by London theatre critics. UK-Scotland: Edinburgh. 1997. Lang.: Eng. 2230

Celedon, Mauricio
Performance/production
Collection of newspaper reviews by London theatre critics. UK-England: London. 1997. Lang.: Eng. 1978

Céline, Louis-Ferdinand
Performance/production
Performative theory and potentially offensive characterizations on stage. USA: Santa Cruz, CA. France: Paris. 1992-1997. Lang.: Eng. 2336

Cenci, The
Performance/production
Collection of newspaper reviews by London theatre critics. UK-England. 1997. Lang.: Eng. 2082

Cendrars, Blaise
Performance/production
The body and gender in Parisian dance performance. France. 1911-1924. Lang.: Eng. 1069

Censor, The
Performance/production
Collection of newspaper reviews by London theatre critics. UK-England: London. 1997. Lang.: Eng. 1970

Collection of newspaper reviews by London theatre critics. UK-England: London. 1997. Lang.: Eng. 1978

Collection of newspaper reviews by London theatre critics. UK-England: London. 1997. Lang.: Eng. 2057

Censorship
Administration
Censorship in early English theatre. England. 1581. Lang.: Eng. 19

The development by a group of fourth graders of a play about child labor. USA: Ridgewood, NJ. 1997. Lang.: Eng. 57

Censorship in the Federal Theatre Project. USA. 1935-1936. Lang.: Eng. 131

Censorship and self-censorship on American television. USA. 1920-1965. Lang.: Eng. 3708

Analysis of a Supreme Court decision regarding indecency and cable television. USA. 1995. Lang.: Eng. 3710

Institutions
History of the Théâtre de Porte Saint-Martin. France: Paris. 1802-1830. Lang.: Ita. 310

Official and unofficial iconography of the Théâtre Italien. France: Paris. 1653-1697. Lang.: Eng. 1405

Performance/production
The effect of war on Croatian theatre. Croatia. 1990-1996. Lang.: Eng. 495

Censorship and Teater Koma's production of *Suksesi* by Rendra. Indonesia: Jakarta. 1977-1993. Lang.: Eng. 558

The production of *The Mannequin's Ball* by Bruno Jasieński. Russia. 1931. Lang.: Eng. 591

The emergence of modern American theatre. USA. 1914-1929. Lang.: Eng. 683

Matthew Krouse, formerly an actor in the entertainment corps of the South African Defence Force. South Africa, Republic of. 1982. Lang.: Eng. 1911

Performative theory and potentially offensive characterizations on stage. USA: Santa Cruz, CA. France: Paris. 1992-1997. Lang.: Eng. 2336

Early Shanghai filmmaking. China, People's Republic of: Shanghai. 1896-1937. Lang.: Eng. 3568

Profile of Taiwanese opera, *Gezaixi*. China: Taiwan. 1895-1997. Lang.: Eng. 3892

Plays/librettos/scripts
Analysis of *Das Mädel aus der Vorstadt (The Girl from the Suburbs)* by Johann Nestroy. Austria: Vienna. 1841-1995. Lang.: Eng. 2383

Censorship and Shakespeare's *Richard II*. England. 1595. Lang.: Eng. 2503

Playwrights' discussions of censorship in prefaces to their work. England. 1790-1820. Lang.: Eng. 2507

Censorship and satire in the eighteenth century. England. 1710-1789. Lang.: Eng. 2617

Censorship and editing of sexual and bawdy language in variorum editions of Shakespeare's plays. England. 1598-1997. Lang.: Eng. 2620

Interview with playwright Wole Soyinka. Nigeria. 1986-1996. Lang.: Eng. 2980

Relation to other fields
Theatre and war. Germany. 1914-1918. Lang.: Ger. 754

Censorship, power, and performance. Kenya: Nairobi. 1938-1997. Lang.: Eng. 771

Controversy over the videotaping of creative works by students. USA: St. Louis, MO. 1994-1997. Lang.: Eng. 829

Research/historiography
Renaissance drama, censorship, and contemporary historical methods. England: London. 1588-1980. Lang.: Eng. 3446

Theory/criticism
Othello, censorship, and public swearing. England: London. 1215-1622. Lang.: Eng. 3470

Centaur Theatre (Montreal, PQ)
Institutions
Centaur Theatre's new artistic director Gordon McCall. Canada: Montreal, PQ. 1997. Lang.: Eng. 1383

Interview with Gordon McCall, artistic director, Centaur Theatre. Canada: Montreal, PQ. 1997. Lang.: Eng. 1389

Centaur Theatre, Montreal's oldest English-language theatre. Canada: Montreal, PQ. 1969-1997. Lang.: Eng. 1399

Center for Contemporary Opera
Institutions
Downsizing American opera companies. USA. 1997. Lang.: Eng. 4059

Center for Theatrical Practice (Gardzienice)
SEE
Ośrodek Praktyk Teatralnych.

Center of Puppetry Arts (Atlanta, GA)
Performance/production
Interview with puppeteer John Ludwig. USA: Atlanta, GA. 1996. Lang.: Eng. 4376

Center Stage (Baltimore, MD)
Plays/librettos/scripts
James Magruder on his translation of *Le Triomphe de l'amour (The Triumph of Love)* by Marivaux. USA: Baltimore, MD. 1986-1995. Lang.: Eng. 3230

Characters/roles — cont'd

Ideas of selfhood and slavery reflected in Shakespeare's *Othello*. England. 1604. Lang.: Eng.   2736

The sympathetic villain on the early modern stage. England. 1594-1621. Lang.: Eng.   2763

The significance of Don Juan in works of Tirso, Mozart, and Molière. Europe. 1612-1787. Lang.: Eng.   2786

The character of the traveler in plays of the Irish Renaissance. Ireland. 1910-1930. Lang.: Eng.   2938

The Greco-Roman parasite character. Roman Empire. 200-500. Lang.: Eng.   2988

Transvestism in English pantomime. UK-England. 1870-1995. Lang.: Eng.   3754

The African 'other' in early French musical drama. France. Africa. 1600. Lang.: Eng.   3887

Opera and gender stereotypes. Europe. 1607-1997. Lang.: Eng.   4287

Neapolitan character types in Italian opera. Italy. 1792. Lang.: Fre. 4301

The origin of the Russian puppet character Petruška. Russia. Lang.: Rus.   4381

Charlap, Mark (Moose)
Performance/production
A lesbian reading of Mary Martin's performance as Peter Pan. USA. 1950-1959. Lang.: Eng.   3978

Charlton, James Martin
Performance/production
Collection of newspaper reviews by London theatre critics. UK-England: London. 1997. Lang.: Eng.   2120

Charnock, Nigel
Performance/production
Collection of newspaper reviews by London theatre critics. UK-England: London. 1997. Lang.: Eng.   2006

Charpentier, Marc-Antoine
Performance/production
Excerpt from biography of opera singer Mary Garden. France: Paris. 1875-1957. Lang.: Eng.   4144

Charpentier, Réjane
Plays/librettos/scripts
Childhood fears in children's plays of Emmanuel Bilodeau and Réjane Charpentier. Canada: Montreal, PQ. 1996-1997. Lang.: Fre.   2420

Chaste Maid in Cheapside, A
Performance/production
Collection of newspaper reviews by London theatre critics. UK-England. 1997. Lang.: Eng.   2098
Plays/librettos/scripts
Calvinism in the city comedies of Thomas Middleton. England. 1604-1611. Lang.: Eng.   2570

Domestic cultural and social struggle in Elizabethan theatre. England. 1592-1621. Lang.: Eng.   2571

Chaudhuri, Una
Relation to other fields
Theatre artists' responses to the debate on multiculturalism of August Wilson and Robert Brustein. USA. 1997. Lang.: Eng.   789

Chaurette, Normand
Plays/librettos/scripts
Self-reflexivity in Quebec drama. Canada. 1981-1988. Lang.: Fre. 2397

Critique of homophobia in Normand Chaurette's *Provincetown Playhouse, July 1919, I Was 19 Years Old)*. Canada. 1982. Lang.: Eng.   2407

Analysis of *Fragments d'une lettre d'adieu lus par des géologues (Fragments of a Farewell Letter Read by Geologists)* by Normand Chaurette. Canada. 1986. Lang.: Fre.   2427

Chavittunátakam
Performance/production
Chavittunátakam, the music drama of Kerala Christians. India: Kerala. 1500-1997. Lang.: Eng.   3871

Chejfec, Leonid
Institutions
Director Leonid Chejfec on director training at RATI. Russia: Moscow. 1990-1997. Lang.: Rus.   1455

Chekhov, Anton
SEE
Čechov, Anton Pavlovič.

Chekhov, Michael
SEE
Čechov, Michajl A.

Chelsea Theatre Centre (London)
Performance/production
Collection of newspaper reviews by London theatre critics. UK-England: London. 1997. Lang.: Eng.   2001

Collection of newspaper reviews by London theatre critics. UK-England: London. 1997. Lang.: Eng.   2038

Collection of newspaper reviews by London theatre critics. UK-England: London. 1997. Lang.: Eng.   2119

Collection of newspaper reviews by London theatre critics. UK-England: London. 1997. Lang.: Eng.   2140

Cher Olivier (Dear Olivier)
Performance/production
The TV series *Cher Olivier (Dear Olivier)* on actor Olivier Guimond. Canada. 1997. Lang.: Fre.   3718

Chéreau, Patrice
Plays/librettos/scripts
The work of playwright Bernard-Marie Koltès. France. 1948-1989. Lang.: Eng.   2806

Chernov, Matthew
Performance/production
Documentation of work by the late choreographer Robert Ellis Dunn. USA: Milwaukee, WI. 1945-1997. Lang.: Eng.   1202

Cherns, Penny
Performance/production
Collection of newspaper reviews by London theatre critics. UK-England: London. 1997. Lang.: Eng.   2139

Cherry Orchard, The
SEE
Višněvyj sad.

Cherry Pickers, The
Plays/librettos/scripts
Analysis of Aboriginal drama. Australia. 1967-1997. Lang.: Eng.   2376

Chesney, William
Design/technology
Teaching theatrical design and production in the context of the liberal arts. Canada: Waterloo, ON. 1997. Lang.: Eng.   143

Chesnutt, Charles W.
Administration
Oscar Micheaux's entreneurship in financing *The House Behind the Cedars*. USA. 1920-1922. Lang.: Eng.   3523

Chester Cycle
Plays/librettos/scripts
Middle English religious drama and audience participation. England. 1400-1550. Lang.: Eng.   2576

Analysis of medieval plays about Jesus and the doctors. England: York, Towneley, Coventry. 1420-1500. Lang.: Eng.   2618

Chevaliers de la Table Ronde, Les (Knights of the Round Table)
Plays/librettos/scripts
Gendered identity in plays of Cocteau and García Lorca. France. Spain. 1930-1937. Lang.: Eng.   2807

Chicago
Performance/production
Collection of newspaper reviews by London theatre critics. UK-England: London. 1997. Lang.: Eng.   2140

Handelian countertenor David Sabella, currently performing in musical theatre. USA: New York, NY. 1996. Lang.: Eng.   3960

Profile of director Walter Bobbie. USA. UK-England. 1971-1997. Lang.: Eng.   3971
Plays/librettos/scripts
Interviews with authors of Tony Award-winning shows. USA: New York, NY. 1997. Lang.: Eng.   3985

Songwriting team John Kander and Fred Ebb. USA: New York, NY. 1927-1997. Lang.: Eng.   4001

Chicago by Sam Shepard
Performance/production
The Sam Shepard season of the Signature Theatre Company. USA: New York, NY. 1976-1997. Lang.: Eng.   2346

Chicago Opera Theatre (Chicago, IL)
Institutions
Downsizing American opera companies. USA. 1997. Lang.: Eng.   4059

Chicano theatre
SEE ALSO
Hispanic theatre.

Ethnic theatre.

Chichester Festival Theatre
Performance/production
Collection of newspaper reviews by London theatre critics. UK-England. 1997. Lang.: Eng.   2033

Collection of newspaper reviews by London theatre critics. UK-England. 1997. Lang.: Eng.   2043

Collection of newspaper reviews by London theatre critics. UK-England. 1997. Lang.: Eng.   2058

Choreography — cont'd

Profile of choreographer Eske Holm. Denmark. 1964-1997. Lang.: Dan.
1177

Choreographer Kenneth Kvarnström. Finland: Helsinki. 1997. Lang.:
Eng. 1180

Choreographer Hans van Manen. Netherlands. 1932-1997. Lang.: Dut.
1182

Mats Ek's *A Sort of* produced by Nederlands Dans Theater.
Netherlands: The Hague. 1997. Lang.: Swe. 1183

Problems of creating and preserving new dance works. Sweden. 1950.
Lang.: Swe. 1184

Choreographer Lena Josefsson. Sweden: Örebro, Stockholm. 1997.
Lang.: Swe. 1185

TV performances of young choreographers. Sweden. 1997. Lang.: Swe.
1186

Interview with dancer/choreographer Gunilla Witt. Sweden:
Gothenburg. 1970. Lang.: Swe. 1187

Interview with choreographer Anne Külper of Tiger. Sweden:
Stockholm. 1968-1997. Lang.: Swe. 1188

Cultural stereotyping and the Shobana Jeyasingh Dance Company. UK-
England. 1997. Lang.: Eng. 1189

Career of choreographer Rosemary Butcher. UK-England. 1976-1997.
Lang.: Eng. 1190

Lea Anderson, founder of The Cholmondeleys and The
Featherstonehaughs. UK-England. 1984-1994. Lang.: Eng. 1191

Dance and the representation of the body in a technological world. UK-
England. 1997. Lang.: Eng. 1192

Choreographers Twyla Tharp and Rosemary Butcher. UK-England.
USA. 1997. Lang.: Eng. 1194

Profile of choreographer Shobana Jeyasingh. UK-England. 1988-1997.
Lang.: Eng. 1195

Choreographer Claire Russ. UK-England. 1997. Lang.: Eng. 1196

Solo performances and audience reception of Isadora Duncan and
Blondell Cummings. USA. Europe. 1910-1990. Lang.: Eng. 1197

Analysis of Martha Graham's Greek cycle of dance dramas. USA. 1926-
1991. Lang.: Ita. 1198

History and the work of choreographer Mark Morris. USA. 1997. Lang.:
Eng. 1199

Assessment of the Altogether Different dance series, Joyce Theatre.
USA: New York, NY. 1997. Lang.: Eng. 1200

The Black male body in concert dance. USA. 1980-1995. Lang.: Eng.
1201

Documentation of work by the late choreographer Robert Ellis Dunn.
USA: Milwaukee, WI. 1945-1997. Lang.: Eng. 1202

Black dance, white dance, and the choreography of Twyla Tharp. USA.
1997. Lang.: Eng. 1205

Gender in choreographies of Mark Morris. USA. 1980-1995. Lang.: Eng.
1206

Dancer, actor, choreographer Benjamin Zemach. USA. 1902-1997.
Lang.: Eng. 1207

Analysis of *Education of the Girlchild* by Meredith Monk. USA. 1980-
1995. Lang.: Eng. 1208

Interview with choreographer Neil Greenberg. USA: New York, NY.
1997. Lang.: Eng. 1209

Choreographer, composer, and director Birgitta Egerbladh. Sweden:
Gothenburg. 1996. Lang.: Swe. 1960

Work of choreographer Susan Stroman on *Steel Pier*. USA: New York,
NY. 1975-1997. Lang.: Eng. 3956

Plays/librettos/scripts
Dance adaptations of Joachim Schlömer. Switzerland: Basel. 1990-1997.
Lang.: Ger, Fre, Dut, Eng. 1014

Relation to other fields
One of three student choreographers on a joint dance project. USA:
Long Beach, CA. 1997. Lang.: Eng. 1211

One of three student choreographers on a joint dance project. USA:
Long Beach, CA. 1997. Lang.: Eng. 1212

One of three student choreographers on a joint dance project. USA:
Long Beach, CA. 1997. Lang.: Eng. 1213

Theory/criticism
Japanese analysis of Western choreography. Japan. USA. 1970-1979.
Lang.: Eng. 1030

Seminar on dance, text, and theatre. Sweden: Stockholm. 1997. Lang.:
Swe. 1032

Choreography and criticism. UK-England. 1997. Lang.: Eng. 1033

Feminist analysis of the ballet *Coppélia*. France. 1870. Lang.: Eng. 1134

Theory and interpretation in *Laughter After All* by Paul Sanasardo and
Donya Feuer. USA. 1995. Lang.: Eng. 1215

Dance history and cultural studies: works of Martha Graham and
Eugene O'Neill. USA. 1913-1933. Lang.: Eng. 1216

Analysis of *American Document* by Martha Graham. USA. 1938. Lang.:
Eng. 1217

Movement analysis on modern dance. USA. 1995. Lang.: Eng. 1218

Training
Teachers and choreographers Soile Lahdenperä and Ervi Siren. Finland.
1997. Lang.: Fin. 1040

Chorus Line, A
Performance/production
History of American musical theatre. USA. UK-England. 1912-1995.
Lang.: Eng. 3954

Chouinard, Marie
Performance/production
The body and cultural identity in contemporary dance. USA. 1985-1995.
Lang.: Eng. 996

Christenson, Jonathan
Institutions
Interview with Joey Tremblay and Jonathan Christenson. Canada:
Edmonton, AB. 1995-1996. Lang.: Eng. 1395

Christian Slave, The
Performance/production
Stage adaptations of *Uncle Tom's Cabin*. USA. 1853-1857. Lang.: Eng.
2250

Christiani Wallace Brothers Combined
SEE
Wallace Brothers Circus.

Christopher, James
Performance/production
Collection of newspaper reviews by London theatre critics. UK-England:
London. 1997. Lang.: Eng. 2036

Chubb, Justin
Performance/production
Collection of newspaper reviews by London theatre critics. UK-England:
London. 1997. Lang.: Eng. 2069

Chumley, Dan
Performance/production
San Francisco Mime Troupe's *13 Días/13 Days*. USA: San Francisco,
CA. 1997. Lang.: Eng. 2335

Chung, Myung-Whun
Performance/production
Opera conductor Myung-Whun Chung. USA: New York, NY. 1953-
1997. Lang.: Eng. 4235

Churchett, Stephen
Performance/production
Collection of newspaper reviews by London theatre critics. UK-England:
London. 1997. Lang.: Eng. 2030

Collection of newspaper reviews by London theatre critics. UK-England:
London. 1997. Lang.: Eng. 2128

Churchill, Caryl
Institutions
Impressions of the Edinburgh Festival. UK-Scotland: Edinburgh. 1997.
Lang.: Ger. 391

Performance/production
Collection of newspaper reviews by London theatre critics. UK-England:
London. 1997. Lang.: Eng. 1983

Collection of newspaper reviews by London theatre critics. UK-England:
London. 1997. Lang.: Eng. 2017

Collection of newspaper reviews by London theatre critics. UK-England:
London. 1997. Lang.: Eng. 2077

Collection of newspaper reviews by London theatre critics. UK-England:
London. 1997. Lang.: Eng. 2105

Collection of newspaper reviews by London theatre critics. UK-England:
London. 1997. Lang.: Eng. 2140

Productions of plays by Caryl Churchill. UK-Scotland: Edinburgh. UK-
England: London. 1997. Lang.: Eng. 2233

Director and dramaturg Jayme Koszyn. USA: Boston, MA,
Philadelphia, PA. 1992-1995. Lang.: Eng. 2290

Harriet Power, director and dramaturg for Churchill's *Mad Forest* at
Venture Theatre. USA: Philadelphia, PA. 1992. Lang.: Eng. 2319

Plays/librettos/scripts
Female characters in plays of contemporary British women. UK-
England. 1980-1995. Lang.: Eng. 3077

Clandestine Marriage, The
Plays/librettos/scripts
Frances Sheridan's *The Discovery* in the context of eighteenth-century theatre. England. 1740-1780. Lang.: Eng. 2451

Cimarosa's *Il matrimonio segreto* and the clandestine marriage on the eighteenth-century stage. Italy. 1766-1792. Lang.: Fre. 4304

Clapham Common (London)
Performance/production
Collection of newspaper reviews by London theatre critics. UK-England: London. 1997. Lang.: Eng. 2074

Clara
Plays/librettos/scripts
Playwright Arthur Miller's collaborations with his wife Inge Morath. USA. 1980-1989. Lang.: Eng. 3272

Clark, Anthony
Performance/production
Collection of newspaper reviews by London theatre critics. UK-England: London. 1997. Lang.: Eng. 2066

Clark, Breena
Basic theatrical documents
Anthology of plays by women of color. USA. 1992-1996. Lang.: Eng. 1338

Clark, Rodney
Performance/production
Collection of newspaper reviews by London theatre critics. UK-England: London. 1997. Lang.: Eng. 2095

Clarke, George Elliott
Plays/librettos/scripts
Analysis of *Whylah Falls* by George Elliott Clarke. Canada. 1997. Lang.: Eng. 2393

Clarke, Margaret
Plays/librettos/scripts
Analysis of *Gertrude and Ophelia* by Margaret Clarke. 1993-1997. Lang.: Eng. 2364

Clarke, Martha
Institutions
The Sundance Institute Playwright's Lab. USA: Salt Lake City, UT. 1997. Lang.: Eng. 1512

Clarke, Mary Carr
Plays/librettos/scripts
Analysis of plays by Mary Carr Clarke. USA. 1815-1833. Lang.: Eng. 3220

Clary, Julian
Performance/production
Collection of newspaper reviews by London theatre critics. UK-England: London. 1997. Lang.: Eng. 2156

Classic Stage Company
SEE
CSC Repertory.

Claus, Hugo
Performance/production
Playwright, dramaturg, and director Hugo Claus. Belgium. 1997. Lang.: Afr. 1569

Clausen, Andrea
Performance/production
Actress Andrea Clausen. Germany. 1960-1997. Lang.: Ger. 1693

Clavadista, El
Plays/librettos/scripts
Analysis of *El Clavadista* by Colleen Curran. Canada. 1990. Lang.: Fre. 2410

Clavigo
Performance/production
Updated classics at Schauspiel Leipzig. Germany: Leipzig. 1996-1997. Lang.: Ger. 1712

Cleage, Pearl
Performance/production
Collection of newspaper reviews by London theatre critics. UK-England: London. 1997. Lang.: Eng. 2061

Community-based dramaturgy and Pearl Cleage's *Flyin' West* at Intiman Theatre. USA. 1994-1995. Lang.: Eng. 2349
Plays/librettos/scripts
Black female culture in plays of Pearl Cleage. USA: Atlanta, GA. 1992-1997. Lang.: Eng. 3197

Cleary, Ann
Performance/production
Collection of newspaper reviews by London theatre critics. UK-England: London. 1997. Lang.: Eng. 2063

Collection of newspaper reviews by London theatre critics. UK-England: London. 1997. Lang.: Eng. 2155

Clements, Mark
Performance/production
Collection of newspaper reviews by London theatre critics. UK-England: London. 1997. Lang.: Eng. 1998

Collection of newspaper reviews by London theatre critics. UK-England: London. 1997. Lang.: Eng. 2140

Clemenza di Tito, La
Performance/production
Background material on Metropolitan Opera radio broadcast performances. USA: New York, NY. 1997-1997. Lang.: Eng. 4237
Plays/librettos/scripts
Analysis of *La Clemenza di Tito* by Mozart. Austro-Hungarian Empire. 1791-1997. Lang.: Eng. 4282

Cléo de 5 à 7 (Cleo from 5 to 7)
Performance/production
Analysis of *Cléo de 5 à 7 (Cleo from 5 to 7)* by Agnès Varda. France. 1997. Lang.: Eng. 3572

Cleveland Ballet Dancing Wheels (Cleveland, OH)
Performance/production
The body and cultural identity in contemporary dance. USA. 1985-1995. Lang.: Eng. 996

Cleveman, Lars
Performance/production
Interview with tenor Lars Cleveman. Sweden: Stockholm. 1980. Lang.: Swe. 4217

Clever, Edith
Institutions
Recent productions of Schaubühne. Germany: Berlin. 1996-1997. Lang.: Ger. 1426

Clizia, La
Plays/librettos/scripts
Comparison of classical Roman, Renaissance Italian, and Shakespearean treatments of similar stories. Europe. 200 B.C.-1610 A.D. Lang.: Eng. 2799

Closer
Performance/production
Collection of newspaper reviews by London theatre critics. UK-England: London. 1997. Lang.: Eng. 2055

Cloud Nine
Performance/production
Collection of newspaper reviews by London theatre critics. UK-England: London. 1997. Lang.: Eng. 2017
Plays/librettos/scripts
Ghosts and patriarchy in plays by Caryl Churchill. UK-England. 1980-1990. Lang.: Eng. 3119

Women and theatrical collaboration. USA. UK-England. 1930-1990. Lang.: Eng. 3264

Clowning
Plays/librettos/scripts
The background and early career of Dario Fo. Italy. 1952-1972. Lang.: Swe. 2960

Clune, Jackie
Performance/production
Collection of newspaper reviews by London theatre critics. UK-England: London. 1997. Lang.: Eng. 2152

Clytemnestra
Performance/production
Analysis of Martha Graham's Greek cycle of dance dramas. USA. 1926-1991. Lang.: Ita. 1198

Coates, George
Performance/production
Multi-media design in George Coates's *20/20 Blake*. USA: Berkeley, CA. 1997. Lang.: Eng. 670

Coburn, D.L.
Design/technology
Kirk Bookman's lighting design for *The Gin Game* directed by Charles Nelson Reilly. USA: New York, NY. 1978-1997. Lang.: Eng. 1368

Coburn, Lesley
Performance/production
Collection of newspaper reviews by London theatre critics. UK-England: London. 1997. Lang.: Eng. 2130

Cocaine Lil
Performance/production
Theatrical vocal music of Nancy Van de Vate. USA. 1945-1995. Lang.: Eng. 3884

Cochrane Theatre (London)
Performance/production
Collection of newspaper reviews by London theatre critics. UK-England: London. 1997. Lang.: Eng. 2020

Cock and Bull
Performance/production
Collection of newspaper reviews by London theatre critics. UK-England: London. 1997. Lang.: Eng.								2089
Cocke, Dudley
Relation to other fields
Theatre artists' responses to the debate on multiculturalism of August Wilson and Robert Brustein. USA. 1997. Lang.: Eng.								789
Cockpit Theatre (London)
Performance/production
Collection of newspaper reviews by London theatre critics. UK-England: London. 1997. Lang.: Eng.								1969
Cockroach Who?
Performance/production
Collection of newspaper reviews by London theatre critics. UK-England: London. 1997. Lang.: Eng.								1993
Cocktail Party, The
Performance/production
Collection of newspaper reviews by London theatre critics. UK-Scotland: Edinburgh. 1997. Lang.: Eng.								2231
Cocteau, Jean
Performance/production
The body and gender in Parisian dance performance. France. 1911-1924. Lang.: Eng.								1069
Collection of newspaper reviews by London theatre critics. UK-England: London. 1997. Lang.: Eng.								2094
Jacques Nichet's staging of the opera *L'épouse injustement soupçonnée* by Jean Cocteau and Valérie Stephan. France: Paris. 1996. Lang.: Eng.								4141
Plays/librettos/scripts
Collection of articles on French avant-garde culture, including theatre. France. 1937-1989. Lang.: Eng.								2805
Gendered identity in plays of Cocteau and García Lorca. France. Spain. 1930-1937. Lang.: Eng.								2807
Jean Cocteau's adaptations of works of Sophocles. France. 1922-1937. Lang.: Eng.								2811
Cocu imaginaire, Le
SEE ALSO
Sganarelle.
Coeur à coeur (Heart-to-Heart)
Plays/librettos/scripts
Childhood fears in children's plays of Emmanuel Bilodeau and Réjane Charpentier. Canada: Montreal, PQ. 1996-1997. Lang.: Fre.								2420
Coeur à Gaz, Le (Gas Heart, The)
Theory/criticism
Analysis of *Le Coeur à Gaz (The Gas Heart)* by Tristan Tzara. France. 1916. Lang.: Eng.								893
Coffee
Performance/production
Collection of newspaper reviews by London theatre critics. UK-England: London. 1997. Lang.: Eng.								2056
Coghlan, Lin
Performance/production
Collection of newspaper reviews by London theatre critics. UK-England: London. 1997. Lang.: Eng.								2012
Cohen, Rob
Design/technology
Benjamin Fernandez's production design for *Daylight*. Italy: Rome. 1996. Lang.: Eng.								3543
Cohen, Sarah Blacher
Plays/librettos/scripts
Texts of plays by Jewish American women. USA. 1985-1995. Lang.: Eng.								3164
Coleman, Chris
Performance/production
Actor's Expression production of an unauthorized version of the musical *Oklahoma!*. USA: Atlanta, GA. 1997. Lang.: Eng.								3959
Plays/librettos/scripts
Sandra Deer's play about W.B. Yeats, *Sailing to Byzantium*. USA: Atlanta, GA. 1997. Lang.: Eng.								3249
Coleman, Cy
Design/technology
Richard Pilbrow's lighting design for the musical *The Life*. USA: New York, NY. 1997. Lang.: Eng.								3918
Performance/production
Actress/singer Lillias White. USA: New York, NY. 1981-1997. Lang.: Eng.								3949
Plays/librettos/scripts
Parody and satire in musical theatre. USA. UK-England. 1727-1990. Lang.: Eng.								3986

Coleridge, Samuel Taylor
Plays/librettos/scripts
Playwrights' discussions of censorship in prefaces to their work. England. 1790-1820. Lang.: Eng.								2507
Relation to other fields
Early criticism of Shakespeare's 'Venus and Adonis'. England. 1593. Lang.: Eng.								3330
Collected Stories
Performance/production
Director Lisa Peterson. USA: Los Angeles, CA. 1997. Lang.: Eng.	2279
College of Theatre Arts (Warsaw)
SEE
Panstova Akademia Sztuk Teatralnych.
Collie, Justin
Design/technology
Lighting design for tour of musicians Kenny G and Toni Braxton. USA. 1997. Lang.: Eng.								270
Collins, John
Performance/production
John Collins, artistic and technical director of Elevator Repair Service. USA: New York, NY. 1991-1997. Lang.: Eng.								684
Colman, George
Plays/librettos/scripts
Frances Sheridan's *The Discovery* in the context of eighteenth-century theatre. England. 1740-1780. Lang.: Eng.								2451
Cimarosa's *Il matrimonio segreto* and the clandestine marriage on the eighteenth-century stage. Italy. 1766-1792. Lang.: Fre.								4304
Relation to other fields
A painting of backstage during a production of Colman's *The Poor Gentleman*. England: London. 1750-1802. Lang.: Eng.								731
Colomo, Fernando
Performance/production
Collection of newspaper reviews by London theatre critics. UK-Scotland: Edinburgh. 1997. Lang.: Eng.								2230
Colony Theatre (Los Angeles, CA)
Institutions
Profile of the Colony Theatre. USA: Los Angeles, CA. 1996-1997. Lang.: Ger.								402
Performance/production
Colony Theatre production of *The Matchmaker* by Thornton Wilder. USA: Los Angeles, CA. 1997. Lang.: Eng.								2307
Color Struck
Plays/librettos/scripts
Analysis of *Color Struck* by Zora Neale Hurston. USA. 1891-1995. Lang.: Eng.								3160
The voices of African-American women. USA. 1840-1994. Lang.: Eng.								3309
Colored Minister of the Gospel, A
Plays/librettos/scripts
The voices of African-American women. USA. 1840-1994. Lang.: Eng.								3309
Colored Museum, The
Plays/librettos/scripts
Black playwrights' subversive approaches to character. USA. 1986-1997. Lang.: Eng.								3184
Colosseum (Essen)
Design/technology
Scenic machine control systems used in musical productions at the Colosseum. Germany: Essen. 1997. Lang.: Ger.								3907
Performance spaces
The history of the Colosseum and its new interior design. Germany: Essen. 1900-1997. Lang.: Ger.								3930
Columbia Opera Workshop
Performance/production
American chamber opera. USA. 1868-1997. Lang.: Eng.								4258
Columbia Theatre (New Westminster, BC)
Administration
Efforts to refurbish the historic Columbia Theatre. Canada: New Westminster, BC. 1927-1997. Lang.: Eng.								9
Combustibles, Les (Combustibles, The)
Plays/librettos/scripts
Analysis of *Les Combustibles (The Combustibles)* by Amélie Nothomb. Belgium. 1994. Lang.: Fre.								2386
Comden, Betty
Performance/production
A lesbian reading of Mary Martin's performance as Peter Pan. USA. 1950-1959. Lang.: Eng.								3978
Comédie (Genf)
Institutions
Profiles of Comédie Genf and Théâtre Vidy. Switzerland. 1989-1997. Lang.: Ger.								384

Comédie (Play)
Plays/librettos/scripts
Analysis of German translations of plays by Samuel Beckett. Germany. 1967-1978. Lang.: Eng.　　2842

Comédie de Genève (Geneva)
Basic theatrical documents
French translation of Tony Kushner's *Angels in America, Part II: Perestroika*. USA. France: Paris. 1996. Lang.: Fre.　　1333

Comédie-Française (Paris)
Design/technology
François Melin, chief electrician of Comédie-Française. France: Paris. 1997. Lang.: Eng.　　1356

Performance/production
Royal and commercial audiences and the Comédie-Française. France. 1700-1800. Lang.: Eng.　　1657

Productions of the Paris theatre season. France: Paris. 1996-1997. Lang.: Ger.　　1668

History and politics on the Parisian stage. France: Paris. 1997. Lang.: Ger.　　1669

Collection of newspaper reviews by London theatre critics. UK-England: London. 1997. Lang.: Eng.　　2113

Comedy
Administration
Protection of comic intellectual property. USA. 1995. Lang.: Eng.　　67

Audience
Early modern comedy and the mixing of classes in the audience. England. 1590-1615. Lang.: Eng.　　1248

Basic theatrical documents
Texts of three comedies on the sociopolitical situation by Tone Partljič. Slovenia. 1997. Lang.: Slo.　　1300

Design/technology
Allen Branton's lighting design for TV festival of comedy. USA: Aspen, CO. 1997. Lang.: Eng.　　3714

Performance/production
History of Italian light entertainment. Italy. 1850-1996. Lang.: Ita.　　565

Comedy and social criticism. USA. 1960-1967. Lang.: Eng.　　648

Changes in women's comedy performance. USA. 1950-1995. Lang.: Eng.　　654

Southern humor and minstrelsy. USA. 1835-1939. Lang.: Eng.　　677

As You Like It and the Chamberlain's Men's move to the Globe. England: London. 1594-1612. Lang.: Eng.　　1619

Ethnography of artists of popular theatre in Tamilnadu. India. 1950-1995. Lang.: Eng.　　1783

Comic actor Ettore Petrolini. Italy. 1886-1936. Lang.: Ita.　　1793

Actor, director, comedian Billy Graham. USA. 1997. Lang.: Eng.　　2286

Subversive potential in comedy of Phyllis Diller and Roseanne Barr. USA. 1985-1997. Lang.: Eng.　　3773

Plays/librettos/scripts
The characteristics of comedy. Lang.: Slo.　　2367

The ideology of Restoration comedy. England. 1660-1710. Lang.: Eng.　　2492

Analysis of Shakespeare's *As You Like It*. England. 1599. Lang.: Eng.　　2596

Shakespeare's comic art in *The Two Gentlemen of Verona* and *Twelfth Night*. England. 1594-1602. Lang.: Eng.　　2597

Bibliography of humor in English theatre. England. 1300-1700. Lang.: Eng.　　2682

Love lyrics in Shakespeare's comedies. England. 1590-1613. Lang.: Eng.　　2691

The influence of Plautus and his comic themes. Europe. 259 B.C.-1997 A.D. Lang.: Ita.　　2784

Analysis of the early comedies of Pierre Corneille. France. 1628-1638.　　2822

The city comedy of Pierre Corneille. France: Paris. 1631-1640. Lang.: Eng.　　2828

Comic techniques of the playwright Aristophanes. Greece. 445-399 B.C. Lang.: Ita.　　2867

Out-of-court legal settlements in Greco-Roman new comedy. Greece. Rome. 500 B.C.-200 A.D. Lang.: Eng.　　2886

Analysis of Strindberg's comedy *Brott och Brott (Crimes and Crimes)*. Sweden. 1888. Lang.: Eng.　　3054

Theory/criticism
The possibilities for a contemporary theory of comedy. 1997. Lang.: Slo.　　3459

Gesture and comedy as interpreted by Bergson and Deleuze. Europe. 1928-1983. Lang.: Ger.　　3697

Comedy of Errors, The
Performance/production
Collection of newspaper reviews by London theatre critics. UK-England: London. 1997. Lang.: Eng.　　1975

Plays/librettos/scripts
Analysis of Shakespeare's *Comedy of Errors*. England. 1594. Lang.: Eng.　　2464

Theatrical antecedents in Shakespeare's *The Comedy of Errors*. England. 1594. Lang.: Eng.　　2474

Themes and structures of Shakespeare's *Comedy of Errors*. England. 1594. Lang.: Eng.　　2480

Food in Shakespeare's *Comedy of Errors*. England. 1594. Lang.: Eng.　　2491

Shakespeare's use of *commedia* in *The Comedy of Errors*. England. 1594. Lang.: Eng.　　2504

Coleridge on Shakespeare's *Comedy of Errors*. England. 1594. Lang.: Eng.　　2505

Early criticism of Shakespeare's *The Comedy of Errors*. England. 1594. Lang.: Eng.　　2535

Early feminist criticism of Shakespeare's *The Comedy of Errors*. England. 1594. Lang.: Eng.　　2548

Comparison of Shakespeare's *Winter's Tale* and *Comedy of Errors*. England. 1591-1611. Lang.: Eng.　　2552

Slavery and servitude in Shakespeare's *Comedy of Errors*. England. 1590. Lang.: Eng.　　2589

Doubles in Shakespeare's *The Comedy of Errors*. England. 1594. Lang.: Eng.　　2616

Feminist analysis of Shakespeare's *Comedy of Errors*. England. 1594. Lang.: Eng.　　2627

Analysis of *The Comedy of Errors* by Shakespeare. England. 1594. Lang.: Eng.　　2630

The double plot structure of Shakespeare's *Comedy of Errors*. England. 1594. Lang.: Eng.　　2633

Feminist critique of Shakespeare's *The Comedy of Errors*. England. 1594. Lang.: Eng.　　2646

Introduction to essays on Shakespeare's *Comedy of Errors*. England. 1594. Lang.: Eng.　　2665

The use of poetry and meter in Shakespeare's *The Comedy of Errors*. England. 1594. Lang.: Eng.　　2685

Shakespeare's use of farce in *The Comedy of Errors*. England. 1594. Lang.: Eng.　　2772

Comparison of classical Roman, Renaissance Italian, and Shakespearean treatments of similar stories. Europe. 200 B.C.-1610 A.D. Lang.: Eng.　　2799

Survey of musical adaptations of Shakespeare. USA: New York, NY. 1938-1997. Lang.: Eng.　　3987

Comedy Theatre (Budapest)
SEE
Vigszinház.

Comedy Theatre (London)
Performance/production
Collection of newspaper reviews by London theatre critics. UK-England: London. 1997. Lang.: Eng.　　2009

Collection of newspaper reviews by London theatre critics. UK-England: London. 1997. Lang.: Eng.　　2093

Collection of newspaper reviews by London theatre critics. UK-England: London. 1997. Lang.: Eng.　　2122

Comfort of Strangers, The
Plays/librettos/scripts
British Library holdings of filmscript material of Harold Pinter. UK-England. 1963-1994. Lang.: Eng.　　3647

Analysis of Harold Pinter's film script *The Comfort of Strangers*. UK-England. 1990. Lang.: Eng.　　3650

Comical History of Don Quixote, The
Plays/librettos/scripts
Female 'mad' songs in seventeenth-century English drama. England. 1685-1700. Lang.: Eng.　　2638

Coming Into Passion/Song for a Sansei
Performance/production
Interview with solo artist Jude Narita. USA: Los Angeles, CA. 1987-1989. Lang.: Eng.　　2341

Composing — cont'd

Theatrical vocal music of Nancy Van de Vate. USA. 1945-1995. Lang.:
Eng. 3884

Kurt Weill's collaborations with playwrights. Germany: Berlin. USA:
New York, NY. 1927-1945. Lang.: Eng. 3934

Restaging the score of Stephen Sondheim's *A Little Night Music*. USA.
1973. Lang.: Eng. 3951

The reconstructed orchestration for the revival of *The Boys from
Syracuse* by Encores!. USA: New York, NY. 1938-1997. Lang.: Eng.
3970

Composer/lyricist Maury Yeston. USA: New York, NY. 1945-1997.
Lang.: Eng. 3975

Versions of Falla's *El amor brujo*. 1915-1924. Lang.: Fre. 4072

Analysis of Mozart's *Die Zauberflöte*. Austria. 1791. Lang.: Eng. 4095

Musical disguises in Mozart's late comic operas. Austria. 1786-1790.
Lang.: Eng. 4101

Analysis of arias in the last act of Mozart's *Le Nozze di Figaro*. Austro-
Hungarian Empire: Vienna. 1786-1997. Lang.: Eng. 4102

Composer Calixa Levallée. Canada. 1842-1891. Lang.: Eng. 4116

Problem of staging the works of Janáček. Czech Republic. 1854-1928.
Lang.: Cze. 4118

Interview with composer György Ligeti. Europe. 1997. Lang.: Fre. 4132

Composer György Ligeti. Europe. 1923-1997. Lang.: Fre. 4133

Composer Jacques Leguerney. France. 1906-1997. Lang.: Eng. 4138

Opera composer Charles Gounod. France: Paris. 1818-1893. Lang.: Eng.
4140

Influences on Dukas' opera *Ariane et Barbe-Bleue*. France. 1885-1936.
Lang.: Eng. 4143

The scandalous premiere of Wagner's *Das Rheingold*. Germany:
Munich, Bayreuth. 1869-1876. Lang.: Eng. 4150

Symbolism and reality in Wagnerian opera. Germany. 1813-1883.
Lang.: Dut. 4155

Hans Werner Henze's opera *Das Mädchen mit den Schwefelhölzern*.
Germany: Hamburg. 1921-1997. Lang.: Ger. 4156

Harmonic analysis of music of Sieglinde in Wagner's *Ring*. Germany.
1853-1874. Lang.: Eng. 4161

Historical introduction to *Palestrina* by Hans Pfitzner. Germany. 1917-
1997. Lang.: Eng. 4162

Speculations about Puccini's unfinished *Turandot*. Italy. 1867-1957.
Lang.: Eng. 4187

The influence of Mascagni, Leoncavallo, and Franchetti on Puccini's *La
Bohème*. Italy: Milan. 1894-1898. Lang.: Eng. 4190

The critical reception of compositions by Saverio Mercadante. Italy.
1852-1995. Lang.: Eng. 4193

Puccini's use of the key of A major. Italy. 1836. Lang.: Eng. 4194

Historical and literary influences on Verdi's operas. Italy. 1813-1901.
Lang.: Eng. 4195

Giordano's opera *Fedora* and its reputation. Italy. 1898-1997. Lang.:
Eng. 4198

Wagner's influence on Čajkovskij's operas. Russia. 1877-1884. Lang.:
Eng. 4208

Analysis of the opera *Eugene Onegin* by Čajkovskij. Russia. 1879-1997.
Lang.: Eng. 4209

Life of composer Manuel de Falla. Spain. 1876-1946. Lang.: Fre. 4211

Musical development of composer Manuel de Falla. Spain. 1876-1926.
Lang.: Fre. 4212

Gottfried von Einem's opera *Der Besuch der alten Dame*. Switzerland.
1918-1996. Lang.: Eng. 4222

Profile of opera composer Peter Lieberson. USA: New York, NY. 1947-
1997. Lang.: Eng. 4241

Anthony Davis' opera *Amistad*. USA: Chicago, IL. 1997. Lang.: Eng.
4242

The Ballad of Baby Doe by Douglas Moore as the quintessential
American opera. USA. 1957-1997. Lang.: Eng. 4269

Plays/librettos/scripts
La Balade du Grand Macabre by Ghelderode and its operatic
adaptation by György Ligeti. Belgium. 1934. Lang.: Fre. 2385

Idealism and the work of Stephen Sondheim. USA. 1956-1996. Lang.:
Eng. 3984

Analysis of Stephen Sondheim's *Pacific Overtures*. USA. 1976. Lang.:
Eng. 3990

The chorus in musicals by Stephen Sondheim. USA. 1962-1996. Lang.:
Eng. 3991

The relationship of lyricists Stephen Sondheim and Oscar Hammerstein
II. USA. 1945-1968. Lang.: Eng. 3996

Songwriting team John Kander and Fred Ebb. USA: New York, NY.
1927-1997. Lang.: Eng. 4001

Symbolism in Wagner's *Ring*. Germany. 1853-1874. Lang.: Eng. 4298

Thomas Jennefelt's new opera *Farkosten*. Sweden. 1985-1997. Lang.:
Swe. 4313

Theory/criticism
The reaction of Hector Berlioz to Donizetti's *La Fille du régiment*.
France. 1840. Lang.: Fre. 4328

Computers—administration
Administration
Directory of available software for non-profit organizations. USA. 1997.
Lang.: Eng. 118

Design/technology
Theatrical uses of computers and the internet. Germany. 1997. Lang.:
Ger. 167

Computers—design/technology
Design/technology
Emerging technology for theatre design and scenography. Canada. USA.
1997. Lang.: Eng. 152

Theatrical uses of computers and the internet. Germany. 1997. Lang.:
Ger. 167

Big Image Systems' theatrical use of computer-generated projections.
Sweden: Täby. 1987. Lang.: Swe. 186

Ratings of lighting design software. USA. 1994. Lang.: Eng. 198

Survey of lighting design software. USA. 1996. Lang.: Eng. 203

Survey of lighting design software. USA. 1997. Lang.: Eng. 206

Ratings of lighting design software. USA. 1995. Lang.: Eng. 218

Internet technology for communication among design staffs. USA. 1997.
Lang.: Eng. 241

Design conferences in cyberspace. USA. 1997. Lang.: Eng. 280

The need for an advanced common-protocol high-speed network for
lighting. USA. 1997. Lang.: Eng. 290

Performance/production
Profile of television series *The Wubbulous World of Dr. Seuss*. USA:
New York, NY. 1997. Lang.: Eng. 4397

Computers—internet
Administration
International copyright law and current technology. 1997. Lang.: Eng. 1

Preparing for new media and technologies in the theatre. Europe. 1997.
Lang.: Ger. 22

The crucial importance of the internet for not-for-profit organizations.
USA. 1997. Lang.: Eng. 127

Design/technology
Theatrical uses of computers and the internet. Germany. 1997. Lang.:
Ger. 167

List of websites for lighting resources. USA. 1997. Lang.: Eng. 210

Performance/production
The Non-Traditional Casting Project's on-line artist files. USA. 1997.
Lang.: Eng. 625

List of opera-related websites. 1997. Lang.: Eng. 4073

Plays/librettos/scripts
Internet marketing of plays. USA. 1997. Lang.: Eng. 703

Relation to other fields
Teaching Shakespeare and the World Wide Web. USA. 1997. Lang.:
Eng. 3404

Teaching Shakespeare with the aid of the internet. USA. 1997. Lang.:
Eng. 3407

Teaching Shakespeare in the high-tech classroom. USA. 1997. Lang.:
Eng. 3431

Computers—performance/production
Design/technology
David Z. Saltz on his installation *Beckett Space*. USA. 1996. Lang.: Eng.
3702

Performance/production
Virtual reality and the death of entertainment. USA. 1993-1996. Lang.:
Eng. 3832

Current work of performance artist Laurie Anderson. USA. 1960-1997.
Lang.: Eng. 3833

Plays/librettos/scripts
Computer-based interactive drama. USA. 1996. Lang.: Eng. 707

Cosimi, Enzo
Performance/production
Choreography in the second half of the twentieth century. Italy. USA. 1950-1997. Lang.: Ita. 981

Cossa, Roberto
Performance/production
Collection of newspaper reviews by London theatre critics. UK-England: London. 1997. Lang.: Eng. 2146

Cosson, Steven
Performance/production
The making of *Tailings* by Erik Ehn and Smart Mouth Theatre. USA: San Francisco, CA. 1995-1997. Lang.: Eng. 636

Costello, Hugh
Performance/production
Collection of newspaper reviews by London theatre critics. UK-England: London. 1997. Lang.: Eng. 2089

Costigan, George
Performance/production
Collection of newspaper reviews by London theatre critics. UK-England. 1997. Lang.: Eng. 2125

Costuming
Design/technology
Design in Ontario theatre. Canada. 1914-1979. Lang.: Eng. 142

Photos of scenographic exhibition, Musée d'art contemporain. Canada: Montreal, PQ. 1997. Lang.: Eng. 144

Ariel's costume in the original staging of *The Tempest*. England: London. 1570-1612. Lang.: Eng. 156

Costume in Renaissance theatre. England. 1100-1500. Lang.: Eng. 157

The history of costume and the structure of Western European dress. Europe. 250 B.C.-1995 A.D. Lang.: Eng. 161

Scenery and costume designer Eric Vogel. Hungary. 1907-1996. Lang.: Hun. 172

Scene and costume designer Attila Csikós. Hungary. 1960-1997. Lang.: Hun. 173

Costume designs of Boris I. Anisfeld, soon to be exhibited. Russia: St. Petersburg. USA. 1994-1997. Lang.: Eng. 180

Theatrical costumes of Kalmykija. Russia. 1990-1997. Lang.: Rus. 181

The actor, the costume, and the audience. Russia. 1700-1950. Lang.: Rus. 183

Theatrical training for tailors and dressers at the Swiss Technical College for Women. Switzerland: Zurich. 1989-1997. Lang.: Ger. 191

Costumer, choreographer, director Bernard Johnson. USA: New York, NY. 1997. Lang.: Eng. 234

Profile of Tech Expo '97. USA: Pittsburgh, PA. 1997. Lang.: Eng. 235

Costume designer Freddy Wittop. USA. 1911-1997. Lang.: Eng. 249

Interview with costume designer Judit Gombár. Hungary. 1955-1996. Lang.: Hun. 941

Exhibition of scenery and costumes for Ballets Russes productions. Russia. France. 1909-1929. Lang.: Eng. 1048

Houston Ballet Company's *Dracula*—costumes, sets, lighting. USA: Houston, TX. 1897-1997. Lang.: Eng. 1049

Design and community theatre. Canada. 1990-1997. Lang.: Eng. 1355

Costume design for *Warrior* by Shirley Gee. USA: Long Beach, CA. 1997. Lang.: Eng. 1374

Film costume designer Ruth Myers. USA. 1997. Lang.: Eng. 3548

Production and costume design for the film adaptation of *The Crucible*. USA. 1995-1996. Lang.: Eng. 3549

Costuming for film and video. USA. 1997. Lang.: Eng. 3552

The significance of costume in Beijing opera. China, People's Republic of: Beijing. 1996. Lang.: Eng. 3890

Design elements of *On the Town* for New York Shakespeare Festival. USA: New York, NY. 1997. Lang.: Eng. 3915

Roland Topor's costume designs for a production of *Le Grand Macabre* by Ligeti. Italy: Bologna. 1979. Lang.: Fre. 4026

Kungliga Operan's costume collection. Sweden: Stockholm. 1954-1997. Lang.: Swe. 4030

Opera costume designer Martin Pakledinaz. USA: Santa Fe, NM, New York, NY. 1997. Lang.: Eng. 4035
Performance/production
CD-ROM presentation of all aspects of *kutiyattam*. India. 1000-1997. Lang.: Eng. 557

Essays on practical theatre problems. Slovenia. 1765-1914. Lang.: Slo. 604

Practice wear of dancers. Sweden: Stockholm. 1997. Lang.: Swe. 986

The effect of costuming on ballet technique. France. 1830-1850. Lang.: Eng. 1071

Hoods and masks in the original production of Shakespeare's *Measure for Measure*. England: London. 1555-1604. Lang.: Eng. 1626

Videodisc of Ibsen's *Et Dukkehjem (A Doll's House)* combining performance and commentary. Norway. USA. 1879-1997. Lang.: Eng. 1830

Conductor's performance guide to the Stuart masque. England. 1500-1640. Lang.: Eng. 3796

Opera Atelier's production of Purcell's *Dido and Aeneas*. Canada: Toronto, ON. 1994-1995. Lang.: Eng. 4112
Relation to other fields
Boydell's 'Shakespeare Gallery' and the eighteenth-century stage. England. 1757-1772. Lang.: Eng. 732

Côté, Lorraine
Plays/librettos/scripts
Adaptations of French classics for contemporary audiences. Canada: Montreal, PQ. France. 1997. Lang.: Fre. 2421

Lorraine Côté's adaptation of Voltaire's *Candide* for Sous-Marin Jaune puppet theatre. Canada: Montreal, PQ. 1997. Lang.: Fre. 4394

Cotgrave, John
Performance/production
Collection of newspaper reviews by London theatre critics. UK-England: London. 1997. Lang.: Eng. 1976

Cottesloe Theatre (London)
SEE ALSO
Design/technology
Design for three productions of Tony Kushner's *Angels in America*. USA: New York, NY, Los Angeles, CA. UK-England: London. 1992-1994. Lang.: Eng. 1363
Performance/production
Collection of newspaper reviews by London theatre critics. UK-England: London. 1997. Lang.: Eng. 1973

Collection of newspaper reviews by London theatre critics. UK-England: London. 1997. Lang.: Eng. 1983

Collection of newspaper reviews by London theatre critics. UK-England: London. 1997. Lang.: Eng. 1999

Collection of newspaper reviews by London theatre critics. UK-England: London. 1997. Lang.: Eng. 2023

Collection of newspaper reviews by London theatre critics. UK-England: London. 1997. Lang.: Eng. 2055

Collection of newspaper reviews by London theatre critics. UK-England: London. 1997. Lang.: Eng. 2114

Collection of newspaper reviews by London theatre critics. UK-England: London. 1997. Lang.: Eng. 2122

Collection of newspaper reviews by London theatre critics. UK-England: London. 1997. Lang.: Eng. 2144

Cottis, David
Performance/production
Collection of newspaper reviews by London theatre critics. UK-England: London. 1997. Lang.: Eng. 2056

Cottrell, Richard
Performance/production
Collection of newspaper reviews by London theatre critics. UK-England: London. 1997. Lang.: Eng. 1987

Collection of newspaper reviews by London theatre critics. UK-England. 1997. Lang.: Eng. 2043

Coulbois, Jean-Claude
Plays/librettos/scripts
Jean-Claude Coulbois' video documentary on Quebec theatre *Un miroir sur la scène (A Mirror on the Stage)*. Canada. 1997. Lang.: Fre. 3734

Couleur de cerne et de lilas (Color of Bruises and Lilac, The)
Basic theatrical documents
Text of *Couleur de cerne et de lilas (The Color of Bruises and Lilac)* by Yoland Simon. France. 1996. Lang.: Fre. 1276

Coulter, Clare
Performance/production
Collection of newspaper reviews by London theatre critics. UK-England: London. 1997. Lang.: Eng. 1974

Council of Resident Stock Theatres (New York, NY)
Administration
New company category in the Council of Resident Stock Theatres agreement. USA. 1997. Lang.: Eng. 100

Country Wife, The
Plays/librettos/scripts
Theoretical knowledge and action in plays of Wycherley. England. 1671-1676. Lang.: Eng. 2590

Danielsson, Ronny — cont'd

Institutions
The closing of Göteborgs Stadsteatern. Sweden: Gothenburg. 1996.
Lang.: Swe.   1480
Interview with Ronny Danielsson, manager of Göteborgs Stadsteatern.
Sweden: Gothenburg. 1997. Lang.: Swe.   1486
The closing of Göteborgs Stadsteatern. Sweden: Gothenburg. 1995.
Lang.: Swe.   1488

Danny and Me
Performance/production
Collection of newspaper reviews by London theatre critics. UK-England:
London. 1997. Lang.: Eng.   1995

Dans la solitude des champs de coton (In the Solitude of the Cotton Fields)
Performance/production
Collection of newspaper reviews by London theatre critics. UK-England:
London. 1997. Lang.: Eng.   2017

Dansaren och tystnaden på 100 decibel (Dancer and the Silence of 100 Decibels, The)
Performance/production
TV performances of young choreographers. Sweden. 1997. Lang.: Swe.
                                                                 1186

Dansens Hus (Stockholm)
Theory/criticism
Dansens Hus seminar on postmodern American dance. Sweden:
Stockholm. USA. 1997. Lang.: Swe.   1214

Dansereau, France
Performance/production
Children's theatre actress France Dansereau. Canada: Montreal, PQ.
1974-1997. Lang.: Fre.   1579

Dante, Nicholas
Performance/production
History of American musical theatre. USA. UK-England. 1912-1995.
Lang.: Eng.   3954

Dantons Tod (Danton's Death)
Basic theatrical documents
Slovene translations of plays by Georg Büchner. Germany. 1835-1837.
Lang.: Slo.   1278
Performance/production
The new season at Bochumer Schauspielhaus. Germany: Bochum. 1997.
Lang.: Ger.   1747
Collection of newspaper reviews by London theatre critics. UK-England:
London. 1997. Lang.: Eng.   2110

Dark at the Top of the Stairs, The
Plays/librettos/scripts
The personal and professional relationship of playwrights Tennessee
Williams and William Inge. USA. 1943-1957. Lang.: Eng.   3128

Dark Meadows
Performance/production
Analysis of Martha Graham's Greek cycle of dance dramas. USA. 1926-
1991. Lang.: Ita.   1198

Dark Voices Ring
Plays/librettos/scripts
Postcolonialism and early plays of Zakes Mda. South Africa, Republic
of. 1979-1997. Lang.: Eng.   3029

Darling, Pet
Performance/production
Collection of newspaper reviews by London theatre critics. UK-England:
London. 1997. Lang.: Eng.   1971

Dart, Philip
Performance/production
Collection of newspaper reviews by London theatre critics. UK-England:
London. 1997. Lang.: Eng.   2105

Dartnell, Guy
Performance/production
Collection of newspaper reviews by London theatre critics. UK-England:
London. 1997. Lang.: Eng.   1988

Dashwood, Robin
Performance/production
Collection of newspaper reviews by London theatre critics. UK-England:
London. 1997. Lang.: Eng.   1982

Daszewski, Władysław
Relation to other fields
Stage designer Władysław Daszewski and actions taken against Polish
writers. Poland: Lvov. 1940. Lang.: Pol.   775

Date, The
Basic theatrical documents
Text of *The Date* by Kym Moore. USA. 1997. Lang.: Eng.   1336

Dattani, Mahesh
Performance/production
Interviews with writer-directors K.N. Pannikkar, Mahesh Dattani, and
Tripurari Sharma. India. 1997. Lang.: Eng.   1781

Daugherty, Michael
Plays/librettos/scripts
Material for contemporary opera. UK-England: London. 1960-1997.
Lang.: Eng.   4314

Daughters of Heaven
Plays/librettos/scripts
Analysis of *Daughters of Heaven* by Michelanne Forster. New Zealand.
1954-1996. Lang.: Eng.   2979

Daulac
Plays/librettos/scripts
Indigenous peoples in Canadian historical drama. Canada. 1886-1997.
Lang.: Eng.   2424

Davenant, William
Administration
Analysis of a legal agreement involving the Red Bull Company.
England: London. 1660-1663. Lang.: Eng.   16
Research/historiography
Proposal for a revised history of English opera. England. 1639-1711.
Lang.: Eng.   4325

Davenport, Marcia
Performance/production
Opera critic, novelist and biographer Marcia Davenport. USA. 1904-
1996. Lang.: Eng.   4262

Davey, Patrick
Performance/production
Collection of newspaper reviews by London theatre critics. UK-England:
London. 1997. Lang.: Eng.   2132

David Copperfield
Performance/production
Collection of newspaper reviews by London theatre critics. UK-England:
London. 1997. Lang.: Eng.   2155

David, Anthony
Performance/production
Anthony Davis' opera *Amistad*. USA: Chicago, IL. 1997. Lang.: Eng.
                                                                 4242

David, John
Performance/production
Collection of newspaper reviews by London theatre critics. UK-England:
London. 1997. Lang.: Eng.   2160

Dávid, Zsuzsa
Performance/production
Four productions of the musical *A Dzsungel könyve (The Jungle Book)*.
Hungary. 1996-1997. Lang.: Hun.   3936

Davids, Colin
Performance/production
Collection of newspaper reviews by London theatre critics. UK-England.
1997. Lang.: Eng.   2142

Davidson, Eric
Performance/production
Collection of newspaper reviews by London theatre critics. UK-England:
London. 1997. Lang.: Eng.   1995

Davies, Howard
Performance/production
Collection of newspaper reviews by London theatre critics. UK-England:
London. 1997. Lang.: Eng.   1977
Collection of newspaper reviews by London theatre critics. UK-England:
London. 1997. Lang.: Eng.   2000

Davies, Lindy
Performance/production
Collection of newspaper reviews by London theatre critics. UK-England:
London. 1997. Lang.: Eng.   2089

Davila Roa
Plays/librettos/scripts
Analysis of *Davila Roa* by Alessandro Baricco. Italy. 1997. Lang.: Ita.
                                                                 2972

Davis, Alison
Performance/production
Collection of newspaper reviews by London theatre critics. UK-England:
London. 1997. Lang.: Eng.   1986

Davis, David
Basic theatrical documents
Text of *Five Exits* by David Davis. USA. 1995. Lang.: Eng.   1323

Davis, Jack
Plays/librettos/scripts
Analysis of Aboriginal drama. Australia. 1967-1997. Lang.: Eng. 2376

Davis, Thulani
Performance/production
Anthony Davis' opera *Amistad*. USA: Chicago, IL. 1997. Lang.: Eng.
                                                                 4242

Dawson, Andrew
  Performance/production
    Collection of newspaper reviews by London theatre critics. UK-England:
    London. 1997. Lang.: Eng.   2002
    Collection of newspaper reviews by London theatre critics. UK-England:
    London. 1997. Lang.: Eng.   2149
Daylight
  Design/technology
    Benjamin Fernandez's production design for *Daylight*. Italy: Rome.
    1996. Lang.: Eng.   3543
Dayton Playhouse (Dayton, OH)
  Plays/librettos/scripts
    Statement of an adjudicator for a new-play competition. USA: Dayton,
    OH. 1997. Lang.: Eng.   3268
De Angelis, April
  Performance/production
    Collection of newspaper reviews by London theatre critics. UK-England:
    London. 1997. Lang.: Eng.   2008
    Collection of newspaper reviews by London theatre critics. UK-England:
    London. 1997. Lang.: Eng.   2101
De Beauvoir, Simone
  SEE
    Beauvoir, Simone de.
De Berardinis, Leo
  Performance/production
    Leo De Berardinis' production of Shakespeare's *King Lear*. Italy:
    Naples. 1996. Lang.: Ita.   1799
De Céspedes, Alba
  Plays/librettos/scripts
    Analysis of Alba De Céspedes' stage adaptation of her novel *Quaderno
    proibido (Forbidden Notebook)*. Italy. 1952. Lang.: Ita.   2950
De Filippo, Eduardo
  Plays/librettos/scripts
    Analysis of *Non ti pago (I Don't Pay You)* by Eduardo De Filippo.
    Italy. 1940-1997. Lang.: Ita.   2951
de Guevara, Lina
  Plays/librettos/scripts
    Account of *Sisters/Strangers*, a community play about immigrant
    women. Canada: Victoria, BC. 1994. Lang.: Eng.   2398
de Jongh, Nicholas
  Performance/production
    Collection of newspaper reviews by London theatre critics. UK-England:
    London. 1997. Lang.: Eng.   2036
De Keersmaeker, Anne Teresa
  Performance/production
    Choreographer Anne Teresa De Keersmaeker. Belgium: Brussels. 1980-
    1997. Lang.: Eng.   1174
De La Guarda (London)
  Performance/production
    Collection of newspaper reviews by London theatre critics. UK-England:
    London. 1997. Lang.: Eng.   2076
De Molina, Tirso
  SEE
    Molina, Tirso de.
De Niro, Robert
  Plays/librettos/scripts
    Analysis of films by Martin Scorsese. USA. 1976-1982. Lang.: Eng. 3676
De Palma, Brian
  Plays/librettos/scripts
    Generic hybridization in the gangster film. USA. 1932-1983. Lang.: Eng.
                                                                           3688
De Roberval
  Plays/librettos/scripts
    Indigenous peoples in Canadian historical drama. Canada. 1886-1997.
    Lang.: Eng.   2424
de Silva, David
  Performance/production
    Collection of newspaper reviews by London theatre critics. UK-England:
    London. 1997. Lang.: Eng.   2137
De Simone, Roberto
  Performance/production
    Italian productions of D'Annunzio's *La Figlia di Iorio (Iorio's
    Daughter)*. Italy. 1904-1983. Lang.: Ita.   1797
De Veaux, Alexis
  Plays/librettos/scripts
    The Black woman's body in *The Tapestry* by Alexis De Veaux. USA.
    1976-1997. Lang.: Eng.   3281
de Vere, Edward
  Plays/librettos/scripts
    The anti-Oxfordian position in the 'who was Shakespeare' debate.
    England. 1590-1616. Lang.: Eng.   2607

De Virués, Cristóbal
  Plays/librettos/scripts
    The figure of Dido in works of the Italian Renaissance and Spanish
    Golden Age. Italy. Spain. 1542-1616. Lang.: Ita.   2957
de Vries, Marion
  Basic theatrical documents
    Text of *big face* by Marion de Vries. Canada. 1995. Lang.: Eng.   1257
De Wet, Reza
  Plays/librettos/scripts
    Analysis of *A Worm in the Bud* by Reza De Wet. South Africa,
    Republic of. 1990. Lang.: Eng.   3023
De-Ba-Jeh-Mu-Jig Theatre Group (Manitoulin Isand, ON)
  Performance/production
    Native Canadian playwrights and theatre groups. Canada. 1979-1997.
    Lang.: Eng.   1597
Dead Class, The
  SEE
    Umerla Klasa.
Dead End
  Plays/librettos/scripts
    Postcolonialism and early plays of Zakes Mda. South Africa, Republic
    of. 1979-1997. Lang.: Eng.   3029
Deaf theatre
  Performance/production
    Julianna Fjeld's *The Journey*, performed in American Sign Language.
    USA. 1997. Lang.: Eng.   669
    Interview with actor and director Tom Fjordefalk. Sweden. 1972-1997.
    Lang.: Swe.   1948
    Deaf playwright Raymond Luczak on Deaf theatre. USA. 1997. Lang.:
    Eng.   2293
Dean, Charlotte
  Performance/production
    Shaw Festival production of *In Good King Charles's Golden Days*.
    Canada: Niagara-on-the-Lake, ON. 1997. Lang.: Eng.   1582
Dean, Dazz
  Performance/production
    Collection of newspaper reviews by London theatre critics. UK-England:
    London. 1997. Lang.: Eng.   2006
Dear Brutus
  Performance/production
    Collection of newspaper reviews by London theatre critics. UK-England:
    London. 1997. Lang.: Eng.   2123
  Plays/librettos/scripts
    Time travel in English-language drama. USA. Canada. UK-England.
    1908-1993. Lang.: Eng.   3171
Dearest Daddy ... Darling Daughter
  Performance/production
    Collection of newspaper reviews by London theatre critics. UK-England:
    London. 1997. Lang.: Eng.   2156
Dearly Beloved
  Performance/production
    Collection of newspaper reviews by London theatre critics. UK-England:
    London. 1997. Lang.: Eng.   2059
Death and the Maiden
  SEE ALSO
    Muerte y la doncella, La.
  Performance/production
    Analysis of Robert North's choreography for Schubert's *Death and the
    Maiden*. USA. 1945-1992. Lang.: Hun.   1122
Death in Venice
  Performance/production
    Lyric tenor Philip Langridge. UK-England: London. 1997. Lang.: Eng.
                                                                           4225
Death of a Princess
  Plays/librettos/scripts
    Interview with documentary filmmaker Anthony Thomas. USA. 1980-
    1997. Lang.: Eng.   3678
Death of a Salesman
  Institutions
    Management and productions of Schauspiel Nürnberg. Germany:
    Nuremberg. 1997. Lang.: Ger.   1431
  Performance/production
    Actor Al Waxman. Canada: Stratford, ON. 1967-1997. Lang.: Eng. 1576
  Plays/librettos/scripts
    The figure of the prodigal son in American family drama. USA. 1946-
    1962. Lang.: Eng.   3254
    Analysis of *Death of a Salesman* by Arthur Miller. USA. 1949. Lang.:
    Eng.   3265

Directing — cont'd

Directing — cont'd

Directing — cont'd

Atom Egoyan's staging of *Salome*, Canadian Opera Company. Canada: Toronto, ON. 1996. Lang.: Eng. 4111

Problem of staging the works of Janáček. Czech Republic. 1854-1928. Lang.: Cze. 4118

Interview with opera director Judit Galgóczy. Hungary. 1987-1997. Lang.: Hun. 4168

László Márkus, former general director of Royal Hungarian Opera House. Hungary: Budapest. 1923-1944. Lang.: Hun. 4173

Profile of tenor and opera stage director György Anthes. Hungary. 1863-1922. Lang.: Hun. 4179

Interview with opera director Balázs Kovalik. Hungary: Budapest. 1995-1997. Lang.: Hun. 4185

Pierre Audi's production of Wagner's *Ring* for Nederlandse Opera. Netherlands: Amsterdam. 1997. Lang.: Dut. 4200

Opera director Boris Pokrovskij. Russia. 1980-1997. Lang.: Rus. 4205

Interview with puppeteer John Ludwig. USA: Atlanta, GA. 1996. Lang.: Eng. 4376

Obituary for Jon Stone of *Sesame Street*. USA: New York, NY. 1997. Lang.: Eng. 4398

Plays/librettos/scripts
Playwright and director Juha Lehtola. Finland. 1997. Lang.: Eng, Fre. 2800

Interview with playwrights Tankred Dorst and Ursula Ehler. Germany. 1997. Lang.: Fin. 2849

Romeo Castellucci's adaptation of the *Oresteia*. Italy: Cesena. 1995. Lang.: Ger, Fre, Dut, Eng. 2947

Interview with playwright/director Fernando Arrabal. Spain. 1932-1996. Lang.: Eng. 3048

Interview with director and author Margarete Garpe. Sweden: Stockholm. 1960-1997. Lang.: Swe. 3063

Interview with Emily Mann, author and director of documentary theatre. USA: Princeton, NJ. 1981-1996. Lang.: Eng. 3139

East Asian influences on writing and directing of Anne Bogart. USA. 1984-1994. Lang.: Eng. 3223

Interview with screenwriter and director Shirley Barrett. Australia. 1997. Lang.: Eng. 3632

Interview with screenwriter and director Atom Egoyan. Canada. 1997. Lang.: Eng. 3633

Richard Loncraine and Ian McKellen's film adaptation of *Richard III*. UK-England. 1995. Lang.: Eng. 3651

Profile of director and screenwriter Joseph L. Mankiewicz. USA. 1909-1993. Lang.: Eng. 3659

David Mamet as screen writer and director. USA. 1975-1995. Lang.: Eng. 3672

Film adaptation of Eric Bogosian's *Talk Radio*. USA: Hollywood, CA. 1988. Lang.: Eng. 3673

Critique of Franco Zeffirelli's film adaptation of *Hamlet*. USA. 1990. Lang.: Eng. 3675

Relation to other fields
Director Einar Schleef on his life in East Germany. Germany, East. 1964-1997. Lang.: Ger. 3356

Theory/criticism
Director Esa Kirkkopelto on the impact of a theatrical performance. Finland. 1997. Lang.: Fin. 881

Hungarian translation of an essay on rhythm in stage direction by Patrice Pavis. France. 1985. Lang.: Hun. 892

Hungarian translation of essays on criticism by Herbert Jhering. Germany. 1918-1933. Lang.: Hun. 896

Polemic on theory and directing. Hungary. 1997. Lang.: Hun. 902

Critique of theoretical approach to analysis of directing. Hungary. 1990. Lang.: Hun. 903

Seminar on dance, text, and theatre. Sweden: Stockholm. 1997. Lang.: Swe. 1032

Methods of notation for the recording of theatrical productions. 1901-1997. Lang.: Eng. 3456

Speech and writing in various aspects of theatre. France. 1997. Lang.: Fre. 3486

Training
The career of Jerzy Grotowski and notes on one of his seminars. Poland. Italy. 1959-1991. Lang.: Ita. 931

The teaching of performance composition. USA: New York, NY. 1997. Lang.: Eng. 937

Directories
Design/technology
Source directory for lighting equipment. USA. 1994. Lang.: Eng. 199

Source directory for lighting equipment. USA. 1995. Lang.: Eng. 200

Source directory for lighting equipment. USA. 1996. Lang.: Eng. 202

Directory of IESNA membership. USA: New York, NY. 1997. Lang.: Eng. 207

Directory of lighting industry resources. USA. 1997. Lang.: Eng. 209

List of websites for lighting resources. USA. 1997. Lang.: Eng. 210

Directory of manufacturers of lighting equipment. USA. 1997. Lang.: Eng. 217

Directory of USITT members. USA. 1997-1998. Lang.: Eng. 281

Institutions
Directory of small Canadian opera companies. Canada. 1997. Lang.: Eng. 4040

Reference materials
European performing arts yearbook. Europe. 1997. Lang.: Eng. 713

Yearbook of British performing arts. UK-England. 1996-1997. Lang.: Eng. 719

Directory of African-American theatre. USA. 1824-1960. Lang.: Eng. 721

A biographical directory of Hispanic presence in American film. USA. 1911-1995. Lang.: Eng. 3690

Directory of television musicals. USA. 1944-1996. Lang.: Eng. 3736

Dirty Tricks
Performance/production
Collection of newspaper reviews by London theatre critics. UK-England: London. 1997. Lang.: Eng. 2133

Disco Pigs
Performance/production
Collection of newspaper reviews by London theatre critics. UK-England: London. 1997. Lang.: Eng. 1977

Discographies
Performance/production
Performer and songwriter Anthony Newley: profile and discography. USA: New York, NY. 1945-1967. Lang.: Eng. 3962

Singer/actress Liliane Montevecchi. USA. France. UK-England. 1933-1996. Lang.: Eng. 3963

Singer/actor Ron Husmann: profile and discography. USA: New York, NY. 1956-1997. Lang.: Eng. 3964

Recordings of Bellini's *La sonnambula*. 1899-1996. Lang.: Fre. 4083

Recordings of Cimarosa's *Il matrimonio segreto*. 1949-1992. Lang.: Fre. 4084

Recordings of *La Fille du régiment* by Donizetti. 1940-1989. Lang.: Fre. 4085

Recordings of Ligeti's *Le Grand Macabre*. 1979-1998. Lang.: Fre. 4087

Recordings of Manuel de Falla's opera *El retablo de Maese Pedro*. 1953-1975. Lang.: Fre. 4088

Listing and evaluation of complete recordings of Boieldieu's *La Dame Blanche*. 1961-1996. Lang.: Fre. 4091

Recordings of Manuel de Falla's opera *La vida breve*. 1913-1995. Lang.: Fre. 4092

Discovery, The
Plays/librettos/scripts
Frances Sheridan's *The Discovery* in the context of eighteenth-century theatre. England. 1740-1780. Lang.: Eng. 2451

Disney Corporation (Hollywood, CA)
Administration
Copyright law and videocassettes. USA. 1997. Lang.: Eng. 3709

Design/technology
Design of Disneyland's show *Light Magic*. USA: Anaheim, CA. 1997. Lang.: Eng. 260

Institutions
The impact of the Disney Corporation on Broadway. USA: New York, NY. 1990-1997. Lang.: Eng. 400

Performance spaces
The New Amsterdam Theatre and the redevelopment of Times Square. USA: New York, NY. 1920-1997. Lang.: Eng. 454

Dispute, La (Dispute, The)
Performance/production
Collection of newspaper reviews by London theatre critics. UK-England: London. 1997. Lang.: Eng. 2133

Diss, Eileen
Performance/production
Harold Pinter's performance in his own play *The Hothouse*. UK-England: Chichester. 1996. Lang.: Eng. 2205

Dissident, Va Sans Dire (Dissident, Goes Without Saying)
Performance/production
Collection of newspaper reviews by London theatre critics. UK-England: London. 1997. Lang.: Eng.   2136

Dits et Inédits (Tales and Unpublished Stories)
Institutions
Solo performance at the Festival de Théâtre des Amériques. Canada: Montreal, PQ. 1997. Lang.: Fre.   1392
Plays/librettos/scripts
Analysis of *Dits et Inédits (Tales and Unpublished Stories)* by Yvan Bienvenue. Canada: Montreal, PQ. 1997. Lang.: Fre.   2394

Divadlo Husa na Provázku (Brno)
Performance/production
Interpretations of Czech classics by Petr Lébl and Vladimír Morávek. Czech Republic. 1997. Lang.: Cze.   1609

Divadlo Jokai (Komarno)
SEE
Jókai Színház.

Divadlo Mimů Alfred ve dvoře Praha (Prague)
Institutions
The Czech pantomime theatre 'Alfred ve dvoře'. Czech Republic: Prague. 1961-1996. Lang.: Cze.   3742

Divadlo na Zábradlí (Prague)
Performance/production
Interpretations of Czech classics by Petr Lébl and Vladimír Morávek. Czech Republic. 1997. Lang.: Cze.   1609

Divadlo pod Palmovkou (Prague)
Performance/production
Productions of Pinter's plays in Prague. Czech Republic: Prague. 1994-1996. Lang.: Eng.   1613

Divadlo Spirála (Prague)
Performance spaces
Description of technically innovative Divadlo Spirála. Czech Republic: Prague. 1991-1997. Lang.: Ger.   419

Divine David, The (London)
Performance/production
Collection of newspaper reviews by London theatre critics. UK-England: London. 1997. Lang.: Eng.   1990

Divorce Me, Darling!
Performance/production
Collection of newspaper reviews by London theatre critics. UK-England. 1997. Lang.: Eng.   2082

Do Not Go Gentle
Theory/criticism
The effect of feminism on children's theatre. USA. 1995-1996. Lang.: Eng.   914

Do You Come Here Often?
Performance/production
Collection of newspaper reviews by London theatre critics. UK-England: London. 1997. Lang.: Eng.   1979

Doating Lover, or the Libertine Tam'd, The
Performance/production
Scottish plays on the London stage. England: London. Scotland. 1667-1715. Lang.: Eng.   1635

Dobay, Dezső
Institutions
Pictorial history of alternative theatre group R.S. 9. Hungary: Budapest. 1990-1997. Lang.: Hun.   1441

Dockteater Tittut (Stockholm)
Institutions
Profile of puppet theatre group Dockteater Tittut. Sweden: Stockholm. 1977. Lang.: Swe.   4353

Doctor Devine Presents: Baby Zoe's Midway Spectacular and Cabinet of Curiosities
Basic theatrical documents
Text of *Doctor Devine Presents*, a carnival scenario by Len Jenkin and John Arnone. USA. 1993. Lang.: Eng.   3781

Doctor Faustus
Plays/librettos/scripts
The nature of Christopher Marlowe's dramaturgy. England. 1585-1593. Lang.: Eng.   2454

Sex and gender in plays of Christopher Marlowe. England. 1587-1593. Lang.: Eng.   2522

Solipsism in Marlowe's *Doctor Faustus*. England. 1551-1616. Lang.: Eng.   2561

Subjectivity and discourse in medieval and early modern drama. England. 1250-1642. Lang.: Eng.   2579

Doctor Faustus and the rise of tragedy. England. 1604. Lang.: Eng. 2690

Documentary theatre
Plays/librettos/scripts
Interview with Emily Mann, author and director of documentary theatre. USA: Princeton, NJ. 1981-1996. Lang.: Eng.   3139

Interview with documentary filmmaker Anthony Thomas. USA. 1980-1997. Lang.: Eng.   3678

Dodi, Gideon
Performance/production
Collection of newspaper reviews by London theatre critics. UK-England: London. 1997. Lang.: Eng.   2087

Dodin, Lev Abramovič
Institutions
Malyj Dramatic Theatre under Lev Dodin. Russia: St. Petersburg. 1983-1996. Lang.: Eng.   1465

Dodson, Owen
Performance/production
Poet, playwright, director Owen Dodson. USA. 1914-1983. Lang.: Eng.   2274

Interview with playwright, director Owen Dodson. USA. 1975. Lang.: Eng.   2328

Dog in the Manger, The
SEE
Perro del hortelano, El.

Dog Opera
Plays/librettos/scripts
Interview with playwright Constance Congdon. USA. 1997. Lang.: Eng.   3163

Dogeaters
Institutions
The Sundance Institute Playwright's Lab. USA: Salt Lake City, UT. 1997. Lang.: Eng.   1512

Doggett, Thomas
Performance/production
The suppression of Thomas Doggett's troupe of strolling players. England: Cambridge. 1690-1701. Lang.: Eng.   507

Dogtroep (Amsterdam)
Institutions
Photographic history of Dogtroep. Netherlands: Amsterdam. 1991-1996. Lang.: Dut, Eng.   3759

Doishvili, David
Performance/production
Profile of recent Georgian theatre. Georgia: Tbilisi. 1993. Lang.: Swe.   1682

Dolce, Ludovico
Plays/librettos/scripts
The figure of Dido in works of the Italian Renaissance and Spanish Golden Age. Italy. Spain. 1542-1616. Lang.: Ita.   2957

Dolgačev, Vjačeslav
Performance/production
Moscow Art Theatre productions. Russia: Moscow. Estonia: Tallinn. 1996-1997. Lang.: Rus.   1861

Doll's House, A
SEE
Dukkehjem, Et.

Dom Aktera (Moscow)
Institutions
Profile of the Dom Aktera (Actors' House). Russia: Moscow. 1990-1997. Lang.: Rus.   368

Dom Juan (Don Juan)
Performance/production
Sociocultural analysis of recent French productions. France. 1993-1994. Lang.: Eng.   1678
Plays/librettos/scripts
The significance of Don Juan in works of Tirso, Mozart, and Molière. Europe. 1612-1787. Lang.: Eng.   2786

Domingo, Plácido
Performance/production
Interview with tenor Plácido Domingo on reviving the *zarzuela*. USA. 1941-1997. Lang.: Eng.   3980

Dominion Theatre (London)
Performance/production
Collection of newspaper reviews by London theatre critics. UK-England: London. 1997. Lang.: Eng.   2046

Don Carlo
Performance/production
Production history of Verdi's *Don Carlo*. Europe. USA. 1867-1997. Lang.: Eng.   4131

Historical and literary influences on Verdi's operas. Italy. 1813-1901. Lang.: Eng.   4195

Economics — cont'd

The importance of a company repertory in early English theatre. England. 1595-1603. Lang.: Eng.   504

The replacement of patronage by regular fees and ticket prices. England. 1580-1610. Lang.: Eng.   506

Compilation of records of early drama in Bristol. England: Bristol. 1255-1642. Lang.: Eng.   510

Reaction to Standard Bank's conference on economic aspects of the arts. South Africa, Republic of: Grahamstown. 1996. Lang.: Afr.   605

The emergence of modern American theatre. USA. 1914-1929. Lang.: Eng.   683

Early Shanghai filmmaking. China, People's Republic of: Shanghai. 1896-1937. Lang.: Eng.   3568

Plays/librettos/scripts

Radicalism in John Walker's melodrama *The Factory Lad*. England. 1820-1832. Lang.: Eng.   2591

Renaissance theatre and the marketplace. England. 1580-1620. Lang.: Eng.   2657

Racial and national meanings and economic practice in Renaissance theatre. England. 1590-1650. Lang.: Eng.   2693

The gift and money economies in plays of Shakespeare. England. 1590-1613. Lang.: Eng.   2706

Playwrights on capitalism: Funtek and Cankar. Slovenia. 1920. Lang.: Slo.   3016

The key role of sentimentalism in English melodrama. UK-England. 1800-1880. Lang.: Eng.   3082

Eda Theatre (Nigeria)
Plays/librettos/scripts

West African popular theatre: texts and analysis. Ghana. Togo. Nigeria. 1995-1997. Lang.: Eng.   2866

Eddie Goes to Poetry City
Design/technology

The scenography of Richard Foreman. USA. 1990-1996. Lang.: Eng.   1362

Eddy, Nelson
Performance/production

Nelson Eddy's career as an opera singer. USA. 1901-1967. Lang.: Eng.   4268

Edelstein, Gordon
Institutions

Seattle's theatrical renaissance. USA: Seattle, WA. 1980-1997. Lang.: Eng.   396

Eden, Mark
Performance/production

Collection of newspaper reviews by London theatre critics. UK-England: London. 1997. Lang.: Eng.   2059

Edgar, David
Plays/librettos/scripts

Medieval theatre as reflected in contemporary drama. UK-England. 1970-1990. Lang.: Eng.   3067

The relationship of creators and their work in devised theatre. UK-England. 1989. Lang.: Eng.   3083

Analysis of *Pentecost* by David Edgar. UK-England: Stratford. 1994-1997. Lang.: Eng.   3086

Masculinity in playwriting. UK-England. 1990-1996. Lang.: Eng.   3108

Edinburgh Festival
Institutions

Profile of the Edinburgh Festival on its fiftieth anniversary. UK-Scotland: Edinburgh. 1947-1997. Lang.: Eng.   390

Impressions of the Edinburgh Festival. UK-Scotland: Edinburgh. 1997. Lang.: Ger.   391

Report on the Edinburgh Festival. UK-Scotland: Edinburgh. 1997. Lang.: Eng.   393

Performance/production

Collection of newspaper reviews by London theatre critics. UK-Scotland: Edinburgh. 1997. Lang.: Eng.   2230

Collection of newspaper reviews by London theatre critics. UK-Scotland: Edinburgh. 1997. Lang.: Eng.   2232

Productions of plays by Caryl Churchill. UK-Scotland: Edinburgh. UK-England: London. 1997. Lang.: Eng.   2233

Editions
Basic theatrical documents

Critical edition of two versions of *El Alcalde de Zalamea*. Spain. 1642. Lang.: Spa.   1307

Performance/production

Attempt to reconstruct performances of plays by Massinger and Fletcher. England. 1628-1633. Lang.: Eng.   1622

Plays/librettos/scripts

The slaying of Polonius in editions of Shakespeare's *Hamlet*. England. 1603-1997. Lang.: Eng.   2498

Shakespearean text and editorial mangling in versions of *King Lear*. England. 1623-1993. Lang.: Eng.   2520

The performability of the first quarto of Shakespeare's *Hamlet*. England. 1603. Lang.: Eng.   2529

The 'bad quartos' of *The Merry Wives of Windsor* as abridged touring editions. England. 1597-1619. Lang.: Eng.   2598

Significant textual variants in Shakespeare's *King Lear* III.i. England. 1605-1623. Lang.: Eng.   2619

Censorship and editing of sexual and bawdy language in variorum editions of Shakespeare's plays. England. 1598-1997. Lang.: Eng.   2620

Proposed later date for a passage in Shakespeare's *Hamlet*. England. 1601-1709. Lang.: Eng.   2621

Analysis and bibliography of performance editions of Shakespeare's *Twelfth Night*. England. 1774-1992. Lang.: Eng.   2688

The significance of early performance editions of Shakespeare's plays. England. 1589-1613. Lang.: Eng.   2689

Critical edition of *King Edward the Fourth* by Thomas Heywood. England. 1600-1626. Lang.: Eng.   2699

History of the printings of Jonson's *Every Man in His Humour*. England: London. 1601-1616. Lang.: Eng.   2711

Analysis of versions of Shakespeare's *Hamlet*. England. 1600-1623. Lang.: Eng.   2767

The numerous versions of Büchner's *Woyzeck*. Germany. 1875-1981. Lang.: Eng.   2852

Continued debate on Shakespearean editorial practice. UK-England. 1592-1996. Lang.: Eng.   3080

The debate over different versions of Shakespeare's *Troilus and Cressida*. UK-England. 1995. Lang.: Eng.   3093

The chronology of Shakespeare's plays according to Chambers. UK-England. 1911-1930. Lang.: Eng.   3101

The classification, editing, and dissemination of early playscripts. UK-England. 1906-1996. Lang.: Eng.   3118

Theory/criticism

Career of Samuel Badcock, literary critic. England. 1779-1789. Lang.: Eng.   3471

Edmunds, Kate
Performance/production

Tony Kushner's *Angels in America* as epic theatre. USA. 1992-1995. Lang.: Eng.   2324

Education
Administration

The development by a group of fourth graders of a play about child labor. USA: Ridgewood, NJ. 1997. Lang.: Eng.   57

Marketing model for university graduate programs in theatre and dance. USA: Lubbock, TX. 1994-1996. Lang.: Eng.   126

Design/technology

Report on design education and training programs. USA. 1997. Lang.: Eng.   219

Institutions

Theatre training in Transylvania. Hungary. Romania. 1792-1997. Lang.: Hun.   330

Minutes of Columbia University Seminar on Shakespeare. USA: New York, NY. 1997. Lang.: Eng.   1515

Performance/production

Staged representations of AIDS. 1980-1997. Lang.: Eng.   461

Dancer Lulli Svedin. Sweden: Stockholm. 1920. Lang.: Swe.   1115

Dramaturgy in the American university. USA. 1997. Lang.: Eng.   2246

A picture book to introduce shadow puppet theatre to children. Slovenia. 1997. Lang.: Slo.   4403

Plays/librettos/scripts

American drama as represented in higher education. USA. 1710-1995. Lang.: Eng.   3279

Relation to other fields

Performing arts education and methods of investigation. Botswana: Serowe. 1997. Lang.: Eng.   727

History of open-air theatre since Rousseau. Europe. 1750-1997. Lang.: Ger.   742

Education, politics, and the amateur play movement. Germany. 1935-1940. Lang.: Ger.   753

Development of amateur theatre during the National Socialist period. Germany. 1935-1940. Lang.: Ger.   760

Education — cont'd

Conflicts in teaching literary criticism and theory. USA. 1612-1997. Lang.: Eng. 797

Innovations in collegiate theatrical instruction. USA. 1900-1945. Lang.: Eng. 798

Strategies for supporting theatre arts teachers in secondary school. USA. 1994-1996. Lang.: Eng. 802

Instructional techniques and needs of secondary theatre teachers. USA. 1996-1997. Lang.: Eng. 803

Case study of a high school theatre teacher. USA. 1995. Lang.: Eng. 805

The Advocacy Committee of the Association for Theatre in Higher Education. USA. 1996. Lang.: Eng. 810

Parental attitudes toward arts education for children. USA. 1980-1997. Lang.: Eng. 815

Joni L. Jones's performance piece *sista docta*. USA. 1994-1997. Lang.: Eng. 819

Controversy over the videotaping of creative works by students. USA: St. Louis, MO. 1994-1997. Lang.: Eng. 829

Analysis of rural arts program in schools. USA. 1997. Lang.: Eng. 838

Fine and performing arts programs in New Jersey community colleges. USA. 1994-1996. Lang.: Eng. 839

The meaning and recognition of dramatic talent in children. USA. 1997. Lang.: Eng. 840

Eurocentric bias in major theatre history textbooks. USA. 1720-1994. Lang.: Eng. 841

Advantages of teaching for playwrights. USA. 1997. Lang.: Eng. 842

Theatre of the Oppressed in the classroom. USA. 1994-1996. Lang.: Eng. 844

Analysis of dance concerts as an educational tool. USA: Long Beach, CA. 1996. Lang.: Eng. 1020

Call for a more comprehensive anthology of eighteenth-century drama. England. 1701-1800. Lang.: Eng. 3327

Shakespeare in the college classroom. England. 1997. Lang.: Eng. 3334

Approaches to teaching Shakespeare. Israel: Tel Aviv. 1993-1995. Lang.: Eng. 3372

Teaching Shakespeare at the University of Haifa. Israel: Haifa. 1994. Lang.: Eng. 3373

Theatre as a tool for moral instruction. Italy. England. 1551-1997. Lang.: Eng. 3375

The failure of study guides to impart critical theory to students of Shakespeare. UK-England. 1990-1996. Lang.: Eng. 3381

Shakespeare and English education. UK-England. 1990. Lang.: Eng. 3383

Analysis of clowns and wordplay as a means of engaging students in teaching Shakespeare. USA. 1997. Lang.: Eng. 3388

Evaluation of educational technology for the teaching of Shakespeare. USA. 1997. Lang.: Eng. 3390

Comparing video versions of *Macbeth* in the classroom. USA. 1997. Lang.: Eng. 3391

Pros and cons of using film and video in teaching Shakespeare. USA. 1995. Lang.: Eng. 3392

Role-playing and journal writing in teaching Shakespearean plays. USA. 1997. Lang.: Eng. 3393

Race, *Othello*, and the high school classroom. USA. 1997. Lang.: Eng. 3394

Teaching Shakespeare's *King Lear*. USA. 1997. Lang.: Eng. 3395

Film as a way of enhancing student understanding of Shakespeare. USA. 1995. Lang.: Eng. 3396

Using film and video to teach Shakespeare. USA. 1985-1996. Lang.: Eng. 3397

The use of film and video to teach the plays of Shakespeare. USA. 1997. Lang.: Eng. 3398

Using video to teach Shakespeare's *Julius Caesar*. USA. 1997. Lang.: Eng. 3399

Review of teaching texts of Shakespeare's *King Lear*. USA. 1995. Lang.: Eng. 3400

Improvisational theatre games in the teaching of Shakespeare. USA. 1997. Lang.: Eng. 3402

Collaboration of teachers and theatre professionals to teach Shakespeare. USA. 1997. Lang.: Eng. 3403

Teaching Shakespeare and the World Wide Web. USA. 1997. Lang.: Eng. 3404

Reader-response theory and the teaching of Shakespeare. USA. 1997. Lang.: Eng. 3405

Teaching Shakespeare with the aid of the internet. USA. 1997. Lang.: Eng. 3407

Feminist and performance techniques for teaching Shakespeare's *Hamlet*. USA. 1997. Lang.: Eng. 3408

The use of textual studies in teaching Shakespeare. USA. 1997. Lang.: Eng. 3409

Teaching students to distinguish between action and narrative in Shakespeare. USA. 1995. Lang.: Eng. 3410

'Playgrounding' in the teaching of Shakespeare's plays. USA. 1997. Lang.: Eng. 3411

The sense of wonder and the teaching of Shakespeare's *Hamlet*. USA. UK-England. 1995. Lang.: Eng. 3412

Team-teaching Shakespeare in an interdisciplinary context. USA. 1997. Lang.: Eng. 3413

Nontraditional methods of teaching Shakespeare's *Romeo and Juliet*. USA. 1997. Lang.: Eng. 3414

Teaching a scene from *Hamlet* using different interpretations on video. USA. 1997. Lang.: Eng. 3415

Shakespeare and the teaching of close reading and theory. USA. 1997. Lang.: Eng. 3416

Using video to teach Shakespeare's *Henry V*. USA. 1997. Lang.: Eng. 3417

Paraphrasing Shakespeare in the classroom. USA. 1997. Lang.: Eng. 3419

Possibilities and limitations of using Shakespearean performance in the classroom. USA. 1997. Lang.: Eng. 3420

Informal survey of high school teachers of Shakespeare. USA. 1995. Lang.: Eng. 3421

Teaching Shakespeare through educational programs at theatres and festivals. USA. 1997. Lang.: Eng. 3422

Review of books on teaching Shakespeare. USA. 1995. Lang.: Eng. 3424

Using performance techniques to teach Shakespeare's sonnets. USA. 1997. Lang.: Eng. 3425

Teaching students to develop their own inquiries into the plays of Shakespeare. USA. 1997. Lang.: Eng. 3426

The multicultural classroom and the teaching of Shakespeare. USA. 1995. Lang.: Eng. 3428

Teaching Shakespeare in dramatic fashion. USA. 1995. Lang.: Eng. 3429

Using historical fiction as background for the teaching of Shakespeare. USA. 1985. Lang.: Eng. 3430

Teaching Shakespeare in the high-tech classroom. USA. 1997. Lang.: Eng. 3431

The benefits of performing Shakespeare in the classroom. USA. 1995. Lang.: Eng. 3432

The importance of openness to new interpretations in teaching Shakespeare. USA. 1997. Lang.: Eng. 3434

Using transhistoricism to teach Shakespeare. USA. 1997. Lang.: Eng. 3435

Georgetown University's decision to drop Shakespeare from its curriculum. USA: Washington, DC. 1997. Lang.: Eng. 3436

Suggestions for effective writing assignments in teaching Shakespeare. USA. 1997. Lang.: Eng. 3437

Whole-language approach to teaching Shakespeare's comedies. USA. 1997. Lang.: Eng. 3438

Process drama in the classroom and the teaching of Shakespeare. USA. 1997. Lang.: Eng. 3439

Description of course on film and visual anthropology and sociology. South Africa, Republic of. 1997. Lang.: Eng. 3692

Graduate seminar on narrative film. USA. 1997. Lang.: Eng. 3695

Drama, technology, and role-playing in the video conference Electric Bedroom. Canada. UK-England. 1997. Lang.: Eng. 3738

Shakespeare: The Animated Tales: educational videos, based on Shakespeare's plays. UK. Russia. 1991-1997. Lang.: Ger. 3741

Use of puppetry in a high school science classroom. USA. 1997. Lang.: Eng. 4384

Creation of marionettes based on historical figures as an educational tool. USA: Atlanta, GA. 1996. Lang.: Eng. 4395

Theory/criticism

History of American performance studies. USA. 1890-1996. Lang.: Eng. 926

Education — cont'd

The effect of contemporary theory on the teaching of Shakespeare. 1997. Lang.: Eng. 3457

Theories of film study. USA. 1968-1997. Lang.: Eng. 3701

Training

Information on theatre training. UK-England. 1997. Lang.: Eng. 934

Modern dance, dance education, and dance training. USA. Europe. 1920-1929. Lang.: Ger. 1222

Education of the Girlchild

Performance/production

Analysis of *Education of the Girlchild* by Meredith Monk. USA. 1980-1995. Lang.: Eng. 1208

Educational theatre

Audience

The involvement of the audience in performance. Sweden. USSR. 1900. Lang.: Swe. 1251

Institutions

Profile of creative drama institute Rosteriet. Sweden: Luleå. 1979. Lang.: Swe. 1492

Performance/production

Use of Boal's 'joker' system in a production of Euripides' *Bákchai (The Bacchae)*. USA. 1995-1996. Lang.: Eng. 632

The use of theatre students as classroom performers at Calvin College. USA: Pittsburgh, PA. 1995-1996. Lang.: Eng. 638

Directing a stage adaptation of *The Smell of Death and Flowers* by Nadine Gordimer. USA. 1995-1996. Lang.: Eng. 647

Active learning and community-based theatre. USA. Croatia. Serbia. 1995-1996. Lang.: Eng. 653

Integration of intellect and emotion in a graduate-level theatre course. USA. 1995-1996. Lang.: Eng. 664

Psychophysiological training of actors in a production of Beckett's *Act Without Words I*. USA. 1995-1996. Lang.: Eng. 687

Report on Performance Art, Culture and Pedagogy Symposium. USA. 1995-1996. Lang.: Eng. 3848

Edwall, Allan

Performance/production

Actor Allan Edwall and his theatre Brunnsgatan Fyra. Sweden: Stockholm. 1949-1997. Lang.: Swe. 1935

Edward II

Plays/librettos/scripts

The appropriation of Shakespeare by the dispossessed and marginalized. 1590-1995. Lang.: Eng. 2366

The nature of Christopher Marlowe's dramaturgy. England. 1585-1593. Lang.: Eng. 2454

Sex and gender in plays of Christopher Marlowe. England. 1587-1593. Lang.: Eng. 2522

Narcissism in Renaissance tragedy. England. 1450-1580. Lang.: Eng. 2609

Homosexual friendship in plays of Shakespeare, Fletcher, and Marlowe. England. 1595-1613. Lang.: Eng. 2697

Comparison of Marlowe's *Edward II* and Shakespeare's *Richard II*. England. 1592-1597. Lang.: Eng. 2735

Edward IV

Plays/librettos/scripts

Civic pride in the anonymous *Edward IV 1 and 2*. England: London. 1599-1600. Lang.: Eng. 2626

Analysis of the anonymous *Edward IV*. England. 1599-1600. Lang.: Eng. 2765

Edwards, Gale

Performance/production

Collection of newspaper reviews by London theatre critics. UK-England: London. 1997. Lang.: Eng. 1973

Edwards, Sherman

Plays/librettos/scripts

Interview with playwright Peter Stone. USA: New York, NY. 1997. Lang.: Eng. 3981

Edwy and Elgiva

Plays/librettos/scripts

Feminist analysis of *Edwy and Elgiva* by Frances Burney. England. 1752-1840. Lang.: Eng. 2518

Edyvean, Anne

Performance/production

Collection of newspaper reviews by London theatre critics. UK-England: London. 1997. Lang.: Eng. 2000

Efremov, Oleg

SEE

Jéfremov, Oleg.

Efter repetitionen (After the Rehearsal)

Performance/production

Moscow Art Theatre productions. Russia: Moscow. Estonia: Tallinn. 1996-1997. Lang.: Rus. 1861

EFX!

Design/technology

Technical aspects of *EFX!* at MGM Grand Hotel. USA: Las Vegas, NV. 1996. Lang.: Eng. 3854

Egan, Robert

Performance/production

Analysis of *Like I Say* by Len Jenkin. USA: San Diego, CA. 1997. Lang.: Eng. 2315

Egan, Susan

Performance/production

Singer/actress Susan Egan. USA: New York, NY. 1991-1997. Lang.: Eng. 3976

Egerbladh, Birgitta

Performance/production

Choreographer, composer, and director Birgitta Egerbladh. Sweden: Gothenburg. 1996. Lang.: Swe. 1960

Eggert, Moritz

Performance/production

Productions at the Munich Biennale. Germany: Munich. 1997. Lang.: Ger. 4148

Plays/librettos/scripts

Interview with opera composer Moritz Eggert. Germany: Munich. 1997. Lang.: Ger. 4293

Eggerth, Mária

Performance/production

Film careers of Hungarian dancers. Hungary. 1929-1945. Lang.: Hun. 976

Église, L' (Church, The)

Performance/production

Performative theory and potentially offensive characterizations on stage. USA: Santa Cruz, CA. France: Paris. 1992-1997. Lang.: Eng. 2336

Egoyan, Atom

Basic theatrical documents

Script of *The Sweet Hereafter* by Atom Egoyan. Canada. 1997. Lang.: Eng. 3525

Design/technology

Lighting design for the film *The Sweet Hereafter*. Canada. 1997. Lang.: Eng. 3542

Performance/production

Atom Egoyan's staging of *Salome*, Canadian Opera Company. Canada: Toronto, ON. 1996. Lang.: Eng. 4111

Plays/librettos/scripts

Interview with screenwriter and director Atom Egoyan. Canada. 1997. Lang.: Eng. 3633

Reactions to *The Sweet Hereafter* by the author of the novel on which the film was based. Canada. 1997. Lang.: Eng. 3634

Ehe des Herrn Mississippi, Die (Marriage of Mr. Mississippi, The)

Performance/production

Playing the role of Saint-Claude in *Die Ehe des Herrn Mississippi (The Marriage of Mr. Mississippi)* by Dürrenmatt. USA: Long Beach, CA. 1996. Lang.: Eng. 2345

Ehler, Ursula

Performance/production

Performances of *Harrys Kopf (Harry's Head)* by Tankred Dorst and Ursula Ehler. Germany. 1968-1997. Lang.: Ger. 1748

Plays/librettos/scripts

Interview with playwrights Tankred Dorst and Ursula Ehler. Germany. 1997. Lang.: Fin. 2849

Ehn, Erik

Performance/production

The making of *Tailings* by Erik Ehn and Smart Mouth Theatre. USA: San Francisco, CA. 1995-1997. Lang.: Eng. 636

Eigsti, Karl

Design/technology

Interview with scene designer Karl Eigsti. USA. 1962-1997. Lang.: Eng. 233

Einem, Gottfried von

Performance/production

Dürrenmatt's *Der Besuch der alten Dame (The Visit)* and its American adaptation. Switzerland. 1921-1990. Lang.: Eng. 1965

Gottfried von Einem's opera *Der Besuch der alten Dame*. Switzerland. 1918-1996. Lang.: Eng. 4222

Einen Jux will er sich machen

SEE

Jux will er sich machen, Einen.

Elizabethan theatre — cont'd

Plays/librettos/scripts

Evil women in early modern English tragedy. England. 1590-1613. Lang.: Eng. 2452

History of pre-Restoration English theatre. England. 965-1660. Lang.: Ita. 2456

The publication of early English playbooks. England. 1583-1642. Lang.: Eng. 2476

Subversion and Shakespeare's older female characters. England. 1590-1613. Lang.: Eng. 2502

Introduction to essays on early English drama. England. 1100-1500. Lang.: Eng. 2513

Feminist analysis of the place of women in Shakespeare's plays. England. 1590-1613. Lang.: Eng. 2519

Philosophical analysis of early English drama. England. 1100-1500. Lang.: Eng. 2521

Models of sexual behavior in Elizabethan theatre. England. 1680-1900. Lang.: Eng. 2545

Homoerotic desire in Elizabethan theatre. England. 1580-1620. Lang.: Eng. 2569

Domestic cultural and social struggle in Elizabethan theatre. England. 1592-1621. Lang.: Eng. 2571

Violence and representation in Renaissance literature. England. 1590-1610. Lang.: Eng. 2614

Shakespeare's Roman history plays in the context of contemporary history and politics. England. 1599-1608. Lang.: Eng. 2615

Collaborative authorship in early English theatre. England. 1580-1610. Lang.: Eng. 2650

Renaissance theatre and the marketplace. England. 1580-1620. Lang.: Eng. 2657

Iambic pentameter and Shakespearean performance. England. 1598-1997. Lang.: Eng. 2671

The forced marriage plot in early English drama. England. 1584-1642. Lang.: Eng. 2675

Love lyrics in Shakespeare's comedies. England. 1590-1613. Lang.: Eng. 2691

Racial and national meanings and economic practice in Renaissance theatre. England. 1590-1650. Lang.: Eng. 2693

Race and colonialism in Shakespeare's *The Merchant of Venice*. England. 1596. Lang.: Eng. 2716

Unconventional relationships in Shakespeare's *Love's Labour's Lost*. England. 1593. Lang.: Eng. 2749

Annotations on a script of *The Two Merry Milkmaids*. England. 1620. Lang.: Eng. 2754

Racial aspects of colonialism in Shakespeare's *Titus Andronicus*. England. 1590-1594. Lang.: Eng. 2760

Death, immortality and punishment in plays of Shakespeare. England. 1590-1616. Lang.: Eng. 2762

The classification, editing, and dissemination of early playscripts. UK-England. 1906-1996. Lang.: Eng. 3118

Bearbaiting and colonialism. England. 1450-1600. Lang.: Eng. 3774

Theory/criticism

New historicism, feminist criticism, and gender roles in Renaissance literature. USA. UK-England. 1987. Lang.: Eng. 916

Recent criticism regarding the purpose and place of theatre in early modern England. USA. UK-England. 1988-1995. Lang.: Eng. 917

The function of evidence in structuring Shakespearean criticism. 1997. Lang.: Eng. 3454

Racism, *Othello*, and South African criticism. England. South Africa, Republic of. 1604-1987. Lang.: Eng. 3473

Elkins, Doug
Performance/production
Survey of recent dance performances. USA: New York, NY. 1997. Lang.: Eng. 1001

Ellington, Duke
Performance/production
The development of *Play On!*, a musical adaptation of Shakespeare's *Twelfth Night*. USA: New York, NY. 1997. Lang.: Eng. 3953
Plays/librettos/scripts
Survey of musical adaptations of Shakespeare. USA: New York, NY. 1938-1997. Lang.: Eng. 3987

Elliott, Kenneth
Performance/production
Collection of newspaper reviews by London theatre critics. UK-England: London. 1997. Lang.: Eng. 2105

Collection of newspaper reviews by London theatre critics. UK-England: London. 1997. Lang.: Eng. 2132

Elliott, Michael
Performance/production
The map of England in productions of Shakespeare's *King Lear*. Europe. USA. 1909-1994. Lang.: Eng. 1650

Elliott, Scott
Design/technology
Derek McLane's set design for *Present Laughter*. USA: New York, NY. 1996-1997. Lang.: Eng. 1365

Ellis, Brett Easton
Performance/production
The opening of the Deutsches Schauspielhaus season. Germany: Hamburg. 1997. Lang.: Ger. 1688

Ellis, Scott
Plays/librettos/scripts
Songwriting team John Kander and Fred Ebb. USA: New York, NY. 1927-1997. Lang.: Eng. 4001

Ellsworth, Angela
Performance/production
Angela Ellsworth and Tina Takemoto's *Her/She Senses Imag(in)ed Malady*. USA. 1991-1997. Lang.: Eng. 3844

Ellwood, Colin
Performance/production
Collection of newspaper reviews by London theatre critics. UK-England: London. 1997. Lang.: Eng. 1996

Collection of newspaper reviews by London theatre critics. UK-England: London. 1997. Lang.: Eng. 2146

Elmhurst Ballet School
Institutions
Professional connections between Elmhurst Ballet School and the Hungarian Dance Academy. UK-England. Hungary. 1996-1997. Lang.: Hun. 1060

Elovich, Richard
Basic theatrical documents
Text of *Someone Else from Queens Is Queer* by Richard Elovich. USA. 1992. Lang.: Eng. 1325
Performance/production
Solo artist Richard Elovich. USA. 1993. Lang.: Eng. 3834

Elsa Edgar
Performance/production
Collection of newspaper reviews by London theatre critics. UK-England: London. 1997. Lang.: Eng. 2118

Elsineur (Elsinore)
Performance/production
Collection of newspaper reviews by London theatre critics. UK-England: London. 1997. Lang.: Eng. 1972

Elsner, Hannelore
Performance/production
Actors on working in theatre, film, and television. Germany. 1941-1997. Lang.: Ger. 3576

Elton, Ben
Performance/production
Collection of newspaper reviews by London theatre critics. UK-England: London. 1997. Lang.: Eng. 1970

Director Laurence Boswell. UK-England: London. 1997. Lang.: Eng. 2214

Elufowoju, Femi, Jr.
Performance/production
Collection of newspaper reviews by London theatre critics. UK-England: London. 1997. Lang.: Eng. 2018

Elverket (Stockholm)
Performance spaces
Dramaten's new stage, Elverket. Sweden: Stockholm. 1997. Lang.: Swe. 1530

Elvis—The Musical
Performance/production
Collection of newspaper reviews by London theatre critics. UK-England: London. 1997. Lang.: Eng. 2068

Ember tragédiája, Az (Tragedy of Man, The)
Design/technology
Stage designs for *Az ember tragédiája (The Tragedy of Man)* by Imre Madách. Hungary: Budapest. 1883-1915. Lang.: Hun. 1357
Performance/production
Provincial productions of *Az ember tragédiája (The Tragedy of Man)* by Imre Madách. Hungary. 1884-1918. Lang.: Hun. 1762

The stage career of Madách's *Az ember tragédiája (The Tragedy of Man)* in Voivodship. Hungary. Yugoslavia. 1884-1965. Lang.: Hun. 1765

Ember tragédiája, Az (Tragedy of Man, The) — cont'd

Jenő Janovics and Imre Madách's *Az ember tragédiája (The Tragedy of Man)*. Hungary: Kolozsvár. Romania: Cluj. 1894-1945. Lang.: Hun.
1767

Music in the premiere of *Az ember tragédiája (The Tragedy of Man)* by Imre Madách. Hungary: Budapest. 1883. Lang.: Hun. 1768

Analysis of the premiere of *Az ember tragédiája (The Tragedy of Man)* by Imre Madách. Hungary: Budapest. 1883. Lang.: Hun. 1779

Géza Blattner's puppet adaptation of *Az ember tragédiája (The Tragedy of Man)* by Madách. Hungary. 1918-1954. Lang.: Hun. 4365

Plays/librettos/scripts

Comparison of works by Madách and Dostojévskij. Hungary. 1860-1900. Lang.: Hun. 2896

Arany's revisions to Madách's *Az ember tragédiája (The Tragedy of Man)*. Hungary. 1842-1862. Lang.: Hun. 2898

Female characters in plays of Imre Madách. Hungary. 1824. Lang.: Hun. 2899

Reception and analysis of *Az ember tragédiája (The Tragedy of Man)* by Imre Madách. Hungary. 1850-1860. Lang.: Hun. 2900

Embers
Performance/production
Collection of newspaper reviews by London theatre critics. UK-England: London. 1997. Lang.: Eng. 2134

Emig-Könning, Christina
Performance/production
Recent activities and productions of Schauspielhaus Rostock. Germany: Rostock. 1994-1997. Lang.: Ger. 1711

Emigration
Plays/librettos/scripts
Hubert O'Grady's melodramas based on the Potato Famine. Ireland. 1879-1886. Lang.: Eng. 2937

Emmons, Beverly
Design/technology
Lighting designer Beverly Emmons. USA: New York, NY. 1960-1997. Lang.: Eng. 254

Emperor Jones, The
Theory/criticism
Dance history and cultural studies: works of Martha Graham and Eugene O'Neill. USA. 1913-1933. Lang.: Eng. 1216

Empire Writes Back, The
Performance/production
Collection of newspaper reviews by London theatre critics. UK-England: London. 1997. Lang.: Eng. 2148

Empty Space (Seattle, WA)
Institutions
Seattle's theatrical renaissance. USA: Seattle, WA. 1980-1997. Lang.: Eng. 396

En attendant Godot (Waiting for Godot)
Performance/production
Interview with members of Sarajevo Youth Theatre. Bosnia: Sarajevo. 1993. Lang.: Eng. 1572

Susan Sontag's Sarajevan production of *Waiting for Godot*. Bosnia: Sarajevo. 1993. Lang.: Eng. 1573

German reactions to the work of Samuel Beckett. Germany. 1953-1976. Lang.: Eng. 1699

Collection of newspaper reviews by London theatre critics. UK-England: London. 1997. Lang.: Eng. 2069

Plays/librettos/scripts
Representational practices of mid-twentieth century avant-garde theatre. North America. Europe. 1950-1990. Lang.: Eng. 696

Contemporary playwrights and the adaptation process. Europe. 1900-1993. Lang.: Ita. 2793

Analysis of German translations of plays by Samuel Beckett. Germany. 1967-1978. Lang.: Eng. 2842

Comparison of a novel by James Kelman to Beckett's *En attendant Godot (Waiting for Godot)*. Ireland. France. 1953-1995. Lang.: Eng. 2907

The leg wound in Beckett's *Waiting for Godot* in the context of Western literary tradition. Ireland. France. 1953. Lang.: Eng. 2909

Classical Taoism in Beckett's *En attendant Godot (Waiting for Godot)*. Ireland. France. 1953. Lang.: Eng. 2934

En Garde Arts (New York, NY)
Performance/production
Deborah Warner and Fiona Shaw on their adaptation of *The Waste Land* by T.S. Eliot. USA. UK-England. 1980-1997. Lang.: Eng. 2251

En-knap (Ljubljana)
Institutions
Pictorial history of the modern dance group En-knap. Slovenia: Ljubljana. 1993-1997. Lang.: Eng. 1165

Enchanted Land, An
Performance/production
Collection of newspaper reviews by London theatre critics. UK-England: London. 1997. Lang.: Eng. 2101

Encore cinq minutes (Five More Minutes)
Plays/librettos/scripts
Analysis of *Encore cinq minutes (Five More Minutes)* by Françoise Loranger. Canada. 1967. Lang.: Fre. 2403

Encores! (New York, NY)
Performance/production
The reconstructed orchestration for the revival of *The Boys from Syracuse* by Encores!. USA: New York, NY. 1938-1997. Lang.: Eng. 3970

Encyclopedias
Reference materials
Encyclopedia of African theatre. Africa. 1700-1996. Lang.: Eng. 710

Encyclopedia of dramatic plots. 500 B.C.-1997 A.D. Lang.: Slo. 3311

Encyclopedia of circus genres. Russia. 1997. Lang.: Rus. 3786

End of the Affair, The
Performance/production
Collection of newspaper reviews by London theatre critics. UK-England: London. 1997. Lang.: Eng. 2143

Endgame
SEE
Fin de partie.

Endlich Schluss (At Last the End)
Performance/production
Major productions of the Vienna theatre season. Austria: Vienna. 1997. Lang.: Ger. 1563

Endre, Béla
Institutions
Profile of Vígopera (Comic Opera). Hungary: Budapest. 1946-1948. Lang.: Hun. 4049

Enemy of the People, An
SEE
Folkefiende, En.
Plays/librettos/scripts
Comparison of Arthur Miller's *The Crucible* and his adaptation of Ibsen's *An Enemy of the People*. USA. 1950-1984. Lang.: Eng. 3126

Eng, Alvin
Basic theatrical documents
Text of plays performed at the Nuyorican Poets Cafe. USA: New York, NY. 1973-1990. Lang.: Eng. 1322

Engberg, Christer
Institutions
Profile of creative drama institute Rosteriet. Sweden: Luleå. 1979. Lang.: Swe. 1492

Engel, Erich
Performance/production
The 'deconstructive potential' of Brecht's own production of *Mother Courage*. Germany: Berlin. 1949. Lang.: Ger. 1696

Engel, Lisa
Performance/production
Productions of plays by Katharina Thanner and Lisa Engel. Switzerland: Zurich, Basel. 1995-1997. Lang.: Ger. 1963

Engel, Wolfgang
Performance/production
Updated classics at Schauspiel Leipzig. Germany: Leipzig. 1996-1997. Lang.: Ger. 1712

Contemporary plays at Schauspiel Leipzig. Germany: Leipzig. 1996-1997. Lang.: Ger. 1736

Comparison of productions of Shakespeare's *Richard III*. Germany. Switzerland. 1996. Lang.: Ger. 1745

English National Opera (London)
Performance/production
The difficulty of performing 'Sempre Libera' in Verdi's *La Traviata*. Italy. USA: New York, NY. 1886-1996. Lang.: Eng. 4186

Recent performances and changes at British opera houses. UK-England: London. UK-Wales: Cardiff. 1996-1997. Lang.: Eng. 4227

English Stage Company (London)
SEE ALSO
Royal Court Theatre (London).

English Touring Opera
Design/technology
Giuseppe Di Iorio's lighting designs for the English Touring Opera. UK-England. 1997. Lang.: Eng. 4032

English Touring Theatre (London)
Performance/production
Actors Timothy and Sam West. UK-England: London. 1997. Lang.: Eng. 2212

Equipment — cont'd

Product review of Leprecon lighting consoles. USA. 1997. Lang.: Eng. 264

Description of the electrodeless lamp Fusion Lighting Solar 1000. USA. 1997. Lang.: Eng. 265

New products at Lighting Dimensions International trade show. USA: Las Vegas, NV. 1997. Lang.: Eng. 266

The Icon automated luminaire and control system of Light & Sound Design. USA. 1975-1997. Lang.: Eng. 268

John Broderick's lighting design for the rock band Metallica. USA. 1988-1997. Lang.: Eng. 269

The lighting industry and federal and local regulation. USA. 1994. Lang.: Eng. 275

Construction and use of flown-in flats. USA. 1997. Lang.: Eng. 279

Design conferences in cyberspace. USA. 1997. Lang.: Eng. 280

Theatrical lighting for a traveling museum exhibit on dinosaurs. USA: New York, NY. 1997. Lang.: Eng. 282

Martin Professional's MAC 600 fresnel lighting instrument. USA: New York, NY. 1997. Lang.: Eng. 283

'Pouncing' gels to make them last longer. USA. 1997. Lang.: Eng. 285

A method of distributing power to a wagon or slip-stage. USA: San Diego, CA. 1997. Lang.: Eng. 288

The need for an advanced common-protocol high-speed network for lighting. USA. 1997. Lang.: Eng. 290

Permanent dimmer-per-circuit systems in theatres. USA. 1990-1997. Lang.: Eng. 291

Call for the entertainment industry to draft safety standards for electrical equipment. USA. 1997. Lang.: Eng. 292

Lighting design for flamenco dancer Joaquim Cortes and his troupe. Spain: Madrid. 1995-1997. Lang.: Eng. 1141

Theatrical lighting at Museum of Science & Industry. USA: Chicago, IL. 1996. Lang.: Eng. 3703

Motorized lighting system and grid used in TV studios. USA: New York, NY. 1997. Lang.: Eng. 3712

Lighting used to recreate a large city fire. USA: Milwaukee, WI. 1994. Lang.: Eng. 3758

Advice to puppeteers regarding public address systems. USA. 1997. Lang.: Eng. 4346

Performance spaces

Celestial effects of the seventeenth-century stage. Europe. 1600-1700. Lang.: Eng. 429

The history of the Colosseum and its new interior design. Germany: Essen. 1900-1997. Lang.: Ger. 3930

Erényi, Béla
Performance/production
Interview with dancer Béla Erényi of the Budapest Opera House ballet ensemble. Hungary: Budapest. 1974-1997. Lang.: Hun. 1092

Ergen, Mehmet
Performance/production
Collection of newspaper reviews by London theatre critics. UK-England: London. 1997. Lang.: Eng. 2065

Collection of newspaper reviews by London theatre critics. UK-England: London. 1997. Lang.: Eng. 2112

ERIC
SEE
Educational Resources Information Center.

Eriksson, Gunilla
Performance/production
Plays based on refugee experiences. Sweden: Gothenburg. 1997. Lang.: Swe. 1927

Erkel Színház (Budapest)
Institutions
Yearbook of the Hungarian State Opera House. Hungary: Budapest. 1995-1996. Lang.: Hun. 4050

Yearbook of the Hungarian State Opera House. Hungary: Budapest. 1996-1997. Lang.: Hun. 4051

Performance/production
Report on a dance concert in honor of ballet soloist Ildikó Pongor. Hungary. 1997. Lang.: Hun. 1081

Ildikó Pongor's performance in the ballet *Anna Karenina*. Hungary: Budapest. 1997. Lang.: Hun. 1082

Interview with opera director Judit Galgóczy. Hungary. 1987-1997. Lang.: Hun. 4168

Interview with opera director Balázs Kovalik. Hungary: Budapest. 1995-1997. Lang.: Hun. 4185

Erkel, Ferenc
Performance/production
Tenor József Simándy. Hungary. 1917-1997. Lang.: Hun. 4170

Erkel, Gyula
Performance/production
Music in the premiere of *Az ember tragédiája (The Tragedy of Man)* by Imre Madách. Hungary: Budapest. 1883. Lang.: Hun. 1768

Erlbruch, Wolf
Plays/librettos/scripts
Children's theatre festival productions. Germany: Berlin. 1997. Lang.: Ger. 2845

Ernani
Performance/production
Historical and literary influences on Verdi's operas. Italy. 1813-1901. Lang.: Eng. 4195

Erpenbeck, Fritz
Relation to other fields
The Communist view of Brecht. Germany: Berlin. 1920-1956. Lang.: Ger. 3351

Error in Judgement, An
Performance/production
Collection of newspaper reviews by London theatre critics. UK-England: London. 1997. Lang.: Eng. 2063

Eschenbach, Christoph
Performance/production
Opera conductor Christoph Eschenbach. USA: Houston, TX. 1997. Lang.: Eng. 4270

Esclarmonde
Plays/librettos/scripts
Representations of the Orient in nineteenth-century French opera. France. 1863-1894. Lang.: Eng. 4290

Esclave du démon, L' (Slave of the Devil)
Basic theatrical documents
Text of *L'Esclave du démon (Slave of the Devil)* by Louise Doutreligne. France. Spain. 1612-1996. Lang.: Fre. 1269

Esdaile, Sarah
Performance/production
Collection of newspaper reviews by London theatre critics. UK-England: London. 1997. Lang.: Eng. 2015

Espace GO (Montreal, PQ)
Performance/production
Martine Beaulne's production of *Albertine en cinq temps (Albertine in Five Times)* by Michel Tremblay. Canada: Montreal, PQ. 1995. Lang.: Fre. 1593

Plays/librettos/scripts
Adaptations of French classics for contemporary audiences. Canada: Montreal, PQ. France. 1997. Lang.: Fre. 2421

Esperando al italiano (Waiting for the Italian)
Basic theatrical documents
Anthology of Latin American women's plays. Latin America. 1981-1989. Lang.: Eng. 1291

Esperpento de las galas del difunto (Dead Man's Duds, The)
Plays/librettos/scripts
Word avoidance and disclosure in plays of O'Neill and Valle-Inclán. USA. Spain. 1926-1959. Lang.: Eng. 3257

Esterházy, Peter
Institutions
A congress on current Hungarian drama. Hungary. 1997. Lang.: Ger. 1437

Estorino, Abelardo
Plays/librettos/scripts
The 'Black Madonna' in Cuban theatre. Cuba. 1925-1990. Lang.: Spa. 2444

Eström, Vivi
Plays/librettos/scripts
Author Astrid Lindgren. Sweden. 1944-1997. Lang.: Swe. 3060

Eszterhas, Joe
Basic theatrical documents
Script of *Telling Lies in America* by Joe Eszterhas. USA. 1997. Lang.: Eng. 3530

Plays/librettos/scripts
Interview with screenwriter Joe Eszterhas. USA. 1997. Lang.: Eng. 3663

ETA Creative Arts Foundation (Chicago, IL)
Institutions
Abena Joan Brown, ETA Creative Arts Foundation, and Black performing arts institutions. USA: Chicago, IL. 1996. Lang.: Eng. 397

Etcetera Theatre Club (London)
Performance/production
Collection of newspaper reviews by London theatre critics. UK-England: London. 1997. Lang.: Eng. 1971

SUBJECT INDEX

Etcetera Theatre Club (London) — cont'd

Collection of newspaper reviews by London theatre critics. UK-England: London. 1997. Lang.: Eng. 1972

Collection of newspaper reviews by London theatre critics. UK-England: London. 1997. Lang.: Eng. 2006

Collection of newspaper reviews by London theatre critics. UK-England: London. 1997. Lang.: Eng. 2009

Collection of newspaper reviews by London theatre critics. UK-England: London. 1997. Lang.: Eng. 2019

Collection of newspaper reviews by London theatre critics. UK-England: London. 1997. Lang.: Eng. 2027

Collection of newspaper reviews by London theatre critics. UK-England: London. 1997. Lang.: Eng. 2038

Collection of newspaper reviews by London theatre critics. UK-England: London. 1997. Lang.: Eng. 2055

Collection of newspaper reviews by London theatre critics. UK-England: London. 1997. Lang.: Eng. 2056

Collection of newspaper reviews by London theatre critics. UK-England: London. 1997. Lang.: Eng. 2087

Collection of newspaper reviews by London theatre critics. UK-England: London. 1997. Lang.: Eng. 2093

Collection of newspaper reviews by London theatre critics. UK-England. 1997. Lang.: Eng. 2098

Collection of newspaper reviews by London theatre critics. UK-England: London. 1997. Lang.: Eng. 2104

Collection of newspaper reviews by London theatre critics. UK-England: London. 1997. Lang.: Eng. 2106

Collection of newspaper reviews by London theatre critics. UK-England. 1997. Lang.: Eng. 2125

Collection of newspaper reviews by London theatre critics. UK-England. 1997. Lang.: Eng. 2142

Eternal Road, The
Performance/production
Kurt Weill's collaborations with playwrights. Germany: Berlin. USA: New York, NY. 1927-1945. Lang.: Eng. 3934

Eternity Lasts Longer
Performance/production
Passage Nord's production of *Eternity Lasts Longer*. Italy: Rome. 1997. Lang.: Ita. 1818

Etherege, George
Plays/librettos/scripts
Analysis of conversations of 'Wit' couples in Restoration comedy. England. 1660-1700. Lang.: Eng. 2453

Foreshadowing of the comedy of manners in Etherege's *She Would If She Could*. England. 1670. Lang.: Eng. 2601

Etherington, Mark
Performance/production
Collection of newspaper reviews by London theatre critics. UK-England: London. 1997. Lang.: Eng. 2160

Ethics
Institutions
Jan Lauwers' theatre group Needcompany. Belgium: Antwerp. 1996. Lang.: Eng. 1382

Plays/librettos/scripts
Subjectivity, ethics, and the body in contemporary drama. USA. Europe. 1940-1990. Lang.: Eng. 3229

Ethnic dance
SEE ALSO
Classed Entries under DANCE—Ethnic dance.
Performance/production
Dance history textbook. Lang.: Rus. 953

The influence of folk-derived dance forms on ballet. Europe. 1830-1850. Lang.: Eng. 1064

Profile of choreographer Shobana Jeyasingh. UK-England. 1988-1997. Lang.: Eng. 1195

Black dance, white dance, and the choreography of Twyla Tharp. USA. 1997. Lang.: Eng. 1205

Ethnic theatre
Basic theatrical documents
Anthology of plays by women of color. USA. 1992-1996. Lang.: Eng. 1338

Institutions
History of Hungarian theatre in Oradea, formerly Nagyvárad. Hungary: Nagyvárad. Romania: Oradea. 1798-1975. Lang.: Hun. 333

Hungarian amateur theatre in Slovenia. Slovenia. 1920-1970. Lang.: Hun. 375

Performance/production
Brazilian folk-theatre forms. Brazil. 1500-1995. Lang.: Eng. 473

Performance and identity politics on the Quebec stage. Canada. 1901-1995. Lang.: Eng. 477

Analysis of Asian Indian performance in the United States. USA: New York, NY. 1994-1996. Lang.: Eng. 662

Polish theatrical activities in Soviet camps and prisons. USSR. Lithuania. Poland. 1939-1947. Lang.: Pol. 688

Ethnography of artists of popular theatre in Tamilnadu. India. 1950-1995. Lang.: Eng. 1783

Interview with solo artist Jude Narita. USA: Los Angeles, CA. 1987-1989. Lang.: Eng. 2341

Interview with playwright Nilo Cruz. USA: San Francisco, CA. 1995-1997. Lang.: Eng. 2356

History in recent Chicano/a theatre. USA. 1964-1995. Lang.: Eng. 2360

A methodology of theatrical creation based on native performance culture. Canada. 1991-1996. Lang.: Eng. 3865

Plays/librettos/scripts
The features of Hungarian-language theatre in Romania. Hungary. Romania. 1960-1970. Lang.: Hun. 2894

Reference materials
Sourcebook on women playwrights of diversity. USA. 1970-1996. Lang.: Eng. 3320

A biographical directory of Hispanic presence in American film. USA. 1911-1995. Lang.: Eng. 3690

Relation to other fields
African masked performance. Africa. 1997. Lang.: Eng. 723

Theatre and South Africans of Indian descent. South Africa, Republic of. 1950-1995. Lang.: Eng. 778

Ethnography
Performance/production
The development of the production *Casing a Promised Land* by Linda Welker and H.L. Goodall. USA. 1997. Lang.: Eng. 685

Research/historiography
An ethnography of which the form and content are determined by the informant. Africa. 1997. Lang.: Eng. 852

Theory/criticism
Translating performance events into ethnographic scholarship. Nigeria. 1993-1996. Lang.: Eng. 909

A model of historical performance ethnography. USA. 1997. Lang.: Eng. 922

Eugene Onegin
Design/technology
Critique of minimalist scenic design for opera. Canada: Toronto, ON. USA: New York, NY. 1975-1997. Lang.: Eng. 4019

Jean Kalman's lighting design for *Eugene Onegin*, Metropolitan Opera. USA: New York, NY. 1997. Lang.: Eng. 4033

Performance/production
Analysis of the opera *Eugene Onegin* by Čajkovskij. Russia. 1879-1997. Lang.: Eng. 4209

Background material on Metropolitan Opera radio broadcast performances. USA: New York, NY. 1997. Lang.: Eng. 4238

Actor Sam Waterston on Metropolitan Opera performance of *Eugene Onegin*. USA: New York, NY. 1996-1997. Lang.: Eng. 4251

Eulogies
Basic theatrical documents
Text of *Eulogies* by Marc Kornblatt. USA. 1997. Lang.: Eng. 1332

Eumenides
Performance/production
Théâtre du Soleil's *Les Atrides*. France: Paris. 1992. Lang.: Eng. 1676

Interviews with the cast of Théâtre du Soleil's *Les Atrides*. France: Paris. 1992. Lang.: Eng. 1677

Intercultural signs in Mnouchkine's *Les Atrides (The Atridae)*, Théâtre du Soleil. France: Paris. 1990-1997. Lang.: Eng. 1679

Euphoria
Performance/production
Collection of newspaper reviews by London theatre critics. UK-England: London. 1997. Lang.: Eng. 1997

Euripides
Performance/production
Use of Boal's 'joker' system in a production of Euripides' *Bákchai (The Bacchae)*. USA. 1995-1996. Lang.: Eng. 632

Interview with members of Sarajevo Youth Theatre. Bosnia: Sarajevo. 1993. Lang.: Eng. 1572

Théâtre du Soleil's *Les Atrides*. France: Paris. 1992. Lang.: Eng. 1676

Fame
Performance/production
The representation of social dancing in mass media. USA. 1980-1990.
Lang.: Eng. 1008

Collection of newspaper reviews by London theatre critics. UK-England:
London. 1997. Lang.: Eng. 2137
Plays/librettos/scripts
Social issues of the seventies in works by Arthur Miller. USA. 1970-
1979. Lang.: Eng. 3173

Familie Schroffenstein (Feud of the Schroffensteins, The)
Institutions
Staatstheater Darmstadt under the direction of Gerd-Theo Umberg.
Germany: Darmstadt. 1996-1997. Lang.: Ger. 1412

Familie Selicke, Die (Selicke Family, The)
Plays/librettos/scripts
Johannes Schlaf, Arno Holz, and German naturalism. Germany. 1888-
1892. Lang.: Eng. 2858

Family Circles
Performance/production
Collection of newspaper reviews by London theatre critics. UK-England:
London. 1997. Lang.: Eng. 2096

Family Devotions
Plays/librettos/scripts
Analysis of Asian American drama. USA. 1970-1997. Lang.: Eng. 3225

Family Values
Performance/production
Collection of newspaper reviews by London theatre critics. UK-England:
London. 1997. Lang.: Eng. 2089

Famine, The
Plays/librettos/scripts
Hubert O'Grady's melodramas based on the Potato Famine. Ireland.
1879-1886. Lang.: Eng. 2937

Fanfare
Performance/production
Performance of the Győri Balett. Hungary. 1997. Lang.: Hun. 1093

Fanke, Maya
Performance/production
Productions of plays by Katharina Thanner and Lisa Engel.
Switzerland: Zurich, Basel. 1995-1997. Lang.: Ger. 1963

Fanning, Hilary
Performance/production
Collection of newspaper reviews by London theatre critics. UK-England:
London. 1997. Lang.: Eng. 2115

Fantomsmerter—Det virkelige liv 2 (Phantom Pains—Real Life 2)
Plays/librettos/scripts
Interview with actress Katrine Wiedemann. Denmark. 1997. Lang.: Dan.
2447

Farabough, Laura
Plays/librettos/scripts
Interview with playwright Laura Farabough. USA. 1985. Lang.: Ita.
3142

Farau, Massimiliano
Performance/production
Collection of newspaper reviews by London theatre critics. UK-England:
London. 1997. Lang.: Eng. 2035

Farce
Performance/production
Comedian Ralph Lynn's work on *Wild Horses* by Ben Travers. UK-
England: London. 1953. Lang.: Eng. 2191
Plays/librettos/scripts
Molière, farce, and *La Jalousie du Barbouillé*. France. 1450-1820. Lang.:
Eng. 2821

Fargeau, Jean-Pôl
Basic theatrical documents
English translation of the filmscript *J'ai pas sommeil (I Can't Sleep)* by
Claire Denis and Jean-Pôl Fargeau. France. 1994. Lang.: Eng. 3527
Plays/librettos/scripts
Interview with screenwriter Claire Denis. France. 1994. Lang.: Eng. 3640

Faris, Scott
Design/technology
Technical aspects of *EFX!* at MGM Grand Hotel. USA: Las Vegas, NV.
1996. Lang.: Eng. 3854

Farkosten
Plays/librettos/scripts
Thomas Jennefelt's new opera *Farkosten*. Sweden. 1985-1997. Lang.:
Swe. 4313

Farmer's Bride, The
Performance/production
Collection of newspaper reviews by London theatre critics. UK-England:
London. 1997. Lang.: Eng. 2101

Farndon, John
Performance/production
Collection of newspaper reviews by London theatre critics. UK-England:
London. 1997. Lang.: Eng. 2037

Farquhar, George
Plays/librettos/scripts
Numbers and counting in plays of George Farquhar. England. 1677-
1707. Lang.: Eng. 2586

The body in plays of George Farquhar. England. 1660-1700. Lang.:
Eng. 2587

Farr, David
Performance/production
Collection of newspaper reviews by London theatre critics. UK-England:
London. 1997. Lang.: Eng. 2047

Collection of newspaper reviews by London theatre critics. UK-England:
London. 1997. Lang.: Eng. 2075

Collection of newspaper reviews by London theatre critics. UK-England:
London. 1997. Lang.: Eng. 2110

Farrar, Geraldine
Performance/production
Interpreters of Bizet's heroine Carmen. France: Paris. USA: New York,
NY. 1875-1997. Lang.: Eng. 4139

Opera superstar Minnie Hauk. USA. 1851-1929. Lang.: Eng. 4243

Farrar, John
Performance/production
Collection of newspaper reviews by London theatre critics. UK-England:
London. 1997. Lang.: Eng. 1999

Farrar, Paul
Performance/production
Collection of newspaper reviews by London theatre critics. UK-England:
London. 1997. Lang.: Eng. 2013

Fascinating Aida (London)
Performance/production
Collection of newspaper reviews by London theatre critics. UK-England:
London. 1997. Lang.: Eng. 1986

Fassbinder, Rainer Werner
Basic theatrical documents
English translation of *Nur eine Scheibe Brot (Just a Slice of Bread)* by
Rainer Werner Fassbinder. Germany. 1971. Lang.: Eng. 1280
Performance/production
Profile of actress Traute Hoess. Germany. Austria. 1969-1997. Lang.:
Ger. 1741

The films of Rainer Werner Fassbinder. Germany. 1945-1989. Lang.:
Eng. 3575

Fastia
Basic theatrical documents
Text of *Fastia* by Diane Ney. UK-England. 1997. Lang.: Eng. 1314

Fat Janet Is Dead
Performance/production
Collection of newspaper reviews by London theatre critics. UK-England:
London. 1997. Lang.: Eng. 2041

Fat Men in Skirts
Performance/production
German productions of plays by Terrence McNally and Nicky Silver.
Germany. 1996-1997. Lang.: Ger. 1721
Plays/librettos/scripts
The popularity in Denmark of playwright Nicky Silver. USA. Denmark.
1994-1997. Lang.: Dan. 3224

Fatal Falsehood, The
Plays/librettos/scripts
Playwrights' discussions of censorship in prefaces to their work.
England. 1790-1820. Lang.: Eng. 2507

Faucher, Jean
Performance/production
Interview with TV director Jean Faucher. Canada. 1952-1997. Lang.:
Fre. 3719

Faucher, Martin
Performance/production
Interview with director Martin Faucher. Canada: Montreal, PQ. 1996-
1997. Lang.: Fre. 1599

Faucit, Helena
Plays/librettos/scripts
Actress Helena Faucit on playing Rosalind in Shakespeare's *As You
Like It*. England. 1598-1893. Lang.: Eng. 2539

Fausses confidences, Les (False Confessions, The)
Performance/production
Collection of newspaper reviews by London theatre critics. UK-England:
London. 1997. Lang.: Eng. 2113

Faust by Goethe
    Institutions
        Kölner Schauspiel under the direction of Günter Krämer. Germany:
        Cologne. 1985-1997. Lang.: Ger.   1425
    Performance/production
        Productions of plays by Shakespeare and Goethe at Zürcher
        Schauspielhaus and Theater Neumarkt. Switzerland: Zurich. 1997.
        Lang.: Ger.   1964
        Collection of newspaper reviews by London theatre critics. UK-England:
        London. 1997. Lang.: Eng.   2005
Faust by Gounod
    Performance/production
        Opera composer Charles Gounod. France: Paris. 1818-1893. Lang.: Eng.
        4140
        Background material on Metropolitan Opera radio broadcast
        performances. USA: New York, NY. 1997. Lang.: Eng.   4238
        Novelist Ira Levin on Gounod's *Faust*. USA: New York, NY. 1997.
        Lang.: Eng.   4250
Faustina
    Relation to other fields
        Opera and social decline. England: London. 1698-1737. Lang.: Eng.
        4321
Fearon, Ray
    Performance/production
        Profile of actor Ray Fearon. UK-England: London. 1997. Lang.: Eng.
        2185
Featherstone, Vicky
    Performance/production
        Collection of newspaper reviews by London theatre critics. UK-England:
        London. 1997. Lang.: Eng.   2130
        Profile of Vicky Featherstone, the new artistic director of Paines Plough.
        UK-England: London. 1997. Lang.: Eng.   2179
        Collection of newspaper reviews by London theatre critics. UK-
        Scotland: Edinburgh. 1997. Lang.: Eng.   2232
Featherstonehaughs, The
    Performance/production
        Lea Anderson, founder of The Cholmondeleys and The
        Featherstonehaughs. UK-England. 1984-1994. Lang.: Eng.   1191
Febrile Fiber Phantoms
    Performance/production
        Account of a performance of *Febrile Fiber Phantoms* by Ken and Flo
        Jacobs. USA: Cleveland, OH. 1945-1995. Lang.: Eng.   3826
Fedáh, Sári
    Performance/production
        Film careers of Hungarian dancers. Hungary. 1929-1945. Lang.: Hun.
        976
Feder, Abe
    Design/technology
        Tony Walton's tribute to scene designer Abe Feder. USA: New York,
        NY. 1956-1997. Lang.: Eng.   1380
Federal Theatre Project (Washington, DC)
    Administration
        Censorship in the Federal Theatre Project. USA. 1935-1936. Lang.: Eng.
        131
    Institutions
        The Midwest Play Bureau of the Federal Theatre Project. USA:
        Chicago, IL. 1936-1938. Lang.: Eng.   1516
    Performance/production
        Workers' theatre and the American labor movement. USA. 1929-1940.
        Lang.: Eng.   2281
        Black actors and writers and the Negro Units of the Federal Theatre
        Project. USA: Washington, DC, New York, NY. 1935. Lang.: Eng. 2350
        Modern theatre and American national identity. USA. 1910-1940. Lang.:
        Eng.   2362
Fedora
    Performance/production
        Interviews with and concerning soprano Mirella Freni. Italy. 1935-1997.
        Lang.: Eng.   4191
        Giordano's opera *Fedora* and its reputation. Italy. 1898-1997. Lang.:
        Eng.   4198
        Soprano Aïnhoa Artetoa. Spain. 1997. Lang.: Eng.   4213
        Background material on Metropolitan Opera telecast performance. USA:
        New York, NY. 1997. Lang.: Eng.   4233
        Background material on New York City Opera telecast performance.
        USA: New York, NY. 1997. Lang.: Eng.   4234
        Background material on Metropolitan Opera radio broadcast
        performances. USA: New York, NY. 1997. Lang.: Eng.   4238

Fefu and Her Friends
    Plays/librettos/scripts
        Postmodern feminist theatre practice and Fornes' *Fefu and Her Friends*.
        USA: New York, NY. 1977-1997. Lang.: Eng.   3185
Fehér, Miklós
    Design/technology
        Stage designer Miklós Fehér. Hungary. 1929-1994. Lang.: Hun.   170
Fehling, Jürgen
    Performance/production
        German theatre during and after the Nazi period. Germany: Berlin,
        Dusseldorf. Switzerland: Zurich. 1933-1952. Lang.: Eng.   1704
Feijoo, Fray Benito Jerónimo
    Plays/librettos/scripts
        The work of theatre critic and writer Fray Benito Jerónimo Feijoo.
        Spain. 1950-1990. Lang.: Spa.   3038
Feld, Merle
    Plays/librettos/scripts
        Texts of plays by Jewish American women. USA. 1985-1995. Lang.:
        Eng.   3164
Feliciano, Gloria
    Basic theatrical documents
        Text of plays performed at the Nuyorican Poets Cafe. USA: New York,
        NY. 1973-1990. Lang.: Eng.   1322
Felipe, Carlos
    Plays/librettos/scripts
        The 'Black Madonna' in Cuban theatre. Cuba. 1925-1990. Lang.: Spa.
        2444
Feluettes, Les (Lilies)
    Plays/librettos/scripts
        John Greyson's film adaptation of *Les Feluettes (Lilies)* by Michel Marc
        Bouchard. Canada. 1996. Lang.: Fre.   3635
Female Prelate, The
    Plays/librettos/scripts
        Dramatic satire of the exclusion crisis. England. 1680-1683. Lang.: Eng.
        2714
Feminist criticism
    Performance/production
        Feminist analysis of performance and theatricality. Europe. USA. 1960-
        1979. Lang.: Eng.   517
        Gender on the Italian stage. Italy. 1526-1995. Lang.: Eng.   564
        Street theatre in Punjab province. Pakistan. 1979-1996. Lang.: Eng.   572
        Female rock bands and the performance of ugliness. USA. 1970-1996.
        Lang.: Eng.   637
        The performance of birth stories. USA. 1997. Lang.: Eng.   666
        Marriage and domesticity in *La Sylphide* choreographed by Filippo
        Taglioni. France. 1830-1835. Lang.: Eng.   1068
        Feminist analysis of the ballet *Giselle*. France. 1830-1835. Lang.: Eng.
        1070
        Analysis of Filippo Taglioni's ballet *La Révolte des femmes*. France.
        1830-1840. Lang.: Eng.   1076
        Modern dance and feminist criticism. Europe. USA. 1906-1930. Lang.:
        Eng.   1179
        Gender in choreographies of Mark Morris. USA. 1980-1995. Lang.: Eng.
        1206
        Analysis of *Education of the Girlchild* by Meredith Monk. USA. 1980-
        1995. Lang.: Eng.   1208
        The actress in Russian theatre. Russia. 1845-1916. Lang.: Eng.   1893
        Reactions to modern performances of *Antony and Cleopatra*. UK-
        England. North America. 1827-1987. Lang.: Eng.   2178
        Shakespeare in his own historical context and in ours. USA. 1996.
        Lang.: Eng.   2269
        Screen adaptations of Shakespeare's *The Taming of the Shrew*. UK-
        England. USA. 1908-1966. Lang.: Eng.   3594
        Subversive potential in comedy of Phyllis Diller and Roseanne Barr.
        USA. 1985-1997. Lang.: Eng.   3773
        Work and artists of the Fluxus retrospective. USA. 1960-1996. Lang.:
        Eng.   3835
    Plays/librettos/scripts
        Analysis of *Gertrude and Ophelia* by Margaret Clarke. 1993-1997. Lang.:
        Eng.   2364
        Analysis of *Siete lunas y un espejo (Seven Moons and a Looking Glass)*
        by Albalucía Angel. Colombia. 1991. Lang.: Spa.   2441
        Fantasies of maternal power in Shakespeare's *Macbeth*. England. 1606.
        Lang.: Eng.   2449

Feminist criticism — cont'd

Women's Romantic 'closet' drama as an alternative theatrical space. England. 1790-1820. Lang.: Eng.　　2486

Masculine and feminine in *Bonduca* by John Fletcher. England. 1613. Lang.: Eng.　　2488

Shakespeare's *Antony and Cleopatra* as a romance. England. 1607. Lang.: Eng.　　2496

Feminist analysis of wordplay in Shakespeare's *Antony and Cleopatra*. England. 1607. Lang.: Eng.　　2510

Feminist analysis of *Edwy and Elgiva* by Frances Burney. England. 1752-1840. Lang.: Eng.　　2518

Feminist analysis of the place of women in Shakespeare's plays. England. 1590-1613. Lang.: Eng.　　2519

Sex and gender in plays of Christopher Marlowe. England. 1587-1593. Lang.: Eng.　　2522

Shakespeare's *The Taming of the Shrew* and 'modern' techniques for the subordination of women. England. 1551-1594. Lang.: Eng.　　2527

The role of Lavinia in Shakespeare's *Titus Andronicus*. England. 1593-1594. Lang.: Eng.　　2532

The female voice in *The Winter's Tale* by Shakespeare. England. 1610-1611. Lang.: Eng.　　2537

Early feminist criticism of Shakespeare's *The Comedy of Errors*. England. 1594. Lang.: Eng.　　2548

A female critic's view of Shakespeare's *As You Like It*. England. 1598. Lang.: Eng.　　2557

Domestic cultural and social struggle in Elizabethan theatre. England. 1592-1621. Lang.: Eng.　　2571

Gender and racial politics in Shakespeare's *Othello*. England. 1605. Lang.: Eng.　　2572

Male patronage and maternal power in Shakespeare's *Timon of Athens*. England. 1607-1608. Lang.: Eng.　　2603

Feminist analysis of Shakespeare's *Comedy of Errors*. England. 1594. Lang.: Eng.　　2627

Shakespeare's Cressida as a victim of sexual assault. England. 1600. Lang.: Eng.　　2632

Feminist critique of Shakespeare's *The Comedy of Errors*. England. 1594. Lang.: Eng.　　2646

Transvestism in Beaumont and Fletcher's *Philaster*. England. 1609. Lang.: Eng.　　2664

Madness and gender in the plays of Shakespeare. England. 1589-1613. Lang.: Eng.　　2677

Shakespeare's *Othello* and early modern precepts of wifely conduct. England. 1605. Lang.: Eng.　　2687

Shakespearean tragedies and history plays and the possible roles for women. England. 1589-1613. Lang.: Eng.　　2704

Marital equality and subordination in Shakespeare's *Othello* and Webster's *The Duchess of Malfi*. England. 1605-1613. Lang.: Eng.　2715

Feminist analysis of female characters in Shakespearean tragedy. England. 1589-1613. Lang.: Eng.　　2743

Analysis of *The Witlings* by Fanny Burney. England. 1778. Lang.: Eng.　　2753

Feminist analysis of women in Ibsen's plays. Finland. 1855-1905. Lang.: Eng.　　2802

The depiction of women in ancient Greek theatre. Greece. 500-200 B.C. Lang.: Eng.　　2884

Analysis of *Daughters of Heaven* by Michelanne Forster. New Zealand. 1954-1996. Lang.: Eng.　　2979

Feminist analysis of Wilde's *Salomé* and Shaw's *Saint Joan*. UK-England. Ireland. 1891-1923. Lang.: Eng.　　3116

Ghosts and patriarchy in plays by Caryl Churchill. UK-England. 1980-1990. Lang.: Eng.　　3119

The female body in plays of Moraga, Fornes, and Cruz. USA. 1980-1991. Lang.: Eng.　　3228

Sisterhood and female bonding in *Crimes of the Heart* and *Sisters*. USA. 1986-1996. Lang.: Eng.　　3511

Analysis of films by Martin Scorsese. USA. 1976-1982. Lang.: Eng. 3676

Female characters in Mozart's *Don Giovanni* and *Die Zauberflöte*. Austria. 1756-1791. Lang.: Eng.　　4280

Relation to other fields

Joni L. Jones's performance piece *sista docta*. USA. 1994-1997. Lang.: Eng.　　819

Feminist psychology and drama therapy. USA. 1997. Lang.: Eng.　　823

Feminine masquerade in Mary Kay Cosmetics. USA. 1993-1997. Lang.: Eng.　　846

Theory/criticism

Feminist critique of Plato and mimesis. France. 1985. Lang.: Eng.　886

New historicism, feminist criticism, and gender roles in Renaissance literature. USA. UK-England. 1987. Lang.: Eng.　　916

A model of historical performance ethnography. USA. 1997. Lang.: Eng.　　922

Feminist analysis of postmodern dance. Europe. 1980-1995. Lang.: Eng.　　1027

Feminist theory and choreographer Pina Bausch. Germany: Wuppertal. 1978-1991. Lang.: Eng.　　1029

Feminist analysis of the ballet *Coppélia*. France. 1870. Lang.: Eng.　1134

Critique of feminist dance criticism. USA. 1995. Lang.: Eng.　　1219

Introduction to theatrical applications of literary theory. USA. Europe. 1997. Lang.: Eng.　　3499

Feminist disenchantment with Shakespeare. USA. 1950-1956. Lang.: Eng.　　3500

The female performer in Australian circus. Australia. 1801-1900. Lang.: Eng.　　3787

Feminist theatre

Institutions

Program of women's arts festival. Slovenia: Ljubljana. 1997. Lang.: Slo.　　374

Performance/production

Feminist aspects of the 'model theatre' of the Cultural Revolution. China, People's Republic of. 1965-1976. Lang.: Eng.　　490

Autobiographical performances of Elizabeth Robins. USA. 1862-1952. Lang.: Eng.　　656

Feminist analysis of dance and the representation of the female body. USA. Europe. 1801-1997. Lang.: Eng.　　997

Elizabeth Robins' *Votes for Women!*. UK-England: London. 1907. Lang.: Eng.　　2219

Playwright and performer Eve Ensler. USA: New York, NY. 1980-1997. Lang.: Eng.　　2354

Desire in performance art of Shawna Dempsey. Canada. 1992-1997. Lang.: Eng.　　3816

The female body in performance art. USA. Europe. 1960-1995. Lang.: Eng.　　3837

Performance analysis of *The Constant State of Desire* by Karen Finley. USA. 1988-1990. Lang.: Eng.　　3846

Plays/librettos/scripts

Analysis of *A Woman from the Sea* by Cindy Cowan. Canada. 1986. Lang.: Eng.　　2392

Feminist solo performance in Quebec. Canada: Montreal, PQ. 1970-1993. Lang.: Eng.　　2402

Analysis of *Encore cinq minutes (Five More Minutes)* by Françoise Loranger. Canada. 1967. Lang.: Fre.　　2403

The significance of rape in *The Rover* by Aphra Behn. England. 1660. Lang.: Eng.　　2744

Theatrical representations of the Holocaust. Europe. North America. 1950-1996. Lang.: Eng.　　2789

Feminist aspects of plays by Elfriede Jelinek. Germany. Austria. 1989-1997. Lang.: Pol.　　2854

Report from women playwrights conference. Ireland: Galway. 1997. Lang.: Swe.　　2930

Interview with director and author Margarete Garpe. Sweden: Stockholm. 1960-1997. Lang.: Swe.　　3063

Role playing in feminist theatre. UK-England. 1982-1995. Lang.: Eng.　　3090

Analysis of *Basin* by Jacqueline Rudet. UK-England. 1985-1997. Lang.: Eng.　　3106

The theme of nurturing in plays of Wolff, Treadwell, and Wasserstein. USA. 1996. Lang.: Eng.　　3136

Critical history of American feminist drama. USA. 1772-1995. Lang.: Eng.　　3151

The theme of hope in postwar American theatre and writing. USA. 1914-1929. Lang.: Eng.　　3153

Mimesis, feminism, theatre, and performance. USA. 1997. Lang.: Eng.　　3176

Postmodern feminist theatre practice and Fornes' *Fefu and Her Friends*. USA: New York, NY. 1977-1997. Lang.: Eng.　　3185

Festivals — cont'd

Performance spaces

Performance/production

Figurative arts — cont'd

Critic Rolf-Dieter Eichler on theatre draughtsman Ingeborg Voss. Germany: Berlin. 1960-1990. Lang.: Ger. 756

Berlin Stadtmuseum's collection of theatre drawings by Ingeborg Voss. Germany: Berlin. 1962-1996. Lang.: Ger. 757

Theatrical draughtsmen and their profession. Germany: Berlin. 1843-1993. Lang.: Ger. 761

Catalogue of exhibition on Italian Futurism. Italy. 1909-1944. Lang.: Ita. 768

Exhibition catalogue regarding Italian Futurism in Liguria. Italy: Genoa. 1920-1942. Lang.: Ita. 770

Theatrical influences on painter Jan Steen. Netherlands. 1640-1690. Lang.: Eng. 773

Ibsen Society of America meeting on Ibsen and the visual arts. USA: New York, NY. 1996. Lang.: Eng. 792

Theatrical protests of Art Institute exhibitions. USA: Chicago, IL. 1988-1997. Lang.: Eng. 801

Performative criticism of photo exhibits by Nan Goldin and Lyle Ashton Harris. USA: New York, NY. 1996-1997. Lang.: Eng. 849

Exhibitions dealing with dance at Kunsthalle Bremen. Germany: Bremen. 1900-1925. Lang.: Ger. 1017

The Ballets Russes and the arts. Europe. 1909-1929. Lang.: Ger. 1131

An engraving of Edward Alleyn dressed as Tamburlaine. England. 1603. Lang.: Eng. 3325

The Ashbourne portrait, formerly believed to be of William Shakespeare. England. 1611-1979. Lang.: Eng. 3343

Visual representations of Greek drama. Greece. 500-250 B.C. Lang.: Eng. 3357

The inspiration of Botticelli in D'Annunzio's *Sogno d'un mattino di primavera (A Spring Morning's Dream)*. Italy. 1895-1897. Lang.: Ita. 3374

Füssli's Shakespearean paintings: exhibition catalogue. Switzerland. 1775-1825. Lang.: Ita. 3379

Museums' new approach to presentation of materials. USA: New York, NY. 1996. Lang.: Eng. 3707

Burlesque theatre as seen in artwork of Reginald Marsh. USA. 1920-1950. Lang.: Eng. 3777

Research/historiography
Eighteenth-century theatrical portraits. England. France. 1700-1800. Lang.: Eng. 3445

Research in theatre iconography. Europe. 1600-1995. Lang.: Eng. 3447

Fil'štinskij, Venjamin
Performance/production
Ostrovskij's *Žadov i drugie (Žadov and Others)* at the Globus. Russia: Novosibirsk. 1997. Lang.: Rus. 1884

Filatov, Leonid
Basic theatrical documents
Writings of actor Leonid Filatov. Russia. 1960-1997. Lang.: Rus. 1295

Fille du régiment, La
Basic theatrical documents
Libretto for Donizetti's opera *La Fille du régiment*. France. 1840. Lang.: Fre. 4010

Performance/production
Productions of Donizetti's *La Fille du régiment*. 1840-1996. Lang.: Fre. 4079

Recordings of *La Fille du régiment* by Donizetti. 1940-1989. Lang.: Fre. 4085

Performances of Donizetti's *La Fille du régiment* on video. 1965-1986. Lang.: Fre. 4086

Plays/librettos/scripts
Analysis of *La Fille du régiment* by Donizetti. France. 1840. Lang.: Fre. 4292

Theory/criticism
The reaction of Hector Berlioz to Donizetti's *La Fille du régiment*. France. 1840. Lang.: Fre. 4328

Film
SEE ALSO
Classed Entries under MEDIA—Film.
Administration
Illustrator Giorgio Tabet's playbills and cinema posters. Italy. 1904-1997. Lang.: Ita. 39

Copyright law and videocassettes. USA. 1997. Lang.: Eng. 3709

Basic theatrical documents
Writings of actor Leonid Filatov. Russia. 1960-1997. Lang.: Rus. 1295

Design/technology
History of *TCI* and its new coverage of design and technology beyond theatre. USA. 1967-1997. Lang.: Eng. 212

The filming of *Millennium* in Vancouver. Canada: Vancouver, BC. 1996. Lang.: Eng. 3711

Institutions
Synthesis of theatre and film at Laterna Magika. Czechoslovakia: Prague. 1959-1997. Lang.: Eng. 305

Report on Strindberg festival. Sweden: Stockholm. 1996. Lang.: Eng. 1494

Fundraising strategies of American Movie Classics. USA. 1997. Lang.: Eng. 3715

Performance/production
Actor Gian Maria Volonté. Italy. 1933-1994. Lang.: Ita. 563

Space in site-specific performance. UK-England. 1960-1997. Lang.: Eng. 619

The public persona of actress Mae West. USA. 1913-1943. Lang.: Eng. 642

Interviews and documents on performance concepts and practices. USA. 1952-1994. Lang.: Eng. 649

The early stage career of actor Buster Keaton. USA. 1916-1917. Lang.: Eng. 651

Constraints and opportunities for Asian-American actors. USA. 1990-1997. Lang.: Eng. 655

The competition between tent repertory theatre and film. USA. 1920-1929. Lang.: Eng. 667

Film careers of Hungarian dancers. Hungary. 1929-1945. Lang.: Hun. 976

The representation of social dancing in mass media. USA. 1980-1990. Lang.: Eng. 1008

Performance history of the ballet *Agon* by Stravinskij and Balanchine. USA. 1959-1997. Lang.: Eng. 1130

Recent productions of Elizabethan theatre. Europe. 1997. Lang.: Ger. 1649

The map of England in productions of Shakespeare's *King Lear*. Europe. USA. 1909-1994. Lang.: Eng. 1650

Interview with theatre and film director Péter Gothár. Hungary. 1947-1997. Lang.: Hun. 1754

Interview with director János Szász. Hungary. 1980-1997. Lang.: Hun. 1758

Writings of actor Valentin Gaft. Russia. 1960-1997. Lang.: Rus. 1867

Actor Innokentij Smoktunovskij. Russia. 1925-1994. Lang.: Rus. 1883

Portraits of stage and film actors. Russia. 1960-1997. Lang.: Rus. 1896

The accessibility of Shakespeare's plays to today's audiences. UK-England: London. 1997. Lang.: Eng. 1968

Actor Dustin Hoffman on theatre and film. USA. UK-England. 1997. Lang.: Swe. 2323

How film and video versions of Shakespeare's plays may reinforce textual authority rather than challenge it. UK-England. 1979-1991. Lang.: Eng. 3510

Rock group U2's use of video and interactive technology. USA. 1997. Lang.: Eng. 3732

Nelson Eddy's career as an opera singer. USA. 1901-1967. Lang.: Eng. 4268

Plays/librettos/scripts
Hamlet, revenge tragedy, and *film noir*. 1600-1996. Lang.: Eng. 2365

The appropriation of Shakespeare by the dispossessed and marginalized. 1590-1995. Lang.: Eng. 2366

Terrains Vagues (Wastelands), Michel Nadeau's stage adaptation of *Rashomon*. Canada: Quebec, PQ. 1997. Lang.: Fre. 2422

Homoeroticism and the challenge to bourgeois society in works of Pasolini and Genet. Italy. 1942-1950. Lang.: Ita. 2964

Interview with playwright and film-maker William Kentridge. South Africa, Republic of. 1986-1994. Lang.: Eng. 3025

Social issues of the sixties in plays and films of Arthur Miller. USA. 1960-1969. Lang.: Eng. 3131

The theme of hope in postwar American theatre and writing. USA. 1914-1929. Lang.: Eng. 3153

Communism and the stage and screen plays of John Howard Lawson. USA. 1933-1947. Lang.: Eng. 3159

Tennessee Williams' plays on film. USA. 1950-1969. Lang.: Eng. 3245

The rhetoric of victimization in *The Glass Menagerie* by Tennessee Williams. USA. 1945-1994. Lang.: Eng. 3298

Relation to other fields
The fear of infection in American popular art and culture. USA. 1997. Lang.: Eng. 848

Film — cont'd

Evaluation of educational technology for the teaching of Shakespeare. USA. 1997. Lang.: Eng. 3390

Pros and cons of using film and video in teaching Shakespeare. USA. 1995. Lang.: Eng. 3392

Film as a way of enhancing student understanding of Shakespeare. USA. 1995. Lang.: Eng. 3396

Using film and video to teach Shakespeare. USA. 1985-1996. Lang.: Eng. 3397

The use of film and video to teach the plays of Shakespeare. USA. 1997. Lang.: Eng. 3398

Possibilities and limitations of using Shakespearean performance in the classroom. USA. 1997. Lang.: Eng. 3420

Theory/criticism

Interview with literary critic Giovanni Macchia. Italy. France. 1997. Lang.: Ita. 906

Performance theory applied to Laurie Anderson's *Home of the Brave*. USA. 1990-1995. Lang.: Eng. 3852

Filmographies

Reference materials

Filmography of African-Americans. USA. 1978-1994. Lang.: Eng. 3691

Fils naturel, Le (Natural Son, The)

Plays/librettos/scripts

Incest and familial taboos in *Le fils naturel (The Natural Son)* by Diderot. France. 1757. Lang.: Eng. 2830

Fin de partie (Endgame)

Performance/production

German reactions to the work of Samuel Beckett. Germany. 1953-1976. Lang.: Eng. 1699

Plays/librettos/scripts

Representational practices of mid-twentieth century avant-garde theatre. North America. Europe. 1950-1990. Lang.: Eng. 696

Shakespeare's *King Lear* as an inspiration for Beckett's *Fin de partie (Endgame)*. England. Ireland. France. 1606-1958. Lang.: Eng. 2750

Analysis of German translations of plays by Samuel Beckett. Germany. 1967-1978. Lang.: Eng. 2842

The chess metaphor in Beckett's *Fin de partie (Endgame)*. Ireland. France. 1957. Lang.: Eng. 2918

Financial operations

Administration

Australian cultural policy. Australia. 1968-1997. Lang.: Eng. 4

Canadian producers Jeffrey Follows and Lawrence Latimer. Canada. 1992-1997. Lang.: Eng. 6

Bell Canada's financial support of the Stratford Festival. Canada: Stratford, ON. 1953-1997. Lang.: Eng. 7

Efforts to refurbish the historic Columbia Theatre. Canada: New Westminster, BC. 1927-1997. Lang.: Eng. 9

Report of forum on unsubsidized theatre. Canada: Montreal, PQ. 1997. Lang.: Fre. 11

Model of financing for theatres in the Czech Republic. Czech Republic. 1997. Lang.: Cze. 12

Real costs and real values of theatrical production. Europe. 1997. Lang.: Ger. 23

Corporate sponsorship of art. Europe. 1992-1997. Lang.: Eng. 24

The effect of budget cuts and theatre closings on surviving theatres. Germany. 1997. Lang.: Ger. 35

Government funding and live performance. Italy. 1980-1990. Lang.: Ita. 40

Money and Swiss theatre. Switzerland. 1917-1997. Lang.: Ger. 51

Basic principles of not-for-profit fundraising. USA. 1997. Lang.: Eng. 56

The fiduciary responsibilities of nonprofit boards. USA. 1997. Lang.: Eng. 58

Investment advice for small non-profits. USA. 1997. Lang.: Eng. 61

An appropriate tax program for theatre personnel. USA. 1997. Lang.: Eng. 71

Guide for actors faced with a tax audit. USA. 1997. Lang.: Eng. 72

The availability of unemployment insurance for artists. USA. 1997. Lang.: Eng. 77

Direct-mail fundraising. USA. 1997. Lang.: Eng. 78

Vision care benefits of Equity health plan. USA. 1997. Lang.: Eng. 84

Changes in Equity bonding policy. USA. 1997. Lang.: Eng. 86

Equity's role in defending government funding of the NEA. USA. 1997. Lang.: Eng. 106

Successful fundraising strategies. USA. 1997. Lang.: Eng. 119

Advice on funding and promoting the arts. USA: New York, NY. 1997. Lang.: Eng. 120

Technical aid in fundraising and marketing for small arts groups. USA. 1997. Lang.: Eng. 121

The Easter Bonnet competition, a fundraiser for Broadway Cares/Equity Fights AIDS. USA. 1997. Lang.: Eng. 128

The erosion of support for classical art forms such as ballet. USA. 1997. Lang.: Eng. 1047

Report on the English theatre scene. UK-England. 1995-1997. Lang.: Ger. 1242

Oscar Micheaux's entreneurship in financing *The House Behind the Cedars*. USA. 1920-1922. Lang.: Eng. 3523

Opera companies and the practice of hiring celebrity singers. Europe. USA. 1960. Lang.: Swe. 4003

State patronage and control of opera in the Duchy of Lucca. Italy: Lucca. 1817-1847. Lang.: Eng. 4004

Institutions

Swedish theatre and cultural policy. Sweden. 1997. Lang.: Swe. 382

Report on Göteborgs Stadsteatern's financial crisis. Sweden: Gothenburg. 1997. Lang.: Swe. 1479

The closing of Göteborgs Stadsteatern. Sweden: Gothenburg. 1996. Lang.: Swe. 1480

Interview with Ronny Danielsson, manager of Göteborgs Stadsteatern. Sweden: Gothenburg. 1997. Lang.: Swe. 1486

The closing of Göteborgs Stadsteatern. Sweden: Gothenburg. 1995. Lang.: Swe. 1488

Swedish directors on the financial crisis. Sweden. 1990. Lang.: Swe. 1490

Guthrie Theatre's new artistic director Joe Dowling. USA: Minneapolis, MN. Ireland: Dublin. 1963-1997. Lang.: Eng. 1513

Performance/production

Interview with director Ragnar Lyth. Sweden: Stockholm, Gothenburg. 1990. Lang.: Swe. 1943

Finborough Arms (London)

Performance/production

Collection of newspaper reviews by London theatre critics. UK-England: London. 1997. Lang.: Eng. 1970

Collection of newspaper reviews by London theatre critics. UK-England: London. 1997. Lang.: Eng. 1981

Collection of newspaper reviews by London theatre critics. UK-England: London. 1997. Lang.: Eng. 1992

Collection of newspaper reviews by London theatre critics. UK-England: London. 1997. Lang.: Eng. 2018

Collection of newspaper reviews by London theatre critics. UK-England. 1997. Lang.: Eng. 2039

Collection of newspaper reviews by London theatre critics. UK-England: London. 1997. Lang.: Eng. 2053

Collection of newspaper reviews by London theatre critics. UK-England: London. 1997. Lang.: Eng. 2069

Collection of newspaper reviews by London theatre critics. UK-England: London. 1997. Lang.: Eng. 2100

Collection of newspaper reviews by London theatre critics. UK-England: London. 1997. Lang.: Eng. 2114

Collection of newspaper reviews by London theatre critics. UK-England: London. 1997. Lang.: Eng. 2131

Collection of newspaper reviews by London theatre critics. UK-England: London. 1997. Lang.: Eng. 2146

Find Me

Performance/production

Collection of newspaper reviews by London theatre critics. UK-England: London. 1997. Lang.: Eng. 2031

Findley, Timothy

Performance/production

Paul Thompson's production of *The Piano Man's Daughter* based on a novel by Timothy Findley. Canada: Ottawa, ON. 1995-1997. Lang.: Eng. 1606

Finger, Gottfried

Institutions

Music in productions of Lincoln's Inn Fields. England. 1695-1705. Lang.: Eng. 307

Fink, Michael

Design/technology

Architectural and entertainment lighting at Life performance space, formerly the Village Gate. USA: New York, NY. 1997. Lang.: Eng. 251

Folklore — cont'd

Relation to other fields
A folk analogue to the *Play of the Sacrament*. USA. England. 1400-1997. Lang.: Eng.   822

Folkoperan (Stockholm)
Institutions
The funding of three Swedish opera companies. Sweden: Gothenburg, Stockholm. 1994. Lang.: Swe.   4057

Performance/production
Interview with Staffan Waldemar Holm, artistic director of Malmö Dramatiska Ensemble. Sweden: Malmö. Denmark: Copenhagen.1984-1997. Lang.: Swe.   1928

Folkteatern i Gävleborg (Gävle)
Institutions
Swedish directors on the financial crisis. Sweden. 1990. Lang.: Swe. 1490

Folkteatern—En Trappa Ner (Gothenburg)
Administration
Protests against budget cuts affecting children's theatre. Sweden: Gothenburg. 1997. Lang.: Swe.   50

Performance/production
Interview with dramaturg Lena Fridell. Sweden: Gothenburg. 1985-1997. Lang.: Swe.   1932

Folkwang-Hochschule (Essen)
Training
Interview with Lutz Försten of Folkwang-Hochschule. Germany: Essen. 1927-1997. Lang.: Ger.   1043

Follies
Plays/librettos/scripts
Sociopolitical themes in Stephen Sondheim's *Follies*. USA. 1971. Lang.: Eng.   3988

Follows, Jeffrey
Administration
Canadian producers Jeffrey Follows and Lawrence Latimer. Canada. 1992-1997. Lang.: Eng.   6

Fomenko, Pĕtr
Institutions
Pĕtr Fomenko's students at Rossiskaja Akademija Teatral'nogo Iskusstva. Russia: Moscow. 1990-1997. Lang.: Rus.   1457

The actors of Masterskaja Petra Fomenko. Russia: Moscow. 1986-1996. Lang.: Rus.   1459

Performance/production
Two productions of *Tanja-Tanja* by Ol'ga Muchina. Russia: St. Petersburg, Moscow. 1997. Lang.: Rus.   1863

Fomenko's production of Puškin's *Pikovaja Dama (Queen of Spades)*. Russia: Moscow. 1996. Lang.: Rus.   1876

A production by Pĕtr Fomenko's directing students at RATI. Russia: Moscow. 1996. Lang.: Rus.   1895

Fomin, William
Performance/production
Performance of the Győri Balett. Hungary. 1997. Lang.: Hun.   1093

Fonteyn, Margot
Performance/production
The artistic partnership of Rudolf Nureyev and Margot Fonteyn. UK-England. 1962-1997. Lang.: Rus.   1118

Food Chain, The
Performance/production
German productions of plays by Terrence McNally and Nicky Silver. Germany. 1996-1997. Lang.: Ger.   1721

Fool House
Performance/production
Collection of newspaper reviews by London theatre critics. UK-England: London. 1997. Lang.: Eng.   2102

Foote, Horton
Plays/librettos/scripts
Analysis of *Only the Heart* by Horton Foote. USA. 1943. Lang.: Eng.   3307

Foote, Samuel
Plays/librettos/scripts
Censorship and satire in the eighteenth century. England. 1710-1789. Lang.: Eng.   2617

Footfalls
Performance/production
The interior I/eye in later plays of Samuel Beckett. Ireland. France. USA. 1978-1997. Lang.: Eng.   1785

Collection of newspaper reviews by London theatre critics. UK-England: London. 1997. Lang.: Eng.   2134

Xerxes Mehta's approach to directing Beckett. USA. 1993. Lang.: Eng. 2305

Plays/librettos/scripts
Analysis of German translations of plays by Samuel Beckett. Germany. 1967-1978. Lang.: Eng.   2842

Analysis of Beckett's *Footfalls, Ohio Impromptu* and *Rockaby*. Ireland. France. USA. 1976-1981. Lang.: Eng.   2928

for colored girls who have considered suicide/when the rainbow is enuf
Plays/librettos/scripts
The voices of African-American women. USA. 1840-1994. Lang.: Eng. 3309

Forbidden Broadway
Plays/librettos/scripts
Gerard Alessandrini's *Forbidden Broadway*. USA: New York, NY. 1981-1997. Lang.: Eng.   4000

Forced Entertainment (Sheffield)
Plays/librettos/scripts
Changing relationships of writing, text and performance. UK-England. USA. 1980-1996. Lang.: Eng.   698

Ford Centre for the Performing Arts (Toronto, ON)
Design/technology
Lighting design for *Ragtime* at the Ford Centre for the Performing Arts. Canada: Toronto, ON. 1975-1997. Lang.: Eng.   3905

Performance/production
Comparison of productions of *Ragtime* and *Jane Eyre*. Canada: Toronto, ON. 1997. Lang.: Eng.   3932

Ford Centre for the Performing Arts (Vancouver, BC)
Performance spaces
Lighting and design of the Ford Centre for the Performing Arts. Canada: Vancouver, BC. 1997. Lang.: Eng.   415

Ford, John
Performance/production
Student production of John Ford's *The Broken Heart*. Australia: La Trobe. 1997. Lang.: Eng.   1559

Plays/librettos/scripts
John Ford's *The Broken Heart* and the prose of Sir Philip Sidney. England. 1629. Lang.: Eng.   2582

History and rhetoric in John Ford's *Perkin Warbeck*. England. 1634. Lang.: Eng.   2674

The forced marriage plot in early English drama. England. 1584-1642. Lang.: Eng.   2675

Foreman, Richard
Basic theatrical documents
Text of *Pearls for Pigs* by Richard Foreman. USA. 1995. Lang.: Eng. 1326

Text of *The Universe* by Richard Foreman. USA. 1996. Lang.: Eng. 1327

Design/technology
The scenography of Richard Foreman. USA. 1990-1996. Lang.: Eng. 1362

Institutions
Ontological-Hysteric Theatre and its influence. USA: New York, NY. 1997. Lang.: Eng.   1501

Performance/production
Interviews and documents on performance concepts and practices. USA. 1952-1994. Lang.: Eng.   649

Collection of newspaper reviews by London theatre critics. UK-England. 1997. Lang.: Eng.   2072

Bertolt Brecht's influence on Richard Foreman. USA. 1950-1997. Lang.: Eng.   2239

Ontological-Hysteric Theatre's production of *Pearls for Pigs* at Hartford Stage. USA: Hartford, CT. 1995. Lang.: Eng.   2270

Directing methods of Richard Foreman, Ontological-Hysteric Theatre. USA. 1968-1997. Lang.: Dan.   2351

Plays/librettos/scripts
Analysis of *Pearls for Pigs* by Richard Foreman. USA. 1995. Lang.: Eng.   3262

Forgách, József
Training
Ballet soloist, teacher, and choreographer József Forgách. Hungary. 1941-1970. Lang.: Hun.   1138

Former Coach Station (London)
Performance/production
Collection of newspaper reviews by London theatre critics. UK-England: London. 1997. Lang.: Eng.   2071

Fornes, Maria Irene
Basic theatrical documents
Text of *Terra Incognita* by Maria Irene Fornes, the libretto for an opera by Roberto Sierra. USA. 1992. Lang.: Eng.   4017

Plays/librettos/scripts
Maria Irene Fornes' *Promenade* as text and performance. USA. 1969-1994. Lang.: Eng.   3147

Fornes, Maria Irene — cont'd

Critical history of American feminist drama. USA. 1772-1995. Lang.:
Eng.   3151

Postmodern feminist theatre practice and Fornes' *Fefu and Her Friends*.
USA: New York, NY. 1977-1997. Lang.: Eng.   3185

Analysis of *Mud* by Maria Irene Fornes. USA. 1983-1995. Lang.: Eng.
                                                                   3192

The female body in plays of Moraga, Fornes, and Cruz. USA. 1980-
1991. Lang.: Eng.   3228

Analysis of *Enter the Night* by Maria Irene Fornes. USA. 1990-1993.
Lang.: Eng.   3255

Critical history of American drama. USA. 1960-1997. Lang.: Eng.   3267

Forrell, Lisa
Performance/production
Collection of newspaper reviews by London theatre critics. UK-England:
London. 1997. Lang.: Eng.   2002

Collection of newspaper reviews by London theatre critics. UK-England:
London. 1997. Lang.: Eng.   2135

Forrest, Edwin
Performance/production
Stage imagery in productions of Shakespeare's *Coriolanus*. England.
1754-1901. Lang.: Eng.   1634

Forrest, Robin
Performance/production
Collection of newspaper reviews by London theatre critics. UK-England:
London. 1997. Lang.: Eng.   2141

Forster, Ewan
Performance/production
Space in site-specific performance. UK-England. 1960-1997. Lang.: Eng.
                                                                    619

Forster, Michelanne
Plays/librettos/scripts
Analysis of *Daughters of Heaven* by Michelanne Forster. New Zealand.
1954-1996. Lang.: Eng.   2979

Forsyth, Margarete
Performance/production
Collection of newspaper reviews by London theatre critics. UK-England:
London. 1997. Lang.: Eng.   2042

Fort Beaver
Performance/production
Collection of newspaper reviews by London theatre critics. UK-England:
London. 1997. Lang.: Eng.   2089

Fortinbras
Plays/librettos/scripts
Lacanian reading of plays by Lee Blessing. USA. 1989-1991. Lang.:
Eng.   3140

Fortune Theatre (London)
Administration
Philip Henslowe's move from the Rose to the Fortune. England:
London. 1576-1616. Lang.: Eng.   20

Performance spaces
Early modern performance spaces. England. 1600-1650. Lang.: Eng. 424

The debate over the stage design and pillars of Shakespeare's Globe.
England: London. 1599-1995. Lang.: Eng.   1525

The building of the Fortune Theatre. England: London. 1600. Lang.:
Eng.   1526

Forza del Destino, La
Performance/production
Historical and literary influences on Verdi's operas. Italy. 1813-1901.
Lang.: Eng.   4195

Foscolo, Ugo
Plays/librettos/scripts
Greek mythology in tragedies of Ugo Foscolo. Italy. 1795-1811. Lang.:
Ita.   2954

Fosse, Bob
Performance/production
Collection of newspaper reviews by London theatre critics. UK-England:
London. 1997. Lang.: Eng.   2140

Foster, Frances
Performance/production
Actress Frances Foster. USA. 1924-1997. Lang.: Eng.   2359

Foster, Gerard
Performance/production
Collection of newspaper reviews by London theatre critics. UK-England:
London. 1997. Lang.: Eng.   1982

Found spaces
Performance spaces
Early English household theatre. England. 1400-1550. Lang.: Eng. 427

Performance spaces in Renaissance Spain. Spain. 1550-1750. Lang.:
Eng.   449

Elena Siemens' performance as a walker in Moscow. Russia: Moscow.
1996. Lang.: Eng.   3762

Production of Harry Schürer's *Space Dream* in a hangar of Tempelhof
Airport. Germany: Berlin. 1997. Lang.: Ger.   3929

Fountain, Tim
Performance/production
Collection of newspaper reviews by London theatre critics. UK-England:
London. 1997. Lang.: Eng.   2038

Four Saints in Three Acts
Plays/librettos/scripts
Comparison of works by Gertrude Stein and Thornton Wilder. USA.
1934-1938. Lang.: Eng.   3127

Analysis of opera librettos by Boito, Da Ponte, and Gertrude Stein.
Europe. 1770-1915. Lang.: Eng.   4289

Fourberies de Scapin, Les (Tricks of Scapin, The)
Performance/production
Collection of newspaper reviews by London theatre critics. UK-England:
London. 1997. Lang.: Eng.   2113

Fővárosi Operettszínház (Budapest)
Performance/production
Colleagues' recollections of director László Vámos. Hungary. 1928-1996.
Lang.: Hun.   1763

Projects of the competitors for the managerial post of the Budapest
Operetta Theatre. Hungary. 1900-1990. Lang.: Hun.   3935

Cabaret and operetta artist Hanna Honthy. Hungary. 1893-1950. Lang.:
Hun.   4338

Fővárosi Operettszínház Tánckara (Budapest)
Performance/production
A joint production of Budapest Operetta Theatre dance company and
Madách Dance Workshop. Hungary: Budapest. 1996-1997. Lang.: Hun.
                                                                   3937

Fox, Michele
Performance/production
Video choreographer Michele Fox. UK-England. 1997. Lang.: Eng. 995

Foxworthy, Jeff
Administration
Protection of comic intellectual property. USA. 1995. Lang.: Eng. 67

Foyn Bruun, Ellen
Performance/production
Collection of newspaper reviews by London theatre critics. UK-England:
London. 1997. Lang.: Eng.   2059

Fragments d'une lettre d'adieu lus par des géologues (Fragments of a Farewell Letter Read by Geologists)
Plays/librettos/scripts
Analysis of *Fragments d'une lettre d'adieu lus par des géologues
(Fragments of a Farewell Letter Read by Geologists)* by Normand
Chaurette. Canada. 1986. Lang.: Fre.   2427

Franchetti, Alberto
Performance/production
The influence of Mascagni, Leoncavallo, and Franchetti on Puccini's *La
Bohème*. Italy: Milan. 1894-1898. Lang.: Eng.   4190

Francis, Matthew
Performance/production
Collection of newspaper reviews by London theatre critics. UK-England:
London. 1997. Lang.: Eng.   2088

Collection of newspaper reviews by London theatre critics. UK-England:
London. 1997. Lang.: Eng.   2155

Frank, Niklas
Performance/production
Reviews of Bochumer Schauspielhaus productions. Germany: Bochum.
1997. Lang.: Ger.   1730

Frank, Otto
Plays/librettos/scripts
The stage adaptation of the diary of Anne Frank. USA. 1947-1950.
Lang.: Eng.   3234

Frankcom, Sarah
Performance/production
Collection of newspaper reviews by London theatre critics. UK-England:
London. 1997. Lang.: Eng.   1980

Frankenstein
Performance/production
Interview with puppeteer John Ludwig. USA: Atlanta, GA. 1996. Lang.:
Eng.   4376

Frankfurt Ballet
Performance/production
The dramaturg and dance production. Germany: Frankfurt. 1993-1997.
Lang.: Eng.   1077

Frankfurter Schauspiel (Frankfurt)
Performance/production
Plays of Botho Strauss and Peter Handke carried over into a second season. Germany: Berlin, Frankfurt. 1996-1997. Lang.: Ger.   1746

Frankly Scarlett
Performance/production
Collection of newspaper reviews by London theatre critics. UK-England: London. 1997. Lang.: Eng.   2038

Franks, Philip
Performance/production
Collection of newspaper reviews by London theatre critics. UK-Scotland: Edinburgh. 1997. Lang.: Eng.   2231

Fraser, Ronnie
Performance/production
Life and career of television actor Ronnie Fraser. UK-England. 1930-1997. Lang.: Eng.   3724

Fraser, Sonia
Performance/production
Collection of newspaper reviews by London theatre critics. UK-England: London. 1997. Lang.: Eng.   2041
Collection of newspaper reviews by London theatre critics. UK-England: London. 1997. Lang.: Eng.   2100

Frau ohne Schatten, Die
Design/technology
Technical description of Semperoper's production of *Die Frau ohne Schatten*. Germany: Dresden. 1997. Lang.: Ger.   4021

Frayn, Michael
Performance/production
Collection of newspaper reviews by London theatre critics. UK-England: London. 1997. Lang.: Eng.   2047

Fréchette, Carole
Plays/librettos/scripts
Quebec playwrights on the body in their work. Canada: Montreal, PQ. 1992-1996. Lang.: Fre.   2431

Fredén, Sofia
Performance/production
Involving youth audiences in theatre. Sweden: Stockholm, Uppsala. 1995-1997. Lang.: Swe.   1949

Fredro, Aleksander
Plays/librettos/scripts
The image of Lvov in Polish drama. Poland. 1700-1939. Lang.: Pol. 697

Freeborn, Mark
Design/technology
The filming of *Millennium* in Vancouver. Canada: Vancouver, BC. 1996. Lang.: Eng.   3711

Freedman, Gerald
Performance/production
Productions of Shakespeare's *Titus Andronicus*. UK-England. USA. 1955-1995. Lang.: Hun.   2225

Freedom Theatre (London)
Performance/production
Collection of newspaper reviews by London theatre critics. UK-England: London. 1997. Lang.: Eng.   2002

Freeman, David
Performance spaces
Profile of Shakespeare's Globe Theatre. UK-England: London. 1970. Lang.: Swe.   1541
Performance/production
Collection of newspaper reviews by London theatre critics. UK-England: London. 1997. Lang.: Eng.   2060

Freie Bühne (Los Angeles, CA)
Relation to other fields
German émigré director Walter Wicclair. USA: Los Angeles, CA. Germany: Berlin. 1921-1997. Lang.: Ger.   3418

Freie Volksbühne (Berlin)
SEE ALSO
Volksbühne.

Freischütz, Der
Plays/librettos/scripts
Nature in Apel's *Der Freischütz* and its operatic adaptations. Germany. 1811-1990. Lang.: Ger.   2856

Fremdes Haus (Stranger's House)
Performance/production
Collection of newspaper reviews by London theatre critics. UK-England: London. 1997. Lang.: Eng.   2143

French Classicism
SEE
Neoclassicism.

French Lieutenant's Woman, The
Plays/librettos/scripts
British Library holdings of filmscript material of Harold Pinter. UK-England. 1963-1994. Lang.: Eng.   3647

French, Beth
Plays/librettos/scripts
Beth French's *Life Sentences*. Canada: Toronto, ON. 1989-1997. Lang.: Eng.   2390

Freni, Mirella
Performance/production
Interviews with and concerning soprano Mirella Freni. Italy. 1935-1997. Lang.: Eng.   4191
Soprano Mirella Freni. Italy. 1935-1997. Lang.: Eng.   4199

Frenkiel, Mieczysław
Performance/production
Guest performances in Polish cities. Poland: Cracow, Lvov, Warsaw. 1810-1915. Lang.: Pol.   583

Frey, Barbara
Performance/production
World premieres at Mannheimer Nationaltheater. Germany: Mannheim. 1997. Lang.: Ger.   1697

Freyer, Achim
Performance/production
Opera productions from Salzburger Festspiele. Austria: Salzburg. 1997. Lang.: Ger.   4096
Interview with director and scene designer Achim Freyer. Austria: Salzburg. 1997. Lang.: Ger.   4097
Hans Werner Henze's opera *Das Mädchen mit den Schwefelhölzern*. Germany: Hamburg. 1921-1997. Lang.: Ger.   4156

Fria Teatern (Stockholm)
Performance/production
Interview with actor Dan Johansson of Fria Teatern. Sweden: Stockholm. 1993. Lang.: Swe.   1930

Frida K.
Design/technology
Background on Ken Garnhum's set design for *Frida K.* Canada: Toronto, ON. 1997. Lang.: Eng.   1354

Fridell, Lena
Administration
Protests against budget cuts affecting children's theatre. Sweden: Gothenburg. 1997. Lang.: Swe.   50
Performance/production
Interview with dramaturg Lena Fridell. Sweden: Gothenburg. 1985-1997. Lang.: Swe.   1932

Friedman, Maria
Performance/production
Actress/singer Maria Friedman. UK-England: London. 1983-1997. Lang.: Eng.   3945

Friedrich, Ernst
Relation to other fields
Actors' political convictions and activities in the German Revolution. Germany. 1917-1922. Lang.: Eng.   763

Friedrich, Götz
Performance/production
Götz Friedrich's production of Gershwin's *Porgy and Bess*. Austria: Bregenz. 1997. Lang.: Eng.   4098
Impressions of opera performances in several German cities. Germany. 1997. Lang.: Ger.   4147

Friel, Brian
Performance/production
Actor and director Peter Luckhaus of Dramaten. Sweden: Stockholm. 1974-1997. Lang.: Swe.   1939
Collection of newspaper reviews by London theatre critics. UK-England: London. 1997. Lang.: Eng.   2086
Irish plays and characters on the New York stage. USA: New York, NY. Ireland. 1874-1966. Lang.: Eng.   2277
Plays/librettos/scripts
Identity and the use of multiple actors to portray a single character in postcolonial drama. Australia. Ireland. Samoa. 1997. Lang.: Eng.   2380
Transformations of Irish society as reflected in its drama. Ireland. 1959-1993. Lang.: Eng.   2913
Analysis of plays by Brian Friel and Tom Murphy. Ireland. UK-Ireland. 1961-1995. Lang.: Eng.   2925
Comparison of Friel's *Molly Sweeney* and Synge's *The Well of the Saints*. Ireland. UK-Ireland. 1997. Lang.: Eng.   2935
Problems of language in plays of Brian Friel. UK-Ireland. 1994-1997. Lang.: Eng.   3121
Postmodern and postcolonial concepts of identity and the plays of Brian Friel. UK-Ireland. 1980-1994. Lang.: Eng.   3122

Fringe theatre
SEE ALSO
Alternative theatre.

Gabily, Didier-Georges — cont'd

Performance/production
Collection of newspaper reviews by London theatre critics. UK-England: London. 1997. Lang.: Eng.   2133

Gábor, Miklós
Performance/production
Excerpts from the diary of actor Miklós Gábor. Hungary. 1955-1957. Lang.: Hun.   1764

Gabriel
Performance/production
Collection of newspaper reviews by London theatre critics. UK-England: London. 1997. Lang.: Eng.   2042

Gabrijel in Mihael (Gabriel and Michael)
Plays/librettos/scripts
Analysis of plays by Jože Snoj and Ivo Svetina. Slovenia. 1900-1996. Lang.: Slo.   3008

Gade, Svend
Performance/production
Asta Nielsen's performance as Hamlet. Denmark. 1920. Lang.: Eng.   3569

Gaft, Valentin
Performance/production
Writings of actor Valentin Gaft. Russia. 1960-1997. Lang.: Rus.   1867

Gaiety Theatre (Budapest)
SEE
Vígszínház.

Gaines, Reg E.
Plays/librettos/scripts
Bring in 'Da Noise, Bring in 'Da Funk and the Black audience. USA: New York, NY. 1996-1997. Lang.: Eng.   4002

Gaja (Gaia)
Performance/production
The musical production of *Gaja (Gaia)*, which used puppets and live actors. Poland: Zusno. 1997. Lang.: Eng, Fre.   3875

Galati, Frank
Design/technology
Lighting design for *Ragtime* at the Ford Centre for the Performing Arts. Canada: Toronto, ON. 1975-1997. Lang.: Eng.   3905
Performance/production
Comparison of productions of *Ragtime* and *Jane Eyre*. Canada: Toronto, ON. 1997. Lang.: Eng.   3932

Gale, Brian
Design/technology
Design of Disneyland's show *Light Magic*. USA: Anaheim, CA. 1997. Lang.: Eng.   260

Gale, Zona
Plays/librettos/scripts
The theme of hope in postwar American theatre and writing. USA. 1914-1929. Lang.: Eng.   3153

Galerie du palais, La (Palace Gallery, The)
Plays/librettos/scripts
The city comedy of Pierre Corneille. France: Paris. 1631-1640. Lang.: Eng.   2828

Galgóczy, Judit
Performance/production
Interview with opera director Judit Galgóczy. Hungary. 1987-1997. Lang.: Hun.   4168

Galibin, Aleksand'r
Performance/production
The work of director Aleksand'r Galibin. Russia: St. Petersburg. 1980-1997. Lang.: Rus.   1887

Galin, Aleksand'r Michajlovič
Institutions
Malyj Dramatic Theatre under Lev Dodin. Russia: St. Petersburg. 1983-1996. Lang.: Eng.   1465
Performance/production
Galin's *Anomalja (Anomaly)* at Sovremennik. Russia: Moscow. 1996. Lang.: Rus.   1875

Gallacher, Tom
Performance/production
Recent Irish productions. Ireland: Sligo, Dublin. 1997. Lang.: Swe.   1788

Gallaire, Fatima
Basic theatrical documents
Text of *Les Richesses de l'hiver (The Riches of Winter)* by Fatima Gallaire. France: Ajaccio. 1996. Lang.: Fre.   1272

Gallasch, Keith
Performance/production
Performance pieces of Open City. Australia: Sydney. 1987-1997. Lang.: Eng.   3815

Galliot, Gil
Basic theatrical documents
Text of *Aimez-moi les uns les autres (Love Me One and All)* by Alex Métayer. France. 1996. Lang.: Fre.   1274

Gallo, Joseph
Design/technology
Lighting designer Jeff Nellis. USA: New York, NY. 1997. Lang.: Eng.   224

Gallo, Paul
Design/technology
Lighting design for the Broadway musical *Titanic*. USA: New York, NY. 1992-1997. Lang.: Eng.   3917

Gambaro, Griselda
Relation to other fields
Performance of gender, nationality, and motherhood in various Argentine plays. Argentina. 1976-1983. Lang.: Eng.   725

Ganelin, Jévgenij
Performance/production
Notes from the actors' master class of Jévgenij Ganelin and Vladimir Bogdanov. Russia: St. Petersburg. 1960-1997. Lang.: Rus.   1868

Gans, Roger
Design/technology
Sound design problems of San Francisco Opera's temporary home. USA: San Francisco, CA. 1996. Lang.: Eng.   4036

Gao, Xingjian
Performance/production
Sally Sussman's adaptation of *xiqu* to Australian performance. Australia. 1988-1996. Lang.: Eng.   3891

Garas, Dezső
Performance/production
Interview with actor Dezső Garas. Hungary. 1960-1997. Lang.: Hun.   1775

García Lorca, Federico
Performance/production
Hanan Snir's productions of Lorca's *Blood Wedding (Bodas de sangre)*. Israel: Tel Aviv. 1990. Lang.: Eng.   1791
Collection of newspaper reviews by London theatre critics. UK-England: London. 1997. Lang.: Eng.   2001
Collection of newspaper reviews by London theatre critics. UK-England. 1997. Lang.: Eng.   2039
Plays/librettos/scripts
Gendered identity in plays of Cocteau and García Lorca. France. Spain. 1930-1937. Lang.: Eng.   2807
Analysis of *Bodas de sangre (Blood Wedding)* and *Yerma* by Federico García Lorca. Spain. 1920-1936. Lang.: Eng.   3050

García Moreno, Angel
Performance/production
Angel García Morena, artistic director of Teatro Fígaro. Spain: Madrid. 1996. Lang.: Eng.   1915

García, Manuel (the elder)
Performance/production
Tenor Manuel García the elder and his son. Europe. 1817-1943. Lang.: Eng.   4127

García, Manuel (the younger)
Performance/production
Tenor Manuel García the elder and his son. Europe. 1817-1943. Lang.: Eng.   4127

García, Rodrigo
Plays/librettos/scripts
Interview with playwright Rodrigo García. Spain. 1964-1996. Lang.: Eng.   3037

Garden, Mary
Performance/production
Excerpt from biography of opera singer Mary Garden. France: Paris. 1875-1957. Lang.: Eng.   4144

Gardner, Mary Lu Anne
Basic theatrical documents
Text of *Margaret Durham* by Mary Lu Anne Gardner. Canada. 1996. Lang.: Eng.   1258

Gárdonyi Géza Színház (Eger)
Performance/production
Four productions of the musical *A Dzsungel könyve (The Jungle Book)*. Hungary. 1996-1997. Lang.: Hun.   3936

Gardzienice Theatre Association (Poland)
SEE
Ośrodek Praktyk Teatralnych.

Garfield, Leon
Performance/production
The power of images to communicate the plays in *Shakespeare: The Animated Tales*. Russia. 1997. Lang.: Eng.   3721

Garland, Patrick
Performance/production
Collection of newspaper reviews by London theatre critics. UK-England: London. 1997. Lang.: Eng.   1989

Garland, Patrick — cont'd

Collection of newspaper reviews by London theatre critics. UK-England: London. 1997. Lang.: Eng.   2018

Garnhum, Ken
Basic theatrical documents
Text of *One Word* by Ken Garnhum. Canada. 1997. Lang.: Eng.   1259

Text of *New Art Book* by Ken Garnhum. Canada. 1997. Lang.: Eng.   1260

Design/technology
Background on Ken Garnhum's set design for *Frida K.* Canada: Toronto, ON. 1997. Lang.: Eng.   1354

Background on Ken Garnhum's set design for *The House of Martin Guerre*. Canada. 1997. Lang.: Eng.   3906

Performance/production
Ken Garnhum's *One Word* at Tarragon Theatre. Canada. 1994-1997. Lang.: Eng.   1602

Garnier, Robert
Plays/librettos/scripts
Garnier's *Hippolyte* and its source, Seneca's *Phaedra*. France. 1635. Lang.: Eng.   2813

Garpagonida (Harpagonia)
Performance/production
A production by Pëtr Fomenko's directing students at RATI. Russia: Moscow. 1996. Lang.: Rus.   1895

Garpe, Margareta
Plays/librettos/scripts
Interview with director and author Margarete Garpe. Sweden: Stockholm. 1960-1997. Lang.: Swe.   3063

Garrard, Rose
Relation to other fields
Space in feminist performance art and political protest. UK-England. 1980-1997. Lang.: Eng.   3850

Garrick, David
Performance/production
Actresses and the adaptation of Shakespeare. England. 1660-1740. Lang.: Eng.   1623

Changes in Shakespearean production under David Garrick. England. 1747-1776. Lang.: Eng.   1627

Iconographic analysis of visual records of actors. Germany. UK-England. 1608-1918. Lang.: Eng.   1683
Plays/librettos/scripts
Frances Sheridan's *The Discovery* in the context of eighteenth-century theatre. England. 1740-1780. Lang.: Eng.   2451

Cimarosa's *Il matrimonio segreto* and the clandestine marriage on the eighteenth-century stage. Italy. 1766-1792. Lang.: Fre.   4304
Research/historiography
Eighteenth-century theatrical portraits. England. France. 1700-1800. Lang.: Eng.   3445

Gärten des Grauens (Garden of Horror)
Plays/librettos/scripts
Playwright Daniel Call and TV aesthetics. Germany. 1967-1997. Lang.: Ger.   2862

Garth Fagan Dance (Rochester, NY)
Institutions
Garth Fagan Dance at the Kennedy Center. USA: Washington, DC. 1997. Lang.: Hun.   1172

Gas I
Basic theatrical documents
English translations of German Expressionist plays. Germany. 1900-1920. Lang.: Eng.   1284

Gas II
Basic theatrical documents
English translations of German Expressionist plays. Germany. 1900-1920. Lang.: Eng.   1284

Gaskell, Sonja
Institutions
Profile of Nederlands Dans Theater and Het National Ballet. Netherlands: Amsterdam, The Hague. 1959-1989. Lang.: Hun.   1164

Gasman, Ira
Design/technology
Richard Pilbrow's lighting design for the musical *The Life*. USA: New York, NY. 1997. Lang.: Eng.   3918

Gaster, Dan
Performance/production
Collection of newspaper reviews by London theatre critics. UK-England: London. 1997. Lang.: Eng.   2089

Gate Theatre (London)
Performance/production
Collection of newspaper reviews by London theatre critics. UK-England: London. 1997. Lang.: Eng.   1982

Collection of newspaper reviews by London theatre critics. UK-England: London. 1997. Lang.: Eng.   1996

Collection of newspaper reviews by London theatre critics. UK-England: London. 1997. Lang.: Eng.   2017

Collection of newspaper reviews by London theatre critics. UK-England: London. 1997. Lang.: Eng.   2032

Collection of newspaper reviews by London theatre critics. UK-England: London. 1997. Lang.: Eng.   2047

Collection of newspaper reviews by London theatre critics. UK-England: London. 1997. Lang.: Eng.   2054

Collection of newspaper reviews by London theatre critics. UK-England: London. 1997. Lang.: Eng.   2075

Collection of newspaper reviews by London theatre critics. UK-England: London. 1997. Lang.: Eng.   2096

Collection of newspaper reviews by London theatre critics. UK-England: London. 1997. Lang.: Eng.   2110

Collection of newspaper reviews by London theatre critics. UK-England: London. 1997. Lang.: Eng.   2129

Collection of newspaper reviews by London theatre critics. UK-England: London. 1997. Lang.: Eng.   2148

Gateway Theatre (Edinburgh)
Performance/production
Collection of newspaper reviews by London theatre critics. UK-Scotland: Edinburgh. 1997. Lang.: Eng.   2230

Collection of newspaper reviews by London theatre critics. UK-Scotland: Edinburgh. 1997. Lang.: Eng.   2231

Collection of newspaper reviews by London theatre critics. UK-Scotland: Edinburgh. 1997. Lang.: Eng.   2232

Gathering, The
Basic theatrical documents
Text of *The Gathering* by Rachael Van Fossen *et al.* Canada: Fort Qu'Appelle, SK. 1997. Lang.: Eng.   3903
Plays/librettos/scripts
Rachael Van Fossen's playwriting for community theatre. Canada: Fort Qu'Appelle, SK, Regina, SK. 1990-1997. Lang.: Eng.   2434

Gatti, Armand
Plays/librettos/scripts
Metatheatrical techniques of Weiss, Gatti, and Stoppard. Europe. 1964-1982. Lang.: Eng.   2783

Gaucher, David
Design/technology
Scenography of David Gaucher. Canada: Montreal, PQ. 1992-1997. Lang.: Fre.   149

Gautier, Théophile
Performance/production
Giselle and the aesthetics of classical ballet. France. 1800-1900. Lang.: Eng.   1067

Feminist analysis of the ballet *Giselle*. France. 1830-1835. Lang.: Eng.   1070

The Hungarian stage career of the ballet *Giselle*. Hungary: Budapest. 1841-1996. Lang.: Hun.   1079

Choreographer Elena Tchernichova on the ballet *Giselle*. USA. 1950-1997. Lang.: Eng.   1129

Gavronski, Aleksander
Performance/production
Interview with actor Tamara Petkevich, former concentration camp inmate. USSR. 1950-1997. Lang.: Swe.   2363

Gay Sweatshop (London)
Plays/librettos/scripts
Women and theatrical collaboration. USA. UK-England. 1930-1990. Lang.: Eng.   3264

Gay theatre
Institutions
History of the Jewel Box Revue, a touring drag show. USA: Miami, FL. 1939-1975. Lang.: Eng.   3760
Performance/production
Choreographer Matthew Bourne. UK-England: London. 1997. Lang.: Eng.   1119

Interview with playwright Barry Lowe and actor Alex Harding on gay theatre. Australia: Sydney. 1997. Lang.: Eng.   1557

Sexuality on stage in the National Theatre production of Tony Kushner's *Angels in America*. UK-England: London. 1992. Lang.: Eng.   2176

Gay theatre in the British mainstream theatre. UK-England. 1986-1997. Lang.: Eng.   2227

Gay theatre — cont'd

Tony Kushner's *Angels in America* in the context of queer performance.
USA. 1992-1994. Lang.: Eng.   2245

Shakespeare and queer cinema. USA. UK-England. 1977-1991. Lang.:
Eng.   3607

Solo artist Richard Elovich. USA. 1993. Lang.: Eng.   3834

Plays/librettos/scripts
Critique of homophobia in Normand Chaurette's *Provincetown
Playhouse, July 1919, I Was 19 Years Old)*. Canada. 1982. Lang.: Eng.
                                                                             2407

Theatrical representations of the Holocaust. Europe. North America.
1950-1996. Lang.: Eng.   2789

Analysis of *The Prisoner of War* by J.R. Ackerly. UK-England. 1925.
Lang.: Eng.   3075

The character Roy Cohn in Tony Kushner's *Angels in America*. USA.
1992-1994. Lang.: Eng.   3154

Gay eroticism in Tennessee Williams' *Cat on a Hot Tin Roof*. USA.
1955. Lang.: Eng.   3202

Identity, cultural transformation, and Tony Kushner's *Angels in
America*. USA. 1992-1994. Lang.: Eng.   3221

Tony Kushner's *Angels in America* and the AIDS crisis. USA. 1992-
1994. Lang.: Eng.   3235

Representations of race and gender in Tony Kushner's *Angels in
America*. USA. 1992-1994. Lang.: Eng.   3236

Analysis of *My Queer Body* by Tim Miller. USA: New York, NY. 1993.
Lang.: Eng.   3251

Analysis of the final scene of *Angels in America, Part II: Perestroika* by
Tony Kushner. USA. 1992-1994. Lang.: Eng.   3271

Reference materials
Sourcebook on women playwrights of diversity. USA. 1970-1996. Lang.:
Eng.   3320

Theory/criticism
Queer performativity and its relation to performance. Australia. 1997.
Lang.: Eng.   862

Bodily functions in gay performance. Australia. 1997. Lang.: Eng.   863

Ramifications of queer theory for theatre critics. USA. 1993. Lang.: Eng.
                                                                             3502

Gay theory

Performance/production
The experience of cross-gender role-playing. USA. 1971-1997. Lang.:
Eng.   2268

Actress Mary Martin and gay/lesbian historiography. USA. 1913-1997.
Lang.: Eng.   3979

Plays/librettos/scripts
The representation of homosexuality in Brendan Behan's *The Hostage*.
Ireland. 1958. Lang.: Eng.   2904

Theory/criticism
Representation of the male body on stage. Australia. 1997. Lang.: Eng.
                                                                             861

Queer performativity and its relation to performance. Australia. 1997.
Lang.: Eng.   862

Bodily functions in gay performance. Australia. 1997. Lang.: Eng.   863

Desire in gay male pornography. USA. 1997. Lang.: Eng.   915

Queer criticism of Shakespeare. UK-England. 1997. Lang.: Eng.   3497

Ramifications of queer theory for theatre critics. USA. 1993. Lang.: Eng.
                                                                             3502

Gay, John

Performance/production
Collection of newspaper reviews by London theatre critics. UK-England:
London. 1997. Lang.: Eng.   1987

Collection of newspaper reviews by London theatre critics. UK-England:
London. 1997. Lang.: Eng.   2099

Plays/librettos/scripts
Parody and satire in musical theatre. USA. UK-England. 1727-1990.
Lang.: Eng.   3986

Gazooka

Basic theatrical documents
Collection of one-act plays by Welsh writers. UK-Wales. 1952-1996.
Lang.: Eng.   1321

Gazza ladra, La

Plays/librettos/scripts
The sources of Rossini's opera *La Gazza ladra*. USA. 1815. Lang.: Eng.
                                                                             4317

Gedda, Nicolai

Performance/production
Profile of tenor Nicolai Gedda. Sweden. 1926-1997. Lang.: Eng.   4219

Gédéon

Basic theatrical documents
Text of *Page 27* by Jean-Louis Bauer. France. 1996. Lang.: Fre.   1268

Gee, Shirley

Design/technology
Costume design for *Warrior* by Shirley Gee. USA: Long Beach, CA.
1997. Lang.: Eng.   1374

Performance/production
Collection of newspaper reviews by London theatre critics. UK-England:
London. 1997. Lang.: Eng.   2117

Gefors, Hans

Plays/librettos/scripts
Hans Gefors' opera *Vargen kommer*, libretto by Kerstin Klein-Perski.
Sweden: Malmö. 1997. Lang.: Swe.   4310

Geheimnis des Lebens (Secret of Life)

Performance/production
World premieres at Mannheimer Nationaltheater. Germany: Mannheim.
1997. Lang.: Ger.   1697

Gehring, Paul

Relation to other fields
Profile of theatre draughtsman Paul Gehring. Germany: Berlin. 1917-
1992. Lang.: Ger.   749

Critic Heinz Ritter recalls theatre draughtsman Paul Gehring. Germany:
Berlin. 1946-1981. Lang.: Ger.   750

The Paul Gehring theatre collection at Berlin Stadtmuseum. Germany:
Berlin. 1946-1981. Lang.: Ger.   751

Gehülfe, Der (Assistant, The)

Performance/production
Productions of Schauspiel Stuttgart. Germany: Stuttgart. 1997. Lang.:
Ger.   1715

Geier-Wally (Vulture-Wally)

Performance/production
Productions of Schauspiel Stuttgart. Germany: Stuttgart. 1997. Lang.:
Ger.   1715

Geiser, Jamie

Basic theatrical documents
Storyboard scenario of *Evidence of Floods* by Jamie Geiser. USA. 1994.
Lang.: Eng.   4387

Gel'man, Aleksand'r

Plays/librettos/scripts
Playwright Aleksand'r Gel'man describes dramatists' conference. Russia.
1996. Lang.: Rus.   2994

Gelbart, Larry

Plays/librettos/scripts
Parody and satire in musical theatre. USA. UK-England. 1727-1990.
Lang.: Eng.   3986

Gémes, Katalin

Performance/production
Mezzo-coloratura Katalin Gémes. Hungary. 1988-1997. Lang.: Hun.
                                                                             4178

Gems, Pam

Design/technology
Lighting by Peter Mumford for Broadway productions of London
shows. USA: New York, NY. 1997. Lang.: Eng.   1367

Performance/production
Collection of newspaper reviews by London theatre critics. UK-England:
London. 1997. Lang.: Eng.   2024

Collection of newspaper reviews by London theatre critics. UK-England:
London. 1997. Lang.: Eng.   2116

Interview with actress Sian Phillips. UK-Wales. UK-England: London.
1930-1997. Lang.: Eng.   2234

Plays/librettos/scripts
Female characters in plays of contemporary British women. UK-
England. 1980-1995. Lang.: Eng.   3077

Linguistic analysis of plays by Delaney, Pinter, Orton, and Gems. UK-
England. 1956-1984. Lang.: Spa.   3100

Gender studies

Audience
Women in the Renaissance theatre audience. England. 1567-1642.
Lang.: Eng.   1247

Design/technology
Lighting designer Jean Rosenthal. USA: New York, NY. 1932-1969.
Lang.: Eng.   228

Audio and visual representation in Tarkovskij's film *Offret (The
Sacrifice)*. Russia. 1932-1986. Lang.: Eng.   3544

Institutions
Judson Dance Theatre and dancing autobiography. USA. 1960-1965.
Lang.: Eng.   952

Gender studies — cont'd

History of the Jewel Box Revue, a touring drag show. USA: Miami, FL. 1939-1975. Lang.: Eng.   3760

Performance/production

Cross-dressing in Chinese theatre and society. China. 1200-1997. Lang.: Eng.   489

Feminist aspects of the 'model theatre' of the Cultural Revolution. China, People's Republic of. 1965-1976. Lang.: Eng.   490

Theatrical representations of female poets—performative aspects of literary culture. England. 1790-1850. Lang.: Eng.   509

Feminist analysis of performance and theatricality. Europe. USA. 1960-1979. Lang.: Eng.   517

Odes for female choruses in Greek theatre. Greece. 500-100 B.C. Lang.: Eng.   549

Gender on the Italian stage. Italy. 1526-1995. Lang.: Eng.   564

The women's performance genre *gidayu*. Japan. 1888-1997. Lang.: Eng.   567

Industrial technology and the display of women's bodies in performance. UK-England. 1870-1954. Lang.: Eng.   616

Race, gender, and nation in nineteenth-century performance. USA. Europe. 1855-1902. Lang.: Eng.   633

The public persona of actress Mae West. USA. 1913-1943. Lang.: Eng.   642

Augusto Boal's forum theatre and the transformation of gender scripts. USA. 1997. Lang.: Eng.   650

Changes in women's comedy performance. USA. 1950-1995. Lang.: Eng.   654

Interculturalism in the work of Lee Breuer. USA: New York, NY. 1980-1995. Lang.: Eng.   678

The emergence of modern American theatre. USA. 1914-1929. Lang.: Eng.   683

Gender and nationalism: Maud Allan's *Vision of Salome*. UK-England: London. USA. 1908. Lang.: Eng.   994

Feminist analysis of dance and the representation of the female body. USA. Europe. 1801-1997. Lang.: Eng.   997

Analysis of three 'dance cultures'. USA. Ghana. 1995-1997. Lang.: Eng.   998

Dance, history, representation, spectatorship, and gender. USA. 1987-1997. Lang.: Eng.   1004

The representation of social dancing in mass media. USA. 1980-1990. Lang.: Eng.   1008

Analysis of a multi-ethnic dance rehearsal. USA: San Francisco, CA. 1996. Lang.: Eng.   1013

Giselle and the aesthetics of classical ballet. France. 1800-1900. Lang.: Eng.   1067

The body and gender in Parisian dance performance. France. 1911-1924. Lang.: Eng.   1069

Gender, authenticity, and flamenco. Spain: Seville. 1975-1995. Lang.: Eng.   1151

Female beauty and American modern dance. USA. 1930-1940. Lang.: Eng.   1204

Gender in choreographies of Mark Morris. USA. 1980-1995. Lang.: Eng.   1206

Essays on gender and performance. 250 B.C.-1995 A.D. Lang.: Eng.   1551

Actresses and the adaptation of Shakespeare. England. 1660-1740. Lang.: Eng.   1623

Anne Oldfield's performance as Lady Townly in *The Provoked Husband* by Colley Cibber. England. 1720-1730. Lang.: Eng.   1632

Reactions to modern performances of *Antony and Cleopatra*. UK-England. North America. 1827-1987. Lang.: Eng.   2178

Victorian ideas of womanhood in productions of Shakespeare's *The Merchant of Venice*. UK-England. 1832-1903. Lang.: Eng.   2188

The performance of Jewish characters on the American stage. USA. 1860-1920. Lang.: Eng.   2261

Argument for reconsideration of gender roles by dramaturgs. USA. 1997. Lang.: Eng.   2265

Shakespeare in his own historical context and in ours. USA. 1996. Lang.: Eng.   2269

Workers' theatre and the American labor movement. USA. 1929-1940. Lang.: Eng.   2281

National and gender identity in productions of Congreve's *The Way of the World*. USA. 1924-1991. Lang.: Eng.   2285

Biography of actress Laurette Taylor. USA. 1884-1946. Lang.: Eng.   2300

The performance of race, gender, sexuality, and power. USA. Europe. 1590-1995. Lang.: Eng.   2309

Early Shanghai filmmaking. China, People's Republic of: Shanghai. 1896-1937. Lang.: Eng.   3568

Asta Nielsen's performance as Hamlet. Denmark. 1920. Lang.: Eng.   3569

Screen adaptations of Shakespeare's *The Taming of the Shrew*. UK-England. USA. 1908-1966. Lang.: Eng.   3594

Representations of Black women on stage and screen. USA. 1939-1995. Lang.: Eng.   3605

The film *Bugsy* as an adaptation of Shakespeare's *Antony and Cleopatra*. USA. 1991. Lang.: Eng.   3613

Voyeurism in Jonathan Miller's TV version of Shakespeare's *Othello*. UK-England. 1981. Lang.: Eng.   3725

Television versions of Shakespeare's *Othello*. UK-England. 1987-1996. Lang.: Eng.   3726

Women in *commedia dell'arte*. Italy. 1545-1650. Lang.: Eng.   3793

Gender, color, and nationalism at the Tropicana. Cuba: Havana. 1959-1997. Lang.: Eng.   3856

The construction of female beauty in popular entertainment. USA. 1920-1930. Lang.: Eng.   3961

A lesbian reading of Mary Martin's performance as Peter Pan. USA. 1950-1959. Lang.: Eng.   3978

Production guide for a performance of *The Medium* by Gian Carlo Menotti. USA. 1996. Lang.: Eng.   4259

Plays/librettos/scripts

American theatrical culture. USA. 1825-1860. Lang.: Eng.   701

Female characters in *kyōgen*. Japan. Lang.: Eng.   1227

Fantasies of maternal power in Shakespeare's *Macbeth*. England. 1606. Lang.: Eng.   2449

Evil women in early modern English tragedy. England. 1590-1613. Lang.: Eng.   2452

Defense of Jonson's character Celia in *Volpone*. England. 1607. Lang.: Eng.   2455

Masculinity in Shakespeare's *Romeo and Juliet*. England. 1595. Lang.: Eng.   2457

Race and gender in Shakespeare's *Antony and Cleopatra*. England. 1607-1707. Lang.: Eng.   2458

Male expectations of women's role in society in Fletcher's *The Woman's Prize*. England. 1633. Lang.: Eng.   2469

The representation of women by boy actors. England. 1450-1600. Lang.: Eng.   2475

Montaigne and heterosexual male desire in Shakespeare's comedies. England. 1593. Lang.: Eng.   2479

Female homoeroticism on the early English stage. England. 1594-1632. Lang.: Eng.   2482

Women's Romantic 'closet' drama as an alternative theatrical space. England. 1790-1820. Lang.: Eng.   2486

Masculine and feminine in *Bonduca* by John Fletcher. England. 1613. Lang.: Eng.   2488

Gender ambiguity in Shakespeare's *Twelfth Night*. England. 1600. Lang.: Eng.   2495

Shakespeare's *Antony and Cleopatra* as a romance. England. 1607. Lang.: Eng.   2496

Gender ideology and the occult in Shakespeare's plays. England. 1590-1613. Lang.: Eng.   2499

Theatrical reflections of the marital double standard. England. 1598-1650. Lang.: Eng.   2501

Subversion and Shakespeare's older female characters. England. 1590-1613. Lang.: Eng.   2502

Domestic conflict in early modern English drama. England. 1590-1633. Lang.: Eng.   2508

Feminist analysis of wordplay in Shakespeare's *Antony and Cleopatra*. England. 1607. Lang.: Eng.   2510

The representation of female virtue in early modern England. England. 1580-1615. Lang.: Eng.   2514

Shakespeare's *Cymbeline* and the attainder of Katherine Howard. England. 1542-1610. Lang.: Eng.   2515

Gender studies — cont'd

Feminist analysis of the place of women in Shakespeare's plays. England. 1590-1613. Lang.: Eng. 2519

Sex and gender in plays of Christopher Marlowe. England. 1587-1593. Lang.: Eng. 2522

Analysis of Nicholas Rowe's *Tragedy of Jane Shore*. England. 1714. Lang.: Eng. 2523

Accusations of rape in English Renaissance drama. England. 1550-1630. Lang.: Eng. 2526

The role of Lavinia in Shakespeare's *Titus Andronicus*. England. 1593-1594. Lang.: Eng. 2532

Gendered power relations, law, and revenge in early English drama. England. 1590-1640. Lang.: Eng. 2540

Models of sexual behavior in Elizabethan theatre. England. 1680-1900. Lang.: Eng. 2545

Homoerotic desire in Elizabethan theatre. England. 1580-1620. Lang.: Eng. 2569

Gender and racial politics in Shakespeare's *Othello*. England. 1605. Lang.: Eng. 2572

Male and female power in *The Changeling* by Middleton and Rowley. England. 1622. Lang.: Eng. 2583

Virginity in *Love's Metamorphosis* by John Lyly. England. 1599. Lang.: Eng. 2593

Male patronage and maternal power in Shakespeare's *Timon of Athens*. England. 1607-1608. Lang.: Eng. 2603

Sexual slander in early modern England and Shakespeare's *The Winter's Tale*. England. 1536-1610. Lang.: Eng. 2604

Class and sex in the plays of Shakespeare. England. 1592-1616. Lang.: Eng. 2605

Female 'mad' songs in seventeenth-century English drama. England. 1685-1700. Lang.: Eng. 2638

Women's silence in Renaissance drama. England. 1601-1613. Lang.: Eng. 2642

Gender and performance in Shakespeare's *All's Well That Ends Well*. England. 1602-1603. Lang.: Eng. 2655

Shakespeare's *Cymbeline* and early modern English nationalism. England. 1609-1610. Lang.: Eng. 2662

Ambivalence toward a female sovereign reflected in plays of Shakespeare and Middleton. England. 1600-1607. Lang.: Eng. 2672

Madness and gender in the plays of Shakespeare. England. 1589-1613. Lang.: Eng. 2677

Woman as commodity in Shakespeare's *The Merchant of Venice*. England. 1596. Lang.: Eng. 2680

Love and sex in Shakespeare's *Troilus and Cressida*. England. 1601-1602. Lang.: Eng. 2686

Shakespeare's *Othello* and early modern precepts of wifely conduct. England. 1605. Lang.: Eng. 2687

Blood and bleeding in Shakespeare's *Julius Caesar*. England. 1599. Lang.: Eng. 2696

Shakespearean tragedies and history plays and the possible roles for women. England. 1589-1613. Lang.: Eng. 2704

Shakespeare's exploration of race, gender, and sexuality in *The Tempest*. England. 1611. Lang.: Eng. 2705

Marital equality and subordination in Shakespeare's *Othello* and Webster's *The Duchess of Malfi*. England. 1605-1613. Lang.: Eng. 2715

Witchcraft and female sexuality in the plays of Shakespeare. England. 1590-1613. Lang.: Eng. 2717

The idea of the self in the English Renaissance. England. 1580-1620. Lang.: Eng. 2728

Masculinity and feminine disruption in Shakespeare's history plays. England. 1590-1599. Lang.: Eng. 2732

Masculine and feminine men in Shakespeare's *Troilus and Cressida*. England. 1601-1602. Lang.: Eng. 2741

Feminist analysis of female characters in Shakespearean tragedy. England. 1589-1613. Lang.: Eng. 2743

Analysis of *The Tragedy of Mariam* by Elizabeth Cary. England. 1695. Lang.: Eng. 2761

Masculinity in Marlowe's *Tamburlaine*, Part II. England. 1587. Lang.: Eng. 2774

The significance of Don Juan in works of Tirso, Mozart, and Molière. Europe. 1612-1787. Lang.: Eng. 2786

Feminist analysis of women in Ibsen's plays. Finland. 1855-1905. Lang.: Eng. 2802

Gendered identity in plays of Cocteau and García Lorca. France. Spain. 1930-1937. Lang.: Eng. 2807

Analysis of *La Dame aux Camélias (Camille)* by Alexandre Dumas *fils*. France. 1848. Lang.: Eng. 2817

Attitudes about rhetoric in Greek and Roman drama. Greece. Roman Empire. 450-350 B.C. Lang.: Eng. 2873

The depiction of women in ancient Greek theatre. Greece. 500-200 B.C. Lang.: Eng. 2884

Gender in Beckett's *Not I*. Ireland. USA. 1973. Lang.: Eng. 2906

Samuel Beckett, music, and gender. Ireland. France. USA. 1955-1989. Lang.: Eng. 2908

Gender in *Rockaby* by Samuel Beckett. Ireland. USA. 1981. Lang.: Eng. 2916

Analysis of Beckett's *Footfalls, Ohio Impromptu* and *Rockaby*. Ireland. France. USA. 1976-1981. Lang.: Eng. 2928

Gender and ideology in Tom Stoppard's *The Real Thing*. UK-England. 1983. Lang.: Eng. 3069

Playwright Noël Coward's life as a gay man. UK-England. 1880-1940. Lang.: Eng. 3073

Gender and sexuality on the Victorian stage. UK-England. 1830-1900. Lang.: Eng. 3085

Analysis of *A Mouthful of Birds* by Caryl Churchill. UK-England. 1986-1997. Lang.: Eng. 3109

Sex, gender, and eroticism in plays of Tennessee Williams. USA. 1956-1959. Lang.: Eng. 3161

Analysis of *Oleanna* by David Mamet. USA. 1992-1997. Lang.: Eng. 3200

Male identity in contemporary American drama. USA. 1915-1995. Lang.: Eng. 3232

Representations of race and gender in Tony Kushner's *Angels in America*. USA. 1992-1994. Lang.: Eng. 3236

Simultaneous discourse in works by African-American women. USA. 1900-1993. Lang.: Eng. 3260

Women and theatrical collaboration. USA. UK-England. 1930-1990. Lang.: Eng. 3264

Gender analysis of plays by Susan Glaspell. USA. 1876-1948. Lang.: Eng. 3269

The Black woman's body in *The Tapestry* by Alexis De Veaux. USA. 1976-1997. Lang.: Eng. 3281

Sisterhood and female bonding in *Crimes of the Heart* and *Sisters*. USA. 1986-1996. Lang.: Eng. 3511

Film adaptations of Shakespeare's *The Taming of the Shrew*. USA. 1929-1966. Lang.: Eng. 3668

Cinematic versions of the Pygmalion myth. USA. 1938. Lang.: Eng. 3682

Transvestism in English pantomime. UK-England. 1870-1995. Lang.: Eng. 3754

Race and gender in masque: *Mr. Moore's Revels*. England. 1636. Lang.: Eng. 3775

Representations of women in Stephen Sondheim's musicals. USA. 1956-1996. Lang.: Eng. 3992

Female characters in Mozart's *Don Giovanni* and *Die Zauberflöte*. Austria. 1756-1791. Lang.: Eng. 4280

Opera and gender stereotypes. Europe. 1607-1997. Lang.: Eng. 4287

Gender in Lully's opera *Armide*. France. 1686. Lang.: Eng. 4291

Relation to other fields

Women and the veil in colonial Algeria. Algeria. 1967. Lang.: Eng. 724

Performance of gender, nationality, and motherhood in various Argentine plays. Argentina. 1976-1983. Lang.: Eng. 725

The female body and the spiritualist movement. USA. 1840-1901. Lang.: Eng. 821

Feminist psychology and drama therapy. USA. 1997. Lang.: Eng. 823

Patriarchal response to the violent woman and Shakespeare's poem 'The Rape of Lucrece'. England. 1592-1595. Lang.: Eng. 3342

Feminist and performance techniques for teaching Shakespeare's *Hamlet*. USA. 1997. Lang.: Eng. 3408

Burlesque theatre as seen in artwork of Reginald Marsh. USA. 1920-1950. Lang.: Eng. 3777

Gender studies — cont'd

Theory/criticism

Representation of the male body on stage. Australia. 1997. Lang.: Eng.
861

New historicism, feminist criticism, and gender roles in Renaissance literature. USA. UK-England. 1987. Lang.: Eng. 916

A model of historical performance ethnography. USA. 1997. Lang.: Eng.
922

Gender and classical ballet. Europe. 1700-1990. Lang.: Eng. 1132

Analysis of *American Document* by Martha Graham. USA. 1938. Lang.: Eng. 1217

Critique of feminist dance criticism. USA. 1995. Lang.: Eng. 1219

Introduction to theatrical applications of literary theory. USA. Europe. 1997. Lang.: Eng. 3499

Feminist disenchantment with Shakespeare. USA. 1950-1956. Lang.: Eng. 3500

Gender, theatre, and 'butch'. USA. 1993. Lang.: Eng. 3505

The female performer in Australian circus. Australia. 1801-1900. Lang.: Eng. 3787

Opera and eroticism. USA. Europe. 1996. Lang.: Eng. 4335

General from America, The

Performance/production

Collection of newspaper reviews by London theatre critics. UK-England: London. 1997. Lang.: Eng. 2000

James Laurenson's role in *The General from America* by Richard Nelson, RSC. UK-England: London. 1997. Lang.: Eng. 2223

Genet, Jean

Performance/production

Visit to Grotowski and Compagnia della Fortezza. Italy: Volterra, Pontedera. 1986-1997. Lang.: Ger. 1805

Collection of newspaper reviews by London theatre critics. UK-England: London. 1997. Lang.: Eng. 2068

Interview with director JoAnne Akalaitis. USA. 1970-1996. Lang.: Eng. 2331

Plays/librettos/scripts

Power in *Le Balcon (The Balcony)* by Jean Genet. France. 1956. Lang.: Ita. 2812

The concept of self in plays of Jean Genet. France. 1950-1975. Lang.: Eng. 2834

Homoeroticism and the challenge to bourgeois society in works of Pasolini and Genet. Italy. 1942-1950. Lang.: Ita. 2964

Subjectivity, ethics, and the body in contemporary drama. USA. Europe. 1940-1990. Lang.: Eng. 3229

Gengangere (Ghosts)

Performance/production

Collection of newspaper reviews by London theatre critics. UK-England: London. 1997. Lang.: Eng. 2064

Genres

Performance/production

The Ensemble for Early Music's production of the Fleury Mary Magdalene play. USA: New York, NY. 1997. Lang.: Eng. 676

Brief history of opera-ballet. France. 1717-1997. Lang.: Eng. 4136

Plays/librettos/scripts

'Bush melodrama' of E.W. O'Sullivan. Australia: Sydney. 1906. Lang.: Eng. 2375

Generic hybridization in the gangster film. USA. 1932-1983. Lang.: Eng. 3688

Relation to other fields

The Neo-Chautauqua and Louisiana Voices. USA. 1874-1996. Lang.: Eng. 796

The 'new theatre' in comparison with other arts and media. USA. 1995-1996. Lang.: Ita. 799

Theory/criticism

The distinctions among music-theatre genres. Canada. 1997. Lang.: Eng. 4326

Gentry, Kenneth

Administration

Equity protest of non-union production of *State Fair*. USA. 1997. Lang.: Eng. 3899

Successful negotiations between Actors' Equity and producers of *State Fair*. USA. 1997. Lang.: Eng. 3900

Geoghegan, Edward

Performance/production

Metatheatricality in melodrama. UK-England. 1840-1900. Lang.: Eng.
618

Geography of Haunted Places, The

Performance/production

Collection of newspaper reviews by London theatre critics. UK-England: London. 1997. Lang.: Eng. 2073

George, Philip

Performance/production

Collection of newspaper reviews by London theatre critics. UK-England: London. 1997. Lang.: Eng. 2022

Collection of newspaper reviews by London theatre critics. UK-England: London. 1997. Lang.: Eng. 2038

Georges Dandin

Performance/production

Roger Planchon's production of *Georges Dandin* by Molière. France: Villeurbanne. 1958. Lang.: Pol. 1675

Georgeson, Richard

Performance/production

Collection of newspaper reviews by London theatre critics. UK-England: London. 1997. Lang.: Eng. 2089

Georgian Academic Theatre (Tbilisi)

SEE

Gruzinskij Akademičeskij Teat'r im. Kote Mordžanišvili.

Gericke, Katharina

Plays/librettos/scripts

Account of new German plays with historical themes. Germany. 1997. Lang.: Ger. 2837

Gershwin Theatre (New York, NY)

Design/technology

Lighting design for *Show Boat*, Gershwin Theatre. USA: New York, NY. 1994. Lang.: Eng. 3922

Gershwin, George

Performance/production

Francesca Zambello directs *Lady in the Dark* at the National. UK-England: London. 1997. Lang.: Eng. 3947

Götz Friedrich's production of Gershwin's *Porgy and Bess*. Austria: Bregenz. 1997. Lang.: Eng. 4098

Gershwin, Ira

Design/technology

Rick Fisher's lighting design for *Lady in the Dark* at the Lyttelton. UK-England: London. 1941-1997. Lang.: Eng. 3908

Performance/production

Collection of newspaper reviews by London theatre critics. UK-England: London. 1997. Lang.: Eng. 2012

Götz Friedrich's production of Gershwin's *Porgy and Bess*. Austria: Bregenz. 1997. Lang.: Eng. 4098

Gertrude and Ophelia

Plays/librettos/scripts

Analysis of *Gertrude and Ophelia* by Margaret Clarke. 1993-1997. Lang.: Eng. 2364

Geschichten aus dem Wiener Wald (Tales from the Vienna Wood)

Performance/production

Recent productions of plays by Horváth. Germany. Austria. 1996-1997. Lang.: Ger. 1722

Gesher Theatre (Jaffa)

Performance/production

Collection of newspaper reviews by London theatre critics. UK-England: London. 1997. Lang.: Eng. 2071

Geszti, Péter

Performance/production

Four productions of the musical *A Dzsungel könyve (The Jungle Book)*. Hungary. 1996-1997. Lang.: Hun. 3936

Get Out of Here

Performance/production

Collection of newspaper reviews by London theatre critics. UK-England: London. 1997. Lang.: Eng. 2003

Gewandter, Holly

Performance/production

Collection of newspaper reviews by London theatre critics. UK-England: London. 1997. Lang.: Eng. 2154

Gezaixi

Performance/production

Profile of Taiwanese opera, *Gezaixi*. China: Taiwan. 1895-1997. Lang.: Eng. 3892

Ghelderode, Michel de

Basic theatrical documents

Libretto of Ligeti's opera *Le Grand Macabre*. Europe. 1978-1997. Lang.: Fre, Eng. 4008

Performance/production

Collection of newspaper reviews by London theatre critics. UK-England: London. 1997. Lang.: Eng. 2139

Glover, Stephen
Performance/production
American chamber opera. USA. 1868-1997. Lang.: Eng.   4258

Glover, Sue
Performance/production
Collection of newspaper reviews by London theatre critics. UK-England: London. 1997. Lang.: Eng.   1989
Collection of newspaper reviews by London theatre critics. UK-England: London. 1997. Lang.: Eng.   1997

Glowacki, Janusz
Plays/librettos/scripts
Shakespearean themes in contemporary plays and productions. Europe. 1965-1995. Lang.: Pol.   2798

Glub! Glub!
Performance/production
Collection of newspaper reviews by London theatre critics. UK-England: London. 1997. Lang.: Eng.   1977

Gluck, Alma
Performance/production
Opera critic, novelist and biographer Marcia Davenport. USA. 1904-1996. Lang.: Eng.   4262

Gluvić, Goran
Basic theatrical documents
Texts of plays by Goran Gluvić. Slovenia. 1980-1997. Lang.: Slo.   1296

Glyndebourne Opera (Lewes)
Institutions
Report on OISTAT meeting of architects. UK-England: London. 1996. Lang.: Swe.   388
Performance/production
Recent performances and changes at British opera houses. UK-England: London. UK-Wales: Cardiff. 1996-1997. Lang.: Eng.   4227

Glynne, William
Performance/production
Collection of newspaper reviews by London theatre critics. UK-England: London. 1997. Lang.: Eng.   2143

Go-Between, The
Plays/librettos/scripts
British Library holdings of filmscript material of Harold Pinter. UK-England. 1963-1994. Lang.: Eng.   3647

Goblin Market
Plays/librettos/scripts
Survey of one- or two-character musicals. USA: New York, NY. 1964-1997. Lang.: Eng.   3989

God's Heart
Design/technology
Robert Brill's set design for *God's Heart* by Craig Lucas, Mitzi E. Newhouse Theatre. USA: New York, NY. 1997. Lang.: Eng.   1372

Godard, Jean-Luc
Performance/production
The map of England in productions of Shakespeare's *King Lear*. Europe. USA. 1909-1994. Lang.: Eng.   1650

Goddard, Janet
Performance/production
Collection of newspaper reviews by London theatre critics. UK-England: London. 1997. Lang.: Eng.   2085

Godfather, The
Performance/production
Francis Ford Coppola and the influence of *The Godfather*. USA. 1972-1997. Lang.: Eng.   3624

Godmilow, Jill
Performance/production
Interview with filmmaker Jill Godmilow. USA. 1967-1997. Lang.: Eng.   3621

Goebbels, Heiner
Plays/librettos/scripts
The development of non-literary opera. Germany. 1970-1997. Lang.: Ger.   4296

Goerden, Elmar
Performance/production
Productions of Schauspiel Stuttgart. Germany: Stuttgart. 1997. Lang.: Ger.   1687
Recent productions of Čechov's *Ivanov*. Germany: Dusseldorf, Stuttgart. 1996-1997. Lang.: Ger.   1706

Goethe-Theater (Bad Lauschstädt)
Performance spaces
History of Goethe-Theater. Germany: Bad Lauchstädt. 1768-1997. Lang.: Ger.   433

Goethe, Johann Wolfgang von
Institutions
Kölner Schauspiel under the direction of Günter Krämer. Germany: Cologne. 1985-1997. Lang.: Ger.   1425

Performance/production
Goethe's aestheticism and his abuse of actors. Germany: Weimar. 1793-1808. Lang.: Eng.   546
Emma Lyon, Goethe, and the *tableau vivant*. Italy: Naples. Germany. 1786-1791. Lang.: Eng.   566
Updated classics at Schauspiel Leipzig. Germany: Leipzig. 1996-1997. Lang.: Ger.   1712
Significant productions in Swabia. Germany: Stuttgart. 1997. Lang.: Ger.   1726
Productions of plays by Shakespeare and Goethe at Zürcher Schauspielhaus and Theater Neumarkt. Switzerland: Zurich. 1997. Lang.: Ger.   1964
Collection of newspaper reviews by London theatre critics. UK-England: London. 1997. Lang.: Eng.   2005
Plays/librettos/scripts
Text and performance in the Romantic period. Europe. 1800-1851. Lang.: Pol.   2790

Gogol Theatre (Moscow)
SEE
Dramatičéskij Teat'r im. N. Gogolja.

Gogol, A Mystery Play
Plays/librettos/scripts
Televisual dramaturgy in the work of some contemporary playwrights. USA. 1990-1997. Lang.: Eng.   3191

Gogol, Nikolaj Vasiljévič
Performance/production
Collection of newspaper reviews by London theatre critics. UK-England: London. 1997. Lang.: Eng.   2158
Use of Mejerchol'd's techniques in a production of Gogol's *The Government Inspector (Revizor)*. UK-England: Northampton. 1997. Lang.: Eng.   2216
Research/historiography
Early attempts to record performance photographically. Russia. USA. 1865-1900. Lang.: Eng.   3451
Theory/criticism
The possibilities for a contemporary theory of comedy. 1997. Lang.: Slo.   3459

Gold, Murray
Performance/production
Collection of newspaper reviews by London theatre critics. UK-England: London. 1997. Lang.: Eng.   2075

Goldberg, Whoopi
Performance/production
History of the one-woman show. USA. 1890-1995. Lang.: Eng.   646

Golden Own Goal
Performance/production
Collection of newspaper reviews by London theatre critics. UK-England: London. 1997. Lang.: Eng.   2006

Goldin, Nan
Relation to other fields
Performative criticism of photo exhibits by Nan Goldin and Lyle Ashton Harris. USA: New York, NY. 1996-1997. Lang.: Eng.   849

Goldman, Lisa
Performance/production
Collection of newspaper reviews by London theatre critics. UK-England: London. 1997. Lang.: Eng.   1970
Collection of newspaper reviews by London theatre critics. UK-England: London. 1997. Lang.: Eng.   2053
Collection of newspaper reviews by London theatre critics. UK-England: London. 1997. Lang.: Eng.   2113

Goldmines
Performance/production
Collection of newspaper reviews by London theatre critics. UK-England: London. 1997. Lang.: Eng.   2038

Goldoni, Carlo
Performance/production
The role of the implied spectator in productions of Omri Nitzan and Hillel Mittelpunkt. Israel: Tel Aviv. 1993. Lang.: Eng.   1792
Plays/librettos/scripts
The influence of French culture on the plays of Carlo Goldoni. Italy: France. 1761-1793. Lang.: Ita.   2952
Piccinni's *La Cecchina*: English translations and analysis. Italy. USA. 1766-1996. Lang.: Eng.   4305

Goldsmith, Martin
Basic theatrical documents
Script of *Detour* by Martin Goldsmith. USA. 1945. Lang.: Eng.   3531
Plays/librettos/scripts
Profile of playwright and screenwriter Martin Goldsmith. USA. 1913-1994. Lang.: Eng.   3656

Goldsmith, Martin — cont'd

Martin Goldsmith and the style of the film *Detour*. USA. 1945. Lang.: Eng.   3658

Goldstein, David Ira
Performance/production
The dramaturg and *One Crazy Day*, an adaptation of Beaumarchais' *The Marriage of Figaro*. USA: Tucson, AZ. 1992. Lang.: Eng.   2322

Goliath
Performance/production
Collection of newspaper reviews by London theatre critics. UK-England: London. 1997. Lang.: Eng.   2086

Goll, Iwan
Plays/librettos/scripts
Analysis of *Methusalem oder der ewige Bürger (Methuselah or the Eternal Bourgeois)* by Iwan Goll. Germany. 1918-1927. Lang.:Ita.   2843

Gombár, Judit
Design/technology
Interview with costume designer Judit Gombár. Hungary. 1955-1996. Lang.: Hun.   941

Gombrowicz, Witold
Institutions
Criticism of productions of Gombrowicz festival. Poland: Radom. 1997. Lang.: Hun.   1452
Performance/production
Report on Gombrowicz festival. Poland: Radom. 1997. Lang.: Eng.   582
Jerzy Jarocki's productions of *Ślub (The Wedding)* by Witold Gombrowicz. Poland. 1960-1991. Lang.: Pol.   1842
Collection of newspaper reviews by London theatre critics. UK-England: London. 1997. Lang.: Eng.   2027
Plays/librettos/scripts
Playwright Witold Gombrowicz—extracts from plays and journal. Poland. 1935-1969. Lang.: Fre.   2984

Gómez-Peña, Guillermo
Performance/production
Performance artists Guillermo Gómez-Peña and Roberto Sifuentes. Mexico. UK-Wales. 1996. Lang.: Eng.   3821
'Confessions' elicited by Guillermo Gómez-Peña and Roberto Sifuentes' *Temple of Confessions*. Mexico. 1994-1997. Lang.: Eng.   3822
Excerpts from diaries of performance artist Guillermo Gómez-Peña. USA: Los Angeles, CA. 1979-1989. Lang.: Eng.   3828
Plays/librettos/scripts
Performance artist Guillermo Gómez-Peña on intercultural collaboration. USA. 1985-1995. Lang.: Eng.   3849

Gómez, José Luis
Performance/production
Directors José Luis Gómez, José Sanchis Sinisterra, and Etelvino Vázquez. Spain. 1975-1996. Lang.: Eng.   1917

Gomez, Marga
Basic theatrical documents
Anthology of plays by women of color. USA. 1992-1996. Lang.: Eng. 1338

Gomorrah!
Institutions
Interview with Pule Hlatshwayo of Market Theatre. South Africa, Republic of: Johannesburg. 1975. Lang.: Swe.   1472

Gončarov, Andrej Aleksandrovič
Institutions
Director training at Russian Academy of Theatrical Art. Russia: Moscow. 1997. Lang.: Rus.   1456
Performance/production
Director Andrej Gončarov. Russia: Moscow. 1970-1997. Lang.: Rus.   1871

Gonne, Maude
Research/historiography
Irish theatre critics' focus on text rather than performance. Ireland: Dublin. 1897-1907. Lang.: Eng.   3450

Gonzales, Mario
Performance/production
Interview with actor, director, and teacher Mario Gonzales. Europe. Guatemala. 1967. Lang.: Swe.   1648

Good as New
Plays/librettos/scripts
Interview with playwright Peter Hedges. USA. 1997. Lang.: Eng.   3258

Good Person of Szechwan, The
SEE
Gute Mensch von Sezuan, Der.

Good, Jack
Performance/production
Collection of newspaper reviews by London theatre critics. UK-England: London. 1997. Lang.: Eng.   2068

Goodall, H.L., Jr.
Performance/production
The development of the production *Casing a Promised Land* by Linda Welker and H.L. Goodall. USA. 1997. Lang.: Eng.   685

Goodbye Girl, The
Performance/production
Collection of newspaper reviews by London theatre critics. UK-England: London. 1997. Lang.: Eng.   2032

Goodman Theatre (Chicago, IL)
Institutions
Educational and community programs involving dramaturgs at Goodman Theatre. USA: Chicago, IL. 1996-1997. Lang.: Eng.   1509
Performance/production
Director and dramaturgs on translating, adapting and producing Molière's *Misanthrope*. USA: La Jolla, CA, Chicago, IL. 1989-1990. Lang.: Eng.   2263
The Goodman Theatre production of *The Black Star Line* by Charles Goodman. USA: Chicago, IL. 1997. Lang.: Eng.   2278
Career of Goodman Theatre dramaturg. USA: Chicago, IL. 1990-1997. Lang.: Eng.   2318
Interview with director David Petrarca. USA: Chicago, IL. 1997. Lang.: Eng.   2329

Goodman, Henry
Performance/production
The world premiere of Brecht's *The Caucasian Chalk Circle*. USA: Northfield, MN. 1948. Lang.: Eng.   2253

Goodnight Children Everywhere
Performance/production
Collection of newspaper reviews by London theatre critics. UK-England. 1997. Lang.: Eng.   2163

Goodnight Desdemona (Good Morning Juliet)
Performance/production
Collection of newspaper reviews by London theatre critics. UK-England: London. 1997. Lang.: Eng.   2085
Plays/librettos/scripts
Time travel in English-language drama. USA. Canada. UK-England. 1908-1993. Lang.: Eng.   3171

Goodrich, Frances
Plays/librettos/scripts
Adaptations of the diary of Anne Frank. Netherlands. USA. 1945-1997. Lang.: Eng.   2978
The stage adaptation of the diary of Anne Frank. USA. 1947-1950. Lang.: Eng.   3234

Goodwoman of Sharkville, The
Performance/production
Collection of newspaper reviews by London theatre critics. UK-England: London. 1997. Lang.: Eng.   2130

Goold, Rupert
Performance/production
Collection of newspaper reviews by London theatre critics. UK-England: London. 1997. Lang.: Eng.   2143

Goong Hay Kid, The
Basic theatrical documents
Text of plays performed at the Nuyorican Poets Cafe. USA: New York, NY. 1973-1990. Lang.: Eng.   1322

Göranzon, Marie
Performance/production
Interview with actress Marie Göranzon. Sweden: Stockholm. 1964-1997. Lang.: Swe.   1958

Gorčakova, Galina
Performance/production
Soprano Galina Gorčakova. Russia: St. Petersburg. 1962-1997. Lang.: Eng.   4206

Gordimer, Nadine
Performance/production
Directing a stage adaptation of *The Smell of Death and Flowers* by Nadine Gordimer. USA. 1995-1996. Lang.: Eng.   647

Gordon, Ain
Performance/production
The use of silent films in theatrical productions. USA: New York, NY. 1997. Lang.: Eng.   2342

Gordon, David
Performance/production
The use of silent films in theatrical productions. USA: New York, NY. 1997. Lang.: Eng.   2342

Gordon, Janet
Performance/production
Collection of newspaper reviews by London theatre critics. UK-England. 1997. Lang.: Eng.   2039

Grace Theatre (London) — cont'd

Collection of newspaper reviews by London theatre critics. UK-England: London. 1997. Lang.: Eng. 2161

Graeper's Egyptian Theatre (Portland, OR)
Performance spaces
The building of Graeper's Egyptian Theatre. USA: Portland, OR. 1924. Lang.: Eng. 3566

Graham, Billy
Performance/production
Actor, director, comedian Billy Graham. USA. 1997. Lang.: Eng. 2286

Graham, Martha
Performance/production
Dancer Dorothy Bird and her work with Martha Graham. USA: New York, NY. 1930-1937. Lang.: Eng. 1121

Analysis of Martha Graham's Greek cycle of dance dramas. USA. 1926-1991. Lang.: Ita. 1198

Female beauty and American modern dance. USA. 1930-1940. Lang.: Eng. 1204
Theory/criticism
Dance history and cultural studies: works of Martha Graham and Eugene O'Neill. USA. 1913-1933. Lang.: Eng. 1216

Analysis of *American Document* by Martha Graham. USA. 1938. Lang.: Eng. 1217

Graham, Tony
Performance/production
Collection of newspaper reviews by London theatre critics. UK-England: London. 1997. Lang.: Eng. 2162

Gramss, Eike
Design/technology
The staging and scenic concept for the premiere of the opera *Schlachthof 5*. Germany: Munich. 1997. Lang.: Ger. 4022

Gran circo Eukraniano, El (Great USkrainian Circus, The)
Basic theatrical documents
Anthology of Latin American women's plays. Latin America. 1981-1989. Lang.: Eng. 1291

Granath, Björn
Performance/production
Actor Björn Granath. Sweden: Stockholm. 1970-1997. Lang.: Swe. 1936

Granatov, Boris
Performance/production
Director Boris Granatov of Vologodskij Youth Theatre. Russia: St. Petersburg. 1980-1997. Lang.: Rus. 1882

Grand English Opera Company (USA)
Performance/production
Grand opera in Denver. USA: Denver, CO. 1864-1881. Lang.: Eng. 4260

Grand Hotel
Performance/production
Composer/lyricist Maury Yeston. USA: New York, NY. 1945-1997. Lang.: Eng. 3975

Grand Macabre, Le
Basic theatrical documents
Libretto of Ligeti's opera *Le Grand Macabre*. Europe. 1978-1997. Lang.: Fre, Eng. 4008
Design/technology
Roland Topor's costume designs for a production of *Le Grand Macabre* by Ligeti. Italy: Bologna. 1979. Lang.: Fre. 4026
Performance/production
Productions world wide of Ligeti's opera *Le Grand Macabre*. 1978-1998. Lang.: Fre. 4080

Recordings of Ligeti's *Le Grand Macabre*. 1979-1998. Lang.: Fre. 4087

Opera productions from Salzburger Festspiele. Austria: Salzburg. 1997. Lang.: Ger. 4096

Peter Sellars' production of Ligeti's *Le Grand Macabre* at the Salzburg Festival. Austria: Salzburg. 1997. Lang.: Fre. 4099

Interview with composer György Ligeti. Europe. 1997. Lang.: Fre. 4132

Composer György Ligeti. Europe. 1923-1997. Lang.: Fre. 4133
Plays/librettos/scripts
La Balade du Grand Macabre by Ghelderode and its operatic adaptation by György Ligeti. Belgium. 1934. Lang.: Fre. 2385

Analysis of *Le Grand Macabre* by György Ligeti. Europe. 1978-1990. Lang.: Fre. 4285

György Ligeti on his opera *Le Grand Macabre*. Sweden. 1978. Lang.: Fre. 4312

Grand Night For Singing, A
Performance/production
Collection of newspaper reviews by London theatre critics. UK-England: London. 1997. Lang.: Eng. 2161

Grand Night Out: Wallace & Gromit Alive on Stage, A
Performance/production
Collection of newspaper reviews by London theatre critics. UK-England: London. 1997. Lang.: Eng. 2149

Grant, William H., III
Design/technology
Lighting designer William H. Grant III. USA. 1950-1997. Lang.: Eng. 296

Granville-Barker, Harley
Performance/production
Collection of newspaper reviews by London theatre critics. UK-England: London. 1997. Lang.: Eng. 2017

Shakespearean production in the age of actor-managers. UK-England. 1840-1914. Lang.: Eng. 2193

Recent roles of actor Michael Pennington. UK-England: London. 1997. Lang.: Eng. 2196

Graser, Jorg
Performance/production
Collection of newspaper reviews by London theatre critics. UK-England: London. 1997. Lang.: Eng. 2011

Graset, Esteve
Performance/production
Interview with installation artist Esteve Graset. Spain. 1978-1996. Lang.: Eng. 610

Grass, Günter
Relation to other fields
Interview with novelist Günter Grass about Bertolt Brecht. Germany: Berlin. 1953-1997. Lang.: Ger. 3353

Grauman's Egyptian Theatre (Los Angeles, CA)
Performance spaces
Documentation of Grauman's Egyptian Theatre. USA: Los Angeles, CA. 1922-1997. Lang.: Eng. 3562

Grave Plots
Performance/production
Collection of newspaper reviews by London theatre critics. UK-England: London. 1997. Lang.: Eng. 2091

Gravel, Robert
Institutions
Robert Gravel and improvisation. Canada: Montreal, PQ. 1977-1997. Lang.: Fre. 303
Performance/production
Theatrical projects of actor/writer Robert Gravel. Canada: Montreal, PQ. 1977-1996. Lang.: Fre. 475

Work of Robert Gravel in improvisation and experimental theatre. Canada: Montreal, PQ. 1976-1996. Lang.: Fre. 480

Actor Robert Gravel. Canada: Montreal, PQ. 1973-1996. Lang.: Fre. 481

Obscenity as social criticism in work of Robert Gravel. Canada. Belgium. 1973-1996. Lang.: Fre. 482

Graven, A.S.
Performance spaces
History of the Minneapolis, later the Radio City Theatre. USA: Minneapolis, MN. 1928-1997. Lang.: Eng. 3565

Gray, Ramin
Performance/production
Collection of newspaper reviews by London theatre critics. UK-England: London. 1997. Lang.: Eng. 2008

Gray, Simon
Performance/production
Collection of newspaper reviews by London theatre critics. UK-England: London. 1997. Lang.: Eng. 2084

Gray, Spalding
Performance/production
Collection of newspaper reviews by London theatre critics. UK-England. 1997. Lang.: Eng. 2072

Interviews on acting with actors, teachers, and directors. USA. 1997. Lang.: Eng. 2352
Theory/criticism
Ideas about mimesis and critical responses to the staging of reality. USA. 1990-1997. Lang.: Eng. 928

Gray, Terence
Performance/production
The work of director Terence Gray. UK-England: Cambridge. 1925-1940. Lang.: Eng. 2210

Grazzini, Antonfrancesco
Plays/librettos/scripts
Sexuality and witchcraft in plays of Antonfrancesco Grazzini. Italy: Florence. 1500-1600. Lang.: Eng. 2956

Guerin, Isabelle
Performance/production
Stars of the Paris Opera Ballet. France: Paris. 1983-1997. Lang.: Eng.
1074

Guerrasio, John
Performance/production
Collection of newspaper reviews by London theatre critics. UK-England:
London. 1997. Lang.: Eng.
1999

Guggi, Thomas
Performance/production
Interview with director, producer, and choreographer Thomas Guggi.
Germany. 1967-1997. Lang.: Ger.
965

Guglielmi, Pietro Alessandro
Plays/librettos/scripts
The dialect operas and *opera seria* of Alessandro Guglielmi. Italy. 1750-
1804. Lang.: Eng.
4303

Guid Sisters, The
SEE
Belles-soeurs, Les.

Guidi, Firenza
Performance/production
Collection of newspaper reviews by London theatre critics. UK-England:
London. 1997. Lang.: Eng.
2015

Guimond, Olivier
Performance/production
The TV series *Cher Olivier (Dear Olivier)* on actor Olivier Guimond.
Canada. 1997. Lang.: Fre.
3718

Gunshy
Design/technology
Lighting for Humana Festival by Ed McCarthy and Greg Sullivan.
USA: Louisville, KY. 1997. Lang.: Eng.
1370

Gunter, Gregory
Performance/production
Interview with dramaturg Gregory Gunter on his collaboration with
Anne Bogart. USA. 1995-1997. Lang.: Eng.
2275

Günther, Rickard
Performance/production
Interview with director Richard Günther. Sweden: Stockholm. 1990-
1997. Lang.: Swe.
3943

Gupta, Tanika
Performance/production
Collection of newspaper reviews by London theatre critics. UK-England:
London. 1997. Lang.: Eng.
2055

Gustave III
Performance/production
Analysis of the original production book of *Un Ballo in Maschera*. Italy:
Milan. 1856-1888. Lang.: Eng.
4197

Gute Mensch von Sezuan, Der (Good Person of Szechwan, The)
Performance/production
Collection of newspaper reviews by London theatre critics. UK-England:
London. 1997. Lang.: Eng.
2130
Plays/librettos/scripts
Brecht's influence on the plays of Howard Barker. UK-England. 1987-
1997. Lang.: Eng.
3084
Mimesis, feminism, theatre, and performance. USA. 1997. Lang.: Eng.
3176

Guthrie Theatre (Minneapolis, MN)
Institutions
Guthrie Theatre's new artistic director Joe Dowling. USA: Minneapolis,
MN. Ireland: Dublin. 1963-1997. Lang.: Eng.
1513
Performance/production
Educational initiatives involving dramaturgs and play production. USA.
1990-1996. Lang.: Eng.
2288

Guthrie, Tyrone
Performance/production
Shakespearean production before national subsidy. UK-England. 1914-
1959. Lang.: Eng.
2175

Guy Mannering
Plays/librettos/scripts
Analysis of melodramas based on novels of Walter Scott. England.
1810-1830. Lang.: Eng.
2681

Guy, Ray
Plays/librettos/scripts
Analysis of plays by Ray Guy. Canada. 1948-1951. Lang.: Eng.
2404

Gyimesi, Kálmán
Performance/production
Opera singer Kálmán Gyimesi of the Szeged National Theatre.
Hungary. 1945-1997. Lang.: Hun.
4172

Gynaikeion, or The History of Women
Plays/librettos/scripts
Livy's influence on Shakespeare, Heywood, and Peele. England. 1569-
1624. Lang.: Eng.
2629

Gyngell, Michael
Performance/production
Collection of newspaper reviews by London theatre critics. UK-England:
London. 1997. Lang.: Eng.
2080

Győri Balett (Győr)
Design/technology
Interview with costume designer Judit Gombár. Hungary. 1955-1996.
Lang.: Hun.
941
Institutions
Interview with János Kiss and Éva Afonyi of Győri Balett. Hungary:
Győr. 1970-1997. Lang.: Hun.
1052
Performance/production
Performance of the Győri Balett. Hungary. 1997. Lang.: Hun.
1093
Győri Balett's production of *Carmen* by Robert North and Christopher
Benstead. Hungary: Győr. 1997. Lang.: Hun.
1094

HaBimah (Tel Aviv)
Performance/production
Hanan Snir's productions of Lorca's *Blood Wedding (Bodas de sangre)*.
Israel: Tel Aviv. 1990. Lang.: Eng.
1791
The role of the implied spectator in productions of Omri Nitzan and
Hillel Mittelpunkt. Israel: Tel Aviv. 1993. Lang.: Eng.
1792

Hachioji City Art and Cultural Hall (Hachioji City)
Design/technology
Interior lighting of Hachioji City Art and Cultural Hall. Japan: Hachioji
City. 1996. Lang.: Eng.
177

Hackett, Albert
Plays/librettos/scripts
Adaptations of the diary of Anne Frank. Netherlands. USA. 1945-1997.
Lang.: Eng.
2978
The stage adaptation of the diary of Anne Frank. USA. 1947-1950.
Lang.: Eng.
3234

Hackney Empire Theatre (London)
Performance/production
Collection of newspaper reviews by London theatre critics. UK-England:
London. 1997. Lang.: Eng.
1977
Collection of newspaper reviews by London theatre critics. UK-England:
London. 1997. Lang.: Eng.
2130
Collection of newspaper reviews by London theatre critics. UK-England:
London. 1997. Lang.: Eng.
2141
Collection of newspaper reviews by London theatre critics. UK-England:
London. 1997. Lang.: Eng.
2160

Haddigan, Mark
Performance/production
Collection of newspaper reviews by London theatre critics. UK-England:
London. 1997. Lang.: Eng.
2080

Hader, Josef
Performance/production
The opening of the Deutsches Schauspielhaus season. Germany:
Hamburg. 1997. Lang.: Ger.
1688

Hadley, Jerry
Performance/production
The background of a new opera, *The Conquistador*, by Myron Fink.
USA: San Diego, CA. 1997. Lang.: Eng.
4236
Tenor Jerry Hadley's New York City Opera debut. USA: New York,
NY. 1979. Lang.: Eng.
4247

Hagedorn, Jessica
Institutions
The Sundance Institute Playwright's Lab. USA: Salt Lake City, UT.
1997. Lang.: Eng.
1512

Haifa Municipal Theatre
SEE
Teatron HaIroni (Haifa).

Haig, David
Performance/production
Collection of newspaper reviews by London theatre critics. UK-England:
London. 1997. Lang.: Eng.
2119

Hailer, Peter
Performance/production
The new season at Düsseldorfer Schauspielhaus. Germany: Dusseldorf.
1997. Lang.: Ger.
1731

Haines, David
Performance/production
Collection of newspaper reviews by London theatre critics. UK-England:
London. 1997. Lang.: Eng.
2108

Hairy Ape, The
Performance/production
Collection of newspaper reviews by London theatre critics. UK-England:
London. 1997. Lang.: Eng.
2107

Hamlet — cont'd

Wordplay and disorder in Shakespeare's *Hamlet*. England. 1600-1601. Lang.: Eng. 2472

The slaying of Polonius in editions of Shakespeare's *Hamlet*. England. 1603-1997. Lang.: Eng. 2498

Subversion and Shakespeare's older female characters. England. 1590-1613. Lang.: Eng. 2502

Feminist analysis of the place of women in Shakespeare's plays. England. 1590-1613. Lang.: Eng. 2519

The performability of the first quarto of Shakespeare's *Hamlet*. England. 1603. Lang.: Eng. 2529

Analysis of Shakespeare's *Hamlet*. England. 1600. Lang.: Slo. 2558

The evolution of the character Gertrude in versions of Shakespeare's *Hamlet*. England. 1600-1604. Lang.: Eng. 2608

Proposed later date for a passage in Shakespeare's *Hamlet*. England. 1601-1709. Lang.: Eng. 2621

Religion in Shakespeare's *Hamlet*. England. 1601. Lang.: Eng. 2651

Principles of Shakespearean dramaturgy. England. 1590-1613. Lang.: Eng. 2658

The poetics of vision in tragedies of Shakespeare. England. 1600-1606. Lang.: Ita. 2667

Ambivalence toward a female sovereign reflected in plays of Shakespeare and Middleton. England. 1600-1607. Lang.: Eng. 2672

Madness and gender in the plays of Shakespeare. England. 1589-1613. Lang.: Eng. 2677

Suicide in English Renaissance tragedy. England. 1590-1625. Lang.: Eng. 2724

Analysis of versions of Shakespeare's *Hamlet*. England. 1600-1623. Lang.: Eng. 2767

Analysis of Sophocles' and Smole's treatments of Antigone and Shakespeare's *Hamlet*. Slovenia. 500 B.C.-1960 A.D. Lang.: Slo. 3005

Analysis of Kenneth Branagh's films *A Midwinter's Tale* and *Hamlet*. UK-England. 1995-1996. Lang.: Eng. 3644

Analysis of Kenneth Branagh's film adaptation of *Hamlet*. UK-England. 1996. Lang.: Eng. 3645

Critique of Franco Zeffirelli's film adaptation of *Hamlet*. USA. 1990. Lang.: Eng. 3675

Sexual aberration in film adaptations of *Hamlet*. USA. UK-England. 1920-1996. Lang.: Eng. 3680

Freudian psychology in film adaptations of *Hamlet*. USA. UK-England. 1910-1996. Lang.: Eng. 3687

Relation to other fields

The influence of *Hamlet* on William Godwin's novel *Caleb Williams*. England. 1600-1794. Lang.: Eng. 3336

Politics in Joyce's *Ulysses* and his references to *Hamlet*. Ireland. 1920. Lang.: Eng. 3363

Teaching Shakespeare with the aid of the internet. USA. 1997. Lang.: Eng. 3407

Feminist and performance techniques for teaching Shakespeare's *Hamlet*. USA. 1997. Lang.: Eng. 3408

'Playgrounding' in the teaching of Shakespeare's plays. USA. 1997. Lang.: Eng. 3411

The sense of wonder and the teaching of Shakespeare's *Hamlet*. USA. UK-England. 1995. Lang.: Eng. 3412

Teaching a scene from *Hamlet* using different interpretations on video. USA. 1997. Lang.: Eng. 3415

Theory/criticism

Nietzsche, *Hamlet*, and modern criticism. England. Germany. 1601-1997. Lang.: Eng. 3472

The theatrical representation of death in the context of contemporary theory. Europe. 1997. Lang.: Eng. 3477

Hamlet: A Monologue

Performance/production

Treatments of Shakespeare's *Hamlet* by Robert Wilson and Benno Besson. Italy. 1995. Lang.: Ita. 1808

Hamletmaschine, Die (Hamletmachine)

Plays/librettos/scripts

Wolfgang Rihm's operatic adaptation of *Die Hamletmaschine (Hamletmachine)* by Heiner Müller. Germany. 1978. Lang.: Swe. 4300

Hamletmaschine, Die (opera)

Plays/librettos/scripts

Wolfgang Rihm's operatic adaptation of *Die Hamletmaschine (Hamletmachine)* by Heiner Müller. Germany. 1978. Lang.: Swe. 4300

Hamlisch, Marvin

Performance/production

Collection of newspaper reviews by London theatre critics. UK-England: London. 1997. Lang.: Eng. 2032

History of American musical theatre. USA. UK-England. 1912-1995. Lang.: Eng. 3954

Hammerschlag, Tamantha

Performance/production

Collection of newspaper reviews by London theatre critics. UK-England: London. 1997. Lang.: Eng. 1993

Hammerstein, Oscar, II

Design/technology

Lighting design for *Show Boat*, Gershwin Theatre. USA: New York, NY. 1994. Lang.: Eng. 3922

Performance/production

Collection of newspaper reviews by London theatre critics. UK-England: London. 1997. Lang.: Eng. 2152

Collection of newspaper reviews by London theatre critics. UK-England: London. 1997. Lang.: Eng. 2161

History of American musical theatre. USA. UK-England. 1912-1995. Lang.: Eng. 3954

Actor's Expression production of an unauthorized version of the musical *Oklahoma!*. USA: Atlanta, GA. 1997. Lang.: Eng. 3959

Plays/librettos/scripts

The relationship of lyricists Stephen Sondheim and Oscar Hammerstein II. USA. 1945-1968. Lang.: Eng. 3996

Hampstead Theatre (London)

Performance/production

Collection of newspaper reviews by London theatre critics. UK-England: London. 1997. Lang.: Eng. 1987

Collection of newspaper reviews by London theatre critics. UK-England: London. 1997. Lang.: Eng. 2008

Collection of newspaper reviews by London theatre critics. UK-England: London. 1997. Lang.: Eng. 2029

Collection of newspaper reviews by London theatre critics. UK-England: London. 1997. Lang.: Eng. 2062

Collection of newspaper reviews by London theatre critics. UK-England: London. 1997. Lang.: Eng. 2083

Collection of newspaper reviews by London theatre critics. UK-England: London. 1997. Lang.: Eng. 2100

Collection of newspaper reviews by London theatre critics. UK-England: London. 1997. Lang.: Eng. 2110

Collection of newspaper reviews by London theatre critics. UK-England: London. 1997. Lang.: Eng. 2119

Collection of newspaper reviews by London theatre critics. UK-England: London. 1997. Lang.: Eng. 2128

Hampton, Christopher

Performance/production

Collection of newspaper reviews by London theatre critics. UK-England: London. 1997. Lang.: Eng. 2104

Plays/librettos/scripts

Christopher Hampton—playwright, translator, and adaptor. UK-England. 1967-1994. Lang.: Eng. 3089

Handel, George Frideric

Design/technology

Opera costume designer Martin Pakledinaz. USA: Santa Fe, NM, New York, NY. 1997. Lang.: Eng. 4035

Performance/production

Handelian countertenor David Sabella, currently performing in musical theatre. USA: New York, NY. 1996. Lang.: Eng. 3960

Stylistic similarities in Baroque and nineteenth-century opera. Europe. 1705-1997. Lang.: Eng. 4128

Soprano Susannah Waters. UK-England. 1997. Lang.: Eng. 4226

Cutting operas for performance. USA. 1997. Lang.: Eng. 4240

Handke, Peter

Basic theatrical documents

English translation of *Die Stunde da wir nichts voneinander wussten (The Hour We Knew Nothing of Each Other)* by Peter Handke. Germany. 1992. Lang.: Eng. 1281

Institutions

Staatstheater Darmstadt under the direction of Gerd-Theo Umberg. Germany: Darmstadt. 1996-1997. Lang.: Ger. 1412

Performance/production

Interview with actor Gert Voss. Austria: Vienna. 1975-1997. Lang.: Ger. 1561

Premieres of new plays by Handke, Krausser, and Enzensberger. Austria. Germany. 1996-1997. Lang.: Ger. 1567

Handke, Peter — cont'd

Hartmut Wickert's production of Handke's *The Hour We Knew Nothing of Each Other*. Germany: Hannover. 1993. Lang.: Eng. 1728

Plays of Botho Strauss and Peter Handke carried over into a second season. Germany: Berlin, Frankfurt. 1996-1997. Lang.: Ger. 1746

Handke's *Die Stunde da wir nichts voneinander wussten (The Hour We Knew Nothing of Each Other)* at Teatr Studio. Poland: Warsaw.1997. Lang.: Eng, Fre. 1840

Collection of newspaper reviews by London theatre critics. UK-England: London. 1997. Lang.: Eng. 2126

Plays/librettos/scripts

Analysis of *Die Stunde da wir nichts voneinander wussten (The Hour We Knew Nothing of Each Other)* by Peter Handke. Germany. 1992. Lang.: Eng. 2844

Trends in contemporary German-language drama. Germany. Austria. Switzerland. 1997. Lang.: Ger. 2859

Handmaid's Tale, The
Plays/librettos/scripts

British Library holdings of filmscript material of Harold Pinter. UK-England. 1963-1994. Lang.: Eng. 3647

Hanes, Mary
Plays/librettos/scripts

Mary Hanes on her play *The Crimson Thread*. USA. 1997. Lang.: Eng. 3205

Hanging Tree, The
Performance/production

Collection of newspaper reviews by London theatre critics. UK-England: London. 1997. Lang.: Eng. 1979

Hankinson, David
Performance/production

Collection of newspaper reviews by London theatre critics. UK-England: London. 1997. Lang.: Eng. 2025

Hannan, Chris
Performance/production

Collection of newspaper reviews by London theatre critics. UK-England: London. 1997. Lang.: Eng. 2137

Hannum, Tim
Design/technology

Tim Hannum's theatrical lighting designs for nightclub settings. USA: Houston, TX. 1997. Lang.: Eng. 231

Hans Otto Theater (Potsdam)
Plays/librettos/scripts

Children's theatre festival productions. Germany: Berlin. 1997. Lang.: Ger. 2845

Hansberry, Lorraine
Plays/librettos/scripts

The figure of the prodigal son in American family drama. USA. 1946-1962. Lang.: Eng. 3254

Margaret Wilkerson and the biography of playwright Lorraine Hansberry. USA. 1982-1997. Lang.: Eng. 3261

Critical history of American drama. USA. 1960-1997. Lang.: Eng. 3267

Hansel and Gretel
Performance/production

Collection of newspaper reviews by London theatre critics. UK-England: London. 1997. Lang.: Eng. 2162

Hänsel und Gretel
Performance/production

Background material on Juilliard Opera's telecast performance of *Hänsel und Gretel*. USA: New York, NY. 1997. Lang.: Eng. 4232

Hänsel, Andreas
Performance/production

Performances of the classics in Franconia. Germany. 1997. Lang.: Ger. 1737

Hansen, Bo Hr.
Performance/production

Profile of author Bo Hr. Hansen. Denmark. 1985-1997. Lang.: Dan. 499

Hänseroth, Albin
Institutions

Interview with Albin Hänseroth of Staatsoper. Germany: Hamburg. 1997. Lang.: Ger. 4046

Happenings
Performance/production

Allan Kaprow on Happenings. USA. 1980-1996. Lang.: Eng. 3831

Happy Days
Performance/production

Collection of newspaper reviews by London theatre critics. UK-England: London. 1997. Lang.: Eng. 2145

Plays/librettos/scripts

Analysis of German translations of plays by Samuel Beckett. Germany. 1967-1978. Lang.: Eng. 2842

Happy End
Performance/production

Kurt Weill's collaborations with playwrights. Germany: Berlin. USA: New York, NY. 1927-1945. Lang.: Eng. 3934

Happy Star (Lomé)
Plays/librettos/scripts

West African popular theatre: texts and analysis. Ghana. Togo. Nigeria. 1995-1997. Lang.: Eng. 2866

Hard Nut, The
Performance/production

Gender in choreographies of Mark Morris. USA. 1980-1995. Lang.: Eng. 1206

Hard Times
Performance/production

Collection of newspaper reviews by London theatre critics. UK-England: London. 1997. Lang.: Eng. 1992

Hardcastle, Angela
Performance/production

Collection of newspaper reviews by London theatre critics. UK-England: London. 1997. Lang.: Eng. 2059

Hardie, Victoria
Performance/production

Collection of newspaper reviews by London theatre critics. UK-England: London. 1997. Lang.: Eng. 2097

Hardin, Herschel
Plays/librettos/scripts

Indigenous peoples in Canadian historical drama. Canada. 1886-1997. Lang.: Eng. 2424

Harding, Alex
Performance/production

Interview with playwright Barry Lowe and actor Alex Harding on gay theatre. Australia: Sydney. 1997. Lang.: Eng. 1557

Hardman, Christopher
Performance/production

Interview with experimental theatre artist Christopher Hardman. USA. 1985. Lang.: Ita. 631

Hare, David
Performance/production

Collection of newspaper reviews by London theatre critics. UK-England: London. 1997. Lang.: Eng. 1976

Collection of newspaper reviews by London theatre critics. UK-England: London. 1997. Lang.: Eng. 2001

Collection of newspaper reviews by London theatre critics. UK-England: London. 1997. Lang.: Eng. 2067

Collection of newspaper reviews by London theatre critics. UK-England: London. 1997. Lang.: Eng. 2070

Directing *The Secret Rapture* by David Hare. UK-England. 1988-1995. Lang.: Eng. 2206

Plays/librettos/scripts

Nostalgia and morality in plays of David Hare. UK-England: London. 1947-1997. Lang.: Eng. 3113

Harfouch, Corinna
Performance/production

Profile of actress Corinna Harfouch. Germany. 1989-1997. Lang.: Ger. 1735

Harman, Barry
Performance/production

Collection of newspaper reviews by London theatre critics. UK-England: London. 1997. Lang.: Eng. 2008

Harmon, Peggy
Plays/librettos/scripts

Survey of one- or two-character musicals. USA: New York, NY. 1964-1997. Lang.: Eng. 3989

Harmston, Joe
Performance/production

Collection of newspaper reviews by London theatre critics. UK-England: London. 1997. Lang.: Eng. 2127

Harriet Tubman
Plays/librettos/scripts

The voices of African-American women. USA. 1840-1994. Lang.: Eng. 3309

Harris, Lyle Ashton
Relation to other fields

Performative criticism of photo exhibits by Nan Goldin and Lyle Ashton Harris. USA: New York, NY. 1996-1997. Lang.: Eng. 849

Harris, Richard
Performance/production

Collection of newspaper reviews by London theatre critics. UK-England: London. 1997. Lang.: Eng. 2132

Harris, Simon
Performance/production
Collection of newspaper reviews by London theatre critics. UK-England:
London. 1997. Lang.: Eng.   2016
Harrison, Tony
Performance/production
Production of Tony Harrison's *The Labourers of Herakles*. Greece:
Delphi. 1995. Lang.: Eng.   1750

Collection of newspaper reviews by London theatre critics. UK-England:
London. 1997. Lang.: Eng.   2006
Harrison, Will
Performance/production
Collection of newspaper reviews by London theatre critics. UK-England:
London. 1997. Lang.: Eng.   2013
Harrys Kopf (Harry's Head)
Performance/production
Performances of *Harrys Kopf (Harry's Head)* by Tankred Dorst and
Ursula Ehler. Germany. 1968-1997. Lang.: Ger.   1748
Hart, Dee
Performance/production
Collection of newspaper reviews by London theatre critics. UK-England:
London. 1997. Lang.: Eng.   2030
Hart, Lorenz
Performance/production
Francesca Zambello directs *Lady in the Dark* at the National. UK-
England: London. 1997. Lang.: Eng.   3947
Plays/librettos/scripts
Analysis of musical adaptations of Shakespearean plays. USA. 1938-
1997. Lang.: Ger.   3983

Survey of musical adaptations of Shakespeare. USA: New York, NY.
1938-1997. Lang.: Eng.   3987
Hart, Moss
Design/technology
Rick Fisher's lighting design for *Lady in the Dark* at the Lyttelton. UK-
England: London. 1941-1997. Lang.: Eng.   3908
Performance/production
Collection of newspaper reviews by London theatre critics. UK-England:
London. 1997. Lang.: Eng.   2012

The reconstructed orchestration for the revival of *The Boys from
Syracuse* by Encores!. USA: New York, NY. 1938-1997. Lang.: Eng.
                                                                    3970
Plays/librettos/scripts
Analysis of *Merrily We Roll Along* by George S. Kaufman and Moss
Hart. USA. 1934. Lang.: Eng.   3190
Hartford Stage Company (Hartford, CT)
Performance/production
Ontological-Hysteric Theatre's production of *Pearls for Pigs* at Hartford
Stage. USA: Hartford, CT. 1995. Lang.: Eng.   2270
Hartley, Jan
Design/technology
Thomas Hase's lighting design for *After Sorrow (Viet Nam)* by Ping
Chong and Company. USA: New York, NY. 1997. Lang.: Eng.   942
Hartmann, Matthias
Performance/production
Major productions of the Vienna theatre season. Austria: Vienna. 1997.
Lang.: Ger.   1563

The opening of the Deutsches Schauspielhaus season. Germany:
Hamburg. 1997. Lang.: Ger.   1688

Recent productions of plays by Horváth. Germany. Austria. 1996-1997.
Lang.: Ger.   1722
Harvey, Jonathan
Performance/production
Collection of newspaper reviews by London theatre critics. UK-England:
London. 1997. Lang.: Eng.   2110
Harwood, Ronald
Design/technology
Howell Binkley's lighting design for *Taking Sides* by Ronald Harwood.
USA: New York, NY. 1997. Lang.: Eng.   1366
Hase, Thomas
Design/technology
Thomas Hase's lighting design for *After Sorrow (Viet Nam)* by Ping
Chong and Company. USA: New York, NY. 1997. Lang.: Eng.   942
Hasenclever, Walter
Basic theatrical documents
English translations of German Expressionist plays. Germany. 1900-
1920. Lang.: Eng.   1284
Haslewood, Joseph
Administration
Analysis of a legal agreement involving the Red Bull Company.
England: London. 1660-1663. Lang.: Eng.   16

Hatcher, Jeffrey
Performance/production
Collection of newspaper reviews by London theatre critics. UK-England:
London. 1997. Lang.: Eng.   2140
Hauk, Minnie
Performance/production
Opera superstar Minnie Hauk. USA. 1851-1929. Lang.: Eng.   4243
Hauptman, William
Design/technology
A raft for use in a production of the musical *Big River*. USA. 1997.
Lang.: Eng.   3923
Hausbesuch, Der (Visit, The)
Institutions
Recent productions of Schaubühne. Germany: Berlin. 1996-1997. Lang.:
Ger.   1426
Hauser, Frank
Performance/production
Collection of newspaper reviews by London theatre critics. UK-England:
London. 1997. Lang.: Eng.   2062

Collection of newspaper reviews by London theatre critics. UK-England.
1997. Lang.: Eng.   2098
Hausman, Constance
Performance/production
Constance Hausman's performance in Berg's *Lulu*. Denmark:
Copenhagen. 1997. Lang.: Eng.   4120
Haussmann, Leander
Performance/production
Interview with actor/director Leander Haussmann on Brecht's influence.
Germany: Bochum. 1997. Lang.: Ger.   1694

The style of productions at Bochumer Schauspielhaus. Germany:
Bochum. 1995-1997. Lang.: Ger.   1732

The new season at Bochumer Schauspielhaus. Germany: Bochum. 1997.
Lang.: Ger.   1747
Hauteroche, Noël Le Breton de
Plays/librettos/scripts
Actor, playwright, and theatre manager Noël Le Breton de Hauteroche.
France. 1620-1680. Lang.: Eng.   2816
Have-Little, The
Basic theatrical documents
Anthology of plays by women of color. USA. 1992-1996. Lang.: Eng.
                                                                    1338
Havel, Václav
Plays/librettos/scripts
The victimized female character in plays by Václav Havel. Czech
Republic. 1963-1997. Lang.: Eng.   2445

Analysis of *Pokoušení (Temptation)* by Václav Havel. Czechoslovakia.
1985. Lang.: Eng.   2446
Having Our Say
Plays/librettos/scripts
Interview with Emily Mann, author and director of documentary theatre.
USA: Princeton, NJ. 1981-1996. Lang.: Eng.   3139
Hawtrey, Anthony
Administration
Theatre manager Anthony Hawtrey. UK-England: London. 1940-1954.
Lang.: Eng.   1243
Hay, Deborah
Institutions
Judson Dance Theatre and dancing autobiography. USA. 1960-1965.
Lang.: Eng.   952
Hayashi, Michiyo
Performance/production
Interview with dancer Michiyo Hayashi. Sweden: Gothenburg. 1997.
Lang.: Swe.   1110
Haygarth, Tony
Performance/production
Harold Pinter's performance in his own play *The Hothouse*. UK-
England: Chichester. 1996. Lang.: Eng.   2205
Hayton, Richard
Performance/production
Collection of newspaper reviews by London theatre critics. UK-England:
London. 1997. Lang.: Eng.   2013
Hazel, Spencer
Performance/production
Collection of newspaper reviews by London theatre critics. UK-England:
London. 1997. Lang.: Eng.   1985
Hazelwood, C.H.
Plays/librettos/scripts
Gender and sexuality on the Victorian stage. UK-England. 1830-1900.
Lang.: Eng.   3085

Headstate
Performance/production
Collection of newspaper reviews by London theatre critics. UK-England: London. 1997. Lang.: Eng. 2080

Health/safety
Administration
Instructions for actors regarding worker's compensation. USA. 1997. Lang.: Eng. 75
Vision care benefits of Equity health plan. USA. 1997. Lang.: Eng. 84
Design/technology
New government standards for machinery and technical devices. Sweden. 1995. Lang.: Swe. 190
Profile of Lighting Research Center. USA: Troy, NY. 1988-1997. Lang.: Eng. 267
The lighting industry and federal and local regulation. USA. 1994. Lang.: Eng. 275
Call for the entertainment industry to draft safety standards for electrical equipment. USA. 1997. Lang.: Eng. 292
Institutions
Profile of a retirement home for actors. Germany: Weimar. 1893-1997. Lang.: Ger. 324
Actress Marie Tempest's campaign for a hospital ward for actors. UK-England: London. 1935-1937. Lang.: Eng. 387
Interview with Barry Kohn, founder of Physician Volunteers for the Arts. USA: New York, NY. 1997. Lang.: Eng. 405
Performance/production
Support services for older or retired dancers. Scandinavia. 1997. Lang.: Fin. 985
Problems and fears of the contemporary opera singer. Sweden. 1995. Lang.: Swe. 4218
Relation to other fields
Theatre and psychotherapy. Finland. 1997. Lang.: Fin. 744
Stress and the performing artist. Sweden. 1997. Lang.: Swe. 780

Heaney, Seamus
Plays/librettos/scripts
Greek myth in contemporary drama. 1970-1990. Lang.: Eng. 2369

Heart of the Earth, A Popol Vuh Story
Performance/production
Ralph Lee's production of *Heart of the Earth* by Cherríe Moraga. USA: New York, NY. 1995. Lang.: Eng. 2238

Heart's Desire
Performance/production
Collection of newspaper reviews by London theatre critics. UK-England: London. 1997. Lang.: Eng. 2105
Productions of plays by Caryl Churchill. UK-Scotland: Edinburgh. UK-England: London. 1997. Lang.: Eng. 2233

Heartbreak House
Performance/production
Collection of newspaper reviews by London theatre critics. UK-England: London. 1997. Lang.: Eng. 1976

Heartlanders
Plays/librettos/scripts
The relationship of creators and their work in devised theatre. UK-England. 1989. Lang.: Eng. 3083

Heathcliff
Performance/production
Collection of newspaper reviews by London theatre critics. UK-England: London. 1997. Lang.: Eng. 1999

Heathen Valley
Plays/librettos/scripts
Analysis of plays by Romulus Linney. USA. 1967-1995. Lang.: Eng. 3275

Hebbel-Theater (Berlin)
Administration
Hebbel-Theater under Nele Hertling. Germany: Berlin. 1988-1997. Lang.: Ger. 32

Hebbel, Friedrich
Performance/production
The new season at Bochumer Schauspielhaus. Germany: Bochum. 1997. Lang.: Ger. 1747
Plays/librettos/scripts
The treatment of the Biblical character Judith in plays by Hebbel and Giraudoux. Germany. France. 1841-1931. Lang.: Ita. 2841

Hecht, Ben
Performance/production
Collection of newspaper reviews by London theatre critics. UK-England: London. 1997. Lang.: Eng. 2157

Analysis of the war pageant 'Fun To Be Free' by Ben Hecht and Charles MacArthur. USA: New York, NY. 1941. Lang.: Eng. 3807

Hedberg, Frans
Plays/librettos/scripts
Frans Hedberg, director, manager, and librettist. Sweden: Stockholm. 1828-1908. Lang.: Swe. 4311

Hedda Gabler
Plays/librettos/scripts
Ibsen and early modernist theatre. Finland. 1885-1905. Lang.: Eng. 2801
The single-parent family in plays of Ibsen and Strindberg. Norway. Sweden. 1888-1890. Lang.: Eng. 2983

Hedges, Peter
Plays/librettos/scripts
Interview with playwright Peter Hedges. USA. 1997. Lang.: Eng. 3258

Hedley, Philip
Institutions
Profile of Theatre Royal, Stratford East. UK-England: London. 1953-1997. Lang.: Ger. 1498

Hefferon, Erin
Performance/production
Collection of newspaper reviews by London theatre critics. UK-England: London. 1997. Lang.: Eng. 2073

Hegedűs, D. Géza
Performance/production
Four productions of the musical *A Dzsungel könyve (The Jungle Book)*. Hungary. 1996-1997. Lang.: Hun. 3936

Heggie, Iain
Performance/production
Collection of newspaper reviews by London theatre critics. UK-England: London. 1997. Lang.: Eng. 2089

Heide, Christopher
Performance/production
Tessa Mendel's production of *Home at Last* by Christopher Heide. Canada: Halifax, NS. 1996. Lang.: Eng. 1589

Heidi Chronicles, The
Plays/librettos/scripts
The theme of nurturing in plays of Wolff, Treadwell, and Wasserstein. USA. 1996. Lang.: Eng. 3136

Heighes, Christopher
Performance/production
Space in site-specific performance. UK-England. 1960-1997. Lang.: Eng. 619

Heilige Johanna der Schlachthöfe, Die (Saint Joan of the Stockyards)
Performance/production
Major productions of the Vienna theatre season. Austria: Vienna. 1997. Lang.: Ger. 1563

Heimfeld, Leona
Performance/production
Collection of newspaper reviews by London theatre critics. UK-England: London. 1997. Lang.: Eng. 2011

Heinrich Heine vs. Nikolai Gogol
Performance/production
Collection of newspaper reviews by London theatre critics. UK-England: London. 1997. Lang.: Eng. 2035

Heinrich V. (Henry V)
Plays/librettos/scripts
Children's theatre festival productions. Germany: Berlin. 1997. Lang.: Ger. 2845

Heinz, Gerd
Performance/production
German productions of plays by Terrence McNally and Nicky Silver. Germany. 1996-1997. Lang.: Ger. 1721

Helle Nächte
Performance/production
Productions at the Munich Biennale. Germany: Munich. 1997. Lang.: Ger. 4148
Plays/librettos/scripts
Interview with opera composer Moritz Eggert. Germany: Munich. 1997. Lang.: Ger. 4293

Helle, Michael
Performance/production
Performances at Staattheater Mainz's new venue. Germany: Mainz. 1997. Lang.: Ger. 1743

Hellman, Jerome
Performance/production
Interview with Jerome Hellman, producer of the film *Midnight Cowboy*. USA. 1969. Lang.: Eng. 3602

Hellman, Lillian
Plays/librettos/scripts
The stage adaptation of the diary of Anne Frank. USA. 1947-1950.
Lang.: Eng.   3234

Hello and Goodbye
Performance/production
Collection of newspaper reviews by London theatre critics. UK-England:
London. 1997. Lang.: Eng.   2135

Hello Out There
Performance/production
American chamber opera. USA. 1868-1997. Lang.: Eng.   4258

Hello Pizza
Performance/production
Collection of newspaper reviews by London theatre critics. UK-England:
London. 1997. Lang.: Eng.   2067

Helsinki City Theatre
SEE
Helsingin Kaupunginteatteri.

Helsinki Youth Theatre (Helsinki)
Performance/production
Report on Finnish theatre productions. Finland: Helsinki, Tampere.
1997. Lang.: Eng, Fre.   1654

Hen & Chickens Theatre (London)
Performance/production
Collection of newspaper reviews by London theatre critics. UK-England:
London. 1997. Lang.: Eng.   1982

Collection of newspaper reviews by London theatre critics. UK-England:
London. 1997. Lang.: Eng.   2057

Collection of newspaper reviews by London theatre critics. UK-England:
1997. Lang.: Eng.   2092

Henderson, Don
Performance/production
Actor Don Henderson. UK-England. 1970-1997. Lang.: Eng.   2192

Henderson, Luther
Performance/production
Broadway orchestrator Luther Henderson. USA: New York, NY. 1997.
Lang.: Eng.   3973

Henley, Beth
Plays/librettos/scripts
Critical history of American drama. USA. 1960-1997. Lang.: Eng.   3267

Sisterhood and female bonding in *Crimes of the Heart* and *Sisters*. USA.
1986-1996. Lang.: Eng.   3511

Henry IV
Performance/production
Collection of newspaper reviews by London theatre critics. UK-England:
London. 1997. Lang.: Eng.   1991

Actors Timothy and Sam West. UK-England: London. 1997. Lang.:
Eng.   2212

The experience of cross-gender role-playing. USA. 1971-1997. Lang.:
Eng.   2268

Film actor Emil Jannings. Germany. 1929-1945. Lang.: Eng.   3574

Shakespearean elements in Gus Van Sant's film *My Own Private Idaho*.
USA. 1993. Lang.: Eng.   3629
Plays/librettos/scripts
Economic metaphors in Shakespeare's Lancastrian tetralogy. England.
1595-1599. Lang.: Eng.   2542

The metaphor of Icarus in Shakespeare's plays about Henry VI.
England. 1589-1595. Lang.: Eng.   2562

The English view of Ireland reflected in Shakespeare's history plays.
England. 1590-1599. Lang.: Eng.   2678

Shakespeare's Falstaff and Puritanism. England. 1596-1599. Lang.: Eng.
                                                                     2701

Physical orientation in the world in Shakespeare's *Henriad*. England.
1596-1599. Lang.: Eng.   2708

Masculinity and feminine disruption in Shakespeare's history plays.
England. 1590-1599. Lang.: Eng.   2732

Analysis of Prince Hal in Shakespeare's *Henry IV*, Parts 1 and 2.
England. 1596-1597. Lang.: Eng.   2773

Falstaff, continuity, and Shakespeare's *Henry IV* and *Henry V*. England.
1596-1599. Lang.: Eng.   2775
Research/historiography
Renaissance drama, censorship, and contemporary historical methods.
England: London. 1588-1980. Lang.: Eng.   3446

Henry IV by Pirandello
SEE
Enrico IV.

Henry IV, Part One
Plays/librettos/scripts
Law, justice, and criminology in plays of Shakespeare. England. 1590-
1613. Lang.: Eng.   2756

Henry V
Performance spaces
The inaugural season of the rebuilt Shakespeare's Globe. UK-England:
London. 1997. Lang.: Eng.   1539

Profile of Shakespeare's Globe Theatre. UK-England: London. 1970.
Lang.: Swe.   1541
Performance/production
Collection of newspaper reviews by London theatre critics. UK-England:
London. 1997. Lang.: Eng.   2060

Collection of newspaper reviews by London theatre critics. UK-England.
1997. Lang.: Eng.   2109

Collection of newspaper reviews by London theatre critics. UK-England:
London. 1997. Lang.: Eng.   2136

The theatricalization of war in Kenneth Branagh's film version of
Shakespeare's *Henry V*. USA. 1989. Lang.: Eng.   3593

Analysis of Kenneth Branagh's film adaptation of Shakespeare's *Henry
V*. UK-England. 1989. Lang.: Eng.   3595

Interview with actor/director Kenneth Branagh. UK-England: London.
1989-1997. Lang.: Eng.   3597

The chorus in film adaptations of Shakespeare's *Henry V* by Olivier and
Branagh. UK-England. 1944-1989. Lang.: Eng.   3598

Interview with actor Michael Maloney about roles in Shakespearean
films. USA. 1995. Lang.: Eng.   3625

Shakespearean elements in Gus Van Sant's film *My Own Private Idaho*.
USA. 1993. Lang.: Eng.   3629
Plays/librettos/scripts
Economic metaphors in Shakespeare's Lancastrian tetralogy. England.
1595-1599. Lang.: Eng.   2542

The metaphor of Icarus in Shakespeare's plays about Henry VI.
England. 1589-1595. Lang.: Eng.   2562

The idea of nationhood in Shakespeare's *Henry V*. England. 1599.
Lang.: Eng.   2656

Principles of Shakespearean dramaturgy. England. 1590-1613. Lang.:
Eng.   2658

Comparison of Shakespeare's *Henry V* and Plutarch's account of
Alexander the Great. England. 1599. Lang.: Eng.   2669

The English view of Ireland reflected in Shakespeare's history plays.
England. 1590-1599. Lang.: Eng.   2678

Shakespeare's Falstaff and Puritanism. England. 1596-1599. Lang.: Eng.
                                                                     2701

Physical orientation in the world in Shakespeare's *Henriad*. England.
1596-1599. Lang.: Eng.   2708

Witchcraft and female sexuality in the plays of Shakespeare. England.
1590-1613. Lang.: Eng.   2717

Masculinity and feminine disruption in Shakespeare's history plays.
England. 1590-1599. Lang.: Eng.   2732

Falstaff, continuity, and Shakespeare's *Henry IV* and *Henry V*. England.
1596-1599. Lang.: Eng.   2775

The ambiguity of Shakespeare's *Henry V* in Kenneth Branagh's film
adaptation. UK-England. 1989. Lang.: Eng.   3648
Relation to other fields
Team-teaching Shakespeare in an interdisciplinary context. USA. 1997.
Lang.: Eng.   3413

Using video to teach Shakespeare's *Henry V*. USA. 1997. Lang.: Eng.
                                                                     3417

Henry VI
Institutions
Minutes of Columbia University Seminar on Shakespeare. USA: New
York, NY. 1997. Lang.: Eng.   1515
Performance/production
Directors Michael Kahn and Karin Coonrod on their productions of
Henry VI. USA: New York, NY, Washington, DC. 1950-1996. Lang.
:Eng.   2312
Plays/librettos/scripts
Gender ideology and the occult in Shakespeare's plays. England. 1590-
1613. Lang.: Eng.   2499

The metaphor of Icarus in Shakespeare's plays about Henry VI.
England. 1589-1595. Lang.: Eng.   2562

Shakespeare's *Henry VI* and treason trials. England. 1585-1592. Lang.:
Eng.   2635

Henry VI — cont'd

The English view of Ireland reflected in Shakespeare's history plays. England. 1590-1599. Lang.: Eng.   2678

Shakespeare's characterization of Richard of Gloucester in *Richard III* and *Henry VI*. England. 1590-1593. Lang.: Eng.   2698

Masculinity and feminine disruption in Shakespeare's history plays. England. 1590-1599. Lang.: Eng.   2732

Henry VI, Part Two
Plays/librettos/scripts
Witchcraft and female sexuality in the plays of Shakespeare. England. 1590-1613. Lang.: Eng.   2717

Henry VIII
Performance/production
The work of director Terence Gray. UK-England: Cambridge. 1925-1940. Lang.: Eng.   2210
Plays/librettos/scripts
The metaphor of Icarus in Shakespeare's plays about Henry VI. England. 1589-1595. Lang.: Eng.   2562

Shakespeare's *Henry VIII* and the debasement of honorable titles. England. 1612-1613. Lang.: Eng.   2624

Politeness in Shakespeare's *Henry VIII*. England. 1612-1613. Lang.: Eng.   2644

Visual imagery and the two queens in Shakespeare's *Henry VIII*. England. 1612-1613. Lang.: Eng.   2660

Henry, Niall
Performance/production
Collection of newspaper reviews by London theatre critics. UK-England: London. 1997. Lang.: Eng.   2052

Hensel, Kerstin
Performance/production
World premieres at Mannheimer Nationaltheater. Germany: Mannheim. 1997. Lang.: Ger.   1697

Playwright Kerstin Hensel. Germany. 1961-1997. Lang.: Ger.   1705

Henslowe, Philip
Administration
Philip Henslowe and the conjurer/astrologer Simon Forman. England: London. 1590-1600. Lang.: Eng.   17

Philip Henslowe's move from the Rose to the Fortune. England: London. 1576-1616. Lang.: Eng.   20
Performance spaces
The debate over the stage design and pillars of Shakespeare's Globe. England: London. 1599-1995. Lang.: Eng.   1525

The building of the Fortune Theatre. England: London. 1600. Lang.: Eng.   1526
Performance/production
Rivalry between acting companies and its influence on plays. England: London. 1594-1600. Lang.: Eng.   1625

Henze, Hans Werner
Institutions
Andreas Delfs, General Music Director of Niedersächsische Staatsoper. Germany: Hannover. 1996-1997. Lang.: Ger.   4047
Performance/production
Productions at the Munich Biennale. Germany: Munich. 1997. Lang.: Ger.   4148

Hans Werner Henze's opera *Das Mädchen mit den Schwefelhölzern*. Germany: Hamburg. 1921-1997. Lang.: Ger.   4156

Hepta epì Thebas (Seven Against Thebes)
Plays/librettos/scripts
Ambivalence about rhetoric in Greek tragedy. Greece. 500-250 B.C. Lang.: Eng.   2877

Her Sister's Tongue
Performance/production
Collection of newspaper reviews by London theatre critics. UK-England: London. 1997. Lang.: Eng.   2085

Her/She Senses Imag(in)ed Malady
Performance/production
Angela Ellsworth and Tina Takemoto's *Her/She Senses Imag(in)ed Malady*. USA. 1991-1997. Lang.: Eng.   3844

Herbal Bed, The
Performance/production
Collection of newspaper reviews by London theatre critics. UK-England: London. 1997. Lang.: Eng.   2031

Michael Attenborough's production of *The Herbal Bed* by Peter Whelan. UK-England: London. 1997. Lang.: Eng.   2198
Plays/librettos/scripts
The character Shakespeare in *The Herbal Bed* by Peter Whelan. UK-England. 1997. Lang.: Eng.   3120

Herbert, Victor
Performance/production
The Metropolitan Opera premiere of Victor Herbert's *Madeleine*. USA: New York, NY. 1907-1995. Lang.: Eng.   4271

Herczog, István
Performance/production
Pécsi Balett's performance of choreographies by István Herczog to music of Bartók. Hungary: Pécs. 1997. Lang.: Hun.   1080

Bartók's stage works presented by Pécsi Balett. Hungary: Pécs. 1992-1997. Lang.: Hun.   1088

Here Lies Henry
Performance/production
Daniel Brooks on his collaboration with Daniel MacIvor on *Here Lies Henry*. Canada: Toronto, ON. 1994-1995. Lang.: Eng.   1578
Plays/librettos/scripts
Playwright Daniel MacIvor. Canada: Halifax, NS. 1990-1997. Lang.: Eng.   2400

Analysis of *Here Lies Henry* by Daniel MacIvor and Daniel Brooks. Canada. 1994-1996. Lang.: Eng.   2437

Herfurthner, Rudolf
Plays/librettos/scripts
Interview with children's theatre playwright Rudolf Herfurthner. Germany. 1947-1997. Lang.: Ger.   2851

Heritage
Performance/production
Collection of newspaper reviews by London theatre critics. UK-England: London. 1997. Lang.: Eng.   2128

Héritage, L' (Inheritance)
Performance/production
History and politics on the Parisian stage. France: Paris. 1997. Lang.: Ger.   1669

Herman, Judy
Performance/production
Collection of newspaper reviews by London theatre critics. UK-England: London. 1997. Lang.: Eng.   2030

Hernandez Espinoza, Eugenio
Plays/librettos/scripts
The 'Black Madonna' in Cuban theatre. Cuba. 1925-1990. Lang.: Spa.   2444

Heroes and Saints
Basic theatrical documents
Anthology of plays by women of color. USA. 1992-1996. Lang.: Eng.   1338

Performance/production
History in recent Chicano/a theatre. USA. 1964-1995. Lang.: Eng.   2360

Herr Puntila und sein Knecht Matti (Herr Puntila and His Man Matti)
Performance/production
Einar Schleef's Berliner Ensemble production of Brecht's *Herr Puntila*. Germany: Berlin. 1996. Lang.: Ger.   1701

Herrell, Heather
Basic theatrical documents
Text of *The Gathering* by Rachael Van Fossen *et al.* Canada: Fort Qu'Appelle, SK. 1997. Lang.: Eng.   3903

Herringbone
Plays/librettos/scripts
Survey of one- or two-character musicals. USA: New York, NY. 1964-1997. Lang.: Eng.   3989

Herrmann, Keith
Performance/production
Collection of newspaper reviews by London theatre critics. UK-England: London. 1997. Lang.: Eng.   2008

Hersey, David
Design/technology
David Hersey's lighting design for revival of *Jesus Christ, Superstar* at the Lyceum. UK-England: London. 1997. Lang.: Eng.   3909

Hertling, Nele
Administration
Hebbel-Theater under Nele Hertling. Germany: Berlin. 1988-1997. Lang.: Ger.   32

Hertzberg, Bertil
Institutions
Funding and the threat to regional theatre. Sweden: Kalmar. 1975-1997. Lang.: Swe.   1475

Hesford, Martyn Edward
Performance/production
Collection of newspaper reviews by London theatre critics. UK-England: London. 1997. Lang.: Eng.   2022

Hesse, Ulrich
Performance/production
Productions at Mülheimer Theatertage. Germany: Mülheim. 1997. Lang.: Ger.   1718

Hesse, Volker
Plays/librettos/scripts
Analysis of Urs Widmer's *Top Dogs*. Germany: Berlin. 1997. Lang.: Ger. 2846

Urs Widmer's *Top Dogs* at Theater Neumarkt. Switzerland: Zurich. 1996. Lang.: Ger. 3066

Heyward, Sandra Ryan
Performance/production
Collection of newspaper reviews by London theatre critics. UK-England. 1997. Lang.: Eng. 2072

Heywood, Thomas
Plays/librettos/scripts
Domestic conflict in early modern English drama. England. 1590-1633. Lang.: Eng. 2508

Accusations of rape in English Renaissance drama. England. 1550-1630. Lang.: Eng. 2526

Domestic cultural and social struggle in Elizabethan theatre. England. 1592-1621. Lang.: Eng. 2571

Narcissism in Renaissance tragedy. England. 1450-1580. Lang.: Eng. 2609

Livy's influence on Shakespeare, Heywood, and Peele. England. 1569-1624. Lang.: Eng. 2629

Critical edition of *King Edward the Fourth* by Thomas Heywood. England. 1600-1626. Lang.: Eng. 2699

Suicide in English Renaissance tragedy. England. 1590-1625. Lang.: Eng. 2724

Analysis of the anonymous *Edward IV*. England. 1599-1600. Lang.: Eng. 2765

Relation to other fields
Conflicts in teaching literary criticism and theory. USA. 1612-1997. Lang.: Eng. 797

Higgs, Timothy
Performance/production
Collection of newspaper reviews by London theatre critics. UK-England: London. 1997. Lang.: Eng. 2059

Highway, Tomson
Performance/production
Native Canadian playwrights and theatre groups. Canada. 1979-1997. Lang.: Eng. 1597

Highways Performance Space (Los Angeles, CA)
Performance/production
Home: The Last Place I Ran to Just About Killed Me by Sacred Naked Nature Girls. USA. 1996. Lang.: Eng. 635

Hikétides (Suppliant Women, The) by Aeschylus
Plays/librettos/scripts
Problems of historical interpretation in Greek tragedy and comedy. Greece. 500-400 B.C. Lang.: Eng. 2887

Hikétides (Suppliant Women, The) by Euripides
Plays/librettos/scripts
Greek history as interpreted in plays of Sophocles and Euripides. Greece. 400-200 B.C. Lang.: Eng. 2870

Rhetoric in Euripidean drama. Greece. 500-300 B.C. Lang.: Eng. 2871

Hilaire, Laurent
Performance/production
Stars of the Paris Opera Ballet. France: Paris. 1983-1997. Lang.: Eng. 1074

Hildegard, Saint
Performance/production
A possible motivation for the writing of *Ordo Virtutum* by Hildegard of Bingen. Germany. 1100-1200. Lang.: Eng. 3870

Hill, Amanda
Performance/production
Collection of newspaper reviews by London theatre critics. UK-England: London. 1997. Lang.: Eng. 2057

Hill, Daniel
Performance/production
Collection of newspaper reviews by London theatre critics. UK-England: London. 1997. Lang.: Eng. 2029

Hill, Gary
Plays/librettos/scripts
Changing relationships of writing, text and performance. UK-England. USA. 1980-1996. Lang.: Eng. 698

Hill, The
Plays/librettos/scripts
Postcolonialism and early plays of Zakes Mda. South Africa, Republic of. 1979-1997. Lang.: Eng. 3029

Hillern, Wilhelmine von
Performance/production
Productions of Schauspiel Stuttgart. Germany: Stuttgart. 1997. Lang.: Ger. 1715

Hillje, Jens
Institutions
Deutsches Theater's venue Baracke and its management. Germany: Berlin. 1997. Lang.: Ger. 1417

Hilpert, Heinz
Performance/production
German theatre during and after the Nazi period. Germany: Berlin, Dusseldorf. Switzerland: Zurich. 1933-1952. Lang.: Eng. 1704

Hindemith, Paul
Plays/librettos/scripts
Analysis of *Sancta Susanna* by Paul Hindemith and August Stramm. USA. 1922-1997. Lang.: Eng. 4318

Hinton, Peter
Design/technology
Background on Ken Garnhum's set design for *Frida K*. Canada: Toronto, ON. 1997. Lang.: Eng. 1354

Hippolyte
Plays/librettos/scripts
Garnier's *Hippolyte* and its source, Seneca's *Phaedra*. France. 1635. Lang.: Eng. 2813

Hippolytos
Plays/librettos/scripts
Translation and the study of Greek tragedy. Greece. 458-400 B.C. Lang.: Eng. 2882

Hiraeth
Basic theatrical documents
Collection of one-act plays by Welsh writers. UK-Wales. 1952-1996. Lang.: Eng. 1321

Hirschfeld, Al
Performance/production
Al Hirschfeld's caricature illustrations of historic musicals. USA: New York, NY. 1903-1997. Lang.: Eng. 3966

Hirst, Steven
Performance/production
Collection of newspaper reviews by London theatre critics. UK-England: London. 1997. Lang.: Eng. 2161

Hispanic theatre
Basic theatrical documents
Text of *Stuff* by Coco Fusco and Nao Bustamante. USA. 1997. Lang.: Eng. 1328

Performance/production
Report on Spanish-American theatre festival. Spain: Cádiz. 1996. Lang.: Spa. 611

Interview with playwright Nilo Cruz. USA: San Francisco, CA. 1995-1997. Lang.: Eng. 2356

History in recent Chicano/a theatre. USA. 1964-1995. Lang.: Eng. 2360

Excerpts from diaries of performance artist Guillermo Gómez-Peña. USA: Los Angeles, CA. 1979-1989. Lang.: Eng. 3828

Plays/librettos/scripts
The female body in plays of Moraga, Fornes, and Cruz. USA. 1980-1991. Lang.: Eng. 3228

Playwright Luis Alfaro. USA: Los Angeles, CA. 1991-1997. Lang.: Eng. 3306

Reference materials
Sourcebook on women playwrights of diversity. USA. 1970-1996. Lang.: Eng. 3320

A biographical directory of Hispanic presence in American film. USA. 1911-1995. Lang.: Eng. 3690

Histoire de France (History of France)
Performance/production
History and politics on the Parisian stage. France: Paris. 1997. Lang.: Ger. 1669

Historiography
SEE
Research/historiography.

Hitchcock, Alfred
Basic theatrical documents
Text of filmscript *North by Northwest* by Ernest Lehman. USA. 1959. Lang.: Eng. 3535

Performance/production
Self-reflexivity in the films of Alfred Hitchcock. USA. 1936-1980. Lang.: Eng. 3604

Plays/librettos/scripts
Interview with screenwriter Ernest Lehman. USA. 1995. Lang.: Eng. 3670

HIV Ensemble (New York, NY)
Institutions
Profile of the educational theatre group HIV Ensemble. USA: New York, NY. 1993-1996. Lang.: Eng. 1503

I Do, I Do
Plays/librettos/scripts
Survey of one- or two-character musicals. USA: New York, NY. 1964-1997. Lang.: Eng. 3989

'I Doubt It', Says Pauline
Performance/production
Collection of newspaper reviews by London theatre critics. UK-England: London. 1997. Lang.: Eng. 2012

I Shall Never Return
SEE
Nigdy tu już nie powrócę.

I Was Real—Documents
Performance/production
Collection of newspaper reviews by London theatre critics. UK-England: London. 1997. Lang.: Eng. 2076

I'll Be Your Dog
Performance/production
Collection of newspaper reviews by London theatre critics. UK-England: London. 1997. Lang.: Eng. 1972

I've Got the Shakes
Design/technology
The scenography of Richard Foreman. USA. 1990-1996. Lang.: Eng. 1362

Ibelhauptaite, Dalia
Performance/production
Collection of newspaper reviews by London theatre critics. UK-England: London. 1997. Lang.: Eng. 2102

Ibrahim, George
Performance/production
Collection of newspaper reviews by London theatre critics. UK-England: London. 1997. Lang.: Eng. 2076

Ibrahim, Ramli
Institutions
Report on Natya Kala festival/conference. India: Chennai. 1996. Lang.: Swe. 950

Ibsen, Henrik
Basic theatrical documents
Slovene translation of Ibsen's *Brand*. Norway. 1865. Lang.: Slo. 1294
Design/technology
Lighting by Peter Mumford for Broadway productions of London shows. USA: New York, NY. 1997. Lang.: Eng. 1367
Performance/production
Autobiographical performances of Elizabeth Robins. USA. 1862-1952. Lang.: Eng. 656
Productions of the Paris-Bruxelles Exhibition. Belgium: Brussels. 1997. Lang.: Eng. 1570
Report on Finnish theatre productions. Finland: Helsinki, Tampere. 1997. Lang.: Eng, Fre. 1654
Productions of Ibsen's *Peer Gynt* by Luca Ronconi and Stéphane Braunschweig. France: Paris. 1996. Lang.: Eng. 1659
Productions of the Paris theatre season. France: Paris. 1996-1997. Lang.: Ger. 1668
Interview with director Stéphane Braunschweig. France: Paris. 1996. Lang.: Eng. 1674
Report on the Paris theatre scene. France: Paris. 1997. Lang.: Swe. 1680
The opening of the Deutsches Schauspielhaus season. Germany: Hamburg. 1997. Lang.: Ger. 1688
Director Frank Castorf. Germany: Berlin. Sweden: Stockholm. 1976. Lang.: Swe. 1700
Performances at Staattheater Mainz's new venue. Germany: Mainz. 1997. Lang.: Ger. 1743
Paolo Sperati, composer of stage music for Ibsen. Italy. Norway. 1856. Lang.: Ita. 1812
Videodisc of Ibsen's *Et Dukkehjem* (*A Doll's House*) combining performance and commentary. Norway. USA. 1879-1997. Lang.: Eng. 1830
Survey of Ibsen stage festival. Norway: Oslo. 1996. Lang.: Eng. 1831
Report on Ibsen festival. Norway: Oslo. 1996. Lang.: Eng. 1832
Collection of newspaper reviews by London theatre critics. UK-England: London. 1997. Lang.: Eng. 2019
Collection of newspaper reviews by London theatre critics. UK-England: London. 1997. Lang.: Eng. 2064
Collection of newspaper reviews by London theatre critics. UK-England: London. 1997. Lang.: Eng. 2104
Collection of newspaper reviews by London theatre critics. UK-England: London. 1997. Lang.: Eng. 2158

The influence of Ibsen and Brecht on Shakespearean staging. UK-England. 1900-1960. Lang.: Eng. 2180
Interview with actor/director Austin Pendleton. USA. 1980-1995. Lang.: Eng. 2266
Productions of plays by Ibsen. USA. France. UK-England. 1996-1997. Lang.: Eng. 2306
Plays/librettos/scripts
Dialectical interaction and visual perception in Ibsen, Strindberg, and Brecht. Europe. 1900-1956. Lang.: Eng. 2797
Ibsen and early modernist theatre. Finland. 1885-1905. Lang.: Eng. 2801
Feminist analysis of women in Ibsen's plays. Finland. 1855-1905. Lang.: Eng. 2802
The single-parent family in plays of Ibsen and Strindberg. Norway. Sweden. 1888-1890. Lang.: Eng. 2983
Interview with director and author Margarete Garpe. Sweden: Stockholm. 1960-1997. Lang.: Swe. 3063
Comparison of Arthur Miller's *The Crucible* and his adaptation of Ibsen's *An Enemy of the People*. USA. 1950-1984. Lang.: Eng. 3126
Mimesis, feminism, theatre, and performance. USA. 1997. Lang.: Eng. 3176
The influence of Ibsen and Greek tragedy on the plays of Arthur Miller. USA. 1915-1996. Lang.: Eng. 3240
Relation to other fields
Ibsen Society of America meeting on Ibsen and the visual arts. USA: New York, NY. 1996. Lang.: Eng. 792

ICA Theatre (London)
Performance/production
Collection of newspaper reviews by London theatre critics. UK-England: London. 1997. Lang.: Eng. 1988
Collection of newspaper reviews by London theatre critics. UK-England: London. 1997. Lang.: Eng. 2019
Collection of newspaper reviews by London theatre critics. UK-England: London. 1997. Lang.: Eng. 2071

Iceman Cometh, The
Plays/librettos/scripts
O'Neill, Williams, and the limits of mimesis. USA. 1913-1980. Lang.: Eng. 3186
Black characters in plays of Eugene O'Neill. USA. 1920-1940. Lang.: Eng. 3248

Ichikawa, Miyabi
Theory/criticism
Japanese analysis of Western choreography. Japan. USA. 1970-1979. Lang.: Eng. 1030

Iconography
Performance spaces
Iconography and the interior design of Shakespeare's Globe Theatre. UK-England: London. 1992-1996. Lang.: Eng. 1538
Performance/production
The effect of costuming on ballet technique. France. 1830-1850. Lang.: Eng. 1071
Relation to other fields
Physical and moral deformity in the Renaissance. England. 1588-1677. Lang.: Eng. 3338

Ideal Husband, An
Performance/production
Collection of newspaper reviews by London theatre critics. UK-England: London. 1997. Lang.: Eng. 2084

Idiot's Delight
Performance/production
The grotesque on the American stage during the Depression. USA. 1929-1940. Lang.: Eng. 2264

Idomeneo
Design/technology
Scenery for Mozart's *Idomeneo* at Bayerische Staatsoper. Germany: Munich. 1996. Lang.: Ger. 4023

If Mr. Frollo Finds Out
Performance/production
Collection of newspaper reviews by London theatre critics. UK-England: London. 1997. Lang.: Eng. 2115

Iizuka, Naomi
Design/technology
Lighting for Humana Festival by Ed McCarthy and Greg Sullivan. USA: Louisville, KY. 1997. Lang.: Eng. 1370

Ikebana
Performance/production
Director Lisa Peterson. USA: Los Angeles, CA. 1997. Lang.: Eng. 2279

Jacob, Abe
  Design/technology
    Amplified sound and the Broadway musical. USA. 1961-1997. Lang.:
    Eng.   3925
Jacobean theatre
  SEE ALSO
    Geographical-Chronological Index under: England, 1603-1625.
  Audience
    Women in the Renaissance theatre audience. England. 1567-1642.
    Lang.: Eng.   1247
  Performance/production
    The doubling and tripling of casting on the early modern stage.
    England. 1598-1610. Lang.: Eng.   1621
  Plays/librettos/scripts
    Sam Shepard's unproduced film adaptation of *The Changeling* by
    Middleton and Rowley. England. USA. 1622-1971. Lang.: Eng.   2490
    The bubonic plague and Shakespeare's plays. England. 1603-1607.
    Lang.: Eng.   2534
    Male and female power in *The Changeling* by Middleton and Rowley.
    England. 1622. Lang.: Eng.   2583
    The Italian palazzo on the Jacobean stage. England. 1603-1625. Lang.:
    Eng.   2625
    Twentieth-century adaptations of Jacobean plays. England. 1604-1986.
    Lang.: Eng.   2673
    Social mobility in Jacobean drama. England. 1618-1640. Lang.: Eng.
                                                                       2745
    Annotations on a script of *The Two Merry Milkmaids*. England. 1620.
    Lang.: Eng.   2754
Jacobi, Derek
  Performance/production
    Derek Jacobi's reception of the Gielgud Award. USA: Washington, DC.
    1997. Lang.: Eng.   2298
Jacobs, Flo
  Performance/production
    Account of a performance of *Febrile Fiber Phantoms* by Ken and Flo
    Jacobs. USA: Cleveland, OH. 1945-1995. Lang.: Eng.   3826
Jacobs, Ken
  Performance/production
    Account of a performance of *Febrile Fiber Phantoms* by Ken and Flo
    Jacobs. USA: Cleveland, OH. 1945-1995. Lang.: Eng.   3826
Jacques Brel Is Alive and Well and Living in Paris
  Performance/production
    Production of *Jacques Brel Is Alive and Well...*, California State
    University. USA: Long Beach, CA. 1996. Lang.: Eng.   3955
Jacques, Brigitte
  Basic theatrical documents
    French translation of Tony Kushner's *Angels in America, Part II:
    Perestroika*. USA. France: Paris. 1996. Lang.: Fre.   1333
Jaguar Jokers (Ghana)
  Plays/librettos/scripts
    West African popular theatre: texts and analysis. Ghana. Togo. Nigeria.
    1995-1997. Lang.: Eng.   2866
Jahn, Burkhard
  Performance spaces
    Production of Harry Schürer's *Space Dream* in a hangar of Tempelhof
    Airport. Germany: Berlin. 1997. Lang.: Ger.   3929
Jahn, Claudia
  Performance/production
    Profile of actress Claudia Jahn. Germany. 1988-1997. Lang.: Ger.   1725
Jakob Ruda
  Plays/librettos/scripts
    Maeterlinck's influence on playwright Ivan Cankar. Slovenia. Lang.: Slo.
                                                                       3007
Jakub a jeho pán
  SEE
    Jacques et son maître.
Jakubowska, Wanda
  Performance/production
    Interview with filmmaker Wanda Jakubowska. Poland. 1948-1997.
    Lang.: Eng.   3582
Jalousie du Barbouillé, La (Jealousy of Barbouillé)
  Plays/librettos/scripts
    Molière, farce, and *La Jalousie du Barbouillé*. France. 1450-1820. Lang.:
    Eng.   2821
Jam session
  Basic theatrical documents
    Texts of plays by Goran Gluvić. Slovenia. 1980-1997. Lang.: Slo.   1296

James, Henry
  Basic theatrical documents
    Text of Hossein Amini's film adaptation of *The Wings of the Dove* by
    Henry James. UK-England. 1995-1997. Lang.: Eng.   3528
  Performance/production
    Interview with director Iain Softley. UK-England. 1995-1997. Lang.:
    Eng.   3589
  Plays/librettos/scripts
    Interview with Hossein Amini, author of the filmscript *The Wings of the
    Dove*. UK-England. 1995-1997. Lang.: Eng.   3643
  Relation to other fields
    Theatrical aspects of fiction by Henry James. USA. 1870-1910. Lang.:
    Eng.   3433
James, Polly
  Performance/production
    Collection of newspaper reviews by London theatre critics. UK-England:
    London. 1997. Lang.: Eng.   2066
Jameson, Karin
  Training
    Interview with dancer/teacher Karin Jameson. Sweden: Stockholm.
    USA: New York, NY. 1992. Lang.: Swe.   1044
Jamieson, Daniel
  Performance/production
    Collection of newspaper reviews by London theatre critics. UK-England:
    London. 1997. Lang.: Eng.   2004
Janáček, Leoš
  Performance/production
    Problem of staging the works of Janáček. Czech Republic. 1854-1928.
    Lang.: Cze.   4118
Jančar, Drago
  Basic theatrical documents
    Text of *Halštat (Halstatt)* by Drago Jančar. Slovenia. 1994. Lang.: Slo.
                                                                       1297
    English translations of plays by contemporary Slovenian playwrights.
    Slovenia. 1980-1997. Lang.: Slo.   1301
  Plays/librettos/scripts
    Analysis of Drago Jančar's *Veliki briljantni valček (Grande Polonaise
    Brillante)*. Slovenia. 1985. Lang.: Slo.   3019
Jane Eyre
  Performance/production
    Collection of newspaper reviews by London theatre critics. UK-England:
    London. 1997. Lang.: Eng.   2111
    Comparison of productions of *Ragtime* and *Jane Eyre*. Canada:
    Toronto, ON. 1997. Lang.: Eng.   3932
  Plays/librettos/scripts
    Stage adaptations of novels. USA. 1997. Lang.: Eng.   702
Janek's Tale
  Performance/production
    Collection of newspaper reviews by London theatre critics. UK-England:
    London. 1997. Lang.: Eng.   2011
Janin, Jules
  Theory/criticism
    Ballet criticism of Jules Janin. France. 1832-1850. Lang.: Eng.   1135
Jannings, Emil
  Performance/production
    Film actor Emil Jannings. Germany. 1929-1945. Lang.: Eng.   3574
Janovics, Jenő
  Performance/production
    Jenő Janovics and Imre Madách's *Az ember tragédiája (The Tragedy of
    Man)*. Hungary. Kolozsvár. Romania: Cluj. 1894-1945. Lang.: Hun.
                                                                       1767
Janovskaja, Genrietta
  Institutions
    Groza (The Storm), based on works of Ostrovskij, directed for young
    audiences at Teat'r Junogo Zritelja. Russia: Moscow. 1996. Lang.: Rus.
                                                                       1463
Janssen, Thomas
  Institutions
    Staatstheater Darmstadt under the direction of Gerd-Theo Umberg.
    Germany: Darmstadt. 1996-1997. Lang.: Ger.   1412
Jansson, Olle
  Performance/production
    Interview with actor Olle Jansson. Sweden: Stockholm. 1985-1997.
    Lang.: Swe.   1950
Jaoui, Agnès
  Audience
    The audience for Sortie 22's *Un air de famille (A Family Resemblance)*.
    Canada: Montreal, PQ. 1997. Lang.: Fre.   1244
Jarman, Derek
  Performance/production
    How film and video versions of Shakespeare's plays may reinforce
    textual authority rather than challenge it. UK-England. 1979-1991.
    Lang.: Eng.   3510

Jarman, Derek — cont'd

Plays/librettos/scripts

The appropriation of Shakespeare by the dispossessed and marginalized. 1590-1995. Lang.: Eng. 2366

Re-evaluation of Jarman's screen version of *The Tempest*. UK-England. 1979. Lang.: Eng. 3649

Jarocki, Jerzy

Performance/production

Analysis of Jerzy Grotowski's *Apocalypsis cum figuris*. Poland. 1964-1992. Lang.: Pol. 581

Biography of actress Anna Dymna. Poland: Cracow. 1950-1997. Lang.: Pol. 1835

Jerzy Jarocki's productions of *Ślub (The Wedding)* by Witold Gombrowicz. Poland. 1960-1991. Lang.: Pol. 1842

Actor Jan Nowicki. Poland: Cracow. 1939-1997. Lang.: Pol. 1850

Čechov's *Platonov* adapted by Jerzy Jarocki, Teatr Polski. Poland: Wrocław. 1993-1997. Lang.: Eng, Fre. 1854

Jarry, Alfred

Basic theatrical documents

Libretto of Ligeti's opera *Le Grand Macabre*. Europe. 1978-1997. Lang.: Fre, Eng. 4008

Performance/production

Collection of newspaper reviews by London theatre critics. UK-England: London. 1997. Lang.: Eng. 2032

Plays/librettos/scripts

György Ligeti on his opera *Le Grand Macabre*. Sweden. 1978. Lang.: Fre. 4312

Jarvis, Andrew

Performance/production

Collection of newspaper reviews by London theatre critics. UK-England: London. 1997. Lang.: Eng. 1975

Jasager, Der (He Who Says Yes)

Plays/librettos/scripts

Contemporary playwrights and the adaptation process. Europe. 1900-1993. Lang.: Ita. 2793

Jasieński, Bruno

Performance/production

The production of *The Mannequin's Ball* by Bruno Jasieński. Russia. 1931. Lang.: Eng. 591

Poet and playwright Bruno Jasieński. Russia. 1901-1977. Lang.: Eng. 592

English translation of Lunačarskij's introduction to *Bal Manekinov (The Mannequin's Ball)* by Bruno Jasieński. Russia. 1931. Lang.: Eng. 597

Játékszín (Budapest)

SEE

Magyar Játékszín.

Jealous Wife, The

Plays/librettos/scripts

Frances Sheridan's *The Discovery* in the context of eighteenth-century theatre. England. 1740-1780. Lang.: Eng. 2451

Jedermann (Everyman)

Performance/production

Max Reinhardt's productions of *Jedermann (Everyman)* by Hugo von Hofmannsthal. Austria: Salzburg. Germany: Berlin. 1911-1920. Lang.: Pol. 1565

Jefferies, Annalee

Performance/production

Actress Annalee Jefferies. USA: Houston, TX. 1986-1997. Lang.: Eng. 2237

Jefferson, Margo

Relation to other fields

Theatre critic and theorist Margo Jefferson on the Robert Brustein/August Wilson debate. USA: New York, NY. 1960-1997. Lang.: Eng. 791

Jefford, Barbara

Performance/production

Reactions to modern performances of *Antony and Cleopatra*. UK-England. North America. 1827-1987. Lang.: Eng. 2178

Jeffrey

Plays/librettos/scripts

Analysis of *Jeffrey* by Paul Rudnick. USA. 1992. Lang.: Eng. 3239

Jeffries, Chris

Performance/production

Seattle Children's Theatre's production of *Bunnicula*. USA: Seattle, WA. 1979-1996. Lang.: Eng. 2311

Jefimov, Andrej

Performance/production

Puppeteer and director Andrej Jefimov. Russia: Ekaterinburg. 1990-1997. Lang.: Rus. 4369

Jefimovskaja, E.

Performance/production

Portraits of actors in children's theatre. Russia: Volgograd. 1990-1997. Lang.: Rus. 589

Jéfremov, Oleg Nikolajévič

Performance/production

Current productions of plays by Čechov. Russia: Moscow. 1940-1997. Lang.: Eng. 1856

Memoirs of director Oleg Jéfremov. Russia. 1960-1997. Lang.: Rus. 1874

Její pastorkyňa (Jenůfa)

Performance/production

Interpretations of Czech classics by Petr Lébl and Vladimír Morávek. Czech Republic. 1997. Lang.: Cze. 1609

Jekyll & Hyde: The Musical

Design/technology

Lighting designer Beverly Emmons. USA: New York, NY. 1960-1997. Lang.: Eng. 254

Beverly Emmons' lighting design for the Broadway musical *Jekyll & Hyde*. USA: New York, NY. 1886-1997. Lang.: Eng. 3924

Jelinek, Elfriede

Institutions

Bruncken directs Jelinek at Theatertreffen. Germany: Berlin. 1997. Lang.: Swe. 1419

Performance/production

Interview with director George Tabori. Austria: Vienna. 1997. Lang.: Ger. 1562

Productions at Mülheimer Theatertage. Germany: Mülheim. 1997. Lang.: Ger. 1718

Contemporary plays at Schauspiel Leipzig. Germany: Leipzig. 1996-1997. Lang.: Ger. 1736

Plays/librettos/scripts

Playwright Elfriede Jelinek on her use of philosophical quotations. Austria. 1750-1997. Lang.: Ger, Fre, Dut, Eng. 2382

Feminist aspects of plays by Elfriede Jelinek. Germany. Austria. 1989-1997. Lang.: Pol. 2854

Trends in contemporary German-language drama. Germany. Austria. Switzerland. 1997. Lang.: Ger. 2859

Jenkin, Len

Basic theatrical documents

Text of *Like I Say* by Len Jenkin. USA. 1997. Lang.: Eng. 1330

Text of *Doctor Devine Presents*, a carnival scenario by Len Jenkin and John Arnone. USA. 1993. Lang.: Eng. 3781

Performance/production

Analysis of *Like I Say* by Len Jenkin. USA: San Diego, CA. 1997. Lang.: Eng. 2315

Plays/librettos/scripts

Televisual dramaturgy in the work of some contemporary playwrights. USA. 1990-1997. Lang.: Eng. 3191

Jennefelt, Thomas

Plays/librettos/scripts

Thomas Jennefelt's new opera *Farkosten*. Sweden. 1985-1997. Lang.: Swe. 4313

Jenness, Morgan

Performance/production

Interview with dramaturg Morgan Jenness. USA. 1979-1996. Lang.: Eng. 2338

Jensen, Julie

Plays/librettos/scripts

Profile of playwright Julie Jensen. USA: Las Vegas, NV. 1970-1997. Lang.: Eng. 3180

Jepson, Paul

Performance/production

Collection of newspaper reviews by London theatre critics. UK-England: London. 1997. Lang.: Eng. 2069

Jermyn Street Theatre (London)

Performance/production

Collection of newspaper reviews by London theatre critics. UK-England: London. 1997. Lang.: Eng. 1984

Collection of newspaper reviews by London theatre critics. UK-England: London. 1997. Lang.: Eng. 1997

Collection of newspaper reviews by London theatre critics. UK-England: London. 1997. Lang.: Eng. 2030

Collection of newspaper reviews by London theatre critics. UK-England: London. 1997. Lang.: Eng. 2091

Collection of newspaper reviews by London theatre critics. UK-England: London. 1997. Lang.: Eng. 2111

Jerrold, Douglas
Plays/librettos/scripts
Nautical melodrama and traditional authority structures. UK-England. 1804-1850. Lang.: Eng. 3072

Jesse H. Jones Hall for the Performing Arts (Houston, TX)
Performance spaces
The renovation of the Jesse H. Jones Hall for the Performing Arts. USA: Houston, TX. 1966-1997. Lang.: Eng. 459

Jessner, Irene
Performance/production
Obituary for soprano Irene Jessner. Canada. 1901-1994. Lang.: Eng. 4105

Jesuit theatre
Plays/librettos/scripts
Analysis of *Regnum Humanitatis* by Jacob Grester. Germany. 1585-1600. Lang.: Eng. 2840

Jesus Christ Superstar
Design/technology
David Hersey's lighting design for revival of *Jesus Christ, Superstar* at the Lyceum. UK-England: London. 1997. Lang.: Eng. 3909
Performance spaces
The renovation of the Lyceum Theatre for *Jesus Christ Superstar*. UK-England: London. 1904-1997. Lang.: Eng. 3931

Jeune femme cherche homme, désespérément (Young Woman Desperately Seeking Man)
Plays/librettos/scripts
Characters in recently produced plays of Carole Tremblay and Michel Marc Bouchard. Canada. 1997. Lang.: Fre. 2417

Jévstignejév, Jévgenij
Performance/production
Portraits of stage and film actors. Russia. 1960-1997. Lang.: Rus. 1896

Jew of Malta, The
Plays/librettos/scripts
The nature of Christopher Marlowe's dramaturgy. England. 1585-1593. Lang.: Eng. 2454
Racial and national meanings and economic practice in Renaissance theatre. England. 1590-1650. Lang.: Eng. 2693

Jewel Box Revue (Miami, FL)
Institutions
History of the Jewel Box Revue, a touring drag show. USA: Miami, FL. 1939-1975. Lang.: Eng. 3760

Jewell, Nelson
Institutions
Profile of the educational theatre group HIV Ensemble. USA: New York, NY. 1993-1996. Lang.: Eng. 1503

Jewish theatre
SEE ALSO
Yiddish theatre.
Performance/production
Jewish themes on Czech stages in recent years. Czech Republic. 1997. Lang.: Cze. 1616
Politics and Michal Weichert, director of Jewish theatre. Poland. 1939-1958. Lang.: Pol. 1851
The performance of Jewish characters on the American stage. USA. 1860-1920. Lang.: Eng. 2261
Plays/librettos/scripts
Jewish persecution and identity in works of Max Frisch and Arthur Miller. Switzerland. 1961. Lang.: Eng. 3064
Texts of plays by Jewish American women. USA. 1985-1995. Lang.: Eng. 3164

Jewish Theatre of New York (New York, NY)
Performance/production
Tuvia Tenenbom's staging of *Love Letters to Adolf Hitler* for Jewish Theatre of New York. USA: New York, NY. 1938-1996. Lang.: Eng. 2337

Jeyasingh, Shobana
Performance/production
Cultural stereotyping and the Shobana Jeyasingh Dance Company. UK-England. 1997. Lang.: Eng. 1189
Profile of choreographer Shobana Jeyasingh. UK-England. 1988-1997. Lang.: Eng. 1195

Jitney
Plays/librettos/scripts
Interview with playwright August Wilson. USA. 1985-1997. Lang.: Eng. 3276
Playwright August Wilson's views on the northward migration of Blacks. USA. 1997. Lang.: Eng. 3277

Jó tündér, A (Good Fairy, The)
Performance/production
István Verebes' production of Molnár's *A Jó tündér (The Good Fairy)*. Hungary: Budapest. 1996. Lang.: Hun. 1772

Jobling, Ed
Performance/production
Collection of newspaper reviews by London theatre critics. UK-England: London. 1997. Lang.: Eng. 2015

Jocasta
Performance/production
Collection of newspaper reviews by London theatre critics. UK-England: London. 1997. Lang.: Eng. 2119

Jodelle, Etienne
Plays/librettos/scripts
Male and female Renaissance writers. Europe. 1400-1590. Lang.: Eng. 2785

Jodorowsky, Brontis
Performance/production
Interviews with the cast of Théâtre du Soleil's *Les Atrides*. France: Paris. 1992. Lang.: Eng. 1677

Joe Turner's Come and Gone
Plays/librettos/scripts
African-American cultural archetypes in the plays of August Wilson. USA. 1982-1995. Lang.: Eng. 3179
Playwright August Wilson's views on the northward migration of Blacks. USA. 1997. Lang.: Eng. 3277

Joglars, Els (Barcelona)
Performance/production
Politics in Barcelona theatre. Spain: Barcelona. 1996. Lang.: Eng. 608
Catalan drama on the Madrid stage. Spain: Madrid. 1996. Lang.: Eng. 1919

Johan Gabriel Borkman
Performance/production
Performances at Staattheater Mainz's new venue. Germany: Mainz. 1997. Lang.: Ger. 1743
Interview with actor/director Austin Pendleton. USA. 1980-1995. Lang.: Eng. 2266
Productions of plays by Ibsen. USA. France. UK-England. 1996-1997. Lang.: Eng. 2306

Johansson, Dan
Performance/production
Interview with actor Dan Johansson of Fria Teatern. Sweden: Stockholm. 1993. Lang.: Swe. 1930

John and Jen
Plays/librettos/scripts
Survey of one- or two-character musicals. USA: New York, NY. 1964-1997. Lang.: Eng. 3989

John Gabriel Borkman
SEE
Johan Gabriel Borkman.

Johnny Johnson
Performance/production
Kurt Weill's collaborations with playwrights. Germany: Berlin. USA: New York, NY. 1927-1945. Lang.: Eng. 3934

Johnson, B.S.
Plays/librettos/scripts
Hans-Ulrich Becker's production of *Lebensabend (Life's Evening)*. Germany. 1933-1997. Lang.: Ger. 2848

Johnson, Bernard
Design/technology
Costumer, choreographer, director Bernard Johnson. USA: New York, NY. 1997. Lang.: Eng. 234

Johnson, Charles
Basic theatrical documents
Text of *Love in a Forest*, an adaptation of *As You Like It* by Charles Johnson. England. 1723. Lang.: Eng. 1265
Plays/librettos/scripts
Comparison of Shakespeare's *As You Like It* and Charles Johnson's adaptation *Love in a Forest*. England. 1598-1723. Lang.: Eng. 2654

Johnson, Georgia Douglas
Plays/librettos/scripts
Simultaneous discourse in works by African-American women. USA. 1900-1993. Lang.: Eng. 3260

Johnson, Samuel
Plays/librettos/scripts
Samuel Johnson on Shakespeare's *As You Like It*. England. 1598. Lang.: Eng. 2599
Relation to other fields
Opera and social decline. England: London. 1698-1737. Lang.: Eng. 4321

Johnson, Terry
Performance/production
Collection of newspaper reviews by London theatre critics. UK-England: London. 1997. Lang.: Eng. 2029

Johnson, Yvonne A.K.
Performance/production
Collection of newspaper reviews by London theatre critics. UK-England: London. 1997. Lang.: Eng. 2086

Joint Stock Theatre Group (London)
Plays/librettos/scripts
The relationship of creators and their work in devised theatre. UK-England. 1989. Lang.: Eng. 3083

Women and theatrical collaboration. USA. UK-England. 1930-1990. Lang.: Eng. 3264

Jonas, Joan
Performance/production
Interviews and documents on performance concepts and practices. USA. 1952-1994. Lang.: Eng. 649

Jonas, Peter
Institutions
Nationaltheater under Peter Jonas' leadership. Germany: Munich. 1997. Lang.: Ger. 323

Jonathan, Mark
Design/technology
Lighting designer Mark Jonathan. UK-England: London. 1997. Lang.: Eng. 1360

Jones, Alex
Performance/production
Collection of newspaper reviews by London theatre critics. UK-England: London. 1997. Lang.: Eng. 2021

Jones, Bill T.
Performance/production
The body and cultural identity in contemporary dance. USA. 1985-1995. Lang.: Eng. 996
Theory/criticism
The debate over what does and does not constitute dance. USA. 1995-1996. Lang.: Eng. 1037

Jones, Charlotte
Performance/production
Collection of newspaper reviews by London theatre critics. UK-England: London. 1997. Lang.: Eng. 1991

Jones, Cherry
Performance/production
Actress Cherry Jones. USA: Washington, DC. 1992-1996. Lang.: Eng. 2317

Jones, David
Performance/production
Harold Pinter's performance in his own play *The Hothouse*. UK-England: Chichester. 1996. Lang.: Eng. 2205

Jones, Gari
Performance/production
Collection of newspaper reviews by London theatre critics. UK-England: London. 1997. Lang.: Eng. 1990

Collection of newspaper reviews by London theatre critics. UK-England: London. 1997. Lang.: Eng. 2156

Jones, Inigo
Design/technology
Review of *The Stage Designs of Inigo Jones* by John Peacock. England. 1605-1995. Lang.: Eng. 155

Jones, Jeffrey M.
Performance/production
Collection of newspaper reviews by London theatre critics. UK-England: London. 1997. Lang.: Eng. 1999

Jones, Joni L.
Relation to other fields
Joni L. Jones's performance piece *sista docta*. USA. 1994-1997. Lang.: Eng. 819

Jones, LeRoi
SEE
Baraka, Imamu Amiri.

Jones, Margo
Plays/librettos/scripts
Tennessee Williams' relationship with directors of his plays. USA. 1944-1980. Lang.: Eng. 3241

Jones, Marie
Performance/production
Collection of newspaper reviews by London theatre critics. UK-England: London. 1997. Lang.: Eng. 2005

Jones, Richard
Design/technology
Stewart Laing's set and costume designs for the musical *Titanic*. USA: New York, NY. 1997. Lang.: Eng. 3914

Jones, Tom
Plays/librettos/scripts
Survey of one- or two-character musicals. USA: New York, NY. 1964-1997. Lang.: Eng. 3989

Jonson, Ben
Audience
Early modern comedy and the mixing of classes in the audience. England. 1590-1615. Lang.: Eng. 1248
Performance/production
The festive context of Jonson's *Bartholomew Fair*. England. 1600-1608. Lang.: Eng. 1628

Collection of newspaper reviews by London theatre critics. UK-England. 1997. Lang.: Eng. 2163
Plays/librettos/scripts
The domination of a king by his counselors in Jacobean political tragedy. England: London. 1603-1610. Lang.: Eng. 2448

Defense of Jonson's character Celia in *Volpone*. England. 1607. Lang.: Eng. 2455

Female homoeroticism on the early English stage. England. 1594-1632. Lang.: Eng. 2482

Analysis of Ben Jonson's *The Devil Is an Ass*. England. 1616. Lang.: Eng. 2538

Analysis of plays of Ben Jonson. England. 1598-1637. Lang.: Eng. 2592

Jonson's reference to a 'madam with a dildo' in *The Alchemist*. England. 1593-1632. Lang.: Eng. 2602

Dryden's prologue to *Albumazar* by Thomas Tomkis. England. 1612-1668. Lang.: Eng. 2643

History of the printings of Jonson's *Every Man in His Humour*. England: London. 1601-1616. Lang.: Eng. 2711

Jonson's *Tale of a Tub* as a political critique. England. 1633. Lang.: Eng. 2723

The idea of the self in the English Renaissance. England. 1580-1620. Lang.: Eng. 2728

The Tempest as Shakespeare's response to *The Alchemist* by Ben Jonson. England: London. 1600-1610. Lang.: Eng. 2733

Ben Jonson's view of himself in *The Poetaster*. England. 1601. Lang.: Eng. 2734

Male and female Renaissance writers. Europe. 1400-1590. Lang.: Eng. 2785

Relation to other fields
Ben Jonson's personal copy of Petrarch's *Opera omnia*. England. 1581-1994. Lang.: Eng. 3339

Jordan, Neil
Performance/production
History of Irish filmmaking. Ireland: Dublin. 1896-1996. Lang.: Eng. 3578

Jordán, Tamás
Performance/production
Interview with actor Tamás Jordán, founder of Merlin Színház. Hungary. 1960-1997. Lang.: Hun. 1776

Jory, Jon
Design/technology
Set designer Paul Owen. USA: Louisville, KY. 1997. Lang.: Eng. 1378

Josefsson, Lena
Performance/production
Choreographer Lena Josefsson. Sweden: Örebro, Stockholm. 1997. Lang.: Swe. 1185

Joseph and the Amazing Technicolor Dreamcoat
Design/technology
Scenic machine control systems used in musical productions at the Colosseum. Germany: Essen. 1997. Lang.: Ger. 3907
Performance spaces
The history of the Colosseum and its new interior design. Germany: Essen. 1900-1997. Lang.: Ger. 3930

Joseph Papp Public Theatre (New York, NY)
SEE
Public Theatre.

Joseph, Nick
Performance/production
Collection of newspaper reviews by London theatre critics. UK-England: London. 1997. Lang.: Eng. 2054

Joseph, Phillip
Performance/production
Collection of newspaper reviews by London theatre critics. UK-England: London. 1997. Lang.: Eng. 2116

Jussi Björlingmuseet (Borlänge)
  Institutions
    Profile of the Jussi Björling Museum. Sweden: Borlänge. 1994. Lang.:
    Swe. 4056

Just the Boys
  Basic theatrical documents
    Text of plays performed at the Nuyorican Poets Cafe. USA: New York,
    NY. 1973-1990. Lang.: Eng. 1322

K'Far
  Performance/production
    Collection of newspaper reviews by London theatre critics. UK-England:
    London. 1997. Lang.: Eng. 2071

Kabale und Liebe (Intrigue and Love)
  Performance/production
    Updated classics at Schauspiel Leipzig. Germany: Leipzig. 1996-1997.
    Lang.: Ger. 1712

Kabuki
  SEE ALSO
    Classed Entries under DANCE-DRAMA—*Kabuki*.
  Performance spaces
    Profile of the renovated *kabuki* theatre Kanamaru-za. Japan: Kotohira.
    1830-1995. Lang.: Eng. 1230
  Performance/production
    Exhibition catalogue and essays on the influence of Japanese theatre.
    Japan. 1997. Lang.: Eng. 569
    The development of Japanese theatrical genres. Japan. 500-1997. Lang.:
    Eng. 1224
    Contrast and comparison of Eastern and Western acting styles. Japan.
    Europe. 1150-1997. Lang.: Eng. 1822
  Plays/librettos/scripts
    Nō and *kabuki* elements in plays of Edward Bond. UK-England. 1980-
    1990. Lang.: Eng. 3105

Kacsóh, Pongrác
  Plays/librettos/scripts
    The development of operetta. Austro-Hungarian Empire: Vienna,
    Budapest. 1850-1930. Lang.: Hun. 4339

Kádár, János Miklós
  Design/technology
    Interview with opera set designer János Miklós Kádár. Hungary. 1954-
    1997. Lang.: Hun. 4024

Kafka, Franz
  Performance/production
    Collection of newspaper reviews by London theatre critics. UK-England:
    London. 1997. Lang.: Eng. 1998
  Plays/librettos/scripts
    Elizabeth Albahaca's *Le Procès (The Trial)* an adaptation of Kafka's
    Der Prozess. Canada: Montreal, PQ. 1997. Lang.: Fre. 2435

Kagel, Mauricio
  Plays/librettos/scripts
    The development of non-literary opera. Germany. 1970-1997. Lang.:
    Ger. 4296

Kahan, Bente
  Performance/production
    Collection of newspaper reviews by London theatre critics. UK-England:
    London. 1997. Lang.: Eng. 2059

Kahn, Barbara
  Plays/librettos/scripts
    Texts of plays by Jewish American women. USA. 1985-1995. Lang.:
    Eng. 3164

Kahn, Michael
  Performance/production
    Directors Michael Kahn and Karin Coonrod on their productions of
    Henry VI. USA: New York, NY, Washington, DC. 1950-1996. Lang.
    :Eng. 2312

Kaiser, Georg
  Basic theatrical documents
    English translations of German Expressionist plays. Germany. 1900-
    1920. Lang.: Eng. 1284
  Performance/production
    Kurt Weill's collaborations with playwrights. Germany: Berlin. USA:
    New York, NY. 1927-1945. Lang.: Eng. 3934

Kaitaisha (Tokyo)
  Performance/production
    Women in Japanese theatre. Japan: Tokyo. 1970-1996. Lang.: Eng. 568

Kalidasa
  Performance/production
    Collection of newspaper reviews by London theatre critics. UK-England:
    London. 1997. Lang.: Eng. 1996
  Plays/librettos/scripts
    Translations of the verse drama of Kalidasa. Slovenia. 1885-1908.
    Lang.: Slo. 3020

Kalkutta, 4. Mai. (Calcutta, May 4)
  Plays/librettos/scripts
    Portrayals of colonial governor Warren Hastings in plays of
    Feuchtwanger and Brecht. Germany. 1916-1927. Lang.: Eng. 2836

Kálmán, Imre
  Plays/librettos/scripts
    The development of operetta. Austro-Hungarian Empire: Vienna,
    Budapest. 1850-1930. Lang.: Hun. 4339

Kalman, Jean
  Design/technology
    Jean Kalman's lighting design for *Eugene Onegin*, Metropolitan Opera.
    USA: New York, NY. 1997. Lang.: Eng. 4033

Kálmán, Oszkár
  Performance/production
    Bass Oszkár Kálmán of the Budapest Opera House. Hungary: Budapest.
    1887-1971. Lang.: Hun. 4174

Kamal Theatre
  SEE
    Tatarskij Gosudarstvénnyj Akademičéskij Teat'r im. Kamala.

Kameneckij, V.
  Performance/production
    Portraits of actors in children's theatre. Russia: Volgograd. 1990-1997.
    Lang.: Rus. 589

Kameri (Tel Aviv)
  Performance/production
    The role of the implied spectator in productions of Omri Nitzan and
    Hillel Mittelpunkt. Israel: Tel Aviv. 1993. Lang.: Eng. 1792

Kamiński, Jan Nepomucen
  Plays/librettos/scripts
    The image of Lvov in Polish drama. Poland. 1700-1939. Lang.: Pol. 697

Kamiński, Kazimierz
  Performance/production
    Guest performances in Polish cities. Poland: Cracow, Lvov, Warsaw.
    1810-1915. Lang.: Pol. 583

Kammerspiele (Magdeburg)
  Performance/production
    Russian, Hungarian and Bulgarian plays at Kammerspiele. Germany:
    Magdeburg. 1989. Lang.: Ger. 1710

Kamondi, Zoltán
  Performance/production
    Zoltán Kamondi's experimental theatre at Csarnok Kultusz Motel.
    Hungary: Miskolc. 1996-1997. Lang.: Hun. 554

Kampen, Claire van
  Performance spaces
    Profile of Shakespeare's Globe Theatre. UK-England: London. 1970.
    Lang.: Swe. 1541

Kampnagel-Fabrik (Hamburg)
  Institutions
    Independent and avant-garde theatre at Kampnagel-Fabrik. Germany:
    Hamburg. 1997. Lang.: Ger. 318

Kamraterna (Comrades)
  Performance/production
    Reviews of Bochumer Schauspielhaus productions. Germany: Bochum.
    1997. Lang.: Ger. 1730

Kanamaru-za (Kotohira)
  Performance spaces
    Profile of the renovated *kabuki* theatre Kanamaru-za. Japan: Kotohira.
    1830-1995. Lang.: Eng. 1230

Kandel, Karen
  Performance/production
    Career of performer Karen Kandel. USA: New York, NY. 1977-1997.
    Lang.: Eng. 663

Kander, John
  Performance/production
    Collection of newspaper reviews by London theatre critics. UK-England:
    London. 1997. Lang.: Eng. 2140
    Work of choreographer Susan Stroman on *Steel Pier*. USA: New York,
    NY. 1975-1997. Lang.: Eng. 3956
    Handelian countertenor David Sabella, currently performing in musical
    theatre. USA: New York, NY. 1996. Lang.: Eng. 3960
  Plays/librettos/scripts
    Interviews with authors of Tony Award-winning shows. USA: New
    York, NY. 1997. Lang.: Eng. 3985
    Songwriting team John Kander and Fred Ebb. USA: New York, NY.
    1927-1997. Lang.: Eng. 4001

Kane, David
  Performance/production
    Collection of newspaper reviews by London theatre critics. UK-England:
    London. 1997. Lang.: Eng. 2091

Kane, Sarah
Performance/production
Collection of newspaper reviews by London theatre critics. UK-England: London. 1997. Lang.: Eng.   2129

Kanin, Garson
Plays/librettos/scripts
Adaptations of the diary of Anne Frank. Netherlands. USA. 1945-1997. Lang.: Eng.   2978

Kantor, Tadeusz
Institutions
The work of Théâtre Demodesastr. France. 1995. Lang.: Eng.   315
Performance/production
Analysis of Jerzy Grotowski's *Apocalypsis cum figuris*. Poland. 1964-1992. Lang.: Pol.   581
The life and work of theatre artist Tadeusz Kantor. Poland. 1915-1992. Lang.: Pol.   584
Archival materials relating to director Tadeusz Kantor. Poland: Cracow. 1943-1997. Lang.: Pol.   585
Plays/librettos/scripts
Representational practices of mid-twentieth century avant-garde theatre. North America. Europe. 1950-1990. Lang.: Eng.   696
Temporality in theatrical production. Europe. 1990-1997. Lang.: Ger, Fre, Dut, Eng.   2791

Kapoor, Ravi
Performance/production
Collection of newspaper reviews by London theatre critics. UK-England: London. 1997. Lang.: Eng.   2031

Kaprow, Allan
Performance/production
Allan Kaprow on Happenings. USA. 1980-1996. Lang.: Eng.   3831
Plays/librettos/scripts
Representational practices of mid-twentieth century avant-garde theatre. North America. Europe. 1950-1990. Lang.: Eng.   696

Karamazov Brothers, Flying
SEE
Flying Karamazov Brothers.

Karantanska tragedija (Carinthian Tragedy)
Plays/librettos/scripts
Analysis of *Karantanska tragedija (Carinthian Tragedy)* by Radivoj Rehar. Slovenia. 1836-1996. Lang.: Slo.   3015

Karasek, Daniel
Performance/production
Productions of Staatstheater Wiesbaden. Germany: Wiesbaden. 1997. Lang.: Ger.   1709

Karbus, Oliver
Performance/production
Performances of the classics in Franconia. Germany. 1997. Lang.: Ger.   1737

Karl Marx
Performance/production
Productions of the Paris theatre season. France: Paris. 1996-1997. Lang.: Ger.   1668

Karl Marx Theatre (Saratov)
SEE
Oblastnoj Dramatičeskij Teat'r im. K. Marksa.

Karlstad Teater
Performance spaces
Profile of the restored Karlstad Teater. Sweden: Karlstad. 1876. Lang.: Swe.   4069

Karmakar, Romuald
Performance/production
Significant productions in Swabia. Germany: Stuttgart. 1997. Lang.: Ger.   1726

Karnad, Girish
Performance/production
Profile of Prasanna, director and teacher. India: New Delhi, Heggodu. 1970. Lang.: Swe.   1782

Karter, Tommy
Institutions
Unions in Copenhagen's theatres. Denmark: Copenhagen. 1997. Lang.: Swe.   1400

Kartun, Mauricio
Performance/production
Collection of newspaper reviews by London theatre critics. UK-England: London. 1997. Lang.: Eng.   2146

Kasimir und Karoline (Kasimir and Karoline)
Performance/production
Major productions of the Vienna theatre season. Austria: Vienna. 1997. Lang.: Ger.   1563

The theatre of director Christoph Marthaler. Germany. 1980-1997. Lang.: Ger, Fre, Dut, Eng.   1692
Actor Josef Bierbichler. Germany: Hamburg. 1997. Lang.: Ger.   1707
Recent productions of plays by Horváth. Germany. Austria. 1996-1997. Lang.: Ger.   1722
Interview with director Christoph Marthaler and set designer Anna Viebrock. Germany. Switzerland. 1980-1997. Lang.: Ger.   1723

Kassai Thália Színház
SEE
Thália Színház (Kosiče).

Kassai, Amy
Performance/production
Collection of newspaper reviews by London theatre critics. UK-England: London. 1997. Lang.: Eng.   2044

Kat and the Kings
Performance/production
Collection of newspaper reviews by London theatre critics. UK-England: London. 1997. Lang.: Eng.   2115

Katatsumuri no Kai (Japan)
Basic theatrical documents
English translation of *Ashi no Aru Shitai (A Corpse with Feet)* by Minoru Betsuyaku. Japan. 1937-1995. Lang.: Eng.   1290

Kathakali
Performance/production
Interview with actor and director Tom Fjordefalk. Sweden. 1972-1997. Lang.: Swe.   1948

Katona József Színház (Budapest)
Institutions
Remarks on a recent book on the Katona József Theatre. Hungary: Budapest. 1982-1996. Lang.: Hun.   332
Interviews and reviews relating to the Katona József Theatre. Hungary: Budapest. 1982-1996. Lang.: Hun.   1439
Pictorial history of Katona Jószef Chamber Theatre. Hungary: Budapest. 1982-1997. Lang.: Hun.   1442
Performance/production
Interviews with singer Magda Varga and her son, actor György Cserhalmi. Hungary. 1922-1996. Lang.: Hun.   551

Katona József Színház (Kecskemét)
Institutions
Response to jubilee album of Katona József Theatre. Hungary: Kecskemét. 1896-1996. Lang.: Hun.   1438
Performance/production
Four productions of the musical *A Dzsungel könyve (The Jungle Book)*. Hungary. 1996-1997. Lang.: Hun.   3936

Katona József Színház, Kamra (Budapest)
Institutions
Pictorial history of Katona Jószef Chamber Theatre. Hungary: Budapest. 1982-1997. Lang.: Hun.   1442
Performance/production
Andrea Fullajtár's performance in *Csendet akarok (I Want Silence)* by Zsolt Csalog. Hungary: Budapest. 1996. Lang.: Hun.   1771

Katunarić, Leo
Performance/production
The reemergence of melodrama on the Croatian stage. Croatia. 1995-1996. Lang.: Eng.   496

Katz, Natasha
Design/technology
Technical aspects of *EFX!* at MGM Grand Hotel. USA: Las Vegas, NV. 1996. Lang.: Eng.   3854

Katz, Zulema
Performance/production
Women directors in Spanish theatre. Spain. 1990-1996. Lang.: Eng. 612

Kauffmann, Bernd
Administration
Profiles of theatre festivals in Bad Hersfeld and Weimar. Germany: Bad Hersfeld, Weimar. 1997. Lang.: Ger.   33

Kaufman, George S.
Plays/librettos/scripts
Social criticism in plays of George S. Kaufman. USA. 1889-1961. Lang.: Eng.   3132
Analysis of *Merrily We Roll Along* by George S. Kaufman and Moss Hart. USA. 1934. Lang.: Eng.   3190

Kaufman, Moisés
Basic theatrical documents
Text of *Gross Indecency: The Three Trials of Oscar Wilde* by Moisés Kaufman. USA: New York, NY. 1997. Lang.: Eng.   1331
Design/technology
Betsy Adams' lighting design for *Gross Indecency: The Three Trials of Oscar Wilde*. USA: New York, NY. 1997. Lang.: Eng.   1377

Kaufman, Moisés — cont'd

Plays/librettos/scripts
Recent plays about Oscar Wilde. UK-England. 1997. Lang.: Eng.　　700

Kaukasische Kreidekreis, Der (Caucasian Chalk Circle, The)
Institutions
The National's season of theatre in the round at the Olivier. UK-England: London. 1997. Lang.: Eng.　　1499

Performance/production
Collection of newspaper reviews by London theatre critics. UK-England: London. 1997. Lang.: Eng.　　2034

Simon McBurney on his production of *The Caucasian Chalk Circle*, Théâtre de Complicité. UK-England: London. 1983-1997. Lang.: Eng.　　2218

Théâtre de Complicité's production of Brecht's *Caucasian Chalk Circle*. UK-England: London. 1997. Lang.: Ger.　　2226

The world premiere of Brecht's *The Caucasian Chalk Circle*. USA: Northfield, MN. 1948. Lang.: Eng.　　2253

Kaupunginteatteri (Helsinki)
SEE
Helsingin Kaupunginteatteri.

Kaut-Howson, Helena
Performance/production
Collection of newspaper reviews by London theatre critics. UK-England: London. 1997. Lang.: Eng.　　2063

Collection of newspaper reviews by London theatre critics. UK-England: London. 1997. Lang.: Eng.　　2075

Kavanaugh, Rachel
Performance/production
Collection of newspaper reviews by London theatre critics. UK-England: London. 1997. Lang.: Eng.　　2053

Collection of newspaper reviews by London theatre critics. UK-England: London. 1997. Lang.: Eng.　　2126

Kavčič, Vladimir
Plays/librettos/scripts
Analysis of plays by Vladimir Kavčič and Vitomil Zupan. Slovenia. 1900-1996. Lang.: Slo.　　3010

Kavi-Kavya (Heggodu)
Performance/production
Profile of Prasanna, director and teacher. India: New Delhi, Heggodu. 1970. Lang.: Swe.　　1782

Kaye Playhouse (New York, NY)
Performance/production
Guest performance of Cooperativo Teatroarte Cuticchio at Kaye Playhouse. USA: New York, NY. 1997. Lang.: Eng.　　4393

Kazan, Elia
Performance/production
Reconstruction of Elia Kazan's production of *A Streetcar Named Desire* by Tennessee Williams. USA: New York, NY. 1947. Lang.: Pol.　　2330
Plays/librettos/scripts
Tennessee Williams' relationship with directors of his plays. USA. 1944-1980. Lang.: Eng.　　3241

Films based on works of stage playwrights. USA. 1951-1972. Lang.: Pol.　　3681

Relation to other fields
Politics and Elia Kazan's film *Pinky*. USA. 1948. Lang.: Eng.　　3694

Kdo to poje Sizifa (Who's Singing Sisyphus?)
Basic theatrical documents
Text of Dušan Jovanović's Balkan trilogy. Slovenia. 1997. Lang.: Slo.　　1299

Kean, Charles
Performance/production
Shakespearean production in the age of actor-managers. UK-England. 1840-1914. Lang.: Eng.　　2193

Kean, Edmund
Performance/production
Staging Shakespeare in the Romantic period. UK-England. 1800-1840. Lang.: Eng.　　2166

Keane, Dillie
Performance/production
Collection of newspaper reviews by London theatre critics. UK-England: London. 1997. Lang.: Eng.　　1986

Keane, Fergal
Performance/production
Collection of newspaper reviews by London theatre critics. UK-England: London. 1997. Lang.: Eng.　　2006

Keane, John B.
Performance/production
Collection of newspaper reviews by London theatre critics. UK-England. 1997. Lang.: Eng.　　2142

Collection of newspaper reviews by London theatre critics. UK-England: London. 1997. Lang.: Eng.　　2151
Plays/librettos/scripts
Transformations of Irish society as reflected in its drama. Ireland. 1959-1993. Lang.: Eng.　　2913

Keates, John
Performance/production
Collection of newspaper reviews by London theatre critics. UK-England: London. 1997. Lang.: Eng.　　2128

Keatley, Charlotte
Performance/production
Collection of newspaper reviews by London theatre critics. UK-England: London. 1997. Lang.: Eng.　　2046
Plays/librettos/scripts
Female characters in plays of contemporary British women. UK-England. 1980-1995. Lang.: Eng.　　3077

Keaton, Buster
Performance/production
The early stage career of actor Buster Keaton. USA. 1916-1917. Lang.: Eng.　　651
Plays/librettos/scripts
The theme of hope in postwar American theatre and writing. USA. 1914-1929. Lang.: Eng.　　3153

Keeffe, Barrie
Plays/librettos/scripts
Twentieth-century adaptations of Jacobean plays. England. 1604-1986. Lang.: Eng.　　2673

Keeling, Stephen
Performance/production
Collection of newspaper reviews by London theatre critics. UK-England: London. 1997. Lang.: Eng.　　2112

Account of new musical *Maddie*. UK-England. 1997. Lang.: Eng.　　3948

Keen, Greg
Performance/production
Collection of newspaper reviews by London theatre critics. UK-England: London. 1997. Lang.: Eng.　　2089

Keene, Christopher
Performance/production
Interview with Paul Kellogg, manager of the New York City Opera. USA: New York, NY. 1996. Lang.: Eng.　　4276

Keene, Laura
Performance/production
Biography of actress/manager Laura Keene. USA. UK. 1826-1873. Lang.: Eng.　　634

Keiller, Patrick
Performance/production
Space in site-specific performance. UK-England. 1960-1997. Lang.: Eng.　　619

Keir Wright, David
Performance/production
Collection of newspaper reviews by London theatre critics. UK-England: London. 1997. Lang.: Eng.　　2059

Keith-Albee Palace (Rochester, NY)
Performance spaces
History of the Keith-Albee Palace. USA: Rochester, NY. 1928-1965. Lang.: Eng.　　3558

Kékesi, Mária
Training
Mária Kékesi, ballet mistress of the Hungarian Dance Academy. Hungary. 1950-1997. Lang.: Hun.　　1137

Kékszakállú herceg vára, A (Bluebeard's Castle)
Performance/production
Pécsi Balett's performance of choreographies by István Herczog to music of Bartók. Hungary: Pécs. 1997. Lang.: Hun.　　1080

Bartók's stage works presented by Pécsi Balett. Hungary: Pécs. 1992-1997. Lang.: Hun.　　1088

Keller, Marcel
Performance/production
Significant productions in Swabia. Germany: Stuttgart. 1997. Lang.: Ger.　　1726

Kellman, Scott
Administration
Interview with producer/performer Scott Kellman. USA: Los Angeles, CA. 1982-1991. Lang.: Eng.　　124

Kellogg, Paul
Performance/production
Interview with Paul Kellogg, manager of the New York City Opera. USA: New York, NY. 1996. Lang.: Eng.　　4276

King Lear — cont'd

Review of teaching texts of Shakespeare's *King Lear*. USA. 1995. Lang.:
Eng.   3400

King of Comedy, The
Plays/librettos/scripts
Analysis of films by Martin Scorsese. USA. 1976-1982. Lang.: Eng. 3676

King of Coons
Plays/librettos/scripts
Black playwrights' subversive approaches to character. USA. 1986-1997.
Lang.: Eng.   3184

King, Denis
Performance/production
Collection of newspaper reviews by London theatre critics. UK-England:
London. 1997. Lang.: Eng.   2132

King, Woodie, Jr.
Performance/production
Interview with actor/director Woodie King, Jr. USA: Detroit, MI, New
York, NY. 1937-1997. Lang.: Eng.   2332
Relation to other fields
Theatre artists' responses to the debate on multiculturalism of August
Wilson and Robert Brustein. USA. 1997. Lang.: Eng.   789

King's Company (London)
Performance/production
Shakespeare on the Jacobean and Caroline stage. England. 1605-1640.
Lang.: Eng.   1637

King's Head Theatre (London)
Performance/production
Collection of newspaper reviews by London theatre critics. UK-England:
London. 1997. Lang.: Eng.   2022

Collection of newspaper reviews by London theatre critics. UK-England:
London. 1997. Lang.: Eng.   2038

Collection of newspaper reviews by London theatre critics. UK-England:
London. 1997. Lang.: Eng.   2090

Collection of newspaper reviews by London theatre critics. UK-England:
London. 1997. Lang.: Eng.   2105

Collection of newspaper reviews by London theatre critics. UK-England:
London. 1997. Lang.: Eng.   2123

Collection of newspaper reviews by London theatre critics. UK-England:
London. 1997. Lang.: Eng.   2129

Collection of newspaper reviews by London theatre critics. UK-England:
London. 1997. Lang.: Eng.   2152

King's Men, The (London)
Administration
Business practices of the Globe and Drury Lane theatres. England:
London. 1599-1743. Lang.: Eng.   18
Design/technology
Ariel's costume in the original staging of *The Tempest*. England:
London. 1570-1612. Lang.: Eng.   156

King's Theatre (Edinburgh)
Performance/production
Collection of newspaper reviews by London theatre critics. UK-
Scotland: Edinburgh. 1997. Lang.: Eng.   2231

Kingdom, Bob
Performance/production
Collection of newspaper reviews by London theatre critics. UK-England:
London. 1997. Lang.: Eng.   2118

Kings
Performance/production
Collection of newspaper reviews by London theatre critics. UK-England:
London. 1997. Lang.: Eng.   2026

Kingsbury, Michael
Performance/production
Collection of newspaper reviews by London theatre critics. UK-England:
London. 1997. Lang.: Eng.   2075

Kingshill, Sophia
Performance/production
Collection of newspaper reviews by London theatre critics. UK-England:
London. 1997. Lang.: Eng.   2114

Kingston, Jeremy
Performance/production
Collection of newspaper reviews by London theatre critics. UK-England:
London. 1997. Lang.: Eng.   2036

Kinnaman, Melina
Performance/production
Interview with actress Melinda Kinnaman. Sweden: Stockholm. 1985.
Lang.: Swe.   1944

Kirby, Michael
Performance/production
Interviews and documents on performance concepts and practices. USA.
1952-1994. Lang.: Eng.   649

Profile of the late Michael Kirby, critic and theatre artist. USA. 1935-
1996. Lang.: Eng.   673

Kirk, Alexander
Performance/production
Collection of newspaper reviews by London theatre critics. UK-England:
London. 1997. Lang.: Eng.   2093

Kirkkopelto, Esa
Performance/production
Report on Finnish theatre productions. Finland: Helsinki, Tampere.
1997. Lang.: Eng, Fre.   1654
Theory/criticism
Director Esa Kirkkopelto on the impact of a theatrical performance.
Finland. 1997. Lang.: Fin.   881

Kirkwood, James
Performance/production
History of American musical theatre. USA. UK-England. 1912-1995.
Lang.: Eng.   3954

Kirov Opera and Ballet Theatre (Leningrad/St.Petersburg)
SEE
Akademičéskij Teat'r Opery i Baleta im. S.M. Kirova.

Kishida, Rio
Performance/production
Collection of newspaper reviews by London theatre critics. UK-England.
1997. Lang.: Eng.   2125

Kiss Me, Kate
Performance/production
Collection of newspaper reviews by London theatre critics. UK-England:
London. 1997. Lang.: Eng.   2086
Plays/librettos/scripts
Film adaptations of Shakespeare's *The Taming of the Shrew*. USA.
1929-1966. Lang.: Eng.   3668

Analysis of musical adaptations of Shakespearean plays. USA. 1938-
1997. Lang.: Ger.   3983

Kiss the Boys Goodbye
Performance/production
The grotesque on the American stage during the Depression. USA.
1929-1940. Lang.: Eng.   2264

Kiss, Csaba
Performance/production
Conversation with director Csaba Kiss and playwright Lajos Parti Nagy.
Hungary. 1980-1996. Lang.: Hun.   1753

Kiss, János
Institutions
Interview with János Kiss and Éva Afonyi of Győri Balett. Hungary:
Győr. 1970-1997. Lang.: Hun.   1052

Kitchen (New York, NY)
Performance/production
Reviews of *Hot Keys* and *Sally's Rape*. USA: New York, NY. 1991-
1992. Lang.: Eng.   2347

Kitchensink
Performance/production
Collection of newspaper reviews by London theatre critics. UK-England:
London. 1997. Lang.: Eng.   1994

Klabund
SEE
Henschke, Alfred.

Kleban, Edward
Performance/production
History of American musical theatre. USA. UK-England. 1912-1995.
Lang.: Eng.   3954

Klein-Perski, Kerstin
Plays/librettos/scripts
Hans Gefors' opera *Vargen kommer*, libretto by Kerstin Klein-Perski.
Sweden: Malmö. 1997. Lang.: Swe.   4310

Klein, Jon
Performance/production
Seattle Children's Theatre's production of *Bunnicula*. USA: Seattle, WA.
1979-1996. Lang.: Eng.   2311

Klein, Susan
Training
Interview with dancer/teacher Karin Jameson. Sweden: Stockholm.
USA: New York, NY. 1992. Lang.: Swe.   1044

Kleine Zweifel (Little Doubts)
Plays/librettos/scripts
Playwright Theresia Walser. Germany. 1990-1997. Lang.: Ger.   2864

Kleist, Heinrich von
Institutions
Staatstheater Darmstadt under the direction of Gerd-Theo Umberg.
Germany: Darmstadt. 1996-1997. Lang.: Ger.   1412

Kopit, Arthur
Plays/librettos/scripts
Critical history of American drama. USA. 1960-1997. Lang.: Eng. 3267

Koppel, Annisette
Institutions
Unions in Copenhagen's theatres. Denmark: Copenhagen. 1997. Lang.: Swe. 1400

Koppel, Thomas
Institutions
Unions in Copenhagen's theatres. Denmark: Copenhagen. 1997. Lang.: Swe. 1400

Koppen (Faces)
Performance/production
Ivo van Hove, new artistic director of the Holland Festival. Netherlands: Amsterdam. 1969-1997. Lang.: Eng. 1826

Kops, Bernard
Performance/production
Collection of newspaper reviews by London theatre critics. UK-England: London. 1997. Lang.: Eng. 2011

Collection of newspaper reviews by London theatre critics. UK-England: London. 1997. Lang.: Eng. 2088

Korf, Kristiana
Institutions
Unions in Copenhagen's theatres. Denmark: Copenhagen. 1997. Lang.: Swe. 1400

Kornblatt, Marc
Basic theatrical documents
Text of *Eulogies* by Marc Kornblatt. USA. 1997. Lang.: Eng. 1332

Korondi, Anna
Performance/production
Interview with soprano Anna Korondi. Germany: Berlin. 1990-1997. Lang.: Hun. 4157

Kortner, Fritz
Performance/production
German theatre during and after the Nazi period. Germany: Berlin, Dusseldorf. Switzerland: Zurich. 1933-1952. Lang.: Eng. 1704

Non-literary realism in Shakespeare productions. UK-England. Germany. 1958-1995. Lang.: Ger. 2170

Korun, Mile
Performance/production
Director Mile Korun on directing the plays of Ivan Cankar. Slovenia. 1965-1995. Lang.: Slo. 1904

Kossenkova, Nika
Performance/production
Sociocultural analysis of recent French productions. France. 1993-1994. Lang.: Eng. 1678

Kostelanetz, Richard
Plays/librettos/scripts
Changing relationships of writing, text and performance. UK-England. USA. 1980-1996. Lang.: Eng. 698

Kostumassinfonia (Kostumas Symphony)
Performance/production
Report on Finnish theatre productions. Finland: Helsinki, Tampere. 1997. Lang.: Eng, Fre. 1654

Kostzer, Kado
Performance/production
Collection of newspaper reviews by London theatre critics. UK-England. 1997. Lang.: Eng. 2058

Koszyn, Jayme
Performance/production
Director and dramaturg Jayme Koszyn. USA: Boston, MA, Philadelphia, PA. 1992-1995. Lang.: Eng. 2290

Kotarbiński, Józef
Performance/production
Guest performances in Polish cities. Poland: Cracow, Lvov, Warsaw. 1810-1915. Lang.: Pol. 583

Kótsi Patkó, János
Institutions
Theatre training in Transylvania. Hungary. Romania. 1792-1997. Lang.: Hun. 330

Koufogiannis, Kimon
Performance/production
Collection of newspaper reviews by London theatre critics. UK-England: London. 1997. Lang.: Eng. 2017

Kovalik, Balázs
Performance/production
Interview with opera director Balázs Kovalik. Hungary: Budapest. 1995-1997. Lang.: Hun. 4185

Kozincev, Grigorij
Performance/production
The map of England in productions of Shakespeare's *King Lear*. Europe. USA. 1909-1994. Lang.: Eng. 1650

Kozlov, Christine
Relation to other fields
The distinction between the live and the mediatized. Canada. USA. 1977-1997. Lang.: Eng. 3706

Kozma Zacharič Minin, Suchoruk (Kozma Zacharič Minin)
Performance/production
Ostrovskij's *Kozma Zacharič Minin* at Moscow Art Theatre. Russia: Moscow. 1997. Lang.: Rus. 1885

Kraemer, Jacques
Basic theatrical documents
French translations of Strindberg's *Fröken Julie (Miss Julie)* and *Den Starkare (The Stronger)*. Sweden. France. 1888-1996.Lang.: Fre. 1309

Kramer, David
Performance/production
Collection of newspaper reviews by London theatre critics. UK-England: London. 1997. Lang.: Eng. 2115

Krämer, Günter
Institutions
Kölner Schauspiel under the direction of Günter Krämer. Germany: Cologne. 1985-1997. Lang.: Ger. 1425
Performance/production
Profile of actress Traute Hoess. Germany. Austria. 1969-1997. Lang.: Ger. 1741

Impressions of opera performances in several German cities. Germany. 1997. Lang.: Ger. 4147

Kramer, Larry
Plays/librettos/scripts
Account of seminar on writing about AIDS. USA: Key West, FL. 1984-1997. Lang.: Eng. 704

Death and dying in plays about AIDS. USA. 1997. Lang.: Eng. 3134

Kramer, Victor
Performance/production
Collection of newspaper reviews by London theatre critics. UK-England: London. 1997. Lang.: Eng. 1981

Krantz, Peter
Performance/production
Maria Lang's *3 små gummor (Three Little Old Ladies)* directed by Peter Krantz. Sweden: Mora. 1997. Lang.: Swe. 1952

Krapp's Last Tape
Performance/production
Staging and Beckett's *Not I* and *Krapp's Last Tape*. France. Ireland. 1960-1973. Lang.: Eng. 1671
Plays/librettos/scripts
Analysis of German translations of plays by Samuel Beckett. Germany. 1967-1978. Lang.: Eng. 2842

Memory and the self in Beckett's *Not I* and *Krapp's Last Tape*. Ireland. France. 1958-1972. Lang.: Eng. 2924

Language and silence in short plays of Samuel Beckett. Ireland. France. USA. 1960-1981. Lang.: Eng. 2929

Krasiński, Zygmunt
Performance/production
Director Leon Schiller. Poland. 1907-1954. Lang.: Eng. 586
Plays/librettos/scripts
Text and performance in the Romantic period. Europe. 1800-1851. Lang.: Pol. 2790

Kráska a Zvíře (Beauty and the Beast)
Performance spaces
Theatre structures used at Prague Quadrennial. Czech Republic: Český Krumlov. 1995. Lang.: Eng. 1518

Profile of Měsíčník Ceských Divadel, a revolving auditorium theatre. Czech Republic: Český Krumlov. 1947-1996. Lang.: Eng. 1519

Krasnaja Žizel' (Red Giselle)
Performance/production
Boris Ejfman's ballet *Krasnaja Žizel' (Red Giselle)*. Russia: St. Petersburg. 1997. Lang.: Rus. 1099

Kraus, Alfredo
Performance/production
The Alfredo Kraus International Competition. Spain. 1990-1997. Lang.: Eng. 4214

Krausser, Helmut
Performance/production
Premieres of new plays by Handke, Krausser, and Enzensberger. Austria. Germany. 1996-1997. Lang.: Ger. 1567

Kreitzer, Carson
Performance/production
Collection of newspaper reviews by London theatre critics. UK-England: London. 1997. Lang.: Eng. 2002

Kungliga Operan (Stockholm) — cont'd

Performance spaces
Kungliga Operan's new rehearsal space. Sweden: Stockholm. 1996.
Lang.: Swe.   4067
Performance/production
Interview with dancer Rennie Mirro. Sweden: Stockholm. 1981. Lang.:
Swe.   990

Sweden's summer opera and musical entertainments. Sweden. 1997.
Lang.: Eng.   4216

Realistic productions at the Royal Swedish Opera. Sweden: Stockholm.
1862-1997. Lang.: Swe.   4220

Kungliga Teatern (Stockholm)
SEE
Kungliga Operan.

Kunju
Performance/production
The classical theatre genre *kunju* and its revival. China, People's
Republic of. 1950-1960. Lang.: Eng.   3893

Kupfer, Harry
Performance/production
Interview with opera singer Noemi Nadelmann. Germany: Berlin. 1997.
Lang.: Ger.   4146

Harry Kupfer's staging of *Lucia di Lammermoor*. Germany: Berlin.
1997. Lang.: Swe.   4154

Kurhaustheater (Göggingen)
Performance spaces
Presentation of Kurhaustheater. Germany: Göggingen. 1885-1997.
Lang.: Ger.   432

Kurich, Hadi
Plays/librettos/scripts
Analysis of *Malinche* by Inés M. Stanger and *Opus Primum* by Hadi
Kurich. Chile. Spain. 1993. Lang.: Spa.   2439

Kurosawa, Akira
Plays/librettos/scripts
Terrains Vagues (Wastelands), Michel Nadeau's stage adaptation of
Rashomon. Canada: Quebec, PQ. 1997. Lang.: Fre.   2422

Animal imagery in *King Lear* and Akira Kurosawa's film adaptation
Ran. England. Japan. 1605-1984. Lang.: Eng.   3636

Kurt, Stefan
Performance/production
Actors on working in theatre, film, and television. Germany. 1941-1997.
Lang.: Ger.   3576

Kürthy, György
Design/technology
Stage designs for *Az ember tragédiája (The Tragedy of Man)* by Imre
Madách. Hungary: Budapest. 1883-1915. Lang.: Hun.   1357

Kurtz, Ronald
Design/technology
Designers of the steamboat *American Queen*. USA. 1997. Lang.: Eng.
                                                                        205

Kusej, Martin
Performance/production
Productions of Schauspiel Stuttgart. Germany: Stuttgart. 1997. Lang.:
Ger.   1687

Productions of Schauspiel Stuttgart. Germany: Stuttgart. 1997. Lang.:
Ger.   1715

Comparison of productions of Shakespeare's *Richard III*. Germany.
Switzerland. 1996. Lang.: Ger.   1745

Kushner, Tony
Basic theatrical documents
French translation of Tony Kushner's *Angels in America, Part II:
Perestroika*. USA. France: Paris. 1996. Lang.: Fre.   1333
Design/technology
Projection techniques for *Angels in America* at Stockholms Stadsteater.
Sweden: Stockholm. 1800-1997. Lang.: Ger.   1358

Design for three productions of Tony Kushner's *Angels in America*.
USA: New York, NY, Los Angeles, CA. UK-England: London. 1992-
1994. Lang.: Eng.   1363
Performance/production
Sex and gender in recent Stockholm productions. Sweden: Stockholm.
1996. Lang.: Eng.   1925

Analysis of Declan Donnellan's production of *Angels in America* by
Tony Kushner. UK-England: London. 1992. Lang.: Eng.   2168

Sexuality on stage in the National Theatre production of Tony
Kushner's *Angels in America*. UK-England: London. 1992. Lang.: Eng.
                                                                       2176

Tony Kushner's *Angels in America* in the context of queer performance.
USA. 1992-1994. Lang.: Eng.   2245

Tony Kushner's *Angels in America* as epic theatre. USA. 1992-1995.
Lang.: Eng.   2324

Comparison of productions of Tony Kushner's *Angels in America, Part
I: Millennium Approaches*. USA: New York, NY. UK-England. 1992-
1993. Lang.: Eng.   2326

The presidential election and the Los Angeles premiere of *Angels in
America*. USA: Los Angeles, CA. 1992. Lang.: Eng.   2327

Interview with director Robert Altman on filming *Angels in America*.
USA. 1995. Lang.: Eng.   -   3603
Plays/librettos/scripts
Account of seminar on writing about AIDS. USA: Key West, FL. 1984-
1997. Lang.: Eng.   704

Death and dying in plays about AIDS. USA. 1997. Lang.: Eng.   3134

The character Roy Cohn in Tony Kushner's *Angels in America*. USA.
1992-1994. Lang.: Eng.   3154

Social debate reflected in Tony Kushner's *Angels in America*. USA.
1988-1996. Lang.: Eng.   3172

Ethnicity in Tony Kushner's *Angels in America*. USA. 1992-1994. Lang.:
Eng.   3189

Tony Kushner's *Angels in America*, postmodernism, and millenarianism.
USA. 1992-1994. Lang.: Eng.   3193

Insanity and prophecy in Tony Kushner's *Angels in America*. USA.
1992-1994. Lang.: Eng.   3195

The supernatural in Tony Kushner's *Angels in America*. USA. 1992-
1994. Lang.: Eng.   3206

Analysis of *Angels in America* by Tony Kushner. USA. 1994-1996.
Lang.: Eng.   3207

Interview with playwright Tony Kushner. USA. 1989-1995. Lang.: Eng.
                                                                      3211

Identity, cultural transformation, and Tony Kushner's *Angels in
America*. USA. 1992-1994. Lang.: Eng.   3221

Tony Kushner's *Angels in America* and the AIDS crisis. USA. 1992-
1994. Lang.: Eng.   3235

Representations of race and gender in Tony Kushner's *Angels in
America*. USA. 1992-1994. Lang.: Eng.   3236

Tony Kushner's *Angels in America* and U.S. history. USA. 1992-1994.
Lang.: Eng.   3270

Analysis of the final scene of *Angels in America, Part II: Perestroika* by
Tony Kushner. USA. 1992-1994. Lang.: Eng.   3271

Jewish identity in *Angels in America* by Tony Kushner. USA. 1992-
1994. Lang.: Eng.   3280

Collection of interviews with playwright Tony Kushner. USA. 1989-
1997. Lang.: Eng.   3294

Interview with playwright Tony Kushner on the influence of Brecht.
USA. 1997. Lang.: Ger.   3300
Relation to other fields
The effect of AIDS on contemporary drama. USA. 1991-1997. Lang.:
Ger.   3406

Kutiyattam
Performance/production
CD-ROM presentation of all aspects of *kutiyattam*. India. 1000-1997.
Lang.: Eng.   557

Parate Labor's teaching of *kutiyattam* Sanskrit drama in France. France.
India. 1989-1997. Lang.: Eng.   1673

Kuvarin, V.
Performance/production
Bolšoj Drama Theatre production of Anouilh's *Antigone*. Russia: St.
Petersburg. 1996. Lang.: Rus.   1862

Anouilh's *Antigone* at the Bolšoj Drama Theatre. Russia: St. Petersburg.
1996. Lang.: Rus.   1897

Kvarnström, Kenneth
Performance/production
Choreographer Kenneth Kvarnström. Finland: Helsinki. 1997. Lang.:
Eng.   1180

Kvetch
Institutions
Report from the Tampere theatre festival. Finland: Tampere. 1997.
Lang.: Swe.   309

Kyd, Thomas
Performance/production
Collection of newspaper reviews by London theatre critics. UK-England.
1997. Lang.: Eng.   2051

Collection of newspaper reviews by London theatre critics. UK-England:
London. 1997. Lang.: Eng.   2151

Lady Windermere's Fan — cont'd

Collection of newspaper reviews by London theatre critics. UK-England. 1997. Lang.: Eng. 2043

Lady's Last Stake, The
Plays/librettos/scripts
Marriage in early plays of Colley Cibber. England. 1696-1730. Lang.: Eng. 2563

Lagodny koniec smierci (Gentle End of Death, The)
Institutions
Teatr Biuro Podrózy and its founder Pawel Szkotak. Poland: Poznań. 1988-1996. Lang.: Eng. 1453

Lagos de San Vicente, Los (Lakes of Saint Vincent, The)
Plays/librettos/scripts
Conversion plays of Tirso and Calderón. Spain. 1600-1681. Lang.: Eng. 3043

Lahdenperä, Soile
Training
Teachers and choreographers Soile Lahdenperä and Ervi Siren. Finland. 1997. Lang.: Fin. 1040

Laing, David
Basic theatrical documents
Text of *The Difficulty of Crossing a Field* by Mac Wellman, music by David Laing. USA. 1997. Lang.: Eng. 1348

Laing, Stewart
Design/technology
Stewart Laing's set and costume designs for the musical *Titanic*. USA: New York, NY. 1997. Lang.: Eng. 3914

Laki, Krisztina
Performance/production
Soprano Krisztina Laki. Hungary. 1970-1996. Lang.: Hun. 4181

Lakmé
Plays/librettos/scripts
Representations of the Orient in nineteenth-century French opera. France. 1863-1894. Lang.: Eng. 4290

Lament for Arthur Cleary, The
Plays/librettos/scripts
Analysis of *The Lament for Arthur Cleary* by Dermot Bolger. Ireland. 1984-1989. Lang.: Eng. 2927

Lamers, Jan Joris
Performance/production
Director Jan Joris Lamers and his influence on contemporary theatre. Netherlands. 1968-1997. Lang.: Eng, Fre. 1824

Lamming, George
Plays/librettos/scripts
New world adaptations of Shakespeare's *The Tempest*. England. Latin America. Caribbean. 1612-1994. Lang.: Eng. 2549

Lampe, Jutta
Performance/production
The deconstruction of femininity in Jutta Lampe and Isabelle Huppert's performances of *Orlando*. Europe. 1923-1997. Lang.: Eng. 1643

Lan, David
Performance/production
Confession, reconciliation, and David Lan's *Desire*. South Africa, Republic of: Pietermaritzburg. 1993-1995. Lang.: Eng. 1908

Lanari, Alessandro
Administration
State patronage and control of opera in the Duchy of Lucca. Italy: Lucca. 1817-1847. Lang.: Eng. 4004

Lancashire Witches, The
Plays/librettos/scripts
Dramatic satire of the exclusion crisis. England. 1680-1683. Lang.: Eng. 2714

Lancaster, Sarah
Performance/production
Interview with television actress Sarah Lancaster. UK-England. 1997. Lang.: Eng. 3727

Land of Fog and Whistles, The
Basic theatrical documents
Text of *The Land of Fog and Whistles* by Mac Wellman. USA. 1992. Lang.: Eng. 1349

Landestheater (Coburg)
Performance/production
Performances of the classics in Franconia. Germany. 1997. Lang.: Ger. 1737

Landestheater Tübingen
Plays/librettos/scripts
Children's theatre festival productions. Germany: Berlin. 1997. Lang.: Ger. 2845

Landon-Smith, Kristine
Performance/production
Collection of newspaper reviews by London theatre critics. UK-England: London. 1997. Lang.: Eng. 1975

Collection of newspaper reviews by London theatre critics. UK-England: London. 1997. Lang.: Eng. 1993

Collection of newspaper reviews by London theatre critics. UK-England: London. 1997. Lang.: Eng. 2023

Collection of newspaper reviews by London theatre critics. UK-Scotland: Edinburgh. 1997. Lang.: Eng. 2230

Lanfang, Mei
Theory/criticism
Brecht's misunderstanding of Chinese theatre as interpreted by Mei Lanfang. Germany. 1925-1959. Lang.: Eng. 900

Lang, Alexander
Performance/production
History and politics on the Parisian stage. France: Paris. 1997. Lang.: Ger. 1669

Lang, Elke
Performance/production
Productions of Staatstheater Wiesbaden. Germany: Wiesbaden. 1997. Lang.: Ger. 1709

Lang, Maria
Performance/production
Maria Lang's *3 små gummor (Three Little Old Ladies)* directed by Peter Krantz. Sweden: Mora. 1997. Lang.: Swe. 1952

Langdahl, Peter
Performance/production
Peter Langdahl's production of *The Cherry Orchard* at Dramaten. Sweden: Stockholm. 1997. Lang.: Swe. 1938

Lange-Müller, Katja
Basic theatrical documents
Text of *Schneewittchen im Eisblock. Ein Spiegelbild (Snow White in the Block of Ice: A Reflection)* by Katja Lange-Müller. Germany. 1997. Lang.: Ger. 1282

Langella, Frank
Design/technology
Derek McLane's set design for *Present Laughter*. USA: New York, NY. 1996-1997. Lang.: Eng. 1365
Performance/production
Presentation of Actors' Equity awards. USA: New York, NY. 1997. Lang.: Eng. 660

Transcript of seminar by actor Frank Langella. USA. 1997. Lang.: Eng. 661

Langham, Michael
Performance/production
Reactions to modern performances of *Antony and Cleopatra*. UK-England. North America. 1827-1987. Lang.: Eng. 2178

Langhoff, Thomas
Institutions
Deutsches Theater under the direction of Thomas Langhoff. Germany: Berlin. 1996-1997. Lang.: Ger. 1428
Performance/production
The current status of Berlin opera and theatre. Germany: Berlin. 1997. Lang.: Ger. 547

Plays of Botho Strauss and Peter Handke carried over into a second season. Germany: Berlin, Frankfurt. 1996-1997. Lang.: Ger. 1746

Langridge, Philip
Performance/production
Lyric tenor Philip Langridge. UK-England: London. 1997. Lang.: Eng. 4225

Language
Plays/librettos/scripts
Iambic pentameter and Shakespearean performance. England. 1598-1997. Lang.: Eng. 2671

Linguistic analysis of plays by Delaney, Pinter, Orton, and Gems. UK-England. 1956-1984. Lang.: Spa. 3100

Text and music in operas by Robert Ashley and by Gertrude Stein with Virgil Thomson. USA. 1925-1980. Lang.: Eng. 4315
Theory/criticism
Sociolinguistic analysis of English medieval drama. England. 1300-1600. Lang.: Eng. 874

Language Roulette
Performance/production
Collection of newspaper reviews by London theatre critics. UK-England: London. 1997. Lang.: Eng. 2021

Lansbury, Angela
Performance/production
National Medal of Arts recipients Angela Lansbury and Jason Robards. USA. 1997. Lang.: Eng. 659

Länsteatern i Skövde
Institutions
Profile of Länsteatern i Skövde. Sweden: Skövde. 1964. Lang.: Swe. 1481

Lavine, Michael
  Performance/production
    Collection of newspaper reviews by London theatre critics. UK-England: London. 1997. Lang.: Eng.   2022
Lavrovskij, Leonid
  Performance/production
    The Hungarian stage career of the ballet *Giselle*. Hungary: Budapest. 1841-1996. Lang.: Hun.   1079
Lawlor, Joe
  Basic theatrical documents
    Text and photos of *Photogrammetry* by Christine Molloy and Joe Lawlor of desperate optimists. Ireland: Dublin. 1997. Lang.: Eng.   1286
  Performance/production
    Experimental theatre group desperate optimists. Ireland: Dublin. 1993-1997. Lang.: Eng.   560
Lawrence, Jerome
  Performance/production
    Collection of newspaper reviews by London theatre critics. UK-England: London. 1997. Lang.: Eng.   2068
Lawson, John Howard
  Plays/librettos/scripts
    Communism and the stage and screen plays of John Howard Lawson. USA. 1933-1947. Lang.: Eng.   3159
Le Gallienne, Eva
  Performance/production
    Actress and director Eva Le Gallienne. USA. 1997. Lang.: Eng.   2343
    Eva Le Gallienne's biographer on her work. USA. 1920-1996. Lang.: Eng.   2344
Le Guillerm, Johann
  Performance/production
    Collection of newspaper reviews by London theatre critics. UK-England: London. 1997. Lang.: Eng.   2074
Le Mar, Angie
  Performance/production
    Collection of newspaper reviews by London theatre critics. UK-England: London. 1997. Lang.: Eng.   2035
Leach, Karoline
  Performance/production
    Collection of newspaper reviews by London theatre critics. UK-England: London. 1997. Lang.: Eng.   2093
Lear
  Performance/production
    Career of performer Karen Kandel. USA: New York, NY. 1977-1997. Lang.: Eng.   663
    Non-literary realism in Shakespeare productions. UK-England. Germany. 1958-1995. Lang.: Ger.   2170
Lear, Evelyn
  Performance/production
    The role of Marie in Berg's *Wozzeck*. Germany. USA. 1923-1996. Lang.: Eng.   4145
Leave Taking
  Plays/librettos/scripts
    Female characters in plays of contemporary British women. UK-England. 1980-1995. Lang.: Eng.   3077
Lebedinoje osero (Swan Lake)
  Performance/production
    Stage interpretations of Čajkovskij's *Swan Lake*. Finland: Helsinki. 1997. Lang.: Fin.   1066
    Vladimir Vasiljév's new version of *Swan Lake* at the Bolšoj Teat'r. Russia: Moscow. 1996. Lang.: Swe.   1107
    Choreographer Matthew Bourne. UK-England: London. 1997. Lang.: Eng.   1119
Lebensabend (Life's Evening)
  Plays/librettos/scripts
    Hans-Ulrich Becker's production of *Lebensabend (Life's Evening)*. Germany. 1933-1997. Lang.: Ger.   2848
Lébl, Petr
  Performance/production
    Interpretations of Czech classics by Petr Lébl and Vladimír Morávek. Czech Republic. 1997. Lang.: Cze.   1609
Leblanc, Maurice
  Basic theatrical documents
    Text of *Le Secret de l'Aiguille creuse (The Secret of the Hollow Needle)*, Gilles Gleizes' adaptation of an Arsène Lupin mystery novel. France. 1996. Lang.: Fre.   1273
Lebow, Barbara
  Plays/librettos/scripts
    Texts of plays by Jewish American women. USA. 1985-1995. Lang.: Eng.   3164

Lechtenbrink, Volker
  Administration
    Profiles of theatre festivals in Bad Hersfeld and Weimar. Germany: Bad Hersfeld, Weimar. 1997. Lang.: Ger.   33
LeCompte, Elizabeth
  Performance/production
    Interviews and documents on performance concepts and practices. USA. 1952-1994. Lang.: Eng.   649
Leçon d'anatomie (Anatomy Lesson)
  Plays/librettos/scripts
    Language in monodramas of Larry Tremblay. Canada. 1989-1995. Lang.: Fre.   2423
    Shift in power relations among author, director, and actors. Canada. 1986-1992. Lang.: Fre.   2428
Leçon, La (Lesson, The)
  Plays/librettos/scripts
    Teachers and students in plays of Walker, Mamet, and Ionesco. USA. Canada. France. 1951-1997. Lang.: Eng.   3296
Lecouvreur, Adrienne
  Research/historiography
    Eighteenth-century theatrical portraits. England. France. 1700-1800. Lang.: Eng.   3445
Ledesma, Michael
  Design/technology
    Lighting designs of Michael Ledesma. North America. Europe. 1996-1997. Lang.: Eng.   178
Lee Atwater: Fixin' to Die
  Performance/production
    Robert Myers's *Lee Atwater: Fixin' to Die*. USA: New York, NY. 1990-1997. Lang.: Eng.   2313
Lee, Chris
  Performance/production
    Collection of newspaper reviews by London theatre critics. UK-England: London. 1997. Lang.: Eng.   2131
Lee, Don L.
  SEE
    Madhubuti, Haki R.
Lee, Eddie Levi
  Institutions
    Seattle's theatrical renaissance. USA: Seattle, WA. 1980-1997. Lang.: Eng.   396
Lee, Jenny
  Performance/production
    Collection of newspaper reviews by London theatre critics. UK-England: London. 1997. Lang.: Eng.   1989
    Collection of newspaper reviews by London theatre critics. UK-England: London. 1997. Lang.: Eng.   1997
    Collection of newspaper reviews by London theatre critics. UK-England: London. 1997. Lang.: Eng.   2019
Lee, Kang-Baek
  Plays/librettos/scripts
    Analysis of plays by Lee Kang-Baek. South Korea. 1961-1997. Lang.: Pol.   3034
Lee, Nathaniel
  Plays/librettos/scripts
    Social practice and convention in Tudor-Stuart drama. England. 1571-1670. Lang.: Eng.   2567
    Female 'mad' songs in seventeenth-century English drama. England. 1685-1700. Lang.: Eng.   2638
Lee, Ralph
  Performance/production
    Ralph Lee's production of *Heart of the Earth* by Cherrie Moraga. USA: New York, NY. 1995. Lang.: Eng.   2238
Lee, Robert E.
  Performance/production
    Collection of newspaper reviews by London theatre critics. UK-England: London. 1997. Lang.: Eng.   2068
Lefevre, Robin
  Performance/production
    Collection of newspaper reviews by London theatre critics. UK-England: London. 1997. Lang.: Eng.   2001
Left Breastless
  Performance/production
    Collection of newspaper reviews by London theatre critics. UK-England: London. 1997. Lang.: Eng.   2087
Legal aspects
  Administration
    International copyright law and current technology. 1997. Lang.: Eng.   1

390   International Bibliography of Theatre: 1997

Legal aspects — cont'd

Levin, Ira
  Performance/production
    Novelist Ira Levin on Gounod's *Faust*. USA: New York, NY. 1997.
    Lang.: Eng.   4250
Levin, Meyer
  Plays/librettos/scripts
    The stage adaptation of the diary of Anne Frank. USA. 1947-1950.
    Lang.: Eng.   3234
Levin, Ruth
  Performance/production
    Collection of newspaper reviews by London theatre critics. UK-England:
    London. 1997. Lang.: Eng.   2060
Levine, James
  Performance/production
    James Levine's production of Wagner's *Ring*. Germany: Bayreuth. 1997.
    Lang.: Eng.   4151
    Conductor James Levine and the Metropolitan Opera Orchestra. USA:
    New York, NY. 1950-1997. Lang.: Eng.   4277
Levine, Michael
  Design/technology
    Theatre in the new millennium. 1997. Lang.: Eng.   138
    OISTAT's conference on theatre technology of the future. USA:
    Pittsburgh. 1997. Lang.: Swe.   227
    Critique of minimalist scenic design for opera. Canada: Toronto, ON.
    USA: New York, NY. 1975-1997. Lang.: Eng.   4019
Levinson, Barry
  Performance/production
    The film *Bugsy* as an adaptation of Shakespeare's *Antony and
    Cleopatra*. USA. 1991. Lang.: Eng.   3613
Levitin, Michajl
  Performance/production
    Cvetajeva's *Sonečka i Kazanova* (*Sonečka and Casanova*) at Teat'r
    Ermitaž. Russia: Moscow. 1996. Lang.: Rus.   1879
Levstik, Fran
  Plays/librettos/scripts
    Analysis of plays about the Slovene tragic hero Tugomer. Slovenia.
    1875-1996. Lang.: Slo.   3012
Levy, Jacques
  Performance/production
    Collection of newspaper reviews by London theatre critics. UK-England:
    London. 1997. Lang.: Eng.   2137
Lewis, Brenda
  Performance/production
    The role of Marie in Berg's *Wozzeck*. Germany. USA. 1923-1996.
    Lang.: Eng.   4145
Lewis, Henry
  Performance/production
    Collection of newspaper reviews by London theatre critics. UK-England:
    London. 1997. Lang.: Eng.   1972
Lewis, M.G.
  Performance/production
    Collection of newspaper reviews by London theatre critics. UK-England:
    London. 1997. Lang.: Eng.   2144
    Collection of newspaper reviews by London theatre critics. UK-England:
    London. 1997. Lang.: Eng.   2153
Lewis, Marcia
  Performance/production
    Successful cabaret performers and their techniques. USA. 1975-1997.
    Lang.: Eng.   3780
Libraries
  SEE
    Archives/libraries.
Librettos
  Basic theatrical documents
    Music and libretto of the musical *In Dahomey*. USA. 1903. Lang.: Eng.
                                                                       3904
    Libretto of Ligeti's opera *Le Grand Macabre*. Europe. 1978-1997. Lang.:
    Fre, Eng.   4008
    Scribe's libretto for Boieldieu's opera *La Dame Blanche*. France. 1825.
    Lang.: Fre.   4009
    Libretto for Donizetti's opera *La Fille du régiment*. France. 1840. Lang.:
    Fre.   4010
    Libretto for Bellini's opera *La sonnambula*. Italy. 1831. Lang.: Fre, Ita.
                                                                       4012
    Text of the libretto to *Il matrimonio segreto* by Domenico Cimarosa.
    Italy. 1792. Lang.: Fre, Ita.   4013
    Libretto for Falla's opera *La vida breve*. Spain. 1913-1914. Lang.: Fre,
    Spa.   4014

    Libretto for Falla's opera *El amor brujo*. Spain. 1915-1916. Lang.: Fre,
    Spa.   4015
    Manuel de Falla's libretto to his opera *El retablo de Maese Pedro*.
    Spain. 1923. Lang.: Fre, Spa.   4016
    Text of *Terra Incognita* by Maria Irene Fornes, the libretto for an opera
    by Roberto Sierra. USA. 1992. Lang.: Eng.   4017
Libussa
  Performance/production
    Peter Stein's production of *Libussa* by Franz Grillparzer. Austria:
    Salzburg. 1997. Lang.: Ger.   1566
Licensing
  Administration
    Copyright law and videocassettes. USA. 1997. Lang.: Eng.   3709
    Licensing performance rights for musicals. USA. 1997. Lang.: Eng. 3897
Lickers and Kickers
  Performance/production
    Collection of newspaper reviews by London theatre critics. UK-England:
    London. 1997. Lang.: Eng.   2019
Lie of the Mind, A
  Performance/production
    Plays by Shepard and Albee at Nederlands Toneel Gent. Netherlands:
    Ghent. 1996. Lang.: Eng.   1825
Lieberson, Peter
  Design/technology
    Opera costume designer Martin Pakledinaz. USA: Santa Fe, NM, New
    York, NY. 1997. Lang.: Eng.   4035
  Performance/production
    Profile of opera composer Peter Lieberson. USA: New York, NY. 1947-
    1997. Lang.: Eng.   4241
  Plays/librettos/scripts
    Peter Lieberson's opera *Ashoka's Dream*. Canada. 1997. Lang.: Eng.
                                                                       4283
Life According to Agfa
  Performance/production
    Contemporary plays at Schauspiel Leipzig. Germany: Leipzig. 1996-
    1997. Lang.: Ger.   1736
Life and Repentaunce of Marie Magdalene, The
  Plays/librettos/scripts
    Middle English religious drama and audience participation. England.
    1400-1550. Lang.: Eng.   2576
Life During Wartime
  Basic theatrical documents
    Text of plays performed at the Nuyorican Poets Cafe. USA: New York,
    NY. 1973-1990. Lang.: Eng.   1322
Life Is a Dream
  SEE
    Vida es sueño, La.
Life of Galileo, The
  SEE
    Leben des Galilei.
Life of the Land, The
  Basic theatrical documents
    Collection of plays about Hawaii by Edward Sakamoto. USA. 1993-
    1994. Lang.: Eng.   1341
Life Sentences
  Plays/librettos/scripts
    Beth French's *Life Sentences*. Canada: Toronto, ON. 1989-1997. Lang.:
    Eng.   2390
Life Support
  Performance/production
    Collection of newspaper reviews by London theatre critics. UK-England:
    London. 1997. Lang.: Eng.   2084
Life, The
  Design/technology
    Richard Pilbrow's lighting design for the musical *The Life*. USA: New
    York, NY. 1997. Lang.: Eng.   3918
  Performance/production
    Actress/singer Lillias White. USA: New York, NY. 1981-1997. Lang.:
    Eng.   3949
Ligeti, György
  Basic theatrical documents
    Libretto of Ligeti's opera *Le Grand Macabre*. Europe. 1978-1997. Lang.:
    Fre, Eng.   4008
  Design/technology
    Roland Topor's costume designs for a production of *Le Grand Macabre*
    by Ligeti. Italy: Bologna. 1979. Lang.: Fre.   4026
  Performance/production
    Productions world wide of Ligeti's opera *Le Grand Macabre*. 1978-1998.
    Lang.: Fre.   4080

Lighting — cont'd

Literature — cont'd

The influence of Shakespeare's *Richard III* on a poem of Wilfred Owen. England. 1593-1919. Lang.: Eng. 3329

Early criticism of Shakespeare's 'Venus and Adonis'. England. 1593. Lang.: Eng. 3330

Disputes the recent attribution of the lyric poem 'Shall I Die' to Shakespeare. England. 1604-1637. Lang.: Eng. 3332

Analysis of Shakespeare's 'Venus and Adonis'. England. 1593. Lang.: Eng. 3333

Criticism of Shakespeare's 'Venus and Adonis'. England. 1593. Lang.: Eng. 3335

The influence of *Hamlet* on William Godwin's novel *Caleb Williams*. England. 1600-1794. Lang.: Eng. 3336

Introduction to collection of essays on Shakespeare's 'Venus and Adonis'. England. 1593. Lang.: Eng. 3337

Ben Jonson's personal copy of Petrarch's *Opera omnia*. England. 1581-1994. Lang.: Eng. 3339

Analysis of sonnets to determine Shakespearean authorship. England. 1599-1616. Lang.: Eng. 3341

Patriarchal response to the violent woman and Shakespeare's poem 'The Rape of Lucrece'. England. 1592-1595. Lang.: Eng. 3342

The dedication to Shakespeare's sonnets. England. 1609. Lang.: Eng. 3345

Playwright Elizabeth Cary and the historical account of King Edward II. England. 1627. Lang.: Eng. 3346

The source of an allusion in Beckett's *Murphy*. Ireland. France. 1938. Lang.: Eng. 3359

Analysis of Samuel Beckett's novel *Comment c'est (How It Is)*. Ireland. France. 1961. Lang.: Eng. 3360

Source of a phrase in Beckett's *Dream of Fair to Middling Women*. Ireland. France. 1932. Lang.: Eng. 3361

Leopardi's influence on works of Samuel Beckett. Ireland. France. 1929-1985. Lang.: Eng. 3362

Politics in Joyce's *Ulysses* and his references to *Hamlet*. Ireland. 1920. Lang.: Eng. 3363

Narrative in Beckett's novels. Ireland. France. 1997. Lang.: Eng. 3364

James Joyce's opinions on the authorship of the plays of Shakespeare. Ireland. 1900-1939. Lang.: Eng. 3365

An illegal chess move in the English edition of Beckett's *Murphy*. Ireland. France. 1938. Lang.: Eng. 3366

Novelist and playwright George Moore. Ireland: Dublin. UK-England: London. 1852-1933. Lang.: Eng. 3367

Autobiographical elements in novels of Samuel Beckett. Ireland. France. 1947-1979. Lang.: Eng. 3368

The structure of Samuel Beckett's novel *Watt*. Ireland. France. 1942-1963. Lang.: Eng. 3369

Theatricality in Samuel Beckett's trilogy of novels. Ireland. France. 1960-1965. Lang.: Eng. 3370

Analysis of fiction by Samuel Beckett. Ireland. France. 1930-1985. Lang.: Eng. 3371

Theatre in nineteenth-century American theatre. USA. 1850-1910. Lang.: Eng. 3387

Shakespeare's influence on detective fiction. USA. UK-England. 1995. Lang.: Eng. 3389

Computer-aided testing of writings attributed to Shakespeare. USA: Claremont, CA. 1997. Lang.: Eng. 3401

Theatrical aspects of fiction by Henry James. USA. 1870-1910. Lang.: Eng. 3433

The influence of theatre on novelist and adapter Louisa May Alcott. USA. 1832-1888. Lang.: Eng. 3442

Proust and Wagner's *Tristan und Isolde*. France: Paris. 1897-1927. Lang.: Eng. 3888

Representation and reception of the *castrato*. France. 1830-1970. Lang.: Eng. 4322

Little Clay Cart, The
SEE
Shākuntala.

Little Comedy, The
Performance/production
Collection of newspaper reviews by London theatre critics. UK-England: London. 1997. Lang.: Eng. 2008

Little Fight Music, A
Performance/production
Collection of newspaper reviews by London theatre critics. UK-England: London. 1997. Lang.: Eng. 2147

Little Night Music, A
Performance/production
Restaging the score of Stephen Sondheim's *A Little Night Music*. USA. 1973. Lang.: Eng. 3951

Little Satire on the 1997 General Election, A
Performance/production
Collection of newspaper reviews by London theatre critics. UK-England: London. 1997. Lang.: Eng. 2047

Little Theatre (Leningrad)
SEE
Malyj Dramatičeskij Teat'r.

Little Theatre (Moscow)
SEE
Malyj Teat'r.

Littlewood, Joan
Institutions
Profile of Theatre Royal, Stratford East. UK-England: London. 1953-1997. Lang.: Ger. 1498

Liturgical drama
Institutions
The theatre of Umbrian confraternities. Italy. 1300-1578. Lang.: Ita. 346
Performance spaces
The English church as performance space. England. 1100-1300. Lang.: Eng. 426
Performance/production
Resurrection drama in the medieval church. Germany: Gernrode. Netherlands: Maastricht. 1500-1996. Lang.: Eng. 1695

Social hierarchy in *Corpus Christi* pageantry. England. 1419-1490. Lang.: Eng. 3801

Enactments of the descent from the cross. Mexico. 1600-1997. Lang.: Eng. 3803

Chavittunátakam, the music drama of Kerala Christians. India: Kerala. 1500-1997. Lang.: Eng. 3871

A performance of the Beauvais *Ludus Danielis*. Netherlands: Maastricht. 1996. Lang.: Eng. 3872

A collaborative production of the medieval *Ludus Danielis*. Netherlands: Maastricht. 1996. Lang.: Eng. 3873
Plays/librettos/scripts
History of pre-Restoration English theatre. England. 965-1660. Lang.: Ita. 2456

The Coventry *Corpus Christi* as a dramatic expression of the Apostles' Creed. England. 1535-1568. Lang.: Eng. 2713
Relation to other fields
Changes in religious drama and practices. England. 1450-1560. Lang.: Eng. 735
Theory/criticism
Critique of the application of carnival to the analysis of late medieval religious drama. England. 1513-1556. Lang.: Eng. 873

Live and Kidding
Performance/production
Collection of newspaper reviews by London theatre critics. UK-England: London. 1997. Lang.: Eng. 2011

Live Entertainment (Livent, New York, NY)
Administration
Equity's contract with Livent. USA. 1997. Lang.: Eng. 92

Live from Boerassic Park
Performance/production
Collection of newspaper reviews by London theatre critics. UK-England: London. 1997. Lang.: Eng. 2063

Livermore, Steve
Performance/production
Collection of newspaper reviews by London theatre critics. UK-England: London. 1997. Lang.: Eng. 2022

Living Theatre (New York, NY)
Performance/production
Analysis of countercultural theatre. USA. 1960-1970. Lang.: Eng. 672

Livingston, Jennie
Theory/criticism
Analysis of criticism of Jennie Livingston's documentary film *Paris Is Burning*. USA. 1991. Lang.: Eng. 3700

Lizzie Borden
Performance/production
American chamber opera. USA. 1868-1997. Lang.: Eng. 4258

Lloyd Webber, Andrew
Design/technology
Work of cinematographer Darius Khondji on film adaptation of musical *Evita*. USA. 1997. Lang.: Eng. 3546

Scenic machine control systems used in musical productions at the Colosseum. Germany: Essen. 1997. Lang.: Ger. 3907

Lloyd Webber, Andrew — cont'd

David Hersey's lighting design for revival of *Jesus Christ, Superstar* at the Lyceum. UK-England: London. 1997. Lang.: Eng. 3909

Howell Binkley's lighting design for *Whistle Down the Wind* at the National Theatre. USA: Washington, DC. 1997. Lang.: Eng. 3920

Performance spaces

The history of the Colosseum and its new interior design. Germany: Essen. 1900-1997. Lang.: Ger. 3930

The renovation of the Lyceum Theatre for *Jesus Christ Superstar*. UK-England: London. 1904-1997. Lang.: Eng. 3931

Lloyd-Evans, Martin

Performance/production

Collection of newspaper reviews by London theatre critics. UK-England: London. 1997. Lang.: Eng. 2149

Lloyd, Jonathan

Performance/production

Collection of newspaper reviews by London theatre critics. UK-England: London. 1997. Lang.: Eng. 2023

Collection of newspaper reviews by London theatre critics. UK-England: London. 1997. Lang.: Eng. 2055

Collection of newspaper reviews by London theatre critics. UK-England: London. 1997. Lang.: Eng. 2089

Lloyd, Phyllida

Performance/production

Collection of newspaper reviews by London theatre critics. UK-England. 1997. Lang.: Eng. 2039

Lo Savio, Gerolamo

Performance/production

The map of England in productions of Shakespeare's *King Lear*. Europe. USA. 1909-1994. Lang.: Eng. 1650

Loane, Tim

Performance/production

Collection of newspaper reviews by London theatre critics. UK-England: London. 1997. Lang.: Eng. 2021

Lobel, Adrianne

Design/technology

Design elements of *On the Town* for New York Shakespeare Festival. USA: New York, NY. 1997. Lang.: Eng. 3915

Lochhead, Liz

Performance/production

Collection of newspaper reviews by London theatre critics. UK-England: London. 1997. Lang.: Eng. 1980

Loera, Paula

Performance/production

San Francisco Mime Troupe's *13 Días/13 Days*. USA: San Francisco, CA. 1997. Lang.: Eng. 2335

Loewe, Frederick

Plays/librettos/scripts

Cinematic versions of the Pygmalion myth. USA. 1938. Lang.: Eng. 3682

Löfgren, Lars

Institutions

Lars Löfgren's eleven years as manager of Dramaten. Sweden: Stockholm. 1986-1997. Lang.: Swe. 1491

Loftus, Cissie

Performance/production

History of the one-woman show. USA. 1890-1995. Lang.: Eng. 646

Logue, Christopher

Performance/production

Collection of newspaper reviews by London theatre critics. UK-England: London. 1997. Lang.: Eng. 2026

Loher, Dea

Performance/production

Collection of newspaper reviews by London theatre critics. UK-England: London. 1997. Lang.: Eng. 2143

Lohinszky, Lóránd

Performance/production

Interview with actor Lóránd Lohinszky. Hungary. Romania: Târgu-Mureș. 1946-1997. Lang.: Hun. 1766

Lok Rehas (Punjab)

Performance/production

Street theatre in Punjab province. Pakistan. 1979-1996. Lang.: Eng. 572

Loncraine, Richard

Performance/production

Loncraine and McKellen's *Richard III* from stage to screen. UK-England. 1995-1996. Lang.: Eng. 3590

Analysis of *Richard III*, film version by Loncraine and McKellen. UK-England. USA. 1993-1996. Lang.: Eng. 3596

Plays/librettos/scripts

Richard Loncraine and Ian McKellen's film adaptation of *Richard III*. UK-England. 1995. Lang.: Eng. 3651

London

Performance/production

Space in site-specific performance. UK-England. 1960-1997. Lang.: Eng. 619

London Bubble

Performance/production

Collection of newspaper reviews by London theatre critics. UK-England: London. 1997. Lang.: Eng. 2085

London Coliseum

Performance/production

Reception of Mark Morris's *L'Allegro, il Penseroso ed il Moderato*. UK-England: London. 1997. Lang.: Eng. 1193

London Merchant, The

Plays/librettos/scripts

Biblical and literary influences on *The London Merchant* by George Lillo. England: London. 1731. Lang.: Eng. 2746

Lone Star

Performance/production

Collection of newspaper reviews by London theatre critics. UK-England: London. 1997. Lang.: Eng. 2145

Lonesome West, The

Performance/production

Collection of newspaper reviews by London theatre critics. UK-England: London. 1997. Lang.: Eng. 2087

Long Day's Journey Into Night

Plays/librettos/scripts

New historicist analysis of O'Neill's *Long Day's Journey Into Night*. USA. 1939-1941. Lang.: Eng. 3146

O'Neill, Williams, and the limits of mimesis. USA. 1913-1980. Lang.: Eng. 3186

The figure of the prodigal son in American family drama. USA. 1946-1962. Lang.: Eng. 3254

Word avoidance and disclosure in plays of O'Neill and Valle-Inclán. USA. Spain. 1926-1959. Lang.: Eng. 3257

The interaction of gazes in *Long Day's Journey Into Night* by Eugene O'Neill. USA. 1939-1941. Lang.: Eng. 3274

Long, Adam

Performance/production

Collection of newspaper reviews by London theatre critics. UK-England: London. 1997. Lang.: Eng. 2094

Long, Yu

Performance/production

Beijing production of Carmen's *Bizet*. China, People's Republic of: Beijing. 1982-1997. Lang.: Eng. 4117

Looke About You

Plays/librettos/scripts

Theatrical reflections of the marital double standard. England. 1598-1650. Lang.: Eng. 2501

Looking for a Bride

SEE

Ženitba.

Looking for Richard

Performance/production

Analysis of Al Pacino's film *Looking for Richard*. USA. 1996. Lang.: Eng. 3606

Looking Out to See

Basic theatrical documents

Collection of one-act plays by Welsh writers. UK-Wales. 1952-1996. Lang.: Eng. 1321

LookOut (Glasgow)

Institutions

Scottish theatres run by women. UK-Scotland. 1996. Lang.: Eng. 392

Lope de Vega

SEE

Vega Carpio, Lope Félix de.

Lopez Martinez, Eduardo

Performance/production

San Francisco Mime Troupe's *13 Días/13 Days*. USA: San Francisco, CA. 1997. Lang.: Eng. 2335

López Rubio, José

Plays/librettos/scripts

The life and career of playwright José López Rubio. Spain. 1903-1996. Lang.: Eng. 3042

Lopez, Sabatino

Plays/librettos/scripts

Playwright Sabatino Lopez and his friendship with writer Federico De Roberto. Italy: Catania. 1896-1897. Lang.: Ita. 2959

Lyceum Theatre (London) — cont'd

Performance spaces

The renovation of the Lyceum Theatre for *Jesus Christ Superstar*. UK-England: London. 1904-1997. Lang.: Eng.   3931

Lyddiard, Alan
Performance/production

Collection of newspaper reviews by London theatre critics. UK-England: London. 1997. Lang.: Eng.   2029

Lyly, John
Plays/librettos/scripts

Female homoeroticism on the early English stage. England. 1594-1632. Lang.: Eng.   2482

Virginity in *Love's Metamorphosis* by John Lyly. England. 1599. Lang.: Eng.   2593

The forced marriage plot in early English drama. England. 1584-1642. Lang.: Eng.   2675

Lyne, Adrian
Performance/production

The representation of social dancing in mass media. USA. 1980-1990. Lang.: Eng.   1008

Lynn, Eva
Performance/production

Collection of newspaper reviews by London theatre critics. UK-England: London. 1997. Lang.: Eng.   2003

Lynn, Judanna
Design/technology

Houston Ballet Company's *Dracula*—costumes, sets, lighting. USA: Houston, TX. 1897-1997. Lang.: Eng.   1049

Lynn, Ralph
Performance/production

Comedian Ralph Lynn's work on *Wild Horses* by Ben Travers. UK-England: London. 1953. Lang.: Eng.   2191

Lyon, Emma (Emma, Lady Hamilton)
Performance/production

Emma Lyon, Goethe, and the *tableau vivant*. Italy: Naples. Germany. 1786-1791. Lang.: Eng.   566

Lyric Hammersmith (London)
Performance/production

Collection of newspaper reviews by London theatre critics. UK-England: London. 1997. Lang.: Eng.   1987

Collection of newspaper reviews by London theatre critics. UK-England: London. 1997. Lang.: Eng.   2006

Collection of newspaper reviews by London theatre critics. UK-England: London. 1997. Lang.: Eng.   2025

Collection of newspaper reviews by London theatre critics. UK-England: London. 1997. Lang.: Eng.   2037

Collection of newspaper reviews by London theatre critics. UK-England: London. 1997. Lang.: Eng.   2049

Collection of newspaper reviews by London theatre critics. UK-England: London. 1997. Lang.: Eng.   2064

Collection of newspaper reviews by London theatre critics. UK-England: London. 1997. Lang.: Eng.   2071

Collection of newspaper reviews by London theatre critics. UK-England: London. 1997. Lang.: Eng.   2099

Collection of newspaper reviews by London theatre critics. UK-England: London. 1997. Lang.: Eng.   2104

Collection of newspaper reviews by London theatre critics. UK-England: London. 1997. Lang.: Eng.   2131

Collection of newspaper reviews by London theatre critics. UK-England: London. 1997. Lang.: Eng.   2156

Lyric Opera of Chicago (Chicago, IL)
Institutions

Chamber opera and the Lyric Opera Center for American Artists. USA. 1997. Lang.: Eng.   4062

Performance/production

Background material on Lyric Opera of Chicago radio broadcast performances. USA: Chicago, IL. 1997. Lang.: Eng.   4231

Anthony Davis' opera *Amistad*. USA: Chicago, IL. 1997. Lang.: Eng.   4242

Lyric Studio (London)
Performance/production

Collection of newspaper reviews by London theatre critics. UK-England: London. 1997. Lang.: Eng.   1979

Collection of newspaper reviews by London theatre critics. UK-England: London. 1997. Lang.: Eng.   1985

Collection of newspaper reviews by London theatre critics. UK-England: London. 1997. Lang.: Eng.   2005

Collection of newspaper reviews by London theatre critics. UK-England: London. 1997. Lang.: Eng.   2015

Collection of newspaper reviews by London theatre critics. UK-England: London. 1997. Lang.: Eng.   2024

Collection of newspaper reviews by London theatre critics. UK-England: London. 1997. Lang.: Eng.   2032

Collection of newspaper reviews by London theatre critics. UK-England: London. 1997. Lang.: Eng.   2044

Collection of newspaper reviews by London theatre critics. UK-England: London. 1997. Lang.: Eng.   2054

Collection of newspaper reviews by London theatre critics. UK-England: London. 1997. Lang.: Eng.   2085

Collection of newspaper reviews by London theatre critics. UK-England: London. 1997. Lang.: Eng.   2095

Collection of newspaper reviews by London theatre critics. UK-England: London. 1997. Lang.: Eng.   2106

Collection of newspaper reviews by London theatre critics. UK-England: London. 1997. Lang.: Eng.   2112

Collection of newspaper reviews by London theatre critics. UK-England: London. 1997. Lang.: Eng.   2118

Collection of newspaper reviews by London theatre critics. UK-England: London. 1997. Lang.: Eng.   2126

Collection of newspaper reviews by London theatre critics. UK-England: London. 1997. Lang.: Eng.   2144

Collection of newspaper reviews by London theatre critics. UK-England: London. 1997. Lang.: Eng.   2149

Lysistrata
Performance/production

Essays on gender and performance. 250 B.C.-1995 A.D. Lang.: Eng.   1551

Early modern interpretations of Aristophanes' *Lysistrata*. Europe. USA. 1892-1930. Lang.: Eng.   1647

Lyssas, Alison
Plays/librettos/scripts

Report from women playwrights conference. Ireland: Galway. 1997. Lang.: Swe.   2930

Lyth, Ragnar
Performance/production

Interview with director Ragnar Lyth. Sweden: Stockholm, Gothenburg. 1990. Lang.: Swe.   1943

Lyttelton Theatre (London)
SEE ALSO

National Theatre Company.

Design/technology

Rick Fisher's lighting design for *Lady in the Dark* at the Lyttelton. UK-England: London. 1941-1997. Lang.: Eng.   3908

Performance/production

Collection of newspaper reviews by London theatre critics. UK-England: London. 1997. Lang.: Eng.   1972

Collection of newspaper reviews by London theatre critics. UK-England: London. 1997. Lang.: Eng.   1977

Collection of newspaper reviews by London theatre critics. UK-England: London. 1997. Lang.: Eng.   1986

Collection of newspaper reviews by London theatre critics. UK-England: London. 1997. Lang.: Eng.   2012

Collection of newspaper reviews by London theatre critics. UK-England: London. 1997. Lang.: Eng.   2067

Collection of newspaper reviews by London theatre critics. UK-England: London. 1997. Lang.: Eng.   2113

M. Butterfly
Plays/librettos/scripts

Authenticity and stereotype in David Henry Hwang's *M. Butterfly*. USA. 1988. Lang.: Eng.   3208

Theatrical representations of Asia and Asians. USA. 1990-1997. Lang.: Eng.   3218

Ma Rainey's Black Bottom
Plays/librettos/scripts

African-American cultural archetypes in the plays of August Wilson. USA. 1982-1995. Lang.: Eng.   3179

Playwright August Wilson's views on the northward migration of Blacks. USA. 1997. Lang.: Eng.   3277

Maan, Shakila
Performance/production

Collection of newspaper reviews by London theatre critics. UK-England: London. 1997. Lang.: Eng.   2055

Mabou Mines (New York, NY)
Performance/production
Career of performer Karen Kandel. USA: New York, NY. 1977-1997. Lang.: Eng. 663

Interculturalism in the work of Lee Breuer. USA: New York, NY. 1980-1995. Lang.: Eng. 678

Maboungou, Zab
Performance/production
The body and cultural identity in contemporary dance. USA. 1985-1995. Lang.: Eng. 996

MacArthur, Charles
Performance/production
Collection of newspaper reviews by London theatre critics. UK-England: London. 1997. Lang.: Eng. 2157

Analysis of the war pageant 'Fun To Be Free' by Ben Hecht and Charles MacArthur. USA: New York, NY. 1941. Lang.: Eng. 3807

Macbeth
Design/technology
Lighting design for productions at New York City Opera and Glimmerglass Opera. USA: New York, NY, Cooperstown, NY. 1997. Lang.: Eng. 4034
Institutions
Management and productions of Schauspiel Nürnberg. Germany: Nuremberg. 1997. Lang.: Ger. 1431
Performance/production
Robert Lepage's approach to directing Shakespeare. Canada: Quebec, PQ. 1993. Lang.: Eng. 1595

Interview with members of Théâtre Repère. Canada: Quebec, PQ. 1993. Lang.: Eng. 1596

Changes in Shakespearean production under David Garrick. England. 1747-1776. Lang.: Eng. 1627

Recent activities and productions of Schauspielhaus Rostock. Germany: Rostock. 1994-1997. Lang.: Ger. 1711

Reviews of Bochumer Schauspielhaus productions. Germany: Bochum. 1997. Lang.: Ger. 1730

Conversation with director Csaba Kiss and playwright Lajos Parti Nagy. Hungary. 1980-1996. Lang.: Hun. 1753

Ingmar Bergman's productions of Shakespeare's plays. Sweden. Germany. 1944-1994. Lang.: Ita. 1934

Collection of newspaper reviews by London theatre critics. UK-England. 1997. Lang.: Eng. 2125

Black actors and writers and the Negro Units of the Federal Theatre Project. USA: Washington, DC, New York, NY. 1935. Lang.: Eng. 2350

Trevor Nunn's television production of Shakespeare's *Macbeth*. UK-England. 1976-1978. Lang.: Eng. 3729
Plays/librettos/scripts
Fantasies of maternal power in Shakespeare's *Macbeth*. England. 1606. Lang.: Eng. 2449

Evil women in early modern English tragedy. England. 1590-1613. Lang.: Eng. 2452

Gender ideology and the occult in Shakespeare's plays. England. 1590-1613. Lang.: Eng. 2499

Feminist analysis of the place of women in Shakespeare's plays. England. 1590-1613. Lang.: Eng. 2519

Mundane language and theatrical spectacle in Shakespeare's *Macbeth*. England. 1606. Lang.: Eng. 2584

Excessive violence and political power in plays of Shakespeare. England. 1604-1611. Lang.: Eng. 2610

Madness and gender in the plays of Shakespeare. England. 1589-1613. Lang.: Eng. 2677

Law, justice, and criminology in plays of Shakespeare. England. 1590-1613. Lang.: Eng. 2756

Director and translator on the actuality of Shakespeare. Europe. 1985-1997. Lang.: Ger, Fre, Dut, Eng. 2796

Polanski's *Macbeth* and the reclamation of high art by the thriller genre. USA. 1971. Lang.: Eng. 3674
Relation to other fields
Comparing video versions of *Macbeth* in the classroom. USA. 1997. Lang.: Eng. 3391

Reader-response theory and the teaching of Shakespeare. USA. 1997. Lang.: Eng. 3405

Macbeth and the Beanstalk
Performance/production
Collection of newspaper reviews by London theatre critics. UK-England: London. 1997. Lang.: Eng. 2160

Macbeth—Stage of Blood
Performance/production
Collection of newspaper reviews by London theatre critics. UK-England: London. 1997. Lang.: Eng. 2096

MacDonald, Ann-Marie
Performance/production
Collection of newspaper reviews by London theatre critics. UK-England: London. 1997. Lang.: Eng. 2085
Plays/librettos/scripts
Time travel in English-language drama. USA. Canada. UK-England. 1908-1993. Lang.: Eng. 3171

MacDonald, Bryden
Performance/production
Collection of newspaper reviews by London theatre critics. UK-England. 1997. Lang.: Eng. 2043

Macdonald, James
Performance/production
Collection of newspaper reviews by London theatre critics. UK-England: London. 1997. Lang.: Eng. 2037

Collection of newspaper reviews by London theatre critics. UK-England. 1997. Lang.: Eng. 2150

MacDonald, John
Performance/production
John MacDonald's production of Pinter's *Old Times*, Washington Stage Guild. USA: Washington, DC. 1994. Lang.: Eng. 2325

MacDougall, Delia
Performance/production
Erin Cressida Wilson on her performance piece *Hurricane*. USA. 1996. Lang.: Eng. 2357

MacDuff, Pierre
Administration
Interview with Pierre MacDuff, general manager of Deux Mondes. Canada: Montreal, PQ, Quebec, PQ. 1960-1997. Lang.: Fre. 1233

Macfarlane, Gaynor
Performance/production
Collection of newspaper reviews by London theatre critics. UK-England: London. 1997. Lang.: Eng. 2054

Collection of newspaper reviews by London theatre critics. UK-England: London. 1997. Lang.: Eng. 2154

MacGregor, Roy
Performance/production
Collection of newspaper reviews by London theatre critics. UK-England: London. 1997. Lang.: Eng. 2120

Machado, Eduardo
Relation to other fields
Theatre artists' responses to the debate on multiculturalism of August Wilson and Robert Brustein. USA. 1997. Lang.: Eng. 789

Machiavelli, Niccolò
Plays/librettos/scripts
Comparison of classical Roman, Renaissance Italian, and Shakespearean treatments of similar stories. Europe. 200 B.C.-1610 A.D. Lang.: Eng. 2799

Machinal
Plays/librettos/scripts
The theme of nurturing in plays of Wolff, Treadwell, and Wasserstein. USA. 1996. Lang.: Eng. 3136
Theory/criticism
Critical perceptions of female violence in plays of Glaspell, Treadwell, and Kesselman. USA. 1922-1997. Lang.: Eng. 3504

Machine Room (London)
Performance/production
Collection of newspaper reviews by London theatre critics. UK-England: London. 1997. Lang.: Eng. 2053

Collection of newspaper reviews by London theatre critics. UK-England: London. 1997. Lang.: Eng. 2080

Collection of newspaper reviews by London theatre critics. UK-England: London. 1997. Lang.: Eng. 2102

Collection of newspaper reviews by London theatre critics. UK-England: London. 1997. Lang.: Eng. 2119

Collection of newspaper reviews by London theatre critics. UK-England: London. 1997. Lang.: Eng. 2141

MacInnis, Allen
Performance/production
Shaw Festival production of *In Good King Charles's Golden Days*. Canada: Niagara-on-the-Lake, ON. 1997. Lang.: Eng. 1582

MacIvor, Daniel
Performance/production
Daniel Brooks on his collaboration with Daniel MacIvor on *Here Lies Henry*. Canada: Toronto, ON. 1994-1995. Lang.: Eng. 1578

MacIvor, Daniel — cont'd

Daniel Brooks' production of *The Soldier Dreams* by Daniel MacIvor. Canada: Toronto, ON. 1997. Lang.: Eng. 1603

Plays/librettos/scripts
Playwright Daniel MacIvor. Canada: Halifax, NS. 1990-1997. Lang.: Eng. 2400

Analysis of *Here Lies Henry* by Daniel MacIvor and Daniel Brooks. Canada. 1994-1996. Lang.: Eng. 2437

Mack and Mabel
Performance/production
Actress/singer Bernadette Peters. USA. 1961-1997. Lang.: Eng. 3957

Mackay, Constance D'Arcy
Performance/production
Constance D'Arcy Mackay's *The Pageant of Sunshine and Shadow*. USA. 1900-1918. Lang.: Eng. 3771

Mackerel Sky
Performance/production
Collection of newspaper reviews by London theatre critics. UK-England: London. 1997. Lang.: Eng. 2115

Macklin, Charles
Plays/librettos/scripts
Censorship and satire in the eighteenth century. England. 1710-1789. Lang.: Eng. 2617

Mackmin, Anna
Performance/production
Collection of newspaper reviews by London theatre critics. UK-England: London. 1997. Lang.: Eng. 1991

MacLiammoir, Michael
Performance/production
Collection of newspaper reviews by London theatre critics. UK-England: London. 1997. Lang.: Eng. 2018

MacMillan, Hector
Performance/production
Collection of newspaper reviews by London theatre critics. UK-England: London. 1997. Lang.: Eng. 1981

MacMillan, Kenneth
Performance/production
The work of choreographer Kenneth MacMillan at the Royal Ballet. UK-England: London. 1955-1992. Lang.: Eng. 1116

MacNaughton, Ian
Performance/production
Productions at the Munich Biennale. Germany: Munich. 1997. Lang.: Ger. 4148

Macready, William Charles
Performance/production
Stage imagery in productions of Shakespeare's *Coriolanus*. England. 1754-1901. Lang.: Eng. 1634

Shakespearean production in the age of actor-managers. UK-England. 1840-1914. Lang.: Eng. 2193

Mácsai, Pál
Performance/production
Interview with actor-director Pál Mácsai. Hungary. 1980-1997. Lang.: Hun. 1777

Mad Couple Well Match'd, A
Plays/librettos/scripts
Theatrical reflections of the marital double standard. England. 1598-1650. Lang.: Eng. 2501

Mad Dog Killer Leper Fiend
Performance/production
Collection of newspaper reviews by London theatre critics. UK-England: London. 1997. Lang.: Eng. 2040

Mad Forest
Performance/production
Director and dramaturg Jayme Koszyn. USA: Boston, MA, Philadelphia, PA. 1992-1995. Lang.: Eng. 2290

Harriet Power, director and dramaturg for Churchill's *Mad Forest* at Venture Theatre. USA: Philadelphia, PA. 1992. Lang.: Eng. 2319

Mad World, My Masters, A
Plays/librettos/scripts
Calvinism in the city comedies of Thomas Middleton. England. 1604-1611. Lang.: Eng. 2570

Twentieth-century adaptations of Jacobean plays. England. 1604-1986. Lang.: Eng. 2673

Implications of mirth in plays of Shakespeare and Middleton. England. 1594-1605. Lang.: Eng. 2780

Madách Színház (Budapest)
Performance/production
Colleagues' recollections of director László Vámos. Hungary. 1928-1996. Lang.: Hun. 1763

Excerpts from the diary of actor Miklós Gábor. Hungary. 1955-1957. Lang.: Hun. 1764

Madách Táncműhely (Budapest)
Performance/production
A joint production of Budapest Operetta Theatre dance company and Madách Dance Workshop. Hungary: Budapest. 1996-1997. Lang.: Hun. 3937

Madách, Imre
Design/technology
Stage designs for *Az ember tragédiája (The Tragedy of Man)* by Imre Madách. Hungary: Budapest. 1883-1915. Lang.: Hun. 1357

Performance/production
Provincial productions of *Az ember tragédiája (The Tragedy of Man)* by Imre Madách. Hungary. 1884-1918. Lang.: Hun. 1762

The stage career of Madách's *Az ember tragédiája (The Tragedy of Man)* in Voivodship. Hungary. Yugoslavia. 1884-1965. Lang.: Hun. 1765

Jenő Janovics and Imre Madách's *Az ember tragédiája (The Tragedy of Man)*. Hungary: Kolozsvár. Romania: Cluj. 1894-1945. Lang.: Hun. 1767

Music in the premiere of *Az ember tragédiája (The Tragedy of Man)* by Imre Madách. Hungary: Budapest. 1883. Lang.: Hun. 1768

Analysis of the premiere of *Az ember tragédiája (The Tragedy of Man)* by Imre Madách. Hungary: Budapest. 1883. Lang.: Hun. 1779

Géza Blattner's puppet adaptation of *Az ember tragédiája (The Tragedy of Man)* by Madách. Hungary. 1918-1954. Lang.: Hun. 4365

Plays/librettos/scripts
Comparison of works by Madách and Dostojévskij. Hungary. 1860-1900. Lang.: Hun. 2896

Arany's revisions to Madách's *Az ember tragédiája (The Tragedy of Man)*. Hungary. 1842-1862. Lang.: Hun. 2898

Female characters in plays of Imre Madách. Hungary. 1824. Lang.: Hun. 2899

Reception and analysis of *Az ember tragédiája (The Tragedy of Man)* by Imre Madách. Hungary. 1850-1860. Lang.: Hun. 2900

Madama Butterfly
Performance/production
Puccini's use of the key of A major. Italy. 1836. Lang.: Eng. 4194

Madame de Sade
SEE
Sado Koshaku fujin.

Mädchen mit den Schwefelhölzern, Das
Performance/production
Hans Werner Henze's opera *Das Mädchen mit den Schwefelhölzern*. Germany: Hamburg. 1921-1997. Lang.: Ger. 4156

Maddie
Performance/production
Collection of newspaper reviews by London theatre critics. UK-England: London. 1997. Lang.: Eng. 2112

Account of new musical *Maddie*. UK-England. 1997. Lang.: Eng. 3948

Madeira, Jean
Performance/production
Interpreters of Bizet's heroine Carmen. France: Paris. USA: New York, NY. 1875-1997. Lang.: Eng. 4139

Mädel aus der Vorstadt, Das (Girl from the Suburbs, The)
Plays/librettos/scripts
Analysis of *Das Mädel aus der Vorstadt (The Girl from the Suburbs)* by Johann Nestroy. Austria: Vienna. 1841-1995. Lang.: Eng. 2383

Madeleine
Performance/production
The Metropolitan Opera premiere of Victor Herbert's *Madeleine*. USA: New York, NY. 1907-1995. Lang.: Eng. 4271

Maeterlinck, Maurice
Performance/production
Interview with director Julien Roy. Belgium: Brussels. 1997. Lang.: Eng. 1568

Productions of the Paris-Bruxelles Exhibition. Belgium: Brussels. 1997. Lang.: Eng. 1570

Claude Régy's production of *La Mort de Tintagiles (The Death of Tintagiles)* by Maeterlinck. France: Paris. Belgium: Ghent. 1997. Lang.: Eng. 1658

Recent productions of works by Maeterlinck. France: Paris. 1997. Lang.: Swe. 1664

Plays/librettos/scripts
Analysis of *Les Aveugles (The Blind)* by Maurice Maeterlinck. Belgium. 1890. Lang.: Ita. 2384

Maeterlinck's influence on playwright Ivan Cankar. Slovenia. Lang.: Slo. 3007

Magyar, Éva
Institutions
Profile of Sámán Színház. Hungary. 1993-1997. Lang.: Hun. 1161

Mahabharata, The
Performance/production
Peter Brook's production *The Mahabharata*. UK-England. France. 1985. Lang.: Pol. 2164
Plays/librettos/scripts
Brook, Mnouchkine and intercultural theatre. France: Paris. 1988-1992. Lang.: Eng. 2832

Mahoney, Mick
Performance/production
Collection of newspaper reviews by London theatre critics. UK-England: London. 1997. Lang.: Eng. 2000

Mai, The
Performance/production
Collection of newspaper reviews by London theatre critics. UK-England: London. 1997. Lang.: Eng. 2007

Maid of Honour, The
Plays/librettos/scripts
Social mobility in Jacobean drama. England. 1618-1640. Lang.: Eng. 2745

Maid of Orleans, The
SEE
Orleanskaja Deva.

Maid's Tragedy, The
Performance/production
Collection of newspaper reviews by London theatre critics. UK-England. 1997. Lang.: Eng. 2098
Plays/librettos/scripts
Evil women in early modern English tragedy. England. 1590-1613. Lang.: Eng. 2452

Maids, The
SEE
Bonnes, Les.

Maienschlager (May Pop-Song, A)
Plays/librettos/scripts
Account of new German plays with historical themes. Germany. 1997. Lang.: Ger. 2837

Maillet, Alain
Basic theatrical documents
Text of *Potins d'enfer (Hellish Gossip)* by Jean-Noël Fenwick. France: Paris. 1996. Lang.: Fre. 1270

Maillet, Antonine
Plays/librettos/scripts
Analysis of *La Sagouine (The Slattern)* by Antonine Maillet. Canada. 1971. Lang.: Fre. 2399

Mailman, Deborah
Performance/production
Collection of newspaper reviews by London theatre critics. UK-England: London. 1997. Lang.: Eng. 2073

Mair, Charles
Plays/librettos/scripts
Indigenous peoples in Canadian historical drama. Canada. 1886-1997. Lang.: Eng. 2424

Maison Théâtre (Montreal, PQ)
Performance spaces
Architectural changes to the Maison Théâtre. Canada: Montreal, PQ. 1997. Lang.: Fre. 418

Maitland, Sara
Plays/librettos/scripts
Women and theatrical collaboration. USA. UK-England. 1930-1990. Lang.: Eng. 3264

Majakovskij, Vladimir Vladimirovič
Performance/production
Actor and director in Russian cinema. USSR. 1917-1958. Lang.: Ita. 3630

Majcen, Stanko
Plays/librettos/scripts
Analysis of *Alenčica, kraljica Ogrska (Alenčica, Queen of Hungary)* by Stanko Majcen. Slovenia. 1912. Lang.: Slo. 3021

Major Barbara
Plays/librettos/scripts
Women's expanding role in society seen in plays of George Bernard Shaw. UK-England. 1893-1923. Lang.: Eng. 3091

Major Problems
Design/technology
The scenography of Richard Foreman. USA. 1990-1996. Lang.: Eng. 1362

Major, Leon
Design/technology
Lighting design for productions at New York City Opera and Glimmerglass Opera. USA: New York, NY, Cooperstown, NY. 1997. Lang.: Eng. 4034

Makai, Péter
Performance/production
Miklós Gábor Kerényi's production of *Der Fliegende Holländer*, Budapest Opera House. Hungary: Budapest. 1997. Lang.: Hun. 4184

Makejév, Michajl
Performance/production
Russian productions of plays by Harold Pinter. Russia: Moscow. 1996. Lang.: Eng. 1864

Makeup
Performance/production
CD-ROM presentation of all aspects of *kutiyattam*. India. 1000-1997. Lang.: Eng. 557
Videodisc of Ibsen's *Et Dukkehjem (A Doll's House)* combining performance and commentary. Norway. USA. 1879-1997. Lang.: Eng. 1830

Makhene, Ramolao
Institutions
Interview with Ramolao Makhene, founder of Performing Arts Workers Equity. South Africa, Republic of. 1976-1996. Lang.: Eng. 378

Maladie de la Mort, La (Sickness of Death, The)
Audience
Robert Wilson's staging of *La Maladie de la Mort (The Sickness of Death)* by Marguerite Duras. France: Paris. 1997. Lang.: Fre. 1249
Performance/production
Robert Wilson's production of *La Maladie de la Mort (The Sickness of Death)* by Marguerite Duras. Switzerland: Lausanne. 1970-1997. Lang.: Hun. 1962
Collection of newspaper reviews by London theatre critics. UK-England: London. 1997. Lang.: Eng. 2135

Malcontent, The
Performance/production
John Marston and children's theatres. England. 1598-1634. Lang.: Eng. 1631
Plays/librettos/scripts
John Webster's malcontents and the reaction to theatricality. England. 1600-1634. Lang.: Eng. 2466
The Italian palazzo on the Jacobean stage. England. 1603-1625. Lang.: Eng. 2625

Malgrave Road Theatre (Halifax, NS)
Performance/production
Malgrave Road Theatre production of *The Company Store* by Sheldon Currie. Canada: Halifax, NS. 1996-1997. Lang.: Eng. 1590

Malin, David
Performance/production
Collection of newspaper reviews by London theatre critics. UK-England: London. 1997. Lang.: Eng. 2059

Malina, Jaroslav
Performance spaces
Theatre structures used at Prague Quadrennial. Czech Republic: Český Krumlov. 1995. Lang.: Eng. 1518
Profile of Měsíčník Ceských Divadel, a revolving auditorium theatre. Czech Republic: Český Krumlov. 1947-1996. Lang.: Eng. 1519

Malinche
Plays/librettos/scripts
Analysis of *Malinche* by Inés M. Stanger and *Opus Primum* by Hadi Kurich. Chile. Spain. 1993. Lang.: Spa. 2439

Malmö AmatörteaterForum
Institutions
Profile of Malmö AmatörteaterForum. Sweden: Malmö. 1995. Lang.: Swe. 1487

Malmsjö, Jan
Performance/production
Interview with actress Marie Göranzon. Sweden: Stockholm. 1964-1997. Lang.: Swe. 1958

Maloney, Michael
Performance/production
Interview with actor Michael Maloney about roles in Shakespearean films. USA. 1995. Lang.: Eng. 3625

Malpede, John
Performance/production
Interview with John Malpede of the homeless performing group Los Angeles Poverty Department. USA: Los Angeles, CA, New York, NY. 1972-1991. Lang.: Eng. 3840

Management, top — cont'd

Performance/production
Colleagues recall Metropolitan Opera general manager Rudolf Bing.
USA: New York, NY. 1950-1972. Lang.: Eng.   4255

Rudolf Bing's tenure as general manager of the Metropolitan Opera.
USA: New York, NY. 1950-1972. Lang.: Eng.   4266

Mandragola, La (Mandrake, The)
Plays/librettos/scripts
Comparison of classical Roman, Renaissance Italian, and Shakespearean
treatments of similar stories. Europe. 200 B.C.-1610 A.D. Lang.: Eng.
                                                                   2799

Manen, Hans van
Performance/production
Choreographer Hans van Manen. Netherlands. 1932-1997. Lang.: Dut.
                                                                   1182

Manhattan Class Company (New York, NY)
Design/technology
Scene designs of Neil Patel. USA. 1996. Lang.: Eng.   1373

Manhattan School of Music (New York, NY)
Institutions
Downsizing American opera companies. USA. 1997. Lang.: Eng.   4059

Manhattan Theatre Club (New York, NY)
Design/technology
Work of lighting designer Kenneth Posner. USA: New York, NY. 1997.
Lang.: Eng.   1364

Manitoba Theatre Centre (Winnipeg, MB)
Administration
Interview with Steven Schipper, artistic director, Manitoba Theatre
Centre. Canada: Winnipeg, MB. 1996. Lang.: Eng.   8

Mankell, Henning
Institutions
Profile of Mutembela Gogo, Henning Mankell, director. Mozambique:
Maputo. 1987-1997. Lang.: Swe.   1447
Performance/production
Interview with principals of joint production *Berättelse på tidens strand
(A Tale on the Shore of Time)*. Sweden. Mozambique. 1997. Lang.: Swe.
                                                                   1959

Mankiewicz, Joseph L.
Basic theatrical documents
Script of *All About Eve* by Joseph L. Mankiewicz. USA. 1950. Lang.:
Eng.   3536
Performance/production
Playwright Christopher Durang on Joseph Mankiewicz's *All About Eve*.
USA. 1950. Lang.: Eng.   3612
Plays/librettos/scripts
Profile of director and screenwriter Joseph L. Mankiewicz. USA. 1909-
1993. Lang.: Eng.   3659

Mankiewicz, Tom
Plays/librettos/scripts
Profile of director and screenwriter Joseph L. Mankiewicz. USA. 1909-
1993. Lang.: Eng.   3659

Mankind
Performance/production
Creating roles in medieval theatre in the absence of psychological
motivation. Italy: Camerino. 1996. Lang.: Eng.   1814

Mann, Charlotte
Performance/production
Collection of newspaper reviews by London theatre critics. UK-England:
London. 1997. Lang.: Eng.   2141

Collection of newspaper reviews by London theatre critics. UK-England:
London. 1997. Lang.: Eng.   2153

Mann, Emily
Plays/librettos/scripts
Interview with Emily Mann, author and director of documentary theatre.
USA: Princeton, NJ. 1981-1996. Lang.: Eng.   3139

Mann, Middleton
Performance/production
Collection of newspaper reviews by London theatre critics. UK-England:
London. 1997. Lang.: Eng.   2115

Mannheimer Nationaltheater (Mannheim)
Administration
Ulrich Schwab's public relations strategy at Mannheimer
Nationaltheater. Germany: Mannheim. 1996-1997. Lang.: Ger.   1239
Performance/production
Productions of Bruno Klimek at Mannheimer Nationaltheater.
Germany: Mannheim. 1996-1997. Lang.: Ger.   1689

World premieres at Mannheimer Nationaltheater. Germany: Mannheim.
1997. Lang.: Ger.   1697
Plays/librettos/scripts
Account of new German plays with historical themes. Germany. 1997.
Lang.: Ger.   2837

Mānoa Valley
Basic theatrical documents
Collection of plays about Hawaii by Edward Sakamoto. USA. 1993-
1994. Lang.: Eng.   1341

Manon
Performance/production
Impressions of opera performances in several German cities. Germany.
1997. Lang.: Ger.   4147

Månrenen (Moondeer, The)
Performance/production
Interview with dancer Michiyo Hayashi. Sweden: Gothenburg. 1997.
Lang.: Swe.   1110

Mansouri, Lotfi
Design/technology
Sound design problems of San Francisco Opera's temporary home.
USA: San Francisco, CA. 1996. Lang.: Eng.   4036

Many Hands
Plays/librettos/scripts
Ideology in community plays seen at Blyth Festival. Canada: Blyth, ON.
1993. Lang.: Eng.   2418

Manzel, Dagmar
Performance/production
Interview with actress Dagmar Manzel. Germany: Berlin. 1997. Lang.:
Ger.   1708

Maponya, Maishe
Plays/librettos/scripts
Interview with playwright Maishe Maponya about his work teaching
theatre at the university level. South Africa, Republic of. 1996. Lang.:
Eng.   3026

Marat/Sade
Institutions
The National's season of theatre in the round at the Olivier. UK-
England: London. 1997. Lang.: Eng.   1499
Performance/production
Collection of newspaper reviews by London theatre critics. UK-England:
London. 1997. Lang.: Eng.   2048
Plays/librettos/scripts
Metatheatrical techniques of Weiss, Gatti, and Stoppard. Europe. 1964-
1982. Lang.: Eng.   2783
Theory/criticism
Typologies of performance analysis. UK-England. USA. 1963-1997.
Lang.: Eng.   911

Marber, Patrick
Performance/production
Collection of newspaper reviews by London theatre critics. UK-England:
London. 1997. Lang.: Eng.   2055

Marceau, Marcel
Performance/production
Collection of newspaper reviews by London theatre critics. UK-England:
London. 1997. Lang.: Eng.   2045

Marcello, Helena
Performance/production
Guest performances in Polish cities. Poland: Cracow, Lvov, Warsaw.
1810-1915. Lang.: Pol.   583

Marchant, Tim
Performance/production
Collection of newspaper reviews by London theatre critics. UK-England:
London. 1997. Lang.: Eng.   2044

Marchant, Tony
Performance/production
Collection of newspaper reviews by London theatre critics. UK-England:
London. 1997. Lang.: Eng.   2018

Marchi, Virgilio
Performance spaces
The work of Virgilio Marchi in the restoration of the Casa d'Arte
Bragaglia. Italy: Rome. 1921-1923. Lang.: Ita.   444
Performance/production
Italian productions of D'Annunzio's *La Figlia di Iorio (Iorio's
Daughter)*. Italy. 1904-1983. Lang.: Ita.   1797

Marcus, Neil
Performance/production
Collection of newspaper reviews by London theatre critics. UK-England:
London. 1997. Lang.: Eng.   1997

Margallo, Juan
Performance/production
Juan Margallo's production of *La tuerta suerte de Perico Galápago (The
One-Eyed Luck of Perico Galápago)* by Jorge Márquez. Spain: Madrid.
1996. Lang.: Eng.   1920

Margaret Durham
Basic theatrical documents
Text of *Margaret Durham* by Mary Lu Anne Gardner. Canada. 1996.
Lang.: Eng.   1258

Margolin, Deb
Performance/production
Essays on gender and performance. 250 B.C.-1995 A.D. Lang.: Eng.
1551

Training
The teaching of performance composition. USA: New York, NY. 1997.
Lang.: Eng.
937

Margoshes, Steven
Performance/production
Collection of newspaper reviews by London theatre critics. UK-England: London. 1997. Lang.: Eng.
2137

Margulies, Donald
Design/technology
Scene designs of Neil Patel. USA. 1996. Lang.: Eng.
1373
Performance/production
Director Lisa Peterson. USA: Los Angeles, CA. 1997. Lang.: Eng.
2279

Maria Antonia
Plays/librettos/scripts
The 'Black Madonna' in Cuban theatre. Cuba. 1925-1990. Lang.: Spa.
2444

Maria Magdalena
Performance/production
The new season at Bochumer Schauspielhaus. Germany: Bochum. 1997.
Lang.: Ger.
1747

Mariage Blanc
SEE
Biale małżeństwo.

Mariage de Figaro, Le (Marriage of Figaro, The)
Performance/production
The dramaturg and *One Crazy Day*, an adaptation of Beaumarchais' *The Marriage of Figaro*. USA: Tucson, AZ. 1992. Lang.: Eng.
2322
Plays/librettos/scripts
Analysis of opera librettos by Boito, Da Ponte, and Gertrude Stein.
Europe. 1770-1915. Lang.: Eng.
4289

Marichal, Teresa
Basic theatrical documents
Anthology of Latin American women's plays. Latin America. 1981-1989.
Lang.: Eng.
1291

Marie and Bruce
Plays/librettos/scripts
Analysis of plays by Wallace Shawn. USA. 1970-1996. Lang.: Eng. 3215

Playwright and actor Wallace Shawn. USA. 1981-1997. Lang.: Eng.
3303

Mariinskij Teat'r (St. Petersburg)
SEE
Akademičéskij Teat'r Opery i Baleta im. S.M. Kirova.

Marinetti, Filippo Tommaso
Plays/librettos/scripts
Futurism and the myth of the Medusa. Italy. 1909-1935. Lang.: Ita.
2953

Marinier, Robert
Institutions
Solo performance at the Festival de Théâtre des Amériques. Canada: Montreal, PQ. 1997. Lang.: Fre.
1392

Marionettes
SEE ALSO
Classed Entries under PUPPETRY—Marionettes.

Marivaux, Pierre Carlet de Chamblain de
Performance/production
Productions of the International Istanbul Theatre Festival. Turkey: Istanbul. 1980-1997. Lang.: Eng.
1966

Collection of newspaper reviews by London theatre critics. UK-England: London. 1997. Lang.: Eng.
2025

Collection of newspaper reviews by London theatre critics. UK-England: London. 1997. Lang.: Eng.
2113

Collection of newspaper reviews by London theatre critics. UK-England: London. 1997. Lang.: Eng.
2133
Plays/librettos/scripts
Adaptations of French classics for contemporary audiences. Canada: Montreal, PQ. France. 1997. Lang.: Fre.
2421

James Magruder on his translation of *Le Triomphe de l'amour (The Triumph of Love)* by Marivaux. USA: Baltimore, MD. 1986-1995.
Lang.: Eng.
3230

Mark Morris Dance Group (New York, NY)
Performance/production
Reception of Mark Morris's *L'Allegro, il Penseroso ed il Moderato*. UK-England: London. 1997. Lang.: Eng.
1193

Mark Taper Forum (Los Angeles, CA)
Design/technology
Design for three productions of Tony Kushner's *Angels in America*.
USA: New York, NY, Los Angeles, CA. UK-England: London. 1992-1994. Lang.: Eng.
1363

Mark, Zane
Plays/librettos/scripts
Bring in 'Da Noise, Bring in 'Da Funk and the Black audience. USA: New York, NY. 1996-1997. Lang.: Eng.
4002

Market Theatre (Johannesburg)
Institutions
Interview with Pule Hlatshwayo of Market Theatre. South Africa, Republic of: Johannesburg. 1975. Lang.: Swe.
1472
Plays/librettos/scripts
Interview with Market Theatre actor and playwright Barney Simon. South Africa, Republic of. 1976-1992. Lang.: Eng.
3027
Theory/criticism
Critical response to a production of Euripides' *Medea* by Mark Fleishman and Jenny Reznek. South Africa, Republic of. 1994-1996.
Lang.: Eng.
3494

Marketing
Administration
Interviews with theatrical poster artists. Poland. 1931-1997. Lang.: Eng, Fre.
44

Polish theatre poster art. Poland. 1949-1997. Lang.: Eng, Fre.
47

Presenting theatre in exhibitions. Poland. 1960-1997. Lang.: Eng, Fre. 48

Interview with marketing expert George Fenmore. USA: New York, NY. 1961-1997. Lang.: Eng.
59

Technical aid in fundraising and marketing for small arts groups. USA. 1997. Lang.: Eng.
121

Marketing model for university graduate programs in theatre and dance. USA: Lubbock, TX. 1994-1996. Lang.: Eng.
126

The crucial importance of the internet for not-for-profit organizations.
USA. 1997. Lang.: Eng.
127

Advertising and marketing campaigns for the musical *Ragtime*. USA: New York, NY. Canada: Toronto, ON. 1997. Lang.: Eng.
3901

Marketing techniques of opera companies. USA. 1997. Lang.: Eng. 4005
Institutions
Profile of poster museum. Poland: Wilanów. 1966-1997. Lang.: Eng, Fre.
357

Marketing strategies of Orlando/Peabody Alliance for the Arts and Culture. USA: Orlando, FL. 1997. Lang.: Eng.
410

Independent theatre meeting on new models of promotion. Germany: Berlin. 1997. Lang.: Ger.
1433
Plays/librettos/scripts
Internet marketing of plays. USA. 1997. Lang.: Eng.
703

Interview with publisher about contemporary drama. Germany. 1997.
Lang.: Ger.
2865
Relation to other fields
Marketing techniques of the interactive show *Tamara: The Living Movie*. USA. 1987. Lang.: Eng.
813

Markgrafentheater (Erlangen)
Performance/production
Performances of the classics in Franconia. Germany. 1997. Lang.: Ger.
1737

Markham, Jehane
Performance/production
Collection of newspaper reviews by London theatre critics. UK-England: London. 1997. Lang.: Eng.
2139

Marking Time
Performance/production
Collection of newspaper reviews by London theatre critics. UK-England: London. 1997. Lang.: Eng.
2131

Marknadsafton (Market Eve)
Performance/production
The work together of actors Solveig Tännström and Börje Ahlstedt. Sweden: Stockholm. 1967. Lang.: Swe.
1961

Markó, Iván
Performance/production
Choreography of Iván Markó performed by Magyar Fesztivál Balett. Hungary: Budapest. 1997. Lang.: Hun.
1086

Márkus, László
Performance/production
László Márkus, former general director of Royal Hungarian Opera House. Hungary: Budapest. 1923-1944. Lang.: Hun.
4173

Marleau, Denis
Institutions
Impressions of the Festival d'Avignon. France: Avignon. 1997. Lang.: Ger.
313
Performance/production
The body and the text in productions of the Festival de Théâtre des Amériques. Canada: Montreal, PQ. 1997. Lang.: Fre.
1583

Marleau, Denis — cont'd

Denis Marleau's production of Lessing's *Nathan der Weise (Nathan the Wise)*, Avignon festival. France: Avignon. 1997. Lang.: Eng. 1665

Marlene
Performance/production
Collection of newspaper reviews by London theatre critics. UK-England: London. 1997. Lang.: Eng. 2024

Interview with actress Sian Phillips. UK-Wales. UK-England: London. 1930-1997. Lang.: Eng. 2234

Marlowe, Christopher
Plays/librettos/scripts
The appropriation of Shakespeare by the dispossessed and marginalized. 1590-1995. Lang.: Eng. 2366

The nature of Christopher Marlowe's dramaturgy. England. 1585-1593. Lang.: Eng. 2454

The influence on Shakespeare of Marlowe's *Tamburlaine*. England. 1587-1616. Lang.: Eng. 2497

Sex and gender in plays of Christopher Marlowe. England. 1587-1593. Lang.: Eng. 2522

Solipsism in Marlowe's *Doctor Faustus*. England. 1551-1616. Lang.: Eng. 2561

Subjectivity and discourse in medieval and early modern drama. England. 1250-1642. Lang.: Eng. 2579

Narcissism in Renaissance tragedy. England. 1450-1580. Lang.: Eng. 2609

Doctor Faustus and the rise of tragedy. England. 1604. Lang.: Eng. 2690

Racial and national meanings and economic practice in Renaissance theatre. England. 1590-1650. Lang.: Eng. 2693

Homosexual friendship in plays of Shakespeare, Fletcher, and Marlowe. England. 1595-1613. Lang.: Eng. 2697

Comparison of Marlowe's *Edward II* and Shakespeare's *Richard II*. England. 1592-1597. Lang.: Eng. 2735

Masculinity in Marlowe's *Tamburlaine*, Part II. England. 1587. Lang.: Eng. 2774

Relation to other fields
An engraving of Edward Alleyn dressed as Tamburlaine. England. 1603. Lang.: Eng. 3325

Marnas, Catherine
Performance/production
History and politics on the Parisian stage. France: Paris. 1997. Lang.: Ger. 1669

Marosvásárhelyi Nemzeti Színház, Magyar Társulat (Târgu-Mureş)
Performance/production
Interview with actor Lóránd Lohinszky. Hungary. Romania: Târgu-Mureş. 1946-1997. Lang.: Hun. 1766

Marowitz, Charles
Performance/production
Charles Marowitz on his approach to directing Shakespeare. USA. 1987. Lang.: Eng. 2302

Márquez, Jorge
Performance/production
Juan Margallo's production of *La tuerta suerte de Perico Galápago (The One-Eyed Luck of Perico Galápago)* by Jorge Márquez. Spain: Madrid. 1996. Lang.: Eng. 1920

Marquis de Sade
Performance/production
The style of productions at Bochumer Schauspielhaus. Germany: Bochum. 1995-1997. Lang.: Ger. 1732

Marquis Theatre (New York, NY)
Administration
Equity-sponsored Phyllis Newman Women's Health Initiative and its benefit performances. USA: New York, NY. 1997. Lang.: Eng. 85

Marriage à la Mode
Plays/librettos/scripts
Analysis of conversations of 'Wit' couples in Restoration comedy. England. 1660-1700. Lang.: Eng. 2453

Marriage of Figaro, The by Mozart
SEE
Nozze di Figaro, Le.

Marriage, The
SEE ALSO
Ženitba.

Maršak, Samuil
Performance/production
Productions of *Gudbai Amerika (Goodbye America)* before and after perestrojka. Russia. 1933-1996. Lang.: Eng. 1898

Marseillaise, La
Performance/production
Excerpt from biography of opera singer Mary Garden. France: Paris. 1875-1957. Lang.: Eng. 4144

Marsh, Gerry
Performance/production
Collection of newspaper reviews by London theatre critics. UK-England: London. 1997. Lang.: Eng. 1996

Marsh, Reginald
Relation to other fields
Burlesque theatre as seen in artwork of Reginald Marsh. USA. 1920-1950. Lang.: Eng. 3777

Marshall Fisher, Ian
Performance/production
Concert versions of neglected American musicals in the 'Discover the Lost Musicals' series. UK-England: London. 1990-1997. Lang.:Eng. 3944

Marshall, E.G.
Performance/production
Interview with actor/director Austin Pendleton. USA. 1980-1995. Lang.: Eng. 2266

Marshall, Ewan
Performance/production
Collection of newspaper reviews by London theatre critics. UK-England: London. 1997. Lang.: Eng. 2061

Marstall Theater (Munich)
Plays/librettos/scripts
Playwright Albert Ostermaier. Germany. 1967-1997. Lang.: Ger. 2853

Marston, John
Performance/production
John Marston and children's theatres. England. 1598-1634. Lang.: Eng. 1631

Plays/librettos/scripts
John Webster's malcontents and the reaction to theatricality. England. 1600-1634. Lang.: Eng. 2466

The Italian palazzo on the Jacobean stage. England. 1603-1625. Lang.: Eng. 2625

Women and household labor in *The Dutch Courtesan* by John Marston. England. 1604. Lang.: Eng. 2748

Martha Clarke's Narrative Project
Institutions
The Sundance Institute Playwright's Lab. USA: Salt Lake City, UT. 1997. Lang.: Eng. 1512

Marthaler, Christoph
Performance/production
Christoph Marthaler's *Stunde Null (Zero Hour)*. Canada: Montreal, PQ. Germany: Berlin. 1997. Lang.: Eng. 1604

Interview with actor Josef Bierbichler. Germany. 1985-1997. Lang.: Ger. 1691

The theatre of director Christoph Marthaler. Germany. 1980-1997. Lang.: Ger, Fre, Dut, Eng. 1692

Actor Josef Bierbichler. Germany: Hamburg. 1997. Lang.: Ger. 1707

Recent productions of plays by Horváth. Germany. Austria. 1996-1997. Lang.: Ger. 1722

Interview with director Christoph Marthaler and set designer Anna Viebrock. Germany. Switzerland. 1980-1997. Lang.: Ger. 1723

Christoph Marthaler's production of Čechov's *Tri sestry (Three Sisters)*. Germany: Berlin. 1997. Lang.: Eng. 1738

Collection of newspaper reviews by London theatre critics. UK-England: London. 1997. Lang.: Eng. 2074

Plays/librettos/scripts
Temporality in theatrical production. Europe. 1990-1997. Lang.: Ger, Fre, Dut, Eng. 2791

Martial arts
Training
Acting, dance, and martial arts teacher Henry Smith. USA. UK-England. 1968-1997. Lang.: Eng. 938

Martin Keller
Plays/librettos/scripts
Interview with playwrights Lars Arrhed and Kjell Abrahamsson. Sweden: Malmö. 1995-1997. Lang.: Swe. 3056

Martín Recuerda, José
Plays/librettos/scripts
Violence in Spanish drama after the Civil War. Spain. 1939-1975. Lang.: Eng. 3035

Martin, Andrea
Performance/production
Singer/actress Andrea Martin. USA: New York, NY. 1947-1997. Lang.: Eng. 3972

Martin, George
Performance/production
Harold Pinter's performance in his own play *The Hothouse*. UK-England: Chichester. 1996. Lang.: Eng. 2205

Master Class
Performance/production
German productions of plays by Terrence McNally and Nicky Silver. Germany. 1996-1997. Lang.: Ger. 1721

Elisabeth Rath's performance in Terrence McNally's *Master Class*. Germany: Munich. 1997. Lang.: Hun. 1742

Collection of newspaper reviews by London theatre critics. UK-England: London. 1997. Lang.: Eng. 2042

Zoe Caldwell and Robert Whitehead on Terrence McNally's *Master Class*. USA: New York, NY. 1996. Lang.: Eng. 2258

Master i Margarita (Master and Margarita, The)
Performance/production
Teat'r na Jugo-Zapade's production of work based on plays of Bulgakov. Russia: Moscow. 1996. Lang.: Rus. 1878

Masterskaja Petra Fomenko (Moscow)
Institutions
Profiles of Teat'r na Pokrovke and Masterskaja Petra Fomenko. Russia: Moscow. 1990-1997. Lang.: Rus. 1458

The actors of Masterskaja Petra Fomenko. Russia: Moscow. 1986-1996. Lang.: Rus. 1459
Performance/production
Two productions of *Tanja-Tanja* by Ol'ga Muchina. Russia: St. Petersburg, Moscow. 1997. Lang.: Rus. 1863

Ženovač's production of Turgenjěv's *Mesjac v derevne (A Month in the Country)*. Russia: Moscow. 1996. Lang.: Rus. 1873

Masterson, Guy
Performance/production
Collection of newspaper reviews by London theatre critics. UK-England: London. 1997. Lang.: Eng. 2034

Mastroianni, Marcello
Performance/production
Actor Marcello Mastroianni. Italy. 1924-1996. Lang.: Ita. 3580

Matchmaker, The
SEE ALSO
Jux will er sich machen, Einen.
Performance/production
Colony Theatre production of *The Matchmaker* by Thornton Wilder. USA: Los Angeles, CA. 1997. Lang.: Eng. 2307

Máté, Gábor
Performance/production
Conversation with director Csaba Kiss and playwright Lajos Parti Nagy. Hungary. 1980-1996. Lang.: Hun. 1753

Mathias, Sean
Performance/production
Collection of newspaper reviews by London theatre critics. UK-England: London. 1997. Lang.: Eng. 2024

Matines: Sade au petit déjeuner (Matins: Sade at Breakfast)
Performance/production
The body and the text in productions of the Festival de Théâtre des Amériques. Canada: Montreal, PQ. 1997. Lang.: Fre. 1583

Mátray, Ferenc
Performance/production
Operatic couple Ferenc Mátray and Ágnes Vámos. Hungary. 1943-1990. Lang.: Hun. 4169

Matrimonio segreto, Il
Basic theatrical documents
Text of the libretto to *Il matrimonio segreto* by Domenico Cimarosa. Italy. 1792. Lang.: Fre, Ita. 4013
Performance/production
Productions of Cimarosa's opera *Il matrimonio segreto*. 1792-1996. Lang.: Fre. 4075

Recordings of Cimarosa's *Il matrimonio segreto*. 1949-1992. Lang.: Fre. 4084

Plays/librettos/scripts
Analysis of Cimarosa's opera *Il matrimonio segreto*. Italy. 1792. Lang.: Fre. 4302

Cimarosa's *Il matrimonio segreto* and the clandestine marriage on the eighteenth-century stage. Italy. 1766-1792. Lang.: Fre. 4304

Mattaliano, Christopher
Institutions
Profile of the Music Academy of the West. USA: Santa Barbara, CA. 1946-1997. Lang.: Eng. 4064

Matthes, Ulrich
Performance/production
Actors on working in theatre, film, and television. Germany. 1941-1997. Lang.: Ger. 3576

Mattsson, Per
Performance/production
Interview with actor Per Mattsson. Sweden: Stockholm. 1965. Lang.: Swe. 1940

Maugham, W. Somerset
Performance/production
Collection of newspaper reviews by London theatre critics. UK-England. 1997. Lang.: Eng. 2092

Maupin, Armistead
Performance/production
Collection of newspaper reviews by London theatre critics. UK-England: London. 1997. Lang.: Eng. 1995

Maurer, Jürgen
Performance/production
Comparison of productions of Shakespeare's *Richard III*. Germany. Switzerland. 1996. Lang.: Ger. 1745

Mauzóleum (Mausoleum)
Performance/production
Conversation with director Csaba Kiss and playwright Lajos Parti Nagy. Hungary. 1980-1996. Lang.: Hun. 1753

Maxim Gorki Theater (Berlin)
Performance/production
Recent productions of plays by Schiller. Germany. 1996-1997. Lang.: Ger. 1716

Maxwell, Diana
Performance/production
Collection of newspaper reviews by London theatre critics. UK-England: London. 1997. Lang.: Eng. 2048

May, Jacquetta
Performance/production
Collection of newspaper reviews by London theatre critics. UK-England: London. 1997. Lang.: Eng. 2085

May, William
Design/technology
Hildegard Bechter's design for the musical *Always*. UK-England: London. 1997. Lang.: Eng. 3910
Performance/production
Collection of newspaper reviews by London theatre critics. UK-England: London. 1997. Lang.: Eng. 2062

Mayakovsky Theatre (Moscow)
SEE
Teat'r im V. Majakovskogo.

Mayakovsky, Vladimir Vladimirovich
SEE
Majakovskij, Vladimir Vladimirovič.

Mayer, Håkan
Performance/production
Interview with dancer/choreographer Håkan Mayer. Sweden. 1970. Lang.: Swe. 988

Mayer, Hans
Relation to other fields
Brecht's disgust with bureaucracy and political quarrels. Germany: Berlin. 1943-1956. Lang.: Ger. 3352

Mayer, Max
Institutions
Profile of New York Stage and Film, in residence at Vassar College. USA: Poughkeepsie, NY. 1930-1997. Lang.: Eng. 398

Mayer, Michael
Institutions
The Sundance Institute Playwright's Lab. USA: Salt Lake City, UT. 1997. Lang.: Eng. 1512

Mayfair Marionettes (Cleveland, OH)
Performance/production
Obituary for Nellie Braithewaite of Mayfair Marionettes. USA: Cleveland, OH. 1997. Lang.: Eng. 4390

Mayger, A.G.
Performance spaces
History of the Minneapolis, later the Radio City Theatre. USA: Minneapolis, MN. 1928-1997. Lang.: Eng. 3565

Mazeppa
Performance/production
Wagner's influence on Čajkovskij's operas. Russia. 1877-1884. Lang.: Eng. 4208

Mazer, Cary M.
Performance/production
Roles of director and dramaturg in updating plays for contemporary performance. USA. 1995-1997. Lang.: Eng. 2303

Mazlowe, Kenny
Performance/production
Collection of newspaper reviews by London theatre critics. UK-England: London. 1997. Lang.: Eng. 2052

Mazzolà, Caterino
Plays/librettos/scripts
Analysis of *La Clemenza di Tito* by Mozart. Austro-Hungarian Empire. 1791-1997. Lang.: Eng. 4282

McBroom, Amanda
  Performance/production
    Successful cabaret performers and their techniques. USA. 1975-1997.
    Lang.: Eng.   3780
McBurney, Frank
  Performance/production
    Collection of newspaper reviews by London theatre critics. UK-England:
    London. 1997. Lang.: Eng.   2034
McBurney, Simon
  Institutions
    The National's season of theatre in the round at the Olivier. UK-
    England: London. 1997. Lang.: Eng.   1499
  Performance/production
    Collection of newspaper reviews by London theatre critics. UK-England:
    London. 1997. Lang.: Eng.   2147
    Simon McBurney on his production of *The Caucasian Chalk Circle*,
    Théâtre de Complicité. UK-England: London. 1983-1997. Lang.: Eng.
                                                                     2218
    Théâtre de Complicité's production of Brecht's *Caucasian Chalk Circle*.
    UK-England: London. 1997. Lang.: Ger.   2226
McCall, Gordon
  Institutions
    Centaur Theatre's new artistic director Gordon McCall. Canada:
    Montreal, PQ. 1997. Lang.: Eng.   1383
    Interview with Gordon McCall, artistic director, Centaur Theatre.
    Canada: Montreal, PQ. 1997. Lang.: Eng.   1389
McCallum, Robbie
  Performance/production
    Collection of newspaper reviews by London theatre critics. UK-England:
    London. 1997. Lang.: Eng.   1972
McCarron, Ace
  Performance/production
    Collection of newspaper reviews by London theatre critics. UK-England:
    London. 1997. Lang.: Eng.   2148
McCarthy, Ed
  Design/technology
    Lighting for Humana Festival by Ed McCarthy and Greg Sullivan.
    USA: Louisville, KY. 1997. Lang.: Eng.   1370
McCartney, Nicola
  Institutions
    Scottish theatres run by women. UK-Scotland. 1996. Lang.: Eng.   392
  Performance/production
    Collection of newspaper reviews by London theatre critics. UK-England:
    London. 1997. Lang.: Eng.   1979
    Collection of newspaper reviews by London theatre critics. UK-England:
    London. 1997. Lang.: Eng.   1981
    Collection of newspaper reviews by London theatre critics. UK-England:
    London. 1997. Lang.: Eng.   2007
McCauley, Robbie
  Performance/production
    The development and reception of *Mississippi Freedom* by Robbie
    McCauley. USA. 1990-1992. Lang.: Eng.   2304
    Reviews of *Hot Keys* and *Sally's Rape*. USA: New York, NY. 1991-
    1992. Lang.: Eng.   2347
    The body of the actor on stage. USA. 1997. Lang.: Eng.   3829
  Relation to other fields
    Theatre artists' responses to the debate on multiculturalism of August
    Wilson and Robert Brustein. USA. 1997. Lang.: Eng.   789
McClellan, Kenneth
  Performance/production
    Collection of newspaper reviews by London theatre critics. UK-England:
    London. 1997. Lang.: Eng.   2045
McClymont, Ken
  Performance/production
    Collection of newspaper reviews by London theatre critics. UK-England:
    London. 1997. Lang.: Eng.   2006
    Collection of newspaper reviews by London theatre critics. UK-England:
    London. 1997. Lang.: Eng.   2047
    Collection of newspaper reviews by London theatre critics. UK-England:
    London. 1997. Lang.: Eng.   2091
    Collection of newspaper reviews by London theatre critics. UK-England:
    London. 1997. Lang.: Eng.   2127
McColl, Hamish
  Performance/production
    Collection of newspaper reviews by London theatre critics. UK-England:
    London. 1997. Lang.: Eng.   1979
McCord, Louisa
  Basic theatrical documents
    Writings of Louisa McCord. USA. 1810-1879. Lang.: Eng.   1334

McCullough, Mark
  Design/technology
    Lighting design for productions at New York City Opera and
    Glimmerglass Opera. USA: New York, NY, Cooperstown, NY. 1997.
    Lang.: Eng.   4034
McCurrach, Ian
  Performance/production
    Collection of newspaper reviews by London theatre critics. UK-England:
    London. 1997. Lang.: Eng.   2063
    Collection of newspaper reviews by London theatre critics. UK-England:
    London. 1997. Lang.: Eng.   2155
McDermott, Phelim
  Performance/production
    Collection of newspaper reviews by London theatre critics. UK-England:
    London. 1997. Lang.: Eng.   1988
    Collection of newspaper reviews by London theatre critics. UK-England:
    London. 1997. Lang.: Eng.   2032
McDonagh, Martin
  Performance/production
    Report on the Fourth International Women Playwrights Conference.
    Ireland: Galway. 1997. Lang.: Eng.   559
    Interview with director Peter Dalle. Sweden: Stockholm. 1970-1997.
    Lang.: Swe.   1941
    Collection of newspaper reviews by London theatre critics. UK-England:
    London. 1997. Lang.: Eng.   1973
    Collection of newspaper reviews by London theatre critics. UK-England:
    London. 1997. Lang.: Eng.   2087
  Plays/librettos/scripts
    Profiles of younger English playwrights. UK-England. 1990. Lang.: Swe.
                                                                     3081
McDowell, John
  Training
    John McDowell, teacher of theatre history. USA. 1997. Lang.: Eng. 935
McGinley, P.T.
  Plays/librettos/scripts
    The character of the traveler in plays of the Irish Renaissance. Ireland.
    1910-1930. Lang.: Eng.   2938
McGovern, Jimmy
  Plays/librettos/scripts
    Account of stage adaptation of Jimmy McGovern's screenplay *Priest*.
    Canada. 1996. Lang.: Eng.   2391
McGrath, Joe
  Performance/production
    Collection of newspaper reviews by London theatre critics. UK-England:
    London. 1997. Lang.: Eng.   1995
McGrath, John
  Audience
    The importance of the audience to 7:84 (England). UK-England. 1971-
    1985. Lang.: Eng.   1252
  Plays/librettos/scripts
    Voice in *Watching for Dolphins* by John McGrath. UK-England. 1991.
    Lang.: Eng.   3110
McGuinness, Frank
  Basic theatrical documents
    French translation of *Observe the Sons of Ulster Marching Towards the
    Somme* by Frank McGuinness. Ireland. France. 1985-1996. Lang.: Fre.
                                                                     1285
  Design/technology
    Lighting by Peter Mumford for Broadway productions of London
    shows. USA: New York, NY. 1997. Lang.: Eng.   1367
  Performance/production
    Collection of newspaper reviews by London theatre critics. UK-England:
    London. 1997. Lang.: Eng.   2034
    Collection of newspaper reviews by London theatre critics. UK-England.
    1997. Lang.: Eng.   2109
    Collection of newspaper reviews by London theatre critics. UK-England:
    London. 1997. Lang.: Eng.   2127
    Collection of newspaper reviews by London theatre critics. UK-England:
    London. 1997. Lang.: Eng.   2144
  Plays/librettos/scripts
    Political analysis of *Someone Who'll Watch Over Me* by Frank
    McGuinness. Ireland. 1992. Lang.: Eng.   2914
McIntosh, Bruce
  Performance/production
    Robert Myers's *Lee Atwater: Fixin' to Die*. USA: New York, NY. 1990-
    1997. Lang.: Eng.   2313
McIntosh, Robert
  Performance/production
    Collection of newspaper reviews by London theatre critics. UK-England:
    London. 1997. Lang.: Eng.   1978

McKay, Malcolm
Performance/production
Collection of newspaper reviews by London theatre critics. UK-England.
1997. Lang.: Eng. 2098

McKellen, Ian
Performance/production
John Caird's adaptation of *Peter Pan*. UK-England: London. 1997.
Lang.: Eng. 2215

Loncraine and McKellen's *Richard III* from stage to screen. UK-
England. 1995-1996. Lang.: Eng. 3590

Analysis of *Richard III*, film version by Loncraine and McKellen. UK-
England. USA. 1993-1996. Lang.: Eng. 3596
Plays/librettos/scripts
Richard Loncraine and Ian McKellen's film adaptation of *Richard III*.
UK-England. 1995. Lang.: Eng. 3651

McKenna, Ged
Performance/production
Collection of newspaper reviews by London theatre critics. UK-England:
London. 1997. Lang.: Eng. 2101

McKenna, Shaun
Performance/production
Collection of newspaper reviews by London theatre critics. UK-England:
London. 1997. Lang.: Eng. 2112

Account of new musical *Maddie*. UK-England. 1997. Lang.: Eng. 3948

McKenzie, Julia
Performance/production
Collection of newspaper reviews by London theatre critics. UK-England:
London. 1997. Lang.: Eng. 2132

McKewley, Robert
Performance/production
Collection of newspaper reviews by London theatre critics. UK-England:
London. 1997. Lang.: Eng. 2079

McKim, Andy
Performance/production
Ken Garnhum's *One Word* at Tarragon Theatre. Canada. 1994-1997.
Lang.: Eng. 1602

McLane, Derek
Design/technology
Derek McLane's set design for *Present Laughter*. USA: New York, NY.
1996-1997. Lang.: Eng. 1365

McLaren, Robert
Plays/librettos/scripts
Robert McLaren and Experimental Theatre Workshop. South Africa,
Republic of: Johannesburg. 1972-1976. Lang.: Eng. 3030

McLaughlin, Ellen
Performance/production
Collection of newspaper reviews by London theatre critics. UK-England:
London. 1997. Lang.: Eng. 2133

McLean, Kristen
Institutions
Kristen McLean, executive director of Puppet Showcase Theatre. USA:
Boston, MA. 1997. Lang.: Eng. 4356

McLeish, Kenneth
Performance/production
Collection of newspaper reviews by London theatre critics. UK-England:
London. 1997. Lang.: Eng. 2032

Collection of newspaper reviews by London theatre critics. UK-England:
London. 1997. Lang.: Eng. 2144

McLellan, Lucy
Performance/production
Collection of newspaper reviews by London theatre critics. UK-England:
London. 1997. Lang.: Eng. 1981

McLure, James
Performance/production
Collection of newspaper reviews by London theatre critics. UK-England:
London. 1997. Lang.: Eng. 2145

McMillan, Ross
Performance/production
Ross McMillan's performance of *The Fever* by Wallace Shawn. Canada:
Winnipeg, MB. 1997. Lang.: Eng. 1577

McNally, Terrence
Basic theatrical documents
Text of *A Perfect Ganesh* by Terrence McNally. USA. 1993. Lang.: Eng.
1335

Design/technology
Lighting design for *Ragtime* at the Ford Centre for the Performing Arts.
Canada: Toronto, ON. 1975-1997. Lang.: Eng. 3905
Performance/production
German productions of plays by Terrence McNally and Nicky Silver.
Germany. 1996-1997. Lang.: Ger. 1721

Elisabeth Rath's performance in Terrence McNally's *Master Class*.
Germany: Munich. 1997. Lang.: Hun. 1742

Collection of newspaper reviews by London theatre critics. UK-England:
London. 1997. Lang.: Eng. 2042

Zoe Caldwell and Robert Whitehead on Terrence McNally's *Master
Class*. USA: New York, NY. 1996. Lang.: Eng. 2258

Comparison of productions of *Ragtime* and *Jane Eyre*. Canada:
Toronto, ON. 1997. Lang.: Eng. 3932
Plays/librettos/scripts
Stage adaptations of novels. USA. 1997. Lang.: Eng. 702

McPherson, Conor
Performance/production
Collection of newspaper reviews by London theatre critics. UK-England:
London. 1997. Lang.: Eng. 2002

Collection of newspaper reviews by London theatre critics. UK-England:
London. 1997. Lang.: Eng. 2081

McVicar, David
Performance/production
Productions at the Munich Biennale. Germany: Munich. 1997. Lang.:
Ger. 4148

McWilliams, Randhi
Performance/production
Collection of newspaper reviews by London theatre critics. UK-England:
London. 1997. Lang.: Eng. 1991

Mda, Zakes
Plays/librettos/scripts
Postcolonialism and early plays of Zakes Mda. South Africa, Republic
of. 1979-1997. Lang.: Eng. 3029

Zakes Mda on the current state of South African theatre. South Africa,
Republic of. 1990-1996. Lang.: Eng. 3031

Me and My Friend
Performance/production
Collection of newspaper reviews by London theatre critics. UK-England:
London. 1997. Lang.: Eng. 2065

Meacher, Harry
Performance/production
Collection of newspaper reviews by London theatre critics. UK-England:
London. 1997. Lang.: Eng. 1985

Collection of newspaper reviews by London theatre critics. UK-England.
1997. Lang.: Eng. 2121

Measure for Measure
Performance/production
Possible staging for a scene from Shakespeare's *Measure for Measure*.
England. 1604. Lang.: Eng. 1624

Hoods and masks in the original production of Shakespeare's *Measure
for Measure*. England: London. 1555-1604. Lang.: Eng. 1626

Collection of newspaper reviews by London theatre critics. UK-England:
London. 1997. Lang.: Eng. 2093

Collection of newspaper reviews by London theatre critics. UK-England:
London. 1997. Lang.: Eng. 2148

Collection of newspaper reviews by London theatre critics. UK-
Scotland: Edinburgh. 1997. Lang.: Eng. 2230
Plays/librettos/scripts
The prisoner Barnardine in Shakespeare's *Measure for Measure*.
England. 1604. Lang.: Eng. 2459

Accusations of rape in English Renaissance drama. England. 1550-1630.
Lang.: Eng. 2526

Social practice and convention in Tudor-Stuart drama. England. 1571-
1670. Lang.: Eng. 2567

Social practice and theatrical meaning in Shakespeare's *Measure for
Measure*. England. 1604. Lang.: Eng. 2568

Excessive violence and political power in plays of Shakespeare. England.
1604-1611. Lang.: Eng. 2610

Twentieth-century adaptations of Jacobean plays. England. 1604-1986.
Lang.: Eng. 2673

Dramatic representations of spectatorship. England: London. 1580-1642.
Lang.: Eng. 2676

Analysis of Shakespeare's *Measure for Measure* as a performance text.
England. 1604. Lang.: Eng. 2719

Law, justice, and criminology in plays of Shakespeare. England. 1590-
1613. Lang.: Eng. 2756

Implications of mirth in plays of Shakespeare and Middleton. England.
1594-1605. Lang.: Eng. 2780

Meckler, Nancy
Performance/production
Collection of newspaper reviews by London theatre critics. UK-England:
London. 1997. Lang.: Eng. 1989

Mejerchol'd, Vsevolod Emiljévič
Performance/production
Use of Mejerchol'd's techniques in a production of Gogol's *The Government Inspector (Revizor)*. UK-England: Northampton. 1997. Lang.: Eng. 2216
Theory/criticism
Theatre criticism of productions by Mejerchol'd. Russia. 1892-1918. Lang.: Rus. 3491
Training
Work on the body in its theatrical context. Europe. 1900-1997. Lang.: Ita. 929
Gennadij Bogdanov's workshop on biomechanics, Sotenäs Teateratelje. Russia. Sweden. 1920-1996. Lang.: Swe. 932

Mejor mozo de España, El (Best Youth in Spain, The)
Plays/librettos/scripts
Analysis of Lope de Vega's Fernando and Isabel plays. Spain. 1579-1626. Lang.: Eng. 3046

Melançon, André
Performance/production
The TV series *Cher Olivier (Dear Olivier)* on actor Olivier Guimond. Canada. 1997. Lang.: Fre. 3718

Melander, Björn
Performance/production
Transferring a stage production to television. Sweden: Stockholm. 1996. Lang.: Swe. 3722

Meldegg, Stephan
Basic theatrical documents
French translation of *Communicating Doors* by Alan Ayckbourn. UK-England. France. 1995. Lang.: Fre. 1310
French translation of *Retreat* by James Saunders. UK-England. France: Paris. 1995. Lang.: Fre. 1318

Mele, Lorenzo
Performance/production
Collection of newspaper reviews by London theatre critics. UK-England: London. 1997. Lang.: Eng. 2010

Meliès, Georges
Performance/production
Documentation of the relationship between nineteenth-century theatre and film. UK-England. France. USA. 1863-1903. Lang.: Eng. 621

Melin, François
Design/technology
François Melin, chief electrician of Comédie-Française. France: Paris. 1997. Lang.: Eng. 1356

Melodrama
Performance/production
The reemergence of melodrama on the Croatian stage. Croatia. 1995-1996. Lang.: Eng. 496
Metatheatricality in melodrama. UK-England. 1840-1900. Lang.: Eng. 618
Anti-intellectualism on the American stage. USA. 1920-1940. Lang.: Eng. 639
Melodramas of Václav Praupner. Austro-Hungarian Empire: Prague, Bohemia. 1700-1799. Lang.: Cze. 3864
Plays/librettos/scripts
The parlor melodrama. England. 1840-1900. Lang.: Eng. 693
'Bush melodrama' of E.W. O'Sullivan. Australia: Sydney. 1906. Lang.: Eng. 2375
The Boer War, Australian melodrama, and the colonial legacy. Australia. 1899-1901. Lang.: Eng. 2377
Social and political themes in Bulgarian melodrama. Bulgaria. 1880-1910. Lang.: Eng. 2388
Radicalism in John Walker's melodrama *The Factory Lad*. England. 1820-1832. Lang.: Eng. 2591
Analysis of melodramas based on novels of Walter Scott. England. 1810-1830. Lang.: Eng. 2681
French melodramas about Martin Guerre. France. 1800-1850. Lang.: Eng. 2810
Representations of women in Parisian melodrama theatres. France. 1830-1870. Lang.: Eng. 2825
Hubert O'Grady's melodramas based on the Potato Famine. Ireland. 1879-1886. Lang.: Eng. 2937
Spanish melodrama and the roots of modern Spanish theatre. Spain. 1870-1900. Lang.: Eng. 3049
Melodrama as the enactment of cultural tensions resulting from British imperialism. UK-England. 1850-1900. Lang.: Eng. 3071

Nautical melodrama and traditional authority structures. UK-England. 1804-1850. Lang.: Eng. 3072
Ideological discourse in nautical melodrama. UK-England. 1794-1830. Lang.: Eng. 3078
The key role of sentimentalism in English melodrama. UK-England. 1800-1880. Lang.: Eng. 3082
Gender and sexuality on the Victorian stage. UK-England. 1830-1900. Lang.: Eng. 3085
American melodrama and realism. USA. 1880-1915. Lang.: Eng. 3253
Relation to other fields
The marginalization of drama on the American West. USA. 1939-1997. Lang.: Eng. 3427

Melody Sisters (Barcelona)
Performance/production
Spanish *commedia* troupes. Spain: Barcelona. 1996. Lang.: Eng. 3794

Melville, Herman
Performance/production
Milwaukee Repertory Theatre and Ko-Thi Dance Company's adaptation of *Benito Cereno*. USA: Milwaukee, WI. 1996. Lang.: Eng. 2316
Background on Britten's opera *Billy Budd*. England. 1797. Lang.: Eng. 4123

Memoricido, El (Memory-Killer, The)
Basic theatrical documents
Text of *El Memoricido (The Memory-Killer)* by Jorge Díaz. Chile. 1994. Lang.: Spa. 1263

Memory of Two Mondays, A
Plays/librettos/scripts
Social issues of the seventies in works by Arthur Miller. USA. 1970-1979. Lang.: Eng. 3173

Memory Tricks
Basic theatrical documents
Anthology of plays by women of color. USA. 1992-1996. Lang.: Eng. 1338

Men on the Verge of a His-Panic Breakdown
Design/technology
Lighting designer Jeff Nellis. USA: New York, NY. 1997. Lang.: Eng. 224

Menaechmi
Plays/librettos/scripts
Comparison of classical Roman, Renaissance Italian, and Shakespearean treatments of similar stories. Europe. 200 B.C.-1610 A.D. Lang.: Eng. 2799

Menander
Plays/librettos/scripts
Out-of-court legal settlements in Greco-Roman new comedy. Greece. Rome. 500 B.C.-200 A.D. Lang.: Eng. 2886

Menaphon
Relation to other fields
The source of an allusion in Beckett's *Murphy*. Ireland. France. 1938. Lang.: Eng. 3359

Mendel, Tessa
Performance/production
Tessa Mendel's production of *Home at Last* by Christopher Heide. Canada: Halifax, NS. 1996. Lang.: Eng. 1589

Mendelssohn-Bartholdy, Felix
Performance/production
László Seregi's choreography for Mendelssohn's *A Midsummer Night's Dream*. Hungary: Budapest. 1864-1989. Lang.: Hun. 1091

Mendes, Sam
Performance/production
Collection of newspaper reviews by London theatre critics. UK-England: London. 1997. Lang.: Eng. 2045
Collection of newspaper reviews by London theatre critics. UK-England: London. 1997. Lang.: Eng. 2103
Collection of newspaper reviews by London theatre critics. UK-England: London. 1997. Lang.: Eng. 2157

Meneghelli, Pierantonio
Plays/librettos/scripts
Trento's opera *Bianca de'Rossi* and its sources. Italy. 1790-1799. Lang.: Eng. 4306

Menken, Adah Isaacs
Performance/production
Race, gender, and nation in nineteenth-century performance. USA. Europe. 1855-1902. Lang.: Eng. 633
The life and writings of actress Adah Isaacs Menken. USA. 1835-1868. Lang.: Eng. 2339

Menken, Adah Isaacs — cont'd

Research/historiography
Early attempts to record performance photographically. Russia. USA.
1865-1900. Lang.: Eng.   3451

Menken, Alan
Performance/production
Collection of newspaper reviews by London theatre critics. UK-England:
London. 1997. Lang.: Eng.   2046

Mennicken, Rainer
Institutions
Profile of Stadttheater Konstanz. Germany: Konstanz. 1609-1997.
Lang.: Ger.   1432

Menotti, Gian Carlo
Design/technology
Technical aspects of YstadsOperan's production of *The Saint of
Bleecker Street*. Sweden: Ystad. 1997. Lang.: Swe.   4029
Performance/production
Background material on Lyric Opera of Chicago radio broadcast
performances. USA: Chicago, IL. 1997. Lang.: Eng.   4231

American chamber opera. USA. 1868-1997. Lang.: Eng.   4258

Production guide for a performance of *The Medium* by Gian Carlo
Menotti. USA. 1996. Lang.: Eng.   4259

Meola, Tony
Design/technology
Amplified sound and the Broadway musical. USA. 1961-1997. Lang.:
Eng.   3925

Mephisto
Institutions
Kölner Schauspiel under the direction of Günter Krämer. Germany:
Cologne. 1985-1997. Lang.: Ger.   1425

Mérante, Louis
Performance/production
John Neumeier's choreography of Delibes' *Sylvia*. France: Paris. 1997.
Lang.: Hun.   1073

Mercadante, Saverio
Performance/production
The critical reception of compositions by Saverio Mercadante. Italy.
1852-1995. Lang.: Eng.   4193

Merchant of Venice, The
Performance/production
151 Theatre Group's production of *The Merchant of Venice*. Brazil:
Brasília. 1993. Lang.: Eng.   1574

Recent productions of plays by Shakespeare. Poland. 1997. Lang.: Eng,
Fre.   1834

Collection of newspaper reviews by London theatre critics. UK-England.
1997. Lang.: Eng.   2163

Victorian ideas of womanhood in productions of Shakespeare's *The
Merchant of Venice*. UK-England. 1832-1903. Lang.: Eng.   2188

Performative theory and potentially offensive characterizations on stage.
USA: Santa Cruz, CA. France: Paris. 1992-1997. Lang.: Eng.   2336
Plays/librettos/scripts
Historical background for Shakespeare's *The Merchant of Venice*.
England: London. 1588-1596. Lang.: Eng.   2471

Gendered power relations, law, and revenge in early English drama.
England. 1590-1640. Lang.: Eng.   2540

Social practice and convention in Tudor-Stuart drama. England. 1571-
1670. Lang.: Eng.   2567

Educated women and the plays of Shakespeare. England. 1596-1603.
Lang.: Eng.   2594

Business and law in Shakespeare's *The Merchant of Venice*. England.
1596. Lang.: Eng.   2659

Woman as commodity in Shakespeare's *The Merchant of Venice*.
England. 1596. Lang.: Eng.   2680

Love lyrics in Shakespeare's comedies. England. 1590-1613. Lang.: Eng.
                                                                    2691

Racial and national meanings and economic practice in Renaissance
theatre. England. 1590-1650. Lang.: Eng.   2693

Homosexual friendship in plays of Shakespeare, Fletcher, and Marlowe.
England. 1595-1613. Lang.: Eng.   2697

The gift and money economies in plays of Shakespeare. England. 1590-
1613. Lang.: Eng.   2706

Race and colonialism in Shakespeare's *The Merchant of Venice*.
England. 1596. Lang.: Eng.   2716

Cross-dressed heroines in works of Shakespeare and Spenser. England.
1590-1596. Lang.: Eng.   2731

Literary closure in comedies of Shakespeare. England. 1595-1605.
Lang.: Eng.   2747

Law, justice, and criminology in plays of Shakespeare. England. 1590-
1613. Lang.: Eng.   2756

Merchant, Ishmail
Performance/production
Analysis of the Merchant Ivory film *Shakespeare Wallah*. India. UK-
England. 1965. Lang.: Eng.   3577

Mercier, Paul
Performance/production
Collection of newspaper reviews by London theatre critics. UK-England:
London. 1997. Lang.: Eng.   1994

Mercy, Dominique
Performance/production
Interviews with members of Tanztheater Wuppertal. Germany:
Wuppertal. 1996. Lang.: Eng.   974

Méré, Charles
Performance/production
The style of productions at Bochumer Schauspielhaus. Germany:
Bochum. 1995-1997. Lang.: Ger.   1732

Merge opera
Performance/production
Productions at the Munich Biennale. Germany: Munich. 1997. Lang.:
Ger.   4148

Mérimée, Prosper
Performance/production
Győri Balett's production of *Carmen* by Robert North and Christopher
Benstead. Hungary: Győr. 1997. Lang.: Hun.   1094

Interpreters of Bizet's heroine Carmen. France: Paris. USA: New York,
NY. 1875-1997. Lang.: Eng.   4139

Merlin Színház (Budapest)
Performance/production
Interview with actor Tamás Jordán, founder of Merlin Színház.
Hungary. 1960-1997. Lang.: Hun.   1776

Mermekides, Alex
Performance/production
Collection of newspaper reviews by London theatre critics. UK-England:
London. 1997. Lang.: Eng.   1985

Merriam Theatre (Philadelphia, PA)
Administration
Equity protest of non-union production of *Grease*. USA: Philadelphia,
PA. 1997. Lang.: Eng.   3898

Merrily We Roll Along
Plays/librettos/scripts
Analysis of *Merrily We Roll Along* by George S. Kaufman and Moss
Hart. USA. 1934. Lang.: Eng.   3190

Merry Wives of Windsor, The
Performance/production
Collection of newspaper reviews by London theatre critics. UK-England:
London. 1997. Lang.: Eng.   2159

Film actor Leslie Phillips' roles at the Royal Shakespeare Company.
UK-England: Stratford. 1997. Lang.: Eng.   2182
Plays/librettos/scripts
Witchcraft and impotence in Shakespeare's *The Merry Wives of
Windsor*. England. 1597. Lang.: Eng.   2512

The date of composition of Shakespeare's *The Merry Wives of Windsor*.
England. 1597-1602. Lang.: Eng.   2547

Homoerotic desire in Elizabethan theatre. England. 1580-1620. Lang.:
Eng.   2569

The 'bad quartos' of *The Merry Wives of Windsor* as abridged touring
editions. England. 1597-1619. Lang.: Eng.   2598

Shakespeare's *The Merry Wives of Windsor* and the law of fraudulent
conveyance. England. 1596-1603. Lang.: Eng.   2718

Shakespeare's *Merry Wives of Windsor* as a comedy of humors.
England. 1597. Lang.: Eng.   2755

Merschmeier, Michael
Institutions
Contemporary German theatre and the Theatertreffen selection.
Germany: Berlin. 1997. Lang.: Ger.   1408

Meschke, Michael
Basic theatrical documents
Libretto of Ligeti's opera *Le Grand Macabre*. Europe. 1978-1997. Lang.:
Fre, Eng.   4008
Institutions
Profile of puppet theatre group Dockteater Tittut. Sweden: Stockholm.
1977. Lang.: Swe.   4353
Performance/production
Interview with composer György Ligeti. Europe. 1997. Lang.: Fre.   4132
Plays/librettos/scripts
La Balade du Grand Macabre by Ghelderode and its operatic
adaptation by György Ligeti. Belgium. 1934. Lang.: Fre.   2385

Meschke, Michael — cont'd

Analysis of *Le Grand Macabre* by György Ligeti. Europe. 1978-1990. Lang.: Fre. 4285

György Ligeti on his opera *Le Grand Macabre*. Sweden. 1978. Lang.: Fre. 4312

Měsíčník Ceských Divadel (Český Krumlov)
Performance spaces
Theatre structures used at Prague Quadrennial. Czech Republic: Český Krumlov. 1995. Lang.: Eng. 1518

Profile of Měsíčník Ceských Divadel, a revolving auditorium theatre. Czech Republic: Český Krumlov. 1947-1996. Lang.: Eng. 1519

Mesjac v derevne (Month in the Country, A)
Performance/production
Ženovač's production of Turgenjév's *Mesjac v derevne (A Month in the Country)*. Russia: Moscow. 1996. Lang.: Rus. 1873

Message, The
Performance/production
Collection of newspaper reviews by London theatre critics. UK-England: London. 1997. Lang.: Eng. 2006

Messager, André
Performance/production
Excerpt from biography of opera singer Mary Garden. France: Paris. 1875-1957. Lang.: Eng. 4144

Messe solennelle pour une pleine lune d'été (Solemn Mass for a Full Moon in Summer)
Audience
Reaction to a production of Michael Tremblay's *Messe solennelle pour une pleine lune d'été (Solemn Mass for a Full Moon in Summer)*. Canada: Quebec, PQ. 1996. Lang.: Fre. 1245

Messingham, Simon
Performance/production
Collection of newspaper reviews by London theatre critics. UK-England: London. 1997. Lang.: Eng. 2093

Městské divadlo (Zlín)
Performance/production
Interpretations of Czech classics by Petr Lébl and Vladimír Morávek. Czech Republic. 1997. Lang.: Cze. 1609

Métachorie, La
Plays/librettos/scripts
Futurist playwright Valentine de St.-Point. France. 1875-1953. Lang.: Eng. 2827

Metastasio, Pietro
Plays/librettos/scripts
Analysis of *La Clemenza di Tito* by Mozart. Austro-Hungarian Empire. 1791-1997. Lang.: Eng. 4282

Metatheatre
Performance/production
Metatheatricality in melodrama. UK-England. 1840-1900. Lang.: Eng. 618

Plays/librettos/scripts
Metatheatrical techniques of Weiss, Gatti, and Stoppard. Europe. 1964-1982. Lang.: Eng. 2783

Metatheatre in works of Samuel Beckett. Ireland. France. 1947-1989. Lang.: Eng. 2911

Postmodernism and metatheatricality in the plays of Tom Stoppard. UK-England. 1967-1995. Lang.: Eng. 3070

Metatheatre in plays of Timberlake Wertenbaker. UK-England. 1988-1995. Lang.: Eng. 3079

Métayer, Alex
Basic theatrical documents
Text of *Aimez-moi les uns les autres (Love Me One and All)* by Alex Métayer. France. 1996. Lang.: Fre. 1274

Metcalfe, Carol
Performance/production
Collection of newspaper reviews by London theatre critics. UK-England: London. 1997. Lang.: Eng. 2028

Collection of newspaper reviews by London theatre critics. UK-England: London. 1997. Lang.: Eng. 2159

Methodology
Research/historiography
Problems of distinguishing dramatic from other activities. Lang.: Eng. 850

Collections of articles on research in performing arts archives, libraries, and museums. 1997. Lang.: Ger, Fre, Eng. 851

Introduction to articles on medieval historiography. Europe. 1208-1400. Lang.: Eng. 853

Proposed historiographical methodology. Hungary. 1960-1990. Lang.: Hun. 854

Paradigms for national theatre historiography and multiculturalism. USA. 1997. Lang.: Eng. 855

Postpositivist theatre historiography. USA. 1974-1997. Lang.: Eng. 856

Contemporary American dance research. USA. 1977-1997. Lang.: Ger. 1024

Eighteenth-century theatrical portraits. England. France. 1700-1800. Lang.: Eng. 3445

Research in theatre iconography. Europe. 1600-1995. Lang.: Eng. 3447

Using Greek tragedy as a historical source. Greece. 500-250 B.C. Lang.: Eng. 3448

Irish theatre critics' focus on text rather than performance. Ireland: Dublin. 1897-1907. Lang.: Eng. 3450

Early attempts to record performance photographically. Russia. USA. 1865-1900. Lang.: Eng. 3451

Archaeology and performance in site-specific productions. UK-Wales. 1997. Lang.: Eng. 3851

Theory/criticism
The function of evidence in structuring Shakespearean criticism. 1997. Lang.: Eng. 3454

Methusalem oder der ewige Bürger (Methuselah or the Eternal Bourgeois)
Plays/librettos/scripts
Analysis of *Methusalem oder der ewige Bürger (Methuselah or the Eternal Bourgeois)* by Iwan Goll. Germany. 1918-1927. Lang.:Ita. 2843

Metropolitan Opera (New York, NY)
Administration
Survey of the publication *Opera News*. USA: New York, NY. 1933-1997. Lang.: Hun. 4006

Design/technology
Critique of minimalist scenic design for opera. Canada: Toronto, ON. USA: New York, NY. 1975-1997. Lang.: Eng. 4019

Jean Kalman's lighting design for *Eugene Onegin*, Metropolitan Opera. USA: New York, NY. 1997. Lang.: Eng. 4033

Institutions
Interview with Metropolitan Opera President, Bruce Crawford. USA: New York, NY. 1997. Lang.: Eng. 4058

Performance/production
Soprano Isabel Bayrakdarian. Canada. 1997. Lang.: Eng. 4115

Production history of Verdi's *Don Carlo*. Europe. USA. 1867-1997. Lang.: Eng. 4131

James Levine's production of Wagner's *Ring*. Germany: Bayreuth. 1997. Lang.: Eng. 4151

Historical introduction to *Palestrina* by Hans Pfitzner. Germany. 1917-1997. Lang.: Eng. 4162

Interview with opera singer and teacher Gábor Carelli. Hungary. USA: New York, NY. 1916-1997. Lang.: Hun. 4183

Soprano Aïnhoa Artetoa. Spain. 1997. Lang.: Eng. 4213

Background material on Metropolitan Opera telecast performance. USA: New York, NY. 1997. Lang.: Eng. 4233

Background material on New York City Opera telecast performance. USA: New York, NY. 1997. Lang.: Eng. 4234

Background material on Metropolitan Opera radio broadcast performances. USA: New York, NY. 1997-1997. Lang.: Eng. 4237

Background material on Metropolitan Opera radio broadcast performances. USA: New York, NY. 1997. Lang.: Eng. 4238

Soprano Antonietta Stella. USA: New York, NY. 1954-1997. Lang.: Eng. 4244

A child's first visit to the Metropolitan Opera. USA: New York, NY. 1988-1997. Lang.: Eng. 4246

André Bishop, artistic director of Lincoln Center Theatre, and his personal reactions to opera. USA: New York, NY. 1997. Lang.: Eng. 4248

Reaction to a production of Mozart's *Così fan tutte* at the Metropolitan Opera. USA: New York, NY. 1997. Lang.: Eng. 4249

Novelist Ira Levin on Gounod's *Faust*. USA: New York, NY. 1997. Lang.: Eng. 4250

Actor Sam Waterston on Metropolitan Opera performance of *Eugene Onegin*. USA: New York, NY. 1996-1997. Lang.: Eng. 4251

Colleagues recall Metropolitan Opera general manager Rudolf Bing. USA: New York, NY. 1950-1972. Lang.: Eng. 4255

Rudolf Bing's tenure as general manager of the Metropolitan Opera. USA: New York, NY. 1950-1972. Lang.: Eng. 4266

Metropolitan Opera (New York, NY) — cont'd

The Metropolitan Opera premiere of Victor Herbert's *Madeleine*. USA: New York, NY. 1907-1995. Lang.: Eng. 4271

Metropolitan Opera Guild annual report. USA: New York, NY. 1996-1997. Lang.: Eng. 4272

Singers Carmela and Rosa Ponselle. USA: New York, NY. 1889-1981. Lang.: Eng. 4273

New York premiere of *Wozzeck* at the Metropolitan Opera. USA: New York, NY. 1959. Lang.: Eng. 4274

Conductor James Levine and the Metropolitan Opera Orchestra. USA: New York, NY. 1950-1997. Lang.: Eng. 4277

The work of a rehearsal pianist at the Metropolitan Opera. USA: New York, NY. 1996. Lang.: Eng. 4279

Meyer, Bettina
   Performance/production
   World premieres at Mannheimer Nationaltheater. Germany: Mannheim. 1997. Lang.: Ger. 1697

Meyer, Hartmut
   Performance/production
   Two productions of the annual Strindberg festival at Stockholms Stadsteater. Sweden: Stockholm. 1997. Lang.: Eng. 1957

Meyerbeer, Giacomo
   Plays/librettos/scripts
   Representations of the Orient in nineteenth-century French opera. France. 1863-1894. Lang.: Eng. 4290

Meyerhold, V.E.
   SEE
   Mejerchol'd, Vsevolod Emiljévič.

Mežulis, A.
   Performance/production
   Interview with actor A. Mežulis. Russia: Moscow. 1990-1997. Lang.: Rus. 1889

MGM Grand Hotel (Las Vegas, NV)
   Design/technology
   Technical aspects of *EFX!* at MGM Grand Hotel. USA: Las Vegas, NV. 1996. Lang.: Eng. 3854

Mhlophe, Gcina
   Performance/production
   Collection of newspaper reviews by London theatre critics. UK-England: London. 1997. Lang.: Eng. 2130

Miami City Ballet (Miami, FL)
   Administration
   The erosion of support for classical art forms such as ballet. USA. 1997. Lang.: Eng. 1047

Michaelmas Term
   Plays/librettos/scripts
   Calvinism in the city comedies of Thomas Middleton. England. 1604-1611. Lang.: Eng. 2570

Michajlova, Olga
   Plays/librettos/scripts
   Profile of young Russian playwrights. Russia: Moscow. 1960-1997. Lang.: Swe. 2993

Micheaux, Oscar
   Administration
   Oscar Micheaux's entreneurship in financing *The House Behind the Cedars*. USA. 1920-1922. Lang.: Eng. 3523

Michell, Roger
   Performance/production
   Collection of newspaper reviews by London theatre critics. UK-England: London. 1997. Lang.: Eng. 1986

Michoéls, Solomon Michajlovič
   Performance/production
   Actor and director Solomon Michoéls remembered by his son. Russia: Moscow. 1890-1948. Lang.: Rus. 1899

Mickiewicz, Adam
   Performance/production
   Director Leon Schiller. Poland. 1907-1954. Lang.: Eng. 586
   Plays/librettos/scripts
   Text and performance in the Romantic period. Europe. 1800-1851. Lang.: Pol. 2790

Micone, Marco
   Performance/production
   Negative reception of Marco Micone's adaptation of Shakespeare, *La Mégère de Padova (The Shrew of Padua)*. Canada: Montreal, PQ. 1995-1997. Lang.: Eng. 1584
   Plays/librettos/scripts
   The 'Black Madonna' in works of Italian-Canadian authors. Canada. 1950-1990. Lang.: Eng. 2396

Microscope Stage (Budapest)
   SEE
   Mikroszkóp Szinpad.

Middle-Class Tendency, The
   Performance/production
   Collection of newspaper reviews by London theatre critics. UK-England. 1997. Lang.: Eng. 2142

Middleton, Thomas
   Performance/production
   Collection of newspaper reviews by London theatre critics. UK-England. 1997. Lang.: Eng. 2098
   Plays/librettos/scripts
   Female homoeroticism on the early English stage. England. 1594-1632. Lang.: Eng. 2482

   Sam Shepard's unproduced film adaptation of *The Changeling* by Middleton and Rowley. England. USA. 1622-1971. Lang.: Eng. 2490

   Accusations of rape in English Renaissance drama. England. 1550-1630. Lang.: Eng. 2526

   Protestantism in early English drama. England. 1559-1612. Lang.: Eng. 2528

   Gendered power relations, law, and revenge in early English drama. England. 1590-1640. Lang.: Eng. 2540

   Calvinism in the city comedies of Thomas Middleton. England. 1604-1611. Lang.: Eng. 2570

   Domestic cultural and social struggle in Elizabethan theatre. England. 1592-1621. Lang.: Eng. 2571

   Male and female power in *The Changeling* by Middleton and Rowley. England. 1622. Lang.: Eng. 2583

   Analysis of *The Roaring Girl* by Middleton and Dekker. England. 1610. Lang.: Eng. 2612

   Women disguised as men in seventeenth-century drama. England. 1602-1674. Lang.: Eng. 2653

   The language of vagrants and criminals in *The Roaring Girl* by Middleton and Dekker. England. 1608-1611. Lang.: Eng. 2661

   Analysis of Middleton's *Women Beware Women* and its adaptation by Howard Barker. England. 1621-1986. Lang.: Eng. 2666

   Ambivalence toward a female sovereign reflected in plays of Shakespeare and Middleton. England. 1600-1607. Lang.: Eng. 2672

   Twentieth-century adaptations of Jacobean plays. England. 1604-1986. Lang.: Eng. 2673

   The forced marriage plot in early English drama. England. 1584-1642. Lang.: Eng. 2675

   Possible revisions by Shakespeare to *The Second Maiden's Tragedy* by Thomas Middleton. England. 1611-1991. Lang.: Eng. 2707

   The ideological function of music and song in plays of Thomas Middleton. England. 1580-1627. Lang.: Eng. 2727

   Social mobility in Jacobean drama. England. 1618-1640. Lang.: Eng. 2745

   Transvestism, desire, and psychosexual displacement in early modern theatre. England. 1590-1619. Lang.: Eng. 2766

   Implications of mirth in plays of Shakespeare and Middleton. England. 1594-1605. Lang.: Eng. 2780

Midnight Cowboy
   Basic theatrical documents
   Script of *Midnight Cowboy* by Waldo Salt. USA. 1969. Lang.: Eng. 3539
   Performance/production
   Interview with director John Schlesinger. USA. 1969. Lang.: Eng. 3601

   Interview with Jerome Hellman, producer of the film *Midnight Cowboy*. USA. 1969. Lang.: Eng. 3602
   Plays/librettos/scripts
   Interview with Jennifer Salt, daughter of screenwriter Waldo Salt. USA. 1969. Lang.: Eng. 3662

Midsummer Night's Dream, A
   Performance/production
   Textual versions and revisions as reflections of performances. England. 1590-1615. Lang.: Eng. 511

   László Seregi's choreography for Mendelssohn's *A Midsummer Night's Dream*. Hungary: Budapest. 1864-1989. Lang.: Hun. 1091

   Production history of Shakespeare's *A Midsummer Night's Dream*. 1594-1995. Lang.: Eng. 1552

   Changes in Shakespearean production under David Garrick. England. 1747-1776. Lang.: Eng. 1627

   The style of productions at Bochumer Schauspielhaus. Germany: Bochum. 1995-1997. Lang.: Ger. 1732

Miller, Arthur — cont'd

Plays of cummings, Miller, and Shepard and the American theatrical aesthetic. USA. 1940-1995. Lang.: Eng.   3304

Film adaptations of plays by Arthur Miller. USA. 1960-1997. Lang.: Eng.   3677

Theory/criticism

Playwright Arthur Miller and criticism. USA. 1940-1995. Lang.: Eng.   3498

Miller, Danny

Performance/production

Collection of newspaper reviews by London theatre critics. UK-England: London. 1997. Lang.: Eng.   2052

Miller, Jonathan

Performance/production

The map of England in productions of Shakespeare's *King Lear.* Europe. USA. 1909-1994. Lang.: Eng.   1650

Productions of Shakespeare's *Titus Andronicus.* UK-England. USA. 1955-1995. Lang.: Hun.   2225

Voyeurism in Jonathan Miller's TV version of Shakespeare's *Othello.* UK-England. 1981. Lang.: Eng.   3725

Miller, Marilyn

Performance/production

Broadway and musical film dancer Marilyn Miller. USA. 1929. Lang.: Eng.   3620

Miller, May

Plays/librettos/scripts

Simultaneous discourse in works by African-American women. USA. 1900-1993. Lang.: Eng.   3260

The voices of African-American women. USA. 1840-1994. Lang.: Eng.   3309

Miller, Monique

Performance/production

Interview with actress Monique Miller. Canada: Montreal, PQ. 1940-1997. Lang.: Fre.   476

Miller, Posy

Performance/production

Collection of newspaper reviews by London theatre critics. UK-England. 1997. Lang.: Eng.   2082

Miller, Roger

Design/technology

A raft for use in a production of the musical *Big River.* USA. 1997. Lang.: Eng.   3923

Miller, Tim

Performance/production

Account of a workshop by performance artist Tim Miller. USA. 1995-1996. Lang.: Eng.   3836

Interview with solo artist Tim Miller. USA: Los Angeles, CA. 1991. Lang.: Eng.   3838

Plays/librettos/scripts

Analysis of *My Queer Body* by Tim Miller. USA: New York, NY. 1993. Lang.: Eng.   3251

Millette, Jean-Louis

Performance/production

Jean-Louis Millette's performance in Larry Tremblay's one-man show *The Dragonfly of Chicoutimi.* Canada: Montreal, PQ. 1996. Lang.: Fre.   1586

Monodramas by Louisette Dussault and Larry Tremblay. Canada: Montreal, PQ. 1997. Lang.: Eng.   1605

Milligan, James

Performance/production

Baritone James Milligan. Canada. 1928-1961. Lang.: Eng.   4106

Milloss, Aurél

Performance/production

Early work of choreographer Aurél Milloss. Hungary. 1906-1942. Lang.: Hun.   1089

Mills, Matthew

Performance/production

Collection of newspaper reviews by London theatre critics. UK-England: London. 1997. Lang.: Eng.   2090

Milton, John

Plays/librettos/scripts

Dramatic works of John Milton. England. 1630-1660. Lang.: Eng.   2484

Violence and representation in Renaissance literature. England. 1590-1610. Lang.: Eng.   2614

Milwaukee Repertory Theatre (Milwaukee, WI)

Performance/production

Milwaukee Repertory Theatre and Ko-Thi Dance Company's adaptation of *Benito Cereno.* USA: Milwaukee, WI. 1996. Lang.: Eng.   2316

Mime

SEE ALSO

Classed Entries under MIME.

Pantomime.

Performance/production

Interview with movement and performance artist Jan Munroe. USA: Los Angeles, CA. 1991. Lang.: Eng.   3841

Interview with teacher and performance artist Rachel Rosenthal. USA: Los Angeles, CA. 1926-1991. Lang.: Eng.   3842

Training

Work on the body in its theatrical context. Europe. 1900-1997. Lang.: Ita.   929

Mineola Twins, The

Basic theatrical documents

Text of *The Mineola Twins* by Paula Vogel. USA. 1995-1997. Lang.: Eng.   1345

Plays/librettos/scripts

Interview with playwright Paula Vogel. USA: New York, NY. 1997. Lang.: Eng.   3181

Minerva Studio Theatre (Chichester)

Performance/production

Harold Pinter's performance in his own play *The Hothouse.* UK-England: Chichester. 1996. Lang.: Eng.   2205

Minerva Theatre (Chichester)

Performance/production

Collection of newspaper reviews by London theatre critics. UK-England. 1997. Lang.: Eng.   2058

Collection of newspaper reviews by London theatre critics. UK-England. 1997. Lang.: Eng.   2072

Collection of newspaper reviews by London theatre critics. UK-England: London. 1997. Lang.: Eng.   2089

Collection of newspaper reviews by London theatre critics. UK-England. 1997. Lang.: Eng.   2098

Collection of newspaper reviews by London theatre critics. UK-England. 1997. Lang.: Eng.   2109

Minghella, Anthony

Performance/production

Collection of newspaper reviews by London theatre critics. UK-England: London. 1997. Lang.: Eng.   2021

Miniature Theatre (Moscow)

SEE

Teat'r Minjatjur.

Minkowski, Marc

Performance/production

Interview with conductor Marc Minkowski. Europe. 1997. Lang.: Fre.   4124

Minks, Wilfried

Performance/production

Performances of *Harrys Kopf (Harry's Head)* by Tankred Dorst and Ursula Ehler. Germany. 1968-1997. Lang.: Ger.   1748

Plays/librettos/scripts

Postwar German portrayals of customs in East and West Germany. Germany. 1945-1997. Lang.: Ger.   2860

Minkus, Leon

Performance/production

Budapest production of the ballet *Don Quijote* by Marius Petipa and Leon Minkus. Hungary: Budapest. 1997. Lang.: Hun.   1083

Minneapolis Theatre (Minneapolis, MN)

Performance spaces

History of the Minneapolis, later the Radio City Theatre. USA: Minneapolis, MN. 1928-1997. Lang.: Eng.   3565

Minstrelsy

Performance/production

Compilation of records of early drama in Bristol. England: Bristol. 1255-1642. Lang.: Eng.   510

Anti-intellectualism on the American stage. USA. 1920-1940. Lang.: Eng.   639

Africanism in American performance. USA. 1840-1995. Lang.: Eng. 641

Southern humor and minstrelsy. USA. 1835-1939. Lang.: Eng.   677

Ontario's numerous variety acts. Canada. 1914-1979. Lang.: Eng. 3855

The paradox of blackface minstrelsy. USA. 1821-1915. Lang.: Eng. 3861

Analysis of blackface minstrelsy. USA. 1800-1875. Lang.: Eng.   3881

Minter, Tom

Performance/production

Collection of newspaper reviews by London theatre critics. UK-England: London. 1997. Lang.: Eng.   1967

Mixed media — cont'd

Design/technology
OISTAT's conference on theatre technology of the future. USA: Pittsburgh. 1997. Lang.: Swe.   227

Performance/production
Documentation of work by the late choreographer Robert Ellis Dunn. USA: Milwaukee, WI. 1945-1997. Lang.: Eng.   1202

Rock group U2's use of video and interactive technology. USA. 1997. Lang.: Eng.   3732

Memory in the work of video and performance artist Arnold Dreyblatt. Germany. 1997. Lang.: Eng.   3818

Theory/criticism
The roots of contemporary multimedia in Wagnerian aesthetics. Germany: Bayreuth. 1850-1997. Lang.: Fre.   4331

Mloda śmierć (Young Death)

Plays/librettos/scripts
Plays by Grzegorz Nawrocki at Teatre Współczesny. Poland. 1996-1997. Lang.: Hun.   2986

Mnouchkine, Ariane

Institutions
Political and artistic strategies of Théâtre du Soleil. France: Paris. 1970-1997. Lang.: Eng.   1407

Kölner Schauspiel under the direction of Günter Krämer. Germany: Cologne. 1985-1997. Lang.: Ger.   1425

Performance/production
Théâtre du Soleil's production of Molière's *Tartuffe*. France: Paris. 1996. Lang.: Eng.   1672

Théâtre du Soleil's *Les Atrides*. France: Paris. 1992. Lang.: Eng.   1676

Interviews with the cast of Théâtre du Soleil's *Les Atrides*. France: Paris. 1992. Lang.: Eng.   1677

Intercultural signs in Mnouchkine's *Les Atrides (The Atridae)*, Théâtre du Soleil. France: Paris. 1990-1997. Lang.: Eng.   1679

Plays/librettos/scripts
Brook, Mnouchkine and intercultural theatre. France: Paris. 1988-1992. Lang.: Eng.   2832

Moberg, Vilhelm

Performance/production
The work together of actors Solveig Tännström and Börje Ahlstedt. Sweden: Stockholm. 1967. Lang.: Swe.   1961

Plays/librettos/scripts
On the correspondence of author Vilhelm Moberg and Dramaten manager Pauline Brunius. Sweden: Stockholm. 1931-1942. Lang.: Swe.   3058

Mocart i Saljeri (Mozart and Salieri)

Performance/production
Amateur theatre production of Puškin's *Mocart i Saljeri (Mozart and Salieri)*. Russia: Skopina. 1990-1997. Lang.: Rus.   1860

Moch, Cheryl

Performance/production
Collection of newspaper reviews by London theatre critics. UK-England: London. 1997. Lang.: Eng.   2154

Model Apartment, The

Design/technology
Scene designs of Neil Patel. USA. 1996. Lang.: Eng.   1373

Modern dance

SEE ALSO
Classed Entries under DANCE.

Institutions
Judson Dance Theatre and dancing autobiography. USA. 1960-1965. Lang.: Eng.   952

Performance/production
Dance history textbook. Lang.: Rus.   953

Classicism as crucial to the beauty of dance. Europe. 1997. Lang.: Eng.   959

Modern Jazzdans Ensemble (Stockholm)

Performance/production
Jazz in Sweden and the Modern Jazzdans Ensemble. Sweden. 1900. Lang.: Swe.   987

Modjeska, Helena

Performance/production
Guest performances in Polish cities. Poland: Cracow, Lvov, Warsaw. 1810-1915. Lang.: Pol.   583

Modrzejewska, Helena

SEE
Modjeska, Helena.

Moffat, Peter

Performance/production
Collection of newspaper reviews by London theatre critics. UK-England: London. 1997. Lang.: Eng.   2067

Moffo, Anna

Performance/production
The difficulty of performing 'Sempre Libera' in Verdi's *La Traviata*. Italy. USA: New York, NY. 1886-1996. Lang.: Eng.   4186

Moher, Frank

Plays/librettos/scripts
The writing of *Supreme Dream* by Frank Moher and actress Rhonda Trodd. Canada: Toronto, ON. 1997. Lang.: Eng.   2425

Moholy-Nagy, László

Theory/criticism
The influence of László Moholy-Nagy on theatrical practice. Germany. 1924-1930. Lang.: Ger.   894

Moissi, Alexander

Relation to other fields
Actors' political convictions and activities in the German Revolution. Germany. 1917-1922. Lang.: Eng.   763

Moj bednyj Marat (Promise, The)

Performance/production
Collection of newspaper reviews by London theatre critics. UK-England: London. 1997. Lang.: Eng.   2102

Mol'jer (Molière)

Performance/production
Teat'r na Jugo-Zapade's production of work based on plays of Bulgakov. Russia: Moscow. 1996. Lang.: Rus.   1878

Molière (Poquelin, Jean-Baptiste)

Institutions
Molière productions of Théâtre du Nouveau Monde. Canada: Montreal, PQ. 1951-1997. Lang.: Fre.   1391

Performance/production
Productions of Molière's *Tartuffe* by Benno Besson and Lorraine Pintal. Canada: Montreal, PQ, Quebec, PQ. 1996-1997. Lang.: Fre.   1601

Productions of the Paris theatre season. France: Paris. 1996-1997. Lang.: Ger.   1668

Théâtre du Soleil's production of Molière's *Tartuffe*. France: Paris. 1996. Lang.: Eng.   1672

Roger Planchon's production of *Georges Dandin* by Molière. France: Villeurbanne. 1958. Lang.: Pol.   1675

Sociocultural analysis of recent French productions. France. 1993-1994. Lang.: Eng.   1678

Collection of newspaper reviews by London theatre critics. UK-England: London. 1997. Lang.: Eng.   1998

Collection of newspaper reviews by London theatre critics. UK-England: London. 1997. Lang.: Eng.   2027

Collection of newspaper reviews by London theatre critics. UK-England: London. 1997. Lang.: Eng.   2056

Collection of newspaper reviews by London theatre critics. UK-England: London. 1997. Lang.: Eng.   2113

Collection of newspaper reviews by London theatre critics. UK-Scotland: Edinburgh. 1997. Lang.: Eng.   2231

Director and dramaturgs on translating, adapting and producing Molière's *Misanthrope*. USA: La Jolla, CA, Chicago, IL. 1989-1990. Lang.: Eng.   2263

Plays/librettos/scripts
The significance of Don Juan in works of Tirso, Mozart, and Molière. Europe. 1612-1787. Lang.: Eng.   2786

Authenticity and the plays of Molière. France. 1660-1666. Lang.: Eng.   2803

Language, emotional tone, and characterization in French classical drama. France. 1601-1700. Lang.: Eng.   2815

Molière, farce, and *La Jalousie du Barbouillé*. France. 1450-1820. Lang.: Eng.   2821

Analysis of Polish translations of plays by Molière. Poland. 1664-1973. Lang.: Pol.   2987

Molina, Sara

Performance/production
Women directors in Spanish theatre. Spain. 1990-1996. Lang.: Eng.   612

Molina, Tirso de

Plays/librettos/scripts
The significance of Don Juan in works of Tirso, Mozart, and Molière. Europe. 1612-1787. Lang.: Eng.   2786

Conversion plays of Tirso and Calderón. Spain. 1600-1681. Lang.: Eng.   3043

Ideology in *El Burlador de Sevilla (The Trickster of Seville)* by Tirso de Molina. Spain. 1622. Lang.: Eng.   3051

Molinari, Nadia

Performance/production
Collection of newspaper reviews by London theatre critics. UK-England: London. 1997. Lang.: Eng.   2038

Moraga, Cherríe — cont'd

Plays/librettos/scripts
The female body in plays of Moraga, Fornes, and Cruz. USA. 1980-
1991. Lang.: Eng.   3228

Morahan, Christopher
Performance/production
Collection of newspaper reviews by London theatre critics. UK-England:
London. 1997. Lang.: Eng.   2122

Morality plays
Performance/production
A possible motivation for the writing of *Ordo Virtutum* by Hildegard of
Bingen. Germany. 1100-1200. Lang.: Eng.   3870
Relation to other fields
Order and justice in early Tudor drama. England. 1490-1550. Lang.:
Eng.   3340

Morath, Inge
Plays/librettos/scripts
Playwright Arthur Miller's collaborations with his wife Inge Morath.
USA. 1980-1989. Lang.: Eng.   3272

Morávek, Vladimír
Performance/production
Interpretations of Czech classics by Petr Lébl and Vladimír Morávek.
Czech Republic. 1997. Lang.: Cze.   1609

Mörder, Hoffnung der Frauen (Murderer, Hope of Women)
Basic theatrical documents
English translations of German Expressionist plays. Germany. 1900-
1920. Lang.: Eng.   1284

Mordillat, Gérard
Performance/production
Films about Antonin Artaud by Gérard Mordillat and Jérome Prieur.
France. 1993. Lang.: Eng.   3573

Mordžanišvili Theatre (Tbilisi)
SEE
Gruzinskij Akademičéskij Teat'r im. Kote Mordžanišvili.

More Grimm Tales
Performance/production
Collection of newspaper reviews by London theatre critics. UK-England:
London. 1997. Lang.: Eng.   2154

More Stately Mansions
Performance/production
Ivo van Hove, new artistic director of the Holland Festival. Netherlands:
Amsterdam. 1969-1997. Lang.: Eng.   1826

More, Hannah
Plays/librettos/scripts
Women's Romantic 'closet' drama as an alternative theatrical space.
England. 1790-1820. Lang.: Eng.   2486
Playwrights' discussions of censorship in prefaces to their work.
England. 1790-1820. Lang.: Eng.   2507

More, Thomas
Theory/criticism
Othello, censorship, and public swearing. England: London. 1215-1622.
Lang.: Eng.   3470

Moreland, Donald
Performance/production
The background of a new opera, *The Conquistador*, by Myron Fink.
USA: San Diego, CA. 1997. Lang.: Eng.   4236

Moreton, Peter
Performance/production
Collection of newspaper reviews by London theatre critics. UK-England:
London. 1997. Lang.: Eng.   2078

Morgan, Edward
Performance/production
Milwaukee Repertory Theatre and Ko-Thi Dance Company's
adaptation of *Benito Cereno*. USA: Milwaukee, WI. 1996. Lang.: Eng.
    2316

Morgenstern, Maia
Performance/production
Interview with actress Maia Morgenstern. Romania: Bucharest.
Hungary: Győr. 1997. Lang.: Hun.   1855

Morgia, Pepi
Design/technology
Lighting designer Pepi Morgia. Italy. 1960-1997. Lang.: Eng.   176

Moriconi, Valeria
Performance/production
The first Italian production of Tennessee Williams's *The Rose Tattoo*.
Italy. 1996. Lang.: Ita.   1795

Moritz, Dennis
Basic theatrical documents
Text of plays performed at the Nuyorican Poets Cafe. USA: New York,
NY. 1973-1990. Lang.: Eng.   1322

Morley, Sheridan
Performance/production
Collection of newspaper reviews by London theatre critics. UK-England:
London. 1997. Lang.: Eng.   2111

Mörner, Alexandra
Performance/production
Involving youth audiences in theatre. Sweden: Stockholm, Uppsala.
1995-1997. Lang.: Swe.   1949

Morris dance
Performance/production
Morris dance and the study of medieval theatre. England. 1570-1590.
Lang.: Eng.   956

Morris, Abigail
Performance/production
Collection of newspaper reviews by London theatre critics. UK-England:
London. 1997. Lang.: Eng.   2012

Morris, Joshua
Performance/production
Collection of newspaper reviews by London theatre critics. UK-England:
London. 1997. Lang.: Eng.   2148

Morris, Mark
Performance/production
Reception of Mark Morris's *L'Allegro, il Penseroso ed il Moderato*. UK-
England: London. 1997. Lang.: Eng.   1193
History and the work of choreographer Mark Morris. USA. 1997. Lang.:
Eng.   1199
Gender in choreographies of Mark Morris. USA. 1980-1995. Lang.: Eng.
    1206

Morris, Peter
Performance/production
Collection of newspaper reviews by London theatre critics. UK-England:
London. 1997. Lang.: Eng.   2038

Morrison, Connall
Performance/production
Report on recent Dublin productions. Ireland: Dublin. 1997. Lang.: Eng.
    1786

Mort de Tintagiles, La (Death of Tintagiles, The)
Performance/production
Claude Régy's production of *La Mort de Tintagiles (The Death of
Tintagiles)* by Maeterlinck. France: Paris. Belgium: Ghent. 1997. Lang.:
Eng.   1658
Recent productions of works by Maeterlinck. France: Paris. 1997. Lang.:
Swe.   1664

Mortier, Gérard
Performance/production
The Salzburg Festival under Gérard Mortier. Austria: Salzburg. 1997.
Lang.: Eng.   4094
Opera productions from Salzburger Festspiele. Austria: Salzburg. 1997.
Lang.: Ger.   4096

Morton, Billy
Basic theatrical documents
Text of *The Gathering* by Rachael Van Fossen *et al.* Canada: Fort
Qu'Appelle, SK. 1997. Lang.: Eng.   3903

Morton, Carlos
Performance/production
History in recent Chicano/a theatre. USA. 1964-1995. Lang.: Eng.   2360

Moscow Art Theatre
SEE
Moskovskij Chudožestvénnyj Akademičéskij Teat'r.

Moscow Puppet Theatre
SEE
Gosudarstvénnyj Central'nyj Teat'r Kukol.

Moscow Theatre Institute, GITIS
SEE
Gosudarstvénnyj Institut Teatral'nogo Iskusstva.

Moskovskij Chudožestvénnyj Akademičéskij Teat'r (Moscow Art Theatre)
Institutions
The studios of the Moscow Art Theatre. Russia. 1905-1927. Lang.: Eng.
    365
Dictionary of the Moscow Art Theatre. Russia: Moscow. 1897-1997.
Lang.: Rus.   1466
Performance/production
Early modern interpretations of Aristophanes' *Lysistrata*. Europe. USA.
1892-1930. Lang.: Eng.   1647
Current productions of plays by Čechov. Russia: Moscow. 1940-1997.
Lang.: Eng.   1856

Moskovskij Chudožestvénnyj Akademičéskij Teat'r (Moscow Art Theatre) — cont'd

Moscow Art Theatre productions. Russia: Moscow. Estonia: Tallinn. 1996-1997. Lang.: Rus.   1861

Memoirs of director Oleg Jéfremov. Russia. 1960-1997. Lang.: Rus. 1874

Ostrovskij's *Kozma Zacharič Minin* at Moscow Art Theatre. Russia: Moscow. 1997. Lang.: Rus.   1885

Moskovskij Teat'r Junogo Zritelja (Moscow)
Performance/production

Productions of *Gudbai Amerika (Goodbye America)* before and after perestrojka. Russia. 1933-1996. Lang.: Eng.   1898

Moss, Piotr
Basic theatrical documents

Text of *Page 27* by Jean-Louis Bauer. France. 1996. Lang.: Fre.   1268

Moss, Victoria
Performance/production

Collection of newspaper reviews by London theatre critics. UK-England: London. 1997. Lang.: Eng.   2106

Mossoux, Nicole
Performance/production

Collection of newspaper reviews by London theatre critics. UK-England: London. 1997. Lang.: Eng.   1988

Mossovét Theatre
SEE

Teat'r im. Mossovéta.

Mother Courage and Her Children
SEE

Mutter Courage und ihre Kinder.

Mother Hicks
Theory/criticism

The effect of feminism on children's theatre. USA. 1995-1996. Lang.: Eng.   914

Mother of Us All, The
Plays/librettos/scripts

Text and music in operas by Robert Ashley and by Gertrude Stein with Virgil Thomson. USA. 1925-1980. Lang.: Eng.   4315

Motton, Gregory
Performance/production

Collection of newspaper reviews by London theatre critics. UK-England: London. 1997. Lang.: Eng.   2047

Mottram, Stephen
Performance/production

Collection of newspaper reviews by London theatre critics. UK-England: London. 1997. Lang.: Eng.   1988

Mouawad, Wajdi
Plays/librettos/scripts

Quebec playwrights on the body in their work. Canada: Montreal, PQ. 1992-1996. Lang.: Fre.   2431

Mount, Lisa
Administration

Lisa Mount, managing director of 7 Stages. USA: Atlanta, GA. 1989-1997. Lang.: Eng.   68

Mourning Becomes Electra
Theory/criticism

Dance history and cultural studies: works of Martha Graham and Eugene O'Neill. USA. 1913-1933. Lang.: Eng.   1216

Mourning Song
Performance/production

Collection of newspaper reviews by London theatre critics. UK-England: London. 1997. Lang.: Eng.   2020

Moussorgsky, Modeste
SEE

Mussorgskij, Modest Pavlovič.

Mouthful of Birds, A
Plays/librettos/scripts

Analysis of *A Mouthful of Birds* by Caryl Churchill. UK-England. 1986-1997. Lang.: Eng.   3109

Moveable Feast (London)
Performance/production

Collection of newspaper reviews by London theatre critics. UK-England: London. 1997. Lang.: Eng.   2016

Movement
Performance/production

Physical work in actor training. Denmark: Holstebro. 1950-1997. Lang.: Eng.   497

Emma Lyon, Goethe, and the *tableau vivant*. Italy: Naples. Germany. 1786-1791. Lang.: Eng.   566

Movement and physical image in South African theatre. South Africa, Republic of. 1997. Lang.: Eng.   1909

Training

Work on the body in its theatrical context. Europe. 1900-1997. Lang.: Ita.   929

Movement training and modern dance. Germany: Hamburg. 1992-1993. Lang.: Ger.   1220

Mowatt, Anna Cora
Performance/production

History of the one-woman show. USA. 1890-1995. Lang.: Eng.   646

Plays/librettos/scripts

Critical history of American feminist drama. USA. 1772-1995. Lang.: Eng.   3151

Moynet, Georges
Performance/production

Documentation of the relationship between nineteenth-century theatre and film. UK-England. France. USA. 1863-1903. Lang.: Eng.   621

Mozart, Wolfgang Amadeus
Design/technology

Critique of minimalist scenic design for opera. Canada: Toronto, ON. USA: New York, NY. 1975-1997. Lang.: Eng.   4019

Scenery for Mozart's *Idomeneo* at Bayerische Staatsoper. Germany: Munich. 1996. Lang.: Ger.   4023

Interview with opera set designer János Miklós Kádár. Hungary. 1954-1997. Lang.: Hun.   4024

Performance/production

Analysis of Mozart's *Die Zauberflöte*. Austria. 1791. Lang.: Eng.   4095

Opera productions from Salzburger Festspiele. Austria: Salzburg. 1997. Lang.: Ger.   4096

Interview with director and scene designer Achim Freyer. Austria: Salzburg. 1997. Lang.: Ger.   4097

Musical disguises in Mozart's late comic operas. Austria. 1786-1790. Lang.: Eng.   4101

Analysis of arias in the last act of Mozart's *Le Nozze di Figaro*. Austro-Hungarian Empire: Vienna. 1786-1997. Lang.: Eng.   4102

Stylistic similarities in Baroque and nineteenth-century opera. Europe. 1705-1997. Lang.: Eng.   4128

Interview with opera director Judit Galgóczy. Hungary. 1987-1997. Lang.: Hun.   4168

Moral conflicts in Mozart's *Così fan tutte* and Britten's *Billy Budd*. UK-England. Austro-Hungarian Empire. 1790-1951. Lang.: Eng.   4228

Background material on Lyric Opera of Chicago radio broadcast performances. USA: Chicago, IL. 1997. Lang.: Eng.   4231

Background material on Metropolitan Opera radio broadcast performances. USA: New York, NY. 1997-1997. Lang.: Eng.   4237

Background material on Metropolitan Opera radio broadcast performances. USA: New York, NY. 1997. Lang.: Eng.   4238

Cutting operas for performance. USA. 1997. Lang.: Eng.   4240

Reaction to a production of Mozart's *Così fan tutte* at the Metropolitan Opera. USA: New York, NY. 1997. Lang.: Eng.   4249

Opera critic, novelist and biographer Marcia Davenport. USA. 1904-1996. Lang.: Eng.   4262

Plays/librettos/scripts

The significance of Don Juan in works of Tirso, Mozart, and Molière. Europe. 1612-1787. Lang.: Eng.   2786

Female characters in Mozart's *Don Giovanni* and *Die Zauberflöte*. Austria. 1756-1791. Lang.: Eng.   4280

Unclear stage directions in Act I of Mozart's *Don Giovanni*. Austria. 1787. Lang.: Eng.   4281

Analysis of *La Clemenza di Tito* by Mozart. Austro-Hungarian Empire. 1791-1997. Lang.: Eng.   4282

Opera and gender stereotypes. Europe. 1607-1997. Lang.: Eng.   4287

Analysis of opera librettos by Boito, Da Ponte, and Gertrude Stein. Europe. 1770-1915. Lang.: Eng.   4289

Direct address in *Don Giovanni* and *La Bohème*. Italy. 1864-1881. Lang.: Eng.   4308

Mozíček (Jumping Jack)
Performance/production

Ballet on the Slovenian stage. Slovenia. 1635-1944. Lang.: Slo.   1108

Mr. Joyce Is Leaving Paris
Performance/production

Recent Irish productions. Ireland: Sligo, Dublin. 1997. Lang.: Swe. 1788

Mr. Moore's Revels
Plays/librettos/scripts

Race and gender in masque: *Mr. Moore's Revels*. England. 1636. Lang.: Eng.   3775

Multiculturalism — cont'd

Performance artist Guillermo Gómez-Peña on intercultural collaboration. USA. 1985-1995. Lang.: Eng. 3849

Relation to other fields

Theatre artists' responses to the debate on multiculturalism of August Wilson and Robert Brustein. USA. 1997. Lang.: Eng. 789

Introduction to articles on the Wilson-Brustein debate. USA: New York, NY. 1997. Lang.: Eng. 790

Theatre critic and theorist Margo Jefferson on the Robert Brustein/August Wilson debate. USA: New York, NY. 1960-1997. Lang.: Eng. 791

Commentary on the Wilson-Brustein debate. USA: New York, NY. 1996-1997. Lang.: Eng. 793

Critique of August Wilson's call for a separate Black American theatre. USA: New York, NY. 1997. Lang.: Eng. 807

Analysis of the Wilson-Brustein debate. USA. 1997. Lang.: Eng. 820

The debate on multiculturalism of August Wilson and Robert Brustein. USA. 1997. Lang.: Eng. 825

The Wilson/Brustein debate on African-Americans and theatre. USA. 1995-1997. Lang.: Eng. 826

August Wilson and the history of African-American theatre. USA. 1926-1997. Lang.: Eng. 828

Robert Brustein and August Wilson debate multiculturalism. USA: New York, NY. 1997. Lang.: Eng. 830

Reflections on European cultural diversity and integration. Europe. 1997. Lang.: Eng. 3350

Multiculturalism and playwright Ebrahim Hussein. Tanzania. 1966-1997. Lang.: Eng. 3380

The multicultural classroom and the teaching of Shakespeare. USA. 1995. Lang.: Eng. 3428

August Wilson's address to the National Black Theatre Festival. USA: Winston-Salem, NC. 1997. Lang.: Eng. 3440

Research/historiography

Paradigms for national theatre historiography and multiculturalism. USA. 1997. Lang.: Eng. 855

Theory/criticism

The river as a metaphor of cultural exchange. India. 1938-1997. Lang.: Eng. 904

Mum's the Word

Performance/production

Collection of newspaper reviews by London theatre critics. UK-England. 1997. Lang.: Eng. 2082

Mumford, Peter

Design/technology

Lighting by Peter Mumford for Broadway productions of London shows. USA: New York, NY. 1997. Lang.: Eng. 1367

Münchner Festspiele (Munich)

SEE

Bayerische Staatsoper im Nationaltheater.

Münchner Kammerspiele (Munich)

Performance/production

Recent productions of Elizabethan theatre. Europe. 1997. Lang.: Ger. 1649

Dieter Dorn's production of *Ithaka* by Botho Strauss. Germany: Munich. 1996. Lang.: Swe. 1720

Non-literary realism in Shakespeare productions. UK-England. Germany. 1958-1995. Lang.: Ger. 2170

Plays/librettos/scripts

Playwright Theresia Walser. Germany. 1990-1997. Lang.: Ger. 2864

Munich Opera

SEE

Bayerische Staatsoper im Nationaltheater.

Municipal Theatre (Haifa)

SEE

Teatron HaIroni (Haifa).

Municipal Theatre (Helsinki)

SEE

Helsingin Kaupunginteatteri.

Munro, H.H.

Performance/production

Collection of newspaper reviews by London theatre critics. UK-England: London. 1997. Lang.: Eng. 2006

Munroe, Jan

Performance/production

Interview with movement and performance artist Jan Munroe. USA: Los Angeles, CA. 1991. Lang.: Eng. 3841

Munrow, Julia

Performance/production

Collection of newspaper reviews by London theatre critics. UK-England: London. 1997. Lang.: Eng. 2019

Murat, Bernard

Basic theatrical documents

Text of *Une Puce à l'Oreille (A Flea in Her Ear)* by Georges Feydeau. France. 1902-1996. Lang.: Fre. 1271

Murder and murder

Basic theatrical documents

Text of *Murder and murder* by Yvonne Rainer. USA. 1996. Lang.: Eng. 3538

Murder in the Cathedral

Institutions

Productions of the theatre festival Kontakt '97. Poland: Toruń. 1997. Lang.: Hun. 354

Murder of Edgar Allan Poe, The

Performance/production

Collection of newspaper reviews by London theatre critics. UK-England: London. 1997. Lang.: Eng. 2114

Murdock, George

Performance/production

Obituary for puppeteer George Murdock. USA. 1996. Lang.: Eng. 4371

Murmuring Judges

Plays/librettos/scripts

Nostalgia and morality in plays of David Hare. UK-England: London. 1947-1997. Lang.: Eng. 3113

Murphy

Relation to other fields

The source of an allusion in Beckett's *Murphy*. Ireland. France. 1938. Lang.: Eng. 3359

Murphy, Arthur

Performance/production

Collection of newspaper reviews by London theatre critics. UK-England: London. 1997. Lang.: Eng. 2145

Plays/librettos/scripts

Frances Sheridan's *The Discovery* in the context of eighteenth-century theatre. England. 1740-1780. Lang.: Eng. 2451

Murphy, Jimmy

Performance/production

Report on recent Dublin productions. Ireland: Dublin. 1997. Lang.: Eng. 1786

Murphy, Tom

Performance/production

Collection of newspaper reviews by London theatre critics. UK-England: London. 1997. Lang.: Eng. 2037

Plays/librettos/scripts

Transformations of Irish society as reflected in its drama. Ireland. 1959-1993. Lang.: Eng. 2913

Analysis of plays by Brian Friel and Tom Murphy. Ireland. UK-Ireland. 1961-1995. Lang.: Eng. 2925

Murray, Braham

Performance/production

Collection of newspaper reviews by London theatre critics. UK-England: London. 1997. Lang.: Eng. 2026

Murray, Brendan

Performance/production

Collection of newspaper reviews by London theatre critics. UK-England: London. 1997. Lang.: Eng. 2005

Murray, Lavinia

Performance/production

Collection of newspaper reviews by London theatre critics. UK-England: London. 1997. Lang.: Eng. 2038

Murrell, Andrew

Performance/production

Collection of newspaper reviews by London theatre critics. UK-England: London. 1997. Lang.: Eng. 2035

Murx

Performance/production

The theatre of director Christoph Marthaler. Germany. 1980-1997. Lang.: Ger, Fre, Dut, Eng. 1692

Muses orphelines, Les (Orphan Muses, The)

Performance/production

Analysis of audio recordings of plays by Michel Marc Bouchard and Michel Tremblay. Canada. 1995-1997. Lang.: Fre. 3516

Museums

Design/technology

Theatrical lighting for a traveling museum exhibit on dinosaurs. USA: New York, NY. 1997. Lang.: Eng. 282

National Endowment for the Arts (NEA, Washington, DC) — cont'd

Religion, gay and lesbian arts, and the NEA. USA: Washington, DC. 1997. Lang.: Eng. 832

Celebrity supporters of the NEA. USA: Washington, DC. 1997. Lang.: Eng. 833

ARTNOW demonstration in support of national arts funding. USA: Washington, DC. 1997. Lang.: Eng. 834

Debate on public support for the arts. USA. 1981-1997. Lang.: Eng. 835

National Festival of Art (Grahamstown)
Theory/criticism
Critical response to a production of Euripides' *Medea* by Mark Fleishman and Jenny Reznek. South Africa, Republic of. 1994-1996. Lang.: Eng. 3494

National Performance Network (New York, NY)
Institutions
Profile of the National Performance Network. USA. 1984-1997. Lang.: Eng. 407

National School of Drama (New Delhi)
Performance/production
Profile of Prasanna, director and teacher. India: New Delhi, Heggodu. 1970. Lang.: Swe. 1782

National Theatre (Bratislava)
SEE
Slovenske Narodni Divadlo.

National Theatre (Budapest)
SEE
Nemzeti Szinház.

National Theatre (Dublin)
SEE
Abbey Theatre.

National Theatre (Helsinki)
SEE
Suomen Kansallisteatteri.

National Theatre (Miskolc)
SEE
Miskolci Nemzeti Szinház.

National Theatre (Munich)
SEE
Bayerische Staatsoper.

National Theatre (Pécs)
SEE
Pécsi Nemzeti Szinház.

National Theatre (Prague)
SEE
Národní Divadlo.

National Theatre (Szeged)
SEE
Szegedi Nemzeti Szinház.

National Theatre (Tel Aviv)
SEE
HaBimah (Tel Aviv).

National Theatre (Washington, DC)
Design/technology
Howell Binkley's lighting design for *Whistle Down the Wind* at the National Theatre. USA: Washington, DC. 1997. Lang.: Eng. 3920

National Theatre Company (London)
SEE ALSO
Design/technology
Lighting designer Mark Jonathan. UK-England: London. 1997. Lang.: Eng. 1360

Design for three productions of Tony Kushner's *Angels in America*. USA: New York, NY, Los Angeles, CA. UK-England: London. 1992-1994. Lang.: Eng. 1363

Institutions
Interview with Jatinder Verma of Tara Arts. UK-England. 1977-1997. Lang.: Eng. 1496

The National's season of theatre in the round at the Olivier. UK-England: London. 1997. Lang.: Eng. 1499

Profile of Richard Eyre of the National Theatre. UK-England: London. 1960-1997. Lang.: Eng. 1500

Performance/production
Productions of the International Istanbul Theatre Festival. Turkey: Istanbul. 1980-1997. Lang.: Eng. 1966

Collection of newspaper reviews by London theatre critics. UK-England: London. 1997. Lang.: Eng. 1977

Collection of newspaper reviews by London theatre critics. UK-England: London. 1997. Lang.: Eng. 2023

Collection of newspaper reviews by London theatre critics. UK-England: London. 1997. Lang.: Eng. 2034

Collection of newspaper reviews by London theatre critics. UK-England: London. 1997. Lang.: Eng. 2048

Collection of newspaper reviews by London theatre critics. UK-England: London. 1997. Lang.: Eng. 2055

Collection of newspaper reviews by London theatre critics. UK-England: London. 1997. Lang.: Eng. 2103

Collection of newspaper reviews by London theatre critics. UK-England: London. 1997. Lang.: Eng. 2104

Collection of newspaper reviews by London theatre critics. UK-England: London. 1997. Lang.: Eng. 2114

Collection of newspaper reviews by London theatre critics. UK-England: London. 1997. Lang.: Eng. 2144

Analysis of Declan Donnellan's production of *Angels in America* by Tony Kushner. UK-England: London. 1992. Lang.: Eng. 2168

Two productions of Tom Stoppard's *Rosencrantz and Guildenstern Are Dead*. UK-England: London. Italy: Forlì. 1966-1996. Lang.:Ita. 2172

Shakespearean production before national subsidy. UK-England. 1914-1959. Lang.: Eng. 2175

Sexuality on stage in the National Theatre production of Tony Kushner's *Angels in America*. UK-England: London. 1992. Lang.: Eng. 2176

The Shakespearean acting and directing career of Judi Dench. UK-England: London. 1957-1995. Lang.: Eng. 2177

The reception of Robert Lepage's production of *A Midsummer Night's Dream* at the National. UK-England: London. 1992-1993. Lang.:Eng. 2189

History of contemporary Shakespeare performances. UK-England. 1989-1997. Lang.: Eng. 2190

John Caird's adaptation of *Peter Pan*. UK-England: London. 1997. Lang.: Eng. 2215

The effect of nationalization and subsidy on Shakespearean production and reception. UK-England. 1960-1988. Lang.: Eng. 2220

Actor David Bradley. UK-England: London. 1997. Lang.: Eng. 2222

Vocal expert Patsy Rodenburg. USA. 1997. Lang.: Eng. 2259

Francesca Zambello directs *Lady in the Dark* at the National. UK-England: London. 1997. Lang.: Eng. 3947

National Theatre of China (Beijing)
Performance/production
Margaret Booker on directing August Wilson's *Fences* in Beijing. China, People's Republic of: Beijing. 1983-1997. Lang.: Eng. 1608

National Theatre of Vietnam (Hanoi)
Performance/production
Ellen Stewart and Theodora Skipitares' collaboration with Vietnamese puppetry troupes. Vietnam: Hanoi. 1996-1997. Lang.: Eng. 4380

National Theatre School (Montreal, PQ)
Design/technology
The scenography program of the National Theatre School. Canada: Montreal, PQ. 1997. Lang.: Eng. 145

National Youth Music Theatre (London)
Performance/production
Collection of newspaper reviews by London theatre critics. UK-England: London. 1997. Lang.: Eng. 2099

Collection of newspaper reviews by London theatre critics. UK-England: London. 1997. Lang.: Eng. 2146

National Youth Theatre (London)
Performance/production
Collection of newspaper reviews by London theatre critics. UK-England: London. 1997. Lang.: Eng. 2099

Nationalist theatre
Performance/production
National identity and Croatian theatre. Croatia. 1900-1996. Lang.: Eng. 494

Nationalism in Estonian theatre. Estonia. 1960-1979. Lang.: Eng. 514

The importance of amateur theatre for Polish cultural identity at the time of the partitions. Poland: Lublin. 1866-1918. Lang.: Pol. 587

Plays/librettos/scripts
Shakespeare's *Coriolanus* and contemporary nationalism. Europe. 1990-1994. Lang.: Eng. 2782

Patriotism in early American drama. USA. 1775-1817. Lang.: Eng. 3187

Theory/criticism
The critical reception of Augusta Holmès' opera *La Montagne noire*. France: Paris. 1881-1901. Lang.: Eng. 4329

Nationaltheater (Munich)
Institutions
Nationaltheater under Peter Jonas' leadership. Germany: Munich. 1997. Lang.: Ger. 323

Nationaltheatret (Oslo)
Performance/production
Report on Ibsen festival. Norway: Oslo. 1996. Lang.: Eng.   1832
Natsuki, Mari
Performance/production
Collection of newspaper reviews by London theatre critics. UK-England:
London. 1997. Lang.: Eng.   2019
Natural World
Performance/production
Collection of newspaper reviews by London theatre critics. UK-England:
London. 1997. Lang.: Eng.   2000
Naturalism
Plays/librettos/scripts
Johannes Schlaf, Arno Holz, and German naturalism. Germany. 1888-
1892. Lang.: Eng.   2858
Nawrocki, Grzegorz
Plays/librettos/scripts
Plays by Grzegorz Nawrocki at Teatre Współczesny. Poland. 1996-1997.
Lang.: Hun.   2986
Neal, Larry
Performance/production
Analysis of countercultural theatre. USA. 1960-1970. Lang.: Eng.   672
Neale-Kennerly, James
Performance/production
Collection of newspaper reviews by London theatre critics. UK-England:
London. 1997. Lang.: Eng.   2055
Neat
Plays/librettos/scripts
Solo performer Charlayne Woodard. USA: New York, NY. 1997.
Lang.: Eng.   3308
Nederlander Theatre (New York, NY)
Design/technology
Blake Burba's lighting design for *Rent*. USA: New York, NY. 1996-
1997. Lang.: Eng.   3919
Nederlands Dans Theater (The Hague)
Institutions
Profile of Nederlands Dans Theater and Het National Ballet.
Netherlands: Amsterdam, The Hague. 1959-1989. Lang.: Hun.   1164
Performance/production
Mats Ek's *A Sort of* produced by Nederlands Dans Theater.
Netherlands: The Hague. 1997. Lang.: Swe.   1183
Nederlands Toneel Gent (Ghent)
Performance/production
Plays by Shepard and Albee at Nederlands Toneel Gent. Netherlands:
Ghent. 1996. Lang.: Eng.   1825
Nederlandse Opera (Amsterdam)
Performance/production
Pierre Audi's production of Wagner's *Ring* for Nederlandse Opera.
Netherlands: Amsterdam. 1997. Lang.: Dut.   4200
Nedivadlo (Prague)
Performance/production
The 'non-theatre' (Nedivadlo) of Ivan Vyskočil. Czech Republic:
Prague. 1963-1990. Lang.: Cze.   1615
Needcompany (Antwerp)
Institutions
Interviews with and texts by Needcompany. Belgium: Antwerp. 1996.
Lang.: Eng.   1381
Jan Lauwers' theatre group Needcompany. Belgium: Antwerp. 1996.
Lang.: Eng.   1382
Plays/librettos/scripts
Director and translator on the actuality of Shakespeare. Europe. 1985-
1997. Lang.: Ger, Fre, Dut, Eng.   2796
Nègres, Les (Blacks, The)
Performance/production
Visit to Grotowski and Compagnia della Fortezza. Italy: Volterra,
Pontedera. 1986-1997. Lang.: Ger.   1805
Plays/librettos/scripts
The concept of self in plays of Jean Genet. France. 1950-1975. Lang.:
Eng.   2834
Negro Ensemble Company (New York, NY)
Institutions
The Negro Ensemble Company and the poor conditions of Black
theatre. USA: New York, NY. 1997. Lang.: Eng.   1506
Neher, Caspar
Design/technology
The importance of Caspar Neher in the work of Bertolt Brecht.
Germany. 1897-1962. Lang.: Ger.   168
Performance/production
Kurt Weill's collaborations with playwrights. Germany: Berlin. USA:
New York, NY. 1927-1945. Lang.: Eng.   3934

Neher, Erika
Performance/production
Kurt Weill's collaborations with playwrights. Germany: Berlin. USA:
New York, NY. 1927-1945. Lang.: Eng.   3934
Neil, Chris
Performance/production
Collection of newspaper reviews by London theatre critics. UK-England:
London. 1997. Lang.: Eng.   2089
Neilson, Anthony
Performance/production
Collection of newspaper reviews by London theatre critics. UK-England:
London. 1997. Lang.: Eng.   1970
Collection of newspaper reviews by London theatre critics. UK-England:
London. 1997. Lang.: Eng.   1978
Collection of newspaper reviews by London theatre critics. UK-England:
London. 1997. Lang.: Eng.   2057
Neinsager, Der (He Who Says No)
Plays/librettos/scripts
Contemporary playwrights and the adaptation process. Europe. 1900-
1993. Lang.: Ita.   2793
Nekrošius, Eimuntas
Performance/production
The body and the text in productions of the Festival de Théâtre des
Amériques. Canada: Montreal, PQ. 1997. Lang.: Fre.   1583
Ghosts in theatrical productions. Poland. Lithuania. 1997. Lang.: Pol.
          1838
Nellie Boyd Dramatic Company (USA)
Institutions
The Nellie Boyd Dramatic Company. USA. 1879-1888. Lang.: Eng.   399
Nellis, Jeff
Design/technology
Lighting designer Jeff Nellis. USA: New York, NY. 1997. Lang.: Eng.
          224
Nelson, Richard
Performance/production
Collection of newspaper reviews by London theatre critics. UK-England:
London. 1997. Lang.: Eng.   2000
Collection of newspaper reviews by London theatre critics. UK-England.
1997. Lang.: Eng.   2163
James Laurenson's role in *The General from America* by Richard
Nelson, RSC. UK-England: London. 1997. Lang.: Eng.   2223
Nelson, Tim Blake
Design/technology
Scene designs of Neil Patel. USA. 1996. Lang.: Eng.   1373
Németh, Ákos
Performance/production
Russian, Hungarian and Bulgarian plays at Kammerspiele. Germany:
Magdeburg. 1989. Lang.: Ger.   1710
Plays/librettos/scripts
Interview with playwright Ákos Németh about Hungarian life and
politics. Hungary. 1964-1997. Lang.: Ger.   695
Németh, Mária
Performance/production
Soprano Mária Németh. Hungary. 1897-1967. Lang.: Hun.   4165
Nemirovič-Dančenko, Vladimir Ivanovič
Performance/production
Early modern interpretations of Aristophanes' *Lysistrata*. Europe. USA.
1892-1930. Lang.: Eng.   1647
Nemo: Jenseits von Vulkania
Performance/production
Theatrical vocal music of Nancy Van de Vate. USA. 1945-1995. Lang.:
Eng.   3884
Nemzeti Színház (Budapest)
Design/technology
Stage designs for *Az ember tragédiája (The Tragedy of Man)* by Imre
Madách. Hungary: Budapest. 1883-1915. Lang.: Hun.   1357
Performance spaces
The national theatre architecture competition. Hungary: Budapest. 1996-
1997. Lang.: Hun.   438
Performance/production
Colleagues' recollections of director László Vámos. Hungary. 1928-1996.
Lang.: Hun.   1763
Music in the premiere of *Az ember tragédiája (The Tragedy of Man)* by
Imre Madách. Hungary: Budapest. 1883. Lang.: Hun.   1768
Analysis of the premiere of *Az ember tragédiája (The Tragedy of Man)*
by Imre Madách. Hungary: Budapest. 1883. Lang.: Hun.   1779
Nemzeti Színház (Miskolc)
SEE
Miskolci Nemzeti Színház.

North, Robert — cont'd

Győri Balett's production of *Carmen* by Robert North and Christopher Benstead. Hungary: Győr. 1997. Lang.: Hun. 1094

Analysis of Robert North's choreography for Schubert's *Death and the Maiden*. USA. 1945-1992. Lang.: Hun. 1122

North, The
Institutions
Solo performance at the Festival de Théâtre des Amériques. Canada: Montreal, PQ. 1997. Lang.: Fre. 1392

Northern Broadsides (Halifax, Yorkshire)
Performance/production
Criticism of productions at Shakespeare's Globe Theatre. UK-England: London. 1996. Lang.: Eng. 2187

Norwid, Cyprian Kamil
Plays/librettos/scripts
Text and performance in the Romantic period. Europe. 1800-1851. Lang.: Pol. 2790

Nost Milan, El (Our Milan)
Performance/production
Materialism in Brecht's plays and a Piccolo Teatro performance. France: Paris. Italy: Milan. 1977. Lang.: Eng. 1656

Nostalghia (Nostalgia)
Performance/production
Music in films by Andrej Tarkovskij. Russia. 1979-1983. Lang.: Eng. 3585

Not I
Performance/production
Staging and Beckett's *Not I* and *Krapp's Last Tape*. France. Ireland. 1960-1973. Lang.: Eng. 1671

Collection of newspaper reviews by London theatre critics. UK-England: London. 1997. Lang.: Eng. 2134

Xerxes Mehta's approach to directing Beckett. USA. 1993. Lang.: Eng. 2305

Plays/librettos/scripts
Gender in Beckett's *Not I*. Ireland. USA. 1973. Lang.: Eng. 2906

Memory and the self in Beckett's *Not I* and *Krapp's Last Tape*. Ireland. France. 1958-1972. Lang.: Eng. 2924

Not Just an Asian Babe
Performance/production
Collection of newspaper reviews by London theatre critics. UK-England: London. 1997. Lang.: Eng. 2055

Notebooks of a Cameraman, Serafino Gubbio
SEE
Quaderni di Serafino Gubbio operatore.

Nothomb, Amélie
Plays/librettos/scripts
Analysis of *Les Combustibles (The Combustibles)* by Amélie Nothomb. Belgium. 1994. Lang.: Fre. 2386

Nourrit, Adolphe
Performance/production
Marriage and domesticity in *La Sylphide* choreographed by Filippo Taglioni. France. 1830-1835. Lang.: Eng. 1068

Nouveau Théâtre Expérimental (Montreal, PQ)
Performance/production
The body and the text in productions of the Festival de Théâtre des Amériques. Canada: Montreal, PQ. 1997. Lang.: Fre. 1583

Nouvelle Compagnie Théâtrale (Montreal, PQ)
Performance/production
Monodramas by Louisette Dussault and Larry Tremblay. Canada: Montreal, PQ. 1997. Lang.: Eng. 1605

Nova Schola Cantorum (Amsterdam)
Performance/production
A performance of the Beauvais *Ludus Danielis*. Netherlands: Maastricht. 1996. Lang.: Eng. 3872

A collaborative production of the medieval *Ludus Danielis*. Netherlands: Maastricht. 1996. Lang.: Eng. 3873

Novosadsko Pozorište (Novi Sad)
SEE
Újvidéki Színház.

Now Eleanor's Idea
Plays/librettos/scripts
Analysis of Robert Ashley's opera *Now Eleanor's Idea*. USA. 1961-1994. Lang.: Eng. 4316

Now There's Just the Three of Us
Performance/production
Collection of newspaper reviews by London theatre critics. UK-England. 1997. Lang.: Eng. 2050

Nowakowski, Roman
Plays/librettos/scripts
Analysis of plays shown on Polish television. Poland. 1929-1997. Lang.: Pol. 3735

Nowe Wyzwolenie (New Deliverance, The)
Performance/production
Witkiewicz productions directed by Grzegorz Horst d'Albertis. Poland: Warsaw. 1997. Lang.: Eng, Fre. 1853

Nowicki, Jan
Performance/production
Actor Jan Nowicki. Poland: Cracow. 1939-1997. Lang.: Pol. 1850

Nowra, Louis
Plays/librettos/scripts
Identity and the use of multiple actors to portray a single character in postcolonial drama. Australia. Ireland. Samoa. 1997. Lang.: Eng. 2380

Radio plays of Louis Nowra. Australia: Sydney. 1975-1993. Lang.: Eng. 3519

Nozze di Figaro, Le
Performance/production
Musical disguises in Mozart's late comic operas. Austria. 1786-1790. Lang.: Eng. 4101

Analysis of arias in the last act of Mozart's *Le Nozze di Figaro*. Austro-Hungarian Empire: Vienna. 1786-1997. Lang.: Eng. 4102

Interview with opera director Judit Galgóczy. Hungary. 1987-1997. Lang.: Hun. 4168

Background material on Metropolitan Opera radio broadcast performances. USA: New York, NY. 1997. Lang.: Eng. 4238

Plays/librettos/scripts
Analysis of opera librettos by Boito, Da Ponte, and Gertrude Stein. Europe. 1770-1915. Lang.: Eng. 4289

Nuevo mundo descubierto por Cristóbal Colón, El (New World Discovered by Christopher Columbus, The)
Plays/librettos/scripts
Analysis of Lope de Vega's Fernando and Isabel plays. Spain. 1579-1626. Lang.: Eng. 3046

Nuevo mundo, El (New World)
Performance/production
Collection of newspaper reviews by London theatre critics. UK-England: London. 1997. Lang.: Eng. 2146

Nüganen, Elmo
Institutions
Profile of Tallinna Linnateater, Elmo Nüganen, artistic director. Estonia: Tallinn. 1967. Lang.: Swe. 1401

Nugent, Daniel
Performance/production
San Francisco Mime Troupe's *13 Días/13 Days*. USA: San Francisco, CA. 1997. Lang.: Eng. 2335

Nuitter, Charles
Theory/criticism
Feminist analysis of the ballet *Coppélia*. France. 1870. Lang.: Eng. 1134

Nunn, Trevor
Design/technology
Lighting design for the tenth anniversary of *Les Misérables* on Broadway. USA: New York, NY. 1987-1997. Lang.: Eng. 3916

Performance/production
Collection of newspaper reviews by London theatre critics. UK-England: London. 1997. Lang.: Eng. 2104

Collection of newspaper reviews by London theatre critics. UK-England: London. 1997. Lang.: Eng. 2144

Collection of newspaper reviews by London theatre critics. UK-England: London. 1997. Lang.: Eng. 2158

Television versions of Shakespeare's *Othello*. UK-England. 1987-1996. Lang.: Eng. 3726

Trevor Nunn's television production of Shakespeare's *Macbeth*. UK-England. 1976-1978. Lang.: Eng. 3729

Nur Du (Only You)
Design/technology
Peter Pabst's stage design for Tanztheater Wuppertal's *Nur Du (Only You)*. Germany: Wuppertal. 1996. Lang.: Eng. 940

Performance/production
Analysis of Pina Bausch's *Nur Du (Only You)*. Germany: Wuppertal. 1996. Lang.: Eng. 964

Interview with Matthias Schmiegelt, company manager of Tanztheater Wuppertal. Germany: Wuppertal. 1996. Lang.: Eng. 966

The creation of Pina Bausch's *Nur Du (Only You)*. Germany: Wuppertal. 1996. Lang.: Eng. 969

Review of U.S. tour of Pina Bausch's *Nur Du (Only You)*. USA. 1960-1991. Lang.: Eng. 1000

Nur eine Scheibe Brot (Just a Slice of Bread)
Basic theatrical documents
English translation of *Nur eine Scheibe Brot (Just a Slice of Bread)* by Rainer Werner Fassbinder. Germany. 1971. Lang.: Eng. 1280

Old Red Lion Theatre (London) — cont'd

Collection of newspaper reviews by London theatre critics. UK-England. 1997. Lang.: Eng. 2082

Collection of newspaper reviews by London theatre critics. UK-England: London. 1997. Lang.: Eng. 2091

Collection of newspaper reviews by London theatre critics. UK-England: London. 1997. Lang.: Eng. 2102

Collection of newspaper reviews by London theatre critics. UK-England: London. 1997. Lang.: Eng. 2115

Collection of newspaper reviews by London theatre critics. UK-England: London. 1997. Lang.: Eng. 2127

Collection of newspaper reviews by London theatre critics. UK-England: London. 1997. Lang.: Eng. 2145

Old Settler, The
Plays/librettos/scripts
Analysis of *The Old Settler* by John Henry Redwood. USA. 1997. Lang.: Eng. 3297

Old Times
Performance/production
John MacDonald's production of Pinter's *Old Times*, Washington Stage Guild. USA: Washington, DC. 1994. Lang.: Eng. 2325

Plays/librettos/scripts
Mystery in the plays of Harold Pinter. UK-England. 1965-1995. Lang.: Eng. 3092

Old Vic Theatre (Bristol)
SEE
Bristol Old Vic Theatre.

Old Vic Theatre (London)
Institutions
The Old Vic's 1997 season under artistic director Peter Hall. UK-England: London. 1997. Lang.: Eng. 1497

Performance/production
Collection of newspaper reviews by London theatre critics. UK-England: London. 1997. Lang.: Eng. 1967

Collection of newspaper reviews by London theatre critics. UK-England: London. 1997. Lang.: Eng. 1991

Collection of newspaper reviews by London theatre critics. UK-England: London. 1997. Lang.: Eng. 2017

Collection of newspaper reviews by London theatre critics. UK-England: London. 1997. Lang.: Eng. 2044

Collection of newspaper reviews by London theatre critics. UK-England: London. 1997. Lang.: Eng. 2049

Collection of newspaper reviews by London theatre critics. UK-England: London. 1997. Lang.: Eng. 2069

Collection of newspaper reviews by London theatre critics. UK-England: London. 1997. Lang.: Eng. 2078

Collection of newspaper reviews by London theatre critics. UK-England: London. 1997. Lang.: Eng. 2095

Collection of newspaper reviews by London theatre critics. UK-England: London. 1997. Lang.: Eng. 2101

Collection of newspaper reviews by London theatre critics. UK-England: London. 1997. Lang.: Eng. 2106

Collection of newspaper reviews by London theatre critics. UK-England: London. 1997. Lang.: Eng. 2110

Collection of newspaper reviews by London theatre critics. UK-England: London. 1997. Lang.: Eng. 2120

Collection of newspaper reviews by London theatre critics. UK-England: London. 1997. Lang.: Eng. 2137

Non-literary realism in Shakespeare productions. UK-England. Germany. 1958-1995. Lang.: Ger. 2170

Shakespearean production before national subsidy. UK-England. 1914-1959. Lang.: Eng. 2175

Actor Dominic West. UK-England: London. 1997. Lang.: Eng. 2195

Recent roles of actor Michael Pennington. UK-England: London. 1997. Lang.: Eng. 2196

Dominic Dromgoole's new play season at the Old Vic. UK-England: London. 1997. Lang.: Eng. 2213

Oldfield, Anne
Performance/production
Anne Oldfield's performance as Lady Townly in *The Provoked Husband* by Colley Cibber. England. 1720-1730. Lang.: Eng. 1632

Oleanna
Plays/librettos/scripts
Analysis of *Oleanna* by David Mamet. USA. 1992-1997. Lang.: Eng. 3200

Critical response to misogyny in David Mamet's *Oleanna*. USA. 1992. Lang.: Eng. 3238

Sexual harassment in David Mamet's *Oleanna*. USA. 1993. Lang.: Eng. 3292

Teachers and students in plays of Walker, Mamet, and Ionesco. USA. Canada. France. 1951-1997. Lang.: Eng. 3296

David Mamet as screen writer and director. USA. 1975-1995. Lang.: Eng. 3672

Oliveras, José Cheo
Institutions
Interview with José Cheo Oliveras, artistic director, La Compañía Teatro Círculo. USA: New York, NY. 1996. Lang.: Spa. 1510

Olivier Theatre (London)
SEE ALSO
National Theatre Company.
Institutions
The National's season of theatre in the round at the Olivier. UK-England: London. 1997. Lang.: Eng. 1499

Performance/production
Collection of newspaper reviews by London theatre critics. UK-England: London. 1997. Lang.: Eng. 2034

Collection of newspaper reviews by London theatre critics. UK-England: London. 1997. Lang.: Eng. 2048

Collection of newspaper reviews by London theatre critics. UK-England: London. 1997. Lang.: Eng. 2103

Collection of newspaper reviews by London theatre critics. UK-England: London. 1997. Lang.: Eng. 2104

Collection of newspaper reviews by London theatre critics. UK-England: London. 1997. Lang.: Eng. 2141

Collection of newspaper reviews by London theatre critics. UK-England: London. 1997. Lang.: Eng. 2158

John Caird's adaptation of *Peter Pan*. UK-England: London. 1997. Lang.: Eng. 2215

Olivier, Laurence
Performance/production
Shakespearean production before national subsidy. UK-England. 1914-1959. Lang.: Eng. 2175

The chorus in film adaptations of Shakespeare's *Henry V* by Olivier and Branagh. UK-England. 1944-1989. Lang.: Eng. 3598

Olivier, Richard
Institutions
The first season of Shakespeare's Globe Theatre. UK-England: London. 1996. Lang.: Swe. 1495

Performance spaces
Profile of Shakespeare's Globe Theatre. UK-England: London. 1970. Lang.: Swe. 1541

Performance/production
Collection of newspaper reviews by London theatre critics. UK-England: London. 1997. Lang.: Eng. 2060

Olivo, Pierre de
Performance/production
Interview with character dance teacher Pierre de Olivo. Sweden: Stockholm. 1940. Lang.: Swe. 1114

Olsson, Anders
Institutions
Profile of Riddarhyttans Industriteater, Anders Olson artistic director. Sweden: Riddarhyttan. 1985. Lang.: Swe. 1474

Om smekningar (About Caresses)
Performance/production
Choreographer Lena Josefsson. Sweden: Örebro, Stockholm. 1997. Lang.: Swe. 1185

On Baile's Strand
Performance/production
Collection of newspaper reviews by London theatre critics. UK-England: London. 1997. Lang.: Eng. 2048

On the Couch with Chrissie
Performance/production
Collection of newspaper reviews by London theatre critics. UK-England: London. 1997. Lang.: Eng. 1969

On the Razzle
SEE ALSO
Jux will er sich machen, Einen.

On the Rim of the Curve
Plays/librettos/scripts
Indigenous peoples in Canadian historical drama. Canada. 1886-1997. Lang.: Eng. 2424

Ostermeier, Thomas — cont'd

Performance/production
German productions of plays by Terrence McNally and Nicky Silver.
Germany. 1996-1997. Lang.: Ger.   1721
Ostrovskij, Aleksand'r Nikolajévič
Institutions
Groza (The Storm), based on works of Ostrovskij, directed for young
audiences at Teat'r Junogo Zritelja. Russia: Moscow. 1996. Lang.: Rus.
                                                                  1463
Performance/production
Ostrovskij's *Žadov i drugie (Žadov and Others)* at the Globus. Russia:
Novosibirsk. 1997. Lang.: Rus.   1884
Ostrovskij's *Kozma Zacharič Minin* at Moscow Art Theatre. Russia:
Moscow. 1997. Lang.: Rus.   1885
Plays/librettos/scripts
Ostrovskij's efforts to create a Russian national theatre. Russia. 1823-
1886. Lang.: Eng.   3003
Oswald, Peter
Performance/production
Collection of newspaper reviews by London theatre critics. UK-England.
1997. Lang.: Eng.   2039
Collection of newspaper reviews by London theatre critics. UK-England:
London. 1997. Lang.: Eng.   2154
Oswick, Ralph
Performance/production
Collection of newspaper reviews by London theatre critics. UK-England:
London. 1997. Lang.: Eng.   2159
Otello
Plays/librettos/scripts
Analysis of opera librettos by Boito, Da Ponte, and Gertrude Stein.
Europe. 1770-1915. Lang.: Eng.   4289
Othello
Performance/production
Gabriele Lavia's production of Shakespeare's *Othello*, in which Iago is
the hero. Italy: Novara. 1995. Lang.: Ita.   1813
Collection of newspaper reviews by London theatre critics. UK-England:
London. 1997. Lang.: Eng.   2103
Collection of newspaper reviews by London theatre critics. UK-England:
London. 1997. Lang.: Eng.   2120
Non-literary realism in Shakespeare productions. UK-England.
Germany. 1958-1995. Lang.: Ger.   2170
Shakespeare's *Othello* in Liz White's film version. USA. 1980. Lang.:
Eng.   3611
Interview with actor Michael Maloney about roles in Shakespearean
films. USA. 1995. Lang.: Eng.   3625
Voyeurism in Jonathan Miller's TV version of Shakespeare's *Othello*.
UK-England. 1981. Lang.: Eng.   3725
Television versions of Shakespeare's *Othello*. UK-England. 1987-1996.
Lang.: Eng.   3726
Plays/librettos/scripts
Race in Shakespeare's *Othello*. England. 1604. Lang.: Eng.   2450
Verse, prose, and the title character in Shakespeare's *Othello*. England.
1604. Lang.: Eng.   2489
Protestantism in early English drama. England. 1559-1612. Lang.: Eng.
                                                                  2528
Shakespeare's dramatization of the effects of gender bias on both sexes.
England. 1604-1613. Lang.: Eng.   2565
Gender and racial politics in Shakespeare's *Othello*. England. 1605.
Lang.: Eng.   2572
Psychoanalysis of racism in Shakespeare's *Othello*. England. 1604.
Lang.: Eng.   2639
Language and power in Shakespeare's *Othello*. England. 1604. Lang.:
Eng.   2645
The poetics of vision in tragedies of Shakespeare. England. 1600-1606.
Lang.: Ita.   2667
Analysis of Shakespeare's *Othello*. England. 1604. Lang.: Eng.   2679
Shakespeare's *Othello* and early modern precepts of wifely conduct.
England. 1605. Lang.: Eng.   2687
Aging in plays of Shakespeare. England. 1590-1613. Lang.: Eng.   2700
Marital equality and subordination in Shakespeare's *Othello* and
Webster's *The Duchess of Malfi*. England. 1605-1613. Lang.: Eng. 2715
Witchcraft and female sexuality in the plays of Shakespeare. England.
1590-1613. Lang.: Eng.   2717
Ideas of selfhood and slavery reflected in Shakespeare's *Othello*.
England. 1604. Lang.: Eng.   2736

The handkerchief in Shakespeare's *Othello*. England. 1605. Lang.: Eng.
                                                                  2740
Law, justice, and criminology in plays of Shakespeare. England. 1590-
1613. Lang.: Eng.   2756
Analysis of Oliver Parker's screen adaptation of *Othello*. USA. 1995.
Lang.: Eng.   3683
Analysis of opera librettos by Boito, Da Ponte, and Gertrude Stein.
Europe. 1770-1915. Lang.: Eng.   4289
Relation to other fields
The expansion of the Turkish and Islamic empires and Shakespeare's
Othello. England. 1453-1604. Lang.: Eng.   3349
Race, *Othello*, and the high school classroom. USA. 1997. Lang.: Eng.
                                                                  3394
The use of film and video to teach the plays of Shakespeare. USA.
1997. Lang.: Eng.   3398
The importance of openness to new interpretations in teaching
Shakespeare. USA. 1997. Lang.: Eng.   3434
Theory/criticism
Othello, censorship, and public swearing. England: London. 1215-1622.
Lang.: Eng.   3470
Racism, *Othello*, and South African criticism. England. South Africa,
Republic of. 1604-1987. Lang.: Eng.   3473
Other Place, The (Stratford)
SEE ALSO
Royal Shakespeare Company.
Performance/production
Report on experimental theatre and the Grass Roots Festival. UK-
England: Cambridge, Stratford-on-Avon. 1996. Lang.: Hun.   617
Collection of newspaper reviews by London theatre critics. UK-England.
1997. Lang.: Eng.   2014
Collection of newspaper reviews by London theatre critics. UK-England:
London. 1997. Lang.: Eng.   2134
Collection of newspaper reviews by London theatre critics. UK-England.
1997. Lang.: Eng.   2150
Collection of newspaper reviews by London theatre critics. UK-England.
1997. Lang.: Eng.   2163
Otrabanda Theatre Company (New York, NY)
Performance/production
Analysis of countercultural theatre. USA. 1960-1970. Lang.: Eng.   672
Ottawa Lyra Opera (Ottawa, ON)
Institutions
Planning a season at five Canadian opera companies. Canada. 1997.
Lang.: Eng.   4038
Otten, Willem-Jan
Plays/librettos/scripts
Playwright Willem-Jan Otten. Netherlands. 1996-1997. Lang.: Dut. 2977
Otter, Anne Sofie von
Performance/production
Mezzo-soprano Anne Sofie von Otter. Sweden: Stockholm. 1997. Lang.:
Eng.   4215
Ottone, David
Performance/production
Collection of newspaper reviews by London theatre critics. UK-England:
London. 1997. Lang.: Eng.   1977
Otway, Thomas
Plays/librettos/scripts
Dramatic satire of the exclusion crisis. England. 1680-1683. Lang.: Eng.
                                                                  2714
Our Betters
Performance/production
Collection of newspaper reviews by London theatre critics. UK-England.
1997. Lang.: Eng.   2092
Our Country's Good
Plays/librettos/scripts
Metatheatre in plays of Timberlake Wertenbaker. UK-England. 1988-
1995. Lang.: Eng.   3079
Our Town
Plays/librettos/scripts
Comparison of works by Gertrude Stein and Thornton Wilder. USA.
1934-1938. Lang.: Eng.   3127
Time travel in English-language drama. USA. Canada. UK-England.
1908-1993. Lang.: Eng.   3171
Out Cry
Performance/production
Collection of newspaper reviews by London theatre critics. UK-England:
London. 1997. Lang.: Eng.   2037

Out of Joint (London)
    Plays/librettos/scripts
        The influence of Čechov's *Tri sestry (Three Sisters)* on plays of
        Sadowski and Wertenbaker. Russia. UK-England. 1901-1997. Lang.:
        Eng.   2992
Outside, The
    Performance/production
        Collection of newspaper reviews by London theatre critics. UK-England:
        London. 1997. Lang.: Eng.   2020
    Plays/librettos/scripts
        Gender analysis of plays by Susan Glaspell. USA. 1876-1948. Lang.:
        Eng.   3269
Ováder (Storm, The)
    Performance/production
        Collection of newspaper reviews by London theatre critics. UK-England:
        London. 1997. Lang.: Eng.   1982
Oval House Theatre (London)
    Performance/production
        Collection of newspaper reviews by London theatre critics. UK-England:
        London. 1997. Lang.: Eng.   1983
        Collection of newspaper reviews by London theatre critics. UK-England:
        London. 1997. Lang.: Eng.   1993
        Collection of newspaper reviews by London theatre critics. UK-England:
        London. 1997. Lang.: Eng.   2000
        Collection of newspaper reviews by London theatre critics. UK-England:
        London. 1997. Lang.: Eng.   2031
        Collection of newspaper reviews by London theatre critics. UK-England:
        London. 1997. Lang.: Eng.   2061
        Collection of newspaper reviews by London theatre critics. UK-England:
        London. 1997. Lang.: Eng.   2123
        Collection of newspaper reviews by London theatre critics. UK-England:
        London. 1997. Lang.: Eng.   2128
Overbay, Craig
    Design/technology
        Work of engineers for rock band Foo Fighters. UK-England. 1997.
        Lang.: Eng.   196
Overmyer, Eric
    Performance/production
        Partial transcript of panel discussion involving dramaturgs and
        playwrights. USA. 1990. Lang.: Eng.   2235
    Plays/librettos/scripts
        Televisual dramaturgy in the work of some contemporary playwrights.
        USA. 1990-1997. Lang.: Eng.   3191
Ovid
    Plays/librettos/scripts
        A reference to Ovid in Shakespeare's *Coriolanus*. England. 1607. Lang.:
        Eng.   2722
        Ovid's Narcissus reflected in Shakespeare's *Twelfth Night*. England.
        1602. Lang.: Eng.   2751
Owen/Penomee, Kari Ann
    Plays/librettos/scripts
        Kari Ann Owen/Penomee on her play *Terms of Surrender*. USA. 1997.
        Lang.: Eng.   3244
Owen, Paul
    Design/technology
        Set designer Paul Owen. USA: Louisville, KY. 1997. Lang.: Eng.   1378
Owl Answers, The
    Plays/librettos/scripts
        Analysis of *The Owl Answers* by Adrienne Kennedy. USA. 1965-1997.
        Lang.: Eng.   3233
Pablo
    Plays/librettos/scripts
        The style of playwright Eduardo Pavlovsky. Argentina. 1962-1993.
        Lang.: Spa.   2374
Pabst, Peter
    Design/technology
        Peter Pabst's stage design for Tanztheater Wuppertal's *Nur Du (Only
        You)*. Germany: Wuppertal. 1996. Lang.: Eng.   940
    Performance/production
        Interviews with members of Tanztheater Wuppertal. Germany:
        Wuppertal. 1996. Lang.: Eng.   974
Pacific Overtures
    Plays/librettos/scripts
        Analysis of Stephen Sondheim's *Pacific Overtures*. USA. 1976. Lang.:
        Eng.   3990
Pacino, Al
    Performance/production
        Analysis of Al Pacino's film *Looking for Richard*. USA. 1996. Lang.:
        Eng.   3606

Paco, Lucrécia
    Performance/production
        Interview with principals of joint production *Berättelse på tidens strand
        (A Tale on the Shore of Time)*. Sweden. Mozambique. 1997. Lang.: Swe.
            1959
Pade, Christian
    Performance/production
        Significant productions in Swabia. Germany: Stuttgart. 1997. Lang.: Ger.
            1726
Padmore, Elaine
    Institutions
        Interview with Elaine Padmore, opera manager of Det Kongelige
        Teater. Denmark: Copenhagen. 1980. Lang.: Swe.   4044
    Performance/production
        Opera and culture in Copenhagen area. Denmark: Copenhagen. 1997.
        Lang.: Eng.   4121
Page 27
    Basic theatrical documents
        Text of *Page 27* by Jean-Louis Bauer. France. 1996. Lang.: Fre.   1268
Page, Anthony
    Performance/production
        Collection of newspaper reviews by London theatre critics. UK-England:
        London. 1997. Lang.: Eng.   2124
        Anthony Page's production of *A Delicate Balance* by Edward Albee.
        UK-England: London. 1997. Lang.: Eng.   2211
Page, Louise
    Plays/librettos/scripts
        Female characters in plays of contemporary British women. UK-
        England. 1980-1995. Lang.: Eng.   3077
Pageant of Sunshine and Shadow, The
    Performance/production
        Constance D'Arcy Mackay's *The Pageant of Sunshine and Shadow*.
        USA. 1900-1918. Lang.: Eng.   3771
Pageants/parades
    SEE ALSO
        Processional theatre.
        Classed Entries under MIXED ENTERTAINMENT—Pageants/parades.
    Institutions
        Participating in events of Bread and Puppet Theatre. USA: Plainfield,
        VT. 1972-1997. Lang.: Eng.   4355
    Performance/production
        Checklist of Tudor and Stuart entertainments. England. 1625-1634.
        Lang.: Eng.   505
        Compilation of records of early drama in Bristol. England: Bristol. 1255-
        1642. Lang.: Eng.   510
        Essays on carnival. Europe. Lang.: Ita.   3782
        History of Neapolitan carnival. Italy: Naples. 1500-1800. Lang.: Ita.
            3783
    Plays/librettos/scripts
        History of Catalan *Corpus Christi* play. Spain-Catalonia. 1437-1997.
        Lang.: Eng.   3052
Paget, Clive
    Performance/production
        Collection of newspaper reviews by London theatre critics. UK-England:
        London. 1997. Lang.: Eng.   2059
        Collection of newspaper reviews by London theatre critics. UK-England:
        London. 1997. Lang.: Eng.   2159
Pagliacci, I
    Performance/production
        Background material on Metropolitan Opera radio broadcast
        performances. USA: New York, NY. 1997. Lang.: Eng.   4238
Paines Plough Theatre Company (London)
    Performance/production
        Profile of Vicky Featherstone, the new artistic director of Paines Plough.
        UK-England: London. 1997. Lang.: Eng.   2179
Paisiello, Giovanni
    Plays/librettos/scripts
        Neapolitan character types in Italian opera. Italy. 1792. Lang.: Fre.   4301
Pakledinaz, Martin
    Design/technology
        Opera costume designer Martin Pakledinaz. USA: Santa Fe, NM, New
        York, NY. 1997. Lang.: Eng.   4035
Palace Theatre (London)
    Performance/production
        Gender and nationalism: Maud Allan's *Vision of Salome*. UK-England:
        London. USA. 1908. Lang.: Eng.   994
Palace Theatre (Louisville, KY)
    Performance spaces
        Renovation of the Palace Theatre. USA: Louisville, KY. 1996-1997.
        Lang.: Eng.   3554

Palace Theatre (Watford)
Performance/production
Collection of newspaper reviews by London theatre critics. UK-England.
1997. Lang.: Eng.   2142

Palestinian Nights
Performance/production
Collection of newspaper reviews by London theatre critics. UK-England:
London. 1997. Lang.: Eng.   2087

Palestrina
Performance/production
Historical introduction to *Palestrina* by Hans Pfitzner. Germany. 1917-
1997. Lang.: Eng.   4162

Paliashvili Opera Theatre (Tbilisi)
SEE
Teat'r Opery i Baleta im. Z. Paliašvili.

Paliès, Jean-Luc
Basic theatrical documents
Text of *L'Esclave du démon (Slave of the Devil)* by Louise Doutreligne.
France. Spain. 1612-1996. Lang.: Fre.   1269
Performance/production
Sociocultural analysis of recent French productions. France. 1993-1994.
Lang.: Eng.   1678

Pandur, Tomaž
Performance/production
Pictorial history of productions by director Tomaž Pandur. Slovenia.
1989-1996. Lang.: Eng, Ger.   1906

Pane, Gina
Theory/criticism
Performance art and the photographic document. USA. Europe. 1970-
1979. Lang.: Eng.   3853

Panigrahi, Sanjukta
Performance/production
Julia Varley on the work of Sanjukta Panigrahi. India. 1952-1996.
Lang.: Ita.   1223

Pankov, P.P.
Performance/production
Actor P.P. Pankov of the Bolšoj Drama Theatre. Russia: St. Petersburg.
1970-1997. Lang.: Rus.   1880

Pannikkar, Kavalam Narayana
Performance/production
Interviews with writer-directors K.N. Pannikkar, Mahesh Dattani, and
Tripurari Sharma. India. 1997. Lang.: Eng.   1781

Analysis of *Teyyateyyam* by K. N. Pannikkar. India: Trivandrum. 1993.
Lang.: Eng.   1784

Pánti, Anna
Performance/production
Interview with soprano Anna Pánti of the Budapest Opera House.
Hungary. 1980-1997. Lang.: Hun.   4164

Pantomime
SEE ALSO
Mime.

Classed Entries under MIME—Pantomime. English Pantomime.
Performance/production
Enactments of the descent from the cross. Mexico. 1600-1997. Lang.:
Eng.   3803

Pants on Fire
Performance/production
Ken Garnhum's *One Word* at Tarragon Theatre. Canada. 1994-1997.
Lang.: Eng.   1602

Papa Hamlet
Plays/librettos/scripts
Johannes Schlaf, Arno Holz, and German naturalism. Germany. 1888-
1892. Lang.: Eng.   2858

Paper Husband
Basic theatrical documents
English translation of *Paper Husband* by Hannan Al-Shaykh. Middle
East. 1997. Lang.: Eng.   1292
Performance/production
Collection of newspaper reviews by London theatre critics. UK-England:
London. 1997. Lang.: Eng.   1987

Paper or Plastic: A Homeless Round Up
Administration
Production of *Paper or Plastic: A Homeless Round Up* by Teresa A.
Dowell. USA. 1996. Lang.: Eng.   63

Papp, Joseph
Performance/production
Analysis of New York Shakespeare Festival's productions. USA: New
York, NY. 1997. Lang.: Eng.   2249

Personal recollections of New York Shakespeare Festival productions.
USA: New York, NY. 1987-1997. Lang.: Eng.   2297

Pappano, Antonio
Performance/production
Opera conductor Antonio Pappano. USA. 1960-1997. Lang.: Eng.   4253

Par-dessus bord (Overboard)
Performance/production
Collection of newspaper reviews by London theatre critics. UK-England:
London. 1997. Lang.: Eng.   2117

Parades
SEE
Pageants/parades.

Paradis (Paradise)
Performance/production
Interview with Nikolaj Cederholm of Dr. Dante's Aveny. Denmark:
Copenhagen. 1997. Lang.: Dan.   1618

Parate Labor (France)
Performance/production
Parate Labor's teaching of *kutiyattam* Sanskrit drama in France. France.
India. 1989-1997. Lang.: Eng.   1673

Paravents, Les (Screens, The)
Plays/librettos/scripts
The concept of self in plays of Jean Genet. France. 1950-1975. Lang.:
Eng.   2834

Parichy, Dennis
Design/technology
Dennis Parichy's lighting design for *Sympathetic Magic* by Lanford
Wilson at Second Stage. USA: New York, NY. 1997. Lang.: Eng.   1369

Paris Is Burning
Theory/criticism
Analysis of criticism of Jennie Livingston's documentary film *Paris Is
Burning*. USA. 1991. Lang.: Eng.   3700

Park Theatre (London)
SEE
Battersea Park Theatre.

Park, Nick
Performance/production
Collection of newspaper reviews by London theatre critics. UK-England:
London. 1997. Lang.: Eng.   2149

Park, Steve
Performance/production
Political activism of actor Steve Park. USA. 1997. Lang.: Eng.   658

Parker, Alan
Performance/production
Collection of newspaper reviews by London theatre critics. UK-England:
London. 1997. Lang.: Eng.   2146

Parker, Lynne
Performance/production
Collection of newspaper reviews by London theatre critics. UK-England:
London. 1997. Lang.: Eng.   2027

Collection of newspaper reviews by London theatre critics. UK-England:
London. 1997. Lang.: Eng.   2101

Parker, Oliver
Plays/librettos/scripts
Analysis of Oliver Parker's screen adaptation of *Othello*. USA. 1995.
Lang.: Eng.   3683

Parkert, Cecilia
Performance/production
Plays based on refugee experiences. Sweden: Gothenburg. 1997. Lang.:
Swe.   1927

Parks, Suzan-Lori
Basic theatrical documents
Text of *Imperceptible Mutabilities in the Third Kingdom* by Suzan-Lori
Parks. USA. 1989. Lang.: Eng.   1337
Plays/librettos/scripts
Analysis of *The Death of the Last Black Man in the Whole Entire World*
by Suzan-Lori Parks. USA. 1995. Lang.: Eng.   3138

Introduction to *Imperceptible Mutabilities in the Third Kingdom* by
Suzan-Lori Parks. USA. 1993. Lang.: Eng.   3177

The principles of Gertrude Stein in the works of contemporary
playwrights. USA. 1993. Lang.: Eng.   3263

Analysis of *Venus* by Suzan-Lori Parks. USA. 1996. Lang.: Eng. 3310

Parlor theatricals
Plays/librettos/scripts
The parlor melodrama. England. 1840-1900. Lang.: Eng.   693

Parnell, Peter
Plays/librettos/scripts
Stage adaptations of novels. USA. 1997. Lang.: Eng.   702

Parody

Performance/production

Resistance and parody in African-American theatre. USA. 1895-1910. Lang.: Eng.   652

Parra, Alexandre

Design/technology

Lighting designer Alexandre Parra. USA: New York, NY. 1997. Lang.: Eng.   274

Parrado, Flora Diaz

Plays/librettos/scripts

The 'Black Madonna' in Cuban theatre. Cuba. 1925-1990. Lang.: Spa.   2444

Parsifal

Performance/production

Impressions of opera performances in several German cities. Germany. 1997. Lang.: Ger.   4147

Theory/criticism

Luciano Berio on Wagnerian opera. Europe. 1880-1995. Lang.: Eng.   4327

Pártay, Lilla

Performance/production

Ildikó Pongor's performance in the ballet *Anna Karenina*. Hungary: Budapest. 1997. Lang.: Hun.   1082

Parti Nagy, Lajos

Performance/production

Conversation with director Csaba Kiss and playwright Lajos Parti Nagy. Hungary. 1980-1996. Lang.: Hun.   1753

Partljič, Tone

Basic theatrical documents

Texts of three comedies on the sociopolitical situation by Tone Partljič. Slovenia. 1997. Lang.: Slo.   1300

Party Line, The (Sydney)

Performance/production

Interview with director Gail Kelly of The Party Line. Australia: Sydney. 1997. Lang.: Eng.   1560

Paryla, Katja

Performance/production

Recent productions of plays by Schiller. Germany. 1996-1997. Lang.: Ger.   1716

Pascal, Julia

Performance/production

Collection of newspaper reviews by London theatre critics. UK-England: London. 1997. Lang.: Eng.   1967

Paseo al atardecer (Evening Walk)

Basic theatrical documents

Anthology of Latin American women's plays. Latin America. 1981-1989. Lang.: Eng.   1291

Pasión Gitana (Gypsy Passion)

Design/technology

Lighting design for flamenco dancer Joaquim Cortes and his troupe. Spain: Madrid. 1995-1997. Lang.: Eng.   1141

Pasja (Passion)

Performance/production

Wojciech Misiuro's Teatr Ekspresji. Poland: Sopot. 1987-1997. Lang.: Eng, Fre.   575

Paso de dos (Pas de deux)

Plays/librettos/scripts

The style of playwright Eduardo Pavlovsky. Argentina. 1962-1993. Lang.: Spa.   2374

Pasolini, Pier Paolo

Plays/librettos/scripts

Homoeroticism and the challenge to bourgeois society in works of Pasolini and Genet. Italy. 1942-1950. Lang.: Ita.   2964

Passage Nord (Oslo)

Performance/production

Passage Nord's production of *Eternity Lasts Longer*. Italy: Rome. 1997. Lang.: Ita.   1818

Passer la nuit (Spending the Night)

Plays/librettos/scripts

Self-reflexivity in Quebec drama. Canada. 1981-1988. Lang.: Fre.   2397

Passion

Plays/librettos/scripts

Analysis of Stephen Sondheim's musical *Passion*. USA. 1994. Lang.: Eng.   3994

Passion plays

SEE ALSO

Mystery plays.

Performance/production

The depiction of the Passion of Christ on the medieval stage. Europe. 1400-1550. Lang.: Eng.   1641

Plays/librettos/scripts

Analysis of a medieval account of a Passion play. England. 1208. Lang.: Eng.   2461

History of Catalan *Corpus Christi* play. Spain-Catalonia. 1437-1997. Lang.: Eng.   3052

Passionate Englishman, A

Performance/production

Collection of newspaper reviews by London theatre critics. UK-England: London. 1997. Lang.: Eng.   2057

Pasta, Giuditta

Performance/production

Outstanding performances of Bellini's opera *La sonnambula*. 1831-1984. Lang.: Fre.   4082

Pataki, András

Institutions

The reorganization of Szegedi Kortárs Balett. Hungary: Szeged. 1987-1997. Lang.: Hun.   1163

Patel, Neil

Design/technology

Scene designs of Neil Patel. USA. 1996. Lang.: Eng.   1373

Paterson, Stuart

Performance/production

Collection of newspaper reviews by London theatre critics. UK-England: London. 1997. Lang.: Eng.   2162

Patria

Plays/librettos/scripts

The environmental music theatre of R. Murray Schafer. Canada. 1966-1996. Lang.: Eng.   3886

Patronerna på Ahlquittern (Squires at Ahlquittern, The)

Design/technology

Outdoor production of *Patronerna på Ahlquittern (The Squires at Ahlquittern)*. Sweden: Bjurtjärn. 1997. Lang.: Swe.   1359

Patroni Griffi, Giuseppe

Performance/production

The work of director Giuseppe Patroni Griffi. Italy. 1948-1997. Lang.: Ita.   561

Paul Taylor Dance Company (New York, NY)

Institutions

Profile of the Paul Taylor Dance Company. USA: New York, NY. 1950-1997. Lang.: Hun.   1171

Paulay, Ede

Performance/production

Music in the premiere of *Az ember tragédiája (The Tragedy of Man)* by Imre Madách. Hungary: Budapest. 1883. Lang.: Hun.   1768

Analysis of the premiere of *Az ember tragédiája (The Tragedy of Man)* by Imre Madách. Hungary: Budapest. 1883. Lang.: Hun.   1779

Paulin, Anders

Performance/production

Two productions of the annual Strindberg festival at Stockholms Stadsteater. Sweden: Stockholm. 1997. Lang.: Eng.   1957

Pauls, Irina

Institutions

Irina Pauls and her dance company at Schauspielhaus Leipzig. Germany: Leipzig. 1990-1997. Lang.: Ger.   943

Pavitt, Paul

Performance/production

Collection of newspaper reviews by London theatre critics. UK-England: London. 1997. Lang.: Eng.   2006

Pavlov, Konstantin

Performance/production

Russian, Hungarian and Bulgarian plays at Kammerspiele. Germany: Magdeburg. 1989. Lang.: Ger.   1710

Pavlovsky, Eduardo

Performance/production

Collection of newspaper reviews by London theatre critics. UK-England: London. 1997. Lang.: Eng.   2146

Plays/librettos/scripts

The style of playwright Eduardo Pavlovsky. Argentina. 1962-1993. Lang.: Spa.   2374

Pavolini, Corrado

Performance/production

Italian productions of D'Annunzio's *La Figlia di Iorio (Iorio's Daughter)*. Italy. 1904-1983. Lang.: Ita.   1797

Pawlik, Peter

Design/technology

Technical aspects of Neue Oper Wien's production of *Maschinist Hopkins* by Max Brand. Austria: Vienna. 1997. Lang.: Ger.   4018

Payne, Tom

Performance/production

Collection of newspaper reviews by London theatre critics. UK-England: London. 1997. Lang.: Eng.   2108

Payroll
Administration
Instructions for actors regarding worker's compensation. USA. 1997.
Lang.: Eng.   75

Pazi, Vladislav
Performance/production
Work of director Vladislav Pazi. Russia: St. Petersburg. 1990-1997.
Lang.: Rus.   1886

Peacock Theatre (Dublin)
Performance/production
Report on recent Dublin productions. Ireland: Dublin. 1997. Lang.: Eng.
                                                                                                     1786

Peacock Theatre (London)
Performance/production
Collection of newspaper reviews by London theatre critics. UK-England:
London. 1997. Lang.: Eng.   1981

Collection of newspaper reviews by London theatre critics. UK-England:
London. 1997. Lang.: Eng.   2133

Collection of newspaper reviews by London theatre critics. UK-England:
London. 1997. Lang.: Eng.   2135

Collection of newspaper reviews by London theatre critics. UK-England:
London. 1997. Lang.: Eng.   2149

Peacock, David
Performance/production
Collection of newspaper reviews by London theatre critics. UK-England:
London. 1997. Lang.: Eng.   2053

Pearce, Harry
Performance/production
Collection of newspaper reviews by London theatre critics. UK-England.
1997. Lang.: Eng.   2098

Pearls for Pigs
Basic theatrical documents
Text of *Pearls for Pigs* by Richard Foreman. USA. 1995. Lang.: Eng.
                                                                                                     1326

Performance/production
Ontological-Hysteric Theatre's production of *Pearls for Pigs* at Hartford
Stage. USA: Hartford, CT. 1995. Lang.: Eng.   2270
Plays/librettos/scripts
Analysis of *Pearls for Pigs* by Richard Foreman. USA. 1995. Lang.:
Eng.   3262

Pearson, Sybille
Institutions
The Sundance Institute Playwright's Lab. USA: Salt Lake City, UT.
1997. Lang.: Eng.   1512

Peate, Mary
Performance/production
Collection of newspaper reviews by London theatre critics. UK-England:
London. 1997. Lang.: Eng.   1993

Collection of newspaper reviews by London theatre critics. UK-England:
London. 1997. Lang.: Eng.   2143

Pêcheurs de perles, Les
Design/technology
Giuseppe Di Iorio's lighting designs for the English Touring Opera. UK-
England. 1997. Lang.: Eng.   4032
Plays/librettos/scripts
Representations of the Orient in nineteenth-century French opera.
France. 1863-1894. Lang.: Eng.   4290

Pécsi Balett (Pécs)
Institutions
Modern tendencies in Hungarian ballet. Hungary: Pécs, Szeged. 1964-
1970. Lang.: Hun.   1054
Performance/production
Pécsi Balett's performance of choreographies by István Herczog to music
of Bartók. Hungary: Pécs. 1997. Lang.: Hun.   1080

Imre Eck's ballets for works by Hungarian composers. Hungary: Pécs.
1977-1978. Lang.: Hun.   1087

Bartók's stage works presented by Pécsi Balett. Hungary: Pécs. 1992-
1997. Lang.: Hun.   1088

Pécsi Nemzeti Színház (Pécs)
Institutions
Interview with Tamás Balikó, actor, director, and manager of Pécs
National Theatre. Hungary. 1980-1996. Lang.: Hun.   340

Pedrero, Paloma
Performance/production
Profile of director Paloma Pedrero. Spain. 1957-1996. Lang.: Eng.   1916

Peele, George
Audience
Early modern comedy and the mixing of classes in the audience.
England. 1590-1615. Lang.: Eng.   1248

Plays/librettos/scripts
Livy's influence on Shakespeare, Heywood, and Peele. England. 1569-
1624. Lang.: Eng.   2629

Peer Gynt
Performance/production
Productions of Ibsen's *Peer Gynt* by Luca Ronconi and Stéphane
Braunschweig. France: Paris. 1996. Lang.: Eng.   1659

Interview with director Stéphane Braunschweig. France: Paris. 1996.
Lang.: Eng.   1674

The opening of the Deutsches Schauspielhaus season. Germany:
Hamburg. 1997. Lang.: Ger.   1688

Productions of plays by Ibsen. USA. France. UK-England. 1996-1997.
Lang.: Eng.   2306

Peery's Egyptian Theatre (Ogden, UT)
Performance spaces
History of Peery's Egyptian Theatre. USA: Ogden, UT. 1924-1997.
Lang.: Eng.   3561

Peine y el espeio, El (Comb and the Mirror, The)
Plays/librettos/scripts
The 'Black Madonna' in Cuban theatre. Cuba. 1925-1990. Lang.: Spa.
                                                                                                     2444

Pelikanen (Pelican, The)
Performance/production
Two productions of the annual Strindberg festival at Stockholms
Stadsteater. Sweden: Stockholm. 1997. Lang.: Eng.   1957

Pelléas et Mélisande
Performance/production
Interview with director Julien Roy. Belgium: Brussels. 1997. Lang.: Eng.
                                                                                                     1568

Productions of the Paris-Bruxelles Exhibition. Belgium: Brussels. 1997.
Lang.: Eng.   1570

Recent productions of works by Maeterlinck. France: Paris. 1997. Lang.:
Swe.   1664

Pelléas et Mélisande (opera)
Performance/production
Excerpt from biography of opera singer Mary Garden. France: Paris.
1875-1957. Lang.: Eng.   4144

Pellet, Christophe
Performance/production
Collection of newspaper reviews by London theatre critics. UK-England:
London. 1997. Lang.: Eng.   2143

Pelletier, Gilles
Performance/production
Interview with actor Gilles Pelletier. Canada: Montreal, PQ. 1950-1997.
Lang.: Fre.   1587

Pelletier, Pol
Institutions
Solo performance at the Festival de Théâtre des Amériques. Canada:
Montreal, PQ. 1997. Lang.: Fre.   1392

Pellew, Philip
Performance/production
Collection of newspaper reviews by London theatre critics. UK-England:
London. 1997. Lang.: Eng.   2147

Pelly, Laurent
Institutions
Report from the Festival d'Avignon. France: Avignon. 1997. Lang.:
Swe.   1403

Pen, Polly
Plays/librettos/scripts
Survey of one- or two-character musicals. USA: New York, NY. 1964-
1997. Lang.: Eng.   3989

Pendleton, Austin
Performance/production
Interview with actor/director Austin Pendleton. USA. 1980-1995. Lang.:
Eng.   2266

Interviews on acting with actors, teachers, and directors. USA. 1997.
Lang.: Eng.   2352

Penhall, Joe
Basic theatrical documents
Text of *Love and Understanding* by Joe Penhall. UK-England. 1997.
Lang.: Eng.   1315
Performance/production
Collection of newspaper reviews by London theatre critics. UK-England:
London. 1997. Lang.: Eng.   2040
Plays/librettos/scripts
Profiles of younger English playwrights. UK-England. 1990. Lang.: Swe.
                                                                                                     3081

Penick, Douglas
Design/technology
Opera costume designer Martin Pakledinaz. USA: Santa Fe, NM, New
York, NY. 1997. Lang.: Eng.   4035

Performance studies — cont'd

The meaning of performance in the late twentieth century. USA. 1955-1997. Lang.: Ger. 919

History of American performance studies. USA. 1890-1996. Lang.: Eng. 926

Performing Arts Council of the Transvaal
Institutions
Origins and work of the Performing Arts Council of the Transvaal. South Africa, Republic of. 1963-1995. Lang.: Eng. 379

Performing Arts Workers Equity (South Africa)
Institutions
Interview with Ramolao Makhene, founder of Performing Arts Workers Equity. South Africa, Republic of. 1976-1996. Lang.: Eng. 378

Pericles
Plays/librettos/scripts
Witchcraft and female sexuality in the plays of Shakespeare. England. 1590-1613. Lang.: Eng. 2717

Defense of Shakespeare's *Pericles*. England. 1607-1609. Lang.: Eng. 2730

Periodo Villa Villa
Performance/production
Collection of newspaper reviews by London theatre critics. UK-England: London. 1997. Lang.: Eng. 2076

Perkin Warbeck
Plays/librettos/scripts
History and rhetoric in John Ford's *Perkin Warbeck*. England. 1634. Lang.: Eng. 2674

Perkins, Anthony
Plays/librettos/scripts
Analysis of filmscript *The Last of Sheila* by Stephen Sondheim and Anthony Perkins. USA. 1973. Lang.: Eng. 3667

Permanent Brain Damage (Risk It! Risk It!)
Design/technology
The scenography of Richard Foreman. USA. 1990-1996. Lang.: Eng. 1362

Performance/production
Collection of newspaper reviews by London theatre critics. UK-England. 1997. Lang.: Eng. 2072

Directing methods of Richard Foreman, Ontological-Hysteric Theatre. USA. 1968-1997. Lang.: Dan. 2351

Permskij Akademičeskij Teat'r Opery i Baleta (Perm)
Institutions
Portrait of the Perm Opera and Ballet Theatre. Russia: Perm. 1945-1997. Lang.: Rus. 4053

Permskij Teat'r Dramy (Perm)
Institutions
Profile of Permskij Teat'r Dramy. Russia: Perm. 1927-1997. Lang.: Rus. 1464

Permutt, Stewart
Performance/production
Collection of newspaper reviews by London theatre critics. UK-England: London. 1997. Lang.: Eng. 2041

Actor/playwright Stewart Permutt. UK-England: London. 1950-1997. Lang.: Eng. 2224

Perotti, Lisa
Performance/production
Collection of newspaper reviews by London theatre critics. UK-England. 1997. Lang.: Eng. 2039

Perrier, Didier
Basic theatrical documents
Text of *Couleur de cerne et de lilas (The Color of Bruises and Lilac)* by Yoland Simon. France. 1996. Lang.: Fre. 1276

Perriera, Michele
Institutions
Michele Perriera's theatre workshop. Italy: Palermo. 1995-1996. Lang.: Ita. 1446

Perrot, Jules
Performance/production
Giselle and the aesthetics of classical ballet. France. 1800-1900. Lang.: Eng. 1067

Feminist analysis of the ballet *Giselle*. France. 1830-1835. Lang.: Eng. 1070

The Hungarian stage career of the ballet *Giselle*. Hungary: Budapest. 1841-1996. Lang.: Hun. 1079

Choreographer Elena Tchernichova on the ballet *Giselle*. USA. 1950-1997. Lang.: Eng. 1129

Perrott, Clive
Performance/production
Collection of newspaper reviews by London theatre critics. UK-England: London. 1997. Lang.: Eng. 2031

Perry, Jann
Performance/production
Interviews with members of Tanztheater Wuppertal. Germany: Wuppertal. 1996. Lang.: Eng. 974

Persai (Persians, The)
Plays/librettos/scripts
History and Aeschylus' *Persai (The Persians)*. Greece. 500-450 B.C. Lang.: Eng. 2883

Persephone
Performance/production
Robert Wilson's performance piece *Persephone*. Germany: Munich. 1997. Lang.: Eng. 536

Persifedron
Performance/production
Russian, Hungarian and Bulgarian plays at Kammerspiele. Germany: Magdeburg. 1989. Lang.: Ger. 1710

Personal Fictions
Basic theatrical documents
Text of *Personal Fictions* by Tim Benzie. Australia. 1994. Lang.: Eng. 1255

Plays/librettos/scripts
Introduction to Tim Benzie's play *Personal Fictions*. Australia. 1997. Lang.: Eng. 2378

Personkrets 3:1 (Personal Circle 3:1)
Performance/production
Interview with playwright and director Lars Norén. Sweden: Stockholm. 1980-1997. Lang.: Swe. 1942

Interview with actress Melinda Kinnaman. Sweden: Stockholm. 1985. Lang.: Swe. 1944

Personnel
Administration
The growth of performing arts administration. Australia. 1975-1995. Lang.: Eng. 3

Thoughts on the status and significance of the ensemble theatre. Germany. 1997. Lang.: Ger. 27

Recent activities of the Non-Traditional Casting Project. USA. 1997. Lang.: Eng. 69

The availability of unemployment insurance for artists. USA. 1997. Lang.: Eng. 77

John Holly, Equity's Western Regional Director. USA: Los Angeles, CA. 1997. Lang.: Eng. 89

Report on unemployment among theatre artists. USA. 1997. Lang.: Eng. 91

Announcement of regional meetings of Actors' Equity. USA. 1997. Lang.: Eng. 93

Intervention of National Labor Relations Board in Equity's collective bargaining agreements. USA. 1997. Lang.: Eng. 94

The merger of the Actors' Fund with the Actors' Work Program. USA. 1997. Lang.: Eng. 95

Statements of candidates for Equity elections. USA. 1997. Lang.: Eng. 96

The National Labor Relations Board's approval of Equity-only auditions. USA. 1997. Lang.: Eng. 101

Actors' Fund support of low-cost housing for people with HIV/AIDS. USA: Hollywood, CA. 1997. Lang.: Eng. 105

New California location for Actors' Equity. USA: Los Angeles, CA. 1997. Lang.: Eng. 107

Equity report: employment in the entertainment industry. USA. 1997. Lang.: Eng. 117

The process of selecting Actors' Equity's regional directors. USA. 1997. Lang.: Eng. 125

Interviews with managers of Göteborgs Stadsteatern and Kungliga Dramatiska Teatern. Sweden: Gothenburg, Stockholm. 1997. Lang.: Swe. 1241

Relation to other fields
Stress and the performing artist. Sweden. 1997. Lang.: Swe. 780

Pesti Színház (Budapest)
Performance/production
Four productions of the musical *A Dzsungel könyve (The Jungle Book)*. Hungary. 1996-1997. Lang.: Hun. 3936

Peter and Wendy
Performance/production
Career of performer Karen Kandel. USA: New York, NY. 1977-1997. Lang.: Eng. 663

Peter Pan
Performance/production
Collection of newspaper reviews by London theatre critics. UK-England: London. 1997. Lang.: Eng. 2158

Peter Pan — cont'd

John Caird's adaptation of *Peter Pan*. UK-England: London. 1997.
Lang.: Eng.   2215

A lesbian reading of Mary Martin's performance as Peter Pan. USA.
1950-1959. Lang.: Eng.   3978

Plays/librettos/scripts
Time travel in English-language drama. USA. Canada. UK-England.
1908-1993. Lang.: Eng.   3171

Peters, Bernadette
Performance/production
Actress/singer Bernadette Peters. USA. 1961-1997. Lang.: Eng. 3957

Peters, Emma Gene
Basic theatrical documents
Text of *Southern Bells: Voices of Working Women* by Emma Gene
Peters. USA. 1997. Lang.: Eng.   1339

Petersen, Taliep
Performance/production
Collection of newspaper reviews by London theatre critics. UK-England:
London. 1997. Lang.: Eng.   2115

Peterson, Lisa
Design/technology
Scene designs of Neil Patel. USA. 1996. Lang.: Eng.   1373
Performance/production
Director Lisa Peterson. USA: Los Angeles, CA. 1997. Lang.: Eng. 2279

Petherbridge, Edward
Performance/production
Interview with actor Edward Petherbridge. USA. 1998. Lang.: Eng. 2340

Petherbridge, Jonathan
Performance/production
Collection of newspaper reviews by London theatre critics. UK-England:
London. 1997. Lang.: Eng.   2160

Petipa, Marius
Performance/production
The Hungarian stage career of the ballet *Giselle*. Hungary: Budapest.
1841-1996. Lang.: Hun.   1079

Budapest production of the ballet *Don Quijote* by Marius Petipa and
Leon Minkus. Hungary: Budapest. 1997. Lang.: Hun.   1083

Petkevich, Tamara
Performance/production
Interview with actor Tamara Petkevich, former concentration camp
inmate. USSR. 1950-1997. Lang.: Swe.   2363

Petrarca, David
Performance/production
Interview with director David Petrarca. USA: Chicago, IL. 1997. Lang.:
Eng.   2329

Petras, Armin
Performance/production
Performances of Schauspiel Leipzig. Germany: Leipzig. 1997. Lang.:
Ger.   1713

Petrolini, Ettore
Performance/production
Comic actor Ettore Petrolini. Italy. 1886-1936. Lang.: Ita.   1793

Petronio, Stephen
Institutions
Survey of the Fall Festival of Dance. USA: Chicago, IL. 1997. Lang.:
Eng.   1169

Petrouchka
Performance/production
Performance of the Győri Balett. Hungary. 1997. Lang.: Hun.   1093

Petrov, Nicolas
Performance/production
Choreographer Nicolas Petrov. USA. 1996. Lang.: Hun.   1127

Petrovics, Emil
Plays/librettos/scripts
Special features and characters of operetta. Hungary. 1900-1990. Lang.:
Hun.   4340

Petruševskaja, Ljudmila
Performance/production
Collection of newspaper reviews by London theatre critics. UK-England:
London. 1997. Lang.: Eng.   2046

Pettengill, Richard
Performance/production
Director and dramaturgs on translating, adapting and producing
Molière's *Misanthrope*. USA: La Jolla, CA, Chicago, IL. 1989-1990.
Lang.: Eng.   2263

Pettersson, Stefan
Institutions
The closing of Göteborgs Stadsteatern. Sweden: Gothenburg. 1995.
Lang.: Swe.   1488

Petticoat-Plotter, The
Performance/production
Scottish plays on the London stage. England: London. Scotland. 1667-
1715. Lang.: Eng.   1635

Peu Plus de Lumière, Un (Little More Light, A)
Performance/production
Collection of newspaper reviews by London theatre critics. UK-England:
London. 1997. Lang.: Eng.   2073

Peymann, Claus
Performance/production
Interview with actor Gert Voss. Austria: Vienna. 1975-1997. Lang.: Ger.
                                                              1561

Major productions of the Vienna theatre season. Austria: Vienna. 1997.
Lang.: Ger.   1563

Premieres of new plays by Handke, Krausser, and Enzensberger.
Austria. Germany. 1996-1997. Lang.: Ger.   1567

Pfaff, Walter
Performance/production
Parate Labor's teaching of *kutiyattam* Sanskrit drama in France. France.
India. 1989-1997. Lang.: Eng.   1673

Pfeffer, Dahlia
Performance/production
Collection of newspaper reviews by London theatre critics. UK-England:
London. 1997. Lang.: Eng.   2059

Pfitzner, Hans
Performance/production
Historical introduction to *Palestrina* by Hans Pfitzner. Germany. 1917-
1997. Lang.: Eng.   4162

Pfüller, Volker
Design/technology
Set design and the influence of new media. Germany. 1990-1997. Lang.:
Ger.   166

Phaedra
Plays/librettos/scripts
Garnier's *Hippolyte* and its source, Seneca's *Phaedra*. France. 1635.
Lang.: Eng.   2813

Rhetoric in Euripidean drama. Greece. 500-300 B.C. Lang.: Eng. 2871

Phantom
Performance/production
Composer/lyricist Maury Yeston. USA: New York, NY. 1945-1997.
Lang.: Eng.   3975

Phavorin, Stéphane
Performance/production
Stars of the Paris Opera Ballet. France: Paris. 1983-1997. Lang.: Eng.
                                                              1074

Phelps, Samuel
Performance/production
Stage imagery in productions of Shakespeare's *Coriolanus*. England.
1754-1901. Lang.: Eng.   1634

Phenomenology
Relation to other fields
Existential drama thearapy. USA. 1997. Lang.: Eng.   806
Theory/criticism
The voice in theatrical representation. France. 1977. Lang.: Eng. 883

Introduction to theatrical applications of literary theory. USA. Europe.
1997. Lang.: Eng.   3499

Theorists of the phenomenology and semiotics of theatre. USA. 1964-
1967. Lang.: Eng.   3506

Similarities and differences of film and theatre. Germany: Berlin. 1900-
1913. Lang.: Ger.   3698

Philaster
Plays/librettos/scripts
Representations of virginity on the early modern English stage. England.
1490-1650. Lang.: Eng.   2640

Transvestism in Beaumont and Fletcher's *Philaster*. England. 1609.
Lang.: Eng.   2664

Philippines Educational Theatre Association (PETA, Manila)
Audience
The role of theatre in Philippine culture. Philippines. 1905-1993. Lang.:
Eng.   1250

Philippou, Nick
Performance/production
Collection of newspaper reviews by London theatre critics. UK-England:
London. 1997. Lang.: Eng.   2005

Collection of newspaper reviews by London theatre critics. UK-England:
London. 1997. Lang.: Eng.   2144

Phillips, Leslie
Performance/production
Film actor Leslie Phillips' roles at the Royal Shakespeare Company.
UK-England: Stratford. 1997. Lang.: Eng.   2182

Plautus, Titus Macchius
Plays/librettos/scripts
The influence of Plautus and his comic themes. Europe. 259 B.C.-1997 A.D. Lang.: Ita. 2784

Comparison of classical Roman, Renaissance Italian, and Shakespearean treatments of similar stories. Europe. 200 B.C.-1610 A.D. Lang.: Eng. 2799

Out-of-court legal settlements in Greco-Roman new comedy. Greece. Rome. 500 B.C.-200 A.D. Lang.: Eng. 2886
Theory/criticism
The possibilities for a contemporary theory of comedy. 1997. Lang.: Slo. 3459

Play
Performance/production
Xerxes Mehta's approach to directing Beckett. USA. 1993. Lang.: Eng. 2305
Plays/librettos/scripts
Language and silence in short plays of Samuel Beckett. Ireland. France. USA. 1960-1981. Lang.: Eng. 2929

Play It Again, Sam
Plays/librettos/scripts
Films based on works of stage playwrights. USA. 1951-1972. Lang.: Pol. 3681

Play of Love and Chance, The
SEE
Jeu de l'amour et du hasard, Le.

Play of the Sacrament, The
Performance spaces
The English church as performance space. England. 1100-1300. Lang.: Eng. 426
Relation to other fields
A folk analogue to the Play of the Sacrament. USA. England. 1400-1997. Lang.: Eng. 822

Play On!
Design/technology
Technical designs for the Shakespearean musical Play On!. USA: San Diego, CA. 1997. Lang.: Eng. 3921
Performance/production
The development of Play On!, a musical adaptation of Shakespeare's Twelfth Night. USA: New York, NY. 1997. Lang.: Eng. 3953
Plays/librettos/scripts
Survey of musical adaptations of Shakespeare. USA: New York, NY. 1938-1997. Lang.: Eng. 3987

Play's the Thing, The
SEE
Játek a kastélyban.

Playbills
Administration
The design of nineteenth-century playbills. UK-England. 1804-1850. Lang.: Eng. 53

Playboy of the Western World, The
Plays/librettos/scripts
Cultural translation and The Playboy of the Western World by J.M. Synge. Ireland. 1898-1918. Lang.: Eng. 2910

Players
SEE
Club, The.

Players Theatre (London)
Performance/production
Collection of newspaper reviews by London theatre critics. UK-England: London. 1997. Lang.: Eng. 2161

Playhouse at St. Clement's (New York, NY)
Performance/production
The use of silent films in theatrical productions. USA: New York, NY. 1997. Lang.: Eng. 2342

Playhouse Creatures
Performance/production
Collection of newspaper reviews by London theatre critics. UK-England: London. 1997. Lang.: Eng. 2101

Playhouse Theatre (London)
Performance/production
Collection of newspaper reviews by London theatre critics. UK-England: London. 1997. Lang.: Eng. 2066

Collection of newspaper reviews by London theatre critics. UK-England: London. 1997. Lang.: Eng. 2118

Playhouse, The (Vancouver, BC)
Performance/production
Susan Cox's production of Pinter's Betrayal at The Playhouse. Canada: Vancouver, BC. 1996. Lang.: Eng. 1592

Playing for Time
Plays/librettos/scripts
Playwright Arthur Miller's collaborations with his wife Inge Morath. USA. 1980-1989. Lang.: Eng. 3272

Playland Blues
Basic theatrical documents
Text of plays performed at the Nuyorican Poets Cafe. USA: New York, NY. 1973-1990. Lang.: Eng. 1322

Playten, Alice
Performance/production
New York premiere of Wozzeck at the Metropolitan Opera. USA: New York, NY. 1959. Lang.: Eng. 4274

Playtexts
Basic theatrical documents
Text of Personal Fictions by Tim Benzie. Australia. 1994. Lang.: Eng. 1255

English performance translation of Nestroy's Der Talisman. Austria. 1833-1849. Lang.: Eng. 1256

Text of big face by Marion de Vries. Canada. 1995. Lang.: Eng. 1257

Text of Margaret Durham by Mary Lu Anne Gardner. Canada. 1996. Lang.: Eng. 1258

Text of One Word by Ken Garnhum. Canada. 1997. Lang.: Eng. 1259

Text of New Art Book by Ken Garnhum. Canada. 1997. Lang.: Eng. 1260

Text of None Is Too Many by Jason Sherman. Canada. 1997. Lang.: Eng. 1261

Text of Girl Who Loved Her Horses by Drew Hayden Taylor. Canada. 1990-1997. Lang.: Eng. 1262

Text of El Memoricido (The Memory-Killer) by Jorge Díaz. Chile. 1994. Lang.: Spa. 1263

English translation of the Yuan drama Reunion with Son and Daughter in Kingfisher Red County. China. 1280-1994. Lang.: Eng. 1264

Text of Love in a Forest, an adaptation of As You Like It by Charles Johnson. England. 1723. Lang.: Eng. 1265

English translation of Mielen kieli (Mind Speak) by Juha Lehtola. Finland. 1997. Lang.: Eng. 1266

Text of Le Voyage (The Journey) by Gérald Aubert. France. 1996. Lang.: Fre. 1267

Text of Page 27 by Jean-Louis Bauer. France. 1996. Lang.: Fre. 1268

Text of L'Esclave du démon (Slave of the Devil) by Louise Doutreligne. France. Spain. 1612-1996. Lang.: Fre. 1269

Text of Potins d'enfer (Hellish Gossip) by Jean-Noël Fenwick. France: Paris. 1996. Lang.: Fre. 1270

Text of Une Puce à l'Oreille (A Flea in Her Ear) by Georges Feydeau. France. 1902-1996. Lang.: Fre. 1271

Text of Les Richesses de l'hiver (The Riches of Winter) by Fatima Gallaire. France: Ajaccio. 1996. Lang.: Fre. 1272

Text of Le Secret de l'Aiguille creuse (The Secret of the Hollow Needle), Gilles Gleizes' adaptation of an Arsène Lupin mystery novel. France. 1996. Lang.: Fre. 1273

Text of Aimez-moi les uns les autres (Love Me One and All) by Alex Métayer. France. 1996. Lang.: Fre. 1274

Text of Les Oiseaux d'Avant (The Birds from Before) by Robert Poudérou. France. 1996. Lang.: Fre. 1275

Text of Couleur de cerne et de lilas (The Color of Bruises and Lilac) by Yoland Simon. France. 1996. Lang.: Fre. 1276

English translation of La Demande d'emploi (The Interview) by Michel Vinaver. France. 1994. Lang.: Eng. 1277

Slovene translations of plays by Georg Büchner. Germany. 1835-1837. Lang.: Slo. 1278

French translation of Büchner's Leonce und Lena (Leonce and Lena). Germany. France. Belgium. 1838-1996. Lang.: Fre. 1279

English translation of Nur eine Scheibe Brot (Just a Slice of Bread) by Rainer Werner Fassbinder. Germany. 1971. Lang.: Eng. 1280

English translation of Die Stunde da wir nichts voneinander wussten (The Hour We Knew Nothing of Each Other) by Peter Handke. Germany. 1992. Lang.: Eng. 1281

Text of Schneewittchen im Eisblock. Ein Spiegelbild (Snow White in the Block of Ice: A Reflection) by Katja Lange-Müller. Germany. 1997. Lang.: Ger. 1282

Text of Totentrompeten II (Dead Trumpets II) by Einar Schleef. Germany. 1997. Lang.: Ger. 1283

Playtexts — cont'd

Script of *All About Eve* by Joseph L. Mankiewicz. USA. 1950. Lang.:
Eng.   3536

Script of *Midnight Cowboy* by Waldo Salt. USA. 1969. Lang.: Eng. 3539

Text of Stacey Callaghan's performance piece *still raw.* Australia. 1994.
Lang.: Eng.   3813

Text of *Object/Subject of Desire* by Shawna Dempsey. Canada. 1987.
Lang.: Eng.   3814

Text of *The Gathering* by Rachael Van Fossen *et al.* Canada: Fort
Qu'Appelle, SK. 1997. Lang.: Eng.   3903

Music and libretto of the musical *In Dahomey.* USA. 1903. Lang.: Eng.
                                                                                     3904

Storyboard scenario of *Evidence of Floods* by Jamie Geiser. USA. 1994.
Lang.: Eng.   4387

Plays/librettos/scripts
West African popular theatre: texts and analysis. Ghana. Togo. Nigeria.
1995-1997. Lang.: Eng.   2866

Texts of plays by Jewish American women. USA. 1985-1995. Lang.:
Eng.   3164

Piccinni's *La Cecchina*: English translations and analysis. Italy. USA.
1766-1996. Lang.: Eng.   4305

Playwright's Center (Minneapolis, MN)
Institutions
Profile of Carlos Questa of the Playwright's Center. USA: Minneapolis,
MN. 1997. Lang.: Eng.   1507

Playwright's Theatre (New York, NY)
Institutions
Manager Edna Kenton on the Provincetown Players. USA:
Provincetown, MA, New York, NY. 1915-1922. Lang.: Eng.   1504

Playwrights Horizons (New York, NY)
Performance/production
Theoretical foundations for the job of literary manager. USA. 1984-
1996. Lang.: Eng.   2333

Playwriting
Administration
Report on the English theatre scene. UK-England. 1995-1997. Lang.:
Ger.   1242

Performance/production
Obscenity as social criticism in work of Robert Gravel. Canada.
Belgium. 1973-1996. Lang.: Fre.   482

Involving youth audiences in theatre. Sweden: Stockholm, Uppsala.
1995-1997. Lang.: Swe.   1949

Partial transcript of panel discussion involving dramaturgs and
playwrights. USA. 1990. Lang.: Eng.   2235

Plays/librettos/scripts
Jungian archetypes and the rules of fiction and drama. Lang.: Ita.   690

Internet marketing of plays. USA. 1997. Lang.: Eng.   703

Account of seminar on writing about AIDS. USA: Key West, FL. 1984-
1997. Lang.: Eng.   704

Networking for playwrights. USA. 1997. Lang.: Eng.   706

History of professional advice to playwrights. 350 B.C.-1997 A.D. Lang.:
Eng.   2370

Playwriting in Ontario. Canada. 1914-1979. Lang.: Eng.   2414

The writing of *Supreme Dream* by Frank Moher and actress Rhonda
Trodd. Canada: Toronto, ON. 1997. Lang.: Eng.   2425

The work of playwright Bernard-Marie Koltès. France. 1948-1989.
Lang.: Eng.   2806

Report from women playwrights conference. Ireland: Galway. 1997.
Lang.: Swe.   2930

Analysis of *O vremja! (Oh, These Times!)* by Catherine the Great.
Russia: St. Petersburg. 1772. Lang.: Eng.   2998

Argument in favor of the one-minute play. USA. 1997. Lang.: Eng. 3175

Profile of playwrights' alliances. USA. 1930-1996. Lang.: Eng. 3226

Criticism of one-minute and ten-minute play contests. USA. 1997. Lang.:
Eng.   3256

Statement of an adjudicator for a new-play competition. USA: Dayton,
OH. 1997. Lang.: Eng.   3268

Playwright Alfred Uhry. USA. 1987-1996. Lang.: Eng.   3278

Scripting narrative for interactive multimedia. USA. 1997. Lang.: Eng.
                                                                                     3705

Relation to other fields
Controversy over the videotaping of creative works by students. USA:
St. Louis, MO. 1994-1997. Lang.: Eng.   829

Training
The teaching of performance composition. USA: New York, NY. 1997.
Lang.: Eng.   937

Pleasance Theatre (London)
Performance/production
Collection of newspaper reviews by London theatre critics. UK-England:
London. 1997. Lang.: Eng.   1991

Collection of newspaper reviews by London theatre critics. UK-England:
London. 1997. Lang.: Eng.   2010

Collection of newspaper reviews by London theatre critics. UK-England:
London. 1997. Lang.: Eng.   2024

Collection of newspaper reviews by London theatre critics. UK-England:
London. 1997. Lang.: Eng.   2056

Collection of newspaper reviews by London theatre critics. UK-England:
London. 1997. Lang.: Eng.   2116

Collection of newspaper reviews by London theatre critics. UK-England:
London. 1997. Lang.: Eng.   2149

Collection of newspaper reviews by London theatre critics. UK-England:
London. 1997. Lang.: Eng.   2160

Pleasure Man
Basic theatrical documents
Texts of three plays by Mae West. USA. 1926-1928. Lang.: Eng.   1350

Pleijel, Lina
Performance/production
Interview with actress Lina Pleijel. Sweden: Stockholm. 1981. Lang.:
Swe.   1946

Plenty
Plays/librettos/scripts
Nostalgia and morality in plays of David Hare. UK-England: London.
1947-1997. Lang.: Eng.   3113

Plester, Tim
Performance/production
Collection of newspaper reviews by London theatre critics. UK-England:
London. 1997. Lang.: Eng.   2040

Plotnick, Alice
Performance/production
New York premiere of *Wozzeck* at the Metropolitan Opera. USA: New
York, NY. 1959. Lang.: Eng.   4274

Plowman, Gillian
Performance/production
Collection of newspaper reviews by London theatre critics. UK-England:
London. 1997. Lang.: Eng.   2065

Plumes in the Dust
Plays/librettos/scripts
Sophie Treadwell and her play *Plumes in the Dust.* USA. 1917-1936.
Lang.: Eng.   3183

Podbrey, Maurice
Institutions
Centaur Theatre, Montreal's oldest English-language theatre. Canada:
Montreal, PQ. 1969-1997. Lang.: Eng.   1399

Podleś, Ewa
Performance/production
Contralto Ewa Podleś. Poland. 1997. Lang.: Eng.   4202

Poe
Plays/librettos/scripts
Sophie Treadwell and her play *Plumes in the Dust.* USA. 1917-1936.
Lang.: Eng.   3183

Poel, William
Performance/production
Shakespearean production in the age of actor-managers. UK-England.
1840-1914. Lang.: Eng.   2193

Elizabethan stage semiotics in twentieth-century Shakespearean
productions. UK-England. 1905-1979. Lang.: Eng.   2203

Poetaster, The
Plays/librettos/scripts
Ben Jonson's view of himself in *The Poetaster.* England. 1601. Lang.:
Eng.   2734

Poetry
Performance/production
Traditional oral poetry and political change. South Africa, Republic of.
1980-1989. Lang.: Eng.   606
Theory/criticism
Playwright Mac Wellman on political and poetic theatre. USA. 1993.
Lang.: Eng.   3507

Pohjanen, Bengt
Institutions
Profile of the Third Theatre Biennale. Sweden: Luleå. 1997. Lang.: Swe.
                                                                                     1478

Poirier, Gregory
Basic theatrical documents
Text of *Rosewood* by Gregory Poirier. USA. 1997. Lang.: Eng.   3537

Politics — cont'd

Politics — cont'd

Politics — cont'd

Politics — cont'd

The relationship between TV journalism and politics. Europe. 1997. Lang.: Ita. 3739

Political satire of Pieter-Dirk Uys. South Africa, Republic of: Johannesburg. 1981-1997. Lang.: Eng. 3740

The performance of 'heritage tourism'. UK-Wales. 1994-1996. Lang.: Eng. 3811

Space in feminist performance art and political protest. UK-England. 1980-1997. Lang.: Eng. 3850

Opera and social decline. England: London. 1698-1737. Lang.: Eng. 4321

Wagner, *Gesamtkunstwerk*, and cultural politics. USA. Germany. 1875-1920. Lang.: Eng. 4324

History of indepedent theatre company Zinnober. Germany: Berlin. 1980-1997. Lang.: Ger. 4383

Theory/criticism

Recent criticism regarding the purpose and place of theatre in early modern England. USA. UK-England. 1988-1995. Lang.: Eng. 917

Performativity, language and sound, and surveillance tapes and videos in the courtroom. USA. 1997. Lang.: Eng. 923

Shakespeare, *The Tempest*, and colonialist ideology. 1997. Lang.: Eng. 3458

Racism, *Othello*, and South African criticism. England. South Africa, Republic of. 1604-1987. Lang.: Eng. 3473

New media, transnationalism, and Shakespearean criticism. Europe. 1990-1994. Lang.: Eng. 3479

Ramifications of queer theory for theatre critics. USA. 1993. Lang.: Eng. 3502

Polk County

Plays/librettos/scripts

Women and theatrical collaboration. USA. UK-England. 1930-1990. Lang.: Eng. 3264

Polka Theatre (London)

Performance/production

Collection of newspaper reviews by London theatre critics. UK-England. 1997. Lang.: Eng. 2121

Collection of newspaper reviews by London theatre critics. UK-England: London. 1997. Lang.: Eng. 2161

Pollock, Alan

Performance/production

Collection of newspaper reviews by London theatre critics. UK-England: London. 1997. Lang.: Eng. 1990

Pollock, Sharon

Institutions

Sharon Pollock's community theatre work. Canada: Calgary, AB. 1981-1997. Lang.: Eng. 304

Plays/librettos/scripts

Historical background of *Blood Relations* by Sharon Pollock. Canada. 1892-1997. Lang.: Eng. 2438

Feminism and murder in plays of Wendy Kesselman and Sharon Pollock. USA. Canada. 1982-1984. Lang.: Eng. 3286

Polunin, Slava

Performance/production

Collection of newspaper reviews by London theatre critics. UK-England: London. 1997. Lang.: Eng. 1981

Collection of newspaper reviews by London theatre critics. UK-England: London. 1997. Lang.: Eng. 2106

Pomeroy, Sue

Performance/production

Collection of newspaper reviews by London theatre critics. UK-England: London. 1997. Lang.: Eng. 1992

Pongor, Ildikó

Performance/production

Report on a dance concert in honor of ballet soloist Ildikó Pongor. Hungary. 1997. Lang.: Hun. 1081

Ildikó Pongor's performance in the ballet *Anna Karenina*. Hungary: Budapest. 1997. Lang.: Hun. 1082

Poniž, Denis

Plays/librettos/scripts

Analysis of plays by Denis Poniž. Slovenia. 1976-1996. Lang.: Slo. 3014

Ponselle, Carmela

Performance/production

Singers Carmela and Rosa Ponselle. USA: New York, NY. 1889-1981. Lang.: Eng. 4273

Ponselle, Rosa

Performance/production

The difficulty of performing 'Sempre Libera' in Verdi's *La Traviata*. Italy. USA: New York, NY. 1886-1996. Lang.: Eng. 4186

Soprano Rosa Ponselle. USA: New York, NY. 1920-1927. Lang.: Eng. 4245

Singers Carmela and Rosa Ponselle. USA: New York, NY. 1889-1981. Lang.: Eng. 4273

Ponto, Erich

Relation to other fields

Erich Ponto's tenure as *Generalintendant* of Dresden theatre. Germany: Dresden. 1945-1947. Lang.: Ger. 762

Poor Gentleman, The

Relation to other fields

A painting of backstage during a production of Colman's *The Poor Gentleman*. England: London. 1750-1802. Lang.: Eng. 731

Popay, Brian

Performance/production

Collection of newspaper reviews by London theatre critics. UK-England: London. 1997. Lang.: Eng. 2159

Popcorn

Performance/production

Collection of newspaper reviews by London theatre critics. UK-England: London. 1997. Lang.: Eng. 1970

Director Laurence Boswell. UK-England: London. 1997. Lang.: Eng. 2214

Pope, Alexander

Performance/production

Collection of newspaper reviews by London theatre critics. UK-England: London. 1997. Lang.: Eng. 1987

Popular entertainment

SEE ALSO

Classed Entries under MIXED ENTERTAINMENT.

Performance/production

The paradox of blackface minstrelsy. USA. 1821-1915. Lang.: Eng. 3861

Plays/librettos/scripts

Bearbaiting and colonialism. England. 1450-1600. Lang.: Eng. 3774

Theory/criticism

Similarities and differences of film and theatre. Germany: Berlin. 1900-1913. Lang.: Ger. 3698

Popular Mechanicals, The

Performance/production

Collection of newspaper reviews by London theatre critics. UK-England: London. 1997. Lang.: Eng. 2138

Popular theatre

Institutions

Compagnie de Théâtre Longue Vue's strategies for attracting new audiences. Canada: Montreal, PQ. 1995-1997. Lang.: Fre. 1385

Por Amor Al Arte (Mexico)

Plays/librettos/scripts

New world adaptations of Shakespeare's *The Tempest*. England. Latin America. Caribbean. 1612-1994. Lang.: Eng. 2549

Porch Monkey

Plays/librettos/scripts

Black playwrights' subversive approaches to character. USA. 1986-1997. Lang.: Eng. 3184

Porgy and Bess

Performance/production

Götz Friedrich's production of Gershwin's *Porgy and Bess*. Austria: Bregenz. 1997. Lang.: Eng. 4098

Porter, Cole

Performance/production

Collection of newspaper reviews by London theatre critics. UK-England: London. 1997. Lang.: Eng. 2086

Plays/librettos/scripts

Film adaptations of Shakespeare's *The Taming of the Shrew*. USA. 1929-1966. Lang.: Eng. 3668

Analysis of musical adaptations of Shakespearean plays. USA. 1938-1997. Lang.: Ger. 3983

Positive Hour, The

Performance/production

Collection of newspaper reviews by London theatre critics. UK-England: London. 1997. Lang.: Eng. 2008

Posner, Kenneth

Design/technology

Work of lighting designer Kenneth Posner. USA: New York, NY. 1997. Lang.: Eng. 1364

Posner, Lindsay

Performance/production

Collection of newspaper reviews by London theatre critics. UK-England: London. 1997. Lang.: Eng. 1992

Collection of newspaper reviews by London theatre critics. UK-England: London. 1997. Lang.: Eng. 2078

Public relations — cont'd

Call for national arts marketing plan. USA. 1997. Lang.: Eng. 122

Ulrich Schwab's public relations strategy at Mannheimer Nationaltheater. Germany: Mannheim. 1996-1997. Lang.: Ger. 1239

Survey of the publication *Opera News*. USA: New York, NY. 1933-1997. Lang.: Hun. 4006

Performance/production

Public relations and the dramaturg. Germany. 1997. Lang.: Ger. 537

Relation to other fields

Athol Fugard receives Paul Robeson Award. USA: New York, NY. 1997. Lang.: Eng. 3423

Public Theatre (New York, NY)

Design/technology

Design elements of *On the Town* for New York Shakespeare Festival. USA: New York, NY. 1997. Lang.: Eng. 3915

Performance/production

Analysis of New York Shakespeare Festival's productions. USA: New York, NY. 1997. Lang.: Eng. 2249

Personal recollections of New York Shakespeare Festival productions. USA: New York, NY. 1987-1997. Lang.: Eng. 2297

Report on colloquium devoted to the 'language of Shakespeare in America'. USA: New York, NY. 1997. Lang.: Eng. 2299

Directors Michael Kahn and Karin Coonrod on their productions of *Henry VI*. USA: New York, NY, Washington, DC. 1950-1996. Lang.:Eng. 2312

Interview with dramaturg Morgan Jenness. USA. 1979-1996. Lang.: Eng. 2338

Público, El (Public, The)

Plays/librettos/scripts

Gendered identity in plays of Cocteau and García Lorca. France. Spain. 1930-1937. Lang.: Eng. 2807

Puccini, Giacomo

Design/technology

Technical aspects of a production of *Tosca* at GöteborgsOperan. Sweden: Gothenburg. 1996. Lang.: Swe. 4031

Performance/production

Impressions of opera performances in several German cities. Germany. 1997. Lang.: Ger. 4147

Interview with opera director Balázs Kovalik. Hungary: Budapest. 1995-1997. Lang.: Hun. 4185

Speculations about Puccini's unfinished *Turandot*. Italy. 1867-1957. Lang.: Eng. 4187

The influence of Mascagni, Leoncavallo, and Franchetti on Puccini's *La Bohème*. Italy: Milan. 1894-1898. Lang.: Eng. 4190

Puccini's use of the key of A major. Italy. 1836. Lang.: Eng. 4194

Background material on New York City Opera telecast performance of *La Bohème*. USA: New York, NY. 1997. Lang.: Eng. 4230

Background material on Lyric Opera of Chicago radio broadcast performances. USA: Chicago, IL. 1997. Lang.: Eng. 4231

Background material on Metropolitan Opera radio broadcast performances. USA: New York, NY. 1997-1997. Lang.: Eng. 4237

Background material on Metropolitan Opera radio broadcast performances. USA: New York, NY. 1997. Lang.: Eng. 4238

A child's first visit to the Metropolitan Opera. USA: New York, NY. 1988-1997. Lang.: Eng. 4246

New York City Opera's seventy-city tour of *La Bohème*. USA. 1994. Lang.: Eng. 4264

Puce à l'Oreille, La (Flea in Her Ear, A)

Basic theatrical documents

Text of *Une Puce à l'Oreille (A Flea in Her Ear)* by Georges Feydeau. France. 1902-1996. Lang.: Fre. 1271

Pugačeva, Alla

Performance/production

Biography of singer Alla Pugačeva. Russia. 1970-1997. Lang.: Rus. 3876

Materials about singer Alla Pugačeva. Russia. 1970-1997. Lang.: Rus. 3877

Pulci, Antonia

Basic theatrical documents

English translations of sacred plays by Antonia Pulci. Italy. 1452-1501. Lang.: Eng. 1288

Pullman, Philip

Performance/production

Collection of newspaper reviews by London theatre critics. UK-England: London. 1997. Lang.: Eng. 2161

Punoz, Armando

Performance/production

Visit to Grotowski and Compagnia della Fortezza. Italy: Volterra, Pontedera. 1986-1997. Lang.: Ger. 1805

Punter, Michael

Performance/production

Collection of newspaper reviews by London theatre critics. UK-England: London. 1997. Lang.: Eng. 2010

Puppet Showplace Theatre (Boston, MA)

Institutions

Kristen McLean, executive director of Puppet Showcase Theatre. USA: Boston, MA. 1997. Lang.: Eng. 4356

Puppetry

SEE ALSO

Classed Entries.

Performance/production

Popular entertainment in Budapest's municipal park. Hungary: Budapest. 1860-1938. Lang.: Hun. 3767

The musical production of *Gaja (Gaia)*, which used puppets and live actors. Poland: Zusno. 1997. Lang.: Eng, Fre. 3875

History of Czech puppet theatre. Czech Republic. 1912-1997. Lang.: Eng, Fre. 4362

Plays/librettos/scripts

Interview with playwright and film-maker William Kentridge. South Africa, Republic of. 1986-1994. Lang.: Eng. 3025

Puppets

Design/technology

Design and community theatre. Canada. 1990-1997. Lang.: Eng. 1355

Puppet designer and puppeteer Suse Wächter. Germany: Berlin. 1997. Lang.: Ger. 4342

Handbook of puppet construction. Slovenia. 1996. Lang.: Slo. 4343

Instructions for hand puppet construction. Slovenia. 1997. Lang.: Slo. 4344

Instructions for flat puppet construction. Slovenia. 1997. Lang.: Slo. 4345

Instructions for muppet construction. Slovenia. 1997. Lang.: Slo. 4396

Performance/production

Chinese theatre and the actor in performance. China, People's Republic of. 1980-1996. Lang.: Eng. 491

Career of performer Karen Kandel. USA: New York, NY. 1977-1997. Lang.: Eng. 663

Live actors and puppets in contemporary theatre. USA. 1996. Lang.: Eng. 4374

Purcarete, Silviu

Performance/production

Collection of newspaper reviews by London theatre critics. UK-England: London. 1997. Lang.: Eng. 2049

Purcell Room (London)

Performance/production

Collection of newspaper reviews by London theatre critics. UK-England: London. 1997. Lang.: Eng. 1988

Collection of newspaper reviews by London theatre critics. UK-England: London. 1997. Lang.: Eng. 1998

Collection of newspaper reviews by London theatre critics. UK-England: London. 1997. Lang.: Eng. 2027

Collection of newspaper reviews by London theatre critics. UK-England. 1997. Lang.: Eng. 2072

Collection of newspaper reviews by London theatre critics. UK-England: London. 1997. Lang.: Eng. 2102

Collection of newspaper reviews by London theatre critics. UK-England: London. 1997. Lang.: Eng. 2159

Purcell, Henry

Performance/production

Opera Atelier's production of Purcell's *Dido and Aeneas*. Canada: Toronto, ON. 1994-1995. Lang.: Eng. 4112

Plays/librettos/scripts

Female 'mad' songs in seventeenth-century English drama. England. 1685-1700. Lang.: Eng. 2638

Purgatorio de San Patricio, El

Plays/librettos/scripts

Conversion plays of Tirso and Calderón. Spain. 1600-1681. Lang.: Eng. 3043

Purgatory

Performance/production

Collection of newspaper reviews by London theatre critics. UK-England: London. 1997. Lang.: Eng. 2048

Plays/librettos/scripts

Landscape and the supernatural in *Purgatory* by W.B. Yeats. Ireland. 1938. Lang.: Eng. 2931

Puritani, I

Performance/production

The premiere of Rossini's *I Puritani*. France: Paris. 1835. Lang.: Eng. 4137

Puritani, I — cont'd

Background material on Metropolitan Opera radio broadcast performances. USA: New York, NY. 1997. Lang.: Eng. 4238

Purkey, Malcolm
Institutions
Brecht's influence on Malcolm Purkey's Junction Avenue Theatre Company. South Africa, Republic of: Johannesburg. 1976-1997. Lang.: Eng. 1471
Performance/production
Junction Avenue Theatre Company and the evolution of South African theatre. South Africa, Republic of: Johannesburg. 1988-1989. Lang.: Eng. 1913

Purple Flower, The
Plays/librettos/scripts
The theme of hope in postwar American theatre and writing. USA. 1914-1929. Lang.: Eng. 3153

Pushkin Theatre (Leningrad)
SEE
Akademičéskij Teat'r Dramy im. A.S. Puškina.

Puškin, Aleksand'r Sergejévič
Performance/production
Amateur theatre production of Puškin's *Mocart i Saljeri (Mozart and Salieri).* Russia: Skopina. 1990-1997. Lang.: Rus. 1860

Fomenko's production of Puškin's *Pikovaja Dama (Queen of Spades).* Russia: Moscow. 1996. Lang.: Rus. 1876

Analysis of the opera *Eugene Onegin* by Čajkovskij. Russia. 1879-1997. Lang.: Eng. 4209

Puss in Boots
Performance/production
Collection of newspaper reviews by London theatre critics. UK-England: London. 1997. Lang.: Eng. 2161

Putnam, Ashley
Performance/production
The difficulty of performing 'Sempre Libera' in Verdi's *La Traviata.* Italy. USA: New York, NY. 1886-1996. Lang.: Eng. 4186

Py, Olivier
Institutions
Impressions of the Festival d'Avignon. France: Avignon. 1997. Lang.: Ger. 313

Report from the Festival d'Avignon. France: Avignon. 1997. Lang.: Swe. 1403

Report on the Avignon Festival. France: Avignon. 1997. Lang.: Swe. 1406

Performance/production
Jean-Damien Barbin in Olivier Py's *La Servante (The Servant)*, a twenty-four-hour performance. France: Paris. 1997. Lang.: Swe. 1663

Interview with director Olivier Py. France. 1995-1997. Lang.: Swe. 1681

Pygmalion
Performance/production
Collection of newspaper reviews by London theatre critics. UK-England: London. 1997. Lang.: Eng. 2088
Plays/librettos/scripts
Women's expanding role in society seen in plays of George Bernard Shaw. UK-England. 1893-1923. Lang.: Eng. 3091

Cinematic versions of the Pygmalion myth. USA. 1938. Lang.: Eng. 3682

Pynkoski, Marshall
Performance/production
Opera Atelier's production of Purcell's *Dido and Aeneas.* Canada: Toronto, ON. 1994-1995. Lang.: Eng. 4112

Pyrotechnics
Design/technology
Design and construction of an actor-controlled pyrotechnic device. USA. 1997. Lang.: Eng. 255

Qu'ils crèvent les artistes
SEE
Niech sczezną artyści.

Quaderno proibido (Forbidden Notebook)
Plays/librettos/scripts
Analysis of Alba De Céspedes' stage adaptation of her novel *Quaderno proibido (Forbidden Notebook).* Italy. 1952. Lang.: Ita. 2950

¿Que he hecho yo para merecer esto? (What Have I Done to Deserve This?)
Plays/librettos/scripts
Analysis of Pedro Almodóvar's film *¿Qué he hecho yo para merecer esto? (What Have I Done to Deserve This?).* Spain. 1984. Lang.: Spa. 3642

Queen Amarantha
Plays/librettos/scripts
Interview with drag actor and playwright Charles Busch. USA. 1997. Lang.: Eng. 3259

Queen Christina
Performance/production
Collection of newspaper reviews by London theatre critics. UK-England: London. 1997. Lang.: Eng. 2116
Plays/librettos/scripts
Female characters in plays of contemporary British women. UK-England. 1980-1995. Lang.: Eng. 3077

Queen Elizabeth Hall (London)
Performance/production
Collection of newspaper reviews by London theatre critics. UK-England. 1997. Lang.: Eng. 2072

Collection of newspaper reviews by London theatre critics. UK-England: London. 1997. Lang.: Eng. 2074

Collection of newspaper reviews by London theatre critics. UK-England: London. 1997. Lang.: Eng. 2076

Collection of newspaper reviews by London theatre critics. UK-England: London. 1997. Lang.: Eng. 2146

Queen of Corinth, The
Plays/librettos/scripts
Accusations of rape in English Renaissance drama. England. 1550-1630. Lang.: Eng. 2526

Representations of virginity on the early modern English stage. England. 1490-1650. Lang.: Eng. 2640

Queen of Spades (opera)
SEE
Pique Dame.

Queen of Spades by Puškin
SEE
Pikovaja Dama.

Queen's Garden, The
Basic theatrical documents
Anthology of plays by women of color. USA. 1992-1996. Lang.: Eng. 1338

Queen's Theatre (London)
Performance/production
Collection of newspaper reviews by London theatre critics. UK-England: London. 1997. Lang.: Eng. 2042

Collection of newspaper reviews by London theatre critics. UK-England: London. 1997. Lang.: Eng. 2097

Collection of newspaper reviews by London theatre critics. UK-England: London. 1997. Lang.: Eng. 2146

Questa sera si recita a soggetto (Tonight We Improvise)
Performance/production
Productions of Staatstheater Wiesbaden. Germany: Wiesbaden. 1997. Lang.: Ger. 1709

Questa, Carlos
Institutions
Profile of Carlos Questa of the Playwright's Center. USA: Minneapolis, MN. 1997. Lang.: Eng. 1507

Question of Mercy, A
Basic theatrical documents
Text of *A Question of Mercy* by David Rabe. USA: New York, NY. 1997. Lang.: Eng. 1340

Quick Eternity, A
Performance/production
Collection of newspaper reviews by London theatre critics. UK-England: London. 1997. Lang.: Eng. 1971

Quilico, Gino
Performance/production
Baritone Gino Quilico. Canada. 1970-1997. Lang.: Eng. 4103

Quilligan, Denis
Performance/production
Collection of newspaper reviews by London theatre critics. UK-England: London. 1997. Lang.: Eng. 2049

Quills
Design/technology
Scene designs of Neil Patel. USA. 1996. Lang.: Eng. 1373

Quinault, Philippe
Plays/librettos/scripts
Gender in Lully's opera *Armide.* France. 1686. Lang.: Eng. 4291

Quintavalla, Letizia
Performance/production
Two productions of Tom Stoppard's *Rosencrantz and Guildenstern Are Dead.* UK-England: London. Italy: Forlì. 1966-1996. Lang.: Ita. 2172

Quintero, José
Plays/librettos/scripts
Tennessee Williams' relationship with directors of his plays. USA. 1944-1980. Lang.: Eng. 3241

Randall, Paulette
Performance/production
Collection of newspaper reviews by London theatre critics. UK-England.
1997. Lang.: Eng. 2033

Collection of newspaper reviews by London theatre critics. UK-England:
London. 1997. Lang.: Eng. 2089

Rao, Maya Krishna
Performance/production
Collection of newspaper reviews by London theatre critics. UK-England:
London. 1997. Lang.: Eng. 2073

Rao, Savrithri Jagannatha
Performance/production
Choreography and *Bharata Natyam*. India. 1997. Lang.: Swe. 979

Rapacki, Wincenty
Performance/production
Guest performances in Polish cities. Poland: Cracow, Lvov, Warsaw.
1810-1915. Lang.: Pol. 583

Rape of Lucrece, The
Plays/librettos/scripts
Accusations of rape in English Renaissance drama. England. 1550-1630.
Lang.: Eng. 2526

Suicide in English Renaissance tragedy. England. 1590-1625. Lang.:
Eng. 2724

Raphael, Anat
Performance/production
Collection of newspaper reviews by London theatre critics. UK-England:
London. 1997. Lang.: Eng. 2157

Rapp, Adam
Performance/production
The brothers Rapp: actor Anthony and playwright Adam. USA. 1997.
Lang.: Eng. 640

Rapp, Anthony
Performance/production
The brothers Rapp: actor Anthony and playwright Adam. USA. 1997.
Lang.: Eng. 640

Rapp, Richard
Training
Richard Rapp of the School of American Ballet. USA: New York, NY.
1997. Lang.: Eng. 1139

Rasga coração (Rend Your Heart)
Plays/librettos/scripts
Playwright Oduvaldo Vianna Filho. Brazil. 1934-1974. Lang.: Eng. 2387

Rashomon
Plays/librettos/scripts
Terrains Vagues (Wastelands), Michel Nadeau's stage adaptation of
Rashomon. Canada: Quebec, PQ. 1997. Lang.: Fre. 2422

Rath, Elisabeth
Performance/production
Elisabeth Rath's performance in Terrence McNally's *Master Class*.
Germany: Munich. 1997. Lang.: Hun. 1742

Ratnam, Anita
Institutions
Report on Natya Kala festival/conference. India: Chennai. 1996. Lang.:
Swe. 950

Rau, Krysztof
Performance/production
The musical production of *Gaja (Gaia)*, which used puppets and live
actors. Poland: Zusno. 1997. Lang.: Eng, Fre. 3875

Ravalec, Vincent
Performance/production
Collection of newspaper reviews by London theatre critics. UK-England:
London. 1997. Lang.: Eng. 2133

Ravenhill, Mark
Performance/production
Collection of newspaper reviews by London theatre critics. UK-England:
London. 1997. Lang.: Eng. 2005

Collection of newspaper reviews by London theatre critics. UK-England:
London. 1997. Lang.: Eng. 2069

Ravinia Opera (Chicago, IL)
Institutions
History of Ravinia Opera. USA: Chicago, IL. 1904-1931. Lang.: Eng.
4060

Performance/production
List of Ravinia Opera productions. USA: Chicago, IL. 1912-1926. Lang.:
Eng. 4267

Raw Space (New York, NY)
Performance/production
The use of silent films in theatrical productions. USA: New York, NY.
1997. Lang.: Eng. 2342

Raw Women and Cooked Men
Performance/production
Collection of newspaper reviews by London theatre critics. UK-England:
London. 1997. Lang.: Eng. 2015

Rawlins, Trevor
Performance/production
Collection of newspaper reviews by London theatre critics. UK-England:
London. 1997. Lang.: Eng. 2045

Rayment, Mark
Performance/production
Collection of newspaper reviews by London theatre critics. UK-England:
London. 1997. Lang.: Eng. 2128

Rayner, Julia
Performance/production
Collection of newspaper reviews by London theatre critics. UK-England:
London. 1997. Lang.: Eng. 2100

Raznovich, Diana
Basic theatrical documents
Anthology of Latin American women's plays. Latin America. 1981-1989.
Lang.: Eng. 1291
Relation to other fields
Performance of gender, nationality, and motherhood in various
Argentine plays. Argentina. 1976-1983. Lang.: Eng. 725

Re in Ascolto, Un
Performance/production
Background material on Lyric Opera of Chicago radio broadcast
performances. USA: Chicago, IL. 1997. Lang.: Eng. 4231

Re Pastore, Il
Design/technology
Critique of minimalist scenic design for opera. Canada: Toronto, ON.
USA: New York, NY. 1975-1997. Lang.: Eng. 4019

Re(membering) Aunt Jemima: A Menstrual Show
Basic theatrical documents
Anthology of plays by women of color. USA. 1992-1996. Lang.: Eng.
1338

Reach
Performance/production
Collection of newspaper reviews by London theatre critics. UK-England:
London. 1997. Lang.: Eng. 2132

Ready or Not
Performance/production
Collection of newspaper reviews by London theatre critics. UK-England:
London. 1997. Lang.: Eng. 2079

Collection of newspaper reviews by London theatre critics. UK-England:
London. 1997. Lang.: Eng. 2152

Real Estate
Plays/librettos/scripts
Female characters in plays of contemporary British women. UK-
England. 1980-1995. Lang.: Eng. 3077

Real Thing, The
Plays/librettos/scripts
Metatheatrical techniques of Weiss, Gatti, and Stoppard. Europe. 1964-
1982. Lang.: Eng. 2783

Gender and ideology in Tom Stoppard's *The Real Thing*. UK-England.
1983. Lang.: Eng. 3069

Reason Why, The
Plays/librettos/scripts
Social issues of the seventies in works by Arthur Miller. USA. 1970-
1979. Lang.: Eng. 3173

Rebellato, Dan
Performance/production
Collection of newspaper reviews by London theatre critics. UK-England:
London. 1997. Lang.: Eng. 1980

Reception theory
Theory/criticism
Reception theory and contemporary theatre research. Europe. 1900-
1997. Lang.: Eng. 3483

Reckless
Plays/librettos/scripts
Televisual dramaturgy in the work of some contemporary playwrights.
USA. 1990-1997. Lang.: Eng. 3191

Reconstruction, performance
Performance/production
Attempt to reconstruct performances of plays by Massinger and
Fletcher. England. 1628-1633. Lang.: Eng. 1622

The reconstruction of medieval plays and productions. Europe. 1900-
1997. Lang.: Ita. 1642

A performance of the Beauvais *Ludus Danielis*. Netherlands: Maastricht.
1996. Lang.: Eng. 3872

Regional theatre — cont'd

Musical theatre in Tatarstan. Russia. 1800-1997. Lang.: Rus.   3938

Branson's theatrical tourism. USA: Branson, MO. 1906-1996. Lang.: Eng.   3958

Plays/librettos/scripts

Argument for a broader range of subjects for women playwrights. USA. 1997. Lang.: Eng.   3287

History of southern drama. USA. 1681-1997. Lang.: Eng.   3299

Relation to other fields

Finnish regional theatre policy. Finland. 1990-1997. Lang.: Fin.   743

Theatre, regional culture, and colonialism. Kenya: Lamu. 1800-1925. Lang.: Ger.   772

Theatre in Galicia. Spain. 1996. Lang.: Eng.   779

Regnum Humanitatis (Reign of Humanity, The)

Plays/librettos/scripts

Analysis of *Regnum Humanitatis* by Jacob Grester. Germany. 1585-1600. Lang.: Eng.   2840

Regulations

Administration

The rivalry between the theatre and the music hall. England: London. 1865-1867. Lang.: Eng.   21

The availability of unemployment insurance for artists. USA. 1997. Lang.: Eng.   77

Legal protection of individuals depicted in altered images. USA. 1997. Lang.: Eng.   130

Shakespeare's early development and the policies of the Lords Chamberlain. England: London. 1592-1594. Lang.: Eng.   1235

Sponsorship and control of medieval French religious drama. France: Paris. 1402-1548. Lang.: Eng.   1237

Design/technology

The lighting industry and federal and local regulation. USA. 1994. Lang.: Eng.   275

Call for the entertainment industry to draft safety standards for electrical equipment. USA. 1997. Lang.: Eng.   292

Performance/production

The production of Canadian radio drama. Canada. 1920-1995. Lang.: Eng.   3517

Performance, mass media, and the regulation of *wayang golek purwa*. Indonesia. 1994-1995. Lang.: Eng.   4399

Régy, Claude

Performance/production

Claude Régy's production of *La Mort de Tintagiles (The Death of Tintagiles)* by Maeterlinck. France: Paris. Belgium: Ghent. 1997. Lang.: Eng.   1658

Recent productions of works by Maeterlinck. France: Paris. 1997. Lang.: Swe.   1664

Rehar, Radivoj

Plays/librettos/scripts

Analysis of *Karantanska tragedija (Carinthian Tragedy)* by Radivoj Rehar. Slovenia. 1836-1996. Lang.: Slo.   3015

Rehearsal process

Performance/production

Staging and Beckett's *Not I* and *Krapp's Last Tape*. France. Ireland. 1960-1973. Lang.: Eng.   1671

Videodisc of Ibsen's *Et Dukkehjem (A Doll's House)* combining performance and commentary. Norway. USA. 1879-1997. Lang.: Eng.   1830

The development of dramaturgy at Yale. USA. 1997. Lang.: Eng.   2247

The collaboration of director Travis Preston and dramaturg Royston Coppenger. USA. 1983-1997. Lang.: Eng.   2254

Rehearsal and performance of a stage adaptation of *Neuromancer* by William Gibson. USA: Santa Fe, NM. 1996. Lang.: Eng.   2355

Production guide for a performance of *The Medium* by Gian Carlo Menotti. USA. 1996. Lang.: Eng.   4259

Theory/criticism

Speech and writing in various aspects of theatre. France. 1997. Lang.: Fre.   3486

Reichel, Käthe

Performance/production

Interview with director Benno Besson. Germany. Switzerland. 1949-1997. Lang.: Ger.   1727

Reidinger, Jiří

Institutions

The Czech pantomime theatre 'Alfred ve dvoře'. Czech Republic: Prague. 1961-1996. Lang.: Cze.   3742

Reilly, Charles Nelson

Design/technology

Kirk Bookman's lighting design for *The Gin Game* directed by Charles Nelson Reilly. USA: New York, NY. 1978-1997. Lang.: Eng.   1368

Reinhardt, Max

Performance/production

Max Reinhardt's productions of *Jedermann (Everyman)* by Hugo von Hofmannsthal. Austria: Salzburg. Germany: Berlin. 1911-1920. Lang.: Pol.   1565

Early modern interpretations of Aristophanes' *Lysistrata*. Europe. USA. 1892-1930. Lang.: Eng.   1647

Director Max Reinhardt's influence on Polish theatre. Poland. 1903-1914. Lang.: Ger.   1849

Theory/criticism

Hungarian translation of essays on acting by Max Reinhardt's literary manager Arthur Kahane. Germany. 1872-1932. Lang.: Hun.   897

Reisch, Linda

Administration

German cultural policy and the theatre. Germany. 1997. Lang.: Ger.   30

Reisz, Karel

Performance/production

Karel Reisz's production of Pinter's *Moonlight*, Roundabout Theatre Company. USA: New York, NY. 1994-1996. Lang.: Eng.   2273

Rejane, Gabrielle

Performance/production

Early modern interpretations of Aristophanes' *Lysistrata*. Europe. USA. 1892-1930. Lang.: Eng.   1647

Relapse, The

Plays/librettos/scripts

The 'Lord of Misrule' in Vanbrugh's *The Relapse*. England. 1677-1696. Lang.: Eng.   2533

Religion

Administration

Censorship in the Federal Theatre Project. USA. 1935-1936. Lang.: Eng.   131

Analysis of a Supreme Court decision regarding indecency and cable television. USA. 1995. Lang.: Eng.   3710

Performance spaces

The English church as performance space. England. 1100-1300. Lang.: Eng.   426

Performance/production

Tradition and African theatre. Africa. 1800-1996. Lang.: Eng.   466

Survey of Afro-Caribbean religious dances. Cuba: Havana. 1700. Lang.: Swe.   1144

The ecstatic dance of Sufi mystics, the 'whirling dervishes'. Syria: Damascus. 1996. Lang.: Eng.   1152

Hoods and masks in the original production of Shakespeare's *Measure for Measure*. England: London. 1555-1604. Lang.: Eng.   1626

The decline of the mystery play in Lille. Flanders: Lille. 1480-1690. Lang.: Eng.   1655

Tendencies of modern Asian theatre. Sri Lanka. 1956-1997. Lang.: Eng.   1921

History of Roman civic and religious festivities. Italy: Rome. 1500-1860. Lang.: Ita.   3802

Analysis of a religious street celebration, the Giglio. USA: Brooklyn, NY. 1880-1997. Lang.: Eng.   3808

Contemporary regional theatre and its origins in ancestor worship. China: Quanzhou, Fujian. 714-1994. Lang.: Eng.   4388

The southern form of *wayang kulit* shadow puppet theatre. Indonesia. 1900-1995. Lang.: Eng.   4401

Changes in traditional *wayang kulit* shadow puppet theatre. Indonesia. 1300-1995. Lang.: Eng.   4402

Plays/librettos/scripts

Religious ambivalence in Greek tragedy. Ancient Greece. 500-250 B.C. Lang.: Eng.   2373

The 'Black Madonna' in Cuban theatre. Cuba. 1925-1990. Lang.: Spa.   2444

Arden of Faversham and *A Warning for Fair Women* as morality plays. England. 1591-1599. Lang.: Eng.   2462

Gender ideology and the occult in Shakespeare's plays. England. 1590-1613. Lang.: Eng.   2499

Medieval drama and stereotypes about Jews. England. 1400-1500. Lang.: Eng.   2531

Community and religious identity in late medieval texts. England. 1400-1500. Lang.: Eng.   2543

Social practice and theatrical meaning in Shakespeare's *Measure for Measure*. England. 1604. Lang.: Eng.   2568

Calvinism in the city comedies of Thomas Middleton. England. 1604-1611. Lang.: Eng.   2570

Religion — cont'd

Renaissance theatre — cont'd

The development and dissemination of theatrical stage space. Italy. 1550-1650. Lang.: Eng.   441

Performance spaces in Renaissance Spain. Spain. 1550-1750. Lang.: Eng.   449

The theatrical space of the Buen Retiro. Spain: Madrid. 1638-1812. Lang.: Eng.   450

Comments of panelists from the Theatre Symposium on Theatrical Spaces and Dramatic Places. USA. 1995. Lang.: Eng.   453

Methods of studying sixteenth-century playhouses. Europe. 1500-1600. Lang.: Eng.   1527

The effect of *commedia erudita* on theatre design and stage use. Italy. 1500-1700. Lang.: Eng.   1528

Mannerism in the performance spaces of early *commedia dell'arte*. Italy. 1520-1620. Lang.: Eng.   3790

Performance/production

The importance of a company repertory in early English theatre. England. 1595-1603. Lang.: Eng.   504

The replacement of patronage by regular fees and ticket prices. England. 1580-1610. Lang.: Eng.   506

The development of the professional theatre company. England. 1550-1620. Lang.: Eng.   512

Acting styles in early English drama. England. 1595-1615. Lang.: Eng.   513

Gender on the Italian stage. Italy. 1526-1995. Lang.: Eng.   564

As You Like It and the Chamberlain's Men's move to the Globe. England: London. 1594-1612. Lang.: Eng.   1619

Renaissance theatre performances in Ferrara. Italy: Ferrara. 1486-1502. Lang.: Eng.   1794

Recent productions of Renaissance drama. UK-England. 1996-1997. Lang.: Eng.   2209

Political significance of court entertainments. England. 1490-1660. Lang.: Eng.   3795

Plays/librettos/scripts

The representation of women by boy actors. England. 1450-1600. Lang.: Eng.   2475

The publication of early English playbooks. England. 1583-1642. Lang.: Eng.   2476

Introduction to essays on early English drama. England. 1100-1500. Lang.: Eng.   2513

Philosophical analysis of early English drama. England. 1100-1500. Lang.: Eng.   2521

Solipsism in Marlowe's *Doctor Faustus*. England. 1551-1616. Lang.: Eng.   2561

Analysis of Shakespeare's *As You Like It*. England. 1599. Lang.: Eng.   2596

Narcissism in Renaissance tragedy. England. 1450-1580. Lang.: Eng.   2609

Livy's influence on Shakespeare, Heywood, and Peele. England. 1569-1624. Lang.: Eng.   2629

Collaboration and authorship of Renaissance drama. England. 1550-1620. Lang.: Eng.   2649

Collaborative authorship in early English theatre. England. 1580-1610. Lang.: Eng.   2650

Renaissance theatre and the marketplace. England. 1580-1620. Lang.: Eng.   2657

Ovid's *Narcissus* reflected in Shakespeare's *Twelfth Night*. England. 1602. Lang.: Eng.   2751

The influence of Plautus and his comic themes. Europe. 259 B.C.-1997 A.D. Lang.: Ita.   2784

Male and female Renaissance writers. Europe. 1400-1590. Lang.: Eng.   2785

Analysis of *Regnum Humanitatis* by Jacob Grester. Germany. 1585-1600. Lang.: Eng.   2840

The classification, editing, and dissemination of early playscripts. UK-England. 1906-1996. Lang.: Eng.   3118

Reference materials

Bibliography of recent Renaissance drama studies. Europe. North America. 1945-1996. Lang.: Eng.   712

Research/historiography

Renaissance drama, censorship, and contemporary historical methods. England: London. 1588-1980. Lang.: Eng.   3446

Theory/criticism

Theatre and the critical analysis of injured or traumatized bodies. Europe. North America. 1993-1995. Lang.: Eng.   878

Renaissance Theatre Company (London)

Performance/production

The Shakespearean acting and directing career of Judi Dench. UK-England: London. 1957-1995. Lang.: Eng.   2177

Renaissance-Theater (Berlin)

Performance/production

Premieres of new plays by Handke, Krausser, and Enzensberger. Austria. Germany. 1996-1997. Lang.: Ger.   1567

Rendra

Performance/production

Censorship and Teater Koma's production of *Suksesi* by Rendra. Indonesia: Jakarta. 1977-1993. Lang.: Eng.   558

Renovation, theatre

Administration

Efforts to refurbish the historic Columbia Theatre. Canada: New Westminster, BC. 1927-1997. Lang.: Eng.   9

Design/technology

Lighting designer for Arthur Miller's *The American Clock*, Signature Theatre Company. USA: New York, NY. 1997. Lang.: Eng.   1371

Institutions

Problems of the newly renovated Teatro Real. Spain: Madrid. 1997. Lang.: Eng.   4054

Performance spaces

Technical profile of the Prinzregententheater. Germany: Munich. 1901-1997. Lang.: Ger.   434

Performances of the vaudeville era. USA: Washington, DC. 1924-1992. Lang.: Eng.   457

The renovation of the Jesse H. Jones Hall for the Performing Arts. USA: Houston, TX. 1966-1997. Lang.: Eng.   459

Profile of the renovated *kabuki* theatre Kanamaru-za. Japan: Kotohira. 1830-1995. Lang.: Eng.   1230

Renovation of the Palace Theatre. USA: Louisville, KY. 1996-1997. Lang.: Eng.   3554

The renovation of the Lyceum Theatre for *Jesus Christ Superstar*. UK-England: London. 1904-1997. Lang.: Eng.   3931

The proposed renovation of the Royal Opera House, Covent Garden. UK-England: London. 1997. Lang.: Swe.   4070

Rent

Administration

Broadway theatre manager John Corker. USA: New York, NY. 1997. Lang.: Eng.   73

Copyright case involving the musical *Rent*. USA: New York, NY. 1991-1997. Lang.: Eng.   3895

Design/technology

Blake Burba's lighting design for *Rent*. USA: New York, NY. 1996-1997. Lang.: Eng.   3919

Institutions

Problems of New York Theatre Workshop. USA: New York, NY. 1996-1997. Lang.: Eng.   3928

Performance/production

The brothers Rapp: actor Anthony and playwright Adam. USA. 1997. Lang.: Eng.   640

Interview with Michael Greif, director of *Rent*. USA. 1996-1997. Lang.: Eng.   3969

Renz, Frederick

Performance/production

The Ensemble for Early Music's production of the Fleury Mary Magdalene play. USA: New York, NY. 1997. Lang.: Eng.   676

Repertory

Institutions

Yearbook of the Hungarian State Opera House. Hungary: Budapest. 1995-1996. Lang.: Hun.   4050

Performance/production

The importance of a company repertory in early English theatre. England. 1595-1603. Lang.: Eng.   504

Requiem por Yarini (Requiem for Yarini)

Plays/librettos/scripts

The 'Black Madonna' in Cuban theatre. Cuba. 1925-1990. Lang.: Spa.   2444

Research methods

Performance spaces

Methods of studying sixteenth-century playhouses. Europe. 1500-1600. Lang.: Eng.   1527

Research tools

Research/historiography

Eighteenth-century theatrical portraits. England. France. 1700-1800. Lang.: Eng.   3445

Research/historiography

SEE ALSO

Classed Entries.

Research/historiography — cont'd

Plays/librettos/scripts
Repertory of titles of plays compiled in the eighteenth century. Italy. 1795-1800. Lang.: Ita. 2948
Reference materials
Annual bibliography of modern drama studies. North America. 1899-1997. Lang.: Eng. 3318
Theory/criticism
A model of historical performance ethnography. USA. 1997. Lang.: Eng. 922

Residenztheater (Munich)
Performance/production
Recent productions of plays by Horváth. Germany. Austria. 1996-1997. Lang.: Ger. 1722

Resistible Rise of Arturo Ui, The
SEE
Aufhaltsame Aufstieg des Arturo Ui, Der.

Reskamraten (Traveling Companion, The)
Performance/production
Jarl Kulle's one-man show Reskamraten (The Traveling Companion). Sweden. 1997. Lang.: Swe. 1937

Resnikoff, Charles
Performance/production
Collection of newspaper reviews by London theatre critics. UK-England: London. 1997. Lang.: Eng. 2006

Restless Years, The
Performance/production
Analysis of television serial The Restless Years. Australia. Germany. 1977-1993. Lang.: Eng. 3716

Restoration theatre
SEE ALSO
Geographical-Chronological Index under England 1660-1685.
Performance/production
Actresses and the adaptation of Shakespeare. England. 1660-1740. Lang.: Eng. 1623
Political significance of court entertainments. England. 1490-1660. Lang.: Eng. 3795
Plays/librettos/scripts
Analysis of conversations of 'Wit' couples in Restoration comedy. England. 1660-1700. Lang.: Eng. 2453
History of English theatre from the Restoration to the late nineteenth century. England. 1668-1895. Lang.: Ita. 2473
The ideology of Restoration comedy. England. 1660-1710. Lang.: Eng. 2492
The 'Lord of Misrule' in Vanbrugh's The Relapse. England. 1677-1696. Lang.: Eng. 2533
Marriage in early plays of Colley Cibber. England. 1696-1730. Lang.: Eng. 2563
Theoretical knowledge and action in plays of Wycherley. England. 1671-1676. Lang.: Eng. 2590
Foreshadowing of the comedy of manners in Etherege's She Would If She Could. England. 1670. Lang.: Eng. 2601
Dryden's prologue to Albumazar by Thomas Tomkis. England. 1612-1668. Lang.: Eng. 2643
The significance of rape in The Rover by Aphra Behn. England. 1660. Lang.: Eng. 2744
Biblical and literary influences on The London Merchant by George Lillo. England: London. 1731. Lang.: Eng. 2746
Analysis of The Witlings by Fanny Burney. England. 1778. Lang.: Eng. 2753
Restoration drama and printed propaganda. England. 1678-1683. Lang.: Eng. 2757
Theory/criticism
Restoration dramatic theory. England. 1650-1700. Lang.: Eng. 3475

Restoration, theatre
Performance spaces
The work of Virgilio Marchi in the restoration of the Casa d'Arte Bragaglia. Italy: Rome. 1921-1923. Lang.: Ita. 444
The history and restoration of the New Amsterdam Theatre. USA: New York, NY. 1903-1997. Lang.: Eng. 458
Critique of the architecture of the restored Shakespeare's Globe Theatre. UK-England: London. 1997. Lang.: Eng. 1540
Sam Wanamaker and the rebuilding of Shakespeare's Globe. UK-England: London. 1997. Lang.: Eng. 1546
Profile of the restored Karlstad Teater. Sweden: Karlstad. 1876. Lang.: Swe. 4069

Restpaar (Pair of Remains)
Plays/librettos/scripts
Playwright Theresia Walser. Germany. 1990-1997. Lang.: Ger. 2864

Reszke, Jean de
Performance/production
The difficulty of performing 'Sempre Libera' in Verdi's La Traviata. Italy. USA: New York, NY. 1886-1996. Lang.: Eng. 4186

Retablo de Maese Pedro, El
Basic theatrical documents
Manuel de Falla's libretto to his opera El retablo de Maese Pedro. Spain. 1923. Lang.: Fre, Spa. 4016
Performance/production
Productions of Manuel de Falla's opera El retablo de Maese Pedro. 1923-1993. Lang.: Fre. 4077
Recordings of Manuel de Falla's opera El retablo de Maese Pedro. 1953-1975. Lang.: Fre. 4088

Retablo de Yumbel (Altarpiece of Yumbel)
Basic theatrical documents
Anthology of Latin American women's plays. Latin America. 1981-1989. Lang.: Eng. 1291

Retallack, John
Performance/production
Collection of newspaper reviews by London theatre critics. UK-England: London. 1997. Lang.: Eng. 2020

Retreat
Basic theatrical documents
French translation of Retreat by James Saunders. UK-England. France: Paris. 1995. Lang.: Fre. 1318

Return Journey
Basic theatrical documents
Collection of one-act plays by Welsh writers. UK-Wales. 1952-1996. Lang.: Eng. 1321

Reunion
Plays/librettos/scripts
British Library holdings of filmscript material of Harold Pinter. UK-England. 1963-1994. Lang.: Eng. 3647

Reunion in Vienna
Performance/production
The grotesque on the American stage during the Depression. USA. 1929-1940. Lang.: Eng. 2264

Reunion with Son and Daughter in Kingfisher Red County
Basic theatrical documents
English translation of the Yuan drama Reunion with Son and Daughter in Kingfisher Red County. China. 1280-1994. Lang.: Eng. 1264

Revenger's Tragedy, The
Performance/production
Recent productions of Elizabethan theatre. Europe. 1997. Lang.: Ger. 1649
Plays/librettos/scripts
Gendered power relations, law, and revenge in early English drama. England. 1590-1640. Lang.: Eng. 2540
Narcissism in Renaissance tragedy. England. 1450-1580. Lang.: Eng. 2609
The Italian palazzo on the Jacobean stage. England. 1603-1625. Lang.: Eng. 2625
Ambivalence toward a female sovereign reflected in plays of Shakespeare and Middleton. England. 1600-1607. Lang.: Eng. 2672
Suicide in English Renaissance tragedy. England. 1590-1625. Lang.: Eng. 2724

Revivals
Performance/production
Concert versions of neglected American musicals in the 'Discover the Lost Musicals' series. UK-England: London. 1990-1997. Lang.:Eng. 3944

Revizor (Inspector General, The)
Performance/production
Collection of newspaper reviews by London theatre critics. UK-England: London. 1997. Lang.: Eng. 2158
Use of Mejerchol'd's techniques in a production of Gogol's The Government Inspector (Revizor). UK-England: Northampton. 1997. Lang.: Eng. 2216

Révolte des femmes, La (Revolt of the Women, The)
Performance/production
Analysis of Filippo Taglioni's ballet La Révolte des femmes. France. 1830-1840. Lang.: Eng. 1076

Revolution Theatre
SEE
Teat'r im. V. Majakovskogo.

Richards, Beah — cont'd

Plays/librettos/scripts
The evolution of solo performance in African-American one-person plays. USA. 1972-1996. Lang.: Eng. 3293

Richards, Thomas
Performance/production
Visit to Grotowski and Compagnia della Fortezza. Italy: Volterra, Pontedera. 1986-1997. Lang.: Ger. 1805

Richesses de l'hiver, Les (Riches of Winter, The)
Basic theatrical documents
Text of *Les Richesses de l'hiver (The Riches of Winter)* by Fatima Gallaire. France: Ajaccio. 1996. Lang.: Fre. 1272

Richmond Theatre (London)
Performance/production
Collection of newspaper reviews by London theatre critics. UK-England: London. 1997. Lang.: Eng. 1989

Collection of newspaper reviews by London theatre critics. UK-England: London. 1997. Lang.: Eng. 1992

Richmond, Robert
Performance/production
Collection of newspaper reviews by London theatre critics. UK-England: London. 1997. Lang.: Eng. 2149

Richter, Axel
Performance/production
Russian, Hungarian and Bulgarian plays at Kammerspiele. Germany: Magdeburg. 1989. Lang.: Ger. 1710

Rickson, Ian
Performance/production
Collection of newspaper reviews by London theatre critics. UK-England: London. 1997. Lang.: Eng. 2081

Riddarhyttans Industriteater (Riddarhyttan)
Institutions
Profile of Riddarhyttans Industriteater, Anders Olson artistic director. Sweden: Riddarhyttan. 1985. Lang.: Swe. 1474

Ride Down Mount Morgan, The
Plays/librettos/scripts
Recent work of playwright Arthur Miller. USA. 1990-1997. Lang.: Eng. 3145

Ridiculous Theatrical Company (New York, NY)
Performance/production
Tony Kushner's *Angels in America* in the context of queer performance. USA. 1992-1994. Lang.: Eng. 2245

Rieser, Ferdinand
Performance/production
German theatre during and after the Nazi period. Germany: Berlin, Dusseldorf. Switzerland: Zurich. 1933-1952. Lang.: Eng. 1704

Riga Russian Drama Theatre
SEE
Teat'r Russkoj Dramy.

Rigby, Jonathan
Performance/production
Collection of newspaper reviews by London theatre critics. UK-England: London. 1997. Lang.: Eng. 1985

Rigoletto
Design/technology
Giuseppe Di Iorio's lighting designs for the English Touring Opera. UK-England. 1997. Lang.: Eng. 4032

Rihm, Wolfgang
Plays/librettos/scripts
Wolfgang Rihm's operatic adaptation of *Die Hamletmaschine (Hamletmachine)* by Heiner Müller. Germany. 1978. Lang.: Swe. 4300

Rimskij-Korsakov, Nikolaj Andrejevič
Plays/librettos/scripts
Russian opera and Symbolist poetics. Russia. 1890-1930. Lang.: Eng. 4309

Ring des Nibelungen, Der
Performance/production
The scandalous premiere of Wagner's *Das Rheingold*. Germany: Munich, Bayreuth. 1869-1876. Lang.: Eng. 4150

James Levine's production of Wagner's *Ring*. Germany: Bayreuth. 1997. Lang.: Eng. 4151

Profile, interview with soprano Hildegard Behrens. Germany. 1997. Lang.: Eng. 4160

Harmonic analysis of music of Sieglinde in Wagner's *Ring*. Germany. 1853-1874. Lang.: Eng. 4161

Pierre Audi's production of Wagner's *Ring* for Nederlandse Opera. Netherlands: Amsterdam. 1997. Lang.: Dut. 4200

Analysis of a digital CD-ROM of Wagner's *Ring*. USA. 1996. Lang.: Eng. 4256

Plays/librettos/scripts
Symbolism in Wagner's *Ring*. Germany. 1853-1874. Lang.: Eng. 4298

Ring Round the Moon
SEE
Invitation au château, L'.

Ringling Brothers and Barnum & Bailey Circus (Sarasota, FL)
SEE ALSO
Barnum and Bailey Circus.

Rios, Alicia
Performance/production
Collection of newspaper reviews by London theatre critics. UK-England: London. 1997. Lang.: Eng. 2073

Interview with performance artist Alicia Rios. UK-Wales. 1994-1997. Lang.: Eng. 3824

Ripley Bogle
Performance/production
Collection of newspaper reviews by London theatre critics. UK-England: London. 1997. Lang.: Eng. 2116

Rise and Fall of the City of Mahagonny
SEE
Aufstieg und Fall der Stadt Mahagonny.

Rising Tide Theatre (Trinity, NF)
Institutions
Rising Tide Theatre and Newfoundland cultural policy. Canada: Trinity, NF. 1973-1997. Lang.: Eng. 1390

Risorgimento
SEE
Geographical-Chronological Index under Italy 1815-1876.

Ristori, Adelaide
Performance/production
Guest performances in Polish cities. Poland: Cracow, Lvov, Warsaw. 1810-1915. Lang.: Pol. 583

English acting careers of Eleonora Duse and Adelaide Ristori. UK-England. 1850-1900. Lang.: Eng. 2169

Rite of Spring, The
SEE
Vesna svjaščennaja.

Ritual-ceremony
Performance/production
Mask and disguise in ritual, carnival, and theatre. 1997. Lang.: Eng. 465

Tradition and African theatre. Africa. 1800-1996. Lang.: Eng. 466

African theatre in a global context. Africa. 1800-1996. Lang.: Eng. 469

Odes for female choruses in Greek theatre. Greece. 500-100 B.C. Lang.: Eng. 549

The role of the mask in non-Western ritual performance. India. Papua New Guinea. Indonesia. 1800-1995. Lang.: Eng. 556

Survey of Afro-Caribbean religious dances. Cuba: Havana. 1700. Lang.: Swe. 1144

Malian wedding dances. Mali: Bamako. 1997. Lang.: Swe. 1149

The defeat and return of Moctezuma in traditional dances. USA. Mexico: Oaxaca. 1550-1997. Lang.: Eng. 1154

Analysis of *Teyyateyyam* by K. N. Pannikkar. India: Trivandrum. 1993. Lang.: Eng. 1784

Confession, reconciliation, and David Lan's *Desire*. South Africa, Republic of: Pietermaritzburg. 1993-1995. Lang.: Eng. 1908

Ceremonial theatrical forms *gigaku* and *bugaku*. Japan. 646-1997. Lang.: Eng. 3798

The development of pageants and processionals. England. 1392-1599. Lang.: Eng. 3800

History of Roman civic and religious festivities. Italy: Rome. 1500-1860. Lang.: Ita. 3802

Analysis of opening and closing ceremonies of the 1995 Rugby World Cup. South Africa, Republic of. 1910-1995. Lang.: Eng. 3804

Analysis of the Pageant of Union. South Africa, Republic of. 1910. Lang.: Eng. 3805

Analysis of a Day of the Dead ritual. USA: New Orleans, LA. 1867-1996. Lang.: Eng. 3809

Contemporary regional theatre and its origins in ancestor worship. China: Quanzhou, Fujian. 714-1994. Lang.: Eng. 4388

Plays/librettos/scripts
Representation and story-telling in African and Caribbean theatre. Africa. Caribbean. 1970-1997. Lang.: Eng. 2371

Greek drama and mimesis. Greece. 500-400 B.C. Lang.: Eng. 2876

East Asian influences on writing and directing of Anne Bogart. USA. 1984-1994. Lang.: Eng. 3223

Rock music — cont'd

Marilynn Lowey's lighting design for Neil Diamond's concert tour. USA. 1996-1997. Lang.: Eng. 3757

Performance/production

Female rock bands and the performance of ugliness. USA. 1970-1996. Lang.: Eng. 637

Rock group U2's use of video and interactive technology. USA. 1997. Lang.: Eng. 3732

Rockaby

Performance/production

The interior I/eye in later plays of Samuel Beckett. Ireland. France. USA. 1978-1997. Lang.: Eng. 1785

Collection of newspaper reviews by London theatre critics. UK-England: London. 1997. Lang.: Eng. 2134

Xerxes Mehta's approach to directing Beckett. USA. 1993. Lang.: Eng. 2305

Plays/librettos/scripts

Gender in *Rockaby* by Samuel Beckett. Ireland. USA. 1981. Lang.: Eng. 2916

Analysis of Beckett's *Footfalls, Ohio Impromptu* and *Rockaby*. Ireland. France. USA. 1976-1981. Lang.: Eng. 2928

Language and silence in short plays of Samuel Beckett. Ireland. France. USA. 1960-1981. Lang.: Eng. 2929

Rodenburg, Patsy

Performance/production

Critique of voice training in contemporary Shakespearean production. UK-England. North America. 1975-1995. Lang.: Eng. 2201

Vocal expert Patsy Rodenburg. USA. 1997. Lang.: Eng. 2259

Training

Vocal training and the split between academics and practitioners. UK-England. USA. 1973-1994. Lang.: Eng. 933

Voice teachers defend their work. UK-England. USA. 1973-1994. Lang.: Eng. 3508

Rodenburgh, Theodore

Plays/librettos/scripts

Diplomat and playwright Theodore Rodenburgh. Netherlands. 1574-1644. Lang.: Dut. 2974

Rodgers, Mary

Performance/production

Collection of newspaper reviews by London theatre critics. UK-England: London. 1997. Lang.: Eng. 2088

Rodgers, Richard

Performance/production

Collection of newspaper reviews by London theatre critics. UK-England: London. 1997. Lang.: Eng. 2088

Collection of newspaper reviews by London theatre critics. UK-England: London. 1997. Lang.: Eng. 2152

Collection of newspaper reviews by London theatre critics. UK-England: London. 1997. Lang.: Eng. 2161

History of American musical theatre. USA. UK-England. 1912-1995. Lang.: Eng. 3954

Actor's Expression production of an unauthorized version of the musical *Oklahoma!*. USA: Atlanta, GA. 1997. Lang.: Eng. 3959

The reconstructed orchestration for the revival of *The Boys from Syracuse* by Encores!. USA: New York, NY. 1938-1997. Lang.: Eng. 3970

Plays/librettos/scripts

Analysis of musical adaptations of Shakespearean plays. USA. 1938-1997. Lang.: Ger. 3983

Survey of musical adaptations of Shakespeare. USA: New York, NY. 1938-1997. Lang.: Eng. 3987

Rodo, José Enrique

Plays/librettos/scripts

New world adaptations of Shakespeare's *The Tempest*. England. Latin America. Caribbean. 1612-1994. Lang.: Eng. 2549

Roempke, Gunilla

Performance/production

Dancer and director Gunilla Roempke. Sweden: Stockholm. 1950. Lang.: Swe. 1111

Rogers, Alex

Basic theatrical documents

Music and libretto of the musical *In Dahomey*. USA. 1903. Lang.: Eng. 3904

Rogers, Ted

Performance/production

Collection of newspaper reviews by London theatre critics. UK-England: London. 1997. Lang.: Eng. 1995

Rogoff, Gordon

Relation to other fields

Theatre artists' responses to the debate on multiculturalism of August Wilson and Robert Brustein. USA. 1997. Lang.: Eng. 789

Rohde, Jokum

Plays/librettos/scripts

Interview with actress Katrine Wiedemann. Denmark. 1997. Lang.: Dan. 2447

Roisman, Lois

Plays/librettos/scripts

Texts of plays by Jewish American women. USA. 1985-1995. Lang.: Eng. 3164

Rojos globos rojos (Red Globes Red)

Plays/librettos/scripts

The style of playwright Eduardo Pavlovsky. Argentina. 1962-1993. Lang.: Spa. 2374

Rökk, Marika

Performance/production

Film careers of Hungarian dancers. Hungary. 1929-1945. Lang.: Hun. 976

Roles

SEE

Characters/roles.

Rollins, Doug

Performance/production

Collection of newspaper reviews by London theatre critics. UK-England. 1997. Lang.: Eng. 2050

Romani, Felice

Basic theatrical documents

Libretto for Bellini's opera *La sonnambula*. Italy. 1831. Lang.: Fre, Ita. 4012

Performance/production

Productions world wide of Bellini's opera *La sonnambula*. 1831-1994. Lang.: Fre. 4078

Outstanding performances of Bellini's opera *La sonnambula*. 1831-1984. Lang.: Fre. 4082

Recordings of Bellini's *La sonnambula*. 1899-1996. Lang.: Fre. 4083

Plays/librettos/scripts

Background information on Bellini's *La Sonnambula*: sleep disorders. Europe. 1831. Lang.: Fre. 4286

Sources of Bellini's opera *La Sonnambula*. Italy. France. 1831. Lang.: Fre. 4307

Romanticism

SEE ALSO

Geographical-Chronological Index under Europe 1800-1850, France 1810-1857, Germany 1798-1830, Italy 1815-1876, UK 1801-1850.

Plays/librettos/scripts

Text and performance in the Romantic period. Europe. 1800-1851. Lang.: Pol. 2790

Romeo and Juliet

Institutions

Profile of street theatre Grupo Galpão. Brazil: Belo Horizonte. 1982-1997. Lang.: Eng. 299

Minutes of Columbia University Seminar on Shakespeare. USA: New York, NY. 1997. Lang.: Eng. 1515

Performance/production

Collection of newspaper reviews by London theatre critics. UK-England: London. 1997. Lang.: Eng. 2090

Collection of newspaper reviews by London theatre critics. UK-England: London. 1997. Lang.: Eng. 2099

Collection of newspaper reviews by London theatre critics. UK-England: London. 1997. Lang.: Eng. 2136

Non-literary realism in Shakespeare productions. UK-England. Germany. 1958-1995. Lang.: Ger. 2170

Profile of actor Ray Fearon. UK-England: London. 1997. Lang.: Eng. 2185

Franco Zeffirelli's film adaptations of Shakespearean plays. Italy. 1966-1990. Lang.: Eng. 3579

Baz Luhrmann's film adaptation of *Romeo and Juliet*. USA. 1997. Lang.: Eng. 3627

Plays/librettos/scripts

Evil women in early modern English tragedy. England. 1590-1613. Lang.: Eng. 2452

Masculinity in Shakespeare's *Romeo and Juliet*. England. 1595. Lang.: Eng. 2457

Argument for 1595 as the date of composition of Shakespeare's *Romeo and Juliet*. England. 1595-1596. Lang.: Eng. 2581

Romeo and Juliet — cont'd

Shakespeare's frequent use of oxymoron in *Romeo and Juliet*. England. 1595-1596. Lang.: Eng. 2641

Principles of Shakespearean dramaturgy. England. 1590-1613. Lang.: Eng. 2658

Analysis of a crux in Shakespeare's *Romeo and Juliet*. England. 1595-1596. Lang.: Eng. 2703

Poetry and action in Shakespeare's *Romeo and Juliet*. England. 1595-1596. Lang.: Eng. 2771

Relation to other fields
Reader-response theory and the teaching of Shakespeare. USA. 1997. Lang.: Eng. 3405

Nontraditional methods of teaching Shakespeare's *Romeo and Juliet*. USA. 1997. Lang.: Eng. 3414

Theory/criticism
The relationship between theatre and criticism, originals and derivatives. France. 1997. Lang.: Eng. 3488

Romeo e Giulietta
Theory/criticism
The relationship between theatre and criticism, originals and derivatives. France. 1997. Lang.: Eng. 3488

Roméo et Juliette
Performance/production
Opera composer Charles Gounod. France: Paris. 1818-1893. Lang.: Eng. 4140

Romeril, John
Plays/librettos/scripts
Playwright John Romeril on the state of Australian theatre. Australia: Melbourne. 1996. Lang.: Eng. 2379

Romero, George
Performance/production
The horror genre and the American film industry. USA. 1953-1968. Lang.: Eng. 3617

Romero, Mariela
Basic theatrical documents
Anthology of Latin American women's plays. Latin America. 1981-1989. Lang.: Eng. 1291

Ronconi, Luca
Performance/production
Productions of Ibsen's *Peer Gynt* by Luca Ronconi and Stéphane Braunschweig. France: Paris. 1996. Lang.: Eng. 1659

Luca Ronconi's production of *Hamlet*. Italy: Rome. 1995. Lang.: Ita. 1802

Plays/librettos/scripts
Analysis of *Davila Roa* by Alessandro Baricco. Italy. 1997. Lang.: Ita. 2972

Ronde, La
SEE
Reigen.

Ronfard, Alice
Plays/librettos/scripts
Adaptations of French classics for contemporary audiences. Canada: Montreal, PQ. France. 1997. Lang.: Fre. 2421

Rønne, Hans
Performance/production
Interview with playwright and director Hans Rønne. Denmark. 1997. Lang.: Dan. 1617

Rose Tattoo, The
Performance/production
The first Italian production of Tennessee Williams's *The Rose Tattoo*. Italy. 1996. Lang.: Ita. 1795

Plays/librettos/scripts
Tennessee Williams' plays on film. USA. 1950-1969. Lang.: Eng. 3245

Stemma for versions of *The Rose Tattoo* by Tennessee Williams. USA. 1937-1997. Lang.: Eng. 3246

Rose Theatre (London)
Administration
Philip Henslowe's move from the Rose to the Fortune. England: London. 1576-1616. Lang.: Eng. 20

Performance spaces
Early modern performance spaces. England. 1600-1650. Lang.: Eng. 424

Shakespeare's plays on the Elizabethan stage. England. 1590-1615. Lang.: Eng. 1520

Work of historical adviser to Shakespeare's Globe project. UK-England: London. 1979. Lang.: Eng. 1542

Theory/criticism
Theatre and the critical analysis of injured or traumatized bodies. Europe. North America. 1993-1995. Lang.: Eng. 878

Rose, Richard
Relation to other fields
Marketing techniques of the interactive show *Tamara: The Living Movie*. USA. 1987. Lang.: Eng. 813

Roseanne (Barr, Roseanne)
Performance/production
Changes in women's comedy performance. USA. 1950-1995. Lang.: Eng. 654

Rosemary Branch (London)
Performance spaces
The Rosemary Branch's entry into the world of fringe theatre. UK-England: London. 1993-1997. Lang.: Eng. 452

Performance/production
Collection of newspaper reviews by London theatre critics. UK-England: London. 1997. Lang.: Eng. 1994

Collection of newspaper reviews by London theatre critics. UK-England: London. 1997. Lang.: Eng. 2139

Rosen, Elsa Marianne von
Performance/production
Dancer/choreographer Elsa Marianne von Rosen. Sweden. Denmark. 1936. Lang.: Swe. 1112

Rosen, Steven
Design/technology
Theatrical lighting for a traveling museum exhibit on dinosaurs. USA: New York, NY. 1997. Lang.: Eng. 282

Rosencrantz and Guildenstern Are Dead
Performance/production
Two productions of Tom Stoppard's *Rosencrantz and Guildenstern Are Dead*. UK-England: London. Italy: Forlì. 1966-1996. Lang.:Ita. 2172

Rosenthal, Jean
Design/technology
Lighting designer Jean Rosenthal. USA: New York, NY. 1932-1969. Lang.: Eng. 228

Rosenthal, Rachel
Performance/production
Interview with teacher and performance artist Rachel Rosenthal. USA: Los Angeles, CA. 1926-1991. Lang.: Eng. 3842

Rosewood
Basic theatrical documents
Text of *Rosewood* by Gregory Poirier. USA. 1997. Lang.: Eng. 3537

Design/technology
Paul Sylbert's production design for *Rosewood*. USA. 1996. Lang.: Eng. 3550

Plays/librettos/scripts
Interview with screenwriter Gregory Poirier. USA. 1997. Lang.: Eng. 3652

Rosmersholm
Performance/production
Collection of newspaper reviews by London theatre critics. UK-England: London. 1997. Lang.: Eng. 2019

Plays/librettos/scripts
Ibsen and early modernist theatre. Finland. 1885-1905. Lang.: Eng. 2801

Ross, Herb
Plays/librettos/scripts
Films based on works of stage playwrights. USA. 1951-1972. Lang.: Pol. 3681

Ross, Jerry
Performance/production
Collection of newspaper reviews by London theatre critics. UK-England: London. 1997. Lang.: Eng. 2057

Ross, Steve
Performance/production
Successful cabaret performers and their techniques. USA. 1975-1997. Lang.: Eng. 3780

Rossi, Vittorio
Plays/librettos/scripts
The 'Black Madonna' in works of Italian-Canadian authors. Canada. 1950-1990. Lang.: Eng. 2396

Rossini, Gioacchino
Institutions
Profile of the Music Academy of the West. USA: Santa Barbara, CA. 1946-1997. Lang.: Eng. 4064

Performance/production
Stylistic similarities in Baroque and nineteenth-century opera. Europe. 1705-1997. Lang.: Eng. 4128

The premiere of Rossini's *I Puritani*. France: Paris. 1835. Lang.: Eng. 4137

Background material on Metropolitan Opera radio broadcast performances. USA: New York, NY. 1997-1997. Lang.: Eng. 4237

Royal Court Theatre (London) — cont'd

Collection of newspaper reviews by London theatre critics. UK-England: London. 1997. Lang.: Eng. 2037

Collection of newspaper reviews by London theatre critics. UK-England: London. 1997. Lang.: Eng. 2056

Collection of newspaper reviews by London theatre critics. UK-England: London. 1997. Lang.: Eng. 2057

Collection of newspaper reviews by London theatre critics. UK-England: London. 1997. Lang.: Eng. 2073

Collection of newspaper reviews by London theatre critics. UK-England: London. 1997. Lang.: Eng. 2074

Collection of newspaper reviews by London theatre critics. UK-England: London. 1997. Lang.: Eng. 2076

Collection of newspaper reviews by London theatre critics. UK-England: London. 1997. Lang.: Eng. 2077

Collection of newspaper reviews by London theatre critics. UK-England: London. 1997. Lang.: Eng. 2081

Collection of newspaper reviews by London theatre critics. UK-England: London. 1997. Lang.: Eng. 2087

Collection of newspaper reviews by London theatre critics. UK-England: London. 1997. Lang.: Eng. 2105

Collection of newspaper reviews by London theatre critics. UK-England: London. 1997. Lang.: Eng. 2122

Collection of newspaper reviews by London theatre critics. UK-England: London. 1997. Lang.: Eng. 2143

Collection of newspaper reviews by London theatre critics. UK-England: London. 1997. Lang.: Eng. 2147

Productions of plays by Caryl Churchill. UK-Scotland: Edinburgh. UK-England: London. 1997. Lang.: Eng. 2233

Plays/librettos/scripts

Survey of English drama by a retired theatre reviewer. UK-England. 1959-1995. Lang.: Eng. 3117

Royal Dramatic Theatre (Stockholm)

SEE

Kungliga Dramatiska Teatern.

Royal Family, The

Plays/librettos/scripts

Social criticism in plays of George S. Kaufman. USA. 1889-1961. Lang.: Eng. 3132

Royal Festival Hall (London)

Performance/production

Collection of newspaper reviews by London theatre critics. UK-England: London. 1997. Lang.: Eng. 2045

Collection of newspaper reviews by London theatre critics. UK-England. 1997. Lang.: Eng. 2072

Royal London Hospital

Performance/production

Collection of newspaper reviews by London theatre critics. UK-England: London. 1997. Lang.: Eng. 2070

Royal Lyceum Theatre (Edinburgh)

Performance/production

Collection of newspaper reviews by London theatre critics. UK-Scotland: Edinburgh. 1997. Lang.: Eng. 2230

Royal National Theatre (London)

SEE

National Theatre.

Royal Opera House (Stockholm)

SEE

Kungliga Operan.

Kungliga Teatern.

Royal Opera House, Covent Garden (London)

Institutions

The touring repertoire of the Royal Ballet. UK-England: London. 1997. Lang.: Eng. 1059

Performance spaces

The proposed renovation of the Royal Opera House, Covent Garden. UK-England: London. 1997. Lang.: Swe. 4070

Performance/production

The artistic partnership of Rudolf Nureyev and Margot Fonteyn. UK-England. 1962-1997. Lang.: Rus. 1118

Historical introduction to *Palestrina* by Hans Pfitzner. Germany. 1917-1997. Lang.: Eng. 4162

The Royal Opera House Verdi festival. UK-England: London. 1997. Lang.: Eng. 4223

Recent performances and changes at British opera houses. UK-England: London. UK-Wales: Cardiff. 1996-1997. Lang.: Eng. 4227

Royal Shakespeare Company (RSC, Stratford & London)

Performance/production

The accessibility of Shakespeare's plays to today's audiences. UK-England: London. 1997. Lang.: Eng. 1968

Collection of newspaper reviews by London theatre critics. UK-England: London. 1997. Lang.: Eng. 1973

Collection of newspaper reviews by London theatre critics. UK-England: London. 1997. Lang.: Eng. 1975

Collection of newspaper reviews by London theatre critics. UK-England: London. 1997. Lang.: Eng. 1987

Collection of newspaper reviews by London theatre critics. UK-England: London. 1997. Lang.: Eng. 2000

Collection of newspaper reviews by London theatre critics. UK-England: London. 1997. Lang.: Eng. 2013

Collection of newspaper reviews by London theatre critics. UK-England. 1997. Lang.: Eng. 2014

Collection of newspaper reviews by London theatre critics. UK-England: London. 1997. Lang.: Eng. 2031

Collection of newspaper reviews by London theatre critics. UK-England. 1997. Lang.: Eng. 2051

Collection of newspaper reviews by London theatre critics. UK-England. 1997. Lang.: Eng. 2109

Collection of newspaper reviews by London theatre critics. UK-England: London. 1997. Lang.: Eng. 2134

Collection of newspaper reviews by London theatre critics. UK-England: London. 1997. Lang.: Eng. 2136

Collection of newspaper reviews by London theatre critics. UK-England: London. 1997. Lang.: Eng. 2149

Collection of newspaper reviews by London theatre critics. UK-England. 1997. Lang.: Eng. 2150

Collection of newspaper reviews by London theatre critics. UK-England: London. 1997. Lang.: Eng. 2151

Collection of newspaper reviews by London theatre critics. UK-England: London. 1997. Lang.: Eng. 2158

Collection of newspaper reviews by London theatre critics. UK-England: London. 1997. Lang.: Eng. 2159

Collection of newspaper reviews by London theatre critics. UK-England. 1997. Lang.: Eng. 2163

Non-literary realism in Shakespeare productions. UK-England. Germany. 1958-1995. Lang.: Ger. 2170

Everyman and *The Mysteries* at RSC. UK-England: Stratford. 1996-1997. Lang.: Ger. 2171

The use of amateurs as extras at the Royal Shakespeare Theatre. UK-England: Stratford. 1879-1995. Lang.: Eng. 2174

Film actor Leslie Phillips' roles at the Royal Shakespeare Company. UK-England: Stratford. 1997. Lang.: Eng. 2182

Michael Boyd's production of Kyd's *Spanish Tragedy* at the Swan. UK-England: Stratford. 1997. Lang.: Eng. 2183

Actress Derbhle Crotty at the Royal Shakespeare Company. UK-England: Stratford. 1997. Lang.: Eng. 2184

Profile of actor Ray Fearon. UK-England: London. 1997. Lang.: Eng. 2185

History of contemporary Shakespeare performances. UK-England. 1989-1997. Lang.: Eng. 2190

Michael Attenborough's production of *The Herbal Bed* by Peter Whelan. UK-England: London. 1997. Lang.: Eng. 2198

Report on meeting of young European directors. UK-England: Stratford. 1997. Lang.: Swe. 2199

John Caird's adaptation of *Peter Pan*. UK-England: London. 1997. Lang.: Eng. 2215

The effect of nationalization and subsidy on Shakespearean production and reception. UK-England. 1960-1988. Lang.: Eng. 2220

James Laurenson's role in *The General from America* by Richard Nelson, RSC. UK-England: London. 1997. Lang.: Eng. 2223

Peter Brook's RSC production of Shakespeare's *King Lear*. UK-England: Stratford, London. 1970. Lang.: Pol. 2228

Plays/librettos/scripts

Women's silence in Renaissance drama. England. 1601-1613. Lang.: Eng. 2642

Relation to other fields

Shakespeare, the RSC, and political ideology. UK-England. 1990-1996. Lang.: Eng. 3386

Royal Shakespeare Theatre (Stratford)
Performance/production

Collection of newspaper reviews by London theatre critics. UK-England: London. 1997. Lang.: Eng. 2013

Collection of newspaper reviews by London theatre critics. UK-England. 1997. Lang.: Eng. 2109

Collection of newspaper reviews by London theatre critics. UK-England. 1997. Lang.: Eng. 2150

Collection of newspaper reviews by London theatre critics. UK-England. 1997. Lang.: Eng. 2163

The use of amateurs as extras at the Royal Shakespeare Theatre. UK-England: Stratford. 1879-1995. Lang.: Eng. 2174

Actress Derbhle Crotty at the Royal Shakespeare Company. UK-England: Stratford. 1997. Lang.: Eng. 2184

Royal Swedish Ballet
SEE

Kungliga Teaterns Balett.

Royal Swedish Opera
SEE

Kungliga Operan.

Kungliga Teatern.

Rózsahegyi, Kálmán
Performance/production

Biography of actor Kálmán Rózsahegyi. Hungary. 1873-1961. Lang.: Hun. 1774

Ruanne, Patricia
Performance/production

Interview with dancer Patricia Ruanne. USA. 1997. Lang.: Eng. 1125

Rubasingham, Indhu
Performance/production

Collection of newspaper reviews by London theatre critics. UK-England: London. 1997. Lang.: Eng. 1996

Rubin, Joel E.
Design/technology

Former OISTAT presidents Helmut Grosser and Joel E. Rubin. USA: Pittsburgh, PA. 1997. Lang.: Eng. 284

Rubinstein, Ida
Performance/production

The body and gender in Parisian dance performance. France. 1911-1924. Lang.: Eng. 1069

Rudet, Jacqueline
Plays/librettos/scripts

Analysis of *Basin* by Jacqueline Rudet. UK-England. 1985-1997. Lang.: Eng. 3106

Rudkin, David
Performance/production

Collection of newspaper reviews by London theatre critics. UK-England: London. 1997. Lang.: Eng. 2068

Rudman, Michael
Performance/production

Collection of newspaper reviews by London theatre critics. UK-England. 1997. Lang.: Eng. 2033

Collection of newspaper reviews by London theatre critics. UK-England. 1997. Lang.: Eng. 2072

Collection of newspaper reviews by London theatre critics. UK-England. 1997. Lang.: Eng. 2092

Rudnick, Paul
Plays/librettos/scripts

Analysis of *Jeffrey* by Paul Rudnick. USA. 1992. Lang.: Eng. 3239

Rudolph, Niels Peter
Performance/production

German productions of plays by Terrence McNally and Nicky Silver. Germany. 1996-1997. Lang.: Ger. 1721

Ruffian on the Stair, The
Plays/librettos/scripts

Analysis of *The Ruffian on the Stair* by Joe Orton. UK-England. 1998. Lang.: Eng. 3076

Rules of the Game, The
SEE

Giuoco delle parti, Il.

Rundgång (Vicious Circle)
Performance/production

Interview with director Kajsa Isakson. Sweden: Stockholm. 1986-1997. Lang.: Swe. 1951

Runnicles, Donald C.
Design/technology

Sound design problems of San Francisco Opera's temporary home. USA: San Francisco, CA. 1996. Lang.: Eng. 4036

Ruohonen, Laura
Plays/librettos/scripts

Report from women playwrights conference. Ireland: Galway. 1997. Lang.: Swe. 2930

Rush, Geoffrey
Performance/production

Collection of newspaper reviews by London theatre critics. UK-England: London. 1997. Lang.: Eng. 2138

Russ, Claire
Performance/production

Choreographer Claire Russ. UK-England. 1997. Lang.: Eng. 1196

Ruud, Sif
Performance/production

Interview with actors Sif Ruud and Thorsten Flinck. Sweden: Stockholm. 1934-1997. Lang.: Swe. 1922

Ruzzante
SEE

Beolco, Angelo.

Rylance, Mark
Performance spaces

Artistic policy and practices of Shakespeare's Globe Theatre. UK-England: London. 1996. Lang.: Eng. 1544

Performance/production

Mark Rylance of Shakespeare's Globe. UK-England: London. 1997. Lang.: Eng. 2197

Soprano Susannah Waters. UK-England. 1997. Lang.: Eng. 4226

Saarinen, Juho
Performance/production

TV performances of young choreographers. Sweden. 1997. Lang.: Swe. 1186

Sabella, David
Performance/production

Handelian countertenor David Sabella, currently performing in musical theatre. USA: New York, NY. 1996. Lang.: Eng. 3960

Sabrina
Plays/librettos/scripts

Cinematic versions of the Pygmalion myth. USA. 1938. Lang.: Eng. 3682

Sacre du printemps, Le
SEE

Vesna svjaščennaja.

Sacred Naked Nature Girls (Santa Monica, CA)
Performance/production

Home: The Last Place I Ran to Just About Killed Me by Sacred Naked Nature Girls. USA. 1996. Lang.: Eng. 635

Sad Lament of Pecos Bill on the Eve of Killing His Wife, The
Performance/production

The Sam Shepard season of the Signature Theatre Company. USA: New York, NY. 1976-1997. Lang.: Eng. 2346

Sada, Yacco
SEE

Kawakami, Sadayacco.

Sado koshaku fujin (Madame de Sade)
Institutions

Recent productions of Schaubühne. Germany: Berlin. 1996-1997. Lang.: Ger. 1426

Sado Koshaku fujin (Madame de Sade)
Performance/production

Collection of newspaper reviews by London theatre critics. UK-England: London. 1997. Lang.: Eng. 2143

Sadowitz, Jerry
Performance/production

Collection of newspaper reviews by London theatre critics. UK-England: London. 1997. Lang.: Eng. 2009

Sadowski, Andrzej
Performance/production

Collection of newspaper reviews by London theatre critics. UK-England: London. 1997. Lang.: Eng. 2027

Plays/librettos/scripts

The influence of Čechov's *Tri sestry (Three Sisters)* on plays of Sadowski and Wertenbaker. Russia. UK-England. 1901-1997. Lang.: Eng. 2992

Safety
SEE

Health/safety.

Sagouine, La (Slattern, The)
Plays/librettos/scripts

Analysis of *La Sagouine (The Slattern)* by Antonine Maillet. Canada. 1971. Lang.: Fre. 2399

Scenery — cont'd

A method of distributing power to a wagon or slip-stage. USA: San Diego, CA. 1997. Lang.: Eng. 288

The influence of Jo Mielziner on scene designer Tony Walton. USA. 1936-1960. Lang.: Eng. 294

Broadway scene designer Tony Walton. USA. UK-England. 1934-1997. Lang.: Eng. 295

Peter Pabst's stage design for Tanztheater Wuppertal's *Nur Du (Only You)*. Germany: Wuppertal. 1996. Lang.: Eng. 940

Exhibition of scenery and costumes for Ballets Russes productions. Russia. France. 1909-1929. Lang.: Eng. 1048

Houston Ballet Company's *Dracula*—costumes, sets, lighting. USA: Houston, TX. 1897-1997. Lang.: Eng. 1049

Analysis of a nineteenth-century work on stage effects in *kabuki* theatre. Japan. 1858-1859. Lang.: Eng. 1229

Background on Ken Garnhum's set design for *Frida K.* Canada: Toronto, ON. 1997. Lang.: Eng. 1354

Design and community theatre. Canada. 1990-1997. Lang.: Eng. 1355

Stage designs for *Az ember tragédiája (The Tragedy of Man)* by Imre Madách. Hungary: Budapest. 1883-1915. Lang.: Hun. 1357

Outdoor production of *Patronerna på Ahlquittern (The Squires at Ahlquittern)*. Sweden: Bjurtjärn. 1997. Lang.: Swe. 1359

The scenography of Richard Foreman. USA. 1990-1996. Lang.: Eng. 1362

Design for three productions of Tony Kushner's *Angels in America*. USA: New York, NY, Los Angeles, CA. UK-England: London. 1992-1994. Lang.: Eng. 1363

Derek McLane's set design for *Present Laughter*. USA: New York, NY. 1996-1997. Lang.: Eng. 1365

Robert Brill's set design for *God's Heart* by Craig Lucas, Mitzi E. Newhouse Theatre. USA: New York, NY. 1997. Lang.: Eng. 1372

Scene designs of Neil Patel. USA. 1996. Lang.: Eng. 1373

Realistic set design and the plays of William Saroyan. USA. 1939-1943. Lang.: Eng. 1375

Set designer Paul Owen. USA: Louisville, KY. 1997. Lang.: Eng. 1378

Benjamin Fernandez's production design for *Daylight*. Italy: Rome. 1996. Lang.: Eng. 3543

Production and costume design for the film adaptation of *The Crucible*. USA. 1995-1996. Lang.: Eng. 3549

Paul Sylbert's production design for *Rosewood*. USA. 1996. Lang.: Eng. 3550

Technical aspects of *EFX!* at MGM Grand Hotel. USA: Las Vegas, NV. 1996. Lang.: Eng. 3854

Background on Ken Garnhum's set design for *The House of Martin Guerre*. Canada. 1997. Lang.: Eng. 3906

Hildegard Bechter's design for the musical *Always*. UK-England: London. 1997. Lang.: Eng. 3910

Design elements of *On the Town* for New York Shakespeare Festival. USA: New York, NY. 1997. Lang.: Eng. 3915

Technical designs for the Shakespearean musical *Play On!*. USA: San Diego, CA. 1997. Lang.: Eng. 3921

A raft for use in a production of the musical *Big River*. USA. 1997. Lang.: Eng. 3923

Technical aspects of Neue Oper Wien's production of *Maschinist Hopkins* by Max Brand. Austria: Vienna. 1997. Lang.: Ger. 4018

Critique of minimalist scenic design for opera. Canada: Toronto, ON. USA: New York, NY. 1975-1997. Lang.: Eng. 4019

Catalogue of exhibition on Parisian opera scene design. France: Paris. 1850-1997. Lang.: Ita. 4020

Technical description of Semperoper's production of *Die Frau ohne Schatten*. Germany: Dresden. 1997. Lang.: Ger. 4021

The staging and scenic concept for the premiere of the opera *Schlachthof 5*. Germany: Munich. 1997. Lang.: Ger. 4022

Scenery for Mozart's *Idomeneo* at Bayerische Staatsoper. Germany: Munich. 1996. Lang.: Ger. 4023

Interview with opera set designer János Miklós Kádár. Hungary. 1954-1997. Lang.: Hun. 4024

Opera scenography of Felice Casorati. Italy. 1933-1954. Lang.: Ita. 4025

Kungliga Operan's set transport system. Sweden: Stockholm. 1995. Lang.: Swe. 4027

GöteborgsOperan's faux-marble floor. Sweden: Gothenburg. 1996. Lang.: Swe. 4028

Technical aspects of YstadsOperan's production of *The Saint of Bleecker Street*. Sweden: Ystad. 1997. Lang.: Swe. 4029

Technical aspects of a production of *Tosca* at GöteborgsOperan. Sweden: Gothenburg. 1996. Lang.: Swe. 4031

Performance spaces

Profile of Měsíčník Ceských Divadel, a revolving auditorium theatre. Czech Republic: Český Krumlov. 1947-1996. Lang.: Eng. 1519

The history of the Colosseum and its new interior design. Germany: Essen. 1900-1997. Lang.: Ger. 3930

Performance/production

The importance of amateur theatre for Polish cultural identity at the time of the partitions. Poland: Lublin. 1866-1918. Lang.: Pol. 587

Visual performance aspects of Greek tragedy. Greece: Athens. 500 B.C. Lang.: Ita. 1749

Videodisc of Ibsen's *Et Dukkehjem (A Doll's House)* combining performance and commentary. Norway. USA. 1879-1997. Lang.: Eng. 1830

Involving youth audiences in theatre. Sweden: Stockholm, Uppsala. 1995-1997. Lang.: Swe. 1949

The construction of the Middle East on the British stage. UK-England. 1798-1853. Lang.: Eng. 2229

Tony Kushner's *Angels in America* as epic theatre. USA. 1992-1995. Lang.: Eng. 2324

Presentation of *Skrattrevyn i Brevens Bruk (The Brevens Bruk Revue)*. Sweden: Brevens Bruk. 1993. Lang.: Swe. 3859

Interview with director and scene designer Achim Freyer. Austria: Salzburg. 1997. Lang.: Ger. 4097

Opera Atelier's production of Purcell's *Dido and Aeneas*. Canada: Toronto, ON. 1994-1995. Lang.: Eng. 4112

László Márkus, former general director of Royal Hungarian Opera House. Hungary: Budapest. 1923-1944. Lang.: Hun. 4173

Plays/librettos/scripts

Letters from playwright Salvatore Di Giacomo to stage designer Luca Postiglione. Italy. 1908-1927. Lang.: Ita. 2958

Relation to other fields

Boydell's 'Shakespeare Gallery' and the eighteenth-century stage. England. 1757-1772. Lang.: Eng. 732

Stage designer Władysław Daszewski and actions taken against Polish writers. Poland: Lvov. 1940. Lang.: Pol. 775

Play competition involving immigrants in Malmö's suburbs. Sweden: Malmö. 1996. Lang.: Swe. 3378

Schade, Michael

Performance/production

Lyric tenor Michael Schade. Canada. 1977-1997. Lang.: Eng. 4109

Schafer, R. Murray

Plays/librettos/scripts

The environmental music theatre of R. Murray Schafer. Canada. 1966-1996. Lang.: Eng. 3886

Schall, Heinz

Performance/production

Asta Nielsen's performance as Hamlet. Denmark. 1920. Lang.: Eng. 3569

Schandelmeier, Cathleen

Performance/production

A puppeteer's experience writing and performing a play commissioned for a child's party. USA: Melrose Park, CA. 1997. Lang.: Eng. 4378

Schaub, Catherine

Performance/production

Interviews with the cast of Théâtre du Soleil's *Les Atrides*. France: Paris. 1992. Lang.: Eng. 1677

Schaubühne (Berlin)

Administration

Interview with Jürgen Schitthelm of Schaubühne. Germany: Berlin. 1970-1997. Lang.: Ger. 34

Institutions

Statements about the current status of Berlin theatres. Germany: Berlin. 1997. Lang.: Ger. 325

Interview with actor Peter Simonschek of Schaubühne. Germany: Berlin. 1979-1997. Lang.: Ger. 1411

The situation of ensemble theatre, with reference to Göteborgs Stadsteatern and Schaubühne. Sweden: Gothenburg. Germany. 1900. Lang.: Swe. 1484

Performance/production

Interview with director Luc Bondy. Germany. France. 1948-1997. Lang.: Ger. 1684

The term 'intonation' in German theatrical theory and practice. Germany. 1806-1991. Lang.: Ger. 1733

Screenplays — cont'd

Script of *Donnie Brasco* by Paul Attanasio. USA. 1997. Lang.: Eng.
3529

Script of *Addicted to Love* by Robert Gordon. USA. 1997. Lang.: Eng.
3532

Text of filmscript *North by Northwest* by Ernest Lehman. USA. 1959. Lang.: Eng.
3535

Text of *Rosewood* by Gregory Poirier. USA. 1997. Lang.: Eng. 3537

Text of *Murder and murder* by Yvonne Rainer. USA. 1996. Lang.: Eng.
3538

Script of *Breaking Away* by Steve Tesich. USA. 1979. Lang.: Eng. 3540

Script for *Scream* by Kevin Williamson. USA. 1996. Lang.: Eng. 3541

Scribe, Eugène
Basic theatrical documents
Scribe's libretto for Boieldieu's opera *La Dame Blanche*. France. 1825. Lang.: Fre.
4009
Performance/production
Productions of Boieldieu's *La Dame Blanche*. 1825-1997. Lang.: Fre.
4074

Listing and evaluation of complete recordings of Boieldieu's *La Dame Blanche*. 1961-1996. Lang.: Fre.
4091

Interview with conductor Marc Minkowski. Europe. 1997. Lang.: Fre.
4124

Analysis of the original production book of *Un Ballo in Maschera*. Italy: Milan. 1856-1888. Lang.: Eng.
4197
Plays/librettos/scripts
Background information on Bellini's *La Sonnambula*: sleep disorders. Europe. 1831. Lang.: Fre.
4286

Franz Liszt's comments on *La Dame Blanche* by Boieldieu. Europe. 1825-1854. Lang.: Fre.
4288

Sources of Bellini's opera *La Sonnambula*. Italy. France. 1831. Lang.: Fre.
4307

Sea of Faces
Performance/production
Collection of newspaper reviews by London theatre critics. UK-England: London. 1997. Lang.: Eng.
2004

Seagull, The
SEE
Čajka.

Seal Wife, The
Performance/production
Collection of newspaper reviews by London theatre critics. UK-England: London. 1997. Lang.: Eng.
1989

Collection of newspaper reviews by London theatre critics. UK-England: London. 1997. Lang.: Eng.
1997

Seattle Children's Theatre (Seattle, WA)
Performance/production
Seattle Children's Theatre's production of *Bunnicula*. USA: Seattle, WA. 1979-1996. Lang.: Eng.
2311

Seattle Repertory Theatre (Seattle, WA)
Institutions
Seattle's theatrical renaissance. USA: Seattle, WA. 1980-1997. Lang.: Eng.
396

Second Maiden's Tragedy, The
Plays/librettos/scripts
Possible revisions by Shakespeare to *The Second Maiden's Tragedy* by Thomas Middleton. England. 1611-1991. Lang.: Eng.
2707

Second Shepherd's Play
SEE
Secundum Pastorum.

Second Stage Theatre (New York, NY)
Design/technology
Dennis Parichy's lighting design for *Sympathetic Magic* by Lanford Wilson at Second Stage. USA: New York, NY. 1997. Lang.: Eng. 1369

Seconde Surprise de l'amour, La (Second Surprise of Love, The)
Plays/librettos/scripts
Adaptations of French classics for contemporary audiences. Canada: Montreal, PQ. France. 1997. Lang.: Fre.
2421

Secret de l'Aiguille creuse, Le (Secret of the Hollow Needle, The)
Basic theatrical documents
Text of *Le Secret de l'Aiguille creuse (The Secret of the Hollow Needle)*, Gilles Gleizes' adaptation of an Arsène Lupin mystery novel. France. 1996. Lang.: Fre.
1273

Secret Is Out, The
Plays/librettos/scripts
West African popular theatre: texts and analysis. Ghana. Togo. Nigeria. 1995-1997. Lang.: Eng.
2866

Secret Rapture, The
Performance/production
Directing *The Secret Rapture* by David Hare. UK-England. 1988-1995. Lang.: Eng.
2206
Plays/librettos/scripts
Nostalgia and morality in plays of David Hare. UK-England: London. 1947-1997. Lang.: Eng.
3113

Secundum Pastorum (Second Shepherd's Play, The)
Plays/librettos/scripts
Subjectivity and discourse in medieval and early modern drama. England. 1250-1642. Lang.: Eng.
2579

Seed Carriers, The
Performance/production
Collection of newspaper reviews by London theatre critics. UK-England: London. 1997. Lang.: Eng.
1988

Seeking the Genesis
Plays/librettos/scripts
Interview with playwright Kia Corthron. USA. 1997. Lang.: Eng. 3162

Seidel, Georg
Plays/librettos/scripts
Analysis of plays by Georg Seidel. Germany. 1980-1990. Lang.: Ger.
2847

Sejanus
Plays/librettos/scripts
The domination of a king by his counselors in Jacobean political tragedy. England: London. 1603-1610. Lang.: Eng.
2448

Sekhon, Parminder
Performance/production
Collection of newspaper reviews by London theatre critics. UK-England: London. 1997. Lang.: Eng.
2055

Selby, Charles
Performance/production
Metatheatricality in melodrama. UK-England. 1840-1900. Lang.: Eng.
618

Selch, Grant Melville
Performance/production
Puppeteer Grant Melville Selch, the 'Puppeteering Parson'. USA. 1997. Lang.: Eng.
4389

Šeligo, Rudi
Basic theatrical documents
English translations of plays by contemporary Slovenian playwrights. Slovenia. 1980-1997. Lang.: Eng.
1301

Selimovic, Jasenko
Performance/production
Plays based on refugee experiences. Sweden: Gothenburg. 1997. Lang.: Swe.
1927

Sellars, Peter
Performance/production
Opera productions from Salzburger Festspiele. Austria: Salzburg. 1997. Lang.: Ger.
4096

Peter Sellars' production of Ligeti's *Le Grand Macabre* at the Salzburg Festival. Austria: Salzburg. 1997. Lang.: Fre.
4099

Selzer, Richard
Basic theatrical documents
Text of *A Question of Mercy* by David Rabe. USA: New York, NY. 1997. Lang.: Eng.
1340

Semiotics
Audience
Reality and fictionality in theatre in education. UK-England. 1960-1994. Lang.: Eng.
1253
Performance/production
Twentieth-century theatre as a signifying practice. Europe. North America. 1900-1995. Lang.: Eng.
515

Intercultural signs in Mnouchkine's *Les Atrides (The Atridae)*, Théâtre du Soleil. France: Paris. 1990-1997. Lang.: Eng.
1679

Hartmut Wickert's production of Handke's *The Hour We Knew Nothing of Each Other*. Germany: Hannover. 1993. Lang.: Eng.
1728

Hanan Snir's productions of Lorca's *Blood Wedding (Bodas de sangre)*. Israel: Tel Aviv. 1990. Lang.: Eng.
1791

The role of the implied spectator in productions of Omri Nitzan and Hillel Mittelpunkt. Israel: Tel Aviv. 1993. Lang.: Eng.
1792
Plays/librettos/scripts
Non-linear approaches to the reading of texts. Canada. 1997. Lang.: Fre.
2419

Analysis of Middleton's *Women Beware Women* and its adaptation by Howard Barker. England. 1621-1986. Lang.: Eng.
2666

Ibsen and early modernist theatre. Finland. 1885-1905. Lang.: Eng.
2801

Shakespeare, William: Part 1 — cont'd

Shakespeare, William: Part 1 — cont'd

Gendered power relations, law, and revenge in early English drama. England. 1590-1640. Lang.: Eng. 2540

Economic metaphors in Shakespeare's Lancastrian tetralogy. England. 1595-1599. Lang.: Eng. 2542

The date of composition of Shakespeare's *The Merry Wives of Windsor.* England. 1597-1602. Lang.: Eng. 2547

New world adaptations of Shakespeare's *The Tempest.* England. Latin America. Caribbean. 1612-1994. Lang.: Eng. 2549

The importance of gender in Shakespeare's *Titus Andronicus.* England. 1590-1594. Lang.: Eng. 2556

Analysis of Shakespeare's *Hamlet.* England. 1600. Lang.: Slo. 2558

The metaphor of Icarus in Shakespeare's plays about Henry VI. England. 1589-1595. Lang.: Eng. 2562

The myth of Narcissus and Shakespeare's *Antony and Cleopatra.* England. 1607. Lang.: Eng. 2564

Shakespeare's dramatization of the effects of gender bias on both sexes. England. 1604-1613. Lang.: Eng. 2565

Social practice and convention in Tudor-Stuart drama. England. 1571-1670. Lang.: Eng. 2567

Social practice and theatrical meaning in Shakespeare's *Measure for Measure.* England. 1604. Lang.: Eng. 2568

Homoerotic desire in Elizabethan theatre. England. 1580-1620. Lang.: Eng. 2569

Gender and racial politics in Shakespeare's *Othello.* England. 1605. Lang.: Eng. 2572

Shakespeare's *Antony and Cleopatra* as a romance. England. 1607. Lang.: Eng. 2578

Argument for 1595 as the date of composition of Shakespeare's *Romeo and Juliet.* England. 1595-1596. Lang.: Eng. 2581

Dance in Shakespeare's plays, especially *A Midsummer Night's Dream.* England. 1594-1595. Lang.: Eng. 2585

Legitimacy and illegitimacy in Shakespeare's *Richard III.* England. 1593. Lang.: Eng. 2588

Educated women and the plays of Shakespeare. England. 1596-1603. Lang.: Eng. 2594

The 'bad quartos' of *The Merry Wives of Windsor* as abridged touring editions. England. 1597-1619. Lang.: Eng. 2598

Verbal contracts in Shakespeare's *Cymbeline.* England. 1608-1610. Lang.: Eng. 2600

Male patronage and maternal power in Shakespeare's *Timon of Athens.* England. 1607-1608. Lang.: Eng. 2603

Sexual slander in early modern England and Shakespeare's *The Winter's Tale.* England. 1536-1610. Lang.: Eng. 2604

Class and sex in the plays of Shakespeare. England. 1592-1616. Lang.: Eng. 2605

The evolution of the character Gertrude in versions of Shakespeare's *Hamlet.* England. 1600-1604. Lang.: Eng. 2608

Narcissism in Renaissance tragedy. England. 1450-1580. Lang.: Eng. 2609

Excessive violence and political power in plays of Shakespeare. England. 1604-1611. Lang.: Eng. 2610

Metaphor and reality in Shakespeare's *Titus Andronicus.* England. 1590-1594. Lang.: Eng. 2611

Violence and representation in Renaissance literature. England. 1590-1610. Lang.: Eng. 2614

Shakespeare's Roman history plays in the context of contemporary history and politics. England. 1599-1608. Lang.: Eng. 2615

Significant textual variants in Shakespeare's *King Lear* III.i. England. 1605-1623. Lang.: Eng. 2619

Proposed later date for a passage in Shakespeare's *Hamlet.* England. 1601-1709. Lang.: Eng. 2621

Shakespeare's *Henry VIII* and the debasement of honorable titles. England. 1612-1613. Lang.: Eng. 2624

Representations of class in the plays of Shakespeare. England: London. 1590-1613. Lang.: Eng. 2631

The death of the heroine in Shakespeare's *Antony and Cleopatra.* England. 1607. Lang.: Eng. 2634

Shakespeare's *Henry VI* and treason trials. England. 1585-1592. Lang.: Eng. 2635

The source of Shakespeare's *Titus Andronicus.* England. 1550-1594. Lang.: Eng. 2636

Rhetoric and subversion in *The Two Noble Kinsmen* by Shakespeare and Fletcher. England. 1612-1613. Lang.: Eng. 2637

Psychoanalysis of racism in Shakespeare's *Othello.* England. 1604. Lang.: Eng. 2639

Shakespeare's frequent use of oxymoron in *Romeo and Juliet.* England. 1595-1596. Lang.: Eng. 2641

Women's silence in Renaissance drama. England. 1601-1613. Lang.: Eng. 2642

Politeness in Shakespeare's *Henry VIII.* England. 1612-1613. Lang.: Eng. 2644

Psychological analysis of Antony in Shakespeare's *Antony and Cleopatra.* England. 1607. Lang.: Eng. 2647

Religion in Shakespeare's *Hamlet.* England. 1601. Lang.: Eng. 2651

Women disguised as men in seventeenth-century drama. England. 1602-1674. Lang.: Eng. 2653

Gender and performance in Shakespeare's *All's Well That Ends Well.* England. 1602-1603. Lang.: Eng. 2655

The idea of nationhood in Shakespeare's *Henry V.* England. 1599. Lang.: Eng. 2656

Principles of Shakespearean dramaturgy. England. 1590-1613. Lang.: Eng. 2658

Business and law in Shakespeare's *The Merchant of Venice.* England. 1596. Lang.: Eng. 2659

Visual imagery and the two queens in Shakespeare's *Henry VIII.* England. 1612-1613. Lang.: Eng. 2660

Shakespeare's *Cymbeline* and early modern English nationalism. England. 1609-1610. Lang.: Eng. 2662

The depiction of Roman characters in Shakespeare's history plays. England. 1599-1608. Lang.: Eng. 2663

The poetics of vision in tragedies of Shakespeare. England. 1600-1606. Lang.: Ita. 2667

Comparison of Shakespeare's *King John* and Bale's *King Johan.* England. 1539-1596. Lang.: Eng. 2668

Comparison of Shakespeare's *Henry V* and Plutarch's account of Alexander the Great. England. 1599. Lang.: Eng. 2669

Ambivalence toward a female sovereign reflected in plays of Shakespeare and Middleton. England. 1600-1607. Lang.: Eng. 2672

The forced marriage plot in early English drama. England. 1584-1642. Lang.: Eng. 2675

Dramatic representations of spectatorship. England: London. 1580-1642. Lang.: Eng. 2676

Madness and gender in the plays of Shakespeare. England. 1589-1613. Lang.: Eng. 2677

The English view of Ireland reflected in Shakespeare's history plays. England. 1590-1599. Lang.: Eng. 2678

Analysis of Shakespeare's *Othello.* England. 1604. Lang.: Eng. 2679

Woman as commodity in Shakespeare's *The Merchant of Venice.* England. 1596. Lang.: Eng. 2680

Love and sex in Shakespeare's *Troilus and Cressida.* England. 1601-1602. Lang.: Eng. 2686

Shakespeare's *Othello* and early modern precepts of wifely conduct. England. 1605. Lang.: Eng. 2687

Analysis and bibliography of performance editions of Shakespeare's *Twelfth Night.* England. 1774-1992. Lang.: Eng. 2688

The significance of early performance editions of Shakespeare's plays. England. 1589-1613. Lang.: Eng. 2689

Love lyrics in Shakespeare's comedies. England. 1590-1613. Lang.: Eng. 2691

Russia in Shakespeare's *The Winter's Tale.* England. Russia. 1610-1611. Lang.: Eng. 2692

The influence of Plato's *Republic* on Shakespeare's *Julius Caesar.* England. 1599. Lang.: Eng. 2694

Analysis of Shakespeare's *Love's Labour's Lost.* England. 1593. Lang.: Eng. 2695

Blood and bleeding in Shakespeare's *Julius Caesar.* England. 1599. Lang.: Eng. 2696

Homosexual friendship in plays of Shakespeare, Fletcher, and Marlowe. England. 1595-1613. Lang.: Eng. 2697

Shakespeare's characterization of Richard of Gloucester in *Richard III* and *Henry VI.* England. 1590-1593. Lang.: Eng. 2698

Shakespeare, William: Part 1 — cont'd

Aging in plays of Shakespeare. England. 1590-1613. Lang.: Eng. 2700

Shakespeare's Falstaff and Puritanism. England. 1596-1599. Lang.: Eng. 2701

Analysis of a crux in Shakespeare's *Romeo and Juliet*. England. 1595-1596. Lang.: Eng. 2703

Shakespearean tragedies and history plays and the possible roles for women. England. 1589-1613. Lang.: Eng. 2704

The gift and money economies in plays of Shakespeare. England. 1590-1613. Lang.: Eng. 2706

Possible revisions by Shakespeare to *The Second Maiden's Tragedy* by Thomas Middleton. England. 1611-1991. Lang.: Eng. 2707

Orlando Furioso as a source for Shakespeare's *Much Ado About Nothing*. England. 1591. Lang.: Eng. 2710

Marital equality and subordination in Shakespeare's *Othello* and Webster's *The Duchess of Malfi*. England. 1605-1613. Lang.: Eng. 2715

Witchcraft and female sexuality in the plays of Shakespeare. England. 1590-1613. Lang.: Eng. 2717

Shakespeare's *The Merry Wives of Windsor* and the law of fraudulent conveyance. England. 1596-1603. Lang.: Eng. 2718

The meaning of dismemberment in Shakespeare's *Titus Andronicus*. England. 1590-1594. Lang.: Eng. 2720

The meaning of 'goodyear' in Shakespeare's plays. England. 1590-1616. Lang.: Eng. 2721

Suicide in English Renaissance tragedy. England. 1590-1625. Lang.: Eng. 2724

Biographical information in Shakespeare's plays and sonnets. England. 1591-1616. Lang.: Eng. 2725

The idea of the self in the English Renaissance. England. 1580-1620. Lang.: Eng. 2728

Analysis of a line from Shakespeare's *King Lear*. England. 1605-1606. Lang.: Eng. 2729

Defense of Shakespeare's *Pericles*. England. 1607-1609. Lang.: Eng. 2730

Cross-dressed heroines in works of Shakespeare and Spenser. England. 1590-1596. Lang.: Eng. 2731

Masculinity and feminine disruption in Shakespeare's history plays. England. 1590-1599. Lang.: Eng. 2732

Substitution and delay in Shakespeare's *All's Well That Ends Well*. England. 1599-1600. Lang.: Eng. 2738

The importance of names in Shakespeare's *All's Well That Ends Well*. England. 1602-1603. Lang.: Eng. 2739

Masculine and feminine men in Shakespeare's *Troilus and Cressida*. England. 1601-1602. Lang.: Eng. 2741

Feminist analysis of female characters in Shakespearean tragedy. England. 1589-1613. Lang.: Eng. 2743

Social mobility in Jacobean drama. England. 1618-1640. Lang.: Eng. 2745

Literary closure in comedies of Shakespeare. England. 1595-1605. Lang.: Eng. 2747

Unconventional relationships in Shakespeare's *Love's Labour's Lost*. England. 1593. Lang.: Eng. 2749

Shakespeare's *Merry Wives of Windsor* as a comedy of humors. England. 1597. Lang.: Eng. 2755

Law, justice, and criminology in plays of Shakespeare. England. 1590-1613. Lang.: Eng. 2756

Rhetoric and Shakespeare's *Troilus and Cressida*. England. 1601-1602. Lang.: Eng. 2759

Death, immortality and punishment in plays of Shakespeare. England. 1590-1616. Lang.: Eng. 2762

The sympathetic villain on the early modern stage. England. 1594-1621. Lang.: Eng. 2763

The conflict between body and speech in Shakespeare's *Coriolanus*. England. 1608. Lang.: Eng. 2764

Transvestism, desire, and psychosexual displacement in early modern theatre. England. 1590-1619. Lang.: Eng. 2766

Analysis of versions of Shakespeare's *Hamlet*. England. 1600-1623. Lang.: Eng. 2767

Poetry and action in Shakespeare's *Romeo and Juliet*. England. 1595-1596. Lang.: Eng. 2771

Analysis of Prince Hal in Shakespeare's *Henry IV*, Parts 1 and 2. England. 1596-1597. Lang.: Eng. 2773

The evolving notion of performance in the plays of Shakespeare. England. 1592-1616. Lang.: Eng. 2776

The enclosure of the commons reflected in Shakespeare's *As You Like It*. England. 1598-1600. Lang.: Eng. 2777

The difference between reading and hearing Shakespeare. England. 1590-1613. Lang.: Eng. 2779

Implications of mirth in plays of Shakespeare and Middleton. England. 1594-1605. Lang.: Eng. 2780

Shakespeare's *King Lear* as a reaction to the death of Elizabeth I. England. 1605. Lang.: Eng. 2781

Male and female Renaissance writers. Europe. 1400-1590. Lang.: Eng. 2785

Comparison of classical Roman, Renaissance Italian, and Shakespearean treatments of similar stories. Europe. 200 B.C.-1610 A.D. Lang.: Eng. 2799

Analysis of Sophocles' and Smole's treatments of Antigone and Shakespeare's *Hamlet*. Slovenia. 500 B.C.-1960 A.D. Lang.: Slo. 3005

The debate over different versions of Shakespeare's *Troilus and Cressida*. UK-England. 1995. Lang.: Eng. 3093

Analysis of opera librettos by Boito, Da Ponte, and Gertrude Stein. Europe. 1770-1915. Lang.: Eng. 4289

Reference materials

1992 Shakespeare bibliography. 1992. Lang.: Eng. 3312

1994 Shakespeare bibliography. 1994. Lang.: Eng. 3313

1993 Shakespeare bibliography. 1993. Lang.: Eng. 3314

1991 Shakespeare bibliography. 1991. Lang.: Eng. 3316

1986 annual Shakespeare bibliography. 1986. Lang.: Eng. 3317

Relation to other fields

Shakespeare as a character in fiction and drama, and as a subject of biography. UK-England. 1987. Lang.: Eng. 786

Desire in Shakespeare's poem 'Venus and Adonis'. England. 1593. Lang.: Eng. 3326

Information on the father of William Shakespeare. England: Stratford, Warwickshire. 1592. Lang.: Eng. 3328

Disputes the recent attribution of the lyric poem 'Shall I Die' to Shakespeare. England. 1604-1637. Lang.: Eng. 3332

Shakespeare in the college classroom. England. 1997. Lang.: Eng. 3334

Analysis of sonnets to determine Shakespearean authorship. England. 1599-1616. Lang.: Eng. 3341

Patriarchal response to the violent woman and Shakespeare's poem 'The Rape of Lucrece'. England. 1592-1595. Lang.: Eng. 3342

The Ashbourne portrait, formerly believed to be of William Shakespeare. England. 1611-1979. Lang.: Eng. 3343

Approaches to teaching Shakespeare. Israel: Tel Aviv. 1993-1995. Lang.: Eng. 3372

Teaching Shakespeare at the University of Haifa. Israel: Haifa. 1994. Lang.: Eng. 3373

Füssli's Shakespearean paintings: exhibition catalogue. Switzerland. 1775-1825. Lang.: Ita. 3379

Shakespeare's influence on nineteenth-century authors. UK-England. 1840-1870. Lang.: Eng. 3385

Shakespeare's influence on detective fiction. USA. UK-England. 1995. Lang.: Eng. 3389

Evaluation of educational technology for the teaching of Shakespeare. USA. 1997. Lang.: Eng. 3390

Comparing video versions of *Macbeth* in the classroom. USA. 1997. Lang.: Eng. 3391

Pros and cons of using film and video in teaching Shakespeare. USA. 1995. Lang.: Eng. 3392

Race, *Othello*, and the high school classroom. USA. 1997. Lang.: Eng. 3394

Teaching Shakespeare's *King Lear*. USA. 1997. Lang.: Eng. 3395

Film as a way of enhancing student understanding of Shakespeare. USA. 1995. Lang.: Eng. 3396

The use of film and video to teach the plays of Shakespeare. USA. 1997. Lang.: Eng. 3398

Using video to teach Shakespeare's *Julius Caesar*. USA. 1997. Lang.: Eng. 3399

Review of teaching texts of Shakespeare's *King Lear*. USA. 1995. Lang.: Eng. 3400

SUBJECT INDEX

Shakespeare, William: Part 1 — cont'd

Teaching Shakespeare and the World Wide Web. USA. 1997. Lang.:
Eng. 3404

Teaching Shakespeare with the aid of the internet. USA. 1997. Lang.:
Eng. 3407

Feminist and performance techniques for teaching Shakespeare's
Hamlet. USA. 1997. Lang.: Eng. 3408

Teaching students to distinguish between action and narrative in
Shakespeare. USA. 1995. Lang.: Eng. 3410

The sense of wonder and the teaching of Shakespeare's *Hamlet.* USA.
UK-England. 1995. Lang.: Eng. 3412

Nontraditional methods of teaching Shakespeare's *Romeo and Juliet.*
USA. 1997. Lang.: Eng. 3414

Teaching a scene from *Hamlet* using different interpretations on video.
USA. 1997. Lang.: Eng. 3415

Using video to teach Shakespeare's *Henry V.* USA. 1997. Lang.: Eng.
3417

Informal survey of high school teachers of Shakespeare. USA. 1995.
Lang.: Eng. 3421

Teaching Shakespeare through educational programs at theatres and
festivals. USA. 1997. Lang.: Eng. 3422

Review of books on teaching Shakespeare. USA. 1995. Lang.: Eng. 3424

The multicultural classroom and the teaching of Shakespeare. USA.
1995. Lang.: Eng. 3428

Teaching Shakespeare in dramatic fashion. USA. 1995. Lang.: Eng. 3429

Using historical fiction as background for the teaching of Shakespeare.
USA. 1985. Lang.: Eng. 3430

Teaching Shakespeare in the high-tech classroom. USA. 1997. Lang.:
Eng. 3431

The benefits of performing Shakespeare in the classroom. USA. 1995.
Lang.: Eng. 3432

Process drama in the classroom and the teaching of Shakespeare. USA.
1997. Lang.: Eng. 3439

Research/historiography

The debate over a signature attributed to William Shakespeare. USA:
Washington, DC. 1938-1992. Lang.: Eng. 3452

Theory/criticism

New historicism, feminist criticism, and gender roles in Renaissance
literature. USA. UK-England. 1987. Lang.: Eng. 916

Shakespeare and performance theory. 1996. Lang.: Eng. 3455

New historicist criticism of Shakespeare's *The Tempest.* 1985-1989.
Lang.: Eng. 3461

Shakespeare, textual authority, and contemporary performance. 1977-
1996. Lang.: Eng. 3463

A critic's approach to the Stratford Festival. Canada: Stratford, ON.
1993. Lang.: Eng. 3465

Career of Samuel Badcock, literary critic. England. 1779-1789. Lang.:
Eng. 3471

Racism, *Othello,* and South African criticism. England. South Africa,
Republic of. 1604-1987. Lang.: Eng. 3473

Feminist disenchantment with Shakespeare. USA. 1950-1956. Lang.:
Eng. 3500

Shakespeare, William: Part 2

Administration

Philip Henslowe's move from the Rose to the Fortune. England:
London. 1576-1616. Lang.: Eng. 20

Audience

Audience reception of Shakespeare productions in Quebec. Canada.
1978-1993. Lang.: Eng. 1246

Basic theatrical documents

Text of *Love in a Forest,* an adaptation of *As You Like It* by Charles
Johnson. England. 1723. Lang.: Eng. 1265

Design/technology

Ariel's costume in the original staging of *The Tempest.* England:
London. 1570-1612. Lang.: Eng. 156

Technical designs for the Shakespearean musical *Play On!.* USA: San
Diego, CA. 1997. Lang.: Eng. 3921

Institutions

Profile of the International Shakespeare Association. UK-England:
Stratford. 1997. Lang.: Eng. 386

The rise of the Shakespeare theatre festival. Europe. USA. Canada.
1946-1997. Lang.: Eng. 1402

Management and productions of Schauspiel Nürnberg. Germany:
Nuremberg. 1997. Lang.: Ger. 1431

The first season of Shakespeare's Globe Theatre. UK-England: London.
1996. Lang.: Swe. 1495

The newly founded Shakespeare Society. USA: New York, NY. 1997.
Lang.: Eng. 1508

Record of Shakespearean studies seminar. USA: New York, NY.
England. 1997. Lang.: Eng. 1514

Minutes of Columbia University Seminar on Shakespeare. USA: New
York, NY. 1997. Lang.: Eng. 1515

Performance spaces

Totus Mundus Agit Histrionem—the motto of Drury Lane, not the
Globe. England: London. 1599-1720. Lang.: Eng. 425

Shakespeare's plays on the Elizabethan stage. England. 1590-1615.
Lang.: Eng. 1520

History of attempt to reconstruct the Globe Theatre. England: London.
1599-1995. Lang.: Eng. 1522

The debate over the stage design and pillars of Shakespeare's Globe.
England: London. 1599-1995. Lang.: Eng. 1525

The archaeological excavation of the original Globe Theatre. UK-
England: London. 1989. Lang.: Eng. 1532

Details of the timber framing of Shakespeare's Globe Theatre. UK-
England: London. 1992-1996. Lang.: Eng. 1536

The inaugural season of the rebuilt Shakespeare's Globe. UK-England:
London. 1997. Lang.: Eng. 1539

Profile of Shakespeare's Globe Theatre. UK-England: London. 1970.
Lang.: Swe. 1541

Work of historical adviser to Shakespeare's Globe project. UK-England:
London. 1979. Lang.: Eng. 1542

The interior design of Shakespeare's Globe Theatre. UK-England:
London. 1992-1996. Lang.: Eng. 1543

Sam Wanamaker and the rebuilding of Shakespeare's Globe. UK-
England: London. 1997. Lang.: Eng. 1546

Account of Shakespeare's Globe Theatre. UK-England: London. 1997.
Lang.: Fre. 1547

Performance/production

Performances of Shakespeare's *Twelfth Night* as objects of study.
England. 1808-1850. Lang.: Eng. 508

Textual versions and revisions as reflections of performances. England.
1590-1615. Lang.: Eng. 511

Interview with Norbert Kentrup of Bremer Shakespeare Company.
Germany: Bremen. 1983-1997. Lang.: Ger. 540

Northern and southern reactions to Edwin Booth's production of
Shakespeare's *Richard II.* USA. 1865-1875. Lang.: Eng. 675

Framing, montage, and race in works of Shakespeare, Baraka, and
Eisenstein. 1997. Lang.: Eng. 1548

Production history of Shakespeare's *A Midsummer Night's Dream.* 1594-
1995. Lang.: Eng. 1552

The 'authority' of Shakespearean texts and performances. 1590-1997.
Lang.: Eng. 1553

Interview with director John Bell. Australia: Melbourne. 1995. Lang.:
Eng. 1558

Interview with director and adaptor Robert Lepage. Canada. 1992-1997.
Lang.: Ger, Fre, Dut, Eng. 1594

As You Like It and the Chamberlain's Men's move to the Globe.
England: London. 1594-1612. Lang.: Eng. 1619

Hoods and masks in the original production of Shakespeare's *Measure
for Measure.* England: London. 1555-1604. Lang.: Eng. 1626

The Globe Theatre and the plays performed there. England: London.
1599-1613. Lang.: Eng. 1629

Research on Shakespeare's memory of roles. England. 1996. Lang.: Eng.
1633

As You Like It, transvestism, and early modern sexual politics. England.
1599. Lang.: Eng. 1636

Recent productions of Elizabethan theatre. Europe. 1997. Lang.: Ger.
1649

The map of England in productions of Shakespeare's *King Lear.*
Europe. USA. 1909-1994. Lang.: Eng. 1650

Shakespearean commentary and the relationship between actors and
academics. Europe. North America. 1985-1996. Lang.: Eng. 1652

German theatre during and after the Nazi period. Germany: Berlin,
Dusseldorf. Switzerland: Zurich. 1933-1952. Lang.: Eng. 1704

Recent activities and productions of Schauspielhaus Rostock. Germany:
Rostock. 1994-1997. Lang.: Ger. 1711

494 International Bibliography of Theatre: 1997

Shakespeare, William: Part 2 — cont'd

Plays/librettos/scripts

Shakespeare, William: Part 2 — cont'd

Shakespeare, William: Part 2 — cont'd

Shakespeare, William: Part 2 — cont'd

Suggestions for effective writing assignments in teaching Shakespeare. USA. 1997. Lang.: Eng. 3437

Whole-language approach to teaching Shakespeare's comedies. USA. 1997. Lang.: Eng. 3438

Shakespeare, Hollywood, and American cultural ambivalence. USA. 1990-1997. Lang.: Eng. 3693

Shakespeare: The Animated Tales: educational videos, based on Shakespeare's plays. UK. Russia. 1991-1997. Lang.: Ger. 3741

Research/historiography

Renaissance drama, censorship, and contemporary historical methods. England: London. 1588-1980. Lang.: Eng. 3446

Theory/criticism

Survey of postmodern Shakespearean criticism. 1997. Lang.: Eng. 3453

The function of evidence in structuring Shakespearean criticism. 1997. Lang.: Eng. 3454

The effect of contemporary theory on the teaching of Shakespeare. 1997. Lang.: Eng. 3457

Shakespeare, *The Tempest*, and colonialist ideology. 1997. Lang.: Eng. 3458

The lacunae of contemporary Shakespeare scholarship. 1997. Lang.: Eng. 3460

Othello, censorship, and public swearing. England: London. 1215-1622. Lang.: Eng. 3470

Nietzsche, *Hamlet*, and modern criticism. England. Germany. 1601-1997. Lang.: Eng. 3472

John Kynaston, literary critic. England. 1728-1783. Lang.: Eng. 3474

The theatrical representation of death in the context of contemporary theory. Europe. 1997. Lang.: Eng. 3477

New media, transnationalism, and Shakespearean criticism. Europe. 1990-1994. Lang.: Eng. 3479

Spirituality and consciousness in Western theatre. Europe. North America. 1900-1996. Lang.: Eng. 3480

The relationship between theatre and criticism, originals and derivatives. France. 1997. Lang.: Eng. 3488

Early twentieth-century views on the authorship of Shakespearean plays. UK-England. 1908-1930. Lang.: Eng. 3496

Queer criticism of Shakespeare. UK-England. 1997. Lang.: Eng. 3497

Shakespeare and the 'spirit of history'. USA. 1800-1997. Lang.: Ger, Fre, Dut, Eng. 3501

Training

Voice training, Shakespeare, and feminism. UK-England. USA. 1973-1994. Lang.: Eng. 3509

Shakespeare: The Animated Tales

Performance/production

The power of images to communicate the plays in *Shakespeare: The Animated Tales*. Russia. 1997. Lang.: Eng. 3721

Analysis of cartoon adaptation for children: *Shakespeare: The Animated Tales*. UK. Russia. 1992. Lang.: Eng. 3723

Relation to other fields

Shakespeare: The Animated Tales: educational videos, based on Shakespeare's plays. UK. Russia. 1991-1997. Lang.: Ger. 3741

Shakespeare's Globe Theatre (London)

Institutions

OISTAT's meeting on Shakespeare's Globe Theatre. UK-England: London. 1996. Lang.: Swe. 389

The first season of Shakespeare's Globe Theatre. UK-England: London. 1996. Lang.: Swe. 1495

Performance spaces

History of attempt to reconstruct the Globe Theatre. England: London. 1599-1995. Lang.: Eng. 1522

The debate over the stage design and pillars of Shakespeare's Globe. England: London. 1599-1995. Lang.: Eng. 1525

The structural design of Shakespeare's Globe. UK-England: London. 1997. Lang.: Eng. 1531

The archaeological excavation of the original Globe Theatre. UK-England: London. 1989. Lang.: Eng. 1532

The design process in the rebuilding of the Globe Theatre. UK-England: London. 1980-1995. Lang.: Eng. 1535

Details of the timber framing of Shakespeare's Globe Theatre. UK-England: London. 1992-1996. Lang.: Eng. 1536

Possible stagings at the reconstructed Shakespeare's Globe Theatre. UK-England: London. 1995-1996. Lang.: Eng. 1537

Iconography and the interior design of Shakespeare's Globe Theatre. UK-England: London. 1992-1996. Lang.: Eng. 1538

The inaugural season of the rebuilt Shakespeare's Globe. UK-England: London. 1997. Lang.: Eng. 1539

Critique of the architecture of the restored Shakespeare's Globe Theatre. UK-England: London. 1997. Lang.: Eng. 1540

Profile of Shakespeare's Globe Theatre. UK-England: London. 1970. Lang.: Swe. 1541

Work of historical adviser to Shakespeare's Globe project. UK-England: London. 1979. Lang.: Eng. 1542

The interior design of Shakespeare's Globe Theatre. UK-England: London. 1992-1996. Lang.: Eng. 1543

Artistic policy and practices of Shakespeare's Globe Theatre. UK-England: London. 1996. Lang.: Eng. 1544

The reconstruction of the Globe Theatre. UK-England: London. 1985-1997. Lang.: Dut. 1545

Sam Wanamaker and the rebuilding of Shakespeare's Globe. UK-England: London. 1997. Lang.: Eng. 1546

Account of Shakespeare's Globe Theatre. UK-England: London. 1997. Lang.: Fre. 1547

Performance/production

Collection of newspaper reviews by London theatre critics. UK-England: London. 1997. Lang.: Eng. 2060

Collection of newspaper reviews by London theatre critics. UK-England: London. 1997. Lang.: Eng. 2090

Collection of newspaper reviews by London theatre critics. UK-England. 1997. Lang.: Eng. 2098

Criticism of productions at Shakespeare's Globe Theatre. UK-England: London. 1996. Lang.: Eng. 2187

Mark Rylance of Shakespeare's Globe. UK-England: London. 1997. Lang.: Eng. 2197

Shakuntala

Performance/production

Collection of newspaper reviews by London theatre critics. UK-England: London. 1997. Lang.: Eng. 1996

Shale, Kerry

Performance/production

Collection of newspaper reviews by London theatre critics. UK-England: London. 1997. Lang.: Eng. 2100

Shallow End, The

Performance/production

Collection of newspaper reviews by London theatre critics. UK-England: London. 1997. Lang.: Eng. 2001

Shalwitz, Howard

Design/technology

Scene designs of Neil Patel. USA. 1996. Lang.: Eng. 1373

Shamanism

Performance/production

The development of Japanese theatrical genres. Japan. 500-1997. Lang.: Eng. 1224

Shanahan, Julie

Performance/production

Interviews with members of Tanztheater Wuppertal. Germany: Wuppertal. 1996. Lang.: Eng. 974

Shange, Ntozake

Plays/librettos/scripts

The voices of African-American women. USA. 1840-1994. Lang.: Eng. 3309

Shanghai Opera House

Performance/production

Beijing production of Carmen's *Bizet*. China, People's Republic of: Beijing. 1982-1997. Lang.: Eng. 4117

Sharkey, Stephen

Performance/production

Collection of newspaper reviews by London theatre critics. UK-England: London. 1997. Lang.: Eng. 2024

Sharma, Tripurari

Performance/production

Interviews with writer-directors K.N. Pannikkar, Mahesh Dattani, and Tripurari Sharma. India. 1997. Lang.: Eng. 1781

Shaw, Fiona

Performance/production

Collection of newspaper reviews by London theatre critics. UK-England: London. 1997. Lang.: Eng. 2157

Deborah Warner and Fiona Shaw on their adaptation of *The Waste Land* by T.S. Eliot. USA. UK-England. 1980-1997. Lang.: Eng. 2251

Shaw, George Bernard

Performance spaces

History of attempt to reconstruct the Globe Theatre. England: London. 1599-1995. Lang.: Eng. 1522

Shaw, George Bernard — cont'd

Performance/production

Shaw Festival production of *In Good King Charles's Golden Days.*
Canada: Niagara-on-the-Lake, ON. 1997. Lang.: Eng.   1582

Collection of newspaper reviews by London theatre critics. UK-England:
London. 1997. Lang.: Eng.   1976

Collection of newspaper reviews by London theatre critics. UK-England:
London. 1997. Lang.: Eng.   2035

Collection of newspaper reviews by London theatre critics. UK-England:
London. 1997. Lang.: Eng.   2088

Collection of newspaper reviews by London theatre critics. UK-England.
1997. Lang.: Eng.   2098

Irish plays and characters on the New York stage. USA: New York,
NY. Ireland. 1874-1966. Lang.: Eng.   2277

Plays/librettos/scripts

Theatrical representations of the Holocaust. Europe. North America.
1950-1996. Lang.: Eng.   2789

Women's expanding role in society seen in plays of George Bernard
Shaw. UK-England. 1893-1923. Lang.: Eng.   3091

Critical biography of playwright George Bernard Shaw. UK-England.
1890-1950. Lang.: Eng.   3103

Feminist analysis of Wilde's *Salomé* and Shaw's *Saint Joan.* UK-
England. Ireland. 1891-1923. Lang.: Eng.   3116

Cinematic versions of the Pygmalion myth. USA. 1938. Lang.: Eng.
                                                                      3682

Shaw, Peggy

Performance/production

Essays on gender and performance. 250 B.C.-1995 A.D. Lang.: Eng.
                                                                      1551

Plays/librettos/scripts

Mimesis, feminism, theatre, and performance. USA. 1997. Lang.: Eng.
                                                                      3176

Shaw, Robert

Performance/production

Collection of newspaper reviews by London theatre critics. UK-England:
London. 1997. Lang.: Eng.   2066

Shawn, Wallace

Performance/production

Ross McMillan's performance of *The Fever* by Wallace Shawn. Canada:
Winnipeg, MB. 1997. Lang.: Eng.   1577

Collection of newspaper reviews by London theatre critics. UK-England:
London. 1997. Lang.: Eng.   1974

Plays/librettos/scripts

Analysis of plays by Wallace Shawn. USA. 1970-1996. Lang.: Eng. 3215

The principles of Gertrude Stein in the works of contemporary
playwrights. USA. 1993. Lang.: Eng.   3263

Playwright and actor Wallace Shawn. USA. 1981-1997. Lang.: Eng.
                                                                      3303

Shayna Maidel, A

Plays/librettos/scripts

Texts of plays by Jewish American women. USA. 1985-1995. Lang.:
Eng.   3164

She Knows, You Know!

Performance/production

Collection of newspaper reviews by London theatre critics. UK-England:
London. 1997. Lang.: Eng.   2079

Collection of newspaper reviews by London theatre critics. UK-England:
London. 1997. Lang.: Eng.   2124

Jean Fergusson's *She Knows, You Know!*, about music-hall star Hylda
Baker. UK-England. 1996-1997. Lang.: Eng.   2207

She Would If She Could

Plays/librettos/scripts

Foreshadowing of the comedy of manners in Etherege's *She Would If
She Could.* England. 1670. Lang.: Eng.   2601

She'll Be Wearing Silk Pyjamas

Performance/production

Collection of newspaper reviews by London theatre critics. UK-England:
London. 1997. Lang.: Eng.   2107

Sheader, Timothy

Performance/production

Collection of newspaper reviews by London theatre critics. UK-England:
London. 1997. Lang.: Eng.   2161

Sheen, Michael

Performance/production

Collection of newspaper reviews by London theatre critics. UK-England:
London. 1997. Lang.: Eng.   2016

Sheer Madness

Performance/production

Collection of newspaper reviews by London theatre critics. UK-England:
London. 1997. Lang.: Eng.   2126

Sheikh, Farhana

Performance/production

Collection of newspaper reviews by London theatre critics. UK-England:
London. 1997. Lang.: Eng.   2085

Shelf Life

Performance/production

Collection of newspaper reviews by London theatre critics. UK-England:
London. 1997. Lang.: Eng.   2108

Shepard, Sam

Performance/production

Plays by Shepard and Albee at Nederlands Toneel Gent. Netherlands:
Ghent. 1996. Lang.: Eng.   1825

Interview with actor Per Mattsson. Sweden: Stockholm. 1965. Lang.:
Swe.   1940

The Sam Shepard season of the Signature Theatre Company. USA:
New York, NY. 1976-1997. Lang.: Eng.   2346

Plays/librettos/scripts

Sam Shepard's unproduced film adaptation of *The Changeling* by
Middleton and Rowley. England. USA. 1622-1971. Lang.: Eng.   2490

Plays of Shepard and Mamet and the myth of Narcissus. USA. 1980-
1988. Lang.: Eng.   3152

Subjectivity, ethics, and the body in contemporary drama. USA. Europe.
1940-1990. Lang.: Eng.   3229

Male identity in contemporary American drama. USA. 1915-1995.
Lang.: Eng.   3232

Critical history of American drama. USA. 1960-1997. Lang.: Eng. 3267

Analysis of Sam Shepard's revisions to *Buried Child.* USA. 1975-1996.
Lang.: Eng.   3282

The father-son conflict in plays of Sam Shepard. USA. 1965-1993.
Lang.: Eng.   3288

Analysis of plays of Sam Shepard. USA. 1943-1996. Lang.: Eng.   3295

Plays of cummings, Miller, and Shepard and the American theatrical
aesthetic. USA. 1940-1995. Lang.: Eng.   3304

Postmodernism and Sam Shepard's *True West.* USA. 1997. Lang.: Eng.
                                                                      3305

Shepphard, Nona

Performance/production

Collection of newspaper reviews by London theatre critics. UK-England:
London. 1997. Lang.: Eng.   2154

Sheridan, Frances

Plays/librettos/scripts

Frances Sheridan's *The Discovery* in the context of eighteenth-century
theatre. England. 1740-1780. Lang.: Eng.   2451

Sheridan, Jim

Performance/production

History of Irish filmmaking. Ireland: Dublin. 1896-1996. Lang.: Eng.
                                                                      3578

Sheridan, Richard Brinsley

Performance/production

Collection of newspaper reviews by London theatre critics. UK-England:
London. 1997. Lang.: Eng.   1998

Interview with composer Peter Schickele. USA: New York, NY. 1965-
1997. Lang.: Eng.   2252

Plays/librettos/scripts

Social status in plays of Medwall, Sheridan, and Tyler. England.
Colonial America. 1500-1700. Lang.: Eng.   2559

Sheridan, Thomas

Performance/production

Stage imagery in productions of Shakespeare's *Coriolanus.* England.
1754-1901. Lang.: Eng.   1634

Sherin, Mimi Jordan

Design/technology

Mimi Jordan Sherin's lighting design and use of old instruments for
American Silents and *The Medium.* USA: New York, NY. 1997. Lang.:
Eng.   1379

Sherman, Jason

Basic theatrical documents

Text of *None Is Too Many* by Jason Sherman. Canada. 1997. Lang.:
Eng.   1261

Sherrin, Ned

Performance/production

Collection of newspaper reviews by London theatre critics. UK-England:
London. 1997. Lang.: Eng.   2088

Sherwood, Robert

Performance/production

Collection of newspaper reviews by London theatre critics. UK-England:
London. 1997. Lang.: Eng.   2129

Sierens, Arne
Performance/production
Collection of newspaper reviews by London theatre critics. UK-England:
London. 1997. Lang.: Eng.   2118
Sierra, Roberto
Basic theatrical documents
Text of *Terra Incognita* by Maria Irene Fornes, the libretto for an opera
by Roberto Sierra. USA. 1992. Lang.: Eng.   4017
Siete lunas y un espejo (Seven Moons and a Looking Glass)
Plays/librettos/scripts
Analysis of *Siete lunas y un espejo (Seven Moons and a Looking Glass)*
by Albalucía Angel. Colombia. 1991. Lang.: Spa.   2441
Sifuentes, Roberto
Performance/production
Performance artists Guillermo Gómez-Peña and Roberto Sifuentes.
Mexico. UK-Wales. 1996. Lang.: Eng.   3821

'Confessions' elicited by Guillermo Gómez-Peña and Roberto Sifuentes'
Temple of Confessions. Mexico. 1994-1997. Lang.: Eng.   3822
Siglo de oro
SEE
Geographical-Chronological Index under Spain 1580-1680.
Signature Theatre (Arlington, VA)
Performance/production
Signature Theatre's production of *Three Nights in Tehran* by John
Strand. USA: Arlington, VA. 1986-1997. Lang.: Eng.   2348
Signature Theatre Company (New York, NY)
Design/technology
Lighting designer for Arthur Miller's *The American Clock*, Signature
Theatre Company. USA: New York, NY. 1997. Lang.: Eng.   1371
Performance/production
The Sam Shepard season of the Signature Theatre Company. USA:
New York, NY. 1976-1997. Lang.: Eng.   2346
Silbert, Roxanna
Performance/production
Collection of newspaper reviews by London theatre critics. UK-England:
London. 1997. Lang.: Eng.   2143
Silence
Plays/librettos/scripts
Space in Pinter's dramas, especially *Silence*. UK-England. 1971-1993.
Lang.: Eng.   3074
Silent Time, The
Performance/production
Collection of newspaper reviews by London theatre critics. UK-England:
London. 1997. Lang.: Eng.   2065
Silja, Anja
Performance/production
The role of Marie in Berg's *Wozzeck*. Germany. USA. 1923-1996.
Lang.: Eng.   4145
Sills, Beverly
Performance/production
The difficulty of performing 'Sempre Libera' in Verdi's *La Traviata*.
Italy. USA: New York, NY. 1886-1996. Lang.: Eng.   4186
Silver, Cameron
Performance/production
Successful cabaret performers and their techniques. USA. 1975-1997.
Lang.: Eng.   3780
Silver, Nicky
Performance/production
German productions of plays by Terrence McNally and Nicky Silver.
Germany. 1996-1997. Lang.: Ger.   1721
Plays/librettos/scripts
The popularity in Denmark of playwright Nicky Silver. USA. Denmark.
1994-1997. Lang.: Dan.   3224
Relation to other fields
The effect of AIDS on contemporary drama. USA. 1991-1997. Lang.:
Ger.   3406
Silver, Steve
Performance/production
Collection of newspaper reviews by London theatre critics. UK-England:
London. 1997. Lang.: Eng.   2052
Silverman, Jeffry Lloyd
Basic theatrical documents
Text of *What Comes From Hitting Sticks* by Jeffrey Lloyd Silverman.
USA. 1994-1996. Lang.: Eng.   1342
Simándy, József
Performance/production
Tenor József Simándy. Hungary. 1917-1997. Lang.: Hun.   4170
Simard, Louise
Performance/production
Interview with members of Théâtre Repère. Canada: Quebec, PQ. 1993.
Lang.: Eng.   1596

Simcox, Symantha
Performance/production
Collection of newspaper reviews by London theatre critics. UK-England.
1997. Lang.: Eng.   2082
Simkin, Dmitrij
Performance/production
Performance of the Győri Balett. Hungary. 1997. Lang.: Hun. 1093
Simkins, Michael
Performance/production
Collection of newspaper reviews by London theatre critics. UK-England:
London. 1997. Lang.: Eng.   2007
Simon, Barbara
Performance/production
Collection of newspaper reviews by London theatre critics. UK-England:
London. 1997. Lang.: Eng.   2091
Simon, Barney
Performance/production
Township musical, the Black musical theatre genre. South Africa,
Republic of. 1976-1994. Lang.: Eng.   3941
Plays/librettos/scripts
Interview with Market Theatre actor and playwright Barney Simon.
South Africa, Republic of. 1976-1992. Lang.: Eng.   3027
Simon, Neil
Performance/production
Collection of newspaper reviews by London theatre critics. UK-England:
London. 1997. Lang.: Eng.   2032

Collection of newspaper reviews by London theatre critics. UK-England:
London. 1997. Lang.: Eng.   2099
Simon, Paul
Performance/production
Marc Anthony's role in *The Capeman*. USA. 1968-1997. Lang.: Eng.
                                                             3977
Simon, Yoland
Basic theatrical documents
Text of *Couleur de cerne et de lilas (The Color of Bruises and Lilac)* by
Yoland Simon. France. 1996. Lang.: Fre.   1276
Simone avait des ailes (Simone Had Wings)
Plays/librettos/scripts
Childhood fears in children's plays of Emmanuel Bilodeau and Réjane
Charpentier. Canada: Montreal, PQ. 1996-1997. Lang.: Fre.   2420
Simons, David
Performance/production
Collection of newspaper reviews by London theatre critics. UK-England.
1997. Lang.: Eng.   2142
Simonschek, Peter
Institutions
Interview with actor Peter Simonschek of Schaubühne. Germany: Berlin.
1979-1997. Lang.: Ger.   1411
Simpson, Lee
Performance/production
Collection of newspaper reviews by London theatre critics. UK-England:
London. 1997. Lang.: Eng.   1988

Collection of newspaper reviews by London theatre critics. UK-England:
London. 1997. Lang.: Eng.   2126
Sinclair, Colin
Performance/production
Collection of newspaper reviews by London theatre critics. UK-England:
London. 1997. Lang.: Eng.   2006
Sinclair, Iain
Performance/production
Space in site-specific performance. UK-England. 1960-1997. Lang.: Eng.
                                                             619
Relation to other fields
The influence of topography and geography on the arts. UK-England.
1997. Lang.: Eng.   787
Sing and Dance
Plays/librettos/scripts
Survey of one- or two-character musicals. USA: New York, NY. 1964-
1997. Lang.: Eng.   3989
Singer's Boy
Plays/librettos/scripts
Playwright Leslie Ayvazian. USA: New York, NY. 1995-1997. Lang.:
Eng.   3198
Singh Kalirai, Harmage
Performance/production
Collection of newspaper reviews by London theatre critics. UK-England:
London. 1997. Lang.: Eng.   2025
Singher, Martial
Institutions
Profile of the Music Academy of the West. USA: Santa Barbara, CA.
1946-1997. Lang.: Eng.   4064

Singing

Administration

Opera companies and the practice of hiring celebrity singers. Europe. USA. 1960. Lang.: Swe.   4003

Institutions

Directory of small Canadian opera companies. Canada. 1997. Lang.: Eng.   4040

Profile of the Jussi Björling Museum. Sweden: Borlänge. 1994. Lang.: Swe.   4056

Performance/production

Interviews with singer Magda Varga and her son, actor György Cserhalmi. Hungary. 1922-1996. Lang.: Hun.   551

Interview with dancer Rennie Mirro. Sweden: Stockholm. 1981. Lang.: Swe.   990

Profile of cabaret singer Ute Lemper. Germany. 1986. Lang.: Swe. 3779

A methodology of theatrical creation based on native performance culture. Canada. 1991-1996. Lang.: Eng.   3865

Biography of singer Alla Pugačeva. Russia. 1970-1997. Lang.: Rus. 3876

Materials about singer Alla Pugačeva. Russia. 1970-1997. Lang.: Rus.   3877

HK Gruber on songs of Kurt Weill. Germany. 1997. Lang.: Eng.   3933

Singer Aleksand'r N. Vertinskij. Russia. 1889-1957. Lang.: Rus.   3940

Performer and songwriter Anthony Newley: profile and discography. USA: New York, NY. 1945-1967. Lang.: Eng.   3962

Singer/actress Liliane Montevecchi. USA. France. UK-England. 1933-1996. Lang.: Eng.   3963

Singer/actor Ron Husmann: profile and discography. USA: New York, NY. 1956-1997. Lang.: Eng.   3964

Music hall performer Libby Holman. USA: New York, NY. 1920-1995. Lang.: Eng.   3968

Singer/actress Susan Egan. USA: New York, NY. 1991-1997. Lang.: Eng.   3976

Marc Anthony's role in *The Capeman*. USA. 1968-1997. Lang.: Eng.   3977

Forgotten operas of Donizetti. 1997. Lang.: Eng.   4081

Outstanding performances of Bellini's opera *La sonnambula*. 1831-1984. Lang.: Fre.   4082

Excerpt from memoir of soprano Astrid Varnay. 1918-1997. Lang.: Eng.   4093

Baritone Gino Quilico. Canada. 1970-1997. Lang.: Eng.   4103

Soprano Frances Ginzer. Canada. 1995-1997. Lang.: Eng.   4104

Obituary for soprano Irene Jessner. Canada. 1901-1994. Lang.: Eng.   4105

Baritone James Milligan. Canada. 1928-1961. Lang.: Eng.   4106

Profile of opera singer Béatrice La Palme. Canada. 1898-1919. Lang.: Eng.   4107

Profile of countertenor Daniel Taylor. Canada. 1997. Lang.: Eng.   4108

Lyric tenor Michael Schade. Canada. 1977-1997. Lang.: Eng.   4109

Soprano Manon Feubel. Canada. 1996. Lang.: Eng.   4114

Soprano Isabel Bayrakdarian. Canada. 1997. Lang.: Eng.   4115

Opera singer Luděk Vele. Czech Republic. 1951-1997. Lang.: Cze. 4119

Constance Hausman's performance in Berg's *Lulu*. Denmark: Copenhagen. 1997. Lang.: Eng.   4120

The Giulia Grisi-Pauline Viardot controversy. England: London. 1848-1852. Lang.: Eng.   4122

Comparison of sopranos Astrid Varnay and Birgit Nilsson. Europe. 1918-1973. Lang.: Eng.   4125

Opera singers and the sometimes conflicting demands of the director and the music. Europe. 1597-1997. Lang.: Swe.   4126

Tenor Manuel García the elder and his son. Europe. 1817-1943. Lang.: Eng.   4127

Stylistic similarities in Baroque and nineteenth-century opera. Europe. 1705-1997. Lang.: Eng.   4128

The transposition of pitch in opera singing. Europe. 1900-1997. Lang.: Eng.   4129

Production history of Verdi's *Don Carlo*. Europe. USA. 1867-1997. Lang.: Eng.   4131

List of summer opera festivals. Europe. Asia. 1997. Lang.: Eng.   4134

The premiere of Rossini's *I Puritani*. France: Paris. 1835. Lang.: Eng.   4137

Interpreters of Bizet's heroine Carmen. France: Paris. USA: New York, NY. 1875-1997. Lang.: Eng.   4139

Excerpt from biography of opera singer Mary Garden. France: Paris. 1875-1957. Lang.: Eng.   4144

The role of Marie in Berg's *Wozzeck*. Germany. USA. 1923-1996. Lang.: Eng.   4145

Interview with opera singer Noemi Nadelmann. Germany: Berlin. 1997. Lang.: Ger.   4146

Interview with baritone Falk Struckman. Germany. 1997. Lang.: Eng.   4149

Soprano Waltraud Meier. Germany. 1957-1997. Lang.: Eng.   4153

Interview with soprano Anna Korondi. Germany: Berlin. 1990-1997. Lang.: Hun.   4157

The life of opera singer Wilhelmine Schröder-Devrient. Germany. 1804-1863. Lang.: Eng.   4159

Profile, interview with soprano Hildegard Behrens. Germany. 1997. Lang.: Eng.   4160

Interview with soprano Anna Pánti of the Budapest Opera House. Hungary. 1980-1997. Lang.: Hun.   4164

Soprano Mária Németh. Hungary. 1897-1967. Lang.: Hun.   4165

Soprano and ceramist Etelka Csavlek. Hungary. 1980-1997. Lang.: Hun.   4166

Interview with mezzo-soprano Olga Szőnyi of the Budapest Opera House. Hungary. 1933-1997. Lang.: Hun.   4167

Operatic couple Ferenc Mátray and Ágnes Vámos. Hungary. 1943-1990. Lang.: Hun.   4169

Tenor József Simándy. Hungary. 1917-1997. Lang.: Hun.   4170

The career of tenor Miklós Szabó. Hungary. 1930-1989. Lang.: Hun.   4171

Opera singer Kálmán Gyimesi of the Szeged National Theatre. Hungary. 1945-1997. Lang.: Hun.   4172

Bass Oszkár Kálmán of the Budapest Opera House. Hungary: Budapest. 1887-1971. Lang.: Hun.   4174

The career of tenor János Halmos. Hungary. 1887-1954. Lang.: Hun.   4175

Interview with baritone István Berczelly of the Hungarian State Opera House. Hungary. 1960-1996. Lang.: Hun.   4176

Interview with tenor Róbert Ilosfalvy. Hungary. 1946-1997. Lang.: Hun.   4177

Mezzo-coloratura Katalin Gémes. Hungary. 1988-1997. Lang.: Hun.   4178

Profile of tenor and opera stage director György Anthes. Hungary. 1863-1922. Lang.: Hun.   4179

Profile of soprano Ingrid Kertesi. Hungary. 1970-1997. Lang.: Hun.   4180

Soprano Krisztina Laki. Hungary. 1970-1996. Lang.: Hun.   4181

Interview with opera singer and teacher Gábor Carelli. Hungary. USA: New York, NY. 1916-1997. Lang.: Eng.   4183

The difficulty of performing 'Sempre Libera' in Verdi's *La Traviata*. Italy. USA: New York, NY. 1886-1996. Lang.: Eng.   4186

Opera singer Fedora Barbieri. Italy. Hungary. 1940-1997. Lang.: Hun.   4188

Tenor Marcello Giordano. Italy. 1965-1997. Lang.: Eng.   4189

Review of a new CD entitled 'Famous Italian Baritones'. Italy. 1996. Lang.: Eng.   4192

Soprano Mirella Freni. Italy. 1935-1997. Lang.: Eng.   4199

Interview with bass Oddbjørn Tennfjord. Norway: Oslo. 1970. Lang.: Swe.   4201

Contralto Ewa Podleś. Poland. 1997. Lang.: Eng.   4202

Soprano Angela Gheorghiu. Romania. 1997. Lang.: Eng.   4203

Mezzo soprano Irina Archipova. Russia: Moscow. 1925-1997. Lang.: Eng.   4204

Soprano Galina Gorčakova. Russia: St. Petersburg. 1962-1997. Lang.: Eng.   4206

Memoirs of the Russian opera star Fëdor Šaljapin. Russia. France. 1873-1938. Lang.: Rus.   4207

Interview with tenor Johan Botha. South Africa, Republic of. 1996. Lang.: Eng.   4210

Soprano Aïnhoa Artetoa. Spain. 1997. Lang.: Eng.   4213

Singing — cont'd

Interview with tenor Lars Cleveman. Sweden: Stockholm. 1980. Lang.: Swe. 4217

Problems and fears of the contemporary opera singer. Sweden. 1995. Lang.: Swe. 4218

Interview with opera singer Hillevi Martinpelto. Sweden. Europe. 1979. Lang.: Swe. 4221

Lyric tenor Philip Langridge. UK-England: London. 1997. Lang.: Eng. 4225

Soprano Susannah Waters. UK-England. 1997. Lang.: Eng. 4226

Interview with opera singer Bryn Terfel. UK-Wales. 1989. Lang.: Swe. 4229

Opera superstar Minnie Hauk. USA. 1851-1929. Lang.: Eng. 4243

Soprano Rosa Ponselle. USA: New York, NY. 1920-1927. Lang.: Eng. 4245

A child's first visit to the Metropolitan Opera. USA: New York, NY. 1988-1997. Lang.: Eng. 4246

Tenor Jerry Hadley's New York City Opera debut. USA: New York, NY. 1979. Lang.: Eng. 4247

Reaction to a production of Mozart's *Così fan tutte* at the Metropolitan Opera. USA: New York, NY. 1997. Lang.: Eng. 4249

Novelist Ira Levin on Gounod's *Faust*. USA: New York, NY. 1997. Lang.: Eng. 4250

Actor Sam Waterston on Metropolitan Opera performance of *Eugene Onegin*. USA: New York, NY. 1996-1997. Lang.: Eng. 4251

Survey of recordings by opera stars. USA. UK-England. 1897-1997. Lang.: Eng. 4252

Contralto Lili Chookasian. USA: Chicago, IL. 1921-1997. Lang.: Eng. 4254

Grand opera in Denver. USA: Denver, CO. 1864-1881. Lang.: Eng. 4260

Interview with soprano Renée Fleming. USA. 1959-1997. Lang.: Eng. 4261

Opera critic, novelist and biographer Marcia Davenport. USA. 1904-1996. Lang.: Eng. 4262

Soprano Lauren Flanigan. USA. 1958-1997. Lang.: Eng. 4263

The Schubert series at the 92nd Street Y. USA: New York, NY. 1988-1998. Lang.: Eng. 4265

Nelson Eddy's career as an opera singer. USA. 1901-1967. Lang.: Eng. 4268

Singers Carmela and Rosa Ponselle. USA: New York, NY. 1889-1981. Lang.: Eng. 4273

Opera and luxury record packaging. USA. 1996. Lang.: Eng. 4278

Plays/librettos/scripts
Classical soprano roles in works of Stephen Sondheim. USA. 1959-1996. Lang.: Eng. 3998

Relation to other fields
Opera and social decline. England: London. 1698-1737. Lang.: Eng. 4321

Research/historiography
Proposal for a revised history of English opera. England. 1639-1711. Lang.: Eng. 4325

Singleton, John
Design/technology
Paul Sylbert's production design for *Rosewood*. USA. 1996. Lang.: Eng. 3550

Sinkó, László
Performance/production
Interview with actor László Sinkó of Új Színház. Hungary. 1960-1997. Lang.: Hun. 1778

Sir Barnaby Whigg
Plays/librettos/scripts
Dramatic satire of the exclusion crisis. England. 1680-1683. Lang.: Eng. 2714

Sir John Van Olden
Performance/production
Attempt to reconstruct performances of plays by Massinger and Fletcher. England. 1628-1633. Lang.: Eng. 1622

Siren, Ervi
Training
Teachers and choreographers Soile Lahdenperä and Ervi Siren. Finland. 1997. Lang.: Fin. 1040

sista docta
Relation to other fields
Joni L. Jones's performance piece *sista docta*. USA. 1994-1997. Lang.: Eng. 819

Sister Son/ji
Plays/librettos/scripts
The evolution of solo performance in African-American one-person plays. USA. 1972-1996. Lang.: Eng. 3293

Sisters
Plays/librettos/scripts
Sisterhood and female bonding in *Crimes of the Heart* and *Sisters*. USA. 1986-1996. Lang.: Eng. 3511

Sisters Jouet, The
Plays/librettos/scripts
Ilse Aichinger's radio play *The Sisters Jouet*. USA. 1967-1997. Lang.: Eng. 3521

Sisters/Strangers
Plays/librettos/scripts
Account of *Sisters/Strangers*, a community play about immigrant women. Canada: Victoria, BC. 1994. Lang.: Eng. 2398

Sisters, The
Plays/librettos/scripts
The influence of Cechov's *Tri sestry (Three Sisters)* on plays of Sadowski and Wertenbaker. Russia. UK-England. 1901-1997. Lang.: Eng. 2992

Site-specific performance
Plays/librettos/scripts
Interview with playwright Laura Farabough. USA. 1985. Lang.: Ita. 3142

Relation to other fields
Analysis of a performance for the Young Presidents Organization. India: Mumbai. 1996. Lang.: Eng. 1228

Identity, cultural exchange, and tourism. Spain-Catalonia. 1950-1997. Lang.: Eng. 3810

The performance of 'heritage tourism'. UK-Wales. 1994-1996. Lang.: Eng. 3811

Space in feminist performance art and political protest. UK-England. 1980-1997. Lang.: Eng. 3850

Research/historiography
Archaeology and performance in site-specific productions. UK-Wales. 1997. Lang.: Eng. 3851

Sive
Performance/production
Collection of newspaper reviews by London theatre critics. UK-England. 1997. Lang.: Eng. 2142

Collection of newspaper reviews by London theatre critics. UK-England: London. 1997. Lang.: Eng. 2151

Six Characters in Search of an Author
SEE
Sei personaggi in cerca d'autore.

Sizwe Bansi Is Dead
Performance/production
Collection of newspaper reviews by London theatre critics. UK-England: London. 1997. Lang.: Eng. 2076

Plays/librettos/scripts
The acting of everyday life in plays of Athol Fugard. South Africa, Republic of. 1960-1974. Lang.: Eng. 3024

Sjöberg, Hans
Institutions
Swedish directors on the financial crisis. Sweden. 1990. Lang.: Swe. 1490

Skådespelarnas klassiker (Classics Actors)
Plays/librettos/scripts
Interview with playwrights Lars Arrhed and Kjell Abrahamsson. Sweden: Malmö. 1995-1997. Lang.: Swe. 3056

Skank
Performance/production
Collection of newspaper reviews by London theatre critics. UK-England: London. 1997. Lang.: Eng. 2022

Skarbek, Stanisław
Administration
Stanisław Skarbek and the building of theatres. Poland: Lvov. 1818-1842. Lang.: Pol. 46

Performance spaces
Teatr im. Fr. Skarbka, a gift to the city of Lvov from a private citizen. Poland: Lvov. 1842-1902. Lang.: Pol. 447

Skazanie o nevidimom grade Kiteže
Plays/librettos/scripts
Russian opera and Symbolist poetics. Russia. 1890-1930. Lang.: Eng. 4309

Skeleton
Performance/production
Collection of newspaper reviews by London theatre critics. UK-England: London. 1997. Lang.: Eng. 2055

Smith, Henry
   Training
      Acting, dance, and martial arts teacher Henry Smith. USA. UK-
      England. 1968-1997. Lang.: Eng.   938
Smith, Jackie
   Performance/production
      Interview with actress Moira Finucane. Australia: Melbourne. 1997.
      Lang.: Eng.   1556
Smith, Simon
   Performance/production
      Collection of newspaper reviews by London theatre critics. UK-England:
      London. 1997. Lang.: Eng.   2041
Smoktunovskij, Innokentij
   Performance/production
      Actor Innokentij Smoktunovskij. Russia. 1925-1994. Lang.: Rus.   1883
Smole, Dominik
   Plays/librettos/scripts
      Analysis of Sophocles' and Smole's treatments of Antigone and
      Shakespeare's *Hamlet*. Slovenia. 500 B.C.-1960 A.D. Lang.: Slo. 3005
Snail Inside, The
   Performance/production
      Collection of newspaper reviews by London theatre critics. UK-England:
      London. 1997. Lang.: Eng.   1982
Snake in the Grass
   Performance/production
      Collection of newspaper reviews by London theatre critics. UK-England:
      London. 1997. Lang.: Eng.   2120
Snake Theatre (San Francisco, CA)
   Performance/production
      Interview with experimental theatre artist Christopher Hardman. USA.
      1985. Lang.: Ita.   631
Snakesong Trilogy
   Institutions
      Interviews with and texts by Needcompany. Belgium: Antwerp. 1996.
      Lang.: Eng.   1381

      Jan Lauwers' theatre group Needcompany. Belgium: Antwerp. 1996.
      Lang.: Eng.   1382
Snape, Sam
   Performance/production
      Collection of newspaper reviews by London theatre critics. UK-England:
      London. 1997. Lang.: Eng.   2127

      Collection of newspaper reviews by London theatre critics. UK-England:
      London. 1997. Lang.: Eng.   2128
Sneeuw, Een (Snow)
   Plays/librettos/scripts
      Playwright Willem-Jan Otten. Netherlands. 1996-1997. Lang.: Dut. 2977
Snelgrove, Mike
   Performance/production
      Collection of newspaper reviews by London theatre critics. UK-England:
      London. 1997. Lang.: Eng.   2131
Snir, Hanan
   Performance/production
      Hanan Snir's productions of Lorca's *Blood Wedding (Bodas de sangre)*.
      Israel: Tel Aviv. 1990. Lang.: Eng.   1791
Snoj, Jože
   Plays/librettos/scripts
      Analysis of plays by Jože Snoj and Ivo Svetina. Slovenia. 1900-1996.
      Lang.: Slo.   3008
Snowshow
   Performance/production
      Collection of newspaper reviews by London theatre critics. UK-England:
      London. 1997. Lang.: Eng.   1981

      Collection of newspaper reviews by London theatre critics. UK-England:
      London. 1997. Lang.: Eng.   2106
So Saddle Like a Horse Why Don't You?
   Performance/production
      Collection of newspaper reviews by London theatre critics. UK-England:
      London. 1997. Lang.: Eng.   2013
So What's New?
   Plays/librettos/scripts
      Fatima Dike on her play *So What's New?*. South Africa, Republic of.
      1990. Lang.: Eng.   3028
Sobchak, Victor
   Performance/production
      Collection of newspaper reviews by London theatre critics. UK-England:
      London. 1997. Lang.: Eng.   2139
Sobel, Bernard
   Performance/production
      Productions of the Paris theatre season. France: Paris. 1996-1997. Lang.:
      Ger.   1668

Sobol, Yehoshua
   Performance/production
      Reviews of Bochumer Schauspielhaus productions. Germany: Bochum.
      1997. Lang.: Ger.   1730

      Collection of newspaper reviews by London theatre critics. UK-England:
      London. 1997. Lang.: Eng.   2071
Societas Raffaello Sanzio (Cesena)
   Performance/production
      The body and the text in productions of the Festival de Théâtre des
      Amériques. Canada: Montreal, PQ. 1997. Lang.: Fre.   1583

      Societas Raffaello Sanzio's production of Shakespeare's *Julius Caesar*.
      Italy: Prato. 1997. Lang.: Ita.   1803

      Review of Societas Raffaello Sanzio's children's theatre production of
      Hansel and Gretel. Italy: Cesena. 1997. Lang.: Ita.   1817

      The *Oresteia* of Aeschylus as performed by Societas Raffaello Sanzio.
      Italy: Cesena. 1981-1997. Lang.: Eng.   1820

      Societas Raffaello Sanzio's production of the *Oresteia* of Euripides.
      Italy: Cesena. 1995. Lang.: Ita.   1821
   Plays/librettos/scripts
      Romeo Castellucci's adaptation of the *Oresteia*. Italy: Cesena. 1995.
      Lang.: Ger, Fre, Dut, Eng.   2947
Sociology
   Administration
      Australian cultural policy. Australia. 1968-1997. Lang.: Eng.   4

      Nationalism in International Day of Theatre. Canada: Montreal, PQ.
      1962-1997. Lang.: Fre.   10

      Philip Henslowe and the conjurer/astrologer Simon Forman. England:
      London. 1590-1600. Lang.: Eng.   17

      The erosion of support for classical art forms such as ballet. USA. 1997.
      Lang.: Eng.   1047
   Audience
      Women in the Renaissance theatre audience. England. 1567-1642.
      Lang.: Eng.   1247

      The role of theatre in Philippine culture. Philippines. 1905-1993. Lang.:
      Eng.   1250

      Reality and fictionality in theatre in education. UK-England. 1960-1994.
      Lang.: Eng.   1253
   Institutions
      The creation of the Canada Council and increased demand for
      performing arts. Canada. 1957-1997. Lang.: Eng.   301

      Sharon Pollock's community theatre work. Canada: Calgary, AB. 1981-
      1997. Lang.: Eng.   304

      Changes in Hungarian theatre and the new generation of artists.
      Hungary. 1989-1997. Lang.: Hun.   334

      Amateur theatre in Slovene political and cultural life. Slovenia: Celje.
      1896-1914. Lang.: Slo.   371

      Theatrical activities in the Ptuj Reading Society. Slovenia: Ptuj. 1864-
      1942. Lang.: Slo.   373

      The impact of the Disney Corporation on Broadway. USA: New York,
      NY. 1990-1997. Lang.: Eng.   400

      Interview with Dieter Görne of Staatsschauspiel Dresden. Germany:
      Dresden. 1997. Lang.: Ger.   1420

      Slovene drama at the National Theatre, Maribor. Slovenia: Maribor.
      1919-1941. Lang.: Slo.   1470
   Performance spaces
      History of the parterre and the audience that occupied it. France. 1600-
      1700. Lang.: Eng.   431

      Power, Elizabethan theatre, and the Shakespearean stage. UK-England.
      1590-1610. Lang.: Eng.   1534
   Performance/production
      Staged representations of AIDS. 1980-1997. Lang.: Eng.   461

      Political and cultural changes reflected in the Festival de Théâtre des
      Amériques. Canada: Montreal, PQ. 1997. Lang.: Eng.   479

      Cross-dressing in Chinese theatre and society. China. 1200-1997. Lang.:
      Eng.   489

      English theatre and popular culture. England. 1590-1610. Lang.: Eng.
                                                                       501

      History of French shadow theatre. France. 1750-1995. Lang.: Eng. 534

      The women's performance genre *gidayu*. Japan. 1888-1997. Lang.: Eng.
                                                                       567

      Women in Japanese theatre. Japan: Tokyo. 1970-1996. Lang.: Eng. 568

      Community movement in theatre. Poland. 1920-1997. Lang.: Eng, Fre.
                                                                       577

Sociology — cont'd

The waning enthusiasm among Swedish audiences for international guest artists. Sweden. 1980. Lang.: Swe. 613

Industrial technology and the display of women's bodies in performance. UK-England. 1870-1954. Lang.: Eng. 616

The crisis of Black theatre identity. USA. 1997. Lang.: Eng. 643

Comedy and social criticism. USA. 1960-1967. Lang.: Eng. 648

Analysis of Asian Indian performance in the United States. USA: New York, NY. 1994-1996. Lang.: Eng. 662

The performance of birth stories. USA. 1997. Lang.: Eng. 666

Southern humor and minstrelsy. USA. 1835-1939. Lang.: Eng. 677

The emergence of modern American theatre. USA. 1914-1929. Lang.: Eng. 683

Community movement-theatre performance *Joshua's Wall*. USA: Philadelphia, PA. 1994-1995. Lang.: Eng. 686

The early history of the tango. Argentina. USA. 1875-1925. Lang.: Eng. 954

Call for an interdisciplinary approach to dance history. Europe. 1675-1900. Lang.: Eng. 957

Jazz music and dance in Paris. France. 1920-1930. Lang.: Eng. 963

Dance and ideological confrontation. Portugal. 1660-1793. Lang.: Por. 984

Gender and nationalism: Maud Allan's *Vision of Salome*. UK-England: London. USA. 1908. Lang.: Eng. 994

The body and cultural identity in contemporary dance. USA. 1985-1995. Lang.: Eng. 996

Analysis of three 'dance cultures'. USA. Ghana. 1995-1997. Lang.: Eng. 998

The representation of social dancing in mass media. USA. 1980-1990. Lang.: Eng. 1008

Analysis of a multi-ethnic dance rehearsal. USA: San Francisco, CA. 1996. Lang.: Eng. 1013

Marriage and domesticity in *La Sylphide* choreographed by Filippo Taglioni. France. 1830-1835. Lang.: Eng. 1068

Foreign dancers and Italian ballet. Italy: Rome. 1845-1855. Lang.: Eng. 1096

Haitian folklore and national representation. Haiti. 1940-1960. Lang.: Eng. 1146

Rukmini Devi and the revival of South Indian dance. India. 1904-1996. Lang.: Eng. 1147

Gender, authenticity, and flamenco. Spain: Seville. 1975-1995. Lang.: Eng. 1151

The hula as an embodied social practice. USA. 1950-1997. Lang.: Eng. 1153

Dance and the representation of the body in a technological world. UK-England. 1997. Lang.: Eng. 1192

Shakespeare on the Jacobean and Caroline stage. England. 1605-1640. Lang.: Eng. 1637

The use of theatre to advance Ethiopian social goals. Ethiopia: Addis Ababa. 1996. Lang.: Eng. 1639

The map of England in productions of Shakespeare's *King Lear*. Europe. USA. 1909-1994. Lang.: Eng. 1650

The decline of the mystery play in Lille. Flanders: Lille. 1480-1690. Lang.: Eng. 1655

Royal and commercial audiences and the Comédie-Française. France. 1700-1800. Lang.: Eng. 1657

The development of 'théâtre forain'. France. 1700-1730. Lang.: Fre. 1666

Critical assessment of the work of André Benedetto, playwright and director. France: Avignon. 1961-1991. Lang.: Eng. 1667

German productions of Shakespeare after reunification. Germany. 1989-1992. Lang.: Eng. 1703

Interviews with writer-directors K.N. Pannikkar, Mahesh Dattani, and Tripurari Sharma. India. 1997. Lang.: Eng. 1781

Ethnography of artists of popular theatre in Tamilnadu. India. 1950-1995. Lang.: Eng. 1783

Analysis of *Teyyateyyam* by K. N. Pannikkar. India: Trivandrum. 1993. Lang.: Eng. 1784

The psychology and sociology of Slovene acting. Slovenia. 1880-1970. Lang.: Slo. 1907

Tendencies of modern Asian theatre. Sri Lanka. 1956-1997. Lang.: Eng. 1921

Sexuality on stage in the National Theatre production of Tony Kushner's *Angels in America*. UK-England: London. 1992. Lang.: Eng. 2176

Social class in English productions of Čechov's *Višněvyj sad (The Cherry Orchard)*. UK-England. 1977-1995. Lang.: Eng. 2221

The social protest theatre of Luis Valdez and Amiri Baraka. USA. 1965-1975. Lang.: Eng. 2260

The performance of race, gender, sexuality, and power. USA. Europe. 1590-1995. Lang.: Eng. 2309

Black actors and writers and the Negro Units of the Federal Theatre Project. USA: Washington, DC, New York, NY. 1935. Lang.: Eng. 2350

Early Shanghai filmmaking. China, People's Republic of: Shanghai. 1896-1937. Lang.: Eng. 3568

Analysis of the Merchant Ivory film *Shakespeare Wallah*. India. UK-England. 1965. Lang.: Eng. 3577

Representations of Black women on stage and screen. USA. 1939-1995. Lang.: Eng. 3605

The portrayal of Asian characters by non-Asian actors. USA. 1930-1969. Lang.: Eng. 3614

The emergence of the art film theatre in its socioeconomic context. USA. 1946-1970. Lang.: Eng. 3628

Shakespearean elements in Gus Van Sant's film *My Own Private Idaho*. USA. 1993. Lang.: Eng. 3629

Analysis of television serial *The Restless Years*. Australia. Germany. 1977-1993. Lang.: Eng. 3716

Television versions of Shakespeare's *Othello*. UK-England. 1987-1996. Lang.: Eng. 3726

Testimonial 'performance' on television talk shows. USA. 1985-1996. Lang.: Eng. 3731

Identity and the television talk show 'performance'. USA. 1985-1996. Lang.: Eng. 3733

Constance D'Arcy Mackay's *The Pageant of Sunshine and Shadow*. USA. 1900-1918. Lang.: Eng. 3771

Analysis of a religious street celebration, the Giglio. USA: Brooklyn, NY. 1880-1997. Lang.: Eng. 3808

Gender, color, and nationalism at the Tropicana. Cuba: Havana. 1959-1997. Lang.: Eng. 3856

The significance of Johannesburg music hall. South Africa, Republic of: Johannesburg. 1886-1896. Lang.: Eng. 3857

Interview with political satirist Pieter-Dirk Uys. South Africa, Republic of. 1945-1994. Lang.: Eng. 3858

Eighteenth-century Spanish lyric theatre. Spain. 1701-1800. Lang.: Eng. 3878

Influences on Dukas' opera *Ariane et Barbe-Bleue*. France. 1885-1936. Lang.: Eng. 4143

The Czech national character as reflected in contemporary puppet theatre. Czech Republic. 1997. Lang.: Cze. 4363

Plays/librettos/scripts

The image of the African on the London stage. UK-England: London. Africa. 1908-1939. Lang.: Eng. 699

American theatrical culture. USA. 1825-1860. Lang.: Eng. 701

The Boer War, Australian melodrama, and the colonial legacy. Australia. 1899-1901. Lang.: Eng. 2377

Social and political themes in Bulgarian melodrama. Bulgaria. 1880-1910. Lang.: Eng. 2388

The modernization and nationalization of Chinese spoken drama. China, People's Republic of. 1980-1989. Lang.: Eng. 2440

Race in Shakespeare's *Othello*. England. 1604. Lang.: Eng. 2450

Defense of Jonson's character Celia in *Volpone*. England. 1607. Lang.: Eng. 2455

Male expectations of women's role in society in Fletcher's *The Woman's Prize*. England. 1633. Lang.: Eng. 2469

Female homoeroticism on the early English stage. England. 1594-1632. Lang.: Eng. 2482

The Jailer's Daughter in *The Two Noble Kinsmen* by Shakespeare and Fletcher. England. 1612-1613. Lang.: Eng. 2483

Theatrical reflections of the marital double standard. England. 1598-1650. Lang.: Eng. 2501

Domestic conflict in early modern English drama. England. 1590-1633. Lang.: Eng. 2508

Analysis of Nicholas Rowe's *Tragedy of Jane Shore*. England. 1714. Lang.: Eng. 2523

Sociology — cont'd

Shakespeare's *The Taming of the Shrew* and 'modern' techniques for the subordination of women. England. 1551-1594. Lang.: Eng.   2527

Domestic rebellion in *The Tempest* and *Arden of Faversham*. England. 1605. Lang.: Eng.   2530

The bubonic plague and Shakespeare's plays. England. 1603-1607. Lang.: Eng.   2534

The figure of St. Joseph in medieval drama. England. 1440-1550. Lang.: Eng.   2544

Social practice and theatrical meaning in Shakespeare's *Measure for Measure*. England. 1604. Lang.: Eng.   2568

Slavery and servitude in Shakespeare's *Comedy of Errors*. England. 1590. Lang.: Eng.   2589

Educated women and the plays of Shakespeare. England. 1596-1603. Lang.: Eng.   2594

Privacy and gossip in Shakespeare's *Twelfth Night*. England. 1602. Lang.: Eng.   2613

Representations of class in the plays of Shakespeare. England: London. 1590-1613. Lang.: Eng.   2631

Shakespeare's Cressida as a victim of sexual assault. England. 1600. Lang.: Eng.   2632

The language of vagrants and criminals in *The Roaring Girl* by Middleton and Dekker. England. 1608-1611. Lang.: Eng.   2661

Shakespeare's *Cymbeline* and early modern English nationalism. England. 1609-1610. Lang.: Eng.   2662

The place of early English theatre in literary culture. England. 1595-1620. Lang.: Eng.   2670

Ambivalence toward a female sovereign reflected in plays of Shakespeare and Middleton. England. 1600-1607. Lang.: Eng.   2672

The English view of Ireland reflected in Shakespeare's history plays. England. 1590-1599. Lang.: Eng.   2678

Analysis of Shakespeare's *Othello*. England. 1604. Lang.: Eng.   2679

Analysis of melodramas based on novels of Walter Scott. England. 1810-1830. Lang.: Eng.   2681

Love and sex in Shakespeare's *Troilus and Cressida*. England. 1601-1602. Lang.: Eng.   2686

Ideas of selfhood and slavery reflected in Shakespeare's *Othello*. England. 1604. Lang.: Eng.   2736

Masculine and feminine men in Shakespeare's *Troilus and Cressida*. England. 1601-1602. Lang.: Eng.   2741

Women and household labor in *The Dutch Courtesan* by John Marston. England. 1604. Lang.: Eng.   2748

Masculinity in Marlowe's *Tamburlaine*, Part II. England. 1587. Lang.: Eng.   2774

The enclosure of the commons reflected in Shakespeare's *As You Like It*. England. 1598-1600. Lang.: Eng.   2777

The significance of Don Juan in works of Tirso, Mozart, and Molière. Europe. 1612-1787. Lang.: Eng.   2786

Love in French theatre and literature. France. 1600-1699. Lang.: Ita.   2804

French melodramas about Martin Guerre. France. 1800-1850. Lang.: Eng.   2810

Analysis of *La Dame aux Camélias (Camille)* by Alexandre Dumas *fils*. France. 1848. Lang.: Eng.   2817

Brook, Mnouchkine and intercultural theatre. France: Paris. 1988-1992. Lang.: Eng.   2832

The cultural construction of the hero in Greek tragedy. Greece. 500-400 B.C. Lang.: Eng.   2874

Transformations of Irish society as reflected in its drama. Ireland. 1959-1993. Lang.: Eng.   2913

Social morality in the works of Catholic playwrights Janez Evangelist Krek and Fran Saleški Finžgar. Slovenia. 1884-1996.Lang.: Slo.   3013

Analysis of *Karantanska tragedija (Carinthian Tragedy)* by Radivoj Rehar. Slovenia. 1836-1996. Lang.: Slo.   3015

Ideology in *El Burlador de Sevilla (The Trickster of Seville)* by Tirso de Molina. Spain. 1622. Lang.: Eng.   3051

Melodrama as the enactment of cultural tensions resulting from British imperialism. UK-England. 1850-1900. Lang.: Eng.   3071

Ideological discourse in nautical melodrama. UK-England. 1794-1830. Lang.: Eng.   3078

The key role of sentimentalism in English melodrama. UK-England. 1800-1880. Lang.: Eng.   3082

Postmodern and postcolonial concepts of identity and the plays of Brian Friel. UK-Ireland. 1980-1994. Lang.: Eng.   3122

Social issues of the sixties in plays and films of Arthur Miller. USA. 1960-1969. Lang.: Eng.   3131

Social criticism in plays of George S. Kaufman. USA. 1889-1961. Lang.: Eng.   3132

Analysis of *The Death of the Last Black Man in the Whole Entire World* by Suzan-Lori Parks. USA. 1995. Lang.: Eng.   3138

Recent work of playwright Arthur Miller. USA. 1990-1997. Lang.: Eng.   3145

Social debate reflected in Tony Kushner's *Angels in America*. USA. 1988-1996. Lang.: Eng.   3172

Social issues of the seventies in works by Arthur Miller. USA. 1970-1979. Lang.: Eng.   3173

Tony Kushner's *Angels in America*, postmodernism, and millenarianism. USA. 1992-1994. Lang.: Eng.   3193

Theatrical representations of Asia and Asians. USA. 1990-1997. Lang.: Eng.   3218

Identity, cultural transformation, and Tony Kushner's *Angels in America*. USA. 1992-1994. Lang.: Eng.   3221

Analysis of *My Queer Body* by Tim Miller. USA: New York, NY. 1993. Lang.: Eng.   3251

Criticism of one-minute and ten-minute play contests. USA. 1997. Lang.: Eng.   3256

Sexual harassment in David Mamet's *Oleanna*. USA. 1993. Lang.: Eng.   3292

Analysis of Pedro Almodóvar's film *¿Qué he hecho yo para merecer esto? (What Have I Done to Deserve This?)*. Spain. 1984. Lang.: Spa.   3642

Film adaptations of Shakespeare's *The Taming of the Shrew*. USA. 1929-1966. Lang.: Eng.   3668

Generic hybridization in the gangster film. USA. 1932-1983. Lang.: Eng.   3688

Bearbaiting and colonialism. England. 1450-1600. Lang.: Eng.   3774

The African 'other' in early French musical drama. France. Africa. 1600. Lang.: Eng.   3887

Sociopolitical themes in Stephen Sondheim's *Follies*. USA. 1971. Lang.: Eng.   3988

Bring in 'Da Noise, Bring in 'Da Funk and the Black audience. USA: New York, NY. 1996-1997. Lang.: Eng.   4002

Trento's opera *Bianca de'Rossi* and its sources. Italy. 1790-1799. Lang.: Eng.   4306

Relation to other fields

Women and the veil in colonial Algeria. Algeria. 1967. Lang.: Eng.   724

The effect of war on Sarajevan theatre. Bosnia: Sarajevo. 1993. Lang.: Eng.   726

Cultural contexts of Toronto-area theatre. Canada: Toronto, ON. 1980-1997. Lang.: Eng.   728

Popular theatre as a tool of empowerment for former street youths. Canada: Edmonton, AB. 1994-1996. Lang.: Eng.   729

Analysis of letters regarding London theatre. England: London. 1597-1626. Lang.: Eng.   733

Changes in religious drama and practices. England. 1450-1560. Lang.: Eng.   735

Transvestism and antitheatrical discourse. England. 1583-1615. Lang.: Eng.   736

Small-town Finnish theatre. Finland. 1997. Lang.: Eng, Fre.   745

Conference on theatre, audience, and society. France: Perpignan. 1996. Lang.: Spa.   747

Theatre and war. Germany. 1914-1918. Lang.: Ger.   754

Critic Alfred Kerr. Germany. 1890-1919. Lang.: Ger.   759

Ritual and performance in ancient Greek sport and warfare. Greece. Lang.: Eng.   764

The movement of theatre from entertainment to 'efficacy'. Israel: Akko. USA. 1994-1997. Lang.: Eng.   767

Censorship, power, and performance. Kenya: Nairobi. 1938-1997. Lang.: Eng.   771

Actress Ellen Terry's effect on women's roles. UK-England: London. 1880-1909. Lang.: Eng.   783

Theatre as a communal experience. UK-England. 1960-1995. Lang.: Eng.   788

Sociology — cont'd

Theatre artists' responses to the debate on multiculturalism of August Wilson and Robert Brustein. USA. 1997. Lang.: Eng. 789

Introduction to articles on the Wilson-Brustein debate. USA: New York, NY. 1997. Lang.: Eng. 790

Theatre critic and theorist Margo Jefferson on the Robert Brustein/ August Wilson debate. USA: New York, NY. 1960-1997. Lang.: Eng. 791

Commentary on the Wilson-Brustein debate. USA: New York, NY. 1996-1997. Lang.: Eng. 793

Support for August Wilson's views on Black American theatre. USA: St. Paul, MN, Princeton, NJ. 1996-1997. Lang.: Eng. 795

The theatricality of everyday life in nineteenth-century America. USA. 1800-1900. Lang.: Eng. 800

Critique of August Wilson's call for a separate Black American theatre. USA: New York, NY. 1997. Lang.: Eng. 807

Call for white directors to examine their casting policies. USA. 1997. Lang.: Eng. 808

Performativity and the performance of autism. USA. 1964-1996. Lang.: Eng. 812

Marketing techniques of the interactive show *Tamara: The Living Movie*. USA. 1987. Lang.: Eng. 813

The future of African-American theatre. USA. 1997. Lang.: Eng. 816

Performance and the Sand Creek Massacre. USA: Sand Creek, CO. 1860-1997. Lang.: Eng. 817

Analysis of the Wilson-Brustein debate. USA. 1997. Lang.: Eng. 820

The female body and the spiritualist movement. USA. 1840-1901. Lang.: Eng. 821

Art and the artist in contemporary society. USA. 1996. Lang.: Eng. 824

The debate on multiculturalism of August Wilson and Robert Brustein. USA. 1997. Lang.: Eng. 825

August Wilson and the history of African-American theatre. USA. 1926-1997. Lang.: Eng. 828

The funding of the Panhandle-Plains Museum. USA: Amarillo, TX. 1966-1997. Lang.: Eng. 837

Feminine masquerade in Mary Kay Cosmetics. USA. 1993-1997. Lang.: Eng. 846

The fear of infection in American popular art and culture. USA. 1997. Lang.: Eng. 848

Belly dance and cultural borrowing. USA. 1851-1993. Lang.: Eng. 1156

Activities of Borovčani Balkan Dance and Music. USA. 1980-1996. Lang.: Eng. 1157

Women's adoption of Delsarte's principles of movement. USA. 1910-1920. Lang.: Eng. 1210

Demographics and attitudes of Montreal theatre-goers. Canada: Montreal, PQ. 1995. Lang.: Fre. 3323

Role of amateur theatre in contemporary Quebec theatrical production. Canada: Montreal, PQ. 1997. Lang.: Fre. 3324

Order and justice in early Tudor drama. England. 1490-1550. Lang.: Eng. 3340

The relationship of tragicomedy to social change. England. 1601-1700. Lang.: Eng. 3344

Anti-theatrical polemics and drama. England. 1561-1580. Lang.: Eng. 3347

Language and social formation in Shakespeare. England. 1595-1750. Lang.: Eng. 3348

The expansion of the Turkish and Islamic empires and Shakespeare's *Othello*. England. 1453-1604. Lang.: Eng. 3349

Reflections on European cultural diversity and integration. Europe. 1997. Lang.: Eng. 3350

Teaching Shakespeare at the University of Haifa. Israel: Haifa. 1994. Lang.: Eng. 3373

Theatre as a tool for moral instruction. Italy. England. 1551-1997. Lang.: Eng. 3375

Christianity and other sociopolitical models in contemporary Slovene drama. Slovenia. 1900-1996. Lang.: Slo. 3376

Play competition involving immigrants in Malmö's suburbs. Sweden: Malmö. 1996. Lang.: Swe. 3378

Multiculturalism and playwright Ebrahim Hussein. Tanzania. 1966-1997. Lang.: Eng. 3380

Shakespeare and English identity. UK-England. 1990-1996. Lang.: Eng. 3384

The effect of AIDS on contemporary drama. USA. 1991-1997. Lang.: Ger. 3406

The marginalization of drama on the American West. USA. 1939-1997. Lang.: Eng. 3427

Performative politics and Western media coverage of Chinese protests. China, People's Republic of. 1989-1997. Lang.: Eng. 3512

Description of course on film and visual anthropology and sociology. South Africa, Republic of. 1997. Lang.: Eng. 3692

Shakespeare, Hollywood, and American cultural ambivalence. USA. 1990-1997. Lang.: Eng. 3693

Politics and Elia Kazan's film *Pinky*. USA. 1948. Lang.: Eng. 3694

Nontraditional and non-professional uses of video. 1990-1997. Lang.: Eng. 3737

The performance of 'heritage tourism'. UK-Wales. 1994-1996. Lang.: Eng. 3811

Opera and social decline. England: London. 1698-1737. Lang.: Eng. 4321

Opera in mid-nineteenth-century New York. USA: New York, NY. 1815-1860. Lang.: Eng. 4323

Wagner, *Gesamtkunstwerk*, and cultural politics. USA. Germany. 1875-1920. Lang.: Eng. 4324

Research/historiography
Call for new engagement between dance scholarship and cultural studies. USA. 1990-1997. Lang.: Eng. 1023

Theory/criticism
Sociolinguistic analysis of English medieval drama. England. 1300-1600. Lang.: Eng. 874

Theatrical performance and its relation to sex and pornography. Finland. 1997. Lang.: Fin. 880

The river as a metaphor of cultural exchange. India. 1938-1997. Lang.: Eng. 904

Performativity, language and sound, and surveillance tapes and videos in the courtroom. USA. 1997. Lang.: Eng. 923

The continuing controversy over 'victim art'. USA. 1997. Lang.: Eng. 1034

Aesthetics values and dance history. USA. 1990-1996. Lang.: Eng. 1035

Dance history and cultural studies: works of Martha Graham and Eugene O'Neill. USA. 1913-1933. Lang.: Eng. 1216

New historicist criticism of Shakespeare's *The Tempest*. 1985-1989. Lang.: Eng. 3461

Social discourse in francophone theatre. Canada. France. Belgium. 1974-1996. Lang.: Fre. 3468

Othello, censorship, and public swearing. England: London. 1215-1622. Lang.: Eng. 3470

Racism, *Othello*, and South African criticism. England. South Africa, Republic of. 1604-1987. Lang.: Eng. 3473

Analysis of criticism of Jennie Livingston's documentary film *Paris Is Burning*. USA. 1991. Lang.: Eng. 3700

Södra Teatern (Stockholm)
Institutions
Södra Teatern, being turned into a forum for world cultures. Sweden: Stockholm. 1997. Lang.: Swe. 383

Softley, Iain
Performance/production
Interview with director Iain Softley. UK-England. 1995-1997. Lang.: Eng. 3589

Sogno d'un mattino di primavera (Spring Morning's Dream, A)
Plays/librettos/scripts
Analysis of D'Annunzio's *Sogno d'un mattino di primavera (A Spring Morning's Dream)*. Italy. 1895-1900. Lang.: Ita. 2942

Vision and representation in D'Annunzio's *Sogno d'un mattino di primavera (A Spring Morning's Dream)*. Italy. 1898. Lang.: Ita. 2971

Relation to other fields
The inspiration of Botticelli in D'Annunzio's *Sogno d'un mattino di primavera (A Spring Morning's Dream)*. Italy. 1895-1897. Lang.: Ita. 3374

Sogno di un tramonto d'autunno (Dream of an Autumn Sunset)
Plays/librettos/scripts
Psychological analysis of D'Annunzio's *Sogno di un tramonto d'autunno (Dream of an Autumn Sunset)*. Italy. 1898. Lang.: Ita. 2941

Analysis of D'Annunzio's *Sogno di un tramonto d'autunno (Dream of an Autumn Sunset)*. Italy. 1898. Lang.: Ita. 2968

Sohn, Der (Son, The)
Basic theatrical documents
English translations of German Expressionist plays. Germany. 1900-1920. Lang.: Eng. 1284

Soho Theatre Company (London)
Performance/production
Collection of newspaper reviews by London theatre critics. UK-England: London. 1997. Lang.: Eng. 2067

Sojuz Teatral'nych Dejatelej (Moscow)
Institutions
Director of Russian Theatre Union on economic conditions. Russia: Moscow. 1990-1997. Lang.: Rus. 369

Sokolow, Anna
Training
Acting, dance, and martial arts teacher Henry Smith. USA. UK-England. 1968-1997. Lang.: Eng. 938

Solaris
Plays/librettos/scripts
Interview with opera composer Michael Obst. Germany: Munich. 1996. Lang.: Ger. 4294

Solaris Lakota Dance Theatre Company (South Dakota)
Training
Acting, dance, and martial arts teacher Henry Smith. USA. UK-England. 1968-1997. Lang.: Eng. 938

Soldier Dreams, The
Performance/production
Daniel Brooks' production of *The Soldier Dreams* by Daniel MacIvor. Canada: Toronto, ON. 1997. Lang.: Eng. 1603

Soldiers Dancing
Performance/production
Collection of newspaper reviews by London theatre critics. UK-England: London. 1997. Lang.: Eng. 2079

Solid Gold Cadillac, The
Plays/librettos/scripts
Social criticism in plays of George S. Kaufman. USA. 1889-1961. Lang.: Eng. 3132

Solo performance
O SEE
Monodrama.
Basic theatrical documents
Collection of soliloquies. Lang.: Dut. 1254

Text of *big face* by Marion de Vries. Canada. 1995. Lang.: Eng. 1257

Text of *New Art Book* by Ken Garnhum. Canada. 1997. Lang.: Eng. 1260

Text of *No Space on Long Street* by Pieter-Dirk Uys. South Africa, Republic of. 1997. Lang.: Eng. 1306

Text of *Someone Else from Queens Is Queer* by Richard Elovich. USA. 1992. Lang.: Eng. 1325

Text of *Refreshment* by Craig Gingrich-Philbrook. USA. 1997. Lang.: Eng. 1329

Text of *Skins* by Tami Spry. USA. 1993. Lang.: Eng. 1343

Text of *Hurricane* by Erin Cressida Wilson. USA. 1996. Lang.: Eng. 1352

Text of Guillermo Verdecchia's radio play *The Terrible But Incomplete Journals of John D*. Canada: Vancouver, BC. 1996. Lang.: Eng. 3514

Text of *Object/Subject of Desire* by Shawna Dempsey. Canada. 1987. Lang.: Eng. 3814
Design/technology
Lighting designer Jeff Nellis. USA: New York, NY. 1997. Lang.: Eng. 224

Institutions
Solo performance at the Festival de Théâtre des Amériques. Canada: Montreal, PQ. 1997. Lang.: Fre. 1392
Performance/production
The philosophy and requirements of doing one-person shows. Finland. 1997. Lang.: Fin. 527

Solo performance of Carran Waterfield. UK-England: Coventry. 1978-1997. Lang.: Eng. 623

History of the one-woman show. USA. 1890-1995. Lang.: Eng. 646

Changes in women's comedy performance. USA. 1950-1995. Lang.: Eng. 654

Autobiographical performances of Elizabeth Robins. USA. 1862-1952. Lang.: Eng. 656

Julianna Fjeld's *The Journey*, performed in American Sign Language. USA. 1997. Lang.: Eng. 669

Ross McMillan's performance of *The Fever* by Wallace Shawn. Canada: Winnipeg, MB. 1997. Lang.: Eng. 1577

Daniel Brooks on his collaboration with Daniel MacIvor on *Here Lies Henry*. Canada: Toronto, ON. 1994-1995. Lang.: Eng. 1578

Interview with actress and solo performer Louisette Dussault. Canada: Montreal, PQ. 1979-1997. Lang.: Fre. 1580

Jean-Louis Millette's performance in Larry Tremblay's one-man show *The Dragonfly of Chicoutimi*. Canada: Montreal, PQ. 1996. Lang.: Fre. 1586

Monodramas by Louisette Dussault and Larry Tremblay. Canada: Montreal, PQ. 1997. Lang.: Eng. 1605

Andrea Fullajtár's performance in *Csendet akarok (I Want Silence)* by Zsolt Csalog. Hungary: Budapest. 1996. Lang.: Hun. 1771

Jarl Kulle's one-man show *Reskamraten (The Traveling Companion)*. Sweden. 1997. Lang.: Swe. 1937

Jean Fergusson's *She Knows, You Know!*, about music-hall star Hylda Baker. UK-England. 1996-1997. Lang.: Eng. 2207

Robert Myers's *Lee Atwater: Fixin' to Die*. USA: New York, NY. 1990-1997. Lang.: Eng. 2313

Interview with solo artist Jude Narita. USA: Los Angeles, CA. 1987-1989. Lang.: Eng. 2341

Playwright and performer Eve Ensler. USA: New York, NY. 1980-1997. Lang.: Eng. 2354

Erin Cressida Wilson on her performance piece *Hurricane*. USA. 1996. Lang.: Eng. 2357

Mary Louise Wilson on her one-woman show *Full Gallop*. USA: New York, NY. 1997. Lang.: Eng. 2358

Desire in performance art of Shawna Dempsey. Canada. 1992-1997. Lang.: Eng. 3816

Account of Brother Theodore's one-man show. USA: New York, NY. 1980-1997. Lang.: Swe. 3830

Solo artist Richard Elovich. USA. 1993. Lang.: Eng. 3834

Interview with solo artist Tim Miller. USA: Los Angeles, CA. 1991. Lang.: Eng. 3838
Plays/librettos/scripts
Beth French's *Life Sentences*. Canada: Toronto, ON. 1989-1997. Lang.: Eng. 2390

Analysis of *La Sagouine (The Slattern)* by Antonine Maillet. Canada. 1971. Lang.: Fre. 2399

Playwright Daniel MacIvor. Canada: Halifax, NS. 1990-1997. Lang.: Eng. 2400

Feminist solo performance in Quebec. Canada: Montreal, PQ. 1970-1993. Lang.: Eng. 2402

Solo performance in British Columbia. Canada: Vancouver, BC, Victoria, BC. 1997. Lang.: Eng. 2405

Interview with writer/actor Guillermo Verdecchia. Canada. 1993-1997. Lang.: Eng. 2409

The increase in solo performance in Canadian theatre. Canada. 1980-1997. Lang.: Eng. 2412

Language in monodramas of Larry Tremblay. Canada. 1989-1995. Lang.: Fre. 2423

The writing of *Supreme Dream* by Frank Moher and actress Rhonda Trodd. Canada: Toronto, ON. 1997. Lang.: Eng. 2425

Analysis of *Here Lies Henry* by Daniel MacIvor and Daniel Brooks. Canada. 1994-1996. Lang.: Eng. 2437

The proposed term 'apostroplay' to designate a genre of solo performance. USA. 1997. Lang.: Eng. 3150

Manual for solo performance. USA. 1997. Lang.: Eng. 3214

Analysis of *My Queer Body* by Tim Miller. USA: New York, NY. 1993. Lang.: Eng. 3251

The evolution of solo performance in African-American one-person plays. USA. 1972-1996. Lang.: Eng. 3293

Solo performer Charlayne Woodard. USA: New York, NY. 1997. Lang.: Eng. 3308

Survey of one- or two-character musicals. USA: New York, NY. 1964-1997. Lang.: Eng. 3989

Solzhenitsyn, Alexander
SEE
Solženicin, Aleksand'r I.

Some Kind of Love Story
Plays/librettos/scripts
Playwright Arthur Miller's collaborations with his wife Inge Morath. USA. 1980-1989. Lang.: Eng. 3272

Someday
Performance/production
Native Canadian playwrights and theatre groups. Canada. 1979-1997. Lang.: Eng. 1597

Special effects — cont'd

Lighting used to recreate a large city fire. USA: Milwaukee, WI. 1994. Lang.: Eng.　3758

Technical aspects of *EFX!* at MGM Grand Hotel. USA: Las Vegas, NV. 1996. Lang.: Eng.　3854

A raft for use in a production of the musical *Big River*. USA. 1997. Lang.: Eng.　3923
Performance spaces
Celestial effects of the seventeenth-century stage. Europe. 1600-1700. Lang.: Eng.　429

Speck, Jules
Performance/production
The Metropolitan Opera premiere of Victor Herbert's *Madeleine*. USA: New York, NY. 1907-1995. Lang.: Eng.　4271

Spectral Hoedown
Design/technology
Improvisational lighting for *Spectral Hoedown*, St. Mark's Church Danspace. USA: New York, NY. 1997. Lang.: Eng.　1159

Speed-the-Plow
Plays/librettos/scripts
Plays of Shepard and Mamet and the myth of Narcissus. USA. 1980-1988. Lang.: Eng.　3152

Spence, Eulalie
Plays/librettos/scripts
Simultaneous discourse in works by African-American women. USA. 1900-1993. Lang.: Eng.　3260

Spenser, Edmund
Plays/librettos/scripts
Violence and representation in Renaissance literature. England. 1590-1610. Lang.: Eng.　2614

Sperati, Paolo
Performance/production
Paolo Sperati, composer of stage music for Ibsen. Italy. Norway. 1856. Lang.: Ita.　1812

Spewack, Bella
Performance/production
Collection of newspaper reviews by London theatre critics. UK-England: London. 1997. Lang.: Eng.　2086
Plays/librettos/scripts
Film adaptations of Shakespeare's *The Taming of the Shrew*. USA. 1929-1966. Lang.: Eng.　3668

Spewack, Sam
Plays/librettos/scripts
Film adaptations of Shakespeare's *The Taming of the Shrew*. USA. 1929-1966. Lang.: Eng.　3668

Spewack, Samuel
Performance/production
Collection of newspaper reviews by London theatre critics. UK-England: London. 1997. Lang.: Eng.　2086

Spialeck, Hans
Performance/production
The reconstructed orchestration for the revival of *The Boys from Syracuse* by Encores!. USA: New York, NY. 1938-1997. Lang.: Eng.　3970

Spickler, Charlie
Design/technology
Charlie Spickler's lighting design for *An Obituary—Heiner Müller: A Man Without a Behind*. USA: New York, NY. 1997. Lang.: Eng.　1376

Spiderwoman Theater (New York, NY)
Performance/production
The female body in performance art. USA. Europe. 1960-1995. Lang.: Eng.　3837

Spielberg, Steven
Performance/production
Analysis of Steven Spielberg's film *Saving Private Ryan*. USA. 1997. Lang.: Eng.　3618

Spinning
Performance/production
Collection of newspaper reviews by London theatre critics. UK-England: London. 1997. Lang.: Eng.　1993

Spiritata, La
Plays/librettos/scripts
Sexuality and witchcraft in plays of Antonfrancesco Grazzini. Italy: Florence. 1500-1600. Lang.: Eng.　2956

Spiró, György
Plays/librettos/scripts
Interview with playwright György Spiró. Hungary. 1980-1997. Lang.: Hun.　2895

Spiro, Peter
Basic theatrical documents
Text of plays performed at the Nuyorican Poets Cafe. USA: New York, NY. 1973-1990. Lang.: Eng.　1322

Spitalfields Opera (London)
Performance/production
Collection of newspaper reviews by London theatre critics. UK-England: London. 1997. Lang.: Eng.　2133
Split Britches (New York, NY)
Performance/production
Essays on gender and performance. 250 B.C.-1995 A.D. Lang.: Eng.　1551

Plays/librettos/scripts
Mimesis, feminism, theatre, and performance. USA. 1997. Lang.: Eng.　3176

Spöksonaten (Ghost Sonata, The)
Performance/production
Collection of newspaper reviews by London theatre critics. UK-England: London. 1997. Lang.: Eng.　1982
Plays/librettos/scripts
Tradition and modernism in later plays of Strindberg. Sweden. 1894-1907. Lang.: Eng.　3061

Spoleto Festival USA (Charleston, SC)
Institutions
Productions of the Spoleto Festival USA. USA: Charleston, SC. 1976-1996. Lang.: Eng.　403

Spolno življenje grofa Franja Tahija (Sexual Life of Count Franjo Tahi, The)
Plays/librettos/scripts
Analysis of plays by Denis Poniž. Slovenia. 1976-1996. Lang.: Slo.　3014
Spontini, Gaspare
Performance/production
Soprano Rosa Ponselle. USA: New York, NY. 1920-1927. Lang.: Eng.　4245

Sporkmann, Frank
Performance/production
Performances of Schauspiel Leipzig. Germany: Leipzig. 1997. Lang.: Ger.　1713

Sprague, Jason
Design/technology
Hildegard Bechter's design for the musical *Always*. UK-England: London. 1997. Lang.: Eng.　3910
Performance/production
Collection of newspaper reviews by London theatre critics. UK-England: London. 1997. Lang.: Eng.　2062

Spring Awakening
SEE
Frühlings Erwachen.
Sprinkle, Annie
Performance/production
The female body in performance art. USA. Europe. 1960-1995. Lang.: Eng.　3837

Sprung, Der
Basic theatrical documents
Text *Der Sprung*, an opera libretto by Thomas Brasch. Germany. 1997. Lang.: Ger.　4011

Spry, Tami
Basic theatrical documents
Text of *Skins* by Tami Spry. USA. 1993. Lang.: Eng.　1343

Spychalski, Téo
Plays/librettos/scripts
Téo Spychalski's production of *Les Démons (The Demons)*. Canada: Montreal, PQ. 1997. Lang.: Fre.　2426

Squarzina, Luigi
Performance/production
Italian productions of D'Annunzio's *La Figlia di Iorio (Iorio's Daughter)*. Italy. 1904-1983. Lang.: Ita.　1797

Squirrels
Performance/production
Collection of newspaper reviews by London theatre critics. UK-England: London. 1997. Lang.: Eng.　2107

Srebrenica
Performance/production
Collection of newspaper reviews by London theatre critics. UK-England: London. 1997. Lang.: Eng.　2141

St. Denis, Ruth
Performance/production
Modern dance and feminist criticism. Europe. USA. 1906-1930. Lang.: Eng.　1179

St. Joan
Performance/production
Collection of newspaper reviews by London theatre critics. UK-England: London. 1997. Lang.: Eng.　1967

Staging — cont'd

Stage imagery in productions of Shakespeare's *Coriolanus*. England. 1754-1901. Lang.: Eng.										1634

As You Like It, transvestism, and early modern sexual politics. England. 1599. Lang.: Eng.										1636

The use of theatre to advance Ethiopian social goals. Ethiopia: Addis Ababa. 1996. Lang.: Eng.										1639

The depiction of the Passion of Christ on the medieval stage. Europe. 1400-1550. Lang.: Eng.										1641

Interview with actor, director, and teacher Mario Gonzales. Europe. Guatemala. 1967. Lang.: Swe.										1648

Recent productions of Elizabethan theatre. Europe. 1997. Lang.: Ger.										1649

Report on Finnish theatre productions. Finland: Helsinki, Tampere. 1997. Lang.: Eng, Fre.										1654

The decline of the mystery play in Lille. Flanders: Lille. 1480-1690. Lang.: Eng.										1655

Jean-Damien Barbin in Olivier Py's *La Servante (The Servant)*, a twenty-four-hour performance. France: Paris. 1997. Lang.: Swe.		1663

Productions of the Paris theatre season. France: Paris. 1996-1997. Lang.: Ger.										1668

History and politics on the Parisian stage. France: Paris. 1997. Lang.: Ger.										1669

Staging and Beckett's *Not I* and *Krapp's Last Tape*. France. Ireland. 1960-1973. Lang.: Eng.										1671

Roger Planchon's production of *Georges Dandin* by Molière. France: Villeurbanne. 1958. Lang.: Pol.										1675

Théâtre du Soleil's *Les Atrides*. France: Paris. 1992. Lang.: Eng.		1676

Report on the Paris theatre scene. France: Paris. 1997. Lang.: Swe. 1680

Interview with director Luc Bondy. Germany. France. 1948-1997. Lang.: Ger.										1684

The opening of the Deutsches Schauspielhaus season. Germany: Hamburg. 1997. Lang.: Ger.										1688

Productions of Bruno Klimek at Mannheimer Nationaltheater. Germany: Mannheim. 1996-1997. Lang.: Ger.										1689

The theatre of director Christoph Marthaler. Germany. 1980-1997. Lang.: Ger, Fre, Dut, Eng.										1692

The 'deconstructive potential' of Brecht's own production of *Mother Courage*. Germany: Berlin. 1949. Lang.: Ger.						1696

World premieres at Mannheimer Nationaltheater. Germany: Mannheim. 1997. Lang.: Ger.										1697

Israeli guest performances of children's theatre. Germany: Berlin. Israel. 1997. Lang.: Ger.										1698

German reactions to the work of Samuel Beckett. Germany. 1953-1976. Lang.: Eng.										1699

Einar Schleef's Berliner Ensemble production of Brecht's *Herr Puntila*. Germany: Berlin. 1996. Lang.: Ger.						1701

Playwright and director Daniel Call. Germany. 1967-1997. Lang.: Ger.										1702

German productions of Shakespeare after reunification. Germany. 1989-1992. Lang.: Eng.										1703

German theatre during and after the Nazi period. Germany: Berlin, Dusseldorf. Switzerland: Zurich. 1933-1952. Lang.: Eng.			1704

Recent productions of Čechov's *Ivanov*. Germany: Dusseldorf, Stuttgart. 1996-1997. Lang.: Ger.										1706

Productions of Staatstheater Wiesbaden. Germany: Wiesbaden. 1997. Lang.: Ger.										1709

Russian, Hungarian and Bulgarian plays at Kammerspiele. Germany: Magdeburg. 1989. Lang.: Ger.										1710

Updated classics at Schauspiel Leipzig. Germany: Leipzig. 1996-1997. Lang.: Ger.										1712

Performances of Schauspiel Leipzig. Germany: Leipzig. 1997. Lang.: Ger.										1713

Productions of Schauspiel Stuttgart. Germany: Stuttgart. 1997. Lang.: Ger.										1715

Recent productions of plays by Schiller. Germany. 1996-1997. Lang.: Ger.										1716

Director Andreas Kriegenburg. Germany. 1985-1997. Lang.: Ger.	1717

Dieter Dorn's production of *Ithaka* by Botho Strauss. Germany: Munich. 1996. Lang.: Swe.										1720

German productions of plays by Terrence McNally and Nicky Silver. Germany. 1996-1997. Lang.: Ger.										1721

Recent productions of plays by Horváth. Germany. Austria. 1996-1997. Lang.: Ger.										1722

Interview with director Christoph Marthaler and set designer Anna Viebrock. Germany. Switzerland. 1980-1997. Lang.: Ger.		1723

Significant productions in Swabia. Germany: Stuttgart. 1997. Lang.: Ger.										1726

Interview with director Benno Besson. Germany. Switzerland. 1949-1997. Lang.: Ger.										1727

Hartmut Wickert's production of Handke's *The Hour We Knew Nothing of Each Other*. Germany: Hannover. 1993. Lang.: Eng.		1728

Directors Tom Kühnel and Robert Schuster. Germany. 1970-1997. Lang.: Ger.										1729

Reviews of Bochumer Schauspielhaus productions. Germany: Bochum. 1997. Lang.: Ger.										1730

The new season at Düsseldorfer Schauspielhaus. Germany: Dusseldorf. 1997. Lang.: Ger.										1731

Contemporary plays at Schauspiel Leipzig. Germany: Leipzig. 1996-1997. Lang.: Ger.										1736

Performances of the classics in Franconia. Germany. 1997. Lang.: Ger.										1737

The directorial style of Jo Fabian. Germany: Berlin. 1987-1997. Lang.: Ger.										1739

Brecht's production of *Mother Courage*. Germany: Berlin. 1949. Lang.: Pol.										1740

Performances at Staattheater Mainz's new venue. Germany: Mainz. 1997. Lang.: Ger.										1743

Interview with director Jo Fabian. Germany: Berlin. 1989-1997. Lang.: Ger, Fre, Dut, Eng.										1744

Plays of Botho Strauss and Peter Handke carried over into a second season. Germany: Berlin, Frankfurt. 1996-1997. Lang.: Ger.		1746

The new season at Bochumer Schauspielhaus. Germany: Bochum. 1997. Lang.: Ger.										1747

Visual performance aspects of Greek tragedy. Greece: Athens. 500 B.C. Lang.: Ita.										1749

Production of Tony Harrison's *The Labourers of Herakles*. Greece: Delphi. 1995. Lang.: Eng.										1750

The interior I/eye in later plays of Samuel Beckett. Ireland. France. USA. 1978-1997. Lang.: Eng.										1785

Hanan Snir's productions of Lorca's *Blood Wedding (Bodas de sangre)*. Israel: Tel Aviv. 1990. Lang.: Eng.						1791

Renaissance theatre performances in Ferrara. Italy: Ferrara. 1486-1502. Lang.: Eng.										1794

The first Italian production of Tennessee Williams's *The Rose Tattoo*. Italy. 1996. Lang.: Ita.										1795

Mario Fumagalli's production of Shakespeare's *King Lear*. Italy: Rome. 1908. Lang.: Ita.										1796

Italian productions of D'Annunzio's *La Figlia di Iorio (Iorio's Daughter)*. Italy. 1904-1983. Lang.: Ita.						1797

Luca Ronconi's production of *Hamlet*. Italy: Rome. 1995. Lang.: Ita.										1802

Societas Raffaello Sanzio's production of Shakespeare's *Julius Caesar*. Italy: Prato. 1997. Lang.: Ita.							1803

I Magazzini's production of Brecht's *Im Dickicht der Städte (In the Jungle of Cities)*. Italy: Messina. 1995. Lang.: Ita.			1804

Massimo Castri's production of *La Ragione degli altri (The Reason of the Others)* by Pirandello. Italy: Messina. 1996-1997. Lang.: Ita.	1806

Federico Tiezzi's production of Brecht's *Im Dickicht der Städte (In the Jungle of Cities)*. Italy: Messina. 1995. Lang.: Ita.		1807

Treatments of Shakespeare's *Hamlet* by Robert Wilson and Benno Besson. Italy. 1995. Lang.: Ita.										1808

Massimo Castri's staging of Euripides' *Orestes* at Teatro Fabbricone. Italy: Prato. 1995. Lang.: Ita.							1810

Giorgio Strehler's staging of Pirandello's *I Giganti della montagna (The Mountain Giants)*. Italy: Milan. 1966-1994. Lang.: Ita.		1811

Gabriele Lavia's production of Shakespeare's *Othello*, in which Iago is the hero. Italy: Novara. 1995. Lang.: Ita.					1813

Creating roles in medieval theatre in the absence of psychological motivation. Italy: Camerino. 1996. Lang.: Eng.					1814

Letters from director Anton Giulio Bragaglia to playwright Nino Savarese. Italy. 1926. Lang.: Ita.										1816

Staging — cont'd

Review of Societas Raffaello Sanzio's children's theatre production of *Hansel and Gretel*. Italy: Cesena. 1997. Lang.: Ita.   1817

Passage Nord's production of *Eternity Lasts Longer*. Italy: Rome. 1997. Lang.: Ita.   1818

The *Oresteia* of Aeschylus as performed by Societas Raffaello Sanzio. Italy: Cesena. 1981-1997. Lang.: Eng.   1820

Societas Raffaello Sanzio's production of the *Oresteia* of Euripides. Italy: Cesena. 1995. Lang.: Ita.   1821

Japanese productions of plays by Samuel Beckett. Japan. 1960-1994. Lang.: Eng.   1823

Analysis of manuscript containing ten vernacular plays. Netherlands. 1405-1410. Lang.: Eng.   1828

Tadeusz Bradecki's activity as an actor, director, and playwright. Poland. 1983-1995. Lang.: Pol.   1836

Ghosts in theatrical productions. Poland. Lithuania. 1997. Lang.: Pol.   1838

Shakespeare's *The Winter's Tale* at Teatr Nowy. Poland: Poznań. 1997. Lang.: Eng, Fre.   1841

Jerzy Jarocki's productions of *Ślub (The Wedding)* by Witold Gombrowicz. Poland. 1960-1991. Lang.: Pol.   1842

Director Max Reinhardt's influence on Polish theatre. Poland. 1903-1914. Lang.: Ger.   1849

Current productions of plays by Čechov. Russia: Moscow. 1940-1997. Lang.: Eng.   1856

Amateur theatre production of Puškin's *Mocart i Saljeri (Mozart and Salieri)*. Russia: Skopina. 1990-1997. Lang.: Rus.   1860

Moscow Art Theatre productions. Russia: Moscow. Estonia: Tallinn. 1996-1997. Lang.: Rus.   1861

Bolšoj Drama Theatre production of Anouilh's *Antigone*. Russia: St. Petersburg. 1996. Lang.: Rus.   1862

Two productions of *Tanja-Tanja* by Ol'ga Muchina. Russia: St. Petersburg, Moscow. 1997. Lang.: Rus.   1863

Director Farid Bikčantajév of Teat'r im. Kamala. Russia: Kazan. 1997. Lang.: Rus.   1866

Report on the Moscow theatre scene. Russia: Moscow. 1997. Lang.: Swe.   1870

Ženovač's production of Turgenjév's *Mesjac v derevne (A Month in the Country)*. Russia: Moscow. 1996. Lang.: Rus.   1873

Galin's *Anomalja (Anomaly)* at Sovremennik. Russia: Moscow. 1996. Lang.: Rus.   1875

Fomenko's production of Puškin's *Pikovaja Dama (Queen of Spades)*. Russia: Moscow. 1996. Lang.: Rus.   1876

Teat'r na Jugo-Zapade's production of work based on plays of Bulgakov. Russia: Moscow. 1996. Lang.: Rus.   1878

Cvetajeva's *Sonečka i Kazanova (Sonečka and Casanova)* at Teat'r Ermitaž. Russia: Moscow. 1996. Lang.: Rus.   1879

Vladimir Anšon's production of Čechov's *Pianola*. Russia: St. Petersburg. 1995. Lang.: Rus.   1881

Ostrovskij's *Žadov i drugie (Žadov and Others)* at the Globus. Russia: Novosibirsk. 1997. Lang.: Rus.   1884

Ostrovskij's *Kozma Zacharič Minin* at Moscow Art Theatre. Russia: Moscow. 1997. Lang.: Rus.   1885

The work of director Aleksand'r Galibin. Russia: St. Petersburg. 1980-1997. Lang.: Rus.   1887

A production by Pëtr Fomenko's directing students at RATI. Russia: Moscow. 1996. Lang.: Rus.   1895

Anouilh's *Antigone* at the Bolšoj Drama Theatre. Russia: St. Petersburg. 1996. Lang.: Rus.   1897

Actor and director Solomon Michoéls remembered by his son. Russia: Moscow. 1890-1948. Lang.: Rus.   1899

Ionesco's *Rhinocéros* at Teat'r na Jugo-Zapade. Russia: Moscow. 1996. Lang.: Rus.   1901

Movement and physical image in South African theatre. South Africa, Republic of. 1997. Lang.: Eng.   1909

Plays based on refugee experiences. Sweden: Gothenburg. 1997. Lang.: Swe.   1927

Ingmar Bergman's productions of Shakespeare's plays. Sweden. Germany. 1944-1994. Lang.: Ita.   1934

Interview with director Peter Dalle. Sweden: Stockholm. 1970-1997. Lang.: Swe.   1941

Interview with director Kajsa Isakson. Sweden: Stockholm. 1986-1997. Lang.: Swe.   1951

Interview with principals of joint production *Berättelse på tidens strand (A Tale on the Shore of Time)*. Sweden. Mozambique. 1997. Lang.: Swe.   1959

Choreographer, composer, and director Birgitta Egerbladh. Sweden: Gothenburg. 1996. Lang.: Swe.   1960

Peter Brook's production *The Mahabharata*. UK-England. France. 1985. Lang.: Pol.   2164

Psychological interpretation of Tennessee Williams' *Suddenly Last Summer*. UK-England: Birmingham. 1996. Lang.: Eng.   2165

Analysis of Declan Donnellan's production of *Angels in America* by Tony Kushner. UK-England: London. 1992. Lang.: Eng.   2168

Non-literary realism in Shakespeare productions. UK-England. Germany. 1958-1995. Lang.: Ger.   2170

Everyman and *The Mysteries* at RSC. UK-England: Stratford. 1996-1997. Lang.: Ger.   2171

Two productions of Tom Stoppard's *Rosencrantz and Guildenstern Are Dead*. UK-England: London. Italy: Forlì. 1966-1996. Lang.:Ita.   2172

Criticism of productions at Shakespeare's Globe Theatre. UK-England: London. 1996. Lang.: Eng.   2187

Victorian ideas of womanhood in productions of Shakespeare's *The Merchant of Venice*. UK-England. 1832-1903. Lang.: Eng.   2188

Report on meeting of young European directors. UK-England: Stratford. 1997. Lang.: Swe.   2199

Elizabethan stage semiotics in twentieth-century Shakespearean productions. UK-England. 1905-1979. Lang.: Eng.   2203

A student production of *Time and the Room (Die Zeit und das Zimmer)* by Botho Strauss. UK-England. 1996. Lang.: Eng.   2204

The work of director Terence Gray. UK-England: Cambridge. 1925-1940. Lang.: Eng.   2210

Use of Mejerchol'd's techniques in a production of Gogol's *The Government Inspector (Revizor)*. UK-England: Northampton. 1997. Lang.: Eng.   2216

Elizabeth Robins' *Votes for Women!*. UK-England: London. 1907. Lang.: Eng.   2219

Théâtre de Complicité's production of Brecht's *Caucasian Chalk Circle*. UK-England: London. 1997. Lang.: Ger.   2226

Gay theatre in the British mainstream theatre. UK-England. 1986-1997. Lang.: Eng.   2227

Peter Brook's RSC production of Shakespeare's *King Lear*. UK-England: Stratford, London. 1970. Lang.: Pol.   2228

The construction of the Middle East on the British stage. UK-England. 1798-1853. Lang.: Eng.   2229

Ralph Lee's production of *Heart of the Earth* by Cherríe Moraga. USA: New York, NY. 1995. Lang.: Eng.   2238

Interview with actor/director Austin Pendleton. USA. 1980-1995. Lang.: Eng.   2266

Ontological-Hysteric Theatre's production of *Pearls for Pigs* at Hartford Stage. USA: Hartford, CT. 1995. Lang.: Eng.   2270

Director Lisa Peterson. USA: Los Angeles, CA. 1997. Lang.: Eng.   2279

Charles Marowitz on his approach to directing Shakespeare. USA. 1987. Lang.: Eng.   2302

The development and reception of *Mississippi Freedom* by Robbie McCauley. USA. 1990-1992. Lang.: Eng.   2304

Productions of plays by Ibsen. USA. France. UK-England. 1996-1997. Lang.: Eng.   2306

Directors Michael Kahn and Karin Coonrod on their productions of *Henry VI*. USA: New York, NY, Washington, DC. 1950-1996. Lang. :Eng.   2312

Comparison of productions of Tony Kushner's *Angels in America, Part I: Millennium Approaches*. USA: New York, NY. UK-England. 1992-1993. Lang.: Eng.   2326

Reconstruction of Elia Kazan's production of *A Streetcar Named Desire* by Tennessee Williams. USA: New York, NY. 1947. Lang.: Pol.   2330

Reviews of *Hot Keys* and *Sally's Rape*. USA: New York, NY. 1991-1992. Lang.: Eng.   2347

Black actors and writers and the Negro Units of the Federal Theatre Project. USA: Washington, DC, New York, NY. 1935. Lang.: Eng. 2350

Directing methods of Richard Foreman, Ontological-Hysteric Theatre. USA. 1968-1997. Lang.: Dan.   2351

Staging — cont'd

Loncraine and McKellen's *Richard III* from stage to screen. UK-England. 1995-1996. Lang.: Eng.   3590

Baz Luhrmann's film adaptation of *Romeo and Juliet*. USA. 1997. Lang.: Eng.   3627

Staging techniques in video installations. Canada. 1978-1997. Lang.: Fre.   3717

Work in Slovakia of Czech mime Ctibor Turba. Czechoslovakia. 1975-1982. Lang.: Cze.   3744

Roman festivities of the Baroque period. Italy: Rome. 1585-1700. Lang.: Ita.   3768

Roman festivities. Italy: Rome. 1700-1870. Lang.: Ita.   3769

Role-playing, audience-free, interactive theatre. Sweden. 1990. Lang.: Swe.   3770

Chronicle of court entertainment at Versailles. France: Versailles. 1668. Lang.: Ita.   3797

Desire in performance art of Shawna Dempsey. Canada. 1992-1997. Lang.: Eng.   3816

The significance of Johannesburg music hall. South Africa, Republic of: Johannesburg. 1886-1896. Lang.: Eng.   3857

Melodramas of Václav Praupner. Austro-Hungarian Empire: Prague, Bohemia. 1700-1799. Lang.: Cze.   3864

Interview with director Robert Wilson. Europe. 1969-1997. Lang.: Ger, Fre, Dut, Eng.   3866

The theatrical productions of Robert Wilson. USA. Europe. 1964-1996. Lang.: Ita.   3883

Comparison of productions of *Ragtime* and *Jane Eyre*. Canada: Toronto, ON. 1997. Lang.: Eng.   3932

Four productions of the musical *A Dzsungel könyve (The Jungle Book)*. Hungary. 1996-1997. Lang.: Hun.   3936

Interview with director Richard Günther. Sweden: Stockholm. 1990-1997. Lang.: Swe.   3943

Concert versions of neglected American musicals in the 'Discover the Lost Musicals' series. UK-England: London. 1990-1997. Lang.:Eng.   3944

Restaging the score of Stephen Sondheim's *A Little Night Music*. USA. 1973. Lang.: Eng.   3951

Work of choreographer Susan Stroman on *Steel Pier*. USA: New York, NY. 1975-1997. Lang.: Eng.   3956

Actor's Expression production of an unauthorized version of the musical *Oklahoma!*. USA: Atlanta, GA. 1997. Lang.: Eng.   3959

Opera productions from Salzburger Festspiele. Austria: Salzburg. 1997. Lang.: Ger.   4096

Interview with director and scene designer Achim Freyer. Austria: Salzburg. 1997. Lang.: Ger.   4097

List of summer opera festivals. Canada. USA. Europe. 1997. Lang.: Eng.   4110

Opera director Robert Carsen. Canada. Europe. 1995-1997. Lang.: Eng.   4113

Problem of staging the works of Janáček. Czech Republic. 1854-1928. Lang.: Cze.   4118

Productions at the Munich Biennale. Germany: Munich. 1997. Lang.: Ger.   4148

Miklós Gábor Kerényi's production of *Der Fliegende Holländer*, Budapest Opera House. Hungary: Budapest. 1997. Lang.: Hun.   4184

Opera productions directed by Erwin Piscator. Italy: Florence. 1963-1964. Lang.: Ger.   4196

Realistic productions at the Royal Swedish Opera. Sweden: Stockholm. 1862-1997. Lang.: Swe.   4220

Background material on New York City Opera telecast performance of *La Bohème*. USA: New York, NY. 1997. Lang.: Eng.   4230

Background material on Lyric Opera of Chicago radio broadcast performances. USA: Chicago, IL. 1997. Lang.: Eng.   4231

Background material on Juilliard Opera's telecast performance of *Hänsel und Gretel*. USA: New York, NY. 1997. Lang.: Eng.   4232

Background material on Metropolitan Opera telecast performance. USA: New York, NY. 1997. Lang.: Eng.   4233

Background material on New York City Opera telecast performance. USA: New York, NY. 1997. Lang.: Eng.   4234

Background material on Metropolitan Opera radio broadcast performances. USA: New York, NY. 1997-1997. Lang.: Eng.   4237

Background material on Metropolitan Opera radio broadcast performances. USA: New York, NY. 1997. Lang.: Eng.   4238

American chamber opera. USA. 1868-1997. Lang.: Eng.   4258

Review of Ronnie Burkett's puppet play *Tinka's New Dress*. Canada: Winnipeg, MB. 1997. Lang.: Eng.   4361

The Czech national character as reflected in contemporary puppet theatre. Czech Republic. 1997. Lang.: Cze.   4363

Géza Blattner's puppet adaptation of *Az ember tragédiája (The Tragedy of Man)* by Madách. Hungary. 1918-1954. Lang.: Hun.   4365

Analysis of Bread and Puppet Theatre's *Domestic Resurrection Circus*. USA: Plainfield, VT. 1970-1997. Lang.: Eng.   4372

Contemporary regional theatre and its origins in ancestor worship. China: Quanzhou, Fujian. 714-1994. Lang.: Eng.   4388

Guest performance of Cooperativo Teatroarte Cuticchio at Kaye Playhouse. USA: New York, NY. 1997. Lang.: Eng.   4393

Profile of television series *The Wubbulous World of Dr. Seuss*. USA: New York, NY. 1997. Lang.: Eng.   4397

Plays/librettos/scripts

Identity and the use of multiple actors to portray a single character in postcolonial drama. Australia. Ireland. Samoa. 1997. Lang.: Eng.   2380

Solo performance in British Columbia. Canada: Vancouver, BC, Victoria, BC. 1997. Lang.: Eng.   2405

Adaptations of French classics for contemporary audiences. Canada: Montreal, PQ. France. 1997. Lang.: Fre.   2421

The dramatic power of *The Conversion of St. Paul*. England. 1500. Lang.: Eng.   2726

Analysis of a line from Shakespeare's *King Lear*. England. 1605-1606. Lang.: Eng.   2729

The handkerchief in Shakespeare's *Othello*. England. 1605. Lang.: Eng.   2740

Annotations on a script of *The Two Merry Milkmaids*. England. 1620. Lang.: Eng.   2754

Text and performance in the Romantic period. Europe. 1800-1851. Lang.: Pol.   2790

Shakespearean themes in contemporary plays and productions. Europe. 1965-1995. Lang.: Pol.   2798

The genesis and stage history of Čechov's *Čajka (The Seagull)*. Russia. 1892-1996. Lang.: Hun.   2999

Relation to other fields

The social and political context of Dario Fo's theatre. Italy. 1959-1975. Lang.: Pol.   769

Theory/criticism

Methods of notation for the recording of theatrical productions. 1901-1997. Lang.: Eng.   3456

Critical response to a production of Euripides' *Medea* by Mark Fleishman and Jenny Reznek. South Africa, Republic of. 1994-1996. Lang.: Eng.   3494

Stalker

Performance/production

Music in films by Andrej Tarkovskij. Russia. 1979-1983. Lang.: Eng.   3585

Stallone, Sylvester

Design/technology

Benjamin Fernandez's production design for *Daylight*. Italy: Rome. 1996. Lang.: Eng.   3543

Stanger, Inés Margarita

Plays/librettos/scripts

Analysis of *Malinche* by Inés M. Stanger and *Opus Primum* by Hadi Kurich. Chile. Spain. 1993. Lang.: Spa.   2439

Staniewski, Wlodzimierz

Institutions

Wlodzimierz Staniewski's experimental theatre group Ośrodek Praktyk Teatralnych. Poland: Gardzienice. 1976-1996. Lang.: Pol.   358

Stanisic, Gordana

Performance/production

Space, place, and travel in performance art and installations. UK-England: London. Germany: Kassel. 1997. Lang.: Eng.   3823

Stanislavskij, Konstantin Sergejevič

Institutions

The studios of the Moscow Art Theatre. Russia. 1905-1927. Lang.: Eng.   365

Performance/production

Twentieth-century theatre as a signifying practice. Europe. North America. 1900-1995. Lang.: Eng.   515

Italian translation of *The Actor's Work on Himself* by K.S. Stanislavskij. Russia. 1863-1938. Lang.: Ita.   601

Suomen Kansallisoopera (Helsinki) — cont'd

Performance/production
Finland's numerous opera festivals. Finland. 1997. Lang.: Eng. 4135

Suor Angelica
Performance/production
Background material on Lyric Opera of Chicago radio broadcast performances. USA: Chicago, IL. 1997. Lang.: Eng. 4231

Super-Beasts
Performance/production
Collection of newspaper reviews by London theatre critics. UK-England: London. 1997. Lang.: Eng. 2030

Supple, Tim
Performance/production
Collection of newspaper reviews by London theatre critics. UK-England: London. 1997. Lang.: Eng. 1975

Collection of newspaper reviews by London theatre critics. UK-England: London. 1997. Lang.: Eng. 2154

Support areas
Performance spaces
Profile of the renovated *kabuki* theatre Kanamaru-za. Japan: Kotohira. 1830-1995. Lang.: Eng. 1230

The debate over the stage design and pillars of Shakespeare's Globe. England: London. 1599-1995. Lang.: Eng. 1525

The renovation of the Lyceum Theatre for *Jesus Christ Superstar*. UK-England: London. 1904-1997. Lang.: Eng. 3931

Kungliga Operan's new rehearsal space. Sweden: Stockholm. 1996. Lang.: Swe. 4067

Musikteater i Värmland's new shop and rehearsal spaces. Sweden: Karlstad. 1996. Lang.: Swe. 4068

Supreme Dream
Plays/librettos/scripts
The writing of *Supreme Dream* by Frank Moher and actress Rhonda Trodd. Canada: Toronto, ON. 1997. Lang.: Eng. 2425

Suréna
Plays/librettos/scripts
Analysis of Corneille's *Suréna*. France. 1674. Lang.: Eng. 2829

Surfing
Performance/production
Collection of newspaper reviews by London theatre critics. UK-England: London. 1997. Lang.: Eng. 1970

Collection of newspaper reviews by London theatre critics. UK-England: London. 1997. Lang.: Eng. 2113

Surrealism
Plays/librettos/scripts
Analysis of *Camino Real* by Tennessee Williams. USA. 1953-1990. Lang.: Eng. 3129

Survival
Plays/librettos/scripts
Robert McLaren and Experimental Theatre Workshop. South Africa, Republic of: Johannesburg. 1972-1976. Lang.: Eng. 3030

Suschitzky, Peter
Design/technology
Technical challenges in shooting the film *Crash*. USA. 1997. Lang.: Eng. 3551

Suspect Culture (Glascow)
Institutions
Impressions of the Edinburgh Festival. UK-Scotland: Edinburgh. 1997. Lang.: Ger. 391

Sussman, Sally
Performance/production
Sally Sussman's adaptation of *xiqu* to Australian performance. Australia. 1988-1996. Lang.: Eng. 3891

Sutcliffe, Mike
Design/technology
Lighting design for the live telecast of the Brit Awards for music. UK-England. 1980-1997. Lang.: Eng. 194

Sutherland, Joan
Performance/production
The difficulty of performing 'Sempre Libera' in Verdi's *La Traviata*. Italy. USA: New York, NY. 1886-1996. Lang.: Eng. 4186

Sutherland, Malcolm
Performance/production
Collection of newspaper reviews by London theatre critics. UK-England: London. 1997. Lang.: Eng. 2104

Sutto-Deyglun, Janine
Performance/production
Interview with actress Janine Sutto-Deyglun. Canada: Montreal, PQ. 1921-1997. Lang.: Fre. 1598

Suzanna Adler
Performance/production
Collection of newspaper reviews by London theatre critics. UK-England: London. 1997. Lang.: Eng. 2089

Suzman, Janet
Performance/production
Collection of newspaper reviews by London theatre critics. UK-England. 1997. Lang.: Eng. 2050

Collection of newspaper reviews by London theatre critics. UK-England: London. 1997. Lang.: Eng. 2130

Reactions to modern performances of *Antony and Cleopatra*. UK-England. North America. 1827-1987. Lang.: Eng. 2178

Television versions of Shakespeare's *Othello*. UK-England. 1987-1996. Lang.: Eng. 3726

Svarta fanor (Black Banners)
Performance/production
Director Frank Castorf. Germany: Berlin. Sweden: Stockholm. 1976. Lang.: Swe. 1700

Two productions of the annual Strindberg festival at Stockholms Stadsteater. Sweden: Stockholm. 1997. Lang.: Eng. 1957

Plays/librettos/scripts
Tradition and modernism in later plays of Strindberg. Sweden. 1894-1907. Lang.: Eng. 3061

Sved, Nikki
Performance/production
Collection of newspaper reviews by London theatre critics. UK-England: London. 1997. Lang.: Eng. 2004

Svedin, Lulli
Performance/production
Dancer Lulli Svedin. Sweden: Stockholm. 1920. Lang.: Swe. 1115

Svenska Balettskolan (Stockholm)
Performance/production
Interview with character dance teacher Pierre de Olivo. Sweden: Stockholm. 1940. Lang.: Swe. 1114

Svenska Riksteatern (Norsborg)
Institutions
Account of a theatre festival/conference of young Scandinavian playwrights. Sweden: Stockholm. 1997. Lang.: Swe. 1493

Performance spaces
Svenska Riksteatern's directory of performance spaces. Sweden. 1990. Lang.: Swe. 451

Svetina, Ivo
Basic theatrical documents
English translations of plays by contemporary Slovenian playwrights. Slovenia. 1980-1997. Lang.: Eng. 1301

Text of *Tako je umrl Zaratuštra (Thus Died Zarathustra)* by Ivo Svetina. Slovenia. 1995. Lang.: Slo. 1302

English and German translations of *Babylon* by Ivo Svetina. Slovenia. 1997. Lang.: Eng, Ger. 1303

Plays/librettos/scripts
Analysis of plays by Jože Snoj and Ivo Svetina. Slovenia. 1900-1996. Lang.: Slo. 3008

Svoboda, Josef
Design/technology
Italian translation of scenographer Josef Svoboda's autobiography. Czechoslovakia. 1920-1997. Lang.: Ita. 154

Survey of classes, demonstrations, and exhibitions at OISTAT conference. USA: Pittsburgh, PA. 1997. Lang.: Eng. 221

Swaggers
Performance/production
Collection of newspaper reviews by London theatre critics. UK-England: London. 1997. Lang.: Eng. 2000

Swamp Gravy (Colquitt, GA)
Relation to other fields
The movement of theatre from entertainment to 'efficacy'. Israel: Akko. USA. 1994-1997. Lang.: Eng. 767

Swan Lake
SEE ALSO
Lebedinoje osero.

Swan Song
Performance/production
Collection of newspaper reviews by London theatre critics. UK-England: London. 1997. Lang.: Eng. 2110

Swan Theatre (London)
Performance spaces
Shakespeare's plays on the Elizabethan stage. England. 1590-1615. Lang.: Eng. 1520

Swan Theatre (Stratford)
Performance/production
Report on experimental theatre and the Grass Roots Festival. UK-England: Cambridge, Stratford-on-Avon. 1996. Lang.: Hun. 617

Collection of newspaper reviews by London theatre critics. UK-England. 1997. Lang.: Eng. 2014

Collection of newspaper reviews by London theatre critics. UK-England. 1997. Lang.: Eng. 2051

Collection of newspaper reviews by London theatre critics. UK-England. 1997. Lang.: Eng. 2109

Collection of newspaper reviews by London theatre critics. UK-England. 1997. Lang.: Eng. 2163

Michael Boyd's production of Kyd's *Spanish Tragedy* at the Swan. UK-England: Stratford. 1997. Lang.: Eng. 2183

History of contemporary Shakespeare performances. UK-England. 1989-1997. Lang.: Eng. 2190

Swarte, Rieks
Performance/production
The visual theatre of director Rieks Swarte. Netherlands. 1989-1997. Lang.: Eng, Fre. 1829

Sweeney Todd
Plays/librettos/scripts
Psychological themes in Stephen Sondheim's *Sweeney Todd* and their effect on audiences. USA. 1976. Lang.: Eng. 3999

Sweeney, Jim
Performance/production
Collection of newspaper reviews by London theatre critics. UK-England: London. 1997. Lang.: Eng. 2126

Sweet Bird of Youth
Plays/librettos/scripts
Sex, gender, and eroticism in plays of Tennessee Williams. USA. 1956-1959. Lang.: Eng. 3161

Tennessee Williams' plays on film. USA. 1950-1969. Lang.: Eng. 3245

Sweet Hereafter, The
Basic theatrical documents
Script of *The Sweet Hereafter* by Atom Egoyan. Canada. 1997. Lang.: Eng. 3525

Design/technology
Lighting design for the film *The Sweet Hereafter*. Canada. 1997. Lang.: Eng. 3542

Plays/librettos/scripts
Interview with screenwriter and director Atom Egoyan. Canada. 1997. Lang.: Eng. 3633

Reactions to *The Sweet Hereafter* by the author of the novel on which the film was based. Canada. 1997. Lang.: Eng. 3634

Swinarski, Konrad
Performance/production
Analysis of Jerzy Grotowski's *Apocalypsis cum figuris*. Poland. 1964-1992. Lang.: Pol. 581

Biography of actress Anna Dymna. Poland: Cracow. 1950-1997. Lang.: Pol. 1835

Swinburne, Algernon Charles
Relation to other fields
Politics in Joyce's *Ulysses* and his references to *Hamlet*. Ireland. 1920. Lang.: Eng. 3363

Swinton Massacre, The
Plays/librettos/scripts
Analysis of plays by Ray Guy. Canada. 1948-1951. Lang.: Eng. 2404

Swiss Christmas
Performance/production
Productions of plays by Katharina Thanner and Lisa Engel. Switzerland: Zurich, Basel. 1995-1997. Lang.: Ger. 1963

Swiss Union of Theatre Makers
SEE
Vereinigte Theaterschaffenden der Schweiz.

Swyer, Sharon
Performance/production
Collection of newspaper reviews by London theatre critics. UK-England: London. 1997. Lang.: Eng. 2132

Sydney Theatre
Performance spaces
Study of the Sydney Theatre. Australia: Sydney. 1796-1820. Lang.: Eng. 414

Sylbert, Paul
Design/technology
Paul Sylbert's production design for *Rosewood*. USA. 1996. Lang.: Eng. 3550

Sylphide, La
Performance/production
Marriage and domesticity in *La Sylphide* choreographed by Filippo Taglioni. France. 1830-1835. Lang.: Eng. 1068

Sylvia
Performance/production
John Neumeier's choreography of Delibes' *Sylvia*. France: Paris. 1997. Lang.: Hun. 1073

Symbolism
Plays/librettos/scripts
The significance of paper in Tennessee Williams' *A Streetcar Named Desire*. USA. 1940-1997. Lang.: Eng. 3217

Symo, Margit
Performance/production
Film careers of Hungarian dancers. Hungary. 1929-1945. Lang.: Hun. 976

Symo, Mihály
Performance/production
Film careers of Hungarian dancers. Hungary. 1929-1945. Lang.: Hun. 976

Sympathetic Magic
Design/technology
Dennis Parichy's lighting design for *Sympathetic Magic* by Lanford Wilson at Second Stage. USA: New York, NY. 1997. Lang.: Eng. 1369

Symphonic Variations
Performance/production
Interview with choreographer Michael Somes. USA: New York, NY. 1992. Lang.: Eng. 1120

Syndrome de Cézanne, Le (Cézanne Syndrome, The)
Plays/librettos/scripts
Self-reflexivity in Quebec drama. Canada. 1981-1988. Lang.: Fre. 2397

Synge, John Millington
Performance/production
Irish plays and characters on the New York stage. USA: New York, NY. Ireland. 1874-1966. Lang.: Eng. 2277

Plays/librettos/scripts
Cultural translation and *The Playboy of the Western World* by J.M. Synge. Ireland. 1898-1918. Lang.: Eng. 2910

Comparison of Friel's *Molly Sweeney* and Synge's *The Well of the Saints*. Ireland. UK-Ireland. 1997. Lang.: Eng. 2935

The character of the traveler in plays of the Irish Renaissance. Ireland. 1910-1930. Lang.: Eng. 2938

Syrener (Lilacs)
Performance/production
Sex and gender in recent Stockholm productions. Sweden: Stockholm. 1996. Lang.: Eng. 1925

Szabó, Miklós
Performance/production
The career of tenor Miklós Szabó. Hungary. 1930-1989. Lang.: Hun. 4171

Szász, János
Performance/production
Interview with director János Szász. Hungary. 1980-1997. Lang.: Hun. 1758

Szczęśniak, Malgorzata
Performance/production
Shakespeare's *The Winter's Tale* at Teatr Nowy. Poland: Poznań. 1997. Lang.: Eng, Fre. 1841

Szegedi Kortárs Balett (Szeged)
Institutions
Modern tendencies in Hungarian ballet. Hungary: Pécs, Szeged. 1964-1970. Lang.: Hun. 1054

Profile of Szegedi Kortárs Balett. Hungary: Szeged. 1987-1997. Lang.: Hun. 1162

The reorganization of Szegedi Kortárs Balett. Hungary: Szeged. 1987-1997. Lang.: Hun. 1163

Performance/production
Career of dancer and choreographer Zoltán Imre. Hungary. 1943-1997. Lang.: Hun. 1078

Szegedi Nemzeti Színház (Szeged)
Performance/production
The career of tenor Miklós Szabó. Hungary. 1930-1989. Lang.: Hun. 4171

Opera singer Kálmán Gyimesi of the Szeged National Theatre. Hungary. 1945-1997. Lang.: Hun. 4172

Székely, Gábor
Institutions
Pictorial history of Katona Jószef Chamber Theatre. Hungary: Budapest. 1982-1997. Lang.: Hun. 1442

Színház- és Filmművészeti Főiskola (Budapest)
Institutions
Interview with Péter Huszti of Budapest's High School of Theatre Arts. Hungary: Budapest. 1987-1997. Lang.: Hun. 336
Performance/production
Colleagues' recollections of director László Vámos. Hungary. 1928-1996. Lang.: Hun. 1763

Szirmai, Albert
Plays/librettos/scripts
The development of operetta. Austro-Hungarian Empire: Vienna, Budapest. 1850-1930. Lang.: Hun. 4339

Szkotak, Pawel
Institutions
Teatr Biuro Podrózy and its founder Pawel Szkotak. Poland: Poznań. 1988-1996. Lang.: Eng. 1453

Szőnyi, Olga
Performance/production
Interview with mezzo-soprano Olga Szőnyi of the Budapest Opera House. Hungary. 1933-1997. Lang.: Hun. 4167

Szulkin, Piotr
Plays/librettos/scripts
Analysis of plays shown on Polish television. Poland. 1929-1997. Lang.: Pol. 3735

Szyfman, Arnold
Performance/production
Director Max Reinhardt's influence on Polish theatre. Poland. 1903-1914. Lang.: Ger. 1849

Ta veseli dan ali Maticek se ženi (This Merry Day, or Maticek Gets Married)
Performance/production
Account of a production of Linhart's comedy about Maticek. Slovenia: Novo mesto. 1848. Lang.: Slo. 1903

Tabard Theatre (London)
Performance/production
Collection of newspaper reviews by London theatre critics. UK-England: London. 1997. Lang.: Eng. 2117

Tabarro, Il
Performance/production
Background material on Lyric Opera of Chicago radio broadcast performances. USA: Chicago, IL. 1997. Lang.: Eng. 4231

Tabet, Giorgio
Administration
Illustrator Giorgio Tabet's playbills and cinema posters. Italy. 1904-1997. Lang.: Ita. 39

Tableaux vivants
Performance/production
Emma Lyon, Goethe, and the tableau vivant. Italy: Naples. Germany. 1786-1791. Lang.: Eng. 566

Tabori, George
Performance/production
Interview with director George Tabori. Austria: Vienna. 1997. Lang.: Ger. 1562

Interview with director George Tabori about Bertolt Brecht. North America. 1947-1997. Lang.: Eng. 1645

Tábori, György
SEE
Tabori, George.

Tábori, Nóra
Performance/production
Album devoted to actress Nóra Tábori. Hungary. 1928-1996. Lang.: Hun. 1773

Tabucchi, Antonio
Institutions
Impressions of the Festival d'Avignon. France: Avignon. 1997. Lang.: Ger. 313

Tacoma Theatre (Tacoma, WA)
Performance spaces
History of the Tacoma Theatre. USA: Tacoma, WA. 1888-1963. Lang.: Eng. 3763

Taganka Theatre
SEE
Teat'r na Tagankė.

Taglioni, Filippo
Performance/production
Marriage and domesticity in La Sylphide choreographed by Filippo Taglioni. France. 1830-1835. Lang.: Eng. 1068

Analysis of Filippo Taglioni's ballet La Révolte des femmes. France. 1830-1840. Lang.: Eng. 1076

Taglioni, Marie
Performance/production
Analysis of Filippo Taglioni's ballet La Révolte des femmes. France. 1830-1840. Lang.: Eng. 1076

Taglioni, Salvatore
Performance/production
Dancer, choreographer, and composer Salvatore Taglioni. Italy: Naples. 1830-1860. Lang.: Eng. 1095

Tailings
Performance/production
The making of Tailings by Erik Ehn and Smart Mouth Theatre. USA: San Francisco, CA. 1995-1997. Lang.: Eng. 636

Tainted Dawn, A
Performance/production
Collection of newspaper reviews by London theatre critics. UK-England: London. 1997. Lang.: Eng. 1975

Collection of newspaper reviews by London theatre critics. UK-Scotland: Edinburgh. 1997. Lang.: Eng. 2230

Takemoto, Tina
Performance/production
Angela Ellsworth and Tina Takemoto's Her/She Senses Imag(in)ed Malady. USA. 1991-1997. Lang.: Eng. 3844

Taking Sides
Design/technology
Howell Binkley's lighting design for Taking Sides by Ronald Harwood. USA: New York, NY. 1997. Lang.: Eng. 1366

Tako je umrl Zaratuštra (Thus Died Zarathustra)
Basic theatrical documents
Text of Tako je umrl Zaratuštra (Thus Died Zarathustra) by Ivo Svetina. Slovenia. 1995. Lang.: Slo. 1302
Plays/librettos/scripts
Analysis of plays by Jože Snoj and Ivo Svetina. Slovenia. 1900-1996. Lang.: Slo. 3008

Takwakin Theatre (Edmonton, AB)
Performance/production
A methodology of theatrical creation based on native performance culture. Canada. 1991-1996. Lang.: Eng. 3865

Talbot, Ian
Performance/production
Collection of newspaper reviews by London theatre critics. UK-England: London. 1997. Lang.: Eng. 2086

Tale of a Tub, A
Plays/librettos/scripts
Jonson's Tale of a Tub as a political critique. England. 1633. Lang.: Eng. 2723

Tales My Lover Told Me
Performance/production
Collection of newspaper reviews by London theatre critics. UK-England: London. 1997. Lang.: Eng. 2129

Tales of Hoffmann, The
SEE
Contes d'Hoffmann, Les.

Tales of the Lost Formicans
Plays/librettos/scripts
Interview with playwright Constance Congdon. USA. 1997. Lang.: Eng. 3163

Talisman oder die Schicksalsperucken, Der (Talisman or the Wigs of Fate, The)
Basic theatrical documents
English performance translation of Nestroy's Der Talisman. Austria. 1833-1849. Lang.: Eng. 1256

Talk Radio
Performance/production
Collection of newspaper reviews by London theatre critics. UK-England. 1997. Lang.: Eng. 2092
Plays/librettos/scripts
Film adaptation of Eric Bogosian's Talk Radio. USA: Hollywood, CA. 1988. Lang.: Eng. 3673

Tallchief, Maria
Institutions
Ballerina Maria Tallchief on the founding of the New York City Ballet. USA: New York, NY. 1946. Lang.: Eng. 1062
Performance/production
Ballerina Maria Tallchief: interview and photos. USA: Washington, DC. 1997. Lang.: Eng. 1128

Tallinna Linnateater (Tallinn)
Institutions
Profile of Tallinna Linnateater, Elmo Nüganen, artistic director. Estonia: Tallinn. 1967. Lang.: Swe. 1401

Tate, Nahum
  Performance/production
    Opera Atelier's production of Purcell's *Dido and Aeneas*. Canada:
    Toronto, ON. 1994-1995. Lang.: Eng.   4112
  Plays/librettos/scripts
    The ideology of Restoration comedy. England. 1660-1710. Lang.: Eng.
                                                                           2492
    Analysis of Nahum Tate's adaptation of Shakespeare's *Coriolanus*.
    England. 1682. Lang.: Eng.   2712
Taxes
  Administration
    Effect of new tax rules on actors and the entertainment industry. USA.
    1997. Lang.: Eng.   70
    An appropriate tax program for theatre personnel. USA. 1997. Lang.:
    Eng.   71
    Guide for actors faced with a tax audit. USA. 1997. Lang.: Eng.   72
    New law exempts theatrical productions from city tax on set and
    costume expenses. USA: New York, NY. 1997. Lang.: Eng.   111
Taxi Driver
  Plays/librettos/scripts
    Analysis of films by Martin Scorsese. USA. 1976-1982. Lang.: Eng. 3676
Taylor-Wood, Sam
  Performance/production
    Collection of newspaper reviews by London theatre critics. UK-England:
    London. 1997. Lang.: Eng.   2059
Taylor, Daniel
  Performance/production
    Profile of countertenor Daniel Taylor. Canada. 1997. Lang.: Eng.   4108
Taylor, Drew Hayden
  Basic theatrical documents
    Text of *Girl Who Loved Her Horses* by Drew Hayden Taylor. Canada.
    1990-1997. Lang.: Eng.   1262
  Performance/production
    Native Canadian playwrights and theatre groups. Canada. 1979-1997.
    Lang.: Eng.   1597
Taylor, Jeremy James
  Performance/production
    Collection of newspaper reviews by London theatre critics. UK-England:
    London. 1997. Lang.: Eng.   2099
    Collection of newspaper reviews by London theatre critics. UK-England:
    London. 1997. Lang.: Eng.   2146
Taylor, Judy
  Performance/production
    Collection of newspaper reviews by London theatre critics. UK-England:
    London. 1997. Lang.: Eng.   1989
Taylor, Laurette
  Performance/production
    Biography of actress Laurette Taylor. USA. 1884-1946. Lang.: Eng.
                                                                           2300
Taylor, Paul
  Institutions
    Profile of the Paul Taylor Dance Company. USA: New York, NY.
    1950-1997. Lang.: Hun.   1171
  Theory/criticism
    Movement analysis on modern dance. USA. 1995. Lang.: Eng.   1218
Taylor, Tony
  Performance/production
    Collection of newspaper reviews by London theatre critics. UK-England:
    London. 1997. Lang.: Eng.   2138
Tazewell, Paul
  Design/technology
    Design elements of *On the Town* for New York Shakespeare Festival.
    USA: New York, NY. 1997. Lang.: Eng.   3915
Tchaikovsky, Peter Ilich
  SEE
    Čajkovskij, Pëtr Iljič.
Tchernichova, Elena
  Performance/production
    Choreographer Elena Tchernichova on the ballet *Giselle*. USA. 1950-
    1997. Lang.: Eng.   1129
Teaching methods
  Institutions
    Profile of children's cultural center The Ark. Ireland: Dublin. 1982-
    1997. Lang.: Eng.   342
    Robert Spillman of Lyric Theatre program, University of Colorado.
    USA: Boulder, CO. 1940-1997. Lang.: Eng.   4061
  Performance/production
    Use of Mejerchol'd's techniques in a production of Gogol's *The
    Government Inspector (Revizor)*. UK-England: Northampton. 1997.
    Lang.: Eng.   2216

Beijing production of Carmen's *Bizet*. China, People's Republic of:
Beijing. 1982-1997. Lang.: Eng.   4117
Relation to other fields
  Innovations in collegiate theatrical instruction. USA. 1900-1945. Lang.:
  Eng.   798
  Strategies for supporting theatre arts teachers in secondary school. USA.
  1994-1996. Lang.: Eng.   802
  Instructional techniques and needs of secondary theatre teachers. USA.
  1996-1997. Lang.: Eng.   803
  Case study of a high school theatre teacher. USA. 1995. Lang.: Eng. 805
  Eurocentric bias in major theatre history textbooks. USA. 1720-1994.
  Lang.: Eng.   841
  Approaches to teaching Shakespeare. Israel: Tel Aviv. 1993-1995. Lang.:
  Eng.   3372
  Teaching Shakespeare at the University of Haifa. Israel: Haifa. 1994.
  Lang.: Eng.   3373
  Analysis of clowns and wordplay as a means of engaging students in
  teaching Shakespeare. USA. 1997. Lang.: Eng.   3388
  Evaluation of educational technology for the teaching of Shakespeare.
  USA. 1997. Lang.: Eng.   3390
  Comparing video versions of *Macbeth* in the classroom. USA. 1997.
  Lang.: Eng.   3391
  Pros and cons of using film and video in teaching Shakespeare. USA.
  1995. Lang.: Eng.   3392
  Role-playing and journal writing in teaching Shakespearean plays. USA.
  1997. Lang.: Eng.   3393
  Race, *Othello*, and the high school classroom. USA. 1997. Lang.: Eng.
                                                                         3394
  Film as a way of enhancing student understanding of Shakespeare.
  USA. 1995. Lang.: Eng.   3396
  The use of film and video to teach the plays of Shakespeare. USA.
  1997. Lang.: Eng.   3398
  Using video to teach Shakespeare's *Julius Caesar*. USA. 1997. Lang.:
  Eng.   3399
  Improvisational theatre games in the teaching of Shakespeare. USA.
  1997. Lang.: Eng.   3402
  Teaching Shakespeare and the World Wide Web. USA. 1997. Lang.:
  Eng.   3404
  Reader-response theory and the teaching of Shakespeare. USA. 1997.
  Lang.: Eng.   3405
  Teaching Shakespeare with the aid of the internet. USA. 1997. Lang.:
  Eng.   3407
  Feminist and performance techniques for teaching Shakespeare's
  Hamlet. USA. 1997. Lang.: Eng.   3408
  Teaching students to distinguish between action and narrative in
  Shakespeare. USA. 1995. Lang.: Eng.   3410
  'Playgrounding' in the teaching of Shakespeare's plays. USA. 1997.
  Lang.: Eng.   3411
  Team-teaching Shakespeare in an interdisciplinary context. USA. 1997.
  Lang.: Eng.   3413
  Nontraditional methods of teaching Shakespeare's *Romeo and Juliet*.
  USA. 1997. Lang.: Eng.   3414
  Teaching a scene from *Hamlet* using different interpretations on video.
  USA. 1997. Lang.: Eng.   3415
  Shakespeare and the teaching of close reading and theory. USA. 1997.
  Lang.: Eng.   3416
  Using video to teach Shakespeare's *Henry V*. USA. 1997. Lang.: Eng.
                                                                         3417
  Paraphrasing Shakespeare in the classroom. USA. 1997. Lang.: Eng.
                                                                         3419
  Informal survey of high school teachers of Shakespeare. USA. 1995.
  Lang.: Eng.   3421
  Teaching Shakespeare through educational programs at theatres and
  festivals. USA. 1997. Lang.: Eng.   3422
  Review of books on teaching Shakespeare. USA. 1995. Lang.: Eng. 3424
  Using performance techniques to teach Shakespeare's sonnets. USA.
  1997. Lang.: Eng.   3425
  Teaching students to develop their own inquiries into the plays of
  Shakespeare. USA. 1997. Lang.: Eng.   3426
  The multicultural classroom and the teaching of Shakespeare. USA.
  1995. Lang.: Eng.   3428

Teaching methods — cont'd

Teaching Shakespeare in dramatic fashion. USA. 1995. Lang.: Eng. 3429

Using historical fiction as background for the teaching of Shakespeare. USA. 1985. Lang.: Eng. 3430

Teaching Shakespeare in the high-tech classroom. USA. 1997. Lang.: Eng. 3431

The benefits of performing Shakespeare in the classroom. USA. 1995. Lang.: Eng. 3432

Using transhistoricism to teach Shakespeare. USA. 1997. Lang.: Eng. 3435

Georgetown University's decision to drop Shakespeare from its curriculum. USA: Washington, DC. 1997. Lang.: Eng. 3436

Suggestions for effective writing assignments in teaching Shakespeare. USA. 1997. Lang.: Eng. 3437

Whole-language approach to teaching Shakespeare's comedies. USA. 1997. Lang.: Eng. 3438

Process drama in the classroom and the teaching of Shakespeare. USA. 1997. Lang.: Eng. 3439

Theory/criticism
The effect of contemporary theory on the teaching of Shakespeare. 1997. Lang.: Eng. 3457

Training
Polemic on theatre training. Finland: Helsinki. 1997. Lang.: Fin. 930

Gennadij Bogdanov's workshop on biomechanics, Sotenäs Teateratelje. Russia. Sweden. 1920-1996. Lang.: Swe. 932

Vocal training and the split between academics and practitioners. UK-England. USA. 1973-1994. Lang.: Eng. 933

John McDowell, teacher of theatre history. USA. 1997. Lang.: Eng. 935

The legitimation crisis in academic theatre. USA. 1997. Lang.: Eng. 936

The teaching of performance composition. USA: New York, NY. 1997. Lang.: Eng. 937

Acting, dance, and martial arts teacher Henry Smith. USA. UK-England. 1968-1997. Lang.: Eng. 938

Self-awareness in dance training. Europe. 1997. Lang.: Ger. 1039

Interview with Lutz Försten of Folkwang-Hochschule. Germany: Essen. 1927-1997. Lang.: Ger. 1043

Interview with dancer/teacher Karin Jameson. Sweden: Stockholm. USA: New York, NY. 1992. Lang.: Swe. 1044

Conversation between teacher Joan Skinner and choreographer Gaby Agis. UK-England: London. 1996. Lang.: Eng. 1045

New approaches to dance training. USA. 1990-1996. Lang.: Eng. 1046

Movement training and modern dance. Germany: Hamburg. 1992-1993. Lang.: Ger. 1220

Modern dance, dance education, and dance training. USA. Europe. 1920-1929. Lang.: Ger. 1222

Voice teachers defend their work. UK-England. USA. 1973-1994. Lang.: Eng. 3508

Voice training, Shakespeare, and feminism. UK-England. USA. 1973-1994. Lang.: Eng. 3509

Profile of mime Etienne Decroux. France. 1945-1992. Lang.: Eng. 3750

Etienne Decroux's classes at l'École du Vieux-Colombier. France: Paris. 1968-1972. Lang.: Eng. 3751

Corinne Soum's recollections of Etienne Decroux. France. UK-England. 1997. Lang.: Eng. 3752

Etienne Decroux's project to revitalize theatre through mime. France. 1945-1992. Lang.: Eng. 3753

Teague, Anthony
Performance/production
Collection of newspaper reviews by London theatre critics. UK-England: London. 1997. Lang.: Eng. 2067

Teale, Polly
Performance/production
Collection of newspaper reviews by London theatre critics. UK-England: London. 1997. Lang.: Eng. 2111

Teat'r Dramy i Komedii (Moscow)
SEE
Teat'r na Taganke.

Teat'r Ermitaž (Moscow)
Performance/production
Cvetajeva's *Sonečka i Kazanova (Sonečka and Casanova)* at Teat'r Ermitaž. Russia: Moscow. 1996. Lang.: Rus. 1879

Teat'r im. Je. Vachtangova (Moscow)
Performance/production
Fomenko's production of Puškin's *Pikovaja Dama (Queen of Spades)*. Russia: Moscow. 1996. Lang.: Rus. 1876

Teat'r im. Kamala
SEE
Tatarskij Gosudarstvénnyj Akademičéskij Teat'r im. G. Kamala.

Teat'r im. M.P. Musorgskogo (St. Petersburg)
Performance/production
Interview with N. Bojarčikov, chief ballet instructor of the Mussorgskij Theatre. Russia: St. Petersburg. 1990-1997. Lang.: Rus. 1105

Teat'r im. Mossovéta (Moscow)
Performance/production
Interview with actor A. Mežulis. Russia: Moscow. 1990-1997. Lang.: Rus. 1889

Andrej Žitinkin, director of Mossovét Theatre. Russia: Moscow. 1990-1997. Lang.: Rus. 1900

Biography of actress Ljubov' Orlova. Russia. 1902-1975. Lang.: Rus. 3584

Teat'r im. V. Majakovskogo (Moscow)
Institutions
Director training at Russian Academy of Theatrical Art. Russia: Moscow. 1997. Lang.: Rus. 1456
Performance/production
Director Andrej Gončarov. Russia: Moscow. 1970-1997. Lang.: Rus. 1871

Teat'r Junogo Zritelja (Moscow)
Institutions
Groza (The Storm), based on works of Ostrovskij, directed for young audiences at Teat'r Junogo Zritelja. Russia: Moscow. 1996. Lang.: Rus. 1463

Teat'r Komedii im. M.P. Akimova (Leningrad)
Performance/production
Actress E.A. Uvarova of Teat'r Komedii. Russia: St. Petersburg. 1990-1997. Lang.: Rus. 1872

Teat'r na Jugo-Zapade (Moscow)
Institutions
Interview with director Valerij Beljakovič of Teat'r na Jugo-Zapade. Russia: Moscow. 1977-1997. Lang.: Rus. 1460

Profile of Valerij Beljakovič's Teat'r na Jugo-Zapade. Russia: Moscow. 1980-1997. Lang.: Rus. 1467
Performance/production
Teat'r na Jugo-Zapade's production of work based on plays of Bulgakov. Russia: Moscow. 1996. Lang.: Rus. 1878

Ionesco's *Rhinocéros* at Teat'r na Jugo-Zapade. Russia: Moscow. 1996. Lang.: Rus. 1901

Teat'r na Maloj Bronnoj (Moscow)
Institutions
Interview with director Sergej Ženovač. Russia: Moscow. 1990-1997. Lang.: Rus. 1461

Teat'r na Pokrovke (Moscow)
Institutions
Profiles of Teat'r na Pokrovke and Masterskaja Petra Fomenko. Russia: Moscow. 1990-1997. Lang.: Rus. 1458

Teat'r Rev'liucii
SEE
Teat'r im. V. Majakovskogo.

Teat'r Satiry na Basiljevskom Ostrove (St. Petersburg)
Performance/production
Two productions of *Tanja-Tanja* by Ol'ga Muchina. Russia: St. Petersburg, Moscow. 1997. Lang.: Rus. 1863

Teater Får302 (Copenhagen)
Plays/librettos/scripts
The popularity in Denmark of playwright Nicky Silver. USA. Denmark. 1994-1997. Lang.: Dan. 3224

Teater Galeasen (Stockholm)
Institutions
Report from the Tampere theatre festival. Finland: Tampere. 1997. Lang.: Swe. 309

Teater Koma (Jakarta)
Performance/production
Censorship and Teater Koma's production of *Suksesi* by Rendra. Indonesia: Jakarta. 1977-1993. Lang.: Eng. 558

Teater Salieri (Stockholm)
Performance/production
Interview with director Kajsa Isakson. Sweden: Stockholm. 1986-1997. Lang.: Swe. 1951

Teater Satori (Stockholm)
Institutions
Profile of the independent Teater Satori. Sweden: Stockholm. 1989-1997. Lang.: Swe. 1483

Teater Schahrazad (Stockholm)
Performance/production
Interview with actor and director Tom Fjordefalk. Sweden. 1972-1997. Lang.: Swe. 1948

Teatro La Fenice (Venice)
Performance spaces
Profile of Teatro la Fenice, recently destroyed by fire. Italy: Venice.
1792-1997. Lang.: Ger. 4066
Teatro La Memoria (Santiago)
Performance/production
Alexander Stillmark on directing Müller's *Der Auftrag (The Mission)*.
Chile: Santiago. 1996-1997. Lang.: Ger. 1607
Plays/librettos/scripts
The *Trilogía Testimonial (Trilogy of Witness)* of Alfredo Castro, Teatro
La Memoria. Chile. 1986-1997. Lang.: Ger. 692
Teatro Lirico (Milan)
Performance/production
Italian productions of D'Annunzio's *La Figlia di Iorio (Iorio's
Daughter)*. Italy. 1904-1983. Lang.: Ita. 1797
Teatro Lliure (Barcelona)
Performance/production
Politics in Barcelona theatre. Spain: Barcelona. 1996. Lang.: Eng. 608
Teatro Marquina (Madrid)
Performance/production
Catalan drama on the Madrid stage. Spain: Madrid. 1996. Lang.: Eng.
1919
Teatro Mercadante (Naples)
Performance/production
Leo De Berardinis' production of Shakespeare's *King Lear*. Italy:
Naples. 1996. Lang.: Eng. 1799
Teatro Nuevo Apolo (Madrid)
Performance/production
Catalan drama on the Madrid stage. Spain: Madrid. 1996. Lang.: Eng.
1919
Teatro Olimpia (Madrid)
Performance/production
Juan Margallo's production of *La tuerta suerte de Perico Galápago (The
One-Eyed Luck of Perico Galápago)* by Jorge Márquez. Spain: Madrid.
1996. Lang.: Eng. 1920
Teatro Olimpico (Vicenza)
Performance spaces
Methods of studying sixteenth-century playhouses. Europe. 1500-1600.
Lang.: Eng. 1527
Teatro Real (Madrid)
Institutions
Problems of the newly renovated Teatro Real. Spain: Madrid. 1997.
Lang.: Eng. 4054
Teatro San Carlo (Naples)
Performance/production
Dancer, choreographer, and composer Salvatore Taglioni. Italy: Naples.
1830-1860. Lang.: Eng. 1095
Teatro Sociale (Alba)
Performance spaces
The reconstruction of the Teatro Sociale. Italy: Alba. 1932-1997. Lang.:
Ita. 440
Teatro Stabile dell'Umbria (Spoleto)
Performance/production
Massimo Castri's production of *La Ragione degli altri (The Reason of
the Others)* by Pirandello. Italy: Messina. 1996-1997. Lang.: Ita. 1806
Teatro Stabile di Roma (Rome)
Performance/production
Mario Fumagalli's production of Shakespeare's *King Lear*. Italy: Rome.
1908. Lang.: Ita. 1796
Teatro Vascello (Rome)
Performance/production
Passage Nord's production of *Eternity Lasts Longer*. Italy: Rome. 1997.
Lang.: Ita. 1818
Teatro Vittorio Emanuele (Messina)
Performance/production
I Magazzini's production of Brecht's *Im Dickicht der Städte (In the
Jungle of Cities)*. Italy: Messina. 1995. Lang.: Ita. 1804
Federico Tiezzi's production of Brecht's *Im Dickicht der Städte (In the
Jungle of Cities)*. Italy: Messina. 1995. Lang.: Ita. 1807
Teatrul de Nord Secţia Harag György (Satu-Mare)
SEE
Szatmárnémeti Északi Színház, Harag György Társulat.
Teatrul de Stat (Oradea)
SEE
Nagyváradi Állami Színház.
Teatrul de Stat Secţia Tamási Áron (Sfîntu-Gheorghe)
SEE
Tamási Áron Színház.
Teatrul Maghiar de Stat (Cluj-Napoca)
SEE
Állami Magyar Színház (Cluj-Napoca).

Teatrul Naţional (Craiova)
Performance/production
Collection of newspaper reviews by London theatre critics. UK-England:
London. 1997. Lang.: Eng. 2049
Teatrul Naţional Târgu-Mureş secţia maghiara (Târgu-Mureş)
SEE
Marosvásárhelyi Nemzeti Színház, Magyar Társulat (Târgu-Mureş).
Teatteri Takomo (Helsinki)
Performance/production
Report on Finnish theatre productions. Finland: Helsinki, Tampere.
1997. Lang.: Eng, Fre. 1654
Teatterikorkeakoulu (Helsinki)
Performance/production
Report on the 'Helsinki Act' festival and symposium. Finland: Helsinki.
1997. Lang.: Eng. 523
Theatre researcher, teacher, and performer Juha-Pekka Hotinen.
Finland: Helsinki. 1997. Lang.: Fin. 526
Technicians/crews
Administration
Real costs and real values of theatrical production. Europe. 1997. Lang.:
Ger. 23
Design/technology
Theatre technician Gert-Ove Vågstam. Sweden. Cuba. South Africa,
Republic of. 1976. Lang.: Swe. 185
Theatrical training for tailors and dressers at the Swiss Technical
College for Women. Switzerland: Zurich. 1989-1997. Lang.: Ger. 191
A tuffet for use by technicians performing low floor work. USA. 1997.
Lang.: Eng. 256
Call for the entertainment industry to draft safety standards for electrical
equipment. USA. 1997. Lang.: Eng. 292
Costuming for film and video. USA. 1997. Lang.: Eng. 3552
Technology
SEE
Design/technology.
Tectonic Theater Project, Inc. (New York, NY)
Design/technology
Betsy Adams' lighting design for *Gross Indecency: The Three Trials of
Oscar Wilde*. USA: New York, NY. 1997. Lang.: Eng. 1377
Tecumseh
Plays/librettos/scripts
Indigenous peoples in Canadian historical drama. Canada. 1886-1997.
Lang.: Eng. 2424
Teenage Vitriol
Performance/production
Collection of newspaper reviews by London theatre critics. UK-England:
London. 1997. Lang.: Eng. 2069
Telarañas (Spiderwebs)
Plays/librettos/scripts
The style of playwright Eduardo Pavlovsky. Argentina. 1962-1993.
Lang.: Spa. 2374
Television
SEE
Video forms.
Telling Lies in America
Basic theatrical documents
Script of *Telling Lies in America* by Joe Eszterhas. USA. 1997. Lang.:
Eng. 3530
Plays/librettos/scripts
Interview with screenwriter Joe Eszterhas. USA. 1997. Lang.: Eng. 3663
Telson, Bob
Performance/production
Analysis of three productions of *The Gospel at Colonus*. USA. 1983-
1990. Lang.: Eng. 3882
Temesvári Csiky Gergely Színház
SEE
Csiky Gergely Színház (Timişoara).
Temperate Meal, A
Performance/production
Interview with performance artist Alicia Rios. UK-Wales. 1994-1997.
Lang.: Eng. 3824
Tempest, Marie
Institutions
Actress Marie Tempest's campaign for a hospital ward for actors. UK-
England: London. 1935-1937. Lang.: Eng. 387
Tempest, The
Design/technology
Ariel's costume in the original staging of *The Tempest*. England:
London. 1570-1612. Lang.: Eng. 156

Tempest, The — cont'd

Institutions
Record of Shakespearean studies seminar. USA: New York, NY.
England. 1997. Lang.: Eng.   1514
Performance/production
Robert Lepage's approach to directing Shakespeare. Canada: Quebec,
PQ. 1993. Lang.: Eng.   1595

Interview with members of Théâtre Repère. Canada: Quebec, PQ. 1993.
Lang.: Eng.   1596

The new season at Düsseldorfer Schauspielhaus. Germany: Dusseldorf.
1997. Lang.: Ger.   1731

Recent productions of plays by Shakespeare. Poland. 1997. Lang.: Eng,
Fre.   1834

Collection of newspaper reviews by London theatre critics. UK-England:
London. 1997. Lang.: Eng.   1989

Collection of newspaper reviews by London theatre critics. UK-England:
London. 1997. Lang.: Eng.   2029

How film and video versions of Shakespeare's plays may reinforce
textual authority rather than challenge it. UK-England. 1979-1991.
Lang.: Eng.   3510

Analysis of *Prospero's Books*, Peter Greenaway's film adaptation of *The
Tempest*. UK-England. 1991. Lang.: Eng.   3591
Plays/librettos/scripts
The appropriation of Shakespeare by the dispossessed and marginalized.
1590-1995. Lang.: Eng.   2366

Monstrosity and portent in Shakespeare's *The Tempest*. England. 1611.
Lang.: Eng.   2485

Domestic rebellion in *The Tempest* and *Arden of Faversham*. England.
1605. Lang.: Eng.   2530

New world adaptations of Shakespeare's *The Tempest*. England. Latin
America. Caribbean. 1612-1994. Lang.: Eng.   2549

Italian tragicomedy and the late plays of Shakespeare. England. 1609-
1613. Lang.: Eng.   2573

Shakespeare's exploration of race, gender, and sexuality in *The Tempest*.
England. 1611. Lang.: Eng.   2705

The Tempest as Shakespeare's response to *The Alchemist* by Ben
Jonson. England: London. 1600-1610. Lang.: Eng.   2733

Post-apartheid readings of *The Tempest*. South Africa, Republic of.
1994. Lang.: Eng.   3032

Interview with director Peter Greenaway. Europe. 1995. Lang.: Ger, Fre,
Dut, Eng.   3639

Analysis of Peter Greenaway's film adaptation of *The Tempest*,
Prospero's Books. UK-England. 1991. Lang.: Eng.   3646

Re-evaluation of Jarman's screen version of *The Tempest*. UK-England.
1979. Lang.: Eng.   3649
Theory/criticism
Shakespeare, *The Tempest*, and colonialist ideology. 1997. Lang.: Eng.
                                                              3458

New historicist criticism of Shakespeare's *The Tempest*. 1985-1989.
Lang.: Eng.   3461
Tempête, Une (Tempest, A)
Plays/librettos/scripts
New world adaptations of Shakespeare's *The Tempest*. England. Latin
America. Caribbean. 1612-1994. Lang.: Eng.   2549
Tender Land, The
Performance/production
American chamber opera. USA. 1868-1997. Lang.: Eng.   4258
Tenenbom, Tuvia
Performance/production
Tuvia Tenenbom's staging of *Love Letters to Adolf Hitler* for Jewish
Theatre of New York. USA: New York, NY. 1938-1996. Lang.: Eng.
                                                              2337
Tenerife
Performance/production
Collection of newspaper reviews by London theatre critics. UK-England:
London. 1997. Lang.: Eng.   2013
Tennant, Neil
Performance/production
Collection of newspaper reviews by London theatre critics. UK-England:
London. 1997. Lang.: Eng.   2059
Tennant, Veronica
Performance/production
Paul Thompson's production of *The Piano Man's Daughter* based on a
novel by Timothy Findley. Canada: Ottawa, ON. 1995-1997. Lang.:
Eng.   1606
Tennessee Theatre (Knoxville, TN)
Performance spaces
History of the Tennessee Theatre. USA: Knoxville, TN. 1929-1997.
Lang.: Eng.   3563

Tennfjord, Oddbjørn
Performance/production
Interview with bass Oddbjørn Tennfjord. Norway: Oslo. 1970. Lang.:
Swe.   4201
Tent theatre
Performance/production
The competition between tent repertory theatre and film. USA. 1920-
1929. Lang.: Eng.   667
Terayama, Shuji
Performance/production
Collection of newspaper reviews by London theatre critics. UK-England.
1997. Lang.: Eng.   2125
Terence
SEE
Terentius Afer, Publius.
Terence, David
Performance/production
Collection of newspaper reviews by London theatre critics. UK-England:
London. 1997. Lang.: Eng.   2112
Terentius Afer, Publius
Plays/librettos/scripts
Out-of-court legal settlements in Greco-Roman new comedy. Greece.
Rome. 500 B.C.-200 A.D. Lang.: Eng.   2886
Terfel, Bryn
Performance/production
Interview with opera singer Bryn Terfel. UK-Wales. 1989. Lang.: Swe.
                                                              4229
Terms of Surrender
Plays/librettos/scripts
Kari Ann Owen/Penomee on her play *Terms of Surrender*. USA. 1997.
Lang.: Eng.   3244
Terra Incognita
Basic theatrical documents
Text of *Terra Incognita* by Maria Irene Fornes, the libretto for an opera
by Roberto Sierra. USA. 1992. Lang.: Eng.   4017
Terrains vagues (Wastelands)
Plays/librettos/scripts
Terrains Vagues (Wastelands), Michel Nadeau's stage adaptation of
Rashomon. Canada: Quebec, PQ. 1997. Lang.: Fre.   2422
Terrible But Incomplete Journals of John D., The
Basic theatrical documents
Text of Guillermo Verdecchia's radio play *The Terrible But Incomplete
Journals of John D*. Canada: Vancouver, BC. 1996. Lang.: Eng. 3514
Terry Titter's Full Length
Performance/production
Collection of newspaper reviews by London theatre critics. UK-England:
London. 1997. Lang.: Eng.   2099
Terry, Daniel
Plays/librettos/scripts
Analysis of melodramas based on novels of Walter Scott. England.
1810-1830. Lang.: Eng.   2681
Terry, Ellen
Performance/production
Shakespearean production in the age of actor-managers. UK-England.
1840-1914. Lang.: Eng.   2193
Relation to other fields
Actress Ellen Terry's effect on women's roles. UK-England: London.
1880-1909. Lang.: Eng.   783
Terry, Megan
Plays/librettos/scripts
Critical history of American drama. USA. 1960-1997. Lang.: Eng. 3267
Terselius, Lill
Performance/production
Transferring a stage production to television. Sweden: Stockholm. 1996.
Lang.: Swe.   3722
Teshigawara, Saburo
Performance/production
Interview with dancer and choreographer Saburo Teshigawara. Japan.
Europe. 1992-1997. Lang.: Ger.   983

Collection of newspaper reviews by London theatre critics. UK-England:
London. 1997. Lang.: Eng.   2076
Tesich, Steve
Basic theatrical documents
Script of *Breaking Away* by Steve Tesich. USA. 1979. Lang.: Eng. 3540
Performance/production
Interview with film director Peter Yates. USA. 1929-1997. Lang.: Eng.
                                                              3600
Plays/librettos/scripts
Screenwriter, playwright, and novelist Steve Tesich. USA. 1942-1996.
Lang.: Eng.   3653

Theatres — cont'd

Performance/production

Theatro Technis (London)
Performance/production

Theatrum Mundi
Institutions

Theme parks
SEE
Amusement parks.

Then Again.
Performance/production

Theodore, Brother
Performance/production

Theory/criticism
SEE ALSO
Classed Entries.
Institutions

Performance/production

Theory/criticism — cont'd

Metatheatricality in melodrama. UK-England. 1840-1900. Lang.: Eng.
618

Modernism and postmodernism in American theatre. USA. 1960-1990.
Lang.: Eng. 627

Directing a stage adaptation of *The Smell of Death and Flowers* by
Nadine Gordimer. USA. 1995-1996. Lang.: Eng. 647

Profile of the late Michael Kirby, critic and theatre artist. USA. 1935-
1996. Lang.: Eng. 673

The Ensemble for Early Music's production of the Fleury Mary
Magdalene play. USA: New York, NY. 1997. Lang.: Eng. 676

The theory and practice of play direction. USA. 1997. Lang.: Eng. 681

Video dance performance and criticism. UK-England. 1997. Lang.: Eng.
992

Dance notation systems and their reflection of concepts and styles. USA.
1700-1995. Lang.: Eng. 1006

Dance and the representation of the body in a technological world. UK-
England. 1997. Lang.: Eng. 1192

Performance theory analysis of *Trio A* by Yvonne Rainer. USA. 1968.
Lang.: Eng. 1203

Essays on gender and performance. 250 B.C.-1995 A.D. Lang.: Eng.
1551

The affective power of the body onstage. England. 1589-1613. Lang.:
Eng. 1620

As You Like It, transvestism, and early modern sexual politics. England.
1599. Lang.: Eng. 1636

Sociocultural analysis of recent French productions. France. 1993-1994.
Lang.: Eng. 1678

Reactions to modern performances of *Antony and Cleopatra*. UK-
England. North America. 1827-1987. Lang.: Eng. 2178

The reception of Robert Lepage's production of *A Midsummer Night's
Dream* at the National. UK-England: London. 1992-1993. Lang.:Eng.
2189

The social protest theatre of Luis Valdez and Amiri Baraka. USA. 1965-
1975. Lang.: Eng. 2260

Theatrical theory, theatrical practice, and the dramaturg. USA. 1997.
Lang.: Eng. 2295

Report on colloquium devoted to the 'language of Shakespeare in
America'. USA: New York, NY. 1997. Lang.: Eng. 2299

Tennessee Williams on Broadway—critical response. USA: New York,
NY. 1944-1982. Lang.: Eng. 2314

Performative theory and potentially offensive characterizations on stage.
USA: Santa Cruz, CA. France: Paris. 1992-1997. Lang.: Eng. 2336

The difficulties of recording and preserving live theatrical performance
on video. Europe. 1912-1997. Lang.: Pol. 3720

Performance art and catharsis. USA. 1977-1997. Lang.: Eng. 3845

The critical reception of compositions by Saverio Mercadante. Italy.
1852-1995. Lang.: Eng. 4193

Plays/librettos/scripts

Jungian archetypes and the rules of fiction and drama. Lang.: Ita. 690

Non-linear approaches to the reading of texts. Canada. 1997. Lang.:
Fre. 2419

Dramatic representations of spectatorship. England: London. 1580-1642.
Lang.: Eng. 2676

Theatre and the representation of death and dying. Europe. 1997. Lang.:
Eng. 2794

Samuel Beckett and postmodernism. France. Ireland. USA. 1942-1982.
Lang.: Eng. 2818

The actions of characters as a basis for scene analysis. France. 1997.
Lang.: Fre. 2831

The numerous versions of Büchner's *Woyzeck*. Germany. 1875-1981.
Lang.: Eng. 2852

Translation and the study of Greek tragedy. Greece. 458-400 B.C.
Lang.: Eng. 2882

Reception and analysis of *Az ember tragédiája (The Tragedy of Man)*
by Imre Madách. Hungary. 1850-1860. Lang.: Hun. 2900

Early critical and theoretical essays by Samuel Beckett. Ireland. France.
1929-1989. Lang.: Eng. 2903

Jacobin playwright and theoretician Francesco Saverio Salfi. Italy. 1759-
1832. Lang.: Ita. 2969

Problems of definition in Pinter criticism. UK-England. 1960-1997.
Lang.: Eng. 3107

Survey of English drama by a retired theatre reviewer. UK-England.
1959-1995. Lang.: Eng. 3117

Collection of essays on plays of Tennessee Williams. USA. 1940-1982.
Lang.: Eng. 3167

Mimesis, feminism, theatre, and performance. USA. 1997. Lang.: Eng.
3176

O'Neill's *Strange Interlude* and its critical and popular reception. USA.
1926-1927. Lang.: Eng. 3201

Authenticity and stereotype in David Henry Hwang's *M. Butterfly*. USA.
1988. Lang.: Eng. 3208

Critical response to misogyny in David Mamet's *Oleanna*. USA. 1992.
Lang.: Eng. 3238

Interview with playwright August Wilson. USA. 1985-1997. Lang.: Eng.
3276

Choosing the ten best operas. Canada. 1997. Lang.: Eng. 4284

Reference materials

Annual bibliography of modern drama studies. North America. 1899-
1997. Lang.: Eng. 3318

Relation to other fields

Conflicts in teaching literary criticism and theory. USA. 1612-1997.
Lang.: Eng. 797

Art and the artist in contemporary society. USA. 1996. Lang.: Eng. 824

Eurocentric bias in major theatre history textbooks. USA. 1720-1994.
Lang.: Eng. 841

The nature of collaboration in dance. USA. 1996. Lang.: Eng. 1021

Language and social formation in Shakespeare. England. 1595-1750.
Lang.: Eng. 3348

The failure of study guides to impart critical theory to students of
Shakespeare. UK-England. 1990-1996. Lang.: Eng. 3381

Reader-response theory and the teaching of Shakespeare. USA. 1997.
Lang.: Eng. 3405

Shakespeare and the teaching of close reading and theory. USA. 1997.
Lang.: Eng. 3416

Representation and reception of the *castrato*. France. 1830-1970. Lang.:
Eng. 4322

Research/historiography

Aristotle's *Poetics* and performative aspects of Athenian culture. Greece:
Athens. 600-300 B.C. Lang.: Eng. 3449

Theory/criticism

Shakespeare, *The Tempest*, and colonialist ideology. 1997. Lang.: Eng.
3458

Magic as defining trope of modern drama. Europe. 1910-1950. Lang.:
Eng. 3482

Playwright Arthur Miller and criticism. USA. 1940-1995. Lang.: Eng.
3498

Analysis of criticism of Jennie Livingston's documentary film *Paris Is
Burning*. USA. 1991. Lang.: Eng. 3700

Training

Corinne Soum's recollections of Etienne Decroux. France. UK-England.
1997. Lang.: Eng. 3752

They That Sit in Darkness

Plays/librettos/scripts

The theme of hope in postwar American theatre and writing. USA.
1914-1929. Lang.: Eng. 3153

Thicker Than Water

Performance/production

Collection of newspaper reviews by London theatre critics. UK-England:
London. 1997. Lang.: Eng. 2089

Things Change

Plays/librettos/scripts

David Mamet as screen writer and director. USA. 1975-1995. Lang.:
Eng. 3672

Things Fall Apart

Performance/production

Collection of newspaper reviews by London theatre critics. UK-England:
London. 1997. Lang.: Eng. 2074

Think No Evil of Us: My Life with Kenneth Williams

Performance/production

Collection of newspaper reviews by London theatre critics. UK-England:
London. 1997. Lang.: Eng. 2106

Think of a Garden

Plays/librettos/scripts

Identity and the use of multiple actors to portray a single character in
postcolonial drama. Australia. Ireland. Samoa. 1997. Lang.: Eng. 2380

Third Person Included

Performance/production

Collection of newspaper reviews by London theatre critics. UK-England:
London. 1997. Lang.: Eng. 2146

Tichenor, Austin
Performance/production
Collection of newspaper reviews by London theatre critics. UK-England: London. 1997. Lang.: Eng. 2094

Tickets and Ties: The African Tale
Performance/production
Collection of newspaper reviews by London theatre critics. UK-England: London. 1997. Lang.: Eng. 2018

Tides of Night
Performance/production
Collection of newspaper reviews by London theatre critics. UK-England: London. 1997. Lang.: Eng. 2077

Tieste (Thyestes)
Plays/librettos/scripts
Greek mythology in tragedies of Ugo Foscolo. Italy. 1795-1811. Lang.: Ita. 2954

Tiezzi, Federico
Performance/production
I Magazzini's production of Brecht's *Im Dickicht der Städte (In the Jungle of Cities)*. Italy: Messina. 1995. Lang.: Ita. 1804

Federico Tiezzi's production of Brecht's *Im Dickicht der Städte (In the Jungle of Cities)*. Italy: Messina. 1995. Lang.: Ita. 1807

Tiger (Stockholm)
Performance/production
Interview with choreographer Anne Külper of Tiger. Sweden: Stockholm. 1968-1997. Lang.: Swe. 1188

Till Damaskus (To Damascus)
Plays/librettos/scripts
Tradition and modernism in later plays of Strindberg. Sweden. 1894-1907. Lang.: Eng. 3061

Till, Benjamin
Performance/production
Collection of newspaper reviews by London theatre critics. UK-England: London. 1997. Lang.: Eng. 2056

Tiller Girls (Manchester)
Performance/production
Industrial technology and the display of women's bodies in performance. UK-England. 1870-1954. Lang.: Eng. 616

Tilly, François
Plays/librettos/scripts
Collection of articles on French avant-garde culture, including theatre. France. 1937-1989. Lang.: Eng. 2805

Time of Your Life, The
Design/technology
Realistic set design and the plays of William Saroyan. USA. 1939-1943. Lang.: Eng. 1375

Time Out
Performance/production
Collection of newspaper reviews by London theatre critics. UK-England: London. 1997. Lang.: Eng. 2077

Timeless
Institutions
Impressions of the Edinburgh Festival. UK-Scotland: Edinburgh. 1997. Lang.: Ger. 391
Performance/production
Collection of newspaper reviews by London theatre critics. UK-Scotland: Edinburgh. 1997. Lang.: Eng. 2232

Timon of Athens
Performance/production
Collection of newspaper reviews by London theatre critics. UK-England: London. 1997. Lang.: Eng. 1975
Plays/librettos/scripts
The bubonic plague and Shakespeare's plays. England. 1603-1607. Lang.: Eng. 2534

Male patronage and maternal power in Shakespeare's *Timon of Athens*. England. 1607-1608. Lang.: Eng. 2603

Punctuation and the interpretation of speeches in Shakespeare's *Timon of Athens*. England. 1607. Lang.: Eng. 2752

Tingler, The
Performance/production
The horror genre and the American film industry. USA. 1953-1968. Lang.: Eng. 3617

Tinka's New Dress
Institutions
Solo performance at the Festival de Théâtre des Amériques. Canada: Montreal, PQ. 1997. Lang.: Fre. 1392
Performance/production
Review of Ronnie Burkett's puppet play *Tinka's New Dress*. Canada: Winnipeg, MB. 1997. Lang.: Eng. 4361

Tinline, Phil
Performance/production
Collection of newspaper reviews by London theatre critics. UK-England: London. 1997. Lang.: Eng. 2046

Collection of newspaper reviews by London theatre critics. UK-England: London. 1997. Lang.: Eng. 2107

Tiplady, Steve
Performance/production
Collection of newspaper reviews by London theatre critics. UK-England: London. 1997. Lang.: Eng. 1988

Tipton, Jennifer
Design/technology
Theatre in the new millennium. 1997. Lang.: Eng. 138

OISTAT's conference on theatre technology of the future. USA: Pittsburgh. 1997. Lang.: Swe. 227

Tirén, Ing-Mari
Institutions
Profile of puppet theatre group Dockteater Tittut. Sweden: Stockholm. 1977. Lang.: Swe. 4353

Titanic
Design/technology
Stewart Laing's set and costume designs for the musical *Titanic*. USA: New York, NY. 1997. Lang.: Eng. 3914

Lighting design for the Broadway musical *Titanic*. USA: New York, NY. 1992-1997. Lang.: Eng. 3917
Performance/production
Composer/lyricist Maury Yeston. USA: New York, NY. 1945-1997. Lang.: Eng. 3975
Plays/librettos/scripts
Interview with playwright Peter Stone. USA: New York, NY. 1997. Lang.: Eng. 3981

Interviews with authors of Tony Award-winning shows. USA: New York, NY. 1997. Lang.: Eng. 3985

Titus Andronicus
Performance/production
Collection of newspaper reviews by London theatre critics. UK-England: London. 1997. Lang.: Eng. 2049

Productions of Shakespeare's *Titus Andronicus*. UK-England. USA. 1955-1995. Lang.: Hun. 2225
Plays/librettos/scripts
Accusations of rape in English Renaissance drama. England. 1550-1630. Lang.: Eng. 2526

The role of Lavinia in Shakespeare's *Titus Andronicus*. England. 1593-1594. Lang.: Eng. 2532

Gendered power relations, law, and revenge in early English drama. England. 1590-1640. Lang.: Eng. 2540

The importance of gender in Shakespeare's *Titus Andronicus*. England. 1590-1594. Lang.: Eng. 2556

Metaphor and reality in Shakespeare's *Titus Andronicus*. England. 1590-1594. Lang.: Eng. 2611

Livy's influence on Shakespeare, Heywood, and Peele. England. 1569-1624. Lang.: Eng. 2629

The source of Shakespeare's *Titus Andronicus*. England. 1550-1594. Lang.: Eng. 2636

The meaning of dismemberment in Shakespeare's *Titus Andronicus*. England. 1590-1594. Lang.: Eng. 2720

Racial aspects of colonialism in Shakespeare's *Titus Andronicus*. England. 1590-1594. Lang.: Eng. 2760

The sympathetic villain on the early modern stage. England. 1594-1621. Lang.: Eng. 2763

To Blusher with Love
Performance/production
Collection of newspaper reviews by London theatre critics. UK-England: London. 1997. Lang.: Eng. 2105

Today Is My Birthday
SEE
Dziś są moje urodziny.

Todd, Carole
Performance/production
Collection of newspaper reviews by London theatre critics. UK-England: London. 1997. Lang.: Eng. 2068

Todd, Paul
Performance/production
Collection of newspaper reviews by London theatre critics. UK-England: London. 1997. Lang.: Eng. 1984

Tokyo Ghetto December 1996
Performance/production
Women in Japanese theatre. Japan: Tokyo. 1970-1996. Lang.: Eng. 568

Tourneur, Cyril
Performance/production
Recent productions of Elizabethan theatre. Europe. 1997. Lang.: Ger.
1649

Plays/librettos/scripts
Narcissism in Renaissance tragedy. England. 1450-1580. Lang.: Eng.
2609

The Italian palazzo on the Jacobean stage. England. 1603-1625. Lang.:
Eng. 2625

Suicide in English Renaissance tragedy. England. 1590-1625. Lang.:
Eng. 2724

Tovstonogov, Georgij Aleksandrovič
Performance/production
Actress Zinajda Šarko on the work of director G.A. Tovstonogov.
Russia: St. Petersburg. 1960-1989. Lang.: Rus. 1891

Towarzstwo Wierzsalin Teatr (Białystok)
Performance/production
Ghosts in theatrical productions. Poland. Lithuania. 1997. Lang.: Pol.
1838

Town, Joanna
Design/technology
Joanna Town, head lighting designer of the Royal Court Theatre. UK-
England: London. 1986-1997. Lang.: Eng. 1361

Towneley Cycle
Plays/librettos/scripts
Analysis of medieval plays about Jesus and the doctors. England: York,
Towneley, Coventry. 1420-1500. Lang.: Eng. 2618

Trafieri, Giuseppe
Plays/librettos/scripts
Trento's opera *Bianca de'Rossi* and its sources. Italy. 1790-1799. Lang.:
Eng. 4306

Tragaluz, El (Skylight, The)
Plays/librettos/scripts
Analysis of *El Tragaluz (The Skylight)* by Antonio Buero Vallejo. Spain.
1967. Lang.: Spa. 3045

Tragedy
Performance/production
Visual performance aspects of Greek tragedy. Greece: Athens. 500 B.C.
Lang.: Ita. 1749
Plays/librettos/scripts
Hamlet, revenge tragedy, and *film noir*. 1600-1996. Lang.: Eng. 2365

Religious ambivalence in Greek tragedy. Ancient Greece. 500-250 B.C.
Lang.: Eng. 2373

Fantasies of maternal power in Shakespeare's *Macbeth*. England. 1606.
Lang.: Eng. 2449

Shakespeare's *Antony and Cleopatra* as a romance. England. 1607.
Lang.: Eng. 2496

Feminist analysis of wordplay in Shakespeare's *Antony and Cleopatra*.
England. 1607. Lang.: Eng. 2510

The role of Lavinia in Shakespeare's *Titus Andronicus*. England. 1593-
1594. Lang.: Eng. 2532

The importance of gender in Shakespeare's *Titus Andronicus*. England.
1590-1594. Lang.: Eng. 2556

Gender and racial politics in Shakespeare's *Othello*. England. 1605.
Lang.: Eng. 2572

Shakespeare's *Antony and Cleopatra* as a romance. England. 1607.
Lang.: Eng. 2578

Male patronage and maternal power in Shakespeare's *Timon of Athens*.
England. 1607-1608. Lang.: Eng. 2603

Madness and gender in the plays of Shakespeare. England. 1589-1613.
Lang.: Eng. 2677

Shakespeare's *Othello* and early modern precepts of wifely conduct.
England. 1605. Lang.: Eng. 2687

Doctor Faustus and the rise of tragedy. England. 1604. Lang.: Eng. 2690

Shakespearean tragedies and history plays and the possible roles for
women. England. 1589-1613. Lang.: Eng. 2704

Marital equality and subordination in Shakespeare's *Othello* and
Webster's *The Duchess of Malfi*. England. 1605-1613. Lang.: Eng. 2715

Feminist analysis of female characters in Shakespearean tragedy.
England. 1589-1613. Lang.: Eng. 2743

Restoration drama and printed propaganda. England. 1678-1683. Lang.:
Eng. 2757

Tragedy and the unity of time in Racine's *Mithridate*. France. 1673.
Lang.: Eng. 2808

The cultural construction of the hero in Greek tragedy. Greece. 500-400
B.C. Lang.: Eng. 2874

The objectives of Greek tragedy. Greece. 500-400 B.C. Lang.: Dut. 2875

Greek drama and mimesis. Greece. 500-400 B.C. Lang.: Eng. 2876

Ambivalence about rhetoric in Greek tragedy. Greece. 500-250 B.C.
Lang.: Eng. 2877

Problems of historical interpretation in Greek tragedy and comedy.
Greece. 500-400 B.C. Lang.: Eng. 2887

Ancient Greek tragedy and religion. Greece. 500-250 B.C. Lang.: Eng.
2888

Foreigners in Athenian tragedy. Greece. 400-250 B.C. Lang.: Eng. 2890

Comparative anthropological approach to Greek tragedy. Greece. 600-
300 B.C. Lang.: Slo. 2892

Greek mythology in tragedies of Ugo Foscolo. Italy. 1795-1811. Lang.:
Ita. 2954

Trento's opera *Bianca de'Rossi* and its sources. Italy. 1790-1799. Lang.:
Eng. 4306
Relation to other fields
Howard Barker on illumination and tragedy. UK-England. Germany.
1996. Lang.: Dan. 782
Theory/criticism
Myth and utopia in tragedy. 1984. Lang.: Eng. 858

Freud and the analysis of tragedy. France. 1979. Lang.: Eng. 885

Tragedy of Jane Shore
Plays/librettos/scripts
Analysis of Nicholas Rowe's *Tragedy of Jane Shore*. England. 1714.
Lang.: Eng. 2523

Tragedy of Man, The
SEE
Ember tragédiája, Az.
Tragedy of Mariam, The
Plays/librettos/scripts
Analysis of *The Tragedy of Mariam* by Elizabeth Cary. England. 1695.
Lang.: Eng. 2761

Tragedy of Philotas, The
Plays/librettos/scripts
The domination of a king by his counselors in Jacobean political
tragedy. England: London. 1603-1610. Lang.: Eng. 2448

Tragical History of Doctor Faustus
SEE
Doctor Faustus.
Tragicomedy
Plays/librettos/scripts
Italian tragicomedy and the late plays of Shakespeare. England. 1609-
1613. Lang.: Eng. 2573
Relation to other fields
The relationship of tragicomedy to social change. England. 1601-1700.
Lang.: Eng. 3344

Training
SEE ALSO
Classed Entries.
Relation to other fields
Case study of a high school theatre teacher. USA. 1995. Lang.: Eng. 805
Training aids
Relation to other fields
Review of teaching texts of Shakespeare's *King Lear*. USA. 1995. Lang.:
Eng. 3400
Training methods
Institutions
Account of a visit to French theatre schools. France: Paris. 1997. Lang.:
Eng. 314
Training, actor
Institutions
Pëtr Fomenko's students at Rossiskaja Akademija Teatral'nogo
Iskusstva. Russia: Moscow. 1990-1997. Lang.: Rus. 1457

The musical comedy program at RATI. Russia: Moscow. 1996. Lang.:
Rus. 3927
Performance/production
Guide to stage combat. 1996. Lang.: Eng. 464

Canadian university theatre. Canada. 1914-1979. Lang.: Eng. 484

The effect of war on Croatian theatre. Croatia. 1990-1996. Lang.: Eng.
495

Physical work in actor training. Denmark: Holstebro. 1950-1997. Lang.:
Eng. 497

Description of cross-cultural actor training project. Finland: Tampere.
1997. Lang.: Fin. 528

Training, singer — cont'd

Performance/production

Obituary for soprano Irene Jessner. Canada. 1901-1994. Lang.: Eng.
4105

Beijing production of Carmen's *Bizet*. China, People's Republic of: Beijing. 1982-1997. Lang.: Eng.
4117

Tenor Manuel García the elder and his son. Europe. 1817-1943. Lang.: Eng.
4127

Excerpt from biography of opera singer Mary Garden. France: Paris. 1875-1957. Lang.: Eng.
4144

The current generation of young opera singers. UK-England. USA. 1997. Lang.: Eng.
4224

Soprano Antonietta Stella. USA: New York, NY. 1954-1997. Lang.: Eng.
4244

Training, voice
Performance/production

Critique of voice training in contemporary Shakespearean production. UK-England. North America. 1975-1995. Lang.: Eng.
2201

John Barrymore's vocal coach Margaret Carrington. USA. 1919-1923. Lang.: Eng.
2308

Transit
Performance/production

Plays based on refugee experiences. Sweden: Gothenburg. 1997. Lang.: Swe.
1927

Translations
Basic theatrical documents

English performance translation of Nestroy's *Der Talisman*. Austria. 1833-1849. Lang.: Eng.
1256

English translation of the Yuan drama *Reunion with Son and Daughter in Kingfisher Red County*. China. 1280-1994. Lang.: Eng.
1264

English translation of *La Demande d'emploi (The Interview)* by Michel Vinaver. France. 1994. Lang.: Eng.
1277

Slovene translations of plays by Georg Büchner. Germany. 1835-1837. Lang.: Slo.
1278

French translation of Büchner's *Leonce und Lena (Leonce and Lena)*. Germany. France. Belgium. 1838-1996. Lang.: Fre.
1279

English translation of *Nur eine Scheibe Brot (Just a Slice of Bread)* by Rainer Werner Fassbinder. Germany. 1971. Lang.: Eng.
1280

English translation of *Die Stunde da wir nichts voneinander wussten (The Hour We Knew Nothing of Each Other)* by Peter Handke. Germany. 1992. Lang.: Eng.
1281

English translations of German Expressionist plays. Germany. 1900-1920. Lang.: Eng.
1284

French translation of *Observe the Sons of Ulster Marching Towards the Somme* by Frank McGuinness. Ireland. France. 1985-1996. Lang.: Fre.
1285

English translation of *Incontro Ravvicinato di Tipo Estremo (An Uncomfortably Close Encounter)* by Luigi Lunari. Italy. 1995. Lang.: Eng.
1287

English translations of sacred plays by Antonia Pulci. Italy. 1452-1501. Lang.: Eng.
1288

English translation of *La festa e storia di Sancta Caterina*. Italy. 1380-1400. Lang.: Eng.
1289

English translation of *Ashi no Aru Shitai (A Corpse with Feet)* by Minoru Betsuyaku. Japan. 1937-1995. Lang.: Eng.
1290

English translation of *Paper Husband* by Hannan Al-Shaykh. Middle East. 1997. Lang.: Eng.
1292

Slovene translation of Ibsen's *Brand*. Norway. 1865. Lang.: Slo.
1294

English translations of plays by contemporary Slovenian playwrights. Slovenia. 1980-1997. Lang.: Eng.
1301

English and German translations of *Babylon* by Ivo Svetina. Slovenia. 1997. Lang.: Eng, Ger.
1303

English translation of *Una hoguera en al amenecer (Bonfire at Dawn)* by Jaime Salom. Spain. 1986-1992. Lang.: Eng.
1308

French translations of Strindberg's *Fröken Julie (Miss Julie)* and *Den Starkare (The Stronger)*. Sweden. France. 1888-1996. Lang.: Fre.
1309

French translation of *Communicating Doors* by Alan Ayckbourn. UK-England. France. 1995. Lang.: Fre.
1310

French translation of *Retreat* by James Saunders. UK-England. France: Paris. 1995. Lang.: Fre.
1318

French translation of *The Importance of Being Earnest* by Oscar Wilde. UK-England. France: Paris. 1895-1996. Lang.: Fre.
1320

French translation of Tony Kushner's *Angels in America, Part II: Perestroika*. USA. France: Paris. 1996. Lang.: Fre.
1333

English translation of the filmscript *J'ai pas sommeil (I Can't Sleep)* by Claire Denis and Jean-Pôl Fargeau. France. 1994. Lang.: Eng.
3527

Performance/production

Translations and non-English-language productions of Shakespeare. Asia. Africa. Europe. 1975-1995. Lang.: Eng.
1554

Negative reception of Marco Micone's adaptation of Shakespeare, *La Mégère de Padova (The Shrew of Padua)*. Canada: Montreal, PQ. 1995-1997. Lang.: Eng.
1584

Interview with director Martin Faucher. Canada: Montreal, PQ. 1996-1997. Lang.: Fre.
1599

Interview with director George Tabori about Bertolt Brecht. Europe. North America. 1947-1997. Lang.: Eng.
1645

Director and dramaturgs on translating, adapting and producing Molière's *Misanthrope*. USA: La Jolla, CA, Chicago, IL. 1989-1990. Lang.: Eng.
2263

The dramaturg and *One Crazy Day*, an adaptation of Beaumarchais' *The Marriage of Figaro*. USA: Tucson, AZ. 1992. Lang.: Eng.
2322

The state of translation in American theatre. USA. 1997. Lang.: Eng.
2353

Plays/librettos/scripts

Characters of Edward Thomas' *House of America* as translated by René-Daniel Dubois. Canada. UK-Wales. 1997. Lang.: Fre.
2436

Orlando Furioso as a source for Shakespeare's *Much Ado About Nothing*. England. 1591. Lang.: Eng.
2710

Jean Cocteau's adaptations of works of Sophocles. France. 1922-1937. Lang.: Eng.
2811

French translation of the plays of Shakespeare. France. UK-England. 1997. Lang.: Eng.
2814

Analysis of German translations of plays by Samuel Beckett. Germany. 1967-1978. Lang.: Eng.
2842

Translation and the study of Greek tragedy. Greece. 458-400 B.C. Lang.: Eng.
2882

Samuel Beckett, bilingualism, and translation. Ireland. France. USA. 1958-1989. Lang.: Eng.
2915

Analysis of Polish translations of plays by Molière. Poland. 1664-1973. Lang.: Pol.
2987

Translations of the verse drama of Kalidasa. Slovenia. 1885-1908. Lang.: Slo.
3020

Problems of translating drama, particularly Shakespeare. Sweden. 1847-1997. Lang.: Swe.
3059

Christopher Hampton—playwright, translator, and adaptor. UK-England. 1967-1994. Lang.: Eng.
3089

James Magruder on his translation of *Le Triomphe de l'amour (The Triumph of Love)* by Marivaux. USA: Baltimore, MD. 1986-1995. Lang.: Eng.
3230

Paul Schmidt on translating and adapting plays of Čechov. USA. 1994-1997. Lang.: Eng.
3273

Piccinni's *La Cecchina*: English translations and analysis. Italy. USA. 1766-1996. Lang.: Eng.
4305

Transvestism
Performance/production

Cross-dressing in Chinese theatre and society. China. 1200-1997. Lang.: Eng.
489

Interview with actress Moira Finucane. Australia: Melbourne. 1997. Lang.: Eng.
1556

As You Like It, transvestism, and early modern sexual politics. England. 1599. Lang.: Eng.
1636

The experience of cross-gender role-playing. USA. 1971-1997. Lang.: Eng.
2268

Interview with political satirist Pieter-Dirk Uys. South Africa, Republic of. 1945-1994. Lang.: Eng.
3858

Plays/librettos/scripts

Cross-dressing in *Alda* by William of Blois. England. 1159. Lang.: Eng.
2487

Gender ambiguity in Shakespeare's *Twelfth Night*. England. 1600. Lang.: Eng.
2495

Women disguised as men in seventeenth-century drama. England. 1602-1674. Lang.: Eng.
2653

Transvestism in Beaumont and Fletcher's *Philaster*. England. 1609. Lang.: Eng.
2664

Cross-dressed heroines in works of Shakespeare and Spenser. England. 1590-1596. Lang.: Eng.
2731

Transvestism — cont'd

Transvestism, desire, and psychosexual displacement in early modern theatre. England. 1590-1619. Lang.: Eng. 2766

Interview with drag actor and playwright Charles Busch. USA. 1997. Lang.: Eng. 3259

Transvestism in English pantomime. UK-England. 1870-1995. Lang.: Eng. 3754

Relation to other fields
Transvestism and antitheatrical discourse. England. 1583-1615. Lang.: Eng. 736

Political satire of Pieter-Dirk Uys. South Africa, Republic of: Johannesburg. 1981-1997. Lang.: Eng. 3740

Theory/criticism
Analysis of criticism of Jennie Livingston's documentary film *Paris Is Burning*. USA. 1991. Lang.: Eng. 3700

Opera and eroticism. USA. Europe. 1996. Lang.: Eng. 4335

Trap, The
SEE
Pulapka.

Traute, Hoess
Performance/production
Profile of actress Traute Hoess. Germany. Austria. 1969-1997. Lang.: Ger. 1741

Travelogue
Performance/production
Dance theatre artist Sasha Waltz. Germany. 1993-1996. Lang.: Eng. 967

Travers, Ben
Performance/production
Comedian Ralph Lynn's work on *Wild Horses* by Ben Travers. UK-England: London. 1953. Lang.: Eng. 2191

Traverse Theatre (Edinburgh)
Institutions
Impressions of the Edinburgh Festival. UK-Scotland: Edinburgh. 1997. Lang.: Ger. 391

Performance/production
Collection of newspaper reviews by London theatre critics. UK-Scotland: Edinburgh. 1997. Lang.: Eng. 2232

Productions of plays by Caryl Churchill. UK-Scotland: Edinburgh. UK-England: London. 1997. Lang.: Eng. 2233

Traviata, La
Performance/production
The difficulty of performing 'Sempre Libera' in Verdi's *La Traviata*. Italy. USA: New York, NY. 1886-1996. Lang.: Eng. 4186

Soprano Aïnhoa Arteoa. Spain. 1997. Lang.: Eng. 4213

Background material on Metropolitan Opera radio broadcast performances. USA: New York, NY. 1997. Lang.: Eng. 4238

Travis, Sarah
Performance/production
Collection of newspaper reviews by London theatre critics. UK-England: London. 1997. Lang.: Eng. 2129

Tre sull'altalena (Three on the Swing)
Plays/librettos/scripts
Interview with playwright Luigi Lunari. Italy. 1990. Lang.: Swe. 2963

Treadwell, Sophie
Plays/librettos/scripts
The theme of nurturing in plays of Wolff, Treadwell, and Wasserstein. USA. 1996. Lang.: Eng. 3136

Research and production sourcebook on playwright Sophie Treadwell. USA. 1885-1970. Lang.: Eng. 3178

Sophie Treadwell and her play *Plumes in the Dust*. USA. 1917-1936. Lang.: Eng. 3183

Theory/criticism
Critical perceptions of female violence in plays of Glaspell, Treadwell, and Kesselman. USA. 1922-1997. Lang.: Eng. 3504

Treasure Island
Performance/production
Collection of newspaper reviews by London theatre critics. UK-England: London. 1997. Lang.: Eng. 2156

Tree, Herbert Beerbohm
Performance/production
The influence of Herbert Beerbohm Tree on G. Wilson Knight. UK-England. 1904-1952. Lang.: Eng. 2173

Shakespearean production in the age of actor-managers. UK-England. 1840-1914. Lang.: Eng. 2193

Tree, Maria
Performance/production
Performances of Shakespeare's *Twelfth Night* as objects of study. England. 1808-1850. Lang.: Eng. 508

Treherne, Nicola
Performance spaces
The history of the Colosseum and its new interior design. Germany: Essen. 1900-1997. Lang.: Ger. 3930

Tremblay, Carole
Plays/librettos/scripts
Characters in recently produced plays of Carole Tremblay and Michel Marc Bouchard. Canada. 1997. Lang.: Fre. 2417

Tremblay, Joey
Institutions
Interview with Joey Tremblay and Jonathan Christenson. Canada: Edmonton, AB. 1995-1996. Lang.: Eng. 1395

Tremblay, Larry
Performance/production
Jean-Louis Millette's performance in Larry Tremblay's one-man show *The Dragonfly of Chicoutimi*. Canada: Montreal, PQ. 1996. Lang.: Fre. 1586

Monodramas by Louisette Dussault and Larry Tremblay. Canada: Montreal, PQ. 1997. Lang.: Fre. 1605

Plays/librettos/scripts
Language in monodramas of Larry Tremblay. Canada. 1989-1995. Lang.: Fre. 2423

Shift in power relations among author, director, and actors. Canada. 1986-1992. Lang.: Fre. 2428

Quebec playwrights on the body in their work. Canada: Montreal, PQ. 1992-1996. Lang.: Fre. 2431

Tremblay, Michel
Audience
Reaction to a production of Michael Tremblay's *Messe solennelle pour une pleine lune d'été (Solemn Mass for a Full Moon in Summer)*. Canada: Quebec, PQ. 1996. Lang.: Fre. 1245

Performance/production
Martine Beaulne's production of *Albertine en cinq temps (Albertine in Five Times)* by Michel Tremblay. Canada: Montreal, PQ. 1995. Lang.: Fre. 1593

Collection of newspaper reviews by London theatre critics. UK-England: London. 1997. Lang.: Eng. 2036

Analysis of audio recordings of plays by Michel Marc Bouchard and Michel Tremblay. Canada. 1995-1997. Lang.: Fre. 3516

Trenne byar (Three Villages)
Performance/production
Role-playing, audience-free, interactive theatre. Sweden. 1990. Lang.: Swe. 3770

Trento, Vittorio
Plays/librettos/scripts
Trento's opera *Bianca de'Rossi* and its sources. Italy. 1790-1799. Lang.: Eng. 4306

Tretjakov, Sergej Michajlovič
Training
The gymnastic training methods of Rudolf Bode. Germany. 1881-1971. Lang.: Ita. 1042

Tri sestry (Three Sisters)
Performance/production
The body and the text in productions of the Festival de Théâtre des Amériques. Canada: Montreal, PQ. 1997. Lang.: Fre. 1583

Sociocultural analysis of recent French productions. France. 1993-1994. Lang.: Eng. 1678

Christoph Marthaler's production of Čechov's *Tri sestry (Three Sisters)*. Germany: Berlin. 1997. Lang.: Eng. 1738

Current productions of plays by Čechov. Russia: Moscow. 1940-1997. Lang.: Eng. 1856

Collection of newspaper reviews by London theatre critics. UK-England: London. 1997. Lang.: Eng. 2047

Collection of newspaper reviews by London theatre critics. UK-England: London. 1997. Lang.: Eng. 2087

Plays/librettos/scripts
Čechov's personality as discerned through his plays. Russia. 1993. Lang.: Eng. 2990

The influence of Čechov's *Tri sestry (Three Sisters)* on plays of Sadowski and Wertenbaker. Russia. UK-England. 1901-1997. Lang.: Eng. 2992

Tri-Cities Opera
Institutions
Downsizing American opera companies. USA. 1997. Lang.: Eng. 4059

Triad, The
Plays/librettos/scripts
British Library holdings of filmscript material of Harold Pinter. UK-England. 1963-1994. Lang.: Eng. 3647

Ungdomscirkus (Norsholm)
  Institutions
    Technical aspects of touring circus Ungdomcirkus. Sweden: Norsholm.
    1979. Lang.: Swe.   3785
Ungrateful Dead
  Performance/production
    Collection of newspaper reviews by London theatre critics. UK-England:
    London. 1997. Lang.: Eng.   2025
Unicorn Theatre (London)
  Performance/production
    Collection of newspaper reviews by London theatre critics. UK-England:
    London. 1997. Lang.: Eng.   2162
United States Institute for Theatre Technology (USITT)
  Design/technology
    USITT technical standard for stage pin connectors. USA. 1997. Lang.:
    Eng.   215
    Preview of professional development workshops of USITT conference.
    USA: Long Beach, CA. 1997. Lang.: Eng.   216
    Survey of classes, demonstrations, and exhibitions at OISTAT
    conference. USA: Pittsburgh, PA. 1997. Lang.: Eng.   221
    Profiles of USITT awards recipients. USA: Pittsburgh, PA. 1997. Lang.:
    Eng.   222
    Survey of OISTAT conference events. USA: Pittsburgh, PA. 1997.
    Lang.: Eng.   226
    The organization of USITT's annual conference and trade show. USA.
    1997. Lang.: Eng.   229
    Preview of USITT conference and OISTAT world congress. USA:
    Pittsburgh, PA. 1997. Lang.: Eng.   237
    Winners of the USITT architecture awards. USA. 1997. Lang.: Eng. 243
    Report on USITT conference and exhibition. USA: Pittsburgh, PA.
    1997. Lang.: Swe.   278
    Directory of USITT members. USA. 1997-1998. Lang.: Eng.   281
    The site of the upcoming USITT conference. USA: Long Beach, CA.
    1997. Lang.: Eng.   286
Universe, The
  Basic theatrical documents
    Text of *The Universe* by Richard Foreman. USA. 1996. Lang.: Eng.
                                                                     1327
University of Maryland Performing Arts Center (College Park, MD)
  Performance spaces
    The mission of the Maryland Performing Arts Center, under
    construction. USA: College Park, MD. 1997. Lang.: Eng.   460
Unlucky for Some
  Performance/production
    Collection of newspaper reviews by London theatre critics. UK-England:
    London. 1997. Lang.: Eng.   2123
Unt, Aimé
  Performance/production
    Moscow Art Theatre productions. Russia: Moscow. Estonia: Tallinn.
    1996-1997. Lang.: Rus.   1861
Untitled ... Naturally
  Performance/production
    Collection of newspaper reviews by London theatre critics. UK-England:
    London. 1997. Lang.: Eng.   1990
Unvernünftigen sterben aus, Die (Reckless Are Dying Out, The)
  Institutions
    Staatstheater Darmstadt under the direction of Gerd-Theo Umberg.
    Germany: Darmstadt. 1996-1997. Lang.: Ger.   1412
  Performance/production
    Collection of newspaper reviews by London theatre critics. UK-England:
    London. 1997. Lang.: Eng.   2126
Unwin, Stephen
  Performance/production
    Collection of newspaper reviews by London theatre critics. UK-England:
    London. 1997. Lang.: Eng.   1991
    Collection of newspaper reviews by London theatre critics. UK-England:
    London. 1997. Lang.: Eng.   2094
    Actors Timothy and Sam West. UK-England: London. 1997. Lang.:
    Eng.   2212
Up from Paradise
  Plays/librettos/scripts
    Social issues of the seventies in works by Arthur Miller. USA. 1970-
    1979. Lang.: Eng.   3173
Upton, Judy
  Performance/production
    Collection of newspaper reviews by London theatre critics. UK-England:
    London. 1997. Lang.: Eng.   2053

Collection of newspaper reviews by London theatre critics. UK-England:
London. 1997. Lang.: Eng.   2105
  Plays/librettos/scripts
    Profiles of younger English playwrights. UK-England. 1990. Lang.: Swe.
                                                                     3081
Uptown Theatre (Chicago, IL)
  Performance spaces
    The Uptown Theatre sign. USA: Chicago, IL. 1925-1997. Lang.: Eng.
                                                                     3555
Urdang, Leslie
  Institutions
    Profile of New York Stage and Film, in residence at Vassar College.
    USA: Poughkeepsie, NY. 1930-1997. Lang.: Eng.   398
Usher, Simon
  Performance/production
    Collection of newspaper reviews by London theatre critics. UK-England:
    London. 1997. Lang.: Eng.   1982
    Collection of newspaper reviews by London theatre critics. UK-England:
    London. 1997. Lang.: Eng.   2010
    Collection of newspaper reviews by London theatre critics. UK-England:
    London. 1997. Lang.: Eng.   2064
Utah Shakespearean Festival (Cedar City, UT)
  Relation to other fields
    Collaboration of teachers and theatre professionals to teach
    Shakespeare. USA. 1997. Lang.: Eng.   3403
Uvarova, E.A.
  Performance/production
    Actress E.A. Uvarova of Teat'r Komedii. Russia: St. Petersburg. 1990-
    1997. Lang.: Rus.   1872
Uys, Pieter-Dirk
  Basic theatrical documents
    Text of *No Space on Long Street* by Pieter-Dirk Uys. South Africa,
    Republic of. 1997. Lang.: Eng.   1306
  Performance/production
    Collection of newspaper reviews by London theatre critics. UK-England:
    London. 1997. Lang.: Eng.   2063
    Interview with political satirist Pieter-Dirk Uys. South Africa, Republic
    of. 1945-1994. Lang.: Eng.   3858
  Relation to other fields
    Political satire of Pieter-Dirk Uys. South Africa, Republic of:
    Johannesburg. 1981-1997. Lang.: Eng.   3740
Vacis, Gabriele
  Performance/production
    The first Italian production of Tennessee Williams's *The Rose Tattoo*.
    Italy. 1996. Lang.: Ita.   1795
Vagina Monologues, The
  Performance/production
    Playwright and performer Eve Ensler. USA: New York, NY. 1980-1997.
    Lang.: Eng.   2354
Vågstam, Gert-Ove
  Design/technology
    Theatre technician Gert-Ove Vågstam. Sweden. Cuba. South Africa,
    Republic of. 1976. Lang.: Swe.   185
Vaillancourt, Lise
  Plays/librettos/scripts
    Playwright Lise Vaillancourt on creating characters. Canada. 1997.
    Lang.: Fre.   2432
Vakhtangov Theatre
  SEE
    Teat'r im. Je. Vachtangova.
Valdez, Luis
  Performance/production
    The social protest theatre of Luis Valdez and Amiri Baraka. USA. 1965-
    1975. Lang.: Eng.   2260
    History in recent Chicano/a theatre. USA. 1964-1995. Lang.: Eng. 2360
Valency, Maurice
  Performance/production
    Dürrenmatt's *Der Besuch der alten Dame (The Visit)* and its American
    adaptation. Switzerland. 1921-1990. Lang.: Eng.   1965
Valentinian
  Plays/librettos/scripts
    Representations of virginity on the early modern English stage. England.
    1490-1650. Lang.: Eng.   2640
    Suicide in English Renaissance tragedy. England. 1590-1625. Lang.:
    Eng.   2724
Valle-Inclán, Ramón María del
  Plays/librettos/scripts
    Parody in the plays of Valle-Inclán. Spain. 1899-1936. Lang.: Spa. 3047

Valle-Inclán, Ramón María del — cont'd

Word avoidance and disclosure in plays of O'Neill and Valle-Inclán. USA. Spain. 1926-1959. Lang.: Eng. 3257

Vallet Kleiner, Danielle
Performance/production
Space, place, and travel in performance art and installations. UK-England: London. Germany: Kassel. 1997. Lang.: Eng. 3823

Valló, Péter
Performance/production
The career of director Péter Valló. Hungary. 1970-1997. Lang.: Hun. 1756

Vámos, Ágnes
Performance/production
Operatic couple Ferenc Mátray and Ágnes Vámos. Hungary. 1943-1990. Lang.: Hun. 4169

Vámos, László
Performance/production
Colleagues' recollections of director László Vámos. Hungary. 1928-1996. Lang.: Hun. 1763

Vampilov, Aleksand'r V.
Institutions
Festival of plays by Aleksand'r Vampilov. Russia: Irkutsk. 1996. Lang.: Rus. 1468

Van de Vate, Nancy
Performance/production
Theatrical vocal music of Nancy Van de Vate. USA. 1945-1995. Lang.: Eng. 3884

Van Fossen, Rachael
Basic theatrical documents
Text of *The Gathering* by Rachael Van Fossen *et al.* Canada: Fort Qu'Appelle, SK. 1997. Lang.: Eng. 3903
Plays/librettos/scripts
Rachael Van Fossen's playwriting for community theatre. Canada: Fort Qu'Appelle, SK, Regina, SK. 1990-1997. Lang.: Eng. 2434

van Hemert, Ilse
Performance/production
Collection of newspaper reviews by London theatre critics. UK-England: London. 1997. Lang.: Eng. 2135

van Hove, Ivo
Performance/production
Ivo van Hove, new artistic director of the Holland Festival. Netherlands: Amsterdam. 1969-1997. Lang.: Eng. 1826

van Nostrand, Amy
Performance/production
Harold Pinter's performance in his own play *The Hothouse*. UK-England: Chichester. 1996. Lang.: Eng. 2205

Van Randwyck, Issy
Performance/production
Collection of newspaper reviews by London theatre critics. UK-England: London. 1997. Lang.: Eng. 1986

Van Sant, Gus
Performance/production
Shakespearean elements in Gus Van Sant's film *My Own Private Idaho*. USA. 1993. Lang.: Eng. 3629

Van Welie, Georgina
Performance/production
Collection of newspaper reviews by London theatre critics. UK-England: London. 1997. Lang.: Eng. 1969
Collection of newspaper reviews by London theatre critics. UK-England: London. 1997. Lang.: Eng. 1982

Vanbrugh, Sir John
Performance/production
Collection of newspaper reviews by London theatre critics. UK-England: London. 1997. Lang.: Eng. 2078
Recent roles of actor Michael Pennington. UK-England: London. 1997. Lang.: Eng. 2196
Plays/librettos/scripts
The 'Lord of Misrule' in Vanbrugh's *The Relapse*. England. 1677-1696. Lang.: Eng. 2533

Vancouver Opera (Vancouver, BC)
Institutions
Planning a season at five Canadian opera companies. Canada. 1997. Lang.: Eng. 4038

Vandekeybus, Wim
Performance/production
Choreographer Wim Vandekeybus and the Eurocrash movement. Belgium. 1989-1997. Lang.: Eng. 1173

Vandenbroucke, Russell
Plays/librettos/scripts
Interview with Russell Vandenbroucke, author of *Atomic Bombers*. USA: Evanston, IL. 1984-1997. Lang.: Eng. 3166

Vandervell, W.F.
Performance/production
American chamber opera. USA. 1868-1997. Lang.: Eng. 4258

Vanya on 42nd Street
Plays/librettos/scripts
Analysis of plays by Wallace Shawn. USA. 1970-1996. Lang.: Eng. 3215

Varda, Agnès
Performance/production
Analysis of *Cléo de 5 à 7 (Cleo from 5 to 7)* by Agnès Varda. France. 1997. Lang.: Eng. 3572

Varför kysser alla Solveig? (Why Does Everyone Kiss Solveig?)
Performance/production
Choreographer, composer, and director Birgitta Egerbladh. Sweden: Gothenburg. 1996. Lang.: Swe. 1960

Varga, Magda
Performance/production
Interviews with singer Magda Varga and her son, actor György Cserhalmi. Hungary. 1922-1996. Lang.: Hun. 551

Vargas, Enrique
Performance/production
Collection of newspaper reviews by London theatre critics. UK-England: London. 1997. Lang.: Eng. 2071

Vargas, Margarita
Basic theatrical documents
Anthology of Latin American women's plays. Latin America. 1981-1989. Lang.: Eng. 1291

Vargen kommer
Plays/librettos/scripts
Hans Gefors' opera *Vargen kommer*, libretto by Kerstin Klein-Perski. Sweden: Malmö. 1997. Lang.: Swe. 4310

Variety acts
Performance/production
The official Polish theatre in occupied Cracow. Poland: Cracow. 1939-1945. Lang.: Pol. 588
Branson's theatrical tourism. USA: Branson, MO. 1906-1996. Lang.: Eng. 3958

Varley, Julia
Performance/production
Julia Varley on the work of Sanjukta Panigrahi. India. 1952-1996. Lang.: Ita. 1223

Varnay, Astrid
Performance/production
Excerpt from memoir of soprano Astrid Varnay. 1918-1997. Lang.: Eng. 4093
Comparison of sopranos Astrid Varnay and Birgit Nilsson. Europe. 1918-1973. Lang.: Eng. 4125

Városi Színház (Budapest)
Performance/production
Cabaret and operetta artist Hanna Honthy. Hungary. 1893-1950. Lang.: Hun. 4338

Városliget (Budapest)
Performance/production
Popular entertainment in Budapest's municipal park. Hungary: Budapest. 1860-1938. Lang.: Hun. 3767

Vasiljév, Vladimir Viktorovič
Performance/production
Vladimir Vasiljév's new version of *Swan Lake* at the Bolšoj Teat'r. Russia: Moscow. 1996. Lang.: Swe. 1107

Västanåteatern (Värmland)
Performance/production
Leif Stinnerbom's production of *Hamlet*. Sweden: Värmland. 1996. Lang.: Eng. 1947

Vaudeville
SEE ALSO
Classed Entries under MIXED ENTERTAINMENT—Variety acts.
Performance spaces
Performances of the vaudeville era. USA: Washington, DC. 1924-1992. Lang.: Eng. 457
Performance/production
The public persona of actress Mae West. USA. 1913-1943. Lang.: Eng. 642
Ontario's numerous variety acts. Canada. 1914-1979. Lang.: Eng. 3855

Vaudeville Theatre (London)
Performance/production
Collection of newspaper reviews by London theatre critics. UK-England: London. 1997. Lang.: Eng. 1986
Collection of newspaper reviews by London theatre critics. UK-England: London. 1997. Lang.: Eng. 2005

Vernoy de Saint-Georges, J.H. — cont'd

Plays/librettos/scripts
Analysis of *La Fille du régiment* by Donizetti. France. 1840. Lang.: Fre.
4292

Verse drama
Basic theatrical documents
English and German translations of *Babylon* by Ivo Svetina. Slovenia.
1997. Lang.: Eng, Ger. 1303
Plays/librettos/scripts
Greek mythology in tragedies of Ugo Foscolo. Italy. 1795-1811. Lang.:
Ita. 2954
Analysis of *Voranc* by Dane Zajc. Slovenia. 1960. Lang.: Slo. 3006
Translations of the verse drama of Kalidasa. Slovenia. 1885-1908.
Lang.: Slo. 3020

Vertinskij, Aleksand'r N.
Performance/production
Singer Aleksand'r N. Vertinskij. Russia. 1889-1957. Lang.: Rus. 3940

Vestale, La
Performance/production
Soprano Rosa Ponselle. USA: New York, NY. 1920-1927. Lang.: Eng.
4245

Viaggio a Reims, Il
Institutions
Profile of the Music Academy of the West. USA: Santa Barbara, CA.
1946-1997. Lang.: Eng. 4064

Vianna Filho, Oduvaldo (Vianinha)
Plays/librettos/scripts
Playwright Oduvaldo Vianna Filho. Brazil. 1934-1974. Lang.: Eng. 2387

Viardot, Pauline
Performance/production
The Giulia Grisi-Pauline Viardot controversy. England: London. 1848-
1852. Lang.: Eng. 4122

Vicharév, Sergej
Performance/production
Interview with dancer Sergej Vicharév. Russia: St. Petersburg. 1997.
Lang.: Eng. 1102

Vickery, Frank
Basic theatrical documents
Collection of one-act plays by Welsh writers. UK-Wales. 1952-1996.
Lang.: Eng. 1321

Victims of Duty
SEE
Victimes du devoir.

Victoria Palace (London)
Design/technology
Hildegard Bechter's design for the musical *Always*. UK-England:
London. 1997. Lang.: Eng. 3910
Performance/production
Collection of newspaper reviews by London theatre critics. UK-England:
London. 1997. Lang.: Eng. 2062
Collection of newspaper reviews by London theatre critics. UK-England:
London. 1997. Lang.: Eng. 2137

Victorian theatre
SEE
Geographical-Chronological Index under England 1837-1901.

Victory
Plays/librettos/scripts
British Library holdings of filmscript material of Harold Pinter. UK-
England. 1963-1994. Lang.: Eng. 3647

Vida breve, La
Basic theatrical documents
Libretto for Falla's opera *La vida breve*. Spain. 1913-1914. Lang.: Fre,
Spa. 4014
Performance/production
Productions of Manuel de Falla's *La vida breve*. 1913-1995. Lang.: Fre.
4076
Recordings of Manuel de Falla's opera *La vida breve*. 1913-1995. Lang.:
Fre. 4092

Vida es sueño, La (Life Is a Dream)
Performance/production
Collection of newspaper reviews by London theatre critics. UK-England:
London. 1997. Lang.: Eng. 2045
Collection of newspaper reviews by London theatre critics. UK-England:
London. 1997. Lang.: Eng. 2060

Video forms
SEE ALSO
Classed Entries under MEDIA—Video forms.
Design/technology
Design for Tina Turner concert tour. USA. 1996. Lang.: Eng. 277

Costuming for film and video. USA. 1997. Lang.: Eng. 3552
David Z. Saltz on his installation *Beckett Space*. USA. 1996. Lang.: Eng.
3702
Performance/production
CD-ROM presentation of all aspects of *kutiyattam*. India. 1000-1997.
Lang.: Eng. 557
The work of director Giuseppe Patroni Griffi. Italy. 1948-1997. Lang.:
Ita. 561
Collection of essays on director Mario Missiroli. Italy. 1956-1995. Lang.:
Ita. 562
Actor Gian Maria Volonté. Italy. 1933-1994. Lang.: Ita. 563
Interviews and documents on performance concepts and practices. USA.
1952-1994. Lang.: Eng. 649
Constraints and opportunities for Asian-American actors. USA. 1990-
1997. Lang.: Eng. 655
Video dance performance and criticism. UK-England. 1997. Lang.: Eng.
992
Video choreographer Michele Fox. UK-England. 1997. Lang.: Eng. 995
Dance-related events in the New York area. USA: New York, NY.
1996-1997. Lang.: Eng. 1007
The representation of social dancing in mass media. USA. 1980-1990.
Lang.: Eng. 1008
TV performances of young choreographers. Sweden. 1997. Lang.: Swe.
1186
The map of England in productions of Shakespeare's *King Lear*.
Europe. USA. 1909-1994. Lang.: Eng. 1650
Interview with actress Lina Pleijel. Sweden: Stockholm. 1981. Lang.:
Swe. 1946
The performance of race, gender, sexuality, and power. USA. Europe.
1590-1995. Lang.: Eng. 2309
How film and video versions of Shakespeare's plays may reinforce
textual authority rather than challenge it. UK-England. 1979-1991.
Lang.: Eng. 3510
The debate on the White Paper on South African Cinema. South Africa,
Republic of. 1996-1997. Lang.: Eng. 3587
Screen adaptations of Shakespeare's *The Taming of the Shrew*. UK-
England. USA. 1908-1966. Lang.: Eng. 3594
Interview with video and performance artist Charles Atlas. USA: New
York, NY. 1990-1997. Lang.: Eng. 3825
Survey of recordings by opera stars. USA. UK-England. 1897-1997.
Lang.: Eng. 4252
Obituary for television puppeteer Morey Bunin. USA. 1997. Lang.: Eng.
4375
Profile of television series *The Wubbulous World of Dr. Seuss*. USA:
New York, NY. 1997. Lang.: Eng. 4397
Obituary for Jon Stone of *Sesame Street*. USA: New York, NY. 1997.
Lang.: Eng. 4398
Plays/librettos/scripts
Analysis and bibliography of performance editions of Shakespeare's
Twelfth Night. England. 1774-1992. Lang.: Eng. 2688
Playwright Daniel Call and TV aesthetics. Germany. 1967-1997. Lang.:
Ger. 2862
Comparison of Arthur Miller's *The Crucible* and his adaptation of
Ibsen's *An Enemy of the People*. USA. 1950-1984. Lang.: Eng. 3126
Television simulation and Ronald Ribman's *Buck*. USA. 1983. Lang.:
Eng. 3216
The influence of Ibsen and Greek tragedy on the plays of Arthur Miller.
USA. 1915-1996. Lang.: Eng. 3240
The rhetoric of victimization in *The Glass Menagerie* by Tennessee
Williams. USA. 1945-1994. Lang.: Eng. 3298
Radio plays of Louis Nowra. Australia: Sydney. 1975-1993. Lang.: Eng.
3519
Film adaptations of plays by Arthur Miller. USA. 1960-1997. Lang.:
Eng. 3677
Text and music in operas by Robert Ashley and by Gertrude Stein with
Virgil Thomson. USA. 1925-1980. Lang.: Eng. 4315
Relation to other fields
Controversy over the videotaping of creative works by students. USA:
St. Louis, MO. 1994-1997. Lang.: Eng. 829
The fear of infection in American popular art and culture. USA. 1997.
Lang.: Eng. 848

Wajda, Andrzej
Performance/production
Biography of actress Anna Dymna. Poland: Cracow. 1950-1997. Lang.:
Pol.   1835

Analysis of Andrzej Wajda's Stary Theatre production of *Hamlet*.
Poland: Cracow. 1989. Lang.: Eng.   1843

Actor Jan Nowicki. Poland: Cracow. 1939-1997. Lang.: Pol.   1850
Waking
Performance/production
Collection of newspaper reviews by London theatre critics. UK-England:
London. 1997. Lang.: Eng.   2012
Walburg, Lars-Ole
Performance/production
The opening of the Deutsches Schauspielhaus season. Germany:
Hamburg. 1997. Lang.: Ger.   1688
Walcott, Derek
Performance/production
Collection of newspaper reviews by London theatre critics. UK-England:
London. 1997. Lang.: Eng.   1971
Waldkinder (Children of the Wood)
Plays/librettos/scripts
Interview with children's theatre playwright Rudolf Herfurthner.
Germany. 1947-1997. Lang.: Ger.   2851
Walker, Aida Overton
Performance/production
Race, gender, and nation in nineteenth-century performance. USA.
Europe. 1855-1902. Lang.: Eng.   633

Resistance and parody in African-American theatre. USA. 1895-1910.
Lang.: Eng.   652
Walker, George
Performance/production
Race, gender, and nation in nineteenth-century performance. USA.
Europe. 1855-1902. Lang.: Eng.   633

Resistance and parody in African-American theatre. USA. 1895-1910.
Lang.: Eng.   652
Walker, George F.
Plays/librettos/scripts
Analysis of *The Power Plays* by George F. Walker. Canada. 1980-1997.
Lang.: Eng.   2408

Teachers and students in plays of Walker, Mamet, and Ionesco. USA.
Canada. France. 1951-1997. Lang.: Eng.   3296
Walker, John
Plays/librettos/scripts
Radicalism in John Walker's melodrama *The Factory Lad*. England.
1820-1832. Lang.: Eng.   2591
Walker, Timothy
Performance/production
Collection of newspaper reviews by London theatre critics. UK-England:
London. 1997. Lang.: Eng.   2037
Walker, Trevor
Performance/production
Collection of newspaper reviews by London theatre critics. UK-England:
London. 1997. Lang.: Eng.   2079
Walküre, Die
Plays/librettos/scripts
Symbolism in Wagner's *Ring*. Germany. 1853-1874. Lang.: Eng.   4298
Wallace, Michele
Relation to other fields
Theatre artists' responses to the debate on multiculturalism of August
Wilson and Robert Brustein. USA. 1997. Lang.: Eng.   789
Wallace, Naomi
Performance/production
Collection of newspaper reviews by London theatre critics. UK-England:
London. 1997. Lang.: Eng.   2009
Wallop, Douglass
Performance/production
Collection of newspaper reviews by London theatre critics. UK-England:
London. 1997. Lang.: Eng.   2057
Walser, Martin
Performance/production
The style of productions at Bochumer Schauspielhaus. Germany:
Bochum. 1995-1997. Lang.: Ger.   1732
Walser, Robert
Performance/production
Productions of Schauspiel Stuttgart. Germany: Stuttgart. 1997. Lang.:
Ger.   1715
Walser, Theresia
Plays/librettos/scripts
Playwright Theresia Walser. Germany. 1990-1997. Lang.: Ger.   2864

Walsh, Enda
Performance/production
Collection of newspaper reviews by London theatre critics. UK-England:
London. 1997. Lang.: Eng.   1977
Walsh, Thommie
Performance/production
Collection of newspaper reviews by London theatre critics. UK-England:
London. 1997. Lang.: Eng.   2062
Walter Kerr Theatre (New York, NY)
Design/technology
Derek McLane's set design for *Present Laughter*. USA: New York, NY.
1996-1997. Lang.: Eng.   1365
Wälterlin, Oskar
Performance/production
German theatre during and after the Nazi period. Germany: Berlin,
Dusseldorf. Switzerland: Zurich. 1933-1952. Lang.: Eng.   1704
Walters, Jess
Performance/production
Collection of newspaper reviews by London theatre critics. UK-England:
London. 1997. Lang.: Eng.   1993
Walters, Sam
Performance/production
Collection of newspaper reviews by London theatre critics. UK-England:
London. 1997. Lang.: Eng.   2003

Collection of newspaper reviews by London theatre critics. UK-England:
London. 1997. Lang.: Eng.   2096

Collection of newspaper reviews by London theatre critics. UK-England:
London. 1997. Lang.: Eng.   2117

Collection of newspaper reviews by London theatre critics. UK-England:
London. 1997. Lang.: Eng.   2145
Walton, Tony
Design/technology
The influence of Jo Mielziner on scene designer Tony Walton. USA.
1936-1960. Lang.: Eng.   294

Broadway scene designer Tony Walton. USA. UK-England. 1934-1997.
Lang.: Eng.   295

Tony Walton's tribute to scene designer Abe Feder. USA: New York,
NY. 1956-1997. Lang.: Eng.   1380
Waltz, Sasha
Performance/production
Dance theatre artist Sasha Waltz. Germany. 1993-1996. Lang.: Eng. 967
Wanamaker, Sam
Performance spaces
History of attempt to reconstruct the Globe Theatre. England: London.
1599-1995. Lang.: Eng.   1522

Profile of Shakespeare's Globe Theatre. UK-England: London. 1970.
Lang.: Swe.   1541

Work of historical adviser to Shakespeare's Globe project. UK-England:
London. 1979. Lang.: Eng.   1542

Sam Wanamaker and the rebuilding of Shakespeare's Globe. UK-
England: London. 1997. Lang.: Eng.   1546
Wanamaker, Zoë
Performance spaces
Sam Wanamaker and the rebuilding of Shakespeare's Globe. UK-
England: London. 1997. Lang.: Eng.   1546
Wandor, Michelene
Plays/librettos/scripts
Women and theatrical collaboration. USA. UK-England. 1930-1990.
Lang.: Eng.   3264
Wang, Luoyong
Performance/production
Profile of actor Luoyong Wang. USA: New York, NY. 1984-1997.
Lang.: Eng.   3967
Wanson, Lorent
Performance/production
Productions of the Paris-Bruxelles Exhibition. Belgium: Brussels. 1997.
Lang.: Eng.   1570
War Memorial Opera House (San Francisco, CA)
Design/technology
Sound design problems of San Francisco Opera's temporary home.
USA: San Francisco, CA. 1996. Lang.: Eng.   4036
Warchus, Matthew
Performance/production
Collection of newspaper reviews by London theatre critics. UK-England.
1997. Lang.: Eng.   2051

Collection of newspaper reviews by London theatre critics. UK-England:
London. 1997. Lang.: Eng.   2089

Weiss, Peter — cont'd

Performance/production

Collection of newspaper reviews by London theatre critics. UK-England: London. 1997. Lang.: Eng. 2048

Plays/librettos/scripts

Metatheatrical techniques of Weiss, Gatti, and Stoppard. Europe. 1964-1982. Lang.: Eng. 2783

Theory/criticism

Typologies of performance analysis. UK-England. USA. 1963-1997. Lang.: Eng. 911

Weiss, Samuel

Performance/production

Portrait of actor Samuel Weiss. Germany: Stuttgart. 1967-1997. Lang.: Ger. 1714

Welker, Linda S.

Performance/production

The development of the production *Casing a Promised Land* by Linda Welker and H.L. Goodall. USA. 1997. Lang.: Eng. 685

Well of the Saints, The

Plays/librettos/scripts

Comparison of Friel's *Molly Sweeney* and Synge's *The Well of the Saints*. Ireland. UK-Ireland. 1997. Lang.: Eng. 2935

Weller, Michael

Performance/production

Collection of newspaper reviews by London theatre critics. UK-England. 1997. Lang.: Eng. 2050

Welles, Orson

Performance/production

Black actors and writers and the Negro Units of the Federal Theatre Project. USA: Washington, DC, New York, NY. 1935. Lang.: Eng. 2350

The television adaptation of Shakespeare's *King Lear* by Peter Brook and Orson Welles. USA. 1953. Lang.: Eng. 3730

Wellman, Mac

Basic theatrical documents

Text of *Cat's-Paw* by Mac Wellman. USA. 1997. Lang.: Eng. 1347

Text of *The Difficulty of Crossing a Field* by Mac Wellman, music by David Laing. USA. 1997. Lang.: Eng. 1348

Text of *The Land of Fog and Whistles* by Mac Wellman. USA. 1992. Lang.: Eng. 1349

Plays/librettos/scripts

Interview with playwright Mac Wellman. USA. 1997. Lang.: Eng. 3194

Introduction to *The Difficulty of Crossing a Field* by Mac Wellman. USA. 1997. Lang.: Eng. 3250

The principles of Gertrude Stein in the works of contemporary playwrights. USA. 1993. Lang.: Eng. 3263

Theory/criticism

Playwright Mac Wellman on political and poetic theatre. USA. 1993. Lang.: Eng. 3507

Wells, Fred

Performance/production

Collection of newspaper reviews by London theatre critics. UK-England: London. 1997. Lang.: Eng. 2161

Welsh National Opera (Cardiff)

Performance spaces

History and construction of Cardiff Bay Opera House. UK-Wales: Cardiff. 1986-1995. Lang.: Eng. 4071

Performance/production

Recent performances and changes at British opera houses. UK-England: London. UK-Wales: Cardiff. 1996-1997. Lang.: Eng. 4227

Welsh, Irvine

Performance/production

Collection of newspaper reviews by London theatre critics. UK-England: London. 1997. Lang.: Eng. 2080

Wembley Arena (London)

Performance/production

Collection of newspaper reviews by London theatre critics. UK-England: London. 1997. Lang.: Eng. 1973

Wendkos, Gina

Plays/librettos/scripts

Interview with playwright Gina Wendkos. USA. 1985. Lang.: Ita. 3141

Went Down to the Crossroads

Basic theatrical documents

Text of *Went Down to the Crossroads* by Philip Goulding. UK-England. 1997. Lang.: Eng. 1313

Wentworth, Scott

Performance/production

Collection of newspaper reviews by London theatre critics. UK-England: London. 1997. Lang.: Eng. 2103

Werfel, Franz

Performance/production

Kurt Weill's collaborations with playwrights. Germany: Berlin. USA: New York, NY. 1927-1945. Lang.: Eng. 3934

Werner, Olivier

Performance/production

Recent productions of works by Maeterlinck. France: Paris. 1997. Lang.: Swe. 1664

Werner, Rainer

Performance/production

Profile of actress Traute Hoess. Germany. Austria. 1969-1997. Lang.: Ger. 1741

Werner, Sarah

Training

Vocal training and the split between academics and practitioners. UK-England. USA. 1973-1994. Lang.: Eng. 933

Wertenbaker, Timberlake

Performance/production

Collection of newspaper reviews by London theatre critics. UK-England. 1997. Lang.: Eng. 2092

Plays/librettos/scripts

The influence of Cechov's *Tri sestry (Three Sisters)* on plays of Sadowski and Wertenbaker. Russia. UK-England. 1901-1997. Lang.: Eng. 2992

Female characters in plays of contemporary British women. UK-England. 1980-1995. Lang.: Eng. 3077

Metatheatre in plays of Timberlake Wertenbaker. UK-England. 1988-1995. Lang.: Eng. 3079

Wertheimer, Elemér

Institutions

The dispossession of a private theatre owner after the Communist takeover. Hungary: Budapest. 1911-1949. Lang.: Hun. 339

Wesker, Arnold

Performance/production

Collection of newspaper reviews by London theatre critics. UK-England: London. 1997. Lang.: Eng. 1977

Collection of newspaper reviews by London theatre critics. UK-England: London. 1997. Lang.: Eng. 1995

Plays/librettos/scripts

Interview with playwright Arnold Wesker. UK-England. 1958-1997. Lang.: Hun. 3115

West Side Story

Plays/librettos/scripts

Analysis of musical adaptations of Shakespearean plays. USA. 1938-1997. Lang.: Ger. 3983

West, Cheryl L.

Design/technology

Technical designs for the Shakespearean musical *Play On!*. USA: San Diego, CA. 1997. Lang.: Eng. 3921

Performance/production

The development of *Play On!*, a musical adaptation of Shakespeare's *Twelfth Night*. USA: New York, NY. 1997. Lang.: Eng. 3953

Plays/librettos/scripts

Survey of musical adaptations of Shakespeare. USA: New York, NY. 1938-1997. Lang.: Eng. 3987

West, Dominic

Performance/production

Actor Dominic West. UK-England: London. 1997. Lang.: Eng. 2195

West, Mae

Basic theatrical documents

Texts of three plays by Mae West. USA. 1926-1928. Lang.: Eng. 1350

Performance/production

The public persona of actress Mae West. USA. 1913-1943. Lang.: Eng. 642

West, Nathanael

Plays/librettos/scripts

The film adaptation of Nathanael West's *Miss Lonelyhearts*. USA. 1933. Lang.: Eng. 3686

West, Sam

Performance/production

Actors Timothy and Sam West. UK-England: London. 1997. Lang.: Eng. 2212

West, Timothy

Performance/production

Actors Timothy and Sam West. UK-England: London. 1997. Lang.: Eng. 2212

Weston, Dick

Performance/production

Ventriloquist Dick Weston. USA. 1997. Lang.: Eng. 4379

Wetterleuchten (Sheet Lightning)

Plays/librettos/scripts

Playwright Daniel Call and TV aesthetics. Germany. 1967-1997. Lang.: Ger. 2862

Wilson, August — cont'd

The debate on multiculturalism of August Wilson and Robert Brustein. USA. 1997. Lang.: Eng.   825

The Wilson/Brustein debate on African-Americans and theatre. USA. 1995-1997. Lang.: Eng.   826

August Wilson and the history of African-American theatre. USA. 1926-1997. Lang.: Eng.   828

Robert Brustein and August Wilson debate multiculturalism. USA: New York, NY. 1997. Lang.: Eng.   830

August Wilson's address to the National Black Theatre Festival. USA: Winston-Salem, NC. 1997. Lang.: Eng.   3440

August Wilson's TCG speech on the Black artist in American theatre. USA. 1996. Lang.: Eng.   3441

Wilson, Edward
Performance/production
Collection of newspaper reviews by London theatre critics. UK-England: London. 1997. Lang.: Eng.   2099

Wilson, Erin Cressida
Basic theatrical documents
Text of *Hurricane* by Erin Cressida Wilson. USA. 1996. Lang.: Eng.   1352

Performance/production
Erin Cressida Wilson on her performance piece *Hurricane*. USA. 1996. Lang.: Eng.   2357

Wilson, Jacqueline
Performance/production
Collection of newspaper reviews by London theatre critics. UK-England: London. 1997. Lang.: Eng.   2128

Wilson, Josephine
Performance/production
Collection of newspaper reviews by London theatre critics. UK-England: London. 1997. Lang.: Eng.   2073

Wilson, Lanford
Design/technology
Dennis Parichy's lighting design for *Sympathetic Magic* by Lanford Wilson at Second Stage. USA: New York, NY. 1997. Lang.: Eng.   1369
Plays/librettos/scripts
Critical history of American drama. USA. 1960-1997. Lang.: Eng.   3267

Wilson, Mary Louise
Performance/production
Mary Louise Wilson on her one-woman show *Full Gallop*. USA: New York, NY. 1997. Lang.: Eng.   2358

Wilson, Richard
Performance/production
Collection of newspaper reviews by London theatre critics. UK-England: London. 1997. Lang.: Eng.   2030

Wilson, Robert
Audience
Robert Wilson's staging of *La Maladie de la Mort (The Sickness of Death)* by Marguerite Duras. France: Paris. 1997. Lang.: Fre.   1249
Performance/production
Twentieth-century theatre as a signifying practice. Europe. North America. 1900-1995. Lang.: Eng.   515

Robert Wilson's performance piece *Persephone*. Germany: Munich. 1997. Lang.: Eng.   536

Robert Wilson's Swedish guest performance. Sweden: Stockholm. USA. 1976. Lang.: Swe.   614

Profile of writer/director Robert Wilson. USA. Europe. 1960-1996. Lang.: Swe.   679

The deconstruction of femininity in Jutta Lampe and Isabelle Huppert's performances of *Orlando*. Europe. 1923-1997. Lang.: Eng.   1643

Recent productions of works by Maeterlinck. France: Paris. 1997. Lang.: Swe.   1664

Treatments of Shakespeare's *Hamlet* by Robert Wilson and Benno Besson. Italy. 1995. Lang.: Ita.   1808

Robert Wilson's production of *La Maladie de la Mort (The Sickness of Death)* by Marguerite Duras. Switzerland: Lausanne. 1970-1997. Lang.: Hun.   1962

Collection of newspaper reviews by London theatre critics. UK-England: London. 1997. Lang.: Eng.   2135

Interview with director Robert Wilson. Europe. 1969-1997. Lang.: Ger, Fre, Dut, Eng.   3866

Interview with composer Hans Peter Kuhn, collaborator of Robert Wilson. Europe. 1978-1997. Lang.: Ger, Fre, Dut, Eng.   3867

The theatrical productions of Robert Wilson. USA. Europe. 1964-1996. Lang.: Ita.   3883

Interview with director Richard Günther. Sweden: Stockholm. 1990-1997. Lang.: Swe.   3943
Plays/librettos/scripts
Changing relationships of writing, text and performance. UK-England. USA. 1980-1996. Lang.: Eng.   698

Temporality in theatrical production. Europe. 1990-1997. Lang.: Ger, Fre, Dut, Eng.   2791

Nature in Apel's *Der Freischütz* and its operatic adaptations. Germany. 1811-1990. Lang.: Ger.   2856

Wilson, Robert McLiam
Performance/production
Collection of newspaper reviews by London theatre critics. UK-England: London. 1997. Lang.: Eng.   2116

Wilson, Sandy
Performance/production
Collection of newspaper reviews by London theatre critics. UK-England. 1997. Lang.: Eng.   2082

Wilson, Snoo
Performance/production
Collection of newspaper reviews by London theatre critics. UK-England: London. 1997. Lang.: Eng.   2118

Wilson, Wils
Performance/production
Collection of newspaper reviews by London theatre critics. UK-England: London. 1997. Lang.: Eng.   1982

Wilton's Theatre (London)
Performance/production
Collection of newspaper reviews by London theatre critics. UK-England: London. 1997. Lang.: Eng.   2157

Wimbledon Studio Theatre (London)
Performance/production
Collection of newspaper reviews by London theatre critics. UK-England: London. 1997. Lang.: Eng.   1974

Collection of newspaper reviews by London theatre critics. UK-England: London. 1997. Lang.: Eng.   1984

Collection of newspaper reviews by London theatre critics. UK-England: London. 1997. Lang.: Eng.   1997

Collection of newspaper reviews by London theatre critics. UK-England: London. 1997. Lang.: Eng.   2019

Collection of newspaper reviews by London theatre critics. UK-England: London. 1997. Lang.: Eng.   2035

Collection of newspaper reviews by London theatre critics. UK-England: London. 1997. Lang.: Eng.   2087

Collection of newspaper reviews by London theatre critics. UK-England: London. 1997. Lang.: Eng.   2113

Collection of newspaper reviews by London theatre critics. UK-England. 1997. Lang.: Eng.   2142

Wing-Davey, Mark
Performance/production
Collection of newspaper reviews by London theatre critics. UK-England: London. 1997. Lang.: Eng.   1983

Tony Kushner's *Angels in America* as epic theatre. USA. 1992-1995. Lang.: Eng.   2324

Wings of the Dove, The
Basic theatrical documents
Text of Hossein Amini's film adaptation of *The Wings of the Dove* by Henry James. UK-England. 1995-1997. Lang.: Eng.   3528
Performance/production
Interview with director Iain Softley. UK-England. 1995-1997. Lang.: Eng.   3589
Plays/librettos/scripts
Interview with Hossein Amini, author of the filmscript *The Wings of the Dove*. UK-England. 1995-1997. Lang.: Eng.   3643

Winter's Tale, The
Performance spaces
The inaugural season of the rebuilt Shakespeare's Globe. UK-England: London. 1997. Lang.: Eng.   1539

Profile of Shakespeare's Globe Theatre. UK-England: London. 1970. Lang.: Swe.   1541
Performance/production
Shakespeare's *The Winter's Tale* at Teatr Nowy. Poland: Poznań. 1997. Lang.: Eng, Fre.   1841

Ingmar Bergman's productions of Shakespeare's plays. Sweden. Germany. 1944-1994. Lang.: Ita.   1934

Collection of newspaper reviews by London theatre critics. UK-England: London. 1997. Lang.: Eng.   2060

Woman Killed with Kindness, A — cont'd

Narcissism in Renaissance tragedy. England. 1450-1580. Lang.: Eng.
2609

Woman Who Thought She Was a Dog, The
Performance/production
Collection of newspaper reviews by London theatre critics. UK-England:
London. 1997. Lang.: Eng. 2054

Woman, The
Plays/librettos/scripts
Greek myth in contemporary drama. 1970-1990. Lang.: Eng. 2369

Woman's Prize, The
Plays/librettos/scripts
Male expectations of women's role in society in Fletcher's *The Woman's Prize*. England. 1633. Lang.: Eng. 2469

Women Beware Women
Plays/librettos/scripts
Accusations of rape in English Renaissance drama. England. 1550-1630.
Lang.: Eng. 2526

The Italian palazzo on the Jacobean stage. England. 1603-1625. Lang.:
Eng. 2625

Analysis of Middleton's *Women Beware Women* and its adaptation by
Howard Barker. England. 1621-1986. Lang.: Eng. 2666

Twentieth-century adaptations of Jacobean plays. England. 1604-1986.
Lang.: Eng. 2673

Women in theatre
Administration
Equity-sponsored Phyllis Newman Women's Health Initiative and its
benefit performances. USA: New York, NY. 1997. Lang.: Eng. 85
Basic theatrical documents
Anthology of Latin American women's plays. Latin America. 1981-1989.
Lang.: Eng. 1291

Writings of Louisa McCord. USA. 1810-1879. Lang.: Eng. 1334

Anthology of plays by women of color. USA. 1992-1996. Lang.: Eng.
1338
Design/technology
Lighting designer Beverly Emmons. USA: New York, NY. 1960-1997.
Lang.: Eng. 254
Institutions
Program of women's arts festival. Slovenia: Ljubljana. 1997. Lang.: Slo.
374

Scottish theatres run by women. UK-Scotland. 1996. Lang.: Eng. 392

Interview with Anna Badora, director of Düsseldorfer Schauspielhaus.
Germany: Dusseldorf. 1996-1997. Lang.: Ger. 1418

Edna Kenton and Eleanor Fitzgerald, managers of the Provincetown
Players. USA: New York, NY. 1916-1924. Lang.: Eng. 1502
Performance/production
Interviews with women in Icelandic theatre and government. Iceland.
1980-1996. Lang.: Eng. 555

Report on the Fourth International Women Playwrights Conference.
Ireland: Galway. 1997. Lang.: Eng. 559

Women in Japanese theatre. Japan: Tokyo. 1970-1996. Lang.: Eng. 568

Women directors in Spanish theatre. Spain. 1990-1996. Lang.: Eng. 612

Solo performance of Carran Waterfield. UK-England: Coventry. 1978-
1997. Lang.: Eng. 623

Changes in women's comedy performance. USA. 1950-1995. Lang.:
Eng. 654

Autobiographical performances of Elizabeth Robins. USA. 1862-1952.
Lang.: Eng. 656

The emergence of modern American theatre. USA. 1914-1929. Lang.:
Eng. 683

Feminist analysis of dance and the representation of the female body.
USA. Europe. 1801-1997. Lang.: Eng. 997

Rukmini Devi and the revival of South Indian dance. India. 1904-1996.
Lang.: Eng. 1147

Female beauty and American modern dance. USA. 1930-1940. Lang.:
Eng. 1204

Tessa Mendel's production of *Home at Last* by Christopher Heide.
Canada: Halifax, NS. 1996. Lang.: Eng. 1589

Actresses and the adaptation of Shakespeare. England. 1660-1740.
Lang.: Eng. 1623

Changes in Shakespearean production under David Garrick. England.
1747-1776. Lang.: Eng. 1627

Actress, theatre director, and teacher Caroline Neuber. Germany. 1697-
1760. Lang.: Ger. 1685

The actress in Russian theatre. Russia. 1845-1916. Lang.: Eng. 1893

Profile of director Paloma Pedrero. Spain. 1957-1996. Lang.: Eng. 1916

Staging Shakespeare in the Romantic period. UK-England. 1800-1840.
Lang.: Eng. 2166

English acting careers of Eleonora Duse and Adelaide Ristori. UK-
England. 1850-1900. Lang.: Eng. 2169

The Shakespearean acting and directing career of Judi Dench. UK-
England: London. 1957-1995. Lang.: Eng. 2177

Edith Craig and the Pioneer Players. UK-England: London. 1907-1947.
Lang.: Eng. 2181

Victorian ideas of womanhood in productions of Shakespeare's *The Merchant of Venice*. UK-England. 1832-1903. Lang.: Eng. 2188

Shakespearean production in the age of actor-managers. UK-England.
1840-1914. Lang.: Eng. 2193

Elizabeth Robins' *Votes for Women!*. UK-England: London. 1907.
Lang.: Eng. 2219

Stage adaptations of *Uncle Tom's Cabin*. USA. 1853-1857. Lang.: Eng.
2250

Mary Louise Wilson on her one-woman show *Full Gallop*. USA: New
York, NY. 1997. Lang.: Eng. 2358

Representations of Black women on stage and screen. USA. 1939-1995.
Lang.: Eng. 3605

Women in *commedia dell'arte*. Italy. 1545-1650. Lang.: Eng. 3793

Work and artists of the Fluxus retrospective. USA. 1960-1996. Lang.:
Eng. 3835

The female body in performance art. USA. Europe. 1960-1995. Lang.:
Eng. 3837

The construction of female beauty in popular entertainment. USA. 1920-
1930. Lang.: Eng. 3961

Contemporary regional theatre and its origins in ancestor worship.
China: Quanzhou, Fujian. 714-1994. Lang.: Eng. 4388
Plays/librettos/scripts
Female characters in *kyōgen*. Japan. Lang.: Eng. 1227

Female dramatists before the Restoration. England. 1590-1660. Lang.:
Eng. 2467

The representation of women by boy actors. England. 1450-1600. Lang.:
Eng. 2475

Women's Romantic 'closet' drama as an alternative theatrical space.
England. 1790-1820. Lang.: Eng. 2486

Female 'mad' songs in seventeenth-century English drama. England.
1685-1700. Lang.: Eng. 2638

The significance of rape in *The Rover* by Aphra Behn. England. 1660.
Lang.: Eng. 2744

Analysis of *The Witlings* by Fanny Burney. England. 1778. Lang.: Eng.
2753

Representations of women in Parisian melodrama theatres. France.
1830-1870. Lang.: Eng. 2825

Strong women in the *Oresteia* of Aeschylus. Greece. 500 B.C. Lang.:
Eng. 2868

The depiction of women in ancient Greek theatre. Greece. 500-200 B.C.
Lang.: Eng. 2884

Female characters in plays of contemporary British women. UK-
England. 1980-1995. Lang.: Eng. 3077

The theme of nurturing in plays of Wolff, Treadwell, and Wasserstein.
USA. 1996. Lang.: Eng. 3136

Critical history of American feminist drama. USA. 1772-1995. Lang.:
Eng. 3151

Analysis of *Color Struck* by Zora Neale Hurston. USA. 1891-1995.
Lang.: Eng. 3160

Mimesis, feminism, theatre, and performance. USA. 1997. Lang.: Eng.
3176

Interview with playwright Paula Vogel. USA: New York, NY. 1997.
Lang.: Eng. 3181

Postmodern feminist theatre practice and Fornes' *Fefu and Her Friends*.
USA: New York, NY. 1977-1997. Lang.: Eng. 3185

Black female culture in plays of Pearl Cleage. USA: Atlanta, GA. 1992-
1997. Lang.: Eng. 3197

The female body in plays of Moraga, Fornes, and Cruz. USA. 1980-
1991. Lang.: Eng. 3228

Simultaneous discourse in works by African-American women. USA.
1900-1993. Lang.: Eng. 3260

Women in theatre — cont'd

Wozzeck — cont'd

Introduction to *Wozzeck* by Alban Berg. Germany: Berlin. 1914-1997. Lang.: Eng. 4158

Background of the opera *Wozzeck* by Alban Berg. Germany. Austria: Vienna. 1925. Lang.: Eng. 4163

Background material on Metropolitan Opera radio broadcast performances. USA: New York, NY. 1997. Lang.: Eng. 4238

Wren, Christopher
Performance/production
Collection of newspaper reviews by London theatre critics. UK-England: London. 1997. Lang.: Eng. 2079

Collection of newspaper reviews by London theatre critics. UK-England: London. 1997. Lang.: Eng. 2124

Wrentmore, Stephen
Performance/production
Collection of newspaper reviews by London theatre critics. UK-England: London. 1997. Lang.: Eng. 1976

Wright, Doug
Design/technology
Scene designs of Neil Patel. USA. 1996. Lang.: Eng. 1373

Wright, John
Performance/production
Collection of newspaper reviews by London theatre critics. UK-England: London. 1997. Lang.: Eng. 2032

Wubbulous World of Dr. Seuss, The
Performance/production
Profile of television series *The Wubbulous World of Dr. Seuss*. USA: New York, NY. 1997. Lang.: Eng. 4397

Württembergische Staatstheater (Stuttgart)
Administration
Württembergische Staatstheater under Friedrich Schirmer's leadership. Germany: Stuttgart. 1993-1997. Lang.: Ger. 1238

Wuthering Heights
Performance/production
Collection of newspaper reviews by London theatre critics. UK-England: London. 1997. Lang.: Eng. 1983

Wuttke, Martin
Institutions
Interview with Martin Wuttke of Berliner Ensemble. Germany: Berlin. 1989-1997. Lang.: Ger. 1424

Problems at Berliner Ensemble. Germany: Berlin. 1989. Lang.: Swe. 1429

Wycherley, William
Plays/librettos/scripts
The ideology of Restoration comedy. England. 1660-1710. Lang.: Eng. 2492

Theoretical knowledge and action in plays of Wycherley. England. 1671-1676. Lang.: Eng. 2590

Women disguised as men in seventeenth-century drama. England. 1602-1674. Lang.: Eng. 2653

Wylde, Martin
Performance/production
Collection of newspaper reviews by London theatre critics. UK-England: London. 1997. Lang.: Eng. 2020

Wymark, Olwen
Performance/production
Collection of newspaper reviews by London theatre critics. UK-England: London. 1997. Lang.: Eng. 2031

Wyndham's Theatre (London)
Performance/production
Collection of newspaper reviews by London theatre critics. UK-England: London. 1997. Lang.: Eng. 2089

Xerxes
Design/technology
Opera costume designer Martin Pakledinaz. USA: Santa Fe, NM, New York, NY. 1997. Lang.: Eng. 4035
Performance/production
Soprano Susannah Waters. UK-England. 1997. Lang.: Eng. 4226

Yang, William
Institutions
Solo performance at the Festival de Théâtre des Amériques. Canada: Montreal, PQ. 1997. Lang.: Fre. 1392

Yankee Dawg You Die
Plays/librettos/scripts
Analysis of Asian American drama. USA. 1970-1997. Lang.: Eng. 3225

Yanqui (Yankee)
Basic theatrical documents
Anthology of Latin American women's plays. Latin America. 1981-1989. Lang.: Eng. 1291

Yassour, Penny
Performance/production
Space, place, and travel in performance art and installations. UK-England: London. Germany: Kassel. 1997. Lang.: Eng. 3823

Yates, Peter
Performance/production
Interview with film director Peter Yates. USA. 1929-1997. Lang.: Eng. 3600

Year of the Dragon, The
Plays/librettos/scripts
Analysis of Asian American drama. USA. 1970-1997. Lang.: Eng. 3225

Yearbooks
Institutions
Yearbook of the Hungarian State Opera House. Hungary: Budapest. 1995-1996. Lang.: Hun. 4050

Yearbook of the Hungarian State Opera House. Hungary: Budapest. 1996-1997. Lang.: Hun. 4051
Reference materials
Yearbook of Italian theatre. Italy. 1997. Lang.: Ita. 715

Yearbook of Dutch performing arts. Netherlands. 1996-1997. Lang.: Dut. 717

Yearbook of Slovenian theatre. Slovenia. 1995-1996. Lang.: Slo. 718

Yeats, William Butler
Performance/production
Recent Irish productions. Ireland: Sligo, Dublin. 1997. Lang.: Swe. 1788

Collection of newspaper reviews by London theatre critics. UK-England: London. 1997. Lang.: Eng. 2048
Plays/librettos/scripts
Asian influence on European theatre. Europe. Asia. 1915-1997. Lang.: Pol. 694

Landscape and the supernatural in *Purgatory* by W.B. Yeats. Ireland. 1938. Lang.: Eng. 2931

Landscape in plays of W.B. Yeats. Ireland. 1916-1919. Lang.: Eng. 2932

The character of the traveler in plays of the Irish Renaissance. Ireland. 1910-1930. Lang.: Eng. 2938

Sandra Deer's play about W.B. Yeats, *Sailing to Byzantium*. USA: Atlanta, GA. 1997. Lang.: Eng. 3249
Relation to other fields
Novelist and playwright George Moore. Ireland: Dublin. UK-England: London. 1852-1933. Lang.: Eng. 3367
Research/historiography
Irish theatre critics' focus on text rather than performance. Ireland: Dublin. 1897-1907. Lang.: Eng. 3450
Theory/criticism
Magic as defining trope of modern drama. Europe. 1910-1950. Lang.: Eng. 3482

Yellow Fever
Plays/librettos/scripts
Analysis of Asian American drama. USA. 1970-1997. Lang.: Eng. 3225

Yerma
Plays/librettos/scripts
Analysis of *Bodas de sangre (Blood Wedding)* and *Yerma* by Federico García Lorca. Spain. 1920-1936. Lang.: Eng. 3050

Yeston, Maury
Design/technology
Stewart Laing's set and costume designs for the musical *Titanic*. USA: New York, NY. 1997. Lang.: Eng. 3914
Performance/production
Composer/lyricist Maury Yeston. USA: New York, NY. 1945-1997. Lang.: Eng. 3975
Plays/librettos/scripts
Interview with playwright Peter Stone. USA: New York, NY. 1997. Lang.: Eng. 3981

Interviews with authors of Tony Award-winning shows. USA: New York, NY. 1997. Lang.: Eng. 3985

Yiddish theatre
SEE ALSO
Ethnic theatre.

Jewish theatre.

Ying hsi
SEE
Shadow puppets.

Yllana (Spain)
Performance/production
Collection of newspaper reviews by London theatre critics. UK-England: London. 1997. Lang.: Eng. 1977

York Cycle
Plays/librettos/scripts
Middle English religious drama and audience participation. England. 1400-1550. Lang.: Eng. 2576

Zauberflöte, Die — cont'd

Background material on Lyric Opera of Chicago radio broadcast performances. USA: Chicago, IL. 1997. Lang.: Eng. 4231

Plays/librettos/scripts
Female characters in Mozart's *Don Giovanni* and *Die Zauberflöte*. Austria. 1756-1791. Lang.: Eng. 4280

Zeami, Motokiyo
Theory/criticism
Signs in theatrical representation. France. 1977. Lang.: Eng. 890

Zech, Rosel
Performance/production
Actors on working in theatre, film, and television. Germany. 1941-1997. Lang.: Ger. 3576

Zeder, Suzan
Theory/criticism
The effect of feminism on children's theatre. USA. 1995-1996. Lang.: Eng. 914

Zeffirelli, Franco
Performance/production
Non-literary realism in Shakespeare productions. UK-England. Germany. 1958-1995. Lang.: Ger. 2170

Franco Zeffirelli's film adaptations of Shakespearean plays. Italy. 1966-1990. Lang.: Eng. 3579

Plays/librettos/scripts
Hamlet, revenge tragedy, and *film noir*. 1600-1996. Lang.: Eng. 2365

Film adaptations of Shakespeare's *The Taming of the Shrew*. USA. 1929-1966. Lang.: Eng. 3668

Critique of Franco Zeffirelli's film adaptation of *Hamlet*. USA. 1990. Lang.: Eng. 3675

Zeit und das Zimmer, Die (Time and the Room)
Performance/production
A student production of *Time and the Room (Die Zeit und das Zimmer)* by Botho Strauss. UK-England. 1996. Lang.: Eng. 2204

Zelwerowicz, Aleksander
Performance/production
Wartime and postwar activities of actor and director Aleksander Zelwerowicz. Poland. 1925-1979. Lang.: Pol. 1848

Zemach, Benjamin
Performance/production
Dancer, actor, choreographer Benjamin Zemach. USA. 1902-1997. Lang.: Eng. 1207

Zemljic, Elizabeta
Relation to other fields
Play competition involving immigrants in Malmö's suburbs. Sweden: Malmö. 1996. Lang.: Swe. 3378

Ženovač, Sergej
Institutions
Interview with director Sergej Ženovač. Russia: Moscow. 1990-1997. Lang.: Rus. 1461

Performance/production
Ženovač's production of Turgenjėv's *Mesjac v derevne (A Month in the Country)*. Russia: Moscow. 1996. Lang.: Rus. 1873

Zhang, Yuan
Institutions
Impressions of the Edinburgh Festival. UK-Scotland: Edinburgh. 1997. Lang.: Ger. 391

Performance/production
Collection of newspaper reviews by London theatre critics. UK-Scotland: Edinburgh. 1997. Lang.: Eng. 2231

Zhejiang Kunju Troupe (Beijing)
Performance/production
The classical theatre genre *kunju* and its revival. China, People's Republic of. 1950-1960. Lang.: Eng. 3893

Zhou, Chuanying
Performance/production
The classical theatre genre *kunju* and its revival. China, People's Republic of. 1950-1960. Lang.: Eng. 3893

Zich, Otakar
Theory/criticism
Introduction to dramaturgical study by Otakar Zich. Czechoslovakia. 1922. Lang.: Cze. 868

Text of an unknown dramaturgical study by Otakar Zich. Czechoslovakia. 1922. Lang.: Cze. 869

Ziegfeld Follies (New York, NY)
Performance/production
The construction of female beauty in popular entertainment. USA. 1920-1930. Lang.: Eng. 3961

Zijlstra, Marcel
Performance/production
A performance of the Beauvais *Ludus Danielis*. Netherlands: Maastricht. 1996. Lang.: Eng. 3872

A collaborative production of the medieval *Ludus Danielis*. Netherlands: Maastricht. 1996. Lang.: Eng. 3873

Zimmerman, Mary
Performance/production
Mary Zimmerman's adaptation of the Chinese epic *Journey to the West*. USA. China. 1997. Lang.: Eng. 2271

Zimmerschlacht (Home Front)
Performance/production
The style of productions at Bochumer Schauspielhaus. Germany: Bochum. 1995-1997. Lang.: Ger. 1732

Zingg, Jeannette
Performance/production
Opera Atelier's production of Purcell's *Dido and Aeneas*. Canada: Toronto, ON. 1994-1995. Lang.: Eng. 4112

Zinner, Hedda
Relation to other fields
The Communist view of Brecht. Germany: Berlin. 1920-1956. Lang.: Ger. 3351

Zinnober (Berlin)
Relation to other fields
History of indepedent theatre company Zinnober. Germany: Berlin. 1980-1997. Lang.: Ger. 4383

Ziolo, Rudolf
Performance/production
Recent productions of plays by Shakespeare. Poland. 1997. Lang.: Eng, Fre. 1834

Zippel, David
Plays/librettos/scripts
Parody and satire in musical theatre. USA. UK-England. 1727-1990. Lang.: Eng. 3986

Žitinkin, Andrej
Performance/production
Andrej Žitinkin, director of Mossovêt Theatre. Russia: Moscow. 1990-1997. Lang.: Rus. 1900

Zloof, Fouad
Performance/production
Collection of newspaper reviews by London theatre critics. UK-England: London. 1997. Lang.: Eng. 2003

Zodiak Presents (Helsinki)
Institutions
Zodiak Presents and its center for contemporary dance. Finland: Helsinki. 1986-1996. Lang.: Eng. 1160

Performance/production
History of dance group Zodiak Presents. Finland: Helsinki. 1980-1997. Lang.: Eng. 1065

Zollar, Jawole Willa Jo
Performance/production
The body and cultural identity in contemporary dance. USA. 1985-1995. Lang.: Eng. 996

Zoltowski, Rick
Performance/production
Collection of newspaper reviews by London theatre critics. UK-England: London. 1997. Lang.: Eng. 2003

Zorin, Leonid
Plays/librettos/scripts
Memoirs of playwright Leonid Zorin. Russia. 1934-1994. Lang.: Rus. 3004

Zsámbéki, Gábor
Institutions
Pictorial history of Katona József Chamber Theatre. Hungary: Budapest. 1982-1997. Lang.: Hun. 1442

Performance/production
Andrea Fullajtár's performance in *Csendet akarok (I Want Silence)* by Zsolt Csalog. Hungary: Budapest. 1996. Lang.: Hun. 1771

Zsóter, Sándor
Institutions
A congress on current Hungarian drama. Hungary. 1997. Lang.: Ger. 1437

Ztížená možnost soustředění (Increased Difficulty of Concentration, The)
Plays/librettos/scripts
The victimized female character in plays by Václav Havel. Czech Republic. 1963-1997. Lang.: Eng. 2445

Zuckersüss und Leichenbitter (Sugar-Sweet and Mournful)
Plays/librettos/scripts
Playwright Albert Ostermaier. Germany. 1967-1997. Lang.: Ger. 2853

Zuckmayer, Carl
Performance/production
Castorf's production of *Des Teufels General (The Devil's General)* at Theatertreffen festival. Germany: Berlin. 1996. Lang.: Eng. 1690

GEOGRAPHICAL - CHRONOLOGICAL INDEX

Belgium — cont'd

1980-1997. **Performance/production.**
Choreographer Anne Teresa De Keersmaeker. Brussels. Lang.:
Eng. 1174
1985-1996. **Performance/production.**
Voice and voicelessness in the theatre of Jan Fabre. Lang.: Eng.
472
1989-1997. **Performance/production.**
Choreographer Wim Vandekeybus and the Eurocrash
movement. Lang.: Eng. 1173
1991-1997. **Performance/production.**
Choreographer Meg Stuart. Lang.: Eng. 955
1994. **Plays/librettos/scripts.**
Analysis of *Les Combustibles (The Combustibles)* by Amélie
Nothomb. Lang.: Fre. 2386
1996. **Institutions.**
Interviews with and texts by Needcompany. Antwerp. Lang.:
Eng. 1381

Jan Lauwers' theatre group Needcompany. Antwerp. Lang.:
Eng. 1382
1997. **Performance/production.**
Interview with director Julien Roy. Brussels. Lang.: Eng. 1568
Playwright, dramaturg, and director Hugo Claus. Lang.: Afr.
1569

Productions of the Paris-Bruxelles Exhibition. Brussels. Lang.:
Eng. 1570

Claude Régy's production of *La Mort de Tintagiles (The Death
of Tintagiles)* by Maeterlinck. Paris. Ghent. Lang.: Eng. 1658

Bohemia
1892-1957. **Performance/production.**
Puppetry of Josef Skupa. Lang.: Eng, Fre. 4360
Bosnia
1992-1997. **Performance/production.**
Interviews with Bosnian actors. Sarajevo. Lang.: Swe. 1571
1993. **Performance/production.**
Interview with members of Sarajevo Youth Theatre. Sarajevo.
Lang.: Eng. 1572
Susan Sontag's Sarajevan production of *Waiting for Godot.*
Sarajevo. Lang.: Eng. 1573
1993. **Relation to other fields.**
The effect of war on Sarajevan theatre. Sarajevo. Lang.: Eng.
726
Botswana
1997. **Relation to other fields.**
Performing arts education and methods of investigation. Serowe.
Lang.: Eng. 727
Brazil
1500-1995. **Performance/production.**
Brazilian folk-theatre forms. Lang.: Eng. 473
1934-1974. **Plays/librettos/scripts.**
Playwright Oduvaldo Vianna Filho. Lang.: Eng. 2387
1967. **Performance/production.**
Interview with actress and producer Regina Braga. Lang.: Swe.
1575
1982-1997. **Institutions.**
Profile of street theatre Grupo Galpão. Belo Horizonte. Lang.:
Eng. 299
1993. **Performance/production.**
151 Theatre Group's production of *The Merchant of Venice.*
Brasília. Lang.: Eng. 1574
1997. **Institutions.**
Profile of Hungarian folk dance festival. São Paulo. Lang.: Hun.
1142
Bulgaria
1880-1910. **Plays/librettos/scripts.**
Social and political themes in Bulgarian melodrama. Lang.: Eng.
2388
1992-1997. **Performance/production.**
Account of the Varna summer theatre festival. Varna. Lang.:
Eng. 474
1997. **Design/technology.**
OISTAT conference on training. Varna. Lang.: Swe. 141
Canada
1842-1891. **Performance/production.**
Composer Calixa Lavallée. Lang.: Eng. 4116
1886-1997. **Plays/librettos/scripts.**
Indigenous peoples in Canadian historical drama. Lang.: Eng.
2424
1892-1997. **Plays/librettos/scripts.**
Historical background of *Blood Relations* by Sharon Pollock.
Lang.: Eng. 2438

1898-1919. **Performance/production.**
Profile of opera singer Béatrice La Palme. Lang.: Eng. 4107
1901-1994. **Performance/production.**
Obituary for soprano Irene Jessner. Lang.: Eng. 4105
1901-1995. **Performance/production.**
Performance and identity politics on the Quebec stage. Lang.:
Eng. 477
1904-1997. **Theory/criticism.**
Realism in Quebec drama. Lang.: Fre. 3464
1908-1993. **Plays/librettos/scripts.**
Time travel in English-language drama. USA. UK-England.
Lang.: Eng. 3171
1914-1979. **Design/technology.**
Design in Ontario theatre. Lang.: Eng. 142
1914-1979. **Performance/production.**
Amateur and community theatre in Ontario. Lang.: Eng. 478
History of professional performers and companies in Ontario.
Lang.: Eng. 483
Canadian university theatre. Lang.: Eng. 484
Summer theatre and festivals in Ontario. Lang.: Eng. 485
Ontario's numerous variety acts. Lang.: Eng. 3855
1914-1979. **Plays/librettos/scripts.**
Playwriting in Ontario. Lang.: Eng. 2414
1914-1979. **Reference materials.**
Resources for Ontario theatre history. Lang.: Eng. 711
1914-1979. **Theory/criticism.**
Theatre criticism in Ontario. Lang.: Eng. 865
1917-1997. **Institutions.**
Profile of Orpheus Musical Theatre Society. Ottawa, ON. Lang.:
Eng. 3926
1920-1995. **Performance/production.**
The production of Canadian radio drama. Lang.: Eng. 3517
1921-1997. **Performance/production.**
Interview with actress Janine Sutto-Deyglun. Montreal, PQ.
Lang.: Fre. 1598
1927-1997. **Administration.**
Efforts to refurbish the historic Columbia Theatre. New
Westminster, BC. Lang.: Eng. 9
1928-1961. **Performance/production.**
Baritone James Milligan. Lang.: Eng. 4106
1940-1997. **Performance/production.**
Interview with actress Monique Miller. Montreal, PQ. Lang.:
Fre. 476
1946-1997. **Institutions.**
The rise of the Shakespeare theatre festival. Europe. USA.
Lang.: Eng. 1402
1948-1951. **Plays/librettos/scripts.**
Analysis of plays by Ray Guy. Lang.: Eng. 2404
1949-1997. **Institutions.**
Quebec drama at Théâtre du Nouveau Monde. Montreal, PQ.
Lang.: Fre. 1388
1950-1990. **Plays/librettos/scripts.**
The 'Black Madonna' in works of Italian-Canadian authors.
Lang.: Eng. 2396
1950-1997. **Performance/production.**
Interview with actor Gilles Pelletier. Montreal, PQ. Lang.: Fre.
1587
1951-1954. **Institutions.**
Productions of Canadian plays at Juniper Theatre. Toronto, ON.
Lang.: Eng. 1394
1951-1997. **Institutions.**
Molière productions of Théâtre du Nouveau Monde. Montreal,
PQ. Lang.: Fre. 1391
History of Théâtre du Nouveau Monde and its performance
spaces. Montreal, PQ. Lang.: Fre. 1393
1951-1997. **Plays/librettos/scripts.**
Teachers and students in plays of Walker, Mamet, and Ionesco.
USA. France. Lang.: Eng. 3296
1952-1997. **Performance/production.**
Interview with TV director Jean Faucher. Lang.: Fre. 3719
1953-1997. **Administration.**
Bell Canada's financial support of the Stratford Festival.
Stratford, ON. Lang.: Eng. 7
1957-1997. **Institutions.**
The creation of the Canada Council and increased demand for
performing arts. Lang.: Eng. 301
1960-1997. **Administration.**
Interview with Pierre MacDuff, general manager of Deux
Mondes. Montreal, PQ. Quebec, PQ. Lang.: Fre. 1233

Chile — cont'd

1972-1995.   **Performance/production.**
The literary interview as public performance. Lang.: Eng.   487
1986-1997.   **Plays/librettos/scripts.**
The *Trilogía Testimonial (Trilogy of Witness)* of Alfredo Castro, Teatro La Memoria. Lang.: Ger.   692
1993.   **Plays/librettos/scripts.**
Analysis of *Malinche* by Inés M. Stanger and *Opus Primum* by Hadi Kurich. Spain. Lang.: Spa.   2439
1994.   **Basic theatrical documents.**
Text of *El Memoricido (The Memory-Killer)* by Jorge Díaz. Lang.: Spa.   1263
1996-1997.   **Performance/production.**
Alexander Stillmark on directing Müller's *Der Auftrag (The Mission)*. Santiago. Lang.: Ger.   1607

China
714-1994.   **Performance/production.**
Contemporary regional theatre and its origins in ancestor worship. Quanzhou. Fujian. Lang.: Eng.   4388
1200-1997.   **Performance/production.**
Cross-dressing in Chinese theatre and society. Lang.: Eng.   489
1280-1994.   **Basic theatrical documents.**
English translation of the Yuan drama *Reunion with Son and Daughter in Kingfisher Red County.* Lang.: Eng.   1264
1842-1949.   **Institutions.**
Traveling Western opera troupes in Shanghai. Shanghai. Lang.: Eng.   4042
1895-1997.   **Performance/production.**
Profile of Taiwanese opera, *Gezaixi.* Taiwan. Lang.: Eng.   3892
1900-1997.   **Performance/production.**
Experimental theatre in Beijing. Beijing. Lang.: Ger.   488
1918-1982.   **Theory/criticism.**
Analysis of the concept of *mo* in Chinese theatre. Lang.: Eng.   867
1997.   **Performance/production.**
Mary Zimmerman's adaptation of the Chinese epic *Journey to the West.* USA. Lang.: Eng.   2271

China, People's Republic of
1896-1937.   **Performance/production.**
Early Shanghai filmmaking. Shanghai. Lang.: Eng.   3568
1950-1960.   **Performance/production.**
The classical theatre genre *kunju* and its revival. Lang.: Eng.   3893
1965-1976.   **Performance/production.**
Feminist aspects of the 'model theatre' of the Cultural Revolution. Lang.: Eng.   490
1968-1989.   **Relation to other fields.**
The theatricalization of protest. Europe. USA. Lang.: Eng.   740
1980-1989.   **Plays/librettos/scripts.**
The modernization and nationalization of Chinese spoken drama. Lang.: Eng.   2440
1980-1996.   **Performance/production.**
Chinese theatre and the actor in performance. Lang.: Eng.   491
1982-1997.   **Performance/production.**
Beijing production of Carmen's *Bizet.* Beijing. Lang.: Eng.   4117
1983-1997.   **Performance/production.**
Margaret Booker on directing August Wilson's *Fences* in Beijing. Beijing. Lang.: Eng.   1608
1989-1997.   **Relation to other fields.**
Performative politics and Western media coverage of Chinese protests. Lang.: Eng.   3512
1996.   **Design/technology.**
The significance of costume in Beijing opera. Beijing. Lang.: Eng.   3890

Colombia
1991.   **Plays/librettos/scripts.**
Analysis of *Siete lunas y un espejo (Seven Moons and a Looking Glass)* by Albalucía Angel. Lang.: Spa.   2441

Colonial America
1500-1700.   **Plays/librettos/scripts.**
Social status in plays of Medwall, Sheridan, and Tyler. England. Lang.: Eng.   2559
1713-1753.   **Plays/librettos/scripts.**
Addison's *Cato* as the source of the poem *The Maid's Soliloquy.* England. Lang.: Eng.   2442

Congo
1995.   **Performance/production.**
Sony Labou Tansi on Congolese theatre. Lang.: Eng.   492

Croatia
1900-1996.   **Performance/production.**
National identity and Croatian theatre. Lang.: Eng.   494

1950-1997.   **Performance/production.**
Report on Croatian summer festivals. Dubrovnik. Split. Lang.: Eng.   493
1990-1996.   **Performance/production.**
The effect of war on Croatian theatre. Lang.: Eng.   495
1990-1996.   **Plays/librettos/scripts.**
War in contemporary Croatian theatre. Lang.: Eng.   2443
1995-1996.   **Performance/production.**
The reemergence of melodrama on the Croatian stage. Lang.: Eng.   496
Active learning and community-based theatre. USA. Serbia. Lang.: Eng.   653

Cuba
1700.   **Performance/production.**
Survey of Afro-Caribbean religious dances. Havana. Lang.: Swe.   1144
1925-1990.   **Plays/librettos/scripts.**
The 'Black Madonna' in Cuban theatre. Lang.: Spa.   2444
1959-1997.   **Performance/production.**
Gender, color, and nationalism at the Tropicana. Havana. Lang.: Eng.   3856
1976.   **Design/technology.**
Theatre technician Gert-Ove Vågstam. Sweden. South Africa, Republic of. Lang.: Swe.   185

Czech Republic
1854-1928.   **Performance/production.**
Problem of staging the works of Janáček. Lang.: Cze.   4118
1912-1969.   **Performance/production.**
Puppeteer, film director, and illustrator Jiři Trnka. Lang.: Eng, Fre.   4364
1912-1997.   **Performance/production.**
History of Czech puppet theatre. Lang.: Eng, Fre.   4362
1924-1997.   **Performance/production.**
Playwright Pavel Kohout recalls the late director Luboš Pistorius. Lang.: Cze.   1612
1947-1996.   **Performance spaces.**
Profile of Měsíčník Ceských Divadel, a revolving auditorium theatre. Český Krumlov. Lang.: Eng.   1519
1951-1997.   **Performance/production.**
Opera singer Luděk Vele. Lang.: Cze.   4119
1958.   **Performance/production.**
Piccolo Teatro's guest performance. Lang.: Cze.   1614
1961-1996.   **Institutions.**
The Czech pantomime theatre 'Alfred ve dvoře'. Prague. Lang.: Cze.   3742
1963-1990.   **Performance/production.**
The 'non-theatre' (Nedivadlo) of Ivan Vyskočil. Prague. Lang.: Cze.   1615
1963-1997.   **Plays/librettos/scripts.**
The victimized female character in plays by Václav Havel. Lang.: Eng.   2445
1968-1997.   **Performance/production.**
The current status of Czech theatre. Lang.: Cze.   1610
1972-1997.   **Institutions.**
Profile of puppetry museum. Chrudim. Lang.: Eng, Fre.   4347
1990-1997.   **Performance/production.**
Recent stagings of Czech classics. Lang.: Cze.   1611
1991-1997.   **Performance spaces.**
Description of technically innovative Divadlo Spirála. Prague. Lang.: Ger.   419
1994-1996.   **Performance/production.**
Productions of Pinter's plays in Prague. Prague. Lang.: Eng.   1613
1995.   **Performance spaces.**
Theatre structures used at Prague Quadrennial. Český Krumlov. Lang.: Eng.   1518
1997.   **Administration.**
Model of financing for theatres in the Czech Republic. Lang.: Cze.   12
1997.   **Performance/production.**
Interpretations of Czech classics by Petr Lébl and Vladimír Morávek. Lang.: Cze.   1609
Jewish themes on Czech stages in recent years. Lang.: Cze.   1616
The Czech national character as reflected in contemporary puppet theatre. Lang.: Cze.   4363

Czechoslovakia
1920-1997.   **Design/technology.**
Italian translation of scenographer Josef Svoboda's autobiography. Lang.: Ita.   154

Estonia — cont'd

1967.   **Institutions.**
Profile of Tallinna Linnateater, Elmo Nüganen, artistic director.
Tallinn. Lang.: Swe.   1401
1996-1997.   **Performance/production.**
Moscow Art Theatre productions. Moscow. Tallinn. Lang.: Rus.
                                        1861

Ethiopia
1996.   **Performance/production.**
The use of theatre to advance Ethiopian social goals. Addis
Ababa. Lang.: Eng.   1639

Europe
                        Performance/production.
Essays on carnival. Lang.: Ita.   3782
259 B.C.-1997 A.D.   **Plays/librettos/scripts.**
The influence of Plautus and his comic themes. Lang.: Ita. 2784
250 B.C.-1995 A.D.   **Design/technology.**
The history of costume and the structure of Western European
dress. Lang.: Eng.   161
200 B.C.-1610 A.D.   **Plays/librettos/scripts.**
Comparison of classical Roman, Renaissance Italian, and
Shakespearean treatments of similar stories. Lang.: Eng. 2799
850-1552.   **Relation to other fields.**
The labyrinth in medieval literature and theatre. Lang.: Ita. 741
1150-1997.   **Performance/production.**
Contrast and comparison of Eastern and Western acting styles.
Japan. Lang.: Eng.   1822
1208-1400.   **Research/historiography.**
Introduction to articles on medieval historiography. Lang.: Eng.
                                        853
1300-1650.   **Performance spaces.**
The development and impact of the roofed theatre. Lang.: Eng.
                                        430
1400-1550.   **Performance/production.**
The depiction of the Passion of Christ on the medieval stage.
Lang.: Eng.   1641
1400-1590.   **Plays/librettos/scripts.**
Male and female Renaissance writers. Lang.: Eng.   2785
1400-1950.   **Theory/criticism.**
Artaud's theatre of cruelty and the passion play. Lang.: Eng.
                                        3478
1500-1600.   **Performance spaces.**
Methods of studying sixteenth-century playhouses. Lang.: Eng.
                                        1527
1590-1920.   **Plays/librettos/scripts.**
Analysis of the nature of drama. North America. Lang.: Eng.
                                        2795
1590-1995.   **Performance/production.**
The performance of race, gender, sexuality, and power. USA.
Lang.: Eng.   2309
1597-1997.   **Performance/production.**
Opera singers and the sometimes conflicting demands of the
director and the music. Lang.: Swe.   4126
1598-1994.   **Plays/librettos/scripts.**
Collection of essays on Shakespeare's *Love's Labour's Lost*.
North America. Lang.: Eng.   2792
1600-1699.   **Plays/librettos/scripts.**
Essays on late Baroque drama. Lang.: Ita.   2787
1600-1700.   **Performance spaces.**
Celestial effects of the seventeenth-century stage. Lang.: Eng.
                                        429
1600-1957.   **Theory/criticism.**
Lecture by Kurt Jooss on dance history and style. Lang.: Ger.
                                        1025
1600-1995.   **Research/historiography.**
Research in theatre iconography. Lang.: Eng.   3447
1600-1997.   **Theory/criticism.**
Theatre semiotics and media studies. Lang.: Ger.   3513
1607-1997.   **Plays/librettos/scripts.**
Opera and gender stereotypes. Lang.: Eng.   4287
1612-1787.   **Plays/librettos/scripts.**
The significance of Don Juan in works of Tirso, Mozart, and
Molière. Lang.: Eng.   2786
1640-1800.   **Performance/production.**
Introduction to issue of *Comparative Drama* dedicated to drama
and opera of the Enlightenment. Lang.: Eng.   1644
1675-1900.   **Performance/production.**
Call for an interdisciplinary approach to dance history. Lang.:
Eng.   957
1700-1990.   **Theory/criticism.**
Gender and classical ballet. Lang.: Eng.   1132

1705-1997.   **Performance/production.**
Stylistic similarities in Baroque and nineteenth-century opera.
Lang.: Eng.   4128
1750-1997.   **Relation to other fields.**
History of open-air theatre since Rousseau. Lang.: Ger.   742
1770-1915.   **Plays/librettos/scripts.**
Analysis of opera librettos by Boito, Da Ponte, and Gertrude
Stein. Lang.: Eng.   4289
1800-1851.   **Plays/librettos/scripts.**
Text and performance in the Romantic period. Lang.: Pol. 2790
1800-1997.   **Theory/criticism.**
Theatre as artifact. Lang.: Ger.   876
1801-1997.   **Performance/production.**
Feminist analysis of dance and the representation of the female
body. USA. Lang.: Eng.   997
1817-1943.   **Performance/production.**
Tenor Manuel García the elder and his son. Lang.: Eng. 4127
1825-1854.   **Plays/librettos/scripts.**
Franz Liszt's comments on *La Dame Blanche* by Boieldieu.
Lang.: Fre.   4288
1830-1850.   **Performance/production.**
The influence of folk-derived dance forms on ballet. Lang.: Eng.
                                        1064
1831.   **Plays/librettos/scripts.**
Background information on Bellini's *La Sonnambula*: sleep
disorders. Lang.: Fre.   4286
1855-1902.   **Performance/production.**
Race, gender, and nation in nineteenth-century performance.
USA. Lang.: Eng.   633
1867-1997.   **Performance/production.**
Production history of Verdi's *Don Carlo*. USA. Lang.: Eng.
                                        4131
1870-1994.   **Plays/librettos/scripts.**
Shakespeare on the European continent. Lang.: Eng.   2788
1872-1966.   **Design/technology.**
Gordon Craig's theory of 'scene'. Lang.: Ger.   159
1880-1995.   **Theory/criticism.**
Luciano Berio on Wagnerian opera. Lang.: Eng.   4327
1884-1985.   **Relation to other fields.**
Psychoanalytic analysis of opera and musical theatre. USA.
Lang.: Eng.   3889
1890-1970.   **Theory/criticism.**
The role of photographs in theatre criticism. Lang.: Eng. 3476
1892-1930.   **Performance/production.**
Early modern interpretations of Aristophanes' *Lysistrata*. USA.
Lang.: Eng.   1647
1892-1996.   **Performance/production.**
Film techniques in dance works of Loie Fuller and Oskar
Schlemmer. USA. Lang.: Ger.   1010
1899-1927.   **Performance/production.**
Isadora Duncan's efforts to raise the level of dance from
entertainment to art. Lang.: Ita.   1178
1900-1956.   **Plays/librettos/scripts.**
Dialectical interaction and visual perception in Ibsen,
Strindberg, and Brecht. Lang.: Eng.   2797
1900-1993.   **Plays/librettos/scripts.**
Contemporary playwrights and the adaptation process. Lang.:
Ita.   2793
1900-1995.   **Performance/production.**
Twentieth-century theatre as a signifying practice. North
America. Lang.: Eng.   515
1900-1996.   **Theory/criticism.**
Spirituality and consciousness in Western theatre. North
America. Lang.: Eng.   3480
1900-1997.   **Performance spaces.**
Avant-garde opera and the limits of the proscenium stage.
Lang.: Ger.   4065
1900-1997.   **Performance/production.**
The reconstruction of medieval plays and productions. Lang.:
Ita.   1642

The transposition of pitch in opera singing. Lang.: Eng.   4129
1900-1997.   **Theory/criticism.**
Reception theory and contemporary theatre research. Lang.:
Eng.   3483
1900-1997.   **Training.**
Work on the body in its theatrical context. Lang.: Ita.   929
1906-1930.   **Performance/production.**
Modern dance and feminist criticism. USA. Lang.: Eng.   1179
1909-1929.   **Relation to other fields.**
The Ballets Russes and the arts. Lang.: Ger.   1131

France — cont'd

1888-1904. **Plays/librettos/scripts.**
A possible source of Frank Wedekind's *Lulu*. Germany. Lang.:
Ita. 2826

1888-1996. **Basic theatrical documents.**
French translations of Strindberg's *Fröken Julie (Miss Julie)* and
Den Starkare (The Stronger). Sweden. Lang.: Fre. 1309

1895-1910. **Theory/criticism.**
Challenge to theory of the relationship between theatre and
film. UK-England. USA. Lang.: Eng. 3699

1895-1996. **Basic theatrical documents.**
French translation of *The Importance of Being Earnest* by Oscar
Wilde. UK-England. Paris. Lang.: Fre. 1320

1895-1997. **Institutions.**
The work of Le Théâtre du Peuple. Bussang. Lang.: Eng. 316

1897-1927. **Relation to other fields.**
Proust and Wagner's *Tristan und Isolde*. Paris. Lang.: Eng.
3888

1897-1997. **Performance/production.**
Antonin Artaud's continuing influence on modern drama. Lang.:
Eng. 1661

Life, career, and influences of Antonin Artaud. Lang.: Eng.
1670

1900-1997. **Institutions.**
Profile of Théâtre National de Strasbourg. Strasbourg. Lang.:
Ger. 1404

1902-1996. **Basic theatrical documents.**
Text of *Une Puce à l'Oreille (A Flea in Her Ear)* by Georges
Feydeau. Lang.: Fre. 1271

1906-1989. **Plays/librettos/scripts.**
Biography of playwright Samuel Beckett. Ireland. Lang.: Eng.
2917

1906-1996. **Plays/librettos/scripts.**
Essays on the plays and productions of Samuel Beckett. Ireland.
Lang.: Ita. 2912

1906-1997. **Performance/production.**
Composer Jacques Leguerney. Lang.: Eng. 4138

1908-1911. **Performance/production.**
Jacques Copeau's stage adaptation of *The Brothers Karamazov*.
Lang.: Ita. 1662

1909-1929. **Design/technology.**
Exhibition of scenery and costumes for Ballets Russes
productions. Russia. Lang.: Eng. 1048

1911-1924. **Performance/production.**
The body and gender in Parisian dance performance. Lang.:
Eng. 1069

1916. **Theory/criticism.**
Analysis of *Le Coeur à Gaz (The Gas Heart)* by Tristan Tzara.
Lang.: Eng. 893

1918-1970. **Performance/production.**
Dancer/choreographer Carina Ari. Sweden. Lang.: Swe. 1113

1920-1930. **Performance/production.**
Jazz music and dance in Paris. Lang.: Eng. 963

1920-1945. **Performance/production.**
The relationship of Antonin Artaud and Etienne Decroux. Paris.
Lang.: Eng. 531

1920-1992. **Performance/production.**
Jacques Copeau, Etienne Decroux, and corporeal mime. Paris.
Lang.: Eng. 3745

1922-1937. **Plays/librettos/scripts.**
Jean Cocteau's adaptations of works of Sophocles. Lang.: Eng.
2811

1929-1985. **Relation to other fields.**
Leopardi's influence on works of Samuel Beckett. Ireland.
Lang.: Eng. 3362

1929-1989. **Plays/librettos/scripts.**
Early critical and theoretical essays by Samuel Beckett. Ireland.
Lang.: Eng. 2903

1929-1994. **Theory/criticism.**
The late theatre critic and essayist Bernard Dort. Lang.: Ita.
3485

1930-1937. **Plays/librettos/scripts.**
Gendered identity in plays of Cocteau and García Lorca. Spain.
Lang.: Eng. 2807

1930-1945. **Plays/librettos/scripts.**
The convergence of fascism and avant-garde theatre aesthetics.
Lang.: Eng. 2833

1930-1985. **Relation to other fields.**
Analysis of fiction by Samuel Beckett. Ireland. Lang.: Eng. 3371

1932. **Relation to other fields.**
Source of a phrase in Beckett's *Dream of Fair to Middling
Women*. Ireland. Lang.: Eng. 3361

1933-1996. **Performance/production.**
Singer/actress Liliane Montevecchi. USA. UK-England. Lang.:
Eng. 3963

1935-1949. **Theory/criticism.**
Derrida's analysis of the theatre of cruelty. Lang.: Eng. 882

1935-1984. **Plays/librettos/scripts.**
Narrative and parents in the work of Samuel Beckett. Ireland.
Lang.: Eng. 2920

1937-1989. **Plays/librettos/scripts.**
Collection of articles on French avant-garde culture, including
theatre. Lang.: Eng. 2805

1938. **Relation to other fields.**
The source of an allusion in Beckett's *Murphy*. Ireland. Lang.:
Eng. 3359

An illegal chess move in the English edition of Beckett's
Murphy. Ireland. Lang.: Eng. 3366

1941-1953. **Plays/librettos/scripts.**
Samuel Beckett's creative surge. Ireland. Lang.: Eng. 2923

1942-1963. **Relation to other fields.**
The structure of Samuel Beckett's novel *Watt*. Ireland. Lang.:
Eng. 3369

1942-1977. **Theory/criticism.**
Psychoanalysis and representation. Lang.: Eng. 888

1942-1982. **Plays/librettos/scripts.**
Samuel Beckett and postmodernism. Ireland. USA. Lang.: Eng.
2818

1945-1987. **Performance/production.**
Interview with Maximilien Decroux, son of mime Etienne
Decroux. Paris. Lang.: Eng. 3746

1945-1992. **Training.**
Profile of mime Etienne Decroux. Lang.: Eng. 3750

Etienne Decroux's project to revitalize theatre through mime.
Lang.: Eng. 3753

1946-1997. **Plays/librettos/scripts.**
Samuel Beckett's report on the Irish hospital at Saint-Lô. St. Lô.
Dublin. Lang.: Eng. 3520

1947-1979. **Relation to other fields.**
Autobiographical elements in novels of Samuel Beckett. Ireland.
Lang.: Eng. 3368

1947-1986. **Plays/librettos/scripts.**
The cathartic effects of failure in Samuel Beckett's *Eleutheria*.
Ireland. Lang.: Ger. 2905

1947-1989. **Plays/librettos/scripts.**
Metatheatre in works of Samuel Beckett. Ireland. Lang.: Eng.
2911

1948-1989. **Plays/librettos/scripts.**
The work of playwright Bernard-Marie Koltès. Lang.: Eng.
2806

1948-1997. **Performance/production.**
Interview with director Luc Bondy. Germany. Lang.: Ger. 1684

1950-1975. **Plays/librettos/scripts.**
The concept of self in plays of Jean Genet. Lang.: Eng. 2834

1950-1989. **Plays/librettos/scripts.**
Open-endedness in works of Samuel Beckett. Ireland. USA.
Lang.: Eng. 2922

1951-1997. **Plays/librettos/scripts.**
Teachers and students in plays of Walker, Mamet, and Ionesco.
USA. Canada. Lang.: Eng. 3296

1953. **Plays/librettos/scripts.**
The leg wound in Beckett's *Waiting for Godot* in the context of
Western literary tradition. Ireland. Lang.: Eng. 2909

Classical Taoism in Beckett's *En attendant Godot (Waiting for
Godot)*. Ireland. Lang.: Eng. 2934

1953-1995. **Plays/librettos/scripts.**
Comparison of a novel by James Kelman to Beckett's *En
attendant Godot (Waiting for Godot)*. Ireland. Lang.: Eng. 2907

1955-1989. **Plays/librettos/scripts.**
Samuel Beckett, music, and gender. Ireland. USA. Lang.: Eng.
2908

Irish rhythms in the writing of Samuel Beckett. Ireland. Lang.:
Eng. 2936

1956. **Plays/librettos/scripts.**
Power in *Le Balcon (The Balcony)* by Jean Genet. Lang.: Ita.
2812

1957. **Plays/librettos/scripts.**
The chess metaphor in Beckett's *Fin de partie (Endgame)*.
Ireland. Lang.: Eng. 2918

1958. **Performance/production.**
Roger Planchon's production of *Georges Dandin* by Molière.
Villeurbanne. Lang.: Pol. 1675

Development of amateur theatre during the National Socialist period. Lang.: Ger.   760
1936-1997.   Performance/production.
Gerhard Bohner's choreography *Angst & Geometrie (Fear and Geomety).* Lang.: Ger.   971
1938-1997.   Relation to other fields.
Profiles of German theatre photographers. Lang.: Ger.   758
1941-1997.   Performance/production.
Actors on working in theatre, film, and television. Lang.: Ger.
                                                                    3576
1943-1956.   Relation to other fields.
Brecht's disgust with bureaucracy and political quarrels. Berlin. Lang.: Ger.   3352
1944-1994.   Performance/production.
Ingmar Bergman's productions of Shakespeare's plays. Sweden. Lang.: Ita.   1934
1945-1947.   Relation to other fields.
Erich Ponto's tenure as *Generalintendant* of Dresden theatre. Dresden. Lang.: Ger.   762
1945-1989.   Performance/production.
The films of Rainer Werner Fassbinder. Lang.: Eng.   3575
1945-1997.   Plays/librettos/scripts.
Postwar German portrayals of customs in East and West Germany. Lang.: Ger.   2860
1946-1981.   Relation to other fields.
Critic Heinz Ritter recalls theatre draughtsman Paul Gehring. Berlin. Lang.: Ger.   750
The Paul Gehring theatre collection at Berlin Stadtmuseum. Berlin. Lang.: Ger.   751
1947-1997.   Plays/librettos/scripts.
Interview with children's theatre playwright Rudolf Herfurthner. Lang.: Ger.   2851
1948-1997.   Performance/production.
Interview with director Luc Bondy. France. Lang.: Ger.   1684
1949.   Performance/production.
The 'deconstructive potential' of Brecht's own production of *Mother Courage.* Berlin. Lang.: Ger.   1696
Brecht's production of *Mother Courage.* Berlin. Lang.: Pol. 1740
1949-1997.   Institutions.
Profile of Dresdner Staatsschauspiel. Dresden. Lang.: Ger.   320
1949-1997.   Performance/production.
Actor Traugott Buhre. Lang.: Ger.   1686
Interview with director Benno Besson. Switzerland. Lang.: Ger.
                                                                    1727
1950-1997.   Relation to other fields.
Theatre photographer describes his work. Munich. Lang.: Ger.
                                                                    755
1951.   Relation to other fields.
Dance and politics in postwar Germany. Lang.: Ger.   1016
1953-1976.   Performance/production.
German reactions to the work of Samuel Beckett. Lang.: Eng.
                                                                    1699
1953-1997.   Relation to other fields.
Interview with novelist Günter Grass about Bertolt Brecht. Berlin. Lang.: Ger.   3353
1955.   Theory/criticism.
Adorno's ideas about opera. Lang.: Swe.   4330
1957-1997.   Performance/production.
Soprano Waltraud Meier. Lang.: Eng.   4153
1958-1995.   Performance/production.
Non-literary realism in Shakespeare productions. UK-England. Lang.: Ger.   2170
1960.   Theory/criticism.
Hungarian translation of an essay on drama by Willi Flemming. Lang.: Hun.   895
1960-1987.   Performance/production.
The performance art of Wolf Vostell and Joseph Beuys. Lang.: Eng.   3819
1960-1990.   Relation to other fields.
Critic Rolf-Dieter Eichler on theatre draughtsman Ingeborg Voss. Berlin. Lang.: Ger.   756
1960-1996.   Plays/librettos/scripts.
German adaptations and appropriations of Shakespeare. Lang.: Eng.   2857
1960-1997.   Performance/production.
Actress Andrea Clausen. Lang.: Ger.   1693
1961-1997.   Performance/production.
Interview with actor Thomas Holtzmann. Munich. Lang.: Ger.
                                                                    541

Playwright Kerstin Hensel. Lang.: Ger.   1705
1962-1996.   Relation to other fields.
Berlin Stadtmuseum's collection of theatre drawings by Ingeborg Voss. Berlin. Lang.: Ger.   757
1967-1978.   Plays/librettos/scripts.
Analysis of German translations of plays by Samuel Beckett. Lang.: Eng.   2842
1967-1997.   Performance/production.
Interview with director, producer, and choreographer Thomas Guggi. Lang.: Ger.   965
Playwright and director Daniel Call. Lang.: Ger.   1702
Portrait of actor Samuel Weiss. Stuttgart. Lang.: Ger.   1714
1967-1997.   Plays/librettos/scripts.
Playwright Albert Ostermaier. Lang.: Ger.   2853
Playwright Daniel Call and TV aesthetics. Lang.: Ger.   2862
1968-1997.   Performance/production.
Performances of *Harrys Kopf (Harry's Head)* by Tankred Dorst and Ursula Ehler. Lang.: Ger.   1748
1969-1997.   Performance/production.
Profile of actress Traute Hoess. Austria. Lang.: Ger.   1741
1970-1997.   Administration.
Interview with Jürgen Schitthelm of Schaubühne. Berlin. Lang.: Ger.   34
1970-1997.   Performance/production.
A tour of the German and Austrian independent theatre scene. Austria. Lang.: Ger.   538
Directors Tom Kühnel and Robert Schuster. Lang.: Ger.   1729
1970-1997.   Plays/librettos/scripts.
The development of non-literary opera. Lang.: Ger.   4296
1970-1997.   Relation to other fields.
German reunification and theatre draughtsman Ingeborg Voss. Berlin. Lang.: Ger.   748
1971.   Basic theatrical documents.
English translation of *Nur eine Scheibe Brot (Just a Slice of Bread)* by Rainer Werner Fassbinder. Lang.: Eng.   1280
1976.   Performance/production.
Director Frank Castorf. Berlin. Stockholm. Lang.: Swe.   1700
1977-1993.   Performance/production.
Analysis of television serial *The Restless Years.* Australia. Lang.: Eng.   3716
1978.   Plays/librettos/scripts.
Wolfgang Rihm's operatic adaptation of *Die Hamletmaschine (Hamletmachine)* by Heiner Müller. Lang.: Swe.   4300
1978-1991.   Theory/criticism.
Feminist theory and choreographer Pina Bausch. Wuppertal. Lang.: Eng.   1029
1979-1997.   Institutions.
Interview with actor Peter Simonschek of Schaubühne. Berlin. Lang.: Ger.   1411
1980-1990.   Plays/librettos/scripts.
Analysis of plays by Georg Seidel. Lang.: Ger.   2847
1980-1997.   Institutions.
The difficult relationship between theatre and newspapers. Lang.: Ger.   1436
1980-1997.   Performance/production.
The influence of Pina Bausch and Johann Kresnik on German choreography. Lang.: Ger.   970
The theatre of director Christoph Marthaler. Lang.: Ger, Fre, Dut, Eng.   1692
Interview with director Christoph Marthaler and set designer Anna Viebrock. Switzerland. Lang.: Ger.   1723
1980-1997.   Relation to other fields.
History of indepedent theatre company Zinnober. Berlin. Lang.: Ger.   4383
1981-1997.   Administration.
Profile of Bremer Theater. Bremen. Lang.: Ger.   31
1983-1997.   Performance/production.
Interview with Norbert Kentrup of Bremer Shakespeare Company. Bremen. Lang.: Ger.   540
1985.   Plays/librettos/scripts.
Analysis of Heiner Müller's *Bildbeschreibung (Description of a Picture).* Lang.: Ger.   2850
1985-1997.   Institutions.
Kölner Schauspiel under the direction of Günter Krämer. Cologne. Lang.: Ger.   1425
1985-1997.   Performance/production.
Interview with actor Josef Bierbichler. Lang.: Ger.   1691

Germany — cont'd

Memory in the work of video and performance artist Arnold Dreyblatt. Lang.: Eng. 3818

Space, place, and travel in performance art and installations. London. Kassel. Lang.: Eng. 3823

HK Gruber on songs of Kurt Weill. Lang.: Eng. 3933

Interview with opera singer Noemi Nadelmann. Berlin. Lang.: Ger. 4146

Impressions of opera performances in several German cities. Lang.: Ger. 4147

Productions at the Munich Biennale. Munich. Lang.: Ger. 4148

Interview with baritone Falk Struckman. Lang.: Eng. 4149

James Levine's production of Wagner's *Ring*. Bayreuth. Lang.: Eng. 4151

Interpretations of the title role in Alban Berg's *Lulu*. Lang.: Eng. 4152

Harry Kupfer's staging of *Lucia di Lammermoor*. Berlin. Lang.: Swe. 4154

Profile, interview with soprano Hildegard Behrens. Lang.: Eng. 4160

1997.   Plays/librettos/scripts.
Account of new German plays with historical themes. Lang.: Ger. 2837

Children's theatre festival productions. Berlin. Lang.: Ger. 2845

Analysis of Urs Widmer's *Top Dogs*. Berlin. Lang.: Ger. 2846

Interview with playwrights Tankred Dorst and Ursula Ehler. Lang.: Fin. 2849

Trends in contemporary German-language drama. Austria. Switzerland. Lang.: Ger. 2859

Interview with playwright Albert Ostermaier. Lang.: Ger. 2861

Interview with playwright Oliver Bukowski. Lang.: Ger. 2863

Interview with publisher about contemporary drama. Lang.: Ger. 2865

Interview with opera composer Moritz Eggert. Munich. Lang.: Ger. 4293

1997.   Theory/criticism.
A reviewer's reservations about the operas of Wagner. Lang.: Eng. 4333

Germany, East
1949-1956.   Institutions.
Exhibition on East German dance. Lang.: Ger. 947
1964-1997.   Relation to other fields.
Director Einar Schleef on his life in East Germany. Lang.: Ger. 3356

Ghana
1995-1997.   Performance/production.
Analysis of three 'dance cultures'. USA. Lang.: Eng. 998
1995-1997.   Plays/librettos/scripts.
West African popular theatre: texts and analysis. Togo. Nigeria. Lang.: Eng. 2866

Greece
**   Relation to other fields.**
Ritual and performance in ancient Greek sport and warfare. Lang.: Eng. 764
600-300 B.C.   Research/historiography.
Aristotle's *Poetics* and performative aspects of Athenian culture. Athens. Lang.: Eng. 3449
500 B.C.   Performance/production.
Visual performance aspects of Greek tragedy. Athens. Lang.: Ita. 1749
500 B.C.   Plays/librettos/scripts.
Strong women in the *Oresteia* of Aeschylus. Lang.: Eng. 2868
500-450 B.C.   Plays/librettos/scripts.
History and Aeschylus' *Persai (The Persians)*. Lang.: Eng. 2883
500-400 B.C.   Performance/production.
The honorary position of *khoregos* or choral leader in Greek tragedy. Lang.: Eng. 1751
500-400 B.C.   Plays/librettos/scripts.
The cultural construction of the hero in Greek tragedy. Lang.: Eng. 2874

Problems of historical interpretation in Greek tragedy and comedy. Lang.: Eng. 2887
500-300 B.C.   Plays/librettos/scripts.
Rhetoric in Euripidean drama. Lang.: Eng. 2871

500-250 B.C.   Plays/librettos/scripts.
Ambivalence about rhetoric in Greek tragedy. Lang.: Eng. 2877

Ancient Greek tragedy and religion. Lang.: Eng. 2888
500-250 B.C.   Relation to other fields.
Visual representations of Greek drama. Lang.: Eng. 3357
500-250 B.C.   Research/historiography.
Using Greek tragedy as a historical source. Lang.: Eng. 3448
500-200 B.C.   Plays/librettos/scripts.
The depiction of women in ancient Greek theatre. Lang.: Eng. 2884
500-100 B.C.   Performance spaces.
The meaning of performance space in ancient Greek theatre. Lang.: Eng. 437
500-100 B.C.   Performance/production.
Odes for female choruses in Greek theatre. Lang.: Eng. 549
500-100 B.C.   Plays/librettos/scripts.
Political theory in the plays of Sophocles and Aeschylus. Lang.: Eng. 2885
500 B.C.-200 A.D.   Plays/librettos/scripts.
Out-of-court legal settlements in Greco-Roman new comedy. Rome. Lang.: Eng. 2886
500 B.C.-476 A.D.   Reference materials.
History of ancient Greek and Roman theatre. Rome. Lang.: Ita. 714
496-406 B.C.   Plays/librettos/scripts.
Collection of essays on Sophocles as a dramatist. Lang.: Eng. 2881
458 B.C.   Plays/librettos/scripts.
Aeschylus' characters Orestes and Electra as enduring archetypes. Lang.: Ita. 2878

Clytemnestra's binding spell in Aeschylus' *Agamemnon*. Lang.: Eng. 2879

References to clothing in Aeschylus' *Agamemnon*. Lang.: Eng. 2880
458 B.C.   Relation to other fields.
Psychoanalysis and Aeschylus' *Oresteia*. Lang.: Eng. 3358
458-400 B.C.   Plays/librettos/scripts.
Translation and the study of Greek tragedy. Lang.: Eng. 2882
425 B.C.   Plays/librettos/scripts.
Analysis of Aristophanes' *Acharnēs (The Acharnians)*. Lang.: Eng. 2872
400-250 B.C.   Plays/librettos/scripts.
Foreigners in Athenian tragedy. Lang.: Eng. 2890
400-200 B.C.   Plays/librettos/scripts.
Greek history as interpreted in plays of Sophocles and Euripides. Lang.: Eng. 2870
400 B.C.-100 A.D.   Plays/librettos/scripts.
Speech within speech in Attic drama. Lang.: Eng. 2869
445-399 B.C.   Plays/librettos/scripts.
Comic techniques of the playwright Aristophanes. Lang.: Ita. 2867
450-425 B.C.   Plays/librettos/scripts.
Analysis of Euripides' *Cyclops*. Lang.: Eng. 2893
450-350 B.C.   Plays/librettos/scripts.
Attitudes about rhetoric in Greek and Roman drama. Roman Empire. Lang.: Eng. 2873
500-400 B.C.   Plays/librettos/scripts.
The objectives of Greek tragedy. Lang.: Dut. 2875

Greek drama and mimesis. Lang.: Eng. 2876
500-400 B.C.   Relation to other fields.
Mimesis and the aesthetic experience. Lang.: Slo. 765
525-456 B.C.   Plays/librettos/scripts.
The role of Clytemnestra in the *Oresteia* of Aeschylus. Lang.: Slo. 2891
600-400 B.C.   Plays/librettos/scripts.
The myth of Dionysus in Greek literature and theatre. Lang.: Ita. 2889
600-300 B.C.   Plays/librettos/scripts.
Comparative anthropological approach to Greek tragedy. Lang.: Slo. 2892
1995.   Performance/production.
Production of Tony Harrison's *The Labourers of Herakles*. Delphi. Lang.: Eng. 1750
1997.   Performance spaces.
Greek and Roman amphitheatres and their reconstruction: exhibition catalogue. Lang.: Eng, Gre. 436
1997.   Performance/production.
Thessaloniki's year as cultural capital. Thessaloniki. Lang.: Swe. 550

Hungary — cont'd

1995-1997. Performance/production.
Interview with opera director Balázs Kovalik. Budapest. Lang.: Hun. 4185

1996. Design/technology.
Open-air productions of summer 1996. Lang.: Hun. 171

1996. Institutions.
Report on the festival of modern Polish arts, Polonia Express. Poland. Budapest. Lang.: Hun. 356

1996. Performance/production.
Andrea Fullajtár's performance in *Csendet akarok (I Want Silence)* by Zsolt Csalog. Budapest. Lang.: Hun. 1771

István Verebes' production of Molnár's *A Jó tündér (The Good Fairy)*. Budapest. Lang.: Hun. 1772

The millecentennial gala of the Friends of Budapest Opera. Budapest. Lang.: Hun. 4182

1996-1997. Institutions.
Professional connections between Elmhurst Ballet School and the Hungarian Dance Academy. UK-England. Lang.: Hun. 1060

Yearbook of the Hungarian State Opera House. Budapest. Lang.: Hun. 4051

1996-1997. Performance spaces.
The national theatre architecture competition. Budapest. Lang.: Hun. 438

1996-1997. Performance/production.
Zoltán Kamondi's experimental theatre at Csarnok Kultusz Motel. Miskolc. Lang.: Hun. 554

Four productions of the musical *A Dzsungel könyve (The Jungle Book)*. Lang.: Hun. 3936

A joint production of Budapest Operetta Theatre dance company and Madách Dance Workshop. Budapest. Lang.: Hun. 3937

1997. Institutions.
Response to children's theatre productions of Kolibri Színház. Budapest. Lang.: Hun. 328

Report on children's theatre festival. Budapest. Lang.: Hun. 329

Survey of children's and youth theatre festival. Budapest. Lang.: Hun. 337

Account of the National Theatre Meetings. Szeged. Lang.: Hun. 341

The role of the literary manager or dramaturg. Bucharest. Lang.: Hun. 361

The graduation performances of the Hungarian Dance Academy. Budapest. Lang.: Hun. 1051

A congress on current Hungarian drama. Lang.: Ger. 1437

Reactions to a festival of new Hungarian plays. Lang.: Hun. 1440

1997. Performance/production.
Hungarian summer theatre offerings. Lang.: Hun. 553

Pécsi Balett's performance of choreographies by István Herczog to music of Bartók. Pécs. Lang.: Hun. 1080

Report on a dance concert in honor of ballet soloist Ildikó Pongor. Lang.: Hun. 1081

Ildikó Pongor's performance in the ballet *Anna Karenina*. Budapest. Lang.: Hun. 1082

Budapest production of the ballet *Don Quijote* by Marius Petipa and Leon Minkus. Budapest. Lang.: Hun. 1083

Choreographies by Balanchine performed by Magyar Nemzeti Balett. Budapest. Lang.: Hun. 1084

Choreography of Iván Markó performed by Magyar Fesztivál Balett. Budapest. Lang.: Hun. 1086

Performance of the Győri Balett. Lang.: Hun. 1093

Győri Balett's production of *Carmen* by Robert North and Christopher Benstead. Győr. Lang.: Hun. 1094

Recent dance performances of Josef Nadj. France. Budapest. Lang.: Hun. 1181

Interview with actress Maia Morgenstern. Bucharest. Győr. Lang.: Hun. 1855

Miklós Gábor Kerényi's production of *Der Fliegende Holländer*, Budapest Opera House. Budapest. Lang.: Hun. 4184

1997. Theory/criticism.
Polemic on theory and directing. Lang.: Hun. 902

Iceland

1952. Performance/production.
Dance in Iceland and Íslenski Dansflokkurinn. Reykjavik. Lang.: Swe. 978

1980-1996. Performance/production.
Interviews with women in Icelandic theatre and government. Lang.: Eng. 555

India

1000-1997. Performance/production.
CD-ROM presentation of all aspects of *kutiyattam*. Lang.: Eng. 557

1500-1995. Performance/production.
Analysis of *tol pava kuttu* shadow puppetry, performed without an audience. Lang.: Eng. 4400

1500-1997. Performance/production.
Chavittunátakam, the music drama of Kerala Christians. Kerala. Lang.: Eng. 3871

1700-1995. Plays/librettos/scripts.
Representations of India in French theatre. France. Lang.: Eng. 2824

1800-1995. Performance/production.
The role of the mask in non-Western ritual performance. Papua New Guinea. Indonesia. Lang.: Eng. 556

1850-1980. Plays/librettos/scripts.
Cross-cultural adaptations of Shakespeare on the Parsi stage. Lang.: Eng. 2902

1880-1995. Performance/production.
Appropriations of Shakespeare's plays in postcolonial India. Lang.: Eng. 1780

1904-1996. Performance/production.
Rukmini Devi and the revival of South Indian dance. Lang.: Eng. 1147

1938-1997. Theory/criticism.
The river as a metaphor of cultural exchange. Lang.: Eng. 904

1950-1995. Performance/production.
Ethnography of artists of popular theatre in Tamilnadu. Lang.: Eng. 1783

1952-1996. Performance/production.
Julia Varley on the work of Sanjukta Panigrahi. Lang.: Ita. 1223

1965. Performance/production.
Analysis of the Merchant Ivory film *Shakespeare Wallah*. UK-England. Lang.: Eng. 3577

1970. Performance/production.
Profile of Prasanna, director and teacher. New Delhi. Heggodu. Lang.: Swe. 1782

1989-1997. Performance/production.
Parate Labor's teaching of *kutiyattam* Sanskrit drama in France. France. Lang.: Eng. 1673

1993. Performance/production.
Analysis of *Teyyateyyam* by K. N. Pannikkar. Trivandrum. Lang.: Eng. 1784

1996. Institutions.
Report on Natya Kala festival/conference. Chennai. Lang.: Swe. 950

1996. Relation to other fields.
Analysis of a performance for the Young Presidents Organization. Mumbai. Lang.: Eng. 1228

1997. Performance/production.
Choreography and *Bharata Natyam*. Lang.: Swe. 979

Interviews with writer-directors K.N. Pannikkar, Mahesh Dattani, and Tripurari Sharma. Lang.: Eng. 1781

Indonesia

1300-1995. Performance/production.
Changes in traditional *wayang kulit* shadow puppet theatre. Lang.: Eng. 4402

1800-1995. Performance/production.
The role of the mask in non-Western ritual performance. India. Papua New Guinea. Lang.: Eng. 556

1900-1995. Performance/production.
The southern form of *wayang kulit* shadow puppet theatre. Lang.: Eng. 4401

1977-1993. Performance/production.
Censorship and Teater Koma's production of *Suksesi* by Rendra. Jakarta. Lang.: Eng. 558

1994-1995. Performance/production.
Performance, mass media, and the regulation of *wayang golek purwa*. Lang.: Eng. 4399

Indonesia-Bali

1996. Relation to other fields.
The inclusion of tourism in Balinese village traditional performance. Singapadu. Lang.: Eng. 766

Ireland — cont'd

1984-1989.   Plays/librettos/scripts.
Analysis of *The Lament for Arthur Cleary* by Dermot Bolger.
Lang.: Eng.   2927
1985-1996.   Basic theatrical documents.
French translation of *Observe the Sons of Ulster Marching
Towards the Somme* by Frank McGuinness. France. Lang.: Fre.
                                                              1285
1990-1996.   Performance/production.
Recent Irish drama and theatre. Dublin. Lang.: Eng.   1790
1991-1997.   Theory/criticism.
Call for interdisciplinary Irish studies. Lang.: Eng.   905
1992.   Plays/librettos/scripts.
Political analysis of *Someone Who'll Watch Over Me* by Frank
McGuinness. Lang.: Eng.   2914
1993-1997.   Performance/production.
Experimental theatre group desperate optimists. Dublin. Lang.:
Eng.   560
1997.   Basic theatrical documents.
Text and photos of *Photogrammetry* by Christine Molloy and
Joe Lawlor of desperate optimists. Dublin. Lang.: Eng.   1286
1997.   Performance/production.
Report on the Fourth International Women Playwrights
Conference. Galway. Lang.: Eng.   559

Michael Flatley's *Riverdance* at Wolf Trap. Washington, DC.
Lang.: Hun.   1148

Report on recent Dublin productions. Dublin. Lang.: Eng. 1786

Recent Irish productions. Sligo. Dublin. Lang.: Swe.   1788
1997.   Plays/librettos/scripts.
Identity and the use of multiple actors to portray a single
character in postcolonial drama. Australia. Samoa. Lang.: Eng.
                                                              2380

Zen interpretation of Beckett's *Ohio Impromptu*. USA. Lang.:
Eng.   2919

Religion and chaos in plays of Samuel Beckett. France. Lang.:
Eng.   2921

Report from women playwrights conference. Galway. Lang.:
Swe.   2930

Comparison of Friel's *Molly Sweeney* and Synge's *The Well of
the Saints*. UK-Ireland. Lang.: Eng.   2935
1997.   Relation to other fields.
Narrative in Beckett's novels. France. Lang.: Eng.   3364

Israel

1963-1989.   Performance/production.
Budapest guest performance of the Batsheva Dance Group. Tel
Aviv. Budapest. Lang.: Hun.   980
1990.   Performance/production.
Hanan Snir's productions of Lorca's *Blood Wedding (Bodas de
sangre)*. Tel Aviv. Lang.: Eng.   1791
1993.   Performance/production.
The role of the implied spectator in productions of Omri Nitzan
and Hillel Mittelpunkt. Tel Aviv. Lang.: Eng.   1792
1993-1995.   Relation to other fields.
Approaches to teaching Shakespeare. Tel Aviv. Lang.: Eng.
                                                              3372
1994.   Relation to other fields.
Teaching Shakespeare at the University of Haifa. Haifa. Lang.:
Eng.   3373
1994-1996.   Performance/production.
Interview with István Juhos of the Batsheva Dance Group.
Hungary. Tel Aviv. Lang.: Hun.   975
1994-1997.   Relation to other fields.
The movement of theatre from entertainment to 'efficacy'.
Akko. USA. Lang.: Eng.   767
1997.   Performance/production.
Israeli guest performances of children's theatre. Berlin. Lang.:
Ger.   1698

Italy

179 B.C.-476 A.D.   Performance spaces.
Theatres and amphitheatres of ancient Rome. Rome. Lang.: Ita.
                                                              443
1300-1578.   Institutions.
The theatre of Umbrian confraternities. Lang.: Ita.   346
1350-1997.   Performance spaces.
Roman performance spaces. Rome. Lang.: Ita.   439
1380-1400.   Basic theatrical documents.
English translation of *La festa e storia di Sancta Caterina*.
Lang.: Eng.   1289

1400-1499.   Research/historiography.
Humanist historiography and the perception of public life and
spectacle. Lang.: Ita.   3812
1452-1501.   Basic theatrical documents.
English translations of sacred plays by Antonia Pulci. Lang.:
Eng.   1288
1486-1502.   Performance/production.
Renaissance theatre performances in Ferrara. Ferrara. Lang.:
Eng.   1794
1500-1542.   Plays/librettos/scripts.
Essays on the plays of Angelo Beolco (Ruzante). Lang.: Ita.
                                                              2940
1500-1600.   Plays/librettos/scripts.
Sexuality and witchcraft in plays of Antonfrancesco Grazzini.
Florence. Lang.: Eng.   2956
1500-1700.   Performance spaces.
The unity of decor in the Renaissance Italian stage and hall.
Lang.: Eng.   445

The effect of *commedia erudita* on theatre design and stage use.
Lang.: Eng.   1528
1500-1800.   Performance/production.
History of Neapolitan carnival. Naples. Lang.: Ita.   3783
1500-1860.   Performance/production.
History of Roman civic and religious festivities. Rome. Lang.:
Ita.   3802
1500-1997.   Performance spaces.
Roman theatres and theatrical life. Rome. Lang.: Ita.   446
1520-1620.   Performance spaces.
Mannerism in the performance spaces of early *commedia
dell'arte*. Lang.: Eng.   3790
1520-1997.   Performance/production.
Commedia dell'arte and contemporary amateur theatre. Lang.:
Ger.   3791
1526-1995.   Performance/production.
Gender on the Italian stage. Lang.: Eng.   564
1542-1616.   Plays/librettos/scripts.
The figure of Dido in works of the Italian Renaissance and
Spanish Golden Age. Spain. Lang.: Ita.   2957
1545-1650.   Performance/production.
Women in *commedia dell'arte*. Lang.: Eng.   3793
1550-1620.   Performance/production.
The mountebank and the *commedia dell'arte*. Lang.: Eng.   3792
1550-1650.   Performance spaces.
The development and dissemination of theatrical stage space.
Lang.: Eng.   441
1551-1997.   Relation to other fields.
Theatre as a tool for moral instruction. England. Lang.: Eng.
                                                              3375
1565-1620.   Audience.
The audience for *commedia dell' arte*. Lang.: Eng.   3788
1584-1585.   Theory/criticism.
Performativity and text in the works of Saint Maria Maddalena
de' Pazzi. Florence. Lang.: Eng.   907
1585-1700.   Performance/production.
Roman festivities of the Baroque period. Rome. Lang.: Ita.
                                                              3768
1598-1610.   Theory/criticism.
The birth of opera and the Camerata Fioretina. Florence. Lang.:
Swe.   4334
1700-1870.   Performance/production.
Roman festivities. Rome. Lang.: Ita.   3769
1750-1800.   Plays/librettos/scripts.
Nature and artifice on the eighteenth-century Italian stage.
Lang.: Ita.   2946
1750-1804.   Plays/librettos/scripts.
The dialect operas and *opera seria* of Alessandro Guglielmi.
Lang.: Eng.   4303
1759-1832.   Plays/librettos/scripts.
Jacobin playwright and theoretician Francesco Saverio Salfi.
Lang.: Ita.   2969
1761-1793.   Plays/librettos/scripts.
The influence of French culture on the plays of Carlo Goldoni.
France. Lang.: Ita.   2952
1766-1792.   Plays/librettos/scripts.
Cimarosa's *Il matrimonio segreto* and the clandestine marriage
on the eighteenth-century stage. Lang.: Fre.   4304
1766-1996.   Plays/librettos/scripts.
Piccinni's *La Cecchina*: English translations and analysis. USA.
Lang.: Eng.   4305

Italy — cont'd

Jakutija
  1996.   **Institutions.**
    Account of theatre festival in the Republic of Sacha. Lang.: Rus.
                                                                   348
Japan
                             Plays/librettos/scripts.
    Female characters in *kyōgen*. Lang.: Eng.   1227
  500-1997.   **Performance/production.**
    The development of Japanese theatrical genres. Lang.: Eng.
                                                                   1224
  646-1997.   **Performance/production.**
    Ceremonial theatrical forms *gigaku* and *bugaku*. Lang.: Eng.
                                                                   3798
  1150-1997.   **Performance/production.**
    Contrast and comparison of Eastern and Western acting styles.
    Europe. Lang.: Eng.   1822
  1500-1600.   **Plays/librettos/scripts.**
    Nō playwright Kanze Kojiro Nobumitsu. Lang.: Eng.   1232
  1600-1995.   **Performance/production.**
    History of the *Awaji ningyō* puppetry tradition. Awaji. Lang.:
    Eng.   4366
  1605-1984.   **Plays/librettos/scripts.**
    Animal imagery in *King Lear* and Akira Kurosawa's film
    adaptation *Ran*. England. Lang.: Eng.   3636
  1830-1995.   **Performance spaces.**
    Profile of the renovated *kabuki* theatre Kanamaru-za. Kotohira.
    Lang.: Eng.   1230
  1858-1859.   **Design/technology.**
    Analysis of a nineteenth-century work on stage effects in *kabuki*
    theatre. Lang.: Eng.   1229
  1888-1997.   **Performance/production.**
    The women's performance genre *gidayu*. Lang.: Eng.   567
  1937-1995.   **Basic theatrical documents.**
    English translation of *Ashi no Aru Shitai (A Corpse with Feet)*
    by Minoru Betsuyaku. Lang.: Eng.   1290
  1960-1994.   **Performance/production.**
    Japanese productions of plays by Samuel Beckett. Lang.: Eng.
                                                                   1823
  1970-1979.   **Theory/criticism.**
    Japanese analysis of Western choreography. USA. Lang.: Eng.
                                                                   1030
  1970-1996.   **Performance/production.**
    Women in Japanese theatre. Tokyo. Lang.: Eng.   568
  1992-1997.   **Performance/production.**
    Interview with dancer and choreographer Saburo Teshigawara.
    Europe. Lang.: Ger.   983
  1996.   **Design/technology.**
    Interior lighting of Hachioji City Art and Cultural Hall. Hachioji
    City. Lang.: Eng.   177
  1997.   **Performance/production.**
    Exhibition catalogue and essays on the influence of Japanese
    theatre. Lang.: Eng.   569
    Nō theatre at the Holland Festival. Netherlands. Lang.: Hun.
                                                                   1231
Kenya
  1800-1925.   **Relation to other fields.**
    Theatre, regional culture, and colonialism. Lamu. Lang.: Ger.
                                                                   772
  1938-1997.   **Relation to other fields.**
    Censorship, power, and performance. Nairobi. Lang.: Eng.   771
Latin America
  1600-1997.   **Performance/production.**
    History and development of *zarzuela*. Spain. Lang.: Eng.   3879
  1612-1994.   **Plays/librettos/scripts.**
    New world adaptations of Shakespeare's *The Tempest*. England.
    Caribbean. Lang.: Eng.   2549
  1981-1989.   **Basic theatrical documents.**
    Anthology of Latin American women's plays. Lang.: Eng.   1291
Latvia
  1990-1995.   **Performance/production.**
    Trends in recent Latvian theatre. Lang.: Eng.   570
Lithuania
  1939-1947.   **Performance/production.**
    Polish theatrical activities in Soviet camps and prisons. USSR.
    Poland. Lang.: Pol.   688
  1997.   **Performance/production.**
    Ghosts in theatrical productions. Poland. Lang.: Pol. 1838
Madagascar
  1800-1995.   **Performance/production.**
    The popular theatre genre of *Hira Gasy*. Lang.: Swe. 1225

Mali
  1997.   **Performance/production.**
    Malian wedding dances. Bamako. Lang.: Swe.   1149
Mexico
  1550-1997.   **Performance/production.**
    The defeat and return of Moctezuma in traditional dances. USA.
    Oaxaca. Lang.: Eng.   1154
  1600-1997.   **Performance/production.**
    Enactments of the descent from the cross. Lang.: Eng. 3803
  1925-1996.   **Plays/librettos/scripts.**
    Analysis of plays by Emilio Carballido. Lang.: Eng.   2973
  1994-1997.   **Performance/production.**
    'Confessions' elicited by Guillermo Gómez-Peña and Roberto
    Sifuentes' *Temple of Confessions*. Lang.: Eng.   3822
  1996.   **Performance/production.**
    Performance artists Guillermo Gómez-Peña and Roberto
    Sifuentes. UK-Wales. Lang.: Eng.   3821
  1996-1997.   **Administration.**
    The current state of Mexican theatre. Lang.: Ger.   41
Middle East
  1997.   **Basic theatrical documents.**
    English translation of *Paper Husband* by Hannan Al-Shaykh.
    Lang.: Eng.   1292
Mozambique
  1987-1997.   **Institutions.**
    Profile of Mutembela Gogo, Henning Mankell, director.
    Maputo. Lang.: Swe.   1447
  1997.   **Performance/production.**
    Interview with principals of joint production *Berättelse på tidens
    strand (A Tale on the Shore of Time)*. Sweden. Lang.:Swe. 1959
Netherlands
  1405-1410.   **Performance/production.**
    Analysis of manuscript containing ten vernacular plays. Lang.:
    Eng.   1828
  1500-1996.   **Performance/production.**
    Resurrection drama in the medieval church. Gernrode.
    Maastricht. Lang.: Eng.   1695
  1555-1637.   **Performance/production.**
    Visual records of early outdoor performances. Lang.: Eng. 1827
  1574-1644.   **Plays/librettos/scripts.**
    Diplomat and playwright Theodore Rodenburgh. Lang.: Dut.
                                                                   2974
  1640-1690.   **Relation to other fields.**
    Theatrical influences on painter Jan Steen. Lang.: Eng.   773
  1883-1959.   **Institutions.**
    Archival materials on the Wagner Society. Lang.: Dut. 4052
  1932-1997.   **Performance/production.**
    Choreographer Hans van Manen. Lang.: Dut.   1182
  1945-1995.   **Administration.**
    Dutch cultural policy and theatre. Lang.: Dut.   42
  1945-1997.   **Plays/librettos/scripts.**
    Adaptations of the diary of Anne Frank. USA. Lang.: Eng.
                                                                   2978
  1947-1997.   **Institutions.**
    The fiftieth anniversary of the Holland Festival. Lang.: Dut.
                                                                   350
    Profile of the Holland Festival. Lang.: Hun.   951
  1959-1989.   **Institutions.**
    Profile of Nederlands Dans Theater and Het National Ballet.
    Amsterdam. The Hague. Lang.: Hun.   1164
  1968-1997.   **Performance/production.**
    Director Jan Joris Lamers and his influence on contemporary
    theatre. Lang.: Eng, Fre.   1824
  1969-1997.   **Performance/production.**
    Ivo van Hove, new artistic director of the Holland Festival.
    Amsterdam. Lang.: Eng.   1826
  1980-1997.   **Plays/librettos/scripts.**
    Survey of the work of playwright Alex van Warmerdam. Lang.:
    Dut.   2976
  1982-1996.   **Basic theatrical documents.**
    Texts of plays by Alex van Warmerdam. Lang.: Dut.   1293
  1987-1996.   **Institutions.**
    History of Theaterfestival. Amsterdam. Lang.: Dut.   349
  1989-1997.   **Performance/production.**
    The visual theatre of director Rieks Swarte. Lang.: Eng, Fre.
                                                                   1829
  1990-1997.   **Performance/production.**
    Recent developments in opera and musical theatre. Lang.: Eng,
    Fre.   3874

Russia — cont'd

Spain — cont'd

1923. **Basic theatrical documents.**
Manuel de Falla's libretto to his opera *El retablo de Maese Pedro.* Lang.: Fre, Spa. 4016

1923. **Reference materials.**
Explanation of Spanish musical terms. Lang.: Fre. 4319

1926-1959. **Plays/librettos/scripts.**
Word avoidance and disclosure in plays of O'Neill and Valle-Inclán. USA. Lang.: Eng. 3257

1930-1937. **Plays/librettos/scripts.**
Gendered identity in plays of Cocteau and García Lorca. France. Lang.: Eng. 2807

1932-1996. **Plays/librettos/scripts.**
Interview with playwright/director Fernando Arrabal. Lang.: Eng. 3048

1939-1963. **Plays/librettos/scripts.**
The role of 'foreign' theatre on the Spanish stage. UK-England. USA. Lang.: Eng. 3044

1939-1975. **Plays/librettos/scripts.**
Violence in Spanish drama after the Civil War. Lang.: Eng. 3035

1947-1990. **Plays/librettos/scripts.**
The search for identity in the plays of Francisco Nieva. Lang.: Eng. 3040

1948-1996. **Performance/production.**
Interview with playwright Fermín Cabal. Lang.: Eng. 1918

1950-1990. **Plays/librettos/scripts.**
The work of theatre critic and writer Fray Benito Jerónimo Feijoo. Lang.: Spa. 3038

1950-1996. **Performance/production.**
Interview with Alberto Miralles of the theatre group Cátaro. Barcelona. Madrid. Lang.: Eng. 1914

1957-1996. **Performance/production.**
Profile of director Paloma Pedrero. Lang.: Eng. 1916

1964-1996. **Plays/librettos/scripts.**
Interview with playwright Rodrigo García. Lang.: Eng. 3037

1967. **Plays/librettos/scripts.**
Analysis of *El Tragaluz (The Skylight)* by Antonio Buero Vallejo. Lang.: Spa. 3045

1975-1995. **Performance/production.**
Gender, authenticity, and flamenco. Seville. Lang.: Eng. 1151

1975-1996. **Performance/production.**
Directors José Luis Gómez, José Sanchis Sinisterra, and Etelvino Vázquez. Lang.: Eng. 1917

1978-1996. **Performance/production.**
Interview with installation artist Esteve Graset. Lang.: Eng. 610

1984. **Plays/librettos/scripts.**
Analysis of Pedro Almodóvar's film *¿Qué he hecho yo para merecer esto? (What Have I Done to Deserve This?).* Lang.: Spa. 3642

1986-1992. **Basic theatrical documents.**
English translation of *Una hoguera en al amenecer (Bonfire at Dawn)* by Jaime Salom. Lang.: Eng. 1308

1990-1996. **Performance/production.**
Women directors in Spanish theatre. Lang.: Eng. 612

1990-1997. **Performance/production.**
The Alfredo Kraus International Competition. Lang.: Eng. 4214

1993. **Plays/librettos/scripts.**
Analysis of *Malinche* by Inés M. Stanger and *Opus Primum* by Hadi Kurich. Chile. Lang.: Eng. 2439

1995-1997. **Design/technology.**
Lighting design for flamenco dancer Joaquim Cortes and his troupe. Madrid. Lang.: Eng. 1141

1996. **Performance/production.**
Politics in Barcelona theatre. Barcelona. Lang.: Eng. 608

Report on Spanish-American theatre festival. Cádiz. Lang.: Spa. 611

Angel García Morena, artistic director of Teatro Fígaro. Madrid. Lang.: Eng. 1915

Catalan drama on the Madrid stage. Madrid. Lang.: Eng. 1919

Juan Margallo's production of *La tuerta suerte de Perico Galápago (The One-Eyed Luck of Perico Galápago)* by Jorge Márquez. Madrid. Lang.: Eng. 1920

Spanish *commedia* troupes. Barcelona. Lang.: Eng. 3794

1996. **Relation to other fields.**
Theatre in Galicia. Lang.: Eng. 779

1996-1997. **Performance/production.**
Selected theatre listings. Barcelona. Madrid. Lang.: Eng. 607

1997. **Institutions.**
Problems of the newly renovated Teatro Real. Madrid. Lang.: Eng. 4054

1997. **Performance/production.**
Theatre in Andalusia. Seville. Lang.: Eng. 609

Soprano Aïnhoa Artetoa. Lang.: Eng. 4213

Spain-Catalonia
1437-1997. **Plays/librettos/scripts.**
History of Catalan *Corpus Christi* play. Lang.: Eng. 3052

1950-1997. **Relation to other fields.**
Identity, cultural exchange, and tourism. Lang.: Eng. 3810

Sri Lanka
1956-1997. **Performance/production.**
Tendencies of modern Asian theatre. Lang.: Eng. 1921

Sweden
1800-1997. **Design/technology.**
Projection techniques for *Angels in America* at Stockholms Stadsteater. Stockholm. Lang.: Ger. 1358

1828-1908. **Plays/librettos/scripts.**
Frans Hedberg, director, manager, and librettist. Stockholm. Lang.: Swe. 4311

1847-1997. **Plays/librettos/scripts.**
Problems of translating drama, particularly Shakespeare. Lang.: Swe. 3059

1862-1997. **Performance/production.**
Realistic productions at the Royal Swedish Opera. Stockholm. Lang.: Swe. 4220

1876. **Performance spaces.**
Profile of the restored Karlstad Teater. Karlstad. Lang.: Swe. 4069

1880-1912. **Plays/librettos/scripts.**
Theosophy and the plays of August Strindberg. Lang.: Eng. 3062

1888. **Plays/librettos/scripts.**
Analysis of Strindberg's comedy *Brott och Brott (Crimes and Crimes).* Lang.: Eng. 3054

1888-1890. **Plays/librettos/scripts.**
The single-parent family in plays of Ibsen and Strindberg. Norway. Lang.: Eng. 2983

1888-1996. **Basic theatrical documents.**
French translations of Strindberg's *Fröken Julie (Miss Julie)* and *Den Starkare (The Stronger).* France. Lang.: Fre. 1309

1889-1897. **Plays/librettos/scripts.**
The visual imagination in the post-Inferno plays of August Strindberg. Lang.: Eng. 3053

1894-1907. **Plays/librettos/scripts.**
Tradition and modernism in later plays of Strindberg. Lang.: Eng. 3061

1900. **Audience.**
The involvement of the audience in performance. USSR. Lang.: Swe. 1251

1900. **Institutions.**
The situation of ensemble theatre, with reference to Göteborgs Stadsteatern and Schaubühne. Gothenburg. Germany. Lang.: Swe. 1484

1900. **Performance/production.**
Jazz in Sweden and the Modern Jazzdans Ensemble. Lang.: Swe. 987

1911-1945. **Relation to other fields.**
Dance and dancers under Nazism. Germany. Lang.: Swe. 1019

1918-1970. **Performance/production.**
Dancer/choreographer Carina Ari. France. Lang.: Swe. 1113

1920. **Performance/production.**
Dancer Lulli Svedin. Stockholm. Lang.: Swe. 1115

1920-1996. **Training.**
Gennadij Bogdanov's workshop on biomechanics, Sotenäs Teateratelje. Russia. Lang.: Swe. 932

1926-1997. **Performance/production.**
Profile of tenor Nicolai Gedda. Lang.: Eng. 4219

1931-1942. **Plays/librettos/scripts.**
On the correspondence of author Vilhelm Moberg and Dramaten manager Pauline Brunius. Stockholm. Lang.: Swe. 3058

1934-1997. **Performance/production.**
Interview with actors Sif Ruud and Thorsten Flinck. Stockholm. Lang.: Swe. 1922

1936. **Performance/production.**
Dancer/choreographer Elsa Marianne von Rosen. Denmark. Lang.: Swe. 1112

1940. **Performance/production.**
Interview with character dance teacher Pierre de Olivo. Stockholm. Lang.: Swe. 1114

Sweden — cont'd

1940-1941.   **Relation to other fields.**
Excerpt from a dance related novel by Eyvind Johnson.
Stockholm. Lang.: Swe.   1018
1944-1994.   **Performance/production.**
Ingmar Bergman's productions of Shakespeare's plays.
Germany. Lang.: Ita.   1934
1944-1997.   **Plays/librettos/scripts.**
Author Astrid Lindgren. Lang.: Swe.   3060
1945.   **Performance/production.**
Actor Jarl Kulle as a student at Dramatens Elevskola.
Stockholm. Lang.: Swe.   1926
1949-1997.   **Performance/production.**
Actor Allan Edwall and his theatre Brunnsgatan Fyra.
Stockholm. Lang.: Swe.   1935
1950.   **Performance/production.**
Dancer and director Gunilla Roempke. Stockholm. Lang.: Swe.
     1111

Problems of creating and preserving new dance works. Lang.:
Swe.   1184
1950-1995.   **Performance/production.**
Interview with actor Jarl Kulle. Stockholm. Lang.: Swe.   1953
1950-1997.   **Theory/criticism.**
Reflections on theatre reviews. Lang.: Swe.   3495
1954-1997.   **Design/technology.**
Kungliga Operan's costume collection. Stockholm. Lang.: Swe.
     4030
1957-1997.   **Performance/production.**
Interview with Sergej Jurskij. Russia. Lang.: Swe.   1877
1960-1997.   **Plays/librettos/scripts.**
Interview with director and author Margarete Garpe. Stockholm.
Lang.: Swe.   3063
1964.   **Institutions.**
Profile of Länsteatern i Skövde. Skövde. Lang.: Swe.   1481
1964-1997.   **Performance/production.**
Interview with actress Marie Göranzon. Stockholm. Lang.: Swe.
     1958
1965.   **Performance/production.**
Interview with actor Per Mattsson. Stockholm. Lang.: Swe.   1940
1967.   **Performance/production.**
The work together of actors Solveig Tännström and Börje
Ahlstedt. Stockholm. Lang.: Swe.   1961
1968-1997.   **Performance/production.**
Interview with choreographer Anne Külper of Tiger. Stockholm.
Lang.: Swe.   1188
1970.   **Performance/production.**
Interview with dancer/choreographer Håkan Mayer. Lang.: Swe.
     988

Interview with dancer/choreographer Gunilla Witt. Gothenburg.
Lang.: Swe.   1187
1970-1997.   **Performance/production.**
Actor Björn Granath. Stockholm. Lang.: Swe.   1936

Interview with director Peter Dalle. Stockholm. Lang.: Swe.
     1941
1972.   **Performance/production.**
Memories of actor Jarl Kulle. Malmö. Stockholm. Lang.: Swe.
     1955
1972-1997.   **Performance/production.**
Interview with actor and director Tom Fjordefalk. Lang.: Swe.
     1948
1974-1997.   **Performance/production.**
Actor and director Peter Luckhaus of Dramaten. Stockholm.
Lang.: Swe.   1939
1975-1997.   **Institutions.**
Funding and the threat to regional theatre. Kalmar. Lang.: Swe.
     1475
1976.   **Design/technology.**
Theatre technician Gert-Ove Vågstam. Cuba. South Africa,
Republic of. Lang.: Swe.   185
1976.   **Performance/production.**
Robert Wilson's Swedish guest performance. Stockholm. USA.
Lang.: Swe.   614

Director Frank Castorf. Berlin. Stockholm. Lang.: Swe.   1700
1977.   **Institutions.**
Profile of puppet theatre group Dockteater Tittut. Stockholm.
Lang.: Swe.   4353
1977.   **Performance/production.**
Interview with actor Johan Ulveson. Stockholm. Lang.: Swe.
     1929

1977-1997.   **Institutions.**
History of the publication *Nya Teatertidningen*. Lang.: Swe.   381
1978.   **Performance/production.**
Dancer Anders Nordström. Stockholm. Lang.: Swe.   1109
1978.   **Plays/librettos/scripts.**
György Ligeti on his opera *Le Grand Macabre*. Lang.: Fre.
     4312
1979.   **Institutions.**
Profile of creative drama institute Rosteriet. Luleå. Lang.: Swe.
     1492

Technical aspects of touring circus Ungdomcirkus. Norsholm.
Lang.: Swe.   3785
1979.   **Performance/production.**
Interview with opera singer Hillevi Martinpelto. Europe. Lang.:
Swe.   4221
1980.   **Institutions.**
Profile of Angered Nya Teater, Niklas Hjulström, director.
Gothenburg. Lang.: Swe.   1485
1980.   **Performance/production.**
The waning enthusiasm among Swedish audiences for
international guest artists. Lang.: Swe.   613

Interview with tenor Lars Cleveman. Stockholm. Lang.: Swe.
     4217
1980-1997.   **Performance/production.**
Interview with playwright and director Lars Norén. Stockholm.
Lang.: Swe.   1942

Interview with actor Sven Lindberg. Stockholm. Lang.: Swe.
     1954
1981.   **Performance/production.**
Interview with dancer Rennie Mirro. Stockholm. Lang.: Swe.
     990

Interview with actress Lina Pleijel. Stockholm. Lang.: Swe.   1946
1984-1997.   **Performance/production.**
Interview with Staffan Waldemar Holm, artistic director of
Malmö Dramatiska Ensemble. Malmö. Copenhagen. Lang.:
Swe.   1928
1985.   **Institutions.**
Profile of Riddarhyttans Industriteater, Anders Olson artistic
director. Riddarhyttan. Lang.: Swe.   1474
1985.   **Performance/production.**
Interview with actress Melinda Kinnaman. Stockholm. Lang.:
Swe.   1944
1985-1997.   **Performance/production.**
Interview with dramaturg Lena Fridell. Gothenburg. Lang.:
Swe.   1932

Interview with actor Olle Jansson. Stockholm. Lang.: Swe.   1950
1985-1997.   **Plays/librettos/scripts.**
Thomas Jennefelt's new opera *Farkosten*. Lang.: Swe.   4313
1986-1997.   **Institutions.**
Lars Löfgren's eleven years as manager of Dramaten.
Stockholm. Lang.: Swe.   1491
1986-1997.   **Performance/production.**
Interview with director Kajsa Isakson. Stockholm. Lang.: Swe.
     1951
1987.   **Design/technology.**
Big Image Systems' theatrical use of computer-generated
projections. Täby. Lang.: Swe.   186
1989-1997.   **Institutions.**
Profile of the independent Teater Satori. Stockholm. Lang.: Swe.
     1483
1990.   **Institutions.**
Swedish directors on the financial crisis. Lang.: Swe.   1490
1990.   **Performance spaces.**
Svenska Riksteatern's directory of performance spaces. Lang.:
Swe.   451
1990.   **Performance/production.**
The repertory of dance for children. Lang.: Swe.   989

Interview with director Ragnar Lyth. Stockholm. Gothenburg.
Lang.: Swe.   1943

Role-playing, audience-free, interactive theatre. Lang.: Swe.
     3770
1990-1997.   **Performance/production.**
Interview with actor Tommy Andersson. Lang.: Swe.   1931

Interview with director Richard Günther. Stockholm. Lang.:
Swe.   3943
1992.   **Theory/criticism.**
Grotowski, Institutet för Scenkonst, and the possibility of theatre
today. Denmark. France. Lang.: Swe.   910

Sweden — cont'd

Seminar on dance, text, and theatre. Stockholm. Lang.: Swe.
1032

Dansens Hus seminar on postmodern American dance.
Stockholm. USA. Lang.: Swe. 1214

Switzerland

1775-1825. **Relation to other fields.**
Füssli's Shakespearean paintings: exhibition catalogue. Lang.:
Ita. 3379

1917-1997. **Administration.**
Money and Swiss theatre. Lang.: Ger. 51

1918-1996. **Performance/production.**
Gottfried von Einem's opera *Der Besuch der alten Dame*. Lang.:
Eng. 4222

1921-1990. **Performance/production.**
Dürrenmatt's *Der Besuch der alten Dame (The Visit)* and its
American adaptation. Lang.: Eng. 1965

1933-1952. **Performance/production.**
German theatre during and after the Nazi period. Berlin.
Dusseldorf. Zurich. Lang.: Eng. 1704

1949-1997. **Performance/production.**
Interview with director Benno Besson. Germany. Lang.: Ger.
1727

1961. **Plays/librettos/scripts.**
Jewish persecution and identity in works of Max Frisch and
Arthur Miller. Lang.: Eng. 3064

1970-1997. **Performance/production.**
Robert Wilson's production of *La Maladie de la Mort (The
Sickness of Death)* by Marguerite Duras. Lausanne. Lang.: Hun.
1962

1980-1997. **Performance/production.**
Interview with director Christoph Marthaler and set designer
Anna Viebrock. Germany. Lang.: Ger. 1723

1989-1997. **Design/technology.**
Theatrical training for tailors and dressers at the Swiss Technical
College for Women. Zurich. Lang.: Ger. 191

1989-1997. **Institutions.**
Profiles of Comédie Genf and Théâtre Vidy. Lang.: Ger. 384

1990-1997. **Plays/librettos/scripts.**
Dance adaptations of Joachim Schlömer. Basel. Lang.: Ger, Fre,
Dut, Eng. 1014

1995-1996. **Audience.**
Analysis of statistics on German-language theatre and audiences.
Austria. Germany. Lang.: Ger. 132

1995-1997. **Performance/production.**
Productions of plays by Katharina Thanner and Lisa Engel.
Zurich. Basel. Lang.: Ger. 1963

1996. **Performance/production.**
Comparison of productions of Shakespeare's *Richard III*.
Germany. Lang.: Ger. 1745

1996. **Plays/librettos/scripts.**
Urs Widmer's *Top Dogs* at Theater Neumarkt. Zurich. Lang.:
Ger. 3066

1997. **Institutions.**
Profiles of Zurich theatres. Zurich. Lang.: Ger. 385

Profiles of Deutsches Schauspielhaus and Theater Neumarkt.
Hamburg. Zurich. Lang.: Ger. 1410

1997. **Performance/production.**
Account of conference on the future of classical dance.
Lausanne. Lang.: Swe. 991

Productions of plays by Shakespeare and Goethe at Zürcher
Schauspielhaus and Theater Neumarkt. Zurich. Lang.: Ger.
1964

1997. **Plays/librettos/scripts.**
Trends in contemporary German-language drama. Germany.
Austria. Lang.: Ger. 2859

Playwright Urs Widmer on Shakespeare's *Richard III*. Lang.:
Ger. 3065

Syria

1996. **Performance/production.**
The ecstatic dance of Sufi mystics, the 'whirling dervishes'.
Damascus. Lang.: Eng. 1152

Tanzania

1966-1997. **Relation to other fields.**
Multiculturalism and playwright Ebrahim Hussein. Lang.: Eng.
3380

Togo

1995-1997. **Plays/librettos/scripts.**
West African popular theatre: texts and analysis. Ghana.
Nigeria. Lang.: Eng. 2866

Turkey

1980-1997. **Performance/production.**
Productions of the International Istanbul Theatre Festival.
Istanbul. Lang.: Eng. 1966

1997. **Relation to other fields.**
Impressions of Turkish theatre. Istanbul. Lang.: Ger. 781

Uruguay

1992-1997. **Institutions.**
Developments at recent meetings of the International
Association of Theatre Critics. Poland. Finland. South Korea.
Lang.: Fre. 360

UK

1826-1873. **Performance/production.**
Biography of actress/manager Laura Keene. USA. Lang.: Eng.
634

1991-1997. **Relation to other fields.**
Shakespeare: The Animated Tales: educational videos, based on
Shakespeare's plays. Russia. Lang.: Ger. 3741

1992. **Performance/production.**
Analysis of cartoon adaptation for children: *Shakespeare: The
Animated Tales*. Russia. Lang.: Eng. 3723

UK-England

1590-1610. **Performance spaces.**
Power, Elizabethan theatre, and the Shakespearean stage. Lang.:
Eng. 1534

1592-1996. **Plays/librettos/scripts.**
Continued debate on Shakespearean editorial practice. Lang.:
Eng. 3080

1593-1750. **Performance/production.**
Possible misunderstandings arising from role distribution
practices. Lang.: Eng. 2208

1608-1918. **Performance/production.**
Iconographic analysis of visual records of actors. Germany.
Lang.: Eng. 1683

1727-1990. **Plays/librettos/scripts.**
Parody and satire in musical theatre. USA. Lang.: Eng. 3986

1790-1951. **Performance/production.**
Moral conflicts in Mozart's *Così fan tutte* and Britten's *Billy
Budd*. Austro-Hungarian Empire. Lang.: Eng. 4228

1794-1830. **Plays/librettos/scripts.**
Ideological discourse in nautical melodrama. Lang.: Eng. 3078

1798-1853. **Performance/production.**
The construction of the Middle East on the British stage. Lang.:
Eng. 2229

1800-1840. **Performance/production.**
Staging Shakespeare in the Romantic period. Lang.: Eng. 2166

1800-1880. **Plays/librettos/scripts.**
The key role of sentimentalism in English melodrama. Lang.:
Eng. 3082

1804-1850. **Administration.**
The design of nineteenth-century playbills. Lang.: Eng. 53

1804-1850. **Plays/librettos/scripts.**
Nautical melodrama and traditional authority structures. Lang.:
Eng. 3072

1827-1987. **Performance/production.**
Reactions to modern performances of *Antony and Cleopatra*.
North America. Lang.: Eng. 2178

1830-1900. **Plays/librettos/scripts.**
Gender and sexuality on the Victorian stage. Lang.: Eng. 3085

1832-1903. **Performance/production.**
Victorian ideas of womanhood in productions of Shakespeare's
The Merchant of Venice. Lang.: Eng. 2188

1840-1870. **Relation to other fields.**
Shakespeare's influence on nineteenth-century authors. Lang.:
Eng. 3385

1840-1900. **Performance/production.**
Metatheatricality in melodrama. Lang.: Eng. 618

1840-1914. **Performance/production.**
Shakespearean production in the age of actor-managers. Lang.:
Eng. 2193

1850-1900. **Performance/production.**
English acting careers of Eleonora Duse and Adelaide Ristori.
Lang.: Eng. 2169

1850-1900. **Plays/librettos/scripts.**
Melodrama as the enactment of cultural tensions resulting from
British imperialism. Lang.: Eng. 3071

1850-1914. **Administration.**
Changes in music hall entrepreneurship. London. Lang.: Eng.
3755

Yugoslavia
  1884-1965.   **Performance/production.**
  The stage career of Madách's *Az ember tragédiája (The Tragedy of Man)* in Voivodship. Hungary. Lang.: Hun.   1765

Zimbabwe
  1960-1997.   **Relation to other fields.**
  The culture and ethnography of the Amakhosi theatre tradition. Lang.: Eng.   3444

DOCUMENT AUTHORS INDEX

International Bibliography of Theatre: 1997

3407, 3408, 3414, 3415, 3417, 3419,
3420, 3422, 3431, 3437, 3439, 3721
Salt, Waldo.   3539
Salter, Denis.   1555, 1595, 1596, 1676, 1677
Salter, James.   3571
Saltz, David Z.   3107, 3702
Salverson, Julie.   2429
Salzer, Beeb.   153
Salzman, Eric.   3863
Sammler, Ben, ed.   287
Sammons, Laura Gordon.   1213
Samuel, Claude.   4133
Samuels, Steve.   3268
Samuels, Steven.   123, 411
Sanchez Basterra, Gabriela.   3050
Sandberg, Helen.   1145
Sandblad, Fia Adler.   2930
Sander, Lucia Vieira.   3269
Sanders, Julie.   2723
Sanderson, Richard K.   2724
Sandla, Robert.   3924
Sándor, L. István.   1181
Sanford, Tim.   2333
Sannuto, John.   1011
Santoli, Carlo.   2967
Santore, Jonathan C.   4318
Šarko, Zinajda.   1891
Sas, György, intro.   1773
Saternow, Tim.   226
Satin, Leslie.   952, 1208
Sauer, David Kennedy.   3432
Saunders, James.   1318
Sauter, Wilmar.   3483
Savčenko, B.   600
Savran, David.   3270
Sawyer, Robert Eugene.   3385
Sborgi, Franco, ed.   768
Scafuro, Adele C.   2886
Scanlan, Robert.   1549
Scano, Gaetana, ed.   347
Scapp, Ron.   3271
Scappaticci, Tommaso.   908
Scarlat, Ana.   1440
Schachenmayr, Volker.   566, 2852
Schafer, Elizabeth.   2209
Schaik, Eva van.   1182
Schalkwyk, David.   2725
Schandelmeier, Cathleen.   4378
Schartz, Howard, photo.   1167
Schechner, Richard.   767
Schechter, Joel.   1892, 2334
Schecter, Joel.   2335
Scheidler, Antje, transl.   3300
Scheie, Timothy.   2336
Scheier, Helmut.   945
Schelling, Franke.   760
Scheper, Jeanne.   3968
Scher, Herb.   3925
Scherb, Victor I.   2726
Scherer, Barrymore Laurence.   4198, 4202
Schevera, Nicholas.   3433
Schierenberg, Olaf.   160
Schille, Candy B.K.   2442
Schiller, Beatriz.   4237, 4238
Schirmer, Lothar.   750, 761
Schitthelm, Jürgen.   325
Schleef, Einar.   1283, 3356
Schlesinger, Judith.   3999
Schlissel, Lillian, ed.   1350
Schlocker, Georges.   26, 317
Schloff, Aaron Mack.   1512, 2337
Schlueter, June.   545, 3272
Schmidt, Goran.   3021
Schmidt, Jack.   222
Schmidt, Paul.   3273
Schmitt, Natalie Crohn.   2931, 2932
Schmitz-Burckhardt, Barbara.   1428

Schmitz-Gielsdorf.   4066
Schneider, Hansjörg.   762
Schneider, Katja.   1012, 1133
Schneider, Rebecca.   3837
Schob, Ivo.   3907
Schoemaker, George Henry.   534
Schoenfeld, Gerald.   60
Schoëvaërt, Marion, transl.   1277
Scholl, Tim, transl.   1101, 1102, 1103
Schonmann, Shifra.   840
Schra, Emile.   1545
Schrank, Bernice, ed.   2933
Schreiber, Loren.   288
Schuch, József, photo.   1052
Schuler, Catherine.   1893
Schulz, Wilfried.   1440
Schürer, Ernst, ed.   1284
Schwartzman, Eric.   289
Schwendinger, Leni.   240
Schwind, Klaus.   546, 1733
Scolnicov, Hanna.   3372
Scott, Anna Beatrice.   1013
Scott, Iain.   4041, 4284
Scott, Robert B.   483
Scott, Virginia.   431
Scribe, Eugène.   4009
Ščul'c, S.S.   3778
Scullion, Adrienne.   1635
Seabrook, John.   3622
Sediánszky, Nóra, comp.   1442
Sedinger, Tracey.   1636
Seizer, Susan.   1783
Selavie, Sasha.   2234
Selbach, Peter.   742
Selig, Paul.   2338
Seligmann, Raphael.   2727
Sell, Michael Thomas.   672
Selleck, Nancy Gail.   2728
Selling, Jan.   1429, 1430
Selmon, Michael.   3274
Semil, Małgorzata.   2985
Senelick, Laurence.   1550, 1894, 3451
Senker, Boris.   495
Sentilles, Renee Marie.   2339
Serame, Arnold, contrib.   283
Serra, Alessandro, transl.   3739
Servos, Norbert.   946, 970, 1131
Sevilla-Gonzaga, Marylis.   4064, 4121, 4213, 4214
Sevilla-Gonzaga, Marylis, comp.   4134
Seymour, A.   788
Seymour, James C.   3275
Sgroi, Alfredo.   1816
Shafer, Yvonne.   547, 1734, 2340, 3276
Shand, G.B.   2729
Shank, Theodore.   124, 673, 674, 940, 2341, 3838, 3839, 3840, 3841, 3842, 3843, 3969
Shanks, Michael.   3851
Shannon, Sandra G.   3277
Shantz, Valerie.   1395
Sharon, Louise.   2730
Shattuck, Sim Bryam.   2731
Shaughnessy, Robert.   2210
Shaw, Catherine M.   675
Sheare, Sybil.   1169
Sheehan, John D.   3970
Sheehan, Thomas W.   3544
Sheehy, Catherine.   2342
Sheehy, Helen.   2343, 2344
Sheffield, Clarence Burton, Jr.   2306
Sheingorn, Pamela.   676
Shenton, Mark.   1499, 2211, 2212, 2213, 2214, 2215, 3910, 3946, 3947, 3948, 3971
Shepard, John.   2345
Shepherd-Barr, Kirsten.   2801
Sheppard, Richard W.   763

Shepperson, Arnold.   3692
Sherbo, Arthur.   3474, 3492
Sherman, Harold.   4000
Sherman, Howard.   3972
Sherman, Jason.   1261
Shershow, Scott Cutler.   3475
Shevtsova, Maria.   1465, 1678, 2832
Shewey, Don.   2346, 3278
Shewring, Margaret.   1629
Shewring, Margaret, ed.   1522, 1532, 1535, 1536, 1537, 1538, 1542, 1543, 1544, 1629
Shrubsall, Anthony.   2216
Shurgot, Michael W.   3434
Sidorow, Sonja.   932
Sidorow, Sonja, transl.   1107
Sieben, Irene.   971
Siebenhaar, Klaus.   325
Siegel, Marcia B.   1218
Siemens, Elena.   3762
Sierz, Aleks.   3087, 3108
Signoretti, Aldo, ed.   343
Silver, Andrew Brian.   677
Silverman, Jeffry Lloyd.   1342
Silverstein, Marc.   3109
Simara, László, photo.   337, 2225
Simard, Jean-Pierre.   3110
Simerka, Barbara.   3051
Simmons, J. L.   2732
Simmons, James R., Jr.   3680
Simon, Attila, ed.   1441
Simon, John.   1965
Simon, Yoland.   1276
Simonds, Peggy Muñoz.   2733
Simons, Tad.   1513
Simonsen, Majbrit.   1063, 1177
Sinfield, Alan.   2734
Singer, Dana.   705
Singer, Mark.   3623
Singler-Wilson, Juliette Clare.   4289
Singleton, Brian.   1679, 1784
Sinibaldi, Clara.   1015
Sinisi, Silvana.   982, 1817, 1818, 2968
Sitar, Jelena.   4403
Sitas, Ari.   3033
Skånberg, Ami.   1170
Skasa, Michael.   1735
Skelton, Geoffrey, transl.   4008
Skipitares, Theodora.   4380
Sklar, Deidre.   3749
Sklar, Zachary.   3696
Skoog, Martin, photo.   951
Skrebels, Paul.   3435
Skura, Meredith.   2735, 3346
Skura, Meredith Anne.   3461
Slavíková, Jitka, transl.   1610
Slights, Camille Wells.   2736
Slingerland, Amy L.   1049, 1159
Slivnik, Francka.   604
Slobodian, Michael, photo.   1075
Smallwood, Robert.   2217
Smeljanskij, A.A.   1874
Smeljanskij, A.M.   1466
Smith, Bruce R.   3436
Smith, Colleen Altaffer.   1021
Smith, Edward Barton.   928
Smith, Hazel.   516
Smith, Iris L.   678
Smith, Jill Niemczyk.   1514, 1515
Smith, Marian.   1064
Smith, Patrick J.   460, 4102, 4162, 4219, 4275, 4276, 4277
Smith, Susan Harris.   3279
Snelling, Clive, transl.   1287
Snider, Denton J.   2737
Snow, Leida.   1047
Snyder, Susan.   2738, 2739

FINDING LIST OF PERIODICAL TITLES WITH ACRONYMS

Books in Canada	BooksC
Børneteateravisen	BTA
Botteghe della Fantasia, Le	BFant
Bouffonneries	Bouff
Brecht Jahrbuch	BrechtJ
Brecht Yearbook	BY
British Performing Arts Newsletter	BPAN
Britis Theatrelog	BTlog
Budapesti Negyed	BudN
Broadside	Brs
Buenos Aires Musical	BAMu
Bühne, Die	Buhne
Bühne Kursbuch Kultur	BKK
Bühne und Parkett	BPTV
Bühnen- und Musikrecht	BuM
Bühnengenossenschaft	BGs
Bühnentarifrecht	Buhnent
Bühnentechnische Rundschau	BtR
Builder N.S.	BNS
Bulletin	BulS
Bulletin	BulV
Bulletin ASSITEJ	BASSITEJ
Bulletin de la Société Paul Claudel	BSPC
Bulleti Magisch Plätze	BMP
Bulletin of the Comediantes	BCom
Bulletin of the School of Oriental & African Studies	BSOAS
Bulletin: Van het Belgisch Centrum ITI	BelgITI
Bundesverband Studentische Kulturarbeit	BSK
Burlington Magazine	BM
Cabra, La	CRT
Cahiers Césairiens	CahiersC
Cahiers CERT/CIRCE	CahiersCC
Cahiers de la Bibliothèque Gaston Baty	CBGB
Cahiers de la Maison Jean Vilar	CMJV
Cahiers de la NCT	CNCT
Cahiers du Rideau	CdRideau
Cahiers du Théâtre Populaire d'Amiens	CTPA
Cahiers Jean Cocteau	CJC
Cahiers Jean Giraudoux	CJG
Cahiers Renaud Barrault	CRB
Cahiers Théâtre Louvain	CTL
California Theatre Annual	CTA
Californian Shavian	CShav
Call Board	CB
Call Boy, The	CallB
Callahan's Irish Quarterly	CIQ
Callaloo: A Black South Journal of Arts and Letters	Callaloo
Callboard	Callboard
Calliope	Calliope
Cambridge Opera Journal	COJ
Canada on Stage	CS
Canadian Drama/Art Dramatique Canadien	CDr
Canadian Literature/Littérature Canadienne	CanL
Canadian Theatre Review (Toronto)	CTR
Canadian Theatre Checklist	CTCheck
Canadian Theatre Review Yearbook (Downsview)	CTRY
Caratula	Caratula
Carnet	Carnet
Časopis za zgodovino in narodopisje	CZN
Castelets	Castelets
Celcit	Celcit
Celjski zbornik	Celjz
Čelovek	Cel
Central Opera Service Bulletin	COS
Ceskoslovenski Loutkar	CeskL
Čest'imeju	Cesti
Chhaya Nat	Chhaya
Children's Theatre Review	ChTR
Chinese Literature	ChinL
Chronico	Chronico
Cineschedario: Letture Drammatiche	CineLD
Circus Report	CircusR
Circuszeitung, Die	Cz
Cirque dans l'Univers, Le	CU
Città Aperta	CittaA
City Arts Monthly	CAM
City Limits	CityL
Classical and Modern Literature	CLM
Classical Journal, The	ClassJ
Claudel Studies	ClaudelS
Clipper Studies in the American Theater	Clip
CLSU Journal of the Arts	CLSUJ
Club	Club
Coleçao Teatro	ColecaoT
College English	CE
College Language Association Journal	CLAJ
Columbia-VLA Journal of Law & the Arts	ColJL&A
Comédie de l'Ouest	CO
Comédie-Française	CF
Comedy	Comedy
Communications from the International Brecht Society	ComIBS
Comparative Drama	CompD
Confessio	Confes
Conjunto: Revista de Teatro Latinamericano	Cjo
Connoisseur	Con
Contact Quarterly	ContactQ
Contemporary French Civilization	CFT
Contenido	Contenido
Continuum	Contin
CORD Dance Research Annual	CORD
Corps écrit	CorpsE
Costume: The Journal of the Costume Society	Costume
Courrier Dramatique de l'Ouest	CDO
Courrier du Centre international d'études poétiques	CCIEP
Čovaškoe iskusstvo, Voprosy teorii istorii	CoviVt
Creative Drama	CreD
Crépuscule, Le	Crepuscl
Crisis	Crisis
Critical Arts	CrAr
Critical Digest	CritD
Critical Quarterly	CritQ
Critical Review	CritR
Critique	CritNY
Criticism	Criticism
CSA News: The Newsletter of the Costume Society of America	CSAN
Cuadernos El Publico	Cuaderno
Cue New York	CueNY
Cue, The	CueM
Cue International	Cue
Cultural Post	CuPo
Culture et Communication	CetC
Culture	Culture
Current Writing	CW
C'wan t'ong Xiju Yishu/Art of Traditional Opera	CTXY
DABEI	Dabei
Dalnij Vostok: (Far East)	DalVostok
Dance and Dancers	D&D
Dance Australia	DA
Dance Chronicle	DnC
Dance in Canada/Danse au Canada	DC
Dance Magazine	Dm
Dance Research	DRs
Dance Research Journal	DRJ
Dance Theatre Journal	DTJ
Dancing Times	DTi
Danstidningen	Danst
David Mamet Review	DMR
Dekorativnojė Iskusstvo SSR	DekorIsk
Detskaja Literatura	DetLit
Deutsche Bühne, Die	DB
Deutsche Shakespeare Gesellschaft/Deutsche Shakespeare Gesellschaft West, Jahrbuch	DShG
Deutsche Zeitschrift für Philosophie	DZP
Deutsches Bühnenjahrbuch	DBj
Deutsches Institut für Puppenspiel Forschung und Lehre	DIPFL
Devlet Tijatrolari (State Theatres)	Devlet
Dewan Budaya	Dewan
Diadja Vanja. Literaturnij al'manah	DVLa
Dialog: Miesiecznik Poswiecony Dramaturgii Wspolczesnej	DialogW
Dialog	DialogA
Dialog	DialogR
Dialogi	Dialogi
Dialogue: Canadian Philosophical Review	Dialogue
Dialogue (Tunisia)	DialogTu
Dioniso	Dioniso
Directors Notes	DirNotes
Diskurs	Diskurs
Diskurs	DRostock
Divadelni Noviny	DiN
Divadelni revue	DivR
Divadlo: (Theatre)	DTh
Dix-Huitième Siècle	DHS
Dix-Septième Siècle	DSS
Dockteatereko	Dockt
Documentation Théâtrale	DocTh
Documents del Centre Dramatic	DCD
Documents of the Slovenian Theatre and Film Museum	DSTFM
DOE	DOE
Dokumenti Slovenskega Gledaliskega Muzeja	DSGM
Don Saturio: Boletin Informativo de Teatro Gallego	DSat
Dong-Guk Dramatic Art	DongukDA
Drama and the School	DSchool
Drama and Theater	D&T
Drama and Theatre Newsletter	DTN
Drama Review, The	TDR
Drama Review	DrRev
Drama: Nordisk dramapedagogisk tidsskrift	DNDT
Drama: The Quarterly Theatre Review	Drama
Drama	DramaY
Dramat	Dramat
Dramatherapy: SEE: Journal of Dramatherapy (JDt)	Dtherapy
Dramatics	DMC
Dramatists Guild Quarterly	DGQ
Dramatists Sourcebook	DSo
dRAMATURg	dRAMATURg
Dramaturgi: Tedri Og Praksis	DTOP
Dramma	DrammaR
Dramma: Il Mensile dello Spettacolo	DrammaT
Drammaturgia	Drammaturgia
Dress	Dress
Družba	Druzba
Družba Narodov	DruzNar
Dvatisoč 2000:časnik za mišljenje, umetnost, kulturna	Dvat
Early Drama, Art, and Music Review, The	EDAM
East Asian History	EAH
Ebony	Ebony
Echanges	Echanges
Echo Planety	EchoP
Economic Efficiency and the Performing Arts	EE&PA
Economic History Review	EHR
Economist Financial Report	Econ
Editorial Nuevo Grupo	ENG
Educational Theatre News	ETN
Eighteenth-Century Studies	ECS
Eire-Ireland	Eire
Ekran	Ekran
Elet és Irodalom: irodalmi es politkai hetilap	Ell
Eletunk	Elet
Elizabethan Review	ERev
Elizabethan Theatre	ETh

FINDING LIST OF PERIODICAL TITLES WITH ACRONYMS

Empirical Research in Theatre .... ERT
Enact: monthly theatre magazine .... Enact
Encore (Australia) .... EncoreA
Encore (Georgia) .... Encore
Engekikai: Theatre World .... Egk
English Academy Review, The .... EAR
Englis i Africa .... EinA
English Language Notes .... ELN
English Literary Renaissance Journal .... ELR
English Studies .... EnSt
English Studies in Africa .... ESA
English Studies in Canada .... ESC
Entertainment and Arts Manager .... E&AM
Entré .... Entre
Envers du Décor, L' .... ED
Epic Theatre .... EpicT
Equity Journal .... EquityJ
Equity News .... EN
Escena: Informativo Teatral .... EIT
Escena .... Escena
Escenica .... Escenica
Espill, L' .... Espill
Esprit Créateur, L' .... ECR
Esprit .... Esprit
Essays in Criticism .... ECrit
Essays in Theatre .... ET
Essays on Canadian Writing .... ECW
Essence .... Essence
Estafeta Literaria: La Revista .... EstLit
Estrada i cirk .... EiC
Estreno: Journal on the Contemporary Spanish Theater .... Estreno
Estudis Escenics .... EECIT
Etnograjiceskoe obozrenie .... EO
Etoile de la Foire .... Etoile
Etudes Theatrales .... Etudes
Eugene O'Neill Review .... EOR
Európai utas .... Europai
Europe: Revue Littéraire Mensuelle .... Europe
Evento Teatrale .... Evento
Exchange .... Exchange
Ežegodnik MChAT .... MChAT
Farsa, La .... Farsa
Federal One .... FO
Feminist Review .... FemR
Feminist Studies .... FemS
Fight Master, The .... FMa
Figura .... Figura
Figurentheater .... Ftr
Film a Divadlo .... FDi
Film, Szinház, Muzsika .... FSM
Filologičeskije Nauki .... FN
Filológiai Közlöny .... FiloK
Finnish Theatre .... FT
FIRT/SIBMAS Bulletin d'information .... FIRTSIB
Flamboyant .... Flamb
Fliegende Teppich, Der .... fTep
Footnotes .... Fnotes
Forrás .... Forras
Forum Modernes Theater .... FMT
France Théâtre .... FranceT
Freedomways: A Quarterly Review of the Freedom Movement .... Fds
Freilichtbühne, Die .... FreilD
Fremantle Arts Review .... FAR
French Forum .... FrF
French Review, The .... FR
French Studies .... FS
Frontiers: A Journal of Women Studies .... Front
Fundarte .... Fundarte
Fundevogel .... Fundevogel
Fundraising Management .... FundM
Gambit .... Gambit
Gap, The .... Gap
Garcin: Libro de Cultura .... Garcin
Gazette des Beaux Arts .... GdBA
Gazette du Français .... GdF
Gazette Officielle du Spectacle .... GOS
Gazit .... Gazit
George Spelvin's Theatre Book .... GSTB
Georgia Review .... GaR
German Life and Letters .... GL&L
German Quarterly .... GQ
German Studies Review .... GerSR
Gestos: teoria y practica del teatro hispanico .... Gestos
Gestus: A Quarterly Journal of Brechtian Studies .... Gestus
Gewerkschaft Kunst, Medien, Freie Berufe .... KMFB
Gilbert and Sullivan Journal .... GSJ
Giornale dello Spettacolo .... GdS
Goethe Yearbook: Publication of the Goethe Society of North America .... Goethe
Gosteri: Performance .... Gosteri
Gosudarstvo i pravo .... GiP
Grande République .... GrandR
Graumann TZ .... GrTZ
Grimm & Gripps, Jahrbuch für Kinder- und Jugendtheater .... G&GJKJ
Grimm & Gripps. Beilage zum Kritischen kinder Medien Magazin .... G&GBKM
Grupo Teatral Antifaz: Revista .... GTAR
Guida dello Spettacolo .... Guida
Guidateatro: Estera .... GtE
Guidateatro: Italiana .... GtI
Habitat Australia .... HA
Hamlet Studies .... HSt
Harlekijn .... Harlekijn
Hecate: Women's Interdisciplinary Journal .... Hecate
Helikon .... Helik
Heresi Napló .... HevN
Hermes: Zeitschrift für Klassische Philologie .... Hermes
Higeki Kigeki: Tragedy and Comedy .... HgK
High Performance .... HP
Hispanic Arts .... HispArts
Historical Journal of Film, Radio and Television .... HJFRT
Historical Performance .... HistP
Historical Studies .... HisSt
History Workshop .... HW
Horisont .... Horis
Hungarian Journal of English and American Studies .... HJEAS
Hungarian Quarterly .... HQ
Hungarian Theatre/Hungarian Drama .... HTHD
Hungarian Theatre News .... HTN
Ibsen News & Comments .... INC
Ibsenårboken/Ibsen Yearbook .... IA
Il Castello di Elsinore .... IlCast
Impressum .... Impressum
Impuls .... Impuls
In Sachen Spiel und Theatre .... ISST
In the Arts: Search, Research, and Discovery .... InArts
Independent Shavian .... IndSh
Indonesia .... Indonesia
Information du Spectacle, L' .... IdS
Information on New Plays .... Info
Inostrannaja Literatura .... InoLit
Instituto Internacional del Teatro .... IITBI
International Theatre Yearbook .... ITY
Interscena/Acta Scenographica .... IAS
Ireland of the Welcomes .... IW
Irish Drama Selections .... IDSelect
Irish Historical Studies .... IHS
Irish Theatre Archive's Newsletter .... ITAN
Irish University Review .... IUR
Irodalomtörténet .... IHoL
Irodalomtörténeti Közlemények .... IK
Iskusstvo .... Iskusstvo
Iskusstvo Kino .... ISK
Iskusstvo v škole .... Iskv
Island Magazine .... IM
Istituto di Studi Pirandelliani e sul Teatro Contemporaneo .... ISPTC
Jacobean Drama Studies .... JDS
Jahrbuch der Deutsche Shakespeare-Gesellschaft .... JDSh
Jahrbuch der Grillparzer-Gesellschaft .... JGG
Jahrbuch der Städte mit Theater gastspielen .... JahrST
Jahrbuch der Wiener Gesellschaft für Theaterforschung .... JWGT
Jahrbuch für Opernforschung .... Jahrfo
Jahrbuch Tanzforschung .... JahrT
Javisko .... Javisko
JEB Théâtre .... JEBT
Jelenkor .... Jelenkor
Jeu: Cahiers de Théâtre .... JCT
Jeune Théâtre .... JT
JITT .... JITT
Journal de Chaillot .... JdCh
Journal du Grenier de Toulouse .... JGT
Journal du Théâtre Populaire Romand .... JTPR
Journal du Théâtre de la Ville .... JTV
Journal for Stage Directors and Choreographers .... JSDC
Journal Freie Theater .... JFT
Journal of Aesthetic Education .... JAE
Journal of Aesthetics and Art Criticism, The .... JAAC
Journal of African Studies .... JAfS
Journal of American Culture .... JAC
Journal of American Drama and Theatre, The .... JADT
Journal of Arts Management, Law and Society .... JAMLS
Journal of Arts Policy and Management .... JAP&M
Journal of Asian Studies .... JASt
Journal of Beckett Studies .... JBeckS
Journal of Canadian Studies .... JCNREC
Journal of Caribbean Studies .... JCSt
Journal of Cross-Cultural Psychology .... JCCP
Journal of Dramatherapy .... JDt
Journal of Dramatic Theory and Criticism .... JDTC
Journal of Film and Video .... JFV
Journal of Irish Literature .... JIL
Journal of Japanese Studies .... JJS
Journal of Literary Studies: Tydskrif vir Literatuurwetenskap .... JLS/TLW
Journal of Magic History .... JMH
Journal of Midwest Modern Language Association .... JMMLA
Journal of Musicology .... JoM
Journal of New Zealand Literature .... JNZL
Journal of Popular Culture .... JPC
Journal of Research in Singing and Applied Vocal Pedagogy .... JRSAVP
Journal of Social History .... JSH
Journal of the Australian Universities Language & Literature Association .... AULLA
Journal of the Eighteen Nineties .... JENS
Journal of the Illuminating Engineering Society .... JIES
Journal of the Royal Asiatic Society of Malaysia .... JRASM
Journal of the Siam Society .... JSS
Journal of the Warburg & Courtauld Institutes .... JWCI
Journal of Voice .... JOV
Juben: (Playtexts) .... Juben
Jugoslovenske: Pozorišne Igre .... JugoIgre
Junkanoo .... Junkanoo
Kabuki .... Kabuki
Kaekseok .... Kaekseok
Kalakalpam .... Kalak
Kalliope:A Journal of Women's Art .... Kalliope
Kanava .... Kanava
Kassette: Almanach für Bühne, Podium und Manege .... KAPM

Kathakali .... Kathakali
Kazaliste .... Kazal
Keshet .... Keshet
King Pole Circus Magazine .... KingP
Kino .... Kino
Kleine Schriften .... KS
Kleine Schriften der Gesellschaft für
  Theatergeschichte .... KSGT
Klub i Chudožestvennaja Samodejetelnost .... Klub
Kommunist .... Kommunist
Kontinent .... Kon
Korea Journal .... KoJ
Korean Culture & Arts Bi-Monthly .... KCAB
Korean Drama .... KoreanD
Korean Studies Forum .... KSF
Korean Theatre Review .... KTR
Kortárs .... Kortars
Kraj smolenskij .... Krajs
Kritika .... Krit
Kronika .... KZphK
Kulis .... Kulis
Kultur-Journal .... KJ
Kultura és Közösség .... KesK
Kultura i Žizn (Culture and Life) .... KZ
Kulturno-Prosvetitelnaja Rabota .... KPR
Kultuurivihkot .... Kvihkot
Kunst Bulletin .... KB
Kurt Weill Newsletter .... KWN
La Trobe Library Journal .... LLJ
Labour History .... LabH
Laientheater .... Laien
Latin American Theatre Review .... LATR
Lettera Dall'Italia .... LettDI
Lettres Québécoises .... LetQu
Letture: Libro e spettacolo .... Letture
Literaturnaja ucheba .... Letuch
Light .... Light
Lighting Design + Application .... LD&A
Lighting Dimensions .... LDim
Lik Cuvasija .... LikC
Lilith:a Feminist History Journal .... Lilith
Linzer Theaterzeitung .... LinzerT
Lipika .... Lipika
Literator: Journal of Comparative Literature and
  Linguistics .... Literator
Literatura .... Literatura
Literature & History .... L&H
Literature/Film Quarterly .... LFQ
Literature in North Queensland .... LiNQ
Literature in Performance .... LPer
Literaturnaja Gruzia .... LitGruzia
Literaturnojë Obozrenijë .... LO
Litva literaturnaja .... Litva
Live .... Live
Livres et Auteurs Québécois .... LAQ
Loisir .... Loisir
Lok Kala .... LokK
Lowdown .... Lowdown
Ludus .... Ludus
Loutkar .... Loutkar
Lutka .... Lutka
Magazine du TNB .... MdTNB
Magyar Iparművészet .... MagIp
Magyar Múzeum .... MagM
Maksla .... Maksla
Mala Biblioteka Baletowa .... MBB
Mamulengo .... Mamulengo
Manadens Premiärer och Information .... MPI
Manipulation .... Manip
Marges, El .... EIM
Marquee: The Journal of the Theatre Historical
  Society .... MarqJTHS
Marquee .... Marquee
Mask .... Mask
MASKA .... MASKA
Maske und Kothurn .... MuK
Maske .... Maske

Masque .... Masque
Masterstvo .... Mast
Material zum Theater .... MT
Matya Prasanga .... Matya
Meanjin .... Meanjin
Media, Culture and Society .... MC&S
Medieval and Renaissance Drama .... MRenD
Medieval and Renaissance Drama in
  England .... MRDE
Medieval English Theatre .... MET
Medieval Music-Drama News .... MMDN
Meister des Puppenspiels .... MeisterP
Meridian .... Meridian
Merker, Der .... Merker
Mestno gledališče Ljubljansko .... MGL
Miedzynarodowny Rocznik Teatralny .... MRT
Milliyet Sanat Dergisi .... MSD
Mim: Revija za glumu i glumište .... Mim
Mime Journal .... MimeJ
Mime News .... MimeN
Mimos .... Mimos
Minority Voices .... MV
Mitgliederzeitung .... Mit
Mitteilungen der Puppentheatersammlung .. MPSKD
Mitteilungen der Vereinigung .... MdVO
Mobile .... Mobile
Modern Austrian Literature .... MAL
Modern Drama .... MD
Modern International Drama .... MID
Modern Language Review .... MLR
Modern Philology .... MP
Moja Moskva .... MojM
Molodaja Gvardija .... MolGvar
Molodoi Kommunist .... MK
Monographs on Music, Dance and Theater in
  Asia .... MMDTA
Monsalvat .... Monsalvat
Monte Avilia .... MAvilia
Monthly Diary .... MoD
Monumenta Nipponica: Studies in Japanese
  Culture .... MN
Moskovskij Nabljudatel' .... MoskNab
Moskva .... Mosk
Mozgó Világ .... Mozgo
Mühely .... Muhely
Münchener Beiträge zur
  Theaterwissenschaft .... MBzT
Music & Letters .... MLet
Music Hall .... MHall
Musical Quarterly .... MuQ
Musicals Das Musicalmagazin .... MDM
Musical'naja Academija .... MA
Musik & Teater .... M&T
MusikDramatik .... MuD
Musik und Gesellschaft .... MusGes
Musik und Theater .... MuT
Muzsika .... Muzsika
Muzyka .... Muzyka
Muzykal'naja akademija .... MA
Muzykalnaja Žizn: (Musical Life) .... MuZizn
My .... My
Mykenae .... Mykenae
Nadie Journal .... NADIE
Näköpiiri .... Nk
Naš Sovremennik .... NasSovr
Nagyvilág .... Nvilag
Napjaink .... Napj
Narodna tvorchestvo .... NTE
National Center for the Performing Arts .... NCPA
Natrang .... Natrang
Natya Kala .... NKala
Natya Varta .... NVarta
Natya .... Natya
Nauka i Religija (Science and Religion) .... NiR
Nauka v Rossii .... NvR
Navi Prolog .... NP
Naytelmauutiset .... Nayt

Nederlands Theatre-en-Televisie Jaarboek ..... NTTJ
New Theatre Review, The .... NTR
Neohelicon .... Neoh
Nestroyana .... Ns
Netherlands Centraal Bureau voor de Statistiek:
  Bezoek .... NCBSBV
Netherlands Centraal Bureau voor de Statistiek:
  Muziek en Theater .... NCBSMT
Neue Blätter des Theaters in Der Josefstadt ..... NBT
neue Merker, Der .... neueM
Neue Musikzeitung .... NMZ
Neva .... Neva
New Contrasts .... NC
New England Theatre Journal .... NETJ
New Literatures Review .... NLR
New Observations .... NO
New Performance .... NewPerf
New Theatre Australia .... NTA
New Theatre Quarterly .... NTQ
New Theatre Review .... NTR
New York Onstage .... NYO
New York Theatre Critics Review .... NYTCR
New York Theatre Reviews .... NYTR
New Yorker, The .... NewY
NeWest Review .... NWR
News from the Finnish Theatre .... NFT
Newsletter of the ITI of the United States,
  Inc. .... NITI
Nihon-Unima .... NihonU
Nineteenth Century Music .... NCM
Nineteenth Century Theatre .... NCT
Nineteenth Century Theatre Research .... NCTR
Nōgaku-kenkyū .... NoK
Nōgaku Shiryo Shusei .... NoSS
Noh .... Noh
Nohgaku Times .... NTimes
Nordic Theatre Studies .... NTS
Notate .... NIMBZ
Notes on Contemporary Literature .... NConL
Nova revija .... Novr
Novaja Rossija .... NovRos
Novoe Vremija .... NV
Novyj Mir .... NovyjMir
Numero .... Numero
Nya Teatertidningen .... NT
Očag Semejnij Zurnal .... OSZ
O'Casey Annual .... OCA
Obliques .... Obliques
Off-Informationen .... OffI
Ogonek .... Ogonek
Oktiabr .... Oktiabr
Ollantay Theater Magazine .... Ollan
On-Stage Studies .... OSS
Ons Amsterdam .... OnsA
Opal .... Opal
Oper Heute .... OperH
Oper .... Oper
Oper und Konzert .... Opuk
Oper & Tanz .... Op&T
Opera Australia .... OperaA
Opera Canada .... OC
Opera Index .... OperaIn
Opéra International .... OI
Opera Journal .... OJ
Opera News .... OpN
Opera Quarterly .... OQ
Opera (London) .... OperaR
Opera (Cape Town) .... OperaCT
Opera (Milan) .... OperaR
Operaélet/Operalife .... OperaL
Opernglas, Das .... Opern
Opernwelt .... Opw
Opuscula .... Opuscula
Opus Osterreichische Puppenspiel-
  Journalette .... Opus
Organon .... Organon
Orpheus Clauspeter Koscielny .... Orpheus

Theatrum: A Theatre Journal	Theatrum
Themes in Drama	TID
Theoria	Theoria
Thespis	Thespis
Tiyatro Araştirmalari Dergisi (Theatre Research Magazine)	TAD
Tijatro	Tijatro
Tijdschrift voor de Podium Kunst	TvPK
Tijdschrift voor Theaterwetenschap	TvT
Tiszatáj	Tisz
Toneel Teatraal	Toneel
Tournées de Spectacles	Tournees
Tréteaux	Treteaux
Traces	Traces
Tramoya: Cuaderno de teatro	Tramoya
Transforming Art	TransA
Transition: Discourse on Architecture	TDonA
Travail Théâtral	TTh
Trujaman	Trujaman
Tvorchestvo	TVOR
Two Thousand	Twot
Tydskrif vir Letterkunde	TvL
Tydskrif vir Volkskunde en Volkstaal	TvVV
Ufahamu: Journal of the African Activist Association	Ufa
Új Auróra	UjA
Új Forrás	UjF
Új Írás	UjIras
Ukrainskij Teat'r	UTeatr
UNIMA France	UNIMA
Unisa English Studies	UES
Universidad de Murcia Catedra de Teatro Cuadernos	UMurcia
Universitas Tarraconensis	UTarra
University of Dar es Salaam	UDSalaam

University of Toronto Quarterly	UTQ
Unterhaltungskunst	UZ
Upstart Crow, The	UCrow
Ural	Ural
Usbu Al-Masrah	Usbu
USITT Newsletter	USITT
Uusi-Laulu	Uusi
V sovèckom teatrè	VSov
Valóság	Valo
Valiverho	Valivero
Vantage Point: Issues in American Arts	VantageP
Vestnik MGU: Series 9-Filologia	VMGUf
Victorian Historical Journal	VHJ
Victorian Studies	VS
Vigilia	Vig
Világszinház	Vilag
Voice: Newsletter for Chorus America	VCA
Volga	Volga
Voprosy filosofii	VFil
Voprosy istorii KPSS	VoprosyK
Voprosy Literatury	VLit
Voprosy Teatra	Voprosy
Vozrozdénie	Voz
Vstreča	Vstreča
Vyakat	Vyakat
Waiguo Xiju	Waiguo
Washington International Arts	WIAL
Weimarer Beiträge	WB
Wer spielte was	Wsw
West Coast Plays	WCP
Westerly	WEST
Western European Stages	WES
Western Journal of Black Studies	WJBS
White Tops	WTops
Wiener Forschungen zur Theater und Medienwissenschaft	WFTM

Wiener Gesellschaft für Theaterforschung Jahrbuch	WGTJ
WIJ, Poppenspelers	WijP
Women & Performance: A Journal of Feminist Theory	WPerf
Women's Review	WomenR
Women's Studies	WS
Working Papers in Irish Studies	WPIS
World Literature Today	WLT
World of Opera	WOpera
World Premieres Listing	WPList
Writings on Dance	WonD
Xiju Luncong: Selected Essays of Theatre	XLunc
Xiju Xuexi: Theatre	XXuexi
Xiju Yishu: Theatre Arts	XYishu
Xiqu Yanjiu	XYanj
Yorick: Revista e Teatro	Yorick
Young Cinema & Theatre/Jeune Cinéma et Théâtre	YCT
Youth Theatre Journal	YTJ
Zahranicni Divadlo: (Theatre Abroad)	ZDi
Zapad Rossii	ZR
Zeitschrift für Anglistik und Amerikanistik	ZAA
Zeitschrift für Kulturaustausch	ZfK
Zeitschrift für Germanistik	ZG
Zeitschrift für Anglistik und Amerikanistik	ZAA
Zeitschrift für Kulturaustausch	ZfK
Zeitschrift für Germanistik	ZG
Zeitschrift für Slawistik	ZS
Zene-Zene Tanc	ZZT
Znamya	Znamya
Zpravy DILIA	Zpravy
Zreliščnyjè Iskusstva (Performing Arts)	ZreIssk
Zvezda	Zvezda

LIST OF PERIODICALS

The following list is an attempt to provide an updated and comprehensive listing of periodical literature, current and recent past, devoted to theatre and related subjects.

This Bibliography provides full coverage of materials published in periodicals marked "Full" and selected coverage of those marked "Scan".

We have not dropped periodicals that are no longer published for the sake of researchers for whom that information can be valuable. We also note and list title changes.

A&A *The Artist. (Incorporates Art & Artists)*. Freq: 12; Lang: Eng; Subj: Related.
ISSN: 0004-3877
■The Artists' Publishing Company Ltd.; Caxton House, 63-65 High Street Tenderden, Kent TN30 6BD; UK.

A&B *Architect & Builder*. Freq: 12; Began: 1951; Lang: Eng; Subj: Related.
ISSN: 0003-8407
■Laurie Wale (Pty) Ltd.; Box 4591; Cape Town; SOUTH AFRICA.

A&AR *Art and Artists*. Formerly: *Art Workers News; Art Workers Newsletter*. Freq: 10; Began: 1982; Lang: Eng; Subj: Related.
ISSN: 0740-5723
■Foundation for the Community of Artists; 280 Broadway, Ste 412; New York, NY 10007; USA.

A&L *Art and the Law*: Columbia Journal of Art and the Law. Freq: 4; Began: 1974; Ceased: 1985; Cov: Full; Lang: Eng; Subj: Related.
ISSN: 0743-5266
■Volunteer Lawyers for the Arts; 1500 Broadway; Ste. 711 New York, NY 10036; USA.

AAC *Australian Antique Collector*. Freq: IRR; Began: 1966; Cov: Scan; Lang: Eng; Subj: Related.
■Editor, Australian Antique Collector; P.O. Box 5487; West Chatswood 2067; AUSTRALIA.

AAinNYLH *Afro-Americans in New York Life and History*. Freq: 2; Began: 1977; Lang: Eng; Subj: Related.
ISSN: 0364-2437
■Afro-American Historical Assoc. of the, Niagara Frontier; Box 63; Buffalo, NY 14207; USA.

AATTN *AATT News*. Freq: 11; Began: 1976; Lang: Eng; Subj: Theatre.
■Australian Assoc. for Theatre Tech.; 40 Wave Avenue Mountain; 3149 Waverly; AUSTRALIA.

Abel *Abel Value News*. Formerly: *Abel: Panem et Circenses/Bread and Circuses*. Freq: 12; Began: 1969; Lang: Eng; Subj: Theatre.
ISSN: 0001-3153
■Abel News Agencies; 403 1st Ave.; Estherville, IA 51334-2223; USA.

AbhC *Abhinaya*. Freq: 12; Lang: Ben; Subj: Theatre.

■Dilipa Bandyopadhyaya; 121 Harish Mukherjee Road; Calcutta; INDIA.

AbhD *Abhinaya*. Freq: 24; Lang: Hin; Subj: Theatre.
■Yuvamanch; 4526 Amirchand Marg; Delhi; INDIA.

AbqN *Arabesque*: A magazine of international dance. Freq: 6; Began: 1975; Cov: Scan; Lang: Eng; Subj: Related.
ISSN: 0148-5865
■Ibrahim Farrah Inc.; One Sherman Square, Suite 22F; New York, NY 10023; USA.

ACH *Australian Cultural History*. Freq: 1; Began: 1982; Cov: Scan; Lang: Eng; Subj: Related.
ISSN: 0728-8433
■Faculty of Arts, Centre for Australian Studies; Deakin University; Geelong Victoria 3217; AUSTRALIA.

ACCTV *Almanacco della Canzone e del Cinema e della TV*. Lang: Ita; Subj: Theatre.
■Viale del Vignola 105; Rome; ITALY.

ACom *Art Com*: Contemporary Art Communication. Formerly: *Mamelle Magazine: Art Contemporary*. Available only through electronic mail 415/332-4335. Freq: 4; Began: 1975; Lang: Eng; Subj: Related. ISSN: 0732-2852
■Contemporary Arts Press; Box 3123; San Francisco, CA 94119; USA.

ACS *Australian-Canadian Studies: an interdisciplinary social science review*. Freq: 1; Began: 1983; Cov: Scan; Lang: Eng; Subj: Related.
ISSN: 0810-1906
■Department of Sociology; LaTrobe University; Bundoora Victoria 3083; AUSTRALIA.

Act *Act*: Theatre in New Zealand. Formerly: *Theatre*. Freq: 6; Began: 1976; Ceased: 1986; Lang: Eng; Subj: Theatre. ISSN: 0010-0106
■Playmarket Inc.; Box 9767; Wellington; NEW ZEALAND.

ACTA *Acta Classica (Proceedings of the Classical Association of South Africa)*. Freq: 1; Began: 1958; Cov: Scan; Lang: Eng.; Subj: Related.
ISSN: 0065-1141
■Classical Association of South Africa; P.O. Box 392; Pretoria 0001; SOUTH AFRICA.

Acteurs *Acteurs/Auteurs*. Formerly: *Acteurs*. Freq: 10; Began: 1982; Lang: Fre; Subj: Theatre.
ISSN: 0991-949X
■Actes Sud, 18; 75006 rue de Savoie Paris; FRANCE.

ActS *Actualité de Scénographie*. Freq: 6; Began: 1977; Lang: Fre; Subj: Theatre.
■Assoc. Belgique des Scénographes et Techniciens de Théâtre; 58 rue Servan; 75011 Paris et l'editeur; FRANCE.

ActT *Action Théâtre*. Lang: Fre; Subj: Theatre.
■Action Culturelle de Sud-Est; 4 rue du Théâtre Français; 13001 Marseille; FRANCE.

Actualites *Actualités*. Lang: Fre; Subj: Theatre.
■Actualités Spectacles; 1 rue Marietta Martin; 75016 Paris; FRANCE.

AD *After Dark*. Freq: 12; Began: 1968; Ceased: 1983; Lang: Eng; Subj: Theatre.
ISSN: 0002-0702
■Dance Magazine, Inc.; 175 Fifth Avenue; New York, NY 10010; USA.

ADoc *Arts Documentation Monthly*. Freq: 10; Began: 1978; Ceased: 1989; Last Known Address; Lang: Eng; Subj: Theatre. ISSN: 0140-6965
■The Arts Council of Great Britain Library, Information and Research Section; 105 Piccadilly; W1V OAU London; UK.

AdP *Atti dello Psicodramma*. Freq: 1; Began: 1975; Lang: Ita; Subj: Related.
■Astrolabio-Ubaldini, Via Lungara 3, 00165 Rome; ITALY.

ADS *Australasian Drama Studies*. Freq: 2; Began: 1982; Cov: Full; Lang: Eng; Subj: Theatre.
■Australasia Drama Studies, English Dept., University of Queensland; Q 4072 St. Lucia; AUSTRALIA.

AdSpect *Annuaire du Spectacle*. Freq: 1; Began: 1956; Lang: Fre; Subj: Theatre. ISSN: 0066-3026
■Publications Mandel L'Edison; 43 bd. Vauban 78182 St. Quentin-en-Yvelines Cedex; FRANCE.

AdT *Art du Théâtre, L'*. Freq: 3; Began: 1985; Lang: Fre; Subj: Theatre.
■Théâtre National de Chaillot; 1 Place du Trocadéro; 75116 Paris; FRANCE.

AdTI *Annuario del Teatro Italiano*. Freq: 1; Began: 1934; Lang: Ita; Subj: Theatre.
■S.I.A.E. - I.D.I.; Viale della Letteratura 30; 00100 Rome; ITALY.

AETR *AET Revista*. Lang: Spa; Subj: Theatre.
■Associación de Estudiantes de Teatro; Viamonte 1443; Buenos Aires; ARGENTINA.

AfAmArt *African American Art*. Formerly: *Black American Quarterly*. Freq: 4; Began: 1984; Cov: Scan; Lang: Eng; Subj: Related.
ISSN: 1045-0920
■Museum of African American Art; Santa Monica, CA; USA.

AfAmR *African-American Review*. Freq: 4; Lang: Eng; Subj: Related.
■Department of English; Indiana State University; Terre Haute, IN 47809; USA.

Afr *Afreshiya*. Began: 1945; Last Known Address; Lang: Eng; Subj: Theatre.
■42 Commercial Buildings; Shahrah-e-Quaid-e-Azam; Lahore; PAKISTAN.

AfrA *African Arts*. Freq: 4; Began: 1967; Ceased: 1987; Cov: Scan; Lang: Eng; Subj: Related.
ISSN: 0001-9933
■African Studies Center, Univ. of California, Los Angeles; 405 Hilgard Avenue; Los Angeles, CA 90024; USA.

AfricaP *Africa Perspective*. Freq: 2; Began: 1976; Lang: Eng; Subj: Related. ISSN: 0145-5311
■Students' African Studies Society, Univ. of Witwatersrand; 1 Jan Smuts Ave; 2001 Johannesburg; SOUTH AFRICA.

AfricaP *Africa Perspective*. Freq: 2; Began: 1976; Lang: Eng; Subj: Related. ISSN: 0145-5311
AFS

AfricaP *Africa Perspective*. Freq: 2; Began: 1976; Lang: Eng; Subj: Related. ISSN: 0145-5311

Australian Feminist Studies

AfricaP *Africa Perspective*. Freq: 2; Began: 1976; Lang: Eng; Subj: Related. ISSN: 0145-5311

AfricaP *Africa Perspective*. Freq: 2; Began: 1976; Lang: Eng; Subj: Related. ISSN: 0145-5311
Freq: 2;

AfricaP *Africa Perspective*. Freq: 2; Began: 1976; Lang: Eng; Subj: Related. ISSN: 0145-5311

AfricaP *Africa Perspective*. Freq: 2; Began: 1976; Lang: Eng; Subj: Related. ISSN: 0145-5311
Began: 1991;

AfricaP *Africa Perspective*. Freq: 2; Began: 1976; Lang: Eng; Subj: Related. ISSN: 0145-5311
Lang: Eng

AfricaP *Africa Perspective*. Freq: 2; Began: 1976; Lang: Eng; Subj: Related. ISSN: 0145-5311
; Subj: Related.

AfricaP *Africa Perspective*. Freq: 2; Began: 1976; Lang: Eng; Subj: Related.
ISSN: 0816-4649

AfricaP *Africa Perspective*. Freq: 2; Began: 1976; Lang: Eng; Subj: Related.
■Research Centre for Women's Studies

AfricaP *Africa Perspective*. Freq: 2; Began: 1976; Lang: Eng; Subj: Related.
;

AfricaP *Africa Perspective*. Freq: 2; Began: 1976; Lang: Eng; Subj: Related.
University of Adelaide;

AfricaP *Africa Perspective*. Freq: 2; Began: 1976; Lang: Eng; Subj: Related.
South Australia, 5005

AfricaP *Africa Perspective*. Freq: 2; Began: 1976; Lang: Eng; Subj: Related.
; AUSTRALIA

AfricaP *Africa Perspective*. Freq: 2; Began: 1976; Lang: Eng; Subj: Related.

AfTR *African Theatre Review*. Freq: IRR; Began: 1985; Lang: Eng; Subj: Theatre.
■Dept. of African Literature, Fac. of Letters & Social Science; University Yaoumde, PO Box 755; Yaounde; CAMEROON.

AG *An Gael*: Irish Traditional Culture Alive in America Today. Freq: 4; Began: 1975; Lang: Eng; Subj: Related.
■An Claidheamh Soluis, The Irish Arts Center; 553 W. 51st Street; New York, NY 10019; USA.

AHA *Aha! Hispanic Arts News*. Freq: 10; Began: 1976; Lang: Eng/Spa; Subj: Related.
ISSN: 0732-1643
■Association of Hispanic Arts; 200 E. 87 St.; New York, NY 10028; USA.

AHAT *Al-Hayat At-T'aqafiyya*. Lang: Ara; Subj: Theatre.
■Ministère des Affaires Culturelles; La Kasbah; Tunis; TUNISIA.

AHS *Australian Historical Studies*. Formerly: *Historical Studies*. Freq: 2 Began: 1988; Cov: Scan; Lang: Eng; Subj: Related. ISSN: 0018-2559
■Dept. of History; University of Melbourne; Parkville, Victoria 3052; AUSTRALIA.

AICRJ *American Indian Culture & Research Journal*. Freq: 4; Lang: Eng; Subj: Related.
■American Indian Studies Center; 3220 Campbell Hall; UCLA Los Angeles, CA 90095-1548; USA.

AInf *Artists and Influences*. Freq: 1; Began: 1981; Cov: Scan; Lang: Eng; Subj: Related.
■Hatch-Billops Collection, Inc.; 691 Broadway; New York, NY; USA.

AIT *Annuaire International du Théâtre*: SEE: Miedzynarodowny Rocznik Teatralny (Acro: MRT). Freq: 1; Began: 1977; Lang: Fre/Eng; Subj: Theatre.
■Warsaw; POLAND.

AIWAT *Al-Idaa Wa At-Talfaza*. Lang: Ara; Subj: Theatre.
■R.T.T.; 71 Avenue de la Liberté; Tunis; TUNISIA.

AJCS *Australian Journal of Cultural Studies*. Freq: 3; Began: 1983; Ceased: 1987; Cov: Scan; Lang: Eng; Subj: Related. ISSN: 0810-9648
■School of English; Western Australian Institute of Technology; Bentley, Western Australia 6102; AUSTRALIA.

AJChA *Australian Journal of Chinese Affairs*. Freq: 2; Began: 1979; Cov: Scan; Lang: Eng. ISSN: 0156-7365
■Contemporary China Centre, Research School of Pacific Studies, Australia National University; GPO Box 4; Canberra, ACT 2601; AUSTRALIA.

AJFS *Australian Journal of French Studies*. Freq: 3; Began: 1964; Lang: Eng; Subj: Related. ISSN: 0004-9468
■Dept. of Modern Languages; Monash University; Wellington Road, Clayton, Victoria 3168; AUSTRALIA.

AKT *AKT*: Aktuelles Theater. Freq: 12; Began: 1969; Lang: Ger; Subj: Theatre.
■Frankfurter Bund für Volksbildung GmbH; Eschersheimer Landstrasse 2; 6000 Frankfurt/1, W; GERMANY.

AL *American Literature*. Freq: 4; Began: 1929; Lang: Eng; Subj: Related.
ISSN: 0002-9831
■Duke Univ. Press, Box 6697; College Station; Durham, NC 27708; USA.

Alfold *Alföld*. Freq: 12; Began: 1954; Cov: Scan; Lang: Hun; Subj: Related. ISSN: 0401-3174
■Alföld Alapítvány, Csokonai Kft.; Piac u. 26/A. I; 4024 Debrecen; HUNGARY.

Alif *Alif*. Lang: Fre; Subj: Theatre.
■24 rue Gamel Abdel-Nasser; Tunis; TUNISIA.

Alive *Alive*: The New Performance Magazine. Freq: 24; Began: 1982; Lang: Eng; Subj: Theatre.
■New York, NY; USA.

Almanach *Almanach Sceny Polskiej*. Freq: 1; Began: 1961; Lang: Pol; Subj: Theatre. ISSN: 0065-6526
■Wydawnicta Artystyczne i Filmowe; Pulawska 61; 02 595 Warsaw; POLAND.

ALS *Australian Literary Studies*. Freq: 2; Began: 1963; Cov: Scan; Lang: Eng; Subj: Related. ISSN: 0004-9697
■Univ. of Queensland, Dept. of English; Box 88; St. Lucia; Queensland 4067; AUSTRALIA.

Altaj *Altaj*. Began: 1947; Cov: Scan; Lang: Rus; Subj: Related. ISSN: 0320-7447
■Krupskaja Street, Building 91A; Barnaul City; RUSSIA.

AltR *Alternate Roots*. Lang: Eng; Subj: Related.
■1083 Austin Ave., N.E.; Atlanta, GA 30307; USA.

AltT *Alternatives Théâtrales*. Freq: 4; Began: 1979; Cov: Scan; Lang: Fre; Subj: Theatre.
■13 rue des Poissonniers, bte 15-1000 Brussels; BELGIUM.

AmatS *Amateur Stage*. Freq: 12; Began: 1946; Lang: Eng; Subj: Theatre. ISSN: 0002-6867
■Platform Publications Ltd.; 83 George Street; London W1H 5PL; UK.

AmatT *Amateur Theatre Yearbook*. Freq: 1; Began: 1988; Lang: Eng; Subj: Theatre.
■Platform Publications Ltd.; 83 George Street; London W1H 5PL; UK.

AmerD *American Drama*. Freq: 2; Began: 1991; Cov: Full; Lang: Eng; Subj: Theatre. ISSN: 1061-0057
■American Drama Institute; Department of English; ML 69, University of Cincinnati Cincinnati, OH 45221-0069; USA.

AmerM *American Music*. Freq: 4; Began: 1983; Lang: Eng; Subj: Related. ISSN: 0734-4392
■University of Illinois Press; Box 5081, Station A; Champaign, IL 61820; USA.

AMN *Arts Management Newsletter*. Freq: 5; Began: 1962; Lang: Eng; Subj: Related. ISSN: 0004-4067
■Radius Group, Inc.; 408 W. 57th Street; New York, NY 10019; USA.

AmS *Amaterska Scena*: Ochotnicke divadlo. Freq: 12; Began: 1964; Lang: Cze; Subj: Theatre. ISSN: 0002-6786
■Panorama; Halkova 1; 120 72 Prague 2; CZECH REPUBLIC.

AmTh *American Theatre*. Formerly: *Theatre Communications*. Freq: 11; Began: 1984; Cov: Full; Lang: Eng; Subj: Theatre. ISSN: 0275-5971
■Theatre Communications Group; 355 Lexington Avenue; New York, NY 10017; USA.

Amyri *Amyri*. Freq: 4; Lang: Fin; Subj: Theatre.
■Suomen Nayttelijaliitto r.y.; Arkadiankatu 12 A 18; 00100 Helsinki 10/52; FINLAND.

Anim *Animations*: Review of Puppets and Related Theatre. Freq: 6; Began: 1977; Cov: Scan; Lang: Eng; Subj: Theatre. ISSN: 0140-7740
■Puppet Centre Trust, Battersea Arts Centre; Lavender Hill; London SW11 5TN; UK.

Annuel *Annuel de Théâtre*. Freq: 1; Lang: Fre; Subj: Theatre.
■Association Loi de 1901; 30, rue de la Belgique; 92190 Meudon; FRANCE.

AnSt *Another Standard*. Freq: 6; Ceased: 1986; Cov: Scan; Lang: Eng; Subj: Related.
■PO Box 900; B70 6JP West Bromwich; UK.

AnT *Annuaire Théâtral, L'*. Freq: 1; Lang: Fre; Subj: Theatre. ISSN: 0827-0198
■Societe d'histoire du theatre du Quebec; Montreal, PQ; CANADA.

Antipodes *Antipodes*. Freq: 1; Began: 1987; Cov: Scan; Lang: Eng; Subj: Related. ISSN: 0893-5580
■American Association of Australian Literary Studies; 190 6th Avenue; Brooklyn, NY 11217; USA.

Antithesis *Antithesis*. Freq: 3; Began: 1987; Cov: Full; Lang: Eng; Subj: Related. ISSN: 1030-3839
■English Department; University of Melbourne; Parkville Victoria 3052; AUSTRALIA.

ANZSC *Australian and New Zealand Studies in Canada*. Freq: 2; Began: 1989; Cov: Scan; Lang: Eng; Subj: Related. ISSN: 0843-5049
■Dept. of English; University of Western Ontario London ON N6A 3K7 CANADA.

ANZTR *Australian and New Zealand Theatre Record*. Freq: 12; Lang: Eng; Subj: Theatre. ISSN: 1032-0091
■Australian Theatre Studies Centre; University of New South Wales; Sydney NSW 2052; AUSTRALIA.

Apollo *Apollo*: The international magazine of art and antiques. Freq: 12; Began: 1925; Lang: Eng; Subj: Related. ISSN: 0003-6536
■Apollo Magazine Ltd.; 45-46 Poland Street; London W1V 4AU; UK.

Apuntes *Apuntes*. Freq: 2; Began: 1960; Lang: Spa; Subj: Theatre. ISSN: 0716-4440
■Universidad Católica de Chile, Escuela de Artes de la Comunicacion; Diagonal Oriente 3300, Casilla 114D; Santiago; CHILE.

AQ *American Quarterly*. Freq: 24; Began: 1949; Lang: Eng; Subj: Related. ISSN: 0003-0678
■Univ. of Philadelphia; 307 College Hall; Philadelphia, PA 19104 6303; USA.

Araldo *Araldo dello Spettacolo, L'*. Lang: Ita; Subj: Theatre.
■Via Aureliana 63; Rome; ITALY.

Archivio *Archivio del Teatro Italiano*. Freq: IRR; Began: 1968; Lang: Ita; Subj: Theatre. ISSN: 0066-6661
■Edizioni Il Polifilo; Via Borgonuovo 2; 20121 Milan; ITALY.

Arco *Arcoscenico*. Freq: 12; Began: 1945; Lang: Ita; Subj: Theatre.
■Sindacato nazionale autori drammatici; Via Ormisda 10; Rome; ITALY.

AReview *Arts Review*. Freq: 4; Began: 1983; Ceased: 1988; Lang: Eng; Subj: Related.
■National Endowment for the Arts; 1100 Pennsylvania Avenue NW; Washington, DC 20506; USA.

Ariel *Ariel*. Freq: 3; Began: 1986; Cov: Full; Lang: Ita; Subj: Theatre. ISSN: 0901-9901
■Instituto di Studi Pirandelliani; Bulzoni Editore; Via dei Liburni n. 14; 00185 Rome; ITALY.

ArielR *Ariel:Review of International English Literature*; Began: 1970; Cov: Scan; Lang: Eng; Subj: Related.
■University of Calgary; CANADA.

Ark *Arkkitehti*: The Finnish Architectural Review. Freq: 6; Began: 1903; Cov: Scan; Lang: Fin/ Eng; Subj: Related. ISSN: 0004-2129
■The Finnish Association of Architects; Yrjönkatu 11 A; 00120 Helsinki; FINLAND.

ArkSSSR *Arkhitektura S.S.S.R.* Freq: 6; Ceased: 1991; Cov: Scan; Lang: Rus; Subj: Related. ISSN: 0004-1939
■Schuseva Street 7; Room 60; 103001 Moscow; RUSSIA.

ArNy *Arte Nyt*. Lang: Dut; Subj: Related.
■Hvidkildevej 64; 2400 Copenhagen NV; DENMARK.

Arrel *Arrel*. Freq: 4; Cov: Scan; Lang: Spa; Subj: Theatre.
■Disputacio de Barcelona; Placa de Sant Juame 1; 08002 Barcelona; SPAIN.

ArsU *Ars-Uomo*. Freq: 12; Began: 1975; Lang: Ita; Subj: Theatre.

■Bulzoni Editore; Via F. Cocco Ortu 120; 00139 Rome; ITALY.

Art&A *Art and Australia*. Freq: 4; Began: 1963; Cov: Scan; Lang: Eng; Subj: Related. ISSN: 0004-301x;
■Fine Arts Press Pty Ltd; P.O. Box 480; Roseville, NSW 2069; AUSTRALIA.

ArtL *Artlink*. Freq: 6; Began: 1981; Cov: Full; Lang: Eng; Subj: Theatre. ISSN: 0727-1239
■363 The Esplanade; Henley Beach S.A. 5022; AUSTRALIA.

ArtP *Art-Press (International)*. Freq: 12; Began: 1976; Ceased: 1979; Cov: Scan; Lang: Fre; Subj: Related. ISSN: 0245-5676
■Paris; FRANCE.

ArtsAd *Arts Advocate*. Freq: 3; Began: 1988; Lang: Eng Formerly: *In the Arts*; Subj: Theatre.
■Ohio State University College of the Arts; Office of Communications; 30 West 15th Ave. Columbus, OH 43210-1305; USA.

ArtsAtl *Arts Atlantic*: Atlantic Canada's Journal of the Arts. Freq: 4; Began: 1977; Cov: Scan; Lang: Eng; Subj: Related. ISSN: 0704-7916
■Confederation Centre of the Arts; 145 Richmond St.; Charlottetown, PE C1A 9Z9; CANADA.

ArtsRS *Arts Reporting Service, The*. Freq: 24; Began: 1970; Ceased: 1976; Lang: Eng; Subj: Related. ISSN: 0196-4186
■Charles Christopher Mark; PO Box 39008; Washington, DC 20016; USA.

ASabah *As-Sabah*. Freq: Daily; Began: 1951; Lang: Ara; Subj: Theatre.
■Avenue Du 7 Novembre; P.O. Box 441 Tunis 1004; TUNISIA.

ASamvad *Abhnaya Samvad*. Freq: 12; Lang: Hin; Subj: Theatre.
■20 Muktaram Babu Street; Calcutta; INDIA.

ASBelg *Arts du Spectacle en Belgique*. Formerly: *Centre d'Etudes Theatrales, Louvain: Annuaire*. Freq: IRR; Began: 1968; Ceased: 1991; Lang: Fre; Subj: Theatre. ISSN: 0069-1860
■Université Catholique de Louvain, Centre d'Etudes Théâtrales; 1, place de l'Université; 1348 Louvain-la-Neuve; BELGIUM.

AScene *Autre Scène, L'*. Lang: Fre; Subj: Theatre.
■Editions Albatros; 14 rue de l'Amérique; 75015 Paris; FRANCE.

ASCFB *Annuaire du Spectacle de la Communauté Française de Belgique*. Freq: 1; Began: 1981; Lang: Fre; Subj: Theatre.
■Archives et Musée de la Littérature, ASBL; 4 Bd de l'Empereur; 1000 Brussels; BELGIUM.

ASInt *American Studies International*. Freq: 4; Began: 1975; Ceased: 1983; Cov: Scan; Lang: Eng; Subj: Related. ISSN: 0003-1321
■American Studies Program, George Washington University; Washington, DC 20052; USA.

ASO *Avant Scène Opéra, L'*. Freq: 6; Began 1976; Lang Fre Subj Theatre. ISSN: 0764-2873
■15 rue Tiquetonne; 75002 Paris; FRANCE.

ASSAPHc *ASSAPH*: Section C. Studies in the Theatre. Freq: 1; Began: 1984; Cov: Full; Lang: Eng; Subj: Theatre. ISSN: 0334-5963

■Dept. of Theatre Arts, Tel Aviv University; 69978 Ramat Aviv Tel Aviv; ISRAEL.

AST *Avant Scène Théâtre, L'*. Freq: 20; Began: 1949; Cov: Scan; Lang: Fre; Subj: Theatre. ISSN: 0045-1169
■Editions de l'Avant Scène; 6 rue Git-le-Coeur; 75006 Paris; FRANCE.

AStage *American Stage*. Freq: 10; Began: 1979; Lang: Eng; Subj: Theatre.
■American Stage Publishing Company; 217 East 28th Street; New York, NY 10016; USA.

ASTRN *ASTR Newsletter*. Freq: 2; Began: 1972; Cov: Scan; Lang: Eng; Subj: Theatre. ISSN: 0044-7927
■American Society for Theatre Research, C.W. Post College; Department of English; Brookvale, NY 11548; USA.

AT *AkademiceskieTetrady*. Freq: 4; Began: 1996; Cov: Scan; Lang: Rus; Subj: Related.
■20 Ul. Povarskaja; Moscow 121069; RUSSIA.

ATAC *Aujourd'hui Tendances Art Culture*. Formerly: *Partenaires*. Lang: Fre; Subj: Related.
■FRANCE.

ATArg *Annuario del Teatro Argentino*. Freq: 1; Lang: Spa; Subj: Theatre.
■F.N.A.; Calle Alsina 673; Buenos Aires; ARGENTINA.

ATB *Annuario do Teatro Brasileiro*. Freq: 1; Began: 1976; Lang: Por; Subj: Theatre.
■Ministerio da Educacao e Cultura; Service Nacional de Teatro; Rio de Janeiro; BRAZIL.

AtG *Around the Globe*. Freq: 2; Began: 1996; Cov: Scan; Lang: Eng; Subj: Theatre. ISSN: 1366-2317
■Shakespeare's Globe; 1 Bear Gardens; Bankside London SE1 9ED; UK.

ATJ *Asian Theatre Journal*. Formerly: *Asian Theatre Reports*. Freq: 2; Began: 1984; Cov: Full; Lang: Eng; Subj: Theatre. ISSN: 0742-5457
■Univ. of Hawaii Press; 2840 Kolowalu Street; Honolulu, HI 96822; USA.

ATT *Amers Theatrical Times*. Freq: 12; Began: 1976; Lang: Eng; Subj: Related.
■William Amer (Pty) Ltd.; 15 Montgomery Avenue; NSW 2142 South Granville; AUSTRALIA.

Audiences *Audiences Magazine*. Freq: 12; Last Known Address; Lang: Fre; Subj: Theatre.
■55 avenue Jean Jaurés; 75019 Paris; FRANCE.

AuJCom *Australian Journal of Communication*. Freq: 2; Began: 1982; Cov: Scan; Lang: Eng; Subj: Related. ISSN: 0810-6202
■Queensland University of Technology; GPO Box 2434; Brisbane Qld 4001; AUSTRALIA.

AULLA *Journal of the Australian Universities Language & Literature Association*. Freq: 2; Began: 1953; Cov: Scan; Lang: Eng; Subj: Related. ISSN: 0001-2793
■Australasian Universities Language & Literature Association; Monash University; Clayton, Victoria 3168; AUSTRALIA.

Autor *Autor, Der*. Freq: 2; Began: 1926; Cov: Scan; Lang: Ger; Subj: Related. ISSN: 0344-7197
■Dramatiker-Union, Eckhard Schulz; Babelsberger Str. 43; D-10715 Berlin; GERMANY.

Autores *Autores*. Freq: 4; Lang: Por; Subj: Theatre.
■Sociedade Portuguesa de Autores; Av. Duque de Loule, 31; 1098 Lisbon Codex; PORTUGAL.

Avrora *Avrora*. Freq: 12; Began: 1969; Cov: Scan; Lang: Rus; Subj: Related. ISSN: 0320-6858
■4 Millionnaja Ul; St. Petersburg 191186; RUSSIA.

AWBR *Australian Women's Book Review*. Freq: 1; Began: 1988; Cov: Scan; Lang: Eng; Subj: Related. ISSB: 1033-9434
■Carole Ferrier; Dept. of English, University of Queensland; Brisbane 4072; AUSTRALIA.

Bal *Balrangmanch*. Freq: 6; Lang: Hin; Subj: Theatre.
■Post Box No. 37, G.P.O.; Lueknowy; 226001; INDIA.

Bahub *Bahubacana*. Began: 1978; Lang: Ben; Subj: Theatre.
■Bahubacana Natyagoshthi; 11/2 Jaynag Road, Bakshi Bazar; Dhaka 1; BANGLADESH.

Balet *Balet*. Freq: 6; Cov: Scan; Began: 1992; Lang: Rus; Subj: Theatre. ISSN: 0207-4788
■Tverskaja St.; Moscow 103050; RUSSIA.

BALF *Black American Literature Forum*. Formerly: *Negro American Literature*. Freq: 4; Began: 1967; Ceased: 1991; Cov: Scan; Lang: Eng; Subj: Related. ISSN: 0148-6179
■Parsons Hall 237, Indiana State Univ.; Terre Haute, IN 47809; USA.

Balkon *Balkon*. Freq: 12; Began: 1993; Cov: Scan; Lang: Hun; Subj: Related. ISSN: 1216-8890
■Enciklopédia Kiadó; Bartók Béla út 82; 1113 Budapest; HUNGARY.

Bamah *Bamah*: Educational Theatre Review. Freq: 4; Began: 1959; Cov: Full; Lang: Heb; Subj: Theatre. ISSN: 0045-138X
■Bamah Association; PO Box 7098; 910 70 Jerusalem; ISRAEL.

BAMu *Buenos Aires Musical*. Freq: IRR; Began: 1946; Lang Spa; Subj: Theatre. ISSN: 0007-3113
■Calle Alsina 912; Buenos Aires; ARGENTINA.

Band *Bandwagon*. Freq: 6; Began: 1939; Cov: Scan; Lang: Eng; Subj: Theatre. ISSN: 0005-4968
■Circus Historical Society; 2515 Dorset Road; Columbus, OH 43221; USA.

BaNe *Ballet News*. Freq: 12; Began: 1979; Lang: Eng; Subj: Related. ISSN: 0191-2690
■Metropolitan Opera Guild, Inc.; 1865 Broadway; New York, NY 10023; USA.

BANY *Black Arts New York*. Freq: 10; Cov: Scan; Lang: Eng; Subj: Related. ISSN: 1057-4239
■215 West 125th St. Dr. Martin Luther King, Jr. Blvd; 4th Floor New York, NY 10027; USA.

BASSITEJ *Bulletin ASSITEJ*. Formerly: *Bulletin d'Information ASSITEJ*. Freq: 3; Began: 1966; Ceased: 1994; Lang: Fre/Eng/Rus; Subj: Theatre.
■ASSITEJ; Celetna 17; 110 01 Prague 1; CZECH REPUBLIC.

BCl *Beckett Circle/Cercle de Beckett*. Freq: 2; Began: 1978; Lang: Eng/Fre; Subj: Theatre. ISSN: 0732-2224
■Samuel Beckett Society; University of California at Los Angeles; Los Angeles, CA 90024; USA.

BCom *Bulletin of the Comediantes*. Freq: 2; Began: 1949; Lang: Eng/ Spa; Subj: Theatre. ISSN: 0007-5108
■James A. Parr, Dept. of Spa. & Portuguese; University of California; Riverside, CA 92521; USA.

BelgITI *Bulletin*: Van het Belgisch Centrum ITI. Ceased; Lang: Fre; Subj: Theatre.
■Belgisch Centrum van het ITI, c/o Mark Hermans; Rudolfstraat 33; B 2000 Antwerp; BELGIUM.

Bergens *Bergens Theatermuseum Skrifter*. Began: 1970; Lang: Nor; Subj: Theatre.
■Bergens Theatermuseum, Kolstadgt 1; Box 2959 Toeyen; 6 Oslo; NORWAY.

Bericht *Bericht*. Lang: Ger; Subj: Theatre. ISSN: 0067-6047
■UMLOsterreichischer Bundestheaterverband; Goethegasse 1; A 1010 Vienna; AUSTRIA.

BFant *Botteghe della Fantasia, Le*. Last Known Address; Began: 1979; Lang: Ita; Subj: Theatre.
■Via S. Manlio 13; Milan; ITALY.

BGs *Bühnengenossenschaft*. Freq: 12; Began: 1949; Lang: Ger; Subj: Theatre. ISSN: 0007-3083
■Bühnenschriften-Vertriebs-Gesellschaft; Pf. 13 02 70; D-20102 Hamburg; GERMANY.

BGTA *Bibliographic Guide to Theatre Arts*. Freq: 1; Lang: Eng; Subj: Theatre. ISSN: 0360-2788
■G. K. Hall & Co.; 70 Lincoln Street; Boston, MA 02111; USA.

BI *Ballet International/tanz aktuell*: Aktuelle Monatszeitung für Ballett und Tanztheater. Formerly: *Ballet Info*. Freq: 12; Began: 1978; Lang: Ger; Subj: Related. ISSN: 0947-0484
■Friedrich Berlin Verlagsges; mbH, Lützowplatz 7; D-10785 Berlin; GERMANY.

BIINET *Boletin informativo del Instituto Nacional de Estudios de Teatro*. Freq: 10; Began: 1978; Lang: Spa; Subj: Theatre.
■1055 Avenida Cordoba; 1199 Buenos Aires; ARGENTINA.

Biladi *Biladi*. Lang: Ara; Subj: Theatre.
■Parti Socialiste Desourien, Maison du Parti, BP 1033; Blvd. du 9 Avril, La Kasbah; Tunis; TUNISIA.

BiT *Biblioteca Teatrale*. Freq: 4; Began: 1986; Cov: Full; Lang: Ita; Subj: Theatre. ISSN: 0045-1959
■Bulzoni Editore; 14 Via dei Liburni; 00185 Rome; ITALY.

BITIJ *Boletin Iberoamericano de Teatro para la Infancia y la Juventud*. Lang: Spa; Subj: Theatre.
■Associación Española de Teatro para la Infancia y la Juventud; Claudio Coello 141; 6 Madrid; SPAIN.

BJDT *Ballett-Journal/Das Tanzarchiv*. Freq: 5; Began: 1953; Cov: Scan; Lang: Ger; Subject: Related. ISSN 0720-3896

■Zeitung für Tanzpädagogik und Ballett-Theater; Ulrich Steiner Verlag; Obersteinbach 5 a D-51429 Bergisch Gladbach; GERMANY.

BK ***Bauten der Kultur***. Freq: IRR; Began: 1976; Lang: Ger; Subj: Related.
ISSN: 0323-5696
■Institut für Kulturbauten; Clara-Zetkin-Strasse 105; 1080 Berlin; GERMANY.

BKK ***Bühne Kursbuch Kultur***. Freq: 2; Cov: Scan; Lang: Ger; Subj: Related.
■Orac Zeitschriftenverlag GmbH; Schönbrunner Str. 59-61; A-1010 Vienna; GERMANY.

BlackM ***Black Masks***. Freq: 12; Began: 1984; Cov: Scan; Lang: Eng; Subj: Related.
■P.O. Box 2; Bronx, NY 10471; USA.

BlC ***Black Collegian, The***: The National Magazine of Black College Students. Formerly: *Expressions*. Freq: IRR; Began: 1970; Cov: Scan; Lang: Eng; Subj: Related.
ISSN: 0192-3757
■Black Collegiate Services, Inc.; 1240 South Broad Street; New Orleans, LA 70125; USA.

BM ***Burlington Magazine***. Freq: 12; Began: 1903; Cov: Scan; Lang: Eng; Subj: Related.
ISSN: 0007-6287
■Burlington Magazine Publications; 6 Bloomsbury Square; London WC1A 2LP; UK.

BMI ***BMI Music World***. Freq: 4 Began: 1964; Lang: Eng; Subj: Related.
■New York, NY; USA.

BMP ***Bulletin Magische Plätze***. Freq: 12; Cov: Scan; Lang: Ger; Subj: Related.
■B. Kohler Verlag; Wydlerweg 17; CH-8047 Zurich; SWITZERLAND.

BMT ***Biuletyn Mlodego Teatru***. Last Known Address; Began: 1978; Lang: Pol; Subj: Theatre.
■Gwido Zlatkes; Bednarska 24 m; 00 321 Warsaw; POLAND.

BNJMtd ***Biblioteca Nacional José Marti***: Informacion y Documentacion de la Cultura. Serie Teatro y Danza. Freq: 12; Lang: Spa; Subj: Theatre.
■Biblioteca Nacional José Marti, Dept. Info. y Doc. de Cultura; Plaza de la Revolución; Havana; CUBA.

BNS ***Builder N.S.*** Formerly: *Builder N.S.W..* Freq: 12; Began: 1907; Cov: Scan; Lang: Eng; Subj: Related.
■Master Builders Asso. of New South Wales; Private Bag 9; Broadway; N.S.W. 2007; AUSTRALIA.Tel: 660-7188.

Bomb ***Bomb***. Freq: 4; Cov: Scan; Lang: Eng; Subj: Related.
■New Arts Publications; 594 Broadway, 10th Flr.; New York,, NY 10012; USA.

BooksC ***Books in Canada***. Freq: 9; Began: 1971; Cov: Scan; Lang: Eng/Fre; Subj: Related.
ISSN: 0045-2564
■Canadian Review of Books, Ltd.; 130 Spadina Ave.; Suite 603 Toronto, ON M5V 2L4; CANADA.

Bouff ***Bouffonneries***. Began: 1980; Lang: Fre; Subj: Theatre.
ISSN: 028-4455
■Domaine de Lestanière; 11000 Cazilhac; FRANCE.

BPAN ***British Performing Arts Newsletter***. Ceased: 1980; Lang: Eng; Subj: Related.
■London; UK.

BPM ***Black Perspective in Music***. Freq: 2; Began: 1973; Ceased: 1990; Cov: Scan; Lang: Eng; Subj: Related.
ISSN: 0090-7790
■Foundation for Research in the Afro-American Creative Arts; P.O. Drawer One; Cambria Heights, NY 11411; USA.

BPTV ***Bühne und Parkett***: Theater Journal Volksbühnen-Spiegel. Formerly: *Volksbuhnen-Spiegel*. Freq: 3; Began: 1955; Lang: Ger; Subj: Theatre. ISSN: 0172-1321
■Verband der deutschen Volksbühne e.v.; Bismarckstrasse 17; 1000 Berlin 12; GERMANY.

BR ***Ballet Review***. Freq: 4; Began: 1965; Lang: Eng; Subj: Related. ISSN: 0522-0653
■Dance Research Foundation, Inc.; 46 Morton Street; New York, NY 10014; USA.

BrechtJ ***Brecht Jahrbuch***. Freq: 1; Began: 1971; Ceased: 1987; Lang: Ger/Eng/Fre; Subj: Theatre.
■Wayne State University; 5959 Woodward Ave.; Detroit, MI 48202; USA.

Brs ***Broadside***. Freq: 4; Began: 1940; Lang: Eng; Subj: Theatre. ISSN: 0068-2748
■Theatre Library Assoc.; 111 Amsterdam Avenue; New York, NY 10023; USA.

BSK ***Bundesverband Studentische Kulturarbeit***. Freq: 4; Cov: Scan; Lang: Ger; Subj: Related. ISBN: 3-927451-11-8
■BSK, Berliner Platz 31; D-53111 Bonn; GERMANY.

BSOAS ***Bulletin of the School of Oriental & African Studies***. Lang: Eng; Subj: Related. London; UK.

BSPC ***Bulletin de la Société Paul Claudel***. Freq: IRR; Lang: Fre; Subj: Related.13, rue du Pont Louis-Philippe; 75004 Paris; FRANCE.

BSSJ ***Bernard Shaw Newsletter***. Formerly: *Newsletter & Journal of the Shaw Society of London*. Freq: 1; Began: 1976; Lang: Eng; Subj: Related.
■Bernard Shaw Centre, High Orchard; 125 Markyate Road; EM8 2LB Dagenahm, Essex; UK.

BT ***Berliner Theaterwissenschaft***. Freq: 1; Began: 1995; Lang: Ger; Subj: Theatre.
ISSN: 0948-7646
■Vistas Verlag Gmbh; Bismarckstr. 84; D-10627 Berlin; GERMANY.

BTA ***Börneteateravisen***. Freq: 4; Began: 1972; Lang: Dan; Subj: Theatre.
■Teatercentrum i Danmark; Frederiksborggade 20; 1360 Copenhagen; DENMARK.

BTlog ***British Theatrelog***. Freq: 4; Began: 1978; Ceased: 1980; Lang: Eng; Subj: Theatre.
ISSN: 0141-9056
■Associate British Centre of the ITI; 15 Hanover Sq.; London WIR 9AJ; UK.

BtR ***Bühnentechnische Rundschau***: Zeitschrift für Theatertechnik, Bühnenbau und Bühnengestaltung. Freq: 6; Began: 1907; Cov: Scan; Lang: Ger/Eng/Fre; Subj: Theatre.
ISSN: 0007-3091
■Erhard Friedrich Verlag; Postfach 10 01 50; D-30917 Seelze; SWITZERLAND.

BudN ***Budapesti Negyed***. Freq: 4; Began: 1993; Cov: Scan; Lang: Hun; Subj: Related.
ISSN: 1217-5846
■Budapest Fovaros Leveltara; Katona Jozsef u. 24; 1137 Budapest; HUNGARY.

Buhne ***Bühne, Die***. Freq: 11; Began: 1958; Lang: Ger; Subj: Theatre. ISSN: 0007-3075
■Orac Zeitschriftenverlag GmbH; Schönbrunner Str. 59-61; A1010 Vienna; AUSTRIA.

Buhnent ***Bühnentarifrecht***. Freq: 4; Cov: Scan; Lang: Ger; Subj: Related. ISBN: 3-7685-2731-X
■R.v. Decker's Verlag; Hüthig GmbH, Pf. 102869; D-69018 Heidelberg; GERMANY.

BulS ***Bulletin***. Freq: 10; Cov: Scan; Lang: Ger/Fre; Subj: Related.
■Schweizerischer Dachverband der Fachkräfte des künstlerischen Tanzes SDT

BulS ***Bulletin***. Freq: 10; Cov: Scan; Lang: Ger/Fre; Subj: Related.
; Dufourstr. 45; CH-3005 Bern; SWITZERLAND.

BulV ***Bulletin***. Freq: 4; Began: 1974; Cov: Scan; Lang: Ger/Fre/Ita; Subj: Related.
■Vereinigun fü Künstler/innen Theate Veranstalter/innen; Schweiz (KTV); Pf. 3350 CH-2500 Biel 3; SWITZERLAND.

BuM ***Bühnen- und Musikrecht***. Cov: Scan; Lang: Ger; Subj: Related.
■Mykenae Verlag Rossberg KG; Ahastr. 9; D-64285 Darmstadt; GERMANY.

BY ***Brecht Yearbook***. Freq: 1; Lang: Eng; Subj: Theatre.
■German Department; 818 Van Hise Hall; University of Wisconsin Madison, WI 53706; USA.

CahiersC ***Cahiers Césariens***. Freq: 2; Began: 1974; Lang: Eng/Fre; Subj: Theatre.
■Pennsylvania State University, Dept. of French; University Park, PA 16802; USA.

CahiersCC ***Cahiers CERT/CIRCE***. Lang: Fre; Subj: Theatre.
■Centre Etudes Recherches Théâtrale, Université de Bordeaux III; Esplanade des Antilles; 33405 Talence; FRANCE.

Callaloo ***Callaloo***: A Black South Journal of Arts and Letters. Freq: 3; Began: 1976; Cov: Scan; Lang: Eng; Subj: Related. ISSN: 0161-2492
■Department of English; 322 Bryan Hall; University of Virginia Charlottesville, VA 22903; USA.

CallB ***Call Boy, The***: Journal of the British Music Hall Society. Freq: 4; Began: 1963; Lang: Eng; Subj: Theatre.
■British Music Hall Society; 32 Hazelbourne Road; London SW12; UK.

Callboard ***Callboard***. Freq: 4; Began: 1951; Lang: Eng; Subj: Theatre. ISSN: 0045-4044
■1809 Barrington St., Ste. 901; Halifax, NS B3J 3K8; CANADA.

Calliope ***Calliope***. Freq: 12; Began: 1968; Lang: Eng; Subj: Theatre.
■Clowns of America Inc.; 1052 Foxwood Ln.; Baltimore, MD 21221; USA.

CAM ***City Arts Monthly***. Freq: 12; Lang: Eng; Subj: Related.
■640 Natoma St.; San Francisco, CA 94103; USA.

CanL *Canadian Literature/Littérature Canadienne*: A Quarterly of Criticism and Review. Freq: 4; Began: 1959; Cov: Scan; Lang: Eng/Fre; Subj: Related.   ISSN: 0008-4360
■University of British Columbia; 2029 West Mall; Vancouver, BC V6T 1Z2; CANADA.

Caratula *Caratula*. Freq: 12; Last Known Address; Lang: Spa; Subj: Theatre.
■Sanchez Pacheco 83; 2 Madrid; SPAIN.

Carnet *Carnet*. Cov: Scan; Began: 1994; Lang: Eng /Fre; Subj: Related. ISSN: 0929-936x
■Theater Institut Nederland; Herengracht 168-1016 BP Amsterdam; NETHERLANDS.

Castelets *Castelets*. Lang: Fre; Subj: Theatre.
■Centre Provincial de la Marionnette de Namur; Rue des Brasseurs 109; 5000 Namur; BELGIUM.

CB *Call Board*. Formerly: *Monthly Theatre Magazine of TCCBA*. Freq: IRR; Began: 1931; Lang: Eng; Subj: Theatre.
                    ISSN: 0008-1701
■Theatre Bay Area; 657 Mission Street, Ste. 402; San Francisco, CA 94116; USA.

CBGB *Cahiers de la Bibliothèque Gaston Baty*. Lang: Fre; Subj: Related.
■Paris; FRANCE.

CCIEP *Courrier du Centre international d'études poétiques*. Freq: 4; Cov: Scan; Lang: Fre; Subj: Related.
■Archives et Musée de la Littérature; Boulevard de l'empereur, 4; 1000 Bruxelles; BELGIUM.

CDO *Courrier Dramatique de l'Ouest*. Freq: 4; Began: 1973; Ceased; Lang: Fre; Subj: Theatre.
■Théâtre du Bout du Monde, Ctre Dramatique Natl de l'Ouest; 9B Avenue Janvier; 35100 Rennes; FRANCE.

CDr *Canadian Drama/Art Dramatique Canadien*. Freq: 2; Began: 1975; Cov: Full; Lang: Eng/Fre; Subj: Theatre.   ISSN: 0317-9044
■Dept. of English, University of Waterloo; Waterloo, ON N2L 3G1; CANADA.

CdRideau *Cahiers du Rideau*. Freq: 3; Began: 1976; Ceased: Lang: Fre; Subj: Theatre.
■Rideau de Bruxelles; 23 rue Ravenstein; B 1000 Bruxelles; BELGIUM.

CE *College English*. Freq: 8; Began: 1937; Lang: Eng; Subj: Related. ISSN: 0010-0994
■National Council of Teachers of English; 1111 Kenyon Road; Urbana, IL 61801; USA.

Cel *Čelovek*. Lang: Rus; Subj: Related.
                    ISSN: 0236-2007
■RUSSIA.

Celcit *Celcit*. Lang: Spa; Subj: Theatre.
■Apartado 662; 105 Caracas; VENEZUELA.

Celjz *Celjski zbornik*. Freq: 1; Began: 1958; Lang: Slo; Subj: Theatre. ISSN: 0576-9760
■Osrednja knji*07znica Celje; Muzejski trg 1; 3000 Celje; SLOVENIA.

CeskL *Ceskoslovenski Loutkar*. SEE *Loutkar*. Began: 1951; Ceased: 1993; Lang: Cze; Subj: Theatre.

■Panorama; Mrstikova 23; 10 000 Prague 10; CZECH REPUBLIC.

Cesti *Čest'imeju*. Freq: 12; Cov: Scan; Began: 1919; Lang: Rus; Subj: Related.
■D-7 Choroševskoje šosse; 32-A, Building 3 Moscow 123007; RUSSIA.

CetC *Culture et Communication*. Freq: 10; Lang: Fre; Subj: Theatre.
■Min. de la Culture et de la Documentation; 3 rue de Valois; 75001 Paris; FRANCE.

CF *Comédie-Française*. Freq: 4; Began: 1971; Lang: Fre; Subj: Theatre. ISSN: 0759-125x
■1 Place Colette; 75001 Paris; FRANCE.

CFT *Contemporary French Civilization*. Freq: 3; Began: 1976; Cov: Scan; Lang: Fre/Eng; Subj: Related. ISSN: 0147-9156
■Dept. of Modern Languages, Montana State University; Bozeman, MT 59717; USA.

Chhaya *Chhaya Nat*. Freq: 4; Lang: Hin; Subj: Theatre.
■U.P. Sangeet Natak Akademi; Lucknow; INDIA.

ChinL *Chinese Literature*. Freq: 4; Began: 1951; Lang: Eng; Subj: Related. ISSN: 0009-4617
■Bai Wan Zhuang; Beijing 100037; CHINA.

Chronico *Chronico*. Lang: Gre; Subj: Theatre.
■ Horo'; Xenofontos 7; Athens; GREECE.

ChTR *Children's Theatre Review*. Freq: 4; Began: 1952; Cov: Full; Ceased: 1985; Lang: Eng; Subj: Theatre. ISSN: 0009-4196
■c/o Milton W. Hamlin, Shoreline High School; 18560 1st Avenue N.E.; Seattle, WA 98155; USA.

CineLD *Cineschedario*: Letture Drammatiche. Freq: 12; Began: 1964; Lang: Ita; Subj: Related. ISSN: 0024-1458
■Centro Salesiano dello Spettacolo; Via M. Ausiliatrice 32; Turin 10121; ITALY.

CIQ *Callahan's Irish Quarterly*. Freq: 4; Ceased: 1983; Cov: Scan; Lang: Eng; Subj: Related.
■P.O. Box 5935; Berkeley, CA 94705; USA.

CircusR *Circus Report*. Freq: IRR; Began: 1972; Lang: Eng; Subj: Theatre; ISSN: 0889-5996
■525 Oak St.; El Cerrito, CA 94530-3699; USA.

CittaA *Città Aperta*. Freq: 1; Began: 1981; Lang: Ita; Subj: Theatre.
■Associazione Piccolo Teatro; Via Cesalpino 20; 52100 Arezzo; ITALY.

CityL *City Limits*. Freq: 10; Began: 1976; Lang: Eng; Subj: Related. ISSN: 0199-0330
■City Limits, Assoc. of Neighborhood Housing Developers; 424 W. 23rd Street; New York, NY 10001; USA.

CJC *Cahiers Jean Cocteau*. Freq: 1; Began: 1969; Lang: Fre; Subj: Theatre. ISSN: 0068-5178
■6 rue Bonaparte; 75006 Paris; FRANCE.

CJG *Cahiers Jean Giraudoux*. Freq: 1; Began: 1972; Lang: Fre; Subj: Theatre.
■Association des Amis de Jean Giraudoux; Université F. Rabelais; 3 Rue du Tanneus 37000 TOURS; FRANCE.

Cjo *Conjunto*: Revista de Teatro Latinamericano. Freq: 4; Began: 1964; Cov: Full; Lang: Spa; Subj: Theatre.   ISSN: 0010-5937
■Departamento de Teatro Latino Americano, Casa de las Americas; Ediciones Cubanes, Obispo No. 527; Aptdo. 605, Havana; CUBA.

CLAJ *College Language Association Journal*. Freq: 4; Began: 1957; Lang: Eng; Subj: Related.   ISSN: 0007-8549
■College Language Assoc., c/o Cason Hill; Morehouse College; Atlanta, GA 30314; USA.

ClassJ *Classical Journal, The*. Freq: 4; Lang: Eng; Subj: Theatre.
■Department of Classics; 146 New Cabell Hall; University of Virginia Charlottesville, VA 22903; USA.

ClaudelS *Claudel Studies*. Freq: 2; Began: 1972; Lang: Eng; Subj: Related. ISSN: 0900-1237
■University of Dallas, Dept. of French; PO Box 464; Irving, TX 75060; USA.

Clip *Clipper Studies in the American Theater*. Freq: IRR; Began: 1985; Lang: Eng; Subj: Theatre.   ISSN: 0748-237X
■Borgo Press; Box 2845; San Bernardino, CA 92406; USA.

CLSUJ *CLSU Journal of the Arts*. Freq: 1; Began: 1981; Lang: Eng/Phi; Subj: Theatre.
■Central Luzon State University, Publications House; Munoz; Nueva Ecija; PHILIPPINES.

Club *Club*. Began: 1923; Cov: Scan; Freq: 12; Lang: Rus; Subj: Related.
■Stardca'luzzroje šosse, I; Moscow 117630; RUSSIA.

CMJV *Cahiers de la Maison Jean Vilar*. Lang: Fre; Subj: Theatre.
■Avignon; FRANCE.

CM *Classical and Modern Literature*. Freq: 4; Lang: Eng; Subj: Related   ISSN: 0197-2227
■P.O. Box 629; Terre Haute, IN 47808-0629; USA.

CNCT *Cahiers de la NCT*. Freq: 3; Began: 1965; Lang: Fre; Subj: Theatre. ISSN: 1188-1461
■Nouvelle Compagnie Théâtrale; 4353 rue Ste. Catherine est.; Montreal, PQ H1V 1Y2; CANADA.

CO *Comédie de l'Ouest*. Lang: Fre; Subj: Theatre.
■Assoc. des Amis de la Comediede l'ouest; Centre Dramatique National; Rennes; FRANCE.

COJ *Cambridge Opera Journal*.Began: 1989;Cov: Scan;Lang: Eng Subj: Related.
                    ISSN: 0954-5867
■Cambridge University Press; The Edinburgh Building; Shaftesbury Road, Cambridge CB2 2RU; UK

ColecaoT *Coleçao Teatro*. Freq: IRR; Began: 1974; Lang: Por; Subj: Theatre.
■Universidade Federal do Rio Grande do Sul; Porto Alegre; BRAZIL.

ColJL&A *Columbia-VLA Journal of Law & the Arts*. Formerly: *Art & the Law*. Freq: 4; Began: 1985; Cov: Full; Lang: Eng; Subj: Related.   ISSN: 0743-5226
■Columbia University School of Law &, Volunteer Lawyers for the Arts; 435 West 116 Street; New York, NY 10027; USA.

Comedy *Comedy*. Freq: 4; Began: 1980; Lang: Eng; Subj: Theatre. ISSN: 0272-7404
■Trite Explanations Ltd.; Box 505, Canal Street Station; New York, NY 10013; USA.

ComIBS *Communications from the International Brecht Society*: The Global Brecht. Freq: 2; Began: 1970; Lang: Eng/Ger; Subj: Theatre. ISSN: 0740-8943
■Foreign Languages; Maginnes Hall #9; Lehigh University Bethlehem, PA 18015; USA.

CompD *Comparative Drama*. Freq: 4; Began: 1967; Cov: Full; Lang: Eng; Subj: Theatre. ISSN: 0010-4078
■Department of English, Western Michigan University; Kalamazoo, MI 49008-3899; USA.

Con *Connoisseur*. Freq: 12; Began: 1901; Lang: Eng; Subj: Related. ISSN: 0010-6275
■Hearst Magazines, Connoisseur; 250 W. 55th St.; New York, NY 10019; USA.

Confes *Confessio*. Freq: 4; Began: 1976; Cov: Scan; Lang: Hun; Subj: Related. ISSN: 0133-8889
■Református Zsinati Iroda Sajtóosztálya; Abonyi u. 21; 1146 Budapest; HUNGARY.

ContactQ *Contact Quarterly*. Freq: 2; Began: 1975; Lang: Eng; Subj: Related. ISSN: 0198-9634
■Contact Collaborations Inc.; Box 603; Northampton, MA 01061; USA.

Contenido *Contenido*. Lang: Spa; Subj: Theatre.
■Centro Venezolano del ITI; Apartado 51-456; 105 Caracas; VENEZUELA.

Contin *Continuum*. Formerly: *Continuing Higher Education Association*. Freq: 3; Began: 1977 Lang: Eng;; Subj: Related.
■National University of Continuing Education Association; 1 Dupont Circle N.W., Ste. 615; Washington, DC 20036; USA.

CORD *CORD Dance Research Annual*. Lang: Eng; Subj: Related.
■CORD Editorial Board, NYU Dance and Dance Educ. Dept.; 35 W. 4th St., Room 675; New York, NY 10003; USA.

CorpsE *Corps écrit*. Freq: 4; Lang: Fre; Subj: Theatre.
■Presses Universitaires de France; 12, rue Jean de Beauvais; 75005 Paris; FRANCE.

COS *Central Opera Service Bulletin*. Freq: 4; Began: 1954; Lang: Eng; Subj: Theatre. ISSN: 0008-9508
■Metropolitan Opera Nat'l Council, Central Opera Service; Lincoln Center; New York, NY 10023; USA.

Costume *Costume*: The Journal of the Costume Society. Freq: 1; Began: 1967; Cov: Scan; Lang: Eng; Subj: Related. ISSN: 0590-8876
■c/o Miss Anne Brogden; 3 Meadway Gate; London NW11 7LA; UK.

Covivt *Čovašskoe iskusstvo, Voprosy teorri i istorii*. Cov: Scan; Lang: Rus; Subj: Related. ISBN: 5-87677-003-5
■Moscow; RUSSIA.

CrAr *Critical Arts*. Freq: IRR; Began: 1980; Cov: Scan; Lang: Eng; Subj: Related.
■Critical Arts Study Group, c/o Dept. of Journalism & Media; Rhodes University; 6140 Grahamstown; SOUTH AFRICA.

CRB *Cahiers Renaud Barrault*. Freq: 4; Began: 1953; Lang: Fre; Subj: Theatre. ISSN: 0008-0470
■Editions Gallimard; S. Benmussa; 8 rue St. Placide; 75007 Paris; FRANCE.

CreD *Creative Drama*. Freq: 1; Began: 1949; Lang: Eng; Subj: Theatre. ISSN: 0011-0892
■Educational Drama Association, c/o Stacey Publications; 1 Hawthorndene Road; BR2 7DZ Kent; UK.

Crepuscl *Crépuscule, Le*. Ceased: 1979; Lang: Fre; Subj: Theatre.
■Théâtre Varia; rue du Sceptre; 78 à 1040 Bruxelles; BELGIUM.

Crisis *Crisis*. Freq: 6; Began: 1910; Lang: Eng; Subj: Related. ISSN: 0011-1422
■Crisis Publishing Co.; 186 Remsen St.; Brooklyn, NY 11201; USA.

CritD *Critical Digest*. Freq: 24; Began: 1948; Ceased: 1985; Lang: Eng; Subj: Theatre.
■225 West 34th Street, Room 918; New York, NY 10001; USA.

Criticism *Criticism*. Freq: 4; Lang: Eng; Subj: Related.
■Department of English; Wayne State University; Detroit, MI 42802; USA.

CritNY *Critique*. Freq: 4; Began: 1976; Lang: Eng; Subj: Theatre.
■417 Convent Avenue; New York, NY 10031; USA.

CritQ *Critical Quarterly*. Freq: 4; Began: 1959; Lang: Eng; Subj: Related. ISSN: 0011-1562
■Blackwell Publishers; 108 Cowley Road; Oxford OX4 1JF; UK.

CritRev *Critical Review, The*. Freq: IRR; Began: 1965; Lang: Eng; Subj: Related. ISSN: 0070-1548
■University of Melbourn; Department of English, Melbourne; AUSTRALIA.

CRT *Cabra, La*: Revista de Teatro. Lang: Spa; Subj: Theatre.
■Mexico City; MEXICO.

CS *Canada on Stage:The National Theatre Yearbook*. Formerly: *Canada on Stage:Canadien Theatre Review Yearbook*. Freq: 1; Began: 1975; Lang: Eng; Subj: Theatre. ISSN: 0380-9455
■PACT Communications Centre; 64 Charles St. E.; Toronto, ON M4Y ITI; CANADA.

CSAN *CSA News: The Newsletter of the Costume Society of America*. Formerly *Newsletter Quarterly and Dress*. Began: 1975; Lang: Eng; Subj: Related. ISSN: 0361-2112
■The Costume Society of America; 55 Edgewater Drive; P.O. Box 73 Earleville, MD 21919; USA.

CShav *Californian Shavian*. Freq: 6; Began: 1958; Ceased: 1966; Lang: Eng; Subj: Theatre. ISSN: 0008-154X
■Shaw Society of California; 1933 S. Broadway; Los Angeles, CA 90007; USA.

CTA *California Theatre Annual*. Ceased: 1986; Freq: 1; Lang: Eng; Subj: Theatre. ISSN: 0733-5806
■Performing Arts Network; 9025 Wilshire Blvd.; Beverly Hills, CA 90211; USA.

CTCheck *Canadian Theatre Checklist*. Formerly: *Checklist of Canadian Theatres*. Freq: 1; Began: 1979; Ceased: 1983; Lang: Eng; Subj: Theatre. ISSN: 0226-5125
■University of Toronto Press; 63A St. George Street; Toronto, ON M5S 1A6; CANADA.

CTL *Cahiers Théâtre Louvain*. Formerly *Cahiers Théâtre*. SEE *Etudes Théâtrales*. Freq: 4; Began: 1968; Ceased: 1991; Cov: Full; Lang: Fre; Subj: Theatre. ISSN: 0771-4653
■q. 1450 Fr. Ferme de Blocry, Place de l' Hocaille; B-1348 Louvain-La-Neuve; BELGIUM.

CTPA *Cahiers du Théâtre Populaire d'Amiens*. Began: 1984; Lang: Fre; Subj: Theatre.
■Amiens; FRANCE.

CTR *Canadian Theatre Review*. Freq: 4; Began: 1974; Cov: Full; Lang: Eng; Subj: Theatre. ISSN: 0315-0836
■Department of Drama; University of Guelph; Guelp, ON N1G 2WI; CANADA.

CTRY *Canadian Theatre Review Yearbook*. Freq: 1; Began: 1974; Ceased; Lang: Eng; Subj: Theatre. ISSN: 0380-9455
■Canadian Theatre Review Publications, York University;, P.O. Box 1280 1011 Sheppard Ave. Downsview, ON M3J 1P3; CANADA.

CTXY *C'wan t'ong Xiju Yishu/Art of Traditional Opera*. Freq: 4; Began: 1979; Lang: Chi; Subj: Theatre.
■Institute of Traditional Chinese Opera; Beijing; CHINA.

CU *Cirque dans l'Univers, Le*. Freq: 4; Began: 1950; Lang: Fre; Subj: Theatre. ISSN: 0009-7373
■lub du Cirque; 11, rue Ch-Silvestri; 94300 Vincennes; FRANCE.

Cuaderno *Cuadernos El Publico*. Freq: 10; Began: 1985; Ceased: 1989; Lang: Spa/Cat; Subj: Theatre. ISSN: 8602-3573
■Centro de Documentacion Teatral, Organismo Autonomo Teatros Ncnl; c/ Capitan Haya 44; 28020 Madrid; SPAIN.

Cue *Cue International*. Formerly: *Cue: Technical Theatre Review*. Freq: 6; Began: 1979; Ceased: 1987; Cov: Full; Lang: Eng; Subj: Theatre. ISSN: 0144-6088
■Twynam Publishing Ltd.; Kitemore;, Faningdon, Oxfordshire SN7 8HR; UK.

CueM *Cue, The*. Freq: 2; Began: 1928; Ceased; Cov: Scan; Lang: Eng; Subj: Theatre. ISSN: 0011-2666
■Theta Alpha Phi Fraternity, Dept. of Speech/ Theatre; Montclair State College; Upper Montclair, NJ 07043; USA.

CueNY *Cue New York*. Freq: 26; Began: 1932; Ceased: 1978; Lang: Eng; Subj: Theatre. ISSN: 0011-2658
■North American Publishing Company; 545 Madison Avenue; New York, NY 10022; USA.

Culture *Culture*. Freq: 4; Lang: Fre; Subj: Theatre.
■Maison de la Culture de La Rochelle; 11 rue Chef-de-Ville; 17000 La Rochelle; FRANCE.

CuPo *Cultural Post*. Freq: IRR; Began: 1975; Ceased: 1983; Lang: Eng; Subj: Related.
■National Endowment for the Arts; 1100 Pennsylvania Avenue N.W.; Washington, DC 20506; USA.

CW *Current Writing*. Freq: 2; Began: 1989; Cov: Scan; Lang: Eng; Subj: Related.
ISSN 1013-929X
■English Dept.; University of Natal; King George V Ave, Durban 4001; SOUTH AFRICA.

Cz *Circuszeitung, Die (Circus-Parade)*. Freq: 12; Began: 1955; Lang: Ger; Subj: Theatre.
■Gesellschaft für Circusfreunde; Klosterhof 10; 2308 Preetz; GERMANY.

CZN *Časopis za zgodovino in narodopisje*. Freq: 2; Began: 1904; Lang: Slo; Subj: Theatre. ISSN: 0590-5968
■Založba Obzorja d.d.; Partizanska 3-5; 2000 Maribor; SLOVENIA.

D&D *Dance and Dancers*. Freq: 12; Began: 1950; Lang: Eng; Subj: Related.
ISSN: 0011-5983
■214 Panther House; 38 Mount Pleasant; London WCIX OAP; UK.

D&T *Drama and Theater*. Freq: 3; Began: 1968; Ceased: 1980; Lang: Eng; Subj: Theatre. Dept. of English, State University; Fredonia, NY 14063; USA.

DA *Dance Australia*. Freq: 4; Began: 1980; Cov: Scan; Lang: Eng; Subj: Related.
ISSN: 0159-6330
■Dance Australia; GPO Box 606; Sydney, NSW 2001; AUSTRALIA.

DABEI *Dabei*. Freq: 6; Cov: Scan; Lang: Ger; Subj: Related. Gewerkschaft Kunst, Medien, Freie Berufe; Maria-Theresienstr. 11; A-1090 Vienna; AUSTRIA.

DalVostok *Dalnij Vostok*: (Far East). Freq: 12; Began: 1933; Cov: Scan; Lang: Rus; Subj: Related. ISSN: 0130-3028
■Kniznoe izdatel'stvo; Khabarovsk; RUSSIA.

Danst *Danstidningen*. Freq: 4; Began: 1991; Cov: Scan; Lang: Swe; Subj: Related.
ISSN: 1102-0814
■Box 20 137; 104 60 Stockholm; SWEDEN.

DAT *Andere Theatre, Das*. Freq: 4; Began: 1990; Lang: Ger; Subj: Theatre.
ISSN: 0936-0662
■Union Internationale de la Marionette; Zentrum Brd e.V., Die Schaubude; Greifswalder Str. 81-84 D-10405 Berlin; GERMANY.

DB *Deutsche Bühne, Die*. Freq: 12; Began: 1909; Lang: Ger; Subj: Theatre.
ISSN: 0011-975X
■Erhard Friedrich Verlag; Postfach 10 01 50 D-30917 Seelze; GERMANY.

DBj *Deutsches Bühnenjahrbuch*. Freq: 1; Began: 1889; Lang: Ger; Subj: Theatre.
ISSN: 0070-4431
■Genossenschaft Deutscher Bühnen Angehöriger; Buhnenschriften-Vertriebs Gmbh; Pf. 13 02 70; D-20102 Hamburg; GERMANY.

DC *Dance in Canada/Danse au Canada*. Freq: 4; Began: 1973; Ceased: Lang: Eng/Fre; Subj: Theatre. ISSN: 0317-9737
■Dance in Canada Association; 4700 Keele St.; Downsview, ON M3J 1P3; CANADA.

DCD *Documents del Centre Dramàtic*. Freq: 4; Ceased: Lang: Spa; Subj: Theatre. c/o Hospital, 51, 1er; Barcelona 08001; SPAIN.

DekorIsk *Dekorativnojë Iskusstvo SSR*. Freq: 12; Began: 1957; Cov: Scan; Lang: Rus; Subj: Related. ISSN: 0418-5153
■Soveckij Chudožnik; Moscow; RUSSIA.

DetLit *Detskaja Literatura*. Freq: 12; Began: 1932; Cov: Scan; Lang: Rus; Subj: Related. ISSN: 0130-3104
■Moscow; RUSSIA.

Devlet *Devlet Tijatrolari (State Theatres)*. Freq: 4; Lang: Tur; Subj: Theatre.Genel Mudurugu; Ankara; TURKEY.

Dewan *Dewan Budaya*. Freq: 12; Began: 1979; Lang: Mal; Subj: Theatre. ISSN: 0126-8473
■Peti Surat 803; Kuala Lumpur; MALAYSIA.

DGQ *Dramatists Guild Quarterly*. Freq: 4; Began: 1964; Cov: Full; Lang: Eng; Subj: Theatre. ISSN: 0012-6004
■The Dramatists Guild, Inc.; 234 W. 44th St.; New York, NY 10036; USA.

DHS *Dix-Huitième Siècle*. Freq: 1; Began: 1969; Lang: Fre; Subj: Related. ISSN: 0070-6760
■Soc. Française d'Etude du 18e Siecle; 23 Quai de Grenelle; 75015 Paris; FRANCE.

DialogA *Dialog*. Freq: 10; Began: 1973; Lang: Ger; Subj: Theatre. ISSN: 0378-6935
■Verlag Sauerländer; Laurenzenvorstadt 89; CH 5001 Aarau; SWITZERLAND.

Dialogi *Dialogi*. Freq: 12; Began: 1965; Lang: Slo; Subj: Theatre. ISSN: 0012-2068
■Založba Aristej d.o.o.;

Dialogi *Dialogi*. Freq: 12; Began: 1965; Lang: Slo; Subj: Theatre. ISSN: 0012-2068
Dialogi, Šentilj 119a; 2212 Šentij; SLOVENIA.

DialogR *Dialog*. Freq: 12; Lang: Rus; Subj: Theatre. ISSN: 0236-0942
■Miusskaja Square, 6; 125267 Moscow; RUSSIA.

DialogTu *Dialogue*. Lang: Fre; Subj: Theatre. Parti Socialiste Desourien, Maison du Parti, BP 1033; Blvd. du 9 Avril, La Kasbah; Tunis; TUNISIA.

Dialogue *Dialogue*: Canadian Philosophical Review/Revue Canadienne de Philosophie. Freq: 4; Began: 1962; Lang: Eng; Subj: Related. ISSN: 0012-2173
■Ste. 46, 1390 Sherbrooke St. West; H3G 1K2 Montreal, PQ; CANADA.

DialogW *Dialog*: Miesiecznik Poswiecony Dramaturgii Wspolczesnej. Freq: 12; Began: 1956; Cov: Full; Lang: Pol; Subj: Theatre.
ISSN: 0012-2041
■Teatr Współczesny, ul. Mokotowska 13; 00670 Warsaw; POLAND.

DiN *Divadelni Noviny*. Freq: 26; Began: 1992; Cov: Scan; Lang: Cze; Subj: Theatre.
ISSN: 0012-4141
■Svaz Ceskoslovenskych Divadelnich a Rozhlasovych Umelcu; Valdstejnske nam. 3; Prague 1; CZECH REPUBLIC.

Dioniso *Dioniso*. Freq: 1; Began: 1929; Lang: Ita/Eng/Fre/Spa; Subj: Theatre. Instituto Nazionale del Dramma Antico; Corso Matteoti 29; Siracusa; ITALY.

DIPFL *Deutsches Institut für Puppenspiel Forschung und Lehre*. Freq: IRR; Began: 1964; Last Known Address; Lang: Ger; Subj: Theatre. ISSN: 0070-4490

■Deutsches Institut für Puppenspiel; Bergstrasse 115; 4630 Bochum; GERMANY.

DirNotes *Directors Notes*. Lang: Eng; Subj: Theatre. American Directors Institute; 248 W. 74th St., Suite 10; New York, NY 10023; USA.

Diskurs *Diskurs*. Freq: 4; Last Known Address; Lang: Ger; Subj: Theatre. Schauble Verlag; Waldgurtel 5; 506 Bensberg; GERMANY.

DivR *Divadelni revue*. Freq: 4; Began: 1990; Cov: Scan; Lang: Cze; Subj: Theatre.
ISSN: 0862-5409
■Theatre Institute; Divadelni Ústav; 110 01 Prague 1 Celetna 17; CZECH REPUBLIC.

Dm *Dance Magazine*. Freq: 12; Began: 1926; Lang: Eng; Subj: Related. ISSN: 0011-6009
■Dance Magazine, Inc.; 33 W. 60th St.; New York, NY 10023; USA.

DMC *Dramatics*. Freq: 9; Began: 1929; Lang: Eng; Subj: Theatre. ISSN: 0012-5989
■Educational Theatre Association; 3368 Central Parkway; Cincinnati, OH 45225; USA.

DMR *David Mamet Review*. Cov: Scan; Lang: Eng ; Subj: Theatre. Box 455076; Las Vegas, NV 89154-5076; USA.

DnC *Dance Chronicle: Studies in Dance & the Related Arts*. Freq: 2; Began: 1978; Lang: Eng; Subj: Theatre. ISSN: 0147-2526
■Marcel Dekker Journals; 270 Madison Avenue; New York, NY 10016; USA.

DNDT *Drama*: Nordisk dramapedagogisk tidsskrift. Freq: 4; Began: 1963; Lang: Nor/Swe/Dan; Subj: Theatre. ISSN: 0332-5296
■Landslaget Drama i Skolen, Kongensgt. 4.; 0153 Oslo; NORWAY.

Dockt *Dockteatereko*. Freq: 4; Began: 1971; Lang: Swe; Subj: Theatre. ISSN: 0349-9944
■Dockteaterforeningen; Sandavagen 10; 14032 Grodinge; SWEDEN.

DocTh *Documentation Théâtrale*. Began: 1974; Lang: Fre; Subj: Theatre. Centre d'Etudes Théâtrales, Université Paris X; 200 Avenue de la République; 92001 Nanterre Cedex; FRANCE.

DOE *DOE*. Formerly: *Speel*. Freq: 24; Began: 1951; Lang: Dut; Subj: Theatre.
ISSN: 0038-7258
■Stichting Ons Leekenspel'; Gudelalaan 2; Bussum; NETHERLANDS.

DongukDA *Dong-Guk Dramatic Art*. Freq: 1; Began: 1970; Cov: Full; Lang: Kor; Subj: Theatre. Department of Drama & Cinema, Dongguk University; Seoul; SOUTH KOREA.

Drama *Drama: The Quarterly Theatre Review*: Third Series. Formerly: *Drama*. Freq: 4; Began: 1919; Ceased: 1989; Cov: Scan; Lang: Eng; Subj: Theatre. ISSN: 0012-5946
■Cranbourne Mansions; Cranbourne Street; London WC2H 7AG; UK.

Dramat *Dramat*. Freq: 4 Began: 1993; Cov: Full; Lang: Swe; Subj: Theatre. ISSN: 1104-2885
■Kungliga Dramatiska Teatern; Nybrogatan2; P.O. Box 5037 S-102 41 Stockholm; SWEDEN.

DrammaR *Dramma*. Freq: 12; Began: 1925; Cov: Scan; Lang: Ita; Subj: Theatre. ISSN: 0012-6004

■Romana Teatri s.r.l.; Via Torino 29; 00184 Rome; ITALY.

DrammaT *Dramma*: Il Mensile dello Spettacolo. Freq: 12; Lang: Ita; Subj: Theatre. I.L.T.E.; Corso Bramante 20; Turin; ITALY.

dRAMATURg *dRAMATURg*. Freq: 2; Began: 1970; Cov: Scan; Lang: Ger; Subj: Theatre. ISSN: 1432-3966
■Nachrichtenbrief; Dramaturgische Gesellschaft e.V.; Tempelherrenstr. 4 D-10961 Berlin; GERMANY.

Drammaturgia *Drammaturgia*. Freq: 2; Cov: Scan; Began: 1994; Lang: Ita; Subj: Theatre. ISSN: 1122-9365;
■Salerno Editrice Via di Donna Olimpia; 20-Roma; ITALY.

DramaY *Drama*. Lang: Slo; Subj: Theatre. Erjavceva; Ljubljana; SLOVENIA.

Dress *Dress*. Freq: 1; Began: 1975; Lang: Eng; Subj: Related. ISSN: 0361-2112
■Costume Society of America; 55 Edgewater Drive; P.O. Box 73 Earleville, MD 21919; USA.

DRJ *Dance Research Journal*. Freq: 2; Began: 1967; Lang: Eng; Subj: Related. ISSN: 0149-7677
■Congress on Research in Dance, Department of Dance; State University of New York College at Brockport, Brockport, NY 14420-2939; USA.

DRostock *Diskurs*. Freq: 4; Began: 1973; Ceased: 1980; Lang: Ger; Subj: Theatre. Volkstheater Rostock; Patriotischer Weg 33; 25 Rostock; GERMANY.

DrRev *Drama Review*. Freq: 2; Began: 1970; Last Known Address; Lang: Kor; Subj: Theatre. Yonguk-pyongron-sa; 131-51 Nokbun-dong, Eunpyong-ku; 122 Seoul; SOUTH KOREA.

DRs *Dance Research*. Freq: 2; Lang: Eng; Subj: Related. c/o Dance Books Ltd.; 9 Cecil Court; London WC2N 4EZ; UK.

Druzba *Družba*. SEE *Rossijane*. Freq: 6; Began: 1977; Ceased: 1992; Cov: Scan; Lang: Rus/Bul; Subj: Related. ISSN: 0320-1031
■Moscow-Sofija; RUSSIA.

DruzNar *Družba Narodov*. Freq: 12; Began: 1939; Cov: Scan; Lang: Rus; Subj: Related. ISSN: 0012-6756
■Sovetskii pisatel; Izvestiia Sovetov narodnykh deputatov SSSR; Moscow; RUSSIA.

DSat *Don Saturio: Boletin Informativo de Teatro Gallego*. Last Known Address; Lang: Spa; Subj: Theatre. Coruna 70-30; Esda; SPAIN.

DSchool *Drama and the School*. Freq: 2; Began: 1948; Last Known Address; Lang: Eng; Subj: Theatre. Whitehall Productions; 63 Elizabeth Bay Road; NSW 2011 Elizabeth Bay; AUSTRALIA.

DSGM *Dokumenti Slovenskega Gledaliskega Muzeja*. Freq: 2; Began: 1964; Lang: Slo; Subj: Theatre. Slovenski Gledaliski in Filski muzej; Cankarjeva 11; Ljubljana; SLOVENIA.

DShG *Deutsche Shakespeare Gesellschaft/Deutsche Shakespeare Gesellschaft West, Jahrbuch*. Freq: 1; Began: 1993; Lang: Ger; Subj: Theatre. ISSN: 0945-5094

■Ferdinand Kamp Verlag GmbH; Widumestr. 6-8; D-44787 Bochum; GERMANY.

DSo *Dramatists Sourcebook*. Formerly: *Information for Playwrights*. Freq: 1; Began: 1981; Cov: Scan; Lang: Eng; Subj: Theatre. ISSN: 0733-1606
■Theatre Comm. Group, Inc; 355 Lexington Ave.; New York, NY 10017; USA.

DSS *Dix-Septième Siècle*. Freq: 4; Began: 1949; Last Known Address; Cov: Scan; Lang: Fre; Subj: Related. ISSN: 0012-4273
■Commission des Publications, c/o Collège de France; 11 Place M. Berthelot; 75005 Paris; FRANCE.

DSTFM *Documents of the Slovenian Theatre and Film Museum*. Began: 1979; Cov: Scan; Lang: Slo; Subj: Theatre. Slovenian Theatre and Film Museum; Ljubljana; SLOVENIA.

DTh *Divadelní ústar*. Freq: 2; Lang: Slo; Subj: Theatre. Celetná 17; 11001 Prague 1; CZECH REPUBLIC.

Dtherapy *Dramatherapy*: SEE: Journal of Dramatherapy (JDt). Lang: Eng; Subj: Theatre. The Old Mill, Tolpuddle; Dorchester; Dorset DT2 7EX; UK.

DTi *Dancing Times*. Freq: 12; Began: 1910; Lang: Eng; Subj: Theatre. ISSN: 0011-605X
■Dancing Times Ltd., Clerkenwell House; 45-47 Clerkenwell Green; London EC1R 0BE; UK.

DTJ *Dance Theatre Journal*. Freq: 4; Began: 1983; Cov: Scan; Lang: Eng; Subj: Theatre. ISSN: 02464-9160
■Laban Centre for Movement & Dance, Laurie Grove; London, SE14 6NH; UK.

DTN *Drama and Theatre Newsletter*. Freq: 4; Began: 1975; Ceased: 1982; Lang: Eng; Subj: Theatre. British Theatre Institute; 30 Clareville Street; London SW7 5AW; UK.

DTOP *Dramaturgi: Tedri Og Praksis*. Lang: Dan; Subj: Theatre. Akademisk Forlag; St. Kannikestraede 8; 1169 Copenhagen; DENMARK.

Dvat *Dvatisoč 2000: časnik za mišljenje, umetnost, kulturna*. Began: 1969; Lang: Slo; Subj: Related. Društvo izdajateljev časnika 2000; Ljubljana; SLOVENIA.

DVLa *Diadja Vanja. Literaturnij al'manah*. Began: 1994; Lang: Rus; Subj: Related. ISSN: 0132-8204
■Gertsen Street 50/5; Room 44; 121069 Moscow; RUSSIA.

DZP *Deutsche Zeitschrift für Philosophie*. Freq: 12; Began: 1953; Cov: Scan; Lang: Ger; Subj: Related. ISSN: 0012-1045
■VEB Deutscher Verlag der Wissenschaften; Johannes-Dieckmann-Str. 10, Postfach 1216; 1080 Berlin; GERMANY.

E&AM *Entertainment and Arts Manager*. Formerly: *Entertainment and Arts Management*. Freq: 4; Began: 1973; Ceased: 1989; Cov: Scan; Lang: Eng; Subj: Theatre. ISSN: 0143-8980
■Assoc. of Entertainment & Arts Mangement, T.G. Scott and Son Ltd.; 30-32 Southampton St., Covent Garden; London WC2E 7HR; UK.

EAH *East Asian History*: Formerly: *Papers on Far Eastern History*. Freq: 2; Began: 1991; Cov: Scan; Lang: Eng; Subj: Related. ISSN: 1036-6008
■A.C.T.: Division of Pacific and Asian Histor; Research School of Pacific Studies; Australian National University, Canberra; AUSTRALIA.

EAR *English Academy Review, The*. Began: 1983; Cov: Scan; Lang: Eng; Subj: Related. English Academy of Southern Africa, Bollater House; 35 Melle St., Braamfontein; 2001 Johannesburg; SOUTH AFRICA.

Ebony *Ebony*. Freq: 12; Began: 1945; Lang: Eng; Subj: Related. ISSN: 0012-9011
■Johnson Publishing Co., Inc.; 820 S. Michigan; Chicago, IL 60605; USA.

Echanges *Echanges*. Freq: 12; Lang: Fre; Subj: Theatre. Théâtre Romain-Rolland; rue Eugène Varlin; 94 Villejuif; FRANCE.

EchoP *Echo Planety*. Freq: 52; Began: 1988; Lang: Rus; Subj: Related. ISSN: 0234-1670
■State Union Publishing; 103009; Tversko Boulevard 10-12 Moscow K-9; RUSSIA.

Econ *Economist Financial Report*. Freq: 48; Began: 1976; Cov: Scan; Lang: Eng; Subj: Related. ISSN: 0013-0613
■Economist Newspaper Ltd.; 25 St. James St.; London SW1A 1HG; UK.

ECr *Esprit Créateur, L'*. Freq: 4; Began: 1961; Lang: Fre; Subj: Theatre. ISSN: 0014-0767
■John D. Erickson; Box 222; Lawrence, KS 66044; USA.

ECrit *Essays in Criticism*. Freq: 4; Began: 1951; Lang: Eng; Subj: Related. ISSN: 0014-0856
■6A Rawlinson Rd.; Oxford OX2 6UE; UK.

ECrit *Essays in Criticism*. Freq: 4; Began: 1951; Lang: Eng; Subj: Related. ISSN: 0014-0856

ECS *Eighteenth-Century Studies*
. Freq: 4 Cov: Scan; Lang: Eng; Subj: Related. Johns Hopkins Univ. Press; 2715 North Charles St.; Baltimore, MD 21218; US.

ECW *Essays on Canadian Writing*. Freq: IRR; Began: 1974; Cov: Scan; Lang: Eng; Subj: Related. ISSN: 0313-0300
■1980 Queen St. E.; Toronto, ON M4L 1J2; CANADA.

ED *Envers du Décor, L'*. Freq: 6; Began: 1973; Lang: Fre; Subj: Theatre. ISSN: 0319-8650
■Théâtre du Nouveau Monde; 84 Ouest, Rue Ste-Catharine; Montreal, PQ H2X 1Z6; CANADA.

EDAM *The Early Drama, Art, and Music Review*. Formerly *EDAM Newsletter*. Freq: 2; Began: 1978; Cov: Scan; Lang: Eng; Subj: Theatre. ISSN: 0196-5816
■Medieval Institute Publications; Western Michigan University; Kalamazoo, MI 49008; USA.

EE&PA *Economic Efficiency and the Performing Arts*. Lang: Eng; Subj: Theatre. Association for Cultural Economics, University of Akron; Akron, OH 44235; USA.

EECIT   *Estudis Escenics*. Freq: 2; Began: 1979; Lang: Cat; Subj: Theatre. ISSN: 0212-3819
∎Inst. del Theatre de Barcelona, c/o Nou de la Rambla; 08001 Barcelona 3; SPAIN.

Egk   *Engekikai*: Theatre World. Freq: 12; Began: 1940; Lang: Jap; Subj: Theatre. Engeki Shuppan-sha, Chiyoda-ku; 2-11 Kanda-Jinpo-cho; Tokyo 101; JAPAN.

EHR   *Economic History Review*. Freq: 4; Began: 1927; Lang: Eng; Subj: Related. ISSN: 0013-0117
∎Blackwell Ltd.; 108 Cowley Rd; Oxford OX4 1JF; UK.

EiC   *Estrada i cirk*. Freq: 12; Began: 1992; Cov: Scan; Lang: Rus; Subj: Theatre. ISSN: 0131-6769
∎Moscow; RUSSIA.

EinA   *English in Africa*. Freq: 2; Began: 1974; Cov: Scan; Lang: Eng; Subj: Related. ISEA, Rhodes University; Grahamstown; 6140; SOUTH AFRICA.

Eire   *Eire-Ireland*. Freq: 4; Began: 1966; Cov: Scan; Lang: Eng; Subj: Related. ISSN: 0013-2683
∎Irish American Cultural Institute; 2115 Summit Avenue; College of St. Thomas Box 5026, St. Paul, MN 55105; USA.

EIT   *Escena*: Informativo Teatral. Freq: 4; Began: 1979; Lang: Spa; Subj: Theatre. Universidad de Costa Rica, Teatro Universitario, Apt. 92; San Pedro de Montes de Oca; San José; COSTA RICA.

Ekran   *Ekran*. Formerly *Sovetski Ekran*. Freq: 4; Began: 1992; Cov: Scan; Lang: Rus; Subj: Related. A-319 Ul. Chasavaja 5-6; Moscow 125319; RUSSIA.

Elet   *Életűnk*. Freq: 12; Began: 1963; Cov: Scan; Lang: Hun; Subj: Related. ISSN: 0133-4751
∎Arany János Lap- és Könyvkiadó Kft.; Forgó u. 1; 9701 Szombathely; HUNGARY.

ElI   *Elet és Irodalom*: irodalmi es politkai hetilap. Freq: 52; Began: 1957; Lang: Hun; Subj: Related. ISSN: 0424-8848
∎Ft. Lapkiado Vallalat; Széchenyi rkp. 1; 1054 Budapest V; HUNGARY.

ElM   *Marges, El*. Freq: 4; Cov: Scan; Lang: Cat; Subj: Related. ISSN: 0210-0452
∎Curial Edicions Catalanes SA; carrer del Bruc 144; 08037 Barcelona; SPAIN.

ELN   *English Language Notes*. Freq: 4; Cov: Scan; Lang: Eng; Subj: Related. ISSN: 0013-8282
∎Department of English, Campus Box 226; University of Colorado at Boulder; Boulder, CO 80309-0226; USA.

ElPu   *Publico, El*: Periodico mensual de teatro. Freq: 12; Began: 1983; Lang: Spa; Subj: Theatre. ISSN: 0213-4926
∎Centro de Documentación Teatral; c/ Capitán Haya, 44; 28020 Madrid; SPAIN.

ELR   *English Literary Renaissance Journal*. Freq: 3; Began: 1971; Lang: Eng; Subj: Related. University of Massachusetts; Department of English; Amherst, MA 01003; USA.

EN   *Equity News*. Freq: 12; Began: 1915; Cov: Scan; Lang: Eng; Subj: Theatre. ISSN: 0013-9890

∎Actors Equity Association; 165 W. 46 St.; New York, NY 10036; USA.

Enact   *Enact*: monthly theatre magazine. Freq: 12; Began: 1967; Lang: Eng; Subj: Theatre. ISSN: 0013-6980
∎Paul's Press, E44-11; Okhla Industrial Area, Phase II; 110020 New Delhi; INDIA.

Encore   *Encore*. Lang: Eng; Subj: Theatre. Fort Valley State College; Fort Valley, GA 31030; USA.

EncoreA   *Encore*. Freq: 12; Began: 1976; Lang: Eng; Subj: Theatre. PO Box 247; NSW 2154 Castle Hill; AUSTRALIA.

ENG   *Editorial Nuevo Grupo*. Lang: Spa; Subj: Theatre. Avenida La Colina, Prolongación Los Manolos; La Florida; 105 Caracas; VENEZUELA.

EnSt   *English Studies*. Freq: 6; Cov: Scan; Lang: Eng; Subj: Related. ISSN: 0013-838X
∎Swets & Zeitlinger; P.O. Box 825; 2160 SZ Lisse; NETHERLANDS.

Entre   *Entré*. Freq: 6; Began: 1974; Cov: Full; Lang: Swe; Subj: Theatre. ISSN: 0345-2581
∎Svenska Riksteatern, Swedish National Theatre Centre; S-145 83; Norsborg; SWEDEN.

EO   *Etnograjicesko obozrenie*. Freq: 6; Began: 1992; Cov: Scan; Lang: Rus; Subj: Related. ISSN: 0038-5050
∎Ulica D. Uljanova 19; B 36 Moscow; RUSSIA.

EOR   *Eugene O'Neill Review*. Freq: 3; Began: 1977; Cov: Full; Lang: Eng; Subj: Theatre. Formerly: *Eugene O'Neill Newsletter, The*. ISSN: 0733-0456
∎Suffolk University, Department of English; Boston, MA 02114; USA.

EpicT   *Epic Theatre*. Freq: 4; Lang: Ben; Subj: Theatre. 140/24 Netaji Subhashchandra Bose Road; Calcutta; INDIA.

EquityJ   *Equity Journal*. Freq: 4; Began: 1931; Lang: Eng; Subj: Theatre. ISSN: 0141-3147
∎British Actor's Equity Association; Guild House, Upper St. Martin's Lane; London WC2H 9EG; UK.

ERev   *Elizabethan Review*. Freq: 2; Cov: Scan; Lang: Eng; Subj: Related. ISSN: 1066-7059
∎8435 62nd Drive, #T41; Middle Village, NY 11379; USA.

ERT   *Empirical Research in Theatre*. Freq: 1; Began: 1971; Ceased: 1984; Cov: Full; Lang: Eng; Subj: Theatre. ISSN: 0361-2767
∎Center for Communications Research; Bowling Green State University; Bowling Green, OH 43403; USA.

ESA   *English Studies in Africa: A Journal of the Humanities*. Freq: 2; Began: 1958; Cov: Scan; Lang: Eng; Subj: Related. ISSN: 0013-8398
∎Witwatersrand Univ. Press; Jan Smuts Ave.; Johannesburg 2001; SOUTH AFRICA.

ESC   *English Studies in Canada*. Freq: 4; Began: 1975; Cov: Scan; Lang: Eng; Subj: Related. Association of Canadian College and University Teachers of English; c/o Dept. of English; Carleton University Ottawa, ON K1S 5B6; CANADA.

Escena   *Escena*. Lang: Spa; Subj: Theatre. Departamento de Publicaciones, Consejo Nacional de la Cultura; Calle Paris, Edificio Macanao 3er. Piso; 106 Caracas; VENEZUELA.

Escenica   *Escénica*. Began: 1990; Lang: Spa; Subj: Theatre. Universidad Nacional Autónoma de México; Coordinación de Difusión Cultural; Centro Cultural Universitario Ciudad Universitaria, C.P. 04510; MEXICO.

Espill   *Espill, L'*. Freq: 4; Lang: Cat; Subj: Related. Editorial 3 i 4, c/o Moratin 15; Porta 3; 46002 Valencia; SPAIN.

Esprit   *Esprit*. Freq: 12; Began: 1932; Lang: Fre; Subj: Related. ISSN: 0014-0759
∎19, rue Jacob; 75006 Paris; FRANCE.

Essence   *Essence*. Freq: 12; Began: 1970; Lang: Eng; Subj: Related. ISSN: 0014-0880
∎Essence Comm., Inc.; P.O. Box 53400 Boulder, CO 80322-3400; USA.

EstLit   *Estafeta Literaria*: La Revista Quincenal de Libros, Artes i Espetáculos. Freq: 24; Began: 1958; Lang: Spa; Subj: Theatre. ISSN: 0014-1186
∎Avda. de José Antonio, 62; 13 Madrid; SPAIN.

Estreno   *Estreno*: Journal on the Contemporary Spanish Theater. Freq: 2; Began: 1975; Cov: Full; Lang: Eng/Spa; Subj: Theatre. ISSN: 0097-8663
∎Penn State University; 350 N. Burrowes Bldg; University Park, PA 16802; USA.

ET   *Essays in Theatre*. Freq: 2; Began: 1982; Cov: Full; Lang: Eng; Subj: Theatre. ISSN: 0821-4425
∎University of Guelph, Department of Drama; Guelph, ON N1G 2W1; CANADA.

ETh   *Elizabethan Theatre*. Began: 1968; Lang: Eng; Subj: Theatre. ISSN: 0071-0032
∎Archon Books; 995 Sherman Avenue; Hamden, CT 06514; USA.

ETN   *Educational Theatre News*. Freq: 6; Began: 1953; Lang: Eng; Subj: Theatre. ISSN: 0013-1997
∎Southern California Education Theatre Association; 9811 Pounds Avenue; Whittier, CA 90603; USA.

Etoile   *Etoile de la Foire*. Freq: 12; Began: 1945; Ceased: 1982; Lang: Fle/Fre; Subj: Theatre. ISSN: 0014-1895
∎15 rue Vanderlinden; Brussels 3; BELGIUM.

Etudes   *Etudes Theatrales*. Formerly *Arts du Spectacle en Belgique*. Freq: 2; Began: 1992; Lang: Fre; Subj: Theatre. ISSN: 0778-8738
∎Centre d'études théâtrales; Université catholique de Louvain; place de l'Hocaille 5 1348 Louvain-la-Neuve; BELGIUM.

Europai   *Európai utas*. Lang: Rus; Subj: Related. Moscow; RUSSIA.

Europe   *Europe*: Revue Littéraire Mensuelle. Freq: 8; Began: 1923; Lang: Fre; Subj: Related. ISSN: 0014-2751
∎146, rue du Fg. Poisonnière; 75010 Paris; FRANCE.

Evento   *Evento Teatrale*. Freq: 3; Began: 1975; Lang: Ita; Subj: Theatre. A.BE.TE.spa; Via Presentina 683; 00155 Rome; ITALY.

Exchange   *Exchange*. Freq: 3; Began: 1975; Lang: Eng; Subj: Theatre. University of Missouri: Columbia, Dept. of Speech/Drama; 129 Fine Arts Centre; Columbia, MS 65211; USA.

FAR   *Fremantle Arts Review: monthly arts digest*. Freq: 6; Began: 1986; Cov: Full; Lang: Eng; Subj: Related. ISSN: 0816-6919
■Fremantle Arts Centre; P.O. Box 891; Fremantle 6160; AUSTRALIA.

Farsa   *Farsa, La*. Freq: 20; Last Known Address; Lang: Spa; Subj: Theatre. Pza. de los Mostenses 11; 9 Madrid; SPAIN.

FDi   *Film a Divadlo*. Freq: 26; Lang: Cze; Subj: Related. Theatre Intitute in Bratislava; Obzor, Ceskoslovenskej Armady 35; Bratislava 815 85; SLOVAKIA.

Fds   *Freedomways*: A Quarterly Review of the Freedom Movement. Freq: 4; Began: 1961; Lang: Eng; Subj: Related. ISSN: 0016-061X
■Freedomways Assoc., Inc.; 799 Broadway; New York, NY 10003 6849; USA.

FemR   *Feminist Review*. Freq: 3; Began: 1979; Lang: Eng; Subj: Related. ISSN: 0141-7789
■11 Carleton Gardens, Brecknock Rd.; London N19 5AQ; UK.

FemS   *Feminist Studies*. Freq: 3; Lang: Eng; Subj: Related. c/o Women's Studies; 2101 Woods Hall; University of Maryland College Park, MD 20742; USA.

Figura   *Figura. Zeitschrift für Theater und Spiel mit Figuren*. Formerly: *Puppenspiel und Puppenspieler*. Freq: 4; Began: 1993; Cov: Scan; Lang: Ger;; Subj: Related. ISSN: 1021-3244
■Brigitta Weber; Pf. 501; CH-8401 Winterthur; GERMANY.

Fikr   *Al Fikr*. Lang: Ara; Subj: Theatre. Rue Dar Eg-gild; Tunis; TUNISIA.

FiloK   *Filológiai Közlöny*. Freq: 4; Began: 1955; Cov: Scan; Lang: Hun; Subj: Related. ISSN: 0015-1785
■Akadémiai Kiadó; Ameriki út 96; 1145 Budapest V; HUNGARY.

FIRTSIB   *FIRT/SIBMAS Bulletin d'information*. Freq: 4; Began: 1977; Lang: Fre/Eng; Subj: Theatre. Fédération Internationale pour la Recherche Théâtrale; c/o van Eeghenstraat 11311, 1071 EZ Amsterdam; NETHERLANDS.

Flam   *Flamboyant. Schriften zum Theater*. Freq: 4; Began: 1995; Cov: Scan; Lang: Ger; Subj: Theatre. ISBN: 3-9804764-3-X
■Studio 7, International Theatre Ensemble e.v.; Vitalisstr. 386; D-50933 Köln; GERMANY.

FMa   *Fight Master, The*. Freq: 4; Cov: Scan; Lang: Eng; Subj: Theatre. Society of American Fight Directors; 1834 Camp Avenue; Rockford, IL 61103; USA.

FMT   *Forum Modernes Theater*. Freq: 2; Began: 1986; Cov: Scan; Lang: Ger/Eng/Fre; Subj: Theatre. ISSN: 0930-5874
■Gunter Narr Verlag; Pf. 2567 D-72015 Tübingen; GERMANY.

FN   *Filologičeskije Nauki*. Freq: 6; Began: 1958; Cov: Scan; Lang: Rus; Subj: Related. ISSN: 0130-9730

■Izdatelstvo Vysšaja Škola; Prospekt Marksa 18; 103009 Moscow K-9; RUSSIA.

Fnotes   *Footnotes*. Freq: 1; Began: 1975; Lang: Eng; Subj: Theatre. Stagestep; Box 328; Philadelphia, PA 19105; USA.

FO   *Federal One*. Freq: IRR; Began: 1975; Cov: Scan; Lang: Eng; Subj: Related. George Mason University; 4400 University Dr.; Fairfax, VA 22030; USA.

Forras   *Forrás*. Freq: 12; Began: 1969; Cov: Scan; Lang: Hun; Subj: Related. ISSN: 0133-056X
■Petőfi Lap- és Könyvkiadó Kft.; Május 1. tér 3; 6001 Kecskemét; HUNGARY.

FR   *French Review, The*. Freq: 6; Began: 1927; Lang: Fre/Eng; Subj: Related. ISSN: 0016-111X
■American Association of Teachers of French; 57 E. Armory Ave.; Champaign, IL 61820; USA.

FranceT   *France Théâtre*. Freq: 24; Began: 1957; Lang: Fre; Subj: Theatre. ISSN: 0015-9433
■Syndicat National des Agences; 16 Avenue l'Opéra; 75001 Paris; FRANCE.

FranceT   *France Théâtre*. Freq: 24; Began: 1957; Lang: Fre; Subj: Theatre. ISSN: 0015-9433

FreilD   *Freilichtbühne, Die*. Freq: 2; Began: 1956; Cov: Scan; Lang: Ger; Subj: Related. Verband deutscher Freilichtbühnen e.V.

; Gebrüder-Funke-Weg 3; D-59073 Hamm; GERMANY.

FrF   *French Forum*. Freq: 3; Began: 1976; Lang: Fre/Eng; Subj: Related. ISSN: 0098-9355
■French Forum Publishers, Inc.; Box 5108; Lexington, KY 40505; USA.

Front   *Frontiers: A Journal of Women Studies*. Freq: 3; Lang: Eng; Subj: Related. Wilson 12; Washington State University; Pullman, WA 99164-4007; USA.

FS   *French Studies*: A quarterly review. Freq: 4; Began: 1947; Lang: Eng; Subj: Related. ISSN: 0016-1128
■Society for French Studies, c/o Dr. J.M. Lewis; Dept. of French; Queen's University Belfast BT7 1NN; NORTHERN IRELAND.

FSM   *Film, Szinház, Muzsika*. Freq: 52; Began: 1957; Ceased: 1990; Cov: Scan; Lang: Hun; Subj: Theatre. ISSN: 0015-1416
■Lapkiadó Vállalat; Erzsébet körút 9-11; 1073 Budapest VII; HUNGARY.

FT   *Finnish Theatre*. Formerly *News From the Finnish Theatre*. Freq: 1 Began: 1995; Cov: Full; Lang: Fin/Eng; Subj: Theatre. ISSN 1238-6057
■Finnish Theatre Information Centre; Meritullinkatu 33; 00170 Helsinki; FINLAND.

fTep   *fliegende Teppich, Der. Zeitung für Kinderkultur und Kindertheater*. Freq: 5; Cov: Scan Lang; Ger; Subj: Theatre. Verein IchduwirAnimation und Mitspieltheater für Kinder; Hockegasse 40/27; A-1180 Vienna; AUSTRIA.

Ftr   *Figurentheater*. Freq: IRR; Began: 1923; Ceased; Lang: Ger; Subj: Theatre. ISSN: 0430-3873
■Deutsches Institut für Puppenspiel; Hattingerstr. 467; D-4630 Bochum; GERMANY.

Fundarte   *Fundarte*. Lang: Spa; Subj: Theatre. Edificio Tajamar, P.H., Parque Central; Avenida Lecuna; 105 Caracas; VENEZUELA.

Fundevogel   *Fundevogel. Kritisches Kinder-Medien-Magazin*. Freq: 4; Began: 1984; Cov: Scan; Lang: Ger; Subj: Related. ISSN: 0176-2753
■dipa-Verlag, Nassauer Str. 1-3; D-60439 Frankfurt/M; GERMANY.

FundM   *Fundraising Management*. Freq: 12; Began: 1972; Cov: Scan; Lang: Eng; Subj: Related. Hoke Communications Inc.; 224 7th Street; Garden City, NY 11530-5771 USA.

Funoun   *Al Funoun*: The Arts. Freq: 12; Lang: Ara; Subj: Theatre. Ministry of Information, Dept. of Culture and Arts; PO Box 6140; Amman; JORDAN.

G&GBKM   *Grimm & Grips. Beilage zum Kritischen Kinder-Medien Magazin-Fundevogel*. Freq: 4; Cov: Scan; Lang: Ger; Subj: Related. ISSN: 0176-2753
■Assitej e.V. Bundesrepublik Deutschland; Schützenstr. 12; D-60311 Frankfurt/M; GERMANY.

G&GJKJ   *Grimm & Grips. Jahrbuch für Kinder- und Jugendtheater*. Freq: 1; Began: 1987; Cov: Scan; Lang: Ger; Subj: Related. ISSN: 0933-4149
■Assitej e.V. Sektion BRD; Schützenstr. 12; D-60311 Frankfurt/M; GERMANY.

Gambit   *Gambit*. Freq: IRR; Began: 1963; Ceased: 1986; Cov: Scan; Lang: Eng; Subj: Theatre. ISSN: 0016-4283
■John Calder, Ltd.; 9-15 Neal Street; London WC2H 9TU; UK.

Gap   *Gap, The*. Lang: Eng; Subj: Related. Washington, DC; USA.

GaR   *Georgia Review*. Freq: 4; Began: 1947; Lang: Eng; Subj: Related. ISSN: 0016-8386
■University of Georgia; Athens, GA 30602; USA.

Garcin   *Garcin: Libro de Cultura*. Freq: 12; Began: 1981; Lang: Spa; Subj: Related. Acali Editoria; Ituzaingo 1495; Montevideo; URUGUAY.

Gazit   *Gazit*. Lang: Heb; Subj: Theatre. 8 Brook Street; Tel Aviv; ISRAEL.

GdBA   *Gazette des Beaux Arts*. Freq: 12; Began: 1859; Lang: Fre; Subj: Related. ISSN: 0016-5530
■Imprimerie Louis Jean, B.P. 87; Gap Cedex 05002; SWITZERLAND.

GdF   *Gazette du Français*. Freq: 12; Began: 1983; Lang: Fre; Subj: Related. ISSN: 0759-1268
■Paris; FRANCE.

GdS   *Giornale dello Spettacolo*. Freq: 52; Lang: Ita; Subj: Theatre. ISSN: 0017-0232
■Associazione Generale Italiana dello Spettacolo; Via di Villa Patrizi 10; 00161 Rome; ITALY.

GerSR   *German Studies Review*. Freq: 3; Began: 1978; Cov: Scan; Lang: Ger; Subj: Related. ISSN: 0149-7952
■German Studies Association, c/o Prof. Gerald R. Kleinfeld; Arizona State University; Tempe, AZ 85281; USA.

Gestos *Gestos*: teoría y práctica del teatro hispánico. Freq: 2; Began: 1986; Cov: Scan; Lang:Eng /Spa; Subj: Theatre. ISBN: 0-9656914-1
■University of California, Irvine, Department of Spanish and Portuguese; Irvine, CA 92697; USA.

Gestus *Gestus*: A Quarterly Journal of Brechtian Studies. Freq: 4; Began: 1985; Cov: Full; Lang: Eng/Ger/Fre/Ita/Spa; Subj: Theatre. ISSN: 0749-7644
■Brecht Society of America; 59 S. New St.; Dover, DE 19901; USA.

GiP *Gosudarstvo i pravo*. Freq: 12; Began: 1992; Cov: Scan; Lang: Rus; Subj: Related. ISSN: 0132-0769
■Akad. Nauk S.S.S.R.; Inst. Gosudarstva i Prava; Izdatel'stvo Nauka; Podsosenskii Per., 21; Moscow K-62; RUSSIA.

GL&L *German Life and Letters*. Freq: 4; Began: 1936; Cov: Scan; Lang: Eng; Subj: Related. ISSN: 0016-8777
■Basil Blackwell Publisher, Ltd.; 108 Cowley Road; Oxford 0X4 1JF; UK.

Goethe *Goethe Yearbook: Publication of the Goethe Society of North America*. Freq: IRR; Lang: Eng /Ger; Subj: Related. Department of German; University of California; Irvine, CA 92717; USA.

GOS *Gazette Officielle du Spectacle*. Freq: 36; Began: 1969; Lang: Fre; Subj: Theatre. Office des Nouvelles Internationales; 12 rue de Miromesnil; 75008 Paris; FRANCE.

Gosteri *Gosteri*: Performance. Freq: 12; Lang: Tur; Subj: Theatre. Uluslararasi Sanat Gosterileri A.S.; Narlpbahce Sok. 15; Cagaloglu-Istanbul; TURKEY.

GQ *German Quarterly*. Freq: 4; Began: 1928; Last Known Address; Cov: Scan; Lang: Ger; Subj: Related. ISSN: 0016-8831
■American Assoc. of Teachers of German; 523 Building, Suite 201, Rt. 38; Cherry Hill, NJ 08034; USA.

GrandR *Grande République*. Formerly: *Pratiques Théâtrales*. Freq: 3; Began: 1978; Ceased: 1981; Lang: Fre; Subj: Theatre. ISSN: 0714-8178
■University of Québec; 200 Rue Sherbrooke Ouest; Montreal, PQ H2X 3P2; CANADA.

GrTZ *Graumann TZ*; Freq: 4; Cov: Scan; Lang: Ger; Subj: Related. GraumannEigenArt, Theaterverlag Wien-Hamburg; Wipplingerstr. 34; A-1001 Vienna; AUSTRIA.

GSJ *Gilbert and Sullivan Journal*. Freq: 3; Began: 1925; Ceased: 1986; Lang: Eng; Subj: Theatre. ISSN: 0016-9951
■Gilbert and Sullivan Society; 23 Burnside, Sawbridgeworth; Hertfordshire CM21 OEP; UK.

GSTB *George Spelvin's Theatre Book*. Freq: 3; Began: 1978; Lang: Eng; Subj: Theatre. ISSN: 0730-6431
■Proscenium Press; Box 361; Newark, NJ 19711; USA.

GTAR *Grupo Teatral Antifaz: Revista*. Freq: 12; Lang: Spa; Subj: Theatre. San Addres 146; 16 Barcelona; SPAIN.

GtE *Guidateatro: Estera*. Freq: 1; Began: 1967; Ceased; Lang: Ita; Subj: Theatre. Edizione Teatron; Via Fabiola 1; 00152 Rome; ITALY.

GtI *Guidateatro: Italiana*. Freq: 1; Began: 1967; Lang: Ita; Subj: Theatre.La guidateatro è venduta direttamente dall 'Théatron'; Via Fabiola 1; 00152 Rome; ITALY.

Guida *Guida dello Spettacolo*. Lang: Ita; Subj: Theatre. Via Palombini 6; Rome; ITALY.

HA *Habitat Australia*. Freq: 6; Began: 1973; Lang: Eng; Subj: Related. ISSN: 0310-2939
■Australian Conservation Foundation; 340 Gore St. Fitzroy; Melbourne, Victoria; AUSTRALIA.

Harlekijn *Harlekijn*. Freq: 4; Began: 1970; Ceased; Lang: Dut; Subj: Theatre. Kerkdijk 11; 3615 BA Westbroek; NETHERLANDS.

Hecate *Hecate: Women's Interdisciplinary Journal*. Freq: 2; Began: 1975; Cov: Scan; Lang: Eng; Subj: Related. ISSN: 0311-4198
■Hecate Press; English Dept., University of Queensland; P.O. Box 99 St. Lucia, Qld. 4067; AUSTRALIA.

Helik *Helikon*. Freq: 4; Began: 1955; Lang: Hun; Subj: Related. ISSN: 0017-999X
■Argumentum Kiadó; Ménesi út 11-13 1118 Budapest; HUNGARY.

Hermes *Hermes: Zeitschrift für Klassische Philologie*. Freq: 4; Began: 1866; Lang: Eng/Ger/Fre/Ita; Subj: Related. ISSN: 0018-0777
■Franz Steiner Verlag Wiesbaden GmbH; Birkenwaldstr. 44; D-70191; Stuttgart; GERMANY.

Hev *Hevesi Napló*Freq: 4;Began: 1991;Lang: Hun; Subj: Related. ISSN: 1217-3746

Hev *Hevesi Napló*Freq: 4;Began: 1991;Lang: Hun; Subj: Related.
■András Farkas; Vörösmarty út 26; 3300 Eger; HUNGARY.

HgK *Higeki Kigeki*: Tragedy and Comedy. Freq: 12; Began: 1948; Lang: Jap; Subj: Theatre. Hayakawa-Shobo, Chiyoda-ku; 2-2 Kanda-Tacho; 101 Tokyo; JAPAN.

HispArts *Hispanic Arts*. Freq: 5; Began: 1976; Last Known Address; Lang: Spa/Eng; Subj: Theatre. ISSN: 0732-1643
■Association of Hispanic Arts Inc.; 200 East 87th Street; New York, NY 10028; USA.

HisSt *Historical Studies*. Formerly: *Historical Studies: Australia and New Zealand*. SEE *Australian Historical Studies*. Freq: 2; Began: 1940; Ceased: 1988; Lang: Eng; Subj: Related. ISSN: 0018-2559
■University of Melbourne, Dept. of History; Parkville 3052; AUSTRALIA.

HistP *Historical Performance: Journal of Early Music America*. Freq: 2; Began: 1988; Lang: Eng; Subj: Related. ISSN: 0898-8587
■Early Music America; New York, NY; USA.

HJEAS *Hungarian Journal of English and American Studies*. Cov: Scan; Subj: Related. HUNGARY.

HJFTR *Historical Journal of Film, Radio and Television*. Freq: 2; Began: 1980; Lang: Eng; Subj: Related. ISSN: 0143-9685

■Carfax Pulbishing Co.; Box 25; Abingdon OX14 3UE; UK.

Horis *Horisont*. Freq: 6; Began: 1954; Lang: Swe; Subj: Related. ISSN: 0439-5530
■c/o Landsleapsförburden; Handelsesplanaden 23A; F 651 00 VASA; FINLAND.

HP *High Performance*. Freq: 4; Began: 1978; Lang: Eng; Subj: Related. ISSN: 0160-9769
■Astro Artz; 240 S. Broadway, 5th Floor; Los Angeles, CA 90012; USA.

HQ *Hungarian Quarterly*. Freq: 4; Began: 1959; Cov: Scan; Lang: Hun. Subj: Related.ISSN: 0028-5390MTI;Naphegy tér 8;1016 Budapest; HUNGARY.

HSt *Hamlet Studies*. Freq: 2; Began: 1978; Lang: Eng; Subj: Related. ISSN: 0256-2480
■Vikas Publishing House Ltd.; 5 Ansari Road; 110 002 New Delhi; INDIA.

HTHD *Hungarian Theatre/Hungarian Drama*. Freq: 1; Began: 1981; Cov: Scan; Ceased: 1988; Lang: Eng; Subj: Theatre. ISSN: 0230-1229
■Hungarian Theatre Institute; Krisztina körút. 57; 1016 Budapest; HUNGARY.

HTN *Hungarian Theatre News/ Ungarische Theaternachrichten*. Freq: 2; Began: 1985; Cov: Scan; Lang: Eng; Subj: Theatre. ISSN: 0237-3963
■Hungarian Centre of the International Theatre Institute; Krisztina krt. 57; 1016 Budapest; HUNGARY.

HW *History Workshop*. Freq: 2; Began: 1976; Lang: Eng; Subj: Related. ISSN: 0309-2984
■Oxford University Press; Pinkhill House; Southfield Road Eynsham, Oxford OX8 1JJ; UK.

IA *Ibsendrboken/Ibsen Yearbook*: Contemporary Approaches to Ibsen. Freq: 1; Began: 1952; Cov: Full; Lang: Nor/Eng; Subj: Theatre. ISSN: 0073-4365
■Universitetssorleget; Box 2959; 0608 Oslo 6; NORWAY.

IAS *Interscena/Acta Scenographica*. Freq: 2; Ceased: 1984; Lang: Eng/Fre/Ger; Subj: Theatre. Divadelni Ustav; Celetna 17; Prague 1; CZECH REPUBLIC.

IdS *Information du Spectacle, L'*. Freq: 11; Lang: Fre; Subj: Theatre. 7 rue du Helder; 75009 Paris; FRANCE.

IDSelect *Irish Drama Selections*. Freq: IRR; Began: 1982; Lang: Eng; Subj: Theatre. ISSN: 0260-7964
■Colin Smythe Ltd., Box 6; Gerrards Cross; Buckinghamshire SL9 8XA; UK.

IHoL *Irodalomtörténet*. Freq: 4; Began: 1912; Cov: Scan; Lang: Hun; Subj: Related. ISSN: 0324-4970
■Magyar Irodalomtörténeti Társaság; Piarista köz 1. I. 59; 1052 Budapest; HUNGARY.

IHS *Irish Historical Studies*. Freq: 2; Began: 1938; Lang: Eng; Subj: Related. ISSN: 0021-1214
■Irish Historical Society, Dept. of Modern Irish History; Arts-Commerce Bldg, University College; Dublin 4; IRELAND.

IITBI *Instituto Internacional del Teatro, Centro Espanol*: Boletin Informativo. Freq: 4; Last Known Address; Lang: Spa; Subj: Theatre. Paseo de Recoletos 18-60; 1 Madrid; SPAIN.

IK *Irodalomtörténeti Közlemények*. Freq: 6; Began: 1891; Cov: Scan; Lang: Hun; Subj: Related. ISSN: 0021-1486 ■Balassi Kiadó; Ménesi út 11-13; 1118 Budapest; HUNGARY.

IlCast *Il Castello di Elsinore*. Freq: 3; Began: 1988; Cov: Scan; Lang: Ita; Subj: Related. ISSN: 0394-9389 ■Rosenberg & Sellier; Via Andrea Doria, 14; 00192 Torino; ITALY.

IM *Island Magazine* Formerly: *Tasmanian Review;*. Freq: 4; Lang: Eng Cov: Scan;; Subj: Related. ISSN: 1035-3127 ■c/o Univ. of Tasmania; P.O. Box 207; Tasmania 7005; AUSTRALIA.

Impressum *Impressum*. Freq: 4; Lang: Ger; Subj: Related. Henschelverlag Kunst und Gesellschaft; Oranienburger Strasse 67/68; 1040 Berlin; GERMANY.

Impuls *Impuls*. Freq: 3; Cov: Scan; Lang: Ger; Subj: Related. Internationales Theaterinstitut; Schloss str. 48; D-12165 Berlin; GERMANY.

InArts *In the Arts*: Search, Research, and Discovery. Began: 1978; Ceased: 1988; Lang: Eng; Subj: Related. Ohio State University, College of the Arts; Columbus, OH 43210; USA.

INC *Ibsen News & Comments*. Freq: 1; Began: 1980; Cov: Scan; Lang: Eng; Subj: Theatre. Ibsen Society in America, Mellon Programs, Dekalb Hall 3; Pratt Institute; Brooklyn, NY 11205; USA.

Indonesia *Indonesia*. Freq: 2; Began: 1966; Lang: Eng; Subj: Related. ISBN: 0-87727 ■Cornell University, Southeast Asia Program Publications; East Hill Plaza; Ithaca, NY 14850; USA.

IndSh *Independent Shavian*. Freq: 3; Began: 1962; Lang: Eng; Subj: Theatre. ISSN: 0019-3763 ■The Bernard Shaw Society; Box 1159, Madison Square Station; New York, NY 10159-1159; USA.

Info *Information on New Plays*. Freq: IRR; Lang: Eng; Subj: Theatre. ISSN: 0236-6959 ■Hungarian Information Service; Krisztina krt. 57; H-1016 Budapest; HUNGARY.

InoLit *Inostrannaja Literatura*: (Foreign Literature). Freq: 12; Began: 1955; Cov: Scan; Lang: Rus; Subj: Related. ISSN: 0130-6545 ■Izvestija; Moscow; RUSSIA.

ISK *Iskusstvo Kino*. Freq: 12; Cov: Scan; Lang: Rus; Subj: Related. ISSN: 0130-6405 ■Moscow; RUSSIA.

Iskusstvo *Iskusstvo*. Freq: 12; Last Known Address; Began: 1918; Cov: Scan; Lang: Rus; Subj: Related. ISSN: 0130-2523 ■Tsvetnoi Bulvar 25; K 51 Moscow; RUSSIA.

Iskv *Iskusstvo v škole*. Began: 1927; Cov: Scan; Lang: Rus; Subj: Related. ISSN: 0869-4966 ■State Union Publishing; Kedrov Street 8; 117804 Moscow; RUSSIA.

ISPTC *Istituto di Studi Pirandelliani e sul Teatro Contemporaneo*. Freq: 1; Began: 1967; Lang: Ita; Subj: Theatre. ISSN: 0075-1480 ■Casa Editrice Felice le Monnier; Via Scipione Ammirato 100; 50136 Florence; ITALY.

ISST *In Sachen Spiel und Theater*. Formerly *Bunte Wagen*. Freq: 6; Began: 1949; Lang: Ger; Subj: Theatre. Höfling Verlag, Dr. V. Mayer; Str. 18-22; 6940 Weinheim; GERMANY.

ITAN *Irish Theatre Archive's Newsletter*. Freq: 2; Began: 1993; Lang: Eng; Subj: Theatre. Irish Theatre Archive, Archives Division; City Hall; Dublin 2; IRELAND.

ITY *International Theatre Yearbook*: SEE: Miedzynarodowny Rocznik Teatralny (Acro: MRT). Lang: Pol; Subj: Theatre. Warsaw; POLAND.

IUR *Irish University Review*. Freq: 2; Began: 1970; Cov: Scan; Lang: Eng; Subj: Related. ISSN: 0021-1427 ■University College; Room K203; Arts Building; Dublin 4; IRELAND.

IW *Ireland of the Welcomes*. Freq: 6; Began: 1952; Cov: Scan; Lang: Eng; Subj: Related. ISSN: 0021-0943 ■Bord Failte - Irish Tourist Board; Baggot St. Bridge; Dublin 2; IRELAND.

JAAC *Journal of Aesthetics and Art Criticism, The*. Freq: 4; Began: 1941; Lang: Eng; Subj: Related. ISSN: 0021-8529 ■114 N. Murray St.; Madison, WI 53715; USA.

JAC *Journal of American Culture*. Freq: 4; Began: 1978; Cov: Scan; Lang: Eng; Subj: Related. ISSN: 0191-1813 ■American Culture Association, Bowling Green State University; Bowling Green, OH 43403; USA.

JADT *Journal of American Drama and Theatre, The*. Freq: 3; Began: 1989; Cov: Full; Lang: Eng; Subj: Theatre. ISSN: 1044-937X ■CASTA, Grad. School and Univ. Centre, City University of New York; 33 West 42nd Street; New York, NY 10036; USA.

JAE *Journal of Aesthetic Education*. Freq: 4; Cov: Scan; Lang: English; Subj: Related. ISSN: 0021-8510 ■University of Illinois Press; 1325 S. Oak St.; Champaig, IL 61820-6903; USA.

JAfS *Journal of African Studies*. Freq: 4; Began: 1974; Lang: Eng; Subj: Related. ISSN: 0095-4993 ■Heldref Publications; 4000 Albemarle St, N.W.; Wasington, DC 20016; USA.

JahrfO *Jahrbuch für Opernforschung*. Cov: Scan; Lang: Ger; Subj: Related. ISSN: 0724-8156 ■Verlag Peter Lang GmbH; Eschborner Landstr. 42; D-60489 Frankfurt; GERMANY.

JahrST *Jahrbuch der Städte mit Theatergastspielen*. Freq: 1; Began: 1990; Cov: Scan; Lang: Ger; Subj: Related. ISSN: 0938-7943 ■Interessengemeinschaft der Städte mit Theatergastspielen; Mykenae-Verlag, Ahastr. 9; D-64285 Darmstadt; GERMANY.

JahrT *Jahrbuch Tanzforschung*. Freq: 1; Cov: Scan; Lang: Ger; Subj: Related. ISSN: 0940-1008 ■Florian Noetzel Verlag; Valoisstr. 11; D-29382 Wilhelmshaven; GERMANY.

JAML *Journal of Arts Management, Law and Society*. Formerly *Journal of Arts Management and Law*. Freq: 4; Began: 1969; Cov: Full; Lang: Eng; Subj: Related. ISSN: 1063-2921 ■Heldref Publications; 1319 Eighteenth Street, NW; Washington, DC 20036-1802; USA.

JAP&M *Journal of Arts Policy and Management*. Freq: 3; Began: 1984; Ceased: 1989; Cov: Full; Lang: Eng; Subj: Theatre. ISSN: 0265-0924 ■City University, Dept. of Arts Policy and Management; Level 12, Frobisher Crescent; Barbican, Silk Street; London EC2Y 8HB; UK.

JASt *Journal of Asian Studies*. Freq: 4; Began: 1941; Cov: Scan; Lang: Eng; Subj: Related. ISSN: 0021-9118 ■Association for Asian Studies, Inc., University of Michigan; One Lane Hall; Ann Arbor, MI 48109; USA.

Javisko *Javisko*. Freq: 12; Lang: Cze; Subj: Related. ISSN: 0323-2883 ■Vydavatel'stvo tosveta; Osloboditelov 21; 036-54 Martin; SLOVAKIA.

JBeckS *Journal of Beckett Studies*. Freq: 2; Began: 1976; Cov: Full; Lang: Eng; Subj: Theatre. ISSN: 0309-5207 ■John Calder Ltd.; 9-15 Neal Street; London WC2H 9TU; UK.

JCCP *Journal of Cross-Cultural Psychology*. Freq: 6; Cov: Scan; Lang: Eng; Subj: Related. ISSN: 0022-0221 ■SAGE Publications, Inc.; P.O. Box 5084; Thousand Oaks, CA 91359; USA.

JCNREC *Journal of Canadian Studies/ Revue d'études canadiennes*. Freq: 4; Began: 1966; Cov: Scan; Lang: Eng/Fre; Subj: Related. ISSN: 0021-9495 ■Trent University; Box 4800; Peterborough, ON K9J 7B8; CANADA.

JCSt *Journal of Caribbean Studies*. Freq: 2; Began: 1970; Lang: Eng/Fre/Spa; Subj: Related. ISSN: 0190-2008 ■Association of Caribbean Studies; Box 248231; Coral Gables, FL 33124; USA.

JCT *Jeu*: Cahiers de Théâtre. Freq: 4; Began: 1976; Cov: Full; Lang: Fre; Subj: Theatre. ISSN: 0382-0335 ■Cahiers de Theatre Jeu Inc.; C.P. 1600 Succursale E.; Montreal, PQ H2T 3B1; CANADA.

JdCh *Journal de Chaillot*. Freq: 8; Began: 1974; Lang: Fre; Subj: Related. Théâtre National de Chaillot; Place du Tracadéro; 75116 Paris; FRANCE.

JDS *Jacobean Drama Studies*. Freq: IRR; Began: 1972; Ceased: 1987; Lang: Eng; Subj: Theatre. Universität Salzburg, Institut für Englische Sprach; Akademiestr. 24; A 5020 Salzburg; AUSTRIA.

JDSh *Jahrbuch der Deutsche Shakespeare-Gesellschaft*. SEE: *Deutsche Shakespeare Gesellschaft/Deutsche Shakespeare Gesellschaft West*. Cov: Scan; Lang: Ger; Subj: Theatre. Deutsche Shakespeare-Gesellschaft West; Rathaus; D 4630 Bochum; GERMANY.

JDt *Journal of Dramatherapy*. Formerly: *Dramatherapy*. Freq: 2; Began: 1977; Lang: Eng; Subj: Related. ISSN: 0263-0672

■David Powley, British Association for Dramatherapy; PO Box 98; Kirkbymoorside YD6 6EX; UK.

JDTC *Journal of Dramatic Theory and Criticism*. Freq: 2; Began: 1986; Cov: Full; Lang: Eng; Subj: Theatre. ISSN: 0888-3203
■University of Kansas, Dept. of Theatre and Film; 356 Murphy Hall; Lawrence, KS 66045; USA.

JEBT *JEB Théâtre*. Lang: Fre; Ceased: 1982; Subj: Theatre. Documentation Générale de la jeunesse, des Loisirs; Galerie Ravenstein 78; 1000 Brussels; BELGIUM.

Jelenkor *Jelenkor*. Freq: 12; Began: 1958; Cov: Scan; Lang: Hun; Subj: Related. ISSN: 0447-6425
■Jelenkor Irodalmi és Müvészeti Kiadó; Széchenyi tér 17 7621 Pécs; HUNGARY.

JENS *Journal of the Eighteen Nineties Society*. Freq: 1; Began: 1970; Lang: Eng; Subj: Related. ISSN: 0144-008X
■28 Carlingford Rd., Hampstead; London NW3 1RQ; UK.

JFT *Journal Freie Theater*. Freq: 1; Cov: Scan; Lang: Ger; Subj: Related. Bundesverband Freier Theater e.V.; Mykenae-Verlag, Ahastr. 9; D-64285 Darmstadt; GERMANY.

JFV *Journal of Film and Video*. Freq: 4; Cov: Scan; Lang: Eng; Subj: Related. ISSN: 0724-4671
■University Film and Video Association;; USA.

JGG *Jahrbuch der Grillparzer-Gesellschaft*. Freq: IRR; Began: 1897; Lang: Ger; Subj: Related. ISBN: 3-273-00043-4
■Grillparzer-Gesellschaft; Gumpendorfer Strasse 15/1; A 1060 Vienna; AUSTRIA.

JGT *Journal du Grenier de Toulouse*. Freq: 12; Lang: Fre; Subj: Theatre. Grenier de Toulouse; 3, rue de la Digue; 31300 Toulouse; FRANCE.

JIES *Journal of the Illuminating Engineering Society*. Freq: 1; Lang: Eng; Subj: Related. ISSN: 0099-4480
■Illuminating Engineering Society of North America; 120 Wall Street, 17th Floor; New York, NY 10005-4001; USA.

JIL *Journal of Irish Literature*. Freq: 3; Began: 1972; Ceased: 1994; Lang: Eng; Subj: Related. P.O. Box 361; Newark, DE 19711; USA.

JITT *JITT*. Lang: Jap; Subj: Theatre. Japanese Institute for Theatre Technology; 4-437 Ikebukuro, Toshima-ku; Tokyo; JAPAN.

JJS *Journal of Japanese Studies*. Freq: 2; Began: 1974; Lang: Eng; Subj: Related. ISSN: 0095-6848
■Society for Japanese Studies, University of Washington; Thomson Hall DR-05; Seattle, WA 98195; USA.

JLS/TLW *Journal of Literary Studies/ Tydskrif vir Literatuurwetenskap*. Freq: 4; Began: 1985; Cov: Scan; Lang: Eng/Afr; Subj: Related. ISSN: 0256-4718
■South African Society for General Literary Studies; Department of Theory of Literature Unisa P.O. Box 392 Pretoria 0001; SOUTH AFRICA.

JMH *Journal of Magic History*. Began: 1979; Lang: Eng; Subj: Related. ISSN: 0192-9917

■Toledo, OH; USA.

JMMLA *Journal of the Midwest Modern Language Association*. Freq: 2; Began: 1959; Cov: Scan; Lang: Eng; Subj: Related. ISSN: 0742-5562
■302 English-Philosophy Building; University of Iowa; Iowa City, IA 52242; USA.

JNZL *Journal of New Zealand Literature*. Lang: Eng; Subj: Related. Wellington; NEW ZEALAND.

JoM *Journal of Musicology*. Freq: 4; Cov: Scan; Lang: Eng; Subj: Related. ISSN: 0277-9269
■University of California Press; 2120 Berkeley Way; Berkeley, CA 94720; USA.

JOV *Journal of Voice*. Freq: 4; Began: 1987; Cov: Scan; Lang: Eng; Subj: Related. Raven Press Books, Ltd.; 1185 Avenue of the Americas; New York, NY 10036; USA.

JPC *Journal of Popular Culture*. Freq: 4; Began: 1967; Cov: Scan; Lang: Eng; Subj: Related. ISSN: 0022-3840
■Popular Culture Association, Bowling Green State University; Bowling Green, OH 43403; USA.

JRASM *Journal of the Royal Asiatic Society of Malaysia*. Freq: 2; Began: 1936; Lang: Eng; Subj: Related. Kuala Lumpur; MALAYSIA.

JRSAVP *Journal of Research in Singing and Applied Vocal Pedagogy*. Freq: 2; Lang: Eng; Subj: Related. Texas Christian University; Department of Music; P.O. Box 32887 Fort Worth, TX 76129; USA.

JSDC *Journal for Stage Directors and Choreographers*. Freq: 2; Began: 1996; Cov: Scan; Lang: Eng; Subj: Theatre. SDC Foundation; 1501 Broadway, Suite 1701; New York, NY 10036; USA.

JSH *Journal of Social History*. Freq: 4; Began: 1967; Cov: Scan; Lang: Eng; Subj: Related. ISSN: 0022-4529
■Carnegie-Mellon University Press; Schenley Park; Pittsburgh, PA 15213; USA.

JSS *Journal of the Siam Society*. Began: 1926; Lang: Eng/Tha/Fre/Ger; Subj: Related. 131 Soi Asoke; Sukhumvit 21 Road; Bangkok 10110; THAILAND.

JT *Jeune Théâtre*. Began: 1970; Ceased: 1982; Lang: Fre; Subj: Theatre. ISSN: 0315-0402
■Assoc. Québecoise du, Jeune Théâtre; 952 rue Cherrier; Montreal, PQ H2L 1H7; CANADA.

JTPR *Journal du Théâtre Populaire Romand*. Freq: 8; Began: 1962; Lang: Fre; Subj: Theatre. Case Postale 80; 2301 La Chaux-de-Fonds; SWITZERLAND.

JTV *Journal du Théâtre de la Ville*. Freq: 4; Began: 1968; Lang: Fre; Subj: Theatre. Theatre de la Ville; 16 quai de Gesvres; Paris; FRANCE.

Juben *Juben*: (Playtexts). Freq: 12; Began: 1952; Lang: Chi; Subj: Theatre. ISSN: 0578-0659
■Zhongguo Xiju Chubanshe, 52; Dongsi Ba (8), Tiao 100700 Beijing; CHINA.

JugoIgre *Jugoslovenske*: Pozorišne Igre. Began: 1962; Lang: Ser; Subj: Theatre. Sterijino Pozorje; Zmaj Jovina 22; Novi Sad; SERBIA.

Junkanoo *Junkanoo*. Freq: 12; Lang: Eng; Subj: Theatre. Junkanoo Publications; Box N 4923; Nassau; BAHAMAS.

JWCI *Journal of the Warburg & Courtauld Institutes*. Freq: 1; Began: 1937; Cov: Scan; Lang: Eng; Subj: Related. Woburn Square; London WC1H OAB; UK.

JWGT *Jahrbuch der Wiener Gesellschaft für Theaterforschung*. Freq: 1; Lang: Ger; Subj: Related. Vienna; AUSTRIA.

Kabuki *Kabuki*. Lang: Jap Cov: Scan; Lang: Jap; Subj: Theatre. 4-12-15 Ginza; 104 Chuo-ku, Tokyo; JAPAN.

Kaekseok *Kaekseok*. Freq: 12; Began: 1992; Cov: Scan; Lang: Kor; Subj: Related. 58-1 Chung Jung-No 1 Ga; Jung Ku; Seoul;SOUTH KOREA.

Kalak *Kalakalpam*. Freq: 2; Began: 1966; Lang: Eng; Subj: Theatre. Karyalaya Matya Kala Institute; 30-A Paddapukur Road; 20 Calcutta; INDIA.

Kalliope *Kalliope*. Freq: 3; Began: 1995 Lang: Eng; Subj: Theatre. 3939 Roosevelt Blvd.; Jacksonville, FL 32205; USA.

Kanava *Kanava*. Formerly: *Aika*. Freq: 9; Began: 1932; Lang: Fin; Subj: Related. ISSN: 0355-0303
■Yhtyneet Kuvalehdet Oy; Hietalahdenranta 13; 00180 Helsinki 18; FINLAND.

KAPM *Kassette*: Almanach für Bühne, Podium und Manege. Freq: 1; Lang: Ger; Subj: Theatre. Berlin; GERMANY.

Kathakali *Kathakali*. Freq: 4; Began: 1969; Lang: Eng/Hin; Subj: Theatre. ISSN: 0022-9326
■International Centre for Kathakali; 1-84 Rajandra Nagar; New Delhi; INDIA.

Kazal *Kazaliste*. Freq: 26; Began: 1965; Ceased; Lang: Yug; Subj: Theatre.
■Prolaz Radoslava Bacica 1; Osijek; CROATIA.

KB *Kunst Bulletin*. Freq: 12; Cov: Scan; Subj: Related.
■Fr. Hallwag AG; Nording 4; 4001 Bern; SWITZERLAND.

KCAB *Korean Culture & Arts Bi-Monthly*. Freq: 6; Cov: Scan; Began: 1974; Lang: Kor; Subj: Related.
■Hankug Munhwa Yeasul Jinhyeng Won; 1-130 Chongrogu Dongsun Dong; Seoul; SOUTH KOREA.

Keshet *Keshet*. Last Known Address; Began: 1982; Lang: Heb; Subj: Theatre.
■9 Bialik Street; Tel Aviv; ISRAEL.

KesK *Kultúra és Közösség*. Freq: 6; Began: 1974; Ceased: 1990; Cov: Scan; Lang: Hun; Subj: Related. ISSN: 0133-2597
■Arany János Lap- és Könyvkiadó Kft.; Corvin tér 8; 1011 Budapest; HUNGARY.

KingP *King Pole Circus Magazine*. Freq: 4; Began: 1934; Cov: Scan; Lang: Eng; Subj: Theatre.
■Circus Fans' Assoc. of UK, c/o John Exton; 20 Foot Wood Crescent; Shawclough Rochdale, Lancaster OL12 6PB; UK.

Kino *Kino*. Freq: 4; Cov: Scan; Lang: Eng; Subj: Theatre;

■Australian Theatre Historical Society; P.O. Box 447; Campbelltown New South Wales 2560; AUSTRALIA.

KJ *Kultur-Journal*. Freq: 4; Lang: Ger; Subj: Related.
■Mykenae-Verlag; Ahastr. 9; D-64285 Darmstadt; GERMAN.

KJAZU *Kronika*: Zavod za povijest hrvatske knjizevnisti. Began: 1975; Lang: Cro; Subj: Theatre. ISSN: 0023-4929
■kazalista i glazbe Hrvatske akademije znanosti i umjetnosti; Opaticka 18; 41.000 Zagreb; CROATIA.

Klub *Klub i Chudoẑestvennaja Samode-jetelnost*. Freq: 26; Lang: Rus; Subj: Theatre.
■Profizdat; Ulitza Korova 13; Moscow; RUSSIA.

KMFB *Gewerkschaft Kunst, Medien, Freie Berufe*. Freq: 11; Began: 1945; Lang: Ger; Subj: Theatre.
■UMLOsterreichischer Gewerkschaftsbund, Gewrkshft. Kunst, Medien, Freie, Berufe; Maria-Theresienstrasse 11; A 1090 Vienna; AUSTRIA.

KoJ *Korea Journal*. Freq: 4; Began: 1961; Cov: Scan; Lang: Eng; Subj: Related. ISSN: 0023-3900
■Korean National Commission for UNESCO; P.O. Box Central 64; Seoul; SOUTH KOREA.

Kommunist *Kommunist*. Began: 1924; Cov: Scan; Lang: Rus; Subj: Related. ISSN: 0131-1212
■Svobodnaja mysl'; Moscow; RUSSIA.

Kont *Kontinent*. Freq: 4; Cov: Scan; Lang: Rus; Subj: Related. ISSN: 0934-6317
■Čistoprudnij Boulevard, 8A; 101923 Moscow; RUSSIA.

KoreanD *Korean Drama*. Last Known Address; Lang: Kor; Subj: Theatre.
■National Drama Association of Korea, Insadong, Jongno-gu; Fed. of Arts & Cult. Org. Building; 110 Seoul; SOUTH KOREA.

Kortars *Kortárs*. Freq: 12; Began: 1957; Cov: Scan; Lang: Hun; Subj: Related. ISSN: 0023-415X
■Magyar Irószövetség; Bajza u. 18; 1062 Budapest; HUNGARY.

KPR *Kulturno-Prosvetitelnaja Rabota*. SEE *Vstreča*. Freq: 12; Ceased: 1990; Lang: Rus; Subj: Related.
■Sovéckaja Rossija; Bersenevskaja Naberež-naja 22; Moscow; RUSSIA.

Krajs *Kraj smolenskij* Began: 1996; Cov: Scan; Subj: Related.
■Dom Sovietov k. 163; Smolensk 214008; RUSSIA.

Krit *Kritika*. Freq: 12; Began: 1963; Cov: Scan; Lang: Hun; Subj: Related. ISSN: 0324-7775
■Népszabadság Rt; Bécsi út 122-124; 1034 Budapest; HUNGARY.

KS *Kleine Schriften*. Freq: 1; Began: 1992; Cov: Scan; Lang: Ger; Subj: Related. 3-925191-95-X
■Gesellschaft für unterhaltende Bühnenkunst e.V.; Grupellellostr. 21; D-40210 Dusseldorf; GERMANY.

KSF *Korean Studies Forum*. Freq: 2; Began 1976; Last Known Address; Lang: Kor; Subj: Related. ISSN: 0147-6335

■Korean-American Educ. Commission, Garden Towers; No. 1803, 98-78 Wooni-Dong, Chon-gro-Ku; Seoul 110; SOUTH KOREA.

KSGT *Kleine Schriften der Gesellschaft für Theatergeschichte*. Freq: 1; Cov: Scan; Lang: Ger; Subj: Theatre.
■Gesellschaft für Theatergeschichte e.V.; Mecklenburgische Str. 56; D-14197 Berlin; GERMANY.

KTR *Korean Theatre Review*. Freq: 12; Lang: Kor; Cov: Scan; Subj: Theatre.
■National Theatre Association of Korea; Ye-chong Bldg; 1-117 Dongsoon-dong; Chongno-ku Seoul 110; SOUTH KOREA.

Kulis *Kulis*. Freq: 12; Began: 1946; Lang: Arm; Subj: Theatre.
■H. Ayvaz; PK 83; 10 A Cagaloglu Yokusu; TURKEY.

Kvihkot *Kultuurivihkot*. Freq: 8; Began: 1973; Last Known Address; Lang: Fin/Swe; Subj: Theatre.
■Kultuurityontekijain Liitto; Korkeavuorenkatu 4 C 15; 00130 Helsinki; FINLAND.

KWN *Kurt Weill Newsletter*. Freq: 2; Began: 1983; Cov: Scan; Lang: Eng; Subj: Related. ISSN: 0899-6407
■Weill Foundation for Music; 7 East 20th Street; New York, NY 10003-1106; USA.

KZ *Kultura i Žizn*. (Culture and Life). Freq: 12; Began: 1957; Cov: Scan; Lang: Rus/Eng/Ger/Fre/Spa; Subj: Related. ISSN: 0023-5199
■Sovéckaja Rossija; Projézd Sapunova 13-15; Moscow K-12; RUSSIA.

L&H *Literature & History*. Freq: 2; Began: 1975; Lang: Eng; Subj: Related. ISSN: 0306-1973
■Ohio State University, Dept. of English; 421 Denney Hall; 164 W. 17th Ave. OH 43210; USA.

LabH *Labour History*. Freq: 2; Began: 1963; Cov: Scan; Lang: Eng; Subj: Related. ISSN: 0023-6942
■Economic History Department; HO4, University of Sydney; NSW 2006; AUSTRALIA.

Laien *Laientheater*. Freq: 12; Began: 1972; Lang: Ger; Subj: Theatre.
■Schweizerischen Volkstheater; 30 Bern; SWITZERLAND.

LAQ *Livres et Auteurs Québecois*. Freq: 1; Began: 1969; Ceased; Lang: Fre; Subj: Related. ISSN: 0316-2621
■Presses de l'Université Laval, Cité Universitaire; Québec, PQ G1K 7R4; CANADA.

LATR *Latin American Theatre Review*. Freq: 2; Began: 1967; Cov: Full; Lang: Eng/Spa/Por; Subj: Theatre. ISSN: 0023-8813
■University of Kansas, Center of Latin American Studies; 107 Lippincott Hall; Lawrence, KS 66045; USA.

LD+A *Lighting Design + Application*. Freq: 12; Began: 1906; Cov: Scan; Lang: Eng; Subj: Theatre. ISSN: 0360-6325
■Illuminating Engineering Society; 120 Wall Street; 17th Floor New York, NY 10005-4001; USA.

LDim *Lighting Dimensions*: For the Entertainment Lighting Industry. Freq: 6; Began: 1977; Cov: Scan; Lang: Eng; Subj: Theatre.

■Lighting Dimensions Publishing; 1590 S. Coast Highway, Suite 8; Laguna, CA 92651; USA.

LetQu *Lettres Québécoises*. Freq: 4; Began: 1976; Lang: Fre; Subj: Related. ISSN: 0382-084X
■Editions Jumonville; 1781 rue Saint-Hubert; Montreal, PQ, H2L 3Z1; CANADA.

LettDI *Lettera Dall'Italia*: Bollettino trimestrale realizzato dall'Istituto dell'Enciclopedia Italiana. Freq: 4; Began: 1985; Lang: Ita; Subj: Related. ISSN: 0393-64457
■Piazza dell'Enciclopedia Italiana, 4; 00186 Rome; ITALY.

Letture *Letture*: Libro e spettacolo, mensile di studi e rassegne. Freq: 10; Began: 1946; Lang: Ita; Subj: Related. ISSN: 0024-144X
■Edizioni Letture; Piazza San Fedele 4; 20121 Milan; ITALY.

Letuch *Leteraturnaja ucheba*. Freq: 6; Lang: Rus; Subj: Related. ISSN: 0203-5847
■Novodmitrovskaja Street, 5A; 125015 Moscow; RUSSIA.

LFQ *Literature/Film Quarterly*. Freq: 4; Began: 1973; Lang: Eng; Subj: Related. ISSN: 0090-4260
■Salisbury State University; Salisbury, MD 21801; USA.

Light *Light*. Freq: 24; Began: 1921; Lang: Eng; Subj: Theatre.
■Ahmadiyya Building; Brandreth Road; Lahore; PAKISTAN.

LikC *Lik Čuvašija*; Freq: 6; Began: 1994; Cov: Scan; Lang: Rus; Subj: Related.
■Dom Pečaty k. 613; 13 pr. I. Jakovleva; Cheboksary 428019; CHUVASHIA.

Lilith *Lilith: a Feminist History Journal*. Freq: 1; Began: 1984; Cov: Scan; Lang: Eng; Subj: Related; ISSN: 0813-8990
■Lilith Collective; P.O. Box 154; Fitzroy, Victoria 3065; AUSTRALIA.

LiNQ *Literature in North Queensland*. Freq: 2; Began: 1971; Cov: Scan; Lang: Eng; Subj: Related.
■Dept. of English; James Cook University of North Queensland; Townsville, 4811; AUSTRALIA.

LinzerT *Linzer Theaterzeitung*. Freq: 10; Began: 1955; Lang: Ger; Subj: Theatre. ISSN: 0024-4139
■Landestheater Linz; Promenade 39; A 4010 Linz; AUSTRIA.

Lipika *Lipika*. Freq: 4; Began: 1972; Lang: Eng; Subj: Theatre.
■F-20 Nizzamudin West; 10013 New Delhi; INDIA.

Literator *Literator: Journal of Comparative Literature and Linguistics*. Freq: 3; Began: 1980; Cov: Scan; Lang: Afr/Eng; Subj: Related; ISSN: 0258-2279
■Bureau for Scholarly Journals; Private Bag X6001; Potchefstroom 2520; REPUBLIC OF SOUTH AFRICA.

Literatura *Literatura*. Freq: 4; Began: 1974; Lang: Hun; Subj: Related. ISSN: 0133-2368
■Balassi Kiadó; Ménesi út 11-13; 1118 Budapest; HUNGARY.

LitGruzia *Literaturnaja Gruzija*. Freq: 12; Began: 1957; Cov: Scan; Lang: Rus; Subj: Related. ISSN: 0130-3600 ∎Sojuz pisatelej Gruzii; Tbilisi, Georg. SSR; GEORGIA.

Litva *Litva literaturnaja*. Freq: 12; Cov: Scan; Lang: Rus; Subj: Related. ISSN: 0206-296X ∎Labdaryu Street, 3; 232600 Viln'yus; LITHUANIA.

Live *Live*. Freq: 4; Lang: Eng; Subj: Related. ∎New York, NY; USA.

LLJ *La Trobe Library Journal*. Freq: 2; Began: 1968; Cov: Scan; Lang: Eng; Subj: Related. ISSN: 0041-3151 ∎Friends of the State Library of Victoria; State Library of Victoria; Swanston Street; Melbourne, 3000; AUSTRALIA.

LO *Literaturnoje Obozrenije*. Freq: 12; Began: 1973; Cov: Scan; Lang: Rus; Subj: Related. ISSN: 0321-2904 ∎Sojuz Pisatelej SSSR; 9/10 ul. Dobroliubova; 127254 Moscow I-254,; RUSSIA.

Loisir *Loisir*. Freq: 4; Began: 1962; Lang: Fre; Subj: Theatre. ∎Comédie de Caen; 120 rue St. Pierre; 1400 Caen; FRANCE.

LokK *Lok Kala*. Freq: 2; Ceased: 1977; Lang: Hin; Subj: Theatre. ∎Bhartiya Lok kala Mandal; Udaipur 313001 Rajasthan; INDIA.

Loutkar *Loutkar*. Formerly Ceskoslovensky loutkar. Freq: 12; Began: 1993; Lang: Cze; Subj: Related. ISSN: 0323-1178 ∎Nina Malikova, Divadelni ustav; Celetna 17; 110 01 Praha 1; CZECH REPUBLIC.

Lowdown *Lowdown*. Freq: 6; Began: 1979; Cov: Scan; Lang: Eng; Subj: Theatre. ∎Youth Performing Arts Assoc.; 11 Jeffcott St.; Adelaide SA 5000; AUSTRALIA.

LPer *Literature in Performance*. SEE *Text and Performance Quarterly*. Freq: 2; Began: 1980; Ceased; Lang: Eng; Subj: Theatre. ISSN: 0734-0796 ∎Inter. Div.,Speech Comm. Assoc., Dept. of Speech Communication; U. of NC, 115 Bingham Hall; Chapel Hill, NC 27514; USA.

LTR *Theatre Record*. Freq: 26; Began: 1981; Cov: Full; Lang: Eng; Subj: Theatre. ISSN: 0261-5282 ∎4 Cross Deep Gardens; Twickenham TW1 4QU Middlesex; UK.

Ludus *Ludus*: List Udruženja Dramskih Umetnika Srbije. Freq: 6; Began: 1983; Lang: Ser; Subj: Theatre. ∎Udruženja Dramskih Umetnika Srbije; Terazije 26; Belgrade; SERBIA.

Lutka *Lutka*: Revija za lutkovno kulturo. Freq: 3; Began: 1966; Lang: Slo; Subj: Theatre. ISSN: 0350-9303 ∎Zveza kulturnih organizacij Slovenije; Kidričeva 5; Ljubljana; SLOVENIA.

M&T *Musik & Teater*. SEE *Teater Et*. Freq: 6; Began: 1979; Ceased: 1989; Lang: Dan; Subj: Theatre. ∎Bagsvard Horedgade 9914E; 2800 Bagsvard; DENMARK.

MA *Muzykal'naja akademija*. Freq: 6; Began: 1957; Cov: Scan; Lang: Rus; Subj: Related. ISSN: 0869-4516 ∎Gadovaja Triumfal'naja uliča; #14/12;, Moscow 103006; RUSSIA.

MagIp *Magyar Iparművészet*. Freq: 6; Began: 1994; Cov: Scan; Lang: Hun; Subj: Related. ISSN: 1217-839X ∎Forka Tömegkommunikációs Kft.; Nádor u. 32; 1051 Budapest; HUNGARY.

MagM *Magyar Múzeum*. Formerly *Új Erdélyi Múzeum*. Freq: 4; Began: 1991; Lang: Hun; Subj: Related. ISSN: 0866-4625 ∎Akadémiai Kiadó és a Közép-Európai Múzeum; Alapítvány; Meredek u. 25 1124 Budapest; HUNGARY.

Maksla *Maksla*. Began: 1959; Lang: Lat; Subj: Related. ISSN: 0455-3772 ∎Riga; LATVIA.

MAL *Modern Austrian Literature*. Freq: 4; Began: 1961; Lang: Eng/Ger; Subj: Related. ISSN: 0026-7503 ∎Intl A. Schnitzler Research Assoc., c/o Donald G. Daviau, Ed.; Dept. of Lit. & Langs, Univ. of CA; Riverside, CA 92521; USA.

Mamulengo *Mamulengo*. Lang: Por; Subj: Theatre. ∎Assoc. Brasileira de Teatro de Bonecos; Rua Barata Ribeiro; 60 C 01 Guanabara; BRAZIL.

Manip *Manipulation*. Last Known Address; Lang: Eng; Subj: Theatre. ∎Mrs. Maeve Vella; 28 Macarthur Place; 3053 Carlton, Victoria; AUSTRALIA.

MarqJTHS *Marquee*: The Journal of the Theatre Historical Society. Freq: 4; Began: 1969; Cov: Scan; Lang: Eng; Subj: Theatre. ISSN: 0025-3928 ∎624 Wynne Rd; Springfield, PA 19064; USA.

Marquee *Marquee*. Freq: 8; Began: 1976; Last Known Address; Lang: Eng; Subj: Related. ISSN: 0700-5008 ∎Marquee Communications Inc.; 277 Richmond St. W.; Toronto, ON M5V 1X1; CANADA.

Mask *Mask*. Freq: 6; Began: 1967; Lang: Eng; Subj: Theatre. ISSN: 0726-9072 ∎Simon Pryor, Executive Officer, VADIE; 117 Bouverie Street; 3053 Carlton; AUSTRALIA.

MASKA *MASKA*. Freq: 4; Began: 1991; Lang: Slo/Eng; Subj: Theatre. ISSN: 1318-0509 ∎Dunajska 22; 61000 Ljubljana; SLOVENIA.

Maske *Maske*. SEE *Maska*. Began: 1985; Ceased: 1991; Lang: Slo/Eng; Subj: Theatre. ISSN: 0352-7913 ∎Zveza kulturnih organizacij Slovenije; Ljubljana; SLOVENIA.

Masque *Masque*. Freq: 24; Began: 1967; Lang: Eng; Subj: Theatre. ISSN: 0025-469X ∎Masque Publications; Box 3504; 2001 Sydney NSW; AUSTRALIA.

Mast *Masterstvo*. Freq: 6; Lang: Ukr; Subj: Theatre. ∎Pouchkineskaia Street 5; Kiev; UKRAINE.

Matya *Matya Prasanga*. Freq: 12; Lang: Ben; Subj: Theatre. ∎54/1 B Patuatola Lane; Emherst Street; Calcutta; INDIA.

MAvilia *Monte Avilia*. Freq: 12; Began: 1980; Lang: Spa; Subj: Theatre. ∎Apartado 70-712; 107 Caracas; VENEZUELA.

MBB *Mala Biblioteka Baletowa*. Began: 1957; Ceased: 1981; Lang: Pol; Subj: Theatre. ∎Polskie Wydawnictwo Muzyczne; Al. Krasińskiego 11a; 31-111 Kraków; POLAND.

MBzT *Münchener Beiträge zur Theaterwissenschaft*. Cov: Scan; Lang: Ger; Subj: Related. ISSN: 0343-7604 ∎J. Kitzinger oHG, Schellingstr. 25; D-80799 Munich; GERMANY.

MC&S *Media, Culture and Society*. Freq: 4; Began: 1979; Lang: Eng; Subj: Related. ISSN: 0163-4437 ∎Sage Publications; 6 Bonhill Street; London EC2A 4PU; UK.

MChAT *Ežegodnik MChAT*. Freq: 1; Lang: Rus; Subj: Theatre. ∎Association of Soviet Writers; Hertsen 49; Moscow; RUSSIA.

MD *Modern Drama*. Freq: 4; Began: 1958; Cov: Full; Lang: Eng; Subj: Theatre. ISSN: 0026-7694 ∎Univ. of Toronto Press; 5201 Dufferin Street; Downsview, ON M5T 2Z9; CANADA.

MDM *Musicals—Das Musicalmagazin*. Freq: 6; Began: 1986; Lang: Ger; Subj: Related. ISSN: 0931-8194 ∎Balanstr. 19; D-81669 Munich; GERMANY.

MdTNB *Magazine du TNB*. Lang: Fre; Subj: Theatre. ∎Theatre National De Bretagne; 1, rue St. Helier; 35008 Rennes Cedex BP 675; FRANCE.

MdVO *Mitteilungen der Vereinigung Österreichischer Bibliotheken*. Lang: Ger; Subj: Related. ∎Vienna; AUSTRIA.

Meanjin *Meanjin*. Formerly: *Meanjin Quarterly* Freq: 3; Began: 1940; Cov: Scan; Lang: Eng; Subj: Related. ISSN: 0025-6293 ∎Meanjin Co. Ltd.; 211 Grattan Street; Parkville, Victoria 3052; AUSTRALIA.

MeisterP *Meister des Puppenspiels*. Freq: IRR; Began: 1959; Lang: Ger; Subj: Theatre. ISSN: 0076-6216 ∎Deutsches Institut für Puppenspiel; Hattingerstr. 467; 4630 Bochum; GERMANY.

Meridian *Meridian*. Began: 1982; Cov: Scan; Lang: Eng; Subj: Related. ISSN: 0728-5914 ∎Dept. of English, La Trobe University; Bundoora; Victoria 3083; AUSTRALIA.

Merker *Neue Merker, Der*.Oper in Wien und aller welt. Freq: 12; Lang: Ger; Subj: Theatre. ISSN: 1017-5202 ∎Dr. Sieglinde Pfabigan; Merker-Verein; Peitglasse 7/3/4 A 1210 Vienna; AUSTRIA.

MET *Medieval English Theatre*. Freq: 2; Began: 1979; Cov: Full; Lang: Eng; Subj: Theatre. ISSN: 0143-3784 ∎c/o M. Twycross, Dept. of English; University of Lancaster; Lancaster LA1 4YT; UK.

MGL *Mestno gledališče Ljubljansko*. Freq: IRR; Began: 1959; Lang: Slo; Subj: Theatre. ∎Ljubljana Čopova 14; 61000; SLOVENIJA.

MHall *Music Hall*. Freq: 6; Began: 1978; Lang: Eng; Subj: Theatre.

■Tony Barker; 50 Reperton Road; London SW6; UK.

MID *Modern International Drama*: Magazine for Contemporary International Drama in Translation. Freq: 2; Began: 1967; Cov: Full; Lang: Eng; Subj: Theatre. ISSN: 0026-7856
■State University of NY; P.O. Box 6000; Binghamton, NY 13902-6000; USA.

Mim *Mim: Revija za glumu i glumište*: Glasilo Udruženja dramskih umjetnika Hrvatske. Freq: 12; Began: 1984; Lang: Cro; Subj: Theatre.
■Udruž. Dramskih Umjetnika Hravatske; Ilica 42; Zagreb; CROATIA.

MimeJ *Mime Journal*. Freq: 1; Began: 1974; Cov: Full; Lang: Eng; Subj: Theatre. ISSN: 0145-787X
■Pomona College Theater Department, Claremont Colleges; Claremont, CA 91711; USA.

MimeN *Mime News*. Freq: 5; Began: 1983; Cov: Scan; Lang: Eng; Subj: Theatre. ISSN: 0892-4910
■National Mime Association; Box 148277; Chicago, IL 60614; USA.

Mimos *Mimos*. Freq: 3; Began: 1949; Lang: Ger; Subj: Theatre. ISSN: 0026-4385
■Schweizerische Gesellschaft für Theaterkultur; Theaterkultur-Verlag; Pf. 1940 CH-4001 Basel; SWITZERLAND.

Mit *Mitgliederzeitung*. Freq: 4; Cov: Scan; Lang: Ger; Subj: Related.
■Gesellschaft für unterhaltende Bühnenkunst e.V.; Hertzbergstr. 21; D-12055 Berlin; GERMANY.

MK *Molodoi Kommunist*. SEE *Perspektiva*. Freq: 12; Began: 1918; Ceased: 1990; Cov: Scan; Lang: Rus; Subj: Related. ISSN: 0131-2278
■Izdatel'stvo Molodaya Gvardija, Ul.; Sushevskaya, 21; Moscow A-55; RUSSIA.

MLet *Music & Letters*. Freq: 4; Began: 1920; Lang: Eng; Subj: Related. ISSN: 0027-4224
■Oxford University Press; Walton Street; Oxford OX2 6DP; UK.

MLR *Modern Language Review*. Freq: 4; Began: 1905; Lang: Eng; Subj: Related. ISSN: 0026-7937
■King's College London; Strand; London WC2 R 2LS; UK.

MMDN *Medieval Music-Drama News*. Freq: 2; Began: 1982; Ceased: 1991; Lang: Eng; Subj: Related. ISSN: 0731-0374
■Kalamazoo, MI; USA.

MMDTA *Monographs on Music, Dance and Theater in Asia*. Freq: 1; Began 1971; Last Known Address; Lang: Eng; Subj: Theatre.
■The Asia Society, Performing Arts Program; 133 East 58th Street; New York, NY 10022; USA.

MN *Monumenta Nipponica*: Studies in Japanese Culture. Freq: 4; Began: 1938; Cov: Scan; Lang: Eng; Subj: Related. ISSN: 0027-0741
■Sophia University, 7-1 Kioi-cho; Chiyoda-ku; 102 Tokyo; JAPAN.

Mobile *Mobile*. Freq: 12; Lang: Fre; Subj: Theatre.

■Maison de la Culture d'Amiens; Place Léon Gontier; 80000 Amiens; FRANCE.

MoD *Monthly Diary*. Lang: Eng; Subj: Theatre.
■Sydney; AUSTRALIA.

MojM *Moja Moskva*. Lang: Rus Subj: Related.
■ul. Tverskaja, 13 Moscow 103032 RUSSIA

MolGvar *Molodaja gvardija*. Freq: 12; Began: 1922; Cov: Scan; Lang: Rus; Subj: Related. ISSN: 0131-2257
■ Moscow; RUSSIA.

Monsalvat *Monsalvat*. Freq: 11; Began: 1973; Lang: Spa; Subj: Theatre.
■Ediciones de Nuevo Arte; Plaza Gala Placidia 1; 6 Barcelona; SPAIN.

Mosk *Moskva*. Freq: 12; Began: 1957; Cov: Scan; Lang: Rus; Subj: Related. ISSN: 0132-2382
■Chudozestvennaja Literatura; 24 Rub. Sojuz pisatelej Rossiiskoi; Moscow; RUSSIA.

MoskNab *Moskovskij Nabljudatel'*. Began: 1991; Cov: Scan; Lang: Rus; Subj: Related. ISSN: 0868-8524
■Arbat, 35; 121835 Moscow; RUSSIA.

MoskZ *Moskovskij Žurnal*. Cov: Scan; Lang: Rus; Subj: Related.
■RUSSIA.

Mozgo *Mozgó Világ*. Freq: 12; Began: 1971; Ceased; Cov: Scan; Lang: Hun; Subj: Related.
■Münnich F. u. 26; 1051 Budapest V; HUNGARY.

MP *Modern Philology*: Research in Medieval and Modern Literature. Freq: 4; Began: 1903; Cov: Scan; Lang: Eng; Subj: Related. ISSN: 0026-8232
■University of Chicago Press; 5720 S. Woodlawn Avenue; Chicago, IL 60637; USA.

MPI *Manadens Premiärer och Information*. Lang: Swe; Subj: Related.
■Svenska Teaterunionen; Svenska ITI; Nybrokajen 13 S-111 48, Stockholm; SWEDEN.

MPSKD *Mitteilungen der Puppentheatersammlung der Staatlichen Kunstsammlungen Dresde*. Freq: 32; Began: 1958; Lang: Ger; Subj: Theatre. ISSN: 0323-7567
■Puppentheatersammlung; Hohenhaus; Barkengasse 6 01445 Radebeul; GERMANY.

MRenD *Medieval and Renaissance Drama*. SEE *Medieval and Renaissance Drama in England*. Freq: IRR; Lang: Eng; Began: 1984; Ceased: 1996; Cov: Full; Subj: Theatre. ISSN: 0731-3403
■AMS Press; 56 E. 13th Street; New York, NY 10003; USA.

MRDE *Medieval and Renaissance Drama in England*. Freq: IRR; Began: 1996; Cov: Full; Subj: Theatre. ISSN: 08386-37035
■Associated University Press; 56 East 13th St.; New York, NY 10003; USA.

MRT *Miedzynarodowny Rocznik Teatralny*: Annuaire Intl. du Théâtre/Intl. Theatre Yearbook. Freq: 1; Began: 1977; Ceased: 1982; Lang: Pol/Fre/Eng; Subj: Theatre.
■International Association of Theatre Critics; ul. Moliera 1; 00 076 Warsaw; POLAND.

MSD *Milliyet Sanat Dergisi*. Freq: 26; Lang: Tur; Subj: Theatre.
■Aydin Dogan; Nurosmaniye Cad. 65/67; Cagaloglu-Istanbul; TURKEY.

MT *Material zum Theater*. Freq: 12; Began: 1970; Lang: Ger; Subj: Theatre.
■Verband der Theaterschaffended der DDR; Hermann-Matern-Strasse 18; 1040 Berlin; GERMANY.

MuD *MusikDramatik*. Freq: 4; Cov: Full; Lang: Swe; Subj: Theatre. ISSN: 0283-5754
■Box 4038; 5102 61 Stockholm; SWEDEN.

Muhely *Műhely*. Freq: 6; Began: 1978; Lang: Hun; Cov: Scan; Subj: Related. ISSN: 0138-922X
■Hazánk Kft.; Árpád u. 32; 9021 Győr; HUNGARY.

MuK *Maske und Kothurn*: Internationale Beiträge zur Theaterwissenschaft. Freq: 1; Began: 1955; Lang: Ger/Eng/Fre; Subj: Theatre. ISSN: 0175-1611
■Universität Wien; Institut für Theaterwissenschaft; Böhlau Verlag Sachsenplatz 4-6 A-1201 Vienna; AUSTRIA.

MuQ *Musical Quarterly*. Freq: 4; Began: 1915; Last Known Address; Lang: Eng; Subj: Related. ISSN: 0027-4631
■GoodKind Indexes, Pub.; 866 Third Avenue; New York, NY 10022; USA.

MusGes *Musik und Gesellschaft*. Freq: 12; Began: 1951; Lang: Ger; Subj: Related. ISSN: 0027-4755
■Henschelverlag Kunst und Gesellschaft; Oranienburger Str. 67/68; 1040 Berlin; GERMANY.

MuT *Musik und Theater*. Die Internationale Kulturzeitschrift. Freq: 10; Began: 1979; Lang: Ger; Subj: Theatre. ISSN: 0931-8194

MuT *Musik und Theater*. Die Internationale Kulturzeitschrift. Freq: 10; Began: 1979; Lang: Ger; Subj: Theatre.
■Meuli & Masüger Media GmbH; Pf. 16 80 CH-8040 Zurich; SWITZERLAND.

MuZizn *MuzykalnajaŽizn*: (Musical Life). Freq: 24; Began: 1957; Cov: Scan; Lang: Rus; Subj: Related. ISSN: 0131-2383
■Moscow; RUSSIA.

Muzsika *Muzsika*. Freq: 12; Began: 1958; Cov: Scan; Lang: Hun; Subj: Related. ISSN: 0027-5336
■Pro Musica Alapítvány; Károly krt. 7; 1075 Budapest; HUNGARY.

Muzyka *Muzyka:Bibliografičeskaja informacija*. Freq: 12; Began: 1974; Cov: Full; Lang: Rus; Subj: Related. ISSN: 0208-3086
■Gos. Biblioteka SSSR im. Lenina; NIO Informkultura; Prospekt Kalinina 101000 Moscow; RUSSIA.

MV *Minority Voices*: An Interdisciplinary Journal of Literature & Arts. Freq: 2; Began: 1977; Ceased: 1989; Lang: Eng; Subj: Theatre.
■Paul Robeson Cultural Center, 114 Walnut Bldg.; Pennsylvania State Univ.; University Park, PA 16802; USA.

My *My*. Freq: 12; Began: 1990; Cov: Scan; Lang: Rus; Subj: Related.
■B-5 ab. 1; Moscow 107005; RUSSIA.

Mykenae *Mykenae Theater-Korrespondenz*. Freq: 24; Began: 1951; Lang: Ger; Subj: Theatre.
■Der aktuelle Theaternachrichtenund Feuilletondienst; Mykenae Verlag Rossberg KG; Ahastr. 9 D-64285 Darmstadt; GERMANY.

NADIE *Nadie Journal*. Formerly: *Drama in Education*. Freq: 2; Began: 1981; Cov: Scan; Lang: Eng; Subj: Related. ISSN: 0159-6659
■National Assoc. for Drama in Education; P.O. Box 168; Carlton Victoria 3054; AUSTRALIA.

Napj *Napjaink*. Freq: 12; Began: 1962; Ceased: 1990; Cov: Scan; Lang: Hun; Subj: Related. ISSN: 0547-2075
■Borsod Megyei Lapkiadó Vállalat; Korvin Ottó u. 1; 3530 Miskolc; HUNGARY.

NasSovr *Naš sovremennik*. Freq: 12; Began: 1933; Cov: Scan; Lang: Rus; Subj: Related. ISSN: 0027-8288
■Souz pisatelej RF; Moscow; RUSSIA.

Natrang *Natrang*. Freq: 4; Lang: Hin; Subj: Theatre.
■I-47 Jangoura Extension; New Delhi; INDIA.

Natya *Natya*. Freq: 4; Began: 1969; Last Known Address; Lang: Eng; Subj: Theatre. ISSN: 0028-1115
■Bharatiya Natya Sangh; 34 New Central Market; New Delhi; INDIA.

Nayt *Näytelmäuutiset (Drama News)*. Lang: Fin; Subj: Theatre.
■Näytelmäkulma, Drama Corner; Meritullinkatu 33; 00170 Helsinki; FINLAND.

NBT *Neue Blätter des Theaters in Der Josefstadt*. Freq: 6; Began: 1953; Lang: Ger/Eng/Fre; Subj: Theatre. ISSN: 0028-3096
■Theater in der Josefstadt, Direktion; Josefstaedterstrasse 26; A 1082 Vienna; AUSTRIA.

NC *New Contrast*. Freq: 4; Cov: Scan; Lang: Eng; Subj: Related. ISSN: 1017-5415
■P.O. Box 3841; Cape Town, 8000; SOUTH AFRICA.

NCBSBV *Netherlands Centraal Bureau Voor de Statistiek*: Bezoek aan Vermakelukheidsinstellingen. Freq: 1; Began: 1940; Ceased: 1963; Lang: Dut/Eng; Subj: Related. ISSN: 0077-6688
■Centraal Bureau voor de Statistiek; Prinses Beatrixlaan 428; Voorburg; NETHERLANDS.

NCBSMT *Centraal Bureau voor de Statistiek (Statistics Netherlands)*: Muziek en theater. Formerly: *Statistiek van het Gesubsidieerde Toneel*. Freq: 1; Began: 1977; Lang: Dut; Subj: Theatre. ISSN: 0168-3519
■Statistics Netherlands; Postbox 428; 2270 AZ Voorburg; NETHERLANDS.

NCM *Nineteenth Century Music*. Freq: 3; Began: 1977; Lang: Eng; Subj: Related.
■University of California Press; 2120 Berkeley Way; Berkeley, CA 94720; USA.

NConL *Notes on Contemporary Literature*. Freq: 4; Began: 1971; Lang: Eng; Subj: Related. ISSN: 0029-4047
■English Department, West Georgia College; Carollton, GA 30118; USA.

NCPA *National Center for the Performing Arts*: Quarterly Journal. Freq: 4; Began: 1972; Lang: Eng; Subj: Related.
■Natl Ctr for the Performing Arts; Nariman Point; 400021 Bombay; INDIA.

NCT *Nineteenth Century Theatre*. Formerly: *Nineteenth Century Theatre Research*. Freq: 2; Began: 1987; Cov: Full; Lang: Eng; Subj: Theatre. ISSN: 0893-3766
■University of Massachusetts; Department of English; Amherst, MA 01003; USA.

NCTR *Nineteenth Century Theatre Research*. Freq: 2; Began: 1973; Ceased: 1986; Cov: Full; Lang: Eng; Subj: Theatre. ISSN: 0316-5329
■Department of English, University of Arizona; Tuscon, AZ 85721; USA.

Neoh *Neohelicon/Acta Comparationis Litterarum Universarum*. Freq: 2; Began: 1974; Cov: Scan; Lang: Eng /Ger /Fre; Subj: Related. ISSN: 0324-4652
■Akadémiai Kiadó; Ménesi út 11-13; 1118 Budapest; HUNGARY.

NETJ *New England Theatre Journal*. Freq: 1; Lang: Eng; Subj: Theatre.
■School of Fine and Performing Arts; Roger Williams College; 1 Old Ferry Road Bristol, RI 02809-2921; USA.

neueM *neue Merker, Der*. Freq: 12; Lang: Ger; Subj: Related. ISSN: 1017-5202
■Dr. Sieglinde Pfabigan; Peitlgasse /III/4; A-1210 Vienna; AUSTRIA.

Neva *Neva*. Freq: 12; Began: 1955; Cov: Scan; Lang: Rus; Subj: Related. ISSN: 0130-741X
■3 Nevskij Pr.; St. Petersburg 191186; RUSSIA.

NewPerf *New Performance*. Freq: 4; Began: 1977; Lang: Eng; Subj: Theatre. ISSN: 0277-514X
■One 14th Street; San Francisco, CA 94103; USA.

NewY *New Yorker, The*. Freq: 50; Cov: Scan; Lang: Eng; Subj: Related. ISSN: 0028-792X
■The New Yorker Magazine, Inc.; 20 West 43rd Street; New York; NY 10036; USA.

NFT *Theatre*: News from the Finnish Theatre. Formerly: *News from the Finnish Theatre*. SEE *Finnish Theatre*. Freq: IRR; Began: 1958; Ceased: 1995; Cov: Scan; Lang: Eng/Fre; Subj: Theatre. ISSN: 0358-3627
■Finnish Center of the ITI; Teatterikulma Meritullinkatu 33 00170 Helsinki; FINLAND.

NihonU *Nihon-Unima*. Lang: Jap; Subj: Theatre.
■Taoko Kawajiri, Puppet Theatre PUK; 2-12 Yoyogi, Shibuya; 151 Tokyo; JAPAN.

NIMBZ *Notate*: Informations-und-Mitteilungsblatt des Brecht-Zentrums der DDR. Lang: Ger; Subj: Theatre.
■Brecht Zentrum der DDR; Chausseestrasse 125; 1040 Berlin; GERMANY.

NITI *Newsletter of the International Theatre Institute of the U.S., Inc.*. Freq: 4; Began: 1988; Lang: Eng; Subj: Theatre.
■220 West 42nd Street; New York, NY 10036; USA.

NiR *Nauka i Religija*: (Science and Religion). Freq: 12; Began: 1959; Cov: Scan; Lang: Rus; Subj: Related. ISSN: 0130-7045
■Moscow; RUSSIA.

Nk *Näköpiiri*. Ceased: 1983; Lang: Fin; Subj: Theatre.

■Osuuskunta Näköpiiri; Annakatu 13 B; 00120 Helsinki 12; FINLAND.

NKala *Natya Kala*. Freq: 12; Lang: Tel; Subj: Theatre.
■Kala Bhawan; Saifabad; Hyderabad; INDIA.

NLR *New Literatures Review*. Freq: 2; Began: 1975; Cov: Scan; Lang: Eng; Subj: Related. ISSN: 0314-7495
■English Department, University of Wollongong; P.O. Box 1144; Wollongong NSW 2500; AUSTRALIA.

NMZ *Neue Musikzeitung*. Freq: 6; Began: 1951; Cov: Scan; Lang: Ger; Subj: Related. ISSN: 0944-8136
■Verlag Neue Musikzeitung GmbH; Pf. 100245; D-93047 Regensburg; GERMANY

NO *New Observations*. Freq: 10; Lang: Eng; Subj: Related.
■144 Greene Street; New York, NY 10012; USA.

Noh *Noh*. Freq: 12; Lang: Jap; Subj: Theatre.
■Ginza-Nohgakudo Building; 6-5-15 Ginza, Chuo-Ku; 104 Tokyo; JAPAN.

NoK *Nōgaku-kenkyū*. Freq: Irreg. Began: 1916; Lang: Jap; Subj: Related. ISSN: 0029-0874
■Hosei University; JAPAN.

NoSS *Nōgaku Shiryo Shusei*. Freq: Irreg. Began: 1973 Lang: Jap; Subj: Related.
■Hosei University; JAPAN.

Novr *Nova revija*: mesečnik za kulturo Freq: 12; Began: 1982 Cov: Scan; Lang: Slo; Subj: Theatre. ISSN: 0351-9805
■ČZP Nova revija d.o.o.; Dalmatinova 1; 1001 Ljubljana; SLOVENIA.

Novr *Nova revija*: mesečnik za kulturo Freq: 12; Began: 1982 Cov: Scan; Lang: Slo; Subj: Theatre. ISSN: 0351-9805
NovRos

Novaja Rossija. Freq: 4; Began: 1930; Lang: Rus; Subj: Related.
■GSP, 8 Moskvina K-31; Moscow 103772; RUSSIA.

NovyjMir *Novyj Mir*. Freq: 12; Began: 1925; Cov: Scan; Lang: Rus; Subj: Related. ISSN: 0130-7673
■Moscow; RUSSIA.

Ns *Nestroyana*: Blätter der Internationalen Nestroy-Gesellschaft. Freq: 4; Began: 1979; Cov: Scan; Lang: Ger; Subj: Theatre.
■Internationale Nestroy-Gesellschaft, Volkstheater; Neustiftgasse 1; A 1070 Vienna; AUSTRIA.

NT *Nya Teatertidningen*. SEE: *Teatertidningen*. Freq: 4; Began: 1977; Ceased: 1990; Cov: Full; Lang: Swe; Subj: Theatre. ISSN: 0348-0119
■Box 20137 S10460 Stockholm; SWEDEN.

NTA *New Theatre Australia*. Freq: 6; Began: 1987; Ceased: 1989; Lang: Eng; Subj: Theatre. ISSN: 1030-441X
■New Theatre Australia Publications; P.O. Box 242 Kings Cross, NSW, 2011; AUSTRALIA.

NTE *Narodna tvorchestvo*. Freq: 12; Began: 1925; Lang: Ukr; Subj: Related. ISSN: 0023-219x
■Starokaluzhskoe shosse, I. 117630; Moscow; RUSSIA.

NTimes *Nohgaku Times*. Freq: 12; Began: 1953; Lang: Jap; Subj: Theatre.
■Nohgaku Shorin Ltd.; 3-6 Kanda-Jinpo-cho, Chiyoda-ku; 101 Tokyo; JAPAN.

NTQ *New Theatre Quarterly*. Freq: 4; Began: 1985; Cov: Full; Lang: Eng; Subj: Theatre. ISSN: 0266-464X
■Cambridge University Press, Edinburgh Bldg.; Shaftesbury Rd.; Cambridge CB2 2RU; UK.

NTR *New Theatre Review*. Freq: 3; Lang: Eng; Subj: Theatre.
■Lincoln Center Theater; 150 West 65 Street; New York NY 10023; USA.

NTS *Nordic Theatre Studies*: Yearbook for Theatre Research in Scandinavia. Freq: 1; Began: 1988; Cov: Full; Lang: Eng; Subj: Theatre.
■Munksgaard; Postbox 2148; 1016 Copenhagen K; DENMARK.

NTTJ *Nederlands Theatre-en-Televisie Jaarboek*. Freq: 1; Lang: Dut; Subj: Theatre.
■Amsterdam; NETHERLANDS.

Numero *Numero*. Freq: 12; Lang: Spa; Subj: Related.
■Apt. Post. 75570; El Marques; Caracas; VENEZUELA.

NV *Novoe Vremija*. Cov: Scan; Lang: Rus; Subj: Related. ISSN: 0137-0723
■Moscow; RUSSIA.

NVarta *Natya Varta*. Freq: 12; Lang: Hin; Subj: Theatre.
■Anakima; 4 Bishop Lefroy Road; Calcutta; INDIA.

Nvilag *Nagyvilág*. Freq: 12; Began: 1956; Cov: Scan; Lang: Hun; Subj: Related. ISSN: 0547-1613
■Arany János Lap- és Könyvkiadó Kft.; Széchenyi u. 1 1054 Budapest; HUNGARY.

NvR *Nauka v Rossii*. Freq: 6; Began: 1961; Cov: Scan; Lang: Rus; Subj: Related.
■Maranovskij Per., 26; 117810 Moscow GSP-1; RUSSIA.

NWR *NeWest Review*: A Journal of Culture and Current Events in the West. Freq: 6; Began: 1975; Cov: Scan; Lang: Eng; Subj: Theatre. ISSN: 0380-2917
■NeWest Review Co-operative; Box 394, RPO University; Saskatoon, SK S7N 9Z9; CANADA.

NYO *New York Onstage*. Freq: 12; Lang: Eng; Subj: Theatre.
■c/o Theatre Development Fund; 1501 Broadway; Room 2110 New York, NY 10036; USA.

NYTCR *New York Theatre Critics Review*. Freq: 30; Began: 1940; Cov: Full; Lang: Eng; Subj: Theatre. ISSN: 0028-7784
■Critics Theatre Review; 52 Vanderbilt Avenue, 11th Floor; New York, NY 10017; USA.

NYTR *New York Theatre Reviews*. Began: 1977; Ceased: 1980; Lang: Eng; Subj: Theatre.
■Ira J. Bilowit; 55 West 42nd Street; New York, NY 10036; USA.

Obliques *Obliques*. Freq: 4; Last Known Address; Began: 1972; Lang: Fre; Subj: Related.
■Roger Borderie; BP1, Les Pilles; 26110 Lyons; FRANCE.

OC *Opera Canada*. Freq: 4; Began: 1960; Cov: Scan; Lang: Eng; Subj: Related. ISSN: 0030-3577
■Foundation for Coast to Coast, Opera Publication; 366 Adelaide Street E., Suite 434; Toronto, ON M5A 3X9; CANADA.

OCA *O'Casey Annual*. Freq: 1; Began: 1982; Ceased; Cov: Scan; Lang: Eng; Subj: Theatre.
■MacMillan Publishers Ltd.; Houndmills Basingstoke; Hampshire RG21 2XS; UK.

ODG *Österreichische Dramatiker der Gegenwart*. Lang: Ger; Subj: Theatre.
■Inst. für Österreichische Dramaturgie; Singerstrasse 26; A 1010 Vienna; AUSTRIA.

OffI *OFF-Informationen*. Bundesverband Freier Theater e.V.. Freq: IRR; Began: 1984; Lang: Ger; Subj: Theatre.
■Kooperative Freier Theater NRW; Güntherstr. 65; D-44143 Dortmund; GERMANY.

Ogonek *Ogonek*. Cov: Scan; Lang: Rus; Subj: Related.
■RUSSIA.

OI *Opéra International*. Freq: 1; Began: 1963; Lang: Fre; Subj: Related.
■10 Galerie Vero-Dodat; 75001 Paris; FRANCE.

Oik *Otrok in knjiga*: Revija za vprašanja mladinske književnosti in knjižne vzgoje. Freq: 2; Began: 1972; Cov: Scan; Lang: Slo; Subj: Theatre. ISSN: 0351-5141
■Mariborska knjižnica; Rotovški trg 2; 2000 Maribo; SLOVENIA.

OJ *Opera Journal*. Freq: 4; Began: 1968; Cov: Scan; Lang: Eng; Subj: Theatre. ISSN: 0030-3585
■National Opera Association, Inc., University of Mississippi; Division of Continuing Ed. and Extension; University, MS 38677; USA.

OK *Oper und Konzert*. Freq: 12; Began: 1963; Lang: Ger; Subj: Theatre. ISSN: 0030-3518
■A. Hanuschik; Ungererstrasse 19/VI (Fuchsbau); 8000 Munich 40; GERMANY.

Oktiabr *Oktiabr*. Freq: 12; Began: 1924; Cov: Scan; Lang: Rus; Subj: Related. ISSN: 0132-0637
■Pravda; Moscow; RUSSIA.

Ollan *Ollantay Theater Magazine*. Freq: 2; Began: 1993; Cov: Scan; Lang: Eng /Spa; Subj: Theatre. ISSN: 1065-805X
■Ollantay Press; P.O. Box 449; Jackson Heights, NY 11372; USA.

OnsA *Ons Amsterdam*. Cov: Scan; Lang: Dut; Subj: Related. ISSN: 0166-1809
■Weekbladpers; Amsterdam; NETHERLANDS.

Op&T *Oper & Tanz*. Freq: 6; Lang: Ger; Subj: Related.
■Vereinigung Deutscher Opernchöre und Bühnentänzer e.V. in der DAG

Op&T *Oper & Tanz*. Freq: 6; Lang: Ger; Subj: Related.
; Oper & Tanz GmbH, Georgstr. 2; D-50374 Erfstadt; GERMANY.

Opal *Opal*. Freq: 6; Began: 1962; Lang: Eng; Subj: Theatre. ISSN: 0030-3062

Oper *Oper*. Freq: 1; Began: 1966; Lang: Ger; Subj: Theatre.
■Zurich; SWITZERLAND.

Opera *Opera*. Freq: 12; Began: 1950; Lang: Eng; Subj: Theatre. ISSN: 0030-3542
■DSB, 2a Sopwith Crescent; Hurricane Way; Shotgate Wickford, Essex SS11 8YU; UK.

OperaA *Opera Australasia*. Freq: 12; Began: 1978; Lang: Eng; Subj: Theatre. ISSN: 1320-9299
■PO Box R361; NSW 2000 Royal Exchange; AUSTRALIA.

OperaCT *Opera*. Freq: 4; Began: 1974; Ceased; Lang: Eng/Afr; Subj: Theatre.
■Cape Performing Arts Board; POB 4107; 8000 Cape Town; SOUTH AFRICA.

OperaIn *Opera Index*. Freq: 1; Lang: Eng; Subj: Related. ISSN: 0030-3526
■Seymour Press Ltd.; Windsor House; 1270 London Road London; SW16 4DH; UK.

OperaL *Operaélet/Operalife*. Freq: 5; Began: 1992; Cov: Scan; Lang: Hun; Subj: Theatre. ISSN: 1215-6590
■Budapesti Operabarát Alapítvány; Hajós u. 19; 1065 Budapest; HUNGARY.

OperaR *Opera*. Freq: 4; Began: 1965; Last Known Address; Lang: Ita/Eng/Fre/Ger/Spa; Subj: Theatre. ISSN: 0030-3542
■Editoriale Fenarete; Via Beruto 7; Milan; ITALY.

OperH *Oper Heute*. Lang: Ger; Subj: Theatre.
■Berlin; GERMANY.

Opern *Opernglas, Das*. Freq: 11; Began: 1980; Cov: Scan; Lang: Ger; Subj: Related. ISSN: 0935-6398
■Opernglas Verlagsgesellschaft mbH; Lappenbergsallee 45; D-20257 Hamburg; GERMAN.

OpN *Opera News*. Freq: 17; Began: 1936; Cov: Full; Lang: Eng; Subj: Theatre. ISSN: 0030-3607
■Metropolitan Opera Guild, Inc.; 70 Lincoln Center Plaza; New York, NY 10023; USA.

OpuK *Oper und Konzert*. Freq: 4 Began: 1963; Cov: Scan; Lang: Ger; Subj: Related. ISSN: 0030-3518
■Ungererstr. 19; D-80802 Munich; GERMANY.

Opus. *Opus. Osterreichische Puppenspiel-Journalette*. Freq: 4; Lang: Ger; Subj: Related.
■Österreichischer Puppenclub; Postfach; A-3130 Herzogenburg; GERMANY.

Opuscula *Opuscula*. Freq: 3; Began: 1976; Last Known Address; Lang: Dan; Subj: Theatre.
■Det Teatervidenskabelige Institot; Fredericingade 18; 1310 Copenhagen; DENMARK.

Opw *Opernwelt*. Freq: 12; Began: 1959; Lang: Ger; Subj: Theatre. ISSN: 0030-3690
■Friedrich Berlin Verlagsges; mbH, Lützowplatz 7; D-10785 Berlin; GERMANY.

OQ *Opera Quarterly*. Freq: 4; Began: 1983; Cov: Full; Lang: Eng; Subj: Theatre. ISSN: 0736-0053
■University of North Carolina Press; Box 2288; Chapel Hill, NC 27514; USA.

■Ontario Puppetry Association; 171 Avondale Avenue; Willowdale, ON M2N 2V4; CANADA.

Organon *Organon*. Freq: 1; Began: 1975; Lang: Fre; Subj: Theatre.
■Ctre de Recherches Théâtrales, Univ. Lyon II; Ensemble Univ., Ave. de l'Universite; 69500 Bron; FRANCE.

Orpheus *Orpheus*. Freq: 12; Began: 1972; Lang: Ger; Subj: Related.   ISSN: 0932-611
■Neue Gesellschaft für Musikinformation mbH; Livländische Str. 27; D-10715 Berlin; GERMANY.

OSS *On-Stage Studies*. Formerly: *Colorado Shakespeare Festival Annual*. Freq: 1; Began: 1976; Lang: Eng; Subj: Theatre.
ISSN: 0749-1549
■Colorado Shakespeare Festival, Campus Box 261; University of Colorado; Boulder, CO 80309 0261; USA.

OSZ *Očag. Semejnij Zurnal*. Began: 1992; Cov: Scan; Lang: Rus; Subj: Related.
ISSN: 0869-5091
■Ist Tverskaja-Tamskaja Street; Building 2, Section 1; Moscow 103006; RUSSIA.

Otecest *Otečestvennije arhivy*. Freq: 6; Began: 1992; Cov: Scan; Lang: Rus; Subj: Related.   ISSN: 0869-4427
■Glavnoe Arkhivnoe Upravlenie; 119817 B. Pirogovskaja 17; Moscow G-435; RUSSIA.

OtK *Otcij kraj*. Freq: 4; Cov: Scan; Lang: Rus;; Subj: Related.
■1 ul Barrykadnaya; Volgograd;; RUSSIA.

Outrage *Outrage*. Freq: 12; Began: 1983; Cov: Scan; Lang: Eng; Subj: Related.
■Gay Publications Co-operative; P.O. Box 21; Carlton South Victoria 3053; AUSTRALIA.

OvA *Overture*. Freq: 12; Began: 1919; Cov: Scan; Lang: Eng; Subj: Theatre. ISSN: 0030-7556
■Los Angeles Musicians' Union, Local 47; 817 Vine Street; Los Angeles, CA 90038; USA.

Over *Overland*. Freq: 3; Began: 1954; Cov: Scan; Lang: Eng; Subj: Related. ISSN: 0043-342X
■P.O. Box 14146; Melbourne Victoria 3000; AUSTRALIA.

P&L *Philosophy and Literature*. Freq: 2; Began: 1976; Lang: Eng; Subj: Related.
ISSN: 0190-0013
■Fine Arts; University of Canterbury; Christchurch; NEW ZEALAND.

PA *Présence Africaine*. Freq: 4; Began: 1947; Lang: Fre/Eng; Subj: Related. ISSN: 0032-7638
■Nouvelle Société Presence Africaine; 25 bis rue des Ecoles; Paris 75005; FRANCE.

Pa&Pr *Past and Present*: A Journal of Historical Studies. Freq: 4; Began: 1952; Lang: Eng; Subj: Related.   ISSN: 0031-2746
■Oxford University Press; Pinkhill House; Southfield Road Eynsham; Oxford OX8 1JJ; UK.

PAA *Performing Arts Annual*. SEE *Performing Arts at the Library of Congress*. Freq: 1; Began: 1986; Ceased: 1990; Cov: Full; Lang: Eng; Subj: Theatre.   ISSN: 0887-8234
■Library of Congress, Performing Arts Library Resources; Dist. by G.O.P.; Washington, DC 20540; USA.

PAaLC *Performing Arts at the Library of Congress*. Formerly *Performing Arts Annual*. Freq: IRR; Began: 1990; Cov: Full; Lang: Eng; Subj: Theatre.   ISSN: 0887-8234
■Library of Congress, Performing Arts Library Resources; Dist. by G.O.P.; Washington, DC 20540; USA.

PAC *Performing Arts in Canada*. SEE *Performing Arts & Entertainment in Canada*. Freq: 4; Began 1961; Ceased: 1991; Cov: Full; Lang: Eng; Subj: Theatre.   ISSN: 0031-5230
■Performing Arts & Entertainment Magazine; 1100 Caledonia Road; Toronto, ON M6A 2W5; CANADA.

PAEC *Performing Arts & Entertainment in Canada*. Freq: 4; Began: 1991; Cov: Full; Lang: Eng; Subj: Theatre.   ISSN: 1185-3433
■Performing Arts & Entertainment Magazine; 1100 Caledonia Road; Toronto, ON M6A 2W5; CANADA.

Pal *Palócföld*. Freq: 6; Began: 1967; Cov: Scan; Lang: Hun; Subj: Related.   ISSN: 0555-8867
■Nógrád Megyei Művelődési Központ Rákóczi út 192; 310 Salgótarján; HUNGARY.

Pamir *Pamir*. Freq: 12; Began: 1949; Cov: Scan; Lang: Rus; Subj: Related.   ISSN: 0131-2650
■Dushanbe; TAJIKISTAN.

Pantallas *Pantallas y Escenarios*. Freq: 5; Last Known Address; Lang: Spa; Subj: Theatre.
■Maria Lostal 24; 8 Zaragoza; SPAIN.

PAR *Performing Arts Resources*. Freq: 1; Began: 1974; Cov: Scan; Lang: Eng; Subj: Theatre.   ISSN: 0360-3814
■111 Amsterdam Avenue New York, NY 10023; USA.

Parergon *Parergon*. Freq: 2; Began: 1971; Cov: Scan; Lang: Eng; Subj: Related.   ISSN: 0313-6221
■Dept. of English; University of Sydney; NSW 2006; AUSTRALIA.

Parnass *Parnass*: Die Österreichische Kunst- und Kulturzeitschrift. Freq: 6; Began: 1981; Lang: Ger; Subj: Theatre.
■C & E Grosser, Druckerei Verlag; Wiener Strasse 290; A 4020 Linz; AUSTRIA.

Parnasso *Parnasso*. Freq: 8; Began: 1951; Lang: Fin; Subj: Theatre.   ISSN: 0031-2320
■Yhtyneet Kuvalehdet Oy; Maistraatinportti 1; 00240 Helsinki; FINLAND.

PArts *Performing Arts*: The Music and Theatre Monthly. Freq: 12; Began: 1967; Lang: Eng; Subj: Theatre.   ISSN: 0031-5222
■Performing Arts Network; 3539 Motor Ave.; Los Angeles, CA 90034-4800; USA.

PArtsSF *Performing Arts Magazine*: San Francisco Music & Theatre Monthly. Freq: 12; Began: 1967; Ceased: 1987; Lang: Eng; Subj: Theatre.   ISSN: 0480-0257
■Theatre Publications, Inc.; 2999 Overland Ave., Ste. 201; Los Angeles, CA 90064; USA.

PasShowA *Passing Show*. Freq: IRR; Began: 1981; Lang: Eng; Subj: Theatre. ISSN: 0706-1897
■Performing Arts Museum, Victorian Arts Centre; 1 City Rd; 3205 S. Melbourne, Victoria; AUSTRALIA.

PasShow *Passing Show: Newsletter of the Shubert Archive*. Freq: 3; Began: 1983; Cov: Full; Lang: Eng; Subj: Theatre.
■Shubert Archive, Lyceum Theatre; 149 West 45th Street; New York, NY 10026; USA.

PaT *Pamiętnik Teatralny*: Poswiecony historii i krytyce teatru. Freq: 4; Began: 1952; Cov: Full; Lang: Pol; Subj: Theatre.   ISSN: 0031-0522
■Institute of the Polish Academy of Sciences; Dluga 26/28; 00950 Warsaw; POLAND.

PaV *Paraules al Vent*. Freq: 12; Lang: Spa; Subj: Related.
■Associació de Joves 'Paraules al Vent'; Casal de Sant Jordi; Sant Jordi Desvalls; SPAIN.

PAYBA *Performing Arts Year Book of Australia*. Freq: 1; Began: 1977; Lang: Eng; Subj: Theatre.
■Showcast Publications Ltd; Box 141; 2088 Spit Junction N.S.W; AUSTRALIA.

Pb *Playbill*: A National Magazine of the Theatre. Freq: 12; Began: 1982; Lang: Eng; Subj: Theatre.   ISSN: 0032-146X
■Playbill Incorporated; 52 Vanderbilt Avenue; 11th Floor New York, NY 10017-3893; USA.

PCD *Premiéry československých divadel*. Freq: 12; Lang: Cze; Subj: Theatre.
■Divadelní ústav; Celetná 17; 110 01 Prague 1; CZECH REPUBLIC.

PdO *Pantuflas del Obispo*. Began: 1966; Lang: Spa; Subj: Theatre.
■Semanario Sabado; Vargas 219; Quito; ECUADOR.

Pe *Performance*. Freq: 6; Began: 1981; Lang: Eng; Subj: Related.
■Brevet Publishing Ltd.; 445 Brighton Road; South Croydon CR2 6EU; UK.

PeM *Pesti Műsor*. Freq: 52; Began: 1957; Lang: Hun; Subj: Theatre.
■Garay u.5; 1076 Budapest VII; HUNGARY.

PerAJ *Performing Arts Journal*. Freq: 3; Began: 1976; Cov: Full; Lang: Eng; Subj: Theatre.   ISSN: 0735-8393
■Performing Arts Journal, Inc.; P.O. Box 260, Village Station; New York, NY 10014; USA.

PerfM *Performance-Management*. Freq: 2; Cov: Scan; Lang: Eng; Subj: Theatre.
■Brooklyn College, Dept. of Theatre; Brooklyn, NY 11210; USA.

PerfNZ *Performance: A Handbook of the Performing Arts in New Zealand*. Freq: 5; Began: 1980; Lang: Eng; Subj: Theatre.
ISSN: 0112-0654
■Association of Community Theatres; P.O. 68-257; Newton, Aukland; NEW ZEALAND.

PerfR *Performance Research*. Freq: 3; Began: 1996; Cov: Scan; Lang: Eng; Subj: Theatre.   ISSN: 1352-8165
■Center for Performance Research; Market Road; Canton Cardiff CF5 1QE; WALES.

Perlicko *Perlicko-Perlacko*. Began: 1950; Last Known Address; Lang: Ger; Subj: Theatre.
■Dr. Hans R. Purschke; Postfach 550135; 6000 Frankfurt; GERMANY.

Perspek *Perspektiva*. Freq: 12; Began: 1990; Cov: Scan; Lang: Rus; Subj: Related.
ISSN: 0131-2278

■Izdatel'stvo Molodaya Gvardiya, Ul.; Sushevskaya, 21; Moscow A-55; RUSSIA.

Pf   *Platform*. Freq: 2; Began: 1979; Ceased: 1983; Cov: Scan; Lang: Eng; Subj: Theatre.
■Dept of Literature, University of Essex; Wivenhoe Park; Colchester; UK.

PFr   *Présence Francophone*. Freq: 2; Began: 1970; Ceased: 1970; Cov: Scan; Lang: Fre; Subj: Related.   ISSN: 0048-5195
■Université de Sherbrooke; Sherbrooke, PQ J1K 2R1; CANADA.

PI   *Plays International*. Formerly: *Plays/Plays International*. Freq: 12; Began: 1985; Cov: Scan; Lang: Eng; Subj: Theatre.   ISSN: 0268-2028
■33a Lurline Gardens; London SW11 4DD; UK.

PInfo   *Puppenspiel-Information*. Freq: 2; Began: 1967; Lang: Ger; Subj: Theatre. ISSN: 0720-7265

PInfo   *Puppenspiel-Information*. Freq: 2; Began: 1967; Lang: Ger; Subj: Theatre.
■Deutsche Puppentheater e.V.; Moorweg 1 D-21337 Lüneburg; GERMANY.

PintR   *Pinter Review*. Began: 1987; Cov: Full; Lang: Eng; Subj: Theatre. ISSN: 0895-9706
■Harold Pinter Society; University of Tampa; Box 11F Tampa, FL 33606; USA.

PiP   *Plays in Process*. Lang: Eng; Subj: Theatre.   ISSN: 0736-0711
■Theatre Communications Group 355 Lexington Avenue; New York, NY 10017; USA.

Pja   *Pipirijaina*. Freq: 6; Began: 1979; Lang: Spa; Subj: Theatre.
■c/o San Enrique 16; 20 Madrid; SPAIN.

Plateaux   *Plateaux*. Formerly: *Bulletin de l'Union des Artistes*. Freq: 4; Began: 1925; Lang: Fre; Subj: Theatre.
■Syndicat Français des Artistes-Interprètes (SFA) 21 bis, rue Victor-Massé; 75009 Paris; FRANCE.

Play   *Play*. Freq: 12; Began: 1974; Lang: Eng; Subj: Theatre.   ISSN: 0311-4031
■Main Street; PO Box 67; 5245 Hahndorf; SOUTH AFRICA.

PlayM   *Players Magazine*. Freq: 22; Began: 1924; Ceased: 1967; Lang: Eng; Subj: Theatre.   ISSN: 0032-1486
■National Collegiate Players, Northern Illinois University; University Theatre; Dekalb, IL 60115; USA.

PlayN   *Playmarket News*. Formerly: *Act: Theatre in New Zealand*. Freq: 2; Began: 1988; Lang: Eng; Subj: Theatre.   ISSN: 0113-9703
■Level 2, 16 Cambridge Terrace; P.O. Box 9767, Te Aro; TeWhanganui-a-Tara Wellington, Aotearoa; NEW ZEALAND.

Plays   *Plays*: (In 1985 became part of *Plays and Players*). Formerly: *Plays/Plays International*. Freq: 12; Began: 1983; Ceased: 1985; Cov: Scan; Lang: Eng; Subj: Theatre.
■Ocean Publications; 34 Buckingham Palace Road; London SW1; UK.

PLL   *PLL: Papers on Language & Literature*; Freq: 4; Cov: Scan; Lang: Eng; Subj: Related.   ISSN: 0031-1294
■Southern Illinois University at Edwardsville; Edwardsville, IL 62026-1434; USA.

PlPl   *Plays and Players*. Freq: 12; Began: 1953; Cov: Scan; Lang: Eng; Subj: Theatre.   ISSN: 0032-1559
■Mineco Design Ltd.; 18 Friern Park London N12 9DA; UK.

PLUG   *PLUG*: Maandelijks informatieblad van het Cultureel Jongeren Paspoort. Freq: 12; Began: 1967; Lang: Dut; Subj: Theatre.   ISSN: 0032-1621
■Cultureel Jongeren Paspoort; Kleine Gartmanplts. 10; 1017 RR Amsterdam; NETHERLANDS.

PM   *Performance Magazine, The*. Freq: 6; Began: 1979; Ceased: 1992; Cov: Scan; Lang: Eng; Subj: Theatre.   ISSN: 0144-5901
■Performance Magazine Ltd.; P.O. Box 717; London SW5 9BS; UK.

PMLA   *PMLA*: Publications of the Modern Language Assoc. of America. Freq: 6; Began: 1929; Last Known Address; Cov: Scan; Lang: Eng; Subj: Related.   ISSN: 0030-8129
■Modern Language Assoc. of America; 62 5th Avenue; New York, NY 10011; USA.

Pnpa   *Peuples noirs, peuples africains*. Freq: 4; Began: 1977; Lang: Fre; Subj: Related.
■82, avenue de la Porte-des-Champs; 76000 Rouen; FRANCE.

Podium   *Podiumkunsten*. Freq: 1 Began: 1987; Lang: Dut; Subj: Theatre.   ISSN: 0922-1409
■Centraal Bureau voor de Statistiek (Statistics Netherlands); Postbox 428; 2270 AZ Voorburg; NETHERLANDS.

PodiumB   *Podium*: Zeitschrift für Bühnenbildner und Theatertechnik. Freq: 4; Lang: Ger; Subj: Theatre.
■Abteilung Berufsbildung; Munzstrasse 21; 1020 Berlin; GERMANY.

Poppen   *Poppenspelbereichten*. Freq: 4; Lang: Dut; Subj: Theatre.
■Mechelen; BELGIUM.

Pozoriste   *Pozorište*: Časopis za pozorišnu umjetnost. Freq: 6; Began: 1959; Lang: Cro; Subj: Theatre.   ISSN: 0032-616X
■Narodno Pozorište; Matija Gupca 6; 75000 Tuzla; BOSNIA AND HERZEGOVINA.

PQ   *Philological Quarterly*: Investigation of Classical & Modern Langs. and Lit. Freq: 4; Began: 1922; Cov: Scan; Lang: Eng; Subj: Related.   ISSN: 0031-7977
■Editor, Philological Quarterly; University of Iowa; Iowa City, IA 52242; USA.

PQCS   *Philippine Quarterly of Culture and Society*. Freq: 4; Began: 1973; Lang: Eng; Subj: Related.   ISSN: 0115-0243
■San Carlos Publications; 6000 Cebu City; PHILIPPINES.

PrAc   *Primer Acto*. Freq: 5; Began: 1957; Last Known Address; Lang: Spa; Subj: Theatre.
■Cervantes, 21-1 Oficina 3; 28014 Madrid; SPAIN.

Preface   *Préface*. Freq: 12; Lang: Fre; Subj: Theatre.
■Centre National Nice-Côte d'Azur; Esplanade des Victoires; 06300 Nice; FRANCE.

Premiere   *Première*. Lang: Ger/Fre; Subj: Related.
■Schweizerischer Bühnenverband; Pf. 9; CH-8126 Zumikon; GERMANY.

Premijera   *Premijera*: List Narodnog Pozorista Sombor. Lang: Ser; Subj: Theatre.
■Koste Trifkovica 2; Sombor; SERBIA.

Presg   *Prešernovo gledališče*. Cov: Scan; Lang: Slo; Subj: Related.
■Glavni trg 6; 6400 Kranj; SLOVENIA.

Pretexts   *Pretexts*. Began: 1989; Cov: Scan; Lang: Eng; Subj: Related.   ISSN: 1015-549X
■University of Cape Town; Private Bag Rondebosch 7700; SOUTH AFRICA.

Primdg   *Primorsko dramsko gledališče*. Cov: Scan; Lang: Slo; Subj: Related.
■Bevkov trg 4; 65000 Nova Gorica; SLOVENIA.

Primk   *Primerjalna književnost*. Freq: 2; Began: 1978; Cov: Scan; Lang: Slo; Subj: Related.   ISSN: 0351-1189
■Slovensko društvo za primerjalno književnost; Aškerčeva 2; 1000 Ljubljana; SLOVENIA.

prinz   *prinzenstrasse. Hannoversche Hefte zur Theatergeschichte*. Freq: 2/3; Began: 1994; Lang: Ger; Subj: Theatre. ISSN: 0949-4049
■Theatermuseum und -archiv Hannover; Prinzenstrasse 9 (im Schasupielhaus); D-30159 Hannover; GERMANY.

Prof   *Profile*: The Newsletter of the New Zealand Assoc. of Theatre Technicians. Freq: 4; Lang: Eng; Subj: Related.
■Ponsonby, Auckland; NEW ZEALAND.

Program   *Program*. Began: 1925; Ceased; Lang: Cze; Subj: Theatre.
■Zemske divadlo; Dvorakova 11; Brno; CZECH REPUBLIC.

Programa   *Programa*. Began: 1978; Lang: Por; Subj: Theatre.
■Grupo de Teatro de Campolide; 43, 20 D. Cde. Antas; Lisbon; PORTUGAL.

Prolog   *Prolog*: Revija za dramsku umjetnost. In 1986 became Novi Prolog. Freq: 2; Began: 1968; Lang: Cro; Subj: Theatre.
■Centar za kulturnu djelatnost; Mihanoviceva 28/1; 41000 Zagreb; CROATIA.

PrologTX   *Prolog*. Freq: 4; Began: 1973; Lang: Eng; Subj: Theatre.   ISSN: 0271-7743
■Theatre Sources Inc., c/o Michael Firth; 104 North St. Mary; Dallas, TX 75214; USA.

Prologue   *Prologue*. Freq: 4; Began: 1944; Lang: Eng; Subj: Theatre.   ISSN: 0033-1007
■Arena Theater; Tufts University; Medford, MA 02155; USA.

Prompts   *Prompts*. SEE *Irish Theatre Archive's Newsletter*. Freq: IRR; Began: 1981; Ceased: 1992; Lang: Eng; Subj: Theatre.
■Irish Theatre Archive, Archives Division; City Hall; 2 Dublin; IRELAND.

Propf   *Pro philosophia füzetek*. Cov: Scan; Lang: Hun; Subj: Related.
■HUNGARY.

ProS   *ProScenium*. Freq: 4; Cov: Scan; Lang: Ger; Subj: Related.
■Schweizer Verband technischer Bühnenberufe; Aescherweg 20; CH-5725 Leutwil; GERMANY.

ProScen   *ProScen*. Freq: 4; Began: 1986; Cov: Full; Lang: Swe; Subj: Theatre. ISSN: 0284-4346

■Svensk Teaterteknisk Förening, Section of OISTT; Mosebacke Torg 1 116 46 Stockholm; SWEDEN.

PrTh *Pratiques Théâtrales*: In 1978 became Grande République. Freq: 3; Ceased: 1978; Lang: Fre; Subj: Theatre.
■200 Ouest rue Sherbrooke; Montreal, PQ H2Y 3P2; CANADA.

PS *Post Script*; Freq: 3; Began: 1981; Cov: Scan; Lang: Eng; Subj: Related. 0277-9897
■Texas A & M University; Literature and Languages Dept; Commerce, TX 75429; USA.

Ptk *Publiekstheaterkrant*. Freq: 5; Began: 1978; Lang: Dut; Subj: Theatre.
■Publiekstheater; Marnixstraat 427; 1017 PK Amsterdam; NETHERLANDS.

PTKranj *Prešeren Theatre of Kranj*. Began: 1945; Cov: Scan; Lang: Slo; Subj: Theatre.
■Prešeren Theatre; Kranj; SLOVENIA.

PTZ *Petersburgskij Teatral'nyj Žurnal*. Began: 1992; Cov: Scan; Lang: Rus; Subj: Related.
■5 Pl. Iskusstv; kv. 56-a St. Petersburg 191011; RUSSIA.

PuJ *Puppetry Journal*. Freq: 4; Began: 1949; Cov: Full; Lang: Eng; Subj: Theatre. ISSN: 0033-443X
■Puppeteers of America; 8005 Swallow Dr.; Macedonia, OH 44056; USA.

PupM *Puppet Master*. Freq: 4; Began: 1946; Lang: Eng; Subj: Theatre.
■British Puppet and Model Theatre Guild, c/o Gordon Shapley (Hon. Sec.); 18 Maple Road, Yeading, Nr Hayes; Middlesex; UK.

Pusp *Puppenspiel und Puppenspieler*. Freq: 2; Began: 1960; Lang: Ger/Fre; Subj: Theatre. ISSN: 0033-4405
■Schweiz. Vereinigung Puppenspiel, c/o Gustav Gysin, Ed.; Roggenstr. 1; Riehen CH-4125; SWITZERLAND.

Pz *Proszenium*. Lang: Ger; Subj: Theatre.
■Zurich; SWITZERLAND.

PZOST *Premiere. Zeitschrift für Oper, Sprech- und Tanztheater*. Freq: 4; Lang: Ger; Subj: Theatre. ISSN: 0933-5390
■Andreas Berger; Berner Str. 2; D-38106 Braunschweig; GERMANY.

QQ *Queen's Quarterly*. Freq: 4; Cov: Scan; Lang: Eng; Subj: Related.
■Queen's University; Kingston, ON K7L 3N6; CANADA.

QT *Quaderni di Teatro*: Rivista Trimestrale del Teatro Regionale Toscano. Freq: 4; Began: 1978; Ceased: 1987; Cov: Full; Lang: Ita; Subj: Theatre.
■Casa Editrice Vallecchi; Viale Milton 7; 50129 Florence; ITALY.

QTST *Quaderni del Teatro Stabile di Torino*. Freq: IRR; Lang: Ita; Subj: Theatre.
■Teatro Stabile di Torino; Turin; ITALY.

Quarta *Quarta Parete*. Freq: 4; Began: 1975; Ceased: 1983; Lang: Ita; Subj: Theatre.
■Via Sant'Ottavio 15; Turin; ITALY.

QuellenT *Quellen zur Theatergeschichte*. Freq: IRR; Began: 1981; Lang: Ger; Subj: Theatre. ISSN: 0259-0786

■Verband der Wissenschaftlichen, Gesellschaften Oesterreichs; Lindengasse 37; A1070 Vienna; AUSTRIA.

Raduga *Raduga*. Freq: 12; Began: 1986; Cov: Scan; Lang: Rus; Subj: Related. ISSN: 0131-8136
■Izd-vo TSKKPE; Kiev; ESTONIA.

Raja *Rajatabla*. Lang: Spa; Subj: Theatre.
■Apartado 662; 105 Caracas; VENEZUELA.

RAL *Research in African Literature*. Freq: 4; Began: 1970; Lang: Eng; Subj: Related.
■Indiana Univ. Press; 10th and Morton Sts.; Bloomington, IN 47405; USA.

Rampel *Rampelyset*. Freq: 6; Began: 1948; Lang: Dan; Subj: Theatre.
■Danske Amatór Teater Samvirke; Box 70; DK 6300 Grasten; DENMARK.

Randa *Randa*. Freq: 2; Cov: Scan; Lang: Spa; Subj: Related. ISSN: 0210-5993
■Editat per Curial Edicions Catalanes S.A.; carrer del Bruc 144; 08037 Barcelona; SPAIN.

Rangarupa *Rangarupa*. Began: 1976; Last Known Address; Lang: Ben; Subj: Theatre.
■Rangarup Natya Academy; 27/76 Central Rd.; Dhanmondi, Dacca; BANGLADESH.

Rangayan *Rangayan*. Freq: 4; Lang: Hin; Subj: Theatre.
■Bhartiya Lok kala Mandal; Udaipur 313001 Rajasthan; INDIA.

Rangyog *Rangyog*. Freq: 4; Lang: Hin; Subj: Theatre.
■Rajasthan Sangeet Natak Adademi; Paota; Jodhpur; INDIA.

Raritan *Raritan*. Freq: 4; Began: 1981; Lang: Eng; Subj: Related. ISSN: 0275-1607
■Rutgers University; 165 College Ave.; New Brunswick, NJ 08903; USA.

Rbharati *Rangbharati*. Freq: 12; Lang: Hin; Subj: Theatre.
■Bharatendu Rangmanch; Chowk;Lucknow; INDIA.

RdA *Revue de l'Art*. Freq: 4; Began: 1968; Lang: Fre; Subj: Related. ISSN: 0035-1326
■Editions du CNRS; Collège de France; 11, Place Marcelin-Berthelot 75005 Paris; FRANCE.

RdArt *Revista d'Art*. Freq: 1; Lang: Spa; Subj: Related.
■c/o Baldiri Reixac, Departament d'Historia de l'Art; Facultat de Geografia i Historia; 08028 Barcelona; SPAIN.

RdD *Rassegna di Diritto Cinematografico, Teatrale e della Televisione*. Lang: Ita; Subj: Theatre.
■Via Ennio Quirino Visconti 99; Rome; ITALY.

RDE *Research in Drama Education*. Freq: 2; Began: 1996; Cov: Full; Lang: Eng; Subj: Theatre.
■Carfax Publishing, Ltd.; P.O. Box 25; Abingdon, Oxfordshire OX14 2UE; UK.

RdS *Rassegna dello Spettacolo*. Began: 1953; Lang: Ita; Subj: Theatre. ISSN: 0033-9474
■Assoc. Gen. Italiana dello Spettacolo; Via di Villa Patrizi 10; 00161 Rome; ITALY.

RE *Revue d'esthétique*. Freq 4; Lang: Fre; Subj: Theatre.
■Privat et Cie; 14, rue des Arts; 31068 Toulouse CEDEX; FRANCE.

Recorder *Recorder, The: A Journal of the American Irish Historical Society*. Freq: 2; Began: 1985; Cov: Scan; Lang: Eng; Subj: Related.
■American Irish Historical Society; 991 Fifth Avenue; New York, NY 10028; USA.

REEDN *Records of Early English Drama Newsletter*. Freq: 2; Began: 1976; Cov: Full; Lang: Eng; Subj: Theatre. ISSN: 0070-9283
■University of Toronto, Erindale College, English Section; Mississauga, ON L5L 1C6; CANADA.

Region *Regionologia*. Began: 1992; Cov: Scan; Lang: Rus; Subj: Related. ISSN: 0131-5706
■Scientific Research Institute of Regionology;Proletarskaj Street 61;430000 Saransk-City RUSSIA

RenD *Renaissance Drama*. Freq: 1; Began: 1964; Cov: Full; Lang: Eng; Subj: Theatre. ISSN: 0486-3739
■Center for Renaissance Studies; Newberry Library; 60 West Walton St. Chicago, IL 60610; USA.

Renmin *Renmin Xiju*: People's Theatre. Freq: 12; Began: 1950; Lang: Chi; Subj: Theatre.
■52 Dongai Batiao; Beijing; CHINA.

RenQ *Renaissance Quarterly*. Freq: 4; Began: 1967; Lang: Eng; Subj: Related. ISSN: 0034-4338
■The Renaissance Society of America, Inc.; 24 West 12th Street; New York, NY 10011; USA.

Repliikki *Repliikki*. Freq: 4; Began: 1970; Lang: Fin; Subj: Theatre.
■Suomen Harrastajateatteriliitto; Minervankatu 1 C 21; 00100 Helsinki; FINLAND.

REsT *Revista de Estudios de Teatro*: Boletin. Freq: 3; Began: 1964; Lang: Spa; Subj: Theatre. ISSN: 0034-8171
■Instituto Nacional de Estudios de Teatro; Av. Córdoba 1199; Buenos Aires; ARGENTINA.

Restor *Restoration and Eighteenth Century Theatre Research*. Freq: 2; Began: 1962; Cov: Full; Lang: Eng; Subj: Theatre. ISSN: 0034-5822
■Loyola University of Chicago, Dept. of English; 6525 North Sheridan Road; Chicago, IL 60626; USA.

RevAS *Review: Asian Studies Association of Australia*. Freq: 3; Began: 1975; Lang: Eng; Subj: Related. ISSN: 0314-7533
■Robin Jeffrey, Dept. of Politics, La Trobe University; Bundoora; Victoria 3083; AUSTRALIA.

RevIM *Review of Indonesian and Malaysian Affairs*. Freq: 2; Began: 1962; Lang: Eng; Subj: Related. ISSN: 0034-6594
■Dept. of Indonesian & Malaysian Studies; University of Sydney; NSW 2006; AUSTRALIA.

Revue *Revue*. Freq: 6; Lang: Fre; Subj: Theatre.
■Theatre de la Commune, BP 157; 2 rue Edouard Poisson; 93304 Aubervilliers; FRANCE.

RHSTMC   *Revue Roumaine d'Histoire de l'Art*: Série Théâtre, Musique, Cinéma. Freq: 4; Began: 1980; Lang: Fre; Subj: Related.
■Ed. Academiei Rep. Soc. Romania; Calea Victoriei 125; 79717 Bucharest; ROMANIA.

RHT   *Revue d'Histoire du Théâtre*. Freq: 4; Began: 1948; Cov: Full; Lang: Fre; Subj: Theatre.   ISSN: 0035-2373
■Société d'Histoire du Théâtre; 98 Boulevard Kellermann; 75013 Paris; FRANCE.

RIDr   *Rivista Italiana di Drammaturgia*. Freq: 4; Began: 1976; Last Known Address; Lang: Ita; Subj: Theatre.
■Istituto del Dramma Italiano; Via Monte della Farina 42; Rome; ITALY.

RLC   *Revue de Littérature Comparée*. Freq: 4; Began: 1921; Cov: Scan; Lang: Fre/Eng; Subj: Related.   ISSN: 0035-1466
■F. Didier Erudition; 6 rue de la Sorbonne; 75005 Paris; FRANCE.

RLit   *Russkaja Literatura: Istoriko-Literaturnyj Žurnal*: (Russian Literature: Historical Literary Journal). Freq: 4; Began: 1958; Cov: Scan; Lang: Rus; Subj: Related. ISSN: 0131-6095
■Inst. Russkoj Lit. Akademii Nauk SSSR, Puškinskij Dom; Nab. Makarova 4; 199164 St. Petersburg; RUSSIA.

RLtrs   *Red Letters*. Freq: 3; Began: 1976; Lang: Eng; Subj: Related.   ISSN: 0308-6852
■A Journal of Cultural Politics; 6 Cynthia Street; London N1 9JF; UK.

RLZ   *Rossijskij Literaturovedčeskij Žurnal*. Began: 1992; Lang: Rus; Subj: Related.
■Krasikov Street 28/21; Union Ran, Literature Section; 117418 Moscow RUSSIA.

RMelo   *Rassegna Melodrammatica*. Last Known Address; Lang: Ita; Subj: Theatre.
■Corso di Porta Romana 80; Milan; ITALY.

RN   *Rouge et Noir*. Freq: 9; Began: 1968; Lang: Fre; Subj: Related.
■Maison de la Culture de Grenoble; BP 70-40; 38020 Grenoble; FRANCE.

Roda   *Roda Lyktan*. Freq: 1; Began: 1976; Ceased: 1980; Lang: Swe; Subj: Theatre.   ISSN: 0040-0750
■Skanska Teatern; Osterg 31; 26134 Landskrona; SWEDEN.

Rodina   *Rodina*. Freq: 52; Began: 1989; Cov: Scan; Lang: Rus; Subj: Related. ISSN: 0235-7089
■Vozdvizenva Street, 4/7 Building; 103728 Moscow; RUSSIA.

Rossp   *Rossiskaja provincija*. Cov: Scan; Lang: Rus; Subj: Related.   ISSN: 0869-8376
■Moscow.; RUSSIA.

RORD   *Research Opportunities in Renaissance Drama*. Freq: 1/2 yrs; Began: 1956; Cov: Full; Lang: Eng; Subj: Theatre. ISSN: 0098-647x
■Department of English; University of Kansas; Lawrence, KS 66045; USA.

RQ   *Romance Quarterly*. Freq: 4; Began: 1953; Cov: Scan; Lang: Eng; Subj: Related.   ISSN: 0883-1157
■Heldref Publication; 1319 Eighteenth Street N.W.; Washington, DC 20036-1802;

RRMT   *Ridotto*: Rassegna Mensile di Teatro. Freq: 12; Began: 1951; Cov: Scan; Lang: Ita; Subj: Theatre.   ISSN: 0035-5186
■Società Italiana Autori Drammatici; Via Po 10; 00198 Rome; ITALY.

RSP   *Rivista di Studi Pirandelliani*. Freq: 3; Began: 1978; Cov: Scan; Lang: Ita; Subj: Theatre.
■Centro Nazionale di Studi Pirandelliani; Agrigento; ITALY.

S&B   *Spiel & B*04uhne (Bund Deutscher Amateurtheater)*. Freq: 3; Cov: Scan; Lang: Ger; Subj: Theatre
■Steinheimer Str. 7/1; D-89518 Heidenheim; GERMANY.

S&D   *Speech & Drama*. Began: 1951; Cov: Scan; Lang: Eng; Subj: Related.
■Society of Teachers of Speech and Drama; 23 High Ash Avenue; Leeds LS17 8RS; UK.

SA   *Screen Actor*. Freq: 4; Cov: Scan; Lang: Eng; Subj: Related.   ISSN: 0036-956X
■Screen Actors Guild; 7065 Hollywood Boulevard; Los Angeles, CA 90028-6065; USA.

SAADYT   *SAADYT Journal*. Formerly: *SAADYT Newsletter*. Began: 1979; Cov: Scan; Lang: Eng/Afr; Subj: Theatre.
■South African Assoc. for Drama and, Youth Theatre; Private Bag X41; Pretoria; SOUTH AFRICA.

SAD   *Studies in American Drama, 1945-Present*. Freq: 2; Began: 1986; Cov: Full; Lang: Eng; Subj: Theatre.   ISSN: 0886-7097
■Ohio State University Press; 1070 Carmack Road; Columbus, OH 43210; USA.

Sage   *Sage*: A Scholarly Journal on Black Women. Freq: 2; Began: 1984; Lang: Eng; Subj: Related.   ISSN: 0741-8369
■Sage Women's Educational Press, Inc.; Box 42741; Atlanta, GA 30311 0741; USA.

Sahne   *Sahne (The Stage)*. Freq: 12; Began: 1981; Lang: Tur; Subj: Theatre.
■Nes'e Altiner; Cagaloglu Yokusu 2; Istanbul; TURKEY.

SAITT   *SAITT Focus*. Freq: IRR; Last Known Address; Began: 1969; Lang: Eng/Afr; Subj: Theatre.
■S. African Inst. for Theatre Technology; Pretoria; SOUTH AFRICA.

SAJAL   *South African Journal of African Languages*. Freq: 4; Began: 1981; Lang: Eng & Afrikaans;; Subj: Related. ISSN: 0257-2117
■African Languages Asso. of Southern Africa; Bureau for Scientific Publications; Box 1758; Pretoria 0001; SOUTH AFRICA.

SanatO   *Sanat Olayi (Art Event)*. Freq: 12; Last Known Address; Lang: Tur; Subj: Theatre.
■Karacan Yayinlari; Basin Sarayi; Cagaloglu-Istanbul; TURKEY.

SATJ   *South African Theatre Journal*. Freq: 2; Began: 1987; Cov: Full; Lang: Eng;; Subj: Theatre.
■SATJ School of Dramatic Art; University of Witwatersrand; WITS 2050; SOUTH AFRICA.

SCagdas   *Sanajans Cagdas*. Freq: 12; Lang: Tur; Subj: Theatre.
■Istiklal Caddesi Botter Han; 475/479 Kat. 3; Istanbul; TURKEY.

Scan   *Scandinavica*. Freq: 2; Lang: Eng/Dan/Ger/Fre/Swe; Subj: Related.

■University of East Anglia; Norwich; NR4 7TJ; UK.

ScCh   *Scene Changes*. Freq: 9; Began: 1973; Ceased: 1981; Cov: Scan; Lang: Eng; Subj: Theatre.   ISSN: 0381-8098
■Theatre Ontario; 8 York Street, 7th floor; Toronto, ON M5R 1J2; CANADA.

Scena   *Scena*:Časopis za pozorišnu umetnost. Freq: 6; Began: 1965; Lang: Ser; Subj: Theatre.   ISSN: 0036-5734
■Sterijino Pozorje; Zmaj -Jovina 22; 21000 Novi Sad; SERBIA.

ScenaB   *Scena*. Freq: 4; Began: 1962; Lang: Ger; Subj: Theatre.   ISSN: 0036-5726
■Institut für Technologie Kultureller Einrichtung; Clara Zetkin-Str. 1205; 108 Berlin; GERMANY.

ScenaM   *Scena*. Freq: 12; Began: 1976; Lang: Ita; Subj: Theatre.
■Morrison Hotel; Via Modena 16; 20129 Milan; ITALY.

ScenaP   *Scena*. Freq: 26; Began: 1976; Ceased; Cov: Scan; Lang: Cze; Subj: Theatre.   ISSN: 0139-5386
■Scena; Valdstejnske nam. 3; Prague 1; CZECH REPUBLIC.

Scenaria   *Scenaria*. Freq: 24; Began: 1977; Cov: Scan; Lang: Eng; Subj: Theatre. ISSN: 0256-002X
■Triad Publishers Ltd.; Box 72161, Parkview 2122; Johannesburg; SOUTH AFRICA.

Scenario   *Scenario*. Freq: 4; Cov: Scan; Lang: Eng; Subj: Related.
■3200 Tower Oaks Blvd.; Rockville, MD 20852; USA.

Scenarium   *Scenarium*. Freq: 10; Began: 1879; Lang: Dut; Subj: Theatre.
■De Walburg Pres; P. O. Box 222; 7200 AE Zutphen; NETHERLANDS.

ScenaW   *Scena*. Formerly: *Poradnik Teatrow, Lirnik Wioskowy*. Freq: 48; Began: 1908; Lang: Pol; Subj: Theatre.
■Wydawnictwo Prasa ZSL; ul. Reja 9; 02 053 Warsaw; POLAND.

Scene   *Scene, De*. Freq: 10; Began: 1959; Lang: Dut; Subj: Theatre.
■Theatercentrum; Jan van Rijswijcklaan 28; B 2000 Antwerpen; BELGIUM.

Scenograf   *Scénografie*. Freq: 4; Began: 1963; Lang: Cze; Subj: Theatre.   ISSN: 0036-5815
■Divadelní ústav; Celetná 17; 110 01 Prague 1; CZECH REPUBLIC.

ScenoS   *Scen och Salong*. Freq: 12; Began: 1915; Ceased: 1990; Lang: Swe; Subj: Theatre.   ISSN: 0036-5718
■Folkparkernas Centralorganisation; Svedenborgsgatan 1; S 116 48 Stockholm; SWEDEN.

Schaus   *Schauspielfuehrer*: Der Inhalt der wichtigsten Theaterstuecke aus aller Welt. Freq: IRR; Began: 1953; Lang: Ger; Subj: Theatre.   ISSN: 0342-4553
■Anton Hiersemann Verlag, Rosenbergstr 113; 70193 Stuttgart 1; GERMANY.

SchwT   *Schweizer Theaterjahrbuch*. Freq: 1; Lang: Ger; Subj: Related.
■Gesellschaft für Theaterkultur; Theaterkultur-Verlag Postfach 1940, CH-4001 Basel; SWITZERLAND.

ScIDI *Scena IDI, La*. Freq: 4; Began: 1971; Lang: Ita; Subj: Theatre.
■Bulzoni Editore; Via Liburni 14; 00185 Rome; ITALY.

SCN *Seventeenth-Century News*. Freq: 4; Lang: Eng; Subj: Theatre.
■English Department; Blocker Building; Texas A & M University; College Station, TX 77843; USA.

Screen *Screen*. Freq: 24; Began: 1959; Lang: Eng; Subj: Related. ISSN: 0036-9543
■Oxford University Press; Pinkhill House; Southfield Road Eynsham Oxford OX8 1JJ; UK.

SCYPT *SCYPT Journal*. Freq: 2; Began: 1977; Ceased: 1986; Cov: Scan; Lang: Eng; Subj: Theatre.
■Standing Conf. on Young People's Theatre, c/o Cockpit Theatre; Gateforth Street; London NW8; UK.

SD *Stage Directions*. Cov: Scan; Lang: Eng; Subj: Theatre.
■SMW Communications Inc.; 3101 Poplarwood Court; Suite 310; Raleigh, NC 27604-1010; USA.

SDi *Slovenské Divadlo*. Freq: 4; Began: 1952; Cov: Full; Lang: Slo; Subj: Theatre.
ISSN: 0037-699X
■Slovanian Acad. of Sciences; Klemensova 19; 814 30 Bratislava; SLOVAKIA.

SdO *Serra d'Or*. Freq: 12; Began: 1959; Cov: Scan; Lang: Spa; Subj: Related. ISSN: 0037-2501
■Publicacions de l'Abadia de Montser, Ausias March 92-98; Apdo. 244; 13 Barcelona; SPAIN.

SEEA *Slavic & East European Arts*. Freq: 2; Began: 1982; Cov: Full; Lang: Eng; Subj: Related. ISSN: 0737-7002
■State Univ. of NY, Stonybrook, Dept. of Germanic & Slavic Lang.; Slavic & East European Arts; Stonybrook, NY 11794; USA.

SEEDTF *Soviet and East European Performance: Drama Theatre Film*. Formerly: *Newsnotes on Soviet & East European Drama & Theatre*. SEE *Slavic and East European Performance*. Freq: 3; Began: 1981; Ceased: 1989; Cov: Scan; Lang: Eng; Subj: Theatre.
■Inst. for Contemporary East European and Soviet Drama and Theatre; Graduate Ctre, CUNY, 33 West 42nd St., Room 1206A; New York, NY 10036; USA.

SEEP *Slavic and East European Performance: Drama, Theatre, Film*. Formerly: *Soviet and East-European Performance: Drama Theatre Film*. Freq: 3; Began: 1989; Cov: Scan;
■Inst. for Contemporary East European and Soviet Drama and Theatre; Graduate Ctre, CUNY, 33 West 42nd St., Room 1206A; New York, NY 10036; USA.

Segmundo *Segismundo*. Freq: 6; Began: 1965; Lang: Spa; Subj: Theatre.
■Consejo Superior de Investigaciones Científicas; Vitruvio 8, Apartado 14.458; Madrid 6; SPAIN.

Sehir *Sehir Tiyatrolari (City Theatre)*. Freq: 12; Began: 1930; Lang: Tur; Subj: Theatre.
■Sunusi Tekiner; Basin ve Halka Iliskiler Danismanligi; Harbiye-Istanbul; TURKEY.

SEL *SEL: Studies in English Literature, 1500-1900*. Freq: 4; Lang: Eng; Subj: Related.
■Rice University; 6100 Main Street; Houston, TX 77005-1892; USA.

Selmol *Sel'skaja molodež*. Freq: 12; Began: 1925; Cov: Scan; Lang: Rus; Subj: Related. ISSN: 0203-3569
■5a Novomitrovskaja ul.; Moscow 125015; RUSSIA.

Sembianza *Sembianza*. Freq: 6; Began: 1981; Last Known Address; Lang: Ita; Subj: Theatre.
■Via Manzoni 14; 20121 Milan; ITALY.

Sentg *Sentjakobsko gledališče*. Cov: Scan; Lang: Slo; Subj: Related.
■Mestni dom; 61000 Ljubljana; SLOVENIA.

SFN *Shakespeare on Film Newsletter*. SEE *Shakespeare Bulletin*. Freq: 2; Began: 1977; Ceased: 1993; Cov: Scan; Lang: Eng; Subj: Related. ISSN: 0739-6570
■Dept. of English; Nassau Community College; Garden City, NY 11530; USA.

SFo *Szinháztechnikai Fórum*. Journal of the Section for Theatre Technology of the Hungarian Optical, Acoustic and Cinematographical Society of the Hungarian Centre of the OISTAT. Freq: 4; Began: 1974; Cov: Scan; Lang: Hun; Subj: Theatre. ISSN: 0139-1542
■OPAKFI; Fő u. 68; 1027 Budapest; HUNGARY.

Sg *Shingeki*. Freq: 12; Began: 1954; Lang: Jap; Subj: Theatre.
■Hakusui-sha, Chiyoda-ku; 3-24 Kanda-Ogawa-cho; 101 Tokyo; JAPAN.

SGfUB *Schriftenreihe, Gesellschaft für Unterhaltende Bühnenkunst e.V.*. Freq: 1; Cov: Scan; Lang: Ger; Subj: Related.
■Hertzbergstr. 21; D-12055 Berlin; GERMANY.

SGIP *Sovetskoe Gosudarstvo i Pravo*. SEE *Gosudarstvo i pravo*. Freq: 12; Began: 1927; Ceased: 1992; Cov: Scan; Lang: Rus; Subj: Related. ISSN: 0132-0769
■Akad. Nauk S.S.S.R.; Inst. Gosudarstva i Prava; Izdatel'stvo Nauka; Podsosenskii Per., 21; Moscow K-62; RUSSIA.

SGT *Schriften der Gesellschaft für Theatergeschichte*. Lang: Ger; Subj: Theatre.
■Berlin; GERMANY.

SGTJ *Schweizerische Gesellschaft für Theaterkultur Jahrbücher*. Freq: IRR; Began: 1928; Lang: Ger; Subj: Theatre.
■Swiss Association for Theatre Research, c/o Louis Naef; Postfach 180; CH-6130 Willisau; SWITZERLAND.

SGTS *Schweizerische Gesellschaft für Theaterkultur Schriften*. Freq: IRR; Began: 1928; Ceased: 1982; Lang: Ger; Subj: Theatre.
■Swiss Association for Theatre Research, c/o Louis Naef; Postfach 180; CH-6130 Willisau; SWITZERLAND.

Shahaab *Shahaab*. Last Known Address; Lang: Ara; Subj: Theatre.
■Hayassat Building; Cooper Road; Rawlpindi; PAKISTAN.

ShakS *Shakespeare Studies*. Freq: 1; Lang: Eng; Subj: Theatre. ISSN: 1067-0823
■Peter Lang Publishers; New York, NY; USA.

ShakSN *Shakespeare Studies*. Lang: Eng; Subj: Theatre.

■Nashville, TN; USA.

Shavian *Shavian*. Freq: 2; Began: 1946; Lang: Eng; Subj: Theatre. ISSN: 0037-3346
■Shaw Society; 6 Stanstead Grove; London SE6 4UD; UK.

ShawR *Shaw*: The Annual of Bernard Shaw Studies. Formerly: *Shaw Review (ISSN: 0037-3354)*. Freq: 1; Began: 1981; Cov: Scan; Lang: Eng; Subj: Theatre. ISSN: 0741-5842
■Penn State Press; Barbara Building; University Park, PA 16802; USA.

ShB *Shakespeare Bulletin:A Journal of Performance Criticism and Scholarship*:Incorporating *Shakespeare on Film Newsletter*. Freq: 4; Began: 1982; Lang: Eng; Subj: Theatre.
■English Department; Lafayette College; Easton, PA 18042; USA.

ShN *Shakespeare Newsletter*. Freq: 4; Began: 1951; Lang: Eng; Subj: Theatre.
ISSN: 0037-3214
■Iona College; New Rochelle, NY 10801; USA.

Show *Show*. Last Known Address; Lang: Eng; Subj: Theatre.
■9/2 Nazimabad; Karachi; PAKISTAN.

ShowM *Show Music*. Freq: 4; Began: 1981; Cov: Scan; Lang: Eng; Subj: Theatre.
■P.O. Box 466; East Haddam, CT 06423-0466; USA.

ShRA *Shakespeare and Renaissance Association: Selected Papers*. Freq: 1; Lang: Eng; Subj: Related.
■Department of English; 400 Hal Greer Blvd.; Marshall University Huntington, WV 25755-2646; USA.

ShS *Shakespeare Survey*. Freq: 1; Began: 1948; Cov: Full; Lang: Eng; Subj: Theatre. ISSN: 0080-9152
■Cambridge University Press, The Edinburgh Building; Shaftesbury Road; Cambridge CB2 2RU; UK.

ShSA *Shakespeare in Southern Africa*. Freq: 1; Began: 1987; Cov: Full; Lang: Eng; Subj: Theatre.
■ISEA; Rhodes University; Grahamstown 6140; SOUTH AFRICA.

Silex *Silex*. Last Known Address; Lang: Fre; Subj: Theatre.
■BP 554 RP; 38013 Grenoble; FRANCE.

Sin *Sightline*: The Journal of Theatre Technology and Design. Freq: 2; Began: 1974; Ceased: 1993; Cov: Scan; Lang: Eng; Subj: Theatre. ISSN: 0265-9808
■Assoc. of British Theatre Technicians; 4 Gt. Pulteney Street; London W1R 3DF; UK.

Sipario *Sipario*. Freq: 12; Began: 1946; Last Known Address; Lang: Ita; Subj: Theatre.
■Sipario Editrice S.R.L.; Via Flaminia 167; 00196 Milan; ITALY.

SiR *Studies in Romanticism*. Freq: 4; Cov: Scan; Lang: Eng; Subj: Related. ISSN: 0039-3762
■Boston U. Scholarly Publications; 985 Commonwealth Ave; Boston, MA 02215; USA.

Sis *Sightlines*. Freq: 4; Began: 1965; Cov: Scan; Lang: Eng; Subj: Related. ISSN: 0065-6311
■USITT; 10 West 19th St., Ste. 5A; New York, NY 10011; USA.

SiSo *Sight and Sound.* Freq: 4; Began: 1932; Cov: Scan; Lang: Eng; Subj: Related. ISSN: 0037-4806
■21 Stephen Street; London W1P 1PL; UK.

SJ *Spielplan Journal.* Freq: 1; Cov: Scan; Lang: Ger; Subj: Related.
■Mykenae-Verlag, Ahastr. 9; D-64285 Darmstadt; GERMANY.

SjV *Sirp ja Vasar.* Freq: 52; Began: 1940; Lang: Est; Subj: Theatre.
■Postkast 388, Pikk t. 40; 200 001 Talin; ESTONIA.

SJW *Shakespeare Jahrbuch.* SEE: *Deutsche Shakespeare Gesellschaft/Deutsche Shakespeare Gesellschaft West, Jahrbuch.* Freq: 1; Began: 1865; Lang: Ger; Subj: Theatre. ISSN: 0080-9128
■Deutsche Shakespeare Gesellschaft; Kamp-Kontor, Ferdinand Kamp Verlag; Widumestr. 6-8 D-44787 Bochum; GERMANY.

SK *Skripicnyj kluch.* Cov: Scan; Lang: Rus; Subj: Related.
■Lyniya, V.O 199053; St. Petersburg;; RUSSIA.

Skript *Skript.* Freq: 10; Last Known Address; Lang: Dut; Subj: Theatre.
■N.C.A.; Postbus 64; 3600 AB Maarssen; NETHERLANDS.

Slav *Slavjanovedenie.* Freq: 6; Began: 1992; Cov: Scan; Lang: Rus; Subj: Related. ISSN: 0132-1366
■Izdatel'stvo Nauka; Podsosenskii Per. 21; K 62 Moscow; RUSSIA.

Slavr *Slavistična revija: časopis za jezikoslovje in literarne vede.* Freq: 4; Began: 1948; Cov: Scan; Lang: Slo; Subj: Related. ISSN: 0350-6894
■Slavistično društvo Slovenij; Aškerčeva 2; 1000 Ljubljana; SLOVENIA.

SlovD *Slovensko narodno gledališče-Drama.* Cov: Scan; Lang: Slo; Subj: Related.
■Erjavčeva o.1; 61000 Ljubljana; SLOVENIA.

Slovl *Slovensko ljudsko gledališče Celje.* Cov: Scan; Lang: Slo; Subj: Related.
■Gledališki trg 5; 63000 Celje; SLOVENIA.

Slovm *Slovensko mladinsko gledališče.* Cov: Scan; Lang: Slo; Subj: Related.
■Vilharjeva o.11; 61000 Ljubljana; SLOVENIA.

SlovO *Slovensko narodno gledališče-Opera in balet.* Cov: Scan; Lang: Slo; Subj: Related.
■Župančičeva 1; 61000 Ljubljana; SLOVENIA.

SM *Spectacles Magazine.* Freq: 12; Lang: Fre; Subj: Theatre.
■42 Blvd. du Temple; 75011 Paris; FRANCE.

Smena *Smena.* Freq: 12; Began: 1924; Cov: Scan; Lang: Rus; Subj: Related. ISSN: 0131-6658
■Pravda ; Moscow; RUSSIA.

SMR *SourceMonthly:* The Resource for Mimes, Clowns, Jugglers, and Puppeteers. Freq: 12; Lang: Eng; Subj: Theatre.
■Mimesource Inc.; 125 Sherman Str.; Brooklyn, NY 11218; USA.

SNJPA *Sangeet Natak:* Journal of the Performing Arts. Freq: 4; Began: 1965; Lang: Eng; Subj: Theatre. ISSN: 0036-4339
■Sangeet Natak Akademi, Rabindra Bhavan; Ferozeshah Rd.; 110001 New Delhi; INDIA.

SobCh *Sobcota Chelovneta.* Lang: Geo; Subj: Theatre.
■Tbilisi; GEORGIA.

Sobesednik *Sobesednik.* Freq: 12; Began: 1949; Cov: Scan; Lang: Rus; Subj: Related. ISSN: 0202-3180
■Moscow; RUSSIA.

SObzor *Scénografický Obzor.* Freq: 6; Began: 1958; Ceased: 1973; Lang: Cze; Subj: Theatre.
■Vinohradska 2; Prague 1; CZECH REPUBLIC.

SocA *Social Alternatives.* Freq: 4; Began: 1977; Cov: Scan; Lang: Eng; Subj: Related. ISSN: 0155-0306
■c/ Department of Government, University of Queensland; St. Lucia Qld 4067; AUSTRALIA.

SocH *Social History.* Freq: 3; Began: 1976; Lang: Eng; Subj: Related. ISSN: 0307-1022
■Routledge Ltd.; 11 New Fetter Lane; London EC4P 4EE; UK.

Sodob *Sodobnost.* Freq: 12; Began: 1953; Cov: Scan; Lang: Slo; Subj: Related. ISSN: 0038-0482
■DZS d.d. Mestni trg 26;; 1000 Ljubljana;; SLOVENIA.

Sog *Soglasije.* Began: 1990; Cov: Scan; Lang: Rus; Subj: Related. ISSN: 0868-8710
■Bakhrušin Street, 28; 113054 Moscow; RUSSIA.

SogogT *Sōgō geijutsu Toshite no nō.* Freq: Irreg; Began: 1994; Lang: Jap; ISSN: 1343-1331
■International Zeami Society, JAPAN.

SoM *Speaking of Mime.* Freq: IRR; Began: 1976; Ceased; Lang: Eng; Subj: Theatre. ISSN: 0381-9035
■Canadian Mime Council; Niagara-on-the-Lake, ON L0S 1J0; CANADA.

Somo *Somogy.* Formerly: *Somogyi Szemle.* Freq: 6; Began: 1970; Cov: Scan; Lang: Hun; Subj: Related. ISSN: 0133-0144
■Somogy Megyei Könyvtár; Május 1. u. 10 7400 Kaposvár; HUNGARY.

SON *Scottish Opera News.* Freq: 12; Ceased: 1987; Lang: Eng; Subj: Theatre. ISSN: 0309-7323
■Scottish Opera Club; Elmbank Crescent; Glasgow G2 4PT; UK.

SoQ *Southern Quarterly, The:* A Journal of the Arts in the South. Freq: 4; Began: 1962; Lang: Eng; Subj: Related. ISSN: 0038-4496
■PO Box 5078 Southern Station; Hattiesburg, MS 39406-5078; USA.

SORev *Sean O'Casey Review, The.* Freq: 2; Began: 1974; Last Known Address; Lang: Eng; Subj: Theatre. ISSN: 0365-2245
■O'Casey Studies; PO Box 333; Holbrook, NY 11741; USA.

SoSaw *Southern Sawdust.* Freq: 4; Began: 1954; Last Known Address; Lang: Eng; Subj: Theatre. ISSN: 0038-4542

■L. Wilson Poarch Jr.; 2965 Freeman Avenue; Sarasota, FL 33580; USA.

SoTh *Southern Theatre.* Began: 1964; Cov: Scan; Lang: Eng; Subj: Theatre. ISSN: 0584-4738
■Southeastern Theatre Conference; University of Carolina; Box 9868 Greensboro, NC 27412-0868; USA.

SOUTHERLY *Southerly: A Review of Australian Literature.* Freq: 4; Began: 1939; Cov: Scan; Lang: Eng; Subj: Related. ISSN: 0038-3732
■Dept. of English; Univ. of Sydney; Sydney N.S.W. 2006; AUSTRALIA.

SouthR *Southern Review.* Freq: 3; Began: 1963; Cov: Scan; Lang: Eng; Subj: Related. ISSN: 0038-4526
■School of Humanities and Social Sciences, Monash University; Gippsland, Chuschill VIC 3842; AUSTRALIA.

SovAr *Sovetskie Arkhivy.* SEE *Otecestvennye arhivy.* Freq: 6; Began: 1966; Ceased: 1992; Cov: Scan; Lang: Rus; Subj: Related. ISSN: 0038-5166
■Glavnoe Arkhivnoe Upravlenie; Pirogovskaya 17; Moscow G-435; RUSSIA.

SovBal *Sovětskij Balet.* SEE *Balet.* Cov: Scan; Ceased: 1992; Lang: Rus; Subj: Theatre.
■Moscow; RUSSIA.

SovD *Sovreménnaja Dramaturgija.* Freq: 4; Began: 1982; Cov: Scan; Lang: Rus; Subj: Theatre. ISSN: 6207-7698
■Moscow; RUSSIA.

SovEC *Sovětskaja Estrada i Cirk.* SEE *Estrada i cirk.* Freq: 12; Ceased: 1992; Cov: Scan; Lang: Rus; Subj: Theatre. ISSN: 0131-6769
■Moscow; RUSSIA.

SovEt *Sovětskaja Ethnografia.* SEE *Etnograjiceskoe obozrenie.* Freq: 6; Began: 1926; Ceased: 1992; Cov: Scan; Lang: Rus; Subj: Related. ISSN: 0038-5050
■Ulica D. Uljanova 19; B 36 Moscow; RUSSIA.

SovKult *Sovětskaja Kultura.* Cov: Scan; Lang: Rus; Subj: Related.
■Novoslobodskaja ul. 73; K 55 Moscow; RUSSIA.

SovMuzyka *Sovětskaja Muzyka:* (Soviet Music). SEE *Muzykal'naja akademija.* Freq: 12; Began: 1933; Ceased: 1992; Cov: Scan; Lang: Rus; Subj: Related. ISSN: 0131-6818
■Moscow; RUSSIA.

SovSlav *Sovětskojě Slavjanovédénjě:* (Soviet Slavonic Studies). SEE *Slavjanovedenie.* Freq: 6; Began: 1965; Ceased: 1992; Cov: Scan; Lang: Rus; Subj: Related. ISSN: 0132-1366
■Izdatel'stvo Nauka; Podsosenskii Per. 21; K 62 Moscow; RUSSIA.

SovT *Sovětskij Teat'r/Soviet Theatre.* Freq: 4; Began: 1976; Cov: Scan; Lang: Rus/Ger/Eng/Fre/Spa; Subj: Theatre.
■Copyright Agency of the USSR; 6a Bolshaya Bronnaya St.; K 104 Moscow 103670; RUSSIA.

Spa *Shilpakala.* Lang: Ben; Subj: Related.
■Dacca; BANGLADESH.

SPC *Studies in Popular Culture.* Freq: 2; Began: 1977; Lang: Eng; Subj: Related.

■Popular Culture Association in the South, Florida State Univ., English Dp.; Tallahassee, FL 32306; USA.

Speak   *Speak*. Began: 1977; Lang: Eng; Subj: Theatre.
■PO Box 126, Newlands; 7725 Cape Town; SOUTH AFRICA.

Spirale   *Spirale: Art, letters, spectacles, sciences humaines*. Freq: 12; Began: 1979; Last Known Address; Lang: Fre; Subj: Theatre.   ISSN: 0225-9004
■C.P. 98, Succ. E; Montreal, PQ; CANADA.

SpIt   *Spettacolo in Italia, Lo*. Freq: 1; Began: 1951; Lang: Ita; Subj: Theatre. ISSN: 0038-738X
■S.I.A.E.; Viale della Letteratura 30; 00100 Rome; ITALY.

Spl   *Spielplan, Der*. Freq: 12; Began: 1954; Lang: Ger; Subj: Theatre. ISSN: 0038-7517
■Die monatliche Theatervorschau, Hg. Löwendruck Bertram GmbH; Pf. 6202; D-38108 Braunschweig; GERMANY.

SpViag   *Spettacolo Viaggiante*. Began: 1948; Lang: Ita; Subj: Theatre.
■Assoc. Naz. Eserc. Spet. Viaggianti; Via di Villa Patrizi 10; 00161 Rome; ITALY.

SQ   *Shakespeare Quarterly*. Freq: 4; Began: 1950; Cov: Scan; Lang: Eng; Subj: Related.   ISSN: 0037-3222
■Folger Shakespeare Library; 201 E. Capitol St. S.E.; Washington, DC 20003; USA.

SR   *SIBMAS-Rundbrief, Hg. Bundesverband der Bibliotheken und Museen für Darstellende Künste e.v.*
. Freq: 2; Cov: Scan; Lang: Ger; Subj: Related.
■c/o Dr. Winrich Meiszies, Theatermuseum Düsseldorf; Jägerhofstr. 1; D-40479 Düsseldorf; GERMANY.

SSSS   *Szene Schweiz/Scène Suisse/ Scena Svizzera*. Freq: 1; Began: 1973; Lang: Ger/Fre/Ita; Subj: Theatre.
■Swiss Association for Theatre Research; c/o Louis Naef; Postfach 180; CH-6130 Willisau; SWITZERLAND.

SSTJ   *Secondary School Theater Journal*. Freq: 3; Began: 1962; Last Known Address; Lang: Eng; Subj: Theatre.
■ATHE; P.O. Box 15282; Evansville, IL 47716-0282; USA.

ST   *Sovetskij Teatr*. Freq: 3; Began: 1983; Cov: Scan; Lang: Rus; Subj: Theatre.
■Vestnik; Moscow; RUSSIA.

Staff   *Staffrider*. Freq: 4; Began: 1982; Cov: Scan; Lang: Eng/Afr; Subj: Related.
■Ravan Press Ltd.; Box 31134; 2017 Braamfontein; SOUTH AFRICA.

StageA   *Stage of the Art*. Freq: 4; Cov: Scan; Lang: Eng; Subj: Related. ISSN: 1046-5022
■American Alliance for Theatre and Education; Tempe, AZ; USA.

StageZ   *Stage*. Freq: IRR; Began: 1956; Lang: Eng; Subj: Theatre.
■Lusaka Theatre Club Ltd; Box 30615; Lusaka; ZAMBIA.

Standpunte   *Standpunte*. Freq: 6; Last Known Address; Began: 1945; Cov: Scan; Lang: Afr;; Subj: Related.   ISSN: 0038-9730
■Tafelberg Publishers; c/o J.C. Kannemeyer, Ed.; P.O. Box 91073; Auckland Park 2006;; SOUTH AFRICA.

Sterijino   *Sterijino Pozorje*: Informativno Glasilo. Freq: IRR; Began: 1982; Lang: Ser; Subj: Theatre.
■Sterijino Pozorje; Zmaj Jovina 22; Novi Sad; SERBIA.

Stikord   *Stikord*. Freq: 4; Began: 1981; Ceased; Lang: Dan; Subj: Theatre. ISSN: 0107-6582
■Foreningen Hidovre Teater; Hidovre Strandvej 70A; 2650 Hvidovre; DENMARK.

Stilet   *Stilet*. Freq: 2; Began: 1989; Cov: Scan; Lang: Afr/Eng; Subj: Related.
■Serva-Uitgewers; P.O. Box 36721, Menlopark 0102; SOUTH AFRICA.

STILB   *STILB*. Freq: 5; Began: 1981; Last Known Address; Lang: Ita; Subj: Theatre.
■Via della Fosse di Castello 6; 00193 Rome; ITALY.

Stol   *Stolica*. Freq: 52; Began 1990; Cov: Scan; Lang: Rus; Subj: Related. ISSN: 0868-698X
■State Union Publishing; Petrovka Street, 16 Moscow 101425; RUSSIA.

STN   *Scottish Theater News*. Freq: 12; Began: 1981; Ceased: 1986; Cov: Scan; Lang: Eng; Subj: Theatre. ISSN: 0261-4057
■Scottish Society of Playwrights; 346 Sauchiehall St.; Glasgow G2 3JD; UK.

STP   *Studies in Theatre Production*. Freq: 2; Cov: Full; Lang: Eng; Subj: Theatre.   ISSN: 1357-5341
■Department of Drama; University of Exeter; Thornlea, New North Road Exeter, Devon EX4 4JZ; UNITED KINGDOM.

StPh   *Studies in Philology*. Freq: 3; Began: 1906; Lang: Eng; Subj: Related.   ISSN: 0039-3738
■University of North Carolina Press; Box 2288; Chapel Hill, NC 27514; USA.

Strind   *Strindbergiana*: Meddelanden från Strindbergssällskapet. Formerly: *Meddelanden från Strindbergssällskapet*. Freq: 1; Began: 1985; Cov: Full; Lang: Swe; Subj: Theatre.   ISSN: 0282-8006
■Strindbergssällskapet, c/o C. R. Smedmark; Drottninggatan 85; 111 60 Stockholm; SWEDEN.

STT   *Sceničeskaja Technika i Technologija*. Freq: 6; Began: 1963; Cov: Full; Lang: Rus; Subj: Theatre. ISSN: 0131-9248
■Serebrianceskij Per. 2/5; 109028 Moscow; RUSSIA.

StudiaP   *Studia i Materialy do Dziejow Teatru Polskiego*. Formerly: *Studia i Materialy z Dziejow Teatru Polskiego*. Freq: IRR; Began: 1957; Lang: Pol; Subj: Theatre. ISSN: 0208-404X
■Polish Academy of Sciences; Rynek 9; Wroclaw; POLAND.

StudiiR   *Studii si Cercetari de Istoria Artei*: Seria Teatru-Muzica-Cinematografie. Freq: 1; Began: 1954; Lang: Rom; Subj: Theatre.
                ISSN: 0039-3991

■Academia Rep. Soc. Romania; Calea Victoriei 125; 79717 Bucharest; ROMANIA.

StudM   *Studenčeskij Meridian*. Freq: 12; Began: 1924; Cov: Scan; Lang: Rus; Subj: Related.   ISSN: 0321-3883
■Moscow; RUSSIA.

StWAusH   *Studies in Western Australian History*. Freq: IRR; Began: 1977; Cov: Scan; Lang: Eng; Subj: Related.   ISSN: 0314-7525
■Department of History; University of Western Australia; Nedlands, WA 6009; AUSTRALIA.

STYol   *STYolainen*. Freq: 6; Began: 1975; Lang: Fin; Subj: Theatre.
■Suomen Teatterityontekijain, Yhteisjarjesto; Maneesikatu 4c; 00170 Helsinki 17; FINLAND.

SuAS   *Stratford-upon-Avon Studies*. Freq: IRR; Began: 1961; Lang: Eng; Subj: Theatre.
■Edward Arnold Ltd; 41 Bedford Square; London WC1B 3DQ; UK.

SuF   *Sinn und Form: Beiträge zur Literatur*. Freq: 6; Began: 1949; Lang: Ger; Subj: Related.   ISSN: 0037-5756
■Aufbau-Verlag Berlin; Französische Str. 32; 10117 Berlin; GERMANY.

Suffloren   *Sufflören*. Last Known Address; Lang: Dan; Subj: Theatre.
■Medlemsblad for Dansk Dukketeaterforening; Vestergrade 3; 1456 Copenhagen; DENMARK.

SuidAfr   *Suid-Afrikaan, Die*. Began: 1985; Cov: Scan; Lang: Afr; Subj: Related.
■Die Suid-Afrikaan; P.O. Box 7010; 7610 Dalsig Stellembosch; SOUTH AFRICA.

SuT   *Spiel und Theater. Zeitschrift f*04ur Amateur-, Jugend- und Schultheater*. Freq: 2; Cov: Scan; Lang: Ger; Subj: Theatre.
■Oberschleissheim u.a., Deutscher Theaterverlag; Pf. 100261; D-69442 Weinheim; GERMANY.

Svet   *Svět a divadlo*. Began: 1990; Cov: Scan; Lang: Cze; Subj: Theatre. ISSN: 0862-7258
■Divadelni obec; Štefánikova 57; 150 43 Prague 5; CZECH REPUBLIC.

SwTS   *Swedish Theater/Théâtre Suédois*. Lang: Eng/Fre; Subj: Theatre.
■Stockholm; SWEDEN.

Sz   *Szinház*: (Theatre). Freq: 12; Began: 1968; Cov: Scan; Lang: Hun; Subj: Theatre.   ISSN: 0039-8136
■Szinház Alapítvány; Báthory u. 10; 1054 Budapest; HUNGARY.

Szab   *Szabolcs-Szatmár-Beregi Szemle*. Freq: 4; Began: 1965; Cov: Scan; Lang: Hun; Subj: Related.   ISSN: 1216-092x
■Móricz Zsigmond Könyvtár; Szabadság tér 2; 4400 Nyíregyháza; HUNGARY.

Szene   *Szene*. Lang: Ger; Subj: Theatre.
■UMLÖsterreichischer Bundestheaterverband; Goethegasse 1; A 1010 Vienna; AUSTRIA.

SzeneAT   *Szene: Fachzeitschrift der DDR Amateur-theater, -kabarett, -puppenspiel und -ntomime*. Freq: 4; Began: 1966; Last Known Address; Cov: Scan; Lang: Ger; Subj: Theatre.   ISSN: 0039-811X
■Zentralhaus für Kulturarbeit, Dittrichring 4; Postfach 1051; 7010 Leipzig; GERMANY.

SzeneS *Szene Schweiz. Eine Dokumentation des Theaterlebens in der Schweiz*. Freq: 1; Cov: Scan; Lang: Ger; Subj: Theatre.
■Hg. Schweizerische Gesellschaft für Theaterkultur; Theaterkultur-Verlag, Pf. 1940; CH-3001 Basel, Schanzenstr. 15; SWITZERLAND.

SzSz *Szinháztudományi Szemle*. Freq: 1; Began: 1977; Cov: Full; Lang: Hun; Subj: Theatre. ISSN: 0133-9907
■Országos Színháztörténeti Múzeum és Intézet; Krisztina körut 57; 1016 Budapest; HUNGARY.

T&P *Text and Performance: Journal of the Comparative Drama Conference*. Freq: 1; Lang: Eng; Subj: Theatre.
■Department of Classics; 3-C Daver Hall; University of Florida Gainesville, FL 32611; USA.

T&R *Theatre and Religion*. Freq: IRR; Lang: Eng; Subj: Theatre.
■Box 727; Goshen College; Goshen, IN 46526; USA.

TA *Theatre Annual*. Freq: 1; Began: 1942; Cov: Full; Lang: Eng; Subj: Theatre. ISSN: 0082-3821
■Department of Theatre and Speech; College of William and Mary; Williamsburg, VA 23187; USA.

TAAm *Theater Across America*. Freq: 5; Began: 1975; Lang: Eng; Subj: Theatre.
■Theatre Sources Inc.; 104 North St. Mary; Dallas, TX 75214; USA.

Tablas *Tablas*: National Council of Performing Art's Journal. Freq: 4; Began: 1982; Lang: Spa; Subj: Theatre.
■San Ignacio #166 e/Obispo y Obrapia; Habana Vieja. C.P. 10100; CUBA.

Tabs *Tabs*. Freq: 2; Began: 1937; Ceased: 1986; Cov: Scan; Lang: Eng; Subj: Theatre. ISSN: 0306-9389
■Rank Strand Ltd., P.O. Box 51, Great West Road; Brentford; Middlesex TW8 9HR; UK.

TAD *Tiyatro Araştirmalari Dergisi (Theatre Research Magazine)*. Freq: 1; Began: 1970; Lang: Tur/Eng/Fre; Subj: Theatre.
■Tiyatro Bölümü, Ankara Universitesi; D.T.C. Fakültesi, Sihhiye; Ankara; TURKEY.

Talent *Talent Management*. Freq: 12; Began: 1981; Lang: Eng; Subj: Related.
■T M Publishing; 1501 Broadway; New York, NY 10036; USA.

Tampereen *TTT-Tampereen Työväen Teatteri*. Lang: Fin; Subj: Theatre.
■Hämeenpuisto 30-32; 33200 Tampere; FINLAND.

Tanc *Táncművészet*. Freq: 4; Began: 1976; Cov: Scan; Lang: Hun;; Subj: Dance. ISSN: 0134-1421
■Táncművészeti Alapítvány; Kerék u. 34; 1035 Budapest; HUNGARY.

Tanecni *Tanecni Listy*. Freq: 10; Began: 1963; Lang: Cze; Subj: Theatre. ISSN: 0039-937X
■Panorama; Halkova 1; 120 72 Prague 2; CZECH REPUBLIC.

TAnim *Théâtre et Animation*. Freq: 4; Began: 1976; Lang: Fre; Subj: Theatre. ISSN: 0398-0049

■Fédération National du Théâtre et d'Animation; 12 Chaussée d'Antin; 75441 Paris Cedex 09; FRANCE.

Tanssi *Tanssin Tiedotuskeskus*. Freq: 4; Began: 1981; Cov: Full; Lang: Fin; Subj: Theatre. ISSN: 0492-4401
■Bulevardi 23-27; 00180 Helsinki; Finland.

TantI *Tantsovo Izkustvo*. Freq: 12; Began: 1954; Lang: Bul; Subj: Theatre.
■Izdatelstvo Nauka i Izkustvo; 6 Rouski Blvd; Sofia; BULGARIA.

TanzA *Tanz Affiche*. Freq: 6; Cov: Scan; Lang: Ger; Subj: Related.
■Publikation für Tanz und Kultur, Hg. Affiche; Verein zur Förderung von Information und Kommunikation in künstlerischen Belangen; Eggerthgasse 10/1; A-1060 Wien; AUSTRIA.

Tanzd *Tanzdrama*. Freq: 4; Began: 1987; Cov: Scan; Lang: Ger; Subj: Theatre. ISSN: 0932-8688
■Erhard Friedrich Verlag; Postfach 100 150 D-30917 Seelze; GERMANY.

TanzG *Tanz und Gymnastik*. Freq: 4; Began: 1944; Last Known Address; Lang: Ger; Subj: Theatre.
■Schweizerischer Berufsverband für Tanz und Gymnastik; Riedbergstrasse 1; 4059 Basel; SWITZERLAND.

TArch *Teatro Archivio*. Formerly: *Bolletino del Museo Biblioteca dell'attore*. Freq: IRR; Began: 1979; Cov: Full; Lang: Ita; Subj: Theatre.
■Bulzoni Editore; Via dei Liburni n 14; 00185 Rome; ITALY.

TArsb *Teaterårsboken*. Freq: 1; Began: 1982; Cov: Scan; Lang: Swe; Subj: Theatre.
■Svenska Riksteatern; 145 83 Norsborg; SWEDEN.

Tatar *Tatarstan Republic*. Freq: 12; Began: 1920; Cov: Scan; Lang: Rus; Subj: Related. ISSN: 0130-2418
■Decabristy Street, #2; 420066 Kazan' City; RUSSIA.

Tatr *Tatr*. Freq: 4; Began: 1985; Cov: Scan; Lang: Ger/Fre; Subj: Related.
■Astej, Gessnerallee 13; CH-8001 Zurich; SWITZERLAND.

TAus *Theatre Australia*. Freq: 12; Began: 1976; Lang: Eng; Subj: Theatre.
■Pellinor Pty Ltd. A.C.N.; 001 713 319, Level 2; 44 Bridge Street NSW 2000 Sydney; AUSTRALIA.

Tbuch *Theaterbuch*. Freq: 1; Lang: Ger; Subj: Theatre.
■Munich; GERMANY.

TCB *Teatro Clásico: Boletín*. Freq: 1; Lang: Spa; Subj: Theatre.
■Teatro Clásico de México; Apartado 61-077; MEXICO.

TCGNWCP *TCG National Working Conference Proceedings*. Freq: IRR; Began: 1976; Lang: Eng; Subj: Theatre.
■Theatre Communications Group; 355 Lexington Ave; New York, NY 10017; USA.

TChicago *Theatre Chicago*. Freq: 12; Began: 1986; Last Known Address; Lang: Eng; Subj: Theatre.
■22 W Monroe, Suite 801; 60603 Chicago, IL; USA.

TCI *TCI: Theatre Crafts International*. Formerly *Theatre Crafts*. Freq: 10; Began: 1995; Cov: Full; Lang: Eng; Subj: Theatre. ISSN: 1063-9497
■Intertec Publishing Corp.; 32 West 18th Street; New York, NY 10011-4612; USA.

TCom *Theatre Communications*. Freq: 12; Began: 1979; Ceased: 1983; Lang: Eng; Subj: Theatre. ISSN: 0275-5971
■Theatre Communications Group Inc; 355 Lexington Avenue; New York, NY 10017; USA.

TCraft *Theatrecraft*. Freq: 12; Began: 1964; Lang: Eng; Subj: Theatre.
■Victorian Drama League, Fifth Floor; 17 Elizabeth Street; Melbourne 3000 Victoria; AUSTRALIA.

TCUG *Theater Computer Users Group Notes*. Began: 1978; Lang: Eng; Subj: Theatre.
■Theatre Sources Inc.; 104 N Saint Mary; Dallas, TX 76214; USA.

TD&T *Theatre Design and Technology*. Freq: 4; Began: 1965; Cov: Full; Lang: Eng; Subj: Theatre. ISSN: 0040-5477
■U.S. Institute for Theatre Technology; 966 East 1030 North; Orem, UT 84057; USA.

TDDR *Theaterarbeit in der DDR*. Freq: 3; Began: 1979; Lang: Ger; Subj: Theatre.
■Verband der Theaterschaffended der DDR; Hermann-Matern-Strasse 18; 1040 Berlin; GERMANY.

TDonA *Transition: Discourse on Architecture*. Freq: 4; Began: 1979; Cov: Scan; Lang: Eng; Subj: Related. ISSN: 0157-7344
■Faculty of Environmental Design and Construction; RMIT GPO Box 2476V Melbourne Victoria 3001; AUSTRALIA.

TDR *Drama Review, The*. Freq: 4; Began: 1955; Cov: Full; Lang: Eng; Subj: Theatre. ISSN: 0012-5962
■Tisch School of the Arts; 721 Broadway, Room 626 New York, NY 10003; USA.

TE *Teater Et*. Freq: 5; Began: 1989; Lang: Dan; Subj: Theatre.
■Købmagergade 5, 3.; Postbox 191; 1006 København K; DENMARK.

Teat *Teatteri*. Freq 8; Began: 1945; Lang: Fin Subj Theatre.
ISSN: 0492-4401

■Kustannus Oy Teatteri; Meritullinkatu 33; 00170 Helsinki; FINLAND.

TeaterD *Teater i Danmark*: Theatre in Denmark. Freq: 1; Began: 1980; Ceased: 1987; Lang: Dan; Subj: Theatre. ISSN: 0106-7672
■Teater i Danmark; Vesterbrogade 26, 3.; DK-1620 København V.; DENMARK.

Teaterf *Teaterforum*. Freq: 6; Began: 1968; Cov: Full; Lang: Swe; Subj: Theatre. ISSN: 0347-8890
■Swedish Society for Amateur Theatres; Von Rosens väg 1 A; 737 40 Fagersta; SWEDEN.

Teatern *Teatern*. Freq: 4; Began: 1934; Lang: Swe; Subj: Theatre. ISSN: 0040-0750
■Riksteatern; Svenska Riksteatern; S 145 83 Norsborg; SWEDEN.

TeatL *Teatr Lalek*. Lang: Pol; Subj: Theatre.

■Warsaw; POLAND.

TeatM *Teatraluri Moambe*. Cov: Full; Lang: Geo; Subj: Theatre.
■Tbilisi; GEORGIA.

Teatoro *Teatoro*. Freq: 12; Began: 1944; Lang: Jap; Subj: Theatre.
■c/o Hagiwara Building, 2-3-1 Sarugaku-cho; Chiyoda-ku; 101 Tokyo; JAPAN.

Teatras *Teatras*. Lang: Lit; Subj: Theatre.
■Vilnius; LITHUANIA.

TeatrC *Teatro Contemporaneo*. Freq: 3; Began: 1982; Last Known Address; Cov: Full; Lang: Ita; Subj: Theatre.
■Via Trionfale 8406; 00135 Rome; ITALY.

TeatrE *Teatro en España*. Lang: Spa; Subj: Theatre.
■Madrid; SPAIN.

TeatrM *Teat'r*. žurnal dramaturgii i teatra. Freq: 12; Began: 1937; Cov: Full; Lang: Rus; Subj: Theatre.   ISSN: 0131-6805
■Izdatel'stvo Iskusstvo; Ul. Gertsena 49; Moscow 49; RUSSIA.

Teatron *Teatron*. Began: 1962; Lang: Heb; Subj: Theatre.
■Municipal Theatre; 20 Pevsner Street; Haifa; ISRAEL.

TeatroS *Teatro e Storia*. Began: 1986; Cov: Scan; Lang: Ita; Subj: Theatre.   ISSN: 1120-9569
■Centro per la Sperimentazione e la Ricerca Teatrale di Pontedera; Societa Editrice Il Mulino, Strada Maggiore 37 40125 Bologna; ITALY.

TeatroSM *TeatroSM*. Began: 1980; Lang: Spa; Subj: Theatre.
■Teatro Municipal General San Martin; Ave. Corrientes 1530, 50 piso; 1042 Buenos Aires; ARGENTINA.

Teatrul *Teatrul*. Freq: 12; Began: 1956; Lang: Rom; Subj: Theatre.
■Consiliul Culturii si Educatiei Socialiste; Calea Victoriei 174; Bucharest; ROMANIA.

TeatrW *Teatr*. Freq: 12; Began: 1946; Cov: Scan; Lang: Pol; Subj: Theatre. ISSN: 0040-0769
■Zarząd Glowny Związku Artystów Scen Polskich; ul. Jakubowska 14; 03-902 Warsaw; POLAND.

TeatterT *Teatterikorkeakoulun Tiedotuslehti*. Freq: 4; Began: 1984; Cov: Full; Lang: Fin; Subj: Theatre.   ISSN: 0781-0164
■Teatterikorkeakoulu; PL 148; 00511 Helsinki; FINLAND.

TeaturS *Teatur*. Freq: 12; Began: 1946; Cov: Full; Lang: Bul; Subj: Theatre.   ISSN: 0204-6253
■Komitet za Izkustvo i Kultura; 7 Levsky St.; 1000 Sofia; BULGARIA.

TeatY *Teatron*: Časopis za pozirišnu istoriju i teatrologiju. Freq: 4; Began: 1974; Cov: Scan; Lang: Ser; Subj: Theatre.   ISSN: 0351-7500
■Muzej Pozorišne umetnosti Srbije; Gospodar Jevremova 19; 11000 Belgrade; SERBIA.

TeatZ *Teatralnaja Žizn*. Freq: 24; Began: 1958; Cov: Scan; Lang: Rus; Subj: Theatre.   ISSN: 0131-6915

■Teatral'noe obschestvo, Theatrical Workers Union; Kiselni Typik dom 1 103031 Moscow; RUSSIA.

TeC *Teatro e Cinema*. Freq: 4; Began: 1968; Last Known Address; Lang: Ita; Subj: Theatre.   ISSN: 0040-0807
■Silva Editore; Viale Salita Salvatore 1; 28 16128 Genoa; ITALY.

TechB *Technical Brief*. Freq: 3; Began: 1982; Cov: Full; Lang: Eng; Subj: Theatre.   ISSN: 1053-8860
■TD&P Dept., Yale School of Drama; 222 York St.; New Haven, CT 06520; USA.

TEJ *Théâtre Enfance et Jeunesse*. Freq: 2; Began: 1963; Lang: Fre/Eng; Subj: Theatre.   ISSN: 0049-3597
■Assoc. du Théâtre pour l'Enfance, et la Jeunesse; 98 Blvd. Kellermann; 75013 Paris; FRANCE.

Telerad *Teleradioephir*. Formerly *Televidenie i Radioveščanie*. Began: 1952; Lang: Rus; Subj: Related.   ISSN: 0869-1932
■Pushkinskaja str. 23/8; 103009 Moscow; RUSSIA.

TEP *Théâtre de l'Est Parisien*: TEP Actualité. Lang: Fre; Subj: Theatre.
■Paris; FRANCE.

TextPQ *Text and Performance Quarterly*. Formerly: *Literature in Performance*. Freq: 4; Began: 1980; Lang: Eng; Subj: Theatre.   ISSN: 1046-2937
■Speech Communication Association; 5774 Stevens; University of Maine; Orono, ME 04469-5774; USA.

Textual *Textual*. Lang: Spa; Subj: Theatre.
■I.N.C.; Ancash; 390 Idma; PERU.

Textuel *Textuel*. Freq: 2; Lang: Fre;; Subj: Related.
■Université de Paris VII; 2, place Jussieu; 75221 Paris CEDEX 05; FRANCE.

TF *Teaterforum*. Freq: 2; Began: 1980; Cov: Scan; Lang: Eng/Afr; Subj: Theatre.
■University of Potchefstroom, Departement Spraakler en Drama; Potchefstroom; SOUTH AFRICA.

TF&TV *Teater Film & TV*. Freq: 8; Began: 1974; Lang: Dan; Subj: Theatre.
■Faellesforbundet for Teater Film & TV; Ny Oestergade 12; DK 1101 Copenhagen; DENMARK.

TGDR *Theatre in the GDR*. Lang: Ger; Subj: Theatre.
■Berlin; GERMANY.

TGlasnik *Teatarski Glasnik*: S. Spisanic na teatrite na Republika Makedonija. Freq: 2; Began: 1977; Lang: Slo; Subj: Theatre.
■MKO, kej Dimitar Vlahov B.B.; 91000 Skopje; REPUBLIC OF MACEDONIA.

TGraz *Theater in Graz*. Freq: 4; Began: 1952; Lang: Ger; Subj: Theatre.
■Vereinigte Bühnen Graz; Burggasse 16; A 8010 Graz; AUSTRIA.

Th *Théâtre*. Formerly: *Théâtre du Trident*. Lang: Fre; Subj: Theatre.
■Théâtre du Trident, Edifice Palais Montcalm; 975 Place d'Youville; Quebec, PQ; CANADA.

THC *Theatre History in Canada/Histoire du Théâtre*. Freq: 2; Began: 1980; Ceased; Cov: Full; Lang: Eng/Fre; Subj: Theatre.   ISSN: 0226-5761
■Graduate Centre for the Study of Drama, University of Toronto; 214 College Street; Toronto, ON M5T 2Z9; CANADA.

ThCr *Theatre Crafts*. SEE TCI. Freq: 9; Began: 1967; Ceased: 1995; Cov: Full; Lang: Eng; Subj: Theatre.   ISSN: 0040-5469
■Theatre Crafts Associates; 135 Fifth Avenue; New York, NY 10010; USA.

ThE *Théâtre en Europe*. Freq: 4; Began: 1984; Lang: Fre; Subj: Theatre.
■Theatre de l'Europe, 1; Place Paul Claudel; 75006 Paris; FRANCE.

TheaterW *TheaterWeek*. Freq: 52; Began: 1987; Cov: Full; Lang: Eng; Subj: Theatre.   ISSN: 0896-1956
■That New Magazine; 28 West 25th St., 4th Floor; New York, NY 10010; USA.

TheatreEx *Theatre: Ex*. Freq: 3; Began: 1985; Lang: Eng; Subj: Theatre.
■104 E. 4th Street; New York, NY 10003; USA.

TheatreF *TheatreForum*. Freq: 2; Began: 1991; Cov: Full; Lang: Eng; Subj: Theatre.   ISSN: 1060-5320
■Department of Theatre; University of California, San Diego; 9500 Gilman Dr La Jolla, CA 92093-0344; USA.

TheatreS *Theatre Studies*. Freq: 1; Began: 1954; Cov: Full; Lang: Eng; Subj: Theatre.   ISSN: 0362-0964
■Ohio State Univ., Lawrence and Lee, Theatre Research Institute; 1430 Lincoln Tower, 1800 Cannon Drive; Columbus, OH 43210 1230; USA.

TheatreT *Theatre Three*. Began: 1986; Ceased: 1991; Lang: Eng; Subj: Theatre.
■Carnegie Mellon, Department of Drama; Pittsburgh, PA 15213; USA.

Theatro *Theatro*. Lang: Gre; Subj: Theatre.
■Kosta Nitsos; Christou Lada 5-7; Athens; GREECE.

Theatron *Theatron*: Rivista quindicinale di cultura, documentazione ed informazione teatrale. Freq: 26; Began: 1961; Lang: Ita/Eng/Ger; Subj: Theatre.   ISSN: 0040-5604
■Quadrimestrale di Cultura, Documentazione e Informazione Teatrale del Centro; Via Fabiola 1; 00152 Rome; ITALY.

Theatrum *Theatrum: A Theatre Journal*. Freq: 3; Began: 1985; Ceased: 1995; Cov: Full; Lang: Eng; Subj: Theatre.   ISSN: 0838-5696
■Theatrum; P.O. Box 688, Station C; Toronto, ON M6J 3S1; CANADA.

Theoria *Theoria*: A Journal of Studies in the Arts, Humanities and Social Studies. Freq: 2; Began: 1947; Cov: Scan; Lang: Eng; Subj: Related.   ISSN: 0040-5817
■University of Natal Press; Box 375; Pietermaritzburg; SOUTH AFRICA.

Thespis *Thespis*. Last Known Address; Lang: Gre; Subj: Theatre.
■Greek Centre of the ITI; Anthinou Gazi 9; Athens; GREECE.

THeute *Theater Heute*. Freq: 12; Began: 1960; Cov: Scan; Lang: Ger; Subj: Theatre.   ISSN: 0040-5507

■Friedrich Berlin Verlagsges; mbH, L*04utzowplatz 7; D-10785 Berlin; GERMANY.

ThIr   *Theatre Ireland*. Freq: 3; Began: 1982; Cov: Full; Lang: Eng; Subj: Theatre. ISSN: 0263-6344
■Theatre Ireland, Ltd; 29 Main St.; Castlerock Co. Derry BT51 4RA; NORTHERN IRELAND.

ThM   *Theater Magazine*. Freq: 3; Began: 1968; Cov: Full; Lang: Eng; Subj: Theatre. ISSN: 0161-0775
■Yale University, School of Theater; 222 York Street Yale Station; New Haven, CT 06520; USA.

ThNe   *Theatre News*. Freq: 6; Began: 1968; Ceased: 1985; Cov: Scan; Lang: Eng; Subj: Theatre. ISSN: 0563-4040
■American Theatre Association; 1010 Wisconsin Ave., NW, Suite 620; Washington, DC 20007; USA.

ThP   *Theater Phönix*:Zeitung für dramatische Kultur. Freq: 5; Lang: Ger; Subj: Theatre.
■Verein Theater Phönix; Wiener Str. 25; A-4020 Linz; AUSTRIA.

ThPa   *Theatre Papers*. Freq: IRR; Began: 1978; Ceased: 1985; Cov: Full; Lang: Eng; Subj: Theatre. ISSN: 0309-8036
■Documentation Unit, Dartington College of Arts; Totnes; Devon TQ9 6EJ; UK.

ThPh   *Theatrephile*. Freq: 4; Began: 1983; Ceased: 1985; Cov: Full; Lang: Eng; Subj: Theatre. ISSN: 0265-2609
■D. Cheshire & S. McCarthy Eds. & Publ.; 5 Dryden Street, Covent Garden; London WC2E 9NW; UK.

ThPu   *Théâtre Public*. Freq: 6; Began: 1974; Lang: Fre; Subj: Theatre. ISSN: 0335-2927
■Théâtre de Gennevilliers; 41, avenue des Gresillons; 92230 Gennevilliers; FRANCE.

Thpur   *Theater pur*. Freq: 10; Lang: Ger; Subj: Theatre. ISSN: 0949-1481
■Pocket Verlag; Alfredstr. 58; D-45130 Essen; GERMANY.

ThR   *Theatre Research International*. Freq: 3; Began: 1958; Cov: Full; Lang: Eng; Subj: Theatre. ISSN: 0307-8833
■Oxford University Press; Pinkhill House; Southfield Road, Eynsham, Oxford OX8 1JJ; UK.

ThS   *Theatre Survey: Journal of the American Society for Theatre Research*. Freq: 2; Began: 1960; Cov: Full; Lang: Eng; Subj: Theatre. ISSN: 0040-5574
■Michael L. Quinn, School of Drama; DX-20 Hutchinson Hall University of Washington Seattle, WA 98195; USA.

Thsch   *Theaterschrift*. Began: 1992; Cov: Scan; Lang: Ger /Dut /Fre /Eng; Subj: Related.
■K*04unstlerhaus Bethanien; Marianneplatz 2; D-10997 Berlin; GERMANY.

ThScot   *Theatre Scotland*. Freq: 4; Cov: Scan; Lang: Eng; Subj: Theatre; ISSN: 0968-5499
■9a Annandale Street; Edinburgh EH7 4AW; UK.

THSt   *Theatre History Studies*. Freq: 1; Began: 1981; Cov: Full; Lang: Eng; Subj: Theatre. ISSN: 0733-2033
■Theatre Dept.

THSt   *Theatre History Studies*. Freq: 1; Began: 1981; Cov: Full; Lang: Eng; Subj: Theatre. ISSN: 0733-2033
; Central College; Pella, IA 50219; USA.

ThSw   *Theatre Southwest*. Freq: 3; Began: 1974; Cov: Full; Lang: Eng; Subj: Theatre.
■Oklahoma State University; 102 Seretean Center; Stillwater, OK 74078; USA.

ThToday   *Theatre Today*. Last Known Address; Lang: Eng; Subj: Theatre.
■Advanced Institute for Development, American Repertory Theatre; 245 West 52nd Street; New York, NY 10019; USA.

ThYear   *Theatre Year*. Freq: 1; Began: 1980; Ceased: 1983; Cov: Scan; Lang: Eng; Subj: Theatre. ISSN: 0261-2348
■In (Parenthesis) Ltd.; 21 Wellington Street; London WC2E 7DN; UK.

TI   *Théâtre International*. Freq: 4; Began: 1981; Ceased: 1984; Lang: Eng/Fre; Subj: Theatre.
■British Centre of the ITI; 31 Shelton Street; London WC2H 9HT; UK.

TID   *Themes in Drama*. Freq: 1; Began: 1979; Cov: Full; Lang: Eng; Subj: Theatre. ISSN: 0263-676X
■Cambridge Univ. Press; Edinburgh Bldg., Shaftesbury Road, Cambridge CB2 2RU; UK.

Tijatro   *Tijatro*. Freq: 12; Began: 1970; Lang: Tur; Subj: Theatre.
■PK 58; Besiktas-Istanbul; TURKEY.

TInsight   *Theatre Insight*: A Journal of Performance and Drama. Freq: 2; Began: 1988; Lang: Eng; Subj: Theatre.
■Department of Theatre and Dance, University of Texas at Austin; Austin, TX 78712-1168; USA.

TiO   *Theater in Österreich*. Freq: 1; Began: 1993; Cov: Scan; Lang: Ger; Subj: Theatre. ISBN: 3-901126-64-3
■Jahrbuch der Wiener Gesellschaft für Theaterforschung; Edition Praesens; Umlauftgasse 3 A-1170 Vienna; AUSTRIA.

Tisz   *Tiszatáj*. Freq: 12; Began: 1947; Cov: Scan; Lang: Hun; Subj: Related. ISSN: 0133-1167
■Tiszatáj Alapítvány Kuratóriuma; Rákóczi tér 1; 6741 Szeged; HUNGARY.

TJ   *Theatre Journal*. Formerly: *Educational Theatre Journal*. Freq: 4; Began: 1949; Cov: Full; Lang: Eng; Subj: Theatre. ISSN: 0192-2282
■Univ./College Theatre Assoc., The Johns Hopkins Univ. Press; 701 West 40th St. Suite 275; Baltimore, MD 21211; USA.

TJV   *Teater Jaarboek voor Vlaanderen*. Lang: Dut; Subj: Theatre.
■Antwerp; BELGIUM.

Tk   *Theaterwork*. Freq: 6; Began: 1980; Ceased: 1983; Cov: Full; Lang: Eng; Subj: Theatre. ISSN: 0735-1895
■Theaterwork; Box 8150; Sante Fe, NM 87504-8150; USA.

Tka   *Theatrika*. Freq: 52; Lang: Eng; Subj: Theatre.

■Athens; GREECE.

TkR   *TamKang Review*: Comparative Studies Between Chinese & Foreign Literature. Freq: 4; Began: 1970; Lang: Eng; Subj: Related. ISSN: 0049-2949
■Tamkang University, Grad. Inst. of West. Langs & Lit.; Tamsui; Taipei Hsien 251; TAIWAN.

Tmaker   *Theatermaker: Vakblad voor de Podiumkunst*. Freq: 10; Lang: Dut; Subj: Related. ISSN: 1385-7754;
■Stichting Vakblad voor de Podiumkunst; Herengracht 174; 1016 BR Amsterdam; NETHERLANDS.

TMJ   *Theatre Movement Journal*. Lang: Eng; Subj: Theatre.
■Ohio State University, Dept. of Theatre; 1849 Cannon Drive; Columbus, OH 43210; USA.

TMK   *Teater, Musika, Kyno*. Lang: Est; Subj: Theatre.
■Talin; ESTONIA.

TN   *Theatre Notebook*: Journal of the History and Technique of the British Theatre. Freq: 3; Began: 1946; Cov: Full; Lang: Eng; Subj: Theatre. ISSN: 0040-5523
■The Society for Theatre Research; c/o The Theatre Museum 1E Tavistock St.; London WC2E 7PA; UK.

Tningen   *Teatertidningen*. Formerly *Nya Teatertidningen*. Freq: 4; Began: 1990; Cov: Full; Lang: Swe; Subj: Theatre. ISSN: 0348-0119
■Box 20137; S10460; Stockholm; SWEDEN.

TNotes   *Theatre Notes*. SEE *Newsletter of the International Theatre Institute of The U.S., Inc.*. Freq: 10; Began: 1970; Ceased: 1984; Lang: Eng; Subj: Theatre.
■US Centre of the ITI; 1860 Broadway, Suite 1510; New York, NY 10023; USA.

TNS   *Théâtre National de Strasbourg*: Actualité. Lang: Fre; Subj: Theatre.
■Théâtre National de Strasbourg; 1, rue André Malraux-BP 184/R5 67005 Strasbourg; FRANCE.

TOE   *Théâtre Ouvert/Ecritures*. Freq: 4; Last Known Address; Began: 1978; Lang: Fre; Subj: Theatre. ISSN: 0181-5393
■21 rue Cassette; 75006 Paris; FRANCE.

Toneel   *Toneel Teatraal*. Formerly *Mickery Mouth and Toneel Teatraal*. Freq: 10; Began: 1879; Cov: Full; Lang: Dut; Subj: Theatre. ISSN: 0040-9170
■Nederlands Theaterinstituut; Herengracht 166-168; 1016 BP Amsterdam; NETHERLANDS.

Tournees   *Tournées de Spectacles*. Freq: 12; Began: 1975; Ceased; Cov: Scan; Lang: Fre; Subj: Theatre. ISSN: 0317-5979
■Conseil des Arts du Canada; Office des Tournées; Ottawa, ON; CANADA.

TP   *Theatre in Poland/Théâtre en Pologne*. Freq: 6; Began: 1958; Cov: Full; Lang: Eng/Fre; Subj: Theatre. ISSN: 0040-5493
■ITI, Polish Center; pl. Piłsudskiego 9; 00-078 Warsaw; POLAND.

TpaedB   *Theaterpaedagogische Bibliothek*. Freq: IRR; Began: 1983; Lang: Ger; Subj: Theatre.
■Heinrichshofen Buecher; Valoisstrasse 11; 2940 Wilhelmshaven; GERMANY.

TProf *Théâtre Professionnel*. Lang: Fre; Subj: Theatre.
■14 rue de la Promenade; Asnieres; FRANCE.

TQ *Theatre Quarterly*: Since 1985 published as New Theatre Quarterly (NTQ). Freq: 4; Began: 1971; Ceased: 1981; Lang: Eng; Subj: Theatre. ISSN: 0049-3600
■TQ Publications, Ltd.; 44 Earlham Street; WC2 9LA London; UK.

TR *Theater Rundschau*. Freq: 12; Began: 1955; Lang: Ger; Subj: Theatre. ISSN: 0040-5442
■Bonner Talweg 10; D-53113 Bonn; GERMANY.

Traces *Traces*. Freq: 6; Lang: Fre; Subj: Theatre.
■Comédie de Rennes; Théâtre de la Parcheminerie; 35100 Rennes; FRANCE.

Tramoya *Tramoya*: Cuaderno de teatro. Freq: 4; Began: 1975; Lang: Spa; Subj: Theatre.
■Universidad Veracruzana; Zona Universitaria; Lomas del Estadio Jalapa; MEXICO.

TransA *Transforming: Art: the arts and self-knowledge*. Freq: 2; Began: 1986; Cov: Scan; Lang: Eng; Subj; Related. ISSN: 0817-2080
■Transforming Art; P.O. Box C168; Sydney, NSW 2000; AUSTRALIA.

TRC *Theatre Research in Canada/ Recherches Theatrales au Canada*. Formerly: *Theatre History in Canada*. Freq: 2; Began: 1991; Cov: Scan; Lang: Eng/Fre; Subj: Theatre.
■Graduate Center for Study of Drama; University of Toronto; Toronto, ON M5T 2Z9; CANADA.

Treteaux *Tréteaux*. Freq: 2; Lang: Eng; Subj: Theatre. ISSN: 0161-4479
■University of Maine at Orono Press; University of Maine; Farmington, ME 04938; USA.

Trujaman *Trujaman*. Last Known Address; Lang: Spa; Subj: Theatre.
■Casilla de Correos 3234; Buenos Aires; ARGENTINA.

TSA *Theatre SA*: Quarterly for South African Theater. Freq: 4; Began: 1968; Lang: Eng; Subj: Theatre.
■PO Box 2153; Cape Town; SOUTH AFRICA.

TSO *Teatro del Siglo de Oro: Ediciones Críticas*. Freq: 2; Began: 1982; Lang: Eng/ Spa/Fre; Subj: Theatre. ISSN: 7188-4400
■Edition Reichenberger; Pfannkuchstr. 4; D 3500 Kassel; GERMANY.

TSOL *Teatro del Siglo de Oro: Estudios de Literatura*. Freq: IRR; Began: 1984; Lang: Spa/Eng; Subj: Theatre. ISSN: 7200-9300
■Edition Reichenberger; Pfannkuchstr. 4; D 3500 Kassel; GERMANY.

TSt *Teatervidenskabelige Studier*. Freq: 1; Began: 1974; Lang: Dan; Subj: Theatre.
■Akademisk Forlag; St. Kannikestraede 8; 1169 Copenhagen; DENMARK.

TT *Theatre Times*. Formerly: *OOBA Newsletter (OOBA Guidebook to Theatre)*. Freq: 6; Began: 1982; Cov: Scan; Lang: Eng; Subj: Theatre. ISSN: 0732-300X
■Alliance of Resident Theatres; 131 Varick Street, Suite 904; New York, NY 10013-1410; USA.

TTh *Travail Théâtral*. Freq: 4; Began: 1970; Lang: Fre; Subj: Theatre. ISSN: 0049-4534
■Editions l'Age d'Homme-la Cite; Case Postale 263; 1000 Lausanne 9; SWITZERLAND.

TTop *Theatre Topics*. Freq: 2; Began: 1991; Cov: Full; Lang: Eng; Subj: Theatre. ISSN: 1054-8378
■Johns Hopkins University Press; 2715 North Charles Street; Baltimore, MD 21218-4319; USA.

TTT *Tenaz Talks Teatro*. Freq: 4; Began: 1977; Last Known Address; Lang: Eng/ Spa; Subj: Theatre.
■University of California-La Jolla, Chicano Studies Program, D-009; La Jolla, CA 92093; USA.

TU *Théâtre et université*. Lang: Fre; Subj: Theatre.
■Centre Universitaire International, Form. & Recherche Dramatique; Nancy; FRANCE.

Tv *Teatervetenskap*. Freq: 2; Began: 1968; Lang: Swe/Eng; Subj: Theatre.
■Inst. för Teater & Filmvetenskap; Box 27026; S 102 Stockholm 27; SWEDEN.

TvL *Tydskri vi Letterkunde*. Freq: 4; Began: 1963; Cov: Scan; Lang: Eng & Afrikaans; Subj: Related. ISSN: 0041-476X
■Elize Botha; Posbus 1758; Pretoria;; SOUTH AFRICA.

TVOR *Tvorchestvo*. Freq: 12; Began: 1957; Cov: Scan; Lang: Rus; Subj: Related. ISSN: 0131-6877
■Izdatel'stvo Sovetskii Khudozhnik; Ul. Chernyakhovskogo; 4A; Moscow; RUSSIA.

TvT *Tijdschrift voor Theaterwetenschap*. Freq: 4; Lang: Dut; Subj: Theatre.
■Instituut voor Wetenschap, Nw.; Doelenstraat 16; 1012 CP Amsterdam; NETHERLANDS.

TvVV *Tydskrif vir Volkskunde en Volkstaal*. Freq: 3; Began: 1944; Cov: Scan; Lang: Eng. & Afrikaans; Subj: Related. ISSN: 0049-4933
■Genootskap vir Afrikaanse Volkskunde; Box 4585; Johannesburg 2000; SOUTH AFRICA.

TWI *Theaterwissenschaftlicher Informationsdienst*. Lang: Ger; Subj: Theatre.
■Theaterhochschule Hans Otto'; Sec. für Theaterwissenschaftliche Dok.; Leipzig; GERMANY.

TWNew *Tennessee Williams Review*. Formerly: *Tennessee Williams Newsletter*. Freq: 2; Began: 1980; Ceased: 1983; Lang: Eng; Subj: Theatre. ISSN: 0276-993X
■Northeastern University, Division of the Arts; 360 Huntington Ave. Boston, MA 02115; USA.

TwoT *Two Thousand (2000)*. Freq: 4; Began: 1969; Cov: Scan; Lang: Slo; Subj: Related. ISSN: 0350-8935
■Journal for Thought, Art, Cultural and Religious Issues; Association 2000 Ljubljana; SLOVENIA.

TZ *Theater der Zeit*. Freq: 6; Began: 1946; Lang: Ger; Subj: Theatre. ISSN: 0040-5418
■Interessengemeinschaft Theater der Zeit e.V., Podewil; Klosterstr. 68/70; D-10179 Berlin; GERMANY.

Tzs *Theaterzeitschrift*: Beiträge zu Theater, Medien, Kulturpolitik. Lang: Ger; Subj: Theatre. ISSN: 0723-1172
■Verein zur Erforschung theatraler Verkehrsformen; Tzs-Wochenschau Verlag; Adolf-Damaschke Str. 103-105 6231 Schawlbach; GERMANY.

UCrow *Upstart Crow, The*. Freq: 1; Began: 1978; Last Known Address; Lang: Eng; Subj: Theatre.
■P.O. Box 740; Martin, TN 38237; USA.

UDSalaam *University of Dar es Salaam: Theatre Arts Department*: Annual Report. Freq: 1; Lang: Eng; Subj: Theatre.
■University of Dar es Salaam, Theatre Arts Department; Box 35091; Dar es Salaam; TANZANIA.

UES *Unisa English Studies: Journal of the Department of English*. Freq: 2; Began: 1963; Cov: Scan; Lang: Eng & Afr; Subj: Related. ISSN: 0041-5359
■S.G. Kossick, Ed.; Dept. of English; Univ. of South Africa; P.O. Box 392; 0001 Pretoria; SOUTH AFRICA.

Ufa *Ufahamu*: Journal of the African Activist Association. Freq: 3; Began: 1970; Cov: Scan; Lang: Eng; Subj: Related. ISSN: 0041-5715
■James S. Coleman African Studies Center; University of California; Los Angeles, CA 90024-1130; USA.

UjA *Új Auróra*. Freq: 3; Began: 1972; Ceased: 1989; Cov: Scan; Lang: Hun; Subj: Related. ISSN: 0133-2295
■Békéscsabai Városi Tanács; István király tér 9; 5600 Békéscsaba; HUNGARY.

UjF *Új Forrás*. Freq: 10; Began: 1968; Cov: Scan; Lang: Hun; Subj: Related. ISSN: 0133-5332
■Komárom-Esztergom Megye Onkormányzata; Március 15. út 2 2800 Tatabánya; HUNGARY.

UjIras *Új Irás*. Freq: 12; Began: 1961; Ceased; Cov: Scan; Lang: Hun; Subj: Related. ISSN: 0041-5952
■Lapkiadó Vállalat; Erzsébet körut 9-11; 1073 Budapest; HUNGARY.

UMurcia *Universidad de Murcia Catedra de Teatro Cuadernos*. Freq: IRR; Began: 1978; Lang: Spa; Subj: Theatre.
■Universidad de Murcia, Secretariado de Publicaciones y Intercambio Cientifico; Santo Cristo 1; 30001 Murcia; SPAIN.

UNIMA *UNIMA France*. Freq: 4; Began: 1962; Lang: Fre; Subj: Theatre.
■Union Internationale de la Marionette, Section Française; 7 Rue du Helder; 75009 Paris; FRANCE.

Ural *Ural*. Cov: Scan; Lang: Rus; Subj: Related. ISSN: 130-5409
■RUSSIA.

Usbu *Usbu Al-Masrah*. Lang: Ara; Subj: Theatre.
■Ministère des Affaires Culturelles; La Kasbah; Tunis; TUNISIA.

USITT *USITT Newsletter*. Freq: 4; Began: 1965; Cov: Scan; Lang: Eng; Subj: Theatre. ISSN: 0565-6311

■US Inst. for Theatre Technology; 10 West 19th Street; Ste. 5A New York, NY 10011; USA.

UTarra   *Universitas Tarraconensis*. Freq: 1; Cov: Scan; Lang: Spa; Subj: Related.
■División de Filologia; Placa Imperial Tarraco, 1; 43005 Tarragona; SPAIN.

UTeatr   *Ukrainskij Teat'r*. Lang: Ukr; Subj: Related.
■Kiev; UKRAINE.

UTQ   *University of Toronto Quarterly*. Freq: 4; Cov: Scan; Lang: Eng; Subj: Related. ISSN: 0042-0247
■University of Toronto Press; 10 St. Mary Street; Toronto, ON M4Y 2W8; CANADA.

Uusi   *Uusi-Laulu*. Lang: Fin; Subj: Theatre.
■Uusi-Laulu-yhdistys; Eerikinkatu 14 A 9; 00100 Helsinki 10; FINLAND.

UZ   *Unterhaltungskunst*: Zeitschrift für Bühne, Podium und Manege. Freq: 12; Began: 1969; Lang: Ger; Subj: Related. ISSN: 0042-0565
■Henschelverlag Kunst und, Gesellschaft; Oranienburger Strasse 67/68; 104 Berlin; GERMANY.

Valivero   *Valiverho*. Freq: 3; Lang: Fin; Subj: Theatre.
■Helsinki; FINLAND.

Valo   *Valóság*. Freq: 12; Began: 1964; Ceased; Cov: Scan; Lang: Hun; Subj: Related.
■Kirlapkiado; Lenin krt. 5; 1073 Budapest VII; HUNGARY.

VantageP   *Vantage Point*: Issues in American Arts. Formerly: *American Arts*. Freq: 6; Began: 1984; Lang: Eng; Subj: Related. ISSN: 0194-1305
■American Council for the Arts; 1285 Ave. of the Americas, 3rd Floor; New York, NY 10019; USA.

VCA   *Voice*: Newsletter for Chorus America. Freq: 4; Cov: Scan; Lang: Eng; Subj: Related.
■Association of Professional Vocal Ensembles; 2111 Sansom Street Philadelphia, PA 19103; USA.

VFil   *Voprosy filosofii*. Freq: 12; Began: 1947; Lang: Eng/Rus;; Subj: Related. ISSN: 0042-8744
■Akademiya Nauk S.S.S.R., Institut Filosofii; Izdatel'stvo Pravda, Ul. Pravdy, 24; Moscow 125047; RUSSIA.

VHJ   *Victorian Historical Journal*. Formerly: *Journal of the Royal Historical Society*. Freq: 4; Began: 1987; Lang: Eng; Subj: Related. ISSN: 1030-7710
■Royal Historical Society of Victoria; Royal Mint; 280 William Street Melbourne Victoria 3000; AUSTRALIA.

Vig   *Vigilia*. Freq: 12; Began: 1935; Cov: Scan; Lang: Hun; Subj: Related. ISSN: 0042-6024
■Vigilia Kiadóhivatala; Kossuth Lajos u. 1 1053 Budapest; HUNGARY.

Vilag   *Világszinház*. Formerly: *Dramaturgical News 1965-1982*. Freq: 4; Began: 1982; Cov: Scan; Lang: Hun; Subj: Theatre. ISSN: 0231-4541

■Országos Szinháztörténeti Múzeum és Intézet; Krisztina körút 57; 1016 Budapest I; HUNGARY.

VLit   *Voprosy literatury*. Freq: 6; Began: 1957; Cov: Scan; Lang: Rus; Subj: Related. ISSN: 0042-8705
■Sojuz Pisatelej SSSR, Inst. Mirovoj Literatury; Bolšoj Gnezdnikovskij per 10; 103009 Moscow; RUSSIA.

VMGUf   *Vestnik Moskovskogo universiteta*. Freq: 6; Began: 1946; Cov: Scan; Lang: Rus; Subj: Related. ISSN: 0201-7385
■Moscow State University; Ul. Gercena 5/7; 103009 Moscow; RUSSIA.

Volga   *Volga*. Began: 1966; Cov: Scan; Lang: Rus; Subj: Related. ISSN: 0321-0677
■Naberežnaja Kosmonautov Street, 3; 410002 Saratov City; RUSSIA.

Voprosy   *Voprosy teatra*. Freq: 1; Began: 1965; Lang: Rus; Subj: Theatre. ISSN: 0201-7482
■Teatral'noe Obshchestvo, Theatre Workers Union; Kiselni Typik doml 103031; Moscow; RUSSIA.

VoprosyK   *Voprosy istorii KPSS*: SEE Kentavr. Freq: 12; Ceased: 1991; Lang: Rus; Subj: Related. ISSN: 0320-8907
■Vil'gel'ma Pika Street; 129256 Moscow; RUSSIA.

Vos   *Vosroždenije*. Began: 1994; Cov: Scan; Lang: Rus; Subj: Related. ISSN: 0869-7930
■Oleg Koševoj Street, 34 a; 367025 Makhačkala City; RUSSIA.

VS   *Victorian Studies*:An Interdisciplinary Journal of Social, Political and Cultural Studies. Freq: 4; Began: 1957; Cov: Scan; Lang: Eng; Subj: Related. ISSN: 0042-5222
■Program for Victorian Studies, Indiana University; Ballantine Hall; Bloomington, IN 47405; USA.

VSov   *V sověckom teatrě*. SEE *Sovetskij Teatr*. Freq: 3; Began: 1978; Ceased: 1982; Cov: Scan; Lang: Rus; Subj: Theatre.
■Moscow; RUSSIA.

Vstreča   *Vstreča*. Freq: 12; Began: 1940; Lang: Rus; Subj: Related.
■Sověckaja Rossija; 3 Krapirenskij per. #2; Moscow 103051; RUSSIA.

Vyakat   *Vyakat*. Freq: 4; Lang: Eng; Subj: Theatre.
■A-28 Nizamuddin West; New Delhi; INDIA.

Waiguo   *Waiguo Xiju*. Freq: 4; Began: 1962; Lang: Chi; Subj: Theatre.
■52 Dongai Ba tiao; Beijing; CHINA.

WB   *Weimarer Beiträge*: Zeitschrift für Literaturwissenschaft, Aesthetik und Kultur Wisssenschafn. Freq: 4; Began: 1955; Lang: Ger; Subj: Related. ISSN: 0043-2199
■Passagen Verlag, Walfischgasse 15/14; A-1010 Wien; AUSTRIA.

WCP   *West Coast Plays*. Freq: 2; Began: 1977; Ceased: 1988; Lang: Eng; Subj: Theatre. ISSN: 0147-4502
■California Theatre Council; 135 N. Grand Ave.; Los Angeles, CA 90014; USA.

WES   *Western European Stages*. Freq: 2; Began: 1989; Cov: Full; Lang: Eng; Subj: Theatre.

■Center for Advanced Study in Theatre Arts; CUNY Graduate School; 33 West 42nd Street New York, NY 10036; USA.

WEST   *Westerly*. Freq: 4; Began: 1956; Cov: Scan;; Subj: Related. ISSN: 0043-342x
■University of Western Australia; Nedlands, WA 6009; AUSTRALIA.

WFTM   *Wiener Forschungen zur Theater und Medienwissenschaft*. Freq: IRR; Began: 1972; Lang: Ger; Subj: Theatre.
■Universitäts-Verlagsbuchhandlung Gmb; Servitengasse 5; A1092 Vienna; AUSTRIA.

WGTJ   *Wiener Gesellschaft für Theaterforschung Jahrbuch*. Freq: IRR; Began: 1944; Ceased: 1986; Lang: Ger; Subj: Theatre.
■Verband der Wissenshaftlichen, Gesellschaften Oesterreichs; Lindengasse 37; A1070 Vienna; AUSTRIA.

WIAL   *Washington International Arts Letter*. Freq: 10; Began: 1962; Last Known Address; Lang: Eng; Subj: Related. ISSN: 0043-0609
■Box 9005; Washington, DC 20003; USA.

WijP   *WIJ Poppenspelers*. Began: 1955; Lang: Dut; Subj: Theatre.
■Wij Poppenspelers; Warmoesstraat 11 NL 2011 HN Haarlem; NETHERLANDS.

WJBS   *Western Journal of Black Studies*. Freq: 4; Began: 1977; Cov: Scan; Lang: Eng; Subj: Related. ISSN: 0197-4327
■Washington State Univ. Press; Pullman, WA 99164 5910; USA.

WLT   *World Literature Today*: a literary quarterly of the University of Oklahoma. Formerly: *Books Abroad*. Freq: 4; Began: 1927; Lang: Eng; Subj: Related. ISSN: 0196-3570
■University of Oklahoma; 110 Monnet Hall; Norman, OK 73019; USA.

WomenR   *Women's Review*. Freq: 12; Began: 1985; Ceased: 1986; Cov: Scan; Lang: Eng; Subj: Related. ISSN: 0267-5080
■1-4 Christina St.; London EC2A 4PA; UK.

WonD   *Writings on Dance*. Began: 1987; Cov: Scan; Lang: Eng; Subj: Related. ISSN: 0817-3710
■Elizabeth Dempster and Sally Gardner; P.O. Box 1172; Collingwood Victoria 3066; AUSTRALIA;.

WOpera   *World of Opera*. Freq: 6; Lang: Eng; Subj: Theatre. ISSN: 0160-8673
■Marcel Dekker Inc.; 270 Madison Avenue; New York, NY 10016; USA.

WPerf   *Women & Performance*: A Journal of Feminist Theory. Freq: 2; Began: 1983; Cov: Full; Lang: Eng; Subj: Theatre. ISSN: 0740-770X
■NYU Tisch School of the Arts, Women and Performance Project; 721 Broadway, 6th Floor; New York, NY 10003; USA.

WPIS   *Working Papers in Irish Studies*. Lang: Eng; Subj: Related.
■Northeastern University; 236 Huntington Avenue; Boston, MA 02115; USA.

WPList   *World Premieres Listing*. Began: 1981; Lang: Eng; Subj: Theatre.
■Hungarian Centre of the ITI; Hevesi Sandor Ter. 2; 1077 Budapest VII; HUNGARY.

WS   *Women's Studies*. Freq: 4; Lang: Eng; Subj: Theatre.

■Department of English; McManus Hall; The Claremont Graduate School Claremont, CA 91711; USA.

Wsw *Wer spielte was? Werkstatistik Deutschland Österreich Schweiz*. Freq: 1; Lang: Ger; Subj: Related. ISSN: 0941-5823
■Mykenae Verlag Rossberg KG; Ahastr. 9; D-64285 Darmstadt; GERMANY.

WTops *White Tops*. Freq: 6; Began: 1927; Lang: Eng; Subj: Theatre. ISSN: 0043-499X
■Circus Fans Assoc. of America; Rt. 1, Box 6735; White Stone, VA 22578; USA.

XLunc *Xiju Luncong*: Selected Essays of Theatre. Freq: 4; Began: 1957; Lang: Chi; Subj: Theatre.
■52 Dongai Ba tiao; Beijing; CHINA.

XXuexi *Xiju Xuexi*: Theatre. Freq: 4; Began: 1957; Lang: Chi; Subj: Theatre.
■Central Institute for Modern Theatre; Jiaonan Qitiao; Beijing; CHINA.

XYanj *Xiqu Yanjiu*. Freq: 4; Began: 1980; Cov: Full; Lang: Chi; Subj: Theatre.
■Cultural and Artistic Publishing; 17 Qianhai Xijie; Beijing; CHINA.

XYishu *Xiju Yishu*: Theatre Arts. Freq: 4; Began: 1978; Cov: Full; Lang: Chi; Subj: Theatre. ISSN: 0257-943X
■Shanghai Theatre Academy; 630 Huashan Lu Road; 200040 Shanghai; CHINA.

YCT *Young Cinema & Theatre/Jeune Cinéma et Théâtre*: Cultural Magazine of the IUS. Freq: 4; Began: 1964; Lang: Eng/Fre/Spa; Subj: Theatre.
■International Union of Students; 17th November Street; 110 01 Prague 1; CZECH REPUBLIC.

Yorick *Yorick*: Revista de Teatro. Lang: Spa; Subj: Theatre.
■Via Layetana 30; 3 Barcelona; SPAIN.

YTJ *Youth Theatre Journal*. Freq: 4; Began: 1986; Cov: Full; Lang: Eng; Formerly: *Children's Theatre Review;* Subj: Theatre. ISSN: 0892-9092
■American Alliance for Theatre and Education;, Theatre Department; Arizona State University; Tempe, AZ 85287-3411; USA.

ZAA *Zeitschrift für Anglistik und Amerikanistik*. Freq: 4; Began: 1953; Lang: Ger/Eng; Subj: Related. ISSN: 0044-2305
■Verlag Enzyklopädie; Gerichtsweg 26; 7010 Leipzig; GERMANY.

ZDi *Zahranicni Divadlo*: (Theatre Abroad). Lang: Cze; Subj: Theatre.
■Prague; CZECH REPUBLIC.

ZfK *Zeitschrift für Kulturaustausch*. Freq: 4; Lang: Ger; Subj: Theatre. ISSN: 0044-2976
■Horst Erdmann Verlag für, Internationalen-Kulturaustausch; Hartmeyerstrasse 117; 7400 Tübingen 1; GERMANY.

ZG *Zeitschrift für Germanistik*. Freq: 6; Began: 1980; Last Known Address; Lang: Ger; Subj: Related. ISSN: 0323-7982
■Verlag Enzyklopädie; Gerichtsweg 26; 7010 Leipzig; GERMANY.

Znamia *Znamja*. Freq: 12; Began: 1931; Lang: Rus; Subj: Related. ISSN: 0130-1616
■Soyuz Pisatelei; Moscow; RUSSIA.

Zpravy *Zprávy DILIA*. Freq: 3; Lang: Cze/Eng; Subj: Theatre.
■Dilia; Polská 1; Prague 2 Vinohrady; CZECH REPUBLIC.

ZR *Zapad Rossii*. Cov: Scan; Lang: Rus; Subj: Related. ISSN: 0132-8166
■Soviet Prospect Street, 21; 236000 Kalingrad City; RUSSIA.

ZreIssk *Zreliscnye iskusstva* (Performing Arts). Freq: 12; Began: 1983; Cov: Full; Lang: Rus; Subj: Theatre. ISSN: 0207-9739
■Gos. Biblioteka SSSR im. Lenina, NIO Informkul'tura; Prospekt Kalinina 3; 101000 Moscow; RUSSIA.

ZS *Zeitschrift für Slawistik*. Freq: 4; Began: 1956; Lang: Ger/Eng; Subj: Related. ISSN: 0044-3506
■Akademie Verlag; Mühlenstr. 33-34; D-13187 Berlin; GERMANY.

Zvezda *Zvezda*. Freq: 12; Began: 1924; Cov: Scan; Lang: Rus; Subj: Related. ISSN: 0321-1878
■Iztadel. Chudožestvennaja Literatura; Mochovaja 20; 192028 St. Petersburg; RUSSIA.

ZZT *Zene-Zene Tánc*. Freq: 2; Began: 1994; Cov: Scan; Lang:·Hun; Subj: Related. ISSN: 1218-6678
■Zene-Zene Tánc Alapítvány; Vörösmarty téri; 1051 Budapest; HUNGARY.

Photocomposition and printing services for this volume
of the *International Bibliography of Theatre* were
provided by Volt Information Sciences Inc.,

Cover Design by Irving M. Brown